The Herries

Chronicle

Hugh Walpole

CONTENTS

ROGUE HERRIES 1
  THE CUCKOO IS NOT ENCLOSED 3
  'FORTY-FIVE 63
  THE WILD MARRIAGE 103
  THE BRIGHT TURRETS OF ILION 160

JUDITH PARIS 187
  ROGUE'S DAUGHTER 189
  WATENDLATH 239
  THE BIRD OF BRIGHT PLUMAGE 292
  MOTHER AND SON 341

THE FORTRESS 381
  MADAME 383
  ADAM AND MARGARET 439
  CUMBERLAND CHASE 484
  MOTHER AND SON 529

VANESSA 589
  THE RASCAL 591
  THE HUSBAND 657
  THE LOVER 712
  THE GHOST 762

ROGUE HERRIES

Over this country, when the giant Eagle flings the shadow of his wing, the land is darkened. So compact is it that the wing covers all its extent in one pause of the flight. The sea breaks on the pale line of the shore; to the Eagle's proud glance waves run in to the foot of the hills that are like rocks planted in green water.

From Whinlatter to Black Combe the clouds are never still. The Tarns like black unwinking eyes watch their chase, and the colours are laid out in patterns on the rocks and are continually changed. The Eagle can see the shadows rise from their knees at the base of Scawfell and Gable, he can see the black precipitous flanks of the Screes washed with rain and the dark purple hummocks of Borrowdale crags flash suddenly with gold.

So small is the extent of this country that the sweep of the Eagle's wing caresses all of it, but there is no ground in the world more mysterious, no land at once so bare in its nakedness and so rich in its luxury, so warm with sun and so cold in pitiless rain, so gentle and pastoral, so wild and lonely; with sea and lake and river there is always the sound of running water, and its strong people have their feet in the soil and are independent of all men.

During the flight of the Eagle two hundred years are but as a day-- and the life of man, as against all odds he pushes toward immortality, is eternal. . .

PART I

THE CUCKOO IS NOT ENCLOSED

THE INN--THE HOUSE

A little boy, David Scott Herries, lay in a huge canopied bed, half awake and half asleep.

He must be half awake because he knew where he was--he was in the bedroom of the inn with his sisters, Mary and Deborah; they were in the bed with him, half clothed like himself, fast sleeping. Mary's plump naked arm lay against his cheek, and Deborah's body was curled into the hollow of his back and her legs were all confused with his own. He liked that because he loved, nay, worshipped, his sister Deborah.

He knew also that he was awake because, lying looking up, he could see the canopy that ran round the top of the bed. It was a dull faded green with a gold thread in it. He could see the room too, very large, with rough mottled white walls and a big open stone fireplace; there was a roaring, leaping fire--the only light in the room--and he could see very clearly the big, shining brass fire- dogs with grinning mouths like dragons and stout curly tails.

He knew, too, that he was awake, because he could see Alice Press sitting there, her clothes gathered up to her knees, warming her legs. He did not like Alice Press, but she always fascinated him, and he wondered now of what she was thinking, so motionless, her head with its red hair pushed forward, her naked neck above her silver brocade.

He knew that he was awake, because he could hear the sounds of the inn, voices calling, doors banging in the wind, steps on the stair, and even the snap-snap of horses' hoofs on the cobbles of the yard. He could hear the wind too, rushing up to the windows and shaking the panes and tearing away again, and then he shivered, pleasantly, luxuriously, because it was so warm and safe where he was and so cold and dangerous outside.

Then he shivered again because he remembered that he, with the others, must soon plunge out again into that same wind and mud and danger.

He would like to stay thus, in this warm bed, for ever and ever.

But, although he was awake enough to know all these things, he must be asleep also--asleep because, for one thing, the room would not stay still, but leapt and rollicked with the fire. All the things in it moved; the fire-dogs grinned and yawned; over a large arm- chair of faded red silk, oddly enough, some harness had been slung, and it lay there in coils of silver and dark brown leather, and these coils turned and stretched and slipped like snakes. Then against the wall there was a long, thin mirror in tarnished silver and, in this, Alice Press was most oddly reflected, the side of her face that was shown there being very thin and red, her hair tawny-peaked like a witch's hat; her eyebrow jumped up and down in a terrifying manner.

Only David was not afraid. He was a very fearless boy. But he thought, as he lay there and watched, how ugly she was in the mirror, and that if his father saw her thus he would not chuck her beneath the chin and so make his mother unhappy. And, although he was not afraid, he was glad nevertheless that Mary's warm arm was against his cheek and the round shape of Deborah's body against his back.

Because it might be that after all Alice Press was a witch. (He had always had his secret suspicions.) The way that she sat there now, so motionless, bending for-ward, was just as though she were making spells--and the silver harness blinked and the glass of the mirror trembled as the flame of the fire rose and fell again.

Then, again, it must be that he was still asleep because, although he knew that he was lying in his bed, he knew also that he was yet bumping and tossing in the coach. In that coach they had surely been for weeks and weeks, or so at least it had seemed to his tired and weary body.

At first when they had set out from Doncaster--how long ago?--he had been all pride and pleasure. It had been a fair and lovely morning--one of the last of the late summer days. The sun was shining, the birds singing, such gay bustle about the cobbled courtyard of the inn, the maids looking down from the windows, the hostlers busy about the horses, the postilions polite and eager to his father, all of them, Mother and Father Roche and Alice Press and Mary and Deborah fitting so comfortably into the soft warm inside of the coach, that had even pictures of hunting painted on the walls and little windows with gold round the edges.

Yes, it had been all gay enough then, but how miserable it had soon become! He could not now divide the days and nights from one another: moreover, he was still there in the coach, bumped up and down, thrown here and there, sleeping, waking with cramp and pins and needles, and Deborah crying and needing comforting, and Mary cross, and his mother frightened, and Alice Press sulky. Only Father Roche, reading in his purple book, or looking steadily in front of him, never perturbed nor upset nor unhappy, always grave and kind, and miles and miles away from them all!

Then the Great North Road, which had sounded so fine and grand when he had first heard of it, how different it was in reality! Not fine and grand at all, but full of deep ruts and mud so fearful that again and again the coach was hopelessly stuck in it, and everyone had to pull and push, cursing and swearing. Once they were almost upset. The coach went right over on its side and the horses went down, and they were all on the top one of another. He, David, had a bruise on his right leg, and his mother's cheek was cut.

The further they went the colder it became. They seemed, almost at once, to leave summer right behind them.

Nor were the inns where they stopped fine and clean like the Doncaster one, but cold, draughty, and the floors and walls often crawling with spiders and other more evil things.

He seemed, lying there in the bed watching the leaping fire, to be transferred suddenly back into one of the worst of them--where, tired and bruised with the rough travelling, he had stumbled into the low-ceilinged, ill-lighted, ill-smelling room, huddled with his mother and sisters at a dirty table in a dim corner, and there stared out into the rude, confused babble--men, women, children, dogs, drinking, shouting and singing, the dogs waiting, mouths agape, while the food was tossed to them, four men playing at some game in a corner, a man with a fiddle and a monkey dressed in a crimson jacket

dancing in the middle of the sandy floor, the heated damp of the room rising to the ceiling and trickling in wet smeary streaks down the walls, a smell of straw and human breath and dung and animals and tallow--and in the middle of this his father standing, in his dark purple riding-coat, his high hat cocked, his waistcoat of silver thread showing between the thick lapels of his coat, his whip with the silver head in his hand--like a god, like a king, demanding a private room, aweing at last the fat landlord, round like a tub, causing all that coarse roomful to feel that a great man had come among them. There was little, tired though he was, that David had not that night noticed, from the painting of the King over the fireplace to a swinging gilt cage with a blue bird, and a man who said he was from the wars and crept to their table on his wooden stumps showing that his right hand had no fingers. . . .

Yes, he remembered everything of that night (was not the man with no legs and no fingers over there now by the fire watching Alice Press, her back of stiff brocade?), because on that night a great happiness had come to him. He had slept with his father. His father and Father Roche and himself had slept in the one small, dirty room, all three on the low, dirty bed. At first it had been almost terrible because his father had been in one of his rages, cursing the place and the dirt and the cold, cursing his family, too, for persuading him to the expense and danger of a private coach, when they would all of them have been so much better on horse-back.

Then, seeing his little son straight and sturdy there in his smallclothes, looking up and waiting for orders as to whether he should go naked to bed or no, with one of his sudden gestures he had caught him up and hugged him, then thrown off only his outer clothing, then taken David and wrapped him, close up against himself, in his great riding-coat--and the two of them stretched out on the bed, Father Roche bodily beside them but spiritually a world away.

How wonderful that night had been! David had slept but little of it. He had lain close against his father's heart, his hands across his father's breast, feeling the great beat of the heart and the iron ribs beneath the thin shirt, his cheek against the smooth softness of his father's neck.

That had been a great happiness, but after that night there had been only trouble. On the high ground towards Kendal they had suffered a fearful storm of wind and rain. It had seemed to them that the end of the world had come; the coach had sunk into the mud so that for hours they could not move it. They had been warned, at the last town, that they must beware of footpads, and at every sound they had started. Quite a crowd of travellers had been accompanying them for safety--farmers, pedlars and other pedestrians. The weather perhaps had saved them. All the footpads were within doors, warm and cosy beside their fires.

In Kendal they had left the coach and had ridden the remainder of their journey on horseback. David, tired though he was, had found that glorious, riding in front of his father, mounting the hills, then dropping under the faint misted morning sun down beside the miraculous waters and mountains, a land of faery such as David had never dreamt of, sheets of white and silver, the mountains of rose and amber and the trees thick with leaves of gold.

They had ridden into Keswick in the afternoon, quite a cavalcade of them, with their possessions on pack-horses, the women and children so desperately fatigued that they could scarcely keep their seats. So, in a dream, to the inn, and the children stripped of their outer clothing and flung into the great bed, the two little girls at once dropping off into heavy slumber.

So should David have done, but instead he had lain there in this strange state of waking sleep. It was, possibly, that he was too greatly excited. For months past, in their home outside Doncaster, he had been anticipating this journey. He had not been happy in the Doncaster home. His father had been so much away, his mother so unhappy, there had been no one save his sisters with whom he could play. He had hated the stuffy little house, the rooms so small and dark, the country surrounding it so dull and uninteresting. And always there had been this unhappiness, his father angry and rebellious, his mother often in tears, Alice Press, whom he hated, supposedly looking after the children but doing nothing for them, gentlemen arriving from Doncaster, drinking, playing cards, singing and shouting all night long. His only interest had been his lesson with Father Roche, who, while teaching him Latin and Greek, would talk to him about many wonderful things, about London with its palaces and theatres and gardens that ran down to the river, and Rome where England's rightful King lived, and then of God and Heaven, and how one must live to please God--to obey Father Roche in all things and to keep secret in his heart everything that Father Roche told him.

The only other entertainment had been the times when he was with Nathaniel and Benjamin, the men-servants. Nathaniel taught him the small-sword and cudgel, and Benjamin taught him to box and to wrestle, and he had been twice with Nathaniel to a cock-fight and once to the village to see a bear baited.

Nevertheless, had it not been for his father and Deborah the days would have been heavy indeed. He was a boy of passionate affections and his whole heart was given to his father and his sister. His love for his father was worship and his love for Deborah was protection.

His father was entirely a being from another world like St. Michael or St. George who came in the Christmas plays. His father who was so handsome and splendid could do no wrong, although when he was drunk he was hard to understand; when he beat Benjamin until the blood ran down Benjamin's back David was sorry for the man, but yet was certain that his father was in the right.

But Deborah was of his own flesh and blood. So, too, was Mary, but he did not care for Mary. She, although she was so young, had already her own independent fashion of living and, because she was so pretty, could have her way when she pleased, which she very well knew. But Deborah was not pretty and was often afraid. Deborah believed that David could do anything, and she always came to him when she was in trouble and trusted him to help her. He could do no wrong in Deborah's eyes, and so he loved her and guarded her as well as he could from every harm.

At the thought of Deborah he turned a little and put his arm about her, which she feeling, although deep in sleep, recognised by a little dreamy murmur of pleasure.

Just then he heard the door (which was behind the canopied bed so that he could not see it) open, and an instant later it was all that he could do to withhold a cry of pleasure. For it was his father who had entered, who was now standing quite close to them, looking down upon them. David closed his eyes--not because he wanted to be deceitful, but because he knew that his father wished that he should be asleep.

Nevertheless, one look had been enough. His father was resplendent! For days and nights now he had seen him soiled and disarrayed with the storms and struggles of that awful journey, muddied and blown and uncaring whether he were neatly kept or no. There were times when his father seemed to prefer dirt and disorder, and they were bad times too. An unkempt wig, tarnished buckles and buttons, a soiled cravat, and David had learnt to know that the disarray and rebellion were more than physical.

Only an hour ago David had seen him striding about the courtyard of the inn, mud-splashed to the thighs, raging and swearing. That had been his last thought before he had fallen into this half-slumber, that his father was still out there in the wind and rain ordering Benjamin and the rest, seeing to the horses that were to carry them the final stage of their weary journey. But now, how resplendent in the white-walled fire-leaping room! David in that one glance had seen it all.

The fine curled chestnut wig, the beautiful claret-coloured, gold- embroidered coat with the long spreading skirts, the claret- coloured breeches and grey silk stockings, the fluted grey-silk waistcoat stamped with red roses, the little sword at his side--ah! glory upon glory, was anything in the world anywhere so glorious as his father thus! No, nothing in London or Rome of which Father Roche had told him--nothing that China or India itself could show!

His heart swelling with pride and happiness he lay there, pretending to be asleep, watching through half-closed eyes. He saw then an odd thing. He saw his father, on tip-toe, approach the fire, steal upon Alice Press, she motionless gazing into the flame, lean forward, put then his hands, deep in their splendid white ruffles, lightly about her face, closely across her eyes.

She gave a little scream, but David knew that at once she was aware who this was.

Laughing, Francis Herries withdrew his hands. She looked up, smiling that strange smile of hers, half pleasure, half rebellious anger.

'Why, sir,' (she was, like David, greatly surprised at his grandeur), 'what fine feathers we're wearing!'

'Hush,' he put his fingers to his lips, 'the children are sleeping.'

'I fancy so. They sound still enough. Poor babies--after such a devilish journey!' She turned again from him and stared back into the fire. 'You are dressed to meet your brother?'

'Why not to meet yourself, beautiful lady?'

He was laughing, that careless, jolly, kindly, good-to-all-the- world laugh that, as David knew, came only when he was happy. So he was happy now! David was glad.

'Myself?' She turned to him fully, showing the deep swell of her bosom beneath the brocaded vest. 'No, I think not. God! that I had not consented to come on this madcap journey.'

For answer he bent down and, still laughing, caught her head in his hands, brought his mouth to hers, kissed her on the lips, the cheeks, the eyes, then, almost violently, flung her away from him, straightening his body as he did so.

'Do you like that better? Does that make you more content with your journey?'

'No, why should it?' She shrugged her shoulders, turning back to the fire. 'Do you love me? No. Then what is a kiss?'

'Love--and love.' He laughed. 'I am no captive to it, if that's your meaning. I visit it, wish it good day, spend a pretty hour in its company--so I am never weary of it nor it of me. Love? And what do you mean by love?'

'I mean,' she answered fiercely, 'those foul, filthy, beggarly days and nights of mud and dung and stinking beds; the pains and bruises that I have known on this journey and the idiocies of your wife and the wailings of your children and the evil dirty tempers of yourself. . . . And what do I receive in return for these things?'

She rose up suddenly and turned to him--a tall broad woman, with scarlet hair and a white face, who would soon be stout.

David, watching her, had never seen her like this, so alive, her big eyes with the fair, faint eyebrows staring, the big bosom under the silver brocade heaving, the big mouth in the pale face half open.

Francis Herries looked at her gently, kindly and with amusement. 'What do you get?' speaking low so that the children should not be waked. He put a hand on her shoulder, and she stood strong and sturdy without moving. David could see her full face now in the mirror and he watched absorbed because it was so awake. Always it had been yawning, the lazy eyes half closed, the cheeks heavy with indolence as she sleepily ate sugar-plums and cakes and sugar figs.

'What do you get? . . . Something. Nothing. And what is there to get? A little hugging and fumbling, sweating and panting, and then satiety.' He looked at her even with more earnest study, as though in truth he had never seen her before, and her eyes did not fall before his. 'You elected to come--to the end of the world. No roads. Savages. A chill house with the rain always falling--and the ghosts of all your sins, my dear.'

She, with a sudden movement that surprised him, caught him round the cheek and with her white face against his ruddy brown one whispered eagerly, furiously in his ear. The fire leapt as though in sympathy with her urgency, and the figures swayed and swelled in the silver mirror.

Francis Herries withdrew from her slowly, carefully, as though he would not hurt her, no, neither her body nor her soul. But he was many, many miles away from her as he answered:

'So that's the way of it. . . . To leave them in the mud and rain and find sunshine, the two of us, alone--alone.' He smiled--a beautiful smile, David, who did not understand the most of this strange conversation, thought. 'Alone with me, Alice, you'd be in despair in a half-hour. No one has been alone with me ever and not suffered the intensest weariness. I have suffered it with myself, recurring agonies of it. And you are not made to be wearied.

'Nevertheless, you will be infinitely dull. Days of rain and mud in a half-tumbled house cut off from everything but the savages. It's your own choice, my dear. And only my body to comfort you. My body without my soul, I fear. My soul has flown. I lost it a week back. I shall find it doubtless on a tree in Borrowdale.'

David saw that she did not understand him, that she gazed at him with a look that he himself did not understand, a look of rage, of love, of uncertainty, of disappointment. She was not very clever, Alice Press. Young though he was, David already had an instinct of that.

His father came softly to the bed and looked down on them. David, his eyes tightly closed, could nevertheless see him, the gold of his coat, the white silk of the lapels, the curling splendour of the chestnut wig. It was as though his father were weaving a spell over him--his eyes so fixedly closed that they burnt. A spell, a spell! The crystal in the silver mirror turning, Alice Press mounting her broomstick and riding through the dark heavy-hung sky, and his father riding on a silver horse into the moon and stars. . . . A spell! A spell!

'Wake up! wake up!'

It was Alice Press's soft white hand shaking his shoulder. He opened his eyes. His father was gone as though he had never been. They were to be up and have their clothes on and see their good uncle and aunt--Uncle Pomfret and Aunt Jannice.

The two little girls, like little round fluffy owls bewildered by their sleep, dazed with the strange light of the leaping fire, fastened their own clothes. Mary was eight years of age, and Deborah seven, and they had been taught from a long time to do for themselves. They had been wearing their winter dresses these last days, and Mary's had dark fur edging the green velvet and Deborah's grey fur upon crimson. David was dressed in a short yellow jacket and long tight breeches, buff-colour, reaching down to his ankles. He tied Deborah's ribbons and points and fastened her shoes. She was very frightened. She was scarcely as yet awake. She did not know what this great room was nor where they were now going. She was terrified of her Uncle Pomfret and Aunt Jannice. She was weary, utterly weary after the days of the journey. She wanted her mother. She, like David, hated Alice Press. She was like a little downy bird, her head covered with soft flaxen curls. She stood there biting her lips so that she would not cry. Had David not been there she MUST have cried. But she stood near him looking up into his face. Where David was no harm could come.

It was now time for them to go down, but they had to delay because Mary must have her horn-book to carry with her. It was a fine one, and its back was of gilded and embossed leather, crimson with silver wire. David knew at once why Mary must have it. It was to show off before Aunt Jannice that she might notice how exceptional a child Mary was.

They searched here and there. Mary had had it with her before she fell asleep. Alice Press swore and threatened. It was of no use. Mary had a marvellous obstinacy when the purpose was concerned with herself. The horn-book was found beneath one of the fire-dogs, and Mary walked out, holding it virtuously by the handle, her head up as though she were leading a procession.

They went down the wooden staircase, which was from Elizabeth's time, very beautiful and broad, the newels thick and strong, the handrails framed into the newels, the balustrade beautifully arcaded, a lovely symmetry of delicacy and strength. In the hall below it was very dark, save in the doorway that looked out into the street where the light of the afternoon still gleamed in pale shadow against black cloud. Great gusts of the gale blew into the hall, at the end of which was a huge stone fireplace with a roaring fire. On broad tables candelabra held many candles that also blew in the wind.

Across the shining floor servants, drawers, maids, men from the kitchen were constantly passing into the wild light and out of it again. Uncertain though the light was, it was enough for David to see his father, standing very stiff and upright, his mother also, and a lady and gentleman who must, David knew, be his uncle and aunt.

The children were brought up to their parents. Mary at once went to her mother, caught her mother's hand, and so stayed, looking very pretty. David kissed his aunt's hand, bowed to his uncle, then stood straight and stiff beside his father. His uncle Pomfret was a big, broad, stout man with a very red face, large wide-open eyes and a little snub nose. He was dressed in rough

country clothes, his long boots were splashed with mud. He smelt strongly of wind, rain, liquor and the stables. He seemed good-natured and friendly, laughed much and struck his leg often with a riding-whip. Aunt Jannice was thin and tall, with a peaked face and a big brown wart in the middle of her cheek. She wore a broad hat and had a curly brown wig which sat oddly about her yellow leathern face. She was very composed, dignified and superior. She contrasted strangely with David's mother, who was always so stout and red and flustered and was given to breaking into odd little hummings of tunes from simple nervousness.

David knew that there was nothing that irritated his father so much as this habit of hers. But David's attention was fixed upon his father. He wished desperately--although he did not know why he wished--that his father had not dressed so grandly. Only half an hour before he had been so proud of his father's grandeur, now he was ashamed of it.

He was sure that Uncle Pomfret and Aunt Jannice were laughing at his father for being in such grand clothes. Not that his father would care, but he, David, cared for him. Uncle Pomfret was much older than his father (he was indeed twenty-two years older; he was the eldest, as Francis Herries was the youngest, he fifty-two years of age and Francis only thirty). He looked as though he might be David's grandfather.

There was indeed no physical resemblance between the two brothers. David discovered also another thing--that they were all striving to persuade his father of something, and his father was very obstinate. He knew how his father looked when he was obstinate, he smiled and was haughty and said little. So it was now.

They were trying to persuade him to stay in his brother's house at least to-night and not to go on in the wind and wet and darkness into Borrowdale. But his father only smiled. He had planned to be in the house to-night and be in the house he would, and the others should be there too.

David saw that his mother was very near to tears, her round mottled face all puckered, and she bit continually at her lace handkerchief. She was desperately weary, poor woman, and afraid and very unhappy.

'Why, blast you and damn you, brother,' said Uncle Pomfret very heartily. 'You must stay with us to-night or prove yourself most unbrotherly. We had always expected it so--Had we not, Janny? There's no road over to Herries. You are going among the savages there, brother. I can swear you were dismayed enough at seeing this griddling little inn after your great Doncaster houses, but this is Paradise to what you're going to. Don't say I didn't warn you now. Damn me for a curmudgeon, brother, if I bottomed you into doing it--but to-night you shall stay with us. There's your lady sunk with weariness, and the babes too, damn me if they're not.'

He shouted all this as though across a windy common, and all that Francis Herries said to it was:

'Herries sees us all to-night, and we'll take our luck with the road.'

'You'll be the rest of this day on horseback,' his brother assured him. 'There's not a cart in Borrowdale, brother, nor a road to carry one. It's all horseback round here. Damn it, you're in Chiney in Borrowdale, but never say I didn't warn you. You wanted cheap living and you've got it. Naked bottom and bare soil! that's life in Borrowdale.'

David had never heard so rough and coarse and hearty a voice, and it seemed to him strange that this big red man should be his father's brother. He jumped, too, from the sharp contrast when a moment later his aunt spoke:

'Come now, Francis. Have some softness for the family. The children can scarce stand with their weariness. Margaret, persuade him. There is room enough with us for so long as you please to remain.'

Her voice was cold and thin like the steady trickle of a determined pump. When she spoke, she stared in front of her, looking neither to right nor left, as though she were reciting a set piece.

David's mother, thus appealed to, very nervously and not looking at her husband, answered:

'Indeed, it's very kindly of you, Jannice. We are weary and 'tis late. To-morrow would be time enough.'

'There, brother!' Sir Pomfret broke in with a roar, 'have you no tender parts? Your wife and the children at least shall stay with us. You shall ride alone if you are resolved--you and the priest,' he added, suddenly dropping his voice.

'There--that's sufficient,' Francis Herries answered sharply. 'My wife will be thankful enough when she's there and settled. In an hour's time the horses will be moving and ourselves on them. Thank you for your goodwill, brother. And now for a meal. It is ready and waiting.'

It was now late for dining. To the children, indeed, it would, before this tremendous journey of theirs, have seemed an incredible hour, for their dinner had been at three of the afternoon ever since they could remember, but now all their customs and habits were in ruin, and they accepted, poor things, blindly and without a murmur what came to them.

They were, however, all three, too tired to have an appetite. In the little private room they were crowded about the small table. David to his distress was next to his uncle, who roared and rattled and laughed as he helped the food, so that it was like being seated next an earthquake.

There was a good baked pie of a leg of mutton, and roasted chickens with pease and bacon, and a fine fruit tart that would, at another time, have made David's mouth water. There was much wine, too, and of this Uncle Pomfret began to drink very heartily indeed, and shouted to the others to do the same. The noisier he became the more upright and magnificent was Aunt Jannice.

Very fine, especially, was she when she rose to wash her spoon in a bowl of water behind the table, so that, having just used it for pease and bacon, it should not now be soiled for the fruit tart. David's mother, who had never seen anyone do this before, could not hide her staring wonder.

David, in spite of his weariness which made everything around him like a dream, fancied that his aunt was storing all things up in her mind, so that for many weeks she would be able to retail to her genteel friends all the strange things that this wild family had done. He did not love her the better for fancying this.

But he was in so dreamy a state that he could be sure of nothing. He, in his half-dream, saw--and he knew that his mother saw this too--that his father was drinking in a defiance of his stout red- faced brother. He knew what his father was like when he was drunken, and he hated his uncle that he should tempt him. Throughout this journey his father had been very fine, drinking nothing, aware perhaps of the charge there was upon him. And in any case he drank little when Father Roche was there.

But in everything that he did, while his brother was present, there was defiance. There had been defiance in his grand clothes, defiance in his refusing to stay in Keswick, defiance now in every gesture. David, because he adored his father, knew all this with a wisdom beyond his years. Meanwhile, in this dreamy state, it was all that he could do with his wits to defend himself against his uncle, who was pushing pieces of meat and of pie on to his plate and even holding his head back and poking food into his mouth. But once when he was about to force some wine down his throat Francis Herries called out quietly:

'Nay, brother, leave the boy alone. He shall have wine when he wishes for it. It shan't be thrust on him.' Pomfret broke out into a flurry of magnificent and filthy oaths. He then thrust David in the ribs and cried at him: 'Why, damn thee, boy, dost thou not follow thy father? He's a lecherous foul-dealing knave enough, I'll be bound--no Herries, an he ain't. Drink thy uncle's health, boy, and be damned to thy father!'

'Pomfret!' said Aunt Jannice. It was enough. The uncle was cowed like a dog under a whip and took some sugar-plums from a plate and swallowed them, three at a time, like a confused child. David looked across to his father. It seemed to him then, as it was to seem to him increasingly in the coming days, that they were younger and elder brother, not father and son. And, indeed, there was only the difference of nineteen years between them.

In his dreamy state it seemed to him that he and his father were circled round with light together, they two, and that his father's crimson and gold shone, and the room burnt against its panelling with a strange and sombre glow.

But his next thought was for Deborah. With every attention that his uncle had permitted him he had watched her and had seen that she was very unhappy.

Poor child, with weariness and fear of her relations and her seated distance from David, she was nearly distraught. She did not understand what had happened to her, but it was something terrible. She understood that more terrible things were shortly to occur. David, watching her, could at last endure it no longer; her frightened eyes, the way that her head bobbed and nodded and then bobbed again, her fashion of pretending to eat and not eating, hurt him as though it were himself.

While his uncle was busy with a long and excited account of his country sports and pastimes, with vociferous curses on the French and praise of the Hanoverian succession, he stepped from his chair and went to her side, bending forward and whispering to her.

But, alas, this kind attention was too much for her; she broke into sobs, not loudly but with a soft titter-witter like a wounded bird.

Uncle Pomfret broke off his account of what he would do to a French Papist an he caught him, to tumble into a bellow of laughter.

'Why, pox on it, here's a little master . . . comforting your sister. . . . Why, damn it, boy, but I like your heart. There's a good one for the ladies. He knows a thing or two, I warrant. But come hither, little Deb. Come to thy old uncle. He'll buy thee a baby, one of your china sorts with pink cheeks, none of your stuffed rags. Come to thy uncle, Deb, and he'll comfort thee.'

'David.' It was his father's voice. 'Leave Deborah. Come to me.' He went up to his father, fearless, but not knowing whether a caress or a blow was to be his fate. Then he looked into his father's eyes and saw that they were soft and humorous and knew that all was well.

'Go, find Benjamin. We must shortly be starting.' Then, turning to his brother, 'She has babies enough, Pomfret; she is weary, and there's a bed at Herries waiting for her.'

He did not hear his uncle's retort, which was something fine and free about beds and ladies and general courtship. He was glad to be away, he didn't care if he never saw his uncle or aunt again; he hated them and Keswick and the inn. But coming into the bustle of the kitchen where serving-men and maids were shouting and pushing, where dogs were waiting for chance pieces of food, and a man with a feather in his broad hat was seated on the corner of a table playing a fiddle, the stir and adventure of it all heartened him and he was glad that he was alive and pushing, shoving forward into this grand new world. The kitchen smelt of everything in the world—meat and drink and the heat of the great fire. He looked around him and found Benjamin seated in a corner near the fire, his arm round a girl. She was feeding him with pieces of meat off his plate.

'Benjamin,' he said, ordering him as though he were a hundred years his master, 'my father says that it's time for the horses.'

Many of them heard him and turned laughing, and a big woman with an enormous bosom would have

made him come to her, and a brawler wanted him to drink, but he fixed his eyes on the stout Benjamin, who put his plate down, gave the girl a kiss, and came without a word. So much power had Francis Herries over his servants.

Benjamin was plump and rosy; he should have been a fine figure of a man, but he could eat all day without ceasing. This was one of the reasons that he was beaten by his master, but he bore his master no grudge. Everything that came his way he took, and over the bad he shrugged his shoulders and over the good he laughed and grunted.

First or all he loved himself, then food, then women (all kinds, young, old, ugly and fair—there was not the ugliest woman in the country who was too ugly for him, and with his round, rosy cheeks, merry eyes, broad shoulders and stout legs he could do what he would), then cock-fighting, dog-fighting, football, bear-baiting, rat-hunting, witch-hunting, all kinds of sport (he was himself not a bad sportsman with the staff and cudgel, and boxing and running and swimming), then every kind of a horse, then young David, for whom he cared, perhaps, more than for any other single human being, but not for him very deeply, only lazily and with easy good-nature. He was from the South, and had, as yet, no good word for this northern country.

He grumbled as they made their way into the dusky yard. 'Pox on it,' he said, 'I'll pepper my own legs with shot, but I thought his honour would give us another hour's quiet and plenty. What's he want riding on to-night for? There's but few like the master for a restless spirit. . . . I'd match that white dog in the kitchen there,' he went on irrelevantly, 'for a hundred guineas against the grey bitch the master had in Doncaster. There's a dog. You could see he never blinked a bird in his life. And you needn't tell master I was kissing Jenny neither! They all say their name's Jenny—'

'I shall not tell him,' said David proudly.

'How many miles is it from this Borrowdale to Keswick?' asked Benjamin.

'Around seven, I fancy,' said David.

Benjamin nodded his head but said nothing. 'It's a little inn as you might say, this,' he remarked. 'Small beside the south-country inns. Not much business in this little town. Kendal's the way the business runs. Not but there won't be some sport in Borrowdale. I may be a poor man and not bred for writing and accounts, but I know a dog when I see one.'

David missed many more of his remarks. For one thing Benjamin was always talking, not like the other man Nathaniel, who was a little spare fellow, very silent and grim, and anyone who was often with Nathaniel must accustom himself to think his own thoughts while Benjamin chattered. Besides this, David again was in his dream state. As he stood in the yard listening to the horses striking the cobbles, hearing the curses of the hostlers, smelling the hay and straw, catching the sharp cold of the breeze about his face, he seemed to move, not on his own feet, but through the air, alighting here and there and then up again, softly, breezily like the wind.

Thus dreaming he found himself standing with the others at the inn door. Father Roche was there, and Alice Press, his father, mother, uncle, aunt, and his sisters--all dreamy and wavering together. A crowd had collected to watch their departure. A great wind was hurrying through the sky above the black gables and chimneys, carrying soft grey clouds with it, and between the clouds once and again a burning star stared and vanished. The horses were stamping and pulling at the heads. Everything was ready for this last ride.

In the doorway stood the stout host of the inn, bowing as Francis Herries very grandly thanked him for his courtesy. Uncle Pomfret laughed and shouted. Then, as it seemed, a moment later one of life's great happinesses had occurred, for David was sitting a horse in front of his father. He had expected that he would be in front of Nathaniel, because all the way from Kendal he had been with his father, and surely such luck would not come to him twice. But here he was pressed against his father's body, and he could feel the movement of his thighs and above his head the throb of his heart, and in his face the wind was beating like a whip.

They were off, trotting over the cobbles, the horse slipping now and then in the mud or refuse, his father stiffening as he pulled at the reins, and at their side seen dimly his mother, pillion behind Father Roche with Mary in her lap, Alice Press with Deborah pillion behind Benjamin, the rest duskily in the rear.

The little town was very still; a light glimmered here and there through a shutter, a watchman going from his warm room, perhaps, to his night-duty passed them swinging his lamp, a chair in which a lady highly muffled could just be seen went swiftly with its bearers round the corner. They turned out of the square to the left, and the clatter that they made as they swept round the corner drew some heads to the window and an aproned man with a candle in his hand to the doorway. Then as they began to clear the town another thing occurred. David was aware that certain figures were running at their side and a man on a little nag was keeping pace with them. The same thing had happened to them on their way to Kendal, when a number of farmers and others had gone with their coach. That had been because of footpads, and now this must be for the same reason.

That made his heart beat faster. They were passing out of the guarded town and were running into dangerous country, dangerous country that, although he did not know it, was to be his country for many a year. He had perhaps some sense of it there under the biting wind, for he shivered a little and drew closer to his father.

They pulled up a little hill and were aware now at once of the open country, for the road beneath them was treacherous. The horses began to walk, and even so they slipped and stumbled in the mud. In the centre the path (it was little more than a path) was hard and well-trodden but on either side a quagmire. There was a faint silver misty light in the sky, but this shifted and trembled with the driving clouds. On the left of them there were thick trees, but on the right the landscape sloped to the mere, and in front of them were black shadows that waited like watchers for their coming, and these, David knew, were the mountains. He was aware then of a further thing, that his father was drunk. Not bestially drunk. Not ferociously drunk. Happily drunk. His body closed a little about his son as he sang softly the children's game:

> 'Lady Queen Anne who sits in her stand,
> And a pair of green gloves upon her hand,
> As white as a lily, as fair as a swan,
> The fairest lady in a' the land.
> Come smell my lily, come smell my rose,
> Which of my maidens do you choose?
> I choose you one, and I choose you all,
> And I pray, Miss Jenny, yield up the ball.
> The ball is mine and none of yours.
> Go to the woods and gather flowers;
> Cats and kittens hide within;
> But all young ladies walk out and in.'

David knew the words very well, because, although this was a girls' game, he had played it to please his sisters. His father repeated again:

'And I pray, Miss Jenny, yield up the ball--And I pray, Miss Jenny, yield up the ball.'

Why had he chosen the name Jenny? Was not that the name by which Benjamin had called the kitchen-maid? Did they, as Benjamin had said, always cry Jenny for a name? His father swayed slightly as he sang, but the horse seemed to understand. In any case they were going slow enough. No harm could come. A little man trotting at their side called up to them:

'I have a fiddle with me, your honour, and will play to you by your fire.'

And Francis Herries answered him happily: 'I'll swear you have a fiddle and know how to play on it too.' Then he began to talk very pleasantly to his young son. The path now was bending down until it almost touched the mere, and David could hear the little waves, driven by the wind, slapping the shore and rippling away again into space.

All his life he was to remember that moment; the clap of the horses' hoofs on the path, the slap and ripple of the water, the little panting breaths of the man running beside them, the warmth and intimacy of his father's body, the dark woods above them, the black hills in front of them, the fiercely moving sky, and the gentle good-humoured voice in his ear.

'And so, David, we are passing into the perilous country where the savages live, where there is only hay to eat and dirty water to drink, where it rains for a hundred days. Dost thou think there will be bears there, David, my son?'

'I don't know, father. I hope so,' said David.

'Bears of one family or another there will be, and snakes in the grass and peacocks on the garden wall. Is it not as though we were escaping? Escaping from what, think you?'

'We are not escaping,' answered David proudly. His voice came in little jolts. They were now on harder ground and were moving more swiftly. 'You would never run away.'

'No, would I not? Art thou so sure, little son? I have run from the lions in my time and then again I have braved them. But this is the most perilous adventure of all. We will not come from this save with our naked skins; and if I am hard pressed will you always stay by me, David?'

'Always,' said David, nodding his head. 'I could never be frightened an you were there.'

'Couldst thou not, couldst thou not, my son? Although the she- devil with the silver hams and the glassy tongue came to down us both?'

'I'm afeared of no woman,' David answered, but the trees now were gathering about him very darkly, and it was cold. In spite of himself he shivered a little.

His father laughed, bent forward and touched ever so lightly with his lips the boy's neck.

'So we are together, side by side, whatever the peril--for ever?'

David straightened his back. 'Yes, sir,' he answered proudly.

'"Twas a maid in the inn said her name was Jenny when I kissed her,' his father said, 'though she's no maid any more. Not by my doing, I had no time to test her virtue. Eh, little son?'

David understood this only vaguely. 'I don't like women,' he said.

'Not your sister Deborah?' His father laughed softly, deeply, as though he were thinking of other things.

'I love Deborah,' David answered.

'And your Aunt Jannice?'

But David did not reply. He could not. He was fast asleep, leaning back against his father's breast.

He woke again with a start to see that all the horses were at a standstill and were gathered about a small stone bridge. At that same moment, as though it had been arranged, a round moon, cherry- coloured, broke out from shadowy banks of cloud.

She stared down at them, and at once, as it seemed in his sleepy half-wakened state to David, the clouds fled away; she sailed gloriously in the sky of shining light scattered with stars. The world around them was like a world seen through glass, pale and unreal, with the trees and hills of ebony sharpness. A hamlet was clustered beyond the bridge and the river, which was running full and throwing up, under the moon, little white waves alive and dancing.

After a consultation they moved on upwards over a little hill with hills on their left side and the flooded gleaming river on their right. It was all very quiet and still. The storm had altogether died away. No one spoke, and the only sound was the hoofs of the horses, now soft, now sharp. The scene was now to David, who had only all his life seen flat and shallow country, incredibly wonderful.

They were passing through a gateway of high rock into a little valley, still as a man's hand and bleached under the moon, but guarded by a ring of mountains that seemed to David gigantic. The moonlight made them larger and marked the shadows and lines of rock like bands of jagged iron. In colour they were black against the soft lighted sky and the myriads of silver stars. A little wind, not sharp and cold as it had been before, but gentle and mild, whispered across the valley.

As they advanced, the only live things in all the world, it seemed that in a moment someone must break the strange moonlit silence with a cry: 'Ahoy! ahoy! who comes to meet us?'

But not even an owl hooted from the listening trees. After a while one mountain detached himself from the skies, coming towards them-- large, sprawling, very dark and solid, with a ragged edge. To the left of this mountain there was a straight thin ledge like a tight-rope, and on the right a very beautiful cluster of hills, in shape like the grouped petals of an opening flower.

Then quite suddenly they stopped. 'That is the house on the left of us,' someone said. It was the first voice for half an hour, and the hills seemed to repeat: 'Yes, that is the house.' The horses trotted over soft, rather boggy, grass, up a little hill, through a thick group of trees, and at once they were all outside a rough stone wall that guarded a ragged, grass-grown courtyard. David looked at the house and was sadly disappointed. Under the black hills it seemed so very small, and in the white moonlight so cold and desolate. It appeared to be two houses: on the right it was high, with a gabled roof and thin latticed windows; then it dropped suddenly to a low rough-seeming building with shaggy farm byres at its hinder end. He noticed, especially, the windows of the higher house, because there were two little attic windows like eyebrows, and he could see, because the moonlight made everything so clear, that the door of this house had handsome carving. But the other building was low and shabby and forsaken.

While they waited at the gate three dogs came out furiously barking, and directly they were followed by a broad thick-set man, walking clumsily, who hurried down to meet them.

Then a light was in the doorway, but still the house watched, cold, desolate, under the moon, with no greeting for them.

'So--we are home,' he heard his father murmur.

Then he felt himself picked up in his father's strong arms, lifted, then carried across the courtyard.

His father set him down, and he ran over the threshold of the doorway. The hall where he stood was flooded with moonlight, and opposite him were two shining suits of armour. People were moving and talking behind him, but he did not hear them.

He was first in the house. As he stood there in the moonlight he, who had been asleep so long, was suddenly awake.

And he made his compact with the house.

THE MOUNTAIN

Charles Francis Herries woke when the light of the fine new day was throwing silver shadows across the misty fields. Pushing back the creaking diamond-paned window, standing there in his purple bed-gown he looked down on the courtyard, the thick clustered yews that guarded, as though with fingers on their lips, the house, the ragged stone wall, then, beyond, the river, the thatched roofs of the nearest yeoman's farm, the fields and the dark sombre hills.

He drew a deep breath, flung off the bed-gown and stood there naked. He did not feel the cold, nor the sharp crisped air; he was at that time impervious to all physical pain and discomfort, a magnificent creature in all bodily force and feeling. He stared out, then looked back into the little, thin, low-ceilinged room. It was furnished scarcely at all--only a narrow truckle-bed on which he and his son had been sleeping--David, his flushed cheek against his arm, still lay there soaked in sleep--a big carved chest with the date 1652 roughly cut upon it, a mirror on the chest, and against the farther wall some old green tapestry (very faded) that flapped and rustled now in the breeze from the open window. There was one high-backed and clumsy chair, and into this his clothes had been carelessly flung. David's little things, carefully folded, were on the top of the chest.

He felt his body, punching it here and there, pinching it, kicking out a leg, stretching an arm. He might have been proud that he was so handsome and in such splendid health--such marvellous health indeed, considering the life that for ten years now he had led. But he was scornful of that as he was of everything else. What good had his beauty, health, strength brought him? Not so much good as that silver moon setting now in a pale rosy sky beyond the latticed window.

He stood there, the breeze blowing on his bare back and thighs, looking down on his little son. Here, too, he was scornful. His young son loved him, but would he love him as the years passed and he grew to realise his father? Would there not develop in him that same withdrawal that seemed to come to every human creature after a short contact with him--yes, even to so poor a thing as Alice Press, who was already beginning to look at him with that strange, surmising glance? David at present trusted and adored him, and in the

centre of Herries' universal scorn, scorn of himself, of all human beings, of the round world and all that moved in it, there stayed this pleasure and pride that his young son so thought of him. That he could neither deny nor reject. But for how long was it to remain? Would he take any steps to retain it? He knew himself too well to fancy that he would.

He turned again to look out of the window on to the scene that was to be his now, he was determined, for evermore. Whatever came of this step that he had taken, whatever misery, ruin, disgrace, he would hold by it. It was final. Only thirty years of age, he yet seemed to see far, far into the future, and something told him that at the very last these dark hills would encircle him.

The hill that chiefly his window faced seemed especially to tell him this. The houses of this time in this country were not built that their tenants might look out on beautiful views, but rather for safety and shelter, tucked tight in under the hill, guarded by heavy yews.

Beyond the fields, in far distance, this humped, lumpish hill, Glaramara, sprawled in the early morning light. Herries knew well its name. For so long as he could remember he had known precisely how this house must stand, and all its history. In 1565, the year following the founding of the Company of Mines Royal, Sir Francis Herries, his great-great-grandfather, had come from his house Seddon, north of Carlisle, in part charge of the 'Almaynes,' the foreign miners, and built him a little house here, called it Herries, and, at last, liking it and the country, had lived in it altogether, giving up Seddon to his younger brother.

In all his young days at Seddon, Francis had heard of Herries, the strange house in the strange country, shut in under the mountains behind rocky barriers, cut off from all the world. His grandfather, Robert Herries, had tried for a while to live in it, but it had been too isolated for him. That, too, his father Matthew had found, and had moved back to Seddon, and after this the old house had been held by a yeoman, Satterthwaite, farm-buildings had been added to it, and much of the older house had been allowed to fall into ruin.

When Francis' elder brother, Pomfret, had made a fortune in speculation (this largely by chance, because Pomfret was no brilliant financier) he had built him his house in Keswick, caring nothing for Herries, which, although so near to him, seemed yet at the very world's end.

Satterthwaite, a clever yeoman above the abilities of his fellows, had done well for himself, and built a farm-house over towards Threlkeld. It was then, after some years of desolate neglect, that Herries had been suggested to Francis by his brother, and, driven both by his romantic love for the notion of it and by his own desperate circumstances, he had accepted with an eagerness that had amazed the unimaginative Pomfret. Yes, an eagerness that was amazing even to himself. What was it that had driven him? That part of him that loved to be alone, that loved to brood and dream and enfold about him, ever closer and closer, his melancholy and dark superstition and defiant hatred of the world. That part of him, too, that felt, as neither Pomfret nor Harcourt, his brothers, felt, his passionate pride in his family. Why that pride? God only knew. There was no reason for it. The Herries men had never done great deeds nor supplied to the world famous figures. For hundreds of years they had been drunken, robbing Border freebooters; only, in Elizabeth's time, his great-great-grandfather, Francis, having some good fortune at the Court, had pushed up a little the family fortunes. That Francis had been a hard-headed fellow, a flatterer, a time-server, a sycophant, but not ungenerous if he got his way, and no fool at any time. Elizabeth had a fancy for him, would have kept him with her, and was none so well pleased when, quite eagerly, he accepted the opportunity of surveying the foreign miners who were sent to Keswick.

Something hurried him thither, that odd strain that was for ever cropping up in every Herries generation, the strain of the dreamer, the romanticist, the sigher for what was not, the rebel against facts; and in that old Elizabethan Herries this romantic dreaming went ill enough with hardness, his pushing ambitions, his desire for wealth.

Between the two stools of temperament he fell to the ground, as many another Herries had done before him. This land in Borrowdale caught his fancy; he stayed on and on there, losing at length his interest in the mines, mooning, a dirty unlaced old man, behind the rocks that bounded that valley, keeping company with the yeomen, pursuing their daughters, drinking, riding, dicing--dying at last in his old tumble-down house, a little soiled rat of a man with ale dribbling at his ragged beard.

That was great-great-grandfather Herries. The place had done something to him, and Francis Herries, gazing now out of his window, thought it an odd fancy that this same sprawling hill, Glaramara, had looked across into that old man's eyes, seeing them grow ever more bleary, more dim, more obstinately sodden.

And so it might be with him! He had come even as that old man had come, in the vigour of his prime and strength, and he had in him those same things--that longing for what was not, dream of Paradise round the corner, belief in a life that could never be. And in him also, riding him full strength, were lechery and drunkenness, lasciviousness and cruelty.

As he stood there, idly gazing, he had a passionate family feeling. Not for individuals. He hated Pomfret, despised Harcourt, cared nothing for his cousins, the children of his uncle Robert, who lived London way, nor for his other two cousins, Humphrey and Maurice Cards and their children, Dorothy, Jeremy, and Henry. Humphrey Cards, a man a good deal the elder of Francis, lived now at Seddon and was said to be a tight-lipped Quaker. Francis had never seen the Cards brothers; they inhabited London when he, as a boy, lived at Seddon, but Pomfret knew them and despised them both.

No, there was not one of the family for whom Francis cared a rap, neither agricultural Pomfret and his yellow-faced wife, nor bachelor Harcourt, there on the edge of that dirty sea-coast at Ravenglass, nor the purse-proud Kensington children of Uncle Robert with their family coach and fine Queen Anne house and garden, nor Humphrey at Seddon, nor ship-owning Maurice (his eyes, they said, so deeply stuck into his business that he could see nothing else) down at Portsmouth--not for a single one of them had he a warm feeling or a kindly thought--they were all rogues and fools together--and yet here he was, new-come to this tumbled old ruin, gazing out on a couple of shabby hills and some grass-greasy fields, and his heart was swelling at the thought of Herries and of the Herries men and women before them, the Scotch and English blood that had gone to the making of them, the English soil that had seen the breeding of them.

He felt suddenly the cold, and with a shiver pulled to the window and took on his bed-gown again.

There was a pump in the yard behind the house--he could hear the handle going; he would go and soak his head under it. He pulled on a pair of breeches, thrust his feet into some slippers, and then softly, lest he should wake his son, stole out.

The morning was deepening now, but the small heavily paned windows let in little light.

The part of the old house that remained had not been ill designed, the rooms lofty and the staircase wide enough for two to go abreast, still something of a wonder in Queen Anne's day and exceedingly unaccustomed in Elizabeth's.

This old house was of two floors, a most unusual thing in that country, the court-room, the dining-hall, the withdrawing-room leading one from the other. Out of the court-room a stair led to a loft that held the three bedrooms, two very small (in one of them he had slept last night with David, in the other Alice Press with the two little girls), and the other larger, containing a grand bed, and in this his wife was still sleeping; Father Roche had a small room below.

On the ground floor there was the entrance-hall and the kitchen, and on to the kitchen abutted the farm-buildings rented by Satterthwaite. These were a diminutive example of the yeoman's dwelling. This building was slated, the ridge made of what were known as 'wrestlers,' slates notched so as to interlock. The rest was primitive enough, the upper floor open to the oaken beams, an oak partition portioning off the sleeping-place for master and mistress.

Below was the house-place, the parlour and the kitchen. A man and his wife called Wilson had been caring for the house ever since the Herries family had forsaken it.

Coming down the rickety stair from the loft in the dim light, Francis Herries could see at once that their care had been neither vigilant nor arduous.

He stood in the dining-hall and looked about him. In that dim air without a sound in the world it seemed forlorn and desolate enough.

At the withdrawing-room end there was a raised dais, and at the court-room end, opposite the dais, some high oak screens, intricately carved.

Along one wall hung a fine spread of tapestry, fresh and living still, worked in colours of red, brown, amber, dark purple, its subject a hunting-scene, so handsomely wrought that all the wall seemed alive with straining hounds and noble horses, huntsmen winding their horns, and for their background dark hills and clustering trees.

This was a fine piece, and Herries, looking at it, wondered that it should be so well preserved. For the rest the hall was furnished barely--one long oak table, some stiff-backed chairs, a carved chest, and a portrait hanging above the dais.

It was this portrait that drew now Herries' attention. In the dim light it seemed marvellously alive. He did not question but that it was the portrait of old great-great-grandfather Herries himself. It had been undoubtedly painted after his coming to Herries, possibly by some wandering artist who had strayed into these wilds or by some London friend passing through Kendal on his way to Scotland--whoever had executed it, he was, in that wavering light, alive and dominating. An old man, his face wrinkled and seamed, his head poked forward out of some dark furs, his eyes dimmed, half closed, and one thin hand stretching forward out of the picture, as though to seize some prize or arrest some attention.

What Francis Herries felt, looking at it, was that there was here an odd resemblance to himself. Was it in the eyes? How could that be when his own were so bright and eager? Or the mouth? But this mouth was puffed and seemed as you looked at it to tremble. Or the skinny neck between the furs? Or the grasping hand? He looked at it, nodded his head as though the sight of it had decided some problem for him, and passed on down the stairs, through the shabby little entrance-hall into the open.

Behind the house he found an old-fashioned pump, and leaning against the wall, scratching his head and yawning, was Benjamin.

By the side of the pump was a wooden bucket. He signed to Benjamin to come and help him, stripped (this was the blind side of the house, and in any case he did not care who might see him). Benjamin splashed him. The water was ice-cold. He pulled on his breeches again, bid Benjamin rub his chest and back. He was in a splendid glow.

Over the low wall he could see the lights of the sky clustering about Glaramara's shoulders. Long swaths of yellow lay across the pale ivory, and the edge of the hills rippled with fire. A bird sang, a little uncertainly, from

the yews, and in the fresh stillness other birds could be heard beating their way through the shining air.

Benjamin, his mouth open, stared at his master, waiting for orders.

'Strip, you devil,' Francis Herries said, laughing. 'You are sodden with sleep.' Benjamin stripped at once, and his plump, stout body began to shiver and quake as the cold air caught his flesh. Francis laughed, then filled the bucket and splashed the water over the man, who did not, however, flinch, but stood there, shaking, but at attention.

'I will repay your courtesy,' Francis said, and seizing him, rubbed his naked body with a ferocious vigour. Then, giving him a kick with his soft slippers, cuffed him on the cheek and bid him put on his clothes.

'How does this place seem to you, Benjamin?'

Benjamin, pulling up his breeches, answered:

'We shall come to a handsome knowledge of one another's customs, hidden here from the world--but 'tis a good place for horses.'

Francis Herries looked about him. 'I haven't seen so clear a water nor smelt so fresh an air for years. But you can leave me when you will. I'll have no man stay who's a grumbler.'

'If I would leave you, master,' Benjamin answered with that odd, half-sulky, half-humorous speech that was so especially his, 'I'd have left you long ago. There's been often reason enough.'

'Why do you stay then?' asked Herries.

Benjamin, rubbing his wet head, answered: 'I can't tell. There's no reason for why I do things.' He paused, then added: 'Where you are, master, there's food and dogs and horses. Day come, day go, life is the same anywhere in the world, I fancy.'

'And when I beat you?'

'All men are beaten,' answered Benjamin, shuffling inside his clothes. 'I'd sooner be beaten by you than another.' He added, looking about him at the hills as though he were seeing them for the first time--' The fellow in the house tells me there's fine bull-baiting, wrestling and other games round these parts. Life's not over for us yet, master,' and, as he shuffled off with his fat walloping walk he grinned at Herries, showing himself half servant, half friend; half hireling, to be kicked, beaten, abused; half equal, knowing secrets and sharing confidences that must breed equal contact.

As he turned to go back into the house Herries saw, looking at him from the corner of the house-wall, an old, bent, infinitely aged woman. She had long, white, ragged hair, and a thin, yellow face. She stood without moving, looking at him.

'Who's that?' he asked Benjamin.

'The house-man's mother.'

The old woman raised her hand as though to feel the wind, then disappeared.

He went into the house to see his wife. The bedroom was dark. He pulled back the curtains and then stood by the window looking across at her. That was a fine bed in which she was lying, the curtains of faded crimson velvet, the woodwork splendidly carved. Crimson velvet, torn and shabby, was tacked also on to some of the panelling of the walls. There was a portrait of a young lady in a green dress and a white ruff over the fireplace.

His wife was yet sleeping. He came to the bed and stood there watching. There was something pathetic in poor Margaret Herries as she lay there, happy for a while at least in dreamless slumber. All the anxieties, woes and bewildered distresses that attacked, so increasingly, her waking life were for the moment stilled.

She looked a fool as she slept. She was a fool, she would always be one, but there was something gentle, kindly, appealing in her stout characterless features. And it might be that there was more character there than anyone, herself most certainly, at this time knew.

Maybe Herries, as he looked at her, felt something of this. Drawing his purple gown closely around him, he gazed at her, lost in his own disappointed ironical thoughts.

Why in folly's name had he ever married her? They had been young enough, he eighteen, she seventeen. They had been idiots enough, he vain beyond all vanity, she adoring beyond all conceivable adoration; she had been pretty, innocent and wealthy. Her father, Ephraim Harden, a very successful City merchant, had died a year before their meeting, her mother being already long-time dead. She was an only child and sent to an aunt in Carlisle on a holiday. They had met at a Carlisle ball, he handsome, without a penny, loathing the dull life at Seddon, where he hung on because he had no means wherewith to live in any other more lively place.

Seddon was still his brother Pomfret's at that time, and Francis and his brother Harcourt were permitted to remain there on a kind of tolerating sufferance. How he had hated that place with its dull grey walls, its poverty and greasy indolence. You might say that this place, Herries, to which he had now come was dull and grey enough, but, from the first moment seen on that moonlit night, he had thrilled to it. It had touched, and he knew this absolutely, some deep fundamental chord in him.

But Seddon and brother Harcourt! Harcourt with his thin, shanky frame, peering eyes and most exasperating cough, his passionate absorption in his books, so that he was only happy when they were piled high around him, sending up their dusty thick smell on every side of him. Harcourt who, in his twenties, had been a gay spark in London, an acquaintance of Swift and Addison and Steele, who had helped in the exposure of the great Psalmanazar, been present at the trial of John Tutchin, and even spent an evening with the infamous Mrs. Manley of the New Atalantis!

But as Harcourt had grown, his zeal for letters had grown with him; he had abandoned the town, buried himself in Seddon with his books, and then, at Francis' marriage, taken himself to the sea-coast, near Ravenglass, where he lived, a contented hermit.

It had not been altogether Francis' desire for money that had driven him into marriage with Margaret Harden. His motives were never unmixed in anything that he did, always there was nobility with his greed, tenderness with his cruelty, humour with his pessimism. He cared for her prettiness and innocence. He might have had her without the marriage ceremony, her body and her money too, she adoring him so that from the first moment she could deny him nothing, and he did not.

Nor was it only his weariness with Seddon. From the first he had realised that it was likely that Margaret Harden would weary him more than ever Seddon had done. He had felt a tenderness (which he might now allow was principally a weak sentiment) for this lonely orphaned girl, tied, until some man should carry her away, to the strings of a dumpy, frowzy aunt whose only interest was in cards and the scandals of the country town.

He had been stung to the venture also by the sharp pleasures of rivalry. The neighbouring squires, the sparks of the little town, even some of the graver, more aged officers of the garrison, had seen in Miss Harden's pretty face and splendid fortune an exciting prize. But from the first moment of Francis Herries' appearance there had been no chance for any other. He had been for her, poor silly fool, the god of all her dreams and maiden longings.

Yes, she had been cheated as vilely as he--nay, in the issue of it, much more vilely. She was no judge of men, poor thing, and had thought him as noble in character as he was handsome in person. The aunt, tired swiftly of the burden of this innocent girl for whom cards were too intricate a pleasure and scandal too distressing a pastime, was delighted to have her off her hands.

Herries had, indeed, considered the thing at some surprising length for a boy so young, but even at that age he had no illusions about himself, knew himself very well for what he was. But he wanted the money, her face pleased him, he had a certain kindness for her, and so the thing had been.

Looking down at her now he could not believe that, so short a while back, she had been that pretty, slender girl. Marriage had at least agreed so far with her that, in the very first year, she had begun to thicken. The three children that had come to her (the only happiness the poor lady had known) had not assisted her beauty; you could not believe that now she was but twenty-nine years of age.

And he would swear that all their quarrels and distress had not been his fault alone. She had never tried at all to grow to his taste and wishes; she had developed in nothing during the twelve years of their life together. She had no curiosity, no inquisitiveness, no sensitiveness, no humour--only sentiment, a liking for good food, a weak indulgence of the children and an infinite capacity for tears. Unfortunately all his ill-temper, his infidelities, his squandering of her fortune had not caused her to love him less; rather she adored him more to-day than when she had married him. Even this last insult, of carrying Alice Press to this place with them, had not stirred her resentment.

It was that above all that irked him. Although he had tried again and again to kill it, he had deep shame at his treatment of her--a shame that never drove him to better behaviour, but that for ever irritated and vexed him. Had she abused him, sworn at him, there would have been some reason for him to despise himself less, but this submission to his unkindness made him, when he was conscious of it, hate her for his reproach of himself.

Not one of his mistresses had ever been anything to him, and Alice Press the least of all. He had taken them in a kind of impatient scorn of their eagerness. What did it matter, one thing more or less, since all had gone so ill?

She was stirring. She raised her arm, let it fall again, sighed in her half-sleep, sighed again and woke. Seeing him, she gave a little cry. He must have looked wild enough standing there in the half-light, his shaven head with its short, bristling hairs, his chest showing bare through the lapels of the bed-gown.

'Francis!' she said, and smiled that trusting, half-deprecating, appealing smile that he so thoroughly detested.

'It is a fair morning,' he answered, 'and time you were about.'

'I know.' She raised herself, putting her hand modestly over her breasts. 'I was dreaming. I dreamt that my aunt Hattie was here again and her dog Pompey, and that she was giving it chocolate.'

'Thank God,' he answered grimly, 'that the reality is more gracious. You are at Herries, and the cesspool below this window is in full odour, and there is a witch in the house.'

'A witch?' she cried, alarmed. She was crammed with superstitions, old wives' tales of warlocks and broomsticks, prophecies and magic spells.

'A witch. I saw her but now alight on her broomstick, scratch a flea from her ear and whisper with her familiar hedgehog.'

Margaret Herries smiled that nervous smile with which she always greeted his pleasantries, not knowing whether he were in jest or earnest; whichever way her conclusion went she was always wrong.

Now she thought that he was jesting and tittered. Also she was but half awake and could not see his face clearly in the half-light. He came nearer to the bed and bent over her. He was moved by one of those sudden and to himself most exasperating impulses of compassion.

'You had best stay where you are,' he said. 'The last week has been exhausting enough for a hide-bound alligator.' He smiled, sat down on the high bed's edge and touched her hand.

'Lie here, and the woman shall bring you some food.'

Margaret was awake enough now. Any kindness from this adored husband set her heart wildly beating, her cheeks flushing, her tongue dry in her mouth.

'If you think it wise--' she stammered. She had a desperate impulse to press his hand, even to put her arm up, pull his head towards her and embrace him, but she knew by bitter experience how dangerous those actions would be. Her hand lay pulsing in his.

'Margaret,' he said, 'if you find that I have done you wrong to bring you here, if you cannot endure the remoteness of the place and the savagery of the inhabitants, you must go for intervals of every year to some town. York is not so far--even Scotland. There is Carlisle . . .' He broke off, remembering certain old scenes in Carlisle.

'And you shall take the children with you. Only you shall not keep David too long. I have done wrong to bring you to this forsaken country.'

The flush yet on her cheeks, she answered:

'Whilst you care to have me here, Francis, I care to stay.'

It was the most aggravating thing that she could have said. It called up in its train a thousand stupidities, placidities, nervousnesses, follies that had, in their time, driven him crazy with irritation. Never a mind of her own, always this maddening acquiescence and sentimental fear of him.

He drew his hand away.

'The rocks that hem us in are not more implacable than your amiability, my dear. I remember that your aunt, prophesying (how truly!) our wedded bliss, said that you had a nature, mild, trustful and clinging. With what knowledge of human character she spoke! Cards and the frailties of her neighbours yielded her human wisdom. Then you shall not go--you shall stay and love and cherish your husband, caring nothing for the odour of the cesspool, the machinations of the household witch, the rustic brutalities of the neighbouring yeomen! I will see that some food comes to you.'

He got up from the bed with that abrupt, impatient movement that she knew so well. She recognised, poor lady, that she had already lost her momentary advantage, how she could not tell.

She looked at him, loving his every feature, then said:

'Yes, Francis, I thank you.'

She was an exasperating woman. As he went from her room he felt that he did not care how unhappy she might be in this desolation to which she had come. She might make friends with the pigs for all that he cared, and good luck to her. And she was but twenty-nine and growing fatter with every hour! Was ever man so cursed?

And yet once again, as, later in the day, he rode out on his black horse, Mameluke, he was affected by his compassion. He had escaped them all; he had not stayed for the meal which now that it was past three o'clock would soon be on the table. He must be alone and facing his own strange thoughts.

At first, as Mameluke trotted quietly along the rough path, he did not notice the country round him. He saw for a while nothing but himself and he saw himself in a mirror, his features caricatured by the distorting glass, his body lengthened to a hideous leanness, his forehead peaked to a white cone-shaped dome. Well, thus he was-- and thus. This sudden quiet, this hush of the fields and sharp, refreshing coldness of the air seemed to bring the issue of the situation before him in sharper form than it had taken for many months.

The issue was this--that unlike all the men and women that he knew, the squires and boon-companions of Doncaster, the women, loose and otherwise--alone of them all he longed for something that he could not touch. He had a vision, a vision that took, when he was with Father Roche, a religious shape, when he was with Alice Press a fleshly, with little David a pride in family, with the beauty of landscape and fine stuffs and rare pieces a poetic, but all these only forms and vestures of a vision that was none of them, but of which thing all were. And with this vision there was the actuality of his life--his life wasteful, idle, cruel, sensual, selfish, vain. He did not, as he rode now on Mameluke, turn his head away from a single aspect of it.

He had once dreamed a dream. It was some five years back at the end of a race-meeting in Doncaster. He had stayed in an inn in the town for the night. Drinking heavily, he was yet not drunk as were his companions. He had shared a room with one of them, pulled his boots off him, flung him down on his bed, where he lay loathsomely snoring. Himself he had gone to the window, pushed it open and stared out on a splendid night flaming with stars.

And there, it had seemed, propped forward on a little chair, his head almost through the window (so that he might easily have tumbled on to the cobbles below), he had fallen asleep. Had he slept or no? How many times since then he had asked himself that question! In any case, through his dream he had seemed to hear the sounds of the night. The slow, lazy call of the watchman, the love duet of cats, the rumbling of a country cart on distant cobbles, the snores of his neighbour, these had been behind and through his dream.

His eyes open, he would have sworn, staring into the stars he had beheld a vision. He was in a region of vast, peaked, icy mountains. Their fierce and lonely purity, as silver-pointed they broke the dark sky, caused him to cry out with wonder. The sky was dark; the mountains glittering white, they ringed round a small mere or tarn, black as steel in shadow.

There was absolute silence in this world. Then as he looked he saw a great white horse, glorious beyond any ever beheld by man, come, tossing his great white mane, to the edge of the mere. He hesitated, lifting his noble head as though listening, then plunged in. He swam superbly, tossing his mane, and Francis could see silver drops glistening in the icy air. He swam to the farther edge; and then Francis was seized with an agonising terror lest he should not be able to climb, out of the mere, up the icy sides of the cliff that ran sheer into the water. That moment of suspense was fearful and compounded of a great love for the splendid horse, a great tenderness, a great reverence and an anguish of apprehension.

Then, tossing his mane once more, the beautiful horse mounted out of the mere, strode superbly across the ice and vanished. Then, again, there was great loneliness.

Waking from this dream and staring back at the little room, stuffy and smelling of drink, the floor tumbled with clothes, his thick, open-mouthed, red-faced companion, he knew an instant of acute, terrible disappointment. For a moment he thought that he would throw himself out, end everything, so as to kill the disappointment; and perhaps it would have been as well had he done so, because, since then, that disappointment had been always with him.

The more that he had hated the noise and filth and confusion of his life in Doncaster, the more he had plunged into it. Now, as he slowly passed along the darkening path that was leading him gradually into the shadow of the hills, he saw one incident after another of the Doncaster life, stretching out their hands to him as though they were figures that kept pace with him. The foolish duel with young Soltery, a quarrel about nothing when they were both drunk, Soltery who was terrified, and then more terrified yet that he should seem terrified. He saw young Soltery's eyes now, as they faced one another in the early morning light on the fields outside Doncaster, eyes of a frightened, bewildered child--and he had shot away one of young Soltery's ears, so that he would be disfigured for life.

Or fat Maitchison the surgeon with his brilliance, his obscenity, his odd beliefs in magic and other humbug--that foolish night in Maitchison's rooms when they had defied the Devil, smashed the mirror, stripped Maitchison's mistress naked and painted her yellow. He could see now the room, furniture overturned, the glass of the big mirror scattered over the floor, and fat Maitchison with gusts of drunken laughter painting the naked back of the swearing girl. . . . And the sudden opening of the door, the breeze blowing in from the street, the candles going out, and someone crying that bats were hanging on the ceiling. . . .

Yes, the races, the cock-fights, the bull and bear baiting, the debauchery and smells and noise--a roaring in his ears, a stink at his nostrils, and always in his heart this longing for the icy peaks of his dream, the black tarn, the splendid horse with the snow-white mane.

He was young, and should do something with his talents. That he was talented he knew. They all told him so. He had infinite courage, splendid physique, an interest and curiosity in many things. What should it be? Which way should he go? And meanwhile the years slipped by, and now, obeying some mad, mysterious impulse, he had cut himself right off, hidden himself among the savages.

Was he to laze here, slouching about, making familiars of the yeomen, riding with them, chaffing their wives, perhaps seducing their daughters?

For what had he come here? He only knew that already the place was working into his veins--the silence, the air with an off-scent of ice in it, the hills that were perhaps only little hills and yet had so strong a power-- witchcraft hills, hiding in their corners and wrinkles magic and spells. As he rode on, the outside world was beginning to slip ever farther and farther away from him. His was the only figure in the landscape; the whole country, as the afternoon shadows lengthened, seemed naked. Above the clustered group of mountains at the end of the valley a little minaret of pale grey clouds was forming, one cloud stealing upon another as though with some quiet purpose; a purple shadow fell over these hills as though a cloak had been suddenly dropped over them.

He saw on his right then a group of buildings.

His empty world was in a moment peopled with life. Near him at the fork of the road was a small crowd gathered about a pedlar who had slung his box off his neck and rested it on a flat stone. Herries drew nearer and, sitting his horse, watched quietly.

The scene that had been a moment before wild and haunted was now absolutely domestic. Three healthy, red-faced girls stood there, their arms about one another's necks, laughing and giggling, one stout yeoman, some farm boys, and a little man, tow-coloured like a wisp of hay, who, by his drab dress, should be one of those itinerant parsons and schoolmen who went from house to house in country districts, taking odd services of a Sunday and teaching the children.

The pedlar was a tall, thin scarecrow of a man, having on his head a peaked faded purple hat, and round his neck some of the coloured ribbons that he was for selling. By his speech, which was cultivated, he was no native, and, indeed, with his sharp nose and bright eyes he seemed a rascal of unusual intelligence.

The little scene was charming in its peace and security. Some cattle were being brought across the long field, two dogs at their heels; a voice calling in rising and falling cadence sounded, as it seemed, from the hills, and in the foreground there was the sharp humorous note of the pedlar, the laughter of the girls and young men and, once and again, the deep Cumbrian accents of the yeoman.

At first they had not noticed Herries, but when one of the girls, looking up, gave a cry of surprise, they were not disturbed, and after a glance went on with their private affairs, governed by a certain dignity and independence of their own.

The pedlar, however, was aware of him although he continued his patter. He had 'Fine thread satins both striped and plain, Persia nets, anterines, silks for scarves and hoods, shalloons, druggets, and some Scotch plaids.' On his tray there were some pieces of fine bone lace, Chinese boxes, necklaces, gold rings set with vermilions, several gold buttons, and red watch bottles ribbed with gold--or he said it was gold. And some books. Chapbooks and calendars, Poor Robin, The Ladies' Diary, some old sheets of the London Gazette, and some bound volumes of Plays. These things of fashion looked strange in the open fields before the little country group, who fingered and laughed and fingered again. The jewellery, indeed, had a false air, but the ribbons and lace were pretty, and above, Herries must fancy, the purses of the locals. Herries noticed, too, that the pedlar did not seem too intent upon his sales or purchases, and that his sharp eyes went everywhere, and especially to Herries and his horse.

He thought to himself that this would not be the last time that he would see that pedlar.

The shadows of the hills now covered the valley; the light flashed palely above Glaramara and then fell. Herries turned his horse towards home. As he moved away the little tow-haired parson detached himself from the others and approached him.

His long parson's coat was green with age, shabby and stained, and his breeches were tied about the knees with string, his bony fingers purple with cold, his nose red; but he had about him a very evident dignity. He bowed, but not subserviently.

'It has been a fine afternoon,' he said, keeping pace with Mameluke's gentle step.

Herries, impressionable ever to the moment's atmosphere, his spirit touched now by some quiet and happiness, answered, as he could when he so pleased, with charm and courtesy.

'The day falls quickly in these valleys.'

'And the light is for ever changing,' the little clergyman answered with pleased eagerness. 'You are newly arrived here, sir?'

'But yesterday.'

'I know everyone in this neighbourhood--man, woman and child. You are the gentleman who has come to Herries by Rosthwaite?'

'I am,' answered Herries.

'There has been much interest in your coming, sir. It will be the wish of everyone that you will find it pleasant here, and stay with us.'

'Do you also belong here?' asked Herries.

'I do the Lord's will and go whither He sends me. For some years now I have taught the children of these villages, assisted at services, done what the Lord has bidden me.'

'You are not a native of Cumberland then?'

'No, sir, I am from the South. I was born in Bideford in Devon. For many years I was chaplain to the Earl of Petersham.'

'Why, then, have you come here? It must seem a severe exile to you.'

'The Lord spoke to me in a dream and ordered me to go North. I was to walk forward until I saw a naked man tied to a tree, and in that place to abide and do His will.'

'Where saw you your naked man?'

'After many months, begging and preaching my way through the country, I came at last to the village of Grange on a summer evening. And above the river where the bridge is, I saw a man naked and bound with ropes to a tree. The men of the village were throwing stones at him: he was near death. He had been caught robbing a yeoman of the place of two hens. I urged them to release him, the Lord prevailed, and afterward I lodged in his house. I lodge there yet.'

'And what, then, do you teach the children?' asked Herries, entertained by this simplicity.

'The Lord's Word, the Catechism, and, when they wish it, Greek and Latin.'

'You have no family?'

'My wife is with God.'

The dark was falling more swiftly now, and it was difficult to see the path. Herries jumped off his horse and walked beside the clergyman.

'What is your name?' he asked him.

'Robert Finch.'

'How shall I like this place? It is cut off from the world.'

There was a sudden odd note of scorn in the little man's voice as he answered:

'It IS the world, sir. Here within these hills, in this space of ground is all the world. I thought while I was with my lord Petersham that the world was there, but in every village through which I have passed since then I have found the complete world—all anger and vanity and covetousness and lust, yes, and all charity and goodness and sweetness of soul. But most of all, here in this valley, I have found the whole world. Lives are lived here completely without any thought of the countries more distant. The mountains close us in. You will find everything here, sir. God and the Devil both walk on these fields.'

'And if I believe neither in God nor the Devil?'

'You are a young man for such confident disbelief. God was speaking to me now, and has told me that you will find everything that you need for the growth of your soul here in this valley. You have come to your own place, sir. You are young and strong, but the day will come when you will remember my words.'

Herries looked back down the path. In the dusk he could see it point like a pale, crooked finger straight at the heavy black hump of Glaramara that was dark against lighter dark. Again he felt ice in the air and shivered.

'They are little hills by your foreign sort,' he said, 'and yet they impress.'

The small voice beside him answered:

'They are the loveliest hills in all God's world.' Then it continued, taking another tone, very mild and a little anxious: 'You have children, sir?'

'Three,' answered Herries.

'If you were in need—' he hesitated. 'My Greek and Latin are good, and I have authority with children. If I could serve you—'

Herries laughed.

'I must warn you,' he said, 'there is a priest in the house.'

There was a pause while the wind, rising, began to blow fiercely, swaying the branches and turning the dead leaves about their feet.

The voice began again: 'He instructs your children?'

'A little.'

'Your own religion—?'

'Nay, I am no Catholic. I have told you I have no religion. How think you, Mr. Finch? In this drunken, debauched world what is your God engaged upon? He is busy elsewhere improving some other planet.'

'Christ died upon the Cross suffering a worse bewilderment.'

Herries laughed again.

'Well, you shall try your luck upon them. But we are a wild house, Mr. Finch, and may, in this desolate country, become yet wilder.'

They had come to the gate that led to Herries.' They paused. To Francis' surprise the little man laid his hand on his arm.

'You are young, sir. I have ten years' advantage of you. I fancy your wildness does not frighten me.'

'On thy head be it then,' Herries cried, as he led Mameluke up the path. The way here was very rough, and he began to curse as he hit the loose stones, plunged into mud, fearing that his horse might stumble and damage his knees. His mood was changing with the swiftness that belonged to his moods. Oddly enough his mind had turned to Father Roche. The little clergyman had reminded him. Why was he burdened with this priest and the risks and penalties connected with his presence? It was true that just now there was a lull in the Catholic agitation, but it might burst out again at any instant. Herries did not doubt but that Roche was busied in a thousand intrigues both political and religious, and they were intrigues with which he had no sort of sympathy. Jacobitism made no appeal to him—he hated the French influence behind it. He wanted no king for England who would be ruled by French money and ambition. Moreover, he took in any case but little interest in politics, and had no romantic feeling for that world. Nor had the Catholic religion attraction for him; he despised what seemed to him its mummery, the child's play, as he saw it, of its tinkling bells and scented air. But Roche's influence over him was strong and subtle. Ever since his first meeting with the man some five years before, it had persisted. And for what reason? Roche was stern, unsympathetic to all Herries' pleasures, showed no warmth of feeling to Herries (no warmth of feeling to anyone, indeed, save little David), used Herries' house quite openly for his own private purposes, had carried on in Doncaster, as Herries well knew, a network of plans and plots with an odd audacity and defiance. When he spoke intimately with Herries it was to rebuke him. And yet Herries would endure from him things that from another he would most furiously resent. Where lay Roche's power? In the continued suggestion that he held somewhere a solution for Herries' sickness of soul? Not in any dogma lay that solution, but in something deeper, something far more profound. . . .

But (and here the house with its lighted windows loomed suddenly up before him as though it had been pushed up through the rough ground) was the priest to remain? Why? He and Alice Press should both be sent packing. One must start fair in this new place--and for a moment before he pushed back the heavy door he had a picture before his eyes of the country group in the fading afternoon light, the coloured scene, the quiet and the animals and the purple-shaded hills. Here in this good land there should be no place for the priest and the woman. . . . Here in this good land--and a moment later he was caught into one of his dark, bestial, frantic rages.

He had left his horse outside the door and, calling Benjamin, pressed up the staircase to the little tapestried dining-hall. A high, thick-clustered candelabrum was burning on the table, all the candles blowing in the winds that came from the floor-cracks, the slits in wall, roof and window.

At the table his wife was seated crying. Alice Press, very gay in a crimson gown, was turning scornfully away from her, even as he entered. The three children were playing together by the oak chest. Over all the room there was a frantic disorder. Some of the boxes, brought by the pack-horses the night before, were there, and scattered about were suits, gowns, china, stuffs, linen, children's toys.

A strange thick scent of burning wax, damp straw and odours from the neighbouring cesspool lay heavy about the candle-shine. He had ordered that the boxes were not to be touched until the morrow, when he could supervise the opening of them.

By whom had he been disobeyed? Both women began to chatter, his wife wailing, Alice Press loud and shrill and defiant. The little girls began to cry. At that moment Benjamin, a foolish smile on his chubby face, appeared at the stair-head.

Francis Herries caught him by the neck, then, raising the riding-whip that was still in his hand, cried:

'What said I to these boxes? Hast thou no wit, thou lubber-pated bastard?'

Benjamin shouted something; everyone began to call aloud at once. The room, the house, the world was filled with shouting and stink and a raging anger.

To come thus, from an afternoon so quiet and promising, to this vileness! Anger boiled in his heart, choking him. He had Benjamin's coat off his back, struck the bare flesh again and again, lashed him about the head, the legs, the thighs, and when suddenly the man hung his head and began to droop in his arms he let fall his whip and began to beat him with his hands, letting him at last drop, a huddled, half-naked heap.

The man had fainted. Raising Benjamin's head, Herries was suddenly remembering how that morning in the fresh air by the pump he had rubbed in friendliness the man's body while the birds wheeled through the sky.

A sickness caught him at the heart. He told David to run for some water, but before the boy had returned the man was reviving. He was lying back, his head on his master's knee. He looked up, then, flicking his eyelids, said:

'It was not by my word, master, that the boxes were opened.'

Clumsily he rose to his feet; he caught his coat to his bare chest--

'I'll be rubbing the horse down,' he said, and stumbled down the staircase.

FAMILY

Pomfret Herries lived at this time in one of the most beautiful houses in Keswick. It was beautiful, not by his own taste or fancy, but because he wished to have a better house than any one of his neighbours.

This has always been a habit with certain of the Herries. Desiring this, he chose for architect that strange, saturnine hermit, old John Westaway, known in Keswick for a madman and the best architect in the North, a desperate traveller who knew Italy as you might know Skiddaw, who had been invited again and again to London, but preferred to live in his little house above the river, seeing no one, liking no one, buried in his books and art treasures. All over the North Westaway's fame ran. He was an old man now, had been, it was said, in his youth the friend and intimate of Chesterman and Van der Vaart and Vanbrugh, a curmudgeon, a surly bachelor, in league, some whispered, with the Devil himself, pottering about that house, with its pictures and statuary, and his dark Italian servant--a devil, but the finest architect, it might be, in England.

He had made Pomfret pay for his fancy, and when it was done Pomfret had grumbled so that you might hear him from John o' Groat's to Land's End--but it was a beautiful house. People came from Kendal and Carlisle and Penrith to look at it, so that at the last Pomfret and his wife had grown proud of it and spoke of it as entirely their doing.

In fine proportion, its roof covered with red tiles, the wrought ironwork across its front showing like lace against the stone, the house was oblong without gables. The windows were for their period most modern. They were sash windows, a great rarity, and they were beautifully spaced. The doorway had fluted columns and over it there was a charming and delicate fanlight.

The house was outside the town near to Crosthwaite Church, and the gardens ran down to the weeds and rushes of the lake-end. The garden held lime trees and the lawn was bordered with tubs of orange and bay trees. There was a little terrace and a rosy wall of red brick, and beyond the formal garden a meadow, the lake and the rising hills. To the right some greenhouses, a flower garden and a kitchen garden.

Inside, the house was wide, spacious and full of light. First a pillared hall, on the right the parlour, on the left a fine, wide staircase opening into a splendid saloon. Beyond the parlour a large bedroom leading to a greenhouse. On the upper floor other bedrooms.

Pomfret's chief pride was the saloon, the decoration of which Westaway had designed and executed--the subject was Paris awarding the apple. Lady Herries had been disturbed by the naked goddesses until it was seen that no one else minded.

In this fine house Pomfret inhabited only one room, a dusky apartment crowded with guns, stuffed animals and fishing-rods. Here he drank merrily with his friends.

Lady Herries' home was the parlour, where she read her medicine books, scolded the maids, suffered in a bitter silence that ancient lady, Pomfret's aunt, fed a screaming macaw, and gave her neighbours tea and chocolate. The three children had their own room far away at the top of the house.

There was a great array of domestics, from Mrs. Bellamy the housekeeper to little Peter the black boy, who had been purchased in London, shivered in the cold, and stole everything that he, with safety, might.

Mrs. Bellamy was of the family of Mrs. Slipslop, and made all the mischief both in the house and in the neighbourhood that time and talents permitted her.

They could scarcely be called a united family, for they were never together. Pomfret diced, drank, rode, hunted with his masculine friends, who liked his company because he was stupid enough for them to rob him at will. Jannice, his wife, bullied him when she was with him, forgot him when she was not. She loved him only when he was ill, and this was often enough, for his intemperate habits and his swinish feeding caused him constant attacks of biliousness and vertigo. There was nothing that Jannice Herries loved like a medical treatise; her familiar and, after Mrs. Bellamy, most constant companion was old Dr. Ellis, who would discuss with her by the hour the whole works of that excellent practical physician, Dr. Thomas Sydenham!

She experimented on her staff, her family and any neighbours who would permit her. Little Peter, who was sick every other day from stealing confitures from the store-room, was her most unhappy patient. And yet, of course, this is not all that can be said about Pomfret and his lady. At heart they were kindly and well-dispositioned. Only they had no imagination, and had been covered with a thin skin of wealth that, like a rash upon their souls, discomforted them, made them uneasy, suspicious, unhappily proud.

Pomfret loved his children, but did not know how to approach them. He cuffed them and spoiled them and cuffed them again. He was generous-natured and desired that his friends should be happy, but he suspected that they laughed at him, and so was pompous and grand when he wished to be easy and familiar.

His money he had made, as he well knew, from his obedience to the advice of a London friend, Hartwell, who, at a certain moment, had directed his affairs. Although his companions robbed him he had wisdom sufficient to leave his affairs in Hartwell's hands. He pretended to a knowledge of commerce and exchange; it was, as he knew in his heart, a bare pretence. He did nothing well, rode badly, shot badly, fished badly. He knew moments of great unhappiness.

Jannice Herries was also without imagination. She was acrimonious and bitter, but she knew that this was not her real life. Somewhere real feeling was hidden, but day succeeded day and nothing was done. She knew that she was unpopular among the ladies of Keswick, but she swallowed every compliment that Mrs. Bellamy gave her, and at the end was more lonely than before.

After her interest in medicine her most active passion was her hatred for Pomfret's Aunt Maria, that very ancient lady, who, born in 1645 and for a time in the fashionable world, was now a hideous remnant of a dead and musty past. She longed for this old lady to die, and would have poisoned her ere this, but alone of the household Aunt Maria refused all of her niece's drugs. She was now eighty-five years of age.

Finally with both Pomfret and his lady there remained a constant uneasiness about their wealth. It had come so oddly, without any true justification. It might go as oddly again. They had witnessed in the last twenty years a series of financial panics. Now with the abominable French ready for any villainy, all this new-fangled independence of servants and labourers, who knew what the next event might be? The Catholics were listening at every window. Why, here was Francis Herries coming to live in the neighbourhood and bringing with him quite openly a rascally priest. Although Walpole and the Whigs were in, who knew how strong was their power?

Jannice Herries' favourite remark to Mrs. Bellamy was: 'Things are not as they were.'

To which Mrs. Bellamy with a shudder would reply: 'No, my lady. If I know my own mind there was never a truer word spoken.'

'And what will you do, Bellamy, if your master is ruined?'

'Heaven strike me dead if I ever desert you, my lady! Marry come up, don't I know a virtuous place when I see one?'

But Bellamy had been lining her pocket for many a year, and being Mrs. Bellamy only by courtesy had her eye on a handsome victualler in Kendal, whose hearth and home she proposed to encompass and govern on the first signs of distress in the Herries country.

The three children, Anabel, Raiseley and Judith, lived in their own world. They, like their father, were Herries of the unimaginative, matter-of-fact breed. They took things as they came, and each, in his or her own fashion, worked quietly and obstinately for personal profit. Anabel was good-natured, plump and easy. Raiseley was clever. It would not be true of him to say that he was without imagination, but it was imagination of an educational kind.

He was studious, priggish, aloof and cold, rarely roused to anger but unforgetful of the slightest injury. He had the wise, calculating side of the Herries blood; he was studious, honest to chilliness, and despised both his father and his mother. Judith would be beautiful; she was dark and slender and already cherished her beauty as her most important asset.

These three were all typical Herries on the stony side of the family character. They saw everything in front of their noses and nothing beyond. They did not mind in the least their social isolation. They might contemn one another, but united at once in condemnation of all other children.

They were waiting now in their high, chilly room for the visit that their cousin in Borrowdale was to pay them. Only the little boy, they understood, was coming with his father and mother. They had already gathered from the conversation of their elders that Uncle Francis was a disgrace.

Of the three of them at this time it may be said that Raiseley and Judith held out no hope of later humanity; for Anabel, because of her good-nature and a certain carelessness that went with it, there were possibilities.

On this afternoon the three children were in their chill room quietly busy. Judith was seated motionless in a high chair, a collar round her neck, a board tied to her back. This was for her figure. She was watching the grandfather clock in the corner. Five minutes of her daily half-hour remained. This half-hour was valued greatly by her, because she knew that this discipline was for the benefit of her beauty. She was only nine years of age, but had already a grave and considered air. Anabel, who was thirteen, was curled up in the window-seat looking at the pictures of some chap-books, Babes in the Wood, Bluebeard, Little Tom Thumb. But she was not reading. She knew the old stories by heart. She was wondering what her little cousin would be like.

She, unlike her brother and sister, was sometimes lonely. She confessed it to no one, but she loved parties and fun. Maybe this little boy would be agreeable.

Raiseley was yawning over his Virgil. Mr. Montgomery, who came every day to teach him Latin and Greek, had but just now gone.

'Jam pater Aeneas . . .' murmured Raiseley, and fingered a little box in which he had a cocoon concealed. He hid this from his parents and Mr. Montgomery, because they would disapprove if they knew. But soon the cocoon would be liberated. No one told him any of the things that he wanted to know about animals, about the stars. Now, when he thought of these things, a new expression came into his eyes. He was suddenly alive with a questioning, investigating alertness. His cold, pale, pointed features gained an interesting sharpness. The book fell from his hand. There were many things that he would know one day; they should not stop him pursuing his knowledge. Mr. Montgomery with his sing-song voice, his perpetual cold at the nose, his eagerness to please, how Raiseley despised him!

He would like to see Mr. Montgomery whipped as little Peter was whipped, or standing as the man they had seen one day in the pillory in the market, his face smeared with the mud and the yellow of the eggs that people had thrown at him. And, as he thought of these things, his face achieved an added sharpness, coldly, intellectually speculative--'Jam pater Aeneas. . . .'

He looked at the little pile of books beside him--A Guide to the English Tongue, by Thomas Dyche, schoolmaster in London; Paul's Scholars' Copy-Book, by John Raynor; The Use of the Globes.

He did not look at them resentfully. He would extract from them everything that they had to give him.

'Judith,' he said, 'I should know more than Mr. Montgomery knows in a year or two. I would think it fine to see him in the pillory as a week back we saw that man.'

Judith, motionless, her eyes on the clock, answered: 'We are to go downstairs when our uncle and aunt come. I am to wear the grey- blue.'

Anabel, from the window, said: 'I like David for a boy's name.'

'I heard them say,' went on Raiseley, 'that Uncle Francis is always drunken and beats Aunt Margaret.'

'But he is very handsome,' said Judith. 'He was wearing such fine clothes the other day that father was shabby beside him.'

'Fine clothes,' said Raiseley scornfully, 'and they living in mud and dirt up to their elbows! They say that Borrowdale is full of witches and giants--wolves too. I would like mightily to see a wolf. I shall ask Uncle Francis to take me.'

The clock struck the half-hour. Judith very carefully separated herself from her board and collar. At that same moment the door opened. They were told that it was time for them to dress.

David and his mother had indeed already arrived.

Poor Margaret Herries had been for weeks dreading this visit. It was now a month since they had come to Herries, and the weather had been so terrible that the ride to Keswick had been impossible. It had rained and rained; not as it rained in Doncaster, with gusts and flurries and pauses and whispering, but in a drenching flood, falling from the grey, lowering sky like sheets of steel.

And the mountains had crept closer and closer, and the cold stolen into the very webbing of the sheets, the torn tapestries beating against the wall, and the mice boldly running for comfort to the peat fire. A horrible month it had been, but with all the courage at her command she had faced the rain, the isolation, her loathing for Alice Press, gathered her children round her as she might and made what she could out of the situation.

Oddly enough she had not been unhappy. Francis had been ever close at hand. He did not go off for nights at a time as he had done at Doncaster. That might come later--but at present it was as though the place cast a spell upon him. He pottered about the house, rode out to Stye Head, walked up Glaramara and the neighbouring hills, wandered along the lake by Manesty and Cat Bells, made himself known to some of the neighbouring yeomen, was silent often enough, drunken at times, angry once and again, but on the whole more her companion than he had been since their first marriage year.

And so there had increased in her heart her ever-constant loyalty to him. What she had suffered watching the degradation of his reputation during these past years no one would ever know. She would never tell. Here it was as though he had begun a new life. Stories long commonplace round Doncaster would here not be known. He would start again, and she would do everything in her power to assist him. Only his brother's family could spoil this fair beginning; she had seen and heard enough already to feel that Pomfret and his wife were Francis' detractors and would from the first take care to be dissociated from any scandal.

She was as fiercely prepared to fight her brother-and sister-in-law as any lioness in defence of her cubs, but her trouble was that she was not a lioness. She was a coward; while she was riding pillion behind her husband and her son, she was aware that at the first sight of Jannice in her own domain she would lose courage, she would tremble, she would show faint-heartedness. Francis had things that he must do in Keswick. He would come later to his brother's house to fetch her. She must face Pomfret and Jannice alone.

So she stood, David at her side, in the little hall with its rounded pillars, its stone floor in black and white squares, its fine picture of an Italian scene, with dim greys and purple for colour, hanging on the right of the staircase.

They were ushered into the parlour. It was lit with candles, and David had never seen such a room. But before he could examine the room he must be startled by the persons in it, by his aunt Jannice, who was dressed superbly in a high wig mounted over a cushion and decorated with roses and daisies, her hoop spread about her, the outer skirt of crimson velvet and the front of her dress white and silver. On one brown cheek she wore a black patch. She was grander than any lady that he had ever seen; no one who came to their house in Doncaster had dressed like that. Young though he was, he realised that her thin, meagre figure and brown complexion ill suited such finery.

But his childish attention was soon drawn from his aunt to the terrific figure who sat in a high chair under the window. This was his great-aunt Maria.

He would never have believed, had he not seen it with his own eyes, that any person could be so old and yet live. Her wig of a bright brown colour was arranged in a fashion of fifty years ago, falling about her strange mask of a powdered, painted face in long curled ringlets. Over one eye was a black patch. Her green bodice was peaked, and her full, open sleeves were caught together with jewelled clasps. Her wide skirt was of purple satin. Her fingers, so thin that they were like the ivory sticks of a fan, were loaded with jewels.

On her lap was a small King Charles spaniel.

She appeared a painted image. Except for her one visible eye nothing in her face moved. David was a polite little boy, but again and again he had to stare. Here was a portent, a revelation in his young life.

The little black boy was standing behind Lady Herries' chair, and as soon as greetings had been exchanged they all sat down. The little black boy handed chocolate; a bright purple macaw in a gilt cage by the window screamed.

For a little while there was a terrible silence. The room was very hot; there was a large log fire. The sky beyond the window was bright with a silver glow.

When the talk had started David could look more easily about him.

He was indeed enchanted with the softness and beauty of everything. Beyond the wide window he could see the trim hedges, the paved path, the fountain with a strange stone bird, long-necked and violent-beaked, rising out of it, and beyond the fountain the line of trees guarding the waters of the lake.

Within the room there were countless objects that he longed to examine more closely, a screen worked in gold thread, a silver casket, a clock with the sun, moon and stars on its face. But more than these, the terrible old woman with her strange ringlets, her painted face, the cascades of her bright purple dress, the sharp-pointed fingers weighted with flashing jewellery. . . .

'Indeed,' his aunt was saying, 'I wonder at Mr. Flammery. 'Tis a poor child that doesn't know its own father, and there's a multitude of his own poor children must be in a fine confusion.'

This puzzled David, who, looking first at his aunt and then at his flustered mother sweating in the face with the heat of the room and the agitation of this her first so important visit, wondered how it could be that any child should not know its own father. He of a certainty knew his well enough.

'Yes, indeed,' his aunt continued, looking, as he was even now old enough to discern, with an odd mixture of curiosity and contempt at his mother. 'You must be well aware, Margaret, of the world into which you have come. In winter I doubt that you'll be able to move a step. You live in the heart of savages, and when the lake is too wild for passage and the roads all of a muck to your armpits the civilised world will be as distant from you as the Indies.'

'I don't doubt,' said Margaret, flushing and perspiring the more, for she knew that it was at her own abandoned Francis that these remarks were made, 'but that the days will pass. There's sufficient to do about the house to take a month of winters. . . .'

David then was aware that his great-aunt's eye had turned in his direction. He was fixed by it as a rabbit by the eye of a snake. . . . It was as though he, sitting on the edge of his chair, and this very ancient lady, both of them motionless, were holding some strange secret communication. Then he was aware of something further--that his great-aunt was about to speak.

In an odd, cracked but exceedingly piercing tone she said: 'God save His Gracious Majesty.'

The worst had happened. The old woman was silent often enough for days together, and this was well, because she was a burning fanatical Jacobite. The terrors into which her dangerous political opinions had again and again plunged Pomfret and his wife were both ludicrous and tragic. Sometimes for weeks she kept to her room, and on every occasion that saw her enter that sanctuary everyone about her breathed the hope that it would be for the last time, but her powers of revival were incredible, and down once more she would come to sit and watch and await her awful moment.

She had been born on the 14th of June 1645, the day of the battle of Naseby, but her great days had been during the last years of Queen Anne, when she had known Godolphin and Marlborough and been received by Lady Masham, having her feet planted in both camps.

But she had been nevertheless, heart and soul, Jacobite, and, it was said, played some part in the intrigues of those last dramatic months. The Elector of Hanover had been for her the Devil himself, and when his cause had been definitely won she had retired from London, professed openly her Jacobite sentiments and chattered and prayed for the coming of the Day.

No one had much regarded her; she had lived in a small house in Winchester, until, her brain softening, Pomfret, driven by one of the kindest and gentlest impulses of his life, had given her shelter and protection.

How many thousands of times since then he had longed for her decease was a secret between himself and his Maker.

Now with terror and dismay Jannice Herries heard her speak. Here was their skeleton clattering straight out from the cupboard and before that fool Margaret Herries. But Margaret was too deeply buried in the warmth of her confusion to pay much regard. Only the little boy felt the power of those few cracked words; something spoke in his heart, some strange sympathy that he suddenly felt, to which he quite blindly and unknowingly responded. He was to remember at a later time this queer muffled moment.

The situation was immediately saved for Jannice Herries by the entrance of her children. The children had beautiful manners. Mrs. Bellamy in black silk, her hands folded across her stomach, stood behind them-- the boy bowed, the little girls curtsied. Anabel's eyes smiled at David. He was quick enough at once to perceive that the other girl was thinking of her own looks. She was like his own sister Mary in that.

And then the eyes of the two boys met, and they knew one another at once for foes. David had as friendly a heart as any boy in the kingdom, but he realised an enemy when he saw one. One straight look at Raiseley's cold reserve and proud consequence and something within him said: 'I hate my cousin.' Just as the cracked voice of the old woman speaking to him five minutes before out of an ancient past was to return to him with significance in years to come, so that first glance exchanged with Raiseley was to influence the Herries family fortunes for many future generations.

Looking at Anabel, David thought to himself: 'That's a friendly girl.' He was uncomfortable among these grown-up persons, and hoped that it would be suggested that he should go with his cousins to see the garden or their toys. He would like finely to inspect more closely that fountain of the beaked bird or to hunt among the reeds at the water's edge.

But no suggestion was made. He too was standing now, his hands stiffly at his side as his father had taught him. The room grew ever hotter and hotter, and with every moment he felt more indignantly Raiseley's scornful eyes upon him.

Margaret Herries must talk to her nephew and nieces. She was never at her ease with children.

'Fine children,' she said nervously to her sister-in-law, 'and seemingly in grand health.'

The word 'health' was the trumpet to sound the charge to Jannice Herries, who answered proudly: 'Fine and sound they are, sister. Six months last sennight Judith here was sorely threatened with the Falling Sickness--hast thou heard of the Antepileptic Crow, sister?'

'I fear not,' said Margaret timidly.

''Tis a perfect cure for the Falling Sickness. Judith was cured by the crow. Deplume and eviscerate a large crow, casting away its Feet and Bill; put into its Belly the Heart, Liver, Lungs, Bladder of the Gall, with Galangal and Aniseeds; bake it in a new Earthen Vessel well shut or closed in an Oven with Household Bread; after it is cooled, separate the Flesh from the Sides or Bones, and repeat this Operation of baking the second or third time, but taking great care that it may not be burnt, then reduce it into a fine powder.' She recited this in a high sing-song as though it were poetry, her eyes almost closed. Opening them she saw that Margaret was gazing at her with great humility and reverence. Maybe the woman was not such a fool after all. She would make, it might happen, something of a companion. A kindliness stole about Jannice Herries' heart. It would be something to have a friendly creature near her whom she could patronise and gratify and instruct. The days in truth were lonely enough. . . .

'You must come and see us at Herries,' Margaret went on to the children.

'Yes, ma'am,' Raiseley answered, gravely bowing. 'It is said that there are wolves in Borrowdale. I would gladly see a wolf.'

Margaret smiled timidly. 'David shall show you the wolves. He has been already in the mountains. Have you not, David?'

Judith, who, since the Falling Sickness had passed as a topic, felt perhaps that she was not receiving sufficient attention, smiled her prettiest smile, so that her aunt, thinking how beautiful a child she was, said, speaking directly to her:

'My little girls, Mary and Deborah, will wish to show you their toys and babies.'

'Yes, ma'am,' said Judith in her softest, gentlest voice, so that her aunt looking at her loved her.

Once more they were interrupted, and this time it was the two men of the family. David waited for his father's entrance. First there was Uncle Pomfret, red-faced, noisy, with his: 'Well, then-- here's all the family! Haste away! Haste away!' and then a sudden look of almost childish discomfort and unease. Quietly behind him David's father, kindly to-day and, for David, so handsome in his dark suit and lace ruffles that all the colour in the room went out before him, dimmed to abasement.

Yes, his father was in good humour to-day, coming forward and kissing the old lady's hand, saluting his sister-in-law's brown cheek, turning then to the children, pinching the cheeks of the girls, tapping Raiseley on his shoulder. . . . How proud of him David was and how ardently longing for the moment to come when he would catch that glance and, perhaps, that smile. But for a while he did not. His father paid him no attention. The parlour was overcrowded with figures and the sound of Uncle Pomfret's demonstrations. Now he was being jolly with his children: 'You will be the death of your poor father . . . I promised your mother to give up half the afternoon to your entertainment, and wasn't I to show you the best pack of dogs in England? But no, Mr. Montgomery don't allow. Pox on Mr. Montgomery--and here's your uncle and little cousin come to visit us--yes, and your aunt too. . . . Pleased to see you, sister . . . and there's no Mr. Montgomery to stop a family welcome, odrabbit it! I am determined upon your being good children now and welcoming your little cousin . . . fine boy, brother Francis. He shall come a-hunting. Canst ride, boy?'

'Yes, uncle,' said David, 'a little.'

'That's more than thy cousin Raiseley can do then. Put him on a horse and he's like the Witch of Endor on a broomstick. . . . Wilt thou learn to ride then, Raiseley, to please thy father?'

This public mockery was anguish to Raiseley, nor did he fail to ledger it in the account against his young cousin. But his pale face did not alter; no shadow of a change was upon it. Looking his father in the face, he answered steadily:

'I will learn, sir, an you wish it.'

'An I wish it!' His father broke into a roar of laughter--'Hark to that now! An I wish it! Have I wished, then, to have a milksop for a son? 'Tis all your Montgomerys and their Latin grammars that have spoilt thee, boy--Here,' catching David suddenly by his breeches and raising him in the air, 'here's the spit of a tree! Here's a lad knows a dog when he sees 'un, that I'll wager! Wilt come with thy uncle hunting, David?'

But he waited not for an answer. He was aware that his wife thought him foolish and noisy. He turned confusedly to chatter to his sister-in-law.

It was then that David had a word with his father. They were standing a little back from the others. 'David, you are to go now. Your mother will ride home with me. You will find Father Roche to the left along the road. He is waiting now at the turn to Crosthwaite Church. You will ride back with him.'

At once David obeyed. He turned, bowed to his great-aunt, kissed his aunt's hand, heard above his head the excuses for his departure, smiled at his girl cousins, exchanged one look with Raiseley and was gone.

How proud he was to be treated thus--as though he were already a man!

He pushed open the heavy house-door, stepped through the courtyard, between the high gates and into the dusky road. It was almost dark; shadows lay about the broad path and little winds ran whispering about his feet.

A great sense of adventure possessed him. Behind him was the lighted town, near him the warm house with its fires and talking company, and outside the house the garden with the bird fountain and all its ordered discipline running to the wild edge of the lake with the clustered reeds. Young though he was, he yet felt the humanity and safety of this world crowded with all its persons so diverse as the ancient lady and little Peter and Cousin Raiseley, his enemy. All this within firelit walls, but, outside, the long road running, as though on a secret purpose, below the mountain that seemed to him huge in the night air, Skiddaw; by now he knew its name. But here, also, there was a church, and men might ride with ease, and at short distance all the traffic of the town. But away from it the road ran on, curving at the lake's end, running up the hill, then above the lake's side until at last it reached that little bridge and the high rocks behind it that were the barrier of his own dark country. There was danger, there, romance and adventure. Cousin Raiseley had said that there were wolves there. He did not know how that might be, but a month's living there had shown him how strange and removed a world it was, and already it was beginning to pull at his boy's heart, so that he was ready to defend it and feel that he was citizen of it. Yes, he would know every tree, every rock, every corner of it before long; he would push his way into every one of the mysteries. . . .

He had been walking swiftly down the road, a little afraid, although he would not have owned it to anyone, of the sound of his own footsteps, when he saw at the parting of the two ways a horse and a figure standing beside it.

The figure came to meet him, and at first he did not recognise it, because Father Roche was dressed as an ordinary gentleman in plain riding clothes.

'Father Roche,' he whispered. He had not intended to whisper, but the silence and loneliness of the road commanded him.

He was taken up and in another moment was seated in the front of the saddle. They started off.

'Not Father Roche any more,' the figure behind him murmured. 'Mr. Roche . . . the times move, and we must move with them.'

His voice had to-night more than ever before the power to move David. He was himself already excited and stirred, and, as they moved over Derwent Hill, through the village of Portinscale and then up over Swinside Hill, with every step they seemed to be moving into some mysterious country, and it was Father Roche's power and spirit that was leading them. Was he then no longer a priest? Could you at one moment be a priest and then, at the next moment, not? Was it at his father's orders that he had ceased to be a priest? But for the moment he was too deeply excited by his own experiences. 'Uncle Pomfret's house is very grand. It is grander than ours at Doncaster. There is a garden with a fountain that is a bird's head, and a clock with the sun and moon on its face. My great-aunt Maria is a very old lady--she looks a hundred years. She has long hair falling about her face. My cousins were present, and my cousin Raiseley is very grave as though he thought well of himself. . . .' He paused, then added: 'We will fight one day. And I shall win.' His little back straightened and his short legs tightened about the horse's neck. 'Uncle Pomfret always speaks at the top of his voice. He lifted me by my breeches and said that I should go hunting with him. Will my father permit me, think you?'

'Yes, David, when you are older.'

David sighed. 'It is always when I am older. My cousin Raiseley asked whether there were wolves in Borrowdale. He said that he wished to see one, but I doubt it. I think he does not care for dogs and horses and wild animals.'

They were going more slowly now, climbing the hill. It was bitterly cold, even a little snow was falling, and a few stars were like points of ice in the sky. They were climbing to high ground. There were three paths on this farther side of the lake, but as Father Roche had been warned in Keswick only one was passable for a horse and that the highest.

'My great-aunt Maria,' David went on, drawing a little back on Father Roche for greater warmth, 'said once "God save His Gracious Majesty." Aunt Jannice was vexed, so that I knew that it could not be the King in London. It is forbidden, is it not, to speak of the other King in Rome?'

Father Roche drew the boy closer to him. The time had come, then, to speak. The boy was now of a sufficient age. For years now he had been waiting for this moment, and he was well pleased that it should be at this instant, cold and sharp under the winter night sky, with the world so silent on every side of them. It had been the lesson of his life that he should have no human passions, and he had learnt it well, but in spite of all his lessons human feeling had grown in his heart for this boy and this boy's father. There were many other plans and schemes in his life that went far beyond his momentary relations with the Herries family. He stayed with them only because it suited his larger purposes to do so, but growing up in his heart in these last years had been the longing to turn this boy on to his own paths. During these weeks since coming to Borrowdale David seemed to have grown in mind and perception. He was already wise in some things beyond his years.

'David, will you listen a little as we ride? I have wished for some time past to speak to you. You are of an age enough now to understand.'

David nodded his head proudly. The only sound in all the world was the clap-clap of the horse's hoofs on the frozen ground.

Father Roche went on: 'There was a King in England once who was a martyr. Wicked men in the malice of their hearts slew him, and so interfered with one of God's most holy laws--the Divine Right that He hath given to those whom He has appointed as His rulers on this earth. This martyr, King Charles of blessed memory, was, perhaps more than any other man on this earth, near in his sufferings to our Saviour Himself. When Christ suffered there was darkness over all the land, and so when King Charles was under trial there were mighty wonders in the sky. You have read of the centurion who was assured that He was the Son of God, and his servant was healed; so with the Blessed Martyr, one of his guards was driven by conviction of sin to repentance. Did they not part our Sovereign's garments among them? Even so have they taken his houses, his possessions, his very garments from our master. . . . And in his life, in his gentleness, his courtesy, his love of his fellow-men, did King Charles approach most closely that blessed prototype.'

Father Roche paused. The road ran now over Cat Bells and Brandelhow; from its bend the land dropped straight to the lake, which could be seen now like a dark mirror of jet below hills that were faintly silver. The horse's breath rose in front of them in clouds of steam; facing them was the hump, black as ebony, of the Castle Crag, and, more gently grey, the hills behind it. For young David, to whom this view was to become one of life's eternal symbols, he was to hear always, when he beheld it, the beautiful, melodious voice of the priest and to see again the scattered steely points of the stars in the velvet sky.

'His was an unrenounced right of sovereignty. None could take it from him. He had been placed there by God, and man had no voice in that choice and circumstance. He was murdered and betrayed by the sons of the Devil. . . .'

A thrill of sympathy touched David's heart. Oh, had he been there, he would have died for that King!

'Even as Christ did, so could he work miracles. Have you ever heard how, being taken by his captors through the town of Winchester, an innkeeper of that city, who was grievously ill and suffocating, flung himself on his knees before His Majesty, crying "God save the King!", and the King said: "Friend, God grant thee thy desire," and the tumours and sores disappeared, and the man was made whole? And the kerchiefs dipped in the King's blood after his death had also this miraculous property.

'His son had also this virtue, and, it is said, touched one hundred thousand persons to cure them. . . . Since this family appointed by God to rule over England have been in exile God's face has been turned away from us. Nothing is so sure and certain in this world as that our beloved country shall not again prosper until our rightful King returns to us. Do you understand what I have been saying to you, David?'

'Yes, sir,' answered David in an awed voice.

They clattered through the little village of Grange. Some woman came to a lighted door to watch them pass. Under the stone bridge the river, flooded with the recent rains, rushed to the lake. They turned into their valley under the dark rocks. 'The time may come, David, when every true man will be challenged. Under which King, God's or man's? What will thy answer be, boy?'

'Under God's King, sir,' answered David.

'Keep silence about what I have said even to your father, but talk to me when you have a mind. Wonder at nothing that you may see me do. I shall come and be gone again, but wherever I may be I shall know that I can trust thee. . . .'

'Yes, sir.'

'You will not be afraid if a day should come . . .'

'No, sir. Only my father . . .' It was not for him then to know how little in later harsh fact this picture of God's King would affect him.

'Your father is my friend. He knows me.'

'Yes, sir. . . . Will he, too, be ready when the day comes?'

Roche hesitated--

'Every true man who loves his God and his country will be ready.'

'Yes, sir,' answered David again, suddenly sleepy and very cold. Loyalties? He now had many. To his father, to Deborah, to this King in Rome. Life was beginning to be filled with great adventure. There was

his father in his dark suit with the silver cuffs, there was the old lady a thousand years old, Cousin Raiseley, whom he would one day fight, his uncle who would take him out hunting, the King in Rome who made people well by touching them, Father Roche who was now no more a priest, his mother whom he loved and Mrs. Press whom he hated, and the old woman in Herries who was a witch, and the hill with the caves, and the more distant hills, where one day he would make great discoveries.

They turned to the house, black and cold under the scattered stars. But it was home, and there would be fire and something to eat, and then falling asleep in the room where his father would afterwards come . . . and then the King in Rome . . .

He was shivering with cold when Father Roche lifted him down from the horse and carried him in.

THE DEVIL

David looked up at the woman whom he so thoroughly detested, with fearless eyes.

'I went out because I wanted.'

'Yes, and the muck and all you've got into,' she answered crossly. 'But it isn't for me to say, I've no authority. And the horses not returned yet from Keswick, and the hills darkening the whole place. I hate this house--from the first instant I set foot in it I've hated it. A nice, pretty kind of life for one who's young enough and handsome enough for a frolic or two.'

She swung the silver chain that lay about her neck and touched the crimson velvet of her sleeves.

'And you fast with the priest all the morning,' she continued, her sharp eyes darting about the shadowy room. 'What is it he must speak so long about with a child like you?'

'He teaches me Latin,' David answered quietly.

'Yes, and many another lesson, I'll swear,' she answered.

He could see that her ears were ever straining for a sound.

'Ugh!' she shivered, 'the rain's coming down again, and all the old tapestries flapping against the wall. It wasn't so in Doncaster, I can promise you, before your father engaged me.'

'No,' said David, hating her.

'No, indeed. There was music there and dancing and the Fair at midsummer and the Plays at Yule. But here . . .'

She broke off. She thought that she had caught the clap of the horses' hoofs on the ragged stones of the little court. She sprang to the darkening window, then turned impatiently back, caught the flickering taper and held it to the leaded pane. Once again she was disappointed. There were no horses there--only the tap of some branches against the wall and the seeping drip of the rain.

'Why did you come here?' asked David.

She struck her hand violently on the table--'Why? why? why?' she answered passionately. 'You are a child. How should you know? And yet--' She came over to him, caught him by the shoulders and stared into his eyes. 'You hate me, do you not? Young though you are, you know enough for that. You all hate me here and wish me gone. And most of all that priest--who has persuaded him against me.'

'He is not a priest now,' answered David. 'He is only Mr. Roche now.'

'No priest? Yes, that is fine talk. Once a priest always a priest. And where has he gone this afternoon, riding away to Keswick? Where is it that he goes for nights together?'

'I don't know,' answered David.

'I'll tell you more,' she continued. 'He can be in prison any day. There are the laws against the Catholics, and he serving Mass in that upper room. Have I no ears nor eyes? So he shall be in prison if he returns and I have my way.'

She stopped again to listen. The house was intensely silent. The two little girls were with their mother in her room. There could be heard even through the rain and the wind the noise of falling water, the swollen stream tumbling down the side of the hill at the house's back. She stood thinking, then came closer again to David. He moved as though he would shrink from her, then firmly stood his ground.

'David, do you not think you could speak to him, to your father? When nobody else is by--he listens to you. I have noticed that when no other can speak to him he can be patient with you. Ask him if he will not ride out with me for an hour--I would tell him certain things. For weeks now I have not been alone with him, and I shall go mad . . . this desire . . . this longing. . . .'

She broke off as though the words choked her, putting one hand to her throat and with the other gripping the boy's arm. David saw that she was in great suffering, and could have been sorry for her had he not hated her so. He remembered that night at the Keswick inn when his father had come in and kissed her. He hated that she should touch him, but he did not move.

'You must speak to him yourself,' he answered. 'My father, these past weeks, has had business in Keswick and in the country here.'

'Business in Keswick!' she answered scornfully, pushing him from her so that he almost fell. 'Fine business! Such as he had in Doncaster. Riding into Keswick to play at cards and look at the women, stumbling about in these mucky country paths to find a girl with bright eyes. . . .'

David cried: 'You shall not speak against my father. When he wishes to talk with you he will tell you. Yes, it is true that we all hate you here and wish you gone. My mother cries because of you. You struck Deborah when she had done no wrong. You should

return to Doncaster, where there are games and music. . . .'

He was trembling with rage and with a desire that in some way he might persuade her to go. Oh, if only she would go away. . . .

But already she had forgotten him. Her ears again had caught a sound, and this time she was not deceived.

The clatter of hoofs was on the stones of the court, and at the same instant Margaret Herries, the two little girls beside her, appeared, holding a light, at the stair's head.

'Is he come? Is he come?' she cried eagerly, and then started down the rickety stairway, moving heavily and awkwardly, the children close behind her.

The hall, that had been only a moment before so dark and drear with the faint light and old Herries sneering from the wall, was now all alive.

Francis Herries in his deep riding-coat, Wilson following him with candles, entered, and his wife and the children ran to him. Alice Press stayed in the dusk. They could see at once that he was in a good mood. He laughed as he saw them, caught Deborah and David to him, bent forward and kissed his wife.

'Yes, something to eat and drink. I'm parched and famished. The rain blew against us like the plague. I thought Mameluke would have fallen twice, and it was such thick darkness along Cat Bells that it was God's miracle we were not in the lake.' He pulled Deborah's hair. 'Thou knowest there's something here for thee and for Mary too--the other pocket for David. . . .' Laughing and shouting with excitement, they felt in the pockets and pulled out the bundles. For Deborah there was a 'baby' with bright flaxen hair and a dress of green silk, for Mary a toy tea-set, cups and saucers decorated with pink roses, and for David battledore and shuttlecock.

With every moment the room grew more lively. A big log-fire was leaping in the open fire-place. Wilson and his daughter were setting the table; Benjamin had come in (Nathaniel had left them at Martinmas), a bottle of wine in either hand, his round face smiling with the pleasantry of the familiar servant who knows that to-night he has nothing to fear from his master's temper. Only Alice Press stood back against the wall, without moving, her hand against her heart.

Francis Herries, his riding-coat flung into a chair, stood before the fire, his legs spread, warming his back.

'Dear brother Pomfret is to visit us tomorrow,' he said. 'He will condescend to take the journey. Keswick was a pool of muck; you couldn't stir for the mud. And so, Deb, you love your baby?'

Deborah was sitting on a stool at her mother's feet, hugging her doll. She was in an ecstasy of happiness, rocking the doll in her arms, then straightening it to smooth its stiff hair, her eyes shining, looking at her brother every once and again to see that he was sharing in her pleasure.

Francis Herries, looking out at them all, hummed in a half-whisper the children's song:

'Lady Queen Anne who sits in her stand,
And a pair of green gloves upon her hand,
As white as a lily, as fair as a swan,
The fairest lady in a' the land.'

To-night he was well content. The mood was upon him when everything seemed fair. It was good thus to come home to his own, to find the candles shining and his own things about him, and his children, whom he loved, longing for him. The devil of restlessness was not with him. That afternoon in Keswick he had won three fine bets at the cock-fighting. He had drunk just enough to make the world glow. Even Margaret, his wife, could seem, close to him, neither so stout nor so foolish. . . . Ah, if they would let him alone, his little pack of demons, he could make a fine thing of this life yet.

His eyes, roaming, found Alice Press, motionless against the wall. His voice changed.

'Have the babies been good?' he asked her.

She came forward into the candlelight.

'Well enough,' she answered, and turning sharply, left the room.

The food came in. The others had dined long ago, but they crowded about him as he ate, and Benjamin stood behind them, smiling beneficently, as though they were all his handiwork.

While he ate and drank he told them little things about his Keswick day--how they had been baiting a bull in the market-place and two dogs had been killed; how there had been a medicine man pulling out teeth, and he had pulled two wrong ones from an old woman, and she had demanded her money back, but he had not given it: the old woman's son had fought him and knocked his tub over; how he had had a talk with old Westaway, the architect of Uncle Pomfret's house, and what a strange old man he was and had been the world over and seen the Pope in Rome and the Czar of all the Russias, and spoke in a shrill piping voice, and trembled with anger, so they said, at the sight of a woman; how there was a little black boy for sale like the one Aunt Jannice had, and some splendid dogs, big and fierce, who would do finely for defending the house in the winter; how there had been in the market-square the day before a gathering of those strange people, the Quakers, and they had been set upon and two of them stripped naked and splashed with tar; how they told him that there was a band of robbers now in Wasdale that came down from Scafell and had murdered two shepherds in the last week; and there was a fine gathering of gentlemen for the cock-fight and he had not done so ill there. . . .

Here he broke off; he knew what Margaret thought of his cock- fighting--another evening he might have teased her and been pleased to see the fear come into her eyes, but not to-night. . . . He was young as David

to-night. He had David on his knee, his hand fingering his hair. His wife, Margaret, was praying: 'Oh, Lord, let this last awhile. Let this last awhile.'

After his supper they played Blind-man's Buff. Francis Herries' eyes were bound with the handkerchief. The children ran, screaming and laughing; Margaret herself played and ran into his arms, and once again-- after how many years--her husband had his arms about her, held her, kissed her cheek. It was David's turn to be blinded, and, as he stood in darkness, he could hear all the sounds-- the crack and tumble of the fire and the hiss of the falling ash, the rain against the window, the breathing of the people about him; and it seemed to him that all the room was lit with red light and old great-great-grandfather Herries came down from his picture-frame and ordered him to come to him. He ran forward; an instant of awful terror came to him. But all was well; it was into Benjamin's arms that he had run, and as he felt the stout, soft body with his hands he screamed with excited relief: 'It's Benjamin! It's Benjamin!'--then Benjamin was blind man.

After breakfast the whole world is filled with light. Everything moves together. Round Herries the entire universe centres itself, spreading out to endless distances that are mysteries--China, Pera, the kingdom of Samarcand--but pouring all its waters into this one deep purple pool--purple of Glaramara, purple of the shadows and eaves and door-post, purple of the feathers in the peacock fan carried by the Princess in Deb's chapbook, purple of the darker river shadows that lie beneath the spume and froth tumbling through Grange to the lake. Through the shadows of this purple February morning, David, standing at the road-bend, Deborah beside him, saw the moving of all the people around him--Alice Press yawning at the window, his father drinking his breakfast ale; Benjamin in the little court, his hand on Mameluke; his mother hearing Mary her morning prayer; the old witch grandmother Wilson silent against the wall, her white kerchief about her chin, leaning on her stick; Wilson himself moving to the cows; then, a little more distantly, Moorcross, the home of the statesman Peel--Peel, the tallest, stoutest man David had ever seen--famous for his wrestling, with a boy of David's own age, whom David would like to know; and beyond the Peels again, all Borrowdale, with the names that were becoming part of him, Rosthwaite and Stonethwaite, Seathwaite and Seatoller, and the hills, glittering on this lovely morning, Glaramara, Scafell, the Gavel; wolves, maybe, above Stye Head, and robbers, his father had said, in Wasdale, and fairies, gnomes, devils, witches. . . .

Deb's hot hand held his more tightly.

'What are you looking for, David?'

What was he looking for? He did not know.

But this was to be a day of days. His happiness last evening, the games, sleeping on the small pallet beside his father's bed and then waking to so wonderful a day! After all the rain and wind, this stillness and shining glitter, small fleecy clouds like puddings or puppies plump against the shadowed softness of the blue, the branch of no tree stirring, so clear that the crowing of a cock far away towards Seatoller could plainly be heard, but, as always here, the sound of running waters, now one, now two, now fast as though an urgent message had come to hasten, now slow with a lazy drawling sound. . . .

He knew that to-day he could have the small shaggy pony, Caesar, that his father had bought from Peel. It was a whole holiday. Mr. Finch would not appear. No one would care what he did nor where he went. He would like to ask the Peel boy to go with him, but he was shy, and the Peel boy spoke so odd a language and then, of course, had his work to do. . . .

At that instant, so miraculous is life, the Peel boy passed them. The Peel boy was bigger and stronger than David, very broad of the chest and thick of the leg; his eyes were blue and his hair very fair; his cheeks were rosy, and he whistled out of tune. He was whistling now, but when he saw Deborah and David he stopped. He paused and smiled.

'Good day,' said David, also smiling.

"Day,' said the boy, shuffling his feet. They grinned and said nothing.

'Have you a knife, please?' David asked.

'Aye.'

David did not need one, but when the large rough cutlass was put in his hand he chipped off the small branch of a tree.

'Thank you.' He tried again. "Tis a fine day.'

'Aye.'

'We have holiday.'

'Aye.'

'I shall ride Caesar to the valley end.'

'Aye.'

Then the Peel boy bobbed his head and went on down the path. He turned back.

'You may have t' knife,' he said.

'Oh, no, I thank you,' said David, very greatly touched. Then seeing disappointment--'Well--if you wish--'

He took the knife, and the Peel boy, delighted, started down the path again, whistling once more out of tune.

The day was well begun.

He walked slowly back to the house, his hand tight in Deb's. She asked: 'David, may I come with you on Caesar?'

'No,' he answered, 'I go alone.' He felt her hand give a little quiver--'Why, you are not afeared? I shall be back by dusk.'

She nodded her head bravely. 'I shall wash my new baby.' But she had something in her mind. She noticed so much more than Mary. She was exceedingly sensitive and would always be. She would always live alone, however many people were near her, and would give herself in passionate devotion to one or two, realising that it was the law of her life that she should give rather than receive.

Already, although she was only seven years of age, she knew of many little things in and around Herries that no one else had seen--the face of a woman, thin and sharp, carved on the oak chest in the dining-hall; a ruby ring that old great-great-grandfather Herries wore on his finger in the picture; the way that Alice Press had of looking scornfully at her finger-nails; the fashion that old Mrs. Wilson had of walking like a blind woman, her eyes tightly shut; the coarse crowing laugh of her grand-daughter--and she knew everything about David: the straightness of his back when he was standing waiting for something, how one leg would rub against the other when he began to be eager in talking about something; his smile, when one end of his mouth seemed to curl more than another; the roughness that a wind would make of his hair when he wore no cap, the beautiful coolness of his forehead when he let her put her hand on it. She did not know that she knew these things--she had as yet no self-consciousness.

The most common sensation for her would always be fear, and the constant duty of her life would be building up sufficient courage with which to meet it. Apprehension would attack her at every turn. It was as though she had three skins less than other folk. Even as a baby she had seen shadows in the room that no one else had seen, heard footsteps that no one else had heard. Things assumed significance for her beyond all fact and reason. There had been a tree in the Doncaster garden, stout in the trunk, thinly carved in its branches. How she had hated that tree, what terrors undefined it had brought to her, how, in all the other excitements of leaving Doncaster, this had been predominant--that she need never see that tree again!

And here at Herries already there were terrors. Alice Press and old Mrs. Wilson of course--these were natural alarms--but also the pump in the yard, the two suits of armour within the house-door that seemed to her to have faces, one white and one yellow, and the steps of someone walking on the floor of the parlour-loft when they were in the dining-hall.

All around her, everyone was insensitive. It was not a time when people noticed such things. There were witches and warlocks, fairies and gnomes, but they were real and active with persons as positive as the serving-man or the night watchman. She kept--as she was always to keep--everything to herself. David alone understood something of her sensitiveness, and this not because he shared it with her, but because he loved her so deeply that she was like part of himself. Only when she was with him she knew no fear. Her confidence in him was as though he were someone divine. Where he was no fear could come, no evil live.

This morning as they neared the house he wanted to go into the yard behind to see whether Benjamin were there. She shrank back.

'Come, Deb. Benjamin hath a new puppy Peel's man gave to him.'

She shook her head and, breaking from him, ran in by the front door. He remembered then that he must see his mother. Every morning he was with her for half an hour, and read out of the Life of King Arthur or the Bible for her. He read very well; he liked books when there were not horses and dogs and games like football and battledore. But to-day he did not want to read. It was not a day for books, and as he moved slowly into the house, he felt impatient with his mother. He shared a little with his father the intolerance of her clumsiness, her habit of tears, her absent-mindedness, and, as with all of us when we are impatient with those who love us, he wished that she did not love him quite so much.

She was so easily hurt. She was always asking him what he was doing, where he was going, with whom he had been; and although there was no reason at all why he should not tell her everything, he inclined to be secret with her because of her curiosity. Then he had seen, so many times, his sister Mary flatter and cheat her mother because of something that she had wanted, and that made him honest to the point of discourtesy. He loved her better when he was not with her; he hated Alice Press because she made his mother unhappy, but he did not mind also making her unhappy. Now, when he went in, he would be forced to tell her about what he was going to do, how he would ride Caesar to the valley's end, and fish in the stream below Stye Head and watch to see if a wolf should be prowling under Glaramara. And he did not want to tell her these things. It would spoil them a little, make them more ordinary and less adventurous.

He found her in her room, alone, the room darkened by the big canopied bed; it was a little chill.

He saw at once that to-day there would be no reading. His mother, dismayed and distraught, was standing in the middle of the room, her hand at her cheek, her eyes crowded with alarm.

So soon as she saw him she began: 'No, David.... Leave me.... This is too vile....' She was not near to tears: no, for once anger had mastered her. She had even a certain grandeur, pulled to her full height, massive, her gaze upon the door. Before he could wonder, someone had come in, and at once a spate of words broke about the place; the room crackled with fury.

He knew, without turning, that it was Alice Press; no need to question that shrill voice that rose in a kind of sweeping tide of temper to a scream.

'And so you mean to banter me, madam--a fine figure before your own children. Was I put here to direct them or no? It is no disparagement to a woman, I suppose, that before all your household I should be told my place and then left to find it by their easy insulting courtesy. Oh, no, indeed--I am not to be averse to every slavish duty that a gentlewoman can be put to, having been dragged from Doncaster by the heels, and then flung into this muck-heap and cesspool to keep proper company with old witches, who by rights should be stripped of every cloth on their backs and then thrown to the river to let them sink or swim! Oh, no, you say, I honour you ever more and more, but I insult you as I may, and as convenience suits me. I do not remember to have ever had the pleasure of witnessing your own rules of law and order in this house or any other. You are quiet enough until the fit moment comes to abuse me properly, and then you have words enough.... I can't express the satisfaction, truly, that it gives me to know the meaning of your feeling towards me, and if I should go naked and be on my knees before you, that would give you satisfaction, perhaps--you who have not your own children to order, nor your husband to bed with you--yet you would teach ME my lesson and my proper order in this house....'

She paused for breath. David saw her now, her pale face crimson, her hands clenched, her breast heaving.

'I will not have you,' Margaret Herries answered, 'abuse my privileges. It was not by my wish nor order that you were here. God knows I have surrendered in these years many of my proper rights, and God He also knows that I have suffered my own bitterness, and such it may be must come to every woman, but yet I am mistress in this house.'

'Mistress!' Alice Press broke in, 'and in a fine house! Mistress when there is such a master here and a house where the mice and rats are the true familiars. Mistress you may be in your own privacy, but mistress, as the veriest hireling on this place knows, in no public fashion. Mistress! Then who is master here? Know you your master and his company? Ask your master his pleasure in Keswick and the drabs that he fumbles, so that after barely a six months' stay in this place his name is a byword! Mistress--'

'I will not,' Margaret Herries broke in. 'This is enough. I have suffered your company long enough, but now it is you or I who go-- and I care not how soon!'

'Go!' Alice Press moved a step forward. 'Yes, though we had been at the same charity school and I had gone the round of neighbours asking for bread, I would not go at your bidding. No, nor do aught else at your bidding. Neither I nor anyone else in this place. You for a weak trembling fool who have neither the courage nor the discipline to bid a mouse go when you would wish it. Oh, I could tell you things, madam, that would make your eyes sore. I have waited in patience, borne your insults and laughed at your silly little pieces of pride, but now at last my silence has lasted long enough....'

Silence fell on the room. Francis Herries stood in the doorway, and David moved towards his mother. He came close to her, scarcely knowing that he did so, and suddenly he felt her trembling hand on his shoulder and steadied himself that he might support it.

'Well,' Herries said quietly, looking about the room, 'here is a scramble . . . the whole house shares in it.'

For once Margaret Herries was not cowed. Her hand tightening on David's shoulder, her voice trembling ever so lightly, she replied to him:

'Mrs. Press has some complaint that I have ordered her unjustly before the servants. She has been impertinent . . .'

David saw, and triumphantly, that it was the other woman who was afraid. In a voice that was strangely stilled after its earlier shrillness, looking straight at Herries, forgetting, it would seem, that there was any other in the room, she answered:

'I have my place here, a place that you have appointed me. Your wife has forgotten . . .'

Herries smiled.

'Your place? No place unless you yourself fulfil it.'

It was possible that in that one quiet word she saw her sentence; she had known, it might be, that for months it had been coming to her. It might be that, beyond that again, she realised now her folly in provoking this scene, in forgetting a patience that it had been, this last year, no easy task to tutor her natural hot temper towards.

'I have fulfilled it,' she answered proudly. 'It is you who have neglected to keep me in it.'

'That may well be,' he answered lightly; 'there is so much to be done and little time to see to it all. And now I advise that you leave us. . . . Wherever your place may be, it is certain that it is not in this room.'

She would, it seemed, speak; then with another glance at him, her colour now very white, she passed through the door.

He looked at his wife with a strange mixture of scorn and kindliness.

'You should know better, Meg, than to suffer her impertinence . . . but at least you shall not suffer it long.'

He went out. David felt still the pressure of his mother's hand. She did not move; then, at last, turned from him, went to the window and stood there looking out. There was nothing that he could do--only he would never speak to Alice Press again. Never! Not though his father whipped him till the blood ran. With this high resolve he left the room, and then, after a pause, the house. He hated it and everyone in it.

He found Benjamin and Benjamin found Caesar. No one prevented him; from the outside court the house within seemed dead. No sound came from it. It was strange that by merely closing a door you shut everything off--anger, fears, greed, joys. Already, at his early years, it seemed to him that one of the ways to secure happiness was to escape from people, to be by yourself in the open.

He wasn't happy as he found his way, past Moorcross, on to the main path, but he was too young and too healthy to be unhappy for long. And there was the consciousness that he was sharing now more in real grown-up life than he had done in Doncaster. But why had his father brought Alice Press with him from Doncaster? That was what he COULD not understand. It was from her that all the trouble came, she who made his mother unhappy, his father angry, Deb frightened, himself in a rage. Were she gone, they would all be tranquil again. But WHY had his father brought her? Why had he kissed her in the inn? There was something strange here that caused his heart to beat and his cheeks to redden. Children then lived from the earliest years in contact with great grossness of word and action. David almost from babyhood had been aware of the physical traffic between men and women, had at the age of seven seen a woman give birth to a child in the streets of Doncaster, but he had as yet translated none of these physical acts to mental or spiritual significance.

Life from the very first was for him far coarser and more brutal than it would be for his great-grandchildren, but for that reason, perhaps, his consciousness of it was purer and less muddled than theirs would be. In any case he drove these things very swiftly from his mind as he drew out from the Rosthwaite hamlet into the open country.

Open country, indeed, it was. At this time it was scarcely cultivated save in a few fields round Seathwaite or Rosthwaite. It lay in purple shadows with splashes of glittering sunlight, a lost land, untenanted by man, no animal anywhere visible, dominated entirely by the mountains that hemmed it in. To David's right ran the path up to Honister, where the mines were; this country was forbidden ground, for here all the rascals and outcasts of the neighbourhood would congregate to scrape among the mine refuse and then sell the scraps of plumbago to the Jews in Keswick, who would meet them at 'The George' or 'The Half-Moon' and then bargain with them. The stories were that titanic battles were fought above Stye Head and on Honister between rival bands of robbers, disputing their plunder, and it was true enough that many a time, walking up Honister, you would find a dead man there, by the roadside, his throat cut or a knife in his belly and often enough stripped naked.

For David, that road up to Honister was the most magical passage of all, and one day he would investigate it, robbers or no robbers, to its very heart; but to-day he was out to catch fish, and it was by the bridge under Stye Head that he would catch them--were he lucky! It was not a great day for fishing with this glittering sun and shining sky.

The farther he got from Herries the happier he became. Of late he had been cluttered about with people. All of them--his father, his mother, Deb, Mary, his cousins, Father Roche, the Press woman, old Mrs. Wilson and her son, Peel and his boy--some of them he loved and some of them he hated, but all of them hindered his perfect freedom.

He, he was wise enough even now to realise, would always be hampered by people--you couldn't be FREE of people, nor did he want to be--but there would be moments and days when you would be free, absolutely, nakedly free, and, oh! how glorious they were!

It was such a moment now.

Caesar was no very magnificent steed, but he was a good enough pony, and quite able to grasp his own moments of freedom. As they came deeper under the hills the path was so rough and uncertain that David let him pick his own way. The group of mountains that closed the valley in were lovely in their wine-grape colour under a sky that had been a stainless blue, but that now, in the fashion of these parts, was suddenly the battlefield for two angry clouds, one shaped like a ragged wheel, the other like a battering ram. The wheel was a thin grey edged with silver and the ram was ebony. The empty valley--the little boy on the pony was the only moving thing in the whole landscape--seemed to wait apprehensively as the wheel and the ram approached one another. The sun appeared to retreat in alarm, but the wheel stretched out a wicked hand with swollen fingers and seized it--then the ram crashed down upon it.

The end of the valley was darkened although behind him, by Castle Crag, the sun was in full glory, and the world blazed like a sheet of dazzling metal. Within the shadow it was cold, and David, shouting to give himself company, kicked Caesar forward.

He came now to three houses, brooding like witches at the side of the rough path, quite deserted, it seemed, open, like many of the other cottages, to the sky.

Before the third cottage stood three men and a girl. David felt his heart beat at the sight of them. They were the wildest-looking men he had ever seen. They were copies the one of another, seemingly of the same height and the same age, the age maybe of his father, broad and strong, and all with dark rough beards. The girl was only a baby, younger than David, slight and dark like the men, but rosy-cheeked, and, as David passed them, she was laughing. One of the men stepped forward and stood in David's way.

'A fine day,' he said.

David nodded. He was frightened, but he wouldn't let anyone, not even Caesar, know it. He wished, though, that the sun would come out again.

'Where'st going?'

The man had a deep, rumbling, husky tone with a rasp in it.

'To fish at the bridge.'

'To fish at the bridge?' All the men laughed.

'Pass, little master.' The man stepped back and ironically doffed a very filthy and greasy hat. Then David, seeing the laughing eyes of the small girl fixed upon him, smiled.

She had in her hand a small switch. She ran into the path, struck Caesar's buttocks and then, as he started forward, laughed with a shrill crying tone like a bird. He looked back and saw her standing in the middle of the path against the sun. He cared nothing for girls--Deb

wasn't a girl, she was his sister--but it did seem to him exciting and adventurous that this small girl should be quite alone with these three wild men, and, apparently, happy with them. She was perhaps the daughter of one of them. It might be that they were some of the robbers who came down from Stye Head and murdered defenceless people and returned. Well, there was nothing about him for them to murder. He had a tin with worms in it, and a home-made fishing rod and a few pence. He was safe enough.

The country now grew ever wilder and wilder. A rough, ragged stream, swollen with the rains and the snow from the tops, rushed along over a deep bed of slabs and boulders. Fragments of rock lay everywhere about him here, so that he had to dismount and lead Caesar. Above his head the two clouds had made truce and after a meeting had separated, one now in the form of a ship that, lined with silver, sailed off into the blue, the other dispersed into a flock of little ivory clouds that stayed lazily, as though playing a game, in lines and broken groups. The sun had burst out again and flooded all the land. David had already learnt that, in this country, the sky was more changeable than in any other in the world, that if you lived here your days were bound up with the sky, so that after a while it seemed to have a more active and personal history than your own. It became almost impossible to believe that its history was not connected with yours, keeping pace with you, influencing you, determining your fate. He had never considered the sky very greatly at Doncaster, but in this world, it drove itself into your very heart. The brilliant sun now struck sparks from every stone, while every splutter of the stream against a boulder flung into the air a shower of light. The whole valley glittered, while above it the mountains, streaked like a wild beast's skin with snow, were black.

He came to the bridge, let Caesar loose, clambered over the smooth wet stones to the deep, green pool under the waterfall, chose his worm and began to fish below the pool. There was shadow here from an overhanging tree and the curve of the bridge. He was exceedingly happy. He had the great gift of complete absorption in the task or play of the moment. He was never to know the divided moods, divided loyalties of his father. His character was not subtle, but steadfast, fearless, unfaltering. He did not realise for how long he fished. He moved below the bridge and then back again. He caught nothing. He never had a bite. The sun was too bright. He sat, his legs apart, his eyes intently fixed on the water. A shadow was flung. He looked up.

Leaning on the bridge, looking down at him very gravely was a pedlar with a coloured hat and a sharp bright face. He had rested his pack on the bridge's wall.

'A fine sun to-day,' said the pedlar.

David nodded.

'Too strong a sun for good fishing,' said the pedlar.

33

David sighed. 'That's true.' He scrambled up to the sward above the stones. He looked at the pack.

'Have you something for me to buy?' he asked, smiling. He had some money in his purse--money his father had given him--and it would be pleasant to buy something for Deborah.

The pedlar shook his head.

'Nothing for you.' Then he felt in a pouch at his waist. 'Do you fancy boxes? I have a little box here . . .' He fumbled, then brought out a small silver box and gave it to David. His hand was nut-brown, with long, thin, tapering fingers. It was a beautiful little box. On one side was carved a picture of girls dancing round a maypole, on the other a picture of gentlemen hunting.

David looked at it, then shook his head. ''Tis a beautiful box, but I have not money enough.'

The pedlar smiled. 'It is yours. Keep it until your marriage- day.'

'Thank you,' said David, dropping it into his pocket. 'But I shall never be married.'

'You will be married,' said the pedlar, 'and have fine sons.'

'How do you know?' asked David, looking into his tin and seeing that the worms that remained were few and poor. He would not fish any more. He found bread and meat in his pocket and offered some to the pedlar, who took more than his share and ate voraciously.

'I know everything,' said the pedlar. 'I am the Devil.'

David believed him. He looked both wicked and gay as he stood there in the sunlight, and Francis Herries had always told him that the Devil was both these things.

'I am not afraid of you,' said David, laughing. 'My father has always told me not to be afraid.'

'I know your father,' said the pedlar, licking his fingers after the bread and meat and looking as though he would like also the piece that David had in his hand. 'Your father is an old friend.'

'He is the finest man in the world,' said David proudly. 'Why will you not show me the things that you have in your pack?'

'I am weary of showing them,' said the pedlar, yawning and displaying a splendid row of sharp white teeth. 'Time enough. You shall see them one fine day.'

'If you are the Devil,' said David, who was always interested in everything, 'you can tell me where there is good fishing.'

'There is good fishing everywhere,' said the pedlar, 'if you have patience. You have patience. It will carry you through the world-- patience and courage, two stupid qualities but valuable.'

'Do you live round here?' David asked.

'Here or anywhere. When you have lived for ever as I have, one place or another is the same.'

'Do you never grow any older?' David asked.

'Never,' said the pedlar. 'A wearisome business. Good day. We shall often encounter one another.

Keep the little box. I am not, in my intentions, always unamiable as people say.'

He shouldered his pack, started up the Stye Head and was quite suddenly lost in the sunlight.

David jogged back happily through the sunny afternoon. He took his time; he saw no human being. The sun falls behind the hills like a stone over this valley, leaving in the sky a long, wide strath of white and blue. When David reached Herries the shadows were straddling giants across the little stone court.

He found his father alone in the shadowed hall; he leant across the long table, on which a map was spread. 'He's looking grand,' David, who relished him in his plum-coloured coat, thought, 'and he has a temper.' So, like a knowing puppy, he slipped quietly past the fading fire. In the room above he heard Deborah's funny little piping voice, singing to herself or her baby. Beyond the leaded window the sky was a lovely pale green like early spring leaves and the low spread of the land was purple again as it had been in the morning. Against this gentle, pure light the room was very dark, although two candles were lit.

His father saw him.

Without looking up from the map: 'Where have you been, David?'

David told him. It might be that there would be a whipping or it might be that there would be a game-- you never could tell with his father.

'Thou hast missed thine uncle, boy.'

David had nothing to say to that--as there was a pause he filled it.

'I saw the Devil by the bridge.'

His father did not answer but suddenly raised himself.

'David, come here.' David came to him.

He put his arm round his neck. 'David, I love no one but you--no one--no one in all the world. And I hate your uncle. Remember this day, for on it I surrender all wishes for a good union between your uncle and me. Silly, patronising fool!' He looked furiously about him at the table which was clustered with a mess of things-- tankards, a platter with bread on it, a riding-whip, a velvet glove with a jewelled clasp. 'I'll twist his neck for him, brother or no brother, an he comes this way again. Aye, you should have seen your uncle riding his fine horse and stepping over the muck and cobbles, he fat as an otter and red as an infant's bum. 'Tis his lady wife sent him to spy the land out--a fine stretch she'll be the wiser for his coming--a dark house, a dull woman and his debauched good-for-nothing brother . . . I'll warrant he's sad that he had me here--a fine tear on his famous reputation. And now that I'm here I'll stay. The place charms me, naked though it is. There's some ale for you, David. Drink to your good-for-nothing rump of a father, naked-bottomed in a cesspool and pleasantly forgot by the gay world.'

But David didn't drink. He felt in his pocket and brought out the little silver box.

'The Devil gave me this,' he said.

His father, his eyes angry yet good-humoured, wandered round the room then came to it.

'A pretty thing. And how did the Devil look?'

'He was a pedlar. He said he knew you.'

'Yes--there is a pedlar here I have spoken with. . . .'

His mind was away, then he caught his son to him and held him close.

'My good brother's son is a damned smug; and gives him no joy--I can beat him there.'

He crooked his son's chin upwards and looked at him. David gazed back at him fearlessly.

'Remember this day,' his father said. 'We shall be alone against the world, you and I.'

CHINESE FAIR

Herries returned, one September morning, after his walk abroad, without his coat. It had been one of his finest, the plum-coloured coat laced with silver. He walked into the house in his white sleeves, and the old witch, Mrs. Wilson, leaned over the top of the stairs and smiled. She never laughed. 'You're grand without your coat,' she said. They seemed to have a kind of understanding, the two of them. He, as did all the valley, believed her to be a witch. He thought none the worse of her for it. He was happy this morning like a boy. It was a bright fresh morning, with clean white clouds leaning negligently on the hills. With the beauty and the youth and the kindly look that he had when he was happy, he was a good sight for an old witch. And she was no misanthrope. Life was too busily interesting for her to despise mankind.

'I'm going to the Fair,' he said like a boy.

She nodded her head, put out her long brown hand, and touched the white linen of his sleeve.

'You're not to give t'coat,' she said. 'It'll be remembered.'

He didn't care whether it were remembered or no. Out on the Watendlath path, looking up at a bright silver waterfall poised like a broken ladder against the green cliff, he had seen by the stones of the beck a dead man with his throat cut and a woman shivering beside him. A dead man was no extraordinary sight; this man was naked save for his shirt, and his white legs stretched stiffly as though they had been carved. The woman did not cry nor ask for alms, but she shivered in the keen September air. He did not speak to her, but obeying the impulse of the instant, took off his plum-coloured coat and threw it over her trembling shoulders. He strode back to the house. Seeing Benjamin in the yard, he leaned from the window and bade him go and fetch the woman to the house. Ten minutes later Benjamin returned to say there was no sign of woman or man.

He did not care. He was too cheerful in spirit to be bothered by a dead man or a shivering woman.

He sat in his sleeves at the window looking out on to the beautifully coloured world, Glaramara plum-coloured like his coat, and the long stretch of green valley.

He was like a schoolboy about this Fair. It was an accidental chance-by-night Fair for Keswick. It had been intended for Kendal and then for Carlisle, a motley company of entertainers and rogues and rascals travelling slowly to Scotland.

But the smallpox was savage this summer in Kendal, and so they had changed to the smaller town. In the past Keswick had had few Fairs but its own. It was too small a place. The chartered Fair on the 2nd of August for the sale of leather, and the Cattle Fairs on the first Thursday in May and on each Thursday fortnight for six weeks after; on the Saturday nearest Whitsuntide and Martinmas for hiring servants, and on the first Saturday after the 29th of October for the sale of cheese and rams. Saturday the year through was market- day for provisions and corn.

But these Fairs were local, and business was their purpose. This present Fair was the maddest, wildest thing in Keswick's memory. It would be generations before the week of it would be forgotten. They said, too, that there was a company of Chinese people travelling with the Fair, and they wore strange clothes, such as had never been seen in that neighbourhood, and they juggled with gold balls and swallowed silver swords, and had an old man with them three hundred years of age. It was always afterwards called the Chinese Fair.

But it was not of the Fair that Herries was now thinking as he sat at the window. He was thinking of how well satisfied he was with this place. He had been here full two years, and his strange instinct that had driven him here had been right. He already loved the valley, and had even now caught some of the sense of its intimacy that led its inhabitants to cling to it with an obstinacy and stubbornness that made them a byword for the rest of the world. It was said that the men of Borrowdale were so stupid as to be scarcely human, and that they did such idiotic things, like building a wall to keep the cuckoo in their valley, that they must be half-witted--that they never stirred from their valley, that some of them had never even seen Keswick, that they spoke a strange language of their own and were like men in a dream.

Herries had heard how the people in Keswick and from Newlands and St. John's and the rest mocked and gibed, but he knew now what it was that held the men of Borrowdale: although he was not yet one of them (they were greatly suspicious of newcomers), one day he would be. Something was in his blood that was in their blood: it was a doom, a judgement, the fulfilment of a prophecy.

He thought of other things too, as he sat there. He was well pleased that he had cut himself off from his brother and his brother's family. Since that day when Pomfret had ridden over to Herries he had never set foot in his brother's house. Margaret and the children had visited--he did not care whether they did or no-- and when he met Pomfret in Keswick he talked with him, but he had never been within his brother's door.

He loved his pride, his fierce intolerance. He cherished it, fed it, adored it. It had been one of his fears, on coming to live in Herries, that perhaps he would find his brother a better fellow than he had thought he was, and so would be forced to see him and keep company with him because his heart drove him.

That was why, on the first evening at the inn, he had worn his finest clothes--because that might annoy his brother, and then Pomfret would appear less pleasant than he was. And so in the event it had been. Now he cherished his scorn of his brother--it was a fine silver flower in his coat.

The thing, however, of which he was mainly thinking now was what he should do to be rid of Alice Press, for rid of her he would be. Although so reckless a man, he knew, as every imaginative Herries has always known, that you can't rid yourself of past deeds. Kill a fox, give your coat to a trembling woman, drink of the water of Sprinkling Tarn, and you are a doomed man. He was doomed because he had kissed Alice Press, doomed because he had shot off that young fool's ear in Doncaster, doomed because on entering Herries he had put the right foot before the left, doomed anyway and a thousand times a day; but to be bored, because he was young and full of life, was a worse thing than to be doomed. And he was bored by Alice Press, bored to the very hilt of his sword. He thought now that he had always been bored with her, although there had been, at the very first, a flashing moment of startling splendour. Now he was bored with everything about her, from her heavy sallow face, her long sad brooding gaze at him, her stealthy eagerness to be alone with him, down to the paste buckles on her scarlet shoes, the scarlet shoes that he had once bought for her on a Fair day in Doncaster, and that she wore now in persistent petulant reminder. Moreover, she had been insulting to Margaret, and he would have no one rude to Margaret but himself. Yes, he must be rid of her, but how?

He looked out at the great shoulder of the hill. 'How, old Glaramara? You are old enough to know. Come and tell me your plan.'

As though in answer to his question, hearing a deep breath he turned round to find Alice Press at his side.

She was very grand in black velvet, with a heavy silver chain and her scarlet shoes.

She came close to him, and the scent that she used, a scent of roses, stifled his nostrils.

'Francis,' she said, her large sombre eyes staring into his. 'You will take me to the Fair, will you not?'

'No,' he answered, smiling at her and patting her white hand. She drew her hand away from the arm of his chair.

'You promised me.'

'I break my promise.'

'You must not. I am bent to go. You have been unkind to me all these months, and I have borne you no grudge. I knew that I could wait. To-day it shall be like one of our old times.'

'Old times never return,' he answered her, looking at her with an intentness that matched her own. How strange it was, this passing of love! A never-ending marvel! At one moment the merest touch of the hand is Paradise, at the next, dead flesh.

'Have you not been selfish in this,' she went on quietly, 'and blind too, perhaps? Because you are tired of loving me you think our intercourse is at an end. But no intercourse is at an end when two have loved one another as we have.'

'Loved!' he interrupted her. 'Love and love! Do you call that love? I have never known what love is. 'Tis a wonder that waits always round the corner. If ever I do know, then I will be faithful. But OUR love! My dear, you use words too lightly.'

He hit her hard there, but she gave no sign. Her eyes did not quiver.

'Of course you are faithless,' she said. 'I have always known that, but I am not quite like the other women you have kissed. I always told you I was not. You cannot rid yourself of me so easily.'

'Can I not?' He looked at her speculatively. 'I have never been false to you. I warned you not to come here. I told you what it would be. Go back to Doncaster, my dear, and find a better man.'

That 'better man' hit her the hardest of all, because, although she thought him rotten, he was yet better for her than any other man in the world. A woman's bitter fidelity is always the honestest thing she has.

'Take me with you to the Fair to-day,' she repeated, 'and we will see. I've made no request for months but have faithfully stayed in this house, suffered every scorn at the hands of your wife, been hated by your children, been faithful to your interests--now, to- day, you will take me to the Fair.'

'I will not,' he answered, smiling up at her. 'David is the only one who goes with me.'

She turned past him and stood facing him, with her back to the window, blotting out the scene as though she thought that the mountain, at which he gazed so persistently, was her enemy.

'Listen, Francis. You are a bad man but a fair one. Here is a bargain. You have spoiled my life, shamed me before everyone, wrecked all my prospects, but I will feel nothing for all this if you will give me this day, one day as we used to have it, as we had it in Doncaster that Fair day when you bought me these shoes.' He knew that she was saying to herself: 'If I can but get him from this house and away with me as he used to be, I can charm him again.'

He answered her unspoken thought. 'You cannot charm me any more, not by one day nor by twenty. It is over. All done. I never promised fidelity. I never loved you. I have never loved anyone save my son. These things are not for our asking, my dear. Nature is rough when she tosses us our moods. "This one for you," she says, "and this for you," and no tears or scarlet slippers will change her indifference. Blame no one. Life is not understood by scolding.' Then he went on very kindly. 'Alice, go back to Doncaster and forget me. There was that fellow--how was he named? Matthew Priestly--he always loved you. He loves you, I doubt not, still. Blow no more on these dead coals. Forgive my indifference. It is the fault of neither of us.'

She saw something in his face that she understood. She gave him one long look and then slowly went. An hour later he was riding with David to Keswick. He could not quite rid his mind of her. Oddly enough it was now in connection with David that he thought of her. David, ever since that quarrel between the two women, had kept his vow. He had refused to speak to Alice Press. The woman had taken it for the most part with a cold, haughty indifference, as though she could not be disturbed by the impertinence of a child, but yesterday there had been a scene. She had demanded of Herries that he should make his son answer her. Herries had ordered him. David, with set face and an odd little frown between his brows that was his father's own, had refused. Herries would whip him for disobedience. David, his body drawn tight together, kept to his refusal. He was stripped and whipped. Herries drew blood from his young son's white back, because he loved him so dearly and was so deeply bored with Alice Press. David put on his shirt and jacket without a word.

'And now will you speak to her?' his father asked him.

'No,' said David.

Then his father kissed him and gave him some fine ointment for his back. To-day it was as though this had never been. David was in perfect happiness as he rode Caesar, laughing and chattering as he did sometimes when he was excited, making Caesar gallop on the free turf of Cat Bells, coming down into Portinscale as though he were heading a charge. The boy was growing. There would soon come a time when he would judge with a man's thoughts. He was a fine boy, of a stiff, brave, honest character, full of courage and obstinate. What would he think of his father?

The Fair was on the farther lake side of Keswick, on the broad meadows that ran to the lake's edge, not far from Pomfret's grand house, and it pleased Francis to think how greatly Pomfret must dislike to have all this rapscallion world at his very door. Keswick, at this time, was a town of one fair street and a huddle of filthy hovels. In the minor streets and 'closes' the cottages, little houses and pig-sties were thronged very largely with a foreign and wandering population--riff-raff of every sort who came to steal plumbago from the mines or were wandering their way northward, off the main route; these houses were crowded with foul middens and encroached on by large open cesspools, pig-sties and cow-sheds. The refuse stagnated and stained the air and tainted the soil. Here were women of ill-fame,

hucksters, thieves, many Jews who paid high prices for the stolen lead. At once on entering the town you were in another world from the honest and independent country of the statesmen and yeomen of the valleys-- these statesmen who for centuries had lived on their own land, their own masters, and owed no man any-thing.

In the former year, 1731, in Keswick, out of a population of some twelve hundred, nearly five hundred persons had died of smallpox, cholera and black fevers. During the summer months the channels of ordure, the cesspools, became intolerable, and in the lower parts of the town respectable citizens could scarcely breathe.

The natural inhabitants of those parts, however, showed no discomfort and made no protest.

On this fine morning the principal street was shining with its white cobble-stones and a throng of people who pressed hither and thither, giving themselves up with complete child-like abandon to the fun of the occasion. The Fair had spread from its proper surroundings out into the street, and David and his father had to push through the groups surrounding booths and cheap-jacks and fancy quacks.

But the Fair itself, when they reached it, was a glory.

So many were the booths and stalls that the waters of the lake were invisible. On every side were announcements of wonders.

'Here is the Dancing on the Ropes, after the French and Italian fashion, by a Company of the finest Performers that ever yet have been seen by the whole World. For in the same Booth will be seen the two Famous French Maidens, so much admired in all Places and Countries where they come, for their wonderful Performance on the Rope, both with and without a Pole; so far outdoing all others that have been seen of their sex, as gives a general satisfaction to all that ever yet beheld them, to which is added Vaulting on the High Rope and Tumbling on the Stage.'

And here again: 'Here is to be seen a little Fairy Woman lately come from Italy, being but Two Foot Two Inches high, the shortest that ever was seen in England, and no ways Deformed, as the other two Women are, that are carried about the streets in Boxes from House to House for some years past, this being Thirteen Inches shorter than either of them. . . . Likewise a little Marmozet from Bengal that dances the Cheshire Rounds and Exercises at the word of Command. Also a strange Cock, from Hamborough, having three proper legs, and makes use of them all at one time.'

Here was a play announced in front of a booth all gay with crimson cloth and gold tinsel--

'An Excellent new Droll called The Tempest or The Distressed Lovers. With the English Hero and the Highland Princess, with the Comical Humours of the Enchanted Scotchman, or Jockey and the three Witches. Showing how a Nobleman of England was cast away upon the Indian Shore, and in his Travels found the Princess of the Country, with whom he fell in love, and after many Dangers and Perils was married to her; and his faithful Scotchman, who was saved with him, travelling through Woods, fell in among Witches, where between them is abundance of Comical Diversion. There in the Tempest is Neptune with his Tritons in his Chariot drawn with Sea-Horses, and Mairmaids singing. . . .'

And then the marvellous animals: 'The true Lincolnshire Ox Nineteen Hands high and Four Yards long, from his Face to his Rump, and never was Calved nor never sucked, and two years ago was no bigger than another Ox, but since is grown to this prodigious Bigness. This noble Beast was lately shown at the University of Cambridge with great satisfaction to all that saw him. . . .

'The large Buckinghamshire Hog above Ten Foot long . . . the wonderful Worcestershire Mare, Nineteen Hands high, curiously shaped, every way proportionable; and A little Black Hairy Pigmey, bred in the Deserts of Arabia, a Natural Ruff of Hair about his Face, Two Foot high, walks upright, drinks a glass of Ale or Wine, and does several other things to admiration; and the Remark from the East Indies; and the little Whifler, admired for his extraordinary Scent.'

Although David did not know it, some of these same animals must have been of an amazing age, because the celebrated Mr. Pinkeman had himself shown them in the days of Queen Anne.

For David, however, hours must pass before he could take in any detail. He did not know that already behind the colour and show there was disgust and discontent on the part of the showmen, because the takings were so small, and there was no one there but gaping country-fellows, the discontent leading in the last day of the Fair to a free fight and riot that spread, before all was over, into the heart of the town.

It all seemed to him so grand and magnificent that there had been nothing in the world like it before. Walking close at his father's side he was caught up into a world of colour and scent--the faint September blue held the flare of the fires that blazed upon roasting meat and fish, popping corn and scented sweetmeats, the thick swaying tendrils of smoke that crawled about the booths, the waving of coloured pennants, the flaunting of flags, and, under this shifting roof of colour, everything broke and mingled again, dogs nosing for food, naked children sprawling in the mud, mummers in gold and blue, women, bare-breasted, shrieking after their men, tumblers somersaulting, a monkey loosed, dragging after him a silver chain, his face weary with age and loneliness, three dwarfs in crimson hose, with huge heads, counting money, a black woman, a yellow kerchief round her head, selling silver rings, clowns, soldiers, girls dressed like angels with white wings, the booths with the drum beating and shrill trumpets blowing, men stripped to the waist, their skin pouring sweat, fighting before a shouting crowd, everywhere eating and

everywhere drinking, men tumbling women and women fingering men--and through these crowds the countrymen, the farmer, the dignified statesman, the gaping yokel moving like strangers, suspicious, aloof, and gradually tempted by ale and women and silver, by noise and food and curiosity, tumbling into the reeking tub and so kicking and shouting and screaming like the rest as the sun went up the sky.

Yes, hours passed. Somewhere, at some time, David had a sudden curious vision of all the colour, reek and noise of the Fair parting like a drawn curtain, and there in the clear space was the lake, misted yellow under a misted sun, cool and still, the line of Cat Bells rising softly above the woods on the farther side, the water still without a ripple, very cool and sweet. Then it closed again, and the stench of roasting meat and uncleanly bodies and painted boards melting in the heat of fires and frying corn and burning wood swept over him again, bringing with it into the very heart of his nostrils the whole pageant of bright colour, purple and gold and saffron, and the odd wildness of a thousand faces, eyes staring, mouths agape, and a roar of bells and whistles, shouts and curses and cries, the neighing of horses and barking of dogs and the shrill human scream of a crimson-pated cockatoo.

He was aware then that he had lost his father. He stood for a moment dismayed. On every side figures were pushing against and around him; now someone would run past him shouting; now two singing, falling from side to side, would lurch drunkenly his way; now with a cry, as though it had come from the ground itself, there would be a rush from a whole group; and all of this dreamlike--a flash of a sword, a trembling coloured flag, a creaking board of a booth, a ringing silver bell, the scream of the crimson-pated cockatoo, the wail of the lost monkey dragging his silver chain, a man bending a woman backwards against a boarded trestle, a naked muddied baby crying for its mother, all in a dream; where the clear, tranquil, golden-misted lake was, there was reality.

But he had no fear; he would see his father again; it was fine to be independent in a noisy world and to hold your own against the Devil. So, looking around him, he saw that he was before the very booth where he had most set his heart, the booth where the Chinamen were. On the outside of the booth a Chinese curtain hung in brilliant splashes of gold and red, a temple, a grove of golden bells, soldiers in armour, a bridge of blue, and in front of the curtain a Chinaman with a yellow face and an ebony pigtail was inviting everyone to enter. A bell clanged, the Chinaman called out in a shrill voice and at the same moment the thick pushing crowd shoved forward. David was caught in it, carried off his feet; he was pressed against smelling clothes and warm sweating flesh; he clutched, that he might not fall, at a man's waist and held to it; his fingers stuck to the damp waist-belt and his arm was driven into a soft belly. For a moment he was almost under a dozen feet, then lifted up again on the sheet of a thousand smells and so almost hurled into the inside of the booth. He did not know whether he should pay money or no, he had lost his breath and found himself enclosed within the thick arm of a huge country-fellow, black-bearded, bare at the neck; their sense of one another was instantaneous, and the black-bearded man laughed, standing him in front of him, pressing him back against his chest, his hot naked arm against David's cheek.

He could see where he was. He was high on some raised boards. Everything around him was quiet. The noise of the Fair had been shut out. On every side of him the people with staring eyes, speechless, stood waiting. A little empty stage was in front of him and above it some curtains idly flapped.

All his senses were centred on this empty stage. It became to him full of omen and suspense. What was about to happen? Who would come there? A very ancient man came with a long face of yellow parchment. He wore a long stiff garment of purple brocaded silk. He sat, quite silently and quite alone, on a little round stool. He was motionless, carved in colours against the dark shadows of the flapping tent. He looked neither to right nor left, was unaware of the sweating crowd. Perhaps he was the Chinaman who was three hundred years old. If you were three hundred years of age you would not pay attention to any crowd; you would have seen so many.

Then the curtains parted, two young men in gold trousers, stripped to the waist, their bodies glistening, came and threw into the air coloured balls. They threw up a dozen balls at once, and the balls, green, yellow, red, made whirls of colour above the head of the old man who never moved.

Then there came two short fat men with very yellow bodies; they were clad only in loin-cloths. Standing in a corner of the stage they began silently to wrestle.

Then six young men came in trousers of gold and jackets of silver; they had poles up which they climbed; they threw ropes to one another and with pointed red slippers on their feet walked on the ropes. Lastly a number of little yellow-faced children, also dressed in bright, shrill colours, ran silently forward, spread their legs and their arms and stood in a pyramid: the child who climbed to the top and stood balancing there with his little feet seemed only a baby with tiny black eyes and a doll's pigtail.

Now all of them--the young men with the balls, the naked wrestlers, the men balancing on the ropes, the pyramid children who suddenly melted to the floor and were turning like bright bales a hundred somersaults and cart-wheels--were moving ceaselessly round the old man who sat motionless on his little stool, never flickering, you could be sure, an eyelid. Faster and faster they turned, but always without a sound, and as they moved the tightly packed crowd moved with them: the crowd began to sway and to murmur: everyone was smiling: the black-bearded countryman who smelt of good fresh dung put his arm tight round David's neck, pressing his body to him. They were all smiling as though they were in a dream, and it must have seemed to many of them that they too were tossing balls into the air, turning somersaults, climbing poles, balancing on ropes. Their bodies must have appeared free to them and clean and strong: the ordure and the filth, the daily toil, the cruelty and sickness and pain, the darkness and rain and cold freezing nights, the life with animals and the wrestle with the hard ungrateful soil, the penury and ignorance and darkness, the loneliness of rejected lovers, the injustice of tyrannous masters, the narrow, constrained horizons, the proud brutalities of a swollen-headed upper class against whom they struggled dumbly, whom one day--and that day was not far distant--they would conquer--all these hard things fell away, the sky was bright and clear, the air fresh like crystal, all for a moment was joy and happiness in a free world where it was always day.

As for David he could see nothing but the silent old man sitting on his stool. The old man seemed to be staring directly into David's eyes. However David moved his head he could not escape that old man. He began to be frightened. He wanted to run away. The old man appeared to have a message especially for him. In another moment something terrible would happen. His father was in danger. And it spread beyond the moment--all his life he would remember that old Chinaman, and whenever he remembered him he would shiver with apprehension. Life was dangerous, and you could only know how dangerous it was when you sat quite still and listened, waiting for a sound to break.

Anyway, he must go. He must find his father.

He wriggled away from his black-bearded friend, then, dropping down from the raised boards, pushing through legs and arms, shoving with his head now this way, now that, at one instant stifled by the human stench, at another brought up against a solid body that would never move again, at last he was by the flap of the tent and tumbled into the free air, leaving behind him, it seemed, a crowd hypnotised, in a trance, a dream. . . .

He was in the open air again and frantically hungry. It must be afternoon. The sun was high in the sky.

So, looking rather desolate and half lost, his father, Francis Herries, saw him. Herries was a little drunk and soon would be more so. Somewhere in the heart of the Fair where they were bargaining about cattle he had discovered an old woman with a store of wine. She sat under an awning, on either side of her a cask of wine. A strange woman, very fat, with a purple face. She did not seem to want to sell her wine, but sat there idly. Once and again she broke into a strange raucous song in a deep, rumbling voice. She ladled the wine out of the casks into long, thin glasses: the wine was a shilling a glass, Portuguese on one side of her, Florence the other. Herries drank the Portuguese. What was it? He neither knew nor cared. Was it White Vianna or Passada or Barabar? Carcavellos or Ribadavia? He drank many glasses. The old woman did not speak to him nor he to the old woman. After that everything entertained him. He had always been very easily amused by little things, and there was something in him that liked the stench and the common crowd and the press of animals human and other--

He watched for a long while two men who, drunk with gin, tumbled about in the mud together. Close beside him was a fellow selling medicines. The two drunkards, suddenly weary, kissed one another and lay there in the mud head by head, looking up at the sunny sky.

The quack, long, thin and brown, like a gnarled tree-branch, with a high black hat--'Here's a plaister will cure old Ulcers and Fistulas, Contusions, Tumours and any Dislocations or Hurts, and when it has performed Fifty Cures 'twill be ne'er the worse but still keep its Integrity.'

He moved leisurely, looking for a pretty face. Where were all the pretty women? Here at least not one. The country girls hanging on the arms of their lovers were each more blowzy than the other. There seemed to be none of his own class here. What was it that gave him a sudden sense of freedom so that he was happy as though he had thrown off bonds?

All these strange faces interested him, wizened and twisted and swollen; he could throw off his fine clothes, put on these tinsel rags and go wandering with them, drinking, wenching. . . . Then looking about him he saw his small son. With a pang of reproach, oddly sharp as he saw his air, half defiant, half frightened, he cursed himself for the rottenest parent. To leave that child in such a place, at such a time! And yet he did not move at once towards him, but watched him, loving him, proud of him, sturdy and self-reliant among all the oddities, the shouting, the flaming fires. Whatever occurred that boy would not cry out, but would stand on his courage to the last, letting endurance father him were no other father there. And was not that because he had no spirit of imagination? Imagination was the devil. Let your fancy move and there, by that booth where the boxing was, you could see the sun roll down from the sky and sweep them all--pimp and trollop, bully and jade, monkey and dwarf, Indian and Chinaman--with its fiery heat, screaming into perdition. As he one day would go. But David would not stir, not till he felt his duty was done.

Then he moved forward and was happy to see the boy's pleasure spring into his eyes at sight of him.

'Did you think me lost?'

'No, father. I've been in the Chinaman's tent.'

'And what did you see there?'

'There was an old man, they say he is three hundred years old, and young men throwing balls.'

Then he added rather wistfully:

'Father, I'm hungry.'

'Come, we'll eat then.'

They moved through the packing crowd and came to a kind of temporary hostelry. It had a grander, larger front than the booths, and, inside, there were long tres-

tle tables with benches stretched on the grass and at the far end a defended fire with a grid. The place was very full with people eating and drinking, and many were already drunk, singing and shouting. David and his father found places at the end of the tent near the fire. A stout jolly man with an apron and a white cap asked them what they would have. There was Pudding and Roast Beef, Boiled Beef and Ox Tripe, Pigeons, well moistened with butter, without larding.

'Pudding and Boiled Beef,' said David. It was then that he saw that his father had been nobly drinking. He was too thoroughly a boy of his time to be disturbed by drunkenness, but, during these last weeks, he had grown greatly and taken a more manly place in the world, and in nothing more than in his attitude to his father. His father was weak where he himself would never be. He did not know this with any priggish sense of virtue: it came to him simply that there were times when he must look after his father just as there were times when he must look after Deborah.

He was a sort of guard to them, not because he was better than they-- all his life and through everything that happened he would always look up to them, but only because he loved them.

He was uneasy now, as looking about the tent he felt that in some way or another this was not a place for his father to be riotous in. The men and women around them were of mixed kinds: there were some sober and solid yeomen and townsmen, eating their meat with grave seriousness, with the Cumbrian air of guarding their own; there were some rascals of the Fair's own company, one of them in a shabby gay jacket of gold thread, another like a pedlar in a crimson cap (he reminded David of the Stye Head Devil who gave him the little box) with a small gibbering monkey sitting on his shoulder. With them were two loose women very gaudily attired, laughing and shouting. One of the women fondled the pedlar, thrusting food into his mouth. Near his father was a group of better-class people. They might be townsmen from Kendal or Penrith. One was very stout with a double chin and little mouse- eyes. He was rather drunken already and spilt his meat on his green velvet waistcoat. Another was a little man, thin as a spider, with a shrill feminine voice. He was over-handsomely dressed with an elaborately curled wig, a full-bottomed coat of bright blue, and many rings on his fingers. He was also drunken, and said many times over that he wanted a full-bosomed woman to go to bed with, that he might wake in the morning and find her near to him.

Herries, as was his way when he was drunk, had become very grand and proud. The wine that now was brought to him, added to the wine that he had already had, increased his grand dignity. David, who very soon had eaten all that he wanted, began to be unhappy and to plan some way of escape out into the air again.

Glancing here and there he knew that there were a number in the tent who had recognised his father. He had long known that there was much curiosity about his father and his father's family, as to why he had chosen to exile himself in Borrowdale, as to his dangerous liking for women, as to his mingling with anyone he met and caring nothing for the quality of his company, as to his having a fine mistress hidden away there in Herries and his flaunting her full in his wife's face--David knew that all these things were said and that already a queer chancy air had grown about the building of Herries, and that they had all become the more suspicious to the outside world because on their first coming they had sheltered a Roman Catholic priest (and who knew on what errand he had vanished less than a year ago?), and had under their roof the most famous witch in Borrowdale.

All this was in David's mind and consciousness. His determination was set on getting his father away before some open scandal occurred, and through all the murk and smell of the crowded tent, stinking of meat, spilt drink and unclean bodies of men, he saw the old Chinaman's eyes, that Chinaman who was three hundred years old and sat like an image.

His father was very haughty, ate and drank without speaking to anyone. He seemed like a god to his son, sitting there so grand and handsome with his thin, brown face, his clear eyes and the silver waistcoat with the ruby buttons.

The spidery man in the full wig buried his nose in his glass, and then, in his shrill high voice, bowing to Herries, said:

'A drink with you, sir.'

Herries drank.

'I am from Kendal,' the little man went on, while the very stout fellow laughed immoderately. 'I have come hither to see the pretty women, but by Jesus there are none!'

'There are several,' Herries replied, eyeing him severely.

'There are several.' The little man tittered: 'You are fortunate, sir. My name is Rosen--may I be honoured by knowing yours, sir?'

'My name,' said Herries very proudly, holding up his glass and looking at the beads of colour in the yellow wine, 'is Charles Henry Nathaniel Winchester, Duke of the Pyrenees and the district of the Amazon.'

Mr. Rosen became very serious. His little brow was puckered.

'I understand you, sir--a secret, between gentlemen.'

'There are women here,' said Herries, 'but no gentlemen--all the gentlemen are at the lake's bottom feasting with the mermaids.'

'I have heard,' said Mr. Rosen, who realised only the last word of Herries' sentence, 'that a mermaid was indeed seen off the northern coast of Scotland a month back. I was told by one who had read of it. I could go to bed with a mermaid,' he hiccuped, and looked gravely distressed, 'were her tail not too long. Could one choose one's mermaid?'

It was then that a terrible thing occurred. David, more and more restless, seeing that the tent was now fully crowded, that several had moved near to them and were listening, had his eye on the tent's door. Through it he could see a patch of bright sunlight, a woman dancing on a tub and many figures passing in shadow. It was clear by the door. Someone entered, a woman, Alice Press.

He stared, first thinking that he was blinded by the sunlight, then that he had mistaken some other woman of a like figure for her-- there was no mistake. She was wearing the black velvet dress of the morning. He could see the silver chain lying against it. And she wore the scarlet shoes. She stood quite by herself, staring about her. She looked up and down the tent. Then she saw Herries. She saw him, looked full at him, then very slowly began to move up the tent.

David's eyes were fixed. He had become an image of apprehension and fear. He could see only the green waistcoat of the fat man and that down it there was trickling a little stream of wine, while his big belly rose and fell in spasms of laughter. He did not look at his father, but he knew, quite suddenly, that his father had seen her. He felt for a moment his father's hand touch his shoulder, then he heard Alice Press' voice.

'I have come, you see. Will you give me something to eat?'

There was a place at Herries' other side. She took it with great ease and composure, but David, who, because of his detestation of her, had her in his very bones, knew as though it had been himself that she was suffering from throbbing nervousness and a devilish fear.

Herries, his face very stern, answered her quietly.

'Yes, since you are come. . . . What will you have?'

She ordered something from the smiling man with the apron, and, attempting a perfect ease, looked about her. She must have seen at once that no women of any quality were there, but only drabs and Fair ladies. All stared at her. At the door-end of the tent a thick rabble was quarrelling and laughing at its own affairs, but at the fire-end all eyes were upon her.

She smiled swiftly at Herries, and then began to talk.

'A kind fellow from Seathwaite brought me. I watched him passing. 'Twas dull at the house and the day bright, so I thought that I would venture for an hour. But I am hungry and 'tis three o'clock. 'Tis a gay Fair and of a size for a little town, as large as the Doncaster Fair. There are things to buy, I can be sure--will you buy me something, Francis?' She put her hand for a moment on his arm, laughing in his face. 'Yes,' he answered slowly, 'I will buy you something.' He did not look at her, but stared in front of him as though he were lost in thought.

Her food was brought, and she began nervously to eat. The heat of the tent, her fear and excitement had brought colour to her sallow cheeks. The black dress

ROGUE HERRIES

suited her and her full half-revealed bosom. The little
spidery man in the blue coat regarded her with all his
eyes, his mouth open, the stout man also.

She continued talking:

'And will you take me to see the sights? There is a
Chinaman three hundred years old and a play . . .' She
broke off. She was gathering courage. ''Tis time you
showed me the world again.'

Herries, for the first time since she had come,
looked at her.

'I will show you the world. It would be ungracious
did I not when you have come so far. First you shall eat
. . .'

It was then that the little Mr. Rosen of Kendal
caught up his courage and spoke to her. He raised his
glass.

'May I drink to you, madam? You honour us by
your company.'

She smiled at him, raising her glass, but her nervous thoughts were fast on Herries.

'We are all friendly together here,' she said. 'Pleasant company. Can you tell me, sir, whether the
Chinaman has truly three hundred years?'

'They say so.'

'A very Methuselah. Are you an inhabitant of
Keswick?'

'My town is Kendal.' The little man's eyes were
now bursting from his head at the sight of the lady's
opulence and beauty.

''Tis a finer town than Keswick.'

'Larger. 'Tis not for me to say that 'tis finer. We
who are citizens of it have our private conceit.' He
sighed, swelled out his chest, felt for the hilt of his
sword.

After a little she looked at Herries. 'I have done
eating,' she said. 'Will you take me to the sights?'

Herries drank his glass, looked at it after, with a
firm hand, he had placed it on the table, then turned to
her gently.

'Alice,' he said, 'as you have taken this on yourself
so you take the consequences. When we leave this tent
we part. . . . You do not return to Herries.'

His voice was quiet, but he had not wished especially to lower it. Mr. Rosen and his stout friend, and
indeed all at that end of the table, heard the words.

The colour in her face deepened. She put her hand
to her bosom, an action of hers that David knew well.

'Come, then,' she said, half rising, 'this is too public
a place . . .'

'Nay.' He put his hand on her arm, holding her
down. 'You have chosen it. Before we move hence you
must tell me that you understand--at the tent door we
part. You go no more to Herries.'

Her rage at the public insult--her temper was always beyond her command--flushed her cheeks. She,
too, had in these ten minutes been drinking to give
herself control. David saw her white hand pressed with
desperate force on the table until the blue veins stood
out.

'Be ashamed,' she murmured. 'In this place. . . .'

'Yes,' he replied. 'In this place. I want your assurance.'

'No, then,' she cried, her voice suddenly rising.
'You bought me. You shall keep me.' It was odd how,
with her anger and the freedom from the drink, the
commonness that was in her blood suffused, like a rising colour, all her body and spirit.

'I bought you. Yes,' he answered quietly. 'Then I
can sell you again.'

Everyone around them was silent. The stout man,
very drunk, rolling his head, suddenly exclaimed:

'Aye, and who would not have her, this beautiful
lady--though she cost him--his--his house and--and--
horses?'

But David saw that she was very afraid.

'Francis, you have been drinking. I did wrong to
come--I confess it--I will do all that you wish. But not
here--not in this place. . . .'

But he went on steadily.

'You have said it. I have bought you, and now, our
bargain being ended, I will sell you again.' He fixed
Rosen with his eye: 'You, sir, how much will you give
me for this lady?'

Several men murmured shame, but everyone here
was very drunken: there was some laughter, and a man
began to sing a song. A woman very gaudily dressed
and painted had come over and, leaning her bosom on
the stout man's back, eagerly watched the scene.

'You insult the lady,' little Rosen began, half rising
from his seat and feeling for his sword: then something
in Herries' face constrained him, and he sat down again.

'I am indeed serious,' said Herries sternly. 'This
lady and I are weary of one another and would part, but
she is mine and I would have compensation. You, sir,'
staring into Rosen's face, 'how much will you give for
her?'

Alice Press rose--'I will pay you for this . . . in good
coin. . . .' She made as though to go, but he rose also,
laid his hand again on her arm, then, his voice clear so
that all heard, said: 'This lady is for sale--for the one
who will bid the highest.'

Cries broke out--some were laughing, some swearing, most too drunken to understand the affair; the
garish woman laughed loudest of all.

A man said: 'Five silver shillings.'

Rosen, fuddled but struggling, in his funny feminine voice screamed: 'You are a filthy dog--you shall be
caned for this--' Nevertheless he could not take his eyes
from Alice Press. His whole body hung towards her.

Herries answered him quietly.

'Come, sir, will you give me forty shillings?'

'He'll give forty shillings . . .' some drunken voice
murmured like a refrain. The garish woman cried
shrilly: 'More than she's worth, the bitch.'

Something happened then to Rosen. With a frenzied gesture he plunged his hand in his pocket, flung
down on the table a heap of silver coin, then leaned
forward, his face almost in Herries'.

'I'll take her. I'll take her. She shall come if she's willing-- I'll care for her--zounds and the devil, I will--an she's willing.'

The money struck the table, and some of the coins, like live things, danced in the air, springing to the ground. A heap, shining there, lay before Herries.

'Have her then,' he said. 'I drink to you both.'

As he did so Alice Press turned to him and struck the glass from his hand. The wine splashed in his face.

She said something to him that no one could hear. Then clearly:

'You shall never be free from this.'

She looked about her once, proudly, and David, who still hated her, nevertheless at that moment mightily admired her.

Then she turned, brushed through the men and was gone.

Mr. Rosen rose and hurried after her.

Herries picked up one of the pieces of silver, looked at it intently, then placed it in the deep pocket of his coat.

Quietly, without any haste, he went out. David, his head up, his eyes shining, followed him.

THE SEA--FATHER AND SON

It was on a windy April night in the year 1737 that David and his father arrived at a new understanding together. The manner of it was on this wise.

The years that had passed since the very public exit of Mrs. Alice Press had suffered this and that figure to rise for a moment before their indifferent background, and then to be whirled like a tumbled leaf into windy space.

There had been the cheerful, friendly Gay, who, dying of an inflammation of the bowels in three days, had drawn this unusual sincerity from Mr. Pope: 'He was the most amiable by far, his qualities were the gentlest. . . . Surely if innocence and integrity can deserve happiness . . .'

It was Mr. Pope's profound opinion that they could not.

On the 13th of March, 1734, one Mr. William Bromley had proposed that 'leave be given to bring in a Bill for repealing the Septennial Act, and for the more frequent meeting and calling of Parliaments'--and the echoes of that appeal were one day to affect even the remotest hearthstones of Borrowdale.

Other figures, oddly contrasted, beckon for a moment on the mirror. Bolingbroke, cursing everyone save himself, takes boat for France on a windy June morning; then Louis of France, making rude gestures, fingers at nose, that he may irritate, polished sophisticate that he is, the barbarian Stanislaus; and a heavy- jowled, good-tempered cynic is fingering women in a gilded London bedroom and refusing most resolutely to be irritated by either Louis or Stanislaus. He has seen, with a smile, the packing of Bolingbroke's boxes, has signed and smiled cynically again because Nature that leaves so many dullards lagging on the stage has taken the great Arbuthnot after only sixty-eight years of noble brilliance, has snorted with his closest friend and intimate, snuff- taking Queen Caroline, over the rude, personally insulting despatches posted indignantly by His Gracious Majesty, the Emperor Charles the Sixth, and has turned with a grunt back to his women and bottles again, strong in this policy of masterly inactivity, this heavy-jowled, good-tempered, massive-bellied cynic Walpole.

One more, before the mirror darkens and the months hurry to a more desperate destiny--a bright-cheeked, rosy boy receiving his baptism of fire at the siege of Gaeta, aged only fourteen, Don Carlos touching the boy's arm with his long hand, and thus angering Caroline and George in their London palace so that they must send to Walpole to soothe them--that boy Charles Edward, whose happiest moment, maybe, is just this when, from that little close-walled flowered garden, he looks across, a fire of ambition at his heart, to a thin line of smoky plum-coloured hills.

In Borrowdale, at Herries, David and his father, on the morning of the 10th of April, 1737, were preparing to ride over to Ravenglass to spend several nights with brother Harcourt.

David, who was almost eighteen now, and had broadened, strengthened, darkened, so that you would not know him for the same little boy who had pretended to sleep in the four-poster at the Keswick inn, knew nothing of Gay or Arbuthnot, of The Beggar's Opera or the malicious devilries of Mr. Pope; but he knew by now a great deal about Borrowdale.

He knew the name of every Statesman in the valley and the faces and bodies of most of the humans there. He knew the innermost, intimate history of every possible fishing locality, the name of every bird, the lair of every fox. He had seen a wolf round the Glaramara caves, he had seen a golden eagle fly in the sun above Castle Crag, he had shared (without shame or shrinking--that sensitiveness did not belong to his time) in nearly every bull- baiting, dog-fighting, cock-fighting that the valley had to offer. He had learnt something of the spinning and weaving, and there had not been a Christmas Feast, a stanging at Twelfth Night, a pace- egging at Easter, a late summer rushbearing, a Hallowe'en or a local wedding at which he had not played his part. He was as popular (although he did not know it and would not have thought of it had he known it) as his father was not.

His whole young life had become absorbed by this valley world and by the close history of his own immediate family. They had been the seven happiest years of his life. He was a boy no longer. He was on the threshold of his manhood.

This journey to Ravenglass was to show him this. He had been anticipating eagerly a visit to his uncle Harcourt ever since he had first come to Herries. Uncle Harcourt was to be different, different from anyone he had seen or known. Harcourt had lived in the great world, he cared for the Arts, he was brilliantly read, a scholar, he could answer many of the questions that, for years now, David had been longing to ask.

For, although he loved everything that had to do with the outside world, he had, too, an intellectual eagerness that was perhaps the growth from seeds that Father Roche had sown. This had not been satisfied.

Simple, gentle little Robert Finch had come and taught the three of them what he could. That had not been a great deal. From the outside world the family at Herries had been more and more shut off.

Here, in spite of his externally happy life, lay the reason for the apprehension and misgiving that were in David's heart. For himself all might be well, for his family and for those whom he loved, all, as he very thoroughly knew, was not well at all.

The clouds had begun to gather after the scandal of the Chinese Fair. That scandal had been in its effects infinitely more public than seemed at the time possible. It had, indeed, been shameful enough for himself, and its effect on him had altered the whole balance of his character. Although five years now intervened he could yet see and feel every detail of it, the close and ill-smelling tent, the leaping fire, the genial host, the garish woman with the painted face, the bright blue coat of the little shrill-voiced man, the silver coins lying on the table, the broad stout hand of Alice Press stark on the table-board--but it had been, it had seemed, a private drama for himself and his father. For months he had caught no outside word of it. All that they had known at home had been that Alice Press was gone, and for ever: that had been relief enough.

Then, even to his boy's ears, bit by bit and piece by piece the story had come to him: the Peel boy knew it, Benjamin knew it, at last, as he found, his mother and his sisters knew it. It was a story incredibly distorted. It seemed to him, when at last he met it face to face, to have no relationship to the truth. Of course he hotly defended his father--but the mischief was done. Here was the man who had sold his woman in public for 'thirty pieces of silver.' Even to that country tradition in that uncouth time the event was memorable.

It clothed his father with a kind of 'apartness'--yes, even for himself. His father had always been for him like no other man, but that had been, in his youngest years, a difference of glory. Now it was a difference of peculiarity.

His was a character that must face everything truly and honestly as it came to him, and now he must face this--that his father could do shameful things and yet feel no shame. This, oddly enough, made him love his father more than he had done before, but it was a love very different from the earlier one. Now he must guard and protect this man who moved under some kind of

influence that was straight from the Devil. David, of course, believed in the Devil--did he not know him as he was in human form?

His father must be loved and guarded because he was different from other men, but no longer could he be worshipped--and this brought him nearer to David. There had been from the beginning something fraternal in their relationship. That was now strengthened.

Other changes had come upon Francis Herries in these five years. He was not the beautiful, young, elegant person that he had been on his first coming to Herries. His body had stoutened, his dress was more slovenly, his air more careless. He bore at times--although he was worlds apart from him--an odd resemblance to his brother Pomfret. At least you could tell now that they were brothers.

In mood he was very much as he had been, gay, charming, sullen, angry, kindly, cruel. He did not appear to feel his apartness. He had his acquaintances in Keswick, men with whom he rode, betted and attended the country events, also women. But David now knew he carried his secret life within him and was never, for an instant, unaware of its presence.

They would have been, as a family, more thoroughly isolated than in winter they were, had it not been for David's country popularity on the one side that made him friends with everyone in the valley and, on the Keswick side, strangely enough, because of David's sister Mary.

Mary was now fifteen years of age and Deborah fourteen. Mary was handsome--she would be a true Herries woman, big-boned, broad-breasted, carrying herself with that mixture of arrogance and confidence and grace--that blending of hardness and courtesy, of indifference and kindly attention, that brought in every country, society, and age such Herries women to the front. She was indeed hard, determined, and ambitious. Of her true feelings for her father she had given as yet no sign, but she must from her very earliest age have felt that he was her enemy, her thwarting opponent in every desire and longing that was hers. In truth, every element in him must have always been distasteful to her, his recklessness, his irony, his grossness, and, above all, his unconsciousness of and disregard for public opinion. For she was cautious, unaware of subtlety, grimly virtuous and alive to every public wind that blew.

Very early, indeed, she must have surveyed the scene and decided that not for her were the isolation of Herries, the mire of Borrowdale, the rusticity of the country company, the coarseness and crudity of living. She had never any eye for any beauty save her own, her only tenderness was to herself, and she had a power of cautious waiting on the event, an ability to spin over months and even years the web of her own secret plans, that was both in its strength and secrecy extraordinary.

Very soon she had begun to turn her eye to Keswick and her cousins there. That was her future world, or rather the stepping-stone to a larger, grander one, and, at once, she began to use it. Very early she won the admiration of her uncle and aunt. She was in truth the very type that they could understand and admire.

She found, as she grew older, ways and means of reaching Keswick that only ruthless determination could have taught her. At first her father had angrily forbidden her his brother's house, but soon he had grown indifferent and lazy. He had never cared for this daughter of his. He did not mind where she went. When she was fourteen she persuaded her mother that she must have dancing- lessons and, riding her own horse, would vanish into Keswick and no one question her.

It may have been that Pomfret and his wife found a certain triumph and pleasure in thus alienating one of the children of Francis, but it is more probable that they had not enough subtlety of mind for this. They gained a certain definite pleasure in hearing the child rail against her father, as she did in quiet, measured, determined tones, but soon it was reason enough that she was there simply because she dominated all the family and had already a kind of social power and authority that neither they nor their children would ever acquire.

Of Deborah, as she grew older, no one save David ever thought. She was not a pretty child. Pale of face, very thin of body, silent. Only her brother knew her and the rare, sweet spirit that she had.

It was from her that he obtained his deeper and more subtle consciousness of the beauty of the country around him. Child though she was, she was sensitive to the minutest beauties--a brown dry tree on a moonlight night, a glittering stream, the softness that snow on the hill-tops gives to the reflective valley, the yellow bunches of leaves on the oak tree, the purple depth of the lake seen beyond a bank of primroses, the low singing of the swallows, the whiteness of frost-bleached stones, the sudden flashing out of lights after a sullen storm, a brown stream running turbulently below a white cottage--above all, the sky of whose pageantry this country seemed more than any other to offer extravagant splendours. She would watch it constantly with a deep enwrapped contemplation, and yet she did not seem a dreamer, helped with a steady unobtrusiveness in all the business of the house; but she was, like her father, although in a very different way, a spirit alone, the only citizen of her mysterious world.

She had a passion for no other human being save David. More than anyone else in the family, she was attentive to Margaret Herries, never irritated by her stupidities or exasperated by her tears; but she had no close contact with her. That was, it might be, her mother's fault. It was her husband whom Margaret Herries loved, ceaselessly, deprecatingly, monotonously, and her daughter Mary whom she admired. She would ask Mary wistfully about Keswick and Pomfret and Jannice. She did not go to see them because she was afraid of them and because her husband would be angry if she did, but theirs was the life that she would have preferred had she had the good fortune--to be in a fine house in a lighted town with company and cards and an occasional ball--but these only if Francis shared them with her.

As he did not choose that life she preferred this isolated one so that he shared it with her. Shared was perhaps too strong a word for anything that he did with her. He told her nothing, approached her always with that same mixture of sarcastic humour and rough careless kindness: she would never understand him at all; perhaps if the moment of comprehension had ever come to her she would not have loved him any longer, so that it was well as it was.

This, however, can at least be said, that, after Alice Press' departure, she was happier than she had been before. If he had other mistresses she did not know of them, and like many another wife, after her and before, so long as she did not know she did not question.

So these years had passed, a strange, slow mist of isolation creeping up around Herries, a mist not of fact but of suggestion, an atmosphere that slowly marked off this family as different from other families, a family of another colour, as though they had been, these Herries, of foreign blood, and had come from some very distant land where odd beasts dwelt and dangerous rivers ran.

It was just about now that, for the first time, someone said in Keswick: 'He's a rogue, Herries--a fantastic rogue.'

Meanwhile, in this April month, Francis and his son David rode together to Ravenglass to stay, for several nights, with brother Harcourt. They rode over the Stye Head Pass and down into Wasdale. David rode on Caesar, and Francis on a little shaggy horse that he called Walpole because he had a belly and was cynically indifferent to any morality. The little horses picked their way very carefully up the hill with deliberate slowness.

No one hurried them. The day was grey and still with little pools of sunlight in a dark sky. The hills had snow on their tops, but in the valleys the larches were beginning to break into intense green flame. As they wound up the Pass, the hills gathered about them, not grandly and with arrogant indifference as larger hills do in other countries, but with intimacy and friendliness as though they liked human beings and were interested in their fates.

By the Stye Head Tarn it was grim and desolate. This Tarn lies, an ebony unreflecting mirror, at the foot of the Gavel--beyond it, to the left, soft green ridges run to Esk Hause and the Langdales and lonely Eskdale.

Above the green stretches there are the harsh serrated lines of Scafell Pike and the thin edge of Mickledore. It was here, however, and on this day that David had his first sharp consciousness of the Gavel, the grand and noble hill that was one day to watch him struggling for his life.

It was not to be seen at its finest here from the Tarn, for it sprawled away to the right almost without shape and form: nevertheless the spirit of it, dauntless, generous and wise, seized and held him. The sunlight, hidden elsewhere, broke above its head and caressed it; long strathes of water, blue like the cold spring streams that ran below the snowdrops, spread about its shoulders.

The whole expanse of land here is wide and strong, so that although no plan or form is visible it makes of itself a form, the Tarn, the green stretches, the grouping hills having their own visible life without any human thought or agency to assist them.

They stayed for a little while beside the black Tarn. Herries, climbing the Pass, had been very genial, speaking of anything that came into his head, of a bull-baiting in Keswick, of funny days in Doncaster and of his old long-ago life near Carlisle. When he was thus he and David were like brothers. But suddenly now beside the Tarn he became morose and gloomy. He withdrew into himself. In silence they rode down into Wasdale, along the road, past the little church to the long lake's edge. Here there was great beauty, the grey lake without a ripple and descending into it the black precipitous Screes, savage and relentless, while on the bank where they rode everything was soft with golden sand, green shelving meadow on which sheep were grazing, and the larches bursting into leaf. All the afternoon they rode in silence turning inland over rough, dull country.

It was not until they came to Santon Bridge that Francis Herries broke the silence.

'Thy uncle Harcourt is Jacobite. He is a romantic jackanapes. Let him not talk thee over.' Then he laughed, twisting himself round on his horse to look at his stolid, thickset, square-shouldered son. 'Not much romantic notion in thy head, David.'

David to his own surprise did not answer. Perhaps it was that the scene had now of itself become romantic. They were riding through thick woods, and between the spaces of the trees the evening sky was faintly rose. A bird, singing, seemed to accompany them. But it was not only the place and the hour. David found that his father had unexpectedly touched something in him that was deep and fervid. Was this the consequence of that ride, seven years ago, with Father Roche? He could hear the melody and worship of the priest's voice now-- 'Even as our Blessed Saviour, so the King . . .'

And, realising this, he was aware that there was something in him here that his father could neither govern nor command--nay, something that his father could not touch. And yet the folly of it! What did he know about Jacobitism, its rights or wrongs? And yet he seemed in those few moments between the dark trees to have started some conflict with his father.

'Where has Father Roche been these years?' he asked.

Herries tossed his head. 'How do I know? He is a fool, a fanatic. He had fine parts but must needs waste them on a mare's nest. . . .' Then he added abruptly: 'He hath been in Rome, tying the Pretender's shoe-strings.'

He went on as the evening gathered under the rosy sky. 'He had a power over me. He has had a power over many. But, believe me, if ever he returns it will be for no good. An ill-omened bird. Yes, a fanatic--better that, though, than a half-nothing like your father. David, have you ever dreamt a recurring dream?'

David shook his head, laughing.

'I am too heavy of nights to dream.'

'I believe that.' Walpole stumbled. Herries pulled at him with a curse.

'I have a dream. . . .' He stopped abruptly. 'There are the lights of Ravenglass. We are almost in.' They came clattering over the cobbles of the little place and smelt the salt sea and heard the sharp questioning cry of the gulls. A fellow standing in a doorway directed them to Harcourt's house.

Although it was now dark David could see the little square white- fronted house thrust back from the street in a small, walled garden. He smelt, as they waited by the door, the sting of the sea and an aromatic scent of herbs and could see here and there the faint yellow of blowing daffodils.

A little old man, very ancient, in a white wig, knee-breeches, and with large silver buckles to his shoes, holding a candle above his head, opened the door cautiously to them, after much unbolting and unbarring and rattling of chains. A moment later Harcourt Herries was there to greet them.

They all went together round with the horses to the stables which were at the back of the garden. The stars were coming out and a strong wind blowing. They returned to the house, and Harcourt, a silver candlestick held high in either hand, led them up to their room.

In the candlelight as he stood and talked to his brother, David could see him clearly. He was a little thin spindle-shanked man very elegantly dressed in an old fashion. He had the high, white forehead and the air of breeding that belonged to the Herries, the breeding that even Pomfret could not quite lose. You could see that he was brother to Francis, but although he was only twelve years older, forty-nine to Francis' thirty-seven, he might have been his brother's father.

His face was thin and drawn and covered with a network of wrinkles; his body was so slight and delicate that as with rare china you might expect to see through it.

Everything about him was refined, from the thin gold ring with a green stone on his finger, to the rich rose-colour of his skirted coat. His voice, when he spoke, was very gentle and kind, and there was in it a note, full and harmonious, that resembled something in Francis' voice.

He looked exceedingly fragile as he stood in the candlelight beside his brother, whose body was beginning to thicken, and his nephew, whose strength and health shone through his young limbs. He had things about him that were like Francis and Father Roche and Deborah, the three people for whom David had, in his life, cared the most.

Harcourt left them to wash off the dirt and weariness of the ride. The jugs and basins in the room were of old beaten silver, and round the top of the four-poster ran a fine tapestry with friezes in rose and old saffron.

Before they went down, Francis said to his son: 'You will find no woman in the house. Harcourt was once in his youth crossed in love. He cannot abide women, and will have none about him.'

Downstairs in a charming panelled parlour they had a meal that was to David a delight. The candlelight trembled before the dark panels.

It was late indeed for dinner, but there was fine fare--a grand salmon, a patty of calf's brains, a piece of roast beef, a dish of fruit with preserved flowers, spinage tarts, sweet with candied orange and citron peel mixed with the spinage, marrow and eggs, and fresh fruit, pears and China oranges and muscadine grapes. There were French wines, Pontack and Hermitage, and later when the table was cleared and showed a pool of splendour under the candles, a bowl of Brunswick Mum, the most intoxicating liquor known to man. Neither Harcourt nor his nephew was drunk. The boy felt perhaps that for the first time, outside his own house, he was treated as a man. Harcourt was a most charming host, telling them in his gentle voice the romantic things about Ravenglass--how its name meant grey-blue river, how three rivers--the Esk, the Irt, and the Mite-- joined here to make the almost landlocked harbour, how once the Romans had been here and made a camp. How in those days it was a place of importance, had its charter in the beginning of the thirteenth century, and at Muncaster Castle near by, the Penningtons would take refuge from the sea raiders, how Henry VI. fleeing there after a lost battle gave his host an enamelled bowl of green glass, 'the Luck of Muncaster,' how still there was traffic in the harbour and much smuggling to and from the Isle of Man, which was but forty miles away. He said that, as he sat there in his room, he could see the Romans and the men of the Middle Ages and all the busy citizens of the place, when it was a prosperous town, come crowding about him with their long, thin faces and strange distant voices--and at that Francis, who was now drunk with the Mum, laughed at him and called him a romantic fool.

It was then that David felt again an odd wave of antagonism to his father sweep over him.

There was something moving between them, something new that had never been between them before: soon it would appear and would be defined.

He became in that first evening attached to his uncle, and it was plain enough that his uncle delighted in him; on the next morning, which was cold and windy, Francis was oddly morose and, saying very little to either of them, went off by himself. Uncle and nephew sat by the coal fire in the parlour.

Harcourt talked of the days when he was a boy in the London of Queen Anne. He had been fourteen years of age when he first went there. He had been present at the sacking of the New Court in the Sacheverell riots and had seen the huge bonfire of its

furniture in Lincoln's Inn Fields; he had had nights on the Folly, the Thames barge opposite Whitehall, although it had already then fallen out of fashion; he described the coffeehouses as though he were still frequenting them--Anderton's, the Bay Tree, Button's, Child's, where you might, an you were lucky, see learned celebrities like Dr. Mead and Sir Hans Sloane; or Don Saltero's, set up by Sir Hans Sloane's servant, where there was a collection of curiosities such as the Queen of Sheba's cordial bottle, Gustavus Adolphus' gloves and King Charles II.'s beard which he wore in disguise in the Royal Oak.

He had been a great lover of the drama, he told David, a faint flush of enthusiastic memory staining his wrinkled cheek.

In the Dorset Gardens Theatre, he had witnessed a performance by the lovely Mrs. Tofts. This theatre was pulled down in 1709, and the world of pleasure knew it no more. In the Theatre Royal, in Drury Lane, he had been thrilled by the performance of the second part of The Destruction of Jerusalem. He would never forget the splendour of Mrs. Rogers as Berenice.

But his chief love had been the Italian Opera. He had himself been present at the great event of its opening on the 9th of April, 1705, when Vanbrugh and Congreve had been there and Mrs. Bracegirdle had spoken the Prologue. The opera on this occasion had been The Triumph of Love.

As he talked he seemed to recreate about him all the distant and vibrating life of that old time, already so quaint and unmodern, with the busy scenes on the river, the perils of the night Mohawks, the chatter of the shops and coffeehouses, and great figures like the Queen and Harley and Marlborough moving in splendid ghostly grandeur.

But what held young David and made this talk memorable to him for ever was the note of wistful and yet acquiescent regret in his uncle's voice. That had been the time when life had been so full of energy and eagerness: everything had been promised then--love and fame and great company--now in this little house, with the sea-coal's thin glow between the fire-dogs, the whisper and rustle of the sea beyond the dark windows, the sense of the little dead and abandoned town once of so busy a prosperity, the remoteness, the half-death-in-life, the eternal melancholy of the indifferent passing of time. . . .

Nevertheless, Uncle Harcourt was cheerful enough. He opened with delicate, reverent fingers his bookcases and produced his Spensers and Miltons and Ben Jonsons. His favourite poet was Mr. Pope. He had Lintot's Miscellany with the first publication of 'The Rape of the Lock,' and the earliest editions of the Iliad as the volumes appeared from 1715 to 1720.

But most of all did he love the 'Elegy to the Memory of an Unfortunate Lady,' and, with tears in his eyes, recited, his voice quivering a little as he spoke:

'By foreign hands thy dying eyes were closed,
By foreign hands thy decent limbs composed,
By foreign hands thy humble grave adorned,
By strangers honoured, and by strangers mourned!
What tho' no friends in sable weeds appear,
Grieve for an hour, perhaps, then mourn a year,
And bear about the mockery of woe
To midnight dances and the public show!
What tho' no weeping Loves thy ashes grace,
Nor polished marble emulate thy face!
What tho' no sacred earth allow thee room,
Nor hallowed dirge be muttered o'er thy tomb!
Yet shall thy grave with rising flowers be drest,
And the green turf lie lightly on thy breast:
There shall the morn her earliest tears bestow,
There the first roses of the year shall blow;
While Angels with their silver wings o'ershade
The ground, now sacred by thy reliques made.'

So long as he lived David was never to forget that scene--the little man, his wig a trifle awry, the volume in one hand, the other hand behind the heavy skirt of his coat, the gentle, melodious voice, the rain, that had now begun to fall, beating on the pane, the distant surge of the sea, the steady friendly murmur of the grandfather's clock. He was not imaginative as his father was; he was never to care very passionately for art and letters, but he made, in this morning, a new friend and acquired for ever some sense of the tragedy of the passing of time and the deep intangible beauty of old loyalties.

His uncle afterwards began to speak of his father. David at once perceived two things, one that his uncle had in his youth deeply loved his father. His older years had given him a protective maternal love of him. There was something very feminine in Uncle Harcourt's nature, and more and more as the morning passed he reminded David of Deborah. And, secondly, Harcourt was greatly distressed at his brother's appearance. He had not seen him for six years and although he said but little and asked but few questions David could see that some unexpressed alarm worked in him.

He spoke of Francis' youth, of how he had been always different from the others, capable of the greatest things, but that some instability had always checked him. 'He hath always imagined more than he grasped, dreamed more than he could realise. There is a wild loneliness in his spirit that no one can reach.'

Then coming and putting his hand most affectionately on David's shoulder he added: 'But he hath bred his greater self in his son, who will fulfil his dearest hopes. I can see that, and it gives me great happiness.'

They were thus affectionately together when Francis Herries came in. He stayed in the doorway then came forward. 'A very pretty picture,' he said. They were both immediately conscious of anger in his voice. David drew away from his uncle, getting up and moving to the window.

'Welcome, brother,' said Harcourt. 'Be warm by the fire and tell us where you have been.'

'Nay,' Francis continued, his voice dry with sarcasm, 'I am one too many. I have a book to read--in my room.' But Harcourt came across to him, laughing, put his hand on his shoulder and drew him to the fire.

Francis was like a child. He sat by the fire, his feet stretched out, and sulked. Their evening meal was not very gay. David felt in every vein antagonism to his father. To repay his brother's courtesy with such childishness! At the age that he had, to sulk and pout like an infant! And yet behind the childishness there was something real. Jealousy? Loneliness? Discontent? Through the evening the antagonism between them grew. By the close of the meal David was miserable. This was none of the old childish quarrels that ended in a beating. And yet what was it about? Where was its growth? A ride through darkening woods, drunkenness over Mum, a flurry of rain. . . .

Sitting there Harcourt raised his glass. "The King!' He crossed the glass in the air.

Francis sprang to his feet. 'None of that humbug, brother! The boy has enough nonsense in his head.'

Harcourt flung his glass behind him. It smashed on the wall.

'I have drunk my toast in my own house,' he answered evenly.

An idiotic moonlight fluttered at the window, very feeble and wavering.

Francis walked to the door, stayed, then came back and put his hand on his brother's shoulder. 'I am become too serious. I have had a day with only ill thoughts for company.' Then, surprisingly, he turned to his son. 'Will you come out with me, David? There is a moon.'

The boy nodded, then turned, smiling, to his uncle: 'You will not be lonely for an hour?'

The little man smiled back at him.

'Mr. Pope will drink a glass with me.' They all smiled at one another. Friendliness had suddenly returned.

Francis and David walked out into the little street, which was quite deserted. There were two sounds, the even whisper of the sea and some drunken fellow at a distance shouting a chorus. The moonlight was a faint, grey, glassy shadow dimming the sharp outline of the houses, but at the sea-edge it was stronger, flooding the water and giving an unreal size and shape to the distant sand-dunes that lay like lazy, grey whales on either side of the harbour.

A little boat stayed very faintly rocking at the shore's edge.

'Shall we take the boat out to the sand?' Francis asked. 'There's no one to prevent us.' They climbed in, Francis took the oars and in silence rowed over the water.

It was not excessively cold, and as they went forward the clouds shredded away, the moon came out riding in a misty, starless heaven. Round her was a ring dark red in colour.

David wondered what his father was going to do. He had some purpose. David on his side felt his own independence resolutely strengthen. Some subservience that there had always been to his father was no longer there. The boat shelved gently on to the sand and they stepped out. The sand was hard and crisp under the feet: the dune was naked save for a thick black post that stood up, like a finger in the moonlight. They walked over the dune and stood on the farther side. The sea was stronger here, coming in fiercely and drawing back with a powerful grating reluctance. They stood together looking out.

'I will not have you play with this Jacobite folly,' Francis said suddenly. 'Understand me in this. You are a child--your uncle is an old dreamer and babbles of Queen Anne.'

David straightened his shoulders. 'I have played with no Jacobite folly,' he said. 'I have only spoken of it once and that for a brief while.'

Francis felt the new tone in the boy's voice. 'You had some fine intimate confidences with your uncle,' he said scornfully. 'I should have remembered that he has a way with young men. Had I remembered I would not have brought you.'

In each of them anger was rising; their isolation, thus standing quite alone in a bare world that was all moonlight and water, increased their sense of opposition.

David said coldly: 'I am no child, father, any longer. I must have my own judgement. My uncle is a generous host. To-day you have left him all afternoon and he has not seen you for six years.'

His father turned to him passionately. 'And so the babe has grown. . . . By Christ, I'll sit meekly by and have my son read me a lesson. Has the hair grown above your belly yet, and how many women are with child by you?'

David stood his ground, but strange old fears, born of whippings and terrors and childish nightmares, crowded over the sand-dune and caught at his feet. 'I am on the edge of manhood and you should know it. I have been child to you long enough. If I find my uncle care-worthy I have a right to care for him. It is time when I must think for myself. I love you, father, as I love no one else alive. There is a bond between us, and, I suppose, will always be, that we can have with none other. You have often recognised it. But I am my own man. I have my own life to carry, and yield my liberty to no one--'

Francis laughed. 'Your liberty--who constrains it? You speak bravely of love, but there is also a word duty. When I say bend you shall bend. When I command you shall go. No doubt but your uncle's flattering enlarges you--but not with me . . . come here.'

David came close to him. Francis caught his cheek and pinched it. 'You are mine, my fine son--strip now.

Here, under this moon. I will run you naked into the sea--cold bathing for a rebellious son. That shall cool thy Jacobite notions. Strip then.'

'I will not,' David said. He was trembling from head to foot, but neither with chill nor with fear.

'You will not? . . . Better for thee far to obey. Strip--naked as you were born.'

'I will not,' David said again.

Francis had in his hand a small cane with a gold-stamped head. He raised it and struck David across the cheek with it. David caught it, flinging it far into the sea.

They stood staring the one at the other.

'That--never again,' David said quietly. The moonlight showed the red weal from his eye to his mouth--'The last time . . .'

Francis stayed without a word. Then he turned and walked away across the sand.

David stood there looking at the red ring around the moon, knowing that something fundamental that would affect all his life had occurred. He had the quality of common sense in melodrama; the unreality of any scene did not lead himself to unreality. This was unreal, the desolate sand, the crazy moon red-ringed, the mildewed sea, his father's assault, his own action--all unreal and yet at their heart a real and true fact, that he was child no longer.

He waited: he was sure that his father would return and that then, perhaps, they would be companions as they had never been before. His father did return, slowly coming across the sand, his figure thin and hard in the soft moonlight.

When he was near David went up to him, holding out his hand and smiling. 'You must know for yourself,' he said, 'that the water is too cold. And for your cane you shall have another.'

Francis caught him, gripped his shoulder, then stood close, his hand against his wounded cheek.

'You are a boy no longer. You are right in that. But I have been jealous to-day, suffering torture for you.

'Always I have been judged to lose anything where I put value, and to catch to me closer than a flea anything that was worthless.

'For years I have been prepared for you to go like the rest. When you were a baby I would watch and say, "Now, in a moment his eyes will change. He will know me for a rogue." And then, as one accident after another passed and still you were the same, I would say, "He is only a child. He hasn't heard. He hasn't years enough to understand." When my temper or my lust has driven me I have thought, "This will take him away the sooner," and I have almost wished for that, because my dread of losing you would be the earlier satiated. And now, to-day, watching your happiness with your uncle, I went out so that he should tell you everything-- how as a child I did this and as a youth that, this way a rogue, that way a villain.

'I thought, "When I return he will know me for what I am, and our time together will be over. Then everything and everyone will have gone from me and I need fear no more."

'And I came in and saw his arm about your neck and hated you, loving you never so dearly as then. Never so dearly--save now.'

He broke off, then drawing David closer to him, waved his hand at the moon. 'The red ring--so it was when I ruffled my first girl, twelve years of age as I was, in a hay-loft.' Then he turned David towards him and looked at him: 'One day you will go from me--but not yet.'

David, smiling, said:

'Why should I ever leave you? I have no light sentiment about persons. You and Deborah I could never leave. You have told me,' he went on, hesitating a little, 'that I have no imagination nor fancy. I think that is true. I see what is before me and only that. But I am the easier faithful. I have noticed that those who have much fancy are but rarely steadfast. But this I know. Were I made more cleverly I would be of less enduring service to you.'

He said this with a very grave air, as though he had long been elderly.

His father answered him: 'There are only nineteen years between us, and as time goes they will lessen. Soon we shall be of an age: then you will pass me and be old before I am weaned. But remember this,' he touched the boy's arm lightly, almost withdrawing from him, 'whatever others say, I have it in me to be faithful--only as yet I have found neither cause nor person nor quality fit for that fidelity. I say this with no arrogance. I know what I am, and that is no fine thing. Nor do I say that with modesty. God may answer, if He is, for it is He that has made a man in a mouldy broken image of a divine ambition. . . . But always with us Herries have been one or two who see farther than they can reach and hope for more than they shall ever get.

'Their place is to break up that pattern formed so beautifully by such as your dear uncle Pomfret. So the strife goes on, and will always go between the marred angels and the belly-filling citizens who have their fine houses and thank God they are not as others.

'The Herries have always been thus, and will always be, so making a fine study for your social observer.

'But I can dream of beauty, and if one day it is put in my hand . . .'

He broke off. 'What I would say,' he added, kicking the sand with his shoe, 'is that crab-apples are deceiving when they shine in moonlight, and the taste is stale.'

Then, almost passionately, he cried:

'Ah, but stay by me, David. I am going the wrong way, and what matters it? It is only another man lost. But one day I may be faithful to something, and then I would have you witness of it.'

David, who only saw the principal fact, that his father needed him, answered, as Ruth once answered:

'I will never leave you.'

His father, looking at him ironically, said:

'Your imagination saves you, Davy. That you have none, I mean. But you have made a vow here. I must have something for the loss of my gold cane.'

And then, the wind once more rising, whipping up the waves, they turned back across the sand.

CHRISTMAS FEAST

The December weeks that winter of 1737 were wonderful. Frost held the valley: Derwentwater Lake was frozen from end to end for thirteen days; the hills were powdered with thin patterns of snow hardening to crystal under a blue sky.

The valley was now truly enclosed. The outer world did not exist for it. The autumnal rains had been very violent, and, after them, Borrowdale barred its door.

The Herries family itself took the fashion. Even Mary deserted her Keswick cousins. As Christmas approached they were all caught into the general eagerness. In every house in the valley such a baking and brewing was going on as the Herries children had never seen in their Doncaster days. And the materials for this were all self- provided. No going into Keswick for town provisions. The valley was sufficient for itself. Down the path below Herries the Statesman Peel would be striding, his hands in huge home-made mittens, his jacket buttoned up to his chin, passing his dairy-maid who, with her piggin in her hand, was hurrying to the cow-house, relishing the warmth and smell of the cows after the bitter cold that descends from the snowy hills; the boys sliding on the little pond beyond Herries in their wooden clogs, the blue sky, the snowy hills over all, the Wise Man with the pink ribbons to his moleskin hat moving up the road to Seathwaite, witches hiding, no doubt, in the Glaramara caves, the Devil warm at a farm-house fire with his pedlar's pack, and all the wives and daughters washing, baking, churning; the puddings and pies will be enough for all Cumberland.

As Christmas approached more nearly David became uneasy and restless. It may have been that there was something ominous for him in the strange isolation of this valley. It was not that he was dull; every moment of the day seemed to be filled. He was now friend to all the valley. Whatever they might feel about his father there was no differing opinion about himself. His handsome looks and splendid body (he promised to be a giant both in breadth and height; he was already as tall as his father), his courage, openness and sincerity, the absence of all conceit and social arrogance, his simplicity, a certain animal lack of subtlety, his kindliness of heart and warmth of feeling--here promised to be a man of no ordinary colour, and everyone realised it. He had that greatest of all powers--he loved his fellows without being conscious that he loved them. Had he been a little less simple he might have seen them more justly, but in the end have judged them more untruly.

With all its simplicity, his character, as it was developing, was not uninteresting. His fearlessness, honesty and warmth of heart gave even his smallest adventures a richness of colour. He was of the race around whom legends grow: already people told stories of his strength, of how he had bent an iron bar in Peel's kitchen, beaten a shepherd from Watendlath, and whacked a Seathwaite farmer at singlestick and he champion of the valley--small stories, but he was already talked of beyond Bassenthwaite and over Buttermere and Loweswater. Borrowdale was the proudest of all the valleys and the stickiest to foreigners, but its natives already showed signs of adopting young Herries. Young Herries, but no other of the Herries, family. It was possibly of this that David was subtly aware, partly this that roused his uneasiness.

It seemed to him that this valley had entrapped them. He was not sorry to be entrapped--he was happier here than he had ever been anywhere--but the sense that they were caught and held roused his fear. It was the only fear that life perhaps could give him--the fear of confinement--and now not so much for himself as for his father. He was growing now to be a man and ever since that night at Ravenglass he had been on shoulder-level with his father. His father seemed to him more alone than anyone in the world. No one in the valley was his friend. He was someone of a different nation from all of them--from his own son as well.

And the valley, because it was at this time almost savage in its isolation, hated and feared, like all savage things, what was different from itself. David loved his father now more than he had ever done, but he understood him less the older he grew, and feared for him more with every day.

He saw with his own eyes once a small child run from his father screaming. He did not yet know that the mothers of the valley told their babies that Rogue Herries would eat them if he caught them.

Nearer to David's father than any other man in the valley was Statesman Peel. He was himself a rather isolated man, gigantic in build but silent, keeping to himself. Rendal Peel, his son, David's dearest friend, was frightened of his father and could manage no contact with him. He too was a silent boy, adoring David, following him like a dog.

So there they were this Christmas that was fated to add another legend to the Herries story. Rogue Herries who sold his woman for thirty silver pieces and Rogue Herries who was slashed in the cheek by young Osbaldistone. . . . Nothing stands still. The course that the lives of Francis Herries and his son David were to take was largely fashioned that winter.

All England was at this time wrapped in superstition: the Age of Reason was only now stirring in that romantic womb--and no valley in England was more superstitious than this little one of Borrowdale. Perhaps you could not call it superstition, so active a part in daily life did they play, pixies and warlocks, gnomes and little green Johnnies, the Devil and his myriad witches. It was not far back that men of Borrowdale, seeing a red deer on the hills, had thought it a horse with horns and pursued it for a magical twist of the Devil; and the wall to keep in the cuckoo would yet have succeeded had it been but a story higher.

It was unlikely that David, a child of his time, would escape this magic. As he sat now, a week before Christmas, with Deborah before the open fire in the Herries hall and saw the snow swirl like twisting worsted beyond the leaded panes, he felt that they were both held there by a spell--the spell, it might be, of his wicked old ancestor hanging on the panelled wall.

His great shoulders and long legs sprawled beyond his chair; his fair head was thrown back; his eyes, warm in spite of their bright blueness, stared into the black beams above him. Deborah, seated at his feet, looking up at him, thought that she had never seen anyone so splendid.

'Deb, why is it that they hate father so?'

For how long now had this question been hovering between them!

'There is a separateness about father.' She stared into the golden cavern that hung, lit with sparks of fire, between the black logs. 'They cannot understand him nor he them.'

'Deb, do you understand him?'

'Yes, I fancy so. He dreams of what life should be and because it falls so far behind his dream he abuses it.'

David let his hand fall on her hair.

'I am no dreamer, but I can see how a man in this life may have ambitions to alter it. I am a poor oaf, Deb. I love every moment of the day. Just to feel the blood in my veins is enough for me. Such a day as yesterday with Rendal on the Gavel when, from the summit, you could look out to the sea like a green shawl and all the tops hushed with snow. . . . That's enough for me, Deb. And always will be. I shall never go from here. I shall never do anything in the world. . . . I cannot be unhappy like my father.' Then he added, dropping his voice: 'I am afraid for our father.'

And she whispered: 'I also.'

They had never, although their lives had been so intimate, confessed so much to one another, and in their young hearts, courageous and generous, there beat a tremendous impulse of loyalty and protection to him.

They offered their young bodies and their strong souls as shields and bucklers for his protection, whatever he might do or be. No matter how valueless his worth they were his guard and would always be.

Deborah looked up to David and clasped his hand; as they looked at one another that was what they meant. Then they both saw, leaning a little heavily against the window-ledge, their mother. Her face was pallid: her hands gripped the wood. She was like a heavy ghost: she had made no sound and her eyes did not move.

'I am unwell,' she suddenly gasped. 'I have a sharp pain at my breast.'

David jumped up and ran to her. He put his arm about her and with his great strength almost carried her up the little stairs to her room. She smiled very faintly as he laid her on the bed.

'The pain is nothing,' then, closing her eyes, she murmured, 'Christ is kind. . . . He moves gently. . . .' She caught her son's hand. 'Don't tell your father. . . . How cold it is in this valley.'

She was better again by Christmas Eve, and was up seated in the hall, watching them dance to the fiddle of old Johnny Shoestring, whose bow squeaked like a dying hen. That was the happiest evening they had yet had in Borrowdale. The hall was bright, the fire leaping, the candles burning, the floor shining. Wilson had hung three old flags that had been buried in the oak chest, one of crimson with a white cross, one of faded purple and one of green. Whose flags? From what wars? No one knew. The holly was thick with red berries that year and hung from the rafters. They could hear the bells ringing from the Chapel above the splash and crackle of the fire. Francis was a child, younger than any. They danced till they sank on the floor with weariness. Margaret Herries never moved her eyes from her husband.

Next night, Christmas night, they were invited to Statesman Peel's. It was not as it was in most parts of England where, at Christmas time, the Squire was the King of the Castle and his subjects were graciously bidden to enjoy his hospitality with a proper sense of his grand benignancy and their inferior peasantry. In Borrowdale every Statesman was master of his own house and owed allegiance to no one. Every Statesman's house was open on Christmas night to all the world, rich and poor. There were the guests, indeed, who had their special places there, but the doors were wide open to the stars and the line of friendly hills and the hard-frosted road.

Peel's kitchen this night was a place of splendour. Its warmth and colour, its happiness and hospitality, stretched to the farthest heavens. Glaramara and the Gavel looked in at the windows, the Derwent rolled its waters past the door, and every star scattered its light over the roof-tree.

There is no house like Peel's house anywhere in England any more, but, as it stood then, in its life and strength and happiness, it was thus. It was a strong place, secured with strong doors and gates, its small windows crossed with bars of iron. It held three rooms on the ground floor and two on the second story.

The front door was covered with a low porch, the entrance from which was called the 'thresh-wood' or threshold, and on this thresh- wood crossed straws, horse-shoes and so on, were laid to hinder the entrance of witches. From this there was a broad passage through the house called the 'hallan'; sacks of corn were deposited here before market-day, pigs were hung after killing, and there was a shelf over the door where sickles hung and carpentry tools were laid.

In Peel's house the hallan opened straight into the 'downhouse'. This was in his case the great common room of the family, the place of to-night's Christmas Feast. Here, in the course of the year, everything occurred, baking, brewing, washing, meals, quarrelling, courting, tale-telling. This downhouse had no second story but was open to the rafters. In later days a second story was often built over the downhouse. The sides of this room were smeared with clay and cow-dung. Joints of meat hung dry for winter use. From the smoky dome of the huge fireplace dropped a black sooty lee called the 'hallan drop'. Under this the women knitted or spun wool or flax, the men sometimes carding the wool, the children learning their lessons, the old men telling their tales. At the opposite end of the passage was the mill-door and beyond this another passage known as the 'heck', and this heck was terminated by a huge octagonal post. Into this post sometimes a hole was bored and in it a piece of cow-hair secured by a wooden peg for the purpose of cleaning combs, and behind the heck was a bench.

The windows were separated by stone munnions, and here were the Bible and Prayer Book, Tom Hickathrift and Sir William Stanley's Garland.

The chimney wing was spacious. Indeed, this was a really vast chamber, for it was the 'house' or dwelling-room and 'downhouse' or kitchen thrown into one. Part of it therefore stood for kitchen with the great chimney and hearth; here, on the heap of wood ashes, was the 'handreth,' an iron tripod on which was placed the 'girdle' for baking oat-bread. Before the fire stood a spit. The two standards, which were three feet high with seven hooks, were hinged, so that they could be folded and put away when not in use. The spit, a slender rod, was six feet in length, and on the rod were two pairs of prongs to hold the meat, and beneath it a dripping-pan. There was a handmill or 'quern,' a malt mill, a spindle and a 'whorl,' a spinning wheel. In the chimney wing were hung hams and sides of bacon and beef, and near the fire-window was an ingle-seat, comfortable most of the year save when the rain or snow poured down on to the hearth, as the chimney was quite unprotected and you could look up it and see the sky above you. Such was the kitchen end of the room. The floor to-night was cleared for the dancing, but at the opposite end trestle-tables were ranged for the feasting. Here was also a large oak cupboard with handsomely carved doors. This held the bread, bread made of oatmeal and water. On the mantel and cupboard there were rush-light holders and brass candlesticks. In other parts of the room were big standard holders for rushlights.

All these to-night were brilliantly lit and blew in great gusts in the wind.

Francis Herries, arriving with his children, David, Mary and Deborah, found that already everything was in a whirl. Peel himself greeted them magnificently, standing his six foot four, splendid in his dark coat of native fleece and buckskin breeches, and Mrs. Peel, stout, very red of face, in russet, all the little Peels (and there were very many) gathered together behind her.

Many were already dancing. It was a scene of brilliant colour with the blazing fire, the red berries of the holly glowing in every corner, old Johnny Shoestring in bright blue breeches and with silver buckles to his shoes perched on a high stool fiddling for his life, the brass gleaming, faces shining, the stamp of the shoon, the screaming of the fiddle, the clap-clap of the hands as the turns were made in the dance--and beyond the heat and the light the dark form of the valley lying in breathless stillness, its face stroked by the fall of lingering reluctant snow.

After the first greeting the Herries family stood quietly by the wall. Fragments of talk, slow cautious words like the repetition of some magic recipe, circled the light.

'Hoo ayre ye to-day? Hey ye hard ony news?' . . .

'Ye say reet, nowt se sartain. Gud day. Ayre ye all weel at heam?' . . .

'Aye, they said she was worth brass. . . .'

'Whya, he's nobbut read about it; what can he knaw? I sud think if he minds his awn job it'll be as weel.'

Peel came and asked Francis Herries to sit by him. His elder girl took Mary and Deborah. David found Rendal.

Francis had come with some of the gaiety and happiness of the preceding night and, as always when he was happy, it seemed to shine in him. He was dressed simply to-night in a suit of grey and silver; although in these last years he had stoutened and broadened he was still handsome beyond all ordinary men. His charm, when he was charming, was so gracious and natural that it won everyone near him.

From the moment of his entering every eye had been upon him. To these people of the valley, although they had talked for months of his wickedness, cruelty, and the strange mystery that led him to isolate himself in this loneliness, he was yet at sight something miraculous and magnificent beyond belief. He was the Dark Angel of their secret dreams.

Romantic--but to himself he was not romantic. As he sat there beside Peel, he could feel the old devilish struggle beginning in him. Partly this was an evening after his heart. He cared nothing for class--all the world was his fellow. He liked to see this common happiness; he could feel in this little, hot, sweating, smelly world all the animal satisfaction that had no ill in it.

He would set them all, had he his way, eating, drinking, fornicating, singing--the whole world singing over its surfeited belly--and mingled with this a tenderness, a kind of familiar protection so that he could love these owl faces, these humped bodies, these spindle legs for their little homely tragedies and satisfactions.

So go we all
Down the dark path,
Alien, to the friendly tomb.

This sense of common luck with the veriest hind was something that had always separated him from Pomfret, Harcourt and the rest--yes, and from his own children.

To-night he could feel it to the full as the rushlights scattered streams of light in the wind and the smell of unwashed bodies, perspiring chaps, dog's offal, burning wood and cooking meat gathered in the air, and all the faces turning in the middle of the room, dilated with the music and the movement--dog faces, horse faces, pig faces, bird faces--but gathering an extra humanity as they felt happiness encouraging them and leading them on to confidence.

He would jump down and share this with them, the drink and the food and the tousling the girls. But he was alone. He could share nothing with anyone. His touch was enough; at the feel of it everything withdrew. Within the heart of the burning candle he was isolated; at its core it was ice. He was ringed with flame and could not get out.

He looked at Peel whom he liked, his big body set back, his broad face spread in laughter: he looked at David whom he loved, moving into the middle of the room crowded now with faces. No one was alone save himself, and he by his own mysterious fault. He was well aware by now of how suspicious they were of him.

This suspicion had blown like a subtle poison through the valley. What had he done to create it? Been drunk once or twice, kissed a girl or two, lost his temper on an occasion--nothing definite save that foolish affair with Alice Press. . . . She had spoken truly. Since that day he had never been rid of her.

But he knew well that it was no positive deed on his part that had separated him. It was something in his spirit. They suspected that battle that was never still in himself, disgust fighting with longing, lechery with an icy purity, a driving dream with sodden reality, the devil in him that would never leave him alone, try as he would to throttle it with self-contempt, irony and the discipline of his impulses.

Sitting now beside Peel he envied that great healthy body, that steady mind, that serene soul, and even as he envied knew that this very thought was separating him, driving him into loneliness and this bitter isolation.

The door would open and the snow blow through in little impatient gusts and all the valley would pour in with it. The room was crowded now against the wall and in the corners. The ale was passing round, and voices were loud and laughter ferocious. But everyone behaved in seemly fashion: a dignity, that seemed to radiate from the grand figure and quiet hospitality of the host himself, pervaded the place. Only--as Francis Herries could feel-- he could sniff it in the air--there was a kind of madness behind the dignity, something that belonged to the witches and old crippled warlocks, to the naked shapes playing under the stars above Seatoller, to the broomsticks flying dimly like thin clouds towards the moon.

Suddenly there was a cry: 'They coom. They're here.' It was the 'Play-Jigg.' This was the drama in verse played by the actors who, tonight, were passing from Statesman's house to Statesman's house.

Johnny Shoestring ceased his playing, the dancers vanished, the centre of the room was clear. Packed against the walls now were bodies and faces, legs and backs. There was whispering and tittering, but quite clearly in the immediate silence could be heard the hiss of the snow hovering down through the open chimney on to the fire.

They came forward. Francis was amused as he saw that the Master of these Ceremonies was his old friend the pedlar, David's Devil. Very roguish he was to-night in a cocked purple hat and purple tights showing his thin, spidery limbs, his face with its crooked ironic smile, and his black shining eyes.

He introduced his little company, Old Giles, a bent old man with a long chin, Pinch, a clown, a stout and jolly fellow, a husband and a wife, and young Go-to-Bed who at once in a high, shrill treble introduced himself:

'My father is old and decrepit,
My mother deceased of late,
And I am a youth that's respected,
Possessed of a good estate.'

The old couple did a little dance of joy at this, and then Pinch the clown came forward and asked young Go-to-Bed if he wanted to increase his fortune. Of course young Go-to-Bed was eager, so Pinch introduced him to Old Giles, who said he would show him how to make money out of nothing. This young Go-to-Bed was delighted to know, so Old Giles told him that he must have his arse kicked a dozen times by friend Pinch, and then he must put his head in a bucket of water and then must sit up a night alone in a churchyard: all these things young Go-to-Bed performed to the infinite delight of the audience, especially in the churchyard when Pinch, dressed as a painful ghost, emptied a sack of flour over young Go-to-Bed and set the dogs on to him.

The 'Jigg' ended in a grand dance and in this the audience soon joined. Go-to-Bed, his face white with flour, led off with Mrs. Peel, and Peel took the Old Lady, and soon all the room was turning to Johnny Shoestring's music.

Still Francis Herries did not move. He was alone on the raised seat near the fire-window. All his children were dancing; even Mary now had forgotten her superior airs and breeding and was smiling at young Curtis, son of a Newlands Statesman. The pedlar came across to Francis.

'Good day.'

'Good day,' said Francis.

'You are not dancing, sir.'

'In my own time,' said Francis.

The pedlar stood there smoothing his hands down the sides of his legs with a look of infinite satisfaction.

'It is very cold up at the valley end,' the pedlar said, 'but the moonlight warms the air. Leave this and take a walk with me.'

Herries felt an impulse to go. The thought of the cold, the black ridge of the hills, and the sky silver-thickened, the freshness, the icy air, was fiercely attractive. His dream--the splendid horse breasting the dark lake under the icy spears--seemed to penetrate the very heart of the thickly smelling, heated room. Close to him the hams and the dried beef swung ever so slightly in the great chimney. A country girl mopped her sweating brow. Beyond the fire-window he fancied that he could hear a cow, desolate in the dark field, lowing for its calf, but of course there would be no cow outside at Christmas. He was about to say that he would go when the pedlar touched his arm.

'Here are strangers,' he said, pointing with his long white finger.

Francis Herries followed his direction and saw pressed near the door at the hallan end a man and a woman and a child. The man was rough, bony, with long black hair that tumbled on to his shoulders, the woman white-faced, crouching a little as though she feared a blow, and pressed against her dress was a very young child. It was the child that held Herries' notice. She could not have been above seven or eight years of age, her face so white that it might have been blanched by moonlight. But it was her hair that was astonishing. She was wearing a little peaked man's cap of grey with a russet feather in it and under this her hair fell almost to her tiny waist. Its colour was flame. Flame. Francis, incredulously smiling at his interest, repeated the word. Flame. As though her head were on fire. Flame smouldering, with a sudden movement of her little shoulders glancing in coloured shadow as though it were alive. It sank into darkness as fire does, then lifted into amber and rolled about her head in smoky sombre red. She pressed farther back against her mother, and the flame seemed to creep across the dress, to move, to stir, then to lie there, idly licking the dull stuff.

Between this fire the little face looked out, the face of a tired baby, weary, scornful, ironically interested and alone.

'I have never seen such hair,' Herries said, as though to himself.

'Come and burn your hand in it,' said the pedlar.

Herries got up and looked about him. The brightness of that baby's hair seemed to have dimmed and hushed the room. The candlelight was smoked, the voices, the laughter, the trampling of feet shut away behind glass. Herries followed the pedlar across the floor. As they approached the man frowned and drew his body together animal fashion. He was all animal, he smelt animal, looking out with sharp suspicious eyes from his shaggy black hair. The woman did not move, but looked up at Herries. The pedlar smiled at her: 'Hey, Jane Starr,' he said.

Then the woman spoke to Herries: he was astonished at her voice, which was soft and musical and without any real accent.

'You have forgot me, sir.'

He smiled down at the child. 'I fear that I have.'

'Once you gave me your coat,' she said softly, staring into his eyes. So that was it! The morning of the day that was to prove so eventful to him, the morning of the Chinese Fair. The tang of that walk came back to him, his happiness, the freshness, the waterfall clinging like a ladder to the rock, the dead man, the patient woman.

'You were welcome to it,' he said, looking at her for the first time. Her face was not comely. White and weary, but there was strength and courage in it.

'And this is your child?' he asked.

'My child,' the woman answered. But the man made no movement, only stared moodily into the whirling room. It was strange that her voice was so soft yet came clearly through all the racket and din of voices, music and stamping feet.

'Of what age is she?'

'Eight,' the woman answered.

Eight!--and so independent and alone in this jostling cruel world. He thirty-seven, and yet already there was some kinship between them. . . .

'What is her name?'

'Mirabell,' and then after a little pause with a quick glance at the man beside her--'Mirabell Starr.'

Mirabell Starr--so he heard for the first time the name that would never leave his consciousness again. He could be very sweet with children. He squatted on his hams, his silver sword trailing on the floor. He put out his strong hand and took her tiny one.

'Mirabell. That is a man's name, you know. . . . Shall we be friends?'

Her strange grey eyes, shining with deep lights, regarded him very gravely. She sighed, then very indifferently answered:

'If my mother wishes.'

Her voice was low, sweet and distant, a little as though it were caught in the echo of a shell. He was charmed with it. Squatting a little lower he put out his arm and drew her in to him, pressing her gently between his knees. The silver thread on his sleeve rubbed her neck, but she did not draw back. Nor did she come to him of her own will.

'Where do you live, my pretty?'

'I live with my mother.'

'And where is that?'

The woman spoke.

'We are from Ennerdale, sir.'

'Ah, from Ennerdale.'

At last, drawing a little breath as though he foretold the emotion that it would give him, he put up his hand and stroked her hair: it seemed that a wave of pleasure passed through his body. Its texture was infinitely soft and lay against the back of his hand like music.

'How come you here? You should be at home on Christmas night.'

The man spoke for the first time. 'We have no settled place. I am a horse-dealer.' His voice was rough and very ungracious, but it had no tang of the North.

Herries caught the child closer. Her head was almost against his breast, and it was as though his heart leapt towards it to greet it. He felt in his pocket and found a charm, a negro's head in gold with ruby eyes--it was a charm against the ague.

'Will you take this from me--a Christmas gift?' he asked.

For a moment, to steady herself, she laid one tiny hand on his thigh while with the other she took the little negro. A thrill of happiness ran through him. She looked at the charm very gravely.

"Tis against the ague,' he told her. 'You will not catch it an you keep this with you.'

She looked up at her mother, then at the man.

'It is very pretty,' she said. 'I thank you.' But although her expression was that of a grown woman her fingers tightened round it as a baby's would.

He kissed her forehead, then straightened himself to his full height.

'I wish you good day,' he said, bowing to the woman very slightly, then turned and walked into the room. He turned confusedly like a man in a dream. For a while he could not see the room clearly. Strange coincidence! That this should be the woman whom carelessly that morning he had for a moment protected! What had been her history? Who was the dead man, who now this present animal, this horse-dealer, horse-thief he did not doubt? She did not look a woman who would pass lightly from man to man--but what did she at all in that company? Mirabell . . . Mirabell. . . . So the child was called. Poor little misery, already bearing in her eyes the knowledge of hardship, cruelty, aloneness. What a life must she have with such a man and his company! Almost he was tempted to turn aside, go back and make some mad demand for the child's protection. A nice affair--to be mixed in such a throng! As though there were not already scandal enough. But he looked back nevertheless. There was no sign of them. They were hidden by the dancers. The Christmas Feast was at its height.

This was a scene from Breughel. The trestle-tables were piled with food, pies and puddings, hams and sides of beef. The drink was for the most part ale, but there was creeping into the valley now that new destroying devil of the English countryside, the demon gin. There were signs of it here to-night--men were pressing the girls now, their faces flushed, their hands fumbling for breast and side. The women were giggling, the dogs snapping at food and legs and one another. An old man with long white hair, thin as a scarecrow, was dancing very solemnly alone in the middle of the floor, twisting his body into corkscrew shapes. At a table near the chimney a group of old people were playing at cards. But wildness was coming in, coming in from the caverns of the hill, and the high, cold spaces round Sprinkling Tarn and the lonely passes above the listening valleys. It was Christ's Day no longer. He had been turned out when the wind had changed, and all the doors and shutters of the house had rattled their shoulders at His going.

Peel himself felt perhaps that his hand was losing its hold on the scene. And perhaps he did not care. He was a man of his time, and that was a rough time, a cruel and a coarse. They had a small, wild, starving dog, strayed in from the valley, and they had tied him to the leg of a table, and were holding meat just beyond his nose, while he yelped in his agony of hunger, and his little fierce protesting eyes darted wildly about the room.

Up in the half-darkness of the hallan one of the shepherds was stripping to a whispering group of men and girls to show his tattooed body, made when he was in the Indies as a boy, marvellous, they say, a whole love-story on his legs and back. Although the night was bitter, couples twined closely together wandered out of the house up the road, kissing to the eternal murmur of the running water.

Then the house-door burst wide and a strange crew broke into the room. They came shouting, singing and very drunk. Their shoulders were powdered with snow, and their frosty breath blew in clouds about them. This was a party that had ridden over from Keswick and Portinscale and Grange, had found their way under the moon to Rosthwaite, and now, drinking at every stage, were turning back again (an they were sober enough to ride) to Keswick. Here was the Lord of Misrule and his followers, a young fellow with very flushed face, a crown awry on his crooked wig, his clothes of purple satin and gold, carried on the shoulders of four half-naked men blacked like Indians and followed by a motley baggage-heap dressed fantastically as jesters, Chinamen and clowns. There was a Hobby-horse and old Father Neptune with his trident. They burst the doors, then paused to arrange their procession. The naked Indians threw off their cloaks in which they had been wrapped against the cold, caught up their young Lord of Misrule and shouldered him, and so marched up the room, followed by the Jester with his bauble, a lady with a flaxen wig and very naked bosom, Neptune and a posturing, shouting throng.

The natives of the valley drew back against the wall. Here were foreigners from the town, and though their intrusion was no new thing at a Christmas time, yet it boded no good. It had ended before in a bloody riot and so might do again. Francis had been looking for his children, and finding them had bidden David take his sisters home, then, if he would, return. So he was once again alone, a great stillness in his heart in the midst of the riot, once or twice looking to see whether he could catch sight of the child and her mother: it seemed that they were gone.

Watching this new invasion he found that he recognised three at least of the company, two from Keswick. The Lord of Misrule himself was young Cuthbertson, son of a wealthy merchant; one of the black men young Fawcett, a Squire's eldest boy; and the Jester himself with his cap and bells Osbaldistone from Threapthwaite, near Whitehaven. Young Osbaldistone was often at Keswick, and Herries had been with him at cards and cock-fighting. There was no love between them. Herries had won his money, which the young fool could ill afford to lose, and Herries had kissed a girl that Osbaldistone had also been pursuing.

At the sight of him a spasm of revolt and disgust caught his heart. He had drunk nothing: he had been moved to-night by the courteous friendliness of Peel, by the happy simplicity of the earlier part of the evening, and, at this last, by his meeting with the child. Apart and reserved as he seemed standing there alone, yet his heart had been filled with kindliness and an almost childlike desire to be friends with the world.

At the sight of this rabble he was tempted to slip away and find his bed. Had he gone, the whole course of his life would have been other. Nevertheless our lives are dictated by character, not by chance. Some foolish pride kept him. He fancied that from the corner by the fire-window the pedlar sardonically watched him. It was true that many eyes were on him, as they had been all the evening; so, because he had some conceit and felt a challenge in the air, he stayed.

Events followed then with dreamlike swiftness. Afterwards if he ever looked back to this night it seemed to him that he had from the very first been trapped. He could not have escaped; he did not pity himself for this (in all his life-history from the first page to the last there was no self-pity), but he did ask himself whether he could have avoided the event: he could not.

The procession settled itself about its Lord: drink was brought: there was much sham ceremony: subjects knelt and sentences were passed; the lady in cloth of gold with the naked bosom was proclaimed Queen. The peasants stood around, mouths agape, the little wild dog, who had been forgotten, yelped dismally, then broke his rope, crawled to a corner where he feasted ravenously. Everyone was at ease again. Dancing took the floor. Figures, fantastic, painted in orange and scarlet and purple, laughing, singing, kissing, whirled and turned; some fell upon the floor and lay there. Still in the farther corner the old people, like characters painted on the wall, played gravely their cards.

Young Osbaldistone, his cap awry, the laced waistcoat unbuttoned, pursued a girl and encountered Herries. He stopped short.

Herries gravely bowed. Osbaldistone looked. The drink cleared from his eyes. He straightened himself. He was a cold-tempered, severe lad in his natural life, debauched enough but ready at any moment to clear debauchery from his system. He stood back fumbling the hilt of his sword.

'Mr. Francis Herries.'

'Mr. Richard Osbaldistone.'

He yet stuttered a little. The drink was not all cleared. 'Dick to my friends,' then added softly, 'but not to you, Mr. Herries.'

No one heard him. Herries frowned. He did not want a quarrel with the boy here, not to-night, Christmas night, and in Peel's house. He bowed.

'I wish you good evening,' he said and turned.

Osbaldistone touched his shoulder. Herries, turning back, was amazed at the hatred that formed and edged the other's face like a mask. To hate him like that! And for what? For nothing--a loss at cards, a girl's kiss. No--for what he himself in his very spirit was. And at the consciousness of that his heart sank and his anger grew.

'You will not wish me good evening,' Osbaldistone said. 'I will have no good evening from you. Since our meeting of last week I have been determined on a word with you. You are a cheat, Mr. Herries, a liar and--it may be--a coward. For the last we will see.'

Then he raised his hand and struck Herries' cheek. Miraculously this, too, no one saw. It gave the dreaminess of this strange hour an added colour--the shrill, discordant music of the violin, the thick steaming air, the great chimney with its smoky fire, the figures confused in colour, unreal in chin and eye and limb, the movement striving, it seemed, to make significant pattern--and yet Herries quite alone in a frozen place with this boy who hated him.

But no man had ever struck him and had no answer. He frowned sternly on young Osbaldistone, who was breathing now fiercely as though driven by some terrific emotion.

'Not here,' he said quietly. 'There is a green behind the house. The moon is bright. I will join you there in an instant. But take care; we must go separately. My host to-night is my friend.'

At once, again as in a dream, young Osbaldistone had disappeared. Herries looked about him. Oh! how desperately he did not wish this to happen! It was from no fear for himself. But he seemed to be haunted to-night by the past; something was pulling him back into that other life that he had abandoned; something would not let him escape.

But he must find a second. It must be, if possible, someone not from Keswick. The less that this was known. . . . He turned towards the door and saw the pedlar standing against the wall, smiling ironically and stroking his thighs with his hands.

'You can do me a service,' Herries said. The pedlar followed him out. The moon was full. No snow was falling.

Against the green behind the house everything was marked as though it had been cut from black paper, the ridge of hill, the roof-line, the thick wall of jagged stones.

Osbaldistone was waiting there and Fawcett, a stout, plump youth, absurd with his blackened face and thick cloak heavily furred. He came to Herries.

'For God's sake, Mr. Herries, this must be avoided. . . .' His teeth were chattering.

'Too damned cold for talk,' said Osbaldistone.

They spoke in whispers.

'If Mr. Osbaldistone will apologise for his insult,' said Herries.

'I will not,' said Osbaldistone.

They faced one another: every detail in the scene was clear under the moon. It was indeed bitterly cold. The frost seemed to creep upon the flat stones that lay about the field. Herries was aware of the tiniest details and would remember them all his days. A snail-track glittered in crystal on the farm wall behind him; a little wind ran over the grass, fluttering the light snow that lay loosely on the ground, and on the path beyond the field he could see the moonlight shine on the ice that the cold was forming on the little pools.

They advanced. At once he knew that Osbaldistone was no swordsman-- and a moment later Osbaldistone knew it too. Again the thought tapped Herries' heart: 'How he must hate me to run this crazy risk!' and again 'Why?' In another moment or two he was aware of the sword's instinct, something much more deadly and determined than his own. He could never strike another's weapon with his and not feel that separate aliveness in his blade, as though it said: 'You have called me out. You have liberated me. Now I am my own master.' And now he was very curiously aware that he must restrain this creature, use all his force and power, otherwise the boy would be hurt. But as they parried and struck and parried again a warmth of companionship with his sword swelled in his throat as though it had said to him: 'Come. We are comrades now. We march together. You wouldn't desert me when you have brought me so far.'

His pride in his accomplishment grew in him. His body grew warm, taut, eager. He forgot his opponent, felt only the moon shining above that cold field, the splendid panoply of stars exulting in his skill.

He had the boy utterly at his mercy, and, at the same moment, the boy's face swung down to him as though it had been lowered from a height. He gazed into it and saw terror there, the certain expectation of instant death.

Death. Yes, one more link in the ridiculous binding chain. This time at least he would be master of his fortune.

He lowered his blade and stepped back. An instant later Osbaldistone's sword had carved his right cheek in two, a deep riven cut from temple to chin.

His face was flooded with blood. Dropping his sword, the field whirring about his ears like a top, he sank to his knee.

He heard young Fawcett cry 'Enough . . .' and a word about honour, then the frosted stones leapt up and hit him into darkness. But before he sank he felt the pedlar's hand on his arm.

DEATH OF MARGARET HERRIES

Deborah found her way one March afternoon through Stonethwaite Valley home.

She had been as far as the Stake Pass, turned back, stayed where the waterfall tumbles over the rocks before the Grasmere turning, looked up at the quiet hills lying against the quiet sky, then down again to the tumbling stream that spread fanwise over the white stones shining in the sun under the water.

Spring was so late here that hardly yet were there signs of it, but Deborah saw every bud and smiled at every pushing green. The spirit of spring was in the faint rain-washed blue of the sky, the purple shadow that hung intangibly about the branches and the pale primrose sunlight that fell in white patterns on rock and stone. The air was cold and snow streaked even the lowest hills.

She was a very slight and lonely child as she walked over the green turf that here in this valley was like the ancient lawns of noble families, so smooth it was and deep. She would soon be fifteen, but children in those years were almost women at fifteen. And she had had much to make her mature. Since her mother had fallen so ill this Christmas, since Mary had grown so proud and was so often with her cousins in Keswick, all the duties of the house had fallen on to Deborah. She was hurrying now for fear of what might have happened while she was away. All last night she had sat with her mother, fighting a thousand terrors, her mother's strange ceaseless talk, the house that was never still, the calling of the owls, but worst of all the anticipated presence of old Mrs. Wilson the witch. Since her mother was ill Mrs. Wilson had been for ever appearing, now here, now there. She spoke little, but at first had offered again and again her remedies. Deborah could hear her now in her odd, croaking voice pressing her herbs, her spells, her incantations. Deb had from the very first been terrified by the old woman, but against her will she had been forced to realise that there was something pathetic and something kind in the old wrinkled face, the little eyes almost hidden by the brown lids, but now anxious and beseeching like an animal's. The old snuff-nosed, wrinkled-faced Doctor Absom, their only resource, once a fine doctor in Carlisle but reduced by liquor to a peddling house-to-house livelihood, had soon stopped her solicitings. He had threatened her in so many words with the gaol for a witch. She had not spoken again after that, but she was always, night and day, hovering there. It seemed, so her son said, that she had formed some affection for Margaret Herries. He

said, almost apologetically, that he had never known her take to anyone before as she took to Mistress Herries; and Deborah, walking now in her cold green valley, seemed still to be haunted by her presence, and, against her fear, something forced her to wonder whether after all Mrs. Wilson's magic might not be of more value than the old doctor's dirty ministrations, he never sober, stinking of snuff, and with bleeding ever his principal remedy.

Poor Margaret! She had been bled enough. There was no more blood left in her. She was dying. Nothing could save her.

The stroke that had slashed her husband's face had struck her down. He had made nothing of it. His face was bound. He had called it a scratch, but from the first instant she had seen deeper than this, had known that here was something predestined.

Child though she was, Deborah had marvellously understood her mother's longing. She was perhaps the only living soul in the world to understand what her mother's love for her father was, how for years she had been praying the God in whom she believed to give her opportunity to show that love without foolishness. Now it might be that the moment had come, and she was too weak to offer it. Not that Herries gave her opportunity: he would have no pity, no tenderness, no allusion to the event. No one spoke to him of it. Everyone pretended that nothing had occurred.

But Deborah knew how her mother ached over him as though he were a child bullied at school and the agony that it was to her, far surpassing her bodily pain, that she could say nothing. She rose to great heights of character in these last days.

But for Deborah life had never yet been so threatening. How would it be when her mother was gone and she alone with her father? Again and again she tried to beat down her fear of him, but it seemed to be something in her very veins. There was David. Had there not been David she might have turned and run back, over the Stake Pass to Langdale and Grasmere, wandered the world and never returned. So long as David was there she could endure any test, but would he always be there? Anyone as wonderful as he must be caught into the outside world. They would call for, shout for him! And then . . . as the light fell and she thought of the darkening house, her father with the fresh purple scar that ran from temple to mouth, catching up one corner of his lip, of her mother's room, of Mrs. Wilson, her white cap, the black stick on which she leaned, she stayed for a moment by the wall of the field and the little chapel looking back to Glaramara, her hand at her throat, her knees trembling.

The thought of David reassured her and she smiled. Where he was no harm could come.

At the turning in of the grassy court two figures made her pause-- two men on horseback. In the fading afternoon light she could not at first tell who they were, then, realising, amazement stayed her: they were her uncle Pomfret and her cousin Raiseley.

They had but now arrived, for they got from their horses as she came to them (she was pleased indeed to see how clumsy Cousin Raiseley was as he climbed down). Uncle Pomfret greeted her with a confusion of heartiness and embarrassment, which showed that he was in no way at ease over his visit. She curtsied and he kissed her, swimming her in an odour of ale and snuff. He was becoming a mountain of flesh. His belly swung before him. Cousin Raiseley, who was pallid and thin as his father was purple and corpulent, bowed to her gravely. She hated her cousin Raiseley because David did. 'Hey, little lass . . .' (her uncle addressed her as though she were a favourite hound) 'here's your old uncle come all the way through the muck to cheer your poor mother up.' He threw a cautious look around him. 'And your father . . . is he about?' She replied quietly. She did not dislike her uncle. There was something kindly and simple about him. She thought: 'He hates coming. . . . It's his good-nature.'

David came out to them, and Deborah flushed with pride as she saw his splendid strength beside his pale shambly-kneed cousin. Benjamin was called to care for the horses, and they all went into the house. What deep shame Deborah felt as they climbed the stairs! She knew Raiseley would be seeing everything, sniffing the farm-smells, the dung and the cesspool, hearing the trickling of water, catching the gleam of the damp on the walls, and, as they came into the upper hall, marking down the holes in the furniture, the bareness of the rafters, the tapestry that was never still against the panelling. She hated Raiseley the more because her home was shabby.

In the hall now there were David and Mary. It was Mary, of course, who at once commanded the scene. She flung her arms around her uncle's short, thick neck and kissed his ill-shaven chin, then with a smiling demureness that was beautiful to witness offered her cheek for Raiseley to kiss, which he did with a very pleasant eagerness.

Uncle Pomfret explained with a great many oaths and confused sentences that he and their Aunt Jannice had been distressed indeed to hear of the grave illness of poor Margaret and that Aunt Jannice had sent with him some cures and recipes.

For himself, would it be possible for him to see her?

The room was dark. The evening glow penetrated the little windows very thinly. Suddenly a figure bearing high two lighted candlesticks appeared on the staircase. It was Francis, his face quivering in the blown flame of the candles. He seemed very tall in that semi-light, in a long, purple dressing-gown, and the scar was leaping on his face.

It might be that Pomfret had not expected that: he stared, his thick legs wide planted, his chin raised. He said afterwards to his wife: ''Twas no man standing there. Someone raised from the dead. The cut lined on his cheek.'

Francis said no word, but came slowly down. Then he placed the candlesticks on the table and holding out his hand said quietly: 'How are you, brother?'

Pomfret began a tumbled and confused explanation, but in a whisper as though he were in church there; finding the whisper arduous, broke into a kind of congested roar, then sank to a whisper again.

Francis nodded his head.

'That was kindly thought . . . Margaret would wish to see you. She is awake--but she is sadly weak.'

He picked up the candles and led the way upstairs again. Pomfret, stepping with his big feet as though on eggs, followed him.

The children, left alone together, were embarrassed. Even Mary, conscious perhaps that the eyes of her brother and sister were upon her, had very little to say. At last Raiseley muttered something about going to see after the horses. He started down the stairs, and David stoutly marched after him. In the dusk, wrapped in the cold air, the two stood stiffly side by side. At last Raiseley, patronage in every word that he uttered, said:

''Tis isolated here . . . and muck at every step.'

David, anger throbbing in his throat, answered:

'It is no place for soft bodies.'

'Nor for active minds,' Raiseley answered.

'Keswick,' David said with a scornful laugh, 'is scarcely the Athens of the world.' (He thought this a fine phrase and told Deb of it afterwards.)

Raiseley sniffed. He had a maddening habit in this as though he suffered from a perpetual cold.

'I wonder, cousin,' he said, 'that you can endure the mud and rain and nothing but yokels for company. But maybe it suits you.'

'It does,' David answered. 'Better than by your looks Keswick might.'

Raiseley laughed. 'Keswick is no abiding-place. I shall be in London in a six-months.'

'Well,' said David, 'for me you can keep your London. There is air here and space, horses to ride and hills to climb. There is no finer spot in England.'

'I can understand that you would find it so,' Raiseley answered.

The poor white worm--David thought--one crack with the singlestick and he'd go over. One push with the thumb and down he'd be! He hated him with every pulse in his body, but at the heart of the hate there was a sort of wistfulness. He would be clever, Raiseley, and getting a fine education. Already he would know so many things that David would never know.

The darkness fell. Benjamin held a flare. The horses clamped with their hoofs on the grassy stones. The two boys stood without speaking, hating one another. Then the two men came out. They were very quiet. Margaret on her death-bed had brought them closer together than they had ever been or would be. Pomfret's simple heart was deeply touched.

'Poor soul,' he said. 'Poor soul . . .'

'She is a woman of great courage,' Francis said.

'Poor Margaret,' their voices echoed on the night air. Pomfret and his son climbed on to their horses.

'That was kindly of you, brother,' Francis said, and held for a moment Pomfret's hand.

'Come and visit us. There is a bed for thee,' Pomfret answered, bent down and kissed his brother's cheek. Then they rode away, their horses stumbling over the dark track.

Francis went back into the house. From these few whispered words both children had realised that their mother was indeed dying. They stood there close together in the dark courtyard, the wind that had suddenly risen whistling about their heads. Deborah began to cry. She clung to David, who put his arm around her, holding her very close. She was a little hysterical with lack of sleep, too incessant labour, fear of the future.

'Oh, David, I'm frightened. Mother will die and you will go into the world and I shall be left here with father. . . . I don't want to be left. . . . I don't want to be left. 'Tis cruel, this valley, when you are alone in it, and there are spirits in the house. The house hates us. There has been no luck for us since we came to it, and I'm weary of the mice and the holes and the shabbiness that will not be cleaned. . . . Oh, David, don't leave me here alone. . . . Don't leave me!'

She sobbed on his breast and he comforted her. 'Deb, little Deb. There's no fear. I'll not leave you. Mother will be happier gone. She was never rightly settled here and the rain and wind destroyed her. Poor mother. She will be warm again and comforted if there's a heaven as they say, and if there's none she'll not be aware of it. But, Deborah, you must not fear father. He's worst with anyone who fears him.

'He will love you an you go to him bravely. He has himself a shyness of spirit. See how happy the three of us will be together-- and you are the bravest of us all. The house is well enough. I'd have it a thousand times before that popinjay place of Uncle Pomfret's in Keswick.

'And I'll not leave you. I'll never leave you. You are the only woman in all the world I love, Deb, save our mother.'

Deborah smiled through her tears.

'There'll be a woman for you one day: every woman who sees you must love you.'

'Ah, but it takes two for that,' David answered laughing. 'There was a girl once up by Seathwaite hit my horse with her stick. Do you know, Deb, it was but a moment and I've never seen her since, but she had a face like a laughing rose. . . . For the rest they are all alike. I warrant marriage is a false tale. I would be free, and who is free with a wife?'

Deborah sighed.

'I shall be left one day. . . . 'Tis so silly, but although I'm fourteen years I'm frightened of the dark. . . . The true dark when there are only owls and mice. And Mistress Wilson. David, is she truly a witch?' She dropped her voice to a low whisper.

David tightened his arm round her. 'I think she's a witch,' he whispered back. 'She never sleeps. She has a fire with blue flame. She makes dolls of wax. I've seen one with a needle through. But she cannot touch thee, Deb. . . . Christ is at the back of thee, and all the holy angels.'

'Maybe,' Deborah answered, shivering against his breast, 'she is a good witch. I'm sure she means no ill to our mother. Maybe she would have cured her.'

But David shook his head. 'Better our mother die than be cured of the Devil,' he answered. Then he folded his little sister yet more closely in his arms and kissed her.

'I will swear an oath, here in this place, never to leave you, Deborah. An I marry, you come also. And if I do not marry, you shall ever keep house for me and father. Now listen, little sister, I will swear. By Christ and His holy angels I, David Scott Herries, will never, while breath is in my body, leave thee, Deborah Herries--unless,' he hurriedly added, 'there is hunting on the hills or travelling to see new countries--an adventure, you understand. You would not hold me from that.'

'I would not hold you from anything,' Deborah answered, standing on tiptoe to kiss him. 'I am not that sort of selfish woman. I know that you will have a grand life, David, of adventure and enterprise, and do you think I would hold you back? I love you too well.'

She was quite happy now, and, their arms around one another, they went into the house.

Francis Herries had gone to his wife's room. He sat there beside the big bed, very patient, staring into the round light of the two candles. Margaret lay, her eyes closed, breathing stertorously. There were beads of sweat on her brow, and her two hands, tightly clenched, lay on the coverlet. Little Absom had gone for a meal but would return. It might well be that Margaret would die before he came back, but it did not matter; he could do nothing.

Herries sat there without moving, looking at his wife. He had never loved Margaret: he did not love her now nor did he let sentiment chafe him, but, as he watched her, he was sorry that her life had been spent with a man whom she could not understand.

It was this lack of comprehension that affected him most deeply as he sat there. She had loved him, but had not understood him at all. He had not loved her, but had understood her only too well.

All human relationships seemed to him miserable things as he sat there--all false, all betraying. Well, for himself, it did not matter. On the Christmas night at the moment when young Osbaldistone had slashed his cheek, he had finished with human beings. As he felt the blood gush over his face he had, at that instant, stepped aside from all his fellows. He had been coming to that point through many months. Now the division was made.

In the weeks that had followed, he had nursed his cut with a quiet sense of completion. He knew that he would be marked for life and terribly, that this would be the first thought that all men would have, the first thing that they would see.

He could look back now and understand that for years he had been slowly separating himself from his fellow-men. His fault or theirs, what mattered it? Their fault because he had a dream that could not be fulfilled, or his because he was ever putting himself wrong with them by loss of temper or arrogance or other passion? So he was done with them. Even poor Margaret was leaving him. Only David remained. David he could not separate himself from, but he was sure that the hour would come when David too would go. But that would be for David to recognise.

And instead of human beings, he would embrace this valley, this soil, this house itself. He had plans that he would get some land from Peel, that he would sow corn, grow trees perhaps, have cattle. He would work with his own hands here. All day and every day during those last weeks he had, when he had not been at Margaret's side, been digging and cutting wood, mending holes, carrying water, Ben, Wilson, David, assisting, but going and coming, whereas he stayed, sweat pouring from him, his nails grimed with dirt, his face raised to Glaramara, then bent again to the ground. And it seemed to him that the soil came and built itself about his heart. He was earthed in: the smell and the tang and the grit of it were in his eyes and his nostrils. He was growing his own hair. Soon it would be long about his brows. His heavy boots were caked with mud, and when he straightened himself this fresh, sharp ache in his back called out to him with a friendly voice.

Margaret stirred. Her hands rose and fell with a little flutter as he had so often seen them do, and a rush of memory swept over him. How badly he had treated her, and how she had asked to be badly treated! What absurd ironic fate had driven them together? Why was life thus, so that you were caught of your own good intentions and held in a trap to which there was no purpose? He had meant to do her kindness and had done her nothing but ill: but was not that indeed the whole motto of his life?

He could think of so many occasions when he had returned from some ride or visit meaning so many courtesies to her, and she, in the very first word, had roused his ironic irritation. And how poor was he that, knowing her love for him and that she was stupid and could not help herself, he had not been kinder to her, more indulgent! His sins had been frightful, thrusting his mistresses under her very nose, coming back drunk to her and forcing her against her will, until in the last matter of Alice Press he had been most evil of all. For all this he must pay, and when the day came for payment he was not to squeal about injustice.

He thought then of her many, many kindnesses and of her great patience, but the thought of her patience only again exasperated him. Why had she been so patient? It would have been better had she been rash with him sometimes and called him what he was. And

so, as most men do who have ill-treated their wives, he came to an odd mixture of feelings, of shame and irritation, of self-blame and wonder that women could be so persistently provoking. At least he was glad that now she suffered no pain.

She stirred and woke. She looked about her without raising her head from the pillow. Then she saw him and smiled, and then, as she had done on a thousand other occasions, checked her smile lest he should think it foolish.

'What hour is it, Francis?' she asked him in a thin, very distant voice.

'Six of the clock,' he said, bending forward and taking her hand. That pleased her and she smiled again.

'My head is very clear . . . I have had strange dreams. I would speak to David. May I?'

He nodded. That 'May I?' touched him deeply. In the first year of their marriage when she had been a young girl and first afraid of him, she had said about this or that little pleasure and excitement, 'May I?' and often enough he had answered: 'No, you may not.'

Now he nodded and went from the room to fetch his son.

He sent David in. The boy came and stood by the bed, his breadth blocking the window. Then a terrible pity and tenderness for his mother, self-reproach for himself, and a consciousness of the imminence of death wrung his heart. He dropped on his knees, put out his great brown hands and took her thin white ones. He seemed for the first time in his life now to realise her. There had always been somebody or something else standing in his view of her. He had caught from early babyhood something of his father's idea of her. Now, when it was too late, she seemed to stand before him as she really was, going on this journey all alone with no one to help her. The room was so dark that it was only by the candlelight that he saw her face, and in that flickering gleam she was not foolish any more--she had courage and dignity, and these things all her life she had never seemed to him to have before.

She put up her hand and stroked his hair. Her voice was faint and he had to lean nearer to her to catch her words. Her arm fell about his neck.

'Davy, I've not been a wise mother to you . . . I've not been a wise woman, but I have loved you with all my heart.'

'I know you have, mother,' he answered.

'I want you to promise me . . . never to leave your father.'

'I will never leave my father.'

'It is strange,' she looked at him rather timidly, 'that love does not bring understanding. I have loved Francis so much but have never known the way to be easy with him.' She paused between the sentences, and David heard the wind tugging at the leaded panes, and in some way the little sound, as of a friendly companion, was comforting and understanding.

'It is too late now for me not to fear your father. Oh, Davy, how have I said again and again, "Now you must not mind him," but I have always minded him and the sight of him has made my heart beat and driven every word from my head. I know so well why he should be irritated with me. How should I not know, being so irritated with myself? But that is all over . . . past . . . away . . .' She stopped, lay back, closed her eyes. David placed his arm around her and held her close to him. He could feel the sweat of her body beneath the nightdress. 'I meant to make him proud of me and I have not. I meant that he should continue in love with me and he was not. I meant many things and have not wrought them, but--' and here her voice grew stronger and she seemed to wake to new life, 'I have given birth to a fine son who will be heard of in the world. Oh, I am proud of you, Davy, my darling, my darling.'

He held her closer, moved to his very soul, because in all these years she had never told him how she loved him.

'And you are strong and grand and fearless. You will be a man among men so that they look up to you and come to you. So, Davy, my darling, you must never leave your father, who is alone and will be more alone as the years go.' She raised herself a little on David's arm.

'Breed sons, my David. Great, strong-limbed men like yourself. Davy, Davy . . .' Her hand clutched his sleeve. 'I am no Herries, but I have borne a son to the Herries. Though they have mocked me, in my womb was carried the finest of them all, and from your seed, David, all the grand Herries shall come.' She sank back and the strangest elfin smile came to her lips. 'Your aunt and your uncle have bred niddering children, but two hundred years hence there shall be Herries who shall know that it was I, Margaret Herries, who gave suck to the man of them all. . . . Your children, Davy . . . . You must have men children to carry the Herries name farther . . . farther . . . farther . . .' She seemed exhausted. She lay back on the pillow and he bent and stroked her forehead. 'Wrong thoughts, Davy,' she whispered, 'for a dying woman, but they have struck your father in the face and your sons must revenge . . . I have loved him so . . . even now to have his cheek against mine, his poor wounded cheek.'

'Shall I call him, mother?' David whispered.

'Nay.' She smiled again. 'He would not know what to do or say. He was ever awkward in a scene. Like a child . . . I would have been mother to him rather than wife, but he would not allow me. Dear Francis . . . Francis, dear . . .'

Then she motioned him to raise her up. Her face was against his. She kissed him. Her lips were damp with sweat.

'Is it not odd that I who have been afraid all my life should not now be afraid? Our good Lord understandeth my awkwardness. His arms are around me. . . . To die is simpler than to live.'

He laid her down again. Her hand closed with exceeding tightness about his.

'Dear Francis. . . . Call him, Davy . . . I am dying.'

Gently he unloosed his hand, went to the door and called softly: 'Father, father.'

Francis came in, and kneeling by the bed put his arms round her and held her as her spirit passed.

Her last word uttered against his cheek: 'Francis, dear.'

END OF PART I

PART II

'FORTY-FIVE

LAUGHTER OF A SPANIEL

Maria Herries died on the morning of February 14, 1745, thus missing by exactly four months the attainment of her hundredth year.

This lamentable failure afforded great grief and a sense of affronted egotism to the whole of the Herries family. Bad news flies apace, and in a surprisingly short time the event was known to, and greatly bewailed by, the children and grandchildren of Robert Herries in Kensington, the family of Maurice in Portsmouth, of Humphrey at Seddon, and the Golds (only far relations-in-law, but nevertheless of a very definite Herries consciousness) in Edinburgh.

They all united in blaming Pomfret and Jannice for this disaster, and indeed very rightly, for who was to blame if they were not? Having kept the old lady alive so long, the least for them to do was to keep her alive that little bit longer. Moreover, it was pleasant to blame Pomfret and Jannice, who had made money in a very sudden and vulgar manner, in a fashion that was not the Herries manner: Herries always inherited, or if they worked, did so slowly and cautiously and with an air of indifference.

Wealth meant little in the Herries blood: they had not at all like certain other famous English families the sense of property. They were indeed quite above and outside this sense, because to be Herries was enough and, rich or poor, you were of an equal and exceptional importance. No, the Herries pride (of which there was always God's plenty) was based on two magnificent foundations: England and Common Sense. When you said English you said Herries, and when you said Herries you said No Nonsense. In this lies any interest that there may be in a study of Herries' family history-- that there was something in the Herries blood demanding that their castle of common sense should be persistently attacked, and almost always from within. Again and again these attacks occur, and with every fresh battle new history is made. 'I am a sensible man,' chanted the first Herries, striding across the naked body of his enemy, Romance or Illusion--and so ever since have his stalwart descendants chanted.

'The man's a fool.' 'The woman's an ass.' 'I can't think what he's after.' 'A madman.' 'A lunatic' 'A dirty dog.' 'Traitor to his country.' 'An artist.' 'A ne'er-do-well.' 'Fantasy.' 'Imagination.' 'An atheist'--such and so have ever been the words and phrases of contempt in the mouths of following generations of Herries.

And rightly so. For just as Common Sense has always served them soundly and well in all their history, so have Imagination, Originality, the hopeless pursuit of the shining star, led them to ruin and disaster, public scandal and disgrace. They have learnt to dread and with justice the dreamer; he has ever haunted the sleep of right-minded Herries men and women.

This Common Sense, on the other hand, has been with them no unstudied art. They have penetrated every nook and cranny of this temple, have studied with hundreds of years of patient learning the shifting features of the God.

At the moment of birth young Herries know precisely the sensible thing to do, how to watch and wait, to avoid all eccentricity, to embrace only those things and persons that are of good report and general repute, to believe only in what they see, to handle only what they can in reality touch, to give their blessing to all that is normal, firmly traditional, safely found. Within the world of common sense they are kindly, generous and open-hearted: let them for a moment stray into that howling wilderness of stars and mandrakes and they are ferocious and bloodthirsty: alarm partly makes them so, the knowledge given to them by history that they are a family especially susceptible to attacks of the dreamer's incongruity, the rebel's immorality. They go, therefore, armed to the teeth: divided as they sometimes are (being yet human) among themselves, they unite instantly at the call of one of their members: "Ware Wolf!" They have made England what it is: they are rightly proud of their magnificent achievement.

But, it must be repeated, their principal interest to the observer of them is that they have, at their heart, the poison of their qualities and intentions. Every generation, it seems, is condemned to this warfare against its own home-born traitors, and from this warfare comes always a stouter, more determined resolve.

The death of Maria Herries, so lamentably previous, offered a fine example of their common sense in action. One thing that had never been understood by them was that Herries men must die so soon. It was natural for the majority, who waste their days in dreams, in pursuit of the thing that is not, in longing for what does not exist, to wear themselves untimely away, their proper punishment and condemnation. But for Herries, who never ran after a vain thing nor stared at the moon, life should be indefinitely extended, and because they believed in a just God (the God of the contemporary majority) it was hard to see why His justness did not perceive exactly this.

There had been already examples in history of what a Herries could do when he tried. Old Polyphemus Herries, barnacled and lichened with tradition, who eight hundred years ago in Fife (the Herries were all Scotch then) had lived to a hundred and sixty-one; old Mary Herries of the Wars of the Roses, who, defending Lancaster Castle, upset pots of boiling pitch on to the heads of invaders, she had lived to a hundred and thirty-nine, and had had fifty-eight grandchildren. Ronald Herries, friend of James I., had lived in sin and iniquity into his hundred and twentieth year--a black sheep, but honoured by the Herries because of his arrogant resolve to beat Death back to Hell, which for a hundred and twenty years at least he succeeded in doing, then drink had him and he died, his head in a butt of Canary!

Since old Ronald no one had passed the century, although Elizabeth Herries of Charles I.'s time had been ninety-three, and little Johnny Herries the hunchback, uncle of Maria and Matthew, had seen ninety-four.

Old Maria as she approached the century had become an object of reverence to all of them, and Pomfret and Jannice, hitherto contemned, had been more honourably considered for preserving her. Here again was something that the Herries did better than anything else--show Death that they would stand no nonsense.

There was nothing that the Herries prided themselves upon more justly than the health and excellence of their bodily vigour. They were not eccentric in this; they did not produce strong men for exhibition at a Fair, or wrestlers at a pageant, but just vigorous, sound Englishmen with no nonsense about them, destined to die calmly in their beds at a ripe old age. And how often in these last years had the words been murmured in Kensington, in Portsmouth, in Carlisle, in Edinburgh, at Seddon, at Hatton, at Brighthelmstone. 'The Herries live long. . . . Maria Herries in Keswick neareth her hundredth year. . . . Nothing ails her. . . . She is bled once and again. . . . She has all her teeth.'

And now she was gone and had missed her goal. A hundred in four months' time! The irony of it!

By an odd coincidence it happened that for Maria's funeral there was a remarkable Herries gathering. Movement over considerable distances was not easy, although easier than it had been, but it was not difficult, of course, for Humphrey Cards, his wife Charlotte, his daughter Dorothy, her husband Anthony Forster, and their little son Will to come over from Seddon, and Grandison, son of Robert, cousin of Pomfret and Francis, had been paying a visit in Edinburgh with Mary his

wife, and Helen and Pelham his children, so they came down: and last but not, of course, least there was Henry, son of Maurice Cards, and Lucilla his wife. In this company three quite separate impulses of the Herries blood could be traced.

Humphrey Cards, hidden away at Seddon, had been suspected of turning Quaker. He had at any rate been oddly religious enough to frighten all decent-minded Herries. His daughter Dorothy, who had married one of the Northumberland Forsters, was grimly religious enough, but not, thank Providence, in any eccentrically dangerous fashion.

Dorothy Forster then (cousin to a more famous Dorothy Forster of this same time) represented the spiritual vein of the Herries body.

Her thin, pale, ramrod-straight body, her dark clothes and quiet misgivings about her other fellow-humans, made this manifest.

Robert's son, Grandison, and his children Pelham and Helen represented fashion. They lived in Kensington, and everything outside London was too odd and peculiar to be true. Grandison had never understood how a Herries could bring himself to live out of London--it was a sort of lèse-majesté against the blood. His eyes, protruding out of his round pale face, expressed perpetual surprise and wonder. He was tall, stout and most elegantly dressed. Clothes were of great concern to him, and food, and the order of entrance and exit. Not greatly distinguished in the village of Kensington, he was an exquisite in Keswick. Aunt Jannice thought him the most marvellous creature in all the world, and had he but allowed himself to be bled more frequently he would have been perfect.

His girl Helen was in no way remarkable, but his son Pelham promised well as the Herries rake of his generation. There must always be a Herries rake, and he must go so far and no farther. He must gamble, drink, womanise to a certain degree, fight duels enough for glory and not enough for scandal, be handsome and dashing and outrageous, but always within the limits of common sense. Other Herries must be able to shake their heads over him, but admire him too, and at last when a new younger rake is maturing he, the elder, must marry a virtuous girl with wealth, settle down and breed a family.

Young Pelham, aged at this time twenty-seven, understood all this perfectly, and had in fact a certain private store of ironic amusement which bewildered at times his fat father and irritated his august mother.

This mother, a magnificent figure, both snobbish and stupid on a large scale, had been a Titchley and, as everyone knows, it is difficult for a Titchley to yield place even to a Herries. She had in fact never quite yielded. She was still just enough rebel against the Herries tradition to need watching; not that she was interesting in her rebellion--she neither thought nor spoke enough to be interesting. Only once and again she would look at a stray Herries with a dumb air of wonder as much as to say: 'In a Titchley world this creature would not be permitted.'

In her quite young days she had known Sarah Marlborough and although now she was in a Kensington set she always got Court news before anyone else.

Henry, son of Maurice, and Lucilla his wife, represented the third strain in the Herries blood. Henry, who was thirty-two years of age, was thin and spare, with eyes gravely fixed. They were fixed upon the markets and he never permitted them to rest anywhere else. For one brief moment of sensual delight he had allowed them to rest upon his wife Lucilla. Ten years ago she had been a beautiful girl. Three years following their marriage she had been attacked by the smallpox, and, quite naturally, after that business had claimed him again. They had no children; the multiplying of coins of the realm was their only increase.

Henry was able and kept his eyes open for all the mechanical improvements and developments that were now beginning to alter the country, how permanently and irretrievably even he did not suspect. He was one of the first men in England to be aware of the deep importance of John Kay's invention of the fly-shuttle in 1733, of John Lombe's discovery in Italy of those improvements in machinery that gave such an impetus to the silk trade, and, in later years, he was to recognise at once the value of Crompton's mule, of Highs' water-frame and the spinning jenny of Hargreaves.

Oddly, with all his cleverness, his attention to business and parsimonious industry, he was never to make a fortune. This too was characteristic of the Herries; they were never in their money- making destined to be middle-men because if, in their tribe, genius showed its head it was instantly suspect and exiled. Henry was no genius, but he was industrious, honest, cross-grained, conceited and quite without poetic fancy. That was well, for had this last been his he would have been unfaithful to Lucilla, who was no woman to endure patiently infidelity.

Gathered there together on some general ground, had they for an outside observer any physical characteristic in common?

Only this: that in them all there was some attribute of the horse-- Pomfret the cart-horse, Dorothy Forster the funeral hack, young Pelham the dashing pony, his father the well-fed favourite of the Countess's barouche, Henry the little dark horse of the race- meeting, and so-and-so . . . these traits of chin, high cheek- bones, long forehead, brooding, patient and unimaginative eyes marking the Herries tribe, giving them their place in English life and history.

And with all this they had great qualities.

They had a great force of fidelity, so that under pain of urgent torture they would not desert their loyalties, their loyalties of creed, of family, of ethics, of social conduct. These loyalties were English, and therefore the easier because no light of imagination was ever let in upon them. Two hundred years ago they had been, to a letter, the same: two hundred years later they would not have changed to a hair's-breadth. They were loyal to their country, to their family, to their loves, to their friends, with a stolid wonder that anybody could be anything else. When those ill- smelling traitors were discovered within their own households (as with every generation they were discovered) that taunt of disloyalty was the first stone that was flung.

As to their country so also to them disloyalty meant everything that was base; abnormality, cowardice, the vilest selfishness, dirty living, obscene thinking. And the certainty of their judgements was only equalled by the swiftness.

It was tragedy for the Herries that they must live in a constantly changing world. When, as now with Maurice's son Henry, these changes were sharply perceived, the Herries strain of orthodox tradition modified the use that was made of them. Loyalty came in there.

The changes were always unfortunate, even when they were most inevitable. The old days were always the good old days for the Herries; that was why, for example, Harcourt, who on this occasion had come over from Ravenglass, was accepted by all of them as a perfect member.

For him only all that was old was worthy. It had been Mr. Pope's only fault that he was not old enough. The thought that old Maria had been born on the day of the Battle of Naseby embalmed her, even though she had so impertinently missed her hundredth birthday, with an especial fragrance.

And behind this reverence there was something very kindly and genial. The Herries men especially were warm of heart. Pomfret and Harcourt, Robert's sons, and in the younger line, Francis' David, young Pelham-- there was strong generous humanity here. Only, faced with what they thought to be heresy, vain worship of false gods, treachery to Church or State, to Country and the Marriage Vows and sound fact, only then they were as fierce, as prejudiced, as bloodthirsty as any Spanish Inquisitor. And for confidence in their own eternal rightness there was no family in Britain to rival them.

Here, then, they were, two days after Maria's funeral, on an afternoon of driving rain, gathered together in Jannice's withdrawing-room: lean Henry and his pale-faced Lucilla, little dainty Harcourt, Mrs. Dorothy black and austere, Pelham's mother stout and frosted, Pelham gay in a coat of orange and silver, Raiseley bitterly envious, Grandison fat and flabby, amiable Anabel and beautiful Judith-the Herries stable--one of these Herries family gatherings that any Herries chronicler is compelled in their history to confront.

Jannice, Lucilla, Grandison, his wife Mary and Helen their daughter, were busy at Ombre. The men, bored with the wet, had come in to take tea with the women. Henry was giving Pomfret a rather patronising lecture on profit and loss (he thought Pomfret the veriest fool), Pelham was tantalising Raiseley with London splendours and besieging the lovely Judith with all his polished arts, and on the crimson sofa the dead Maria's spaniel lay, staring with sad angry eyes at the hated company.

The room was lit with candles, but the curtains were not drawn, and beyond the windows a furious sky tore in sweeping battalions of smoky clouds from horizon to horizon. To-day as so often in this country of clouds the sky imposed itself upon the farthest interior seclusion. The glittering furniture of the room, the gilt of the chairs, the jewellery of the little clocks and boxes, the crimson silk, the shining silver candlesticks, the amber of the fluttering flames of lights and fire surrendered without question to the black shapes of the sky that seemed so vast and threatening, dragging at the distant tops of the hills as though to fling them across the lake on to the houses of the town.

Everyone in the room was irritated by the storm, but no one asked for the curtains to be drawn. There had been also during these last days other irritations.

The friendly scorn felt in different degrees by them all for their host and hostess reacted upon themselves. It was exasperating to feel that a Herries, whose hospitality they had accepted, was below the proper Herries mark, and Pomfret, who was only at his ease when he was out of doors killing something, who was always too uncomfortable in his wife's presence, had flustered through these days, now roaring in a noisy and false good humour, now putting on an air of deep seriousness that his words, alas, only betrayed, now sinking into a schoolboy silence of discomfort.

Jannice too was unhappy. For many years now she had been comfortable here in her own little circle, testing neither her wit nor her beauty against broader standards. But she detested the large pompous body of Grandison's wife after the first half-hour of her arrival. For Mary Herries, Jannice had the double aggravation that she was neither a Titchley nor a worthy Herries. She had indeed, with her provincial airs, her silly cures and recipes, her little conceits and ugly appearance, everything against her. Pomfret had never cared for his wife so protectively as during these last days when 'the Titchley woman,' as he called her, had mocked him with every word. He longed to humiliate fat Grandison, to put him on a horse that would throw him at the first ditch, to fire a gun in his ears, to win his money at a cockfight, even to strip the clothes off his flabby body and soak him in the lake. He would show these Kensington puppies what real life was like up here in the North Country. Even as he listened to Henry Cards' dry words, hoping that he might gather a business wheeze or two, his other ear was on the Ombre table listening to the thick voice of Mary Herries as she instructed the others in the Kensington fine shades of Ombre play.

Mary Herries indeed was indignant with every pulse in her large body at the company that she was forced to keep. The very cards that Jannice had provided seemed to her contemptible with their old-fashioned pictures of 'the Bishops in the Tower, Popish Midwife, Captain Tom, Army going over to the Prince

of Orange,' etc. They were Jannice's best cards, 'the best superfine Principal Ombre cards at 2s. 9d. a Dozen.' She had been playing with them these twenty years. If good enough for anyone in Keswick, why not for anyone in Kensington?

Mary Herries had other causes for dissatisfaction. She knew that her son Pelham was attracted by Jannice's girl Judith. She adored her son; this was the strongest, fiercest motive of life for her. His handsomeness, cleverness, gaiety, made her the proudest woman in all England, and her pride was the more defended because it was mingled with a worshipping fear of an irony in him that she would never understand.

That by any horrible chance he should throw himself away on the girl of these country bumpkins was terrifying to her. Fool though she was she could see that Judith was a dark beauty: dressed properly and educated in Kensington she might make others than her son stare. She knew too that Pelham meant as a rule but little by his gallantries--there was already a fine list of momentary conquests behind him--but the dullness of these last days (was it for ever raining in this pernicious country?), his idleness and something arrogant and distant in Judith might lead to some desperate impetuosity. She could scarcely hold her cards as she thought of some dreadful crisis suddenly exploded before them: her husband, poor fool, would perceive nothing, and would never dream of acting until all was over.

And she had a further irritation. This was the King Charles spaniel on the crimson sofa. This, the last of dead Maria's many spaniels, was the only true mourner of that poor lady. She was missing her now with every wheezy breath that she drew. She was old, fat, the victim of many pains and tortures; life had long ago been misery to her had it not been for the touch of those strange dry fingers, the scratch of those multitudinous rings, the warmth of that thin shrivelled body, a bag of bones under the coloured shining silks. Alone she had shared her mistress's recent life, her longings, her prides, her greeds, her ignorances, her loneliness. Alone she had called out of that aged woman, so nearly deceased long before the actual moment of death, tenderness and unselfishness, the only cause in her of anxiety for another. During those long nights when Maria had lain looking up at a remorseless ceiling, seeing pageants of vanished scenes and figures, her pride her only refuge, the spaniel had breathed against her withered hand, rested its head against her dried bosom.

Together they had faced a world that seemed to them both worthless and ugly; all the old glories were over, but so long as they were together pride would sustain them both.

Now they were no longer together, and the spaniel, only aware that her mistress called her no more, ached her old heart away in angry wasted rebellion. But there was more than despair and loneliness there. There was also a spirit of impotent and sarcastic rage. She was of blood royal, descendant of a line of kings. It had always seemed to her that Jannice and Pomfret, their offspring also, were low and degenerate creatures. She hated that they should touch her, and when Raiseley or Judith teased her, her whole soul rose in affronted disgust. While Maria lived she had been protected, and in sublime confidence of her dear mistress had been able to scorn those others, but now she knew that she was open to the world. . . . Pains racked her, dim fears besieged her, and with these the scorn that she knew her mistress had felt ever increased within her.

She was no Herries: her alliance had been to a single soul, not to the herd. So now as they passed around her with their strange scents and movements and sounds she hated them even as she despised them, and most bitterly of all she hated and despised the stout, crackling, silk-swishing, fan-waving, scent-distilling Mary Herries.

It may have been that in this woman beyond the others she detected false arrogances and knew that of them all it was she who would have most fiercely affronted her mistress. In any case it was upon Mary Herries that she fixed her filmed and fading eyes, concentrated her aching body, curled her upper lip, showing two sharp and yellow teeth.

Mary Herries was telling some tale of a friend: 'But a miserly temper. She is as expressive to her husband as a casket of jewels. Many's the night I've seen her lug out her old green net purse full of old jacobuses while her waiting woman in the room behind is diving into the bottom of her trunk hoping for a stray piece or two . . .' when she was aware of the spaniel's eyes.

She moved her chair ever so slightly and was aware of them the more. The spaniel was laughing at her, or maybe it was the spirit of old Maria that mocked her through the dog.

She felt suddenly an accumulation of miseries: she saw Grandison her husband as he stood in his nightshirt, his ugly naked toes spread, his bristling head bare of its wig, and in that figure, so deeply accustomed that it seemed to be part of her own, she groaned at the weariness of her life. What was all this pretence of Kensington finery, this elaborate mention of old Duchess Sarah, Sir John and the rest, when a yard away Pelham was making eyes at that hoydenish country girl, and her stomach ached beneath her tightened stays and her feet were pinched in their silver shoes, and Grandison, scratching at his wig for the thousandth time, cleared his throat over his cards preparatory to playing the wrong one? What were these Herries but second-rate country bumpkins? Henry with his spare money-calculating eyes, who yet could make no fortune, Dorothy in her thin black with her psalm-singing pieties, Pomfret stinking of drink and the miry road, his miserable Raiseley with his splay feet and mean little nose. Oh! she was sick of the lot, she had messed her life through her own silly folly, storms of rain beat the windows and the spaniel mocked her!

A point had come in the game and she flung her cards on the table. 'I play no more,' she said in her thick soft voice that was like the stirring of suet in the pan.

She had been winning (a fact that until now she had quite honestly not noticed) and at once she was aware that Jannice Herries found in this the reason of her withdrawal.

Jannice had not at sixty improved in appearance. She was thinner, more sallow, more drawn and by her odd unsuited clothes more painfully quartered than ever.

'An old witch,' thought Mary Herries.

'A fat mean cook of a woman,' thought Jannice.

'Why, cousin, you are winning,' said Jannice sharply. 'You must give us our revenge.'

But Mary Herries, raising her stout body painfully, pushing back the chair, feeling freshly the agony of her pinching shoes, answered:

'That dog should be poisoned.'

Everyone felt the unseemliness. A Herries, the oldest of all the Herries, had been but two days buried. This was her dog, all that remained of her, almost you could say a Herries dog. But worse followed.

Mary, her voice quivering to an unexpected plaintiveness: 'I am sick to death of this: it rains and rains again. Maria is happily buried if it was here that she must look out of window.' Then with a toss of her head, the painted flowers in her white wig nodding their petals, she waddled from the room, her little feet protesting with sad little creaks against the weight that they must carry.

Grandison knew what this meant. She was feeling Titchley, and when she felt Titchley he was in for a terrible hour. He hastened after her. The dog still laughed, motionless like a dead dog.

But the men, Henry and Pomfret, young Pelham and Harcourt, like all Herries men when a woman made a scene, came together. Young Pelham, leaning back against the purple brocaded chair near the door, smiling, said: 'My mother has vapours often enough at this hour. She will be happy only in a land where the sun always shines. I appeal to you, sir' (smiling at Pomfret), 'this is a handsome country, but it rains unduly.'

'It would not be so handsome a country,' said Harcourt, 'did it not rain so frequently.' And he turned from them, looking out of window across the lake to the hills where a sudden flash of pale sunlight had pierced the storm, striking an arrow of gold that cleft Cat Bells in two. He loved it, every stick and stone of it! How he loved it! And as he looked, a deep homesickness for his own home at Ravenglass, his little garden, his gleaming book rows, the faint flash of the sea beyond his windows, took him.

All of them in that room caught from him some sense of English soil. The men moved together to the window and stood there side by side looking out. They were Herries in this: that however far they might be drawn from the English soil, they yet belonged to it. Even in Kensington they felt the stirrings of ancient waterways and the tuggings of prehistoric roots. Which partially explains perhaps that they were never good travellers abroad, queasy, irritable, of an arrogant critical mind; and if they must settle in a foreign land they must turn it speedily to a Scotch or English likeness.

They felt now that urgent need to break out into the open air that every Herries feels when his women are badgering him.

Pomfret's indignation at the insult to his wife was mingled with a twofold satisfaction: it was not he who for once was the clown of the occasion and, although he would never confess to this, his own dear Jannice had been found to be less than perfection. There came to him indeed at that moment, gazing out at the steel wall of rain that fell now like a vengeance from the muddy sky, a thought of what life would have been had Jannice never existed. He cast an uneasy backward glance at the spaniel, who was now wheezily sleeping. How many things dogs knew, and how greatly the more at ease he was with them than with humans! Now with a dog . . . !

And he thought again of Jannice, of how to this day, although they had been married so long, he was afraid of her, afraid of that sudden sharp tap in her voice like a knock on the window, that chilly glaze of contempt in her eye when he had been an especial fool. Yes, and his own children. . . . Only Anabel was friendly and easy, and she was easy with all the world.

He was sixty-seven years of age now, a tun of a man with a floating hulk of a belly, and he was lonely as perhaps were all men of sixty- seven. Only with horses and dogs and a drinking parson and a swearing friend or two, killing, hunting those animals that he yet so dearly loved, only thus might he for a driving hour cheat himself of his loneliness. Staring out of window, not hearing anything of the voices in the room behind him, he thought suddenly of his brother Francis. Why, he could not say. He did not think of him more often than he must, partly because he was a scandal, partly because he loved him. At heart it might be that Francis was more to him than anyone else in the world: Francis, digging away in that miry patch of stinking mud in that nook-shotten valley, Francis shouted at by the peasant children, Francis, adulterer and vagabond, known to have sold his woman at a public fair, to have killed his wife with unkindness, to have driven one of his own daughters away from her home, to be sheltering under his roof the most notorious old witch in the country, Francis--'Rogue Herries' to all the world, so that he brought with every hour disgrace on the Herries name-- yet Pomfret loved him. His mind flung back to that first windy evening when Francis and his family arrived in the town, Francis so young and handsome then in all his gay clothes, and to that other time, the day that poor Margaret died, when he had ridden over to Herries and Francis had been so grave and kindly, so noble in spirit, and he, Pomfret, had kissed his brother, loving him and wishing in his own clumsy speechless way to protect him.

Oh! Francis was bad and not to be mentioned, but through the sheets of rain Pomfret had a mad, monstrous wonder of a moment whether, if he had been with him out there in rugged tumbled Herries, life might not have been richer, more valorous, better worth . . .

And so wondering, turning because he heard the door open, saw to his stricken, open-mouthed amazement his brother, Francis Herries, standing in the room.

He had not seen his brother for three years; the last time had been in a Keswick street when Francis, riding past on a huge kind of cart-horse, had patronised Pomfret and sent him home in a fuming fury.

But now how strange he looked standing there, wearing his own black shaggy hair, muddily booted to the thighs, his long brown coat faded and stained, his face brown and spare, the shape and form of it altered by the deep white scar that ran from brow to lip. His face was yet shining with raindrops, water dripped from his boots, the back of his brown hand shone with rain. Years back he had promised to be stout; now he was lean and spare, and seemed of an immense height. He had aged strangely. Pomfret had a quick vision of him that other first time at the inn when glittering in gold and crimson he had been so young and handsome. Now the soil was in the furrows of his cheeks.

To Jannice, staring from above the card-table, it was as though the Devil had sprung out of the floor. Francis was to her as the Devil. Sharing no blood with him, disliking him from the very first, her dislike was now hatred--hatred mingled with deep fear. For years he had threatened everything in which she believed, her morality, her family, her social position. Especially her social position. Every little success in Keswick was threatened with the consciousness that only a mile or two away there was this sinister figure, outlaw, adulterer, vagabond, and, because she never saw him, her sense of his evil power grew and grew with imagination. She was a woman compact of superstition. Witches and warlocks, mandrakes and goblins were as real to her as her own children. The two worlds were, with her, one. Had Francis been arrested for dealings with the Devil and been burnt at the stake she would not have thought it an injustice.

She had sworn that never again should he pass her door. He was here, and it seemed to her as she looked across the room at him that fire and brimstone smoked at his nostrils.

Harcourt was the first to speak. He was enchanted with pleasure. He came forward, holding out both hands: 'Francis, my dear brother!' That explained to the others who this was. Young Pelham, greatly interested, thought: 'So this is my dangerous and exiled relation. This is a man. Worth the lot of us here.' He was drawn naturally to the rebel in life. He had a complete intellectual appreciation of rebellion, although his love of comfort would always keep himself on the side of safety.

Francis looked about him, bowed to Jannice and Dorothy Forster, then, smiling (his smile was odd now because the scar caught his upper lip and twisted it), said:

'Forgive me. I would not have intruded, but, passing, thought that I would greet the family . . . very briefly. It can be so seldom that we are all together. Not, you know,' he continued, smiling more broadly, 'that I enjoy family gatherings, and I fear that I have not impertinence enough to invite you to Herries, unless anyone has an affection for potato-gathering. But I would not wish to be remiss in paying some reverence to my great-aunt.' He looked at the handsome boy by the chair. 'You must be Grandison's boy?'

'How are you, sir?' said Pelham, coming forward and holding out his hand.

Francis rested for a moment his hand on his shoulder. 'You should know my son David,' he said. 'If you care for the country a day or two at Herries. . . . But I suspect that you have better things to do.'

Pomfret here blustered forward. 'Well, brother, damn it, now that thou art here . . . a drink in this damp weather. . . . Why, damn it, man . . .' Then, conscious of his wife behind him, stopped abruptly.

'Nay, nay,' said Francis, smiling. 'My horse is outside and I have business. I heard you were all here. Doubtless you thought of me and wished my presence but were shy of asking me.'

He saw the spaniel, crossed to the sofa, bent down and stroked it. 'Poor bitch. You have as little place here as myself. I'll be coming to see thee one of these days, Harcourt.' Then was gone abruptly as he came.

INTO THE CAVE

Francis Herries rode off into the rain, his mind a strange torment. To enter that house over whose threshold he had not stepped for so many years had been an impulse of the moment. He had been inside before he had known that he was going, and, brushing past the startled manservant, he had entered that room and almost blinked, like an owl, at the unaccustomed light. It had been more than the candlelight; to himself who had been having for so long no intimate contacts save with the wind, the air, the hard grit of unyielding soil and the soft friendliness of the land after rain, these figures were like fish swimming in a strange sea. Like fish, and yet they had tugged at his heart.

He had entered the house in a childish play-acting spirit of dare-devil as though he would say 'Bo!' to a goose, but the very sight of silly Pomfret with his hanging belly and little Harcourt whose eyes had shone with pleasure at sight of him, and that handsome lad Grandison's boy, and all his Herries blood had pressed about his heart. It was to conceal this--which had been as violent as an unexpected blow in the face--that he had moved to the dog, stroked it, said those false sentimental words--the play-actor in him again. But behind the false sentiment there had been that swift ache of loneliness.

He knew it: he could confess it to himself: for all his intolerance and truculence he would have loved to stay with the men, with Pomfret, Harcourt, young Pelham, even with stiff Henry and flabby-faced Grandison, spent the night with them, laughed and drunk and changed bawdy stories with them, felt HERRIES again, felt the family blood in him and all England behind his tread and that ancient old tree-man whispering in his ears the ancient Herries password . . . and then perhaps to have taken the boy Pelham off to Herries and to have shown him David, who was a giant now and the hero of the country-side and the simplest, grandest Herries of them all. Then to have put on his decent clothes again and found a good horse once more (Mameluke buried beneath the yews behind the house) and ridden off to Seddon for a week or two, and then perhaps to stay with Grandison in Kensington. . . . He! He grinned, the rain blinding him as he climbed the steep hill to Cat Bells. That was never again for him nor would he care for it did he have it. In a day he would be quarrelling with Harcourt, mocking Pomfret, laughing at Grandison, corrupting Pelham. But the Herries blood was there. He had been a fool to enter that place.

There was something further for him to consider. In Keswick that afternoon he had talked with Father Roche. He had been crossing the market-place, his head up, looking neither to right nor left, in enemy's country and knowing it, when a country fellow dressed like a carter had touched his arm. He had turned about with his accustomed haughty stare, and that voice, once so powerful over him, came back to him across all the years. He knew him immediately, the voice with its seeming musical resonance, the eyes with their strange commanding glow belonging to one man only in the world. Roche had smiled, his broad hat pulled over his brows. Francis had asked him to Herries. Roche had refused, saying that he was on his way to Carlisle. The business was urgent. Very shortly the world would hear startling things. The hour for which they had all been waiting so long had struck at last. The voice was not raised, but behind it was that old fanatical undoubting spirit, and it had for Francis its ancient power. Standing there in the marketplace, the rain soaking down upon them, the old times swung back, days in Doncaster when it had seemed to him that he would follow Roche anywhere, evenings when it had appeared no odd fancy that, threading the stars, God and all His cohort of angels, the chariots of fire and the horsemen thereof, could plainly be discerned. Roche had given him an address--Walter Frith, in charge of John Stope, English Street. Carlisle. He would be found there. They had parted.

So all the old life was swinging back. You could not escape it, throw it off as you fancied, dig yourself into the very stomach of the soil--one tap on the shoulder, one glance through the dark branches of the yew and you were caught again. As Francis rode down to Grange Bridge the rain cleared. The clouds were rolling away above the Castle Crag, and a faint fair wash of crocus spread in a sea of light over the black pointed hill. On either side above Watendlath and the slow slopes beyond Grange white fleecy mists still lay low like bales of wool, but you could feel the light that burnt behind them, and the soft fields beyond the stream toward the lake were richly green.

He crossed the little bridge, turned to the right, rode between the trees beside the swift river along the track to Rosthwaite. In the village he had not seen a soul. It had been like a dead place. And well it might be. All the valley from Seathwaite to Grange had been cursed that winter. Misfortune had followed misfortune. Cattle had died, agues and fevers and plagues of pests had seemed to choose the valley for their camping-ground, and at the last smallpox had come, had raged right down the valley and only here. None over in Grasmere nor the other way in Newlands nor more than ordinary in the Keswick slums. The valley had been marked out. He knew well enough what the people were saying, that there was a curse, a spell, and he knew further that the old Wilson woman under his own roof was marked as the agent. And he knew that behind her he was himself marked out.

Yes, and he knew more than that: that, had it not been for David, weeks ago the roof would have been burned down over his head, Herries a heap of ashes and himself, perhaps, stoned to death. He did not care for their hatred, but he did not wish to die. There was something in life that was, like the beat of a drum, insistently enthralling. He had always felt it: he would never escape it: and it was as though, did he live long enough, he would discover the answer to this incredible mixture of beauty and filth, wizardry and commonplace, stagnation and unceasing activity. He did not want to die, but he did not want, either, that it should be by permission of his son that he should live.

But this was not for long. David was going: he knew it as though David had told him. And he did not want David to go. No, he did not. . . .

David was now twenty-five years of age, six feet five inches tall, as broad as a wall, the strongest man in the county beyond question, and many thought, with his fair blanched hair, blue eyes and splendid carriage, the handsomest. Let that be as it might. It did not matter. He was simple, modest, a man without words, quite direct in thought and act and with few subtleties. He had, for his years, scarcely stepped farther than Seascale on one side, Penrith on the other, very rarely left his valley, made few friends in Keswick, though all the world was friendly. His own valley loved him and said, as Francis well knew, that Rogue Herries had never fathered him. And yet he was clear Herries enough, the line of his jutting chin, the high strong cheek-bones made him plainly of the 'horse' family. He moved, tossed his head, swung his body like some high-bred animal, held, confined.

For eight years now he had helped his father in the land around Herries, ploughing, planting, digging, all as he very well knew, but never said, to little effect. His constant companions were his father and Deborah; he was friend to all the valley, but had no other close intimacy save that old childhood one with Peel's boy, Rendal, who was now a man almost as big and strong as David himself. Of love affair there had been as yet, it seemed, no sign.

He was a man of few words save possibly with Deborah. When he went to sport or meeting, to hunt or local games, and performed some miracle of strength, he came home afterwards without a word of it. His thoughts were certainly slow in labour: you could almost see them move behind his smooth clear forehead. He had a long, slow laugh that began as a murmur, spread into a long rumble, ended in a roar. He had a slow temper. He had two faults: that he was suspicious of men and, although courteous in manner, desperately hard to make a friend of. And he never forgot nor forgave an injury. When, that is, he had proved it to be one. He paid no attention to gossip, drank as men drink, but kept the effects of it to himself. He showed no resentment at the cruelties, foulnesses, obscenities of his time. He was a man of his time. He did not trade with women because he did not as yet apparently care very greatly for women's company save Deborah's. He was tongue-tied with women and impatient of their ways. He did not care very much for any company and preferred best to be away on the hills alone. He was very Herries in some things: in his passion for England--he had all the Herries' ignorant contempt for and dislike of foreigners; in his interest in the family--he would ask his father many questions about Herries history and relationship; in his inability to see anything that was not in front of his nose.

It was his father who was the rebel, not he. Unless he were passionately roused--a very rare thing--there was something lazy and comfort-loving in his great size and strength. He seemed to be never physically tired, but he liked to lie back staring into fire or sky, seeing nothing, perhaps thinking nothing, letting light and warmth soak into him.

But what were his thoughts of his father? How many times, in the instant of digging or planting, hoeing or carrying, walking or riding, Francis had looked up at the sky, at the long hump of Glaramara, or, from Grange, at the opening flower of Skiddaw, and asked himself that question. David was infinitely kind, ceaselessly patient. Since that night so long ago at Ravenglass no word of impatience had passed his lips, he had shown no angry movement towards his father. But they had moved, these last years, with a sort of mist between, loving one another and yet distrustful: or Francis on his side at least had held distrust. What must David feel about his father's isolation, self-adopted, ironically self-proclaimed, and about the ever thicker wall of hatred built by the world against him?

We love most, perhaps, those of whom we are a little afraid. David was the only creature in the world of whom Francis was afraid, and this was a fear only of a sudden blazing word, a glance of contempt. Then, the word spoken, the glance flung, Francis would pass into the final ostracism.

When Mary, two years earlier, had left him, Francis thought that the word would be spoken. Mary, who had grown increasingly beautiful and contemptuous, had gone without a sign one morning to her aunt in Keswick. She had sent a letter from there saying that she would not return. No other word came from her. They heard that she went afterwards to stay in Carlisle, then that she was back in Keswick, then in London. Then it was said that Francis had beaten and abused her. He smiled at that. In earlier days he had beaten David often and Deborah on occasion: on Mary he had never laid a finger.

Would David blame him for Mary? He did not. David blamed him for nothing. Was his silence criticism? Maybe not. He was always so very silent. Once, when they were together in Langdale, Francis looking down the long green sward and then up to the Pikes, rosy in sunset, said:

'You must hate me, David.' And David, after a long silence while the birds swept above their heads home, answered:

'I have three friends. You are one--and the first.'

But what comfort, his irony urged on him, was he to find in that? David had not answered his question, only asserted his loyalty; and David's loyalty was so unsubtle that it offered no reward to one's pride.

Not that Francis' pride was in question. He was so proud that his son's approval or disapproval altered nothing. He was so proud that he would tell his son to go to the devil did he patronise him. But he did not patronise him. He stood at his side and worked with him. That was all.

So he rode into the little stone court of Herries, shouted to fat Benjamin to come for his horse, and longed, as he stumbled up the dark staircase, to see David waiting for him.

David was there. He was standing in the dark brown room upon whose surface the firelight was very faintly flickering, listening, and so intent was his attitude that Francis also stayed motionless by the door: the only sound in the room was the soft settling of the ash from the piled logs.

'What is it?' Francis asked at last. Then he heard, but so faint that it was like the scratching of mice on the wainscot, a trickling crooning sound; someone, at a distance, behind walls, was singing, singing in a high-pitched murmur of a voice a little tune like an incantation or a prayer monotonously reiterated.

'Mrs. Wilson,' David said, then coming close to his father and laying his hand on his arm: 'She sings to keep herself company. She's afraid.'

'Of whom?' asked Francis, although he knew the answer.

'They are very impatient. . . . I've been telling her she should go from here.'

'Turn her from this roof . . . after these years?'

'No, no. . . . Help her to the Low Countries. At the Hague there is some family she was nurse to once. They would take her. We could secure her a passage.'

'She is old,' Francis answered. He liked the warmth of his son's body close to his. He hoped that David would not move. That visit to the family had made him lonelier. . . .

He put his arm across David's vast shoulders. His long brown fingers pressed a little into the smooth warmth of his son's neck.

'I think she is going mad with terror,' David said. The room too seemed a little mad: the dusk wrote letters on the wall with the firelight and then erased them again. The wind that was getting up and rattling the leaded panes drowned the little song and then by contrast raised it again. It was more dangerous in the dusky room because both men believed in witches and thought that Mrs. Wilson was one.

Then Benjamin came clumping up the staircase, holding the lighted candles in their tall silver candlesticks in either hand, and Deborah came in to lay the table for some supper; there was life and movement and the little song could be heard no more.

Deborah, who was now twenty-two years of age, was little and insignificant until you noticed her eyes, which were large, soft, grey, very beautiful. Her shyness was her trouble. She could not be courageous about people. She was afraid of every person in the world save David, and especially of her father. She had had the same fear for seven years, ever since the death of her mother, that David would go and leave her with her father alone. That fear was now a torture, and no reassurance on David's part could comfort her.

Francis knew, of course, that she was afraid of him, and that exasperated him. Every time that she shrank from him his old ironic dislike of himself increased in him and she was included in that. When the supper had been cleared away and she had gone up to her room, the two men were left alone in front of the fire. The rain had returned and in violence; it slashed the panes, roared with the wind away, then fell again upon the house as though it would batter it to the ground; the fury passed and the rain softly stroked the windows, whispering indecent and chuckling secrets, then ran in a hurry as though it were pattering after someone, burst after that once more into a frenzy of rage and exasperation . . . an evil frustrated old woman, the rain that night.

Secure from it the two Herries drew close together. Suddenly they were intimate as they had not been for months. Francis put his hand on David's broad thigh, drawing his great body a little nearer to him. When he told him about his visit to the family that afternoon David was excited.

'Oh, why did you not stay?' he said. 'The awkwardness would have worn away. How did Cousin Pelham look? And Henry Cards . . . and Cousin Dorothy . . .' He sighed. 'I would that I'd been with you.'

Francis sharply withdrew his hand. 'You could go. . . . Why don't you?'

David shook his head, laughing. 'What would they want with me? I've no head for their company. No, no. It was your opportunity, father. But you frightened them.'

Francis said: 'David, I've been wishing to ask you. We've been working side by side these years. It's come to but little. Everything here must seem to you cursed, the house, the soil, the life, the loneliness. I fancy that it's in that very cursedness of the place that I find some salvation. I would have it hard and ungrateful. Here for the first time in all my days I've found response to my own temper and some aggravating comfort. But for you! Already you are doing good business in Keswick and with your friend in Liverpool. Why should you stay? There's no place in the world where you wouldn't make your way, and you should see the world, find a woman of your own breed, not bury yourself in this windy hole for hinds and pigs. . . . I'm other than you. The dirt of the soil is more to me than any man, aye, or woman either. I am stuck here, my feet in the clay, and am accustomed. But it is not your abiding-place and will never be.'

He was amazed then at how roughly, after he had ended, his heart was beating as he waited for the boy's answer. What would it be here without David? How could he endure it? But better that David should go rather than he should indulge his father by staying. Francis would take no patronage. Yes, but his heart hammered as he waited.

David was slow as always. At last he answered: 'I'm glad you've spoken at last, father. All these months I've wondered what was in your mind. But I can't leave you. We're bound together, I fancy, different though we are. And yet . . . there IS something I should say. Father, why should we stay by Herries? The place has never cared for us. As a boy I ran first into the house and shivered at its greeting. Everything has been wrong for you here. The people have been wrong for you, the soil stubborn; nothing that you have planted has grown: you have been with every year more alone here. Why should we stay? We owe nothing to the house. In the South together, the three of us, where it is warmer and the sun shines and people's hearts are more friendly. . . . Father, let us leave here. Everything has been wrong for you here.'

'No,' his father answered in a strange, low voice, as though he were speaking to something within him. 'Everything is not wrong for me here. Here is my home, the only one I've ever known or shall know. I feel the touch of the peat, the scratch of the dried bracken, and it is my place.'

His voice had its accustomed ironic tone. 'So they've been persuading you, David, my son? "Take your father away, David Herries. He stinks in our noses, he is warlock and dirty liver and murderer maybe. Remove his carcase or we will remove it for you." They've persuaded you, David . . . but there must be more than a word before they can move me. I am stuck fast, and there's my ghost to come after me when they've knocked my head in and scattered my entrails for dung over their fields: there's still my ghost, David.'

David got up. His voice was cold with anger when at last after a long while he spoke.

'That is unjust. No man could persuade me against you save yourself. I am no traitor. But guard yourself against irony with me. I am a fool, you know, and may understand it wrongly.'

He went out.

So that was that. Herries was alone. He got up very early next morning, washed himself at the pump and went off, walking, his head in the air, not caring a damn if he never saw his bullock of a son again. Or he said not. His heart within his heart ached, as it always did, for his son. That heart would have gone, waked the boy, embraced him. The only heart to which David responded, the only one that he understood. For David had all the simple sentimentality of his period; for him there were these actual contrasted powers, God and the horny Satan, Michael and all the angels, dragons and rescuing princes, shepherds, shepherdesses, and the ravening wolf, the good old man by the fireside reading out of the Book to his family clustered at his knees, wedding bells and Innocence wed under roses to Purity and Strength. Yes, David believed in all these things. He saw life like that.

Francis, as he strode off into the early morning rain that sung about his ears in a feathering mist, said aloud: 'I'm done with the boy. What's the use? . . . No ground between us,' and the rain whispered in his ear: 'It's a lie! It's a lie!' Once he almost turned back. It would be very easy to run up those stairs, climb to David's room, see him sunk in sleep there, his chest bare, his knees curled up. Francis knew how he lay, his cheek on his hand, dreaming of his princesses and his shepherdesses. He had no more subtlety than that. The Herries sentimentalist. No, not conscious enough to be called anything. A sweet-breathed, mild- eyed animal, with the obstinacy of a mule, the strength of a horse, the fidelity of a dog. He should be breeding. He should be let out, like a stallion, to the women of the country to get fine sons. All this true enough did you forget his heart, which in its strength, sweetness, sympathy, durability was of another order from the animal. There was his immortality, and, likely enough, the immortality of all of us.

For there was immortality in us! The great white horse of Herries' dream striking up from the ebony lake to the icy peaks. Sentimentality, that again, thought Herries, and arrogance, planning for your little peapod of a marionette so handsome a destiny. But the very fact of the planning. . . . Why this burning, eager, rebellious, longing fury between his miserable bag of bones, the thick coiled entrails, the stringy nerves, the flat-faced pancreas, that silly mechanism that one blow from a fool could tumble as a child tumbles a toy. Burning there between the bones and fat, the blood and gristle, this fierce arrogant ambition, this persistent dream, this lovely vision. . . . 'All we like sheep . . .' Nay, like gods rather, lost in a strange land.

Herries often, as he dug and sweated, cursed the reluctant soil and his aching back and blistered hands, turned back and back to those same common platitudes, fresh to him because they were his own and mingled with so many strange things for which he could find no words. His brain, heart, generative organs: how to reconcile these three in a common harmony and drive them to a fine destiny, his brain that was clogged with lack of education, his heart that led him only to self-contempt, his generative powers that had known their best days, and they nothing to boast over. All keys to some event, but all out of control and discipline, all leading to silly ends.

Not intelligent enough, not kind enough, not even lecher enough. A botched machine set in a country veiled with mist. . . .

He had crossed the fields, passed the little cottages of Seatoller and the yews, and started up the hill to Honister. On the left of him Hause Gill tumbling in miniature cataracts with the recent rain, on the right of him the ever-opening fells. He drew great gulps of air into his lungs. That was for him, that unenclosed fell. As soon as he reached a point where the moss ran unbroken to the sky all his troubles dropped away from him and he was a man. There was no place in the world for open country like this stretch of ground in Northern England and Scotland, for it was man's country: it was neither desert nor icy waste; it had been on terms with man for centuries and was friendly to man. The hills were not so high that they despised you; their rains and clouds and becks and heather and bracken, gold at a season, green at a season, dun at a season, were yours; the air was fresh with kindliness, the running water sharp with friendship, and when the mist came down it was as though the hill put an arm around you and held you even though it killed you. For kill you it might. There was no sentimentality here. It had its own life to lead and, as in true friendship, kept its personality. It had its own tempers with the universe and, when in a rolling rage, was not like to stop and inquire whether you chanced to be about or no. Its friendship was strong, free, unsentimental, breathing courage and humour. And the fell ran from hill to hill, springing to the foot, open to the sky, cold to the cheek, warm to the heart, unchanging in its fidelity. As he breasted the hill and turned back to look across Borrowdale the sky began to break.

He stared, as though the scene were new to him, to Glaramara and then over Armboth to the Helvellyn range. It was new to him: never before had it held those shapes and colours nor would it again: with every snap of the shuttle it changed.

Now across the Helvellyn line the scene was black and against the black hung the soft white clouds. Borrowdale glittered in sun like a painted card, flat, emerald and shining. Above his head all the sky was in motion: beyond him over Honister tenebrous shadows thrust upward to one long line of saffron light that lay like a path between smoking clouds. All the fell smelt of rain and young bracken, and two streams ran in tumult across the grass, finding their way to the beck. The sunlight was shut off from Borrowdale, which turned instantly dead grey like a mouse's back; then the sun burst out as though with a shout over the low fells that lay before the Gavel. A bird on a rock above the beck began to sing.

He was filled with a delicious weariness. He lay down there where he was, his full length on a thin stone above the beck, and on that hard surface fell happily, dreamlessly, asleep.

He woke to a strange sense of constriction. He moved and found amazingly that his arms and legs were tied with rough rope. He raised his head and stared into the eyes of a man who sat motionless on a rock near him. A horse grazed in the grass close by.

Francis stared at the man: the man stared back again.

'You sleep fast,' the man said. 'I bound you and you didn't waken.' He was a man with a thin dry face, long shaggy black hair, a coat and breeches of some colour that had faded into a dirty green. He looked like part of the fell. His legs were thin and long and sharp. He was not young, fifty years of age maybe.

'Why have you bound me?' Herries asked quietly.

'You are my prisoner,' the man replied.

'My body is--for the moment,' Herries answered.

The man was, from his voice, not of the North. His tone was firm, quiet, reflective.

'You are Herries of Herries in Rosthwaite.'

'Yes. How do you know me?'

'I've seen you many times.'

'What have you against me?'

'Nothing.'

'Then why have you bound me?'

'You are my prisoner,' the man answered again.

'Yes; but why?'

'I have a curiosity to ask you some questions. Would you come peacefully with me?'

'Whither?'

'By Honister.'

'Yes,' said Herries.

'You swear it?'

'Yes.'

'Then I will untie you.'

He came forward and, quite gently, with some care, undid the bonds.

Herries sat up and felt his arms and legs where the rope had been, but he had been bound only a moment or so: it was the binding that had waked him. Then he rose and stretched himself. The man also got up. He was of great height and very thin with a long nose. His face was pitted with smallpox marks.

They started to walk together forward to Honister, the man leading the horse. The air was deliciously fresh and the sky filled now with little dancing white clouds.

73

'What is your interest in me?' Francis asked at last. They were on the higher ground, about to turn the corner, and before he turned he looked back and saw, picked up by the sun, on the low ground before Armboth a little wood of silver birch. The sun hung over the little wood in a brooding lighted mist and the thin silver trunks stood up proudly, burnished. Herries, because of what happened afterwards, was never to forget them.

This fellow was a man of not many words, but at last he said, long after Francis' question:

'Can you recall, once, many years gone, you gave your coat to a woman by the road?'

'Yes,' said Herries, his heart beating.

'And once later on a Christmas night you talked with her?'

'I remember,' said Herries.

'I was there, that second time,' the man said.

'There was with her,' Herries said, 'a young child.'

The man nodded. 'The woman was my sister. The child was her child and is with me yet.' He waited awhile and then went on. 'I bound you because you would not have come with me else. Or I thought so. They say in the valley that you are the Devil and eat human flesh.'

Herries looked at the man smiling. 'Do you think so?'

The man looked back at Herries.

'No,' he said. 'When my sister died she said I was to give you the only thing she had. I have kept it for you.'

'But why,' asked Herries, 'must you bind me to give it me?'

The man answered: 'Our place is rough in Honister. We are in bad repute here, my brother and I, though not so bad as yourself. I thought you would fight before you came, and because of my sister I would not strike you. Are you as bad as men say?'

'I am as bad,' answered Herries, 'as other men. And as good. We are as the fancy hits us.'

The man nodded his head gravely. 'That's true. One man's life is this way, another's that. We have little choice.'

They struck up the fell to the left and climbed. The man led the horse patiently and with kindness. When they were high on the moor they could see the guards of the mines pacing on the path below.

All the fell rolled beneath them now like the sea, and the clouds rolled above them, driven by a sunny dancing wind. On the brow of the hill the man took Herries' arm, led him over boulders, dipped down the shelving turf, then pushed up again on the hinder shoulder of Honister.

Then, loosening his grip, he vanished. Herries stood alone, hearing no sound but the wind and running water. He could see, icily blue, the thin end of Buttermere Lake far below. He heard a whistle and saw the black head of the man just below him. He went down.

He saw then the grey opening of a cave in the hill, fenced with dead bracken and furze. He followed the man in. At first he could see nothing, but could smell cooking food, an odd sweet scent of flowers and a musty animal tang. The man had his hand on his arm and very gently, as though he were speaking to a child, said: 'Sit you there. You can sleep if you will. The straw's dry.' Francis turned back, shifting the bracken a little; and the sun flickered on to him, dancing before his eyes.

But he did not wish to look about him. He was oddly incurious and infinitely weary. Why this weariness? It was as though the kind black-haired man had laid a spell upon him. So he slept, long and almost dreamlessly. The nearest to a dream was that he was led again through the incidents of the morning, following the lean man over ever-darkening fell, then was pushed from a height and heard, as he raised himself from a hard cold ground, a voice say to him: 'Into the cave! Into the cave! You have been outside too long.'

With that he woke, wide-eyed, oddly happy, extremely hungry. He sat up and looked about him. The sun streamed in from the fell. He could see all the cave, which was not indeed quite a cave, but rather the opening of some deserted entrance to a long-neglected mine. In the black cavern beyond him there was a fire and on the fire a round black pot. A girl sat on the ground watching the pot.

At once he knew her. Her hair, which fell all about her face and almost to her waist, told him—there was no colour like that anywhere else in the world; but something thin, poised, intent, alert, independent, in her attitude also told him: his eyes saw once again that figure never in all these years lost sight of, the tiny child, crowned with its flaming hair, pressed back against its mother's skirts. Instinctively, he put his hand up to his cheek and felt his scar.

He had found her again. He had the oddest sense of having reached the end of some quest, a sense of rest, of fulfilment, of motionless certainty.

'Well?' he said quietly.

'Well?' she answered, without turning or taking her eyes from the fire. 'So you've waked?'

'I've waked.'

'I never saw a man sleep so sound.' Then after bending forward and stirring the fire she added, but still not looking at him: 'So you've come at last.'

'At last?'

'Yes. I knew that you would come one day.' Her voice, he noticed, had the very same sweet, remote tone that all those years ago it had had. Seven years, and they were as though they were yesterday.

He got up and stretched himself. His clothes were stuck with bracken. He came across to the fire, looking at her hair that was dark in the cave like the sombre shadows in flame when the smoke is thick. Even now she did not look up.

'Well, I have waited for you too,' he said.

At that she turned and looked up at him, and as his eyes met hers he knew two things: that he loved her and that he had never before, in all his ventures, known at all what love was. He knew, instantly afterwards, a third thing: that he meant nothing at all to her and that she would be glad when he went. He knew that by the way that she looked beyond him to the mouth of the cave, a little impatiently, her mind on the fire and also on some possible escape for her.

She was a child, under eighteen. He was over forty. This folly . . .

But he could not take his eyes from her. They were locked there, and all his body moved in its inner spirit towards her so that already, although his hand had not touched hers, his arms were round her, his head, so heavy with fruitless work and anger and impatience, resting on her child's breasts.

'How did you know,' he said at last, his voice husky, 'that I would come one day?'

'Oh,' she answered, 'mother would speak of you, and my uncle, and I would see you in the woods, Borrowdale-way. I begged once of your son by Stonethwaite. He gave me a silver shilling. He is the finest man I have ever seen. He has the grandest body. But I could never love him. He is too thick. But I have seen too much love.'

'You are only a child,' Herries said, 'and cannot know.' The force within him was too strong. Had it meant death in the next moment he could not have prevented himself. He put out his hand and touched her hair. But it did not mean for her anything at all. She did not move her head but allowed him to stroke it as he would.

He felt that, and his hand came back to him. Then she got up from the fire, straightening herself. Her body was very thin and still a child's body, but lovely to him in its slender line, the long legs and high carriage of the head and the lovely bosom, breathing on the very edge of maturity.

'My uncle is out watching,' she said. 'The guards are active to-day. They killed two men last night. Some day soon they will find this place and then we must move on again.'

'What does your uncle do?'

'My two uncles. Oh, they do what they can. Steal from the mines and sell to the Jews in Keswick, or they poach, or my uncle George fights in the Fairs . . . whatever comes. But they are hoping for news soon from France. Then we will go to Carlisle or Scotland maybe.'

'From France?'

She smiled. 'They never tell me anything. Why should I care? It is all the same to me. One day they will be killed, and I shall sell myself to some wealthy man.'

'You would do that?'

'And why not? I must have food. To feed my body, I give my body. What is my body? It is not myself. That I keep for my own.'

'If your uncles are killed, you must come to me. I will take care of you.'

She looked at him, smiling. 'You are very ugly, and they say in Borrowdale that you are very wicked. I don't care if you are wicked--but how rich are you?'

'I am very poor.'

'Then why should I come to you if I don't love you?'

'Because I would care for you and work for you and protect you.'

'Maybe I should lie with your son. Would you still protect me?'

He turned his eyes away from her.

'Yes; even then.'

She put her hand lightly on his shoulder.

'No; if I ever came to you I would be honest. My mother always said a woman must be honest or she is nothing. Men can be as dishonest as they please. That is the difference between men and women.' She smiled at him like a small child, enchantingly. 'I would be honest if I came--but I will never come.'

Her two uncles crossed the light. They were in excellent spirits, amused by some joke they had had with one of the guards. One of them, Anthony, had rabbits and a hare.

They all sat round and ate. The food was excellent: savoury meat cooked in the pot, tasting of herbs and sun and all the rich juices in the world. There was good wine too. The two men--Anthony was round and fat, with a broad chest and short thick neck: he was coloured dark brown and had sharp suspicious eyes like a ferret's-- curled up and went to sleep.

All through the sunny afternoon, while the clouds raced past the cave's entrance driven by the wind, Herries sat where he was, silent, watching the girl. She sat quite near to him, sewing at some garment and then afterwards lying back on the hay, the sun on her cheek, and falling easily, comfortably asleep.

He sat there thinking of nothing, nothing at all. He did not want to move. The air was cold although the sun shone, but he was hot with a kind of fever; once and again he trembled. Once he leaned forward and touched her cheek with his hand. He withdrew abruptly as though he had, by so doing, pledged himself to some awful danger. But he did not think at all, neither of his past nor of his future, nor of himself in any way. He simply knew that his fate had come and that whatever way he turned now he could not escape it.

He did not want to escape it. He, forty-five years, she sixteen. This child who cared nothing for him and perhaps never would care. A child of vagabonds. That did not matter. He was himself a vagabond. They were both outcasts. He sat staring there like a drunken man or an idiot. There was utter silence in the cave; only the wind, rushing by outside, sometimes cried out like a struck harp not quite in tune.

When the shadows began to lengthen and the sky beyond the cave was a pale washed blue with no clouds in it, the men stirred and woke together. George looked gravely at Herries as though he were going to lecture him. Then he got up, found an old green box behind the fire, fumbled in it and brought to Herries a simple rough silver chain with a little crucifix of black wood on its end. 'This was what she left for you,' he said.

Herries expected that he would say more. He had spoken in the morning of questions that he would ask. But he said no more, only stood there as though dismissing him.

Herries took the chain. He did not want to go. He wanted with a desire stronger than any that he had ever known to stay, but the two men stood there waiting for him to go.

The girl had waked, stretched her arms, then walked to the cave opening: the evening wind blew her hair so that it seemed to be fire blowing about her head and against the grey stuff of her dress.

'Hadn't you questions that you would ask me?' he said.

'No,' said the lean man.

'I don't understand why you brought me here.'

'To give you that.'

'Well, then, tell me your names.'

'I am George Endicott. He is Anthony Endicott.'

'And the girl?'

'The girl's name is Mirabell Starr.'

'Maybe we shall meet in another place.'

'Maybe.'

'In Carlisle, perhaps?'

'Maybe.'

Anthony, the fat one, turned back into the cave as though the matter were closed. George held his hand out.

'I bound you because I was afraid you wouldn't come.'

Herries exchanged a handgrasp.

'That's no harm. I shall keep the chain. My thanks for the meal. At Herries there's a meal for you.'

Then he went out of the cave. He held out his hand to the girl.

Lowering his voice, staring into her eyes, he said: 'You have promised to come to me if you are all alone.'

She answered like her uncle.

'Maybe,' she said. She let him hold her hand, and for a moment, in the wind that was now very strong blowing from the sea, his body pressed against hers.

'I will be good to you,' he said.

'So they all say,' she answered, 'until they've got what they wanted.'

'I shall never get what I want,' he answered. He longed to kiss her pale thin cheek, but the indifference in her eyes humiliated him. So he turned, bending his head a little, and went up the fell, not looking back.

WITCH

Mrs. Wilson stood, as was her habit, at the foot of the stairs, listening and looking up. No one was moving in the house. It was after mid-day. She knew that Herries was digging at the back of the house, that his son was away for that day in Keswick, that his daughter was in Rosthwaite and Benjamin the servant at the stable: she was therefore quite alone in the house.

She stood there endeavouring to make up her mind to what was for her a great venture. She was planning to go to Grange. She had not been out of that house for six months: she had not been in the village of Rosthwaite for a year. This enterprise of hers needed immense resolution and courage. Although, since early morning, she had been summoning her will to this expedition, she was not yet completely resolved on it.

Old Tom Mounsey, deaf and dumb, had contrived to send her word that his wife Old Hannah Mounsey was dying and wished to see her before she went. Hannah Mounsey, once Hannah Armstrong, a gay and beautiful young thing, was Katherine Wilson's oldest friend. She was now, like Katherine, so old that she didn't know how old she was. And she was dying. She was the first human who had asked to see Katherine Wilson for more than twenty years.

The old woman had been strangely stirred by the summons. She was so old that the days of her youth were as yesterday. They were very vivid and alive to her. She saw Hannah still with red cheeks, bright flaxen hair, and a blue gown. She heard Hannah laugh as she hid with Katherine in Statesman Armstrong's barn, while young Johnny Turnbull had searched for her to fumble and kiss her. Young Johnny Turnbull had been hanged in Carlisle for stealing a sheep. As everyone knew, it was not he who stole the sheep but Daniel Waugh.

She was very old, but she could make the journey. Her legs could still carry her. It would take her two hours or more to walk to Grange, but she could do it. It was not her legs that frightened her. Something else.

She was frightened of the outside world, and with reason. The outside world hated her. They hated her as much as they were afraid of her.

They said she was a witch. Was she a witch? She did not know. They said that the troubles of the last year were her doing. Were they? She did not know. Sometimes she thought that they were and felt an odd impulse of power. Was it true that by crooking her finger or nodding her head she could kill sheep, scatter the palsy, burn hay-ricks, poison food? It might be so. She did not know.

It was not of course true that she could fly on a broomstick or that she had danced naked with the Devil in Glaramara caves.

But she HAD danced naked in the woods one moonlit night. That was a great many years ago. Many, many years. She had had a child by Joe Butterfield because of that dancing. The child had been happily still-born, and Joe Butterfield had been gored to death by his own bull many years back. . . . He had been a fine big young fellow, with a tattoo of a mermaid on his chest.

She could not remember many things, and many things she remembered in every detail. But all that she wished now was to be let alone: all the passions save fear had died right down in her. Her love of fun and gaiety, her recklessness, her vicious tempers, her courage, her loyalty to those whom she loved, her passion for her son who, after living in this house with her so long, had left her, all these fires had sunk to grey ashes. The only thing remaining to her was fear.

The first time that she had been really afraid was one day shortly before the coming of these Herries, when, walking out on the path to Seathwaite, some boys had thrown stones and shouted 'Witch!' after her. Long before this she had been suspected of witchcraft, she and Mary Roberts and Ellen Wade and Alice Leyland. Alice Leyland had been much older than the others. It may be that Alice had been a witch. She had made an image of Gabriel Caine and burnt it at a slow fire, and he had died within three days.

She had, too, her famous love-philtre, and Katherine herself had mixed this in her own man's drink, a year after their marriage, when he was going with the Hoggarty girl in Keswick. It had not, however, caused him to leave the Hoggarty girl, not until she had had the smallpox and grown ugly.

The old woman sat down at the foot of the stairs. Did she dare to venture into Grange? She sniffed danger in the very air, but that might be her fancy. Much of it might be her fancy. She had stayed alone in this house until she scarcely knew what she believed. But, from the very beginning, there had been something about her that set her apart from the others. She had been a pretty girl: they had all said so. She had cared for men no more and no less than the others, but the difference had been that men were not enough: no, love was not enough, nor courting, nor childbirth, nor any of the dreary, dull, day-by-day life in that dreary, dull valley.

She must have excitement, but then, after that, it was not excitement that she wanted, not excitement only. She was curious, inquisitive. She wanted to see INTO things, and when she had seen Alice Leyland and the others dance naked across the grass under the moon and then vanish into the black wood she had been curious to see what they did there. So she, too, had danced naked into the wood, and all that had happened had been Joe Butterfield's baby.

Had it not been for that odd sense of power that sometimes came to her she would have left it alone.

But there had been hours when she felt that she held all the valley in her hand to do with as she would. She felt that sometimes even now. What was that accompanying her, lifting her up, taking her to the very verge of some discovery? Was it only her fancy? In later years she had yielded to the temptation to see in the eyes of others that look of fear, of terror. . . .

When they came to her, as they used to do, to ask her to heal their cattle, to help them with a lover, to injure an enemy, she had always told them to go away again, that she knew no spells, no charms, had no powers.

But they did not believe her, and she did not believe herself. Had she no power? Why was it then that she would rise in the night and walk to the window and see the shadows under the moon come flocking to her call, and had she not killed Janet Forsse by looking at her after Janet had called her a witch outside Rosthwaite Chapel? Had not Janet gone home, lain down on her bed and died? That had done her much harm, that death of Janet. They had feared and hated her from that moment. She had felt the power rise in her breast, fill her breast, well into her eyes. But was that truth or falsehood? Janet had eaten meat from a poisoned pot and so died. . . .

All her life she had wished others well. Only when they insulted her she must turn and defend herself. And in these last years, from loneliness, desolation, unhappiness, she had scarcely known what she did. She had made wax figures, watched from the window, spoken sometimes with shadows. Why not with shadows when no one else would speak with her?

Everything had been worse with her since the coming of Herries. From the first day she had hated the father and loved the son. The father had something in common with her. Although she was an untaught woman, and he was a grand gentleman, yet they shared something. He had looked at her and she at him. It might be that he was the Devil. Some thought so in the village. It might be. He looked like the Devil once and again. Perhaps he could answer the questions that she never dared to ask. She was afraid of him, and she hated him. She had always loved his son David since, as a little boy, he had run first into the house. All that was simple and good and maternal in her responded to him. He had always been kind to her, talked to her, asked her how she did, and now that he was the finest, grandest man in the valley she was proud of him, as though he had been her work. When his mother had died she had wanted to protect and care for him. He had not needed her--he needed no one--but she prayed for him night and morning.

That had been until the last year, but in the last year fear had grown in her breast, swallowing up everything else in her.

The thing that she feared most now was to dream, because in her dreams she was quite unprotected. So soon as she slept she was outside the house in the naked road, or the house was without walls, or she was on the mountain-side. Then while she waited alone in this awful space she could hear them coming, hundreds of them; the present and past came together--Alice Leyland, Joe Butterfield, Turnbull, Hannah Armstrong, and with them many strangers. But they all looked alike. They had terrible faces, and that look in the eyes of lust and hatred, curiosity and pleasure. Years ago, when a young woman, she had seen a boy stoned to death in Keswick market. They said that he had burnt a rick. That look then had been in their faces. It had been perhaps also in her own.

In her dream they came always nearer and nearer, quite silent, and she had no strength to escape them. Then one had called 'Witch!'

She would awake trembling and the sweat would run down into her eyes; then she would sigh with relief at the respite, and would get up and touch the familiar things, the clock, the settle, the pots and pans, to reassure herself.

When her son had left her he had said nothing, but had looked at her once before he went, and the look in his eyes had held fear, just as her own eyes held fear. She had not tried to keep him. Only after he had gone she sat and remembered all the things he had done as a child and especially when he had sucked at her breast and she had crooned songs to him.

And now should she go in to Grange? It might be that it would break the spell, it might be that she would meet folk who would be kind to her, and, seeing Hannah again, she would recover her courage.

She moved slowly back into the empty kitchen. She was still strong. Her bodily health had been always amazing; she had never known a day's sickness, and that, too, had made her sometimes wonder whether she were not under the Devil's especial protection.

She stirred about the kitchen, raising her head, sniffing the air; her brown face was a network of wrinkles, her hair was snow-white, her eyes dimmed in vision. She moved on her legs easily and with freedom.

Suddenly she knew that she was going into Grange: it was as though someone had bent over and whispered in her ear. The great grey cat, with one eye green and one brown, her only friend in the world, had come and rubbed itself against her legs. It was he, perhaps, who persuaded her.

Every witch must have a cat. She had seen Alice Leyland once take a glove that she had soaked in blood and water and rub it on her cat's belly, murmuring some spell. . . . What were the words? She had known them all once. Words, words, words . . . words from where? They had come to her once, without her own desire: there had been the day when she had seen Statesman Peel's man rubbing between the horns of his oxen the grease from the Paschal Candle, eyeing her as he did so. Yes, then, against her own will, not at all by her agency, the words had come to her lips. He had seen her lips move and had told them in the village.

But her cat. She bent down and stroked it, letting her old dried fingers press into the fur, liking to feel the cat's response as it bent its back a little, stiffening, stretching its legs, its eyes closing with pleasure. She had thought often that her cat knew more than she did. Watching sometimes at night from the high window she had seen it slip off across the fields, moving with quiet secret purpose, just as Alice Leyland had once moved.

The cat and Alice Leyland knew things that she would never know.

She went to the cupboard and found her cloak and high-crowned, old-fashioned hat. She found her crooked, gnarled stick. She started out.

When she came into the path beyond the courtyard her heart beat so furiously that she must stop: it leapt with wild angry stabs as though it were telling her not to go. For a whole year she had not been beyond the courtyard. She was encouraged by the stillness of the world about her, not a sound save the running water that was never silent, and the scrape, from behind the house, of Herries' spade as it struck the hard soil. She was always scornful of Herries' labour; the soil here was like stone or mire, harsh, ungrateful, contemptuous: it hated Herries as she did. A little pleasure stirred her heart as she thought of Herries' labour and the small reward he had for it.

She walked down the path, moving with marvellous strength for an old woman. She thought that she heard the cat following, and she turned to forbid it, but there was nothing there.

It was a grey, overhanging, autumn day with no wind: the light on walls and trees trembled once and again as though thunder was coming, but the leaves that still lingered, brown and shrivelled, on the trees, never shivered.

She walked as she had lived, in a half-dream. Sometimes it seemed to her that figures were walking with her, sometimes that she was alone. When she reached the river she muttered a little with pleasure, as though she were blessing it. Perhaps she was. This river, the Derwent, had been part of her from birth. Her parents' cottage had bordered it: her first instinct as an infant had been to find it, and now, because for so long she had not seen it, she greeted it again as an old friend. There had been a time in her life when, if she did not see it every day, she was miserable. From Seathwaite to the lake she had known every inch of it, its deeps and shallows, its moods of anger, rebellion, calm, blue content, shrill chatter, acquiescence, curiosity; its colours, brown like ale, blue like glass, grey like smoke, white like cloud; she had bathed in it, fished in it, sat beside it. Often, shut up in that house, she had listened to it, especially when it was in flood; then it was happiest, most violent. It was the only thing in the world now that she could trust: it would never harm her. It did not care whether she were witch or no.

As she passed beside it now, happy in a dim confused way at recovering it again, she seemed to speak to it, telling it how sorry she was that it was shrunken, that its stones and boulders must be exposed, and its voice have fallen to a murmur. Never mind. The rains were coming again. Patience, patience. . . . And as she looked her husband rose out of it, his brown tangled beard wet, his eyelashes dripping water, his breast, thick with soaking hair, exposed, his flanks too shining with damp fine yellow hair, his toes crooked about the stones of the river-bed; his bare arm rose up as he brushed his hair from his eyes as he used to do. He called out something to her, and his voice had just the old husky growling note, but she could not hear what he said.

She walked on, resolutely, her stick striking the path, her head in its high black hat, and very far away, beyond Grasmere maybe, the thunder dimly rumbled. She gathered confidence as she went: a silly old woman she had been to stay in that dark house letting fear gather upon her. She would not wonder now but it was that devil Herries that had put those thoughts into her head. It was himself that the people hated, and she had taken his contempt for her own. Just because, forsooth, some boys had thrown stones after her and a labourer cast a word at her, she had hidden away and missed her proper company. It would be good to see Hannah once more. Hannah was dying, they said, but she would be able enough to remind her of the old days when they had both been young and happy together. One kindly look from Hannah's eyes would be a fine thing, and she would walk all the way back to Herries again and show the village that she was no witch, but an old woman who liked company and chatter and friendly faces in candlelight.

As she walked, strength seemed to increase in her. She had no ache nor pain in all her body. She was still good for life. Death had not got her yet. She breathed the air, even though it were close and packed with thunder, and as the hill grew steeper by the Bowder Stone, she set her knees to it and braced her back and climbed bravely to the turning of the road. Then, at the sight of the Grange cottages across the river, again her courage failed her. She was passing Cumma Catta Wood, a place that she had always feared because, when she was a girl, young Broadley had drowned himself in the pool there below the wood. It was a pretty place, a little hill thick with trees hanging over a broad pool, where the river gathered itself together for a while and stayed tranquilly reflecting the sky. But they said that young Broadley haunted it, and that, in ancient days, there had been pagan sacrifices there. You could see the two projecting stones where the sacrifices had been.

The old woman moved on. She paused before she crossed the bridge that raised itself up like a cat's back over the divided strands of the river. The Grange cottages, huddled on the other side, seemed to be waiting, watching for her.

Their faces were white, shining in the grey shadows of the thundery air.

She crossed the bridge, wondering that she saw no human being: she must herself, to those who, behind dark window-panes, watched her, have seemed a curious figure alone in that still grey landscape, in her high hat and black cloak, tapping with her stick.

She knew Hannah's cottage, a little grey dwelling twisted like a crumpled ear over the river. She knocked with her stick on the door. There was no answer, and she had never felt the world so breathlessly still. The rattle of her stick on the door had been so sharp that she would not knock again. She pushed the door back

and went in. The interior was very dark and smelt of damp hay. Some hens ran squawking from under her feet into the open. Her eyes were dim and the light was dusk, but she soon saw that the very old man, Hannah's husband, was sitting in a chair by a black, empty grate and that a large stout woman was bending over him, making signs with her hands. But he did not look: he stared, without any movement, in front of him.

The woman looked up and saw Mrs. Wilson. She stared then with a start of recognition, turned as though she would motion to the old man, then turned again, and, with a muttered explanation, almost hurled her stout body out of the cottage. Mrs. Wilson could hear her feet hastening over the cobbled path; once more there was breathless waiting silence. . . .

The old man could not hear her, could not speak to her. She was as old as he, but he looked infinitely older. He was a little man like a grey nut, and on his head he was wearing a bright-red nightcap. It was of no use to waste time with him, so she fumbled her way up the twisted wooden staircase. Half-way up she paused: she was suddenly very tired. Her legs were aching and she was a hundred years old. The door of the room at the stair-head was open and she went in. A large four-poster bed with faded red hangings occupied most of the room, placed a little unevenly on the crooked wooden floor. Hannah Mounsey was stretched out on the bed in her grave-clothes, her long, thin face, with the closed eyes, looking spiteful, because the mouth had fallen in and the sharp brown chin stuck forward aggressively.

So Hannah was dead, an old grey bag of bones under the long white clothes. This was young Hannah with the flaxen hair and blue gown. There was a faint odour in the room, and a mouse scuttered across the floor. Beyond the dim, diamond-paned window you could hear the Derwent carelessly running.

Death was nothing odd to Mrs. Wilson, yet peering half blindly over the bed she shivered. She would not be greeted by Hannah, then; her journey had been fruitless. Suddenly she felt a deep sorrow for herself. Hannah was gone, the only one who in all these years had sent for her. Nobody now wanted her at all. To pass from this dead house to the dead house Herries was all the same. And yet she had the capacity still to love someone, to take trouble for someone or something. She was not dead, as Hannah Mounsey was, and she had a sudden vision of herself coming out on a sunshiny morning, sitting outside her cottage, other neighbours gathering round, all of them chatting, laughing together.

Then something made her prick up her ears: she did not know what it was, but it was something that caused her altogether to forget the dead woman on the bed. Fear leapt into her body. Her legs were trembling, so that she caught the post of the bed. She had a sense of being trapped, and yet when she listened again there was no sound, only the careless running of the river. Nevertheless, she knew that there was reason for her fear. She looked about the room, at the looking-glass, the wooden box painted with red hearts, a chair with a thin curved back. She listened, her head bent forward, her hat a little crooked. There was a sound behind the soundlessness: the still air was full of it, and the odour of musty decay in the room grew with every second stronger. She must get out, get away, get to Herries.

Although her legs that had been so strong were now trembling like slackening cord, she found her way down the wooden staircase. Nothing was changed in the room below. The old man in the red nightcap still sat there without moving, staring in front of him.

She pulled back the door, peered out on to the ragged garden, and beyond it the grey smooth running water, and beyond that the field rising to Cumma Catta Wood. Then, although no sound reached her, she turned and stared, across the cobbled path, into a group of faces.

Men and women, close together as though for protection, were gathered at the end of the cobbled path. They stood, huddled together, not speaking, staring at her. Although she could not see well and was so deeply frightened that it was as though her heart were beating in her eyes, yet certain faces were very distinct to her. One belonged to a large stout man in a brown wig and green coat and breeches. His face was red as a tomato and his eyes wide and staring. There was the smooth white face of a young woman; a face with a black beard; there was a young girl's face, very fresh and rosy, with a mole on one cheek.

She looked back behind her; there was no way out there, only a thick rough-stone wall. They could easily stop her if she ran in front of the river.

She walked forward towards them, leaning on her stick because her knees trembled so badly, and at her movement a hoarse whisper broke the thick air: 'T'witch . . . t'witch . . . t'witch.' She stopped, rubbing at her eyes with her hand. The people stood and she stood; then, not knowing what she was doing now, she turned back towards the cottage door.

Her movement released them. A second later two had her, one, the big red-faced man, dragging at her arm, the other a little man with a hump who caught her with twisting hands round the waist.

She heard someone cry: 'A trial! A trial!' She tumbled on to her knees, not for supplication but because her legs shaking as they did and the man dragging her, she had no strength. She looked now a ridiculous old woman, her hat knocked sideways, her head bent, one thin arm up as though she were shielding herself. But having gone so far with her they paused. The two men stood away from her. The rabble--for it was now a great crowd, some having run and told the others what was toward--broke into every kind of babel, some shouting one thing, others another.

Meanwhile she stayed there murmuring: 'Oh, Christ save me! Oh, Lord Christ save me! Oh, Christ save me!' but her thoughts were like wild terrified birds flying from one place to another, so that she was think-

ing of her knee that was cut by the sharp stone, of Hannah lying dead, and of a great weariness that had seized her, turning all her body to water. But mostly she was afraid of the large red-faced man. Then, in the pause, life coming a little back to her, she looked up and searched some of the faces to see whether there was kindness in any of them. With a horror that was the most terrible confirmation of all her earlier fears, she realised that all these faces had that look that so often, alone in Herries, she had anticipated: the look of lust and hatred, curiosity and pleasure. And they all seemed strangers to her.

As was perhaps to be expected, it was a woman who took the next step. A long, thin, elderly woman whose head wagged on her neck as though it were loosely tied there.

Crying out something in a shrill, high voice like a bird's, she rushed forward and, bending down, struck the old woman on the cheek. It was as though that had been a signal. The crowd tumbled across the path, loosed, it seemed, by a word of command. A funny babble of sound came from them, not human, not animal: 'Swim her!' 'Swim her!' 'Sink or swim!' A little girl danced delightedly round and round, like a leaf spinning, crying: 'T'witch! . . . T'witch! . . . T'witch!'

Inside the cottage, the widower of Hannah Mounsey sat staring in front of him, hearing nothing, seeing Hannah as a young, laughing, fresh-faced girl. He moved his hand a little, enclosing with his arm her waist.

They dragged Mrs. Wilson along the path, bumping her head on the stones, pulling her by her feet and her hands. They tumbled her out on to the green sward between the bridge and the river.

Then again they stood back from her. She crouched there, her head hanging forward. Her hat was gone, her white hair was loose about her face, her gown was torn, exposing her withered brown breasts; she clasped her arms together over these. Tears trickled down her cheeks.

There was a desperate impulse in her now to say something, but she could not speak. Her terror urged her that if she could only make them listen she would persuade them that she was no witch, but only a harmless old woman who had never done any harm.

But she could not speak: fear constricted her throat, and her tongue moistened her dry, dead lips. Her other thought was that soon they would hit her again. She bent her head over her arms to shelter herself from the blows.

The crowd now had no individual consciousness. Some cried that they must take her to the little house at the back of the village and that she must be tried there all in proper order and decently. But these were the minority. The others must see her swim; then they'd know whether she were witch or no. Then there was a moment's strange silence. Every voice fell. For an instant the only sounds were the very distant rumbling thunder, the running river and the old woman's crying, a whimper like a child's.

Three women ran forward. They bent down over her; shouting they tore her clothes from her. They threw her clothes over their heads into the crowd. They tore her flesh as they dragged her things away. One stood up, tugging at her white hair, and so she pulled the thin, bony body up, raising it to its knees.

Someone threw a stone. It struck the body between the breasts.

Then the stout, red-faced man, shouting as though he were proclaiming some great news, called for order. Everything must be done properly. No one should say that they were out of justice. He strode forward, laughing. He caught the body in his arms, then dropped it again as he felt in his breeches pocket, from there brought faded green cord. He took the body again and roughly, as though he would tear one limb from the other, took the right foot and fastened it to the left hand, the left foot and fastened it to the right hand. So trussed, she lay motionless. Then suddenly raising her face, which now streamed with blood, she sent forth two screeches, wild, piercing, sounding far over the crowd out into the village, down the road. Then her head fell again.

Triumphantly he raised her in his arms, holding her, her head against her knees, as a woman might an infant. He danced her for a moment in his arms. Then he ran forward, the crowd shouting, yelling, laughing, and up the bridge some children ran that they might see better, singing and dancing: 'T'witch . . . t'witch . . . t'witch.'

He lifted his stout arms and flung her out, high into air. The little white body gleamed for a moment, then fell, like a stone, into the water.

Herries straightened his aching body and leaned on his spade. He had been clearing a patch of hard, stiff ground. Later there should be an orchard here: he saw it in his eye, the strong, gnarled trunks, the blossom, the apples hanging in shining clusters, the sun blinking through the leaves.

He spat on his hands and bent again to the spade. Around him nothing had grown well save a strange ruffian-like grass that had sharp-pointed blades like jagged knives. Some stunted blooms, some ragged naked vegetables. It was the wrong place, the wind caught it too fiercely, there was not sun enough, the soil was too resolutely stubborn. Meanwhile, to the house many things should be done. Windows were broken, pipes had fallen; one corner towards the hill had tumbled right in, and stones lay in a careless heap.

Nevertheless, the house looked stout and obstinate, its colour was of a pale gentle ivory, stained here and there with orange and pink, stains of rain and wind. Its feet were dug resolutely in the ground. It was alone but not lonely, defiant but not complaining.

Herries raising himself again, turning to look at it, loved it.

He saw fat Benjamin, sweat pouring from him, hurry towards him.

'They are drowning Mrs. Wilson, by Grange Bridge, for a witch.'

He turned and listened as though he expected to hear something. Only a faint rumble of thunder over Grasmere way. He said nothing to Benjamin, but dragging on his old faded long-skirted coat, strode into the yard. Benjamin, silent as himself, brought out his horse.

At once, without a word to one another, they rode off along the rough track to Grange. Then, after a little, Benjamin, in the husky voice which ale, weather and stoutness of body had produced in him, explained that he had been riding back through Portinscale. Passing Grange he had heard that the old witch Wilson was in Mounsey's cottage, saying spells over his dead woman, and that they were going to have her out and 'swim' her. He had hastened on to his master.

Herries had long been expecting this. He did not doubt but that Mrs. Wilson was a witch. He had a horror of her for that. He was glad that now she would be out of his house. He felt no pity, no sense of a hunted thing, of a crowd lust-baiting. Such feelings were not of his time, class or education.

Had he been a magistrate and she been brought before him with evidence of her dirty dealings, he would have condemned her without hesitation and watched her sentence without a shudder. But here he also was involved. His pride drove him to protect his house. They would touch one of his servants? He would see to it. He hated them as he rode, the whole dirty foul rabble of them.

Then as he went something else moved in him. Since his day in the Honister cave a new element had stirred, a kind of softness, a glow of unanalysed, almost unrealised kindliness. He had not wanted it. He would scorn it if he dragged it into day-light.

But he did not drag it. It stayed within him like a secret fire that burnt stealthily without his feeding it. Every little thing was happier to him now than it had been.

His gaze softened, even now as he stared through the trees at the river, pounded up the hill, saw the humped bridge and the crowd at the water's edge.

He leapt off his horse and came down to them. He spoke to no one. As he came to the stream he saw an old white bundle of flesh with hair that streamed behind it rise, eddy in a little pool, sink again.

He plunged in, waded up to his thighs. The crowd said no word. The body rose again right at his hand. He plunged his arms in and caught it, dragging it to his breast. The head wagged against his coat.

He turned, standing and looking at them all for a moment, then breasted his way back to the bank. On dry ground he felt his hands chill against the bare flesh, so he laid the sodden body delicately on the ground, took off his faded coat, wrapped it round, then, holding the little corpse like a child against his shirt, strode up the hill, all the people silently withdrawing from him.

He mounted his horse and rode away.

THE ROCKING WOOD

As they rode through the rocking wood, the wind tearing at their heels, Herries talked to David.

It was the wild stormy afternoon of Friday, 8th November, 1745. It had been Herries' suggestion that they should be riding to Carlisle. For months now he had been longing for this.

In the Scots Magazine for July, at the barber's in Keswick, David had read:

'There have lately been several rumours of some designs upon Scotland or Ireland by the Pretender's eldest son.' Then, a month later, at that same barber's, it was said that there had been a landing in Scotland.

Now this very morning Keswick was frantically buzzing. The rebels were in Jedburgh. At any moment they would be South. . . .

Francis Herries had shown no interest. His mind was elsewhere. David even was surprised at his own indifference. His principal thought was of Father Roche. After all these years his chance had come! After all these years! David was a child again riding under Cat Bells, his body tight between Roche's thighs, and that beautiful, persuasive voice in his ears: 'Even as our Lord suffered . . .' But he was practical now, was David, a grave and serious man with a liking for the steady security of the reigning dynasty. He had been prospering lately. He had bought land near Cockermouth. He had an interest in two vessels trading from Liverpool. There was a farm at the back-end of Skiddaw that he might buy if things went well. He had no hunger for rebellions. . . .

But the romantic soul still breathed close to his heart. The memory of Roche could stir it, some woman one day, but most of all, now and ever, his love for his father, this strange man, removed in temperament, thought, passion so far from him, so mysterious and alone. Of late so silent, but united to him as no other human being was united.

Therefore when, quite suddenly, in the dark hall at Herries last evening, his father had said: 'Shall we ride to-morrow to Carlisle?' David had at once agreed. No more than that. No reason given. In all these years at Herries David had been only once to Carlisle, his father twice. But it seemed that now, riding alone together, they might come to some fresh intimacy. It must come from Herries. David was a man of few words and deep shyness in close relations. There was something, too, in the isolation of Herries that drove speech deep down. They talked less and less in Herries.

They were silent out of Keswick until they rode into the woods below Skiddaw. A terrific wind was surging among the trees; all the wood was rocking, and light mists spun and shifted over the two humps of the mountain-top that were powdered with snow thin like smoke. Beyond the wood Bassenthwaite Water was whipped into curls of white and an angry spray.

Herries began to speak, his thought that had followed its own secret course ever since they left Herries breaking into spoken word: '. . . When I came to the river's edge she was bobbing, a white bundle, in the water. I strode in and picked her out, and they stood there while I carried her off. At that moment, David, when I held her wet and sodden against my body I felt something new in me. I had been coming to that as I had been coming to many things through these years. . . . She cried against my heart although she was dead. She cried something, telling me a road to go. She was a witch and foul-living. In all those years that she was with us, David, I don't doubt but that she was evil.

'But she had been alone as I also had been alone. They hated her as they hated me. Not that I care at all for their hatred, but there was a bond in our loneliness. I had always known it.' (He thought, as he went on: Why am I telling him this? He can never understand that loneliness. He will never feel this thing that I feel.) '. . . I have had to bear my difference all my life, David, as she had to bear it. By no choice and no wish. I have no faith in God. I have never had; but for those of us who are different there is a compulsion to listen that is almost a faith. Nature, I suppose, chooses once and again to separate a few from the rest. She understands them and speaks to them. But why should we who are thus separated expect human nature to understand? Human nature must protect itself. I perceive that it must be so. Human nature is narrower than Nature, less wise and less secure.

'We who are different cannot come into that general company, however we may desire it. It is our lot. Myself, I do not grumble at it. What have I ever done worse than these others, than Pomfret or Harcourt? But every dice has been loaded against me, every act removed me further. . . . Nothing strange there, since it is understood. Think you that she was a witch, David?'

Through the groaning of the boughs and the rocking wind David's voice came out sturdily:

'Most certainly she was a witch, father.'

'Yes . . . most certainly. They were cruel because they were afraid, and I was compassionate because I, too, have suffered. Do you think it has meant nothing to me that I could not be like other men? I, too, have my pride, my sense of honour, my friendliness, although it does not do to speak of these things. But with them all, my brothers, my wife, my mistresses, my children, that final intimacy has been forbidden. Only with my own kind could I be intimate, and I could not find my kind. Often I have wished to put my case' (Herries thought: I am putting my case to him now and he does not understand it at all, not a word of it), 'but my case has not been their case. I am, in some sense, it must seem to them, against Nature, but it is not against Nature but rather against human nature.

'Nevertheless, there is compensation in loneliness. I am growing to find that. There is strength in it, and a compelled wisdom. I learnt that from the witch. The evil that she knew was not so weighty as the strength that she caught from her isolation. They might stone her, but their stones would not bring her into their company nor would they stay her. Nothing can stay us, no physical death.' (He smiled to himself thinking: All these words go to the wind. He has not caught any of them.)

And David, stolid on his horse, his back broad as a wall, his head finely set, was thinking: 'He is talking to me now as man to man. He has never before done that. But this talk of feelings: I can't be with him there. What's the use of it? I love him whatever he is, different or no, but it's uncomfortable to speak openly about love. . . . Easier here, though, with this wind blowing and the trees creaking. If the Calliope does well this voyage I could pay a price for that farm. It will mean leaving Herries. It must come to that one day. But not yet. I must take Deb with me and that would leave him alone. I can't leave him alone; and he wouldn't go from Herries. But one day if I marry, which I shall . . .'

He felt the cold rain on his face and the wind swooping down and then up again. He threw back his head, stretched his great chest, turned to his father, smiling:

'Maybe, father,' he said, 'you force yourself to be different by thinking that you are. Folks take one for what one says one is. You have always refused them, thought poorly of them, frightened them maybe. Will you never leave Herries, father?'

'Leave Herries?'

'Aye. Maybe I'll buy that farm at the back of Skid-daw-- Penhays. . . . John Tennant and I have done well lately with the Calliope and the Peggy Anne. If this Pretender doesn't upset the world. . . . Herries is a hard place, father. No soil, no sun, rock and mire. They have this thought of you in the valley and will never be rid of it.

'But at Penhays you could have your own land and work it, and it would be brighter for Deb. . . .' He waited, then continued more shyly. 'Uncle Pomfret loves you, father, at heart. I know he does. Aunt Jannice is sick now and has little say. My dear cousin Raiseley is in London. If we were at Penhays we would be more in the world. At Herries . . .' He broke off, afraid suddenly, as he had so often before been afraid, of his father's anger. Some word would be spoken and all the good of their talk be gone, and they would ride on in offended silence. David had his own temper in his own way and it showed most easily with his father, simply because he loved him most.

But to-day he need not have been afraid. His father turned to him with a strangely childlike, ingenuous gaze as though he were David's junior and had been asking advice from him.

'Herries is a bitter place for you and Deborah. I've always known it. But for me there is none other nor ever can be. I'm held there and it's for ever. But you will go, of course, when the right time comes. And, for that, I may not be alone. It may be that, one day, I shall marry again.'

The rocking wind, as though driven by that word to a frenzy of derision, cracked in his ear: 'Marry again! He'll marry again! Crack! Crack! Crack! He'll marry again!' David brushed the rain from his eyes. Marry again! He thought that his father had done with women. For a long time now there had been no sign of any traffic with them.

'Well,' he said, 'have you seen a woman?'

'Yes . . . there is someone. She is a child. She could only need me through weariness and fear of loneliness. But I am in love again. Again! I have never loved before. I am very happy in the mere thought of it.'

David had an instant of deep comprehension and of an aching affection for his father. With a swift vision of imagination, born only through love and exceedingly rare with him, he saw his father as he had been, so handsome and grand. As he was now, his face disfigured, his body gaunt and bent with digging and grubbing. . . . Could a woman care for him now? A sense of his father's isolation came over him as it had never done before.

Now, however, they had come out of the woods and were in open country across which the icy rain was blowing in furious sweeps. On a good day a great stretch of land spread grandly to the Firth and the hills behind it, but now everything was blotted out.

For Herries, although to-day he could not see, this coming into the open was like walking out of a house and closing the door behind him. That was why he chose this route, because he loved it. The regular riding path was by Threlkeld. That little world of hills and lakes was gone in an instant, folded away. On a clear day you could look back and see Skiddaw, the Helvellyn range, the group above Stye Head, Grasmoor and the rest lying gently like lions above the land, their heads resting on their paws. One step and you were in a new world, a world as romantic perhaps in spirit as that other, but not this, as beautiful but not with this beauty. That odd sense of magic, so that with one foot forward you lost it. He would always, on reaching this spot, know a little shiver of fear that when he came back again that lovely country would be gone, a mirage dreamed of by him and by him perhaps alone. But to-day in his head he carried with him the rocking wood. The trees creaked around him long after he had left them.

The wind fell: the rain drew off: the air was colder. The thick sky watched them maliciously and once and again sent down a flake of snow to spatter their eyes.

They had come into new country in another sense. The cottages and farms that they passed gave them a consciousness of agitation. Women stood at the doors. A man called after them some question. A horseman rode past them furiously towards Carlisle. Unconsciously themselves they drove their horses faster, the mud scattering up about them as they went.

'The Pretender may be in Carlisle ere this,' said David suddenly. 'What then?'

'We'll ride back again,' said Herries.

'What do you think, father? Has he a hope? In Keswick they wished him back in France, to a man they did. Disturbing their affairs. It's odd to remember it, but I thought it a fine thing as a boy when Father Roche spoke of it. Now, because I may buy a farm, I see other things. Is Roche in Carlisle, do you think?'

'Yes, so I fancy. When I was a boy at Seddon, in '15, thirty years ago, there was a peacock screamed under the hedge by the pantries. I thought him the finest, most defiant bird in the kingdom, and when they were out in '15 he was like the Old Pretender, that bird. I had a fancy about him that if their foray failed he'd die; and, sure enough, he died. Died of spoilt pride. I've always thought rebellion a grand thing, but now I don't know. . . . I love this ground and the men on it, although they'd thank me little if they knew it. If Charles Edward has his way, every field will be blood- stained. Either way my peacock dies. . . . No, he can't win. He's too late. And if he wins it can be only for a moment. Hanover's a hog by my peacock, but he's made his sty of our home, and it's quieter for him to lie there. I told Roche once that the notion of beauty to a plain people like the English is too upsetting. They stand by their stomachs. They are poets only by protest.'

The scene cleared: the sky lifted and the snow fell faster. A man on a horse passed them, then drew up and waited for them.

He was a short fat man on a short fat horse, hunched forward rather absurdly, not a good rider. He had a dark-crimson coat with silver buttons: his face was round, red and anxious, rather a baby face with open wondering eyes and startled eyebrows.

'I beg your pardon, gentlemen--'

They drew up their horses.

'Are you for Carlisle?'

David said that they were.

'What news have you?'

'None.'

'Ah, things are bad.' The little man looked at them beseechingly, as much as to say: 'Be kind to me. Tell me some good news, even though it's lies. Tell me anything, only that I may calm down and regain my dignity.' It was plain enough that he was frightened of Francis Herries, who, straight on his horse, his scarred face showing pale and impervious under his broad black hat, was silent and grim enough. David, with his health and ruddiness and open smile, reassured him. He confided in him.

'You see, gentlemen, I'm riding out of my way, but I had the news at Sockbridge last night that the rebels were in Jedburgh, and that they were already moving South. My God, they may be in Carlisle at this instant, and my poor wife and Hetty . . . I said to Mr. Wordsworth--Mr. Richard Wordsworth, Superintendent of the

Lowther Estates, I was to-day staying under his roof, my worthy friend; maybe you know him, gentlemen?-- 'Sdeath, Mr. Wordsworth, I said, it can't be that they are in Carlisle already, and our house in English Street, the very centre of the town, my wife sick of a nervous complaint these last five years, ever since William Gray, the best surgeon in the whole of Carlisle, gentlemen, cut her for the bladder. And it isn't as though Hetty had a head on her shoulders neither. The sight of a soldier makes a fool of the child, and these breechless Highlanders are beyond law, as we all know well enough. Eh, gentlemen, forgive this uneasiness, but I fancied that you'd have some good news, maybe of a defeat or a rout and the Pretender taken, or driven back to France again, where, Heaven is witness, it were better for him to have stayed.'

The words came with panting eagerness, but there was a childish simplicity and good nature behind them that won David, who was as childish, simple and good-natured as himself.

'I fear, sir,' he replied, 'we can give you little comfort. We are riding from Keswick where we had only the news that you yourself have had. We know nothing of what is happening in Carlisle.'

The little stout gentleman looked anxiously about him. 'It's cold,' he said, 'and the snow is in our faces. Would you give me the courtesy of your company? With every step we may be meeting danger. I am no coward, but I will confess that this news has quite unnerved me. It is only what I have been expecting these thirty years, but that it should drop on to us when I was away from home and my wife none too well . . .'

'Certainly we will keep company,' said David cheerfully. 'I think you are unduly apprehensive, sir. We should have heard, I am sure, were the Pretender already in Carlisle. I scarcely think that the Royal troops will allow him so much advantage. If one may go by the common feeling in Keswick the sense of the country is against him, and a company of raw Highlanders is hardly a match for an English army. Moreover, the farther they come from their own Highlands the less stomach they'll have for the job.'

This was the kind of comfort that the little man was needing, and in return for it, as they went forward, he gave them all his history. His name was Cumberlege, John Cumberlege of the Moor House, English Street, Carlisle, and he was a corn-dealer like his father before him. He had had three children, and two had died in infancy, one of the staggers and one of the croup. He had been twice married, and Hetty, his only child, was of the second marriage. He was of good standing in Carlisle, and numbered among his friends there the worthy Dr. Waugh; young Mr. Aglionby, Mayor of the City; Thomas Pattinson, Deputy-Mayor; and Colonel Durand, Commander of the City. They might see from this how safely they might trust themselves to his company. He had also much to say of his late host, Mr. Richard Wordsworth, who had but recently been appointed Receiver-General of the County of Westmorland.

Altogether, as they jogged along, he recovered in this general recital of his famous friends a good deal of his natural confidence and genial humour.

David was glad of the little man's companionship. Francis Herries had fallen into one of his grim and arrogant moods again and would vouchsafe not a word. The afternoon was early dark, and there was a spectral air over the scene.

Indeed, the uncertainty of the situation influenced David in spite of himself. Moving thus through the cold dusk over a flat and silent land one could not be sure that at any moment one might not stumble upon the whole of the Prince's army. Where were they? How had they fared? It might be that this adventurer was truly destined for some glorious success and England would fall into his hands like a fine plum? Then back the Catholics would come again and with them the French dominance, and who knows after that the sequel? At this all the Herries English rose rebellious in David's soul. He wanted no French power here nor Catholic either. It was at this moment, perhaps, little Cumberlege pressing near to him, the few chill snowflakes striking his cheek and a great silence on every side of him, that he knew once and for all what he was. Scottish ancestry or no, he was English Herries. Men and women for two hundred years afterwards were to have some consequence in their lives from this moment of conviction.

Little Cumberlege asked them where they were lodging in Carlisle.

David told him that they had no settled place.

'Then, sirs, you must come to us. To be frank with you, I shall relish your company. There's no man in the house but the boy Jeremiah, and he's a witling with a wall-eye. I only took him to pleasure his father, who did me a service in '32, the year they hanged Humpy Dillon for sheep-stealing. You're a man of your inches, sir,' he added, looking appreciatively up at David, 'and might render us a service at a dangerous pinch.'

David looked at his father, who said no word. He smiled at the eager excited little man, the skirts of whose crimson coat stuck out from his fat buttocks as though with an indignant life of their own.

'For to-night at least,' David said, 'we'll take you at your word and thank you.'

A strange world had now come up about them, for the wind had dropped, the snow ceased to fall, and instead a fog rolled in thick grey folds across the fields. This fog was to take a great part in the alarms and fears of the coming days: many, looking back afterwards and telling their story, gave it a personal form and body as though it were a creeping devil of an especial malignancy created by the Pretender himself.

David, who was never given to vague imagination, himself felt it an oddly alive thing. It came creeping towards them, now slipping along the road on its belly, licking the horses' hoofs, then raising a white swollen arm, wreathing their necks with it, then slipping away again, mounting into a wall in front of them, closing about them, stifling them, blinding them, dropping again to a thin shallow vapour that swathed the hedges with spider-web.

For Herries, it filled his dreams. For half an hour now he had not realised where they were nor cared. He rode forward, possessed by his vision. Since the word 'Carlisle' had, carelessly perhaps, passed Mirabell's lips it had been his one thought to go there. But with that burning impulse came also the resolve not to be defeated by it, because he felt that, let him surrender to it, and he would be beaten. Some prevision of the future told him that this journey taken through the fog, into the Lord knew what, was the beginning of a pursuit for him that was far more than physical, and, being spiritual, must fail in its aim.

He stared through the fog, her body, her soul, dancing in front of him. A child who had given him no single thought, a vagabond, ruthless and heartless perhaps, intolerant certainly of any of the bonds that he would put upon her. But all his history had led him to this, his rebellions, scorns, arrogances, dreams, self-contempts, Alice Press and the like, his wife Margaret, every woman whose tongue he had ever twisted beneath his own led him to this. He wanted nothing for himself, only to be good to her, to know that she was happy, that she had what she wanted. That she had what she wanted! Ironic, ironic desire, for it would not be himself that she longed for. . . . And so he rode on.

They came upon Carlisle quite suddenly and were challenged at the gate.

Carlisle had at this time a population of some four thousand persons, the majority of these living within its walls.

The Castle Walls and Citadel had still their original force: the Castle was held by a nonresident governor and a company of invalided veterans: the city gates were shut at the firing of the evening gun. Nevertheless, its life as a centre of warfare was now still and dead. The union of the kingdoms of Scotland and England had silenced the Border warfare, turned guns into knitting needles and cannon-balls into peppermint rock. Here, perhaps, lay the root of the Prince's advantage, that any Scottish invasion of England was by now undreamt of in Carlisle and the town was in no way prepared for it.

On this evening the bustle at the gate was tremendous. The Herries would most certainly not have been admitted had they been alone, but their little friend, Mr. Cumberlege, had not said too much about his popularity in Carlisle. Especially did a large, pompous and terribly flustered military officer appear delighted to see him, even to the extent of embracing him. He was not, Mr. Cumberlege explained, sotto voce, a real and proper military gentleman, but rather a volunteer, in his time and natural state a wealthy bachelor with a taste for wine and a talent for the game of bowls, moreover a relation of good Doctor Bolton, the Dean of Carlisle. He had in his private garden a fountain with a naked mermaid who blew water out of her tail, considered by many a marvel.

At the moment he was thinking of neither bowls nor mermaid, but was in a dreadful flutter of indecision.

Scouting parties had been sent out to discover, if they might, the Rash Adventurer's (such was the title decided on by those who wanted to land safely in the ultimate result) whereabouts. That afternoon, so Mr. Bolton told Cumberlege, Lieutenant Kilpatrick had advanced beyond Ecclefechan and sighted a body of rebels. A Scottish quartermaster, seeking quarters for his troops in Ecclefechan, had been seized and was now in Carlisle Castle. That was as much as was known for the present.

A strange contrast was to be found in Mr. Bolton's manner, he suddenly rapping out most authoritatively a military order, then sinking his voice to a nervous, confidential murmur with John Cumberlege, who was as apprehensive as himself. They made a funny enough pair, their contrast in size, their bodies starting at every sound, and once when a horseman clattered over the cobbles suddenly clutching one another as though for protection.

They rode up English Street to Cumberlege's house, which was a neat little Georgian building with a brass knocker on the door showing a sea-fish swallowing a trident, and a sundial on the lawn by the street, and a fine little gate with small dragons on either side of it. A good light burning in a cresset over the door blew in the wind. The street was deserted. The fog had cleared, and the sky was full of cold and glittering stars.

'Come in. Come in, gentlemen,' said Cumberlege, looking about him before he opened his front door as though he scented a Highlander round every corner. 'It's a poor hospitality I shall offer you, taking me unexpected and my wife an invalid, but--' and here he dropped his voice still further, 'there's wine in the house. Wine too good for the Highland rabble that's coming upon us.' And then to himself, as he unfastened his door: 'Poor Bolton! Poor Bolton! I'll wager he wishes himself back safe with his mermaid.'

Half an hour later they were seated in Cumberlege's gay little dining-room, a beef pie, an apple tart and some of the finest Madeira in front of them. It was a handsome little room with dark-red wallpaper hung with scenes from Mr. Gay's masterpiece, 'The Beggar's Opera,' and a handsome oil painting of Mr. Cumberlege's grandfather in a green coat and ruffles, over the mantelpiece. A noble old gentleman with a face like a codfish and a neck so thick that it was no wonder to hear, later in the evening, that he had died of an apoplexy. Silver candlesticks, a glass bowl of oranges and figs, a fire in the hearth, the curtains warmly drawn, and best of all Cumberlege's daughter Hetty, who was as pretty a dark child as David had ever seen.

Two things were very plainly visible: one that to John Cumberlege this daughter was the life and light of

his being. He sat with one stout arm round her and fed her with figs as though she had been a child in arms, his eyes moving ever and again about her pretty face with its nose a little snub, its eyelashes beautifully dark and long, its rounded chin and soft cheeks, as though all his happiness were there.

The other evident fact was that the child had fallen in love with David at sight. She sat there shyly smiling at him, her cheeks flushed, her eyes burning with pleasure and adventure. She was in a dress of white calico sprayed with pink roses, as David was long after to remember. A pretty face was a pretty face to David. Many times of late he had thought that he must fall in love, but Keswick did not offer so many varieties. Now he wondered whether his fate were not here. It was not, but it was near enough to make his heart beat, his tongue stammer and his big body move clumsily as though, in spite of itself, it must be impelled towards her.

John Cumberlege too, perhaps, as he looked across the table at David, had his dreams. It was true that he knew nothing about these visitors of his, and the elder was alarming in his taciturnity and grim seclusion, but you could not look at the younger Herries and doubt him. Honesty was in every glance, every breath, simplicity, a courageous rectitude.

For Hetty Cumberlege this threat of the Scottish invasion was a grand and enchanting game. Was it true that the Prince was the most beautiful young man? When he came to the city would there be routs and balls as she had heard there had been in Edinburgh? For herself she didn't care what her father thought; she was all for seeing him, and it would be a wicked shame were he stopped before he got to Carlisle. But he would not be. He was already there. He had been at Ecclefechan that day. Perhaps to-morrow he would be in the city, and if there was a ball she had no dress fit to wear. But oh, she was glad her dear father was safe (this with an especial hug of her father, a blushing glance at David). Mother had been in a great way all day and hadn't had her afternoon sleep and had been bled again this evening, and she had run to the window and the door a thousand times to see whether he were not coming, and would there be firing and the windows broken and people wounded?

Why shouldn't the Prince come into the town if he wanted to? That was the feeling of most of the militia anyway, and it was only that old jackanapes Colonel Durand who was for everybody fighting. She was sure that no one wanted to kill anyone else, the idea was perfectly horrid. And as the Madeira mounted into David's head and the weariness bred of his long forty-mile ride dazzled his eyes, it seemed to him that he was already kissing those blushing cheeks and stroking ever so gently that bare and gleaming shoulder.

Francis Herries said no word beyond mere politeness. He could not. He saw the figures of little Cumberlege and his daughter, the silver candlesticks, the glittering glass about the fruit, the portrait of old Cumberlege senior, in a thin and gauzy dream. He was here in Carlisle, and every beat of blood in him urged him, weary though he was, to go out and search for her. It seemed to him that there was more than mere vague urgency in this. Opposite him where he sat was a small round mirror with a dark oak frame. Its glass was blistered and cracked with age, so that the candle- flame flickered and redoubled in it, and the colours of the room, dark crimson, white and green, were a blurred and mellowed fog. Staring in it, half-asleep maybe, the voices coming to him with a faint chirping hum, he seemed to see that child Mirabell step into the mirror, break the misted colours, turn to him that strange, cold, indifferent face, gravely surveying him, oddly and harshly inviting him.

He pushed his napkin and wine-glass from him and asked his host to excuse him while he found a little air in the street. His head was hot and he must cool it before he went to his bed. He was aware that they felt, all three of them, a certain freedom from restraint at his departure.

In the street the wind had now quite fallen and only, as though dropped by the multitudinous shining stars, thin flakes of snow fell lazily as though they were too indifferent to reach the ground. No one was about. There were few lights in the windows. The sense of suspense might have been his own imagining, but it seemed to him that behind the doors and the windows folk were listening. He could hear the hearts throbbing, could see the eyes straining, and over his head and about his body the stems and branches of the rocking wood seemed still to be beating and groaning. He had been in that wood all day. He was not clear of it yet.

As though led by a guide at his elbow he turned up a dark and narrow street that was as silent as an empty pocket. On his right there was a light blowing above the name, 'The Silver Horn.' Here as well as another place. He pushed back the heavy wooden door and stumbled on to the uneven stone floor of an inn-room filled with a rough glare of men, women, smoke, thickly smelling of dried fish, tobacco and stale drink.

He sat down at a long deal table, men, countrymen, farmers, making easy way for him, too deeply intent on their talk to consider him. A thin wasp of a serving-man brought him some ale; a heavy thumping clock, hiccupping once and again as though it had taken in the drink as steadily as its customers, tick-tocked just above his head; a parrot, whose bright-green colour he could just see swaying on a perch through the smoke, called out in a thick husky caw; and still through it all the wind and creaking of the morning's wood kept him company.

He discovered soon enough that there was only one topic and that the natural one. Where was the Pretender and where his Highlanders? Even now they might be at the walls. What would Durand do? What Pattinson the Deputy-Mayor, young Aglionby being safely away in the country somewhere? What would the Dean and Chapter do? What would the Cumberland and Westmorland Militia do? What was everyone going to do? Were they all to be blown to bits? What was Wade going to do? What was the King in London doing that he hadn't sent any reinforcements? Didn't he care what happened to old Carlisle, and if he didn't why should old Carlisle care what happened to the King?

Ah! but those Highlanders! Here fear crept through the smoke, skins went shivering, the tick-tock of the old clock took on a deeper tone. Those Highlanders. . . . Hadn't you heard, then, of what they'd been doing in Edinburgh and Glasgow, of the women they'd been raping and the destruction they'd been causing? The story went tonight that back at Kelso Spital they had shot all the sheep, hanged all the farmers, drunk the warm blood of the sheep like so many cannibals. There was the tale, too, of the farm-wife at Langholm who refused to tell the rebels where her husband had hid the horses and cattle, she lying in bed with a new-born child. She refused, even though the rebel officer threatened her with cutting down the beam that supported the roof of the farm-house. He cut away at the beam, but it stoutly withstood, and the house was spared.

And what of Carlisle? What is the good of holding out, the Castle as rotten as it is, the Gate not covered by any outworks, the Wall over the Lady's Walk very low with neither parapet nor flank to defend it, the old gateway not defended by any flank, and we having nothing to oppose seven thousand rebels save a few invalids? . . . Surely better, then, to let the Pretender come in under guarantee of decent behaviour on both sides. Hick, hick, hick, stammered the clock. It was then that, staring through the smoke into the light of the roaring fire, Herries saw Mirabell.

This gave him no sense of surprise nor question of undue coincidence. It seemed to him the most natural thing in the world that she should be sitting there, and his only sensation was one of great happiness, a happiness oddly tranquil and secure. He had at first no ambition to speak to her, only to sit there and know that she was alive and in the same room with him.

He could not, from where he was, see her very clearly. She was wearing an amber-coloured hat with a feather in it and a deep dark- red cloak with a high collar; he could see, from where he was, that the cloak was faded and old. He could not deny but that she seemed bedraggled and shabby. He could not distinguish her features, only sufficient to know that it was surely she, but indeed where else in the world was there hair of such a colour? It was piled up, burning between the tawny colour of her hat and her white neck, a fire in smoke and under creaking windy trees.

He was half-asleep, perhaps, with weariness, or the heat of the room bemused him, but after a little while it appeared that he and she were quite alone in the wood and that they rode forward silently to some unknown destination.

After a while he wished to see her more clearly, rose from where he was, pushed through the farmers and countrymen and came to another place across the room. He was sitting in a corner now, near the fire, quite close to the bright-green parrot; it was fiercely hot, but he did not feel the heat.

He was beside her now, and at once his heart was shot through by a sharp and intolerable agony. That was no exaggerated figure of speech. It was like that. He felt the pain before he realised the cause. This cause was that, beside her, his arm around her red cloak, was a young man, a fellow of little more than twenty perhaps, yet a boy with a boy's fresh colour, a boy's laugh, a boy's bright eyes. Those eyes were fixed on her and her eyes on his. That they loved one another, and to a pitch that excluded the scene and everything in it, was clear to any casual onlooker. How sharply, deeply clear to Herries, in whose ears might be echoing yet the crash of the derisive boughs. 'Crack-crack! Crack-crack! He means to be married! He means to be married!'

As he watched he saw her hand come out and take the broad brown hand of the young man. Then she smiled at him, a shy, delicate, happy child's smile that drew her, although they did not move, deep into the young man's heart.

Her note for Herries had always been her remoteness; he had never seen her intimate with nor close to anything. He had never dared to imagine how she would look when she was in love. His only hope had been that she had never known what that was, and so he had wondered whether he might not be the first to teach her. For he had taught in his day many lessons in love. Now he knew that that would never be.

When some control came back to him he studied the boy carefully. He was dressed roughly in a dark coarse coat and homespun breeches, and gaitered to the thigh for riding. His body was slim and well-formed, he carried his head high: everything about him was honest and upright, strong and smiling. He was a proper man. It was after concluding this (and his pride allowed him to flinch from no challenging comparisons) that Herries noticed a third figure. This was a thick, short, black-bearded fellow who sat behind the pair, swinging his legs from the table-end. His face was covered with a shaggy black beard and his hair lay in a black tangle over his forehead. There was black hair on the back of his hands. He was dressed soberly and cleanly, and his large, steadily open, black eyes never left the face of the girl.

Once and again he said a word to her, but when he spoke it did not rouse the girl, who smiled at the boy as though it were he who had spoken. But they were all three of them very quiet, not joining at all in the conversation around them, making a little world and history apart by themselves.

For Herries it was as though a new fresh chapter of his life had opened. When we fall in love the desire in us is so strong that we argue like desire in the other, and stay cheated so long as we may. Well, his cheat was over, but he was in no kind of way released from her. He realised at once that he was only the more strongly bound because he would never forget now how she looked when she was in love, and would never again be

able to defend himself against her with a sense of her remoteness.

Often since the day in the cave, lying on his bed, working in the field, riding solitary up Stonethwaite, standing on Esk Hause and seeing the valleys glitter and smile beneath him, he had wondered how she would look at him the first time that she knew she could trust him. For that was what he had meant to do; by great kindliness and patience to make her trust him as she had never trusted anyone before. Now he knew that that would never happen.

He saw, too, how all his actions since the day in the cave had been for her. He had never once been free of her. When he had taken the witch from the river and held her to his heart it had been this child that he had held. All the new compassion and softness that had lately been growing in him so that the sterner, more ironical part of him had been frightened at the change and tried to drive it away, all this had been from her. It had been as though he had been educating himself out of the nastiness and pride of his earlier life, so that he might be ready for her when she came to him: and now she would never come.

She would never come. The trees of the wood gathered about his head very thickly and now with silence because the wind had died. The green parrot swung from bough to bough watching him with beady eyes. Then he heard her speak, and her voice was as deeply familiar to him as though he had been in company with it all his life.

She spoke to the parrot.

'For a penny,' she said,' I'd wring your neck, you evil bird.'

The young man, looking at her as though he would drown her in his love, answered in a voice that was roughly boyish and eager:

'I shall buy the bird for you.'

And she answered, holding his hand very tightly: 'Two is company.'

The black-bearded man behind them swung off the table and stood, thick and stocky, looking up at the parrot. He went up to it and stroked its neck. The parrot bent its head, eyeing him obliquely with a beady eye.

Herries had seen enough. He went out, into the street.

SIEGE IN FOG

Herries woke early the next morning, and under a sharp agitation of disturbance and fear. The room in which he was lying was foreign and strange to him. His eyes slowly picked up one thing after another; the faded green hangings of his bed, the uneven boarding of the floor, a print hanging against the dark panel of the wall, showing apprentices playing football in the Strand, and another with a crudely coloured presentation of Bear-Baiting. On an old chest under the window was a bowl of thick green glass, rough in texture so that the colours of the green glass seemed to shift and change.

The light from the window was dim. There was no sound anywhere.

Where then was he? With a rush as of charging horses, events, pictures, words came back to him. He sprang from his bed as though, at once, he would hasten out into the street and start about his affairs. He went to the little window and pushed it back. A thin, wet, wispy fog met him. He was in the house of Mr. Cumberlege of Carlisle. He was also in the 'Silver Horn,' and close to him Mirabell Starr was looking into the young man's eyes, while the green parrot rocked on its perch. And he was in the ground behind Herries, digging while Glaramara humped its back over him and the light came down in misty ladders over Stye Head, and he was rowing slowly from Lord's Island, while the water slipped in ripples of steel from hill to hill.

He passed the back of his hand across his eyes, pulling himself together. He was here in Carlisle. The Prince and his Highlanders . . . Mirabell . . . this green bowl above whose colours the thin fog shifted. . . . His hand touched his bare chest and felt for the chain and the wooden cross that Mirabell's mother had left for him. He had not been without it since that day, and now, as his hand touched it, a new determination came to him: that he would find the child and talk to her and see how he might serve her. She was not for him and now would never be, but he might help her.

He stretched his legs and his arms, smiled; his face just then was kindly, not sardonic, but a little old and rough, battered and torn above his body, for his skin was fair and delicate like a woman's.

The door creaked open, and David came in. He was in an excitement unusual for his calm temper. He was fully dressed.

'Father, what are we going to do? They say this morning the town's under siege. There's a fine to-do, and half the city's downstairs swearing the militia are going to give in before they are fairly started, and the other half's in the street screaming about the Highlanders, and there's a fog so thick you can't see the back of your hand. Are we going to stay here? I doubt if we can get out now if we want to.'

'Of course we stay,' said Herries, sitting on the bed's end and swinging his bare legs.

'What did you hear last night when you were in the town?'

'Oh, naught, but that a parrot has green eyes.'

'Old Cumberlege loves me like a son this morning. He's plucky enough for himself, but his lady and his lady's woman are raped already by bony Highlanders in their imagination. They can't tell whether to be sorry or glad. The girl's brave, though. She calls me her brother.'

David grinned and put his arm around his father's bare neck.

'So we're to stay here?'

'Of course we're to stay, seeing we can't get out.'

'But who are we for? The Prince and his Highlanders?'

'For ourselves.' Herries stood up, stretching his arms. 'We're in a green city with warlocks and witches. Take care of the witch downstairs, David. Or love her if you wish to. A fog's the place for true love. My stomach's empty. Is there any food in this siege, or do we live from now on upon snails and puppies' tails? And water. There's a tin basin here, but no water.'

'I'll fetch you some.'

David returned with a bucket of water. He watched his father bathe. 'You're strong. Stronger than you used to be.'

'Aye, I'm strong—and damned ugly. The fog's to my advantage. Hast kissed the girl downstairs, Davy?'

'Yes, I kissed her.' David was crimson. 'She liked it.'

Herries, drawing on his hose, laughed.

'Good enough now. There'll be tears later.' They went down the crooked stairs, arm-in-arm.

But that day went for nothing. For the most part father and son were together, walking the town, watching the country people (for it was Martinmas Hiring Day), listening to a thousand silly rumours and stories.

At three in the afternoon there was a real sensation. A party of fifty or sixty horsemen appeared on Stanwix Bank, overlooking the city. The road was crowded with country people going home. When these were cleared away the ten-gun battery of the Castle fired, but the troopers were in safety by then.

Francis was in his little room washing his face in the tin basin when the guns fired. The floor seemed to quiver; the little panes of the windows rattled; a scatter of birds flew past, and there was a woman's scream, shrill and sharp, through the house. Then silence.

He went to the window. The fog was clear and the sky silver with threads of blue above the crooked roofs. He leaned out. On a cobbled corner of the side-street (he could see only a fragment of it) a man stood, looking up. Herries had the oddest fancy, seeing dimly in that faint afternoon light, that it was the pedlar standing there, the pedlar whom he had not seen since that Christmas night of the duel. . . . Oddly like him, with a peaked cap, the thin straining body. He fancied that he could certify the sharp, piercing eyes. He stepped back into the room in whose dusk the green glass bowl was the only light. Of course it was not the pedlar, but the fancy held him.

He yet seemed to have the echo of the guns in his ears, and the woman's scream. What was to happen to him here? An odd burning shiver ran through him like the first warning of a fever: he knew in that second, staring into the green glass of the bowl, that one of the crises of his life was approaching. He knew it quite certainly. He did not care for his life—it was not of so precious a quality to him—but this crisis that was coming was of deep import and would change, whichever way it went, all his fortune, physical and spiritual.

He knew it, as though the guns had blown away a veil from his eyes.

He went out to see what was toward. The country people were all hastening home. There was a stir in the Square like a scare among sheep when a wolf is by. Little groups collected like flies round sugar, and yet over all the bustle and movement there was a strange hush as though no one dared to raise a voice. He heard the names pass back and forth: 'Wade,' 'Durand,' 'Aglionby,' 'Waugh,' 'Pattinson.' The pigeons came strutting at his very feet, and above the roofs the sky suddenly tossed up arms and wreaths of red and gold, proclaiming the setting sun.

He turned his steps towards the Cathedral. In the Close everything was very still. Someone stood in a side door of the Cathedral looking up at the flaming sky. It was as though everyone he saw were straining an ear for the sound of the guns again.

Someone was speaking to him. 'A fine evening, Mr. Herries.'

He turned, as one turns in a dream, because he knew the voice. He passed his hand before his eyes, and in his ears the cannon dimly sounded, for it was Mirabell Starr very quietly standing there.

'I have followed you, Mr. Herries--most indecently. I saw you ten minutes ago.'

She looked at him with that clear-eyed indifference so known to him. But she was pleased, perhaps. The sky sank to smoky grey, and he could scarcely see her face. The bells chimed five o'clock. But she was glad to see him, less indifferent than she had been. He caught that and cherished it. She looked a baby, wearing the same shabby red cloak. His heart throbbed. He held himself sternly at attention, his arms stiff at his sides, lest he should touch her.

'I'm bold to address you.'

'No,' he answered. 'I'm well pleased.'

She saw in his eyes that he was worshipping her, this odd, ugly, elderly, scarred man.

She was frightened, perhaps, and for the honest child that she was wanted to put everything in a clear, defined light.

'I followed you--' she caught her breath a little. 'I wanted to tell you. . . . There at Honister, when we talked, I told you that I didn't believe in love. Well, now, you were kind and asked me to come to you if I needed anything, and my mother trusted you, so you must know I am very happy and I love someone, and he loves me.'

'That is good,' he said sternly. 'And it is a good man you love?'

'Yes, it is a good man.'

'He will care for you?'

'Oh, always.'

'I am happy. But you should not be here. This town will be dangerous now.'

'I have been in danger all my life,' she answered. 'Danger is nothing--for myself,' she added hastily.

Then, smiling at him so sweetly that his heart ached, she said quickly:

'I wished you to know. Good night,' and was gone.

He stood without moving, for how long he did not know.

There was a bitter, almost despairing, pain at his heart, such as he had never known before. He had always been too proud to despair of himself, but now, under the black shadow of the Cathedral, he really despaired. He was isolated, ostracised, hateful to all men. At once, at first sight of him, these Cumberleges had drawn back. . . . That he could face, but now, all pride flung aside, all fear of weakness discarded, he felt the bitterest anguish. Because, for a moment, he had been in touch with a kind of joy, a sort of happiness that he had not known before existed. He had seen it in the distance, stretched his hand, touched its wings; it had flown. Sternly, his back against the Cathedral wall as though he were hammered on to it, he stared in front of him, his palms gripped. He had not known before that his love for her was so deep that the hooks of it were in his very entrails. He knew now, and that he would always love her so.

On the following morning, the Sunday, Francis and David were summoned to the defence of the city. The fog was this morning thicker than ever and added to the general confusion and increasing alarm. Every kind of rumour was about. No one knew where the Prince and his army might be. Some said that he was already inside the city. Some said that Wade and his forces were marching to relieve them, others that they were to be left to their fate, their children would be eaten alive, their women raped and the houses burned to the ground.

Among the most gloomy of Carlisle's citizens was Mrs. Cumberlege, who continued to scream from her bed of sickness. At one moment she succeeded in staggering as far as her doorway (rumour had it that she could have staggered a great deal farther had she so wished) and crying: "The Highlanders are here! The Highlanders are here! Help! Help! We are all to be murdered!'

This was, of course, desperately upsetting for Mr. Cumberlege, who was forbidden by her to leave her defenceless in the house. At the same time he wished to do his duty as a loyal citizen and surrender himself to Colonel Durand's orders. It ended in his slipping, with Herries and David, off into the fog, and leaving her in the care of her beautiful daughter.

They went to the Castle and were enrolled for defence. Prospects were not cheerful. From the room in which they stood, crowded about with an extraordinary tumbled and disorderly mixture of old men, young men and boys, they could hear the echo of trowel and hammer on the city walls. The original garrison was but eighty old 'invalid' soldiers. The guns were so ancient that they were reputed to have been, in the jest of the drinking-bouts and tea-parties, Boadicea's. Durand had augmented them with ten small ship's guns brought from Whitehaven, and the old ruined walls were now in course of being altered that they might fit these.

Forty townsmen were in charge of the Whitehaven guns, and another eighty served the Castle artillery.

Confusion was the more confounded by the bringing from neighbouring towns and villages of small companies of militia, but their arms were of different bores, and every man made his own ball fitting the size of the piece.

All the worst trouble, Herries soon perceived, came from these same militia. Colonel Durand had proposed that the militia officers should do duty by detachment from their several companies, but this they emphatically and turbulently opposed, and drew lots, among themselves, for their posts. The result of this was that there was no order nor discipline, and men wandered where they would and were already demoralised and fatigued.

As the morning drew on, the confusion in the room where Herries was grew ever more active. Men ran about like children, crying out, fingering arms in so uncertain a manner that it was likely at any instant that one would blow another to pieces, starting up and running to the windows, chattering, crying, shouting, now boasting, now bewailing. An old countryman stood near Herries, an ancient man with a long grizzled beard who, again and again, called out: 'Who is for the Lord? Who is for the Lord?' Little Cumberlege walked to the window and back, stopping every other minute by David, whose strength and imperturbability seemed to give him an immense satisfaction. It seemed to be impossible for the present to come near Durand, who was in an inner room.

Then, about mid-day, the fog rolled off, and a young man with a long yellow face like a turnip came in shouting:

'They are upon us. The whole army. At the very walls.'

He had scarcely spoken when the guns were heard to fire. 'That's from Shaddon Gate,' someone cried. There was a moment of transfixion when everyone stood, not seeing what to do, where to go, waiting for they knew not what. Then two men ran in, shouting hysterically:

'We have beat them. They are retreating.' And almost at once the fog came down again, blotting everything out.

Some said now that they had retreated all together, others that it was but a blind, others that they had marched round to the other side of the city and were already creeping about the streets.

Some swore that they could hear the skirl of the Highland pipes. Even for Herries who, in such an affair, had no unsteady nerves, there was an odd thrill from the knowledge that in the brief interval of clarity the whole of the Prince's army had been seen at the very walls. It was true, then. They were in the real heart of this situation, not imagining it. Shortly there might be--nay, surely would be--massacre and bloodshed. And where would she be in this? A chance bullet? A drunken Highlander? His whole body trembled. . . . The old countryman clutched his arm and peered into his face.

'Who is for the Lord? Who is for the Lord?'

It was late in the afternoon before he and David were marched off to the part of the wall that was their post. As they marched through a portion of the town it had a weird effect, because the order had gone out that there were to be lights in all the lower windows, darkness in the upper. The fog, too, hung high, so that they seemed to be stepping along a stream of uncertain watery glow, while above them was a bank of blackness. All was silent; behind the lighted windows there was no sound. Against his will every man was listening for the guns.

No one spoke. They might have been moving to some secret rendezvous. Herries had at his side a short, round, very stout, little man who groaned, panted and seemed to be bursting with some tremendous secret.

They paused at a lighted corner while their destination was settled. At once the little fat man, whose face was beetroot colour (his head trembled with a queer jerky movement), burst into the middle of excited, despairing sentences as though he were continuing a long, already uttered speech. He caught Herries' arm and held it, and this oddly pleased him. There was someone in this foggy world who did not shrink from him.

'. . . The eldest but five and a half. . . . One every year, and the five of them alone in the house with their grandmother, deaf as a post, to mind them. . . . I said to them that I would not be gone a half-hour, and what service can I be with a musket, serving out butter and sugar for the last twenty years? . . . But what do you think, sir? Shall we beat them off, do you think? My sister would have been in to mind them, but only two days back she was on a visit to Allonby to her brother-in-law, as indeed I told her at the time that he was but inviting her to take advantage of her. He was never a man, from his boyhood up, to do a thing and not expect anything back for it, as Margaret my sister has herself said many a time . . . and the children crying their hearts out in the dark. . . .'

The light from a flare that someone carried swung in the breeze, as though a tongue were licking the cheek of the fog. In that sudden illumination Herries saw two things: that David was not with him and that quite close to him, almost in touch of him, was Mirabell's young lover.

At that knowledge he caught his breath as though he expected a blow. The boy (for he was little more) stood stiffly, his head upstaring straight into Herries' face.

He did not, of course, recognise him, but he looked at him as though he would know him. And yet he was looking beyond him. Herries saw now that he was not seeing anyone. He was swimming deep in his own thoughts, and his mouth was smiling.

The order came again to move forward. The young man was very near to him. It was as though he had been placed there in David's stead.

The little fat man stayed close at Herries' side. Whistling ejaculations came from between his lips. 'Eh, sirs! . . . Eh, sirs!' 'The pity of it! The pity!' 'The waste in this town!'

Mirabell's boy, the second coincidence. First the 'Silver Horn' and now this. He felt a dead weight upon him, as though he were caught in some trap. The conviction that had been with him in his room when he heard the first gun, came back to him, that he was moving to some deep crisis in his affairs and that all his future would depend on the way that he now acted.

Oddly, at the very first sight of him under the flare, he knew that he hated him.

Inside the wall they took their places. Someone came round and told them where they were to go, and that at a certain time they would be relieved. At once it was evident that there was no discipline. The fog had lifted again and a few faint, very small stars could be seen.

Men were moving about, talking to one another. The fat man, his hand once more on Herries' arm, was about it again. '. . . Only yesterday, being Martinmas Hiring, I engaged the girl, but when she saw the trouble in the city nothing would stay her. I offered her a double wage if she'd bide with the children. She'd be safer, too, here than out in the country, but when they fired that cannon it frightened her. Not a word would she hear. . . .'

The young man stayed at Herries' side as though he knew that was the place for him. Yes, he had a fine, clear, noble countenance. No fear there, no meanness. His slim body was strung to the full height of discipline and obedience. Still on his lips was that little, happy smile.

Herries, as though under command, spoke:

'The fog clears,' he said.

The young man turned as though he had been recalled from a great distance.

'They must be at our very feet,' he said. 'It will be cold before dawn.' He smiled, then he added: 'I have a friend who was with me until ten minutes back. We wished to be together.'

Three men came past, peering. One of them stopped.

'I have found you,' he said. That thick growling voice was guide enough for Herries. He knew that the company was now completed. The face, with its black hair, peered close at Herries. Herries could see him again as he stepped to the parrot, tickling its neck with his finger.

'I had lost you,' the young man said.

'I am never lost,' he laughed deep as though in the coils of his stomach. 'Well, sir,' he said to Herries, 'this is a play.'

Herries nodded, turned away, looked out to the grey web of the night, its texture dotted with lights that seemed to sway and stagger because the mist came in drives, advancing and retreating.

They took their places, quietly, the three of them together, and stood there without moving. An immense time seemed to pass. The cold grew very intense.

Herries thought: 'Here I am, these two with me, not by my own choice or intention.' He felt growing up in him the old man that he had by now, he thought, discarded. Something seemed to him to come through the night and the fog and the cold and place in him one evil thing after another, as you pile stuff in a cupboard. 'And now this I'll add. And now this. Yes, and this we must have.'

Evil things, lecheries, lusts, cruelties, meannesses, desires to hurt, to maim, purposeless maliciousness. And he himself seemed to look on, coldly and with external deliberation. All his love for the child, Mirabell, was tarnished and coarsened. He now lusted for her in exactly the way that, in his younger days, he had lusted for many women. His hands touched her hair, her small child's face, her little breasts, her waist, her knees, coldly, with desire but no fine passion.

His evil thoughts spread over the walls into the dark plain beyond. He saw the Prince's army encamped, and it seemed to him that he could stare into every tent. Each place was peopled with evil men, men cruel and mean and lascivious as he was. They were crawling over the country, carrying naked women on their backs, naked women whose hair was loose about their bodies and down whose faces tears were pouring. He saw a farm, the house, its windows shuttered for the night, the farm buildings stacked with provender, the animals sleeping in their places, the master in the upper room asleep, his head resting on his wife's breast.

Through the gate, a little bent man, a flare in his hand, crept. He stooped lower, setting the flare now here, now there. The flames sprang up. The byres were caught. The animals screamed. The fire ate the walls of the house with greedy avaricious gestures. White faces were at the windows. There were screams, cries, odour of burning flesh. The woman, held in her man's arms, watched the flames crawl nearer. . . .

The little bent man moved about the country, doing here one evil thing, another there. Herries moved with him, his body cold, like marble, his heart burning.

All the men in the Prince's camp seemed to stir before him. They moved closer to the walls, and in all that army of eyes there was anticipatory lust and longing for suffering in others and destruction and ruin. Herries himself seemed to lead them on, saying: 'Here is a good place. . . . And here are women. . . . Here are houses to burn.'

A shiver of bad desire ran through him. It was as though he had been sleeping there on his feet and wakened. It might be so. Everything was very clear about him, the dark ramparts, the white faces of men.

He could have said: 'I see men crawling like lice, and that is all that they are. Poor, lowest and meanest of all created things.' He tried not to think of anything. He knew that if he went much farther he would face thoughts that were lower and viler than any that he had ever known. But someone went on piling the cupboard high with these. 'Here is a new one. Here is one that I have found. And here another. . . .'

He turned a little and talked to the black, short man at his side, who, like the boy, had neither moved nor spoken all this time.

'What do you think,' he asked, 'of this adventurer's chances? Will he reach London?'

With that odd growl as of an animal roused by some sense of danger, the man answered: 'I neither know nor care. He can take this place when he wishes-- and all England for me.'

'Doesn't it matter to you then?'

'Why should it? There is food and drink under any king. One ruler is like another, unless oneself has the chance of ruling.'

'Are you in Carlisle by hazard?' To Herries it was as though, beneath this conversation, other words were being said and other meanings of deep import were being intended.

'I am anywhere by hazard. One place is as another to me.'

'I have seen you before,' Herries said. 'The other evening at the "Silver Horn."'

'It may be,' the man replied. 'I have been there.' He spat against the wall. 'Some of us may be dead men before morning.'

'Why do you stay here,' asked Herries, 'if you are indifferent? You lose your life, maybe, for nothing.'

'My life!' The man growled a chuckle. 'I have no life. I have only moments. I am hungry, I eat. I am thirsty, I drink. I want a woman, if I can I take her. Life stops. Well, why not--when it has never begun?'

'Then you have no fear of death?'

'No. If there's no life, there's no death. There is only the body. One fills it. One empties it. One seizes with it what one can.'

Herries said: 'Then you regret nothing that you have ever done?'

'Only what I have wanted and have not had.'

'You are fortunate, then,' Herries answered. 'You have no scruples, no regrets.'

'Regrets! No! Why? Where I am strong enough I conquer. Where I am weak I take to my heels.'

'Why, then, I ask again, are you here? In this bleak place, in danger, where nothing is to be gained.'

'Ah, perhaps something is to be gained.'

The thin, faint light was enough for them to see one another's faces, and suddenly, at the same moment, they stared, the one at the other. It was indeed a strange look. Herries, gazing into that shaggy face with the bristling, black hair, the light, fiery little eyes, the low

chill brow, felt that he had seen this face before, and often. He felt, too, that the man was coldly, deliberately, and without interest in anything but his own purpose, asking him to do something. What he could not tell.

'That's a deep scar you've got,' said the man.

'Yes.'

'Did you kill the man who gave it you?'

'No,' said Herries.

'I would have done: drawn and quartered him. You see my hands?' He held them out, hideous hands, the backs thick with black hair, the fingers stumped and gnarled.

'They are strong. I could strangle an ox with them.'

Herries, moved by some curiosity, touched one. It was ice-cold and damp.

'Yes. You have strong hands.'

For the first time the young man spoke:

'He is so strong that he can lift a cart with them. Can you not, Tony?'

The man did not answer. The boy went on: 'Is it not strange, sir, standing here in this cold mist, waiting for we know not what and for no real reason?' His face was charming, as he turned it to Herries. 'I am all for a fight in the open, and when you know the cause, but this chill waiting . . . and I would be loth to die, just now.'

'The boy's in love,' said the man. 'He's thinking always of his beautiful girl. Isn't it so, Harry?'

The boy laughed.

'That is no business for this gentleman,' he said. 'Another man's love affair is dull news.'

And so they would move, these men, stirring so quietly under the wall, their eyes burning, their hearts thick at the thought that with a knock or two this town would surrender. And then what fun there would be for them! No house closed to them, the women cowering in the bed-curtains; their 'Hallo! you there . . . I have you!' Dragging her out, pulling back her head, loosening her hair, tearing her clothes from her--her neck, her breasts, her eyes staring in terror, the crackle of flames, the tramping of men, the warm trembling body slack in their arms. . . .

'And out on the Fell I have seen the shepherd whistling to his dog and the sheep come in a cloud, while the sun strikes the stream like mirror-glass. That's what I want and will have, when this is over.' It was the boy speaking.

The man growled at his side. 'The lad's a poet. He writes reams of it. There's books already enough in the world.'

'But this, sir, too, is wonderful. Can you not feel it to be so? The town so dark behind us and the land so dark before. We standing on so narrow a parapet that one cannon-ball would tumble it to dust. If 'twere only myself I were thinking of . . .' He sighed and turned impulsively to Herries. 'Oh, sir, we standing as we do in this dark, strangers, need not be afraid of rashness. Have you not felt often how unsafe it is to love? The agony of another's safety. . . . The pain of parting . . .' He broke off. They were all very close together, and their voices low.

Herries felt that he was alone there and that these two were but voices of his own different warring selves.

The mist was thick again and the cold very sharp. They stood instinctively the closer.

It was then, with a sudden pang as though an enemy had struck a blade into him, that he realised the intensity of his hatred for this boy. This had been approaching him for a long while, keeping pace with all his other evil thoughts, but now it had outpaced the others and crept all over his body like a fever. His hands shook. He did not trust himself to speak because his voice would shake.

This was the boy loved by Mirabell. Had he not come she would have learnt to love himself. Aye, she would. With what woman had he ever failed? No matter if he were older now and face-scarred, when he chose to put forth his charm what woman resisted him? And most certainly she, a child who, in spite of her boasts, could know so little about men, would have surrendered to him. But now her heart had been taken by a chit of a boy, beardless, simple, a baby poet. She would love him and then rue it, live with him a week and tire of it. A few years and she would be a woman, complex, tyrannous, passionate. And was this boy companion for such a woman?

But, more than conscious thought, his body was moving him towards some action. His hands about the boy's throat in that thick darkness, his hands strong as iron, one throttle, a little murmured cry. There would be no witness save the other fellow, and, with that, Herries, although no word had been spoken, was aware that it was the black-faced fellow's desire that he should do this. He was aware that the man hated the boy as he did. The fellow was very close to him, thigh pressed to thigh, and even as this knowledge came to him he felt the cold, damp, hairy back of that other hand on his.

One squeeze of the fingers about the throat. . . . In the hurry and panic of this especial crisis no one would hear and no one know.

His body shook now so that, touching the thick, hard body close to him, he knew that the man felt this trembling and was aware.

The fellow said to him: 'At what hour did they say they would relieve us?'

But behind the spoken words were these others: ('We understand one another, we two. Do this and there will be no sound. . . .')

He replied: 'At midnight.'

(And his answer: 'I wish for no understanding with you. What I do I do for myself.')

The man growled: 'The cold is more biting with every second.'

(And behind the words: 'Press your fingers into his windpipe. I will keep guard.')

Herries answered: 'The cold will be worse for the second watch.'

('Keep guard for yourself. I am my own guard.')

The man's cold hairy hand touched Herries' fingers.

'This town can stand no siege unless Wade relieves it.'

(And behind the words: 'It will be quickly done. Catch him by the neck. Press his head back.')

Herries said: 'Well, Wade should have been here to-day were he coming.'

('But it is my affair. Leave me alone to my own deed.')

The boy's voice came from what seemed an infinite distance: 'I wonder what the hour should be. I have missed the Cathedral clock.'

And from a greater distance yet some other voice: 'Eh, but it's cold . . . awful cold. There'll be snow before morning.'

Every evil act of Herries' life seemed to come to him there, all that had been unrestrained, uncontrolled, self-willed and cruel. The days in Doncaster, Margaret weeping on her bed, Alice Press at the Fair, and it was he who with his own hands had bound the naked witch. . . .

He seemed to encircle Mirabell, his adored, with one arm and with the other he touched the boy's neck.

The boy turned, but Herries allowed his hand to stay against the warm skin.

('One twist of the head and you have done it. I will keep silence as though it had been myself.')

Then desperately, out of the mist, from some place that was not his own heart, some sort of a prayer issued: 'Oh, God, who dost not exist, help me now for I am in perilous trouble. Oh, God, who art not, save me from this sin.'

He touched barely the boy's neck, but he felt as though he held him in his arms, and all the hatred, all the aching lonely desire for the girl so indifferent to him, all the insistent urge to kill, was in the power behind his hands, his arms, his beating heart, his straining body.

It seemed to him that he threw him over the parapet and that nothing had been done.

The boy laughed.

'Your hand is cold,' he said.

Herries dropped his arms.

'I could wrestle with you to be warm,' he said.

'Well, let us wrestle then,' said the boy laughing.

Herries answered shuddering: 'I must go to find my son.'

He stumbled off into the dark. Figures were moving, voices murmuring. And then there was a great silence as though all the world had been stricken dumb.

He pressed up against the rampart of the wall, his forehead clamped to the cold stone. And so he stayed.

PART II

THE PRINCE

Charles Edward, with his army, entered Carlisle city on Monday, 18th November.

This was the climax of days of panic and despair. There is no need here to recover the episodes of that unhappy week, to recall once again how, after unfortunate Deputy-Mayor Pattinson had gaily sent word to London that the Prince had retreated, and been officially thanked for the news, he discovered only too quickly the error of his judgement; or how, to a growing accompaniment of terror and dismay, the citizens of that gallant town learnt that they were deserted and betrayed; or how on the 15th the Highlanders were within eighty yards of the city wall and answered the disheartened fire of the garrison with scornful jeers, 'their bonnets,' one commentator remarks, 'held high aloft at the end of their trenching spades.'

After this, do what Durand might, there was pandemonium in the city. That brave man did his utmost, 'assuring them,' to quote again the chronicler, 'that they need fear nothing from the rebels, that they were in a very good condition to defend themselves, and that if they would continue to behave with the same spirit and resolution they had hitherto shown, the rebels would never capture the city.'

It was the militia who brought the panic to submission. To the mess-room at the 'King's Arms' they retired, and this was their Declaration:

'The militia of the counties of Cumberland and Westmoreland having come voluntarily into the city of Carlisle for the defence of the said city, and having for six days and six nights successively been upon duty in expectation of relief from His Majesty's forces, but it appearing that no such relief is to be had, and ourselves not able to do duty or hold out any longer, are determined to capitulate, and do certify that Colonel Durand, Captain Gilpin and the rest of the officers have well and faithfully done their duty.'

Durand, after reading this, made one more attempt to reason with them, but they would listen to no reason and no argument.

'The majority of the officers insisted that they were resolved to treat with the enemy for themselves.'

One last attempt was made; the townsmen, having better guts than the poor militia, refused to capitulate, determined to hold the Castle, collected provisions and munition in the Castle, but, alas, the militia 'melted away through the night, and on the morning of the 15th Durand was left with his eighty "invalids" and a capful of brave townsmen.'

On this a messenger who had been sent to the Prince returned with these words: 'That he would grant no terms to the town, nor treat about it at all unless the Castle was surrendered; likewise, if that was done, all should have honourable terms, the inhabitants should be protected in their persons and estates, and every one be at liberty to go where they pleased.'

These terms, better than the citizens had expected, decided the matter. The Duke of Perth entered and took possession of the Castle and city. The capitulation of Carlisle was effected with the loss of one man only, and he a rebel.

On the 16th of November the Duke of Perth, on the steps of the Cross in the centre of the Market Place, proclaimed King James III., and the Town Clerk and members of the Corporation went out to Brampton, where the Prince was, and, on bended knee, yielded him the keys of the city.

So, on the 18th of November, the Prince entered the city, and David Herries and Hetty Cumberlege were among those who saw him enter.

That was a happy day for David. It was for him, and for many thousands of others who were there, like passing out of a nightmare. Strong of purpose, courageous and unflinching as he was, these last days had begun to test his nerves. 'If only,' he had thought (as he was to think many times again in the course of his life), 'folk would keep their mouths shut.' The thick foggy weather, the uncertainty of the future, the possibility of massacre and fire, the sense of futility from beating against all these nerves and ill-controlled passions, were beginning to frighten him.

For himself he did not care, and in his father he had absolute faith, but these trembling and crying women were another matter. Little Hetty Cumberlege was among the bravest of them, but on her, too, the wild stories and frenzied anticipations were having their effect. Had he been in love with her it would have been simpler. A sort of glory would have come from that. But although he wished to be, he could not. He could not understand that. She was pretty and charming, and herself as far in love with him as her childishness and inexperience allowed her to be. A word, a kiss, one passionate movement and she would have been his. But he could not make that movement.

Yet she woke him to a consciousness of women as no one before had ever done. He was twenty-six years of age and had never yet kissed a woman, save in friendliness. Now, even in these few dark troubled days, he looked at the women about and around him with new eyes. Hetty Cumberlege had done that for him. But he did not love her. He was sorry, but he did not.

The consciousness that she was ready to love him at a moment's turn embarrassed him terribly. He wished that he had Deborah there to advise him. Every look from Hetty's eyes (and she gave him a great many) made him feel ashamed. He would have liked to love her. He felt now that it would be delightful to love someone, but that someone would not be Hetty.

He would have spoken to his father about his troubles, but his father had been removed from him in some strange absorption of his own. His father had shown a surprising gentleness and kindliness these last days, but he had been alone. And by his own wish.

So here David and Hetty were watching the Prince enter Carlisle. The crowd by the city gates was so thick that they caught only a glimpse of him. David was far taller than the majority around him. He saw, as a flash of sun struck from the heavy winter clouds, the fine white horse and on the horse a youth with a gallant air, his head up, a smile of pride and courtesy and triumph on his lips. He looked like a king. He was happy that morning as, had they all but known it, he was never to be happy again. The horse tossed its head, a hundred pipers played, and the sun went in again behind the clouds.

So then they went home. There was a very lively company in the parlour. Mrs. Cumberlege had found the general excitement too much for her retirement, and there she was laid out on the sofa. To David she was truly an amazing sight, for her stoutness and shortness of figure gave her, lying there with a handsome China shawl over her knees, the appearance of a bolster. Her face was very red and she had on top of it her best wig, powdered, curled and greased, dressed high over a large cushion and decorated with imitation fruit and a little ship with silken sails. Mr. Cumberlege was there, two ladies, and a jolly old fellow with a wooden leg, who announced himself as Captain Bentley. He was apparently a stranger in the house, and could not be sufficiently polite to Mrs. Cumberlege, whose stout cheeks were all smiles and whose head nodded with pleasure so frequently that the little ship travelled on stormy seas indeed.

The talk was, of course, all of the Prince. An amazing calm, and even gaiety, had for the moment come upon the town. It would not last, but, just now, no one was alarmed any longer. The Prince was here. He was charming, handsome, and who knew but that in a week or two he might be master of the country? Moreover, his Highlanders were here too and were behaving with the greatest propriety. Not a single act of riot or mischief had been reported. It was whispered indeed that a number of ladies were sadly disappointed. .

. .

The white favour was becoming for women with every moment more popular.

As to Captain Bentley, you might think that there was no Prince and no Highland invasion. He sat on the edge of his chair, which creaked beneath his weight and the glory of his plum-coloured breeches and silver buckles, and forced upon Mrs. Cumberlege incidents of his personal experience. He was very honest about his drink, and proud of it too. He declared that he could swallow a bowl of punch and two mugs of bumbo without any difficulty whatever, and told a long tale of how, being in Wapping, he had a fierce toothache and could find no one but a woman to pull the rogue, which she did with so muscular an arm that he thought she must be a man in disguise, until inquiring further he found that she was a woman indeed.

'Fie! Captain,' said Mrs. Cumberlege, laughing most friendlily at him, upon which he would have bent forward to whisper in her ear had not the stink from her wig been too strong for two by no means sensitive nos-

trils. He had also a grand tale of how in London a month or two back he had seen a show of moving pictures. Truly marvellous. You could see a coach roll out of the town, and a gentleman in the coach saluted the company, and you could watch ships sailing upon the sea and a man come to light a lamp in the Tower. In return Mrs. Cumberlege had a sister-in-law who had seen a live griffin at a Fair and he had shot fire from his mouth, which had so sadly frightened her sister-in-law that she had given birth to triplets before her due time.

There was a bowl of punch, and both Mr. Cumberlege and Captain Bentley became very merry indeed, and even the three ladies found their sentences coming none so clearly.

During all the gaiety Hetty and David sat close together in the bow-window. The streets were now dark outside, but many people were about. The cobbles echoed their steps. There was laughter and singing, and everywhere you felt the sudden relief, the freedom from panic.

Romance, too, was in the air. For good or ill this young and beautiful Prince was now in their city. Everything, it seemed, was giving way before him. After all, was he not one of our own people, no foreigner? Had not that sound of 'James III.' cried on the steps of the Market Cross a pleasant echo in the air?

And for Hetty Cumberlege, too, this was the most romantic hour of her life. This huge young man, who sat so close to her, so brave, so strong, so proper a man, she thought that he loved her and presently would say so. It was true that she feared his father, but he would not live always with his father. It seemed to her impossible that they could be related, so different were they. The candles burning in the room, the flickering firelight, her mother for once in a good mood: now surely it was designed that he would speak.

How marvellous a chest he had, how beautiful a neck, what glorious eyes, how direct and honest he was: she could trust herself to him for ever. A little shiver ran through her body. She hung her head. She did not dare to look at him.

And David said never a word. His was not a quick nature, but yet quick enough for him to realise, with an awful sense of horror, that she was waiting for him to speak. He could see it in her hanging head, her trembling hands. This was for him the most terrible moment of his life. He longed to move, but was frozen to his chair. He heard the merry Captain and Mr. Cumberlege trolling a song from an infinite distance. What must he do? By whose fault had he tumbled into this dreadful dilemma? She was so sweet, so young, so pretty. She would be wonderful for any man to hold in his arms, to press his cheek to hers; and yet he did not want to hold her. He wanted only to escape from the room. His great clumsy body seemed to him to fill the room and to swell ever larger and larger as he stayed there.

'There are many people yet abroad,' he said.

She raised her eyes, looked at him, and dropped them again.

'Yes. . . . But it is cold. I think there will be snow.'

'At Herries, where we live . . .' he began desperately.

'Yes?' she said, looking into his eyes again.

'Winter-time the snow lies on the Fell to a great depth. Many sheep are lost in it.'

'Poor things,' she said.

'Sometimes in winter they must carry a corpse over the hills from valley to valley. When the snow is deep 'tis no light matter.'

'I like the summer best,' she answered.

How he longed to say: 'Hetty, dear, I like you so, but I don't love you. I wish I did.' Instead he told her about his sister Deborah. She was not interested. Her hand stole out and nearly touched his breeches. Had she touched him he might have yielded, and all his life, and the lives of many future Herries, been other, but her hand stole back again.

'Father is greatly pleased that you are here,' she ventured.

'I am glad,' he answered.

'And mother too.'

'I am very glad.' She meant that someone else was greatly pleased too, but she did not say so.

'We must be returning home in a day or so,' he said, his face burning. 'I have business, an interest in two vessels in Liverpool. And maybe I shall purchase a farm.'

'You are very young for so much business,' she said, and again she looked at him.

The thought came to him that this proclamation of his prosperity might be considered a foreword to a proposal, so he said hurriedly:

'It is not much. A small venture.'

If something did not happen soon he was lost. Something did happen. His father saved him. The door opened and Francis Herries came in.

David, his heart thumping his deliverance, went to meet him. Hetty, a minute after, left the room and running up the stairs, closing her door, threw herself on her bed in a passion of tears.

Herries meanwhile had had his own strange hour. He felt, because of it, soft and gentle to all the world. That night struggle on the wall had left him first as a wounded, then as a convalescent man and, in this convalescence, he was oddly gentle.

He felt a great and persistent weariness throughout his body, and everything about him--the town, the people, the crisis--was removed behind a sort of dream-curtain. Just now this Mirabell Starr was the only real thing to him in life. She was more real by far than he was to himself.

That same afternoon he had seen and talked to her. He had been wandering through the streets, lost in his own thoughts, but getting behind them an impression of this day's events very different from the one in Cumberlege's warm parlour. There was relief, it was true, but beyond the relief a sulky stiffening, a sense of humiliation and apprehension. It was as though, with a kind of second-sight that he had, he could feel the doom that was coming to this place, could touch Cumberland's swollen cheeks and smell the hot stench of that black hole where nearly four hundred poor wretches, huddled and trampled like cattle, were, in so short a time, to pant their strangled lives away. He could see, it might be (and yet not see), brave Coppock drawn on the smart new sledge through the English Gate to execution, and gaze upon that sad procession now only two months distant, the officers with their legs tied under the bellies of their horses, the privates on foot marching like felons, two abreast, fastened by rope. If he did not see these things he felt them in the air, which was growing with every moment colder and was made bitter by a driving wind that held in its lap a steely sleet.

He had reached the farther end of English Street and was about to turn when Mirabell all but ran against him. Three times now within the week chance had brought him to her, or perhaps it was not chance. There was to be one more . . .

She was cloaked up against the wind and seemed to him infinitely young and fragile. They encountered under a lamp-flare, and she knew him at once. She smiled. He could see that she was in some fear, and that stirred him at once to a sharp passion of protection.

'Mr. Herries,' she said.

'You should not be out alone,' he answered her quickly. 'Not now, toward evening, the streets as they are.'

She did not repulse him. She seemed glad of his company.

'I am going to my lodging,' she said rather breathlessly. 'In Abbey Street. Behind the Cathedral. I have a room there.'

They started along English Street. She looked back.

'You see no one following us?'

'No,' he said. 'Who should be following you?'

'No one . . . but now, the town as it is . . .'

'Take my arm. No one shall touch you while I am here.' The pride he felt as he said that! And the rush of blood to his heart as he knew the touch of her hand on his arm!

'I know who it is,' he went on. 'A short, thick, black-bearded man with a chill hand.'

'You know? Yes. Anthony Thawn. But how do you know?'

'I saw you, a week back, in the "Silver Horn." I was quite near to you. There was a green parrot and this fellow stroked its neck.'

'Yes. He is a friend of Harry's. Harry is my lover. I am greatly afraid of him, Mr. Herries. I have never been afraid of anyone before, and it is not for myself now but for Harry. He pretends to be his friend, but I know that he is not. He was first a friend of my uncles. He was with us here when we first came to Carlisle. Then when my uncles went to Scotland he stayed. He would make love to me if he dared. Harry is so simple that he thinks Thawn is his friend. I have told him no, but he will not believe me. Always when I leave them alone I am afraid of some evil. . . .'

She poured all this out as a little child might, confident in her hearer's interest. And indeed Herries was interested, so deeply that it seemed to be his own history to which he was listening.

'I have seen your lover. He also was at the "Silver Horn." He has a noble face.'

'Harry! Yes, he is noble! When we go from here he will marry me and we will live in London, where he has a brother. Harry is a poet. He is writing a grand poem on "Dido and Aeneas." I can't tell whether I have the names rightly. I have never had any education.'

'But could you live in London, when you have been always in the open? Seeing you on Honister I had thought you could never endure a town.'

'I could live anywhere with Harry. He also loves the country as I do, and when he has made a little money we will come back to the mountains. He will find patrons for his poem. He says that is often done.'

How different, Herries thought, love has made her. She is still a child, but all the wildness and rebellion are gone. His heart ached, but the touch of her hand on his arm consoled him. Perhaps he could help them, these two, and in being a friend to them find his salvation. They were both so very young.

'This fellow Thawn,' he said, 'if he troubles you I will rid you of him.'

But she shook her head. 'That is not so easy. He is very strong.'

'I, too, am strong,' said Herries.

'I have no fear,' she answered confidently, 'when I am with Harry. It is when I am away from him. He trusts everyone. He can see no harm in anyone. If he had had my life he would not be so trusting, as I am always telling him.'

They were skirting the Cathedral. They would not have many more minutes together.

'I told you,' Herries said, 'on Honister that I am always by you if you need me. Will you promise me, if you are afraid, to come to this place? It is in the very middle of the town, only five minutes from here. If I am away I will let them know, so that they can always find me.' He gave her the name of Cumberlege's house. 'Do you promise?'

She looked at him, then nodded her head. 'Yes, I promise.' She sighed, he thought, with some relief. 'Here is my lodging,' she said.

Abbey Street was a quiet, staid place behind Tullie House. It was a thin house with neat stone steps and a light in the upper window.

'Thank you. I am sure that Harry is here. The light is in my room.' Her voice had changed to a radiant happiness. She had already, he thought, almost forgotten him. She ran up the steps and into the house. He watched her until she was gone.

All that night he dreamt of her.

Events moved swiftly with him then. That next day, 19th November, was to be a marked day for him his life long, and for more than one reason. He left Cumberlege's house after three of the afternoon; by six of the evening that had occurred which gave his life a new strain never again to be lost.

By the Market Cross he was confronted with Roche. He had been expecting this meeting. Roche had in Keswick told him where he would be found in Carlisle, but Herries had not sought him out. Roche belonged to his old life, not to this one. But here Roche was and recognising him instantly; indeed Francis Herries, with his proud arrogant carriage, his scar, his high sturdy figure, was not a man easily passed.

Roche's pleasure at the meeting was moving. He was dressed in civil clothes, but as a very grand gentleman. The grandeur suited him well. His black coat was of silk, elaborately laced, and at his side there was a slender gold-hilted sword. He wore a tie-wig and a three-cornered hat of dark felt and laced. His pale, long, aristocratic face was grave and dignified, and not jubilant as Herries would have expected it to be.

He caught Herries' arm and walked with him as though he would never let him go again.

'Well,' said Francis, 'your prophecies have been found true. You must be a happy man.'

But Roche was not altogether a happy man. As they walked, their cloaks close about them because of the bitter wind, Roche, dropping his voice, spoke his doubts. All was not as well as it ought to be. True enough that, with Edinburgh and Carlisle in their hands, the Government forces apparently dismayed, they had prospered to a marvel. But there were dissensions in the camp.

'His Royal Highness is but a boy, and has had little experience as yet of governing men. How could it be otherwise at his age? But there are the Irish. They have great importance, perhaps too great, in his councils. There is Lord George Murray. He is stiff-necked and obstinate and hates the Catholics. He has but now sent in his resignation because His Royal Highness had left the Duke of Perth and Murray of Broughton to arrange the terms of surrender without consulting Lord George.' His Royal Highness had written Lord George a very sharp letter in which he had said that he was glad to hear of his particular attachment to the King, but was sure he would never take anything as a proof of it but his deference to himself. This to Lord George, who considered himself the God Almighty, was a bitter word. But they could (Roche was forced to confess) ill afford to lose Lord George, who had a great sense of strategy and the discipline of armies. The Lord knew they needed discipline (here Roche sighed), and it was hard to come by in such an ill-composed army as theirs.

'There was, too, great division of opinion as to the next steps to be taken. It was said that the Government was sending an army of ten thousand under Sir John Ligonier to Staffordshire. Some were for a return to Scotland, others for remaining here to wait the rising of the North Country Jacobites. The Prince himself was for marching forward.'

Herries could see that Roche was in great perturbation of mind and longing for a confidant. He seemed to have no doubt at all as to the direction in which Herries' sympathies would lie, and was, it appeared, ready to confide to him any secret. He had aged very greatly since Herries had had any long talk with him, but that was natural enough, for a number of years had passed and he had been engaged in much perilous enterprise. But he had changed, too, in spirit. He seemed to have no longer anything of the religious zealot about him, but was completely the man of affairs, and with the discovery Herries also realised that all Roche's old influence over him had gone, his power and his charm.

He was eager to know what Herries felt to be the mood of Carlisle. Were they for the Prince? Had Herries not seen in the reception of the Prince's entry a disposition to enthusiasm? One more success and might it not be that the whole of the North would turn?

Herries said what he could and, snatching at any encouragement, Roche insisted that he should come now to see His Royal Highness and assure him of this. Even though it were only for five minutes. He was himself on his way there.

Herries had no wish to be dragged into any definite partisanship, but against this his curiosity to see the Prince was very great. So he went with him.

The Prince was lodging at the house of Mr. Charles Highmore, Attorney-at-law. This was a white-fronted house on the west side of English Street, standing back some yards from the main thoroughfare.

Roche and Herries passed under an archway, sufficiently wide for a carriage drive. Above the archway was a big bay-window, and the whole house seemed spacious. There were glimpses of a fine garden at the back of it.

At the doorway and in the entrance hall there was a great bustle. A big fire burnt in the hall, officers were standing in groups, messengers coming and going. Leaning over the banisters of the wide staircase Herries saw two small children watching wide-eyed all that was going forward. Roche, begging Herries to seat himself for a moment in the hall, vanished behind a green-baize door.

Herries waited there. He realised that his presence caused very considerable interest. One stout, thick-thighed officer, grandly dressed, warming his back at the fire, stared at him persistently. He was always afterwards, for no reason that he could define, to remember this officer with his swollen cheeks, pug nose, legs tight within their sky-blue silk breeches.

It seemed to him, although this impression may have been unwarranted, that there was some carelessness and disorder over the hall bustle, too much shouting and calling out and casual argument. Only a

giant Highlander, who must have been some seven feet in height and was broad in proportion, stood motionless near the entrance. It was at him that the two children, breathless on the stairs, principally gazed.

It was cold and exceedingly draughty. The fire blew out of the open fireplace in flurries of smoke and flame. Some faded green tapestries of gods and goddesses feasting flapped on the wall. Near the baize door a group of young officers stood in whispered consultation.

He had taken this all in (and for the rest of his life it would remain with him), when he saw Roche come through the door and approach him.

'His Royal Highness,' he said, 'is most anxious to see you.'

He followed Roche through the door (pursued, as he knew, by the curious eyes of everyone in the hall) into a small, darkly wainscoted room. There was a table with a bowl of fruit, a finely carved fireplace and some high-backed chairs. On the mantelpiece was a big gold clock, very handsomely mounted, with the moon and stars portrayed and a Cupid with a small gold hammer to strike the hours.

Only two persons were in the room. One was a plump gentleman with a good-natured kindly face, who stood turned to the window that he might see better some papers held in his hand.

The other was warming himself at the fire. This was a lad in a grave handsome dress of dark purple, wearing his own hair, a diamond star at his breast. This boy's face was of a most delicate oval shape, the chin weak, the mouth rather too full. His splendour (for he did that day seem splendid) lay in his eyes of a deep eloquent brown, bold and haughty, brave and inquiring, and in the magnificent carriage of his beautifully shaped head, the carriage by natural right divine of a king and a ruler of men. His hair was of a fair brown, catching the light so that it seemed gold-tipped.

This was Prince Charles Edward.

But he was a boy, a child, an infant! Herries, in that first glance and then as, bending a knee and kissing the hand, he looked up into those eyes, was transfigured by surprise.

He had known that the Prince was but twenty-five, about the age of his own David; he had himself again and again wondered what it must be for such a boy to be in charge of so wild and tumultuous and kenspeckle an army, but in some imaginative fashion the events of these last weeks had altered his vision. The Prince, seen only through event, had grown and aged in the consequence of his successes. But now, face to face, why, beside David himself who could have taken him across his knee and with one gesture broken him, he was unbelievably a child.

And then, rising from his knee and exchanging with him look for look, Herries had a curious moment of vision.

It is an old tale that a drowning man sees in one instant the whole course of his past experience laid out as on a map. So now Herries, looking into that young man's eyes, had, in one moment of time, a vision of a world.

In Paris carts rumbled over the cobbles under a snowy sky, the French King lolled on his bed, scratching his stomach, yawning, then stretching a fat naked leg to see whether last night's drinking had dulled the use of it. A courier, waiting in the cold hall with despatches, shivered and thought tenderly of his new mistress. At Calais the snow was beginning to fall, and along the deserted beach an old man in rags that blew in the wind wandered, searching for sea-trove. On the Dover Road a coach plunged up the hill, while within it, rolling in sleep one against another, two men and a woman dreamed of money, lechery and food.

The clouds gathered ever more thickly over Europe. In Vienna it was a blizzard, by the Hague the sea was rising and tumbling in huge swollen billows along the deserted shore. In London the Hanoverian King stumbled as he climbed the stairs, swore a German oath, wondered for the hundredth time which among his treasures he must take with him to Hanover if a sudden flight caught him. He had a violent cold and that old pain in the left side that hurt him when his nerves were out of order.

All through London that afternoon panic was spreading. No one had any thought but for himself and his. A man swung from ledge to ledge above a back court of the Strand, his pocket stuffed with rings and necklaces. He dropped eight feet, stumbled and was up, running through the falling snow, like a shadow, down to the river. In a room lit only by the firelight a lover was buttoning his smallclothes, a lady arranging her hair before a mirror. The clouds descended ever lower and lower over London. Out of a window and above the river a lady was leaning, looking out to hear whether even now she could catch the Highlanders coming. On the Great North Road the coaches were running, and two miles before Doncaster three footpads were waiting, their horses shivering in the cold. Such a snowy night was good for the trade.

Up on the fells above Brough and Appleby it was desolate indeed. A shepherd, trying to shield himself from the fierce wind, searched for some lost sheep, calling to his dog, glancing up at the sky as though it had some personal and especial message for him.

In Kendal and Penrith and Keswick, men sheltering by fires, busy over their money-making, had only one topic. The Pretender was in Carlisle. Carlisle had fallen. First Edinburgh and now Carlisle. An old man, dying in a farmhouse by Caldbeck, wandered in his delirium and called for the girl of his heart, now forty years dead. Two women, in a rich house by Grange, quarrelling over cards in their high gilded drawing-room, paused suddenly to listen, because above the fall of the stream under the bridge they seemed to hear the tramp of soldiers. . . .

What did Herries see? What did Herries hear? He only knew that before him was a child, ignorant, im-

petuous, brave and tragic, and that as he breathed, as his hand went to finger the lace at his throat, as he felt for the skirt of his purple coat stiff with whalebone, Europe, carrying on its wheeling surface, as on an indifferent turntable, the hearts, the souls of these little men, wheeled another turn in her history, this boy for a single bitter instant the moving force.

Tragedy! Herries could see it in every stir and flicker of the flame behind him. This boy to rule England, this boy to meet those heavy, cumbrous, cruel forces now advancing to encounter him! He could, in that second of understanding, have taken that boy in his arms, hastened with him to deep obscurity, protected him until the crisis was past.

Then the Prince spoke, and it was a king who was speaking.

'Mr. Herries,' he said, smiling most charmingly, 'you are welcome. Mr. Roche here says you are an old friend of his.'

'Yes, sir. It was pleasant to meet again.'

'And what do you think of the feeling in this city? Is it favourable to us?'

'I am a stranger here, sir. From the little I have seen I would say that feeling is divided. Many are waiting to feel the current of the wind.'

The Prince looked at him. Here was a man. Young though he was, he was no poor judge when his prejudices were not already stirred and his liberty not threatened. Years later, in 1771, when he was sheltering shabbily under the roof of the tailor Didelot, hunting round for a wife, the Irishman Ryan introduced him one drunken evening to a tall lean fellow, with a scarred face, a famous ragamuffin duellist. Lolling, paunchy and red-faced, on the shabby sofa, looking up at the fellow, Charles Edward remembered that other man with a scar. Where had it been? And when? In the close, hot, smelly room, thick with smoke and stinking with drink, his bemused mind went back to that other scene: Carlisle, high burning hopes, courage, pure ambitions, England open before him, and that strange, stern, ugly fellow who carried himself and spoke like a leader. The grease dropping from the slobbering candle was mixed with his own maudlin tears. That day . . . and this. . . .

'Sheridan, this is Mr. Herries of Keswick.'

The stout man turned from the window, smiling. They bowed and shook hands.

'What do you advise, Mr. Herries; that we should go forward or stay where we are?'

The unexpected and casual directness of this startled Herries: he fancied that some lack of caution in it had startled Sir Thomas Sheridan, too, and not for the first time.

His natural honesty, as always, drove him.

'I cannot tell what information Your Highness has obtained. I am sure that time is a most important element in your favour. I am sure, too, that many who are secretly on your side are waiting for your success before they join you. If by pressing forward very rapidly you are likely to reach London within a very brief period of time, I should push forward. If your progress is likely to be slower, then I should remain in the North until more of your friends come out to you.'

'Yes, yes . . .' answered the Prince impatiently. Then it seemed that he caught Sheridan's eye, for he turned abruptly back to the fire, stared into it a moment, then wheeled round to Herries again.

'Of what sort of a place is Keswick, Mr. Herries?' he asked.

'It is a small town, sir, very remote from the world.'

'Your place is in the country?'

'Seven miles from Keswick, in a valley beyond the lake.'

'You have much rain there, I have heard.'

Herries smiled. 'It is a changeable climate, sir. We have every sort of weather.'

The Prince shrugged his shoulders. 'Peste! Every sort of BAD weather. I know the changes; hail one fine day, sleet another, snow a third. You should try the south of France, Mr. Herries. There it is all sunshine and beautiful ladies.'

Herries smiled. 'I have no doubt, sir. But I love this cold North Country. It has something magical for those who feel it.'

The Prince laughed.

'Eh, Sherry? Shall we leave this business we're on and settle down in the mountains to shoot bears and frighten the wolves. Poor Sherry! Mountains and bears are not for your stomach. For myself, I don't know. But, Mr. Herries, you had better come with us. We will lead you into the sunshine.'

Herries paused, then looking the Prince between the eyes he answered: 'I am afraid the public world is no longer for me, sir. I am forty-five years of age and no very good company.'

The Prince looked back at him, honestly and quietly. They liked one another.

'Eh bien! Yours is no doubt the better part. We have little choice in our destinies, I believe. Fate is with us, and then, a change in the wind . . .' He shivered, made as though he would kick the fire with his foot, half turned his face.

'At least you wish me well.'

Herries said: 'I will always wish you well, sir.' He hesitated, then went on: 'I would only say that I love England with a passion. I believe that you have the same love. And, were I younger--' He broke off. 'I hope you will believe, sir, in my sympathy.'

The boy looked at him with some touching appeal in his eyes. There was fear there, some hint of dismay and confusion as though, only now, he were beginning to realise the impossibility of the task that he had at first so gaily shouldered. Herries' heart went out to him, just as it might have gone to David in trouble.

He bent the knee and kissed the hand again, bowed and left the room.

In the street again he said good-bye to Roche, promised to meet him shortly, saw him vanish into the dusk. He did not know that he was never to set eyes on him again.

A little bemused, he stood hesitating. Then, as though he could step no other way, he turned down English Street toward the Cathedral. It was not dark yet: there was a queer, green, owlish light through which snowflakes were falling, fragments of ghostly wool. Very few persons were now about. He crossed into Abbey Street, which was quite deserted. He stood in the shadow by the long wall of Tullie House. It was cold, but he did not feel it. There was no wind.

How absurd! He was watching, like any young moon-calf, outside his mistress' window. There was no light in the demure, thin-lipped house, where she was lodging. He could see the number--Thirty--in clear Roman numerals above the door. There was no stir of life anywhere.

But he knew the strangest satisfaction in standing there. It was as though he were protecting her, although, for all he could tell, she might be in the other end of the town. And there was also a sense that he was expiating a little the frantic temptation that he had known on the wall. That gave him, oddly enough, the only conviction of sin that he had ever known. He had done many evil things in his life and had dealt ironically with them all. But this . . . He had stepped farther then into monstrous countries than ever before. Was it only because this had touched her? Or because he was, in his old age, developing a new sense of sin? Time perhaps that he did. Or was it that sentimentalism, a sentimentalism of the very kind that he had always most despised, was creeping over him? Or was it a sort of frustrated lust? Because he would not yet possess Mirabell he imagined a noble aim in himself? Ah, that last, God forbid! He did not want to possess her--or at least not that mainly--he wanted to care for her, be good to her, make her happy. . . . And then, having used her, would he not tire of her and forget all his nobility, as he had with so many women before her? For the instant the picture of Alice Press came back to him; Alice Press when he had first seen her, when he had first had her, when he had tired of her, hated her, sold her. . . .

He nodded his head to himself. Yes, this was most truly something other, something quite new in him, something growing, like a plant, in his soul. If there were indeed a soul. . . . If there were not, there was at least something in him that was not only animal; his great white horse plunging through the black lake, climbing the splintered hills--she was, for him, of the world of that dream.

The door of the house opened. He was almost opposite it, but the shadow, thickening as the early winter darkness crept upon the city, covered him.

Two came out. They were Mirabell and her lover. He caught her face for a moment under the light by the door, and she seemed in an ecstasy of happiness. She was pressed close to the boy, who had his arm around her. He watched them go, quietly, down the street. He was never afterwards to know what still kept him there.

101

His business was over. She was well protected, and, as his constant irony drove him to perceive, by the only protection that she coveted. She had, he could not doubt, lost all awareness of him. Perhaps, after seeing him, she had told her lover, and together they had laughed at the thought of that ugly, elderly courtier, laughed kindly but with the selfish, indifferent confidence of blissful lovers.

He felt the cold now and drew his cloak close about him. Yes, it was cold and he was alone, and the street was very silent. He was conscious again, as he looked at the light above her door, of a sense of doom that lay over the city and over the Prince whom he had just left and, it might be, over himself. For himself he did not very much care.

But for Mirabell . . . Mirabell . . . Mirabell. . . . An absurd name . . . a man's name. He looked back to that Christmas feast so long ago, the woman standing by the door, the child huddled against her skirt. It had been that woman's romantic notion to call the child Mirabell after some play perhaps. Congreve's Way of the World, was it? or perhaps she had heard the name spoken or seen it on a news-sheet. Mirabell . . . Mirabell. . . . Yes, the mother to whom he had once given his coat must have been a romantic creature, filled, he had no doubt, with unsatisfied longings.

The door opened again. A man came out. It was Thawn.

Herries caught his black face in the light, but there was no mistaking the fellow's walk, that lurch, that slouch, that roll from heavy foot to heavy foot. He walked, too, with his head sunk between his thick shoulders as though he had no neck.

An animal, by God, a wild hairy animal, possessed by the Devil. He paused by the door. He was considering something, and his face was as evil as a face may be and yet be in some sort human.

Then he lurched away, moving, in spite of his awkwardness, with great speed.

There began then a strange pursuit. Herries followed as though he had been ordered to do so. But it was like a pursuit in a dream. They seemed to move in a dead city. Herries could never remember afterwards that he passed a living being. As he moved anxiety grew in him. He had no reason, but with every step his fear increased. Thawn never looked back, nor hesitated. He seemed to know exactly his direction and purpose.

They kept to the dark side-streets, came to the Castle, skirted it and, turning a corner near the city wall, saw the girl and boy but a little in front of them.

Then it was they whom Thawn had been following.

The girl was standing folded by her lover's arms. His back was towards them.

There was a sudden alteration in Thawn's movement. He walked more swiftly, but very silently. His feet made no noise at all.

At that same instant Herries understood.

He ran, crying 'Look out! Look out! . . . Take guard!' But he was too late. The boy turned, but with that same movement Thawn struck, his black arm, the pale chill of the back of his hand, the knife shining. Herries caught these and his thick, pulsing, stertorous breath like a bear's grunt.

The boy fell without a cry, and Thawn was gone, moving like a shadow into the shadows of the dusk.

The girl flung herself down, then stared up at Herries, not seeing who he was.

Herries knelt, pulled the shirt down, felt the heart. The boy was dead. His own hands were a mess of blood.

'He's dead,' he said, touching her hair, which fell, loosened, about his hands.

'You lie,' she answered.

Then he bent his will and purpose to do all that should be done.

END OF PART II

PART III

THE WILD MARRIAGE

CANDLELIGHT RESPECTABILITY

On a beautiful summer afternoon, in the year 1756, David and Deborah rode into Keswick. Deborah was proud because, for the first time, she was riding her new horse, Appleseed, that David had given her. Old fat Benjamin had named him. It seemed to Deborah a very pretty name. She was excited, too, because they were riding in to a Ball and were to sleep three nights at Keswick. Although Deborah was now thirty-three years of age, a very great age indeed, she was still wildly excited by a Ball. She could not think how David could remain so calm.

But David was always calm. As she looked at him now, gigantic (he was six foot six inches in height, and broad with it) but placid, smiling to himself at some notion that was, she was quite sure (she thought to herself), to do with ships or tallow or grain, she loved him more than ever, but was a little indignant with him too. She would have liked to stick a large and sharp pin into the rough broadcloth that covered his immense, immovable back.

It was a Ball at the Assembly Rooms (the first of the season), and they were to stay for three nights with, technically, Uncle Pomfret, in reality, Cousin Raiseley and sister Mary.

In the year 1750 Cousin Raiseley had married sister Mary. Deborah who, in spite of her placidity, had some good strong feelings within her, hated her cousin Raiseley and had always disliked her sister Mary. It was, she had thought at the time, a very suitable match, only she had supposed that Mary would have made a smarter one. Heir to a baronetcy though he was, Raiseley was, after all, with his poor health and country background, no very great catch for anyone. It was true that his social value had risen a little after his sister Judith married the Honourable Ernest Bligh, who might, with good fortune, be one day Lord Monyngham, but Judith, after her marriage, disregarded her family entirely, and never again came near Keswick--no, not even when her mother died.

It was well known, too, that neither Raiseley nor Mary had been a grand success in London. That was why, perhaps, they had married one another, a fellow-feeling making them wondrous kind. So back to Keswick they had come, Raiseley to cheer the remaining years of his poor old father, who could not move for the gout, Mary to rule the household, and so much of Keswick as she could ensnare, most tyrannously.

They did not often invite Deborah to come and see them, and Deborah had determined to refuse when they did, because Mary would not see her father, would not come out to Herries, would not speak to him if she saw him in Keswick.

'If father is not good enough for Mary I am not,' said Deborah, and then sighed because there were so many who would not speak to her father.

But now, on this occasion, her father had insisted that she should go. He had kissed her, looking at her with that queer, ironical smile that still, even after all these years, frightened her so strangely.

'Thou'dst best go, Deb. And maybe there'll be some spoiling of the Egyptians. Anyway, it will help Davy.'

So they had left him, standing in the little grass-grown courtyard with fat Benjamin and Benjamin's thin wife Marjorie (whom he had married out of Newlands some ten years ago), standing there gaunt and shabby, grand and lonely, shading his eyes against the sun, then turning back to the old house with that odd, absorbed, dreaming look as though he had already forgotten them, almost, with that one turn of the heel, putting them out of existence.

They were climbing up out of Grange, and soon the lake came into view. It was an early autumn afternoon of crystal clarity; the lake, Skiddaw, and Saddleback behind it, were as though they were enclosed in a series of mirrors. The lake was a bowl of pale-blue glass, cracked here and there with silver splinters. Over a portion of it shadows of rose amber tumbled with a faint, rippling stillness, as though one were breathing on it to stir it. Lord's Island lay on this silver-blue like a ball of ebony ruffled at its edge by the silhouette of its trees. On the farther side the fields, bright green in the sun, rose to the slopes of Saddleback that was beginning gently to change from amber to purple, and behind the dark line of the hill the sky was almost whitewashed, with a little colour.

So, as the eye travelled upwards, it moved from dark to light, from light to dark, but always with the tranquillity of perfect harmony. The air about them, as they rode, shared this crystal purity with the scene. One pale cloud, blown open into the shape of a great white rose, travelled over their heads.

For Deborah this Lake had grown to have almost a magical splendour. Although Rosthwaite was some miles away, she walked continually to Grange, to Manesty, even to Portinscale, to sit beside it, listen to the trees whispering and the broken ripple of the tiny waves against the stones. Even physically she had some kinship with the Lake. In no way beautiful, rather broad and shapeless of figure, her pale gentle face, her hair faintly gold, her steady honest gaze, her spiritual QUIETNESS belonged to the coves and shallows and wooded shelters of the Lake-side. There was strength and force, too, behind her gentleness, just as the Lake had strength and force. She lived securely and proudly within her borders as the Lake lived.

As they rode she noticed all the trees, mountain-ash, holly, ivy, hawthorn, yew; and they were all transformed for her into a sort of glory. Rocks here and there by the side of the lake glittered in the sun. She thought to herself how passionately moving this world would be were she seeing it for the first time on such a day. She would surely say to herself: 'This must be a very holy place.' But now that she knew it so very well it was not less holy, and in every different mood it seemed to have a different holiness.

David broke the beautiful silence.

'We're coming to a new time, Deb, a modern world; with these new toll-roads our valley will be enclosed no longer.'

'It will be better for riding to Keswick.'

'Aye, there'll be good things doubtless, but it will be sad to see the old world go. I doubt that you will find anything grander in the world than our Statesmen--Peel and Elliot, and Curtis and Ramsay, more self-dependent, more self-sufficing, owing nothing to any man. . . .'

'They have been cruel to father,' she answered fiercely, an odd fierceness to come from her placid countenance.

'Nay, not cruel,' he answered with his customary slowness, as though he thought every word out before he uttered it. 'He's strange to them, and I don't wonder. These last eleven years-- we've talked of it many a time-- he's been like a man lost. Since the Rebellion, when we were in Carlisle, he's been a "fey" man. As though he were searching for something he could never mind. He loves me, I know, but he'll tell me nothing. He's as strong and hearty as he was twenty years gone--more hearty for all the walking he does--but it's of no avail to try to keep him to business. He is happier walking the Fell than any other way, he's happier silent than speaking, happier alone than with company. There was something in Carlisle, all those years ago. . . .' He broke off, then turned on his horse towards her, speaking more rapidly: 'I've never told you, Deb. I've never told any man. There was a night in Carlisle--after the Prince made his entry--I was climbing into my bed: I had gone an instant to the window to see whether the snow was

falling. I heard the door open and turned. Our father was in the doorway, white as a cleaned stone. He stumbled and held by the bed-post. I thought he would fall and ran to catch him. He held by my shoulder. His nails dug into the flesh. I asked him what it was, whether he were sick. He nodded his head and looked as though he did not see me. He put his hand flat on my naked heart.

'"Aye, sick," he answered me, "and unhappy, Davy." Then he went out. I did not dare to follow him. I waited, listening for a sound. There was none. In the morning he was as he has been since-- closed, lost and alone. They are right to fear him, Peel, Curtis, and the rest. He's a man lost.'

Deborah answered at last:

'He was never as we were, never like any other. But I love him now as I never did. I always feared him. Now I would be proud to comfort him, would he let me.'

'Aye, but he will not let you--nor anyone.'

They rode on silently for a time. Then David spoke again.

'I have a hard evening, Deb,' he said. 'I've to tell Christina that I'll not be marrying her.'

'Oh!' cried Deborah. 'I'm glad!'

'Yes.' He nodded his head. 'You never liked it, Deb. I fancy you will never care for me to marry. But it must be one day. I must have children. But it'll not be Christina who'll be their mother.'

'What's decided you?' she asked him.

'I do not love her. I have never loved her. I thought she'd be grand for a wife, in all the outward things, you understand. Mellways would be a fine house and there's broad land with it. She's kind, but wearisome. Her voice has a fearful monotony. And she doesn't love me herself. It's her dogs and her horses that have her real fancy. She's been thinking I'd be good for looking after the horses.' He chuckled in his slow, drawling way. 'And her eyes are not even,' he added.

'I'm glad, I'm glad.' Deborah almost sang it. 'I knew that you were not lovers and that she would contemn Herries and would take you away and would think me a dolt. Aye, she does that already.'

David sighed. 'But it will be uneasy telling her. I'm not grand at speeches. Love's a strange thing, Deb. You go to your bed thinking that you love a girl and you wake in the morning to know her eyes are crooked. . . .' He hesitated, then went on: 'I should be marrying. I was six-and-thirty last Martinmas, and I've money enough now. But it's the children rather than the woman I dream of.'

Deborah answered: 'You're in luck, Davy, because you're a man. I'm younger, and yet I'm now an old maid. I could have loved a man, but no man has ever fancied me.'

'To-night, maybe,' said David. 'Don't lose heart, Deb.' But he didn't say it with great conviction. It was true. Deborah had always been an old maid and would always be one. Not like her sister Mary, who had made eyes at men since she was a baby.

As they rode through Portinscale village over the stream by old Crosthwaite Church into Keswick (the shadow of Skiddaw, russet and silver-grey, sprawling above them), he fell into thought.

He had very much to think of. He was a boy no longer, a man of thirty-six. Things were approaching a crisis, and he must come to some man's decision. He could see, looking back over the last ten years, that he had been almost incredibly influenced in his actions by his father's; incredibly because his father had neither by word nor action tried to influence him, had told him indeed, again and again, that he must break away, make his own life now, leave him and even forget him.

His affairs had developed beyond all reasonable expectation during those years. The little enterprise in Liverpool that had started with a share in two small trading vessels had grown until he had his finger now in half a dozen Liverpool ventures. He had bought land in Borrowdale, beyond Keswick towards Troutbeck and at the farther end of Bassenthwaite towards Cockermouth. It was not that he had a brilliant head for commerce, but he was notably honest and upright, very sure if also slow, kindly and agreeable to deal with. He had, too, a wider and deeper sense of the social changes that were moving under his feet than had most of the men around him. He perceived that these years that followed the '45 Rebellion were opening up the North. He could not perceive that he was now living at the commencement of England's great new industrial life, but he understood something of the new inventions and sniffed more in the air. It would be fifty years yet before the world that he foresaw was in true being, but, in his own small individual way, he was part of it.

But, with this new and exciting world of affairs, his father would have no touch; nay, would not, could not. He had been willing, almost eager at first, to help in the little Keswick office that David had now for his own behind the Assembly Rooms toward the Kendal road. He had a brain far abler and more brilliant than David's, but it would not stick into these items of lading and shipping and transport. He did not care: he could not bother with it.

So, after a while, he slipped back to Herries, and David was glad that he went, for not only did he confuse any issue that he touched, but his own unpopularity with the outside world hampered the business at every step. It was not only the old evil reputation that he already had, but the new evil reputation that he was for ever creating. He no longer kissed the women and gambled and drank with the men. It had been better maybe if he had. He held aloof from all social contact; when he met a man he looked at him with his cold ironic eyes and as often as not turned on his heel without a word, and this, as David knew, not from scorn, arrogance or pride—these fires had remarkably died in him—but rather that his mind was altogether elsewhere,

searching for something, dreaming of something, regretting, hoping—at least in no mood for Liverpool trade.

So back to Herries he went. Here, too, he was odd, almost to madness. He would have no stranger in to improve the house. He or Benjamin or David might support a tottering wall, mend a gaping stair, fill in a window—no strangers. Nor would he permit David to buy more land to go with the house. There was at one time a fair lot available that would have made Herries a fine property, but Francis would have none of it. He dug still in his one or two barren fields as he had always done, planted what would not grow, dug to sterility, and was quiescent. This and his rovings gave him a kind of restless contentment. With every year he roved farther—looking for what? for whom? On horse or on foot he had covered all the country from Shap to Gosforth, from Uldale to Stanley Gill. Every stream and every hill he knew. Here, in this soil and rocky fell, lay his passionate devotion. One of two; the other unsatisfied.

To David and Deborah his manner remained always the same, jestingly ironic, scornfully loquacious, lovingly friendly of a sudden, then for a day, two days, a week utterly silent, while his eyes roved, his ears were acock listening for a step. It was keeping company with a haunted man.

But where in this lay his influence? David could not say, except that quite simply he loved him. He loved him, it seemed, more with every year and understood him less. As Deborah had once said, where she and David left off, their father began. He was in country that they had never so much as seen a map of.

But things were reaching a crisis. David hated Herries. He had perhaps always at heart hated it since, the first of that family, he had crossed its threshold and seen those chill suits of armour receive him. He hated the house for its darkness, gloom, damp, moth-eaten, grudging spirit. He hated it because of the things that had happened there—the long-ago evil of Alice Press, his mother's death, old Mrs. Wilson the witch, and all the superstition and avoidance that had grown up around his father there. He wanted to leave it to die its own death. He was convinced that if he could take his father away from there his father would become another man. This odd wearisome passion his father had for finding something that would put everything right and fair would die in another, healthier atmosphere. David loathed everything that was dark and damp, morbid and introspective, superstitious and nightmare-ish. These things, he thought, did not properly belong to his father, but had been bred in him by the place.

At his engagement to Christina Paull he had expected a settlement. They would live near by Penrith, and his father would live with them. But Christina had plainly denied that, and so had his father. His father had loathed Christina, calling her a 'tight-nostrilled bitch,' but had in no way persuaded David against the marriage.

'A mare like that,' he had said, 'cannot step in between our lives together, not though you live in China.'

And David had found that true. Without saying a word, his father had in some way shown him how truly impossible Christina would be.

David had been greatly relieved to see the impossibility; but yet, did it mean that he was never to escape his father, never have his own life, nor children, nor freedom? Why did he love his father so fiercely, when he did not at all understand him and often was infuriated by him? There was some bone in him that was his father's bone. That was the only answer.

As they rode into Keswick he shook his head with a kind of despair, and Deborah, who had been riding quietly on Appleseed beside him, looked up as though she expected him to speak. But he said nothing, only sighed very deeply.

And so they came to old Uncle Pomfret's house.

Externally it had not changed very much in the last twenty-five years. When David, as a small boy, had first seen it on that memorable occasion of his visit with his mother, it had seemed a palace of a shining and a glittering splendour. Now it was a small place. The trees had grown in the garden, the fountain, once of so incredible a beauty, was now diminished and stained with rain: sic transit gloria!

But within Mary had made everything as fine and modern as Raiseley's stingy habits would allow her. She had two footmen, and in the saloon (which appeared now to David amazingly small) a beautiful Bury four-backed settee and some exceedingly handsome Chippendale chairs with cabriole legs.

Although, as David very well knew, she cared nothing at all for literature, she had Sir Charles Grandison, Thomson's epic poem, Liberty, and Glover's tragedy, Boadicea, prominently displayed on her table.

He regarded his sister critically: never having liked her, he had not denied her opulent beauty. She was yet beautiful, but was too thin and haggard, and her eyes and mouth wore a discontented and peevish expression. The Herries, because of their prominent horse- like bones, were not advantaged by thinness. Her cheeks were strongly painted, and her wig very high and decorated with pompoms.

She greeted her brother and sister with the condescension she always used, but, David thought, with a certain anxiety, as though she would, if she knew how, win them to her side. At their entrance the two infants, the boy Pomfret, aged five, and Cynthia, aged two, were in course of display to their reluctant relatives. They were plain children, the girl clear Herries, thin, pale and bony, the boy plump, with the features of his grandfather. They howled lustily, and had to be removed by their fat kindly Aunt Anabel, whose complacency seemed armoured against any vexation.

The little parlour was hot and over-filled with Herries. Grandison, his wife Mary, and Cousin Pelham were there; Uncle Harcourt, now sixty-eight years of age, frail

and delicate like a piece of china; and Dorothy Forster, stiff in creaking black, as gloomy and funereal as ever.

Pelham was the grand one of the party. He was now thirty-eight years of age, still a bachelor, very elegant indeed, and kindly with it. He seemed to Deborah's country eyes the handsomest man she had ever seen, with his slim body, suit of black and silver; he was Herries at its most elegant. All the Herries breeding seemed to have concentrated in his repose of bearing, humorous knowledge of the world, languor, superior indifference. Deborah could not but wonder what it was that had brought him to so rustic a ball in so small a country place.

It was his mother who had brought him, he having gone to her, as on many another occasion, to see whether she had a plan that would relieve him of some of the more tiresome of his debts. These were the only occasions when he did go to her, her maternal solicitude and anxious care of him boring him exceedingly. But he was always courteous to her when he WAS with her, making up in manner what he omitted by his constant absence.

This time she had the excellent notion that Uncle Harcourt might be of use. Here was a source untapped, and, if Herries gossip were to be trusted, a rich source too. It stood to reason that a bachelor, living alone in a world-away seclusion like Ravenglass, with no one but himself to consider, must have a fair sum of money put by. Moreover, little Uncle Harcourt was sixty-eight, and, as things were, could not be expected to live for ever. . . . So Pelham had already suggested to his little uncle that he should come and stay for a while at Ravenglass, and the charm of his manner had been no whit abated by the obvious reluctance of his uncle (who was not born yesterday) to have him.

Mary Herries, stout, overbearing and ill-mannered, had tried to subdue her personality to the desperate needs of her son, and had wooed Harcourt like any sucking-dove. This had been no easy task for her, and the entry of the large handsome David, who was, she knew, Harcourt's favourite nephew, did not please her at all. She gave David the barest of greetings, and poor Deborah no greeting whatever.

Deborah indeed found her ultimate comfort with poor old Uncle Pomfret alone in his room, trophies of the chase mouldering about him, and his leg (already huge enough) swollen to twice its natural size and laid out on a chair in front of him.

Poor Uncle Pomfret, rotten now with gout, and deserted in his own house, seventy-eight years of age, and no one caring whether he lived or died! Gone were all his blustering, hunting years; gone his oaths, his country pastimes, his childish prides, his simple pleasures!

When his wife Jannice had died, he had thought, poor fool, that it was not a bad thing. She had worn him to an irritable thread with her medicines, tempers and dominance. Now, on how many a lonely afternoon he would wish her back again! His gout would have been for her the very thing that she wanted! Would she not have loved to posset him and bleed him and cosset him! Might they not have found in their mutually sick old age a mutual love and comfort?

It was true that his daughter Anabel did for him what she could, but it was Anabel's mania these days to be, of all things incongruous with her stout form and rosy cheeks, a blue-stocking.

She had corresponded with Mrs. Delany and sent a long screed to Lady Mary Montagu on the smallpox, and, on a visit to London, she had attended a meeting in Mrs. Elizabeth Montagu's famous Chinese drawing-room in Hill Street. Nothing would hold her after her return, and although she was kind to her old father when she thought of him, she forgot him for most of the time.

So there poor Uncle Pomfret was, and tears poured down his cheeks as Deborah sat beside him, stroked his puffed and swollen hands and settled his pillows. Huskily he asked her how her father did, and could not hear enough of what she had to tell him.

'Brother Francis! Brother Francis! He was closer to me than any of them. But I was afraid of your aunt, my dear. . . . And Francis didn't want me, didn't want any of us. . . . I mind when I went to see your poor mother afore she died--poor soul! Sitting up in bed for manners' sake when she was almost gone. Francis felt her going, although he was always too clever for her. . . . Here, bend thy head a moment, little darling, and I'll whisper thee something.'

Deborah bent her head and felt his hot liquorish breath and the odd touch of his burning hand against her fresh cheek.

'When thou hast a man, don't take one too clever like thy father, for he'll dream without thee; nor stupid like thy old uncle, for he'll not dream at all. Do thou the dreaming, and he'll never leave thee.' He thought this mighty clever and lay there chuckling until the chuckle brought on the gout, and his pain was a torment to see.

On the third night was the Ball.

They did not go until nearly eleven o'clock, because they were the gentry and it was not genteel to go too early.

The Assembly Room was a small room, even by Carlisle or Kendal standards, but to Deborah it seemed like Paradise indeed.

She would have clapped her hands, had she dared, at the shining candles, the little gallery with its gilded scroll where the musicians were, the alcoves where the food was--jellies, syllabubs, cakes, orgeat, lemonade, fruits and the rest--the gleaming floor, the hangings of red and blue, the rows of benches down the side all covered with persons in the most beautiful dresses.

It was the second ball only of her life, although she was thirty-three, and by contemporary standards an old

maid. But she did not look thirty-three that night in the new dress that David had bought for her in Liverpool. This dress was not grand, with its modest hoop and gentle frills and fichus, but its rose colour went prettily with the freshness of her cheeks and bosom. Her figure was too large and full, but this to-night gave her strength and honesty, and she had always masked gracefully, like the well-born lady that she was.

At first she could see little, because of her terror of the enormous Mary Herries at whose side she seemed remorselessly attached. Mary Herries and Grandison were almost the largest persons in the room, and looked double their natural size because of their magnificent clothes. Mary Herries' hoop was as wide as the globe, and her wig, in which nestled birds, flowers and fruit of the gayest colours, towered to heaven.

Grandison in crimson and silver, as stout as he was tall, as superb in his own estimation as he was stout, was thought by some of the yokels peering in through the door to be the King of England. Well, they were Herries from London, and so must show these country bump-kins!

In a brief while, happily, they forgot Deborah, and she was able to sit on a bench and look at the world.

The townspeople were dancing country dances; the minuets would come later.

Deborah, who had a sharp Herries eye, saw many things: how the townspeople grew demure with the appearance of the gentry, and plainly less happy; how little Mr. Gibbon of the china shop (whom she knew well and liked greatly) was already drunken, and his wife in an agony of alarm; how charming Pelham was, moving about so gracefully, speaking to everyone with such kindness; how greedy and sulky Raiseley was, going to one of the alcoves by himself and helping himself to syllabub; how grand Mary thought herself, moving about among the townspeople as though she owned all of them, but always with that unhappy, discontented look in her eyes; how speedily David had caught a glimpse of Christina Paull and moved hurriedly in another direction (and what a darling, and how handsome and how superior to everyone else in the room!); and what fun the country dances were (her feet were moving to the gay tinkling little tune!), and how she did hope that someone presently would invite her to dance; and what fun balls were, and why had she not been to more of them; and how the girls clustered together and giggled and made eyes at the men (and how odd it was that she had not a girl friend in the world, nor had ever had one), and--

At this moment she was aware that someone was sitting very close to her, and this someone a man. She turned round and saw, next to her on the bench, a short, sturdy little clergyman with a chubby face.

He must, she thought, be someone's private chaplain, perhaps from the Castle at Cockermouth or one of the grand country houses. He looked a gentleman (she stole several very careful glances). Many of the clergymen known to her had been little better than the peas-antry, living a life of the utmost poverty and treated accordingly. Most of the grander clergymen she had heard of never went near their parishes, and visited Bath or Harrogate.

This clergyman--his hair was tinged with grey--looked healthy, strong and a gentleman. She thought him very pleasant. And apparently he thought her so, for presently he shifted his broad shoulders and turned to her, smiling most charmingly. He apologised for not allowing her room and stood up that she might have more. She, blushing, begged that he should sit down again. But he looked very well standing there on sturdy legs, his face a fresh colour, his eyes (as she was ashamed to notice) very large and fine.

'Pray, sir, be seated,' she said, smiling in her turn.

'I fear I incommode you.'

'Why, no, sir, there is room.'

He sat down again.

'The music is excellent,' he remarked.

'For a little place, I agree,' Deborah replied, feeling a proper woman of the world.

Very soon they were talking. He told her that he was but newly come to the neighbourhood, being in charge of a Cockermouth parish. He told her that he had been chaplain to Lord and Lady Padmont in Rut-landshire, and very kind patrons they had been. She discovered, too, that he was greatly interested in Nature and especially in birds, and this was a great link between them, because she was interested in Nature too.

Then he asked her whether she would not care for a little refreshment, and they walked together to the alcove. She did not know whether she were not exceed-ing proper modesty in this, but after all she was thirty-three and he was a clergyman.

Then, over a syllabub, he introduced himself. His name was Gordon Sunwood, the Sunwoods of Glouces-tershire. He was, he told her, thirty-eight years of age and (blushing at the confession) a bachelor.

He then added, touching (quite accidentally) the back of her hand with his, that he was a bachelor be-cause he had not until now seen anyone who combined the qualities of a saintly spirit, a beautiful person and a merry heart. He wasn't sure, he added, whether the last were not the most important of the three. He did enjoy a joke, and had found nothing in Holy Scripture to con-demn such a taste. But there: of course, were he ever so fortunate as to discover the Fair Divinity with the triple merit, it was unlikely that she, on her side, would be ready to share his modest Parsonage and slender sti-pend. But to THAT must add (this he almost whispered, sinking his voice to an incredible roguish-ness) a certain little fortune of his own, left him by a friendly aunt, so that things were not so bad, and in case of offspring . . .

But, at this point, Deborah could only decide that he had been drinking a little. And yet, even though he had, she could not but think him charming. It was true that clergymen were little higher in the social scale than

hostlers or dairymen, but Deborah was no snob and, considering that she lived in a tumbledown manor with a father ostracised by all the country-side, she had no reason to be. In any case she did not care. She liked this little man with the round bullet head and cheeks like a russet apple and thick sturdy back and warm voice and clear twinkling eyes. Nay, although she had spoken with him but ten minutes, she more than liked him already. And this was her first adventure with a man in all her thirty-three years!

David meanwhile was having an experience less agreeable than that of his sister. He noticed neither the shimmering candles nor the fiddle, fife and drum, nor the orgeat and syllabub. He had eyes only for Miss Christina Paull, and they were not, alas, eyes of love.

He wondered as, fixed into a little corner with this lady, he glanced at her, how he could ever have con-templated matrimony with her. And as with many a man before and after him, behind the immediate misery of his horrid task was a glimpse of the glories of later freedom.

Miss Paull made things more easy for him by, most rashly, laying down some laws for their future comfort. She was a very determined young woman, Amazonian in build and colour, smelling freshly and quite pleasantly of the stables and spreading her legs apart as though she were always, in her imagination, astride a horse.

What she wanted to say was that she was very sorry indeed, but that after their marriage David must leave his father behind him. She had heard rumours that he intended to move his father along with him.

David saw his advantage. Like many another who contemplates diplomatically a quarrel, he snatched at any trivial excuse for one.

'My father is not to be moved thus lightly,' he said. 'If he cares to come with me, he will come.'

Christina, with that kindly good-humoured patron-age that she applied to all human beings (regretting that for their own advantage they were not horses or dogs), explained patiently that she meant no criticism of his father; she had no doubt but that he was an excellent man. Nevertheless he was not a comfortable man, not an easy man, not an ordinary man. Married persons were better without relatives in their house.

That was undeniable. David did not contradict it, but, shifting his huge body on the little gilded chair until it creaked again, he remarked that perhaps, maybe, after all it were possible. . . . The words choked in his throat.

But Christina Paull knew well enough what it was that he intended to say. She was not at all sure but that he was right. She was as independent as any of her feminine descendants two hundred years later were likely to be. Her only relation was her old father, who was drinking with the stable-boys most of the day and drunk with the neighbouring Squire all the night. Nev-ertheless she had, since her plighting with David, heard so much of his own scandalous father that she was already half shrinking from her bargain.

She was no very sensual female; men would never mean very much to her, but David had caught her with his strength, health, amazing bodily vigour. But when she had bedded with him a month or two and the novelty of it was worn a little, what then?--there would be the father, the strange family history, witches and adulteries and general vagabondage. . . . She was not so sure.

But David was quite sure. His mind was suddenly clear, his courage certain and undaunted.

He smiled at her charmingly, as though he were offering her a kingdom, and said:

'We'll not be marrying, Christina.'

She took his statement as clearly as he gave it.

'It is, perhaps, wiser.' She looked at him, and liked him better than she had ever done before.

'I think,' she said, 'I'm not a marrying female.'

In his relief David would have offered her the gold of the Indies had his hands contained the treasure.

He nodded his head. 'I also. Marriage is a hampering state.'

She laughed, then bent towards him, tapping his shoulder with her fan, like a horse in skittish mood. It was a frank age. 'There is nothing against going to bed with you, David, on a dark night,' she said.

David crimsoned to his fair hair.

'I doubt that you'd like it,' he said. 'I'm a heavy sleeper.'

So they parted most excellent friends; and, a year later, Christina married Sir Roger Bollinger, who knew more about horses, cock- fighting and the breeding of spaniels than anyone in the north of England. She had nine children, and behaved to them as a bitch does to her puppies, caring for them when they were young and tender, but, when they grew, forgetting them entirely in the odours of the stable and the ardours of the chase.

And David--but that is another story.

The minuet was over. David, watching its last delicate graces, was amazed to see that his Deborah had for her partner a little stout parson, who, strutting, preening, flaunting, bowing, was like a cock before its mate.

The dance concluded, the little parson bowed and retired, after showing Deborah to a seat. There David found her. She was flushed, her bosom heaved, her eyes shone; she was prettier than he had ever seen her. He seated himself beside her.

'Why, Deb,' he said, 'what's this? A clergyman?'

She seemed scarcely to hear him, then turned to him and answered: 'He is the Reverend Gordon Sunwood. He is of a Gloucestershire family. He has now a living in Cockermouth. He has been very attentive, David.'

David took her hand between his. 'Dear Deb. . . . And is he already a suitor?'

She took her hand away. 'That is unkind. He has only talked with me a little. He is interested in Nature, and has a remarkable knowledge of birds.'

David chuckled. 'Beware, then, of his birdnesting.' Then, boyishly happy over his freedom, he went on: 'It is done, Deb. The task is over. She is of the same mind. As I am no horse nor a rare-bred dog, she is to be yet a maid. And we are good friends over it.'

Deborah almost danced on her bench.

'Oh, Davy, I'm so glad. 'Twould never have done. She'd have made you sleep in a kennel and given you a fine bridle. Oh, Davy, I am so happy! I was never so happy before nor saw anything so beautiful as this is! Are not the lights fine?--and although I had not danced since Christmas, Mr. Sunwood found me "exquisite." That is what he said! I--exquisite! But to watch the world and its follies; I swear I could sit here the night through!'

'Yes,' said David, smiling at her, 'with the birdfancier at your side.' As he looked at her, a tender compassion over her happiness pervaded him. She who had for so many years, without grumble or complaint, borne the closed-in, stifling, melancholy life of Herries, making no friends, having no gaiety, fighting her fears and loneliness and depression without a word to anyone, there was courage and character there! And to be so deeply pleased with this little country scene and amateur gaiety! Shame on himself and his father that they could have suffered it so long!

He could have kissed her there where she sat before them all, but they were interrupted by the portentous figure of Aunt Mary Herries, who hung over them like a battleship and finally demanded his company.

But Deborah was not to be alone for long. Of all amazing things, the elegant and wonderful Pelham had sought her out and was sitting at her side.

She would have been afraid of him had she been less happy. As it was, he caught her happiness and her freshness, and to his stale thoughts, plain though in truth he thought his country cousin, there was charm and pleasure here. His heart was good, though his morality was worn.

He was at his most delightful. Timidly she asked about London and the grand world. Gaily he told her tales and anecdotes and adventures, all of a decorous kind. He told her how a friend of his, Mr. Spencer, had married Miss Pointy, and come up to town in three coaches-and-six with a company of two hundred horsemen.

He gave her dreadful details of the Lisbon Earthquake. He described to her the London fashions: how gowns were pinned rather closer than before, hoops as flat as though made of pasteboard and as stiff, the shape sloping from the hips and spreading at the bottom, enormous but not so ugly as the square hoops. Heads now very variously adorned, pompoms with some accompaniment of feathers, ribbons or flowers; lappets in all sorts of sizes; long hoods worn close under the chin, the strings go round the neck and tie with bows and ends behind. Night-gowns worn without hoops. He was as gay and attentive as though she were the only lady in the world. It was true that he did not ask her to dance, but perhaps he was wearied of dancing.

Before he left her, very earnestly looking her in the eyes, he said: 'Dear Cousin Deborah, pray for me on occasion. I wish all the world well, save myself. I have the taste to be a monk, but, alas, not the character. I am going to the devil as fast as may be, but have dreams of another world.'

As he said this, he had, she thought, a strange look of her father, something ironical, regretting and doomed. She felt very, very tender towards him. But when he was gone, the most charming and distinguished person in the room, her eyes were looking, her heart was beating for her little clergyman. She could not help herself. She did not know whether it were right or wrong. She did not care.

And he returned to her. He bent towards her, sinking his voice to the most delicious of confidential whispers. He told her that he had been thinking only of the moment when he might come to her. He offered her his arm. They walked the length of the room together. He complained of the heat. She acquiesced. They passed behind the hanging curtains, pushed a door, and they were in a little yard at the back of the Assembly Rooms, under a sky sheeted with stars, a faint breeze whispering at their ear.

'You will take cold.'

He put his arm about her. She leaned against him, and could feel his heart beat against her arm.

He asked whether he might write; she murmured 'Yes'. And he bent his head and kissed her, the first kiss from a lover that she had ever received.

So the evening had gone well for Deborah.

THE WILD MARRIAGE

They rode off next morning in the pouring rain. This rain was the especial and peculiar property of the district, rain that must often fall behind any chronicle of human lives here.

It was rain of a relentless, determined, soaking, penetrating kind. No other rain anywhere, at least in the British Isles (which have a prerogative of many sorts of rain), falls with so determined a fanatical obstinacy as does this rain. It is not that the sky in any deliberate mood decides to empty itself. It is rain that has but little connection either with earth or with sky, but rather has a life of its own, stern, remorseless and kindly. It falls in sheets of steely straightness, and through it is the rhythm of the beating hammer. It is made up of opposites, impersonal and yet greatly personal, strong and

gentle, ironical and understanding. The one thing that it is not is sentimental.

The newcomer is greatly alarmed by it, and says: 'Oh, Lord! Lord! how can I live under this!'; the citizen of five years' habitation is deprecating to strangers but proud in his heart; the true native swears there is no rain like it in the world and will change it for none other.

Any true chronicler of the Herries family will be forced, frequently, to speak of this rain.

David and Deborah, their horses, Absalom and Appleseed, passed through it as though it were their only wear. The whole country was blotted out by it, the lake quite invisible, the hills smothered in quilted cloud. The path, that could not yet be dignified by the name of road, was in a condition of indescribable mire and ruin. It needed a very little to make it difficult; tomorrow it would be impassable. But the horses plunged and waded their way through, while the trees bent to the deluge and the hammer beat, beat, beat in the clouded barriers of the mist.

David and Deborah were very happy, riding home. They said very little to one another, because it was difficult to talk through the rain and because each had important thoughts to investigate and arrange.

David was happy because he liked (as all true Herries like) his meeting with the other Herries. He had felt a warm companionship with his poor old Uncle Pomfret, with Uncle Grandison, with dear little Uncle Harcourt and especially with Cousin Pelham. With all of them, different as they were, there had been a blood tie which he had recognised and they also.

Pelham had shown especial friendship and had invited him to London. David thought that he would go. It would be good for his business; he felt, too, a sympathy with this world of brocade, silver candlesticks, soft voices, delicately nurtured women. He had been a savage too long. He knew now that he was not much longer for Herries. He was happy, too, because he had escaped from Christina Paull, and escaped so politely, with neither harsh words nor hurt feelings.

And Deborah? Deborah swam through the rain in a streaming and glorious splendour. Her happiness was so great that she was truly and magnificently born again. The kiss of last evening had transformed her. She rode, her head up, her eyes alight, her mouth curved in a retrospective smile. She did not doubt but that she would marry him. He had not asked her, but he would. He was honest and good. A clergyman? Well, but she was very suited to be a clergyman's wife and the mother of a clergyman's children. At the thought of the children her heart hammered with joy to answer the hammer of the rain. How good, how generous, how well-wishing life was!

So they rode, and it was not until they were feeling their way cautiously through the mud below the Bowder Stone that Deborah was suddenly uneasy. What distressed her? She could not say. She was very sensitive to these mysterious, unreasoning impressions, and especially in this valley, which had always seemed to her to have a peculiar, magical quality of its own. She told herself at first that it was her thought of Mrs. Wilson and her horrible death that still, after all these years, lingered with her. She always hated Cumma Catta Wood, with its pagan sacrifices and scent of murder. But soon, as they turned down the lane that led to Rosthwaite, she knew that it was not that.

She was increasingly apprehensive. It might be her dislike of Herries; especially it seemed to her dreary and forbidding after the social brightness of last evening. But it was not Herries alone. On the little mound that rose above the shaggy path that led to the house her father was standing. They could see him, waiting there in the rain, his cape over his head, leaning on his stick.

David said: 'Father is waiting for us. Something has occurred.'

And Deborah, as so often she had felt before at the thought of her father, knew a sickening apprehension of dismay. Some evil thing had come.

Then when she was face to face with him she knew that he was radiantly, wildly happy. She had never seen this light in his face before. It transformed him, even as she herself had been transformed last evening. At the sight of his happiness she, too, was happy again. Her apprehension left her, and when he held her and kissed her wet cheek she stayed with him, letting his arm encircle her.

He was happy and he was shy too. They had dismounted from their horses, but he kept them there. 'Wait!' he said. 'Before you go to the house. . . .' He seemed like a boy, in spite of his grey hair, long about his neck, and his figure, bent a little from his persistent labours.

'There is someone . . . I must tell you . . .' He stammered a little. He put his arms about both of them, drawing them to him, and the rain fell all round them in walls of silver steel.

'There is a lady here in the house; this very day I am to marry her. Davy, Deb, be kind to her. She is strange here. . . . Please me in this.' His voice was triumphant, as though he wanted all the world to hear his news.

They were bewildered; intent upon their own affairs, this sudden transition was amazing, paralysing. Marriage? Their father? Now? At once? At Herries? But whom? Was this some sudden freak, mad gesture, crazy eccentricity?

'Marriage, father? To-day? Here?' David was stammering in his turn.

'Yes--to-day. Here.' His father mocked him, pressing him closer to his side. 'I was in to Keswick yesterday. I have been bustling; have been with the surrogate, and have the licence. And this afternoon there will be the clergyman. Don't be angry with me, Davy, for not telling you. For eleven years now I have served my 'prenticeship, and she has come to me of her own free will. These last months it has gone hard with her. Be gentle with her.'

David was silent. What was he to say? Who was this woman? Another Alice Press? But behind his almost breathless astonishment was the thought that this new move would, whatever else it involved, help him to his own freedom. But then, as they neared the house-door, his love for his father overwhelmed every other emotion.

It might be that this would be some woman who would be good to him, care for him, devote herself to his comfort.

He turned at the house-door and put his hand on his father's arm. 'If this is for your happiness, father,' he said, 'Heaven bless her, whoever she may be.'

He had in his mind (thinking still, possibly, of Alice Press) the image of some large opulent woman who had caught his father's fancy. He mounted the stairs and turned into the dining-hall, which was, even now in this morning hour, brilliantly lit by a high cluster of candles on the broad table and a great fire in the open fireplace. Under all this splendour the tapestries, the portrait of old Herries leapt in the air, and the room was alive with the drumming of the rain on the panes.

A girl in some dress of flaming orange and crimson, seated on a low stool, was crouching towards the fire, her head in her hands.

As they all came in she turned round facing them, and then, seeing them, jumped to her feet as though to defend herself.

The three stood for a moment motionless by the stair-head while the girl confronted them. She made indeed an astonishing picture. For David she would always be the figure of that first moment. But it was not for him the first moment. He recognised her at once as the 'robber-girl' (so he used to call her) whom, in the old long-ago days, he had met up and down the roads, begging of him, mocking him once and again, always--to his Herries sense of order and decency-- the outlaw and vagabond.

But indeed she had changed since then. That had been a child: this was a woman. She was of a bitter thinness, tall, and her small white face like a mask set with fierce hostile eyes. Her wonder, then as now, was her hair, which fell in ringlets about her shoulders and in the firelight was, with that glow, its own lambent flame. Her dress was fantastically over-coloured: a bodice of bright orange with silver buttons, a hooped skirt of the old-fashioned shape a burning crimson, and faded yellow shoes. She was, in her small peaked face, like an angry child, but her body was mature and her hands, long, thin and very white against her dress, those of a grown woman.

Francis Herries went across to her. 'Mirabell,' he said (and David wondered at the gentleness of his voice), 'this is my son, David, and this my daughter, Deborah. They will be loyal to you and devoted as they have been always to their father.'

David went over to her and took her chill, lifeless hand.

111

'We are old friends,' he said smiling, 'so it is not hard to be new friends too. I hope you will be happy with us.'

She did not answer, but looked at him with her fierce, protesting eyes.

Deborah went and kissed her on the forehead. 'Indeed I hope so,' she said.

The girl, at the touch of Deborah's lips on her forehead, trembled, but still said nothing.

Herries said to his son: 'Come away, Davy. I have business with you.' He smiled back at the two girls. 'We will return, but you will be better friends without us.'

He clattered down the stairs, David following him.

Deborah, left alone with this strange hostile creature, had an impulse to turn and flee. A sort of terror seized her, as was often the way with her; but her own deep happiness, which nothing here could touch, reassured her, and there was something in that white, small face and the wide, staring eyes that moved her heart. That her father was to marry this wild girl seemed to her an incredible thing; but everything about her father was incredible to her, and had always been.

She came close to her.

'I did not hear your name,' she said. 'Mine is Deborah.'

'Mirabell.'

'Mirabell! What a pretty name!'

'No, it is a crazy name. My mother had it from a play. It is a man's name.'

Deborah did not know what to say, what question to ask, but the girl broke in fiercely:

'You may hate me as much as you will. It matters nothing.'

'But why should I hate you?' Deborah asked.

'To be here, in your house, a stranger. It is not my will. I have no will any more. I came to your father yesterday because I was hungry. Once, many years ago, he told me to come. If I had had food I would not have come. They put me in prison in Kendal for a wanton. I was three months in their filthy jail. And then for two weeks I have been hungry. Your father has been good to me; therefore because he wishes to marry me I will marry him, and then, when he is weary of me, I will go away again.'

She spoke in a kind of fierce defence of herself, her eyes never still, roaming about the room like those of a captured animal.

Deborah was touched to pity. She put her arm round the girl and drew her down to the settle by the fire.

'Oh . . . in prison! How cruel! And hungry for two weeks!' She caught her cold hand and held it to her.

'Cruel? No. Why? I may have robbed or lain with men, asking them in the streets.'

'Well. . . . If you did. . . . Still it is cruel. Kendal jail. . . . I have heard of it.'

'I did not steal nor lie with men. But only because I was proud. Now I am proud no longer. Anyone can do anything with me.' Her thin body under her gay dress shivered.

'But now you must be happy,' Deborah said. 'We will make you happy, all of us.'

'No, you cannot make me happy. I can never be happy again, but I will work for your father and give him what he needs--if I can.'

'And father has known you a long while?' Deborah said.

'Since I was eight years old. And now I am twenty-seven.'

'You must not be unhappy. . . .'

But the girl drew away from her, rose up, stood looking down on her.

'Happy? Unhappy?' she said scornfully. 'That is nothing. . . . It is only that when you have been hungry long enough you must have food.' She turned her back on Deborah and stood looking into the fire.

They were silent then, until Herries came back. After this he dominated the scene. In their own separate fashions they all surrendered to him. The strange girl seemed to have a driving desire to make herself of use, and, speaking to no one, moved down and up to the kitchen, taking plates from Benjamin's wife, helping with the potatoes, rubbing the silver--all with a kind of hostile fierceness.

Herries showed his wisdom by not attempting to prevent her, nor did he speak to her, but his eyes were never away from her when she was near to him. It was as though he could not believe in his luck. He had thrown off his years. He was almost a boy again. His body was straightened, the thin, pointed face with the high bones had lost its grey pallor and was flushed with colour. His head was up and his voice rang with joy.

He had been shopping in Keswick, raided the neighbouring farms, stirred Mrs. Benjamin (who could cook when she liked) to make pies and puddings. Soon a great feast was laid out on the broad table under the portrait of scornful old Herries. There was a fine paste of almonds with candied cherries, plums and currants. There were two fowls, a splendid pie (for which he must have paid dear, thought David, remembering also that it was his mother's money that bought it), wheaten loaves, China oranges, walnuts and plums, candied Madeiras, citrons and muscadine grapes.

To drink, there was to be a grand bowl of punch made after Major Bird's famous recipe, Batavian arrack and good honest ale.

For whom was all this? Were there to be guests, and if so, who? No questions were asked. Everything went forward.

The little chapel was only a step away. The rain, too, had now ceased to fall, and the sky was filled with little round fleecy clouds stained with blue shadows.

Herries appeared in his grandest dress, a suit that had lain in the big oak chest for many a year, something almost of Queen Anne's reign, strangely out of fashion, its colours faded, fitting oddly with his ugly scarred face and long grey hair. He had a dove- coloured waistcoat woven with gold. His cloth coat was of cinnamon colour, his sword was silver and gold-hilted, with figures on the handle, and he carried a cane with an amber head.

A strange pair the bride and bridegroom made as they started out together down the lane, he walking very proudly, she, her arm through his, hanging her head and looking like a gipsy from a fair. Deborah and David walked behind.

At first no one saw them. Some men and women were working in one of Peel's fields, and looking over the hedge caught a sight of all this glitter and colour. Then an old woman at a cottage door had a glimpse and called out after them. Then some children playing by the great oak tree near the inn had a sight of them, and all came trooping after.

At the door of the inn there was a little wizened, hunch-backed pedlar selling his wares. He, too, came hobbling behind.

Little Rosthwaite Chapel by the village was one of the smallest in England, and passing under the porch Herries and David had to bow their heads.

The clergyman was waiting for them, and almost at once the little place was filled with the children, the pedlar, some old women. For Herries the scene was some dream long dreamt by him, now accomplished in reality. Since the moment when she had come knocking at the door of Herries and he had opened it to her (would that be for ever the most miraculous moment of his life?), his happiness had been so strong, so universal, so overwhelming that he could neither realise nor see objects outside it. There WERE no objects outside it. This joy had covered all the world like a great cloak of surpassing brilliance. The others, David and Deborah, had but just ridden off to Keswick. He had gone back into the house and set about polishing the silver on some harness. The knock had sounded through the still, withdrawn place, mingling with the eternal murmur of running water. He had seemed to know that the knock announced great news, for he had hastened down the old stairs, flung open the door. And there she had been in the little grass-grown court, at fainting-point with hunger, in her bright shabby clothes. He had caught her in his arms and carried her in. From that moment his happiness, unquestioning, undoubting, had risen like a wave all about him and drowned him. He scarcely saw the girl herself in his triumph.

She was here; she needed him, and she would stay. Would she marry him? Yes, she would marry him. At once? Yes, at once if he wished it. Would she stay with him? Yes, she would stay with him. She acquiesced in everything, while he fed her and gave her drink. He placed her in Mrs. Benjamin's care, then went out for the licence, the parson, the grand food, the liquor and a chain of fine gold that he bought off a Jew in Keswick. All that night he lay alone on his naked bed, seeing only her, thinking only of her, staring into radiant bliss. How David and Deborah would take it scarcely stirred his imagination. He loved them. He hoped that they

would be glad; but if they were not, the brilliance of his happiness would not waver.

So now, when he stood in the tiny chapel and took Mirabell Starr for his wedded wife, the shabby little place was ablaze with glory. He bent and kissed her cold unresisting mouth, then passed down the aisle again between the children, the hunch-backed pedlar and the old women. Outside a crowd of people had gathered. He waved his hand to them and, in a voice ringing with joy, told them that they would one and all be welcome at his house. They all followed after, whispering among themselves.

Deborah's memory may be the truest mirror to catch the scene that followed. Into the heart of her old age that scene remained as something framed off by itself, apart in colour and shape and fashion, something wild and fantastic beyond conception.

First, the quiet of the Borrowdale road and the little grey village, the peaceful sky in which all the little clouds were turning rosy as the sun went down, the barking of dogs, the fields softly lit by the gentle sun, Rosthwaite Fell a kindly guardian hovering above them, ducks waddling in silly procession, an old woman sweeping her doorway--and through this placid quietness Herries and his bride in their silver and cinnamon, their orange and crimson, he marching as though he were conqueror of the world, she beside him, looking in front of her, neither to left nor right, her face a mask; then David, striding, towering over the rest but shy of this pageantry; herself, Deborah, feeling the rosy sky, the pale green of the sunlit fields, the dark shadows of the hills and, as she was always to remember, the consciousness of her new life that the kiss of the night before, pervading everything, had given her. And, after them, the whole rabble of the village, gathering force with every step, children running to keep up, farm boys, women from the fields, old dames from the cottages, dalesmen and labourers, headed by the little round fat clergyman and the humpbacked pedlar, all of them crowding along, but, so strangely, not speaking above a whisper, wondering in excited awe what it was now that Rogue Herries would be at.

Deborah knew this well enough, and one question she was soon asking was: Would they step into the house? For many, many years Herries had been forbidden, warlock ground to them. Had not the witch, Mrs. Wilson, lived there, and was it not back there that Rogue Herries had taken her after her drowning? Had he not lived there with his painted woman of the town, had not his poor wife died there?--poor soul, poor soul! Aye, it was a wicked house, evil enough, a place of spells.

But now it was as though they themselves were under a spell. They followed as though the pedlar were piping some magical tune that they could not resist. Deborah knew, too, that they had recognised, well enough, the bride. Already she was aware of the scandal that that would be, only adding to the other scandals.

It seemed that every step that her father took must only be the more fatal to his name. They had seen the girl in the roads, on the Fell, begging, dancing, stealing, one of the robbing gipsies, and now Rogue Herries had married her. And he fifty-six, who should surely now be repenting of his sins (that were so many) and making ready for the next world, where, whatever he did, his place could be no easy one.

She knew so well what they were thinking, and, when they came to the bend of the road where the lane to Herries, turning up to the right over the stream, met it, she felt the pause, the hesitation.

Herries and his bride went on, the pedlar and the clergyman went on, a second's wavering and the crowd followed too. Coming to the gate before the courtyard they waited. Herries turned, his grey head bare in the evening light; he waved, with a sort of joyful gesture, his stick with the amber head in the air. He cried:

'Here is food and drink and no grudging. Welcome, my friends, this day at least. We will drink to the bride.'

He marched on, carrying his hat in one hand, waving his stick in the other. They all followed. An odd and wild scene it was after that. The two old suits of armour had never seen the like. The dark stair was narrow. They crowded up it, pressing upon one another, still whispering, no word above a whisper.

The clergyman, sweating with the pace at which they had gone, and the pedlar were the first to follow into the dining-hall. The pedlar, as though he owned Herries and all in it (he had a crooked body and a pock-marked face and thin strands of carroty hair on his bald poll), laid his pack on the table and scattered the contents. 'A bride's gift!' he called in a funny cracked voice. 'A bride's gift! What will you have, lady? A grain gold watch-chain, cambrics, gold buttons, watch bottles. . . . What will you have? A gift for the beautiful bride!'

Soon they were, most of them, in the room, peering about them, staring at the old chest, the tapestries, the portrait, the wide stone fireplace. They crowded together like animals, but many of them, although they were in the witch's house, remembered their Cumbrian manners, than which there are no finer in dignity and self- respect and courtesy the wide world over. Many of them might have fled, it could be, had it not been for David, but they knew Mr. David Herries, they trusted him to see that they would come to no harm; not his fault that he was the son of the Devil, who had danced with witches and now married a gipsy. And another reason why they did not go was that they could not, for there were so many crowded on the stairs that they could move neither up nor down.

They might have been forgiven that day for thinking that Herries was of another world. He stood at the end of the table, lit by the jumping fire, the scar standing out on his face, even his clothes-- in spite of their grandeur--of another age, and his voice was strange, glorified, filled with a triumphant power as though he

had won a great victory, or, as an old woman said that night, 'made new contract with t'Divil.'

He filled the glasses and the cups with the brandy and the arrack and passed them round. This was fiery stuff, stronger than their accustomed ale, so it was no wonder if soon their voices were loosed.

The feasting began, only the bride, sitting at the table-end with the bridegroom, did not eat and did not speak. Herries seemed not to see her. He pressed those close to him, his children, the clergyman, the pedlar, a stout broad-shouldered dalesman with a vast black beard, a farming woman with crimson face and swelling breasts, already a little drunk, all of them near to him he pressed to eat of the fowls and the pie, the fruit and the mound of beef. Soon they were eating right enough, and as the drink went round they began to pull at the food, the more drunken of them reaching across the table, cracking the nuts and catching the shells in the air, and throwing pieces of flesh to two or three hungry dogs who had crept in with them.

Then Herries rose to make a speech. He had drunk very little, but he seemed a drunken man, his hand trembling, and his eyes, always brilliant, now glittering with an eager fire.

'Friends and neighbours,' he said (and the pedlar, looking round him, echoed in his shrill cracked tones, 'Friends and neighbours'), 'I welcome you all here on this the happiest day of my life. The moon is silver in the sky' (now once again the rain was pouring down torrentially and clattering at the panes), 'and all the good dogs are baying at it. This is the valley of our hearts: in every stream there are fish of gold, and on the hills through the heather the blessed angels are picking the blackberries and singing under their wings as the rabbits run from their holes to listen to them.

'In no other valley in the world can these things be, and to-night, when the stars are blinded by the light of our happiness, the Old Man will be tramping the road, his pack under his elbow, and the stones hard to his stubborn toes. That is what happens in our wonderful valley, so drink to the Bridegroom and the Bride, whose nakedness your loving thoughts will cover and whose roof is your roof, and the snail on the wall has left his silver track for your guidance. Drink, friends and neighbours, and tumble downstairs as you may.'

No one understood a word of it, and for years after there were some who said that Rogue Herries, on his marriage night, had invoked the Devil. They had heard him with their own ears, had they not?

Then an old man, very grave and reverend, with a white beard and a nobly shaped head, stepped forward to make a speech.

'We mun thank Mr. Herries,' he said. 'When I was young, we did varra weel off labscourse en stirabout fur dinner and we'll do varra weel yet. But Mr. Herries has grudged neet.' He wandered off into disconnected reminiscence. 'Folks was harder lang sen. . . . When I was a lad wi' a bit of bluemilk cheese en breed I never ailt nowt. . . . In my opinion ther's nowt bangs good muck . . . good muck wi' plenty o' suction in't 'll bring a crop any time. Anyways it's nobbut dry work talking without summat to sup on, and ther's plenty to sup on here. . . . But cuntra's turned upside-down. It'll be lang afore they see any mair times like t'oad uns . . . any mair times like t'oad uns . . . afore t'Rebellion . . . afore t'Rebellion. . . .'

His voice sank into his beard; moreover, the noise now was too general for him to be heard. The arrack was having its way. There was stamping and singing, some child was crying. They were crowding more and more about the table. A glass fell and crashed. The rain slashed the windows until they rang again.

Deborah had watched the riot growing. In spite of the festivity there was a false element in it. Her father's happiness had something protesting in it, and was made the stranger by the girl's silence. David was doing what he could for friendliness, moving among them all in his quiet natural fashion, but with the heat of the great fire, the strength of the drink, the ferocity of the storm outside, a crisis seemed to be mounting over them.

It came, and with a wild suddenness. The pedlar, whose little skimmy eyes had scarcely left the face of the new Mrs. Herries, had been coming ever closer to her. He seemed himself to be mad with some sort of sensual desire or arrogant conceit. At first he fingered the orange sleeve of her coat, then bent forward, put his hand under her chin, lifted her face. 'A kiss,' he said, 'from the happy bride.'

A moment later Herries' fist had crashed into his misshapen ugly face, and he tumbled backwards into the noisy crowd. Herries, pressing after him, seemed to be seized with an exultant rage. He struck right and left.

Everyone scattered to the door, and, as he pursued them, they turned pell-mell, one upon another; men, women, children were heaped to the door, were stumbling, leaping, flying down the stairs, rushing into the court, away, away through the gate, and down the lane, as though the Devil were after them.

In a leap of the fire the room had been cleared, the table, the floor messy with food, glasses overturned, only the pedlar, unconscious, flat on his back.

'You with the rest!' cried Herries, and, picking him up, threw him down the stairs, ran down the stairs after him, picked him up again, dragged him through the court, threw him over the wall into the lane, returning then, found his pack still on the table, picked it up, stuffing ribbons and chains and gold buttons back into it, ran down with it, and threw that too over the wall. The rain came soaking down upon it.

Back in the hall again he saw that Deborah and Mirabell were gone. Only David stood, tall and considering, above the ruined feast.

Herries broke out, roaring with laughter.

'Well, Davy. . . . Our first hospitality.'

And David answered, picking up an orange from the table and biting into it with his teeth: 'Well, father, you made the punch too mighty for them.'

By evening a quiet contentment seemed to have come to them. No sign of the feast, no sign of the feasters. An hour before, Herries had gone out to look for the pedlar to see whether he were killed or no. There was no glimpse of the pedlar, nor of his pack; only the cold muddied path, the trees sighing under the rain.

Now they were all about the fire, Deborah sewing, David doing his accounts at the table, Herries in the oak chair with the big arms to it, and Mirabell quietly near to him, silent as before but a little flush now in her face, and looking up once and again, first at one of them, then another. The riot had, it seemed, in no way disturbed her. She had known many like it before.

Herries' joy was quiet now and tranquil. He would look at her, an odd smile playing about his lips, then glance away again.

He nursed his knee, bending forward towards the fire. The old house seemed to fit into their mood. Somewhere Benjamin could be heard, beyond the rain, raucously singing a tune. He was drunk a little. The room was dry and warm for once; the firelight played about the brown figures in the tapestry and threw a strange shadowing on the beams. Sometimes a mouse scratched behind the panelling. Deborah was thinking of love, David of business. It was plain of what Herries was thinking. No one knew Mirabell's thoughts.

The evening wore on, the storm died down, and with the cessation of the rain all the rivers and streams of the fields and rocks seemed to rush into the house. The whole valley was vocal with running water, and some little wet stars came out and blinked between the black driving clouds.

Deborah and David went to their beds. Deborah, before going, bent down and kissed Mirabell's forehead.

When they were gone, their doors closed, and all silent again, Herries rose and said to her softly:

'Mirabell . . . speak to me. Say that you have trust in me.'

'Yes,' she said. 'I have trust in you.'

He stooped and picked her up. He carried her, her hair strayed across his breast, up the stairs, along the tumbling passage to the little room where he had slept with small David on their first night in the house.

He laid her on the bed, knelt down beside it, stroked her hair, kissed her eyes and mouth; then, very tenderly, with a gentleness of a woman, he undressed her. When she was naked he took her in his arms again, and, with one hand free, turned down the bed, and laid her in it, smoothing the pillows for her head.

Then he knelt down beside her again.

'My darling,' he said, 'when I saw you in the cave on Honister I loved you so that I knew then and for ever where my haven was. After that day I have had no other desire than that, to worship you and serve you. Many of my days have been evil, but I have had no shame of that. I let things pass me by because my eyes were set on a dream. I knew always that in some place or person or act there lay the fulfilment, so that when I came to it I would find myself. I was always searching. No man has been more lonely than I, and by my own fault. I would receive no pity, that most contemptible of the vices, and I would give none, but I could be honourable could I find a place for my honour, and I could serve if I could see an altar. And now I have found it. I have years left. I am strong. There is no task too hard for me now I have got you, and if you stay with me no unhappiness can touch me.'

She looked at him then, full in the face. Then she put her hand up and, very gently, stroked his cheek where the scar was.

'You know,' she said, almost in a whisper, 'that I loved once and when he was killed I was slain too. I am a dead woman, Francis. I was a child when I talked to you in the cave. I was a woman at that moment in Carlisle. I care for you. I feel sorry for you. But I have no love for you. I told you yesterday. I can never love anyone again, I think. And so I wish that you did not love me so much. But you have shown me more kindness than anyone has ever shown me. I will do my very best to please you. Indeed I will.'

They remained for a while, he kneeling by the bed, she stroking his cheek. Then he took off his clothes and went in with her.

He put his arms round her and held her icily cold body close to his heart. Her head was on his breast and suddenly she began to cry, without sound, but he could feel her tears wet against his arms. She cried for a long time, he consoling her and stroking her long hair.

THE VOICE

It was not strange, when you think of it, that the valley should now determine that it was a witch Herries had married.

It was, after all, only what they had expected him to do. It was, after all, only what they had always expected her to be. After the wild marriage party, so grotesque in its conclusion, every sort of fantastic story was abroad. Some said that Rogue Herries had, all in a moment, shown a fiery tail between his coat-ends and that two brown crooked horns had sprung out from behind his ears. Others that the girl had flown of a sudden above the table and was carrying in her right hand a broomstick. All agreed that they had been beaten with mysterious blows from a hundred invisible arms. The pedlar, who seemed, with his hump and carroty hair, to have settled down in the valley, went about everywhere whispering, in his cracked voice, stories about Herries.

No, this was not odd, but what was strange was that, as the months passed, Mirabell won the name among them of a good witch, almost of a kind of well-wishing fairy. No one could quite say how this idea began to grow. It was not that she did anything for them; she did not, indeed, take any part in the lives of the farmers and dalesmen. It was said (and most of the stories came from Mrs. Benjamin, who was a very talkative woman and had friends in Rosthwaite, Seatoller, Seathwaite, Grange, everywhere in the valley, in fact) that she was busy all day in the house, quietly going about her duties. That she was kindly to everyone, never out of temper, never proud nor haughty, never gay, but never sad either. She was not a bad witch in any case; only a poor gentle woman who had let her spells lie forgotten in their pack. Nevertheless the village children were warned not to speak to her when she went about, walking or riding, with her flaming hair and the brilliant-coloured clothes that she loved to wear.

After a time the village women began to pity her. They could not charge Herries with unkindness to her, although that they would have loved to do. It was plain enough that he worshipped her and would do anything in the world for her. He was a changed man, Mrs. Benjamin declared, when she was about, although he would curse and swear and strike Benjamin with his whip or cane, as he had always done, when she was away.

The story was gradually told that Mirabell Herries had been in love with the Devil himself, who had been disguised as a beautiful young man, and then, when she saw her sin, she had fled from him and been broken-hearted ever since. This, the farm-women said, might happen to any woman. She was not to be blamed for it.

Within the house David and Deborah became greatly attached to her. This did not say that they had any intimacy with her. She remained apart, reserved, secret, but she was in all her ways so gentle, so ungrudging in her service to all with whom she came in contact, that even the old wind-blown house itself seemed to gather a warmth and kindliness from her presence in it.

They must feel, too, their father's worship of her. Oddly they did not resent that nor charge her with taking his love from them. It was her purpose plainly that she should take nothing, but only give, and that shyly, as though she had no right to think that her gifts would be received.

There came a day, a warm dim February day, when Deborah was taken a little closer into this girl's privacy, and that perhaps because of Deborah's own confidence to her.

It was, as often happens in this country, a sudden flash of sun and warmth and promise between storms of wind and rain.

When they saw how it would be the two of them rode out under Cat Bells through little Braithwaite village, up Whinlatter, and then, finding a sheltered corner and letting their horses feed in the grass by the road, seated themselves where they could look down upon Bassenthwaite, smooth under the sun like a gold shield, and across to Skiddaw that opened like a flower of steel and silver against the windy sky.

Deborah, moved by some quick impulse, told Mirabell that she had a lover; Mirabell turned towards her with a gesture of more eager friendliness than she had ever shown to her.

'Oh, tell me about him,' she said. So Deborah, with the sedate deliberation that, even when she was in love, could never leave her, told Mirabell about the Keswick Ball, and the little clergyman and the kiss under the stars.

'And I had a letter yesterday delivered by horse from Cockermouth,' she added, blushing and looking very happy in spite of her sedateness. 'Is it not foolish to be so in love at my years? . . . But then he is not a boy,' she added, smiling with love at the picture of him in her heart. 'I fancy that we are greatly suited,' she said, feeling for the letter in her bosom.

She read the letter, while the breeze rustled over the fell and the shadows passed like wings of gigantic birds across the slopes of the hills.

MY DEAREST FRIEND--When I had read your letter I grumbled, for I would have had it so lengthy that it would stretch the reading of it until I might see you again. I have now read it twelve times and could, were I put to it, read it blindfolded and make no mistake in it. It was a sweet letter nevertheless, and I love you at my heart with so great a devotion that I cannot subscribe to your absence, you resting in my heart and so being never away from me.

And so you being here in my parlour, what do you think of it? Everything is smart and everything elegant. There are the short candles and the long ones, the tea-urn and the two screens with the Chinese figures upon them, of which I have told you already. And even now I have been busy on my sermon, whose text is: 'Suffer the little children,' and I have also a Latin inscription to compose for the tomb of Mr. Harvey, the principal solicitor of Cockermouth, who passed away a sennight back, as I fancy my last letter informed you. There is also my good dog Rufus at my feet, who already loves you who are now his only mistress, and has looked at your letter with an obeisance marvellous in so dumb a beast.

Two chairs also are newly come to the parlour, purchased by me a fortnight back at the sale of poor Mrs. Newbiggin's effects (of this also, I think, I have told you). They have a certain lameness at the moment, but I know how to steady them against your coming. When am I next to EXPECT a letter? They are as careless at the Crown as at every other inn in the country, and the thought that a letter from you may be even now in the wrong hands is a constant anxiety for me.

You know how I love you, my dearest, and that with every hour my love increases. . . .'

'The rest is nothing,' said Deborah, folding it up and looking at Mirabell with a sudden anxiety. After all, how slightly she knew this woman, how different their natures and origins. Such a letter might seem to her the last foolish pettiness, and if she laughed . . .

But Mirabell did not laugh. She turned and drawing Deborah to her, kissed her. This she had never before done of her own accord.

'You are happy,' she said. 'That is a very kind letter. No one has ever written me a letter. He would have--' She broke off, stared down with her strange elfin eyes to Bassenthwaite, that is always from a height like a lake ebbing its life away between marshy strands; then crept closer to Deborah as though she sought protection from something.

'You are all so kind to me. As no one has ever been. And I wish to return your goodness, but I am outside it. I want to be drawn into your friendliness, but my spirit is dead. My mother, after my father had been killed (he was slain by my uncle, who had always hated him), told me that when he was stabbed every other was stabbed also. She lived with dead people after that. I was so young that it meant nothing to me then, but now . . . Oh, how well I understand!'

'Had you some tragedy then?' Deborah asked. She knew, of course, that there had been tragedy here, but she had never asked any question. Her father had told her nothing.

'It has always been tragedy all my life, but never tragedy that touched me--until this last. My father was murdered, struck in the back in the dark by my uncle. My mother died on the Fell in the rain, her feet deep in mire, no one near us but the kites and the sheep. Then I was with my other uncle, wandering, thieving, hiding, escaping, in caves, on the Fell, begging in the street, beaten, always moving from one hill to another, from one road to another. I was ravished when I was twelve. I had seen four men foully murdered before I was sixteen years of age; one was all night dying, his head in my lap, his blood soaking my clothes. But nothing could touch me. I was apart, by myself!' She sprang up, as though inspired, and cried: 'Ohè! Ohè! Ohè!' and her call echoed from hill to hill, perhaps from Grasmoor down Crummock to Red Pike, from Red Pike to Langdale, from Langdale to Coniston Old Man.

'I would call and so thrust them from me. With my call I expelled them. Touch me? I was not there to be touched!' She called again and heard the echo come back. Then she crouched down once more close to Deborah, her hand on her arm.

'Your father came and found me in a cave on Honister Crag. I told him that day that I was myself, free, by myself, and it was true. But I had remembered him. He gave me that when I was a child with my mother.' (She felt in her dress and brought out the golden head with ruby eyes that he had given her at that Christmas feast.) 'He went away, but I still remembered him. He is not easy to forget. He is a Man, not half a man or a piece of one, but a whole one made in one block like a carved stone. I remembered him, but I did not care for him. I cared for no one; only the memory of my mother made me lonely sometimes, and when men wanted me then I was lonely too, because I hated men.

'Then--' (she broke off, caught her thin breasts with a sudden pathetic, driven gesture as though she must control some beating impulse) 'we came to Carlisle. My uncles were much on the Border, thieving, wrestling, carrying messages. They had been for a long time working with the Scottish rebels, you see, and were paid by them as secret agents. After the Prince landed they went to Edinburgh. I was left in Carlisle. There was a man whom they knew there, a devil, he was evil as Satan, and more evil than that; they knew what he was and what he intended to me, but they were still his friends, and for that I will never forgive them, nor speak to them, nor drink with them, neither here nor in eternity.' Her face was suddenly cold and mask-like with hatred.

Deborah had never seen that figure, the white mask-like face, so small, so carven, so cold under the red smoke-gleaming hair. But she was full of pity, and she put her arm out and drew Mirabell closer to her.

'This man said he loved me; he was hideous in his body as in his soul: squat, black, always cold to the touch. He came to my bed and I fought him. I dug my nails into his eyes, and naked as I was I forced him to creep away, under the smoky candle, his tail between his legs, dog as he was. He did not attempt me again, but he watched me; he was always there watching me, waiting until my uncles should return. He thought they would give me to him. Then Harry found me. We loved at the very first sight, as I came to the door of my house on a fine morning, he riding by. It was always a surety. He was beautiful, he was brave and noble-hearted, he was young and a grand poet, he was mine and I was his. . . . And oh! Deborah, Deborah' (she began to weep, tears pouring down her cheeks, beating her hands, clenched, against her breast), 'Thawn killed him, he stabbed him in the back, he fell dead at my feet, and I dead with him! Deborah, Deborah!' (she turned, clinging, holding to Deborah's body) 'what shall I do? I am not alive. I died with him. When he fell, I fell! Oh, how shall I live again if Harry cannot come back to me? He comes. He beats at the window. When I lie beside your father I hear him crying. When I am moving about that dark house he is a light ahead of me, but I can never come to him, and he can never come to me. I want him so, but he is dead on one side of the wall, and I am on the other. What shall I do when you are so kindly to me, and your father loves me so, and I only a ghost in the middle of you? Oh, what shall I do? Oh, what shall I do?'

In all these months Deborah had never seen her display feeling. She had been kind, and had served them all, and been quiet. Now she clung to Deborah, sobbing on her breast, holding Deborah's arms, weeping as though her heart were all tears.

'Hush! Hush!' Deborah kissed her hair, her forehead, keeping her very close. 'It will pass. It will pass. We will all love you and have a home for you. You are not alone any more. We love you. We love you.'

But Mirabell raised her head, staring into the faint pale sky as though she would find some answer there. 'It will never pass,' she said. 'It is eleven years now, and it was yesterday that he died at my feet.'

She quieted as suddenly as she had cried out. The clouds came over, gathering together in fleecy, windy companies, cloud forming with cloud in ribs and ripples of gauzy vapour. Soon all the sky was a ribbed shore of pale ghostly sand. The fells grew black, and little streams that laced their forms were rents in their strong flanks. Bassenthwaite paled, as the sun withdrew, into the curve and colour of a grey shell. The wind raced over the moor and up the fell, suddenly liberated, delighting in its freedom. It was cold and sharp with the tang in it of sheep's dung and new young bracken and coming rain.

'Let us go home,' said Mirabell. 'It is cold.'

They mounted their horses and turned down the hill. For Deborah, Mirabell's story had flung the whole life at Herries into a new, dramatic and, for her timidity and quiet mind, sinister shape. Mirabell was something now apart from all of them; she was to be pitied, cared for, comforted, but she could give none of them anything. She could not give her husband anything. She did not love him at all. Through all these months Deborah had supposed that in her own strange way Mirabell loved her father, and now it appeared that she had no love for him, but thought only of some ghostly young man who had been dead for eleven years. Well, but if she did not love her father who himself adored her so! Why, that must mean torture for her father, despair, misery. What end could it have but disaster?

This was the first moment in Deborah's life, now as their horses were picking their way through the stream that runs through Braithwaite village and starting up the winding hill to Cat Bells, that she truly loved her father without any sense of fear or dismay. She was overwhelmed with pity for him, caught after all his rough and lonely life into this great passion for someone who did not love him, and could not. 'Oh, poor father, poor father!' she thought. 'How he must be suffering, and under what restraint!' She remembered all his goodness and gentleness these last months, and how, when Mirabell was there, so quietly and with such courtesy he waited on her and cared for her. Deborah's heart, that was all softness and tenderness, ached for him. She cared, too, for Mirabell. It was not her fault that she had come, and she was doing all in her power. But so little was in her power! Nothing was in her that he needed, and yet she was his only need!

That evening in the house Deborah watched with a new understanding and sensibility. And Herries seemed to detect that there was some change in her. She went with him to the door of the house before going up to her bed. The wind that had risen while they looked down on Bassenthwaite was now raging through the valley. It carried in its arms a new young slender moon, and seemed to be tossing it from leafless tree to leafless tree. The trees bent with their bare arms to catch it and then tossed it in and out of the rushing clouds. There was a great noise, a noise of streams, of branches cracking, of the wind itself, and the beams and rafters of the old house.

Herries listened, loving it.

'One wind more and everything will tumble,' he said. 'You'd best go, Deborah, before the fall.'

She timidly put her hand through his arm and stood close to him.

'Father, I love Mirabell,' she said.

'I am old for a husband,' he said, seeming not to hear her. 'When I was young I ranged from door to door, and now that I have found her I am old, bent, twisted. . . . Deborah, will you not marry before it is too late?'

She wondered whether he had heard something. She herself had said nothing. It had not yet seemed the right time. She nearly spoke then, but she did not. While he wanted her, she must stay.

'One day, father, . . .' she said, 'but not now.' And then the wind, with a great scream of happiness and freedom, drove them indoors.

The following day Herries took his wife, riding pillion, into Keswick. He was terribly proud of her. He wanted to show her to everyone; he knew what they said of her, that she had been gipsy, tramp, thief. That was nothing. It was the truth for him that she was glorious, extraordinarily, magnificently glorious. She was as glorious to him now as she had been before he married her. And she was also as mysterious. Intimacy had not made her less mysterious. But perhaps, although he did not know it, there had been no intimacy. Did he know that? He was a deep man who knew many things, but often did not realise them.

She rode behind him into Keswick in a crimson dress with gold buttons. He was in his old shabby country clothes, wearing his own hair. When he touched her he was happy so that he could sing, but behind his happiness he was unhappy: he had questions that he wanted to ask her, and he did not dare.

As they drew near to the town, along the path and across the watery meadows, people were walking and riding. In the Town Square there was a thick pressing multitude. He asked a fellow what the matter was, and someone told him it was the Methodists, and then another fellow volunteered that it was George Whitefield, the most remarkable preacher of them all.

Herries was interested in all that he had heard of the Methodists, who had now for a number of years been strengthening their position in the country, and especially of this Whitefield, concerning whom and his extraordinary preaching he had had, like everyone else at this time, many reports.

He knew that this was a courageous man who was ready, for his religion, to meet any form of contempt, abuse and danger. He knew that he was sincere, of deep piety, of constant energy, of selfless industry. Against these things he weighed what he had heard of his emotionalism, theatricality and fanaticism, all qualities to which Herries, by his own reserved and private mind, was deeply hostile.

He had heard that Whitefield had but one desire, to save souls for God, that often he preached fifty or sixty hours in the one week, and that his journeys, involving as they did at that time so much physical discomfort, were ceaseless.

He knew, too, that he was a man free of all meanness; his bitterest adversary did not attribute to him small ambitions, petty jealousies, sly revenges. He appeared to Herries, from what he had heard of him, to be feminine in his hysteria, weak-nerved, histrionic, ill-balanced, but he was, even because of these defects, exactly suited to move great masses of people by impassioned appeals, passing from place to place like a torch of fire.

When he heard that it was Whitefield who was here he decided that he must listen to him. He backed his horse out of the crowd, and, dismounting, took the horse by the bridle and Mirabell by the hand, finding some higher ground where he could watch what was going forward.

He told Mirabell of the reason for the crowd. She did not seem to be greatly concerned, but, as he had noticed before when she was in any crowd of people, to be looking about her searchingly, as though she would find someone.

He stood, his arm around her, holding her close to him. He felt as though some crisis were arriving between her and himself; this was no new feeling, but had been present with him for the last two months or more, and he knew that was because something was urging him with every day more pressingly to ask her certain questions with regard to himself. He was aware, too, that it was better that he should not ask these questions, that her answers might precipitate a crisis that would make him much unhappier than he had ever been before. But he could not help himself. With every hour he was urged farther. He must know, he must know-- whether now, after these months, she did not love him a little, a little, a very little . . . the first stirring of some new emotion in her . . . and at the thought of asking her and of her answer he trembled as though with cold.

Very soon he was aware of a voice coming to him very clearly over the heads of the people. He could see, only indistinctly, any figure. The crowd, of every type and order of person, was packed tightly across the Square; they seemed to press against the houses behind them, as though they would bend them back. It was an intent and silent crowd, so intent that the urgency seemed to spread to the distant line of hills, Causey and

Cat Bells and Maiden Moor, beyond the roofs, so that they, too, were listening.

The figure was indistinct, someone lit with the pale February sun, a body of grace and good proportion, but it was the voice that came straight to Herries, as though it were to him alone that it was appealing. He realised then that every man and woman in that crowd felt as he did, that it was to him or her alone that the voice was speaking. At once, hostile though he was to public emotion and theatrical display, he yielded to the beauty of the voice. It was, beyond any sort of argument, by far and far the most moving and lovely voice that he had ever heard. Every word was distinct and clear, running to him with a separate and special urgency, and the words were bound into a general rhythm most melodious and musical; yes, it was like music, the perfect and rounded notes following one after another, to make, at the fitting moment, a completed harmony. So lovely was the voice that for a little while he did not listen to the words, then they were forced upon his attention with a pressing gentleness, as though someone, very gracious and kindly, were at his elbow, saying, 'You must hear this; this is for you and for you alone. It has great importance for you.'

He listened then with the utmost attention.

'It is simply as an occasional preacher that I am come to preach the Gospel to all that wish to hear me, of whatever denomination. I have nothing to do with denominations, for it is the righteousness of Jesus Christ that I am preaching, and that righteousness has no denominations. You have heard many times of the righteousness of Jesus Christ, and at every time you have been wearied or indifferent to Him or busied with affairs. It may be that this is the last time you will hear of Him and the last time that I shall preach of Him. Here into this town He has come, knowing that it is for the last time, but you do not know. The clouds have circled over your heads, the sun is about to set and, setting to-night, it will not come again. You are returning to your homes, your candles are lit, your children are at your knee, and distantly from over the hills there is the faint sound of a trumpet. The sound is distant, for the hills cover it, and your many daily businesses, the food for gossip, the food for the belly, the food for pride and vanity, these make a babel in your ears and blot out the distant call. But soon,' and here the voice rose to a high bright summoning call, 'the trumpeters have crossed the hills! The trumpeters have crossed the hills! The trumpeters have crossed the hills!'

He paused as though he were listening. It seemed that everyone else was listening too. The crowd was tense and concrete, as though its eager attention had moulded it into one man. Across the silence there struck stray sounds, the crowing of a cock, the sharp bark of a dog, the stamping of some horse's hoofs against cobbles. These emphasised the stillness. They could see the hills where the trumpeters were. They could name them--Skiddaw and Saddleback, Helvellyn and Fairfield, Langdale Pike and the Gavel, Seatallan

and Haycock, and through that circle of grey listening hills they could see the trumpeters moving.

The voice took a personal colour. 'The Trumpeters come first, moving down the valleys, and after them the cohorts of the Saints in their shining armour, and after them the Priests and Prophets with judgements in their hands, and after them'--the voice sank to a whisper and through the crowd there ran a little rustle of apprehension--'after them the Great Judge Himself.'

There was silence again. A stout countrywoman near Herries began to sob.

'Who in this valley shall be ready for that awful army? Now, outside your door, there is one summoning blast. No time for preparation, for hiding the things that should not be seen. THY JUDGE IS THERE . . . THY JUDGE IS THERE. . . . And He is just and He is merciful. Yes, but He is just. Think not only of the mercy; think also of the Justice. . . .' And then, with a sudden agonising, beseeching cry: 'Oh, my hearers, the Wrath to come, the Wrath to come!'

There was a terror and imminent fearful apprehension in that last cry that even a man like Herries, steeled against every sentimental appeal, could not resist. He started as though someone at that instant came running to him, crying out that the end of the world was upon him. He looked hastily around him, as though a wild animal or flaming fire were at his back. And on the crowd the effect of that cry was immediate and tremendous. Superstitious, ignorant, simply and often savagely moved, cut off as they had been for many centuries from all contact with a larger world, they were ready to be seized by any swift emotion, ready and eager. Here Whitefield, however, had won his hardest victory, for these North Country people were not Celts as the Cornish and Welsh were. They were neither dreamers nor fanatics. As Herries knew, five years before they had stoned the Methodist preacher almost to death, and the whole district from Kendal to Carlisle had a name of great danger for the sect.

But they would not stone Whitefield now. He himself began to be moved with the crowd; his body swayed, his arms rose and fell, his voice was torn with distress and urgency. Tears, they said afterwards, were pouring down his cheeks. He picked out men and women from the crowd. 'Oh, sir, are you indeed ready? Have you your garments packed for the journey, your horse harnessed, and your conscience clear? For Heaven and Hell, Death and Judgement are not names only for you. They are real, they are present. Eternity is a true word and Everlasting Punishment is no lie. Can you be led to the Judgement Seat before that awful crowd of Witnesses and not tremble? Your deeds are behind you. There is no hope now that they may be altered, for they are written in the book. There is the pause. You have made your plea. You are waiting for the sentence, and even as you stand here now, so it is certain that you will stand before your God. Eternal Damnation! Damnation for ever and ever more, suffering and torment and the agony of a repentance that is out of time!'

His voice sank again to a pleading whisper, while now his utterance could be heard to be broken with sobs. 'O God, where is Thy mercy? O God, whither shall I turn?' Then, with a great cry that rang, glittering, resonant through the air: 'In Christ Jesus! In Christ Jesus only is there any hope! But even He is Just.' His voice was now of an awful solemnity: 'Sinner, I must do it. I must pronounce sentence upon you.' Again there was a terrible silence, and then, in a voice of thunder as though the very cobbles of the town must rock:

'Depart from me, ye cursed, into everlasting fire!'

The crowd began to cry out: 'O Christ, save me!' 'Christ be kind to me!' 'God have mercy upon me!' Men were pushing against one another to reach nearer to the preacher, tears fell from many eyes, and suddenly, with a great burst of sound that had in it something gloriously strong and victorious, the hymn 'Our God, our help in ages past' broke out and was carried, it must seem, far beyond the confines of the town.

The voice had ended and Herries was freed. He turned to find that Mirabell was clinging to him, her face very white, her eyes closed.

'Come. It is growing dark. We will go home.'

She nodded. He led his horse out of the crowd and then, in a little dusky side-street where there was a deep silence, he lifted her on to the horse and climbed on behind her. With his arms about her he started away. The horse went gently.

Herries thought: 'There is this Damnation then. I, too, shall be damned with the rest.' He had stirred to a consciousness, through this scene, of a general move-ment behind his own personal history, of some new world coming to England. Ten, five years ago those men and women would have driven Whitefield with stones and abuse out of the town. Now he held them, although it might be only by a kind of superstition and sentiment. He felt that all around him there was a new consciousness, a fresh curiosity, a novel enterprise. For himself, he belonged to the old world that was passing. He had still a link with the boy who, sniffing his way through Queen Anne's London, had not been so far removed from the Rebellion, the tumbling of King Charles' head, the Plague and the Great Fire. But David and Deborah had no touch with that world at all; it was a dream, a fairy-tale to them. David's enterprises were consciously engaged, through his vessels and the things that they carried, with other worlds that were not dreamworlds of adventure and romance, as China and India and Russia had been to Francis' childhood, but definite practical places in which men walked on their legs, ate mutton for their dinner and read the news-sheets. Everything was opening up before him, and at the same time closing in about him. This very rough path on which to-night his horse was picking his way would soon be a toll-road that would carry carts and carriages. This modern world so novel, strident, ill-fitting. In the hearts of those people listening to White-field he had detected a new curiosity. And (here his Herries blood drove him) he disliked and distrusted this modernity. Queen Anne's age appeared to him as something infinitely quiet, cosy, picturesque and easy.

They were talking now of inventing things to make the lot of the common people easier. The common people! No one had thought of the common people when he was a boy. Why invent things only to make them restless? He thought of the old London scenes, so dim now in memory; the crowds on holiday all upon pads and hackneys, Mob's Hole where the ox, roasted whole, was eaten, the dancing to a bagpipe, the fiddlers scraping, an old trooper from the Royalist wars tootling upon a trumpet. The shopping in the New Exchange, that he had so adored as a boy, the beautiful ladies in coach or sedan chair, the ladies with their pets, marmo-sets and Barbary doves, scarlet nightingales and milk-white peacocks. And the Coffee Houses which to him, taken there as a boy on a London visit by Harcourt, twelve years his senior, had seemed the great paradise of glory; the Coffee Houses with the fine glass lanterns hanging without, the pretty Phyllis smiling at the bar, the young swells of a morning, whether at Searle's or Squire's or the Grecian, dressed, as Steele had it, 'in gay cap and slippers with a scarf and party- coloured gown.' The drinking, the smoking, the gaming, the singing-- oh, the Life, the Life that it was! . . .

And now, now, how drab and busy this new world, with no respect from youngsters to elders, no romance, only money-making, business, and the whole world in your pocket!

It was his age. How old he was, and only now his true life beginning!

At that his arms tightened about her body, he bent forward and touched her neck with his lips. He fancied that she yielded to him a little. Did she or no? How often, in these last months, he had wondered that!

And then the temptation that had been behind him so fearfully all day rushed to his lips. He could not stay it now. He had run in upon his fate.

'Mirabell,' he said, 'I must ask you a question.' He felt his heart hammering in his breast. His hands trem-bled.

'Yes,' she said, and then, most unexpectedly, asked him one:

'Do you think there can be a God, Francis?'

A God? A God? What did it matter whether there were a God or no now when the only urgency in this world was, had she come to love him a little.

'That Methodist thinks so,' he answered her lightly.

'Those poor people whom he threatened with damnation, what right has God to judge them, having made them so? And yet--' she looked round at him into his eyes. 'He had a great eloquence. I saw the trumpet-ers coming through the valley.'

'Mirabell,' he began again, 'I must ask you a ques-tion.'

'Yes,' she said patiently.

'Am I,' his hands tightened about the reins, 'am I so very old to you?'

'Old! Why, no!'

'I am old. All my life is behind me and yet, loving you, it is but beginning.'

She said nothing.

He went desperately on: 'You told me on your wedding-night that you did not love me, that you could not. I have never questioned you again. But now it is too much for me. I can wait no longer. Have you not, in these months, learnt a little, a very, very little, to have love for me? Or is it, can it never--' He broke off, so terribly agitated that he could not speak.

At last she answered, turning round again, and looking up at him like a little child.

'I do not feel you old. I feel you so very good, better far than I had ever thought. But love . . . are we not friends, good friends, trusting friends? I am not made for love. Only once, and that was a dream. But your friend . . .'

Then he broke out (although he knew very well the fool he was, and that maybe in these words he was breaking up all the foundation of their happiness together): 'Friend, friend, friendship! What is that for a man? I have never had a friend. I do not want a friend. But my love for you is eating me up, tearing at my heart. As that man to-day desired his God so I desire you. It must be. I cannot live if I haven't it. Your cruelty . . . I lie with you in my arms and you are not there. I touch you and you are gone. I must have a little of you, a touch, a breath, a word that is yours meant for me. I am in torment, dying of thirst, of hunger . . .'

He could not make the words, he held her, letting the reins fall, as though he would drag her into his very breast. He felt her body stiffen against his.

'No,' she said, almost beneath her breath, 'I will not lie to you. I cannot. Even though you kill me I will not be dishonest. It is not my fault that I am apart. I am apart from all the world, yes, and from myself.

'Francis, I would give you everything. I have never but once wanted so to give myself, but I cannot. I cannot! Oh, I should never have come! I am wicked, I am a cheat. . . . I care for you so much, I would give everything to make you happy. But love--it escaped me that night. I cannot find a way to get it back.'

He answered nothing. He rode the horse more swiftly. After a long time, fear in her heart, longing to comfort him, she spoke again:

'I would do everything. Teach me. I will learn.'

He said, between his teeth:

'I have my answer. You have so generous a heart. I will be patient.'

As they rode on (and now it was very dark) her unhappiness seemed to her more than she could bear.

SAGA OF DAVID

I. THE YOUNG SARAH

The place has now come for David's story. These events occurred in early May 1758. David was in his thirty-ninth year in the course of them.

David did not appear a man of thirty-eight at this time. His face was very young, unlined, fresh in colour, strong in profile, with the prominent bones of all the Herries, but his forehead was as clear and smooth as a young boy's. Just at this time, because he was working considerably at the little Keswick office, he was beginning to stouten. His huge frame would gather fat very easily. But this did not diminish his strength, which was now, and would be for another fifteen years, prodigious. It was at this time that he picked up Statesman Peel in one hand and Benjamin with the other and held them, without any effort, suspended for a considerable time.

Men would come from Ennerdale and Eskdale to see him wrestle, and they said that he was, if he pleased, a terrible man with his fists. The twisted carroty-haired pedlar, Peter Dolfin, who was now for ever hanging around Rosthwaite and Grange, hated him and said that he would be hanged for murder any day that he lost his temper. But he never did lose his temper these days. There was a certain sluggishness in him at this time (except when he was occupied on his business; then he was wide awake enough). This is the story of how he lost his sluggishness.

The most remarkable thing about him, as he grew, was the sweetness of his nature. This sweetness of temperament has been a continuous strain in the Herries blood. There has been no generation lacking certain examples of it.

This is no merit to its possessor, entails no virtue, deserves no reward. It is a quality of personality extremely vexing to many who think it sentimental and untrue to life. It is not sentimental because it is a quite natural element in the character of the possessor, and the possessor is unaware that he has it. David did not find life gentle, kindly or considerate. He knew that it was fierce, callous and dangerous. It was companionship with a tiger who, with one careless scratch of the paw, produces tragedy, ruin, catastrophe, and then yawns his indifference. But although he knew life to be dangerous and quite heedless of his personal good luck, his nature drove him to choose the better parts of the men and women about him, to enjoy the happy and bright moments, to perceive beauty without having any imagination about it, to wish everyone well and to rejoice at others' good fortune. It was easy for him just now because of his superb health, but afterwards, in bouts of pain, distresses and anxieties, the loss of someone who was dearer to him than all else, this sweetness of nature did not leave him. It came, as it always comes, from something remote and deep, beyond the business of the body, a central radiance of spirit.

He was, of course, no saint. He was exasperated, sulky, unjust, as everyone is, but only for the moment. These moods never dwelt in him. They tried him and found him uncomfortable as a living-place.

During this year 1758 his sluggishness did not prevent him from restlessness. After he had freed himself from Christina the restlessness increased. He began to wish, as he had never wished before, to make love to someone. He had matured very late. In Liverpool on an occasion he had gone with a woman and, after a brief moment of physical excitement, had known that such encounters were for ever barren for him. But his restlessness was not springing only from need of the love of woman. He seemed to have, at this time, no exercise for his warm, affectionate heart. He was, and had always been, quite undemonstrative, but he must have someone to love. He had loved his father and Deborah, and, in lesser degree, Peel's son. But Rendal was dead (killed in a brawl in Penrith), Deborah's mind elsewhere, his father married again.

It was his father's marriage that mainly caused his restlessness. He had never, in his own simple and unexperimenting mind, suspected the possibility of such utter absorption in another as he perceived now was his father's case. He himself realised the attraction of Mirabell, he thought her beautiful and gentle, and strangely different from other women, but he soon saw that she did not love his father, but was doing what she did from a sense of gratitude and duty. He saw, too, that his father was hungry and thirsty for what he could not have, and that his soul was set on this eluding quest. His father had, for the time, forgotten him. And so, because he loved his father with an unanalysed persisting love, having its roots in his very earliest years, he missed increasingly his contact with him. He did not know how to recover it again; he never knew, in his relations with people, how to change anything. He could not analyse nor examine himself. He had never done such a thing in his life, but he felt, as a loving animal feels, isolated and pushed aside. He blamed no one, felt no jealousy, but was increasingly, with every week that passed, lonely. His business, although it interested and occupied him, was nothing to him compared with his relations to one or two people.

So, although he did not know it at this time, he was very lonely and would soon be very unhappy.

More and more it became clear to him that he must marry. Well, what then? Could they all live together at Herries? There was room enough, but the sense of drama, of events that happened always just out of sight, began to bewilder him as though he were beginning to be asked to look in many different directions at once. This was no place for his wife, whoever she might be. There was some money (his mother's, as he often ironically reflected), but everything was shabby, out-at-elbows. It was not that they did not wish to have

everything in fine colour, but there was some movement inside the house itself; as soon as a window was mended a door was off its hinges. Everything blew against the wall and along the floor. There was a draught in every corner, and rats behind the panelling.

In the old kitchen, where Mrs. Benjamin officiated, everything accumulated. Mrs. Benjamin was slatternly and careless. Nobody minded.

His father's wife helped about the house as though she were a servant. Those seemed to be the times when she was happiest, when she was carrying plates, sweeping floors, polishing the brass and silver. She was oddly most at her ease with old Benjamin. It was as though they had some secret friendly understanding. As though they had come from the same place. . . .

Herries would enter and find her scouring the plates. He could not endure that; he would ask her to go and dress in her finest, and then he would sit her in the high-backed chair in the dining-hall, and he would change his clothes (he had been, as usual, digging, trying to turn rock into pasture, plucking up weeds, or simply standing staring at Glaramara, watching as it turned from amber to purple, purple to jet, jet to silver), and then there they would sit, the two of them, she in gold and crimson, he in cinnamon and silver, on either side of the fire, saying nothing at all.

No, all this was too eerie for David. He didn't know what would happen soon; something, he thought, that would make them all unhappy.

And no one wanted him. When he rode in from Keswick, evening time, he would see them sitting like that in the firelight. They were two ghosts to him. Everyone now was just out of his reach. He had never been so alone in his life before.

So one day he rode over to Wasdale. He went to see about some sheep that, he had heard, were for sale, and cheap. They belonged to a man called Denburn. This man Denburn was a gentleman, they said, from London, fallen on evil days. He had a tumble-down farm at Wasdale Head called Scarf Hall, a place half gentleman's house half farm. They told him in Keswick that Denburn was a ruffian, but clever, had a library of books that he set great store by. He had a daughter too.

He had some sheep, and David wanted some for his fields by Herries, so he rode over.

It was dark when his horse (he was riding Deb's Appleseed) had picked its way to the bottom of Stye Head, and it was difficult to find his way. He found his path across Lingmell Beck, and then plunged into a black thicket of trees. Here he stumbled for a long while, hearing water tumbling all about him, and the wind roaring down the pass.

He was not a man to mind wind and tumbling water, but he was uncomfortable nevertheless. This lake-end valley, cut off from the world, was an excellent rendezvous for smugglers from the sea-coast, only a few miles away. The inn at that time, the Wasdale Inn, was a wretched place, as he well knew, both in accommodation and reputation, but it was there that he must pass the night.

As he blundered among the trees, scarcely able to see his thumb before his mouth, he felt for his knife and his pistol. He might need them before the night was through.

He came through the wood and almost stepped on to the inn. There was a light in the window; he banged on the door, which was opened by an old woman with a shawl over her head and a shabby patch over one eye. He called for some one to look after his horse, and a lad went with him to a tumbled stables at the rear.

After seeing to his horse's comfort (poor comfort, but all that he could have) he stood for a moment swallowing the mountain air, looking up at the great shoulders of the Gavel behind him and the black sprawl of Lingmell, the sharp edge of the Pike in front of him. The night was clear. Stars, as the dusk faded into night, were breaking, in their thousands, into the stuff of the sky.

Reluctantly he shouldered his way across the floor of the close- smelling inn-room. All eyes were upon him as they well might be. He was so tall that he could, standing on his toes, touch the ceiling; so broad that he seemed to be at elbows with every man there. It was a small place, dim with the smoke from the fire, smelling of food, ale, dung, human unwashed bodies. The bodies were there, a dozen men, the old woman and another. His eyes were on her instantly. She was turning to go as he came in. She was dressed for riding, and wore a large hat with a feather and a great gold buckle that glittered and flashed in the firelight.

She was a young girl of strong, sturdy build, an open laughing face, broad shoulders, big-breasted, brown-haired. She might be, David thought, of any age from seventeen to twenty. She was tall, carrying her head grandly on her shoulders. As David came in her head was half-turned, she laughing at someone, striking her whip against her thigh.

She was the most natural, open creature David had ever seen. Beside her was a man of some fifty years, very tall and skeleton thin. This man was dressed quietly in grey coat and breeches with a white stock; he wore a brown tie-wig. His face was as sharp and pointed as his body was thin and long. He had very thick, dark, beetling eyebrows and his complexion was sallow, his face deeply furrowed. A very ugly man. As he talked he bent his body about as though he would snap it.

For the rest there was the host of the inn, Sol Beddowes, who was as thick, black, and dirty as a tar-barrel, some rough fellows who might be smugglers, and one or two honest dalesmen. But David's eyes were all for the girl.

He spoke to Beddowes; was, with a brusque word, told that he could have a bed, came to the fire and so was companion to the man and girl. He heard someone say 'Mr. Denburn,' so he spoke:

'Am I speaking to Mr. Denburn?' he asked. The long sallow hatchet of a face wheeled slowly in his direction and the little eyes receded into the eyebrows.

'I am Mr. Denburn.'

'My name is Herries,' said David. 'I have a piece of business with you. May I come and call on you some time to-morrow?'

The body rose, as though on its heels, and leaned towards him like a whip, then the voice, cold, chill, and filled with self- importance, answered:

'Business of moment?'

'To the advantage of both of us, I fancy,' he answered.

'I am at home to-morrow evening.' Then he added, a little more graciously (he had been examining David with great care, and appeared to find him interesting), 'but possibly you prefer to be away before evening. . . . I could arrange a meeting in the morning.'

David, with a thought of the girl, answered that the evening would be a perfect appointment. He knew that the girl had been intently aware of him, and, suddenly, he looked at her, catching her gaze. She did not flinch, but looked at him squarely, then smiled.

'A dark night to come over the Pass,' she said. Her voice delighted him, rich, warm, deep. It was as though he had heard it before, many times, and recognised it, coming home to it. He was excited by the sound of it, as he had never been by a woman's greeting.

Mr. Denburn went to the door. She followed him. Before she went out she looked back, smiling again, and David smiled too.

Until he slept he thought of her. Was he in love at last? He sat by the fire, looking into the flames, his legs stretched out, as he loved to sit, talking to nobody, thinking slowly and steadily.

He remembered the women he had ever made any court to. The woman in Liverpool, a woman in Seatoller, Christina, one or two more. Little approaches that had been amusing, casual, leaving his heart alone. This was different: already it was different.

It seemed to him, poor David, the newest, most unusual experience in the world. It WAS unusual possibly. Strong healthy men in that age were seldom as virgin as he at thirty-eight.

He felt about twenty, and as he thought of her with every thought he was younger. He recalled the tones of her voice again and again with a happy luxury. She was only a child in years, but the voice seemed to him to have in it wisdom, fun, and good health, three splendid things as he saw the world.

When he went to his bed in a little room over the stables he found that he must share it with a stout dalesman. At any other time there would have been trouble. To-night he did not care. The dalesman was asleep and snoring like a pig, his hairy chest heaving under the candle. David shoved him to the wall. He only grunted and turned on his side. Then David lay down, pulling up his knees, as he had to do in most beds, and, instantly, with a happy smile on his face, he was asleep.

He did not, unfortunately, dream of the brown-haired young woman, but he found himself in the little dark wood, lost, bewildered, stung by sharp thorns, his feet in plosh and mire. Beyond and above him on Stye Head someone was waiting for him, someone in peril, and it seemed, oddly enough, that this someone was himself. Did he not reach this figure to rescue him there would be disaster, but with every effort that he made his feet stuck the faster and the thorny trees tore his face more savagely. The voice from Stye Head called to him: 'Help. Help! I can do no more!' He made a last gigantic effort for freedom, and woke to find himself clutching the hairy throat of the stout farmer, his knee planted on his chest. Even this did not wake the slumberer, who, lost in his own pleasures, murmured: 'Coom, lass, pour oot for t' lot.'

David could not sleep after that. He lay there, listening to a first lonely bird, smelling the stuffy odour of straw, blanket, dried cow-dung that the room enclosed. He lay, his arm behind his head, gazing at the grey square of the little window, wondering how now, in clear day-time, he would find her. Was it perhaps only his longing to be in love that had cheated him? Would he discover her now like the rest, ordinary pleasant womanhood, with no magic about her? He didn't know. He wished urgently that he could summon her there, immediately, that he might satisfy that question.

At last he got up and went out. The fresh morning air caressed his eyes, his mouth, as though it loved him. He found the beck and washed his face and hands in it. It was icy cold. The light crept out above the black edge of the Pike, the trees came forth as though rising from their sleep, the hills moved grandly into their places. The few birds and the whispering beck greeted him with a happy, aloof indifference.

He didn't see her again until the evening.

Scarf Hall was hidden in the woods under Green How.

When David came to it the moon sailed out from above the Screes and an owl hooted. The house swam in a pale light that flowed about it like green water. An odd building surely; one old tower and on either side of it bow-windowed circular rooms like ears. The grass and bushes of an entangled nettled garden spread almost to the old door, whose front was lined with thick iron bars, studded with large flat-faced nails. Out of one of the upper windows a garment was hanging to dry, and it flapped humorously in the moonlight. A big white cat came out of the shadows and rubbed itself against David's legs, mewing.

He banged the old knocker, that was an old man's face with nose and chin meeting, against the thick wood. His knock resounded as though it would wake the heart of the Screes, but it didn't disturb the cat that continued to mew and rub against his boots.

After a while an old man, holding a lamp high, unbarred the door and opened it an inch. David must have looked giant-tall in that moonlight, for the old man nearly dropped the lamp in his astonishment. But he had been told maybe that there would be a visitor, so he opened the door wider, and the cat slipped into the hall.

He was a funny old man, bent and hairy, wearing a green apron. He had quite a little company of hairs on the end of his nose. Without a word he led the way, David striding after.

They were seated about a table in a dining-room eating and drinking. Because of the odd uneven shape of the tower this room was like a box with its corners pushed in. It seemed that the corners of the ceiling (which was an ornate one, painted with faded pink-bottomed cherubs festooned with chains of roses) would fall in also, for they bulged as though under a heavy weight. The room was badly lit with two candles in silver candlesticks. There was a spinet in one corner and a large yellow globe like a huge dried melon in another. The white cat was curled up on the broad window-seat.

About the table were Mr. Denburn, Miss Denburn, an ancient lady in rusty black and a high white wig, and a broad thick-set coarse-looking fellow with a round red face like a sun. In the poor light Mr. Denburn was more sallow and hatchet-faced than ever. With his long protruding chin his face had the shape of a yellow-pointed shoe, and his eyebrows looked as though they were made of horsehair and fastened on with glue.

He tried to be genial this evening, but geniality was difficult for him. He bade David welcome, pushed a cold pie towards him, and filled his glass with wine. The thickset man was introduced as Captain Bann. He was drunk quietly, and, it appeared, in no good temper.

'I must offer my apologies,' David said. 'My business is with some of your sheep, Mr. Denburn. I should have told you so last evening. You will be forced to have two visits from me.'

But Mr. Denburn was delighted to speak of his sheep. His self-sufficiency was amazing. To hear him speak you would think that there were no sheep like his in the whole of Northern England--and yet David knew that he was a poor farmer--almost no farmer at all. While he spoke he wriggled his body up and down, as though there were a perpetual itch between his shoulder-blades.

In a very patronising tone he cursed the neighbourhood, the climate, the Hanoverian government, the war with France, and humanity quite in general. He gave David to understand that he had for long led a life in London very different from this present one; that had it not been for certain rogues and vagabonds he would now have his place at court, and that he had rendered this same cursed Hanoverian family much personal service in the '45, but that he could wish now that the Pretender had pushed on to London when he might have done, and thrown the whole London lot into the Thames.

'Aye, aye,' gurgled Captain Bann, his nose in his glass. 'Pox on the lot and into the Thames with the bastards!'

At this point Miss Denburn and the ancient lady rose to retire, and David hurried to open the door. The cat stretched itself and followed them out. At the door he bowed and Miss Denburn curtsied, smiling with the greatest friendship as she did so, and he, as she smiled, felt his body tingle all over.

Returning to the table David found that the two gentlemen were regarding his physique with great interest. Indeed Captain Bann, who was now far gone in liquor, proposed that the two of them should strip there and then and try a fall. There should be stakes which Mr. Denburn should hold. He was beginning immediately, swaying on his stout legs, having taken off his coat, to undo his stock. David, however, firmly declined the honour.

It was shortly plain enough to him that these were two very considerable scoundrels. They had an understanding which hinted at many mutual past knaveries, and Mr. Denburn was the master of the other. Denburn did not drink; his eyes under the absurd eyebrows were never still. He cracked walnuts in his sharp bony fingers as though he were cracking beads.

Captain Bann was made quarrelsome with drink, and wished to provoke David to some argument. He spilled wine on the tablecloth and paddled his fingers in it, even flicking a drop or two into David's face. But David was not to be provoked. It occurred to him, however, that had Denburn been of that mind the two of them would have set upon him without any uneasiness of conscience; it was an unpleasant notion to have Denburn's long fingers at his wind-pipe and the Captain's brawny shoulders pressed on his stomach. That he could manage them both he did not doubt, but it was a lonely spot, lonely and most ominously silent. There was no sound at all but the tapping of a branch against the pane behind the green curtains.

So, very shortly, he made his excuses to depart. Denburn did not attempt to stop him, and they arranged for a morning visit to the sheep.

He had no further word with Miss Denburn.

Quite early, however, next morning he encountered her, and had with her what was for him a very eventful conversation. Waking again very early (this last night he had had his bed to himself) he went down to the lake and stood watching the silver ripples break from the mirror, running out of the glassy stillness as though with childlike delight into the young stiff reeds at the water's edge.

He stood there, looking down, as the light broadened over the Screes, heard steps, looked up and saw Miss Denburn. She had not seen him in the half-light, but was walking along the lake path, her head up, her body beautifully free, taking in the morning air.

He straightened himself and bowed, smiling very shyly. He had read few romances and little poetry, books gave him poor pleasure, but if he had he would have known that this was a fitting time and place for a lovers' meeting. As it was, he did not think of himself as a lover but only as David Henries, delighted at the presence of a most beautiful lady. In actual truth he did not think consciously of anything at all.

She was as little self-conscious as he. To reveal a secret, she had fallen in love with him instantly at first sight in the inn yesterday. It had seemed to her as natural as mounting a horse. She had fallen in love a number of times in her young life already. She thought falling in love exceedingly pleasant. She was by nature impetuous and fond of all natural things--eating, sleeping, hunting, fishing, chattering, loving, hating.

When she saw a handsome thing she went directly towards it. David was by far the handsomest man she had ever seen. She had thought about him incessantly since first meeting him and how she might meet him again without anyone else being by. She had come out this morning on the chance. He was the kind of man she fancied would be up early.

Had he said at once this morning: 'I love you. Marry me,' she would have answered at once: 'Yes, I will,' without a moment's proper hesitation.

All her life she had been with bad, ugly-thinking, vilely-acting men, and she would have followed a tramp to get away from them. It was the mercy of a sometimes benevolent Providence that young Sarah was not by now wedded to a tin kettle and a baked hedgehog with a rabble of ragged children at her skirts. She had no caution whatever. But, as David was shortly to learn, escaping from Mr. Denburn was not so easy as it might be.

As a matter of history David did, within a surprisingly short time, tell her that he loved her. As has been already explained, he was in a state very imminent on declaring his passion to some one or other, and this was a girl most exactly after his physical desire. Whether they were, either of them, after the spiritual needs of one another was something neither gave a thought towards. By good chance for the blood-history of many later Herries they were, both of them, fine creatures. Every once and again these chancy things happen fortunately.

In any case, Sarah looking at him with the smiling eagerness with which a young puppy looks at some human who promises a walk, David naturally advanced in boldness very swiftly.

They walked beside the lake together while the sun came over the hill and worked patterns of gold into the black reflections of the precipitous Screes. Over their shoulders Middle Fell looked down upon them benevolently.

David began with becoming modesty. He explained some facts about himself and that he lived at Rosthwaite in Borrowdale.

'I know Rosthwaite,' she remarked reflectively. Then she added: 'My name is Sarah.'

He told her that he had a business with Liverpool trade, that he was buying land thereabout, and, in fine, that things were going well with him.

'You are married, Mr. Herries?' she asked him, giving him a very quick look and thinking him so handsome that she longed to pull his ears.

No, he was not. He looked at her as he said it, and blushed. Gathering boldness, he asked her whether she lived alone here with her father, and said that it must be bleak enough in the winter-time.

She startled him by the answer:

'Mr. Denburn,' she said, 'is not my father.'

He was astonished indeed.

'No. He is my uncle. My parents are both dead. My father died in the year previous. My uncle is my guardian.'

David was encouraged then to hint that it had not seemed to him natural that Mr. Denburn should be her father. He hinted that he did not like Mr. Denburn.

'Like him indeed!' her voice rang out. 'He is detestable! I have always hated him. He was my father's brother and held a strange influence over my father. In his last years my father was, I fear, quite in my uncle's hands. I inherit some wealth--no great sum-- from my dear mother. I was their only child. My uncle removed to this lonely spot that he might influence my determination. It is his desire that I should marry that pig of a Captain whom you saw besotted at the table last night.

'My resolve for my own independence irritates them vastly. I am only seeking some opportunity to return to London. But this guardianship is strict. Even now the Captain is, I wager, if he is not sleeping off his drunkenness, somewhere on the watch. If not the Captain, then my uncle. You see, Mr. Herries, I am a captive.'

She said it laughing, and he greatly admired her spirit, but he fancied that behind her laughter there was an apprehension. She was not, he imagined, as happy as she seemed.

She told him that she must return. Even now it was dangerous for her to be away.

He offered then his assistance, in any sort, in any kind. And a moment later, without realising the extravagant speed of his progress, he was telling her that he loved her, that he had loved her at the first sight in the inn, that he had never truly loved anyone before, and that he would love her, he fancied, for ever and ever.

'What!' she cried. 'You the age you are and the handsome man you are and never loved anyone before!'

'Never!' he declared, and with more truth than she could dream of. She did perhaps, young as she was, realise that there was something different in the freshness and sincerity of his declaration from the ordinary fashion of men.

Her eyes softened and her face shone with pleasure as she looked at him. She could not help herself. He was so very delightful. She gave him her hand and told

him that she would meet him again that afternoon. She would walk across the fields to a farm at the foot of Lingmell with the old woman who was her duenna. She would see that the old woman did not disturb them.

They parted like two children enchanted with one another's company. He was very young for his years.

He saw Mr. Denburn that morning and Mr. Denburn's sheep. He bought the sheep and hated Denburn. He would in any case have hated him, but now, because he knew that Sarah was oppressed by him, it was difficult for him to keep his hands away from him.

Denburn of course noticed nothing. As with all self-appreciatory persons he was lost in his own glories. Because David said little he discovered him to be good company. His condemnations covered the whole world: no one and nothing escaped them. With his scorn there was mingled a mean anger and an avaricious greed. He would have haggled over the sheep's price for an hour but David gave him at once what he asked. He scarcely saw the sheep, he did not see Denburn at all; he saw only young Sarah with all the glories of heaven about her head and himself in bliss at her feet. He also saw himself as the inevitable father of her children. When he had left him and was back at the inn he went up to the stuffy little chamber, into which the May sun was now pouring, sat on the miserable truckle-bed and endeavoured to control his fire. But he could not. It lapped him around with a burning, shining flame. Never, in his thirty-eight years, had he approached this sensation of worship, happiness and almost agonising wonder. He had not known that love would be like this nor that it could descend with such precipitate suddenness. He had no doubts about its issue. He would shortly marry Sarah and that was enough.

How he would marry her, snatch her from her captivity, did not yet occur to him; nor did he at present think of his father nor Deborah nor Herries. He had never been able to think of more than one thing at a time.

And so when he met her on a sunny meadow under Lingmell he could not at first speak at all.

The ancient lady who accompanied her had been left in the farmhouse asleep. It was her virtue that, placed in a comfortable chair, her handkerchief over her face, she fell instantly asleep, like any bird with a cloth over its cage. Sarah had discovered this pleasant trait in her and profited by it.

So in that meadow, the shadows from the hill gathered about it as they walked, they confessed their love. It was not, it could not be, a very lengthy business, when two are instantly of the same mind, afraid of nothing and regardless either of the present or future.

David, when at last he found words, said: 'I told you this morning. I must repeat it. I cannot help it if you are angry. I have been thinking of you incessantly since the morning and I must tell you again that I love you.'

Sarah replied: 'I am not angry at all. I loved you the first instant in the inn.'

David said (but not meaning it): 'You should consider it. I am very old.'

And Sarah answered: 'Young men never pleased me.'

Then he kissed her, very gently, not as he intended to kiss her later on.

They were both so exquisitely happy that for a long time they could not speak at all but looked at one another, walked a little and looked at one another again.

After a while it occurred to them (the gathering shadows warned them) that the old lady would soon wake and that something must be done.

'Of course,' David said, 'you must come away with me.' He stood drinking in her loveliness. She was none of these thin willowy women that you could crack over your knee, but strong, broad- breasted, of noble carriage, health, vigour, energy, simple directness in every look and gesture. A third, watching them, might have thought them of the same family.

'Of course I must,' said Sarah and then moved, with more practical directness than he, on to the difficulties.

It seemed, at first sight, an easy matter. All, David said, that she had to do was to walk out of the house. He would have a horse at hand, and so, over the Pass and home. Indeed his first suggestion was that she should come with him immediately.

That, so eager and impetuous were they, might have been (and much trouble spared them) were it not for the old woman. Sarah would not leave her to the fury of her uncle. She must go when the old lady was not on duty. From this she would not stir.

David began now to be once more his true, slow, cautious self. This needed thinking of; there was Herries, there was his father. There were his own affairs. He hesitated less than ever as to his purpose, but everything must be soundly based at home, ready for her when she came.

He discovered then that she was being guarded as a prisoner. Although she might laugh with her young indomitable courage, he began to realise that these last months had been torture for her, and that, had he come or no, she would not in any case have endured much more of it. A more suspicious soul than David might at this point have asked himself whether she were not using him only as a means of escape. But with all his simplicity he was astute. He knew that she was in his own state of blissful bewildering love.

They could not, in fact, make any very serious decisions that afternoon. After a sentence they would stop and walk in a world together so magical and removed from argument that all plans were monstrously unreal. The most that it came to was that, early to- morrow morning, he would take his sheep home, and then shortly return to take her after the sheep.

Only it must be soon. For every reason, but chiefly because waiting seemed an incredible folly--it must be soon.

Once again he kissed her, behind the thick body of a chestnut tree (lest they should be observed), and this time it was a long embrace, with all heaven in it. That was the first true kiss of David's life.

Once, as they neared the farm, she turned to him, and there was a new seriousness in her voice. 'Do not think,' she said, 'because I have told you so quickly that I love you that it is a light word. I have been moving to this my whole life long.' She spoke as though she had already lived an eternity. And he very gravely answered: 'I will love you, dear Sarah, for ever.'

They came into the farm and found the old lady fast sleeping under a red handkerchief, and snoring lustily.

SAGA OF DAVID

II. THE FIGHT ABOVE WASDALE

Abductions were common enough at that moment in the world's history; they roused no sort of comment unless the persons concerned were of social or financial splendour. David and Sarah were of neither. It was in fact a completely minor affair to everyone save the few persons concerned.

It was unimportant to David's father. David hinted to him that he had discovered the lady and might, if fortune favoured, bring her home. Herries was digging. He looked up, his face muddy, his eyes angry at withdrawing from their proper business.

He told David to go to hell, find anyone there he fancied, and do with her what he pleased. He was in one of his old moods, cursing the mud that splashed into his face, cursing his aching bones, but happy and tranquil in his occupation.

And David in his turn was angry in the old way. He abused his father handsomely, and going into the house felt a proper relief. He could do as he pleased: whatever way he went his father would be behind him.

In the doorway he met Mirabell. She was standing there watching a flight of birds cutting their way through the fresh spring air.

She was holding in both hands a tub filled with dirty water, her thin spare arms straining to the weight. Her face, beautifully pale like ivory under the tawny hair, was raised to the sky with a childlike pleased curiosity.

She smiled shyly at David. 'You see them best on the Fell,' she said, 'where you may follow them for a fine distance. . . . The hills have taken them.'

He tried to relieve her of the tub but she wouldn't allow him. She was always shy with him, eager to please him without giving him any of herself.

But what he felt now was the amazing contrast that she made with young Sarah. On every occasion that he saw a woman now, Sarah was the more wonderful to him. This fancy of his father's--he liked her, felt kind to her, would be glad to please her, but she was a fade-away unhappy wisp, holding herself in against everybody, while Sarah--!

At the thought of her he was in such a glow of happiness that he could have picked Mirabell up in his arms and tossed her like a feather.

She, with her funny, almost witch-like perception of the moods of others, said:

'You're happy to-day.'

'I am,' he answered, throwing his arms up to the sky. 'I am! I am! I am!'

He was in a mood to tell her of it.

'I have found a maid--over the hill. I'm going to fetch her back, and marry her.'

To his surprise Mirabell was happy, as though good news had come to herself.

'I'm glad. Where will you live?'

'Here.'

'Yes, don't leave your father.' She put down the tub and caught his great hand in her thin bony fingers. She looked up at him, smiling. 'Is she young? And beautiful? And a fine mother for your children?'

'She is young and beautiful, and a fine mother for my children,' he repeated after her, smiling back at her. They had never come so close together before.

'Bring her here, Davy. There is room enough.'

'Oh yes,' he answered, looking up at the old house where in one corner the roof was slipping, and where a chimney cocked sarcastically with a drunken leer. 'There is room. But, Mirabell, why should we not all go from here? There is money enough for a fine place where they can take father newly. Here they have always hated him. Persuade him, Mirabell.'

But she shook her head. 'In that I can't move him. He is stuck in the place.'

'For you he'd do anything.'

'No. That--never.'

Then she picked up the tub again, moved into the court, and over her shoulder, repeated: 'Bring her here, Davy. Good luck to your hunting.'

Next morning he went back to Wasdale. He walked over. After much thinking he had decided that a horse would be a danger, that he must be as little visible as possible before the event. He was inclined at this moment to consider but lightly of the whole business.

For Sarah to escape from two such elderly-ruffians as Denburn and the Captain would be surely no problem. It seemed to him as he walked under a clear blue sky, singing, the very simplest thing in the world. . . .

In the little valley by the beck under the Pass at the foot of Lingmell there was a deserted shepherd's hut that he had marked on the last occasion. This, he thought, would do very well to pass a night in without observation.

He reached it in the late afternoon when the light was failing. The silence was profound, broken only by the gentle running of the beck. There was a sweet air scented with water and fresh grass. He sat in the little hut on a pile of dry bracken while the colours faded and the sky whitened, thinking, happily, triumphantly, of all the joy that was coming to him. He hadn't known that love could so change the world in a second of time.

He stretched his body out, his arms behind his head, and looked up at a little hole in the turfed roof through which the sky was like a crystal cup.

His imagination had Sarah in his arms, and he whispered to her: 'My darling, my little love,' and enjoyed himself hugely.

When it was dark he went out. He met nobody until before he reached the wood of Scarf Hall. The world seemed to be entirely deserted.

When he came to the grass-grown drive he stole carefully to the rear of the tower to see whether a window were open. On the left side he found a window brilliantly lighted. The shine streamed out, illuminating a strange little garden that had once been carefully tended. There was a thick box hedge with animals cut upon it--a cock, a swan, a dog--and in the centre of the little lawn a square sundial. This was all lit with the pale shadowed light from the candles in the room.

Standing in the dark by the box hedge he could see into the room. The table, whose surface shone like a mirror, had on it a large bowl of fruit, a bottle of wine, and a board of red and yellow chessmen set out as though for play. The white cat was curled up near the yellow globe. A large silver candelabrum with many branches threw a fine dazzling radiance over the broad figure of the Captain, who was seated, alone in the room, at the table, his large red face between his hands, staring in front of him, a grand picture of drunken stupor. The room was so still that it might have been a painted scene.

After a while a breeze descended among the trees and, as though he had been roused by that (although he could not have heard it), the Captain took the bottle of wine with a shaking hand, filled a long thin glass, raised it to his mouth, drank it, and then, amazingly, climbed to his feet and shook his fist threateningly and savagely in the air, at nothing in particular.

He was the picture then of a man very angry and very foolish. His rage seemed to possess him for he suddenly, with a curve of his stout arm, swept all the chessmen off the board, raised the board itself and flung it to the ground. Then he stared about him as though he had just awakened from a dream. It was odd enough to see all this in dumb show and hear no sound.

A thin cold rain began to fall, pattering among the leaves.

The door opened, the Captain turned, and, miracle of miracles, Sarah entered. She was dressed exquisitely in a silver dress, and she carried a candle. When she saw the Captain she would retire again, but he stumbled to the door and stood with his back to it.

She blew out the candle, placed it quietly on the table and turned to him, her head raised. She said something to him; he replied, very ludicrously falling on one knee. She came to the window and at that same moment David stepped forward into the light. He stood there in an agony of apprehension lest the Captain should see him, but the Captain, drunken as he was, could not balance himself on his knee and sprawled to the floor.

Sarah laughed (and a fine splendid sight it was to see), stepped over his body and, at the moment that her hand was on the door, looked back into the garden.

She saw him. Heaven be thanked, she saw him! Her face was rosy, she put her hand for an instant to her breast, then left the room. The Captain lay there where he had fallen, his face in the chessboard.

Some window must have been slightly open, for the candles began all hurriedly to blow as though they were laughing at the Captain, and in that same new flurry of wind Sarah had joined David by the hedge.

They exchanged no word. He drew her face to his, his hands were about her neck, the rain blessing both of them.

At last, withdrawing from one another, they began to laugh in sheer joy of seeing each other again. He drew her away into the back of the little garden out of the light, then hurriedly told her his plan: 'It must be to-morrow night. I will be here in this same place. At what hour?'

She whispered back: 'At this same time. But I may not escape at once. I will come from that window. . . .' Then in sheer happiness she caressed his face with her hand, tracing his mouth, his eyes, his nose.

'I hadn't dreamt it would be so soon. I have watched two evenings. I must pull your ears. It was the first thing in the inn I desired.'

'You will be damp. The rain--'

'Kiss me again. Hold me tightly. If I had other clothes I would come now. . . .'

'Do you love me? Have you thought of me?'

'I love you so. . . . I haven't ate a thing these two days. My uncle . . .'

She broke off, listening. The Captain had come through the window, lurched on to the bright square of lawn, took off his wig and lifted his naked scalp to the rain. He stumbled towards them, holding his wig in his hand.

'Water,' they heard him say. 'Damned refreshing . . . cool to the head.' He rocked into the sundial which he clasped with both arms.

They waited, scarcely breathing, while he hugged the dial. Then they kissed again, a long embrace, suddenly not caring for the Captain. She came out into the light, walked right past him, through the window into the house.

He stood, scratching his head, not knowing whether he had seen anything or no. David slipped away.

He slept the sleep of the innocent, the just and the healthy that night in the hut and dreamt of nothing and nobody. He woke to a cold day with a great wind that drove bellying grey clouds in riotous hurry over the hills as though preparing for some grand show when the clouds should be packed away. All day they rolled, leaving the tops clear, sharp and cold beneath their smoky procession. All day David stayed in the little valley, eating the bread and meat that he had brought with him and drinking out of the stream. He climbed the Pass as far as Stye Head then, to warm himself. It was but a little way down into Borrowdale. There could be but little trouble in the affair. They would be at Herries by early morning.

He had but one encounter; a thin wiry choleric Squire with some hounds who, attended by two men, was going up the Pass as he came down. The Squire wanted company and held David by the coat while he enlarged on his affairs. Like another Squire of his time he was all for 'lending' anyone who disagreed with him 'a flick.' He had a long matter in his head about an estate that joined his own, somewhere, David gathered, Eskdale way. 'Join the two and there's no larger estate in the kingdom. I had rather bate something than have the pox of a fellow advising me on my own ground.' He had an especial cursing fury at the towns and London in particular. 'I'd be a Hanoverian 'fore I'd show my arse among their smoking chimneys. Pox on all Hanoverians and Presbyterians either. Thou must come drink a bottle at my table. I'll show thee some trees and some horses also. You show your fancy very plainly. I'm ne'er mistaken in a man. Thou'rt no Hanoverian.'

He would then back with David and drink with him in the Wasdale Inn. Then, to David's consternation, suggested they should impose themselves on Scarf Hall. He knew, it seemed, Denburn. 'He's a mean varlet,' and he'd doff his clothes to give him a lick as soon as spit in his face; nevertheless there'd be wine there and they'd make a rousing night of it.

It took a quarter of an hour's good work to dissuade him from this and to push him on up the hill again, but at last, swearing at his men and his hounds, he vanished round the bend, his little wiry legs the last visible part of him.

The only merit of this adventure was that it was pleasant to realise the general unpopularity of Denburn. All human kind doubtless loathed him. David had through the afternoon some apprehension lest the testy Squire, in search of good liquor, should turn and descend again, and he watched the Pass with some anxiety. But there was no figure on the Pass. Doubtless he had gone, cursing, down into his own place in Eskdale.

The rain threatened all day but never fell. When at last darkness came, the hills were clear and later there would be a moon.

In the little garden again he performed the silliest act of his life. Looking back afterwards he never could see what drove him to it. It may have been the cold, which was bitter, or impatience to bring things to an issue, or sheer childish playfulness.

In any case the garden was chill, half-an-hour's waiting made him stamp his feet with restlessness, the house was dark without a visible light. He stepped over the lawn, brushing against the sundial, felt for the window of the dining-parlour, found it unlatched and was inside.

There he paused, his hand on the table-edge. He listened; there was not a sound but a hysterical clock that giggled somewhere like a schoolgirl. He opened the door, crept into the hall, a wavering candle turned the corner, and in a moment he had the old lady in his arms.

He clasped her to him as though he loved her, his broad hand over her mouth, and pulled her, lighted candle and all, back into the parlour, and closed the door very quietly behind him. The old lady was in a strange garment of faded green, her grey hair about her shoulders and on her lined wrinkled face an expression of such convulsive terror that it touched his compassion. But she did not speak, only gaped at him, her mouth open like a young bird's. He took the candle from her trembling hand and set it down on the table.

'You love Miss Denburn,' he said hurriedly. 'I know you do. Miss Denburn is in great peril and must be away with me to-night. I would not put you to any sort of inconvenience, madam, but every moment has its danger. Assist us and you shall be rewarded magnificently.'

Her mouth opened and shut. She kept plucking at her green gown that it might cover her négligé. The leaping candle made the queerest figure behind her on the wall. She said at last in the oddest voice, between a squeak and a whisper:

'There's the Captain coming down and we're all undone.'

He saw from that that she was on the right side and had probably been already warned by Sarah, but she trembled like a flower and, he feared, might at any moment drop to the ground in a faint.

So he pushed her into a chair, poured some wine from a decanter on the table into a glass and made her drink it. She gasped and gurgled, but, it was plain, enjoyed it.

'Now, madam, you must return to Miss Denburn and tell her that I am waiting for her here. Then go to your chamber and remain there.'

He spoke sternly, but he smiled. And she, to his astonishment, smiled back at him, put her finger to her lip with an evident enjoyment of the conspiracy and, clutching her gown about her, stole softly out of the room again.

A moment later, listening in the darkness, he heard the Captain's voice. The Captain was not drunk to-night. He sounded another man, rallying the old lady with quite a deep dignity and precision.

She, David gathered, was endeavouring to escape up the stairs and he detaining her.

'No shame on your attire, Sister,' he was saying (that plainly his jocular name for her). 'You shall drink a glass with me--a handsome night-cap. The moon will be up and we will salute it through the open window.'

She replied something and then David could hear her hastening upstairs. A second later the Captain was through the door, so near to David that he could feel the hot breath on his cheek.

He was himself pressed back against the wall as flat as his great body would allow, his hand ready on his sword-hilt.

The Captain went past him and began to curse for a light. He had a fashion, it seemed, of talking to himself. 'Curses on the dark! 'Tis a house of no discipline. But I'll not drink this evening. I'll match Ned with his sobriety, blast his superior elegance. And I'll not be longer here neither; it's a job or it's no bargain, nasty skinflint.'

He moved to the window. David could see his broad bulk, in the thin light that preceded the moon, his hands in his breeches pocket, his legs straddling. He continued to talk as an angry boy might: 'I'm no such fool as he'd think me, as he'll find in his own time. The girl's well enough, but she hates me sober and loathes me drunk.

'And there's Jane at Newmarket. . . . A shrew's a shrew however much gold she carries. . . . And this plaguy country where it rains like Egypt's plague, and no company to make a night of it. . . .' He yawned prodigiously, then, with an exclamation, found in his pocket what he wanted. He fingered the tinder-box, struck a light, turned and saw David.

In another second he would have shouted but with a leap David was across the room, had knocked the light from him and hurled him with a crash to the ground, his hand over his mouth. The noise of the crash must surely rouse the house and as, after that, they struggled, David's ears were alert for Denburn's footsteps. But there was nothing save the chattering clock that seemed suddenly to redouble its pace in a violent excitement.

That was no mean struggle. The Captain must in earlier days have been a man of his hands, and even now, weakened by lazy living and drink, his big body had energy. Had David been free it would have been a matter of a few moments, but as it was he must keep his hand over the man's mouth, which hampered him sadly. The Captain wriggled like a worm, now bottom up, then with his legs twisting like a centipede's, then with a sudden force in his belly that turned it into iron, pressing against David's arm. He had his hand in David's eye and was knuckling him lustily until, throwing his body on to the man's stomach, David had a free arm and could press the other's hand back to the floor.

131

Their panting breath and the roll of their bodies on the floor was the only sound.

Then the door was open and there was a light. David could not turn to see and had an awful fear it was Denburn. But it was Sarah's voice:

'Quick,' she said. 'My uncle is on the stairs.'

'The bands from the curtains,' he gasped. 'Fasten his legs.'

With admirable energy and dexterity she had them there and (as she told him later) tied them about those stout ankles with the greatest satisfaction. She was as brisk as though her life had been spent in such tasks.

'The garden-house. . . . Over the lawn. . . .'

They pushed the window and dragged him out. David's wide and deep kerchief was over his nose and mouth, the curtain-bands over his arms and legs. These were temporary enough and would stand little resistance, but for the moment they must do.

David's huge arms dragged him across the lawn (his head bumped the sundial), through the path by the box hedge, and, hidden in thicket, there was the garden-house. It was a small enough place, piled with straw and gardening-tools, but they bundled him in, closed the door and bolted it. Then they ran.

By the path that skirted the lake-end they stopped. She caught his hand and leaned against him, recovering her breath. They listened intently. It was strange after those moments of hot panting struggle to stand still in a world, cold, motionless, at their feet the grey rounding of the lake and about them everywhere the dim shapes of the hills. The house, the room, the heaving body of the Captain, all in China. . . .

A dog barked somewhere. The reeds rustled. He held her to him as though she were part of himself.

'Now . . . how long may that garden-house bolt last?'

'Not long; the wood is rotten.'

David laughed. 'He had an immoderate taste of my fingers . . . Come. We'll do the kissing later. There's no time . . .'

They were off again, through the little gathering of houses, then the wood, then the foot of the Pass.

'Soon there'll be the moon.'

Before they started to climb, in that strange milky glow, they turned toward one another and kissed. Her immediate ready courage of the last half-hour pleased him most divinely. That was the companion that he would have, a man in swiftness, eagerness of perception, a woman when the softer time demanded it.

He was proud of her mettle beyond any personal pride that he had ever known.

'You did that bravely. Oh, I love you a thousand times for it!'

She took his head in her hands, fondling it, bending it to her breast. 'I did not know that love would be thus,' she murmured. Silly stuff to both of them had they heard others whisper it, but they might be allowed it, the night before them being sterner than they knew.

Indeed so little concerned were they that they started up the Pass hand in hand, like two children.

She told him her adventure. The old lady had warned her, she had started down the stairs when she heard the crash of the tumble. Then there was panic for her! What to do? To go forward and risk what she might find below or to turn back and wait? The door of Denburn's room opened. It was dark on the stair and she waited, listening for his movement. He asked her from his door had she heard anything.

'Only an owl,' she had called back to him, her heart thumping. He went in again, closing his door, and once more she listened. Now everything was still save the clock. Only the white cat (that had doubtless slipped through the door when the Captain opened it) slithered up to her, rubbing against her legs. She had taken that as an omen, and so went forward. Then, most foolishly, when she saw the pair of them struggling on the floor she had wanted to laugh. The Captain's broad beam and his knuckle in David's eyes . . .

But at the thought of that she caught David's hand the tighter.

So they walked on, unconscious of anything save the splendour of being in love, of the health of their bodies. One hundred and fifty years later a descendant of theirs would be walking up this same Pass with the lady of his choice to whom he had just declared his passion. She had accepted him, but, as he kicked the rough shale from under his feet, he would be wondering, in the manner of his time, whether he had done wisely. She was pretty enough, but might she not sicken after children? Of course with birth-control methods as safe as they were . . . Her nose certainly went blue with the cold (although to-morrow was the first of May it was damned cold) and her taste in Chinese art was uncertain . . . 'Darling,' he was, a hundred and fifty years later, remarking, 'That book of Breasted's shows quite plainly . . .'

And now at this same moment David, looking back down the milky path and feeling at his sword, said most happily: ''Twould be no bad place for a fight . . . if your uncle has the stomach for it.' Only the wind, whistling by, answered them. There was no suspicion of a pursuer.

He kissed her again. He really couldn't kiss her enough; this kissing was so different from any that he had ever known.

Then the moon peered over the edge of Lingmell. She scarcely showed herself, a fingernail of pale colour, but she was rising; very soon the Pass would be flooded with light, the moon that ushered in May.

But it was not to be just yet. There drifted, in the odd fashion of inconstancy that these hills have, sudden filmy wisps of mist, the edges of the thinnest gauze, having no especial purpose, rising from nowhere, born of nothing, so thin as to be transparent with the dim preface of the moon behind them. And at the same moment a new wind began to shrill up the valley between Lingmell and the Pass.

David after many years knew this country well and something in the wind told him that these vapours would not remain transparent for long. An odd unanalysed anxiety caught him. Mist was the one thing of which he had not thought.

'Oh, look!' Sarah caught his arm and pointed to the valley. ''Tis as though a great kettle were boiling.' The vapour was coming up towards them in spirals of smoke and, you might suppose, little clouds of steam. David was not imaginative, but, in his anxiety to have this adventure safely over, he was ready to fancy some active agency down there in the valley, some enemy raising a huge fire of damp logs to send up a torrent of twisting smoke.

'We must press on,' he said. 'The Pass can be cursedly confusing in the mist.' The thin gauze skirted the Pass like a live thing and as it thickened above them, obscuring the rising moon, the world darkened again and chilled, the wind whispering at their ears.

An odd thing happened then to David. He fancied that his father was walking beside them. He could almost see the man, tall and powerful, with his long hair, his shoulders a little shrunken, his whole body moving forward with that obstinate energy that was so peculiarly his, his eyes staring into some imagined dream of space.

It was as though he said: 'There is trouble for you now, and so I am here. You have taken this girl in a single second, forgetting our bond together. But you will not be permitted to forget it. We are Herries always, and we Herries are always together against the world whether we wish it or no, and so it will always be. Our bond is for no time or termination. It endures infinitely. A weariness, perhaps, but nevertheless a law.'

Indeed David may at this moment have been thinking these things, for he was suddenly conscious of his father, and not very long ago, at Herries, his father had said something of this kind to him when he asked him why he did not marry, and added that marriage would be no escape for him because he was indubitably a Herries, and must always belong to those of his own blood rather than to anyone from outside.

It was only for a second in time that David saw his father striding there beside them, but it was a second that contained many centuries in its form.

The incident thirteen years back, in Carlisle, came to him when he had watched in the fog on the walls. He had lost his father and then, in the early morning, his father had found him. There had been an extraordinary relief in that reunion, something far beyond the immediate circumstance of the incident.

Now again, for nearly two days, he had lost his father, absorbed by his sudden love for this girl. His father had held him once more and, for that moment, it had been as though Sarah did not exist.

He had her again, catching her hand. The Pass was really steep here with a sharp edge, and the mist was now boiling up from the valley in thick rolling masses of cloud.

He stayed her to caution her, and at that same instant the tops cleared, the moon sailed out, full and faintly red-cherry coloured. Everything was illuminated, the Gavel on their left, Lingmell, Scafell, the Pike, the rough track of the Pass winding down into the valley.

They turned to look back, and there, sharply clear in the moonlight, pressing up the Pass were two figures, Denburn and the Captain.

Each saw the other and stood transfixed. David was happy.

'If only the mist holds off I can deal with them. They won't use their pistols so long as you are here. Oh, but I'm longing for a cut at your uncle—'

The distance between them was short. The two men were standing on a green promontory that stretched out of the Pass over the valley, looking to Wasdale and the sea. They were exceedingly clear in the moonlight, first like statues, then beginning with feverish energy to scramble forward up the Pass. Denburn shouted something and David, laughing, shouted back:

'Ohè! Ohè! Ohè! Cut-throat and Captain! I'll buy you both for a farthing.' He was like a boy again at the thought of a fight.

'I could meet them here,' he said reluctantly. 'At this bend. I'd have the command of the path.'

But Sarah urged him on. Her courage, although she would never let him know, had failed her. She didn't want him to fight, she was sick in the stomach, she was suddenly a child of her own really tender years. She had been brave enough in the house because that had been a matter of escape, and her uncle had not shared in it. But now he was almost upon them, and all the terror and sense of malignant power with which he had always possessed her returned to her.

Since she had been an infant in the little house, with her father and mother, in Kensington village, she had known this. She had caught it first, perhaps, from the terror that her father and mother had of him.

When he had reached to her and tried to take her on his knee, she had shivered and gone pale with apprehension. The comfits that he had given to her had always seemed to her poisoned, the touch of his hand the touch of a frog.

The natural buoyancy and health of her disposition had prevented this from breeding in her any permanent unhappiness. Her terror of him was intermittent, only really present when his physical body forced her to realise it. It was his physical body that she realised now. Although he was only a manikin of a figure against those moonlit hills, he was as real and powerful as though he were there beside them. She was sure that he would kill David! He had the evil power. There was something in him that must be stronger than the goodness and courage in David.

So she urged David forward, running ahead of him, and he followed, joy in his heart that now he might at last settle with that dirty fellow who had ill-treated his beloved Sarah, stroking his sword-hilt as though it were the best friend he had.

They had reached the turn, climbed the boulders, came to the point where the signpost now assists the aspiring tourist, saw the tarn lying before them black under the moonlight.

'I will meet them here,' David said, his pistol in one hand, his sword drawn in the other.

Sarah implored him to go on. He saw then her terror and was, privately, disappointed in it.

'I will but make a statement or two,' he said quietly, but with the obstinacy of a small boy. 'Your uncle must understand my feeling for him before I take you from him. That is justice.'

Then he saw the rising ground that leads past Sprinkling Tarn and Allen Crags to Esk Hause. 'That would be better,' and, with her following him, he took the higher fell.

Then, without an instant's warning, the moon was blotted out again. The mist swept up in an array of thin cloud that veiled the hills, the fell, the tarn. Before it thickened into a wall of white muffling vapour they saw the two figures round the corner and start up the fell towards them.

'Now we are caught indeed,' David whispered. He stood listening. He felt for her hand, clutching it. 'Don't move from me,' he cautioned her. "'Tis easy to miss in this cloud. I must listen for their step.'

But, as always in that mountain-mist, listening he heard every imagined sound. Rocks seemed to fall from a great height, water rose in a whirl-wind from the lower ground, voices were everywhere, animals rustled at their feet, there was secret laughing, an army of curses, the ringing of bells, and behind and around all this a dead cold stillness like the grave.

Forgetting his own caution and thinking he heard his enemy, he moved away from her.

Again he listened, and suddenly, quite near to him, so that it was almost at his ear, he heard the Captain's voice: 'I'll not move till this mist thins. It's the Devil's work. . . .'

David turned and there, looming right up at him, and seemingly twice its natural size, was the Captain's body. The Captain saw him at the same instant and immediately a shot struck the wind. The echo of the pistol fire was volcanic, as though the whole system of rock and fell had split with one heave.

Then they were breast to breast and, a moment after, sword to sword. It was the strangest duel, their bodies visible one moment, invisible the next, the swords flashing as though with life of their own, lunging into emptiness, coming up sharply in defence against no opponent, and for David always the agony that he did not know where Denburn was; he might have Sarah in his arms by this; and there was also the part that the mist itself seemed to take in the affair, eddying around him, sweeping by with a swing of the wind's arm, beating against him, as though with a personal meaning.

He realised very quickly that the Captain was in a rage, and that the anger was personal because they had trussed him and piled him in the garden-house.

At first he muttered the dirtiest oaths: his personal vanity had been meanly affronted: but soon his strength began to fail him. The tussle with David earlier that night, the pressure up the Pass, the force of his age and his evil living all swiftly told on him. He made a lunge into cold fog, staggered with the impetus, and David's sword was through his arm. With a gurgle as though he had tumbled into a tub of water, he dropped.

David turned to find that the mist had slipped off the lower slope and was hastening, like a live thing, up the hill, torn away like a theatre curtain and flinging into the moonlight all the higher ground as far as Sprinkling Tarn. He could see the edge of that water a curdled grey against banks of vapour. The clouds were everywhere thinning, and the moon shone behind them with a thin glow, giving the shadows of watery ghosts to every rock and stone. As the mist pulled away Sarah ran to him: at his feet curled unconscious was the Captain; quite near to them Denburn, his sword in his hand, watching them. Phantasmal all these figures were, in a world so shadowy and faint that with every moment and shift of the clouds it was a new world.

So David put his arm about Sarah and thought he would say a word to her uncle.

'Go home, uncle,' he cried. "'Tis cold, and you must be abed. Sarah has said her farewells. She leaves thee the white cat. She is weary of thy company. Go home, go home. Thou art old for the fells at nightfall.'

He saw from where he was that Denburn had no pistols. He was flicking his sword back and forth. The moon was now in full splendour again, and the clouds had rolled back to veil the Gavel and crowd the Pike. The stretch of moor, the edge of the tarn, the Stye Head Tarn below them were brilliantly lit, and all the hills were ebony.

Denburn answered: 'You have killed my friend, ravished my house where you were hospitably entertained, and shall most immediately repent of it.'

The charge of broken hospitality vexed David, for it was, in a manner, true.

'I have not killed your friend,' he answered. 'You had best gather him together and go home with him or he will catch an ague. As to your hospitality I ask you now, with proper deference, have I your leave to wed your niece Sarah Denburn, whom I love and shall cherish always? I have money enough, and prospect of more. I am thirty-eight, and in admirable health. Give us your blessing and I will carry the Captain down myself.'

To this Denburn answered with some foul oaths. His voice had an odd note of surprise in it, as though he could not credit his senses that anyone should treat him with so arrant a disrespect.

'Well then,' said David, 'I will beat thee home for a dirty rascal and bragging bully. Run now, or I'll drive thee down.'

He moved forward. Denburn said nothing, but circled round towards the hills, then ran forward up towards Sprinkling Tarn.

There was something oddly comical in this long man with his waggling moonlit shadow running, but there was method in it. He found his higher ground with the Tarn behind him to the left.

'I'm afraid of no long-legged country bastard,' he cried. 'Leave the girl and go to your own place or I'll slit your ears.' Even here there was yet this odd note of astonished disappointment that he should be so inelegantly treated.

David moved up to him; he saw then that Denburn had been skilful in choosing his place. The moon, richly full, stared down at him; the shadows were baffling and at every step upwards he was under a disadvantage.

Their swords touched and it seemed to Sarah that the hills crowded nearer to watch the better. For her it was indeed the issue of her whole life.

Were David even wounded to unconsciousness she knew that she had no hope of Denburn's mercy after this affront to his pride. She crouched, watching, her hands clasped, her eyes hot and burning. She might possibly have aided him. Already she understood David well enough to realise that if she did he would never forgive her.

But Denburn was no very able swordsman. On higher ground though he was, David, whose reach was tremendous and eye certain, drove him step by step towards the Tarn. Denburn lunged, parried, lunged again with fury, overbalanced, and David had struck his sword from his hand. David himself was no very grand swordsman although he inherited an instinct of it from his father. He had wished all his days to do precisely this, in the manner of all the approved tales and poems.

With joy at his heart he followed the pattern of the romancer. His foot on Denburn's sword, he threw his own on to the turf.

'Now, Mr. Denburn,' he said, 'we'll wrestle for it.'

Very certainly he meant to kill him. The man was a dirty misshapen dog who had done nothing but evil and had no right to be in this beautiful world at all. Especially had he no right to be in a world that contained young Sarah.

So he ran forward and they were locked excellently in one another's arms. Denburn was wiry and his fingers were quickly about David's neck. David too was embarrassed by his height and, whether it were his anxiety for Sarah, his climbing to higher ground, or some extra energy that he had put into his swordplay, certainly he could not find his usual easy strength.

Denburn was strong in two particulars. His fingers would not be dislodged from David's throat, his feet would not be dislodged from the ground.

Sway as they might it seemed that his feet had some magic contact with the soil. The fingers tightened and there was a firm thought in David's brain. What if

after all he were to lose this? His breath began to come pantingly. The fingers dug inwards like live things with their own live purpose. It was as though his eyes were being pushed from their sockets. The moon rose like a flaming disc, hurled itself through the sky and swept back to its place again, while the black shoulders of the hills rocked and bent. His knees began to sag and the turf to run up to him like the swaying deck of a vessel. He released one arm to catch at those hands, tore at them, but they neither bent nor shook. Only pressed deeper. Denburn's head came curiously towards him, the eyes small, detached, the mouth curved and, as always, coldly self-pleased.

'O Christ!' The voice came from far away, from the very heart of the red and fiery moon.

'I am a strangled man. . . .'

He reeled, and with that reel lay the fortune of his destiny. Denburn's hand was shaken. David's body rose; like a dog he shook his throat free. His giant arms crushed the other's in a great grip. He lifted him from his feet, raised him in air, turned staggering with him, and flung him into the Tarn.

The man splashed, sank, did not rise. Heaving with gusts of strangled breath David waited. The ripples died under the moon, but Denburn did not come again. The scene was as still as a glass mirror and the quiet wonderful.

Yet he waited. Then, when he saw that for a certainty Denburn would never return any more, he ran to Sarah.

HERRIES IN 1760

Beauty is aroused by Beauty and change answers to change. But in this valley at this time Beauty was spread in vain for natives. They had not yet learnt to find it in the eyes of the outsider. Poet Gray nine years later, peering to find Castle Crag and Glaramara 'indescribably fearful,' was to open a gate that has grown since then most uncomfortably wide.

As to change; perhaps in no corner of England had the escapades and accidents of history made less stir than here. Looking over the flat green surface sheltered so tenderly by its protecting hills, you may see the monks of Furness Abbey riding their nags on survey of their property, or Sir Wilfred Lawson of Isell protecting his German miners, or Radcliffe of Derwentwater in the Civil War turmoil dredging peasants from the Borrowdale fields to support the King and to meet in that conflict their own near neighbours who, under Lawson of Isell, fought for Parliament, stored munitions on St. Herbert's Island, burnt the Radcliffe house on Lord's Island, and, riding up Borrowdale over the Stake Pass to Rydal, pleasantly sacked Rydal Hall.

And so to present memories, the old men and women of 1760 who could remember well enough the events of '15 when the Radcliffe house was still standing on Lord's Island and the last Lord Derwentwater lost his poor young head, dying by the axe as a last distinction--and so the Rebel Hunts on the hills after the '45, the terrified fugitives hiding behind the kitchen door, and Butcher Cumberland waiting in Carlisle. And now there was the new road, and more new roads after it, and soon Gray's post-chaise and, later, the little boy struggling over his sums at Hawkshead School, and the eyes of the world turning in wondering patronage towards this small square of ground. . . .

On this very afternoon of early November 1760, David Herries was looking out from his fields behind Herries on to a scene that no events could alter, that would for two hundred years to come wear the same quiet face. This November weather is cold and sharp, but the sun is out lying flat upon the fields; some of the sheep are away on the fells, on the lower slopes of Thornythwaite and High Knott and Watendlath, some are cropping the short turf in Stonethwaite, some hiding from the wind in the crannies and coverts of the rocks.

The valley has just learnt that on October 25 old George II. fell down dead in Kensington Palace. No one has been greatly stirred by this. Only some of the women gave a thought to a young Prince, only twenty-two years of age, a Prince who is really English at last, who says in his opening speech that 'he glories in the name of Briton.'

But, for David, this news meant something. He could not see young Charles James Fox, a boy of eleven, standing in front of his father and reciting in a shrill treble and with proud gestures lines from Samson Agonistes, nor John Wesley, in spite of his fifty-five years, preaching at five in the morning and finding it a 'healthy exercise,' nor Joseph Priestley, twenty-seven years of age, nosing his nonconformist way to his principles of oxygen, nor Samuel Johnson, an odd fifty or so, pushing his cumbrous path through the Strand, cracking his fingers as he went--he could not tell what the larger world might be at, nor indeed why it should be at anything at all (he was never a philosopher), but he did know that a crisis was arriving in his own affairs that must be met and met with courage and wisdom, and that, behind his own personal crisis, the solitude and isolation both of this valley and of his own history were passing and could never return again.

What must he do? What was the right thing not only for himself but for all?

He had married Sarah Denburn in May 1758. It was now the fourth of November 1760. From then until now, he and his wife had resided at Herries. Last evening (and here he leant his arms on the little rough stone wall, staring out in front of him, not feeling the cold, so lost was he in his grave anxiety and distress for what had occurred) there had been a terrible scene. It had been, of course, the fault of his father; it had been

only the worst of a number like it that, through this past year, had increasingly occurred.

It came in the first place from this cursed obstinate determination of his father to remain at Herries. When on that early May morning he had brought Sarah down to Herries it had seemed natural enough, even inevitable that they must stay. In the first place they had remained to face any trouble that might arise. The Captain, who on that eventful night had found his own way back to Wasdale, had at once, nursing his wounded arm, ridden off to his own place, wherever that might be, without word to anyone. David, remembering the chessmen scattered on the floor and the futile gestures of vexation, fancied that he had not regretted Denburn.

No one else, it seemed, had regretted him either. His body had been found a week later by some of the smugglers who used the Borrowdale-Ravenglass secret paths for their expeditions and were none too anxious for much investigation. They had left the body at the Wasdale Inn, and ridden away. That Sarah Denburn had married David Herries was proof enough that the Herries family knew something of the matter, but Denburn, it now appeared, was so deeply loathed and David himself was so widely popular, that no more questions were asked. In any case, a murdered man or so found in the hills was no matter for much curiosity.

The only local consequence of it was that once again 'old Rogue Herries' was connected with darkness. His son had killed the father, and married the daughter (as Sarah was in the outer world supposed to be). They skipped David in their superstitions, allowing him to do as he pleased, but the Rogue had another deed to his reckoning--and, as the wives whispered over the kitchen fires, "twould most surely not be the last.'

But for David, worried just now as perhaps he had never been in his life before, there was no superstition or rumoured chatter involved; there were facts, definite and hard.

The main fact was that the stress and odd circumstance of his father's marriage had been increased and aggravated by the arrival of his own beloved Sarah in this dark, damp and tumbledown place. If David had loved her at sight in Wasdale that love was nothing at all compared with what he felt for her now after a year and a half of matrimony.

She was ideally his desire. In her freshness, common sense, cheerfulness, kindness, tenderness she combined for him all the possible virtues. She had with these one fault only, and that would be no fault in any place of her own--it was that she must be putting anything to rights that she saw wrong.

It was not that she was meddlesome, but she was young--even now, after all this matrimony, but twenty-two--and where she saw dirt, incompetence, neglect, she must alter it. Not then with any officiousness or judgement of others, but she must alter it.

What she needed, as David only too clearly saw, was a place of her own. She had done what she could to Herries. She had in a way transformed it. Swept the corners, cleaned the floors, stopped the doors from creaking, ridden pillion with David to Penrith and Kendal to buy a chair, a table, and even, miraculously, a harpsichord. She aired the beds with warming-pans, mended her father-in-law's small-clothes, taught Mrs. Benjamin new dishes (and Mrs. Benjamin didn't thank her for it) and, through it all, was cheerful, merry, never out of temper, always busy and, it seemed, happy. Only David knew that she was not happy.

Deborah adored her (she pining, poor dear, to be married, and crying on Sarah's shoulder over it). Herries himself liked her. He found her merry and pleasant company. He didn't care how often she whisked about the house with a broom, or told Mrs. Benjamin how to keep the kitchen clean, or scrubbed the old worm-eaten floors. He liked to hear her play on the harpsichord, and often, with her, his old humorous ironic nature would return; he would have fits of his old playfulness again, and race her about the house, and hide behind doors to jump out on her. At these times he seemed to have half his sixty years, and they, the girl of twenty-two and the man of sixty, had a wonderful comradeship. Indeed, David was bitterly reflecting, were it not for Mirabell, they might be now a happy family.

Mirabell! Mirabell! Mirabell! He repeated the name, that had always seemed to him a fantastic and stupid one, aloud. He was beginning to hate her.

He hated her (he had always definite and solemn reasons for everything) because she made (wantonly, as it seemed to him) his father so unhappy, and because she, Mirabell, hated Sarah.

Sarah did not hate Mirabell; on the contrary she liked her, was sorry for her, would have made a friend of her had it been possible. It was true that she did not understand her, but who could understand this melancholy, dreamy, unnatural woman who, although she was now thirty-one years of age, was yet a child in so many things?

His exasperation with her began before he had realised her attitude to Sarah. Why could she not give his father more of what he desired? Even though she did not love him could she not pretend it? Women were good at pretending. Even though she had once had a lover must she mourn him for ever? To watch his father's unceasing tender care of her, to feel his unresting devotion, and to discover at the end of it his unhappiness--this was exasperating enough.

But when she began to avoid Sarah, not to speak to her could she help it, to leave a room when Sarah entered it, his exasperation grew to something deeper. It seemed (David was not good at these states of mind) that Mirabell's dislike had its origin in a resentment that Sarah took to herself the management of the house. She fancied, poor silly child, that it had been her affair. On a day she burst out before them all; this was the only thing she could do, the only service she could render, and now this service had been taken from her. Why, she was mad in this! What had she ever done before

Sarah came but carry plates hither and thither, rub the furniture, make the beds? She had had no talent for managing the house at all. How could she, she who had been a gipsy, a liver in caves, a companion of rogues, smugglers?

It was marvellous enough that she had the decency, the decorous manners that she had; how could she hope to be a house-woman in the fashion of Sarah who was gentle-born?

And there was more than this. She must always fancy that Sarah was mocking her, noting her country habits, laughing at words that she used, and the rest. Sarah never mocked her; she could not do anything so unkind. It was true that Sarah felt her difference from the rest of them, but she did not show Mirabell that she felt it.

Still the hostility grew, and with that hostility the girl's unhappiness, and with that unhappiness his father's strange outbursts of rage. They were roused always in the same way, and directed always against Mirabell. He seemed to rush from serving her and loving her directly into a tempest of passion when, before them all, he would abuse her, order her out of the room, surrender to a fit of dreadful violence. Then, after a while, a sort of horror would come into his eyes, as though he had done an awful thing, he would sit silent among them, then leave them and go to her.

When he abused her like this she answered nothing, only her pale face grew paler, and she would hang her head and go. She never disobeyed him, never answered back to him, was indeed submissive to everyone. It was perhaps this very submissiveness that exasperated David, not being himself a submissive man.

Well, it could not continue. Sarah could endure little more of it. If his father would not leave Herries then he and Sarah must leave it. On the other side there was the promise made to his dead mother and made to himself that he would never leave his father.

But against this there was now the strongest reason of all: Sarah was with child. Such a scene as last night's was impossible for her in her condition. The crisis had arrived. There was a fine house, half manor, half farm, to be bought in Uldale, behind Skiddaw. Just the place for him in which to start his family. But to leave his father. . . . What must he do? What must he do?

He turned at a sound and saw Sarah coming across the field to him. He was exceedingly pleased to see her. She would understand precisely the point that he had reached.

She came to him, and put her hand on his broad shoulder. She didn't speak. Clasping her with his arm he drew her closer.

'Dearest, it is cold for thee. We will go in.'

She laid her head on his shoulder.

'I am weary, Davy. Mirabell has tears in every word that she speaks, and your father does not speak at all, and there is a pool of water under the stair.'

He stayed thinking; then, looking down into her face, he said, as though he had at last reached the conclusion of long doubt: 'Yes, we must go.'

She waited, then said: 'It has been wrong here for me from the beginning. Why? I have no immoderate vanity, but I had not intended officiousness. Davy, AM I so officious? How can I know? Deborah says not. . . . In all those ill years after my mother's death what I did for my father was necessary. Anything to protect him against . . .' (She stopped. Inured to any sort of beastliness though she was, that death on the fell still haunted her.) 'But I was a child. I grew to be a woman that night you took me away. And being of a sudden a woman I must justify myself-- for myself, you see, and for you whom I loved. Have I interfered too greatly in this last year? But what could I do? The discomfort, the disorder, the uncomeliness--' She caught him closer to her with her arm about his neck. 'And why should Mirabell grudge it? I would not take her place. I have not, I could not--but to stay still and watch the dirt grow. 'Tis ill enough in a morning when your father, black and half naked in his old robe stained with drink, takes his ale. . . . I would not have you like that, not though you reach a hundred, but I have said nothing, all these months, not a word. But last night--that rage and Mirabell lying speechless at his feet! Oh no, Davy, it's not to be endured. 'Tis not wholesome nor natural. . . .'

'It shall not be endured, dear one,' he said, kissing her. 'I have been in the wrong to persist in this. It is settled. We will go to Uldale for a time at least. I must tell my father.'

But Sarah was an understanding and tenderhearted woman. She realised something of the long history that lay, far back, between those two.

'But you cannot leave him. We must think out a plan. To be at Uldale part, and here part, or for him to come--' She broke off, wrinkling her brow. In her heart at that moment she felt that she could not endure Herries another instant! How she loathed it, with its old musty furniture, its draughts and dripping water and constant disorder and rats and owls! The thought of a good, clean house at Uldale, a house of her own and David's that their children should be born in! Away from these strange underground disturbances that she could not understand any more truly than David. That brought her to her next word:

'Davy, your father and Mirabell are in another world from you and me, from Deborah too. We see things plainly as they are, and always will. A road is a road to us, and a house a house. But Mirabell and your father see nothing as it is. I cannot sit still like a puss in the corner to wonder which way the wind is blowing. For me, give me a fireside and you, a square screen to keep off the draught, a work-basket, and I can do well enough; but for them they see neither screen nor work-basket. But always something beyond the window that they have not, or once had or would have, or will have if they wait long enough.

'We must be doing something, they must only be thinking. Your father is sixty, and has been here these thirty years doing exactly nothing.'

'Yes,' said David, 'because facts are not sufficient for him. He could have done well with them if he would; you may call it an epidemical distemper, a madness, but he bears his condition with grand fortitude. He could not change it. He must have more than facts, and find something that will be a key for him to all existence.'

''Tis well,' said Sarah dryly, 'that he has money sufficient to keep him, even though it is your mother's, and a roof over his head, even though it is full of holes.' Then her heart reproaching her, she went on: 'Nay, I care for him greatly and would for Mirabell too if she would let me. 'Tis their unhappiness that distresses me. If I could bring them together I would never say a word for our going. But our being here separates them the more. They are of another world than ours. They are poets, maybe, and see everything fantastically. We--' she laughed, and pressing her cheek against his, very lightly bit his ear, 'we, Davy, are the farmers of this world, and are for ever taking our eggs to market.'

'And poor Deb,' he added. 'She cries her eyes out to be with HER farmer AND to have a child by him. 'Twill be too late an she does not hasten.'

Sarah looked back at the house, her strong broad body pulsing with health, her cheek glowing with the cold. 'That he can remain here and love it so! What he sees here or feels! If she would but love him as he loves her, then his dream would be fulfilled, I suppose, and he understand the universe . . . As he loves her! But no two love alike. Do we love alike, Davy?'

'I love thee the more.'

'Nay, no man loves a woman the more. You love me but you love also your Liverpool trade, and the fields here, and the sheep, and a cockfight in Keswick and chatter with the Keswick men. . . . Heigh- ho! We women--a poor circumstance to be a woman and a poor end, were it not for the children,' she added more softly. 'What's a man beside a child?'

They turned to go back and saw Herries coming towards them.

When he was near he had the face of a naughty child conscious of guilt. He wore a plum-coloured coat with silver buttons, and at his side a little sword with a chased silver hilt. He had dressed up and shaven properly. Thus, his head high and with that look of a child caught out in his odd angular face, high-boned, crooked with its scar, lined, stern and gentle, scornful and friendly, thus David, knowing that the moment had come at last when he must leave him, loved him. Sarah too wanted, as she saw him come so proudly and yet so submissively, to comfort him, the thing in all the world, as she knew, that he would most resent.

'Well,' he said angrily to David. 'You will kill her of ague in this wind. Bring her in.'

He looked out over the landscape, over the scrubby, stony ground, thick with bush and tree, here cleared for cultivation, there wild again. That was what he loved, that wildness! He looked on to Rosthwaite Fell and Glaramara behind it, greeting them.

'Softly,' said David, laughing. 'Sarah has tolerable strength. She does not faint at sight like the town ladies.'

He turned to them and looked at her with his old ironic smile. He bowed to her gravely. 'Madam my daughter-in-law, I am an old gentleman reaching dotage and beg to be excused for most unhandsome meddling.' He took her hand in his and went on most gently. 'My dear, forgive me. I forget sometimes my place. But soon you will be gone, and free; then you will look back and pardon me because you have a loving heart.'

'Be gone!' she cried. 'Why, in what condition . . . ?'

He shook his head, smiling, at both of them.

'Why, you know, I'm no such fool. I lost my temper painfully last night, my dears, and now you have been saying: "Poor old man, it is too terrible," and David has said "You cannot endure it, my love," and Sarah has said "Nay, my dear, you must stay with your father," but meanwhile there is a fine property at Uldale, and there is a child coming who must have a clean place to be born in, and--there are other things.' His face was suddenly stern. He looked out to Rosthwaite Fell as though to find comfort there. 'Davy has spoken of his promise to stay by his father, and Sarah has told him that he must not break it, and both of them are thinking how a way can be found.' He put a hand on David's shoulder. 'Is it not thus?' he asked.

It had been so exactly thus that they could neither of them answer him. He nodded.

'Yes, and so the property must be bought at Uldale, and I will trot over on my nag for a glass of ale and then--most contentedly trot back again.'

It was done. There was nothing to be said. In the hearts of all three of them they knew that it was the inevitable necessity. No one had spoken of Mirabell, but she was there, the final cause.

So David rode over to Uldale and in a short while was the owner of the manor farm and the land about it.

This was a modern house that had been standing only some ten years or so, charming in spirit and colour, built for comfort rather than display. Above it ran the moor free and unfettered to the skyline, and from that moor you could see behind you the Solway Firth and the Scottish hills, before you across the valley to Skiddaw and Saddleback, and then, curving to the right, the whole range from Helvellyn through the Pike and the Gavel to Robinson and Grasmoor.

Under this glory the house nestled, catching the sun, sheltered from wind and rain.

As David looked upon it, its walls faced with red brick that was already mellowing, the sash windows of happy proportions, the roof with its strong cornice, the dormer windows, the trim garden, the farm buildings, the little orchard, a great pride and happiness filled his heart.

He seemed to know, as though someone had whispered to him, that this was to be the home of his children and his children's children, and that he was beginning here a history that must have eventful consequences far beyond his own small consciousness.

All the world here seemed open and free. Near to Cockermouth, Keswick, Carlisle and Penrith, he was in the main world and was a man of that world. As he rode back to Herries he felt as though he were plunging into the dark bowels of the earth.

Weeks of restraint and discomfort followed. Sarah felt a desperate guilt. Mirabell seemed to show by attempting a shy, awkward friendliness that she was herself to blame, and poor Deborah, when she knew that she was to be forsaken, could not disguise her terror.

Nevertheless, in her heart, when she heard that David was going, she felt certain of her own coming freedom . . .

On the last night that they were together David and Herries sat up late by the fire. They did not speak much. David tried at last to say something.

'Father, it isn't a real parting. There'll be always a room for you and for Mirabell too. 'Tis no distance. It will be a pleasant change for you. And I will come here whenever you need me.'

Herries grinned. 'We are fastened together for life, Davy, but I don't care for having you by. That's the truth. I'm set on another plan from yours. Thou art a fine healthy lump of flesh and wilt breed children like a rabbit, fine children, I don't doubt, with no maggots in their heads. I've always had a maggot and it's made me lonely. By desire, mind you. I prefer it. I love you against my will, Davy, for you are everything that I would not be. To make money, build a house, have land, breed children, honour the King, pay your taxes, leave your mark on the country though it may be but the impression of your bottom on your counting-house chair, I can see 'tis an ambition as good as another. Myself I've stuck in the mud here for thirty years, been given a contemptible name, done nothing whatever save see the house drop over my head, married a wench from the road who doesn't love me, although she'd wish to, poor lass, out of a churchy kind of gratitude. . . . 'Tis as useless a life as a man can find and as pitiful, but I've had moments, Davy, that you will never know, and 'tis by the height of your divining moments that life must be judged. I love this woman that I have got here as you and Sarah will never love, in the entrails, Davy, down among the guts, my boy. And I'll have her yet, struggle as she may, and when I have her I'll know what the stars are for and why the moon's a silver treachery and what God has in His anointed beard. . . . And they'll not drag me from this house till the rats are gnawing at my toes and there's lice in my ears. For this is my home, this spot, this ground, this miry waste, and here I'll die--and the third day I'll rise again. I love thee, Davy, but thou art the damnedest fool of a good fellow that was ever made between sheets. So good-night to thee, my little son.'

After which he yawned loudly, stretched his arms, scratched his thigh and stamped up to his bed.

After this it was Deborah's tragedy. Poor Deb, a woman now of thirty-seven, an age at this time when, still unmarried, you were an old maid and as good as buried. She looked her age too, for she was broad and massive-bosomed, with sturdy arms and haunches, and a wide good-natured double-chinned face. She looked well in a mob cap, aproned and in pattens.

Nevertheless her little clergyman loved with a devoted unfaltering patience. He did not mind how broad she grew--he was no slim beauty himself. He would wait for ever if need be. He told her so again and again in his letters which were filled with love and little snatches of news and pieces about his health and his food.

'Little Love--' (he always addressed her thus, nor saw any humour in it) 'I had a fine visit yesterday to Sir Whickham Partridge's seat at Highloft. The gardens are very fine, of uneven ground diversified with valleys and hills. There is also a monstrous fine dairy with churns of butter, prints and skimming dishes all of the handsomest kind. We had fine weather and a most pleasant journey. . . . I have had three Baptisms in the last four days, but one infant hath died of the croup since and is now safe in the arms of Christ Jesus, which is all the better for the family in that there are nine of them already and the man, a good honest fellow, making little at his business--he is a cordwainer. . . . Little Love, you say nothing in your last letter about our marriage, for which I pray night and morning. I wait on your circumstances, which are, I know, uneasy of settlement. But my sister is ready to receive you here whenever the proper time comes.'

Or again:

'I rejoice at the good account you give of your health, Little Love. You have so cheerful and happy a disposition that you are able to endure the discomforts of your watery valley. . . . The bed in the guest-chamber has gone weak in one leg, and my sister Mary slept there the last two nights and found it unevenly balanced in the morning. . . . Thou knowest how dearly I love thee, Little Love, and wait only thy signal for all to be in readiness here. . . .'

Yes, he could wait for ever, but she could not. Four years gone and nothing done. Four years gone

and not a word said to her father. Whether he guessed or no she could not say. He was a strangely perceptive man and, when he wished, a strangely silent one.

After Mirabell came, for a while Deborah conquered her fear of him. He was softer, gentler, and seemed himself to care for her more openly. Then she might have spoken to him about her little clergyman. She had no reason to suppose that he would be angry. Why should he be? He had never shown any dislike of her marrying, or that he wanted to keep her with him for ever. But he would laugh. He would look at her in that terrible ironical way and, with a word or two, drive her into the very centre of the shyest reserve.

But what of that? He cared for her in his own fashion. He would not be unkind to her, he would even give her his own sort of ironic blessing. But here the accumulated effect of her years with him, of her old frights and old loneliness, her sense of his strangeness, above all, her terror of some sudden outburst of rage, held her back. Again and again she would tell him; again and again she postponed the occasion.

Then after David brought home Sarah it seemed certain that she would go. There was no need for her now that Sarah was here, but then, as the new situation developed so uncomfortably for them all, as Mirabell retired unhappily more and more into herself, Deborah stayed because she seemed to be the only link between Mirabell and Sarah. They liked her, both of them, although Mirabell said very little. But she, out of her own reserves and deep shynesses and perception of tiny things, understood Mirabell's wild, unhappy heart better than any of them, and Mirabell knew it.

But, when Sarah and David departed, her mind was made up. She would wait no longer. Stay in this house alone with the two of them she could not. They did not need her. She could do nothing for them; it was between Mirabell and Sarah that she had been able to help, never between Mirabell and her father.

Another thing also drove her to her decision--the knowledge that Sarah was going to have a child. That was the one ever-present, ever-dominant idea, the children that she would have.

She thought of it, dreamt of it, whispered the names that she would give them (to herself). But she was thirty-seven; soon it might be too late.

So a week after David and Sarah had gone she wrote a little letter:

MY DEAR LOVE--I can wait no longer nor suffer you to wait neither. On Tuesday next I shall be in Keswick at four of the clock standing at the corner by the Assembly Rooms.--Shortly to be your True and Loving Wife,

DEBORAH HERRIES.

I have not told my Father and shall bring only a small Basket fearing to upset him with my Newes.

When the letter was despatched by the carrier, her happiness flooded over her in a radiant shower. Why had she not done this before? She could not tell. A spell seemed to be broken. Surely then it would be easy to tell her father. 'Father, dear, next Tuesday I am going to Cockermouth to be wed with a clergyman.' But she could not say it even now. She knew how he would take it.

'Wed with a clergyman? Bedded with a parson?' and then his eyes, loving her but despising her too, then his shrug of the shoulder as he went out to his digging, or his tramp over the fells, or his riding to some distant valley. She also said nothing to Mirabell lest she should afterwards be charged with deceitfully keeping a secret. But on the last evening she went over to her and kissed her.

'Dear Mirabell, remember I am for ever your friend.'

The girl (for she seemed still a child with her slender body, little breasts, small rounded head) looked at her from under her pile of fiery hair and said, smiling:

'Why, Deborah, are you going on a journey?'

'Maybe,' whispered Deborah, nodding her head. Mirabell suddenly clung to her, resting her little head between Deborah's big breasts.

'Come back again one day. And if you travel think of me who would like to travel too.'

'Aye,' Deborah said, 'I will come back.' They kissed then, very lovingly.

When she kissed her father good-night that evening he was abstracted, reading a play of Shakespeare's, Antony and Cleopatra, and calling it nonsense one minute and miraculous marvel the next, so he nodded good-night, scarcely seeing her.

Next morning she rode into Keswick on Appleseed. Herries was out in the fields, cutting scrub away, and did not see her go. She left on the dining-table a letter:

DEAR FATHER--I have gone to Cockermouth to be wed to a clergyman, Mr. Gordon Sunwood. I have known him these four years but did not tell you, not to weary you with it. He is a Good Man, I am sure. I shall write to you at Cockermouth and then we will come to visit you if you wish us.--Your loving Daughter,
DEBORAH.

Herries did not return until evening. He saw the note on the table and read it. He read it again and then again. He smiled, then he laughed, then he threw back his head, roaring.

Then he called loudly for Mirabell. When she came he shouted:

'We are alone. We are alone. We are alone!'

He strode to her, caught her up, held her high, then kissed her over and over. His old wild joy of his wedding day seemed to have returned.

'Poor Deb! She is wed to a parson, to a stummicky, bottomy, garlic- smelling parson. I love my daughters, I cherish them, I give them all I have, but now they are gone and I have done my duty, my duty, my full and fitting duty. They are gone and we are alone, my Sweet, my beloved, my darling wife. . . . You and I, and there is no one to care for you but I, and no one to watch when we kiss nor when we quarrel. . . . I love my Deborah, but I like her better away sitting on the fat knees of her rummidgy parson, breeding young parsons to fill the pulpits with their precious tidings. . . .' He set her down on a chair, knelt before her, his head bent into her lap. 'Mirabell, there is no one in the whole green world but ourselves.'

When at last he was quiet she said anxiously: 'Is Deborah gone then?'

'Aye, Deborah is gone to wed with a parson.'

'Ah, that was what she meant when she kissed me last evening.' She shivered a little, but he could not see her; then, straightening her thin body against the chair, she said:

'And now if there is no one else you must be served by me.'

'Nay, nay,' he said. 'I shall be server, and you shall be the queen, for you are my love whom I adore. And shall ever adore through this death and the next after it and after that, to eternity again.'

But she, as though she had not heard him, and were following her own thought said: 'The Trumpeters coming through the valley. . . . I know that they must come.'

That evening he would not allow her to do anything, made her sit in the high chair at the end of the table, served her with food and drink, and at last when he had his own, sat on a stool at her feet. 'Deborah is a good woman,' he said once, 'and will make her parson happy,' and that was the only allusion he gave her.

Mirabell seemed to feel his happiness and respond to it. They sat together by the fire and she told him of her adventures with her uncles, and times that she could remember in London, and she let him hold her hand and stroke it, and when he kissed her she returned his kiss.

He rose and went upstairs and came again with a small cedar-wood box. He poured the contents on to her lap. They lay glittering there. There was a gold Moco stone chain set in gold, a necklace with pearls and vermilions, a gold watch, a rumphlet of diamonds set in silver and gilt, a large rose diamond set in silver and fastened to a bodkin, a gold ring with seven diamonds in the form of a rose, and a diamond cross.

She cried out at sight of them, a child now in her pleasure. He told her that they had been his mother's and that he had kept them for a fitting time to give them to her. He did not tell her that he had been storing them for the day when at last she would, freely, of herself, tell him that she loved him. She had not yet told him, but now that they were alone again, with everyone out of the way, soon, soon she would tell him.

He knelt before her and hung them all on her until she glittered and glistened in the firelight, all the stones winking and shining under the flame of her hair. Her fingers were loaded with them, and her neck and bosom, and she wore the diamond cross in her hair.

Then, very friendly together, they sat at the table while he gave her her writing lesson. At this, and at reading, she was very slow and stupid. It seemed that she COULD not learn. But to-night she was docile, and did her utmost to please him, sitting there in her old gown and covered with jewels.

She went to sleep quietly that night in his arms. He slept also. Later he woke to find that in her sleep she had got out from him, and was standing at the window in her nightdress, beating at the panes and crying:

'Harry, Harry! Take me out! I can't get out! Harry, Harry, I can't get out!'

He could hear her sobbing. He lay very still. Later she came into bed again, and he stayed very quietly, longing to touch her and to comfort her, but doing nothing. So he lay for many hours beside her in great trouble.

THE LOVER

Herries and Mirabell were alone in the house.

Except for Benjamin and his slatternly greedy wife there was no human being near them. Herries watched Mirabell as a cat watches a bird, and he watched out of love and terror lest at any moment she should escape.

Now most truly he was paying for all the infidelities of his long life. He knew in the depths of the bitterest truth what the anguish of unrequited love was. He was sixty-two years of age and had never yet known such burning desire of the flesh, burning because it was eternally unsatisfied. Night after night he might lie with Mirabell and do with her what he would, and night after night, when she slept, he would get up from bed and walk the house like a frantic ghost because she did not love him.

But this agony bit far deeper than any unsatisfied desire of the flesh could do. He was ready to surrender any physical connection for ever and ever if only she would love him a very little, and she was ready to give him everything she had out of kindness.

And so they came terribly to fear one another. She was afraid of his rages, his silences, his miseries and his absences. She was so fond of him that when he was away she longed for him to return so that she might be kind to him, and then, when he was there, she longed for him to be away again because she found that she could not give him the love that he desired.

Although she was now thirty-three years of age she was still very much of a child, and she was hoping that suddenly one morning she would find that she loved him. She was so fond of him that she could not understand why that fondness was not love. But it was not. Her heart never beat the harder when he was coming. Her face never flushed when he looked at her with passionate desire; at such times there was terror in her heart and she would wonder whether this night perhaps she would find that she could not surrender her body to him any more, and must tell him so.

That would be fearful, that night when it came. They both trembled at the idea of it. She thought that perhaps after she had shuddered apart from him, he would get up and go out and kill himself. She knew that he was aware of her reluctance, and that he loathed himself for pressing her. Sometimes when he had not, but had only kissed her and turned over to sleep, she almost loved him, put her hand up to caress his cheek and then put it down again lest he should take it as a sign that at last she really loved him.

But, although she guessed so much, she did not guess the half of his real torture; how before every step that he took towards her he hesitated lest she should make some movement, exclamation, sign that showed how she shrank from him.

She was troubled, too, by an increasing stifling sense of imprisonment. It was not only that now he watched her every step. It was also the personality of the house that she had always hated from the first. It watched her even as its master did. There were things in it that were spies, she was sure: the portrait of the old Herries in the dining-hall, the two suits of armour, the drunken tumbling chimneys. She could hear the suits of armour clanking after her at night, and she would stay in her room, the door ajar, listening to them as they whispered about her.

She hated it that always there was the same view from the windows and the yard. All her life long she had wandered, and now, wherever she looked, she must always see those two horrid hills, Rosthwaite Fell and Chapel Fell. The very hills that were Herries' passion were her loathing, and she hated most of all the way that he would talk about them as though they were persons and his very dear friends. They WERE persons and her very dear enemies.

But worst of all for her--and this thing, as the months passed, became an obsession--was her consciousness of all the little stone walls running up the sides of the hills. All her life long these stone walls had been the dearest things in the world to her. When she was an infant and could not walk, they would put her, wrapped in a shawl, under one of these walls out of the wind. As she stayed there, she could see the wall running, like a live thing, first across the turf straight like a taut string, then suddenly turning and leaping upwards until it was lost at the high bend of the hill. Over all this landscape she saw these little walls running, gay, free, vigorous, and when she walked--the wind blowing her hair--pressing up the side of the hill, the wall went with her, keeping her company. Now she was tied to this house. From the back of the yard she fancied that she could see a thin black line on Rosthwaite Fell; this was the wall and it would run to the ridge, then straight with only the sky over it, then it would dip again, catching its breath in the little valley before it mounted up again. Tears would fill her eyes as she gazed, and an impatience that made her heart beat angrily.

'He is kind to me, he loves me, but what would it hurt him if I were gone a week? I would return.' But would she? She could not honestly answer that. She was honest above all else. With all her faults of childishness, temper, rebellion, ignorant boasting, she was immaculately honest. It was because she knew that if she once went away she might never return that she never begged him that he might let her go.

Another thing her honesty showed her to her great distress and pain. She was beginning to forget Harry. This was the cruellest thing of all, because she had nothing with which to replace him. In all her bitterest distress at the agony of having lost him, there was a kind of bitter happiness because her love for him, although he was gone, was so wonderful. A thousand times a day she would recall everything that he had said and done, how he had looked here, how he had smiled there, what his eyes had done when he told her that he loved her. They had not had so very long a time together, so that the collection of her memories must be conned over and over. But the years had passed, and the conning had become almost mechanical; her honesty drove her to discover this and then drove her further, to realise that days and even weeks went by and she did not think of him at all.

She was indeed a strange mixture of childishness and maturity, of anger and submission, of knowledge and ignorance. Her best parts were her kindliness and honesty and a kind of instinctive poetry she had, and her industry. She always wanted to be at work on something, but unfortunately she had no gift for housework or keeping a place clean, or remembering what she must do. Untidiness seemed to follow her; things were broken, forgotten, disordered wherever she was. Nor would she learn. Her stubbornness was terrible. In these two years, Herries had taught her neither to read nor write. She would begin a lesson with him in all docility. He, for so restless and scornful a man, was marvellously patient with her. The lessons would start, both of them in great amiability, then her stupidity would irritate him, she see that he was checking it, and so she would burst into tears and run to her room.

What she liked best was when they sat in front of the fire, she on a cushion at his feet resting her head on his knees and he telling her stories. Then there was a great peace between them; he would forget his passion for her and be only her friend, and she would feel so kindly to him that she thought that in another moment she would love him.

They mingled strangely little with the outside world. Deborah lived, serenely happy, with her little clergyman in Cockermouth. She had only one grief--that as yet she had no children and soon she would be too old. But a Wise Woman had told her that she would have two sons, and Wise Women knew. David rode over often from Uldale although he was so busy a man. He was always urging his father and Mirabell to go and visit them, and Deborah too sent pressing invitations. But Mirabell would not go any more. She was frightened of Sarah, so efficient, businesslike, normal and happy. She thought that Sarah despised her, and so in her heart perhaps Sarah did.

But no. Sarah was of too generous a nature to despise her. She could not understand her. Mirabell with her odd looks, baby face, bright-coloured untidy clothes, sudden silence, odd sayings, was incredible to her. She did not understand her at all, and remembered that she was only a gipsy. Sarah was not a snob, but it was a time when the middle classes thought of the peasants as of another world from themselves, like dogs or cats or horses. Then Mirabell could not bear to see the neatness and grandeur of Uldale. It was not really very grand, but it seemed so to Mirabell with its solid walls and fine fires and trim garden, clocks and pictures and comfortable beds. There the rain did not drip through the roof, nor were the meals thrown anyhow on to the table, nor did the beds stay unmade all the day long. After a day's visit to Uldale she came back to Herries resolved to set everything into marvellous order. The next morning she was up in the dark busy and eager. But nothing would go her way; after she had swept, the dust was still there, the mud seemed to walk of itself into the house and lie about the stairs, the mice would come on to the table and nibble at the bread. And Herries did not care; he did not mind in what disorder he was living. He would curse Benjamin and his wife in a splendid rage, and then forget it all again. He was always dreaming, of the weather, the country, the clouds, the running water, and of herself.

So, this winter of 1762, things went from bad to worse.

A week before Christmas there was a great frost. A frost that holds is, in this district, rare; but round Christmas there is much cold spicy weather, the air nutmeg-scented, the waters running down all the hills with a tinkle of ice in their chuckles, the trees are red, amber to rose, and the sky grey, dove-winged, often very clear and shot with stars.

Mirabell was having a reading lesson in a house as still as the dead. A great fire leapt in the stone fireplace and the light of it clambered about her jewels and her orange-coloured dress. She had a silver shawl over her hair to see what it looked like, and when she should have attended to her lesson she was moving her head

143

against the old round cracked mirror that hung by the window to see how it shone. It was not vanity that moved her, but childishness and restlessness; this last because out in that grey frost-held world she knew that the little walls were running up the iron-clad hills to the grey snow-gathering sky. On such a late winter's afternoon she would be running ahead of her uncles over the turf, through the keen icy wind, to reach the edge of the Tarn. Here the water would lie black under a thin crinkle of silver ice, and the first cold stars would come out, and perhaps the slip of a frozen moon. . . .

Herries, his patience constrained with difficulty, was reading out of Swift's Polite Conversation. He chose this work because the English was good and the words were mostly of one syllable. Also it entertained Mirabell because of the pictures of, as it seemed to her, ridiculous polite society.

It was Herries' plan to read a piece very slowly and with great patience. Then Mirabell was to read it after him. This did not please her. She liked him to read straight on. What did it matter whether she herself should learn to read or no? He was always there to read to her.

Herries read:

'MISS. Lord, Mr. Neverout, you are as pert as a Pear-monger this morning.

NEVEROUT. Indeed, Miss, you are very handsome.

MISS. Poh, I know that already; tell me news.

(Somebody knocks at the Door. Footman comes in.)

FOOTMAN (to Col.). An please your Honour, there's a Man below wants to speak to you.

COL. Ladies, your pardon for a Minute.

(Col. goes out.)

LADY SMART. Miss, I sent yesterday to know how you did, but you were gone abroad early.

MISS. Why, indeed, Madam, I was hunched up in a Hackney Coach with Three County Acquaintance, who called upon me to take the Air as far as Highgate.

LADY SMART. And had you a pleasant Airing?

MISS. No, Madam; it rained all the Time; I was jolted to Death, and the Road was so bad, that I screamed every Moment and called to the Coachman, "Pray, Friend, don't spill us."'

Herries paused. Mirabell was seated beside him, her head screwed round to the mirror.

'You don't attend,' he said sharply.

She looked back quickly to the book like a frightened child. 'I do indeed,' she said hurriedly. 'What a childish Miss, to scream every moment because the coach jolted her! I could make her scream if I had her here.'

'Come,' said Herries sternly. 'Now you shall read.' He did not wish to be stern. His hand was very near her

flaming hair that was now ungathered and fell about her shoulders under the silver shawl and over the orange satin gown. It needed all his strength not to stroke it. His hand would move up and then down again while his heart thumped beneath his waistcoat. He must not touch her. All hope in an ordered lesson would be over if he did. She would sit on the floor in front of the fire and demand a story--a woman, thirty-three years of age. At least she did not look a day more than twenty. So, to check himself, he was stern.

'Cease glancing at that mirror,' he said, 'and read this for me.'

She began, very slowly:

'MISS. Lord! Mr. Nev-er-out, you are as p e r t as a Pea--'

She stopped.

'What is this long word?'

'P e a r,' he answered.

'Pear.'

'M o n g e r.'

She looked at it and shook her head. 'I have never seen such a word before.'

'No, doubtless. But how will you ever learn to read if you see only the same words every time?'

'Why should I learn to read?' she asked. 'Why do you force me? There are many ladies can't read. Besides I am not a lady, and will never be one. There are other things I can do, but not this.'

'You are thirty-three years of age.'

She jumped up.

'And older, older, older! I'm just as young as I was when I was five. I knew everything then and nothing. It is the same now.'

It was true. As he looked at her he saw her both as woman and child and loved her as both.

'Yes, that is true,' he said sadly. 'I am neither old enough nor young enough for you.'

'Oh, don't let us talk of ourselves!' She turned away to the mirror again. Then she softened, coming back with a smile. 'Oh, Francis, take me as I am! I cannot change with your wishing it nor you with mine. We must make what we can with what we've got.' Then she threw the silver shawl on to the table.

'I will go and do some sweeping,' she said. She was interrupted by a noise at the door. It was Benjamin, who said that there were some children there to sing carols. Then there was a strange light in Herries' eye, a curious smile at his scarred mouth. It was many years that the children had not come near his house to sing carols. Proudly he had always said that he did not care whether they came or no. But he did care. It seemed like a good omen that they should come to his old house at last.

So he ordered Benjamin to have them up, and soon in they trooped, some seven or eight boys and a short stout man in a red coat and with a double chin and a big belly.

They stood all together over by the fire, close, as though they were a little frightened. They had doubtless heard things about the house and its owner. But the sight of Mirabell reassured them. She was enchanted with them. She loved children, being a child herself, and now she clapped her hands, and went and stroked their cheeks and asked them their names, speaking in broad Cumberland just as they did.

Then she stood near Herries: his arm was about her, and so they listened to the music. All their years afterwards they remembered this scene and especially one carol. The stout fellow had a little viola on which he played very sweetly. The boys, at a sign from him, all lifted up their heads together like young birds and began to sing.

They sang 'The Three Kings' and 'The Cherry Tree' and others, but it was this one, 'The Angel Gabriel,' that Mirabell never afterwards forgot. The simple sweet tune greatly touched her, and later she learnt the words and remembered them, she who could never get anything that Francis taught her by heart. It was, she would afterwards think, the last scene of her childhood--yes, her childhood, although now she was thirty-three, and the background had always exquisite beauty in her memory--the grey frosted world outside hard like iron, and inside the room everything melting in the coloured firelight, the flickering ceiling, the crimson logs, the faces of the children, and Herries himself, grave and kind and generous-hearted, as she liked best to see him.

So the children sang 'The Angel Gabriel':

The Angel Gabriel from God
Was sent to Galilee,
Unto a Virgin fair and free
Whose name was called Mary:
And when the Angel thither came,
He fell down on his knee,
And looking up in the Virgin's face,
He said 'All Hail, Mary!'
Then sing we all, both great and small
Noël, Noël, Noël;
We may rejoice to hear the voice
Of the Angel Gabriel.
Mary anon looked him upon,
And said, 'Sir, what are ye?
I marvel much at these tidings
Which thou hast brought to me.
Married I am unto an old man
As the lot fell unto me;
Therefore, I pray, depart away,
For I stand in doubt of thee.'
Then sing we all, both great and small,
Noël, Noël, Noël;
We may rejoice to hear the voice
Of the Angel Gabriel.

'Mary,' he said, 'be not afraid,
But do believe in me.
The power of the Holy Ghost
Shall overshadow thee;
Thou shalt conceive without any grief,
As the Lord told unto me;
God's own dear Son from Heaven shall come,
And shall be born of thee.'
Then sing we all, both great and small,
Noël, Noël, Noël;
We may rejoice to hear the voice
Of the Angel Gabriel.
This came to pass as God's will was,
Even as the Angel told.
About midnight an Angel bright
Came to the Shepherds' fold,
And told them then both where and when
Born was the child, our Lord,
And all along this was their song,
'All glory be given to God.'
Then sing we all, both great and small,
Noël, Noël, Noël;
We may rejoice to hear the voice
Of the Angel Gabriel.
Good people all, both great and small,
The which do hear my voice,
With one accord let's praise the Lord,
And in our hearts rejoice;
Like sister and brother, let's love one another,
Whilst we our lives do spend,
Whilst we have space let's pray for grace,
And so let my Carol end.
Then sing we all, both great and small,
Noël, Noël, Noël;
We may rejoice to hear the voice
Of the Angel Gabriel.

When they had ended Herries could not do enough for them. That strange mood of excited gaiety that sometimes swept over him was on him now. He sent old Benjamin to the kitchen for cakes and sweetmeats; he would stuff the children till they were sick. He took the smallest, who would not be older than six or seven, on to his knee, and a great softness of feeling pervaded him when he saw that the child did not shrink but played with his heavy gold chain and told him his name, Richard Watson. Was the legend finished then? Was he no longer Ogre or Rogue? Oh, this was surely a good omen for him, and now everything would be right with Mirabell too. Before they were in bed she would tell him that at last she loved him. . . .

The boys had lost all their shyness, and were moving about the room, filling their mouths with cake, and examining everything. He gave the fat man richly from his purse, and clapped him on the shoulder. He carried little Richard on his shoulder down the stairs when they were all going. He saw them from the door with their lighted lanterns go across the frosty court. He saluted the myriads of stars so bright above the black line of the hills with a wave of his arm before he came back into the house.

He stood in the doorway of the room smiling at her, and she smiled back at him. She was sitting at the fire humming to herself the 'Angel Gabriel' tune.

'Like sister and brother, let's love one another,
Whilst we our lives do spend.'

He went to her at once, made her sit on a cushion at his feet, and, following on the triumphant current of his mood, drawing her head back against his knee, burst into a wild flow of talk:

'It is the first time all these winters that the children have been here. They've gone to every house but this one. Why should I care whether they have come or no? But I have cared, and now that you are here I have wanted everyone to be friendly. Yes, for the first time in my life I've wanted friendship. . . .'

He drew her closer to him, and she felt his hands hot and trembling against her cheek.

'Don't be angry with me. Don't turn me away. You must shrink because my hands are old, old and dry, but there's no age in my heart. I WAS old when I came here first, proud and young. I thought I could do just what I liked then--with anyone or anything. But I've learnt wisdom. Time has taught me. I haven't done what I liked with anything. Even the soil--I haven't even a fine potato out of it. And the trees have all gone crookedly against me, and the wind has blown the hills sideways. But I toiled on, because I knew that there was an answer somewhere to my question if I refused to be beat.

'What's my question been? I don't know myself. That's the odd thing. I don't know either the question or the answer. I puzzle my head sometimes till it breaks. Yes, breaks. Splits like a fig. Then I think the answer will be in there. It must be. That's the thing that spins round and round and asks all the questions. But if it has the questions then it must have the answers too. These questions. Why is the sky grey to-day, my dear, and being grey, with a touch of rose to it, why does my heart thump? Why cannot I leave this place, this tumbled heap of stones, but must hang on always staring at a humped hill and a pocketful of rank grass? Yes, split your brain and dig in the mess with your fingers for the answer.

'Nay, it's not in the brain but in the wind behind the brain and the soft sly voice behind the wind. Ah, that voice! I tell you, Mirabell, there are times when I've almost heard it. I've stood on Honister, where I found you, my darling; I've stood there listening, and He's been almost in my hand. A sly dog, conceited of His power, with all the beauty that He's got and all the strength to frighten us. And at the last, maybe lazily,

out of idleness, He drops a present into our lap, a golden rose, a string of glass beads.

'I say damnation to His power. I care not a rabbit for it, but 'tis the mystery plagues me, Mirabell, the oddity, grotesque like a map of China, bits here and there, offal and star-dust together. That's why I stare and stare, looking at a hill or a tree or a lump of this rotten soil, for the secret may be in any place, and by a hair's-breadth of laziness we may have missed it.

'The Herries have always been like that, one mystery-monger and the rest good sober citizens. David's the sober sort. There have to be both in the world. But David finds nothing odd. It is all as it should be. But for me, until I found you, there's been no answer.

'Now, if you loved me, there'd be an answer to every question. I am your lover, Mirabell. I'm not an old man past sixty, but young and strong, always your lover. Can you love me a little, Mirabell? I have been patient all this time with you here. Is it coming to you a little? I am so hungry for it. I think I must not be without it much longer. Mirabell, Mirabell. Love me a little, a very little. . . . I want you so.'

His voice ended in an almost breathless whisper and she held herself taut so that he should not feel the shiver that was running through her body.

At first while he talked she had been hypnotised by his voice, but had not listened to his words. It was comfortable here by the fire; she liked him when he was kind and friendly. She always loved his voice when he was telling her a story or talking about his ideas. She found his ideas incomprehensible. She did not understand one of them. The things that he said were completely unreal to her. This mystery that there was in life, she could not see any of it. Her own life was clear enough. She had been beaten and ill-treated and must fight for herself, then she had loved a man, as many a poor girl had done before her, and he had been murdered most foully, and after that this man had been kind to her and given her a home. She could not love him; that was not her fault; she was generous, she would give him anything, but that was something that you could not give unless it happened so. There was no mystery here.

He was always talking of staring at stones and trees. When he came to this her mind slipped away and she would think of other things-- of the little walls running away under the frosty air, of old Mrs. Benjamin who was a slattern, of Sarah's fine household gifts (odd how often she thought of Sarah!), and to-night of those children singing their carols. How fresh their voices had been, how fresh and how sweet!

But when he came to his love-making, fear snatched her back to attention. Oh, how she hated it, that now so familiar change from friendliness to love! She was like an animal caught, all her senses alert for any chance of escape.

Everything was changed. The tone of his voice, the touch of his hand; she could feel all his body trembling behind his fingers. Not a simple lustful desire to possess her--that she could have understood and to that she would have submitted--but this thing, far more deadly, this praying, pleading passion that she should love him. How could she when she did not? Oh, how could she? . . . There was danger here, dreadful danger both to herself and to him. Yes, she held herself taut lest that inner revulsion should escape her and rouse his fury. It was, she understood, fury and rage and disgust with himself rather than with her, but that did not make it less awful.

'I love you, Mirabell, dear, dear Mirabell. . . . Give me a little in return. . . . Love me ever so little.'

Stiff against him, her head up, staring into the fire, she answered:

'We are so happy thus, Francis. Let us stay tranquilly. . . .'

'Tranquil!' He caught her closer. 'A fine word to use, but I have never been tranquil. I have not been worthy of any tranquillity.'

She understood that. This man was in reality the shyest and most modest she had ever known. She did not comprehend men who were fighters with themselves. Every man in her life had taken himself for what he was and thought no more about it. But this man was different. She did dimly perceive that everything in his history-- rebellion, outrage, ostracism, irony, sense of beauty--had come from his own restless dissatisfaction, and that if she saw his soul naked it would be a soul on its knees. But she did not want to see his soul bare. Any close terms with him meant violence and the demand for something that she hadn't to give. Moreover on an occasion like this her fear was so great that such wits as she had were away.

'Let us read again,' she said, trying to smile at him. 'I will be cleverer this time.'

He put his hand to her neck and held her head up to him.

'Understand this. I am out of breath now. I can endure no more. You must love me. You can if you will. You have love in you. You could give it to that other man. And have I not done more for you than he could ever do, more in every way? Has a man ever loved you as I love you? I want nothing. . . . Love me and I will never ask you a favour. Love me and I will sleep in another bed. Love me and I will work for you like a dog. We shall leave this place that has always fretted you. We shall go where you will and I will never even kiss your hand. I will not touch you, Mirabell, if you can love me a little. My heart is starved . . . after these years . . . I have no more power to resist.'

He was at her feet, kneeling. All his pride was gone, all his power over himself. His scarred face lifted to hers, if she had been able to see it, was beautiful.

But she could not see it; she was so frightened that she could see nothing. This was the worst that he had ever been. With a little cry she tried to rise. He caught at her dress. He held her round her knees.

'Say that you love me even though you do not. I will cheat myself.'

But she could not. Her lips moved but no words came. He caught her, pressing his face to her bosom. Then he felt her tremble. That flung him into madness. He had been always afraid of this and had been on his guard. Now he guarded himself no longer.

'I will beat you into it. Can you stand outside me and I not compel you to come in? Have I waited so long for naught? Have I no strength?' He caught her and strained her to him. He covered her face, half averted, with kisses. He dragged her head back by the hair and kissed her neck, tore her gown open, burying his face in her breasts, murmuring: 'An you will not come to me, I'll make you . . . I shall conquer your stubbornness, do you see? You are inside me, at my heart . . . shall never escape . . . I carry you with me.'

Her fear was so frantic that she managed to break away from him and crying out: 'Oh, never, never any more!' ran, half naked, across the floor and up the wooden stairs. She heard him stumbling after her, crossed the dark passage, found her room, bolted the door with its wooden bolt and then crouched against the wall, listening. She thought that he meant to kill her, but it was not the fear of death that frightened her, but something far deeper, a mingled terror and sorrow for him was part of it.

He came to the door and battered on it, shouting: 'Come out, then . . . I will end it for us both. . . . Come out that I may finish it.'

He paused, and the silence in the house was terrible; not only in the house but in all the frost-bound, star-shadowed world outside. There was moonlight in her room, splashed against the wall. Her eyes devoured the door.

He battered again, then flung all his weight. The whole house rang to his blows, the door that was very old cracked. He kicked and it fell.

From the doorway he saw her crouched against the wall. He waited, his breast heaving.

She did not speak, she could not. So they stared at one another.

His madness left him. The moonlight seemed to lap it up. He knew that he had done something for which he would never forgive himself.

He turned and with hanging head went away.

MIRABELL IN FLIGHT

There is a work of particular interest to members of the Herries family--Letters in England, 1757-1805-- edited by Dorothea Leyland (Satters and Bonnin, 1876).

This is a book worthy of more general reading. Miss Leyland tells us how, after the purchase by her father of Rockington Hall in Shropshire (the home of the Durward Herries from 1830 to 1854), she discovered in an old oak chest a red leather box stuffed with old letters. They were hard to decipher, yellow and torn, but after some difficulty and the exercise of much patience they were all transcribed.

They included letters preserved and formed into little packets neatly tied with red ribbon by that solemn and serious Mary Titchley, wife of Grandison Herries and mother of the gay Pelham; of all of whom we have already caught glimpses.

They were not of necessity letters written entirely to or by members of the Titchley and Herries families, although these formed the larger portion of them. This, one may suppose, was why Miss Leyland decided against giving the collection a family name. The volume excited very much less attention than it deserved. There was not at the time of its publication the interest in eighteenth- century minutiae that there is to-day. It has been long out of print. In any detailed chronicle of the Herries family during the years included by it, it must be of great value.

There is one letter--dated April 4, 1763--which is pertinent here. It is written to Pelham Herries (at this time a bachelor of forty- five years of age living in King Street, St. James's) by his cousin Frances Titchley, a single lady of middle years who was at the time making a tour of Scotland and the North of England with her brother Reginald and his wife.

After certain details that do not here concern us (the full letter can be found on page 331, in the volume above referred to) it proceeds as follows:

. . . I was about to close my letter without communicating to you my most interesting Adventure, most interesting at least to Yourself who, if you will remember, begged me to ascertain any News of your Cousin whether in Keswick or the Barbarous Wilds of Borrowdale.

In my own solitary Person I had not the courage to invade the Fortress of dear Raiseley and dearer Mary. You know how they are thought of by the Family as a Pair of Unconscionable Ogres from whose Hospitality no Cakes and Ale are to be hoped for, but only the Chilly Fingers of Uneasy and Insincere Politeness. In short, dear Pelham, neither Reginald nor Coelia would accompany me on a Call and I would not go alone, so although we were three whole days in Keswick and expecting momentarily the most Inconvenient of Meetings we escaped without a sight of them.

Blame me if you will, dearest Pelham, but remember that you have not yourself been over Punctilious in your Obedience to Inexorable Duty.

You know that I can always see more faults in my own Performances than I love to think on, but at least You shall not be entirely Disappointed in me; I have something yet to offer you.

You know that Reginald has, from his Cradle, a love of the Horrible and that no Terror is so Great but that he must tickle his Palate with it. We have seen, as I have told you in my other letters, Sights of Superb Splendour and the Grandest Magnificence in Scotland. For my part I felt that I had seen enough and even my Love for You was not Spur sufficient to drive me into the (so rightly named) Jaws of Borrowdale to catch maybe a glance of the ferocious Herries who inhabits there. But you know how 'tis the nature of the Common People to hate all Novelties and the nature of Reginald to be drawn by them, so when the Boots at the Keswick Hotel assured us that there was Nothing in Borrowdale to be seen but Horrid Crags and Violent Waterfalls this decided Reginald immediately. He was ready indeed to go alone, and Coelia, when she heard that the only Transport was on Horseback, decided violently against going but, a little thro' Charity to myself and a great deal thro' Charity to You because I was aware of your Eager Curiosity to hear something of your strange Francis for whom you bear, you always tell me, so odd an Affection, I agreed to accompany Reginald and to share with him whatever Perils and Dangers there might be.

Strong Temptations rise within my heart to make of this a story as fearfully absurd as any thing in the History of Miss Betsy Thoughtless, but I will spare your Sensitive Feelings and I am sure you will consider my Behaviour has been very handsome. In short we set out on the fairest of Young Spring Days and discovered the most lovely of England's uninhabited though Cultivated Vallies. I say Uninhabited but am not quite Literal. Houses and Farms there are scattered here and there in a wilderness of Scrub under the Frowning Eyebrows of horrid Crags and Precipices. Whatever you wish to offer up to your Idol, Taste (and you know that I have ever applauded your taste in the Arts, extravagant tho' some of your Relations have found it) as We saw it under a brilliant Sun with fresh Green glittering from a recent Shower I was not altogether resolved against coming to live in these Regions for the remainder of my Days and indeed might seriously so consider it were it not for the too close Juxtaposition of dear Raiseley and Mary. But now to my Story. Our Guide, who both in his Corpulency and abruptness of Speech reminded me strongly of Uncle Roger (whose Partiality for green corn partridges and ill success at the Oxfordshire Poll you will certainly remember) showed us the Beauties and Curiosities of the district as we passed them, the Ingenuity of the Bowder Stone, the Beauties of the River Derwent, a wood above the river where not so long back they drowned a Witch, but I will not detain you with these, knowing, dearest Pelham, your Unmitigated Impatience with anything that has not to do with a graceful Ankle or a Pack of Cards, and so proceeding over the Wildest Country, all Horrid Boulders and Little Trees growing in grotesque profusion, we approached at length the village of Rosthwaite. You have heard me say that I am a Philosopher only in the fields, and never in the Fields but when the sun shines, so should I have been most surely a Philosopher now, but I confess to a most unphilosophical Tremor when the Guide says, as quietly as you please, 'And that is the House of Herries,' pointing with his stick to a strange Building on a rising Hillock so near to us that only a rivulet and a rustic Bridge divided us.

The Afternoon was gathering in and the Shadows fast falling across the Valley. There was a Purple Light over all the scene and the Mountains had assembled in front of Us as though to close us in with their Black and Jagged Sides. It was a fearful Scene, dear Pelham, and I am thankful indeed that I had Reginald with me Who being destitute of all Imagination suffers no Distress from Nature at her darkest nor the forebodings of Man's untimely End. How Strange, how Abandoned, how Desolate this House of Francis Herries! I have seen you draw a Gothick Hog-sty for a customary Freeholder in Northamptonshire but this would be entirely beyond your Pencil.

From where our horses stayed We could see the deserted grass-grown courtyard, Walls from which the bricks were already falling, windows so Dark that they must be always foreign to the Sun, and the Garden behind a tangle of Weed and Stone. The House must be in part Elizabethan or of an earlier date and it had, in this Shadow that crept about the silent Valley, so unhappy an Air that I have never seen a House speak so eloquently. And now see what follows! We had been watching in silence for some five minutes when of a sudden a Woman comes into the Doorway.

She stands for a moment in Hesitation then crosses the Courtyard and turns down the Path towards us. We had, as You might imagine, a Perfect View of her and I ask you to imagine how Romantick a Picture with this tumbling dark House behind her and the Black Hills on every side and no Sound in the World. As she came toward Us I saw that she was beautiful or so Unusual as to be named a Beauty. She passed us by silently as a Ghost might. She wore nothing over her Head, and her Hair was the Reddest in Hue I ever saw. Over her shoulders she had a Orange Shawl.

Her Face was small and white like a Child's but by her Person I should say she was near thirty Years. Lost in her Thoughts she gave us no Notice. Then, when She was scarcely past us a man came from the same door, walks to the Lane, sees her in front of him and also draws near to us. This was of course your admired Francis.

He also passed Us without the merest Glance, slowly as though He would not accompany the Figure in front of him but yet would keep Her in His Eye.

You have seen Him, Pelham, and so I need not waste Paper in describing Him to you, but how Striking and how Strange is his appearance. His Clothes are Shabby and stained with mire. He had a Black Hat and a Coat with wide old-fashioned skirts of rusty Brown, he was gaitered to the Knee.

But his Face--scarred on one Cheek from brow to lip--his Eyes of a most tender and Romantick Cast,

grave and yet kindly, his Body so straight (save for the slightest stoop of the Shoulder) that although You tell me He is over Sixty it is yet difficult of Belief. There seemed a sort of Desperation in his eye although You, knowing my Romantick Disposition, will attribute this Embroidery to my excess of Sentiment.

He passed Us and followed the Lady but, as I have told You, not to be up with her but rather to keep Her in his Watch. We saw her turn into the shadow of the darkening Road. He slowly behind her and so the two of them out of our Sight.

Forgive, dearest Pelham, the Length of this Epistle but I had resolved that I must give you the fullest details of this Occurrence although Reginald pshaws me and assures me that We have seen nothing at all but a husband and wife on their Daily Walk. For myself there is something more Romantickal and I will confess to you that I have altogether fallen in Love with your Francis and would perhaps try my Fate with Him were he not so obviously already Captured.

My Health is much after the old fashion; yours, I hope however, is quite recovered . . .

There is nothing further in this letter that calls for attention.

The other view of Francis and Mirabell during this month is Deborah's. For a long time past Deborah and her husband had been demanding a visit. Francis had never come near to them since Deb's marriage.

One afternoon towards the end of April, Francis and his wife (riding pillion) appeared outside the little, squat, rosy-faced rectory. The Reverend Gordon Sunwood was cleaning out the pig-sty. Deborah was baking a cake. She arrived at the doorway, her face rosy from the heat of the fire, her hands thick in dough.

She was pleased and frightened at the same time. They looked so strange sitting silently on a large black horse as though they had been conjured out of the ground.

It was altogether the strangest visit. There seemed no actual reason for it. Neither seemed glad to be there. But, by the second day, Deborah seeing that something was terribly amiss between the two of them, her warm heart was deeply touched and she tried to draw close to them. No easy matter. They were like foreigners who are uncertain of the language spoken around them. They looked foreign, too, sitting in Deborah's amazingly neat and bright parlour with its shining brass, its handsome pictures of King George and his Queen, its Chippendale chairs.

But altogether it was the prettiest of little rooms, hung round with India paper, with Chelsea china, and a pagoda, and a looking- glass in a frame of Chinese paling.

This room was Deborah's pride, and how happy she was, sewing by the fire, listening to the steps on the cobbles, and interrupted once and again by the fat, cheerful countenance and round plump person of Mr. Sunwood, who would look in to tell her about the new litter of pigs or how the hens were laying or the text he had chosen for his next sermon or how Mrs. Jameson, the lawyer's wife, was faring in her childbirth.

Deborah had all she wanted in the world, for now she knew that she was to have a child. (She was delivered of boy twins on the morning of October 3, 1763.)

Socially, too, the Sunwoods were very popular. It must be remembered that Deborah had never all her life long known what social popularity was. There had been always over them the atmosphere of her father's sin and social impossibility. She had also been in Doncaster too young to know what society was, and at Herries there was no society.

She yielded herself, therefore, now to all the friendliness and neighbourliness with a full will, and happy were her days. But all her life came back to her full flood in the presence of her father; yes, right back to her infancy when they arrived at Keswick on that stormy afternoon and Alice Press sat beside the fire.

Old shadows, old terrors. She was not afraid of him now quite as she had been; married life had given her independence. Besides, he was strangely kind and gentle. He seemed to have lost all his authority, acquiesced in anything that was suggested; he charmed Deborah the most by his exceeding courtesy to his wife, rising to offer her any attention, always with his eye on her.

But they talked scarcely at all together, only smiled occasionally, and then as though they were strangers.

Deborah did her best to come to close terms with Mirabell and, until the final evening, altogether failed. She took her over the little house, showing proudly all her treasures. Especially the bedstead in which Mr. Sunwood and his lady enjoyed their marital comforts. This was a mahogany bedstead with fluted posts and dark crimson hangings. Other glories of the house were a walnut-tree writing table, three India-back walnut-tree chairs with stuff silk damask seats, a pier-glass in a black and gold frame, blue and white china, and a Turkey carpet.

It may be wondered what contrasts Mirabell made in her heart between this and Herries. Poor woman! A house like this, cosy, warm, clean, bright with frilly things, and an air everywhere of love and safety, had never been, all her life, in her way. Would she have cared for it or would it have driven her wild? If it had been this that she wanted, and she had urged Francis Herries sufficiently towards it, there is little doubt but that he would have tried to get it for her. She did not belong to this comfort.

With every hour Deborah felt the distance between them growing. Physically they were of separate worlds, Deborah plump, with cap and apron, keys at her girdle, with her bright happy face, placid too and yet sensitive with that perception, kept by her from childhood, of small unexpressed things.

It was this perception that made her bond with Mirabell, that separated her from Sarah and David and gave her kinship with her father, although she feared him. She was in that way nearer to her father than to her own husband. She watched Mirabell. She saw her stand near the mirror in the parlour, half reflected in it. Her face was elfish, both tragic and impatient. Under its great burden of hair it was poignant in its loneliness. And at last Deborah, unable to endure the woman's silent suffering any longer, caught her in her arms and held her there.

'Tell me, my dear, what is it? What is wrong? Why are you unhappy?'

Mirabell did not try to escape as Deborah had thought that she would. She stayed there looking down.

'We are both unhappy,' she said at last, 'because I cannot give him what he would have, and he has done something for which he will never forgive himself.'

Deborah drew her to a chair. She felt close, close to her. She suddenly seemed to understand her as she never had before, understand the good honest heart, her wild nature uneasy at captivity, her gratitude for his kindness to her, her misery because she could not love him. These things were all told to her as though Mirabell had spoken.

She did speak; she looked up into Deborah's face, seemed to find comfort in those quiet eyes.

'It is all my own sin, all because I came to him for shelter that first time when I was hungry.' She began to speak passionately as Deborah had seen her do once before above Bassenthwaite Water.

'I could not know then; I was a child in so many ways. I knew that he loved me, but not that for so long, with so much refusal, he would still love me. His love is terrible; it is like a pain in his heart and in mine. If I cared nothing for him it would be easy. I would have told him and left him. But how can I not care for him when for so long he has been so good to me, and for so long asked nothing in return? Now at last he does ask something. He cannot help himself. . . . And then there is more. I am imprisoned in that house. I am a woman now, not a child, and it seems that I am a woman accursed because I cannot rest anywhere. I think that when Harry was killed I was struck a blow here at my heart. I can feel it, a pain that nothing can heal. After all, I am of no family and of no place. I am not in my own world with him. If I loved him, then nothing would matter, but because I cannot. . . .'

She broke off, threw up her head. 'I have a great scorn of women who go about bewailing everything. We had a woman once who was like that; she was mistress of one of my uncles. "Oh," she was always saying, "he has struck me," or "He neglects me," and therefore he did strike her, no blame to him. I would wail about nothing of myself, but to see him so wretched when I care for him. . . .' She broke off again, then turned eagerly to Deborah. 'Oh, you don't know, Deborah, how good he can be! He is quite changed now. Of course he is older, but it is not only age. There is a new gentleness--can you not see it?'

'Yes,' said Deborah, 'but it is because he is unhappy.'

'I know, I know!' Mirabell caught Deborah's arm. 'I cannot endure that quietness, not for much longer. If we could speak together-- but, after Christmas last, he will say nothing concerning the two of us. There was an angry scene. He beat down the door of my room. I thought he would kill me. I would not have cared had he, but the fit passed and since then he has had a shame that has no cause. What is that--beating the door down? He himself has done many things worse--and to me what have they not done? Beaten me and kicked me, and many worse things. I would not have minded if he had beaten me, but it was of a sudden to withdraw, as though he had done some shameful thing.'

'That is because he loves you,' said Deborah.

Then Mirabell said, dropping her voice very low:

'It cannot go on like this. It must have a turn. It were better for him that I were not there.' And then, with the oddest smile, looking close at Deborah again: 'And perhaps I am not there. No woman at all. The real woman is somewhere else and loves him. I feel that I have no soul, that I must go out to find one.'

At that Mr. Sunwood came in and they had supper.

Deborah had one word with her father. After supper he went to the door with her to see the rich red spring moon. He stood there, feeling through all his body the peace of the little town. The cobbled path, the white houses shining in the moonlight, the rooms behind them with their warmth, no sound, and the moon riding through the serene sky. But he turned to her:

'I will not accept this world of ghosts,' he said. 'He has laid it thus, so and so. "And now you take it," says He. "This is good enough for you." But it is not good enough. It is a botch, a mess, a frustration, and man is frustrated in the middle of it. But for every man, one twist and it would be right enough. "Jog this for me a turn to the left," says Man, "and I shall have comfort." "Not I," says God. "Jog it yourself if you can."' He laughed and tweaked Deborah's ear very gently. 'Thou art happy, Deb?'

'Very, father,' she answered.

'Aye, so I see. And I like your parson, even though he likes not me.'

'Oh, but he does,' said Deborah indignantly.

'Nay,' said Herries laughing. 'I am an old serpent in his nest. I can see him wondering, as we sit at table, "Now, how doth my adored Deborah come from that thief's loins?" But 'tis my seed, Deb, that you are, never shame thy mother else.' He sighed, shrugging his long shoulders. 'Poor sainted Margaret! Old days. Think you that she is behind that moon now, Deb, watching us?'

'Where Heaven may be,' said Deborah.

'Aye, where Heaven may be--a plaguy caterwauling place.'

Taking all her courage she said: 'How sweet Mirabell is, father; and she cares for you most deeply.'

He looked at her as though he had not heard, then, very low, staring at the moon and speaking into the air:

'She has no right to care. I have treated her very evilly; everything in me turns to evil.' Then, shrugging his shoulders again: 'Come in. Do you know that I am sixty years old and more? Every part of me from nose to belly, from belly to knee-joint, is aware of it. Only I, I myself, will not recognise it.'

They went inside, and next morning the two rode back to Herries.

As they rode Mirabell knew that he had some fresh plan in his head. She heard him laugh softly to himself, saw him turn to look back at her, then toss his head as though he were proud of making his mind up. And she was intensely miserable. She had never before known such misery. When Harry had been killed, that had been unhappiness of another sort--deep, biting agony with grandeur in it; this was unhappiness that came from failure. Somehow in these years, with all the chances that she had had, she should have made a better job of it. Had Deborah's parson felt passion for her but she no passion in return, would she not have made the best of it, have satisfied him in some way, have 'taken him in' for his own good as so many women must do with their men?

Ah, but Deborah's parson and her Herries, what different men they were! There was no one like her Herries (here she felt a queer sort of pride) for oddity, suddenly stepping inside himself where you could not get him. And herself and Deborah! Here, too, there was a bed-rock difference. Deborah was a lady and she, Mirabell, was not. She did not know what she was-- something for nothing, an absurd misfit belonging to no place, no person. And here such a bitter sense of desolation came to her that it was all she could do to hold back her tears.

It would never do that he should see her weeping, so she turned away blinking at the thin sunshine radiant with promise. Derwentwater lay below them. The air seemed to be filled with the sound of waterfalls, and in contrast to this delicious murmur the lake was softly still. One boat floated upon it, the hills were most delicately reflected in purple shapes, a looking-glass world. Lord's Island was a cloud of green. Everything was freshly green-- the copses, the hawthorns. Birds were singing everywhere-- bullfinches, robins, thrushes--and on all sides the gentle fields sloped lazily up to the rocks and spurs of the hills that would soon have a shadow of green smoke on them from a hint of the new bracken.

Such peace must seem unreal when life is at impossible odds, but for Mirabell this free and open nature had always been the only true certain thing that she knew. She did not analyse it, she could not have described it, because it was part of her, and, just as she was at a loss about her own moods and nature if she were asked for any definition, so she was at a loss here. But the lake, that had slipped so beautifully down between the hills and now lay in perfect peace, rose up to her and for a moment drew her into its own tranquil reassurance.

For some days after their return Francis Herries kept his plan, whatever it was, to himself; then at last one evening he told her.

Herries was at its best in the spring and the early summer. Daffodils blew about its walls, birds were everywhere nesting, the old rooms seemed to take the sunlight more readily, the windows could be flung open; the place lost its musty smell of ancient cobweb and leaking wainscot. Herries himself worked all day on the ground, and now at last, after all these years, it seemed to be responding and yielding to his long care of it. People, too, seemed to be losing some of their long avoidance. Women would greet him at their doors as he passed, men exchange 'Good-day' with him, and sometimes children would hang about the courtyard, stroke the dog and watch Benjamin groom the two horses.

They were standing by the wall at the house's back looking at the light fading over Rosthwaite Fell, when he turned abruptly to her and said:

'Soon we shall be leaving this.'

For a moment she did not understand what he said. He repeated it, looking at her shyly, but watching her to see the surprise of pleasure flash into her eyes.

'Leave Herries?'

'Yes. . . . Since our visit to Deborah I have been thinking. This is no place for you. You have always hated it. We will find a bright trim house like hers, with modern walls and India paper on them, no dripping water, no disorder . . . a proper parlour for you to sit in.'

'Leave Herries? . . . But you love every stone of it.'

'Yes. But you do not. I can do you that service.'

She was terrified. A mature, profound understanding came to her at this moment. There was some crisis at this time when she became a woman. It may have been this. She saw in a flash of intuitive comprehension that this was his last throw. If she had learnt anything about him during these years with him, it was that Herries was everything to him, that it had a power over him, as some places have over some men, deeper than thought, deeper than reason.

She saw in his eyes, in their light dancing attack on her, that he was saying: 'Now--now--you must love me. I have found a way at last. I am giving up everything, the only thing I've ever really cared for. THIS must win you.' And she knew, as she looked about her, at the darkening fells, the stony fields, the house that seemed to grin malignantly at her, with what loathing she regarded it, with what poignancy she felt the pathos of his abnegation, with what wretched certainty she knew the hopelessness of his desire.

A panic seized her. She felt as though she could run to the house and beat on it with her hands until they bled.

'You must not. You shall not. Do you not realise that I have no power to change this, that no giving up of anything can alter it? Oh, I am wretched indeed to have come, wretcheder to stay, cheating you, cheating myself, when I care for you so. If I did not care it would be easy. But I do not love you. I shall never love you. Nothing can change it.'

'This can change it,' he said. 'We will go from here where you will. It is this house and its discomfort that has chilled you. I was a fool not to have seen it before. I know my way.'

She bowed her head. There was only one thing for her to do.

In the four days that followed, she must have gone, again and again, over every aspect of it. By leaving him might she not liberate him? What was her presence to him save a goad, a torture? She was by now obsessed with this sense that she had, from the beginning, only harried him, and that now the harm that she did was touching insanity. Leaving Herries, what could there be for him but continual remorse and regret with no compensation?

Possibly she had never cared for him so tenderly and so regretfully as now. Those last days of April when the sun shone and the water glittered on the rocks, and green burnt like fire, they moved apart, he, it seemed, resolved that he had won her by this last surrender to her, but suffering, it may be fancied, a brutal hurt with every glance that the house gave him. She saw that he dug no longer, nor planted, nor went out to the hills.

During those last nights he never touched her, and she, lying awake at his side, hated with shivers of revulsion this passion that seemed so necessary to men that they must die if they could not have it.

Oddly, the more deeply she cared for him, the more now she detested the thought of his physically possessing her. She wanted no man ever to touch her again.

On the last night of April, a starless, moonless night, about two of the morning, she rose from his side, crept to the other room where some clothes were, wrote on a piece of paper, left it where he should see it, and fled. By seven o'clock she was on the coach for Kendal.

That night by an odd chance he slept heavily, having been much awake other nights. When he woke and saw that she was not with him in bed, he went to the passage and called her.

It was May Day; the light over the house was dim. All the way down the stairs he called her. On the table where he had so often tried to give her lessons was a piece of paper, and very childishly written:

It is beste to goe. You will have Piece better without me.

MIRABELL.

He stood, holding the paper towards the window, reading it over and over, rocking on his feet.

The sun, surmounting the hill, pierced the window, but he saw nothing.

ULDALE

I. FOUNDING OF A FAMILY

Meanwhile David and Sarah had made a fine start of family life at Uldale. They had two children--Francis, born in 1760; and Deborah, born in 1762. They were both grand healthy children.

David, indeed, was at last in his full and proper element. You could see this in the happy confident gaze that he threw over his wife, his children, his square house with its rosy brick set so comfortably in its little walled-in garden, his little farm, his servants, his farm hands, and even over the high and swelling downs stretching towards Scotland and the sea--all, in a sort of fashion, his, because he loved them with a personal love and was proud of them with a personal pride.

This was what he had always been intended to be--patriarchal founder of an English family with his great stature, huge limbs, splendid carriage.

As he strode about the soil, his flaxen head up, his chest spread, his eyes shining with health and vigour and happiness, he was already the Patriarch gathering these men and women, these beasts of the field and birds of the air under his protecting shelter.

He was now forty-three years of age, and had much worldly wisdom hidden in his round solid-looking head. He was beginning to make very real profits through his Liverpool trade, and, had he wished, could have become a wealthy man. He had the talents, the persistence, the courage. But here the real Herries strain came out in him, also the touch of softness of sentiment that belonged to the little boy who had adored to ride in front of his father, who had hated Alice Press and been thrilled by the dreams of Father Roche. The Herries strain in him made him weary of money-getting, just as it began to be important.

Herries did not care for property; they were too proud to think it worth while to amass it. They cared so much for family, for their own standing, their own importance in England, that no vulgar amassing of wealth could do anything but damage their self-approval. But then again their family pride was so unself-conscious, so completely taken for granted, that they never thought of it, talked of it or defended it. The English have always had this quality of confident security, and this makes them remote from the rest of the world and will always isolate them whether their island continues to be

an island or no. It accounts for their universal unpopularity, for their insular stubbornness, their hypocrisy and their profound calm in a crisis. It accounts also for a generous warmth of heart hidden under an absurd armour of frigid suspicion of strangers. It accounts for their poetry, their lack of imagination, their peculiar humour, their irritating conceit and ignorance in foreign countries, and a certain naïve youthfulness which is both absurd and attractive.

Any history of any English family must be concerned with this confident security and the shocks that it receives from time to time. These shocks never ultimately affect it; the history of any English family therefore is, basically, comedy rather than tragedy; comedy decorated with incongruous things like spring flowers, teapots, the Battle of Trafalgar, London fogs, beer and country vicarages. This confident security is the true reason of our magnificent sequence of great poets. Poetry is roused by sheer rebellious indignation, so vilely exasperating is it to anyone with imagination.

David, however, thought in these days little of poetry. He was so busied from early morning (he was up at five-thirty every day) until evening, that life flashed like a meteor before his eyes and was gone.

In actual fact the times were propitious for him. There was possibly no period in the history of the village labourer so black, degraded and hopeless as that between the years 1760 and 1832. Let there follow some items important in the Herries family chronicle. The agricultural labourer at this time earned fourteen pence a day or eight shillings a week, and his wife, were she lucky, might earn sixpence a day. Here are some of the things that the labourer must provide for his family: candles, 3d.; bread or flour, 1s. 8d.; yeast and salt, 4d.; soap, starch, 2 1/2d.; tea, sugar, butter, 1s.; thread, worsted, 3d. The weekly total would be some 8s. 4 1/2d. or £21:15:6 per annum, his earnings being £20:16s.

In addition to the weekly expenses, there were clothing, rent, fuel, amounting to some £8, and leaving the happy villager with a yearly deficiency of nearly £9. He could buy neither milk nor cheese. He could not brew small beer save for some especial occasion. So difficult was it to obtain soap for washing that they burned green fern and kneaded it into balls. A quarter of wheat cost in 1787 forty-eight shillings, and that amount was trebled later.

Everywhere and in every way the labourer was oppressed by the farmer. Landlords and farmers were, at this time, advocating enclosures everywhere. The common field system was utterly wasteful; far better to throw all the fields into large farms.

David found that here in all the country that stretched between Uldale and Carlisle matters were very different from the independence and security of the Statesmen in Borrowdale and Newlands. There a labourer could rise by thrift and diligence until he should be in some sort his own master. In all the country districts about Uldale, by enclosure the labourer was losing his right of cutting fuel on the common, his piece of land, his pig and cow. Privilege of gleaning after harvest, whereby poor families often obtained enough corn to last them through the winter, was also now withdrawn.

Signs of the new world were also to be found in the arrival of the middleman; the farmer sold his corn to the miller, the miller to the mealman, the mealman to the shopkeeper, the shopkeeper to the poor.

In short, the halcyon time for the poor man at work on English fields was over, never, alas, to return.

David was fortunate in that his farm was small and his means were large. His heart was warm and kindly, his character patient, his intelligence shrewd. It was not long before his name began to be known for wise charity and true understanding; it would not be long before 'Squire Herries' was his designation.

His whole heart and soul rose to his new position. He was founding a family, not a new family, but a new branch of the finest family in the world, the Herries of England. Here, from every possible motive, both his spiritual and physical energies were engaged. At the heart of it were his wife and children. Here both his love and his pride knew no bounds. Beyond them were all the Herries (with one very important exception).

After he had been at Uldale a year or so, he wrote to various relations informing them that here he was, and that they were welcome to a bed and a sup any time they passed that way.

In dueness of time he heard from Cousin Pelham, a very gay and frivolous epistle, saying that Uldale was the very place for flight when the bailiffs should become too pressing; a stiff angular letter from Dorothy Forster, complaining of the weather and her rheumatism; a grand document from London from his cousin Judith (now the Hon. Mrs. Ernest Bligh), informing him that her social duties were so onerous that she was sadly afraid that she could spare no time for the bleak North (where, she knew well from her unhappy youth, it always rained); a delightful letter from dear Uncle Harcourt (now seventy-five years of age), wishing his nephew every prosperity, but intimating that gout had him by the leg and David must come to Ravenglass to see him rather than he to Uldale. There were others: Will Forster, now twenty-five years of age, who wrote from Alnwick to inquire about the hunting; an aunt of Pelham's, an ancient Titchley, who, drinking the waters at Bath, begged him to subscribe to her Home for Indigent Sedan Chairmen; and young Morgan Gold of Edinburgh, who wrote to ask David to be a subscriber and patron to his forthcoming epic, The Tower of Babel.

In one way and another David felt his bag had not been a bad one. This was his first step towards bringing the family together, making it a real force and power in the progress and happiness of England.

It was England that he always ultimately saw; England expressed in the downs, streams and hills of his own surrounding country; England in the names so

immediately close to him--Skiddaw Forest, Bassenthwaite Common, Great Calva, Bowscale Fell, Blackhazel Beck, Mungrisdale, Scarness, Jenkin Hill; England in the little streets of Keswick; England spreading and dipping and rising again, through town and country, from county to county, until on every side it claims the sea.

His patriotism was like the patriotism of most men, founded on a stone, a flower, the sound of a stream, a clod of earth, the rustle of a tree, but it spread from these things until it embraced the earth, the moon and stars at one reach, and dug pits in his soul at the other.

All fine enough, but there was one festering strand in his ambition which was not so fine. That was his hatred of and scorn for his dear cousin and brother-in-law, Raiseley Herries.

Raiseley, who was forty-five years of age now, had never been a very fine physical specimen, and now, from idleness, a bad constitution and much early coddling, had developed into as complete a valetudinarian as his mother had ever been. In his youth he had had brains of a rather scientific sort, but for lack of encouragement and because of a bad education they had run to seed. He had not had all the best chances. His health had always been bad: THAT was not entirely imagination. His marriage had been unfortunate. Mary, David's sister, had never cared for him, had indeed never cared for anyone but herself, nor did her two children, Pomfret, aged twelve, and Cynthia, aged nine, care for him either. His appearance was distressing, his long thin face yellow like a turnip, frequently coloured with the ravages of dyspepsia, his lanky body gaudily and untidily clothed, always on his features the malcontentedness of a thoroughly disappointed man. He added to these unamiable qualities an overweening pride in his position and a hasty but cowardly temper.

His quarrel with David had begun at a very early age, from that day, in fact, when David had paid his first Keswick call with his mother so many years ago. For long Raiseley had had the best of it. David, living in disgraceful obscurity with a father who was the scandal of all the world, was no very possible rival. It was true that Raiseley had married David's sister, but this was because Mary had turned her back on her family and disowned them all. Afterwards matters had not been improved by the fact that whenever Mary wished to scorn or abuse her sickly husband (and these occasions were not rare as the intimacies of marriage strengthened) she found an easy weapon in the size and ability of her brother (whom, nevertheless, herself she termed for many years 'clodhopper'). It was not, however, until David came to Uldale that the feud was really proclaimed.

At first when they had heard of David's purchase of the place, both Raiseley and Mary had laughed scornfully. Their position in Keswick was nothing very fine (they were not even contemptuously popular as old Pomfret had been before them), but they nevertheless represented the only kind of Herries of which Keswick socially had any cognisance. It was not so much that English society in the middle of the eighteenth century was snobbish, as that the members of it simply felt that those who were not members of it were not human. It was easy enough. A man who was not a gentleman was hanged for stealing a sheep or whipped at the public stocks until the blood ran, or a child would be imprisoned in a jail too filthy for rats for stealing a loaf of bread, or a woman who was not a lady would suffer the grossest of public indignities for no reason other than that she answered her mistress impertinently.

There was no question but that any Herries was a gentleman; unfortunately Francis Herries had declassed himself completely, and must be therefore doubly disowned. How ridiculous then of his son to expect, because he bought a small property in the neighbourhood, that he would be received or accepted! It was true that Rogue Herries' daughter had been accepted, but that was because she had disowned her monstrous father at the earliest possible moment, and then had been washed, as it were, pure in London's chastening waters before returning to Keswick. David not only approved of his monster of a father, but openly declared his devotion to him, and was seen with him as often as possible, yes, even though the man, after selling his mistress in public and murdering his first wife, had married a common gipsy off the fells.

Oddly enough, none of these things seemed to stand in David's path. After all, he was not new to Keswick; he had done business there since he was a boy; everyone knew his rectitude, his courage, his humour. He was a proper man; he could carry an ox on one shoulder; stripped, he could fight any man in the North Country. Had he not carried off his wife single-handed from the villain of a father and a posse of attendant villains? True, he had killed the man, there under Esk Hause. The thing was already an epic, and ballads had been written about it.

This was the Keswick view, and soon neighbouring squires were calling at Uldale, and David was hunting, fishing, shooting with them, and it began to be noised abroad that some of the jolliest evenings to be enjoyed in Cumberland were to be found at the Fell House, Uldale.

It was then that the bitterness of his hatred for his brother-in-law was felt to the full by Raiseley Herries. His view of life was in any case a bitter one. Ill-health made him bitter, a conviction of wasted brains and opportunities, disappointment both in his wife and his children, hurt vanity, wounded conceit--these all made him bitter.

David's scorn and contempt for Raiseley was a bad, unworthy element in his warm, generous, noble nature, as Sarah well knew and deplored.

'It isn't worthy of you,' she would say after he had boasted to her of some small triumph, 'and one day it will come back badly to you. Our children will suffer for it, if not ourselves.'

'Not they!' said David, laughing, throwing his babies up into the air and catching them. "Tis an old feud, Sarah, my love, and it began with his laughing at my father when we were infants together. With his wheezly, flammering body, I could break him over my head.'

And so in pride and scorn and derision he rode himself over to invite the two of them to his first grand festivity, this May Day, 1763. Sitting his horse outside their door, a magnificent sight for all to see, he gave his messages to young Pomfret, a stout, sturdy boy, who carried his head proudly so that David took to him at sight.

It was plain that young Pomfret had been trained to disapproval of his uncle, but he could not drag his eyes from the horse.

'Wilt have a ride?' asked David, laughing.

But young Pomfret shook his head and ran into the house.

Sarah also shook her head when David returned and laughingly told her of it.

'Why should we breed our children to this? What affair is it of theirs that you and Raiseley Herries have a spite?'

She was nursing her own baby, Deborah, not yet a year old, as she spoke. She looked down, smiling, her eyes bright with love. 'We have had feuds enough in our lives--my uncle and your father; now there must be peace. This is not like you, Davy; it is not your generosity.'

'I feel no generosity,' he answered sharply. 'My sister left us and stayed in Keswick to mock us. Raiseley has been our enemy since he was weaned.'

But Sarah shook her head. 'Then it is the more reason the thing ceased. It has lasted long enough. See that you are not proud, Davy, in your new place. Of all things pride is the worst.'

He bent over the mother and child, himself a child at that instant. 'I have reasons for my pride. Two good reasons.' Then, kissing her, his great hand cupping her chin: 'And how can I not be proud when I love you so? Having such a wife, what is a man worth an he is not stiff with pride?'

So Mary and Raiseley Herries did not come to the May Day Feast at the Fell House. But all the rest of the world came.

It was a grand May Day, soft and warm. David had the downs above his house for his games--for the Archery, the Football, the Wrestling and the Dancing. Upright on the downs, its head proudly lifted to heaven, was the Maypole, its hanging streamers lazily lifting like live things in the breeze. He stood with Sarah on the lawn in the brick-walled garden to receive his guests. He wore a plain suit of mulberry trimmed with silver. His fair hair (he was beginning, as were many others, to wear--save on very state occasions--his own hair) shone in the sun. His rosy face--strong, clear-eyed, broad-browed--beamed happiness. Sarah stood beside him in a pretty grey dress, the hoop sprayed with roses, a fine white wig with cherry ribbons, and she wore silver shoes. She looked as healthy, confident, happy as he.

Around them, too, everything was happy: the pigeons cooed, cows softly lowed, birds sang in the elm-tree, young Francis was sturdy enough in his three years to stand beside his mother holding tightly to her with one hand and with the other cracking his whip.

David and Sarah insisted on receiving all alike; to-day there were to be no class distinctions. David had sent invitations to all his old friends in Borrowdale, and many of them had ridden over--Peels and Satterthwaites and Mounseys and Bells. Sarah, although truly she was no snob, could not but be gratified to see how the gentry and their wives were appearing--Mr. Bonstead from Keswick, Squire Osmaston and his lady from near Troutbeck, Squire Worcester and his lady from the other side of Threlkeld, the Peaches and Sandons and Ullathorpes from Keswick, the Brownriggs all the way from Patterdale, the Newsomes of Newlands, the Robertsons of St. John's in the Vale, the Kendals from the other side of Bassenthwaite.

Soon Sarah found that she was compelled to observe social distinctions, so she led Mrs. Osmaston and Mrs. Worcester and old Miss Mary Peach and the Misses Gwendolyn and Frances Brownrigg out to the seats that had been arranged on the down with an awning to protect them from the wind. The farmers and their wives and children gathered in their own groups, and splendid Statesmen like Richard Bell, towering with his white head and six foot five above all the others, and George Satterthwaite, like a bull for thickness and strength, walked on the springing turf as though they owned the world and were rightly proud of it.

Yes, this was perhaps the happiest day of his life for David. It had come to this: that he had now his true independent place in the world, his place, his wife and children, this turf on which he was treading, this English turf under English hills, watered with English streams--these things were his and he owed them to no man alive. Men of all kinds, from old Osmaston, who was a sort of king of Cumberland at this time, from Richard Bell, as noble-hearted as he was ironically cautious and loyally steadfast, to old Ducken the ploughman, who was now moving towards the Maypole, a string of children at his heels, these men and their womenfolk had greeted him, welcomed him, received him into their world.

And he thought as he stood there, his legs spread, his head up, his face flushed with happiness, of himself as a small boy at Herries listening to Alice Press as she screamed at his mother; of the Chinese Fair and the ancient Chinaman with the old, old face; of that awful scene in the tent when his father sold Alice Press; of how he stood in the courtyard sparring with Raiseley while his mother was dying upstairs; of old Mrs. Wilson the witch; of the ride to Carlisle; of that awful moment when his father, looking a dead man, had come into his room in Carlisle; of the day when Mirabell had met them in Herries--a thousand other scenes were called up

by his memory. He knew now that, in spite of his devotion and loyalty to his father, that strange mist of disgrace and isolation had always been hanging over him, although he was too proud to acknowledge it.

Now at last, at last he was clear of it!

All this while his eye was on the road beneath him to see whether his father and Mirabell would appear. He had, of course, sent word to them--a special letter on horseback--that they must most certainly come. He wanted them to come; it would not be a real complete day for him if his father were not there, but with that, if he were honest with himself, there was a feeling too that they would be strange, his father and Mirabell, in this company. They were always strange, his father with his arrogant look that went so oddly with his scarred face, his silence, his sudden ironical statements, his wandering eye so that his mind seemed to be always elsewhere, and Mirabell like a play-actress with her gaudy clothes and ill-easiness in proper and normal company. He wanted them to come, but he dreaded a little what the result of their coming might be.

Now everything is in movement. The coloured ribbons of the Maypole flash in constant change against the blue of the sky and the green of the turf. The girls pass like notes of music sounding in regular rhythm against the air.

On a grassy mound above the road an old man with two chins and a frizzy white wig stands fiddling, and he has an attendant piper. Birds fly across the sun, bells sound, clouds lighter than smoke, with the soft colour of swan's down, collect and hover and disperse.

Beyond the Maypole there are benches, a barrel of ale, apples soaked in sugar and thick flat cakes crammed with raisins, damp in the middle. Men and women cluster here; there is wrestling, kissing and hugging and drinking, and, beyond them, as the sun slides down the sky, the sloping black side of Skiddaw catches the light: it is as though it rolled its coat off and spread there, basking, while the clouds are shadowed across the shining surface. And David stands, his head up, breathing the air, catching the light, feeling that the whole world is his, joy in his heart.

A farmer passes. He turns, laughing, rolling his thick back towards the Maypole.

'T'dancing is grand,' he says. Osmaston's huge body draws near, seeming to darken the sun with its bulk. He happens very gravely to talk politics with young Herries. 'Now Grenville . . . And these American Colonies . . . ?' They are just beginning, in other places beside Uldale, to seem impertinent.

Sarah's task was harder to-day than her husband's. About her were seated, their hoops spreading wide around them, the Misses Gwendolyn and Frances Brownrigg and the great Mrs. Osmaston. Mrs. Osmaston was a tremendous lady, with her high white wig, her enormous white bosom half naked to the sun, her round white arms. With all this massive flesh her features were small and tightly pinched together. But out of her little mouth a tremendous voice proceeded, deep and bass like a man's, and with this voice she had been accustomed for forty years to give commands to all around her, save only her husband whom she resolutely obeyed. She was like a great white whale lying there in the sun. She had never been out of Cumberland in her life, and had all the knowledge of and confident scorn for the rest of the world that such determined staying-at-home produces. She had been, both in the '15 and the '45, an ardent Jacobite, and could never say enough about the Hanoverian dynasty. Many of her oaths and similes were of an excellent coarseness, and she alluded to all the natural processes of man with much freedom and gusto. When in good humour, as she was to-day, she would slap her friends on the back or pinch their arms or yield them even more familiar gestures. She often made the oddest noises, and was, in honest fact, none too cleanly in her person, so, as her own devoted husband said, "twas best to sit to windward of her.' Better than all else, she loved to discuss the love affairs of her neighbours and friends, and had, as she said, 'a nose for copulation like the nose of a dog for a hare.' She liked Sarah and told her so. Seated there, her great knees wide- planted inside her hoop, her fat arms akimbo, she told one bawdy story after another and was ably abetted by the Misses Brownrigg, who, being supposedly virgins, had their eyes eternally at the keyholes of all their neighbours' bedrooms.

Sarah, a woman of her time, was amused by the bawdy stories when she could keep her ear to them, but she must watch first one side, then another, to see that all went well, that nobody was offended, that everyone, even to the smallest child of the least important labourer, was happy. But everyone was happy. Happiness was everywhere.

Now it was time for the great Football game. Everyone streamed towards the upper down where the game was to be. The goals were distant nearly half a mile the one from the other. There were few rules, if any; all cunning and trickery were at advantage, but brute force was the greatest power of all. There were fifty players a side to start with, although before the game ended there were nearly a hundred a side. It was a match between the Uldale men and the Keswick men, wide latitude allowed for district partisanship.

It was a superb sight to see the hundred men-- farmers, labourers, townsmen, woodsmen, sailors from the coast, dalesmen, shepherds-- stripped to their smallclothes, rush together with great shouts of joy and triumph. The ball rose into the air and at once the battle began, clumps of men binding together, arms locked, rushing head down to meet other bands with a great crash of neck and shoulder.

Soon the giants on either side were to be seen. Willie Peel of Mungrisdale with his two sons, a mountain of a man, his sons as big as he, the three rushing forward, the ball at their feet, lesser men clinging to their sides and buttocks, leaping at their necks, trying to trip them at the feet, while to meet them came John

Ringstraw and his brother George from Threlkeld, men like bullocks, crimson of face, thick of neck, with backs like walls. Willie Peel meeting John Ringstraw, for a while all lesser men drew back and watched them hurl themselves the one at the other, arms interlocked, backs straining, legs planted for a throw, while the air was beaten with the shouting and all the dogs barked and the shadows lovingly stroked the sides of Skiddaw. Then Willie's belt was burst and his smallclothes were flapping about his ankles; nothing mattered that to him, and he played for the rest of the game half naked, but the ball now had passed to a wily little devil, Jock Mounsey from Grange in Borrowdale, who was away across the downs with the thing at his feet, half a hundred men after him.

All the downs now rolled like a sea towards the sun and the hills. Little waves of dark shadows broke the pale primrose glow. Skiddaw and Blencathra grew dark, and seemed to billow with gestures of lazy self-indulgent satisfaction out towards the tender colours of the May Day sky.

And against this fair scene the battle rose and fell. Little Mounsey was for a while detached, a small figure springing along like a deer, controlling the ball as though it were tied to his shoestrings, but then the two Grimshaws, stocky shepherds from Troutbeck, had caught him up. One of them tripped him and he fell, but before the ball had turned back to the goal at Skiddaw end half a hundred men had arrived and thrown themselves upon it.

Here now was a mêlée in the grand old style, no quarter asked and no quarter given. Over the ball in a wriggling, writhing heap twenty men were lying, and over these another thirty were striving, while behind them were the outguards, arriving from every part of the field, and, if they could not reach the central scrimmage, wrestling and boxing on their own. So that now there was a grand and noble sight, this central mass of heaving men, detached groups of fighters, and the spectators shouting, roaring, the dogs barking as though they were mad. The fine ladies themselves cursed and swore in their interest, and it was all that her husband could do to prevent Mrs. Osmaston from rushing on to the field of play and lending assistance.

All is fair in love and war, and no chronicler would dare to catalogue some of the things that were done in that scrimmage; shirts were torn from many a back, once and again a head would rise, as though seeking for the stars, and stare vacantly skywards, blood pouring, eyes blackened, and once and again, a figure for an instant stood completely stark and so faced the world in utter nakedness, like some primeval hero before clothes were.

Then, alive with its own devilry, the ball suddenly emerged and sped forward, pursued by Willie Peel and one of his sons. Willie, his long hair flying, naked to the waist, his shaggy chest broad as a wall, his eyes on fire, crying his war-cry 'Peel! Peel! Hey Peel!' was well away, the ball at his feet. Staggering that so huge a man should run so swiftly and keep the ball at his toe with so astounding an accuracy, but now he was away from them all, the field streaming at his feet, and in his size, strength and beauty he joined partnership with the strength and beauty of the scene, the grand type of all Cumbrian strength, sureness of purpose, largeness of grasp, as good as anything the world has seen, and as lasting.

The only man in his way was Jock Elliot of Crosthwaite, and he was a kind of ogre of a man, almost deformed, so short of stature, so thick, so shaggy, with such long swinging arms.

With a great grin, his little eyes burning under his black bristling eyebrows, he advanced to meet Willie Peel. Peel tried to 'slip' him, but, heavy though Elliot was, he was agile too, and was in front of him. Their bodies met with a shock that would have slain two ordinary men and could have been heard, you would swear, away in the streets of Keswick itself.

The two men drew a breath and closed. A moment later Peel had Elliot in his arms, held him as though he loved him dearer than any woman, and actually raised him from the ground. Elliot's head was up. He seemed to be staring at the heavens as though imploring the gods to do him this last great service, then, his short legs about Peel's thighs, he brought him crashing to the ground, himself on top. That seemed to end their struggle. They lay, full length, one on the other, softly heaving, while the world roared its approval and, gently, quietly, rosy clouds drifted like miniature galleons towards the west.

But the ball was out again. Three men had it and were racing towards the Uldale goal. All Uldale drew its breath; soon most of the remaining audience, save the very aged, were rushing into the field to join the game.

David too. He had been all this time like a dog straining at the leash. Now stripping off his mulberry coat and flowered vest, he rushed into the fray. Peel's two sons were with him. Together they raced the field, and David, as he ran, felt that this was truly the grandest moment of his life, with the wind brushing his cheeks, the mountains crowding to meet him, the turf strong and resilient beneath his feet.

He touched the ball; it passed to young Isaac Peel, then over to Rumney Peel, back to himself again. He could feel the field streaming behind him. Two men were in their way. David feinted; the ball obeyed him like a living thing, and now the three of them, sharing for an instant a comradeship that was as true and strong as though long companionship had made it, were away, away with only the hills to meet them.

Skiddaw smiled; Blencathra clapped his hands; all the rosy clouds sang together; and to the roar of the approving world, the ball slipped between the posts.

Glorious never-to-be-forgotten moment--and David, turning, throwing his arms high for victory, saw, quite near to him, above the road, waiting beside his horse, the figure of his father.

He moved towards him, joyfully greeting him. Then he paused. Something very terrible had occurred. He felt it come, through the lovely evening air, darkening the sky, dimming the sounds of the games, removing him to a circle of silence wherein he stood alone with his father. Afterwards he remembered that he had thought: 'Why, he's old . . . and a terrible thing has come to him.'

In Herries' voice when he greeted him, however, there was no tremor, and his hand, in its long black glove, was hard and firm. His clothes were dark, his face was pale, drawn, as it often was, a little crookedly. Whence did David have his sense of some disaster?

Herries said, very quietly, but holding his son's hand:

'Davy, has she been here?'

'She? . . . But who?'

'My wife.'

'Mirabell? No. Is she not with you?'

'She left me early this morning, and I must find her.' The hand in David's gave a slight quiver.

'Why did she leave you?'

'I cannot say. But I must find her.'

David put his hand on the other's shoulder and felt an odd pride that it should be so hard and strong. All this while he had been looking into his father's face, and now, beneath the customary ironical gaze and twisted mouth, he felt such a force of controlled agony that he dropped his eyes. He had never yet loved his father so deeply as now, when he realised that he was unable to help him.

'She cannot have gone far,' he said urgently, longing to do or say something to assuage that unhappiness. ''Twas a momentary pique or resentment. She had secret moods unlike other women--'

But Herries stopped him, raising his hand and gripping his son's shoulder so fiercely that David winced. He wore only his shirt.

'No, it was no pique,' Herries said quietly. 'I had told her that we would leave Herries because I fancied that she would be happier so. She thought it would kill me to leave Herries, so, for my comfort, she went away. I must find her that she may understand.'

He turned, stroking his horse's neck.

'Father, I will come with you. I will sleep with you to-night, and to-morrow--'

Herries shook his head, smiling.

'Nay, this is my affair. You are a good son, Davy. I shall find her. Nothing in heaven or hell shall stay me.'

He mounted his horse.

'Return to your guests. Farewell.'

He started down the white road and, before he turned the corner, looked back once and waved his hand.

PART III

HERRIES STARTS HIS SEARCH

Very early the next morning, Herries, after bidding
farewell to Benjamin, his servant and friend, started out
on his search.

END OF PART III

PART IV

THE BRIGHT TURRETS OF ILION

RETURN OF A WANDERER

On a sharp clear autumn afternoon of the year 1768, Mr. Simeon Harness, pastor, schoolmaster, and general man-of-all-work in the districts of Rosthwaite, Watendlath and Seatoller, climbed to the top of the Brund Fell and looked appreciatively about him. With so little a climb he had reached an elevation of great splendour. He was a short, pursy man, normally scant of breath, but for the last five years he had walked these tops on his daily occupations, and so friendly and kindly had they come to seem to him that he did not realise any arduousness in surmounting them.

His own home--two rooms of a farmhouse--was in the hamlet of Watendlath, the smoke from whose chimneys he could see now lazily curling beneath him.

He had indeed a fine view. On these tops you could walk for miles and scarcely be compelled to descend. Beloved names came to meet him as he looked. Towards Derwentwater, Brown Dodd and Ashness Fell and High Seat; towards Thirlmere, Armboth and Watendlath Fell; towards the Langdales, Coldbarrow and Ullscarf and High White Stones. The ranges lay all about him in shapes more human than those of his friends, moulded and formed, now sharply with rocks and steeples and slanting cliffs of shining colour, then gently in sheets of flaming bracken lifting to smooth arms and shoulders embossed like shields of metal. Wild profusion, and yet perfect symmetry and order. One colour faded to another, purple cliff above orange sea, deeps of violet under shadow of rose, and a great and perfect stillness everywhere.

When he turned and looked across the valley to Stye Head he saw, falling over the Gavel and Scafell, ladders of sunlit mist that were indeed to his devout soul like steps to heaven. It did not seem strange to him that, on a sudden call, one should climb these ladders and so, to the sound of trumpets, pass into that other glorious company.

He sighed. He did not wish to pass over. He supposed that there was still much work to do, but there were times when his scattered flock seemed to be past all stirring, when, if he looked back, he had achieved exactly nothing at all, when the pain in his side, which had been his constant companion ever since, three years before, some drunken revellers had in the friendliest of spirits thrown him off a hayrick, was sharper than he could silently endure, when his own sins, his ingratitude to God, his liking for ale, the greed of his stomach, and the sudden sharp temptation of a handsome woman, mounted crimson-high--on such occasions, in spite of all fortitude, he sighed for the ladders of God.

He had a round bare face like a baby's, wore a small tie-wig and a coat and breeches of rusty black, and carried in his hand a worn copy of Mr. Chapman's translation of the 'Iliad,' which appeared to him to be, after the Bible, the finest book in the world.

It was his intention, although the afternoon was chill, to sit on the ground, with his beloved hills all around him, and read. He knew that in a short time the peace of the scene would steal about him and quieten his distresses. This magical charm had never failed him. He sat down, facing the silver ladders, and opened his book, gathering the skirts of his coat about him for greater warmth and smiling amiably at the three or four sheep who were tranquilly grazing near him.

He began to read:

Fires round about them shined, As when about the silver moon, when air is free from wind, And stars shine clear, to whose sweet beams, high prospects, and the brows Of all steep hills and pinnacles, thrust up themselves for shows, And even the lowly valleys joy to glitter in their sight, When the unmeasured firmament bursts to disclose her light, And all the signs in heaven are seen that glad the shepherd's heart; So many fires disclosed their beams, made by the Trojan part, Before the face of Ilion, and her bright turrets showed. A thousand courts of guard kept fires, and every guard allowed Fifty stout men, by whom their horse ate oats and hard white corn, And all did wishfully expect the silver-throned morn.

He repeated the phrases aloud that the hills might also enjoy them.

'The lowly valleys joy to glitter in their sight.' The 'bright turrets' of Ilion. The 'hard white corn.' 'The silver-thronéd morn.'

He was himself something of a poet and had once written an 'Elegy to Sophia Countess of Balebury,' his one-time patroness. It had, of course, never been published, but he showed it once and again to an intimate.

All very well to be a poet, but when you had but thirty pounds a year, a pain in your side and a sadly lascivious nature, where was the time for poetry? He was concerned too for the country. The fate of the American Colonies was dwelling just now heavily on his conscience, although no others of his friends seemed to be concerned with it. Grenville's Stamp Act of three years before had appeared to him an injustice unworthy of his country's greatness; but on the other hand he had only now, in a belated news-sheet, been reading of the episode of the sloop Liberty in Boston and the abominable riots that followed the seizure of the cargo. Hard, hard the ways of this world; so easy would men only love one another, but that very thing how difficult, as he could see in his own case, because try as he might he could not love Willie Richards, the farmer in whose house he lodged, as he truly should.

So he sighed and envied the sheep, then smartly abused himself for an ungrateful wretch whom God had placed in this marvellous world, hemming him in with ladders of silver and gold, extending to him with every new day the signs of His grace and favour, while even the pain in his side was troublesome but a little and nothing at all compared with what many poor folk had to suffer. He could not, however, return tranquilly to his Homer. He was sitting on a natural platform of turf, and now he rose and walked back and forth, two hands clasped behind his back, his eyes drinking in the constant change of scene as the light and shadow ran beneath the sun, his mind biting on its troubles, its successes (as when last Sunday forenoon he had preached in Keswick market-place to some hundred souls), its fears and surrenders.

He had just thought that his stomach was queasy and it was time he made his way down to Watendlath for a meal, when, looking in the direction of the Pikes, he perceived someone approaching. This was a man moving with a remarkably easy and resolute stride, and, as he came nearer, Mr. Harness saw that he carried on his back a bundle and in his hand a very stout staff.

The stranger (for Mr. Harness could see at once that it was no one familiar to him) appeared to hesitate as to his choice of descent; then, seeing the little clergyman, he came to meet him.

Now, close at hand, he was clearly remarkable for his height, his strong leanness, his white hair (he wore his own hair, which was cropped to his neck), and for

the unusual character of his features. His eyes were large and brilliant, his countenance haughty and reserved but marked by a deep scar which ran from the forehead to the upper lip.

So soon as he saw the scar Mr. Harness knew who it must be. This was Herries of Herries in Rosthwaite, the extraordinary man who had gone mad after his wife, a common gipsy woman, left him. That at least was the gossip of the valley. Although Mr. Harness had been for five years at Watendlath and Herries had been on several occasions during that period at his home, Mr. Harness had not yet seen him.

Opinion locally differed as to whether the man were mad or no. Some said that he had been always crazy since he first came there; others that he was not mad at all but cursed by God; others that he was not wicked even, but only a poor soul with whom everything had gone wrong. And a few said that he was a good man and generous and very wise. It was true at least that after his wife left him opinion became gentler towards him, and the old term 'Rogue Herries' had a note of kindliness in it; but it was still said everywhere that once he had had league with the Devil, had lived with a witch in his house and, when they drowned her, carried her home and buried her in his garden.

So, for all these opinions, Mr. Harness was greatly interested to meet with him.

'Good-day,' he said, smiling.

Herries took off his broad black hat and wiped his forehead.

'It is warm walking,' he said, looking at Mr. Harness with a very kindly expression in his dark eyes. His hat off, there was something indeed very remarkable in his appearance, for his hair was of a most beautiful snowy whiteness that seemed to catch the afternoon light. His face too was brown and spare with health.

'Have you come far, sir?' asked Mr. Harness.

'From Furness.'

'That is a long distance. By Langdale is shorter.'

The other laughed. 'I am sixty-eight years of age, but have no sense of it.'

'Sixty-eight!' said Mr. Harness in admiration. 'You are accustomed to walking, sir?'

'I never knew what true health was before I adopted it.' Then he added very simply, 'My name is Herries and I am going to my house in Rosthwaite. Perhaps you are yourself going that way?'

'My name is Harness,' answered the other. ''Tis odd that we have not met before.'

'I have heard of you, sir,' said Herries. 'We will go together, then.'

As they turned he went on: 'I have been all day alone and shall be glad of a little company. 'Tis odd how you may walk these hills for a week and meet no human soul. There was a time when I preferred my own company to any man's, but now it may be that I know my own self too well.' Then, after a moment's pause, he added very quietly, 'I have been for a long time in search of my wife who left me in a misunderstanding five years ago.'

'I have heard something of it,' said Mr. Harness, gravely.

Herries nodded his head. 'I speak of it to everyone I meet, for it may by chance happen that they have heard of her.'

Mr. Harness was very sympathetic. He liked this man.

'It is scarcely likely,' he said, 'that she will have remained all these years in the district.'

Herries nodded. 'Nay, it is not likely. But the North Country was her only home. Though she has gone south for a while she will return. Of that I am certain.' Then, very cheerfully: 'But these are personal matters; I know did you have news of her from anyone you would inform me. I am hoping that she may be at my house, waiting for me. I have considerable hope. It is three months since I was here, and as this is the only spot of the whole earth for me it is a great happiness to return.'

'Have you been far, sir?' asked Harness.

'I have been for the first time for many years in London.'

'And pray tell me, sir,' said Mr. Harness, eagerly, 'how did you find the Town? I have, alas, never been there, and must trust to the descriptions of others.'

'I found it grievously altered,' said Herries. 'There is scarce any of the old Town left. They are pulling down here and destroying there until it is pitiful to realise that in a year or two the character of the Town will be gone. 'Tis this craze for modernity. I assure you, sir, there is such a rush and tumble in these days that one must hesitate to cross the street for the fierceness of the traffic.

'But what appears to me the most lamentable is that the Town is losing its character, and might be as modern as the town of New York for its new buildings, the vulgarity of the people, the craze for wealth, and the rest. But indeed, sir, I am an old country cousin, and 'tis a shock to my system to comprehend that Queen Anne is truly dead.'

'You spoke of the town of New York,' said Mr. Harness. 'Pray tell me, did you hear much talk of our American Colonies?'

'Scarce a word. America is too remote for men to worry over.'

Mr. Harness sighed. 'I fear there is a great injustice there. We shall worry before all is done.' He went on more tentatively: 'And you heard no news of your wife in London?'

'No, sir, I did not. I had one evening, however, an odd adventure.'

'Pray let me hear it, sir,' said Mr. Harness.

'I was minded one evening to go to the theatre. They were playing the Othello of William Shakespeare.'

Before the first act was over I was conscious that there was a fellow near to me who was aware of my nearness to him. I looked again and again, but could see only his back. After a while he turned, and I perceived that he bore an odd resemblance to a fellow many years ago in these parts, a pedlar, a vagrant who, by accident rather than any design, had played some part in incidents of my former life here.

'I am a man of no superstitious feeling. This world is interpenetrated, we cannot but doubt, with many others, but it is our business to deal with this one and leave the rest to a future time. But it has ever been my misfortune to be dreaming when I should be most practical, and to see my way cloudily when I should be most exact.

'The lights were blowing, there was a wind stirring in the theatre, and I had a strange conviction that in another moment or so I was to die. I don't know, sir, how it may be with you, but life has so tormented me with its riddle that to die without any answer to it has always seemed to me an exasperating indignity.

'The theatre grew dark to me, the wind blew about my ears, the candles leaping before my eyes, and the fellow of whom I have spoken appeared to come close to me and whisper with malicious amusement in my ear. The theatre was crowded to my eyes with dancing figures grotesquely attired, and in the centre of them I seemed to see my wife begging me to come to her.

'In the increasing uproar of wind and light and many men shouting, I fought my way towards her, this fellow at my side striving to prevent me. With the utmost difficulty, and after much roughness, I reached her, and, at the touch of her hand and the consciousness of the great joy that we both were feeling, everything seemed to be made clear to me. I wondered that for so long it should have been so perplexing. The intensity of that joy made my past life of no account. . . . We fell together, our hands clasped, between a crowd of whirling figures, the candles dancing before our eyes. Such a mutual death was greater than anything that life had been. It was in all the experience of a moment, but so vivid that it was impossible to deny its positive occurrence. Nevertheless I had not vacated my seat, nor missed, I fancy, any detail of the play. When, in my clear mind, I looked for this fellow again he was not there.'

'It was a dream,' said Mr. Harness gravely. 'God has many fashions of making Himself clear to us.'

'Well, well,' Herries answered briskly, with a smile. 'It may be so. But I doubt the benevolence of your God. He is plaguily roundabout in His plans for serving us, nor have I found life so sweet that I am minded to thank Him so heartily for what He has done for me.'

'It may be,' said Mr. Harness, 'that sweetness is not its purpose, but rather a very varied experience for the growth of our poor wisdom. The beauties of Nature and the unexpected nobility of man under severe trial are sufficient justification for living, to my mind.'

Herries answered quietly: 'An God will give me my wife again, I will ask Him for no further justification.'

They were reaching now the foot of the Fell and approaching the road. It was plain that with every step Herries' pleasure at returning to his home was increasing. They turned left towards Rosthwaite, and walked very happily together along the path that ran down above the river bed. It was a beautiful evening of great quietness; the air smelt sweetly, and the sky was rosy above the hills.

Mr. Harness, thoroughly at ease with his companion, talked freely on his affairs, how the pain in his side troubled him, and how his appetite was shamefully strong, and he had been drunk ten days back, and sung, he was afraid, a number of lascivious songs. But the Devil was always round the corner with a remarkable knowledge of each individual's weakness. They parted in great friendliness, and Herries went on up to his house.

At the entrance to the little court he hesitated. Dusk was coming rapidly now, and he could see only dimly the stone wall, and beyond it the huddled dark mass of the house, its line ragged against the sky. A little wind had come with the evening, and was whistling and whining over the ground, a tune so familiar to him in its thin desolation, mingled as it was with the rhythm of running water and the chill of oncoming night, that it was like the hand-grip of a friend. But it was not the wind to which he was now listening. How often, during these last years, he had waited thus on his return!

Sometimes he had been absent only a week, sometimes months, and once, directly after her flight, nearly a year had passed. Always the same. Listening, his hand on the gate that was swinging now on its hinges, because he must postpone a little longer the moment when he would put it to the test whether she were waiting for him or no. One day it would be--of that he had no doubt--but how soon? How soon? Could he endure this time the blow of the disappointment? He set back his shoulders, looked up to the last yellow strands that struck like whips across the darkening sky, then went forward with a firm tread.

The door was open. He could see the familiar things, the old armour, the yellow-faced clock like a moon against the shadow, and he could hear the sounds, the clock's voice, a banging door monotonously complaining, and the stir that there was always about the old house, rats in the wainscot, maybe, and the dust of the years sifting from ceiling to floor.

She was not here. He knew it instantly. Never mind; she would come--if not now, another time. To-morrow, soon, it could not be long delayed. So he went slowly up the old creaking stairs, stood in the dark hall, and then shouted for Benjamin. He was suddenly very weary, dropped his bundle and stick on the floor, and sank into the armchair by the fireplace.

Soon he heard Benjamin come clambering up the stairs. A moment after, Benjamin was in the doorway, holding two lighted candles, his face wreathed in smiles.

'Master! Master! You're back!'

He set the candles on the table, and came over with his old familiar rolling gait like a shapeless porpoise. His face was round like the moon, he had three chins now, and a belly that hung over his stout legs like a pillow, but he was not soft. His hair was short and erect on his head, his eyes wore their old expression of sound surprise, and on his nose there was the same old brown wart. The same! Of course he was the same! It was as though Herries had taken him with him on his travels. He came to his master, and his master greeted him with his old gesture, pulling him towards him, pinching his cheek, then driving him away again with a smack and a gentle kick.

'Well, old ass, old noddle, with us again . . . with us again. . . . The world over, and thy round face always behind the candles-- Satan be thanked for it!'

Benjamin went on his knees and pulled off his boots, looking up once and again into Herries' face with a pleasure that was none the less precious for being simple. Herries rested his hand on the broad back. So she had not come, she was not here. One more delay-- how many yet would he endure?

He drove it from him.

'Food, fire, drink, Benjamin. There has been no one here?'

'Master David, master. Miss Deborah once. Statesman Peel . . .'

'Aye; more of that in a moment. Has Mrs. Benjamin a fowl or can slaughter one? Has she a pie? I could eat thy own chaps, thou monstrous swine.'

The man sat back on his haunches.

'My wife is gone, master.'

'Gone!' Herries sat back astonished. 'What! A-whoring!'

'No, poor woman. She's dead.'

'Dead! Dead! Why? how? when?'

''Twas Midsummer Night. She'd had a pain in her belly. I'd cursed her for a whining woman, and told her I'd take a whip to her, always moaning about her belly as though she'd a child there and was eight months gone. But it was real enough. She wasted day after day to the thinness of a hickory stick. She wouldn't eat, she who could swallow a leg of mutton and a beef pie quicker than any woman. And she was gentle--terribly gentle and forgiving. I cursed her for that too, but she could do nothing with it. "My temper's gone down with my belly," poor soul, she'd say. Mother Dawlish of Stonethwaite physicked her. There's no one finer. She has herbs from Solomon's time, they say. But 'twas no use. Comes Midsummer Night, as fine and warm an evening as you could search for, but she was mortal cold and would lie in my arms, a thing she'd not wished for these many years. She had never been a loving- tempered woman, and would always be in a tantrum if I wanted to press her a bit. But now she was there, with my arms round her and a mighty pain in her belly, poor thing, and as fine and warm a night of stars and moonshine as you'd wish for. She was wandering at the last, wanting a green nettle to tickle Tom Prommice that she'd had a mind to be married to before I plagued her. Aye, all she wanted was a green nettle and I had none for her, and so she passed, with the moon coming in at the window, there in my arms.'

'Why, poor old Benjamin!' Herries drew him closer, enclosing his neck with his hand. 'You are alone--and I also. And since then, there has been no one with you in the house?'

'No one, master, and many's the night I've thought I've heard her tread--lop-lop-lop, heavy-heavy-heavy, and then a kind of skitter- skatter with the flop of her slipper. I've risen from my bed to look for her, but it's been the wind or the rain coming in through the roof at the left end there.'

'So we're alone here.'

'None the worse for that.' Benjamin straightened himself and rose. 'I'll light the fire and have a grand meal for you.'

Herries nodded. 'And you need no woman to help you?'

Benjamin turned near the door. 'We shall do without women. I'm wise now, so that I'd rather have my sleep than a woman. That's what life teaches you.'

Well, thought Herries, life hadn't taught him that yet. Quietly, as he often did, in an attitude of cool dispassion, he considered this longing for Mirabell. What was it that drove him? Certainly not lust. That it had never been. Certainly not self-pity or fear of loneliness. In one sense he had never been lonely, in another he had never been anything else. What was it, this hunger? He supposed that in human beings there was always through life this search for fulfilment, and through life to death most men never found it. They managed well enough without it, had no time to speculate, snatched at whatever substitutes they could find and made the most of them.

But with some men this search was ceaseless. It would for ever be the theme of all their days. The poets made poetry of it, the conquerors hacked kingdoms out of it, the madmen plaited straw in their hair. He had been one of these. It had never let him rest, and when he saw Mirabell the question was answered for him. He had loved her in the only true sense of love, that of finding completion in another soul and remaining settled there like a kernel in the heart of a nut. Everything moved by law whether there were a God or no, and this was a law, as certain and ordered as the movement of the stars, that he should love Mirabell. Did she love him, then the order was completed, and one more fragment of perfect movement was added to the multiplicity of the rest. But she did not. She had never loved him

for a single moment. So here was another jangled piece of disorder added to all the others.

He had had a strange life, not, he thought, an unhappy one. It had been too interesting for that, but it was a fierce business, ferocious in its wildness, surprising in its beauty, ironical in its foolishness, mysterious in its purpose, but always invigorating, powerful, infinitely worth while.

He watched old Benjamin light the fire, smiling to himself to think that after all this life, this struggle, these passions, rebellions, and desires, this should be all that was left to him, this old fat man who was like a dog in appetite, lack of vision, and fidelity. Oh, and David also.

'So my son has been here?' yawning in sleepiness.

'Mr. David has been here, master, and once he brought his babies with him.'

'How do they grow?'

'Grand children, fat and greedy.'

'And how is my son?'

'Not a more content man in the county, master. "Well, Benjamin," says he, "how scrub does this place look! It wants a pail of water," says he, "and the doors are all loose on their hinges!" "Well, Mr. David," says I, "it is a tolerable place for Master and me because we're at ease in it," says I, "and 'tis better to be where you're at ease, however scrub it may be, than in a palace where there's no small-beer nor a bull-baiting." "Why, Benjamin," says Mr. David, "you're a philosopher." "I leave that to the master," says I, "and suit my bottom to my own stool." But he's always friendly. He's a smiling gentleman, and they say he has a fine house. I've not been there myself, though he's asked me.'

'Aye, he has a sound imagination,' said Herries, 'and a sound belly. Phantoms and apparitions are not in his company, and he's the happier for it. I'm glad he's well.'

'So am I too,' said Benjamin, happy to see his master so cheerful, 'for he is a grand strong man, and can wrestle any other in the county, and he's breeding a grand family that will last to Judgement Day, I should think.'

When the food came Herries made Benjamin sit down beside him, and told him of some of his adventures. The old man had a great ear for marvels. Nothing was too miraculous for him to believe. Herries told him how he had seen in London a man with a furry tail that stuck out of his breeches, and a woman with a beard to her waist. Also a mermaid in a tank of water.

Benjamin sighed, watching to see whether Herries was relishing his food.

'A mermaid! That's a woman with a fish tail. I've heard of such. And what would be her issue, master, after lying with a man? Fish, think you?'

'More mermaids,' said Herries. 'They sing so sweetly that no man can resist embracing them.'

'Did the one you saw sing, master?'

'She was melancholy, poor creature, being a captive, and did nothing but sigh, and the tears poured down her cheeks.'

"'Tis a shame,' said Benjamin, banging the table, 'to keep them for a show. Why did you not break the tank, master, and plunge her into the sea again?'

'I'm no knight-errant any more, Benjamin. I have lost my fire.'

'Not a bit of it, master,' said Benjamin cheerfully. 'You shall see how merry the two of us shall be here. I can cook to your fancy, and the trees are growing and I've got bricks round the chimney, and the horses are in fine trim. You shall see how grand everything will be!'

Left alone, Herries lay back and looked at the fire, strange thoughts crowding on to him; the scenes of the last months, lonely hillsides, crowded inns, the noise and smells of streeted towns, lights and flares, clouds and wind, odd voices and shouting strangers, all the bustle of a world. He had not been unhappy in it. There had been something as spectator that had pleased his ironic fancy, and there had been always the driving passion of his unresting search. But that other earlier life, now so remote-- pictures now crowded about him--the mad restless life at Doncaster, the arrival at Keswick, and poor old Pomfret with his oaths and nervous violence, the night ride out to his house, poor Margaret, Alice Press. . . .

His visions stopped there. He drove them back. Of what use? All, all had been a preparation for Mirabell. He saw her, a tiny child clinging to her mother in the noise of the Christmas games, standing beside him on Honister, speaking to him shyly in Carlisle: 'I wanted to tell you . . . I love someone . . .', that fearful moment when, above the dead body of her lover, she turned, not seeing him, staring into the face of her tragedy, the marriage-day, in the little Chapel, afterwards the huddle of the villagers tumbling down the stairs, and again when he had carried her to their bed . . . these too he must drive back. But his longing he could not control. His longing for nothing more than her presence. Were she here now, sitting opposite him at the fire, he would not pester her for love. Were she returned, he would never speak to her of love again--only that she should be there!

He smiled at his old age, his white hair: he as a lover! But this love had nothing to do with age nor with physical strength nor with beauty. He did not love Mirabell for her beauty. She was not beautiful. She was not clever, nor had she the arts of the woman. But she was his wife, his child, his mistress, his friend, and he felt a kind of triumph because nothing could rob him of this, his only feeling for her that death itself would not destroy.

If only for five minutes he might speak to her he was sure that he could persuade her to stay with him. There was nothing now to frighten her. He did not want her now to love him, that is, if she truly could not.

But at the thought of the bliss that it would be if she loved him, his heart beat so thickly that he could sit still no longer. He tried to rise, to find that one of his legs would not stir. The pain was so sharp and so sudden that he cried out. A wave of pain covered his body. He thought that he would faint. Then, while he gritted his teeth, it passed again. Benjamin returning at that moment, he called out to him to help him.

'Why, master, are you lame?' The old man helped him up.

'Aye; take me to bed. I'm old. This leg failed me a sennight back.' But he grinned at the top of the stairs. His leg was better again.

'That won't beat me. But see me to my bed, and talk your nonsense, old fool. I'll not have ghosts in my room to-night.'

And Benjamin, whose mind was literal, told him how the old woman Carpenter of Grange had been chased in Cumma Catta Wood by the ghost of the old witch Wilson, who had barked like a dog, and flame had come from her mouth.

'She will not plague me,' said Herries. 'I carried her in my breast once for all her witchcraft.'

He kept Benjamin at his side far into the night.

ULDALE

II. FAMILY LIFE

Sarah Herries one fine summer day had a tea-party. Not by her own intent. She had but recently risen from the delivery of her third child, William Benedict Herries, who was born on a damp day in June, 1770. Why Benedict, said everyone? No one knew. Sarah thought it a nice name, and David was so happy at having another son that he didn't care what they called him. Why was David so happy? He had two children already, and children are, they say, very expensive. They were not so expensive then. There were more servants, much more space, much more indifference to infant complaints. Children wailed, were not attended to, ceased wailing. But David cared nothing for expense. Here was another Herries. He saw himself in the role of Abraham with Herries scattered about him like the sands of the sea.

Sarah did not mind. This was to be the last of her children and she would have been sad had she known. She was strong, resolute, happy, maternal. This was the grand time of her life.

Squire Osmaston and his wife rode over on this fine summer day, and the O'Briens happened to be out in their new carriage. This was a year or two before the Carlisle Post Coach, which went from Carlisle to London in three days. The world was opening up. You could travel so fast now that there was no escaping a neighbour, did he wish to see you. So fast, but not so securely. The O'Briens had a house between Carlisle and Bassenthwaite. They had come ten miles in their carriage and were shaken to pieces although this was summer weather and the roads were dry. They were shaken but proud. The Squire and his lady had ridden over on two enormous horses who looked, as young Maurice O'Brien whispered to their friend, Colonel Assheton-Bolitho-Carmichael, who had ridden over with them, like 'animals out of the Mythology.' The gentlemen were drinking in the parlour while the ladies sat in the garden sheltered from the winds by a charming little Gothic temple which Sarah, who was sharing the universal taste for Gothic, had had constructed.

So there they were. David was unfortunately in Borrowdale, where he had been staying the night with his father. Sarah, warned by her maid Nellie, who had spied the chaise, had quickly changed her house-work clothes for a large orange hoop and an upper dress of silver which suited her very handsomely. Mrs. O'Brien and her two daughters, Katherine and Olivia, were very finely dressed, so finely that they took up most of the space in the temple, but Mrs. Osmaston had on a muddy riding-suit, her wig awry, and her hat on anyhow. She sat as usual with her legs spread, her hands on her hips, looking like the Wife of Bath, temp. 1770.

Sarah enjoyed it all hugely. She loved to have friends about her, to play hostess, to sit in her own grounds with her house at her back, to know that her children were well, the cows in the paddock not ailing and her own bodily vigour returning to her at last after some very languid weeks. Talk, talk! What were they talking about?

About a boil on the Osmaston back, about clothes in Carlisle, about the incredible impertinence of servants and the high vails that they everywhere demanded, about Miss Nancy Souper of Hardcross and her illegitimate baby that she'd had of a local doctor, about a shepherd who had been hanged last week for stealing two halters and a hammer, about colds and chills, about everything in the world and nothing at all.

The new baby was brought out for inspection and was considered strong, healthy and the spit of his father. The baby, who was withdrawn howling, led to a very animated discussion of the comparative virtues of Doctor James's Powder and Bishop Berkeley's Tar-Water. Dr. James's Fever Powder, nothing could rival it. It had saved the lives of Royalty, was good for everything from smallpox to distemper.

The powder rose in a happy cloud before the ladies' eyes. Of a sudden, life was secure and confident. Incredible that anyone should ever die! Mrs. O'Brien (whose voice was small, very precious, as though every utterance were worth its weight in gold) gave it as definite fact that between the year 1750 (when the powder first began to be in reputation) and the close of the year 1763 fewer had died, upon an average, than in any preceding thirteen years, upon which Mrs. Osmaston, kicking out her leg, scratching her dirty wig and barking like a dog, remarked that this was no virtue in a powder. For her part this business of keeping Inconsiderable People alive when they were greatly better dead was vastly overdone. The world was largely too filled with unnecessary persons. In the good old times, which were better in every way than the present, when someone ailed, if he or she were of a sickly constitution the illness finished them, and a good thing too, for who wished the countryside to be peopled with ailing imbeciles who were for ever about to be ill or recovering from illness and a nuisance to everyone about them? Had she had her way she would have strangled Dr. James at birth and saved this world a monument of trouble and expense.

Mrs. Osmaston always grew vigorous in the open air. Houses stifled her. She was only really happy with dogs and horses, men who told her bawdy stories and ladies with whom she might exchange scandal. Her heart, however, was kindly and generous, her life a constant protest against the conventions of a ridiculous society. It was told of her that when the Squire in her own village had put a girl in the family way, and the girl was turned out by her drunken but virtuous father, she had taken the girl into her own house and nursed her until she was well again.

What was life to her? a succession of following the hounds, tramping the fells after the fox from dawn to dark, eating and drinking vast quantities of everything, bullying and loving her thick-hided husband, scolding her friends, crying over Clarissa, chatting with every huntsman and stable-boy in the district, driving all her household to church of a Sunday and encouraging the parson to be drunk after dinner.

Mrs. O'Brien was a sententious and sentimental woman with all the belief of her time in capital letters. Mrs. Osmaston shocked her very deeply and she could not forbear to say:

'Why, Alicia, to speak so destructively you condemn both our Maker and His Divine Purposes. Why should we practise the virtues of Compassion and Indulgence on behalf of our Fellows if this world is not an Education and an Improver of our frailties? Olivia, my love, turn your cheek. The sun is catching it.'

'I cannot for my part,' said Mrs. Osmaston, 'do with your Sensibilities and Virtues. We are not put here to be Virtuous, but to cause as little trouble to our fellow-mortals as may be. And the proof is that if you have a flea down your back you think nothing of your Sensibility but off with your smock and snap him between finger and thumb.'

Both the O'Brien girls tittered at this. Mrs. Osmaston was so very droll! Olivia was all Sensibility, but Katherine inclined towards dogs and horses and a drink with the gentlemen. They both despised their mother, but feared her. Underneath her sensibilities she had an iron hand.

'We have had,' said Mrs. Osmaston, who enjoyed teasing Mrs. O'Brien, 'the oddest cousin from London. He would have pleased you mightily, Julia. He was all sensibility. He was in raptures over every country sight. He was ever talking of the Elysian fields and "gentle showers" and "rivers of dew." A sheep sent him into ecstasies. He was all for discovering hillocks and haycocks and dusky trees. At the last he was discovered lying under a haycock with a milkmaid, where his processes were, I don't doubt, as ordinary as though he'd been fiddling with a chambermaid in Piccadilly. But his hair was all straw and he was whipped through the fields by a jealous shepherd, so his experiences were at the last sufficiently Arcadian.' Mrs. Osmaston roared with laughter, slapping her thighs. 'The shepherd had his breeches down and whipped his bare skin, so that he could not sit to cards that evening. He returned to town next day and is the less Arcadian for his visit.'

All the ladies laughed and had anecdotes of a similar kind to furnish, and then there must arise the accustomed arguing as to the relative virtues of Mr. Fielding and Mr. Richardson. Those two gentlemen entered the Gothic temple, their spirits comfortably enjoying the salubrious air and the female society. Mr. Fielding liked the pretty Olivia best, with her pink and white, her air of a rakish prude and her fine legs (which, being a spirit, he could plainly discern under the lemon-coloured hoop), and little Mr. Richardson preferred Mrs. O'Brien who was after his own heart.

'But Grandison!' cried Mrs. O'Brien, 'how tenderly imagined, how proudly conceived! What Ideal Behaviour and Constant Fidelity!' and Mr. Richardson planted a kiss on her broad brow which seemed to her like the tickling of a fly so that she brushed the place with her hand.

'A ---- for your Grandison!' said Mrs. Osmaston very coarsely. 'Now Jones is the man for my money and for Katherine's too, I don't doubt. What, Katherine! Would you let Jones touzle you were he here? Would you beat Sophia out of the field, girl? I'll wager if your mother's back were turned you'd not hesitate.'

It was well perhaps that the gentlemen were coming across the lawn. Squire Osmaston was drunk and Mr. O'Brien nearly so. They were singing a hunting catch which rang prettily through the summer air, but they hushed as they drew close to the temple.

Mrs. Osmaston rose to control her lord and master.

'You're drunk, Peter, and will never reach home in safety.'

He staggered a little, then slapped her fat neck with a hearty friendliness.

'I'm a little drunk and a little sober. My good horse Robin knows how to carry me. I have not been drunk for a week past and, for that, my fair hostess will forgive me.'

Everyone was readily forgiven on so lovely a summer evening. They all moved to the road where the fine new chaise was vastly admired and the two enormous horses solemnly held by Ralph, David's farm man. The scene was thick with gold dust like a bee's wing and the trees smelt of honey.

The chaise was away first with a great waving of arms and shouting of good-byes. Before she mounted her charger Mrs. Osmaston put her stout arm round Sarah's neck and embraced her.

'I am fond of you, my dear. I am a foolish, old woman who chatters a world of nonsense, but there's a bed for you and a horse to ride with us any time you desire it. Now then--huppety-hup--' With a leap she was in the saddle and settled there as though she were part of the horse's anatomy. The Squire too, drunk though he might be, had no trouble in mounting, and a fine pair they made, facing the country as though they were king and queen of it.

The Squire had some last confidential word. 'There's a tale,' he said to Sarah, looking at her solemnly from the back of his horse, 'a damnably good tale that I must tell your husband. 'Tis a tale of an orange and Mrs. O'Brien's pet monkey. 'Tis the wittiest, handsomest . . .'

'Whoop!' cried Mrs. Osmaston, giving his horse a whack with her whip, and off they went down the road, a cloud of dust behind them and the sky golden over their heads.

The horses' hoofs rang on the road, then peace resumed its power.

Sarah walked a little while in her garden before going into the house. Although the sun, a smiling gold penny, had almost perched its chin now on the ledge of the hills, the air was yet richly warm and the cool of the evening mingled with it most freshly.

All the sounds were of the summer evening, bees were yet humming, the men were calling to the cows, and a thrush was singing from the thick luxury of an oak tree as though it had but just come into the noblest of fortunes. Sarah's heart beat with the conscious appreciation of the goodness of life. She could not believe that she was thirty-two! Thirty-two! Thirty-two! And she knew old ladies in Keswick with Brussels caps on their heads not a day over thirty. But she was younger now than she had ever been. In those hard years with her uncle she had been old. She saw herself as a child of fifteen, standing before one of his infernal rages and calculating with the wizened wisdom of an old witch how she would drive him into a certain position and make a bargain with him there. Her youth had begun with that almost miraculous appearance of David there in the Wasdale Inn. She had loved him at sight, and thrown herself at his head and won her liberty.

But afterwards, over that last scene on the Pass, a cloud hovered. There had been something evil then. She had hated her uncle, she had owed him nothing, he had not cared what misery he had planned for her, but still in his death there had been a cloud of evil. She would never be quite free of it.

For a moment the garden had been darkened and the humming of the bees dimmed, but she was of too healthy a nature to prolong any morbidity, and so, singing to herself, her strong freshly-coloured body moving freely in its orange and silver, she walked her garden.

She loved this place because it was so open. Although in the manner of the time the garden was a little arranged with its temple, box hedges and ornamental paths, yet it ran boldly into open country, the down rising above it on the one side, the road running under the hills on the other. But she loved it in reality because it was the home of her husband and her babies. She was all maternal.

David was her child more than her lover. She understood him now, she thought, with completeness. She had all the woman's tender irony at the ridiculous things that seemed to him important, at his absorption in minutiae; she had, too, the woman's almost jealous envy at his ability to throw off his moods, to forget his passions, to take everything with a light mind.

Was there anything for which men finally cared? David loved her, of course, but a little as a child loves its mother. If another child calls him to play a game, off he goes, forgetting his mother until he needs her again. But Sarah had a great understanding and a splendid gift for taking things as they were. She did not wish David to be different in anything, but were he different she would suit herself to his condition. Standing under the oak tree, looking over to Skiddaw's sprawling shoulders, she speculated a little as to how it would have been if David had had his father's temperament. She did not understand Francis, and yet felt that perhaps at the last she could have understood him better than did any other.

He was old now, but finer, more striking than he had ever been, with his white hair and long nervous figure, of which every part seemed to be imaginatively alive. She could not understand that he should love someone desperately, without end, for ever. David would not. Did she die he would never forget her, would care for her always, but he would marry again and be happy, and the second wife would listen to his plans and share his activities, and be mother of his children just as she was. The knowledge did not make her sad. All she wanted was that he should be happy, happy always and vigorous always and noble-hearted always.

Smiling at the thought of him, she went into the house to her children. They were brought down to the parlour.

Francis was ten and Deborah eight. Deborah was as sweet-natured and unselfish and happy as Francis was reserved and driven in upon himself. Both were pretty children, Francis very dark, slim, aristocratic, never familiar with anyone, fearless, but oddly tempered. He would be distressed for no reason, happy for no reason. He liked best to be by himself. Whether he was fond of his father Sarah could never be sure. He allowed his father to play with him, responded to his father's demands on him, was for the most part obedient. He did not appear, though, to miss him when he was absent, nor showed excitement on his return.

He adored his mother. With her he was not demonstrative, but you could tell that everything she said or did worked in his own bosom responsively, and he would watch her, when he thought that she was not looking, with loving meditative eyes.

Deborah, on the other hand, loved everyone, and gave herself to everyone. She had no self-consciousness, no pose for effect, no selfish motive in anything. She was like any other child in small things--temper, disappointments, aggravations--but everything was quickly over. The serenity of her temperament carried her always on a calm sea. She was as fair as her brother was dark, like her father in that, although slender and delicately made. David worshipped her.

In the parlour they were endlessly happy. There was the China wallpaper, with the white and blue pagodas, temples, bridges and flowers. There was the spinet at which their mother sang. There was the cabinet with the silver boxes and gold chairs and little Chinese figures. There was the music-box with the King and Queen on its lid, who marched to the tinkling tune. There was the animated carpet with the battle worked on it--cannon firing, horses rearing, Captains waving on their men; and there was the comfit-box with the sugared cherries and the cakes of marzipan.

This evening young Francis stood at the window watching the sunset fall over Skiddaw. He was like his grandfather in this at least, that he could not have enough of this country. He had not as yet seen much of it; but now, as he looked out, he was swearing to himself that he would not rest until every stone and tree of it was revealed to him. What did he see there if he looked hard enough? The mountains opened, and, carried by the wind, you struck with your golden shoes the centre of a group of hills like men watching you. Here was a pool, icy and black, and suddenly into the middle of it there plunges a beautiful white horse. . . .

"Tis the white horse,' he cried excitedly, turning from the window to Deborah.

'A white horse?' asked Sarah, thinking of a new shawl, the gold buttons of David's coat, whether Mrs. Osmaston ever wore a clean wig, and if not why not, and why David was not returned.

'Why, yes, Mama. . . . We told you. The ice breaks and it swims to the shore.'

Some story, she supposed, that Mrs. Monnasett, nurse, housekeeper and general confidante, had been telling them. Mrs. Monnasett needs many pages to herself, but cannot have them--with her passion for plums, her belief in witches and centaurs, and her play-acting, so that, give her a handkerchief and a deal board, and she can be Cleopatra, Jane Shore and Mrs. Elizabeth Montagu without shifting her wig. But did anyone suppose that David or Sarah made Uldale, made the children, made the sun turn grey before an East wind, and the milk sour before thunder? No, no. It was all Mrs. Monnasett.

And now it was time for the children to hear the music-box and to have one sugared cherry apiece. Francis listened to the tune and saw five small negroes in gold-laced jackets dance across the carpet. One carried an ivory cane with a blood-red knob to it, and he had only one eye. Where the other eye should have been. . . . So he suddenly began to shudder, to shudder and shiver and tremble. He knew now that he would see that empty place where the eye should be all night, so quite without warning and quite foolishly he was sick on the carpet.

Sarah could not understand it. She had never been sick in her life. Perhaps Mrs. Monnasett would understand. She was better with Francis than was anyone else.

'After one tune he was sick. . . .'

Francis lay, very small and very white, in his four-poster that had green curtains with roses.

Mrs. Monnasett, so large that she filled the room, her black hoop billowing about her, a silver chain rising and falling on her breast, took his hand, and continued her fairy-story about Queen Anne. 'But the Princess was resolved to see the Queen, although she had only a rag upon her, so she said to the Lord-in-Waiting, who was fingering his snuff-box made of one green emerald, "Sir, there is a spider in the Queen's closet." Now if there was anything that Her Majesty had a distaste for 'twas a spider, as everyone in the Court knew, and only a week back five hundred and thirty-one spiders had been thrown into the kitchen fire, and made such a smoke that the Royal Cook had turned a dish of Peacock into a Canterbury Pudding by the misfortune of the smoke blinding her eye. Therefore the Lord-in-Waiting hastened as swiftly as his stout legs would carry him, and the Princess, following. . . .'

Sarah, sitting awhile to watch that the boy was comfortable, wondered what Mrs. Monnasett's history might be. No one knew. She had been living for several years in a little green cottage outside Keswick when Sarah met her, and had herself suggested that she should come to Uldale, for 'I love children,' said she, 'and am never happier than in their company.' And so indeed it seemed, for she had no interest at all in Society, but cared only for being with the children, and talking to her little white dog, Mr. Pope, and eating as many sweet cakes as she could find. 'Which is the reason of her

great stoutness,' thought Sarah, but she was truly a Blessing for the house, and long might she remain.

David was home. She could hear him calling 'Sarah! Sarah!', so she hurried downstairs, and he was there in the parlour, larger than ever before perhaps. He was delighted to see her, but gave her that kiss which husbands give their wives when they have been a long while married and are thinking of someone else.

'You would not consider him fifty years old,' thought Sarah proudly. His brown tie-wig was pushed back a little from his forehead, and he slapped his great thigh.

'Here is Paradise. Here, come.' He sat down in the big chair and she sat close to him, her hand on his knee. 'I'll tell you, I hope you were frightened out of your senses for me because I did not return.'

Sarah smiled. 'I am never frightened when you are away, but I had a party, and you were sadly missed.'

'Aye, that for certain,' he grinned. 'But I have the ague and the fever and the toothache as well. That house is of paper, and will be blown away with the first wind, and there my father sits with old Benjamin on his hams beside him, listening to every mouse in the passages.'

'How is he, Davy?'

'Oh, well enough. He was but just returned from another of his journeys. He is crazed, and yet he is not crazed. He is as content, I believe, as ever he was in his life, but he will never rest until he has found her, although what he will do with her when he has found her no one can tell. But he will never find her. She is dead or gone abroad or changed into an apple tree. But he is resolved that she will return.'

'He and Benjamin are quite alone?'

'They sit like a pair of quarrelling lovers. "You shall have veal to-day, master," says Benjamin. "I shall not," says my father. "But you shall," says Benjamin, and he gives him veal and my father beats him. And all the while the house rocks and mumbles, and the mice sit on the tables and the rain beats through the ceiling. And next week he will be off again and walk a hundred miles, asking of every sheep has he seen his wife. But he is sane enough. He began with me, examined me on all the family, and confounded me with his knowledge. He has been, too, to see Deb's two boys, and can tell you where they are in Arithmetic, and that Deb has a new China piece in her cabinet and a black cat with no tail.'

'Will he not come here for a week and have good food and a warm bed?'

'He does not want good food nor a warm bed neither.'

Sarah sighed, then, looking up at David, laughed.

'How is it that he is your father and you so different?'

'I am not so different. We have a great bond of common feeling. 'Tis odd, Sarah, but I am more comfortable with him than with any other human on the globe, save yourself. I have a feeling, Sarah, that if Mirabell were to return and give him satisfaction by loving him, and they to settle down together, he would become very like myself.'

That was clever of him, thought Sarah, who, like all loving wives, wanted always to prove him strong in the direction where he was undoubtedly weak.

They began then, sitting very close together, to gather all the tiny important things--Davy's toothache, how Molly the mare had cast a shoe, whether Forrest the head farm man was lazier than was natural, the eternal mystery of Mrs. Monnasett, and so to Francis who had been sick on the carpet for no reason, and thence to the baby Will who had chewed his coral--and through it all their happiness, their security, their mutual trust, their luck that they had one another.

And David the Patriarch--this is the last view of him just now-- staring into the Chinese pagodas, the bridges and the Immortal Temple, sees a Great Tree stretching to heaven, and hanging from its million branches Herries, and Herries, and Herries.

Beneath the tree lies England--her valleys, her rivers, her great cities, and the rocks of her invincible coast--and over England the Tree beneficently stretches its green shade.

There are enough Herries here for a thousand years, and who is that so fatherly protective on the topmost branch?

Who but David himself? He draws Sarah close to him and, with his broad arm around her, kisses her.

But it is England that he is embracing.

THEY MEET IN PENRITH
FEB. 4, 1772

The Peel Towers have faded, the refugees from Culloden are bones beneath the turf, the poet Gray has more than three years back 'dined with Mrs. Buchanan on trout and partridges,' and Herries has stayed, rested his bundle on the slope of the hedge, and stood with his back to a friendly oak to settle in his mind whether there be three roads or one stretching before him in the dim February light.

His fever, which had become by this quite a friendly companion to him, often brought him to such an uncertainty. He called it his Fever because he did not know what other name to give to it. It came and went as it pleased, having quite a cheerful and independent life of its own. You could never tell what it would be about.

It gripped him in its strong arms at any time, and supplied for him the queerest fancies. You could scarcely call it a sickness, because, although it weakened his limbs, dimmed his eyes and beat him about the head,

it provided him also with an odd exhilaration and gave him many phantasies. Sometimes it drove him to bed because his back and legs refused to carry him any longer, and, had his will been less strong, he might have yielded to it then more completely, for nothing pleased him more than to lie, the Fever with him, on his bed in Herries and see the strange sights that the Fever brought him, and hear, always a little removed, the sounds, the running of water, the beating of drums, the rumbling of thunder, that echoed in his ears.

But he was not defeated by it. He would boast to it: 'Nay, Fever, I like your company once and again, but you shall not weaken me. This picture that you are showing me of a chariot filled with monkeys and a bark with gold apples is entertaining enough, but to- morrow I go about my business again.'

And the Fever, being a good-natured fellow, would recognise his stubbornness and let him have his way.

On this dark afternoon it was as stubborn as he. He shivered with the chill, his body was as though bruised by a tumble, his head was on fire. So he stood against the oak tree and wondered whether there were three roads into Penrith or only one.

'Ah, well,' said the Fever, rattling inside his head like a loose button, 'you are seventy-two years of age, you know. You haven't the power over me you once had.'

Yes, but WERE there not three roads? He had walked only from Appleby that day, and he must press on to Herries. But how could he press on when there were so many roads to choose from? They mingled and divided and mingled again. They ran to his nose, leapt skywards, rolled like strips of white boarding down an implacable hill.

He wiped his brow, which was damp with sweat, and that seemed to quieten him, for now there was but one road stretching in a subdued and orderly manner to the foot of the town.

He picked up his bundle and went on. In the main street there was no one about. Near to him was a lighted window (for early though it was, the town was already dark) and over the doorway hung a sign, 'The Green Parrot,' with a painting of a fine green bird with an ironical eye. A parrot? A parrot? Once before there had been a green parrot in a room filled with talk, and a man. . . . But he could not settle the matter. After the Fever had left him he would investigate his memory.

There was a small bare panelled room with a table and a bench, so he sat him down and soon a stout old man in a green baize apron came to attend to him. This old man had a broken nose and a hand without a thumb, but he was pleased to see company. There was something about Herries that always won him attention wherever he might be. He brought him ale and bread and meat, and then sat beside him for fellowship's sake. The old man was called Andrew Greenship, and at once, as though he had spoken with no one for a hundred years, told Herries all his history. He had been a soldier in the old days and fought in the Low Countries. His thumb had been severed by a Hanoverian hatchet, and his nose broken in a fight about a gold piece. He had gout when the weather was bad, and for the most part trade was poor. But mostly he wanted to talk about his son who had gone to make his fortune in London, had returned without making it, and was now a curse to his father. He was in Carlisle at the present, but would soon be back again wanting money from his father, and with a pack of women and dogs at his heels and no place to put them. The old man could not understand it. Why were things as they were? Why were there not cakes and ale for everyone? For his part his only comfort was a dog called Mulberry, who was the cleverest dog in all Cumberland and Westmorland, and once let him set his teeth in another dog . . .

The Fever waved its hand and departed. The room was warm, the fire burnt brightly, and the red curtains were cosy about the windows.

On the wall was a play-bill. At the Theatre Royal, Penrith, they were presenting Othello, by Mr. William Shakespeare, to be followed by a farce, There is No Wife like a New One.

'The Players are here?'

But are they not here? Andrew had not himself seen them, but he had heard them grandly spoken of. To-night was their last performance. But Andrew was inquisitive. Who was this old man, so fierce and so courteous, travelling only with a bundle? He asked many questions. Herries answered them all. He had been far, he was a great traveller, he knew London, he had seen the King, he, too, had a wife and children. But after all he was a mystery. He gave nothing of himself away, and his eyes moved as though he could see a penny through a wall of houses. When he rose from his hard bench Andrew was amazed at his height and strength.

'How old would he be?'

Seventy-two years! and Andrew was but sixty-three come Michaelmas. Andrew had not for many a day seen a man he liked better the look of, but he was one of your gentlemen, a nobleman maybe, taking his exercise for the fun of the thing, as noblemen were apt to do.

There came in a little, stout, self-important apothecary-chirurgeon. He had been his rounds in the country and had his saddle-bags filled with boluses and electuaries. In his skirt pocket he had his sand-glass and wanted to take Herries' pulse with it.

He had had a busy and, it is to be hoped, profitable day; one lady had been treated for the vapours, and one lady, alas! for the itch. He was in a temper, too, for in Appleby he had not heard the 'Gardey Loo,' and some of the contents from an upper window had missed his head indeed, but struck his long-skirted coat, and it would never be clean again.

He recovered over his ale and the warm, close, smelly comfort of the low-ceilinged room. He described with gusto a recent visit to Edinburgh, the ladies in their gigantic hoops, their heads and shoulders covered with green and scarlet plaids, the green paper fans with which they warded off the sun, their red-heeled shoes, the dirt and filth and narrowness of the stairways, the streets crowded with the rude and impertinent 'caddies' carrying messages and parcels, the theatre where he had seen The Mourning Bride and The Country Wife, the cock-fights, the taverns where the advocates drank their morning sherry, and the bacchanalian nights in the meanest of 'oyster cellars,' where you would enjoy raw oysters and porter, and dance with both the lowest and the highest ladies of the town.

Aye, that was a life in Edinburgh, but after a week of it you longed for your work again, and here he was, who had dined a fortnight back with the Bishop in Carlisle, and had to pay a whole guinea in vails to the servants, and was to-morrow night to have a grand feast in Keswick with some fellow apothecaries, and where he would be the following morning no one could tell.

It was this fellow's talk that kept Herries where he was and so led to the events that followed. The apothecary, whose name was Summers, lighted his eye on the play-bill on the wall; and although he asserted that it would be a poor enough affair, and laughed at the 'Theatre Royal' which would be a makeshift of boards in a tent, he licked his lips all the same, for he loved a play and would see one in any place. Very politely he invited Herries to accompany him. Herries meanwhile had been hit by an odd coincidence. He was always catching now at coincidences and omens (having little else to go by) and, while little Summers was talking, had remembered fully what the 'Green Parrot' signified to him. No need now to recall that scene in Carlisle; did he let himself, his fancy would pull him back into the very centre of it. He held himself off from it, but it kept knocking just outside his heart. He would stay the night here. He turned and asked Andrew whether he had a bed. Aye, if he did not mind sharing a room with a post-boy. No, Herries minded no company. His brain was on fire now with the thought that somehow, somewhere, something would come of this coincidence. How many many times before he had trusted to similar coincidences he did not now regard! Every occasion was a new one, filled with hope and happy prospects. His cheeks glowed, his hands trembled.

'The old gentleman,' said the apothecary aside to Andrew, 'has a fever. It would be wise if he permitted me to bleed him.'

But they both of them had a certain fear of this strange old gentleman who sat quietly there by the window, a smile on his lip and the light of eagerness in his eye. When the time came for them to be going, he marched off with Summers as though he were going to his wedding.

The weather now was fine, the air sharp, the evening very dark.

It was a strange theatre that they were introduced to, the arena a stable and the tiring-room a hay-loft, as they could very easily see. Everything was open and exposed. On some wooden steps, leading up to the loft, Othello sat, his face fittingly blackened, wearing a long and very soiled white robe, drinking out of a pot of ale. He would drink, and then start up in a state of very honest fury to instruct with many curses two or three yokels who were learning, even at this late hour, to trail a pike in a soldierly fashion. In spite of his spasmodic rages he did not look to be a bully, having one of the roundest and mildest of faces, with a small snub nose and eyes that, although they rolled whitely in their black disguise, could not deny their essential amiability.

The arena was but poorly filled, dimly lit with candles that guttered in all the breezes of heaven, and very powerfully to the nose came the odours of cows and horses and the pungency of dung.

Little Summers had plenty to say, and fortunately needed no answer, for Herries, sitting very upright, his hands clasped over his staff, his eyes staring straight before him, surrendered to the strange fever of expectation that now, as in times altogether past recording, swept him into breathless excitement. How well he knew, had he dared to reckon, this repetition of circumstance! The omen, a tree, the name of a street, a woman's hair, a printed word, the fire of confident assurance, the bitter unavailing disappointment. Every time he would be cheated, every time make ready for the next occasion.

Presently there was a sharp altercation. A large stout red-faced farmer, two ladies in attendance, came and sat next to the apothecary, and soon, the ladies wishing for more room than was rightly theirs on the bench, the large farmer began to sit all over the little apothecary, who had, it seemed, a temper as fiery as a bantam's.

'You have paid, sir, for TWO seats?'

The farmer slowly shook his head, and his thick sides quivered with laughter. This excited the apothecary to a frenzy, and he most inappropriately called the farmer a puppy.

The two ladies then began to take part in the affair, saying that they supposed the gentleman must be from Keswick or Kendal or some other rough part, and for themselves they did not see why they should lower themselves to speak with common persons; they'd never done so yet, and had no intention of now beginning. Both sides of the dispute appeared to amuse the farmer greatly, for he could do nothing but shake with silent laughter, say 'Aye, Aye,' turning his head from one side to the other, and murmur something about 'Coom back a bit,' moving, however, himself not at all. So the apothecary leant over his broad chest, and was about to make some very rude remarks to the ladies, when what

seemed to him the very great beauty of the younger lady struck him so forcibly that his face was suddenly wreathed in smiles, he was apologising for his abruptness, and was seated at the other end of the bench in no time at all. This, instead of angering the farmer, but appeared to amuse him the more, and, as the young lady was apparently not displeased, all was well. But the little altercation had confused Herries, and he had not realised that the play had begun.

There was a door at the back corner of the stage, and when this was opened a cow could be seen feeding in its stall. The scenery was a piece of tattered cloth hung crookedly from a rafter, an old gilt chair and a green-painted table. Against the front of the stage a number of children and boys had gathered, and were clustered, open- mouthed, in an attentive group watching the antics of the actors. A stout woman in a soiled crimson hoop, with a shawl over her head and a small black dog in her lap, sat on a chair near a candle, holding a prompt-book.

Herries soon lost himself in a mixture of falsehood and reality. The rustic scene, the smell of the cows, and the evening air lifted him back into his own world at home, and he could see the trees blowing in dark fan-like clusters above the familiar gable-end. Shakespeare had always been a glory to him, at a time, too, when he had no great popularity, and soon he was caught up anew into the familiar story and once more felt the ringing beauty of the words.

Othello came down to the candles, and, forgetting the Duke and the attendant senators, addressed his rustic audience, pausing at times for a word and turning impatiently to the lady with the red hoop, who must hesitate before she discovered the place. Nevertheless the atmosphere was caught. Venice and her waters did their business yet once again of tricking a mortal soul or two into a foolish trust in the fidelity of beauty.

The little black dog barked.

'She loved me'--said Othello, wiping his nose with the back of his hand,

> --for the dangers I had pass'd,
> And I loved her that she did pity them.
> This only is the witchcraft I have used;
> Here comes the lady; let her witness it.

and then, from among the cows, holding her long train that it might not be soiled by the dirt, Mirabell came in.

He did not see her. She had spoken her words:

> My noble father,
> I do perceive here a divided duty,

before he realised her.

Then it came to him, quietly, inevitably, as though it had been from the beginning arranged that it should be like that.

That was Mirabell, her hair, her small child's face, her body looking stout and thick beneath the shabby tawdry dress of white satin. On each cheek was a splash of red paint, and behind this her little face was oddly white and her eyes staring.

Yes, this was Mirabell. It was as he had always expected it, if not here, why, then at another place. Soon he would go, when this mummery was over, behind and fetch her away. They would stay the night in Penrith, and to-morrow would be home. At the thought of home and Mirabell there again he began to tremble. It was as though someone were slowly shaking him from head to foot. Someone also was shouting in his ear, and everything in front of him was swimming in a mist of shapeless colour.

It began at once to be incredible to him that she should be there and not recognise him. Why did she not cease all this foolishness and suddenly cry out: 'Francis! Francis! Francis, I am coming home!'? At that he began to wonder why he himself was not crying out. He clasped his staff with a fearful intensity. His arm shook above it, and unknown to himself a tear was trickling down his cheek.

Very soon he would have risen from his seat, pushed his way through the country people, but fortunately she turned, and, as Othello, his eyes on the boys who were teasing the little dog from the front of the stage, said: 'Come, Desdemona,' she gathered up her dress, glancing to see that she did not trip over a hole in the boards, and at his words, 'We must obey the time,' she vanished through the door.

Herries rose instantly and pushed through the crowd, mounting with steady steps the wooden ladder that led to the hay-loft.

Here there was a torn curtain. Shaking it aside he stood just within, leaning a little on his stick. On the floor two children were playing with some stones and string. They had tied the string to one of the stones and were dragging it, bumping, over the cracks in the floor. There was a wooden table piled with theatrical properties, and on the table a long thin man was sitting, powdering his hair, while a woman bent over him mending a hole in his faded sky-blue tights. A little fat man in a full-bottomed wig and red satin breeches was looking at himself in a cracked glass and adjusting on his head a tin helmet. From below came the lowing of a cow for its calf and the voice of Iago, very high-pitched and trembling with dramatic irony.

The woman mending the sky-blue tights was Mirabell.

One of the children cried out. She looked up.

So they looked at one another after these many years. She was old, worn, ill. That was his only thought--that he must take her at once, without an instant's delay, and have her cared for. Her beautiful hair had lost its lustre, the blobs of red paint on her cheeks seemed to sharpen the lines, the shadows, the thinness of that child's face that yet was a child's face no longer, but a woman's, weary, ill-fed and drawn.

And what did she see? An old white-haired man leaning on a stick. But what happiness was in her heart when she saw him! Yes, the shock of it surprised herself. The only friend that she had in the world. Was that ungrateful, perhaps, when the simple, kindly player, Othello, Julius Caesar, Jaffier, Prospero and Falstaff, cared for her, was good to her? Yes; say, then, the only friend that she herself wanted. How much greater the ties of those years that she had lived with him had been than she knew! Had she done right to leave him? Had he been happier without her? Was it by chance that he saw her now? Had he ever seen her, wished for her? Would he want her to return with him, or had he come only to give her a good-day for the sake of old times?

All these thoughts pressed upon her in that first moment as she looked at him.

She dropped the needle and went over to him. Then she was moved to the very depths of her being when she saw that he was so profoundly shaken at the sight of her that he could not speak, but, his hand trembling on his stick, tears falling, turned his head away that she should not see.

She put her hand on his arm and led him to the corner of the room by a little broken window that was stuffed with paper. The two men said nothing, paid no attention. It was nothing to them that an old man should speak to her, or, for that, a young one either.

'Don't cry,' she said. 'How happy I am to see you!'

When he could command himself he put up his hand and touched her hair. Then he said:

'You must come with me. As soon as this is over. We will stay to- night in Penrith, and to-morrow go home.' Then, before she could answer, he went on: 'I have been searching for you ever since you went away. I was in London looking for you.' He was so fiercely excited that his words came breathlessly, as though he had been running. 'But it is no matter--now that I have found you.'

'Yes.' She had to give herself time to settle her own problem of honour and duty. 'I have wondered so many times--whether you thought of me, what you did. But you have been ill. Your hair is white.' She smiled. 'We are both old now.'

His eyes never left her face, never moved. They were as beautiful, as strong and piercing as ever they had been.

'I will come to fetch you as soon as the piece is played.'

But she must postpone telling him how she was placed. Things were not so simple as that. But, for a moment, she wished that they had been. How she wished it! She was so weary, she was so bad an actress, this life was so mean and dirty. To go back with him, to be cared for and loved. . . . She would let him love her now in any way that he wished. One thought of the rest that it would be! To sit in that chair in Herries and hear the running water; Herries that once she had hated! But she drove all the pictures back.

'You have wanted me then? You have missed me? I have so wondered. . . . But listen.' She began to speak quickly, holding his arm with her hand. 'A man here--he is playing Othello--has treated me with great kindliness. I was very sick--it is five years back--dying, I think. He was acting in the town. He is good, most generous-hearted, and I am a shabby actress, but, when he might have had a position in London had he left me, he would not. He is drunk sometimes, but even at that he is kind.

'I have never loved him, but if I leave him now he will lose all-- his interest, his work. He has no one else. Those are his two children by another woman. She is dead of the smallpox. They too, they think I am their mother, poor babies. Francis--'

He broke in fiercely. 'You left me. You can leave him then.'

'I left you because I thought it right for you. You were only unhappy.'

'And what have I been without you?'

'You are strong. Adam is weak. If I left him he would not do anything but die in a ditch, and the children would die. We have so little time. I will see you again, most truly I will. Did you know what it is now to hear your voice. . . .' She broke off. That was not the way. She began to be tormented. She could go with him now, without one word to anyone. When she saw him holding her with his eyes, her own longing to be loved by him again, to be warmed by him, to be protected by him, began to pervade her like a happy faintness. Instinctively she drew nearer to him, and he, suddenly raising his head proudly, put his arm around her.

Othello came in.

At the sight of him Mirabell's torment grew. In his foolishly blackened face, his dirty dishevelled turban, his fat good-natured cheeks, she felt all his commonness and by contrast Francis' aristocracy. This was a spiritual thing, not a social. This heavy fat man who when he was hungry crammed his food into his mouth like an animal, who was so simple and foolish that he knew nothing of the world but the little scandals of the hedgerows and the dirty anecdotes of the roadside inns, who was kindly because he had not the wits to be aught else, who, when he was fuddled, would kneel at her feet, crying and kissing her worn soiled hands until she was ashamed, who was feckless and lazy and vain, boastful and ignorant, weak and little--and Francis who looked now, standing in that dingy attic, a king among men, Francis so mysterious in his breeding, Francis who loved her so that he had searched all England for her!--she did not draw back from his arm as her shabby Othello approached them.

She made them known. She realised that her man, Adam Betty, at once perceived that this newcomer was a patron, someone who might possibly raise them all up in the world. He spoke to him with a mixture of humility and boasting.

'Small quarters, sir, but the Muse must be served. Shakespeare! I kneel to him! So wise a connoisseur as yourself must have some points from which a humble player. . . . But my Othello--the Heart is there, the Heart! The Noble Moor is translated into this rough barn, and Miss Starr's Desdemona--ah, there, sir! you will have a performance of a Natural Sublimity--'

But Mirabell could not endure it. She saw Herries' courtesy, his head a little bowed as he listened, but also his almost mad impatience, so that she feared that at any instant he would break into some desperate declamation.

Othello was a little drunken. He swayed a trifle on his legs, and was now sending a small boy in a shirt and ragged breeches for further liquor. The scene was becoming intolerable to her. The wretched place, the figures pressing about them, the consciousness that soon she must return to the stage, the shock of Herries' presence there, her longing for him (which was by far stronger than she would have supposed), the consciousness of a new dignity and fineness in him as an older man that there had not been before, above all, the ache for the rest and care that he would give her, all these tore at her heart.

Then there was a little incident. One of the children, the smaller, thin and spare, in a shawl and a tattered red kilt, with bow legs and the expression of an aged woman, running to its father, tumbled over a crack in the floor and fell howling to the ground.

At once its father, who had been grandiloquently orating, rather to the general world than to Herries, of his rendering of other rôles in Mr. Shakespeare's plays, lost all quality as actor, and became only a simple and affectionate parent.

As he bent over the child and raised it, speaking to it gently, drying its tears with the corner of his dirty gown, catching it in his arms and kissing it, he was a man of dignity and feeling. He was the man who had been good to her when everyone else had abandoned her, who needed her, who trusted in her. He turned and, smiling through his sooty blackness, gave her the child.

'You see,' she said, turning to Francis, 'that we cannot speak together here. I must tell you of everything more fully. It is not, oh, believe me, it is not so easy a thing. You shall meet me afterwards--yes, yes, I promise you.'

He looked at her as though he would never let her go. He did not care that she was worn and shabby. This was a love that had no dictation from outside things. But he saw that it was true that they could not talk there.

'I have your promise?' he asked, touching again with a shy secret movement her hair.

'Yes, yes. . . . Later. At ten o'clock I can be free. There is a place beyond the Castle on the left of the road towards Keswick. There is a gate there with a deserted cottage. Wait for me there.'

She had spoken in a hurried whisper, rocking the child in her arms. He saw that there was nothing more to be done here. He knew that she would keep her promise, so, with one last look at her, he went.

After that he walked he knew not where. A soft rain began to fall, but he did not realise it. He realised nothing but the hunger to have her with him again. He heard the three-quarters strike on the church clock, and, hurrying as though by chance she might be before her time, went to the place. He found it without difficulty, although the night was very dark.

He stood there by the gate in the rain. He was ill again, although he did not heed it. His legs were trembling and his head was on fire. Many lights were dancing in his eyes. But he thought only of the clock. His heart leaping, he heard it strike the hour, counting aloud the strokes.

Now she would come, in another moment she would be with him. The quarter struck, then the half-hour. The silence grew with every minute more menacing. It was as though the town, the dark night, everything in the world were holding her back to taunt him. He ran into the road, then a little way towards the town. He began to call then, louder and louder. No one came. The clock struck eleven. The silence was not broken.

The quarter struck again, and once more the half-hour.

He began to run. It might be that she had said some other place. He was in the town, which was now utterly black under the rain. He ran, calling her name. Two hours later, a blind, fiery, unconscious impulse leading him back to the 'Green Parrot,' when old Andrew with candle and nightdress opened the door to the knocking, Herries fainting, fell into his arms.

PHANTASMAGORIA IN THE HILLS

Herries lay for six months moving into Death's arms and then slipping out of them again. It seemed to him like that, but Death was no grisly skeleton with grinning bones, but a place of light and space where there was a great singing emptiness and a hooded, brooding sun. He moved and was bathed in a curious lethargic contentment; 'So this is where one goes,' his complacency told him, but he was allowed only to sniff the air and shade his eyes from the light, when pulleys dragged him back to a hot fire, aching limbs and a will to live.

He was a very old man in those times to live at all with such an illness. The town took a sort of obstinate pride in his recovery. Wagers were laid. Sir Humphrey Paddock, an ancient knight whose house was at Cross Trees, a mile outside the town, bet the little black boy that his wife had brought up from London against Squire Bantock's famous mare, Marjorie, that Herries would not die. It was as well that he won, for he did not tell his lady, who was attached to little Pompey, and there would have been the domestic devil to pay had he lost.

Old Andrew obtained quite a notoriety and an added custom from his guest's struggle with death. Old Andrew was prouder of Francis than he had ever been of anyone in his life. Heaven knows where he got his affection for him from. The snob in him perhaps. He had always worshipped Quality quite frankly, and when, twenty years later, in his very old age (he lived to be almost a hundred), men praised the Revolution in France as the beginning of a grand new world, his indignation was a sight to witness.

But his affection for Herries went deeper than that. He tended him like a woman, would scarcely have left his room had it not been for the necessities of his trade and for Benjamin.

In the first delirious weeks Herries was always calling for Benjamin, so Benjamin was sent for. He came and set up a jealous imperious rule that no one could defeat. He had all the unreasoning suspicion that anyone who is accustomed to Keswick has for anything that happens in Penrith. He wore an air of exceeding knowledge. No one understood his master but he. He would talk oracularly, in the inn-parlour, to anyone who cared to listen, about the great man that his master was, and the wise man and the mysterious.

It became after a while bruited abroad that Herries had shut himself up for many years in his lonely house because he was discovering the Philosopher's Stone or some such thing. Benjamin, and indeed many of the citizens of Penrith, had still a mediaeval mind, and any marvel was welcome.

But when Benjamin was in his master's room, caring for him, his tenderness and devotion were wonderful.

'Come now, come now,' he would say, wiping the sweat from the brow, smiling into the staring eyes, smoothing the sheets about the body. 'There's no fear to trouble you. Softly, master, softly. Hold to my hand now and you'll know that there is no one can come after you. Nay, nay. There's no one here but Benjamin. Yes, yes. She'll be with you presently. She has but gone out for a breath of air and so that you may sleep a little. Softly, master, softly. All is very well. Lie still and rest then.'

Being by nature a man of fancy to whom any fable was welcome, he indulged himself by uttering any kind of marvel that might be expected to comfort his master. His fancy was closely allied to his literalness, so that if he stated that Mirabell had been but just now in the room, he must describe her dress that was sweet with sprigs of roses and say that her hair had a silver comb. He would tell Herries that all the town, aye, and the County too, was at the door enquiring how he did, and that coaches packed with Countesses waited in the street, and Marquises and Dukes sent messages of condolence. But nothing mattered to Herries, who lay, for many a day and night, his long thin fingers twitching the sheets, his eyes pitifully staring, his haggard cheeks as white as his hair.

Nothing finer can ever be recorded of old Andrew than that he endured, without too much argument, Benjamin's patronage and superiority. The two old men even achieved finally a kind of alliance together against the rest of the world.

Little Summers always afterwards asserted that it was he who saved Herries. Certainly he bled him often enough, and could be seen many times a day tramping up and down the wooden stairs, his sand- glass, almost as big as himself, in his hand.

But whether it was Benjamin or Summers or Fate or Herries' own constitution, he did, in spite of medical treatment and enough dirt and ignorance to slaughter a cityful of old men, recover. The day came when he was carried downstairs to the back-parlour by Benjamin, where he lay on a sofa in the sun, with canaries in a cage twittering above his head and a distant view of the dim hills through the window.

After that he gained strength amazingly, and it was in mid-July that he stepped with Benjamin into a hired chaise, bade old Andrew farewell, and departed for Herries.

He had become very silent. No one knew now what was in his mind. David, Sarah, Deborah had all been to visit him in Penrith, and they had felt that they were with a stranger. He asked them no questions, heard their news with courteous indifference, seemed to feel no connection with them. His only request was that he should return as speedily as possible to Herries, and there was a glow in his cheek and a smile on his lips when the chaise stumbled up the rough lane (there was path enough now for a carriage), and he was once more inside the little grass-grown courtyard.

He went quietly about the house from the top loft to the dark cellar beneath the kitchen, touching everything and making sure that it was there.

He talked often with great and excited incoherence, then for many days he would be quite sensible and coherent, then for days silent. But he asked no questions about anything, nor mentioned Mirabell's name.

There was an old white horse that he had had for some years, called once ironically by him the Paladin. It was a horse of a rather comic appearance, short in the leg and very bare of feature, with a large black patch over one eye that gave it an extraordinarily innocent and amiably foolish expression. Herries took now a fancy to this horse, and every day rode out on it. But he went no longer for any journeys. Every evening he returned.

No one knew of what he was thinking. You could not say that he was mad, because if you did he would in another moment show so much sense and consciousness of the true life about him that you were (if you were Benjamin) dumbfounded.

But he thought himself that he was growing mad, that he was less certain with every day as to the reality of anything. He had been all his life scornful of other men's acceptance of reality; that had been one of the principal reasons for his division from them. On the other side, he knew that now, for the first time in his life, he was not honest with himself. There was something within him that he would not examine. He had always despised humbug, and now he was himself a humbug, because there was a great hurt and unhappiness in his breast that he would not examine.

He would not glance down at anything that was past. Something was not here, something that he had passionately desired. No matter. Let it lie. He could not procure it. It was gone. To call it up, long for it, stretch out his hands to it, meant madness. And he also would not think of the future. He did not know what was coming. Maybe that lighted chamber of Death with the hooded sun, maybe a man in armour riding him down, maybe old age and food in your belly. He would look only at the present, this rustling tapestry on the wall, this old hill beyond the window-pane, this chair with the crusted gold sunk into its wood, this green slipper with the silver buckle, this halter that gaped from its hook on the wall. But here is your trouble, old man. Who knows what these things are?--the tapestry, the hill, the chair, the slipper, the halter--maybe they are cheating you. They are not what they seem. The tapestry is an old woman whispering, the slipper a fallen leaf, the house and the hills around it a well in which you are sunk up to your very neck. You think you are alive and are not. You were dead months ago and lay stretched out with the sheets to your chin and the candles blowing at your feet, and now that you are dead you have the power to see double, two of everything, and the trees like men walking.

He would catch Benjamin's arm at a time, and would say, chuckling: 'We are both dead, old friend, and no one knows it.' Benjamin did not mind. It was only his master's way.

So Herries would ride out on the Paladin to think of these questions, and would return in the evening, his head none the clearer.

He was always at his most sensible when David or Deborah came to visit him. He would sit in his chair by the fire or walk with them gravely over his territory, showing them an apple tree or a cabbage or the new marigold. But he never asked them questions. He listened with great pleasure to Deborah's stories of her twin boys, of their cleverness, courage and remarkable natures, of Mr. Sunwood's sermons, of how they had been to visit the Bishop, of their friends the Wordsworths and the grand house they had, of the new road to the North, of the many visitors to Cockermouth, and of Lady Freshwater's garden that had three cascades, a Gothick Temple and a statue of Minerva.

He listened, too, when David told him of his farm, of his business, of his hunting, of his children and his horses. He enjoyed it all. He was glad that they should come, but so soon as they were gone he forgot all about them. He walked about the house at night talking to himself. Benjamin would get up and follow him lest he should do himself a mischief. Once he pulled Benjamin out of bed to show him the moon over Rosthwaite Fell. Another night he crept into Benjamin's bed and lay there shuddering, his arms about the other's neck. Once, talking very sensibly and in perfect command of his faculties, he spoke about his wife Margaret, but as though she were there in the house.

'You are not to speak to her of this. She is sensitive to all that I say, poor soul, but if she would not fear me we would do better. You have seen yourself how she trembles if she thinks that I am angry. I cannot bear a trembling woman, and never could. You could say to her not to be afraid, for there is nothing to fear in me. I have not been in a rage since the children were little.'

Nevertheless he would sometimes be in a rage for no reason whatever, and then he would shout and storm just as he did in older days. His best friend and visitor, who seemed altogether to understand him, was little Mr. Harness the clergyman, who came often to see him, and thought nothing that he did or said odd at all.

Mr. Harness, in fact, had a theory that Herries was as sane as any man, but elaborated and fantasied things, in order to hold himself from thinking. He had a hope that religion would assist him. He brought with him certain beloved books from his little library-- Henry Dodwell's Christianity not Founded on Argument, Butler's Analogy, Warburton's Divine Legation, Law's Serious Call and The Way to Divine Knowledge.

It may be that Herries read these works, maybe not. No one will ever know. He did not discuss anything with Mr. Harness so much as throw out casually to him stray observations, as:

'The Planets, I fancy, must have a hearty detestation of their God. To be held by an iron hand in one order, always to obey a Law made without any consultation of them. A Planet having a trifle of Independence would prefer to fall to fiery ruin. . . . So Satan snapped his fingers.'

Mr. Harness had no liking for Chaos.

'No, you would not. You are too good a man. Nor do I fancy that if God walked in this garden, I would myself be doing anything fine or bold. He has had the experience to make Him ready for any occasion. But I would ask Him one thing--whether He is not at some time wearied of His power, and wishing that He could Himself be a rebel once and again against it.'

And he said once to Harness:

'What men call madness is only to have a picture of your own. I make my own vision of things more independently as I grow.'

Had you asked him at this time what his condition was, he would have told you, perhaps, that he saw three things to other men's one-- or perhaps Mr. Harness was right, and he busied his brain with pictures because he did not wish to look into reality.

In any case the great day of his life arrived, coming to him blindly as all our great days come. It was May 16, 1773. He rode out after his early dinner on the Paladin. He sat up very straight and stiff, wearing his old broad-brimmed black hat, his legs reaching far down because the Paladin's legs were short, his eyes staring straight in front of him as though he were setting out on some urgent quest.

Benjamin stood at the top of the path watching him anxiously. He was never certain when he saw his master thus depart whether he would ever welcome him back again.

It is possible that Herries had some notion that this was a great day, or it may have been only that the sun was shining strongly on field and hill, powdering the valley with gold-dust; it is true that his heart beat strongly with expectation. He would not ask himself any longer what it was that he expected, but he smiled sometimes grimly to himself as he went, and, as was his habit, he talked to the Paladin.

'What is your will to-day? Where do we go? Make use of your imagination. You shan't flick your ears at the sun. Unmannerly behaviour. . . . There's no graciousness in you.'

He came to a field off the road near Stonethwaite hamlet where some men and boys were baiting a little bull with two dogs. He got off the Paladin, leaving him to crop the hedge, and went into the field. There was no reason. He had nothing against the baiting of bulls, which was the habit of the time. Or, rather, he had had nothing. It may be that now, seeing three things instead of one, he was in advance of his period. The little animal was mad with terror and pain. One of its legs was torn and bleeding, the skin above one eye was ravaged and the blood poured down its face. But like Wesley's bull it could not be roused to much vengeance against its tormentors, but only pawed the ground, lowered its head, and raised it again.

Herries went up to it, put his hand on it, stroked it, and it did not stir, only stood there trembling. The men knew him well enough, and, thinking him a crazy old man, let him have his way. A stout red-faced farmer promised him that the bull should be let alone, and to his own later surprise kept his promise. He didn't know, he said afterwards, but the bull and the old man seemed to have an understanding. Witchcraft . . .

So then Herries got on to the Paladin again, and they ambled forward until they reached Seathwaite, and then past the hamlet wandered on along the well-known path into the pool of the hills. It was that time of the afternoon when on a fine day in early summer this end of the valley holds all the sun in a blaze of gold, while the hills above it are black. Herries came to Stockley Bridge, where once long ago his son had talked with the Devil, let the Paladin wander, and sat down on a flat stone above the clear green pools that Grain Gill makes for its own sweet pleasure.

From above him and around him Glaramara, his old friend, and Allen Crags and Great End and the Gavel looked down and saw him, far below them though he was, a black figure in that blaze of gold.

Whatever he was at other times, he was not clear in his head just then, for he saw, out of the tumbling stream, from behind the casual rocks, from the green bracken of the fell, figures rise on every side of him. He did not know whether they were men or women, nor did he care. They rose like flopping scarecrows, and came trooping, ambling, appearing and disappearing, making signs at him, passing him without heeding him, flying in the air like jackdaws, until at last an odd old creature with a wrinkled face marked with lines like a map, its texture also of parchment, came and crouched on its thin shanks beside him.

The air was exceedingly peaceful, the green pool between the grey stones pure and still, the sunlight over all, so that Herries did not mind a talk.

'Where are you from?' he asked idly, watching two flies circle above the pool.

'From nowhere at all. But it is a fine evening.'

'It is indeed,' said Herries. 'And your companions. Where do they hail from?' For he could see behind the black cloak of his neighbour the dark cloaks of many others beating like birds' wings in the air.

'Also from nowhere.'

'If I give you something,' said Herries (for the shadow with the parchment face had a begging eye), 'will you go away?'

'What have you of any value?'

'I have only one thing,' said Herries, 'upon which I lay any value, save my house, my son and my servant. That is a silver chain that I wear around my neck. It was left to me once by a lady who was dead. That I will not give you. But I have a spade, some trees, a horse, a

picture of an ancestor and two suits of armour. Also a witch's bones in my garden. To any of these you are welcome.'

The black-cloaked beggar moved his bony hams derisively.

'Poor property,' he said, 'at the end of a long life.'

'Am I then at the end?' asked Herries with interest.

'Not absolutely. Why have you retained so little?'

'I cannot tell,' said Herries. 'I have never had a saving nature. When I was young I scattered my seed like grass--if I may be for a moment poetical. Now I am old and I have only one desire and one dream.'

'What is your dream?' asked the shadow, but more from politeness than interest. He yawned indeed, raised a bony hand, but did not hide a cavernous mouth.

'I have dreamed of a noble white horse who swims a black pool and mounts hills of ice. But I pray your pardon. My dream can interest no one save myself.'

'Not at all,' said the shadow politely. 'And what is your desire?'

'That is no man's business,' said Herries abruptly.

'As with the rest of us,' said the shadow, crouching a little nearer, 'you have found life a silly thing with no meaning.'

Herries nodded at the pool.

'Inconsequent. Without an answer. But I have seen hints that there may be an answer elsewhere. Were men themselves less foolish there is beauty and adventure enough to balance the rest. Not, you understand, that I am of any wider intelligence than my fellows. I have been always beyond ordinary foolish. Nor do I regret it.'

The shadow plainly found his acquaintance uninteresting. He rose like a black beanstalk.

'One thing I will tell you,' he said. 'You are but at the beginning of your journey. My felicitations on your companion. Keep your spade, your scar, your fine white horse. You will need them.'

The company now darkened the air, which was very chill. The sky was grey. The hills shone with ice, and at Herries' very feet was the black still pool that he had so often seen before. It was no surprise to him, therefore, to behold a moment later the beautiful white horse go plunging in.

Once again he saw him, but now he was closer to him than he had ever been before. His great head, with its flowing mane of snow, clove the water, breaking its blackness, and Herries could feel the superb strength of the body as it drove its path. Then came the moment of struggle when the horse must plant his hoof on the slippery slant of the icy rocks. He could see more clearly than ever before how he raised his head in a superb agony of effort, how the hoofs slipped and slipped again, how it seemed as though he must fall back into the icy water, how every muscle was straining, how the glittering hills looked on with stern indifference.

All Herries' own vitality, everything that he had put into life, any past gallantry or courage or discipline, he seemed to give to aid his friend. Then with a great controlled burst of energy, that last effort was made and the ascent was won.

The white mane was shaken in triumph, the water dripped from the white body like rain, and he was off piercing the hills until he was like a silver arrow flying skyward.

Herries smiled and rubbed his hands. And there was no pool, there were no icy hills. Only the fellside, the bubbling stream, and all the valley grey now because the sun had sunk behind the rim of the purple tops. He had slept then. The Paladin was cropping the grass close at hand, and the stars were creeping out into the soft green sky. Between sleeping and waking, now that you were old, it was no great matter. Life melted from one to another, and the dividing wall became with every breath the less opaque.

He supposed that he had slept. Then sleep was more real than waking.

He climbed on to the Paladin and rode dreamily home. But this time, as he came up the path to the house, he could see, dusky though it was, Benjamin waiting at the gate. He ran forward, caught the Paladin's bridle.

He was shaking with the excitement of some news.

'Master! Master!' He pulled, in his quivering eagerness, at Herries' arm. 'She has returned. The mistress is here. She is waiting for you by the fire!'

THEY ARE ALONE AND ARE HAPPY

She was standing against the wall beside the window, straight against it as though she must have something behind her in case of attack. She had a grey shawl over her head, a faded green upper dress and a shabby red hoop. She looked old and monstrously weary. That had been Benjamin's first thought when he saw her come slowly across the courtyard, that she was fearfully weary.

Herries did a very touching thing. He went straight across the room to her, put his hand up, and stroked her pale cheek. Then he bent his head and kissed her hand.

'Forgive me,' he said, 'but I have been dreaming much of late. I supposed this also was a dream.'

They stood very close to one another, looking into one another's faces for what seemed to Benjamin, who stood without moving at the door, a long time.

Then she spoke quickly, and never taking her eyes from his face.

'Before everything I must tell you that I have come here to explain to you. That is why I have come. I can go again as easily. You must know why I broke my promise to you of meeting you on that night.

'After you were gone, my protector—the man you saw, the player— made a scene of great jealousy. He had seen that we were known to one another; he overheard our appointment. He was mad with a strange new anger and fear that I had never before seen in him.'

She caught her breath, putting her hand to her breast. 'It was as though he knew that you were the only friend I had in the world. Often he had seen me with other men and been unmoved. Now he told me that if I went that night to see you he would kill himself. I believe he would have done it. I considered my duty. I thought . . . that if I saw you again . . . I might stay with you. There were the children. So we left Penrith that evening after the play. I sent a messenger to you with a letter, but he never found you or said he did not.

'And a month back Adam left me for a young woman who had lately joined our company, taking the children with him. I had been ill. He left me without money—this was in Salisbury—and I have slowly come back. Let me stay with you to-night, and then if you wish it to-morrow—'

She swayed, reeled, would have fallen had he not caught her.

She was ill from nothing but exhaustion. When she was in bed Herries fed her with strong soup and hot wine. She thanked him with a smile, put her arms around his neck and kissed him, then, sighing with a sense of safety, turned and slept. She slept all that night, all the next day and all the night after. She slept like a young child, her head in her hand.

Herries sat for most of that while at her side. He slept a little, but was always starting out of his sleep to see whether she were there. Very gently he would put his hand out and touch her heart, to be sure that she was breathing.

Benjamin said to Mr. Harness: 'He's in such joy at her return that it's like to turn him crazy altogether.' But that was just what it did not do. He walked directly away from his dreams and fancies, leaving them behind him like discarded clothes. He came down to the door to speak with Mr. Harness.

'It is my wife who has returned, sir,' he said. 'We are friends, I am happy to think, and therefore I would wish you to give me joy, for this is the most cheerful thing that has happened to me in all my life.

'I have been, since my illness, a trifle dazed in my head, the rather I fancy because it was not healthy for me to see things exactly as they were, but now I am very well, and you may wish us a long life together.'

'Indeed I do,' said Mr. Harness, but thinking that seventy-three was an advanced age to begin life at. 'I am most heartily pleased, sir, and will offer my duty to your lady when she is well rested.'

On the morning of the second day, while Herries was sitting beside her bed and the sun was pouring in at the window, she awoke entirely refreshed. For a moment she did not remember where she was; then, when she saw his white hair and eager look, such a shadow of happiness and relief swept her face as was moving to see, for, poor thing, everything was very different from when she had gone away: she had suffered so many hardships and known so little rest that it was not only the added years had aged her.

They talked a little quietly and she had her hand in his.

Then he said, after kissing her cheek: 'There is but one thing that I must say. I pray you not to leave me again, for this time it would be my death.'

'Nay, I will never leave you any more, Francis.'

'For I am not as young as I was. Be angry. Have things as you will. I shall not pester you now to love me. Only you must not go away.'

She repeated again: 'I will never leave you any more.'

He said then in his old way: 'We are a couple of fools to make promises. Was ever a vow kept in this world? But I cannot endure the thought. . . .' He turned his head aside. 'I will not ask you to make a vow. Only do not go--unless you must.'

'And you will not leave Herries?'

'No. I will never leave Herries now.'

It was natural that in the first weeks there should be a certain awkwardness between them. There were the old things to remember and the new things to expect.

Each found the other at first changed. It was only after a while that these superficial alterations dropped away and they discovered that the old spirit shone there.

But there WERE changes, real and true ones. Each was altered by trial. The shock of her going and then his long illness in Penrith had softened Herries to a more patient acquiescence. It was as though he had peeped through a door into another room and seen certain things there that excited his curiosity and so made him less stirred by his present surroundings. It was also that her absence had been so terrible to him that, now he had got her again, he was contented in her mere presence, not wishing her to be this or that, but only near him.

Also it was as though he had found an answer to the question that he had been asking all his life. He had found justification. Finally he was so happy that he asked no more questions. It was enough that she was there and wished to remain there.

The principal difference in Mirabell was that she was a child no longer. It was not only that she was now forty-four years of age, for there are some who carry their childlikeness with them to the grave, but also trou-

ble, loneliness, sickness had given her that kind of sanctification that comes through sorrow.

Not that she was miserable or went about the place with a sad mouth. It was only that at first she could not realise her security.

What occurred was that presently happiness began to seep into the house. It is dangerous to speak of happiness, and cowards knock on wood for protection. But there are times in a man's life when it comes, at first slowly in a trickle, then rising ankle-deep, then flooding the window, at last brimming the chimneys. There is also no source of happiness quite so sure and true as the real love of one human being for another; this too seems at first incredible and very often when it has climbed waist-high sinks again, but real love is a true thing although it needs two fine-natured persons to make it true. One is not sufficient.

Nevertheless, as a matter of history, happiness flooded this old house at last and must therefore be mentioned although many would speak of ague, toothache, blights among the cattle or a hanging in the barn.

The old house soaked it in. A muddled old house it was by this, a jumble of chimneys, gables and crooked corners. What shapeless buildings! Sties like an alderman's coffin, stables like byres and byres like the ruins of Rome. Peat-stacks, dung-hills everywhere, poultry scratching in the grass-grown court, ducks everywhere garrulous, weeds hip-high, and, rather by their own volition than from any care taken of them, in their proper seasons, daisies, marigolds, jonquils, pansies, orange-lilies, gardener's garters and honeysuckle.

The old house with its cocked impertinent chimneys, its wainscots and irregular windows and ghost-haunted stairways sinking, slowly sinking into this growing height of vegetation that, encouraged by the overlooking hills, climbed patiently to heaven.

Into all of this their happiness crept. After a month or two you could feel it everywhere. Deborah and her clergyman, David and Sarah, who came in due time to pay their respects to the returned bride, all felt it. They felt also that they were not really wanted. Mirabell was most happy to see them and was very much more at her ease with them than she had been, but no one else was wanted. Happiness is like that--a cheerfully selfish thing.

Mirabell sat there and in her heart wondered what it was that had, on that other occasion, made her run away. It was as though she looked back upon another woman, a strange, uneasy, restless creature who had not wanted this and had been discontented with that. She did not ask herself yet whether now she loved Herries. Like himself she bothered herself with no questions. She wanted to be sure that she was there.

There were times when they would suddenly look at one another, both needing the same assurance.

It could be said that all that Mirabell felt for a long while was that this was a safe haven and that any other haven would have done as well. No one could tell. She did not examine the question. The haven was Herries and Herries was the haven, both man and house. She could not imagine that there could be any other. This was, after all, the only one that she had known her whole life long.

Slowly, piece by piece, some of the things that she had suffered came out. The poverty, discomfort, dirt, weariness, insult that were the inevitable companions of touring players. To the man himself she was always loyal. He had meant very well by her always. He had loved her in his own way, and the two poor children, sickly, ugly, thrown from one hardship to another, had had only herself to look to. He had on the whole, save for a momentary impulse or two, been faithful to her. After his first passion for her had worn away she had wondered that he had kept her, for, most certainly, she was not beautiful, she was often ill with hunger and cold, and she was an astonishingly bad actress.

She could remember her lines and that was all. She could never imagine herself anything but what she was. The plays seemed to her mostly foolishness, Mr. Shakespeare no better than another. She had not managed well for him. She could not cook anything fit to be eaten nor keep a place in order. Her only merit was her fidelity.

So, when at last the other girl joined them--a black-haired, fierce- tempered woman, a remarkable actress in the more fiery parts--she did not wonder that he went away with her. She would have been happy at her freedom had it not been for the two poor children, who hated the black woman and cried whenever they saw her. Poor Adam! To what miserable end must he come. Poor, stupid, good-hearted Adam to be eaten by a tigress!

Then, as months went, she forgot all the past. This new happiness burnt all the old things as a fire burns straw. They, both of them, she and Francis, went forward into a new world and lived one grand day after another. Oddest of all, he became young again. His brain was unclouded, his limbs vigorous. This was his Indian Summer.

But nothing stands still. Everything now was an inevitable sequel to all that had gone before, but a new sequence was being created.

In the autumn, that was very wet, full of howling winds, and thick at the foot with sodden leaves, Mirabell found that she was watching Francis with an odd anxiety and restlessness. Whenever he left her she was uneasy, and she would stand at the thin window that looked over the court waiting to see him turn the bend, pause at the gate, and then look up to the window, thinking, as she knew, of her. It was not that there was any true reason for uneasiness. All through that year he was strong and well, and although Benjamin, who liked gloomy tales and prophecies, told her fearsome stories about his fever, there was no sign of its return. When

he lay at night with her, putting his arms round her, she falling to sleep in the hollow of those arms, his body was like iron, marvellous for so old a man.

Nor was there any reason, as once there might have been, to fear any outside hostility, for that had died. The 'Rogue' was used in friendly fashion when it was used at all.

Nevertheless she never saw him leave the house without fearing that he would not return. All this time, with Benjamin, she managed the house. The only other was a wild girl called Bethany, of whom a wandering woman, who had died five minutes later, had been delivered in a ditch near Seathwaite.

If she was not quite right in the head, at least she did what she was told, and developed after a time a passionate devotion to Mirabell. So the house went none so badly.

But this anxiety of Mirabell's grew. She did not know what was the matter until on an evening after Christmas it was made clear to her.

That same afternoon Herries had ridden on the Paladin into Keswick to see the lawyer about money matters. She could never but smile when she saw him go, so erect on the fat horse, with his legs so long, his head stiffly set under his broad black hat. So soon as he had turned the corner and was out of sight, with a sigh she left the window and went to the oak chest where there was some linen to be marked. Looking into the chest, under the linen she saw a cedar box, and, opening it, found piled pell-mell together the jewels with which formerly he used to dress her. Gathering them together, she went to the table and sat down with them, and was filled with memories.

She could see herself now seated at the table, the jewels in her ears and hair and round her neck, while he patiently tried to teach her to read. Tears filled her eyes. How good he had been to her! She had never been able to learn anything from him, and that was strange, because she had learnt her lines in the plays easily from Adam. There had been something then between her and Francis that had prevented this contact. Now there was nothing. They stood bare breast to breast.

With that she sprang up in a great terror. She lit candles, piled logs on the fire, and, although it was far too soon, began to listen for his return. It was one of those quiet winter afternoons, so still that you could almost hear a robin's step. She looked out of the window, and a round red sun was sinking over fields and paths that glimmered faintly with a white shadowed frost. There was no sound in the house save the logs on the fire that chattered crisply one moment and then broke into a sort of music like bubbling water, and Bethany who was singing below stairs.

She went to the head of the stairs and listened. Then she tried to work and could not, went down to the kitchen and talked with Benjamin, came back again, going to the window, although beyond it now all was black, then watched the stars come out like very distant fires, then listened to the wind getting up and roaming, whistling about the house. All this time her panic grew. Oh, if he did not come! But he would not. She knew that he would not. Something had happened: he had been suddenly ill. This was a premonition. The house was alive with it. Every board, every rafter creaked with it. There were steps on the stair, and he came in.

She ran to him, flung her arms round him, drew him to the fire. He could feel how she was trembling.

'But what? . . .' He stood smiling down at her. 'You are trembling.'

'I thought you would not come.'

'But why?'

'The house was so still. You were away so long.'

He sat down, drew her to him, laid his hand on her hair.

'It was not so long. There was no one in the town. Not a leaf stirring. I read a tale somewhere once of a Dragon who, very hungry, came to the town for a meal. There was only the King's Prime Minister there--the others were away hunting--an old dry man. The Dragon licked him all over, but found that he was so lacking in juices that he dropped him from his jaws and returned sulkily to his cave. I was such an old man to-day. An old man on an aged horse in a frosty town. . . .'

'I was afraid . . . I am always afraid when you go out.'

'Then you care for me to return?'

'Care!' He felt her body draw closer to his. 'I love you, Francis. I didn't know surely until to-day. I had not thought. But I love you so dearly that I live only when you are near me. I was looking at the old jewels in which you used to dress me. How could I then have been so ungrateful? But we cannot force love. And I was busy with selfish grief for Harry. Then in those years away from you I learned that in the whole world there is no one who is like you. It is a pity that I have learnt it only now when I am old. . . .'

'We are both old,' he said, smiling. 'I have learnt some things too.'

So it had come at last. At last! At last! His happiness prevented any words. Nevertheless, when a moment later Benjamin came in carrying some logs and dropped one, he jumped up and cursed him with all his old fervour, then threw his riding-gloves at him.

But that evening they sat for a long time by the fire hand in hand, saying nothing.

Then, in the spring, Benjamin died.

One evening he had a rheum. Next day a cough tore his chest in two. On the day following, every breath he took cut like a knife. But he would not go to bed. He had a superstition that once you went to bed in the daytime you never got up again.

Illness, too, was new to him. He had had blows and kicks and bruises and cuts, but never an illness like this. This sharp pain in his chest drove him to remember his father, who had had a cake-shop in Taunton. His father had been one of the fattest men in the South of England and one of the best-natured. It was from him that Benjamin had his own good-nature. His cake-shop, which had been a famous one (and Benjamin might have succeeded to it and been a wealthy man to-day had he not thrown a plate at his stepmother and run away to seek his fortune), was very small, and his father filled all of it with his handsome brown peruke, his three chins, and his white apron. It was his father's belief that he was grandson to a nobleman by a country-girl's mistaking her road home on a dark night. In any case he had an 'air,' a tone, a something, and everyone noticed it, and bought his cakes the more readily.

Little Benjamin, sitting in the room behind the shop and smelling the rich plummy smell of good bakery, would wonder whether his grand jolly father wouldn't burst the wall of his shop with his huge shoulders, swinging stomach, roaring laugh.

And then, one evil day, his father caught this pain in the chest. Benjamin, who was then about fourteen years of age, had never seen anyone change as his father did. He suffered so terribly (he said that a hundred knives were slicing him into pieces) that they put him to bed, and there in the big four-poster that had the canary-coloured curtains (Benjamin remembered every aspect of that room-- the two chairs, of which his mother was so proud, of dim gilt, covered with silk embroidery, and on the table in the window a bowl of dried rue and sweet-briar--he could smell its sleepy perfume yet) he lay, his chins grimy with the unchecked beard, and in his eyes a look of terrified surprise.

He lay there and said nothing, save one day that he could no longer smell the thick hot scent from the bakery. They knew then that the end was near, and a day later, staring with that same surprise as though it had been impossible to conceive that it was this had been waiting for him, he died. So, a month later, Benjamin threw a plate at his stepmother and ran off to seek his fortune.

It was going to bed that did it. In spite of the pain from the knives his father should have stood on his two feet and defied them all.

But now when, after all these years, Benjamin had this same pain of the knives in his chest, he felt terror and he felt defiance. So they meant to play him the same trick, did they? He had learnt a thing or two from his old father. He'd defy them by standing on his legs-- yes, let them do their worst. So they did. They knocked him down there on the kitchen floor, where he lay with two broken plates beside him, and Bethany ran crying to her master.

Benjamin was put to bed then whether he wished or no. A doctor was found, a young fellow this time, Parling by name, a tall bony lad with great ambitions and a speculative mind, lodging in Grange because he was reading for a thesis.

When Parling looked at Benjamin, stripped his chest, listened to his lung, two opposite worlds met. Parling was all for the future, Benjamin saw only the past. Benjamin regarded the young doctor with horror. Two hours after his departure (he leaving a very serious report of the old man's condition with Herries) Mirabell, sewing by the fire, hearing a sound, turned to see Benjamin, dressed in his working clothes, swaying on his feet, at the end of the room. She ran to him. He tried to push her off. 'Stand on your feet! Stand on your feet!' he cried, clutching her arm and staring wildly beyond her. 'They can't catch you if you stand on your feet.' A fearful bout of coughing racked him and he fell forward. With great trouble she held him, he so heavy and she so slight, until Herries came and, bearing him in his arms like a baby, laid him back in bed again.

After that he was partly away in Taunton and his childhood, and partly clinging to Herries. His love for Herries came out in him like a child's dependence on its mother. He had stood by his master so long, through so many evil reports and mischances, that to go anywhere now without him seemed an incredible thing. And a great part of the while he confused Herries with his father.

He smelt the bakery. He saw the boy come into the room with the long tray and the dark brown cakes lying on it, all in rows like a game, and he felt the saliva gather in his mouth as though he were a little dog; then he heard his father's thick deep voice (as though he were himself an enormous Cake speaking), 'Chut! Chut! Be careful, boy! . . . I'll flog thee for a stumble,' and then the beneficent smile as he looked at the tray so approvingly and rubbed his fat hands that seemed to have always in their interstices fragments of flour.

But across this vision drove Herries. Herries in his proud youth, Herries stripped in the open waiting to have the water dashed over him Herries riding his fine horse, Herries having his boots pulled off, Herries shouting for his dinner.

In his rambling talk many of his private anxieties that had never risen into expression when he had command of himself came out.

'Master, master, I'm coming . . . Aye hurry, hurry! It is past the hour and no one come . . . If I break it he'll mind, but there's always a stumble or a trick for a man's feet. Coming! Coming! What more can I do? He would have me every place the same time, and then nothing but kicks after all's said. . . . Aye they can name him names, but what do they know? So it is Master Davy, so it is. But you go by the field to the left there. They say there's a fine trout or two. I'll not tell your father.

'Coming, coming, master! That's his joke. Every gentleman has his own fun--and every man too for that. There they go! Tumble them down the stairs! Tumble them down them!

'I'll set a dog to them an they come shouting their bawdy nonsense. . . . Nay, but, father, I said naught. But she's not my mother. I'll do her bidding. She shall let me alone though. If she strikes me I'll not stay. . . . 'Twas a woman with a green petticoat had the paper. She's gone in a coach and had a monkey with her. He's gone a long while. It's lonely, this house . . . If I did tumble her there's no sin. And if there's a child the old man won't know it. I'll be rubbing Unicorn down. There's an hour before sundown. Steady now! Steady! 'Tis dark in this house before you've time for a lantern. . . .'

The day before he died he recovered his senses altogether. He lay very placidly, looking at the ceiling and smiling to himself. On the next evening, which was warm so that the window was open, he heard them calling the cows in.

'The country's a fine place,' he said in a weak, quavering voice. 'Doncaster was not much, master. But here there's always a bustle. Are you happy now, master?'

'Yes,' said Herries, 'I'm happy.'

'I'm glad of it. There has been another look in your face since the mistress came home. And where would I have been without you? Dandering around, coming to no good, for I had always a leching for women. But I wouldn't have bided in one place for any woman. No, I would not. Nor worked for any woman neither. 'Tisn't right for a man to work for a woman. It is against nature. That's what my father always said, and he'd had a multitude of women in his time. . . . You've been a good master to me and I've been a good man to you. There's satisfaction in that certainly.'

Then he began to count slowly to thirty or forty, and then begin again. It may have been cakes that he was counting, or cows or horses. So, counting, he died.

After the funeral they were alone in the house, for Bethany, feeling that a funeral was a festival, had gone merrymaking.

'We are alone in the house, my dear,' said Herries.

She kissed him, then, a happy triumph showing in her face, answered:

'No, we're not alone, Francis. Nor will be again. Old woman though I am, I am to have a child. How am I for a clever woman?'

She danced around the room, and he, looking at her, saw all her youth come back to her. Her hair flamed; she was as she used to be when he implored her to love him. Now he did not need to implore. She was his completely.

DEPARTURE FROM HERRIES

Mrs. Henny came now on the scene.

Mrs. Henny was a southern woman who for ten years had been living a widow in Grange. She was a lady of all trades--nurse, midwife, cook, friend of all the world and, in the modern manner, a witch. One may see how different the modern manner (temp. 1774) is from the old, because whereas, years ago, Mrs. Wilson had been persecuted and drowned, Mrs. Henny was the most popular woman from Seathwaite to Portinscale.

Young women indeed came to ask her advice from districts as distant as Shap and Kendal. There was no one, they said, so successful in promoting a hesitating love-affair, no one with so sound a knowledge of herbs and simples. She sold charms, verses, and prophecies in packets, and kept in cages birds that told your fortune. She was in fact a 'good' witch, and was never known to do anybody any harm.

In appearance she was a little thin-boned woman with bright sharp eyes, a jutting chin, and she liked to wear wide black hoops and long black gloves on her hands.

It was she herself who suggested to Herries that she should come and 'do' for him. She could cook, she told him, she could nurse; there was a child coming and no midwife in Cumberland her equal. It was not strange that he, already most anxiously nervous about his wife's condition, should agree to her proposal; it was only strange that Mrs. Henny, who had a nice little cottage of her own in Grange, just on the farther side of the bridge, where she had a most thriving trade, should wish to come. And there was only one possible explanation. She was the most inquisitive old woman in England.

Her curiosity was her devouring passion. She had been a girl of uncertain morality in her youth, not from any sensual laxity but only because she found that promiscuous affection provided her with more excellent secrets than any other mode of living. She had an amiable nature and did not wish to use these secrets to anyone's hurt, but know them she must.

It was for the same reason that she began, later in life, to dabble in love philtres, prophecies and potions--only that she might be confided in. That it was lucrative was for her an entirely secondary consideration.

It is probable that for years now her bright little eyes had been fixed upon the Herries house and her ears strained to catch the slightest sound from it. The tales about Herries were so many, he and his house were now so legendary that she was not the only one who would look up from the path and see a light burning in a window there and long to know the truth. Mrs. Herries' return must have excited her yet further; when she heard of Benjamin's death, and that there was to be a child, she saw her opportunity.

On a warm spring evening of 1774 she arrived with a black box and a cage of canaries. To do her justice, although she may have come there from curiosity, she very speedily fell in love with both of them.

She was a warm-hearted old woman in any case, but the two things that she loved were power and a satisfied curiosity. Here she very quickly had both. They told her anything that she asked and they let her do what she wished. They were in truth so deeply absorbed the one in the other that they had no energy for asserting their rights.

'She couldn't enough confess,' she confided to her friends in Rosthwaite and Grange, 'the fashion with which they loved. In the heart of male and female,' she declared, 'you will ever find a principle of self-love and vanity, and this makes us very unwilling to give way to one another in anything. It is the desire of most females to have lovers, but for the most part it is because they wish for admiration. It is indeed the only way we females have of raising ourselves in Society.' But in this instance Mrs. Herries appeared to have no appetite for flattery but desired only to serve Mr. Herries, which was the stranger in that, after being married to him, she had left him for many years. His worship for her was odder yet, for she was not an educated woman, was most unskilful about the house, and although her hair was of a fine colour, no one could call her beautiful, nor was she, in strict parlance, a lady. Mrs. Henny had always let it be known in Grange that she was herself a lady, her father a clergyman and she herself early married to a clergyman who, as in the case of Mrs. Laetitia Pilkington, had treated her shamefully and abandoned her. However, she followed the parallel no closer. She was therefore a judge of the Upper Classes and Nobility, and she must observe that never, in all her wide experience, had she known a gentleman of the very finest birth, as Mr. Herries undoubtedly was, accustom himself so admirably to a wife who was not gently born. They suited one another in everything and could not endure to be out of one another's sight.

His, Mrs. Henny considered, can have been no easy nature to subdue, for, old though he was, he had yet a fiery temper and a very ironical tongue, but to his wife he was always the gentlest and most amiable of mortals. Mrs. Herries, poor thing, had the look of one worn out with life. She had ever an air of apprehension if he was not near her. She had been tossed about, Mrs. Henny--who was something of a poet--continued, so fiercely by life's cruel waves that she could not believe that she had reached a haven at last.

As for her child, this was her first, she was very old at forty-four for childbirth and had no strong constitution. It would be an uncertain situation. Meanwhile, they stayed hand in hand by the fire, or went out walking to

,gether, saying but little, wishing only for one another's company.

Such was Mrs. Henny's account, listened to with the greatest interest by the ladies of the neighbouring villages, who had not for a long while had such a first-hand account of doings in Herries. And they on their part revived all the old stories--of the fine rake that he had been when he had come so long ago to Herries, of his selling his mistress at the Fair, killing his wife by unkindness, burying the witch in the garden and the rest. He was a changed man, they reckoned, and it only showed what God's adversities could do.

Nevertheless Mrs. Henny, with all her curiosity, perceived one thing only dimly: the gathering anxiety with which they watched one another as the year advanced.

He had good reason for his care of her. As the child strengthened in her womb, he was more and more reminded of her age and her weakness. She seemed, as he lovingly watched her, to regain the slender childlike features that once had stirred so deeply his tenderness. She was a mature woman now in her control, knowledge of life and patience, but it was a child's face that looked across the table at him. So, lover although he was, he was also increasingly maternal; he could not watch and care for her enough.

This was also the emotion that was growing in her, for she now with every week saw increasingly that he was old. The fever returned to him at nights and he would shiver in her arms. His memory sometimes played him tricks, and his body that had served him so marvellously for so long sometimes betrayed him. The leg that had given him trouble once failed him again. He would pretend that it did not and she would pretend that he was stronger than he had ever been, and each hid the trouble from the other.

In July, Bethany ran away with a soldier she found in Keswick.

The summer was cold and wet; with October there came glorious fiery days, burning with colour, and then, in the first weeks of November, a first powdering of snow on the hills.

He began now to feel a fierce and biting anxiety that never left him. The nine months were past and the child was not born. She appeared to suffer very little discomfort. Possibly at no other time in her difficult life had she shown such courage and hardihood as she did now. She was always cheerful, and when he was there seemed the happiest woman in the country.

Mrs. Henny, who had so vast an experience, said that it was no matter that the child should be delayed; it was often so, and for the best nine times in ten.

On a day in November, Herries took her in a hired chaise to the Lake. The carriage stumbled over the rough path, which was bad for her; but she insisted. They stood for a little while in the woods below Cat Bells, pleased at the scene. The water was as still as glass, and the snow that brokenly covered the hills was reflected in it like a multitude of white fleecy feathers. The bare trees were brown and sunny; the light travelled like a silver arm resting upon hill after hill. Never before had they felt their love so strongly as then. It was love too mature and settled for many words and, most

truly, too deep for tears. It had come out of great sorrow and anxiety, many mistakes, much selfishness, some anger and petulance, and it was now purified of everything save itself.

'I have never known whether there is a God,' said Herries. 'I am no more sure now than I was forty years ago. But I always said that if I had you, and you loved me, I would thank Him.'

'I love you with all my heart.'

'I know it. And so take off my hat to the old monster.'

And he took it off and bowed to the fleecy feathers in the Lake.

'Life has a meaning,' he said. 'At last, at last it has a meaning. One fine hour is enough.'

Then he took her back to the chaise, wrapping her warmly.

'When I am sententious, my dear, you must punish me. To talk about life so is in the worst manner of Mr. Richardson, whom I detest. But even he shall not hinder my telling you that I love you.' And he kissed her cheek.

A few days later, David rode over to see him. He was greatly distressed to see how very ill the old man looked. But he said nothing of it to either of them.

As he stood by his horse before his departure, with his arm around his father's neck, a powerful sense of his love for his father overwhelmed him. It seemed to him that in spite of his affection for his wife and children, his absorption in his affairs, his pride in his position, none of these things truly touched him as deeply as this emotion.

He spoke of Mrs. Henny.

'She cares for you properly, father?'

'Yes, yes.' He looked up laughingly. 'She is distressed to-day because this morning she found her birds dead. She sees an omen in everything.'

'Why will you not bring Mirabell to us? She shall have every comfort and the child shall be born under Sarah's care.'

'No, no,' Herries answered impatiently. 'Of course the child must be born here in Herries.'

'How you love this place!' David looked about him. 'In all these years you have never failed it.'

'Nor has it ever failed me,' answered Herries stoutly.

'And you have never failed me either, father,' said David. 'After all this there is no one in the world I love as I do you.'

But Herries was not feeling sentimental.

'Aye, we've been bound together, different as we are. . . . There, get along. The snow is coming.' He gave his son a friendly push, then turned into the house, not looking back.

That night he was very ill. There was no doubt but that the worry of these last weeks brought it on. They put him to bed and summoned the young doctor. For a fortnight he was delirious and knew nobody. Then he was in his senses again, but was too weak to move. He lay there and Mirabell lay by his bed. He never took his eyes from her face.

The snow was falling heavily. The first day a wind blew and the snow piled up against the house and began softly to climb the windows. There was a still white light all about the house.

Sharply, about mid-day, Mirabell was taken with her first pains. Mrs. Henny put her to bed. They lay in two rooms adjoining and the doors were open that they might speak to one another.

He called to her: 'The snow is climbing the windows. Is it light in your room?'

And she answered very cheerfully, that he should not know what she was suffering:

'Yes. I can see its shadow. Are you better? I would come to you. I shall be stronger tomorrow.'

'Are you warm? Is Mrs. Henny with you?'

Her pain was terrible. She could not answer. Mrs. Henny came to his room and told him that she was sleeping.

But when the spasm had passed, she called out:

'Is your head well now? Soon I will come myself and see.'

His head ached strangely. The snow was coming into the room, mounting higher and higher. Some of it touched his lips and it was bitter like blood, but behind the confusion, the flashing lights, the roar of water, his mind held on to her, and, in a voice very feeble but clear, he answered: 'Yes. . . . Yes . . . I am better . . . but it is dark.'

Her pain rose and swallowed her. She thrust down a shriek of agony lest he should hear her.

She had one last thought. She seemed to cry it triumphantly, although it was truly so faint that the old woman who was delivering her did not hear it.

'Francis . . . dear, dear Francis!'

Her child was delivered, and some moments later she died.

Herries, who was ever a fighter, rose in his bed to come to her. He saw her standing in the doorway, the snow whirling softly about her head.

Gladly he called to her.

'Mirabell! Mirabell!'

Then sank back, as it seemed to him, in her arms.

There was silence in the house for a brief moment. Then there was a thin wailing cry. The old woman and the new-born child were the only living things in the house.

THE END

JUDITH PARIS

FOR J. B. PRIESTLEY

A PREFATORY LETTER

MY DEAR JACK,

There is in general no reasonable excuse for burdening a novel with a Preface or any sort of statement; a novel should show in itself its purport without outside emphasis. But, after the publication of Rogue Herries, I saw that with the next 'Herries' volume there must be a note of explanation. And for these reasons:

First: when a reader sees another instalment of Herries history he may think it necessary that he should read the first in order to understand the second.

Secondly: after Rogue Herries had made some friends it was in some places assumed that 'NOW, of course, I would write a sequel.'

And thirdly: the principal criticism of Rogue Herries was on the ground of its diffuseness.

I must explain then that, firstly, the story of Judith Paris may be followed without any knowledge of her father or curiosity as to her descendants. Then, far from considering a sequel to Rogue Herries for the first time AFTER its publication, I must here confess that I had, more than twenty years ago, the plan of writing the history of an English family that should cover two hundred years and that should have, throughout, the same English scene for its centre. This was, I think (although Mr. Galsworthy may correct me), before the later Forsytes were thought of, or any suspicion of Sagas hung in the literary air.

Thirdly, I hope that when any who are interested realise (possibly with dismay and indignation) that there are to be, in all, four volumes of Herries history, certain details and characters will not seem so unnecessary, nor certain scenes so diffuse.

I would like, very modestly, to defend the fact that I write, and must write, from my own point of view. I can see that the Herries family offers, in its history, subject-matter for every kind of historian. But my view of the Herries in these volumes is frankly a romantic one.

Every historian, whether of a country or a family, is compelled by his temperament to his own individual vision. I can see that there is a Herries history that is realistic, one that is comic, one that is scientific. Any of these might be more broadly convincing than my own, but I must mix my own colours and stand by the result.

As to diffuseness, compression in such a scheme as this is not easy. I might have written a novel, a long one too, only about Jennifer. Even with Judith I have been compelled to squeeze ten years of her life into one chapter. Those ten years could well be the subject of another novel. The Rockages at Grosset fascinate me, but my theme compels me to keep them minor. And how much more I know about Georges Paris in London or Charlie Watson in Watendlath than I have space to tell!

Every scene and character has been deliberately chosen by me because of the book's continuous theme. At the awful word 'Theme,' however, I feel that I am growing altogether too serious and solemn.

My intention is simply to record scenes from the life of an English family during two hundred years of English change and fortune, and beyond that to pay a tribute to a part of England that I dearly love.

Judith Paris may be read as a quite independent novel, but the four books are seen together in my mind as a piece of gaily-tinted tapestry worked in English colours.

Affectionately yours,
Hugh Walpole

I have kept my faith, though Faith was tried,
To that rock-born, rock-wandering foot,
And the world's altered since you died,
And I am in no good repute
With the loud host before the sea,
That think sword strokes were better meant
Than lover's music--let that be,
So that the wandering foot's content.
W. B. Yeats

PART I

ROGUE'S DAUGHTER

The old woman and the new-born child were the only living things in the house.

The old woman, Mrs. Henny, had finished her washing and laying-out of the bodies of the child's father and of the child's mother. She had done it alone because she had been afraid to leave the house with no one alive in it save the new-born child. Now she was exhausted and, in spite of her labour, fearfully chilled, for the snow, although it fell now more lightly, was piled high about the doors and windows as if, with its soft thick fingers, it wished to strangle the house.

She was very cold, so she drank some gin, although it was not as a rule her weakness. The bodies of Mr. and Mrs. Herries lay, the eyes decently closed, the pale hands folded, each in its proper bed.

A fine heat burnt through Mrs. Henny's old body. The gin was good. Then her head fell forward and she slept.

The old house rattled and squealed in the wind that was rising up now that the snow had almost ceased to fall. Feet seemed to creep up and down the stairs, fingers were at the windows, but the dead and Mrs. Henny slept on.

Then, in the room where the old woman, the child, and its mother were, from the window a piece of glass, very old and dark green like weeded water, was loosened with the wind and fell tinkling to the boards. The snow blew in like a live thing and the room was icily chilled.

The child that had been sleeping felt the cold and began to cry, a shrill cry on one note. But Mrs. Henny heard nothing, the gin holding her fast.

Squire Gauntry--little Tom Gauntry--riding along the Borrowdale path just below the house on the farther side of the little bridge, heard the cry. It was strange that from so weak a creature the cry should be so clear. He heard it, and he pulled up his horse; the six hounds who were with him stopped also. The snow had but just ceased to fall and for the first time that day. It was so unusual in that country for there to be so heavy a fall that he halted and looked about him in wonderment. The roofs of Rosthwaite, all the hills, the fields were buried in the white smooth covering, and now, for the first time, light began to break through. The grey stuff of the snowy sky was torn and a faint green field spread over the dim hills, and the snow began shyly to sparkle. The wind blew the top of the snow into little smoking spirals. Some rooks flew, like black leaves, cawing, breaking the sacred silence. The green field spread.

Herries, the house, raised on its little hill, to Gauntry's right, seemed to be overwhelmed by the snow, huddled, shapeless, helpless, and out of that white shapelessness this thin, desolate, tiny cry continued.

Gauntry was eager to be home; his high black riding-coat was heavy with snow, he was weary and chilled, but there was something in that cry that moved him. A hard-bitten little man, leading always his own life and telling everyone else to go to the devil, nevertheless he was sentimental too: so he turned his horse, crossed the bridge over the stream, and, followed by the six hounds, guided the animal through the snow, and, striking with his whip on the gate of the courtyard, holloaed three times.

There was no answer at all. The silence settled down again. There was no sound but the thin persisting cry. He hesitated as to his next step. He had met Herries once and again, but had no intimacy with him. Indeed, no one had. He was said to be a queer customer, one not easy to deal with, one who would not thank you for uninvited interference.

Gauntry was just like that himself, and, for that very reason, had always felt a sympathy with Herries. He liked a man who told the world to go to the devil: it was what the world was meant for. Nevertheless, he was tired, cold, thirsty. Why should he put himself about for a man who would only curse him?

Then something about the stillness of the house hit his attention. The place was but a ruin in any case; under the snow he could fancy how the boards creaked and the chimneys rocked.

He dismounted from his horse, pushed wide the old, grumbling gate, the snow falling thickly from it, then, followed in silence by the hounds, crossed the courtyard.

The house-door was unbarred. The iron handle turned easily. He entered, to be met by two rusted suits of armour stationed at the foot of the stairs. Still there was silence everywhere, save for the lament of the child.

How cold the house was! He shivered, drawing his cloak tighter about him. Then again he holloaed. No answer. Where the devil were they hiding? Not a sound, not even a clock-tick. Up the creaking stairs he went, the dogs padding after him.

He came to a room hung with faded brown tapestries; there was a portrait of a wicked-looking old man in the dress of Elizabethan times, dead ashes in the stone fireplace, remains of a meal, bread, a mutton bone, on the table.

He called again: 'Herries! Herries!' but this time softly. Something in the place constrained him. Lord! how cold the house was!

A narrow wooden stair led higher, so on he went, the hounds following, crowding one another on the stair but making no sound.

At the stair-head there was a room. He pushed the door, entered, then stood there looking.

First he was aware that the snow was blowing in through a broken window, and then that a child lay in a wooden cradle. It was the child's cry he had heard. Then he saw that in a chair near the bed an old woman was asleep, and at her side was a bottle, tumbled over, spilling its contents on the floor. Then, stepping forward, he saw farther. On the bed a woman was lying. He saw at once that she was dead. Her red hair was spread about the pillow, her eyes were closed, and in her face there was a look of great peace and contentment.

Mrs. Herries! He had heard of her many a time, but had never seen her. She had been a gipsy girl when Herries married her. She had run away from him, and then returned. Herries' second wife, the only woman, they said, whom he had ever loved. Gauntry bent forward and touched reverently the cold, thin hands. Yes, she was dead. Where, then, was Herries? Roughly he shook the old woman by the shoulder, but she would not stir. Only her old head rolled. He called softly 'Herries!', then went to the cradle, and the infant, who must be but newly born, at once ceased to cry.

He went to the door and listened, then seeing a room close by pushed softly into it. Herries himself was lying in bed there. Going closer Gauntry saw that he, too, was dead--an old man, his face scarred, but he, too, seemed to smile in great contentment and happiness.

Both, then? Both dead? He turned back to the other room, again shook the old woman, but saw that the drink held her fast. He stood there wondering what he should do, while the hounds sat on their haunches by the door and watched him.

Through the dusk the snow sparkled like diamonds, and somewhere a solitary bird began its chirping. The infant did not cry, but seemed to watch him.

'Old woman!' he cried. 'Wake up! Wake up!'

But she would not wake. What must he do? The child must not be left here in this bitter cold: he could see that it was very warmly wrapped. Every preparation had been made for its coming. Poor woman! Poor Mrs. Herries! Died in childbirth maybe, and Herries himself dying in the next room. Strange end to a strange life!

A tenderness seized him as he looked at that thin childish face, those thin delicate hands! What lovely hair she had! Herries had loved her, they said, almost to madness.

Well, someone must be told. Herries' son, David Herries, at Uldale must be told. Someone in Rosthwaite village must be fetched. But he could not leave that child there to start its melancholy cry so soon as he was gone. No, he could not. Very delicately for so dried and rough a little man he picked up the child, wrapping round it its warm bedding. Were it warm enough it would not suffer. They were hardy children in Gauntry's world. He was pleased that the child did not cry, but lay there in his arms contentedly.

Then he went out, down the stairs, across the courtyard, led the horse with one hand, and so, followed by the hounds, crossed the little bridge.

He knocked on the first cottage-door in Rosthwaite. An old, wrinkled woman opened it. He told her of what he had found. She exclaimed something incoherently of witches and warlocks; another woman came, they chattered together. Two men joined them.

After many wonderings, forebodings and murmurs they started off up the hill to the house, in a group together as though they were afraid.

He stood there, considering. He did not wish to leave the child. It would be late when he was home. He would take it to his own place, Stone Ends, that night, and the family at Uldale should have it in the morning.

Yes, he did not want to leave it. Poor baby; it trusted him and seemed to watch him lest he should go away. Both dead in the one hour! He was helped to his horse, the child lifted to him by a village girl, then he called to the hounds and rode away. The infant, warm under the thick wrapping, uttered no sound.

LIFE AT ULDALE

In the autumn of the year 1785 David Herries was sixty-six years of age, his wife Sarah forty-seven, his children, Francis twenty-five, Deb twenty-three and Will fifteen; his little half-sister, Judith Herries, was eleven.

They all lived at Fell House, Uldale. Uldale is on the farther side of Skiddaw and looks over the moor to the Solway Firth. The sprawling flanks of Skiddaw spread between Uldale and the town of Keswick.

In 1785 Marie Antoinette was playing hide-and-seek with her ladies in the gardens of Versailles, William Pitt was Prime Minister of England, Jane Austen was ten years old, and a Keswick boy of sixteen had just been hanged for stealing a leg of mutton. Nevertheless, this is a poor way of reckoning history, especially at Uldale, where the crops mattered and cock-fighting mattered and old Mrs. Monnasett had only this very moment died.

History, of course, begins anywhere and everywhere. For Judith Herries it began, perhaps, when little Tom Gauntry found her squealing under the closed and lifeless eyes of both her parents. She never reckoned it so; she reckoned that it began on this autumn day when, after looking at Mrs. Monnasett's corpse, she was whipped by her half-brother David.

This at once shows the ludicrousness of her position. She was eleven years old, and yet was sister to David Herries, who was sixty-six, and, yet more absurd, aunt, or at any rate half-aunt, to Francis, who was twenty-five, and Deb, who was twenty-three.

To make the matter more complicated yet and surely most improper, she was in love with her nephew Francis. For excuse you may say that she loved and hated alternately everyone around her a hundred times a day.

One of the disgraceful colours to this first notable event in Judith Herries' life was that Mrs. Monnasett was but just dead and lying in state in the Blue Room. It was, indeed, because Mrs. Monnasett lay there that the trouble began.

Fell House was a pleasant building, square-shaped, its brick rose-coloured, a walled-in garden, many fruit trees, the farm buildings with all the animals and the odours, a Gothic temple beyond the lawn, pigeons in the loft, swelling downs stretching almost to the sea, Skiddaw against the windows, and the road where the coaches ran not so far away that you could not hear the horses.

Life for Judith should have been agreeable there. They all wished to love her, and there was nothing in the world that she liked better than to be loved, but it had all been spoilt for her from the very beginning because she preferred so infinitely the life at Stone Ends, where Uncle Gauntry drank, hunted, beat her, loved her, taught her to ride, to hunt, to prepare the birds for cock-fighting and to learn everything there was to learn about men and women.

She was only eleven, but she knew more, far more, about everything than her half-niece Deb, who was twenty-three, or that other Deborah, her half-sister, who was married to a clergyman at Cockermouth and had two grown sons.

Uldale was by far too tame for her, and yet she loved them all and yearned for them all to love her. She knew, though, even at this age (she had known it long ago), that they could not really love her, for her mother had been a gipsy woman taken by her father off the fells and married by him when he was already an old man. She knew that David and Deborah, his children, had been ashamed of this marriage and had despised him for it. (They had not despised him for it. She would learn that one day.) Oh yes, they could not love her at Uldale, because she was the daughter of a gipsy and had been found one day dancing naked on the roof and could swear most horribly. But at Stone Ends they did not mind whose daughter she was and allowed her to do whatever she pleased.

Now on this afternoon in October they had but just finished dinner, Mrs. Herries, Deb, Will and Judith. Mr. Herries and Francis had ridden to Newlands to see about a piece of land. Mrs. Monnasett was to be buried the following day. The house was quite still. Mrs. Herries went to the China Room to write a letter to her sister-in-law, Mrs. Sunwood of Cockermouth. Deb was for the dairy, Will away on some secret purpose of his own. No one needed Judith. She stood, listening to the stillness of the house, half-way up the staircase, her fingers in her lip, considering. She was an odd little creature, even as odd little creatures go. She was very small, although made in excellent proportion, save that her red hair, which hung in ringlets, seemed weighty for her head. Her complexion was pale and would always be so: she had the horse-features of all the Herries, prominent nose and cheek-bones. She was, in fact, no beauty, but there was very much character in her bright and challenging eyes, the resoluteness of her mouth. When she smiled she could be very winning. She could also look exceedingly impertinent, and, when angry, with her red hair, her pale face, and perfectly balanced, lightly swinging body, she could seem a flying fury. She had tiny hands and feet; of these already she was boastfully proud.

She was dressed in a red bodice with silver buttons and a small orange hoop. She wore red shoes. This was her best dress, bought for her in Carlisle on a birthday by David Herries, who alternately loved and hated her. She was supposed to wear this grand dress only on very special occasions; she put it on most days of the week, but although she wore it so often it was as fresh as when it was new. She had, from the first, that gift of being as clean and spotless in all her circumstances as a piece of china. That was a dirty age, but Judith had always a passion for washing; no water was too cold for her; she was so hardy that nothing ever ailed her. One out of every three children at this time died before it was four years of age. Judith had never known an ache or a pain. They said that it was because Tom Gauntry had carried her on the very day that she was born through all the snow and ice from Borrowdale to Stone Ends. If that hadn't killed her, nothing would.

She stood, swinging a red shoe, sucking her thumb, and considering. She had intended to go to the corner of the road and watch for the return of Mr. Herries and Francis. She loved Francis madly, passionately, although he was her nephew. She loved his thin delicate body, his pale austere face with the dreaming eyes, the soft gentle voice. He should have been a woman, people said, and that was why so few understood him, but Judith understood him and she would willingly (she thought) die for him. She would not, of course, in reality die for anyone, having now and always a fierce and tenacious hold on life. But she fancied that if he said (in his soft dreaming voice) 'Judith, pray jump from yonder window and break all your bones,' she would jump. The fact that he considered her very little, scarcely ever thought of her, made no difference. She loved him only the more fiercely. He and Uncle Gauntry were the gods of her fiery, agitated, dramatic world.

As she stood there the stillness of the house forced itself ever more upon her attention. She had intended to go to the road, but what an opportunity this was to creep in and look at Mrs. Monnasett! She had seen dead people before. There was the boy in Bassenthwaite village who had been beaten by his master and had suddenly (most ungratefully) died; she had been walking with Will and they had come on him lying against the Cross on the Common. There had been the beggar who came to their door one summer night to ask for food, and he had fallen dead while walking away up the hill. She was no stranger to death, and thought, in a general way, little of it. But Mrs. Monnasett was different. Judith had known her all her life. She had been nurse and tyrant and friend to all the children. She had been there for years, ever since Francis and Deborah were born, and what a strange woman she had been, with the hairy mole on her cheek, the strange stories that she used to tell, the songs that she used to sing, the ghosts she had seen and the witches she had known, and, more than all, the little gold box that she carried with the charm of a snake's skin and the queer-smelling foreign root; would she have that little box with her yet, even though she were dead?

Judith had thought that the charm would prevent her from ever dying. She would live for ever. But no, she had not. She was dead now and the worms would eat her. Had she the little box yet with her? Judith

considered. She and Will had been forbidden to go near the room, but that forbidding only made the matter more charming. She would have a whipping, but she had had many, and when David Herries whipped her she had only to sob in a certain strangling way and he was always sorry for her and would kiss her and let her have a pinch of snuff out of his box. Yes, the risk was nothing. Softly she stole up the stairs.

As it happened, Mrs. Sarah Herries was at that same moment writing of Judith to her sister-in-law, Mrs. Deborah Sunwood. She sat in the China Room, pleasant and sunny, the low windows looking across to Skiddaw. The room was handsomely furnished with some pagodas and vessels of Chelsea china, in which were set coloured sprigs of artificial flowers. The walls were hung with a Chinese wallpaper and, to quote an old Herries journal, 'A looking-glass, enclosed in a whimsical frame of Chinese paling, stood upon a Japan table over which was spread a coverlet of the finest chintz.' Yes, a pretty room, burnished now with the last orange glow of the setting sun, for it was after five, and Sarah Herries must light the candles.

She stood there a moment watching the trembling flame, a handsome woman in a rose-coloured hoop, wearing her own hair, a fine bosom, and the face stout a trifle, but kindly, good-humoured and patient.

She was thinking, perhaps, as she held the snuffer in her hand and glanced at her broad figure in the looking-glass, that her life had been cast in pleasant places since that day so many years ago when David had snatched her out of Wasdale and fought her uncle on the Stye Head Pass.

She was thinking of that and of her Will, whom she adored, and her Francis, whom she adored not quite so much, and of her fat good-natured Deborah, whom, because she took a trifle after herself, she loved a little less . . . yes, ever so little less. And then her thoughts turned, as they always did were they given any freedom at all, to her beloved, worshipped David, the fire, the heat, the passion of her happy life, still the most handsome of all human creatures although he might be stout now, still the best of all humans although he might on occasion drink himself under the table or lose at faro with Squire Osmaston and the others the money that he had put aside for the purchase of Brandon's field. Her eyes were wet a trifle, the candle-flame danced mistily as she sat herself down in the dark Irish Chippendale chair to write to her sister Deborah.

There was nothing in the world that she liked better than to write to Deborah, for she understood so precisely the importance of everything that Sarah thought important, was interested in all the cures that Sarah practised on the children, thrilled to the heart when she heard that wicked Cousin Pelham, now nearly seventy and old enough to reform (but he never would), had sent Sarah all the way from London by coach and carrier a Chippendale bookcase with a Gothic design in the cornice and rosettes on the lower panels.

Yes, Deborah understood everything, and most especially did she understand about Judith.

This, then, was the letter's first part, the candle-flame trembling, the China paper dancing, the outer world fading to a silver star and the white tone of the climbing road.

MY DEAREST SISTER--I hope that you were not disappointed of your lodgings in Kendal and that the boys took care for you. I can give but little account of these last days for, as you know, we have had Kate Morris's children with us while the house in Keswick was set to order. Their visit had like to have been fatal to me for they not being acquainted with the Semblance of Manners nor trained indeed to anything but having their own Way perfectly in all things that were bad enough without our Judith's added wickedness to excite them.

There is also now Mrs. Monnasett dead in the House and last Tuesday the new Coachman that we had from Mr. Newsom of Newlands was drunk returning Home from Penrith and the postillions also and like to have overturned us on a gallop against a Post coming through Threlkeld.

However, dearest Deborah, you are aware that my Nature is both Tranquil and Harmonious and that if I might but be sure that the Beneficient Creator is not on occasion busied with His Attention in other more interesting Directions I would not trouble for drunken Coachmen or anything else.

Mrs. Monnasett is to be buried to-morrow forenoon.

I am happy that I consider nothing more disagreeable than Learning in a Female for Mr. Huxtable the Tutor of Kate's children has been here a week and found us all Savages save Francis.

With him he must talk Greek and all the Indian Languages and has Mr. Young's Night Thoughts at his Finger End and Mr. Pope's Essay on Man sprouting from his Eyeballs--a Man heavy of figure and such a Comedy on a Horse that it would do you good to see. But Judith who must always carry everything too far put a Cracker under his Chair and a Mouse in his Wig for which David whipped her, but not I fear so severely as she merited. But Mr. Huxtable showed no Impatience, reminding us that Alexander the Great and Diogenes were Characters alike for their indifference to Trifles the one holding the World as his Tub, the other his Tub as the World or some such Nonsense.

And now in Seriousness, my dearest Sister, I have been so gravely disturbed over Judith that last Tuesday I was blooded and on two occasions my throat has been excoriated.

For the Child has a Devil that there's no exorcising. She is now high and now low and not altogether bad; David indeed swears that she is not bad at all and

has as good a Heart as anyone in this house, which may be in Truth enough save that if she has a Heart she has also a Temper and a Disposition to Evil that I swear poor child is as great a Trouble to Herself as it is to Us.

I have no doubt as I have often said to you before but that it had its commencement in Mr. Gauntry's love for her as a Baby. We have forbidden her his Place for the Present. I have no Need to tell you, Sister, of the scandalous Conduct now current in Stone Ends. It is the Talk of the Countryside. The last Time Judith was there they had been wanting to make her drink with him and I must not be ingreateful to the Squire when I acknowledge that he will not have her contaminated and in any Case she can with a marvellous Discretion for a child of her years manage the whole Establishment at Stone Ends that she has under her little finger. It is Managing that she is always after and has been from a Baby. All the satisfaction that I have is that she has not yet learnt the Fashion of managing me nor ever will, but to see that Chit of a Child with her red hair and Herries Nose giving orders to my Will and Deb is so Unnatural as to be only partly Decent. Monnasett could deal with her and would have it that her Temper was from her Consciousness of and Uneasiness at her unlikely Parentage, but I have not seen her so Sensitive but have found again and again a brutal insensibility to the wants and opinions of others.

For the present she is in a Pretty Tantrum because she is forbidden Mr. Gauntry's and if we do not watch her she will be over there in a trivet. She has found out, I fancy, that I am not to be feared although I am not yet assured that she has found out that I am to be loved. But am I indeed? She is too odd a changeling for either David or myself to be certain of our Hearts towards her. It was the same with her mother, poor Mirabell, who as you will well remember, dearest Sister, never loved me because I was too Settled a Wife and Domestic a Woman for her. And this Child also could be in her turn Domestic when she wished. She is in fact of a Mixture so odd that it needs a more perceiving Woman than myself to fathom her only it is Plain enough that she must have her Way in everything and Dominate all those around her. Then, granted her Desires, she will let her Heart speak and has a Generosity that is not to be checked. Nevertheless I am filled with Fears for the future. As she grows her Nature becomes more clear with every hour and this house is in a Turmoil over her. . . .

As to your Complaint, gentle purging is to be advised; no vomits but if your stomach flags four to eight drops of Elixir of Vitriol is excellent and if feverish three spoonfuls of a decoction of the bark by boyling one ounce and a half in a quart of water to a pint. I must tell you, dearest Deborah, that since the days that Cupid set Hercules to the distaff he has not had a nobler conquest than mine over the straightening of the cupboard-room in the new . . .

193

The remainder of this letter has nothing for our purpose.

It is Herries history, however, that at the moment when Mrs. Sarah Herries was doing her best to place Judith upon paper, the same Judith was with the utmost gentleness and caution opening the door of the Blue Room where Mrs. Monnasett was lying.

Entering, she was both pleased and sensually alarmed by the dim candle-fluttering light that hung about the room, making the blue pagodas on the wall-paper, the high tallboy, seem of infinite mystery, and the blue tester hangings and overlay of the bed sway in some dimly felt stirring of the breeze. Not that she was frightened. Judith did not know now, did not, for many years, know what it was to be afraid. The day would come, and in a room not unlike this present one, when, hearing her beloved Francis enter the hall below, she would know, but that was not yet.

She approached the bed; it was one that had always most especially attracted her with its reeded and fluted columns, delicately carved with acanthus leaves. There were very few things, even at this early age, that she did not notice. The candles were standing at the bed-head, and Mrs. Monnasett, very yellow against the white of the pillow, her black hair spread, her large strong hands neatly folded, lay there, her lips curved in a sardonic smile. So, Judith reflected, often in real life she had smiled as though she knew more, far, far more than anyone around her. And so, indeed, Judith was very sure that she did. If she had not been an actual witch she had been as near to it as not to matter. Judith had known that all the domestics and hands about the farm had thought her one. Yes, she had known everything, and now what did she know? Did Death tell you anything more? She looked as though, behind those closed eyelids, she were seeing a thousand things. A fire burned in the room. It was hot, and there was a faint cloying smell of corruption. Judith came very close, stood on her toes because the bed was high, and touched with her warm fingers the dead hand. It was not only cold like iron but hard like iron. Where was Mrs. Monnasett now? With God? Asking God questions? Telling Him, perhaps, things that He did not know. But, above all, had she the little gold box with her? Judith did not intend to steal it, only to see whether they would bury it with her.

She looked about the dim dark room, sniffing the faint decaying odour like a little dog. The heavy curtains at the windows fluttered, the blue pagodas on the wall seemed to run a race, the fire crackled and sputtered, mice would be behind the wainscot, but none of these disturbed Mrs. Monnasett, who lay there, growing surely with every moment more yellow, and the mole black upon her cheek, smiling her secret smile because of the things she knew that others didn't. But had she the little gold box with her? Had she? Had she? Judith must know.

She stood at her tallest, leaned over and, with a shiver of excitement at her daring, felt with her hand, under the clothes, in the hollow of Mrs. Monnasett's breasts.

She had scarcely touched that chill flesh when there was a voice at the doorway, a voice of horror and disgust.

She nearly lost her balance and, half tumbling, started away from the bed to see Mrs. Herries, holding high a lighted candle, in the doorway. The child assumed at once the attitude that she always had when she was set for trouble. She flung her head back, held her hands behind her and waited.

'Judith! Come out of here.'

She followed Mrs. Herries from the room. In the passage she stood by the door like some small wild animal ringed about with enemies.

'What were you doing there?'

'Nothing.'

'Nothing! That is a lie!'

'I wasn't doing anything.'

'You wicked child! You had been forbidden to enter the room.'

'Yes, ma'am.'

'You confess your disobedience?'

'Yes, ma'am.'

'And at the bed you were touching--'

Sarah Herries' voice broke in her disgust and revulsion.

'I wished to look at Mrs. Monnasett--and bid her farewell.'

Sarah Herries sighed. This strange child! But there was feeling there, tenderness. The child had heart. And all would have been well had not that odd impulse to absolute honesty that would, throughout Judith's life, force from her such inconvenient avowals burst from her now:

'I wished to see whether Mrs. Monnasett had yet with her the gold box with the charms.'

'You wished to see--what?'

'Whether she had yet the little gold box with the charms.'

'You would see . . .' Mrs. Herries broke off. Her nature was kindly, wise, tolerant, but she did not understand this child any better than in the earlier days she had understood the mother. And just as then elements would arise that sickened some sound English normality in her, so now with Judith there would be often moments when she hated this child, in reality hated her so that she wished her out of her house and her family, a thousand miles away, never to return.

She felt this revulsion now, a sort of sickness. To search the corpse for a gold box--a child of eleven. She was afraid of what she might do, so she said: 'Go to your room and wait there until I come to you.'

Judith, without a word, turned and went.

Her room was a small one under the roof. From her window she could see the road, the hills, the woods that stretched towards Bassenthwaite. Here she had her treasures--a candle-stand that Francis had given her, a china jar, old and cracked, but with lovely orange flowers on it, that she had begged from Mrs. Monnasett, two 'babies'--rag dolls from her own babyhood--a fox's brush that Tom Gauntry had sent her, a piece of China silk, a faded and stained battle-piece in a black frame that she had found in a cellar, a treatise on cock-fighting, and a Bible that Reuben Sunwood had presented to her last Christmas-time. Here she would sit on a small oak-panelled arm-chair and watch from the window the outside world that she so desperately loved.

Now she banged the door behind her, kicked off her red shoes and stood scowling. She hated Fell House and everyone in it save Francis. She knew that she had been wrong to go and look at Mrs. Monnasett, and more wrong still to touch her. Her immaculate honesty forbade her to blame Mrs. Herries for any injustice. She had been right to be angry, the punishment that would follow would be just. She was so much wickeder than all the others, as she very well knew. Here was no portrait of a poor, ill-treated little girl. They tried to love her; it was her own fault that they could not. But with every breath that she drew she was longing for Tom Gauntry--the odd, rambling, ill-shaped house with the smell of dogs and horses and drink and dung and cooking food and musty curtains, with the noise and laughter and songs, with the freedom and airy indulgence as though all the doors and windows were for ever open-- that was her life, that the place into which she had been taken on the very first day of her existence, and Uncle Tom with his twisted brown face and twisted brown body, his funny bow-legs and his hoarse whisper and his cry to the hounds and his oaths and angers-- HE understood her as no one else in the world did. . . . And then, cutting across that picture, as so often it did, was another one, quite opposite, that made her understand the Herries decency of Uldale, made her, in certain moods, finely handy about the place, in the store cupboards, the dairies, so that she could sew and bake and clean with the best of them, and understood too when Will (for whom she did not really care) would tell her, with all the gravity of a grown man, of how he would advance the Herries family and have money in all the banks and buy land everywhere--all this she could understand and believe in.

Yes, but at this precise moment she was a little girl of eleven in one of her hellish tempers, one of her incoherent rages, so that she could swear in proper Cumberland just like any of the girls or men about the place, so that she was mad to be out of the house and over the fells, sniffing the peat, hearing the water of the mountain-streams run and the tug of the sheep at the grass and the sharp bark of the sheepdogs. . . .

She turned, her eyes furious and her little feet stamping, at the sound of the open door. Francis Herries had come in.

At the sight of him she forgot for a moment all her trouble. He was still in his riding-clothes. He must have come straight to her after his arrival. His face was so beautifully peaked and serious under his brown wig, his legs in their riding-boots so handsomely shaped and his eyes so far away, so mysterious. . . .

She drew her breath sharply as she always did when she saw anything that seemed to her beautiful. How she loved him! And he, from his great height, looked down gravely to the odd little figure with the defiant mouth and the red hair and rebellion in every inch of her.

He slapped his whip against his thigh.

'Father is coming shortly to beat you. I thought I'd best prepare you.' Then he smiled, a lovely winning smile which, in anyone more self-conscious, must have been artificial. But Francis Herries, as he never thought of himself, never thought of his smile either.

'I know.' Her eyes devoured him. 'I don't care as long as you've come.'

'What have you done, you little devil? Why can't you be good?'

'I can't be good,' she answered defiantly, 'because my father married a gipsy. And I'm happy he did,' she added.

This was an old familiar statement of hers. She was always dragging in the gipsy. It seemed to Francis to be in bad taste, so he said again:

'What have you done this time?'

'I went in to see Mrs. Monnasett.'

The thought and image of death, so familiar as to be less than nothing at all to the men and women of his time, always affected Francis Herries with a queer tremor of mystery and horror. It seemed to him revolting that this child should have been in Mrs. Monnasett's room.

'Why must you do that?' he asked.

'To see if she had her little gold box.'

'What box?'

'A box of spells that she had.'

He said nothing and turned to the door.

With a little tremor in her voice she said: 'Please punish me.'

He turned back. 'Punish you?'

She broke out passionately, an unusual passion for so young a child.

'I didn't know that it was wrong, but if you had told me not I would never have gone. Punish me and you will see. I will do anything you tell me, stand in icy water or let the rats in the cellar gnaw me or sleep in the stable.'

He looked at her, met the intense absorbed devotion of her eyes, and was greatly touched. When he could come out of his dreams and notice human beings he loved them, loved all humanity. He was humble also, and found it strange that anyone should care for him. This small child, standing there, in her stockinged feet and coloured hoop, adoring him, moved him. They were friends from that moment, although neither realised that it was just then that their long alliance was formed. He spoke lamely enough:

'Punish you? No. Why should *I* punish you?'

They could say no more because at that moment David Herries came in. He carried a riding-whip, was in his riding-clothes, looked exceedingly sheepish. He had been always of great size and immense strength. Now, at sixty-six, he was beginning to be corpulent, had a red face and something of a belly, but looked very much the same kindly, obstinate, unimaginative boy who had, nearly thirty years before, carried his Sarah away from the dark house in Wasdale.

He looked sheepish because he hated this business. Francis went out. Judith bent over the chair and he whipped her. Neither said a word until it was over. She replaced her little clothes, then stood, her lip trembling, because she was very near to tears but would not cry, near the window.

Her stockings were crooked, which seemed to David very pathetic, and without knowing it she had her hand on her back where it was sore.

He filled the room with his great bulk, and his red face was creased with kindliness. He scratched his bare head, pushing his wig a little awry. He talked because he saw that she was near to tears.

'Now, Judith, why must you do such a thing? 'Tisn't decent to be in the death-chamber, and it was against all orders, as you very well knew. Now, then, it is over, isn't it? Never to be spoken of again. . . .'

He went and picked her up and kissed her. Had he known it (and it had been always one of David's weaknesses that he was not clever at perceiving things), this was, of everything that he could do, the thing that she detested most.

To be picked up, like a tiny baby, to be dangled in the air, to be held close to this huge man and feel his bristly cheek and smell the odour of liquor and horses, to have her neck pricked by the sharp buttons of his coat, and, worst of all, to have his great heart hammering in her ear, this was the final ignominy!

She stayed passive, only when he would kiss her mouth she turned her head aside. He put her down with a grunting sigh. She was a problem, this child, just as her mother Mirabell had been before her. He did not understand her at all.

He looked at her, smiled an awkward, clumsy smile, muttered, 'We shall say no more about the thing,' and stumped away.

She stood there, considering. She did not want to see any of them ever again, save Francis. Somewhere a clock sounded six. A cart rattled down the Fell road. She went to the window and looked out. It was almost dark; the hills were shadows against shadow.

Then she smiled.

She knew what she would do.

STONE ENDS

She was so made that once a plan came to her nothing in the world was ever going to stop her, and every pulse of her body beat to that one purpose.

She flung back the narrow diamond-paned window, found a cloak and a shawl, left the red shoes for thick country ones. No time was wasted, and as she worked for her purpose her small mouth was set, her chin was out. Nothing was to stop her in such a mood. She didn't think of consequences (she was never to think of them as she should do), recked little that this second disobedience in one evening meant trouble for her more serious, perhaps, than any that she had yet encountered.

She had been out of that window before. There was still light enough for her to see the old crooked water-pipe that jerked an arm round the farther end of her casement, then there was the water-butt, then the stone passage leading to the stable. But she had a long descent on that pipe. She clung to it with hands and feet, her chin and nose rasped by its casing. Her small legs trembled, the shawl blew against her face, she felt (or imagined that she felt) spiders' thread in her hair, then her feet found the water-butt, she held her body together and jumped.

She fell on her hands and knees, and the black cat, Solomon, ran from under her very feet, scrambling up the monkey-tree. Her knees were bleeding, her hoop under her cloak was torn. But she stood, holding her breath like a proper conspirator, to hear whether the noise had made any stir. There was no sound but the owl hooting. It seemed that a breath of light had blown back again into the sky. Over the garden wall, the Caldbeck fells were outlined as though a row of candles were lit behind them.

It was the moon; later that moon would strengthen, and the freshening wind would blow the stars up. All the garden scents were crowding the night air. She was very cheerful indeed, and, pulling the cambric tight about her face again, stepped across the irregular paving of the yard, called very softly, 'Barnabas! Barnabas!' At once the little black horse with the white star on his forehead put his head over the paling. In another moment she had unbarred the door and was leading him out, stroking his nose.

Barnabas understood perfectly what she wanted. She mounted the black outside the gate and, her legs spread very wide, her hair flying, was away up the road. A mile later, the first delirium of freedom passed, she began to consider ghosts, witches and warlocks. She was not afraid, but there was the man with the face like a rat, the woman with two heads, the lost soul of Judas that whimpered like an infant, the old woman with a rat on her shoulder, the lovely lady on the skeleton horse, the old woman with three beards, the soldier who had lost his head in the wars and carried it in his handless arms, the coach with the eight devils and the fiery horses, the lady of Caldbeck who walked searching for the child that she had murdered.

And worse, perhaps, in actual fact, than any of these, the highway robber who had been hung in chains on the path between Thistlebottom and Whelpo, although there were now only his bones remaining.

She was not afraid of any of them, but she repeated aloud to herself the Lord's Prayer and so much of the Creed as she could remember, and then the names of the places near her home--Ireby, Snittlegarth, Binsey, Aughertree, Nevin Tarn, Orthwaite, Over Water, Braefell, Branthwaite. It comforted her that Barnabas trotted comfortably along as though he knew precisely his destination, but it comforted her yet more when she met a cheerful gang of pack-horses, the bell-horse first with his pleasant noise. They were carrying peat from the moors in halts, old-fashioned wicker-baskets that were very soon now to give way to carts.

Judith called out to the men as she passed them, waving her hand, and they talked that night about the witch that had greeted them (on a black horse) and had waved in the air hands shining with flame.

Stone Ends, Tom Gauntry's place, was a mile beyond Caldbeck. She made no further encounter. The clock of Caldbeck Church struck seven as she trotted through the deserted little street.

On the dark road beyond Caldbeck she met two drunken soldiers who stood in the road and waved at her. They had a lantern; one had a wooden leg. She leaned forward on to Barnabas' mane and cursed them in good Cumbrian. She called them 'Hulkers' and 'Lubbers' and 'Dummle-heads.' She told them that they gave her 'a nasty dwallow taste in her mouth' and that they'd better 'jump up and knep a daisy.' She must have astonished them, perched on the horse, her red hair flying about in the uncertain circumference of the lantern that waved in their drunken hands. At any rate, they did nothing, and stood aside to let Barnabas by.

So she arrived at Stone Ends. This was a rough-cast building of no height, with an outside gallery and stair. There were mullioned windows, great trees overhanging the mossy slates and round thick chimneys. There was a garden with a clipped hedge, the fells everywhere beyond, a rough plot of flowers, some outbuildings, a sundial, a little stream.

Lights burnt in the windows, but Judith did not need a light. This little place had been familiar to her since her babyhood, her only true home. She tied Barnabas to the gate and went cautiously to the porch. She was not certain how she would be received. Old Gauntry was not always the perfect host, especially when taken unawares. Riding Barnabas so soon after the beating had not improved the soreness of her seat. She did not want another whipping, nor to be sent directly back to Uldale again. So, with her ear to the heavy door, she listened. Little listening was needed. The chorus of revelry was clear enough. They would have been hunting, she decided, and were now in process of becoming drunk as soon as possible. THAT did not frighten her. She had heard often enough: 'Now this is a fine fox we've killed and it munna be a dry one.' The important thing was to ascertain the STAGE of drunkenness at which they had arrived. She knew that between the first and second hour they would all be in a state of exceeding friendliness.

She was, however, given no time to consider. The door opened and Wull shoved his hairy head out. Wull (or William Flint as was his proper name) stood to Tom Gauntry as the Fool stands to his King. Judith would never forget the agitation with which she had first beheld him. In her babyhood she had been told that he was the Hobthross, the Brownie who lurks in old houses--works all night for the family to whom he has attached himself, stretches himself before the fire, churns the milk for the girls, and can be heard singing at his tasks. A kindly spirit, but wild to look at, with his shock of hair, his broad ugly face, his misshapen limbs. Just so was 'Wull,' and when she was an infant he would love to pull faces at her until she howled with rage. She was never frightened of him, but only angry. Later he became her friend, then her warm ally. He poked his ugly head out at her now.

'Wull! Wull!' she whispered.

Sometimes he was a complete fool, sometimes most intelligent. He would tell her about himself with a broad grin: 'Ah'm nobbut a bit goffish.' It was probable that he was not 'goffish' at all, but knew exactly what he was doing. When he saw who it was he let her in. The house-place was filled with dogs and smelt like a midden. Judith did not mind the smell in the least. The dogs were everywhere; every kind of dog. They ran at her when they saw her, barking and tumbling all over her. Some of the hounds were bigger than she. They all knew her. One, a spaniel bitch, Clara, adored her, had followed her once almost all the way back to Uldale.

When Clara saw her she was in an ecstasy of happiness, springing up and down, yapping on a shrill high note, her beautiful large eyes beaming with joy. Judith asked Wull how many gentlemen there were in there. He didn't know; about twenty maybe. They had had a grand day's hunting and had killed over by High Hesket. He cuffed the dogs and quieted them, but the noise had been heard. The room door opened and Tom Gauntry came out. He stood with his funny crooked legs straddling. He was very fairly drunken. When he saw Judith he gave a loud 'Yoicks! Yoicks! Tally-ho! Tally-ho!' and they came crowding to the door. Judith recognised a number she knew--young Osmaston, Squire Watson, old Birkmyre, Statesman Peel-- also two ladies.

Gauntry came over to her and picked her up and carried her shoulder- high into the room where they were dining. Oddly enough, what she hated in David Herries she liked in Uncle Tom.

'And why the hell have you come?' asked her.

'Because I wanted,' she answered.

From her height she looked over the scene, which was for her no new one. The room was not large. They were crowded about the round table upon whose shining surface the candles guttered grease. Food was piled everywhere--mutton, beef, puddings; wine was spilt on the table, and almost the first thing that Judith noticed was the naked head of old Dunstable, robbed of its wig, lying forward in a puddle of wine. He had succumbed already.

Most of them had not. Sitting now, sharp-eyed, on a chair beside Uncle Gauntry, she saw very quickly that there were two boys there, boys of about her own age. It was not unusual that boys should be there, and one of them she knew, little Johnny Peel, two years younger than herself. It would later be said of him that he was 'lang in the leg an' lish as a lizard,' and someone in the Gentleman's Magazine was to record that 'he seems to have come into this world only to send foxes out of it.' He was of Caldbeck village, but there was no hunt already that he wasn't attending within any radius from Penrith to Cockermouth, Cockermouth to Carlisle. It was said of him already that he could do thirty miles in the day and not be tired of it; later on it was to be fifty. But Judith knew that boy before; he didn't interest her. The other was another matter. She had not hitherto allowed her young life to be much encumbered with boys. On the whole she despised them; of late especially her real worship of Francis Herries had veiled her sight.

But this boy struck through to her deep consciousness. How often afterwards she was to look back to this moment when, as she sat perched up on the chair beside Tom Gauntry, her little sharp eyes flashed across to the table to the equally sharp eyes of that small, black-haired, bullet-headed urchin, who was grabbing any food that he could see. Very characteristic that Judith's first vision of him should be of greedy rapacity! But (also how characteristic of him!) it was not merely greed. While he snatched at meat and bread and the thick pastry of the beef-pie his little black eyes were flashing about him, humorous, contemptuous, but as alive as fire-balls!

'Who's that?' Judith asked of Gauntry. He was, as she had hoped, at the cheerful side of his drinking, singing a catch, shoving food into his mouth, exchanging bawdy stories with all and sundry.

'That!' he laughed, following her eyes. 'That's the Frenchy! There's his mama!' pointing a chicken-bone at a lady farther along the table. There were only two women here, one of them the wife of young Squire Osmaston, a flaxen-haired, broad-bosomed, opulent lady at the moment chucking Sam Newton under the chin. This other was different. She sat upright like a maypole and was black as a raven. Marvellous black eyes, she had, a lovely shapely bosom, and silver ornaments in her dark hair, which was her own and unpowdered. You could see, Judith decided, that she was the little boy's mother. They would be French then. Judith had heard of Paris, where silks and brandy came from. She had seen a print of the French Queen dancing in a great hall lit with flambeaux. This lady looked as though she could be a queen were she given the opportunity.

The noise and confusion now were very great. Old Dunstable had slipped beneath the table.

Wilson of Ireby was standing on his chair proposing healths; fat Dick Conyngham of Penrith and a thin young man with a crooked nose were embracing. Voices rose and fell, then suddenly the chorus, everyone joining together:

> Then chink and clink your glasses round
> And drink to the Devil below the ground.
> The more you drink the better you be
> And kiss the lasses upon your knee.
>   Chink, clink!
>   Chink, clink!
> The Devil himself can't drink like me.

Then young Drayton of Keswick, whose sweet tenor was famous for
miles around, stood up and sang the song of 'Beauty Bathing':

> Beauty sat bathing by a spring
>   Where fairest shades did hide her;
> The winds blew calm, the birds did sing,
>   The cool streams ran beside her.
> My wanton thoughts enticed mine eye
> To see what was forbidden:
> But better memory said, fie!
>   So vain desire was chidden:
>   Hey nonny nonny O!
>   Hey nonny nonny!

> Into a slumber then I fell,
>   When fond imagination
> Seemèd to see, but could not tell
>   Her feature or her fashion.
> But ev'n as babes in dreams do smile,
>   And sometimes fall a-weeping,
> So I awaked as wise this while
>   As when I fell a-sleeping:
>   Hey nonny nonny O!
>   Hey nonny nonny!

The beauty of the words, of the voice, seemed for a moment to sober
them.

> Hey nonny nonny O!
> Hey nonny nonny!

they sang, and down the fat cheeks of Dick Conyngham drunken tears were coursing.

No one appeared to think it strange that the child should be there. Most of them knew her; she seemed to belong to the place, and for many of them that happy time was now approaching when nothing anywhere seemed strange, when the candles on their silver stalks swam like gold roses in a shimmering haze, and the moon, now delicately rising beyond the uncurtained windows, was quadrupled in its pure serenity; now, through the open door, the dogs were coming in to pick up what trifles they might from the scattered floor, and a thousand clocks were ticking their friendly chatter on a thousand walls. No one thought of the child, not even Gauntry himself; only Clara, the spaniel bitch, coming in with the rest, had found her and was sitting behind her chair.

Judith ate very little and drank nothing. It was no unusual thing at that time for a child to be drunk. The children of the poor lay in the gutter drowned with gin. In the back parts of Keswick town Judith herself had seen them. But something in her, connected possibly with her immaculate personal cleanliness, had made her, so long as she could remember, detest liquor. When she was only a baby some friend of Gauntry's had tried to make her drink Madeira, and she had screamed, beaten his face with her hands, torn his nose with her nails. She didn't like the smell of it very much, but in a scene like this the stench of wine and heat and unwashed human bodies, dogs and horses, candle-grease and cooked meats, was so familiar to her that she never thought of it.

What she did think of, though, was that when the drinking and rioting had reached a certain pitch she would leave them, for they were then no longer of any use to anybody.

It neither shocked nor distressed her that they should lie about the floor with their heads in puddles of wine. She preferred in fact the rough-and-tumble riot here to the orderly drunkenness at Fell House, and she had on several occasions watched while Wull and Andy and Matthew had stripped Uncle Gauntry and laid him in his naked bed. What she did mind was that they were all so stupid when they were 'gone.' She was quickly developing that passion, afterwards to be so strong in her and so irritating to her acquaintances, of hating to waste a single moment! Her restless energy was, later, never to leave her for an instant alone. They were a waste of time, these stupid hours when they all lay about, dribbling and drabbling, with the moon high, the wind fresh, blowing the stars about the sky. She might as well be in her bed, which was where, indeed, she WOULD be had she remained at Uldale.

Her bright eyes searched the room. She saw one thing, that the French lady was absorbed by Mr. Drayton, who had sung 'Beauty Bathing.' He was a good-looking man, Mr. Drayton, slender and straight, with yellow hair like a blazing candle, and he wore a beautiful flowered waistcoat. There were gold buckles on his shoes. The French lady liked him, that was plain. They stood, the handsome pair of them, gravely by the window, away from the litter, noise and mess; quite suddenly Mr. Drayton took the French lady's hand. Now was the time, then, for Judith to speak to the little French boy.

She stepped off her chair and, followed by the spaniel, came round to where the French boy was sitting. She touched his shoulder. He turned round and smiled at her.

'Come out,' she said.

He came at once, making a last grab at a handful of raisins before he went. They ran hand in hand, as though they had known one another for ages, into the dark hall, where the fire was blazing, and the dogs, as though they owned the house and everyone in it, were moving about, snapping at one another, yawning, lying down to sleep, climbing the stairs, gnawing bones, scratching for fleas.

The two children sat close together beside the fire.

'I know. You're French,' Judith said.

He spoke without an accent, as though he were English. He gave her, rather reluctantly, some raisins. The truth is, she took them.

'I was born in London,' he told her.

'Oh, I want to see London!'

'Is your hair in truth that fine colour?' he asked, pulling it.

She slapped his face, not lightly but with genuine feeling. He got up, his eyes blazing. He stood there, his sturdy little body trembling with anger. It seemed that he would kill her. But he thought better of it. His hand to his cheek he sat down again.

'Because you are a girl I won't hurt you,' he said.

'Hurt me!' She was indignantly scornful. 'No one can hurt me!' Then she went on: 'I was whipped this noon.'

They were friends again. She, taking more of his raisins, asked him how it was if he were French he had never been in France.

'My papa and my mama are French born,' he told her.

She asked him his name.

'Georges.' And his other name.

'Georges Paris.'

'But Paris is a town.'

He told her there were people called Paris too. He told her then (he always from the very earliest time loved to talk about himself) that his father was dead, that his mother liked England to live in, that they lived for the most part in the village of Hampstead, near London. Hampstead was on a hill, and at night you could see all London lit up from their window. Judith wanted to tell him something about herself. Her name was Judith Herries, her mother had been a gipsy, she lived with her half-brother at Fell House in Uldale. She could ride and swim, had a horse called Barnabas (it wasn't in fact her horse at all, but it made it grander to say so), could stand on her head, train a bird for fighting, and so on, and so on. Mrs. Monnasett was dead and would be buried to-morrow. She had run away and would be whipped on her return.

But he wasn't interested. He could do nothing but look at her hair. He had never seen anything like it in his life before.

Then her mind ran away from him. The place where they were was lovely to her, with the leaping fire, the moonlight, the dogs. She thought of Statesmen and farmers and boys and horses--all friends of hers. She liked to hear the men singing in the distance. All her troubles were far away; to-morrow, the whipping, Fell House. In an impulse of general happiness that had little to do with the boy she put her arm round his neck, drew his head towards her and kissed him. He did not mind that at all and pulled her hair--but gently. And she did not, this time, smack his cheek.

Dreamily she went on: 'Maybe when I'm grown I shall marry you. But I must have dogs and horses, and we must have our house near to this. But you must not be drunken.' Then, pushing his head away from her, she asked sharply: 'But what shall our children be--French or English?'

'French,' he answered her quickly.

'No, they shall not. English.'

'French.'

'No, English.'

'Then I'll not marry you.'

She pinched him in the place where it hurt the most. In another moment they were fighting, rolling on the floor, all the dogs yelping. But they were interrupted by a greater agitation, for the door suddenly swung open, there was a shout and clatter, and into the hall came fat Dick Conyngham riding Judith's Barnabas. Poor Barnabas was in any case overweighted by the huge body that rode him; he was frightened also. He came kicking into the hall, the dogs setting up an infernal din.

'The stairs! The stairs! I'll ride him to the attic!' and Conyngham drove the little horse towards the staircase, waving his fat arms like a madman.

They all came pouring in out of the other room, those of them who could stand, to see Barnabas kicking with his hind legs and Judith raging like a mad thing.

She rushed to little Gauntry, catching him by the arm: "Tis my Barnabas. . . . He has no right . . . He'll break his knees!' and Gauntry, who had been singing the tail-end of some chorus, was suddenly, in the manner of drunken men, in a terrible rage and rushed at Conyngham. The fat man drove the horse at the stairs, but in a moment they had him on the floor and were kneeling on his stomach.

Barnabas, wild now with the lights, the dogs, the fire, began to prance madly hither and thither; and Judith, fearing nothing, had caught him, was carried off her feet as she hung to his mane, crying 'Barnabas! Barnabas! Dear Barnabas! They shall not touch you!' The little horse knew her hand and voice. He snorted, pawing the wood floor with his hoofs; he looked wildly around, then he suffered her to lead him away.

She took him this time to one of the outhouses. She stood there in the soft moonlight wondering whether after all she would not ride home again. Not far from her was the lower end of the garden that held a little pond with a statue of an armless lady. The little pond was like a curved shell of ivory, and the lady was green in the moonlight.

A moment later they all rushed past her, a shouting and singing rabble. Fat Conyngham was to be ducked in the pond for that he had taken a lady's horse without her permission. They were not like men at all, but shadows that the moon had made. They were stripping him; a moment he escaped and ran, a ridiculous pink figure, bald-headed, across the grass. They chased him around the sundial, caught him; there was a splash, and she could see a spray of water dazzle the air.

She rubbed her nose in Barnabas' mane. Should she go home? She was lonely, a little frightened. They had never been so wild before in this place. The house did not seem to be her friend any longer, only the quiet fells that stretched beyond it, with the boggy peat, the sheep cropping, the eternal sound of running water.

It seemed of a sudden comforting to have Sarah Herries' arm around her. She was a child again. She was not TRULY frightened. She had never been frightened. She would not be frightened now. But in absolute truth it would be pleasant to be in her bed with the cherry curtains, to hear the owl hooting and Deborah Herries snoring not too far away.

Then, because she would never grant to either God or Man that she could be afraid of anyone or anything, she threw up her head defiantly at the moon, stroked Barnabas on the nose, whispered to him that she would not be long away and went back to the house.

They were still dancing and singing round the pond. The garden had a fantastic air like a witches' sabbath. The house was now deserted and empty. The dogs were for the most part away, the moonlight stained the floor, the fire was low. No sign of the French boy, no sign of anyone. She peeped through the door, and there were two men, asleep, with their heads on the table. The candles guttered.

She herself felt a fearful weariness. She was aching for sleep. She staggered on her little feet. Her shoes hurt her, her beautiful dress was torn, the place where she had been whipped was smarting. She would find the room upstairs that was generally hers. The thought of sleep was so delicious as to be incredible.

She sat down half-way up the stairs, and with her head in her hand dreamily considered herself. She had learnt to do this early in life, because, observing things and people, she had realised that if you do not consider yourself no one else is going to. But when she began to think of herself it was always to her mother and father that she was led.

Years ago she had persuaded Tom Gauntry to take her, pillion- fashion, to see the house where she was born. They had ridden into the heart of the valley of Borrowdale, and there, on a little hill above the village of Rosthwaite, was standing this strange tumble- down house. She could not credit her own sharp eyesight when she saw it. They had tied the horse to the gate and walked in the grass-grown courtyard. It was late April, and the smaller daffodils were blowing under the wind. A storm was coming up over Glaramara, and flashes of sun glittered in cold sharp gleams and were gone again. Under the wind and the hurrying cloud the house looked desolate enough. Judith, used to the noise and vitality of Stone Ends, the luxury and comfort of Uldale, could not believe that this was where her father had lived for so many years. Some peasant lived there now. Two very dirty children, sucking their thumbs, lurked in the doorway. Behind the house a waterfall glistened against rock. There was the sound of running water everywhere. It looked as though one 'fuff' of wind would blow the place down.

That day 'Uncle Tom' told her to the smallest detail of how he had found her, the snowstorm, her wailing cry, her father and mother dead. But he would never tell her enough about her father. He had not known him, he said. Neither would David and Sarah tell her much, although he had been David's father, and so David must know everything. David would tell her only the grand things, how passionately through many years he had loved her mother, how tall he was and strong, how noble he was, and went his own way whatever people might say. 'Whatever people might say--' Judith nodded her head over that. People had said a good deal, no doubt. She only wished that she could have been there, standing at her father's side, to tell those people what she thought of them. To tell those people what she thought of them--Her head was nodding, and had not the moon been shining straight into her eye she would have fallen into deep slumber. As it was she was suddenly awake. She would find the room and the bed. . . .

She climbed the stairs, looked out of the window on to the outside gallery and the fell beyond, pushed back a door. She stood there. Her heart seemed to stop its beating. The almost bare room, with only the yellow-curtained bed, two chairs, a chest, was sunk in moonshine. In the middle of the moonlit pool the French lady was standing quite naked. Behind her, her clothes were piled on the boards. She stood, her legs together, her arms raised above her head, her black hair loosened about her shoulders. Her breasts were full and firm. She was smiling.

At her feet, clad only in his shirt, young Drayton was kneeling, his hands about her naked waist, his eyes raised in an ecstasy to her face.

They never spoke nor moved. Judith saw that something glittered sharply in the light--the diamond buckle of her shoe, lying on top of her clothes.

Then the child heard him speak:

'Oh, how beautiful you are! Oh, how beautiful you are!'

But the French lady only smiled.

Judith turned away. Her shoes made clop-clop on the boards. She sat down on the top of the stairs.

What had she seen?

Something that she would never forget, something that hurt her.

She began to cry very softly, lest anyone should hear her. She cried and cried. She wanted to go home. She wanted someone to care for her.

Huddled up, now only a baby lost and bewildered, crying and sobbing, there with her head against the banister she fell fast, fast asleep.

SUNWOODS IN COCKERMOUTH

Deborah Herries, the daughter of Francis Herries, sister of David Herries and half-sister of Judith, married, early in 1761, the Reverend Gordon Sunwood, a clergyman who lived in the town of Cockermouth. Mr. Sunwood had no particular cure, but after his marriage published two admirable works--one A Treatise on the Magnificat, the other The Hope of Grace to Come, or Sinners at the Feet of Jesus. This second work had a very real sale throughout the North of England. He was in considerable request as a preacher. In 1765 his aunt, Miss Mercia Sunwood, died in the town of Exeter, bequeathing him a very reasonable fortune.

They had two boys, twins, born in the year 1763, Reuben and Humphrey.

Deborah Herries had been always, unlike her sister Mary and brother David, of a quite unambitious disposition. For the first half of her life she had lived quietly with her father at Herries in Borrowdale, perfectly content to care for him and offer him as much love and affection as he was willing to accept.

After his second marriage, however, which occurred when he was well on in years, she considered that she was no longer needed by him (which was perfectly true), left him and married her clergyman in Cockermouth. She had loved Mr. Sunwood from the first moment of seeing him at a ball in Keswick, and he was indeed exactly suited to her, being as kindly, well-disposed, unenterprising and equable as she. She differed from him greatly in her perceptions; she had a good deal in her of her father's poetry, very much more than had her brother David, who had, however, been always much closer to their father. She had been kept from her father by a sort of terror of him, being never very comfortable with persons who were scornful or sarcastic, or liable to sudden temper or indignation.

Mr. Gordon Sunwood had been a rest and refreshment to her after her life with her father, for, as his rotund body, snow-white hair and kindly rosy face portended, he could with the greatest difficulty be angry with anyone or anything, and then only for a moment at a time. Methodists, Wesleyans, Quakers, Dissenters of any kind-- these were almost the only animals who could rouse him to any sort of genuine indignation.

Marriage with Deborah excited him to a kind of mild ambition, and it is quite certain that he would never have written, or, having written, would never have published his two books had she not stirred his faculties.

Having published them he exhibited a natural pride very evident in most authors, who have, from time immemorial, found it difficult to conceive that theirs are not the only shining fish in the literary ocean.

When Deborah's twins were born the cup of her joy was full. And, as is not the case with all optimistic parents, her joy continued, for as the boys grew in physical stature so also they grew in kindliness of nature and obedience to their parents.

They were, one is happy to record, by no means angels, but their vices were mild ones, and their faults just sufficient to keep them properly human. Humphrey had by far the easier disposition of the two. Tall, slender and flaxen-haired, life was for him one long adventure. He was as restless as he was merry, so popular at the Cockermouth school that it was entirely to his credit that he should wish to be constantly with his parents.

Everyone spoke well of him, and it is not, perhaps, altogether to be wondered at that his charm became his principal asset and an easy substitute for hard work and diligence. His parents succeeded in affording him his residence at St. John's College, Cambridge, and, if he did nothing there but secure the pleasant good wishes of his fellow-men, that was more than many others succeeded in securing.

After Cambridge the question was what should be done with him. He would hear of nothing but London, and to a lawyer's office there he went. On this bright afternoon in early November of the year 1785 his proud mother was excitedly occupied in reading his first letter from the Metropolis.

Humphrey's twin brother Reuben had quite another history. They had only small resemblance to one another whether in character or in physical appearance. And yet the bond between them was almost fantastic. From their first conscious moments they had been all in all the one to the other; theirs, indeed, was a love that nothing in life would be able to influence. Humphrey, volatile, restless, and woman-lover as he was, yet knew no emotion so unyielding and passionate as this for his brother. For Reuben, Humphrey was always and ever in a world apart. Reuben was unlike Humphrey in that he was stout, clumsy and plain. He was not uncleanly in his person, but his clothes never fitted him, nor could he be brought to consider the practical details of daily life. His eyes were good and faithful, his mouth, although too large, kindly and tolerant, but his nose was ludicrously ill-shaped, his hair wild and of a dingy colour, his limbs uncouth and ill-disciplined. From his very early years he had been of an intensely religious mind. It had been always understood that he would be a clergyman. At the age of sixteen he joined the religious society of St. Bees, but was there for a year only, finding that he could not come to the same mind with the authorities.

He returned to his parents' house in Cockermouth, and to their considerable grief had in the last five years shown little progress in anything; his favourite occupation was to walk the hills for days on end by himself, and he could be seen striding along the roads, talking aloud and snapping his fingers in the air.

He was devoted to his parents, amiable and docile. There had, however, been strange rumours of late concerning him, not of any immorality or cock-fighting or gambling, but of something that was, in his father's eyes, very much worse: a suspicion that he was concerting with the Methodists. A well-known Wesleyan itinerant, Mr. Jeremy Walker, had been seen in his company. There was a rumour that he had taken part in some sort of outdoor meeting. His father had not yet dared to ask him whether there was any sort of truth in this. He knew well his son's honesty, but Mr. Sunwood was grievously disturbed in his mind.

Their home on the outskirts of Cockermouth was a pretty place, looking out to the fields and woods, having a garden filled with sweet-williams and pinks and hollyhocks in their due season, and an arbour and a trellis for roses. In the parlour there was a rosy chintz and some fine pieces of mahogany, in Mr. and Mrs. Sunwood's bedroom a grand four-poster and a dressing-chest with a lattice of Chinese decoration. At the corner of the stair there was a round- faced clock of Irish Chippendale. There were spindle-backed chairs, a Bury settee and a fine Turkey carpet in the dining-room. These things were the very pride of Mr. and Mrs. Sunwood's hearts. There was a maid-servant called Rebecca, a cat, Timothy, and a boy, who worked (when he felt inclined) in the garden, named Jacob. Deborah herself cared for the preserving, pickling and daily cooking. She and Rebecca kept the little house as clean and shining as a new saucepan. They were, both of them, so proud of it that they dreamt of it at night.

Deborah had but seldom any time for rest and reflection; she did not, indeed, desire it. On this particular afternoon, however, she was expecting her sister-in-law, Sarah Herries, and some members of her family to dinner at four o'clock; they would remain for the night and return to Fell House on the following day. Everything was ready for them, the Guest Room prepared, the dinner preparing. All day she had had with her Humphrey's letter. Only now was she free to settle herself and read some of it. Her excitement was as intense as though Humphrey himself had made a sudden unexpected appearance.

Mr. Sunwood came in from tending a pig, who led (unwitting his destiny) a greedy and contented life in a sty at the back of the house; close together on the settee, his hand resting often on her plump shoulder, they read the letter. Humphrey began with loving messages to everyone. Then he had many things to tell of London: the eating-house where he had paid a shilling for his dinner of meat and pudding, the Thames with its fine bridges and noble arches, the hackney coaches, the dangers of the streets where the coaches and carts crowded so closely that there was scarcely room to move, and the noise so fierce that you must step into the quiet of a shop if you wanted to converse with a friend, a ship on land near the Tower that was a trap for pressing simple people into being sailors, the signs outside the shops with 'Children educated here,' 'Shoes mended here,' 'Foreign spirituous liquors here,' the general drunkenness, so that the common people were always far gone in gin and brandy. He had visited Vauxhall with the son of his master, Mr. Hodges, and had much to say about the paintings and statues, the rotunda and the orchestra therein.

The most exciting news to his parents, however, was that he had taken dinner with his mother's cousin, Sir Pomfret Herries, who had a fine house in Kensington: Pomfret was the son of Deborah's first cousin Raiseley, who had once owned a fine house in Keswick but was now with God. Deborah's memory flew back to her cousin Raiseley, a sickly and arrogant youth who had been for ever at war with her brother David. It had seemed that there would be a family feud there, but when Raiseley had in later years moved to London, and the Keswick house was sold, communication had altogether dropped.

It seemed, however, that this child Pomfret, whom Deborah remembered as a little stout boy beating David's big black horse with a toy whip, now a man of thirty-four or so, had done well for himself in the City, married a clergyman's daughter, and begotten of her body two healthy children.

Well, feud or no feud, Pomfret Herries had been kind to her boy, and for that she would forgive him all old scores. Young Humphrey described the splendour of the Kensington house, the garden with its fountain and statues, the many servants, the rich food and wine. Cousin Pomfret was large and stout ('like his poor grandfather before him,' sighed Deborah, with a sudden desire to go somewhere and be kind to that poor old man with his red face and pimples, suffering so sadly from gout, sitting alone and deserted in the Keswick house by the Lake). And now there was this new Pomfret with his children and handsome wife sitting in his grand Kensington house, forgetting no doubt that he had ever had a grandfather. Time flies, thought Deborah, and this is a modern world that we are in. Those old days are gone for ever! There was indeed a certain moment's melancholy in this excited acceptance by her son of this new life. She had lost him!--he who only a moment ago had been rolling naked on this Turkey carpet while she turned the tunes in the music-box--and, her eyes a little tearful, she placed her chubby hand on her husband's chubby arm that she might feel securely that he, at any rate, was still with her.

Mr. Sunwood loved his son, but so confusing is this modern life that there were four things in his head all obscuring and dimming the things that Humphrey had to tell him. That was the worst of these days: you never had a moment's peace. There was his friend Mr. Forster, who wanted a midshipman's place for his boy, and hadn't Mr. Sunwood some interest; there was his own wickedness in sitting up almost all night at cards two days back at Mr. and Mrs. Donne's, and although he had lost but a shilling in all it was a habit that must not grow on him; and there was the funeral of Mrs. Hardacre to-morrow and he must see that his black silk hatband had its proper white love-ribband; there was their own dinner, too, this very day. Sarah and David Herries were accustomed to good fare. Deborah had told him that there would be a couple of rabbits smothered in onions, a couple of ducks roasted and an apricot pudding. He himself had seen to the wine, punch and beer. And what was that that Deborah was reading to him? 'A girl staying in the house, Nancy Bone, has a lovely figure, and we laughed and joked much together. I sat beside her when we played Forfeits, and I have bought her to-day a purse made of morocco leather. For dinner we had a turkey roasted, a boiled chicken, blancmange, tarts, a damson cheese. . . .'

Deborah, her eyes shining, said: 'If it should be a match between our Humphrey and this Nancy . . .' upon which, throwing to the wind all the other concerns that had been plaguing him, and realising only her, the best wife God had ever given to man, he put his arm around her broad shoulders, kissed her on the lips and pinched her ear for an audacious matchmaker.

He was about to ask 'And where is Reuben?' when they heard the clatter of the horses on the cobbles. A moment later and there in the doorway were Sarah, David and their youngest boy.

Everyone was very happy; they were sitting in the parlour, and little Rebecca, looking her best in her fresh cap and ribbons, was offering wine and cake, and Jacob was caring for the horses.

Mr. Sunwood, although he would acknowledge it to no man, was always a little shy of his brother-in-law, David Herries. He was always hoping that this hesitation would shortly be conquered and had even prayed to God about it, but on every fresh occasion the shyness was there. For one thing David Herries was now a great man in the county, his influence everywhere felt, and men said that one of these days he would be knighted. Mr. Sunwood could never feel perfectly assured that David had not a little despised his sister for marrying a simple clergyman. Then David was a great man physically too, enormous he looked now as he spread about the settee with his snow-white wig, which he still occasionally wore, his round red face, his full-skirted blue coat and silver waistcoat, his immense thighs and legs in their riding-boots, his silver spurs.

But no one could have been kinder than David was to his brother-in- law. There was no condescension in his heart to anyone, he had no pride anywhere in his heart save that he was a Herries and had done something to raise his branch of the Herries family in the world. It was strange indeed to see how, the moment that David and Deborah his sister were together again, the Herries family feeling was suddenly everywhere.

The house, the furniture, the cake, the wine, Rebecca and the cat, little Mr. Sunwood himself, all became adjuncts of the Herries Family, whether they would or no. That was a way that the Herries people had.

Nevertheless David and his brother-in-law discussed the affairs of the nation in quite a broad general spirit. David had a great deal to say about the recent rejection of Pitt's Reform Bill. He was glad indeed that it had been rejected. If ever there was a true Tory in the world it was David Herries, and Mr. Sunwood agreed with him, being as Tory in Church as David was in State. David's voice had a way of rising to a regular boom when his feelings were roused, and they were roused now. He could not himself see that there was anything wrong with Parliamentary Representation. He would have things left as they were. For all that he could see, this was nothing but a plot on the part of the Yorkshire freeholders to put a check on the authority of their good and wise King. He shook his great head over these new times. Why couldn't we leave things as they were? This discontent of the lower orders boded no good. What was this chatter about their Rights? When he had been a boy they had had no Rights and were contented enough. He recalled the admirable behaviour of a servant his father had had, Benjamin he had been called. The more you whipped him the better he was pleased, and he had died in his father's arms. David never perceived the incongruity of his remarks in that he himself could never beat anyone and was notorious for over-indulging his servants. Mr. Sunwood, however, agreed cordially and sighed over these new times, and was afraid that there were many fresh changes coming.

Sarah and Deborah meanwhile were talking together as eagerly as any two women will who are very old friends and have not seen one another for a while. Sarah, although she did not at present declare it, was paying this visit because, above everything, she wished to discuss with Deborah the urgent matter of Judith. Deborah, on her side, was longing for the moment when she might begin about Humphrey's letter and his visit to the Pomfret Herries.

Sarah had the greatest opinion of Deborah's sound common sense. Judith's escape to Tom Gauntry's on the evening of her whipping had had most momentous consequences. David had ridden over to Stone Ends and brought her home. From then until now her nature was changed. She was obedient, docile, with flashes of fiery temper, strange impetuous affections; Sarah, whose nature was equable and always under control, could not understand her at all: she felt, too, that she was alone in this, for David had not the art of understanding temperaments. Francis could do what he liked with the child, but would not, so there you were. . . .

Meanwhile one member of the household was in his attic room drumming with his fingers on the window. This was Reuben. He could not decide to go down. He had seen them arrive. The one of them that interested and touched him most was not there--Judith. She came in his heart after his brother and his mother, and so warm, so almost passionate, were his affections that she would have been surprised indeed had she known of them. As yet she never thought of him; she had seen him but seldom, and he was no figure to appeal to a child, with his lanky hair, his stout ill-shapen body and his untidiness.

But if she had been there he would have come down. He would have endured his awkward distrust of himself before his grand uncle and his discomfort before the sharp critical eyes of young Will his cousin. Had Judith been with them he could have sat and looked at her lovely hair, and perhaps done her some little service.

But he knew what they thought of him. He could hear his uncle ask why he was not at some work, saving his parents their charges. He had seen his uncle stand by the horse, give his riding-coat to Jacob, revealing the splendid clothes. Why was he never to be like that? Why was everything in him just so turbulent and disordered, as though he heard from a great distance some Call to the obeying of some Order, and yet could not distinguish what that Call might be--and why, oh, why, was something driving him now towards a step that must enrage his father and make his brother grieve?

It had been only a year ago that Mr. Walker had given him an ill- written, exceedingly ill-printed Life of John Wesley, and this book had been for him, since then, almost his Gospel. Everything related in it had seemed to grow into his own nature. When he read that Wesley wore his hair flowing loose upon his shoulders to give the money that would be spent in caring for it to the poor, that seemed to him a divine action. When he read Wesley's words: 'I would as soon expect to dig happiness out of the earth, as to find it in riches, honour, pleasure (so called) or indeed in the enjoyment of any creature. I know there can be no happiness on earth, but in the enjoyment of God, and in the foretaste of those rivers of pleasure which flow at His right hand for evermore. Thus by the Grace of God in Christ I judge of happiness. Therefore I am in this respect a new creature': his soul thrilled within him; it was almost as though he saw God Himself standing before him and the light of His Countenance shining upon him.

When he read of how Whitfield on the afternoon of Saturday, February 17, 1739, stood upon a mound, in a place called Rose Green, his 'first field pulpit,' and preached to the Kingswood colliers, he felt that he would have given all that he had might he but have stood at his side on that great occasion.

He read how Wesley preached at Gwenap, in Cornwall: 'I stood on the wall, in the calm still evening, with the setting sun behind me; and almost an innumerable multitude before, behind and on either hand. Many likewise sat on the little hills, at some distance from the bulk of the congregation. But they could all hear distinctly while I read "The disciple is not above his Master," and the rest of those comfortable words which are day by day fulfilled in our ears.'

Oh, those comfortable words! Why had he not too been there on that beautiful evening, following that great man's counsel?

Above and beyond all there was the necessity for the New Birth. 'One will ask with all assurance, "What! Shall I not do as well as my neighbour?" Yes; as well as your unholy neighbour, as well as your neighbours that die in their sins; for you will all drop into the pit together, in the nethermost hell. You will all lie together in the lake of fire, "the lake of fire burning with brimstone." Then at length you will see (but God grant you may see it before!) the necessity of holiness in order to glory, and, consequently, of the new birth; since none can be holy, except he be born again.'

None can be holy except he be born again! So he was not holy. No, indeed, he was not. He was filled with a loathing and hatred of himself, of his body, but far more of himself, his character and true person. He knew himself for a glutton, a coward, an idler, filled with vanity, sensual thought, ingratitude.

But it was worst of all that he should not know which way he should go. He had seen during the last year something of Mr. Walker and his friends; he had been to some of their meetings and was not happy there. There was something of his father in him, more than he knew; something perhaps of the Herries blood of his mother. The violence and hysteria in the meetings repelled and silenced him. And they, too, felt that he was not with them. What he wanted he could not tell, save that he must serve God, and must in himself bring about some entire change. Poor Reuben! He was just now the loneliest young man in the world.

He leaned from his window and listened to the sounds of the little world about him. Some horse was impatiently pawing the cobbles, a pedlar sharply cried his wares, a flock of sheep came hurrying under the window, pressing together with their wide, startled, stupid eyes; the shepherd, an old man, with a white shaggy beard, wearing a wide black hat, called shrilly and with an absent mind to his sheep-dog. Beyond these movements the wood lay in dark shadow, motionless as though painted on the silver sky. Every fibre in him responded to this lovely world. He must get out into it. He would not go down to his aunt and uncle. He would see them later in the evening. Had little Judith been there--! And at the thought of her, although he had no sensual feeling for her (was she not, ludicrous thought, his aunt?), he became quite suddenly disturbed by consideration of women. They flocked, like a covey of bright shining birds, about him, settling on his head, his shoulders, his hands, ruffling their feathers, crimson and silver and gold, with their sharp beaks pecking at his cheeks, smiling at him out of their hard bright eyes. His body was burning, his heart roughly beating. The Devil himself was with him in the room, which had become hot and airless. The sun was sinking, and the wood, as though stricken by the hand of God, was ebony. The silver sky was a camping-ground for tents of crimson; shadows of approaching evening stole across the brightness of the field. His room was evil and filled with temptation. Not realising that he was hurrying to the turning-point of his life, he hastened softly down the stairs, along the passage, into the path before the house.

The little town was embraced by the rosy light of approaching evening. Fresh breezes from the sea ruffled the hair and wigs of the citizens; not far away the kindly hills caught the light. The streets were narrow, ill-paved and of a certain odour, but it was the time when the labours of the day are drawing to a close, many were at their dinner, children ran playing from door to door.

At the door of Jacob Hilton's Library young Mr. Clementson, flour-dealer, was having a pleasant word with Mr. Fletcher of the 'King's Arms,' and here was the Carrier coming in from Workington.

They all knew young Reuben Sunwood well enough and greeted him kindly, but he had the sense (perhaps with some truth) that they regarded him oddly and avoided too plain a recognition of him for the Methodist company he was keeping.

So he turned off the main street up a dark and narrow way, thinking of his own troubles, his evil temptations, his loneliness, his perplexed opinions, and found himself, almost without knowing it, in the coach-yard at the back of the 'Black Bull.'

He had been attracted here, it might be subconsciously, by the shouts and laughter of a pushing, pressing crowd. He was among them before he knew. He stood there watching. In the middle of the yard there was a cleared space and in the cleared space a post. Chained to the post was an old, ragged and exceedingly weary bear. Near to the bear, held in the arms of two stout young men, was a small brown-faced man, his forehead streaked with blood. It seemed that he was a foreign pedlar of some kind from his long black hair, his brown complexion, a torn jacket of crimson with a silver chain. It was soon clear that he was a foreigner, for he jabbered ceaselessly in a strange tongue, words pouring from him in a tangled, agitated flow. Once and again he would raise his little body as though he would break away, and then his voice jumped into a shrill scream of protest that roused bursts of laughter from the onlookers.

Kneeling on the ground were two men who held in leash a bulldog and a small terrier, and these two dogs were madly straining to be free that they might get at the bear.

Everyone was hurling bets into the air, and close to Reuben a short thick-set man sucking a straw was taking bets down in his book. The excitement was intense; it was months, a tall farmer near Reuben told him, since there had been a bear to be baited.

Above the hubbub and bustle, clouds of saffron sailed tranquilly over the sky that was now white as moonlit water. Two children hung between the balusters of the inn balcony, laughing at the little pedlar.

At first it seemed to Reuben that he was not concerned in the matter. The bustle and noise, the friendly stomach of the large farmer against which he was pressed, the general air of goodwill and happiness was a relief to him after his own silly and selfish perplexities. There was very much of the child in him, and he liked above all to have happy people around him. To see animals baited was no fresh thing to him; he had been accustomed to such sights since he was a baby. The cruelty of his time was natural to his time and so was no cruelty. He pushed himself forward that he might see the better.

Then he encountered the face of the bear. An encounter it was, as though the pale sky, the crowd, the inn buildings had been swept into lumber and only he and the bear remained. The bear raised its old sad wrinkled face and looked at him. Age was there, bewilderment was there, but what was there, beyond all else, was Reuben himself. Reuben looked at Reuben.

The bear was fastened to the post by a rusty chain that went round his middle and his foot. His body was chafed in a number of places, where life had been hard on him. The long brown shaggy hair of his body was tangled with mud and dirt, and above his left eye there was a deep cut from which blood dripped.

It was this that Reuben first saw, how he raised his paw clumsily, slowly, as though he were resolved to be cautious, and wiped the blood that trickled down his nose. From under his thick tangled brows his eyes looked out, melancholy, slow and brooding. It was these eyes that seemed at first to be exactly Reuben's own. He knew how often his gaze had been fixed upon himself and the world in which he moved with exactly that same perplexity and sadness. The bear's loneliness was his own loneliness.

Then the bear began quietly to realise that he was in the middle of his enemies. Carefully, with that same caution, he moved his head to look for his master, and when he saw him held with his coat torn and his brown breast bare he began to be angry. (Just, Reuben thought, as he would himself slowly, in the middle of his enemies, begin to be angry.) But with his anger there rose also slowly his sadness and his bewilderment. He shuffled with his feet; his paw rose and fell again. He began to roll his head. Then he tried to break from his chain, and when he found that he could not, he jerked his head towards his master. Then again rubbed the drops of blood from his nose.

Something very grand entered into him, the grandeur of all captured and ill-treated things. He lifted his head and stared from under his jutting brows at the crowd, and was at once, with that single movement, finer than all of them. He was no longer Reuben. Reuben had been left behind and was now one of the crowd.

Then a large fat man without a hat, his hair tied with a brown ribbon, in red faded breeches, strode forward and undid the chain. Everyone shouted. The bear, bewildered, hesitating, rubbed his nose again, then, like a man in bedroom slippers, shuffled towards his master.

At the same moment the two dogs were loosed. Everyone began to shout together. It seemed to Reuben that it was towards himself that the dogs were running.

The bulldog instantly attacked the bear, caught his leg and hung on there. The smaller dog stayed back, whining.

The world was pandemonium. Men were laughing, yelling, moving, so that the crowd rocked like a wave. But the bear stood doing nothing; he only raised his paw and stroked his nose. He was a very old bear, who had been travelling for an infinity of years; he was very weary and did not understand why things were as they were.

The bulldog loosed his hold, sprang at the bear's throat, missed and rolled over. The bear sank on all fours, and, rolling his head with a blind gesture, seemed to be asking of them all what they were about.

It was then that Reuben, pushing violently his way, broke into the centre and ran to the bear. Then everything happened swiftly and, for the crowd, comically. A bear or a man, it was the same to the crowd. The bulldog bit Reuben's leg. Something struck his face. There were shouts and cries. Lightning broke from heaven, and the multitude of men, faces, heads of hair, hands, rose in a swirl like a shifting canopy of black flies and carried him sky-high. Then he fell, fell into a pit that was black, that had the mouth of a fish, opening, shutting, opening again. But as he fell somewhere, triumph, joy, freedom--things that he had never known--broke like silent fireworks in his heart. . . .

Many generations after, he was sitting in a chair in the parlour of Mr. Candlish the bellman. He knew him well, a short pursy fellow with a wart on his nose. Mrs. Candlish had bound his head. One eye was closed. A little crowd in the doorway surveyed him. Someone held a candle. He smiled feebly on them all, climbed to his feet, found that he could walk, although his body ached and blood trickled from under the bandage.

He said that he would go home now, thank you. No one stayed him. They were silent when he limped past them, and stared after him in silence as he hobbled down the street. He did not know at all why he was happy, but he was.

He had not far to go. Every step was an agony. He opened his house-door and pushed into the parlour, where they were at dinner. With his one eye from under his bandage he saw his uncle David, shining in splendour, his father pouring wine, his mother--her face suddenly springing into terror at the sight of him--his aunt, and his little cousin Will, who watched everything and missed nothing that anyone said.

He saw the table piled with food, the candles that danced in their silver holders and the harpsichord in the corner. Someone cried out; he swayed in the doorway, tried to ask for some wine, could not, fell fainting at his mother's feet. As he tried to catch her hand he smiled.

He was the bear, and none of them knew it.

FIREWORKS OVER THE LAKE

For the evening of June 23, 1787, Mr. Joseph Pocklington of Vicar's Island announced that there would be fireworks discharged from his own ground IF the weather were fine.

IF the weather were fine! How that phrase beat its anxiety in a thousand hearts, for not only was it a question of the fireworks, but the band, organised by Mr. Peter Crosthwaite of Crosthwaite Museum, would play airs from Haydn and Mozart, and there would be dancing in Crow Park, to say nothing at all of the boats that there would be on the Lake itself, the Chinese lanterns, and the dark recesses of the water hidden from the inquisitive glances of the moon.

Would there be a moon? Yes, there would be a moon. Mr. Crosthwaite himself, who, after serving his country for twenty years in the Navy, had but recently returned to his native place with a most interesting collection of curiosities, promised that there should be a full and lustrous moon.

It mattered little where you went on that early morning of June 23. Every riser had the same idea; night-cap after night-cap might be seen hanging from the window, sniffing at the weather. From the windows of the 'Royal Oak' and the 'Queen's Head,' from John Powe's where the Old Club for so many years held its meetings, from the attics of the 'Shoulder of Mutton,' from the Excise Officer at the 'George and the Dragon,' from Abel Graves the hairdresser's and Mr. Lancaster the patten-maker's, from the toll-gate at Brow Top--yes, and much farther afield than these . . . right around the Lake, from Stable Hill and Burrow and Low Low Door, High Low Door and Grange, Borrowdale Common and Manesty Nook, Mutton Pye Bay and Branley, House End and Water End, Finkle Street and Portinskill. Yes, and beyond these again, from Newlands and Rosthwaite, Stonethwaite and Watendlath, Braithwaite and Bassenthwaite, even to Buttermere and Uldale and Caldbeck and Threlkeld--even to Penrith and Grasmere, to Patterdale and Ambleside, the news had run and the night-caps were at all the windows, whether of mansion or Statesman's farm, of shop, of meeting-house or humble cottage.

For these nights on the Lake, IF only the weather were fair, were nights to stir the poets to song, and they DID stir the Keswick poets to song. Are not those poems to be found in Keswick archives to this very day?

Mr. Pocklington himself loved to give pleasure to the people of Keswick, and the people of Keswick loved to have pleasure given them. And was not Mr. Pocklington a fine man, seeing that he owned so much land around the Lake and had his place on Vicar's Island and at Ashness and at Fall Park, and had set up a wonderful Druid's Circle in the pleasantest imitation of the real one above Keswick?

If only the sun would shine, everyone and everything was in favour. And the sun DID shine. It rose above a curtain of mist that cut the Lake into half, turned the islands into clouds of emerald, touched Skiddaw with rose and the sharp edges of Blencathra with ebony.

All the gardens of Keswick--and at that time Keswick was filled with gardens--glittered in the sun. Then as now, no gardens in England could grow sweet peas and pinks and stock better than the Keswick gardens. On a summer day, such as this one, Keswick smelt of flowers, save only in the slums, behind Main Street, where the odour was quite another one. But here dwelt only gipsies and whores and smugglers from St. Bees and Ravenglass, and they didn't matter to anyone.

So the day lengthened; the air was balmy, Mr. Crosthwaite took out his flute and tuned it, Miss Evins the schoolmistress practised her dancing-steps privately in her bedroom; the 'Royal Oak,' the 'Queen's Head,' the 'Shoulder of Mutton' prepared for an infinity of custom;

all the children were beyond human discipline, Mr. Pocklington's gardeners guarded the fireworks, and from distant silent valleys the horses had set out, the ladies riding pillion as happy as though there were not a heartache in the world. All the Herries would be there. It was a proud day for the Sunwoods, for their Reuben was but just returned from France, where he had been these last two years; and all the Herries from Uldale-- David and Sarah, Francis, Deborah, Will and Judith-- rode out in the forenoon and had dinner in state at the 'Royal Oak.'

William Herries, now seventeen years of age, small, short, spindly- legged, an arrogant nose in the proper equine Herries style, a thin rather tight mouth that could, and often did, break into a very charming smile, and clothes neat, correct and most unobtrusive, this William Herries was, as he always had been, exceedingly old for his age.

He himself knew that this was so; he had realised for the last ten years at least that he was quite the oldest of them all. Without any sense of condemnation, without any outward show of superiority, he had long felt a very real contempt for all the other members of his family--for his mother because she was jog-trot, his father because he was conservative, his brother Francis because he was a dreamer (here was his severest contempt), and Judith (could she be reckoned as one of the family) because she was mad and had no control of her emotions. (Strangely, though, here he recognised in Judith some spirit of mastery closely akin to his own.)

He recognised that he was superior to every member of his family but chiefly in this: that he knew so exactly what he wanted to do with his life and how he would do it.

His father, poor man, had a kind of notion that Will would follow himself in his trading business, would work in Liverpool for a while, travel in the East for a while, and finally, having doubled the value of everything, settle down as Squire of Fell House.

Some of this prophecy was, indeed, correct. Will WOULD follow his father in the business, would in truth double it and more than double it, but NOT from Liverpool. It was in London that Will Herries intended to make his career. It was not at all that Will objected to business; that was not the kind of snob that he was. Now, with all England's glorious foreign conquests, with the India Trade, the China Trade and the rest, now was the very time to make a fortune. But it was to be a fortune made in the grand manner, made in the very heart of the universe, made against the very strongest opposition, and made--here was the fount and crown of the whole ambition--made for the HERRIES' glory.

Will was nothing if he was not Herries, and Herries practical, material, of the earth earthy. He was sentimental about nothing; he was most certainly not sentimental about this. He did not know in what distant childish dreams this ambition had not had its birth, to make a fortune and with that to take his place at the head of the Herries family. So that men everywhere might say: "That is a Family, that is. It has houses and barns, gardens and fields, ships and horses and sheep and cattle. THAT is what a Herries can do.'

He saw neither poetry nor romance in this ambition. It seemed to him a perfectly practical logical plan. He would not mind if, at the end of it, one day he returned to Uldale as its master. He cared for this North Country if he cared for any country at all. There was something in its bleak spaces, its coldly blowing winds, its little stone walls running like live things about the fells, its glancing, shining waters, its cleanliness and strength and honesty, that was akin to his own strong unfaltering purpose.

He had, of course, the defects of his qualities like all of us, and it was one of his defects that he made no allowance for the poetic, incalculable quality in human nature. He thought, even now at the young age of seventeen, that he could always calculate with perfect safety. He knew exactly what his father and mother would do and say. His father with his large hearty good-nature, his simple laughter, his ability for seeing what was under his nose, and his stupidity in thinking that that was all that there was; his common sense that stopped just short of real knowledge; his sentimentality (Will, like many another practical man and woman, mistook for sentimentality quite deep and genuine feeling), his boisterous physical life, love of food, of drink, of hunting, of horses, of cock-fighting and card-playing and wrestling and football; his kindliness and satisfaction with small material things. Will knew that most of the business was now left to Mr. Metcalfe and his son, his father's partners in Liverpool, and he despised his father for so leaving it. He had a good-natured regard for his father and he despised him thoroughly.

He really loved his mother; it was perhaps the strongest human feeling that he had, and this was chiefly because he thought that she managed the house very well, ruled the servants and had everything in order, but she was always doing what seemed to him silly sentimental things.

For his elder brother Francis he felt a contempt that was almost savage. Francis stood for everything that he despised; he did nothing, but hung in idleness about the house, reading, dreaming, saying absurd, ridiculous things, seeing poetry in everything, liking to be alone, simply cumbering the ground. He had not even the natural passions of drinking, wenching, gaming. He was nothing, nothing at all.

From them all, with a self-control that argued well for his future success in the world, he completely hid his scorn. To them all he appeared a quiet, obedient, studious boy, who did what he was told and gave no trouble.

Francis possibly had some suspicion of the iron will and determined purpose that was developing there, but no one knew what Francis thought about anything.

The only other person who had any accurate knowledge of Will was Judith. His own attitude to Judith was a peculiar one. He had to confess that Judith perplexed him. He had to confess regretfully enough that to sum her up as wild and foolish was not sufficient. She was, it was true, all of these things, but she appeared to be something else besides.

The relation between them was exceptional. Judith was now approaching thirteen years of age. She, like himself, was older than she looked, except that, at times, she looked old enough to be eighty. She had all the colour, all the oddness, all the uncertainty, irresponsibility, that he distrusted and condemned. It was natural enough, he considered, when you thought of her mother. But besides this was her desire to dominate everyone with whom she came in contact, and this was like his own desire except that she wanted it for other reasons. She wanted power because of PEOPLE, he wanted it because of THINGS. He had sensual feeling like anyone else, and had had already two experiences. She had sensual feeling too, but it was quite different from his, because whenever she cared for anybody (and she cared for fifty different people a week) she threw herself into it as though this were the only affection of her life, while he always knew that people were nothing, that no one ever cared for anyone else very long.

And he told himself this, although right before his eyes were his own father and mother who had loved one another for so many years and would do so to the end. But his father and mother had so much ridiculous Sensibility--and very little Sense at all.

Nevertheless it remained to him puzzling, this relation of his with Judith. Defensive or offensive? She wished to dominate him as well as the rest of her world. It amused him sometimes to allow her to think that she did.

So he remained, this young man of seventeen, watching, waiting, calculating all his chances.

The night was enchantingly warm. They went down to the Lake in a body--David in his fine rose-coloured coat, wearing his own hair clubbed and powdered (an increasing fashion); Sarah in a fine hoop of silver with little roses; Deborah, red in the face with pleasure and happiness ('blowzy,' Will thought her); Judith, a fascinating little hat on the side of her red hair and a little hoop with silver ships painted on it; Will, very soberly dressed in brown, demurely in the rear; Francis, slim, aloof.

Mr. and Mrs. Satterthwaite of Bassenthwaite village walked down with them. Mrs. Satterthwaite's talk was all of servants, a new one, Mary Benson, recommended by Mrs. Blane, five pound a year, tea twice a day, good at cookery and understanding her needle. Well, we hope, don't we, that it will turn out for the best? But they begin so well, don't they, up so early, ready to milk

the cow, and then, where are you? A month later, already in child from the cowman or drunk on the parlour floor. Yes, where are you? All the sky, milky now with golden fleece before the sun's setting, is crowded with maids flying like witches, mocking their mistresses, and men, bare as they were born, down the wind after them. Do what you will, it is all Nature, and what do you say to Mr. Bradby, the new schoolmaster in Keswick? A sensible and good-natured man, unmarried--and at once Mrs. Satterthwaite's two daughters, single and plain, poor things, always left to their own thoughts at every dance in the neighbourhood, staying in Carlisle at this very instant with an aunt to see whether SHE couldn't do something about it, filled the scene and checked the conversation.

Not for Judith. She was so happy that she must dance along the path as she went, chattering to Francis, although she knew that he was listening to nothing that she had to say.

Everywhere, on every side of her, people were moving forward to the Lake, and all of them as happy as she. She loved that people around her should be happy; she was to love that as long as she was alive. If only they were happy and ALSO did what she told them, she asked nothing more of life.

And to-night, everything was perfection. She had had her own way in everything, was wearing the clothes that she wanted, there would be dancing under the trees and they would be in a boat on the Lake, the moon would rise, and then, best of all, there would be Fireworks--Fireworks, of all things in life that she loved best! Could she have seen Mr. Joseph Pocklington, she would have flung her arms around him and kissed him. She did not mind what she did when she was happy. Her soul and body surrendered then completely to the emotion of the moment. Nothing existed for her except that moment.

Even Will, who thought it foolish, indeed, when you were a little short thing with a pale face and so many people around you, to dance along so that all must notice you, was forced to acknowledge to himself that her happiness was infectious. He himself hoped to have his arm around some feminine waist before the evening was over.

When they gained the lakeside it was beautiful indeed. The Lake, whose waters scarcely moved, only a trembling shudder of pleasure once and again mysteriously stirring, had caught flakes and scatterings of gold from the last rays of the sun as it fell behind Cat Bells. Vicar's Island lay like a dark hand upon the water. Under the trees there were booths with many things to buy. Someone was playing a fiddle. Everywhere boats floated, and the oars plashed like music through the air.

Happiness? Happiness? Where is it? Where is it? Here, now, this very moment, with the movement of the people under the trees, the fiddle and the soft distance of the orchestra on the Meadow, before one's eyes the silver stretch of water spreading to the hills that lay like friendly elephants (thought Judith, who had never seen an elephant) humped against the sky. Yes, here is Happiness, because here is Mystery and promise of Adventure. One cannot quite see who is moving beneath the trees. One step and whom may one not encounter?

Two boats were waiting for the Herries family in the charge of old John Blacklock, who was so broad in the waist and thick of the leg that he was like one of the sights at the Fair, two bodies with one head. This head and face, too, were so thickly covered with hair that his eyes shone out like a friendly animal's from a bush. Judith always talked Cumberland to him.

She greeted him now with: 'Noo than what, John?' which pleased him greatly. In his opinion she was a 'gay fewsome lass.' When the weather was bad, he would come out to Uldale and work in the garden for a week or more.

But there was at once a real excitement for her, because Reuben was there. They were waiting for them-- little Mr. Sunwood, very neat in his best parson's clothes; Deborah, always so kind and comfortable; and Reuben, a trifle neater for his two years' sojourn in France, but otherwise very little changed. She liked Reuben, in part because of the power she had over him, in part because of his modesty and warm-heartedness. She even understood his shyness, although it was so far from anything in herself. It was, indeed, part of her character that she should care more for Francis and Reuben, so unlike her in temperament, than any other of her relatives.

And at once her power for having things as she wanted them was apparent. A child of less than thirteen, she was in five minutes seated under an oak tree; the Lake spread in front of her, and settled around her were Reuben, Francis and Will. It was true that they were there to take a breath and look about them before the activities of the evening began for them, and were scarcely conscious, perhaps, that Judith was there, or it was Reuben only who was conscious. Will, as usual, had his sharp eyes fixed on everything at once and was absorbed in considering how he should turn things to his own advantage, and of what Francis was thinking no one could tell, but very quickly Judith had fastened her personality upon all of them and was taking the lead.

So they talked, the background of the fading evening, the faintly rustling trees, the moving people, voices, music forcing from all of them a gentle comfort and well-being that drew them all together in general friendliness. In after days these voices of the lost and ghostly past of this moment would visit them again.

For Judith, as she sat perched on the bole of the tree, a cloak over her shoulders, her shoes shining in the dusk, it seemed to her, as it had seemed to her a thousand times already, that life was at this very moment beginning. She was so happy that she should have been afraid, but she was never afraid when she was happy.

'Reuben, tell us about France. Did you see the King and Queen?'

But Reuben had very little to tell about France. Something about Lourdes, where there was a castle on a rock; state prisoners were sent there by lettres de cachet. Here they died of despair and misery. At Pau he had been shown the cradle of Henry IV., which was the shell of a tortoise. At Bordeaux he had seen Dauberval the famous dancer. He had visited Versailles and had seen men walking in rags of the direst destitution. There was a wonderful botanical garden there. In the Castle at Chambord he had been shown the room where Marshal Saxe had died. It was said that he had been run through the heart by the Prince of Conti in a duel. And so on. And so on. Little things, unalive, related by him in his shy, hesitating voice so that, Will thought impatiently, he turned everything to dullness. But how could it be other? How could he, in this quiet homely comfortable scene, tell them of the things that had been burning in his heart--the filth, oppression, cruelty, suffering? Tell them of the man whom he had seen in Tours beaten to death before his eyes, because he had taken a log from the Seigneur's wood, or the two girls ravished by the son of the Lord of the Manor, one of them within a week of her wedding, or of the horde of starved creatures that he came upon on the road outside Paris, scarecrows, their bodies shivering in the bitter wind? The bear again, lodged now close in his heart, he the protector of it; how could he speak of that to Will or Francis Herries? So his voice died away, and he felt the scornfulness of Will's eyes.

'When I am grown,' Judith cried, 'I shall go to France. I shall see the French Queen and dance in Versailles. I shall see India and China and the savages of the West Indies. What will you do, Will?'

He smiled. It was always his way to be courteous and friendly to everyone. Besides nothing in the world interested him so greatly as to think of what he would do when he grew up, a time that was very near to him already.

'I shall build the Herries fortunes,' he said in that voice, a little mocking, a little ironical, so that if anyone objected to what he said he could declare that he had never meant it. 'I shall have a larger fortune than any other Herries, and then, when I have accumulated it, I will tour the globe and return to make another fortune.'

'And will you not marry?' asked Judith greatly interested.

'I shall marry,' said Will gravely, 'and so increase the Herries stock. I shall have six children,' he added mockingly.

To their surprise an angry voice broke on the scene--surprise because it was the voice of Francis, who seemed never to be disturbed nor to wish to join in their childish conversations. But he was disturbed now, and at the sight of his disturbance two fish- shaped clouds above Vicar's Island joined hurriedly together the better for self-protection.

'There, Will; that's your fancy. It's you, yourself. Money-bags, children, more money-bags. God, what ambition!'

It was a sharp interruption and rather frightened all of them. Francis was twenty-seven years of age and so in another world from their own. He had never mingled with them; he was like a ghost to them with his thin handsome face, his cold blue eyes that could on a sudden so strangely burn, the severe suit of grey and silver that he so generally wore. Will might despise him, but there was fear mingled with that scorn.

And now suddenly he was standing, all shadows around him, his voice that had been always so chill and reserved beating with emotion.

'You shall have your money-bags if you want them. What is easier? And getting them you will have nothing. And is that all life is to you? Are you so blind that you can see no ghosts behind the money- bags and ghosts behind them again? Have you only your physical parts to cram food into your swelling belly?'

('I have no swelling belly,' Will thought complacently. 'I have an admirable figure.')

Francis went on, coming close to them, standing over them. His anger was gone as soon as it had come. He spoke now gently.

'When I was small I had a dream of a grand white horse breaking from an icy pool and breasting the rocks, tossing its mane. I have not dreamt that for a long while, but I know that that dream is more real to me than all the chairs and sofas, the mutton-pies and shoe-buckles. How can you not tell that that only is real in this world, that vision of ice and strength breaking it, and if we have not seen that we have seen nothing? Who can tell what is Reality? But this at least I know, that I shall never know happiness until I have seen more than you will ever see, Will, my young brother.'

'Thank you for nothing, Francis,' Will answered, looking up at him and smiling. 'I prefer my money-bags to your white horses.'

'Aye, I know what you think,' Francis broke out passionately. 'What you all think. That I loaf at home and take what my father gives me. . . . Wasting . . . wasting.' His voice broke. 'Our grandfather was so. He was searching all his days and never found anything. . . . Forgive me, I have been absurd. This world itself is absurd to me, but behind it . . . behind it . . . there are Wonders. Forgive me . . . forgive me,' and to their utter surprise he turned and vanished into the trees.

For a moment they were all in a great discomfort. It was so agreeable an evening. They had not the slightest notion of Francis' meaning and they did not wish to spoil his pleasure. Judith, who loved him, would have wished to have run after him, to have taken his arm and comforted him. But to have comforted him for what? She could not tell.

And at that moment, fortunately, the first fireworks broke like a sigh in the darkening heaven. Everyone said 'Ah!' and then 'Ah!' again, just as a hundred years after, and a hundred years after that again, they would sigh with pleasure and strain their eyes upwards. So now they gazed. Everywhere they were gazing, in the little flower-scented streets of Keswick, lovers waiting among the Druid stones, shepherds on Blencathra, watchers by the Watendlath Tarn, children gathered by the cottages in Newlands and under Castle Crag and by the waving reeds of Bassenthwaite.

A star broke into a silver cluster, another into points of blue, another showered drops of gold. In the hills the echo called and answered. For a flash all the faces were lit with a white radiance, the dancers paused in the Meadow, the trees on the Island were fiery and then the darker for their flame.

For Judith it was a moment of sheer ecstasy. She sat, her head back, her hat behind her neck, her legs uptilted, and at every rush as of wings, at every gentle crackle of sound, at every fresh miracle of blue and gold she murmured, her hands tightly clasped. She forgot everything and everyone in that beauty. A star burst, and showers of silver flecked the sky.

She sprang up and ran to the Lake edge. Others were crowding there, and she stood with them, her head bare, gazing upwards. Three rockets burst together, and the sky was scattered with stars. 'Bravo!' 'Bravo!' 'Bravo!' everyone shouted. She clapped her hands; everyone was clapping with her. Again the hills called and answered. Then the pause came, a sudden deep and mysterious silence. The Lake was now infinite. Far, far away, where the hills were packed together, a faint radiance was gathering, the coming moon. Real stars began to twinkle.

Out of this dark lovely world a voice spoke to her: 'It is better in a boat.'

She knew the voice well; in the last two years she had thought of it very often. It was the French boy of Tom Gauntry's.

The lanterns had been lighted and were swaying from the trees. She could see him quite plainly. He was just the same, only taller, in a very grand coat and breeches with gold braid. Under his hat his hair was as black as ever, and his eyes as black. His mouth was just as impudent. She grinned at him, a childish grin.

'Fetch me a boat then.'

What would Sarah think? It would mean perhaps another beating. She had been ordered not to go near the boats until they told her. The thought of being alone with the French boy was most exhilarating. She watched him while, without another word, he was in a boat, had pushed it towards her and, like a grown man, with fine ceremony, handed her in. As she stepped in she glanced about her to see whether any of the family were near. No sign of any of them. She fancied that she heard Sarah's voice, and in a sudden panic pushed from the shore. Many other boats were now moving, and, in the distance, they were singing.

'Quickly,' she cried, with delight, 'or they will see us.'

They floated away: the oars touched very gently the water as though they were whispering to it their pleasure in the evening. As they moved, the shore behind them came out, with all the dark figures, the lights like jolly smiling faces among the trees, and shadows dancing on the Meadow to a thin faint tune that was reedy like wind through wallpaper.

'Where have you been?'

'In London with an uncle.'

'And your mother?' She saw the room, the beautiful naked woman, her arms raised, the diamond buckle shining.

'My mother is dead.'

Dead? And at the moment a firework broke in the sky again, this time a circle of fierce rasping flame that whistled with the hiss of an angry cat.

Dead? Judith shivered. Then for these two years the picture that had transformed her, that had changed her from a thoughtless baby into something, something very different . . . that picture had been for nothing, of a dead woman.

'Why did she die?'

'What is it? I cannot hear.' He had leaned forward on the oars.

'Why did she die?'

'She died of the smallpox.'

'When was it?'

'A year back.' He spoke quite indifferently.

'Did you not care?'

'No. She was unkind to me.'

'She must have been very gracious; a beautiful lady. Her hair was so dark.' Judith shivered again. She wanted to return to the shore, to be with her own people. And surprisingly something else dominated almost every other feeling, that she wanted to kiss the French boy. Hateful, when his mother, his beautiful mother, had for her, at any rate, only this moment died.

'How old are you now?' he asked her.

'Twelve--nearly thirteen.'

'I am sixteen.'

'What are you doing here? Why are you not with your uncle?'

'My uncle is in Carlisle. I am with Gauntry until he fetches me. I like this country. Soon I shall come to live here.' Then he added, laughing: 'Is your hair yet the same colour? I have thought of your hair often.'

Because she wanted to kiss him and because she mustn't, because she was only twelve and he sixteen, she flipped water in his face. He laid down his oars in the boat, moved near to her and roughly kissed her, cheeks, eyes, mouth. She pulled her head free and smacked his face just as she had done two years before. But he did not move. He sat quietly beside her, his hand at her waist. She did not move either. Fires were burning now on Vicar's Island, the set-pieces of the fireworks. A trellis-work of flame ran like live things from tree to tree. All the Lake near the Island glowed, but in the distance it was very dark, with a smoky sheen on it, the first foreshadowing of the moon.

She sat there in perfect happiness. She hoped that he would kiss her again. He did so. Then she returned his kiss.

'I shall be whipped if they know about it.'

'My mother whipped me, but my uncle dare not. When my mother was angry she could kill a man.'

'Was she long ill of the smallpox?'

'No. A month. I was glad when she died. Do you love me?'

'No.'

'Later you will. You are only a baby. In two years I will write you a letter, and perhaps you will come to London.'

'Will you want to marry me?'

'Perhaps. You have such beautiful hair.'

Judith considered. In two years she would be nearly fifteen. She could marry soon then and leave Fell House and live in France.

'If I married you should we live in France?'

'Maybe.'

'Will you have money and a house and horses.'

'Yes. Of course.'

'And we will have children?'

'Yes. Of course.'

'We will have six children, and I want to see the French Queen dance in Versailles.'

'I want to live in this country and have dogs and horses.'

'But will you not take me to France for a visit?'

'Maybe.'

They kissed again. She kissed him like a child, just as she kissed Francis. Then quite suddenly she knew that she must return to the shore. At once, at once! She was afraid of him and of the Lake that seemed dark now because the fireworks had died away.

She told him to take her to the shore.

'No. We will stay here.'

Then he saw another Judith. She stepped from him, and, the boat rocking under them, went to the oars and began to row. She could do anything with a boat or a horse.

'If you leave me now I will never see you again,' he said to her fiercely. She made no answer, and a moment later had scrambled over the boat's edge and had landed.

That was the last she saw of him, standing up very dimly against the dark water.

She ran in to the trees and, quite breathless, tumbled straight into Reuben and his mother.

'I was lost,' she said. 'Where are they?'

She put her hand under Reuben's arm and smiled at him so sweetly that he was enraptured. She looked such a baby with her pretty hat crooked, a little breathless.

'We will go and find them,' he said.

THE FUGITIVE

How does a house first know that changes are coming to it? or does a house know? Are we not attributing to it emotions, fears, agitations that are not its real property? The answer depends on yourself. What you see, hear and feel is for yourself alone.

It is certain in any case that in that winter of 1788-1789 Sarah Herries, just arrived at her fiftieth birthday, knew that some change was at hand. It was the first unhappy winter for her since-- since when? Since she had lived with David at Herries.

Had she cared for wider issues she might have realised that the change was not only here, but in all the civilised world. She did not, however, care for wider issues, had never done so. It had never meant anything to her that the American rebels had thrown tea into Boston Harbour, that old Chatham had the gout, that Fox made an unholy alliance with North, that young Pitt pored over The Wealth of Nations at Cambridge, that men were trampled to death by the horses of noble carriages on the roads outside Paris, that Necker sat up all night biting his thumbs over the impossible business of turning twice two into five. If she had known of these things she would not have cared.

But she did perceive that nothing now went right in the house, that doors swung on their hinges and refused to close, that the Chinese figures in the Blue Room tumbled, through nobody's fault, and were broken to pieces, that the cows gave no milk and the horses went lame.

Twenty years earlier she would have hunted for witches. Now she could only discover that David was becoming an old man, that she herself was fifty and that everyone in her family was at odds. She was a sensible woman, who refused to surrender to superstition, but things were going wrong, and as she lay at night awake in the big four-poster beside David she could hear the wind come whispering down from Skiddaw and must listen, do what she would, to a hundred steps creeping about the stairs and mysterious voices behind the curtain.

But there were unhappy evidences more material than steps and voices.

The first trouble was on the day after the firework evening on the Lake. At dinner Will had suddenly said to Judith:

'Well, miss, you enjoyed, I trust, your pleasant trip in the boat last night.'

No one knew why he said it. He did not care for Judith, but he bore her no especial malice. He did not himself, perhaps, know why he said it. It came no doubt from his deep restless love of power. He was only a boy, but he could turn them any way he wished.

All might even then have been saved had it not been for Judith's implacable honesty.

'You were in a boat?'

'Yes, ma'am.'

'With whom?'

That she would not say: with a gentleman, yes. For a brief period, to see the fireworks better. David beat her. The child said nothing, only afterwards alone with Will she told him that she would not forget his kindness.

'I wanted to see how it would go,' he told her quite honestly. He admired her then, such a little thing, standing on her toes to make herself seem taller. She bore him apparently no grudge.

'It shall not be for long,' she said, nodding her head like a woman of forty. She turned on her toes, pirouetting. 'I'll be a woman very shortly.'

But for the moment, as the consequence of this indiscretion following many others, she was in great danger of the one and only thing that she dreaded--of being sent to Miss Macdonald's Academy at Carlisle.

She had heard something of this school from Margaret and Hetty Worcester of Threlkeld, who attended this place for a time, and she did not like what she had heard. They rose at six winter and summer, ate a piece of bread and then had an hour's schooling. Then there was 'Punishment Hour,' wherein, it seemed, the Misses Macdonald indulged in an orgy of whipping, six stripes of the rod for a small offence, and a 'proper whipping' meant that you fetched the rod, kissed it, and then, before the school, were stripped, 'mounted' on another girl's back and beaten till the blood came. Hetty Worcester gave an admirably detailed description of it. Judith knew well that before she suffered that ignominy there would be a murder done. Not that Hetty thought much of it, for in her home everyone was whipped, the maids and the grooms, the dairy girls and even the tutor. Nevertheless, Judith knew that a week in Miss Macdonald's Academy and she would be a vagrant loose upon the world, and for that she was not yet ready.

While her fate hung thus in the balance the relations between Sarah and Judith developed uncomfortably. Judith bore her sister-in-law no grudge, she knew herself to be a difficult ill-disciplined child, but the difference between their ages was so great and their characters were so ill-suited that, as Judith grew, trouble was bound to come.

Sarah in her heart cared for nothing at the last resort but David. She loved her children, but David was her adoration. She could not endure to see him vexed, even for a moment, and now she realised that Judith was constantly vexing him. He understood her as little as did Sarah. He was too kindly-natured to exercise his authority sufficiently. Judith was for ever escaping him. After all she was not his child, but his half-sister. There were many times when she seemed to him her mother come alive again.

He was a great deal at home now; went to Liverpool very seldom. He trusted the Metcalfes for everything, and soon Will would be in Liverpool. Therefore he was much at Uldale. He loved every stick and stone of it, and he could be seen, his body casting a vast shadow, pottering over the sunny lawn, looking up as a great hurrying cloud flung its shadow over the Fell, examining the horses, watching the maids working in the dairy, going over accounts with Mr. Matcham the agent, or simply leaning on the stone wall and gazing across the white road at the low sprawling shape of Skiddaw.

So, being at home thus, he was always tumbling upon Judith and Francis; Judith, her ringlets flying, riding Barnabas or sliding down the banister of the great staircase, or, in another mood altogether, standing motionless, watching, waiting--what was the child about and why did she look so damnably like her mother?

Or Francis, twenty-eight years of age now, always so slim, elegant, apart, silent--and doing nothing. Twenty-eight and doing nothing! For you could not call reading Cowley or Milton or Shakespeare anything, or roaming aimlessly the countryside (and greeting no one as he went) anything. His father would catch him writing in a book and when he would ask him of it he would close the book and, secretly, deep in himself, would answer the question by saying:

'Nothing, sir.'

Once David lost his temper, and only once.

'I'll not keep you here idling.'

An hour later Francis came down the stairs in his riding-coat, Andrew the boy carrying his valise. He was going away, and David knew that it was for ever. David found then how deeply he loved him. Afterwards he pleaded with him: why were they drifting so far apart? Could they not open their hearts to one another? And Francis answered: 'Oh, sir, would to God I could! Something silences me. I will work, father, anywhere you place me . . . in your Keswick office . . . I will do all I can.'

What an echo of ghosts was here! For had not David's father once, in the dead years, said the same? For a moment Francis Herries the Elder stood there, that same ironical twist to his lip that his grandson had.

So Francis went to work in the Keswick office, and he was useless. All he cared for was to read poetry and philosophy. Poetry and philosophy! So, loving one another deeply, they drifted farther and farther apart.

But Judith was a greater mystery for poor David, who would sit back in his arm-chair before the fire, his legs spread, his great bulk at ease, but his honest friendly face twisted with perplexity.

He wanted to do what was right by the child. She was his own father's daughter; but the truth was that neither he nor Sarah felt that she had anything to do with him at all. At one moment she was a child of her proper age, at another almost a woman, ordering the men and maids in the place as though she commanded it. She had a good heart, he could tell that, but when she couldn't get her own way she was a devil, not raging nor crying but her sharp, pale, little face cold and savage under her red hair. And he sometimes thought that she hated Sarah. They didn't forbid Gauntry's to her any more. What was the use? She would simply go there, and one day, if they were not careful, she would never come back, and what a scandal that would be! Besides, there was no harm in little Gauntry, and he loved the child like his own daughter.

So David went over all his perplexities, feeling perhaps, as Sarah did, that changes were coming. When things were too difficult for him he would ride over to Worcester's or Osmaston's and play cards all night or get drunk and be carried up to bed.

Meanwhile he clung to Sarah, his wife, ever more deeply. She was his real friend, had always been. He loved Deborah, his daughter, but in his heart found her a little dull; he was a little afraid of Will, who always knew better than he himself did; Francis, whom he loved best of his children, was a mystery. So he stayed with Sarah and was only truly happy when she was by.

In March of the new year they decided that Judith should pay a visit to the Sunwoods in Cockermouth. Maybe they would manage her. Judith was very happy to go. She was very happy to go, but never dreamt before going that when she was there she would be so happy to stay.

She had visited a number of times at the little house, but had had no notion that it would suit her so perfectly to live in it. It was the very size that she liked, small, compact, comfortable. Everything in it went on under her very nose; she could have her fingers in every pie, in Deborah's cooking and preserving, sewing and cleaning, in the dealings with the pig, in all the little affairs of the town, the gossip, the tea-parties, the expeditions on fine days, the cosy conferences round the fire on wet ones. In five minutes she had Mr. Sunwood entirely under her control, he would read his sermons to her, she would listen to his accounts of his Quadrille parties, enjoy by proxy the first piece of roasted swan that he had tasted at a grand party at the Castle, and even advise him as to the right time to take a good dose of rhubarb.

But the element that made this visit so enchanting was her quite unexpected friendship with Deborah. Deborah was nearly sixty-six years of age and Judith only fourteen, yet the difference in their ages seemed to make no division between them at all. Judith was hungering for affection with all the ardour and excitement of her temperament. She was separated from Francis and also (although of this she tried to prevent herself thinking) from Georges, the French boy. So she was ready, in any case, to throw herself upon Deborah and

Reuben. But she soon discovered that she had never been brought into contact before with anyone at all like this stout, soft-eyed, soft-voiced, gentle-hearted woman. The people whom she had hitherto known had not (save for Reuben, and he had been two years away) been gentle-hearted--not Gauntry, nor Sarah, nor Will, nor even Francis.

The first thing that drew her to Deborah was that Deborah let her do anything that she wished, and the second thing was that Deborah told her so much that was new and exciting about her father.

They sat together beside the fire, Deborah sewing and Judith leaning forward, her chin cupped in her hands, and Deborah recovered for the child her own childhood. This gave Deborah herself a surprising happiness and pleasure. No one in her own family had asked her questions about those days. It was her husband's belief that he had rescued her from some wild sort of savagery and the less said about it the better, and her sons had never shown any curiosity. But this strange child with her ardent, eager, impetuous spirit brought her father back to her as though he were with them in the room. HER father! THEIR father! And at the thought that they had, both of them, she nearing the end of her life, the child only beginning hers, the same father, a bond of affection was formed and remained. She soon discovered that she herself loved to recall that long-ago time, the wild Borrowdale valley, so cut-off and remote, the old house rocking to every wind, the death of her mother and her own fear at being left alone with her father, although she loved him. Her devotion to her brother David, such a wonderful boy, the strongest boy and man in the valley (different, she was forced to confess, from the stout, rather lazy monarch of Uldale), the old witch, Mrs. Wilson, who lived with them and was drowned in the Derwent by the villagers, her own lonely thoughts, love of natural things, shyness--then the ball in Keswick and the little clergyman coming to sit beside her and make love to her, her father's strange marriage to Judith's mother, and then the unhappiness of that odd woman, her flight, her father's loneliness and madness and search, and always the tumbledown house and the isolated valley behind and through it all.

She let Judith ask as many questions as she wished and answered all that she asked. Judith recovered the personalities of her father and mother as she never had done before. They became alive to her. She saw Francis, her father, the scar marring his face, tumbling the villagers down the stairs after the wedding. She saw Mirabell, her mother (it was part of her oddness that she should have a man's name), breaking her heart because the man she had loved had been murdered under her eyes in Carlisle. She saw Francis, her father, setting out in search of her, wandering over England looking for her, at last capturing her again, and then the two of them dying together in that lonely house.

Something grew in her as these two ghosts were drawn to her side. HER ghosts and only hers. No one alive in the world had the right to both of them as she had. She was never, after this, to lose the fancy that all her life long there were three of them moving about together through the world.

'Oh, if but I had been there,' she cried. 'I could have made them so happy!'

And Deborah, in her turn, recovering thus her young days, felt her heart warm in her for her dear, lost father. Only she and David in all the world thought of him any more--and now this child. How could she but love her?

Judith was easy enough to love in such a case. She asked nothing better than to love and be loved in return: it was only when someone was an enemy, or she thought was an enemy, that her fierce hostility flamed out. Even then she could be generous and large-hearted. She wished Will no evil because he had betrayed her about the evening on the Lake. She could not be mean nor spiteful about little things.

They were both large-hearted, she and Deborah.

Then something more drew them together. Judith discovered that Deborah was very unhappy. For eight months she had had no word from her son Humphrey. Mr. Sunwood pooh-poohed the whole business. The boy would write when he had leisure; the Post was a very uncertain affair; he, himself, would soon make a journey to London and see the boy.

But none of this could comfort Deborah. They had heard nothing, either, from his master. The last news had been a year ago. At first the boy had written frequently. He had been last home a year and a half ago and had been well and merry, but, even at that, she had fancied that he had said too little about his work. It was all his pleasure, his visits to Vauxhall, how he had seen the good King and Queen, been to a picnic in Twickenham, travelled down the river with the Pomfret Herries, and so on, and so on. But of his work very little. And that was a year and a half ago.

As Judith listened to all this her impatience leapt into flame. But why didn't someone go to London? Why didn't Mr. Sunwood or Reuben? She would go herself. Why should not she and Deborah go? It was a shame to leave it in this uncertainty. . . . She jumped up and ran about the room, tossing her red ringlets in the air.

But Deborah, smiling, shook her head. It wasn't so easy to go to London, a very long journey. Mr. Sunwood felt no alarm, why should she? Reuben had his work at Mr. Stele's the solicitor's. Oh, it was all right. She was sure that all was well. Humphrey was such a good boy. Any day there would be a letter. And she would look across the room at the little bottle-green window and shake her head, and her eyes would swim in tears.

So Judith went to Reuben. Reuben was changed by his two years in France, more remote. He was tidier, but alas! little cleaner. It was not at that time important that you should be clean, and Judith was peculiar in wishing for cleanliness. When Mr. Sunwood came in from attending to the pig he was not very clean and would sit down to his dinner without thinking of it. But Reuben's linen, his small-clothes, oh, they wanted a deal of attention! His hair was not brushed and fell untidily about his shoulders. His shoes were often caked with mud. In his attic there was always a close stuffy smell, terrible untidiness, his bed where he used to lie, his hands behind his head, looking up at the attic roof, staring and thinking, sadly tumbled. Judith never came into the room but she longed to set about it with a scrubbing brush and a pail of water. But she loved him none the less, his fat loose body, his kindly, large, wondering eyes. He was generous and soft-hearted like his mother, but so often like something that had lost its way. He moved at times as though he were blind. He was a dreamer like Francis, but what an incongruous comparison he made with that slim, elegant, severe figure! And he had told her once that if he were afraid of anyone in the world it was of Francis.

Then one evening she came up to his attic and found him lying on his bed, his coat off, his shoes off, his stockings half-way down his legs, and he was talking to himself, while a long drunken candle guttered on a chair beside the bed.

She herself held a candle. She stood for a moment listening to him:

'Oh, Lord! Oh, Lord!' he was saying, 'I am a sinner. I have no courage in my heart. I am a poor wretch. Oh, damnation! Damnation! I long in my heart after women and go the way I should not! Oh, Lord, Lord! . . .'

She stopped this peroration by crying in a very solemn voice: 'I am the Devil and have come for your soul, O Reuben!' and he, hearing her, jumped from the bed and stood blinking at her like an owl.

'Do you truly long after women?' she asked him a little later, when they were both sitting on the bed close together, the candles throwing great shadowy shapes on the wall.

'Yes, I do.'

'Well, then, you should marry.' She nodded her head, swinging her little legs and wishing for the thousand-thousandth time that they were longer.

'No woman would have me.'

'No, not while you are so untidy in your clothes. Why don't you brush your hair and have a new ribbon for it? And there is a hole in your stocking.'

'I hate Mr. Stele and his office,' he said suddenly. 'I was so happy the day I saw the bear. That was a sign, and I did not follow it.'

'They sent you away to France,' she said, 'because of the bear.'

'Yes.' He nodded his head. 'And one day in the road beyond Tours-- a hot glaring day--I saw Jesus Christ standing there. He stood right in my path; the sun was shining in His hair. He looked at me so kindly and said: "Reuben, feed my Lambs." And I have done nothing, nothing.'

'For how long did He stay there?' she asked. She had a very practical mind and no sense of religion at all. She could not help that. She wished to have it, but she found it very difficult to believe in anything that she did not see.

Reuben pulled up his stockings. He was always aware that she disliked his untidiness. She herself looked so neat now in her little orange hoop and brown shoes.

'He did not stay long,' Reuben sighed. 'It was the second time. He came to me once at St. Bees.' He put his hand timidly and took one of hers.

'Judith,' he said. 'You are so brave. Show me what to do.'

'Yes, I will show you,' she answered, coming close to him. 'Go to London and see Humphrey.' She felt him tremble.

'I dream about Humphrey,' he answered her, 'every night. I know that he is in great trouble. One of us always knows when the other is in trouble. I know that mother also is grieving, but I am afraid to go to London. I am afraid of everything. I would not know how to behave in London nor what to do. They would all laugh at me, and I cannot bear to be mocked. London is so vast, and there is so much noise there. . . .' He broke off, plucking with his fingers at his clothes.

'No, but you must go,' she answered. 'I will never speak to you again if you do not. It is your duty to your mother. Do you love me, Reuben?'

'Of course.'

'Then go to London or I will never see you again.'

She began then eagerly to speak of what he would do and just where he should go. She seemed to know everything about London, although she had never been there. His cheeks kindled, there was light in his eyes. Yes, he would go. He would ride into Kendal and take the coach there. He would speak to his father. . . . And then he shrank back. But all the people, so many strangers, the lighted streets, he would be lost.

'Well, if you do not go, I am finished with you.'

She stood in the middle of the floor, her head up, scorning him. And at that moment some of her strength entered into him, entered into him never to leave him again. He went to the window and looked out across the darkness. Then he looked back into the lighted room and saw her standing there. He cried out in a kind of frenzy:

'I'll go! I'll go! I'll go!'

How often in other places, in later times, he remembered that scene! And then she danced about the room like a mad thing, caught his hands and made him dance too. She ended by tying his hair with a new ribbon and finding another pair of stockings for him. She hoped that he would find a woman in London to make him happy, and she also hoped that he would not, because she wanted to have him all to herself.

Howbeit, events moved faster than Reuben. Before he could speak to either his mother or his father something very terrible occurred.

Years and years afterwards Judith would remember that March afternoon and its sudden storm sweeping her off her feet into an adventure that would have its consequences for all her life.

She and Deborah had been shopping in the town. It was market-day and proper March, with a sky that was here pale green, there pale blue, while little busy clouds like torn sheets of grey paper flew and scattered under cross tugs of wind. The sky was swept with streams of light that flooded out into glory, throwing sheets of pale silver colour on to field and wood.

It was one of those days when everyone in the little town was conscious of the near neighbourhood both of the mountains and the sea. The wind had begun with little anticipatory gusts, as though it were trying its forces to see whether they were strong and sound, then, as everything went well, it increased its power, began to find pride in its strength, and soon, doubtless, would be bellowing with vainglory. You could see in your mind's eye Ennerdale, that was not far away, ruffling into little flakes of foam, its waters chocolate-coloured, while the sky above the hills was all busy with its traffic, sending clouds hither and thither, flashing light now on, now off, under order of the March gale. All the hills, black and grim, gathered like conspirators close about the waters. On the other side of the town there was the sea, the wind tugging at St. Bees Head, and all the shipping tossing maliciously in Whitehaven Bay.

The booths of the market were creaking and cracking, cloths blowing about, the pedlar forced to cover his wares, ropes straining, doors rattling, everyone clinging to their hats and wigs.

Then with a shriek of whistling fun the wind and the rain came, driving straight up the street, sweeping the trestles and boards away, carrying the whole town with it as though it would toss it into Ennerdale.

Judith and Deborah went scurrying home, hats, wigs, pieces of cloth, fragments of wood, dogs, cats, shrill voices, laughter, all hurrying through the air, it seemed, with them.

Safe in the little house again, panting for breath, wet, blown, laughing, they looked about them, while the rain rattled on the windows crossly because they had escaped it. They stared under wet eyelashes about them, and the first thing that Judith saw was a letter, lying innocently on the table: it was addressed 'Miss Judith Herries.'

She snapped it up.

'A letter?' asked Deborah.

'Yes.'

'From Uldale, I warrant.'

'Yes,' said Judith. It was not a lie because she had not yet looked at it. It lay warm in her wet hand. She thought it would be from Sarah, summoning her home. Who had left it there? Had David perhaps ridden over, or Francis? It might be that they would spend the night. But she wouldn't go back to Uldale. She was too happy where she was. She wouldn't go back until she had seen Reuben safely away to London. . . . She had got thus far. She was climbing the stair to her room. She saw what it was. It was from Georges Paris. He was in Cockermouth. He asked her to meet him in the parlour of the 'Greyhound,' five o'clock that evening. He would wait until six.

Her first thought was of his impertinence, then that he should have the spunk to leave the letter at her very door where anyone might read it, then that she wouldn't go, nothing should induce her, then that she would greatly like to see him again just to tell him what she thought of him, then that she would take Reuben with her (it would be so amusing to see Georges' face of disappointment), then that this would be the first time of seeing him since the evening on the Lake, then that she would not go but would send a letter by Reuben, then that perhaps she WOULD go just to see what he was like now. . . .

By this time she was in her room and laughing at the thought of an adventure. For it WAS an adventure. Georges was always an adventure. She would wear her orange hoop. . . . But in this weather with the streets swimming in water! She heard the maid calling her to dinner. Three o'clock. There would be plenty of time before five. . . .

By the end of the meal she was uneasy. She was always uneasy when she thought of Georges. She determined that she would take Reuben with her.

Behind the parlour there was a little room with nothing much in it but a large yellow globe, a powder-stand and a shaving-table. It could be turned into a guest-room at a crisis. She pulled Reuben in there after her. The little windows looked out on to a narrow crooked path that ran through fields to a shaggy wood, on fine days a pleasant prospect, but this afternoon you could see nothing but the storm that swung in sheets of rain across the scene, the drops on the panes in the windows rattling like little pellets from a shot-gun. From a side-door of this room there was a short passage and another door opening on to the field.

When she had Reuben in the room with her, she suddenly thought--no, after all, she would not tell him. Why should she not go alone? Georges could not harm her. They would be in a public place. She was not afraid to smack his face again if need be. She was not afraid of Georges nor of anyone. So when she saw Reuben, still wiping his last draught of ale from his mouth and smiling in that uncertain way that he had when he was not sure how she was going to use him next, she burst out laughing.

'Reuben--' she said, and then she paused.

'Yes,' he said obediently.

'It's raining.'

'Yes,' he said again, wondering.

'But I am going out into it.'

He said nothing.

'And no one is to know. I shall go by this door.'

He looked at her in perplexity. She could always do as she liked with him, but after all she was but a child. Her small stature and something innocent in her wide-open eager eyes always made her younger than her age, just as the resolved dominating lines about her mouth made her older. Nevertheless, she was young to be going out into the town alone, and in this weather, and what could she be going for but to see a man?

At the thought his heart beat thickly, his stout cheeks coloured, he plucked at his coat.

'You shall not go alone,' he said. 'I shall accompany you.'

'Oh no, you will not!' she answered laughing. 'You shall stay here and keep them quiet. If they ask where I am you shall say I am busy working--and so I shall be.'

'Busied at what?'

She stood on her toes, pulled his head down, and kissed him.

'Never you mind. I am your aunt.'

'I shall accompany you,' he said firmly.

She looked at him. Would it be better perhaps, after all, that he should? She was NOT safe with Master Georges. She remembered a moment in the boat when, in an instant, at a touch of his hand, she had been warned.

Many visits to Stone Ends had acquainted her with life. Children were not children for long in those days. SHOULD she take Reuben with her? And it would tease Georges so that he should be there. And Reuben was so strong, so safe, so devoted. A sudden impulse of great affection for him, one of those impulses that were often all through her life to rise in her, straight, unalloyed, from her heart, influenced her now. She put her hand on his arm.

As she did so they both heard, quite clearly through the slashing and angry rain, a rap on the window. Her hand tightened on his arm and they turned. The rap came again, urgent, imperative. They stared and at first could see nothing. In any case there would have been only a pale, fading light, but now with the storm all was darkness. Reuben hurried to the window and pressing his face against the pane stared out. He could see a shadowy form.

'There is someone there,' he whispered to Judith, then, hurrying through the little passage, opened the outer door. The wind almost blew the door to, but holding it firmly he looked out.

'Who's there?' he called softly.

A moment later his fingers were grasped by a cold hand, he had been drawn back into the passage, a figure soaking with wet was pressed close to him, and his brother Humphrey's voice was in his ear, nay, at his very heart.

'Reuben . . . for God's sake--no sound. . . .'

'Humphrey!'

'Yes. Is there anyone there?'

'Only Judith.'

But Judith, hearing the whispering voices, had come into the passage. Humphrey, pushing past them, had peered into the little room, seen that there was no one there, hastened to the door and bolted it, then turned to them both:

'No one must know. Not father nor mother. No one. Get me something to eat. Oh, God, I am so weary!'

He sank into the only chair in the room, murmuring again, 'Food. Food, and secretly.'

Reuben didn't question. It was, as it always was with his brother, as though this were part of himself, soaked with rain, fugitive, in some frantic plight, hiding from the world. He moved as though hurrying to save himself, undid the bolt and was gone.

Judith bolted the door again. Her heart was moved at once to eager pity and a desire to help. When she had last seen Humphrey he had been so young, so handsome, so self-confident, so sure of himself and his ability to manage any situation in life; now another man was there, utterly weary, exhausted, his head back, the water dripping from the capes of his coat, his hair long and matted, his face pale, haggard, and his eyes that had been so gay and happy now restless, hunted, brimming with despair.

He seemed to her to be years older, older than himself, older than Reuben, and he seemed, beyond that, to be mysterious, a man from some world that she had never before realised, a man who should, by right, speak to her in a strange language.

He wasted no time, did not ask her why she was there, did not consider her except as an agent of assistance for him.

'I have been an age outside. I could not see clearly who was in the room. I had to risk something. Thank God, it was Reuben!'

His words came in gasps. His hands moved ceaselessly.

'I've had no food for two days. I have tramped from Kendal. . . .'

She was intensely practical, as she always was in a crisis. 'You must take off your coat. It is dripping. You must have dry things.'

He got up from the chair and she helped him to take off the shabby soiled riding-coat. His body was trembling; he was wet through to the skin. The thing that moved her most was that his eyes were never still, searching the globe, the powder-stand, the dull green portrait of some old Sunwood ancestor, the dark bulging window against whose panes the rain, falling now gently, pressed.

She did not stop to ask him why he was there, nor what catastrophe had plunged him into this disaster, but his fear infected her. She was not in the least afraid, but she listened, as he did, to any outside sound. She realised that whatever else happened his mother must not now see him. She did not know the reason, but she understood that he was bitterly ashamed to see his mother, that, beyond any other possible disaster, that was the one he dreaded.

Her sense of this made him still more mysterious to her and touched her heart yet more deeply. Towards anyone pursued she was always to be sympathetic, although there was some true Herries in her that placed her also on the side of justice. In herself she was to be always both pursued and pursuer.

Reuben scratched on the door and came in, not clumsy nor shy any more, but swift, silent, efficient. He was acting for the stronger part of himself. He closed the door very gently behind him, bolted it softly. He had half a cold mutton-pie, bread, cheese, ale.

Humphrey drew to the little table, devoured the food frantically. He seemed just then like an animal, his ears pricked, his eyes everywhere, his hand curved close about the meat.

'Mother is with father,' Reuben whispered, 'listening to his sermon.'

'He is wet to the skin,' Judith answered. 'He must change everything.'

Reuben went out again. She stood by the door, letting him finish his food. Life was like this. She had seen it already countless times. Mrs. Osmaston's maid had stolen stockings, had fled and been caught in Keswick, jailed there; a pedlar had murdered a woman in Keswick for a shilling, he had been chased by a crowd of men and boys to Threlkeld and stoned there to death. . . .

'Yes,' said Humphrey, speaking quite clearly out of the half-light illumined only by one blowing candle. 'And now I must get to the coast. I am so weary. God, if I could sleep for twelve hours.'

'What is it?' she asked. 'What has happened?'

His face, pale, drawn, the hair shaggy on his forehead, looked up at her. She felt as though he were her child.

'I killed a man in London. Over cards.'

'Have you any money?' she asked him.

'Nothing--now. It is all gone.'

She came over to him and stroked his hair back from his forehead. With a gesture of infinite weariness he leaned his head, wet with rain as it was, back against her childish breast.

'I shall sleep,' he murmured. 'How soft your hand is!'

Reuben knocked; she unbolted the door. He came in with clothes on his arm. At once, as though a desperate hurry were now his accustomed state, Humphrey jumped up and stripped. Judith helped him. This was no time for maidenly modesty, and she had seen many a man naked before.

When he was finished he sat there holding Reuben's hand in his. The three of them began a quick whispered conversation. On the one thing he was determined, that his father and mother shouldn't know. Nothing would shake him in that. He told them very little of what had happened. Things had been going badly for a long while. Some fierce love-affair he had had with Nancy Bone: Pomfret had forbidden him the house. After that Judith had a picture of some dark underground London, gutters running with water, sudden flares of light, gambling, little rooms in crooked inns, life by the river, curious interludes of some great man like Mr. Fox or Mr. Burke, a struggle up again to larger rooms, then down again, fights in that same gutter, swinging shop-signs, a narrow street crowded with carriages, a woman looking from a window, a fight, some fat man with a wound in his breast, and all the while it seemed to be rain and fog. . . . She was to have this queer picture of London for years until the reality gave her another one.

But the one thing that stood out clearly was that he must escape from England. Some port . . . Whitehaven. . . . It was then that she had her idea. With a flash of inspiration she thought of Georges Paris. She had long known that young Georges with other friends of Gauntry's had dealings with some sort of traffic on the Cumberland coast. Some kind of smuggling perhaps. She had been too much of a child for them to take her into any kind of confidence, but her last time at Stone Ends there had been a Captain Barnett, a thin green-faced man like a nettle, who had praised young Georges for his enterprise in some Whitehaven or St. Bees expedition.

She did not doubt but that that was what brought Georges into Cockermouth this afternoon. He would do anything for her; he should help to get Humphrey out of the country. Once again in a moment she took the situation into her hands. She acknowledged without a tremor to Reuben that it had been this Georges Paris whom she had been going to meet. Was he to be trusted? Of course, he was to be trusted. He was her friend. She had known him for years. He would do anything that she told him. They followed her. What else? Something had to be done at once. They must not stay in this house. There was no other plan.

Only Reuben said one thing that often afterwards she was to remember: 'If he does this for you, are you under some obligation to him?'

Feverishly eager to be off, as she always was when she had a plan, she tossed her head. She did not even answer, but almost pushed them both in front of her, through the little passage and out of the door.

That brief journey from the house to the 'Greyhound' was the most exciting thing that had yet happened in her life. She was in charge of the expedition; the men followed meekly. That sense of power, the strongest sense in her, drove her like a charm. Without her, Humphrey, all of them, would have been lost. Now she would direct the affair like God Himself. The rain had ceased; the little cobbled streets were gloomy and deserted. They left Humphrey in the shadow of the yard of the inn and went quickly up the wooden staircase to the parlour. No one was about. In the parlour, a small panelled room, a little sea-coal fire was smoking and two candles guttering. Someone came forward. It was Georges, almost hidden in the capes of his riding-coat. She saw at once that he was angry because she was not alone. She felt herself forty years of age at least as she took his hand, introduced Reuben. He had never seen her so beautiful. Indeed he had never thought her beautiful, only strange, unusual, in some antagonistic way appealing to his senses. Now, in the half-lit smoky room, in all her colour, her small hat with a feather, her hair, her little face ivory-coloured and in expression mischievous, kindly, proud, all together, she seemed to him for the first time a woman. He put his riding-whip on the table, clasped his hands behind him. He longed to kiss her. Who was this big clumsy oaf of a fellow with her?

Very quickly Judith explained, keeping him greatly at a distance, very lofty, commanding rather than requesting.

And she saw, a moment later, that he found an opportunity in all this. It was the first real request that she had ever made of him. He asked no questions about Humphrey. A relation of hers in distress . . . He must get to sea swiftly and quietly . . . Had he a friend? . . . Was there a boat? . . .

By chance he had a friend. He paused and looked at her oddly.

'If I do this for you--?' he broke off.

They had both, concerned in their own personal drama, quite forgotten Reuben.

He forced her eyes. She would not be browbeaten by him, so stared proudly back at him, at his dark eyes, black hair, thin, proud, restless face.

She said nothing. He, as though satisfied, nodded his head.

'Where is the gentleman?'

They passed to the staircase. As they went down she whispered to Reuben: 'Have you any money?' He nodded his head: 'I had thought of that.'

They found Humphrey in a panic of nervous anxiety. How strange it was to Judith to see what circumstances could do to a man! He had been so easy, gay-hearted, confident. Her whole being ached for him. She would have liked to go with him, share his adventure wherever it might be, see that he was not cold, hungry, lonely. As they hurried down a dark side-street, stumbling over gutters, holes in the road, refuse, she put out a hand and caught his. For a moment she held it, hot, dry, quivering. . . .

They stopped before a door below the pavement; a little flight of steps went down to it. Georges went ahead of them and knocked. While they waited, a man, swinging a lantern, passed them. He did not look at them, but Judith felt as though it were the whole town staring. Then the door opened a little way, a head peered out, some words were exchanged. They all went in. The place was a large cellar, a lantern hanging from a hook, some farming implements in corners, a pile of hay, and, seated on an overturned barrel, a man of an enormous corpulency. His coat was open at the neck to allow room for his three chins. His cheeks were purple above a yellow beard and his nose had been slightly flattened on one side in some fight, but his eyes were large, clear and merry. His hand was a roll of beef and his thighs so huge that it was a wonder any breeches could ever contain them. He rose to receive them, and standing, his legs wide, he was like a vast amiable monster at home in its cavern. He smelt of oil, fish and whisky, but it was plain that he admired Judith immediately, hanging over her with a merry possessive look as though at any moment he would pick her up and slip her into his deep coat-pocket.

It was clear also that he knew young Georges Paris very well and understood immediately what was wanted. He never looked at Humphrey, who had slipped into the shadow, nor addressed a word to him. His name, it seemed, was Captain Wix. His voice was deep, rolling, and had the same kindliness as his eyes. Those eyes scarcely left Judith. Straddling on his legs he kept looking at her while Georges quickly whispered. He nodded his head several times, took a great chequered handkerchief from his pocket and blew a blast on his nose.

'It will be good enough for charges,' he rumbled to Georges.

Judith, who was adoring this adventure, the dark close cellar, the straw, the swinging lantern, and the sense of having arranged the whole affair, spoke then and said that they had money with them.

'Keep it, lady,' growled Captain Wix. ''Tis no matter.' He became gallant and was inexpressibly comical. 'I have a ship,' he informed her, 'like a daisy. An you come for a trip in her you shall be as safe and trim as in your mama's parlour. I'll have the cabin done up special for you.' He bent towards her, beamed at her with the greatest kindliness: 'Now what do you say to a piece of fine lace? A present from a friend who knows the coast of France like his own hand. What do you say now to a little trip?'

But here Georges intervened. He drew the gigantic creature aside, speaking to him very seriously rather as a king speaks to his subject. The matter, it seemed, was concluded. They were to leave Humphrey in Captain Wix's charge.

Reuben went to his brother. When he rejoined them there were tears on his cheeks. Judith then kissed Humphrey.

He spoke with sudden desperation. 'My mother mustn't know. . . . I will beat them yet. . . .' Then fiercely, catching her hand: 'There's no God. . . . Naught but injustice, no mercy. . . . I shall find my way yet.'

Captain Wix kissed her hand.

When she went up the little steps again with Georges she felt suddenly helpless, very tired, six years old, and so cross with him that she did not thank him, only said 'Good night' quickly and walked up the street.

Georges, before he went downstairs again, looked after her, smiling. He felt very important, very wise, a ruler of men.

DEATH OF DAVID

The July heat bathed the little town in its ardour, but breezes, stealing from the Lake, from the higher woods, from Skiddaw forest and Blencathra shallows, carried the scent of flowers everywhere. The town slept. Some sheep wandered dreamily down Main Street, the dust blew in little spirals between the hedges toward Crosthwaite Church, the post-chaise waited outside the 'Royal Oak,' two young men, with nothing whatever to do, lounged up against the wall of Mr. Crosthwaite's Museum. A little way up the street a small group waited for the arrival of the Good Intent post-coach from Kendal. It was five minutes past four of the afternoon, and nine out of every ten of Keswick's citizens were still discussing their good liquor and digesting the day's dinner.

Francis Herries came down the sunny street, riding from Penrith. He was, in this July of 1789, twenty-nine years of age and as handsome a bachelor as the counties of Cumberland and Westmorland contained. He was, however, as awe-inspiring as handsome. No young lady anywhere, not even the pretty daughters of Mrs. Herring of Bassenthwaite, reputed the most daring young women in the whole of the North of England, had ever attempted a flirtation. He was immensely clever, they said, was for ever reading. It was true in any case that he had no close friend--now, riding down Main Street, he seemed alone with his own shadow.

He may have been half asleep, may have been deeply lost in some speculation, when he felt a hand laid on his bridle. He looked down and saw little Mr. Summerson the Surgeon, short, stout, very gay in a purple coat, looking up at him.

'Have you heard the news, Mr. Herries?' he asked.

'No,' answered Francis. 'What news?'

'The Bastille in Paris has fallen.'

Francis straightened himself. 'The Bastille--?'

'Yes, sir. Fallen to the Revolutionaries. I know no more. I had it from Mr. Jobling, who has just ridden in from Kendal. The news is quite certain.'

Francis smiled. 'Thank God, sir. Thank God. This means a new world.'

Little Mr. Summerson looked as though he were not so sure, but Francis did not wait to hear what he had to say. His heart triumphant, as though it were by his own agency that this great deed had been brought about, he passed along the road to Bassenthwaite now like a conqueror.

The Bastille fallen! The Bastille fallen! It must be true. Summerson had been certain of it, and if it were indeed so, then all the secret wishes of his heart were gratified. Secret indeed, for there had been no one in whom he could confide. The secret history of his mind had been born with him perhaps; he had always, to his own thinking, been different from all the others, but its first real mature food had been the treatise of Helvetius on 'Mind' and 'The System of Nature' of Holbach. Holbach's work especially had seemed to explain the whole of life to him; its system of metaphysics had exactly suited his speculative untrusting nature, his instinctive cynicism, and its eloquent ardour for physical science had become his ardour also.

Voltaire's scepticism and good sense, the absence of all fanaticism and mysticism had carried him yet farther. He delighted in his clear ideas, his ironical banter, and his determination to make the world a wiser place so that ultimately it might become a better one.

His education had then been completed by the influence of Rousseau. The Contrat Social seemed to him the Bible of the new world. This sentence of Rousseau's, 'The moment the Government usurps the sovereignty, the social compact is broken, and all the simple citizens regaining by right their natural liberty are forced, but not morally obliged, to obey,' became his gospel.

Had his youth been spent in a larger and more varied society much of the effects of these doctrines might have been worn away in contact with older and more experienced minds. But there had been few with whom he could discuss anything. His nature was in any case reserved; some inherent shyness forbade confidences; his father had views utterly divorced from these; his father was conservative absolutely in religion, politics, agriculture, everything. Will's mind was quite selfish and practical, his mother was not interested in ideas. Judith was only a child.

He made no friends among the gentlemen of the neighbourhood; there were very few gentlemen to make friends with. He knew that had any of them seen into his mind they would have regarded him as traitor to everything in which they believed.

At Penrith there was a certain Mr. Frederick Moore, an elderly man, a retired Army officer, who thought as he did, but went much farther. Mr. Moore was, indeed, a fanatic, and in that displeased the reasonableness of Francis' mind, a strange man, solitary, embittered, intensely dogmatic. But he lent Francis books and pamphlets, and they had many talks together.

Rousseau was Mr. Moore's god, and he very quickly became Francis' also. They would neither of them see that Rousseau himself recoiled from many of his own opinions and conclusions. Passionately they out-Rousseaued Rousseau. They disregarded such sentences as: 'If there were a people of gods, they would govern themselves as a democracy. So perfect a form of government is not suited for men' and 'The best and most natural order is, that the wise should govern the multitude, provided that one is sure that they govern it for the profit of the multitude and not for their own.'

But Francis, although he thought continually about Government, had only the simplest notions of the matter. Had he been a fanatic like Mr. Moore he would have gone farther, but just as his nature held him back from extravagance so also it prevented inspiration. He felt that he was fortunate that he was born to be a citizen of a new world, but in cruel fact he was neither the child of the old world of reason nor of the new world of feeling. He had the misfortune to sympathise deeply with the unhappiness of a vast multitude of human beings, who were only now growing conscious of their rights, but he was an aristocrat by instinct although a democrat by reason--and was too reserved, too lonely, too self- suspicious to venture into any kind of demonstrative action.

He had followed, as well as news-sheets, pamphlets, books, and Mr. Moore permitted him, every movement in France--the doctrines of the Economists, who contended for the inviolability of private property, the shameful consequences of the stupid despotism of Louis XV., the iniquitous taxes, the brutalities of the upper class, the exemption of the nobles from taxation, Necker's poor attempts at reform in 1780, the monstrous sale of offices, the increase of tyrannies that followed Turgot's fall, Necker's failure in 1781, and after that the growing incompetence of everybody and everything: the luxury and ostentation of the Court of Versailles, the unpopularity of the Queen, the amiable weakness of the King, the Assembly of Notables by Calonne, their dissolution--until at last he had felt that he was almost a personal witness of the most dramatic of the recent events, the coup d'État of May of last year, the convoking of the States-General by Brienne, the strength of the Third Estate, the gradually rising tide of disorder, the flood of revolutionary pamphlets, the bad harvest of '88, and the fearful winter that succeeded it, the freezing of the Seine, the prominence of Mirabeau and Sieyès, of Barnave and Dupont and Bailly, the Oath of the Tennis Court on June 20.

The Oath of the Tennis Court was the last absolute news that he had had until to-day; for the last month he had been living in a ferment of expectation and feverish excitement. He could not understand that the men and women around him took so slight an interest in these events. If they spoke of outside affairs at all it was, at the most, in a late day, of the King's sickness, the possibility of a Regency, some new gambling scandal of

Charles Fox or the eccentricities of Mr. Pitt. The small business of the countryside contented them all.

So he had moved, poor Francis, as though he carried a bomb in his breast. There were times when he thought that he would cross to France and take part in the great crisis that was developing there, but his self-distrust, his natural love of England and his home (cherished passionately in his heart, unguessed at by anyone save possibly Judith) held him where he was.

This great news to-day released him! The world was free! The strongholds of all the tyrants had fallen! This was to be a symbol that would stand to all the world for the new freedom!

These may seem empty phrases enough set down upon paper, but in Francis' heart they were flames and torches. In very truth as he rode now under the July sun beside Bassenthwaite, he felt as though every constriction, every doubt of himself, every shyness and stupid caution were now released.

France would lead the way for all the world. He saw Louis with his fat good-natured face, Marie Antoinette with her gay beauty, seated grandly on their thrones by the will of their people. He could almost hear, beside these quiet sparkling waters, the wild cheers, the frantic shouts of joy that must fill the Paris streets. And now all men would hear them, and would be ashamed of their lethargy, their shameful lazy injustice and indifference.

He was indeed ashamed of himself. As he rode along he felt born again; his life had been most selfish. It should be so no longer. At any cost to himself he would take part now in forwarding the new justice and uprightness that was come into the world. As he rode he could have sung his happiness aloud.

He did not doubt but that his father, with all other men, would see the grandeur of this event. His father was a just man, although an obstinate. He loved his father dearly (who could help but love him?), although he was shy of him. How this new era in France would bring them together, would bring all men together and would lead to a new era in England also! As he turned up the lane to Fell House his eyes were dim with tears of joy.

And at once, so characteristically, he was checked by contact with his fellow human-beings. A maid, coming from the dairy, carrying buckets, Will's tutor seated reading on the lawn, his mother stepping down the staircase as he entered the house, all these drove him at once to silence.

His stout good-humoured sister met him at the turn of the stairs. He had nothing at all in common with Deborah. She had all the good- natured domesticity of a thoroughly contented Herries. So absolutely satisfied was she with herself, her family, all the little circumstances of her surroundings, that in all her twenty- six years she might be said never to have suffered an ache or a pain, whether of body or of soul. She was handsome in a large- boned Herries fashion, was never irritable, never excited, never curious about the nature of other people, always ready to do anything for anyone.

How ridiculous to say to her: 'Deb, the Bastille has fallen!' It would be to her exactly as though you had said: 'Deb, the cat has kittened!'

Having washed, brushed, changed his linen, he came downstairs again, walked into the garden and discovered Judith mocking the tutor. Mr. Langbridge was shortly leaving them. Will was now nineteen and did not need a tutor. Mr. Langbridge was long, gaunt, perpetually hungry, brilliantly founded in the classics (which was of no use at all to Will), hoping to be a clergyman, of a fanatically serious mind. He understood no sort of humour, and it delighted Judith to hold long conversations with him, asking him gravely about his health, his studies and his home in Dorset. For he detested the North, with its dark clouds, its rain, the savagery of its people, its bare strong hills. He was a perpetual exile. She stood in front of him now, her hands behind her back, her eyes twinkling, but her expression very serious.

Francis, coming upon her, realised quite suddenly that she was a woman. She was old for her fifteen years in her self-possession, young in her childish impulses. He knew that she adored him, just as she had always done; it had been a long faithful service on her part for which he had made little return. There was something about her small stature, pale face, and almost savage unlikeness to the average Herries order that frightened him, and yet he had long ago realised that she was the only one in this family who ever remotely understood him.

He realised it again now, for as she turned to him he saw that she immediately recognised him to be under the power of some very strong excitement. Mr. Langbridge pulled his long lanky body together, rose, very solemnly bowed to Francis and stalked away.

She looked at him, half roguishly, half with that affection that she could never keep from her eyes when she was with anyone of whom she was fond.

'Dear Francis,' she said, dancing about the lawn on her very small feet, 'you have got a secret. I can see that you have. And none of the family is worthy of it.'

She turned towards the house and they both saw David, followed by Will, coming towards them. The whole scene, the rosy brick house with its chimneys and gables and pigeon-loft, the dairy and stables behind it, the moor that was like a heaving green curtain moved with the intensity of the sun, the blue sky without cloud, the lawn so brilliant in colour that it hurt the eye, the trimmed hedge, the Gothic temple, the sprawling shadow of Skiddaw, the figures in their gay clothes, David in purple, Judith in green, Francis in silver, this moment of heat and colour would be remembered by all of them for ever.

David, carrying a riding-whip, moved heavily.

'Well, Francis,' he said, 'what news in Penrith?'

'Great news, sir,' Francis answered.

'What! has Pitt a fresh plan for the franchise?' David asked with good-humoured scorn. All Francis' notions seemed to him those of a child. But it was a half-sneer on Will's superior face that drove Francis on.

'No, sir,' he answered. 'The Bastille has fallen to the People in Paris.'

They all stayed, rigid, transfixed. David said at last: 'Where did you have the news?'

'Mr. Summerson told me in Keswick. He had it quite surely from Kendal.'

David raised his head and looked at everything, the buildings, the walls, the garden, as though assuring himself that they were all still there, safe and secure. Then he said slowly: 'If this is true it is terrible news.'

'I think,' Francis broke out, 'that it is the grandest news the world has ever had.'

Judith, who cared nothing for the fall of the Bastille in comparison with the immediate dangers of the scene, saw David's broad hand tremble about his riding-whip.

'Then you advocate rebellion,' he said slowly, 'murder, revolution. . . .'

'Yes,' Francis answered hotly, 'if these things are to bring justice back into the world.'

'Justice!' David's whole body trembled. 'Justice for the dirtiest mob of cut-throats that ever fouled a country. Justice for ingratitude, for disloyalty to a worthy King . . .' He half turned towards the house, then, his face swollen, it seemed, with anger, he came nearer to Francis. 'You are not my son if you find this foul rebellion glorious.'

'Then I am not your son,' Francis cried. 'I have long suspected it. For years I have watched your blindness to the way the world was going. For how much longer do you think a million men will suffer at the orders of one, and of one weaker, more selfish, more tyrannous than they could ever be? Thank God, men are to be free at last, free from tyrants, free. . . .'

'From tyrants like myself?' David cried, his anger now quite uncontrollable. 'A fine thing for a son. . . .'

'Take it as you will,' Francis answered, his words biting on the air. 'There is tyranny everywhere, here as well. . . .'

Some long accumulation of small persistent differences, always unsettled, mingling with the heat of the July day and their deep love, always checked, always running into perverse courses, combined to produce in them both a furious anger.

'By God, for less than that . . .' David cried.

'If your pride is hit,' Francis answered, 'it is by your own will. It is time that your eyes were opened.'

'I'll have no rebellion here,' David shouted. 'No rebellion here. Your gutter-friends may for the moment have their way in Paris. I am yet master in this house.'

'No more!' Francis cried. 'Many masters are falling.'

David raised his riding-whip and struck Francis on the cheek. They were silent then, and the cooing of the pigeons ran like water through the air, the only sound. Francis bent his head. David dropped the whip.

'Francis,' he began in a thick low guttural, turned a step and fell, like a log, to the grass. He was carried in. It was a stroke. Mr. Summerson the Surgeon was fetched from Keswick. David was bled. Consciousness returned to him, but he could not speak, and his left side was paralysed.

Francis went about the place with his head up, his features cold and severe, and agony in his heart. No one, except Judith, knew that he felt anything. His mother would not speak to him. That moment, running out on to the sunlit lawn at the sound of a cry, had changed Sarah Herries from a cheerful normal woman of her world into a creature of one impulse and one impulse only. Nothing now was alive for her in the world save David, her house meant nothing to her, her children meant nothing to her, she meant nothing at all to herself. She would not speak to Francis. She looked through him as though he were not there. She regarded none of them very intently. They were shadows to her. She seemed in one half-hour to become of a thinner, straighter figure; the colour left her cheeks, her eyes held a steely radiance, her voice a hard metallic ring. Something masculine that had been perhaps always in her personality came out now very queerly, save when she was in David's room; there she was soft, gentle, maternal. David had always been her child; now her love for him burnt with twice the earlier intensity because he was altogether dependent on her. He lay there, a huge bulk, beneath the clothes, only his eyes moving.

Judith watched all this with an acute perception, but in the first weeks her thoughts were all for Francis. She longed to tell him what she felt; at last she had her opportunity.

One evening, a cold wet August night drawing on, at the turn of the stairs on the upper passage beyond her room, she ran into him in the half dusk. His hands held her in the first shock of their contact. She could feel how they trembled. And at once, deeply moved by that trembling, she began, not weighing her words nor thinking of anything but that she must comfort him:

'Don't go. Don't go. I have been wanting to speak to you for these weeks past. I know that you have always a little mocked at my affection for you--indeed I have mocked at it a little myself-- but it gives me a right, after all these years, to tell you that I am the only one in all this house who understands you. Don't grieve about him, Francis dear. It was not your fault, indeed, indeed it was not. You had to say what you believed that day, and I know that he admired you for that behind his anger. The stroke must have come in any case--Mr. Summerson says so. And his heart, too, has been weak these years past. So soon as he is better he will send for you and tell you that he loves you--'

'My mother will not allow me to see him,' Francis interrupted her.

'She cannot prevent you if he wishes it. As soon as he can speak he will ask for you. I know that now he is sorry and is grieving for you.'

His voice shook. 'No, I must go and never return. I have been a curse to this place. Only I can't go without a word from him. I am waiting only for that--'

'Yes. He is better to-day. Mr. Summerson thinks that in a week or so he will be able to speak a little. The paralysis is only on one side.'

They were in the dark together; neither could clearly see the face of the other, but Judith knew that Francis was crying. Half a child, she was greatly inclined to cry, but she only stood close to him, her hand on his arm.

'You have always been the best friend I have had here,' he said at last.

'And I will be,' she answered.

Afterwards she could not but reflect that she was always better with anyone who was in distress or desired her help. She liked above everything to feel that she was needed, and yet she had a strong contempt for any weak-willed person who was for ever relying on others. What she liked was to assist or direct those who normally were quite able to assist themselves. What she would have done now to have helped Sarah had Sarah but invited her! But Sarah needed no one's help, and least of all Judith's. She allowed Deborah to do things for her, and very remarkably Deborah began to develop under this crisis, but Judith she completely disregarded.

This, again, was why Judith had no sort of contact with Will. Will relied on no one but himself and took no one into his confidences. He gave the impression that he was watching every move, every phase of the situation, weighing it all that he might turn it in the best way to his advantage.

The house very quickly suited itself to the new circumstances. Everything turned now around the room where David was lying. He had been always greatly popular with his servants; unlike many men of his time he had always seen them as separate individuals, was constantly inquiring about their families and circumstances, had a jolly, natural, healthy interest in all of them. He had been the one of the family for whom they cared, who stabilised their loyalty. His simple animal health and boyish pleasure in little things had always pleased them. He had been an indulgent but not a foolish master; they were very sorry now for his misfortune.

David rose with infinite slowness and caution from a sea of darkness. Wearily he pushed aside fold after fold of heavy clinging cloth that hindered his sight. Then, tired out, he lay back to resist no longer, and saw swaying above his head a gold rose set in a green cloud. He heard, a little after, from an infinite distance a voice speaking to him. Someone touched him, and he sank instantly back into the dark sea whose waters, smooth like oil, lapped him round and lay upon his eyes and mouth. Aeons later he saw again the gold rose on the green ground, and once again heard the voice, and knew that it was Sarah his wife who was speaking to him.

He raised very slowly his right hand and touched the chill flesh of his breast beneath his shirt. Then he would raise his other hand, but he had no other hand. His perceptions moved with infinite slowness. After, as it seemed to him, a lifetime of patient watching he realised that the gold rose was fixed in its place above his head, and that there were other gold roses. Then, after another infinity of time, he knew that these gold roses belonged to the tester of the bed in which he was lying.

His wife's voice was often in his ear. She made a noise like a bird, like a mouse; the noise came and went and came again. He was immensely susceptible to light. A wave of light would slowly sway in front of him, would be withdrawn and then return with greater intensity.

There came a time when he wished to speak about this light, but he could not. He could speak no more than a dead man. But he was not dead at all. An urgent pulsing life began to beat within him. This life was connected with nothing that he saw or heard. It had a wild riotous time of its own within him: it laughed, it sang, it wept, it sighed, but it was imprisoned, and it longed to get out. His eyes began to take everything in--the room with the purple curtains, the piece of green tapestry, the crooked legs of the chairs, Sarah, Deborah, the maid, once and again Will. He saw and recognised them all, but he could not speak, nor had they anything to do with the wild life inside him. When he knew this he pitied himself and them; tears, helpless tears, rolled down his cheeks, and his wife wiped them away.

He knew now all the things that they did to him-- the things the surgeon did, how it was when they turned him in bed (he was a very heavy man and it was not easy), and when they put a new shirt on him, washed his face. Sarah kissed him, and he touched her cheek with his right hand.

He was never by himself. At night candles were burning, and Sarah sat there, sometimes sewing, sometimes reading a book, her eyes continually going to meet his eyes. He was ashamed at some of the things he must do for her, but she was his wife, he had lain with her in her arms; he would lie there staring at the gold roses and think of how often he had buried his hands in her hair.

He was glad that she was always there, because he was lost in that wild turbulent life within himself, and she was all that there was to call him back. Then one night he was far away. He was standing on a deserted beach beside a lonely sea. Someone was beside him, a man, and quite suddenly this man raised a stick to strike him. He seized this stick, broke it in half and flung it into the sea. After that this man never left him. He was very tall, thin of face, and he had a scar that ran from eye to lip. The man stood beside him on a green lawn,

and this time it was he who had the whip; he raised his hand and struck; as he did so the man changed. He was young, and after he was struck he bent his head.

David lay there for a long while striving to reconcile these two figures. They were the same and were not the same. At one time they seemed to be himself; then they were separate, then together again.

One grey ghostly morning he awoke and knew everything. The man who had wished to strike him was his father; the man whom he had struck was his son. He knew everything. He had been ill, and was lying now in his bed, while beyond the window a bird sang, and near him the candles were almost burnt out, and Sarah sat in a high chair, her head forward, asleep. He passed then, struggling all alone, hours of terrible agony. His left side was dead; there was no feeling nor motion in it. His heart bled for his son. He could think of nothing but that. He must see his son. He must see his son. He raised his right arm: he tried to shout and to shout again. No sound would come. His father and his son. He must ask them both to forgive him; until he had done that there was no peace for him.

At last the door opened; someone came in, carrying something. Sarah woke and came to the bedside. His eyes besought her. He raised his hand. His agony of mind was terrible, for he could not reach her. How strange that he could not reach her! After all these years together, their love, their intercourse, their friendship. She was the mother of his children, and he could not reach her. Strange low mutterings came from his mouth. His eyes implored her, begged of her.

The light, grey, webbed, hung like a film about the room, and in this film she moved. At length she bent down to kiss him, and as she did so, his eyes were so near to hers that she must have seen the agony in them. He made sounds that seemed to him explicit prayers, but she could understand nothing.

It was three hours later that the surgeon understood sufficiently to send for a paper. Then David wrote in a large sprawling hand the word 'Francis.' Francis came. They were alone in the room together, and David spoke the first word since his illness. 'Forgive.' His voice was strange, cracked, with a slur in it, but Francis understood and knelt beside the bed. David, with his trembling right hand, stroked his hair.

After that he could not bear to have Francis out of the room, so that the two of them, Francis and Sarah, were there together. But Sarah would not speak to her son nor look at him if she could help it. David began then the slow business of seeing that two and two make four. There were some things that he could not understand at all. He did not know why he had struck his son with a whip, nor why he was sometimes there quite clearly in the room with his wife beside him and at other times he was in the little dark house in Borrowdale, following his father, hearing his father's voice, and behind the voice the wind rustling the tapestry, and the noise of water falling down the rock.

He slept a great deal, and in his dreams he climbed the rocks, ran across the springing turf of the Fell, stood on the Pass with Sarah in his arms, watching his enemy climb the road towards him.

At times again he would be dreadfully unhappy. Tears would roll down his cheeks; he would wipe them feebly with his hand. But why he was so unhappy he could not tell.

But at these times an infinite pity for himself overwhelmed him. 'Poor David. Poor, poor David. Poor, poor David.' Was there ever anything so sad as poor David--and, from a great distance away, he watched this poor David and sympathised so deeply with his loneliness, his helplessness, the injustice of his state.

After a time words came back to him. He could say 'Francis, Sarah. I don't want. Good night.' He mumbled them; his mouth was twisted.

His brain conceived a new map of the world for him. There was the room where he lay. Pieces of furniture became alive and personal to him. A china table, a tea-kettle stand, chairs with faces. He liked especially a ribband-back chair covered with red morocco, a real friend of his, that would smile and wave his leg at him. The tapestry on the wall, its subject Susanna and the Elders, was also his friend. He liked Susanna's kindly breasts and her shining thighs. He was glad that he had not allowed Sarah to make the house in the Gothic style, as she had once planned to do, after Horace Walpole or some other London absurdity. He had an honest scorn for artists and writers. She had wanted a wallpaper printed in perspective, windows with saints in painted glass, and even arrows, long-bows and spears.

Poor Sarah! What a good woman, how wonderful a wife she was to him! He liked her to sit beside the bed and be near to him. He would smile a crooked twisted smile and murmur her name. Yes, all this was real enough. Summerson with his hour-glass, the basins and glasses, old Ballard the man-servant with his handsome white wig, Will, Judith, and, above all, Francis. Deborah too, good girl. She had a genius for moving quietly, big woman though she was: no hand so soft as hers, and--best of all--she breathed good-humour. He wanted no sad faces about him; in Sarah's eyes he detected sometimes a look of terror, and that he would not have because it made himself afraid. . . .

Yes, all this was real enough. But beyond the room he could not be sure where he was. The landscape was the landscape of his young life, and although in this room he was tied to the heavy four-poster, once he was outside the room he could move where he wished. Every part of Borrowdale was open to him. All the old places: beloved Stonethwaite, with its tumbling stream, the springing turf of Stake Pass, the swinging birds above Honister, hundreds more; the wrestling bouts, the high room of old Peel's with its blazing fire and broad rafters, the taste of the dried salted beef and mutton, the oatmeal puddings, the bull-ring in Keswick, when on a grand day in the market-place you must sit on an adjoining roof to get a view, the shearing days with the chairing and the bell-ringing, Twelfth Night when the lighted holly tree was carried from inn to inn-- all had departed from him so long, long ago, killed by the later modern times, but now he was back in them again, all his health and vigour were returned, he was the strongest man in all the valley, and every hill knew him, Glaramara smiled on him, Eagle Crag was his brother, Sprinkling Tarn his sister, Sea Fell his lover. . . .

He lay there, motionless, smiling, his blue eyes fixed on the gold rose. They thought that he was imprisoned there, a helpless hulk. Little they knew! He was free again, as he had not been for many a year.

His father now accompanied him everywhere. His father digging that intractable ground, riding with him to Ravenglass, sitting beside him at the old stone fireplace in Herries, his hand on his thigh, his father and Mirabell, his father and Deborah, his father who had been always closer to him than any other human being.

They wished to pull him back from this happiness, this freedom, this strength of body, and cold running air of the fells, smell of the bracken, sound never stilled of running water. The sheep moved, the sun glistening on their fleecy sides, the shepherd whistled to his dog, the clouds rushed out and covered the sun that yet escaped them, mocking them and flashing a shield of light upon the distant brow. . . .

'Hold on to me, father. They are dragging me back. I will catch your arm. They shall not separate us. . . .'

It was time for him to be washed, to be turned in his bed. The smell of the sick-room was there, the chair with the red morocco, Susanna with her breasts, Sarah's grave face and that look of terror in the eyes. Only Francis and Judith knew his father. That child with her pale face and red hair, hair like Mirabell's. Poor Mirabell . . . but no, she was not to be pitied, for she loved his father at the last. . . .

His mouth crookedly formed the word 'Judith.' She came to the bedside, not frightened like Sarah, smiling, standing on her toes to be level with the bed. He took her hand in his. It lay there warm and soft.

'Judith.' That was the last word that he spoke.

For he was swung away in a great torrent of light. He flew on the air, kicking his limbs free, his head up, his hair tugged at by the wind. Away and away, over Borrowdale and Stonethwaite, over Sea Fell and the Langdales, over Waswater, black like ebony. . . . What freedom, what happiness!

He shouted: 'Oh, hoi! Oh, hoi! Oh, hoi!' He came swinging down until the turf sprang beneath his feet. He was leader in an immortal chase. 'Oh, hoi! Oh, hoi! Away! Away!' The scent of the bracken and the falling leaf, the touch of the stone of the little running walls! He had caught a cloud and swung into the dazzling sun. Old Herries was at his side, the moulded shoulders of the Tops were beneath his hand, the ruffled water of the Lakes spun to the swirl of his great strength.

'Follow! Follow! Away, away!'

His father and he, masters of the air, friends of every hill, laughing with every twist of tarn and river, raced towards the sun. . . .

Watching the bed, they saw his body lie motionless: the eyes stared.

Sarah's scream brought Deborah running into the room.

QUARREL AND FLIGHT

Judith awoke to a sudden consciousness of distress. She had been very happily asleep curled up in the corner of the settee with the green Chinese dragons. These dragons had pursued her very pleasantly in her dream, large amiable creatures with green scales; from their bodies flakes detached themselves (as they ambled along) and lay like green pennies on the hot dry sand.

It was so hot, this sandy country, that she woke with a start to find the warm spring sun shining in through the window on to her face. She looked about her, bewildered, on to the Sheffield-plated candlesticks and the blue and white china in the corner cupboard. With the final release from her dream she pushed a large, fat, beery, and most affectionate dragon away from her and sat up, listening. What she heard was Sarah, in the room across the hall, talking to herself.

Sarah was not talking to herself, she was talking to David. Judith knew exactly how it was; Sarah was walking quietly up and down the room and was begging David to return, was telling David that she could not endure life without him, was asking David how he could have left her.

These outbursts were becoming rarer with Sarah, but they were still constant enough to fill the house with uneasiness. She had been for years the happiest, most normal of women. One man's death had changed her from that into this suffering remote figure, who was battling, who had been battling for months, to recover her security. Soon she would be armoured again safely against life, but the old Sarah was dead, vanished for ever, and happiness was, for the time, gone from that house.

It was part of Judith's character that she had no patience at all with nerves or hysteria. It was a period when women enjoyed and fostered all the artificialities that might give them an important place in a world designed entirely for men. 'Vapours' were the order of the day for the majority of God's females. If they could not rouse attention by one manoeuvre they would rouse it by another.

Judith had never had the 'vapours' nor would she ever have them. Nevertheless, she was near sixteen, and had the understanding, in many things, of a grown woman. Her education in life had been, thanks to Tom Gauntry and his friends, early and thorough. She realised that this was no nonsense nor affectation on Sarah's part. David's death had simply taken away from her all the ground on which for years she had been standing. She was fighting to regain her sure footing; she would regain it. Meanwhile she would allow no one to help her.

Now, as Judith listened to that murmuring voice, she longed to go and help her. She knew, if she did go, the kind of treatment that she would receive. The only person in the world who could assist her now crossed the hall and went in to her. Deborah's soft comforting voice could be heard. A little later the two women passed out into the garden together.

It was one of Judith's deepest chagrins that in all this crisis she had been of no use at all. It was Deborah, of all people, who had saved the situation, stout dull Deborah who was suddenly the principal figure in the house, was kind and tactful with everyone, managed the servants, entertained the local gentry, kept the accounts, prevented Will (when at home) and Francis from open quarrel and understood Judith, it seemed, better than anyone had ever done. This had been that quiet woman's chance and she had seized it.

In the year that followed David's death the situation had demanded exactly such a woman as Deborah. She had always seemed slow, unobservant, uninterested; now it was apparent that she observed much and was never uninterested. She was greatly assisted by limiting her horizon to her own affairs. That France was in revolution, that her mother was in hysteria, these were not her business. She had loved her father as well, possibly, as any of them, but her father was dead, life must go on, the cows must be milked, intercourse with neighbours resumed. She quietly assumed direction of the house.

Had Will been there her domination might not have so quickly succeeded, but Will was in Liverpool, forming new contracts with Mr. Metcalfe. Francis also was away for days at a time. The house became the abode of the three women, and had it not been for Deborah, catastrophe would have rent it from attic to cellar. For Sarah, in the strange unnatural world that she now inhabited, had a fierce and unresting grudge against Judith. Judith's name had been the last word on David's lips, it was into Judith's eyes that David had looked before he turned his head on the pillow and passed. Judith was to Sarah still the strange unaccountable child that she had been ten years ago. At that time a girl of sixteen was often a mature woman, but Judith was for Sarah still a rebellious intriguing child, born of a gipsy. These things are mysteries, but beyond question there mingled now in Sarah's feelings about Judith something of her old uneasiness with Mirabell. Mirabell, Judith's mother, had never liked her, had indeed refused her kindliness and friendliness. Here was Mirabell born again.

But Judith was not Mirabell; she was fiercer, more readily hostile and resentful, far more dominating. She would not let Sarah hate her without making some return for it. It was not her fault that David had said her name before he died. If anyone wished to make a friend of her she was ready, but she was ready--oh, exceedingly ready--for anyone who wanted her as enemy.

Deborah disregarded all this. She was loving to Sarah, loving to Judith, loving to Francis, to whom even now, after these many months, his mother would not speak. Deborah took the situation and kept it, for the moment, safe. She could not keep it safe for long-- it was charged with violence and danger--but what she could do she did. She indulged also her own fancy. Her fancy was, and had always been, for social amenities. She loved tea-drinkings, card- parties, evenings, when some neighbour 'put up' four or six couples for a dance, expeditions of a moderate kind to some interesting site or historic building, and, above all, the chatter that circled around love-affairs and interesting engagements.

She had now entirely her own way in this, for Sarah was living altogether in her own world. When a decent interval had passed since David's death, neighbours came and went at Uldale with an easy frequency unknown for some time past. There were the Redlands of Thornthwaite, the Darlingtons from Whelpo, the Berrys of Roseley, the Carringtons of Forest Hall. It was suddenly a woman's world, and a world that seemed to Judith ridiculous in its obsession with trifles and incredible in its indifference to all outside events.

Deborah's principal friends were the Redlands of Thornthwaite-- Squire Redland, his stout pleasant wife, and the two handsome Miss Redlands--and the two Miss Berrys of Roseley. The elder Miss Berry was the great gossip of the district. She found everything amusing and left everything scandalous. The Miss Redlands, dark, big- boned, handsome women, were the flirts of the district. Their thought was only of men. Mrs. Redland had a genius for the arrangement, in other people's houses, of teas and suppers, parties at cards and little musical occasions.

Hours--and for Deborah most enchanting hours-- would be spent in the discussion of social combinations and permutations. Mrs. Redland had the talent of making any house in which she happened to be visiting appear instantly as her own. She was massive, enjoyed bright colours and had a laugh like a trooper. She would arrange herself on the settee with the green dragons and instantly begin:

'But, my dear Miss Berry, we must not be too nice. Invite them all. Why not? They are a standing example of good humour and amiable intention, and I am sure Mr. Frank Fuller, although he may be the oddest crea-

ture in the world, is a gentleman, which cannot be said for Mr. Beaton, who has a store of underbred finery quite amazing.'

And little Miss Berry, with her sniff that suggested an eternal cold, would observe:

'Mr. Beaton is a coxcomb as everyone knows. But there is nothing to be ashamed of in being a coxcomb. What he enjoys the most is an evening of noisy entertainment, and for my part there are times when noisy entertainment is the thing. Ask Mr. Beaton by all means. That will make six couples exactly.'

'And this time,' Mrs. Redland would say, looking about her, 'we will make the dining-room of use by shifting the pianoforte. Last time there was not room for anyone to have real enjoyment.'

And Judith, listening, would wonder that Deborah had the patience to submit to these ladies who ordered the house as their own. But, indeed, she herself was not at all popular with them. They wondered why this sulky sarcastic girl was there. Was she 'out' or was she not 'out'? Was it true that she was the love-child of some peasant courted in the ditch by that old ruffian of a Herries, who had died in a hut in Borrowdale?

David was only a year dead, and they were dancing in his house. But if Sarah made no objection to it had anyone else a right? Sarah's face was now a mask. She sat in her upstairs room, looking from her window. There were some days when no one came to the house at all, and then, so eerie was the silence, so threatening the atmosphere, that Judith understood why Deborah encouraged her sociabilities.

But with every week the inevitable crisis drew nearer. Francis was absent during all that summer. Will came and went, but in November, two days after Judith's sixteenth birthday, Francis returned--and life was permanently changed for them all for ever after.

His return was innocent and quiet enough. There was a storm of rain. Skiddaw was hid in purple shadow and over its head an ebony lake of cloud hung like a reflection. Beyond it, towards the sea, faint strips of blue sky showed that it was but a shower. The rain fell like thunder. Mrs. Redland and one of her daughters, the two Miss Berrys, Deborah and Judith sat in the parlour and waited for the rain to pass. A dance-- arranged entirely by Mrs. Redland--was to take place in the following week at the Darlingtons'. The Darlingtons were lazy, but good-natured. They did not mind at all that Mrs. Redland should consider their house as hers so long as she did all the work for them. She was now in high feather. All the invitations had been successful. There were to be eight couples.

Mrs. Redland was pretending to be angry with Miss Berry's imitation of old Miss Clynes, whose teeth clicked in her head like castanets. 'For shame, Miss Berry, you shall not mimic her! And as to young Mr. Clynes, he is perfectly satisfied with his sheep and his farm.'

'Yes,' cried Miss Berry in an ecstasy of enjoyment at her own sense of fun and humour, 'and they say that coming in the dark into the house one day he took his aunt for one of his sheep that had been straying all the afternoon. "Shoo! Shoo! Shoo!" he cried. And you know how the good lady, when she is but half awake, baas for anyone who is close to her. . . . Well, well, I've no doubt but the young man will make a match of it with Jane Bastable. Poor thing. She missed the dancing-master last year, although she trudged into Keswick twice a week and oftener. . . . "Baa, baa!", and it wasn't until the young man lit a candle that he saw how things really were.'

Miss Berry's imitation was most lively, and they were all in a roar of laughter over it when the door burst open and Francis Herries, the capes of his riding-coat dripping with water, stood there, glared fiercely for a moment, and was gone.

Judith, who had been sitting by herself in the window watching the black cloud above Skiddaw shred into a dozen fish-tails, hating Mrs. Redland and Miss Berry, wondering what end all this unhappiness in the house could have, seeing him, sprang up and went out.

She saw him standing in the hall, that was dark with a kind of smoky reflection of the rain, as though bewildered. He looked at her, and without a word turned into the little room that had been always David's sanctum, a cold and cheerless little room now; here were cases with old books that David had never read, but his chair was there, a table with some of his papers and the prints of Derwentwater, Keswick, Borrowdale that he had dearly loved.

Judith followed Francis there. He had flung off his cloak and turned to her, his face working with anger and impatience.

'The house is changed,' he said bitterly. 'It is no home for either of us any more. . . . Where is my mother?'

'In her room. Oh, Francis, I am so glad that you have returned!'

'I have come back with a purpose. This cannot continue. My mother must speak to me for there are things that must be settled. This silence has lasted a year, and I will have no more of it.'

He looked so unhappy, so desolate, as he stood there that her heart ached for him, and the anger that had been piling up all these months at the treatment of both himself and her reached at that moment its crisis. She felt that the time had come for a settlement, and she was glad of it.

'Oh, Francis, isn't it the strangest thing! She loved you so. She was always so kind and so good. I have thought that it was a sickness that would pass, but you are right; it must be brought to an issue. . . .'

She recollected in that instant the scene in the cellar at Cockermouth, when Humphrey Sunwood, outcast and fugitive, had said farewell to her. Now she and Francis were outcast and fugitive: for no fault of theirs.

She thought, standing in that room, of David's kindliness and benignity. Were his ghost with them now he must grieve at these circumstances. Oh, if he were only here, if he were only here!

'You do not know,' Francis went on rapidly, his voice trembling with emotion, 'that two weeks ago from Penrith I wrote to my mother. I said everything in that letter, of my love for my father, of my great unhappiness, that I was the cause of his sickness, that I would never, never, so long as I lived, forgive myself for that, but that I loved her too, that I loved her the more for my own fault, that I had borne patiently all these months her silence and that I had well deserved it, but that this must have some limit because I loved her, because I loved our home. . . .' His voice broke. He turned, leaned his head on his arms against the fireplace. For a little the only sound in the room was the driving rain. When he looked up and spoke again his voice was stern and resolved.

'She did not answer my letter. I have waited these two weeks. So now it must end. I must know one way or another.'

'Yes, it must end,' Judith answered. 'For all our sakes. . . .'

'I am going to her now.'

He left the room. She stood there, heard him mount the stairs. In a little while the rain had stopped. She heard the ladies come out, chatter, laugh, depart. Deborah came past the open door, but did not look in, and moved slowly into the servants' part of the house. Still there was no sound from upstairs. Then, quite sharply, Francis' voice rang out, one word cutting the air like a snapped stick. Judith, driven by an impulse that was entirely beyond her governance, ran up the stairs, stayed for a moment, then, her face hardening into resolve, walked down the passage.

She pushed Sarah's door open and went in. The room that Sarah had chosen for herself after David's death was a small bare one. Over the fireplace was a highly coloured, badly painted picture of David. It had been done by some travelling artist some ten years before, and showed David complacent in full wig, a crimson coat and flowered vest, red-cheeked, exceedingly amiable.

He grinned down at Sarah, his wife, who sat in a chair of crimson morocco; her hair, her face, grey, her dress black, a ghost of desperate anger and unhappiness. It was the unhappiness that Judith, standing in the doorway, first saw, then, a second later, she was engulfed in the anger as though she had to push up her head to avoid drowning in it. She closed the door.

'I will not speak either to him or to you!' Sarah cried, her hand trembling on her chair.

Francis, in entire command of himself, was by the window. He came forward.

'I am glad you have come, Judith,' he said. 'I would have a witness to this. After twelve months my mother has at length addressed me. . . .' He went close to her.

His voice was tender and full of affection. 'I cried out at what you said, mother, but you have a right to say what you wish. You have told me to go and never to come back. I will go, but not before you have heard me.'

She did not look at him, but, half rising in her chair, spoke to Judith.

'I know that you are on his side,' she said, 'but that is no new thing. Ever since they brought you to this house as a baby you have made nothing but evil here. You have never belonged here, and it is quite fitting that you should take the part of the son who killed his father, leaving us all desolate.'

Even as her face was a mask hiding some real woman under it, so her voice was not her own. Judith had a queer perception of the old, rather tired, very quiet woman that Sarah would be after this sickness was over, as unlike the woman that she had once been as this present woman was unlike. She had a strange conviction, as though someone spoke to her, that throughout this scene she must keep that old tired woman in her mind, so she would be kinder and more just.

No one could be more just or more decent than Francis.

'Listen, mother,' he said. 'You SHALL attend to me, for later when you look back you will be glad that you heard me. You loved father. God knows I did also. My love is something; you cannot take it from me. But I could not deny my nature, neither for you nor father nor anyone. That nature has always put me by myself, alone. I tell you now so that you may remember it after, that I would change it, God knows how I would change it, if I could. And is it not enough that I must carry with me all my life the knowledge that it was my insane obstinacy that killed father; is not that some punishment for a man? Did he not himself forgive me? Was he not the most generous-hearted of men, and can we not now, who both loved him, find some ground in his generosity and make a peace? Mother--'

He approached her. She drew back violently, almost pushing the chair over. Then she rose, swept by him as though he were not there, and went to the window.

'Very well,' she said, 'if you wish it you shall hear me. I was a happy woman; you have made me an unhappy. I had a home, a husband whom I loved; I have nothing any more. You say it was only your nature. Very well, I am an enemy of that nature. I was your mother. I am so no more. I do not know you. You may remain in this house if you will. You have the right. I believe the house is now yours. I will leave it if you wish. But understand, if you stay and I stay I do not know you. We remain as strangers.'

She beat her hand against her black dress, her fingers scraping the silk as though her control was almost exhausted. Yet her eyes, looking beyond them both into some mysterious distance, seemed to say: 'I am impris-

oned here. These words are not mine. I do not know who is the speaker.'

Francis turned to Judith with a gesture as though of despair.

'No,' he said, 'I will not go like that. I am no stranger to you whatever I have done. You have borne me, suckled me. I have lain on your breast. Things cannot be ended. . . .'

'Listen then,' she interrupted quickly. 'I was once a girl, very unhappy. Your father came and rescued me, fought for me, married me. From the first moment that I saw him I worshipped him. I bore him three children. Now I have but two. Can you understand THAT then? That . . . That . . .'

But Judith, furious with what seemed to her the theatrical falseness of a woman hugging with a sort of selfish joy the self-inflicted tragedy, broke in:

'I have something to say in this. I am a woman, Sarah, as you are a woman. I am a child no longer. What right have you to fancy your grief is yours alone? For a year and more you have walked by yourself, hugging your wrongs, and you have hugged them so long that you are a comic figure, not real at all. We have all endured your nonsense long enough. Oh yes, you can order me to go. I know that I have no place here any more. I am going. But Francis is another matter. For a whole year, with absolute patience, he has endured your tantrums and bewailings. He is offering you now your last opportunity. Lose it, and when you come to your senses again you will whistle for him back and whistle to empty air. If I were your daughter I could show you something. You adore David, yes, but you allow the house to be filled with chattering women, and Mr. Finch comes with his fiddle from Keswick, and the pianoforte is moved to have room for another two couple, and--'

She paused for breath. She was in one of her rages, almost dancing on the Turkey carpet.

Sarah broke into her pause.

'No, you are right, Judith. You are no child of mine. Thank God for it. We, at least, have been strangers always. I see no kind of reason for you to intervene in this. Francis is the master here now. If he wishes you here I have no say. If you think me a comic figure, that also is of no importance. I did not ask you to come and wrangle here. I may be allowed, perhaps, another room where I may be by myself. When you have finished, if you wish to stay here, I will go.'

Then Francis turned to her, his face lit with a most noble generosity and kindness.

'Mother, listen. Why should you cut yourself off? You have been angry with me long enough. Were father here he would laugh at all of us. There are never so many in the world who are our own stock, our own flesh and blood, that we should separate ourselves from those we have. I have told you that all my life long I shall carry with me the burden of my father's death. But life is not over for that. Would my father wish us, because he is gone, to spoil our lives for him? He would be the last, the very last in the world, to tolerate it. He loved life, every piece of it, and he loved friendship and fellowship and the forgetting of injuries. He never grudged an injury his whole life long. You know that he did not. He has forgiven me, although I cannot forgive myself. Dear mother, in his name, forgive me too. Let me be your son again; come out and make this house real. I will be as true a son to you--'

She broke in: 'No. No. Never! You, both of you together, do you think I cannot see into your hearts? Do you think this treachery is a new thing to me? Make no mistake. I know you--and now, perhaps, you will allow me to find another room.'

Judith cried: 'You shall not go like that. Listen. You say that I have been false to you all my life long. I know that I haven't been good. I have always found discipline hard; not YOUR discipline, Sarah. Any discipline. But I think, looking back, that you were always very kind to me. You never saw that I was always older than I should be, that I was disgraced by my own impulse to be for ever making new resolutions that I couldn't fulfil. There was no more evil in it than that. The greatest kindness you could ever show me was to let me have my own way that I might quickly discover how foolish my own way was. But there was no more wilfulness than that. I have always cared for you, Sarah, and now when I leave you, as I shall do this very night, I want you only to remember afterwards that I would tell you truths while I can and wish you well.

'And it is for that, because I wish you so well, that I beg you not to lose Francis. He is right. David's death is no reason for any separation. Keep him with you. His situation should secure your compassion, not your anger--'

Francis broke in: 'Judith, you are not to go.'

But Sarah was already at the door: 'Our worlds are separate, Francis,' she said, more quietly than she had hitherto spoken. 'You have thought me comic, Judith, in my selfishness. There you are doubtless right. Only I pray God that you may never know the unhappiness that I know. I did not think there could be such an unhappiness in the world and anyone live with it.'

She opened the door and went out.

Judith stared at the picture of the rubicund and complacent David.

'When he was alive,' she said, 'Sarah was quiet enough in her affections. She loved him, but not to any desperation. Francis, I hate women with their exaggeration and sentiment. There is something rotten here like a poison.'

He sighed wearily, stroking his forehead with his hand.

'No. There is a reality in it somewhere. I always knew that we were nothing to her compared with my father. He filled her whole vision, and now she is lost.'

'I will never be that for a man,' Judith answered sharply. 'Mark you that, Francis. Never, never, never!'

She went up to him, stood on tip-toe, kissed his forehead.

'Dear Francis, good night.'

He did not attempt to stop her, but stood there, lost in his own problem.

'Even he,' she thought, 'does not want me here.'

Indeed, when she reached her room, she felt more desolate than ever before in her life. She belonged now to exactly no one at all.

She must go at once, this very night, but she had no doubt at all as to what this going meant. She was going now once and for ever. This place was never again to be her home, or so at least she thought, being no witch to see in a glass her future.

She looked about her little room that had been the same ever since her babyhood. There was the oak-panelled arm-chair, the tallboy, the bed with the faded cherry-coloured hangings.

She got out of the drawer her childhood treasures: the fox's brush from Tom Gauntry, the book on cock-fighting, the china jar with the orange flowers, the two rag 'babies' and, best loved of all, the Bible with the wood-cuts that Reuben had given her.

She smiled when she looked at them, but smiled quite without sentiment. Her childhood was over, quite finally, for ever. And she was not sorry. It had been a mischancy ill-fitting time. Yes, that was one thing, but this sudden exile into a vast uncanny world was quite another. Suppose Tom Gauntry didn't want her? He was growing old now and was uneasily under the domination of his cook, Emma Furze. . . . Oh, well, if he didn't want her, there were other places. She could work; she wasn't afraid of anyone.

Then, quite unaccountably, she wanted to cry. Indeed, indignantly, she brushed some tears from her eyes. How she wished that Reuben was here! He loved her, and only he in all the world. Poor clumsy, fat-faced, kindly Reuben. She hadn't seen him for six months. Deborah Sunwood, too, was altered since Humphrey's troubles, not the same bright tranquil woman as before, and Reuben was so restless that he might be away from Cockermouth any time.

Something had happened to them all, just as it was happening to the larger, outside world, breaking up all the old moulds, busily forming new ones that would be, no doubt, very like the old ones when they were settled.

But the thought of the change and of some movement in the world very much larger than her own little trivial affairs stirred her to action. There were no tears any more. She would go to Stone Ends to-night, and if they did not want her there she would move on. What of London? There were Herries there, who would help her. After all she WAS a Herries, whatever they might say. And at that she thought suddenly of Georges Paris. She had seen him once and heard from him twice since the adventure with Humphrey in Cockermouth. The time she had seen him had been at Stone Ends; they had not been alone, had had few words, but there had been something in a kind of mocking proprietary air that he had had that had not altogether pleased her. Nevertheless, he had grown extraordinarily handsome, slender, dark, with a sort of sword-like sharpness and brilliance. He shone among all those befuddled squires and hunting men at Gauntry's like a prince in disguise. Oh no, she was not romantic about him. She knew his selfishness and conceit and laziness well enough, but when he was near to her, looked at her, touched her, he stirred her blood, and she liked her blood to be stirred. She liked anything, any risk, any danger, rather than stagnation. That Georges Paris WAS a danger she never disguised from herself for a single moment.

Well, she must be moving. She wanted to get away from the house, away from Sarah's sickness, from Francis' unhappiness, from Deborah's chattering women, as quickly as might be.

She began to turn everything out, her possessions, clothes, hats and shoes, until they lay all over the room. Then she decided to take nothing with her. She would ride over on the cob to Stone Ends and send for her things.

She smiled as she remembered the time when, years ago, after David's whipping her, she had climbed out of the window and ridden away.

It should not be so dramatic an exit this time.

But, in honest fact, when at last she walked out of the house she heard no sound, she met no one. It was as though she were going out of a dead house.

Out of a dead house into life.

MADAME PARIS

She went along on her horse--clop-clop, clop-clop--and with every ring of the road she was more surely leaving everything behind.

She saw nothing, thought of nothing outside herself. The separate strains fighting for order in her mind slowly, by a kind of reluctant agreement, as though they were obeying commands against their will, sulkily settled themselves.

'I have left everything behind me, and I am going out into nothing-- or perhaps everything. Everyone with whom I have had to do has been showing Sensibility about something, even Will. But I wish to show Sensibility about nothing. I have only myself to consider. Even Francis does not need me. I am nearer to my dead father and mother than I am to anyone else. But there also I will not show Sensibility. They are dead and dead for always. I shall never see them or speak to them. I may have feeling in me that comes from them, but they cannot help me. They will not weep if I come to disaster. They will not answer if I call. Who is in my life? David is dead. Sarah has just thrown me out, Will and Francis think of themselves, Deborah is nothing, Deborah Sunwood has her husband and is grieving for Humphrey, Reuben thinks about God, Tom Gauntry to whom I am going is old and loves his cook, Georges-- Georges wishes to kiss me when he sees me. Otherwise I am nothing to him. There is nobody at all who needs me. So far as I can tell, I have not a penny in the world, although Francis would, I suppose, give me some money if I asked him. I shall not ask him. I have no friends, no money, no work.

'I am sixteen years of age, with fine hair, a poor complexion, a nose too large, and ridiculously small stature. I have no especial intelligence, but I know when persons are speaking to me and I remember something of what they say. I have never been afraid of anybody or anything, but I have not as yet met anybody or anything to be afraid of.

'I have never had a lover, but am very ready to have one. I am curious about love. I expect that love itself is nothing very fine, but I could care for somebody very deeply. I would wish to have children that I might care for them. Is this Sensibility? I do not mind whether it be so or not.

'I know nothing as yet about the outside world, but I am extremely inquisitive concerning it, nor do I believe, like Mrs. Redland or Miss Berry or Deborah, that it spreads no farther than Kendal. I would be interested to see many countries, and the Revolution in France is a very exciting event. I would like to see Mr. Pitt and Mr. Fox and the King and Queen (although they do not appear to be interesting).

'I fancy that I have no very good Disposition. I have a violent temper and dislike to be opposed in anything, but when my affections are roused there is nothing I will not do. Is this Sensibility? I fancy that it is.

'I am not a child any more but a woman. When did this change come to me? I think that day in Cockermouth with Humphrey. I had no concern that day as to what happened. I knew that whatever happened I could master it.

'I love this part of England. This is undoubtedly Sensibility, but I do not mind if it is. I do not wish ever to live anywhere else, although I wish to see other places. I would like to marry a man here, and have children here close to where I was born. . . .

'Because of my father I am very proud to be a Herries. I would like to meet all the different Herries, although I am sure that I should not wish to be with most of them very long. I find that it is in my nature to hate people very much and to love people very much, and also to laugh at everybody and also myself when I am very angry.

'I do not think that there is a God or that Reuben saw Him on the road outside Tours. If there is one He is stupid, because He has so much power and makes very little of it. Neither Francis nor Georges thinks there is a God.

'When I have some money I shall be very good at managing it. I am very good at managing anything if no one is in my way. I am not sorry for Sarah as I should be. She likes to be miserable, because she has never been miserable before. It is a new feeling for her. I am sorry for Francis, because he will remember all his life about David, which is a sad waste of time. I am resolved to make my life very amusing.'

With this she discovered that she was outside the gate of Stone Ends. The house was dead. A thin quarter moon hung like a wisp of pale rag over the end of a dirty silver-edged cloud, and, washed by ghostly mist, the house showed nothing human. She tied the horse to the gate and walked up the irregular stone path to the old worm- eaten door. At the sound of the banging knocker all the dogs in the house set up a fearful yelling and barking.

There was a pause, and Judith felt desperately cold and frightened. Suppose the old man didn't want her? He had been always good to her, but now he was aged and ailing, and under the thumb of his cook, people said. Suppose he didn't want her? And the wind, blowing sharply from Skiddaw, rustled all the plants in the weedy neglected garden in melancholy echo. One thing she noticed. The fountain was no longer playing. That had been Tom Gauntry's great pride, and his boast was that, however badly things went, he would always have enough water for the fountain. An owl hooted.

'You see,' said the owl, 'we haven't water enough any longer.'

There was a great unrasping of bolts from within, and then the door slowly opened. Old Tom Gauntry, holding a blowing candle, stood there, and a comical figure he looked. He was in a nightdress, black stockings and dingy slippers, and he wore a very long nightcap with a red worsted tip to it. Over his nightdress he had flung an old riding-coat. He peered out, shivering, his old wrinkled face like an anxious monkey's. When he saw who it was he gave a cry.

'Judy. By God, 'tis Judy!'

He looked so comical, with his nightcap, his nose dripping, his unshaven chin, that she couldn't help herself. She began to laugh, and then the cold and her own most uncertain situation in some strange way forcing her, once she had begun to laugh she couldn't stop. She pushed past him, to get in out of the cold, and then laughed and laughed and laughed.

'Judy! For Almighty sake shut the damned door. I've a cursed cold on me.'

'I must go and look after the horse first,' she said. 'Where's Wull?'

He began calling 'Wull! Wull! You devil, where are you? Wull! Wull!', and all the dogs began to bark.

While she was standing there she could take in the scene, which was certainly funny enough. The old hall stank of dogs, drink, damp. Dogs as usual were all about the place, scratching, sleeping, suddenly lifting up their heads and howling. In the stone fireplace a great fire was roaring up the chimney. In the ingle two old men, one in an untidy wig, one bald-headed, were sitting. On a table near them was a large bowl with a ladle in it, and, her head resting on the table, slept Emma Furze, a tall woman, snoring lustily.

'Hush!' said Judith. 'You'll wake her.'

'The last trump won't wake her,' cried Gauntry. He was rather drunken, but not badly so. 'Wull! Wull! Where the hell are you?'

Wull appeared, yawning, scratching his untidy head, his shirt hanging out over his breeches.

'Take Miss Judith's horse to the stable.' He put his old horny hand on her arm. 'Come to the fire and get warm, my pretty.'

She came to the fire and was introduced to the old men.

'This is my ancient friend, Mr. Jeremy Cards. He's a relation of yours. And this is Joe Twisset, he's a relation of none but the devil.' He kicked and cuffed the dogs, who, however, knew Judith and jumped about her, licking her hand. She went to the fire and stood in front of it roasting herself. She smiled on the two old men.

She was suddenly happy. She was at home here. The dogs, the smells, the old men, they were all right. She could manage it all very comfortably.

Gauntry was delighted to see her. She was, as he explained to the two old men, his especial pet, his pride, his joy. And although he was rather drunk he meant it all. The two old men were rather drunk too, but blinked their eyes in the firelight, rubbed their hands and looked happy.

'But why, my pretty, have you come so late? You should be abed, a child like you.' Sniff, sniff, sneeze, sneeze. 'I've a hell of a cold, a damnable hellish cold, and I'm not as young as I was.'

Judith explained that she had left Fell House for ever. She said very little about it. She had taken off her hat, and her hair burnt in the firelight. The old men looked at it admiringly.

'Yoicks! Yoicks! Hurray for ever!' Gauntry was delighted. 'Didn't I know it was coming? "Wait a bit, you old devil," I said to myself. "She'll be coming to you. Just be patient a trifle." This is your cousin,' he added, pointing to the old man in the wig, 'and it's certain he's delighted to see you. Aren't you, Jeremy?' he shouted in the old man's ear. 'This is Judy Herries, daughter to Francis. She's your cousin, you old bastard!'

Old Jeremy Cards rose on his trembling legs and made a low bow.

'I knew your father, my dear, and a fine grand man he was. I was born in 1712, I was, and I'm seventy-eight years of age and got my full sight and everything, but my hearing's failing a trifle. My right ear's the one for you to speak into if you'll be so good. It was in 1763 I saw your father last in the town of Kendal, and I remember like yesterday. . . .'

233

'Well enough, well enough,' Gauntry broke in. 'You must drink something, my pretty, and then we'll find a bed for you. Before she wakes,' he added, suddenly dropping his voice. 'Better get settled before she wakes. Although I can manage her, mind you. She's afraid of me, she is, but she's a good soul when she's sober, and an old man like me can't be expecting young beauties at his time o' life. Down, Roger, get out of it, Trixie. . . . The dogs know you well enough. So they should. This is your proper home, my dear. Didn't I find you when you were not a day born? By God and I did! Have something to warm you, my pretty.'

She was glad enough of the hot strong drink. Wull came in to say that the horse was stabled. The old kitchen clock rivalled Mrs. Furze's snores. All was cosy and comfortable.

Judith told the three old men about the scene at Uldale, and they nodded their sympathy, but old Jeremy Cards was galvanised to an extraordinary life by the very mention of the Herries family. So David was dead! Aye, aye--a pity, a pity! He'd known him as a fine young man who could cross-buttock anyone in the country. When would that be now? Aye, 1742, just before the Jacobite troubles, he'd seen David wrestle a man in Newlands, a great bullock of a man he was too, but David was the prettiest lad stripped--and there came before Judith's eyes a David whom she had never known, young, fresh, strong-limbed. Behind him were other Herries, old Maria who had lived to be almost a hundred, Pomfret and Jannice in Keswick, little Harcourt at Ravenglass, and Jeremy's own people, his father Humphrey, who had been born in 1687, and his mother Charlotte, who loved dancing and was a Beauty in the days of Queen Anne. The old man went rambling on, putting his skinny finger to his bare poll and wiping his eyes, that the smoke made to run, with a large yellow handkerchief. The logs fell to crimson ruin in the fire, and all the dogs slept.

Old Jeremy sighed: 'All dead, buried, and the worms have eaten them. But the family goes on. I daresay there'll be Herries sitting in this same spot a hundred years from now.'

He seemed, Judith thought, a brave old man, because he was quite alone in the world and hadn't a penny. He stayed about in the district, in any house that would keep him. He didn't want much, a drink, a bite, and the fire to sit beside. As he told them, most of his days were now swallowed by dreaming. 'It's hard to tell what's a dream.' Yes, that was true. It was hard to tell.

It occurred to Gauntry that the girl might be hungry. She acknowledged that she was, and the old men all said that they were hungry as well, so the host scuttered off in his clop-clop slippers to find them some food. He returned with a mutton ham and a piece of a pie. Some of the dogs woke up and came sniffing round; then Emma Furze woke also. She raised her head slowly from the table, stretched her arms and yawned. Then she saw Judith and stared as though her eyes would burst from her.

'This is little Judy Herries, Emma,' said Tom Gauntry nervously.

She stood up. She was a big woman. She had large black eyes, a fine bosom, and she stood with her legs spread like a trooper.

The old man looked at her apprehensively.

'Oh, is it?' she said.

Judith rose and held out her hand. But Mrs. Furze was uncertain as to whether she saw two Judiths or three, so, to avoid any silly mistake, she walked off a little unsteadily.

'She will be most agreeable,' said Gauntry, 'in the morning. She has a totally different nature in the morning.'

The mutton ham was extremely good.

In the morning, indeed, Mrs. Furze shed tears upon Judith's shoulder. She arrived in Judith's room before Judith was awake and sat for a long while moodily observing her. Judith, before many weeks were out, was to know all Emma Furze's history, was to know, too, that there was much merit in her if also some melodrama. Emma was to play an important part in Judith's story. But for the moment Judith, after a most healthy sleep, awoke to see this big woman balanced on a small chair and tears rolling down her nose. Tears, whether male or female, had always an instant effect upon Judith's heart, so now in a moment she was out of bed and, in her thin shift, was kneeling on the bare boards by Emma's side, imploring her to tell her trouble.

What, now as ever, was not Emma's trouble! At present it was difficult enough to disentangle. Emma, as Judith soon heard, had been an actress, and fine words were her pleasure. Words poured from her like the water from Lodore after heavy rains, and out of all the confusion nothing was immediately to be gathered. There had been a villain somewhere, 'a villain of uncultivated manners and corrupt heart'; there had been 'a smiling innocent babe.' She had been 'tossed on the waves of a sea of sorrows' and so, 'washed up' on Tom Gauntry's 'shores,' had consented to be both his cook and his mistress.

Her tale was so lengthy, so incoherently mingled with tears, the boards of the floor were so hard, that Judith was compelled to rise, whereupon Emma also rose and, folding Judith to her bosom, embraced her very warmly, told her that she would 'worship her for ever' and, becoming instantly practical, asked her what she would have cooked, with what clothes she might supply her; stated that, in fact, she was her servant for life. She was very quickly of the utmost cheerfulness, laughing and plunging about the bare room. It was thus, in this ridiculous manner, that Judith made one of the principal friendships of her life.

The next occurrence was, of all amazing things, the appearance of Will Herries. Two days after Judith's flight he appeared on a grand calm morning when the grass was still silver with frost and the scent of the Fell was stung with the breath of icy running water. The grass of the little tangled garden was crisp and crackling under Judith's heels. She looked up and saw Will, sitting there very stiff and reserved on a fine coal-black horse. She had not seen him for a long while. She thought he was in Liverpool. He looked older, thinner, better pleased with himself than ever, and he had all the pursed-up solemn air of a man who finds himself immensely important.

Their conversation was short. He did not come down from his horse, but was quite friendly. She stood near him, her hand on the bridle, looking up at him and often smiling. He seemed to her so very pompous.

'Where are my things, Will?'

'Your things?'

'My handsome possessions, my marriage portion, my livelihood. There is a dress and a cap, two pairs of shoes, a cracked china jar, the brush of a fox, a Holy Bible. . . .'

He looked severe. 'You must ride back with me, Judith.'

She laughed. He couldn't but feel that she was a lively attractive little thing, standing there in the crisp morning air with the Fell and the old house for her background. He saw, too, with surprise that she had become in the course of a night or so a woman.

'Ride back? Is that your mother's wish?'

He leant over towards her confidentially. He always prided himself on his diplomatic gifts.

'Now, Judith. These are women's quarrels. You know well enough that my mother has been a sick woman since my father's death.' (He said MY Mother and MY Father as though they had been his own most especial private property.) 'A sick woman. . . . But it will pass. It is already passing.'

'Has she spoken of me?'

'No. She has kept to her room.'

'Has she spoken to Francis?'

Will's upper lip, that was thin and tight like whipcord, was sharp.

'Francis is greatly to blame. He is my brother, but I cannot acquit him of fault.' (He said MY Brother as though, rather reluctantly this time, he owned him.)

Judith broke out fiercely:

'He is NOT to blame. . . . David's attack would have followed whether Francis were aggravating or no. You know well what the surgeon said. And after David's death Francis did everything that was possible. Sarah hugs her misfortune. She is not alone in losing a husband.'

Will said severely: 'You forget that she is my mother.'

'I forget nothing at all. Least of all do I forget that I never belonged at Uldale, Will. This is an old shabby place, and there are only old men in it, but it has always been my home more than the other. A poor taste, but my own. And so long as Sarah is living we can never be under the same roof. No, here is my place and here I stay.'

Will looked sternly about him as though he were making a quick business-like survey of the house, grounds, view, and found them of exactly no value at all.

'You know of Gauntry's bad repute?' he asked.

'Oh, Will,' she answered lightly, smiling at him. 'Who shall cast stones? There is not one of us without his detractor--'

This made Will uncomfortable. He looked for a moment as though he were going to ask Judith whether she had heard anything about himself. He had all the sensitiveness to personal reputation that belongs to very selfish men. However, all he said was:

'You yourself are a Herries, Judith, and in this part of the country the Herries have a reputation.'

She interrupted him laughing. 'There's another Herries in the house here already--Jeremy Cards. He knew my father.'

Will's expression was as though he had smelt some strong odour, which, indeed, as they were not far from the midden, he might have done.

'I have heard of him. A disreputable old man. . . .' He saw apparently that there was nothing to be done. He was relieved, perhaps, that it was so. 'So you will not come?'

'No, Will. I am happier here.' She asked him: 'Are things going well with you?'

He looked at her kindlily. He liked anyone who took an interest in his affairs.

'Well enough. . . . I am to go to London very shortly.' (He said London as though it were HIS London, just purchased by him.) 'I'm glad. They say there's a deal of money there.' He nodded very seriously. 'Liverpool is too small a place,' he told her.

He shook her hand, was minded to pat her head, but refrained. Then he rode off, she calling after him:

'Remember that my things must be sent.'

He turned in the saddle, nodded gravely and disappeared.

She went in to find Tom Gauntry huddled in an old bed-gown over a grumbling fire, dogs spread all around him. He looked up at her smiling, but his old face was wrinkled with pain. Her heart ached for him.

'That was Will Herries,' she said cheerfully. 'He asked me to return to Uldale. I say nay, like the girl in the ballad, and that is the end of that.'

'That is the end of that,' whispered the coal in the fire. 'Are you sure that you are wise?'

He put out his dry bony hand and took hers: 'Here has always been your home, and so long as I'm alive it shall be. But maybe that's not so long. My back aches and my head's like a turnip. There's a hunt to-day,

Threlkeld way. Hunting's over for me. And I'll never be on a horse again neither. . . . Strange, strange! I've lived my life on horses. . . . But it's been a long life. Emma likes ye, my pretty. She's got a heart, Emma has, poor silly soul. She'd skin herself for anyone she's fond of--HAS skinned herself a hundred times, poor girl. It's mortal cold this morning. And yet I'm hot in the head, as though there were coals of fire blazing away. It's the devil to be an old man--better go while you're active.'

She nodded her head. 'I think,' she said, 'I could deal with whatever came. I feel that way on a fine crisp morning. Uncle Tom, what am I to do to-day? There are a thousand things--I'll ride over to Bassenthwaite village. There's a woman there a marvel with herbs. David had her once for his leg. . . .'

The old man rolled his head, 'Nay, nay, I'm past everything but dreaming, damn my bones. Don't you worry, my pretty. When you've had a pain in your leg a long while it's a kind of friend.' Then he added quite casually as though he were saying nothing at all: 'Georges may be riding over from Whitehaven to-day.'

Her heart began to hammer. 'Georges Paris?'

'Aye. He's grown a fine young man, but he'll burn his fingers one of these days. He's in with a lot o' rogues. I've told him, but he don't listen. Thinks he can manage them. Very confident young man is Georges.'

Before she could say anything or even reason with herself about her foolish excitement Emma Furze joined them. Judith saw that she had smartened herself. She had a black hoop and a silver band in her dark hair. She looked really handsome as she stood there. There was something both foolish and good in her face; her black eyes were large and always brimming with emotion; at the slightest excuse her breast would heave and swell. She looked at Judith with a childlike smile of pleasure.

'I saw a fine man on a horse and said to myself, "He's come to take her away." I was tortured by the anxiety, my dear.'

'You need be tortured no longer. No fine gentleman shall take me away.'

With a sigh of relief Emma sat down beside them. How pleasant it was for Judith in the fresh quietness of the morning, no sound in the house but the old clock ticking and a mouse scratching behind the wainscot!

Judith asked Emma some questions, and out her history tumbled in an overwhelming flood--some of it at least. As Judith was to discover, there were endless, endless chapters to it; she had led, it seemed, a thousand lives, and was yet, according to her own account, but two and thirty.

Her first part had been that of the Duke of York in Richard the Third at the Birmingham Theatre, then Cupid in The Trip to Scotland, then Prince Arthur in King John, then Bath, where Mr. Palmer gave her five shillings a night. Her first girl's part was Sukey Chitterling in Harlequin's Invasion. She drew from her bosom

a packet of papers, yellow with age and greatly torn; she read to them with every possible dramatic gesture some of her notices.

'On Tuesday night Miss Pomeroy ("My name at that time, my dear") made her appearance in Isabella; and, although the audience went with such strong prejudices in favour of the fashionable Melpomene, yet it never did Mrs. Siddons draw more genuine tears from an audience. It is impossible to conceive what a high-finished picture this lady gave of Isabella's woes, and how nearly she arrived to nature in almost every scene. There were no studied pauses, to purchase, by vacancy of time, the approving hands of the audience, and yet the house echoed with repeated marks of approbation. Her shriek at the discovery of Biron had a good effect, but was rather that of terror without amazement, than of terror and amazement mixed. When the public consider that this Miss Pomeroy is that Miss Pomeroy who performed Cowslip. . . .'

Old Jeremy came stealing down the stairs to join them. He was blinking his eyes and yawning, for he was only now awake, but Emma's dramatic voice, the great rise in it as she came to the word 'terror,' her sudden declamation of Isabella's most moving lines, soon stirred him. It was as good, he declared, as being at the Theatre and with nothing to pay. The dogs barked, Wull came to the door and listened, and Judith, who had never seen a play, was entranced.

Very early in the afternoon the light vanished behind the hills, and the house was a place of shadows. Judith riding in from Caldbeck, and, chilled to the bone, hurrying to the fire, saw Georges Paris standing in the firelight. No one else was there. It was the same as when they had run, that first time, from the supper-room, and she had smacked his cheek.

She would not smack his cheek now. He had grown a man, slim and tall in his riding-coat and riding-boots, his black hair tied in a queue, his handsome self-confident face bright with life, fun, energy, adventure.

He saw, too, a changed Judith. From the child whom he had left there had grown a child-woman, charming in her small buoyant independence, throwing her hat beside her and shaking her red curls just as she used to do, holding out her hand to him at once in their old friendship.

'How d'ye do, Georges? I'm happy to see you again.'

'By heaven,' he thought, 'she's somebody. . . . I'm glad I came.'

For he had been in two minds about it. Stone Ends was in no sort of way the place it had been. Gauntry was ill, only old men there, flea-bitten dogs, and the strange woman, half cook, half play-actress, in command. Georges was profoundly convinced that he could live but once and must waste no time. Had he been present when Gauntry needed he would have helped him to his last shilling, for he was impetuously generous, but he was happy in living for the moment and in finding the moment always exciting.

And now this Moment was Judith. He had not expected to find her here and certainly not supposed that she would, at his very first glimpse of her, affect him so strongly. He had thought of her, forgotten her, thought of her again. He lived for excitement, and only accepted the things and people that could contribute to that. Since he had seen her he had had adventures enough-- on the Cumberland coast, on the Solway, in Holland, in London--to satisfy, he thought, any man. What he did not recognise--as we never recognise the truest things about ourselves--was that all these adventures had been scattered with a thin second-rate dust, as though, with everything that he touched, he robbed it of a degree of fineness. He had first-rate moments and a great quality of happy fearless adventure when things went well, but he had second- rate ambitions, second-rate vision, second-rate reactions. He was a fine young man with a soul, through no fault of his own, inevitably shabby. Was it perhaps in Judith's power to raise him into a finer world? He did not think so, because he was convinced that no world could be finer than the one he was in; and she did not think so, because she never, all her life through, saw herself as a moral agent in anything. She never thought at all about moral qualities in the abstract.

At any rate, simply as a factor in the intricate course of Herries history, it must be recorded that on that afternoon, November 24 of the year 1790, Judith Herries and Georges Paris, standing beside the fire in the hall of Stone Ends, fell in love with one another.

Judith knew at once what had happened to her. She was always extremely clear-sighted about herself. Now if he attempted to kiss her she would not smack his cheek. But she did not intend that he should kiss her. She was in fact very cool to him indeed.

He had intended to stay the one night at Stone Ends and then ride on to Penrith, where he had business of an especially interesting nature. He was by present occupation a smuggler and just now a prosperous one. But his intention was to find a little place somewhere in the district, a rather remote place if possible, and make it his centre. This was not only a business ambition. He had a true love of the country, possibly the truest thing in him; he liked nothing better than the old life of hunting, fishing and the rest that he had had in the earlier days at Stone Ends. Sensuous enough, he nevertheless vastly preferred men to women as companions. He had long pictured to himself a small farm somewhere that could be the centre both of his business and his pleasure. Now that he was in funds was the time to purchase such a place. He certainly would not be in funds for ever.

So, at the very first instant of seeing Judith walk across the floor towards him, in a flash it had come to him: 'Here is the woman you want.' He had always considered her, even as a child, a most sensible capable person. There was some hard common sense in Judith that had always roused his keenest admiration. She knew this country and liked it. She would run a house well, would manage men with authority. She had no ties. She had pluck and courage and, he surmised, would not trouble herself too deeply about transgressions of the law. Now that he beheld her again he remembered how greatly he had been impressed in Cockermouth by her decision and resolution. She was not strictly a beauty, but there was something very attractive to the senses.

When he wanted anything he always, in five minutes, concluded that it was his. He wasted no time at all; before they had been half an hour together he was making ardent love to her.

Emma Furze was in her room that night imploring her to be careful.

'He is not for you--no, never, never!'

She held Judith's hand and spoke as though the fate of nations were in danger.

'What have you against him, Emma?'

'He has no character, no fine feelings. I have known men and been betrayed by them too. They are all false, and this young man is French as well.'

'They are not all false,' said Judith, thinking of Francis and Reuben. 'But you must recollect, Emma, that I am acquainted with Georges Paris since I was a baby.'

'Yes, but now you are in love with him. You were not and now you are. Love blinds poor women. Men are never to be trusted for a single instant. They are filled with cruelty and caprice. On the most vain and frivolous pretexts, whenever their temper is in the least ruffled, they cast you aside. They behave with propriety only when it is to their advantage.'

'Well, my dear, you need not fear. I know myself.'

But did she? She lay in bed looking at the moonlight washing the floor. She was in love--and for the first time. Did she know that? Her cheek was hot as she fell asleep. And her dreams were of a fiery splendour and a happiness that she had never touched before.

It was plain enough to everybody next day that Georges remained at Stone Ends only because of Judith. He carried on his courtship with an impatient ardour that had a great deal of very real passion in it. He was ruthlessly selfish about everyone else. Gauntry he patronised, the two old men he disregarded, Emma Furze he detested. Like many sensual men nothing exasperated him more than having to be in the company of a woman who was most unattractive to him. Emma exasperated him by her apparent vagueness. She seemed to him to live entirely in a world of make-believe. He declared that she did not know where France was nor that Paris was the capital of that country: neither politics nor money meant anything to her at all. She lived entirely in a world of the passions, except when she was cooking. (She was a very excellent cook.) She was vague and ignorant and absent-minded except when someone for whom she cared was in question; then she was as sharp as a needle. He knew at once that she was his enemy so far as Judith went, and he loved her none the better for that knowledge.

So things moved swiftly. Judith was in a strange state. He caught her when she was isolated from all her claims and associations. Everything played into his hands. When her things arrived from Uldale, with them came a letter from Reuben. It was very short.

DEAREST JUDITH--I am going with Humphrey to France. There is the centre of all the movement for the Betterment of Mankind. I shall learn there in that New World how to help Mankind. I shall think of you so often, dearest Judith. I love you with my whole Heart.

REUBEN

SUNWOOD.

France! It had taken Reuben as it had taken Francis. And now it seemed that it must take her too. But what a different France hers! For Georges seemed to care nothing for his parents' country, save that he got lace and brandy from it, nor did it concern him at all that there was a Revolution there. What was Georges in reality? Did she know him? Did she see him as he was? Was Emma in the right about him? But, as the days went on, she could not think any more. She had never been in love before. She had not known that it would be this strange fiery heat, mist before the eyes, all the outside world sounding dim to the ear.

The house, the old men, Emma, all grew faint and unreal to her, and Georges was ever more clear. He seemed to her most beautiful, and now, because he also was in love, he was most tender.

In these chill frosty December days he was at his very best. There were in him somewhere noble instincts; he wanted her so fiercely (as he wanted anything withheld from him) that his very desire brought him close to her and he caught some of her fineness. He had been in love again and again since he could remember, but now three things were united that had perhaps

never been before-- desire, perception of character, and practical advantage. There was wisdom in his choice of her, although the very thing that now attracted him, the strong domination of her will and purpose, would be, when passion had died, the last thing that he would want in her.

She held out against him so long as she could, but he was too strong for her. It seemed to her that this had been foreshadowed since her sharp farewell to him in Cockermouth. He had looked at her then as though he knew that one day she would come to him.

But she was never less assured about him than at the moment before she submitted. Coming down the stairs she saw him standing in the hall that was lit by a blazing fire. He was dark black, standing motionless there, as though he were waiting for her. She paused on the stair, and the thought struck her heart: 'This man is my enemy.' Then she came down, and a moment later she was in his arms.

Afterwards he was speaking in all sincerity when he said:

'My dearest, I will care for you with my whole heart. You can make me noble and fine. This is a new beginning. There is nothing you cannot make of me.'

Lying in his arms she was wildly happy with that fierceness of intensity that was always hers in everything that she did. But she had never surrendered herself before to anyone save the ghost of her father. No one had held her and loved her and stroked her hair and kissed her with passion. She did not know that it could be so sweet. What vows she made of service and devotion! How she would work now that she had someone to work for!

She did not ask him where he would take her, whether he had money to keep her! She could work for them both; at what she did not inquire.

Her cheek against his, she stayed in a trance. Perfect happiness had come. How could she ever have thought that she did not know him? She knew him utterly. She had always known him as she knew herself.

She was so very young.

END OF PART I

PART II

WATENDLATH

FRANCIS RIDES OVER

This book is the history of a country, England (not, of course, the whole history); of a family, Herries (nor the whole history of that); and of certain members of that family especially--Judith Paris first, then, after her, of Reuben, Will and Francis (and not, of course, their whole history either).

But the Herries are English, and Judith, Reuben, Will and Francis are Herries. At the heart of this family there is a struggle and in each of these individuals a struggle. The history of that struggle is the history of this book, is the history, perhaps, of every book that has ever been written.

The history of any country and the history of any family is continually presenting strange underground movements of ebb and flow, and to these movements members of the country and of the family are for ever responding, although they may themselves be quite unconscious of it. Moreover, the actions of one individual will often permeate the whole body of which he or she is a part; even slender characteristics may affect it as the shape of Cleopatra's nose swung Egypt, Napoleon's passion for hot baths France, and Mrs. Fitzherbert's virtuous tenacity England.

So the determination of Will Herries' prominent chin affected just now the fortunes of the whole family of Herries. They may be said to have swung upwards upon it.

In 1791 Will Herries moved to London and married there a Miss Christabel Carmichael, a young woman with a fine waist, something of a fortune, a doting father; against these benefits must be set a slight cast in one eye and a rather hysterical temper. Will cared nothing for the first and soon dominated the second. He was determined to get on, and, as in this life everyone gets what he wants if only he wants it hard enough, he did get on, and speedily.

He was soon known in the City as a man of prudence and enterprise nicely commingled. His business was especially in Indian trade, tea, silks and spices. He had a pretty house in the village of Chelsea, and in February 1792 Mrs. Will Herries gave birth to a son, Walter, who, with his opening shout to the world, proclaimed that he also meant to get on and to waste no time in doing so.

It would, however, be an exaggeration to say that at this time any other members of the Herries family were at all aware that they were about to swing upwards on the point of Will's chin. As was always the Herries characteristic, there was perfect self-confidence everywhere until disintegrating imagination broke in and threatened it. The Family was at this moment divided, unlike Gaul, into four parts. There were the Herries of Uldale, Sarah and her children, Francis and Deborah; the Pomfret Herries of Kensington, with whom poor Humphrey Sunwood once on a time visited; the Cards of Bournemouth, Prosper Cards who married Amelia Trent and had offspring, Jennifer, born in 1770, and Robert, born in 1771; and, fourthly (but in their own opinion absolutely firstly), Lord and Lady Rockage of Grosset Place in Wiltshire. Judith Herries, sister to Raiseley and first cousin to David, had, many years before, bewildered into matrimony the Honourable Ernest

Bligh, who in his gout-ridden and exceedingly ill-tempered old age had become Lord Monyngham, then Viscount Rockage. Of them had been born three children, Frederick, who died, Carey in 1755 and Madeline in 1756. Carey, now Lord Rockage, had two offspring--Carey the younger, born in 1780, and Phyllis, born in 1782.

Lord and Lady Rockage, his sister Madeline, his children Carey and Phyllis, lived all in penniless grandeur at Grosset in Wiltshire, where the rain trickled through the roof, the trees creaked and wailed, and the cold of the stone passages carried rheumatism into the bones of all who suffered it.

Lest these family branches should seem confusing it may be said that the Uldale family stood for Country Life, Pomfret's family for London, the Cards in Bournemouth for Social Intercourse, and the Rockages for the Ruling Classes; yes, and more than that, for two strong elements of the Ruling Classes at the end of the eighteenth century in England, namely the arrogance of a dominating Aristocracy and the narrowness but courage of Methodism.

This book is not, however, in the main the history of the Rockage fortunes. There is a story there, in that odd proud group of the family, that should command a book of its own.

To have suggested to either the Rockages or the Cards of Bournemouth at this time that Will Herries was an important relation would have been to invite derision. But Will's time was approaching.

Possibly Francis, up in Uldale, had more foreknowledge of it than any other. He knew his brother. Indeed, very often, Francis, who was without any personal conceit, felt that he knew everything about his own immediate relations, that he knew too much for anyone's happiness. He had in fact a very special quality of psychological penetration. He was now grown very handsome for those who did not find his figure too slender. His features were sharp but delicate, his colour fresh and gentle; he carried himself with a strongly reserved dignity, was always clothed with perfect simplicity but in absolute taste.

He wore an air of melancholy, no pose of the period, but very real indeed. These years were, in fact, very unhappy.

They might well be so. Uldale was, at this time, no cheerful place. He held himself there because he thought it his duty. A bailiff managed the farm, but Francis managed the bailiff--and everyone else as well. He had far more authority than cheerful stout David had ever had; he was the friend of no one, and would have been unpopular in his remoteness had there not been a very proper pride in him. He was the Aristocrat of the district, and everyone was pleased that there should be an Aristocrat. His melancholy reserve lent not only the house but all the district an air. Unlike his sister Deborah, who was in and out of all the houses of the neighbourhood with her giggle, her two little dogs and her passion for gossip, he went nowhere and entertained only with reluctance.

But it was on his relations with his mother that the whole house hung.

Sarah Herries was now an aged and shrunken woman. In the spring of 1792 she was fifty-four years of age, but she looked another ten. Her hair was white; she dressed always in the deepest black, her shoulders a little bent as she walked slowly, leaning on an ebony cane. Her eyes were scornful, as though she said always to the world: 'You took from me the only thing for which I ever cared. What do you expect of me now?'

Now that her features were more slender there was a resemblance between herself and her son. The stout and chattering Deborah seemed to have no relationship with either of them.

Sarah had not, of course, forgiven Francis; she would never forgive him. She would never forgive him, but she surrendered to his influence. She allowed him to do what he would with the house and everyone in it. She found indeed no interest in either contemporary life or persons. She sat, either in her own upstairs room or in the temple in the garden on a fine day, staring in front of her, at the bad blowzy painting of David or the china figures or across the sunlit lawns to the sweep of Skiddaw or the Scottish hills. Her lips moved; her thin pale hands beat together a little on her lap. She was in no way deranged. Any question asked of her she answered sharply and with a certain shivering impatience.

She allowed Deborah to chatter to her for so long as she would, and Deborah flattered herself that but for her jolly brightness and good-nature the house would fall into ruins. But Deborah also abandoned everything to Francis. She paid visits with increasing avidity among the neighbours. She was a great player of cards, a passionate gossip, surely a destined old maid. But Destiny does not always work to pattern.

Francis behaved to his mother with unfaltering courtesy and an unflinching patience. But it seemed to him that life could not continue for very much longer like this. His real life was imprisoned within him like a fire within an ivory bowl. The bowl would crack, and the fire burn the hand that held it.

He was thirty-two. His life was passing. And a day came when his endurance broke.

In the evening he sat opposite his mother in the China Room, while a thin coal fire whispered grumpily between them. The curtains, with their stamped pagodas and blue tilted bridges, were drawn. A small King Charles spaniel bitch lay at Francis' feet. He realised quite suddenly, with that premonition of coming events, always his special gift, that some crisis was approaching. Everything in the room seemed to share his knowledge.

On his lap, as he was always afterwards to remember, was a copy of Burke's Reflections on the Revolution in France. His mother spoke. She had a fashion, when they were alone together, of speaking, as it were, to herself, so that when he answered her it was as though he were addressing the wall behind her or a picture or a chair. But now she looked at him directly.

'Francis,' she said, and her eyes wandered over his face as though she were seeing him for the first time. 'Why do you stay here? It is not, I know, to give yourself pleasure.'

'Yes, ma'am,' he answered. 'I am happy here.'

'No, you are not. I know exactly why you stay. It is from a sense of duty. You think that you did me a wrong and repay it by this attention to us. That is your duty.'

He made no answer. His heart beat thickly.

'Well, it is no duty. You have your own life to be lived. Will is working in London, but there is money sufficient for you to travel. Herman is honest enough and will see that everything goes smoothly here.'

Herman was the bailiff. The reference to Will was no new one. The inference was that Will was working hard at making money in London while Francis idled. . . . No new inference.

But Francis, tried by much practice, only nodded his head.

'If you wish me to go, ma'am.'

'I wish! I wish! Who cares what I wish? . . . I am a dead woman.' Then a surprising thing happened. She turned to him almost eagerly, as though they were, for an instant, friends. 'You didn't know, did you, that one person can die and quite another take her place within the same skin? That other woman would have long forgiven you had she lived. Besides, she was your mother. She was gay and happy, foolish possibly in her trust of events, but she was only a child, although she bore children. . . . But this other woman here is not your mother, was not even when she was alive. You have often felt her unjust, I know. . . .'

'No, ma'am,' he answered her.

'Oh, but you have, you have! And rightly. . . . Only I am not sorry at any injustice. That belonged to your mother.'

As always a strange mingling of irritation and pity rose in him. He hated a sort of melodrama and extravagance in her speech, and yet he knew that at the heart of the extravagance there was a real cankerous sickness.

He felt deeply sorry for them both, so gently he answered:

'I do not want to go, mother, unless you wish it.'

She got up, felt for her cane, walked towards the door, then turned and said roughly:

'I do wish it. We can have no life together, you and I.'

Then she went out.

He stayed there alone in a kind of impotent fury. So that was all he got for his years of faithful service! He had always had a sharp, keen sense of reality and also a kind of hunger for it. He felt now that ever since

his father's death this house had been completely unreal, and it was his mother who had made it so.

To-night, his mother's last words in his ear, he was moved to a passionate sense of rebellion. He paced up and down the little parlour, the spaniel following his movement with soft anxious eyes. Yes, if she wished him to go he would do so! No word of thanks for all the drudgery of these years! Here he had lamed his life at its most active and promising period to serve her, and all he received was a contemptuous reference to Will. Will, who had never, in all his days, thought of anyone but himself or of anything but his own advantage!

Poor Francis was one of those who are confident about ideas but doubtful about the human race. That Liberty, Equality, Fraternity must ultimately flourish, he was convinced, but he was hurt, with pitiful ease, by any act of human injustice. He found it difficult to believe that human beings were egoistic, jealous, cruel, niggardly, and yet on every day of his life he was injured by proofs that they were.

He COULD not credit that all his years of service went for nothing. They did not go for nothing. Did he but know it, it was his mother's acute knowledge of her own injustice that aggravated her bitterness. But . . . 'Herman will do as well.' Herman, the stout, red-faced bailiff, who was honest only because he was stupid and faithful, only because he was without imagination.

To-morrow, then, he would go. He would show them--He stopped abruptly. Wiser councils were prevailing. First he would ride out to Watendlath and see little Judith. She would help him. She was now, he sighed, his only friend. The spaniel came to him as he sat down by the fire, put her paws on his knee and gazed into his face.

Next morning he rode out. He took a magnificent white mare, Juno, his especial favourite, who knew the country so well that she could find her way over almost trackless paths and climb precipitous hills like a young pony. He was a fine figure in his purple riding-coat with the high collar, his head up, like a king. But he didn't feel like a king. There was something surreptitious in his departure as he turned down over the fell towards Bassenthwaite.

He told no one where he was going. Mention of Judith to the Uldale household was a great deal worse than useless. He had seen her three times in the fifteen months since her marriage, once in Keswick, twice at Watendlath. Watendlath was an exceedingly remote little valley lying among the higher hills above Borrowdale. It could indeed be scarcely named a valley: rather it was a narrow strip of meadow and stream lying between the wooded hills, Armboth on the Grasmere side and King's How and Brund Fell on the other.

It was utterly remote, with some twenty dwellings, a dark tarn and Watendlath Beck that ran down the strath until it tumbled over the hill at Lodore.

Georges Paris had found here exactly the place that he wanted, an old house once a Statesman's but now belonging to a farmer, Ritson, who, owing to a ne'er-do-well son, now dead, was at money odds, but owned two farms. Paris bought one farm from him, but kept him there to maintain both. And there he deposited Judith, while himself, for much of the year, was engaged on all kinds of doubtful adventures on the coast, even in Holland and Scandinavia.

Francis had not seen Judith for some months, but at his last sight of her had been amazed by the happiness that radiated from her. He had regarded the marriage with that ragamuffin Frenchman as most certainly disastrous, had not had spirit even to contradict the self-congratulatory 'I-told-you-so's' of his mother and sister. When he heard that Judith had been banished to Watendlath, disaster seemed even more certain. But when he saw her he found her confident, assured, triumphant. It was true that it was then still the first year of her marriage and for most of that Georges had been away. But she had had six months in Watendlath alone--and had flourished on it. When he rode out there on the last occasion it had been veiled in rain and storm. It had seemed to him simply the end of the world. With the rain lashing his face and the gale tugging at his hair he had looked back to see that small indomitable creature laughing good-bye to him in the narrow doorway. Indomitable, yes! But the happiness was real. It was not assumed to reassure him. His heart was touched, and he loved her more than ever.

He thought, as he rode on this March morning of flushing sun and hovering cloud through Keswick and then beside the Lake water that now tumbled with a shiver of grey and then swam into straths of gold, that she was the only human being now in all the world whom he did love.

In old days, when she had been a child and told him insistently that she adored him, his own shyness and sensitiveness of taste had held him back, but, after his father's death and her flight to Gauntry's, he had realised to the full the courage, fidelity, warmth of feeling in her, yes, and her egotism and passion for power as well. How could that passion for power be satisfied in this lonely place where there were scarcely a hundred souls? He himself, who had no passion for power but only for justice, could not be quiet there. No, he thought, sighing, as he turned Juno away from the Lake up the Fell path, nor anywhere else.

Where in the world now was Equality, where was Freedom? He, who had killed his father with his joy over the fall of the Bastille, must now in this March of 1792 begin to tremble at the things that his Frenchmen were contemplating. After the Flight to Varennes his sympathies, always so easily swayed by human misfor-tune, had begun to turn towards that unhappy King and Queen. Then the news in December of the ultimatum to the Elector of Treves had moved him again towards this brave country beset by so many external, as well as internal, enemies, but the latest news of the quarrels between Delessart and Brissot in the Assembly caused him the bitterest disappointment.

He was afterwards to recollect that it was on that March day of cold sunshine, riding out to Watendlath, that he foresaw something of the cruel confusion that led to the September Massacres.

As he rode into the higher air and crossed the little bridge above the running stream he shook his shoulders with a sort of indignant despair. He had never before felt his life to be so lonely, so aimless, such a failure. He looked about him, and as always the beauty of this beloved country fell on him like a balm. Only a few days before there had been a March snowstorm in the upper dales. He could not yet, riding among the trees, see the rising Fell, but he could scent the snow in the air. He knew that if the snowfall had been deep the shepherds would be anxious for the sheep. He felt suddenly a touch of their anxiety, and with that a kind of shame for bothering about unreal things like politics when there were such real things as sheep close at hand. Soon he would be clear of the trees for a while and see how the sheep were faring.

He had reached now the spot where Watendlath Beck tumbled into Lodore, and as always when he was here he must stop and breathe in deeply that perfect beauty. This was surely one of the loveliest places in all England--English, too, in its qualities of old imperturbable age, a kind of wistful tranquillity, a cosiness of beauty mingled with an almost fierce suggestion of force. Here Vikings had stood, here two hundred years later his descendants would stand, and at every time the cataract (when the rains had fallen) would fling clouds of mist above the turning flower-like whiteness of the water that leapt and fell and leapt again between the thin brown stones. The dark bare stems of the larch and oak stood sentinel on either side, and exactly framed by the delicate pattern Derwentwater lay, in colour now snow upon steel, a thin shadow of stainless white hovering over the silver grey. Skiddaw and Blencathra seemed to sway under the changing passing cloud. Every colour--white and grey and brown--although so delicate, seemed to hint at the coming Spring; there was the promise of saffron and primrose in the stems of the trees, in the leaping water of the Fall.

Francis felt for a moment that here was the answer to all his unrest. With his hand on Juno's back, his eyes leaping with the water, he swore to himself that he would be true to this fragment of English soil, and that so long as he was so no other disappointment, whether in God or man, could deeply touch him. Here was his proof that there was something lovely in the world that made this life worth while.

He rode then higher on to the Fell, Juno picking her way on an almost trackless path, and could see now the sheep gathered into dark groups feeding on the loads of hay that the farmers had sent to relieve them. The whole sweep of the Fell was flooded with thin sunshine, and little rocks stood out in it like islets of ebony. The snow, on the farther Fell, was more scattered and lay in streaks like marking on a tiger's back. The sheep moved in black sequence against the running stone walls. There was silence everywhere, except for the rhythm like a humming voice of the distant falls.

He rode on, through forest again. As he approached Watendlath in his purple coat on his great white horse, the distant white fells, like pummelled pillows, shining down on him, he might have been some knight-at-arms riding into the Forbidden Land. He seemed to be more and more withdrawn from the world. He was high up among the hills, and yet this meadow and stream had the quality of a mysterious valley that would later on be rich with flowers and enchanted with the voices of birds. But to-day ice and snow and rock ringed him inexorably round.

Soon, looking down, he saw the odd dumpy shape of John Green House, Judith's home. A queer little place indeed, crouched into the soil as though it feared a blow, its narrow windows peering blindly on to Armboth Fell that here was split to allow a beck to tumble down the hollow. There was the chattering of the beck, the bark of dogs, the lowing of a calf, but before he had reached the door Judith had seen him, had run out, had almost pulled him off his horse in her eagerness, flung her arms round his neck and dragged him into the house.

John Green House was L-shaped with a double porch. From the 'hallan' or passage there were three doors, one that led into the 'down-house,' now used for farm purposes, baking, brewings and the rest, the second that led to the garden, and the third to the 'house-place' or 'house,' a beautiful room with lovely views, surrendered now entirely to Judith; beyond this room was a smaller panelled one, Judith's bedroom. A small staircase led upstairs to rooms that had been formerly open to the rafters but that were now ceilinged.

Judith took Francis into the 'house-place,' shining now in the pale March sunlight. The walls were plastered. There was a stone mantelpiece over an open hearth; there was a settle, some carved chairs and a large oak table.

There were signs of Judith's passionate cleanliness everywhere. Everything gleamed and shone; china, candlesticks of beaten brass, an old spit with many hooks and a dripping-pan. Some early daffodils were in a china bowl on the oak table.

She stood back and stared at him.

'Now, let me look at you! Oh, how handsome you are, Francis! I had forgotten. You are more beautiful every day!' She stood on tiptoe, pushing back the high hard collar of his riding-coat that she might see the white fall of his neckcloth and the beech-coloured waistcoat with the stamped silver buttons.

'I always put on my best when I come out to see you,' he said, laughing, and taking off his riding-coat.

'That's more than I can do for you,' she answered.

She was wearing the country clothes, an upper-dress of undyed duffel like a man's and a skirt of native wool woven into a sort of serge--wool of the black sheep mixed with red and blue. Her stockings were of blue homespun, and she had clogs of uncurried leather. They were lined with straw to keep her feet warm.

Francis thought she looked extremely well, with her pale excited face and the pile of red-gold hair on top of it. She was, as always, immaculate from head to toe. She had an air of virginal purity as though the wind, the rain, the unchecked sun had cleansed her with an austerity of their own. In fact she was neither austere nor remote. She was wild with excitement at seeing him, could not keep still, went dancing about the room, touching first one thing and then another, talking all the time. Of course, she was yet a child, only seventeen, while he was thirty-two. But it was true what she said, suddenly turning to him and crying: 'You know, Francis, I've always loved you--from the moment that I was born!'

She had to have someone to love, and she had to have someone to dominate too. It amused him to see how at once she took charge of him, telling him where he must go and what he must do. It would soon be the dinner-hour, but first he must see everything, and she danced in front of him, taking him along the 'hallan' into the farmhouse of the Ritsons. He was aware of a great fire roaring in the open fireplace, of a spit turning, of sacks of corn, hams and sides of bacon hanging, the oak settle screened by the 'heck,' the 'rannel-balk' or great wooden beam across the chimney, and a chain with hooks for cooking utensils hanging. The big room seemed filled with men and women, all busied with affairs, but he noticed in especial one magnificent old man with a snow-white beard like a patriarch. Judith introduced him. This was Robert Ritson, the head of the Ritson family, a man of seventy-four, who, in spite of his many troubles, financial and others, was yet above the world, above it and removed a little from it, with that touch of remoteness and austere reserve that is in all true Cumbrians.

Then they went out. She led him over the boulders and the foaming beck down the hill above the meadow to the Churn. The Churn was filled just now with water from the snow off the fells and toiled and tossed and seethed, an odd spot of turmoil above the quiet silence of the long meadow. Judith said a strange thing as they were looking into it.

'If Georges were to leave me I'd throw myself into it,' she said. Then laughing: 'No, I would not. I would stick a knife in his back.'

'Do you love him then so much?' asked Francis.

'I do.'

'And does he love you?'

'He loves no one at all but himself,' she answered.

Then they went and stood by the Tarn in front of the stone wall of the house. All was very grey and silent. The hills streaked with white, thick with naked trees, looked down on them while quilts of wadded cloud rolled heavily across the sky. Francis shivered.

'It's a black piece of water,' he said.

She told him that it could be every colour, that it had so many moods that she could almost believe that it was alive, as Mother West, the witch, said it was.

'Have you a witch then in this small place?' he asked her.

They had, but a good and kindly one who gave the girls love potions and the men cures for the rheumatism. 'She is an immense woman, like a whale.' Then, as they walked back into the house again, Judith told him about all the families in the place, the Ritsons, the Wilsons, the Tysons, the Morrows, the Blythwaites, the Gibsons, the Robsons.

Judith knew everyone and, as Francis soon perceived, governed everyone. She was Mistress of Watendlath, knew it and triumphed in it.

But it was not until after their dinner that they truly talked. For dinner they had oat-bread baked on the girdle, a broth of onions and savoury herbs, and a goose pie that had been made at Christmas. To drink there was ale brewed in the 'down-house.'

When dinner was over they sat over the fire, while the logs hissed and crackled and spat and threw out tongues of flame against the blackened stone. He asked her first whether she were happy. As she replied, telling him everything in her mind with her accustomed honesty, he watched her. She had changed but little, and he thought to himself that her real struggle with Georges was yet to come.

She had all the audacity and self-confidence that she had always had. Nothing in life had frightened her as yet then. She had a woman's knowledge and common sense.

'This Georges of yours,' he said. 'You'd stick a knife in his back if he left you. But he's always leaving you. How long has he been away this time?'

'He has to be away on his business.'

'What is his business?'

'Oh, smuggling, stealing, anything bad. But when he has made money he will settle down here.'

'Such a man settle down?'

'Oh yes. You cannot know him, of course. I often think no one knows him but myself.'

'How much has he been here in the fifteen months of your marriage?'

'Three months. Three months and a half. There was the first month-- oh, that was grand! We did nothing but make love to one another. I was new to him. It couldn't stay. . . . One morning he knocked me down, and before I was myself again he was gone. But he wrote me a beautiful letter from Whitehaven. He was away then six months. He came back one forenoon without any warning and then we loved one another again--two weeks or more. Then he was away five months, and the last time he was here we were good company, not lovers. He had a woman in Whitehaven.'

'You knew all this,' he asked her, 'and didn't care?'

She looked at him with bright eyes. 'Most certainly I cared. Night after night I cried myself sick; then if I made a noise he would go and sleep with the farming men. He has no heart. He is quite cold. When I saw that, I stopped crying.'

'And you love such a man?' he asked, disgusted.

'Certainly. He wants me to love him. And I find him charming. He is the most elegant company in the world. When he is here at home we laugh and laugh for hours together. If I am in love with him and troublesome, he is either in love, too, or he is drunk and doesn't care, or he goes away. He certainly cares for me more than anyone in the world, but not for me very much. He says it is the fault of his mother, who was a bad woman and beat him. Did I ever tell you, Francis,' Judith dropped her voice a little, 'how when I was little and ran away to Uncle Tom's I looked through a door and saw Georges' mother naked and a young man in his shirt kissing her knees?'

'No,' said Francis, 'you never told me.'

'Well, that was the beginning of it.'

'The beginning of what?'

'Of my love for Georges. I love him because he is beautiful and witty and cares for nobody. But one day I will make him think of me so that he can never get me out of his mind. It is almost so now. He is always writing to me . . . and when he has stolen enough money from other people, we shall go to London and steal some more.'

Francis was aghast.

'But, good heavens, child, do you approve of stealing?'

'I would not steal myself. I wouldn't steal a halfpenny. But no one will ever stop Georges from stealing. It is in his blood. He steals my things all the while--and from the Ritsons too. But one thing about Georges--he never tells a lie. If I ask him whether he has had women in Whitehaven he always says Yes. He tells me all about the smuggling. He tells me everything. You cannot change people's natures. Isn't that what your Mr. Rousseau said? I have read the Nouvelle Héloïse and find it too full of sentiment. Well, I love Georges and I cannot change him. He had a bad mother--so what would you?'

'And he beats you?'

'No longer. After the last time I said next time I would kill him. Perhaps I would. He knows my father was mad and my mother a gipsy. That is one thing he cannot understand--that I am so PRACTICAL.' She said the word twice with immense satisfaction. 'And on the other side so wild. I tell him that is the Herries blood; what makes them so interesting a family.'

'But,' cried Francis, still greatly distressed, 'there will be some terrible scandal. He will kill someone or be killed or be put in gaol or be hanged for a thief. . . .'

She nodded her head. 'Georges says he will never die in his bed. I would be for ever anxious while he is away if I were not--what is it?--a fatalist. That's what I am, Francis, a fatalist. What will be will be, and nothing shall beat me.'

Then she went on eagerly. 'I want to go to London. London must be fine. I want to see all the Herries, my relations. Will lives there now, and they say his wife is as proud as a peacock and has a cast in her eye. Georges heard about them. And there is Pomfret, old Raiseley's son. . . . Oh yes, and there are the Rockages in Wiltshire. It was the greatest fun, Emma Furze saw them.'

'Who is Emma Furze?'

'She is my greatest friend. She was Uncle Tom's mistress, and after he died she went back to the theatre again. She had a season in Salisbury, and Lady Rockage had a meeting about the wickedness of the theatre. Emma went, and she says Lady Rockage is like an old pincushion and has two children at her heels, and they have a house always in the rain--'

'It can't always be raining,' Francis interrupted, laughing. Then he asked: 'But how can you endure it so long here alone?'

'I am never alone,' she answered indignantly. 'Never for a moment. I shall prove it to you. I keep a Journal.'

She ran, pulled out the drawer of a cabinet and brought back to him a book bound in dark-green leather with heavy clasps.

He opened it at random and read, in her sprawling childish hand, entries such as these:*

Nov. 3, 1791. Mrs. Ritson had a Haunch of Venison this morning from Mr. Crosthwaite of Keswick. Obliging of him but I think he has an eye on Mary Ritson. While I was in at Tom Blythwaite's this morning their cousin Nancy B. from Mardale was taken in Labour being only a quarter gone and had a Miscarriage. No doctor nearer than Grange and he not arriving till late afternoon.

Nov. 7, 1791. The Carrier, Ned Wilkinson from Keswick, round this forenoon. 2 Sauce Ladles pd twenty shillings. Poor Rate from Lady Day to Michlms pd 1.5.2½. Oh I forgot bought also of Ned Wilkinson a pair of Garters 0.1.0. To Poor Travelling Woman walking over from Grasmere 0.6.0. Mrs. Mary Robson's little Boy by me for an hour while his Mother baked.

Nov. 23, 1791. Mrs. Watson of High Head Grange sent us 2 Tubbs of Geneva. Very kind. The Robsons and Braithwaites--John, Hob, Anne, Henry, came in last evening and we had a Grand Feast. I gave

them Pease Broth, boiled Leg of Mutton and Caper Sauce, Mince Pye. After supper we had Quadrille at which I lost 1d per fish--1.0.0.

Dec. 4, 1791. Mr. Bletson rode up from Rosthwaite--said he wished he could have driven up his new Curricle to show me. Very smart painted Green with Red lines. Walked down to Rosthwaite with him, he leading his horse. Walked back through Snowstorm. Very heavy over the Langdales. Fine Show of Sun betweenwhiles above Armboth. Pd 1.0. per yd for 6 yds of white Cotton for Lining.

* Judith Paris' Journal is still Herries property. See *An Old Border Family*, published by Houghley & Watson, 1894.

'Yes,' said Francis, looking up from the book to her eager face. 'You're not dull--and you ARE practical.'

'It is to show Georges,' she answered, 'if he were ever to ask where the money goes. But he never does. I have enough from the farm, even though,' her voice lowered, her face grew dark, 'Georges were never to return again.'

'Then you don't know . . . whether he comes, when he comes--?'

'No; even though he writes he never says. A while ago I had a letter, and from it you might fancy he would be here any moment. My eye is always on the road by the Tarn. One day without a word he will be coming along.'

She came closer to him, sitting curled up at his feet, her hand on his knee. 'I think so much of my father. I fancy that I am the only person left alive who gives him a thought. Already he has gone so far back for everyone else, but not for me. His house, you know, was just below here at Rosthwaite. It is tumbling down. Poor father! Everyone thought him too mad to be real, but I understand how he felt. He is alive in me still, Francis. Perhaps none of us ever die.'

'Better the dead than the living!' Francis broke in so fiercely that Judith turned to stare at him. 'Put no trust in anyone alive, Judith--not in your Georges nor in me nor in your friends here. The dead are faithful, but the living change with every breath. What was my mother ten years back, Judith? You knew her. No one kinder or more generous ever breathed; but now, although I may break my heart serving her, she can only say that Will is making money in London or that the bailiff manages better than I . . . I am going away from Uldale. I can endure it no longer.'

She could feel his whole body heaving with his distress. She thought that in a moment he would break into tears.

'Nay, nay, it is not so bad. I mustn't speak of Sarah because, God forgive me, I never loved her, but it will be good for you, Francis, to go to London for a while. Perhaps I shall follow you with Georges.'

'Everything has left me,' he murmured. 'I am quite alone. I am not a man to make friends readily. Even Moore, with whom I had an intimacy, has gone too far for me in this French business. And now-- my mother, my sister--'

She kissed him passionately. 'I will never, never leave you, Francis. After Georges I love you most in the world. Do you remember years ago when I crept in to look at Mrs. Monnasett after she was dead and your father beat me, how you came and comforted me? I ever ADORED you!'

'And do YOU remember,' he said, holding her close to him, 'one evening when there were fireworks on Keswick Lake, how we sat together--you and I, Will and Reuben--and talked of our future, how Will said that all he cared for was to make money, and I talked like a ninny, and Reuben--'

He broke off.

'And where is Reuben now? I have not seen him these two years. Someone told me he was an itinerant preacher.'

Judith nodded. 'Yes . . . He preaches in the hills to anyone who will listen. They throw stones and mud at him and set dogs on him from the villages, but he says that he is happy now, and so I hope he may be. Poor Reuben! Francis, will it not be terrible for him if there is no God, and when he is dead he has had all the stones and mud for nothing?'

'There can be no God,' Francis answered. 'This world is too unjust and bitter. No God could suffer Himself to witness it, an it is His own doing. . . . And yet I dream sometimes of a fine Heaven, all mercy and charity, where all men are free and there are no tyrants. . . .' He sighed, rubbing his eyes with his hands. 'Certainly a dream--farther from this world every day. . . . But you, Judith, Will, Reuben and I--we are a mixed lot of Herries. All Herries is in us together. From a study of all of us you would get the Herries quality. All obstinate, all proud, all English, but in nothing else alike. But you are right. You have told me what I came to ask. I will go to London. And yet I doubt that I will be happy there. I love this piece of country like none other in the world.'

She would have answered him, telling him, too, how she loved it; but he saw that she suddenly stiffened. She rose slowly from his feet, straightening her small body as though under a spell. Her eyes were fixed on the window.

He followed her gaze and saw coming on the rough path above the Tarn a group of people.

'It cannot be! It cannot be!' he heard Judith mutter, and then, a moment after, she had broken from him with a cry, had rushed from the room and, her red hair tumbling, had started down the path.

Standing at the window, he saw then a figure detach itself from the group and run ahead of the rest. The figure met Judith, raised her in the air, hugging her.

'This must be Georges,' thought Francis with a quick sensation of sadness and loneliness. It was right that Judith should run to him. It must be marvellous for her after so long an absence, but why must the fellow come just now and spoil the only happy hour that Francis had known for many months?

Judith cared for him, Francis, but at the sight of her husband she could forget him as though he had never been. So it was with him always. Everyone had someone else. He was first with no one. Well, what of it? Had he not courage enough for that rôle? He shrugged his shoulders and went out.

Standing in the little wind-swept garden, he could see that others had been attracted by the noise and had come to the doors. In front of a cottage not far from him stood an enormous woman, yes, like a whale. That must be the witch of whom Judith had spoken.

A wind blew up the little stream that tumbled from the Tarn. Some fat Herdwick sheep wandered like sleep-walkers towards the Fell. The group was near enough now for him to distinguish them. The leader was a slim, handsome, dark fellow, Georges Paris. He had an arm round Judith, who was looking up, talking eagerly. In the other he swung carelessly a gilt bird-cage that contained a bright crimson bird.

Behind were two pack-horses laden with boxes; there were sheep- dogs, some young men, a stout laughing girl with a red ribbon in her hair. Georges Paris was wearing a handsomely cut riding-coat and a broad hat with a silver cord round it. The colours of the gilt cage, the crimson bird, the red ribbon, stood out sharply against the dark Tarn ridged now with the wind like a gridiron, the snow-streaked hills, the heavy-grey sky.

The air quivered with excitement; there were the voices, dogs barking; everyone was laughing. A group of the Ritsons came out eagerly from the farm.

He felt that he could not bear to meet them. He slipped away, found Juno and rode off. No one noticed him. Within a week he had departed for London.

THE CRIMSON BIRD

Georges Paris, running forward to meet Judith, did not know and would not have cared had he known that with those very steps he was influencing the future form and shape of branches of the Herries tree.

He was gay, he was honourably fatigued, he was hungry and thirsty, triumphant with physical health and money in his pocket. He hadn't seen his dear little Judith for many months. He was going to remain with her now and make her happy and make himself happy; but even as he greeted her he was able to notice that one of the Ritson girls, advancing now towards the little bridge, had grown uncommonly pretty while he was away and had exactly the figure that he preferred.

Judith, too, running forward to meet him, was unaware that she was running forward into the first chapter of her mature life, and that when he caught her up, putting the bird-cage for a moment on the stones, and hugged her and rubbed his cheek against hers, this was the opening of a battle that would form her nature and mould it, affecting through her the whole future stock and texture of the Herries family.

That moment when Judith was caught up and felt Georges' arms about her and his mouth on hers was her last of peace. She did not at the time realise that. She was to have weeks now of happiness. But looking back long afterwards she saw clearly that that was so. The steps from that were so gradual, so silent, but the movement was sure. So, to the end of her life, she remembered that heavy grey sky, the snow-flecked hills, the ruffled water of the Tarn, the crimson bird beating against the bars of the cage on the wet shining stones, and that warm amused murmur of Georges' voice.

'My little darling. . . . And is your hair still so lovely?'

Afterwards she thought perhaps that she got what she deserved, because in all her excitement she forgot entirely Francis, never all that afternoon remembered him, sank into her husband's arms that night without a thought of him.

It is of no use, however, to be too solemn about it, for that day and many days after it were exceedingly happy for both Judith and Georges. Georges wanted only for himself to be happy, and if he was happy, why, then, he was charming to everyone. It was only when he began to be less happy that others began to suffer.

And Judith wanted only that Georges should be happy. She could not have believed that the world could be so lovely as it was in the weeks after Georges' return. They were still children, both of them, in their capacity for happiness. They could be happy at a moment's notice and over nothing at all, a bird's cry, a gooseberry pudding, a dance in the road, the sun on the Tarn.

The sun shone during those weeks. All the valley was illuminated. Nor was it ever a constant sun, whose glow can be wearisome. Not in this country. It was a sun attended by flights of happy clouds, and it shone upon all the running streams with the endearing tenderness of a passing hand, glittered in the heart of the bogs of peat and struck fire from the steaming rocks.

For the first weeks Judith had no conception but that she was going to be happy for ever. She knew that Georges was selfish, grabbing, thoughtless of others, a liar and a thief. On the other hand he was delightful to look at, a charming companion when he was pleased, and although a liar about his deeds, quite honest about himself. But beyond these things she loved him. She

loved him with all her being, and when one says that of Judith one means it.

She loved him maternally, because she knew that he was an evil small boy, who had not reached any age of discretion. She loved him physically. She loved him as a comrade. She loved him quite selflessly, never thinking at all of her own advantage in anything, but in her heart she was determined one day to dominate him. She could not help that in herself. It was so in her with everyone whom she met. She must WANT to dominate them.

But she loved him behind and beyond these ways, as only women can love--that is as though she had made him herself. She did not like altogether some of the things in him that she had made, but it was her work. So she loved him with deep tenderness and care, but also with the proprietary pride that a craftsman has for his beautiful creation.

She knew that he did not love her in any sense of the word love as she understood it, but she did not want him to love her in HER way. She wanted him simply as he was. Well, she got him as he was, and the first trouble came when he showed her a little of what he was. This was in March 1793.

The suddenness of that first trouble took her breath away. They had had a merry evening. They had had a 'rocking-night' in the Ritsons' great kitchen, the women spindling while everyone told tales. Wonderful stories were told, stories of the 'Wise Man' and 'Hobthross,' sovereign remedies against witchcraft, stories of the hunting of the 'hiding' men after the 'Forty-five.'

Suddenly Judith was aware that no one there liked her husband. The Cumbrian can hide his true feeling better than any other of God's people; there is no sober reticence anywhere in the world so dignified, so impenetrable as his if he wishes. Judith knew these people; they were her friends; they had taken her in and made her one of them, and when the Cumbrian does that you are safe. They had not, however, taken Georges.

How did she know it? She could not tell, unless perhaps it were something that she saw in the bright unswerving eye of old Ritson, seated in the settle, his body high and taut, his white beard a prophet's. His eye rested on Georges, and Judith was suddenly frightened. They did not like Georges. They none of them liked him.

Later that night she was lying beside Georges in bed. They could hear the tumbling water beyond the house. No other sound. Driven by her queer uneasiness, she began to ask him questions, questions about his life in Whitehaven; he kept always a dark cloud over all his life away from her. It had always been understood between them that she left that alone. But if she asked him anything he must answer her truthfully. As his answers always hurt her she had learnt not to ask.

But to-night she was uneasy. Why did her friends here not like him? He felt strange to her, as though she had never touched him before nor heard his voice. She was very young and knew nothing yet about marriage.

So she said a very foolish thing.

'Next time that you go to Whitehaven, I shall come with you.'

He laughed gently. He put up his hand and buried it in her hair. 'Then I would kill you and throw you into the sea,' he said.

'But when you go to London you say you will take me with you.'

'Yes, I shall need you there.' He tugged at her hair.

'Don't, Georges. You hurt me. . . . But perhaps you need me in Whitehaven.'

'I neither need you nor think of you in White-haven.'

'You don't think of me?'

'But why should I? I have quite another life there.'

'But you write letters to me.'

'Yes. Suddenly you come into my mind. . . . Your smallness, your hair, how you laugh when you are amused. Then I write.'

She sighed with satisfaction.

'Then you do belong to me. I can make you do what I say.'

This was the instant of transformation. He sat up in bed and shook her until her head was, it seemed, separated from her neck. Then he pushed her out on to the floor.

She got up slowly, rubbing her hands in her eyes and staring at him in amazement. Then he jumped out of bed and chased her out of that room into the next. He caught her, dragged her by the hair and threw her on to the floor again. He was trembling with anger. She could see him only dimly in a pale-green moonlight that shadowed the sky and the room. But two stars quivered with laughter above the dark stern trees.

'Never you say that again!' he shouted at her. 'I'll beat you! That you own me! Never you say that again! You miserable! I'll whip you. By God, I shall show you!'

He was dancing with rage. She got up and stood against the wall, staring. She was too angry to speak. She sat all night in a chair under the green moonlight. She was bitterly cold. She couldn't think at all; she was so utterly surprised.

Early in the morning he came to her, kissed her feet and her hair, said that he was so sorry, so very, very sorry. Then he carried her to bed and warmed her cold body. She said not a word. She had never in all her life been so completely surprised.

All that day she was silent, going about her duties with a grave set face, and all day in her eyes there was that look of surprise. But she was not a fool, and she had the great gift that was to serve her again and again of seeing straight in difficult crises. When the situation was sentimental she was unsentimental, as indeed most women are. She was not in the least sentimental now,

and when, in the evening of that day, Georges, made very uncomfortable by her silence, explained himself, she listened gravely, not thinking at all as to how she could snatch compensation from him for her wounded pride, but simply as to whether what he said really explained what had happened.

But, in the middle of the explanation, Judith, looking up, saw the crimson bird, a cockatoo, in the gilt cage hanging from a nail. The bird had its head on one side and, with its beady eyes shining, listened attentively to everything that Georges said.

'I am bad,' he began. 'I always told you that I was. I have never had--what do you say?--any fine sense of morality. I am not at all like your Sir Charles Grandison. I despise the sentiments; they are for women. I have the devil of a temper and I have never tried to check it. My mother had it also. For myself I think that if you understand my temper it is very agreeable. It makes a change.'

'Do you love me?' asked Judith suddenly. She asked not at all from sentiment, but because whether he did or not was a practical question of importance.

'No,' he said. 'No, Judith, I do not. I love nobody. I don't know what it is to love anybody if by love you mean to be in a fever, to give up what you want, to run hurrying to the feet of the beloved. I have never been in a fever about any person except to sleep with a woman, and then it is quickly over. No, I do not love you.'

'I see,' said Judith.

'No, but you must understand. I do not love you, but I care about you more than anyone except myself. I am bad and worthless. Not that I am ashamed. Why should I be? It is the colour I was born, that is all. But I am nearer having virtuous feelings when I am with you than at any other time. I have always thought that I had no heart as my mother had none. The French people are not famous for their heart. But at times I suspect that you are giving me a little. For example, I have been unhappy to-day because I hurt you, and I have never before been unhappy about hurting anybody. I always want to come back to you when I have gone away, and I feel now that if ever I bring everything down about my head--as I shall one day--it is only you in the whole world that I want to come to. You are a wonderful woman, Judith. You have more strength and courage and sense than I have ever seen in a woman. I don't really care for women except for a moment. I prefer greatly men, and that is what I like, to be in danger, to be against the law. More than anything in life I like to be against the law. I cannot bear that anyone should say to me "Do this!" or "Go there!" I am like a bird in a cage. That was why last night, when you said that you could make me do what you wished, I hated you and wanted to kill you. I am no good, Judith, but I do not care. If I want to be in a rage I am in a rage, if I wish to steal I steal. Life is not important, not in the least. You and I are not important. No one is important.

'Only to break the law, to beat someone who plays against you, to take what isn't yours and make it yours, that for a short time is amusing. But I hope my life will not be long.'

After all this Judith nodded her head. 'I think I understand you,' she said. 'You are very honest with me, Georges, and it would be an easier matter if I did not love you. There is no reason for loving you that I can see, but I do. Only I must protect myself. You must not beat me nor drag me by the hair. That is stupid and sentimental. It is like Emma Furze acting in a play.'

He agreed that it was. They were reconciled and were good friends again.

But when two people live together, every struggle between them, however handsomely it is ended, alters the relationship. Judith was now on her guard. She watched Georges, even as the crimson bird watched her. Yes, the crimson bird was very like Georges. It was charming when it wished, and twisted its neck to be scratched and rubbed its beak against your finger. But it surrendered, for no very obvious reason, to the most frantic tempers, screaming its rage and rasping its claws against the cage; it was very proud of itself and its feathers, and its spirit was undaunted, which was also one of the fine qualities in Georges. Judith had no intention of surrendering to Georges; he should not dominate her, but he was now a little distance removed from her. She must be close to him without his knowing it. She thought that she was clever enough for that. But it is difficult for any woman who has a very tender heart and no sentimentality. She is for ever tempted into situations that seem to her foolish. And therefore she keeps back so much that she feels.

As the summer came nearer Georges began to grow very restless.

He was not restless with the place. In his fashion he cared for it almost as deeply as Judith did, and it did not worry him at all that the people did not like him. Ever since he had first come to Cumberland as a little boy, the Cumbrians had disliked and suspected him, and it had never disturbed him at all. That it did not was one of the things that in the old days amused Tom Gauntry about him.

Watendlath was the wildest piece of land that he had yet known. The fells towards the Langdales appeared endless, and in their mingling of peat and heather, ancient rock, strange tumuli in human shape, and sudden streams rushing through the soil as though on some secret mission enchanted his lawlessness. On the other side there was Keswick. All England just then was gambling crazy, and Keswick had its little share.

Georges was a born gambler; one day he was a genius at cards and at another he would be so wild and reckless that he would lose all his advantage. Like Mr. Fox and the superior gentlemen in London he would bet on anything, the fall of a leaf, the approach of a woman round the corner, the wax of a guttering candle. There were plenty of men, from gentlemen like Mr. Osbaldistone and Mr. Kenrew down to ostlers at the 'George' or broken-down wasters like Tom Fawcett, who, in Keswick, would oblige him. At first, after his return from Whitehaven, he was well in funds. Then less and less so.

Judith sometimes rode with him into Keswick. She had a few friends there, a Mrs. Pounder who had come from Bath, a rather blowzy red-cheeked lady, who knew Emma Furze, had a warm heart but an uncertain moral code; a Mrs. Dunn and her husband Henry Dunn, kindly people, crazy about dogs and horses; one or two more. But on the whole Judith did not care for Keswick and would have given thirty of it for one of her beloved Watendlath. What really distressed her as the weeks passed was that Georges might in a gambling fit rid himself of her adored farm. That he was capable of it, in one of his excitements, she well knew.

For her own expenses she needed almost nothing at Watendlath. She shared with the Ritsons food and shelter. She was scrupulous in her record of expenses, chronicling every penny; Georges never looked at her laborious accounts. At first he was ready to shower money on her. He bought her scarves and dresses and shoes and bonnets. She didn't need them in the least. Now he was less ready. She didn't care. There would always be food and shelter for him at the farm.

But if one night he should suddenly tell her that the farm was gone?

On the other hand, she shared with him his excitement about London. She would like to experience that adventure. They were not so cut off in the North as they had been. There was plenty of talk about the old King, the Regent, Mrs. Fitzherbert and the rest.

Beyond this she had a strong Herries feeling. The Pomfrets in Kensington, Will and his ambitions, the Rockages in Wiltshire, she wanted to see them all and maybe, herself, play some part in the Herries fortunes. Half of her was sober Herries--she could understand Will's ambitions--the other half was wild English, born of her mother and father, belonging altogether to these hills and lakes and streams. One half of her looked at the other half of her, partly in mockery, partly in wonder.

By the month of July, which was hot and green with no wind, she knew that a crisis was approaching. Even the crimson bird seemed to know it, for it rapped its nails no longer on the bars of the cage, nor fell into violent rages. It perched, with its head on one side, and listened.

And the crisis came. But before it came, she had a moment with Georges that she would never forget, one of the happiest of her life.

He rode in from Keswick, up the little rough path above the beck that was now thin and placid like a child asleep. The evening sun was deep and fair over all the landscape, and gold-dust was in the air. He came and sat beside her in the window-seat, took her hand, put his arm around her and drew her to him. These gestures were so rare in him that she knew that something critical had happened.

She sat there, her heart trembling lest in his next words he should tell her that he had gambled the farm away. But he did not. He told her nothing, and she, wise through much experience, asked no questions.

They sat in the golden silence for a long time. The little stream that ran down the break in Armboth was only an amber line now after the dry weather.

'Judy, you funny little thing, how can you stay here month after month and be happy?'

'Because I love the place. My father lived below the hill in Rosthwaite, and he was there without moving for years and years.'

'Yes, but your father was crazed.'

'Maybe I'm crazed as well.'

'No, but you're not. You have more sense than anyone in Keswick. I'm proud of you, Judy.' Then after a pause he asked her: 'Do you not hate me for riding into Keswick and gambling, leaving the business in Whitehaven to tumble?'

'No,' she answered. 'I could never hate you.'

'Why not? Cannot you hate?'

'Oh yes, I can hate very well.'

'I could almost love you,' he said, 'if I were quieter. Sometimes I dream of making a handsome fortune, and we have a big house with dogs and horses, and you have all you want. . . .'

'I have all I want.'

He drew her closer, held to her as though someone would tear her away. She did not dare to let him see how happy she was. Wild ideas ran through her head that perhaps always life would be like this now. He would give up his dangerous ventures, they would improve the farm, sometimes they would go to London for a holiday, perhaps there would be children. She would be a hostess, as Sarah used to be in Uldale; on occasion she and Georges would escape from everyone up into the hills, Eskdale or Patterdale, away from everyone. . . .

'How old are you now, Judy?'

She told him. Nineteen in November.

'I should not have married you so young. Indeed, I should never have married you at all.'

She drew his head close to her childish breasts. She sat on the window-seat clutching him to her. She saw her feet dangling. How she wished she were taller! Of course, he could not love her, so small and insignificant. Then as she looked at his dark head and felt the warmth of his cheek against her thin dress she thought that she was as good as another, better than many. But she would love him all her life long, even though she lived to be a hundred. He was worn out. 'He was play-ing cards all night,' she thought-- and he slept there, his head on her breast.

It was her last quiet hour for many a day.

The crisis came a week later, and the cause of it was, of all people in the world, Reuben. She had seen Reuben but thrice since her marriage, once at his mother's house in Cockermouth (little Mr. Sunwood had died a year and a half ago of a chill), once in Keswick, and had once listened to his preaching in Borrowdale beyond Rosthwaite. Poor Reuben! On that last occasion her heart had ached for him. He wandered, so she understood, from place to place, belonging to no especial ministry or sect, simply preaching Christ and His message. Yes, simple enough in intention, but involved in every possible sort of loneliness, hostility, ostracism. Reuben had not even, Judith thought, the gifts or personality of a preacher. He looked clumsy, ill-shapen, in his awkward, ill-fitting black coat, and he had what no public orator must have, lack of confidence in his own gifts, and so he bred lack of trust in his audience. He gazed anxiously around, and, save when he was caught up on the wings of his devotion and imagination, he hesitated for words and moved restlessly on his feet. On the day when she heard him there was a gathering of farmhands, women, boys, who listened, some with a mild, some with an angry, interest, and before the end he had been driven away with mud and stones. She had hurried after him, but had not found him.

Now, on a lovely summer's day, Mrs. Ritson ran in to say that there was an itinerant preacher on the nearer side of Brund Fell and that they were going to hear him. It might, Judith thought, be Reuben. Georges was away at a farm bargaining for a horse.

Indeed, it was Reuben. She saw him at once, standing in his black coat bathed in sun, while all about him the rough tumbled fell wore that rather sinister look that this country has in brilliant sunlight--something too naked and bold, as though the real country were only present in cloud and mist and had given way to some flaunting and scheming intruder. Reuben looked the more helpless, the more dishevelled in the glare, and Judith, her heart always instantly touched by anything at odds, longed to go and stand beside him. He had by now, however, his supporters. Since she had last seen him he had collected apparently a little band of strange and incongruous figures--a large stout woman in a man's jacket and a bedraggled green skirt, two rheumy old men who were so nervous of their audience that they could scarcely stand on their rickety legs, two girls and a boy. Reuben was stouter of body, Judith thought, but younger than ever in face, his eyes wide and anxious like a baby's, his cheeks plump, his chin indeterminate.

A crowd had collected, it had followed him from Seathwaite, Rosthwaite, Grange. It was a rough-looking lot of men, women, children and dogs, some there in evident sympathy, but for the most they were, Judith thought, strangers to the district. She had noticed of late a certain class of foreigner in Keswick and surroundings. There was much distress abroad. Food prices were high, work in many parts scarce. Transportation, too, was so much easier than it had been. This little world was no longer isolated from the older one. The days of its extreme remoteness were over for ever.

Reuben was speaking when Judith, Mrs. Ritson, and two other women drew near. He spoke with a shrill, rather piercing note that dropped suddenly to a low bass. There was something ludicrous about this that almost at once set some of his audience laughing. As he talked he waved his hands in the air and rolled his eyes. Every once and again the little group round him would break into singing with a wavering and unsteady tone. Judith became with every moment more uneasy. He began a passionate evocation of the character of Jesus Christ, speaking of His charity, His unselfishness, His courage. Behind his uncertain voice there was a piercing sincerity, but he had not the power to evoke for others what he himself saw. Judith had the strange notion that the hills, the rocks, the peat seemed to understand him better than the people around him. She fancied that the sun was a little veiled, the colours a little milder. But he could not catch his audience; they were not fish that day for his net. Some of the more scornful men began to laugh. One of the dogs began a fight with another dog. When the quavering voices were raised other voices joined in derisively. And as the opposition grew, Reuben's voice was ever more shrill, and his eyes wandered more beseechingly to the heavens.

Then someone threw a stone, pretending that it was aimed at one of the dogs. Other stones followed. Two men had been drinking gin from a bottle and began to quarrel; a moment later they were rolling on the ground atop of one another. The dogs were barking, the women screaming, figures were running down the hill. Clods of peat were thrown, more stones; something cut Reuben's cheek. His little band clustered close together, and then, as the scene was wilder, the two old men and the stout woman started away quickly over the brow of the hill.

Reuben stood there, his hand on his bleeding cheek, as though he did not quite know what to do. Judith went up to him and put her hand on his arm.

'Reuben dear--' she said.

He started, at first seeming not to recognise her. The crowd was streaming away down the hill.

'Come and rest at the farm,' she said.

He followed her quite passively, like a child. She felt his arm trembling under her hand. Then when they had gone a little way he began to speak.

'They think it finer not to listen . . . to throw mud . . . I cannot hold them. You may laugh, all of you may laugh, but the day is coming when the spirit of the Lord will descend upon me. . . . Stay a moment, Judith, while I fasten my boot.'

He was wearing faded and stained green breeches under his coat. He bent to tie the worn string of his boot. When he raised his head his forehead was bathed in perspiration and his cheek was bleeding again. But he was smiling.

'God has but just spoken to me and told me that I do well. He watcheth over me and will see that I come to no harm.'

'Where are you living?' she asked him; she had to take many quick little steps to keep pace with his almost running strides.

'Like the birds of the air--' Then he shook his head. 'I cannot remember, but I must always be talking in Bible phrases like the Methodists. But with you, Judith, that's folly. I live nowhere. I have no home unless I go to mother. You know,' he began more excitedly, 'now that God is the only real thing in my life, roofs and walls are constricting. I am happier in the open.' She asked him to stay with them for a little while and be rested, but he shook his head. 'No, no . . . I must go on. There is so much to be done.'

While he was sitting beside the big open fire, she brought water, and he washed his face. He took off his coat and his shabby riding- boots and his soiled neck-cloth. He opened his shirt and bathed his breast that was smooth white like a woman's. His hands, too, were soft.

He became more collected and told her of his brother's death in France, how he had joined the first ragged French army and almost at once had been killed in some squabble on the way to the frontier. As he spoke Judith saw again the desperate hunted man in Cockermouth. It had been, it seemed, since that day that both for her and Reuben active consciousness of life had begun. After his brother's death, he told her, he had been always restless, and at last had begun to preach up and down the country, simply by himself, attached to no creed. He didn't know whether he did any good; it seemed to him that he did not. But he must go on. He was the Bear, ordered to play his part. . . .

She realised that he had no great interest in her affairs. He put up his hand once and touched her hair, but he asked her no questions about herself, whether she were happy, how she lived here. . . . Once he broke out about women. They were his great temptation, the temptation of the Devil. He tried to lead his life without them, but they were always breaking in. Often he could not sleep at nights, and in the towns, in the taverns and inns. . . .

She kissed him. 'Reuben, stay here for a little. It is very pleasant here, and I will care for you--'

She broke off. Georges was standing in the doorway, looking at them. She realised at once the evil temper that he was in. Things had gone badly with him over the horse. Reuben rose. His coat and vest were on a chair-back, his long muddy riding-boots on the floor. He looked doubtfully at Reuben.

Judith said: 'Georges, this is Reuben.'

Georges began at once. 'Yes, and we want no canting preachers here. I have heard of your doings, sir. Whatever my wife may say, this is not the place for you.' He was in one of his black rages, trembling with anger.

Reuben at once hurried to pull on his boots, drag on his coat. He said nothing.

Judith burst out: 'Georges, you shall not. Reuben is my relation and my friend--'

'A fine relation. A canting humbugging preacher who steals the chickens and kisses the maids. A fox! A fox--'

But Reuben was clothed and stood for a moment with a very fine dignity. He kissed Judith's cheek. 'Good-bye, dear,' he said, then staying a moment before Georges, quite, as Judith was afterwards to remember, without any fear: 'Good-day, sir; I do not steal chickens, and that I am a preacher is true and is God's will.'

She ran forward with a cry. 'No, no, Reuben--'

But he was gone. She could see him walking swiftly, but still with dignity, along the little path by the Tarn.

She stayed, watching, until he was out of sight, and then she was a proper termagant. Georges knew well that she had a temper, but he had never seen it like this, and had his own rage not been too fierce for him to be clear about anything he would have marvelled.

Although now they were close together, they shouted at one another as though they were at far ends of the valley.

'That is the last time! This is my place. He is my relation, like a brother. He came here weary, soiled--'

'A fine brother with his thieving.'

'You to talk of thieving--'

'Well, at least, I do it in the open. There's no hiding in women's cupboards.'

'You SHALL not! He is more noble than you can ever understand--'

'Well, go to him then! Tie a string to his tail and follow him round the countryside.'

She looked at him, then, moving back to the fireplace, drew her little body to its full height and in a small chill voice, speaking now very low, said:

'You are cruel. I have always known it, but how cruel, not until to-night.'

He came towards her, not for reconciliation. At that moment he hated her: to set up her will against his, and she had been bathing his cheek, that mean canting rat of a preacher--she--his wife--

'Aye,' he said slowly, 'when I have a ranting woman to discipline.'

'Now learn this,' she answered him, looking him in the face as though she had struck him between the eyes. In his rage he was not so angry but that he could see some dignity of anger in her that gave her a dominance he had never suspected in her. 'Learn this. I am not your woman to be disciplined. Here was one who came to me, my kinsman, weary, hungry, beset, and you drove him out with a curse. That I will never forget.'

'And I will never forget,' he answered as fiercely, 'what you have been to me this day. I am master in this place.'

'You shall never be master of me,' she answered.

'We shall see.'

He came towards her as though to strike her. She never moved. Then he remembered something. He was held. She was the elder at that instant as he stood there like an angry boy, his black hair ruffled and damp. He had on still his riding-coat, and he carried a whip in his hand.

They exchanged a long defiant look. Then he turned on his heel.

'I have had enough of this,' he said, and he went up the winding stair.

She never moved. Later--she had no sense of time, but her anger bore her as though on a horse with bright wings, timelessly, through dry air--he came down, pulling after him a box. It bumped on every stair. He stood in the doorway, dark in an evening glow all saffron, with faint blue light in the upper sky.

'I shall never return,' he said.

Still she did not move. She heard him call to young Jacob Ritson. She heard them lead the horse out and its sharp stamp on the stones, very clear on that summer evening. Then she saw him ride off, the box behind him. She saw him climb the Fell beyond the Tarn. And still her anger was so hot that it held her high in fiery space.

Many hours later, at some early morning time, she woke, and her brain was quite clear and her anger all gone. She did not at first realise that he was not there. Half awake, she turned as she was accustomed to do, to settle her small body inside the curve of his arm. She would lay her head on his breast, even in her sleep seeing that her hair was not in his eyes, then her hand would fold inside his palm.

She stretched out her hand and touched only the cold bed. Then she was fully awake. She sat up to hear some bird calling its cry like slipping water beyond the open window. There was a pale light, like stealing smoke over the room, and in her ear as though a voice had called it from over the hill: 'I shall never return.'

She waited weeks for a letter. None came. He was gone; and he meant, no doubt, what he had said. It would be like him. She saw now that she had never had any real hold on him. He did not love her; he had very often told her so. He liked to tell her. She knew nothing about his life without her. She envisaged White-haven and the sea as a strange town, the houses running down to the sea-edge, figures moving on the foreshore, bales loaded in darkness, the firing of a pistol, or some woman, very opposite to herself, tall and dark, coming softly in a candle-lit room, drawing him towards her . . . and outside these scenes a sea always angry, grey and roaring, and some foreign coast, darkness again, men moving on tiptoe. That was what her imagination did for her, and it was to this land that he had returned. He would never come back.

She had great courage. She would show no one that anything had occurred. She went about all her daily business, her head up, poking her nose into every village affair, nothing too trivial for her, deciding always what was best to be done, hypnotising them into believing that she was a woman, although she knew now that she was only a child.

Her business now was to cut out all the outside world. She would not think of Georges nor of anything beyond Watendlath Beck.

All the souls of the village she brought into her world and made them giant-size to fill the space better--old man Ritson, patriarchal, aloof, believing fiercely in God and His angels, whom he expected to descend from the skies at any moment, but practical, too, about money so that he knew where every penny went to; young Tom Ritson, deformed, with a crooked back, a marvel at any job with his hands; Mary Ritson, the beauty who loved some imaginary man of her dreams and would wear a lost far-away look when earthy young men courted her; Giles Braithwaite the wrestler, famous in all Borrowdale already, though he was only twenty, later to be famous through all Cumberland and the North, at present a stupid young man who thought the French lived over Ullswater way; James Wilson, broad, brown-faced, kindly-eyed, the finest Cumbrian of them all, whose wife Jane gave him a child every year so that he now had fourteen; Mother West, the whale, the witch, perhaps at the last, when all was said, Judith's warmest friend in the place; the children, the babies, scattering like ducks, like chickens, like puppies in and out of the becks, the peat, the stony passages--all Cumberland, if you liked, held in this small space, among these few rocks and boulders. Nor so changed from to-day when the Herdwick sheep still pass from descendant to descendant, and the children still go, day after day, rain or shine, down the rocky path to school in Rosthwaite. They did not care that only a mile or two away by the sea the new Industrial England was beginning to show its dusky evil-stained face, nor that there was an old mad King in London. Here, between Armboth and Brund Fell, was, and is, the whole heart of England.

Soon, though, it was not enough for Judith. With all her resolve and courage, unhappiness crept closer and closer to her. She began to dread the waking moment of every day. She began to watch, against her will,

more and more anxiously the path by which the carrier would come on his old fat horse from Keswick.

She realised for the first time for many years how lonely she was. These friends of hers in Watendlath were not enough for her. Reuben, even if she could find him, was not enough. Francis was in London. Deborah, Reuben's mother, was a widow in Cockermouth. Judith thought sometimes of going to visit Deborah Sunwood, but she shrank from it because it was there that she had one of her liveliest memories of Georges. She began to see, with a vividness that appalled her, that she had staked her whole life on Georges. She had not cared so much when he was away, because she had always known that he would come back. Like many another she discovered that true love is irreplaceable. There may be other later experiences as fine, but never THAT one again. There was no one else like Georges. There never would be. His very selfishness, ill-temper, childish reckless independence gave him his colour. And the fact that she had lost him made him twice as precious. She was growing through all this knowledge. Life taught her more now in these few weeks than in years before, but we do not thank life for teaching us WHILE we are being taught.

She became more and more miserable. Sleep forsook her. She lay for hours, watching for the light, and when it came she watched the road. One evening she went to Mother West's dark smoky room that smelt of herbs and bacon, and made her tell the cards.

But the cards told nothing. Then one autumn afternoon her unhappiness was so deep that all her courage left her. She went out on to the peak of the Fell that looks down over Borrowdale and sat there, while the clouds rolled over Scafell in red and smoky splendour and all the bracken was gold. But she saw nothing. She sat there, her head in her hands, and cried her heart out. Only a stone's fall below her her father had lived, crazily alone for years.

'Oh, I cannot endure it any longer,' she cried as though to him. 'I cannot live without Georges. What am I to do?'

She dried her eyes and tried to be sensible. This was what she always despised others for doing, to have the vapours as the women in Keswick did, or to want a man who did not want them. Georges did not want her. Now, here on this hill, with only the sky about her, she must understand that he was never going to return. Her life with him was over, and she must make a new life for herself. 'No one can beat you but yourself.' She was young, strong, full of curiosity and eagerness to see the world.

Georges had never cared very much for her (but had he not always returned to her?), he was not a fine man (but was he not endearing with his dark hair and his sense of fun?), he was for ever in a temper (but was he not enchanting when things went well?), he would be hanged one day (would she not be proud to stand at his side when all the world was against him?), he was

French, and the French were a bad nation (did she truly care WHAT he was so long as he was with her?), she was an independent woman (who would live her life in her own way whatever men did). Perhaps (for queerer things happen in this world than facts allow for) an old man with a scarred face stood beside her then, his arm about her, he looking down through rock and stone to a little house tumbling to ruin.

So she went back over the Fell with her head up, and the first thing that she heard was that there was a letter for her. On the one day that she had not watched! It was scribbled on some rough tea-paper and ran:

DEAR LITTLE QUEEN JUDY--I have got a Fortune and We shall go to London to spend it. I am coming Home to fetch you.--Your loving husband, GEORGES.

She allowed the letter to drop. She ran like a mad thing in to all the Ritsons, and she caught the Patriarch round the neck, crying, 'He's coming home! He's made a fortune! He's coming home!'

She danced like the child that she yet was, into the hallan and over the cobbles, and ran into the whale's parlour and danced all about between the stuffed birds and the snakes in spirits and the bottle with the baby's thumb.

The smoke blew out of the chimney, and old Mother West, smoking her pipe, nodded her head with pleasure, for she loved this child.

The crimson bird in the cage woke up and scraped with its talons on the wires.

HAPPINESS IN LONDON

The only part of Georges Paris that was visible was his nightcap, white with a red tassel that lifted and fell above his nose with the rhythm of his breathing.

Through the open door in the larger room Judith Paris lay, also sunk in sleep, her hair loose about the pillow, and on her lips a happy smile, because she dreamt that she and Georges were alone in a chaise made of silver that drove swiftly through the clouds above Scafell.

All the cocks around Cheapside were crowing. Above London a heavy dark mantle was slowly lifted, and soon over all the mud and running water that clung to the toes of the red-bricked City the sun would ride with an especial triumph, because it had not been seen for so many days. It had rained for nearly a week, and Jackanapes Row and Blowbladder Street were running with water.

Had Georges looked out from his little window into the street below at that first cock-crowing hour, he would have encountered Cheapside at the single moment of either day or night when all life there was still, for the roisterers had roistered to their beds, the 'Charlies' had not yet started their policing day, the watchmen had completed their happy and far-too-easy duties. The cocks, calling from St. Dunstan's in the West to the Strand, from Butchers' Row to the Poultry, were kings of the hour.

Then as the light grew stronger he might have seen one small figure, little Jack Robinson, youngest son of Mr. Jack Robinson, shoemaker, whose premises were on the ground floor under Georges and Judith. Mr. Robinson, senior, had four small boys, who worked on his behalf sixteen hours of the day, and twelve children, fruit of his own loins, so that he was accustomed to children. That Jack, his youngest, should at this moment be earning his wages as 'climbing boy' seemed to him but right and proper, so that there he was with shovel, scraper and brush, and in his cap a brass plate with his master's name and address. He had had some bad chimneys that night, and was so sleepy that he had found his way home as it were blindfold, with chimneys dancing by his side all the way. His lungs were half-choked with soot, his knuckles were in his eyes, but he was home. In another five minutes he would have rolled under the blanket with six other young Robinsons, pushing in among them like a little bird. He was awake enough, though, to see that it was a fine day and to rejoice thereat, for there was to be a cockfight by Bath Street that afternoon, and there would be rich gentlemen to beg pennies of on a fine day.

You can almost see Cheapside sit up, rub its fists in its eyes, give a great yawn and, jumping out of bed, start shaking its rattle. A light air has sprung up with the sun. For days these piles of little red houses, lifted, like boats on a stormy sea, on heaving cobbles, open sewers, sudden little hills that run up and down in the middle of narrow thoroughfares simply for fun, have felt the mud rise higher and higher about their doors. But this is June, and even in Cheapside the country is not far away. You can smell hay and roses as well as sewage and stale cabbage and the offal of cows and dogs and horses. The river, too, is close at hand; you can hear the noise from the steam-engines in the factories of the soap- and oil-makers, the glass-makers and the boat-builders. Were you to stand on the roof above Georges' nightcap, you would see the Pool, a forest of masts, the ships at anchor, the lighters and the barges. . . .

But Cheapside has its own noises, and soon, its face rosy with pleasure, is waving its rattle like the infant that it is, while the sun grows stronger and stronger and the churches are ringing their bells.

The noise is now rocketing about Georges' room. He hears nothing because he is well accustomed. But soon it is ten in the morning, and Cheapside is going to make the best of the splendid day.

First there are the milkwomen, then the baker ringing his bell and calling out 'Hot Loaves,' then the watercress men (three bunches for twopence), then the old lady (at this time there were two old ladies, one with a beard, who made Cheapside their headquarters every day from ten to one) crying 'Baking or Boiling Apples,' charcoal stove and barrow attending them. And now there is the man with bandboxes, carried on either end of a pole (at this time in Cheapside and the neighbourhood a giant negro), then the brickdust man with his small sacks and his donkey (the brickdust men are, after the lamplighters, the great trainers of bulldogs). There are the rat-trap dealers and the bullock-livers man, the basket man, the bellows man, the chair-mender and the door-mat man. All calling together, they are answered by the opening of high windows, the emptying of pots and pans, the rumbling of the country wagons, the first stir in the shops whose glass windows run round-bellied above the cobbles, the barking of dogs, the lowing of cows, the ringing of bells--such a hubbub that, although it is not yet mid- day, a lady with her servant meeting another lady with HER servant must step into Mr. Jordan's the silversmith's to exchange a word or two and, once there, there are clocks to be seen and necklaces, and there is a bull, they say, loose by St. Paul's and a crowd running really for the fun of the thing, because it is a June morning with the sun shining, and here is an Italian with a peep-show and a monkey, and a man caught robbing Mrs. Morris's fruit-stall and no 'Charley' anywhere to be seen so that Mr. Benjamin Morris, fresh from a good night's sleep and fit for anything, has given the thief two between the eyes and he has tumbled into the gutter, and the little Robinsons, thoroughly up and about now, throw choice pieces of dirt at him, and the bull, they say, is really mad, has trampled down two flower-stalls and a Jew's clothes-basket, and in the distance coming in veiled harmonies through the summer air there are the strains of a band, strains that mingle with the scent of the roses and new-mown hay and make the young dandy in his blue and silver, reading his paper in one of the Turk's Head Coffee Houses, think of Apollo Gardens and St. George's Spa.

All this before mid-day, and while Georges and Judith are yet happy dreaming. The room in which Judith was sleeping was a large one, Georges' little more than a closet. A shabby place, Judith's room. The bed in which she was had over it a very heavy mustard-coloured canopy, covered with faded red roses. The mantelpiece was tall and narrow, surmounting a wretched stove, semicircular, with a flat front. There was a bowed fender of perforated sheet brass, a scarred table, and a large china jar filled with roses. There were two cupboards, a mean stand with a wash-hand basin. On one of the stiff high-backed chairs some of Judith's clothing. On another most of Georges'. The crimson bird hung in a gilt cage by the window, but there was now green baize cloth over his head. The sun poured in through Georges' room into Judith's, lighting up patterns of dust and the bare boards of the floor and the bright green silk jacket over the chair and the silver sheen of Georges' white waistcoat with buttons of emerald. There were lying on the floor two masks, a child's drum painted brilliant red and yellow, and a bunch of artificial flowers.

So they slept, but not for long. A door burst open. A woman's voice (it was Mrs. Robinson's, who was at the moment stumbling down rickety stairs, nursing a naked baby, devouring a slice of bread and ham) screamed: 'You can have it your own way, ma'am. . . . You can have it your own way!'

In the doorway stood a lady of magnificent proportions, tall as a grenadier, as broad as tall, with a fine bosom, a grand impassioned eye, an air of ruling the world. How magnificently, too, was she dressed! Over her hair, arranged 'hedgehog' style and powdered a very light yellow, she wore a high-brimmed hat of dark beaver fur, adorned with splendid trimmings of purple silk. The dress that covered her noble form was a long caraco jacket of brown striped silk, a light corselet of black taffeta with white trimming. She carried a cane with an ebony top. She stood, her head high, her large face rubicund and jolly, her arm out resting on her stick in a fine theatrical pose.

Her eyes took in the room. Then she saw the bed and moved nearer to it. She stood looking down on Judith, smiling, her eyes sentimentally soft, for she was a most sentimental woman and had not seen her dear Judith for two years.

Then after a while she tiptoed across the room and looked in upon Georges, who was snoring lustily now with his mouth wide open. She looked out of window and had the pleasure to see a grand coach, wobbling along like a fat woman, stick in a rut between cobbles, little boys run up to the windows, a lady in a beaver hat very like her own push her head out, and a man have his fruit-barrow overturned in the general excitement.

After five minutes of this, back to the bedroom again and back to the bed. With a magnificent gesture that it was a thousand pities there was no one there to see, she bent forward and gave Judith a smacking kiss on the forehead.

Judith woke, sat up, pushed her hair from her eyes, then saw her visitor. With a cry she was out of bed and had her arms around the other's tremendous waist.

'Emma! my darling, darling Emma!'

'Emma it is, my love! Thy Emma, whom Fortune has constrained, but the Heart--'

She could say no more, for Judith kissed her again and again, while Emma's great arms enfolded her in her thin nightdress with the excited fervour of an amatory bear.

'Oh, Emma. Where HAVE you been? I assure you I think it most ungrateful in you--'

But Emma would let her finish no sentence. Words poured from her. She had been in Ireland. She had been in Dublin. She had had the greatest success in the Irish theatres since Venus and Minerva took human form. Especially in The Irish Widow or, maybe yet more, in Dryden's Rival Queens. Tragedy, comedy or farce, as Judith knew, it all came the same to her. And there had been a gentleman in Dublin . . . Oh, a gentleman in Dublin!' Everyone who knew us spoke of marriage as a speedy and certain affair, and I could have cried myself into the vapours had I not Resolution and Character. . . .'

'Well, and what prevented him?'

'An impudent little Toad with the morality of a-- but I shock you, my darling Judith.'

'Never fear,' cried Judith, jumping up and down the floor in her bare feet and the greatest excitement. 'I have stood a good many shocks.'

'But how are you, my dear little love? and how does Mr. Georges?'

'Very well. Very well . . . we are all very well. But why have you been so long away from me? Two years. . .'

All this in jerks, in exclamations, in frenzied pauses while Judith laughs and Emma laughs.

'And he pursued me, the monstrous wretch, through three streets and an alley-way until I was forced to run into a toy-shop and hope to have the fortune to meet with a chair!'

'But you are handsome now, Emma, so handsome! And so grand. You have money. You have wealth.'

'I have a little. Just for the moment. All to spend upon you, my darling. I am hoping to have an engagement at Drury Lane.'

'Georges and I, we too have money, just for the moment. . . .'

'Your Georges, he detests me. I am terrified of him. He finds me impossible.'

'But Georges is changed, as you will discover. He is older, more serious. He has still some bad friends, but I have now a little influence, a very, very little influence. When he is not gambling at the "Salutation" or at Offley's he does very well with the money that he made two years ago; he started a business in Whitehaven with Captain Wix. You know Captain Wix? I forget. He is huge as a barrel, and his heart is as big as his belly. He is all heart. Even his liver is heart. But he is also shrewd, and they have made money. . . . Georges travels from London there and back again. . . . Yes, when he is away from his wicked friends, Mr. Charteris, Mr. Mandable, and there is a Whitehaven young man, Mr. Stane. I like him the least of them all. His father owns a ship that trades to Holland. Georges has a share in it. But Georges is good now. You will see that for a Frenchman he is very well. . . .'

'Oh, God, yes!' cried Emma, throwing her arms abroad in an ecstasy. 'I can see that you are the happiest of women.'

'I am indeed, indeed happy,' Judith cried, 'now that you are come.'

They settled down more quietly after that, and sat down together on the bed under the yellow canopy, Emma's arm around Judith, Judith's red head on Emma's bosom.

There was no insincerity in their affection; there was even a certain relief in their pleasure at being together again, for with neither of them had the success of their fortunes been quite so great as they gallantly pretended.

Emma had great qualities, and one of them was constancy to those whom she loved--for so long, at least, as they loved her! For Judith she had an especial care: there was something brave and reckless and good-humoured that exactly appealed to her. She liked a woman to have both spirit and heart, and a friendship with Judith that extended now over a number of years had proved her both dauntless and passionate.

When Emma had last seen the pair they had but lately descended on London, and their position was hazardous. She suspected, looking about the room, that it was still hazardous. Judith, she thought to herself, had been through something in these two years. She was prettier, her features were maturely formed, her assurance greater, her recklessness also, perhaps.

There was something individual in the dark flame and shadows of amber light of her hair. Emma had never seen any like it--and beneath it the pale vivacity of her small face was so sharply featured. Her body was lit with energy and independence. Covered as it was now with only the lightest of nightdresses, the June sun warming it, there was something virginal, untouched, in its fire and purity. Emma had once again the sense, that she had known before, that there was something in Judith remote and separate. And yet there could be no one more human, more normal in her passion for all the adventure, all the fun, all the experience that life chose to bring to her.

They had talked then, two years before, upon the great things that were to come from the descent upon the Herries relations. Well, what had come of it? How were they all?

Judith jumped off the bed, caught Emma's beaver hat, seized her cane. 'Look, Emma! Look! Now I'll give you Will! He's very tall, you know, very tall. Oh yes, extremely! And he talks like a war-horse. "Oh yes! Ha, ha! Well, well! Dear me! How are you, my dear?"' (Here Judith bent forward, very grand, almost to the ground and shook hands solemnly with an invisible midget.) 'Just as though, you know, we hadn't been brought up as children together. He's the City Man, but he's also moving up. Oh yes, very much up indeed! He can tell you all the latest about the Prince and his bride, and what poor Mrs. Fitzherbert is doing, and why Lady Jersey chose the Prince SUCH a plain partner and what Mr. Fox lost last night at cards. He moves doubly, you know, Emma, darling. There's the Will of the moment and the Will of ten years hence--the Will there's going to be if he has any luck. And Christabel. Oh, Christabel! She's like this!' (Judith rolled her eyes, stood on tiptoe and made her face as vacant as a saucepan.) 'She's so stupid you can't believe it! She's for ever running herself down that you shall run her UP! "I am but an old wife," she'll say. "I have my principles but nobody cares to bother with ME!" And nobody does, you know. But she's kind, poor Christabel. She has a heart. She's all extravagances. "That's a SWEET fellow," she will say. "Oh, a SWEET fellow."' (And Judith gave her voice such a pitch of stupid ecstasy that Emma roared with laughter.)

'And then there are the Herries from Kensington, Pomfret and Rose and dear James and sweet Rodney. Pomfret's kind, but he loves the women, and Rose is so busy catching him that she can think of naught else. Pomfret's stout and dresses grandly. He and Rose are socially finer than Will and Christabel, but they haven't the money. No Herries have as much money as Will, and the house in Kensington costs a deal. I like Pomfret. Georges and I found him the other evening at Ranelagh, with a lady all simpers and jewelry. Oh, it was the loveliest thing! They had a chicken and a dish of ham between them, and he was feeding her with the merrythought. . . . Mr. James Herries puffs himself like a bull when he walks. Like this.' (Here Judith gave an admirable imitation.) 'His voice is all falsetto. He's at the pimple stage.

'Then there are the Cards from Bournemouth. They come every year to London for the Season. Prosper and Amelia and the beautiful Jennifer, their daughter. Prosper is nearly fifty years of age and is most distinguished. He wears a full-bottomed wig, although it's the fashion no longer, and can tell you all about the virtues of Bournemouth. He's so grandly dignified that his knees won't bend, and he has buckles on his shoes as large as saucers. Amelia's a little woman like a rabbit. But I like Amelia. She'd be happier in a cottage with a sampler to work at. But Jennifer, she's a beauty! She really is, Emma. Of the DARK kind! All cloudy splendour and proud as Helen of Troy.

'And then--oh, Emma darling, best of all there are the Rockages. I've stayed there down in Wiltshire. Yes, twice. Without Georges, you understand. Maria likes me--wherefore I can NOT understand! But she does! She thinks I have a soul to be saved, and so I don't doubt that I have. And what a place! They haven't a penny between them, and the family coach has rats in the straw, and they put buckets in the hall when it's raining to catch the water through the ceiling. But Carey--that's Rockage--must have everything as grand as grand, although the footmen have holes in their stockings, and there isn't food to go round. The last time I stayed there I half died of discomfort. You know how it is in a country place where nothing is looked after. Here it was the EXTRAVAGANCE of neglect! All day

long it was nothing but pulling at bell-ropes that brought no answer or always the wrong servant, or a pair of rusty tongs that let slip a coal that is smaller than your head, or an asthmatic pair of bellows, the coals always out, all the pencils with their heads broken off, and SUCH a mess of things in every room that was lived in--phials, fiddles, books and knick-knacks, and the rooms that weren't lived in as cold as tombs with all the family portraits frowning from damp. And the gardens! Oh, Emma, the gardens! All laid out in the ancient taste. You know--a mile's length of clipped trees with spouting lions, fish-ponds as round as a wheel, with six or eight flights of neglected terraces and a summer-house, all broken-down windows and decayed bluebottles.

'And the religion. Oh, Emma, the religion! Early morning, all the maids and the footmen with their patched heels in air, while Carey read a sermon, and trampling through the Wiltshire mud with Maria delivering tracts on the villagers, and Madeline, Carey's sister, mad with enforced virginity, talking to herself in a cupboard. . . . And yet, Emma, it's there that I feel all Herries and want to feel so. Half of me is so Herries that I understand Will's ambition and Carey's pride and am proud of Jennifer's beauty because she's Herries like myself. But the other half of me . . . that's with Francis and Reuben and Georges and is lost in Cumberland peat. That's from my father, Emma, and I doubt it will ruin me in the end. But when I'm at Grosset or Kensington or Will's place I'm ALL Herries, and I would run all the establishment and see how the butter's used and where the beef-bones go to and how every penny fares. Were it not for Georges I'd be mistress of Will's place by now, and Comptroller at Grosset, but they're afraid of Georges. They think he may be hanged any day, and they don't want a hanging relation.'

'Well,' said Emma reflectively, 'I'm glad that there's plenty of money. Money! Money! Judy, my darling, I'd sell my heart and lungs for money. I've never enough.'

'To tell you truth, neither have we,' said Judith, dropping her voice. 'I was speaking a trifle out of order, maybe, when I said that Georges' business was admirable. It might be if he'd attend to it, but we've been put to some odd straits, and it isn't twice or thrice only he's been in the lock-up.'

'But not to-day!' cried Georges, laughing. They looked up. He was standing in the doorway with his nightcap still on his head, a quilted blue bed-gown wrapped around him, rubbing his eyes and yawning.

This was an uneasy moment for Emma. In spite of her size she was a deeply shy woman, ready to burst into tears at any moment from sensitiveness. In the bad old days Georges had hated her; moreover, she was uneasy with anyone who had known her in the raggle-taggle times when she had been poor old Gauntry's mistress. Two years ago Georges had been polite to her and that was all.

Now, however, his regard was amiable. He was stouter than he had been, she reflected, but still very handsome. She was no trivial observer, and at once she realised that Judith's influence over him was now a very real one. Their relations had changed. He was more good-natured, less self-willed, a little lazy, some of his earlier energy dissipated. All this she realised in the next half-hour, and with it her attitude to Judith insensibly altered. Judith had a new power. She was somebody now. Emma surrendered to her, but resisted her too, a mixed attitude that Judith would rouse out of many of her later companions.

They spent the happiest hour. Both Georges and Judith were of a ravenous hunger. In the cupboard there was a cold pie, a rice pudding, beer and cheese. They had everything out on the shabby table and ate as they were, Judith in a yellow jacket, her nightdress, and Emma's hat still on her head. Georges was kind to Emma. He had won money the night before over the contest between Battling Ginger and Monty Punt. He was right now for a day or two. He scattered his winnings on to the table among the pie and the rice pudding, and let Judith take what she wanted. Emma, encouraged, was able to come out with her project, which was that they should both accompany her to the 'Elephant and Castle' at Newington for supper. She had, she told them, a young friend, a Mr. Audley, and the young friend had a coach, and he would drive the three of them, through the fields, to Newington. They should drive back under the moon with the hedges smelling of flowers; at the 'Elephant' there were sheep and cows, and on a June night country-dances on the Green.

So they all gave themselves up to being happy. They had a fine natural capacity for happiness, all three of them, and being in one degree or another all adventurers, happiness brought no kind of obligation with it. Georges dressed there in front of Emma, and there was no false modesty on either side. The bells of St. Mary le Bow had struck three by the time that everyone was ready.

The usual dining hour was anything between three and four, but they would wait now until they could enjoy their supper under the trees of the 'Elephant.'

Georges, when dressed, was a dandy, and Emma sighed romantically, as she always did at thought or vision of a handsome man.

His stoutness, not yet pronounced, added to the impressiveness of his foreign good looks. He was a man now, not a boy, a man with a reckless air, a good-natured mouth, a roving and humorous eye. A man to be trusted? Emma thought not. A man for a woman to love? Of course. A man for Judy to love? Oh, Emma hoped so, but could not be sure. They made a fine pair. The colour of Georges' coat was dark cinnamon, no collar to it, single-breasted; the waistcoat fully seen, of light blue satin cut low under the pockets, under which,

as well as down the front and at the bottom, was a border of rosebuds, jonquils and heart's-ease. He wore a lace frill, called a Chitterling, the ends of his white cravat trimmed with lace, and the ruffles at his wrists the same, his hair powdered, no curls, but brushed back from his face and hanging in a black bag with a rosette behind. Judith wore a jacquette of pale silver-coloured silk and the bodice and underdress were of dark wine colour. Her red hair was unpowdered and fell down behind with curled ends, and perched on it she wore a hat of light straw, also of pale silver. Her shoes had silver buckles.

Judith thought the clothes that she and Georges wore on this day important, for she describes them in her Journal minutely, and at the top of the page has written in a hand that is still very childish: 'The Happiest Day of My Life.'

Mr. Audley's chariot-chaise was to be met in Holborn, so they engaged a hackney carriage and drove there, Judith with her head out of window for there was so much to see on this very fine day. They rattled along with a great deal of bumping, jerking in and out of holes, climbing little hills and running down the other sides again, along Blowbladder Street, past Butcher Hall Lane, Bath Street--sacred to the memory of Charles II.-- Ivy Lane, where Dr. Johnson had his Club, under the ancient gateway beside Giltspur Street, up Snow Hill, past Cock Lane, Cow Lane, Fleet Market, then a steep climb up Holborn Hill, when they moved so slowly that little boys looked in at the window, a gentleman with silver rings in his ears wanted Judith to buy a green parrot, the Bishop of Ely's Palace with his gardens, Thavie's Inn, Staple Inn and so to Holborn. Here, at a corner of Whetstone Park, was Mr. Audley with his coach.

Judith had already asked Emma to tell her all she could about Mr. Audley, but Emma could not tell her very much. It seemed that Mr. Audley was a young man with a very rich City father (here it was Georges who pricked up his ears), that he was a great admirer of Emma's ('A passion for the Play, my dear. He was in Salisbury at the time, buying a horse, and he saw me in Othello. I am free to confess that Emilia is not so splendid a rôle, most especially in the version that we were playing, which was one with music, and Othello, Mr. Barnstaple, had a fine tenor and played the flute in the third act, but I was wearing white satin, and poor little Miss Huxley, who was playing Desdemona, was a chit of a thing that you could fit into a nutshell. To be honest, my dear, he liked my size. He was heard to say loudly in the pit that the Furze was his style and--well, we were friends very shortly after. He is a nice young fellow with most agreeable manners.')

He flushed with pleasure when he saw them. His coach was very smart, of a bright bay colour with silver ornaments on the harness. He was attended by a stout driver in a blue and yellow striped waistcoat who, as they approached, was engaged from the box in a sharp and apparently rather bitter discussion with two gentlemen and a fruit-barrow.

Everything and everyone was very lively, including the June sun, the shopmen standing in their doorways, the glittering glass of the shop-windows, an old man with a fiddle to whose tunes several children were dancing, a stout lady with a bell who was selling pinks and roses, and a church near by ringing peals as though it were mad with joy.

Mr. Audley was introduced, they all climbed in and started off. Judith gave herself up to complete enjoyment. Everything was as she would have it, except that she would have preferred a chaise to a coach, because in a chaise she could see more, but in a chaise there would not be room for them all.

Mr. Audley was exceedingly attentive to her, so attentive that she was afraid lest Emma should be jealous. His method of attention was to ask innumerable questions, to which, however, he appeared to expect no kind of answer. He had a foolish expressionless face, but his questions were for the most part educational, concerning literature and the drama. Judith soon conceived a feeling of maternal care for him, as though he were an infant or a puppy. He seemed to her so very eager, inexperienced and untutored.

'Pray, ma'am, you have read Evelina, of course. Do you not find the Branghtons too amusing? Is it not laughable where the Captain throws Madame Duval into a ditch? Is not the close inexpressibly touching? Is London not dull in June--no Covent Garden, only the Little Theatre? Pray, ma'am, have you been to the Tower lately? Are not the tigers and lions fine? I saw recently Foote's play The Minor. It is all against the Methodists. I laughed myself into hysterics. I was at the Pantheon the other evening. It is never the same since it was burnt. I was at a Masquerade there, as mean as ever you saw. But the fireworks at Marybone! Have you seen the fireworks at Marybone? I hope you find this coach easy. I have a phaeton, bought only last week, but Mrs. Furze told me that friends might accompany her. I trust you are comfortable.'

It was his way, she assured herself, of courtesy and politeness. She need not listen to his questions if she did not wish. She had, once and again, an uneasy feeling that Georges was watching Mr. Audley with a growing conviction that he would, a little later, be an easy friend to win money from. She pushed that from her. She did not care just now to consider that side of Georges' character. Yes, she surrendered herself completely to happiness. There had been many days in the last two years when she had been, it seemed to her, living on the very edge of irretrievable disaster. One touch and she and Georges would both tumble over into a bottomless pit, and no one in the world care that they had gone. She knew Georges so well now that the black side of the account of her life with him was fearfully familiar. But slowly, slowly she was influencing him. Month by

month he was less drunken, attended more steadily to his Whitehaven business, submitted to her will.

By a constant good humour, a perpetual check on her fears and alarms, a refusal to be astonished at any sudden calamity, a trained restraint on her own nerves, temper, moods--by all these things she had gradually governed him, he not knowing that he was governed. The odd thing was that, although she knew now by heart all the iniquities of which he was capable, all his tempers, his violences, his infidelities, his shadinesses, she loved him more than ever. He was still her created work, although she was wise enough now never to show him that it was so. And there was, when all was said, somewhere in his strange character, a strain of sweetness, of loyalty, of liberality, of boyish candour, that made him to her, with reason, endearing. But, when all was said, she loved him, had always loved him, would always love him. There could be no one else for her.

It was enchanting when, after crossing the river, they left the town behind them and passed into the open fields. The blue sky was cloudless. Everything was painted with a shining lustre, and the trees were dark at the heart of their green foliage. They were at the 'Elephant' almost before they knew it.

Here, indeed, there was liveliness! In the centre was the stout sign-post with its four pointers, and round and about it all the world was on the move. There was a countryman on a donkey, driving two other donkeys in front of him, two shouting peasants with whip and dog, urging their stupid but amiable cows, two coaches drawn up at the inn door, and another, loaded with people, nearly riding down a little collection of barrows piled with flowers, fruit and vegetables. There was a private coach crammed with six people, and led by four horses, chariots, hackney--coaches, groups of country-people stood about enjoying the lovely afternoon, a party of very fine ladies and gentlemen, moving as though they were creatures of another planet, brilliant in their colours of red and purple, children outside the gardens playing at ball, dogs everywhere, and a superb solitary gentleman riding his horse, his servant riding behind him on another. Judith's heart beat with ecstasy when she saw all this life. She put her hand through Georges' arm and walked as proud as a duchess with him into the inn.

Here everything was in a bustle with the arrival of the two coaches, so, very soon, they crossed the road to the Gardens on the other side. These were simple Gardens, not like Marybone or Bagnigge Wells, but they were what Judith preferred. There were 'Chinese' benches, rough wooden tables, very childish amusements with a pillory for a gentleman to sit in until he was liberated by a kiss from a lady, a maze in which lovers might be lost and a peep- show rather the worse for wear and weather. But soon Judith was attending to none of these things, for sitting on the bench, her mouth open with excitement at all the things and people to see, her legs swinging, her eyes shining with delight, she was aware that Georges, of his own volition, had come to sit beside her, had his arm around her, was pressing her to him. All the world was forgotten in the heart-beating discovery of that moment. He had come of his own will, there in the public view, he who was so shy of demonstration, of anything that could attract general attention.

Wise from experience she showed no great responsiveness, only moved a little closer to him. But her heart was beating, and within herself she was thinking: 'I must keep this in memory. Whatever comes in the future nothing can take this away!'

All she said aloud was: 'Oh, how hungry I am! It is almost six, and we have eaten nothing all day long.'

'There was the cold pie,' he reminded her; then he whispered in her ear: 'Judy, do you love me?'

'A little,' she answered.

'Are you happy?'

'Yes--but when I have eaten I shall be happier.'

'I think you are charming. I am seeing you to-day with fresh eyes.'

'Your old wife!' She turned round to him, her eyes dancing. 'After so many years you can find that she has charm?'

'You are better. You are vastly improved. You are a woman now and yet you are still a child. Life has taught you something.'

'Marriage with you has taught me something,' she answered, laughing. 'Striving to alter you--'

'I doubt your capacity to amend me,' he said. 'Nobody enjoys better spirits than I--at times. To-day when the sun is shining and my French blood is warmed and you, my little wife, are beside me, and we are in fine clothes and have money. . . . Then I think heigh-ho! how virtuous I could be! But soon it will be Mr. Moss and cold mutton and flying down side-streets to avoid creditors and the fog and rain--'

'Meanwhile,' she cried, 'let us be happy now. We have a happy day. We must enjoy it.'

'We must enjoy it,' he repeated after her. His eyes lighted as he saw Mr. Audley coming towards them.

'Sir,' he cried. 'I would have a wager with you. Guineas that the next person through that gate yonder is a female.'

Mr. Audley looked rather nervous. Judith saw that he was no gambler by nature.

'Why, surely,' he agreed in his silly fluttering voice. 'Guineas it is, sir.'

They watched the gate. Judith saw, with an odd mixture of tenderness and chagrin, that Georges was watching with an eager excitement worthy of some great hazard. His body was tingling with his suspense. For a moment no one came. Then a stout man in a high beaver hat, very solemn in his claret-coloured coat, marched in through the gate.

'Damn!' cried Georges. 'It is against me! But double or quits, Mr. Audley, that the next is a female.'

'No, no,' Judith broke in. 'For shame, Georges. I am famished. Food I must have. . . .'

She saw his brow clouding. He would, in another moment, have forgotten all his recent affection for her had not, fortunately, Emma been seen arriving and with her a serving-man.

She was now in her proper and most happy element, arranging ceremonies that had to do with food and drink. They were to have their meal under a large spreading chestnut. They would have veal cutlets, a small green-goose and asparagus, a damson pie. . . .

Judith was long afterwards to remember that scene, the soft warm air, the cool green benignity of the great tree, the children playing on the sward near to them, the noise of the coaches and the carriages, the voices, sheep bleating--all beyond the gate; the laughter of lovers happily lost in the maze near to them, her own happiness as she sat beside Georges, her hand once and again resting on his knee.

They were all so happy, Mr. Audley so proud of his entertaining, and Emma in her tall hat at almost bursting point with pleasure at the food, the cheerfulness, the general sense of security. Poor dear! Her life did not provide her with so many secure moments!

She complained, of course, of the cooking as in duty bound, being herself so great a connoisseur, but hugely nevertheless she enjoyed it. She shouted orders to the waiters, and herself, at one moment, hurried forward to inspect the green-goose on its way through the gate from the inn opposite.

Then, as the sun sank beyond the garden walls and everything was suffused with a pale shadow of gold, the dark friendly patterns growing lengthy on the grass, a silver star or two winking through the trees, a fiddler drew near and with him a woman, who had a strong sweet voice. She sang:

'Beauty clear and fair,
　　Where the air
Rather like a perfume dwells:
Where the violet and the rose
Their blue veins and blush disclose
And come to honour nothing else;
Where to live near
And planted there
Is to live, and still live new;
Where to gain a favour is
More than light, perpetual bliss--
Make me live by serving you!

'Dear, again back recall
　　To this light,
A stranger to himself and all!
But the wonder and the story
Shall be yours, and else the glory;
I am your servant and your thrall.

'Dear, again back recall
   To this light!'

Oh, that this moment might last for ever, never to change. This voice, this shining light, enclosed in this garden. . . .

Georges, too, must have felt something of it for he rose impetuously and pressed money on the fiddler, then turned back to them a little shamefaced. But he kissed Judith before he sat down. The dusk came; candles were lit. There was dancing on the green.

But, alas, when it was time to go it was found that the coachman was perilously drunk. He greeted them all with a warm and most appreciatory affection. He would have embraced Emma, quarrelled with a little gentleman near by, who had, he fancied, insulted her.

Mr. Audley was greatly ashamed and not of much value in the situation. He twittered like a bird whose nest is in danger, looking at Emma as though to implore her not to like him the less for this accident. Georges was of excellent practical use. It was just the situation for his temperament. He helped to hoist the man on the box, frightened away the interested spectators, quieted the horses and threatened the coachman with such dire penalties were there an accident that for the moment he was sobered. So they started off down the road under the stars. There was a moon, and everywhere a radiant peace.

But not for long. After a while the coachman began to sing; the horses took fright; the coach rocked and rocked again. Georges attempted, with head out of the window, to bring the man to his senses. There he was with throat uplifted, singing to the moon. A moment later there was a fearful heave, and the coach was on its side in the ditch. Georges climbed through the broken door, ran to the horses' heads. The others, uninjured except for a shaking and a bruise or so, climbed painfully after him and sat in the hedge. The coachman, his singing silenced, was perched skywards, fallen almost on to the horses' backs, his thick legs dangling. Georges assisted him down, and he at once began to snivel, his fist in his eyes like a schoolboy's.

The shafts and one wheel were broken. The other wheel raised in mid-air made a fantastic gesture.

At length Mr. Audley and the coachman, still snivelling, set off for the nearest village to find some other conveyance. Emma, Judith and Georges sat in the hedge over a ditch, and a network of fiery stars shone down upon them. There might be highwaymen, an added adventure, but it seemed not; for the whole world was still, holding its breath under the moon.

In the shadow of the fantastic coach with its clamant wheel Georges and Judith sat close together. He seemed to be, in the spirit of that beneficent night, a transformed creature. He declared his love as though this were the first night that he had met her. She held her breath, catching the divine moment that it might be with her for ever.

'Judith, I love you to-night. I have never told you that before.'

'No, never--and I have wanted it so.'

'It has grown in me. Through all my vagaries it has been ever drawing closer to me. YOU have been drawing closer to me.'

'And I love you, Georges. I always shall.'

'Perhaps this is the beginning of a new life for us.'

She shook her head humorously.

'No. Things will be up and down again as they have always been, but I am very happy for this moment.'

She was in a transcendent happiness. The two different strands of her life were suddenly united in one common glory--her practical daily Herries life, and the dream, that which separated her from the rest of her kind. Love had for a moment united them.

The fantastic wheel of the coach against the sky seemed to promise her something:

'Trust this moment.'

And to threaten her something:

'This moment is already almost gone.'

'Oh, let me keep Georges!' was her unuttered prayer. And if in the sequel her prayer was denied her, it was also granted. Her whole nature in that half-hour was fulfilled.

In the hedge, bathed in the warm flower-scented air, for a brief while they were completely united.

THE HERRIES BALL
May 17, 1796

Judith went to the famous Masquerade at Will Herries' house, given there in the month of May of the year 1796, dressed as her mother.

She had never seen her mother, who had died in giving birth to her. She had seen no picture of her; nevertheless it was a link in the strange sequence of events that once there should have been a child sheltering in its mother's skirts at a Christmas games in a Borrowdale farm, that then there should have been a woman crying over her lost lover in Carlisle streets, that again there should have been a weary woman knocking at the door of Herries in Rosthwaite, that now Judith, dressed as a ragged gipsy, her red hair loose about her head, should be waiting in an almost breathless excitement for the coach to take her to another Herries house.

There were to be many consequences from the Masquerade on this night, consequences as important to the whole Herries family as the quarrel that rose out of this occasion, consequences that helped to make Judith's life afterwards what it was, and from that to affect generations and possibly the colour of England itself. For if, on that night, Judith had not been dressed as a gipsy, would the beautiful Jennifer have snapped the ivory stick of Mrs. Will's fan-- that famous fan!

It is still in dispute as to whether the mandarins painted on it were clothed in blue or silver. A letter still extant, written on the day after the Masquerade by Rose, Pomfret's wife, speaks of 'Christabel's BLUE Fan.' On the other hand, in Judith's own Journal, there are these words: '. . . And so, scarcely knowing what she did, so angry was she, she snapped one of the sticks of Christabel's Fan with the Silver Figures that had been lying on the Table at her side. . . .'

We may go back, too, and ask History whether if Francis Herries, senior, had not sold his mistress at a Keswick Fair, would Jennifer Cards have recollected the fable of old Maria and her spaniel, and, if she had not . . . Of all the things of which we are uncertain in this world--and there are more every day--we can at least be sure that History has for one of its subjects the ultimate importance of trifles. A coin rolled on a table, a verse by Mr. Pope, a cabbage grown in a stubborn garden, a foggy night in Carlisle, a players' booth in Penrith, scattered snow reflected like feathers in a lake--such things were the landmarks in the life of Francis Herries of Herries. Such things were to mark the life of his daughter also. And it is in the chronicle of such things that the history of the Herries family finds coherence.

Judith and Georges were ready dressed waiting for the hackney- coach, Judith as her mother and Georges as Mephistopheles. Four of the Robinson children, thumbs in their mouths, stood inside the doorway, wondering at the splendour, and a moment later there was Mrs. Robinson herself, a baby in her arms, to announce that the coach had arrived.

Georges was superb and well aware of it. He wore scarlet shoes, black silk hose and doublet, a crimson cloak, a red peaked hat with a black feather. His costume, tight-fitting, displayed his figure to splendid advantage. He knew that his ankles, his thighs, his chest, could suffer any display. He would, if he did not take care, soon be too stout, but that was not yet.

Judith's dress was orange colour, trimmed with silver; it was ragged a little, showing her neck and arms. She had a wreath of flowers in her hair. She looked a child of ten; her excitement gave her a colour of eager expectation. But although her excitement was great, she was yet able to be practical. She had her anxieties. Georges was in one of his wild moods. They had, during the last three months, been living very precariously. She was not sure--he would not tell her--but she fancied that he had been losing heavily at cards. Young Mr. Stane (whom she hated) had arrived three days before from Whitehaven; in his sinister and complimentary politeness she had imagined threats and bad omens.

She was in the difficult position of attempting to protect Georges, but not knowing from what to protect him. He had been in his most cynical, mocking, restless temper, treating her as though she were a helpless child,

assuming for himself an air of profound wisdom (which was, as she well knew, quite unjustified). She could only control or have any influence over him by asking him no questions. She would not ask Henry Stane anything. The lovely intimacy of that wonderful June day at Newington had never returned. She had been wise to tell herself that day that she must treasure it, for there would not be many like it. Her anxiety over him only made her love him the more, but she was working in the dark, fearing she knew not what, dreading some awful disaster. She never saw Henry Stane without knowing her fear increase. And she was not yet twenty-two years of age.

However, it was her nature to be concerned with the happiness of everyone who came near to her, and, before they started, she was busy with all the Robinson children. They were a dirty little group, as, indeed, necessity forced them to be. Judith, with her passion for cleanliness, had kept her place as decent as she might, but the rest of the house, although some of the rooms were let to gentlemen of means, was a pig-sty. Many of the window-frames were black with soot, windows were stuffed with paper and rag; in one room eleven members of an Irish family slept in two beds; a drunken tailor on the floor above Judith kept a pig in his apartment.

Mrs. Robinson had enough to do with her lodgers, her family and her husband's apprentices. She was not a bad-natured woman, and she had a deep admiration for Judith because she kept her room so clean, was always in a sensible mood and was connected with fine families. She had intended binding out her eldest girl Fanny, a child of eleven, to a tambour-maker, but very reluctantly, for she knew well enough the cruelty that these apprentice children must suffer. And Fanny was a bright, pretty child. But Judith had persuaded her to keep her at home, had even herself employed the child and paid her a wage. Then there was the little chimney-sweep (already out on his work this evening), who was falling into bad ways. Judith had been looking after him a little, letting him come into her room in the early afternoon when he had had his sleep out and was ready for any mischief. He was a funny old little boy and regarded Judith as just of his own age. . . .

So now she pinched the cheek of one child, patted the verminous head of another, smiled at the harassed mother and then, followed by her splendid Mephistopheles, picked her way down the filthy staircase.

Chelsea was a great distance in the coach, and they had plenty of opportunity for conversation. Avoiding any display of sentiment as she always did when she wanted to get at the truth, she challenged him at once as to the position: things were bad? He shrugged his shoulders. He had been unlucky. He was always unlucky now. Henry Stane had come down from Whitehaven with his usual complaints. Henry Stane--she shivered. Why had he so much to do with everything now? Well, he wanted to be a partner with Wix and Georges. He was ambitious. Because his father had once been a simple fisherman, he thought it fine to have risen in the world as he had; now he wanted to rise still further. Judith, trying to think connectedly in the jolting coach, had an impulse to implore Georges to free himself from Stane, buy him out, do anything. She did not know why she dreaded him as she did. Her mind flew back to the night in Cockermouth when she had helped to save Humphrey. That dark cellar, the fugitive, they were connected in some way with Stane and his ambitions. . . . But she said nothing. After the night of that quarrel in Watendlath she had determined not to question Georges about his Whitehaven affairs unless he wished.

'Don't sell the farm,' was all she murmured, as much to herself as to him.

'The farm?'

'Watendlath. You said once that if all else failed you could be happy there, in the life. . . .'

'By God, I could! It's strange, Judy, but when you speak of it I could leave this London and the coin and the stinking candles--all shut up, closed--I'd give a fortune to see that water now tumbling over the stones and watch those smutty-nosed sheep pushing up under the stone wall. . . .'

She, too, had for a moment a vision--the cut in Armboth Fell, the Tarn when the wind played on it, the ridge of the Fell looking over Borrowdale.

But with his French impatience and eagerness for practical things he drove all that from him. He had now an immense confidence in her common sense and a respect for her judgement. It had grown in him through the years. So he began to outline the schemes that he had for making use of all the Herries connections. This was an old topic with him. He often blamed her for not making more of all her Herries family. They liked her. Those old Rockages would do anything for her. Will was like her own brother. Will Herries was becoming a very rich man. Everyone talked of him. Why could they not give up this hand-to-mouth existence? Why should she not get Georges some place in Will's City business? To-night would be a fine time to work something. Will would be in great feather at having so grand a Ball in his house. Judith would be able to do anything with him.

Judith sighed to herself. This was an old, old topic. Georges always raised it when things were going badly. When things went well he loudly despised Will and his business, said that he wouldn't be tied in the dirty City for all India's wealth. It was only when he was in a corner that he thought of it. Yes, Judith sighed. The omens were bad. Georges must be desperate. And she could not tell him what was the truth--that all the Herries family regarded Georges as a wild adventurer, almost as a vagabond. That they would not have Georges, this little gambling Frenchman from nowhere, into any intimate connection with them, not if you offered

them all China! It was bad enough with the country crowded with French refugees as it was. . . .

Georges went on. How clever Will had been about all this French War that was ruining so many men, and he had managed to make his profit out of it! There were rumours that he had been lending the Prince money. Everything that he touched seemed to turn to gold! And Georges was just the man for him! They were much of an age. Will could not be more than twenty-six or so. So young a man must need partners.

'He has partners,' Judith remarked. 'He is the youngest in his firm.'

Well, young or not, he was the lively one. What would he not be at forty? And he had been in the City for so short a time! Georges MUST make some association with him! Surely Judith could manage it. Judith had an impulse to turn to him: 'It's your own fault that I can't--you with your tempers and sudden idleness and bad company and gambling and the rest!' But she might as well have said: 'You, Georges Paris, because you were born Georges Paris.'

Their coach was going very slowly now, for they were approaching Ranelagh and there was much traffic. The road (that had been but a few years before all country, but now buildings were springing up) was crowded with chairs, private coaches, hackneys, boys running with lights, families walking--so much noise of wheels and shouting that Georges and Judith could not hear one another speak. Now, as always, she surrendered at once to all the excitement. She forgot all troubles, financial, domestic, thought only of the Ball and all the fun there would be.

Will's house stood in its own ground. The whining purr of the violins could be heard coming, as it were, from the heart of the trees. Above the wide staircase the long ballroom glittered under the wavering flutter of the candles that blew gently in their hanging silver lustres.

Will had taken a bigger house than his present needs when, at a moment, Sir Frederick Cottenham must sell at a ridiculously low price because of a night's loss at cards. Servants were so cheap as to cost almost nothing, except for mouths to be fed, and although, because of the French War, food was more costly every day, here there seemed to be always an abundance. It came from somewhere, Christabel herself scarcely knew whence.

But the events of that strange evening began for Judith, not as she stood masked watching the fantastic medley of Turks, Nuns, Punchinellos, Italian Ladies of the Renaissance, Devils, Monks, Columbines and the rest, but rather at the sudden sight of Francis, disguised only by his mask, wearing otherwise a plain suit of black and silver. She would have moved at once to his side, but she must first speak to Will and Christabel. They were the only two unmasked in the room. There was something, Judith felt at once, a little pathetic in Will's sense of triumph. She had a divination (how utterly surprised he would be if he knew!) of what this glorious moment would mean to him, and of the jealousies, hatreds, contempts that his very success would rouse up against him.

Yes, even now, this very room would be seething with them! The Herries who were here would be resenting his power, but resolving to make use of it, and those who were not Herries would be scorning him for a City merchant who was pushing into Society. And yet the Herries were as ancient and well-rooted a family as any in England. But it was new, this pushing upwards of the merchant by power of his wealth, this very Ball the symbol of the reluctant yielding of the old world to the new.

Will would have no sense of any of this. She realised, looking at his thin stiff body, marked with the sharp horse-bones of the Herries, his eyes lit with a cold, nevertheless animated pride, that he could feel nothing but his success. He might well be proud. Little more than a boy, he yet had arrived at this power. But Judith felt that in Christabel there was a real uneasiness. In an ugly dress of a pale yellow, her hair done too high for the present fashion, she seemed almost to be expecting sneers and insults. Judith saw that this evening had been both her proud expectation and anxious dread for months before. She was in a state of nervous tension that might lead to anything. And, in fact, at this time moods, tempers, resentments, wild pleasures were very near the surface. There was in the London of that moment much social etiquette, but little social control. The world was turning over, and everyone's foothold was a little insecure.

Neither Will nor Christabel had at that moment very much time for Judith, and after a while she was free to find Francis. A minuet was in progress. The coloured masked figures stirred in the candle-shine like fragments of a pattern moving towards a perfect arrangement. The moment when that arrangement was achieved--would the world stop? But on every occasion something prevented perfection. Tall high windows were covered with curtains of silver brocade. On the distant gallery the musicians played. Judith could see, above the clouded colour that was veiled with a kind of dim smoke, one fiddler, very thin, his arm raised like a stick, a sharp-pointed nose that seemed almost to be directing the whole room. . . .

She found Francis and touched his arm.

'Sir,' she said, 'a word with you,' as though they were strangers. Then she laughed. They stepped back into the curve of the window-place. They had not seen one another for six months.

Francis had, the year previous, made friends with a Mr. Samuel Rogers. This gentleman was a poet, who had become famous with a piece entitled 'The Pleasures of Memory.' He lived at Stoke Newington, and Francis had stayed with him there. In January of this same year he had been involved in some of the troubles connected with what was known as the White Terror, the suspicious and terrified reaction in England of the Terror in France, and Francis had been able to show him some assistance during this anxiety. He was, from Francis' account, a sharp-tongued little man, bitter in speech about everyone, but of great active kindliness in deed. Francis, at least, seemed to understand him, and in his company lately had met many interesting people. Rogers had London rooms in Paper Buildings, and Francis had had wonderful evenings there with men like Horne Tooke, Parr, Sheridan, and even the great Mr. Fox himself. Francis had taken to a sort of sporadic journalism, the political variety. He also had published essays in the Gentleman's Magazine under the pseudonym of Peter Mountain.

But he seemed to-night to have but little interest in his own career. He was making a new life for himself; but Judith soon saw that it was no more the life that he wanted than the earlier Cumberland one had been. He was as alone here in this sounding, moving gaiety as he had been beside the silence of the Watendlath Tarn.

He seized upon Judith with a kind of feverish thirst. His need to-night was for someone who could give him some sort of reassurance. Behind his mask his loneliness seemed for a moment to darken the candles, the coloured clothes, to put out all the splendour. She had her own excitements, her own anxieties, but as always when she was with anyone whom she loved she forgot her own life in her eagerness to benefit the other.

'Judith, let's escape together thousands of miles away--to some island where there are no people.'

'Only the savages,' she answered him, laughing.

'Well, we Herries are savages. I hate us in the mass. Behind the masks you can scent Herries a mile away. There, in that silly black costume, that's Maria Rockage, and near her in the red and gold that's Rockage. There to the right, the Punchinello, that's Montague Cards; there's Amelia, dressed as a Nun, dancing. We are a horrid family, so pleased with ourselves. For ever casting someone into outer darkness. "Oh, he's mad." "She's lunatic." "That's an atheist." And for what are we proud? Because we are English, because we are Herries, as though you said: "Because I'm a cow." Judy, there was old Maria. Have you ever heard of Maria? She died in '45. She lived almost to be a hundred, within a month or two. When she failed her century Herries were angry all over the country. That is a record of the sort that they value. I have heard my father tell how your father visited them in Keswick after old Maria's funeral and found them all at odds. But her dog was there, the only thing that cared for her, and your father said that the scorn of them all in that dog's eyes . . .' He broke off. Looking at her half quizzically, he added: 'You know you have no right here, you and Georges. You are vagabonds. And I am one also.'

'I know,' Judith answered. 'And I had the whim to dress as my mother. I never saw her. But I fancied her at this Ball. What they would all say, if she came in from Borrowdale with the mud on her shoes! But I feel Herries as well, Francis. I would like to be the head of the family, very wealthy, telling them all what to do.' Then, catching his arm: 'Why, see, that must be Jennifer! Did you ever see anyone so lovely?'

Francis turned, looking more closely into the room.

'Do you know,' he said, 'I have never seen Jennifer? My lovely cousin. . . .'

But he broke off. Quite close to them a beautiful girl was passing. Jennifer Cards was in that year when Francis first saw her twenty-six years of age. Francis Herries was thirty-six. That first sight of her was one of the more important moments of Herries history evolved on that eventful evening. She was dressed as Catherine de' Medici in a magnificent robe of slashed crimson, and behind her lovely head a stiff high collar of silver. Ropes of pearls were in her black hair. She was tall, carried herself superbly, her skin had the whiteness of a white rose. She walked lazily as though half asleep. Francis stared. He could not speak. It was as though, after all these years, his dream had been, by some favouring magician, created into fact for him.

'Her dress suits her nobly,' Judith said. But he did not hear her. He stood like a man lost.

Like a man lost! It was from that moment, perhaps, that Judith began to have the sense that this whole affair was a dream, and a dangerous dream too. Her excitement did not leave her, but the happy element in it. She began to feel that there was something evil in the air.

The dance had stopped, and the dancers broken up. A sort of wildness crept into the house. Not far away, in Ranelagh, down the dark alleys, couples were standing in the shadow, body strained against body in deep embrace. Although the music in the room had ceased it still seemed to linger in the trees, and little companies of wanderers gathered at the garden-gates, watching the house so brilliantly lit, heard the lean fiddler. Was he seated among the chimney-pots? Was it some strain from the Ranelagh musicians? Or an old beggar fiddling wildly down the road?

Judith saw that she had lost Francis. He cared no more what she said to him. And then she saw another thing. She saw that her own especial Mephistopheles was attracted just as Francis was. But he was more active. His eyes fixed on the lovely lady, Georges waited until he saw her a moment detached, alone. He went up to her and spoke. How exactly Judith knew what the tone of that voice would be, the softness, the charm! His mother's! She saw again, as she often did when she was with him, that moment of her childhood when in the bare room the young man had knelt to the naked woman! Mother and son. Ah, but he had charm when he spoke like that, when his body seemed to tremble behind his voice. She could fancy how his eyes would shine behind the mask! He spoke. Jennifer turned. She

looked at him and laughed. He spoke again. She smiled, and they both moved away together, she leading, he following.

Judith shivered. She was cold there in the window. Francis and Georges, the two whom she loved best in the world, they would both leave her at any moment for a fine woman. She had done so much for Georges, but at any instant he forgot her. Indeed, it seemed that no one remembered her. She seemed to be as alone in that crowd as though she were by herself on Brund Fell. Her gipsy's dress, how shabby it was beside all these splendours! And her mother would have been shabby, too, had she been here. Once again she knew that sharp pang of alarm at her own insecurity in this harsh, indifferent world. She had no one but herself. Only her own pride to keep her. No one would care if this moment she vanished for ever. Not Georges? No, not Georges. Emma, perhaps, and at the thought of that large, comforting woman the tears stung her eyes, were damp behind the mask. Then she pulled herself up. What did it matter if she WERE alone in the world? So her mother had been, so her father. Oneself was enough. She was aware then that a Mask, dressed as Punchinello, stood motionless at her side. He had been there perhaps for a long while. She turned, and as she did so he spoke:

'You would not expect to find me here,' he said.

She knew at once the voice. It was young Stane. How was young Stane here? She thought he did not know Will. Georges had not brought him. He was always to her uncanny, and his presence now only increased her sense of the strange wildness of the evening.

She said coldly: 'I did not know that you were acquainted with Mr. Herries.'

'Yes. You would not know. I had said nothing to Georges. But I have known Mr. Herries--for some time.'

She might have guessed that he would. It was like him to make use of every advantage, but to tell no one of what he was doing. He would go far. He was not now more than twenty-five. Ten years back on naked feet he had been selling fish in Whitehaven. Georges had told her of his father, a huge man with a white beard, always reciting the Scriptures, who worshipped this his only child. She turned and looked at young Henry Stane. He had large black eyes behind the mask. He was black-haired, sallow like Georges, but tuned, she knew at once, to a far greater determination. He would eat Georges up! She saw at once how Georges' laziness, good-nature, bad temper, self-indulgence, all these would be simply easy material for Stane's advancement. He was an adventurer too, but he was resolved not to remain one.

Meanwhile she had never hated anyone so much; instinct, fear for Georges, and her own innate repulsion. She was not at her best when she hated anyone. She showed her feeling too readily. She showed it now.

'I congratulate you, Mr. Stane,' she said. She saw (and it was to explain very much to her afterwards) that his most maddening quality was his imperturbability. Nothing could touch him. That would infuriate Georges just as now it was angering her. Then his next words amazed her:

'Pardon me. I know how you regard me. All is love or hatred with you. I admire so much your sincerity. But although you dislike me so very much, would you not perhaps allow me to say a word about your husband?'

'No,' she answered.

'Very well. But you have much influence with him.'

'What is it, then?'

'Only that he is making a great mistake to neglect his business so constantly. It is a good business, but it needs attention. He has a good head, Georges, but no discipline.'

She hated the familiarity in his voice. From behind her mask she looked at him.

'I know quite well what you feel about my husband. You wait only to climb over him into his place.'

'No, I assure you, madam--'

'Oh yes, I know very well--'

'Then there is nothing more to say. I meant it civilly.'

As he went it was as though another little Punchinello leapt out of him and sat on his shoulder, its small, puckered, malicious face laughing back at her. How insulting of him!--but there was truth, too, in what he said. And Georges was whispering somewhere in Jennifer's ear.

She had not for many years felt so miserable, so lonely, lost, deserted. Again and again the hot tears gathered behind the mask, and she beat them back. She felt as though some influence separated her from everyone there. She had expected to be so happy, but now that sense of slipping on the very edge of some disaster frightened her so threateningly that all she could do was to start off in search of Georges, to be sure that he was safe. No, she did not care whether he were with Jennifer or no, so long as he were safe.

She was soon caught into the throng. She realised that everything was growing very wild. Couples whirled madly together, colliding with others. Both men and women were elated with their freedom. Many were unmasking. The fiddlers seemed to be playing mad, discordant tunes as though they were drunk.

She had an odd thought as some stout Cardinal tried to catch her by the arm. 'It's because in their hearts they despise Will that they do this. It would not be like this in a really grand house.' She suspected that any of the 'really grand people' who had come had left already.

She was confirmed in her suspicions by having thrown almost into her arms poor Maria Rockage.

Maria and Carey had, she knew, come to the Ball with a great sense of condescension. For one thing, Will was young enough to be their son; for another, he was a City man; for another, nothing in London anywhere was so fine and superior as Grosset. So they had come with condescension, with Methodist suspicion, and with kindliness of heart. Judith, young though she was, knew every motive in Maria Rockage's brain, her poverty, so that often at Grosset there was not food enough, her passion for her offspring, her confused Methodism, her muddled benevolence and her real warmth of heart. It was on this last ground that the two of them met.

But now Maria was frightened. She could not find Carey. She MUST find him, for they must leave at once. Even the servants downstairs were drinking. There was a little black boy on the staircase eating pie out of a dish. The whole affair was tumbling out of control. She must find Carey and take him home, back to their rooms in Berkeley Square. As a matter of fact, Judith knew that the rooms were not in Berkeley Square, but up a mews in Brick Street. Young Phyllis (safely asleep at Grosset) was for ever betraying her mother's tactics. Maria's terror rose. She especially resented that Jennifer Cards should be the belle of the evening. She disliked and condemned the Bournemouth branch of the family. Moreover, her own rather shabby black dress had been, in intention, a Catherine de' Medici. It had a stiff high black collar. 'She paints shockingly high. How Amelia permits her . . . But Amelia wishes to sell her to the finest bidder, and for all they were so grand when Carey stayed at Bournemouth last year, the rain came into the coach and the straw was soaked . . . and I'm sure that Robert (Jennifer's brother) is an effeminate young man as you'd find among the silks and gauzes at a dressmaker's. Judith, WHERE is Carey? Oh, help me to find him! This is, indeed, pandemonium.'

Almost everyone now had unmasked, and the scene had a strange phantasmal beauty.

In the brilliant dusty light, figures moved now to country dances. One followed another, the 'top couple' always 'calling the dance.' There were Chain Figure, Allemand, Triumph, Swing Corners, Poussette and many more. The dancers kept their places, observed their decorum. It was beyond them, in the alcoves, up and down the stairs, in the hall, that the coloured figures, devils and monks, courtesans and milkmaids, Columbines and sea-captains tumbled and laughed, whispered and embraced. Silver and purple, cinnamon and orange, grey and crimson broke, melted, formed, as though from the gilt ceiling with the pink naked cherubs a figure solemn, sad-faced, remote, hiding a gigantic yawn, absent-mindedly pulled the strings.

In any case the Herries strings were pulled that night. By a kind of fate the little Herries figures were drawn together and with disastrous consequences.

For Christabel Herries the evening had become a torture. She was only a girl in years, although tall and gawky of figure. Will's wealth had come suddenly. Of the many persons invited she knew herself not half, and their masquerades made them only more mysterious to her.

At that time in London it was a very general complaint that many persons came to private Balls and Masquerades who were quite unknown to their hosts and hostesses. It was the increasing licence of these London seasons that led to the strict etiquette of Bath and other watering-places. With the divisions at Court, the uncertainty of the war with France, the consciousness of a lower class slowly but increasingly vocal, the new importance of the business man from the City, the advancing licence of Vauxhall, Marybone and the many lesser resorts, no hostess during the last years of that century but knew alarms and terrors that would have horrified her grandmother. No smaller hostess, in any case—and Christabel was a very new hostess indeed. It is an old and very true axiom that nothing can harm a party save the anxieties and alarm of the host and hostess themselves. All would have been well on this especial evening had Christabel been able to command herself. Unfortunately, when the crisis arrived, Will was elsewhere. He in fact saw nothing the matter with his Ball. It would have taken a great deal more than a few riotous spirits to upset his complacent equanimity. He had also enjoyed no small quantity of his own wine, which he thought excellent; he congratulated himself on acquiring it cheaply from a Jewish gentleman in the City. He was dancing the Triumph with a lady quite unknown to him, but, in his eyes, of an especial fascination, when Christabel so desperately needed his support. There were to be many occasions afterwards when he would have given half his wealth had he only been there that he might have prevented what occurred.

Many times in the records of any family it must seem that the stage has been set with especial and malicious purpose. Had Will's house not been an old one of Queen Anne's date there would not have been the small ante-room leading from the ballroom itself, and had there not been the small ante-room . . .

It happened that Rose Herries, Pomfret's wife, from Kensington, began the trouble. Rose Herries was a woman thinned and raddled by incessant jealousy. By birth the daughter of a small Worcestershire clergyman, she had been amazed when the handsome young Pomfret Herries had proposed for her in marriage. Pomfret's father, Sir Raiseley Herries, had married the sister of David, the son of old 'Rogue' Herries, but there had been an old boyhood feud between Raiseley and David that David's sister had certainly done nothing to heal. It was because of their proximity to David's family at Uldale that the Raiseley Herries had moved from Keswick to London. Raiseley, Pomfret's father, had always been delicate and ailing. When Pomfret had been around twenty-five years of age, Raiseley had moved for a summer into Worcestershire because of some doctor or other, taking his two children with him.

It was here that one fine morning young Pomfret had seen the lovely Rose walking down a country lane. He had fallen in love with her on the spot. He had been often in love before, but never considered matrimony. Now he did consider it, and six months later was married.

Rose had never recovered from the shock of it. The most that she had ever expected was a local squire, but now to be a baronet's Lady, to have a grand house in Kensington and, above and beyond that, to be married to a man whose figure was everything that her most romantic imagination could have designed for her! Sir Pomfret was an amiable fellow, contented with all that came his way. He was as good a husband to her as was in his nature. But, after the first month, he was unfaithful, nor was he either then or later able to conceal his infidelities. And, so evilly does fortune arrange, Rose was designed to be jealous. She was made for it. The more jealous the more she loved, and the more she loved the more jealous. Pomfret learned, as all husbands learn, to conceal more skilfully his private life, but the less Rose knew the more she guessed. She was frankly a plague both to herself and to him. A Masquerade such as this was designed to torture her.

Sir Pomfret's stout figure (he had come to the Ball as Henry VIII.) soon escaped her vision. She told herself, as, poor woman, she had told herself a thousand times before, that 'she must permit him his pleasure.' For five minutes she knew a sort of unhappy nobility. She was being fine, generous, the true wife; but the five minutes were as long as a lifetime, and soon, her long thin neck craning (she was dressed in a watery green and considered herself a Naiad), she looked for him everywhere. She had come to the Ball happy and expectant; Pomfret would stay by her side, he would dance with her and then, very handsomely, she would say: 'Now be off. You don't want your old wife at hand all the evening.' But he had left her so quickly; he had given her nobility no opportunity.

It is another of the signs that Providence had its long finger crooked in this affair that the men were all of them absent, Will dancing, Rockage talking of his place in Wiltshire to an elderly baroness, Pomfret making love to a very young but very worldly Nun, and Georges . . . Well, Georges, his head singing with Jennifer's beauty, was betting with some young men on the staircase as to the number of young women's feet you could see moving across the ballroom floor.

So the men were away. This was a woman's affair. Rose Herries met Christabel by chance behind the bronze-coloured curtains that portioned off the ante-room from the ballroom. It was comparatively quiet here: the music, the voices came like water flowing up, ebbing away again. The room had been cleared of furniture; the walls had a blue and white paper recommended to Christabel within the last month as the very latest design. On it were depicted over and over again the sorrows of Werther, an elongated Werther watching a gigantic Lotte beside the spring.

It was unquestioned that Christabel did not, by this time, know what she was doing. It seemed to her that the whole thing was a devastating, world-shaking scandal. To-morrow all London would be speaking of it. She and Will would be disgraced for ever. The scandalous Herries Ball . . . She had been always a delicate woman. Child-bearing had but shaken her nerves the further. Her stupid, wondering features, pale but strangely streaked as though with the marks of someone else's fingers, were puckered and childishly distressed above her ill-fitting yellow dress.

She had convinced herself that it was Jennifer Cards who had disgraced the Ball. She had always disliked Jennifer, always distrusted the Cards branch of the family, who, she was well aware, looked down upon Will and herself. She did not like Rose and Pomfret, the Kensington branch, very much better. Little Judith was the one she especially cared for. She would have liked to have her always with her. It was a thousand pities that she must live up in that rough Cumberland and be married to a scamp of a rascally Frenchman. Poor little Judith! Christabel knew that she would come to some catastrophe. But she liked her; Judith was kind and considerate, despised no one, understood one's troubles. How she wished that Judith were here now! Then she saw her with Maria Rockage and at the same moment Rose, in her ugly green dress, peering about among the crowd.

The four women drew together as though by instinct, standing just inside the ante-room as bathers, soaked with the sea, gather together on a rock for a moment's pause. They were all nervous and uneasy--Christabel because of her social anxiety, Rose because of her errant husband, Maria because she could not find Carey, Judith because the whole evening had been a failure for her.

The big room was thinning. The candles were burning low. The music had lost its vigour. In the distance a crimson Cardinal pursued a Dairymaid, who ran with little screams of pleasure across the shining floor.

'That Baddeley,' said Rose Herries scornfully. 'There is some resemblance to mankind in him. That is as much as you can say. . . .' She was speaking of a Mr. James Baddeley, an acquaintance of Pomfret's.

'It is scandalous,' said Maria Rockage, 'that Jennifer should be so monstrously without a chaperon all the evening. When I was a girl, to leave one's chaperon for an instant, except to dance with an acceptable young man--' She broke off. She thought of her daughter Phyllis at Grosset, and how she could not afford to buy her the dresses . . . that flaunting crimson with the silver collar . . . 'But, of course, the looseness of these Masquerades. . . .'

Christabel felt at once that this was a criticism of her Ball. All over London to-morrow. . . . Her long fingers closed and unclosed about her fan. (The famous fan. Were the figures painted on it of blue or of silver? Who will ever know?)

'I admit . . . 'Tis a failure, a monstrous failure. . . . I am distracted. . . . And Will has assisted me in nothing at all. . . . I have had all the burden myself. . . .' She did not mind now what she said. She was on the verge of tears.

The others were surprised. They had not been thinking of the Ball. They had not thought it out of the way. Everyone knew what these Masquerades were. Once you wore a mask. . . .

'Why, Christabel,' Maria said amiably (for when she could rise above her own worries she was a kindly woman), 'the Ball is well enough. A very fine Ball. A Masquerade must always have a certain licence.' (But nevertheless she thought 'This is a pandemonium.')

Judith, who had been standing looking into the outer room, wondering where Georges was (she could not see with her small stature over the heads of the dancers), thinking that at least he might ONCE that evening have sought her out, felt an instant desire to take Christabel in hand, to reassure her, to persuade her that everything was well, to make her happy again (and behind that she was still wondering about Georges, thinking that her love for him was a sort of poison in her blood, a poison that she would never, never be rid of).

'Yes, Jennifer has no modesty,' Rose said, bending her long neck. (Was THAT Pomfret laughing with that girl in white, there near the window in the farther corner?) 'Her father permits her to do as she pleases. Amelia has been playing cards instead of doing her duty. I never liked the girl: swollen with self-approval. They say that at Vauxhall the other week . . .' She broke off, for Maria Rockage's hand was on her arm. Jennifer was standing, quite close to them, alone, looking into the ante-room.

It must be understood that the girl was elated with her triumph. She had not been so very much in London, and Bournemouth's triumphs were not very satisfactory. This was her first REAL Ball, and, more than that, it was in the very heart of the family. Although the Rockages had been there, yes, and the Herries from Kensington, it was she who had been the evening's sensation. She knew that socially the High World had not been represented here. But Jennifer was true Herries in that. Although she disliked all the other Herries except her own family, yet she thought them as good as anyone in the world--as good as the Pope or the Prince or Queen Charlotte or Lady Jersey. She wanted nothing more than to be the acknowledged Herries Beauty, and that not at all for the outside world but simply for the Herries world.

So here she was, panting with triumph, her mask in her hand, her marvellous dark blue eyes glittering with success and pleasure, her magnificent bosom half bare above the crimson, her carriage superb, her youth, vitality, self-confidence all alive and shining--and she glanced for a moment into the ante-room to see whether her mother were there. She looked and saw the four women, three of them, to her, untidy old frumps, and the fourth that strange girl Judith Paris, whose force of personality she felt. The girl had marvellous hair. She had character too. She didn't like her.

She might in fact have passed on had Judith's gipsy dress in some odd way not challenged her. Judith in her ragged dress with her unpowdered hair was unlike anyone else at the Ball. She had had, Jennifer knew, a vagabond for her mother and a vagabond for her father. Jennifer's grandfather had known 'Rogue' Herries.

So Jennifer stayed. She had not intended to look scornful. She was too happy. But there was an element of cruelty in her. She looked at Christabel's pale face and ugly yellow, at Rose's thin bones and ill-chosen green, at Maria Rockage's untidy hair, and before she moved away, she smiled.

Then she asked:

'Is my mother at cards?'

The smile was, for Christabel, a statement of the whole evening's failure. Her voice trembling, she answered:

'No. But wherever she is, you should be with her.'

Jennifer came forward a little into the room. She wanted these old women to have a full sight of her youth and her beauty. Christabel was her own age, and yet how elderly, how worn, how awkward she seemed! And perhaps Christabel thought: 'This is what I should be! The Ball would have been a success to-night had I been!'

Jennifer stood there, swinging her mask between her fingers.

'Christabel,' she said, 'I must congratulate you on the evening.' She meant a compliment. She had no sense of irony there. But Christabel saw it as only ironical.

'I do not need your compliments,' she answered, 'and least of all when they are not intended. I know what you have felt this evening. I must tell you that you have failed entirely if you wished to conceal your feelings.'

With a shock of surprise Jennifer realised that Christabel was in a hysterical rage. The three girls were standing near to one another, the two older women farther apart. Maria, who wished that everything should be peaceable, but that at the same time she might satisfy a little her own sense that her daughter had not fine clothes and that the evening had lacked decorum, said: 'You should have been more with your mother, Jennifer, or your mother more with you. Chaperons are still in fashion, my child. Yes, your mother is at the card-table. Pray give her my love.'

'Oh,' cried Jennifer, 'so that is what my sweet relatives have been settling with one another. That I need a chaperon!' She curtsied to them, and Judith thought that she had never in her life before seen anyone so beautiful. ('But,' she also thought, 'what a temper! My God, what a temper!')

'But for my own part,' Jennifer went on, addressing Christabel as though no one else were there, 'it appears ridiculous ostentation to me! At a Ball like this--' She paused, staring Christabel in the eyes. She had always hated Christabel, she thought, the mean pudding-faced thing, proud only because her husband had made money as a merchant, a vulgar City merchant.

'And what at a Ball like this?' Christabel whispered. They had come close together as though they were discussing some very intimate secret. Rose interrupted. She was aware that there was a very dangerous element here, something that threatened everyone's comfort. 'There!' she cried, laughing nervously. 'Why, I am certain that Jennifer meant nothing. The Ball is very fine. We have all enjoyed a most handsome evening. Jennifer had no intention--'

'But I had an intention,' Jennifer interrupted hotly, looking only at Christabel. 'If you fancy that I am to have my manners taught me--and my mother her manners also. There is a shabbiness here that one might have expected. Manners learnt from Great-Aunt Maria, I don't doubt, who learnt them at the Battle of Naseby. . . .'

'Manners!' cried Christabel, beside herself with weariness, hysterical exhaustion, jealousy, loneliness. 'Manners from you!'

She moved forward. Jennifer turned aside and, resting her hand on a small table beside her, without knowing what she did, picked up Christabel's fan that was lying there. She raised her head contemptuously; her fingers tightened about the fan, and one of the sticks broke with a little crack that sounded in Christabel's ears like a pistol shot. It was her favourite fan, one of her finest possessions.

She stepped forward and smacked Jennifer's face.

And this, exactly, was the true history of one of the most famous and momentous quarrels in all the Herries history, so long as events have been recorded.

THE HANGING

Judith sat facing old Montague Cards. He was not old in years, being but twenty-nine. He was the only son of Morgan, brother of Prosper and uncle of Jennifer, and was, therefore, the lovely Jennifer's cousin. He was a bachelor and plainly designed from the beginning for that character. He was thin to emaciation, never varied in his dress, a bag-wig, a suit of black silk. His nostrils constantly heaved in a sort of simpering protest, as though he were offended by a bad smell. But he was not. It was a sort of inner nasal irritation. His voice was affected and often rose to a shrill note, but behind these absurdities he was in reality a kindly, nervous, generous soul, who longed to be liked but did not know how to set about it. He had a horror of being made love to by women, although he liked their company, for he adored gossip.

He was tyrannised by his man-servant and his man-servant's wife. He had been, until Will's sudden rise, the wealthiest of all the Herries. His grandfather had left him money, and he, by careful investment, had increased it. He was very cautious and reputed to be miserly. This he quite certainly was not, but he found the reputation useful. Like all the other Herries he thought there was no other family in England so fine and so grand, but he quarrelled with individual members of it. He had not, for instance, spoken to either Carey or Maria Rockage for years until to-day. This cleavage was the result of the bursting of a damaged water-pipe upon him in the middle of a winter night when he was staying at Grosset. He complained that the Rockages thought it an honour to receive the contents of a burst water-pipe at any time, in any place, were it a Grosset water-pipe. He liked to stay with other Herries in the country. Visits saved expense. At once, however, on hearing of the family crisis, he had offered his rooms in Berkeley Square as an unprejudiced meeting-place. The Ball had not, as Christabel had feared, been the subject of any general scandal. It had in fact, in the outside world, made absolutely no mark whatever, but among the Herries themselves the effect had been terrific.

Judith, looking now at the various Herries seated in the fine brocaded chairs round Montague's panelled room, saw, from the barely concealed sentiments of pleasure in the various faces, that here at last was the family battle for which they had all for long been aching.

Carey Rockage, as someone outside the dispute and the titled head of the family, was in charge of the conference, and delighted he was. It had been no easy matter for the Rockages, economically, to be compelled to stay in London an additional week, but their rooms in the Mews were cheap, and young Carey and Phyllis would be living on short rations for many a week after their return to Grosset.

Rockage had a round baby face with dimples. His suit was rusty with age, his hair shabbily powdered, and one stocking had a hole above the heel. But he was a real Herries. There was dignity and discipline there. He could command men, and there was a certain sweetness in his nature, as there was also in his wife's, which had, in spite of their narrowness and Methodism, long ago drawn Judith to them. Maria, his wife, was sitting near to him, and in her excitement it was all that she could

do not to be speaking all the time. She hated so intensely the beautiful Jennifer, jealous of her loveliness, the advantages she had over her own dear Phyllis, but in the main thinking, quite honestly, that the beautiful creature represented all the whoredoms of Babylon.

Jennifer herself was not present. It was thought more fitting that she should not be, but her father and mother, Prosper and Amelia Cards, were there in very truth; it would not be too much to say that their rage and sense of insult was as fine and pure an emotion as ever a Herries had known.

Prosper, in spite of his forty-eight years, was, by far, the finest figure in the room. His suit of crimson and silver, his elaborate wig of shining whiteness, the splendid ruffles at his throat and sleeves only served to emphasise his magnificent physique. He had the chest and neck of a bull, but his features were not common. They had, as Amelia was proud to emphasise, a classical correctness. He was not fleshy as Pomfret Herries was; his frame was gigantic. He carried on the Herries' physical tradition of David, Will's father. Curiously enough he was not proud of his beauty; he had been so, maybe, once, but now he had transferred it all to his lovely Jennifer and it was in her that the whole of his life--physical, material, mental--and his ambitions were centred. She was to marry a Duke. Nothing on this earth was too good for her. And that she should have been struck in the face. . . .

He sat there outwardly calm, his splendid legs in their silk stockings stretched in front of him. Outwardly calm. But, if he lived to a hundred, as he and all the other Herries felt it their right to do, he would never forget this insult. Amelia, his wife, in a dress of canary silk, seated at his side, had the subdued and colourless appearance of a woman who has, her life long, played second to a splendid husband. She was not, however, as he knew, so colourless.

The round shining table between them, on the farther side of the room sat Pomfret, fleshy, unserious, gay in spite of himself; Rose, his wife, thankful that she had Pomfret secure at her side for an hour at least, eagerly excited at the human possibilities of the situation; Will, very stiff, trying to be grand, feeling desperately young, aware at one moment that he was richer than them all, at another that his wife had slapped the face of a guest in her own house, trying to calculate the social and family consequences of the incident, rather as a financier will balance his probabilities. Christabel, gauche, awkward, knowing that the whole family, save possibly Judith, was against her, a sort of rough obstinacy rising to support her, warmed too by an almost frantic hatred of Jennifer; a little farther from them again Francis, elegant, aloof, looking out of window as though he were thinking of something else--and Judith.

She had not intended to come. It was only because Christabel herself, coming all the way to Judith's lodging in a coach, had persuaded her.

Christabel, bursting into tears, had protested that all the world was against her: even Will had scolded her, had told her that her temper had put back his affairs a dozen years at least. True, she had slapped Jennifer's face, but was she to endure impertinence from anyone who offered it her? Rose and Maria had been with her in that. But now--who knows? They were under the thumb of their husbands. . . . Judith must come and support her.

Judith had her own private troubles--worse, she could not but think, than anything that Christabel had to suffer. In the week since the Ball, disaster had crept nearer, and now, for these last two nights and days, Georges had not been home.

He was attempting (how well she knew it!) to repair desperate fortunes with some desperate remedy. At every occasion when he left her she did not know but that she might never see him again. Maybe he was even now at the Thames bottom with his head battered or his throat cut. She thought, sitting in that room warm with the May heat, smelling the scent of the lilac bloom that came up from the Square below, hearing the cry of some vendor in melancholy tuneful cadence, 'Oh, if he would only come. Nothing else matters! It is strange how I love him!'

She had left word at the lodging if he should return there while she was away. Did any of those in this room love anyone as she loved Georges? She clasped her small hot hands together, smoothed her dress, and heard Prosper Cards' deep stern voice come to her as though from the heart of an abysmal pit:

'I am not indicting Mrs. William Herries for anything,' she heard him say. 'That is too strong a word. There must be, however, an apology in writing.'

'Come, come, Prosper, my friend,' Pomfret's easy genial voice interrupted. 'Is there not altogether too much ado about a trivial matter? Nay, nay--' (He raised a fat white hand.) 'We are all one family here. It is among relatives. Jennifer and Christabel are young, life is beginning for them, they had both an intemperate moment. For my part I like a little hot blood. . . .'

'Yes, Pomfret, we know that you do,' Prosper answered drily, crossing one splendid leg over the other. 'But I do not consider it a trivial matter, nor does my wife. We demand an apology in writing.'

Will's voice broke in. It trembled a little and was more human than Judith had ever heard it. 'If one apology is necessary, then so is another. My wife has already agreed that her action was hasty and undisciplined. The more reason that the affair was under her own roof. But what of the cause? Your daughter, sir, used words of gross discourtesy and in her temper destroyed one of my wife's most cherished possessions. . .'

'Cherished possessions!' broke in Amelia Cards. 'Fiddlesticks! A fan, and no extraordinary one neither!'

'Fiddlesticks!' Will cried, now very hot and red in the face. 'Is that a word for a lady . . . ?'

But Rockage interrupted, the dimples on his cheeks deepening so that he looked like a laughing cherub:

'Ladies! Ladies! Gentlemen! Gentlemen! You have invited me to preside over this conversation, simply, it was understood from the first, a friendly conversation that the little incident may be closed finally. It was with the wish of everyone that we met. Let us all part friends. The matter is surely clear enough. There was regrettable temper on both sides. The evidence has proved it. Mrs. Will Herries has stated her own regret. It only remains for my friend Prosper on behalf of his daughter--'

'Not a whit! Not a whit!' answered Prosper, slapping his silken thigh. 'I must have an apology in writing. There is no evidence that my daughter showed temper.'

'She did! She did!' broke in Christabel, on the edge of tears. 'She spoke most insultingly, comparing me with old Great-Aunt Maria of Naseby Battle, and making a play of our entertainment, and all for no reason but her own vanity, because she thought that she was the beauty of the evening--'

'As indeed she was,' Prosper said with deep satisfaction. 'No one within a mile's race of her.'

The lilac, rich, warm, pungent, floated in through the open windows, bathing Judith's eyes with its lovely odour. Oh, why must they squabble about this silly business and her own life on the knife-edge of ruin? She was here, a grown woman, to help her cousin, to aid in the family councils, but she did not feel like a grown woman. She felt like a little girl, shut in a dark room, expecting she knew not what terrible entry. What did they, these comfortable, well-fed Herries, know of the struggle that these last years had been for Judith and Georges, the scrapes for money, the taming of landladies, the corners of Coffee Houses, the night hours when Judith in her shift, her arm around Georges, had again and again persuaded him that all would yet be well? What did they know . . . ?

Then Rose's introduction of her own name caught her attention.

'There can be no question about the impertinence offered. Ask Judith Paris.'

All eyes turned to her. Her head was confused. Her own personal anxiety pressed upon her heart like a hand closing down on it, and the hand seemed to crush lilac bloom in its fingers; lilac swinging through the sky, while the tops of the green trees in the Square flamed on the iridescent air.

She heard Prosper Cards' deep arrogant voice: 'Well, what has little Miss Judith to say?'

Years after, when she looked back and wondered at the sudden temper that she showed now (temper that had immense consequences), it seemed to her that everything rose together to influence her. Just as, had Christabel's fan not been on the table, there would have been no family crisis, so had there been no warm day, no lilac, no anxiety for Georges, nay, even no dimples in

Carey Rockage's cheeks, and, most certainly, no 'little Miss Judith' from Prosper, why then there would have been no temper, no such public taking of sides, binding her, she often afterwards felt, to a whole lifetime of consequences. 'Little Miss Judith' indeed! There was certainly something insufferable about this Cards family!

She heard her own voice, rather shrill, not like her voice at all:

'I think that Christabel had aggravation. Contempt was shown for her Ball, not too civil in a guest who had been so kindly entertained. Christabel should not have slapped her face, maybe . . . but I would have slapped her. I would indeed. One's own guest . . . Oh, there was certainly cause!'

She realised with some satisfaction the surprise that everyone felt. For a moment she forgot even Georges, for she was doing what she loved to do, influencing a situation, a group of persons, above all, a group of Herries! She could feel how Rose Herries was thinking, 'Well I never; who'd have thought it!' and would wonder whether Judith's boldness might possibly titillate Pomfret's sensual side: how grateful Christabel would be, and even Will; how furious Amelia, Jennifer's mother; how scornful Prosper (but in his slow grandeur and handsome pride he would never forget it nor forgive it).

She stole a glance at Francis, who still was staring out of window, staring at the trees that shimmered like green glass in the sun. And what was HE thinking of? She knew at once by a sort of inspired divination. He was thinking of the lovely, lovely Jennifer--had been thinking of her all day. Years later she was to know that her divination was true.

Meanwhile she had to fight to maintain her position. Prosper was regarding her through his large liquid brown eyes with a patronising indulgence.

'Come, come, Miss Judith,' he said. 'Why so unkind to my daughter? How has she offended you?'

'She HAS not offended me!' (Judith thought--does he not know that I'm married, the great pompous ox? Oh, how once again she wished that she were larger, her legs longer, her brow more imposing!) 'I have nothing against your daughter, sir, but I was present, and must say what I think. In my advice it would be more seemly for nothing more to be said of the matter on either side. There was temper shown both ways. It was a late hour, and everyone was weary.' She was surprised at the firmness of her voice. Her personality counted; she knew that they were all impressed with it.

Perhaps Prosper felt that also, for he said, his voice a little more angered than it had been:

'Why do we waste our time? I should be in the country by now. My wife and I are not here for some child's play. I demand from Mrs. Will Herries an apology in writing.'

Will, his face pale with anger, the horse-bones of his cheeks emphasised with his passion, answered:

'It is clear enough from the evidence. . . . I also demand an apology in writing.'

Then everyone began to speak at once:

'No apology on either side.'

'Great rudeness.'

'For my part I'd have a public apology.'

'And what could you know of the matter? If you'd been beside your daughter as you should have been--'

'Most certainly she insulted me. She laughed at my entertainment and broke my fan--'

'I demand an apology in writing. . . .'

'After all, they are both young. Who should mind a slap in the face . . . ?'

'I would call you out, Cousin Prosper, for less.'

'Call me out then. I'll make mincemeat out of you!'

'Pomfret! Pomfret!' (This, shrilly, from Rose.) 'What are you about? And at your age. . . .'

And then a contribution from Cousin Montague, who had said no word until now, had been completely forgotten by everyone:

'The weather is so warm. There are refreshments in the parlour. The other room has a cooler outlook--'

Then from the hubbub, the decisive authority of Carey Rockage. Strange, the dominance of that shabby baby-faced man!

'Friends, friends! This is a family affair. About nothing so outrageous neither. Mrs. Will has agreed that she will offer an apology. As to writing, I am sure, Prosper, that your good-nature will insist--'

'Good-nature be damned!' Prosper interrupted. 'My daughter has had her face slapped and publicly. My wife is with me in this. For the hundredth time--there must be an apology in writing.'

'And I say there shall not!' cried Will, suddenly jumping up and tipping his chair over. 'This is our last and final word. My wife has expressed her regret for her hastiness. We expect the expression of similar regret from Miss Jennifer Cards. Otherwise there is an end to any possible intercourse between this branch of the family and the Bournemouth part of it. Greatly to be regretted-- but this is final.'

The boy, for he was little more, glared across the room at the magnificent Prosper. It was a little, Judith thought, David defying Goliath.

But she was proud of him. She saw now--perhaps for the first time-- why it was that he was making himself a solid figure in London.

Then came the real surprise of the occasion. For Francis, who had hitherto been silent, spoke. 'I should wish to say,' he interjected, 'that I am dissociated from my brother in this. I hold that Miss Jennifer deserves an apology in writing.'

'Oh no, Francis--oh no,' Judith whispered under her breath. She realised with an actual pang of apprehension that this silly dispute about so trivial an affair was going much deeper than she had ever supposed. Her memory spread before her in an instant of vision, scene after scene--Uldale in the old years, Sarah and David, Francis and Will; Francis hardly more than a child, staring at Skiddaw, turning and picking Will up from the long orchard grass, smoothing some fancied hurt; Francis and Will bathing and running naked from the stream; Francis, Will, Reuben, herself, watching the fireworks at the Lake's edge. But Francis must be possessed by this Jennifer! That he should so defy his brother, so publicly. . . .

And it was the last straw for Will. He caught Christabel by the arm, dragging her from her chair.

'No apology!' he shouted; 'neither now nor ever!' He shook his fist across the room. 'You can carry your Bournemouth manners back with you! I wish you good day.' At the door he turned. 'And your own betrayal of me, Francis, I am not likely to forget.'

He pulled Christabel through the door with him. Everyone broke into confusion. Judith could hear Montague urging:

'It is the warm weather . . . refreshments . . . a cool parlour.' And Prosper's measured tones: 'Young puppy! I'd call him out for a penny!' And Maria Rockage: 'Oh dear, oh dear! . . . That's a pity, and Carey so wonderfully discreet.'

Well, the thing was done. Judith sighed, turning away from Francis, who stood with his back to the company, looking out of the window down into the Square. It seemed, Judith thought, as though the beautiful shadow of Jennifer hung over all the room.

A moment later she had forgotten them all, for there, standing just within the door, looking at them all, a half-defiant, half- apologetic smile on his face, was Georges!

He was neat and tidy, in a brown suit, holding his hat in his hand, but--she saw at once--infinitely weary. His round face was ashen. He held himself as though at any moment he might fall.

Rockage knew him. Rose and Pomfret spoke to him. A moment later Judith was tugging at his arm.

'Georges, you had my note. I have waited two days. . . . Where have you been . . . ? What . . . ?'

'I came to fetch you,' he said, looking at her with a great kindliness that caught at her heart. 'We shall talk better outside.'

She took his arm. He bowed to the assembled company. One last impression she had (that was to seem to her afterwards like the closing note on all her old life) of Francis, turning from the window and very gravely regarding them both. Then they were out of the room and down the stairs.

The Square was quite deserted and beautifully still in the dusty golden sunlight of the hastening summer afternoon. They walked along, she still holding his arm.

He spoke very rapidly, but still with a great and considering kindness.

'Listen, Judy. . . . Everything is up. I have been a fool these two days, just as I have been a fool all my life. But worse now, much worse. Listen to what I say. I must be off this instant. There's a boat I know at Greenwich; away tonight for Copenhagen--'

'But what have you done?'

'I've played two nights and a day. Once I was handsomely to the good, then lost it all again. But that's not the thing. There was a scuffle this morning at Jonathan's. I stuck a ninny--no, he's not dead--but they are out against me and several more. London's closed to me for a time at least.'

'And I?' Her mind was active with a thousand possibilities.

'Go back to Watendlath and wait for me.'

They stood at the Square corner, and now she had actually just above her head a thick bush of purple lilac that leaned towards her as though it would brush her cheek. A negro boy, with a silver turban and leading a spaniel by a thin chain, passed them whistling.

He spoke to her most urgently. 'Judy, I know you are brave, and most sensible. I'm sorry indeed that I have brought you to this pass, the more that these years in London have made us friends. I have no friend in the world like you. You've tamed me because I caught my admiration and kept it. . . . Judy, I think I could love you for long now, were we quietly in Cumberland. . . .'

At the word 'Cumberland' she broke out: 'Oh, why could we not go there? Both of us. No one would look for you in Watendlath.'

'No,' he answered sharply. 'I must be out of England. I've come to think that they hate me here. They turn on me and hunt me like dogs a hare if they have the slenderest reason. I'm a man of no country. I'd rather be on the sea than on the land anywhere. Except for you I'd go to sea and never touch land again. . . . But I always have to come back to you, and will come. Go to Watendlath. Be patient there. I shall write and send money if I have any. But you can manage in any case. You have a man's head on you. There's money enough in the lodging--the drawer by the fireplace. Here . . . the key. That will carry you North. I should pay the woman and leave to-night. Stay quietly there. Answer no questions if they ask you. One day, perhaps soon, you'll see me walk up the road. I MUST come back to you. There's no one and nothing else in the world draws me. . . .'

She asked no questions. She hated people who asked tiresome questions at an urgent crisis.

He caught her by the shoulders, as he sometimes did when he was pleased, lifting her a little from her feet. He kissed her.

'Now--good-bye,' and he had turned the corner swiftly and was gone.

She stood there, looking up into the lilac, but not seeing it. Not from sentiment but because she knew that in the future it would often please her to remember, she repeated some of the things that he had said.

'I think I could love you for long now. . . . Except for you I'd go . . . You have a man's head. . . .'

And so she had. She wanted to commit some panicky folly like running down the street to find him and then insisting that wherever he went she would go with him, but she must be practical and do exactly what he had asked her.

She was glad that she must leave London. As though to be in tune with the urgency of her own affairs, the day was clouding. Thunder was behind the houses. She walked on, thinking how, with ease, she could catch the night coach to York. From there across country she might share a post-chaise if she were lucky. The very thought of Watendlath made her heart beat with pleasure. The cool breeze slipping down the mountain-side, the water, green-clear, tumbling into the Punchbowl, the Tarn mirroring one white cloud, while the Fell looked down to Rosthwaite; the Ritsons, the children, the dogs, the smell of the peat, the dung, the Cumberland bracken (now there would be new fresh fronds springing up, curling above the stem) and, most lovely of all, the eternal running streams, so reassuring, so friendly. . . . Why had she left it? Although she was only a step from Berkeley Square all the members of the Herries family, with whom she had so lately been, seemed unreal and unalive.

She hurried on, for her mind was set now on the practical business of doing what Georges had told her--leaving London and catching the night coach.

Soon she was in the poorer streets that hung like spiderwebs about Charing Cross. The heavy day was dark now above her head, and the noise of the traffic on the street, the stench of the gutter, the projecting windows and the roughness of the cobbled road held and confused her.

When she stood it seemed that almost at once people closed in upon her. She was in a narrow street that opened out until it became almost a small cobbled square hemmed in with uneven and overhanging houses. She was aware then that her own thoughts had hindered her from noticing that some event was going forward. Before she knew it or could resist it she found that a mixed and very evil-smelling crowd was pushing her on; then, looking about her, saw that beside a butcher's shop that had above it a large swaying sign a platform had been erected and on the platform a gibbet.

The sight of the gibbet sickened her; it had in its very rough newness and sharp angles a sense of torture and pain about it. She turned as though to go back, but found now to her dismay that the crowd behind her was too thick for her to pass through.

She had heard at one time that malefactors were sometimes hanged by the place of their crime, and she supposed that unwittingly she had tumbled upon some such scene. The odd mixture of emotions in her breast at that moment--her passionate feeling of love for Georges, the excitement of the recent family squabble, the sense of the exceeding importance that she should do at once what Georges asked her--threw her into a special state of nervous apprehension. Her first thought was that she must at once get away from where she was. She realised that in her abstraction she had moved into a crowd that must have been waiting there for a considerable period. All the windows of the neighbourhood were open and were crowded with figures. Boys were clinging to the lamp-posts, and along one side of the street a platform of boards had been arranged on barrows and tubs, and this was thronged. Above the roofs the sky was dark, and she fancied that she could hear distant rumbles of thunder. Whatever happened she must escape, so she turned to go back the way that she had come, but she was at once obstructed by a large man carrying an empty tray round his middle, and a group of women who, so soon as they saw that she wanted to pass them, with laughter prevented her.

'No passage this way,' one woman, who had a huge bosom and her skirt tucked up almost to her knees, cried.

'I beg you,' Judith began. 'It is an urgent matter--if you please.'

'If you please--if you please!' the whole street seemed to echo her. 'Only one thing urgent here, and that is a jerk with the rope and, lady or gentleman, it's all the same, we all go to heaven!'

She was so small that she had no hope of asserting herself. She looked about her to see whether some face were likely to help her, but she thought that she had never seen so many coarse mouths, bright hard eyes. There was in the look of everyone a flutter of the animal--the animal allowed for an hour a little freedom, to prowl into a larger cage and taste handsome food. The sense that she had had for a long time in London that times were changing, that the people themselves were now more actively conscious of possible power and were moving towards it, held her now. For the first time in her life she was afraid of people. She had never before been aware of what a crowd was. Her individuality was lost. If she were not careful she would be trampled down, not her body but something much more real and vivid than that.

She hated any public scene; her reserve and dignity came to her rescue. She turned back and found that she could move forward more easily. She might escape at the broader street-end. But when she had gone some way, jolted, pushed, with much unpleasant contact with clothes and hot breath, legs and arms, she came to a stop again. She saw to her great distress that she was almost under the platform where the gibbet was. Here was a thick ring of people, mostly women; she thought of France. It must have been often like this in France, the women knitting and singing, their ears straining for the rattle of the tumbrils.

She felt faint with the heat and the smells and the noise. Scarcely knowing what she did, she caught at an arm to steady herself and found that she was holding on to a little thin man in a large hat and a rusty black suit. He smiled at her kindly.

'Can you help me out of this, sir?' she asked gently.

He shook his head. 'I fear not, madam. It is best to stay where you are. The crowd grows thicker every moment.'

'Oh, but I don't wish to stay. I have a most urgent appointment.'

He pointed with his finger. She looked and saw that escape was now impossible. The crowd had in the last five minutes flooded in. She could see the shining hats of the 'Charlies' at the crowd's edge.

'Is someone to be hanged?' she asked.

'A young man.'

'What had he done?'

Stolen three shillings from his master's till--the butcher's there.'

She was a woman of her time, she did not feel the injustice of it as a woman of a later day would do, but it was as though, in that moment, looking anxiously into the little man's mild eye, pressed in on every side, stirred perhaps by the drama of her own personal circumstances, she received some especial consciousness, ahead of her time, a sense of cruelty and persecution that pierced her very heart.

'Oh, poor boy . . . I don't want to see. . . . Please cannot you assist me? What are all these people here for? If he must die it should be by himself alone. Oh, help me, please! . . .'

She saw herself the hopelessness of any escape. He was very kind. He put his arm very courteously round her. 'There is no way out. You can see for yourself. It will be over soon now. It was to be at five o'clock. We shall have a storm if they are not quick.'

Something compelled her to look around her. The people near her were decent enough, quiet, grave-faced. They waited indifferently, as though it were a peep-show they had come for. Two women close to her were chatting about their own affairs. A hush spread slowly over the crowd, as though a hand had been laid upon them all. A man, burly and broad, carrying a cane, mounted the steps to the scaffold. He went to the gibbet and felt the rope. A flock of pigeons flew from one side of the street to the other, and a sudden clap of thunder, as though someone had fired a gun, startled them. They rustled their wings like a shower of falling paper.

It seemed to Judith that this was her own personal tragedy, that all her life she would be affected with her memory of it. She was forced now to watch; indeed two opposite impulses seemed to fight in her, one that she should hide her face, the other that she should see every slightest thing.

The crowd was very still in the vicinity of the scaffold, but beyond that, there were laughter and singing and beyond that, in a great distance, all the noisy traffic of the day. The atmosphere was strange, very dark above their heads, but pale beneath with the flat colour of sunlight. The shops were like pale faces staring from darkness, and the thunder muttered like an uncertain drum.

She saw all this with a sickness of anticipation. She really felt sick, as though it were Georges or Francis or Reuben--someone who was very close to her--who was going to suffer. The silence grew and seemed to spread to the farther distance. She saw individuals-- a woman's face with a wart, an old gentleman in a shabby brown wig, a girl with a sharp nose who lifted a child that it might see better, a man, a foreigner surely, wearing a bright green turban-- and all these individuals seemed to belong to her, to know all about her, and to have arranged to come with her to see this sight.

Then, as though obeying some signal, a little procession mounted the steps. There was the stout fellow with the cane, a long thin man bareheaded, three officers in uniform, a clergyman with parson's bands carrying a book, and, last, between the officers, a boy with his hands tied. At once she could not remove her eyes from the boy. He was broad and short and ruddy-faced, like any strong country boy. His hair was cropped, he had large blue staring eyes that, Judith saw, were now mad with an ununderstanding terror. But his mouth, which was a child's mouth, uncertain and tremulous, was trying to be resolved and manly.

She was, against her will, so terribly close that she was forced to see these things; she fancied then (she knew afterwards it could have been only fancy) that as soon as he was on the platform the boy's eyes were seeking hers. What he was doing was searching the crowd, the houses, the sky; a wild animal at bay looking for escape, although he knew that there was none. But Judith fancied that she could help him. Raising herself on her toes she nodded and smiled and nodded again; even (although she did not know it) her lips were forming words: 'Be brave! I'll help you! I want to help you! Be brave!'

Indeed he tried to be, poor lad. Things moved very quickly. The parson, who looked shabby and had mud on his stockings, read from a book. The boy came forward. He was in his shirt and breeches; the shirt, open, had slipped from one shoulder and showed his breast. His face was ruddy in spite of his fear; he looked as though he should have been caught robbing an orchard.

He came forward and began to speak bravely enough. Now an absolute silence froze the scene. Carts could be heard rattling on the Strand cobbles very far away.

'Good people,' he began (his voice was fresh and very young), 'I am told to bid you all farewell and to beg you to stay in peace with God. Good people, it is very true that I took the shillings from the till--I never for an instant denied it. I was tempted by the Devil, good people, for I am very weary of the Town and was hungering for the country again. It was but an instant's temptation, and here I am, so that, good people, all learn by me to resist--' He had begun bravely, held up, perhaps, by the importance of the attention given him by the listening crowd, but suddenly it seemed to come upon him that he was really going to die, that, in a few moments, he would be fighting for breath. . . .

He broke off, his voice rising to a shrill terror. No, no . . . I must not die . . . I must not die. . . .' He moved as though he would throw himself from the platform. The officers caught him, and then began a dreadful struggle. He was young and strong. The three officers wrestled with him all over the platform. His shirt was torn from him and he was bare to the waist. He cried again and again, 'No, no . . . I will not . . .' and other words that no one could distinguish, some private name that sounded like 'Nancy.' Then they had him. His arms were bound behind him; his naked chest, white and shining with sweat, pushed forward, his head, turning, twisting, turning like an animal's in the pen before execution. An agonised whisper came: 'Jesus! Oh, Jesus Christ!' Just before they had the rope round his neck his eyes seemed to find Judith's, blue, staring and asking some question.

Then he was swinging, his legs twisting as though with independent life. The body heaved, then his head hung and he was still.

'Now, madam,' said the little man from an infinite distance, 'I can assist you.'

Judith nodded her head. Reuben had been right. Until the Bear was safe from persecution nothing could be well in the world.

THE CLIPPING

Sarah Herries, widow of David Herries and mother of Francis, Deborah, and Will, died on the 3rd of July 1796, suddenly, at the age of fifty-eight.

She was walking in the garden with her daughter Deborah, wrapped in one of her strange and brooding silences, when she cried out suddenly in a proud and joyful voice: 'Davy! Davy!', ran forward, her arms out-stretched, and fell down on the green sward.

Her heart had failed her, and she was mercifully re-lieved of a life that was only a torment and distress to her. Judith went from Watendlath to the funeral. Will and Francis naturally could not arrive from London. The distance was too great and the time too short. Deborah Sunwood, now an aged, white-haired, and very quiet little woman, long a widow and never the same since the death of her son Humphrey in France, came from Cockermouth, and she and Judith had a very lov-ing meeting. Deborah Herries, a stout, large, rosy-faced, cheerful woman, was now left in sole charge of Uldale and its affairs. She begged Judith to come to her when-ever she wished. They had a friendly regard for one another, but nothing whatever to say, and Judith knew that Deborah, who loved social events and decent be-haviour, regarded Georges in her heart as a rogue and a vagabond, which indeed he was.

The night of her return from the funeral Judith had wild and fantastic dreams. It was a hot airless night, very still, and the streams, thin though they were, seemed to leap in through the open windows and chat-ter about the room. She had been sleeping badly for a long time past. Wise though she was and determined always to be sensible, a foreboding of distress and mis-fortune grew on her day by day, as though a cloud with every hour grew heavier and darker above her head. She had had one letter from Georges since he left her in London. It was addressed from Bergen in Norway, very short, sending his love, telling her that he was busy and would return when he could. She thought that she read between the lines a new sense of care and longing for her, but that, with her usual good sense, might be a willing imagination.

The nights were the bad times. During the day she was surrounded with friends in whose affairs she took ever a more active and dominating interest, but at night she was alone, and that part of herself that she could least easily control--her wild and restless part--seemed to have full power.

On this particular night she suffered especially from the thought of Sarah. Her loving heart could not endure that she had never been reconciled to Sarah. When she was a child she had not thought that she cared for Sarah at all, but as she grew, so she perceived that there was some deep loyalty and submission in her feeling.

She had always been too proud to go to Sarah and ask her forgiveness; besides, she did not think that Sarah had anything to forgive, but she had supposed that some accidental meeting would bring them together again. Now it would never be.

At least, if there was another conscious life, Sarah was now with David, was happy again and understood everything. But this supposition, a very doubtful one, as it seemed to Judith, was poor comfort. She tortured herself, on the ride back from Uldale, with the thought of all the lonely years that Sarah had endured. She could never bear that people could suffer, and especially that they should suffer through her fault, and now there occurred to her a thousand ways in which, with a little courage, she might have approached Sarah and done something for her.

Her dreams that night were wild, entangled and desperate. She was again in the London street, where the boy was to be hanged. Pressed in, tossed about by a wild and revengeful crowd. But it was Georges who was to be hanged. She could do nothing to save him, but must stand there helplessly and watch. The sky was black, the houses ringed with flame, and from a high window Christabel, Will's wife, leaned out and cried that her fan was broken and Georges must suffer for it. Then Georges came sailing towards her in a little boat; waves, hot and angry, with cruel white tongues, filled the street and beat about the scaffolding. Young Stane was in the boat, and Georges suddenly caught him, held him in the air, then flung him into the waves while all the people cried.

She woke, trembling, damp with sweat. At first the deep quiet of the room with only the sound of the singing streams soothed her. She lay there and listened to her heart as it slowly diminished its terrible beating. How good that it had only been a dream! From her bed she could see, in the faint morning light, the shadows of the homely, familiar things, and beyond the open window the friendly breast of the rising hill.

She was in her own house with friends on every side of her. Since her return, although she had said very little to anyone, they had all understood, it seemed, that Georges was in some trouble. They did not like Georges, but with that wonderful silent sympathy that is perhaps the Cumbrian's finest gift, they had closed in around her, showing her their affection and loyalty. She had never been so near to them before as she was now.

Yes, but she wanted Georges. She wanted him with a fierce hunger that was an experience quite new to her. She was doing what he told her, staying here and filling her life with little daily interests, but, in the back of her mind, there was always the fear that after a while, if he did not return, waiting would be too hard for her, and she would run off to Whitehaven and search for news of him.

To conquer her desire for him she lay there, as the new light flowed about the room and a cluster of sharp steel-glittering stars faded out above the black hill line, saying over to herself, aloud, the names of places that she loved, and the names of people whom she loved. She said, as though she were addressing the shapes, with every moment less dim, in her room:

'Stonethwaite, Honister,
Gavel, Watendlath,
Rosthwaite, Uldale,
Bleaberry, High Seat,
Armboth, Grey Knotts,
    Glaramara--'

They had sung her almost to sleep again, mingling with the streams that ran about the boards of her room when, with a sharp stab of awareness, she was conscious of an odd thing--that with every day she was becoming more frightened of leaving her own square of ground.

It was as though someone had told her that did she step over a certain line, something terrible would befall her. She had noticed at the funeral that she had to force herself to face people, even good friends like Deborah Sunwood. It was as though she expected that anyone at a moment's notice would cry: 'I have news for you. Georges--' The people here around her she could trust.

They were her own people--the Ritsons, the Wilsons, all the children and the dogs. And her new great friend, Charlie Watson.

Watson had a farm, New Hope, towards Armboth. He had come there in the last year; he was from the village of Strands, near Wastwater.

He was a Cumbrian of the Cumbrians; that is, he was silent, often churlish, sharp, a marvellous shepherd and utterly loyal. She had met him one day coming up from Rosthwaite. He had two dogs with him. She had been startled by his looks, for he was broad and massive and his hair was of so jet a black, his cheeks of so warm a colour, that at first he seemed a foreigner. He had a short, sharply cut, black moustache that was not like the neighbours'. He was so broad of shoulder and thick of thigh that his height seemed moderate, but he was of good height nevertheless.

He would be thirty-five years of age. They began to talk. You would have said that all he thought of at that time was sheep, that or any time. He thought of other things later, though. He was proud, sensitive, suspicious, and hated foreigners till he knew them. He had worked in Liverpool five years in his youth. He was single; preferred sheep to women, he told Judith once. True enough then--not true later. On their first meeting he said little more than 'Aye!' He looked at her as though he disliked her. He stood, his legs wide apart, striding the fells.

He told her that his sister looked after his comfort, that it was a dry month, that he didn't hold with politics--Regent or King, it was all the same to him, but we'd better not take after the Frenchies.

Judith said: 'My husband's French.'

He said: 'Aye,' looking at her meditatively and without a hint of apology. Then abruptly, still looking at her, he remarked: 'You'll be Mrs. Paris. I mind hearing of you.'

'Nothing bad, I hope,' said Judith.

'For t'matter o' that--nay,' he said, suddenly smiling a slow deep smile. He strode away, not looking back, his dogs after him.

After that first meeting they were always encountering one another. He was a friend of old man Ritson's, but it seemed to her soon that he came to the farm very much more often than he had done.

Once or twice, without any conceit of self-flattery, she wondered whether he were in love with her. He seemed to seek her out so directly, with a simplicity that might elsewhere have caused gossip. But, in a week or two, she realised that the Ritsons and the rest knew just what his feeling for her was. He was sorry for her, but without hurting her pride. They said of him that he was mighty tender with all animals and rough with women and off-hand with men. It seemed that he thought that she needed protection as an animal might. He made himself her protector. There was no sentiment between them. They made a curious pair, he so large and she so small, and she could have disappeared, she used to fancy, into the outer pocket of his coat. He was an unusual man with his intense depths of feeling unexpressed. One day they were standing together near the Tarn, and three strangers, two ladies and a gentleman, rode up on horses. They were sightseers, the first 'tourists,' perhaps, that Watendlath ever beheld. They called Watson 'my good fellow' and, when he had given, very curtly, some information, the gentleman threw him a shilling. The ladies, very grand and speaking with affectation, looked at Judith, who was dressed like Mrs. Ritson or any of the people of the place. When they were gone Watson threw the shilling into the Tarn. He was trembling with anger.

'I'll tell them if 'tis t'right road. If they come again without biddin' they maun stay a bit . . . I'll settle him.'

She laughed and said that she supposed that anyone had a right to the place.

'Nay, they havena . . . the man's a lump of mutton off an auld tup.'

She didn't laugh any more, when she saw how deeply moved he was. It was as though these people had soiled the landscape for him.

Judith went one day and called on his sister. Then one evening, sitting in his kitchen, she told him everything: about her father and mother, her childhood in Uldale, her life at Stone Ends, her marriage with Georges, her time in London, her present distress and ever-growing anxiety, her love for Georges that seemed to grow ever deeper and deeper. He took her hand in his huge one.

'Aye, you want someone to look after you.'

From that evening it seemed to her that he was always at hand, although there were days when she didn't see him. Indeed he was a tremendous worker, had no time for idling with females. But he was behind her and beside her. The thought of him infinitely comforted her.

As, lying there, she considered him, his silence, his tenderness, her fears thinned away. It seemed that it was her fate to have these figures guarding her, protecting--Tom Gauntry, Emma, now Charlie Watson. The strange thing was that she did not want anyone to protect her. She was quite well able to protect herself. But she liked to have friends. She loved to be loved--that is, by the people whom she wanted to love her.

The sun flashed above the purple ridge of the hill. The sky was pale green like the wing of a young paroquet.

The Ritsons had their 'Clipping,' and it was a grand day. The hot weather had lasted for over a fortnight, and this was the hottest day of them all. The sheep panted fit to burst their sides. Armboth Fell shone like a brazen shield and was so slippery dry beneath the bracken that it was flaming ice to the feet. The Tarn was shadowed with an ebony mist under a sky clouded with heat.

The clipping was perhaps the grandest day of the year for the Ritsons. They were farmers in a small way, but very popular. Neighbours came from miles, first to help in the clipping, then to eat of the feast and dance in the Ritson kitchen.

Charlie Watson came. He was the best clipper in Cumberland maybe; a Master. Then there was Tommy Blunden of Smoke, Robert Tyndale of Cardale, Will Bennett of Axholme, Roger Perry of Thunder. They, their wives, their children, their dogs.

Judith was happy again. The night was far behind her. But the thundery weather distressed her; it had been ominous to her ever since that last day in London, and now, in the middle of helping with the great joint of beef, with the huge pease-puddings, with the arranging of the long table, she would go to the porch and look out over the Tarn to the hills and listen. Perhaps it was Georges, also, for whom she was listening.

In the kitchen there was tremendous noise and confusion. Old man Ritson was too aged now to move about, the rheumatism had him fast, and sometimes the pain was so bad that someone inside him yelled loud enough to bring the roof down, but the yell never passed his inside. He sat, his grand head high, his gnarled hands on his knees, watching and saying nothing. His daughters, his grand- daughters and a great-grand-daughter (in a cradle by the window) were all around him. A sea of femininity. But he said nothing. He sat there thinking of his youth, of fighting a man bare-skin in Whitehaven and throttling him, of tending sheep on the hills above Coniston Water, of the fugitives in '45 from Butcher Cumberland and his father hiding one up the kitchen chimney, of sheep and sheep, cows and cows, fine weather and bad, of women whom he had loved, his children and their ways, Armboth and Brund Fell and Glaramara that were live creatures to him, Gods maybe, carrying on their gigantic forms the rocks and tarns and streams that were their splendid properties. Yes, he had plenty to think of. And he sat there, looking straight in front of him, while the pains at his hip made him bellow inside.

When the table was laid, Judith, to escape the kitchen heat, went out to watch the clippers.

As the weather was so grand the clipping could be in the open air instead of in the barn. All the sheep had been brought in. There were eight hundred sheep and five hundred lambs.

Beyond the house in a grand half-circle were fifteen clippers striding the sheep-stools, and each clipper held a sheep, shorn, half shorn, about to be shorn. There was a tremendous noise, for the gate of the farm-yard was packed by five score of wooled sheep penned against it. They would be caught, one after another, by one of the boys, who, in a wild, excited pack, tumbled and fought and shouted, having the day of their lives.

The sheep bleated and their lambs on the fell-side or in the fields bleated as well. The dogs barked and even horses neighed. It was strange to feel, beyond this excited whirlpool of sound, the glazen silence of the Tarn, the road, the hills, pulsating through the shimmering heat, but silent, as though holding their breath for the first peal of thunder that would release them from this spell.

Judith first looked for Charlie Watson, and a splendid sight he was. His shirt was open at the neck, and sweat beaded the thick black hair of his chest. His arms, red-brown to near the elbows then snow-white, bulged with muscle; his legs planted wide to hold the sheep between them seemed to be rooted in the ground; every once and again his head went up and his mouth parted, showing his teeth white under the short thick black moustache. (His perfect teeth were a phenomenon in the dale, for most men lacked one or two.) His short, thick hair had almost a metallic gleam in its blackness.

As always when at work, his dark eyes shone, his parted lips seemed to cry aloud his energy, his body worked in harmony with the fell, the running water. He worked with rhythm, as though the whole of English nature and the wheel of the brazen sky moved, back and forth, with the pulse of his blood; and he handled the sheep as though he loved them.

Tom Ritson was in charge of the clipping; an old man called Benny Held--with two fierce questioning white eyebrows and a face like a wrinkled turnip--kept the pitch pan heated and held the marking iron and the rudd stick. Young Roger Perry of Thunder, a lad nearly as thick and broad as Watson, held the animals while old Benny applied the marking.

Judith forgot her anxieties and trouble for the while. Now there came out in her all her passion for management. She could not be present at a scene like this without burning to 'arrange things.'

She looked fifteen years of age, with a high sun-bonnet tied over her red hair and her legs bare as the other women's were, stamping about in her clogs. Her cheeks were flushed, her eyes shining. Her Cumberland blood exulted in the scene. This was the heart of England and so the heart of the world. Everything was right for her--the scent of the bracken, the still waiting expectancy of the hills, the sun shining on the little stone walls that ran up into the edge of the sky, the rough voices that had a sort of grumbling humorous note in them, the jokes and oaths and laughter, the bleating of lambs and sheep, the strange helpless whiteness of the sheep after they were shorn--knowing that they were so different, so changed that their own lambs did not recognise them--the life of this little community centred here in this circle of fells, so remote from the world but strong, independent, asking nothing from any man (as for centuries they had asked nothing, so for centuries more they would ask nothing), and all of them looking at her, speaking to her as though she were one of themselves (which, indeed, she was), the sun slipping over the sky and, as the afternoon drew on, shadows staining every hill with a different dye, Armboth saffron as though sunlight had soaked into its very heart, Brund Fell orange-red, then sinking, with almost an audible sigh, into a gentle silver-grey, and beyond them the farther hills, violet cloths spread before a sky white with evening haze, and, with the evening, a breeze springing that had every scent of coolness in it, young grass, water over shining stones, and the wet wavering mosses that shadow the Tarn's edge. The sea also was not far away.

Ale was brought out in pots, and there were hunks of fruit pie. Then the sky was green, and the first star winked at a silver moon half full. The fleeces were tied in small bundles, the loft door was closed on them, and everyone moved indoors to the feast.

There were rounds of beef and oat-bread, pease-puddings, gooseberry pies, puddings 'touched' with rum. Soon everyone was very merry. Benny Held had brought his fiddle. Robert Tyndale, who had a fine tenor, sang Ewan Clark's 'Happy Bachelor':

'A bachelor life of all lives is the best;
No cares matrimonial disturb his calm rest;
No lectures called Curtain shake sleep from his eyes,
When tir'd he can rest, and when tir'd he can rise.'

and 'Wey, Ned, Man!':

'Wey, Ned, Man! Thou luiks sae down-hearted,
Yen wad swear aw thy kindred were dead;
For sixpence, thy Jean and thee's parted--
What then, Man, ne'er bodder thy head.'

Then, Charlie Watson, shy but determined, sang in a deep bass:
'What charms has fair Chloe':

'What charms has fair Chloe!
Her bosom's like snow!
    Each feature
    Is sweeter,
Proud Venus, than thine!
Her mind like her face is
Adorned with all graces,
Not Pallas possesses
    A wit so divine.

'What crowds are a-bleeding
While Chloe's ne'er heeding:
    All lying
    A-dying
Thro' cruel disdain:

Ye gods, deign to warm her
Or quickly disarm her;
While Chloe's a charmer,
    Your temples are vain.'

He sang without any expression whatever, and a disdainful look on his face as though he despised the song and himself for singing it, but, when it was over, and the applause had been terrific, he flushed with pleasure and looked down the long table to see whether Judith had approved.

Then the tables were cleared, Benny Held struck up his fiddle and everyone was dancing. Stamp-stamp-stamp, clamp-clamp-clamp along the kitchen floor, the dust rising, faces flushed, bodies a little unsteady with the ale, whispers and protesting laughter, kissing and hugging, and old Ritson, sitting in his chair, looking straight before him, thinking of the time when he had taken the girl of his heart out of the hot room into the cold of the valley and wandering down to the Tarn's edge had kissed her for the first time. He fancied that now, although she had been dead so long, she was standing just behind the hallan, her eyes taunting him. . .

Charlie Watson asked Judith to dance. He clamped round the room with her, staring over her head, saying nothing. He trod on her toes, bundled her about, and his arm held her like an iron rod.

They stayed by the door, and he was about to speak to her. Alice Ritson, the only unmarried Ritson girl remaining, for Mary had died two years before, ran in from the garden path, waited an instant, looking at the crowded room, then went up to Judith, caught her arm and whispered: 'Judith, 'tis Mr. Georges. He's coom back. He's there, in your own place.'

For a moment the room with its figures and haze of heat swayed, in movement, almost it seemed, to the fiddler's tune. She remembered afterwards (looking back as she did so many, many times) that Charlie Watson put out his arm and for a moment held her. She felt (she knew afterwards, although at the time she did not notice it) the beating of his heart against her cheek. What an agony of joy, anticipation, and fear!

'It is my husband,' she said, looking up into his face: then she ran out.

Georges was standing in their living-room, near the staircase, down which he had once bundled his box. She ran to him, and at once knew by the way that he held her that something terrible had happened to him. He had never held her like that before, as though his only safety lay in his contact with her.

'I thought that I would never be here,' he said. He lifted her off her feet and looked into her eyes. Then he put her down and went to the door, which he closed, slowly, surely; then stood for a moment with his back to it. They could hear through the wall the scream of the fiddle and the tramp-tramp-tramp of the dancing figures.

'Will you come down to the Tarn?' he asked her.

'But you must eat.'

'I had food at Keswick.'

'Where's your horse?'

'I've tethered him. He had his corn. He can stay.'

'But here . . . You must be so weary. I can make all comfortable.'

'No, no, no. I must be outside. Away from the music.'

Taking his hand, looking up at him, she said: 'What is it? Are you in trouble?'

'Yes,' he answered. 'I'm in trouble.'

She nodded her head, asking him no more.

They went out together, and the evening was sweet with all the summer scents. One lamb in a fold bleated incessantly; as soon as they came down the hill the music faded to a murmur like a voice in the Fell. The Tarn had a broad path of moonlight that quivered with little shudders of gold.

'Will you be cold?' he asked her. 'If you've been at the dance.'

'No. The air is warm.'

He put his arm around her; she was pressed close against his thigh, and they walked up and down.

'Judy, I've murdered Stane.'

She shivered, and he held her close. When she could steady herself she thought, at once: 'Now he will need me. He shall want me always. He is mine to the end,' and directly afterwards: 'Are they searching for him? I must get him away.' It was odd, but she thought of Humphrey Sunwood and how sensible she had been then.

She asked him at once: 'Are they after you for it?' She had always hated Stane. She didn't care that he was dead.

'No. It was two weeks back. Off Bergen. No one knows.'

'How was it? Was it in a fight?'

'No. Not a fight. I murdered him deliberately. I took him out in the boat to do it.'

'And no one saw?'

'It was evening. A storm got up. After I had drowned him I turned the boat over and swam to land. But do you not shrink from me? First, before all else, I must know that--'

'No. I love you. How could I shrink from you?'

'Because I shrink from myself. It was deliberate, Judy. Planned. Intended. Not a drunken scuffle, not a hand-to-hand struggle. I took him by the throat and squeezed it till I thought my fingers would break. Then I toppled him over. The rain was coming down in torrents, and there was a wild sea. I thought I should myself drown, and I would have been glad of it, but nothing can drown me nor hang me nor stab me. . . . I shall live for ever, Judy, with Stane around my neck--like a dead bird, clammy, with talons scratching my skin.'

His hand was fiery hot in hers. She remembered afterwards that in all her bewilderment, her determination to be sensible, her tenderness for him, her hatred of Stane, which seemed now to be double what it had been, was amazement at this new Georges. He was like a man whom she had never seen before; she loved him as deeply as the other Georges, nay more, because he needed her, which the other Georges had never done. But his French indifference, callous humour, self-sufficiency. . . . Where were they? Was this man a coward?

He seemed to know her thought. He drew a deep sigh of relief.

'Now it is better. If you are with me we will beat that damnable ghost. For he's been a ghost, Judy, keeping step with me all the way. Afterwards it was like a spell. In Bergen they believed every word. His body was beaten on to the rocks the day following, his face disfigured. It seemed natural that his neck was broken. Three days after I set back to Whitehaven. In Whitehaven I saw his father. . . .'

He broke off.

'His father--a giant old man with a beard to his waist. He had a mad worship for his son. You know it. I've told you. I thought that he must suspect, caring so much. . . . But no. He stood there without moving. He went blind, groping with his hands. Then he caught me round the neck and kissed me. He thought I was Stane's best friend. There was water lapping up against the room where we were and a man came in with a sword. I thought young Stane would slip from beside me, catch the sword and stab me with it. I would offer no resistance. But when later old Stane called his son, running up the staircase after him, shouting his name in the rooms, there was no one there.

'But he would not let me go. All night he sat there holding my hand.'

'But how did it come?' Judith asked. 'Stane's death, I mean. What made you do it?'

'You know how it was. You felt it as I did. Stane and I always hated one another. I've been bred in England, Judy. I speak like an Englishman, walk like one, in my behaviour am like one--is that not so?'

'Yes,' she said, but she knew in her heart that it was not so. He had never walked, talked or behaved like an Englishman.

'Yes, but there are times when I am French through and through, when I loathe England and the English. And some Englishmen I hate from the beginning. So I did Stane. So satisfied, arrogant AND ignorant. That mixture of conceit and ignorance that is in all your relations, Judith--the most obvious thing in the English. And he was clever, too; he saw at once how I was, my laziness, excitement, that I was unable to stay with anything for long. He judged me well, truly-- that was partly why I hated him. And he meant to supplant me. He saw that the others, Wix and the rest, were dissatisfied. He manoeuvred me to London and then worked on them. . . . My God, Judy, he was clever! And I a fool! Holy Heaven, the fool I was!'

The words broke from him in a despairing cry such as she had never heard from him before. It seemed to be echoed from the hills. She was afraid lest someone should hear.

'Hush, hush!' she said, leaning up and stroking his cheek as she might with a child. 'Not too loud. And then--?'

'Well, he came to London to work his way into Will Herries' counsels. You saw him at the Ball that night. He gave a black account of me to Herries, worked promises out of him and then returned to Whitehaven to show them that he had power in the City, while I diced and drank. . . . Oh, it was true enough! Every word was true. . . .

'Then when I had fled from London to Christiania he knew all of it. He must have been spying into every corner. I started some business in Bergen. Not much, but something. It was doing fairly, and I meant to return to Whitehaven, show them my steadiness, make all well again. For I knew Wix cared for me in his heart. . . . I hadn't heard that Stane had told him all the London affairs, my debts, the scuffle in the Coffee House, everything. He came over to Bergen, Stane, I mean. He pretended that it was an accident, but I knew well what it was.

'We met in an inn-room above the sea. He was victorious. He had a letter from Wix to say that they were ended with me in Whitehaven, that I had best never return to England. Stane was triumphant. It was the moment for which he had been working so long. His face was lit up. He had a wart on his right eyelid. Behind his head on the green wall there was a map of China and the Indies. I can tell you, Judith, that I all but killed him there, drove his head into that yellow map, there, just where China was. But there were men about, a street with traffic, boats knocking with the tide against the wall.

'I waited. I waited two days. I was most friendly. I licked his hand, asked that I should be the clerk. Then he boasted, how his father had once been a common fisherman and he himself had sold cockles barefoot. And he went further. He paid for my drink and told me how easy I had been, what a simpleton, and then he said something about you, Judy--'

'I always hated him,' she said.

'Yes, but he wanted you. You were his size, he said. He liked small women--and he was haunted by the wish to plunge his hands in your hair--'

She said nothing, only came closer to him.

'So I made my plan. I said I would row him across an inlet to a house where there were paid women--drink, women, dancing. He could be lascivious. Contemptuously he permitted me. As I strangled him he called out for his father thrice. That was his only decency. Physically he had no strength; I could have broken him anywhere.'

He stopped and said hoarsely: 'I have a fearful thirst. My mouth is dry every hour.'

'We will go home,' Judith said, laying her hand for an instant on his brow, 'and sleep.'

THE OLD MAN OF THE SEA

Judith woke, as now she was accustomed to do, to find Georges standing on the floor, wrestling in his sleep with his implacable enemy.

She could see only his shadow. The October night was dark; clouds hid the stars. The words came from him thick and fast: 'No, no. Leave me. I have done with you. That was to end it. Struggle then, and the water's cold. . . . Sharp, sharp. I'll not touch you again. Keep off me. No, no. I'll listen to no whisper. It is useless. Oh, God, keep me free!'

The last was a whisper of intense and gasping weariness. He sank to his bare knees. She knew that he was kneeling on the floor, his head in his hands, while his body trembled.

She got out of their bed, went to him and very gently put her arms round him. He stayed there trembling against her. Then slowly he woke.

'Where am I?' he asked.

'Here with me.' She led him back to bed, he docile as a child. They lay down together, hand in hand. Almost at once he was asleep again. But she remained for a long time awake, wondering what it was best to do.

This was October. He had returned in July--July, August, September, October, and there seemed to be no end to it, no frightening away of the ghosts, no helping him to overcome them. For the first time in her life she wished that she were older-- older and wiser. In the immediate weeks after his return her great fear had been lest in an instant of indiscretion he should confess to somebody what he had done. He never rode into Keswick but she waited in an agonised terror for his return. She never saw him talking to the Ritsons or walking with Watson (for whom he had conceived a great liking) but she expected the end of the talk or the walk to be some terrible revelation. But now, especially when she was weary or lying awake at that time of the early morning when fears are most pressing, she sometimes wondered whether it would not be better that he should confess to someone. The burden of sharing it alone seemed often more than she could bear.

She was not subtle about it. She was not made for subtlety. He had killed Stane, who had tried to bring him to ruin. That seemed to her fair. She would herself kill, if need be, anyone who threatened Georges. She would lie in bed, clenching and unclenching her hot little hands, with such a hatred of Stane in her heart that she would almost swoon of it. He had tried to kill

Georges, to kill in Georges' life everything that was of any value in it: he would have taken from Georges his livelihood, his friends, even his wife. Well, then--what crime had Georges done?

No one had seen. No one guessed. It was over. What then possessed Georges? It was perhaps the hardest part of her task now that this Georges was another man from that careless, wild, courageous, casual Georges, whom she had married and loved. And yet they were the same! She saw dimly how the one had become the other. She could trace back a thousand times when, in the past, he had been afraid of his deeds and then, because he was afraid, had recklessly covered the old fault with the new one. He had never had any stability. He had refused to dig deep into life. She had seen that in him again and again, and now, when he had tumbled into reality, it had been TOO deep for him.

His kindly casualness had always made him live for the moment, but from his childhood--although he would never confess to it because of his pride--he had had an anticipation of fear like a child who is safe only while the lighted candle is in the room.

She did not analyse this. Women of her day did not analyse natures and motives, but she understood him at last.

The irony of it was that now at length she possessed him as she had always longed to do, but as so often when in life we are granted our desires, her gratification was tragic. For, although she possessed him, she could not help him. He relied on her now for everything. He did nothing without asking her. He hated that she should be out of his sight.

There in the half-dark, he uneasily sleeping at her side, she was teased by the odd mixture of her feelings. If she had killed Stane she would see to it that she was not haunted by his ghost. Once done well done! There was impatience in her love for Georges. He must get some work to do: that would worry his ghosts! The farm was theirs and the next farm the Ritsons', both worked by the Ritsons. That just sufficed them for their immediate needs, but she could not endure to see Georges standing about, leaning against a stone wall watching the sheep or the clouds or walking on the uneven stone path beyond the farm outhouses, his hands behind his back, his head down, as though he were a prisoner. His only healthy days were those when he went off on the fells with Charlie Watson.

She was beginning to 'manage' him as she 'managed' old Ritson's rheumatism, Mrs. Ritson's bad clumsy sewing, Tom Ritson's carelessness about money, young Alice Ritson's love-affairs; and like all managing people she always a little despised those who succumbed to her management. It was part of Watson's power over her that she couldn't manage him anywhere.

But her real anxiety was that she did not herself know which way she would go. Part of her--her father's part--shared Georges' terrors to their depths. She knew how real that ghostly world was, how dark its valleys, how awful its inhabitants. But for the other part of her all ghosts were unreal, fantastic, just as her father had been altogether unreal and exaggerated for many people. As though, indeed, someone had said to her about her father: 'Fielding would not have drawn such a character.' No, but there were ghosts outside the books of Mr. Fielding and Mr. Richardson. But were there? Was it not merely the colic? How real were Georges' terrors?' Very real,' whispered a shadow by Rosthwaite. 'I spent my life in fighting them.' 'Balderdash,' said Will Herries and all the Herries.

But if only she herself could go one way or another! At one moment she wanted to shake Georges by the shoulders, to wake him thoroughly from a silly dream; at another she had only to close her eyes, and young Stane, the wart on his eyelid, his mouth curled contemptuously, his clothes wringing wet, crawled from the Tarn and slipped up the field towards her. Two events showed her very sharply the division between her two worlds. One was an unexpected letter from Francis. He wrote from Bournemouth saying that he had intended to send her a letter 'weeks back' but had been so closely occupied . . . Closely occupied in Bournemouth?

He was staying with Prosper and Amelia Cards. He had been there for some weeks. Judith, remembering the Ball, whispered to herself: 'Jennifer.'

. . . At first, dear Judith, I will be honest and confess that I found the country so desolate that I could have drowned myself. But there have been ameliorations, and now I find myself hanging on when the season is inclement and London calls. Moreover, my conscience tells me that I should come North and assist poor Deborah and see my darling Judith. Not that yourself are my conscience, dear Judith, but rather my pleasure. However, I am kept here and by what I will one day tell you.

('By whom rather,' thought Judith.)

The Town is a nest of old women who drink nauseous water and talk gossip by the bushel. We have also had a Menagerie with two Lions and a Bear. I tasted the waters but once. Do you remember how once for a punishment my poor mother gave us a pint basin of thin gruel with a spoonful of salt in it for a week and how it tasted? Well, that's for these waters. I fear that the Dispute that had its commencement with that accursed Ball of Will's shows no abatement but only an increase. Brother Will will have nothing to do with me, and there is indeed now a Division in our family starting with Brother Will and Cousin Prosper and spreading into many directions.

I am myself deeply sorry for it. What a stupid affair to start with a Broken Fan! I console myself with the friendliness of my relations here and especially with my cousin Jennifer.

I fear that yourself, dear Judith, are held here to have taken sides most decisively, and that Amelia, at least, is not to be reconciled to you. Cousin Prosper in his cups is reconciled to all the world, but out of them-- well, he has enough family pride for Sir Charles Grandison. I have been entertained by Godwin's Enquiry concerning Political Justice. You should read it, for if we are going the way of France, which is none too unlikely, there are wise words for us here. I am myself engaged on a paper answering some points in Paine's Age of Reason. We were never, I am convinced, in all our National History, more at the parting of the ways than we now are. All Europe is in an uproar. The People's Voice is making itself felt everywhere and splendid extravagances at Brighthelmstone are not sufficient satisfaction for such a heavy rise in prices.

You know, Judith, that I was always more Dreamer than anything. Now more than ever I dream my dreams. I am thirty-six years of age and have done nothing with my life. See Will, who is adding pound to pound with every breath he draws. Dare I venture into matrimony, little Judith? Is there any woman would be fool enough to take me if I asked her . . . ?

'Any woman?' thought Judith. 'Will Jennifer?'

The thought struck her with an added pang of loneliness and difficulty. If Francis married Jennifer, then he was lost to her, Judith, for ever. And with Francis gone it seemed to her that she would be, indeed, alone. But Jennifer would not have him. She was to make a far finer match than a poor North Country cousin ten years her elder.

Putting the letter down with a sigh, the world contained in its pages slipped into incredibility. How unreal, beside her present actual trouble, seemed that little pasteboard quarrel of the fan. Will's city life, Bournemouth's waters, Paine's Age of Reason, Jennifer's beauty, Prosper's pride and the rest. There WERE two worlds, and the secret of living was to know both to be real! But it was a problem. So she went out and rubbed old Ritson's back with ointment, looked at Tom Ritson's bull that he had bought in Keswick, advised Alice Ritson against young Humblethwath of Rosthwaite and stood, shading her eyes against the October sun, to see Georges ride up the path with Watson.

What she did see was incredible.

Georges was walking along the rocky path leading his horse and beside him was walking--Reuben! Reuben, as she could see, talking, gently, kindly, smiling, and Georges was smiling too.

At the first sight of them she had to recall that last time when she had seen Reuben, proud, master of himself, but driven from the house . . . and now, Georges was walking with him as though he loved him!

Reuben had been often in her mind. She was always thinking of him, but she had never seen him again since that day. Now, as she turned towards them, she loved him for being kind to Georges, and she loved Georges for being kind to Reuben. It was the first time she had had comfort since Georges' return. She met them and kissed them both. They stood there, the three of them, looking down at the Tarn, which was ruffled with little grey bird's feathers that ran in flocks under the pale sun, making the whole sheet of water quiver with life.

Reuben was different. He was far surer, more in command of himself and of everything. He was stouter but harder too. He was wearing black knee-breeches and stout black shoes and a broad black hat, but he was clean and neat; his white stock was clean and the white bands at his wrists. His voice was quiet and assured like his carriage. He moved and spoke like a man who had discovered how to rule himself.

They all went into the house. Reuben said that he would stay with them the night. He had come from Wasdale. To-morrow he had to preach in Mardale. He had walked from Waswater over the Stye Head and up from Rosthwaite.

That evening they had a strange conversation that Judith was never to forget. Oddly now Reuben dominated them both. He had never dominated Judith before, he had always been subservient to her, but now, although he was as loving to her as ever, being with her as though they had never been separated, he had a new power that set him apart. Soon she knew where his power lay. He was no longer afraid of anybody or anything. She saw that Georges submitted to him like a child to an elder. They sat, the three of them, close together by the wood fire that blazed with a sharp exulting power in the hearth. Judith sat at Georges' feet, her head against his thigh. She caught his hand in hers and felt its pulse leap wildly against her palm.

She was always saying to him now with every movement, 'Don't be afraid, I'm here.'

Reuben had not very much to tell them about himself. He went about, just as before, preaching everywhere, anywhere.

'What do you preach?' Georges asked suddenly.

'Jesus Christ,' Reuben said.

'I do not wish to be offensive,' Georges went on slowly. 'May I say what is in my mind with honesty?'

Reuben smiled. 'Yes. If you will.'

'Well, then, Christ is a figure to me who died long since. A Jewish rebel. The times needed a new religion. This was offered them and they took it. I cannot believe in any God, or that Christ was more than a brave man, mistaken. . . . This life is all that we have, and, by God, it is a poor one!' His hand trembled in Judith's.

'I do not think so,' said Reuben. 'I know Jesus Christ. I have talked with Him.'

'But these are words,' said Georges. 'My mother was heathen and her father before. My grandfather was an atheist, famous in his day, in the town of Toulouse. It is true that I was always taught that the Christian influence was a false one, but that has not formed my mind. I have observed men and their actions, and I find that there is no sign of a God in the world.'

'Then life is meaningless.'

'Yes, meaningless.'

'It is a question,' Reuben said quietly, 'that every man must decide by his own experience. Here we are, two men in the world. You are certain of your experience and I of mine. But if I had been to China and seen the Emperor and you had not, you would permit my right to my certainty, would you not?'

'Yes,' answered Georges impatiently. 'But the Emperor of China exists. Many people have seen him. The Christ is a fable.'

'You must permit me my experience. I know that God is in the world.'

'And I know that He is not.'

'Are you as certain,' asked Reuben, 'that He is not, as I that He is?'

Georges raised his eyes, haggard and restless, to Reuben's face.

'Then if He is, how can He permit this cruelty, this pain . . .' He broke off. His whole body was trembling.

'When I was a lad in Cockermouth,' Reuben said, 'I saw one day a bear baited in the street. I suffered torture from its helplessness. Now I know from my own life that all experience adds to one's riches. And pain possibly gives the most.'

'Was the bear the richer?' Georges broke out passionately.

'If the bear knew his gain. This is not the end,' Reuben said. 'Or so I believe. I have an immortal part, and Jesus is my friend to show to me that I have.'

'This world is enough,' Georges cried. 'A vile world in which we have no chance and are buffeted by a hidden enemy.'

Reuben was silent. He bent forward and gazed into the fire.

'Ah, but I have two worlds,' he said at last, 'and there I am richer than you. I must deny neither. I am citizen of both. In the one I am very young, an infant, but with the Grace of God I shall grow. In the other I eat my bread and pay my tax, but my body dies, my tax is paid and I go through the door, out of it, at any time.' Then he added, smiling to himself: 'The great lesson of life is patience.'

'Patience!' Georges broke out. He started to his feet. 'I swear to God, if there be one, that I have no patience. That I refuse to delay. I want my judgement. For my sin . . . for my crime. . . .' He stood over Reuben, bent forward, shaking the other's shoulder.

'Reuben! Your sins, if you've committed any, do they stay with you? In your other world that you speak of, will you be punished for ever? Will there be no release?'

Reuben nodded his head. 'Yes, there is release for sin--after repentance.'

'But I do not repent. I have done no wrong. He merited his death. He . . .' Georges broke off, seeing what he had admitted. There was an intense silence between the three of them. Judith, whose guard over Georges was constant, turned to Reuben with some of her old ferocity, as though she would defend Georges with her claws. But there was no need. Reuben looked down at the floor; then, glancing up, he said:

'What I tell you must seem like empty folly to you. I can only warrant you that nothing is final; there is no end to experience-- and there is no sin too large to keep Christ Jesus from your life.'

He rose and went over to Georges and put his hand on his shoulder. 'Pay for your sin--good worthy coin. Then travel on.'

He went up to his bed.

After he was gone they sat close, hand in hand. Georges said desperately: 'Judith, there must be ghosts. It is true, although I never thought it. He will not leave me. At every corner I think to see him, and now it is months since I broke his neck and he drowned.'

Then after a little he added: 'There must be some end coming to this. I can FEEL it coming. If I could fight someone with my hands, stand my trial, be hanged by the neck--yes, anything rather than this stealthy silence. I, all my life I have never cared what I did nor minded what I did, and I am young and have everything before me. And he's dead and no one knows. It is sentimental imagination, this fancy I have--but I can't be free of it. I can't! I can't! I can't!' He walked desperately about the room. Then he stopped sharp in front of Judith. 'Judith, do YOU think there's a God?'

'I don't know. No one knows.' (But she thought to herself: 'What he said about the two worlds is true. That is the way MY life is going.')

But she rose and then, bending forward, said:

'I shall tell you what I think, Georges. That you are lazy. That you must go somewhere to work and forget Stane. Why should you think of him? If he were here and he had tried to hurt you as he did, and I were strong enough, I should strangle him with my two hands. He was our enemy, and you slew him fairly. Shake off your imagination! Go farming with Charlie Watson for a while. He'll teach you things. He has no business with ghosts--'

Georges looked above her head to the farther wall. 'Stane's father,' he said. 'His heart was broken.'

She herself felt a pang then. Yes, the consequences went, as always, beyond the act. But she faced them. . . . Stane, his father, all his relations--she'd face them all. Let them attack Georges and they attacked her too. But to fight for Georges, she now saw, needed more than physical combat.

A week later Judith lost her temper in the good old fashion of her childhood, and this loss of her temper led to an incident.

There was a man just then, Larry Tod, who was helping Tom Ritson with his cattle. He was a waster, this Larry, no good at all, and he wandered about the district doing odd jobs hither and thither and not much good anywhere. He was famous, though, as a wrestler. He was big, carroty-haired, broken-nosed. He liked to strip to his shirt and drawers and show a chest like a board, and, to quote the old description of the famous French wrestler, Le Boeuf, 'a stomach like a bale of wool.' He was very proud of himself, very sly, up to any mean trick, the right sort of figure for the villain in a wrestling bout. And that, on this occasion, because of Judith's temper he was.

On this day, an October afternoon of driving black cloud when the fells looked twice their natural size, Judith coming into the yard saw Tod bending down and twisting the tiny arm of young Walter Ritson, who was yelling his loudest.

Tod straightened himself when he saw Judith. He was always dirty with manure and mud and the rest. Now he wiped the back of his hand over the flat of his broken nose and said something about the child's laughing at him. Young Walter, the tears drying on his cheeks, stared up at them both in interested amazement.

Judith's temper was fine to see. She enjoyed it herself. She had been living in half-shadows with Georges for months back and she needed a change. Then she hated the huge oaf with the surly eyes, the tangled hair that seemed like a parody of her own. He was a sort of ogre personification of all that threatened Georges. She told him her notions about him. Slowly his brow darkened. What he would have said or done no one will ever tell, for Charlie Watson came by. Tod turned his rage in that direction. He hated Watson anyway.

A minute later Watson was stripping his coat. It was to be a wrestle. The news went round as though a bell had been rung. Everyone came flocking, and the match was moved to the green mound above the farm.

All the little village was there--men, women and children. A ring was formed, Watson and Larry Tod stripped to shirt and drawers. Both men were open at the neck.

It was to be the best of three throws. The little crowd held their breath, while the sky tossed cloud after cloud as though there were some giant juggler over the hill, and the Tarn, black as ink, lay insolently below them.

In the front of the ring, squatting on the grass, was young Walter Ritson, the cause of the trouble, with his mouth open. He hated Larry, but he feared him too, and if Larry won he fancied that there would be trouble for him. Perhaps the others felt the same. Larry Tod had been prominent in the little place these last weeks, and with every day he was becoming more sure of himself and more insolent. And for Judith and Georges, also watching, although neither confessed it to the other, the result of this seemed like an omen. Let the red-haired ogre win, Georges thought, and he was pushed a step farther into his prison.

The men shook hands and got into holds. Larry tried at once the back heel, the simplest and oldest of all 'chips,' for all the wrestler has to do is to lay his foot behind his antagonist's heel and bend him over it. But you must be strong to do it. Larry was strong, but so was Watson, who at once slackened his hold and moving his beautiful firm body with the most delicate grace, turned his side. Watson tried then for a buttock, but Larry's immense strength prevented him. Watson tried to get under him to lift him over his back. Then, when that failed, he stepped away and there they were again, their arms at one another's necks. They began slowly to step round. The little crowd drew their breath. This was to be an even match.

For Georges it was an agony. In his strange, over-nervous, harassed state everything was exaggerated. The dark furry clouds hung low, as though with an especial sinister message for himself. When the sun suddenly struck out from them with bright splinter- like rays, flinging the dry bracken into patches of amber light as though there were a secret flame beneath the soil, that, too, seemed to point the finger at him. Why was he thus persecuted? Could he not bring his mind to order? It was true what Judith had said, that Stane deserved his death. It was only his imagination that dragged with him everywhere the accompanying scene, the rain hissing on to the boards of the boat, the sudden consciousness in Stane's eyes of Georges' intention, the cry lost in the storm, the whip, whip of the wind.

The women were shouting. Watson had tried the right-leg trip, making Larry swing sharply towards his left. With a mighty straining of muscle, his thighs and buttocks forced to their uttermost strength, he lifted Larry up, hoisting Larry's left leg up with his right and-- to a great shout of all and sundry--landing the ogre with a fine bump on his back.

First throw to Watson.

The two men stayed a moment, wiping their brows. The crowd were silent. Did they feel, perhaps, that there was something concerned here more deeply than the personal encounter? The women were all on Watson's side, and yet he was aloof from them. He had never tried to make love to any of them. There was a little feeling that he was 'a bit above himself.' Larry, when he was dressed up and had washed his face, was a great figure of a man and knew what love- making was. One and all, though, in their hearts, they loathed him and perhaps, like little Wallie, feared him too.

At any rate he looked now a man to be feared. As he stood there waiting, scowling between his sullen eyes, he looked as though he would kill Watson had he the chance.

When they came together again Larry tried the hitch-over, that is, he attempted to turn his left side to Watson, curl his left leg round Watson's right and, while Watson was standing on his left leg, cross-buttock him. But Watson was too quick for him, and soon they were moving round, slowly, cautiously, trying for some advantage.

You would not tell from looking at Georges, standing straight and grave, his rather round cheeks composed, his black eyes sombre and still, that his soul was in torment. If he had one! If he had one! That preacher, Reuben Sunwood, with his confidence in his Christ, his quiet happy assurance. . . . Ah well, that was not for Georges! His life had gone for nothing, one silly mistake and foolishness after another! He had begun life with a sense of adventure, with a kind of bravado, as though he could dare the world and bring it tumbling to his feet. But the world had snapped its fingers at him. He had got nothing out of it. Nothing save Judy!

He half turned and looked at her, standing on tip-toe, her mouth a little open, her hair blowing, all excitement like a child. A child! But how courageous and independent! How she had held by him--from the first, through everything, her loyalty never for a moment wavering. If he could but get rid of this present burden and dread he would show her that at last he realised her worth. He had been a long time coming to it, through slow selfish stages, but he knew it now, that he had had the luck of the devil to get her-- yes, luck far better than he deserved.

He heard the deep indrawing breath of the women beside him and saw, with a beat of excitement, Larry Tod turning his back suddenly, getting right under Watson and, with a great heave that had also in it a lightning quickness, sending Watson flying over his back. He had buttocked him, fair and square.

Second throw to Tod.

Then, indeed, Georges' whole life and purpose seemed to be in the match. Watson must win; he must, he must! The very sight of Larry Tod strutting about there like a flaming peacock, pushing out his chest, stroking his arms, throwing glances from his narrow eyes to heaven as though he expected the clouds to acclaim him, that was indeed too much. If Watson lost now all was lost. It was as though Tod with his coarseness and his evil had been sent as a messenger to Georges threatening him with some low, vile dominion for ever.

Watson stood there quietly, no expression in his eyes, waiting. Above them the clouds were stripping the sky, which began to be flooded with a white pale glow. The Tarn, beneath them, was white like the peeled inside skin of an orange; all the houses of the village were black.

The men took hold again. First Tod, setting his teeth, tried the swinging hips, but this, if it is to succeed, must be a swing of great quickness, and Watson was too strong for him. Then Watson, in his turn, tried the chip, getting his knee behind his opponent's so that Larry might lose his balance. It seemed that Watson would succeed. Larry raised his head to the white sky, his teeth clenched, his eyes closed; you could feel that he thought that he was going. But his strength was too much for Watson. He escaped, and suddenly, a moment later, was clicking Watson's right leg with his own right and his left with Watson's left. The struggle now was fearful. Both men put out their uttermost. Watson resorted to the outside click to save himself from falling, placing his leg as near the ground as possible. The two men swung and strained; Watson's neck and upper chest were soaked with sweat. Then Larry's little eyes were triumphant; he crossed both Watson's legs quickly with his own, cross-buttocking, and with a shout, his huge frame seeming to double its natural size, he had Watson on the ground.

He stood there, smiling.

Georges turned. His fate was sealed then. He walked away down the hill. Coming to the little rough bridge he saw someone standing there, someone with his back to him, a man of a great height, in a long dark-blue coat. He knew, before the man turned, who it would be. It was young Stane's father.

A few minutes later Judith noticed that Georges was not at her side. She had been absorbed by the incidents of the last bout, and when she saw Watson beaten she felt, as Georges had felt, that there was some personal omen, intended for them both. That was not like her. She realised it herself, but these last weeks had tried her. Yes, she wished she were older and wiser and, in general, more patient. She wished that she were not so easily excited-- excited by just anything, a piece of silk, a cloud in the sky--and then by a man hanging! It was then that she saw that Georges was not beside her and, at once, apprehension seized her as it always did now. It seemed to hover over her like a black bird--yes, and the sky white behind the bird, the Tarn dead white and all the bracken dead.

Watson was walking slowly towards her, pulling on his coat. She had to speak to him.

'Next time, Charlie,' she said, smiling.

'Aye.' She could see that he was bitterly disappointed. She was not sure that there were not even tears in his eyes.

'I'll whack him--great oaf!' he said, half to himself, half to her. She realised with a quick sharpness of perception that he had done it all for her, all from the first to the last. She put out her hand and it lay in his hot one, damp and sweating from the tussle.

'I'll back you, Charlie Watson, against all the world.' And yet, although she was so grateful to him and friendly, the truth was that she was scarcely aware of him.

Over and over again she was saying: 'Where's Georges? What's he about? Why did he go without telling me?'

She turned and ran down the hill. Pushing open their door, she saw a strange sight. A giant old man stood looking at her. He had long white hair that fell to the blue collar of his long heavy coat, and he had a white beard, like the cleanest, most shining wool. Above his beard a sharp pale nose and two pale-blue eyes. All down his long blue coat were round brass buttons, and he wore tall boots that gaitered him to the thigh. He was so white and clean that he seemed to be wrapped in some mask-like covering, and Judith had the odd sense that with a gesture he could throw off all of this--the hair, beard, face, clothes--and that he would be then a thin naked old man, sharp like a sword.

Another odd thing was that at once she knew him. She did not need to hear Georges' voice:

'Mr. Stane, this is my wife. Judith, this is poor Mr. Stane's father.'

She remembered always her sudden resentment that Georges said 'Poor Mr. Stane.' There was weakness and cowardice there. She would never have said 'Poor Mr. Stane' had a thousand of his fathers been there!

She went forward, holding out her hand.

'How are you, sir? Will you not sit down? You must be weary after your walk.' She saw at once that the old man liked her and that, very strangely, she liked him. It was always Judith's way, her life through, to know in the first instant whether she liked or disliked anyone.

The old man sat down. Georges had not moved from his place, standing against the wall, and Judith did not look at him. Rather she was compelled to notice everything about old Mr. Stane, how, with solemn, dignified, cautious steps, he moved to a chair; how he slowly sat down, spreading on either side of him the long heavy skirts of his coat; how he put up his hand and smoothed his white locks, pinched his white nose, then, very carefully, as though he were dealing with something extremely precious, laid his hands on his immense knees. It was then that she was struck with his great strength. His hands looked as though they could wring the neck of an ox.

'Mr. Stane,' Georges said, 'took a chaise to Keswick and walked from there to see us.'

'Aye,' said the old man. 'I was drawn like. My heart is aching for my son, madam, and your husband was the last to see him. It was a terrible accident and God's will. But he was all I had in the world.'

He spoke with very little accent in a soft mild tone. Then he went on: 'Whoso casteth a stone on high casteth it on his own head. He that worketh mischief, it shall fall on him, and he shall not know whence it cometh.'

Her heart beat wildly. He knew then? He had come here for some kind of vengeance? But he looked up and gave her a smile, so gentle, so friendly, so amiable that she could only smile back at him.

'The Scriptures, madam,' he said, 'have been a comfort to me all my days.'

'Yes,' she said, not knowing what to say. 'And now you must have some food.'

'Thank you kindly, madam. I could enjoy a bit of food. Although I like a walk, you understand.'

'Mr. Stane, Judith,' Georges said, 'will stay here with us to- night.'

'Thank you kindly,' the old man answered, pinching his nose. 'I wouldn't mind.'

He smiled on them both, then sighed a deep heavy sigh.

TUMBLE DOWNSTAIRS

Old Stane stood, as he liked to do, the blue skirts of his coat spread, before the fireplace.

Judith sat on the window-ledge, peeling potatoes from a large 'kist' on her lap, looking out of window at the gold smoke of the bracken that rolled in a low cloud up and up above the thin splintered blue of the Tarn. A late October afternoon, quite still, without a cloud in the sky, and the running everywhere of water, crystal clear.

Within the room, too, everything was sharp and clean; Judith, her lithe figure like a cut jewel, the flames of the fire like painted laths, old Stane's beard like the white of an egg, his blue coat without a spot, his long strong hands washed, you would say, with pumice-stone. Cleanest of all his long nose, always like the nose of a mask.

'Well, madam,' he said, 'I swore that my son should become a great man. I had myself sold fish with my feet bare on the Whitehaven cobbles, and the Lord thought it well for me to do so. My wife, ma'am, died in child-birth. She was a good woman, although with impulses not entirely Christian. When the Lord took her I accepted my rebuke that I could not have made her more godly, and I offered my son, even as Abraham offered Isaac a sacrifice to the Lord--'

('Young Stane,' thought Judith, 'a sacrifice to the Lord!' She could see his face, mean and ambitious, and his hands as they moved towards her . . . if she had allowed him--! She shuddered a little.)

'But as Abraham with Isaac, so with myself and my son. The Lord did not at that time demand the sacrifice. He knew His own good time. . . .'

Oh, when would he stop! She thought that in these last weeks he had managed to creep into her very being. She would never be rid of him again. He had done nothing but hang about the house. He never went farther than the steps beyond the door. He was always there. At night they could hear him move his great body in his bed, yes, although there were a thousand doors between themselves and him! He ate but little,

drank only water, spoke to no one save Georges and herself. He was quite silent if they were not there. Sometimes he would talk to them, sometimes only look at them. He would stare and stare over his long nose.

He had little movements that made her long to scream out. One was when he laid, slowly and almost sacramentally, his thick heavy hands on his thick heavy knees. Then he would stroke his beard with a purposeful meditation as though he were wondering whether, with a quick jerk, he would not tug it off and show it to be a disguise. He would raise a hand as though he would give a blessing. He was always gentle, kindly and patient. She liked him behind her terror of him. Had he not been young Stane's father she might have been his friend.

As it was he must go--and as soon as might be. But Georges would not let him go. He was fascinated by him as the rabbit by the snake.

Two days before this, almost hysterical with irritation (for it was absolutely against her character to be passive in this manner), in their room at night she had attacked Georges.

'Tell him to go!'

'I cannot.'

'Why not?'

'This is the least I owe him.'

'You owe him nothing! Georges, tell him to go!'

'You don't understand. . . . So long as he wishes to remain he must.'

She could have shaken him until his head rolled on his shoulder.

'Georges, wake up! You are dreaming. You killed the man in self- defence. He would have finished you. He wished to. Well, then. The old man has no right over us.'

'I cannot tell him to go.'

'Then I will.'

'Tell him. You will see. Nothing will happen.'

'But what IS it? What spell has he laid on you?'

'No spell. I cannot do otherwise.'

'But is he to be here with us always?'

'So long as he wishes.'

'But he makes you miserable. He reminds you always. If he went away you would forget.'

He came to her, put his arms round her.

'In this you ARE a child. You are too young to understand. It is not because I think I was wicked to kill Stane. I've done many worse things. But I'm not the same man since I did it. I feel that I must confess it to someone. Then it will be over.'

'But you have confessed it--to me.'

'You are part of myself or you have grown to be. We are both in this--as though you had been in the boat too.'

She stood up straight beside him, like man standing by man.

'Well, I shall tell him to go.'

And so, on this golden afternoon, she did.

She was not afraid to tell him; her earlier fear of him seemed to leave her as she spoke.

'Mr. Stane,' she said, coming quite close to him. 'When will you be leaving us?'

He didn't answer: he was pulling at his beard.

'I ask,' she said, smiling up at him, 'because I may have a guest. Mr. Francis Herries. He has written that he may be coming.'

The old man's nose seemed to probe into her, tickling her skin. As a fact he was bending down towards her.

'When you have no place for me,' he said, very gently stroking his beard and almost, it seemed to her, drawing her into the meshes of it, 'I may reside in the village. It is a pleasure for me to be near your husband, who was so good a friend to my son.'

She was on the verge of crying out: 'He was not good to him. They hated one another.' It was one of Mr. Stane's peculiarities that he seemed to draw out of you your most secret thoughts.

He smiled on her very affectionately as he added:

'I am an old man, madam. The Lord has seen fit to take everything from me. These, your husband and yourself, are, it may be, the last affections of my life.'

After that what could she say?

That night they lay awake hearing him walk his room. It was a heavy soft tread like an animal's. They heard him get into his bed at last. Then there was only an owl's cry.

They clung together that night like children.

'Georges, let us run away.'

'Where?'

'Anywhere. London. Paris.'

'He would come after us.'

'Georges, I MUST help you. I must! I must! I'm not a fool. This is a ridiculous thing, to be hemmed in by an old man.'

He sighed, holding her very closely.

'It matters very little. I'm happy because now I love you. Judy, Judy, I love you so.'

'And I love you more and more.'

'But how can you when there is so little in me to love? I have never treated you well from the beginning.'

'Georges, I shall never love anyone again. That is true. I know it absolutely. This is for all my life long.'

He stroked her hair. That, at least, he had loved from the very beginning.

'Judy, if we could be rid of this I know now what we would do. I could settle here now, I wouldn't wish to move. I would farm with Watson. I have lived out all my restlessness. We would have enough. Perhaps you would have children. If only we could be rid of this!'

'But we can, Georges!'

They were whispering as though the old man in his room could hear them.

'He must go, and then you will forget it all.'

'What did he say when you spoke?'

She did not answer.

'Did he say he would go?'

'No.'

'You see.'

'Oh, but I shan't be beaten by an old man.' Her voice rose. She dropped it to a whisper again without knowing that she did so.

'Judy, I love you! I love you! I love you!'

'Oh, Georges, I love you so! It has come at last, both of us loving one another--both of us.'

'Yes--both of us. . . .'

'It is very seldom that two people love with the same strength.'

'I did not know that I could love anyone for long. You have made me by being so good.'

They heard the old man in the other room rise from his bed. The boards creaked. They were silent, their hearts beating the one against the other.

But it was on that night that they both had terrible dreams. Georges dreamt that he was being hanged from a tree that was covered with white moss, and in that last moment before death the moss was alive with worms. Judith dreamt of a white horse that, plunging through dark water, leapt up the black hills beyond, and that, as it leapt, her father (she had never seen him, but she knew that it was her father) ran and jumped on to its back, calling to her to follow. But she could not, because Georges was struggling in the water and she trying to save him. The white horse vanished, a star fell from the sky into the water, and Georges was drowned.

In the dim musk-like shadow of dawn she waked and found Georges sleeping at her side. In her relief she laid her hand on his bare heart and felt its steady beat. Then she looked in his face and saw that he, too, was struggling in dreams.

She brushed his dark hair back from his forehead, kissed his eyes, stroked his breast, gently as a mother her child.

In the morning, however, all her sentiment was gone. They must be rid of this old man. The weather had changed. The sky was a fury of wind and rushing cloud. The clouds ran like messengers, and the sun struck like a whip on the hills, slashed and was gone. The bracken changed in an instant from dun to fire, from fire to sullen death. The clouds, after racing the sky, suddenly gathered into heavy bales of wool and then slipped down, enclosing Watendlath in mist. The rest of the world was shut away. Judith, in spite of her common sense, began to lose her wits, for now she, too, was conscious of a terrible impulse to catch the old man by the beard and tell him everything.

'Yes. It's true. I don't know whether you think it or not, but Georges killed your wretched son, and he deserved it. Now will you go?'

She had never felt any urge like this before. It was exactly as though someone were whispering in her ear. Their nights were broken. They were afraid to sleep because of their dreams. The old man stayed by the house, and they found that they, too, stayed there also. Charlie Watson was away in Carlisle. She did not seem to want to speak to anyone. She never went into the Ritsons' kitchen. The low wet clouds seemed to shut them off, the three of them, from all the rest of the world.

Judith sewed, cooked, sometimes walked to the Fell and looked down to Rosthwaite. That was the farthest she went. Georges sat, walked to the door and looked out, sat down again. It was as though they were both held by a spell. It could not, of course, continue like this. But what would happen? Old Mr. Stane seemed to be perfectly content. He talked much and always about himself and his son. He gave no trouble, stayed for the most part beside the fire.

'You may be sure that I appreciate your kindness. The Lord will not suffer a sparrow to fall to the ground. . . . My boy would have been wealthy had he lived. He had a fine head for business. Aye. Aye. All that I had, but it is the Lord's will, and His mercy must be great in our eyes. . . . But it is a grief to me that he should have perished in foreign waters. Your husband, ma'am, did all that he could, but it was beyond human power to save him. I know that. For an old man it is a hard blow, but it will not be long before the Lord will take me to Himself. . . .' Nevertheless he did not give the impression of great sorrow, but rather of intent watchfulness. He watched with his nose, and when he stroked it with his thick slow finger it was as though finger and nose were communicating together.

One afternoon the rain came. It fell in hard relentless torrents. The country was blinded as though a hood had been drawn over its eyes. That night in the war of water and groaning trees Georges caught Judith's hands and told her that he could hold out no longer. He must tell the old man and be damned to him.

'When I have told him, I can take him by the neck and shove him from the door. He can take what revenge he pleases.'

For a moment she thought that perhaps this would be best. Then she saw what it would mean. Georges would be arrested and hanged. She told him that that would be the end of everything, of herself as well as of him.

'Well, maybe that would be best. Anything's better than this. He is strangling us as though he had a cord round our throats, and he knows it.'

She had a wild notion that they should start out then and there, run for their lives, on and on, reach some foreign country-- China. . . . Even as she said it she knew that it was hopeless. He had strangled all her energy.

On the next night the rain had ceased, and a cold pale stillness lay over everything. They sat around the fire, and Mr. Stane told them about his home, his possessions, his clothes, his Bible, his intimacy with God as he had done a thousand times before. There never was such an egoist.

'The Lord giveth and the Lord taketh away. . . .'

Georges sprang from his seat by the fire, stood up against him, front to front.

'I killed your son. I killed your son. I threw him into the water and watched him drown. I hated him and hate him yet. . . . Now be damned to you both. . . . You and your son . . . both of you.'

It was as though the words had been spat out and then returned into him again. He put his hand to his throat. Judith rose with a startled cry. She came close to him, as though to protect him, so that they were all near together. In the silence she heard the owl's cry that had been haunting her for weeks.

At last, after this great pause, old Stane slowly lifted himself up from his chair, stood above them, then with his white hand pushed them, breaking through between them.

He looked at them, nodded his head.

'I knew it . . . a long time back. I wanted confirmation from your own mouth. Bloody murderer of my son--'

'Well, he had been bent on my ruin for years. He wished to take my place.' Georges panted the words. 'It was an old feud between us. We hated one another from the beginning.'

Old Stane nodded his head. 'Aye--you hated him.'

'Now go!' Georges cried. 'Call in the Justice. I shan't run away.'

He seemed like a man liberated. Judith went to him and put her hand on his arm.

'We shan't run away,' she repeated.

But Stane did not move. Georges felt such a sickness of the sight of him, a sickness that involved himself, his deed, the whole world. He would never be free of all this until Stane was gone.

'Finish it,' he said, and went up the stairs.

Everything happened then with great swiftness. Georges had reached the upper landing, when old Stane turned and was after him. For so heavy a man he moved quickly, as though someone very young and vital were concealed in that bulk.

He was at the stairhead in a moment. Georges turned to face him and they stood close together as though in amity.

Stane shouted:

'I came for this! . . . I came for this! Down you go, murderer--'

His arms shot up, he hugged Georges close to his heart as though he loved him, lifted him like a baby, then hurled him away from the stair, over to the floor below.

He waited, looking down, then rushed down the stair, bent for a moment over the huddled figure, passed out through the door.

It had happened in a flash as lightning strikes a house. Judith had not stirred; now, liberated, she ran to Georges, frantically, crying she knew not what, knelt down beside him.

His head was bleeding and both his legs were bent beneath him. He was quite conscious and he looked at her and smiled.

'My back is broken . . . he has done for me.'

'No. No--' She lifted his head and placed it against her breast.

'There's nothing to do, Judy, my darling. I'll be gone in a moment. The old devil was strong. . . .'

She tried to be clear-headed and wise. This was the crisis of her whole life, something for which she had been always preparing. Her hand was soaked in the blood from his wounded head, but she could think of nothing save his eyes, which stared into hers as though they would never let her go.

'I must fetch someone. They shall ride into Rosthwaite. . . .' She did not know what she said.

'No. Don't go. Don't leave me. Soon I shan't see you.'

She began to cry.

'. . . It is just. . . . Now we had come to love one another. Ugh, I can't speak. I am swimming in water. . . . Sinking. Hold my eyes, Judy. Oh, Judy, darling, how I love you!'

'And I you, Georges. Always. Oh, Christ, for help. Someone to help. . . .'

'Nothing to be done.' His head sank deep against her breast. His voice fell to a whisper.

'I love you--for ever--'

His hand touched hers and he was gone.

END OF PART II

PART III

THE BIRD OF BRIGHT PLUMAGE

FAMILY PAPERS

Letter from Judith Paris to Francis Herries, Esq.

22, Westbourne Place,
London,
16th of May, 1800.

MY DEAREST FRANCIS--Dinner is over, Emma has gone out to visit a friend, the candles are properly trimmed and now is the time to do what I have for several days pledged myself to--write a proper and informing letter. You know well by this time, dear Francis, that I am never as informing as I would wish to be, but on this especial occasion I have real news for you--for, what do you think? I was actually present at Drury Lane Theatre last night when the poor King was shot at by a ruffian and a most providential escape from death.

Mr. Ross with whom Emma has on several occasions acted at Drury Lane, had given her two tickets and, as you may well believe, we were all agog for we were promised that the King and Queen and all the Princesses would be present.

Now fancy the event! Scarcely had the King entered the box, before he had taken his seat and was yet bowing to the audience (myself and Emma were on the floor and had a most excellent view of it) when a wretch in the pit not far from us aimed at the poor King with a horse-pistol and fired.

You can imagine the sensation! Everyone was screaming. It was fortunate that there was not a panic. The King alone was calm, for he turned, said some words to an attendant, took his seat quite tranquilly and sat out the entertainment which was 'She Would and She Would Not' and James Cobb's 'Humourist.'

It was terrible to see the people throw themselves upon the wretched would-be assassin, who was pulled over the spikes and hurried across the stage. Sir William Addington examined him in an adjoining apartment.

After a while up went the Curtain and we all--on the stage and off it--stood up and sang 'God Save the King.' Emma was crying like a child and I must confess that my own eyes were wet. Princess Mary fainted twice they say, but Princess Elizabeth was most brave and we could see how the Queen nodded to the Princesses that they should keep up their spirits.

They say to-day that the name of the man was James Hadfield and that the King was indeed lucky, for one of the slugs from the pistol was found only a foot to the left of the royal chair. The affair is the more mysterious it seems, in that only that same afternoon during his attendance at the field exercises of the Grenadier battalion at Hyde Park a Clerk in the Navy Office was shot while standing only a few feet from the King. It was thought at the time to be an accident but now it looks otherwise.

What times we live in! The whole world is disturbed and the wretched Revolution in France has been, I am convinced, the cause of it. Gold is scarce they say, and I know from my own experience how scarce food is. Everyone is complaining but nothing is done and many well-informed persons fear that we are on the verge of Revolution. Well, after all this public news you will wish to hear something more personal.

This is now my second year with Mrs. Dudeney and her children. I go to her house in Mecklenburgh Square at nine every morning and am there until six, save for Saturdays and Sundays. I take my dinner with them and often drive out with Mrs. Dudeney or her sister Miss Chalpaine.

I must confess that I have grown attached to the children. They are good little things, even a trifle too virtuous, for you know, dear Francis, I never care sufficiently for those I can completely rule.

Poor Mrs. Dudeney misses her husband very sadly and this that we have in common should draw us closely together. But something holds me apart from everyone, even from Emma. It is as though my heart were indeed quite dead and, although time has now passed, I live in a dream. It seems to matter nothing where I am or what I do. My whole movement is external. I speak of this to no one else save yourself--even Emma has no notion of it but thinks that I am well recovered from Georges' death.

But oh Francis, I am not! Something has died in me for ever. That condition of living when one existed only for another is gone never to return.

That catastrophe was a dream. Hunt though they did high and low for old Stane, he was never seen again. Was he imagined by Georges and myself? I sometimes think so. But it is not that I cherish any illusion about Georges. He was neither strong nor faithful; I loved him as he was--not as a Perfect Being, whom, in fact, I should have detested. Forgive these sentiments. You are the only one with whom I ever share them.

Emma has now abandoned the Theatre or possibly it would be more truth to say that the Theatre has at length abandoned her. She is a strange Creature, quite devoted to me until some man crosses her path, when she is for a while like a school-girl. She has still her Charms and is less stout than formerly and as good a woman as ever was known.

Our apartment here is pleasant and looks out to a Square with Trees. There are sparrows, a man with a clarinet, a Poodle that walks every morning in the Square and an Artist up the stairs who quizzes me at every opportunity.

Write soon and tell me all about dear Uldale. Is the Museum still there at Keswick and have there been any Balls? Give Deborah my greetings and nod to every stream, hedgerow and little hill in the neighbourhood. Do the clouds still dance above Skiddaw? How I wish that I were there!--Your loving

JUDITH.

Francis Herries, Esq., to Judith Paris.

Uldale, 14th of June, 1800.

DEAREST JUDITH--I was delighted indeed to have a letter from you, for it was several months since I had heard and I was beginning to feel some anxiety. When I saw you last year in London you had not been sufficiently with Mrs. Dudeney to know how you would find her, and it is very gratifying indeed to discover that at least she is neither a bore nor a bully.

I cannot quite accommodate myself to the necessity of your earning a living in this manner, but quite honestly, dear Judith, I do not feel that it would be altogether wise for you to live with us while Deborah is here, nor would you yourself I think wish it.

Deborah is the best of women and the most kindly of sisters, but she must rule domestically any place where she is and will brook no rival. You also as you admit have a certain ruling capacity and when Greek meets Greek--!

Moreover remembering Georges still as you do, work is I do not doubt the most helpful of Panaceas, and I know that you are of the greatest value to Mrs. Dudeney and her family.

You do not say in your letter whether you have seen Brother Will. I hear that he is with every week a man of greater wealth and more important responsibility. I am told that they are to take a house in Mount Street (my information is from Bournemouth). I hear also that Christabel is no more in love with a grand life than she ever was, poor thing, and has in fact never recovered socially from the unhappy and now historic Ball.

Will will have no dealings with me and breathes fire and slaughter against his Bournemouth relations. Is this not foolish? But Will was always as filled with himself and his affairs as an egg with meat, and an insult to his wife is a snap of the finger in the face of the Almighty.

Nevertheless Will prospers and I do not. He is the other side of the Herries blanket from ourselves, dear Judith, and I think all the interest in our family's history must come from that, that men like Will are being for ever disgraced and made anxious by men like me. We break in upon their solid plans as a horse-thief breaks into their gold. So also on their side they break in upon our dreams. Where, I must ask myself, wandering among these fields and hills, do the two worlds join? Who may bring them together? Last week I rode up Borrowdale to Stonethwaite and wandered for an hour about the little overgrown court and garden of Herries where my grandfather and your father dug for so many years the hard and ungrateful soil. A shepherd, Wilson, now has it and lets it go as it will.

It was almost as though your father were at my elbow. I had forgot him but my father so frequently spoke of him that it is as though I had known him. I have only one memory of him, a tall gaunt black man with a scar on his face, riding up the white road to Uldale. I must confess to you that I was miserable enough that hour in that garden. All has gone wrong with me of late. Deborah's little sociabilities, the neighbours, their tea-parties, cards and small festivities I can take no interest in. My writing such as it was has failed me; even my reading has little power over me. The country seems to me on the verge of ruin, the country people seething with discontent, the towns no better, a crazy king on the throne and a Prince--you do not need me to say anything there.

But you know what it is, dear Judith, that drives me. I am a man now of forty years and should be past such madness and should be master of such folly--but rather I am sunk in it deeper than before. Every breath I draw, waking or sleeping, seems to drag me to Bournemouth. They tell me that she is more beautiful than ever. She should be indeed now in the full flower of her loveliness. I hear also, and this has possibly given strength to my madness, that young Beaminster, the Duke of Wrexe's eldest son, is crazy for her. What a match for her that would be! But if anyone in our age is fitted to be a Duchess it is she! What a triumph for the Herries family if it should be so! I hear too that she is both proud and kind beyond ordinary measure--and truly in every grace and virtue she is over all others. . . .

I will not burden you more with this. You ask whether Skiddaw stands where it did. Indeed it does. This is a perfect month for this country. There is a spot by Portinskill bordering the Keswick Lake where I love to be. The trees are now young flames and when the water is like glass they burn in their reflections. Then a breeze ruffles that glass and the fire is suddenly in the sky carried on the breast of a cloud. Were she with me here to see this beauty I know that I could win her to love me. I know it, Judith, I KNOW it! But what is the value of such vain dreams? If you should hear anything of young Beaminster being at Bournemouth or of their meeting in Town, pray let me know.--Your loving
FRANCIS.

Miss Jennifer Cards to the Hon. Angela Painter.

Grosset Place,
Wiltshire,
September 2, 1802.
MY DARLING ANGELA--Forgive this odious hand for I cannot find my own pen and all the writing-tables here are filled with birds' nests and bones for the dogs. I speak with the utmost literalness for you cannot conceive the disorder in which Maria Rockage loves to confuse everything. But I have told you of this odd

Place before and there is no need to make a repetition save that it is truth itself that there is a Bason on the floor of my bedroom at this instant to catch the drops from a crack in the ceiling, for it has rained for twenty-four hours without ceasing and every room in the Place runs with water. Not that we any of us are disturbed in the slightest degree. We are all True Britons in this respect and discomfort is part of our Birthright. There are but three of us here at the moment, Rockage, Maria and Phyllis, twenty last week and quite pretty in a milk-maid kind of style.

I fancy that she is the principal cause of my invitation here, for she had her Coming Out last Season and then must Go In again for they haven't a Penny amongst them and can make no sort of Show-- while I, they suppose, have everyone in my Handkerchief from Mrs. Fitzherbert downwards. They fancy too that I can give the Child some kind of a 'ton,' but I am too amiable on the one side and too lazy on the other. And indeed she is not so bad in a simple kind of way.

But you know, dearest Angela, of what it is that I would write. Have you seen Beaminster since his return, have you spoken with him, if so did he mention me and what is his attitude now that he has seen China and all the Indies? Perhaps he has brought back with him a young Chinese Woman and I will not care if he has. But will I not? What is my mood? Upon my word it is hard to tell. How perverse is the world! Here am I, thirty-two years of age and still Single. And yet I have had every Element in my favour, have no aversion to Matrimony. At least I have told Beaminster a thousand times that I do not love him and would marry him only to be a Duchess. I like him at least sufficiently to be honest with him and as you know have refused him a hundred times. But now, time passes. It will not be long before I am a Withered Hag. What is Love, Angela? I swear I have never known it. My cousin, Francis Herries, swears that it is the Toothache of the Soul that no dentist can cure. I can only say then that my Teeth have no need of a Doctor. But why are the Virtues and Qualities of men so obstinately dissipated? There is Francis himself, the best and happiest of company, but having nothing better than a small Place in Cumberland where it rains inordinately. There is young Stephen Hailes whose every breath showers gold pieces, but he is so gross in his feeding and thinks of nothing but Horses. There is Beaminster (and I would adore to be a Duchess), but he whines through his Nose like a Parson and cracks at the knees.

And many another all of whom you know, dearest Angela. I'm not boasting that I tell you this, but only that I may remind myself of my Vast Age and how my Opportunities are slipping over me.

There is talk still everywhere of the Peace and it is the fashion only to hasten to Paris. Rockage has heard that Charles Fox is on a visit to Bonaparte and that Mrs. Fox is for the first time publicly acknowledged.

I shall be soon returning to Bournemouth for Wiltshire rusticity is softening my Wits. Moreover there is shortly coming here little Judith Paris whom you have seen I fancy in London. Maria has an odd Affection for her. She is a quaint thing whose French husband was killed some years back in a brawl in the North, since when she must be a Governess or Companion as he left her without a Penny. She is as you will remember, an Oddity, being but a few feet in height and with hair of coarse flaming red.

Maria vows that she is a Noble Creature. I am not myself prepossessed too strongly in her favour as she supports the Will Herries part of the Family in that ridiculous squabble of which I have often told you and over which we have so frequently laughed together. In any case I prefer my Nobility over two foot and a quarter!

Write soon, dearest Angela, and relieve the Anxiety of Your loving Friend,

JENNIFER.

Francis Herries, Esq., to Judith Paris.

Uldale,
Cumberland,
14th of September, 1802.

DEAREST JUDITH--I am following my letter of yesterday with this brief note that I may enclose this silver chain and cross. Last night rummaging in some old drawers, I came upon some effects of my father's, a packet or two of letters, a book or two, a riding-whip, this Chain and a small silver Box. The Box was the one of which he had often told me, decorated with the Picture of girls dancing round a Maypole and gentlemen hunting. It was given him as a Child by a Pedlar. The Chain also he had spoken of, and it seems that your Mother's Mother bequeathed it to your father for some Service he had one time done her.

The Chain then is by right your own and it pleases me greatly that I have discovered it, as also the silver Box by which I know my Father held considerable store.

I have no further news than that of yesterday.--Your loving

FRANCIS.

Judith Paris to Mrs. Will Herries, of 48 Mount Street, London.

Grosset Place,
Wilts.,
December 3, 1802.

MY DEAR CHRISTABEL--It was most kind of you to write to me. I was most grateful. I have been here now for two months and have as yet no regrets at having left Mrs. Dudeney. Phyllis is a charming girl, modest and intelligent, with a sense of fun that enables her to see the Ludicrousness of much in her home and her Parents, and yet in no way impairs her Love for them.

They are indeed Lovable and yet most truly there is also something of the Ludicrous! Had you but now seen Carey peeping over the banisters, his nightcap nodding above his eyebrow, his nightshirt flapping at his bare ankles, shouting for Doggett, the man, because he heard that the sow had but just now littered! Indeed this is no place for early rising, for even now I was downstairs at ten o'clock to find such a confusion in the breakfast room, fender huddled two yards high, into the middle of the room, chairs, tables, shovel, poker, tongs anyhow, carpet thrown back, dust everywhere, dogs everywhere, bees-wax, rubber, brush, broom, mop, pail, and before a cheerless grate Maggie the girl on her knees. All the doors on this house have rusty refractory door-locks of which the hasp invariably flies backward, all chimneys smoke, going to bed the candle at once goes out with a whiff and a stink in the passage and you break your shins at every step, all the corks break and drop in fragments INSIDE the bottles, all keys are lost to all drawers, room after room (there are dozens of unused ones) is piled with broken bricks, scattered chisels and hammers, battered trunks mildewed with neglect. No proper alliance is formed with any butcher, carrier or baker, no salt-cellars have their spoons, no knife its proper fork, every snuffer to every candlestick tilts off and drops its contents on the carpet, every bell-rope breaks, or if it rings, brings the wrong servant, every scissor pinches without cutting . . . and so on, and so on! Dear Christabel, I could continue this for an hour!

Into this chaos it is hoped that I shall bring some kind of order, and indeed I see a good ten years' work in front of me. But after all these are my own people and not strangers, and as I see Maria in an old silk Negligée padding around, her slippers flapping on the carpet, dogs sniffing at her heel, and that kindly amiable smile on her face, knowing that she loves me (as indeed I believe that she does), I must love her in return.

All this must seem terrible to you in your smart Mount Street Mansion, and you can understand what it must be to myself who have, as you know, a Passion for cleanliness, but I have no longer Energy to direct my own path and take what comes. Affection seems to me everything just at present.

Your beautiful Enemy, Miss Jennifer, was staying here in the summer. They report her proud, matter-of-fact, worldly, not over intelligent but kindly and not conceited. They were rather relieved though, I fancy, at her departure. They say that she has any number of times refused Lord Beaminster and that now he, after a visit to the East, is paying attention to Lord Garrison's girl, but I do not know what truth there is in these rumours.

Has Will still the same implacability about Francis? The Monynghams have been here. I dislike the name and am glad that Carey's father after being Lord Monyngham became Viscount Rockage-- a far handsomer title!

What of Pomfret in Kensington? I hear that he has been ill and that James, the monster, is biting his thumb till he can be Baronet. Like his grandfather Raiseley, whom Will's father always so thoroughly hated, I never cared for James.

Love to all in Mount Street and if Mrs. Dudeney pay a call, as I fancy that she may, pray be kind to her for my sake.--Your loving

JUDITH.

Francis Herries, Esq., to Judith Paris. (Portion of letter only.)

Uldale, Jan. 6, 1805.

. . . . You know what it was that I read in the Gazette. And so she has surrendered! Well, it will become her to be a Duchess although I hear that he is sadly spindle-shanked and a dull dog. I will think no more of her. I feel stronger now that the blow has at length fallen. I must build my life on a sounder bottom.

One agreeable thing has occurred. A Mr. and Mrs. Coleridge have for some time past lived at a Keswick house, Greta Hall, and now he is joined by another poet, Mr. Robert Southey, whose sister-in-law he had married. I have met Mr. Southey and find him a most agreeable person of immense learning, but no haughtiness of manner. Mr. Coleridge is an extraordinary man who lives for the most part in other worlds than ours. He is often absent from Keswick and, so gossip says, is on no very easy terms with his wife, but the Southey family is excellent and very friendly towards myself. I am even stirred once more to attempt something with my pen. But more of this later. . . .

William Herries, Esq., of 48 Mount Street, to Judith Paris.

48 Mount Street,
London,
Feb. 20, 1805.

DEAR JUDITH--You must forgive the brevity of this letter. I am but now returned from the City where I was consulted in certain important matters having no indirect connection with His Royal Highness's affairs. Your enquiry on Carey's behalf concerning his City

Investments I will prosecute further and send you information when I have it.

The Budget of two days back causes some concern especially the extra 6d. per bushel of salt which will I imagine greatly hamper the curing of bacon and ham, but on the whole things might I consider be worse.

Have you heard how Jennifer's engagement to Lord Beaminster prospers? I can only say that I pity the foolish fellow from the bottom of my heart. He little knows the Tartar that he has taken to his bosom. After dancing round him for years she has condescended to be his future Duchess without I fancy intending him any return. He will discover his mistake in time. I must however admit that the Match is a fine one for our Family.

There is considerable anxiety in the City about the King's health. Stocks fluctuate accordingly. Christabel would I know send her love were she conscious that I was writing. She is lying in her room; she had a slight stomach affection to-day.

Pray give my regards to Maria and Carey. I am pleased to learn from Christabel that you find your stay with them agreeable. I must confess that I have little love for the Country save for our own Northern portion of it which however for family reasons of which you are well aware I am little likely to see again.

With kindest regards, dear Judith, I remain--Yours most sincerely,

WILLIAM HERRIES.

Judith Paris to Francis Herries, Esq.

Grosset Place,
Wilts.,
Feb. 25, 1805.

DEAREST FRANCIS--I hesitated whether to write after I had seen the news, but I feel that it would not be friendly on my part did I not tell you of my sympathy. She has made her choice and that she can prefer a marriage without love because of its Social Splendour is only proof to me of her unfitness for any marriage with a finer man.

Put her utterly out of your Heart, dear Francis. I do not doubt but that you have done so. I pity her for her unwise decision, for where there is no love there can be neither companionship nor respect. So at least I feel. I wish that I were with you. I myself have often a longing for the pressure of your hand. You remember how as a Child I loved you and how I would watch at the window for hours to see if you came. As it was then so is it still, save that I am a woman now and have learnt something of life and know what it is to be alone.

Do not fancy, however, that they are not all goodness to me here, for indeed they are. I have brought some discipline into affairs here, but the real trouble is lack of means. Poor Carey has no mind for business and he cannot keep more than one thing in his head at a time.

No sooner is he distressed by the loss of a silver spoon than he is told that a dog has the Eczema, and some woman is up from the village to beg something of him, or Squire Somebody or Another has ridden over from Somewhere and must have a Bed.

The Guest Room is always in disorder, there are rats in the wainscot and a window-pane is broken. Still time passes and I am tranquil, refusing to lament over milk that is spilt or a fire that has died. Only maybe the fire is not dead and burns the more fiercely because no one perceives it. . . .

We have had a Visitor this last week and a pleasant one, Warren Forster of Alnwick. You recollect that he is the Grandson of Mrs. Dorothy Forster who used to visit at Keswick. He is a man of some thirty-five years and has been visited by incessant misfortunes. When a child he was kicked by one of his father's horses and has been slightly lame ever after.

He has also, I fear, some affection of the Heart. In addition to these things his wife to whom, as I understand, he had been some four years married, last year abandoned him and ran away to America with a theatrical gentleman and has never since been heard of.

In spite of these visitations he is a man of great Character and much tenderness of Heart, never complaining and always cheerful. Maria dotes upon him and I must confess that I myself have a warm Friendliness toward him. I can see you smile at this point, and prophesy me a second husband, but that will never be--Georges remains with me as though he were yet living. I must go now as I hear Carey calling me.--Your loving
JUDITH.

Francis Herries, Esq., to Judith Paris.

Uldale,
November 9, 1805.
DEAREST JUDITH--By now you must be aware that Jennifer has broken her engagement. Scarcely had the glorious news of Trafalgar reached us and we were in the midst of waving flags and hanging lanterns, when I received a letter written by herself informing me that she had broken off all relations with Lord Beaminster. She begged me to come to Bournemouth and you will not be surprized to learn that I am catching to-night's coach at Kendal.

I will write from there.--Yours in haste,
FRANCIS.

Judith Paris to Mrs. Emma Furze.

Grosset Place,
Wilts.,
Dec. 8, 1805.
MY DEAREST DEAREST EMMA--Late though it is and mean and drunken my candle, I am scribbling a hurried word to you to tell you what I have only myself this evening learnt--that my dear Francis was married to his Jennifer secretly in London three days ago. I have only had the barest word from Francis acquainting me with the fact and that they have already set off for Cumberland. As I sit in this large bare room with the wind howling down the chimney and the mice scratching in the wainscot, it is hard not to be melancholy. How, how can this end? Only badly, I fear. She has but accepted him on the rebound from her trouble with Beaminster. She does not love him and even though she did, could never endure the remoteness of our Cumberland country. I can see that they will move to London and poor Uldale fall into the tea-party chatter of Deborah's domination. And yet I have heard that Jennifer does not love London either and that that is one of the first causes of her quarrel with Beaminster. You know, dearest Emma, that yourself and Francis are now the two human beings whom I love the most deeply and for Francis this affection has existed from my earliest childhood. He has been always a little remote from life and interested in notions more than persons--always, that is, until this passion seized him. He is one of the noblest of men, but reserved in the expression of his feeling. She must be proud and selfish, accustomed to adoration and her own way. What CAN come of this but disaster? I have heard, too, that she is lazy and idle and will sit for hours admiring herself in the glass but this, I confess, comes from Will Herries who detests her.

Where are you now--at Colchester or Nottingham? Is Mr. Edwardes the Knight at Arms that you fancied and is the care of his two little girls as entertaining as you had anticipated? There are times when I am tempted once again towards London and Mrs. Dudeney. She would welcome me with open arms back again any while.

Only my affections hold me here, for try as I may I cannot bring any order into the Place. This Country is at its worst in the Winter, all muck and mist, so unlike my own beloved Cumberland where the Winter is the best, for the hedges sparkle with frost, the hills are powdered with snow and the air smells like wine.

Here, at Grosset, the Country is low and miry and one must walk in high, hard-bottomed fields not to be knee-deep at every step--one is like a frog kicking and sprawling through a welter of water.

My candle is at its last drunken nod and I must go to bed.--Your most loving

JUDITH.

Mrs. Cards of Macklin House, Bournemouth, to her daughter, Mrs.Francis Herries, of Uldale, Cumberland.   (Portion of a letter.)

Macklin House, Bourne-
mouth,   June 8, 1807.

MY DEAR JENNIFER--Your father has requested me to say that we are both anxious at not having had news from you for so long a period. You must really, my dear daughter, try to oblige your loving father and mother more frequently in this respect. It is not kind to continue any sort of grudge against your father because he did not in the first place approve of your marriage. A year and a half have passed since that event and he has become as you know reconciled to it. He wishes only for your happiness and welfare and you know well that there is no human being on the face of the globe for whom he cares as he does for you. You know that it is our wish that you should lie-in in Bournemouth and I have written to Francis asking him his own feelings in this matter.

I have not much News for you. The talk is only of the Princess, whose behaviour since the return of her Champion, Mr. Perceval, into power, has been, they say, outrageous. At a Ball at Mr. Hope's she was truly a sight if eye-witnesses are to be trusted. Her figure is now as round as a drum and she paints monstrously. Her conversation is so wild that she seems often like a madwoman and she is not ashamed to be seen anywhere with her boy 'Billy Austin'. The Prince has broken entirely with the old Whigs and his hatred of Grenville and Grey is fanatical. Sheridan rules him in everything and in your father's opinion is nothing but mischievous.

The London dresses are now so tight that it is almost impossible to walk in them. In my old-fashioned eyes the 'robes en Caleçon' are quite shameless, all the outline of the figure being clearly seen beneath them. Very often there is nothing but a thin petticoat beneath and that is sometimes omitted. The skirt is now in two pieces, a third piece sewn in diagonally as a lateral gusset. . . .

Francis Herries, Esq., to Judith Paris.

Uldale, Dec. 7, 1807.

MY DEAREST JUDITH--I wish you to be the first to know that last evening at seven-thirty of the clock Jennifer was delivered of a fine boy. They are both doing well and my happiness is beyond measure. I am convinced that now with a child in the house all will go well.

I will write later at greater length.--Your loving,
FRANCIS, Father of John
Herries.

Judith Paris to Francis Herries, Esq.

Grosset Place,
March 29, 1808.

DEAREST FRANCIS--This is the first sign of Spring this year and so I write to ask you whether you are yet living or have changed into a Leprechaun or one of the Borrowdale Cuckoos? What I would give to see Keswick Lake or Newlands Valley or the Moor above Uldale on such a day as this--for at home the skies are ever changing and streams are running and the bracken is popping while here even on this Spring day all is Languid and barely stirs.

But do you know, Sir, that of late you have very gravely neglected your Half-Aunt or whatever is my true Relationship to you? It is now some six weeks since I had any word from you and I am feeling very gravely neglected. Two Nights back I had a Dream about you and I awoke distressed, thinking that you had called to me and I could not go to you. Do pray write and tell me how you are and how Jennifer is and little John. I am uneasy in my mind.

At this especial Moment it is necessary that I should write to calm my Feelings, for this morning has witnessed one of my most celebrated Tempers. I fear I give vent to them more frequently than of old, whereas it should be the other way. This morning I stamped and shouted like a Fishwife. I think I had some reason though, and you shall judge. It was over young Carey, who is at home just now and doing no good here. He should have gone for the Navy, as was originally intended, instead of this foolish notion that he should superintend his father's estate. For that he has no more gift than his poor Father has, nor has he his Father's sweetness of nature. He is a thick heavy Oaf as I had the pleasure this morning of telling him, for I had but just, urged by the sweetness of the Spring sunshine, directed the clumsy Maggie to the proper cleaning of the Drawing and Breakfast Room when in Carey must come, knee-deep in mud, cracking a whip and followed by four huge dogs so that he breaks a China Ornament kissing Maggie (not knowing that I was present) and sets the dogs after the cat, crying 'Halloo! Halloo!' and riding the Chairs with all his lanes and bogs clinging to them.

I treated him to a pretty Scene and then, when he laughed, boxed his Ears. Although he is twice my height that flummoxed him and while he stared I told him all I thought of him, that he was a selfish good-for-nothing nincompoop living on his father's Bounty and doing nothing but chase Foxes and set the Dogs on the Cats. And I fear, although I did not tell him so, that he does worse than this with the Girls in the Village and thinks it all Fine Sport.

Well, in upon this comes Maria, who thinks him the Paragon of all Wonders. He went off in a Sulk calling me a fine collection of names, and Maria was altogether at a loss for she loves me and thinks I can do no wrong. But I am sometimes deeply weary of this life here, dear Francis. There is something in me that aches for Cumberland, even though there are scenes there that I could never have the Courage to revisit. This is not my place nor are these in truth my people. But where is my place and where are my people? Like my father before me I have no Home and yet I am truly a domestic creature and could not live except for the affections of those of whom I am fond.

Warren Forster has been here visiting again and we are become the greatest of friends. I think his lonely situation touches me--not that we are melancholy together but rather laugh for most of the time.

Pray write to me soon and tell me how little John fares. In your last letter you mentioned that he was suffering with a Colic.

Francis Herries, Esq., to Judith Paris.

Uldale,
June 10th, 1808.

DEAREST JUDITH--I have not written frequently of late because I have not been in the merriest of spirits--nothing specific but only a Malaise that is, it seems, difficult for me to shake myself free of. But now I have two Items of News that I must give you. One is that Jennifer will be lying-in again this November. We hope that this time it may be a girl. She is well and seems to have no fears of the event. I am afraid that she sometimes finds me a Dull Dog.

My second Item is that Sister Deborah is engaged-- to a Squire Withering of Summerhays by Carlisle. As Deborah is now forty-six years you can fancy that this event was most unexpected but Withering is of her own age and has already been twice married. He is a jolly red-faced Ox, whose interests are entirely bucolic, but he will I think suit Deborah well, for her desires are as you know of an exceeding Sociability, and now she may entertain the Neighbourhood to her heart's desire.

Her relations with Jennifer have been, as I have hinted to you before, of an armed friendliness and I doubt whether there will be many tears shed on either side at parting.

The Cotton Riots at Manchester have been I understand of a serious nature, houses have been broken into, managers burnt in effigy and many rioters lodged in jail. The People are making themselves more and

more felt and I must admit that they and their Cause have increasingly my Sympathy. Jennifer is an Aristocrat of the Old School and would have every Rioter burnt at a public Stake.--Your loving

FRANCIS.

I am becoming good Friends with Mr. and Mrs. Southey and frequently visit them.

Mrs. Francis Herries of Uldale, Cumberland, to Mrs. Judith Paris, at Grosset Place, Wilts.

Uldale, Nov. 10, 1809.

DEAR JUDITH--You will I fancy feel some surprize at receiving a letter from me, but indeed I would have written sooner had we not all been so occupied with the Jubilee which for my part I am most thankful that it is safely over. You would not, however, have recognized your little Keswick. We had grand Fireworks above the Lake, an ox roasted whole in the Market Place and many other Diversions.

It is not however of the Jubilee that I wish to write to you. I am Laziness personified and to write a Letter is always an agony to me so I will come sharp to the point.

It is this--that both Francis and myself wish that you should come and live with us. It is plain enough that Francis should wish it-- he has always wished it-- and therefore I write myself that you may believe in my own independent desire for it. In honesty I discover that, since the departure of Deborah, the two children and the management of the House are more than I can properly sustain. But beyond this I will admit that I consider that it will be of advantage both to Francis and myself that you should be with us. I have grown unaccountably sluggish of late and so I fancy has he. In addition to these things I have a real wish that you should love me--something that may at this present seem to you quite impossible, but juxtaposition and a Good Will may work wonders.--I am, Your sincere friend,

JENNIFER

HERRIES.

Judith Paris to Francis Herries, Esq.

Grosset Place,
Nov. 15, 1809.

DEAREST FRANCIS--I have but now received a Truly Extraordinary Letter from Jennifer which I have answered as honestly as I may. You doubtless know of it. But what am I to say?

Of course I wish to come to you and Uldale. I have wished it all these years when I have been in sober truth a real Exile from my own country. I have developed a fondness for Carey and Maria and Phyllis. I would leave them perhaps for no one else in the world, but you have always been--save for Georges--first in the world to me and I would go anywhere to serve you. Also it is a Happiness to think that I must have the Care in some part of your Children.

But does Jennifer truly wish me to come? Have you not pushed her into that Letter? I must know this before I give any Answer. I had fancied that she had in her Heart no affection for me. I am myself not easy, love to dominate where I am, am often in terrible Rages and am haunted by the past. But you know this, dear Francis, and you know your wife. It seems to me that if I come and things go ill I may imperil all our Happiness. Yet the House at Uldale calls me like a living person. I cannot refuse if you assure me that it is Jennifer's wish as well as your own.--Your loving

JUDITH.

Francis Herries, Esq., to Judith Paris.

Uldale, Nov. 19, 1809.

DEAREST JUDITH--Come. It is Jennifer's wish most certainly. Things are not too Happy here. You can help us to understand one another. Come.--Your loving

FRANCIS.

Judith Paris to Mrs. Emma Furze. (Portion of a letter.)

Grosset Place,
Wilts.,
Nov. 29, 1809.

. . . If you can meet the Coach I shall be most happy. Farewells here are of a quite Tragic Description. Even young Carey weeps down the Barrel of his gun.

Oh Emma to what Adventure am I going? My Life is built on that piece of ground. I have tried to shake myself free of it, but how fruitless was that effort I now know as I feel the excited beatings of my Heart. It may be that I am committing the supreme Folly of my Life. . . .

ULDALE AGAIN

'Let us walk up the hill,' Judith said to Francis.

They got down from the chaise and allowed it to draw slowly ahead of them. She put her arm through Francis'.

She was not going to tell him how frightened she was. This scene so amazingly familiar to her, the trees bright and bare so that the winter sun seemed to be shining in the heart of their branches, the thick soft carpet of leaves, the fresh sharp air with a breath of approaching snow in its stillness, all these were the friendly accompaniments of countless old winters. Soon, at the turn, the first houses of the village would appear, the blacksmith's, the little house with the round bottle-green windows, and beyond them the first comfortable shoulder of the moor. All so familiar that they were part of her own blood, and yet her heart was beating with an almost agonising apprehension.

She wished now that she had not come. Oh! how she wished it! She had been safe there in Wiltshire, safe even though she had not been alive. Now the pain was sharp, as when the blood returns to a limb that has been numb.

At once, on her first sight of Francis in Keswick, she had been sure that he was not the same. She had seen him before he had seen her; he had stood in front of the inn, slim and dark, slapping his thigh with his whip, looking sternly out into a forbidding world.

She had instinctively drawn her shawl more closely about her and shrunk back as though she would prevent him from seeing her. He had kissed her, put his arm about her, given her a hot drink, seen to her baggage and, through the drive out of Keswick along the familiar Carlisle Road, had been infinitely kind. It had been her own fault that she had been so helplessly constrained. He did not know that with every step Georges was approaching more closely to her. Georges, Georges . . .

But that cowardice she had foreseen, and with every strength in her character she had beaten it back. Then, in place of it, as they turned away from the Lake into the heart of the woods, the thought of Jennifer increasingly possessed her. Why had she come? Jennifer did not want her. She COULD not want her. She had yielded to Francis' entreaties, and now she thought that Francis did not want her either. It was true, in fact, that for Francis, too, there had been a little shock. When he had last seen Judith she had been a girl; now she was a woman, and, with that exceptional sensitiveness that was his curse as well as his blessing, he felt, at first sight of her, that she had become a woman whom he did not know.

This resolute, solid little person almost hidden under her shawl and pelisse, her small white face looking out at him from her rose-coloured bonnet with such seriousness, was very different from the fire and impetuosity of his own familiar Judith. He had good reasons--there had from the first been many--for doubting the wisdom of this experiment and now he suffered a sudden panic, foreseeing every kind of trouble and even disaster. He had, Heaven knew, enough already!

So, while they rode, a silence fell between them. Then, as they started on foot up the hill, she stopped, laid her hand on his arm, looked up into his face.

'I am frightened, Francis,' she said. 'I feel as though I cannot go on.'

'I am frightened also,' he confessed.

They looked at one another. Then she laughed, and it was as though a screen were rolled away, the old Judith of all his life was back again.

'Do you remember once when your father beat me and I climbed out of the window?'

He nodded, smiling.

'I thought then that I could never be frightened at anything. I am wiser now. . . . I am frightened of Jennifer.'

It was he now who put his arm through hers, drawing her close to him. They marched now steadily up the hill.

'There's no need to be,' he said. 'You can do so much for Jennifer, Judith. And for myself as well. We are in a tangle. You must clear it.'

'Do you think she will like me? Because if she does—I can do nothing with anyone who dislikes me.'

'You must make her like you,' he answered. 'Everything hangs on that. She is proud, she has been spoilt by much admiration, for which she does not really care. She COULD be happy here. You can make her so.'

'Are you yourself happy?' She stopped again, looking up into his face.

'I, my dear?' He shrugged his shoulders. 'Have I ever been happy save for a moment or two? But I love her very dearly. I am not a wise man,' he added, lowering his voice as though he were speaking to himself, 'I have never been wise all my life. I killed my father. My mother hated me. It is not natural that I should be more fortunate with my wife.'

'I have come into a pretty business,' she thought. 'This will not be easy.'

But they had found one another again. Her resolution, obstinacy and common sense were all active now that she realised that there was something to be done. The dusk had fallen when they reached the house. She could see it only as a white ghost. The lights in the hall confused her, and it was a moment before she could realise that Jennifer was greeting her. Then she was almost shocked by Jennifer's beauty. It was a woman of forty who confronted her, but age here had nothing to say. Jennifer's loveliness came from her superb richness of colour and form. Her hair was dark with the darkness of clouded fire, when the flame is imprisoned by black shadow. Her skin had warmth in its ivory softness. She was very tall, a height that was emphasised by her high close dress with its waist just below the breasts, but her body was moulded by her maturity to a perfect fitness. She stood, her head up, her lovely neck and arms bare, save for a thin Cashmere purple shawl, as though she were receiving a deputation of loyal subjects. Only her eyes were a little sleepy, heavily lidded.

Judith had never in her life before felt so small, so insignificant. It was as though she were a servant coming for a place. She was weary, too, crowded about with old memories, homesick for she knew not what. But it

was not her way to be beaten. Only, as on so many other occasions, she wished passionately that she were taller.

The thought in Jennifer's mind as she bent down to kiss her was: 'Well, I need not be afraid of this little thing.'

Jennifer moved into the little parlour that was thick, for Judith, with pressing memories. She recognised at once gratefully that it was not changed. That was Francis' doing. But also, with a flash of intuition, she realised that Jennifer must be lazy. She would have altered things if she had had a mind for that. Here was the old spinet with the roses on its lid, the music-box with the King in his amber coat and the Queen in her green dress; there was the carpet with the pictures of the Battle, the leaping horses and the cannon firing. For how many years had it been there—and yet it looked even fresher than in earlier days. Best of all, here was the China wallpaper with the blue and white pagodas, the bridges, flowers and temples.

Jennifer helped her to take off her jacket and bonnet.

'You must be weary.'

'Oh no, thank you'; but she was. She sat down on the old brown sofa that was covered with a pattern of red leaves and little rosy apples. Francis had gone to see about the horses. She and Jennifer were alone.

'Did you have an agreeable journey?'

'Yes. The weather was fine. We had only one storm before Kendal.'

'You must rest now and take your ease. Life is very quiet here.'

Judith thought: 'She talks as though I had never been here before. I knew it before she did.' She was in that nervous state of weariness and loneliness that can rouse, very quickly, the Devil, but she had already faced the Devil so often in her life that it was easy to say to him now, as she did, 'Lie down!'

She smiled. She could not help it. Jennifer was so very beautiful.

'What lovely hair you have,' Jennifer said.

'It is sadly tumbled.'

'No, but you will want to go to your room. I will show you.'

They went up the staircase down whose banisters Judith had many times slid. That was something at least that Jennifer had never done. Jennifer moved upwards like a queen.

'I hope you will like this room,' she said, throwing open the door.

Oh heaven! it was Mrs. Monnasett's room, the room where once she had crept up to the bed and touched the cold body, searching for the little box. . . .

'I trust that you will be comfortable here,' Jennifer said, staring with her sleepy eyes about her. 'If you need anything pray tell me.'

'I have known this room,' Judith said, also looking about her, 'all my life.'

The two women looked at one another--one swift appraising glance-- and at once Judith knew it was going to be a battle.

'She is going to let me be happy here,' she thought, 'if I do what she tells me.' Then there was the further thought: 'You've never done what anyone told you-- except Georges.'

But she was so weary that she could have cried if she had been a woman accustomed to crying. She was not.

'Thank you, dear Jennifer,' she said. 'You are very amiable.' She knew that Jennifer was thinking: 'I can manage THIS little thing.'

For several years after Georges' death the terrible time had been the night. If she slept, one horrible dream after another swept over her; if she were awake, loneliness and remorse weighed down her heart. Loneliness because Georges was not there, remorse because again and again she asked herself whether she might not have done something to prevent the calamity. Why had she not driven the old man from the house, driven him, with whips and scorpions? How was it that she had submitted to his presence so passively? It was as though he had cast a spell.

What could she have done? What? What? She tormented herself day after day, night after night. Then as the years had passed quiet sleep had come back to her. She was not one to bewail the past. She had her new life to make. But during the years in London and Wiltshire there had been no life. It had been as though she had walked in her sleep. Now with one step into the lighted hall to- night life had swept back to her. Contact was made again.

She woke in old Mrs. Monnasett's four-poster and looked about her trying to penetrate the darkness. It seemed that she could. Georges was alive again and at her side, and said with his old reckless impudence: 'Soon we'll have this house in our hand.'

So, leaning her head on his breast, she went happily to sleep. In the morning she met the two children, John aged two, Dorothy aged one, in the charge of a fat beetle-browed woman, Mrs. Ponder. Judith knew at once that this was a bad, ill-disposed servant who was resolved to defy her. John was a square-made, sturdy child with the high Herries horse-bones and light blue eyes that reminded her of David. There seemed to be no nonsense about him at all. Dorothy was small and dark and nervous. She hid herself in Mrs. Ponder's dress.

Judith loved children and had a swift power over them, perhaps because she was herself little and was amused by small things that seemed, however, to her important.

For John the only thing that mattered on that day when Judith first saw him was that Matt the stableman had made a ship for him and would take him later to the Tarn to sail it. As soon as he discovered that Judith also wished to see the sailing of the ship, she became part of his world and was never again outside it. He did not as yet talk a great deal, but expressed his emotions with wriggles of the body and small stern frowns.

'Pray, ma'am,' said Mrs. Ponder, 'do not permit the child to be a worrit.'

'I care for children extremely,' answered Judith quickly, looking straight at Mrs. Ponder's black eye-brows. 'To be quite honest, I do not think I can live without them.'

'That is very well, ma'am,' said Mrs. Ponder, who was a woman of one idea at a time. 'But he must not be a worrit.'

Dorothy was another matter. Baby though she was, she was already nervous, suspicious and reserved. Mrs. Ponder was her only haven. When Judith came near to her she screamed, which pleased Mrs. Ponder very much indeed.

Indeed everything that occurred on this first day after Judith's arrival contained the signs and portents of the struggle--a struggle that involved the fates of all of them, and of many more beside them--that was to come. The prophecy of the walk up the hill had been a correct one.

Snow fell all day, snow most unusual for that time of the year, soft, feathery, gentle, at first not lying, then, as the day sharpened, lying with a silver radiance over all the world.

It always seemed to Judith afterwards that she gathered in her complete and final knowledge of Jennifer in that first winter afternoon. They sat after dinner in the parlour, drinking their tea, the two of them one on either side of the fire, where the logs crackled and hissed, the only sound save the gently whispering clock.

Jennifer sat very straight, working at a piece of silver embroidery. Erect, her splendid body, with its soft rounded arms, its swelling breasts, its crown of dark, slumbering hair, gave an odd impression of being on guard. Often Judith was in the future to notice that Jennifer's body seemed to have a life apart from the brain that directed it. Jennifer's brain, she was to discover, was not active. It moved very slowly from point to point and there stayed obstinately without stirring. It was not an animal brain at all--something quite other-- but her body was entirely animal, wanted only to be cared for. That was why, perhaps, Jennifer was not conceited and minded nothing at all when her body was admired; why, too, men had deserted her at the moment of crisis.

But if she was not conceited she was intensely proud. She had all the pride of a woman who has no imagination, the most fundamental pride of all because the owner of it cannot look outside and make comparisons. Her pride had its origin in the fact that she was a Herries (though but a portion of one), and in the fact that she had a father and mother who thought her perfect.

She did not admire herself because they thought her perfect, but admired THEM for that reason, and her pride was all the greater.

There were things that Judith, as she sat by the fire on that first day, wanted to know. First how so gloriously beautiful a creature, who might (so Judith, rather simply and very modestly, thought) have had all London on its knees, could stay year after year in this little distant country place; secondly, whether or no Jennifer loved Francis; thirdly, why Jennifer had asked her, Judith, to come.

Before the hour by the fire was over, Judith had discovered the answer to the three questions. First--Jennifer liked the country better than the town because Herries were of more social value in the country, because she had always lived out of London and was a woman of habit, but in chief because she was lazy. The country demanded less energy than the town.

Second--she did not love Francis in any sense that Judith understood the word. But--she was lazy. That might explain it.

Third--she had asked Judith because, after Deborah was gone, there was too much to do. A housekeeper was impertinent. Judith, to whom, in Jennifer's judgement (she repeated this several times), Francis was quite devoted, would please Francis and keep him quiet. In short she had invited Judith because--she was lazy.

'Pray come nearer to the fire. It is monstrously cold.'

'Thank you. And is Deborah comfortable with her Squire?'

'I believe so indeed, as much as one may be comfortable in this world.'

She raised her slumbering eyes, lifted her white hand on which a great ring with a deep crimson stone glittered, to shield her face from the fire, and said: 'Are we to be friends, Judith?'

Judith bent forward, giving her glance for glance.

'I trust so. It is my own most earnest wish.'

'You will be on my side sometimes?'

'Your side?'

'Yes. You were not on my side in that most unseemly quarrel in London many years ago.'

'I was then quite unformed. . . . And Christabel was then my friend. You were not.'

'Yes, we were young then. I wonder. Is it wise--do you think-- that we have met again?'

Judith answered gravely. 'It is for yourself to decide.'

Jennifer's body became more active. You could see the life stirring through it, as still water is suddenly moved by a breeze.

'Are you passionate?'

'I beg your pardon?'

'Are you passionate? With that hair you should be. I hear that you have a temper that can be monstrously roused. I should like to see it.'

Judith laughed.

'There is time enough,' she said. Moved by a quick impulse and because she wished always to be friends if it were possible (she could be an enemy very easily if that was wanted), she went over to Jennifer, bent across her chair and kissed her. To her own surprise Jennifer put up her arm and with her soft warm hand drew Judith closer, kissing her again.

'It is by far more comfortable to be friends,' she said.

But was it Jennifer's body that had kissed her--or Jennifer?

That evening Jennifer, Judith and Francis sat in the parlour. The little clock with the china dairymaid struck. Jennifer rose, stretched her arms, threw up her lovely head. Her eyes were almost closed. She seemed to be tasting some delicious food or smelling a marvellous scent.

'I am sleepy. I shall go to bed.' She moved, slowly, majestically, to the door. She turned towards them, showing a sleepy smile. She yawned.

'Good-night,' she said.

After a little silence Francis said: 'I am so happy that you are here, dear Judith. Jennifer likes you already.'

'Do you think so? I am afraid that at first I shall be needlessly troublesome. In time things will settle themselves.'

'Is it strange to you to come back here?' He looked at her with eyes of deep affection. Now he had regained his old Judith. It was true that on the outside this was almost a middle-aged woman who sat near to him, a woman, too, who had known the most bitter unhappiness, who had suffered years of the harshest loneliness, but there was there also the child with the light of humour in her eyes, with her pugnacity, eagerness and acceptance of adventure.

'Strange?' She looked into the fire. 'No. But, Francis, with what passion I love this house. I had not forgotten it--no, not a table nor a chair, not a print nor a carpet, and the garden, the high wall, every branch of every tree. But I had not known that I would be so touched by it, nor that it would lead me on into the country beyond it. MY country. . . .' She laughed. 'Perhaps it will be wisest in me to check my feelings while I can; I am determined against too much enthusiasm. In an old woman it is an absurdity.'

'An old woman!' he said fondly. 'Why, Judith, you are not changed.'

'No,' said Judith. 'When I was in my room this evening after dinner and pressed my nose against the pane, standing a little on my toes, just as I did when I was a child, I could see nothing but the snow falling through the darkness. Nevertheless, the country crowded about me--Scarness, Bowscale, Calva, Black-hazel, Mungrisdale.' She said the names like a spell. 'And so leading to Watendlath, which I must face if I am ever to have any peace here. On the first fair day I shall ride over to Watendlath.'

'Why, Judith,' he said, 'you are a poet.'

'Part of me is a poet, and the other part, I fear, most unpoetical.'

He sighed and stretched his long, thin legs to the fire, rubbing his hands in his hair. 'I also. Part poet, and the useless part, the only part for which I have any care. We are a strange family. It seems that the Dreamer must always destroy the Man of Deeds, and so either way you fail. Your father let the practical go and was called a madman. My own father was ultimately all practical and faded spiritually away. Will has always been for the practical--he has never known a conflict and is become a money-bag. There is Reuben who has rejected the practical and is saved, maybe, by his Maker. And you and I, Judith--our fates are yet undecided. But it would be a subject for an Epic, this Herries struggle, with a changing England behind it. Which is real? Is there a soul? Are we for ever to be exiles from our true country? All my life I have been like a man wandering down a road that leads nowhere.'

'You should ask Mr. Southey these things. He is a poet.'

'I have asked him. He is sure of his destiny. His answer is in his books and his family. I never knew a man more confident. But his brother-in-law, Mr. Coleridge, has more genius, and so is more lost. . . .' He drove his fist on to his knee. 'Judith, I must lose myself in something greater than myself. That is the only answer.'

'And your marriage?' She asked at length the question that had been hovering between them all day.

'My marriage is a failure, a damnable, pernicious failure. How could it have been otherwise? Jennifer never loved me. She has never loved anyone. When she dismissed Beaminster she was frightened of her old age and she liked me better than the others. So she took me. And she has done her best with me. But there is a devil of selfishness in her. In a country life some sort of selfishness is, I conceive, a necessity. I also am selfish. But our selfishnesses--hers and mine--do not coincide.'

He stopped. Then went on eagerly, 'Judith, I say these things because all our lives we have been frank with one another, but also since you must live here you must understand what the situation is.'

'Yes,' she said. 'What is the situation?'

'I am as crazy for Jennifer as ever I was. She has a terrible physical spell over me. In a while you will feel it right through the house--the spell of her body. I care for her, too, in other ways; I have a great tenderness, sometimes an almost unspeakable longing to make her happy. And so long as she is comfortable she is happy, but let her comfort once be disturbed and the whole house is wretched.

'She is pure Herries, the unimaginative practical sort. Had she energy she would be the feminine Will of the family, turning everything to practical profit, but she has none and she wants none. She does not love me but she loves no one, not her parents nor her children. But she is proud of everything that is hers, myself as well. She will quickly be proud of you if you serve her. If you do not--'

'Yes--if I do not?'

'She will fight you until you do. And she has many strange weapons. . . .' He went on after a pause. 'I had thought when I asked her to marry me that what she would not be able to endure would be the quiet and silence here. That she would be restless here, want people that would entertain her, admire her. But that has been the slightest of the trouble. She has settled here like a cat by the fire so long as she is comfortable.'

'Then why,' asked Judith slowly, 'did you ask me here? If she is comfortable . . .'

'I had to have you, Judith. I had to. It is turning me mad, this life here. It is not that I have not much to do. I have learnt much of the estate. I have grown a wise countryman. Things are prosperous here. I buy land, sell cattle. So far I have conquered my dreams. But I love her and despise her. I love her and despise myself. I know that she does not care for me, that my children do not care for me. I am in touch with no one here. And therefore I had to send for you. For the last three years I have had this longing, but beat it down. Now it has been too strong for me.'

Judith felt her heart leap. She had loved Francis all her life and at last her reward had come. He needed her and had told her so. This was perhaps the first moment of true happiness that she had had since Georges' death.

But she showed no emotion.

'Yes, but if we care for one another--brother and sister as we are, although, Francis, I am in reality your aunt, you know--what will Jennifer say?'

'There we must be on our guard. I do not know how it will affect Jennifer. If she is against it she will use every weapon to be rid of you.'

'She thinks,' said Judith, 'that I am a meek little thing. I saw it in her eyes to-night. But I am not. Francis, now that I have come, I cannot go again. Nothing can turn me out. I am resolved. This is my country, my home . . . even if Jennifer hates me.'

'You have no true realisation,' he said slowly, 'of Jennifer's obstinacy.'

But she was astonished at herself. She felt rising in her breast a resolved determination on power. That other self--not the self that at her window behind the falling snow had in the gloaming traced every rise and fall of the fell, the peaked line of Skiddaw, the thin haze of the Scottish hills; but the self that had conquered

Georges and these last terrible thirteen years, this obstinate self--was moving her forward to this new conquest.

She would make them all love her, Jennifer, children, servants, even the dogs. But--if they would not love her--then they should obey her. But for Francis she felt an infinite tenderness. She got up and knelt in front of the fire by his chair. She did not touch him. She would never again kneel by a man to embrace him. That had been for Georges alone. But she turned to him, looking at him with so much sweetness that his heart was comforted as it had never been since the day of his marriage.

'Francis,' she said, 'in the way of love I shall never care for any man again, but in the way of ourselves, of all our lives, I love you most dearly. And I will win a victory here.'

He was about to put a hand to her. He stopped and listened.

'Hush,' he said. 'I thought I heard a door opening.'
But there was no sound. The door was fast closed.

PAYING A CALL ON MRS. SOUTHEY

Opening the door of her bedroom on a fine July afternoon, intending to prepare for her visit to Mrs. Southey, Judith stood frozen to the wall.

In the far corner of the room could be seen the broad, ill-shapen back of Mrs. Ponder, its calico covering spread to its utmost as she bent over the drawer of the little spindle-legged escritoire near the window. In these drawers were Judith's papers and personal odds and ends--old letters, legal documents, programmes of dances and concerts, ribbons and faded flowers.

Most of these were now scattered about the floor while Mrs. Ponder, in furious haste and grunting like a pig, burrowed ever deeper.

'Yes,' said Judith. 'Good afternoon.' She had always hated the woman; from the very first she had detested her, and now there was such a rage beating in her throat that she had a most childish impulse to rush across the room and seize the woman by the neck and shake her head off.

Mrs. Ponder's back jumped, then straightened itself; then Mrs. Ponder's pasty-faced, beetle-browed countenance turned round, terror braced by defiance appeared in it.

'Yes, Mrs. Ponder?' Judith said again, her voice small and quivering in her anger.

'I was straightening things, ma'am,' the woman answered in her sulky, deep-toned voice, 'helping to keep your drawers tidy.'

'You are not paid, I think, to keep my drawers tidy.'

Mrs. Ponder was recovering her self-command. She had thought that she was safe enough, had just time enough. What ill luck that the little soft-footed, prying

thing should come creeping up five minutes too soon! Oh well! she wasn't going to be put down by this red-haired left-over of a thief and a vagabond. She knew what she knew.

She put one hand on her hip.

'Excuse me, ma'am. I cannot say I am sure what I am paid for and what I am not paid for, only to do my duty, I should suppose.'

'And is it your duty to decipher my personal letters?'

'I do not know what you mean, ma'am, by deciphering. I was intending for the best.'

'You are very obliging, but it is a dangerous precedent, Mrs. Ponder, as I think you will find. Leave this room! It will not, I trust, be long before you leave this house.'

The woman came forward. She was half of a mind to have her say. It was a year and a bit since this French Madame (for Mrs. Ponder, like many another, confused facts when she wished to) had come to the house interfering and disturbing. She, Mrs. Ponder, had hated her from the first.

She would like to say now all the things that she knew and had picked up from gossip. What was she after all? The daughter of some road gipsy who had married a thief killed in a cheap scramble. If it were not for the Master, poor silly fool, she would not be here another day, with her red hair and standing on her toes to make herself taller! Mrs. Jennifer didn't want her, that was plain enough. And then she was alienating the children. The little boy had never been the same since her coming. . . . Mad she was, going off bareback with no hat on her head all the way to Caldbeck! Mad, as her rascal of a father had been, so she had heard, before her.

All these things Mrs. Ponder would have liked to say, but there was something about Judith, something both in her rage and her dignity, that frightened the woman against her will.

She was about to go through the door when Judith stopped her: 'Why did you do this? For what were you looking?'

'I, ma'am? Looking? . . . Why, for nothing, I assure you.'

'Nonsense. Of course you had some purpose.'

Judith stepped forward, and Mrs. Ponder, thinking she was going to strike her, retreated.

'No. I would not touch you. You are a bad servant. You have always been one. You will leave this house in the morning.'

'That is for my mistress to say.'

Yes. It was true. The woman was right. But Jennifer would not hesitate. After such a thing as this!

'I cannot understand what it was that you wanted. Pray inform me.' The disgust in Judith's eyes was more insulting than the anger. Mrs. Ponder would not quickly forget it. But, for the moment, it would be better to withdraw. So she withdrew.

After she was gone Judith sat in her chair considering. They were to go to take tea with Mrs. Southey at Greta Hall, she, Jennifer and Francis. She had come up to put on her bonnet. But she must speak to Jennifer before they went. She could not calmly join in the social amenities of the Southeys while this was raging in her breast. To break open her drawer and read her letters! There were packets of letters from Georges there. . . . Oh, it was monstrous, it was impossible! The insolence of the woman. But she would go at once-- that was one good thing. The affair would have a good issue, for the woman had been always impossible, and now there would be a fine reason for her dismissal. Jennifer would not hesitate. Of course, she would not. Judith's heart seemed to stop a beat. Jennifer was so strange a woman. They had been friendly enough during these twenty months. She had been delighted for Judith to take the house in her hands; she had given her free rein. But Judith knew her no better than on that first evening.

She could not any more now than then say whether it were War or Peace. The time had gone so swiftly; there had been so much to do-- the house to order, the servants to watch, the children to care for, Francis to make comfortable, new neighbours to know, and sometimes--twice or thrice--strange sudden expeditions into the mountains, to Watendlath, to Newlands, once so far as Ennerdale, when another life altogether had stirred and moved, a life that was not dead, although it was given so little freedom. The time had gone, Judith had even been happy because of Francis, because of the children, because the neighbours were kind, and chiefly because this house and the little village and the Moor were all hers. From Iredale to Caldbeck, from Threlkeld to Mungrisdale it was hers. And so, because of all these things, the central situation, the pivot upon which everything else turned, the relationship between herself and Jennifer, had never been examined.

But it had been growing; all the while it was growing. As she sat there, beside her bed, looking at the dove-grey bonnet that lay upon it, she suddenly shivered. WHAT was Jennifer thinking? Had Jennifer. . . ? And at the very suspicion of that thought, she, to whom honesty and cleanliness and fair dealing were the first rules of life, sprang indignantly from her chair. Oh no! that was monstrous. . . . Monstrous. . . . But she must go, at once, AT ONCE, and speak to Jennifer.

So down she went, and the first thing that she saw was the fat, handsome, sensuous face of Captain Fernyhirst in the hall. Captain Fernyhirst lived near Caldbeck. He had bought, only last year, old Uncle Tom's house, Stone Ends. He had a pale, ill wife there and two lanky children. And he was an admirer and friend of Jennifer's.

He was a fine upstanding man with a broad back and stout legs. His eyes were too small, his nose a trifle too large, but he looked elegant in his green coat, his hair curling above his ears, his spurred heels spread, yes, as though he owned the house and everything in it.

They were a handsome pair, a very handsome pair. He greeted Judith with the courteous patronage that he always used to her. He said something about the weather, and went. Jennifer was dressed in green and white, her lovely hair falling in thick ringlets on her bare neck. Very lovely, Judith thought, was her hair, parted in the middle of her fair smooth forehead, combed towards the sides, falling in curls that seemed to hold in their dark shadows a strange, steely lustre.

'Very lovely hair,' thought Judith, 'but I wonder whether Mrs. Ponder . . .' She was in fact too angry to wait, as she should have done, for a more favourable opportunity, and in that lost an important chance of commanding the situation.

Impetuously she led the way into the parlour.

'Jennifer, I must speak to you.'

'My dear . . . but we are late, and Mrs. Southey is most punctilious. . . .'

Slowly she followed Judith in.

'Jennifer, Mrs. Ponder must be dismissed. At once. To-night.'

'And why?'

'I caught her, now, five minutes back; I went to my room and she was searching my drawers. My papers were scattered about the floor.'

It was not Jennifer's way to speak quickly. It was as though slowly and with practised deliberation she sent a message through all her tall body that it must be prepared for a set of circumstances, that there was no haste required . . . plenty of time.

She sat down, put her hand to her hair, looked out of window.

'Well, Judith, I must inquire. Mrs. Ponder is an admirable servant. She was perhaps making tidy your effects.'

'Making tidy my effects? But who is she to make my things tidy? It is not her business. She had no place in my room. No, indeed. She was making nothing tidy. She was spying.'

'Spying? What is there for her to spy into?'

'Nothing, of course. I have nothing to hide.' Then amazement, increased by her anger, seized her. 'But, Jennifer--are you not yourself indignant? Do you understand what it is? She was SPYING! The woman was in my room, my letters were on the floor. Letters. Letters from my husband . . .' Her voice broke. She was very near to tears.

'Well, it shall be inquired into. I am convinced that you have judged too hastily. It IS your weakness, Judith. You act too immediately on the impulse of the moment. . . .'

'MY fault! My fault!' Judith broke in. 'But, Jennifer, I cannot understand! You appear to be blaming ME! Do you hear what I said? That Mrs. Ponder was discovered by me tossing my private papers about the floor, her hands among my effects. She did not deny it. She could not. She was most insolent. She must go . . . must leave . . . at once, to-morrow morning. You must tell her so. A fine thing to have in the house, a servant who opens drawers and carries her secrets, I have no doubt, to the kitchen-maids and the grooms. You cannot hesitate. Francis would insist. . . .'

She pulled up. For her life she wished that she had not spoken those last words. Her rage had carried her away. The very thought of the woman's ugly thick back and the packets of Georges' letters. . . . But she should not have mentioned Francis. Was she never to learn?

In the short silence that followed, the place seemed to fill with the summer scents, the radiant sun floated the room with shadows of gold. Some man called to his horse, wheels creaked on the road. Then Jennifer spoke:

'Yes. . . . It was I who asked Ponder to search your drawer.'

She looked at Judith, and Judith looked back at her. Judith's pale face slowly flushed. This was an incredible thing. It was as though the spinet had leapt through the ceiling, or the little rosy apples on the sofa had rolled like little live bullets about the floor. An incredible thing. To Judith, in spite of the many events that had been her lot, the most astonishing, the most dumbfounding of them all.

'You . . . told her?'

'Yes. I wished to know what you were writing of me to London.'

'I . . . to London?'

'Indeed, yes. To dear Will and Christabel, who have so true an affection for me.'

'And so . . . you thought that such dishonest behaviour was in my character--that while I lived here and was your friend I would write . . .' She broke off. All words failed her. The sun had died from the room, which was grey in her eyes and chill.

'But why not? We must have common sense. When you first came here I hoped that we should form a friendship, but you had other ideas. You were determined to be mistress here. You alienated my husband, my children, my servants. I was well assured that your friends in London must have the benefit of your experience. Why not? If I had had your ambitions I should have doubtless done the same.'

'You thought that? I have been here for more than a year. All this while you have fancied me indulging in such treachery; you have known me so little that you suspected SUCH things in my conduct? Why, then . . . why, then . . . if your mind has been of such a colour, you must have hated me! . . . And I thought that we were friends. For a year I have suspected nothing. And you have made your servant spy on me. . . .'

She was shaking, quivering with rage, astonishment, but also with a dreadful miserable unhappiness that seemed to strike deep into her very soul. All her life long, through every difficulty and distress, she had been supported always by her sense of her own integrity and the conviction that everyone thought her honest. She had not had pride in that, but it had been her comfort; whatever else went, that remained. And now--to be charged with such treachery and to be hated when she had thought that she was cared for.

Her lip quivered. If she wept now it would be a humiliation for which she would never forgive herself.

Steadying her voice she said quietly: 'I have never suffered any disloyalty to you, Jennifer, in myself or another. I had thought we were friends and so acted. You have wronged me,' and left the room.

Once in her own place any tendency to tears was gone. Tears! No, indeed! She walked the floor like a raging little animal in a cage. The letters, papers, ribbons were still scattered about, where Mrs. Ponder had left them. Mechanically, without knowing it, she bent down and put them back and closed the drawers. She remained, kneeling there, looking in front of her.

Her immediate impulse was, as it had always been in every crisis of her life, to take some dramatic action instantly--to find Francis, to tell him what had occurred, without either self-defence or accusation of anyone, and then to depart--to be, as swiftly as possible, as far from Jennifer as the world allowed her. But very quickly her temper cooled. Her intelligence reasserted itself. There was more in this than a vulgar quarrel. The whole of her own past life was in it, her father, her mother; the whole of the Herries family was in it, for what she was meeting now in Jennifer was the thing in the Herries blood that her father, herself, Francis, Reuben, Georges had always been fighting--the unimaginative, calm, self-assured obstinacy and confidence.

At that she knew that she was herself now calmer. She rose from her knees and, as she looked about the room, realised something with an absolute certainty of its truth, as though someone had whispered it in her ear. Jennifer had intended this quarrel. She did not hate Judith. Hatred was an emotion unknown to her sluggishness. She had decided--perhaps some while back--that Judith made her uncomfortable and that Judith must go. Francis would never allow her to go, unless there were some very obstinate reason or unless Judith herself was provoked to it. She must provoke Judith or she must find a reason. In all probability she was smiling now quietly to herself, thinking that she had succeeded.

At that Judith flung up her head and swore that whatever occurred she would not go. This was her place, and here she would stay. She could be as obstinate as Jennifer, yes, and more obstinate.

There was a knock on the door, and opening it she found Francis there. The carriage was ready. Jennifer was ready. He was smiling, had no consciousness that there had been any trouble. She looked at him and smiled too. She was there to make Francis happy, and make him happy she would, Jennifer or no Jennifer.

She put on her bonnet and shawl and went down with him.

'I like the grey bonnet,' he said.

'I had it in Carlisle,' she said, 'a month ago.'

Jennifer, in her fine green and white bombasine dress and an ostrich feather in her bonnet, stood by the carriage, the moors undulating in hummocks and pools of green on every side of her. She smiled as they came towards her.

'Dear Judith,' she said, 'what a charming bonnet!'

So it was all bonnets, and a more agreeable trio, sitting behind the immense back of Fred the coachman, could surely not be found in Keswick. Francis might complain that Will made the money and that he was a failure, but nevertheless things were very comfortable at Uldale. That land that they had bought towards Caldbeck was turning out very well, and, in spite of the unsettled times, the shares in the Liverpool shipping business were for ever improving. And, in a year, Judith had brought the house to a fine discipline. Mrs. Harper, the housekeeper, a widow from Carlisle, was an excellent woman. Jennifer herself was not at all extravagant. Whatever she wore seemed to be beautiful on her. She had no great taste for entertaining. An occasional little dinner with cards afterwards, a Ball at Christmas. No magnificence even then. Ten couples at the most. Yes, new bonnets could be afforded. They were very generous to Judith or, at least, Francis was. His allowance was most generous. She had never had so much in all her life before; never been so comfortable. . . . Comfortable? A glance across at Jennifer on the opposite seat, and it was as though everything sinister and destructive thickened the summer air.

To be charged with such malice and deceit, to be suspected of the basest treachery. . . .

'They say that Mr. Coleridge dislikes his wife extremely and will never again return to Keswick. He goes often, I believe, to visit Mr. Wordsworth in Grasmere. . . . How cool the woods are! . . . The Southeys always seem to me very pleasant people; Judith, my dear, if the sun is too hot you must change places with me. You know that I am never disturbed by the heat.'

She was not. She basked in it, or like a great bird of brilliant plumage bathed her feathers in it, letting the light strike gold and emerald and sapphire from her loveliness.

'Edith Southey,' said Francis, 'is a very pretty-behaved child, very pretty-behaved, indeed. And little Hartley, Coleridge's boy, is most unusual. But, of course, he is growing now. He must be fifteen, at least. He is at school at Ambleside. Yes, this is a most beautiful day; the air is exceptionally warm.'

Francis was happy to-day. He was always pleased when he was going to see Mr. Southey. That she should set her servant on to spy and then, without a tremor, admit it. . . . How lovely that rather selfish droop of her mouth and the faint warm glow of her cheek, and the softness of her eyes as they looked out so calmly under their heavy lids! . . . The falseness! That Judith had tried to alienate the children! John loved her. That was not Judith's fault. And he was uneasy with his mother. He knew, as children always know, that she did not in her heart care for him. Or did she care? Who could tell for whom she cared?

'Look, Judith, how blue the Lake is! There is not a ripple.'

Yes, she had thought that she had got her way, and that in a week Judith would be gone. She was wrong. As they approached Keswick the air was rich with the scent of the summer flowers. July and August are the bad months for this country. There is rain, everything is heavily green without variety. But days come like this one when all the trees, larch and birch and fir and oak, are so deeply shadowed and so highly lit that fire runs from stem to stem, melting into cloud and climbing into swift eddies of green smoke. If only there are clouds in the sky the hills lie waiting to receive the shadows that slip like birds from shoulder to shoulder. The clouds have a great richness in this month, so proudly filled with white light that they quiver with their intensity, throwing paths of ghostly radiance on to the Lakes that are blue, here and there ruffled darkly like tarnished silver. On such a day the richness of the English scene, when the hay burns in the nostrils and every cottage garden has the dusky odour of snapdragon and sweet-william, is immortal. One summer's day is enough for memory to be enriched for ever.

Keswick was so small a country town that in the summer its gardens dominated all the rest. Greta Hall is at the entrance to it from the Carlisle side, and once they had crossed the little bridge they were almost there, but Judith could smell the flowers mingling with the soft friendliness of the cut hay that lay on the open fields.

She could see the peace of the town, the farmers' carts, Mr. Probus the Apothecary standing at his door enjoying the sun, two young ladies laughing as they came out of Mrs. Gray's, the bonnet shop, old Mr. Fordyce the antiquarian, who was said to sleep half the year on the Roman Wall, with his snuff-coloured wig and old-fashioned breeches. As the carriage turned up the drive she thought: 'It will take more than Jennifer's insults to drive me away from this.'

This was Judith's first visit to the Southeys. Mrs. Coleridge and Mrs. Southey had been to Uldale. They were quiet, comfortable women; certainly Mrs. Southey was a comfortable woman. About Mrs. Coleridge one could not be so sure; there were lines of discomfort about her mouth, restlessness in her eyes. You could see that they were sisters and had lived for most of their lives together.

Yes, the house was charming, a nursery garden on the right as they climbed the hill; then you could see an orchard with plum trees and apple trees behind the house. They were admitted by a cheerful motherly-looking woman, who conducted them into the parlour on the left of the passage. They waited in the parlour, gathered together in a kind of attitude of defence as people are when they are awaiting their hostess.

This was a charming room, with a large green shaped like a horse-shoe in front of the window. The room was comfortably furnished with old furniture, shabby but friendly. There were pictures on the wall-- one really dreadful painting of a staring doll-like Mrs. Coleridge.

Mrs. Southey came in. There were greetings all round, words about the splendid weather, about the hay, the crops, being tired, not being tired, being hot, not being hot. But they must all come upstairs to Mr. Southey's room. That was where tea would be. So upstairs they all went.

Oh! this was a wonderful room, so light, so well-proportioned, so airy! And the views were fine. Were the views not fine? They were indeed. The room had three windows. The large one that looked down upon the green and the flower-beds and away to the Lake and the mountains, the two smaller ones whence you could see the lower part of the town.

The room was lined with books, and there were splendid volumes bound in vellum lying in heaps on the floor. And the family portraits on the wall; before long Judith knew who they all were-- Mr. and Mrs. Southey by Downman, little Edith Southey and little Sara Coleridge by that fine artist Mr. Nash; the other three Southey children, Kate, Isabel and Bertha, also by Mr. Nash.

Much good furniture, Mr. Southey's writing-table piled with books and papers, a screen, a desk. The room was decorated in quiet dignified tones, the curtains of French grey merino, the furniture covered with some buff colour. A noble room, the room of a poet, lit now with the summer sun, and all the summer sounds mingling beyond the open window.

It was, in fact, Mr. Southey himself who showed Judith the portraits and then some of his books. At first she thought him a little alarming with his dark hair, his grave features, the dignified, rather remote way he had of moving, a little as though, she wickedly fancied, he were carrying the offertory plate in church. He was at first the official host, cold and ceremonial. He held up his head as though he knew it was a fine one; she thought that he certainly was aware that he was an important personage. She fancied, too, on their first arrival, that he had thrown an impatient glance or two at his writing-table, where his papers lay, as though he wished his visitors very far away. And he certainly had no idea as to who she was; he took care to give her no name lest he should be in error. She thought that he had difficulty sometimes in seeing her at all and would have spoken with the same grave courtesy if she vanished; he would not know that she had gone.

And then, when they moved to the large window, he became entirely another person. When he spoke of this country, this country that she loved as dearly as he, his voice thrilled, his face was lit, his black hair flung back.

'You know it is hard for me to speak of these things. When I first came to Keswick I assured myself that I should never settle down without a violet--no violet and no nightingale. But now I have long forgot those losses. My brother Tom was settled in the valley of Newlands, and I would not like to confess to you how we have been, the two of us, our childish behaviour. And now with my own children there is no stone or leaf of Walla Crag or Watendlath that we do not know.' (Watendlath--a quiver at the word touched her and fled.) 'And with my books--my books. Are you yourself a bookworm? If so you see in front of you the most impassioned of your clan. Let me show you--' He waved his hand and, eagerly walking to the bookcase, began to pull out volumes for her. 'Have you been ever in Portugal? Do you know Portugal? What! you have never seen Cintra! . . . And is Verbeyst an unknown name to you? Verbeyst of Brussels. He has three hundred thousand volumes. Do you know what it is to open a chest of books? What are you going to find? . . . No, let me show you this--The Revelations of St. Bridget. See, not only are the initial letters illuminated, but every capital through the volume is coloured. . . . Fuller's Church History. . . . Is not Sir Thomas Browne a favourite with you? . . .' A small tortoise-shell cat came and rubbed its back against his leg.

He was quivering now like a boy. His hands shook, his face was all smiles. Then ruefully laughing at himself: 'Ah, I am for ever making collections. It is foolish, is it not, for who will read them if I do not, and they arrive more swiftly than even I can peruse them. Time! Time! Why are the days not twice as long and the nights four times! Come, I must not weary you, but I can see that you have a fancy yourself this way. You have a fancy, have you not? you have a library? I hope that you have a library.' He smiled at her so friendlily and his eyes were so kind that she wished that they could be examining books for ever.

At tea, seated in a half-circle, Mr. Southey, Mrs. Coleridge, pretty Edith Southey, Mrs. Southey behind the tea-table, they were all very gay. Judith had often noticed that when at parties Jennifer was present, everything went well. People were delighted with her beauty. Shadows and shapes of loveliness seemed to radiate from her passivity and composure. Then, being so beautiful, people assumed that she would be haughty and proud. But when she was anywhere the first thing that she did was to secure her comfort and, as she was always the most beautiful person present, she was always the first to be offered a seat, food, drink, whatever it might be. So, assured that she had all that she needed, she was as amiable as anything, listened with apparent attention to everyone's stories (although Judith suspected that she never heard a word of them). There was, however, always a sense of thunder behind the calm. When suddenly out of her comfort she might, Judith thought, snap something in her fingers, even as on that old historic occasion she had snapped Christabel's fan.

But on an afternoon like to-day's she was entirely at her ease. She had had a fight and, as she thought, won it. She had been increasingly uncomfortable during the last six months; now that cause of that discomfort would be removed. Then the weather was hot, which she greatly preferred. Then the Southeys were reputable people; she had herself never read any of Mr. Southey's long poems, but she knew that they were generally respected. What she liked was for the Herries to be gracious and condescending to families that were worthy of graciousness. The Southeys, she thought, were really worthy. Then Francis was happy here; he could here indulge his ridiculous passion for literature; and, although she only cared as to whether he were happy or no because when he was unhappy his sulkiness made her a little uncomfortable, yet, in warm weather like this, she preferred that everyone should pass a pleasant hour.

And lastly there was that little pushing nonentity Judith, who had been this very day told her place and at whom therefore it was agreeable, once and again, to look.

All in all, Jennifer that afternoon was very comfortable at the Southeys'. There would come a day when, looking back, she saw that warm, quiet afternoon as the beginning of all her trouble.

Mrs. Southey was the conversational one; Mrs. Coleridge had a tendency to peevishness (which you could understand, Jennifer lazily pondered, if it were true that her husband was always away from her and was a slave to opium . . .)

'Are you partial to evening visiting?' Mrs. Southey inquired. 'I must confess that we are not. Mr. Southey has so much work in the evening and the roads are so often floated by the rain. Not that I think this is a rainy district in reality. It is only that it seems very hard when it does come down. Does it not rain hard sometimes, Mr. Herries? I have never seen such hard rain anywhere.'

Mr. Southey, who was offering cake and bread and butter with a graciousness that almost demanded the accompaniment of music, answered with gravity: 'It is the rainy hours that give us the opportunity for all our reading. Is it not so, Edith? Or rather, in my little girl's case, the writing out of charades and riddles into our book. Come now, Edith. Confess. How many charades have you copied in to-day?'

'None at all, Papa. I have been in the town with Mama.'

What Judith liked in him, she thought, was the warmth of his affections. As he spoke to his daughter his eyes looked on her as though he would surrender the world for her sake. And, as she knew, there was his boy Herbert whom he loved even more dearly.

'That is what my friend Wordsworth will never do. Copy a charade for a lady. No, he bows and regards her sternly and slips out of door and takes a walk. Are you acquainted with Wordsworth, Mrs. Herries? The greatest man alive in England to-day. Yes, indeed, the greatest man in England, as the world will see one of these times. There has been a young man in Keswick this last winter, a Mr. Shelley, with his wife. A most unusual young man. I have told him that when he is as old as I am he will grant the truth of my prophecy about Wordsworth. He, too, wishes to be a poet. We are all poets these days, Mrs. Herries. . . . Well, he is an unusual young man. Just what I was myself in '94. What it was hard for him to understand was that you may have Five Thousand Pounds a year and yet be a good man; I fancy that there are many young men like him to-day. The Revolution in France is responsible, you know. But I set him upon a course of Berkeley. That should do him good. He does not realise as yet that a man must put a bound upon his desires and work within them. . . . Dear, dear, how sententious I am becoming! Pray, Mrs. Herries, another of Mrs. Southey's tea-cakes. They are quite famous in the neighbourhood, you know. John Wilson declares there are none like them even in Scotland, which is the land of tea-cakes.'

'Yes,' thought Judith. 'But will Francis be on my side? He must not know. He SHALL not know unless Jennifer herself tells him. And I believe that she will not.'

She had a horrible sense that the battle now would be underground, that no one henceforth would tell anyone anything, and that was so against her own character that it was as though she must twist her whole soul to conform to it.

'For my part,' Mrs. Coleridge was saying, 'I would never encourage anyone to marry. There can be so many blunders in matrimony. Although, to be sure, young people must marry. 'Tis only natural for them.'

It was now that Judith saw enter the room a very extraordinary being. This was a boy of some fifteen or sixteen years of age; he had a small restless body dressed in clothes too young for it, the short blue cloth jacket, the white trousers and open frilled shirt of boys junior to him. Dark hair strayed untidily over his forehead, but his eyes were the strangest part of him, burning with intelligence and yet at the same time lost, as he gazed about the room, in a kind of abstract wonder. He saw them all seated about the tea-table and smiled, came towards them, stared at Jennifer as though he were mesmerised, then, pulling himself back with a jerk, nodded, still smiling, and stepped away to the farther part of the room.

'Nay, Hartley,' said Mrs. Coleridge, 'you must wish Mr. and Mrs. Herries good-day.'

He came back to them with an odd stepping dancing movement as though he scarcely touched the floor. Then he stood there, shook hands, seemed as though at any moment he would break into laughter. What was amusing him? It was to Judith exactly as though he had sprung through the wall, coming from another world. He was no resident in this one. All his real life was elsewhere, and as she watched him she became restless. She wanted to get up and run away from all of them--to Watendlath, maybe, find the old house, sit with the Ritsons by the great hearth and hear the lambs bleating beyond the window; then to pass into that other room and to stand watching that staircase, to see again that old man with the white beard as he turned to the stair. Georges would come in, wait beside her as he often did, take her and lift her, pressing her backwards against his breast. Oh, after all these years, after all these years . . . Was she never to be rid of it? If the battle were joined now between Jennifer and herself, it was also joined between the one world and the other. It was almost as though Georges were beside her, fighting Jennifer.

All this disturbance had come from that strange boy there, moving away again, flitting now here, now there, regarding no one and regarding everyone, humming (she fancied, although she could not be sure) some tune to himself. They had all moved away from the tea-table and so she found herself encountering Hartley. He was standing on one foot, one ankle curled around another, and staring at Jennifer. He greeted Judith as though he had known her all her life. Children often did so because she was small and independent.

'That is the most beautiful lady, ma'am, I have ever seen,' he said.

Jennifer was being shown books and manuscripts now by Mr. Southey.

'Yes,' said Judith. 'You are Mrs. Coleridge's boy?'

'Yes, ma'am; there are Derwent and Sara and I. I go to a school at Ambleside. Mr. Dawes is the Master.'

'And what do you learn there?'

(It was the strangest thing, as though behind this outward talk they were conducting a quite different conversation. As though he said to her: 'I have just been with Georges and he told me . . .' It was the boy's air of being not yet awake, of suffering under some enchantment.)

His eyes were never still, nor his feet. He looked at her with the most engaging friendliness.

'Oh, they try their best to teach me, but I cannot learn any of the ordinary things. I shall dream of that lady for weeks and write stories about her. She shall be the Queen of Ejuxria.'

'Where?'

'Ejuxria. It is a country that I discovered many years back. She shall be the next Queen. Oh, ma'am, what a grand Queen she will make.'

Oh yes, she will, and her servants will go spying in the drawers of her Ladies-in-Waiting, reading their letters, undoing the faded ribbons . . .

'Do you like to be here?' she asked him.

'I like to be everywhere. It is all the same, for if a place is ugly one can make one's own picture of it, can one not, ma'am?'

How odd it was to see this small child, with his restless, unexpected gestures (so that he would crack his fingers or move three steps on one foot as though he were playing hop-scotch, or swing his little arms above his head), a child like none other that she had ever seen, and feel that she had so much in common with him. She felt no awkwardness. He understood her absolutely. His smile was the most bewitching part of him; it embraced and included her in his own delight.

'And what will you be when you grow up?' she asked him.

'I shall be nothing,' he answered, twirling round on one foot. 'I shall never grow up, I should think. I cannot learn the things that help one to grow up, and I know such a number of things that one must not mention. I have a secret name for everything. What is your name, ma'am?'

'Judith--Judith Paris.'

'Judith--I shall call you Florindascantinopolis. One day I will show you where Ejuxria is.' Then he added quietly: 'And now I must go and do my Greek lesson. And then we are going to play cricket--when the others come back from the Lake.'

Yes, they were going. Farewells were being said. Good-bye, Good-bye. . . How warm it is! Is it not warm!

'Yes, the laurels are in great profusion here--but the kitchen-garden is not really too extensive. So beautiful at Uldale! So fine a view of the Scotch Hills. . . But certainly we will come . . . very much obliged . . . too kind of you . . . Good-bye. Good-bye.'

So they rode home.

'Most agreeable people,' Jennifer said. 'When you are in London, Judith, you must read Mr. Southey's poems. They are all the thing in London.'

'London!' Francis cried. 'London! But Judith is not going to London.'

'No. I am not,' said Judith.

The two women looked at one another. Upon Jennifer's fine smooth white brow a small, a very small frown appeared, the first, Judith thought, that she had ever seen there.

'Of course not,' said Jennifer. 'But we cannot expect Judith never to wish to leave Uldale.'

'I am very happy at Uldale,' Judith said, smiling at Francis. 'You are so very good to me.'

But afterwards when Jennifer had gone upstairs, slowly, majestically, like a green and white swan floating upwards, to take off her bonnet, Judith had a desperate, almost choking need of reassurance. She caught Francis by the broad lapels of his coat. He paused astonished. He was always shy of demonstrations, she knew. She looked up into his face and he saw that her eyes were filled with tears.

'Francis, you do want me here, do you not?'

'Want you!' He put his thin firm hand on her small one. 'Why, I will never let you go!'

She nodded and said in a low voice: 'I am glad. I wished you to tell me so.'

He added kindly, holding her hand more closely in his: 'You have altered everything here. The servants, the children all love you. And the best of it is Jennifer has grown so attached. I have never known her trust anyone so before. She relies on you completely. I cannot thank you sufficiently.'

'I am glad,' said Judith, moving towards the stairs, 'that you are pleased.'

GONE TO EARTH

On a lovely October afternoon a post-chaise drew up outside Fell House and from it stepped a little short man in a brown hat.

He wore a dark brown 'carrick' with many capes, breeches of a light grey and very smart and shining top-boots. He was something of a dandy. He opened the gates, walked up the tiled path and pulled the bell-rope. He walked with a slight limp.

There was complete stillness round him. The thick, gold leaves of the trees in the garden, the little heads of amber chrysanthemums, never stirred in the blue air. Only the pigeons rustled in a flock above the pigeon-house at the sound of the bell, then settled again.

While he waited he sniffed the sharp beauty of the autumn weather and savoured the great spaces surrounding him on all sides. The edges of the hills were clear as though they had been cut out of paper. He could hear the sheep cropping on the moor beyond the garden wall.

A manservant opened the door and he inquired for Mrs. Paris. He was shown into the hall bathed in sun, then after a pause into the parlour, where he stood holding his hat and looking anxiously at the door.

A moment later it opened and Judith stood astonished. Then she ran forward, holding out both her hands.

'Warren!' she cried.

He laughed and was so glad to see her that his little grey eyes, bright and restless like a bird's, twinkled with pleasure. He had not seen her for four years.

'You are not changed in the least,' he said, holding both her hands in his.

'Why, of course not,' she said, leading him to the sofa. His limp made her seem protective towards him. 'And why should I be?'

'I have thought at times,' he said, looking at her very closely, 'from your letters, that you were.'

'In which way?'

'Oh, more serious, more grave.'

'I am a most serious person,' she said. 'You have never granted me that sufficiently.'

She was enchanted to see him. He was exactly what she was needing, an easy, good friend who cared for her, who was outside all the increasing perplexities and complications of this house and her position in it.

'But why are you here? And where have you come from?'

'I have been in Keswick a week.'

'In Keswick a week and only just come!'

'I had some business there and I would not come to see you until it was concluded.'

'But why not?'

'Because it concerns you.'

'Concerns me?'

'Yes. Wait an instant until I have seen you. I have been looking forward so impatiently to this moment.'

He was holding her hand a little harder than she wished. Very gently she withdrew it. He must be her friend, nothing more. But her FRIEND! She had never in her life wanted a friend so badly as she did just now.

His face was very charming, ugly because the nose was too large and the mouth too small, but eyes and mouth both were wrinkled and lined with kindliness and humour. His looks had also that sense of strain common to everyone who has had a life of pain and ill-health. But he did not appear a weakling. His body was broad and sturdy, and he was alert and active save for his limp. He was now forty-three years of age.

'Well, what is your great news? I can tell that you are bursting with it.'

'Yes. You may not care for it when you hear it.'

She was quickly apprehensive; recent events had made her so.

'I had thought that you might have got wind of it.'

She suddenly knew. Of course! he was to be married! She was disappointed.

'I know--you are to be married!'

He looked straight into her eyes, so that she dropped them.

'No . . . not yet,' he answered quietly. 'Nothing like that. Will has bought Westaways and I am to be manager of the estate.'

She drew back, erect with amazement.

'What!'

'Yes; Will has bought Westaways. The purchase was concluded last evening.'

Westaways was the house that old Pomfret, Raiseley's father and David Herries' uncle, Francis' and Will's great-uncle, had had built for him between Keswick and

Crosthwaite Church. It was called Westaways because it was one of the best examples of the work of an old crazy genius of an architect who, a hundred years ago, had lived in Keswick. It had been built for Pomfret and his wife at great expense and it was a beautiful house. When Raiseley had moved with his wife, Mary, to London, he had sold the house to a Colonel Grant, who, however, had infrequently resided there. Six months earlier Colonel Grant had died in Spain and there had been much local speculation as to its next owner.

Will had bought Westaways! Will was coming here to live, eight miles from his brother with whom he was not on speaking terms! Will was coming back to Keswick. Will with his money and pride and scorn of everything outside London! Will . . . !

'Oh no, no!' she broke out. 'It is impossible! Westaways and Will! Will and Keswick!'

'I know. But it is so. I have concluded the purchase myself.'

'And he is to live here?'

'He will come up occasionally. I fancy that Christabel and Walter will be here more frequently. She has not been well of late. Young Walter loves the country. He is mad on horses.'

'How old is Walter now?'

'Twenty-one. He was born in 'Ninety-two. He will make as good a business man as his father. But different. He loves power even more than Will. I never saw a young man so arrogant. He must have his own way in everything.'

'But I cannot believe it. It is incredible. Does he mean to be reconciled with Francis? He will not find it so easy.'

'No. I am afraid not. He is very bitter against Francis, and young Walter carries on the feud.'

'Then--' Judith waited. Suddenly she cried: 'Oh, he is coming here to show off! To triumph over Uldale! I see it all. Oh! it is shameful, shameful! With his money he thinks that he will humiliate Francis!'

'Remember,' Warren said, 'Francis married Jennifer.'

Judith could not grasp it. The change in everything that it would make, the unpleasantness, the rivalries, jealousies, personalities! The difficulties for herself, a friend of Will's and Christabel's as she was. She could not cut herself off from poor Christabel. That would be a disloyalty that no one would command in her . . . but how otherwise was her life with Francis and Jennifer to be possible, difficult as it was already?

In her perplexities she burst out: 'Warren, you should not have taken this. It is going to lead to nothing but hatred and ill- feeling--'

He nodded his head.

'Perhaps I should not. I hesitated, I will confess, but there was one thing that decided me.'

She said nothing. He went on.

'That you were here.'

'Oh no, Warren, please--'

He persisted.

'No, you have to hear me. I came to say this. From now we shall be living near to one another, and I do not care what you or any other may think. For four years I have tried to conquer my love for you, but it will not die. No, listen . . . listen . . . please do not send me away! No, Judith, please--please!'

She had risen and stood there looking at him: 'Warren, it is quite useless. You know that it is. We settled that four years ago. We were to be friends. You promised it.'

'I know, I know,' he answered. 'And so I intended it to be. But I cannot command it, try as I may. It is the last of my life. I shall have no more. My life has been always broken, everything has failed in it. This too will fail. I see that it must. But I am compelled to tell you.'

As she looked at him she longed to be kind to him, to give him anything that he wanted. What she had always desired, what she would always desire, was to give people what they wanted. And for seventeen years now no one had wanted anything very much. At Grosset it had been a carpet brushed, a window mended, a consoling word to Maria, a humorous word to Carey, and here it had been comfort for Francis, who after all was not comforted.

As she looked at Warren whom she liked so greatly, who was so courageous and bore pain without flinching, who never made complaint, she longed to give him anything. But how could she? She did not love him. He wanted passion, and she had no passion left for anyone in the world. And then it was absurd; she was thirty-nine.

'Dear Warren,' she said gently. 'I care for you very greatly. With Francis here you are the best friend I have. But love--love of the sort that you mean, I have none for anyone. It is true although it may sound fantastic, but I love Georges after all these years as dearly as I did when he was alive. Is that false, a sentimentality? I think not. Or, if so, I am myself deceived. And then I am so old. I am near forty.'

He got up and stood beside her, but did not touch her.

'Yes, I know everything. Nothing has altered since we talked at Grosset. You are not old to me. Besides, I am not myself young. There is nothing to do--I did not ask you to do anything. But I could not come here to live and not show you that there is no change in my feeling. I shall not do anything but what you would wish.'

He kissed her hand, gave a little bow, and limped away out of the room. She heard the carriage rattle off down the road.

The light was failing, and the little room was shadowed with yellow dusk. She stood there, her hand on the lid of the spinet, looking at the dim garden and the white road beyond it. Her head whirled. Will coming to Keswick! Will only eight miles away! Will and his family hanging over Uldale and flicking Francis' sensitiveness, Jennifer's pride, with every hour that passed! Oh, but it was impossible! The situation was impossible!

The door opened, and Jennifer came in.

'Who was that who was here?' she asked. She was wearing a dress of deep crimson that fitted very close to her body. She walked wearily. During the last months Judith had seen that something was distressing her, something that had nothing to do with her comfort. A curious perception of life was slowly, slowly waking in her. One could see it tremble in her like a faint flutter in a white sky before dawn. Her battle with Judith continued, but this was not the cause of her disturbance. It was from some other direction.

'That was Warren Forster.'

'Warren Forster? Why did he not stay?'

'He had a piece of news--' Judith hesitated. This same news was going to shake Jennifer's placid laziness as nothing else could do. Judith longed to see that shaken; in part Judith hated Jennifer as she had never hated anyone before. But, beyond that, there was something further. Jennifer's anger would include Francis' discomfort. They were all included in this.

'Well,' Jennifer said slowly. 'Cautious little Judith. You ARE cautious, are you not? With your own plans and purposes--'

She always, now, when the two of them were alone, tried any kind of irritation that seemed to her clever, but like all unimaginative women she could only think of the taunts and teasings that would goad herself if someone applied them. Quite different ones would be needed for Judith.

'No, I am not cautious!' Judith answered, smiling. 'But this is rather astonishing news that Warren brought. Prepare yourself for a shock.'

Jennifer, who was standing, drawn to her full height, looking out of window, had her mind only half on Judith's words. She was watching or waiting or listening. . . .

'Well, my dear? What is your great news?'

'Will has bought Westaways at Crosthwaite and is coming to reside there with Christabel and the family.'

Judith had her reward. Jennifer turned; her eyes for once were wide and awake, her beautiful mouth open, her whole body stung to attention. 'What? What do you say?'

'It is true. Warren has just completed the purchase. He is to be Will's bailiff.'

At that same moment Francis came in. He had been riding and looked immensely handsome in his many-caped coat. His face was splendid now, very sharp and set, thinner than it had ever been; his whole body was drawn fine and alert.

'Francis? Do you hear? It is impossible, fantastic. Oh, no . . . he cannot . . . he would not dare. No, no. There must be a mistake.'

It was astonishing enough to see Jennifer pacing the room, her head up, waving her arms, in a flurry of agitation.

'Judith, what is it? What's amiss?'

'Only that Warren Forster has been here and has told me that Will has bought Westaways and is to come there with Christabel.'

'Will! Bought Westaways!'

'Yes.'

Jennifer turned sharply upon Judith.

'You knew of this. You had heard of this already. You knew this was coming.'

She was so frantically disturbed that for once she forgot the caution that she always kept before Francis.

He at once turned to her. 'Jennifer! Certainly Judith did not know--' He stared at her as though he were seeing something new.

'Well, then,' she cried, tossing up her head and moving towards the door, 'it is at least just what Judith would have. Her dear friends, Will and Christabel, next door. No one can wonder at her pleasure.'

Before she went, her voice shaking with rage, she said to Francis: 'You have brought me to this--to be humiliated before that City merchant and his chicken-faced wife, but I shall not sit under it patiently, you shall see.'

When she was gone he put his arm around Judith and drew her down in front of the fire.

'You are sure of this?'

'Quite sure.'

'Warren himself came to tell you?'

'Yes.'

'And of course you had not an idea of it?'

'Why, no--of course not.'

He sighed deeply, leaning his head on his hand, looking into the fire. He was still wearing his heavy coat. She slipped it off his shoulders.

At last he said: 'Will is doing it only to humiliate me. He could have no other purpose.'

She tried to reassure him. 'No. Why should you take it so? After all this is his home. He lived here all his childhood. He must care for it. He will come to make friends.'

Francis struck his knee with his hand, his favourite gesture when he was excited.

'Never, never. He hates me and Jennifer too. And besides--if he wished to be friends I would not agree. He has insulted Jennifer in every way, and now it only needs this--'

She said what she could, but what was there to say? It was quite true. She knew that there was only one reason why Will had bought Westaways.

Then quite suddenly Francis asked her a surprising question. Dropping his voice a little he said:

'Judith, has Fernyhirst been here this afternoon?'

'No. Why?'

'Oh, for no reason. I wondered. He seems to ride this way frequently.' After another pause he asked her: 'Why did Jennifer speak to you like that?'

'Speak to me?'

'Yes, in that manner--unfriendly, angry. Is she offended with you?'

'Sometimes a little.'

'I have thought lately--'

After a while he said: 'Everything is turning wrongly. I feel as though some great misfortune were coming.'

She must get away. That, when she awoke the next morning, was her first and most dominating impulse. This was no new passion for escape. It had been constant with her all her life long. She was for ever wanting to escape--but never in the end escaping! That might be the just epitaph on her tomb were she ever to have one! Now she was going to escape almost exactly as she had escaped to Tom Gauntry's out of the window all those years ago after David Herries had beaten her. Only now she would not escape out of the window!

No one in the house seemed astir. It was as still as the lovely October morning around and above it. She left a note for Francis, laying it on his table in his study. She went round to the stables and brought out Peggy, who whinnied with delight at her approach.

Peggy was a small and very strong mare that Francis had given her, a brown mare with a most human expression, for she could look wicked and evil at the approach of Jennifer and most affectionate and engaging when Judith was near.

As she turned the corner at the bottom of the hill, leaving the house and the village behind her, her spirits rose with every clatter of Peggy's hoofs. She had told Francis that she would be a night away in Watendlath; but now she thought that it would be very pleasant were she to extend the one night into two. She wished to wipe Uldale and everyone in it out of her mind, yes, even Francis.

For two days she would not be the woman of Uldale, but someone quite different--the woman of Watendlath.

As her spirits rose she was like a girl of twenty instead of a woman of almost forty. Peggy, who was also, by mares' standard, a middle-aged female, became a very conscienceless child, pricking up her ears at sounds of birds and rustlings in the trees, although she knew that they meant nothing at all, and striking the stones of the road with an especially youthful gaiety because this piece of freedom was quite unexpected and the thing that most of all she enjoyed.

Judith was once more reminded with especial clearness of that evening when she had climbed out of window and ridden to Tom Gauntry's. It seemed only yesterday, and she remembered how lively she had been,

swearing in good strong Cumberland at the men in the road. It was as though nothing of any importance had occurred in her life between that ride and this, except Georges. And yet she was middle-aged, riding off like a girl. Something very ridiculous about that, but then she often found herself ridiculous! Women rode on horseback very much less than they had done when she was a child. They went now sedately in chaises or barouches; it was quite a common thing now to go to Edinburgh or even to London, whereas in her girlhood it had been quite an adventure.

And how formal and careful in these days the women of her age were! Mrs. Osmaston of Troutbeck (very far from sedate her old mother-in- law had been!), Mrs. Worcester from Threlkeld, Alice Sandon of Keswick and Mary Robertson of St. John's in the Vale, Mrs. Southey, Mrs. Coleridge--all stout, careful, sedate women who would never dream of riding on horseback from Uldale to Watendlath!

The matter with her, Judith, was that she was a trifle vulgar and common. It had always been so, always divided her from people. She had it, she supposed, from her mother. How enchanting it would be to see her mother appear suddenly now out from the hedge, with her hair about her face, her gay ragged clothes, her wild behaviour!

'I am your daughter,' Judith would say, jumping off Peggy, and then they would sit down in the hedge together and talk about everything. Judith would show her the silver chain that Francis had sent her; she always wore this under her clothes.

'Come away with me,' her mother would say. And away at once they would go for ever! No question of a real escape then!

She had never been a proper lady; even Francis, she suspected, found it so. That was why she had been so easily friends with people like Georges and old Tom Gauntry, Emma Furze, Charlie Watson, who were not ladies and gentlemen either. If only she had looked a little different!--here Judith, in spite of herself, sighed. To be so small, to have such unimportant features--and now she was a little stouter and her hair had lost some of its lustre.

She could not understand how Warren Forster could be in love with her! Nobody had ever been in love with her for her looks; Georges had only come to love her through propinquity. But that was her greatest triumph, the triumph of her life!

But to return to the vulgarity of her nature, that was the reason, no doubt, of her struggle with Jennifer. Jennifer detested anyone who was not a lady. She had hoped that Judith was a lady, and then, when she found that she was not . . .

Well, Judith could not help it. She was not to worry her head on this beautiful morning about Jennifer. She bore Jennifer no kind of malice--only why was she, Judith, in that house at all? Some part of her was always dragging her back into Herries affairs. She did not want to go back. How splendid it would be if she could stay in Watendlath for ever--then her real life would begin!

She would not go through the town, but took the bridle-path at the back of it, along the lanes under Skiddaw until at last she joined the path that led up to the stream above Lodore.

Here at a clearing between the trees she was compelled to stop Peggy and watch, for a moment, the storm that struck the Lake. It had been, when she left Uldale, a perfect October morning, without one cloud to mar the pale delicate blue. But, with the dramatic splendour that makes these skies the most wonderful in the world, a rolling black cloud, like a great funnel of smoke, had rushed over from the sea, pouring over Cat Bells and Robinson like the issue of a conflagration. The Lake was yet blue, the hills still gold with their burnished bracken. But this cloud hurried with the gait of a drunken man. It had been a funnel of smoke, but now, even as Judith watched, it swung outwards as that same drunken man might wave his cloak in a gesture of defiance. Then it spread with ferocity, eating up the sky, frothing at its edge in spumes of grey vapour, its black heart catching a purple light, the stain of blackberries.

It ate the sun. The Lake shivered and fell into a trembling agitation of tones and circles; the hills, that had been so bright, raised their heads; they seemed before Judith's eyes to increase their stature, and shadowed gulfs of purple rent their sides. Around her still the bracken was gold, the sun beat upon her face. Then with a quick whirr of wind the raindrops fell. The woods sighed. Where, only a moment before, there had been gentle stillness, there was now a sibilation like the whisper of a thousand gossips.

Soon the rain was falling as though a huge bowl had been opened over her head, but already, above Robinson, a thin line of gold cut the black wedge; light, mysterious and lonely, fell on one of the small islands and lit it with an unearthly glow. The black cloud began to break.

This moment's storm seemed to mark her passage from one world into another. As she moved on up to the road above Lodore, she felt that all her other life was closed to her, and she was so happy that it was absurd to think that she had ever been otherwise.

It seemed a moment later that she was in the Ritsons' kitchen. What a welcome she had! She had been to Watendlath three times in the last two years, but only for very short visits. She had not slept a night there, and, on one occasion, Francis had been with her. Now she WAS to sleep a night there, maybe two, and she was quite alone. With all Cumbrians, when, after long years, much silent watchfulness and infinite caution, they decide that you may be trusted, the fidelity and affection is all the more fervent because of the earlier testing. But Judith was quite unique in the lives of the people of Watendlath. Her appearance, her history,

her marriage with its extraordinary end, her long years with the 'Grand Folk' down South, her character with its odd mixture of fiery temper and great patience, of humour and seriousness, of youth and old wisdom, half a lady, half anything but a lady, her character honoured them by being both so strange and yet so ordinary. In a way they took her quite for granted now after all those years with them, but in another way they never took her for granted. They were never sure what she would do next. And, in addition to all these things, most of them loved her (there are always grumblers everywhere who do not love anybody) because she made them laugh, because she washed dishes and scrubbed floors, because she was interested in everybody and everything, because she could talk the broadest Cumberland and often did, because she knew as much about sheep as anyone, because she could lose her temper with a man like any good woman, because her rascal of a husband (they had always hated Georges) neglected her, because she continued to be fond of him long after he was dead, because she had no pride and someone in one class was the same to her as someone in another, because she was shocked at nothing that they did, whether they were dirty, mean, lecherous, drunken, cruel, spiteful (and at times as with all other of God's creatures they were one or another of these things), because she was a plain-looking little woman but also unusual, so that you always looked at her twice--but chiefly they loved her because they trusted her, which, with a Cumbrian, is first and last the principal thing. She kept her word; her heart was warm; she was not 'stuck on herself'.

Old Man Ritson had died two years back, his daughter-in-law last year; now Tom Ritson and Alice shared the farm. Tom had married a girl from Cockermouth, a simple little woman who was a good cook, and Alice had married young Roger Perry of Thunder, who was so thick through, broad across and short of leg, that he resembled the small stone wall above the Tarn. He had a round red freckled face and was a very silent man. However, he liked Tom Ritson, loved Alice, had three small boys who rolled about the kitchen floor like little ninepins and was excellent with cattle and sheep. The Ritsons were now a very happy household.

They all rushed at Judith, even the three small Perry boys, who had not the least notion as to who she was, but, like puppies, felt that she was part of a good and friendly world. Alice was perhaps the best pleased of them all. She had an almost reverential love for Judith. Although now a quiet pale-faced woman who went about her work with little comment, she saw further into character than did the others. She understood a little of what Judith's feeling for Georges had been; he had not been for her merely the foreign rogue and rascal that the others had thought him.

As Judith sat down beside the huge open fireplace, realising with deep pleasure that all the busy life of the kitchen was going on around her just as though she were not there, the men stumping in and out, the women in their clogs clattering about, baking, working at the butter, going after the chickens, shooing geese out of the doorway, looking into the sunny yard to see whether the men were coming for their dinner, Alice Perry quietly watched her. She was anxious for her, thinking of what none of the others would consider-- for Judith had not slept the night here since the night of her husband's death; more than that, she had never since then entered that room. Alice knew that now, this time, she would enter it.

Then, just as the men came clattering across the yard, hungry and thirsty, Charlie Watson rode in on his horse.

'It's Charlie!' Alice cried. 'Charlie Watson!'

Judith ran to the door and then out to meet him. He jumped off his horse and stood there, his legs spread, his mouth twisted in that strange, shy, almost angry smile so peculiarly his. It was as though he said: 'Well, it's a foolish thing to feel this pleasure and one is an idiot to set one's affections on anything but a sheep-- still, I can't help myself.'

It was a year and a half since she had last seen him. He had stoutened, but otherwise was little changed from the man she had met on the road from Rosthwaite seventeen years ago. His skin was as clear, his teeth as white, his colour as ruddy, his body as strong--and his tongue as silent.

'Aye. 'Tis good to see ye. Lookin' fine.'

Then they walked into the kitchen together.

While they were all eating, Charlie sitting among the farm-hands and with one small Perry on his broad knee, she watched him with exceeding pleasure. She knew from all that she had heard in the last year that he was growing to be a very important person, not only in that neighbourhood but beyond, as far as Ravenglass on one side and Mardale on the other. One thing for which he was becoming famous was his fighting the cause of the farmers against the cattle- dealers. In those days, when there were no railways and few newspapers, cattle-dealers did much as they pleased, naming their own prices and seeing that they got what they demanded.

He was already beginning to buy cattle himself at fair prices, and send them to Liverpool. At present only in a small way; it was, later on, to become a famous thing. Then he was a great arbitrator in all local disputes. His scrupulous fairness, his evenness of judgement, made him ideal for the settling of boundaries, squabbles about sheep and cattle, even domestic troubles. He was himself growing wealthy, but lived always in the simplest fashion on his farm. Although he was older now he was still a great wrestler and player at any and every game. She had heard also that he refused to marry, laughing at every suggestion. Many liked him but he had no intimates; he seemed to prefer to be alone. He liked her, she knew, but she could not flatter

herself that she knew him. She was even at times afraid of him.

But now as she sat there watching the October afternoon fall behind the kitchen windows, hearing all the sounds that she loved, sheep slipping like a flock of anxious old women up the path, water being drawn from the well, the soft crooning song of little Mrs. Perry as she rolled the dough on the long kitchen table, the screeching of the turkeys on the field above the farm, her own fear gathered about her. Because she knew that she was soon to do that of which she was most in the world afraid. The first time, after coming up from the South, that she had ridden over, she had intended to force her will, but Francis had been with her and that had been her excuse. The second time Alice Perry had been sick, and that, she told herself, had been her excuse. But to-day there was nothing to prevent her.

Her pale face grew weary and strained. Her hands were clenched on her lap. She answered Mrs. Perry's chatter without an idea of what she was saying.

Then she nodded her head as though something spoke to her, commanding, and she submitted. She got up and went out into the yard. Watson stood there speaking to Perry. She nodded to him, and he came across to her.

'Charlie, will you come with me?'

He seemed to know at once what she meant and walked off with her without another word.

The distance was nothing, but at the door she hesitated.

'I have never been inside--since it happened.'

Gently he put his hand through her arm.

'Come in,' he said.

She felt as though she were leaving everything living behind her. The air was suffused with a purple dusk, and she turned back to see the Tarn one blaze of fierce white light. The hills seemed gigantic. She heard, exactly as though she were leaving them all for ever, all the sounds of life, the animals, the human voices, the running water; then they went in together.

The room that had once been her sitting-room was used now for lumber, and one end of it was piled with sacks. An old kitchen table, rickety on three legs, was in the middle of the room and on it stood a large swinging mirror whose glass was cracked. The glass reflected the staircase. Some hens were rooting about on the floor. The place was dusky, but everything was as clear to her as though flooded with sunlight. And everything had happened yesterday, that night, only a few hours ago.

'Old Mr. Stane stood there in front of the fire. Suddenly Georges went up, as close as to touch him, and cried out: "I killed your son! I hated him! I killed him, I tell you, and you can do what you like." Then he went up the staircase and the old man ran after him and caught him and threw him down. Then he ran down the stairs again and went out. I saw that Georges was dying. There was nothing to be done--nothing at all. But before he died he caught my hand and he told me he loved me. He died at once. There was nothing I could do. No one could have helped. It was too late.'

'Aye,' said Charlie. 'It must have been terrible for you.'

She began to cry, hiding her head in his coat, holding to him, and he put his arm round her. He stood looking over her into the cracked mirror.

At last she whispered, so faintly that he could scarcely hear her: 'This is my home. . . . I shall never have any other.'

She cried on, then went and sat upon the stairs, looking all round at everything, taking every piece of it into her so that she need never fear to come again. And he stood gazing at her and knowing that she had altogether forgotten him.

They stayed so long without moving that the hens grew bold and scratched in the dirt at their very feet.

GHOSTLY IDYLL

But, as everyone knows, just when Fate seems to have a fine bouncing climax in his hand he shakes his head, changes his mind (which is not nearly so settled a one as people seem to think) and puts the climax back into his pocket again.

It was so with Judith now. She came back from her two nights in Watendlath happier than she had been for many a year. She had slept in her old room again. Whether she had truly slept or no she could not say, but, without either sentiment or nonsense, it had seemed to her that Georges kept her company. Therefore she returned to Uldale in a state of great happiness. She settled down into all the Uldale affairs again as though she were for a moment pitching her tent there. Very soon she would be back at Watendlath. Nothing should keep her. But everything kept her. It was to be months, and then even years, before she saw Watendlath once more. Members of the Herries family never escape so easily as that.

Her time now at Uldale was difficult, and it was the difficulties that kept her. Feeling that she must stay, she did not dare go even for an hour to Watendlath lest it should keep her for ever and her duty be broken. The first difficulty was Jennifer. Strange! Can one be so secret a woman without being secret at all? For although Jennifer had now her mysterious preoccupation that caused her to twist her brows and bite her thumb, yet she was not really secret. She was wondering, Judith knew, whether to go further with Fernyhirst.

Judith suspected that Jennifer was moved, as a woman stirred by a man, for the first time in her life; that she was as uncomfortable, bewildered and disturbed as a child wakened up from a deep sleep by sunlight. She was finding one discomfort after another press in upon her. Always before she had been able to deal with discomfort. Now she could not. She had told Judith to depart, but she had not departed. She had tried to make Francis a convenient figure in her life and nothing more, but of late he had begun to frighten her. She had told Fernyhirst to cease to make love to her, and he had not ceased. She had told herself to be indifferent to him, but she was not indifferent. Even with Mrs. Ponder she was beginning to be uncomfortable, for Mrs. Ponder now was often insolent. Even with her children she was not comfortable, for they were growing and insisted on having lives and personalities of their own.

Because of all these unsettled discomforts Jennifer was at last beginning to live. Her eyes were no longer half-closed. She was often alert, as though she were listening for some sound.

One thing for which she was listening was the arrival of Will and Christabel at Westaways; but the months passed, one year closed and another year opened. Still they did not come.

Warren Forster, who was often at Uldale, although Jennifer disliked him and showed it, said that This, That and the Other prevented them. . . . They would come. . . . Surely they would come. . . . A pity. . . . He had endeavoured to persuade Will to alter his mind. Westaways was not the house for him. But Will was obstinate. He did not know why he was so obstinate.

Francis, however, knew; Francis was an altered man. Biting, sarcastic, silent, even with men of his own mind, like Southey, he appeared to have lost all his sweetness.

'He's gone sour,' said Fernyhirst to Jennifer, and he stretched his broad chest and pinched his strong neck with a smile of satisfaction. It was a long business, this siege, but she was the handsomest woman in the county and it was a fine occupation for a dull country life. It could have but one end to it. He was an extremely patient man, as his training of horses and dogs (for which, in the North, he was famous) showed.

Worst of all, Francis had now shut himself away from Judith. If he spoke his mind to her he must speak of Fernyhirst, and that he was resolved not to do. He was now entirely alone, even as his grandfather and namesake had been before him. He was going the same road.

It was on a winter morning towards the close of '14 that family history took a stealthy step forward. Young John Herries, aged now seven, was the cause. He was a very typical Herries child, square and strong like his grandfather, rather sensitive, but with a more plentiful allowance of humour and less sentiment about his father than David had had about his.

In fact at this time he had no sentiment about either his father or his mother. His mother he quite honestly disliked. He knew that she did not care for him. He hated to be embraced by her. In his father he was more truly interested; but this was a bad period for anyone to be interested in Francis. John saw him as a thin, severe, august figure moving about the place giving orders. He admired his father, but was happier when his father was not present. For Dorothy, his sister, he had a feeling of mixed contempt and protection. She cried a great deal, and she clung to Mrs. Ponder, whom he, John, without extenuation or limitation, detested. No, he thought very little of Dorothy.

His whole heart was given to Judith, and had been ever since she had gone to the Tarn with him to sail his boat. He was very tenacious of ideas and affections. He loved Judith because he trusted her, because she talked to him like a human being, because she did not mess him about with embraces, because she was always so clean and neat (he was already fastidious about these things), because she thought the things in which he was interested important, because she considered the things funny that he considered funny. He treated her as he would have treated another boy who was a friend of his (he had no boy friends). He never gave any sign that he was glad to see her. He would look at her, a little frown gathered between his eyebrows, and he would ask her opinion. When he was going to laugh, the laugh came first in his eyes, which would be twinkling with merriment while the rest of his face was quite grave. He liked to rub the flat of his hand up and down the side of his breeches. Another pleasure was to put on a sudden very deep bass voice which was supposed to be an imitation of Mrs. Ponder's.

'Boney's coming to eat you!' he would say out of his boots. It was her favourite threat, but instead of fearing he would chuckle with laughter.

He would walk up to Judith with great gravity and say, with his chin sunk into his neck so as to bring out his deep voice better: 'Boney's coming to eat you!'

It was John on this winter morning who made history. Judith had dressed and was ready for the day. She came out of her room on to the landing. On this landing the rooms of both Jennifer and Francis opened. Stairs led up to Mrs. Ponder's sacred chamber and attics; stairs led down to the main hall. Standing there for a moment before she descended, Judith thought of all that she had to do. She looked what at that instant she was, a very competent housewife, with keys at her waist, a green apron, and a spotless lace cap on her head. She had much to do: there was Mrs. Harper, there were the kitchen-maids, there was the dairy. Mrs. Birket and some London friends of hers were coming to supper and cards. . . . She heard then, from a large ancient cupboard that had stood for many a day in a corner under the stairway, strange sniffs, and then-- a most startling sneeze.

Opening the cupboard door she beheld an odd sight. Seated on the dusty floor was John, absorbed in the feeding of a large, and, it seemed, very greedy brown rabbit.

'Why, John--' she cried.

He jumped to his feet, catching the rabbit by its long ears. As always, in any situation, now or ever, he stood his ground, but he was very red in the face and his cheeks were marked with dust. The rabbit squirmed in terror.

'Oh, but, ma'am,' he said in his husky confidential voice, 'I was intending--'

She could see that he was really frightened. But why? She could not think that there was anything very terrible in feeding a rabbit. . . . But why a cupboard? Why this furtive secrecy? She asked him. He stepped out of the cupboard, holding the rabbit in his arms.

He dropped his voice so that it became even more husky.

'You see, ma'am, Mrs. Ponder had forbidden me to keep it. Yesterday. You see,' he dropped his voice yet lower, 'she has an exceptional distaste for rabbits. She ordered Jim to have it killed, and so I have been hiding it in this cupboard--'

'But why did you not tell your father?'

'Why, ma'am, he says that I must do as Mrs. Ponder orders. It is only,' he whispered, coming very near to her, 'for to-day. I have found a place in the field--' He broke off. She realised that he did not want her to know where the hiding-place was lest she should be inconvenienced by questions. She whispered back to him, smiling:

'My indulgence shall be given. I shall tell no one.'

Greatly relieved, he went back to the cupboard.

She remembered something in her room that she had forgotten, and, for a moment, was back there, opening and shutting a drawer. Before she had reached the door again she heard a clamour. A woman's voice, muffled as though she were endeavouring not to be overheard, but so passionate that it shook the air. Hastening out, she was horrified to see Mrs. Ponder, her face all black eyebrow, hurry across the floor and, with a vindictive gesture, fling open the window and throw the rabbit out. John gave a cry, then stood there, his face twisted with anguish. Not seeing Judith, Mrs. Ponder threw herself upon the boy and, in a convulsion of passion, dragged him by the hair towards the stairway. She moved so swiftly in her rage that she had knocked his knees against the lowest step before Judith could move. Then she was stopped by something else, for Francis had come out. Mrs. Ponder heard him and stayed. She let John go, and he, as though driven by a sort of wild fury, uttering little sobs, his eyes staring, ran past them all down the stairs.

'What is this?' Francis asked.

Judith had once heard him described by one of the ladies of the neighbourhood as 'a pleasant gentlemanlike man.' He had, she thought, never deserved the description less than at this moment. To speak in the terms of the author of The Italian, he was 'cold fury nobly seething.' Mrs. Ponder felt this, and for once in her courageous life was alarmed.

'Not at all, sir. Nothing, I mean. Master John has been disobedient.'

He moved towards her as though he would strike her. Judith remembered that she had once done the same. Mrs. Ponder appeared to have that effect on her critics.

He drew up and, looking at her as though she should, were he magician enough, change into a rat at his feet, said:

'You will leave this house within the morning.'

And she, recovering some of her confidence, answered, as once before she had answered Judith:

'That is for my mistress to say, sir.'

It happened then (for this landing was as public a place as that generally chosen in the theatre for intimate confidences) that Jennifer came from her room, looking very lovely in some loose garment of a rosy shade and a white cap with rosy ribbons covering her dark hair.

'Well, Ponder--' she said, and, seeing Francis and Judith, stopped.

'This woman,' Francis said, 'will leave the house to-day.'

Judith then saw Mrs. Ponder give Jennifer a very strange look.

Jennifer said: 'Why, what has she been doing?'

'She has been in a bestial temper and has dragged John by the hair.'

Mrs. Ponder folded her arms as much as to say: 'You have not the smallest chance of moving me.'

'And what has John been doing?' Jennifer asked.

'If you please, ma'am, he has been most disobedient. He had concealed a nasty filthy rabbit in the cupboard, and after my telling him that of all filthy animals and filled with diseases, and my doing all for the best, ma'am, as I always do--'

'She had thrown the rabbit,' Judith broke in, 'out of window and was beating John against the stair.'

It had been better, as usual, if she had not interfered.

Jennifer, looking only at Francis, said: 'Mrs. Ponder was in the right if John disobeyed her.'

'I have said what is to be done,' Francis answered, his face cold with disgust. 'The woman goes to-day.'

'I shall do what I think right,' Jennifer answered.

They looked at one another, a strange long look. His unspoken words were: 'She has the command of you. You do not dare to let her go.'

But he would have no scramble before servants.

At the top of the stairs he said again: 'She goes to-day,' and went down.

Mrs. Ponder began: 'I assure you, ma'am, I had no thought but for the best. I would always do my duty--'

But Jennifer returned without a word into her room.

This little scene, so swift and so impromptu, was to have a deep and lasting effect on all the persons concerned in it, but on the life of Judith most of all.

After it the house was as silent as a valley in the moon. The winter day was sharp and sunny. The hedge sparkled with crystal and the lawn was laced with silver frost. A very fat robin at the parlour window sang. He was the only live thing. Francis rode out. Jennifer stayed in her room.

Judith went about her work and felt very lonely. What would happen? Would Mrs. Ponder go? Whatever happened she had for a long time to come lost Francis, who would now keep more within himself than ever, and John, whose look of terror and anguish as he ran down the stairs she would never forget. Meanwhile the rabbit lay, with its back broken, on the stones below.
. . .

While she was in the storeroom, marking in a book the jams, jellies and preserves while Mrs. Harper, a small thin woman like an amiable radish, chattered along, she thought impatiently: 'I cannot endure this much longer. I can't stay in a house where nobody cares for me.' Although she was forty years of age she was as childish as that. But perhaps what she really meant was that she needed to be close to somebody, close in affection and sympathy. This house to- day was a prison.

So that when, an hour later, Warren Forster arrived on horseback, her reaction from that early morning scene was terrific. She had never before been so glad to see him. Had it not been for that early disturbance she would never have gone riding with him, and had she not gone riding with him everything in later Herries history would have been different.

As it was, she did not care. She was reckless that day, reckless through exasperation and a longing for someone who was not angry, was not hurt, was not deceitful.

Warren, his little figure so dapper on his large horse, was not angry nor hurt nor deceitful. He was enchanted to see Judith, who was kinder to him, more responsive to him, than she had ever been. The house was quite still. She looked around her and found nothing alive in it but the robin. The air was filled with distress and anger. So she gave the robin crumbs, took Peggy out of her stable and rode off with Warren.

Often, when afterwards she looked back upon this eventful day and tried to see how one step had so determinedly led to another, it seemed that it had all been planned. But it was not in reality so. Nothing was planned. They just rode into the cold and crystal air.

At first they talked lightly of general things: of how Napoleon had tumbled down at last, of the quarrels among the Allies at Vienna, and the clever man that Talleyrand was; that it looked as though France, Austria and England would soon be fighting Russia and Prussia; of Napoleon's exile on Elba, and whether he would be there for the remainder of his days. They talked of those things, but they did not really care any more than their descendants would care for similar figures and intrigues. Napoleon, Talleyrand, the Czar of Russia were as remote from them as they rode along the Cumberland lanes as figures on a Chinese screen. They talked about affairs in England: of the King and the Regent, and the high prices and the uncertainty of everything and everybody; of how the world was changing as it had never changed before; of how interesting it was to live in a time of transition, but also how unsettling; of how there were no great figures in the world any more, no great literature, although Mr. Wordsworth's poems were pleasant and Childe Harold had some fine writing (and was it true that Lord Byron was both so beautiful AND so wicked, Judith asked), just as their descendants afterwards would talk. Warren said that Will Herries said that trade was going soon to recover and that everyone would be wealthy again, that there would be wonderful new industries, and that everyone would soon be living in towns because the country was too dull.

'That would be a pity,' said Judith, looking about her at the grey hills, their tops scattered with snow like sifted sugar. 'There is nothing so beautiful as the country.'

'I think so also,' said Warren, looking at her. He was madly in love with her that day. He was never to know why his love for Judith was so much fiercer and more sharp than any other emotion of his life, his greatest happiness and his greatest distress.

It had been so from the first moment of his seeing her at Grosset, although that had not been a good occasion, for it had been a stormy wet afternoon and she had been standing in the hall rating a servant when he came in. Her voice had had a sharp and dominating note in it, as though she were telling all the world to go to Hades. The fire in the hall had been smoking, there were dogs all about the place and one of Maria Rockage's garments hanging up to dry. Judith had turned on him like a cross, exasperated child and had been anything but gracious. So perverse are men, and so beyond all rules is love, that he had liked her the better for her mood. He preferred, perhaps, women who were of the ruling kind. Then as he came to know her more truly he found that, although she wished to dominate, she could be led by her affections almost anywhere. She could not indeed be led to love him, but would do almost anything for him out of kindness.

He was a man of great courage, humour and spirit, and his pains, physical and other, had taught him patience. So he waited for a long time, and at last he had his reward.

They had no plan of direction, but they rode through Keswick (where Judith did a little shopping), then out, above the Lake, to the Grange Bridge and on into Borrowdale.

'My father lived here,' Judith said, 'all his life. They could not persuade him to move away. His house tumbled about his ears, but he died in it and I was born in it. Here,' she waved her whip to a broad bend of the little river, 'they drowned a witch. My father went before

them all and took her out of the water and carried her away.'

The trees, bare above the chattering river, had a rosy edge to them in the cold air. The top of Castle Crag played with little wreaths of mist that crowned its head with a thin light, behind which the black rocks gleamed. His hopes began to rise, he knew not why. She was so friendly to-day. There seemed to be a new current of intimacy running behind her words. He did not know that he was indebted to a rabbit for his happiness.

'Would you have an objection,' she asked, 'if we paid a visit to that old house of my father's where I was born? I have not for a long while visited it. There is only a shepherd there. It must be bare and deserted.'

They turned off the road and across the little bridge.

In the little graveyard near here Georges had been buried, and here her father and mother had died.

The house that stood behind a little courtyard, defended by a rough stone wall, seemed quite dead against the pale blue sky. It had been, Warren thought, two houses; on the right it was of some height, with latticed windows and a gabled roof. From this attempt at grandeur it fell away to a low rough place that had what seemed to be farm buildings attached to it.

But all was now in utter desolation. As they led their horses in through the gate, shabby and broken, their feet struck the rime from the stiffened grass. Birds rose in a whir of agitation from the thin stems of the bushes; a large white cat with malevolent eyes slunk across the fast disappearing stones. Yet it was a scene of great beauty. Rosthwaite Fell and Glaramara in further distance rose above the fields in purple grandeur. Water ran in silver skeins down the rocks, and its tumbling was the only sound.

Warren had got down from his horse to lead it in, and now, standing in front of the old door, he cried, 'Is anyone here?'

There was no answer. They heard some animal stamping in a byre close by. They pushed the door back and entered.

A musty odour of decay, straw, animal dung, met them, but they persevered and, climbing the stair, found themselves in a large room.

This, it appeared, was the place where the shepherd was at home. A sort of couch made from boxes, and a decayed chair that had great arms from which the stuffing protruded like a disease, had been arranged with cushions and a blanket before the wide stone fireplace. There were remains of a meal--a loaf, some cheese, a plate--on the table that was the only other piece of furniture there.

Judith stood looking about her. 'It is strange,' she said. 'It is as though I had lived here. I know where everything was. There are the marks on the wall yet where that picture hung. It was a picture of an old man of Elizabeth's time. It hangs in the house at Uldale now. When I was a small child he terrified me. Here they would sit, my father and mother, before the fire, and upstairs they died and I was born.'

'Ugh! It's cold,' said Warren, shivering. 'We will not stay.'

'We will make a fire,' Judith said. 'Why not? Perhaps we will bring their ghosts back with the warmth.'

He was eager to do anything that she asked. They climbed the rickety stairs, rotten now with holes, creaking at every step, into the upper storey. The rooms here were pitifully small, but had a more human air, for one of them was plainly used for sleeping by the shepherd and his wife.

'It was here I was born.' Judith stared about her. 'Uncle Tom has often told me. How he was riding through the snow and heard an infant crying. He came up here with all his dogs, and in the bed my mother lay dead, in a cradle myself, and on a chair the old woman asleep with drink. And in the next room my father dead. So he picked me up in his arms and rode off with me home.'

Warren would have wished to come close to her and put his arm around her. She looked so small and by herself. But he did not dare. In the next room they found a pile of logs. They carried some down and made a great fire in the open hearth.

They sat down near to it, close together, warming their hands. The house was filled with her father and mother. Georges seemed there too. Only dead people. And for that reason, because she could not get at the dead and her heart was so moved that she longed to be kind to the living, almost without knowing that she did it, she laid her hand on Warren's knee, and then, when she felt it throb in response, she did not care to take the hand away again.

It was the first demonstration that, unurged, she had ever made to him; after a little he, as though he were moving mountains or the heavens would fall, laid his hand on hers.

'The fire makes me sleepy--the fire and the cold air.' She took off her riding-hat and shook her red curls about her face. 'Warren,' she said, 'you look most solemn. Well, I should also feel solemn. Perhaps I do, but I have often noticed that whenever I feel most solemn I want to laugh.' She went on talking as though she would cover the emotion that she knew he was feeling. 'This house, deserted as it is, is better than Uldale just now. Everyone is at odds there, and I am weary of trying to make them better. I want a life of my own, Warren.'

'Come away with me, then,' he said.

'But that would be no life of my own. Since Uncle Tom carried me out of this place in his arms I have been for ever mixed with the lives of other people.'

'You can go to a nunnery,' he said, laughing. He came a little closer to her. The fire was burning with splendid energy and roaring up the chimney.

'No. I am mixed with other people because I want to be. I am not such a coxcomb as to suppose that I am inhuman. I am inquisitive; I must know just what their lives are, and then I must tell them what they ought to be. And yet I wish to be by myself. I am only happy in one place, and that is Watendlath.'

'Are you not happy now?'

'I shall soon be warm, and then, when I am, I will tell you whether I am happy.'

He put his arm around her; she did not move away. Why should she if it pleased him? And he was alive. His heart was beating against her breast. She was tired of anger and disappointment. Her heart ached to be kind.

She went on talking. At last he said (his hand was trembling under hers):

'Judith, I love you every day more. . . . What shall be done about it?'

In ordinary times she would have checked him, but now--what did it matter? Was she not too particular in guarding herself? After all, was she so important? She had only in all her life been important to one person, and that was to Georges, and even to him for only a little of a time. How much she was making of her life, considering herself this way and that way, when in reality she was nothing. The mother of no one, the lover of no one, scarcely the friend of anyone. . . . She was not pitying herself--rather laughing at herself--with a little interest and tenderness, because she knew herself better than she knew anyone else.

So she let him hold her hand, then tenderly kiss her cheek, then with great gentleness stroke her hair. The trembling of his body touched her infinitely. Warren, who had faced so many things with such courage, needed her now to help and befriend him.

'Oh, Warren!' She liked him close to her, the fire was very pleasant, and figures, friendly figures, seemed to be in the room. 'It is so long since Georges died. I wish I could let him go in peace. I shall not be a free woman until I can be friends with everyone and yet be independent. Does it make you happy to be sitting here, the two of us beside the fire?'

'Desperately happy.'

'I want you to be happy.'

Why not? Oh, in God's name why not? There was Reuben's bear, and the boy hanged on the gibbet, and Georges thrown down the stair, and John's rabbit. . . . Why not be kind while one may? So soon it is all over and nothing done, no kindness remembered, no indulgence or charity. She thought, looking into the fire and feeling perhaps the figures in the room gather more closely about her, that she had never been charitable enough. If this life had a purpose (which she gravely doubted), it was for us to learn charity. A dangerous lesson, because the more charitable we became the less free we became, and this desire for freedom was becoming with her a passion. But the bear danced in the

Square, the rope swung on the gibbet, Georges lay with his back broken, little Hartley Coleridge was a prisoner, the rabbit was flung out of window, Warren had a bad leg, and his wife had left him, and he loved HER, poor man--although why he loved her she couldn't conceive.

'I have never been happy until now,' he said, resting his head on her lap. It seemed as though Georges, and the child that she had never had, and maybe her mother and father whom she had never seen, were all represented in that little damaged body holding her as though she were its only hope.

She smiled, looking out above his head. Why should she be so proud of herself? Why should she not be kind? Why should she not give anything she could that would make him happy? She sighed, touched his cheek and then surrendered, giving him all he asked--

WILL HERRIES DINES AT WESTAWAYS

She knew early in February that she was to have a child. For some time she had been happy, and, when she was certain of this new circumstance, it was as though life beat up in her like a released fountain.

For years after Georges' death there had been no life, then slowly, slowly it had returned, always finding its source in Watendlath. Now she was going really to live again, and all she had to do was to fight for her freedom. That she had not yet secured, but she would secure it now that the child had come to help her.

She was beginning at last to understand something about life. A woman is made for the love and protection of someone or something else; this is the mainspring of her nature. But in order to employ this love and protection at its fullest she must be free of any bond that is simply a tyranny without love. All the women around Judith at this time were so bound--it would be generations before they would begin to be free--and Judith would have been held in the same way had it not been for the lives and natures of her father and mother whom she had never seen or known. The whole history of being a Herries is learning to be free.

She took things as they came. What was coming was her child. What was also coming was Will Herries to Westaways. What was also coming was some decisive crisis between Francis and Jennifer. And it seemed that all these things were arriving together.

Since the ride to Borrowdale, Forster had seen Judith less frequently. He was shy now and uncomfortable, for he had never realised so sharply that Judith did not and could not love him as at the moment of her surrender to him. He did not know that she was to have a child, but he did know that, on that day, she did not surrender to him but to her memories. She had begun by wishing to be kind to him, and then had recalled the voice and movements of a man who was dead. That hour had been filled with ghosts.

So, although he loved her with a fire that really ate into the very nerves of his small and ailing body, he came to visit her less often and, when he was with her, saw her as someone always just beyond reach.

She was resolved that he should not know about the child. It did not seem to her that it would be Forster's child at all, so filled had the ruined house been with others on that winter afternoon.

Passionately she wished that it should be born in Watendlath, in that room where Georges had died, but her practical mind saw beyond the sentiment of that desire. That her child should be born in Watendlath would involve too many others beside herself--the Ritsons, Charlie Watson, Jennifer, Francis. . . . She must go away, and the child must be born with only herself for its guardian. She did not know at present where she would go or what she would do.

There were more immediate necessities, for, in this same month, on a gusty evening of February 1815, Will Herries with his wife, his son and a vast deal of impedimenta arrived at Westaways.

On the morning after his arrival Judith and Francis had a talk.

Francis looked a man twenty years more than his real age. He was so thin that his facial bones, always prominent in the Herries fashion, gave shadows and lines to his cheeks and eyes. His dark, thick hair emphasised his pallor. He looked a man with his back to the wall. Judith knew that, besides his trouble with Jennifer, he was in great distress about the condition of the people around him. The long years of the French wars had brought hunger and unhappiness everywhere; in the agricultural parts of Cumberland and Westmorland, where life was largely self-supporting and where the narrow and remote valleys led to seclusion, the pinch was not so severe as in many parts of England, but in the last twenty years industrial life was beginning to make itself felt, a new phenomenon, and towns like Kendal, Whitehaven, Cockermouth knew something that was close to starvation.

He, who had been always on the side of the people against privilege, of the rebel, the underdog, found himself now a rich man with a fine house and a body of servants. He would like to give away all that he had, but he was not free--he had a wife, children, dependants. More than that he saw that this new growing England did not want his charity. He was held to be an aristocrat, and to be responsible for taxes, bread prices and all the other evils. Of his class he found no one in sympathy with his ideas. The squires and landholders round him thought that a sign of encouragement to a poor man meant that the poor man would rule, as he had been doing in France. The French example was before every eye. So Francis was once more alone, as all his life he had been. But he was not only alone--he was inarticulate. He had the great misfortune of seeing the justice of both sides. He, who had once proclaimed exultantly the fall of the Bastille, now feared any kind of revolution for his own country that he loved so dearly.

Until now there had been no riots in Cumberland, as in the Midlands and the South, but only a week or two ago rioters had burnt some ricks and stable-buildings of Osmaston's, and he himself had received several threatening anonymous letters.

If only, Judith thought, he would speak to me, say frankly all that was in his mind, as he used to do. But it was years now since he had been honest with her. Silence had grown upon him. He was shut up within himself.

But now to-day he began frankly enough.

'Judith,' he said at once, 'I want you not to avoid Will and Christabel because you are living here.'

That, unfortunately, produced a feeling of irritation in her--all in a moment when she had intended to be so kind and understanding. She was suddenly tired of the lot of them--Francis, Jennifer, Will, Christabel, all of them.

'What do you wish me to do, Francis?'

'Why . . . to go to Westaways . . . when you wish . . . as often as you prefer.'

'And Jennifer?'

He shook his head impatiently.

'What has that to do--' He broke off. 'I often think you hate Jennifer.'

She sat down, suddenly weary.

'Oh no--hate?--oh no, dear Francis. Perhaps I am a little tired. What would you say, Francis, if I went away altogether?'

'Went away!' His thin pale face was aghast. He put his hand up to his forehead in a movement of bewilderment.

'Oh no! You to desert us! It would be shameful!'

Then she was angry. There was the implied right here that had always irritated her in him, as though, if he decided that she was necessary for him, why, that was reason enough for anything. It was not selfishness but rather an obstinate preoccupation with his own ideas.

Her anger gave her the opportunity to say some things that had long been in her mind. She looked up at him, and part of her thought, 'Oh, poor Francis, how weary and despondent he looks!' But the other part thought, 'How insensitive he is! I have endured this long enough.'

'Listen, Francis. I am going to say one or two things. One is that I have been here for over five years and have been a failure. Yes--don't protest--it's true. I have been a failure with you. Do you know that you have not spoken out your heart to me for three years? No, not once. I have loved you all my life. You are the only friend I have beside Emma and Reuben, whom I never see nor hear of, and one other. But of late you have shown me no friendship. You have never thought of me at all, never inquired how I did nor how things went with me. You have been filled with your own troubles. I have been the housekeeper here. Good enough.

'Then I have failed because Jennifer hates me. Oh yes, she does! When I first came she was too languid to hate anyone. But now she is not languid any more and is perfectly capable of hatred. Do you know that when I had been here a year or so I discovered Mrs. Ponder searching my drawer for my private letters? No, you did not know. But I begged Jennifer that Mrs. Ponder should depart. Mrs. Ponder did not depart. Later, YOU ordered that Mrs. Ponder should depart--but Mrs. Ponder is still here. I have not failed with the children-- John loves me, I know, but even that has been an added aggravation to Jennifer. Yet, although for five years Jennifer and Mrs. Ponder have done all that could be done to make me miserable (and I am not happy, you know, when people near me dislike me), I have stayed because I love you and I love your children. Or no-- maybe there is too much sentiment in that. If I am strictly truthful, I have stayed in part because I like to make people do as I wish. I have stayed even because Jennifer has wished me to go. I have stayed, perhaps, because I would not be defeated by a fat snake like Mrs. Ponder.

'But you, dear Francis, have never given these things one thought. You have not asked yourself whether I were lonely or unhappy. In fact, I am almost frantic for my freedom. There is a place but a few miles from here where I could be happy for ever. But, although it is so near by, I do not seem to be able to reach it. My father, by all that I hear, was the same. But he was not a complacent female as I am.'

She smiled up at him then, feeling quite friendly again now that she had said her mind.

But he, in a voice of horrified disgust, said:

'Mrs. Ponder searched your private papers. You told Jennifer of it and yet Mrs. Ponder stayed?'

'Well, but YOU told Jennifer about the rabbit, and yet Mrs. Ponder stayed.'

She wanted then to rise and throw her arms around his neck, so terribly unhappy did he look.

'You are right,' he said at last. 'Dreadfully right. I have been most fearfully to blame.'

Then, of course, she repented of having said anything. She did not want to add to his distresses. What she DID want, however, was to be free of them all and to have her life to herself!

She went on quietly: 'You see, Francis, I am the only one in this house who is friendly with Will and Christabel. What complications will come now from my being here! I cannot abandon Christabel, who was so good to me in London. And of course I cannot abandon you! I think it shameful of Will to have come here, and so I shall tell him, but I shall be a shuttlecock between the two houses. I am nearly forty-one years of age, and that is too old for a shuttlecock!'

'You say you cannot abandon Christabel and you cannot abandon myself--but a moment ago you were implying that you wished to be free of all of us!'

'And so I do.' She shrugged her shoulders. 'And so I will. I am for ever promising myself. To-morrow--the day following . . .'

She had risen and, instinctively, they came together. He drew her to him and they exchanged a long embrace, the first of real intimacy for years.

'Judith,' he whispered, stroking her cheek, 'do not leave me, I beg you. I beg you. I am unhappy. No one understands--'

She thought of the child alive within her, and then she was so happy that she thought humorously, 'Was ever a woman in so many complications? But this is living--every moment has excitement.' At that instant she was so much a child that she could have sat down at the spinet and strummed any discordant noise. For she loved Francis to love her. Never mind if she could not be free just yet. Time for that! She LOVED Francis to love her! He had not for so long!

'Oh, Francis, I love you!' she murmured. What would he say if he knew that she was to have a child, she who was, he thought, so faithful to Georges' memory? Well, so she was. But Georges would be glad for her to have a child. Then she could not have Francis back again without at once wanting to manage him. She drew him down on to the sofa beside her, holding his hand. She wanted at once, without delay, to make him happy! Somehow to make him happy! Her eyes were so glowing with life and eagerness and vitality that she did not seem like a small, round, middle-aged female in a grey spencer, but rather she was the daughter of a gipsy, telling fortunes.

She held his hand lightly.

'Now listen, Francis. Here is what you must do--'

And at that moment Jennifer came in.

They were both silenced. They had nothing whatever to say. Jennifer, brilliantly attired, stood there and looked at them. She was dressed for going out.

Francis thought, 'She is going to meet Fernyhirst' and was at once miserable.

Judith thought, 'I really hate this woman at last.' But did she? There was something IGNORANT about Jennifer, as though with all her beauty, her husband, admirers, children and the rest, she had never learnt anything about life at all. Just as you pity a selfish, wilful child because of the trouble that is in store for it, so Judith pitied Jennifer. And where you pity you cannot hate.

She was dressed in a crimson spencer with long sleeves that she wore open. It was lined with white fur. Over it she had a delicate Cashmere shawl and under it a long, tight-fitting dress of grey. On her head was a tiny crimson bonnet, close-fitting to the head, decorated with an upright ostrich feather. Her low boots, ankle high, showed the beautiful elegance of her little feet.

Remarkably, at this critical moment--for it was the only one at which the three of them together discussed the Westaways situation-- scarcely a word was said.

Jennifer, looking at Judith as a bird of Paradise might look at a sparrow, said:

'So I hear that Will has arrived at Westaways. You know, Judith, that your visits there will inconvenience us in no way whatever. Pray visit there when you feel inclined.'

Judith got up and, simply because she knew that it would annoy Jennifer, rested her hand on Francis' shoulder.

'Thank you, Jennifer.'

Mrs. Ponder was in the doorway. 'Fred is there with the carriage, ma'am,' she said. She gave her two enemies, Francis and Judith, a dark look. Yes, she had stayed there although they had told her to go. And she would stay so long as she pleased.

Jennifer, her head high, her ostrich feather nodding, swung her way out.

When the door had closed, Francis said: 'Judith, do you think. . . ?' Then he stopped.

'And now,' said Judith, pointing to the sofa, 'I will tell you what you must do, Francis--'

The first occasion on which Judith dined at Westaways was on a wild, stormy afternoon in March. She was generously allowed the closed barouche by Jennifer, who was for ever making attempts to suggest that Judith was a sort of poor relation. (And indeed was she not just that in reality?)

'Dear Judith, I pray that you may have an entertaining evening. Do not encourage Christabel to call on us here.'

'I am sure that she will not wish to,' said Judith.

Jennifer looked at her closely. Was she beginning to suspect the child? Then Jennifer was clouded by a glance of apprehension. She looked back to the stairs as though to be sure that no one was there.

'Judith,' she said. 'If they talk scandal of me at Westaways--as of course they will--even though you dislike me, well, I am Francis' wife.'

'Scandal?' said Judith. 'What scandal?'

'There is always scandal in a country neighbourhood.' She looked most beautiful in the candle-light. Her dark ringlets gleamed on the soft orange texture of her Cashmere shawl.

Judith smiled, compelled by that beauty to which she was always surrendering wherever she saw it.

'How little even now you know me,' she said.

But as she climbed into the dark carriage she stubbed her shoe against the step. In the dark she nodded to herself. 'I cannot ENDURE these people!' It was as though her mother, puzzled and bewildered at Herries fifty years earlier, had spoken.

But it was a most interesting evening. Judith stepped, in a moment, back into her old place. There was James, son of Pomfret and Rose, great-grandson of old Pomfret, who had built the house; he was a short, stubborn-looking fellow of thirty-six, very silent, and, everybody said, waiting for his father to die that he might succeed to the baronetcy. There was Montague Cards, in whose London rooms the famous arbitration had once taken place. He was now forty-eight, looked as though his cheeks were painted and wore most affected clothing. He spent as much of his time as possible in staying with relations free of charge. He planned to remain at Westaways longer than Will had any idea of. Carey Rockage, now sixty, was a splendid old fellow, wearing loose garments that seemed to have been made for someone else, most absent-minded but always finding something interesting and amusing to entertain himself with. Maria was now an old woman of sixty-one and looked like a haystack on wheels. She moved with a kind of rolling motion. She had peculiar habits; she would whistle to herself or, at table, make little pellets of bread and flick them about. She was so untidy that no one of her garments seemed to belong to any other. Her hair was white and she wore a lace cap, none too clean and set rakishly at an angle. For Judith, who had such a passion for cleanliness, her untidiness was an agony. She found herself, before she had been at Westaways ten minutes, running after Maria, picking up her handkerchief, fastening a button, tying a ribbon.

Will Herries was not greatly changed, save that he was a wealthy man now of forty-five, and so had swollen in importance. Not physically swollen; he was as thin and stiff as a water-pipe, and he spoke like Moses delivering the Ten Commandments to the people of Israel. Christabel also was now a middle-aged woman, dressed better than of old, and was not so deeply terrified of functions and ceremonies.

She was, however, one of those people whose anticipation of catastrophe spoils every occasion. And expectation of disaster attracts it as surely as mountains attract rain.

Walter was now their only remaining child, his sister having died some years previously of smallpox.

Walter was terrific. He was, Judith thought, the largest young man she had ever seen. Horse-like as all the Herries were one way or another, he resembled a charger for whom no general, however famous, could ever be grand enough. He had all the splendour of bone and muscle united to a supreme self-confidence and determination. He was the absolute symbol of Herries, blood, bone, and soul, all mingled together, engaged upon the same pursuit. He was neither dour nor aloof like his father. He laughed often, and his laughter, Judith thought, must make the inner confines of Borrowdale quake. His chest was the broadest, his

legs the thickest, his neck the strongest, his arms the most muscular that she had ever seen. Set in all this splendour were very small eyes that had a strange meditative stare, even when he was most jolly. Later in the evening she was to perceive how instantly he could change from pleasure to business. She decided that he would become the most important of all the Herries family, and she was correct in her prophecy.

Already he dominated everyone there. He wore a huge stock, a vast purple coat and immense trousers, just then coming into fashion. His hair was a dark curly brown, and he had a snuffbox as big almost as a bandbox.

He ordered the servants, arranged the details of the party as though he were master of the house. Two years previously he had married Agnes Bailey, daughter of a rich City merchant. She was not present this evening because she was expecting very shortly her first child. So Walter, roaring and laughing, informed Judith, adding that if the child were not a boy he would let his wife know of it! She was a little bit of a woman, he informed Judith, whom he could slip easily into his pocket. He spoke of her with all the pride that the Herries feel for any woman who has been wise enough to marry one of them. As always, when she was with anyone of great height, she was embarrassed by her own smallness. But she soon recovered. He at once chaffed her.

'Why, you are the pocket Venus!' he cried.

'Oh, Walter!' cried Christabel. 'Pray, pray--'

But Judith laughed.

'How much brain is there in all that muscle, Cousin Walter? I've seen bullocks at a fair--'

He thought that immensely good. She found that he laughed at almost everything. She rather liked him. After the restraints of Uldale this was rather refreshing. She discovered very shortly that it was he who had persuaded his father to come to Westaways. He was all for carrying on the family feud, partly from rancour and scorn of Francis, partly from pride and physical good health. And he had never been in Cumberland before, although it was his home. Of course it was his home. His grandfather had been the best fighter in the district, and his father had been born here. That was enough for him. She saw that he was determined to get Uldale into his hands before he had done.

She was happy at once when she saw how greatly pleased Christabel and Maria were to see her. Then speedily also the light of battle was in her eye. For she perceived that they were all there, that everything was done, to impress her. She was the spy from the enemy camp, and the intention was that she should return and tell them all at Uldale that they had no chance, that they had better surrender at once, pack up and go. Well, she was going to tell them nothing of the kind. She was fond of Christabel, but she loved Francis. Poor Francis, growing old now, with nothing to show for life at all save his children, who did not know him. Yes, she was on his side, and so she would let that great hulking elephant of a Walter know before the evening was over.

The house she had never been inside before. She knew well its charming exterior; she had often walked and ridden past it, its roof covered with rosy tiles, the beautiful wrought ironwork, the door with the fluted columns and the delicate fanlight.

Within it was by far grander than Uldale, with the pillared hall, and up the wide staircase to the grand saloon that had been decorated by old Westaway himself. The subject of the decorations was Paris awarding the apple, and there were three fine, plump, rosy goddesses. In this fine room, glittering and gleaming with the candle-light and the swinging splendours of the glass candelabra, they were all gathered. Soon they went down to dinner.

Judith was seated between Walter Herries and his father, who, his back erect, his thin neck raised like a hen's, should have commanded the assembly. He did not. Walter praised the food, guaranteed the liquor, chaffed old Maria, scolded and commanded the servants.

At the last moment Warren Forster slipped in and, with a nod and a smile to them all, took his place.

'You have nothing, I wager,' Walter said to her, 'like this at Uldale.'

Judith looked about her: a very grand room with a massive fireplace, the table piled with food, perfect organisation.

'I prefer Uldale.'

'You prefer Uldale? But, come now, Cousin. I may call you Cousin? What can you prefer? There is no space at Uldale, no light--'

'No light! We have all the light in the world!'

'Well, well--so has a barn. I know what I know. You shall have your Uldale.'

She looked at him with great calmness.

'You have come here, Cousin Walter, to crow over Uldale. Well, you shall not do it for me. I am old enough to be your mother, Cousin Walter, and there are one or two things I shall teach you before we are done.'

He looked at her with admiration. He liked her. He had heard that this little woman had spirit. What was she? Born in a barnyard out of a gipsy? No matter. She had pluck.

'Is Jennifer as lovely as they say?'

'She is very lovely.'

'I would go a long way for a beautiful woman. But Francis, now--he is vexed, is he not, at our taking Westaways?'

'He has other things to think of.'

'Ha, ha! . . . I warrant he has, and there will be more before long. Jennifer insulted my mother, you know . . . in a public place too.'

'That is an old story--and there are two sides to it.'

'Not so old that I have forgot it. And you would smack my face if there were cause, Cousin Judith. By gad, I believe you would too.'

'Certainly,' said Judith gravely, 'if there were cause.'

'Well, I drink your health, Cousin. We are to be friends.'

'I am in the other camp,' she said, smiling at him.

'It will be all one camp one day,' he answered her.

She heard Will saying with great gravity:

'I have heard my father tell many a time how as a small boy he came to this house. It was your great-grandfather Pomfret, James, who had it then, you know. Yes, and he sat there with my poor grandmother--she died shortly, poor thing--and stared and stared. For it was a grand house to him. He had never seen the like of it. And there were all the things in the room that are here yet. I will show them to you afterwards, Maria. We had them in London and brought them up with us. Out of the parlour window the fountain with the bird that has been here from the beginning. The screen with the gold work on it, the clock with the sun and moon. We had them in our London house. You must have seen them often, Maria. But what frightened my father-- he was only a small boy, you know-- was his great-aunt Maria, sitting there with a spaniel on her lap. He often told us children of it. She had a wig with flowers and a hoop as large as a tent, a black patch on her cheek, and her fingers covered with jewelry. She was born in the year of the battle of Naseby, you know. So here we are back to the battle of Naseby.'

Will, Judith thought, was quite human all of a sudden. He was so proud of being here, back in his rightful place. Yes, she understood him and sympathised with him. Then he looked at her, as though he would say: 'Here we are, you see, and we shall remain.' Then her cheeks flushed. So would Francis remain AND his children. She would see to that while she had breath left in her body. (Odd that only an hour or two ago, in the carriage, she had wanted to be free of the lot of them! Now she was in the very middle of the battle, and glad to be!)

More and more food appeared. (They had not dinners like this at Uldale.) More and more wine was drunk. James began, in his stubborn determined way, to talk of the present discontents. He had nothing good to say of anyone--King, Regent, Parliament, Army-- but the villains of every piece were the working-classes. Oh! these working-classes! What was it they wanted, the dirty dogs? Why were they NEVER content? They complained of the price of food. Well, let them work harder and earn more. They said that their homes were not fit to live in! What did they expect? Palaces?

Nearly everyone joined in. At Manchester and at Liverpool there were disorders every day. Of course it would be right enough now that Napoleon was safe in Elba. But would it be? Someone said that we would be fighting Russia next. . . . Wars were endless. One led to another. And while there were so many wars, of course trade would be bad. . . . At the word 'trade' Will lifted up his sharp blue-tinted chin and told them all what he thought about Trade.

Money would be in the towns--Birmingham, Liverpool, Manchester. . . . This new machinery. . . . The country would be a dead place in another thirty years. Cotton? Had any of them thought about cotton? Well, he had. India and the East were all very well, but wise men were turning their attention to home products. Now that Napoleon was shut up and the Allies were in Vienna. . . . In another thirty years there would be no country in England, no TRUE country.

Why, when his grandfather had come first to Keswick his father, as a little boy, had ridden into Borrowdale on horseback as though you were riding into China. His father had often told him. Why, nothing on wheels had ever been seen in Borrowdale a hundred years ago, and now he wouldn't be surprised but that one day they would be driving carriages with steam. He looked at them all grimly, just like an angry and emaciated Moses.

'They'd better look out,' he seemed to say, 'or they would have the surprise of their life!' For a brief moment he dominated all of them; even Walter disappeared.

Old Maria Rockage, on his other side, listened to him and thought what nonsense he was talking. She had drunk some wine--not her customary habit--and her head was a little fuddled. To tell the truth, she was homesick for Grosset. Oh yes, she knew that this was all fine, with the fountain in the garden, and the painting of the naked women upstairs and all the shining candles. Everything was very orderly, the servants moved most quietly. There was enough food to feed the village at Grosset for a week (and that when all the countryside was starving!), but she wasn't really comfortable here. She didn't care for that big shouting Walter, and Will wasn't kind to Christabel, and the large four-poster that enshrouded herself and Carey at night was not truly a FRIENDLY bed, and she missed her children; even though Carey the Younger WAS fond of doing nothing, she would rather have him than this hulk of a Walter, and Phyllis was a SWEET child. . . . She began to feel very melancholy indeed. A tear fell into the goose on her plate. Then she looked up and changed a smile with Judith.

She felt better. What a pity that Judith had ever left them! They had all been very happy together! And now she heard the strangest things about Jennifer. Judith surely was not happy there. But the child (for although Judith was over forty, Maria thought of her as a child) LOOKED happy. She had grown stouter. What a sensible woman! Grosset had been in pieces ever since she had left them! And it was neither nice nor kind of Will to come here simply to triumph over Francis, all because years ago Christabel had slapped Jennifer's face. Not that she had ever liked Jennifer, beautiful though she was. And they said that Francis was most unhappy. . . . It was not as though he were a boy any longer. . . . He must be fifty-five or so, and had

done nothing with his life, poor man. . . . She piled up little pellets of bread beside her plate.

Behind the wall of talk and laughter they were moving on their secret ways. Will was stiff with triumph. This was a grand dinner. He would show brother Francis at Uldale. . . . Christabel longed to have a real talk with Judith. She wanted that somehow, in one way or another, they should understand at Uldale that she was not their enemy. . . . In her heart she would rejoice to have a reconciliation with Jennifer.

Walter was hot and thick and turbulent with the pride of life. He saw himself as a conqueror. Of what? Of whom? It did not matter. James had in his heart contempt for all these country bumpkins, the grand Walter included. The old-maidish bachelor with the painted cheeks was enjoying the food and the wine. Here was the place for him! He would stay . . . one month, two, three? Old Carey was thinking of a dog of his, Pluto, who was as game a dog . . .

Warren Forster, who had scarcely spoken, sat, his eyes secretly fixed on Judith. Judith, placed so demurely there, once in his arms while the logs crackled in the stone fireplace. Judith, the passion of his whole life. . . .

And Judith herself began to wish to escape. She felt unwell, some great uneasiness at her heart. She WAS in the camp of the enemy! It was as though she could foretell in some secret way all the consequences that were to come out of this move into Westaways, a move made from vanity and vainglory. She had sympathised with Will, but now she felt that he was there only that he might snub Francis. And as for his son! He seemed to be more overbearing with every minute that passed, as the room grew more heated, the food more grossly devoured, the wine more carelessly drunk, the lights more brilliant. He seemed to grow and hang over her in a vast imposing shadow. He had drunk great quantities of wine, but it had not affected him. Will's speech was already clouded, poor old Carey was waving his glass with uncertain hands, Monty Cards was calling for a song in a shrill high tone, James scowled. . . . It was time for the ladies to be gone.

They rose. Walter got up, bowed, then kissed her hand.

'Adieu, Cousin Judith!'

His purple coat with its high collar strained across his tremendous shoulders, his stock seemed scarcely to confine the muscles of his neck--but his eyes were very small. She looked up at him, glance to glance. What she would give for a few more inches! But his little eyes closed before hers. In a majestic procession the ladies left the room.

Upstairs, seated beneath the rosy goddesses, Christabel at once drew Judith aside. From where Judith sat, under the swinging glittering glass on the gilt sofa, she could look out through the curtains that were not yet drawn, to the Lake darkening now in the gathering dusk. Its bosom was shaken with trembling; its surface was crossed with paths of pale opalescent light, and one rosy shadow hung on to the green skirts of the hill. It moved Judith most strangely to see how the Lake was trembling; however, in another moment she was looking about the room and thinking how she would arrange it were it hers. That cabinet would be best in the corner and the large clock with the marble pillars. . . .

'And so, Judith,' Christabel was saying in that hushed anxious voice of hers, while old Maria nodded her head, jumped awake and then fell off again, 'you must understand that I have no animosity. Bygones must be bygones.'

'No, YOU have no animosity,' said Judith, nodding her head and swinging her legs as well as she could in her long gown (for the sofa was a trifle high). 'Of course YOU have none, dear Christabel. But what of Will and Walter?'

'Oh! yes!' Christabel admitted, her brow wrinkling with anxiety. 'Should not the curtains be drawn? It is almost dark. Ah, here comes Wiggins with the tea.--I am half afraid of Wiggins. We brought him from London. Monty found him for us!'

Judith looked at Wiggins, who was almost as mountainous as his master, Walter. Poor Christabel--to be crushed among all these huge men! But she would like to have the managing of Wiggins. He would be child's play beside Mrs. Ponder.

'Yes, Wiggins. Here, if you please. You understand, Judith, that men look upon these things quite differently. Walter regards it as a sort of a game. He does indeed, and he is very chivalrous about any insult to myself. . . . And Jennifer WAS rude to me, you know. . . .'

'So long ago!' said Judith scornfully. (Yes, and the spinet would be better nearer the window. What a lovely pattern of flowers and leaves on its cover! And then you could have the sofa. . . . Sofas were still rare and this was one of the finest Judith had ever seen.) What a lot of money Will must be making! Well, it was what he had always wanted. . . .

'At least,' Christabel went on, 'you will not leave me, dear Judith. I must see you sometimes. I must indeed. It was my only comfort in coming here. You must not hate me because Jennifer does!'

'Hate you! Dear Christabel!' Touched as always by any appeal to her affection, she leaned forward and kissed Christabel's dry cheek. 'Alas, I hate nobody! Hatred is so difficult to sustain. Even Mrs. Ponder--'

'Who is Mrs. Ponder?'

'An odious female.'

'And Jennifer?' Christabel looked to see that Wiggins was gone and Maria fast asleep. 'They are saying very odd things about Jennifer, Judith.'

'What things?'

'Is there not a Captain Fernyhirst? And they say that Francis--'

'I suppose Walter brings you this gossip,' Judith broke in indignantly. 'Remember, Christabel, that I love Francis more than anyone in the world. I will not hear a word against him--'

'No, no,' Christabel cried, frightened of offending Judith. 'It is only that it is common talk--'

'There is always common talk,' said Judith. 'In every country place they talk.'

She was thinking: 'Well, there you are, now it has all begun. Christabel is different already, sniffing out things about Uldale. And soon Jennifer will be saying things about Christabel.' She saw Walter on a huge horse riding deliberately past Uldale and making rude gestures, mocking the smallness of the place and the bareness of the garden. Oh! it would be impossible! She had an impulse to rise there and then and run for her life.

Indeed, she did shortly run, but not before she had heard some astonishing news. The door burst open; all the men were there, Walter in front of them. They were shouting and crying out. Old Maria woke up, Christabel thought the house was on fire, Judith wondered whether Walter's wife upstairs was suddenly delivered of a child. But no! Walter was roaring out:

'What do you think? What do you think? Boney has escaped from Elba! Escaped from Elba, by God! He's in Paris, and the French are with him to a man! Esthwaite has looked in to tell us. There's news for you! Boney escaped from Elba! Whoop! Whoop! . . . What a fellow! By gad, I admire him! Escaped from Elba, by gad!'

They were all in a frantic excitement, even James, and Monty Cards was crying out like a woman:

'He'll be in London yet! We shall all be French before the year's out.'

Judith, standing by herself, beside the window, felt the news run inside her like wine. That marvellous fat little man, whose corpulent shadow had hung over them, almost all their lives as it now seemed, had done it again! Yes, it was wonderful. He was a wonder. She could see, looking through the haze of the candles, all Europe in a hurry and a scurry, hastening like ants, hither, thither, everywhere. Stiff and conceited Talleyrand, and the sentimental weak Russian, their own mountain of flesh, the Regent, the old mad King, all the bourses and the shops and the theatres, the country lanes, cottages, mountains, lakes--all suddenly quivering again under the shadow of that little indomitable monster!

The others in the room had for the moment forgotten her. They were all talking together; in the doorway Wiggins and another man-servant stood listening.

Bonaparte free again! You could hear the cry from China to Peru! Well, if Napoleon could free himself so easily why should not she?

The news and a sudden glimpse of Warren Forster's anxious, pale face (even in the excitement he did not forget her) made her almost mad with eagerness to get away. Away! Anywhere. . . . To have her child somewhere by herself. No Herries. No relations or duties or scandals. Napoleon had done it. She had as strong a will.

Moved by an irresistible impulse she was out of the room and had slipped down the stairs. They were not thinking of her. She felt as though she had the energy to escape down the road just as she was, and in a moment she would be in Paris! Well, why not? Anything to escape. However, she found her bonnet and shawl, ran out into the garden, and then in the courtyard at the back discovered Fred. She told him that she wanted the carriage. At once! At once!

While she waited for him she smiled up at the stars that were beginning to break into the sky.

If Napoleon had done it she could! And it was as though the child in her womb laughed its approval.

JUDITH IN PARIS

This time Judith escaped some distance; she ran from Westaways to Paris.

In June the battle of Waterloo was fought and Napoleon's escape was concluded.

Judith told Francis and Jennifer that she would take a little holiday. She was going to stay with Emma Furze in London. Jennifer was kind to her and kissed her good-bye. Judith did not know whether she was aware of the increase in her figure or no. No one else seemed to notice anything. Francis was grave and reserved again. All he said was:

'It is not for long, Judith. Have you sufficient money?'

'Yes, thank you. . . . No, it is not for long,' she answered him. She did not know whether she were lying or no. It might be for ever.

But John made a scene. Quiet as he usually was, on this occasion he made a scene. He cried himself into being sick and scratched Mrs. Ponder's cheek. Then, two hours after Judith's departure, he ran away. He was found on the road to Bassenthwaite in a hedge, fast asleep. . . .

On a very hot summer afternoon, in the middle of the Café des Mille Colonnes, sat La Belle Limonadière, dressed in crimson velvet and covered with jewels, serenely looking down on her hundreds of clients, like an empress, but very accurate in the change that she gave to the waiters. Spread before her were dozens of portions of broken sugar, five or six pieces in each portion, arranged in little silver saucers like wine-funnel stands.

This was the remnant of the respect for sugar induced by the period when Napoleon closed Europe against English commerce. There were at this moment no sugar-basins in Paris.

La Belle Limonadière, although perhaps her best time was now over, was indeed a brilliant creature. A contemporary--a gentleman certainly to be trusted--describes her as having a complexion of Parian marble. He goes on (his letter is in the Herries' archives): "Her black hair and eyes were in striking contrast with her complexion. The usual aids of colour to the cheeks were not forgotten, but quite what the French call au naturel--a word merely meaning something less artificial than the last stage of artifice. La Belle has an air and expression of great good nature; and, what most amused me, a most solemn attitude of correctest propriety. Nobody presumes to address her without previous formal presentation, and it is found impossible to give any coffee orders to her majesty except through the medium of a gentleman-in-waiting!"

To Judith and Emma, sitting almost under her nose, this brilliant, black-haired, crimson-clad creature was infinitely fascinating. They could not take their eyes off her! She reminded Judith a little of Jennifer, only that she was not so beautiful. She always afterwards seemed to Judith to be the symbol, the decorated figurehead of this strange Paris adventure--to have the colour, the audacity and also the sordidness and underground thunder of this fantastic Paris scene. During all that followed in these exciting weeks, La Belle Limonadière was marching just in front, the presiding deity of this affair.

On this especial afternoon she was very gracious to a noble-looking gentleman (plainly not a Frenchman) who sat with some friends near to her, eating an ice and smiling up at the queen's throne. This gentleman, someone confided to Emma, was no other than Mr. Walter Scott, the famous poet. Judith looked at him with all her eyes, and loved him at once for his grand high forehead, his eyes beaming with kindness under their shaggy eyebrows, the courtesy of his mien. He was like a very noble sort of sheep-dog. When he got up and, limping on his stick, passed down the hall, she felt as though all were indeed well with this strange world, which was neither so fantastic nor so threatening as she had thought it.

For although she was greatly enjoying it all she was also rather frightened. For one thing they had not very much money, she and Emma, for another she was not very well, she who had always been so strong and so healthy. And then she was taken with strange waves of homesickness, wondering whether Francis were in health, whether the meals at Uldale were served properly, whether John missed her and what the clouds were doing to Skiddaw.

However you cannot, as she was for ever discovering, both have your cake and eat it, and this was most truly a fascinating scene. Paris was now a hotch-potch of all the nations of the world. This splendid hall, mirrored all round, divided by fluted Corinthian pillars, made the company seem innumerably multiplied. Here were English officers, then Highlanders with their plumed bonnets, now Prussian hussars, and again Brunswickers in their sombre uniforms. The French ladies, in their walking dresses and in high-crowned, plume-covered bonnets and shawls, were attended by their beaux, who were as gay, lively and noisy as though there had been no revolutions, no devastating wars, and as though their country were not at the moment occupied by the triumphant foe.

But how dazzling this scene, thought Judith, and how unreal the figure of the strange crimson hostess, her figure, solemn, correct, almost austere, multiplied in all these mirrors, herself entrenched with peaches, sugar and nosegays of flowers!

Beneath all the gaiety and sparkle you felt that the ground trembled. The English were popular, but the Prussians were hated. She saw on every side of her the Prussian arrogance. She had heard that when Wellington had protested about some outrageous piece of conduct, Blücher had replied: 'Yes, but remember--the French were never in England.' The very fact that the French found it so difficult to submit to the domination of a people whom they had so long despised, caused those people to be more arrogant. In the cafés their behaviour made Judith, who, when the English were not in question, was, because of Georges, more French than the French, tremble with indignation. And the whole public life of the French, so that they seemed to be never at home but spent their whole time in the cafés, the theatres, or on the boulevards, made this trouble with the Prussians the more prominent.

But then, as she by this time thoroughly realised, the French themselves were scarcely, as yet, disciplined. They had not suffered a revolution in their country so long a while for nothing. The French boys in the street, for instance, were insolent beyond belief, and she and Emma were for ever encountering both men and women who seemed to them like dangerous animals just let loose from their cages.

She found evidence enough of it in the lodgings; they were in the Rue Vivienne. They had two rooms in the apartment of Monsieur and Madame Dufresne. Little M. Dufresne, thin as a stick, with a funny black toupee and a tiny black moustache, had suffered some terror in his earlier years from which he seemed to find it impossible ever to escape. His chief pleasure was in animals, so that he had in his room a cockatoo, a monkey, three dogs, two cats and a tortoise. For animals he had, it would seem, a very special gift, but for human beings no gift at all. His wife, on the other hand, was a large brawny woman, whom Judith could well imagine knitting in front of the scaffold while the tumbrils rolled up. Her great muscular arms were always bared to the elbow and she had a deep bass voice like a man's. They

were a pair who led their own lives-- they interfered with neither Judith nor Emma in any way, but at night one could hear the thick, low rumble of Madame's voice through the wall; it seemed to threaten every sort of vengeance.

However, here they were in the Café des Mille Colonnes and enjoying every moment of it. For Emma, indeed, this stay in Paradise was simply heaven. She had her darling Judith to look after and care for, and there rolled all around her the very life that Fate should have designed for her. She was now a woman between fifty and sixty, handsomer than she had ever been, for her figure, tall and majestic, had thinned, and her grey hair, her sparkling eager eyes, her vitality attracted attention wherever she went.

She was more ready now to be spectator than actor, but the sight of almost any man stirred her blood and excited her curiosity. And had ever a city in the world's history been so grandly filled with splendid men as was Paris at this moment? Glorious men, and most especially the Highlanders, who, in their intriguing costume, simply had the French ladies at their feet!

She was always on the move, for ever seeing the sights. They went to the Opera, saw the King, a most benevolent-looking gentleman, the Emperor of Austria and the Duke of Wellington. They witnessed a ballet in which some of the performers were dressed as Highlanders, and heard the building ring with cries of 'Vivent les Écossais!'--a glorious moment. There were constant processions, and one morning they saw pass no less than thirty thousand Russian soldiers. They went to the Théâtre des Variétés and saw 'Jean Bool' most amusingly caricatured. Best of all, perhaps, were their visits to the encampment of the English troops--the 95th Rifles, 52nd Light Infantry, and 71st Highlanders--in the Champs Elysées. This was one of the sights of Paris and immensely Emma enjoyed it. The world seemed only to exist to provide handsome military forms and fine ladies to gaze upon them.

She would, in fact, have known perfect happiness had it not been for a certain anxiety about Judith. Judith had been the one constant and unchanging devotion of her life. She would never have claimed for herself that she had a constant nature. She had not one herself, nor did she, any longer, expect constancy of others. She knew, she said, human nature too well.

But Judith was changed. You must expect it, of course. Judith was over forty and the child coming. It was no light matter to have your first child when you were over forty. But there was more in it than this. In the first place, Emma could not understand Judith's devotion to Georges. No, she certainly could not! It was true that Georges had never really liked her, but it was not that she was prejudiced. She could never have fallen in love with Georges herself; but one of the things that life taught one was that everyone must have, and be permitted to have, their own taste!

No, but Georges had not been good to Judith; he had been a thoroughly worthless, selfish fellow; and here she still was, after all these years, adoring him as though he had been a paragon!

But she was filled with contradictions. She adored Georges' memory, but some other man was father of her child. She had always seemed to Emma one of the most virtuous of women, possessing in fact a virtue that poor Emma herself could never hope to command. And yet she had apparently given herself to a man for whom she did not greatly care, simply from an impulse of kindness. Emma herself was kind, but she was also passionate, even now when she was nearing sixty. But Judith was passionate only in relation to Georges. And how ironical that she had offered all that love to Georges, who was never to give her a child, but that now, when she was almost past child-bearing, a chance moment with someone whom she did not love should accomplish everything! But life was like that. Emma herself could remember . . .

Beyond her nostalgia for Georges there was a deeper nostalgia, and this Emma could not understand at all. For it seemed from Judith's brief and broken confidences—Judith talked very little about herself even to Emma—that she thought that could she only get away to Watendlath, leave for ever all her Herries relations, and hide herself in the hills for the rest of her days, all would be well.

'Surely then,' cried Emma, 'in heaven's name, go! You are your own mistress!'

But that, it seemed, was exactly what Judith was not. She was for ever being dragged back into Herries affairs.

'But you are not so weak!' cried Emma.

'But don't you see,' Judith answered, 'it is a struggle inside myself. And one day it will be too late. I shall be compelled to choose, and shall make the wrong choice. And then I shall be inside the Herries for the rest of my days. And the worst of it will be that I shall like it—and I shall have lost all my real life for ever.'

Not that Judith often talked like this. But she was brooding, Emma knew, too much within herself. If Emma made a fool of herself, which she often did, she burst into a rage or a flood of tears and it was all over. But Judith took things to heart. And then of course you did brood when you were having your first child. Poor women! What a time they had! And then Emma would see a Highlander pass by, with a great swing of the haunches, and be glad indeed that she was a woman!

On this particular afternoon Judith was in the highest spirits. They came out into the Palais-Royal, chattering and laughing. Judith was full of Mr. Walter Scott—what fine eyes, how kindly an expression, how interesting his limp made him! Emma had never read one of his poems—they looked so very long—but she was prepared to find anyone noble whom Judith thought to be so.

The Palais-Royal was a place of enchantment. Under the hot afternoon sun it glittered and glowed with its life and splendour. It was a little city in itself. In shape an oblong quadrangle with piazzas completely around it, a garden planted with rows of trees, laid with gravel, with flowers and grass plots enclosed. Under the piazzas were countless shops, far more brilliant, as it seemed to Judith and Emma, than the shops of London. On the ground-floor, coffee-houses and restaurants; on the principal floor upstairs, coffee-houses, gaming-houses, exhibitions; higher up again, what a Herries traveller of the period calls in his Journal 'the abodes of vice and profligacy.' (This is from the Journal of Rodney Herries, the very pious younger brother of James, who in middle life took orders, and was ultimately Archdeacon of Polchester.) He goes on: 'The attics are inhabited by filth, misery, and crime, in endless variety and in a manner that renders it much safer to take that fact on hearsay than on actual reconnaissance. I should have mentioned,' he piously continues, 'that below the pavement are places much corresponding in character to the attics, though many of them are only cheap cafés, traiteurs, or pastry-cooks, of fair respectability.' He ends in a passage of particular eloquence by calling the Palais-Royal 'This immense gangrene.'

It was for Judith wonderful in all its mingled life, its wealth and poverty, fine ladies and scoundrels, triumphant soldiers and washerwomen, ordinary quiet Frenchmen and ruffians almost in rags, clerics and flower-sellers, tourists and solemn officials. They had been in it so often, Emma and she, that she wondered why it seemed to-day to have some special significance for her.

She stood for a moment under the burning sun, jostled on every side, trying to define her impression. She was being reminded of something. The broad space around her seemed to narrow. The dazzling sunlight on the white walls darkened. She was suddenly chilled. The movement was frozen. She heard a voice in her ear: 'No, madam, I fear the crowd is too great. . . . Yes, he stole from his master's till . . . a butcher . . .'

She caught Emma's arm. 'Let us go home, Emma. We must rest before this evening.'

'Why, my dear, you are pale. You are unwell.'

'No, but I was reminded of something.'

Afterwards, in the dark little room in the Rue Vivienne, she said to Emma:

'Emma, I am sure that something will happen to us in the Palais-Royal. I shall not return there.'

And Emma thought to herself: 'It is beginning. These fancies that women get at such a time!'

She made her lie down, and sat beside her, telling her lively improper stories of her own past life. Through the wall they heard the odd plaintive chatter of M. Dufresne's monkey. It chattered like a child, then broke into an angry scream. Then the dogs barked.

Then could be heard the deep menacing rumble of Madame Dufresne.

Their window was open because of the heat, and from far below them came the rattle of carriages, the crying of wares, the distant dreamy cadence of a band. In the air was the smell of Paris, the scent of carnations, the tang of baking bread, the hot touch of the iron trellises before the balconies, the sniff of crumpled paper, dry almost to burning-point. Judith was almost asleep. Once opening her eyes, looking at Emma, she said: 'I saw a boy hanged once in London. I thought of it to-day.'

'I know; you have told me of it often,' said Emma composedly. 'What is a hanging? You are too sensitive, my darling.'

'Perhaps I shall die when the child is born.'

'Nonsense. Nonsense. Die! I never heard such folly!'

'I know how cool it is now up Newlands, and how the breeze blows above the turf of Maiden Moor. . . . I rode once, but only once, with Francis to Hawkshead, and then up the hill to where the two little tarns lie. Oh, Emma, you never saw a thing so quiet and so cool when a great white cloud floats overhead and Fairfield and Helvellyn watch over you. . . . Oh, how hot it is, and how sorry I am for Monsieur Dufresne's monkey. . . . Madame Dufresne will murder us one night in our beds. She hates us for Waterloo. And she will hide our bodies in that vast cupboard with the creaking door. I am sure there are rats in the wainscot. . . . Emma I KNOW that something will happen to us in the Palais-Royal, and that great woman with the black hair and the crimson dress will sit above us and watch us torn to pieces while she arranges pieces of sugar. . . . I wonder how Francis is, and whether he has that blackberry preserve that he loves. They are always forgetting to have it on the table unless I am there. . . . I wonder if you can see the Scottish hills clearly to-day, and what they are doing at Westaways. . . . That crimson woman has Jennifer's air. . . . Jennifer would be fine in a café with mirrors multiplying her. . . . How I wish I knew Mr. Scott! He has stayed, I know, with Mr. Southey. Francis may have met him. . . .'

She dropped away to sleep while Emma, her eyes full of devotion, watched her and listened to M. Dufresne's monkey.

That evening they went to the Tivoli Gardens. Judith, after a long sleep, had recovered all her spirits and was ready for any amusement. Here there was plenty. They had quite agreed that the place could not compare with Vauxhall for size and splendour; but the summer evening was so lovely, the crowd so diverse and so intent upon enjoyment, that it was impossible not to be merry. There was a great crowd on this especial night, for it was said that the King and the Duchesse d'Angoulême were to be present to see the floating of an illuminated balloon. Emma had said that the Duchess would not be there, because she was so devout that she considered all amusement harmful. In fact no Crowned Heads were present, nor could they persuade the balloon to rise, although a great many people paid five francs to stand within the ropes to see it do so.

There were all the regular diversions. One of the principal of them was to guess who were French officers; for in spite of Blücher's order that any discovered should be at once apprehended and treated as prisoners of war, Paris was filled with them. Then there was the gaiety of going around in a circle--the gentlemen on wooden horses, the ladies in chairs--in order to carry off with a small sword a ring hung out upon a post for the purpose; or you might get into a boat and ride about on a small artificial pond scarcely larger than the boat; or you might watch Mlle. Sachi, elevated sixty feet on a tightrope; or there were the fireworks, QUITE as good as Vauxhall; or you might simply laugh at the costume of the French ladies, which seemed to Judith and Emma very ugly, with the high headdress, the hair drawn tight from the temples and forehead over a coif, or hid with a high-crowned bonnet covered with feathers, no perceptible waist, but a loose robe hanging like a sack from the throat to the ankles, carefully collected about the wrists, and a shawl worn three-corner-wise. Emma and Judith thought these styles most absurd and laughed together a great deal.

However, the grand feature of the Tivoli, as of every other place of entertainment in Paris, was the dancing.

Everyone formed a circle round the dancers, who did everything possible to be as widely observed as might be. One gentleman was pirouetting round on his wooden leg and vastly enjoying it.

Soon a grave French gentleman with a square black beard invited Emma to dance, and, old though she was, she eagerly agreed, giving Judith a nod and a wink and setting off into the middle of the ring as though she were not a day more than twenty.

Judith was tired and sat down on a little wooden bench. The green of the trees was as brilliant as fresh paint under the illuminations, and between the leaves the evening sky showed, soft and delicate and tender. She loved to see people happy, to hear their cries of pleasure, to see the children running, to watch the sturdy simple faces of the English soldiers as they walked about in pairs, gravely considering the French girls, to catch the quick coloured flash of the fireworks, blue and green and red, above the dark water of the little pond. . . . She was tranquil. She was waiting for the delivery of her child. She felt at peace with all the world; she owed no one a grudge. When she thought of how hazardous and desolate had been her entrance into the world she was fortunate indeed to have had so full and adventurous a life. When her child came she would see that it had all that she could give it. Poor Warren! She thought of him with warm kindliness and affection. She was glad that he did not know what had happened to her.

She heard a familiar voice say 'Judith,' looked up and saw Warren Forster standing in front of her.

At once she cried: 'Oh, Warren, how ill you look! Sit down. Sit down here beside me!'

That was at first all that she could think about. He did look very ill. His sharp face, always strained with the memory of past suffering, was grey and haggard. He was so frail that, although when she began to think of all that his being there in Paris would mean, she would be intensely aggravated, she wanted now to put her arm around him and protect him. He sat down beside her. She patted his knee. He thought, as he looked at her, Had she any idea of what his finding her meant to him, of what burning dizzy happiness it was to him to look at her small child-like face with its honest eyes, its rather sharp ironical mouth, its clear smooth brow, the whole energy of her sturdy compact body, the independence, courage, humour that her poise always implied? No, she did not know. Had she known she would not have had the heart to leave him without a word.

'Well, Warren. What are you doing in Paris?'

'I have been searching for you for a whole fortnight, every day, all the time--'

'But how did you know that I was in Paris?'

'Francis told me.'

'Francis!--but he did not know my address.'

'No; that is why I have been searching for a fortnight. I have been looking everywhere. I had a feeling that to-day I should find you.'

'But what did you want to find me for?'

'Oh, Judith, you should not have left England without telling me! That was not kind of you. And the other also was not kind.'

'What other?'

'I know everything. Jennifer told me. . . . Yes. I went one day to Uldale. I had not seen you for three weeks. I must see you, so I went to Uldale. Jennifer was in a temper. She had been furious. When I stood in the hall, asking for you, she leaned over the stair and said, quite loud, anyone could have heard, "Judith has run away because she is going to have a child!"'

'Oh!' cried Judith. 'Did she?'

'Yes. And so I then at once understood everything. How could I have been so blind, so selfish?'

'So now they all know,' said Judith slowly. 'Well--it does not matter.'

'I was crazy with anger at myself. All these months and I had never thought! I went to Francis and demanded to know where you were. All he could tell me was that you were in Paris.'

'Poor Warren,' said Judith, patting his knee with her gloved hand. 'You look so very unwell.'

'So then I went to Will Herries and said that I must be permitted a holiday. He made some demur, but

Walter said that it would be right. It did not matter. Walter is staying at Westaways through the summer. So then I came to Paris.'

'But why do you look so ill, Warren?' she asked again. 'What have you been doing to yourself?'

'It is my heart--nothing at all. I have been so anxious about you. Oh, Judith, you should not have gone without saying anything to me!'

'Why not? It was no one's affair.'

'No one's affair! It is my child as well as yours. And I love you so. Ah, let me say that once again. For a whole fortnight I have been searching for you. I deserve to be allowed to tell you that I love you. And now you are going to be mother to my child. That is so wonderful that I cannot believe it is true.'

'It is true enough.' She sighed. Here she was--caught again! But he looked so unwell that she could think of nothing else. She would take any trouble now, when he looked so unwell, not to hurt him. She began to be very practical. 'Now listen, Warren. I am here with a friend--Emma Furze. You have heard me speak of her. We are in lodgings in the Rue Vivienne together.'

'I am in a hotel near the Palais-Royal.'

'Near the Palais-Royal. Very good. Then to-morrow morning--'

'Oh, not to-morrow morning!' he broke in. 'I have been two weeks looking for you. Allow me to stay with you for a little while this evening.'

'Our rooms are very small.'

'I do not mind what they are. I must see that you are comfortable. You must have better rooms. You must allow me--'

'Nonsense, Warren. Everything is very nice where we are.'

A moment later Emma arrived, very heated. She smiled at the square-bearded gentleman, who bowed significantly, as though they had agreed on a further meeting, and went away.

'Oh, such a charming man! And he speaks perfect English! He is a Professor of Languages, and his wife has been dead five years. He has a--'

'Emma, this is a friend of mine from England. Mr. Warren Forster.'

So this is the father of Judith's child, thought Emma, this little pale insignificant man!

She was inclined to be resentful, because he had provided all this trouble for Judith, but when she saw how ill he looked her heart was melted and she was as eager as was Judith that he should be comfortable.

They hailed a carriage and drove to the Rue Vivienne. Oh, dear! thought Emma, how he does love her, poor man! For he continued to look at her as a dog looks at its mistress, a fashion that always irritated Judith, who thought that everyone should be equal.

Warren insisted that he should pay the carriage. That Judith permitted him. Then they went through the courtyard, climbed the dark and smelling stairs.

In the close little sitting-room Warren said: 'What is that?'

'It is the monkey and the cockatoo in the next room.'

Emma was very tactful and went away. She knew that they would want to talk to one another. There were only two chairs. He insisted that Judith should take the larger. So she sat there, her hands behind her head. She felt her child move beneath her heart, her child and his. He sat very erect in the stiff-backed chair, leaning forward, his thin fragile hands tightly clasped together.

'Oh, I am so glad that I have found you!' he said. 'If you knew how happy it makes me. And that you are to be the mother of my child--that is the proudest thing that has ever happened to me!' Then as he saw that she was going to speak: 'No, don't say anything yet--pray, pray do not. I know that you do not love me, that you have never loved me. But you have given me such great kindness, and now that we are to have a child, I do not know--I do not know--' He broke off, twisting his hands nervously together. He looked up at her, smiling like a child asking a favour. 'It is a bond.'

But that was exactly what she would not have it. How was she to be honest with him without hurting him?

'No--Warren. I must be free. I am bound to no one, and the child will not be bound either.' She got off the chair and came to him and stood close to him. She put her arm round him, and he, like a child with its mother, bent his head against her.

'You know, Warren, I have told you before. I have only touched life deeply once. I have only once loved and I never shall again. At that time I was so young that I did not know that that would be the only time. But I could not have valued it more highly even if I had known. And at the end when he was dying and said that he loved me . . . No, no,' she broke off, her hand trembling on his shoulder. 'That was my real life. Nothing, my dear friend, has been quite real to me since. And I came to France because I wished my child to be born in Georges' country, and if I have been unfair to you, forgive me. I did not mean it--'

'No, no,' he broke in, 'never unfair. You have been only good.'

He bent forward and kissed her. She went on eagerly:

'We will make you comfortable, Emma and I. We will all be together. I was wrong, Warren dear, not to see you more frequently in England. That was most reprehensible, but now we will make you well. We will all be so happy together--'

For he looked so ill, poor little man. He had sunk against the hard back of his chair. His fingers clutched her hand. His face was the colour of ash. His lips were purple.

'Yes . . .' he murmured. 'I am ill . . . my heart. . . . In my coat . . . drops.'

She rushed to his carriage-coat that he had flung off when he came in. In a pocket she found a little bottle. He murmured directions. She thought that he was going to die. There seemed nothing so important in all her life as to save him. Little by little he came to himself. His lips were less blue. He even smiled a timid nervous smile.

'The pain,' he murmured. 'The pain is very terrible.'

'Oh, you must remain here!'

She knelt by him, stroking his hair, holding him close to her.

'Are you better? Are you better now?'

'Yes, I am better now.'

'Of course, you must remain.'

She thought what she could do. One of the beds must be moved out of the other room. She and Emma could sleep together. Reassuring him that she would return in a moment she went out to find Madame Dufresne, and behold that woman, who had been so fierce and so sinister, was now the very soul of kindness.

Emma also was there. All together they moved the bed. Then alone Judith helped Warren to undress, as a mother her son. She gave him one of her own nightdresses. Very small and wan he looked lying there, never taking his eyes from her face. The doctor had been sent for.

She sat down beside the bed, sewing at something for the child.

She could hear very faintly the street noises. The candle flickered and threw great shadows on the wall. He put his hand out, took hers and kissed it.

'Now, now . . . you are to sleep. That is what you are to do.'

But she bent forward, leaned over the bed and kissed his forehead. He closed his eyes as though in an ecstasy of happiness. She continued quietly to sew, to listen for the doctor. She felt the child move in her womb. How strange life was! That she should be sitting here in Paris, waiting for her child to be born, Warren in bed in her room!

How strange, incongruous, foolish and touching! She felt a strong pride as though she had her hand on life, a mettlesome steed, restive under her touch, restive but obedient!

PALAIS-ROYAL

'Son Altesse le Prince de Benevento!'

'That is Talleyrand,' whispered Emma, who was in so frantic a state of excitement that the feather in her head-dress wobbled like a live thing.

Oh! thought Judith, how I wish they were all here to see us--Will, Christabel, Walter, Pomfret, Rose, Maria, Carey, Francis, Jennifer and the children, John and Dorothy. How they would adore it--the brilliant colours of the uniforms, the flash of the decorations, the silks, satins, shawls, diamonds of the ladies!

It was not Judith's natural disposition to want to show off, even to the members of her family whom she disliked most; but this was one of the great Balls of History!

How was it that they were there at all? Well, Warren had encountered (on the first day that he was able to go out after his recovery from his heart attack) a business friend of Will's, a Monsieur Rakonitz of the famous Viennese jewellers, and he knew everyone: had supped with Blücher and shown rubies to the King of Prussia, and sold a bracelet to Fouché. He had suggested that he could find three tickets for Warren. In all probability he had some deal with Will in hand, or wanted Will's influence for something. In any case, he was a grand jolly fellow, with a big beard and his hat cocked on one side. Then, unlike so many men with their hats cocked on one side, he had remembered his promise, and Warren had had his tickets.

So here they were, as merry and excited as three children. Judith was very near her time, and, in consideration of her age and that this was her first child, it had been wiser of her perhaps not to have come, but she could not resist it. She could never refuse to have fun, nor could she refuse to be kind to anyone, and she knew that Warren's evening would be nothing were she not there with him.

Not so Emma. She was devoted to Judith; but whether Judith were there or no she would enjoy herself. Her purple gown, her splendid turban, gave her a fine dramatic air, as of a prophetess given to acting tragic rôles at occasional moments. This was her pose while she remembered, but when she forgot she was simply a tall jolly libertine, ready to smile at anything and eager for every kind of attention, with a heart that Warren, who did not really like her, described as 'incredibly open.'

Judith stood beside her, insignificant in the white gown that hid her figure, a little, very ordinary, middle-aged woman, but to Warren more magnificent and splendid than any one there.

They stood against the wall under a huge galaxy of candelabra, and Warren told them who everyone was.

Talleyrand was an old, powdered, old-fashioned gentleman. He might have been any card-playing, gently-flirting, fussy-about-his-food- and-his-bottle, old gentleman--one of the milder, politer Herries, Judith thought. But when you looked at him more closely (and they had an excellent opportunity, for he stood near to them, smiling, bowing, his sharp eyes ceaselessly darting now into this face, now on to that stubborn back, now beyond the other ingratiating desire for recognition) you could see an elaborate calm, a dangerous mildness. . . .

'Le Duc d'Otrante!'

Fouché, the villain of the piece, the super-policeman, sly devil, malicious tyrant, admirable teller of indecent stories. . . .

'Sa Majesté le Roi de Prusse--leurs Altesses Royales les Princes Royaux de Prusse--le Duc de Mecklembourg.'

The Prince of Orange, pale from his recent wound, Lady Castlereagh, General Alava, the Prussian King, plain, kindly, stout, melancholy, the princes his boys, also melancholy. . . . Oh yes, it would be agreeable to have Francis here, DEAR Francis whom, now that one was away from him, one loved as deeply as ever . . . he would enjoy this and would look so distinguished and for a moment would forget Jennifer . . . and oh! if Jennifer suddenly entered how startled everyone would be! What a wonderful entrance she would make, moving lazily like a queen, ever so slightly smiling in her consciousness of the great beauty that she was, and Talleyrand would bend his little figure forward and inquire of Lady Castlereagh, and Fouché would turn his sharp eyes, and the Prussian King would stroke his melancholy cheek. Yes, Jennifer should have been a queen in some country where everyone admired her, where there would be little work. . . .

And then followed the great thrill of the evening. An important body of officers and aides-de-camp, a rather aged, not very interesting officer at their head, and the announcement:

'Son Altesse Sérénissime--le Prince Blücher.'

Everyone pushed forward to stare at him, and then what a moment! half-way down the salon, Wellington moved forward and, meeting with smiles, the two great heroes shook hands.

But for Judith even that was not the final climax, for, just behind her, she heard a voice say 'Look at that-- a few weeks ago those two men delivered Europe'--and, half turning, saw standing quite close to her, whom but Mr. Walter Scott?

His expression was one of rapt and intense fervour. His eyes, from under their heavy eyebrows, glittered with emotion. She thought there were tears in them. As he leaned forward, his high-domed forehead rising into an odd peak, his strong shoulders set, the nobility of his mouth speaking of all the kindness (and yet firmness and stiff obstinacy too) that a Scottish gentleman is capable of, she felt that she MUST speak to him, wisdom, folly, or no.

'Is it not wonderful to be present at such a moment?'

He turned and saw a modest, stout little body in a white gown. As he greatly preferred modest and simple people to any other, he smiled like a brother and gave a little bow.

'It is indeed, madame.'

He turned his eyes back to Wellington and Blücher. She did not venture any more, but she pulled

Warren away to a little distance and whispered in a voice husky with excitement:

'I have just spoken with Mr. Walter Scott.'

She was so happy and Warren was so happy that they were united in this hour more than they had ever been. For some weeks she had been looking after him, and he had needed her so; she had grown as a sister, as a mother, fonder and fonder of him. And he WAS someone to be fond of. She had not known that he had so tender and gentle a nature, one so honest and sincere. And in knowing him better she perceived a new and a better side of the Herries character, something more generous, easy, and kind. Francis had had that strain, Maria and Carey had some of it, even Pomfret and Rose. If only their wretched ridiculous family quarrels did not obscure it!

She said to Warren one day:

'Although you are but QUARTER Herries you are the RIGHT quarter! You are what we all ought to be!'

He flushed with pleasure.

'You can say that when yourself--'

'Oh no, I am all wrong. I shall turn into the most awful old woman if I live. Always grab, grab at people, and they will all run--and then I shall blame them and not myself.'

So to-night they both forgot Emma (who was quite capable of entertaining herself) and wandered about in blissful excitement together. Every once and again, laying her hand on his arm, she would say: 'Are you certain that you are quite well? You feel nothing? You are sure?'

And he would answer radiantly: 'I am too happy to feel ill.'

His features were very pale, she thought, but otherwise he had filled out again. His body was sturdy and firmly set once more.

They saw many interesting things. They saw a portrait of Napoleon resting against the wall, the stern fixed eyes gazing out upon this scene that emphasised his defeat. They saw in the ante-chamber of the great supper-room Wellington himself slip across to a small supper-table and join Lady Castlereagh and Mr. Scott. They were all very gay and merry, Lady Castlereagh indeed screaming like a peahen.

They themselves went out into the gardens, where long supper-tables were laid and hundreds of people were supping. They sat down at a table under the trees from which lights were shimmering. Everywhere there was a flood of noise like the sea, multitudinous voices, laughter, knives, forks, plates, the popping of corks, the rhythm and pattern of the distant band.

'Oh, Warren, I feel as though something wonderful were going to happen with the birth of our child. Will it, do you think? Am I cheating myself? I have not been so happy since I was with Georges. You know I came to Paris because of Georges, do you not? You are not angry, are you? Because now I am so glad that you came. I wasn't glad at first. I was so SICKENED of

Herries. All quarrels and temper, and no one caring for anyone. I wanted to be rid of it all. But now you are yourself, dear Warren. We are splendid friends. I care for you so much. I am glad that it is your child. Is it not ridiculous that it cannot be always like this, you and I and the child? I don't WANT to go back to all the Herries character. It will catch me up, and I shall like it and become a managing, NASTY old woman, and be too old to know that I am. . . . You must save me from that, Warren.'

He put his hand on hers. 'You are so good, Judith. . . .'

'No, I am NOT good. I have never done anyone good. Emma said that the other day, and that when I met her first she was drunken and lost. But Emma would never be lost. She has too great a vitality. And I did Georges no good neither. But now perhaps, if I choose rightly and stay outside the Herries family--'

'You must eat some of this chicken,' said Warren. 'This chicken is excellent.' Then added inconsequently: 'I have not long to live. Another attack like that last one will finish me. But I want you to know, Judith, that you have given me the happiest days of my life. I did not know I could be so happy. . . .'

'Yes, is not this chicken excellent? It would be nice to have Francis here, and Maria--'

'Ah, now you want others--'

'No. It is beautiful as it is. But I want everyone to be happy to- night. Imagine! All the Kings eating chicken only a yard away! And I spoke to Mr. Scott, and I heard the Duke say "Damnation." Would it not be funny, Warren, if I suddenly had my baby here on the grass, in a corner under the tree? And then we would ask Mr. Scott to be its godfather. I do hope that it is a boy. What shall we name him? Some new name. Not a Herries name, like Francis or Pomfret.'

She sucked a chicken-bone, holding it in her fingers.

There was a 'grimacier' entertaining a crowd on the lawn away from the tables. At his side were the long windows flooded with light, phantasmal figures moving within, beyond him; behind him shadows pooled with dancing candle-shine, and into the pools figures moved with white, excited, laughing faces. The King of Prussia's two boys were there, laughing at his antics. He was a long cadaverous man and wore a sheepskin cap. He made the most extraordinary faces, pulling his chin down, wrinkling his forehead, closing his eyes. He imitated the English, did a Highlander making love to a French girl, 'Jean Bool' and his wife eating at a restaurant, Napoleon running from Waterloo, Mlle. George singing a song.

Judith began to laugh.

'He is so clever. Is he not clever? Oh, Warren, see--look what he does with his cap! Is not that marvellous?'

She laughed till she cried. They stood close together and then hand in hand, while Emma, in another part of the garden, told a stout Frenchman how comic he was; and Fouché took the leg of a chicken in his fingers and cracked the bones with his teeth as though they were so many condemned criminals.

Then came the fearful day, never to be forgotten by Judith as long as she lived, September 4, 1815.

On the early afternoon of that day they walked, the three of them, to view the site of the famous Bastille. At first they had all been in the highest spirits. Judith had, in the last few days, been feeling almost incredibly weary, but heavy though her body was, her heart was light. Since the day of the famous Ball she had known a new relationship with Warren, a deeper intimacy. They were now like brother and sister; she could care for him, watch over him without any falseness on her side or irritation on his. On these days he poured out everything from his heart, talked and talked as though he could never tell her enough, and she loved to listen. It was all thrilling and exciting to her as though she had shared in it. Emma, occupied with many romances of her own, left them much to themselves.

Then, early on this morning of the Fourth of September, Judith awoke in a panic. She lay on her bed, feeling the child kick in her womb, wondering whether it were a bad dream that she had. Some figure seemed to be in the room with her, now it was young Hartley Coleridge twisting one leg round the other, now Reuben, now young Stane, and now, more definitely, La Belle Limonadière from the Palais-Royal with her black hair and crimson dress, arranging the lumps of sugar.

The figures faded as the light in the room grew clearer. There was no one there. The panic remained.

They started to walk in the afternoon, but it was very hot, and they called a carriage. Little light silver clouds flecked the sky, the buildings were pigeon-colour, the air full of the scent of flowers, there was the echo of bands, distant as though from behind closed doors.

They crossed the bridge of Austerlitz, drove gently along the boulevards and then came to the site. Here they got out, dismissed the carriage and walked about, seeing, from every angle, where the famous attacks of 1789 had been made. For Judith this was an event of poignant memories. She could see now David advancing across the bright shining grass of the Uldale lawn to meet Francis, then the talk, the quarrel, the uplifted stick. If David had lived, had Sarah not 'gone crazy ' . . . Ah well, what was the use of that kind of memory? Every link in the chain must be there; she would not be here now had she not ridden over to Stone Ends and struck a small boy because he loved her hair; she would not be the woman she was had she not rescued Reuben's brother in Cockermouth, had she not. . . .

She dragged herself wearily after the other two (how tired she was, how hot the day, how heavy the child within her!), but she smiled when Emma, who was being very dramatic over the Revolution, turned to her; she put her hand through Warren's arm, and was interested in everything.

What they especially were interested in was an immense wooden shed, in the middle of the site, and a half-finished colonnaded tower of freestone. This was enclosed with a wooden paling and had a gate. Inside the gate on a stool was sitting a slim, pale-faced, elderly woman, one of whose cheeks had a painful twitch. Her eyes were sad and staring, as though she were looking for something that she could not find. She was clothed very decently with a shawl over her thin shoulders.

She begged them to enter and see the 'Elephant.'

'The elephant?' said Warren. 'Pray, what elephant? This is not the Jardin des Plantes?

But it seemed that Napoleon had determined to erect a huge fountain on the Bastille site that its waters might wash away the memory of the awful events that had occurred there. This fountain was to spout its waters through the trunk of a great elephant. The melancholy woman, her eyes staring far beyond them while she spoke, pressed them to enter. Judith did not want to go; she did not know why, but she did not want to go.

However, Emma was all for seeing everything, so in they went.

The model was built of clay, indurated and whitened, exactly in figure and size what the bronze was intended to be, and it stood at the tremendous height of sixty feet. It had been intended that it should be placed on a stone pedestal and that then the water should pour out of its trunk into a succession of basins all round.

The woman, in a dreary unhappy voice, said that the English intended to finish this work, so she had heard.

'They have a number of other things to finish first,' said Warren laughing. But nothing at all seemed to amuse the woman.

She asked them gravely, as though she were accusing them personally:

'What have YOU done with the Emperor?'

'He is in charge of the Allies.'

'Will he ever return?'

'Never! . . . Never!'

'Tant mieux! Mais l'Éléphant!'

For some reason this huge white towering beast affected Judith with nausea. It looked so bare, so savage, so revengeful. With its great trunk it seemed to be ready to catch them, throw them up, and then, when they had fallen at its feet, riotously trample on them. In the hot quivering summer air it appeared to move, there was life in its vast body. The woman became more sinister, her cheek twitching, her hands moving; they would be prevented from escaping and the elephant would pursue them, trumpeting, within the palings. The air was so close that it was stifling.

She felt that in a moment she would be hysterical.

'Quickly. I cannot endure it. It is horrible. It is moving, cannot you see that it is moving?'

'Why, Judith--'

'No, no. I must get out. I cannot endure it.'

In a moment she would be laughing and screaming. She ran out into the street.

They followed her, wondering what the matter was.

'No. It is nothing. The heat was terrible. And the elephant . . . its trunk . . . And the woman hated us. Could you not see? Of course, she hated us.'

They sat down at a little table on the boulevard and ordered coffee. Judith was surprised to discover that she was trembling.

'But did you not feel it? I cannot understand why you did not. The elephant was alive. Oh yes, I know. . . . But it WAS alive. In another moment . . .'

She drank her coffee, feeling that she had been too foolish for anything. She to give way to nerves! So that when they suggested that they should go to the Palais-Royal, although she hated to do so, she agreed.

Arrived there, they sat at a little table beneath a wide awning and watched the scene. The ladies with their high hats, their long sumptuous dresses, some of them with canes, all of them painted, vivacious and, it seemed, without a care in life, smiled at the men as anglers throw their baited hooks. The shops glittered, the sun shone down relentlessly; the moving crowds were like players in a game where something has to be found, now suddenly hurrying forwards as though the scent were 'hot', now hesitating, halting, the scent lost.

Judith's uneasiness increased. It was the heat, it was the noise, it was the smell of hot iron and dried dung and clothes. The long stretches of the square shone like glass. Some toy balloons, red and green and yellow, were floating like swollen puff-balls in the air. In one place a 'grimacier' held a little crowd, throwing on and off his headgear, changing his coat, dancing, bending backwards. Nearer her there was a Punch and Judy, and from within the little coloured box came the sharp rasping cry and the quick bark of the little frilled dog.

It seemed to her that everyone was hostile, and this was not all her imagination, for at this time in Paris, behind the gaiety and laughter, all nerves were taut, no one knew what was to happen next, no one could trust his neighbour. There was great hostility to the Prussians. French officers in disguise were everywhere waiting to pick a quarrel. One of the means was to sit in a public place with your feet stretched and trip up a Prussian. Duels were fought every day. Two Prussians had been murdered the night before in a dark street behind the Opéra.

Judith sat there wondering what was the matter. She was not exactly ill, but felt a deep apprehension.

Was her time imminent? Perhaps she had best go home, but she did not wish to spoil Warren's pleasure. She knew that he would insist on going with her.

She looked at him while he talked to Emma; how fond she had become of him, what good companions they were! She liked to be fond of people, especially when they were not weak and yet did what she advised. The pleasantest people in the world were the selfish ones who were also kindly, so that in the middle of their selfishness they thought of you and did something for you. Unselfish people who were always eager to do something for you were so irritating. . . .

A group of French people, eagerly laughing and talking, came out of the restaurant behind Judith and, not noticing her, bumped against her and almost knocked her chair over. She felt her heart leap, the shops and chairs and coloured clothes danced before her eyes. She could not drive that horrible white elephant out of her mind. It would not surprise her to see it come trumpeting and trampling, the crowd running before it. She would not be able to move; she would be held in her place as one is in a nightmare. Something had warned her not to come to the Palais-Royal.

Then she noticed sitting near to her a young Prussian officer, quite alone. He had large melancholy eyes and was little more than a boy. He stared out into the pageant with unseeing gaze. What was it? Was he sick for home? Was he thinking of someone he loved and wishing that she were with him, wondering what he did there?

Warren turned to her smiling. He was watching the 'Punch,' laughing at the little dog. Always after she would remember every detail of the next few minutes. A tall very handsome lady, in a high green fur hat, was leaning across her little table, gazing into the eyes of a stout frog-faced gentleman choked by a huge stock. Some band was coming nearer, the music grew louder and louder as though a door were opening. Two more crimson balloons floated into the air; a small poodle, ridiculously naked, ran forward into the crowd, lost, and a shrill feminine voice cried 'Dédé . . . Dédé!' It heard the voice and eagerly ran back again.

Emma was exclaiming: 'But the air was so ravishing that I could not endure to return, so I waved my hand and he came, running, such ecstasy painted on his features. . . .'

Then everything happened in a moment. The band just entered with a blare of sound, someone laughed, the lady in green pinched the gentleman's chin. . . .

A young Frenchman with a black moustache and sharp beady eyes moved against the chair in which the young Prussian was sitting; a glass fell with a clash, the Prussian was almost tumbled from his seat. The Prussian started up, his hand on his sword. The two faced one another. A pistol-shot cracked; the young Prussian, his legs bent oddly beneath him, lay huddled against the iron legs of the table.

At the sound of the shot the sky seemed to swing, the buildings to bend forward.

Everyone came out running from the restaurant. There were shouts and cries. Two officers in Uhlan uniform approached the Frenchman.

Judith saw him struggling with them. She was quite near to him, and could observe how, although his face was white, he expressed a rage that was like a mad cat's. He repeated, in a shrill treble voice, over and over again the word 'L'Empereur!'

He pushed back the men who were attacking him, turned with a swing of his body and looked straight into Judith's eyes--without of course seeing her, but, in the fiery meeting of sun, sky, roofs, and floor that seemed now to whirl in a wheel of flame before her, she saw the face of the hanging boy from London.

She felt herself now, just as she had done then, sick from a kind of claustrophobia, the crowd shutting her in. She had lost sight of both Emma and Warren. She was alone, as she always seemed to be in every crisis.

Then the young Frenchman, brushing his cheek with one hand, as though a fly had bothered him, flung out the other, and again a pistol-shot crashed like a stone flung through glass.

At that it was as though the Palais-Royal had been a plate in a second tilted forward, spilling its contents downwards into some abyss. The screams and shouts were detached. One shout was deep like a drum, another was shrill like the knock on a high gong.

Judith, struggling to escape from chairs and tables, saw Warren endeavouring to push through an absurd clump of bodies that clung together like plants in a storm. Behind them the whole Palais-Royal, still tilted, swarmed with figures as unreal as puppets worked by strings.

He called 'Judith! Judith!' He beat the bodies in front of him frantically aside with his arms. He reached her, fell against her. Horses were rising. A horse, mounted by a soldier, came charging through fallen furniture. Glass fell with a crash. A dog barked, and on that bark she caught Warren in her arms, for his face was purple. He could not speak. He dropped limp against her, so that she stumbled to the ground.

Kneeling there, her arms around him, she saw that he was dead, heard a bell ring just above her head, saw the horse (shaped like an elephant) go charging into the sun.

A wave of pain caught her, so frightful that some other person broken to pieces inside herself screamed. Everything was black.

She sank down on a descending shaft of pain. She slowly mounted again, to find that she was quite clear-sighted, was lying on a hard, dry sofa, her head on a pillow that smelt of cheese. She hated the smell, but also the row of lofty shining mirrors that reflected again and again the long room with empty tables, chairs piled high.

Somewhere in the distance shouting fell against the mirrors and died on the floor. She felt the sweat tumble into her eyes, wiped it away, and saw a vast Emma towering above her.

'Warren is dead,' Judith murmured.

A little stout man with two chins, who seemed also to smell of cheese, advanced to her. She saw that he was greatly agitated. A big silver ring trembled as his hand trembled. She heard him say:

'A screen! A screen! . . . Where is a screen!'

Then she had one more absolute moment of clear vision.

Warren was dead. Her child was being born. She would die also, and history would repeat itself, for even as she had been born at the instant of her parents' death, so now would her child be born of their death.

The little man leaned over her. She saw the silver ring tremble. A cascade of pain hovered in the air--but before it broke over her she screamed out, 'I will not die! . . . I will not die!'

'It is a boy,' said the doctor to Emma, quarter of an hour later.

They were bringing the bodies of the wounded into the restaurant and laying them in the shadow where the room was coolest.

END OF PART III

PART IV

MOTHER AND SON

THE HILLS

Walter Herries rode up the hill from Hawkshead one fine summer's evening to get some air before spending the evening with his friend, Squire Thistleton, at High Grange. He had come over from Grasmere more swiftly than he had intended, having already eaten his dinner with the Bordens there, not wishing to invade High Grange before nightfall. Squire Thistleton's lady bored him most desperately: stay the night with Thistleton he must, for he had important business matters to discuss with him, but be bored by Mrs. Thistleton he would not. Although he was so genial, for ever laughing at the jokes of others, yes, roaring and slapping his vast thigh at them, yet, like all very self-centred men, he had a watchful eye. If he must suffer at the jokes of others there must be excellent reason for it. He did nothing at all without an admirable reason. Immense in build though he was, he was not yet corpulent for his twenty-eight years. He looked exceedingly handsome in his green riding-coat as the white horse picked its way carefully up the rough stone-strewn path. The summer is the worst time of the year in which to see this country: the naked blue sky does not suit its shape and size; the hills dwindle beneath the sun; the green carpet of field and brow has neither shade nor variety. But to-night fragments of orange cloud floated across a blue so faint as to be almost without colour, and the hills were so clearly outlined that they forced themselves, dark rocks of a mysterious country, out of a sea with no ripple.

Walter had no eyes for scenery; he left that to the romantic writers, now ever more numerous. But, pausing on the brow, and looking down to the left where the waters of Coniston lay bronzed and still, he felt all the pride of one who owns a fine property. For he had

come now to feel that he, and he alone, possessed the whole of this charming and fruitful land. It was a natural and happy evolution of circumstance. He was at this moment well beyond his own actual territory, which was not as yet a very large one, but he felt himself to be so infinitely the most important person alive in the combined counties of Cumberland and Westmorland, and what he felt himself to be, that he was.

It was now over three years since Will Herries, his father, had departed back to London. He was to be seen very seldom at Westaways. It had been made clear to him (Walter had assisted in the demonstration) that the City was the place for him. For one thing, there was nothing in life so pleasant for Will as the making of money, and although now much of his wealth had its richest foundations in Manchester and the Midlands, London was inevitably the heart of affairs. For another, Walter had helped him to perceive that, although Cumberland society did not object to wealth, it still objected to the City. The time was coming when a City man, granted that he had retired and had pocketed plenty of gold before retiring, would be admitted into good company, but that time was not quite yet. Moreover, Will had no intention whatever of retiring. He was now only fifty years of age and in excellent health. Business had never been so interesting as now when it was beginning to rouse itself, in the promise of so much fresh industrialism, out of the depression that followed the French Wars. The chimneys of the Midlands were gallantly smoking, and Will must be there to see that they were properly supplied.

Walter's ambitions were quite other. He disclaimed now all connection with business. With his handsome person, his geniality, his ruthless selfishness, his happy disregard of the interests of any but his own, his fine place (but he already felt Westaways far too small for him) and, above all, his almost insane pride in the Herries name, he was excellently placed to dominate his country world. The men and women around him, he would say, had judged of Herries by the miserable specimens hitherto offered to them. HE would show them what a Herries really was. Indeed, his earlier scorn of Francis and Jennifer had by now grown to an irritated and festering hatred. He would never dominate this country properly until Uldale and its occupants were wiped from the face of the land. They had not a chance against him; Francis weak and idle, Jennifer dull and scandalous. Only in their children could they rival him. At that thought, which constantly peered up at him out of the dark recesses of his mind like a malicious stinging animal, his whole body would tremble. For, in the spring of 1815, his wife had presented him with twins, a boy and a girl, and the boy was a weak and ailing cripple. Moreover, his wife would give him no more children, and, unless she died, Uhland must be his only son.

In his disgust at the puny and deformed baby he had not cared what they called him, and Mrs. Herries, moved perhaps by the increasing wave of German Romanticism, or hoping, it may be, that the child thus named might make some escape from the Herries nature, had had this outlandish fancy. The boy was Uhland, marked in this way, as in all others, from the common kind.

And Francis' children, John and Dorothy, were healthy and strong. Elizabeth and Uhland--John and Dorothy. He was beset by the contrast.

The horse moved forward. He turned down the hill to the two small pools that lay, in blue translucent stillness, under the dark guardianship of the wood. Behind the trees Helvellyn and Fairfield kept sleepy tolerant guard.

The day had been hot; their purple shadows slumbered.

There was perfect stillness all about Walter Herries as he sat on his horse and looked into the pool. There were other little things that had exasperated him to-day. He had been slowly riding by Grasmere Lake when he encountered that crazy old poet, William Wordsworth, and his mad sister as they walked along.

Walter, with his accustomed geniality, had stopped his horse to speak to them, as a king might to his subjects. Everyone knew that Wordsworth as a poet was a mock and a derision, and his sister, Dorothy, was as mad as a hatter. Wordsworth wrote poems about donkeys and daffodils. He was a joke to the neighbourhood, and that little sister of his, with her shabby clothes and fiery eye . . . And yet, speaking to them with all courtesy, he had been in some way rebuked. The comical pair! Wordsworth was going fishing; his sister said something about a bird on a tree. They did not seem at all gratified that he had spoken to them.

'Good day to you, Mr. Herries . . . Good day to you,' Wordsworth had said, as though he were impatient to be gone, and his sister had wandered about the road,

following some bird with her glittering eye. . . . Oh, mad, mad both of them! But mad or no they should have been impressed by his greeting.

Another vexation had been a queer one. As he left home that morning little Uhland, five years old, had limped to wish him farewell. He had felt a sudden pride in his heart at sight of him. Proud of that white-faced bony little cripple! But it was pride that he had felt; he had been moved; he had bent down to embrace him. That was an absurd emotion--although, after all, when all was done, the child WAS a Herries . . . his only heir. . . . In spite of himself he sighed, rested his hand on his great thigh and looked about him, breathing in the sweet-scented summer air.

At that same moment there rushed past him, out of the wood, the most astonishing figure, a small naked child. It was a boy, and, straight in front of Herries' horse, he splashed into the pool. Another moment and he was swimming vigorously, tossing his head and uttering cries of delight. The pool was deep--the two pools would be a fine small lake one later day--and this midge of a boy, screaming like a little shrill bird, dived, appeared a moment later at the pool's edge, and then sprang out, dancing about and waving his arms in front of Herries' horse.

The horse, alarmed by this unusual adventure, reared, and Herries, in anger, snapped his whip, catching the child's bare leg. The child laughed and plunged into the pool again; a moment later a peasant woman appeared at the wood's edge, then ran down to Herries.

'What are you doing, whipping a baby! Have you nothing better--'

She broke off. They had recognised one another. This woman was Judith. She was dressed like a peasant in some rough material of red and green. On her red hair she wore no covering. On her bare feet she had wooden shoes. She stood, her small body set, her little face grinning.

'Why, Cousin Walter, I did not know that it was you. . . . It is a long time since we met.'

So it was. Years and years. He had not set eyes on her since that night in '15, when she had dinner with him, and they had heard of Napoleon's flight from Elba. None of them had seen her. She had been living in the hills with her bastard child. She had gone back to her origin.

'Well, well. Cousin Judith.' He took off his hat.

'Yes, and don't you whip my son or I shall have something to say.'

She was laughing, and he felt that in some way she was mocking him.

'Your son?'

'Yes. Adam, Adam, come here!'

The child seemed to spring from nowhere and stood, naked and dripping, by the horse. Yes, this would be her child. It would not be a day more than five, born in the same year as his own. He saw, with satisfaction, that the boy was ugly. The small body was brown with sun, the hair--that lay thick and matted above his eyes-- jet black. He had a short snub nose and a large grinning mouth, a strong sturdy body, but the legs and arms were too long. Yes, an ugly and common-looking child. He did not seem to feel cold, but Judith drew him to her, put her green shawl over him and her arm around him. He leant against her, wet as he was. She did not seem to care.

'This is Mr. Walter Herries, a relation of ours,' she said to him.

How strong and sturdy the woman seemed! She must be between forty and fifty now. What a queer pair they made.

At that he recovered his self-command which, for a moment, he seemed to have lost. He leaned lazily toward her, resting one hand on his hip. The horse shifted a little and, bending down, began to pluck the grass. The stillness was exquisite. A cloud, like a bronze chrysanthemum, jagged at its edges, floated over the wood and darkened, like a hand, the little pool.

'Where have you been all these years?' he asked her, friendly and patronising.

'You know well enough.'

What clear bright eyes she has! he thought, and wondered whether there were specks of dust on his clothes. His hand moved down the lapel of his coat.

'And when will you return to civilisation?'

'It is quite civilised enough where I am.'

'Have you seen Francis and Jennifer lately?'

'Francis has come to see me at Watendlath.'

'Well, I must be off to my supper.' He looked at the infant, and the infant looked back at him. 'So your name is Adam, young man?'

The child grinned up at him, looking at him fearlessly.

'Adam Paris,' he said. Then he added most unexpectedly: 'I could make your horse jump more if I tried.'

'You try--that's all!' said Walter, suddenly angry again.

'Now you leave the child alone, Cousin Walter,' said Judith. 'He is not afraid of you nor of anything else in the world. But I will give you something to be afraid of if you touch him with your whip.'

He had a sharp consciousness (which he was to recall one day) of the force and vitality of her personality. Whenever he encountered her she compelled him to remember it, small though she was. While she was away he created, if he thought of her at all, his own picture of her as an insignificant sort of poor-relation-governess. But when he was with her it was another matter. And now he suddenly thought: 'I had forgotten HER! Suppose that she should come back to Uldale!'

However, all that he did was to be gracious again. He took off his hat, bowed, invited her to bring her boy to see them at Westaways.

Judith was not ungracious. She always returned courtesy for courtesy. 'Yes, I will come one day, Cousin Walter. I hope Mrs. Herries is well.'

'Oh yes. Well enough.'

Then Walter rode away, his figure for a moment gigantic at the top of the bend against the soft glow of the milk-white sky. Judith, her hand in her son's, started along the little path that skirted the pool. Adam was wrapped up entirely in the shawl; the end of it trailed on the ground behind him. He danced along.

'What a fat man!' he said.

'That is your Uncle Walter.'

'In truth my uncle?'

'Near enough.'

'I could have made his horse jump.' He skipped a few paces and nearly tumbled. But she did not move to catch him nor did she ask him whether he were cold, as any other child would have been.

'Was the water agreeable?'

He wrinkled his nose like a little dog. 'I can smell the fire burning.' He shouted and cried aloud with happiness. The shawl fell off him, and bare as a young foal he ran towards the wood. Judith walked soberly after him. She was thinking deeply about Walter.

A small nondescript dog ran out to meet them. This was a mongrel dog who, coming from nowhere, had attached himself to them. He first ran eagerly towards Adam, moving awkwardly on legs that were longer than they should have been, but with eager excited joy. Then, just before he reached Adam, it occurred to him that he might not perhaps be so popular as he had hoped, so he crawled on all fours, dragging himself along with a bright supplicating eye.

'Dog! Dog!' Adam cried, and picked him up and ran into the wood, hugging the animal to his bare stomach; the dog's tail wagged in an ecstasy of happiness.

Just inside the wood a bright fire was burning, and on the other side of the fire sat a stout man in black, reading a book, and with an absent-minded hand once and again stirring with a stick the pot that hung over the fire.

Adam, who was now almost dry, flung himself, dog and all, into the stout man's lap.

'Uncle Reuben, a fat man on a horse tried to whip me, but he could not. Can we eat now?'

'You must dress yourself,' Reuben said, putting his book down and reaching out to a pile of minute clothes near to him.

Adam stood up on Reuben's thighs, putting his hands round Reuben's neck. Reuben clasped him round his small naked body, holding him lest he should fall.

'And who was this fat man?' he asked, moving his face a little; the small dog, when he saw what Adam was doing, was trying the same with the addition that he would lick Reuben's cheeks. The fire threw a shining colour on Adam's body. He seemed to be surrounded with a nimbus of light.

'Mother said he was my Uncle Walter. . . . Can we not eat now?'

He jumped suddenly off Reuben's thigh and had scuffled into a shirt and a pair of diminutive blue trousers. His legs were bare.

'Mother, can we not eat now?' He ran towards Judith, who stopped to look into the pot.

'Whom do you think I have seen?' she asked Reuben.

'I know. Adam told me.'

He spread his black riding-coat for her and she sat down, leaning her head against his knee. She looked up and could see the dark fans and wheels of the trees flecked with cool shell-white sky.

'Yes, Walter. After all these years. He looked huge and mightily satisfied. Do you know what he said to himself as he looked at me, Reuben?'

'No.'

'Here is slattern Judith and her bastard. . . . Adam laughed at him. . . .' She pushed Walter away for a moment and went on: 'You had a grand meeting this noon. The grandest I've seen.'

'Yes, praise the Lord!'

'But Reuben, you talked more of political things than religious. You were trying to make them discontented.'

'They are discontented already. They have been starving for years and now their masters will bring in machinery and they work in the dark like slaves.'

Judith shook her head.

'No. Not here. They are farmers and shepherds. There is no discontent in Kendal or Keswick.'

'No, but a little way out--at Whitehaven, Cockermouth. . . .'

She looked up at him and put up her hand. He took it in his.

'I like it better when you talk about God. Although I do not believe in Him I like others to. At least . . . believe or not . . . I haven't the wits to be so certain. But I like to hear you speak of Him. You bring Him so close. You are so sure of yourself now, Reuben, and yet as kind and good as ever you were. I had rather people were kind than anything else. Yet I detest a fool, and so many kind people are half-witted.' She let herself run on, looking up and seeing that a little evening breeze moved, as a tiny boat moves on a pond, through the trees. She looked down and saw that Adam was playing with the dog.

'Reuben, are you still bothered with women?'

He laughed. 'No. I am too old.'

'Nonsense. You are not sixty. When did they cease to torment you?'

'I will tell you. It was in Kendal some ten years ago. It was in the winter-time and I had been preaching out on the hills. It was perilously cold, and in the inn after supper a large red-faced girl invited me to her room. Then, to be warm and to be comforted by someone (for I was much alone at that time) I went into bed with her. And she had but just blown out the candle when I saw the Lord, a young man in silver armour standing on the floor. The fire shone on him and he was glorious. He cried to me, "Reuben, the pleasure is not worth the pain." And I answered "Nay, Lord, I was so cold." And he came to the bed and touched my forehead with his hand. I lay by the girl all night but neither of us was harmed.'

'And do you truly think it was the Lord?' asked Judith.

'Who else could it have been?' said Reuben.

'No, no one else.'

'Well, then--'

'But maybe you were already asleep--'

'Not before embracing the girl. No. It was the Lord. I have seen him in such armour at other times too--'

'And women are nothing to you since then?'

'I like women,' he said. 'But the temptation is over.'

'What are your temptations still?'

He answered gravely, counting on his fingers. 'One, I am a coward; two, I am greedy; three, I like a warm bed; four, I tell tales; five, I hate the Methodist preacher at Cockermouth; six, I am lazy-- I can sleep all day--'

She interrupted him. 'Look up. There is a red cloud like a crimson bird that Georges once had, hanging between two trees.'

But it was one of Reuben's defects that natural scenery meant nothing to him. Any human thing, but a tree, a cloud, a mountain-- nothing. The pot was boiling. Judith commanded the whole situation. The three of them and the dog sat and had a splendid meal.

'We will go up the hill and see the sunrise as you promised?' Judith asked.

'Yes,' Reuben said, but in spite of himself he yawned behind his hand.

She had an impulse to be cross, as she always had when things were not to be as she wished them. Then she conquered her crossness. She had been expecting for months this evening with Reuben. About twice a year they spent a night together. Once before they had ridden up into the Langdales and seen the sunrise. And now he was sleepy. His head was nodding. It had been a grand meeting and must have wearied him, but she had been looking forward passionately to a long talk with him. It was so seldom now that she could talk with her own kind, and to-night, most especially, she wanted his advice, for she was about to pay a visit to Uldale again for the first time since her return from France. She was taking Adam with her. The sudden vision of Walter had been like an omen. She was not frightened, but she needed help and only Reuben could give it her. And now Reuben was sleepy. Only Adam was not. He was dancing about with the dog, eager for the next adventure now that his hunger was satisfied.

Reuben turned round, knelt on the grass and said his prayers. Then he leaned against a tree-trunk and in another moment was asleep.

'He's asleep,' said Adam, laughing.

The night was so warm and the scent of the trees so comforting, the uncertain flicker of the fading fire so bewitching that, standing there, she felt that she was under a spell.

She was in magnificent health because of the life that she had been leading since coming to Watendlath, the life of a peasant, harvesting, digging, helping with the sheep, riding off with Watson for a whole day on the fells, ploughing for hours through the quagmires at the top of the Fell after a lost or strayed lamb—and always in perfect content. That was the life to which part of her temperament entirely responded; but the other part would not have been content had she not had Adam. Adam now was her whole life, her soul, her body, her past, her future, her God and her destiny.

She had been waiting always for some such passion as this. Her love for Georges had possessed her, but it had not been returned until the last and, say what one may, a love that is not returned is only half a love.

Moreover, although she had not known it, she was a woman to whom motherhood was the only possible complete fulfilment. Her love for Georges, her affection for Reuben, Francis, Maria, Warren, Emma Furze, Watson, had been in its impulse maternal. But they had not been her own. Now she had something that was her own, and anyone watching her might have been frightened of the fiery, possessive, passionate element at the heart of her love for her son.

But she was not a fool. She kept her love in control as yet. And Adam was not at present difficult. His mother was his companion; he knew none other as good. He loved her quite naturally without thinking of it. He was independent but warm-hearted and, at present, he had no feeling that she threatened his liberty. There was as yet no cloud on his sky. The first five years of his life, two in France, three at Watendlath, had known no blemish. She had been able to give him all he wanted, because when Warren's will was read it was found that he had left her all his own small means—not much, but enough for her needs. The boy was of amazing health, and, so long as he was not shut up in a room for too long, asked for no attention. He trusted everyone as a puppy trusts everyone before his first betrayal. He was fearless, truthful and gay, the three best things a small boy can be. He would defend his mother against anyone or anything; he was obedient so long as she did not hamper his liberty. Once, for some small crime, she had locked him in a room; he had broken the window and disappeared until nightfall. She understood that because she had once climbed out of a window herself.

Their relationship was, at present, perfect.

Now as the light faded and the stars came out she tried to persuade him to sleep. She would not wake Reuben. She would walk up the hill and see the sunrise by herself. But she almost hesitated to speak because the silence was so glorious, broken only by the running water that is to be heard everywhere in this country, the gentle friendly crackle of the burning wood as it fell into crimson embers, the occasional movement of the horses behind her.

Adam, too, seemed to feel the silence, for he stood without moving, his legs spread, looking up.

'Now you must sleep, Adam.'

He shook his head, not saying anything.

'Oh no. . . .' He looked at her, smiling. 'There's the moon.'

And there it was, sailing very calmly with a sort of smiling conceit between the trees.

She knew that he wouldn't sleep. 'Come. And we shall see the sunrise.'

So he took her hand and they started off, the small dog following. Adam was never very talkative. To be out at night was no very new thing to him. They left the little wood behind them and started to climb. They were now on the open moor. The Langdale Pikes, Fairfield, Helvellyn were beyond, and across Yewdale loomed the hump of the Old Man. The light about and around him was diffused as though shed by the multitude of stars. The pools of shadow, neither brown nor grey, lay below them like lakes of sleeping water. Fairfield and Helvellyn were marked with crags and precipices like the tearing made by some giant's fingers. How black, how black the hills against the luminous sky! A little higher on the moor and they were suddenly staring into the moon's face. They could see now the two little pools which seemed to blaze with moon-silver among the surrounding vapour. No wind stirred; somewhere some sheep were moving and the air was warm like the breath of a flower.

They sat down against a gigantic boulder; the stones around them rose in that moonshine like monolithic sacrificial monuments. As they sat in that stillness the hills seemed to approach them. Helvellyn, always a beneficent hill, leaned towards them, Fairfield embraced them, the pools below smiled at them. Somewhere in that wood Reuben was lying against a tree snoring with his mouth open. Adam curled in against Judith's side, the little dog curled in against Adam.

With her arm around her son Judith sat staring into the moon. She did not often think of the past, but tonight it came crowding towards her, figures issuing from the hills, events stealing up from the mist—the day that she had looked at Mrs. Monnasett and David had beaten her, the moment when she had seen Georges' mother, the night of the fireworks when Will and Francis and Reuben had talked, the escape of Reuben's brother, David's stroke and death, Sarah's passion—and then all her life with Georges, from the first week (what a baby then she had been!) to the last awful scene with

Stane's father! And then the dead quiescence of the years at Grosset, the semi-life with Jennifer and Francis, Will's coming to Westaways, the friendship with Warren leading to the drama in Paris-- drama of death, drama, thank God, of life.

She did not believe in God, but she did feel tonight that every event, every character, had led her to this--this question that was now the dramatic crisis of her whole life--which world was she to choose, the world of Uldale or the world of Watendlath?

She had thought that it was settled. Only a month or two ago she had said to Charlie Watson that her Herries life was finished for ever; she would not leave Watendlath until Adam was grown. Then he should choose for himself, but she would remain.

She had thought that it was settled. Then came a letter from Francis. He implored her to come to Uldale. He gave no reasons. She was to come, if only for a night, and bring Adam with her. The most touching thing was that Jennifer had scrawled at the bottom of the page: 'The two of us need you.'

Well, she would go, but only for a few nights, only to show them that she was out of Herries affairs for ever. But was she? The invitation had stirred her. She wanted to see Uldale again--the dairy, the housekeeping, the servants. She was sure that it would be in a mess. And Jennifer, John, Dorothy. . . . She was too proud to come to see them, after all the scandal about her, without an invitation . . . but if they asked her. . . . For a brief moment Watendlath had seemed small, shut in, her domination there a poor thing, even her beloved Charlie a rough ignorant farmer. . . . Then she had been ashamed, and in a day or two her true nature had recovered itself. For she knew that this was her true nature, the nature that she derived from her mother, the nature that outlawed her from the Herries blood.

Had she not written to Francis and said that she would come she would now have refused his appeal. But she had given her word.

Then the sight of Walter Herries this evening had revived all the struggle again. How proud and conceited he had been! It was thus, seated on his horse, gigantic against the skyline, that he remained for her, and, at the thought of him, her whole proud obstinate passion for dominating returned.

It was thus that he meant to wipe out Francis and Jennifer, John and Dorothy. She saw them helpless and cowering under his whip. She knew suddenly why Francis had sent that letter to her. How amusing to return to Uldale--she, the outlaw with her bastard boy-- and fight Walter, make Adam--illegitimate though he was--head of all the Herries! Her heart beat triumphantly; she drew her arm more closely about him; he was sleeping.

She looked up at the stars as though to defy them. And the answer came back without question. 'Here is your country. Here is your place.'

But why? All the rebels were killed or disgraced. Georges had been murdered, Warren killed, Francis humiliated, her father an outcast, Reuben--well, Reuben talked more of social things now than of God. What of the bear, the boy hanged, young Hartley Coleridge? She was not sentimental about outlawry, but it seemed that if you fought against the laws of the House--if you broke the windows, rushed downstairs with no clothes on, rang the bells in the belfry, refused the common food or drink, brought the mongrel dog into the parlour--they all together, with one loud cry, threw you into the street; and then, how were you better?

For three years in Watendlath she and her boy had been outlawed; and how was she better?

'You ARE better,' the little dog, the cherry-faced moon, the scar like a sword on Helvellyn's flank answered her. 'You have never been at peace before. THIS is your world, not the other.'

But she was practical and not given to hearing voices. To beat Walter, to dominate all the Herries, to place Adam at the head of them. He would have, she was sure, all Will's genius for money, all Walter's physical strength, all Francis' brains. . . .

Which way was she going? Her whole life led to this crisis--or so she fancied, as we like to fancy that there is a line and a course and a climax, when it may not be so at all.

She remembered the way that the hens scratched in the room when she had first returned to it after Georges' death, the elephant in Paris, and that woman bending over, searching among her letters, and Adam trailing in the shawl, Reuben licking his fingers after the meal from the pot. . . .

Perhaps there is no line, only a gesture here; a leaf falling, the sheep huddling up the path outside the farm. But there was Adam. . . . She was responsible for the life that he would have. Would he be like Charlie Watson, blowing on his fingers for the cold, or Will sitting in his counting-house, or Walter at the head of his table, or Francis waiting for his wife's lover and pretending not to see . . . ? No, not that. Adam, even now, was as brave as a lion. Poor Francis. . . .

But before she fell asleep she was aware that the decision that she would make must affect many lives, much Herries history. She knew what she could do if she tried. She had never as yet tried with her whole heart. She had always been divided. Her son had united her. She saw him, as her eyes closed, reaching up with his hand, catching the stars and joining, with the light that streamed from them, her divided heart.

She woke to see one bright bar of gold above the ridge. The edge of the bar sparkled and quivered. Behind it a fleet of tiny pink clouds trembled, hovered, then merged into a fan-shaped shadow of rosy light.

She bent down and kissed Adam. 'Wake up,' she said, 'and see the sun.'

He looked up, rubbed his eyes with his knuckles, then jumped to his feet, caught her by the hand and pulled her to a higher ridge of the moor.

Little winds, little fingers passing over an instrument, blew against their faces. The sky was beyond depth, without end, but was flecked now with fire. Thick white mist lay like water beneath them, but this soon was touched and lightened, thinned; the rocks and the spear-tops of the trees rent and tore it. They, too, caught the gold, and Helvellyn was, as though it had rolled its shoulder towards the light, purple.

The mist broke everywhere, and the sky was showered with flecks of gold. The cloven mist streamed down the hills like rain. Light was everywhere. The valleys ran with sun.

'Now I'll race you!' Adam shouted, and started tearing down to the little wood.

JUDITH RETURNS TO ULDALE

When Judith stood again in the so-familiar hall at Uldale she was deeply excited. It was her nature to be excited, and that nature had not changed although she was forty-six years of age.

A stranger would have seen only a little ordinary pale-faced, middle-aged woman, bewildered perhaps by the sudden light, dressed in bonnet and shawl, faded but scrupulously clean, holding by the hand a very small, rather ugly boy. No romance there. Nevertheless the situation was romantic, for Judith was returning to the home of her childhood, after behaviour so scandalous that it should have ostracised her for ever, holding her illegitimate child by the hand--and she was there by invitation! She would not, she proudly assured herself, be there in any other way!

Her emotions were mixed and confused: she could never enter this house without a hundred memories crowding upon her, but it was characteristic of her that the first thing that interested her was that there were signs of neglect and untidiness everywhere. She saw that at once, and her fingers itched to put everything to rights.

For a moment the only person who greeted her was the very decent woman who opened the door. She knew that her ancient enemy, Mrs. Ponder, had been dead now three years of a fever. She gave the woman a quick friendly glance.

'Thank you,' she said, smiling.

Then her very next move, instinctive, almost unknown to herself, was to step forward, still holding Adam by the hand, and put a picture that hung crooked on the wall straight again.

'That's better,' she said.

It was an old picture that she knew well, of a huntsman leaping a little ditch. She gave it a friendly little pat.

Then Jennifer came out from the parlour. 'Judith! I didn't know--' she cried; but even then she came forward a little slowly, a little lazily, as though she were but half awake.

She was not as handsome as she had been; she was middle-aged now, as Judith was, but she was still a very remarkable woman, carrying herself with the same old dignity and grandeur, and her hair, untouched with grey, was of the same superb darkness. She was wearing a coloured bodice of orange over a white skirt. The orange sleeves, puffed and slashed, were very fine. But Judith saw at once that the dress was a little slatternly, and that her cheeks were painted. Her eyes, too, were weary, not with quite the old affectation of sleepiness. There was real fatigue, disappointment, unhappiness there.

She towered over Judith and the little boy. She bent down and kissed Judith.

'Is this Adam?'

'Yes. This is Adam.'

She kissed him, and he returned the kiss with fervour. She was quite the most beautiful lady he had ever seen, as this was the most beautiful house he had ever been in. He stared at the wallpaper with its Chinamen and castles, at the silver candlesticks, at the broad staircase, at the tall grand lady with the wonderful orange sleeves. From that first moment he and Jennifer were friends.

'Here is Francis! Francis, Francis, Judith is come!'

Francis was coming down the stairs, and Judith, looking up at him, felt a shock of dismay. He had been over to Watendlath to see her a year ago, and she had thought then that he looked old and ill, but now--how thin he was, how tired he seemed; he was an old man, and yet he was not more than sixty!

In a way he was more handsome than he had ever been. His extreme thinness suited him; his high collar, frilled shirt, and dark blue trousers showed his figure to the greatest advantage.

Judith was proud of him and deeply sorry for him; she longed to put her arms around him and mother him. He took both her hands in his.

'Judith, this is famous! . . . After all this time! And is this Adam? How do you do, Adam?'

'Very well, I thank you, sir,' said Adam in his shrill piping voice that was apt to end in a squeak.

They all laughed to relieve the tension of the meeting. There was a bustle about the baggage.

Judith went out into the dark garden. Charlie Watson had driven them out from Keswick. He leaned over and held her hand. For a moment she clung to his touch. All Watendlath seemed to be personified by him.

'Good-bye, Charlie,' she said, raising herself on tiptoe. 'We shall soon be back.'

'I am not so sure about leaving you.'

'Nonsense.' His face was close to hers. She let her hand rest for a moment on his rough coat and thick strong arm.

'Watendlath is not far away.'

''Tis a world away,' he answered her gruffly, and at once drove off.

She went back into the house. Her thought was, before everything, of Adam. He must go to bed. They had left Watendlath early that morning and, wild with excitement, he had been awake at four. Then, too, putting him to bed would give her some excuse to be alone a little before coming down.

On the landing they met the two children. John was now thirteen and Dorothy twelve. John was oddly like his father in face, but would be broader and thicker in body. Judith knew that he had a most charming character, kindly, affectionate, loyal--a little weak perhaps, a little dreamy like father and great-grandfather before him. How strange! John's great-grandfather had been her father! She thought of it as she kissed him. Dorothy was good-natured, obedient and conventional, something like her Aunt Deborah, fair- haired, at present plump, at the moment conscious of her 'pantalettes,' which were only fastened with tapes above her knee and gave her much anxiety. Such things were always to make her anxious.

Both children were delighted to see their Aunt Judith as they had always called her. Life at home had not been too pleasant of late; now that Aunt Judith had come it would be more gay.

They were exceedingly interested to see Adam. He was at once at his ease with them. He was always at his ease with everyone, because he trusted everyone.

He threw off his little riding-coat, letting it be where it fell, and showed John how the horse that Charlie Watson was driving had thrown up its head and snorted, but in the middle of this exhibition he was excited by the sight of the room where he and his mother would sleep. He had been too young during those first years in France to notice or remember things, and since then the farm at Watendlath had been all that he had known.

Certainly the room at the Keswick Inn to-day had been grand, but that had been a public place with men drinking and a man playing a harp, and there had been a dog with a lame leg. This was HIS room and his mother's!

He ran round and round it, shouting cries of joy. For Judith it was strange enough. For, once again it was her old room, the room where Mrs. Monnasett had died.

'I thought you would wish to be in the same room,' said Jennifer, standing in the doorway.

It was indeed the same room! In all these years the wallpaper had not been changed. Still there were those blue pagodas, there was the tallboy that had seemed to her as a baby so infinitely high, over the bed the blue

tester hangings and overlay, the bed itself with the columns fluted and reeded and so charmingly carved with acanthus leaves. There Mrs. Monnasett, with her yellow face, had lain, the candles flickering in the breeze, her lips fixed in a sardonic smile. . . . The room of all Judith's life. Nothing had occurred. Only yesterday she had bent forward to find the little box. . . .

'I will leave you,' said Jennifer. 'Come, children. Aunt Judith will soon come down.' There was a new note in Jennifer's voice, as though behind her words she was pleading for something.

But Judith now could think only of Adam. She undressed him and washed him. He would hardly keep still. She held him naked in her arms and kissed him. He lay back against her watching the leaping flames of the fire. His small dark head against her breast (he was quite suddenly sleepy), he asked her questions.

'Is that gentleman my uncle?'

'Yes, dear.' Impossible to explain now why and how he was not!

'Was my father like him?'

'No; your father was not so tall nor so old.'

'This gentleman is very, very old.'

'No. Not truly. He will not appear old when you know him.'

'Is that boy called John?'

'Yes.'

He yawned a huge yawn.

'I like him. . . .' Then he added, blinking his eyes at the fire: 'Is the beautiful lady his mother?'

'Yes.'

'But he called her ma'am.'

'Many boys and girls call their mother ma'am and their father sir.'

He thought about this. 'I cannot call my father sir because I haven't one, and I have never called you ma'am.'

'No, and you never will,' said Judith resolutely. She put on his shirt and carried him to the big four-poster.

He looked so small in it that she laughed. Then they both laughed. The touch of the cool sheets woke him up again and he rolled all over the bed. Then he lay still, watching her with wide-open eyes while she changed her dress, washed her face and hands, brushed her hair.

'This is a very grand house,' he said at last.

'Yes. I lived in it when I was a little girl, younger than you are.'

But the strangeness of it! In that bed, where her small son was lying, old Mrs. Monnasett had once lain! She looked at him, her heart bursting with love, but her voice was quite severe when she said:

'Now go to sleep, Adam. Are you hungry?'

He could not be. He had eaten a tremendous dinner at Keswick.

'Yes, yes. I am! I am!' he cried, although until his mother had mentioned it he had not thought of it. But how wonderful he thought her in her evening dress! The colours of her gown were rose and lavender grey, and she had a turban with a plume of feathers.

When she bent down to kiss him he hugged her and pinched her nose, a favourite game of theirs.

'If I do not eat soon I shall be asleep,' he answered, grinning at her. Yes, he was ugly as proper standards went, but she would not alter him by a hair's breadth.

'Do I look fine?' she asked him.

He nodded and watched her with all his eyes until she was out of the door.

But she did not feel fine at supper. They had dined at three in the afternoon but she at five in the Keswick Inn, so they were hungry and she was not. It seemed very natural that Jennifer should enjoy her food. However severe the crisis her appetite was strong.

Judith was strongly conscious of her clothes. That was not like her, but for three years the rose-lavender dress and the turban had lain in a box under the stair at John Green House. Fashions had changed. Evening dresses were shorter and had a padded 'rouleau' at the bottom. Waistbands were directly above the hips. Nevertheless, although she was in fashion, Jennifer was not smart. She looked as though she had put on her clothes in her sleep. Jennifer was untidy, Judith was dowdy; that's what they were. Francis was the grand one, seated gravely at the end of the table, his head thin now, as though carved of a fine stone. The ruffles at his neck were of a peerless whiteness.

Their talk was stiff and awkward. They spoke of general affairs. People were still discussing the Cato Street business, although it was eight months since its occurrence. Judith noticed at once with what feverish excitement Francis spoke, as though ignorant desperadoes like Thistlewood and Edwards were in every town, hiding down every lane, concealed in every corner.

She noticed, too, that when he went on in this exaggerated sensational strain Jennifer's lips stiffened and her eyes were scornful. She looked at Judith once, as though to say: 'You see now what he has come to. Can you wonder if I despise this man?' and Judith thought again that there was an appeal for help there.

Matters became even more personal when they discussed the Coronation that was to be celebrated in the following year, the King's efforts for a divorce, and the Queen's eccentric behaviour.

Francis, who had been drinking, Judith saw, very much more than was his habit in the old days, broke into a demonstrative, emotional defence of the Queen. The King was a blackguard; he did not care who heard him say it. He was surely old enough now to say what he pleased. Besides, everyone knew what the King was. It was disgraceful that the country should have to suffer under such a man. And the poor Queen--well, she had been, perhaps, a little imprudent at times. She was eccentric, emotional. But who had driven her to her eccentricities? Brougham was a hero. He would drink to Brougham. They must all drink to Brougham. Judith

noticed then Jennifer's irritation. She saw that such scenes as these were part of every evening's programme. Jennifer, looking across the table at Francis scornfully, praised the King, said that he had been much calumniated. At least he was no prig nor Methodist. For her part she liked a jolly fellow, a man who knew what life was and lived it to the full . . . not a half-alive pedant who skulked about the house. . . . She stopped abruptly. Then smiled at Francis.

'I am fortunate,' she said softly, 'to have a husband who strikes the mean. Judith, do you not think that Francis is looking well?'

'Very well,' said Judith, and she put out her hand and touched his. He looked at her with a glance that had in it so much of apology and unhappiness that her heart was wrung.

The food was badly cooked and warm when it should have been hot. The meal dragged on interminably. No allusion was made to anyone's private affairs. At last they sat there in silence while the candles trembled and the old clock ticked like a miser counting his money.

What was the matter with the house? There was more in this than the relations of Francis and Jennifer, more than Jennifer's infidelity, more than Francis' self-disgust. An air of apprehension was everywhere. She had detected it, even in the faces of the two children.

When at last they got up to move into the parlour, Judith thought of Watendlath with a longing that was almost irresistible. She had an impulse to run out into the dark cool garden. She would be closer to the hills there and would hear water running somewhere. She felt the touch of her hand on Charlie Watson's strong arm. Oh, there everything was so simple, so happy!

In the hall she stopped for an instant to hear whether there was any sound from Adam. No, he would be sleeping quietly. She was comforted again.

In the parlour the three of them sat like images. The outburst was soon coming, but until it did they must be silent. Judith herself was affected by the stillness that was so vocal. Seated with her back to the window she had a sudden fancy that Walter Herries was standing outside, watching them, peering in. It was all that she could do not to get up and see.

Then Jennifer rose, said that she was going to bed, kissed Judith and went out, her eyes half closed, yawning a little, just as she had used to do.

'Well, Judith,' said Francis.

'Well, Francis.'

He got up with a quick impetuous movement and came to where she was sitting. He knelt down by her chair, put his arms around her, rested his head on her breast.

'Oh, I am so weary, so weary,' he murmured.

She thought of the time when she was a baby and had adored him, when David had whipped her, and she had not cared so long as Francis loved her. She smiled a little wryly above his head. Poor Francis!

Then to her distress he began to weep. He seemed to be completely broken down. He wept as though all his control must be abandoned or he would die. She had never seen Francis cry. She could not bear it.

'Oh no, Francis. No.... No, no!'

Then at last he looked up at her, his cheeks stained with tears.

'Forgive me, my dear. It is many years since I wept last. I am not given to weeping. But seeing you come back to-night, after all this time, the same, so familiar, the only friend I have left--it has been too much for me. Truly, Judith, I am desperate. I don't know which way to turn.'

'Now sit here beside me.' She motioned to a place on the sofa. 'Let us talk over things quietly. They are never so urgent when one talks over them quietly. We will discuss everything just as we have always done.'

He came and sat beside her.

'But you are going to stay now that you are here, are you not? ... You are not going away?'

'For a few days. Of course, we will stay for a few days.'

'For a few days? Oh, but that is nothing. Judith, you must live here again--for a while at least--you and your boy....'

'Live here?' She laughed. 'Francis, do you not realise that I am now a scandalous person? I have had a child out of wedlock as everyone knows. With Jennifer and the children--'

'Scandalous!' he broke out. 'We are all scandalous now! Yes, I will say anything tonight. I have held myself in long enough. Jennifer has been that man's mistress for years now--quite an old family affair. As soon as I am away at Kendal or Carlisle he comes here, and everyone knows it. Everyone knows it, I tell you. It is the common joke! Walter sees to that.... And all these years I have done nothing. I, the fine Francis who started the world with such grand ideas. I have done nothing, nothing at all.

'I have skulked in corners, taken his hand, offered him drink, while he makes my wife a common whore... . Oh, my God, my God, I am the most despicable man on this earth, the most despicable and the most unhappy!'

She tried to calm him. He was trembling from head to foot.

'She hates me. She despises me. And, God forgive me, I love her yet. It is because I love her that I have been able to do nothing, because with my cursed nature I have always seen two sides of everything. She never loved me. I forced her into marriage. Why should I have denied her all opportunity of love?'

He caught her hand.

'Judith, do you remember that Ball all those years ago, the Ball when Jennifer broke Christabel's fan? Of course, you do. It all started from that. It has all come from that. You remember that I was talking to you when she first came by! How lovely she was that night! Do you remember? Catherine de' Medici with the collar of pearls and her white neck and the crimson dress? Her excitement at the Ball--do you remember? ...

'And after--the meeting in Berkeley Square. Do you remember? When I sat in the window and it was so hot and the scent of the lilac came up from the street. I sat in the window thinking of Jennifer, and then do you remember how I broke in upon Will and how angry he was? Our separation dated from that.'

Did she not remember? And how, a moment after, Georges stood there in the doorway, Georges in his brown suit, spent and done ... ?

'Before that,' Francis went on eagerly, 'everything had been well-- for all of us and for the country too, I think. What a good old country it was when I was a child, so quiet and so cosy! Everyone drank ale, and there was "oat clap bread," and no one came to disturb us. The children would help in the spinning or drive the sheep on the fells. Everyone was happy together. But now there are visitors peering and fingering, and in the towns children of six and seven years work in the dark, and the machines have come to take the bread out of men's mouths. The sky is blackening with smoke, we have a King too drunk to sit on the throne, and class is against class....'

He broke off. 'No, by God, what do I care for the country any more? There was a time when I cared. Did I not kill my own father and cause my mother to hate me, because the Bastille fell?'

He laughed bitterly, striking his knee with his hand.

'But now what should a cuckold think of his country--a cuckold plain to all his neighbours, and any who do not know of it kind Cousin Walter will tell them of it.'

She tried to calm him. He was so dreadfully excited that she thought that at any moment he might raise the house.

'Dear Francis, the country is well enough. This is a time of transition, and such times always seem hard to those who are in them. There is a grand new world coming....'

'And I don't care if there is!' he interrupted her. 'You can have your fine new world! If I could but get my fingers round dear Walter's large throat!' He stopped himself with a tremendous effort. 'You see how it is with me to-night, my dear. I am excited at seeing you again. For you are the only one I have left, the only one who understands me. I killed my father. My mother hated me. My brother and wife hate me yet. God knows but my children hate me too. But I ask for no pity. It is all my own doing. You and I, my dear, are misfits; and to be a misfit in the Herries family is to be slain.'

'We are neither of us slain,' she said, looking up at him quickly. 'It is perhaps true that we are misfits. But it is the misfits, I fancy, who give the value to the world.

What would the Herries family be without us? A dull, poor lot. We are the ones who understand and because we suffer have charity. We can see into both worlds. We travel into strange countries where the others cannot go, and bring back the news.' She laughed. 'I am turning very poetical,' she said. 'It is not my ordinary fashion. But I must tell you, Francis, that if I am a misfit I am a very happy one. And so may you be too if you will. I am certain that Jennifer does not hate you. She must be long weary of that other affair. All will soon be forgotten. . . .'

'Forgotten!' he broke in. 'Not with Walter Herries there! Ah, you do not yet know the villain of the piece!'

'Walter?' she asked. 'What can he do?'

'What can he do? What has he not-done? He hates us, has always done, because, firstly, he says Jennifer insulted his mother, secondly, he must be king of the castle here and wants no other Herries round, and, thirdly, he has a deformed son, and my children make him mad. . . .'

'But he can do nothing.'

'Do nothing? He can do everything. He is my perpetual enemy and has been these five years. He is so proud that he will burst his skin one of these days. He has all the neighbourhood in his pocket.'

He calmed himself that he might give the value to his words. 'Do you know what for five years he has been doing? There are spies all around me, and every small action of mine is repeated to him. It has been so for five years now. Fancy to yourself what it would be if a good friend of yours, who had known you well for a long while, drew a caricature of you in a book, using all your external habits, your tricks of speech, your eccentricities, and then, with a diabolic cleverness, twisted them all to mean and sordid motives? You would be yourself bewildered. You would say yes, that it was true; you had done this and that, you wore your hair so, you laughed thus, and like all men you had your weaknesses, your follies. Was this perhaps a true picture? And if you saw it as partly true how much more would others, who know you but externally, judge of your true self? And you would begin to doubt yourself and to suspect every movement, every gesture. I tell you, Judith, that my neighbours here who have known me all my life long take rather Walter's picture of me now than their own. There is nothing goes on in this house that he does not know, nothing that he does not use. . . .'

Yes, he would be like that. She knew instinctively that what Francis said was true. She felt, even here in the warm safe room, the force and danger of his overbearing vitality.

But she answered firmly:

'Listen, Francis. No one can traduce you but yourself. Even your bitterest enemy knows that a satire is a satire. Its very exaggeration must make him consider the opposite. One is alone in this world. No one knows one save oneself, and then it is only a glimpse of

the truth that one has. Forget Walter, and if you cannot forget Walter fight him!'

She jumped to her feet.

'I could fight him! He should have enough of his spying and traducing if I got at him!'

'Yes, yes,' he cried eagerly. 'You must stay, Judith. Remain here. With you to help me I can be another man. Although I am old--' His voice faltered. 'Sixty is an age. . . .'

She had had enough. She was infinitely weary. Francis' request that she should stay gave her a sudden flick of terror. She did not want to stay. She must get back to Watendlath. She and Adam safe in Watendlath, away from all these Herries. . . .

She kissed him.

'Good-night, Francis, dear. All will come right.'

But as she climbed slowly the stair she thought, in spite of herself, 'But how COULD he not have challenged Fernyhirst? How COULD he let it go on as he has--all these years?' But she was too weary to consider it further. However, her evening was not yet done with. As she passed Jennifer's door a voice called her.

She went in.

Jennifer was sitting on her bed in her shift, her long white legs dangling to the floor. Her room was in a disorder. Clothes were flung about the floor, drawers were pulled open, the curtains were roughly drawn, a lamp by the bed was smoking to the ceiling.

Judith closed the door.

'What has he been saying?'

'Oh, it is so late!' Judith sighed. 'Dear Jennifer--'

'No, I must know.'

'He has been saying nothing, only that he is unhappy--'

Jennifer put out a long white arm and drew Judith to the bed.

'I am unhappy too! Oh, so dreadfully unhappy! It is all his fault. I hate him. . . . I have hated him for years. Why was I such a fool as to marry him? He has been speaking to you of Edward.'

'Edward?'

'Fernyhirst. But that is all finished. Finished long ago. I hate him too.'

Judith looked at her, and again her tiresome maternal impulse that was for ever preventing her real action interfered. But what was she to do? This poor, tired, aged woman! And once there had been that brilliant happy girl, radiant with beauty and success, in the crimson dress, the collar with the pearls?

But she had still lovely legs and feet! How different might Judith's own story have been had she had such wonderful feet and ankles! She put her arm round her, but how she longed for her bed!

'Francis spoke for the most part of Walter!'

'That devil! He is determined to ruin us, Judith, all of us--my poor children--' and even then, when she should have wept, she yawned, kicking her feet a little, looking at her silver slippers. And in that yawn Judith saw once and for ever exactly what she was. She was true Herries. She had no imagination, none whatever. Had she had any she would never have married Francis, never have lived in Cumberland, never have suffered an intrigue with Fernyhirst, never have stayed here for years, doing nothing, understanding nothing, seeing nothing! And it was against the Herries in her that Francis had beaten in vain! Had she been of an age it was Walter that she should have married. They would have suited one another to perfection.

It was from that moment of comprehension that Judith's complete domination of Jennifer began.

'Dear Judith. You are such a consolation. There was a time when I was jealous of you. I know how shockingly I behaved. You need not tell me of my behaviour. But now I would do anything for you--and Francis too. It is the one point on which we are agreed. You must stay for a long, long while.'

Judith smiled and shook her head.

'I am an abandoned woman, Jennifer--myself and my little bastard. We do not belong to good society any more.'

'What foolishness! I am sure that an illegitimate child is nothing. Everyone is so free in these days. And I am as bad as you. Everyone knows about Edward. Certainly you must stay.'

'I have grown unused to society. I am a peasant, digging and ditching, watching the sheep. You cannot think how strange these clothes seemed to me to-night.'

Jennifer, looking at her naked legs with approval, answered:

'I am sure that is a very good costume. But we are two old women. What does it matter what we wear? My legs are still fine, although there is no one who cares any more. Nor do I wish there to be. Love is the most wearying thing I know.'

Judith said good-night.

'Then you will stay?'

'For a day or two at least.'

'No, for always. The children worship you, and little Adam is a love.' She stood up in her shift that fell in folds to her silver slippers. For a moment there was something genuine and touching in her fine eyes that looked out above her painted cheeks in a true and human appeal.

She said what Francis had said:

'You are my only friend.'

Judith undressed and lay down beside Adam. She stared into the dark. She WOULD not, no, she WOULD not be caught by these two. She WOULD not come back into these Herries affairs. . . . But they were so alone. Francis had no one--Jennifer only her brother, who was a fat careless bachelor in Bournemouth. Both Prosper and Amelia were dead.

But she WOULD not be caught. . . . She seemed to hear beyond the window the water of Watendlath. She could see the Tarn lying in ebony silence under the stars. The sheep were pressing up the road, the cows were to be milked; here came Tyson, his arms loaded with hay for the cattle. Armboth touched the stars. . . .

She was near to tears; she was so homesick.

She was too old, too settled in her quieter life to take up these quarrels again. Ah, but Walter, riding his white horse, striking at Adam with his whip. . . .

With a gesture of protection she stretched out her arm and drew Adam to her. He was deep in sleep but he grunted like a little pig and nestled into her side.

ROUND OF THE MOON

The house was bathed in sunlight and ladders of dust quivered in the air. No room had been swept for months; the kitchen was a disgrace; the dairy--ah, how beautiful it had once been with its gleaming cleanliness, the stone floor like a mirror--and now! In the stables there were but three horses, two of them fit for little but to drag the carriage at a funeral pace along the rocky, uneven roads.

Judith swept through the place like a whirlwind. Mrs. Quinney, the housekeeper, Martha Hodgson, the woman who had opened the door on Judith's arrival (she was cook and maid both), Doris, a stupid country girl, and Mr. Winch, the thin cadaverous little tutor, were, in addition to Bennett the coachman and Jack the stable-boy, all the servants. Very different from David's day, different even from Jennifer's early day, but Judith must make the best of it. And make the best of it she did. In no time she had them all at her call, all save Mr. Winch, of whom more in a moment.

She summed them up instantly. Mrs. Quinney was lazy, greedy, gossipy, weak, amiable, gossipy, greedy and lazy. Martha was earnest, plain, silent, faithful, opinionated and earnest. Doris was little, if anything, removed from the beasts of the field and like them was hungry, obedient, and responsive to overtures of love from the opposite sex. Bennett had always reminded her a little of her dear Charlie. She liked him because of that. He was stouter, less intelligent, had far less personality, but was a man--that is, he was a Cumberland man and therefore silent, suspicious, obstinate, faithful and courageous.

Jack the stable-boy pleased her best of all. He was only a lad and had come from the depths beyond Mardale, but he had the makings of a grand gentleman. He, from the first, would do anything for her.

There they were, ready to her hand. For years they had been neglected. Francis had scarcely spoken to them, Jennifer had let them do as they would. Before the week was out the house looked a different place, the floors shone, the silver glittered, the food came hot to the table, the horses trotted, Caesar the dog barked at night when he heard a strange step, the spiders were broomed away, the carpets were dusted, the grass of the lawn was cut, a dead cat was removed from the Gothic temple, a mouse was found in the chaise, chrysanthemums, bronze and orange, lighted the parlour, the drawers in Jennifer's bedroom were tidied, Dorothy had fresh ribbons to her dress, and the holes in John's stockings were mended.

Judith was to stay only a day or two. It was nearly Christmas before she had the house entirely to her liking.

Then, one winter's day when the sun like a swollen red penny rolled between shifting orange clouds over Skiddaw, she looked out through the bottle-green glass of the parlour window and saw Mr. Winch creeping round the corner of the house toward the stables.

Creeping he was. His thin lanky body was bent almost to all-fours. There was a moment when in actual fact he knelt on the path and looked ludicrous enough in that position.

Abruptly round the corner came Francis, his head bent, his arms behind his back, and almost stepped on Mr. Winch, who was diligently brushing his trousers. Francis said a word to him and came on, lost in thought as he always was in these days.

Now what had Mr. Winch been doing? With her accustomed impetuosity Judith had disliked him from the first moment of meeting him, and, it is to be feared, for no better reason than that his hands were damp. Afterwards there were other reasons. Whence had he come? He had been in the house for four years and yet both Francis and Jennifer were exceedingly vague about him. He had tutored Lord Somebody's son once somewhere; he said himself that he came from Warwickshire; Jennifer disliked him and behaved as though he were not there. Francis talked to him on a day, and then on another day disregarded him. It seemed that he taught the children something. John at least said that he did. Judith disliked him increasingly, and the more she disliked him the more obsequious he became. His appearance was most certainly not prepossessing, for his narrow grey eyes were so placed that you could not be sure whether he had a squint or no, his suit was always a shiny black and he was for ever blowing his nose.

This vision out of the window woke Judith to life. She had been alive indeed all these weeks, engaged on a business that she adored, but the house had swallowed her. She had not seen outside its affairs. Except in one matter, and that was the emotion that never left her, night or day, her love for her son, Adam. She was suffering for the first time in her life from jealousy.

For Adam, when he had been in the house two days, fell in love with John. He was in love so completely and absolutely that he forgot his mother altogether. For five years she had been everything to

him, and now she was, in the flash of an instant, it seemed, nothing to him at all. Of course it was not so. It was simply that he was at the age when he could not think of two things at the same time. He had never, as yet, in his life had an older boy for companion, and he found it simply enchanting.

John was kind, amiable and easy. He had not had in these last years a happy life. The house had been smoky with unhappiness. The two children had been quite neglected. He had followed the hounds at a time, but then the horse had been sold. He went out shooting rabbits with Bennett. He witnessed an occasional wrestling or cock-fight. But he was 'soft' for his time. He hated cruelty of any kind. It made him sick. It was hard to say at present what he cared for. He was not a student like his father, he did not roam the country. He liked to stay at home, work in the garden, read stories. Although he was no student he could read tales and poetry to himself by the hour. He would sit curled up in a corner somewhere and pray that he would not be noticed. He had always detested Mangnall's Questions and Butler's Guide to Useful Knowledge--for such things he had no use whatever, but Goldsmith's History of England he devoured in all its four volumes because of the thrilling detail in it. Then there was Vicesimus Knox's Elegant Extracts in Prose and Verse, then Marmion, The Lay, the Waverleys, The Parents' Assistant, The Fairchild Family and, secretly, obtained from some of the Forresters who lived in Bassenthwaite, many volumes of the Minerva Press, The Mysterious Hand, The Demon of Society and the rest.

He read, he dreamed, his life was intensely solitary. It was an amazing thing for him when this ugly baby, so fearless, so interested and so happy, came into it. The two great characteristics of Adam Paris, then and always, were his interest and his happiness. In later years he was to exasperate many persons by these two qualities, for most human beings quite naturally call extensive interests selfishness, and happiness complacency.

John had not known much happiness yet in his life, and few persons had cared very actively whether he were happy or no. He was shy of his father as his father was shy of him, and afraid of his mother. Dorothy was a girl. Mr. Winch was nothing. Only Bennett was his friend, and Bennett had never much to say. Now this small boy came and worshipped, thought him a god, believed everything that John told him, trusted him utterly. Soon they were inseparable.

Adam did not forget his mother, but she was always there, while John was something new and showed him everything that he wanted to see.

When Judith realised that she was jealous she was amazed at herself. She liked John and trusted him; Adam could not be with anyone better. But her jealousy would not let her alone. She showed it to no one, but something told her that the first stage of her life with her son was over. She would never again have him so completely her own as she had had him during those first five years. She was alone again. It seemed to be the one lesson that life was for ever teaching her. Alone she was; alone she must ever be. She did not yet realise that it was the lesson that every other human being was also, with exasperated tears and helpless gestures, learning.

The fire of her love for Adam burnt her heart, it seemed to her. She stood listening for him. She called softly, then louder, then louder again. At last he would appear at the stairhead or at the stable door, John beside him. She would smile and wave to him and go away.

At night she had him. He would dance into bed, ask her one question after another on the wonders of the past day, and then instantly fall asleep. Then her time came. She would fold his small body in her arms and, with his head against her breast, would tell him how she loved him, how he was everything to her, how he was all that she had, how she loved him as no mother had ever loved her son, and the shadows of the fire would leap ironically on the wall and Adam would breathe softly in his sleep, lost to her even then.

But he was not really lost to her. In the depth of her being she knew it and was comforted. Meanwhile the discovery of Mr. Winch on all-fours on the garden path woke her to important issues.

Having the house now tidied and disciplined, she was aware that, in spite of herself, Walter Herries' shadow was hanging over her as it was over the others. Not so grimly perhaps, nor so tragically, for she still maintained to herself with all her energy that her stay here was only temporary and that in another fortnight-- after Christmas for certain--she would be free, in Watendlath, of the pack of them, never to return. She was not very sensitive as to her social position--she had never been sensitive--but she was aware that the visitors to Uldale in these last months had all regarded her with a very lively curiosity, and she thought that, behind their politeness, there was a kindly ostracism. They did not, she was aware, invite her to their houses, but that might have been as easily because of Jennifer's scandal as her own.

Only good, kind Mrs. Southey invited her. She went with the secret hope that she would see again that strange boy Hartley. But Hartley was not there. None of the children were present. Mr. Southey was very kind and a little distant.

Of Walter himself and his family she had seen nothing. The two households were cut off from one another as though they were as remote as China from Spain. But, rightly or wrongly, she heard the loud voice and saw the broad back of Walter behind everything and, in spite of her own good common sense, began to catch something of the superstition that Francis and Jennifer had of him--as a sort of malicious devil, horns on his head, hoofs instead of feet, and an eye in the middle of his back.

Seeing Mr. Winch, one thing at least became plain to her: Mr. Winch was Walter's spy. Assured of that, she was, in a moment, alive to a whole blazing bundle of circumstances, as suddenly bright and crackling as though she had seen it burst into flame before her eyes.

On looking back afterwards it appeared to her that everything and everyone sprang into action from that moment when she saw Mr. Winch on all-fours. It was, in any case, very soon after that day that some of the worst and unhappiest moments of her life confronted her.

The awful day opened for her quietly enough. It was a fortnight before Christmas, and in the morning the sky was a bright shrill blue, the tops had a powdering of snow and the roads were hard with frost.

Adam was to go on some grand Christmas expedition into Keswick with John and Dorothy. She accompanied them, riding her own sturdy little mare, Phyllis, that she had brought with her from Watendlath. She thought that after she had seen them safely into the town she would ride on into Borrowdale and have a glimpse of Herries again. She had woken that morning with her head full of Warren. She could not tell why. She had not thought of him, she was ashamed to confess to herself, for months. But now, without warning, he had returned as the dead do unexpectedly return.

They had an agreeable ride into Keswick, passing many enchanting things on the way--a pedlar, a blind man with a trumpet, two drunken men fighting, a flock of sheep and a herd of cows. Adam had had his eyes and nose pressed to the windows of the chaise and was asking questions as fast as he could breathe, not waiting for any answers. The vast broad back of Bennett bobbed up and down on the box outside, the inside smelt of straw and mice, and Judith tried to feel no jealousy as she watched John holding Adam that he should not fall.

Then she rode on into Borrowdale. The road was still wild and uneven and unfit for a carriage, although carriages often used it, for it was the thing now to tour the Lakes and see 'the horrid precipices' and 'the thunderous waterfalls' that had so terribly frightened Mr. Gray. To-day, however, Judith had the scene to herself. Not a human being did she see, save an old man gathering sticks in a field. The Lake embraced the blue sky with a little tremor of excitement, and very lovely were the reflections of the snow-sprinkled hills in that blue water, hill-tops trembling like shadows in a swaying mirror.

The village of Grange was dead, and when at last she came to the Herries house, that was dead also. As before, when she had been with Warren, no one was there, but there were the remains of a meal on the table and a crumbling fire in the kitchen.

She sat on the old mildewed couch in the upper room for a while. Here she and Warren had sat . . . how long, long ago! Had they not sat there that day Adam would not be sucking lollipops (as she was sure that he was doing) in Keswick at this moment. Once again she asked herself why she had surrendered to Warren? For love of Georges' shadow?--and then with a sharp pang she realised for the first time how swiftly Georges was now fading from her mind. All the pain of losing him was gone. She did not miss him any more! Adam had taken his place.

She was not a sentimentalist. Facts were facts, and Georges, who had always wanted everyone else to be happy so long as he himself was not uncomfortable, would be glad. But Adam! She stood before the dead stone fireplace and pressed her hands before her eyes. Her passion of possession was terrific. She must govern it, guard it. Adam as he grew must be free. Looking into darkness, seeing into the future, she was afraid of herself.

The house dripped with damp and was of a fearful cold. She listened. Were there ghosts about? No; to-day Adam had slain them all. Father, mother, husband--one crick of her son's finger and they were fled.

She visited Georges' grave, then stopped at one of the cottages in Rosthwaite and ate and drank there. She knew every man, woman and child in Rosthwaite. It needed all her control not to push Phyllis up the well-known track. She was so near to Watendlath that, had Adam been with her, she must have gone--and then never have come down again! It was just over her head! If she listened she could hear Mrs. Ritson calling and Molly the cow lowing for her calf!

She would not come this way again. It was dangerous. But she would not need to come, for in a fortnight Christmas would be here, and directly after Christmas she and Adam would leave Uldale for ever.

She started homewards and saw that the weather was changing. She looked back and beheld how over Scafell and the Gavel great black clouds were climbing. They were piling up as though out of a vast vat. The blue sky above her head seemed to tremble in anticipation of its destruction. The clouds had a sort of boiling rage and fury in their blackness. She turned on her horse to watch as though at some show or pageant. Then she saw a small white cloud, like a puff of smoke from a cannon, spring above the hill and start to fly from the enemy. The little white cloud spread across the blue, and the black clouds pursued it. She could almost hear them roaring in their fury. 'I hope it will escape! I hope it will escape,' she could fancy the bare trees around her, that were all beginning to tremble, were saying. But of course the little cloud had no escape. The vanguard of the black army put out an ebony feeler, as an octopus might do, and the little white cloud was instantly swallowed. The landscape around her went dead as though a hand had struck it. The trees were shaking violently. A drop of rain smacked her cheek. She whipped Phyllis up and ran for it. By Grange she was caught. The rain slapped the earth like a woman beating a carpet. The drops danced on the

ground with exultant joy. There was an empty outhouse off the road opposite the bridge. Pulling Phyllis after her, she ran in--and found Walter Herries filling the little place with his bulk!

They were at first very polite. His eyes twinkled with amusement. The noise of the rain on the roof was so loud that they had to shout. Then, quite suddenly, she sprang in.

'Walter Herries, you should know that shortly I intend to wring the neck of your shabby little spy and throw him into the stable.'

'My spy!'

'Nasty Mr. Winch.'

He laughed, throwing his great head back and slapping his thigh.

'Cousin Judith, come and stay at Westaways for a little. Food and drink are better than at Uldale.'

She looked at him contemptuously.

'I would marry Mr. Winch sooner than sleep under your roof.'

'I am not inviting you to share my bed, Cousin Judith.'

She flushed.

'That was worthy of you,' she said. 'But remember you cannot touch ME anywhere. It may be in the end I can harm YOU the more.'

He seemed contrite. 'I said a dirty thing. For once you see me ashamed. Make the most of it.'

She looked at him with a quiet inspection that made him, she saw, uncomfortable.

'I believe I could be your match if I cared, but I have done with all the Herries affairs. I never was in truth part of them and I never will be. But you must understand that I have loved Francis all my life, and something will come of your persecution of him.'

They had to shout, and there was something very ludicrous in that. In spite of herself, and although she was feeling exceedingly angry and had never hated him more, she smiled. He smiled too.

'I think we could be very good friends,' he said.

'Never! Never!' she answered passionately. 'I hope very much I can do you some harm before I die.' Then, to her great vexation, she smiled again, for a little trickle of rain, coming in from the roof, fell down his cheek and made him look absurd.

'Why do you persecute Francis? It is a very small game and not at all worth all the energy you put into it.'

'Jennifer insulted my mother,' he said like a sulky schoolboy.

'What! You are going back all that way--because years ago at a stupid Ball Jennifer broke your mother's fan?'

'They can leave Uldale and go elsewhere. Francis is doing no good there. Jennifer is the countryside scandal. They do the Herries name harm.'

'The Herries name! And what good do YOU do the Herries name?'

That touched him. He started up.

'By God! I do the Herries name more good than your rascally father, or HIS miserable puling grandson.' He grew calm again, came near to her and would have taken her arm had she not moved away.

'Now listen, Judith. I have but begun. I am a young man, strong and healthy. I shall wipe your Uldale family out as though they had never been. I have wealth and power, but nothing at all in comparison with what I shall have. I am here for ever--I and my son after me.'

'I have not seen your children,' she said quietly.

It was cruel of her. She touched him there. His stout red face grew more crimson. For a moment she felt almost kindly towards him.

'Never mind,' he said, so low that she scarcely caught the words. 'My son has one leg that is shorter than the other, but he will have a headpiece that Francis' boy will one day fear.'

'So you carry the feud into a later generation,' she said scornfully.

'Not if they leave Uldale. Let them go South. I will not bother them.'

'I see!' She looked him in the eyes. They were now very close together and she could smell the stuff of his handsome brown riding- coat.

'Had I not other plans for myself I should like to stay and fight you, Cousin Walter. . . . I, too, have a son, you know. His father was Herries, even though distantly.'

'Yes. Poor Warren.' He laughed contemptuously. 'An illegitimate Herries, my dear.'

'But Herries blood,' she answered.

He caught her arm then, whether she liked it or no.

'We should be friends, Judith. We are of the same sort.'

'But we are enemies, Cousin Walter,' she answered. 'Good, sound, rock-bottom enemies. Good-day to you.'

The rain had almost ceased. She mounted Phyllis and rode away. It was nearly dark when she reached Keswick, but the sky had cleared again. There were a few stars already and a fine frosty tang in the air. Soon there would be a grand full moon. The thought of the moon stayed her. There would be plenty of light to ride home by if she returned later. Francis had gone to Cockermouth for the night on a piece of business and she shrank from an evening quite alone with Jennifer. There was nothing more dreary, for Jennifer would either yawn and say nothing, or seek to abuse Francis, when Judith must stop her, or retrace the by now desperately familiar path of her affair with Fernyhirst, her weariness of him, the unfairness of everything and what would Judith advise her to do?

When Francis was present things were better, but without him--no, she could not endure it! Moreover, she was herself tired. She was not so young as she had been. It had been a long ride to Borrowdale; the visit to Herries, the encounter with Walter had for the moment exhausted her.

So she stepped in to see the only two friends that she had now in Keswick. They were a quaint pair, Miss West and Miss Pennyfeather. They were one of the scandals of Keswick, and about them Keswick was never weary of talking. They lived in a very small house in Main Street, next to a smithy. They were indeed an eccentric pair, devoted, original, entirely indifferent to public opinion, clever and sarcastic.

Miss West dressed as near a man as to be no matter. She wore a powdered wig and a coat with brass buttons. It was said that in the evening in her parlour she wore trousers. She drank and, it was rumoured, smoked a long clay pipe. She had a thin dried face with a long nose and very bright keen eyes. Miss Pennyfeather was very feminine, round and plump, pink and white. But she was even more sarcastic and cruel than Miss West in a quiet soft way. In reality they were neither of them cruel, but gave much in charity. They hated men and would not, it was said, have one in the house. They liked Judith greatly and would have seen much of her had she wished it. She liked them also, but was not in Keswick sufficiently.

She knocked on the door, was admitted by their little maid Betty, and found them by the fire in the parlour, Miss West reading to Miss Pennyfeather from one of the novels of Mrs. Cuthbertson.

They were enchanted to see Judith.

Miss West threw Mrs. Cuthbertson on to the floor, crying in a deep bass voice: 'This is Stuff!'

Then they had supper off cold chicken, rhubarb pie and cheese and, after that, played cards very frivolously. Miss West told some scandalous stories about the curate of Crosthwaite, about the wife of a coal-merchant who had recently come into money and set up his carriage, and a French poodle owned by the eccentric Mrs. Mason, a widow. They all laughed very much and Miss West imitated the Crosthwaite curate looking for his handkerchief in the middle of his sermon.

When Judith at last departed she wondered what had happened to her lately. It seemed so long since she had last laughed with real abandon.

Phyllis was thinking of her stable and under a full moon trotted with enthusiasm. It was late. The Crosthwaite Church struck the hour of eleven as they turned into the Carlisle road.

As she went along she was happy and confident. 'Three old women! Never mind. We know how we can enjoy ourselves without the men-- and I stood up to Walter. I enjoy standing up to Walter. I shall do it again.' She would tempt Miss West and Miss Pennyfeather up to Watendlath after Christmas. They were great riders. They should stay a day or two with her at the farm. They would enjoy the Ritsons. . . .

When she reached the house it was five minutes to twelve by the round-faced clock above the stables. The moon shone with such brightness that the whole world of hill, fell and dead white road was recreated into unreality. The stars were fiery--all else was icy cold and like a dried bone in colour.

She put Phyllis into her box, patted her nose and then, almost startled by the sound of her own steps on the cobbles in the still world, crossed over to the house.

She let herself in and with soft tread went straight to her room. The stair was flooded with moonlight.

She lit the candles and, with one raised in her hand, went over to see that Adam was sleeping. With his cheek on his hand, his mouth a little open, he looked so entirely hers and hers alone that she gave a little gasp of happiness, put down the candle and sat on the bed-edge gazing at him.

She blew out the candle, drew back the curtain and let the moonlight spread a pool of liquid shadow about the carpet. She did not feel sleepy. She was immensely content. She sat at the window looking at the frosted slope of Skiddaw, the friend of her life.

She was thus idly watching and had listened to the clocks tell the half-hour when, muffled by the window but sharp on the frosted road, she heard the hoofs of a horse. She bent forward and saw, to her amazement, the horse stop at the gate and a heavily-cloaked rider, whom she quickly knew to be Francis, dismount. Francis! Here! Now! She stood up, her hand at her heart. Something told her at once that there was trouble. She saw him open the gate and lead the horse round to the stable.

Driven by some instinct, unreasoning but imperative, she softly went from her room on to the landing, and, as she did so, at the same moment Jennifer's door opened and she appeared, in her nightdress, her ringlets about her shoulders, a candle in her hand, and on her feet her silver slippers.

'What was that?' she said, her finger to her

'Francis is returned.'

'Oh, my God!'

Even as she breathed that they heard the outer door of the house open. Jennifer seized Judith's wrist. She never spoke, but pushed Judith into her room.

Six candles were blazing, a table with wine and the remains of a chicken was near the bed, which was tumbled and in disorder, and Fernyhirst in his shirt and trousers, his shirt open at the neck, his rather long grey hair untidily over his forehead, sat sprawling in a large crimson chair.

'What is it?' he asked, looking up; then saw Judith and his mouth stayed open. She thought that she had never seen a more unattractive creature, purple-veined, double-chinned, with a heavy stomach and thick unwieldy legs. Her disgust with both of them was so intense that for a moment it covered everything else. That they should thus--these two elderly lovers--have been philandering in the room next to her sleeping son seemed to her a foul thing. That Jennifer should thus have gone back on her word--

But beyond her personal sense of affront she knew at once was something more important. Francis

must not find them there. He must not. And once this hateful discovery of hers was passed she would see to it that Fernyhirst came to the house no more.

But they remained, frozen into silence. The room seemed chilled by an icy wind from the cold world outside, although the fire blazed in the grate. They waited, the two women standing where they were, Fernyhirst sitting up in his chair.

Jennifer only whispered once: 'He always goes to his room.'

They heard nothing, for the door was closed: then, as though the house crashed about their ears, the door opened and he stood there.

Judith saw at once from his face that he had known what he would find. Instantly he flung himself across the room and fell upon Fernyhirst, pulling at his shirt, beating his face with his hand and crying:

'At last! At last! . . . You bloody rat. . . . You whoring, filthy . . .'

Jennifer ran to them, pulled feebly at Francis' coat and screamed. The table with the chicken and wine fell over, making a terrible crash.

Judith ran in among them.

'Francis! Francis! Listen! . . . Be quiet! Be still! The house must not hear, it must not wake . . . Francis! Francis!'

Francis seemed to hear her, for he stopped clawing at Fernyhirst and walked away, trembling from head to foot, his breath coming with a strange shrill sob.

The scene indeed was very quickly over, for Fernyhirst, silent and, it seemed, unmoved, rose, felt the blood that trickled on his cheek, put on very calmly his waistcoat and coat, picked up from the chair his hat and riding-coat and walked to the door.

There he turned and, looking at Francis, said heavily, 'You shall answer me for this.' He seemed not at all disturbed, and even looked at the decanter on the floor as though he had half a mind to pick it up. Then he went out.

Francis came forward, and, speaking very rapidly and, Judith thought, as though he had made up his speech in his head beforehand, addressed Jennifer, who was now sitting on the bed and crying very wildly.

'I go now,' he said, 'and I shall never return. Thank God I have seen the last of you. . . . I shall attend to your lover. . . .'

He stammered, as though he would say something to Judith, but suddenly hung his head and went swiftly out of the room.

He dragged his horse out of the stable and clattered up the road in pursuit of Fernyhirst, who was but a little ahead of him. He had but paused to take two rapiers from the corner of his room--the small room behind the parlour that was cluttered with guns, fishing-tackle, books, papers, swords and these rapiers. No one had touched them for many a year.

As he rode he did not feel the cold; he was rather bathed in a damp heat that was also dry, so that, although his forehead was wet with sweat, his hands had no moisture. That afternoon, walking along the street in Cockermouth to see some fellow on a land transaction, he had been touched on the elbow by a ragged man with a black patch over one eye, who had given him a dirty piece of paper. On this was scrawled in a rough unfamiliar hand: 'The Captain is with your wife to-night and don't leave till morning.'

Reading it, he walked on mechanically until he was almost out of the town without knowing it. He was no longer Francis Herries-- that weak, lily-livered creature was gone for ever. He was a fiery man of action, but cautious withal, a crafty vengeful devil, murderous in intent, brilliant in device. This sly fiery devil waited until night at the Cockermouth inn, sitting in a room there, with a plate before him, but not eating. Once and again he held scornful converse with the pitiful Francis, who was imprisoned in a cage and could not get out.

'Let me out!' cried Francis.

But the fiery devil only grinned, while his hand trembled on the table and his eyes were blind.

Later he found them just as the dirty piece of paper had said, and now he was going to kill Fernyhirst.

He came upon him a quarter of the way to Stone Ends. He rode past him at a gallop and then turned and faced him. There was bare moor on either side and the moon cynically observant. Everything was as bright as day, and the smoke from the horses' nostrils clouded the air.

'Off your horse, Fernyhirst,' Francis said. 'We will finish this here.'

'Let me pass, you blackguard,' Fernyhirst cried. But he was a coward at a pinch, had always been. He did not know whether Francis had not a pistol. He climbed off his horse and began blustering.

Francis showed him the rapiers.

'We will fight here and now,' he said.

'This is monstrous,' Fernyhirst said. 'No seconds. No arrangements. I protest. I refuse--'

'We will fight here and now,' Francis repeated.

Perhaps it occurred to Fernyhirst that here would be a good opportunity to teach this puling husband a lesson, for although a coward he had been a skilled duellist in younger days, and the rapier was his favourite weapon. He knew, too, that this business would be scandalous if he let it go on. The quickest over the less said.

His hesitation swung to bluster.

'If you wish it,' he said scornfully. 'You are a poor husband, Herries, and poor husbands always make shabby fighters.'

Herries said not a word.

They drew the horses up the moor and over the ridge to a hollow where they could not be seen from the road. They fought in their shirts, although the cold was intense. Francis was a good swordsman, but it was years since he had had any practice. He fought in what

was known as the Neapolitan style, with straight arm and straight back, his knees bent. Fernyhirst fought with a flourish, sweeping his rapier in the air. He knew instantly that Francis was a good swordsman, and cursed his own lack of condition, for he was fat and had been drinking heavily that same night. The scene was strange enough. Sheep came up the moor and stood bewildered. The two horses cropped the grass, and across a cloudless sky the full moon proudly sailed. The hills cut the sky sharply in the frosty air and seemed to bend their brows in attention.

They fought for a while without advantage to either side; then suddenly Francis, lowering his rapier a little, pressed upon his enemy. Fernyhirst retreated a step or two, then Francis made a short lunge in tierce. Fernyhirst backed again, but, after some clever feints, came forward and himself began to challenge Francis.

This extra exertion told on him. His breathing distressed him, and soon two moons circled in his vision, swinging about the shining length of Francis' weapon. Was he to be killed? In this bitter air with no witness? A sudden fear of Francis' intensity caught him. He lunged, his breath coming in pants, but he could not find Francis' body. Everywhere that stiff wall of steel met him. His legs were trembling, the ground rocking. The fear of death, of imminent and dreadful death, leapt at his throat like an animal from the moon.

He gave a yell that made the sheep scatter down the slope, turned and fled for his life. Panting, he flung himself on his horse, threw the rapier away from him and rode off as though all the Furies were beside him.

And Francis stood under the moon without moving. This had been the creature to whom for all these years he had surrendered his wife.

The agonised bitterness of a self-contempt that now would never find a cure stole slowly, quietly down upon him.

Gently his head bent; he went towards his horse.

FRANCIS IN LONDON
Spring 1821

From the window of his little lodging off St. James' Street Francis could see a pale green sky floating between the clouds of two smoking chimneys, a curricle waiting outside the bow-window of Ashton's, the hosier's, and a very elegant dandy picking his way through the puddles as though his life depended on the dryness of his boots. Both before and behind him spouts, charged with the rain that the flat roofs had collected, were pouring out their floods. He had navigated one. Now he paused before the other as though collecting all his resources. Soon the lamps on the little elevated posts that dotted the street would be lighted. The sun was almost set. One star, freshly washed, so bright it was, by the recent rain, hovered in the green sky. So agreeable was the spring air that Francis had his window open. He could hear the rattle of the carriage-wheels on the cobbles of St. James', could smell the damp and soot and sea-coal and the cooking that was going on in Mrs. Morland's room downstairs.

In his melancholy depressed mood, to watch the dandy gave him some occupation. The man in his light pantaloons (surely his calves were padded!) his absurdly exaggerated hat, his ridiculous collar à la guillotine, his monstrous waist (he was wearing beyond question Cumberland corsets), seemed scarcely human.

As he paused, looking at the water-spout, raising first one foot and then another, Francis, in spite of his dejection, could scarcely forbear to laugh. Then there hurried past, his coat up to his ears, a little man with a pile of books under his arm, who, Francis fancied, might be Mr. Lamb, to whose house his friend Daintry, the water-colour painter, had one evening taken him. Francis thought, for a wild moment, that Mr. Lamb might be coming to pay him a call. Why not? He had been most pleasant to him, talked to him of old plays and actors, asked him whether he had thought of play-writing, had appeared to be interested, had inquired his address . . . but no, it was not Mr. Lamb. Of course not. No one ever came to visit him.

The green sky faded, the old lamp-lighter whom Francis knew so well by now, with his funny step that was a kind of dot-and-carry walk, passed down the street. Francis closed the window, drew the curtains, lit the candles, went to the table, drew out his papers; he was writing an article on Malthus which he hoped (very faintly) that the Evening Chronicle might look upon kindly. He wrote a few lines and threw down his pen. It was no good; the thing was a farce. He sat there, his head between his hands, muttering to himself that the end had come.

He had taken of late to talking to himself, for indeed he had for the most part no one else to talk to. Mrs. Morland told Morland that the poor old gentleman was wrong in his head; she hoped he would do no one a mischief. Morland, who was a coal merchant by trade and as kind-hearted as any man in London, shook his head and said that he thought that Mr. Herries had lived too long in the country. He had lost touch with the Town. 'London's a big wild place these days, Maria, and not good for a gentleman who has no friends seemingly and is accustomed to country fields.' This was perhaps true. Francis HAD lost touch with the Town. He had been here now for nearly five months. After the wretched farcical fight with Fernyhirst he had ridden to Penrith, slept the night there and taken the London coach on the following day.

He had found rooms with the Morlands, and for a week or two had fancied that he might begin a new life. He had written a brief letter to Jennifer, saying that he would never return, but that proper provision would be made for her and the children. He had sought out some of his old friends, avoiding, however, any possible contact with any Herries relations. His principal success here had been with his old acquaintance, Samuel Rogers, who, only a year or two younger than Francis, welcomed him with the warm kindliness and good heart that that crabbed old poet hid under his sneers and oddities.

He welcomed Francis to his famous house in St. James's Place, with its view of the Green Park, its collections of prints, its Etruscan vases. Here Francis could have found exactly the society suited to his taste, and many happy contacts might have come of it. He had real literary feeling, could talk excellently when he was in the mood. He had, however, developed an almost crazy spirit of suspicion and self-detraction. It seemed to him that everyone must know of the disgrace and misery that weighed so heavily upon him. No one knew and no one cared; but, after a few visits, some fancied slights, some momentary irritations on the part of old Rogers, he slipped away and hugged his loneliness. He had thought that writing would be his great recourse. He thought that now at last he had the freedom and independence. But always his own wretched thoughts broke into his imagination and shattered it.

He walked mile upon mile of London streets, but here, too, he was unhappy, for the old London that he had known was gone or going. The stucco of Mr. Nash was rapidly covering with its pallid cloak the red and brown and grey of the earlier houses. A passion for building seemed to have sprung upon the town, and the suburbs were eating fields and lanes and trees as fast as they could be devoured. This was a busier, more serious London than he had known, and it seemed to have no place for him. Everywhere new shops were opening, no one appeared to have leisure any more, all were thinking of making a fortune or seeing some new invention. House-building, experiments with machinery, expeditions to America, a visit to Paris and back, a tour on the Continent--all these were everyday adventures. It was a world in which he was lost. He was altogether a lost man; he had no foothold anywhere any more. On the little ink-stained desk near the window lay a pile of letters from Judith unopened. He had not read one of them; he did not dare to. She would implore him to return, would tell him of John and Dorothy, of himself and, worst of all, of Jennifer.

The awful thing, the poison that in his loneliness devoured him, was that he still loved Jennifer. He loved her as ardently and as hopelessly as at the beginning, yes, as madly as on that first occasion when he had seen her at the Herries Ball. The thing that had ruined him, apart from his own indecision of character, was that his love had never been returned. That had not been Jennifer's fault--she had been honest with him--but from that misery of tantalisation he had died. For now he was as good as dead. Had he once captured her he would have found, likely enough, that the thing captured was neither interesting nor valuable, but he had been able neither to catch her nor leave her, neither to admire her nor despise her, neither to fight for nor against her; she had completed the ruin that his own miserable weakness had begun. As he sat there he did not pity himself nor curse himself. He did not feel that he was altogether to blame. He was a piece of pottery in whom the potter had carelessly set a flaw.

He might be, as Judith had said, one of the hopes of the Herries; but they had been too strong for him and the hope was lost. From the very beginning he had been frightened of Will's efficiency, a rebel against his father, acquiescent in things as they were, a slave to his mother's melodrama, subservient again to his wife's lazy indifference. The Herries had beaten him every time. He might have been a success in any other family. Judith alone had understood him. Judith . . . dear, darling Judith . . . so kind, so wise, so brave, so friendly and true. . . .

He got up, made a step towards the desk. He had almost those letters in his hand. But no, he must not. If he read them he would return and there would begin again that wretched half-life, with Walter's spying and bullying. . . .

Walter! He called the name aloud as though he were challenging it. He could see that swollen, redfaced, confident boaster. . . . There was a knock on the door. Mrs. Morland looked in.

'A lady to see you, sir,' she said.

'A lady?' He turned back, smoothing his hair that had grown too long and tumbled over his forehead. His heart beat nervously, as it did now when anyone approached him. There was a pause, and then who should come in? Who but old Maria Rockage?

He was so greatly surprised that he could not speak, but could only stare at her with his mouth open. She was an odd enough figure. She must be, he thought, nearly seventy. She was wearing a black, rather faded costume of a fashion quite ten years earlier, all in one piece, tied with a band of ribbon immediately under her ample breasts. Her shoes were muddy and she had a black poke-bonnet. Her face wore its accustomed expression of anxiety, nervousness, kindliness and assurance.

Her nervousness was for the actual moment, her assurance for her general state. But, as always, kindliness was the predominating note. As a matter of fact, she was not so old as Francis thought her--she was sixty-six--and she felt a great deal younger than that.

'Cousin Maria! . . . But I never expected. . . . Pray come in. . . . I am delighted. . . . But how did you know my lodging?'

She smiled at him with great beneficence.

'Mr. Rogers told me. Carey and I were at a party in St. James's Place the other evening, a very fine party . . .' (The odd thought came to him that, in spite of her Methodist proclivities, she was ever going to parties.) 'I

had Phyllis and Carey with me. Literature and the Arts. . . . And then Judith wrote to me. She begged me to search you out. She is so greatly distressed--'

She was looking at him, and biting the fingers of her worn gloves, and putting up her hand to pat the hair under her bonnet, and screwing her mouth round in a strange way that she had. What a funny old thing she was!

He cleared the papers away and sat her down at the table. Of course, he said to himself, she was looking around her and seeing how shabby everything was. She would tell Will and Christabel, and everyone would know. How was he certain that she had not come to spy out for Walter? She had but recently been staying at Westaways. Tiresome old thing! And then, to his amazement, he saw that tears were trickling down her cheeks! When he saw that, it was all that he could do not to cry himself, so tired and wan and miserable he was. She began to chatter with little gulps and stammers.

'Francis, we have never known each other very well. We are almost of an age. I fear it is an impertinence my coming like this and intruding on your privacy. But I had to come. The Lord told me to come; and although I know that you think me foolish about my religion, still we are both old people now and can be tolerant about one another. I have not come to interfere in any way, dear Francis. Indeed I have not. But I could not bear to think of your being all alone and away from Jennifer and your lovely children-- although I have never quite agreed with Jennifer, yet she is no longer as young as she was neither, and the pomps and vanities of our life fade away, leaving us often much alone. I know that, although I have the best husband in the world and dear Carey and dear Phyllis, I know what it is to be lonely and have only the Lord to depend upon--' She broke off and looked at him with mild kindly eyes, beseeching him not to be rude to her.

She smiled at him over her handkerchief, a watery but encouraging smile. He wished to be kind--but what was he to say?

'Dear Cousin Maria, this is very good of you. I fear I have no hospitality to offer you.'

'Oh,' she broke in, 'I want nothing. I want nothing at all, I assure you. Too good of you--and your room is very cosy, very cosy indeed. And right on the street, so that you have people passing. You cannot really be lonely. Always something going on--a carriage accident or a fire or a Punch and Judy. I would go anywhere myself to see a Punch and Judy. Carey is for ever laughing at me for it. "Why, Maria," he says, "I believe you'd run down the street if there were a Punch and Judy about"--and I believe I would, you know. So very amusing. . . . One never tires. . . .' She broke off and then said abruptly: 'And when was the last time you heard from dear Judith?'

'I haven't heard,' he said in a very low voice, 'for quite a while.'

She put out her gloved hand and laid it on his.

'Francis,' she said, 'go home. Think of your dear children. Forgive Jennifer and go home. We must all forgive one another. I am certain that Carey and I have forgiven one another a hundred times. Go home, Francis.'

He caught his hands one within another and looked straight in front of him.

'I cannot, Cousin Maria. I cannot. You do not know--'

She came closer to him, putting her hand on his arm.

'No, of course I do not know, but I cannot endure to see you looking so unhappy. We are not young any longer, Francis, you and I; and when we are old it is not at all easy to be alone. No, it is not easy. Carey and I miss one another if we are apart a day. What will you do here in this lodging alone? Come to us at Grosset for a while if that will assist you. And then go home. Jennifer means very well. She means very well indeed. She had a selfish upbringing. Poor Rose never had a notion of how to bring up a family. She is the mother of your children, Francis.'

He was deeply touched. Her sincerity and true longing to be good to him were beyond any question. But he wished that she would go. No one could help him any more. He smiled at her and laid his hand on hers.

'Thank you, Cousin Maria. You are exceeding kind. But I must shoulder my own troubles. What you say is very true. We are growing old, and nothing is of very much importance any more. Thank you, Cousin Maria, but indeed I must stand on my own feet.'

There was something in his face that told her that it was so.

She hesitated, stammered, then broke out: 'Well, then--would it trouble you. . . . You would not laugh, I am sure . . . but it might be a help to you. The Lord is always nigh. If I offered a prayer. . . .'

Her eyes gazed at him with the eager moisture in them of a puppy begging for a biscuit.

'Certainly, Cousin Maria. It is good of you--'

At once she knelt down on the floor beside him and, her bonnet falling back a little from her head, her gloved hands clasped, prayed.

'Oh Lord God, I pray Thee to look down on this Thy servant who has been sore troubled and in deep distress. Thou knowest what are our faults and failures, but there is in Thy heart an infinite patience and an all-preserving Wisdom. Take this Thy servant into Thy care and show him the way that he may find once again those whom he best loves and be restored into their company. Thou knowest what is best for him, and Thy will be done. In the name of Thy Son who was crucified for us on the Cross and whose Divine Example we would eternally follow. Amen.'

She waited a moment, her head between her hands, then she rose. There was thick dust on her black gown, but she did not notice. She stroked her nose with her hand.

'And now I must really be off,' she said briskly. 'Phyllis and I am to spend a little evening alone together. We are reading The Task. Remember, pray, Cousin Francis, that we are most eager to have you with us at Grosset, if you care to come. You have only to send us word. Yes, we shall all be delighted to see you.'

She bent and kissed him on the forehead; then murmuring something to the effect that she did hope that it was not raining, she gave him a smile at the door and went out.

He sat on, lost in thought. In what was he lost? The candles flickered, the shadows leapt on the wall, carriages rumbled beyond the window, steps hurried by, voices rose and fell, but he was engulfed in his sense of utter disaster. Good old woman! She had wished to help him, but it would need more than Maria Rockage to help him now.

At last he rose, found his hat and coat and went out. He walked up St. James' Street and into Piccadilly. He did not know why he was walking nor whither, but it seemed to him that a figure was at his side, keeping pace with him, murmuring in his ears: 'This is your farewell to the world. Soon, when the lights have dazzled your eyes sufficiently, you will return into your dark house.'

In the nervous state in which he was, it seemed to him that there was a babel of sound all about him. The lamps were lit, but there was still a great deal of traffic and business, and the fine spring evening after the rainy afternoon encouraged everyone to be out. London, although it was so rapidly growing in size and energy, had still something of the village about it. In this central part at least there was much recognising of acquaintances, the cheerful intimacy of shopmen who knew their customers and, only a yard away, big houses, silent squares with lawns and gardens, the grandeur of the great mansions on the Park, footmen standing on doorsteps, coachmen from the boxes of their carriages looking down upon this world as though they commanded, shopmen filling their doorways, their legs spread, their noses sniffing the fresh evening.

To all this Francis was a stranger; he passed like a shadow, hurrying nowhere. At every moment something occurred to infuriate him. For some while a cart accompanied him. It contained, it seemed, a thousand iron bars that rattled and rumbled and screamed above the cobbles. A drunken sailor, rolling by, ejected a shoot of tobacco and missed his shoes by an inch: an odour of meat seemed everywhere; the hackney coaches rattled his brains to pieces.

Infuriated by the noise, but still, as it seemed at him, driven on by this companion at his side, he turned up a side street hoping to find quiet, but first on a doorstep a footman was practising 'Paddy Whack' on a small fife, execrably out of tune, a headlong butcher's boy rushed by uttering a shrill cat-call; in a room just above his head there was a dancing lesson being held. The window was open and he could hear the 'One--Two--Three' and then 'Now then--Left-- Right,' and the shrill discordant wail of a fiddle. . . .

Despairing of freeing himself from all these miseries, he turned back, found Piccadilly again and ventured into Mr. Hatchard's bookshop; there would be silence, the friendliness of books, the courtesy of good Mr. Sumner who, although he looked like a prize- fighter, had all the delicacy and sensitiveness of one who knew Byron and Scott and Coleridge, and had often, under Mr. Sheridan's direction, supplied the Prince, in earlier days, with the best literature.

So Francis stepped in--and there was old Mr. Rogers!

Yes, old Mr. Rogers, the very last man in the world whom he wished to see. Nor was he alone. He was attended by a stout thick-set young man, badly dressed, with an untidy neckcloth and a very supercilious air.

Mr. Rogers gave him a finger and introduced him to his friend.

'This is Mr. Macaulay, who is at Cambridge and soon will be having the world at his feet. Come, come, Macaulay. You know you will. You know you will. You are as confident of it as I am.'

The thick-set untidy youth raised a pair of very remarkable piercing eyes and began to talk with great eloquence and volubility. It was clear that he did not suffer from shyness.

Francis meanwhile hated the confident young man and hated Rogers. He was sure that they were mocking him; indeed, that everyone in the shop was mocking him. It was true enough, perhaps, that Rogers was not over-pleasant, because he had gone out of his way to be kind to this fellow who, of late, had treated him casually.

'Well, Mr. Herries,' he said in his sharp restless voice, 'it is well met and farewell, for I am shortly taking a sister and niece with me on to the Continent--Switzerland and Italy. I have been trying to persuade Tom Macaulay here to accompany me, but he has better things to concern himself with. . . . Well, well, Mr. Herries--good-day to ye. Good-day to ye.'

The loquacious young man had already forgotten him and was talking eagerly to Sumner about a book that he held in his hand. Sumner also (who was, as a rule, so courteous) had not noticed him. In a tumult of irritation Francis left the shop. So Rogers had had enough of him? Even Sumner did not care to speak with him, and so old and insignificant was he that an untidy young man from Cambridge could turn his back on him. It was true enough. He was old and shabby. He had no place in the world any longer.

At the corner of St. James' Street he met a man whom he slightly knew, an effeminate bore, and this fellow would not let him go, but with one finger on his coat must, in a shrill piping voice, talk about the coming Coronation. It was all that anyone was thinking of, it was the finest and grandest the world had ever seen, no expense was to be spared, and they said that the Queen, poor thing-- At last Francis broke away. As he hastened down the street he fancied that the man was looking after him, wondering what madness had taken possession of him. Well, he was mad if they liked. He had no place in this absurd world any longer--this absurd, monstrous crazy world.

When he entered his little room again and lit the candles once more, a sense of disgust took him. What a mean little place it was, with its smell of soot and cooking food! How grimy and foul the world had grown!

He went into his little bedroom, filled his basin with water, stripped, washed from head to foot, put on clean linen and another suit. Then he returned to his table, took out paper and pen and began to write:

DEAREST JUDITH--You have all your life forgiven me for my many faults and failings; once again--and this is the last time that I shall ask you--you must forgive me. For many weeks your letters arrived here and now they are lying in a pile on a table near me unopened. For it is only a part of my general weakness that I have not opened them. I did not dare, for I know that if I had done so you would have tempted me back. But I must not go back, dear Judith. Were you not so noble and generous to me you would be honest with me and tell me what I know well to be the truth--that I must never come back again. You have known me all my life long and once when you were a baby you loved me. Perhaps you love me still, for your heart is so generous that it can pass over all weaknesses and all mistakes. But I myself cannot pass them over. In these last weeks I have learnt to face myself and to see what is there. You will think that there is too much self-pity in what I have written, but it is not so. I have never pitied myself. I have had every chance to make something of life and I have thrown every chance away.

When I was a young man and you were a child I used to talk to you about all the things that I intended to do. I had great faith in myself, and because I have none any more is not a reason for pity, but rather for acceptance. I have failed everyone--my father, my mother, my wife, my children and my ideals.

I think that there are other men in like case. Men of our time have some of them been unfortunate because they have lived in an age of transition. The Great Time was behind them. The Great Time is coming again--but some of us have had our faith taken from us and have not been given, or have not found, a new one. I thought once that all men would be free now. I thought once that the poor man would have Justice. But the poor man is more a slave than before, and we are all of us in prison. I cannot write clearly; I see everything darkly, but I know that for myself I took the wrong path.

I am writing this only because you must not, YOU MUST NOT, dearest Judith, take the wrong path also. Return to your own life, take your boy, have nothing to do with the fortunes of our family. For such as you and I there can never be any happiness in Herries affairs. They are ruin and damnation to us. They deprive us of all that our souls need. I have been no good friend to you. I have not given you assistance when you sorely needed it. I have left you alone when you were most lonely. In this as in everything else I have betrayed myself. But now I am speaking truth from the heart. Your life is not with Will and Walter and Jennifer and the rest. They are strangers to you and you to them. Because I married a stranger and, God help me, love her now as dearly as I ever did, I have worked my own Destruction.

I know that you will be good to Jennifer and my children, but they are provided for, and YOU MUST NOT STAY WITH THEM. Be true to yourself. You know well enough what you should do. . . . Go back to Watendlath. I can see the light over the hill, hear the streams running . . . the streams running. My hand shakes. Tell Jennifer that I love her, I love her, just as I did . . . as I always . . . Embrace the children. John will be a fine boy . . . and your Adam. Go back to the light over the hill. There is so terrible a noise in this town. Dear Judith, think of me kindly, but better to forget me. I could not find a Balance. I was always fearful of Action. God be with you, but there is no God--none for me. Nothing. . . .

He broke off; his pen rattled on to the table. He sat there for a long while, his head buried in his hands. Then he got up, folded the letter and addressed it. He went to the window, pulled back the blind and looked out. Two ladies were talking, laughing. A little dog came sniffing up to the lamp-post. Another dog saw him from the other side of the street and came slowly across. A boy, carrying some parcels, stood idly and watched them.

Francis went to the drawer of his little ink-stained desk and took from it a pistol.

He crossed to the mirror, cracked and seamed with age. He saw with great clearness the faded green paper, the print of the fight between Gully and the Chicken, the copy of Drayton's Poems, that he had been reading, on the table. Then he put the pistol to his mouth.

Mrs. Morland, fancying that she heard someone tumble or the distant firing of a gun or the collision of two carriages, went to her window and looked out. But no: in the street there was nothing to be seen but two ladies laughing together and the cautious intimacies of a Newfoundland and a King Charles.

MONEY

'Will you not come in and pay us a visit, Cousin Judith?' Walter Herries asked. He was standing at the high pillared entrance to Westaways. The wind was blowing with a kind of innocent child-like caprice and turning back the leaves of a giant beech to a duller chillier gold. Judith, with Adam beside her, felt the wind tugging at her big velvet-lined feathered hat. Her hands were warm inside their muff. Her face for once was rosy; the sharp air, the wild sky, the scudding fragments of blue and the harp-like swing of the wind across the bare fields, the ridges of snow on the brown range of fell, all exhilarated her.

Moreover, it was four days before Christmas and directly Christmas was past she was returning with Adam to Watendlath--yes, for ever and ever!

She had passed Westaways as she had done a thousand times before, walking from Crosthwaite to Keswick. The carriage was in Keswick for the day; Jennifer was paying visits and after their three o'clock dinner at the inn they would drive home.

It was now mid-day. The Crosthwaite Church clock had but just told the hour. She had intended to take Adam to show to her friends, Miss West and Miss Pennyfeather. The last thing that she had expected or wished was to be caught by Walter Herries.

Westaways looked gleaming and polished in the wet windy sunlight. On the eastern corner there were ladders and men working. Walter was for ever doing something to the place.

'Do come inside now, Cousin Judith, and taste a glass of sherry.'

She knew that he had a family party for Christmas--Will, Christabel, old Monty Cards, Rodney, the pious second son of Pomfret and Rose from Kensington, old Pomfret himself and his ancient old-maid sister Cynthia, and best of all, Maria's Phyllis with her husband, Mr. Stephen Newmark, and two of their children; Phyllis had been married in 1818 and had already three babies!

It was Phyllis whom she would like to see; Christabel too, Will even. But she shrank from the crowd of them, all gathered in the parlour, talking scandal, most of it of the family order. In she would march with Adam, and Will's neck would tighten in its collar, and fat, over-decorated, 'Regency' old Pomfret would wink at her (she could bet on it!), and silly kind old Monty would stroke his powdered cheek while his corsets creaked, pious Rodney would look down his nose--only dear Phyllis, untidy like her mother, with some of the Grosset disorder clinging to her, only Phyllis would really welcome her, would be enchanted to see her. She had a curiosity, too, to behold Phyllis' husband, Mr. Stephen Newmark. Maria, in letters, had informed her that he was a very fine man indeed, a wealthy religious landowner from Warwickshire. Wealthy AND religious--not a very promising combination!

There was the other temptation, too, that this was her last opportunity for spying out Westaways. Was it not absurd, perhaps, to say that, when Watendlath was only a mile or two away? But Watendlath was more than a mile or two away, it was a world away. As poor Francis had said in that last despairing letter.

Strange to pass from the thought of that letter to that great brilliantly-coloured body straddling there in the gateway! But, looking at him, she suddenly wondered whether he were not already a trifle old-fashioned? The thought gave her a malicious pleasure. He was certainly over-dressed for the present times, with his billowing stock and its jewelled pin, his claret-coloured coat with the exaggerated waist (he was corseted--and what immense corsets they must be!), the fawn-shaded pantaloons fitting so tightly over the calves. There were rings on his fingers. And yet he was a man! Do Walter all the injustice in the world, but you could never name him effeminate. He was the prize bull of the stock. Already, young as he was, there was a purple tinge to his cheek, but his eyes were hard and clear and his mouth firmly and confidently set.

'Come inside and drink a glass of sherry with us, Cousin Judith.'

She looked up at him from under her broad-brimmed hat with that air of humorous impertinent defiance that they seemed always to use to one another.

'I have Christmas shopping and calls to pay. Have we not, Adam?'

Adam, who was holding a little toy whip, had never taken his eyes from Walter since he had first seen him.

'Why, young man, you have some clothes on at last, I see.'

'Yes, sir.'

'And how old are you since I saw you last?'

'Six, sir.'

'Six, are you? Well, your mother shall bring you in out of the wind. Not too young for a glass of sherry, are you?'

'Of course he is, Walter. A glass of sherry indeed!'

'Why, I was drinking sherry before I was weaned, and look at me! Come along in! Come along in!'

So Judith went and Adam also, his eyes still following Walter's back as though he had never before seen anything like it.

She knew that he had been doing things to the house, and when she stood in the hall her astonishment was vivid at the changes that he had made. Everywhere were riches. On the wall facing the front door a great piece of purple tapestry showing Diana hunting, on either side of the door pieces of sculpture, one of a Pan playing his flute, another of a stout naked goddess

drinking. (What, oh, what would Maria Rockage say to this paganism?)

At the stairhead, over the door of the saloon, was a sumptuous painting of a French king (Louis XIV. perhaps) dining with his ladies, and, beside the door, a silver pedestal with a black bust of some Roman Emperor--and Walter, as he walked slowly up the stairs, gave the impression even in his back-view that it was he and no one else who had wrought all these splendours.

They were gathered about a blazing fire in the saloon--Will, Christabel, Monty Cards, Rodney and his father, Phyllis, Carey her brother, and a thin upright man with a hooked nose who must be her husband, Mr. Newmark.

As Judith crossed the long shining slippery floor, holding Adam by the hand, she felt that both herself and her son were midgets. She was not frightened but she could feel their intense interest as they all turned towards her. She was helped by Adam's absolute confidence. He nearly tripped and fell as he bent his head back to look at the gods and goddesses in their brilliant nakedness. He feared no one.

Christabel and Phyllis rose with cries of pleasure to greet her. Everyone made a display over Adam. Old Pomfret (still a very gay and brightly set-up dog in spite of his years) was the most pleased with him. He took him between his knees and looked into his ugly little face with a very lively interest. He asked him questions, and Adam, in his funny high voice, answered them all instantly.

Judith, sitting with her hand in Phyllis', thought: 'This grows grander every month. Up, up, up. And at Uldale we go down, down, down! Never mind. The battle is not ended yet. . . . Yes, Adam is ugly. His mouth is too large by far--but he charms everyone. . . .' That strange pang at her heart again! He charms everyone! He always will--and I shall be left. . . . 'But I WISH him to charm everyone, to be happy and honest and brave as he is now--always.' And then, following quickly on this, cutting across the self-sufficient tones of Rodney, who would be one day Archdeacon of Polchester and patroniser of the very Black Bishop, came this thought:

'In ten days we shall be in Watendlath, eating food with the Ritsons, and Adam will be mine, mine, mine!'

She could almost hear the sheep shuffling with the noise of the rustle of leaves across this shining floor. She could see the sun strike the flint in those rocks until they shone like spearheads, dulling the painted goddesses. 'Oh, if anything should hinder my reaching there! But nothing can, now surely nothing can!' It was as though she were planning to get as far as China!

They were still discussing that now so wearily worn topic, the Coronation and the Queen's beating on the Westminster doors. Will, who was strangely aged now and thinner than ever, so that he looked like a stork standing on one leg and protecting his nest (only his eggs were money-bags), was all for upholding the Crown.

'What we want,' he said with his usual air of delivering judgement, 'is stable conditions. To counteract the lower classes. Relax, and we shall have another Peterloo. . . . But the country is recovering its Balance. I am glad to be able to say that the country is recovering its Balance.'

Everyone looked greatly relieved. It was pleasant to hear from Will, who must know, that all was well.

Adam was passed round from hand to hand. They were all kind to him although he was a little bastard. But Judith knew that it was for the moment only, and that her presence made them uncomfortable, yes, even poor Christabel, who was restless under the eye of her lord and master. The thought came to her as she saw Rodney's eyes meditatively resting upon her: 'Oh, if Adam could grow into the master of them all, rule the pack of them! He could. He has even now twice their spirit. . . .' But she was going to Watendlath, and Adam with her, leaving the Herries behind them for ever, and Adam would be a farmer like Charlie Watson, and one day he would come down into Keswick, driving his sheep, and he would encounter Walter's children in their fine carriage, and the coachman would shout to him to clear his sheep from the road. . . . And after Adam would return, riding up the road to see the Tarn shining with the evening sun, and he would call to his dog, and the fields would smile up at him, the hills look kindly down. . . .

'Well, my little friend,' said Rodney Herries to Adam (he spoke as though to a little black child newly rescued from the heathen), 'and what is the game you enjoy the most?'

'To cut men out of wood,' said Adam with complete assurance, but his eyes wandering a little. 'I have cut Mr. Noah and the Duke of Wellington and Mr. Winch.'

'Very praiseworthy. Very praiseworthy indeed,' said Rodney, looking, however, bewildered.

'He is commencing,' said Judith, 'to carve figures. He has a true disposition towards carving.'

'Yes,' went on Adam eagerly, looking at everyone with an enthusiastic smile. 'And I colour them also. And Bennett gives me the wood. He says--'

'Hush, Adam, hush,' said Judith, drawing him towards her. He came to her, but with one last look round him and pointing at old Cynthia Herries, Pomfret's sister, who had a nose like a door-knocker:

'That old lady would be very fine for cutting.'

His manners, Judith could see them deciding, were not at all of the best, but what could you expect when his mother . . . ?

Then Walter came forward.

'Judith, you must see my improvements. Forgive me for taking you away an instant. I must show you the improvements.'

She knew that he wished to speak to her alone. She had known it all the time. The drama of the scene, the implication of it all, had been rising in her with increasing force. Poor Francis was dead, Jennifer bewildered, like a woman lost in a wood, the children helpless--and this power, this force, destructive and remorseless, hung over them. And something told her that she was the only one whom Walter feared; it had always been so. And it might be that she was the only one whom, of all that company, Walter respected.

She looked back and saw that Adam was safe with Phyllis' arm around him. Then she followed Walter out.

He preceded her into a little parlour off the saloon, a room so small that, when he had motioned her into a red morocco chair and himself stood, with his legs straddled, in front of the fire, the two of them filled it. There was nothing in the room save a Chippendale cabinet on which was a bowl of Christmas roses. They were full-blown and wore that look of patient expectancy that precedes death.

Walter began at once:

'Judith--how long will you remain at Uldale?'

'I cannot see that that is any business of yours, Cousin Walter,' she answered sharply. She had retained her white fur muff, and her fingers in it clasped one another with self-congratulation. What was it in her that made her love a battle? She was at the moment perfectly happy, all her faculties widely awake, her eyes on the rich panelling, the Christmas roses, and the brilliant person of Mr. Walter Herries.

'No business of mine,' he went on. 'Well, perhaps not. And yet because I have a regard for you, Cousin Judith, I would wish you out of Uldale. That place and all in it are doomed.' He said this, a little swell of importance rising in his great chest.

'Really! That is exceedingly interesting. And by whom are they doomed, pray?'

'By myself.'

'Are you so powerful?' He was, she reflected, like a giant schoolboy fallen from some star where everyone was twice as big as nature.

'I am indeed,' he answered. 'And growing more powerful every day. It is my father's wish that our family should be the chief figures in this country. Natural enough, when you think of it. He was born here, and his father lived here till the end of his life. He has developed an affection for the place.'

'An affection so deep,' interrupted Judith, 'that he never comes near it save on Saints' Days and Festivals! No, no, Cousin Walter,' she went on, 'there are the two of us alone here, and we may be frank. I belong to this country far more than you ever can. My mother may not have been of the country, but at least for generation upon generation my ancestors have lived and thieved here, stolen cattle and ladies only too ready to be stolen. I love this country, and so will my son after me. I love it because it is dark and full of storms and rains every other day, and smells of bracken and sheep and cow-dung. But you have none of these reasons. You love it because you wish to impress it, and I can tell you, Cousin Walter, it is not so easily impressed. What have you got? You have one thing--money. Nothing else. You are not especial clever that I have heard; you are too stout to be beautiful; you are a bully of those weaker than yourself; you are as conceited as a peacock. I am almost old enough to be your mother, Walter. In fact, in Eastern countries I believe I might have been--so forgive me for my frankness.'

'Go on,' he said, smiling at her.

There were moments when she thought that she rather liked him. Hatred would make everything easier.

'Very well, then, I will. You have nothing but money. At Uldale they have much. Poor Francis, who took his life because he had so much more perception and understanding than you, loved this country with all his heart. He made an unhappy marriage. Oh! I am not blaming Jennifer. There was a time when I hated her, but it is hard to hate anybody long. It was not her fault that she could not love him. Now that is all over, and there are two very fine children who are NOT doomed, dear Walter, however much you may say it. They have more right to this country than you have. Money can't beat them, and don't you think it.'

Walter nodded.

'Very well, then. We know where we are. You have said nothing, though, of the scandals that we have all suffered for years past. It may be foolish' (again his immense chest swelled), 'but if I am proud of one thing in this world it is of being an Englishman and a Herries. I have as much right as yourself to any part of England, Cousin Judith, even though your ancestors WERE cattle-thieves. How agreeable has it been to us, do you think, that for years past, under our very noses, we should have a Herries who is too weak to challenge his wife's lover, who allows adultery any day or night under his roof; a woman so lost to shame that she receives her lover in the room next to her children; a man so lily-livered that he challenges that same lover, and then before the duel is fought runs to London--?'

'I do not believe that,' Judith broke in, her eyes flashing. 'We have only the word of that miserable oaf whom everyone knows for a coward--'

'Yes; and what about Uncle Francis for a coward, who let such things be year after year?'

'And who are you,' she broke in hotly, 'to be so virtuous? How have you treated YOUR wife all these years? And what of milkmaids in Keswick and loose women in Kendal? Do you suppose that you are so sacred that no one talks of you?'

He threw his head back and laughed.

'I am no hypocrite, Cousin Judith. Nor are you. I am as other men. You had your little come-by-chance in Paris. But I have not allowed my wife a lover, nor have you blown off the top of your head with a pistol. But come . . . that is not the point. You may say that

there is no power in money. But I say there is. And more. Money is going to be powerful in England as it has never been before. I am no such fool as I look, Judith. In spite of my size I have a trifle of my father's brains. But the long and short of it is just this. They must leave Uldale. It is my obsession that they should. I hate Jennifer, for she was rude to my mother; but beyond that they are a blot on the Herries name. I will pay them a good price for the house, but they must quit this part of the country!'

'Never!' cried Judith, springing up. 'Never! Never! Never!'

'Now come, Judith. Why should you care? What are they to you? You loved Uncle Francis. Good. I have nothing against it. But he is gone. Jennifer is a dull, heavy, stupid woman. You have never liked her. What is all this to you?'

'It is this to me! These are Francis' children. You would bully them out of existence. Well, you shall not.'

'What will you do to prevent it?'

'Never mind. You shall not.'

He shrugged his great shoulders.

'It may be true that I am a bully,' he said slowly. 'I hate the weak. They have no place here if they cannot stand up for themselves. You are the only one whom I admire, and you have put yourself out of court with your little bastard. Not that I have anything against bastards; but you are a little public with yours, are you not? It was worth seeing just now the way that prig Rodney's nose curved down his cheek. So leave them alone, Judith! Be quiet with your boy in some place and we will be good friends. But leave Uldale alone.'

It was on the edge of her tongue to tell him that he need not be disturbed, for in ten days she would be in Watendlath and free of him for ever. But she did not speak. As she faced him the dominating part of her longed to oppose him, to fight him, and beat him, to defend John and Dorothy, to show him that the little bastard was not so negligible as he pretended. She COULD fight him! And what a fight that would be!

Meanwhile there was Watendlath. She almost sighed as she turned away and saw a smooth white petal of the Christmas roses flutter to the ground.

'Good friends?' she repeated. 'Not if you touch Uldale.'

'Well I SHALL touch Uldale,' he said, moving towards the door. 'I have told you. And now, come up and see the children. Bring your boy with you.'

But at the door she paused.

'This is not a game, Cousin Walter.'

He stood over her.

'No. I have told you. It is a chapter in family history.'

'What have you ever done,' she asked scornfully, 'to be so proud of our family history?'

'Non mi ricordo,' he answered in the phrase that had been the popular catchword ever since Majocchi's evidence in the Queen's trial. He was determined to be amiable.

But, with her hand on the door, and with a passion that in these days she rarely showed, she burst out: 'I tell you, Walter, you must leave Jennifer and the children alone'; and he, smiling, murmured lightly that popular epigram:

Most gracious Queen, we thee implore
To go away, and sin no more;
But if that effort be too great,
To go away, at any rate.

They looked into the saloon and found Adam diving into old Pomfret's pockets and producing treasures-- a gold snuff-box, some seals and a small watch set with diamonds. The old man was watching him with delighted pleasure, and Judith at once forgave him all his pomposities, sensualities, infidelities to Rose, every other crime or weakness.

Adam came at once running when she called him. He turned when he was half-way to the door and waved his hand to the figures at the fire. Pomfret and Christabel waved back. Phyllis got up from her chair.

'Are you going up to see the children? You shall see my babies too.'

Judith knew how deeply intrigued they all were. What had Walter been saying to her? How much part did she play now in family affairs? She knew that Will was regarding her with secret alarm. She had always been a signal of danger to him, representing everything that was lawless and unsanctified. And she had been always Francis' ally. Perhaps he thought now of that old scene in Monty Cards' house when Francis had defied him . . . lured by Jennifer's beauty. . . . Well, he had never been lured by anyone's beauty, and he was glad of it. But this pain in his leg was vexatious. This Northern air did not suit him. He was truly well only in the City. But she knew by this time that she was in the camp of the enemy and, as she went out of the room with her head up and trying not to slip ignominiously on the polished floor, her hand went quietly to the silver chain, her father's, that she always wore beneath her clothes.

So the four of them went upstairs, Walter leading. It was a fine high room where the children were. Almost a hundred years ago old Pomfret's children, Raiseley and Anabel and Judith, had sat there, the girls with boards down their backs to keep them straight, learning their Latin. But much had been done to the room since then. The windows were fine and high, with a great view over the Lake and Scafell, and the Gavel grouped handsomely at the end of it. The waves were running across it now as though in a race, and the woods by Manesty were black as jet.

Inside the room everything was warm and cosy--a great fire roaring, a decent-looking elderly woman sitting beside it sewing. On the carpet Elizabeth, one of Walter's twins, was playing with Phyllis' two babies; Uhland, the other, was sitting on a small chair by himself, his face absorbed as he pulled the hair out of the tail of a painted wooden horse.

Many, many times afterwards she was to look back to this moment when she first saw Uhland. (Poor child, that he should be burdened his life long with so outlandish a name!) How characteristic that he should be sitting gravely by himself pulling something to pieces! But, at the moment, she felt nothing but pity. He had already, although he was but six years old, the face of an old man, the high forehead lined and the corners of the mouth bitter, and those strange grey penetrating eyes. His legs were dangling over the chair, but she noticed immediately that, absorbed as he was, at once, when he heard someone enter, he drew them up so that no one should observe their inequality. His body was too small for his head; his hands, she saw, were very beautiful, and, later, when she had reason to know how proud he was of them, she was interested to remember how quickly she had perceived them.

What followed touched her deeply. Walter, in his magnificent claret coat and resplendent pantaloons, hurried forward to his son, caught him up in his arms and held him close to his breast. The child seemed unmoved. His face did not change. Only one hand rested on his father's big one. Walter kissed him many times, oblivious of everyone else there.

'You must say How do you do?' he commanded him, and brought him to Judith. The child's cold grey eyes rested on her and, she fancied, with an expression of instant dislike.

'How do you do, ma'am?' he said in a small, remote voice. She bent forward and kissed his cheek, which was chill and dry. It was odd to touch that pallid, small face and feel Walter's great red one just above it. Walter took him back to his chair and, kneeling on the floor beside him, talked to him about the horse.

Walter had shown no attention to his daughter Elizabeth. This was a charming child with fragile, delicate features and pale flaxen hair.

She glanced once at her father as though she would have liked his attention, but she did not seem at all unhappy; she talked eagerly, made friends with Adam, played games with the babies, who already, Judith thought, bore, both of them, resemblance to Mr. Newmark.

After a little while they came away, but Judith saw that, as they left the room, Uhland stood up and gazed after them with an almost frightening intensity.

Judith, with Adam holding tightly to her hand, walked into Keswick. Even the road was alive with the stir of Christmas, but she moved for some while with unseeing eyes; she had a sense of danger--as though did she let Adam out of her sight for an instant Walter would get him.

The touch of his warm little hand in hers comforted her; but that was not enough. In one hand she held her muff, but with the other arm, had it not been so public a place, she would have encircled him that she might be the more secure.

He meanwhile had observed everything and had a hundred questions to ask. Why did no one wear any clothes in the pictures? Why was the floor so slippery? Who was the old gentleman with the diamond watch? The little boy upstairs had one leg longer than another. Why was the big man who had tried to hit him with the whip so red in the face? Why.... Why.... Why...?

Then suddenly he was aware, with the perception that came from their long-continued intimacy together, that she was disturbed and wanted his help. He always knew when she needed him, although he might not understand what it was that she needed. Even at the time of his greatest intimacy with John (he was as deeply devoted to John as ever, but the novelty was gone) he would look up and run off to find her, although he could not himself tell why.

She walked more slowly. She wanted him to understand something:

'Adam, would you wish to live in a house like Uncle Walter's, so grand and rich, with everything you could need?'

He put out his tongue at two small boys who were mocking him from the hedge, then he applied his whole intelligence to the question.

'I would like that rocking-horse,' he said at last.

'Yes. But besides--' Her step was slower. So soon she would be in Keswick, and there would be Jennifer and gossip and the outside world. At this moment she felt for him so overpowering a love that it was as though she were saying goodbye to him before he departed to America or the incredible South Sea Islands.

'Besides--would you wish to live there--always?'

'Would you come and John and Dorothy and Bennett, and might I cut things?'

'No. We would not come.'

He considered it.

'I should LIKE the rocking-horse,' he said slowly. 'But, OF COURSE, you would be in the house.'

'No, I would not.'

'But you will be everywhere I am always.'

'No.' She shook her head. 'No.'

He laughed, for the two little boys were running along in the hedge making faces at him, and one of them, not being able to see in two places' at once, fell down.

'The boy fell down,' he said, screwing his head round to see better.

She stopped at the little stream that was now coffee and now a froth of foam.

'Listen, Adam. I wish you to hear this. No one will ever love you as your mother does now. No one can take you from me. No one. We will soon be in Watendlath with Charlie and Mrs. Perry again. I could make you a fine man in a grand house, and everyone would do what you say, but I am going to make you a

farmer like Watson, and when you are in the road with your sheep, the carriage that you should have ridden in will order you to clear the way. You will be walking and you might have been riding. You will be rough and poor and you could have been grand and rich.

'But we will be happy, you and I and Charlie and Alice; but the little sick boy will be rich and powerful, and you will be poor and nobody.'

He did not mind at all. He was looking to see a fish jump in the river.

But she put her hand under his chin and looked into his eyes.

'I want you to remember this, because all my life I have been making this choice. You cannot understand now, but one day you will look back and perhaps be angry with me.'

He knew that she was wanting him to understand something, so he screwed his forehead into a hundred wrinkles and did his best.

'Would you prefer that you were Charlie Watson or big Uncle Walter?' she said.

He laughed at the thought of being Uncle Walter and, then and there, puffed out his cheeks, swelled out his chest, and began to strut about. Then his face was grave. He turned, looking back down the road.

'If he hits me with his whip again,' he said, 'I'll BEAT him.'

The change was so swift that she was astonished.

'But you like Uncle Walter,' she said. 'He was very kind to you.'

'Why does the little boy have one leg bigger than the other?'

'He was born like that.'

His mind seemed to jump.

'It's Christmas! It's Christmas!' he cried, and began to run down the road in front of her. She walked after him. He turned back to meet her.

'Boneyparte was beat at Waterloo, Mr. Winch says,' he remarked very gaily, dancing about. Then catching her hand again and dragging her along he shouted:

'And I will beat Uncle Walter when I am bigger!'

He ran, pulling her hand, calling like a song:

'And I love you better than everybody--better than John, better than Dorothy, better than Bennett, better than Jack, better than--'

But even as the litany continued, something caught his attention, a goat dragged along by a cord, and a very small girl in charge of it. He pulled his hand away and ran on to see this phenomenon, but as he ran he chanted in a high absent-minded refrain:

'Better than Bennett. Better than Jack. Better than--'

And she, feeling that it was an omen, followed after.

PART IV

MOB

Judith in a state half sleep, half wakening, heard a voice say: 'Dig deep here. The deeper you may dig the richer the loam.' She recognised that she had a choice either to stay in that square of country, hemmed in by hills, and dig down and down--for what? treasure perhaps--or to fasten to her shoulders a pair of very elegant gold wings and fly the country over, but, of course, be for ever on the surface. She had to make a choice, and she made it without hesitation. With a sense of great relief and satisfaction she shouldered a spade, and as she did so saw the pair of wings be drawn up on a gold wire through the dark sky.

With confused notions of Mrs. Radcliffe, a novel that the night before she had been reading, The Last Step; or The History of Mrs. Brudenal, Rousseau's Confessions, and Isabella; or The Rewards of Good Nature, she woke to see the thin January light covering the floor with a sort of pale mildew and to realise that Adam, having thrown off the clothes, was sleeping upside down with his feet on her breast. She turned him round, heard him sigh happily in his sleep, and staring up at the bed-hangings, thought: 'He--She--It was right. She must dig and remain faithful to the--' To what? That question woke her. She realised that the crisis of her life had come.

How often before it had seemed to be upon her--when David had beaten her, when Georges had married her, when old Stane had robbed her, when Jennifer had insulted her, when Warren had kissed her, when Adam had kicked his way out of her, when Francis had called her back to Uldale, when Francis had written a last letter to her, when Walter had challenged her--but now at last the crisis had truly come, for to-day she must make Jennifer realise that within a week she was positively and for ever departing and that no prayers, no beseechings could alter her resolve.

She moved restlessly on the bed as she thought of it. No wonder that she had woken early with this in front of her! Again and again in the last year she had attempted the break; but first there had been poor Francis alive, and then there had been poor Francis dead, and then Jennifer had kept to her bed for weeks, and when at last she had been driven out of her bedroom had refused to attend to her affairs, refused to see Mr. Bertram, the solicitor from Keswick, refused to do anything unless Judith were there to force her to do it.

During the last three months it had come to this. Again and again she had said:

'Well, Jennifer, I will do this for you' (speak to Mr. Winch or Bennett, or talk business with Mr. Bertram, or write to London about some shares or discuss with Mrs. Quinney the fare for the coming week). 'But you had far better yourself, you know, for a week after Christmas I am off, and you will have to manage it all then.'

'Oh, a week after Christmas--besides, you will change your mind.'

'I shall not change my mind.'

After the discovery of Fernyhirst (who had never put in another appearance), Francis' refusal to return, and then his suicide, Jennifer's sluggishness had swallowed all the rest of her. Once she had been lazy because she was proud; now she was lazy because she was humiliated. She tumbled into a slattern over whom Judith had absolute command. Judith had seen her as lovely girl, proud and overbearing wife, self-satisfied mistress, betrayed beauty (her attitude after Francis' departure), and now she was humble, but yawning, slattern. Poor Jennifer! Parents who had adored her too deeply to educate her or to force her to anything that she avoided had begun her ruin. Her lazy and stupid indifference completed it. She cared now only for her food, an occasional fine gown, and sometimes to dress Dorothy up and take her into Keswick. (But when there always fancied that she was insulted, and returned in a state of indignation and confused panic.)

She went to bed of an evening ever earlier and earlier; the time would surely come when she would never rise at all.

She had, however, one increasing terror, and that was of Walter Herries. He had assumed now quite gigantic proportions for her. He could do, she was convinced, any horrible thing that he chose. He was bent on her destruction. And in that last she was perfectly correct.

Poor Jennifer! She might have been, Judith thought, a brilliant, successful beauty at an earlier time. She was born too late for her period. Like many of her contemporaries, she was the victim of a transition world.

She would, however, now be forced to action. When Judith was gone, Mrs. Quinney, horrid little Mr. Winch, kindly but saturnine Bennett, would do as they pleased. And then John would grow and take his place. He was now fourteen years of age and as nice a boy as you could find--gentle and kind, thoughtful for others, but manly also; more resolute in character than his father. He was reticent; no one had ever known what were his real feelings about his father's suicide, or how much he knew about the scandal in the house. Judith suspected that he had suffered with intensity. She fancied, too, that he had a sort of irritated pity for his mother.

But John against Walter? That was the only thought that gave her obstinate departure a touch of treachery.

To-day she must tell Jennifer that the matter was final, and, three days from now, she would be safe with Adam in Watendlath.

It was a kind of fate, as things developed, that before mid-day she should encounter Watson.

He stopped his horse by the Uldale gate. He would not come in. She came out to him.

Why did her heart beat so when she saw him? She was not in love with him. She had never been. He was a fine thick figure of a man, but it was not his figure that made her heart beat. Did a shadow pass? Behind him the hollows under Skiddaw filled like wine in a jade bowl--but it was not the hollow valleys. He did not love her, or at least had never given her reason to think that he did. They were two elderly people now, she nearing fifty, he over sixty. Was it their friendship and mutual trust that made her heart beat? But when she put her hand in his all the nonsense was over. He never had much to say. She had many things to do and could not waste precious time standing there in the cold.

Besides, after three days, she would be seeing him six times a week! There was a joy! It was so intense that she burst out:

'Now there's no need, Charlie, to keep me in the cold. I am busy this morning--and in three days I shall be in Watendlath, for good.'

'Truly, you're coming?'

'Truly, I'm coming.'

'Aye, but you've said it so many times. . . .' Then he added, smiling, speaking his broadest, as he did when he was happy: 'I willn't believe tha, not without thou'll swear 't.'

'Oh, I'll swear it. In three days.'

'Aye, I'm glad!'

This was too much emotion for both of them, so she asked him what he was doing so early in their direction. He could give no connected account of himself, mumbled something about visiting for an account in Caldbeck, but she was aware instantly that he was troubled and had come to tell her something. He talked on about agricultural distresses--the old grievance of cash payments, the abundant harvest of '20 that had led to over-supply, the wet autumn of '21 that had destroyed the crops, the new contemplated Corn Law, Huskisson's speech in the House of Commons, all uninteresting enough to her with the wind driving down the road in icy gusts. Then at last he came out with:

'There's trouble about.'

'Trouble?'

'Aye. They burnt Squire Forrester's ricks last night over at Deddon.'

'Who did?'

'Oh, some of t'wild lads and men with no work, and others egging them on!'

'Poor Mr. Forrester!'

'Aye. 'Hope they'll hev a long wait in gaol. Well, I must be moving. 'Tis true you're coming in three days?'

'Yes--true enough. And never going away again. Adam is to be a farmer like yourself, Charlie.'

'Reet.' He smiled a tremendous smile, his teeth as white and perfect as they had been twenty years before. 'I'll gang down and mak' all ready for him.' He gave her one of his long protecting looks as though he thought she was only safe when he had his eyes upon her; then he lifted his hat and rode away.

All day she remained troubled. Charlie was so cautious that you had to guess from one spoken word the twenty that he had intended. But the remark about Forrester's could have no application to them. No one would want to burn THEIR barns. Nevertheless she knew that this was a day of fate. She set back her shoulders as though a shadow had warned her that before nightfall she would need all her endurance.

In any case, without any shadowy whispers, she needed all her endurance for her talk with Jennifer. All her life she had detested scenes, but she was aware that Jennifer fell into them and out of them as easily as she washed her hands. A scene there would be--but it would be good to have it behind her, and, although there would be, in all probability, three days of silence and sulks, after that--liberty!

She chose her time well--six o'clock in the parlour, following an excellent dinner, the curtains drawn, Jennifer languidly--with a painted hand-screen to shade her face--before the fire, thinking of her food and the handsome flock-gauze gown that she was wearing.

'Jennifer,' said Judith, 'I think that you should realise that in three days Adam and I will be gone.'

'Oh dear,' Jennifer, stifling a yawn, answered. 'Not this evening, Judith, pray. You are for ever speaking of going. "Jennifer, to-morrow I am going--the day after to-morrow I shall be gone, Jennifer," but, thank Heaven, it is only a bagatelle like Mr. Hume and his grey top-hat.'

Judith sighed. This would be indeed a tiresome affair.

'This time it is no bagatelle. It has been one often enough. I had intended to go a year and a half back, and I have remained on and on until I do not wonder that you hesitate to believe me. But this time it is true and certain.'

'But you cannot go in three days. Mr. Bertram is coming from Keswick next Wednesday.'

'Well, it will be practice for you in something you will have to do very often--talk business with Mr. Bertram.'

'Oh, but it is absurd! Of course I cannot talk business with Mr. Bertram.'

'Really, Jennifer. A woman of your age and unable to talk business.'

Jennifer smiled and put her hand on to Judith's arm.

'Oh well, you do it so very much better than ever I can. You are made for business, Judith. Why, only last Tuesday--'

This would be interminable. She rose from her chair and stood between Jennifer and the fire.

'I am very serious. You MUST understand. I am going to Watendlath in three days' time to LIVE. This was always temporary--my stay here. You have been very good. I have been happy here; but it is not, it has never been, my real life. I have been running away from this house since I was a baby, since I can remember, and I am for ever returning to it. Now I am running away for the last time.'

Something in Judith's grave serious gaze, something in the determined set of her small body, caused Jennifer to put down her screen and move her head uncomfortably.

'It grows wearisome, Judith, this everlasting talk about Watendlath. What you should want to go to the place for at all I cannot conceive; but if you MUST go-- for a visit, to see your farmers and their wives--well, I cannot prevent you. Only, pray return as soon as may be.'

Judith stamped her foot with irritation.

'Jennifer, listen! I am going to Watendlath in three days and I am not returning. I am NOT returning. Now, do you understand?'

'You will leave me?'

'Yes, yes, yes. I have told you a hundred times.'

'Leave me?' The screen fell to the ground. Her big blue eyes widened, her hand began to beat on her dress. 'Leave us? Oh, but, Judith, you cannot! You cannot indeed!'

The note of terror was there. Jennifer was awake to reality; fright was the only thing that awoke her. Judith was suddenly compassionate. She put her arm around the large trembling woman:

'Listen, Jennifer. I have been trying to escape from this house ever since I was a baby, and I am now a woman of middle age and STILL I haven't succeeded! From the house, not from Francis or you or John. I have never been permitted to lead a life of my own. When I was with Georges I was devoured with love for him, so that I was not myself. Now I have Adam, and Adam shall not lead this false life, nor will I any longer.'

But Jennifer did not understand a word of it. She had no imagination, and she saw only things that concerned herself.

'False life? But this is not a false life here.'

'No,' said Judith, striving to be patient. 'The tables and curtains and chairs are real, but it is a false life to me, nevertheless, occupied with fears and ambitions that do not matter. You see, Jennifer, I am only half Herries. My mother was a gipsy. And even that Herries half is wild. You know what my father was. So now I am going away where there are no Herries, and I shall take my son with me.'

But Jennifer had not heard a word of it. Slowly, while Judith was speaking, her brain had been taking in this fact--that Judith was going away and that she would be alone and defenceless.

She gripped Judith's arm and cried out, her body trembling again and her cheek white where it was not painted.

'No, no . . . you are going away, to leave me and my children to Walter Herries! You cannot. . . . You must not!'

Now the terror was real enough, and the strange thing was that Judith felt it also. She looked for an instant at the darkened window-pane. She had been troubled all day. She was, in her final resources, alone in this house with this crying, hysterical woman. Of course Walter could do nothing, nor did he wish to. He was at this moment kneeling on the nursery floor embracing his pale little boy. Nevertheless. . . .

'Now, Jennifer. Come, this is absurd. Walter can do nothing. You have Walter Herries on the brain. Everything is well here. There is money enough, you have Mr. Bertram in Keswick, you have most devoted servants, John is growing a fine boy. You cannot wish me to stay here and cosset you for ever. Besides, I am blown on. Everyone knows that I have an illegitimate child and that poor Warren was its father. What good can that do you? You will discover when I am really gone that it is much better so.'

But Jennifer, in full realisation now that Judith meant what she said, was past all control. She clung to Judith, holding her with a frantic grasp.

'What can you mean? You cannot be so cruel. You were never cruel even when I was stiff with you in the old days. Walter is a devil. You have seen it for yourself. All the scandal about me everywhere is his doing. He will poison my children and--'

'Jennifer, don't be so absurd.'

'No, but it is not absurd. I am certain he will poison all the water here before he is done. I see him at every turn. I dare not walk alone unless I should see him. I am quite alone here. I have not a friend but you. Everyone hates me. Walter sees to it that they do. He is everywhere whispering. . . . If you go, Judith, I shall kill myself and then you will have to come and see to my poor children, my poor deserted children. I know that Walter forced Francis to kill himself. I am sure of it. He wrote him a letter or something, and only because years ago I broke his mother's cheap little fan. Oh! how I wish that I had never left my dear father and mother. There has never been anything but unhappiness since I left Bournemouth. But I will not be alone in this house. . . . If you go I kill myself. . . .'

'Come, come, Jennifer. You must not be so foolish. You are like a child.'

Jennifer was now in floods of tears. She waved her hands, beat with her feet on the ground and behaved like a madwoman. Part of this was stupid and lazy histrionics, but part of it was the true bewildered apprehension of a slow, but not evilly intentioned, woman who might, had she married a rich warm husband in a safe comfortable place, never have been exposed. It was because Judith knew this and by now understood her so well that she was touched.

'Come, Jennifer. Come upstairs and lie down.' (Always the recipe for Jennifer's distresses.) 'We will talk quietly. There is nothing for you to be so distressed over. Nothing at all. You have an obsession about Walter. He can do you no harm. Come and lie down.'

She surrendered as though hypnotised. Judith led her away.

On the stairs she said:

'Well, but you were only laughing at me, Judith. You are not going away?'

Judith patted her shoulder.

'You will see in the morning it does not look so terrible. After all it is only a few miles. I shall be close at hand.'

But when at last Jennifer had been laid down and petted and quietened and she, Judith, stood in the still hall with the clock ticking the only sound:

'Phew!' she said to herself. 'THAT was something.' But she was resolute. Nothing now could turn her. However, half an hour later she had to suffer another attack. There was a knock on the parlour door and John appeared.

He looked at her shyly. Of late she had noticed in herself a certain embarrassment which she was for ever trying not to show him. Was she not going to desert him? A look that he had of his father, although he was more firmly built, a look of delicate sensitiveness and courtesy, deeply touched her. Then there was his love for Adam.

He had fair hair, blue eyes, a very white skin and a proud mobile mouth. His worst fault was his modesty and his lack of self-assurance. Perhaps the unhappy history of his parents had encouraged that. She knew that his sense of honour was so scrupulous that decisions, their rights and wrongs, were often an agony to him.

'John,' she said. 'Come in.'

He came in and stood near her, twisting and un-twisting his hands.

'Aunt Judith, mother is crying. She says that you are going away.'

'John, dear, come here,' Judith said, drawing him to the sofa where so often she had sat with his father. He sat close to her, very erect, his thin white hands resting on his knees. She looked at him and loved him dearly. In that one look the foolish childish jealousy that she had had because Adam loved him too vanished alto-gether.

'I want you to understand. Adam and I are going away because it is best for you all that we should. I have managed everything for too long here. I am a managing old woman, you know. I cannot see a thing without wishing to arrange it. Now you are growing into a man, and this is your position, not mine. And then--' she hesitated for a moment, 'you know that I was not mar-ried to Adam's father, and people gossip. So--it is better for me to go.'

He gave a small gulp in his throat, staring into the fire.

'Yes, Aunt Judith.'

'You do understand, do you not?'

It was harder than she had expected.

'Yes, Aunt Judith. . . . But will you never come back any more?'

'You and Dorothy will come to visit us--only we shall be farmers, you know.'

'Yes.' He hesitated, then said: 'You and Adam are my best friends. I know Mr. Winch says that I am not one that others can like very much--'

'What does Mr. Winch say?' she burst out indig-nantly.

'Oh, he means it very well. And it is true. I like to be by myself unless it is someone I understand. And I do understand you and Adam. So--if you go--'

And then to her utter dismay he broke into tears, hid his head in his hands and sobbed most bitterly. She put her arms around him (a thing that she seemed to be doing to everyone to-day). He leaned against her for a little, then looked up, deeply ashamed and rubbing his eyes with his knuckles.

'I never cry,' he said. 'I don't know why now. . . . Mother was so unhappy . . . and she is afraid of Uncle Walter. She says that if you go he will destroy us . . . and I am not very old yet. . . .'

'John, John. Listen to me. Uncle Walter can do nothing to you. You are here to care for your mother and sister. You are on guard over them. There is noth-ing to fear, and Adam and I will only be a few miles--'

She was interrupted by a loud banging at the door, a furious, impatient knocking.

They both started up, and she was never to forget that John put out his hand on to her arm as though he intended to begin, at once, to guard her from danger.

The knocking was repeated, more impatiently than before. She hurried out and opened the door. There was a figure against the dark, and then as he moved forward she saw who it was--it was Reuben.

'Reuben!' she cried, astonished. Then she saw that he was in the very greatest agitation. He closed the door behind him. Mrs. Quinney was coming towards him.

'Quick, Judith,' he said, 'I must see you alone.'

She drew him into the dining-room, something in her saying: 'This is what you have been expecting all day long.'

When the door was closed she caught his arm. 'Reuben, what is it? I thought you were at Whitehaven.'

There was perspiration on his forehead, and his breath came in gasps until he was calmer.

'Have you not heard anything?'

'Heard anything? No, of course not. What is it?'

'I have ridden as swiftly as I could. I got away only in time. . . . My own men. . . . My own people. . . .

They would not listen to me. They knocked me down, threw things at me. I tell you, Judith, they have thrown me over and it is because I have deserted God. I have been drawn more and more into earthly things, politics, money . . . and now--'

He was incoherent, staring about him; scarcely, it seemed to her, recognising her at all.

'No, but, Reuben, what IS it? Please, please. . . .'

'Yes, you are right. I scarcely know what I am saying. Listen, Judith; they are on their way now to burn this place down. I had dinner in Cockermouth and it was there that by chance I learnt of it. Holroyd, Atkinson, Bell, Wood--no, but of course their names mean nothing to you. There is a mob of them on their way now. Someone had put them up to it. They have been out of hand the last month. Last night some of them burnt Squire Forrester's ricks. . . .'

'Yes, yes, I know. But why here? We have done nothing.'

'No. No. I don't understand.' He wiped the sweat from his forehead. 'It was about Jennifer--some vastly improper things that they were saying.'

'Jennifer?'

'Yes--and Fernyhirst.' He seemed to waken then to the sense of the urgency. 'No, but no matter. They can be only a mile or so away. A good hundred of them. What are you going to do? What have you here in the way of servants?'

He stood staring about him. Then he went on quickly: 'Someone should ride for one of the Magistrates. Mr. Fox at Holtby is the nearest. He is old but courageous. Only last year he wished to have me whipped off his grounds. Is there anyone can go? He should be there in an hour.'

'Yes. Jack. He's a brave boy. He'll go.'

She seemed to be transformed. This was a situation that she could understand. No tears and vapours and horror of some vague unknown danger. Something definite.

'We must have all the servants in'--and from that spoken word until the end of the affair she was in absolute command. She went out into the hall and found John and Mrs. Quinney there, wondering.

'John--will you do a thing for me?'

'Anything,' and she knew that he too was glad that action had come at last.

'Go up to your mother. Sit beside her bed. Read to her. Anything. She must be kept quiet and tranquil in her room for the next hour.'

He gave her one look, asked no questions, and went.

'Now, Mrs. Quinney, I want all the servants. Everyone. In here. I have something to say to them. Will you fetch them, please?'

Mrs. Quinney went. Judith returned to Reuben.

'Reuben, you must have something to eat and drink.'

He nodded. He was sitting down and in his eyes was a look of utter dejection. Once again she was carried back to that day when she had given succour to his brother. The same incident--the same command. She brought him bread and meat and ale, and he ate and drank eagerly.

'But I cannot understand,' she repeated. 'Why here? Why Jennifer? Jennifer has done no one any harm but herself, poor thing.'

'Oh, they are mad. They have been so for months--indeed for years. This is only a little sequel to Peterloo, and there will be many another before all is done. But the wretchedness of this is that it is I who have been urging them to it. . . . Oh no, not here, of course, nor to any violence. I have preached peace, but of late I have been filled with their material harshness and have forgot their souls. You yourself saw it when we were at Hawkshead. You spoke to me of it. And now to-day they would not listen to a single word from me. Bell and Holroyd are the worst. And only a year back Holroyd would have done anything for me.'

The door opened and they came in: Mr. Winch, Mrs. Quinney, Martha Hodgson, Doris, Jack Turner, Bennett.

At the sight of Bennett Judith's heart warmed. With his broad thick bulk, his utterly unperturbed air, his kindly protective eyes (just as Charlie Watson was protective), he would be the man for her now.

They stood in a group together, Mr. Winch, with his pallor and nervous shifting eyes, a little apart from the others.

'Listen!' she said, smiling to reassure them. 'Mr. Sunwood has ridden on to tell us that some rioters are on their way here from Cockermouth. It seems they mean mischief. Well, they shall find us ready for them. Jack, I want you to take Peggy and ride off at once to Squire Fox at Holtby. He is a Magistrate. Ask him to come as speedily as possible. You should be back with him in two hours. You know his place?'

Jack nodded.

'Well, go then. Be as quick as you can.'

With another nod he was off.

'Fred' (this was Bennett), 'have we any firearms?'

'There's two guns and an old pistol. I don't know if 'tis firing yet.'

'Good. Get anything you can. So soon as we hear them we will make the whole house dark. Do not disturb Mrs. Herries or the children until we must. It should be an hour or more yet before they are here. They may not come at all. Now, Mrs. Quinney, Martha, Doris, no fuss, now. At the worst it is only a few rough boys and men. Mr. Fox will be here as soon as they--that is, if they come at all. You be quiet in the back of the house, will you?'

They smiled and nodded proudly. They were Cumbrian women and not lightly disturbed. Nor were they garrulous. They showed no agitation at all. Bennett remained alone with Judith and Reuben.

'Dusta think,' he asked, 'there'll be many of them?'

'A good few, I reckon,' said Reuben.

'Aye,' said Bennett slowly. 'T' height of wickedness. And they'll suffer.' Then he added: 'Foreigners likely.' That was his principal sentiment--that he was shocked. He did not know, as he was often fond of declaring, what had come to the country. However, he was really only unhappy when he was puzzled as to which way he should act. It was the fear of his life that he should act the wrong way and look a fool. Happily in this present case his duty and his pleasure were clear.

He went off to the stables.

Reuben looked at her admiringly. This was how he liked to see her.

'Judith, you should be the Captain of a pirate.'

She laughed. 'Perhaps they will not come after all, Reuben.'

'Oh yes,' he said. 'They will come.'

'Let us go out and listen.'

They went into the garden and then on to the road. Then up on the moor. It was a fine night now, with a thin moon and quivering sheets of dim smoky stars. On the ridge of the moor the frosty air stung. Hills and valleys lay, under the deep shadows of the moon, in up-and-down disorder like a quilt shaped by the limbs of a recumbent giant. They listened, but there was only the thin whistle of the wind, smell of earth and sheep and rabbits, and the peaceful sleeping land.

'Maybe they will not come.'

'Oh, they will come. Not a doubt of it. Holroyd shouted filth at me; I had lost all touch with him. Do you remember one night when I came to Watendlath and Georges asked me about God? I was in touch then. It was as though I had Him under my cloak; but the world tempted me again, and I lost Him. First, when I was a boy, it was my fear of being a fool; then it was women; then I climbed over that and saw God as plainly as I see you; then their politics tempted me, and I lost Him. So I lose them as well.'

'You have done a good, kind thing coming to tell us, Reuben. God will be pleased with that. For myself, if there is a God, I will be grateful one moment and defy Him the next. It is no use to be always on your knees.'

She was talking to cover her own fears. She was thinking at that moment only of Adam. Her heart was wild with fear for him. Had she not been ashamed she would have snatched him out of bed, caught him up in her arms and run away with him out of the back door. When she was in the house and there was plenty to be done it was one thing, but out here in the cold and silence quite another. An owl hooted. A little wind pulled at their feet. The anaemic moon was enveloped by a thin cloud of gauze, and the world was veiled.

'Hark! Can you not hear something?'

She caught his arm. They both listened. The breeze rose and fell; a church bell from a great distance could be heard echoing the half-hour. On the wind for a moment there seemed to be the crack of horses. But it died.

'No. That was the church clock.'

They listened again. It seemed as though all the landscape were listening with them.

'Yes. I am certain I hear something.'

She stood close to him. He put his arm around her. The breeze came up the slope again and the moon rode out, her light stroking Skiddaw's shoulder.

'Yes. Listen. Listen.'

Then above the beating of their hearts they heard it beyond any question, the strike of horses' hoofs on the winter road.

'Quick! Quick! Back to the house!'

They ran down the fell, along the road and through the gate. As Judith turned in she saw a figure come out of one of the village houses; the black shadow stood looking down the hill. It was beyond doubt now, a clatter of horses, laughter and voices.

She ran into the house and up the stairs. First she went into Jennifer's room. It was in darkness. John came towards her.

'She is asleep.'

She went to the bed and shook Jennifer's shoulder.

'Jennifer! Jennifer! Wake up!'

When she was awake she told her as quickly as possible.

'Now, Jennifer, it is nothing. Only some drunken boys. But you must stay here. Don't move from here. It will be soon over.'

'Drunken boys? . . . But what do they want?'

'Reuben is here, and Bennett has a gun, and Mr. Fox of Holtby is coming over.'

'Oh dear. Oh dear. . . .'

But she had no time for Jennifer's 'Oh dears!'

'John, you remain with your mother. Adam and Dorothy had best be here as well. I will bring them.'

When she went into her own room her heart for a moment failed her. Adam was lying, his head on his arm, fast asleep. She woke him, wrapped him in a blanket so that he looked a young bewildered Indian, and told him quietly:

'Adam, there are some noisy men in the garden. If they shout and throw stones, it is no matter. Mother is here and Bennett and Mr. Winch and Uncle Reuben. You stay with John, darling, in Aunt Jennifer's room.'

He nodded his head, yawning and rubbing his eyes with his knuckles. 'Where will you be?' he asked.

'I shall return very soon. Now, go to John, darling.'

'Can't I see the men throwing stones?'

'No. Not now. Be a good boy.'

He was always a good boy if his mother thought that it was serious. He saw that she thought that this was serious, and obeyed. She took him into the next room, saw that Dorothy was also there, and Jennifer sitting up in bed and asking John questions. She gave Adam to John and left them.

When she came downstairs another world had already burst upon them. The house was in darkness, save for the candles in Jennifer's room. The women were in the kitchen. Bennett and Reuben, each with a gun, were in the hall. They all three moved into the parlour.

She looked between the curtains and almost cried out at the scene. At least a hundred men, women and boys were gathered in the road, dark and shadowy in the moonlight, but some of them carried torches whose flames, leaping in the wind, jumped from shadow to shadow. About a dozen men were on horseback.

She recognised at once a number of villagers among them. Since Francis' death the men and women of the village had held aloof from Jennifer, whom in fact they had always disliked.

There was the strangest contrast between the black silence of the house and the shouts, laughter, cries that came from the crowd. She saw that one of them, a long thin bearded man on a white horse, was their leader.

'That is Holroyd!' Reuben whispered to her. The crowd moved backwards and forwards as though stirred by some impetus within themselves. Through the closed window she could not hear what they were crying. White faces leapt into torchlight and out again. Arms rose and fell. Suddenly the gates swung back and they all tumbled pell-mell into the garden. Then there was a pause and silence. They stood transfixed, as though a spell had been cast on them, staring at the house.

That was queer--to stand behind the curtains with that familiar room all about her, to look out and see that multitude, faces like fish-scales in the moonlight, all still and waiting. All for no reason! These were familiar things, the furniture, the walls, the pictures, and yet these strangers had the impertinence to break through the gate, to trample on the garden, to insult the shadows of David, of Francis, of Sarah--perhaps to frighten the spirit of her own son, Adam! A furious indignation began to rise within her.

The silence cracked. A stone was flung and smashed through the parlour window, missing Judith by a breath.

'Take care!' Reuben whispered, pulling her back.

The throwing of that stone released them. They all began to shout at once. More stones were thrown. Figures were running down the lawn, others towards the stables. Meanwhile the thin man with a beard sat motionless on his horse.

'I must go out to them!' Reuben said.

'No. No. They will throw stones. Wait--'

'No. I cannot wait.'

He went out. She heard him open the door of the hall, and, before he shut it, a roar of voices reached her, like a sudden ripple of thunder. What had she better do? Her impulse was to go with him. The parlour door

had closed, but now it opened to show the meagre black figure of Mr. Winch, who entered with a lighted candle.

'Blow out that candle!' she ordered him sharply.

But he could not. He stood there, his mouth open, his eyes shifting from place to place, the candle shaking in his hand. He was in a sweat of terror. Indignantly she snatched the candle from him and blew it out, saying:

'No one will harm YOU, Mr. Winch. Your place is with the children upstairs.' She heard him slip away.

From the intervals where the curtains were not drawn the glare of the torches, falling and rising, lit the room--the coloured top of the spinet, the crimson chair, the sofa with the red apples. She could also hear now through the break in the window that the stone had made. Reuben's voice came across to her, and it seemed that they were listening:

'. . . and if I had done so you might have charged me with a fault, but for many years now I have had only your interests at heart. What others could I ever have had? Have I not given my whole life to your friendship? . . .' She lost it again. Then it returned. '. . . and this house has never harmed you. It has not starved you as some have done, nor ill-treated your children as some have done, nor thrown you out of employment like some. But even though it had, this would not be your Court of Appeal. Violence of this sort has never won anyone any good, and well you know it. Cruelty to women and children has never been our Cumberland way. . . .'

'A little too much of the orator,' she thought. 'I'D speak to them!'

But he was not to speak much longer. She caught the words: '. . . and be for ever ashamed of as dastardly an action. . . .'

Perhaps someone was stirring up trouble from the road. In any case, there was a sudden rush from the rear of the crowd, shouts and screams, and someone threw a lighted torch, whirling through the dark until it fell with a hiss on the lawn and lay there blazing. The man on the horse made as though he would ride on to Reuben and so past him into the house; but, in spite of his furious movement, his voice was sharp and controlled as he cried:

'Enough words, Sunwood! Back to the stables, lad. And we'll see them blaze!'

'Shall I fire? Shall I fire?'

Judith heard a voice in her ear, and putting out a hand felt Bennett's breast and his heart beating like a clock.

'No. . . . Wait, Fred. Oh, the devils! I cannot endure this. And with the children upstairs. Oh, when will Mr. Fox come? I must go out to them! I cannot endure this here!'

'No, no, ma'am. Stay where you are!'

'No. I must go.' She tore herself from Bennett's hand and ran from the room, he following her. She could never quite clearly remember afterwards what occurred in that outside pandemonium. The air was cold and yet the heat seemed intense. There was smoke in her nostrils. Reuben was shouting. She saw that his forehead was bleeding, and that seemed to loose a fury inside her. She never knew what she cried, but she drove into the middle of them; then, nearly stumbling over a mounting-block by the door, she climbed on to it.

'Be ashamed of yourselves. Attacking women and children who have done you no harm. Go back to your homes, you bullies. . . .'

The ineffectiveness of her words enraged her yet more. They swept past her and around her, not even seeing her, shouting, some of them singing, the horses rising in the moonlight like white seahorses. Then, as though it were a banner unfurled, a shuddering, quivering flame leapt up into the sky from the stables. The fire lit the whole scene; all faces were white, the house like a black wall with the pale glass squares of the windows. A woman's cry came from inside the house.

'The horses! The horses!' Judith cried, and began to push and fight through the mob, who, at sight of the fire, seemed dimmed and quieted as though they sank from the scene. Some man struck her in the breast. She turned, gasping for breath, and saw Bennett behind her, his gun raised.

'You shall have it then!' he cried, and fired.

Holroyd on his horse half turned, raised an arm, shivered and slowly fell. Reuben sprang forward, was for a moment illuminated by the fire; a shot rang from the road, and he too jumped as though, with arms lifted, he would touch the moon, and collapsed on the horse-steps.

The two shots, the crackle and gesture of the fire, the riderless horse plunging, seemed in a moment to change the scene. Men and women all turned. They fled through the gate.

A woman, her hair loose, turned and shouted in a shrill broken voice: 'Curse you . . .' and something more about Jezebel and vengeance.

Then panic had caught them all, for they were flying down the road-- horses, men, women--the white moonlit stretch was black with fleeing figures. . . . Then, save for Reuben's huddled body on the steps, there was nothing in the garden. Only the flames of the stable chattered, hissed, rose and fell as though they were busy with their own private important business.

Judith, with Reuben's head in her lap, looked desperately around her.

'Quick, quick, Fred. Someone fetch Doctor Borden from the village. He'll be hiding in his house. Tell him' (her voice was fierce and bitter) 'that it is safe now. He must come. The women must get buckets for the fire. . . .' She caught sight of some slinking figures in the gateway. Villagers who, now that the riot was over, had crept out. 'Force them. They must help. The house must not burn.'

Bennett answered. 'The house is safe. It is only the outside sheds. The fire is burning itself out. Oh, Mr. Reuben, are you hurt, sir? Are you hurt?'

'He's dying, Fred.' She bent over him. His eyes were open, looking at her. He smiled.

'Good-bye, Judith. I did my best.'

She knew that he was dead. Her hands were soaked in blood. She stared out above him to the quiet sky and the stables lit by fire. She felt a hand on her shoulder and looked up. It was Mrs. Quinney.

'He is dead,' she said quietly. 'Help me to carry him in.'

THE CHOICE

Reuben was buried five days later in Ireby Church-yard. As Judith drove in the carriage, away back to the house again, she was so weary that the whole world was quite unreal.

A great crowd had been at the funeral. Men and women had come from all parts, for Reuben was in general much beloved, and the riot, the disorder and his death had made the greatest possible stir. Nothing else was talked of. Holroyd (who had only a flesh-wound in the arm) and Bell were in Kendal gaol; other arrests were expected to be made.

All of this could do poor Reuben very little good; but Judith was aware as, a lonely little black figure, she moved through the courtyard gate into her carriage, that she was surrounded with sympathy. She had known already that Uldale village was properly ashamed and anxious to make amends. She did not care. Reuben was gone--and, very soon, oh, very, very soon, she would be away from them all, safe with Adam in Watendlath.

It was a most curious day, she thought, as she drove up the road. For three days and nights there had been unceasing rain, and as, night after night, she had lain awake the rain had seemed to shroud her in as though it were weaving for her a great suit of silver armour, and in this she could live, safe and protected, for ever after.

But this rain in the valleys had meant snow on the hills. They were more thickly covered than they had been for many years. To- day the landscape was shrouded in mist. There seemed to be three veils, one upon another, and these were always shifting. The middle veil was faintly radiant and orange in colour, for it held the sun, sunlight enfolded and shrouded. The farthest veil was of a very dim blue, cold, with snow in it. The first veil was almost transparent, of the thinnest gauze.

All the land moved in mystery behind these veils, for it was the land that appeared to be moving as the veils shifted. Everything was on the edge of discovery, but nothing was clear, only the stones under your feet, trunks of birch and larch and oak at your hand. In the corner of a field leaves were burning, a blazing fire in smoke.

So, sitting in the carriage, only half-awake, in this shrouded world, it did not seem strange to her that the forms of her four friends, all dead from violence, should be sitting beside her-- Francis, Georges, Warren, Reuben--one of whom she had loved and still loved, one the father of her son, two the friends of her lifetime.

They none of them, she thought, looked at her with any reproach. She had in a way been the cause of death in all of them--at least she had been in the minds and hearts of all of them when they died. But, unsentimental as ever, she did not intend in any way to reproach herself. She had been honest with them all, and she knew that they wished her well. They had all died fighting--Georges fighting discipline, Francis his own soul, Warren convention, Reuben fighting his way back to God. They had all, in fact, been fighting Herries one way or another--if you took Herries for fact against fancy, as she did.

However, she was too weary to do more than smile upon them and assure them that they need not look at her with such anxiety. She and her little son were on the very point of escaping. The Herries would not get her, try as hard as they might. Nevertheless, she knew that when she was alive again she would discover that the unfair savage death of Reuben had placed something hard and bitter in her heart that had never been there before.

When she had taken off her bonnet and cloak, washed her face and brushed her hair, she thought that she would finish the thing once and for all. Jennifer was down in the parlour looking at the mist that trailed past the window. A small block of wood had been placed where the stone had crashed; they would come very shortly from Keswick and mend the window. Indeed, very little damage had been done: two windows broken, a shed or two destroyed--that was all there was to show for the flaring torches, the flaming sky, the shouts and curses and Reuben's death.

Jennifer looked very fine in her black gown. There was no paint on her face, and her magnificent black hair gave her to-day some nobility. But the shock of that night had done something to her. She was more properly controlled than she had been for years.

'There is a letter come for you,' she said.

Judith took it and saw that it was from Emma Furze. Emma! As she read it her heart glowed. And then, when she found that Emma was in London, was well and happy and gay, and wished to come up and spread some of her happiness around the Watendlath farm, it was as if the sun had broken into the room. She should, indeed she should. In another week Judith and

Adam would be there. Then there would be Emma and Charlie and Alice Perry. . . .

'Were there many at the funeral, Judith dear?' Jennifer asked.

Judith told her of the funeral.

Jennifer nodded to all the details.

'I am glad that I did not go. I am very unrestrained at funerals. And I do not know that I shall ever have the courage to go out again. Do you not know what they were calling . . . some of the women. . . ? Doris heard them. "Jezebel." One woman wanted to burn me in the stable.'

'Nonsense, Jennifer. You must not think of it. They are very kindly disposed to us. They are ready to do anything.'

'To us? To you, you mean. So long as you are here we are safe. But I want to tell you. I have been thinking deeply and I see how weak and wretched I have been. I am terribly ashamed. And I mean to be a help to you, Judith, in the future as I have never been. And to John and Dorothy too. Yes, I am most wretchedly ashamed, and John, that evening, was so brave and so good. I am sure no boy of his age anywhere is so brave. You will find, Judith, that I shall be quite another woman--'

'Well, that is excellent,' said Judith cheerfully. 'It is what I have always told you, Jennifer. You have been frightened by shadows.' Then she went on more gently, but with great firmness. 'Next week Adam and I are going. My mind is quite made up. You will find everyone here as kind as possible--everyone in the village. Eager to make friends.'

'Oh no,' said Jennifer in a voice so low that Judith could scarcely hear her. 'Oh, please Judith--it will kill me if you go away.'

They had had it out already so many times. There was to be no more discussion of it. But as she bent to kiss Jennifer's cheek she had an appalling sense of weakness.

Oh, let her waste no time! Let her slip out now, this moment! Jennifer was harder to resist now that she was so quiet, and there was John who had been so brave and Dorothy who, on that awful night, had been so good to Adam, telling him stories. As she kissed Jennifer and felt the cold touch of her hands she cared for her as she had never done before.

Another moment and she would surrender, moved and softened as she had been by the funeral. She would surrender and be lost, all hope of her happiness gone! She murmured something and hastened out, almost expecting to find Walter Herries barring the door of the house with his huge body, defying her to escape.

But in the hall, instead of Walter Herries, she found Mr. Winch.

'May I speak to you a moment, madam?' he said.

'Yes, Mr. Winch,' she said. She had a new gravity. She had noticed it herself. She did not dislike it so long as she was in Uldale. It would not do at all for Watendlath. She led the way into the small room that had been Francis'. Mr. Winch, very pale, his hands clasped, his head up, looked at her.

'Well, Mr. Winch?'

'I thought I should tell you. . . .' He hesitated. '. . . I wish to resign my duties here.'

She felt a relief. It would be easy to find some far better tutor, someone who did not go down on his knees on the gravel path. Indeed, had she had her way he would have gone long ago. Jennifer had some weakness for him. He read Minerva Press novels to her.

'But why?' she asked. In spite of herself she was scornful. 'Have the rioters been too much for you? You remained safely in the back of the house for the greater part.'

'I know,' he stammered. 'You must despise me--and rightly. But you do not know all. If . . .'

Then to her amazement he burst into sobs, threw himself down on his knees, held up his hands.

'Mr. Winch!' she exclaimed, stepping back, thinking he must be out of his senses, that the fear of the other night had unsettled his wits.

'No, no. Listen to me. I have been miserable for a very long time, and this terrible catastrophe, with the death of Mr. Sunwood, has destroyed me. I was his murderer.'

'You!' She could have laughed at the little figure in the shiny black with the rather grubby hands. But his distress was real, his fear was real. She saw that this was a matter of importance.

'Please rise,' she said. 'Please get up. You cannot be Mr. Reuben Sunwood's murderer, for I myself saw the shot fired that killed him.'

He was sobbing. He buried his head in his hands.

'I cannot speak to you unless you get up.'

He rose. He composed himself. His head bent a little, as though he were making a confession, he went on:

'No, not in positive fact his murderer. I did not fire the gun. But in everything else--Mrs. Paris, ever since I came to you I have been spying upon everyone in this house. Mr. Walter Herries of Westaways has paid me for that odious business.'

'I know it,' she said quietly.

'You knew it?'

'I saw you one day on your knees in the garden spying on Mr. Francis.'

'You knew it and you did nothing?'

'I did nothing because, once I knew it, you were safer than someone I did not know.'

He went on a little more confidently.

'I have no excuse. None. I did not need the money. All my life I have avoided shabby actions. But Mr. Walter Herries had a strange power over me. He could do anything with me that he pleased. I do not urge that in my defence; there is no defence. But so it was. He overtook me one day walking to Keswick and

from the first I was his slave. I brought him news of everything that happened at Uldale--everything. It was I who found a man that should carry the note to Mr. Francis when he was in Cockermouth, telling him that Captain Fernyhirst was here that night.'

'You did that?' He thought she would strike him and he moved back, but she had not stirred.

'Yes, I. It was Mr. Walter Herries' plot, entirely arranged by him.'

Her face was so terrible that he could not look at it. He turned away.

'Yes. And so with everything here. Every day he had news. It was he, by my agency, who brought the rioters here.'

'Yes,' she said (but she was not addressing him). 'I understand.'

'He intended, I think, only to give you a fright. I was in Cockermouth and saw Holroyd and Bell and the others. They were given money. There was to be no real damage to life or property. But they had drink on that afternoon. They went further than they intended.'

'Yes,' she said. 'They went far.'

'I have been very miserable ever since I have been here. Again and again I have gone to him to tell him that I would do his work no longer but when I saw him . . . I cannot explain. . . . He had a power. . . .'

He was trembling.

'Forgive me,' he said. 'I must sit.' He sat down, his head so bent that she could scarcely catch his words. 'Again and again I have tried to say to you that I must go. Something prevented me. And at the beginning of this week when I knew what was in hand I was in hell. I could not sleep nor eat. A hundred times I was on the edge of breaking it to you. But his presence seemed always behind me. I thought that he would kill me if I betrayed him. He has often said, in his jolly laughing way, that he would. But he did not mean it to be murder. I did not intend. . . . But it is too late. You may give me up to the Justice, Mrs. Paris. You may indeed. I would be happier. . . .'

'You!' She turned to the window. Francis and Reuben both killed by Walter!

Her stomach was sick. Her knees trembled. She also sat down, but with her back to him. For a long while there was silence. Could she bring the thing home to Walter? She half turned, as though she would speak, but turned back again. No! there was no help there. He would have seen to it that nothing could be carried to him. Who would believe a creature like Winch? Walter's power . . . ! And suddenly she saw him, as though he were there with them in the room, vast, blazing with colour and jewels, laughing, but so bent from conceit and arrogance on his purpose that nothing was too terrible for him, too mean, too cruel. And yet he was a jolly man and loved his son even as she loved hers. She got up.

'Pray go away, Mr. Winch,' she said. 'Go away in the morning. What is due to you will be sent to you. I would be happier not to see you again.'

Without a word he got up, and, head still bent, went out.

Very slowly she went upstairs to her room. No one was there. She looked out. Behind the mist the moon of five nights ago was now full, but it was like a flat stone ridged with light and wrapped in wool.

She had been caught. Now she had no doubt. She could not go. She had been able to defeat everything but this. Now a hard determined anger such as she had never felt had come and would abide. Francis . . . Reuben . . . killed by that laughing man. How could she now leave Jennifer and John and Dorothy defenceless?

Oh, but the other life! Watson was expecting her. In the Ritson kitchen Alice at this moment perhaps would be speaking of her. And her home, the room where Georges had died. And Adam to be a farmer, to grow up knowing nothing of this world of money, deceit, jealousy, unkindness. The Tarn, wrapped in mist, would be waiting for the moon to break. Or, perhaps, there was no mist there to-night and the slopes of the fells, snow-clad, glittered.

'I cannot . . . I cannot. . . .'

She turned, possessed by some strange madness, pulled drawers open, found a box beneath the bed, began, on her knees, to cram it.

Adam came running in. He was shouting and dancing.

'Jack says there will be a new barn. They will begin to-morrow, and the windows--'

He stopped, seeing what she was doing. She shook her head as though the battle were hopeless. Once as a little girl she had climbed out of window, but now--to leave them, Jennifer weak, John, Dorothy, so young, to that determined remorseless purpose. . . .

'They are doomed, you know,' Walter had said, and even as he said it, he was aware that he had killed Francis, was planning this.

She got up from her knees and went to the window again. As she looked the moon broke the mist. Skiddaw started up in dazzling white. Like a white rose, like a glorious white rose from heaven, she lifted her head, and the mist sank to lie in waves across the valley.

She looked and she wept. The tears blinded her. She said farewell.

She came and sat down by the bed and drew Adam to her. She had command of herself.

'Tell me something,' he said. 'Tell me about Uncle Tom.'

It was his favourite story. While her mind was fiercely working on her future, hers and his, mechanically she went on with the familiar words:

'Although it had snowed so bitterly Uncle Tom got off his horse because he heard the baby crying, and he rode over the little bridge--'

'Don't forget the dogs! Don't forget the dogs!' Adam cried.

'Yes. They were all there and they followed him solemnly over the courtyard and into the house. And they went up the stairs. And they went into a room, the dogs sat down by the door, the old woman was sleeping--'

Oh, who was moving in the hills? What Rogue was wandering, calling for her, telling her that here was her home? The dry bones of the dead were alive. They were calling for her, those two old ghosts, and she could not come. . . .

She had now complete command of herself. She drew him closer.

'Adam, I want you to listen. You may not understand, but do you remember that one day going to Keswick I talked to you about being a farmer?'

'Yes,' he said. He drew himself up very straight because she was reposing a confidence in him and he was proud. He stood up straight with all the pride of a very small boy, that pride that is perhaps the small boy's most lovely quality.

'Now everything is changed. I have had to make the most important decision of my life--a decision for you also. You and I are to fight, Adam. I had thought that it would all be quiet and at peace, but now we are going to fight.'

'Who will we fight?' Adam asked with great interest. 'Uncle Walter?'

'You are too young to understand, but later you will see that I could do nothing else than this. We have to be very strong, you and I, and very wise, Adam. We will beat them all, and you shall be the head of them. No, you cannot understand now. But you must trust me.'

He threw his arms round her neck. She was small, and it was easy for him to draw her head down; he could kiss her and lay his cheek against hers. Now, if she wished to fight someone, he would help her. He thought that perhaps she was sorry that she had made him stay in Aunt Jennifer's room when they came to burn the stables. Now, this next time, he would go with her and help her.

While he hugged her, her pride was rising. Her pride, her deep and unchangeable hatred of Walter Herries. In that hour the second half of her life began.

She got up. Now she would take command. A fierce bright delight flowed in her veins. She would make Adam the master of them all. Walter's boy. . . . She saw him in his little chair, his deformity, his old, pale face, and the big man kneeling at his side. She caught Adam to her, kissing him passionately. Adam should be King.

With her head up, as though she already commanded a kingdom, she stepped downstairs.

She opened the parlour door. Jennifer was standing at the window. When she heard the door open she turned. She looked and saw a short pale woman in a plain black gown. But she saw also a woman on fire with determination, with pride and an almost fanatical purpose.

'Why, Judith--!' she began.

'All is well,' Judith said quietly, coming forward and stroking the red apples of the sofa. 'I shall not leave you, Jennifer. It is better I remain.'

THE END

THE FORTRESS

FOR MY FRIENDS

GERTRUDE AND MUIRHEAD BONE

Thy gentlest dreams, thy frailest, Even those that were Born and lost in a heart-beat, Shall meet thee there. They are become immortal In shining air.

The unattainable beauty, The thought of which was pain, That flickered in eyes and on lips And vanished again; That fugitive beauty Thou shalt attain.

Those lights innumerable That led thee on and on, The masque of time ended, Shall glow into one. They shall be with thee for ever, Thy travel done.

A.E.

Part One

Madame

THE SHADOW AGAINST THE SKY

'All is well,' Judith said quietly, coming forward and stroking the red apples of the sofa. 'I shall not leave you, Jennifer. It is better I remain.'

As her hand mechanically stroked those same rosy apples, so friendly and familiar, she reflected.

Yes, this simple sentence declared the crisis of her whole existence. Nothing ever again could matter to her so deeply as this decision. With it she had cut away half her life, and perhaps the better half. She was not by nature a dramatic woman; moreover, she had but lately returned from the funeral of the best friend she had, and she was forty-seven years of age in this month of January 1822. So--for women then thought forty-seven a vast age--she should be past drama. Quietly she sat down on the sofa, leaned forward, looking into the fire. Jennifer Herries was speaking with eager excitement, but Judith did not hear her. Jennifer was fifty- two and should also be past drama but, although a lazy woman, she liked sensation when it did not put herself to dis-comfort.

Judith at that moment heard and saw nothing but the past, the past that she was irrevocably forsaking. Strange how the same patterns were for ever returning! Her father had been a rogue and a vagabond, a rebel against all the order and material discipline of the proper Herries. In his early years he had married Convention and of her had had a son, late in life he had married a gipsy and of her had had a daughter in his old age, when he was over seventy. David at one end of his life, Judith at the other.

In their histories again the pattern had been re-peated. David of his marriage had had two sons: Will

the money-maker, Francis the dreamer. Will prospered even now in the City; Francis was a failure, dead of his own hand.

And with their children again the pattern was re-peated. For Will's son Walter was triumphant near by in his house at Westaways, and Francis' widow, Jennifer, and Francis' children, John and Dorothy, remained, undefended, here at Uldale.

It was here that she, Judith, came into the pattern. Daughter of two vagabonds, mother of an illegitimate boy, she should be vagrant. Half of her--the finer, truer, more happy and fortunate half--(she nodded at the fire in confirmation) was so. But the other half was proper, managing, material, straight-seeing Herries. She threw her wild half into the blaze (her hand flickered towards the fire). It was gone. She remained to fight for Jenni-fer, Jennifer's children, John and Dorothy, and, maybe who knows? . . . her own boy Adam.

To fight whom? Here Jennifer's voice broke through:

'. . . That will be most agreeable. I have always said that the Yellow Room needs but a trifle altering and it will make . . . but Francis would never see it. And with a new wallpaper . . . We must certainly have a new wallpaper . . .'

To fight Walter Herries, and all that were his. As 'Rogue' Herries in his tumble-down house in Borrow-dale had fought all the world, as Francis his grandson had tried to fight the world and failed, so now would she fight Walter, flamboyant, triumphing Walter, made of Will and his money-bags, sworn to extinguish Jenni-fer and her children and all that were in Fell House, Uldale.

It had been the wish of her whole life to flee from all the Herries and live in the hills as her mother had lived before her, but Walter Herries had challenged her and she had taken up the challenge.

'. . . Not that it should be difficult,' Jennifer was saying, 'to find another girl to work with Doris. Girls will come willingly enough now that you are going to remain, Judith, dear . . .'

Walter and his two children, Uhland and Elizabeth, with all the money in the world, against Jennifer and HER children, undefended and helpless, Judith and her Adam, fatherless and by law without a name . . .

Jennifer was going on: 'And Walter will not DARE, now that you are remaining, Judith . . . You are the only one of us all of whom he is afraid . . . He will not DARE . . .'

Would he not, so large and confident and powerful? Had he not said that he would snuff them out-- Jennifer, John, Dorothy--raze Fell House to the ground? And what had SHE, small, elderly, alone, with no one in the world belonging to her save Adam, to oppose to that strength?

Nevertheless, she looked across to Jennifer triumphantly.

'We will give Walter something to think about,' she said.

'And you can go to Watendlath when you wish,' Jennifer said.

'Oh no. Watendlath is over for me. Watendlath is ended, a closed valley.'

'But how foolish, Judith. It is only a mile or two.'

'It is the other end of the world.'

She did not tell anyone how that night, with Adam asleep beside her, she cried. She lay awake for half the night, hearing the owl hoot, a mouse scuttle, and seeing a slow, lonely moon trace with her silver finger a question mark across the floor.

Her thoughts were wild, incoherent, most mingled. At one moment she was fiercely rebellious. She sat up, staring about her. No, she would not remain! She would tell Jennifer in the morning that she revoked her decision. She allowed her fancy then to play with the lovely sequence of events if she went. Tom Ritson should arrive in his cart. She and Adam would be packed into it, and, after tearful farewells, they would be off, down the hill with one last backward wave at the bottle-green windows of the Uldale shop and the slow friendly shoulder of the moor, along the road to Bassenthwaite, beside the Lake, Keswick, then up the hill again, above Lodore, and then--Oh, happiness! Oh, joy! The little valley closing them in, the long green field, the tumbling Punchbowl, the two farms, her own, John Green House, and the Ritsons'; below the farm the round scoop of the Tarn, black or silver or blue, the amphitheatre of the hills, the sheep nosing at the turf, the cattle moving in the byre, and best of all, Charlie Watson, straight as an arrow in spite of his years, riding towards her over the stones . . . the fresh sweet air, tang

of soil and bracken, glitter of stones, sweep of the changing sky . . . she had to catch the sheets between her hands.

That life was for ever surrendered. Then, at once, her other practical self came running in. She was mistress of Fell House now. They would all do anything that she told them. Jennifer was her slave. She had seen, at the Ireby funeral, what the neighbours and villagers thought of her. Yes, in spite of her illegitimate son. Many things would have to be done. Had she strength enough? It was the convention that a woman over forty was an 'old thing' without savour. It was true that she had been aware, for some time past, of the troubles, melancholies, miasmas peculiar to her time of life, but she had refused to surrender to them. She felt within her a wonderful vitality and energy, as though she were at the beginning of life rather than more than half through the course of it. Just as in earlier days her love for her husband Georges had filled her with fire and splendour, so now her love for her son Adam glorified her. She was such a woman.

Yes, many things needed to be done. Walter Herries thought that Fell House was at an end, did he? She would show him. Jennifer had money. They could purchase the piece of land towards Ireby . . . four more cows, two more horses. The dairy must be enlarged. They were lucky in their servants. Bennett was devoted, would do anything for her. Jack was a good boy. Mrs Quinney was honest and hard-working, although she had a tongue when she was put out. Martha Hodgson was a good God-fearing cook, who never grumbled so long as she was not interfered with, and Doris would do well if they had a child in from the village to help her.

They must entertain more than they had done. John and Dorothy were growing now. John was fourteen and Dorothy thirteen. It was right that they should take their proper place in the County . . . She must find a tutor for John and Adam. Someone who would have no dealings with Walter. There was Roger Rackstraw in Keswick, a friend of Miss Pennyfeather's. He had a broken nose and looked altogether like a prize-fighter, but he had been for two years tutor to the Osmaston children and had done well there. She would see about that in the morning. She would lose no time. And, maybe, she might, after all, shortly pay a visit to Watendlath, stay with the Ritsons for a week, ride over to Watson's farm . . . No, no . . . Better leave that alone until she was settled here, settled deep, deep down so that she could never pull herself up again.

Then once more desolation caught her. She lay back on her pillow sobbing. She could not help it. She had given up all that she loved best in the world, all save Adam. And for what? She had been considering Walter Herries as too serious a figure? What was he after all but a big, blundering bully? What could he have done to Jennifer and the children? John would soon be able to protect his mother . . . But no. John was soft, sensitive, gentle. She remembered how years ago Mrs Ponder, a servant in the house, had thrown his pet rabbit out of the window. She had thought then that he would have died of misery. And yet he had courage. Only a few days before, when the rioters had set fire to the stables, he had sat with his mother through all the noise and confusion, reading to her, trying to comfort her . . . He had courage, but he was no match for his Cousin Walter. She, and she alone . . . At that she fell, at last, asleep.

It was natural that the world of Judith's son, young Adam, should be very different in shape, colour and contents from his mother's.

He was now in his seventh year and as strong as a young colt. He was, most certainly, not handsome. Even his mother could not think so. His hair was black and straight without a suspicion of a wave in it, his nose snub, his mouth large, his legs and arms too long for his body as yet. Nevertheless, he gave promise of both height and breadth. His grey eyes held both humour and caution, and he was brown with health. He was clumsy in his movements--indeed he was to move all his life short-sightedly, and this not because he was short-sighted but because he was absent-minded.

Were his interest thoroughly caught, absent-minded was the last thing that he was, but he was often thinking of the unexpected instead of the customary.

It seemed that his character would be warm and loyal, but he was sparing of words. He hated to show feeling or express it. He was independent, always venturing off on his own, busy on his own purposes. Whether he liked or disliked anyone he never said, but he had a very especial connexion with his mother and would, on a sudden, leave what he was doing and search for her because he thought that she needed him.

When he did this his intuition was always right. He was quite fearless and could be very pugnacious, but he would attack someone without warning and often when he had been smiling but a moment earlier. He was inquisitive, would ask questions and remember carefully the answers given him, although he would not always believe their truth. On the whole, his independence, his loyalty, his taciturnity and his courage were at present his strongest characteristics. He walked very much by himself.

His horizon was larger than that of many boys of his age, for his first years had been spent in France and after that he had lived like a young peasant in the Watendlath valley. His friends had been farmers like Charlie Watson and the Ritsons, farmers' wives like Alice Perry, farmers' boys like the young Perrys.

Then on coming to Fell House he had known the first attachment of his life (he was never to know very many). His mother was part of himself and he of his mother, so that did not figure as an attachment, but at the moment that he saw John Herries he adored him.

John, Jennifer's boy, who was eight years older than Adam, was fair, slender, handsome and an aristocrat. He walked with his head up, as though he were made to rule the earth. But he was too gentle and unselfish to wish to rule anyone, and it soon happened that the young black ruffian Adam did all the commanding. John was impetuous until checked, then was hurt and silent. He had a very occasional stammer that added to his shyness. He had most beautiful natural manners and was over-aware of the feelings of others. He loved to be liked, hated to be disapproved of, while Adam did not care whether anyone liked him or no. Nevertheless, Adam responded deeply to affection, although he said nothing that showed this. He forgot neither kindness nor injury, but John was always eager to heal a quarrel; John was wretched in an atmosphere of unfriendliness. Adam enjoyed a fight if he felt that the cause was a worthy one.

John's sister, Dorothy, was fair, plump and amiable. She was a type that was always recurring in the Herries families. She had some of her mother's laziness, but took a livelier interest in the outside world than her mother did.

Adam's world seemed sufficiently filled with these figures--his mother, Jennifer whom he called his aunt although she was not, John, Dorothy, Mrs Quinney the housekeeper, Mrs Hodgson the cook, Bennett the coachman, Jack the stable-boy, Doris, two dairy-maids. Until now there had also been Mr Winch the tutor, but Mr Winch was gone for ever.

Geographically his world held first the house, the garden, the stables, then the moors that fell to the very edge of the garden, Skiddaw and Blencathra under whose shadows all the life of the house passed, and beyond them Keswick, and beyond that the world of Watendlath becoming speedily to him now a dream world, a sort of fairy kingdom where all the glories and wonders of life were enclosed.

However, he had then (and he was always to have) the great gift of accepting what he was given and making the best of it. It is true that did he feel he was being given something that he ought not to be given, he would fight relentlessly to change it. He had, for instance, felt that he was NOT given Mr Winch, and he had fought Mr Winch most gallantly. It seemed only in the proper nature of things that Mr Winch should be removed.

His attitude to John changed as time passed. He did not love him less, but when he found that he could make John and Dorothy do as he wished he had his way with them. Although he was only six he knew very well on every occasion what it was that he wanted to do. The only trouble was that others did not always want to do likewise.

Like a stone flung into a pool so the fearful adventure of the rioters had broken into the settled pattern of

Adam's life. That had been one of his proudest moments when his mother had told him to go into Aunt Jennifer's room and wait there until 'the men who were throwing stones at the windows' had gone away. He had known that there was more in his mother's mind than she expressed in words. She had in fact said to him: 'I shall have occupation enough. I trust YOU to guard all that I have no time for.' A strange scene that was in Aunt Jennifer's bedroom with all the familiar things, the high bed with the crimson curtains, and Aunt Jennifer's lovely black hair in a lace cap, her silver shoes and a green turban with a feather in it lying on the floor, Dorothy sitting virtuously on a chair pretending that she listened to John who was reading from Goldsmith's History of England (Adam did not, of course, know what the book was), John with his gentle voice reading on and on, never taking his eyes from the book--all this so quiet and ordinary, while the reflection from the flames of the burning stables played like living figures on the wallpaper, and the muffled echoes of shouts and cries came from below. He would never forget the white tenseness of John's face, the little exclamations of Aunt Jennifer: 'Oh dear! Oh dear!' 'Listen to that!' 'We shall all be murdered!' 'Children, we shall all be murdered!', the ridiculous aspect of the leather cushions that had been pushed up against the windows, the way in which everything in the room jumped and sank and jumped again in accordance with the fiery hands that stroked the walls. He himself sat on a low chair near the bed and had no doubt but that he was there on guard over them all. He was prepared that at any moment Aunt Jennifer should jump out of bed and run as she was into the passage and down the stairs. It was privately his opinion that she showed great cowardice to remain there while his mother and Bennett and Mrs Quinney were defending the house, but he had a patronizing, forgiving affection for Aunt Jennifer, as though she were a pony gone at the knees, or a dog that wouldn't fight other dogs, or a doll whose stomach oozed sawdust.

It was all that he himself could do to sit there thus quietly, but his mother had given him that piece of work and so without question there he was!

The worst moment of all was when Aunt Jennifer suddenly cried (just as John was reading about the Princes who were murdered in the Tower): 'Oh, it is me that they are after! I know it is! . . . They have always hated me! They will burn the house over us! . . . We mustn't remain here, children . . . We must fly or we shall have the house burnt over our heads!'

Although Adam was too young to be aware of it, it was perhaps the serious regard that the three children bestowed upon her that forced her to lie back again upon her pillow, to close her eyes and await, as best she might, the outcome.

Indeed the affair was soon at an end. Quiet fell in a moment. The shadows and tremblings of the flames'

reflections continued to play upon the walls of the room. John opened the door and listened. Below there were shufflings of feet, whispers, someone was weeping. They waited . . . At last Judith herself came, and Adam learnt that Uncle Reuben was dead.

The news was the first real crisis in young Adam's life, the first occasion on which he had been close to a death that was real and actual to him. In France the old Curé of the village had died when paying them a call, but Adam had been too young to understand. In Watendlath a cow had died and one of Charlie Watson's horses. But Uncle Reuben had been his friend. He had spent whole days with him in the hills and, although he had been fat and puffed as he climbed a hill, he had been able to talk to hundreds of people at the same time and had known stories about Abraham, the Lord Jesus, the Giant of Poland, King Arthur's Round Table and scores of others. He had never bothered Adam with making him do things he did not want to do, as Charlie Watson sometimes did, and he carried gingerbread and lollipops in the pocket of his gown.

Now Uncle Reuben was dead, shot with a gun that had been fired by one of the wicked men who wanted to burn the house down. As the consciousness of this absolute fact, positive, not in any circumstances to be changed, sank into Adam's mind, something affected him for ever. He was, his whole life afterwards, to remember the moment when his mother, breaking off from some story that she was telling him, drew him towards her and said to him that now they were to remain at Fell House, not go to Watendlath as she had promised, and they were to remain to fight . . . To fight whom? . . . Was it Uncle Walter?

He suggested Uncle Walter because he himself wanted to fight him. Once in the hills when he had been bathing, Uncle Walter had ridden past on a white horse and tried to strike him with his whip. He had not forgotten that. He would never forget. So it seemed to him quite natural that he and his mother should fight Uncle Walter. And now when his mother said that they would remain here and not go to Watendlath he connected that with Uncle Reuben's death and concluded at once that it was Uncle Walter who had shot him. That being so, he, Adam, would one day shoot Uncle Walter. The sequence of ideas was quite natural and inevitable. He said nothing. He asked no questions. But he did one thing. He had a black doll, a black doll with a red coat and brass buttons. He hung the doll from a nail on the wall and threw marbles at it. Within a week he could hit the doll from a great distance. The doll's face that had been made of painted clay was no longer a face.

Then on an afternoon late in February, John and Adam had a curious adventure. Adventures were for ever happening to Adam, whether watching a carriageful of ladies tumbled into the ditch on the Carlisle Road, seeing a drunken old man fall off the top of the Kendal coach, looking at the gipsies who came and pitched with their caravans painted orange and blue on the moor above the house until they were ordered away (they had brown babies, two monkeys and a basketful of snakes; a woman in a crimson kerchief with silver coins through her ears invited Adam to join them: had it not been for his mother he would have done so). Adventures for him were perpetual, but this one had for him a new quality, terrifying had he allowed himself to be terrified.

It had been a strange day. In the forenoon there had been showers of rain that had filled the road with puddles of silver. Then Skiddaw about two of the afternoon took a step or two and came face to face with the house, dragging a stream of clouds over his shoulder with him. He had a way of doing this: a shrug of shoulders, a quiver of his sides and there he was staring in at the parlour window. The air was fresh with a sniff of spring (although spring would not be with them for a month or two). Adam walked out as far as the stream in the hollow below the Tarn; the water glided and leapt. The moss was wet on the gleaming stones above the brown water; the Fell rose straight from the hollow and was thronged with little moorland streams, for there had been heavy rains. He thought that he saw an eagle and he looked up and up into the sky that was whitish blue and empty until the clouds that clung on to Skiddaw's shoulders. All these little things belonged to the adventure. As he entered the house again Skiddaw receded and the clouds turned rose; the road beyond the garden wall was very hard and white. He could hear a young owl hooting. He climbed the stairs to find two large marbles, one crystal white, one purple, that he liked to carry in his pocket. Then slid down the banisters to the parlour. He knew that his mother and Aunt Jennifer were paying a visit. They had gone in the carriage with Bennett.

In the doorway of the parlour he found John and saw at once that he was shaking with some event. He pulled Adam by the arm into the room, which was lit only with the dusk of the falling day and the sharp jumping flames from the fire.

He spoke in a whisper.

'Adam! . . . Cousin Walter has been here!'

Adam looked to the window.

'No,' said John, 'he has gone.'

'He came into the house?'

The two boys whispered like conspirators.

'No. Not so far as the house. He was on a white horse. He got down and stood at the gate. Then he opened it and stood in the garden. He stayed looking at the house without moving, for a long while. Then he went out and rode away. I saw him through the window.'

Adam drew a deep breath and clutched the two marbles in his pocket.

'Did he look angry?' he asked at length.

'I could not see his face. Everything was so still. I thought he would knock at the door, but when he was inside the gate he never moved. He stood there look-

ing. I thought he could see me through the window and I hid behind the curtain.'

Adam went to the window and peered out. The glow in the sky was bright and shredded now with little yellow clouds like goslings.

'He is gone,' he said, his nose pressed against the cold pane.

'Yes--but a moment back. He rode slowly up the hill. Oh, Adam, why did he come?'

'To spy on us.' Adam nodded his head. 'I shall go after him.'

'Oh, Adam, will you?'

'Yes, why not? Perhaps he has a gun and is waiting to shoot someone.'

John must go too if Adam went, but he felt an overwhelming fear, sprung from years of his mother's dread. Adam was too angry just then to be frightened. When he was angry he was possessed with rage; there was no room for any other emotion. When he had been a baby his anger had sometimes almost choked him because it boiled inside him and he could not shout nor cry. He took John by the hand, and together, as quietly as might be, they stole out of the house, closing the big heavy door gingerly behind them. The owl hooted at them as they hurried on to the road.

Outside the gate Adam halted. Something in the whiteness of the road pulled him up. But he knew what it was. A week ago he had been walking up the hill and had come upon a fat and distended frog. This frog was croaking in a despairing manner; around its neck were folded the thin spiry legs of two smaller frogs who clung thus, motionless, without sound. From the mouth of the large distended frog protruded a tip of tongue scarlet red.

Adam came the next day and found that the swollen frog was dead (the red tongue still protruding), but the two live frogs were still there, their legs interlaced, while another frog, small and green, squatted near by on guard and to see that justice had been done.

Adam was too young to feel spiritual disgust: his original instinct had been one of interest and curiosity, but now the scene around him was ghostly with evening mist, and out of the mist sprang the sharp white road; by the side of the road was a yellow-bellied frog with a tongue like blood and around him croaked a chorus of green frogs. The moor was filled with green frogs. He stood staring intently in front of him.

'What is it?' whispered John. 'He will be gone in an instant.' They stood very close together and listened. All was still. The lights of the little village we're coming out; Fell House was a black mass against the mist.

It was perhaps the cold that drove them forward. They walked on the turf at the side of the road so that they should make no noise. They turned from the road and began to climb the moor, stumbling over the unevenness of the turf. Suddenly, John caught Adam's arm: 'Keep down . . . He's there!'

Just in front of them a shelf of turf rose above a cutting. To the right of them, very close to them, three sheep, aware of them, held together, their sides panting. But quite clearly the boys could see the figure on the hill. He seemed gigantic in that light, his white horse colossal. The mist, into whose vapours the moon would soon pour her light, made a ghostly background to that motionless horseman, great of bulk, in a black overcoat with a high black collar. His thighs, his riding-boots, were jet against the whiteness of his horse's flanks. Neither he nor his horse moved. The sheep too seemed to be carved against the moor, and the two boys, kneeling behind the rising of turf, their hearts thumping as it seemed to them into their throats, waited to see what he would do.

He did nothing. He stayed there looking down on to Fell House. Then, as darkness fell, he turned his horse's head and rode away.

AT WESTAWAYS

Westaways was a very different place from Fell House, Uldale.

Fell House would have always, whatever were done to it, the atmosphere of the farm from which it had sprung. David Herries, John's grandfather, had in his time made certain enlargements. He was greatly proud--and so was Sarah his wife--of his dairies, the garden with its fine lawn and Gothic temple, the parlour and the best bedroom, but both David and Sarah had been simple people, nor, since their marriage, had they travelled far afield. Sarah, for a brief while, had been bitten with the London fashion, fostered by Horace Walpole, The Castle of Otranto, Mrs Radcliffe and the rest, for pseudo-medievalism, suits of armour, stained-glass windows and plaster gargoyles, but she was not by nature romantic and the craze had soon passed. Fell House, nestling its warm cheek against the breast of the moor, was an improved farmhouse and no more.

Utterly different from its very inception was Westaways. In the early years of the eighteenth century old Pomfret Herries, brother of 'Rogue' Herries, and so uncle to David, young John's grandfather, had had it built, not because he wanted a beautiful house but because he wished to go one better than his neighbours. However, it WAS a beautiful house because he chose for architect old John Westaway, saturnine and melancholy hermit, one of the finest architects then alive, trained in Italy, the friend of Vanbrugh and Chesterman, famous through all the north of England not only for his skill but also for his eccentricities and savage temper.

Old Pomfret had to pay for his ambitions and grumbled at the cost for years after, but he had, in the end, a lovely house. It is true that the only room in it of any value to himself was his own apartment thronged with guns and fishing-rods. He was proud, nevertheless, for people came from miles to see the house.

It was situated between Crosthwaite Church and the town of Keswick. At that time the gardens ran down to the fringe of the Lake. The virtues of the house were its beautiful tiles of rosy red, the delicate wrought-ironwork across its front, the sash windows--at that time a great rarity--the pillared hall, and especially the saloon, whose decorations were designed and executed by John Westaway himself. The subject of the design was Paris awarding the apple, and the three goddesses were painted with extreme vigour.

After old Pomfret's death the house passed out of the family for a while, but Will, David Herries' money-making son, bought it back again and thought to live in it. However, London, and especially the City, held him too strongly. He found the country both dull and fruitless. His son Walter reigned in Westaways in his stead.

Walter, who had little taste but great energy and a readiness to take the advice of others (for his own profit), enlarged and improved Westaways. For a number of years workmen were always about the place. He added a wing towards Crosthwaite, doubled the stables, extended the gardens and had a grand conservatory. He also put fine things inside the house; he had a famous piece of tapestry that showed Diana hunting, some excellent sculpture, and a Van Dyck and a small but most valuable Titian. There was also over the door of the saloon a painting of the Watteau school in deep rich colours of some French king dining with his ladies--a picture all purples, oranges and crimson that the Keswick citizens thought the finest thing they had ever seen. Only old Miss Pennyfeather laughed at it and called it 'stuff', and Mr Southey, after dining with Walter, was said never even to have noticed it.

Walter Herries himself cared for none of these things for themselves, but only in so far as they represented strength and power.

At this time he was thirty years of age and his children, Uhland and Elizabeth, who were twins, were seven; they were born in the same year as young Adam and were a few months older than he.

Walter was large in girth and limb, but could not at this period be called stout. He was in appearance a survival of the days of the Regency, now swiftly slipping into limbo. He seemed already something of an anachronism with his coats of purple and red, his high thick stock with its jewelled pin, his capacity for eating and drinking, his roaring laugh, his passion for sport. But he was not really such an anachronism as he seemed. In politics, when he bothered to speak of them, he appeared as reactionary Tory as Wellington or old Lord Eldon, but in reality he stood closer to Huskisson and Canning. The fact was that he learnt much from his father, who, one of the astutest men in the City, had his eye more firmly fixed on the past. Walter, caring for nothing but his personal power and the aggrandizement of his family, loving only in all the world his crippled little son, building his edifice in part for himself but in the main for Uhland's future, considered that future very much more deeply than anyone supposed. He suffered from the fact that no one in his immediate surroundings was of any use to him in these things. He reigned in a passionate loneliness and perhaps in that had more in common with his great-grandfather, old 'Rogue' Herries, than he would ever have dreamed possible. His wife Agnes he held to be an imbecile, and she was truly as terrified of him as all timid wives are supposed to be of tyrannous, loud-voiced husbands.

On a certain fine September morning of this year, 1822, a long- legged, supercilious individual named Posset (William Posset, son of William Posset, coachman at Levons Hall) brought into Walter Herries' dressing-room a large tin bath. The floor of this dressing-room drooped in its centre into a hollow and in the floor of this hollow was a small iron grating. Over the hollow the bath was inserted. A pinch-faced youth in a uniform of dark red and brass buttons then arrived with two vast pitchers so large as almost to conceal him. With an air of extreme relief and under the cold eye of the lengthy Posset, young Albert emptied the pitchers into the bath. Posset then with delicate tread stepped into the next room, pulled back the curtains and approached the four-poster. Walter, his mouth wide open, his chest bare, his nightshirt pulled down over one shoulder, was snoring loudly. Posset, with a gravity worthy of a tax-collector, shook the bare arm. Walter woke, gave one glance at Posset, sprang from his bed, tugged his nightshirt over his head, rushed in to the next room and plunged into the bath. Young Albert, accustomed to the fierce eruption of water, always at this point retired to the farthest corner of the room, where he stood, towels over his arm, admiring, with an amazement that custom never seemed to lessen, that great body, that splutter of exclamations, grunts and oaths, and that sudden magnificent figure of a man withdrawn from the water, suffering the lusty (but always reverent) towelling of Posset--and water dripping everywhere, running in little streams and eddies into the hollow and away safely through the iron grating. Albert always informed those less privileged that there was no sight in the world quite so fine as he plunged into his bath--no lion in a show, no tiger in Indian jungle, could have the energy and vigour of his master at this moment. It was Albert's top moment of his day--a pity that it came so early; every event was a decline from it.

Walter had long ago insisted that any visitor in the house--his mother, his wife, very definitely included--must, unless a doctor forbade them, be present at the family breakfast table. It was the beginning of his patriarchal day. Only thirty years of age, he already felt himself founder of the whole of the Herries stock, and nothing pleased him better than to have Herries collected from all over the country and seated at his table.

This was not at present easy, for Keswick was tucked away in the North and travelling was difficult. Nevertheless, this was not a bad halting-place on the way to Scotland, and the number of Herries 'bagged' for Walter's dining-table in the last five years was remarkable.

Walter liked further to collect Herries who were oddities and to encourage them in their idiosyncrasies--granted, of course, that these idiosyncrasies did not inconvenience himself. Here he was instigated by the old motive of the King and his Court Jester. Walter might be said to have a great sense of fun, if no very strong sense of humour. He liked, for example, to indulge old Monty Cards in his femininities (Monty painted his cheeks and powdered his nose), in his little meannesses and his nervous terrors. He enjoyed the company of old Maria Rockage (for whom he had a real liking) that he might shock her Methodist principles. He even was childish enough to play on his wife's terrors by laying a book on a door that it should fall on her when entering a room. He was not at all above practical jokes and horseplay. They were part of his 'Regency' manner.

He had just now as his guests, Phyllis, Maria Rockage's daughter, her husband, Stephen Newmark, and three of her children--Horace aged three, Mary aged two, and Phyllis only one. She was anticipating a fourth. They were all very healthy children and Mr Newmark looked upon them as just rewards tendered to him by a grateful Deity.

For Stephen Newmark, tall, long-nosed, sanctimonious, was a perpetual joy to Walter. He took life seriously. He enjoyed Family Prayers. Walter, therefore, indulged his fancy and insisted that all of them, Agnes his wife, his mother (who was staying just then with him), his own two children, and all the household should be present on the stroke of eight and offer up, under the leadership of Mr Newmark, thanks to the Creator for the dangers of a night safely past and the glories of another day vouchsafed. It puzzled Mr Newmark a little that Walter should be so truly determined on Family Prayers. This determination did not altogether 'go' with his cock-fighting, horse racing, card-playing, but Newmark had long ago decided (and confided to Phyllis) that his Cousin Walter was 'a strange fish'. In that conclusion he was perfectly correct.

On this morning, however, Walter had a small matter of business to discharge before breakfast. Rosy, scented, his stock starched until it glittered, his pantaloons of dark purple hiding his magnificent legs, 'rings on his fingers and bells on his toes', he descended, like Jove from Olympus, to the study where he transacted his affairs.

Here his agent, Peach, was waiting for him. Peach was a short, stocky, beetle-browed little man who had been in the service, for most of his days, of the Duke of Wrexe. He came, therefore, from the South and hated the North AND the Northerners with a dreadful passion. He would not have stayed here a day had it not been for the odd power that Walter Herries exercised over him. He could not be said to LOVE his master-- he was not known to love any human being; he was not deferential, showed no servitude, disputed his master's wishes hotly and was grudging in thanks for benefits, but he seemed to have found in Walter Herries a man who had stung, reluctantly, his admiration--the only man in the world it might be. He appreciated Herries' dominating roughness, coarseness, liking for horseplay, and then something more--outside and beyond these.

In any case he made a wonderful servant and was hated cordially throughout the countryside.

He was standing now, his legs, that were slightly bowed, apart, his hand gripping the shoulder of a slim fair-haired boy who, his hands tied behind him, his eyes wide open with fear and apprehension, stayed there, his heart beating like a terrified rabbit's.

'This is the boy,' Peach said.

'Yes,' said Walter, looking at him.

The boy's eyes drooped. In his heart was the terror of death. He knew that he could be hanged for what he had done.

'I discovered him,' Peach went on, 'last evening. He had a small wheelbarrow and was placing in it some logs from the pile outside the further stables.'

'What did he say?' Walter asked.

'He said nothing. At least not then. Later when he was shut into the cellar for the night he admitted that he was hungry and had a mother who was hungry and a small brother who was hungry.' Peach gave a click in his throat, a favourite noise of his, and it resembled a key turning in a door. 'They all say they're hungry now.'

'What's your name?' asked Walter.

'Henry Burgess.'

'Well, Henry Burgess . . . You know what the Keswick Justices will say?'

The boy was understood to mutter that he didn't care.

'You don't care? Well, all the better. It's a hanging matter, you know.'

'I gave him food and drink,' Peach remarked reluctantly. 'He wouldn't have held up else.' Then he added: 'His mother's been waiting outside all night.'

There was an interruption. The door opened and Uhland came in. It was his habit to find his father here before breakfast. For a boy of seven he was tall and very spare and his face was grave and sadly lined for a child. One leg was longer than the other and he walked aided by a little ebony cane. When he saw that there was company he stopped at the door. It was characteristic of him that he stood there looking at them solemnly and said nothing.

'Well, what's your defence?' asked Walter.

The boy was understood to say they were all hungry.

'All hungry, were you? That's not much of an excuse. Couldn't you work?'

No work to be found. Hard times. Had been working for a hostler. Turned away for fighting another boy who insulted his mother.

'Young ruffian,' said Walter complacently. He stood, his chest thrust out, his thumbs in his armholes. Then he nodded to Uhland, who came limping forward. Walter put his arm round his son and held him close to him.

'Uhland, this boy has been stealing my wood. He says he did it because he was hungry. If he goes before the Justices it will be a hanging matter. Shall I send him or no?'

Uhland stared at the boy, who suddenly raised his eyes, glaring at them all.

'He doesn't LOOK hungry,' he said quietly.

'No, upon my word he doesn't,' said Walter with boisterous good humour. 'That's good for a child, Peach, is it not? He does not look hungry. You are right, Uhland, my boy.' He laughed, throwing back his handsome curly head. 'Well, what shall we do with him?'

'Let him go, Papa,' said Uhland. His voice was cold, but he looked at the boy with interest. 'We have plenty of wood.'

'Yes, but we shall not have,' said Walter, 'if all the young vagabonds--Very well, let him go, Peach. He shall have the dogs on him if he comes this way again.'

Without a word Peach, pushing the boy in front of him, took him from the room.

Walter laughed, yawned, stretched his great arms.

'Well, my boy, how are you?'

'Very well, Papa, thank you.'

'Slept? No headache?'

'No, Papa, thank you.'

'Will you come with me into Keswick this morning?'

'Yes, Papa.'

There was a pause; then Uhland said:

'Elizabeth wishes to come.'

'She can go with Miss Kipe.'

'Yes, Papa.'

A roar like a wild beast's cry for his food filled the room. It was the ceremonial gong--a gong brought from India, purchased by Will and given by him to his son, a superb gong of beaten brass and carved with the figures of Indian deities.

So they went to breakfast, Uhland's small bony hand in his father's large one.

They were all assembled in the bright, high room whose wide windows looked out on to the garden with the splashing fountain, the Lake and the hills beyond. Stephen Newmark was there, standing behind a reading-desk; Phyllis his wife; two of her children; Elizabeth with her governess, Miss Kipe; Christabel Herries, Walter's mother; Agnes, Walter's wife; Montague Cards and the whole household-- Posset, young Albert, the cook, the maids and the little kitchen- help.

Walter took his place beside his wife and instantly they all knelt. A long row of upturned boots met the interested gaze of two robins on the window sill. After a while, with creaking of knees, rustling of aprons, they all rose and sat down while Mr Newmark read a selection from the New Testament. The sun flooded the room. A large fat tortoiseshell cat came stealthily down the garden path, its green eyes fixed on the robins. On the bright road beyond the house the Burgess family began to trudge in silence towards Carlisle, Walter put out his hand and laid it on Uhland's shoulder. The cook, who was fat and had trouble with her heart, began to breathe heavily, Posset caught the eye of the prettiest of the maids and instantly looked away again. Little Elizabeth, looking out, saw the cat and the birds. Her eyes widened with apprehension.

'Let us Pray,' said Mr Newmark, and down on their knees they all went again.

'May the blessing of the Lord rest upon us all this day,' said Mr Newmark. There was a pause, then a rustle, a knee-cracking, a boot- scraping, and they were all on their feet again.

The domestics were in line--Mrs Rains the cook, Posset, the maids, Albert, the little kitchen-maid who had a round rosy face and a neat waist--all in their proper order.

'Fresh country girls you succeed in getting, Walter,' said Newmark after they were gone, his mind meditatively on the kitchen-maid.

'Anybody wanting the barouche this fine morning?' said Walter genially. He was in an excellent temper, which fact the three ladies perceived and brightened accordingly. Christabel Herries, Walter's mother, was fifty years of age and thin to emaciation. She wore gowns of black silk with a purple Indian shawl thrown about her narrow shoulders. She moved with timidity, as though she were ever expecting a rude word. She adored her son but feared him. She had been, all through her married life, under the domination of Herries men. Her husband had never treated her with unkindness, but the City had swallowed him, leaving Christabel alone on shores of domesticity so barren that she occupied half her London evenings talking to herself in a large drawing-room all yellow silk and mirrors. Will, her husband, had hoped to make her a social success. But after a disastrous Ball that they gave in the summer of '96, a Ball that had ended with a scene between Christabel and Jennifer, then a radiant young beauty, Will, with a shrug of his shoulders, had reconciled himself to her disabilities. He very quickly saw that the thing for him to do was to make the money so that his son Walter might carry on the family glory.

Walter had always been kind to his mother, but for family rather than personal reasons. He thought her 'a poor fish', but then he had no opinion of women unless they were handsome. Christabel was, however, the mother of Walter Herries; she must therefore be honoured by the outside world. And he saw that it was so.

Agnes, as the wife of Walter Herries and the mother of his children, should also have secured honourable treatment had the thing been at all possible. But in this Walter saw that the world was not to blame, for a more miserable woebegone sickly female was not, he was assured, to be found in the civilized globe. When he married her she had been something of the type of that new rosy- cheeked kitchen-maid (whom he had noticed, and saw also that Newmark had noticed). She had been merry at first with a certain rather kittenish charm. But she was 'cold'. Marital relations had terrified her from the first. Their marriage night had been a horror, and after the birth of the twins they had occupied separate bedrooms. Then she had had one sickness after another, now did not choose to trouble to talk; 'sulky', Walter told himself. She pretended to be fond of the children but, he was happy to say, Uhland had already as much scorn of her as his father had.

He felt (and with justice surely) that Fate had dealt unfairly in giving so magnificent a man so wretched a partner. He was fair to her, he gave her everything that she needed; all that he asked of her was that she should keep out of his way and not interfere with his plans for Uhland. With Elizabeth she should do as she pleased.

Phyllis Newmark was tall, of a charming pink and white complexion, and had a laughing eye.

Her father, Lord Rockage, in his place, Grosset in Wiltshire, had given her love and kisses combined with general disorder, poverty and Methodism. On these mixed virtues she had thrived. She was kindly, cheerful, intelligent and quite uneducated. She was born to be a mother, and a mother she was most assuredly proving. She did not mind how many children she had. She adored them all. Newmark, having helped to provide her with three, must receive her grateful thanks. She gave him her obedience, laughed at his foibles and understood him better than anyone else in the world. She too had noticed his glance at the kitchen-maid although at the same time she was murmuring (with real devotion) the Lord's Prayer and observing a pimple on the neck of little Horace and wondering whether Walter would allow them the barouche that morning or force them into the post-chaise or order them to walk. She knew, however, exactly how to deal with the kitchen-maid, the pimple and the walk (if that were compulsory). Nothing could defeat her; she inherited from both her parents courage, honesty and an insatiable zest for life.

Soon they were all around the breakfast-table and set to with an eagerness that spoke well for their digestions. Rounds of beef; pies; fish, broiled and fried; eggs, baked, fried, boiled; hams, tongues, jams, marmalades, buns, scones--everything was there, and tankards of ale, tea, coffee . . . Agnes Herries alone pretended to eat but did not.

'Yes, you may have the barouche,' Walter observed, 'and Phyllis shall have the barouche box if she chooses-- I know that it gives her the greatest gratification both to see and be seen.' Then, having paused sufficiently to catch all their attention, he added:

'But first I have a visitor.'

'A visitor?'

'Yes. At ten o'clock precisely a lady is to come and see me.'

'A lady?'

'A friend of you all--Mrs Judith Paris.'

He allowed his words to sink in. And indeed they caused a stir. Both Christabel and Phyllis Newmark had the deepest affection for Judith. To Phyllis she had been a familiar friend since her babyhood, for Judith had once lived at Grosset, and to Christabel she was perhaps the only woman in the world who had never failed her, the one human being who did not patronize her, cared for her as she was, knew with tenderness and perception the barrenness of her life.

Yet Christabel had only seen her once in seven years. Only once since the night when Judith had dined at Westaways, the night of the news of Napoleon's escape from Elba. After that Judith had fled to Paris, borne her illegitimate son there. Since her return to Uldale there had been war between the two houses. Whenever Christabel came up from London to stay with her son she hoped that there would be some chance meeting, in a lane, in a street. She had not dared herself to prepare a meeting.

'Oh, Judith!' Phyllis cried joyfully. 'I had been intending to ask . . .'

'She is coming,' Walter said, greatly amused at the disappointment that his womenkind would suffer, 'solely on a business matter. The visit is only to myself.'

Then Christabel showed courage.

'Walter, you should invite Judith to dinner. Bygones are bygones. You should most certainly invite her to dinner.'

'And Jennifer?' asked Walter, laughing.

Christabel's pale cheek flushed. No, she could never forgive Jennifer. That old quarrel, twenty-six years old, could never be forgotten. It had too many consequences. It had split the family; it had been the close of Christabel's social life. She had never had the courage to give a real party again. And then Jennifer had behaved scandalously. She had been another man's mistress under her husband's nose. That poor Francis had shot himself in London was all Jennifer's fault. No, Jennifer was another matter.

'Well, then,' said Walter, observing his mother's silence. 'You see, ma'am. And you cannot have Judith here without Jennifer. Judith rules that house. She has become, I hear, a perfect Turk . . . Well, well, it may not be for long.'

He added these last words in a half-murmur to himself. With a final pull at his tankard of beer, wiping his mouth, with a bow to the ladies, he got up, walked for a moment to the window and stood there, looking out, then left the room.

As soon as he was gone the children broke out into little pipings and chirrupings. The two Newmark children (who should have been in the nursery, but their father wished them to take their part, even thus early, in the morning ceremony) rolled decorously on the floor at their mother's feet. You felt that already their infant eyes were cautiously on their father. Uhland sat without moving, one leg over the other, an attitude protective of his deformity. Elizabeth, shyly crossed the room. She was a beautiful child, most delicate in colour and build. She had none of the high bones of the Herries tribe. She did not seem like a Herries until suddenly with a lift of her head you saw pride and resolve, two of the finer Herries characteristics. Her mother took her hand and they stayed quietly together, remote, in a world of their own, without speaking . . .

Judith was shown into the little parlour next the saloon. It had not been long since she had had a talk with Walter there--last Christmas-time it had been. Now, as she sat on the red morocco chair waiting for him, she thought of that, and how there had been a bowl of Christmas roses. A petal had fallen lazily, wistfully to the carpet. Their talk then had been almost friendly. She had gone with him afterwards to the nursery to see the children, and she had been touched by his protective love for his son.

But now all was changed. In the interval between that meeting and this she had had proof enough of the serious danger that this big laughing man offered to her and to hers.

She was here to defend her own, and a wave of hot fierce pride beat into her cheeks as she sat there, a small unobtrusive woman in a black bonnet, her hands in a black muff, waiting for him to come in. It was he who had written to her, a short polite note asking her whether she could give him a few moments on an important matter. She would not have come, but she also had something of her own to say. She would see that she said it.

When he came in she got up and bowed, but did not offer her hand.

'Well, Cousin Walter,' she said grimly. 'What do you wish to see me about?'

His own tone changed when he saw her attitude. He had intended to be friendly, jolly, a mood that he preferred, for he liked himself in that role. But he was like a child if anyone affronted him. It might be, too, that Judith was the only person in the world of whom he had some fear. Still, his ground was sure and he began confidently enough.

'Forgive my asking you to take this trouble, Cousin Judith. You will agree, however, that I should be deceiving myself if I fancied that my presence would be welcome at Uldale.'

'Nevertheless,' she answered, 'you have paid us already at least one visit this year.'

'Indeed?'

'Last February I believe it was. You did us the honour to ride over and even to inspect our garden.'

He was confused. He had not thought that she knew of it.

'Well--it happened that I rode that way . . . But come, Cousin Judith. I am certain that we have neither of us time to waste . . .' Then he, added, a little awkwardly: 'I am sorry that you are already determined that our talk shall be unfriendly.' (What was there, he asked himself, about the little plain woman in the homely bonnet that made him feel like a scolded schoolboy? She had, in the last six months, acquired the devil of a manner--as though she were already Queen of Cumberland. Well, he would show her that she was not.)

She regarded him sternly.

'Cousin Walter, I was in this same room Christmas last. We had a conversation that was not altogether unfriendly. Since then facts have come to my knowledge. I know that it was through you that Francis Herries left home and put an end to his life in London. I know that it was because you bribed and suborned that the riot occurred at Fell House--the riot that ended in the undeserved death of the best friend I had in the world--Reuben Sunwood. And since then,'--she spoke without emotion and without removing her eyes from his face--'since I have been in charge of things at Fell House, your hand has been everywhere. Those fields towards Ireby that we intended to purchase--you paid an absurd price for them, although you could not need the ground. You bribed the cattle-man whom we had last March from Mungrisdale to poison our cows. Within the last month you have attempted to bribe Mr Rackstraw, who has been with us all this year as tutor, to spy upon us as Mr Winch did before him. Mr Rackstraw has been gentleman enough to show us loyalty. After these things--and I have no doubt that there are many more with which your conscience can charge you--it is perhaps a little without meaning to speak of friendliness between us.'

Walter did not move, did not shift his great bulk, did not turn his eyes away. He admired her. By God, he admired her! There was someone here worth fighting.

'Very well, then,' he said at last. 'We know at least where we stand, you and I. I will not, however, admit responsibility either for Francis' weakness or Sunwood's rashness. Francis would not have shot himself had he been another sort of man. It was his whole life condemned him, not I. As to the riot, no one regretted more than myself its most serious consequences. And what evidence have you that I was concerned in that matter?'

'The evidence of Mr Winch,' Judith answered.

'Faugh! A wretched little time-server who cheated me quite as steadily as he cheated yourself, Judith. As to other more recent matters, well--do you recollect our last conversation in this room?'

'Perfectly.'

'Then you will remember the challenge I laid down. I told you-- what I trust you sincerely believe--that I had no animosity whatever towards yourself. I told you also that for reasons both private and public I was resolved that Jennifer and her children should vacate Fell House, and that if I could not see to it by fair means that they went, then I would see to it by unfair. I was honest in that. I gave you warning.'

'And on what ground,' Judith cried indignantly, 'had you the right? Fell House is Jennifer's place. It is where her husband was born and his children after him.'

'My father also was born there,' said Walter quietly. 'As you may have observed, Judith, I have a great sense of family. It is perhaps the greatest quality in me. Jennifer with her rotten public history offends my sense of family. There is also an old quarrel between her and my mother that possibly you have not forgotten. In any case, I made you a fair offer then. I make you a fair offer now. Let Jennifer and her children leave Fell House and go to live in the South--and the matter is for ever ended.'

'We are only beating the old ground,' answered Judith impatiently. 'There is nothing to be said on that score. We defy you now, Cousin Walter, as we defied you then. There is only now this difference--that they have me to fight for them, and life has made me a determined woman, not easily moved.'

'No,' he answered quickly. 'I am aware that you are not. We are alike at least in that. But you know that my quarrel is neither with you nor your boy. Indeed, it has never been. That is one matter on which I wish to speak to you.'

He hesitated, then went on:

'It seems that my boy, Uhland, has met your boy Adam on several occasions.'

'Yes, I know it.'

'They are only babies, but Uhland is old for his age. He has taken an unaccountable liking for your Adam.' He paused, laughed, continued: 'Forgive me for that word "unaccountable". But for children as young as they are--' He broke off.

She felt herself, against her will, touched. When Walter mentioned his son a different character seemed to speak from his eyes, his mouth, his very hands. He was young and proud when he spoke of his son. Some better light shone through his coarse texture. But she did not want to be touched.

'You must know,' she said impatiently, 'that it was through no wish of mine that they met. It was in the woods beyond Portinscale-- pure accident.'

'Oh, I know, I know . . . I was not charging you with any intention. But my boy speaks of him, wishes to see him--'

'Yes,' Judith answered, 'that is a mischance that we must correct.'

'A mischance?'

'Yes. It would be good for neither of them, things being as they are, that they should be better acquainted.'

Walter choked back some reply that he was about to make. His control was remarkable.

'I had hoped,' he said steadily, 'that you would allow the children occasionally to meet. We elders may have our divisions. There is no reason--'

She broke in, jumping impetuously to her feet:

'No reason! No reason! There is THIS reason, Cousin Walter--that you are our enemy. You have killed Francis Herries, you would rob his children of the very roof over their heads. Only a moment ago you threatened me. And yet you wish that my son and your son--'

She stopped, sat down quietly, smoothing her skirt.

'I have still some of my old temper remaining although I am near fifty . . . In fact, I may tell you, Cousin Walter, that I was never in better health in my life. Aye,' she nodded her bonnet, 'that is what I had come to say. You may think me an old woman, but I am young enough yet to keep my son from your influence and, pray God, I ever will be.'

He was angry; she had touched him. His hand fingered the jewelled pin in his stock. But his voice was level as he answered: 'Very well, then. You are confident, Cousin Judith. I am an impatient man by blood, but in this case I can school myself to waiting.

'Now hear my offer. It was to make it that I asked you to visit me. Last week I purchased the land at High Ireby. It was my intention, unless we come to some agreement together, to build a house there.'

High Ireby? At once she grasped the implication. The High Ireby land was on the hills above Uldale. It was at some distance, but nevertheless it overlooked Fell House. Walter there in some big place of his planning, with his fields, his cattle, his servants . . . In spite of herself she showed some agitation.

'That would be done,' she said at length slowly, 'to spite us.'

'It would be done,' he answered, smiling (for he saw that she grasped the consequences), 'because I admire the view. It would not be perhaps altogether happy for Jennifer and her children to have me so neighbourly.' He looked at her closely. She gave him back look for look. 'But,' he went on, 'you have not heard my proposition. This house here is now too small for me, but there are other sites that I could choose, other than High Ireby. Then it is one of two things. Either Jennifer sells me Fell House--I will give her a good price for it--and removes herself South. And in that case I would make you the offer of it. You should be my tenant at a most moderate rental. Or I build on High Ireby. There is no necessity for an immediate decision. I only wished that you should know what I had in mind.'

Judith saw then his plan; that this should hang over them night and day. If Walter built a house at High Ireby, it would kill Jennifer. And John? His nature being as it was, he could not endure it. Nor would it stop at Walter's living there. He would be able, in a thousand ways, to molest them at Fell House, to spy upon them, to break their privacy . . . Yes, it was a clever notion.

'At any time, Cousin Judith,' he said, moving towards the door, 'that Jennifer is ready for me to have Fell House at a good price--'

She got up, putting her hands in her muff.

'You are clever, Walter,' she said. 'I grant you that. You are clever.'

'I am flattered,' he said, bowing. 'I must be clever to fight so brilliant an adversary.'

'Stuff!' she answered, tossing her head. 'None of your fine manners. Time's wasted by them.'

Outside the door she turned.

'You are a strange man. So much trouble to persecute two weak women.'

'One weak woman,' he corrected her.

At the top of the stairs he said: 'You understand my offer?'

'Oh yes, I understand.'

'Well, good day.'

'Good day to you, Walter.'

As she climbed into the chaise she was surprised to find herself trembling. Her desire at that moment was to hasten home and find them safe. Then to gather them all into her arms--Jennifer, John, Dorothy and Adam.

But all she said aloud for the benefit of Bennett's broad back was, once again, 'Stuff!'

ADAM'S WORLD

It might be claimed that in spite of all that happened to him afterwards, the most important years of Adam Herries' life were from 1822 to 1826, from the age of seven to the comparative maturity of eleven.

It was true that the French years and the Watendlath years were important, but it was Mr Rackstraw who really woke him into active conscious life, and Mr Rackstraw didn't come to Uldale until after the riot at the beginning of 1822.

The five years that followed had for Adam three outstandingly influential personalities--his mother, Mr Rackstraw and John. Looking back, in later years, he sometimes fancied that everything that he did afterwards, all the things that brought him into trouble, all the things that gave him happiness, sprang in reality from those three people. At least, it is true that afterwards one person only was to influence him so deeply, and for two others only was he to care with such strong endurance as he did for his mother and for John Herries. But it was his character that was, in the main, to settle the result of events for him, as it does with all of us. What he was he was partly born, partly formed by people and events, partly fashioned by his own free will.

During those five years he lived, as all small boys do, a kind of under-water life with his own particular anemones, sea-horses, coloured weeds and stones for his absorbed attention. Of the traffic of the waters above his head he knew nothing; it mattered to him not at all, of course, that Mr Canning, staying with John Gladstone in his Liverpool home, watched a small boy called William Ewart playing on the lawn, or that there was a skirmish at Missolonghi, or that taxation grew ever higher and higher, that men and women cursed the machines that were taking the bread from their mouths, that the word 'Reform' was becoming an ever-louder battle- cry on men's lips . . .

He was always to have a great capacity for choosing at once the things that would, he thought, be useful to him and rejecting all the rest. From the very first he went his own way, and this independence was the beginning of all his trouble with his mother.

On the first occasion when he went off for a whole day without warning, indeed without word to anyone, he was on his return in the evening, tired, dirty and triumphant, beaten, and by his mother. She could not but remember, as she watched him adjusting his small trousers, the occasion so long ago when David Herries had beaten herself, hating it more than she did. The memory made her catch Adam to her breast and cover his face with kisses, an act of sentimentality that was to be, on the occasions of these punishments, her last. For she saw that he thought poorly of her for relenting, and for a day or two despised her a little.

She fought her first serious battle with him over this affair. He would neither tell her where he had been nor would he promise her not to do it again. For an awful week it seemed to her that her whole relationship with him was broken to pieces, until she discovered that she was now more intimate with him than ever before. For, when she said that she no longer wished to hear where he had been, he told her everything. He had been in the woods beyond Ireby, had had food with a farmer, had stroked a wild dog that everyone else feared, had found birds' eggs and fought a boy about tying a cat to a log and throwing stones at it. He told her everything and then tried to convey to her that he would always do so, but that he must have his freedom. He was to be always very inarticulate, and when now he found that she did not understand what he wanted, he simply fell into a complete and unyielding silence.

She explained to him that if he really loved her he could not give her anxiety and unhappiness by disappearing without telling anyone first. He wanted to say that if he told anyone he would be prevented from going and that therefore it was plain that no one must be told, but this was too deeply complicated for him, so he said nothing. Then she, the least sentimental of women,

descended, in her distress, to the desperate expedient of asking him whether he loved her or no, and he, who loved her with all his being, disliked so profoundly to speak about his feelings that he said nothing at all. He, being seven, was not, of course, aware of his reasons for these things. He simply knew that he was hungry, that his posterior was sore where his mother had struck him, that he hated to be questioned, that he had had a grand day, and that he would go off again in a similar manner as soon as opportunity offered itself.

Judith was a sensible woman and she had an especial talent for understanding other people. This was not 'other people' but her own flesh and blood, and, just as forty years ago she had climbed out of the window and ridden away to Uncle Tom Gauntry at Stone Ends, so now her son Adam must also be free.

She did the wisest thing--she left the whole matter to Mr Rackstraw. This was, in fact, very remarkable on her part, for at this time in England the great parental movement for the proper discipline and benefit of the children was just beginning to achieve force and power. All the children of England were learning to say 'Sir' and 'Ma'am' to their parents, never to speak before they were spoken to, and to ask questions in the manner of Little Henry--but Judith was never like other people, and their ways would never be hers.

Mr Rackstraw had from the first a strong influence over Adam. He was a man made up of very striking opposites. In appearance he was a little, wiry fellow with a face like a slumbering coal, red, dusky and shadowed ash-colour. He had a broken nose and sparse sandy hair. No beauty, but with clear bright eyes and a lively mouth. He wore always rough country clothes, his legs were a little bowed, and did he wear a straw in his mouth would have been the perfect hostler. Nevertheless, he was beyond mistake or question a gentleman. His rather sharp voice that would crack in moments of excitement, his eyes, the way that he carried his head, and the fine aristocratic shape of his hands told you that. He was, in fact, of a very good family, the Rackstraws of Rackstraw Manor in Rutlandshire, and his elder brother was Sir Wilfred Rackstraw, 14 Mount Street, London, and some minor official in the Foreign Office. He told you these things if you asked him, said the Rackstraws were poorer than mice, and that he had also a brother a smuggling trader on the Whitehaven coast. Whether this last were so no one ever knew. But he certainly had some very odd friends and some very mixed tastes. There was not a farmer, hostler, stableman, huntsman, poacher in the district he didn't know. But he was on social terms too with the County families--the Osmastons, the Derricks, the Tennants. He was an intimate friend of old Miss Pennyfeather, and they cracked jokes continually: he often took a dish of tea with Mr Southey and they, said, knew as much about his library as he did himself. There was not a cock fight, a football match, a boxing match that he did not attend, and yet he gave himself nobly to the two boys, John and

Adam. His passion was for Homer, and Adam owed that at least--that the Iliad and the Odyssey were to be ever friendly companions to him because of Roger Rackstraw. He had a pretty sense too of the virtues of Virgil, Horace, Thucydides and the Greek dramatists, and could make them live under his fingers. He had a poor opinion of contemporary English Letters, although he said a good word for the Waverley romances and told everyone that there was a young poet, John Keats, who would be remembered. For Mr Wordsworth he had more praise than was locally considered reasonable, but when alone with a friend confessed that he thought Southey's poetry 'fustian'.

However, his great and abiding passion was for this country in which he lived, and it was here that he and Adam had their great meeting-place. He was not a local bumpkin, of course, and his principal charm for Jennifer was that he seemed to have ever at his fingers' ends all the London gossip. He was always very courteous and tender to Jennifer, as though he felt that she needed protection and guarding. It might be too that she appealed to him, for, over fifty though she was, she was yet beautiful in a sort of tumbling-to-pieces, letting-herself-go fashion, and he would say, to the end of his days, that he never anywhere else saw dark hair and fair complexion to match Jennifer Herries'.

He would sit in the parlour and tell her things, how Brougham after the Queen's death, defending his not going with the body to Brunswick, had said: 'It was well known through the whole of the business he had never been much for the Queen' (and a dirty tyke Brougham was, said Mr Rackstraw); how Castlereagh's suicide was because of a pernicious blackmail that he had suffered under, how the King now is become an awful bore and talks about nothing but his old age, how Lady Holland persecuted her guests with her odious cats that were for ever scratching and clawing, how the King was seen somewhere walking with his arm round Canning's neck, how scarcely anyone went now to Lady Jersey's parties, and that the gambling saloon in St James' Street was the most splendid ever known and that young William Lennox and others were certainly being ruined there . . .

These were Jennifer's happiest hours, when lazily sitting before the fire, warming her beautiful hands, she could, without moving, transport herself into a world where indeed she did not wish herself to be, but about whose movements she was never weary of hearing.

Nevertheless, it was to Adam and Judith that Rackstraw was closest. He seemed to understand Judith exactly, submitted to her domination but treated her with a sort of quizzical honesty that she found delightful.

It was Adam, perhaps, whom he really loved, although he never showed him much liking, treated him often with roughness, lost his temper with him completely (and then he would shout and swear like a trooper) and ordered him about when he wished as

though the boy were his slave. He understood, however, the child's passion for independence, and it was he who persuaded Judith to buy him his pony, Benjamin, and never, after one of the boy's disappearances, did he reproach or punish him. It was the rule, as Adam well understood, that if he went off alone he must be always back again by nightfall. He made, himself, many expeditions with the boy. These were the grandest occasions of Adam's life. Rackstraw taught him to see the country rightly. It was a country, he said, of CLOUDS and STONES. Stone walls, grey clouds, stone-coloured seagulls on dark fields like fragments of white stone, streaks of snow in winter thin cloth of stone, and above these stony crags pinnacles of stone, needles of stone, piercing a stony sky. He learnt to see a small imprisoned valley, wind-swept, as a living thing subject to growth and decay like himself. Through this vale twisted the mountain torrent, fighting with stones, letting its life be dominated by these piling stones that heaped themselves one on another, that fell in showers down the hillside, that at length perhaps choke the life of the stream and form a stony pathway that leads at last to new shapes of grass and moss and fern. The clouds feeding the streams, the streams fighting the stones, life moving ceaselessly from form to form, from pattern to pattern.

He learnt that it was impossible to live in this country, loving it, without having always in his heart the colour and shape of clouds. When, later, the drive of his life carried him to the South, he brought the clouds with him: he was never again to be rid of them. He knew all their patterns, forms and vagaries. He knew the clouds that flew in flags and pinions of flame and smoke over the brow of the hill, driven forward as though by gigantic bellows, he knew the moth-coloured clouds that with soft persistence gathered like great boneless birds around the peak of a hill, he knew the clouds of rose and silver that lay in little companies against a sky of jade in winter above sun-drenched snow, he knew the fierce arrogant clouds of jet and indigo that leapt upon a pale sky and swallowed it, he knew the gay troops of cloud that danced and quivered around the sun, he knew the shining clouds that the moon, orange-ringed, gathered round her on a frosty night when the hoar glittered on the grass and the only sound under the black trees was the chatter of the running streams. The clouds were of themselves reason enough why this country was first for him in the world.

But Rackstraw taught him also detail and reality. He learnt to know ash and oak, birch and thorn, holly and hazel. He knew about the cutting of the coppice woods for firewood and for 'spills' and how it was 'coaled', and what was a 'stander' and what a 'yarding', and from what woods houses of 'crucks' were made, and what 'dotard' oaks were. He learnt to know every variety of rain, from the stampede when it comes down like animals rushing a thicket to the murmur and whisper of a hesitating shower. He knew how sudden gusts would come as though someone threw a bucket of water at you, and again how it would be as though you walked down a staircase of rain, catching your breath for a pause, slowing up on the step's very edge while the water trickled under you.

During those five years he went on many rides with Rackstraw, and sometimes they would be away two nights, sometimes three, and once and again a whole week, he on Benjamin, and Rackstraw on his bony ugly horse Satan. He remembered all that he saw. He had in his heart and brain for evermore the Brathay, set in its circumference of meadowland, the view like a crumpled handkerchief from Pike o' Stickle, the cold, haunting loneliness of Black Sail, the glassy perfection of Small Water, the fall of screes from Melbreak, the sudden flight of birds so that the sky seemed darkened at Ravenglass, the long stretch of shore pale and lucent towards Whitehaven, the evil cleft of Simon Nick whose ghost seemed ever to be watching from the thin darkness, the great view from Yewdale to the Old Man, the Roman Fort on Hard Knott, the grand silence of Waswater where the Screes, the proudest of all the hills, plunge scornfully into unknown depths--these and hundreds more were to be his companions for ever.

He knew the dalesmen, their wives, sons, daughters, dogs, horses and cows; he knew the Herdwick sheep as though he were one of them. He knew the birds, the golden eagles, soon to be gone for ever, the osprey, the dull heavy kite, the redshanks and larks, the fishing cormorant. He felt like his own the flight of the peregrine, the black-and-white wheat-ear, and the mocking little cry of the sandpiper as it flitted in front of him along the Lake's edge. The kingfisher and the moorhen spoke to him, one of rushing water, the other of pools so still that the reflection of a cloud on their surface was like a whisper.

And all the singers--the willow-wren, the chiffchaff, the blackcap, the whitethroat, the tree-pipit--he mocked and imitated and whistled to.

From all this life there came three lives--one, the life of the outer country; two, the life of his home, the building of Fell House, the village and the moor; three, the personal life with the human beings around him; and from all the events that occurred to him during those five years three were of particular importance. One, the affair at Watendlath, was the matter of a moment--and it was thus.

In all these five years he went over only on three occasions to Watendlath. This abstention was proof of itself of his love for his mother; it was because of her that he did not go more often, for he loved Watendlath more than any other place on earth. Judith never once told him that she did not wish him to go, but he knew from the first that it made her unhappy. Why, he wondered, would she herself never go? She cared for Charlie Watson and the Ritsons and the Perrys. Once, looking out of window and he standing at her side, after

some trouble that she had had with Mrs Quinney, she burst out: 'Why am I tied here? I am missing my whole life!' and he knew that she was thinking of Watendlath. She never mentioned the place. Once or twice Charlie Watson rode over to Uldale, but his visits were very brief. He seemed constrained, and even to Adam he was sharp and curt.

It was on the third occasion--a week after Adam's ninth birthday-- that the strange thing happened. It was early autumn, the hills were on fire with colour above the grey stone, the dead bracken flamed, and the Tarn, rocked by a little wind, was scattered with tiny feathery waves. Adam and Mr Rackstraw had ridden over and stayed the night with the Ritsons. Charlie Watson never appeared, although the Ritsons said that they had told him that Adam was coming. So it was an unsatisfactory visit, for without Watson Watendlath was only half alive. Moreover, even the Ritsons seemed to be not quite so friendly as they had been. Adam, who was quick for a little boy, fancied that they were offended because his mother had not been to see them, and in arms as he always was if he thought that his mother was attacked, he attempted some sort of defence, but only made things the worse, for Alice Perry smiled and said she knew that Mrs Paris was busy, she had heard that she had much to do: they all called her 'Madame' now, she had heard, a kind of foreign way of calling a person, and, of course, were she busy they could not expect her to come all the way to Watendlath, and so on, and so on. Everyone began to speak of other things.

This made Adam angry and he went down, a rather desolate little figure, in the late afternoon to the Tarn alone. The wind had died; mists were rising. The sky that had been cloudless all day was frosty white, and the amber of the hills was fading into dun. Behind him sheep moved, like a concrete part of the dusk, up the slope. He was cold, lonely and disturbed by a sense of having betrayed his mother in coming here. He wanted to go home: he would rather not stay the night in the farm. The Perry boys, although they had known him since he was a baby, were stiff with him. And where was Charlie Watson? Why had he not ridden over? He wanted to go home.

Standing there, looking at the Tarn, he had the sense for the first time (it was to return to him very often) of being outside himself. He could see every movement that he made and he felt that, if that boy threw himself into the Tarn and disappeared, Adam Paris would still be there, nor would he feel any loss. It went so far that he pinched his arm to see whether he were real. Then he threw stones into the Tarn. The noise of the splash echoed in his ears, but even that was unreal--as though someone else, far from himself and having no relation to himself, had thrown the stones.

It was then that directly in front of him, rising from the Tarn, he saw a figure on a white horse. While he looked the figure grew clearer--a man in odd clothes, a black hat, and under the hat a wig. He wore a long, heavy, purple riding-coat, and down one spare thin cheek ran a deep scar. This man was quite clear to him in every detail to the silver buttons on his coat. He was not looking at Adam but away, gravely, up into the hills. Neither horse nor rider made any movement. They were like coloured shapes painted on the mist. Then they vanished. That was his grandfather, who had lived, years ago, below the hills at Rosthwaite. He had talked of him to his mother so often and had asked so many questions about him that he knew exactly how he would look, and in later days he might realize that it was his own imagination, at that moment of loneliness and longing for his mother, that had conjured up the figure.

But now he was only a small boy who believed in ghosts and pixies, warlocks and witches. So for once in his life he took to his heels and ran and ran until he arrived breathless in the warm and lighted kitchen.

He never told anyone of what he thought he had seen, but that night in bed, listening to the snores of Mr Rackstraw, he was comforted as though he had made a new friend.

The second affair concerned John, and this was one of the most dreadful half-hours of Adam's life, dreadful because he was not at this time old enough to meet the emotion that he encountered. When mature things break in upon childhood a picture is broken, a view destroyed; the picture and view never quite return.

Adam was nearly ten when this thing happened, and John seventeen and a half.

Their friendship had by now grown so close that they were more than brothers. They had the intimacy with that edge of strangeness and interest belonging to a friendship that has no blood relationship.

John had caught and held Adam in the only way that he could catch and hold him--by demanding his protection. He did not consciously demand it: this had grown out of Adam's fearlessness and John's sensitiveness. John was handsome beyond all ordinary standards; he was the best-looking young fellow, it was generally admitted, in the County. He was tall, slender, fair, with a straight carriage and an air of such breeding that when he moved both men and women unconsciously watched him, feeling perhaps that he was of a different strain from the rest of mankind.

When he came into a place he walked haughtily and seemed proud, his head erect, his mouth sternly set, but at once, when he was in contact with another human being, his smile shone out, lighting up his face. His proud carriage sprang from an intolerable shyness that he could never overcome. It was agony to him to meet new people or anyone of whose kindliness he was not sure. At any unfriendliness he flung on instantly an armour of reserve. With the men and women about the place he was in perfect relations; they all loved him and would do anything for him. His beauty seemed to them something rare and wonderful, and when they knew him also to be so gentle and kind they served him without further question. Nevertheless, he was no commander of men; any tale of distress touched him, however false it might be. He believed what he was told, and when he was deceived thought that it was some wrong in himself that had caused the deceit.

It was here that Adam, whom even when he was so young a child he trusted and loved as he trusted and loved none other, protected him. Adam was uncouth and rough beside him. He did not grow more handsome as he grew older. The darkness of his hair, the brown of his face and body, made him seem someone foreign and apart. He wore always the roughest country clothes. He spoke, when he did speak, with a slight Cumberland 'burr', he was often silent when he ought to speak and would look at people with a sort of frown as though he were summing them up. His worst fault was exactly the opposite of John's, namely, that he suspected everyone until he had proved his case.

It became plain to him soon that John was his charge. In spite of the difference of their ages he was already wiser about the world than John and, because he was not sensitive and because hostility only made him hostile in return and because he was afraid of no one, he was a good bodyguard.

Only one thing at this time came between the two of them. A chance meeting brought them into contact with Uhland, Walter's son. Adam had long ago decided that Walter Herries was his enemy and the enemy of all those whom he loved. He was not aware, during these years, of the developing battle between Walter Herries and his mother, but he did know that everything round Westaways was enemy country.

The queer thing was that Uhland, who was Adam's age, never missed an occasion of an encounter with Adam if one were possible. They met but seldom, in the Keswick street, once and again at the Hunt, at a sheep trial, at a running-match: once when Adam was fishing by himself beyond Crosthwaite Church, Uhland, unattended, came limping through the field. He stood looking at Adam, apparently afraid to speak. Adam would have had nothing to do with him, but the boy was lame, his face was pale, he seemed so sickly that it was a wonder he could move at all. So he spoke, and Uhland came and sat beside him. What followed was most uncomfortable, for Uhland sat there, staring out of large protruding eyes, and said nothing.

At last he felt in his jacket and offered Adam a top, a large one coloured green and crimson. Adam did not wish to take it, but Uhland clambered to his feet and went limping away across the field without another word . . .

Now John had from the very first the strangest fear of Uhland. There was something about his deformity and sickliness that affected him as though the boy had a disease that he could convey to others. He saw him on the rarest occasions, but he was often conscious of him, would, in the middle of the night, think of that leg longer than the other, those protruding eyes, the little body that seemed to be bent by a head too big for it.

Once he burst out passionately to Adam and wished him to promise never to speak to Uhland again.

'But I don't speak to him,' said Adam, astonished.

'You meet him. He talked to you in Keswick a fortnight back.'

'He has a horse,' said Adam irrelevantly. 'It is called Caesar. It's coal black with a white star on its forehead.'

'I tell you,' John repeated, 'you are not to talk with him.'

'Why not?' asked Adam.

John could not say. The boy and his father hated them, would do them any harm . . .

But Adam fell into one of his silences. John would not speak to him for days.

Then came this terrible distressing thing.

It came like a door banging on to a silent room. It was in the early summer. Adam had been riding, had shut Benjamin into his box, stroked his nose and talked some nonsense to him, then very happy, whistling out of tune, had wandered into the house. He had a room to himself now, one that he had chosen, an attic with a slanting roof and a fine view over the moor to the slopes of Skiddaw. He and Skiddaw were now on speaking terms, and there was nothing about Skiddaw that Adam didn't know--or so he thought.

He had but just sat down upon his bed and was thinking of the coach that had passed him with a fine tantivy and a grand cloud of dust from the horses' hoofs, thinking perhaps that he would like to see the world a bit, when the door opened and John came in. He stood without moving. He had been paying some visit and was dressed very smartly in a claret-coloured coat, the hips and chest padded, a white frill, his dark chestnut trousers strapped under his boots. Adam remembered then that, urged by Judith, John had been to call on some people with a house on the border of Bassenthwaite Lake. They were called Sanderson and were new arrivals in the neighbourhood.

He stood there, his face pale, his lips quivering. He crossed to the bed, sat down by Adam, then to Adam's horror burst out crying, his head in his hands.

Adam put his arm around him and sat there, not knowing what to do or say. He had never seen John cry before, and that a man should shed tears seemed to him an awful thing.

'What is it? . . . What's the matter, John?' he said at last, his voice a funny broken bass from his emotion. For a long while John, crying desperately, made no answer.

Adam stared out of the window at Skiddaw and watched birds flying slowly, dreamily, across the faint glassy sky.

This is what it is . . .' John caught Adam's hand. 'My mother--' He hesitated, then the words poured out of him. 'I had visited the Sandersons. Young Robert Sanderson was there. He is a friend of Cousin Walter's, and I could not abide him from the first. He was affronted by something I had said in the house about the Catholics in Ireland, that the Catholic laws were monstrous and that we should have shame for our treatment of Ireland . . . He answered hotly, and when I left came out with me to my horse. He sneered at something I said. You know how it is--I hate a quarrel. I answered him gently, and then he said something about the fine man Cousin Walter was, and that by what he had heard Fell House here should be his. That was too much for me and I called Cousin Walter what he is--a damnable blackguard. Then Sanderson told me . . . he said . . . he said it was common knowledge that because my mother had been a man's mistress here and because my father had found them together, therefore my father had killed himself in London. Because my father had been a coward and allowed that man to come to this house, to sleep here . . . he knew of it. The whole world knew . . . I struck Sanderson in the face--and I rode away.'

Telling his story had calmed him. He caught his breath. His face now was as white as a peeled stick, his body trembled, but he wept no longer.

'Everyone knows--has known for years. Only I didn't know . . .'

They were quiet for a long time. Adam's hand tightened on John's. He could not bear to feel John's body tremble. He longed to do anything for him, to rush out and trample on Sanderson, to burn Uncle Walter's house down, to . . . Oh! He knew not what! But he could neither do anything nor say anything. He was not ignorant, young though he was. He knew--in a child's way--about men and women, without feeling that all those things, the making of love, the birth of children, were real in a real world. But he understood that this was a disgraceful and terrible thing. Nevertheless his own active feelings were those of rage against Sanderson and a passionate instinct to defend John.

He said at last in a husky voice:

'I expect he's a liar. They are all liars, friends of Uncle Walter's.'

'No--it's true . . . I have known for a long while that mother was afraid, afraid of everything, of Cousin Walter and people in Keswick--and that my father had shot himself in London, but this . . .'

Then he added, still shivering as though with an intense cold:

'I must fight Sanderson.'

'Yes, you must kill him,' Adam answered eagerly. Here was something that he could do. 'Mr Rackstraw shall help us.'

'Cousin Walter put him on to this: I know he did. Everything we do, everywhere we go, Walter Herries is at our back. Oh, God, if I could do him an injury for all he's done to us! And now I know. I know why he has so much power over us, why my mother fears him as she does . . . My father was a coward, my mother . . .'

He stopped.

'Adam, you must speak of this to no one. We will settle Sanderson's affair ourselves. But that everyone should know, that they have known for years . . .'

Adam said, nodding his head:

'If it's pistols, John, you can kill him. Mr Rackstraw says you're the best shot with a pistol for your age in Cumberland. We'll practise in the barn. We'll go now . . .'

But nothing came of it then. They learnt that young Sanderson had gone South. He never answered John's letter, and later, joining his regiment, went abroad. The consequences were not so easily settled. After that summer afternoon nothing was the same again.

Adam's third affair concerned his mother.

As those years passed, Judith dominated Fell House and its neighbourhood ever more completely.

When Adam was eleven, in 1826, Judith was nearly fifty-two. Now fifty-two was considered in those days a great age for a woman. There were old women like Mrs Tennant of Ireby who were old women, sat in a chair and had the air of prophetesses. There were old women like Mrs Summerson in Keswick who played cards night and day but were nevertheless old women. There were old women like Mrs Clare of Portinscale who rode to hounds, cursed and swore, drank and gambled, chaffed with the stable-boys, but were still old women. Judith Paris was unique. After settling in command at Fell House she seemed with every month to grow younger. Her body, taut, neat, active, appeared not to know fatigue. Her hair, once so lovely an auburn, was now grey, her face, always pale in colour (and she would use no paint as most of the older women did), knew no wrinkle. She rode a horse like a commander. She was austere and direct when about her business, but she could behave suddenly like a girl. She went to dances, card-parties, hunts, balls in Keswick. She was known everywhere as 'Madame,' famous for her kindness, her sharp and direct speech, her common sense. She had not changed in her impulsiveness, her attention to business, her loyalty, her childish pleasure in little things. Only those who knew her well were aware that something she had had was now, to all appearance, gone. It might be dead, it might be hidden. Miss Pennyfeather in Keswick knew, Jennifer unperceptively was aware . . . Jennifer said that Judith was no longer romantic.

Another thing that everyone knew about her was that she was 'mad' about her boy. Of course the boy was illegitimate, although everyone could name his father, but his illegitimacy and the fact that Judith herself was the daughter of old 'Rogue' Herries (now a legend: they said that his ghost 'walked' in Borrowdale) and a gipsy, made the mother and son something apart. 'Madame' was becoming a legend like her father. Every kind of tale was told of her. When she came into a room people stared and whispered. But they invited her, they admired her; she was a 'character' and did the neighbourhood a sort of credit.

We are in part what our friends and neighbours make us and, unconsciously, Judith began at this time to respond to the demand for her to be 'queer'. Her dress was a little extravagant. Her skirts were very full in the Dutch fashion. She liked gay colours and was often seen in a shawl of red cashmere. She had hats of fine straw worn over a lace cap--far too young for another of her age, but in some way not ridiculous for her. Her turbans of figured gauze at an evening party were magnificent. She already carried the cane of white ivory that was, later, to be so famous. People in Keswick said, 'Madame is coming,' and gathered at shop doors and windows to look.

She ruled everyone in Fell House save her son Adam. It was at the beginning of his twelfth year that she put her power over him to the test and failed. This occasion was one of the great crises that marked his boyhood.

No one knew with what passionate emotion she loved this child. Everything else that was dear to her she had surrendered--save her love of power and her love of son. As he grew her feeling for him developed into a mingling of love, admiration and exasperation. She had always wished for him to be independent and apart from other boys. His father, poor Warren, had had but too little character. Adam seemed to have no resemblance at all to his father; he was his mother and then himself as well. He reminded her continually of what she had been as a child, and it was a curious irony that she should so often feel the same bewilderment and irritation in dealing with him felt long ago by David and Sarah Herries about herself. She learnt, very soon in their relationship, that he hated any kind of demonstration. Did he love her or did he not? She knew that he did, and with all his heart, but any expression of affection silenced and removed him. But he MUST obey her. When she had surrendered her domination of his movements (no one knew what this cost her) she consoled herself with the right to order him in all other ways.

The exercise of power grows with what it feeds on. People succumbed to her so easily that she came to expect it as her right. Adam always obeyed her when he felt that her demand was just. She had one thing more to learn--that, if he thought her unjust, he was quite beyond her power.

The incident had minute beginnings. One fine morning she had driven with Adam in the chaise to Keswick. Mr Carrick the haberdasher came on to the pavement to receive her orders, and after he was gone, before she could move forward, tiresome old Major Bellenden must limp forward and, his wide-brimmed hat gallantly in hand (although the day was cold), commence one of his interminable conversations. Major Bellenden, who lived alone on the road to Threlkeld, was a purple-faced old bachelor, tyrannized over by a peevish manservant. He had served abroad, knew the East, had had an amusing adventure or two, but all these were swallowed up by the fact that he had been actually present at the famous performance on February 13th, 1820, at the Paris Opera of Le Carnaval de Venise when the Duc de Berry had been assassinated. Nay, more, he had by a lucky chance left the Opera for a moment and returned at the very instant when Louvel planted his dagger 'up to the hilt', had heard the Duke cry 'What a ruffian!' and then 'I have been murdered!' Later, he had listened to the screams of pain that came from the poor Duke as Dupuytren probed the wound, had seen Decazes enter to examine the murderer, and best of all had even been witness of Louis XVIII himself as, tossed about between the banisters of the stairs and the wall, they had tried to push his chair that he might get to the Duke. He told over and over again how the Duke, dying, raised himself and said: 'Forgive me, dear Uncle, forgive me'; and Louis answered: 'There is no hurry, dear Nephew. We will talk later about this.' And then how, at the very last, when the Duchess was filling the room with her lamentations, the Duke said: 'My dearest, control yourself for the sake of our child,' and so gave France the first news that there would be an heir to the Bourbons . . .

So often had the Major told this very long story with all the details of it exactly repeated, that the Duc de Berry's assassination seemed to many persons to have occurred in Keswick. However, 'The Old Bore and his Murder' was the general summary of Major Bellenden.

It chanced that on this very morning the Major mentioned his Duke. Some remark of Judith's about the weather reminded him. 'It was weather like this . . . that horrid affair of the Duc de Berry, of which I expect I have told you . . .', and looking up caught young Adam smiling at him in a very irritating manner. Adam had heard his mother in her lighter moments, imitating the Major: 'I had my foot on the stair . . . Louvel must have brushed my arm . . .' and giving then the very half-choked, half-important guffaw that was the Major's.

Adam smiled, and the Major saw him smiling. His mother also saw him. The Major was deeply hurt and went limping away.

During the drive homewards Judith scolded him, speaking of reverence to age, of impertinence and other kindred matters.

'But, Mama, you yourself laughed . . .'

'Not to his face. That is bad manners.'

'I am sorry, Mama. Look, there is Mr Southey with--'

'Now listen, Adam. You are to listen. You must apologize to the Major.'

Adam sat grimly silent. Of all things in the world he hated most to apologize. The matter might on an ordinary day have stopped there, but Judith had been irritated by a number of small things, by the failure of Miss Pritchett, the little dressmaker whom she patronized, to have a dress ready; by Mrs Quinney's cold; by the customary sluggishness of Jennifer.

So she pursued it.

'Promise me, then, that you will apologize.'

Adam said nothing. He sat there, his mouth pursed in an exasperating manner.

'Promise me that you will apologize.'

At last he murmured:

'It is unfair, Mama. You yourself laugh at him.'

'That is different. He was not present.'

Then again, as the chaise drew slowly up the hill to the village:

'Say that you will apologize.'

No answer.

'Well, then, I must punish you.'

Adam was enclosed in his attic for the rest of the day without food.

In the evening Judith came in to him, her head held high, her heart aching with love. She had been quite wretched all the afternoon. She had realized with a pain that was deeper than any emotion felt by her for many days that without Adam there was nothing. All this business of defying Walter, of managing the house, the servants, Jennifer, of corresponding with various Herries all over the country, of visiting and dining and being sociable--it was all nothing, nothing at all without Adam. She had loved her husband, she loved Adam. There was nothing else. And with a sudden shudder, as though a hateful wrinkled hag in a bonnet had bowed to her in the glass, she saw her old age, of which until now she had scarcely thought--her old age, empty, ugly and cruel.

She came into his room and found him standing looking out of the window, just as, centuries ago, she had stood at her window when David was to beat her. He did not turn. She put her hand on his shoulder. She was, not by much, taller than he, but when he turned her heart leapt, for he was so lovely to her, so utterly her own, so proud and so strong, just as she would have him be.

But he was relentless--and he was utterly beyond her reach. She said something. She asked him to come downstairs. No, he would not come down. Did he not see that he was wrong, that he had hurt the feelings of an old man, that it was proper to offer an apology when one had shown bad manners?

'I did not show bad manners,' Adam said, not looking at her.

She did not know it, but he himself was terrified--terrified at this resentment that he felt to her, his rebellion as though he were fighting for something very serious and important. He had never felt like this to her before. He almost hated her.

'Well, then, you will see it later on. You will see that I am right. Come down now and we will not speak of it.'

But it could not be settled in that way. His dreadful silence which he himself hated dominated him. She put her arm around his neck.

'Come, Adam.'

He dragged himself away from her and went back to the window, looking out. That infuriated her and she surrendered to one of her old tempests of passion. She stormed and stamped her feet. He was ungrateful, hard, unloving, disobedient. She had done everything for him, and thus he repaid her. Well, he should see. She was not to be insulted by a child. He should be beaten. Maybe that would teach him . . .

'Beat me,' he said, turning round upon her.

They looked at one another, each with hatred. The look was so terrible, so new, so far from anything that either of them had thought possible, that in another moment they would have been in one another's arms.

But she did nothing, said nothing, and after a moment left the room.

When she had gone he sat, swinging his legs, the unhappiest boy in the United Kingdom.

THE SUMMER FAIR

The scarlet cloak of Oberon cast hastily on the daisied sward of the meadow, the laughter of the fairies as they fled towards the wood, the young men as they waited by the church gate, straining forward, listening for the word to go, the strange orange turban of Miss Pennyfeather, the breaking lights of violet and crimson as the fireworks burst above the Lake, the clown standing on his head in the market-place, his calves brown as berries against the sunlight, the line of chaises, barouches, waggons, the gauze and linen of the coloured dresses shining as the ladies leant forward from their carriages to watch the runners pass, the roseate haze on Skiddaw as the reflection of the setting sun threw great lines of colour across the crowded meadow, the peal of the bells from Crosthwaite Church, the gipsies with gaudy rings, crimson kerchiefs, white teeth flashing as they told fortunes in their encampment below the wood, Titania tearing her frail petticoat as she climbed the cart to ride through the town, the riot of men and women after dusk under the stars when a kind of madness

seized the place, sunlight, bells, babel of voices, scents of flowers, neighing of horses, the plashing of oars upon the water, the stars and the flare of torches-- for days and months and years the smoking shadow of this life was to hang about Keswick.

It was in August of 1827 that the famous Summer Fair came, blazed, vanished. For years afterwards it was remembered; for years now it has been as though it never was. And yet the town had known nothing like it before unless it were the famous Chinese Fair of nearly a century earlier. There is no record of it. Search contemporary journals and you will find nothing. For it came, it went, as many of the finest things in life come and go, by accident; it is only a background to the history of certain private lives; a handkerchief was dropped, a horse stumbled, a word was spoken. In a week the meadow was itself again, the waters of the Lake were calm, the gipsies were in Carlisle, the booths were piled boards, the bell-ringers were practising for another ceremony, the Strolling Players were drinking in a Kendal inn.

Nevertheless, there was never anything like it again. Chance, Mrs Bonaventure, sunshine, the accidental passing of the gipsies and the Players, stars and a full moon made this thing.

Mrs Bonaventure had come to Keswick six months before. She was a large stout lady with a red face, a roaring voice, and a wealthy husband almost as large as herself. They were a jolly pair, vulgar, if you like, with their loud voices and carelessness of social divisions, but it was known that she was the daughter of a Lancashire baronet, so, as Mrs Osmaston said, 'You can be sure she can speak quietly when she wishes,' and they were generous, crazy for parties and picnics and dances, and thought there was no place in the world like Keswick . . .

It was she who first had the notion of a Fête. It was in some way to be connected with the hand-loom weaving, and in some way with the birth of a baby boy to her sister who lived in Rutlandshire, and in some way with the Duke of Wellington, and in some way with a prize that Mr Bonaventure was giving for a race for young men under twenty-five, a race from Crosthwaite Church to the Druids' Circle.

In any case, there must be a Fête.

There should be booths along Main Street with gingerbread and apples and toffee. There should be dancing in the moonlight. There should be no nasty sports like bull-baiting or cock-fighting. There should be decorated boats on the Lake, and fireworks. She did not know that some Strolling Players chanced to be performing in Penrith. She did not know about the gipsies. All these delights were added unto her.

Suppose that old Herries, remembering as he must that Chinese Fair, when in an eating booth he had sold his lady for a few pieces of silver, were present, perched cross-legged on a chimney, standing upright against a tree top, what would he think of it all? A hundred years gone (but time is of course nothing to him now), and yet here was his daughter, like a little general, marshalling her family forces, and here his great-grandson Walter commanding HIS battalions, and behind them, around them, all the lively consequences, male and female, of that wild turbulent life by which HE had once been surrounded! Yes, wild and turbulent that Chinese Fair had been, civilized and gentle THIS Fair must seem to him--but the same battle was joined now as then, and so will be, for ever and ever, change the background as you may, for ever and ever, amen!

As his long sardonic person wanders now skywards, now mingling unseen with the crowd, now peering sardonically from behind the chimneypot, he watches that same daughter with tenderness maybe, and young John and Adam and Elizabeth with concern, and great- grandson Walter with humorous sarcasm, watches and grimly smiles and vanishes into a star, wondering why they should all be so serious over a matter so brief and trivial.

For the rest, how are they, in reminiscence, to break that confusing fantastic day into some sort of shape and order: morning, afternoon, evening and the moonlight night?--or, better than that, they divide it by event--the boats on the Lake, the race through the town, the Midsummer Night's Dream, the dancing on the meadow-- four cantos of a happy poem.

THE BOATS ON THE LAKE

By eight of the morning the booths were lining Main Street, the children were dancing like mad things down the road, the sun was blazing (for they had all the luck that day) and boats were putting out from the Islands, from Manesty, from Lodore, from Grange. By ten o'clock the carriages were rolling up, from Penrith and Ullswater and Newlands and Bassenthwaite, from Carlisle even, from Grasmere and Rydal, from Shap and Hawkshead. Very early in the morning for some of them the horses must have been led from their stables and the coaches loaded. Many came in pillion-riding as for hundreds of years they had done, while the grander farmers were proud in the 'shandy-carts'. Keswick, although Crosthwaite Church had not yet begun its peal, was ringing with bells, for teams of pack-horses, used for the carrying of pieces from the hand-loom weaving, came jingling in. Many of the women who were spreading their apples, nuts, cakes and bottles of herb beer on the trestles had been many a time to Hell Gill Bridge for the Brough Hill Fair, and with that same jingling of bells came the scents and sounds from Shaw Paddock and Aisgill and the old Thrang Bridge in Mallerstang.

But it was down by the Lake that the day was to begin. The sun lay on the water like a caressing hand, and the hills, from Walla Crag, from the Borrowdale peaks, from Cat Bells and Robinson, reflected their colour and proud forms as though they had another life beneath their glassy waters.

Mrs Bonaventure, attended by husband and friends, was soon seated like a queen on the commanding perch of Friar's Crag. She loved fine colours. She wore a hat as broad nearly as her shoulders, and from it waved four large ostrich feathers. Her dress, magnificently full, was a brilliant orange.

Very soon the borders of the Lake were thronged with figures, and the water whispered with the soft splash of oars. Across the meadows and trees suddenly broke out the bells from Crosthwaite, and from the landing-stage the blast of the Town Band. A gun was fired from the Island. The Fête was begun.

It was just before midday, when every eye was straining to see the first boat round the corner of the Island, that the party from Westaways arrived. Walter himself drove his coach from the house to the end of the Lake Road, and as his four horses galloped up Main Street everyone cheered and the little boys turned cartwheels and the pigeons flew in exulting circles above their heads.

Walter was elegant indeed as he flourished his whip decorated with coloured streamers, his many-caped riding-coat of green high above his thick neck, his chest thrust out, his head up as though to say: 'You may claim this or that for your glory today, but here is the true centre of the affair!' He had in the coach with him his wife, his children and his relations. It was a piece of fortune that these relations were present to witness his splendour, for it was only chance that the young sons of Durward Herries were passing through from Edinburgh and that James Herries (at length, after many years of weary waiting, succeeding to his old father's baronetcy) had come over from York.

But there they were: the two boys with two Oxford undergraduate friends from a house near Carlisle, and Sir James Herries, Bart., puffed out with solemn pride and complacent satisfaction. Agnes was there too, and also Uhland and Elizabeth.

After leaving the coach they walked, a cluster of splendour, to the Lake's edge.

No one could be more genial with all the world than Walter when things went as they ought to. He had left his riding-coat in Posset's care, for the day would be hot, and now at the age of thirty-five his great frame was beginning to yield at last to the stoutness that it had so long resisted. His high hat with the broad brim, rough in texture, was a dark wine-colour; his claret- coloured coat, the tails sewn on separately that it might fit his sides the better, followed the lines of his body exactly. His neckcloth was shaped at the sides and stiffened with pig's bristles, rising to a kind of arch at the cheeks, and at its centre was the accustomed jewelled pin. He wore two waistcoats, one of dark purple, the other dark grey; his trousers, tight at the knees, widening downwards, were fawn. This must have been a warm costume for the middle of summer, but the stuff was all of a light material, and it was only at the neck as the day advanced that he was uncomfortable--which may possibly have accounted for his excitement at the end of the day: by such slender threads do human actions hang!

With his clothes, his bulk, his carriage, his merry arrogance, his vitality and bonhomie, he was by far the most remarkable figure on that day. Men said afterwards that to them this appeared the turning-point of his life--his last public appearance before the beginning of the Fortress!

He stationed himself with his wife, children and friends--a kind of resplendent patriarch--on a little green mound whence he could watch, above the vulgar crowd, the procession of the boats.

Scarcely, however, had the first two boats rounded the corner of the Island before the party from Fell House arrived--'Madame', Mrs Jennifer Herries, Adam, John and Dorothy, with Mr Rackstraw in the background.

They had come almost to the water-edge before they realized that Walter Herries and his company were stationed above them. The people of Keswick could not be ignorant of the family warfare, had indeed for many years now been aware of it. The most fantastic stories were abroad: that Walter Herries had put poisoned wine in the Fell House cellar, that he had hired ruffians from Whitehaven to kidnap young John, that 'Madame' herself in the dead of night had climbed in at a Westaways window armed with a carving-knife--no tale was too absurd. Even though the procession of boats had begun, everyone watched to see what 'Madame' would do. But 'Madame', after a moment's glance, did nothing at all. Her Leghorn hat, trimmed with dahlias and ears of corn, her muslin dress of lilac, should have seemed ridiculous in a woman of her years. But she was not ridiculous, rather wonderfully imposing, her little figure neat and strong, her hand resting on her ivory cane, her head raised as though she ruled the world. Jennifer Herries, in a white muslin, towered above her, but was less impressive. Everyone said how handsome John Herries was, that Dorothy Herries had a fresh complexion, and that Madame's boy looked very French--the same comments were always made.

If Walter had noticed Judith, he gave no sign of it. So there they all were to watch the procession. Round the bend came the boats, the first four with twelve oars apiece. They were all decorated with flowers, and in three of the boats girls in white sang to the accompaniment of harps. The oarsmen were in white with crimson sashes at the waist. The sixth boat was a barge, and in it seated on a throne was the Guardian of the Lake. He was a stout old gentleman (Mr Barleycorn the hosier, in fact) with neck bare, garlanded, his fat legs bare to above the knees, and he carried a trident, thereby causing many of the spectators to suppose him Neptune.

In the boat that followed him was enthroned the Queen of the Lake with attendant maidens. This, as everyone knew, was Mrs Armstrong who kept the sweet-shop just below Greta Hall. She was a commanding woman, full-breasted, and even on quite ordinary occasions, when selling a stick of liquorice to a small boy, stiff with dignity. It was because of her dignity that she had been chosen for this office.

In the boats that followed some licence of costume had been permitted: there were sailors, pirates, clowns, village maidens and Columbines. At the last there were small children carrying bouquets of flowers and watching with uneasy glances lest at any moment they should be precipitated into the water.

Oh, but it was a GRAND procession. The sun gave them his glory, the mountains wished them well, the church bells rang and the Town Band blared, the voices sang, and through it all the plash, plash of the oars gave rhythm and movement to the pattern of flowers and water and shadowed reflection.

They swept in a great circle, then drew up in line before the shore. The Guardian of the Lake rose a little unsteadily in his throne and delivered an address, not a single word of which could be heard by anyone. Then planks were thrown from boat to boat, and the goddess (Mrs Armstrong), 'every movement a symphony,' walked most majestically if uncertainly to the land, followed by her maidens, then by the little children, and last by the shouting rabble of sailors, clowns and Columbines.

Everyone now was shouting, everyone was singing; everyone rushed in unison together up to the field behind, where Mrs Bonaventure was to receive the King and Queen.

'Very pretty,' said Judith. 'Very pretty indeed.'

'Very handsome,' said Walter Herries, coming from his green mound. He took off his wine-coloured hat and bowed.

'Good day, Walter,' said Judith, looking him steadily in the face.

He smiled and seemed a boy of eighteen.

'I hope you are well,' he said.

'Never felt better,' answered Judith.

'We have a fine day.'

'An excellent day.'

Sir James bowed. Judith inclined her head. Walter's party moved on.

Young Garth Herries asked a question.

'That, my boy,' answered Walter, 'is a relation of yours--and the most remarkable woman in England.'

THE RACE THROUGH THE TOWN

PART I

As everyone knows, the men and women of the North Country have never believed in the display of their emotions unless there is good ground for it. They prefer to wait and see what is really occurring before they venture an opinion. When they say a thing they mean it, but they mean a great many things that they never say.

The more extraordinary, then, was the outburst of singing and joy as the flowery boats circled the shore. It was a spontaneous cry as though some especial genial deity were abroad that day who, wishing for a song and laughter, saw that it was so. (In parenthesis: there had been up to this midday very little drinking. That came after.)

Adam found himself with his mother, Dorothy and John perched on a mound outside the churchyard wall, waiting with a great crowd of other spectators for the race to begin. He was, if he had cared to think of it, possibly the happiest boy in England that day. This was what he loved--the sun, the crowds, his own familiar country, every kind of sport and, as instinctively he knew, his mother as happy as he was.

In spite of the difference in their ages, mother and son were just now children together. This too was what Judith loved. She had a child's passion for small things, she adored to see other people happy. Adam's hand was in hers, and she had enjoyed her moment's challenge with Walter. There was no sign anywhere of the Westaways party, and she was quite certainly just then monarch of all she surveyed. Because she was so small of stature she stood once and again on tiptoe so that she might miss nothing. Nearly everyone around her knew who she was, and if anyone didn't he was certain to inquire; you couldn't catch a glimpse of her and not be conscious of her personality. But they were all proud of her, although they didn't quite know why. Farmers and their wives, townsmen and statesmen and better-class smiled, nodded, said it was a fine day, and she smiled and nodded back at all of them.

Adam, as was customary with him, said little but noticed everything. Dorothy stayed close beside her mother. At that time young ladies stayed as close to their mothers as though they were glued to them lest something evil should occur to them. John, very handsome in his plum-coloured coat, was apart, as he so often seemed to be. He was enjoying himself, but quietly and with that slight nervous social tremor that never quite left him when he went abroad. He did not know that within half an hour the greatest event of his life was to occur.

Across the road were lined the runners, twelve of them. They wore thin shirts open at the neck and short drawers. They were young, strong, tanned most of them by their outdoor labour. The two favourites were John Graham of Threlkeld, a tall, stringy young man with a head shaped like a hammer; and Will Leathwaite of Grange, who was short, thick and simple-eyed like a baby. Two of the men, Tom Trimble from St John's in the Vale and Harry Pender of Keswick, were famous runners but were older than the others. Trimble was a giant and as broad as he was tall. His legs and arms were hairy and his chest hirsute beneath his shirt. Good nature beamed from him and he looked round him smiling on everyone, although his brow was wrinkled with his serious purpose. He towered above the others. Pender was thin and cadaverous. He was an ill-tempered man and hated to be beaten. Mrs Pender in the hedge near at hand waited with anxiety, for she knew that were he defeated he would be none too pleasant a companion that evening. Trimble's mother, an old rosy-faced woman with a basket on her arm, kept calling out to her son to encourage him, and he would look across the road and smile at her and shout: 'Aye, mother, I'll do my best.'

Old Major Bellenden had been appointed starter, and very self-important he was. At the stroke of the half-hour from Crosthwaite Church clock he would shout 'One. Two. Three,' wave the handkerchief, and off they would go.

Adam's hopes were resting on Will Leathwaite, the thick simple-faced young man. He knew Will a little, for Will's father was a friend of Bennett the coachman, and Will would on occasion ride over from Grange or drive with a calf or farm produce. Will was Adam's kind of a man because he spoke little, was good-natured and afraid of nothing.

Then, just as all eyes were staring at the clock--it wanted but two minutes to the half-hour--up the road came Walter and his friends. They were hastening along, laughing and talking, making a great deal of display. Walter strode in front; his wife, children and the two young men followed. Room was made for them behind the Major, who began hurriedly explaining to Walter Herries a number of things, very important things, involved in his official business.

And it was then that something happened to John. He saw, as though for the first time, Elizabeth, Walter's young daughter.

It was not, of course, for the first time. He had seen her on several other occasions, but he had never spoken to her, and never considered her at all. Now her loveliness rose at him from the crowd, the cries, the fields and road as Venus rises (constantly, we may believe) from the sea.

Elizabeth Herries was at this time only twelve, but she was tall for her years. Her fair colouring, her air of shyness, her slim erect body, above all her quietness, enchanted John. But he could give no reasons for that sudden thundering of his heart, that queer sense of being urged by some force around him, the very air about him, to run forward, to touch her hand . . . He had seen her before and she had meant nothing to him. He could not understand it. It was an enchantment, a magical turning of flowers and hedge, dusty road and churchyard wall into shining glass, feathered clouds and raining gold. To run, to touch her hand, to speak . . .

Then, as though he had wheeled upwards on a rising sphere from sunlit underworlds, he caught his own state again, heard the voices, saw the lilac stuff of Aunt Judith's dress. Walter Herries' daughter! He raised his head and stared at the sun.

The clock struck, the handkerchief was waved, they were off! And Adam was off too. A moment before he had been holding his mother's hand, as docile a boy as you could find. She thought that she had him for the rest of the day. But he was gone before he knew that he was going. As the white figures flashed like birds towards the town, he, driven by an impulse entirely irresistible, was after them. His mother, his amiable placidity, were lost as though they had never been. Others were running too; there were shouts and cries, and then suddenly he was aware of a known voice and there was Farmer Leathwaite, father of Will, trotting on his black horse beside him.

'Hup! Hup!' Farmer Leathwaite cried, and a moment later had Adam in his arms, then held tightly in front of him. That was a glorious ride! Leathwaite had completely lost his Cumbrian caution. As the horse trotted on, from Leathwaite's big stomach into the very pit of Adam's back came continual cries, adjurations, shouts and cheers: 'That's it, Will, my lad! Keep goin'! Keep goin'! Not so fast through t'town . . . Gently, gently, my boy. You'll beat 'em! You'll beat lot of 'em . . . Keep joggin' . . . That's the fancy! Go to it, my lad! Fine lad! Fine lad! Gently, gently! . . .'

And Adam was caught by the same fever, crying in a cracked voice: 'Go it, Will! Keep going, Will! Hurray! . . . You're winning! . . .'

But the gallant horse was also stirred by the splendour of the event and, do what the farmer would, refused to be stayed, so before they knew it they had galloped up Main Street, horses and shops, booths, women, dogs and shouting boys all left behind.

'Woh! Wey! Wey! Woh!' cried Leathwaite, trying to look back and see how his son was faring, but the mare with her ears pricked back was racing all the other mares in the world, and before they knew it they were out of the town and climbing the hill.

With shouts and curses the horse was at last pulled up. Small groups were gathered about the path. Leathwaite mopped his brow with a large yellow handkerchief.

'Do you think Will is going to win?' asked Adam breathlessly.

'Can't say . . .' Leathwaite panted. 'He's in grand condition . . . Hope so . . . Hope so . . . They'll be coming shortly . . .'

It was very quiet here. After the dust, heat, shouts and cries it was as though a heavy door had closed on the world. The trees were darkly thick above their heads, the hills like blue clouds beyond the town.

'How's he doing?' someone called from the waiting group.

'A' reet . . . a' reet,' Leathwaite shouted back.

'I think he'll win, don't you?' Adam said.

Oh, but he HAD to win! The whole of the world's happiness depended upon it. Then, after what had seemed an infinity of time, the white figures appeared, two in front neck and neck, then three, then at a considerable distance four or five. They were going more slowly now; the hill was telling on them, and they had the hardest task yet before them.

The first two were Trimble and a lad called Sawston. Trimble's big body was almost done. The sweat poured down his face, his breast was half bare, and on his face there was a set mechanical smile. But Will was in the next three and running strong . . . With him were John Graham and Pender. Leathwaite rose on his horse and waving his arms roared encouragement. Adam shouted too.

'Go on, Will . . . Go on, Will . . . You'll win! You'll win!'

He was one with Will then. He and Will were running together. He was inside Will, knew all his thoughts, his determination, his measuring of the hill beside him, his calculation of his strength, knew the maddening irritation of Trimble's great back in front of him, the temptation to make the spurt before it was time.

Now the horse went with them, and up the hill Adam and father and son charged together.

Trimble was giving way. Young Sawston passed him. Graham and Will drew level with him. Now Graham and Sawston were neck and neck. Here began the real steepness of the hill. The sun blazed down, the trees had drawn back as though refusing shelter.

'Now, Will, my lad! Now!' shouted his father.

'NOW, WILL, NOW!' screamed Adam.

Sawston, Graham and Will were together. Graham, his head more than ever like a hammer, was running well. He was fresh as a skylark and breasted the hill as though he loved it. Sawston seemed on a sudden to lose heart; he looked back, missed his stride. Will passed him. At the hill-top where the path ran level to the Circle, Graham and Will were ahead.

THEN, thrust on, it may be, by his father's fierce energy, Will Leathwaite made his spurt. He was ahead; Graham caught him. Graham was ahead. Will was level.

The Circle, calm, dignified, gazed indifferently out to Helvellyn and Scawfell and the Gavel. Will threw up his head; he seemed to catch all that country into his heart and, fiercely, like a swimmer fronting a terrific wave, flung himself across the string, the winner by a head.

Adam tumbled off the horse. Leathwaite, shouting his joy, caught Adam's small hand and wrung it as though he had never seen him before.

THE 'MIDSUMMER NIGHT'S DREAM'

PART I

The play was to begin at four o'clock. A platform had been erected on the rising shoulder of the fields where now St John's spire raises its finger for the friendly communion of the clustering hills. Up the slope climbed the meadows, striding to woods and sky. To the left the town, below them the Lake now richly dark under this sun with a sheen like the gloss on a blackberry; on benches raised roughly in four tiers sat the Quality. Beneath them and on either side of them crowded the citizens of England, for, although at this very moment of four o'clock of a fine afternoon in August 1827, all the Keswickians might be said to have been hovering before landing in a new world--a world of light, grime, noise, motion and confusion--yet the decencies were to be observed for a long time yet. Man still doffed his cap to Master, heads of families WERE heads of families, a mile was a mile when you had to walk it, and amusements were still simple enough and rare enough to be amusements. The little town, above whose roofs there hung a violet haze, shared in the happiness of its inhabitants as even to this day it yet does. From the days when the monks of Fountains were permitted a mill-dam on the Greta, through the stages of a weekly market in the thirteenth century over the old bridge at Portinscale, past the dark slumbering church of Crosthwaite, from the thirty citizens of Keswick in 1303, it had had its strong identity and kept it. Spirit and body were from the first lusty and self-confident. St Herbert saw to the first, the weekly market saw to the second. Through the wars of Scots and English, when Threlkeld and Millbeck must be fortified, when beacons flamed on Skiddaw, through the German invasion in Elizabeth's time until in middle seventeenth century the last smelting-house fell into ruin, comforted by the bleating of its sheep, the lowing of its cattle, resisting the constant rising of the waters that threatened to overwhelm it, Keswick stayed compact, pastoral and proud.

Then came Mr Gray riding in his post-chaise, then came the poets, and the world outside discovered it. Nevertheless, neither then nor now has that outside world even scratched the lustre of its peculiar beauty. Now it was not minerals that the invaders demanded, but scenery, so scenery Keswick would give them. Let them come and take it, for they could not diminish by a leaf, a flower or a swollen silver stream the soul of the place itself. At first wool, then shoes, then pencils, then Conventions--Keswick with an agreeable smile was generous, and could afford to be, because its soul was, and must be, intact.

But it liked best its own affairs, the fun that it had made itself for its own people, and so today it was especially happy and its chimneys purred with pleasure. There was an air of casual enjoyment about everything, and most especially about the play of Mr Shakespeare's. You would not perhaps have recognized it for Mr

Shakespeare's play if you had seen it, for that was the time when actors did what they pleased to the plays that had the honour to offer them performances, and to none more than to Mr Shakespeare's.

These Players were here entirely by chance. They had been in the town from Penrith for several days, so that Mr William Greene--the chief of them--a gentleman as round as Falstaff and as jolly too, was by now almost a friend, and there was his wife, Mrs Greene, a tall lady with a deep bass voice, and his daughter Isabella, but these were known as friends always ready for a drink and none too certain about the paying for their charges.

Rain would have ruined everything, but rain for once was far, far away. It seemed, as you looked out across the purple Lake to that stainless sky, that it would never rain again.

The Quality, sitting most contently on the hard boards (for the Quality was easily pleased if there was any kind of fun toward), shared in the general cheer. Among the Keswickians there was considerable anxiety (although a happy anxiety), for a number of the Keswick children had been called in to be fairies, and no one knew how they would behave or what they would do--the children least of all--for there had been but one rehearsal, when the confusion had been so great that the final orders simply were 'to keep their eye on Titania and Oberon and follow them around'.

While they waited, the superior people held distinguished conversation together. There was not a great deal of room. Walter was pressed against James Herries, and his stout knees pushed into the thin backs of Misses Mary and Grace Pendexter, two maiden ladies who were ready to enjoy anything at any time and at any sacrifice. Evening after evening they would be out in their pattens, their old servant lighting them with a lantern, to play cards with Miss Pennyfeather or Major Bellenden, and now to have the handsome knees of the master of Westaways pressing their bones was a joy indeed. It happened, so close were they all together, that Westaways and Fell House were at last neighbours. It was as though the whole day had been working for this end, and, indeed, important consequences were to come of it. For John was near to Elizabeth Herries. When he saw how close he was to her, none of his customary shyness or caution could restrain him. In her primrose gown, sitting beside her mother, not speaking but her lips a little parted at her enjoyment of the scene, she seemed to him like a lovely bird from some Paradisal forest. It was arranged for him by some especial destiny that he should be near her. He knew that her mother, Mrs Herries, was a gentle lady who would wish him no harm. Her father, laughing and slapping his knee, was at a distance. Only one thing prevented him--Uhland, her brother, who sat staring in front of him, his brow wrinkled, his eyes like little stones, one knee--as always--crooked over the other. As always, John was affected by a sort of cold nausea at his proximity, but today this new emotion of joy and happiness, as though like a

407

great explorer, from the deck of his ship, over the track-less waste, he had seen the gold sands gleaming, was too strong for him to be checked.

If he moved a little from where he was sitting he would almost touch her. He rose up, stood back as though not to prevent the others' view, then raising his hat said:

'Good afternoon, Mrs Herries.'

She must have been greatly astonished that he should speak to her, but she, poor lady, bore no animosity to anyone in the world and was delighted at kindliness, so she smiled timidly and said:

'Good afternoon.' ('What a splendidly handsome boy,' she thought.)

John's eyes (he could not help himself) were fastened on Elizabeth, but he said:

'Yes, ma'am. We are fortunate in the weather.'

'It is indeed a splendid day,' Mrs Herries replied to him.

Then, boldly, he spoke to Elizabeth.

'I trust you can see well where you are sitting,' he said.

She looked up at him, and to her also he appeared as something new and wonderful. He was standing in the sunlight, very erect and tall, the sun shining on his hair. She wondered why she had never noticed before how beautiful he was. Although she was frightened of her father and had been forced all her life into the background, she was not nervous. She smiled.

'I can see most excellently, thank you.'

At her smile he could have gone on his knees and worshipped her.

'You will tell me if I am in your view,' he said, bowing. Then, just as he was moving away, he realized that two eyes were looking at him with a malignant force that seemed impossible for so small a boy. Elizabeth's brother's . . . Something cold struck his heart.

The play had begun. From the first it was invalidated by the fact that Mr Greene, who was playing Bottom, wished to be in the forefront throughout, and that his wife, who was Titania, had the same desire.

So Theseus and his Court were soon bustled off the scene and the pairs of lovers were permitted to love and bicker only in brief moments while Bottom found his breath. Titania (very fine in shining ermine with a helmet--a perfect conception of Britannia) was meanwhile hovering with her attendant elves ('There's Lucy,' cried Mrs Bucket, 'her with the daisies.' 'That's our Liz--standing on one foot,' cried Mrs Ellis) near the platform and suddenly pushed forward and began, in her deep voice, to shout her lines.

'First, good Peter Quince, say what the play treats on,' shouted Mr Greene.

'What, jealous Oberon! Fairies, skip hence. I have forsworn his bed and company,' cried Mrs Greene.

For a moment it seemed that there would be trouble, but Bottom had his way, and Titania retired to sit on the grass near by and throw daisies at the children, for in spite of her size and voice she was a merry and kindly woman.

When, however, the time for the fairies was really come, they had their triumph. For one thing Oberon was a splendid young man, with a handsome red cloak and a noble pair of legs. Then the children, loving the sunshine and the freedom, exalted by the presence of parents and relations, behaved as fairies should, dancing everywhere, joining hands and singing, tumbling head over heels, running races, plucking at Oberon's cloak. The gaiety that had been in the air all day possessed the company and the audience together.

When Bottom became an ass and laid his great form on Titania's big lap everyone roared with applause, and the fairies pinched his legs, and Titania took off her helmet because it was so hot. There were fairies everywhere. When Theseus and his Court returned the sun was lower in the sky and long shadows lay across the grass. Some of the fairies, tired out, were sleeping, but behind Bottom and his companions, as they played their Play, the children danced and sang, Titania, carrying a baby in her arms, walked with half a dozen infants at her skirts (she had by now flung away most of her armour), and Bottom and Peter Quince, Theseus and Helena romped to the fiddle of an old man of the company who worked at his music in an ecstasy of enjoyment.

Puck came forward to speak his Epilogue and a sudden silence fell:

If we shadows have offended,
Think but this (and all is mended)
That you have but slumber'd here
While these visions did appear.
And this weak and idle theme,
No more yielding but a dream . . .

The cheers and shouts echoed from Main Street to Cat Bells. The gipsies under the wood heard it; an old man, driving his cart home to Watendlath, heard it and in a piping voice began to sing . . .

THE DANCING ON THE MEADOW

The moon rose, triumphantly full, made of light and crystal, lucent in a sky fiery with stars. The evening was so warm that everyone brought food in baskets, in napkins and bags, and sat about on the meadow waiting for the Town Band.

Judith, Jennifer and the children had planned to stay and see the dancing and the fireworks, but now Jennifer wished to go home. They had all been resting at Miss Pennyfeather's and had started towards the Lake to see the fireworks when Jennifer caught Judith's arm.

'I think I will go home, Judith.'

They were standing under the trees. Adam, John and Dorothy had gone on to the margin of the Lake that they might watch the trembling path of the moon on the water, and the boats like dark fragments of cloud that floated into the light and out again.

'But why, Jennifer?' Judith asked. 'Are you unwell?'

'No,' said Jennifer. 'I have a foreboding.'

'A foreboding? Of what?'

'I cannot say . . . Perhaps it is being so near to that wicked man all day--the murderer of my husband.'

'Nonsense, Jennifer. You must not have these fancies, you must not. Come. The fireworks will shortly commence.'

'No. I prefer to go home.'

'But we cannot find Bennett . . . And I have no notion where Mr Rackstraw has gone. Jennifer, dear . . . Here is a seat. Rest here for a moment.'

The two women sat down together. Judith took Jennifer's hand, but the gaiety and happiness that had accompanied her all day were gone. Once (what years ago it seemed!) in Paris she had been with her friend Emma Furze, watching the dancing, and suddenly, without warning, Warren Forster, the father of Adam, who was shortly then to be born, appeared in front of her. She remembered now the sharp sense that she had had of Fate stepping up through the dark trees beside her. She had the same sense now.

'What is it, Jennifer? . . . It has been a most beautiful day. Everyone has been happy.'

'I cannot help it, Judith. I am growing an old woman now, but whenever I see that man I am afraid. He has been close to me all day--and the nearer he comes to me the greater terror I feel. And I am sure that one day he will build a house in Uldale and he will look into our windows. He will kill me; yes, he will kill me just as he murdered Francis. And then he will kill John and Dorothy.'

Judith started. Could Jennifer know of Walter's threat to build on High Ireby? She herself had never spoken of it, but someone else might have done. Walter had held his hand now for a long while; of late he had let them be except that there was a story of John's that he had looked out of window one night and seen Walter on his horse, motionless, staring at the house. But that may have been dream or fantasy. John had all the imagination of his father.

'No, no, Jennifer . . . Listen--you must not think about Walter. He has forgotten us. He has not been near us for years. Really he has not. And I am looking after you. While I am there no harm can come to you.'

Judith felt as though she had a large overgrown child beside her. Jennifer was as usual untidy, her turban was a little askew. Her fine dress of white muslin that went wonderfully with her dark hair trailed at the skirt: her cashmere shawl was torn in one place. Through how many differing stages of relation she had been with Jennifer, Judith thought! From that first vision of her at

Christabel's Ball in their youth when Jennifer, in her Medici dress, had been the loveliest creature in the world, through jealousy and anger, almost to hatred (she recalled vividly still that day at tea at Mrs Southey's), to this complete, kindly, but a little scornful domination!

'Come, Jennifer . . . Do not go home . . . It will make the children unhappy. They are having such a wonderful day. There will be the fireworks and then the dancing. It is so warm a night!'

Jennifer laid a trembling hand on Judith's.

'Judith, I know something dreadful will occur.'

'Nonsense. Nonsense . . . Now this truly is nonsense. We must not spoil the children's amusement.' ('And my own amusement as well,' thought Judith. 'I have never enjoyed a day so much.')

But she had made this one appeal to Jennifer that must be successful. Selfish, apprehensive, sluggish though she was, she wished the children to be happy, and especially John, whom she adored.

So they went, arm-in-arm, to the Lakeside.

The fireworks were a great success, and when they had watched them they walked slowly up the hill to the meadow. Adam went with Judith. They were of a size now. Adam was as tall as his mother.

'Are you happy, Adam?'

'Yes, Mama.' He gave her arm a little squeeze. 'I AM glad Will won the race.'

'Yes, so am I--but you should have told me that you were going . . . I had no notion where you were.'

'Yes, Mama . . . Can we go and see the gipsies?'

'Yes, if you stay beside me.'

When they came to the field the theatre was cleared away, and where the audience had sat the Town Band was. The great moon shone down on them all like a kindly benevolent hostess who had arranged the festivity and saw that it was good.

Young John had but one thought. His eyes roamed the scene. But poor John! He moved as we move in a nightmare seeking some person or place, but baffled at every moment by figures, mists and sudden catastrophes. The moonlight was now bright enough, the space wide enough for an army of young lovers, but fate played with him, catching him now here, now there, as though it were warning him that it would be better for him to ride home, find his bed and hide there. First he encountered one of the Miss Pendexters, who at once drew him into a babble of chatter: '. . . Well, now, that's a true saying about an ill wind, for only a moment ago I was asking your mother how you were finding it all. "John's enjoying himself, you may be sure," I said to her, "for this is just a night . . ." Oh, there's Major Bellenden. I was going to ask him . . . and a perfect little house my sister and I have moved into. We insist that you come to see us. Perfect situation, near the road so that there's always something passing, and dear

Crosthwaite Church only half a mile . . . Yes, I was telling your mother--how lovely she is in the white muslin, to be sure--I was telling your mother that it will be no trouble of an evening to find our way to Miss Pennyfeather's for a game, for on a dark night Maria with a lantern is all we need, and often enough we can make up a table for ourselves. For our friends are so obliging--so very good . . .'

Escaping from this he ran into a confusion of happy life. So dry was the night that everyone sat on the grass, watching the dancing and exchanging all the gossip. The town, the countryside, all was represented. The music of the band came gently through the air.

And more turbulent every moment was the evening becoming, for there were rough fellows from Cockermouth and Whitehaven, there were the gipsies, and bottles were passing from hand to hand. The dancing was growing wilder. Stout wives picked up their skirts and romped. Old grandfathers with a 'tee-hee-hee' pinched the arms of young girls, babies cried, dogs barked, but the woods made a dark frontier, the sky a star-fretted canopy, the mountains kept guard.

Through this whirling, noisy scene John found his way, looking into every face, thinking that maybe her mother had taken her home, praying that that might not be.

Then, mounting the hill towards the gipsy encampment, he saw the whole party. They had found some trestle seats--Walter, James and the young men were exceedingly gay; Mrs Walter Herries and Elizabeth were a little apart, quietly watching. John waited, taking in with all his soul Elizabeth as she stood, a dark cloak now over her shoulders; the rest of the world, the dancers, the lighted fires, the stars that sparkled above the heavy wood, vanished. She was alone and in her silence and quiet, a saint in a chapel secret and remote for his own single worship. He stayed there a long while. In his twenty years he had known no feeling like this, nothing that made him both so proud and so humble, so resolute and so brave, but so timid also with a shy foreboding.

She was a child, eight years younger than himself; she was the daughter of his greatest enemy. He was conscious then of Walter, who was being very merry and noisy, so that you could hear his laughter above all the rest. He was aware too of Uhland, who sat like a little ghost beside his father.

Without knowing it, he had moved nearer and then nearer again. On any other occasion nothing could have compelled him to approach those figures who stood to him for everything in life that he hated and feared the most.

He had come up behind them, and then, as though she had known, Elizabeth turned round to look at the downward slope of the hill and the light on the water. They were all absorbed in the dancing, and the two, as though in a trance, came together.

They had exchanged only two sentences of convention in all their lives, but it seemed to her quite natural that he should say, looking at her but coming no closer:

'I have been searching for you everywhere.'

'Oh!' she said with a little cry of warning, looking back.

'Yes, I know . . . But I must see you again. I must, I must.'

'One day--yes . . . I would like it--'

'Where?' He came nearer until he almost touched her.

She shook her head.

'We must not--'

'Listen,' he said quickly. 'I will write. Our coachman will find a way to give it you--'

She stared at him as though she must see him so intensely that she would remember afterwards all his features. She nodded as though they had made a compact, then slowly she turned back.

No one can say what he would have done then, of what madness he might not have been capable, had he not seen, with a dismay that thrust him in an instant from one world into another, his mother, Judith and Dorothy approaching.

To his horror he saw that they, quite unconsciously, were walking directly into the Westaways group. He would have thought that for some mad reason they were doing this deliberately, had it not been that they were so plainly unaware. For Judith was laughing, pointing with her stick to some dancers, and Dorothy was teasing Adam as though she were trying to make him dance. He did dance a few steps, looking in the moonlight like a little animal, with his long arms and short body. They all laughed. John heard Judith say: 'Here is a fine place. We can see well from here.' He would have started forward to warn them, but it was too late.

In another moment Judith had almost stumbled on the bench where Walter was sitting.

John came forward as though to protect his mother. Walter Herries stood up. It was plain that he had been drinking heavily, for he lurched a little on his great legs as he stood.

Jennifer was transfixed with terror. In all the years since her husband's death she had never until now been face to face with him.

Walter took off his hat.

'Good evening, ladies! How agreeable a surprise! Not unexpected too. Will you not join us?'

Jennifer caught at Judith's arm.

'Oh, come, Judith. Come away!'

But Walter was delighted. Such scenes he fancied. The young Durward Herries boys, who saw something strange was abroad, stared, their laughter checked.

'Well, Jennifer,' Walter said. 'It is a long time since we met. It was my mother you knew, I think. I hope that you cherish no ill- will, though, for I assure you that I do not.'

'Thank you, Walter,' Judith broke in. 'This is too public for your wit. Jennifer, we will turn back--'

But he strode forward so that he almost touched Jennifer's arm. He made no sign that anyone existed for him but Jennifer, who shrank back against Judith.

'No, no. Why so unfriendly? We must be friends, we must indeed. For we are to be neighbours. Very near neighbours indeed. You didn't know? But, of course . . . At High Ireby. I am to start building in a month or so.'

'You cannot--' Jennifer answered. That would be terrible. I could not--'

'Why, yes,' said Walter. He took a step nearer. Then John, seized with a wild fury, struck him in the chest. Walter tottered, for he was not at all steady, almost fell. There were cries, exclamations. Little Uhland had rushed forward, hitting at John's legs.

It was, in fact, a most ludicrous, lamentable scene, for the other young Herries men, themselves rather drunk, came forward (not very aware of what they would do). Judith lifted her stick, Agnes Herries caught Walter's arm . . .

Then in a moment the publicity of it hit them all. They stood transfixed in a frozen group. Two gipsies approached and one of them, a young woman with an orange kerchief and a cage of little green birds said: 'Lady . . . Pretty lady . . . The birds will tell your fortune . . . Happy luck, lady.'

Walter steadied himself.

'Here,' he said, 'you can tell my fortune, my girl, and give me a fine one.'

With great dignity, very slowly, Judith and Jennifer, their children following them, turned down the hill.

THE BEGINNING OF THE FORTRESS

Walter Herries had told Jennifer that the building of his house on High Ireby was at once to begin. It was not, however, until the month of March 1830 that the foundations were first laid--and it happened that Jennifer was there to see.

Jennifer never recovered from that shock of the encounter with Walter on the night of the Summer Fair. It was the climax to a series of events that stretched back to that old Ball of her youth, and possibly, behind that again, to her earliest nursery escape from reality. She did not know now--she had not an analytic mind-- what had happened to her or indeed why anything had ever happened to her at all. She was an old woman--this year saw her sixtieth birthday--but for all her years she felt herself to be still a young girl most unjustly treated by everyone.

In the early days--they seemed to her to be as recent as last evening--she had never had justice. Her beauty had brought her nothing: everything had been always just awry. She would have been the Duchess of Wrexe and a great woman of the world had not the Duke been so unpleasant a young man and the position of great lady so tedious and wearisome. She would have been a quiet beauty in the country had not Francis, her husband, been a weakling. She would have been a splendid Mistress had not her lover been a clod. She would have been a triumphant Mother had her children loved her. She would be now mistress of her house had not Judith taken selfishly everything out of her hands. Always injustice, everywhere injustice. No one saw what she was and no one cared.

The sluggish slackness in her that had ruined her life she did not perceive, for we never catch the causes of our fate, so clear to everyone around us. She might even now have been a fine tragic figure had she had the intelligence to look noble, the energy to tidy her hair, the wisdom to have reticence.

She had never had dignity or wisdom; she had been always the slave of trifles, small jealousies, degrading idleness, lazy avoidances of trouble.

But the terror of Walter struck into her character as a snake strikes. She was poisoned in all her being. The infection spread slowly, but from the moment that Judith consented to stay and took the house into her hands, Jennifer was lost. She had now nothing to do but brood over Walter. She cowered beneath his shadow, unable to move, waiting the awful moment.

As his shadow grew ever more terrible the figures immediately around her became themselves shadows. John had once been her darling, Judith's Adam a pleasure, the servants agreeable, her daughter Dorothy 'a good girl', Judith herself, although a tyrant, exceedingly useful and a safeguard.

After her scene with Walter all these were as unsubstantial to her as figures on a tapestry. She might have been still a fine woman; she had yet all her height, her hair (once so lovely) was white with, if she had cared, a fine lustre in its silver. But she was untidy, careless, a slattern. Any old clothes did for her, her hair escaped its pins, she would tap-tap in loose slippers, an old shawl over her shoulders, from room to room. Only her eyes were good, and the blaze in them, their intensity, belied all the rest of her, so that they were like a bright fire in a lumber-room. She would begin sentences and not finish them, eat food greedily and suddenly abandon it, pet John and Adam eagerly and then look at them as though she did not know them. The servants disregarded her; they took their orders from Madame.

Judith knew that terror was of an especial danger to anyone of even part Herries blood. She had seen, in all her active varied life, that the history of the Herries, as of so many British families, was that of a building impregnable, as its builders thought, to the attacks of all outside forces. But the outside forces are strong and immortal. Nothing tempts their malicious humour so thoroughly as the complacency of the builders. Here they twist a chimney, there a window rattles, now the wind sweeps wildly up the ordered garden, the iron-sheathed door shudders, a picture falls, the carpet rises on the floor.

Jennifer's parents had been typical Herries, good, complacent, satisfied, laughing at imagination. Jennifer, so lovely, their pride, their joy, must be safe if any Herries was. Who would dare to touch her? So, in their love for her, they took from her all her defences. Now, when a vision of another world more real than the Herries one might have saved her, she had no vision. And Judith could not help her.

From the moment of Walter's threat, for two years and a half, she waited. But life does not allow you to wait. No one knew what the matter with her was and, more tragically, no one cared. Her children had loved her, but Dorothy was all for comfort and found her uncomfortable, while John, after he knew of the reasons for his father's suicide, shrank, against all his will and wish, from contact. Moreover, he had now something so absorbing in his life that his mother was dim to him, as he was to her.

Judith could have loved her because she pitied her and pity, with Judith, was maternal; but daily contact with Jennifer's laziness, carelessness, selfishness, turned pity into impatience, and when Judith was impatient she was at her worst.

So Jennifer was alone with her terror.

As the time advanced, that terror took strange forms. High Ireby became a place of extraordinary fascination for her. It was several miles from Uldale and uphill for most of the way, but day after day she walked through the fields, climbed the slope and then stood, under the trees, gazing at the lovely scene--the walls of a ruined cottage, a small wood of whispering trees, remnants of a garden patch, and the long slope of the melancholy fields with the village and house of Uldale tucked into the hollow.

To the right were the sprawling slopes of Blencathra and Skiddaw. They lay against the sky like the careless limbs of a giant sleeper under an enormous coverlet tossed into casual shapes. She knew here all weathers, all seasons. She would stand against the ruined wall, under the trees, a tall, motionless old woman in a tawdry hat, clutching her shawl, staring in front of her. She became a familiar figure to the inhabitants of the village near by. It was not strange that she should soon have a reputation for madness, but she was not mad in the least. She would stand there, or sit on a tumbled stone, and reflect, in a lazy way, on her misfortune--not on any very definite misfortune but on the general way in which she was ill-treated and neglected. Sometimes she would determine that on her return to Uldale that day she would tell them all what she thought

of them--Judith, John, Dorothy, even Mr Rackstraw--but she never did. Partly it was too much trouble, partly when she was once again in the comfortable parlour at Uldale drinking tea before the fire or, in the summer, sitting under the tree on the lawn in the sunshine, she was cosy like a cat and smiled, lazily, on everyone.

She had too, all this time, marvellous health. Nothing ailed her.

She had perhaps the idea, as she stood in the little wood, day after day, that thus she was defying Walter. During all these two years she never saw him in the flesh. He became the more monstrous because she did not see him.

Then one day at last the thing happened. That March there was a late fall of snow. During the first week of that month a blizzard blew across the North, adding discomfort to all the hardships that the poor people were, at that time, already suffering. Waters were frozen, the sun, when it broke through, turned the snow-ridges into shining marble, the crows were spots of ink on the virgin fields.

She had had a cold for a week, and Judith had kept her in bed, but as soon as she was up she strode across the fields again, her shawl flapping behind her, climbed the hill and walked into a multitude of men.

Trees were falling. It seemed that on every side of her the trees were tumbling. The walls of the ruined cottage were no more. Men walked measuring the ground. A fire was lit on the snow and illuminated the broken whiteness of the scene that stretched back into the farther shadows of the wood.

As she stood back in the road hidden by two huge horses from whose nostrils steam struck the air, a tree fell with a great crash and a groan that seemed to come from her own heart. Men shouted joyfully, and some boys, muffled against the cold, danced round the fire.

She stepped into the middle of the road and several of them saw her. Two gentlemen on horseback, attended by little Peach, Walter's agent, were watching the proceedings: one of them was the architect, Mr Humphrey Carstairs from London, the other, young Julius Hopper, a clever lad working in old Mr Bonner's office in Keswick. Old Mr Bonner was the oldest, stupidest and laziest architect in the North of England, and no one despised him quite so deeply as did young Julius. Young Julius was slim and dark and exceedingly handsome in his high-collared dark green overcoat; Carstairs was squat, thick, his head almost hidden in the curves of his plum-coloured capes. He bent low in his saddle; he suffered severely from rheumatism.

He turned and saw the strange woman in the old-fashioned hat, drawn to her full height in the middle of the snowy road. He stared, then turned to young Julius. 'Who's the old body in the shawl?' he asked.

Young Julius stared also. He knew who she was: his first thought was that this would be amusing for Walter Herries if he rode over that afternoon. His second was of alarm. She looked crazy; he knew, of course, of the feud. She might have a pistol under that shawl of hers. He was a warm young man, fond of life, very ambitious. He had no desire to die as yet. Another tree fell; men were dragging branches across the snow that blew in little smoky spirals of silver into the air. The flames of the fire leaped, and an old man sitting by it, with a great red comforter round his neck and yellow mittens, began to play on a fiddle. The mittens made his fingers clumsy, but the men liked the music and worked with a better will.

'She's a Mrs Herries from Uldale yonder,' young Julius whispered. 'She's a sort of cousin of Walter Herries.' Then he added: 'I'll go speak to her.'

With what he felt to be exceptional bravery (for it was possible enough that she concealed a pistol) he dragged his horse's head round and rode towards her. She never moved, but stood there in the road, staring at the men, the fallen trees, the old man in the bright red comforter. Young Julius raised his hat.

'Good afternoon, Mrs Herries.' Then he said, smiling: 'Very wintry for March, ma'am.'

He wasn't sure that she saw him. He moved his horse a little to the right.

Then she said: 'What is going on here?'

He was able now to see her eyes, the pallor of her face, something dignified in her isolation. He spoke with the greatest politeness as he answered:

'Why, ma'am, Mr Walter Herries of Westaways is to build a house here.'

'Indeed?' She nodded her head. 'A house of some size?'

'Oh, yes. It is to be a very fine place indeed--gardens and a fountain, magnificent stables. A lonely spot, though, to have chosen. Mr Carstairs there from London is the architect.'

'What is your name?'

She looked at him directly and there was something in her eyes that touched him very truly.

'My name, ma'am, is Hopper--Julius Hopper. I am assistant to Mr Bonner, the architect in Keswick. I know your son, Jack Herries, well. We are very good friends.'

'Ah, yes, my son.' Her eyes went back to the fire that seemed to have a great fascination for her. The thin, reedy, uncertain squeak of the fiddle came whining through the sharp air.

'And how long will it be in the building?'

'A considerable while, ma'am. Mr Herries wishes everything to be of the best . . .'

'Ah . . . He wishes everything to be of the best . . .'

'Yes, ma'am. And these are not easy times. Although so many are without employment, it is not easy to get good workmen and wages are high. As soon as we have Reform things will be better.'

'You believe in Reform?'

'I do indeed, ma'am. We shall have Revolution else, like the French.'

'You are wrong.' She spoke with slow consideration, as though she beat every word upon the ground. 'Reform itself is Revolution. The country will be ruined. The country is in any case ruined.'

'I hope not indeed.'

'Ah, you are young . . .'

She moved away from him up the road. His horse stepped beside her. He would never forget that odd, tall, black figure with the crazy hat, moving against the snow. He thought after that it had been a kind of omen, but he was a sane practical young man who did not believe in omens, although out of habit he avoided walking under a ladder.

She came so far and then saw Peach. Mr Carstairs had come down from his horse and now he and Peach were studying a plan. Jennifer scarcely knew Peach, and yet his short bow-legged figure was in some way familiar to her. She looked up at Julius, and he, not knowing what to say, remarked:

'The snowdrops are doing bravely in spite of the snow.' There was a great patch of them under the trees. Some of them were already trodden down and, as he looked, two men, carrying a log, tramped upon the patch.

'Oh, the snowdrops!' She put her hand on his knee, leaning up to him. 'Tell Walter Herries what he is destroying.'

She turned and walked swiftly down the road, catching her shawl more closely about her. The three men turned to watch her.

Meanwhile at Uldale, as it happened on that same afternoon, Judith assisted by Dorothy Herries was entertaining four lady callers--old Miss Pennyfeather, Mrs Leyland of The Ridge, Bassenthwaite, and her two daughters Nancy and Bella.

Miss Pennyfeather had been driven over by Judith, who had been taking luncheon with her in Keswick; the Leylands had come over from Bassenthwaite in their barouche. All the ladies were very pleasantly animated: the three elders, their heads together, near the fire, and the girls laughing and chattering by the window.

For the Leyland girls this was an adventure. Dorothy Herries, blooming with health and good temper, was two years older than Nancy and Bella, who were twins and were wanting to be married, for they were already twenty years of age and soon it would be too late. They were nice simple girls who had never been to London and only visited the theatre in Newcastle and were eager for gossip and adventure. They were pale, flaxen, tall and slim, and dressed alike. They wore dresses of poplin, colour violette de Parme, with heart-shaped bodices, and the corsages long and tight at the waist. They had hats of rice straw with very wide brims, trimmed with anemones. Each thought the other looked bewitching, for they were generous and warm-hearted by nature.

They had never been to Uldale before on a visit, and this was a great adventure. 'Madame' was a 'character' through the whole countryside, and it was wonderful to be entertained in her parlour. Or was it Mrs Herries' parlour? People said that she was mad and walked about the country singing songs to herself--mad, poor thing, because her husband had discovered her with her lover and he had killed himself. Very shocking, but HOW romantic! And then her son John was so handsome, the best-looking young man in the North, a little sad and pensive as a good-looking young man ought to be. (For they adored Thaddeus of Warsaw and Mrs Cuthbertson's Santo Sebastiano and Mrs Meeke's Midnight Weddings.) Dorothy on the other hand--whom they loved at sight--was not melancholy at all and laughed all the while.

Then there was 'Madame's' boy whom they did hope they'd get a sight of. He was, of course, illegitimate, which made him so interesting, although everyone knew who the father had been. He SHOULD have been romantic and melancholy, but people said that he was ugly and silent and kept to himself. Nevertheless, it would be ADORABLE to see him!

While they laughed and chattered by the window they tried to keep an ear open for the company by the fire. For Miss Pennyfeather did say such SHOCKING things and their mother (Mrs Leyland was stout and jolly) had told them that on no account were they to listen to Miss Pennyfeather's wickedness, so they were naturally all ears.

But the ladies seemed to be talking of nothing but Reform, Lord John Russell, and of Brougham's attack on Lady Jersey in The Times, and how bitter she was against Reform, and so on, and so on--dull stuff!

Then Dorothy let it out that next month 'Madame' and her son were to go to London to stay with some relations. THAT was exciting! To go to London! To see the great Simpson at Vauxhall, to visit the New Zoological Gardens in Regent's Park, to attend a Masquerade in the Argyll Rooms, to catch a glimpse of the Duke, and best of all the Theatre, the Surrey, the Royalty, or Sadler's Wells.

They knew all about it; it was as though they had been in London all their lives. They looked across to the fire and that little upright dominating woman in her crimson dress with the huge sleeves; they stared (as unobtrusively as politeness insisted) at her small pale face, her neat grey hair, her ivory cane, and watched her bright eyes, her smile, the tapping of her small foot on the carpet. People said that she was the daughter of a gipsy and that her father, although of the finest family, had been a rogue and vagabond. And here she was, with her illegitimate boy, behaving as though she were Queen of England. Ah! WHAT a romantic afternoon they were having!

It was made yet more splendid by the entrance of John Herries. Both girls, at sight of him, had the same

thought. What a LOVER he would make! But there was something that told them at once that he was not for them. He came over to them and made himself very charming. His voice was soft and gentle. Yes, he WAS melancholy, although he teased his sister and chaffed them about their beaux at a recent Ball in Keswick. But they felt that his mind was elsewhere.

What a HERO of a novel he would make! He was too gentle to be truly Byronic, but he would suit The False Step exactly! How beautifully he went and paid his devoir to their mother, with what ease! And yet he was in no way effeminate, quite unlike that horrid William d'Arcy of Threlkeld, or, on the other hand, that oaf, young Osmaston.

Well, it was time for them to be going. Darkness would soon swallow the pale saffron twilight. Already the candles were lit in the room. Mrs Leyland rose to make her adieux when the door opened and the strangest figure stood in the doorway.

Jennifer stood there, her hat a little askew, her long thin fingers clutching her shawl. She could see but indistinctly. The candlelight blinded her, coming in as she did from the dark snow- shine road. But she saw Judith.

'Judith! Judith! He has begun to build!'

The cry, shrill, poignant, broke the comfortable cosiness of the room into fragments. Jennifer had awaked at last.

'Judith! They are trampling on the snowdrops . . . The trees are falling!'

She stumbled forward, her hat ever more askew as she moved, and Judith, coming to her, caught her hand.

'Wait, Jennifer. There are guests here . . .'

Mrs Leyland, good and kind woman as she was, did the right thing. She chattered:

'Well, I'm sure . . . How do you do, Mrs Herries? A cold afternoon to be out in. You must be weary, and a cup of tea will be the very thing. And now we must be going. So very dark, although William is a most careful driver. We brought him from Newcastle with us. He was always careful from a boy. Might William be summoned, Mrs Herries? Thank you. Most kind. Come, girls. William will have the horses in an instant. He is always so prompt. It has been truly most delightful. I'm sure . . .'

But Jennifer was not to be silenced by any chatter. She saw only one thing, one terrible thing, before her eyes--and she must declare it. Judith had seated her on the sofa, had pulled the bell- rope, was pouring a cup of hot tea. Dorothy had come round to her mother. The girls stood in the window, not knowing quite what they should do but enthralled by what they saw and heard. John had gone to hasten Mrs Leyland's horses.

'Yes, he has begun at last, Judith. All his men are there, measuring the ground, and it is to be a huge place with a fountain and fine stabling. All the trees are falling, and they have lit a fire in the snow.'

'It is Walter Herries,' Judith explained sotto voce. 'He has been threatening for a long while that he would build on High Ireby that he may overlook us--and now it seems that he has done it.'

'Well,' cried old Miss Pennyfeather. 'Let him, and much good may it do him! I cannot endure Walter and I don't care who hears me. Fat overgrown bully! Let him build with his limping child and puny wife! Don't you worry, Judith. 'Tis all stuff and nonsense! He can't harm you and he knows it!'

'Yes, indeed,' said Mrs Leyland, gazing anxiously at the door for news of her horses. 'I should think so indeed. So he's to be our neighbour at Ireby, is he? A pretty neighbour, and so Mr Leyland will prove to him if he comes bothering our way. Come, girls-- William must have brought the horses round.'

But Jennifer looked at them all with startled, staring eyes.

'He will not be content until he has destroyed us. I knew it from the first. All his windows will look down on us. We must leave Uldale. I always said that he would have his way!'

Judith was sitting beside her. She had one of her hands in hers.

'Jennifer, Jennifer . . . You must not be so distressed. Cousin Walter will do us no harm. How can he? What if he does build a house at Ireby? That can do us no harm. Come, come, Jennifer . . .'

How soft and gentle her voice was, thought the girls, and how crazy Mrs Herries looked, poor woman, with her hat on one side!

Mrs Leyland beamed comfortably on them. 'I am sure Ireby is no place for a house, no place at all. I cannot think why he should choose such a spot, and Westaways good enough for anyone, I should have thought. I always said he was a strange man, and Mr Leyland, who is downright if any man is, remarked to me only a week back that he was growing far too stout for his health. If he could but give some of his size to his wife, poor woman . . .'

John appeared in the doorway.

'Come, girls. Here's Mr Herries to say that William has the horses round. Has he not, Mr Herries? That's excellent. William is always so prompt. Good day to you. Good day. Good day. MOST delightful. Never enjoyed anything more. Come, girls. TOO kind of you, Mrs Herries. It's time we were moving on, with the snow and everything . . . You must all come over to Bassenthwaite at the nearest opportunity. Oh, I insist. I take no refusal. So very good of you, Mrs Herries--'

When the Leylands were out of the room a silence fell. Jennifer drank her tea. Then she rose.

'There is no peace for us any more here,' she said. 'You may laugh, Judith, but it is so. He will destroy us all.' Then, staring at Miss Pennyfeather as though she were seeing her for the first time, she added: 'They were trampling on the snowdrops. It is to be a tremendous place with rows of windows. I think I will go to my room.'

She walked out.

Judith sighed.

'If that isn't unfortunate! Poor Jennifer! And the Leylands will talk for weeks!' Then taking Miss Pennyfeather's arm she added: 'Janet, come up with me. You are the most sensible woman I know. Talk to her. I'm of no service when she's like this.'

So Dorothy and John were left alone. Dorothy saw at once that her brother was greatly disturbed; he stood there, fingering his high stock and looking, as she remembered her father had sometimes looked, as though he were going to be sick. At such a time she could not help him. She was good about sensible practical things like a broken leg, a bloody head, a cold in the chest, but when John was in a mood she was uncomfortable as though he were improper. Although she was the soul of good nature and almost always in a good temper, she resented the states into which her mother and brother sometimes tumbled.

John said at last:

'Nothing can help mother. Now that she has this in her head.'

'I'll see about some linden tea,' Dorothy said. 'It has soothed her many a time.' And relieved at an opportunity of escape, she bustled out.

She had been gone but a moment when Adam came in. Adam was now fourteen and a half. He had filled out in the last two years and was deep of chest, thick across the shoulders. His black hair was always untidy; a lock hung now over his forehead. He was ruddy with health, with the brown colour that made so many who didn't know him think him a foreigner, but he was English enough all the same, with the broad brow, snub nose, large mouth, square body, short sturdy legs, bright eyes like his mother's. He was English, too, in his reticence and hatred of demonstration. This affected him now, for he saw at once that John was worried and would need his help. John liked demonstrations: there were times when he wanted Adam to show him that he loved him, and although Adam did love him more than any human thing save his mother, he hated to show it. Oh! how he hated it!

He was in rough country things and his high boots were muddy, for he had been out with Rackstraw, Bennett and the dogs rabbiting and had had a glorious afternoon. When he saw that John's distress was so real he thought to himself, 'Let John do what he likes to me if it helps him.' With a backward glance he threw reluctantly behind him all the happiness of the afternoon, the crisp air, the scent of the snow, the yelping of the dogs, the sunlight breaking in silver across the slow fields.

'Adam, Mother has been to High Ireby. Walter Herries has begun to build.'

'I knew it,' Adam said quickly. 'Bennett told me.'

'Mother is very unhappy. She came in while the Leylands were here and spoke as though she were crazy.

This will SEND her crazy! If I could do something! How I hate him! He comes nearer and nearer with his sneer and his crooked son and--' He broke off.

'Pooh!' said Adam, cracking his whip against his boot as grown men did. 'It's fun, John--fine fun! Why should you care? And your mother will be better now that it's happened. It has been the waiting for it . . .'

'I am afraid of nothing else,' John went on. 'Nothing but this. I'm no coward. You know that I'm not. But Cousin Walter, since the days when we were small . . . Do you remember that evening when he rode up to the house and we watched him? And now that I'm managing the estate it brings me closer to him. Oh, Adam, I wish that you and Aunt Judith were not going to London--'

'It's grand!' Adam cried, throwing out his chest. 'There'll be the coach and the lights, chimneys smoking and everyone shouting, and mother says we shall go to a theatre--'

'Adam,' John broke in. 'There's something else. I must tell you. I have been intending so for three months past, but no one knows. It makes everything so difficult--' He broke off and began to pace the room. Adam, his legs straddling, waited. 'It's this. You're to tell no one, Adam.'

'No one,' repeated Adam, and meant it.

It's Elizabeth--Walter's daughter. We are in love. We have been so for more than two years. It began the night of the Summer Fair.'

'What!'

'Yes, yes . . . Why should it not be? There is no one so lovely, so good, so lovely--'

'But she is a child, a little girl--'

'She is your own age, Adam. In two years she will be seventeen--'

'Elizabeth! HIS daughter!'

'Yes, yes . . . I know all that you can say. I have said it all to myself again and again. But it happened at sight, and now it is for ever. Nothing can change it.'

Love--love of girls and women--as yet seemed to Adam an absurdly inexplicable business, a waste of time, a ludicrous sentimentality. And now this, for a child who was a baby, the daughter of their greatest enemy whom they had sworn always to hate, the sister of the loathsome, deformed Uhland . . . An impulse to despise John rose in his heart and was at once loyally driven down again.

'Oh, John!'

'Do not pity me. Do not laugh. We love one another for ever, and so soon as she is old enough we shall marry.'

'No, no, you must not!' Adam caught his arm. 'Uncle Walter's daughter! . . . I shall never speak to you again if you do!'

'Well, then, don't! I don't care!'

'But, John, how CAN you? For two years? And you've been meeting?'

'Sometimes. But not often. We write.'

Adam turned, with a gesture of disgust as though he would leave the room, but John gripped his shoulder.

'Adam, you must listen. You MUST. You are the only friend I have. The only one. I love you more than anyone in the world save Elizabeth. Again and again we have sworn that nothing should separate us--'

'Yes, but this--'

'No; you are young. You don't understand--'

'I'm not young.' Adam broke away. 'If you wish to love a girl you can, but not HIS daughter.'

'But don't you see? I could not help it. As I breathe so I love her. You will yourself one day--'

John's eyes caught Adam's and held him. There was an expression in them that struck to the very depths of Adam's loyalty and devotion. He knew then that he could never desert John, never, whatever the crisis.

He muttered something, looking away.

'Mind--it is our secret.'

Adam nodded his head, then said gruffly:

'I must go to the stables. Caesar has a sore leg. Coming?'

JUDITH AND ADAM IN LONDON

They--Judith and Adam--had spent the most glorious night at the George, Stamford, in the very room, so the landlord himself informed them, occupied by his Sacred Majesty, King Charles the First, when he slept there on his way from Newark to Huntingdon on the night of August 23rd, 1645. This Judith, in ordinary circumstances, would never have believed (although the room was splendid with oak beams and a huge four-poster and a small closet off it where Adam slept and snored), but the fact was that she was so greatly excited by her journey and by the expectation of London (where she had not been for so long a time) and by the temporary escape from Uldale, that she behaved like a child of ten and was ready to believe anything. One of the drawers remarked to another of the drawers that he'd never yet seen an old lady like it. They had had to wait for their adventure for it was not until the second week in October that they left Uldale.

Adam was quite as deeply excited as his mother and expressed his emotions in sudden fiery little sentences, like shots from a gun, that seemed to have little or no relation to one another.

Everything was glorious, the long ride in the coach the day before (Adam had insisted on sitting outside, although it was terribly cold and there was a place for him inside), the sound of the horn, the spanking pace of the horses, the incidental humours of the road and, most especially, the powers and personality of Mr Joe

Dorset, the Coachman, with whom Adam was utterly and entirely in love.

Then had come the falling dusk, the lights of the town, the bustling courtyard of the George, the wonderful dinner when, like a gentleman, Adam had drunk his mother's health in marvellous claret, sitting up in his chair so straight that he nearly broke his back in two (he and his mother so grand at a table all to themselves, while the old gentleman with three chins and two daughters entertained the table in the middle of the room with his anecdotes of Tom Hennessey and his shooting adventures in Scotland), and then the great bedroom in which King Charles had slept, and his mother going upstairs to it in such stately fashion, the landlord himself in front with two candles, that you would have thought her Royalty.

But all this was nothing at all to the glory of the next day when they started in a pale golden dawn, frost in the air, and the roans stamping their hoofs to be off. Adam, wrapped in a hundred coats, had the glory of sitting beside the great Joe with the old three- chinned gentleman on his other side.

He could observe everything and listen to everything too. He saw the gold fade from the sky and give place to one of the loveliest mornings of the year. The fields were yet frosted, the road was hard; only once had they to travel through water, which gave Joe (who had a voice like a gurgling water-pipe) occasion to describe what had happened once to the Stamford Regent when going through St Neot's, fifty-six miles out of London-- how the Ouse had overflowed its banks there, and although an extra pair of leaders were put on, ridden by a horse-keeper, yet the water was up to the axle-trees and even, for a while, the Regent was afloat, to the dreadful peril of some ladies inside it. And that led the stout gentleman to talk of Tom Hennessey's famous whip, which, as everyone knows, was a crooked one so that it could tickle the lagging wheelers in a fashion no other whip could achieve. And that led Joe to show what he could do with HIS whip, and a stout lady behind them BEGGED him to be careful and not to hurt the horses, which Adam thought the funniest thing he'd ever heard. (But then women WERE peculiar, all of them, even his mother.)

There came a glorious moment, later in the morning, when Joe actually entertained Adam himself in conversation.

'And what might YOUR age be, young gentleman?'

'Fifteen.'

'Fifteen! Deary me! Think of that now! . . . Learnt to fight yet?'

'A little.' (Adam was modest. Rackstraw had taught him well.)

'Going to see a Fight in London?'

'I hope so.'

'Next week, come Friday, there's the Nottingham Pet and John Willis at Islington. That'll be something.' Then, after a pause, 'Going to school in London?'

'No; just for a visit.'

'Ever been to London afore?'

'No, never.'

'Ah! That's a treat for a young lad. That's a treat, that is. All the same the country's better. Live in the North?'

'Yes, in Cumberland.'

'Ever seen the Crusher?'

'No. I'm afraid I haven't.'

'Never seen the Crusher--and live in Cumberland? Why, think of that now! I remember his fight in Newcastle when he smashed Foxy Rundle in twenty rounds-- in '23 I think it was.' But here the old gentleman broke in; he hadn't seen the fight himself but he had heard . . . and here the coach had to be stopped for a lady with enough baggage for a journey to China, who didn't like this, and wouldn't have that, until Joe's temper was as purple as the capes of his riding-coat. And then-- somewhere early in the afternoon-- the foretaste of London began to creep upon Adam. London! London at last! How faint suddenly were Uldale, Skiddaw, the village shop with the green bottle window . . . Dorothy and the way she'd take the jars of preserve out of the cupboard and examine them one by one with a seriousness . . . old Bennett and the way he'd pinch his leg . . . even John standing there, looking at Adam, telling him that horrid hateful news, that he loved Walter's daughter . . . all figures as dim now as the faded pinks and blues on the Chinese screen in his mother's bedroom! London!

Already they were at the Peacock at Islington, and the hostler was shouting, doors were slamming, old Joe Dorset taking up parcels, answering silly questions from nervous ladies, drinking out of a jug, examining the horses, reassuring a nervous old gentleman wrapped in a vast white muffler--and then, in another moment-- Tantivy! Tantivy! Tantivy!--they were off again.

'Are you comfortable, dear?' his mother had asked him, poking her head out of the window. 'Not too cold?'

'He's all right, ma'am,' Joe Dorset had answered, 'as right as a 'edge'og'; and Adam had been proud all down his spine. Certainly he was all right. What a pity his mother hadn't come outside! She would have enjoyed it. Now, after Islington, lights flared on the country road, for the dusk is creeping up and out of it suddenly loom drovers and a herd of cattle. Then Smithfield and Cow Lane, then up Holborn Hill. But these places were, of course, nothing to Adam. What did he see? In detail very little, for mist is everywhere, noise is everywhere--through the mist lights and flares, a blazing window, a crooked chimney, a barrow alive with flame. And the noises--hackney cabriolets, drays, waggons, wheelbarrows, shouting boys, bawling men, screaming women, ringing bells--and through it all, above it all, beyond it all, his heart beating like an African drum!

He was never one to show his excitement. He sat now in absolute silence, his hands tightly clenched together under his coat, his mouth firmly closed, but his eyes staring, staring as though they would pierce this foggy, noisy mystery through to the other side.

Tantivy! Tantivy! Tantivy! He felt now Joe's pride that he was bringing his coach in on time. How they dashed over the cobbles, how the roans tossed their heads, how through the murk and gloom one could dimly feel figures sliding, horses slipping, voices shouting to be out of the way. Then, one more blast and into a courtyard of light and splendour the Stamford Regent dashes. The George and Blue Boar, Holborn: London's heart is touched at last.

He discovered then, quite to his own surprise, that he was extremely sleepy; he discovered, too, for the first time in his young life, what every traveller discovers, that once at a destination and the life that only a moment earlier had been pulsating with fire and energy is collapsed at your feet like a spent balloon.

Even Joe Dorset was fading. Not that he wouldn't be pleased to meet Joe again somewhere, but his figure was shrunk and his voice sounded miles away.

No, his mother was once again the centre of his world. She dominated the place, sending hostlers here and stable-boys there, collecting their luggage, standing over it, ordering a hackney cabriolet, and all as quietly but as imperiously as though London were at her feet and knew it.

'Now, Adam,' she commanded. 'In you get!' And in he did get, into the mustiest, smelliest, darkest interior that his enterprising life had yet known. Mice, straw, newspapers, stale beer and damp cloth all seemed to have gone to the making of that hackney cab. There was indeed straw on the floor of it and old newspaper squeezed into the hinge of one of the windows. The driver was a little man with a pinched white nose and no eyebrows. He seemed to be terrified of Judith, for when she said, 'Number Nine, Cadogan Place,' he almost bowed to the ground.

They were crushed together inside the cab, for they were piled round with parcels and small boxes. Judith put her arm around him, and so they bumped and jumped and swayed and sank as though on a tempestuous sea. Houses rose and fell beyond the misty windows, horses loomed gigantic, figures sprang up before them and vanished again, and in Adam's nostrils was that smell with which he would associate London all his life long--straw, ale, and the faint scent of violets that stole from his mother's clothes.

They had arrived. The cab had stopped with a jerk, the door creaked open, and a little boy with a large broom was there on the pavement, his hand out, begging.

When Judith had given the little boy a shilling (which astonished him very much and led the driver of the cabriolet to wet his lips in anticipation) the big solemn door (supported by black marble pillars) was slowly opened and a very thin footman with powdered hair and

an ornamental waistcoat stood there staring at them. It seemed from his expression that he could not believe that anyone should be arriving in a hackney cab at that particular moment, but Judith walked straight past him as though she were the Queen of Egypt, and then, remembering that the driver had not yet been paid, hurried down again, directed the bringing-in of the luggage, smiled at the footman, said her name in a very determined manner, and entered the house a second time, on this occasion followed closely by Adam.

The hall was so extremely dark and a lamp by the staircase so exceedingly dim that a white bust of a gentleman with a lot of hair and naked shoulders, and a large picture of Moses addressing the Children of Israel, were the only things for a long while visible.

'Madame Paris,' said Judith again. 'We are expected.'

The footman disappeared and returned to say, 'This way, Madame,' disregarding Adam altogether. He, however, was determined not to be left alone in that darkness, and setting his face into its ugliest scowl (his manner when he was 'against the world') stumped along behind her. They were shown into a very large drawing room that seemed to Adam, accustomed to the bright colour of Uldale, the most funereal he had ever seen. There were two large white marble pillars at one end, dark brown curtains across the windows, a huge portrait of a gentleman with a white stock and an immense watch-chain over the white marble mantelpiece, a long bookcase buried in glass, and a marble pedestal with a simpering bust of a lady's head on it between the windows.

All this he quickly observed, and then he noticed the people present. (He had ample time for this because no one spoke to him during the first five minutes.) Mr Newmark he knew already, his high stock, his large nose, his long legs. He seemed more dignified than was possible for a flesh-and-blood human being to be. Mrs Newmark he knew too. He liked her. He noticed that she had grown very stout. There was an elderly gentleman in a brown wig, an elderly lady in a vast hat, and a very pretty young lady in a most bewitching poke-bonnet of the lightest blue. So, standing near the door, rubbing one leg against the other, he watched the greetings.

'Judith! . . . Judith!' Phyllis Newmark ran forward, kissed her again and again, dragged her to the fire. There was nothing false or affected about Phyllis.

'Oh, you are here! You have arrived! After all that DREADFUL journey! You must be frozen indeed. Frozen. Simply frozen. We have been expecting you these ages, have we not, Stephen?'

Mr Newmark, unbending in a slow solemn process from the crown of his head to the middle of his extremely thin waist, greeted them with the manner of one of England's Ambassadors receiving a deputation from a foreign tribe. He hoped that the journey had not been too positively inclement. Judith, her eyes twinkling, assured him that it had not.

'And this is Mr Pomeroy.'

The gentleman in the brown wig kissed her hand.

'And Mrs Pomeroy.'

'And this is Sylvia--Sylvia Herries, Garth's wife. You know Durward's son.'

The eyes of the young lady in the poke-bonnet-- eyes alive with merriment and impudence--and the eyes of Judith--also, although so much older, alive with merriment--met, and in that instant the two of them, the girl of twenty and the woman of fifty-six, were friends for life. Judith seldom made a mistake. She had not made one now.

'Is not that perfect that you are here at last? Is it not wonderful, Mrs Pomeroy? All the way from Cumberland. Oh, I must embrace you once more. I am so VERY glad to see you. Stephen, is it not excellent that they have arrived safe and sound?'

'And there is my Adam,' said Judith, turning round. She knew that it must mean some real sacrifice of his principles that Stephen should receive a little bastard into the very heart of his sanctified family. It had been Phyllis' doing, of course. Nevertheless, it was good of him. She would not forget it. Adam came forward. Although there was always something clumsy in his movements, Judith had taught him good manners. He bowed and said: 'How are you, sir?' 'How are you, ma'am?' 'Very well, I thank you, ma'am.'

What the next step might have been no one could tell, for there came, suddenly, a portentous and dramatic knocking on the door--in fact, two knocks, most solemnly delivered, with a proper interval between.

'Come in!' cried Mr Newmark.

The door slowly opened and a procession entered. First, a tall, severe woman in black silk, then in order, it seemed, of ages, all the Newmark children. When Judith had last seen them at Westaways there had been but three; now there were seven if you included (as indeed you must) an infant who, in the arms of a stout, bonneted nurse, brought up the rear. The procession assembled itself at the door and waited.

'Good evening, Miss Trindle,' said Mr Newmark in his deep bell-like tones.

'Good evening, sir. Good evening, ma'am.'

'Come, children,' said Mr Newmark. 'You may bid us goodnight.'

Then they all advanced--Horace, aged eleven, first, then Mary, aged ten, Phyllis nine, Katherine seven, Stephen five, Emily four and the infant Barnabas of almost no age at all.

The Ceremony was magnificent.

Horace was a thin, pale-faced boy, large spectacles covering wide- open, anxious eyes. He advanced timidly to his father, gave an absurd little bow, 'Goodnight, Papa.'

Mr Newmark bent down and in a dignified but kindly fashion kissed his cheek. Horace then went round and bowed to the others. 'Goodnight, sir.' 'I wish you a goodnight, ma'am.' He came to Judith, who caught him up and kissed him on both cheeks, disarranging his spectacles. He looked at her quickly, then carefully straightened his glasses. He paused before Adam and gave him a comical twinkling look, as much as to say: 'This is all very absurd. Don't think I'm taken in by it.' His mother hugged him in a quite human manner.

The others followed. Mary was stout and plain. Phyllis slender and pretty. Katherine stolid. Stephen nervous of his father. Emily yawning. Barnabas from the arms of the nurse gazed at his father as though he had never seen anything so droll in his life. They were all marshalled at the door and, together, standing in a row, made a simultaneous bow.

'And now,' said Phyllis (she was blushing a little), 'let us come upstairs and I will show you and Adam your apartments. Mrs Pomeroy, pray, forgive. We shall speedily return.'

Their rooms that night were of an icy chill, but English men and women were hardened--not for them the soft and effete comforts of more degenerate nations. Nevertheless, both Judith and Adam slept like the dead, bathed next morning in round tin baths brought in elaborately by a heavily breathing, muscle-straining maidservant. They were both in time for Family Prayers, held in the long, cold dining room. Beyond the windows as Mr Newmark read (as it seemed to Judith) almost the whole of the first Epistle to the Corinthians, a yellow fog wriggled and bridled up and down the Square.

But it was afterwards, over empty eggcups, vast cold hams and two terrific coffee-pots that Judith heard a most interesting discourse from Stephen Newmark. As Judith sat there listening she decided that she liked him better, far better, than she could ever have supposed that she would. He was at his best, serious, informed and exceedingly interesting. As he propelled his long, thin body up and down the breakfast-room, speaking in his deep, measured voice, he was like some prophet of old proclaiming woe to all the world. And yet he was not unduly sensational, did not, she was convinced, go further than the facts warranted. Being an intelligent, active- minded woman, she had, even in the confines of Cumberland, realized the critical time through which England was passing--and not only England but all the civilized world. The Revolution in France that very summer had been sufficient to point a packet of morals. The riot at Uldale ending in poor Reuben Sunwood's death had driven home all the local lessons. She had felt, for years past, what every other thinking man and woman had felt, that one cry, one lifted rifle, one more revelation of the filth, degradation, misery in which half England was living, might precipitate here a Revolution worse than any France had ever known. But Newmark dealt with facts, and facts only. Huskisson's death on September 15th, at the opening of the Liverpool and Manchester Railway, seemed to him a sort of omen. He returned to it again and again: such a fine man, one of the few men of intelligence in the country, such a foolish accident! These Railways--you were at the mercy of these horrible engines. One day it would be all engines. Human beings would be crushed by them. Will Herries had been there, had been standing quite close to Mr Huskisson at the time. He would tell her all about it.

'I don't suppose that I shall be seeing Will,' said Judith grimly.

'No?' said Stephen, surprised. 'You will find him now a man of very great importance.'

'I don't doubt,' said Judith.

After that the general lawlessness, the riots at Otmoor in Oxfordshire, followed by the calling out of the military at Oxford, Captain Swing and his rick-burning, the hanging of three men by the High Sheriff in Somersetshire, an execution witnessed by fifteen thousand people, the stirring up of the people everywhere by Cobbett and Carlyle, outrages in Kent and Wilts, in Bucks and Surrey, followed always by summary executions.

Then to London--dirt and starvation and wretchedness cheek by jowl with a luxury, extravagance and heartlessness that had never been witnessed before in any living man's memory. Materialism, immorality of the grossest, an utter scoffing disregard of religion.

'They say,' Stephen burst out, 'that all this is still the effect of the wars. But, good God, this is 1830--Waterloo was in '15!'

He passed on, growing ever more agitated beneath his cold and pedantic exterior, to the King, the Court and the burning question of Reform. The King was an old fool. They had hoped, in the summer when George, unregretted by anyone alive, had at last seen fit to die, that this honest, worthy old man who succeeded him would save his country. But this honest, worthy old man was nothing but a fool, nay, a maniac. Everyone had been pleased at first by his easy, simple manners. He was crazy from the first, wouldn't have his own servants in mourning, but had ordered Mrs Fitzherbert to put hers into black, put on his plain clothes and went wandering into the streets where he was followed all the way up St James's by a mob until a woman, outside White's, pushed her way through and kissed him; had a party at Buckingham House and dismissed the people by saying: 'Time you were off. Come along to bed, my Queen.'

'Well, you know, Judith, it isn't amusing. No, indeed, it is not. In such times to have such a crazy old monarch. A bad effect on anybody.'

And for the rest where was a man we could trust? The Duke, Peel, Lord John Brougham--all mad about this Reform one way or another. What's the Cabinet to do? It spends all its time sitting to concoct proclamations offering rewards for the discovery of rioters, rick-

burners. That's not the way a country ought to be governed.

Stephen's agitation was truly genuine. You could not listen to him and not respect him. You could not listen to him and not think of that little procession of the night before nor see that it was in his mind that all of them from Horace to young Barnabas might have their throats cut by the mob any of these days. And meanwhile, the candles guttered within, outside the yellow fog went sliding and whispering among the tall black houses. Judith, in spite of herself, shivered. The room was so desperately cold.

'We have forgotten God!' cried Stephen, 'and God will punish us.'

But then he cheered up a little, and, pouring himself out a cup of what must have been very chilly coffee, lifted his voice a tone and began to talk about 'Our Family'.

It amused Judith greatly to discover that he considered himself completely a Herries and his children Herries too. They were the nephews and nieces of Lord Rockage and cousins to all the Herries tribe and that was enough for him. Whoever the Newmarks were or had ever been they were now altogether behind the curtain. She saw that it was his idea that the Herries were going to save the country, if not in the foreground of affairs, why, then, very active in the background.

But Will Herries WAS in the foreground; it was expected that he would be a baronet any day. And there was Carey Rockage a peer, James Herries ('stupid pompous Ass HE is') a baronet, Sylvia Herries, Garth's wife, 'one of the loveliest, wittiest girls in town,' Walter adding field to field in the North, Jennifer's boy (as he had heard) one of the handsomest young fellows in England, and she, Judith, herself--

'And I, Stephen?' asked Judith, laughing.

'Well, anyone with half an eye--'

In short, she became aware that she had, in a very few hours, made a strong impression upon Stephen. It was idle to pretend that she was not pleased. All her old love of power came surging up within her. She began already to realize that this visit to London was going to rouse in her another crisis, a crisis not unsimilar to the one that had driven her to abandon Watendlath. She had been too long up there buried in the country. Here were the Herries going up, up, up. Here was she, even though she WAS fifty-six (and she didn't feel a day more than thirty), with all these conquests ready to her hand. A sudden violent distaste attacked her--a distaste of Jennifer with her crazy imaginings, the stout bullying form of Walter, the littleness and gossip of Keswick, the long slow curve of the Uldale hills--

'We are becoming every day more powerful as a family,' proclaimed Stephen. 'Will is intimate with Peel. He is throwing himself into these new Railways. He grows richer every hour. Carey's boy, Roger, is only nineteen but shows excellent political ambitions. My own boy Horace--' He broke off as though this were too personal. Then added: 'These are the times for people like ourselves. The best class in England, the soundest, the most solid. Money, brains, beauty--and a proper fear of God.'

He broke off and finished his cup of coffee. Strange, she thought, considering him, how although he was not a Herries he was proclaiming himself so curiously a cousin to Will, Walter, the Venerable Archdeacon Rodney, Jennifer's father and the others. All the qualities that her own father had so sadly lacked, and Francis and Reuben and now, she feared, young John. And she herself--she was a combination of the two opposites, the only one in the family who was so, which was exactly why she could, if she liked, dominate the lot of them!

'Stephen!' she cried. 'I shall enjoy my time in London!'

From the moment of that breakfast-hour she never ceased to realize that this visit was a crisis for her and for her Adam as well. Adam himself had indeed the most glorious time. It was as though Stephen relaxed his pomposity and Phyllis her housewifely burdens under the influence of their visitors. The children-- Horace, Mary, Phyllis--had never known such a time. Either with their mother or with the grim Miss Trindle they discovered all the glories of the Town for Adam's benefit. They went to Miss Linwood's Exhibition of Needlework Pictures, and saw the Malediction of Cain and Jeptha's Vow, to Barford's Panorama where were wonderful displays of foreign scenes. One of the most marvellous of all things was the Panorama of London at the Colosseum in Regent's Park, where, raised in a lift (the wonder of the Town), you saw the Conservatories, Swiss Cottage, Alpine Scenery. In St Martin's Lane was the pavilion of the gigantic whale which was found dead off the coast of Belgium on November 3rd, 1827. This skeleton was ninety-five feet long and eighteen broad, and for another shilling you might sit 'in the belly of the whale'. This both Horace and Adam were permitted to do. But better still were the Zoological Gardens in Regent's Park (only opened in 1828 and therefore still a sensation) and (best, oh, far best of all for Adam and Horace) 'Weeks' Mechanical Exhibition' in Tichborne Street, where you might see an automaton tarantula spider made of steel which moved its claws and horns, an animated white mouse formed of oriental pearls that ran about a table 'feeding at pleasure', a caterpillar of enamelled gold and brilliants feeding on the foliage of a golden tree, and an old woman who, at a call, came forth from her cottage, walked about supported by crutches 'while the joints in her arms and legs are all in apparently natural motion'.

For Judith, too, her progress about London during that first week was one thrilling adventure. All her ear-lier doings there rushed up to her as though they had occurred but yesterday, a strange haphazard married life with Georges, money one day, none the next, the visit to the 'Elephant' when the coach had overturned, the famous Ball, the awful moment in the Square when Georges told her that he must flee for his life--that other world, a London so different from this, so ancient, gone like a dream with its colours, its fans and powder and elegance, and Georges, dear, dear Georges, so feckless, so venturesome, so unreliable, beside her now at every step, his hand through her arm in the old persuasive way, forcing her to agree to something weak or hopeless or mad.

Georges, Georges . . . And here she was an old lady of fifty-six with a boy of fifteen who ought to have been Georges' son but wasn't, in this Town that Mr Nash had covered with whitewash, where poverty of the most hideous mingled with riches of the most extravagant, where the very pavement seemed to threaten, at any moment, an earthquake.

At the beginning of the second week she encountered Will.

She was sitting before a small, smoky, cold fire in the marble- pillared drawing room, her feet on the fender, plucking up her energy to go up to her icy bedroom and dress for dinner, when the footman opened the door, murmured something and withdrew. She looked round to see Will standing there. The same old Will, only grander. He carried his years well. He did not look sixty nor anything like it. Sixty! And it was only yesterday that, a boy on a horse outside Stone Ends, he had listened to a child, Judith, declaring firmly that she would not return to Uldale, no, not if she died for it! He did not look sixty and he did not look as though he could conceivably be Walter's father. He was dressed most handsomely in black. His coat was so waisted that it gave him an almost feminine appearance, but he was not feminine. Oh, dear me, no!

If he was startled at seeing Judith, he gave no sign of it. Her pale face was yet paler. She looked at him with all the distant haughtiness that she could command, but in her heart she wished that she did not instantly once again feel like a child in pantalettes.

'Why, Judith!' he said. He came forward and gravely shook her hand. 'I thought that I should see you. I heard that you were in Town.' Then he added, smiling a little: 'It has been unkind of you not to pay Christabel a visit.'

She did not answer that but said:

'Phyllis has not yet returned. Won't you sit down?'

He did--with great care and dignity.

'Well--how are you, Judith?'

'In excellent health, thank you, Will.'

'I am glad to hear it. And your boy?'

'Also in excellent health.'

'Good.'

There was a pause.

'And how are all at Uldale?'

'Admirable, thank you.'

'Good. I hear that John is a fine boy. You yourself, Judith, look younger than ever.'

She said nothing to that, but wished for the millionth time that God had made her taller. Then he went on--his voice was now exceedingly measured and assured as though he were always accustomed to speaking to people of the utmost importance:

'I am glad that Phyllis has not yet returned. It gives us a moment for speaking together, Judith. You are fifty-six' (how characteristic of him to remember her age!) 'I am sixty. Is it not rather childish of us to continue this feud?'

'I am continuing no feud,' she answered. 'You had better ask Walter about feuds.'

'Ah, Walter!' he sighed. 'Walter is very headstrong. I admit that that has been in part my fault--my fault and his mother's. But he would have his own way from earliest childhood. And are you not imagining things, my dear Judith? You also, if I may say so, have always had plenty of character.'

'Imagining!' she broke out. 'Imagining!' Then, controlling herself, she went on: 'You know, perhaps, that he is building on a hill above Uldale simply that he may overlook us and interfere with us in every possible way.'

'He told me that he was to build,' Will said quietly. 'I advised him against it.'

'He murdered Francis,' she said, 'and he is frightening Jennifer into her grave.' She saw then that she touched him. At the mention of Francis a faint flush coloured his sallow cheeks.

'Francis,' he said at last. 'Poor Francis! He was his own enemy.'

'He need not have been,' she answered hotly. 'It was because of Walter's spies that Francis learnt of Jennifer's infidelity.'

But he was not to be stirred.

'Is not this all rather old history, Judith, my dear? There are two strains in our family--let us face it--and they are never at peace together. I was never at one with Francis myself. We sought different things out of the world. What he sought for was perhaps harder to obtain than what I sought for. He never found it, and in his disappointment--No, no, my dear. You cannot lay all that upon Walter. You know the world too well. You are altogether too wise.'

She considered that. There was something in what he said. Then she began in another more friendly, more impetuous tone.

'Will--cannot you persuade Walter to cease this building? Cannot you persuade him to leave Jennifer and her children in quiet? Then we will be friends. I shall be only too happy.'

He looked at her with a strange, almost human, smile.

'Persuade Walter? My dear, he has gone far beyond MY persuading. I have no influence over him whatever. He would even rather that his mother and I did not come to Westaways.' He waited a moment and then continued: 'You know, Judith, I have all my life been pursuing money--money and power. I have got both. I do not regret it. But in that pursuit one loses other things. I have lost human relationships. I have no time for them. As I say, I do not regret it. But it is so.'

She felt herself being drawn closer to him than she had ever been before.

He went on: 'Once, years ago, when we were children--do you remember?--we were watching fireworks on the Lake, you, Francis, Reuben Sunwood and I. We all said what we would do with our lives. I have fulfilled almost exactly those early ambitions. I would not, however, say that I am a happy man. But who is happy? I have my moments. That is, I suppose, as much as one may ask.'

She heard the opening of the outer door and then the comfortable friendly tone of Phyllis's voice, so hurriedly she said:

'Will, I have no unfriendliness to yourself or Christabel--none whatever--but I will fight like a tiger to keep Jennifer and her children safe. I may be an aged tiger and not a very large one, but I can still be fierce. I am Walter's enemy so long as he is Jennifer's and John's and Dorothy's, so now you know.'

Will looked at her gravely and opened his mouth as though he would speak, but Phyllis' entry in a bustle of welcome prevented him. There was some chatter, and Will got up to depart. It was only then that he said to them with great solemnity:

'My reason for calling--I should have told you before--I thought that you would like to know. His Majesty has graciously offered me a Baronetcy which I shall accept.'

Yes, indeed, the Herries were going up, and Judith shared now in all the drama of family life to the full. It took her only a fortnight to be considered the most impressive figure among them all.

The Family Letters of this time are filled with references to her:

> Madame Paris has been the Family Sensation this week. Your father is laid up with the gout but he PERMITTED me (you know what he is) to dine at Lady Rosbey's. Our cousin, Judith (IS she a cousin?) arrived with the Newmarks and in FIVE MINUTE Shad the whole room

laughing. She must be ANY AGE and wears the most outrageous colours. Nevertheless, she was sprightly as a kitten and without losing her dignity an instant. She was as up in everything as though she'd never moved out of Belgravia and kept us all vastly amused with her Paris adventures in '15 where it appears that she . . .

And another:

Judith Paris is the rage. I must confess that I find her charming for she is kindly as well as intelligent, enjoys everything as though she were born yesterday (she's fifty if a day!), and is no SNOB like dear William and others of our relations. She has with her an illegitimate boy (they say he is Warren Forster's son. You remember Warren--a little PEAKED man with a nervous habit of snapping his fingers) and takes him about with a great deal of pride. It is a thousand pities that she should be buried in the North for we sadly need her esprit and intelligence . . .

And a third:

We dined last night at the Bulwers in Hertford Street. That amusing young man, whom you enjoyed so greatly at Barnet last year, was there, Mr Disraeli. Rosina Bulwer was a sight! Plastered with jewels and painted to the eyes, while Bulwer himself glittered all over! There were plenty of the Family as you may suppose and of all people the solemn Newmark and his fat dowdy Phyllis. However, the excuse for their coming was our cousin Judith from Cumberland. I had heard of her often enough and was all eagerness to behold her. Well she is a little short pale-faced thing with grey hair and had a dress of brocaded pink gauze (of all things for a woman over fifty!). She carried an ivory cane and should have been altogether absurd. But she was not! Disraeli was enchanted with her and Rosina talked to her an immense deal and even Miss Landon admitted her 'ton'. I can tell you how she does it. By being perfectly natural, having plenty of humour and common sense. I never saw anyone enjoy herself so completely . . .

Indeed she did. She went everywhere, did everything, and knew, for the moment, no weariness. Sylvia Herries was her principal companion. That girl, with her eagerness, sense of adventure and gaiety that had at its heart some undefined melancholy, was designed for her affections. Then suddenly Judith woke. That 'unhappiness' was everywhere, hidden by a superficial eagerness that had no stability.

She saw that she was in a society where nothing was real, where no one believed in anything at all, where everyone feared what the morrow would bring. The 'Silver Fork' novels of fashionable life, just then beginning to be so popular, were symptomatic of the falsehood and sham, while cruel and malicious sheets like the Age and the John Bull of Theodore Hook showed where the rottenness was hidden.

Prolonged war had killed sincerity, every kind of faith, social behaviour. The world of London that she, for a moment, invaded was dominated by a new aristocracy of wealth, an aristocracy without tradition, without breeding, an aristocracy that in its aggressive uneasiness suffered itself to be blackmailed by the vilest panders and the most worthless adventurers. Most of the great houses in London were occupied by 'new men' who hurried to learn manners that could never truly be theirs and sought with drink, gambling, orgies and ostentation, to give a semblance of splendour and security. The roads to prominence lay through scandal, back-biting and jealousy. Sport, jewels, wild expenditure covered meanness and vice. All was fake; for a woman to be virtuous proclaimed her dowdy. Men lived by their wits and climbed relentlessly over the backs of their dearest friends.

Such was the fashionable world of which Judith had a glimpse. But it was in just such a world that the opportunities of such a family as the Herries--sober, careful, traditional--lay.

The Herries in London were separated into three parts--the business Herries, Will at their head, James the baronet following rather clumsily, and Amery Herries, Sylvia's brother-in-law, very able and sharp, a possible successor when Will was in his dotage. There were secondly the religious Herries, headed by Stephen Newmark, who, as Judith soon perceived, when he was not sensible, was VERY tiresome indeed. Stephen had his pet clergyman--Mr Aubrey Grant of St Anne's, Pimlico--a gentleman very often at Stephen's table, a stout effeminate, purring gentleman, adored by the ladies and detested by Judith. There was also in the Newmark household the Methodist tradition of the Rockage family in which Phyllis had been brought up. Maria Rockage was still alive, a kindly rheumatic old Dowager in the place in Wiltshire. She was for ever sending the Newmark family pamphlets--'The Miner's Lament', 'The Royal Road to Hell', 'The Shopman's Vision'--interspersed with delightful, gay and very human epistles. She lamented grievously that she could not come up to London to see Judith, who had once lived with her for nearly ten years and whom she adored. Many of Mr Aubrey Grant's congregation came to Cadogan Place--old Mr and Mrs Pomeroy were very prominent--and quite awful Judith found them all. The scent on Mr Grant's handkerchief alone was enough to send her out of the room when he was there.

The third division was the social one. Into this, at times, the other two divisions penetrated, but Will and Christabel, Newmark and Phyllis, various Newmark cousins, did not truly belong.

Sylvia Herries, young though she was, was mistress here. She knew the London social, literary, Bohemian world completely. She laughingly declared that all the adventurers in London came to her tiny house in Brook Street. Indeed she did not care who came. She kept open house. Neither she nor Garth--now a very elegant, charming young man--seemed to have much money. They were for ever in desperate straits. Will--who was in these days more generous than of old--must have helped them again and again. They reminded Judith constantly of herself and Georges in those old, mad, adventurous days. That was perhaps why she came to care for them more than any other of the Herries relations, and why she made her alliance with them. Sylvia was her own kind--audacious, reckless, pleasure-loving, but also serious, practical and wise about other people.

It soon became obvious that Stephen disliked her constant visits to the little house in Brook Street, a little house that was all light colours, jingling pianos, poodle dogs and noise. There were authors like the Bulwers, Letitia Landon, Theodore Hook, young Ainsworth, of whom he could not possibly approve. There were dancers, opera singers, racing men and ladies of extremely doubtful reputation. Judith had, alas, no more of those fine serious conversations with which on the first morning she had been honoured. It seemed to him really lamentable that a woman of her years should care for such a world. He had been right, as he constantly told Phyllis in the sacredness of their huge four-poster, in wondering whether anyone so brazen about her bastard child was a suitable guest for them, and poor Phyllis, who loved Judith with all her heart, tried to keep the peace. But what Phyllis really did not understand was that Judith should be so deeply horrified at the present state of the London world and yet enjoy the parties in Brook Street so greatly. She seemed like two different women in one.

Then the climax arrived. On an afternoon of the third week of Judith's stay, Sylvia Herries was alone with Judith in the Newmark drawing-room. Sylvia was looking most bewitching with her ringlets, rose-coloured tulle, a waist so small as to be almost invisible, and a printed satin scarf. She danced about the room like a fairy, she bowed with mock ceremony to the pedestal and the lady's head thereon, she imitated Stephen, whom she found entirely ridiculous. Judith also was seized with a devil. She valsed with Sylvia round and round the room. The 'valse' was still new enough to be divine. They danced ever more madly. They danced into a small table that held a large preposterous vase of the brightest green. It tumbled with a crash to the ground, and, of course, at that precise moment Stephen entered with old Mr Pomeroy.

There was nothing to be said, nothing to be done. There the vase was in a thousand pieces. There were the two ladies--one of them old enough to be the other's mother--hot, dishevelled, and Judith had, a moment before, lost one of her shoes. Stephen gave one of his grim sacrificial smiles, Sylvia departed with a private moue of amusement for Judith's benefit (seen, however, by Stephen). Judith did her best to become, quickly again, an elderly dignified lady.

'Oh, it is of no importance, no importance at all,' said Stephen, bending stiffly to pick up some pieces. 'An old family heirloom-- but still--no matter, no matter.'

But he never forgave Judith that broken vase. An ivory fan, a green vase: these are the things of which family histories are made. It was quite clear--Stephen now made it plainly apparent-- that it was time that the visit of Judith and Adam came to an end.

'Come and stay with us, darling,' said Sylvia. 'For as long as you please.'

'No,' said Judith. 'Cumberland is my proper place.'

And it WAS. She would not, she knew, be happy in the little house in Brook Street. THAT was not her home, any more than was Stephen's. Her holiday (and oh! how she had enjoyed it!) was at an end.

So she looked round her to collect herself and her things, and found Adam. Not that she at all had forgotten him. It had been wonderful to see him against this new background and with new people. She found that he was enterprising, reserved and extraordinarily generous. She had known all these things about him since the beginning of time, but they wore a fresh dress in this fresh world. His generosity was surely astonishing, for he had very little money unless his London relations gave him some. In any case he was always buying things for the little Newmarks, for his mother, for Phyllis. To Sylvia, whom he worshipped, he gave nothing. All the little Newmarks loved him, even the spectacled Horace, who was not lavish with his affections. Mary and her sister Phyllis would be demonstrative, but he shrank from their demonstrations with horror. He allowed no one any physical approach. He produced a toy, a doll, a horse, a rattle for the baby, flowers or whatever, and he said 'Here!' or 'That's for you, ma'am'. He looked at you sternly while he presented it, forbidding you to thank him. Then he escaped. He escaped very often, went off on his own affairs. He was, in fact, very happy during this visit.

The visit came to a close, both for Judith and Adam, with an adventure that it was not likely that they would forget. It was the recurrent adventure of Judith's life: once, in London, a boy hanging; twice, in Paris, an elephant escaping; and now, the third time.

On the evening of Monday the eighth of November, Amery Herries took Judith, Adam and his sister-in-law Sylvia to the Adelphi Theatre to witness a performance of The Heart of London, or A Sharper's Progress, by William Thomas Moncrieff. This was a glorious play, and although not intended for the young did Adam no kind of harm.

The play over, they stepped from one melodrama into another.

The Strand, lit with the flares of burning stakes carried head- high, and in the distance towards Covent Garden by an overturned cart that had been set alight, showed a wild fantasy of faces, a mob that now was stagnant like a dead pond and then broken as though by a whipping wind, all this driven by a roar that had nothing human in it save an occasional woman's scream.

The citizens of London, excited by Mr Hunt at a meeting at the Rotunda in Blackfriars Road, were making their way to the West End that they might assist the cause of Reform. As soon as the shouts were heard the doors of the Adelphi were closed, but Amery's party had slipped out five minutes earlier, to secure a hackney coach. The doors were closed behind them; before they could consider their position they were swung forward into the street. Judith, Adam's arm through hers, saw neither Amery nor Sylvia again that night.

It was as though Judith and Adam fell into a jungle of undergrowth. Above them bodies towered and whether they wished it or no they were carried forward to the cries of 'Down with the Police!' 'Reform!' 'No Peel!' 'No Wellington!'

Down there in the undergrowth they conversed:
'Never mind, Mother: I'm here,' said Adam.

'Now, don't you let go!' Judith said crossly. This was impertinence, to treat her and her son in this fashion. A light swung to the sky, and stars escaping, a golden net scattered among the chimney-pots. Then the sky was darkened, and a large face attached to a stout body in moleskins was rosy in the glare of a burning stake stinking of tar.

'No Wellington! Down with Wellington!' roared the moleskins most good-naturedly. He stank of gin, and his hand, roughened with honest toil, stroked Judith's cheek.

At that touch fear, that she had known so seldom in her life, caught her and pressed against her. A bear tortured, a boy hanged, Adam's father clinging to her while the horses' hoofs pranced in the air, these once again encompassed her.

'Reform! Reform!' shrieked a woman, her hair about her face and a basket on her arm. Judith looked at Adam and saw that he was quite unafraid and greatly enjoying everything.

'Adam, in a moment there should be a turning to the river. Watch for it!'

But the impetuous movement ceased. Staring around her she saw that their progress had been far more rapid than she had supposed, for they were in Downing Street and had halted in front of Lord Bathurst's residence. She knew the house well, for Garth Herries had taken her to a reception there. By squirming her body through a funny jumble of legs, chests, arms and hands she found a corner for Adam and herself against some railings, and was able to observe from there how a gentleman, his face crimson with rage, came out on to the balcony. He was armed with a brace of pistols and, shouting in a voice thick with anger, told them that if they committed any illegal act he would fire. Groans, yells, shouts of 'Go it! Go it!' answered him, whereupon another gentleman arrived on the balcony and took the pistols from him. Then everyone cheered and seemed suddenly radiant with good spirits.

At that same moment Judith perceived that Adam was gone. She became at once a frenzied woman. Any self-control that she had ever learnt, any caution or reserve, was lost. She screamed like a madwoman, 'Adam! Adam!', tried to move and found that she could not, beat on some stout manly chest: 'Let me go! Let me go! Let me through! Can't you see? My boy . . . Adam! Adam!'

But it happened that a strong body of the new police had just arrived from Scotland Yard that they might form themselves into a line at the end of King Street to prevent the mob from proceeding to the House of Commons. At once a great shout went up: 'The Peelers!' 'The Peelers!' 'Down with the Peelers!' As though the ground were agitated with earthquake, the crowd rocked forward and back, seeming to rise in places like a bulging floor about to crack. A line of wavering flame ran against the walls of the houses where men with lighted wood were ranging themselves in a line of defence. But Judith saw and heard nothing. Adam was lost, Adam might be crushed underfoot, she would never see Adam again; and at that frantic thought all the world that had seemed so important, social, political, religious--yes, and all the Herries, all Uldale, all her individual life and desires, blew like scraps of burnt paper into the air. Her shawl was torn from her, her wide-puffed sleeves rent. She beat on some face with her hands, she tore some cheek with her nails. 'Let me go! Let me go! Can't you see? My boy's gone!'

But no one saw and no one cared. A general fight was toward. Inspector Lincoln of the E Division had arrived with seventy men. The tri-coloured flag that had 'Reform' painted on it--the banner of the riot--was captured by the Peelers. There was a rush to recapture it. A man, bare-breasted, his shirt hanging in ribbons from his back, black-haired, brawny, his chest tattooed with a ship in violet and green, hung above the mob like a sign. He had in his hand a hatchet. Judith, seeing him with a strange and memorable distinctness, beheld him, as it seemed to her, trample on her boy. The crowd rose and fell; she was swept off her feet and would, it may be, have ended all her adventures there and then for ever had not some man caught her to him so that she was soaked, as it were, in his sweat and ale and dripping clothes, her head against his beard, his hand upon her breast. A fine thing for an old lady of fifty-six! But it saved her. Crushed, with her face in his rough hair, seeing nothing, frantic for Adam, she heard around her the strange sough and sigh of a mob suddenly terrified, resolved to run, the wind beating from under their feet, as though it would raise them to the sky. 'Reform!' 'Reform!' 'Reform!' 'The Peelers!' 'The Peelers!'

And then sudden quiet, a child crying, a whistle sharply blown, and she herself, her cheek bleeding, was half sitting, half crumpled on the pavement. But she was up in a moment. She could run now; there was nothing to stop her. As though God had crooked His little finger, there was no one there. Some man leant against the railings moaning and nursing his head, a beaver hat lay in the roadway, a burning faggot sent up a twist of smoke, and the silence was like a miracle. A yard away there was Adam, crying 'They're on the run! They're on the run! Mother, look, look!'

He had never been more than a yard away, then. She was furious with him and, her hair about her face, did what she had never done before--slapped his face.

'You careless boy! You careless boy!'

But he was enchanted. It was the best adventure of his life so far. His mouth was bleeding, his coat and trousers torn, but he laughed and laughed as though he'd never have done.

Then she hugged and kissed him.

'I thought you were killed,' she said. She felt an old, old woman, an ache in every bone and her head like a turnip. Very characteristically, she recovered her dignity.

'Now we'll find a hackney coach,' she said.

The watchman was calling up from the street below two o'clock of the morning before Adam came in to wish her goodnight. She was sitting up, a very old lady indeed she felt, propped up with pillows and telling her different aches to mind their business and behave. There was a bruise on her forehead, one knee was lamentably swollen, but there was no real harm done . . . only she was very old of a sudden. Nine hundred and ninety.

'Come here and kiss me,' she said.

Adam was in his nightdress, and, with a purple lump the size of a lemon over one eye, looked no beauty.

He laughed and sat on the bed, her arm around him. She made him put on her furred dressing-gown and furred slippers, for the room was viciously cold. There was a warming-pan inside the bed now, and she made him slide his feet inside against hers.

So he slipped into the circle of her arm, lay there with his black hair in his eyes, too eagerly excited to sleep yet. The panic of her fear that she had lost him was still with her. She had never loved him with such passionate intensity and she had never felt so old. Her brain formed odd confused pictures for her, nothing tangible, nothing consecutive. In the big stone fireplace a baby fire leapt as though it were trying its first steps in life so that it might really be a fine grown-up fire one day. An impenetrably black picture of a forest, a lonely tower, and some horsemen swayed a little on its cord, blown by all the draughts of heaven, some of whom whistled through the wallpaper like lonely spirits trying to keep their courage up. Three candles guttered on the table beside the four-poster with the green hangings; a mirror topped with heavy gilt feathers reflected the light. And under and above all this was the dreadful cold, a cold worse than Arctic, for it was damp. Soon Adam was lying inside the bed folded in his mother's arms as he had not been since he was a tiny boy at Watendlath.

Without words they reached a loving intimate security that daylight and Adam's dislike of manifestation had hindered at Uldale. It had always been there, but for long now she had not had his heart beating, as it were, inside her very body.

Idly she watched the pictures come and go: Stephen saying 'And now let us pray'; Sylvia Herries imitating some ballet-dancer at the Opera; young Mr Harrison Ainsworth (so handsome but wearing too many rings and his curls too heavy with Macassar oil) telling her about his recent Italian journey, and how he had found a rouge-pot at Pompeii; gossip about Ball Hughes and the Bulwers and Lady Blessington and Holland House--and then, over all this nonsense, the figure of the man with the ship of violet on his chest, raising his hatchet . . .

She held Adam closely to her, kissed him, stroked his forehead. He did not resist nor move away as he would normally have done, but sleepily murmured: 'Down with the Peelers!' 'Down with Wellington!' 'Down with the Peelers!'

'Hush, dear. Don't think of the horrid thing. I wonder how Amery and Sylvia are! Dear me! how incredibly selfish! I have never thought of them until this instant!'

Then the dancing pictures vanished. She saw something else and with extraordinary clearness. She raised herself on her pillows. Adam tickled her foot with his.

'Adam, wake up! There is something that I must say!'

He took her hand in his.

'Adam--you will shortly be a grown man and I shall be an old woman. I had not thought of it until this moment. How dreadful to be old! And I shall not be a nice old woman. I shall want my way. I made the mistake of my whole life when I stayed at Uldale. We should have gone to Watendlath. I have become Herries and made you Herries and shall wish you to be more and more Herries. Adam, promise me that, however I wish it, you will keep your independence. You are not to be Herries. You are illegitimate anyway, and your father was so little Herries as not to matter. I shall want to keep you later. You will be all I shall have. But you are not to permit me. Do you hear? However much I love you . . . Dear me, dear me, what a nasty old woman I am going to be!'

Then, as there was no response, she said again:

'You are not to allow me to swallow you, do you understand? Fight me, if need be. In another ten years I shall be completely Herries, from head to toe. How horrible! Adam, do you hear me.'

'What, Mama?'

'You are to keep your independence. I love you too much for it to be good for either of us.'

'And when the Peelers were coming . . .' he murmured.

The vision passed. She saw nothing, but gathered him closer into her arms, and he slept, holding her hand tightly in his, while she gazed out into the room and watched the little fire surrender its life, and the candles blow unsteadily in the wind.

WESTAWAYS: FATHER AND SON

It was not true to say that Walter Herries was without imagination. He could see very vividly things that were not actually in front of him, only they must, those things, if they were going to act on him powerfully, SPRING from facts. Then, his imagination once started, he could be obsessed, obsessed by his own grandeur, by his sense of power, by the thought that he was a Herries, and, above all, by the knowledge that he was Uhland's father.

At this very time that Judith was in London breaking vases, meeting Mr Disraeli, and scratching the cheeks of rioters, Walter was taking his son Uhland day after day up the hill to Ireby to watch the Fortress growing. Uhland was now fifteen years of age, and the Fortress was half its way to heaven.

It must be remembered that it was not yet called the Fortress--that name came to it later--but already it was beginning to be grim of aspect. Mr Carstairs, bothered by rheumatism and this cursed Northern climate, was not in the best of tempers. And he was beginning to dislike Walter Herries extremely. He had never been bullied before, being a man of some personality and temper. Walter Herries often spoke to him as he would to his groom, and Carstairs would have given the job up long ago were it not that he was aware that the Herries

were now important people in London and a useful connexion, that Walter threw money about, and (this the most important with Carstairs, who was, finally, a man of feeling) that Walter could show, at times, an extraordinary and even pathetic charm.

He wanted the place to look like a castle. It was to have battlements and towers, towers from whose summit a flag could fly. That was the moment of Romanticism, of the Waverley Novels, of Weltschmerz, of Pelham and (a little late) Childe Harold and Werther. There was no Weltschmerz in Walter, but he would have his battlements and a flag flying. So the place was going up, grim and grey and forbidding. Its half-grown walls could already be seen from all the country round.

Nearly every day Walter and Uhland rode up there, Walter on a big white horse, Uhland on a small black pony. As you watched them together (as Carstairs watched them) you might sometimes think their positions reversed, that Uhland was the father and Walter the son. There WAS, Carstairs decided again and again, something most truly pathetic in their relationship, for Walter dearly loved his son. It was the one true, selfless, generous instinct in him. Selfless? That perhaps not, for an intense family pride was at the root of it. But pride? Pride in that queer, misshapen, white-faced ancient child, whose sharp countenance was always grave, whose voice was so cold and detached, whose chilly eyes watched you so solemnly, with so deep and questioning a gaze. Only once had Carstairs seen the boy moved by some human emotion, and that was when, by a chance, having met young Adam in Keswick and had a chat with him, he had said something about him to Walter. Young Uhland had been listening; colour had crept into his cheeks, light into his eye. Walter had made a scornful gesture, and it seemed that Uhland was going to say something in protest. He checked himself.

It was, thought Carstairs, an interesting thing to see that stout, red-faced man with his bright waistcoats, his pins and his rings, his confidence and his pride, surrender to that colourless child in his black suit, so silent, so neat and so watchful. Yes, watchful! That was what Uhland was, watchful and waiting. Meanwhile his sister Elizabeth, the prettiest child, Carstairs thought, that he had ever seen, never shared her father's company. It was as though he had no daughter.

That was a month of chills and mists, of sudden winds and gleaming suns. One afternoon when the sun ran in and out of the clouds like a jester, Walter and Uhland rode up to Ireby.

'Father,' said Uhland, 'why are you building this house?'

Why was he building this house? What a question! Nevertheless, this was the first occasion on which Uhland had shown any interest in the affair. Day after day they had ridden up there, and Walter, in a flood of talk, had shown his son how this would be there, and that here, that the ballroom would be so long, and the dining-room catch the sun at such a time, that he should have a room to himself, in one of the towers if he liked, so that he could look over the whole country, over to Keswick, over to Scotland . . .

And Uhland had watched him gravely and plucked at his upper lip in a way that he had, but said no word.

'Why am I building this house?' Walter explained. 'For you, my son, and for the glory of the family, so that when you marry, my son . . .'

'I shall never marry,' said Uhland.

'Ah, you think that now, Uhland, but the time will come when you will see a lady so beautiful . . .'

But Uhland shook his head.

'I don't care about women,' he said.

But, of course, he must marry. Did he not wish to carry on the family?

He looked at his father sardonically. There were plenty of people to do that--all the lot at Uldale, all his relations in London.

Walter felt a chill at his heart. Of course, Uhland must have sons, and they must have sons, and sons and sons!

'Look, Father--there is Mrs Herries!'

She was there again then, standing on the edge of the rough bare field, her tall black figure framed by the rough bare hills. A sensation of disgust caught him. He had not seen her for several weeks and thought that she had at last wearied of this crazy, imbecile watching. For crazy and imbecile she was! At first he had been rather pleased at the sight of her. He was having his revenge, although a revenge for what he by now would have found it rather difficult to say. Jennifer and her children had shrunk to rather poor game, although he hated the boy for his health and good looks, while his own son . . .

'Why does she come here, Father, day after day?' Uhland asked.

'She's mad,' Walter answered brusquely.

'But how mad? I thought mad people screamed and broke things.'

'She shall scream well enough before I have finished with her.' He felt vindictive today and would like to hurt someone. And yet he was not by nature cruel. If things only went well with him he could be as jolly and generous as anyone. But what was all this, what his treasures in Westaways, his position in the County, this new place of his, if Uhland were not to take pleasure in them? His big body throbbed sometimes with a savage desire to take his boy and squeeze him into some sort of life of response and activity. Here was he doing so much, striving so hard, and for what kind of return? He turned back on his horse and, seeing that dark figure against the skyline, thought for a moment of what it would be to have, indeed, John Herries for a son. He hated that young Herries. Yes, he would drive them all to perdition before he'd done.

He drew his horse closer to Uhland's pony and, speaking very gently, he asked him:

'Will you not care, Uhland, to have a son to succeed to all this when you are gone?'

'No, Father. Why should I?'

Walter sighed. 'If you cannot see that, I cannot make you.'

Uhland, after a pause, said quietly:

'I should be glad to have a brother like Adam Paris.'

'Adam Paris?' Walter, in his impatience, made his horse rear. 'That boy! Why do you think of him so much? He cares nothing for you.'

'I like him--just as I hate John Herries.' He looked about him, then asked: 'Father, when you have built this, will John Herries hate it?'

'Yes, my boy, he will.'

'Ah--then I am glad you are building it, Father.'

'Why do you hate young Herries so much? You scarcely see him.'

Uhland considered it.

'Why do people hate one another, Father?'

'Because of something they have done, some injury or harm they have done.'

'Well--that's the reason then.'

'But young Herries has never harmed you.'

'No. But I will harm HIM.'

An incomprehensible boy! But Walter had never been clever at analysing other people and, in any case, his clear view of his son would be fogged by his blinding absorbing love for him. He did not know it, but he would never have cared for a strong healthy son as he loved this weakling.

They arrived at the place. A great bustle was toward, men moving with barrows and carts, climbing ladders, shouting, hammering, cutting stone, filing and sawing. The house, half raised, lifted blind eyes to the sky. It was built of Cumberland stone, beautiful in its dim blues and greens and greys with here a soft blush of rose, there a strand of gold, but the effect of the whole was nevertheless grim and cold. It promised to be strong; nothing, it seemed, would conquer it.

Walter climbed over into the interior and Uhland stood and watched him. Within, on that misty day, everything was in a half-light. The men, accustomed to his presence, went about their work. Through a gap where a window would be, Walter could see the sharp fall of the hill. There, in the cup of the ground, would be Uldale. He savoured in his nostrils, for a moment, the especial blend of rough soil, sharpened with the grey-stone of some solitary farm blending with the bare outline of the rising hills beyond, cold and bleak but strong and deeply true--that meeting of strength and austerity and richness that is Cumberland's gift to those who love her. He loved her as an animal loves its home. But today he was restless and dissatisfied. He climbed his way out again, and after a word or two to the foreman, rode down the hill. He went a little ahead and Uhland, watching, as he always did, for everything, saw something very strange. His father had turned the corner by the little wood into the road that ran from Uldale to Bassenthwaite. Out of the wood came two people: Walter was already gathered into the dusk, but they saw Uhland, and he saw them before they turned back into the wood again.

They were his sister Elizabeth and John Herries.

He rode on after his father.

Uhland's room at Westaways was as bare as a monastic cell. The walls held no pictures; the only furniture was a bed, two chairs, a bookcase, a washstand and a cupboard.

There was, however, more in this room than this stiff furniture. There were the animals.

Uhland, since a very small child, had shown a strong interest in any animal wounded, hurt or deformed. A very pretty little picture might be elaborated of a pale-faced, limping little boy sorry for hurt animals because he was himself hurt. But you could not think of sentiment in connexion with Uhland--it froze at his touch.

Nevertheless, in this lonely world through which we pass, each of us shadowed from the other, who knows or can truly discern the instincts of the human mind? It was enough, in the case of Uhland, that in a cold, undemonstrative fashion he cared for any damaged animal that came his way. The animals, on their side, appeared to recognize him as one of themselves. They never showed him that especial attention given by animals to human beings who are kind to them; sometimes, we may suspect, with a sense of conventional duty. They showed Uhland just as much feeling as they would to another animal. They did not trust him any more than they would trust one another. Yes, he was one of themselves.

At this particular time, there was in his bedroom a bright parrot with pink feathers, in a gilt cage. His claw was bandaged. Uhland had bought him of a sailor in Keswick. There was a dog, mostly spaniel, in a basket. It wore, with an air of comic but patient protest, a large yellow silk handkerchief over one eye. Uhland had found it dying in a ditch near Threlkeld, minus an eye, after suffering torture at the hands of some farm-children. In another basket was a wild cat, minus a leg, that had been caught in a trap on Cat Bells. This animal, black, with fierce burning eyes, spent most of its time gathered on its haunches and spitting, but it allowed Uhland to do what he wished with it.

In vain had Walter protested that it was unwholesome to keep animals in the room where you slept. Uhland briefly stated that he would see to it that they were clean, that he would trust no one but himself to look after them. Walter submitted. If they made the boy happy there they must remain. And Uhland saw to it that they WERE clean. The room was spotless, with

an odd, dried, mummified scent of the cloistered cell about it. Its only sign of life was the sudden chattering of the parrot, who would gibber unintelligibly to himself and rattle the bars of his gilt cage.

Today, coming in from his ride, Uhland squatted down on the floor and examined the dog's eye. Very skilfully, and with fingers that were strangely delicate, he undid the yellow silk handkerchief, washed the angry red eye-socket, put some ointment on a long tear above the right temple. The dog, a black spaniel with a touch of sheepdog, waited calmly while this was done. When it was over he lay down in his basket and licked his paws. Uhland gave him some water, then squatted down beside him, staring in front of him. There was a lamp on the chest of drawers near him that gave an ivory patina to his pale cheek. The black cat crouched in his basket and watched him with fiery eyes.

When he thought, he thought not like a little boy but like a man for whom all illusions are over. He had never had any illusions. He saw the things in front of him with cold clarity. He was only a small boy, but he knew an intensity of controlled feeling that was quite mature. He knew shame because he was not as other boys, haughty pride because he was the son of his father. His father was rich, powerful, had servants, horses, lands. He would have respected and cared for his father more deeply had his father cared for him less and showed less that he cared. The only two human beings who entered at all at this time into his emotions were Adam and John Herries. He loved the one and hated the other. He hated John Herries because he had been brought up from a baby to do so, because John was handsome and strong, but chiefly because he was gentle and submissive. Anyone who was submissive roused in him, child though he was, something wild and savage. To be submissive when you were strong enough to be otherwise, to bend your neck like a woman when you were hearty enough to be a proper man! It was as though someone preferred to be lame when he need not! He caught a sense perhaps also of John's dislike and fear of himself. He KNEW that John Herries was afraid of him, child though he was, and the contempt he felt for fear was closely allied to hatred.

For these same reasons he had always loved and admired Adam Paris. That stout, rough, untidy brown body with its independence, freedom, absence of all sentiment, caught and held for ever his admiration. Adam Paris did not care whether he, Uhland Herries, lived or died, and so Uhland loved him.

As he squatted there on the floor his thoughts were dark. He had guessed for a long while that his sister Elizabeth had some secret. They had nothing at all in common, he and his sister. She was afraid of him, and he thought her pretty but uninteresting. But now-- she and John Herries! Uhland knew as yet nothing about the love of men and women, although the gossip of stable-boys and farm-hands had long ago told him all that there was to learn about the physical facts of conception and generation. The thing did not interest him. In any case Elizabeth was only a child as he himself was. But that John Herries should be on any kind of terms with a member of his family, roused, slowly, steadily, all his coldest anger. He looked like a little old brooding man as he sat there on the hard floor in the light of the lamp.

On the very next afternoon, as it happened, Uhland encountered John Herries.

Riding out on his pony (he was always happy when riding because his deformity was not apparent) he met John Herries walking alone on the road beyond Portinscale. John was strolling along, thinking deeply, his hands behind his back. As he walked his lips moved. He was very handsome in the dark-blue coat, fawn pantaloons, a brown beaver hat. Uhland pulled up the pony.

'Excuse me, sir,' he said in his queer grave child's voice.

John looked up and at once was seized with the chill of apprehension and discomfort that always attacked him whenever this boy was near him. He had been thinking of charming things--of the faint pallor of the dried bracken against the hill, of the fact that soon Aunt Judith and Adam would be back from London, of a party that they had had at Uldale for his sister when they had practised archery on the lawn--yes, and of Elizabeth whom he loved with all his soul, and for whom he was waiting until she should be old enough for marriage. And then--this hobgoblin! To be afraid of a small boy on a fat pony! But he was afraid.

Uhland did not get down from his pony. He simply said in his clear chill voice:

'If I see you with my sister again, you shall be beaten by my father's servants.'

John replied contemptuously:

'How is it you are out, young Uhland, without your governess?'

But Uhland went on:

'I mean it. I saw you both at Ireby.'

John stood there looking at him. He was determined to conquer this causeless apprehension. Gentle and courteous though he was, he had a manly spirit; it was true, perhaps, that this child was the only creature of the world of whom he was afraid. He might even if he looked at him long enough pity him for his pale face, his meagre body that could not keep itself straight even on a pony. But he looked--and dropped his eyes. He was rooted there as one is in a nightmare.

'Now look here, young man,' he said lightly, 'you keep to your own business, which is firing paper bullets out of pop-guns, I should think. This is a fine day; I'm walking for my health, you're riding for yours. We go opposite ways.'

'Then you leave my sister alone,' Uhland repeated. 'Your family and my family hate one another, and I'm glad they do. When I'm a man I'll do you a hurt if I can.'

'When you're a man--' John laughed. 'That's a long way. Good afternoon.'

He passed on, but he knew in his heart that it was all he could do to prevent himself from running.

Meanwhile Uhland rode up the hill a little way and then back to Westaways. He would have a word or two to say to Elizabeth. He found her in her room sewing 'or some such nonsense'. He limped in, sat on a corner of the sofa near to her, crossed his legs and looked at her. He recognized, of course, that she was a beautiful girl; he had all the Herries quality of perceiving things as they were, and he saw her fairness and delicacy, so that every colour from the pale shadowed gold of her hair to the warm pallor of her neck and arms was in perfect harmony; he saw all this, her fragility and strength, the gentleness of her eyes, the humour of her mouth. He admired her as a valuable family possession, and the thought that young Herries should be familiar with her revolted him-- but revolted him in his own quiet child's way. Nevertheless, there is no one more determined than a child when he HAS an obsession.

'I saw you and John Herries at Ireby,' he remarked.

They were twins, but to Elizabeth he had never seemed like a relation at all. They had never done anything together, never cared for the same things nor thought the same thoughts. Elizabeth had many faults but they were not Uhland's. Her worst fault just now perhaps was her almost sulky reserve. This was the result of her father's ignoring of her. That had eaten deeply into her. She would let either her father or Uhland torture her to the last point of endurance and not utter a cry. She loved John Herries, but he was a man and she was only a child. She met him secretly, wrote to him and the rest chiefly because she knew what her father and Uhland thought of him. It was therefore not probable that Uhland would get anything from her now.

'Yes?' she said, continuing her sewing.

'You are never to speak to him again,' Uhland went on.

'Who said so?'

'I say so.'

'Indeed?' She looked at him, smiling. Then she bit off her thread. 'I shall speak to exactly whom I please.'

'You shall not. If you do I shall tell your father.'

'Tell him, then.'

'He'll beat you.'

She smiled again. 'You don't think I care for that . . . Uhland, what a baby you are!'

That stung him, but he showed no signs. He nursed his knee in his hands, leaning forward and looking at her.

'Those people at Uldale are our enemies,' he said. 'They will have to leave there and go somewhere else when father's house is finished.'

'Yes?' she said.

'Father will send you away to school if he knows,' he went on.

'I shall be glad to go away,' she answered. 'I am always asking him to send me to school.'

'Well,' said Uhland, getting up, 'if I see John Herries talking to you again I shall shoot him.'

'Then you'll be hung,' she said, smiling.

'Perhaps it's Herries that will be hung,' he answered. Then he limped away.

But he had no intention whatever of saying anything to his father. He liked to keep his secrets.

Walter on his side was driven, after that little talk with his son on Ireby, by a strange restlessness. What had the child meant about never marrying? He WAS, of course, a child. He knew nothing of women or marriage . . . but the thin echo of that small cold voice, like the whistle of wind through the wallpaper, frightened Walter. The boy was growing. He had now his own thoughts and plans. Walter ought to know what these were. He discovered with angry resentment that he knew almost nothing about his son. The resentment may be said to have been directed against the Deity, Who was not at that moment paying all the attention to Walter Herries' affairs that He should do.

So Walter went in to say goodnight to his son. He was sitting up in bed, propped against his pillows, reading, by the light of a candle, a book. A dark cloth was over the parrot's cage, the dog was curled up asleep, the cat sat blinking at the candle.

Uhland was reading Ivanhoe.

'What a silly book, Papa!' he said. 'I am certain that people never talked like that'

Walter placed his great bulk on the bed and put his arm round his son. Under Uhland's nightdress there was a sharp rigid spine-bone that seemed to protest against the caressing warmth of Walter's hand.

'Why, not, my boy?' said Walter, who had never read Ivanhoe. 'Sir Walter Scott is a very great man.'

'Have you ever read a book called Frankenstein, Papa?'

'No, my boy.'

'That's better than this stuff. Frankenstein creates a Monster and cannot escape it. There is too much fine writing, however.'

Walter sighed. Although this room was so clean yet you were oppressively conscious of the animals in it. Their very silence was alarming. He drew Uhland closer to him and felt the hard casing of ribs on that bony little body. He kissed him. Uhland resigned himself. He knew so well, oh, so very, very well what this was, this having his face pushed into the thick hot vast territory of his father's waistcoat with its hard brass buttons. Beneath his thin cheek his father's heart pounded like an imprisoned thumping fist. If his hand slid down to the hard warm expanse of his father's thigh it was as though he touched hot steel. Moreover, he detested sentiment.

'Uhland,' said Walter, 'I was hearing this evening that they are ordering fresh troops into Carlisle. There is fear of riots over all this Reform.'

'Yes, Papa.'

'Do you understand about Reform?'

'Oh yes, Papa.' Uhland allowed his hand to be held and imprisoned in his father's. 'Parliament has chosen its members from the wrong places--little places have many representatives and big places have few. The people are not at all represented.'

('Good God!' thought Walter. 'Who IS this son of mine?')

'Yes, Uhland,' he went on, rather heavily. 'The people want to throw us out, my boy. They want the country to belong to THEM. They're tired of seeing us have the best of everything, and I don't blame 'em. All the same it would never do if they had their way. Think what England would be like if the working-man did what he liked with it. Imagine if you had Posset in power in London instead of--well, instead of the Duke of Wellington, for example.'

Uhland agreed that it would be ridiculous. But, he added, interested:

'You see, Papa, there would be five Possets, not one Posset.'

Walter asked him to explain.

'Well, in Keswick there are hundreds of men think they're as good as Posset. But if it's you or the Duke of Wellington they KNOW they're not so good, so while you or the Duke of Wellington rule there's only one of you, but if Posset were to rule all the others would want to as well.'

'Well,' said Walter after a pause, 'remember you're a Herries and belong to the finest family in England.'

'Are we the finest family in England?'

'Most certainly we are.'

'Then they are fine at Uldale too?'

'Yes,' he answered, laughing, 'so long as they go somewhere else to live.'

Then Uhland asked a strange question.

'Papa--is it part of you what your great-grandfather was?'

'What DO you mean?'

'Well--your great-grandfather was a wicked man and married a gipsy, who was Adam Paris' grandmother. Are you and Adam and I partly like we are because of what your great-grandfather did?'

'I can't say . . . I suppose so . . . Something.'

'But we are so different.'

'Now you go to sleep, Uhland . . . Do you love your old father?'

'Yes, Papa.'

'You are all he has, you know. All he has in the world.'

'Yes, Papa.'

'He would do anything for you.'

'Yes, Papa.'

The dog began to move restlessly in his sleep, and he snapped his teeth at the flies of his dreams.

'I am sorry that you like to keep these animals in your room, Uhland. It is not good for your health.'

Uhland threw Ivanhoe on to the floor; then he turned over to sleep.

'Goodnight, Papa.'

'Goodnight, my boy.'

There was a pathos in the manner of Walter's exit: the heavy man, brilliant in his claret-coloured coat and rich brown pantaloons fitting tightly to his thighs, elaborately stepping softly on his toes that he might not disturb his son. He had blown out the candle. At the door he turned back to look. He could see nothing, and the only sound in the room was the dog in his dreams snapping at flies.

ENTRY OF THE FORTRESS

He stood on the black edge of the rock and stretched his arms. He could have shouted with joy, for today was the great day of his life.

Near him, around him, subservient to him were many of the Family. There were present his father, Sir William Herries, Bart; his son Uhland; Sir James Herries, Bart, and the Venerable Rodney Herries, his brother, Archdeacon of Polchester in Glebeshire; Carey, Lord Rockage, and his wife Cecily and their son Roger; Stephen Newmark and his wife Phyllis; Garth Herries, his wife Sylvia, and Amery his brother; and, after these, more distant cousins, cousins by marriage or anything you like, Cards and Garlands and Golds and Ildens and Titchleys--only nobody from Uldale.

It was April 2nd, 1832, and his house on Ireby was triumphantly open.

It was six in the morning of the happiest day of Walter's life. The day, which was to end with a grand dinner and a magnificent ball to which the whole County had been invited, had begun with a run with the Blencathra Pack, and now here they were on the flanks of Helvellyn, so that the sun and the hills, the whole world as God had made it, might see the mighty glories of the Herries family and Walter Herries in particular.

Walter was as happy as a child. It was not conceit that he felt; he had no small vanities because of what he had done. Everything was inevitable. Because he was English and Herries and Walter, therefore he was King of the North. No force of heaven or earth could have helped it. No especial credit to himself that it was so.

Everything was well. God had seen to it that the weather should be right. There had been early in March a very heavy fall of snow, then towards the end of the month ten days of the loveliest possible weather, when the sun had burnt through a warm rosy mist, the cro-

cuses had flowered in the Keswick gardens, the lambs gambolled in the meadows, the waters of Derwentwater, Bassenthwaite and Thirlmere shone with a blue as deep as any Italian lake, then colder again with a further snowfall on the tops, and now, in this early-morning misty air, a blue cloudless sky spread like a field of young violets above their heads.

As his eye covered the scene he saw that all the members of his party were there. Those staying with him were of course present, save only his mother and his wife, too delicate, poor women, for such an expedition. But the others whom he had lodged in Keswick and Bassenthwaite, in Braithwaite and Portinscale, were there also, not one of them was missing. It was a grand assemblage, headed by the great John Peel himself, whose tall bony figure, clad in his grey rough garment that descended almost to his knees, could be seen on a green knoll not far away.

Yes, it was a marvellous day: weather, scent and all would be right. The morning was as still as though it held its breath for very rapture. The hills in the distance were softly coloured in every shade from the faintest mauve to that dark indigo that has the bloom of the richest plums. On the rough ground below him he could see the huntsman's scarlet coat (the huntsman alone was permitted the scarlet), and near him the hounds, little white dots, rose and fell like shining pebbles.

His heart was moved, so that there were tears in his eyes as he caught a faint note of music. Then the music swells, running like a living human voice through the still air. Somewhere hounds have struck a 'drag'. The white pebbles draw together and all move upwards towards him.

A tall gaunt shepherd at his side in his excitement catches his arm and cries: 'Sista . . . Sista . . . Yonder, yonder he goes!'

Then scream and scream again bursts the silence, echoing back from valley and hill. The world that had been so still is broken with movement and shouting and the stir of action. It is good. Oh yes, it is very good indeed to be alive!

Walter had with him his father, Rodney the Archdeacon, Garth Herries and Sylvia his wife, but he was at that moment conscious of none of them. The hounds, in a kind of jolly frenzy, were answering to the holloa, and he too now had to answer, for he began to pound upwards, plunging into the boggy places, knocking his stout legs against stones and boulders. The leaders have struck the line, the hounds rush past Walter as though driven by a wild windy flurry; the music of the horn, of the cries, sweet and lovely, is all about him. He is himself crying 'Holloa! Holloa! Away! Away!'

Then the hounds were hidden by a breast of the hill and he paused, puffing a bit, blowing a trifle--for he was a big man and this ground was no light stuff to cover.

Unfortunately he found that he had Rodney the Archdeacon at his side, even clinging to his arm and blowing down his neck.

'Whoof! Whoof! Walter! Deary me! Deary me!. . . Most exhausting! So early in the morning too! Whoof . . . Now tell me, pray, my dear Walter, in this ridiculous hunting of yours there were some quite small dogs with the huntsman . . .'

'Terriers! Terriers, my dear Rodney.'

'Really! Really! Is that so? Indeed!'

'Yes, yes. We'd never get a fox out of his hole without them--'

'Indeed! . . . Do you think we shall SEE a fox?'

'We did see one just now. Down below us. There they are! There they are! Out on the brow. Come on, Rodney! Stir your hams. Now we're off!'

He went pounding off and fell headlong into a lake of mist. He was quite suddenly alone. No sound. No cry. The mist eddied and whirled.

He stayed where he was and was conscious of a foreboding, as though some whispering figure had crept close to his side. Why was he, who a moment ago had been so happy and confident, now helpless? A hand had been laid on his shoulder that he should stop to hear some judgement. He looked about him, but he was blind and, it seemed, deaf as well. How unforeseen a country this was, always, when you least expected it, coming up to assert its power over you. He did not put it like that, but he was like a little boy, blundering unexpectedly into the dark. The mist clung to him like thin lawn, then moved from him and faced him in a wall of blankness, then eddied like smoke, creeping along the ground, then pressed in upon him again filling his mouth and nose. He stared, dumbfounded, as though he expected to hear a voice . . .

It broke: a gap was there no bigger than a hand; a crag leapt into air, shaped like a face, black as jet. The ground, brown and then faintly green, came sliding from space, and then, in a second of time, swimming in a wall of bright and airy colour, the whole landscape was back again; the voices were there, calling, shouting. Only a little above him was the huntsman's red coat and the hounds in a broken sequence of white and brown and grey silhouetted against the blue of the morning sky. He wiped his face. 'Dammit!' he thought. 'It don't do to be alone here,' then laughed and ran like a schoolboy again up the slope.

All the world was alive and so fresh and bright that he could shout for joy. There is the sharp call of a raven; near him to the left on the slopes of the Fell are the small bodies of the Herdwick sheep--and there, just in front of him, can it really be, is the fox himself!

He is running with a slouching, slinking movement, first straight then with a jerk upwards again, stopping for an instant by some borran where he might hide, thinking better of it, round the crag, seen for an instant, running to higher ground, then vanishing.

The sight of that fox fired Walter as though he had himself created him. He began to pound upwards again. The hills rose with him, leading him on. They were bathed now in crystalline light, purer than the purest glass, alive with their own vibrant force, stronger than any human life and far more confident of their eternity. And then another miracle! For, reaching a higher slope, he was above the mist that lay below him in a sea of white shifting cloud while he himself trod on a firm sparkling floor of brilliant snow. The snow carpeted the ground for a space, glittering with points of fire, then the rock broke from it, hard and black, only to surrender to higher fields of brightness.

He crossed the snow as though on wings, the sun and the air lifting him, rounded a boulder and had the whole pack in view. Now a dreadful fear possessed him that he would be too late for the kill. He saw Garth and Sylvia swinging along not far from him and he waved his arms crying, 'Come on! Come on! Holloa! Holloa!'

Sylvia waved back to him and, great though the excitement of the moment was, his natural instinct about women, hot and strong in him, murmured: 'That's the loveliest female . . .'

His heart hammered as he leaped a low stone wall and found himself on bracken and in the thick of the mob. They had shut the fox away from an earth near by; you could just see him tracking for the rocks. But the hounds have edged him lower and lower.

'Aye,' said a little purple-faced man to Walter. 'What he's after is that borran yonder. The terriers'll have to be after him from below. That's what he likes.'

The little purple-faced man was trembling with excitement. He smelt oddly of bracken and snuff; he was a stranger to Walter, who felt a sort of indignation that he SHOULD be a stranger. Everyone today was a kind of dependant of the Herries family. No one should exist who was not. The little purple-faced man began frantically to run, and Walter ran with him. The fox had gone to earth, into a borran where he was 'head on' to his adversaries.

This was a big dog-fox and worth the fighting. The excitement now was terrific: the ground seemed to quiver with it. The air shuddered with shouts and cries and the snap-snapping of the hounds. The terriers were mad to get at him; one small animal, crazy with young pride and ambition, had struggled its way far into the borran. Suddenly it emerged, looking foolish. All the terriers stopped marking, and the hounds began to rush madly round the borran, yelping, yowling, bellowing. The huntsman and the whipper-in were cursing and swearing, and John Peel himself, with his funny, ill-fitting long coat, could be heard muttering his own particular Cumberland oaths. And this was where none of the Herries were of any use at all. They hung on to the fringe of the outside world--Will and Walter, Rodney and James, Garth and Amery-- all of no importance. They might just as well be dead.

For the fox had slipped away underground and bolted. He was already at a considerable distance. The fear now was that he would find a borran so deep that it would be impossible to get at him or they would lose a terrier or two there. But no! He is out again, and the hounds have steered him away from the rocks. The hounds move now as though they have absolute command of the game and are certain of the end of it. The fox is out; he is tracing a thin trod through the bracken. The hounds, running from scent to view, are hard upon him. A moment later, Mischief or Satan or Hamilton has him by the throat; he vanishes beneath a flurry of white and brown and swinging tails. Walter drew a deep sigh; he stood, his legs planted wide, his chest out, burning satisfaction in his eyes. That had been a great hour, and now he must recover his dignity and gather his family about him again.

Rodney was at his elbow, but he did not want Rodney nor that fat idiot James his brother. He despised them both, because when he was short with them (as he often was) they took it like lambs. He moved among the Herries cousins--those of them stout enough of wind and strong enough of limb to achieve the 'kill'--with an air of fine and genial patronage. He felt like a king and thought it quite natural that they should feel that he was one. But the members of the family who really attracted him were Garth, Amery, and Sylvia. Amery, slender, stern-faced, grave, was the coming 'money' man of them all, already an important figure in the City, and Garth was jolly, careless and handsome: young though he was, he could drink anyone under the table and was ready for any escapade or devilry. But Sylvia! Her eyes shining, her cheeks rosy with health and excitement, framed by the hills and the glassy blue of the morning sky, she was the loveliest thing he had ever seen. She was ready, he was sure, for any gay adventure. Harmless, of course; but tonight when the splendid house was shining with light and colour, a laugh, a smile, a pressure of the hand . . .

He moved towards them. Then he remembered Uhland. How could he have forgotten him? The whole day was to be Uhland's! This day had no meaning unless it were all for Uhland. He turned back and began to search for his son on the faint green shadows of the lower slopes . . .

Two Titchley cousins--old maids from Carlisle and so entirely unimportant that nobody ever learnt their names from the beginning to the end of the affair--sat on the corner of an almost concealed sofa in the ballroom and considered the sight presented to them. One was stout and one was thin; as no one ever learnt their names that is as far as the historian can go. They were dressed in the fashions of 1820, with high waists, drapery of silk netting over their busts, their ball-dresses short, with padded rouleaux at the bottom. One was in rose and the other in mignonette-green. Their first cousin, an eminent doctor in Carlisle, had brought them and, having brought them, completely forgot them. However, they did not care; they had rooms in Keswick but were determined not to return to them until the festivities were entirely concluded. They were in a state of ecstatic and almost drunken excitement and pleasure. A footman brought them ices and orangeade. No one else spoke to them the night long.

It was the loveliest sight they had ever beheld. They were at first inclined to be shocked by the naked goddesses displayed in the famous tapestries, they thought some of the costumes 'bare in the extreme', they discovered a young man, quite drunk, behind one of the gold curtains in a corner near to them, but soon as the air grew more heated, the noise of the band in the gallery more strident, they threw away convention and, their mouths a little open, sipping their ices, surrendered to their ecstasy.

Above their turbans of figured gauze, above the high ceiling painted with the stars of heaven and naked cherubs hanging garlands, climbed one of the two towers of the Fortress. In the highest room of the tower (which by his own choice was Uhland's room) a monkey with one eye and a face of the deepest melancholy scratched his chest; a small terrier with a broken leg whined, paused to listen, whined again; the parrot, under its green baize covering, its head on its shoulder, slept a deep, philosophic sleep. The moonlight soaked the room in a pale green light and, very faintly, the sound of the fiddles, the bassoon and the drums whispered in the air.

In the gardens everything was still and cold. Everything was new-- the stone walls, the steps, the fountain whose waters flashed under the moon, the naked beds where the flowers would soon be so splendid. The trees beyond the garden walls were old; here daffodils were in bud, and the snowdrops dying. An owl cried; the music, muffled but determined, drowned its cries. Then from the heart of the trees a little wind rose and went whistling and lamenting about the garden-beds and the paths as though looking for its familiar friends who were gone. Beyond the high road the landscape, falling to the valley, spreading to the smoky hills, was soaked in moonlight and lay there as still as a pattern on glass. A man from Ireby village walking out to meet his sweetheart stayed for a moment in the road to listen to the music, to stare at the blaze of lighted windows, then some sudden apprehension--as though he feared that his girl would not be there to meet him-- hurried him on.

Around and about the lighted ballroom many of the rooms were yet empty; some of them had ladders and pots of paint and buckets. Here a chair lay on its face, there pictures were piled against the wall; in one room workmen had left cheese and a hunk of bread.

The ballroom blazed with colour like the page of an illuminated missal. Agnes Herries sat with Christabel, Walter's mother, on a little sofa, and everyone came and talked to them. Agnes was feeling dreadfully ill; at her heart was a pain like a hand clutching and unclutching. She did not know what to say to Walter's mother, with whom she had never been familiar. She could not say that she liked this new house, for she hated it; nor that she was sorry to have left Westaways, for she had hated that too; nor that she was glad that Walter was happy, because she was not glad. The sight of so many people whom she did not know, whom she feared, made her sick. She knew that her little shrivelled body looked absurd in its gaudy ball-dress with the huge sleeves like epaulettes. She knew that everyone despised her. Her only happiness was to catch a glimpse once and again of her lovely daughter Elizabeth, who in her dress of silver silk was, in her mother's eyes, beautiful beyond compare. Once her son Uhland, resting on an ebony cane that he now carried, came and spoke to her. When he was gone Christabel said: 'What a clever face Uhland has!'

'Yes, he is very clever.'

'I have never,' continued Christabel, who was longing for her bed, 'seen so many of the family together in one room--never since a Ball I once gave in London.'

She was no longer distressed by the memory of that eventful Ball. It seemed to her now, on looking back, to have been a very successful affair. She sought anxiously for Will, her husband. Ah! there he was, talking to Amery Herries, a clever young man. They would be talking about money, always Will's favourite topic. Perhaps soon she might slip away to bed. Why, she wondered sleepily, had her son chosen so poor a specimen as Agnes for his wife? But her wonderings were never very active. She had long ago learnt that it was wiser not to wonder about anything very deeply.

The band broke into one of the newest valses. The floor swam with colour, green and white, purple and rose. Laughter, music, the movement of so many happy persons filled the air with a golden haze; the owl's cry could not penetrate the thick walls of Cumberland stone.

It was nearly midnight. At Uldale, John, Dorothy, Adam had all gone to bed, but Judith sat in Jennifer's room looking after Jennifer. Looking after Jennifer! An exasperating thing to do! Jennifer had been ill for weeks, but they had had to set a guard about her door to keep her in bed. She was there now, propped up with pillows, her eyes shining like fireflies. Her face was as white as dough. Even in her bed she looked dishevelled, her heavy breasts exposed, her nightdress torn above her right elbow, her lace nightcap tilted over one ear. She wanted to get up.

'You can't!' said Judith.

Judith was in a violently bad temper. All day she had ordered the maids about as though they were dirt, rapping with her stick on the floor. It had been all that she could do not to box Dorothy's ears. They had all been on edge that day. Was it because of the Ball at Ireby? Were they, in spite of themselves, conscious of it? In any case, you did not know of what the children were thinking. John had been melancholy for a while now, and Adam--Adam was silently fighting her desires. Adam wanted to get away and she knew it. She was determined to prevent it.

Meanwhile Jennifer was very ill. She had caught a chill walking in the country lanes in a thin dress with black satin shoes and silk mittens. Her heart also was bad. Her legs were swollen. She was deaf in one ear.

'You are keeping me in bed against my will. I insist on getting up.' She looked across the sheets with hatred at the neat, pale-faced woman in the red morocco chair. She listened. The house was as still as a bottomless well.

She poured out a torrent of mild, lazy abuse:

'Yes, you keep me here and think it very fine. You have grown into a bully, Judith. That's what you are. Everyone knows it. You are impossible with everyone . . . impossible . . . Why the maids stay in the house I don't know. I insist that I get up.'

'Don't be foolish, Jennifer. It's past midnight. You must go to sleep. I will give you your drops.'

'I don't wish for my drops. They are poisoning me. I expect that Walter has bribed the doctor to put poison in them.'

'Don't be foolish. You know that he has done nothing of the kind.'

'Oh, this woman!' thought Judith.

Jennifer slowly raised herself on her hands, climbed out of the clothes and sat on the edge of the bed, her swollen legs hanging heavily.

'So Walter has opened his house. All the country-side save ourselves is dancing there tonight. The next thing he will build a house just outside our garden.' She looked up with lazy maliciousness. 'You may say what you like; he has poisoned all our life here. John is not the same, you are not the same, Adam is not the same.'

Judith said nothing. Jennifer went on:

'You love Adam more than anyone in the world, do you not?'

'Yes, of course I do. Jennifer, get back into bed. You will catch your death--'

'Well, he is going to leave you. I can tell. I know. He will soon be seventeen and is not of such a character as to remain in a country place--'

A sharp pain, like the touch of a knife, struck Judith's heart, but she got up and, very gently, went to the bed. She patted Jennifer on the shoulder as though she were a child and urged her back into bed again. Quite placidly Jennifer obeyed.

'Oh, dear! I have such a pain in my chest! How they will be dancing now on Ireby! Everyone from Keswick will be there!' She sighed, a deep childish sigh.

'How still this house is! Only the clocks . . . Judith, what do you think life is for?'

'What is it FOR?' Judith was listening. It was, of course, only her imagination, but it seemed to her that she could hear very faintly drums and fiddles and a dim bassoon. One did fancy that one heard things in a quiet house at night.

'Yes. Why are we born? Why do we live? Why do you love Adam so intensely when it is all for nothing?'

'It is not for nothing.'

'Oh, but of course it is. He will grow up and marry and forget you just as I forgot my own mother and father. I should never have left them. I should never have come North. I should never have married Francis. My children don't care for me. No one cares for me. You are all waiting for me to die.'

'Nonsense, Jennifer.'

'No, but it is not nonsense. I cannot understand it, all the bother and the worry. People are born and they die, and other people are born and it is all for nothing.'

'It is not for nothing,' Judith repeated. 'It is that we may have some experience, that we may learn--'

'Yes, but learn what? I am sure that I have never learnt anything except to be disappointed and to be afraid of Walter.'

Judith, who was half asleep, struggled to comfort Jennifer.

'You have learnt more than you know, my dear. There is something immortal in us that must grow, and it grows with experience.'

But did it? Did she mean what she said? Her love for Adam was immortal. Her love for Georges was so-- it would never die. There was something to FIGHT in life, something strong and glorious . . .

She covered a yawn with her hand. 'Now, Jennifer, you must sleep.'

Jennifer lay back in the bed. 'I have such a pain near my heart. My throat is sore. I can see Walter come dancing down the hill when I am buried. And then he will finish John and Dorothy as he has finished me.'

There was something so truly pathetic in her voice; she was like a small child who is suffering she does not know why. Judith bent over the bed and smoothed her pillow. Jennifer caught her hand.

'You are good to me, Judith, although I know that you wish that I were dead.'

'Of course I don't wish that you were dead.'

'Oh yes, you do. You have never forgiven me for preventing you from living in Watendlath. Had you lived in Watendlath you would not have wanted everything your own way so.'

This was so true that Judith felt as though it were her own voice that was speaking. But she showed no signs: she stroked Jennifer's hair.

'Judith, do you not hear something?'

'Hear what?'

'Music--violins and a drum.'

'No--of course not.'

'Oh, but I do. Go to the window and pull back the curtain.'

She went. She looked out.

'What do you see?'

'I see nothing. Only the trees and the moonlight.' But that was not true. Quite clearly she could see in the far distance Walter's house on Ireby. The windows shone like little stars.

'Can you not see the house?'

'Yes; very dimly.'

'Ah . . . Judith, Judith!' It was a cry. 'He will kill John as he is killing me! I can see him. I can hear him. He is coming!'

She hastened back to the bed.

Jennifer was very ill and the perspiration glistened on her forehead. Her hand was at her heart.

'Oh, I am in such pain! Such terrible pain!'

'Quiet, dear. It will soon pass. I will fetch the drops--'

'Don't leave me . . . Oh! Oh! I am going to die! The room is dark . . . Judith, where are you?'

'Sir Roger' was over; some of the older people were departing, Miss Pennyfeather among others. She greeted Walter with dignity and thanked him for a very enjoyable evening. Indeed, she had had one, and Mrs McCormick was to drive her back in her barouche. Mrs Walter Herries had gone to bed; Miss Elizabeth, standing beside her father, did the honours.

The old lady, who was feeling roguish, whispered in his ear:

'You have a most beautiful daughter.'

And then, to be more roguish yet, whispered:

'But I miss Judith Paris. She is a great friend of mine, you know.'

He agreed to both these propositions as perhaps he would have agreed to anything tonight in his happiness and triumph. But he was surprised at the loveliness of Elizabeth. He did not feel that he was her father any more strongly than he had ever done, but she WAS beautiful. And he would have been delighted had Judith been there. He bore her no grudge. A little later Sylvia Herries found herself beside Elizabeth and spoke to her.

'Are you enjoying yourself, Elizabeth?'

The girl smiled shyly. She thought Sylvia Herries the loveliest woman she had ever seen. She had heard that she was a beauty in London and had a Salon attended by famous men, and yet she looked little older than herself.

'Oh yes,' she said.

'Do you like the new house?'

She did not say that she hated it, that she was miserable there, that she was afraid lest her mother should die and leave her defenceless, but her colour rose in her cheeks and she answered:

'I am not perhaps accustomed . . . Later on perhaps.'

The oddest feeling rose in Sylvia's breast. This child seemed to rebuke her by her innocence and inexperience. Suddenly she hated all her London life, with Rosina Bulwer storming angrily at her overdressed husband, and young Mr Ainsworth such a coxcomb, the tables after a party scattered with cards and overturned glasses and the grease from candles.

She looked at Elizabeth with great affection. 'Be happy while you may. You are so young and so beautiful.'

At that moment up came Walter, a little drunk. He took her away. They were dancing the valse again. He asked her to dance. He was not a bad performer for so big a man, but why had he not even looked at his daughter? His breath smelt of wine, his heavy body was pressed close to hers.

'This is a triumph for you, Cousin Walter,' she said. 'I have never seen so many of our relations before.'

His arm tightened about her slender waist.

'I'll tell you a thing,' he said. 'I have been looking forward to this day all my life.'

'The house is magnificent,' she said. But she did not think so. She found it cold and bleak. There was too much grey stone about it, and the towers and sham battlements were hideous. It was like a fortress.

But he did not pay attention. He whispered in her ear:

'I'll tell you another thing. I think that I am in love with you.'

This was no new thing to her. Men were for ever whispering it in her ear; moreover, with his physical vitality, size and strength there was something attractive . . . also tonight he was like a boy in his happiness. So she did not answer him, but said instead:

'The hunting this morning was the grandest adventure. I never enjoyed anything so much in my life.'

His hand rested on her arm; truly he danced well for so big a man.

'Yes, was it not? Glorious weather. And, do you know, this is a strange country. I took a step and was blinded by mist with sun all about me. For a moment I was lost.'

'Yes? Indeed?' She had not heard him. She saw that her husband was watching them. She fancied that he did not care for Walter, although he had not said so.

The valse was ended, and he led her away to an alcove near the window where they were hidden by curtains, hidden from everyone save the two Titchley cousins, whose eyes were more active than ever.

She sat down, and he stood leaning over her chair, his hand very near her lovely neck. To make conversation she said:

'Is it not comic, Cousin Walter, to see so many Herries together? What do you think of us as a family?'

'What do I think? . . . Well, well . . . Sylvia, how lovely you are! I am sure that I have never seen anyone so lovely.'

'I hate our family when it is together in big numbers. We are all hard and material and self-seeking. When one of us is not he is gored to death by the others, like a sick animal in a herd.'

'Sylvia, would you make an objection if I kissed you? Only a cousinly kiss, you know.'

'I should certainly object most strongly. I am married, you know.'

'So am I,' he murmured laughing, and, bending forward, kissed the back of her neck.

Her husband, Garth, had seen them dancing. Sylvia was right; he did not like Walter; he wished that they had not come. He was vaguely unhappy, a rare experience for his lively, careless temperament, and, turning, found that Elizabeth, near to him at that moment, was being left with many bows by her partner, a fat, pursy little man.

'This is a grand sight,' he said. 'Who was your elderly partner, Elizabeth?'

'A doctor from Keswick.'

'Are you very happy? You should be.'

Some restraint that she had been fighting all the evening broke down. She liked Garth; he was gay and young and kind.

'No, Garth, I am not.' She held her head high, but he saw that her eyes were bright with tears. They were away by themselves, and he wanted to put his arm round her and protect her.

'Why not?' he asked her.

'Oh, this house--do you like it? It is hard and cold. And my mother is ill. And--and--'

'You are in love?' he asked her quickly.

'Yes, I am,' she said softly. 'I have been ever since I was a child.'

She was only a child now, he thought.

'Well--is there no hope of marrying?'

'None. A year ago we agreed that we would not meet any more. It is quite, quite hopeless. But I love him the same and so I always shall.'

'That is something,' he answered gravely. 'Fidelity. That is very rare, and the best way to maintain it is never to meet. Propinquity, my dear, kills love.'

'Why!' said Elizabeth, her eyes open and startled. 'Do you not love your wife?'

'I can be jealous of her. I am proud of her. I wish to be near her. Is that an answer to your question?'

'Oh!' whispered Elizabeth, staring at him and longing for John Herries with such a desperate ache that she thought that everyone must see it. Would you bring me some orangeade, cousin? I am thirsty.'

The band struck up a quadrille. They moved to their places. It was the climax of all the splendour and pageantry of the evening.

'Oh, did you see--?' said one of the Titchleys to the other.

Walter, his countenance shining with wine, health, exercise, success, love and triumph, led Cecily Rockage to her place in the dance.

There was a moment's pause. Then the band struck up again and all the coloured figures moved, softly, gracefully, about the shining floor.

At Uldale, Judith, her arms about Jennifer, gazed around her desperately for help. But no help could be forthcoming, for with a sigh Jennifer bent her head and, falling forward, died against Judith's breast.

END OF PART I

Part Two

Adam and Margaret

THE BATTLE

Adam, on the morning of his twenty-second birthday, rode alone to Manesty Woods.

At breakfast, there had been the customary festivities. His mother had given him a riding-whip mounted in silver, John had given him Captain Marryat's Mr Midshipman Easy, Dorothy had sent some silk handkerchiefs, and Rackstraw the French Revolution of Thomas Carlyle. They had all been very kind. Especially had the love shown him by his mother moved and affected him. He had ridden over alone to Manesty that he might think, that he might resolve his strong determination into unchangeable fact.

He intended, before another twenty-four hours were past, to tell his mother that he must leave Uldale and seek his fortune in the world. It was a fierce resolve, one towards which it seemed to him that his whole life had been tending. It needed some girding of the loins! The scene with his mother would be terrific!

In the quiet autumn weather he rode through Portinscale, up the hill towards Braithwaite, then turned to the left, followed the leaf-strewn paths until the woods closed about him and, tying his horse to a tree, plunged down to the Lake's very edge.

There was breeze enough to run a slight murmuring ripple to his feet: for the rest the silence was complete. Opposite him Skiddaw rose like a dividing flower in purple shadow to a shadowed sky. Shadow veiled the Lake. Fields, hills and houses were dim.

He sat there, his hands pressed on his broad knees, and thought things out. Yes, there would be a devil of a row! His mother, as she now was, was not easy to oppose--and yet, if only because he loved her, he must oppose her. He was twenty-two today and, as he saw it, he had wasted five years of his life. For a young man five years seem an immense time. Ever since, at the age of fifteen, he had visited London with his mother he had resolved to leave Uldale, and yet here he was--seven years later, and he was still there!

It was not that he was not resolute enough! As he sat there with his mouth set and his thick broad shoulders squared, he was the very image of resolution, and yet his mother had been too much for him!

He had begun, he remembered, five years back, when Walter Herries had given his first Ball at Ireby and Aunt Jennifer had died, his Grand Rebellion. He had said, his legs apart and his hands in his pockets, that he was going. And his mother had answered him: 'Well--go!'

But she had not intended for a moment that he should go. She had used Roger Rackstraw and John to assist her. Adam was greatly attached to Rackstraw in spite of his drinking, his wenching and his gambling. Rackstraw had taught him everything that he knew--how to ride, how to fight, how to read. It was from Rackstraw that he had got more than from any other the love of this country that he so deeply worshipped. Stones and clouds! Clouds and stones! He looked up at the small vaporous clouds browsing like sheep on the fields of misty sky above him. The long white stone upon which he was sitting, the boulders that lay about him, these were his intimate companions because Rackstraw had introduced him to them. Yes, he owed Rackstraw a great deal, and it was Rackstraw who had persuaded him that he must remain, for a while at least, to help John with the property, the farm at Uldale, the land towards Skiddaw, the business affairs in Keswick. Well, he had remained. He loved John Herries very dearly; there were things that he could do that John could not. He was more easily friends with the farmers and the labourers and the Keswick people. There was something in John, some reserve and shyness, that kept him apart; he inherited that from his father. But everyone liked Adam and trusted him, which was something in these days of rick-burnings in the country and starvation in the towns.

Then, two years ago, he had tried again.

'I am wasting my life here, Mother. I want to go to London.'

This time she did not say 'Go!' She had looked at him as though she would burst into a torrent of rage. She was by then over sixty; her hair was white, but her small body was as taut and erect as ever. Nevertheless, she was not quite as strong as she had been. She sat down more frequently, would take his arm when they walked in the garden. It was not so easy as it had been the first time. Nevertheless, she had not said 'No'. Dorothy had but just become engaged to a Mr Bellairs of Ryelands, near Seascale. An excellent match. Bellairs was Dorothy's age, would succeed to a fine estate, was a good, solid sound-bottomed Englishman with no nonsense about him. So Adam must wait until Dorothy was married. Dorothy DID marry in June of 1836 and had gone to Ryelands to live. Well, then, Judith was all alone now with John. Of course, Adam must stay. Not that Judith minded in the least being the only woman in the house. She adored it. She had always had an affection for Dorothy, but of late the girl had grown into a very common-sensible house-keeping woman and had had ideas of the way that Fell House should be managed. She had married, Adam was of the private opinion, in the very nick of time.

So then it had gone on, and Adam could just see his mother nodding her little head to herself, her mouth curved in a triumphant smile. 'Now I've got him for ever! I shall marry John off, and then the two of us will be alone here together.' (Adam knew that she would never marry John off. There had ever been only one woman for him. There would never be another.)

But there was more in it than this. There was Walter Herries at Ireby.

Adam was extremely practical and saw things as they were. He was not, as John was, frightened by unsubstantial fears. But he could not deny that part of his resolve to run away to London was founded on Walter and the house at Ireby.

After Jennifer Herries' death they--Judith, Adam, John and Dorothy-- had decided altogether to disregard dear Cousin Walter and his big, ugly grey house. And so in a kind of way they had. They never mentioned Walter except to joke about him, his growing corpulency, his absurd airs and the rest. When Agnes his wife died,

Judith attended the funeral, and Walter spoke to her in a very friendly manner.

Nevertheless, what Jennifer had prophesied was partly true. The Fortress (as everyone in the countryside now called the place) came ever nearer to Uldale. One reason of this was that Mr Peach, Walter's agent, seemed to be on terms with all of the Uldale dependants. Even old Bennett was seen chatting with him. Mr Rackstraw drank and betted with him, and one night was deposited, dead drunk, at Fell House gates with an ironic note in Peach's handwriting.

Then Adam knew that John was always thinking of Elizabeth. He did not, Adam believed, meet her any more nor correspond with her, but John was certain that she was unhappy, in especial since her mother's death, and the thought tortured him.

Then there was the matter of Uhland Herries, his liking for Adam, his hatred of John. For a while he was continually meeting Adam, in the roads, in Keswick, by the Lake; until at last Adam told him that he did not wish to speak to him nor have anything to do with him, that his father was the enemy of all of them at Uldale, and that, so long as it lasted, there could be no intercourse between them. Uhland just stared at him out of his strange grey eyes, nodded, and rode away. But John had the fantastic, unreal notion that Uhland was always following him, waiting for him round corners and so on, would one day do him a hurt.

Finally, Adam believed it to be true that his mother was slowly more and more conscious of Walter. When little things went wrong she attributed it to Walter, just as Jennifer used to do. Adam caught her sometimes standing in the garden, staring over at the Fortress. Of course, she was becoming an old lady now, and fancies would have more power over her than they used to do.

For Adam there was a growing atmosphere in the Uldale house that seemed to him sickly and false. He must escape from it.

There was, however, much more behind his resolve than this. He was determined to do something fine in the world.

Although his reticence hindered him from declaring his thoughts to anyone, he was filled with idealism and love for his fellow human beings. On this day, as he sat there, looking over the shadowy Lake, he felt perhaps some of the sentiment that was stirring in England just then. There was a new young Queen on the throne; all the debauchery, mismanagement, selfishness of those fat old men who had pretended to govern England had passed away. With this child who already in a few months had shown strength and honesty of purpose and purity of mind there was a new hope in the land. Adam had pictures in his mind, as all Englishmen had just then, of that girlish figure on horseback in the Park, or advancing with perfect dignity and command to meet her Ministers, so that all the old men who had known that other régime, the Duke and Peel and Melbourne, were ready to kneel down and worship her. Melbourne was already her slave. Might it not mean that a New Age of Knight-Errantry and the Brotherhood of Man was to begin?

If so, Adam meant to have his share in it. He was very young, had had little experience of the world, but it seemed to him then--as it was to seem to him all his life through--that a very little was needed to make the earth a glorious place where everyone loved his fellow-man and worked, unselfishly, for the general good of mankind.

There was nothing selfish in his desires as he sat there that morning. He never thought of himself at all. His heart swelled in him as he formed pictures of life as it ought to be, as surely it would be in time to come. It seemed to him that it would be a fine thing if himself and others of a like mind were to band together and work all with a common will for the good of the world. He was proud of his family, although he himself was illegitimate, but he was not proud of individual members of the family. Something was always taking them in the wrong direction. Even he perceived, in spite of his intense loyalty, that something had happened to his mother. It might be that she had, as she once told him, made the wrong decision when she had stayed at Uldale instead of going to live at Watendlath. Then there were Francis and Jennifer, John's father and mother, Walter and Uhland, Will and Garth and Sylvia in London. He did not feel himself better than any of them--there was never anyone with less conceit--but it seemed that in life one was for ever being tempted to take a wrong step: a quick decision and one was moving down the wrong road, never again to be in the right one.

He felt life to be good; it could not hold such beauty as he saw before him that morning and not be good. Yet so many things were wrong with it--so much poverty, suffering of women and children, dirt and shame and crime. Surely, if one worked hard enough, and if enough people in the world cared for justice and equality, everything would swing round--not to perfection, perhaps, but to something in unison with this beauty, this sense of God active and moving in men's hearts?

In any case, he meant to see what he could do; so he must go out into the world, fight his way, find others of like mind with himself. He got up, stretched his arms, felt an infinite strength and hope in him. He hated this struggle with his mother. But, if he was resolute, it would be sharp, brief, soon over, and then she would see how right he was. He smiled as he looked about him and untethered his horse. How lovely and perfect this place was! Perhaps one day he would return and have a cottage here, with the hills above him, and the Lake at his feet. Nothing the world could hold would be so good as that would be! He rode home.

But alas! How noble and ideal are we at one moment; how peevish and unkind the next! Adam stopped in Portinscale for a bottle of stout and some cold beef. There was nothing better than to sit in the window of the Inn, drinking the stout and eating the beef while the grey stillness of field and Lake bound with the hedges of the cottage gardens spread like a fan before him, to sit there and think of the world opening, of the great deeds to be performed therein, of the fights to be fought, the weak to be protected, the books, maybe, to be written! He had no thought that he was a genius, but Keats (whose Lamia and St Agnes' Eve Rackstraw had introduced to him) had not thought himself one, and Mr Carlyle had been a peasant, and there was the author of Sketches by Boz . . .

So he rode slowly home through the mist and the yellow leaves, dreaming of what was coming. What immediately came to him was the Reverend Mr Bland, the new curate at Cockermouth, who had had a London curacy and bore a letter from Stephen Newmark. A stout wife was with him and a stout daughter. The visitors had been asked whether they would take port or sherry, and the glasses, biscuits and decanters were laid out on the table. The candles shone (gas was not yet introduced into Fell House), a table near by was ready with the round, lacquered Pope Joan board and the mother-o'-pearl counters, for Judith adored Pope Joan. And she sat there like a queen in a beautiful shawl with long fringes and her snow-white hair in long ringlets, enjoying herself tremendously.

The Reverend Mr Bland stayed an eternity. He had endless things to say about his new church, how the Psalms were read 'too quick,' and the red cloth on the reading-desk was faded to a dirty brown, and how at St Mary's in Islington . . . No, they would never be gone, for Farmer Wilson had driven them over and had gone on to some farms about some business of his own and . . . Oh! there was Farmer Wilson at last, and soon the Bland family was lifted into his cart, and the dusk closed down upon their rumbling.

He followed her up to her room, watched her shake her curls, change her shawl, do a little pas seul up and down her floor in imitation of Mr Bland's mincing steps, laugh and sing a note or two from 'Speed on, my mules, for Leila WAITS for me,' which was one of the popular ballads of the day. It was very difficult for him to attack her at such a moment, and yet he could not wait. Although so thickly and sturdily built he was nervous as a young girl when he confronted his mother. The memory of that first awful quarrel following his laugh at old Bellenden in Keswick never left him; there was, too, something dismaying in her swift transition from mood to mood. Then she was sixty-three, and, let her pretend as she might, was not as strong as she had once been. And then-- hardest of all--he loved her better than anyone alive.

So he burst out at once that he might get it over quickly.

441

'Mother--I'm going to London. I've been thinking it over. I'm going to earn my living like other men. I must, I must . . .'

Like other men! She stopped in her invocation of 'Leila', stood there in the middle of the floor and laughed at him. Like other men! To her he was still an infant, or at most a small boy who stole jam from the cupboard and bought bull's-eyes at the shop in the village. And yet he was not! She looked and saw him standing there, stolid and square, in his man's blue coat with the velvet collar and the strapped pantaloons, a lock of his black hair falling over his forehead, whiskers sprouting on his cheeks, his grave eyes confronting her without flinching. No, he was not a child any longer. This was what Jennifer had foretold. She reached out for her ivory cane that was leaning against the four-poster.

'Not on your birthday, Adam,' she said, and moved towards the door.

But he did not budge. He felt his knees shake, but now that he had begun he would go through with it.

'Yes, Mother, I must.' He cleared his throat. 'Listen, Mother, dear. I'm twenty-two today.'

'And what has that to do with it?'

'Everything. I am a man and should do a man's work.'

'You have a man's work here.'

'No, I have not. You know quite well that for all I do here I might be shut up in a cupboard. John and Rackstraw can manage everything.'

'That is not true. John is too dreamy, and Rackstraw drinks in the village.' She felt that her legs were trembling, so with great dignity she walked to the chair near the fireplace and sat down.

The devil of it was that words never came easily to him! He could think clearly enough, but when it came to words! . . . He stood nearer to her.

'Mother, pray listen. I am not being rebellious or wicked. You know how . . . how . . . devotedly I love you--'

'So devotedly that you want to break my heart,' she said.

(Something sarcastic in her said: 'Break my heart! My dear, what stuff!')

He began to be angry, which was a help to him. When he was angry his lower lip jutted out, a sign that she knew very well.

'This is a resolve,' he said. 'Nothing shall turn me from it.'

'Well--if it is a resolve--what will you live upon?'

'I have fifty pounds I've saved, thirty I got for those sheep at Threlkeld, twenty Uncle Will sent me . . .'

'Fifty! Thirty! . . . Nonsense! . . . That will last you a month or so. And then what?'

'I shall find work.'

'Yes, but what will you do? What will you do?' She stamped her cane on the floor. 'You've been trained to nothing.'

'I can find work,' he said doggedly. (He thought of saying: 'Whose fault is it that I've not been trained?' but fortunately kept it back.) 'I'm ready to do anything.'

'And starve in a gutter,' she answered contemptuously. Then her voice softened. 'Now, Adam, this is folly. You HAVE work here, your proper work. John loves you. I am sure he would not know what to do without you. You are necessary to all of us here.'

As she softened so did he.

'We can soon test whether I'm necessary or no,' he said, laughing. 'I will go to London for three months, and you shall see how well you do. Why, mother, in a week you will have forgotten all about me!'

She saw then that he meant to go. She bent her head for a moment. She wanted to deal with this quietly, but she had less control of herself now than the other day. Something leapt up within her, crying, 'I want to get out!' and out it came, disclosing itself as a nasty piece of temper that took herself by surprise quite as much as anyone else. She had always had a hasty temper, but now it was as though she had her own and someone else's as well.

She was determined on two things: not to let him go and not to be angry. So she got up and walked to the door; as she passed him she laid her hand for a moment on his shoulder, smiled at him and said:

'Now you must not be naughty, Adam. Some time--later on--you shall go to London. Perhaps I shall come with you,' and left the room. There for once her tactics were altogether wrong. Those words, as it happened, were all that were needed to stiffen him. She was still treating him like a child; she WOULD not see that he was a grown man. That just showed how hopeless everything would be if he stayed.

But he must go at once. He could not endure that this relationship with his mother should continue. She would beat him down if she had time; her ruthlessness had all the old history of their lives together to harden it.

Very soon, in fact, the battle was renewed. Next day at breakfast alone with John, drinking beer and gobbling beef pie, he told him his decision.

'John, I've got to go.'

'Got to go?' asked John.

'Yes, to London. I'm wasting my time here. You know that as well as I do. I've got to be of some use in the world.'

'Well, aren't you being of use here?'

'No, nothing to matter. You see, John, there's a dreadful lot of injustice everywhere. Look at these women in the factories and the children in the mines. Look how people are starving. Why, they say in White-haven--'

'Yes, I know. But couldn't you improve things and stay here as well? And is it your business? I mean--'

'You think I'm a bit of a prig,' said Adam. 'But I don't want to consider myself at all. I may be a prig or not. I don't care--' He broke off, laughing. 'Yes, I do care. I don't want to be a prig. But I find it so difficult to say what I mean. What I MEAN is that I think that a number of men are feeling that they want to help to make England a grand place--without all this injustice and division between the rich and the poor. And I want to stand with them.'

'And you're on the side of the poor?' asked John.

'Of course I am. I haven't much myself, I'm illegitimate, I'm nobody. Who should be on the side of the poor if I'm not? But I don't want to preach, you know. There's none of the parson in me. I only want that they should have more to eat and better homes, that young children shouldn't go down the mines and be in the dark all day--'

'I daresay they like it--being in the mines, I mean.'

'Like it! How can they like it? Would YOU like it?'

'No, but I'm not accustomed to it.'

Adam had been unusually eloquent, so now he was quiet again although he had not, even now, said what was really in his heart. John got up, came round to him and put his arm around him.

'I expect you're right,' he said. 'Only what it will be here without you--'

'You need not disturb yourself,' said a sharp voice in the doorway. 'Adam is NOT going to London.'

They both looked up, and there was 'Madame' in the doorway, shaking on her cane with anger. 'No, I will not have it,' she said, her voice quivering. 'You get this notion out of your head, Adam, once and for all. Your duty is here. There's been enough of this nonsense.' And she went.

The two looked at one another.

'By Caesar!' said John, 'I never knew she was there.'

Adam said in a low voice: 'It's no good. She can't stop me. But it's awful fighting her.'

'Yes,' said John. 'No one likes it. That's why she always has her way.'

Meanwhile Judith went about her household duties, and the maids had a dreadful morning of it. She felt as though she were fighting for her very life. If Adam left her, what remained? Oh yes, of course she was fond of Uldale--but to be alone here with John, the stupid neighbours, Walter on the hill . . . All the morning she was closer to weeping than she had been for years. This would not have happened had she done what she should have done--gone to live in Watendlath with Adam. He would have become a fanner and she would have lived with him.

She went up to her room. She stared out at Skiddaw, veiled now by dirty, swollen clouds. What was she to do? How was she to influence him? Behind her anger and indignation was admiration of his obstinacy. She would have behaved once just as he was behaving.

But she beat these thoughts back. No weakening on her part. If she softened she was lost.

So that at dinner in the afternoon she was severe, aloof, the grand lady, the Empress. And Adam, unfortunately, because of his knowledge that he had that forenoon ridden into Keswick and drawn his money from the bank, was not at his best.

If she knew that! But she did not know it. In her heart she was quaking, but as the meal proceeded she became reassured again. She addressed most of her remarks to Mr Rackstraw, who, with his dry, red face and weather-beaten figure, seemed to promise her that nothing here at least could change. Adam sat there, eating and drinking as though this day were like any other day. So it must be! She had been agitated by absurd alarms.

Once she said: 'The Hunt Ball in Carlisle is to be the twenty- third of October. You and John, Adam, can have a bed at the Witherings'. They will be going for sure.'

No one said anything.

'I have been hearing,' said Rackstraw, 'about this new postal scheme. All our letters to cost us but a penny wherever we send them. We live in modern times.'

She discussed the postal scheme and Lord de Ros' gambling scandal. His manner of cheating at cards had been to have a coughing fit under the table. And there had been the massacre in New Zealand-- one hundred and twenty people murdered--but really so far away that one could not visualize it. She was ALMOST reassured; as she moved in a manner a little more stately than usual from the room she gave Adam a quick look and thought that she had never before found him so exasperating and never loved him so dearly.

Adam told Rackstraw that same afternoon that he was going. They were in the stables and it was growing dark. A storm of rain was blowing up, and the light in the lantern that Rackstraw carried flickered.

Rackstraw nodded his head.

'I knew you would,' he said.

'I must. I can't help myself,' said Adam.

'No, of course you cannot.'

'Care for my mother, Roger. This will hit her for the moment, but she'll see it's right later.'

'Yes, she will,' said Rackstraw. 'She's a damnably sensible woman, your mother.'

He shook Adam's hand as though he were going that moment.

'Good luck to you.' He fumbled in his deep pocket, pulled out a little book and gave it to him. 'It's the Iliad. Grandest book in the world. I always carry it with me. Think of me sometimes.'

'But I'm not going now--' began Adam. Then stopped. He knew suddenly that he was.

By suppertime he had made his plans. He would leave the next day, drive one way or another to Manchester, then take the new railway. The very thought of this railway made his heart beat. Yes, he would certainly be seeing the world.

443

After supper he went out to the stables, wearing his riding-coat and hat because the storm was so fierce. As soon as he was indoors he heard his mother's voice calling him from upstairs. He went up, his spirits heavy with foreboding. She was sitting in her bedroom by the fire, wrapped in two fine cashmere shawls and looking a very amiable and kindly old lady.

'That's well, Adam,' she said, smiling. 'Come and talk to your old mother.'

No, she was not an old lady. She was as young as Eternity and vigorous. So, in order that he might be entirely honest, he stood by the door.

'I've been vexed all day by your nonsense,' she said. 'Very foolish. Now sit beside me and I'll tell you what I've arranged. You want more to do, my son. That's the trouble. Well, I've thought of that farm at Crossways. I think, with a tightening or two, it can be purchased--'

'No, Mother,' he said. 'It's no use. I'm as resolved as last night. I must go and at once. Tomorrow.'

'And why tomorrow precisely?' she asked him, her voice trembling.

'I cannot wait and have this trouble with you. I cannot endure it. Anyone else--'

She got up. 'Never mind me,' she said. 'Don't be a hypocrite, Adam.'

'I'm no hypocrite,' he answered fiercely. 'I'm your son.'

'You are not my son if you go,' she answered as fiercely as he. 'If you go I disown you.'

'Now this is nonsense,' he fought back. 'Have you no ambition for me? If I'd been another I should have gone to school and then to some business--'

She came nearer to him.

'So you reproach me?'

'No, I do not reproach you. I cannot understand that you who have so much strength of mind can never have had any ambition for me. You--'

She came close to him.

'Take care, Adam, or I'll teach you!'

She was shaking, and that touched him so deeply that his voice grew tender.

'Mother, listen. You MUST listen. You remember that once when we were in London at the Newmarks', after the riot, I was in bed with you. You told me then that if ever you threatened my liberty I was to defy you. You said that this would happen. You urged me then--'

But she had not listened to a single word. She caught hold of him and began to shake him so furiously that she drove him back against the door.

'Take off that hat and coat.'

He was now as angry as she. Anyone looking at them would have seen well enough that they were mother and son.

'No, I will not.'

'Take off that hat and coat.' Her small body had in it an extraordinary vigour.

'No.' He put out his hand to prevent her doing herself a hurt. 'You cannot use me like this. You shall not.'

'Oh, will I not?' Her words came in little passionate sobs. 'When I was a girl--we whipped our--disobedient sons--'

He tore himself away from her.

'Well, then,' she panted, 'if it is so--you shall remain here--and consider it.'

She went out, pulling the door behind her with a bang that echoed all over the house. He heard the key turn in the lock.

'By God! She's locked me in!' he heard a voice that did not seem like his own exclaim aloud. He sat down on the bed, and the room sank back into silence like a pool after a stone has splashed it. He heard the rain beating on the window. He was more angry than he had ever been in his life, and he did not care whether his mother broke her heart or whether, indeed, the whole world blew up. He looked at the window, went over to it, stared out.

Here anyhow was a way out. He could walk to Penrith, get the morning coach . . . Thank heaven, he had his money.

He climbed over the sill, felt the rain sweep against his cheek, fumbling, found the water-pipe. It was the same water-pipe that his mother, escaping years ago, had used.

THE CHARTISTS

It was while watching the return of the Procession from Westminster-- the Procession on June 27th, 1838, of the Coronation of Her Gracious Majesty Queen Victoria--that the life of Adam Paris was changed. He had exactly thirty shillings in the world. After arriving in London he had found a job reading to an old blind gentleman in Bayswater, things like Pope's Homer and Scott's Lady of the Lake. The old gentleman had died, and Adam had found, after some weeks of starving, another job with Fisher and Taylor, publishers of infidel writers like Paine. For a time all was well, then Fisher took a dislike to him and dismissed him. After that he sank to starvation. He had a room in a lodging-house off the Strand, 'Wheeler's'. No one was ever to know how lonely he was and how desperately homesick he was during those months. He wrote to his mother once a month, giving an address, but had no reply. He wrote to no one else; he was too proud. He was sick and hungry for the smell of dry bracken and the tune of running water, for the small bodies of his Herdwick sheep and the little white farms . . . And, by the day of the Procession, he was so hungry that he could think of nothing but food. He scarcely saw the Procession. Afterwards he had a picture of coloured fragments--horses tossing their heads, grand splashes of crimson caught and lost again, pennons waving, spurs and bridles jingling and glittering, cries and shouts: 'Here he is! . . . That's the Duke! . . . That's Marshal Soult! . . . Who's that little man? . . .' soldiers and again soldiers, backs erect, heads up behind the tossing manes of their chargers, a blare of music, a moment of deafening brass and thunder dying to a distant melody, and the air still save for the clatter of hooves; then a vague roar like a wind in the air, louder and louder, more and more personal, then 'She's here! That's her! . . . Oh, how young she looks!'--and, with an odd beating of the heart and mist at the eyes, for a moment his hunger forgotten, he caught the face and figure, tiny in the great gold coach, of a girl so young and unprotected that there was something deeply appealing in the risks that she was taking. Why, she was no more than a baby! She was bowing to them. She smiled. She was gone. 'She's but a child,' Adam murmured, turning away--then thought that, for the first time in his life, he was going to faint. The street and the people were spinning up to him. He lurched sideways and was held in the arms of a tall, broad-shouldered, smiling fellow in a plain, brown beaver hat and a black coat,

'What's up, friend?'

'I'm hungry,' said Adam simply. So the tall man in the brown beaver hat took him home. This man was called Caesar Kraft and he lived with his daughter Margaret in three rooms off the Seven Dials. Kraft and Adam knew, within an hour of their first meeting, that they had that deep emotional affection for one another that men, often the manliest and strongest, sometimes experience. There was a little room on the other side of the passage from the Krafts that Adam hired. The Krafts were Chartists, and within twenty-four hours Adam was a Chartist too. By the spring of 1839, indeed, Adam was a more thorough and convinced Chartist than Caesar Kraft himself.

On the morning following his first night with them he had had a long and critical conversation with Kraft. He knew afterwards that this conversation was one of the turning-points of his life. It came at a time when he was exactly ready for it--growing from boy into man, ignorant of the world, lonely and longing for affection. As a child he had loved John Herries, but with that exception, and of course his devotion to his mother, which was part of himself, he had revealed his heart to no one. Now he opened it to Kraft, for Kraft, too, needed a friend. Adam made no mistake here. Caesar Kraft was the noblest, purest, most selfless human being he was ever to know.

Their alliance formed, the rest followed.

'Do you think you can write?' Kraft asked him.

'I have no idea,' Adam answered.

'Remain here for a week and study some of these.'

Kraft put in front of him a mass of documents, pamphlets, letters, appeals, protests, from every part of the country. It was a very remarkable collection, and Adam devoured the whole of it.

This is no place to go in detail into that documentary evidence. It can be found in many volumes easy of access, but some things are worth recording because of the effect that they had upon Adam's life and outlook.

He knew that children in the mines, descending a shaft six hundred feet deep, went along a subterranean road three miles in length, and that at the 'workings' on either side of them the hewers were employed in a state of complete nudity because of the great heat. The child, sometimes not more than six years of age, was employed there to keep the doors or 'traps' shut against the flow of inflammable air. Here, then, the child would sit in the dark all day opening and shutting those doors. At first he was given a candle, but after a while when he was accustomed to the dark the candle was taken away.

Later the child would be promoted to be a drawer or 'thrutcher' and then, clad only in a pair of trousers, a belt round the waist, a chain attached to the belt at one end and the truck at the other, the chain passing between his legs, often on all-fours because of the lowness of the gallery, he would, hour after hour, act his part as beast of burden. The 'thrutchers' would push the truck along with their heads and, although they were protected with a cap, were soon bald. The women 'thrutchers' wore nothing but a pair of short trousers.

He learnt that a hedger in the country would receive seven-pence a day for six days of the week to find him clothes, food and lodging. He learnt that the soldiers in barracks had for urinal wooden tubs, and in those same tubs they must afterwards wash.

He learnt that in the Navy the sailors lived entirely on salt beef, salt pork and maggoty biscuit, and that they would bet with one another as to which piece of biscuit would, unaided, crawl across a table faster than another. He learnt that a labourer lived almost entirely on tea (often made of crusts or twigs) and potatoes. For months together he would not taste meat. A young man had been asked how he lived on half a crown a week. He replied that he did not live on it. 'I poach,' he said, 'for it is better to be hanged than to starve to death.'

Children did not go home to dinner because there was none. A man, working in a factory, told this story: 'Up at five in the morning to get to the factory, work till eight, half an hour for breakfast, work till noon, dinner an hour, then work till four, half an hour for tea, then work till nine. The master's strap, six feet long, was kept at his right hand, two cuts at a stroke, and every day some of it.'

The injuries of the bread-tax were beginning to be poignantly felt. Bread was made from barley-meal. Families lived for days on swede turnips, roasted, baked and boiled. A man had a wife and six children to keep when flour was twelve shillings a bushel. To have a red herring, to be shared by several, was a great treat. If a father obtained a penny white loaf, his children would trudge miles to meet him that they might see it the sooner. A man would, in his hunger, eat the pig-pease and horse-beans that he was threshing. The children would steal the cabbage-stalks and swedes from the fields. Some families would go early out and eat the snails. Bread was soon to be at one-and-sixpence the loaf.

So it was in factory, mine and field, in small village and large town.

Adam's nature, the more that it was so restrained, was deeply stirred by suffering, but hitherto the suffering that he had known had belonged to separate incidents and individual persons. Now it seemed to him that the whole country was spread with a cloud. It was hard to believe that there was anyone who was aware and yet would do nothing about it. But it was so; not only were there thousands who did not stir a finger, but he soon came to realize that everyone who had any power in the country was against any change. This girl who was Queen--he heard of nothing but her rides in the Park with Melbourne, that she danced in her Palace until two of the morning, that at her dinner parties the plates were of gold and the cutlery of silver.

It was good for him that he fell under the influence of such people as the Krafts or he might have become a violent agitator like Henry Lunt, Kraft's friend. But Caesar and Margaret had spent their lives among these questions. Their natures were sweet and tolerant although they were as determined in the Cause as any fanatic, and it may be said that they saved Adam at this time.

One thing, however, did happen to him, and that was a suspicion of his own family. He thought of Walter and Uhland at Ireby, of Sylvia and her gay parties, of Will and his money, of James and his greedy stomach, of the Newmarks and (as it appeared to him now) their hypocrisy, of the Rockages and their snobbery, even--in his new bitterness--of Dorothy and John. Uldale with its farm, its ordered garden and orchard, its stables with the fat horses, the lawn gleaming so smoothly under the morning sun--how could they suffer it all so easily when men, their stomachs empty, bled from the master's strap, when children of six years old sat naked hour after hour, day after day, in the dark, when women and children went into the fields and grubbed for cabbage-stalks, when in the streets outside his window the stench was so terrible that you fainted under it and fever was in every house?

He began to have an obsession about the Herries. He saw them with their horse-faces bending forward with malicious pleasure to watch the sufferings of the crawling figures beneath them, Walter guzzling, Will seated on his money-bags, Sylvia with her poodle dancing across the shining floor of her boudoir. He thanked God that he was illegitimate. He was another Herries rebel--the bull that 'Rogue' Herries saw baited, Reuben's bear and the boy hanged of his mother's youth, the falling Bastille with which Francis killed his father--these were unknown to Adam, but he was forging a new link in that strong chain of protest.

And then in the middle of this he received a letter from his mother, the first that he had had since he had left Uldale.

MY DEAR ADAM--You have been very good in writing to me with such regularity. Do not think that I have not appreciated your letters but I was DETERMINED that I would not WEAKLY submit to your self- will and OBSTINACY. Nevertheless, for a long time now I have known that you were right to do as you did and I was too OBSTINATE myself to confess to my mistake. You have doubtless heard from Mr Rackstraw who tells me that he has written to you and you have all the NEWS but now that I have broken the ICE I must further tell you that I am LONGING to see you again and that there is no day since your departure that I have not been of the same MIND. I am growing an old woman now, Adam. I am sixty-five years of age although I must say I am extremely VIGOROUS and save for a stiffness in my right arm which only comes out in damp weather I am in excellent health. All are well here. John has bought two more cows. We have been very GAY these last weeks and Dorothy with her boy and little girl has been staying this fortnight with us. Veronica (a most FOOLISH name in my opinion) is a very ENGAGING baby and Timothy a good child when MANAGED. Dorothy has much common-sense but is anxious to have the command, even here at Uldale, which of course, as you can suppose, I do not ALLOW. John is not so cheerful as I would wish. He had an encounter with Peach, Walter's man, last week up at Bogshaw and they came I fancy to some hot words. I have of course seen nothing of the people at Ireby but I hear that Walter refuses to have Elizabeth's name mentioned since her disappearance, of which of course you've heard. Poor child! No one seems to CARE what has happened to her. It would not have been so if Agnes were still living.

I will not write more now because you are a DISOBEDIENT son and do not deserve a long letter but I am nevertheless (LONGING to see you soon)-- Your loving mother,
    JUDITH PARIS.

Adam's first impulse after reading this letter was to go at once North, by coach, railway, or any other means that offered. This was no new impulse. Scarcely a day of the last six months that he had not known it, but he had always driven it back as a weakness that he must not feel. But now with the letter in his hands his love for his mother was for a while overwhelming. Behind the words he saw her pride, her obstinacy, her sweetness, her humour, her gaiety, her tenderness. It was as though she were with him in the room. He realized, once again, that they were part of one another, bone of bone and flesh of flesh. But for that very reason he would not leave the work to which he had set his hand. If he returned to her even for a day her influence over him would be so strong that she might persuade him to remain with her. He MUST be himself, develop his own life, create his own pattern. In the end that is what she would wish him to do.

So he sat down and wrote her the most loving letter he had ever penned and then turned to his work again.

They had soon discovered that he could write. He was, in fact, just what they needed, for he was honest, indignant and accurate. His youth gave his words freshness and his sincerity prevented any fustian or melodrama.

The fanatics--one of the wildest was this man called Henry Lunt-- complained that he was not strong enough. They soon discovered that he was of no use at all as a speaker. He had no power over words, and the sight of an audience was appalling to him.

He went on one occasion with a number of delegates from London to Manchester and they put him on the platform. It was one of the most horrible experiences of his life. He stood there, his brown healthy cheeks pale, fumbling his hair with his hand, moving his thick legs as though he would kick the place down. He stammered, stopped, stammered again, strung some sentences together and sat down, a lamentable failure.

When he came back to London he told Margaret about it.

'I felt as though they stripped my clothes off my back.'

'Yes,' she said, 'they say it was the worst speech ever made in Manchester.'

'They'll never ask me to do it again--that's one good thing.'

'But you can write about the bread-tax and the shilling loaf and the fever here in Seven Dials,' she answered, 'better than anyone we've had since Tom Colman.'

She was standing near to him, and he put out his hand, resting it on her shoulder. She did not move away.

'Margaret, how old are you?' he asked her.

'Let me see. I was born in February 1820. This is March 1839. I am nineteen.'

'You are not like a girl,' he said, his hand holding her arm more strongly. 'You are a woman.'

'I have been a woman ever since mother died. That night when she went and father was in my arms I thought he would die too. I never knew two people love one another as he and mother did. I grew up that night.'

'It was a happy thing for me that afternoon when Caesar spoke to me.'

'It was a happy thing for us too,' she answered.

That night in bed he knew that he loved Margaret. He had loved her, he perceived, since the first moment that he saw her. She was the first woman he had ever cared for, and this excitement and tenderness was quite new to him. He lay there thinking of her, of her unselfishness, honesty and integrity. But he realized that he knew nothing about her feeling for himself. She was as quiet as he was; he had never seen her show any interest in men, but they were not very much together. She was out at her dressmaking all day and was often kept to very late hours. She might have a lover somewhere. There might be another side to her, a side that she never showed at home. He was extremely ignorant about women. Although he was approaching twenty-four years of age he had never kissed any woman save his mother, Jennifer and Dorothy. With the exception of his mother his deepest feelings of affection and loyalty had been roused by men--John, Rackstraw, Caesar Kraft. So this feeling for Margaret was something quite new, and that night, as he lay awake, listening to the drunken shouts in the street below, it grew and grew until he felt that he had Margaret in his arms. That seemed to him the happiest wonder, something that awed him with its mingling of worship and desire; lost in this new experience he fell asleep.

He was as cautious and careful in this as in everything else. His shyness made him shrink from any rebuff. He had nothing to offer her, no position, no prospects. And here for the first time his illegitimacy troubled him. Kraft perhaps would not want his daughter to marry a bastard. He was proud of his family, talked of his German grandfather as though he had been the grandest man in Germany. But when that seed of love is sown in a nature like Adam's nothing can hinder it.

But this new desire made life difficult for him. He was pulled in two quite opposite directions: his love for Margaret as the days went by filled itself increasingly with light and colour like a glass ball that becomes with every hour more radiant. But his discontent with the sickness and starvation all round him was something fierce and hostile, dark, jagged like lightning.

He remembered that once at home when he was on his favourite place at the bottom of Cat Bells, in Manesty, by the Lake a wind had come up, the sky had been darkened with hot saffron-edged clouds. All in a moment the breeze had lifted, and the Lake that had been placidly blue was edged with little frothy white waves. The whole expanse of water was mulberry-coloured and the islands were black- green, the tint of leaves turned backwards by the wind. Behind this angry scene Skiddaw and Blencathra and the fields below them rose drenched in light and sun--a wall of sun flashing and sparkling. As the Lake was dyed ever deeper and deeper with its mulberry stain and the little waves jumped with tongues of a dead white, the wall of light seemed to exult in its own glory: it shouted its strength aloud. Then, as a shutter closes, a hand swept wiping out all colour. Hills and lake together were dun.

He had never forgotten this scene. He had thought of it often in his first homesick days in London; now his experience seemed to be thus mixed--an exulting wall of light, a tossing discontented floor of stain. For the first time he was touching forces very much stronger and deeper than himself.

Then one of the great evenings of his life came. He went with Caesar Kraft and Margaret to a Chartist meeting in Seven Dials. Lunt and another, Philip Pider, were with them. Lunt was worked up to more than his customary indignation because a family living in the cellar of his building had been sick of the fever: two of them, an old man and a child, had died, and their bodies had been left there in the cellar two days and a night before anyone attended them. Adam noticed that behind his indignation was a kind of fierce joy because he had been given some more evidence to use in his damning account against all authority. He described with angry gusto the filthy state of that cellar, the pools of moisture, the loathsome stench, the rats.

He was this night like an animal himself, his strong dark hairy body moving like an animal's, his words, growls, mutters, little snatches of ferocity. The surroundings that evening were strange and fantastic. There had been a thick yellow fog all day, but now it had thinned, hanging in discontented wisps about the streets and buildings. The lamps in the street were damp and mildewed with moisture; the shops were for the most part closed, but some were yet open and you could see, in the candlelight, figures like shapes in the fire cross-legged over a boot or shoe, arms raised to fetch down some garment, a butcher standing with blood on his apron above slabs of red meat and dark amber-coloured entrails. Everyone moved through the wispy fog as though in secret, and there was that faint scent of sulphur in the air that a thick London fog leaves behind it.

For Adam that walk to the hall where the meeting was to be held was one of his most blissful moments. Margaret's hand was through his arm; he could feel the soft swell of her breast against his sleeve, she was so close to him. She spoke in a voice that was quiet and happy. He knew that she was happy, he could feel it in every word that she spoke. Once and again he could catch under her bonnet the gleam of her eyes, the shadow of her cheek above her dark green shawl. He was terribly anxious not to cheat himself (all this experience was so new to him), but he began to believe that his company must have something to do with her happiness--and then quite suddenly she told him that it was so.

'You know, Adam, since you came to us father and I have been happier than we used to be.'

His heart hammered with delight. He thought that she must feel its beatings against her arm. And as always when he was deeply moved, he could say nothing.

'Um--' he muttered.

'Are you not glad?'

'Of course, I am glad--if it's true, Margaret.'

'But, of course, it's true. Why should I say it if it was not? Father was often very lonely before you came. He can be passionate in his affections, and I think he loves you more than he ever loved anyone except mother.'

'And yourself?'

'Oh, myself--I am always there, you know. He has become accustomed to me.'

He plucked up his courage, although his tongue was dry in his throat.

'And some day you will marry, Margaret?'

'Yes,' she answered quietly. 'I hope so--some day.'

'Perhaps there is someone--already--'

'Oh, I don't know,' she answered, laughing. 'There is Mr Hooper--a friend of Madame's at the shop . . .'

'Oh, is there?' he said, his heart dropping to a dreadful deadness.

'I think he likes me,' she went on quietly. 'He wears two waistcoats and I am certain he has a corset. He speaks like this: "Oh, Miss Kraft . . . I'm sure . . . most exquisite . . . Pray, turn that I may see the back. I'm quite in raptures!"' She imitated him and burst out laughing. '*I* like him, but I fear father would not. But he has a fine little villa in Islington, and he sings to his own accompaniment on the pianoforte.'

He supposed that she was teasing him, but he could not be sure. Now they had arrived at the hall, and the other world of fire and tumult drove down upon them.

The hall was a large one, and when they entered they found it packed with people. The air was thick with the warm smell of human bodies, the odour from the oil lamps; figures were indistinct--here a face, there an arm, a body flung forward--everywhere an almost ecstatic excitement and attention. Kraft, Lunt and Pider went to sit on the platform, Adam and Margaret were pressed into the wall near the door. Adam had been to many meetings by now, but thought that he had never seen such eye-strained faces, men and women and some children, one baby held aloft and waving its chubby fists in the air.

It had just begun when they entered. The Chairman, a round tubby man with thick grey side-whiskers, was speaking. The atmosphere was at present quiet and controlled. He said something about the conditions of the time, the oppression of the authorities, the iniquities of the Bread Tax, the Six Points of the new Charter. He sat down, and a long thin fellow with a straggly beard got up. He had a rather weak, piping voice and no very impressive manner: he began quietly, so there were voices from the hall; 'Speak up! We can't hear!' and a rough growl from someone: 'Sit down, damn ye, if yer can't talk.'

That last seemed to rouse him, for he raised his rather pale, watery eyes and stared down into the hall: 'If you listen you'll 'ear all right,' he said at last. 'I ain't 'ad food in my belly for the last six months, what yer can call food.' They listened. He had control over them. He had come, he said, to tell them what it was like now to work on the land. 'We're slaves to the farmer's body, slaves like they were in the old Roman times. For ten years I served Farmer Wellin in my county--aye, you don't know 'is name likely, but one name does as well as another. Then one fine day he tells me he ain't no more work for me nor my two boys--so then I goes here, I goes there. No work. Then I goes to Manchester, starves there a bit, comes 'ome again, put in the Union, turned out after a day or two, lays abed a bit, gets a day's work, then on board-day goes to them again, gets a day's work, starves a bit, lays abed a bit, goes searching for work again, eats stuff they've given the pigs because I'm that 'ungry. My boys, as good lads as ever you see, 'anging around gets into bad ways, one of 'em roots up a turnip or two and gets gaoled. 'Is mother breaks 'er 'eart and dies of weakness. That's why I'm not speaking so 'earty, begging your pardon, friends.

'I say a poor man's a slave. He can't leave his own parish--for why?--because in a foreign parish they've plenty of their own to give work to. And what are our masters doing? They're wasting of the land, that's what I say they're doing. Give me an acre of land and I'll live well and decent on it AND give my boys a proper life. I was out of work last spring from Christmas to barley-sowing. I goes to the farmer and asks for a scrap of land to grow potatoes on. "Oh no, you don't," says he. "Give you potatoes and you'll want straw and a pig and I don't know what all. And one day, maybe, I'll be wanting you to work for myself," he says. "Oh yes," he says, "prices be so low I must lower your wages," he says, but when prices goes up does he raise the wages again? Not if he knows of it. What I say is, if the loaf's cheap we're ruined, but if the loaf's dear we're starved. For myself I'm ready enough to die, but my boys . . .'

His piping voice suddenly stopped. He wiped his eyes with the back of his hand. Then he went on:

'The farmers say they can't live without they make four rents--one for stock, one for rent, one for labour, one for theirselves. Times is bad and they can't make their four rents. Well, does the landlord as does nothing give up his rent? Of course not. Then corn falls two pound a load and worse--farmer's forty shilling out o' pocket on every load of wheat--eight shilling on every acre of his land on a four-course shift. Where's that to come from? He can't stint the landlord so he stints the labourer. Tell the landlord, friends, what you think of him and do justice to your fellow-men.'

He stopped, his voice ending in a funny little whistle, and he sat down, his legs almost giving way beneath him. The majority of the men and women in the hall had for the most part never seen a green field in their lives--the facts and figures meant nothing to them-- but the sincerity and urgency of his starved and feeble body stirred and moved them. You could feel it run through the hall like a message. There was a murmur, a restlessness, voices cried out. They were all brothers together, in field and factory, street and mine. Adam could see the faces around him change from a vague listening absorption to a personal human activity. A little man like a terrier leaped to his feet. He was plainly a practised orator. He brought the personal case of the labourer into the more general cause of them all. A woman broke out from the centre of the hall:

'They would part me from my children!' she cried in a shrill, agonized wail. 'How did I leave them this morning? Crying for their breakfasts. I've had no bread to give them for the last month and more. I've no bread. I've no fire. How can I have with one shilling and sixpence a hundred for coals? If I snatch a bit of wood from a hedge they'll gaol me. It's the women and children you should be thinking on! Oh, if I was a man I know what I'd be doing! I know what I'd be doing!'

Another woman, on that, cried out, waving an arm hysterically: 'Ax the Queen. Go and ax the Queen to come and see for herself. She's got a heart same as us . . .' And a man near her roared out: 'Why, the Queen-- she's all locked up. They've got the dragoons guarding her. Do you think the Queen wants to be frightened with the like of we? She's got Melbourne, she has. What is it to him or her if poor labourers suffer and our women are stripped naked in the mines and bread's one-and-sixpence the loaf? Ax the Queen! Aye, go and ax her and see what her soldiers do to you!'

A confused babel of voices broke out. You could feel that the temperature of men's blood was rising as though with every word they moved closer together and closer and closer, so that at last they seemed to be one man, a man with eyes red and burning, a mouth hard set, cheeks hollow with hunger--a man with his hand clenched to strike.

Someone leaped up and cried shrilly: 'Let us take what is ours! Let us take what is ours! Let us take what is ours!'

Anything might have happened then. Adam, not knowing that he did it, put his arm around Margaret and drew her nearer to protect her; they were pressed against the wall. No one thought of his or her neighbour; a stout woman in an orange shawl had her hand, without knowing it, on Adam's arm, and in a kind of strangled sob was saying over and over: 'Aye--it's the People's right--it's the People's right--it's the People's right . . .'

Adam knew that in another moment there would be that strong, swaying movement beneath their feet as though the floor were stirring under them, and that then all would be swept together in some mob-hysteria beyond control.

But it did not come. Instead the rotund little Chairman in some way made himself heard. He said that Mr Kraft would speak to them and, as Caesar rose to his feet, quiet came over everyone again. How proud Adam was of him at that moment! His square shoulders were set like those of a man carrying a banner; his eyes spoke to some distance far beyond the hall and its occupants; his voice, rich, warm, sincere, had no arrogance in it and no self-seeking.

'I do not believe in disorder,' he said. 'Neither now nor at any time. I know that our cause is just, but I find it so just that it must have victory--but victory by law and not by riot. Patience--'

At the word 'Patience' someone shouted out: 'We have been patient long enough!'

Caesar went on: 'We have not been patient long enough. We can never be patient long enough so long as we are moving. And we ARE moving! We have our Six Points of our Charter, and they are so right and so just that all the world will yield to them. We are working for a prize greater and more lasting than our immediate troubles. We are working for our children and our children's children. What do we gain by fire and murder? We place ourselves in the same case as our oppressors. We must believe in justice, for there is justice in the world. Men may be unjust, but behind them moves something stronger, finer and wiser than man.'

He went on then to tell them what the heads of the movement were doing, showed them their plans in detail, and was so comprehensive, clear and wise that soon the hall was as quiet as a vestry, and you could hear the rumble of the carts on the cobbles outside. All then might have moved peacefully to its close, but as soon as Kraft, to a hubbub of applause and clapping of hands, had sat down, Lunt sprang to his feet. He stood swaying on his short, strong legs, his body a little forward, his dark face with its shock of black hair alive with indignation and an almost mad impetuosity.

'I am Caesar Kraft's friend!' he called out. 'I HAVE been and shall be! But I say that his advice to you is the advice of a dreamer! Wait, he says! Patience, he says! Yes, we are patient, and meanwhile what happens! Our old men and children, our wives and daughters, die in cellars swimming in filth, as I have seen two dead today; our women starve naked in the fields grubbing roots that pigs would refuse. Our men are beaten by their masters until their backs drop blood. We starve. We starve. Half the men in this room are starving now! And the Government says--let them starve! The less work for us, the Government says. Let them eat one another, the Government says, if they're hungry. Let them lie closer to one another if they're cold! Why should they interfere between slave and slave?'

He began to pace the platform, his face turned to them, his body shaking with his vehemence.

'Why do we give opium to our little children? So that they may forget their hunger! We entreat the Government to have mercy on us, we send it petitions, we show it our naked backs and our fever- dying comrades. "Oh yes," they say, and send us an answer: "Sorry to say that it is altogether out of the power of Her Majesty . . ." Her Majesty! And she feeding off gold plate and riding in the Park of a morning! What does she know or care? Patience, Caesar Kraft tells you, but *I* tell you that we have had enough of patience, that they won't listen although we call, that they laugh at our tears. The Towns must win the Charter for England--men and women like yourselves--and not by patience, not by sitting down and waiting while we starve, but by rising and showing our power, by driving fear into their souls, by putting those same dragoons out of the way that we may meet the Queen face to face and say to her: "Here are your people! You haven't seen them before, but take a good look at them--see their backs how they bleed, how their stomachs are empty, their children crying for food--"'

He was interrupted by a roar of voices. 'Aye! Aye! . . . We'll go now. We'll go to the Queen . . . We've been patient enough! To the Palace! To the Palace!'

Like a wind through trees the roomful swayed, then broke. Men shouted, women called. The din was fearful, threatening, with that note in it that no individual man can recognize as his own and, after catastrophe, denies as his own.

They broke and rushed to the doors, Adam holding Margaret, who, however, was almost as strong as he.

The noisy, shouting mob tumbled into the street to be met with a fog as thick as a wall of suet. It was comic, that sudden dropping of voices, that check on the rush and impulse as though they had all found themselves on the edge of a precipice with the sea booming below them. The street was quiet and chill; the fog blew through the air in thick, yellow folds, laying its clammy touch on every mouth. Figures shot up out of the dark, some of them with flares, flamed and vanished. The crowd from the hall passed like smoke into smoke.

Adam laughed. He put his hand through her arm and they walked forward.

'Well--that is the end of THAT rioting. We must go forward, trust our luck. We will reach a clearer patch soon.' The fog was the one thing in all the world that could give him courage to speak, for they were close together, but in darkness.

So, when they had gone only a little way, he said outright:

'Margaret, I love you. Will you marry me?'

'Yes,' she said.

He stopped where he was, put his arms round her and kissed her. She did not move so he did not either. They seemed in a trance, protected by the fog, her lips on his, his arms tightly round her. At last when, very slowly, they moved on again he said:

'I must tell you, Margaret, that I have no money, no home, nothing.'

'Yes,' she said. 'Your home is with us.'

'And I have a mother whom I love more dearly than anyone but you.'

She held his hand more tightly.

'I have no father, as you know. I have no family. I am illegitimate.'

She laughed.

'You belong all the more to me for that,' she said.

Then a long while afterwards, when the fog in front of them was clearing, she said, sighing:

'Oh, I did hope, Adam, that you loved me, for I loved you from the first moment.'

HISTORY OF ELIZABETH

Adam would have been greatly surprised had he realized that not far from where he was standing that June day in 1838 Uhland and Elizabeth had also witnessed the return of the Procession from Westminster Abbey. Will had invited them to London for the Coronation and they had accepted his invitation.

'Do you wish to go?' Walter had asked them. He also had been invited, but an affair upon which he was just then engaged (a highly exciting amorous affair with a lady who lived near Cockermouth) prevented his acceptance. Moreover, he did not wish to go; he found, if he were honest, his father a dull dog and his mother a quite unspeakable bore. Yet in his own way he loved them, wrote to his mother every month and sent his father presents of game.

When Elizabeth heard of the invitation she waited breathlessly to know whether she would be allowed to accept it. It was upon just such an invitation that she had been counting, for she was determined to escape from her father, from Ireby, from her brother, and, if possible, never return.

She was now a beautiful girl, twenty-three years of age. Her mother had died in the autumn of 1835, and since then she had not known one moment's happiness.

When, so long ago, she and John had agreed to separate and not to see one another again she had been but a child. She had forced the separation upon John because she had been certain that marriage with her would be for him a disaster. She was perhaps wrong there. Had they at that time run away and married, the whole course of their lives might have been altered to happiness, but how could he run away when he was responsible for everything at Uldale? Since then his

sister had married Bellairs, but now there was something stronger than any practical reason that drove Elizabeth.

She believed--and had more reason for her belief than anyone outside the house at Ireby could know-- that Uhland would kill John if she married him. Wherever they went Uhland would find them out. She had a terror of her father and brother that went far beyond actual day-by-day fact.

Uhland's hatred of John became fanatical after he learnt that Elizabeth cared for him. It became so fanatical that he did nothing about it, as though he knew that he had only to bide his time, as though he knew that there was no need for him to do anything yet because John at Uldale was well aware of it; it was as though he could see inside John's heart and feel the fear and apprehension growing there. It was as though he felt that if he did YET anything positive in word or deed it would hinder the full flavour of his act when the real time for it arrived.

There the two of them were, Uhland at Ireby and John at Uldale, very near together, and, like a spell in witchcraft, the power of the one over the other, although they never met, always increased.

And in the same way, on the other side of the account, Elizabeth's love for John never lessened, but increased.

She went about, saw many people in the County, made friends, led outwardly a quiet normal life; she tried with all her force (and she had much strength of character) to kill her love for John. She seldom saw him in public, for people, knowing well the old feud, took care that the two households did not meet. Sometimes in the Keswick street, at a hunt, at a public ball, they would catch sight of one another and turn away. John, on his side, thought that he was only waiting until Elizabeth was old enough. He knew that she was beautiful and rich and should make a fine marriage. If she married him, when her father and brother hated him so, it meant exile for her and, perhaps, disgrace. But when she was of age she had only to make him a sign and he would act. Nevertheless, although he was no coward in any other way, the thought of Uhland made him sick. Often when he was busy about the house or the farm or riding or paying a visit some dreaminess would overtake him, it would seem to him as though with one step, by unlocking some door he would pass into another world infinitely more beautiful than this one. He had dreamt once as a child of a marvellous white horse plunging through an icy tarn and climbing, his mane flowing, the steep mountainside. He had never forgotten the dream although it had never returned. If he could ride that horse he would spring forward into regions of splendour and eternal life! But again and again when such images came to him, asleep at night, walking the fells, sitting half awake by the fire, he seemed to hear a step behind him and would start up, expecting to see the cold malicious face of Uhland watching him.

So there they were, the three of them, in this summer of 1838. Again and again afterwards Elizabeth would look back to this time at Ireby and ask herself whether she did anything that fostered later events. But she could not see that she was responsible. She held on during that time to the principles, first that her father's neglect of her and his scandalous behaviour should not touch her, secondly that Uhland's taunts should not touch her, thirdly that her love of John should not touch her. It was the last of the three that at length drove her to flight. She COULD not, she COULD not be so near to him and not see him. Her father's behaviour she was by now accustomed to; Uhland's taunts she could endure, but they were ingenious. He would test her suddenly, unexpectedly. He would say: 'I hear young Herries has made a fool of himself over that farm . . .' 'They are saying that John Herries has put a girl at Jocelyn's by Troutbeck in the family way. He can't leave farm girls alone. He has a low taste,' or 'They say that Herries goes to Cockermouth and gambles night after night--gambling all the estate away, poor fool . . . Hard on old Madame.' All lies of course! Walter Herries would chuckle and shake his shoulders (he was growing immense now although still handsome in a florid three-chin fashion). But Elizabeth would not stir. She had all the Herries pride. She would look at Uhland and smile very faintly, and he would look gravely back at her. There would be at that moment a strange subconscious alliance between them.

But by the summer of this year, 1838, she had reached the limit of all her endurance. How she hated the Fortress no words of hers could express. Even to the outside unprejudiced person it was not a happy house as Westaways had been. Westaways had been created by an artist, and it was a thousand pities that in the autumn of 1836 it was pulled down by the purchasers of the land; they had a plan for building an Almshouse there but this never came to anything. All the eighteenth-century colour and glitter, all the ambitions of Pomfret and Jannice, the childish hopes of Raiseley and Judith and Anabel, the early ambitions of Walter--all gone at the flourish of a hand, a little cloud of dust rising slowly over the tumbling brick! And the Fortress was not built by an artist! It was intended to stand for Herries independence, strength and superiority. Good English material power. Most certainly it looked strong enough with its battlements and towers, its broad high rooms, its walls and garden-paths and fountain. But it was never gay, never light-hearted, never alive! Even Walter felt this. He entertained there lavishly, had dinners and hunting- parties, dances and drinking-bouts and, after Agnes' death, made it open house for all the squires of the County. But it refused to come alive! Half the rooms 'died on him', do what he would. He complained that there was not sufficient feminine society in it. Elizabeth entertained and she was a lovely hostess, quiet, dignified, kindly. Everyone liked her, but everyone said that the place was sad. They whispered that Walter beat her when he was in a drunken temper. He did not beat her: he never ill-treated her: he gave her everything that she asked. He simply did not consider her. A Mrs Fergus, a genial stout widow, was housekeeper there during these years. She was common, voluble, gossipy, a good manager. She liked Elizabeth and tried to win her trust. But she did not. She confided to everybody that something was the matter in that house. It was as though a ghost were in every room in spite of the drinking-parties and dinners.

It may have been that Uhland was the ghost. He had certainly grown into a very severe, silent young man. Friendship with Adam might have saved Uhland at this time. He showed from a conversation that he had with Elizabeth in London that he was as lonely as she. Adam was certainly the only human being in the world to whom he would have disclosed himself. There was no doubt but that during those years from 1832 to 1838 he was as unhappy as Elizabeth was. It may be that at the end of it all he despised and hated himself quite as much as he despised and hated John Herries. No one will ever know.

Walter meanwhile, being really a foolish soul with very little understanding of other human beings, continued to persuade himself that Uhland adored him, adored the Fortress, adored the fine fortune that Walter preserved for him (already not quite so fine as it had once been: the Fortress like a heavy dull grey monster swallowed greedily all that was offered it). His love for Uhland was pathetic. He was like a big lumbering elephant cherishing a morose young wolf.

And that was how things were when Elizabeth and Uhland went to London.

When they arrived, late one evening, in Hill Street, where was Will's present town house, Uhland was in a monstrous temper because of the bad time that they had had in the coach. They had booked for the inside, of course, but there had been an asthmatic gentleman with a cough so tiresome, and an old lady with so many small packages that she was for ever undoing to see whether the contents were safe, that Uhland had sought the roof. There were not many passengers, and with extra money he had secured the box- seat, and there wrapped in the leather-covered rug might have been fairly comfortable, but then a storm had come on and the rain had driven down his neck, his overcoat was soaked, and the coachman was for ever thrusting his rein-elbow into his (Uhland's) ribs. The day following had not been much better, for the food at the inns was atrocious, and the manners of everyone appalling. Why had they not tried the new railway? It was so erratic. You never knew where it began and where it left off. Worst of all, their hackney cab, when at last they got into it, collided with a dray, and they were in perilous chance of immediate death.

So they arrived at Hill Street and discovered that a grand party was in progress. A tall gorgeously dressed footman hurried them up the stairs as though they were very criminal indeed. Everywhere were flowers; there was the distant music of a band and the crackle of many voices. Elizabeth had not been in her large cold room five minutes before a maid knocked, came in, and asked her whether she should unpack for her.

'Her ladyship is unfortunately most unwell. She has been confined to her bed for several weeks. She hopes to see you, Miss, in the morning.'

Was she supposed to come down to the party, Elizabeth wondered. Would she get anything to eat? She was inordinately hungry. The maid, who looked a nice girl, Elizabeth thought, was on her knees unpacking.

'Would you tell me your name?' Elizabeth asked.

'Ellen,' said the girl.

Elizabeth shivered. HOW hungry she was! And then, miracle of miracles, the door burst open, and in came Sylvia Herries looking radiant and lovely in pink tulle and carrying a tray!

'Oh, my dearest Elizabeth!'

'Dear Sylvia!'

'But of course I knew that you would be STARVING, and Frederick is bringing a warming-pan. You can place it under those cushions and sit on it. How are you feeling, my sweetest Elizabeth? But of course you must be DEAD! But how lovely you are looking! A little thin . . . Was the journey quite, quite dreadful? Ah, here is Frederick! There, Frederick-- place it beneath those cushions . . . Oh, dear little Elizabeth! I am RAVISHED to see you, and Cousin Will is giving the grandest party. Mr Macaulay is here and Lady Brownlow and Lady Euston and the Bishop of Oxford and EVER so many more, and James' wife is doing the honours. You never saw anything so amazingly odd. She's wearing a turban like a pastry-cook's shop! But there's no one so lovely as you are, so you must hurry, my dearest, and eat this chicken and drink this champagne and wear your LOVELIEST costume . . . Now sit on the warming-pan, dearest, QUITE still for five minutes. That will warm the under part of you in any case. There's the most enravishing band and I've danced five waltzes already . . .'

So Elizabeth sat on the warming-pan and then with the assistance of Ellen and Sylvia put on her dress of white organdie with a rose at her girdle, which, although it HAD been made by little Miss Trent in Keswick, suited her exactly.

When she came into the big room, blazing with lights, swimming in music, a kind of exultation seized her. How wonderful to have escaped from that cold, grey Fortress with the heavy grey clouds hanging over it, the stern dark landscape hemming it in, to this scene of splendour and magnificence! Ah! If only John were here! But one day he would be! They would be here together! She deserved some life and some fun, surely.

Will came up to her and was very kind. He was of course stiff and pompous a little, but he meant well and this was a big occasion for him. He led her up to Lady Euston who, in satin, a green turban and splendid diamonds, was the most terrifying lady she had ever seen.

'Well, my dear, and so you have come for the Coronation?'

'Yes, ma'am.'

'Let us trust that Providence will favour us with good weather. It is very cold for the summer.'

'Yes, indeed, ma'am.'

'This is your first visit to London?'

'Yes, ma'am.'

'Your cousin must bring you to Almack's, and you must visit the Opera. How do you do, Sir Henry? I hear that Mr Croker has written the most offensive article about Soult in the Quarterly . . .'

Soon she was dancing, once with Garth, once with Amery, once with Roger, Carey Rockage's son. Then with a gentleman whose dress-coat was so extremely waisted that she was afraid lest he should break in two at any moment. He wanted, very solemnly, to tell her about the Park: 'Until recently the Park has been most sombre and I assure you most unsafe for ANYONE after nightfall. However, lamps with gas have now been introduced and throw a noontide splendour. They combine in fact ornament with utility, and vice has been banished from her wonted haunts . . .' She supposed that he had something to do with the Parks, he seemed so very serious about it.

Then Garth introduced her to a stout rather plethoric young man, a Mr Temple, she understood. She had not waltzed with him once around the room before she realized that he was greatly charmed with her. He told her so; he led her away to a corner behind a mass of begonias and, breathing hard to recover his wind, said in a sort of wondering whisper that she was, upon his life, the most lovely girl that he had ever seen. He begged her, he implored her, not to take offence. The admission had been, to his own amazement, compelled upon him. She could not take offence. There was nothing offensive about him; he was like a baby in his tight clothes, with a large diamond in his shirt and his hair excessively pomaded. She wanted to laugh and, when he left her for a moment to bring her some champagne, she did laugh. She could not help it. She was happy. She was free. She would never go back to Ireby again, and John would come to her.

'You have made a conquest, my dear cousin,' said Garth, a little later.

'A conquest?' she asked.

'Edward Temple. He is the richest young man in London.'

In the course of the next week or so Elizabeth discovered a number of curious and amusing things. Poor Christabel was, alas, too ill to see her. She sent her loving messages and hoped that she was enjoying herself. Elizabeth was chaperoned either by Sylvia or by James' wife, Lady Herries, poor Beatrice. She was known as 'poor Beatrice' because she said such silly things, wore such hideous clothes, and tumbled into such foolish blunders, but like many who are pitied by their fellows she was a great deal happier than those who pitied her. She was good-natured, most indiscreet, and admired Elizabeth's beauty with a sincerity that was touching.

Will lived with much splendour. When they went to a ball or a theatre or Vauxhall of an evening they were carried in a fine painted 'chariot' with Frederick, the footman, in silk stockings, plush breeches and hair-powder, standing behind; the Herries family arms were on the panels. But the house in Hill Street could not be said to be comfortable. That there were often unpleasant 'whiffs' from the drains meant nothing. People even preferred that the drains should 'smell' occasionally because then they could tell which way the wind was blowing and whether 'there would likely be rain'. The furniture was fine, heavy and impressive, but the passages and rooms were dreadfully chill, and there was an air of mortality everywhere save when there was a party. Elizabeth had some very dreary days and evenings. Will was in the City all day, Uhland out and about on his own affairs, as men, lucky creatures, were able to be, but unless Sylvia or Lady Herries came for her she was sadly alone. All the Herries were good and kind to her, but she soon perceived that they were, nearly all of them, living above their means, reaching up to the new grand position that Will's money and Sylvia's social successes had brought to them. It said much for Will's dignity and tact that, having made his position by business, he and his should be admitted to Almack's and allowed the honours of Holland House. But the Herries were a very old family, and the Rockages had most certainly not made their money in business--having exactly no money at all. Roger, Carey's boy, and his wife Janet had a house in Mayfair during the Season and ordered little dinners from the caterer (and WHAT scrapes they went through in order to pay the caterer no one knew but themselves); then as soon as the Season was over they disappeared, with their only child Carey, into two very shabby rooms in Pimlico, and Janet did the cooking. The life of Sylvia and Garth, too, was one long and exciting piratical adventure--a very thrilling volume of hairbreadth peril and escape it would make. Garth spent much of his time at Crockford's, which was not on the face of it a very foolish thing to do, for the subscription was but ten guineas a year, and in the gambling-rooms there was served a splendid supper free, with excellent wine for all Mr Crockford's guests.

Behind this were, of course, for many a man ruin and despair. But Garth was not a fool; he had some of his brother Amery's astuteness, and he knew his world.

Elizabeth, however, was not like Judith. She could not throw herself into whatever fun was going forward. She was quiet, reserved and shy. All she wanted of life was that she should be allowed to live quietly in a corner with John somewhere and never be disturbed by anyone again.

She sat of an evening in the great drawing room or in her bedroom, a book on her lap, and meditated her escape. For escape she must. She knew that Uhland had some plan; she felt as though with every hour he was the more closely driving her to some purpose of his own.

There came an evening at Vauxhall when she began to realize what his plan for her was. She went with Sylvia, Garth, Uhland and Phyllis Newmark. It was all very splendid. There were the 'twenty thousand lamps' shining against the soft velvety sky of a July evening, Ducrow and his horses, the famous bandstand round which, if you were an unattached gentleman out for the evening, you might swirl with the loveliest, if not the most virtuous, ladies of the town, the fireworks and the vocal concerts.

For a while she enjoyed herself, listening to Sylvia's chatter, liking the general gaiety and abandon; nevertheless, she wondered, as she always did on these occasions, why she could not throw herself into things as the others did. They must find her dreadfully stupid, she thought, and, in fact, Garth that same evening confided to Sylvia behind the bed-curtains that he thought that little cousin of theirs mighty handsome, by Jove, but she seemed to be feared of her life lest someone should kiss her or chuck her under the chin; and Sylvia was forced to confess with a sigh that she didn't come out as she'd hoped. She was more at home, she suspected, in the country.

Well, later young Mr Temple joined them and, after that, poor Elizabeth's evening was a ruin. Everyone beamed upon Mr Temple, and soon he was seated with Elizabeth as his especial charge, feeding her with chicken and ham. He had a great deal to say to her, admired her gown and told of his place in Surrey where he had horses, dogs and a piano. He said he was prodigiously fond of music and the Italian opera. Very tenderly he helped her to a 'sliced cobweb'--the famous Vauxhall ham. His favourite expression, the phrase of the moment, was, when he saw anything amusing: 'What a bit of gig!'

Soon his absorption of the famous Vauxhall punch led him to closer intimacies. He pressed her hand and wished to take her up one of the shaded walks. From this Sylvia saved her, but she observed with terror that Uhland watched these proceedings with approval.

She did not sleep that night in her huge bed. What was she to do? She felt utterly defenceless. She had not a friend in the world. Strangely, she thought of Judith and Adam. What it would have been to her just then to have seen that little old lady with her sharp nose and kind bright eyes entering at the door, or Adam with his strong, ugly, honest face standing beside her! But they seemed far away, and John farther. She had no one to whom she might turn. Beatrice Herries was too foolish and indiscreet, Sylvia too flighty, Christabel too unwell. Of Will she was afraid, Garth she did not trust. She was inexperienced in the world's ways, and London seemed now like a great web in whose sticky threads she was entangled.

Then one evening Uhland came to her room. She had but just lit the candles. Bulwer's Last Days of Pompeii was in her hand, but her mind was with John, running as it so often did over those earlier days when they had written and met . . . He was like her, she thought, shy, not caring for the world, uneasy with others. Why could they not be together in some place where no one else could come? Uhland sat near her and was kinder to her, at first, than he had ever been. He wore black; his thin sharp features had in them a shadow of suffering. She knew that he was often in pain, and that feeling of some companionship between them, something that lay deep, deep down below all this strife and antagonism, stirred in her. They COULD be friends if only . . .

He told her about some of the things that he had been doing. He seemed to be as out of everything as she.

'I hate London. I do not belong here. They laugh at us as country cousins.'

'Oh no,' she protested. 'They are so very kind.'

'Kind! Do you know what they say of us? They find us most desperately dull, sister, and that's a fact. I hate drinking. I won't play at cards. They swagger-- Lord, how they swagger! And then to be up all night and for nothing--women, drink, gambling-- gambling, women, drinking. Why, Ireby were better!'

He looked at her, one of those quiet speculative looks that always made her afraid.

'I am different from everyone!' he burst out. 'They mock my lameness!'

'Oh no,' she said gently. 'They don't think of it. Why, Sylvia said--'

'Yes. Sylvia said--Sylvia said--' he answered contemptuously. 'Dear Sylvia had better take care or she'll have the bailiffs in that pretty house of hers and Garth will be in the Marshalsea . . . No,' he went on more quietly. 'It is my own fault; I am no company for anyone here, not even for myself. There's a devil in me that won't let me alone. We Herries are a poor lot unless we take what's in front of our noses. We were not made to be exceptional. Not that I'm exceptional, you know, except in my temper. I despise their smugness. What do they know of what it is to have a needle stab your leg every other minute, and to be something that every

woman pities? . . . No matter though. I shall show them all one day . . .'

She did not dare to show pity. She knew how deeply he resented it. But she said:

'We should go somewhere together, Uhland, the two of us. We could go to the Colosseum or the Panorama. I should adore to see the Panorama.'

But he did not answer her. He sat there brooding, looking down, nursing his leg. There was something, she thought, twisted, wizened about him, his thin small body bent, throwing strange humped shadows on the wall in the candlelight.

He looked up.

'You are secure at least, Elizabeth.'

'Secure?' she asked him.

'Yes. Temple is crazy about you. He will be proposing for you one of these days.'

'Oh no,' she whispered.

'Oh yes,' he answered. 'It is a fine match. There couldn't be a better. He's something of a fool, of course. But that's his age. He'll improve. I never knew a man more deeply in love.'

She said nothing. He went on:

'He is fabulously wealthy. He has his house in Belgravia and a place in Surrey. Only an old mother to care for. He doesn't play at cards and is afraid of loose women. You can do what you will with him.'

'That, Uhland, you can dismiss altogether from your mind. I should not marry him if there were no other man in the world.'

He looked at her.

'Still thinking of your friend in Cumberland?' he asked her.

'No . . . But I would never marry Mr Temple.'

He got up and walked, limping, about the room.

'Never is a long story. It would be a fine thing. Our father would think so.'

She smiled.

'There I am my own mistress.'

'Not entirely,' he said quietly. 'I think you had better consider Temple.'

'And why?'

He stood by the door, his pale eyes gravely regarding her.

'Dear sister, consider what a fine husband Temple would make. Consider it. Be wise,' and left her.

She was afraid after that and despised herself for being so. What was there about Uhland that made everyone who knew him apprehensive? Even the stable-boys at Ireby dropped their voices when he was approaching, and she knew that people in Keswick called him 'Little Mischief', although no one accused him of any actual cruelties. On the contrary, that habit of kindness to injured animals was still with him. He would be in a rage if he saw a horse ill-used or a dog tied by the tail. And yet it was not as though he cared for animals!

No, what they all felt about him was the potentiality of an outburst. Society is built up on the convention that we all INTEND to behave. That is the bargain we make the one with the other. Then, if there is one who hasn't made the bargain! . . .

In any case, Elizabeth felt some ring closing round her. She was perhaps at that time young for her age. She had been always with her mother, had known no other girls intimately. But this was a situation in which other girls than herself might have been frightened, for she knew that her father would regard this match as a heaven-sent chance. He had always wanted to be rid of her. Like so many men who are for ever making love to women he despised them heartily and wanted them for one thing only. He preferred greatly men's company, and the only chance that a woman had with him as friend was for her to have something of the downright and fearless about her as Judith had. Now Elizabeth had nothing of the downright about her whatever. She was proud and brave, but it was a pride that was too real to reveal itself and a courage that was too real for cheap display.

It was a misfortune for her that Christabel was so ill, but she did have one strange little conversation with her grandfather which was to have important after-consequences for her.

Sir William Herries was now sixty-eight years of age and as straight as a flag-pole. His hair was grizzled and he was very thin of body with a sharp nose, high Herries cheek-bones, and a severe, rather chilly eye that came from considering sums, additions, subtractions, multiplications for sixty-five years. It was at the age of three, his father David used long ago to declare, that he had added his first sum, accurately, and without assistance. He was dressed immaculately, always in black with none of those gaudy waistcoats, diamonds, pins and gold chains that ornamented the bodies of the Disraelis, the Bulwers and the Ainsworths of the day. But he was a splendid sight as you saw him step out of the carriage that had brought him up from the City, in the high hat, high stock, coat fitting perfectly at the slender waist, and tightly strapped trousers. A fine sight as, inside the cold hall with a marble statue of a goddess, handsomely robed, holding aloft a lamp, he gives his hat, gloves and cane to Frederick, passes his hand for a moment over his grey locks, pinches his side-whiskers, and walks slowly, slowly up the broad staircase.

'How is Lady Herries?' he asks Warren, the fat butler. 'Has Doctor Salter paid his visit?'

'Doctor Salter has been, Sir William. Her ladyship is much the same.'

'Ah . . . Ah. Ha! . . . Thank you, Warren.'

So one late afternoon, he came into the drawing room, ornamented as was the earlier drawing room in the earlier smaller house with oil-paintings of David his father and Sarah his mother, and a huge marble clock that had Virtue seated in a toga on the top of it, window hangings of a very grave mustard colour, a table or two scattered with 'Beauty Books' and 'Keepsakes', the po-

ems of Felicia Hemans and a book of engravings of Greece and Italy--all this as chill and as damp as a mausoleum, all this bringing pride and comfort to his soul.

Today he moved about, putting a 'Keepsake' straight on a table, arranging the hanging of one of the curtains, looking out for a moment into the summer evening that was coquetting with Hill Street. Then only was it that he discovered Elizabeth seated on a sofa.

'My dear!' he exclaimed. 'I never saw you!'

'Good evening, Grandfather.'

He was weary, he was lonely, he had a pain in his side. He sat down beside her. He had never been blind to feminine beauty although he HAD married Christabel. His daughter, Alice, who had died of a chill in 1812, had been as plain as her mother. He was proud and pleased that his grand-daughter should be so beautiful. Elizabeth's beauty lay in the perfection of her delicacy, the rosy bloom of her colouring; her shoulders and arms, revealed by the low cut of her cream-coloured dress, had the soft firmness of a child's unawareness. Her hands, exquisitely shaped, were both gentle and strong. She had the fairness of a rose scarcely daring to open.

'I am afraid, my dear,' he said, 'that I have not seen so much of you during this visit as I should have wished. I am growing an old man, but I have never, all my life, learnt how to delegate business to others. If I do not see to it myself it's done wrong. I trust that you have been happy.'

'Oh yes, Grandpapa.'

'That's good. And Uhland?'

'I think he has been very happy.'

She longed to burst out: 'I am not happy at all! They want to marry me to a young man I detest. You must prevent them.' But she did not dare. She knew him so little, and he looked so very imposing with his legs spread out in front of him and his long, thin hands with the tapering fingers laid on his bony knees.

'It is a misfortune that your grandmother has been so unwell.'

'I hope she is getting better,' Elizabeth said gently.

'No, my dear, I fear not. Doctor Salter is doing all he can, but, as he constantly says, she will not make a sufficient effort. A great pity! A great pity! Your grandmother is a wonderful woman, my dear, but she has never had quite the courage needed for a life like ours. After all, she is a woman.'

'Yes, Grandpapa.'

'And what have you been doing with yourself, my dear?'

Elizabeth told him some of the things that she had been doing.

He nodded, rubbed his hands together, rose.

'Very good. Very good. I trust your grandmother will soon be sufficiently well for you to see her. It is delightful for us to have you here.'

But as he went out of the room and climbed the stairs he was vaguely uncomfortable. Was she happy? She appeared lonely. That brother of hers was a queer fish. Very queer. But then he was crippled, poor child. Odd for Walter, big and healthy as he was, to have a crippled son. What a beautiful girl! It did one good . . . But he was vaguely uneasy, and the uneasiness remained.

Two days later Mr Temple came and proposed, and after that events followed swiftly. He came with Sylvia Herries and they drank tea together in the mustard-coloured drawing room. Sylvia said that she must go and ask Mrs Arnold, the housekeeper, about some silks that she wished to match. No sooner was she out of the room than Mr Temple fell on his knees. It was a proposal in the conventional fashion!

'Dearest Miss Herries! Oh, if I may only call you Elizabeth! From the first moment I saw you I have been in a dream. You are the only woman in the whole world for me. All that I have is yours . . .' and so on and so on.

Elizabeth also behaved in the traditional manner.

'Pray, Mr Temple, rise from the floor.'

He caught her hand. He kissed it.

'I shall have to call for someone if you persist in this ridiculous--'

'Adorable Elizabeth! Most heavenly--'

He climbed on to the sofa beside her and tried to kiss her cheek.

'Please, Mr Temple.' Then she broke into sheer disgust. 'Oh, go away! No, I do not love you. I can never love you. I do not even care for you. No, not even with friendly feelings. This is absurd. This is too absurd--'

She freed herself and stood with her hand on the bell-rope.

He was amazed. He could not believe his ears. This was the first proposal of his life, for he had always believed that himself and his riches were irresistible and that when the time did come for him to honour anybody there could be but one possible result.

He was deeply chagrined. Even a tear rolled on to his fat little cheek.

'Oh, dammit!' he cried, and went indignantly from the room.

Next morning Uhland came to her in her room. His look of cold, resolved anger terrified her; she felt as though he had imprisoned her and would do what he pleased. The sense of power that he spread about him was extraordinary.

'Elizabeth--what is this I hear? Temple has proposed and you have refused him.'

'Yes.'

'You silly little fool! You are to write to him immediately and say that you have reconsidered it.'

She shook her head.

'But I say Yes. It is the very thing for you. Father will wish it. All of us.'

'No, Uhland. I don't love him. I dislike him extremely.'

'Love? What is love? It is because you have still some sentimental longing for that young prig in Cumberland.'

'You know,' she answered, 'that that was over long ago.'

'I know nothing of the kind. If you will not accept Temple I shall charge your refusal to John Herries--and I shall know what to do--'

'You can't harm him!' she answered fiercely, all her dread of him gone. 'You can't touch him and you know it. But threats can't serve you. Nor your bullying. I should never marry Mr Temple if you starved me!'

'You SHALL marry him,' he answered.

He came up to her and put his cold, damp hand on her bare shoulder. 'I know what is good for you and I will see to it.'

He looked at her and left the room.

After that she had only one thought--flight. She had already for weeks been contemplating it. She had plenty of spirit, and the thought that at last she would escape from Ireby, from this house, from her father, from all these Herries relations gave her wings. That afternoon she searched The Times and at last found what she wanted. A Mrs Bohun Winstanley of 21A Sloane Street had an agency for 'Governesses, Companions, Situations for Genteel Persons'. Ellen, the maid, was her next resource. She had, in these weeks, won Ellen's devoted affections, not difficult considering her beauty, charm and gentleness. It seemed too that Ellen hated her place here, hated Mrs Arnold, the housekeeper, and was only waiting an opportunity to give her notice. Elizabeth told Ellen everything, even her love for John, and Ellen's eyes grew moist with sentiment as she drank in the details of such a romance. Ellen was sworn to secrecy. On the following day, having packed Elizabeth's box, she was to take a hackney-cab and meet Elizabeth outside St Clement Danes Church at midday. To this Ellen swore: she also protested that the most horrible tortures man (Ellen's natural enemy) could devise would not tempt her to betrayal. Elizabeth kissed her.

Early the next morning, wearing her quietest bonnet, she slipped out of the house into Hill Street. It was a fine morning and she walked out of her way to Charing Cross, taking her time lest Mrs Bohun Winstanley should not yet be at work. No one interfered with her. A cheap dandy with a sham diamond pin and a double-breasted waistcoat ogled her, a policeman in a blue swallow-tailed coat and white trousers glanced at her with some curiosity, but for the most part everyone was busy about his or her own business. There was a great deal of noise with the bell of the crier, the horn of the omnibus, the Italian boy and his hurdy-gurdy, and the shops with their small-paned bow-windows were opening, somewhere church bells were ringing. Everywhere everything was entrancing, for at last, at last, she was free!

When she thought the time was come she mounted inside an omnibus and at length was put down at the top of Sloane Street. Soon Number 21A was found, a dingy door, a still dingier staircase. One flight up, in faded green letters, was Mrs Bohun Winstanley's name. Entering she found a room, grimy and disordered, with a shabby canary moulting in a shabby cage by the very dirty window, and a lady in a bonnet and mittens seated at a table strewn with papers. Standing in front of the empty grate was another lady, wearing a very gay bonnet covered with flowers, and a bright emerald-green shawl. This lady was tall, thin, and plainly in the worst of tempers. The lady at the table was small, and, at the moment, alarmed. A dewdrop trembled at the end of her nose, her mittens quivered with a life of their own, and she murmured again and again: 'Oh dear! Oh dear! But it is so EARLY . . . so early, Mrs Golightly . . .'

'Early! Early!' cried the other lady, while all the flowers trembled in her bonnet in sympathy. 'Don't speak to me of "early", Mrs Winstanley. A promise is a promise!'

'But her little girl has the croup.'

'And what of MY little girls, Mrs Winstanley? What of MY little girls? Here have they been these three weeks, and Mr Golightly in Bath and returning tomorrow--'

It was then that both ladies together noticed Elizabeth.

'Well?' said Mrs Winstanley.

'I beg your pardon, I am sure,' said Elizabeth. 'I can wait outside--'

'But what IS it?' said Mrs Winstanley, plainly near to tears.

'I read your advertisement in The Times,' said Elizabeth. 'I am looking for a place as governess or companion--'

Both ladies stared at Elizabeth. They had obviously never seen anyone so beautiful before.

'Sit down, pray,' Mrs Winstanley said at last (and it was clear that she saw, in Elizabeth, the ship of rescue). 'Now, Mrs Golightly, this is a young lady of whom I intended to have spoken yesterday--'

Mrs Golightly stared and stared.

'You are looking for a place?' she said at last.

'Yes. ma'am.'

'What is your name?'

'Mary Temple.' (Oh, how absurd! She had taken Mr Temple's name after all!)

'How old are you?'

'Twenty-three, ma'am.'

'What experience have you had?'

'I think,' broke in Mrs Winstanley, 'that you will find that she has had excellent experience.'

'Has she?' said Mrs Golightly doubtfully. 'She looks very superior, I must say.' Then she added: 'And your references?'

'I will speak for her references,' said Mrs Winstanley quickly.

'Ours is a very agreeable family,' Mrs Golightly said in a kind of dream. 'My two little girls are angelic--less than no trouble at all . . . When could you come?' she asked abruptly.

'This afternoon,' said Elizabeth.

'Very odd. Very odd, indeed. Have you French, Arithmetic, the Pianoforte, Dancing, Deportment? . . .'

'I think you will find that Miss Temple has everything that you require,' Mrs Winstanley quickly inserted.

'Indeed!' Mrs Golightly still stared in a kind of dream. 'Very distinguished!' she murmured. 'You are familiar with the Poets?'

'I beg your pardon?' Elizabeth said.

'Shakespeare, Milton, Lord Byron, Mrs Hemans--'

'Oh yes,' said Elizabeth, 'I think so.'

'You THINK so,' said Mrs Golightly. 'Don't you KNOW?'

'She is especially familiar with the Poets,' said Mrs Winstanley, speaking very gently and nodding her head.

Mrs Golightly stared and stared.

'You can come this evening?' she said at last.

'Yes, ma'am.'

'Of course,' Mrs Golightly said, turning to Mrs Winstanley, 'she may be a thief in collusion with all the thieves of the Metropolis. Pray, don't think me rude,' she went on, turning to Elizabeth again, 'but it is so very odd. I know nothing whatever about you. With whom were you last?'

'I am sure that you will find everything perfectly correct,' said Mrs Winstanley.

Mrs Golightly stared a little more.

'Well, I don't know, I'm sure. If Mr Golightly had any liking for young ladies the idea would be absurd, but as he has never given one a thought, being far too closely occupied by his beetles and butterflies . . .' She nodded her head. 'Very well, then. This evening. Mrs Winstanley will explain the terms,' and without another word she left the room, banging the little door behind her.

'And now,' said Mrs Winstanley gently, and blowing her nose, 'pray, tell me, my dear, who you are.'

THE GOVERNESS

Elizabeth read her letter over again. In a few minutes she must go to Mrs Golightly's boudoir, where she must read for an hour while the moths buzzed about the lamp, the silly clock ticked, and the words of the novel in her hand moved in a mist of confusion before her

PART II

heavy eyes. For she was very weary, as indeed she was always weary at this hour in the evening. Clarissa and Francesca were happily asleep in bed, lost in slumber, although safe neither from suffocation (for their bedroom would be hermetically sealed) nor from bugs. The little house in Islington crawled with animals, bugs and beetles and cockroaches (Alice the kitchen-maid, who slept in the kitchen, spent most of her day killing them: she was too tired at night to care), while spiders hung in every corner and dust lay on tables, sills and shelves as thick as the sand of the desert. In the meantime Mrs Golightly, surrounded with emerald- green curtains, ottomans and 'Keepsakes', sat in her evening yellow silk, her ringlets bound by her 'arcade' (a wonderful arrangement of wires twined with rosebuds, lace and ribbon), waiting for Elizabeth to continue her reading of Agnes Serle by Miss Ellen Pickering.

This was Elizabeth's letter:

4 Praed Street,
Islington,
March 4th, 1839

BELOVED JOHN--I cannot, try as I may, refrain any longer from writing to you. The thought of your anxiety for me (for I do not think flatter myself that you must be anxious) has been a motive ever more constant with me. But this I could have resisted were it not that your dear image, for so many many years now the dearest to me in all the word, refuses to leave to me the proper control of my feelings.

I know only too well, dearest John, that I am breaking all the vows that I have made and upon which I was myself formerly the most insistent. I am aware that all the reasons that kept us apart must keep us apart still: indeed their influence must be stronger with us than before since the irrevocable nature of my own desperate deed! How desperate it must seem to my own family you will realize from the fact that neither my father nor brother have made the slightest effort to find me out. I will admit to you that it is the increasing sense of my own loneliness that compels me to write to you. I had hoped that, cut off from all family ties, I might learn to forget you, but, dear John, true love is not so easily set aside and however dearly I have loved you in the past I must confess that it is only in these last weeks that I have realized to the full how deep and constant that love must be.

Perhaps it is shameful of me to make this confession to you, but shameful or not it must be made, for without some word from you I truly think that I shall die. I have not formerly been weak. I am weak now and must detest my weakness even while I yield to it.

I would not wish you to think that I am unhappy with Mrs Golightly, the lady in whose house I live and to whose little girls I am governess. She is not indeed at all unkind, only rather foolish and unable to keep her house clean or manage it with any efficiency. The two little girls are good and patient, poor little things, although entirely neglected. Mrs Golightly reads novels, recites poetry, has evening parties and attends concerts in Hanover Square, while Mr Golightly, who is fat and absentminded but also kindly, collects moths and butterflies, which takes him very often into the country. Meanwhile the house is a ruin, the cooks come and go every week and only poor Alice, the kitchen-maid, is faithful and does all the work of the place.

Dear John, I think I have grown into a woman in these last months and see life more sanely than I did. I had, I do not doubt, an exaggerated picture of my father and my brother and although I know they do not love me and have never loved me, they are neither so hard nor so unkind as I at one time thought them. But do not think me cowardly, dear John, in thus writing to you. I am not thinking of changing my life but only that you should sometimes write me a letter and give me the opportunity to write to you. You understand, do you not, that no one is to know of where I am nor of what I am doing. No one save yourself. It is to be a secret from everyone, but I love you so much that I think I shall be insane if I do not hear from you. Later on perhaps you will come to London and we shall meet again. Only to think of such a meeting sends me crazy with joy and happiness. But I know that you will answer this letter and that is all the happiness I wish for at this present time. Your most loving

ELIZABETH

She folded it up and sealed it.

'I am very wicked,' she thought. 'I have never done anything so really wrong as this before. But I don't care.' She further thought that she had been stupid not to have done this long ago. Her months with Mrs Golightly had made her begin to wonder whether she had not paid altogether too much attention to the decencies. She did not realize that it was the escape from the Cumberland house that had changed her, the fact that she was emerging from the influence both of her father and brother, who until now had dominated her whole life.

She put on her bonnet and shawl, opened the door, listened, ran downstairs, down the front steps, then along the lamp-lit street to the post office. She hesitated a moment before dropping the letter in. Was it right? No, it wasn't right. Nevertheless, in it went. She stared defiantly about the street, but there was only one hackney-cab crawling along and an Italian organ-grinder with a shivering monkey in a crimson coat. She dropped a sixpence into the little monkey's cup as a sort of oblation. The monkey looked at her with eyes so old and so sad that she could not resist a little shudder. It was as though the monkey said: 'We are all cold. All lost. All doomed. There's nothing to be done about it . . .'

On the other hand, Alice, with a large smut across her nose, was looking up from the bottom of the area steps. She had a large broom in her hand which she waved in a cheerful fashion as much as to say: 'We're friends, we are. I know what you've been doing and wish you all the luck.' The thin strains of the barrel-organ echoed down the empty street as though they, too, wished her good fortune.

She ran quietly up the stairs, took off bonnet and shawl, brushed her ringlets and, with Agnes Serle in hand, marched down to the boudoir.

'Aren't you a little late, my love?' asked Mrs Golightly, who was reclining at ease with her velvet slippers toasting at the fire. The pug, Levilla, was on her lap, choking as usual.

'Yes, I think I am, a little,' said Elizabeth gently, and, opening her book, began to read.

She had remarked to herself again and again in these months how completely now she was separated from the Herries world. It was as though they lived, all of them, in another continent. Mrs Golightly did on occasion read out from the newspaper some social item, and once she remarked with a great deal of unction that she saw that Sir William Herries had been doing this or that. 'Let me see,' she went on. 'He is a cousin, I fancy, of Lady Rockage, and there is that lovely Mrs Garth Herries whose name you see everywhere. They are all the same family, I imagine.'

But Mrs Golightly and all her friends spoke of Gore House or Almack's as one speaks of Paradise. But with no envy. She had her world and was perfectly content with it, but the division between her world and that other one was quite complete. Mrs Golightly was a generous, unenvious person altogether. She thought her husband, children, friends and home all quite perfect. It was the fashion, moreover, for herself and her friends to be romantic about everything, and this same Romance gave them every kind of satisfaction. They liked their literature, their painting, their music, their religion to be romantic. They felt deeply and sincerely for all Oppressed Peoples. Mrs Golightly was for ever attending meetings for the poor Poles, for the Negro (whom they went so far as to call their brother), for the unhappy Greek and the neglected Hottentot. That her house was in a mess and that the slums, factories and mines quite close to home needed attention-- these things were never discussed because they were NOT romantic.

Mrs Golightly enjoyed entertaining her friends in the evening (a little music on the pianoforte, a little 'dance' in the very small drawing room), she enjoyed a walk with Mr Golightly when he was at home, a visit to the theatre or a concert--but perhaps more than anything else she enjoyed sitting with her toes in front of the fire of an evening and listening to Elizabeth's read-ing of a novel. That original inquiry at the Agency about the Poets had been genuine enough, but when it came actually to READING--well, the novel was the thing! Elizabeth had a beautiful, quiet, cultivated voice, as Mrs Golightly told all her friends. It was a pleasure indeed to listen to her. So Elizabeth read, night after night, from the works of Bulwer, Ainsworth, that delightful new writer Charles Dickens, Theodore Hook, Mrs Gore, Miss Austen ('a LITTLE dull, my love--not enough Event') and even some of the old 'Minerva Press' romances--Mandroni, Rinaldo Rinaldini and The Beggar Girl and her Benefactors, the last in seven volumes.

Meanwhile the two little girls went on as best they might. It would not be true to say that Mrs Golightly did not love her children. She loved them very dearly. But they, too, must be romantic. She dressed them in very bright colours, showed them to her friends with pride and left Elizabeth to do the rest. They became deeply attached to Elizabeth. They never had seen anyone so lovely and, in fact, would never see anyone so lovely again. Although she dressed in the quietest way, never raised her voice and never lost her temper, they obeyed her and told her everything. Alone with her they chattered and chattered, asking her innumerable questions. She taught them what she could with the aid of Butter's Exercises on the Globes, Lindley Murray's English Grammar and Goldsmith's Poems for Young Ladies, but she had never had very much education herself and was appalled at her own ignorance.

Although a strong offshoot of the City ran past Sadler's Wells through the High Street, Islington was nevertheless a little country town of its own, filled with trees and gardens. The Golightlys had their carriage and drove into Town on necessary occasions, but, socially, their world was their own world and they gave little thought to any other. Elizabeth's arrival here was a sensation and, during the first weeks, the bachelors, handsome young men, and gay old married ones attempted every kind of flirtation. They found her, however, so unapproachable that she achieved the reputation of an Islington mystery. It was soon asserted that she was the child of a noble lord who had attempted to marry her to a villain, that she was the child-bride of an aged marquis who violently ill-treated her, that she was heiress to a vast property and had fled from unwelcome suitors.

She was too kind and gentle to be disliked by them; she gave herself no airs; she listened to their stories and was grieved for their misfortunes. Mrs Golightly did her utmost to discover her secret, and even Mr Golightly would look up from his butterflies, smile in a mysterious manner, nod his head and say: 'We expect you to be carried off from us in a gilt chariot any day, my dear.'

Mrs Golightly's methods were more subtle. On one of the reading evenings she would break out with:

'You mentioned, did you not, my love, that your brother was in the Army?'

'Oh no,' Elizabeth would reply. 'I have no relations in the Army.'

'Indeed! Well, fancy that! It must have been the Navy you said.'

'Nor in the Navy,' Elizabeth would reply, smiling.

Or Mrs Golightly would look at her with great tenderness, remarking:

'That must have been a sweetly pretty Ball at Lady Carrington's yesterday evening. Young Lady Hermione Blossom was looking her loveliest, I understand . . . You doubtless know her, Mary, my love.'

'No,' Elizabeth would murmur. 'I have never seen her.'

'Ah, so you say!' Mrs Golightly would reply, looking very arch. 'We know what we know.'

The children were pressed into service, but they, poor dears, were so simple and innocent that they had no wiles.

'Oh, Miss Temple,' Francesca would say. 'Mama says that everyone knows that you are not Miss Temple really, and that you will be leaving us very shortly.'

'I have no intention of leaving you, Francesca.'

'Mama says that you have fled from persecuting parents.'

'Does she, Francesca? I have not fled from anyone.'

And Clarissa, who loved Elizabeth with passion, would hold her hand as though it were a pump-handle and exclaim: 'I am certain that you are a Princess in disguise, dear Miss Temple, and I DO love you so!'

'There are no real Princesses,' Elizabeth would answer. 'Only in fairytales.'

She managed for a while well enough. They were kind to her, and it was not their fault that she knew with every week more and more unbearable loneliness and longing. Then came the egregious and appalling Mr Roberts. Mr Frederick Roberts was a stout, cheerful, noisy young man who was the practical joker of the group. He was absent during the first part of Elizabeth's sojourn, in Scotland. Everyone spoke of him with rapture.

'Wait, my love, until Mr Fred Roberts returns!' Mrs Golightly cried. 'Islington is not the same without Mr Roberts. Mr Roberts has the life of a thousand. He is the wittiest young man in London.'

Elizabeth awaited his arrival with some eagerness. He could do everything--play the pianoforte, sing a song, shoot birds, hunt the fox, dance like an angel and join anyone for any length of time at Commerce, Vingt-et-Un or Speculation. He could imitate Webster or Buckstone or Fanny Kemble as though they were in the room with you. He was the soul of good nature, and all the young ladies in Islington wanted to marry him.

When he did arrive Elizabeth found him truly terrible. He was fat, coarse, common, self-satisfied, exceedingly conceited and as noisy as the fireworks at Vauxhall. But, worst of all, he must for ever be playing practical jokes. Practical jokes were 'the thing' in Islington; everyone loved them, but no practical-joker anywhere was as inexhaustible in his energies, as fertile in his resources as Fred Roberts.

He marked down Elizabeth at once as his future bride. He proposed to her on the second evening after meeting her and, when she indignantly refused him, roared with laughter and would have slapped her on the back had she not eluded him. His 'jokes' were endless. You never knew when you were safe from him. One of his most famous was the occasion when at supper at Mrs Preedy's he poured melted butter into all the gentlemen's pockets. He loved to tie two doors together, ring both bells and watch the result round a corner. On one most laughable occasion he arrived at the Livingstone-Jones' with a tray of medicated sweets so that everyone was ill. He came to a Masquerade with mice in his pocket, let them loose and returned in another costume to enjoy the results. When Mrs Bonnington lost her husband he appeared by her bedside as the ghost of her departed (she was ill after this for weeks). Mrs Green had a stout and elderly butler into whose shoes he fastened tin-tacks so that poor James, putting them on unsuspectingly, fell down a flight of stairs and was nearly killed. How Frederick laughed when he heard of it! And the odd thing was that everyone liked him for these games! They thought him the funniest, jolliest fellow and declared that any girl who 'caught' him would be lucky indeed!

He had never, it seemed, been 'seriously inclined', although he was 'something good' in the City and could marry whenever he wished. Now he WAS 'caught', and it was Elizabeth who had 'caught' him.

Poor Elizabeth! Mr Temple had been nothing to this!

It was, however, her terror of Mr Roberts that drove her to write to John. It seemed that there was no safety for her anywhere--if not one, then another. She even discovered herself thinking of the Fortress as a place of security.

If she left the Golightlys and went elsewhere it would be the same-- danger everywhere.

A few days after posting her letter a worse thing than Mr Roberts occurred--Mr Golightly fell in love with her. She had never thought of him save that he was kindly and that he passed a dazzled, bewildered existence in a maze of coloured insects. He had means of his own that he had inherited from his father, a wealthy merchant who had dealt in candles or something of the kind. He had never been known to look at a woman save Mrs Golightly, at whom, moreover, he, on the whole, looked as little as might be. His fidelity to his butterflies was absolute.

There came then an evening. Mrs Golightly went to join her two friends, Miss Sanders and Mrs Witsun, at the house of their mutual friend, Mrs Peters, for a game of Commerce. The girls had gone to bed, and Elizabeth sat in her room pretending to read and thinking of John. She thought now of John every moment of the day. How was her letter faring? How soon might there be a reply? And, surrounding John, encompassing and enveloping him, was the country of her home, the silver river through the flat Portinscale fields, Main Street in Keswick with Miss Hazlitt's bow-window and the coach standing . . .

A knock on the door. Enter Mr Golightly. She was so deeply amazed that she could not speak. There he stood with his round stomach in a flowered waistcoat, his coat-tails spreading fan-wise over his fat thighs, buckles on his shoes and spectacles on the end of his nose.

He closed the door firmly.

'This is an opportunity,' she heard him say to himself. He came forward and without another word fell immediately on his knees in front of her. His spectacles jerked to the ground and he gazed up at her with blue eyes, childlike and innocent, eyes dimmed because they had seen the world for so long behind glasses, eyes that had gazed for years upon butterflies. She tried to rise, but he put his fat hand on her knee and burst out at once:

'Miss Temple--Mary, I am well aware that this is disgraceful. I am proud that it is. I have wished for years to do something disgraceful. I doubt whether anything could be more disgraceful than this. I am old enough to be your father, but I love you passionately. I may say that I have never loved anyone passionately before. And when I say passionately I mean passionately.'

'But, Mr Golightly--this is shameful--'

'I know that it is shameful. I have been struggling against it for several weeks. At least I have been struggling against NOT struggling against it.'

She did manage to rise.

'But this is abominable. In Mrs Golightly's absence--'

'Oh, damnation take Mrs Golightly!' he burst out, clasping her skirts and holding her firmly. 'What do you think it is to sleep year after year with Mrs Golightly in a four-poster? What do you think it is to wake early in the morning and see Mrs Golightly beside you? Were it not for my butterflies I should have gone mad long ago. And you, loveliest of virgins, what do you know of four-posters? Do you realize what a four-poster MIGHT be? Even I, old as I am, could . . .'

But that was enough. She tore herself from his clinging hands and went, even as she had done in Hill Street, to the bell-rope.

'One word more, Mr Golightly, and I summon Alice.'

He rose to his feet. He was trembling and there were beads of perspiration on his nose. Without his spectacles he seemed oddly undressed.

'Yes,' he murmured. 'I must appear revolting to you. It is natural that I should. It is my fate that I must appear revolting to everyone save Mrs Golightly.'

He bent down and picked up his spectacles. She thought that he was near to tears.

'Forgive me,' he said. 'I could not help myself and I am glad that I could not. I am still a man, not a mummy. Oh! how beautiful you are!'

And he went, wiping his spectacles in a large orange handkerchief, from the room.

After this there was nothing for it but flight. Mr Golightly AND Mr Roberts! And if Mrs Golightly discovered . . . But she did not want to go before she had had her letter from John. ONE letter from him and she would be better prepared to face the world again. Days went by. The beetles crawled in the kitchen. Agnes Serle came to her conclusion and was immediately followed by Adelaide or the Countercharm, the odious Mr Roberts proposed to her three times, on every occasion with peals of laughter--and still there was no letter from John.

Then came the party. This was the grandest party that Mrs Golightly had yet given in Islington--dancing, music, Commerce and Speculation, everything that the heart could desire. The whole house was 'cleared' for the event. The dining room was not far from the drawing room. In the drawing room there would be music and then dancing. Mr Fortescue would play on the violin, Mrs Porter's two daughters would sing duets, Mr Fred Roberts would give his Imitations and comic songs. It was also confidently expected that Mr Roberts had some special 'joke', a secret from everyone but himself.

The supper came from the caterer's, who also provided two long, thin men with immense side-whiskers to serve as waiters. Poor Alice was driven from one pillar to another post all day and all night, while Mrs Thackeray, the at-the-moment cook (she had given notice and was to leave directly AFTER the party), for a brief while permitted herself to be amiable because, like every other servant in the world, she enjoyed a party.

When the guests were all assembled the sight was very impressive. The house was swollen with the guests. They were in the hall, on the stairs, hanging out of window, flooding dining room and drawing room. The gentlemen, many of them with long and wavy hair, had high black stocks enriched with massive pins; the white shirt-cuffs were neatly turned over the wrists, dress-coats buttoned, trousers tight with straps and pumps. The ladies either wore curls neatly arranged on each side, or their hair dropped in a loop down the cheek and behind the ear, and then fastened in some kind of band with ribbons at the back of the head. Pink was the favourite colour, pink with plenty of lace and artificial flowers. The older ladies were magnificent in turbans, and some of the younger wore across the forehead a band of velvet or silk decorated with a gold buckle, or something in pearls and diamonds. Miss Sanders, who was sixty if a day, had a black ribbon across her brow, the ribbon containing in the middle a steel buckle.

Every lady, of course, wore cleaned kid gloves, and the turpentine that had gone to the cleaning of them gave off a pungent and powerful odour. Quadrilles were still danced and even the Country Dance lingered, but the Valse was the true enchantment, although in Islington it was still considered rather advanced and daring, and always everyone was afraid to be the first to commence. Once and again the dancing was stopped for a little music, and Miss Merryweather sang in her piercing soprano or the Misses Porter gave one of their delightful duets. At first everyone was as polite as polite could be. The gentlemen stood by themselves and the ladies by THEMSELVES, but soon the punch-bowl had been mixed--a lovely mixture of rum, brandy, Curacao, lemon, hot water, sugar, grated nutmeg, cloves and cinnamon. There was also rum-shrub. And above all, for the gentlemen, Bishop. Bishop was a kind of punch made of port wine instead of rum, and exceedingly potent it was. It was the Bishop, possibly, that accounted in the end for Elizabeth's terror and distress.

Very soon everyone became very jolly, and of course the jolliest of them all was Fred Roberts. Before the evening had exhausted an hour of its splendour he had fastened three girls into a cupboard, let off a squib under Miss Merryweather's skirts (and her shriek was of a more violent soprano than any betrayed by her singing!), piled three plates on the lintel of the door so that they crashed on to the head of one of the long, thin waiters; but his great feat was that he had brought a live grass-snake in his pocket, and this he sent crawling over fair arms and necks until ladies stood on chairs and one Miss Porter fainted (or was it, as some said, that she had enjoyed the rum-shrub?).

He was the greatest success. Everyone voted that they had never seen him in so splendid a humour, and he WAS in fine form, for he had a bet with six of his Islington cronies that before the evening was over he would be able to announce to all the world that the beautiful Miss Temple had consented to be his bride.

During the earlier hours, however, he left Elizabeth to others, although his merry eye was always upon her. At first things were not so terrible. She sat with Mrs Devizes, a lady who was vastly proud of her house, 'twice the size of this, my dear'. And must describe with perfect happiness her mahogany table and curtains of crimson rep, her gilt fleur-de-lis wallpaper and the way that she preserved her gooseberries and currants.

How Elizabeth prayed that she might be left alone with her, for she was tranquil and calm, and, as her words flowed on, it seemed that life somewhere must be secure--an enclosed world under a glass bell, mahogany, crimson rep and gooseberries.

But she was not allowed to stay where she was. For, in the first place, Mrs Golightly was so happy at the social success of her party that she was talking about Elizabeth to everyone, how she was certain that she was the daughter of a Duke, how good she was and beautiful she was, and how indebted she was to Mrs Golightly, who 'treated her just like one of her own daughters'. So naturally the young men came up and besought her to dance with them, and then, while valsing, paid her fatuous compliments and fought with one another over the honour of claiming her. Everyone began to be greatly excited, the ladies as well. Games were proposed, Forfeits, and Blind Man's Buff and Catch-in-a-Corner.

Elizabeth slipped out of the room only to find Mr Golightly, the worse for Bishop, standing in a corner near the window, staring quite desperately in front of him.

He caught her arm and drew her to the window.

'You must not tremble,' he assured her. 'You are safe with me. Indeed, indeed you are. I only wish you to be the first to know that I am leaving Mrs Golightly.'

'Oh no, no!' she cried, deeply distressed.

'I am determined, quite, quite determined. Before you came into my life I was asleep. But now I am awake and I know that my existence with Mrs Golightly is a sham!'

Oh, those poor little girls, she thought. And Mrs Golightly, who is so happy and confident. If only she could have taken him away and talked to him, for she liked him in spite of his absurdities. But she did not dare to go apart with him, and here they were besieged on all sides--people were running up and down stairs. It was quite pandemonium.

'You will feel quite differently tomorrow,' she assured him.

'Oh no, I shall not. You have changed my life. You have--'

But worse followed, for Mr Roberts appeared, carrying a glass of punch, his red face shining with happiness, his eyes fixed upon her as though she were already his bride.

Paying no attention to Mr Golightly, he caught Elizabeth's hand, dragged her with him into the room where everyone was valsing madly, and began to swing her round, dropping his glass on to the floor. She thought it better not to resist lest worse should befall.

'We are designed for one another!' he cried. 'It is Fate! I am rich, you are beautiful! Let me tell them all that you will have me! I have been waiting all my life for this moment! I am the happiest of men! . . .' Then, before them all, suddenly, ceasing to dance, he caught her in his stout arms and kissed her.

She broke from him, ran among the dancers, found her way to the door and, on the verge of tears, half tumbled down the stairs into the hall. At the moment there was no one there, but the house-door was open, Alice was on the step, and beside her someone was standing. Alice came in.

'It is for you, miss. A gentleman asking for you--'

She went forward, trying to calm her agitation. Before her, visible enough in the pale, smoky lamp of the little hall, was John.

She was in his arms; HIS arms were round her.

'Oh, John--John--John,' was all she could hysterically cry. She was sobbing on his shoulder.

'My love . . . my adored one . . . my only, only love!'

Alice was in an ecstasy. She was practical as well.

'Oh, miss, come into the Master's room. There's no one there. Only the coats and hats.'

Into Mr Golightly's room they went, and there, among the butterflies and beetles, John told her that he had come as swiftly as he could and for one purpose only. At the first possible moment they would be married.

'Married, John?'

'Yes, married, my love. We have been too ridiculous. We have been wasting our lives.'

(Uhland? Her father? Oh, no matter. Let come what might!)

'Oh, John--I have longed for you so!'

'And I for you! When I received your letter . . .'

Mrs Golightly was in the doorway, behind her Miss Porter and others.

'Mary! Why, my love . . .'

Elizabeth, holding John's hand, and looking more beautiful than ever in her life before, said:

'Mrs Golightly--allow me to introduce you--Mr John Herries. The gentleman to whom I am to be married. He has come all the way from Cumberland--'

It was the supreme, the loveliest moment of her life.

FAMILY LETTERS

6 Acacia Road,
Marylebone,
London,
April 20th, 1839

MY DEAR FATHER--Yesterday morning John and I were married at St Mary's Church, Phillamont Street, Marylebone.

I am afraid that this may make you angry and I am sorry indeed that it should do so, but as you have made no inquiry after my whereabouts I am hardened in the belief that nothing that may happen to me can give you very great concern. I am sorry indeed for this, but from my very earliest years you have shown me that you would have preferred never to have had a daughter. I find it very difficult in these unhappy circumstances to appeal to your forgiveness because indeed I do not feel that there has been anything on my part very blamewor-

thy. I studied to love you, but you wished for the love neither of my dear mother nor myself. You are not responsible, dear father, for that. If you could not love us you could not, but neither am I responsible for wishing to make some kind of life for myself where I could be happy.

Perhaps now that I am away from you I may not cause you so much aggravation and one day you may wish to see me again. I know how greatly you have always disliked the family at Uldale but they on their part have, I am sure, felt nothing but friendliness and it is the great hope of John and myself that our marriage may heal the division between the two families. John has some means of his own and we shall be in no need of assistance from anyone. Our cousins, Garth and Sylvia, are most kind, and Carey has invited me into the country. I have written to grandfather acquainting him with our marriage. I am afraid that grandmother is no better.

With every respect, dear father. I am, Your loving daughter,

ELIZABETH

John Herries to Judith Paris

6 Acacia Road,
Marylebone,
London,
April 22nd, 1839

MY DEAR AUNT JUDITH--Elizabeth and I were married on April 19th at twelve noon at St Mary's Church, Phillamont Street, Marylebone.

Dear Aunt Judith, are you very angry with me? I did wrong perhaps to leave you so suddenly with that brief letter of farewell, but I am enclosing (by her own wish) Elizabeth's letter to me that she wrote from London. Now read that and I am assured that with all your tenderness and love of others you will not be able to wish my actions other than they were. Indeed I could not help myself and arrived, as it turned out, only just in time, for my beloved Elizabeth was in the very act of escaping from an Islington ruffian when I stepped in at the door. Can you imagine it? She had been a Governess, having run away from her grandfather's, to two little girls of a lady with the astounding name of Golightly! They were kind to her, I fancy, although I cannot force very much out of her. She was never communicative about herself as you know.

But you do NOT know, dear Aunt Judith! You know one another so slightly that it will be one of my happiest pleasures to make you better acquainted! Seriously you have been so long more than a mother to me (more than my own mother ever was to me I fear) that you will, I know, rejoice in my happiness. I have not, I think, ever been truly happy before. I have been always apprehensive, fearing disasters that have never arrived. In the strangest way that house at Ireby and the inhabitants in it have hung over me like a doom. You have perceived this and thought me often faint-hearted and absurd, I know--yet these things are the spirit and I have much of my poor father's lack of self-confidence. A Herries without conceit of himself is worse off than any other man in the world, I think! If you but knew how often I have urged myself forward to some act that I feared simply because I feared it! It seems to me now fantastic that I should have so dreaded Uhland's crooked body and the coarseness of his father--but now I have rescued Elizabeth from them, and myself as well! Do you know how, for so many years, he neglected and despised her and how patiently she bore that neglect? The end of the story is not yet. I will make myself so famous that they shall crawl on their knees to me before all is done! Now is not that an unworthy sentiment?

Elizabeth has but now entered and the kettle is on the fire and the toasting-fork ready! Our happiness is surely greater than that of any other two in the world! And yet how many lovers are there in this city at this same moment swearing the same thing. But we are such old lovers and have waited so long--longer, far longer than there was any need! How clearly I see that now!

My only unhappiness is that I have left you alone at Uldale-- Dorothy, Adam, myself, all gone! And yet I am not sure that you will not be happier without us--all of us save Adam of course! I shall be seeing him tomorrow I trust. He is all Chartist now, I suppose, but he cannot think ill of me, for Elizabeth and myself are as poor as church mice and happy to be so. Sylvia came to see us last evening. She was exceedingly kind and says that Garth will soon find work for me. There will be my share of the Uldale money, but I would prefer that you send me nothing--until I ask for it.

Elizabeth is at my side. She sends her love. As she sits beside me I wonder what I have done to deserve this fortune. I have done nothing. I have been a poor feckless creature all my life but now, please God, there shall come something very different out of me. Our love for one another is beyond utterance. Dear Aunt Judith, wish us well and write to tell us that you are not angry. Your loving

JOHN

Judith Paris to Adam Paris

Uldale,
February 8th, 1840

MY DEAREST SON--Your letter received last evening. I am SORRY indeed that you should imagine that I am not PLEASED with your marriage. I am pleased with anything that gives you HAPPINESS but I am an old woman with only one passion left me and

that is for my SON. If you fancy that there is any mother in the world who gives her son willingly to ANOTHER WOMAN then you betray only once again that ignorance of my sex which, I fear, has been always your portion and will be so to the end.

You say that I need not fear that I shall lose you. NO, INDEED, I CANNOT LOSE YOU, for you are a part of myself, more perhaps than you will ever realize. You will return to me. You will bring her with you, but she can never have that part of you that is mine. You can tell her so if you wish. I am prepared to love her for as we grow old THE MORE ONE CAN LOVE THE BETTER FOR ONE'S HEALTH. I have no PATIENCE with old women who complain of being LEFT. I have always been standing on my own legs and intend to continue so. I like the name Margaret. She sounds sensible. I enclose with this my present to her. This silver box was left me by my brother who had it from a pedlar when he was a boy, and the silver chain was my grandmother's. I always intended them for your wife. Bring her soon to see me. I am quite alone here at the present although Dorothy and the children shall pay me a visit very shortly.

Bellairs is not in good health. It is his STOMACH. I am for ever telling him that he overeats but he answers that I am fanatical about food and eat like a SPARROW. Certainly all our neighbours eat and drink far too much and I attribute my own astonishing good health to my careful feeding. Why should we behave like swine at a trough? I remember when I was a young woman in London that Georges had INCREDIBLE stories of the amount that his friends consumed and I can remember Christabel and Jennifer in their youth guzzling like PIGS. Well, they are all dead and here am I feeling twenty. How I run on, but I enjoy talking to my son who is now a Chartist and a husband and I don't know what! Only yesterday he was pulling cows' tails in the orchard.

John and Elizabeth were at poor Christabel's funeral. Will was a very dignified figure they say. But Sylvia writes to say that a young Mrs Morgan, widow of an Army captain, is already setting her cap at him. Is not that revolting? He is seventy this year if I am not mistaken, and she not a day over thirty! And what comedy if our fat five-chinned purple-faced Walter has a baby brother, a new uncle for our pretty Uhland! Since John left here we have had no great trouble with Ireby.

Uhland spoke to me in Keswick some days back and asked most politely after you. He has eyes like Cumberland stone and his lame leg is as lively as a spiteful old woman. I think Walter has no spite against myself but would do any hurt that he could to John and Dorothy. He and Uhland have already stories circulated in Keswick about John, and John himself seems apprehensive for in his last letter to me he says that he fancied that he saw Uhland looking at him out of a hackney coach. It may be that he was right, for Uhland has been twice to London.

All is well at Uldale. Rackstraw manages to a MARVEL. He is now at war with Peach, Walter's man. They detest one another and so carry on this ridiculous feud a stage further. We have built a new Barn in the upper field. Flossie the mare is too old for the carriage and has been put in the Paddock. I told you I think that Dorothy is coming shortly for a visit. You know me well enough to understand me when I say that I do not mind at all that I am in SOLE command here. I seem to know so very much better than anyone else the way things OUGHT to be done. And I was sixty-five years of age last November!--Your most loving

MOTHER

John Herries to Adam Paris

6 Acacia Road,
Marylebone,
October 25th, 1840

MY DEAR ADAM--The fact that you and Margaret (to whom give every loving message from Elizabeth and myself) are at Uldale encourages me to write a long letter, some of which I would wish for them all to see. Other parts of it I shall mark Private and they are for your ears alone.

Well, first to my great piece of personal news. The writer of this Epistle has pleasure in informing you, dear Adam, that he has been now for two days personal and private Secretary to Sir Edward Mitcham, Bart, MP for Great Cottenham. What say you to that and to whose services think you I owe it? To whom but to Grandfather Will! This is, you will all at Uldale allow, a most remarkable feat and three in the eye to my dear father-in-law and four in the nose to my beloved brother-in-law. What they will say to this villainous backsliding on old Will's part I have infinite delight in imagining. It seems that I owe this as I owe every other happiness in life to my beloved Elizabeth, for it appears that a long while back when she was staying with him he was moved by her loveliness and by her loneliness, coming in one evening and seeing her all by herself and sufficiently dejected. So he has had it in his mind for some time to do something for us and this is what he has done.

Old Mitcham is a stout claret-coloured old boy who lives in Bryanston Square with a fat wife and two plain daughters. He is amiable enough so long as he is flattered and is saved from an extravagant personal vanity by his adoration of Palmerston. Palmerston can do no wrong in his eyes and already I am myself beginning to see with a similar vision and watch the affairs in Syria as though my life depended upon it. They say that it is the Syrian business that has killed Lord Holland and that his dying word was: 'Mehemet Ali will kill me'.

I do not know that I have any Parliamentary ambitions myself. Elizabeth says that I would make a good orator, but she has a certain prejudice and I am altogether too nervous and shy to thrust myself into public notice. Meanwhile old Lady Mitcham is quite in love with Elizabeth as indeed is all the world. Sylvia says that she has come out amazingly and is another creature from when she was staying with grandfather. As well she may be, for she was at that time a lonely and deserted creature.

You have heard, I suppose, the gossip about grandfather. It is certain that this Mrs Morgan is for ever in Hill Street. She is a lively, gay, light-headed little woman, all bright colours, tinkling laughter and sharp acquisitiveness. She already touches everything in the house as though she owned it. I imagine myself that grandfather would not be averse to a child in his old age, for it is my private belief that he has suffered a long and bitter disappointment over Walter, who pays him less and less regard. I suggest that grandfather sees in Mrs Morgan a possible instrument rather than a personal pleasure.

Private. I have marked this Private because I should be ashamed were anyone but yourself to see it. But you have known me from babyhood, dear Adam, and loved me as long, I think. Listen then, brother and friend. Elizabeth and I love one another more dearly with every hour that passes. Our intimacy, our trust, our devotion is perfect. And yet there IS one thing of which we will not speak to one another. We have both a fear, an unreasonable, foolish, crazy fear of Uhland. That she has it I know well. She speaks of him in her sleep and always in terror. By the way that she so deliberately avoids his name I know that she thinks of him. She fancies that because I married her he will do me some hurt and still more now that grandfather has volunteered this last kindness. Living with him so long has bred in her a fear of him that is beyond reason and is the stronger for its vagueness. And I must confess to you, dear Adam, that all my old terror of him persists. How often you have chided me for that! How foolish to your logical and consistent mind are such fears, but I have this from my father, who had it, perhaps, from HIS grandfather--that I live partly in a world of shadows. For a Herries that is fatal and there are times when I feel caught--held in a trap--and for no cause, no reason. How you must despise me. But no, you love me and are the most faithful and unswerving friend. Otherwise I would not have the courage to tell you. But there is more than that. The other evening at dusk coming from Bryanston Square I am certain that Uhland himself followed me.

Walking towards the Park down a narrow and ill-lit street I heard that tap of his stick and the hesitation of his step with which I have been so long dreadfully familiar. For a while, I dared myself not to turn, but at length my curiosity was too strong for me and, looking around,

I saw in the light of a lamp the thin figure of Uhland, his dark beaver hat, pale face, black clothes. He stood there, without moving, leaning on his stick. I hurried on through a street now absolutely silent. He seemed to follow me now incorporeally.

Pray do not laugh at me in this. Your sturdy mind cannot imagine what such fears and terrors may be. You remain undaunted by that other world so far more real than this one. Between the Haunted and the Unhaunted there is a gulf that can only be bridged by love, and I am not one who can love more than one or two. Why does he hate me so, Adam? What have I ever done to him? What is this strange Feud in our family that is for ever forcing its way in?

But, for a moment to be practical, pray discover for me if you can, while you are at Uldale, whether Uhland has been recently in London. It would relieve my mind greatly if it had not been he. Meanwhile this is the one only subject about which Elizabeth and I do not speak. There is a shadow here, the size of a man's hand . . .

But to be cheerful and DAYLIGHTY again, pray when you write tell me all the news of Uldale, of Aunt Judith, Roger, and in especial Margaret and yourself. When do you return to Town? You know that I do not think your Charter the cure for all our ills but times seem to become with every week more serious--the rick-burnings, riots and the rest--and I have little confidence in either Melbourne or Lord John. Your loving friend,

JOHN

Judith Paris to Sir William Herries, Bart

Uldale,
January 10th, 1841

DEAR WILL--I write to congratulate you on your MARRIAGE and, with that, to be as HONEST with you as I have always been. What do old people like you and me want with marriage? There is something INDECENT in it, do you not yourself think so? For you have always been the most COMMONSENSICAL of all our Family and I cannot believe that, sitting in a corner, you do not laugh to yourself and wonder at your own action. You were lonely I must suppose. Well, so indeed are all of us. What do you say to an old woman of sixty-six sitting ALL BY HERSELF in a house under a MOUNTAIN miles from anywhere--or from ANYONE except your beastly Walter in his stone prison? Well, have it your own way--only I refuse to tell you that you have done a FINE thing. If we cannot LAUGH at ourselves we are lost souls and although your sense of the COMIC has never been very strong in you, still you have a certain DRY picture of yourself I know. I TRUST your widow will give you every SATISFACTION. Do not think me unkind nor un-friendly, dear Will. I am neither, and I have an especial

GRATITUDE to you just now for what you have done for dear John and Elizabeth. That was especially noble of you seeing that your Walter hates them so (although WHY I cannot understand. Now that poor Christabel is gone he cannot STILL be thinking of that broken Fan). Moreover we were BABIES together and that I can NEVER forget although you were a dry and calcu-lating child with a passion for SUMS (that I always detested) from the very start. Do you remember how you rode over to STONE ENDS to fetch me back home and how I snapped my fingers at you? Yes, and would do it again if the same occasion rose. I am in marvellous health, thank God (although I doubt whether it is His doing). Dorothy comes with her babies to see me. She has now three GIRLS-- one born this last November--Veronica, Amabel and Jane. Timothy is four--a fine child. Bellairs is in poor health--some dis-order of the STOMACH.

I must close. I am sending you a CUMBERLAND HAM as a wedding present. You have everything in the world that you need, save only a Cumberland Ham--and there are no other Hams so good in the world any-where. Your most affectionate

JUDITH

Margaret Paris to her father, Caesar Kraft

(This letter was never posted but was found, many years later, by   Adam Paris among his wife's papers.)

Uldale,
Cumberland,
April 6th, 1841

MY DEAR FATHER--It is very likely that this let-ter will never be posted. I am writing it at two of the morning, sitting under a candle in my dressing gown while Adam sleeps in the bed close behind me, sleeps so soundly as he always does, sleeps as I alas just now so seldom do!

For, Father dear, that is why in the morning I shall not post this letter, because I shall be ashamed of my mood. I am unhappy tonight, desperately unhappy, unhappy as I have never been in my life before. Now listen, father. I know that Adam loves me, I know that they all wish me well here, I know that Adam is as proud and ambitious for our work as you and I. I am well in health and so is he. We have money enough. Best of all I have you, dearest, dearest father--and yet tonight my courage is all gone. I have at the moment no resistance.

I think perhaps that my marriage has been the most dreadful mistake. I love Adam more, far, far more than when I married him and I am well assured that he loves me. I think his character noble, strong and generous. I was not mistaken in thinking it so when I married him. But, father, I think there is no woman in England so lonely as I am at this moment.

They are all so strange. This wild rough country is so strange. Adam's mother is so strange. Adam's mother! Perhaps that is where all the trouble lies! On my first visit here with Adam she was, as I told you, most friendly. She wanted to love me as a daughter, she said, and that is I know what she intended. But love does not come like that. She was resolved to feel no jealousy of me and in that very resolve felt it. You know how quiet I am, father. You have always understood that I feel more than I can say and that I cannot force myself to any feeling if it is not there. 'Madame' (as they all call her here) is the opposite of this. I have never said much about her to you. You have never seen her. You cannot imagine her. She is unlike anyone else in the world, a little tiny woman with snow-white hair, a pale brown complexion, wearing the brightest colours, her eyes sparkling, carrying an ivory cane, and alive in every inch of her! I cannot convey to you how alive she is! I do not know her exact age but it is certainly between sixty and seventy and yet she is more living than anyone else in the neighbourhood. Everyone knows it. Everyone recognizes it. She is a great figure here. She is compounded of two opposites. Her mother was I believe a gipsy and thence she has her gay colours, her restlessness, her laughter, her generosity, her tempers, her childlike pleasure in little things. She will dance to a music-box tune or pick up her skirts and run down the road, or rate a tramp like Queen Elizabeth, or play Backgammon like a baby, kiss and stroke the cheek and love you in a passion! And on the other hand she has a good business head, runs the house and property like a lawyer, disciplines the servants, has her finger in every pie.

But her passion is for Adam. Adam is everything to her. She would like to possess him, every bone and vein of him, and his soul beyond. But she is wise enough to know that she cannot and that she can only take from him what he voluntarily gives her. That is a great deal. They have the strongest bond, the two--almost without knowing it, without wishing it. It is not only a bond of mother and son but a bond of family too. All the Herries I have met, whether in London or here, have something in common although they are all so different. What it is I cannot say. It is as though, inside the family, they are all against one another, but that against the outside world they are all united. Even Adam has something of this, although he is for ever saying that he is illegitimate and does not belong to them and disapproves of their worldliness and pride and materialism. For they ARE material, grossly so AND proud--proud with the worst kind of English pride as though they were God's people. John Herries in London is the only exception I have seen--yes, and PART of Madame. Part of HER is non- Herries, hates that blood and would like to escape from it.

In any case I am shut out, father, however kind they WISH to be, I am shut out. I am shut out by them all and by this hateful hard, raining, hostile country. It is all sodden hills and grey cloud and stone walls here. When the sun shines everything is harder than ever. The stones have a hard face, the people look as though they would like to kill you, the cattle lower their heads at you. I know that it is only on visits that we are here and that Adam will never leave his work in London, but I am afraid lest one day his mother will win and bring him back here for ever. He is so silent. He cannot express his feelings at all. When I lie in his arms I know that he loves me, but he will never say so. He is so shy of expression and when others are there I sometimes think that he almost hates me. Of course he does not. He is true and loving and noble, but why cannot he say something to me once and again, only some little things to reassure me? Then he goes off--for a whole day, leaving me with his mother and without a word to any of us. He loves this country so passionately that I do not count for anything beside it. I was so happy with you, dearest father, living with you, working with you. I needed no one. And then he came and at the first sight I loved him with all my soul as I shall always love him. But here I seem to fight every stone wall, every little stream, every sulky cloud. If only he would speak to me, tell me once that he loves me, defend me against my fears . . . Oh, father, why . . .

Judith Paris to Adam Paris

Uldale,
March 4th, 1842

MY DEAR SON--Dorothy and the children arrived last week. I cannot say I am sure how this EXPERIMENT may turn out. I confess that I am not altogether easy in my mind. When Bellairs died two months back Dorothy certainly had no IDEA of it, nor had I. But she found the house more and more melancholy and longed every day more ardently for Uldale so she must have her way. We can but see and I admit that it is agreeable to have company again.

Dorothy has grown very STOUT but is kind and much IMPROVED I think. She was always AMIABLE as you know, but had a strong conviction that she must MANAGE. I have explained to her that the children are HER business and the house MINE. She was at first inclined somewhat to think me an OLD LADY. She discovers that I am not so ancient as she supposed!

And now, Adam, I have had a great ADVENTURE. I have spent two nights in Watendlath! What do you say to that! I have stayed in the old house, eaten at the old table, walked the old ways. I have seen where Charlie Watson is buried and will confess to you that I shed a TEAR or two. I have seen again my Georges. Yes, standing by the Tarn, just as he used, smiling at me, because he had done something that he should not, and today was yesterday. I was a young girl again and all LIFE was in front of me. Well, that is over, my son. As I looked across the water to the hills and down to Rosthwaite where your grandfather lived, I knew what I had THROWN AWAY when I remained at Uldale. I sold my SOUL perhaps that day but what does it matter? There are too many souls already in space for the loss of one little one to be of importance.

Alice Perry's son reigns and a fine fellow he is, with four fine CHILDREN. His wife I thought a poor feckless creature and her HODGE-PODGE a disgrace, but for once I kept my old tongue quiet and told her only COMPLIMENTS. For an hour I was WILD again, old woman though I am. But the wildness passed. Here I am at my table adding accounts and the cows are going to milking beyond the window and Skiddaw is as mild and stout as Dorothy herself.

They all thought me MAD to go. I have still a touch of madness, but it diminishes. Rackstraw has the GOUT, Mary--the new maid (from Cockermouth--a good girl)--the toothache, her face swollen twice its size. I shall never see Watendlath again.

I LONG to have you here. It seems to be the ONLY THING I live for now, but I will not force you. You will come in your own good time. I passed Walter in the road last week. We did not speak. He is IMMENSELY fat and is not as careful in his dress as he was. There are awful doings at Ireby from all I hear, and many people refuse to go there any longer. I hear that he vows vengeance on us all because John and dear Elizabeth are happy in London--a poor sort of reason-- but he cannot harm us. Give my love to Margaret. I am sending you some of my own PRESERVES, two HAMS and a WOOL-WORK OTTOMAN that I bought at old Mr Chancey's sale in Keswick as a present to Margaret. Your loving

MOTHER

Adam Paris to Judith Paris

7 Farrimond Street,
London,
April 3rd, 1842

MY DEAREST MOTHER--This must be only the briefest of notes as I go this afternoon to a meeting in Manchester, but I thought you would like to know how we find our new rooms.

We think them exceedingly comfortable when we have time to consider them. I was never before as busy as now. People are still talking of Peel's Income-Tax and we Chartists will most certainly not oppose it. It is a small step in our own direction but the state of the country is with every week worse and the conditions among the poor frightful.

We have seen none of our relations save John and Elizabeth. I am happy to say that Elizabeth and Margaret have become the greatest friends. I am most happy for that. Margaret has not been so well of late.

In great haste. Your loving son,

ADAM

Very many thanks for the Cheeses and Butter you so kindly sent. They are most welcome.

HOMECOMING IN WINTER

The little town shivered under the breath of the helm-wind that, beating down from the icy caverns and hollows of Helvellyn, threw dark quivering shadows of cloud on the garden walls, set Main Street trembling with a half-worshipping, half-shuddering agitation, and caused Mrs Constantine, who had Mrs Trevelyan of Bournemouth as guest, to rub the tip of her nose with her muff a hundred times.

Fortunately at this moment of English history ladies were, by the dictates of fashion, more warmly clad than at any time before or after. So many petticoats, with solid padding, indeed did they wear that the crinoline must come in very shortly and assist them. Mrs Constantine was wearing four petticoats, and her poke-bonnet was lined with fur. Her peaked and animated face was for ever hiding itself in an enormous snowy muff. But it was right that it should be cold. Mrs Constantine, wife of one of the doctors in Keswick, told Mrs Trevelyan (whose heart, if the truth were known, was sick for Bournemouth) that it was right that it should be cold. She exulted in it, she revelled in it. It was but a week before Christmas and what was Christmas if not cold? The coach rattled down the street, old Tom Rawson blowing his horn with a fine Christmas flourish. The boys were just out of school and, wrapped up almost to the eyes in mufflers, rushed along the street screaming like sea-birds, playing 'shinny' as they went, the wooden ball lathe-turned, the 'shinny' sticks cut from the hedges. Keswick was its own quiet self in these winter months, lying peacefully beneath the purple wind-scarred hills. In the summer, as Mrs Constantine explained, it was now 'the rage', college youths from Cambridge, every house letting lodgings, the pencil-makers selling to every visitor enough black-lead pencils to last a lifetime; spar-dealers, curiosity-mongers, boatmen making a fortune; coaches tearing in and out, picnics everywhere, and until lately Mr Southey to be seen at any time, taking his walk. Poor gentleman, nothing but tragedy now. So many things to see! So MANY things to see! . . . But now all is quiet. Soon sheep, their wool blown a little by the wind, move up the street, the boys with their 'shinny' sticks racing in and out among them, there is a sudden flash of sun from the wrack of cloud, piercing like a sword drawn from its scabbard the cobbles, the sheep, the boys, slashing into sudden colour the cold flanks of Blencathra.

But Mrs Constantine was historical. History was her passion. Oh, Keswick was full of history! There was Acorn Street where the Royal Oak had been (oak--acorn--did Mrs Trevelyan see the quaintness?) and the Friars Inn where Lord Derwentwater quaffed a flagon of ale before riding to the '15, and Crosthwaite Vicarage where the tithes--the wool, the pigs, the geese, the dairy produce-- were brought and a grand dinner with hodge-podge followed. Here Mrs Trevelyan sneezed.

'You are not chill, my dear, I trust?'

'Oh no, not at all, not at all--'

And the old Moot Hall and the--Here she broke off to murmur:

'My dear Eliza! This is most fortunate. Here coming towards us is the most interesting person in Keswick.'

Mrs Trevelyan, blinded by the sharp wind and knowing that she had caught a cold that would endure for weeks, stared a little uncertainly.

But there was no doubt as to whom Mrs Constantine intended, for, stepping out of a barouche, standing for a moment, resting on a cane and looking about, then slowly walking up the street towards them, was a most remarkable woman. She was small of figure, but her step was astonishingly alert. She carried her head as though she commanded the town. As she approached them more nearly Mrs Trevelyan saw that her hair was snow-white under her poke-bonnet, that was of a rich blue and decorated with a feather. She wore a purple silk mantlet trimmed with a shaded ribbon. She was distinguished, most dainty, most determined. Her hands were hidden in a purple muff. She tapped with her cane, she looked about her eagerly, as though she were sniffing the fragrant, frosty air. Some boys with their ball, racing up the street, slowed down as they saw her. She smiled benignly upon them. A gentleman, riding a splendid roan, touched his hat. She bowed like a queen. A bearded farmer, driving a cow, touched his hat and she bowed again. She arrived at the two ladies.

'Oh Mrs Constantine, how DO you do?'

'Very well indeed, thank you, Madame Paris. Will you permit me to introduce to you my friend, Mrs Trevelyan, from Bournemouth.'

'With the greatest pleasure . . . I hope you are well? You are paying a lengthy visit?'

Here Mrs Trevelyan unfortunately sneezed and was so deeply aggravated that instead of paying compliments, as she had intended, she could only stutter:

'The air in Bournemouth is more balmy--'

'It is indeed. But here, I fancy, it is more bracing. I am on my way to visit old Miss Pennyfeather. She has not been so well, you know. Pray, remember me to the Doctor, Mrs Constantine. If you would be so good . . .'

She moved on.

'A most remarkable woman,' said Mrs Constantine eagerly. 'They say her mother was a gipsy. She has a house at Uldale and is a relation of the Herries family. Her father was a Herries--long ago here in Keswick. She has had a most remarkable history--'

They passed on to the more sheltered side of the street, but not before Mrs Trevelyan, who felt her chill gaining upon her with every cut of the wind, had remarked: 'She appears to enjoy most excellent health. I never saw such spirits!'

No, indeed. She had not and she would not, for Judith was at the height of happiness. This evening, by the Lancaster Coach, Adam her son was arriving for the Christmas festivities. Adam was coming home. She had not seen him for nearly a year; he was bringing his wife with him and that was very pleasant, but for Judith no one and nothing mattered but Adam.

She was in splendid health. This wild wind, these steel-grey hills suited her. She was exalted, lifted up. Between a break in the wall, over a dry and wind-tossed garden, she could see the distant Lake, the small waves in feathered hurry racing before the tongue of the flicking air. Were her hands not so warmly in the purple muff she could have stretched them out and embraced it all--sky, hill, water, stone and tree. The freshness, the strength, the flashing scornful sun! Snow was in the air! Snow! And Adam was coming home, Adam was coming home. She saw Dr Constantine, very thin-waisted, in his high beaver hat, riding his cob. She bowed. He bowed. It was all she could do not to give a little hop, skip and jump for sheer joy of living! Adam was coming home! Even as she rapped Miss Pennyfeather's knocker she gathered him to her heart, felt herself lost in his embrace, knew once again that neither wife nor work could take him from her. He was yet in her womb!

Little Nancy, Miss Pennyfeather's treasure, opened the door to her and she was in the parlour. It remained unchanged through all these years just as the rooms at Uldale remained unchanged, although Dorothy was for ever talking of 'new furniture'. New furniture! Judith detested the great ugly, heavy, clumsy stuff such as you saw at the Osmastons' or the Applebys'. No, this delicacy was what she loved and her eye rested with gratitude on dear Miss Pennyfeather's blue Chinese wallpaper, the nodding mandarins on the mantelpiece, the delicate harpsichord with its painting of violets on the lid, and the pretty delicate chairs with their faded gilt. But she did not look for more than a moment, for there, dancing from foot to foot in front of Miss Pennyfeather, who was sunk deep in an armchair and all wrapped up in shawls, was the strangest figure!

He was an odd little man, scarcely five feet high, his head on one side as though he had a crick in his neck, his shoulders humped; he had (Judith saw at once and recognized from olden days) the most marvellous eyes, dark, luminous, living every life in their orbs, at one moment enraged, at another amazed, at a third delighted, at a fourth swimming in fun. He had long white locks, unbrushed, dishevelled, and they seemed to have a breath of their own as they moved. He was wearing a blue-lapelled swallow-tailed coat with brass buttons, two waistcoats, a black stock and a high white collar above it. As Judith came in upon him he was dancing round like a top, his white hair waving, and nursing in his arms two white kittens, while Miss Penny-feather's spaniel, Bonaparte, barked at his heels. Yes, Judith knew at once who he was! Back, without a moment's interval, to that afternoon at Southey's when, her heart sore and indignant at Jennifer's unkindness, that boy with the flashing eyes had broken in . . . and now . . . this old man . . . and she . . . She had never seen him between then and now . . .

She bent down and kissed Miss Pennyfeather. Then she held out her hand.

'Mr Hartley Coleridge! You will not remember me . . . And, indeed, of course, you cannot. It is--oh, I fear to say how many years! I was a young woman, you a boy, tea at Mr Southey's . . .'

He did not remember her in the least, but he put down the kittens and held her hand and looked into her eyes with his own lambent ones and pretended that he remembered her perfectly well. They stood together, hand in hand, much of a height.

'Remember you! Why, of course, dear lady, of course, of course. Hey-diddle-diddle, but that is a long time ago--sad things, many sad things since then. So many gone, so many failing of high hopes. But we won't be sad. We refuse to be sad. I can see that you are never sad. We are like these kittens, you and I. Here-- the reel of cotton--I have lost it. Here, help me!' He was down on his knees searching under the harpsichord.

He looked up pleadingly at Miss Pennyfeather.

'Claribella, Isabella, Rosamunda--may I request a glass of beer?'

She looked at him sternly, then shook her head at him.

He sat back on the floor, his hand on a kitten's back.

'Well, a glass of water then.'

She pulled the bell-rope.

Then he was on his feet again. He danced about the room, talking all the time.

'Willie and Nannie Coates; you know, Lord and Lady Bacon because they kept so many pigs . . . They used to say . . . And Dinah Fleming--dear, dear Dinah--and you know the Mr Briggs and the Branckens and the Hustlers--at Tail End. Oh, you know them all, Claribella, and love them, and we'll go together! We'll pay calls together! We'll go round in a gig drawn by a goat all set up with lanterns. We'll stop on Dunmail and have goat's milk and I'll write a poem . . .'

He caught up the kitten, held it in front of him murmuring,

> Our birth and death alike are mysteries,
> And thou, sweet babe, art a mysterious thing.

'Jeanette,' he murmured. 'That was to Jeanette.'

He almost ran to the door. 'I must be away! Off! Gone! Vanished!'

He ran back and, with the utmost tenderness and delicacy, bent down and kissed the very old lady in the chair.

'Perhaps for the last time, Claribella, Rosamunda,' he said. 'Who knows but that beer may finish me one of these warm, spidery days?'

He stood in front of Judith and smiled so enchanting, engaging a smile that there were tears in her eyes.

'You saw me last,' he said, 'as a boy with everything in front of me. Now I can leap a brook and dance a hornpipe--not bad for an old man.'

He bent forward, kissed her hand, went to the door, bowed to both of them and was gone.

To Judith, his appearance, so unexpected, so brief, was the most extraordinary omen. He had been that to her on the only other occasion that she had met him. It had been then as though they had known one another always, sharing some secret life private to themselves. It had been so then. It was so now. All that he had lost, all that she had lost, rushed to her heart. She stared at the closed door as though it concealed a mystery. Then she recovered herself and was busy in cheering her old friend, who now was paralysed, whose doom was upon her, whose spirits were as brave and cheerful as those of the kittens that played with the ends of her shawl.

'Oh! He never had his glass of water!' Judith cried.

'Nancy will give it him. He is an old friend of Nancy's. He is with her in the kitchen now, chucking her under the chin. But she knows that she is never to give him beer--that I shall never forgive her if she does.'

Miss Pennyfeather lay back exhausted, her hands helpless, the yellow skin drawn sheath-like over the ridge of bones, only her eyes brave, defiant and amused. For an hour or more Judith made her happy.

'I enjoy seeing you so cheerful, my dear.'

'I enjoy it myself. But Adam is coming. I have not seen him this year.'

'And his wife?'

'Yes.'

'You should bring her to see me one day. I am curious. You don't care for her.'

'Oh, I do!' Judith shrugged her shoulders. 'Or I would. If she'd let me. She is a great calm, quiet woman. All the same I think she is a little afraid of me.'

Miss Pennyfeather said nothing.

'And you know that I am never my best with anyone who is afraid of me.'

'Now, Judith.' Miss Pennyfeather's eyes sought the other's very seriously. 'We have been the greatest friends for many years, have we not? Well, then, I can speak my mind. You must be good and generous to Adam's wife. Any other way lies catastrophe. Make her love you.'

'I have tried.'

'Yes--with reservations. "I will love you," you have said, "if you recognize that I come first with my son."' Then suddenly, with an odd galvanic energy: 'Possessive love--I detest it.'

Judith bent over her friend.

'Very well, dearest . . . You are right. I will make Margaret love me.' She laid her warm white hand on the dead yellow one.

After a pause Miss Pennyfeather said:

'There is another thing, my dear. Gossip. They come in here and gossip although I tell them not to. Is it true that you are having John and Elizabeth for Christmas?'

'Yes. And Sylvia and Garth Herries also. They are coming down from Edinburgh.'

'Look out, then, for trouble from Mr Walter. I hear that he is enraged beyond all measure that you should have John and Elizabeth.'

'Why should I not have them?'

'After his casting Elizabeth off--and after John marrying Elizabeth. Oh, my dear, you are not as a rule so slow!'

'Yes . . . I see. Well, I am not afraid of him.'

'They say that young Osmaston and Fred Kelly and others are always at the Fortress--card-playing, drinking . . . Gossip. But no decent person goes to the Fortress any more.'

Judith smiled.

'I told Walter years ago that he could not do it. From the moment he laid the first stone of that building everything has gone wrong with him. Jennifer's ghost haunts him. And Uhland's ingratitude. And now his father's marriage . . . Do you know that old Will may be a father any day now?'

'Never!' cried Miss Pennyfeather.

'Yes, and he is seventy-two years old. Well, my father was the same. They are strong men, the Herries . . . Goodbye, my dear. I shall be in again very shortly and shall bring Adam's wife with me.'

When Judith was in the barouche again and turning towards home the afternoon was already gathering in. A pallid bar of shuttered light lay between heavy clouds above Skiddaw. The wind had died, but little sobbing breaths rose and fell among the bare trees. The hills were cold, clothed in an ashen shadow, and over the long, thin fields a chill, hard and remorseless, laid its hand. A few hesitating flakes of snow were already falling.

Halfway along Bassenthwaite they approached a horseman and, in the half-light, Judith saw that it was Walter. She would have had old Bennet drive past him, but Walter, at once recognizing her carriage, rode his horse in front and across it. Bennett pulled up the horses and Walter came close, laying his gloved hand on the back of Judith's seat. She had not spoken with him for over two years.

'Good evening, Judith,' he said.

His voice was thick and husky. Now that he was close to her she could see the gross double-chinned face, the purple veins in nose and cheeks, the little eyes half closed under the heavy lids. He was very large in his riding-coat. He towered above her. He looked rather pathetic, she thought, and she was not in the least afraid of him.

'Good evening, Walter.'

'I shall not detain you a moment,' he went on, turning to curse his horse that it did not keep still. 'I have only a question to ask.'

'And what is that? We shall have snow, I fancy.'

'Yes. My question is not about the weather.'

He leaned closer to her, and his breath was coarse and hot.

'Is it true, as I hear, that you are entertaining my daughter at Uldale this Christmas?'

'Perfectly true.'

'You are aware that she disobeyed me flagrantly and that by entertaining her you are insulting me before the whole countryside?'

His voice quivered and again she thought: 'Poor Walter!'

'Now, Walter, this is a cold, chilly moment to discuss such a matter. I shall invite whom I please to my house.'

His big hand quivered on the board.

'Then you must take the consequences,' he said very low.

'I can look after myself--and my guests.'

'Well--I have warned you.'

She rested her hand for a moment on his.

'Come, Walter. This is foolishness. Forgive Elizabeth. Pay us a visit. Let us slay this stupid feud that has lasted so long. Hatred never did any good.'

He shouted: 'By God, No! . . . By God, No!'--dug spurs into his horse and charged away down the road.

Old Bennett drove on. His broad back (shoulders now bent and round) represented his proper emotions. He served Madame. If anyone did her a hurt, he would see to it. But words--words break no windows. That Herries of Ireby was crazed, and the way, so they said, that he carried on with women was shameful. Bennett, with all the virtue and fidelity of the unimaginative, scornfully flicked his horses' ears.

Judith was only for a moment perturbed. It had been strange, that dual recurrence of little Coleridge and of Walter--her past breaking in. But as she grew older she found that past, present and future began to merge. Time was becoming of less and less importance. There were these facts: her visit with Warren to Rosthwaite, the awful birth in Paris, Adam the baby teasing Walter on his white horse, Reuben as he fell mortally wounded in the lighted garden, Jennifer crying 'They've begun to build! They've begun to build!' or, long long ago, a beautiful naked woman and a young man on his knees, old Uncle Tom and Emma sitting by the fire at Stone Ends, David dropping, as though a stone had struck him, on the bright green grass, Georges throwing her out of bed at Watendlath, Georges falling, falling while the Old Man with the white beard . . . She looked up through the trees to the dark sky. All these things had occurred together, at the same moment of time, and meant but this--that they had been signs to light Judith Paris the way to salvation--and she had not gone . . . There was somewhere a Door . . . and somewhere a Key . . . and all History, whether of Nations or Families, was but this . . . Have you found it? Are you in touch? Have you made the Connexion? . . .

She sat back, drawing her mantlet more closely about her. No, they meant but this, all these shining moments, these figures woven into her tapestry--that she adored her son Adam, that he was coming home tonight, and her head would for a moment rest on his breast, that they would be together, together . . .

Her heart began to beat so that she must lay her muff against it.

The house was alight with candles. They had not gas yet, although Dorothy was always urging it Judith refused. Candles and lamps. This gas hurt the eyes. It was dangerous. And how pretty the candleshine against the Chinese wallpaper, or lighting you up the twisted stair.

'How modern you are!' she said, pinching Dorothy's fat cheek. Then added: 'I shall be gone soon. Then you may have gas.'

She was managing very well with Dorothy, who had grown in experience as well as in physical size. She was now a great woman with big breasts and wide beam and a face like a dairy-maid. Having children had taught her a deal; she managed them well. They obeyed her, indeed, better than they obeyed their Great-aunt Judith, as they were taught to call her. Timothy was a normal lively boy already like his father. The three little girls-- Veronica, Amabel and Jane--were docile, happy-natured. Veronica was the pretty one. She had dimples and dark hair like her grandmother's. Yes, they were good children.

By eight o'clock the whole house quivered with excitement. For one thing, with the coming of Adam and Margaret the stir of the Christmas festivities might be said to commence. John and Elizabeth were arriving tomorrow, Sylvia and Garth Herries two days later. Christmas Night there was to be a dance. The children could scarcely contain themselves, and the little girls

were busy, secretly, all day long, painting, sewing, cutting out, making their presents.

Adam and Margaret would take a post-chaise from Kendal, so one could not be sure when they would arrive. Judith walked all over the candlelit house, seeing that everything was right. She pushed open a window a moment and listened to the bell-ringers practising at the church a mile and a half away. She could hear the running water, and felt, with a thrill of contrasted warmth, the cold dark paths running up the mountain-sides, the gullies down whose flanks the wind was tearing. One cold flutter, then another, touched her cheeks. It was snowing.

She lingered especially in the room where Adam and Margaret would sleep. This had been Jennifer's. Here Francis had surprised Jennifer, here Jennifer had lain while John read to her and the reflection of the flames that the rioters had lighted danced on the walls. Yes, everything was well. The four-poster was ready, there were flowers (Christmas roses) on the davenport, the stamped fleur- de-lis wallpaper looked fine in the candlelight. Dorothy would like tall pier-glasses and grates of shining steel and heavy cornices. Not while Judith was in command! She came out and stood at the top of the stairs, holding a candle and listening. The house was very still, only the ticking of the clocks, a door opening and closing. Stillness, peace. A great wave of thankfulness flowed over her. She had not done so badly then. After all the turmoil of her life it had come to this--that, hale in health, honoured and trusted, in this old house that she loved, she stood there waiting for her son whom, by wise dealing, she had kept in her heart. She smiled to herself, thinking of the moment when, in that room close to her, he had defied her. He had climbed out of the window just as she had once done. Bone of her bone, flesh of her flesh . . .

The bell pealed through the house. The knocker shook the door. They were here, they were here!

She ran down the stairs, across the hall, flung open the door, was out on the paved path. Bennett and the boy had come from the stable with lanterns and all the dogs with them, barking, yelling, yelping. And there beyond the gates, like a visitant from another ghostly country, was the post-chaise. A moment later Judith was in her son's arms.

Half an hour later Margaret stood alone in the bedroom, hesitating to blow out the candles before she went down. Adam had already preceded her. She stood there beating down her fear. She saw herself in the glass, her image flickering uncertainly in the blown candlelight. Yes, she was tall, broad, plain; clear straight eyes, dark hair brushed carefully, cleanly, strong, but-- dull! Oh, dull, dull, dull! And this little woman with all her oddity, liveliness, sharpness would find her with every visit more dull.

It was all she could do to keep the tears back from her eyes. The journey had been very long, the train stinking of oil from the ill- trimmed lamps, the last drive in the chaise chill and rough. She was terribly weary. Had she had her way she would have gone to bed, then and there, and slept for a night and day, but Madame would think that weak and foolish.

'What! A strong woman like Margaret! What a wife for my son!'

And Adam--why had he not FELT her isolation, dread, loneliness? Her father would have known in an instant what she was feeling, but Adam seemed to have no intuition. Oh! he loved her, of course! But he never seemed to wish to tell her so. She scolded herself here as she had already done a thousand times. What was this need in her for reassurance? It had not been so before her marriage. She and her father had never spoken about their love. But Adam was so strange. Even now, after their years of marriage, she did not understand him. Perhaps no one understood him except his mother. He would escape from her--at any moment. At one time he was there, and then, in a second, he was gone! And it never occurred to him to suit himself to her mood, to ask what SHE was thinking! Maybe all Englishmen were like that! It was her German blood that made her ASK for sentiment, sympathy, little loving words and actions. At night, in the dark, his heart beating against her heart, her arm around him as though he were her child--ah, then he was hers! But why with the first flash of daylight must he cease all demonstration as though he were afraid of the light? Oh, these Englishmen--but they were difficult as husbands!

He was downstairs now with his mother, and here was she trembling at the smell and feel of this hostile house, at the thought of the dark cold hills that closed in, at the anticipation of that little cold woman with her sharp eyes, her way of suddenly looking at you as though she wondered that you COULD be such a fool!

Well, she must fight it. Adam was so happy to come home. She must make him think that she was happy too.

She came down and found them as she had expected, in the parlour seated on the sofa with the roses (Margaret HATED that sofa), Madame's white sharp hand resting on Adam's broad knee with so proprietary an air!

Adam jumped up.

'Come here, my dear,' said Judith, patting the sofa. 'I am sure that you must be tired. Come and sit beside me.'

'Thank you,' said Margaret, feeling large and awkward and clumsy in all her limbs. 'I am not tired at all, thank you.'

She sat down beside her. There was a pause then, as though Margaret had interrupted a very intimate conversation. Then Judith continued again the excited narration of people and events that she had been pouring on to Adam before Margaret's entrance.

Then Dorothy came in, red-faced, smiling, her corsage of puckered taffeta too tight for her figure, her hair a trifle untidy. Margaret liked Dorothy. She was kind and unalarming--somehow rather German.

They went in to supper. How happy Adam was! Margaret's heart ached with love of him as she watched him across the table. He was like a small boy again, asking about everything, the dogs, the horses, the cows, the dairy, Dorothy's children, all the neighbours. He had forgotten, she saw, all his distress about the poor, the Corn Laws and the rest--the things that would make him so unhappy in London that he would walk the room, tossing his head, beating his hands against one another, crying out . . .

She saw, too, Judith's happiness, how the small lady, sitting so straight at the head of the table, was almost breathless with happiness at having her son home again. How excitable she was at her age, what a child still in many ways! She would rap out an order to the parlour-maid like a general addressing a soldier, and then in a moment would forget it all and clap her hands at some joke, or throw to one of the four dogs--that sat with staring eager eyes near her chair--something from the table, or laugh at Rackstraw. And once she jumped up and walked, strutting with an affected gait to show them the absurdity of some old man in Keswick.

'Yes,' thought Margaret, 'what a poor creature I am to grudge them their happiness in being together! I will win her heart, make her love me.' But the words would not come. She could only answer in monosyllables. Some reserve stuck in her throat. 'Oh, what a fool and a spoil-sport they must think me!' she cried to herself.

After supper, the Waits came. First they could be heard behind the closed windows, faint shrill voices and the sudden plaintive squeak of a fiddle. They were summoned into the hall and stood there in a semi-circle--three boys, an old man with a white beard, a stout countryman in a smock, and a thin tall man with spectacles who was the fiddler. The servants came to listen. The dogs sat solemnly on their haunches in a group, yawning once and again.

The boys sang in piercing trebles while the old bearded man had one of the deepest voices, surely, in the world. They sang their carols without fear or hesitation, looking at no one but holding their heads up and staring into the ceiling with a kind of ecstatic frenzy. When it was over they were given money and hot drinks. They vanished into the night, and a flurry of snow blew in through the open door.

Afterwards they sat around the blazing fire in the parlour talking, listening to the wind that had sprung up and now was howling round the house.

When they all went up to bed Adam followed his mother into her room. When the door was closed she held him in her arms as though she would never let him go.

They sat down close together at the foot of the bed.

'It has been a long time, Adam.'

'Yes, Mother, I know. It is not easy. There is so much to do.'

'Are you happy?' She looked at him sharply.

'Happy? Who is happy?'

'Then you are not. Why not?'

He stared, under frowning brows, into the fire.

'The state of the country is dreadful. Never been so bad. No employment, trade fearful, no faith in Parliament, living conditions frightful--and everyone helpless. What is coming, Mother? Surely something disastrous.'

She put her arm around him, and he his around her.

'Yes,' she said. 'But I know something about life now. Nothing is so bad as you expect.'

'No. Perhaps.' He hesitated. 'I come in for a good deal of criticism, Mother. Many of them think me priggish, snobbish, out for my own hand. It was a shock the first time that I realized it. I had thought that I was so genuine, really moved by the love of my fellowmen, truly believing in them. And then when I heard myself called a self-seeker I was miserable for a while. I allowed no one to see it--not Margaret even-- but I thought, "Well, perhaps I am this. I am deceived in myself." There's a little man, rather a power in London, he believes in nothing and in nobody. He says frankly that if you say that you love your fellowmen or trust your friends you are a hypocrite. He hates and despises me. I know the sort of picture he draws of me behind my back, amiable, filled with noble sentiments, but a snob because I am a Herries and making my own career under a cloak of caring for others. Yes, I was unhappy for a while--so long as I thought it might be true. But it is NOT true. There is something in me stronger and deeper than my intentions or my words or my acts. I DO believe in my fellowmen, I DO love them. I know that most of them intend the best. I know that Henry Cray is wrong with his bitterness and cynical mind. I have ceased to disturb myself. I am tranquil again.'

'Yes.' She drew his hand into hers.

'That is hard--the first time you really see yourself as your detractors see you. But it is grand too. At last you are seeing the whole picture. You are a spectator of yourself. That happened to me years ago in this very house, when Jennifer hated me. I could not BELIEVE that anyone could see me as that--mean, sly, intriguing. But only those who love you know you. There is good criticism, though, in the view of your detractors. You take yourself too seriously, Adam, I don't doubt. Pompous, sentimental! No, you are not, but you think perhaps too much of nobility and fine living. Life's a magpie's hoard--an occasional gold piece quite by accident among the broken glass and bits of coal. Take life lightly, my son. Believe in it, but laugh at it and at yourself.'

He kissed her. 'Later on. I'm too solemn, I know. I am always feeling it. But I live so much by myself, in my own thoughts . . .'

'And Margaret?' she asked him.

'I think I love Margaret more every day--but I don't grow closer to her. She wants something from me. I don't know what it is. Something I cannot give her. I have never been able to say in words what I feel. I'm tongue-tied. It seems to threaten my freedom if I speak too much. She is very quiet, too, of course. We are both too quiet together perhaps.'

'I am going to make Margaret love me this Christmas-time,' Judith said. 'She is lonely, Adam, and she loves you more than anyone else ever has--except myself.'

'You and she, Kraft, and John,' Adam said slowly, 'the four in my life who have loved me. But for the most part men cannot come close to me. I used to dream of helping to make a great Brotherhood in England. Now I know that I never shall. I am not the man.'

'No,' she answered. 'Maybe you are not. It is not for us to choose what we shall be. We have to accept and without protest.'

She kissed him most lovingly, and he went to his wife.

THE WILD GOOSE

The wild goose, the same bird that Orlando was afterwards to see, flew over the house as the light was just breaking. The whirr of its wings stirred the perfect stillness of the crystal scene. The early sun was dim, but a pale glitter showed every tree and blade of grass sparkling with crystal. The whiteness of the snow, even in that thin light, dazzled the eye.

The sun rose higher--the wild goose was gone--the sheathed snow, stretching in a translucent glory to the line where Skiddaw cut the sky, now faintly blue, ran to the very foundations of the house and was marked only by the tiny feet of birds.

They were all going to church--Madame, Adam, Margaret, Elizabeth, John, Sylvia, Garth, Dorothy, Veronica, Amabel, Timothy, Jane, Rackstraw, Bennett, old Mrs Quinney, Martha Hodgson, Jack Turner, Alice, Clara, Wilson, Mrs Wilson. Nearly two miles to the church. Some had walked ahead, some were driving, all the dogs had gone charging across the field, little clouds of shining iridescent powder rose up above the purple shadows that darkened the snow.

John and Elizabeth walked.

'Oh, I'm so happy!' said John. 'This is the loveliest Christmas!' But was he speaking truly, for over his head, frowning down upon him, was the Fortress? It looked sardonically threatening with its battlements and turrets;

the walls met above the hill like a great hanging eyebrow; the stone was dull, heavy, squat, but snow fell in a sheet of dazzling light from its grey shoulders and it could not disown, however it might wish, the blue peerless sky that overlooked it. Light struck the walls and the preen of the two peacocks that Walter had bought. They stretched their tails on the miniature battlements.

'Is not Aunt Judith wonderful?' said John.

'I love her so much,' said Elizabeth.

She thought that it must be impossible to be happier than she was at that moment. And perhaps--who knows?--she would meet her father in the road, all would be forgiven, he would come to the Christmas party . . .

Was that, John thought, Uhland sitting his black horse under the yews? There! There! Cannot you see? His heart was chilled. No. There is no one there . . .

They were approaching the church, and the bells were ringing like mad. The quire were in a small gallery and were almost throttled with evergreens, holly and ivy and mistletoe. There was fiddler and a clarionet. The young ladies in delightful bonnets, some small boys shining with soap, the village postmaster, Mr Collins, Farmer Twistle, Farmer Donne, young Donne--they all played and sang with such a vigour that some of the holly fell with a rattle and clatter from the old beam. There was an anthem in which all the parts went wrong and nobody cared. Two of the dogs from the Hall-- Satan and Mischief--strolled up the aisle and pushed with their noses at the door of Madame's high-walled pew. Then they lay down, their tongues hanging out, their eyes fixed in front of them. How everyone sang 'Oh, Come, all ye Faithful'! . . .

In the churchyard afterwards, old Mr Summers, the Vicar, stood and shook hands with everybody.

They all walked home, and it was passing through the second field that one of the important events of Adam's life occurred to him. He was to remember afterwards, with a rich sense of gratitude, that shiny expanse of snowy field, and how in the sunlight the snow turned to rills of sparkling water that glittered through the grass, and how over the hedge Sam Longford's cottage that he knew so well sent up a banner of purple smoke that fluttered against the stainless sky.

For a thick-set, broad-shouldered man, touching his cap, spoke to him.

'You won't remember me, sir?' he said. 'I've been working Penrith way the last five years--Will Leathwaite.'

Adam stopped and smiled but looked bewildered.

'You will think me very uncivil,' he said.

'Why, sir,' said the man, smiling all over his rather simple countenance. 'The Summer Fair of 'twenty-seven, when I won t'race up to Druids' Circle. Why, sir, you rode with my poor old fayther on his mare, Jessamy, and you was shouting for me fit to burst your lungs. And I won, sir, I won! Bit too heavy now, I reckon!'

Why, of course, Adam remembered! He saw the whole scene, how their horse charged the village street, and how they must pause on the road until the runners caught them up. He heard his eager cry to the old farmer: 'Do you think Will will win, Mr Leathwaite? Do you think Will will win?' And here was Will! And Adam, looking at him, liked him.

They talked a little while. Will stood there, awkwardly, kicking the snow with his boot. Then he looked up, his face red.

'Not wanting any kind of servant, sir, are you?'

'Why, no,' said Adam. 'I'm a poor man, Leathwaite, a poor man.'

'I'd come to you,' said Leathwaite, looking Adam straight in the eyes, 'just for my keep.'

'What! Aren't you married?'

'No--nor likely to be.'

Adam nodded his head and smiled.

'Well, if I ever do want one--I'll tell you.'

They shook hands and Adam moved on. The wild goose, flying in from the sea, circled over Skiddaw, then swerved towards the water of the Lake, already thinly crusted with silver, dark in the shadow under the hills.

As the afternoon lengthened excitement grew. All life was INSIDE the house now. The dining room was filled with the long extended table; it was a place of mystery. Behind closed doors the preparations for the ceremony went on. On every fire all over the house the great logs blazed. Sylvia poked her head through the door of Judith's room.

'That's right, my dear. Come in.'

Sylvia came in.

'I must go and make myself grand.' She stood and looked at the old lady who sat toasting her toes at the fire. Sylvia considered her. She loved Judith, had done so from the first moment of their meeting. She would not have spent her Christmas in this outlandish place had it not been for Judith. Yes, and her curiosity. She had now, for so many years, intrigued, manipulated in her London world that she was intensely curious and inquisitive. She took it for granted that everyone intrigued, that no one was what he or she seemed, that all private lives trembled for ever on the edge of crises. And there was something--should she speak of it to Judith or no? Judith also loved her, but, considering her, now, found that she was not so lovely as she had once been. She had aged lines on her forehead, had something hard and even a little desperate about the corners of her mouth. So many Herries, she reflected, aged before their due time.

'Oh, Judith, I have never had a happier Christmas.'

'That's good. Sit down for five minutes. We have plenty of time.'

'It must make you happy to have Adam and Margaret.'

'It does,' said Judith, kicking a shoe against the fender.

'I do wish that we saw them more often in London. But with Adam's views . . .'

'Yes, I know.'

'*I* of course do not care in the least, but some of our friends think the Chartists would murder us all in our beds had they the chance--'

'Yes, dear. Absurd.'

Sylvia sighed. 'It is so restful here. I dote on the country. I hate my London life.'

'Then why do you lead it?'

'Oh, I don't know. What else should one do? Garth would be bored to death in the country.'

'I suppose he would.'

'You know that Will's wife may be brought to bed at any moment?'

'Yes, my dear.'

'Fancy--at his age! And how provoking for Walter!'

There was a pause and then Sylvia said:

'I suppose that Walter still keeps up this ridiculous feud?'

'Yes,' said Judith. 'He is furious, I believe, that I have John and Elizabeth here.'

Sylvia said:

'I saw him yesterday.'

Judith looked up sharply.

'Saw whom? Walter?'

Sylvia nodded.

'I was out walking. I had got on to the moor and was standing looking around me when he rode up behind me. You cannot imagine the start it gave me! You know--or maybe you do not know--in any case a few years back he was attracted to me. It began years ago when I stayed at Ireby for their opening Ball--the time when poor Jennifer died. I have seen him since once or twice--not for a considerable while though.'

Judith looked at her. How far had that gone? A strange shiver of repugnance--the consciousness of herself being in any close contact with Walter--for an instant held her. But Sylvia's beautiful face was quite unmoved. She was absolutely calm.

'How altered he is! Quite shocking! So gross--I must confess that I was uncomfortable. Dusk was falling and although the house was not far distant--' She broke off. 'Well, I can look after myself of course. However, he did not get down from his horse. We exchanged only a few words.'

'What did he say?' Judith asked.

'He inquired how I did, said it was long since we had met. Then he asked whether Elizabeth was staying at Uldale. I said she was.'

'Well?'

'He was very strange. Most odd. Judith, I think he may be coming here tonight.'

'Coming here?'

'Yes; he said something about it, something about a surprise visit. He said that it would make a fine bonfire if he burned this house down and everyone in it.'

Judith smiled grimly.

'We will manage him if he does come.'

Sylvia bent and kissed Judith, then went, but at the door she turned. 'The Herries men are so very peculiar,' she said. 'If they cannot have what they want they rush to destruction. Garth is just like that.'

In another room Elizabeth lay in John's arms. She murmured:

'Darling, I must dress.'

He stroked her hair, kissed her eyes, held her passionately close to him.

'Oh, Elizabeth,' he whispered, 'we must never be parted, never, never, never, never.'

'Nothing can part us,' she said.

'Nothing? No one? Never?'

'Nothing. No one. Never.'

'I could not believe that love could grow when it was from the beginning so intense. But when I look back to even a year ago it does not seem that THAT was love at all.'

They held one another in an embrace that, they thought, defied Death itself.

Before she went down to dinner Margaret looked into the nursery. Dorothy, when Margaret had asked her permission, had suddenly kissed her.

'I am fond of you, Margaret, I am indeed. We are more alike than anyone else in this house is like either of us.'

Perhaps they were. Two large, plain domestic women. Margaret had not thought that she was domestic. She had lived so long working happily with her father for a Cause. Now she was domestic. She wanted a child. It might be that all German women were so.

So she went into the nursery. When John and Dorothy had been children, there had been no nursery, but now, on the top floor, they had knocked down a wall and bludgeoned a passage. The room had sloping roofs, and wide windows stared out to Scotland. You could see the Firth stir under the sun like a slippery silver snake. When Margaret came in the four children were in bed, but of course not asleep; Timothy was five, Veronica four, Amabel three, Jane only two: Dorothy had been faithful to her duties, and then Bellairs, having planted his seed, had incontinently died.

Timothy was typical Bellairs, brave, stupid, kind and greedy. But the girls were all Herries, Veronica and Amabel of one kind and poor little Jane of the other. Veronica and Amabel were proud, sensible, determined and self-satisfied. Nice little girls, they already gave the impression that Herries little girls were much the best. But Jane, dear Jane, was the true descendant of the Rogue, of Francis, of all their cloudy ancestors before them. She dreamt dreams, she cried for no reason, brokenly she tried to explain that she saw things, a white horse, frozen water, a lady with red hair; she was a nervous, sensitive child, shy but most responsive to affection. It was to her cot that Margaret went. The children lay, their eyes staring, their cheeks hot, thinking of the marvellous day that it had been. In a heap near the window were the new toys. There was a rocking-horse, a doll's house, a 'shinny' stick and ball for Timothy.

They gave cries and shouts when they saw Margaret. They did not know who she might be, but today everyone was a friend. She talked to them, kissed them, but she knelt down beside Jane's cot. Jane, whose head was covered with yellow curls like a duckling's, smiled, stroked Margaret's cheek with a fat finger and fell asleep, and Margaret knelt there, her heart aching as though she were the loneliest woman in the world.

Down in the hall the boys from the village had arrived, Mumming, and it was a great pity that they had chosen so bad a time, for soon guests would be here and the ladies of the house were dressing.

However, Madame miraculously appeared to have time for everything, and there she was, sitting at the foot of the stairs, almost under the mistletoe, dressed in her best and beating her hands to the music. The boys, in the middle of their play, could not but look at her, she was so very fine. Her white hair gleamed, her naked shoulders shone (amazingly white for so old a lady). Her dress had three skirts--cream, silver, cream again--and was decorated with crimson roses. She wore silver shoes.

'Bravo! Bravo!' she cried, tapping with her stick. The boys were without coats and their white sleeves were tied with ribbons, their hats decorated with evergreen, and they carried thick staves.

There was a fiddle and a drum. Their dance was clever and most intricate, advancing, retreating, advancing again and striking their sticks the one against the other. They shouted Cumberland shouts and brought with them into the candlelit hall the rough tang of the mountain-stream running under grass, the windswept 'top' bare under the rushing cloud.

'Excellent! Most excellent!' Madame cried, thinking that they must go to the kitchen for beef and ale, and the kitchen in confused disorder because of the great Dinner.

One stout boy wore a fox's head and carried a fox's tail. Another boy wore a mask with a huge nose and bulbous cheeks.

'I know!' cried Madame. That's Willy Caine . . . you can't deceive me. How is your Aunt, Willie? She's up again, I hear.'

She drove them, hot, flushed and happy, off into the kitchen.

Then the guests began to arrive. The Reverend Mr Summers and his old, old wife, although they had the shortest way to come, were of course the first. There were the Osmastons, the Applebys, poor old Miss Keate from Keswick, a dry old maid, but she had nowhere to go for her Christmas dinner, the two Miss Blossoms all the way from Penrith (friends of Dorothy's), and Deborah's grandchildren, Fred and Anne Withering, from near Carlisle.

They would sit down twenty altogether--quite as many as the dining- room would hold--but Judith was bound to acknowledge that she was proud of her table when, seated at the head of it with stout Mr Osmaston on one side of her and old Mr Summers on the other, she looked around her. She had her dear Adam near to her and quite enough Herries to make her feel patriarchal. As you looked down the two sides of the table you could pick without any trouble the members of that family--Adam, Dorothy, John, Elizabeth, Garth, the two Witherings. Unlike though they might be, they were yet alike in these two things--in the high prominent bones, the tall erect heads and straight shoulders--and in their consciousness that they were dominating the rest of the company and came first wherever they might be.

The room is looking beautiful, she thought. The old dark green wallpaper was a fine setting to all the candlelight; the fruit, piled high between the silver candlesticks, had a hard brilliant edge of colour as though it were made of metal. Everyone smiled, laughed. There was not a care in the world.

Old Bennett, dressed up in a green coat with silver buttons, came in carrying a silver dish, and on it was a pig's head with a lemon in its mouth. Everyone stood up: there was a great clapping of hands; then, after an interval, attended by the stable-boy (also dressed in a green coat with silver buttons), who carried two lighted candles in silver candlesticks, old Bennett was back again bearing the Wassail Bowl. This was a magnificent china dish, crimson and gold, and the recipe of the drink had come all the way from old Pomfret of Westaways and he had it from the old Elizabethan Herries of the Mines. Roasted apples floated on its surface, and the aromatic scent of it was as the spices of Arabia.

Speeches were made, healths were drunk. Before the ladies left the table Madame gave the speech of the evening; proud, happy, her eye passing once and again to Adam, she was said by them all to resemble Queen Elizabeth--Queen Elizabeth in an amiable mood, be it understood.

When at last the gentlemen joined the ladies the Wassail Bowl was empty and the house was flaming with jollity. To Fred Withering it seemed there were three staircases, and old Mr Summers confided to Osmaston an affair of his in his Oxford days that was anything but clerical. Only John seemed apart from the others ('Oh, the most beautiful man I have EVER set eyes on!' Miss Keate confided to Sylvia), his eyes resting constantly on Elizabeth with an adoration that had something poignant in its heart as though he were well aware that all was illusory, vanishing at the touch, doomed to destruction.

'Cheer up, old boy,' cried Garth, who was completely drunk but very charming.

John smiled and laughed; he was happier than he had ever been in all his life.

While the dining-room was cleared for dancing they played games-- Cumberland games moreover. Instead of Oranges and Lemons there was the Penrith Down the Long Lonnins:

Down the long lonnins we go, we go,
To gather some lilies, heigho, heigho!
We open the gates so wide, so wide,
To let King George and his men go by.

And then Sandy O.

Here Judith, Dorothy, John and Adam, who had been all brought up on it, sang the words with all their youth in their eyes:

My delight's in Sandy O,
My delight's in Brandy O,
My delight's in the red, red rose,
Come along, my Annie O.
Heigho for Annie O,
Bonny Annie O.
All the world would I give
For my bonny Annie O.

For this game there is a girl in the middle, and she chooses one from the ring; the tune is Hops and Peas.

And another 'ring' game, Hops and Peas and Barley-corn:

Hops and peas and barley-corn,
Hops and peas and barley-corn,
Hops and peas, hops and peas,
Hops and peas and barley-corn.
This is the way the farmer stands;
This is the way he folds his arms,
Stamps his feet, claps his hands,
Turns around to view his land.

How they all stamped and clapped!

'Yes, well,' said Miss Keate, who was wearing, quite out of fashion, a turban, 'I never imagined for a moment--'

But best of all was Green Gravel.

Round the green gravel the grass grows green,
All the fair maidens are shame to be seen;
Wash them in milk,
And dry them in silk;
Last down wedded--

At the word 'down' all slip to the ground, the last down is married. Then she stands in the middle, and they sing a song about her. Then she is asked which she likes best, butter or sugar. If she says 'sugar' it is her sweetheart she likes; if 'butter' it is some other.

After a while Margaret slipped from the room. It was very hot. She could not help it, but she felt isolated, alone. Everyone knew everyone so well. Adam had been placed some distance from her at the supper-table, and he was enjoying himself so greatly that he had thought of nothing but his enjoyment. Men were like that: children when they were happy. And she loved to see him so; that was the desire of her heart, but once she caught John's eyes as they rested on Elizabeth's young enchanting beauty and that glance stabbed her. Elizabeth was so beautiful, so young and virginal and good. Margaret seemed to herself old and soiled with all her hard life with her father, the shabby places in which she had lived, the poor desperate rebellious people who had been her companions. She had been proud of the new dress that she had been wearing, but now it seemed heavy and coarse. In the wild extravagance of her mood it appeared to her that she had lost Adam for ever . . .

She slipped upstairs and found her room. She threw herself on to her bed and burst into tears. This was, perhaps, the first time in her life that she had ever shed bitter tears; she had been always calm, controlled, and had wondered, often enough, that women should weep so readily and in front of those whom they loved. She was in years only twenty-two, but she seemed to herself to be so much older. She had felt often like a mother to Adam, to her father even, and now that she should, like a little child abandon herself to her grief! But she could not stop. Faintly she heard, coming up to her from below, the singing and laughter. Her curtains were not drawn, and she could see the snow falling in a thick tide beyond her window. How cold and desolate those hills, how bleak this North Country, how harsh the loneliness that lay like an icy hand on her heart!

The door opened and, turning on her bed, she saw that Adam had come in. He came in, happy and sweating. He was laughing, and his black hair lay damp on his forehead. His eyes shone in his brown face. His blue evening-coat with its dark velvet collar was waisted almost to effeminacy, as was the fashion of those years, and the tails of it stood out over his thick sturdy thighs. He looked always better in rather rough loosely fitting clothes. He came in laughing and humming the last notes of the Green Gravel; then he saw Margaret. He stopped dead, and the change in his face was almost ludicrous. Neither he nor anyone else had ever seen her cry before. No, not her father when her mother died.

'Margaret!'

It seemed to him in his astonishment that his heart turned over in his chest.

'Margaret! What is it?'

She sat up, found her handkerchief, wiped her eyes and, rather wanly, smiled.

'I suffered from a terrible headache. It was the heat.'

Clumsily, still bewildered, unable to realize what he saw, he sat down on the bed. He took her hand, which was trembling but suddenly lay quiet as it felt the tranquil reassurance and strong bones of his brown one.

'A headache? But why did you not say?'

'Why should I disturb anyone? You were all so happy.'

He looked at her more closely.

'That's not true. You would not weep for a headache.'

As he saw her, whom he loved so dearly, with her hair in disorder and her cheeks stained, his love that was so deeply secure in his heart that he never questioned it, began to be restless and uneasy.

They could neither of them lie to the other ever about anything, so she said quietly:

'No, it was not the headache.'

'Well, what then?'

'I was foolish. Nothing but foolishness.'

He put his arm around her and drew her to him, but they were not really together. He had been twenty-seven in September, so that he was not very old, and he had no experience of women at all. He began to be frightened as though something within him had whispered: 'Take care, you may lose her.'

'But what is it, Margaret?' he repeated. 'Have I done something.'

Then she said, dropping her voice, looking away from him:

'I thought you loved me no longer.'

His agitation increased. Loved her no longer, when he worshipped her? Loved her no longer when only last night? . . . But now his old trouble, that he could never find words to express himself, attacked him.

'Love you?' he stammered. 'But, Margaret, I--I . . . I could not love anyone more,' he ended, looking at her.

'No--I am sure. Of course. But perhaps it has been a great mistake. I am not handsome. I am not clever. This is your world and not mine . . .' Then she burst out with a sudden cry, a note in her voice that he had never heard before. 'Oh, Adam, I have been so lonely!'

The shock to him then was one of the worst of his life. He had taken everything for granted. He had gone quietly on, troubled about his work and his feeble achievement in it, troubled at the state of the world and the general unhappiness, but sure always of two things--

his love for Margaret and his mother, and their love for him. These were so sure that he never dreamed that they needed expression. Like so many other Englishmen he lived in a man's world where expression of feeling was something too foreign to be decent.

The thought of his mother stirred, a recognized solid fact, in the middle of all his bewilderment.

'But my mother? Has she been unkind to you?'

'No. She has been very kind. It is not her fault that she cannot like me.'

'But she does like you. She said so last night.'

Ah, then they had been discussing her! The two of them together wrapped in their own intimacy! But Margaret had a noble nature, above and beyond all smallness or mean jealousy. She put her arm around Adam's neck.

'My love . . . Forget this. I have had so little experience of the world, and all women are foolish sometimes. I have felt sometimes that we could speak to one another more, say more what was in our hearts-- and tonight you were all together, you knew one another so well. I was foolish . . . Forgive me, forgive me.'

Then, with her head against his breast, she cried again, not wishing to stop her tears that, in their flow, seemed to release and set free all her misery of the last weeks, release it so that it would never return again. He held her in his arms as though at any moment she might escape him. The shock and the surprise were to him tremendous and the effect of this would remain with him for the rest of his life. His heart was so tender, he hated so passionately to wound or hurt anything alive (unless it were an enemy, someone or something that he thought cruel and evil) that the knowledge of hurting her was terrible to him.

'Margaret! Margaret! Don't cry. You shall never cry again. What I have done, wrapped in myself, never seeing . . . But I never can say what I feel. I don't deserve that you should love me. I shall make it up to you now all my life long.'

He stroked her hair. They stayed, cheek against cheek, in silence. At last he said:

'We shall understand one another now.'

She kissed him and, holding his head passionately against her breast, looking out to the falling snow beyond the window, murmured: 'Now no one can separate us. I shall never be afraid again.'

A little later, intensely happy, hand in hand they went downstairs and rejoined the company.

Now had it not been for an excellent journal known as The Cumberland Paquet the astonishing events that made this evening for ever memorable (so that years later they were, in a much exaggerated form, often recalled) would never have been known to the outside world. But it happened that there intervened now a short pause in the festivities--a pause between games and the dancing, and Miss Keate, hot in the head with exercise (and some of the Wassail Bowl), and young Mrs Appleby found a place on the corner of the stairs where they might cool. From their position, it must be noted, they had a perfect view of the hall and the hall door. Miss Keate had with her a copy of The Cumberland Paquet of December 13th which she had discovered in a corner of the parlour. She had secretly abstracted it that she might have 'a quiet read with it at home'. She was just such a lady, a kind of magpie, and, being of very slender fortune, picked up once and again 'things that she was sure no one else could want'. But now being with Mrs Appleby cooling on a corner of the stairs it was natural that they should look over it together. Had they not done so they would certainly have joined the company in the dining-room and shared in the dancing.

The Cumberland Paquet was, however, of surpassing interest. There was a leader about the Emperor of China and the vast sum of money that he had paid to the British (most gratifying to British pride), something about India, and something about the very mild season so that a 'blackbird had been heard in the neighbourhood of Springfield making the neighbouring woods echo with his melodious strains'.

'Poor blackbird,' sighed Miss Keate, whose heart was most tender, 'he must be quite dead by now.'

There was a fascinating advertisement which both ladies, their heads close together, read with absorbed interest, that 'Mrs Taylor begs most respectively to inform the ladies of Ulverston and its vicinity that she has just received an assortment of SIMISTER'S PATENT WOVE STAYS, which are now ready for inspection.

'To those Ladies who have made trial of the Patent Wove Stay comment is unnecessary, but to those Ladies who have not--'

'Have you, my dear?' asked Miss Keate.

'Well, no,' answered Mrs Appleby. 'You see . . .' and then followed five minutes of delightful intimacy.

The real news, however, that kept them glued to the stairs and so made them witness of what followed was a thrilling account of the doings at the Whitehaven Theatre. It was headed: Theatrical Fracas, and it began: 'We stated in the last number of the Paquet that Mrs Paumier, the wife of the Manager of our Theatre, would take her benefit on Friday evening, and expressed the hope that the play-going public of this town would, as they had done on a former occasion, give her a bumper.' Unfortunately the bumper was prevented because, just before the rise of the curtain, the rest of the company struck for higher wages, the audience grew restive at the delay, and 'some sharp words passed between Mrs Paumier and the performers'. Something very like a riot followed. There was in another part of the Paquet a public statement: 'indeed Mr and Mrs Paumier seemed in universal trouble'.

'Why, just listen!' murmured Miss Keate, and she read to her companion:

'It being currently reported that Mr Gilfillan has signified to all persons visiting his wife for beneficial purposes, that he has received from Mr Paumier little or nothing on account of his (Mr Gilfillan's) services at the Theatre, Mr Paumier deems it his duty to publish the following receipt bearing Mr Gilfillan's signature, in order that his (Mr Paumier's) character may in some measure be redeemed until a full and printed statement of his outlay shall be given.'

'Well, did you ever?' said Miss Keate. 'Actors and actresses! What a life they lead! Quite another world from ours! Living on the edge of a volcano. I dare say if the truth were known--'

Miss Keate always afterwards said that it was at this moment (she would remember the name of the Paumiers, she said, so long as she lived) that she had the strangest premonition that something dreadful was about to happen. There was certainly no reason for any premonition, for a more perfect Christmas scene could not be imagined. Everyone now was dancing and the screech of the violin could be heard through the closed doors. Both hall and parlour were deserted; the ladies had only the mistletoe and holly for cheerful company.

But Miss Keate would for ever swear that she had her premonition. She put up her head, caught Mrs Appleby's hand, dropping the Paquet, and listened. Immediately after there came a terrific banging at the house-door. You would have thought that everyone within a mile would have heard it, but the door of the dining-room was closed and inside the room the music, the laughter, the tramp of feet as the country dances went their way made it a world enclosed.

Miss Keate and Mrs Appleby sprang to their feet; after a short interval the knocking was repeated and now more violently than before. Soon a maid came to the door, hesitated and then, as the knocking was renewed a third time, opened it. It was then that the two ladies knew the sensation of their lives, for with the open door the wind, carrying with it a flurry of snow, blew into the hall, set the mistletoe rocking; with the wind came a man. The ladies did not, in the first moment, see who it was, for his riding-coat blew about his face, but a second after he looked up and about, stared at the ladies, and they instantly recognized him. It was Mr Walter Herries.

The door banged behind him, and he stood there, his bulk filling the hall, his face red and angry. The little maid did not know what to do, nor for the matter of that did the two ladies either. Then he cried out in a voice like a bull's:

'I've come for my daughter!'

Miss Keate was very good, in after years, as she pictured the scene. She had a sense of the dramatic. She described the holly and mistletoe, the sound of music and dancing, the frightened eyes of the maid, and then, about Mr Herries, she would say:

'Oh, you never saw a more enraged man! His face was crimson. You could conceive him bursting. You would have supposed that he would pull the house down. Clara Appleby trembled all over; I had to place my arm around her to steady her or she would have fainted, I am sure.'

There is something absurd, of course, in a man roaring out that he wanted his daughter, and Miss Keate, who had quite a satiric turn when she liked, saw that clearly:

'He was standing right under the mistletoe. Too absurd when you come to think of it!'

He said no more, but stood there waiting. The maidservant went to the dining-room and returned, an instant later, with Judith. THAT was a moment for the two ladies--a very great moment indeed.

'Madame,' Miss Keate would afterwards relate, 'must have known whom to expect. She came out to him like the Queen of England and she said, in a voice as clear as a bell and as though it were the most ordinary thing in the world, "Well, Walter? Good evening. And what can I do for you?"

'"Do for me! You can fetch me my daughter and be damned to the lot of you!"

'"Yes--we had better discuss it in here, I think."'

To the exquisite disappointment of the two ladies Judith and Walter vanished into the parlour. Miss Keate always afterwards said that from the very beginning Judith Paris appeared to have some power over the man. The two ladies stood there staring, and listening with all their ears. For some while there was little to hear or see. A maid knocked on the parlour door. Then the dining-room door opened, throwing into the hall a burst of music and gaiety, and out came John and Elizabeth. They had been given some message. They hesitated in the hall, then, hand in hand, went into the parlour, closing the door behind them. For a while again there was silence, and then--

But Miss Keate was never to know what exactly occurred INSIDE the parlour.

And what occurred was this:

'Sit down, Walter,' said Judith, when they were both inside. He stood just by the door, glowering at her, his head thrust a little forward. Judith saw that he had been drinking, that he had a smear of mud on his chin, and that he held, in one gloved hand, a riding-whip. The room was in complete confusion, the carpet turned up, a chair on its side, holly dripping over the mantelpiece, a lady's ribbon on the ground, a lace handkerchief.

'Sit down, Walter, pray,' said Judith. 'And tell me why--'

'You know why,' he answered, his eyes shifting up and down the room. She sat on the sofa and twirled a large white feather fan in her fingers. Her ivory cane (which she was not at all sure she might not have to make use of before the end of the interview) rested near her.

'Indeed I do not, Cousin Walter.'

He came nearer to her.

'I warned you. I told you that you could go too far. Too far! By God, you've always gone too far!'

He was, she supposed, about fifty years of age and he looked sixty with the heavy black pouches under his eyes, the purple veins in cheeks and nose. Oddly, the strain of liking that, in spite of all that he had done, she had always had for him, still, she discovered, survived. Poor Walter! What a mess he had made of everything!

'I have come for my daughter.'

'Elizabeth? Certainly you shall see her.'

'She returns with me to Ireby tonight.'

Judith looked at him impatiently.

'But, Walter, that is absurd. She is no longer a child. She is a married woman.'

'We can soon stop THAT marriage. It shall be dissolved. She was married by force.'

'Indeed she was not!' answered Judith indignantly. 'If ever anyone married freely she did. The marriage has been the greatest success.'

She was listening with all her ears. At any moment dancing revellers might break from the dining-room into the hall and the parlour. She had seen Miss Keate and Mrs Appleby on the stairs. She was determined to finish this scene as quickly as possible.

'It has, has it?' said Walter, coming yet closer to her.

She saw that he was in a confused drunken rage, uncertain as to what he would do or say but determined to assert his power.

'And I know who contrived that marriage. It was you, my fine lady. It has been a long battle between us. You think I forget, but I forget nothing. Do you remember how I whipped your naked little bastard up at Hawkshead years ago? Well, I'd whip him again--'

'It is Elizabeth that we are speaking about,' Judith answered quietly.

He paused to pull himself together. Word slipped from word, sentence from sentence. There was a fog in his brain.

'I demand to see my daughter,' he muttered.

'Certainly you shall,' she answered briskly, pulling the bell at her side.

He was swaying a little on his feet.

'Why don't you sit down, Cousin Walter?' she asked him again. 'You don't look at all well.'

'I am in perfect health,' he answered furiously. 'Never better.'

'And Uhland?' she asked politely.

But this politeness bewildered him. He shook his whip at her.

'Look here, Judith!' he said. 'You're damned clever. You always were. But you don't get round me this way. Do you hear? You can't abduct my daughter from under my nose and I have nothing to say. No, I'm damned if you can. And then marry her to that young swine . . . I always swore that I'd finish him, and by

God I will. The whole lot of you. Rude to my mother, was she? I told her she'd repent it.'

He was referring now apparently to Jennifer, and a picture rose before Judith of that poor bewildered lady walking in her black dress across the fields.

The maid appeared.

'Please tell Mr John and Mrs Herries to come to me here immediately.'

She turned to Walter.

'Now, Walter, pray let us have no scenes. These are old, old quarrels that should have been long ago buried. Elizabeth is a sweet girl. She and John are devoted. What else is there left to build enmity upon? I am sure that you are not angry with me. You never were. And, although you have behaved badly once and again, I forgive you everything. Now let us be friends--'

John and Elizabeth entered the room. Inside the door they released hands and Elizabeth came forward, her head up. She held out her hand.

'She was the loveliest creature,' Judith afterwards said, 'I ever saw. There were roses all over her silk skirt, roses in her cheeks. Her curls were untidy with her dancing and she had the face of an angel. Any father would have been moved by it.'

Walter, however, was not moved. He disregarded her hand and, swaying on his heavy feet, said: 'You are to come back with me.'

She looked round at John for a moment, then smiling said:

'But I am married, Father.'

She, who had been afraid of him all her life, had no fear at all.

Then he began to storm.

'You shall obey your father, do you hear? It was no marriage. You're not married to him. You disobedient . . . disobedient . . .' He began to choke and he put his hand to his throat. He continued to look past Elizabeth to John; all his great body was increasingly agitated. Judith rose from the sofa and went up to him, putting her hand on his arm.

'Walter, this is absurd. You must see that it is. John and Elizabeth are married and have been for a long while. And why not? They love one another, and John has a fine position in London. You don't know him. You've scarcely ever seen him. All your silly hatred is built up upon nothing. Now make the best of it. Shake hands with them . . .'

But he had not been listening to her at all and, suddenly, he rushed forward catching John by the shoulder with one hand, raising the whip with the other.

'You damned puppy! I'll teach you a lesson. I'll teach you a lesson. I'll kill you for stealing my daughter. Steal my daughter, will you? I'll teach you.'

He raised his arm and, clawing John's collar, slashed at him with the whip. No one but Elizabeth saw that in that moment John turned white as the mistletoe berries above them, or that, at Walter's touch, his body seemed to collapse as though his bones had melted. She saw that and, knowing John's courage, realized even at that moment of touch that there was some additional horror here, something old and inborn, quite beyond physical terms.

But it was Judith who had the centre of the stage. Walter's touch on John seemed to swing her into one of those old rages of hers that had for long now been disciplined, for she rushed and threw herself on Walter with so much vehemence that the surprise of it tumbled him forward. She caught his arm and, small though she was, swung him right round and then slapped his face as though she were tearing paper. The whip fell; Walter put up his hand to his cheek and stood there staring.

'You dare! You dirty bully! You come into MY house again! You blackguard! I'll show you where you are in MY house. Go! . . . There's the door! You show your face again! You dare! You . . .'

She stamped her foot; she raged like a fishwife, glaring into him as though she would tear his nose out of his face.

He turned, bent half down as though he would pick up the whip, but let it lie there.

'Pick it up! Pick it up!' she stormed. 'I won't have any of your filthy things in MY house! Christmas Day too! Where are your feelings? Where's your decency? Never you dare to set your foot . . .'

He picked up the whip, stared at her still in a dazzled, confused fashion, muttered something, fumbled for the door.

As he opened it they were all suddenly aware of social conventions; they heard, with an immediate pressing clarity, the murmur of the music and the dancing feet. They all three followed him into the hall.

Judith herself opened the big door for him and stood there, with John just behind her, while the snow whirled in the wind that blew the light over the porch.

'Goodnight, Walter . . . Goodnight,' Judith said.

Miss Keate saw him go out, his head down. 'As though she'd whipped him,' she always ended her story.

Elizabeth went to John, putting her arm through his; the dining-room door opened and someone ran out.

'John! Elizabeth! You must come for "Sir Roger".'

'Don't mind, John. Don't mind,' Elizabeth whispered. She was beginning a new relation with him from that moment.

But he whispered back: 'There was Uhland there-- standing in the porch under the light.'

She didn't hear. She pressed his arm with her hand. 'It's nothing,' she said again. 'I have finished with my father for ever.'

But John stared at the door. It was not Walter Herries but Uhland that he was seeing.

END OF PART II

483

Part Three

Cumberland Chase

IREBY, January 5th, 1843

Finished tonight that stuff-and-nonsense book Carlyle's Heroes. Wonder that I had the patience to read it on to the end, but I fancy that I was always going further to see whether all his tall words and German sentences would lead to anything. They do not any more than does this damnably silly Journal of mine. There is just this difference. Carlyle is a hypocrite and I am not. He knows he is no hero but says he is one--I know that I can be a hero as suitably as any of his Fredericks and Cromwells, but prefer not to be one. And why do I prefer? Because the world is so crammed with fools and conceited coxcombs that it is a finer thing to sit by and watch--to watch, if you like, the decline and fall of the house of Herries and myself with it. Bang--Bang--Bang--Whiskers--Whiskers-- Whiskers. This is nothing but the sound a blind man makes seeing himself to bed with the light of a thick stick and the smell of the candle-end. And it is also, if you like, the noise that my beloved father and Sam Osmaston are making just under this floor of my room, both as drunk as cockchafers in lamplight, on their knees most likely, searching for a goose's feather.

But this Journal is supposed to say what I do. Well, what do I do? Get up, you lamentable cripple, and look at yourself in the glass, examine once again your ugly wry face, your ribs, like an old mans' counting-board, and your white bit of twisted bone politely called a leg. Good, good! That's the thing, my boy! That's the way to bring your conceit down and sit on the floor to talk about Heroes. But the soul's the thing, is it not? Does not old Carlyle say so? The soul! The soul! Where may you be, soul? Stuck in that leg of mine? Hiding like a rabbit behind a rib or two? Well, come out for once! Let's have a look at you! Where are you, green, crimson or mulberry; and your shape? Are you

tortoise-like with a shell like a snuff-box, or thin and spidery, catching flies for your food, or just a pincushion with pink lace and a blue silk bow?

What a week I've had too!

They've all been here. The Newmarks with all their brood, Phyllis a female Alderman, Newmark the prize prig of the market, Horace as long in the leg as a pair of stilts and as wooden, DEAR little Emily and DEAR little Barnabas. All with the latest news of my good grandfather's new offspring. 'Oh, WHAT a sweet infant! the dearest little boy!' until I thought my father would throttle the lot of them. Amery Herries too with eyes like gooseberries, the merriest drunken bachelor, and old Rodney from Polchester, sixty if he's a day, touring the Lakes and Scotland with one eye on his clerical dignity and the other on the destiny of every halfpenny! Lord, how I hate the lot of them and how they hate me! Didn't I make little Emily cry by blowing out the candle, and isn't old Rodney afraid of my humours? A family sinking to rot, my masters, cursed because, between too much money-bag on the one side and too much indecisive dreaming on the other, the way to Salvation is missed every time. Not that there IS any Salvation, even though you search for it. Nothing but madness or death from over-eating whichever way you go.

But now when the house is silent and every stone in this building can be heard scraping its reproaches, I wonder at my indignation. Indignant? No, I have not blood enough for so bold a word. I sit here, sneezing, rubbing my knees the one against the other, healing Rob's ear in the basket, raising my perpetual theme of hatred of my dear John brother-in-law and do nothing, positively nothing. Neither lust urges me nor greed nor envy nor desire for knowledge: only if I had John's neck here I would twist it until his eyes were in his back, and even that is a fancy--nurtured lust, something bred of years of coddling. It HAD a reason once and now I've fed my brain with so many centuries of imagination that to see him tortured in my fancy is as good as the actual deed.

And yet it could have been otherwise. Only this stupid mutton- faced Journal shall know how otherwise it might have been! Another father, flat-faced Adam for a brother and a pair of legs like anyone's, and I had the power, the wish, the ambition. I could have written a book or two, I fancy, better than Bulwer at any rate, or played in a laboratory and made a discovery, or talked as wittily as any Disraeli or Palmerston of them all. I have more brains in my toenail (those on the withered foot have an especial brilliancy) than all my Herries cousins lumped together. But from the very first I was outcast. THAT at least is no imagination. I make no claim for it and I ask for no pity, but to be different from birth, to have the street children mock at you and the dogs bark, and visitors to the house look the other way--it is a kind of allowance for hatred. They say Carlyle has dyspepsia and yet he thinks himself a Hero. Well, am I not a Hero that I sit here and think, and think, and wish myself a villain? And my father still loves me. He thinks me a miracle of brilliance and perversity. All that is left to him, poor man, for his brain is fuddled with drink, the ladies won't call, his fine house is a stony desert, and they flourish at Uldale like the righteous!

Ah! there's the rub! Cousin Judith as lively as a flea, Cousin Dorothy and her children fat as good cattle, John and Elizabeth like sucking-doves. There! He is singing. I can hear him under the floor. And Sam Osmaston with him--a fine out-of-tune chorus . . .

Ireby, November 13th, 1843

Rob's ear has this canker again. It's his perversity, I well believe, for he knows truly that once his ear is well, out he'll go, to be stoned by the Keswick boys again, I suppose. And the odd thing is, I shan't care. He's been with me almost a year now. I enjoy his face like the parson's, with its side-whiskers and a slobbery white patch like spilt milk on his nose. He's fonder of me than any dog's ever been, but I hate that sycophancy. I'm near shooting him at times or hanging him from the beam with a rope-- yes, even while I wash and clean his ear with the tenderness of a woman.

And now what do you think, O my Journal? What has our dear father done but buy a piece of the moor just above Uldale and build a small cottage on it and into that shove Peach and his dirty brood. There is just one patch, it seems, that great-grandfather David neglected to buy, a measly brown bit that even the sheep neglect. He has done it to vex Aunt Judith of course, and vex her it must to have the filthy little Peaches at her garden gate, and Peach at war with her drunken Rackstraw.

Since she scratched dear father's cheeks last Christmas-time he's been all bent on vexing her, although in my view he thinks her a damnably fine old woman. So she is! She and Adam--another brood from the rest of them.

November 22nd

I am just back from Rosthwaite where I have been limping about all day like an old woman looking for eggs. But something or someone (Algebraical formula? $x + y = xy^2 = God?$) had put it into my mind of late to be interested in my old Great-great-grandfather, the Rogue. It seems that he spent half his life longing for a gipsy girl (Aunt Judith's mother by oddity) who, when he got her at last, incontinently died. I like the smell of that old man and have picked up a pack of curiosities about him, how he sold a stout mistress at Keswick Fair, was given a scar in a duel, fought for the Pretender outside Carlisle or some such thing, married his gipsy at Rosthwaite and cuffed and kicked the guests down his stairs, how she ran away and he roamed the hills for years looking for her; then, catching her at last, gave her Judith whom she died of. There is something deeply sympathetic to me here, for he was outcast as I am, a rebel as I, if I had the guts, would be, a hater too, I fancy, only he would not play Hamlet by the year as I have done.

His old house is a ruin, some tumbled barns swallowed in weed and swiftly vanishing. I sat on some broken mouldy stairs this afternoon and could have sworn to seeing the old fellow watching me ironically. It's his irony I like the taste of. None of the Herries have irony save Aunt Judith. I would like a picture of him, but father says there is none; however, an old cottager well over ninety years with whom I talked today--a lively cursing old man with no teeth, so that he must hiss like a snake when he talks, but his hearing is mighty sharp--he remembers him, how he came striding over the little bridge by Rosthwaite, in a plum-coloured coat with a scar down his cheek, and how he and his gipsy lay both dead in the house together and an old man rode up on a horse and carried the new-born child (Judith, by all that's comic) away on his horse with him. The only man of our family with whom I have any touch, and he dead these seventy years! Grandfather Will must remember him. Next time in London I shall harry his wits over him . . .

I am planning a long London visit. This house is the devil. It is colder than any crypt, and the stone, cover it as you may, breaks through and snarls at you. Every wind in the country whips it and the trees moan like kitchen-maids with the toothache. Also I have the ambition to touch up Cousin John a trifle. I could look in at his window and give him a queasy stomach. What is this hatred? Contempt of his mealy-mouthed propriety? Rage at his impertinent marriage with my sister? Jealousy of his strength and whole limbs? Something taught to me in my cradle by my father? Yes, and more than all this. I hate him because I have always done so, because of what he is and because he is happy and I am not. These are honest reasons, but behind these there is the pleasure of the pursuit. As my old roguish ancestor pursued his gipsy so I pursue my John. We freaks in the Herries stock must have our revenge on the normal ones; there is a warfare there that has necessity in it. And I have no other emotions. I have never lusted after a woman in all my days, nor cared for a human being save Adam. Is that my own fault? I could have asked for quite another destiny, but I had no say in it. So, to my only pleasure, to see him start at the sound of my step and flinch under my hand. My leg aches in sympathy.

12 Granger Street, London February 12th, 1844

Three weeks in London. What a folly! Dinner at Richmond or Blackwall, the Cave of Harmony, the Coal Hole and such; the inner sanctities of Meadows' and 'Seven's the main' of the caster, and 'Gentlemen, make your game' of the groom-porter. Cards everywhere and, even without the perils of lansquenet, with a pony on the rubber, five pound points and betting on the odd trick, you are caught before you are hooked. There is scarcely a quiet respectable house in all London where they won't rook you if you give them half a chance.

All the same there's a strange curtain of hypocritical respectability over this town since my last visit. They say it is our good little Queen and our handsome German Prince. No nonsense at Court, they say. All heading now for the Virtues.

Last night a party at my grandfather's where, if you please, we sat round in a circle and a woman with teeth like a grinning hag's read us the poems of Mr Tennyson. Poor old grandfather would have slumbered happily in his corner had not Mrs Will in a pink dress with 'volants' almost up to her waist (and there must have been at least eight rows of them) pinched him after every melancholy verse. She had time too for elegant flirtation with a fat young man whose whiskers were as long as a horse's mane! I have never disliked anyone more and her loathing of myself is badly concealed by her extreme endearments. She was frightened of me, I believe and hope. But I perceive that I throw a gloom on to every party that I encounter. All the better. This London is a meeting-place of all the snobs, hypocrites, sharps and idiots of Christendom.

But I remain, for I have my own quiet amusements. One of these is the clearing of Cousin Garth's pockets, for such a juggins at cards deserves clearing.

Another is to listen to the bombast of old James or Carey who both have the fancy that THEIR England (THEIRS, mark you) is the most Christian and at the same time the most commercial miracle that this weary planet has ever beheld! To hear them talk of old Pam or of Peel you would fancy that we had no Chartists nor starving populace whatever, and to listen to their con-

tempt of ANY foreign country is to realize to the full ONE side of the beautiful Herries shield!

I listen and then with one remark blow their soap-bubbles to air-- and don't they hate me for it too! It is worth the boredom of London to see old James flush his double-chin and stutter: 'But, my dear sir--my DEAR young friend . . .'

I have a deeper pleasure than these mild amusements, though. I have discovered Cousin John's hours: he leaves Bryanston Square five of an evening and for the good of his precious health walks across the Park. Thrice a week at least I see to it that he shall encounter me. We never speak; indeed one glimpse of me is enough to destroy his peace for the rest of the day. He would take a cab were it not that he fights his cowardice, and it has happened twice that when he has taken one I have followed him in another, coming from mine as he issues from his. This game gives me a wild and sensual pleasure. There are certain streets and houses that are marked with the colour of our meetings. Best of all I learnt from Sylvia Herries last week that he and Elizabeth would be at the theatre. They had a box and I in the pit enjoyed my evening to the full. At every meeting it seems to me that we come closer together even as my father grows closer to Uldale. I am contented to bide my time, for there is no pleasure for me in life like this chase. Is this madness? It may be that it is, for it seems to me that I am now two persons and when the one is not with him the other is. I sleep but little and walk the streets at night, hearing my own step in pursuit of myself, that same halting stumble that must, I know, haunt the bowels of Cousin John. I would swear that last night, dressing for grandfather's party, I saw two figures in the mirror and neither shadowy . . .

March 13th

I have had an encounter that has moved me oddly. Yesterday afternoon in the Strand I walked straight into Adam. He was brown and ruddy and sturdy, dressed roughly, books under his arm, his eyes serious and kindly as they ever were. May the Devil forgive me, but I was pleased to see him. Our talk was thus:

'Why, Adam!'

'Why, Uhland!'

'Are you well?'

'And you?'

His hand was on my arm and I felt, for a foolish minute, that I would have followed him anywhere. He is the only one in the world not to glance at my leg, to be perfectly at ease with me, to give me some glimpse of a normal world where men are honest and mean their words. Yet I doubt not he is a prig and thinks highly of his own virtues. Yet he was kind without hypocrisy. He asked me to visit them and he meant it, I think. But I turned away. I could have struck him for moving me as he did. I could have struck him, but I looked back after him as though I were letting my best chance go. He is still on my mind today. He has given me his address and I have half an impulse to visit him. But for what? I should but despise his amiability and suspect his seriousness. There is no place where we can move side by side and I do not know that I wish that there should be.

Ireby, April 7th, 1845

I am so much better that I can at last get to my Journal again. Not that I hunger for it, but it is at least a testimony to some energy. And today has been a day as warm as milk and so still that you can hear the cows munching. There was all morning a mist like thick honey with the light breathing behind it a glorious exultant spirit. The sun has been dim all day and Blencathra and Skiddaw have been like whales, unicorns, blankets of soft down, and this afternoon when the sun came fully out and the air was blue they rolled over in delight as puppies do when, deliciously expectant, they want their stomachs stroked. It is not like me to write of the weather, but I have been ill for so long and have smelt nothing but candle-ends, slops and the horsey grain of my blankets.

Last evening I had an odd talk with my father that needs recording. He came in wobbling a candle, in a bed-gown, his chest exposed, but in spite of this very sober. I have been dimly conscious of him the last months, coming in and out of my fantasies. And WHAT fantasies! Myself hanging, bare save for a thin shift, from a beam, my toes turned in, and my second self exuding like milk from an udder out of my left ear-- and I was Grandfather Will's infant, guzzling at a bottle and clutching a money-bag, and the room was on fire and myself in the middle of it frying like an acorn, or I hobbled on Stye Head, the mists chasing me until I fell headlong into Eskdale, and once a white horse, flashing up a frozen mountainside, caught me with its teeth and flung me down into ice. In and out of this, then, has come my good father, but only last evening did we have any serious conversation.

He tells me that he has not had a drop of liquor for the last six months, during my illness. And I can believe him. For once he does not look more than his fifty odd years. His fat is dropped from him--yes, and his spirits have gone too. He is a little crazed, I think, as I am. This house has the seeds of craziness in its bones. For he says that Aunt Judith has poisoned me, some insane story about her bribing the cook to spoil my food! There's real craziness as I told him, for whatever that old lady may be about it will never be poisoning. He tells me, however, that Rackstraw whipped one of the Peach children within an inch of its existence for stealing out of the Uldale kitchen window and that one of the Uldale barns has been set on fire. He wants to have Aunt Judith in jail, but I tell him that the countryside would burn the jail down to get her out.

When all this loose talk of revenge and the rest had died away he besought me not to leave him. He has a fear, it seems, that I shall steal away just as Elizabeth did. He moved me for he loves me with the strongest mingling of pride, fear and egotism. God knows I don't want his love. I have no regard for him except that it seems to me we are caught in the same trap. My illness has left my head clear and empty. I am imprisoned and cannot be free until some act frees me. Death, perhaps, of which I have no fear. But death liberates only one of myself. The other remains imprisoned.

My father held my body in his arms. How lonely and isolated an act! No one has ever held me close to their breast since I was an infant, and my father is not a man of sentiment, but he sees everything else going-- health, reputation, wealth--save his love for me and his hatred of the Uldale lot. I tell you we Herries are lost men if we let our dreams go too far, be they good or bad, and this old folly of hating one another is a dream like the rest, for there is no satisfaction to be found in any egoistic desire. I can see that we are intended to lose ourselves altogether in something impersonal, and once Cousin John, the pretty, were gone I could be lost, I fancy, turning with what relief into the thick honeyed air like a child loosed from school . . . But what a couple the two of us, my gross father straining my bony wasted fretfulness against his bare chest, and our eyes refusing to meet! And myself, round the corner, peering and grinning at the idiocy of the scene from behind the wardrobe.

When he kissed me I shrank into my twitching leg and he felt me shrink and for once I hated my unkindness. He is a very simple man, my father. He meant this Fortress to be a great symbol of Herries power--just as Cousin James and Rodney and Grandfather and Amery are building up their fine Victorian England--but to lay stone upon stone is not enough. That is a thing that the building Herries have never understood. I do not believe in God but I do not think that you can build anything without Him.

My father wishes me to take my proper place here when I am recovered. He is reformed, he says--no more the rake. We will attend to farms and property. Yes, but no Herries has ever wanted to accumulate property. We do not care for it enough. We think too much of ourselves and will not yield our personal conceit to anything, not even to property.

And we must get Aunt Judith out of Uldale, he says. And we must make this house warm, he says. It is always so devilish cold. He does not know that there is a rat eating away the foundations. And, when all is said, he loves me like a dog, not knowing why, and I care for nothing and nobody, not I. It is something though to see the gold light again lying evenly over the hills and to hear the stream running down the hill. I have grown, during my illness, a pale forked beard. I look, in the glass, like a green radish.

487

London, January 14th, 1846

Yesterday I had a half-hour of sanity that is worth recording. I spent it with Grandfather Will. He requested me to pay him a visit. Why? Even now I do not know. Some intention perhaps of compensation because he has thrown my father and myself aside for ever and young Ellis reigns in our stead. (Why Ellis? A dreary, dry-as-dust, left-over-from-yesterday pantry kind of name, but its mother has rich cousins thusly.) Nor do I blame him for that. We are not a pair to be proud of, I suppose. And so I went. Appalling that house in Hill Street. No rain-washed air sweeping Blencathra here, but furniture spawning everywhere, masses of it, heavy and despondent, groaning between thick rep and treading down the thick Turkey. There are pallid sightless statues and old Herries gilt-edged on every wall. I was alone in a vast room with my grandfather, and we crept together for safety. 'Keepsakes' were our only company. But I am modern for my time. I am a hundred years hence. I am sickly with the odour of 1950. He is bent now, his hair white, his clothes fitting him, black and stiff, as though they were made in a Bank. But in his old age he is kind and eager. I should judge that this baby is the only human soul for whom he has ever cared, although he spoke of Elizabeth's beauty and seeing her alone in this room one day in the past 'like a vision'. He meant, I fancy, that it could not be true that she was my sister. He thinks me misshapen and dangerous and cannot understand that I should be descended from his loins. Something has gone wrong somewhere and he is bewildered because he has always done the sensible thing. But he intended to be kind, sat close to me although I made him creep, and by not looking at my twitching leg he only looked the more intently. He asked me how I did. He had heard that I had been ill. He feared that he would never see Cumberland again although in his youth he had seen eagles sailing over Glaramara. He has a trick of fingering his coat-buttons as though they were counting-house money. He wanted me to tell him something. But what? That things have not turned out as they should do, his brother Francis a suicide, his son a drunken fool, his grandson a deformity? Well, there is little Ellis, and I see as though under glass his heart beat up again and his old eyes, weary with gazing on figures, open out at the new hope. Then he is proud of England. It is as though he had made it, put a hump on Skiddaw here, added a tomb to Westminster, straightened the Strand, bidden the sea halt in Norfolk, and run the railway to Newcastle. He is tired, he explains to me, and then with great courage lays his hot bony hand on mine.

'For I am seventy-five,' he tells me, 'and have worked hard all my days.'

He hopes that we are all now reconciled, for there was once a silly quarrel. Something about a fan. His wife, 'your grandmother,' was concerned. But that is all so old, so very very long ago, and he hopes that now all is well. Do I see Judith Paris often? A remarkable woman with much spirit and character. And I think of the little Peach children setting a match to Aunt Judith's parlour, and Aunt Judith slapping my father's face.

But he hopes that all is well. We must be friends, all of us. Our family must stand together. They mean something to England. He talks of Palmerston and Peel and the Corn Law crisis and says the 'rotten potatoes have done it,' and how angry the Duke is and that Melbourne told the Queen 'that it was a damned dishonest act,' and that John Russell has come out of it all 'damned poorly', but they are all dim figures to him now. Ellis aged three has swallowed up the firmament. He has a little rheumatism in his legs, he tells me, but otherwise he is well enough, and so he pulls himself up and slowly, slowly, very stiff and straight, stamps from the room. And I go down into the street to meet my waiting double . . .

Ireby, October 9th, 1846

I have seen the 'Barguest'. I am a haunted man. I was lost yesterday afternoon in the wilds between Blencathra and Skiddaw, Skiddaw Forest way. I do not know where exactly I was. I could not find the same place again. I had plunged upward, limping and running and limping again in my own ridiculous fashion, treading down the dried bracken that in certain lights has almost a glow of fire running through it. I had looked back and seen Ireby with its stone turrets, its frowning eyebrow, squat like a discontented image staring down at Uldale. I looked forward and the rocks closed me in. They have that fashion here. They move forward of their own will; you can see them almost scratching their craggy sides. A moment before there had been the long swinging slope of bracken, fields below marked off and smelling rain, the stone wall running straight up into air, a round tufted tree holding the light, cottages and farms--and now only this pressing crowding observant rock, the ridge of the hill black against the October sky save for some little white clouds that like spies crowded to the ridge and looked over down into the amphitheatre. I am noting it down thus minutely because of what then occurred.

I seemed to be able to move neither up nor down; my leg limits me and I felt as though the slope of rock on which I was standing would slide down with me--maliciously, while the rocks round me shook with laughter. And then I saw the Barguest. An old man shaped like a whale-bone. He came along towards me on his hands and knees, and once and again he would stop, stare at me, and bite his long fingernails. But I could see through him; he swayed like water-mist, was at one time so hazily defined that there were wisps of him like clouds about the rock, then so sharp that I could count every button. It was no imagination--or I am mad perhaps with want of sleep. I stayed transfixed, and he came right up to me. I could smell his breath, an odour of mushroom and sodden leaves. He touched me with his long yellow fingernail and then dispersed into vapour. I know this is so. It is no dream and, if I am crazy, which for some months now I have suspected, what is reality? But I am sure that I shall see this place again and at some fatal time. When the Barguest had vanished I climbed a stone and all the scenery was restored again, the fields green in the October sun, and rain-clouds gathering up above the sea.

WAX FLOWERS AND THE REVOLUTION

Adam tried, with all the self-control that belonged to his training, to forget what the day after tomorrow meant to him, but, try as he would, again and again something repeated inside himself: The day after tomorrow . . . The day after tomorrow. Everything hangs on Monday, my whole life . . . everything I've worked for.'

Margaret, in a brown bonnet, hanging on his arm, caught sight of the magnificent Beadle, whiskered, gold-laced, standing superbly at the door of the Pantheon Bazaar.

'Oh, let us go into the Pantheon . . . I can find something there for poor little Daisy Bain, whose foot was crushed by that wagon last week. It won't occupy us a minute. Do you mind, Adam?'

They were both making a sublime attempt at proving that nothing was toward. Today was like any other day. And yet, with how many thousands around them, they were, it might be, on the eve of a new era, a new world, a world of light, justice and brotherhood. All London was making preparation for Monday's great Chartist rising. All clerks and officials were ordered to be sworn garrisons. Every gentleman in London was become a constable. (What a very grand carriage outside the Princess Theatre, and what a hideous befrilled Pug in the window!)

After all, what an incredible year! In the month of March alone fearful street fighting in Berlin, flight of the Prince of Prussia, riots in Vienna and Milan, Hungary in revolt, revolution in Austria, and, above all, France tumbling either into a chaos of disaster or a triumph of a new grand order!

And on Monday--Monday, April 10th, 1848--England too might see the turning-point of all her history. But Margaret had always a child-like desire for pleasure, and Adam was, nowadays, a great deal more easily pleased than he had once been. They had walked out into the mild spring air that they might quiet some of their almost trembling agitation. How odd it was to see the bird-stuffer's shop with the birds of paradise and parrots, crimson and gold and violent green, a statuary shop, with Canova's Graces, the staymaker's, the fitter's

shop with the little cork ball bounding up and down on the perpendicular jet of water, the provision shop with the Durham mustard, the Abernethy biscuits, Iceland moss, Narbonne honey, Bologna sausages--these and many many more, and to think that in another two days all these splendours might be at the mercy of the mob, that the poor might have their wrongs righted, the just come to their own . . . It must be truthfully added that any stranger seeing Adam and Margaret as they passed the bowing Beadle at the Pantheon door would have been astonished indeed at such revolutionary sentiments, for never did a pair look more respectable and kindly--Adam, set and solid, with his dark side-whiskers, his handsome high hat and gentlemanly cravat, and Margaret in her brown bonnet and overjacket of white embroidered muslin. Revolutionaries? Surely not this respectable pair!

In fact they did forget for ten minutes inside the Pantheon that they WERE revolutionaries. Margaret was so happy to be alone with Adam for a little that she forgot all else. Adam was changed since that Christmas at Uldale, more thoughtful, more demonstrative, but he was constantly preoccupied with his work, and their rooms were from morning to night crowded with other people. She did not often have him to herself. She was so happy that it had been HIS suggestion that they should take this walk! He did not often suggest that they should go off somewhere alone. She sometimes almost wished that there WAS no Charter, that that flamboyant boastful Feargus O'Connor had never been heard of, that she and Adam and her father need not so continually be considering the wrongs of other people! And the Pantheon, when they were inside it, was enchanting! First they went up to the gallery where they might look down on that exciting coloured maze of babbling children, beautiful ladies, attendant footmen and subservient shopmen. Behind them (and they glanced in for a moment) was that queer neglected little picture-gallery with the dusty twentieth-rate pictures and tragic Haydon's enormous spectre-like 'Lazarus' dominating with its fruitless ambition and almost emerging misconceived genius the atmosphere not only of the Pantheon but the street beyond it, the people, the carriages, the houses. Once this was a theatre; here were the Grand Staircase, the Rotunda, the green room, the conservatories, dressing rooms. Here were Ariadne in Naxos, Daphnis and Chloe, Bellerophon, The Cruelty of Nero. Old Will, a stiff prosperous conceited young man of the City, must here have applauded and Christabel feebly clapped her gloved hands and old Carey have slumbered! Even the lovely radiant Jennifer, with her proud parents, must here have been the beauty of the evening. Judith's Georges must have looked in with a companion to observe the legs of the chorus; Guimard danced in a hoop that reached nearly to her ankles. Those were the pigtail days of Duvernay and Ellsler and Taglioni! Here George III's eldest son met the lovely

Perdita, and Charles Fox in a domino shouted a tipsy applause!

A church, a waxwork show, an opera, and then one night, in the middle of Don Giovanni, twelve demons bearing torches of resin rose to seize the guilty hero, and behold there were THIRTEEN demons, one of them carrying TWO torches and disappearing in a flame of real fire while the audience fainted and the manager vanished into a madhouse!

But Margaret and Adam were not thinking of the past: the present and the future were THEIR concern! They were very young--Adam young for his almost thirty-three years, Margaret only twenty- eight. Everything was in front of them.

Before they descended from the gallery Adam turned.

'Margaret, are you happy?'

'Very, Adam.'

'You know that you are everything to me now. Whatever happens on Monday, whatever way things go, nothing can alter that.'

'Yes, I know.'

He kissed her and they went down the stairs like a couple of children. To purchase something for little Daisy Bain was no easy task, for the variety of toys was extraordinary and the young ladies at the stalls so VERY polite and superior. Margaret was always easily dashed by patronage and had she been alone would have fled from those elegant young women in dismay, but Adam confronted them so calmly and with so agreeable a smile that they were ready to do anything for him. There was the monkey on a stick, the serpent made of elastic (a compound of glue and treacle), a centipede at the end of an indiarubber string, and many another; but best of all were the wax flowers. Oh! how lovely they were! Margaret clapped her hands when she saw a whole stall of them! She had no eyes then for the tortoiseshell card-cases, the pink scented invitation cards with 'on dansera' in the corner, the muslin slips, the volumes of polkas with chromo-lithographed frontispieces, the sandalwood fans, the mother-of-pearl paper-knives with coral spring handles--all these could be bought at the Pantheon, but she saw only that blazing bank of colour--crimson, orange, violet, silver-- the flowers smiling from their stalks--carnations, pansies, roses, lilies-of-the-valley, peonies--their wax petals soft and iridescent, as fresh, as vernal as though but a moment ago they had opened their smiling faces to the sun!

'Oh, Adam, are they not marvellous!' she cried. Something then touched his heart, as though he had never truly loved her before and as though he were warned that, without realizing his treasure, it might be, at a moment, lost to him. He would buy the whole store-load for her! Revolutions, tumbling thrones, the rights of the poor, these things fell down before the wax flowers like pasteboard castles!

She chose an assorted bunch--purple pansies, icily white lilies-of- the-valley, a crimson rose.

'They will live for ever!' she said, smiling into his eyes.

They were packed very carefully into a box, and lying on tissue paper looked, Margaret thought, worthy of the Queen.

'They should be kept under glass to preserve them from the dust,' she said.

The stately young woman who served her smiled with an exquisite dignity.

'That is generally considered wise, madam,' she remarked.

'Oh, Adam, how kind you are!' Margaret whispered as they walked away. 'I shall have these all my life long.' Then dropping her voice, looking at him shyly but with a deep intensity: 'I do love you so'.

They passed the refreshment counter and enjoyed, each, an arrowroot cake. Daisy Bain had been quite forgotten, so hurriedly a doll with flaxen hair was purchased for her. They enjoyed the conservatory with the fountain that contained the gold and silver fish, the exotic plants and gay flowers. But it was very hot in the conservatory, and the parrots and cockatoos made an intolerable screeching. One cockatoo, as Margaret could not help observing, strangely resembled Mr Feargus O'Connor and, for a moment, a dread caught at Margaret's heart. What would happen on Monday? Was this their last peaceful day? Would they ever be so happy again? She looked at the box that she carried in her hand and sighed. She held Adam's arm yet more closely as they passed out through the waiting-room where some grand ladies were waiting for their carriages, and so into the light and fresh air of Great Marlborough Street.

On their return home they found themselves in another world. Adam discovered suddenly, looking at the room's disorder, the bottles of beer, the smoke from pipes, books thrown on to the floor, that he wanted to be out of it all, that his enthusiasm was dead, that he did not care what happened on Monday, that there was no Cause any longer. As he saw Margaret moving quietly into the farther room, carrying the box that held her precious wax flowers as carefully as though it were glass, he discovered that with her departure all the light seemed to have gone out of his world. He had reached some new relation with her during that half-hour in the Bazaar. She was more precious to him than ever before.

So with that rather stumbling, halting movement that made him seem short-sighted, but that was only in reality because his thoughts were elsewhere, he turned and took in his company. He saw at once that Henry Lunt held the floor. He would of course in any place where he was. He was in no way different from the day when Adam had first met him, still shabby, black, fierce, denunciatory, self-confident. Adam knew that he was brave and honest, but he knew also that he was narrow-visioned, foolishly impetuous, and that his temper was so violent that it was extremely dangerous. He had been twice gaoled for his share in riots and disorders: this had not made him either wiser or more tolerant. He was more conceited than he had been, thought he knew everything and had all the gifts of leadership; tonight he seemed to Adam a noisy, tiresome demagogue. There were now too many of his sort in the movement, and, in fact, the whole impetus seemed to be slipping away from the Chartists. The Irish potato famine, the Anti-Corn Law League, above all the exciting spectacular troubles in Europe, made the Chartist movement a little old-fashioned. Louis Philippe's fall in February still possessed men's minds to the diminution of all else. After all, people said, bad though things were, they were not as bad as in France. We English are too sensible for Revolutions. We are not of that kind. Adam agreed with them. The Chartists, especially men of Lunt's type, appeared now something foreign and affected.

Undoubtedly everyone in the room this evening felt a little of this. Lunt talked the louder because of it, and, sitting on the edge of the table, swinging his stout legs, harangued Kraft, Pider, and Ben Morris and a young Jew, Solomon, as though he were, with wonderful magnanimity, screwing their courage to the striking-point.

Pider, it seemed, had said something mildly deprecatory before Adam came in, and Lunt was all on fire over it.

'Aye,' he was shouting, 'that's just what I was expecting to hear, Pider. There are too many of your sort about, and that's the truth. Here we are slaving for years back to bring this thing about and at last the moment has arrived. The great, magnificent moment, the climax of all our efforts, and what do you do but--'

'Yes, but,' Pider broke in, 'suppose the moment hasn't arrived after all? Suppose Monday's abortive and there's nothing done? Look at O'Connell!'

'Yes, look at O'Connell!' cried Lunt fiercely, jumping from the table and waving his short arms. 'He's dead, isn't he? And deserved to die. They may have given him a fine funeral in Dublin, but we know what he was, a faint-heart whose courage failed him just when it was needed. Feargus O'Connor's quite another sort of man--'

'I don't know,' said Pider doubtfully. 'I've heard men say of O'Connor--'

'And what have you heard men say of O'Connor?' Lunt shouted. 'There are always men jealous of their leaders, but I tell you that any man who says O'Connor will fail us is lying in his throat, and so I'd tell him to his face. I know O'Connor. I've eaten and slept with him, and a grander, finer leader of men the world doesn't hold! Answer me that, Pider, and tell me that you know

O'Connor better than I do and I'll tell you it's a falsehood.'

Pider, who was not lacking in courage and was in no way afraid of Lunt, started fiercely forward. Kraft came quietly in between them.

'Now, now,' he said, smiling. 'Where's the good of our arguing about what will happen on Monday? Who can say how things will turn? We've done the best we can and must leave the rest to God.'

'God! God!' Lunt shouted fiercely. 'It isn't God we're wanting, but confidence in ourselves. I tell you--'

But Kraft gave a sign to Adam and turned off into a little side-room that he used as a study. Adam followed him and closed the door behind him. He put his arm round Adam and drew him close.

'You look weary,' Adam said.

'Yes, I am weary. Their shouting makes me weary. There are times when I'm sick at heart of the whole thing, times when I wish that I'd never heard of the Cause at all, and had spent my days mending watches or keeping sheep in a field.'

'It's not like you,' Adam said, 'to be down.'

'No, maybe it's not. But tonight I have a kind of foreboding, a sinking of the heart.' He pressed Adam's shoulder. 'What is it, Adam, creeps into all Causes alike, a kind of worm that eats the heart out of them? It's a sort of egotism, I suppose. You grow to think of your own part in it all, to admire your own energy, your fine speeches, to be jealous of others who are praised, to want personal rewards. To be impersonal, to care nothing for yourself, it is the only lesson of life, and no one can learn it!'

'Yes. If there is a lesson!' Adam's dark eyes slowly clouded. 'When you watch the Churches fighting as they are, when you see Jews like Disraeli bringing off their clever fireworks, while you watch a sot like Walter Herries at home trying to frighten women . . . It may be there's no lesson, no plan, no future, no God--'

Kraft shook his head.

'I feel my immortality,' he said. 'I cannot doubt it, but it is perhaps a poor kind of immortality. God MAY be a sort of flash Jew like Disraeli or a dandy like D'Orsay or a storyteller like Charles Dickens or a ranter like Lunt--it may be one long swindle--but it goes on, I KNOW that it goes on.'

'Yes,' Adam continued, nodding his head, 'and emotions like my present love of Margaret. That's no present from a cheap Jew; or walking down by Sour Milk Ghyll on a summer evening when the water is whiter than snow and the hills clouds--D'Orsay couldn't make SUCH a gift to anyone. But this, Caesar, all this that we have been working for for years--I see no New Heaven and New Earth THIS way. Men don't change. Why do they not change, Caesar, that's what I want to know? Why do I not change with all the experience I get? I can remember when I was a tiny boy bathing one evening in a tarn above Hawkshead. My mother was there, and an old fat fellow, my uncle Reuben, a sort of itinerant preacher, who told me stories. He was a wonderful man as I remember--I daresay he was not in reality. He was killed after a riot when they tried to burn Uldale down, set on by Walter Herries. I owe Walter Herries something, you see. But what was I saying? Oh yes--that night. What was I? Four, five? I don't know. We lit a fire under the trees, there was a dog, and Uncle Reuben told me stories. All beauty, all loveliness is in that night as I look back. Not now. Not here. Not then as I knew it. I was happy, of course, but recognized nothing extraordinary. But looking back I see now that there was something divine in that wood that night. Why,' he burst out, laughing, 'there was something divine in Pantheon Bazaar this afternoon. My love for Margaret. Hers for me. Let me recognize it now and offer D'Orsay-Disraeli-Dickens-Jupiter my thanks for it.'

Kraft smiled.

'What has happened to you, Adam? You are usually so silent. Words are pouring from you.'

'I know. I'm living at an extra intensity tonight. As though there were only a thin strip of paper between myself and discovery-- discovery of what? I don't know. D'Orsay's rouge-pots?'

'I know,' Kraft answered quietly. 'I am the same. It is our excitement about Monday, I suppose. A Scotsman would say I am "fey". I can see my shroud, Adam.'

Sunday night he slept so little and woke so early that while it was still dark he slipped from Margaret's side, dressed hurriedly, and went out. He walked through the quiet streets for some while without thinking of his direction, then found that he was in the City. Here it was as cool and silent as an oyster. The wall of the Custom House was a dead wall, the Coal Exchange was sleeping, but soon he was down on the wharfs where life was already active and earnest. Here were tubs smelling of oranges, shops--already opened--packed with salt fish, dried herrings, Yarmouth bloaters, mussels and periwinkles, dried sprats and cured pilchards. For he was in Billingsgate. Here the Billingsgate marketeers were drinking from massive blue and white earthenware mugs filled to the rough brims with coffee; here porters were busied clearing piles of baskets away, putting forms and stools in order, in eager preparation for the fish auction. The wharf is covered with fish, and the great clock of Billingsgate booms forth five o'clock. The stands are laden with salmon, shoals of fresh herring, baskets full of turbot, while the crowds are gathering thickly, and everyone is shouting and crying at once.

Adam watched with increasing pleasure. Close to him a fine fellow stood, a hat tall and shiny as though he were a habitué of Aldridge's Repository, his sporting neckcloth fastened with a horseshoe pin, while round his giant stomach was bound the conventional blue apron; he was wearing galligaskins and straight tight boots of sporting cut. Here were the eight auctioneers; here Bowler's, Bacon's and Simpson's, the noisiest taverns (at this hour) in the whole of London. Now was the excited selling of the 'doubles' and the 'dumbarees'. Fish, fish, fish! Plaice, soles, haddocks, skate, cod, ling . . . Suddenly he recollected. My God, this very afternoon, and the gentleman in the galligaskins and blue apron might find all his occupation gone! By five of the evening of this very day, all the soles and cods and haddocks might swim peacefully in the sea for the attention paid to them! This very street, instead of its stream of fish-scales, bones and dirty water, might be running in blood! Instead of gaiety, laughter, money business, there might be death, ruin, a blaze of fire, smoking catastrophe!

There was a sick dismay at his heart. He had been working for years with an earnestness and eagerness that had possessed every energy he had. He had lost in these years much of the fantasy and humour that had been part of his childhood. At this stage he was grimly serious, taking nothing lightly. At that moment in the Billingsgate Market he saw himself as someone fantastically absurd, working like a labourer at piling brick upon brick, and as he laboured the bricks turned, before his eyes, to straw.

A joke, a farce, iridescent fish-scales floating down the teeming gutter. He hurried home.

This morning, Monday, April 10th, was a lovely day, the sun streaming down with that soft mild radiance that brings a spring scent of flowers into the London streets. The Chartist detachment to which Kraft and Adam belonged moved off very early to Kennington Common. There was no definite procession to the Common; the Procession, presenting the great Petition, was to march at least a hundred thousand strong, under the leadership of Feargus O'Connor, to the Houses of Parliament.

Here the Petition was to be presented, and what would follow after was the question on everybody's lips. Men like Lunt declared that what would follow be the greatest Revolution in England since 1688. But how precisely that Revolution would take place, no one precisely knew. It was true that the Queen and her Consort were not supremely popular, but no one had anyone to propose in their place, and even the Lunts of the movement could not claim that the whole of England was at all ready as yet for a President or a Dictator.

The very troubles that the rest of Europe were battling with made many Englishmen proud of their own passivity.

Nevertheless, a Revolution there would be, some sort of a Revolution. What the average man, both Chartist and non-Chartist, feared was that, simply through ill-directed and undisciplined contact, there would be riot and bloodshed, meaning nothing, leading nowhere; men perceived, from the recent Paris example, that one small unexpected event could lead to vast and unexpected consequences. Let fifty thousand shouting Chartists reach Westminster . . . Why, then, both sides being armed, some horrible catastrophe might take the whole civilized world by surprise. No one in London was happy on that lovely spring morning and, if the truth were known, most certainly not Mr Feargus O'Connor himself, who, in spite of his descent from Irish kings, had no wish to find himself in gaol before the evening.

Neither Adam nor Kraft was happy. They had one last word together before they set out.

'I have the oddest feeling,' Kraft said. 'I dreamt last night, of what I don't know, but I woke saying to myself, "Yes, that's the answer." Now, I know what it all means. I seemed, in that brief dream, to have passed through all experience and to have realized that envy, greed, jealousy, disappointment, lust, bodily sickness-- it was not until I had known them all and tranquilly accepted them all, that I began to live. Tranquility. I tell you, Adam, I am as tranquil this morning as a pond-weed. My anxiety is gone, but my desire too. I cannot imagine what it is that has agitated me so deeply all these years.'

Adam frowned.

'I am not tranquil. I am afraid of what a parcel of fools are likely to do before the day's out.'

It was still very early when the three of them reached the Common. On their way thither they had been impressed by the silence of the town, as of something strongly on its guard. There was little traffic in the streets, very few people about and many of the shops closed. Adam learnt afterwards that many of the important official buildings round Westminster were defended with guns and that Whitehall was in reality an armed camp.

When they arrived at the Common they saw that there was the crowd that had been confidently expected. There were many banners flaunting devices like 'The Charter, the whole Charter, and nothing but the Charter,' 'Justice for All Men and No Favour,' 'Up! Up for O'Connor!' and there were a number of brass bands.

Men, women and children sat and walked about, rather listlessly, dressed, some of them, in their Sunday clothes, while others seemed to boast their poverty. There were many pale, thin, with angry, restless eyes and hungry faces; others appeared to have come to enjoy the sights. There were some booths with food and drinks.

Everything was very quiet, there was a murmur of voices, a sense of expectant waiting as though at any moment a miracle might break out in the sky above their heads.

Soon after their arrival Lunt joined them.

'Not so many as were expected,' Adam said.

'Pooh,' Lunt answered. 'They'll turn up. It will take many of them time to get here. And this is noth-

ing. You wait until the Procession starts for Parliament and see how many join us. You listen to O'Connor when he makes his speech and you'll hear something.'

Soon it happened that everybody began to press together towards the centre of the Common and the crush became uncomfortable; toes were stepped on, umbrellas and sticks poked into innocent faces, women lost their children, and children were crying, pockets were freely picked.

Adam saw that it was towards O'Connor and one or two gentlemen near him that the crowd was thronging, and soon, owing to Kraft's important position in the movement and the badge that he wore, he found that they were enclosed in the magic circle. He was so close to Feargus O'Connor that he could observe him well. A wild theatrical gentleman, he seemed both over-decorated and shabby, for he had on the breast of his blue coat a number of ribbons and medals, but his pantaloons were older than they ought to be and stained with mud. His hair fell in untidy ringlets from under his high hat, and he waved with a great deal of excited gesture the cane that he was carrying. In the other hand he had a stout roll of paper that was supposed by everyone to be the famous Petition. He was, it was clear, excellently conscious of the attention that he was receiving. Once and again he would put up his hand to his rather soiled cravat, the cane would drop to the ground and be obsequiously lifted by someone. He would dart his head up rather as a suspicious hen might do, stare with proud and melancholy indignation at some small boy who, open-mouthed, was gazing at him with all his eyes.

It appeared that he had some reason for indignation, for it seemed that his pocket had been picked. Had anyone ever heard the like? The leader of the country against tyranny and oppression, and his pocket had been picked! How much had there been in his purse? He could not be sure, but a very considerable sum; also a blue silk handkerchief to which he attached sentimental value.

But Adam quickly realized that Mr O'Connor was not at all at his ease. While he talked with an excited and incoherent fervour his eyes were for ever searching the horizon and searching it with a kind of terrified preoccupation as though he expected at any moment to see a large scaly dragon, vomiting fire, issue from the Kennington trees.

He greeted Kraft absent-mindedly and shook a finger with Adam (the rest of his hand clutching the sacred roll of paper) without seeing Adam at all.

He became with every moment more deeply agitated. Beside him was a long, thin, cadaverous man who looked like a Methodist clergyman, and a stout, rubicund fellow like a butcher. There was no sign, however, of any organization or leadership. From time to time someone broke through into the magic circle, whispered mysteriously to O'Connor and vanished again. He on his part would nod his head with great self-importance or shake it or look up to the heavens or wave his cane.

He alluded again and again to the fact that his pocket had been picked, and once and again would burst into a fine frenzy, invoking the Deity: 'My God, have I been chosen to lead these people at this great hour? Have they come to me hungry and shall they not be fed?' Then, dropping his voice: 'What is it, Forster? Has Cummin not arrived? Where is Whitstable? Have they got the thief that has my purse? March to Westminster? But where are the others? This is not the half of them! And my toes trodden on and my pocket picked . . .'

The crowd waited with a most exemplary patience. They were, it seemed, ready to picnic on the Common for the day if necessary. Many of them, Adam was convinced, were not Chartists at all. Many were rogues and vagabonds who had come to gather what they might out of so large a crowd. He saw, as he looked about him, many incongruous figures, here a rather shabby young dandy in pea-green gloves and a shirt embroidered with dahlias and race-horses, then a stout serious-looking gentleman with peg-top trousers, chin-tuft and eye-glass, and close beside him a sturdy fellow who might have come straight from the Billingsgate of the morning, green apron and galligaskins all complete. It could not be said to be a very murderous crowd, and, as Adam looked, his fears of red revolution died away. There would be no revolution here. But for what then all these years had he been working? Not for revolution certainly, but also not for a contented humorous crowd like this. He drew Margaret's arm through his and waited for what might come.

What soon came was an excited stir through the crowd. It whispered like wind through corn. Someone had arrived. Something had occurred. Two men pushed through and spoke to O'Connor; at once his countenance turned red and then white again. He dropped his cane and no one picked it up. He stood, hesitating, his head turning first this way, then that.

The crowd was dividing; it was the Constable, Mr Mayne, followed by three of his inspectors. Mayne, a fine, resolute-looking man, took his stand a little way from Adam, and sent one of his inspectors forward to O'Connor. It was clear that O'Connor was in a terrible fright. 'Afraid of arrest,' whispered Kraft contemptuously to Adam. O'Connor, after a second's hesitation, clutched his cane and roll of paper and went to meet Mr Mayne. The two men made a striking contrast, and in that moment of seeing them together, it seemed to Adam that any alarms or hopes on the part of anyone that Revolution would ever again break out in England were finally dissolved.

'Mr O'Connor,' said Mayne, 'I am here to inform you that the meeting on this Common is permitted, but no procession to Westminster.'

O'Connor said something.

'No. No procession whatever.'

O'Connor spoke again.

'Certainly, Mr O'Connor, I am very pleased to hear it.'

O'Connor held out his hand; Mr Mayne shook it.

The Revolution was over.

Mayne, with his inspectors, disappeared, and O'Connor came forward to address the crowd. There were stands with flags and banners for him to appear on, and he did step up on to one of them, attended by some half a dozen gentlemen, but very little that he said could be heard. It appeared that he himself was going to the Home Office that he might present the famous Petition there; there would, however, be no procession; in fact, everything was over, or rather, the Meeting might continue as long as it pleased, but he, Mr O'Connor, would not appear in it.

He vanished, and there followed an extraordinary scene. Many of the more peaceful citizens, laughing and jeering, turned to leave the Common, but at the same time crowds of roughs and hooligans, urged on by the more violent Chartists, drove their way towards the stands with shouts and threats. Women were screaming, children crying, men shouting, no one seemed to be in command, someone tore down two of the banners.

'We had best be out of this,' Adam said, turning to Margaret. Then he saw Lunt. The man seemed to be in a frenzy and was orating, waving his hands, his hat off, his face congested with anger. In his hand he carried a short, thick club.

'Come,' said Kraft sadly. 'The curtain is down. The play is over.'

They turned together, but at the same moment Lunt caught sight of them. Like a madman he rushed at them, stopped in front of Kraft and shouted:

'Now where are you? You white, shaking coward! You and your friends! This is your work, with your psalm-singing, chicken-hearted caution! You have brought England to her knees, sold us like slaves!'

Kraft said quietly: 'Come, Henry. This is a farce.'

'Farce!' Lunt screamed. 'Yes! and who has turned it into a farce?'

'You and others like you,' Kraft answered sternly, his voice ringing out so that all heard him. 'I have warned you again and again, but you would not listen. With your violence you have frightened most decent men away. Aye, and lost most of our battles before they were even fought.'

Lunt's shouts had drawn a large crowd about them. Some excited men pressed forward, shouting incoherently, some laughed, some agreed with Kraft. But Lunt was beside himself; he moved in a whirlwind of passion in which he could distinguish nothing but his own disappointment, the failure of all that his egotism, yes, and his melodramatic self-sacrifice had for years been planning. He closed up to Kraft, who did not move.

'By heaven!' he shouted, 'I will show you who is a traitor! I'll teach your dirty cowardice!'

Kraft caught his arm.

'Be ashamed, man!' he cried. 'Go home to your wife and children!'

The touch infuriated Lunt, who thrust himself free, swung his club and brought it crashing on to Kraft's head. Kraft fell, his hand catching at Margaret's dress as he went down. Instantly there was silence. It was as though a hand caught the Common, the crowd, the sunlight, and, crushing it all into nothing, flung it away. There was emptiness and the sun shining on Kraft's white shirt and his twisted hand.

Adam was on his knees, his arm under Kraft's head that was crooked and veiled in blood. He looked up. 'A surgeon!' he said. 'For God's sake, someone, quickly, a surgeon.'

But he knew that Kraft was dead--the finest man in the world was gone. Tears blinded his sight as he bent again to the ground.

CHILDE ROLAND TO THE DARK TOWER

This was one of Judith's good days. This year, 1850, had not opened too well for her. For one thing in January she had had a splendid quarrel with Dorothy, had slapped Amabel (now a big stout girl of eleven) for riding one of the calves, had ordered Dorothy out of the house, had been told by Dorothy that she would not go, had discovered old Peach talking to one of her maids, had dismissed the maid and been of a mind to go up to the Fortress and tell Walter what she thought of him.

When this lively afternoon was over she had gone to bed, lain on her back and laughed aloud at her own bad temper. Dorothy had come in later to make the peace and discovered the old lady sitting up in bed, her lace cap a little askew on her snow-white hair, laughing and doing household accounts. They had embraced, as they always did after a quarrel, and Judith had settled down to the reading of Mr Thackeray's Vanity Fair. She had a passion now for novels, although she considered Thackeray too sentimental and something of a hypocrite. Becky, however, she could thoroughly enjoy and considered that there, but for the grace of God, went Judith Paris. Amelia and Dobbin she could not abide, but Rawdon had quite a deal in common with her dear Georges, who was as close to her still as he had been in 1790.

At the end of a chapter she had blown out the candle and lain down to sleep. She had slept for an hour or so and then woken suddenly to a sharp pain in the side. It was the first sharp pain she had ever known and she greeted it humorously as much as to say, 'Well, I knew you would come sometime. Now that you are here, behave as a gentleman.' The pain behaved badly at first and then, like a new acquaintance, having left his card, departed. But in the morning she felt very unwell indeed, tried to get up but could not, was finally in bed

for a week. She was attended by Dr Fairchild from Keswick, a little wizened sarcastic man of middle age. They got on very well, were rude to one another, gossiped a good deal, and found that they had much in common.

He told her that she had the rheumatics and he put her on a diet. It was from this moment that she began to care about food. Food had never, all her life, been very important to her. She had always had a healthy appetite and took what came. But now that she was forbidden, she lusted. She liked to forbid herself, but hated that anyone else should forbid her anything. Moreover, Dr Fairchild, with a deliberate maliciousness, as it seemed to her, forbade her the very things for which she cared the most, and especially meat. She had encountered at odd times cranky persons who pretended to live entirely on vegetables. There was poor young Ivison, son of Mr Ivison the bookseller in Keswick, whose pale earnest countenance both amused and irritated her. It was said that he ate nothing but carrots and cabbage, and once, when she met the poor thin boy beside Mr Flintoft's Model of the Lake District, he had incontinently fainted there at her feet! So much for carrots and cabbages.

Nevertheless, she did on the whole as she was told, and now, at the beginning of March, was in fine vigour again. Her spirits were all the livelier, because just at this time John was given a holiday and came up with Elizabeth on a visit. It was a year and a half since they had been at Uldale. The house was very full and she adored it to be full. Dorothy's children were growing-- Timothy was thirteen, Veronica twelve, Amabel eleven, and Jane (Judith's especial pet) was nine. Old Rackstraw taught Timothy Latin, and there was a governess, Miss Meredith. Miss Meredith Judith did not like at all, but she could not deny that she was an excellent governess. Miss Meredith, who was round and plump like a barrel, had all the present popular conventionalities. It was Judith's constant delight to shock her, for Judith could not in the least understand this great wave of propriety that had swept over the country. To allude to legs or bosoms or ardent young men or any of the processes of human creation seemed to Miss Meredith like death, and Judith perceived that not only Dorothy but the little girls themselves approved of these reticences.

'But, my dear Dorothy,' Judith would say, 'what is there shocking about being born? Why, I remember at Stone Ends when I was a girl--'

'When you were a girl, Aunt Judith,' Dorothy answered firmly, 'the world was a very different place. Not civilized at all.'

'I am sure,' Judith retorted, 'I can't say about being civilized, but babies are born in exactly the same way now as they were then. It would do Miss Meredith all the good in the world to be flung into a hedge by a tramp--'

But Dorothy was so greatly distressed that Judith desisted.

'PLEASE, Aunt Judith,' Dorothy said. 'Do not offend Miss Meredith. She is the best governess in the world. Exactly right for the children. I don't know where we'd ever find such another.'

So Judith refrained, and only teased Miss Meredith when the temptation was quite irresistible.

She loved the house to be full, for she knew that she was a miracle for her age. Dorothy, with all her energy and obstinacy, had no say whatever in the running of the house. And Judith was not at all the conventional tyrannical old woman so common in works of fiction from the days of the Egyptians and maybe long before them. Everyone loved her. She was cared for now as she had never been in all her life before. How in the past she had longed to be liked! How it had hurt her when Will had disapproved and Will's mother hated her and Jennifer plotted against her! But now, when she had all the love that she could possibly desire, she did not greatly care for it. She hated sentiment and always preferred common sense.

Adam, of course, was a thing apart; she was deeply fond of John and Elizabeth, had an affection for Dorothy and the children, but, with the possible exception of little Jane, Adam was the only human being in the world whom she loved.

She certainly did not love herself, but she was proud of her age, her strength, her capability and, above all, her scorn for and successful battles over everyone at Ireby.

Of late Walter had been trying to irritate her in every way that he knew. Things were stolen, her house was spied upon, her servants were bribed, if there was any malicious story possible about anyone at Uldale it was spread in every direction. But Judith and Dorothy were exactly the women to fight a campaign like Walter's. They had much common sense and a strong feeling for the ludicrous. Dorothy was lacking in a sense of humour, but her sense of fun was so strong that to see a gentleman slip on the ice or a lady lose her bonnet in the wind made her stout sides ache with laughter.

So Walter seemed to her silly and Uhland unwholesome.

On this sunny day in March the weather was so warm that John and Elizabeth could walk comfortably up and down the lawn together. Judith, looking at them for a moment out of the parlour window, smiled with approval. John the night before had been most entertaining. If not of Parliament he was near it enough to have plenty of inside information. Both Judith and Dorothy were thrilled with interest as he told them of the hatred that the Queen and Prince Albert felt for Palmerston. Palmerston was John's hero, so he was a trifle malicious about the Queen and the Prince. Lord Clarendon, it seemed, had, a few weeks ago, dined at the Palace, and now it was all over the Town that the Queen in the drawing room after dinner had lost all control and spoken with so much vehement bitterness that Lord Clarendon had not known where to look; and when she had done the Prince had begun and, when Clarendon had visited him next day, had orated about Palmerston for two hours without stopping.

This gave the two ladies great pleasure to hear, not because they wished the Queen or Palmerston or anyone else any harm; simply that it brought the lawns and hedges of Uldale straight into the Palace.

So Judith looked out of the window at John and nodded her approval. It was so fine a morning that she had put on a new dress for the first time, a dress made especially for her by Miss Sampson in Keswick. She wore more sombre colours now, although she still loved a touch of brightness here and there. As she was wearing long drawers trimmed with lace, a flannel petticoat, an under-petticoat, a white starched petticoat, and two muslin petticoats under the dress, she had, for an old lady, a good deal to carry. Very soon now the stiff bands of the crinoline were to relieve ladies of their outrageous burden. Judith was wearing a dress of grey taffeta with twelve flounces all of a dark shade of green. Out of this 'like a lily-stem out of a flower-tub' rose her dark-green bodice with pagoda sleeves and a very lovely white lace collar (this last a present from Sylvia Herries the preceding Christmas). Her only concession to her years was her white lace cap. Her small, alert, vigorous body carried its cumbrous clothes with grace and ease; her eyes sparkled like little fires. She had, as she had always had, an air of crystalline spotlessness. The muslins, the collar, the cap were new minted as though direct, that minute, from some most perfect laundry. And so in fact they were. Everything was laundered in the house and Mrs Kaplan the housekeeper (Judith's slave) saw that all was perfection.

They were rich now at Uldale. Dorothy had money from Bellairs and her portion of Herries money. Judith's own investments, shares in Liverpool concerns inherited from David Herries, land and property round Uldale excellently supervised for many years by Rackstraw, all mounted to an income well beyond their needs. Judith had no desire for wealth, but she liked to have everything handsome about her. Everything WAS handsome. On this lovely March morning Uldale glistened like a jewel.

She went her rounds of the house, tapping with her stick and humming a tune. She visited everything, the high-ceilinged kitchen, pantry, servants' hall, housekeeper's room complete with black cat, work-basket and flowered footstool. Then, perhaps, after the dairy the place that she loved best, the still-room. Here were cakes, jams, preserves made; here was the china washed and the dessert set out. Then the lamp-room, the storeroom, the meat-larder where were the weighing machine and the great pickling jars. Then the wood and coal stores, the laundry, the pump-room and the dairy. She stayed for an especial time this morning in the kitchen, for its brick-floored spaciousness bathed in sun was exceedingly pleasant. She stood there, smiling at the maids, leaning on her stick, looking at the roasting-spits, the Dutch oven, the chopping-block, the sugar-nippers, the coffee-grinder, the pot and pan racks, everything shining, gleaming, glittering as though active and happy with conscious, individual life.

All was good; all was well; still humming her tune she went out on to the sunlit lawn to find John and Elizabeth.

For a moment she looked back at the house--dear house to whose safety and comfort she had, through all her long life, returned again and again. There had been terrible hours here. She could see David Herries fallen, stricken on this very lawn, she could catch again Sarah Herries' distracted glance, could see Jennifer waiting for her lover, Francis' mad return and frantic exit, the rioters and poor Reuben's slaughter, her own tragic surrender of Watendlath, the Christmas party and the fracas with Walter. There had been every kind of tragedy, farce, drama here; birth, death, ruin, love, humour, light easy days, pain and laughter. She had come through it all, as one always did come through if one kept on patiently enough, did not take oneself too seriously, saw the sequence of event, of change, decay and birth in proper proportion. One came through to this sunlight, to this lovely landscape, this quiet English calm; then, turning, she saw that John was walking towards her and, with that quick intuition that she always had, wondered instantly whether after all the tale was told, whether there were not a number more of chapters to be added.

For John was alone and, she saw at once, in trouble. She had never quite understood John. She had loved Francis, his father, but had never understood him either. The alarms, fears, superstitions, doubts of those two were foreign to her direct sensible nature. The part of her that had shared them she had deliberately killed.

John's slim, upright body, his pale hair, beautiful almost feminine features, had always marked him apart from other men. She thought, as she saw him approach her: 'John will never be out of trouble. He will never know what it is to rest.'

He came straight up to her and, his voice quivering a little, said:

'Aunt Judith. I have told Elizabeth I am going up to Ireby.'

She was astonished. A long grey shadow seemed to fall across the sunny lawn.

'Yes. Didn't you know? He has written her a letter: that scoundrel Peach brought it half an hour ago.'

'A letter?'

'Yes. Here it is.'

He handed her a large sheet of paper scrawled over in Walter's big clumsy hand.

DEAR ELIZABETH--As a dutiful daughter you are to pay me a visit. If you don't come of yourself I shall fetch you. Your loving father,
WALTER HERRIES

'Loving father!' said Judith, her voice shaking with anger. 'What impertinence!'

'Yes. But of course Elizabeth mustn't go. She wished it, and I forbade her even to think of it. But *I* am going--and at once.'

As she looked at him he was again the small boy when the nurse had thrown the rabbit out of the window. He stood there, his head up, his nostrils quivering (exaggerated pictures of him, she thought, but spiritually true), like a high-bred horse, defiant but afraid of the whip because of the catastrophe that a contact might bring. She, too, was afraid of some disaster. She knew, as she looked at him, that she had always been afraid of it for him.

'No. Don't you go, John. I'll pay him a visit. I've been wishing to for weeks.'

'Nonsense,' John said roughly. Then, recovering himself, added: 'Pardon me, Aunt Judith. I didn't intend to be rude, but this is MY affair. You must see that it is--'

She did not attempt to stop him after this, but only sighed to herself as she saw him mount his bay, wave his riding-whip to her, turning with that charming, rather weak, altogether lovable smile that was so like his father's that it always made her heart ache.

Where would this thing end, she thought, as she entered the house. When had it begun?--back, back, maybe to the days when her father had been a wild young man and sold his woman at the Fair, an old eternal quarrel between beauty and ugliness, normality and abnormality, sense and nonsense--a quarrel born, as all quarrels are in this world, of jealousy and fear. But she did not care for philosophy; she took things as they came, and what immediately came now when she entered the house was a quarrel with Dorothy, who wished to buy a sofa covered with wool-work and fringed with beads that she had seen in Carlisle. To buy this monstrosity and place it in the parlour instead of the lovely old one that had the red apples.

'But it's all the mode!' cried Dorothy. The Osmastons have wool- work everywhere.'

'They may,' said Judith grimly, 'but so long as I'm up and about that sofa remains in the parlour. Why, I was resting my hand on it when I came to the most important decision of my life.' Then she added as she tapped away on her stick: 'It's all Prince Albert and his German taste. I detest the man.'

Meanwhile John rode down the road towards Ireby. It suited his mood that the sky became overcast as he reached the bottom of the Ireby hill. On his left a bubble of seething little white clouds rose on the Skiddaw ridge, and other clouds rushed up to the sun and, with gestures of sulky annoyance, swallowed it. He HATED himself for this fear that had seized all his bones like water. The very thought of Uhland made him sick. But perhaps Uhland would not be there. He did not mind Walter at all; he was simply a gross, quarrelsome, bad-mannered fool. His thoughts went back to that day in his childhood when, with Adam, he had watched Walter on the moor. He had been afraid then, but he saw now that it had been Uhland's shadow behind Walter that had, like a prophecy, frightened him. He had been afraid of Uhland before he was born.

He tried now, as he rode slowly up the hill, to formulate that fear, to bring it into the open. But it would not come. That was the awful thing about it. When he forced himself to think of Uhland, or was compelled to do so, he saw him as a shapeless, boneless animal emitting some sickening odour, as one sees a creature in a dream, lurking in shadow in a dank cave or the corner of a cellar, or behind a stone. The hide-and-seek that Uhland had played with him now for so long had introduced into his own soul and body some sickly element, so that, at times, he believed that Uhland was some part of himself--that part we all have, hidden, shameful, lurking. There was nothing shameful in his life except this one cowardice. In everything else he was brave, and so all the more did he feel this one exception to be real.

He raised his head as he saw the grey stone house squatting, in its trees, on the top of the hill. Today he would force this thing into the open; it should skulk, just out of touch and feeling, no longer.

He tied his horse to the wall outside the garden and walked up the flagged path to the door. Stone frowned at him everywhere.

The gardens were trim but dead. It was late March, and the daffodils were in full golden flood under the rosy Uldale walls. Here, too, beneath the dark trees beyond the flowerbeds they flamed in little cups of fire, but the garden itself was black and gritty. As John stood there banging the knocker of the door, the whole place leered down on him.

It was not that it was so large, but that it was so dead. The windows had no faces, the stone turrets were like clenched fists, and worst of all, there was no sound at all anywhere.

At Uldale there was always sound--laughter, singing, running water and the light chatter of birds. He wondered, above the beating of his heart, that there was not a bird singing in the Ireby gardens.

At last there was a creaking of bolts and the door slowly opened. An old bent man whom John had never seen before stood there; he had bow legs and was dressed in the style of thirty years earlier, black worsted stockings, black knee-breeches, a rather soiled neckerchief, and a dull brown tye-wig that cocked a little over one eye. He had a tooth missing, and his words whistled through his lips.

'Is Mr Walter Herries at home?' John asked.

'If you'll wait I'll see,' said the old man, looking out into the garden as though he expected to see a lion rooting up the bulbs. 'What name shall I say?'

'Mr John Herries.'

His mind seemed to be on other things as he ambled away, leaving John in the hall. The hall was stony and bare. There was a fireplace with grinning fire-dogs and a large stand hung with heavy coats and stacked with whips. There was no carpet on the stone that struck the feet icily. He stood there, wondering whether the old man would not forget him, when a green baize door to his left opened and a woman came out. She was not young but not old either, and very extravagantly dressed in a Russian short jacket of gold brocade figured with bunches of flowers in coloured silks. Her skirt had so many flounces that she appeared to be robed ten times over. She wore a bonnet lined with rosebuds, and her cheeks were rosebuds too, only extremely artificial, for John had never seen a lady more brightly painted. This brilliant person brushed past him as though he were not there, and she was swearing like a trooper. She turned towards the stairs and shouted:

'Hell take your meanness, Walter!'

She was so angry that she stared at John without seeing him.

As though from nowhere a very large stout man in a nightcap and a rich flowered dressing-gown appeared on the stairs. He was grinning, his nightshirt was open at the neck and he carried a very small brown hairy dog in one hand by the scruff of its neck. Very good-humouredly he called out, leaning with his free hand on the banister: 'Au revoir, my dearest,' and threw the dog to the lady. John started forward, but the lady was quicker, caught the dog with wonderful dexterity, and rushed from the house, banging the door behind her.

Walter wiped his large hands in a handkerchief that very deliberately he took from his dressing-gown. He was about to vanish when John called out:

'Cousin Walter.'

He peered forward down into the dark hall.

'Hullo. Who's there?' he asked.

'John Herries. I wish to have a word with you.'

Walter came slowly down the stairs, drawing his dressing-gown about him, his slippers tip-tapping. He came right up to John and bent forward, peering at him.

'Oh, it's you, is it?' he said at last. 'Where's my daughter?'

He was very clean-shaved, and his cheeks, round and rosy, shone like a baby's and smelt freshly of some scent. His face was fat, but his neck and exposed chest were white and firm. His mouth, eyes, and thin hair protruding from the night-cap gave him the look of age, for he was only fifteen years older than John in reality, but looked quite of another generation. His body was of great size and had a balloon-like appearance under the dressing-gown.

'May I speak to you?' asked John.

'You may,' said Walter quite amiably. 'Come upstairs.'

John mounted after him, and Walter led the way into a room that was as untidy and uncomfortable as a room could be. There was a spitting, smoky little fire in the grate; a carpet, red with a buff pattern and a large tear, in front of the fireplace; two pier-glasses; a woolwork ottoman and a large harp leaning against the wall. The room smelt of caraway-seed and was very close.

Walter, his legs stretched, stood in front of the fireplace and motioned John to a seat.

'If you're cold,' he said, 'I can't help it. Didn't know you were coming. Have a brandy.'

'No, thank you,' said John, turning his hat round and round in his hands.

'Well, what do you want now that you are here?'

'You wrote a letter to my wife. I am here to answer it.'

Walter scratched his head under his night-cap and grinned. Then he sat down in a large faded green leather chair and stretched out his thick hairy legs, kicking off one slipper and crinkling up his toes.

'Forgive my attire, Cousin John,' he said. 'That bitch of a woman put me out this morning—and now I've put HER out.' He threw his head back and laughed. 'Have a brandy. Pray, have a brandy,' he said again.

'No, I thank you,' said John very ceremoniously.

'Well, I will.' He pulled an old red worsted bell-rope and so still was the house that the clang of the bell could be heard echoing, echoing into eternity. 'Now then,' he said, 'why isn't my daughter here?'

'She is not here, neither is she coming.'

'Well, that's straight enough. But she IS coming if I want her.'

'You have no sort of right to her,' John answered hotly. He was glad if he was getting angry. That made him less conscious of the silent house, less aware of his own anticipation of Uhland's entrance.

'And why have I no right? I'm her father, aren't I?'

'You ill-treated her, and then when she ran away because she was so miserable you made no kind of inquiry as to her whereabouts. She might have died for all you cared.'

Walter yawned, scratched his breast, leaned forward, shaking a fist.

'Look you here, Cousin John. Let me tell you something. You are in danger, you are. It began with your mother, who was impertinent to my mother. I gave her a warning, but she wouldn't listen, and I frightened her into her grave. When she was gone I warned you that you'd better be after her—all of you. But you wouldn't take the warning, and, more than that, you have the damned impertinence to marry my daughter—'gainst my wishes too. I don't bear you a grudge. I don't bear anyone in this world a grudge except my old father who goes cohabiting with a woman young enough to be his daughter and gets a child by her. Dis-gustin'—simply disgustin'. No, I don't wish you ill, but I've been telling the lot of you these years back to move out of Uldale, and you will not listen. You are in danger, Cousin John, and if you won't drink a brandy like a gentleman you'd better be off. I've had an irritating time already this morning, and I don't want another.'

'You needn't think,' said John, getting up, 'that we are afraid of you. We know all the dirty little games you've been playing, putting Peach on to rob and spy, bribing the servants, but it doesn't affect us, not an atom.'

'Does it not?' said Walter cheerfully. 'No, because you've that old woman in the house. She's a hard-plucked one, she is. I've been fighting her for years, and upon my soul there is no one in the world I admire more. But it won't go on for ever, you know. Dear me, no. There'll be a nasty family crisis one of these days. You can tell the old lady so.'

The old bow-legged man with the brown wig arrived with a bottle and two glasses. Walter filled one tumbler half full and drank it off.

'That's better,' he said. 'And now you'd better be going.'

He got up and shuffled his great body across the room, yawning, scratching his back, his night-cap tilted over one ear.

'Dam' bitch,' he said. 'I wish I'd broken the bones of that dog.' He kicked the harp with the toe of his slipper. 'That was her doing,' he said, jerking his head. Thought she could play on it. Forced me to order the thing from Carlisle . . .' He swung round at the door.

'Uhland hates you, you know,' he said, grinning like a schoolboy. 'Hates you like a poison. Don't know why. Always has.'

John said nothing.

In the passage Walter said:

'Ever been over this house? Chilly place. Draughty as hell.' He threw open a double door. This was the salon where the fine opening Ball had been given. Here were the tapestries, and the decorations, hanging garlands and the dazzling stars of heaven. But the floor was filmed with dust, there was a large patch in the gilded ceiling, a corner of the tapestry flapped drearily against the wall, a chair was overturned, and there were bird-droppings on the long windowsill.

'Fine room,' said Walter. Then, closing the doors behind him, he said: 'There are rooms and rooms in this place. Too many rooms.'

Somewhere a dog was howling and a door banged, monotonously, like a protest.

'Goodbye, then,' said Walter, nodding. 'I am sure I don't know why you came.'

'I came in answer to your letter.'

'Ah, yes. Well, it's my daughter I wish to see. No one else.'

'I came to tell you that. That she will not come.'

'Yes.' He nodded. 'She will, though—if I want her. Damn that dog. There's no peace in this house.' He shuffled off, disappearing quite suddenly. And he was replaced, for John, hearing a sound, looked to the left, and there on the stone step of a little winding stair stood Uhland..

He said nothing. He was dressed in black, with a single flashing diamond in his stock. He said nothing, he turned back up the staircase, tapping with his stick. And John followed him. The silence of the house, broken only by the distant yapping of the dog, compelled him, and the film of dust that seemed to be floating everywhere in the house compelled him. But he went because he was ashamed not to go; the fear that so maliciously squeezed his heart would mock at him all his life long if he did not go. And he went because Uhland wanted him to go.

At the top of the little stone staircase the tapping stick led him through an open door into Uhland's room. This was furnished with a four-poster, a parrot in a cage, a sheepdog lying on the floor by the window, a grand view straight down the hillside to Uldale, a bookcase, a pair of foils and a bare shabby table and two old brown chairs.

Uhland stood in the middle of the room and looked at him.

'And pray what have you come for?' he asked him.

They faced one another for the first time, as it seemed, for many years, and even now John could not bring this face and body to any definite terms. It was indistinct, floating in dust, wavering into space. The room smelt of animals, the bed was unmade, the sheets tossed about. The sheepdog paid them no attention, but slowly licked a paw that was wrapped in very fresh white linen.

John was not indistinct to Uhland. He hated, as he looked, every particle of him; the high aristocratic carriage of his head, his gentle amiable eyes, his handsome clothes and, most of all, he both hated and loved his fear of himself. He drew lines with his stick on the worn dusty carpet.

'What have you come for?' he asked again.

John's words stuck in his throat; he could not help himself. It may have been the close air and animal smell. He forced himself, as though he were beating with his foot on the floor, to speak.

'I came to see your father about a private affair,' he said at last. 'But now I am here I should wish to know what the hell you mean by following me, spying on me in London and elsewhere during these last years?'

'Ah, you've noticed that, have you?' said Uhland.

They both knew that it would need only a gesture, a careless movement, for them to be at one another's throats. If Uhland had not been lame, John must have sprung forward, and oh! the relief that that would be, the clearing away, as one sweeps off cobwebs, of years of dreams, nightmares, shame and terror. But he could not touch a cripple, and, more than that, as Uhland drew lines with his stick on the floor, he seemed to place a barrier between them.

'Well,' Uhland said, 'it has amused me to make you uncomfortable. You are such a coward, so poor a creature, that anything can frighten you. And you had the impertinence to marry my sister.'

'If you were not lame,' said John, 'I would show you whether I am a coward or no.'

'Ah, don't allow that to stop you. Lame though I am, I can look after myself. You have always been a coward. Everyone knows it.'

'If you were not Elizabeth's brother--'

'Another excuse.'

John drew a deep breath. He could not help himself, but this thick close air made the room swing about him. Uhland's stick hypnotized him.

'I'll show you--' he began. 'If I am disturbed by you any more I shall forget your weakness and make you sorry you were ever born. I've warned you. I won't warn you again.'

He turned to go. He saw the dog raise its head, heard the parrot scratch the bars, then knew that the closeness of the room gripped his windpipe, darkened his eyes. The floor swirled up like a wave and struck him. He fainted, sinking limply back against the legs of the chair.

Uhland looked at him, hesitated, then went to the washing-basin, fetched the jug and bent down, his arm under John's body, splashing his forehead with the water.

He had John's body in his arms. He put his hand beneath his shirt and felt the smooth firm warm skin above the heart. He drew the body close to his own, and his long thin fingers passed over the face, the neck, the open shirt. His own heart was beating tumultuously. With one hand he very gently bathed the forehead just as he bathed one of his wounded animals, with the other he pressed his fingers on the mouth, felt the warm lips under his touch, stroked the strong throat, looking always into the eyes.

His hand pressed more intently on the mouth; then he shuddered through all his body. He saw that John's eyes were slowly, dazedly opening, so he drew away, letting the other collapse against the chair. He got up, threw a look about the room, and, very quietly, went out.

EXHIBITION

'I am as excited as a child,' said Judith.

'You ARE a child,' answered Dorothy severely. 'Do wrap your shawl more closely or you will catch the most dreadful chill.'

'Chill--pooh!' said Judith, leaning over the edge of Will's most handsome carriage that she might see the better an extraordinary Frenchman in beard, felt hat and full pantaloons.

They had come to London to stay with Will for the opening of the Great Exhibition.

Long before their departure from Cumberland the Exhibition had penetrated their seclusion. For weeks and weeks no one in Keswick, Bassenthwaite, Cockermouth, Buttermere Valley, Penrith or anywhere else had had any other thought but of the Exhibition and the possibilities of a visit to London. Old Bennett, for example, had received from somewhere in London a plan of a monster lodging-house that would be designed to 'put up' at least a thousand souls from the country at one and the same time 'for one and three per night', and for this small sum each and every person was to be provided 'with bedstead, good wool mattress, sheets, blankets and coverlet; with soap, towels and every accommodation for ablution, a surgeon to attend at nine o'clock every morning and instantly remove all cases of infectious disease'; there was to be 'a smoking room, detached from the main building, where a band of music was to play every evening, gratis' and 'cold roast and boiled beef and mutton, and ditto ditto sausages and bacon, and pickles, salads and fruit pies (when to be procured) were to be furnished at fixed prices', all the dormitories were to be 'well lighted with gas'; to secure the complete privacy of the occupants they were 'to be watched over by efficient wardens and police constables', and finally, 'the proprietor pledged himself that every care should be taken to ensure the comfort, convenience and STRICT DISCIPLINE of so large a body.'

What could be fairer than that? Everyone was going. On a certain morning almost the whole of Uldale and Ireby villages departed in carts and carriages for the 'Travellers' Train' at Cockermouth. Others journeyed to Carlisle and met the train for London there. For hundreds of persons round and about Judith's little world this was the first real journey of their lives.

And it was, in fact, oddly enough, Dorothy's first train journey too. She was never one to allow her emotions to get the better of her, but she did cry a little as she left Timothy, Veronica, Amabel and Jane to the rotund Miss Meredith. She had never before been absent from them for a single day, but Miss Meredith was 'the safest person in the world', nothing could have appeared more secure that morning than the Uldale lawns and rosy walls happy under the soft April sun. When, at the station, she beheld the porters in their green velveteen jackets, heard the engines fizzling, and the large bells announcing the coming of a train that soon arrived, bumping and groaning as though in fearful agony; when, safely in their carriage, they were entertained by a stout gentleman with the grandest whiskers who warned them in a voice, husky and urgent, about the perils of London--the cracksmen, the rampsmen, the snorzers and thimble-screwers, all these exciting varie-

ties of pickpockets and murderers--when at last arriving in the Metropolis and waiting outside the station for their luggage to be brought to them, there occurred, 'under their very noses, just as though they were in a theatre', a 'school of acrobats', and an 'equilibrist' spun plates high in air, balanced burning paper-bags on his chin, and caught cannon-balls in a cup on the top of his head--why, then Dorothy forgot her children entirely and surrendered completely to her adventure.

She had thought that her main occupation in London would be to take care of Judith, but she very quickly discovered that Judith took care not only of her but of everyone else in her company.

During the first evening at the house in Hill Street, Judith put the second Lady Herries in her proper place in exactly five minutes. She laughed at her, pinched her chin and exhorted her thus: 'Now you mustn't mind me, my dear. I'm seventy-seven years of age and nothing ails me. Wonderful, isn't it? I need no looking-after. I came to London as a very young girl and was not at all alarmed by it, so it's most unlikely that I shall be alarmed by it now. I knew Will long before you were born--that is the prettiest cashmere, my dear; where DID you discover it?--yes, and Will knows me too, do you not, Will? So you are not to disturb yourself about me. I shall have EVERYTHING I want, I am certain. And now, may I not see little Ellis? I am dying for a sight of him.'

Dorothy perceived that no one in the large cold house had anything of Judith's fire and vitality, and that that same fire burnt only quietly at Uldale. She realized for the first time how much of her personality Judith subdued in the country, and how patient Judith had often been with herself and her children.

'Judith is a marvellous woman,' said Will that evening. 'More marvellous every time I see her.'

'Yes,' said Dorothy meekly.

That was Will's opinion of Judith; Judith's opinion of Will was that he was pathetic. Will was eighty-one years of age and could only go out for an airing, sitting in his carriage, wrapped up like a mummy and with someone at his side to blow his nose, see that his feet were warm and that his hat was on straight. This 'someone' was never Lady Herries, but rather his attendant, Robins, a thin, severe, black-haired man of very religious principles. Lady Herries paid no attention to her husband whatever. She made a sort of a show on the first night of Judith's visit, gave him his pills and wrapped a shawl around his shoulders, but after that the virtuous Robins did everything, cutting his meat for him, pouring him his wine and suddenly remarking sternly: 'No, Sir William. No potatoes. They are forbidden.'

However, Will did not seem greatly to care. Judith was astonished at his subservience. Was this the stern and austere Will who had commanded so implacably poor weak-jointed Christabel? 'Shall I be like that soon?' thought Judith. 'I prefer death.'

But Will did not care, because he had one constant, eager, unceasing preoccupation--'little Ellis'. Little Ellis was now eight years of age and as small and wizened a boy as you would be likely to find. He was accounted exceedingly sharp, had a moneybox into which he was constantly putting sixpences, and inquired the price of everything. Will thought him wonderful and quite frankly now spoke of Walter and Uhland as ungrateful wretches.

He saw Judith as Walter's principal aggravator and this made him admire her more than ever. He liked to dilate on the riches that he was leaving Ellis--Walter was not to have a penny, nor Uhland, 'that surly peevish cripple', anything either. John and Elizabeth, however, were to receive a good legacy. Elizabeth he now loved. He had her to the house whenever he was able, and she, better than anyone else, seemed to understand and comfort him.

Of his wife he never spoke, but his allusions to 'poor, good Christabel' gave Judith to understand that ghosts can, once and again, have their proper revenge.

Now that it was clear that Will would not live much longer, visits of members of the Herries family to Hill Street were frequent. It was not that they were greedy: they cared neither for money nor poverty. But Will was now the most important member of their family, and the death of an important Herries was, in their eyes, a world affair. Carey Rockage, James Herries (a most tiresome and pompous old bore of seventy-two), Stephen Newmark (who considered himself a Herries and then something), Amery, Fred Ormerod (cousin by marriage of Monty Cards and a gay, drinking bachelor), Bradley Cards (a nephew of Jennifer's), Tim Trenchard (a busybody cousin of Garth's and Amery's), all these men with wives, daughters and appendages drove up to Hill Street, left cards, came and sat in the long, dreary drawing-room and asked Lady Herries to receptions.

Of them all Judith liked best to see Sylvia. She had loved Sylvia from the moment of their first meeting and she loved her still, although the beautiful, bright, impertinent girl she had first known was now a weary, over-painted, discontented middle-aged woman. Sylvia had been fighting too long the battle of living above your means. Had it been her lot to have married a man of large and assured fortune she would have been a brilliant and successful leader of Society and, at the last, a contentedly reminiscent old lady. But Garth was a cheerful, corruptible vagabond. They had neither of them morals nor honesty. They had stolen, cheated, lied all their lives long, always without any desire to hurt or damage, but hurt and damage they had--first their friends and acquaintances, last of all themselves. Moreover, the London that now surrounded them was not their own; the raffish, speculating, bouncing world of the Thirties was succeeded now by the serious, earnest, virtuous and hypocritical world of the Fifties. To be fair to Sylvia and Garth, they did not know how to be hypo-

critical, nor did they think it good manners to be earnest. So they were shabby and left-behind and out at heels.

Sylvia wept on Judith's bosom; the paint ran down her cheeks, and before she left she accepted ten pounds from Judith with a readiness that showed that every day of her life she was accepting small sums from someone.

Elizabeth had one talk with Judith that disturbed her greatly. Elizabeth was now thirty-six but was as remotely lovely as she had ever been. That delicate bloom and fragrance belonged to her still. On the afternoon of this talk she was wearing a costume of the new 'crystallized' gauze so that she seemed the floating cloud to which ladies at that time were so fond of comparing themselves. She was quite unaware of her loveliness: Judith, watching her with sharp, practised eyes, thought that it was as though she lived under a glass bell with John, everything and everybody shut away from them. And she was very unhappy about him.

'He cannot sleep at night,' she said. 'He thinks that I am not awake and he talks to himself. He slips out of bed very quietly and goes into the other room and walks about. I am so frightened, Aunt Judith.'

Judith kissed her, held her hand, but there was always something stiffly independent about Elizabeth. She asked for help but refused to accept it. Also she loved John, Judith thought, too deeply for it to be healthy.

'Is he worrying about your father?'

'I suppose so--or rather it is Uhland. Uhland obsesses him, and since he went up to Ireby that day last year it has been worse.'

'Well, my dear child, I've been fighting your father for years and am none the worse. John should see this sensibly.'

'But it seems like something in his blood, something inside himself. As though he were pursued by Uhland. It is a fantasy, Aunt Judith--not real at all. After all, what can Uhland do?'

'His father had the same, and his great-grandfather; something that would never let them alone. Well,' Judith sighed impatiently, 'I cannot understand it. I never could. When there's a difficulty or a danger, face it. Don't run away from it.'

'John does face it,' Elizabeth answered indignantly. 'You must not think he is a coward, Aunt Judith. He's tremendously brave in everything--but this is like a sickness.'

Judith nodded her head; there were two worlds, she knew, and unless you found the connexion between them you never found peace. Once she had herself had to make a choice. She had made it and was now the old woman she was in consequence.

Then she found that it was a very fine thing to give cheap advice to others, but that she had her own trouble to face. Her trouble-- one that she had never expected nor considered--was that she was plunged, willy-nilly, into a sea of jealousy about Adam. Willy- nilly because, cry out as she might, refuse to be, at her age, so mean and small and petty, there she was in it up to the neck.

Adam had of course been the great central fact of her visit to London. To see the Great Exhibition certainly, but to see it with Adam. To lean on Adam's strong arm everywhere, to have the delicious intimate little talks with him, simply the two of them alone in her room, that had been for many years now her greatest happiness in life, to feel, above all, that no one had the close relationship with him that she herself had. It was not that she wished to shut Margaret out. She was neither so selfish nor so stupid. Moreover, she had fought that battle before and had won a victory. But her later life had been built up on the absolute intimacy of herself and her son, an intimacy that no one and nothing could break. She was, however, becoming greedy, greedy of her vitality, her uniqueness. She was 'Madame', the most marvellous old lady in Cumberland and, if she wished, the most marvellous old lady in London. This was nothing in her as cheap and petty as conceit, but the sort of amused triumph we all feel when we are clever at a game. All this was on the surface, but her very soul was possessed by her love for Adam. No one knew how deep that went. She had only loved two people in all her life, her husband and her son, but she loved them like a tigress. At the same time she had human enough wisdom and tolerance enough to keep the tigress behind bars.

Never before had her relationship with Adam been threatened as it was now. She perceived at once that the reason of it was the sudden and violent death of Margaret's father. She had not known of the scene between Margaret and Adam that Christmastime at Uldale. That would have informed her yet further had she been aware of it. But since Caesar Kraft's death she had seen very little of Adam and Margaret. They had paid only one brief visit to Uldale. She was quite unprepared for this change.

It was not that Adam was not as devoted as ever. He was there at Hill Street to meet her on the first evening. When they were alone in her room, he took her in his arms and hugged and kissed her as though he would never let her go.

'Why, how strong you are, Adam!' she cried, laughing and crying and happy as a queen. It was after this that she perceived that his thoughts were always on Margaret. HE was of course as silent as ever, but her first sight of Margaret told her that there was here a new assurance and certainty. Margaret possessed Adam now and was quietly radiant because of it. They had three rooms in Pimlico. Adam wrote for the papers, knew Dickens and John Forster, Yates and Wilkie Collins. He was not of the writing world, stayed quietly outside it, made few friends, but made those few firmly. He wrote considerably about politics, reviewed books a little, and said cheerfully to his mother that the only things he really wanted to write were fairy stories.

'Fairy stories!' Judith cried, looking at Adam's stocky, thickset frame and ugly unromantic countenance.

'Don't be afraid, Mother,' he said, laughing. 'I shall never write them. I must earn our bread and butter, but a good fairy story-- there must be a handsome satisfaction in writing a good fairy story.'

This was nonsense of course, so she told him sharply, but it annoyed her that Margaret should think it quite a natural thing for him to do. 'Yes,' Margaret explained, 'he has found real life so very absurd.'

'Nonsense,' Judith answered. 'I never listened to such stuff. Fairy stories! A man like Adam! Why, he has a chest like a bull's!'

She soon discovered that her relations with her son and daughter-in- law were complicated by her advancing years. She was a wonderful old lady, but she could not do as she used to do. She took her breakfast in bed every morning and did not rise until midday. She was forced to confess that she returned to Hill Street exceedingly weary after her shopping expeditions. It was necessary, therefore, for Adam and Margaret to come to her rather than that she should go to them, and she thought that Margaret accompanied her husband too frequently.

Being direct and honest, she immediately said so.

'My dear boy, I am in London for a very brief visit. I have one foot in the grave. I love Margaret, of course, but I love you more.'

He said nothing (he never did say anything), but he came alone. Then she fancied that he was thinking of Margaret and wishing that he were with her.

She would interrupt some Cumberland piece of gossip with a sharp: 'Now, Adam, you are not attending. You are thinking of Margaret.'

Jealousy began to mount in her as the tide swells a sea-pool. She slept now but badly, and before had not minded that, for she would lie and think of the old days, of Georges and Reuben and Charlie Watson and Warren, Adam's father, until the room seemed crowded with their figures; but now she could think of nothing but Adam, and, with the fantastic exaggeration that the night hours give, she would beat her thin little hands together and cry to herself that she had lost him for ever, that she was a miserable, deserted old woman, and that she might as well die. It was then that her poignant despair at the choice that so many years ago she had made for the sake of Jennifer, John and Dorothy, would strike her like a voice of doom.

'Ah! if I had but gone with Adam to Watendlath he would have been mine for ever!'

But in the daylight she was by far too sensible and blessed with too strong a sense of humour to tolerate such obvious melodrama. She laughed at herself, her fears, her selfishness. Nevertheless her jealousy mounted. She was as sweet as Tennyson's Miller's Daughter to Margaret, but Margaret was not deceived. The trouble with both Margaret and Adam was that they were so quiet. You could not tell what they were truly thinking!

Poor Judith! Jealousy is from the Devil. It was hard for her that she should have to fight her first real battle with him at so advanced an age!

The Great Day approached. The Great Day arrived!

But the whole of London was by this time an Exhibition. Foreigners were everywhere--Germans, Turks, Americans, French and even Chinamen. On every side amusements were springing up, M. Alexis Soyer opened his Restaurant of All the Nations, there was 'the Black Band of His Majesty of Tsjaddi with a hundred additional bones', the Musicians of Tongoose, the Troubadours of Far Vancouver, the Theban Brothers, and the most celebrated Band of Robbers from the Desert. Barnum provided a splendid entertainment, whereby for a rather costly ticket a guest was provided with 'a bed, a boudoir and a banquet, together with one hour's use per diem of a valet and a private chaplain, free admission to theatrical green-rooms, a seat in the House of Commons, and a cigar on the Bench of Judges'. Mr Catlin reopened his Indian Exhibition, and Mr Wyld would take you on the 'Grand Tour of Europe', or a visit to Australia or New Zealand for threepence a time.

But it was enough for Judith and Dorothy simply to view the crowds in the streets. The road to the Crystal Palace was an amazing scene. Trains of wagons lengthened far away, like an Eastern caravan, each waiting for its turn to be unloaded. Omnibuses, carriages, carts, barrows congested the road. The public houses, of which there were a great number, hung out gay and patriotic flags, and their doors were crowded with loafers, soldiers, beggars and women with shawls over their heads. Along the pavement were lined the hawkers shouting their wares, trays filled with bright silvery-seeming medals of the Exhibition, pictures of it printed in gold on 'gelatine cards', many barrows with ginger-beer, oranges and nuts.

Along Rotten Row troops of riders galloped noiselessly over the loose soft ground at the rear of the Crystal Palace, while in front of it an interminable line of carriages crawled slowly past. Close to the rails were mobs of spectators on tip-toe, their necks outstretched, seeking glimpses of progress. All along the building were ladders with painters perched high upon them and walking on the crystal covering which miraculously sustained them. At the end of the building were steam-engines puffing clouds of steam, and amid the wreckage of thousands of packing-cases were giant blocks of granite, huge lumps of coal, great anchors, the ruins of a prehistoric world. The noise, confusion, turmoil--who, asked Dorothy, could describe them? She was given to

platitudes, and irritated Judith by insisting that 'such chaos is an emblem of man's energy working to a just end'. The Exhibition in fact turned her head a little spiritually, and made her so deeply proud of being a Herries that she seemed to walk like a goddess. All the Herries felt the same, that the Exhibition was their especial work and Queen Victoria the head of the family.

On the Great Day itself, the First of May, the heart of London beat with a pride and exaltation that was to affect the country for at least another fifty years.

Judith, Dorothy, Lady Herries, little Ellis, Adam, Margaret, John and Elizabeth had, all of them, thanks to old Will's power and position, splendid seats for the opening ceremony.

They started early, and that was wise, for the carriage was soon involved in a long, wearisome procession of carriages from whose windows every kind of bonnet and hat was poking and shrill feminine voices exclaiming: 'But this is monstrous! We shall miss the Queen! It is really too bad!'

John and Elizabeth were to join the others inside the building and were already there when Lady Herries, dressed in a magnificent purple bonnet and superb cashmere shawl, her head very much up, led in her little procession. Judith came last, leaning on Adam's arm.

They had excellent places, and the Sight, the Vision, the Glory-- this, as Dorothy remarked, 'exceeded all Expectations and showed what Man could do when guided by the Divine Will'. (Dorothy was not, in her normal Cumberland domesticity, in the least like this. 'You are a little over-excited, my dear,' Judith had told her that morning.)

Yes, it was superb! Their seats were in one of the galleries, the galleries planted like flower-gardens with bonnets of pink, yellow and white. The Great Central Glory was the Glass Fountain. Of this Archdeacon Rodney Herries' son, Captain William Herries, RN, wrote in his A Jolly Tar's Capers (Weston and Mary, 1895): 'This glorious fountain in the centre of the building, shining, as the sun's rays came slanting down upon it through the crystal roof, as if it had been carved out of icicles, or as if the water streaming from the fountain had been made suddenly solid and transfixed into beautiful forms. Although but a rough, careless little Middy at the time, I can remember well that, standing beside my father, at that time Archdeacon of Polchester in Glebeshire, tears welled up into my youthful eyes and pride of my country fired my ambition.

'"It is such families as ours in such a country as ours," I remember my dear father remarking, "that, under God's Grace, can create, for the benefit of the world, such wonders."'

It must be confessed that Judith saw it all less romantically. Rodney Herries she had, incidentally, always detested. But nevertheless she was carried away, forgetting years, jealousies, aches and pains (for this morning she had a little rheumatism). For one thing the noise was terrific. The waiting multitude was quiet enough, but around them, throughout the building, all the machinery had been set in motion--the MACHINERY, key-note of the Exhibition, symbol, relentless, humourless, of the new world that this day, May 1st, 1851, was introducing. There were in the machine-room the 'self-acting mules', the Jacquard lace machines, the envelope machines, the power looms, the model locomotives, centrifugal pumps, the vertical steam-engines, all of these working like mad, while the thousands near by, in their high hats and bonnets, sat patiently waiting, passive, unwitting that the Age of Man on this Planet was doomed.

Judith and Adam, John and Elizabeth, were most certainly unwitting. Judith's little hand was thrust through Adam's thick arm, while John and Elizabeth were holding hands under Elizabeth's shawl. Margaret was thinking of her father and wishing that he were here, Dorothy's mouth was wide open, and Lady Herries was studying a coarse-grained Chambéry gauze near to her and wondering whether she could obtain one like it. Yes, a superb scene! The canopy above the royal seat, adorned with golden cornice and fringe and a small plume of blue and white feathers at each angle, the floors clean and matted, at each corner of the central square stages for illustrious visitors, from the gallery tops magnificent carpets and tapestries hanging, here the Spitalfields Trophy with its gorgeous silks, and there, the supreme triumph for many, the wonderful plaster of Paris statues, so white, so gleaming, their nudity draped so decently with red cloth. A sob rose in many throats, too, at the sight of the splendid equestrian statues of the Prince and the Queen, so large and lifelike that you might imagine that at any moment the horses might start to charge down the central aisle. (This was Dorothy's fine whispered thought.) Here, to quote Captain William once again: 'Behind these was another Fountain' (it appears that he nourished a passion for fountains!) 'that made the stream as it rushed up from the centre and divided itself into a hundred drops, flashing in the sun as they fell, look like a shower of silver sparks--a kind of firework of water; and beside this rose the green plumage of the palm trees embedded in moss, while close at their feet was ranged a bed of flowers, whose tints seemed to have been dyed by the prismatic hues of the water-drops of the neighbouring fountain. Then appeared the old elm trees of the park, looking almost like the lions of the forest caught in a net of glass; and behind them again was a screen of iron tracery, so light and delicate that it seemed like a lace-work of bronze.'

A little later he continues: 'But it was when the retinue of the Court began to assemble that the scene became one--perhaps the most-- gorgeous in colouring and ever beheld; for it was seen in the clear light of the transparent roof above. The gold-embroidered bosoms of the officers seemed to be almost alight with the glitter of their ornaments; there stood all the ministers of state in their glittering suits; the ambassadors of every country, some in light blues and silver, others in green and gold, others in white, with their bosoms' (incidentally a favourite word of the Captain's) 'studded with their many-coloured orders. There was the Chinese mandarin in his red cap, with peacock's feathers dangling behind, and his silken robes with quaint devices painted upon them in front and at the back. There was the turbaned Turk, and the red fez- capped Egyptian; and there were the chocolate-coloured Court suits, with their filigree steel buttons, and long, white embroidered silk waistcoats.

There was the old DUKE too' (these are the Captain's capital letters) 'with his silver hair and crooked back showing most conspicuous amongst the whole. At the back and sides of the throne stood the gentlemen-at-arms, in their golden helmets, with the long plumes of white ribbon-like feathers drooping over them. Beside these were the portly-looking beefeaters, in their red suits and black velvet caps; and near them were the trumpeters, in their golden coats and close-fitting jockey-caps, with silver trumpets in their hands. Near these were the Aldermen, in their red gowns of office, and the Common-Councilmen in their blue silk gowns, and the Recorder in long powdered Judge's wig, the Archbishop in full lawn sleeves and close curly wig, the Musical Director in his white satin-damask robe and quaint-looking black cap, the heralds in their emblazoned robes, the Garter King-at-Arms in his gorgeous red velvet coat becrusted all over in gold--while round all these were ranged sappers and miners, in their red and yellow uniforms; and behind them were seen the dark-blue coats of the police.'

And the brave Captain complacently comments:

'It was a feast of colour and splendour to sit and gloat over--a congress of all the nations for the most hallowed and blessed of objects--one, perhaps, that made the two old soldiers, as they tottered backwards and forwards across the scene, the most noticeable, because in such a gathering for such an object, the mind could hardly help looking upon them as the last of the warriors to whom the nation would owe its future greatness. I could not but reflect,' the Captain adds, 'that my own family that has been proud to call England its mother for so many centuries had, under God's divine direction, helped sensibly by its honest devotion to duty and its consistent patriotism to bring this Great Country into its supreme world-dominating position.'

Then he continues after this little spurt of family pride: 'At a few minutes before the appointed hour the royal carriages with their bright liveries were seen to flash past the windows of the northern entrance; then darted by a troop of the Life Guards, with their steel helmets and breastplates glistening in the sunshine, and immediately after, the glass sides and roof of the Crystal Palace twanged with the flourish of trumpets that announced the arrival of the Queen. At this moment the gates were flung back, and within the crimson vestibule appeared a blaze of gold and bright colours.

'Then advanced the royal retinue, with the ushers and chamberlain in front, bowing as they moved backwards towards the throne; and after them the Prince leading the Princess Royal, and the Queen with the Prince of Wales, and followed by their Court.

'As the Queen moved onwards with her diamond tiara and little crown of brilliants scintillating in the light, the whole assembly rose and, waving their hats and fluttering their handkerchiefs, they shouted forth peal after peal of welcome.'

And here we may leave the excellent Captain in his happy state of obsequious reminiscence. His book is unquestionably of value, quite apart from its Herries interest, and is certainly worthy of a modern reprint. It attained six editions in the 'nineties.

Sad to say, Judith was not at all moved as was Rodney's son. For one thing the seat on which she was sitting was exceedingly hard, for another she was bothered by the noise of the machines, for another she was feeling odd in the head, a little as though she had been drinking. And for another she had never, in all her life, been impressed very greatly by domesticity: the Queen, the Prince, and their two children appeared to her so dreadfully domestic. That was on her father's side. On her proper Herries side she would have been undoubtedly more deeply impressed had she been quite at her ease. But she was distressed about John, about Adam, and a very little about herself. Most certainly she felt queer, as though there were a weight pressing on her heart, as though, unless she were careful, she would see double. She thought that, in all probability, this glittering and scintillating glass disturbed her. Absurd to build so large a place entirely of glass!

She could not resist, however, some beating of the heart when, as the Queen moved forward, wearing her diamond tiara and crown of brilliants, everyone rose and, waving hats, fluttering handkerchiefs, shouted their cries of welcome. Judith rose, fluttered her handkerchief, shouted with the rest. For a moment she was deeply stirred. The sturdy figure of Victoria appeared to divorce itself from all the world around it, as though it said: 'I am lonely. I am a Queen. I represent loneliness, austerity and power.'

She had that quality, was to have it all her life, of sudden dignified remoteness, so that she became a symbol, a promise, a prophecy. Judith, old enough to be that same Queen's grandmother, felt that now. The white head and light-blue coat of the Master of the Queen's Music appeared on the rostrum, he raised his baton, and above what Captain Herries called 'the melodious thunder of the organ', the National Anthem--led by the choristers--filled the glass dome and was caught by the light and glitter and flung into the sunny heavens. The Archbishop asked for a blessing (the Machinery frantically responded), the Queen and Prince walked in procession, and then Her Majesty declared the Exhibition open. And to end once again with Captain William:

'Immediately were heard the booming of the hundred guns without, telling the people of the Metropolis that the Great Exhibition of the Industry of All Nations had been formally inaugurated.'

Judith recovered herself and sat down. That reaction that inevitably follows all climaxes seized her. What, after all, was all this fuss about? It would only make the country and everyone in it exceedingly conceited. And how tiresome the Exhibition had already become! For months in advance of it no one had talked of anything else, and now for months after it no one would have any other topic. She looked down from the gallery, and the mere thought of all the plaster statues, the great organ, the fountain, the machinery, the furniture, the stalls covered with goods, the endless cups of tea, the ferns and plants and blossoming shrubs, the crying children, angry husbands and disappointed wives, all this wearied her beyond measure.

'I think that I will return to Hill Street,' she said to Adam.

'Very well, Mother dear, but first you must see just a few of the sights.'

She did not want to see any of the sights. She would like to be seated safely and privately in her armchair in her room at Hill Street.

Says Captain William Herries: 'Well might the nation be proud of its Crystal Palace. No other people in the world could have raised such a building . . .'

That is exactly what Judith thought, straining up her old eyes to the glitter and the shine. 'All this glass,' she thought, 'so ostentatious', and her dislike of Prince Albert, assuaged for a moment by the National Anthem, returned in full force.

Adam took her by the arm and she walked gaily along, with Dorothy and Lady Herries very patriotic behind her, Margaret on her other side, and John and Elizabeth not exchanging a word.

'Why don't they speak?' she thought. 'Aren't they happy?' She was wearing a soft grey bonnet and a mantilla of shaded grenadine. She walked as though she were twenty, with every once and again a step that was rebellious, originating in some quite other person. She still saw double on occasion, and there was a twinge of pain in her right shoulder.

There were of course a great many things to see, and oh dear! So many people! Bonnets and polkas, polkas and bonnets, green and brown 'wide-awakes' and fluffy beaver hats--and then the People, this time with a capital P! They will be MUCH worse on the shilling days, but there seem to be a great many of them, even as it is, many with babies in their arms, many with baskets, many with fat bursting cotton umbrellas.

'There are too many people,' Judith said to Adam. The pain in her shoulder had spread to her armpit. 'Really,' she thought, 'Lady Herries is an IDIOT!'

Oh dear, there are a GREAT many things to see! Here is a railwayman, family following, his japan pouch by his side, hurrying to see the locomotives; there a carpenter in a yellow fluffy flannel jacket pointing out to two small boys the beauties of a huge top formed of one section of a mahogany tree.

'Ridiculous!' Judith thought. 'No one in the world can wish for a top as big as that!'

Here is a hatless and yellow-stockinged Bluecoat boy mounting the steps of one of the huge prismatic lighthouses to see the way that it is made . . . Look! There is a model of the Italian Opera House, and behold! There is a minute and most extensive model of Liverpool with a looking-glass sea and thousands of cardboard vessels. This last Adam examined with the most serious care. 'Remarkable! Very remarkable indeed!' he repeated again and again.

Judith could not explain it, she was greatly ashamed but she wanted to slap him. As with all mothers in the world there were moments when she wondered whether these very prosaic results were at all worth all the pains that she had taken.

'Did I bring him up for this?' she thought as she watched him so seriously count the cardboard ships. Then she caught Margaret's calm look of devotion and she hated Margaret. There was no doubt but that she was not at all well.

Of course they must see the machinery. For hours Judith had been dreading this moment. Pressed close against the stout limbs of a member of the National Guard--'Really a CHILDISH costume,' she thought as she looked upwards to his conical hat with its little ball on top, and smelt the rough texture of his red worsted epaulettes and full-painted trousers--she was compelled to admire the power-looms, and then there was the steam brewery, then the model carriages moving along the new pneumatic railway, the hemispherical lamp-shades made out of a flat sheet of paper, the exceedingly noisy flax-crushing machine, the splashing centrifugal pump, the whirling of the cylindrical steam-press . . .

'Adam,' she whispered, drawing him a little closer to her, 'I am glad that I am an old woman. All these machines--what a very unpleasant world it is going to be!'

She whispered, because Dorothy and Lady Herries were in a state of fluttering ecstasy. 'Stupendous!' 'What an achievement!' 'Do observe those wonderful little wheels!' 'Man's triumph over Nature!' Dorothy was proving herself a true Herries. She saw Herries everywhere. If it had not been for the Herries family . . . Strange! Judith must certainly be unwell, for she wanted to slap both Dorothy and Lady Herries.

'Adam,' she whispered, 'I fear that I MUST sit down!'

There was no reply and, looking up, she saw that Adam was not there. Looking farther she discovered Adam and Margaret, a distance away, their backs turned to her, close together examining a piece of machinery. That was possibly the worst moment of her life. Absurd--so little a thing! And yet the horror of Georges'

death, the tragedy of Francis' suicide, the awful evening of Adam's birth--none had touched the loneliness, the isolation of this neglect. Lady Herries was examining a miniature engine with a great assumption of technical knowledge, Elizabeth and John had disappeared.

Judith proudly, her bonnet up, walked away. As she reached the outer hall pain seized her, her heart was beating strangely. Her limbs trembled. Everyone around her seemed weary. On the steps of the red-cloth-covered pedestals weary women and children were seated, some of them munching thick slices of bread and meat. Around the fountains were gathered exhausted families drinking out of thick mugs. All over the floor were orange-skins, dirty pieces of paper; Judith sat down on one of the crimson steps, resting her head on her hands. Was she going to die in this ridiculous place with all these strangers around her? The noise of the machines rattled and quivered, piercing her very backbone. 'Am I going to die? Is this the end?'

A stout woman near to her, her legs spread, crooking a baby in one arm, was drinking out of a bottle. Strange, Judith thought, to allow such people in on the day of the Queen's first visit. But that was right. All were equal--all women together. She had read somewhere that after a certain hour the general public would be admitted. The sight of the woman strengthened and comforted her. She was herself a vagabond, born of vagabonds. No Herries, but daughter of a gipsy. Even though her son deserted her, even though all the pains in the world attacked her, even though this horrible machinery invaded the world, destroying peace and privacy, no one could touch her, she was independent.

She looked up, and there was John. He was standing quite near to her but did not see her. On his face was a look of pitiable distress. He held himself taut, his hands to his side, as if he were answering some charge. On every side of him the crowd pushed and thrust, but he was as alone as though no one else were in the world.

The sight of someone in trouble always caused her to forget herself. She rose, although her knees trembled, walked over to him and touched his arm. He started; her touch had drawn him from a dream.

'John, dear. Take me home. I am very tired.'

That charming kindly smile that she loved in him so much warmed her heart.

'Why, of course, Aunt Judith. We will find Elizabeth.'

She had her hand lightly on his arm. No one should know how ill she felt.

'Such a noise! So many people! I am realizing, my dear John, what a very old woman I am.'

'Nonsense, Aunt Judith,' he said, patting her hand. 'This would be too much for anyone.'

But as he looked at her with so kindly an expression, she realized that it was true: she was an old woman at last.

THE FUNERAL

The last visit to London that she was ever to pay was early in 1854, and the occasion was Will's funeral.

They all said that it was defying Providence for her to go, for she was seventy-nine that Christmas, but she was determined: nothing and no one should stop her. In honest fact they all knew a fearful pride in her resolve. Seventy-nine and going to London! No one but a Herries could have done it, but the Herries always lived to a great age and died in their boots! Look at Will! Eighty-four and in the City three days before his death. It was true that he had been strapped up in his carriage like a mummy, and had held a sort of reception there in Threadneedle Street with clerks and people bowing to him on the steps of his offices: nevertheless, eighty- four and working in the City!

Judith was perfectly conscious of all the things that the different Herries, scattered about the country, would be thinking of her enterprise and, being half Herries herself, she was pleased that they should be pleased. Then of course she insisted that she must pay tribute to Will, for Will was part of her whole life, and now, when her youth was for ever present with her, intermingling with all the current events of her day so that it was often impossible to tell which was past and which was present, Will was perhaps nearer to her than he had ever been before. For as a girl she had never liked him; as a woman she had often despised him; but now, joined as they were in their old age together, she almost loved him.

She had, however, two principal motives for her departure. One was that she would see her beloved Adam, a motive sufficient to carry her AND her coffin if necessary to the North Pole; and the other (although this she confessed to no one in the world) her desire to show Walter Herries that she was still alive and kicking.

Now, when she could not move about as she had once done, but must sit, either in the garden when it was sunny and warm, or in the parlour before the fire, or in her bed with her lace cap on her head and mittens on her fingers just like any other old lady (although she was not in the least like any other old lady!) events and persons were inclined, if you did not keep them in order, to acquire a gigantic significance.

On the one hand she was tranquil as she had never been in her life before. Old age certainly did that for you; and on the days when there was no pain to bother her (for pains of one sort and another paid her now quite constant visits), when she was neither wildly excited by some pleasure (like an unexpected dish for dinner or a sudden visit of a friend, or something entrancing that little Jane had been doing, or a piece of gossip) nor exasperated by some bit of foolishness or some alarm about Adam, why, then this tranquillity was marvellous! You just sat there, or lay there, and it lapped you round like a radiant sheet of golden light, light within you, above you, around you, while the trees burnt in gold steadily against the sky and the streams ran murmuring to your feet, and all this lovely world stood still for you. It was at such times (and they were many) that the past became the present and the present the future. Then there was no Time. She was a child again, watching them ride the horse up Tom Gauntry's staircase, and she was eating roast goose at the 'Elephant', she was walking beside dear Charlie Watson at Watendlath--all was alive again, nothing had died, she herself was immortal.

Nevertheless the things that disturbed, disturbed violently, and the thing that disturbed the worst was Walter. No climax had come as yet to their quarrel. That moment when she had turned to Jennifer and said (ah, how many years ago! Poor Jennifer!): 'Do not be distressed, my dear. I am going to remain,' that challenge had as yet reached no climax. But the climax would come. She knew it as though she were a prophetess and could see the future. Already enough unhappiness had been generated by that old, old quarrel. John's life, Elizabeth's life, Jennifer's life, Walter's Life, Uhland's life--all these had been damaged by it, as hatred and jealousy and envy always damaged any lives that they touched. Her own life and Adam's had been changed by it, for she would have been in Watendlath long ago but for it, and still there was worse to come. She had stayed in Uldale and protected them all, but Walter was still there, the Fortress was still there, Peach's cottage (there was now a younger Peach in command) was just over her garden wall; Walter was a sot and Uhland a crazy misanthrope-- but they were not gone, they still remained.

She had been told, only a week or two ago, that Walter had said of her: 'That old bed-ridden gipsy.' Bed-ridden, was she? She would show him! She would go to London if for no other reason!

Nevertheless, it was Will that she was thinking of as she made her departure. Her heart was soft with tenderness.

Dorothy came with her and was full of matronly care and fuss. After the day of her visit to the Great Exhibition, Judith, to everyone's surprise and offering no reason, abandoned her gay colours and adopted a kind of uniform, black with white ruffles and white lace at the throat. With her hair that had the shining softness of snow and the deep white upon white of an evening cloud, with her small pale face, her exquisite neatness and cleanliness, carrying in her hand her cane, she had the air of some austere Mistress of Ceremonies. But then her whole body and nature laughed at austerity. As she grew older her sense of fun, enjoyment of little things and active consciousness of that enjoyment, her eagerness for news, her avidity for sharing in everything, these things constantly increased in her. Her heart--she was warned that she must be careful of her heart. 'My heart?' she laughed. 'It's as sound as one of Dorothy's muffins' (for Dorothy was a good house-keeper but a heavy-handed cook). Then there was the rheumatism, and sometimes she felt faint. Once indeed she fainted in her bedroom, but no one was there with her and no one was told of it. On many days she was as well and strong as Veronica and Amabel--both very healthy girls. One afternoon she slapped Veronica very heartily indeed because that child, aged now sixteen, told her that God disapproved of reading common books on a Sunday.

'You are a prig, the most dreadful animal in Crea-tion,' Judith cried, and when Veronica, losing her temper, shouted, 'And you're a gipsy,' Judith slapped her. Veronica, who was not a bad child, was appalled at what she had done, and Judith walked all the way up-stairs and brought her down a bag of peppermints. (Judith liked peppermints and always kept a store in her bedroom.) All this in one afternoon.

Moreover, with her favourite Jane, now a wisp of a child of thirteen, she would play games by the hour and never tire. They would play backgammon and Pope Joan, and then Jane would read to her--Macaulay's His-tory, Ruskin's Seven Lamps of Architecture, Pendennis, Hypatia. Judith thought Ruskin 'a bit of a prig' but didn't say so, because Jane thought him so beautiful. After Adam, Judith loved most in the world this dream-ing romantic child who was of the tribe of Francis and Reuben and John. 'I am afraid she will be unhappy,' Judith thought, 'but she will have some of the joys none of the others will know.'

When she set off with Dorothy for London it was Jane who came into her room alone, Jane she held to her heart with all that impetuous feeling that years could not dim, Jane who gave her a parcel of three little hand-kerchiefs that she had worked, Jane who stood in the road staring long after the carriage had disappeared. Timothy, now a big stout fellow of seventeen, who bore a strange resemblance to the portraits of his great-grandfather David Herries, teased her:

'She's a nice old lady, but whew! what a temper!' he remarked.

Jane gave him a queer look.

'All right,' he said uneasily, pinching her ear. 'I daresay I like her as much as you do, if all the truth were known.'

She was so weary when she, at last, reached Hill Street that she felt as though her whole body had been crushed under the wheels of the train that had conveyed her.

She saw Lady Herries for a moment, and her ten-derness for poor Will enveloped the stout painted lady, whom she had never liked, who, however, looked better in her full black silk than she had ever looked in gay colours. She was sitting in the vast dismal drawing room and wearing a bonnet of velvet and crêpe. Every-one was wearing velvet just then.

'That's one thing,' said Judith to Dorothy as she began to undress. 'I shall never wear velvet, my dear. Never! I shall die first!' She added: 'I am dead now, I think. The smell of gas in that train was quite awful. Give me Mr Thorpe's Northern Mythology. It's at the top of my bag. It will send me to sleep if anything will.'

The maid who brought her her breakfast in the morning was full of information. There was nothing that Judith liked better than to have someone with whom she might chat while she was having her break-fast.

It seemed that Will had died quite suddenly of heart failure at three o'clock in the morning. He had not felt well and had gone to his wife's room and had fallen down there dead.

The maid did not know, Judith did not know, no one would ever know of the awful little conversation that had taken place on that last morning.

It was true: he had felt very unwell and had stum-bled to Lady Herries' room. He walked with great difficulty, but she had woken to see him standing there, swaying on his feet, a candle in his hand.

'I think I am going to die,' he gasped, his hand at his heart. She had jumped out of bed, found the drops that were to be given to him if there were a heart-attack. He had sunk, blue in the face, into a chair. He recov-ered a little, looked up into her face, and saw in those pale-blue eyes a look of eagerness.

'You are glad that I am dying,' he said.

'Will! Will!' she cried, sinking on to her knees be-side the chair. 'How can you be so cruel?'

'It is very natural,' he replied. 'I don't blame you. It is perfectly right. You never even pretended to love me. No one has ever loved me. Not even Ellis--'

She protested and tried to hold his hand. He waved her away with a gesture of great dignity. Then his face became purple.

'I have wanted the wrong things--' he murmured, and died.

The funeral was to be at twelve. A great many members of the family were expected. Soon Adam came in to see her. She held out her arms and he knelt by the bed, took her small white hand in his and laughed for sheer joy at being with her again. For, when you had said everything, there was something between these two, stronger than life, stronger than death, something that no one shared with them, something that if it could be caught and held, hard and shining in one's hand like a flaming crystal, would explain, quite sufficiently, what everything is about and why we are travelling at all. But of course it can't be caught.

'Isn't this room absurd?' Judith said, laughing. She could never grow accustomed to the fashions of the time. She belonged in taste to the end of the eighteenth century. Looking back, everything of that time seemed to her to have lightness, brilliance and form. Everything in 1854 was huge, heavy and static, wrapped, too, in a sort of damp fog.

In her room there was a sofa covered with red rep, a copper scuttle and scoop (quite gigantic), a huge fender of brass, fire-irons of set steel, a hearthrug of white sheepskin, two great Minton vases with a floral design on a turquoise ground, a picture made out of seaweed in a frame of Tunbridge ware, a work-box--also of Tunbridge ware--that had a lid with a bouquet in mosaic and sides with 'Berlin wool' mosaic, and a vast dressing-table and mirror, trimmed with glazed linen and muslin. All these things and many more jostled one another in the room that was chill with the chill of the grave. In their centre, very bare, very innocent, was a tin bath.

Among these things Adam knelt and held her hand. He was a broad square man now, brown of face. She didn't like his whiskers, although, of course, every man wore them. She loved his eyes, which were bright, shining and most kindly. He had great breadth of shoulders, looked as strong as an ox. He was absent-minded, but not with her. He wrote for one of Dickens' papers, reviewed books. He was happily married. He was thirty-eight years of age. All these things were apparently true. But the only thing that was true for her was that he was a small child running up the path from the Tarn at Watendlath, calling out to her that he had seen a kingfisher.

These glorious moments came to her very seldom, but, after that awful hour at the Exhibition, she had beaten down her jealousy. Killed it? No, perhaps not, but she was nearly eighty years of age and must learn to accept facts. Was there anything else to learn of life?

She stroked his brown cheek, kissed him, chattered, laughed, then sent him away. She must get up and face the family.

It was a moment that they none of them afterwards forgot, her entrance into the big drawing-room where they were all gathered together. The blinds were drawn and the room was lit with gas which giggled like a silly schoolgirl. The gas was, however, the only jester. Everyone was immensely solemn. Lady Herries sat on the sofa, Ellis at her side. All around her were grouped the family. James Herries was the oldest--he was seventy-five. He stood beside the sofa, a vast, swollen, pompous effigy in black. There was Archdeacon Rodney, with his wife Rebecca, one of the Foxes of Ulverston, and their son the naval officer. There was Stephen Newmark, close to him Phyllis, now very stout, and four of their seven offspring, Horace, Mary, Katherine and Emily; there were, of course, Garth and Sylvia and Amery, that gay bachelor Fred Ormerod, Bradley Cards and his little wife who was like a pincushion in

figure, Timothy Trenchard, his wife and two daughters, Carey Rockage, only a year younger than James and almost as stout, with his wife Cecily and their children Roger and Alice. John and Elizabeth stood quietly by themselves in a window. Walter, Will's eldest son, and the new baronet, was not present, nor was his son Uhland. Everyone thought this disgraceful.

When Judith entered, followed by Dorothy and Adam, a wave of emotion swept the whole assembly. Even Lady Herries, who disliked Judith and was eagerly jealous of her position as the centre of this day's ceremony, was moved. For this was what the Herries above all else loved. Survival. Perpetuity. To last longer than anyone else. To have life and vigour when all your contemporaries had failed to last. Even as once upon a time they had made eager bets on the centenary of Great Aunt Maria, so now their excitement and pride were kindled, for Judith Paris was seventy-nine and yet walked with a firm step, her head up, her eyes shining, the most commanding figure of them all.

But there was more than this. Judith had, in all these years, won a great reputation among them for honesty, kindliness and fair charity. They were not, on the whole, very charitable to one another. No members of any family are very charitable to one another. They know all the wrong things. But Judith, because she had lived in the North, had been outside their squabbles, rivalries and jealousies. They thought her a fine generous-hearted woman. She herself, as she saw all those Herries, so solemn and so black, felt a strange mixture of two quite opposite emotions. She thought them absurd and she felt that she would like to mother them all. They WERE absurd--old James so conscious of his baronetcy, so stout, his black legs like pillows, his grizzled whiskers like cauliflowers; Newmark, his head perched above a high stock and collar so that he resembled a dignified but anxious hen; dear Phyllis, so FEARFULLY fat and her dress so voluminous that all her brood could comfortably have nestled beneath it; Sylvia, alas, no longer pretty, badly rouged, the black velvet on her dress cut to resemble pansies; Rockage, with an odd resemblance to dear old Maria, long dead, but living again in her son's untidiness and a kind of shabby good will (how well Judith remembered that occasion when she had slapped his face at the house in Wiltshire for his riding to hounds over the drawing-room chairs!); Horace Newmark, now a plump pale-faced man of thirty-five in large spectacles and resembling a little in his air of high discontent Mr Thackeray--yes, they were absurd and lovable too. How Will would be pleased did he see this great gathering! How he would approve of the black and the dignity and the solemnity! At the memory of him, to her own surprise, a tear stole down her cheek. 'Old ladies cry easily!' she thought, as she kissed the widow's plump cheek.

She walked about among them, and they were all very kind to her. It was all crêpe and black broadcloth.

Robins, followed by a thin young footman with a cold, walked around offering sherry and a biscuit.

She sat down in a chair near the darkened windows, and the low- murmured conversation went on around her like a draught creeping in through the walls and the floor. It was late February and very damp. There was a discontented, peevish fire in the huge fireplace, but as is so often the case with English fireplaces the heat went up the chimney and left the room severely alone. Nearly everyone seemed to have colds; the sneezing was prodigious. It was understood that a thin rain was falling outside.

Soon she had John and Elizabeth beside her chair. Elizabeth looked lovely but not, Judith thought, very happy. When Elizabeth moved away to talk to Margaret, Judith caught John's hand in hers and said:

'Well, dear John, how are you?'

They were away from the others. She felt his hand clutch hers, tightly, and had an impulse to put her arms around him and hold him safe.

'Very well, Aunt Judith, thank you.'

'And the Secretaryship?'

'Oh, splendid! They are so very good to me.'

'And Elizabeth?'

'We are more in love than ever.'

She nodded her head.

'That's right!'

He was the handsomest man in the room by far. But as she looked at him she caught the oddest resemblance in him to his father Francis. Just that way had his father looked at Uldale that night when he had implored her help. Her help against what? Against nightmares, ghosts, his own frustration . . .

'It's odd, isn't it,' John said, 'Walter and Uhland not coming?'

'Very wrong of them.'

'Yes, I suppose so. Have you . . . have you seen them at all?'

'No, my dear.' She smiled grimly. 'They poison our cows once and again. Walter threatened to bring an action against Bennett's boy for stealing his timber. Let him try, that's all!'

'Yes, Aunt Judith . . . You know, Elizabeth wrote a letter to Walter the other day. She thought she ought to. She heard he was ill.'

'Did she, my dear?'

'He never answered her, though.'

The time had arrived. St. Luke's Chelsea, a church that Will had attended for many years because he liked its Gothic and the length of its sermons, was their destination--a long journey at the pace that their carriages would take them. The hearse had plumes, almost as large as palm trees. The array of carriages was magnificent. Judith accompanied Lady Herries and Ellis in the first carriage.

That is always a problem, the conversation on a funeral journey, but Lady Herries made it no problem at all. First she cried, looking out of the carriage window,

pleased and satisfied with the attention that the procession was securing. Then she set about the task of convincing Judith that her life was now at an end, that she had only Ellis to live for, and that she alone, of all God's mortals, had understood Will and given him what he needed. Ellis, who was now eleven years of age, less shrivelled than he had been, but bony, horse-faced like all the Herries, with sharp eyes above a large bony nose, said nothing. Did he care at all, wondered Judith? Did he know that he had been the one comfort and pride of his father's old age? At any rate, he looked like a gentleman. It was extremely difficult for any Herries NOT to look like a gentleman, which was perhaps what was the matter with them. Judith noticed that once and again Ellis stole a sharp look at her. Of what was he thinking? Of her age, in all probability. How old she must seem to him! And yet he had been accustomed to old people! A sudden sympathy for the poor child caught her. She put out her hand and held his. The little hand, in its shiny black glove, was as cold as a seashell.

'Will altered,' Lady Herries was saying. 'Altered immensely in the last years. He depended upon me for everything. I say nothing against his first wife--' ('You'd better not,' thought Judith) '-- but to pretend that she understood him was absurd. Poor Will! Everyone thought--even those nearest to him' (this with a glance at Judith) 'thought that his great interest was money. Erroneous-- quite erroneous. If you had heard the way that he would talk late in the night--'

Judith began to be angry. But she saw her anger coming from a long way off. She had, through many years' practice, trained herself to meet it and turn it back before it reached her heart. Bad for old ladies to be angry, and in any case waste of time. But how she did hate this woman! False and greedy and sham! Poor Will! how lonely in those last years he must have been! Old pictures began to crowd up again--that familiar one when she and Will and Francis had watched the fireworks by the Lake and had prophesied about their lives. Soon she would begin to cry. She MUST not cry. She WOULD not before this woman--all scent, whale-bone and crêpe. She could not see her face for the heavy black veil that covered it, but she knew how small and mean those eyes were, how tight and hard the little mouth! Those were not the thoughts for a funeral, poor dear Will's funeral, so she looked out of window and saw a French poodle walking beside an old lady; he had a peaked nose, woolly wig, leggings and tail-band, and a horrible shaved, salmon-coloured body. The old lady was younger in years than Judith but not half so vigorous. She walked as though she were a hundred.

They were passing slowly through a mean, shabby street. Groups gathered, children ran, men took off their caps--for this moment the Herries dominated the scene. It did not make them proud. It was their right, now and always--so much their right that they gave it scarcely a thought. Here is a gin-palace, here a seedy

French pension, children in torn pinafores gazing at the sweetshop window, here a rag shop with tobacco-pipes crossed in the window and turpentine-infected bundles of firewood. Through all this, drink, poverty, childhood, sweets and tobacco and gin, Will is grandly riding for the last time!

'Without my care and affection I shudder to think what his last years would have been--'

Judith clutched the top of her cane with her two little hands. In all her seventy-nine years, with the single exception of Mrs Ponder, she had never disliked anyone so much. She heard a sniff, a strange little strangled sniff. Ellis was crying, tears were trickling down his bony nose. She put out her arm and drew him closer to her. He stayed against her as stiff as a whalebone. But she was glad that he was crying. He HAD cared for his father then. He HAD cared! She would do something for Ellis. Ask him to Uldale, let him play with Dorothy's children . . . Then she found that she too, under her veil, was crying, and suddenly she wanted to lean forward and take Lady Herries' hand. Perhaps what the woman said was true. She HAD cared for Will--in her own peculiar undemonstrative way.

They have arrived at the church. Herries wing out of carriages like crows from a nesting-tree. But silent. Immensely solemn. How broad and deep the hat-bands on the black hats, how heavy the whiskers, the stocks, the voluminous black skirts, the umbrellas, the thick black boots! A crowd has gathered about the church door. The church has all its attendant offices and officers--the stout, self-important beadle, the neatly grained high boxes, the three- decker pulpit, the wizen-faced pew-openers (two of them). The church is icily cold, and the hassock on which little Ellis kneels is hard as iron. He is miserable and feels a sense of aching loss, although loss of what he has really no idea.

Judith, sitting there, watching the big coffin draped in black, wondering about the pew-opener in the black bonnet who had already retired to a corner behind a pillar to count the pennies, thought that the Herries must have multiplied themselves threefold since they entered the church. She thought--for her imagination was fantastic now with weariness and chill--that the ghosts of departed Herries must have joined the living. Maybe if she looked more closely she would see poor Warren there, gazing at her as he used to do with that dog-like devotion, Francis, Jennifer, even David and Sarah, and Deborah Sunwood whom she had loved so dearly in her childhood, and Jennifer's father and mother, and poor Christabel. When you reached her age the dead and the living were all equally alive--no one was dead, no one was living.

Yes, Adam was living! He sat beside her, and sometimes he would look at her to see that all was well with her. Then quietly, with that solid protection that she loved so in him, he put his strong arm round her:

and then, to her shame, to her great disgrace, she fell fast asleep!

She woke hurriedly to find that the coffin was leaving the church and that she, with Lady Herries and Ellis, must immediately follow it. 'Oh, dear! How disgraceful!' she thought. 'I do hope that nobody saw me!' But she walked down the church, very firmly, all the Herries' eyes upon her. She did not care for the family now. She was thinking only of Will--Will, whose last grand ceremony was over, who would do sums on paper no longer, would be denied potatoes by Robins never again; with the exit of that body out of the church one long chapter of her life as well as his was closed.

Later they were all in the long dining-room. The table was covered with food: drink of every kind was on the vast sideboard that looked as though it had once formed part of a great mahogany mountain and was still marked with the pick-axes of ardent climbers. Judith, dizzy with an almost drunken weariness, sat in a chair near the fireplace. All that she wanted was to go to bed; meanwhile she must listen to the Family. Inhuman furniture and human bodies, high mountains of ham and beef, chickens, pies, great loaves of bread all circled round her together. There was a marble group near the window--'Sir William Herries, Bart, and Lady Herries'-- poor Christabel like an early Christian Martyr in a long icy flowing robe. The fender was of painted mahogany. There were six dessert-stands in ormolu with monkeys carrying silver nuts. On the mantelpiece were some towering vases of Copeland ware, gold on a cobalt blue ground.

'Everything is so large,' she thought, and once again had the old, old wish that her own legs were longer. Soon, however, she forgot both her weariness and the furniture in her interest in the conversation that went on around her. They had forgotten her, all save Adam and Margaret. But, more than that, they had already forgotten Will. Gone were those hushed voices, vanished that sad solemnity. As they crowded about the table, eating like wolves and drinking like the damned, their voices rose ever higher and higher, their excitement, with every moment, keener.

For now, liberated from that momentary consciousness of poor William, aware that he was safely underground and that they could therefore move freely forward with the enterprise and energy that belonged to their Herries blood, they were discussing the War.

It was, she reflected, natural that they should do so, for only yesterday, February 27th, England's ultimatum to Russia had been despatched. She herself detested war, any war, every war. She had been in Paris in 1815 and had borne Adam there, seen his father die there, suffered agonies and terrors that had affected her whole life. Why anyone should be GLAD about war she could not imagine, but not only was everyone in the room GLAD, they were TRIUMPHANT.

She saw, too, with that detached observation that came from her mother Mirabell (who had been quite certainly not at all a Herries) that this was for them not an English war but a HERRIES war. It was the Herries who were indignant at the Massacre of Sinope, the Herries who applauded and supported every action of Lord Stratford, the Herries who had advised Lord Palmerston to resign, the Herries who thought Louis Napoleon a hero, the Herries who mocked poor Mr Cobden and silly Mr Bright for their support of the Peace Society.

As Judith listened she realized with every moment more fully what it was that separated her from the Herries clan and all the other clans in the world like them-- what it was that had separated her father and Francis and Reuben, what it was that gave John his terrors and made little Jane walk apart from her healthy and energetic sisters. Here it was, this quality of the uneasy imagination, this desire for a beauty that was never to be caught, this consciousness, pursuing, relentless, unceasing, of a world BEHIND the world. She could have got up from her chair and, stamping her cane on the floor, have cried: 'You fools! You fools! Will nothing teach you?'--but all she did was to smile a little, refuse a plate of ham courteously offered her by the Archdeacon, and consider pensively the silver monkeys with their silver nuts.

So, over Will's dead body, they sang their Song of Triumph.

Old James, whose chest was congested so that he wheezed like a harmonium, coughing over his plate of chicken, cried to anyone who might listen: 'I tell you, sir, these damned Russians must be put down.' He caught the ear of Cecily Rockage, a thin woman of sixty who greatly admired him (as she admired indeed everyone, for she was a humble woman). 'I can tell you for your private ear, my dear Cecily, that in the Club a day or two back Clarendon himself told me that in his opinion Newcastle had managed Palmerston exceedingly well, getting him to withdraw his resignation without any conditions, you know. Of course, the Radicals are disgusted, and so they may be. But in my opinion--'

'That's just what Carey says,' Cecily Rockage murmured, looking about her in her dim, peering way to see that her beloved son Roger was having plenty to eat and was thoroughly happy.

'They are important,' Judith thought. 'They are beginning to cover the country.'

In her Cumberland retreat she had not realized HOW important the Herries had grown. Once upon a time there were but a few of them, a gambler here, someone there riding a horse into a wilderness, an old man and an old woman drinking over the fire, but now the times had favoured them. They believed in England, they believed--almost terribly--in themselves. Oh! how they believed! What unquestioning confidence they had! Everything, everything was right with Eng-

land from her Government to her furniture, and Judith realized, as she looked about her, as she heard Ormerod's gay laugh, and the Archdeacon's benevolence, and Stephen Newmark's solemn blessing, as she saw the women billowing in happy pride about their men, Sylvia a little elated with wine, Phyllis the proud mother, Rodney's Rebecca the eager listener, that there was something fine and grand in their faith, that these men and women WERE making England what she was, England the dominant Power of the world, the Queen of the Earth!

Only--was it worth the trouble: all this hard work, energy, faith? Queen of the Earth! WAS that really important?

'I am really very tired, darling,' she whispered to Adam. 'I think I'll go up to bed if no one minds.'

No one minded. Earlier in the day, when William was still above ground, she was of importance. Now she was forgotten; England's Glory had taken her place.

Later Adam came to say goodnight to his mother. As he climbed the high stairs, leaving the boom and whisper of voices behind him, he felt a great longing to take his mother and Margaret, wrap them in shawls and whisk them off, with himself, to a desert island--a glorious island of burning sun, coral sand, heat and light and colour. The three of them alone, living for ever, always warm, always private, telling one another stories, and making necklaces of shells. He stopped on the landing opposite a dark engraving of Prince Albert and the Queen, and laughed. Two mice heard him laugh and, surprised out of their lives, whisked away.

He entered his mother's room carefully. There was a fire burning; the copper scuttle-scoop, the brass fender, the steel fire-irons shone resplendently. The old lady was lying, her pillows propped up behind her, apparently staring at a large oil painting entitled 'Little Black Sambo', which showed a small black child daintily covered with the leaf of a palm tree, sitting on the seashore sucking his thumb while two little white girls, clad immaculately in muslin and long pantaloons, stared at him with speculation. The firelight danced on the wall; the rain beat against the pane--it was not an uncheerful scene. She did not turn her head nor move when he entered. In spite of his heavy figure he trod very gently, sat down on a chair beside the bed and waited.

Then suddenly an awful fear seized him that she was going to die. Her face was always pale, but her small hands as they lay on the gay patchwork quilt had a marble pallor. And she lay so very still. She was, after all, of a great age. She should never have made the journey to London; this day must have been of a fearful exhaustion for her.

The thought that he might lose her at any moment now--that she might go out like a candle carelessly blown by the wind--made him catch his breath, constricted his heart. The only three people in the world whom he loved, now that Caesar Kraft was dead, were his mother and Margaret and John. His nature was deeply modest, acutely sensitive. He could not believe that men and women liked him, and it was true that, at present, very few knew him because he was so silent about himself and thought himself a useless, cumbering failure. He had had great ambitions for the good of man and they had all failed. At that moment when Kraft had fallen and died at his feet, all his hope of helping his brother man had died. He had not the confidence nor the power nor the will. He was so shy of thrusting himself forward, so shy of display or self-advertisement, that men thought him proud and arrogant. At the newspaper office, in the little Club to which he belonged, even with a man like Charles Dickens, genial, friendly, exuberant, he could not let himself go. But these two women understood him, his mother and Margaret understood him, and to lose one of them . . .

And there was one more thing. He was only half alive in London. His soul ached for Cumberland, but Margaret did not like it. She was unhappy there. Stones and clouds, clouds and stones . . .

She turned her head and saw him. She put out her hand and caught his.

'Dear me, how nice, Adam! I have been dreaming, I suppose. But I don't know. I never know now whether I am dreaming or not . . . I was very tired, I must say, but bed is most comforting. There is no place like bed. I am sure that I never expected to feel that. I used to be so very energetic. But it's my body that's tired, not my spirit . . . How disgusting old James is, eating such a lot at his age!'

They talked quietly and happily together.

'Mother,' Adam said. 'One thing I hadn't told you. Will Leathwaite is coming to London to be my servant.'

That interested her. 'Is he indeed? What a good thing! I like Will so very much.'

'Of course it's absurd that I should have a servant with the little I make. But he wants to come. He says he doesn't care what I pay him, and it will be a little piece of home.'

'A very big piece,' Judith remarked, chuckling. 'That's nice for you, dear. Are they still guzzling and drinking down there?'

'I suppose so.'

'And what a deal they talk. Chatter, chatter, chatter. They are all delighted there's a war--why, I cannot imagine.' She closed her eyes and dreamt again. She talked as though out of a dream. 'I fancied just now that God was in the room. A God a little like Georges and a little like yourself, Adam. Perhaps that's what God will be--composed of the people we love most. He was so very kind and most reassuring. I have never been a religious woman, you know, Adam. Reuben Sunwood used to be greatly disappointed with me. He was so

very certain. But I suppose an old woman may be allowed her fancies. I find that everyone is very certain about God in these days. Quite different from when I was a girl. It's as though they had made Him themselves.'

She sat up, climbing up out of her dream, full of energy again.

'I do hope you are happy, dear Adam,' she said.

'Yes,' he said. 'When I am with you and Margaret, Mother. But I'm terribly shy. It grows on me, I'm afraid.'

'Yes, your father was the same. But I shouldn't worry. We are different--you and I and poor John and little Jane. And the Herries family is an awkward family to be different in. All my life I have been fighting them. And now I am not fighting anyone any longer, even Walter. Too much trouble.'

She lay back again, closing her eyes.

'How lovely life is, all of it--having a baby, fighting Walter, pains and aches, food and riding up to Watendlath, poor Jennifer, the garden at Uldale, dear Adam, dear, dear Adam . . .'

She had fallen asleep. He sat there for some while watching her, then bent down and kissed, very gently, her forehead, then stole from the room.

CLIMAX TO A LONG SEQUENCE

I JUDITH AND WALTER

Will Leathwaite had come to say farewell. He was going at last, after six months' delay, to London to be Adam's servant. Judith was able to sit on the lawn in the September sunshine, it was so warm. The sun had the shininess of a hot sea and the lawn was like misty waters; the colours seemed gently to roll in shades of pale citron, of silver-grey, from the floor of the little Gothic temple to the walls, faintly pink, of the beloved house. Across the road, beyond the old peach-stained stones, rose the shadowed forms of the mountains, stretching themselves like great luxurious cats in the sunshine. A flight of curlews broke the pale wash of the sky, and you could feel, even though you could not see, the rough grass of the brown moorland, the icy glitter under the warm sun of the running moorland streams. Those green slopes, as yet scarcely purpled with heather, heaped up like a wave above the house answering the plaintive windy cry of the curlews.

In the middle of this peace, listening as always for her delight to the rhythm of running water, water slipping happily under the sunlight, she said goodbye to Will Leathwaite. It was as though she were sending Adam a piece of the North. Will was nearly fifty now and towered above her as he stood, his cap in his hand, staring in front of him. His colouring was very fair and there was a bald patch on the very top of his round bullet-like head. His features were stamped with simplicity, obstinacy, strength and kindliness; his cheeks were russet with good health, and there were little wrinkles at the corners of his very blue eyes that spoke of extreme good-nature. His body was large, broad, clumsy, his shoulders a little bowed. It was plain that he saw only one thing at a time and that once he had an idea in his head, nothing--no earthquake, no thunderbolt--could loosen it. He stood up in the thin Northern sunlight as though he had been created by it.

'Well, Will, you will look after Mr Adam, will you not?'

'I will, ma'am.'

'Will you like town life, do you think? It is very different from anything you've been used to.'

'So long as Mr Adam is satisfied, I'm ready,' he answered.

'It will be a great thing for Mr Adam. He hasn't many friends, you know.'

'Yes. T'nature of him is slow like my own, ma'am.' Then he smiled, a delightful slow, considering smile. 'T'best way, I think, ma'am.'

The children, Amabel and Jane, ran across the lawn, laughing and shouting, with a ball. He turned and watched them with a quiet decorous pleasure.

'Write to me, Will, and tell me how you find everything.'

'Yes, ma'am. Thank you, ma'am.'

He touched his yellow forelock and stepped slowly, steadily away, moving his great body with the ease and dignity of a gentleman in his own right. She sighed happily. It would be nice for Adam to have so trustworthy a man at his side.

She was glad that she was feeling strong and vigorous and that the air was warm, because she had much to think about. Both Margaret and John were staying in the house. Adam had written to say that Margaret was tired with the London air and needed a holiday, so she had been at Uldale a week and, so far, the visit had been a great success.

John had suddenly appeared with only a telegram's warning. No one knew why he had come. Then Elizabeth had written to say that she had sent him because he could not sleep in London. The summer had been hot: his master was in Switzerland. She herself was going to stay with the Rockages at Grosset. It was better that she and John should be apart for a while. This was sufficiently alarming, but John had said nothing until suddenly last evening, wishing Judith goodnight, he had told her that Elizabeth was going to have a baby.

'It's all wrong, Aunt Judith,' he burst out. 'I should not have a child.' He was quivering and his face was strained with distress.

'What nonsense!' she said. 'I never heard greater nonsense. Why, it's splendid for dear Elizabeth to have a baby.'

'It will be a coward--as my father was, as I am.'

He left the room without another word.

After that she slept very badly. Dream followed dream, and every dream was filled with apprehension. Every part of her past life seemed, in her dreams, to be now connected and to point to some inevitable result. She was once again with Georges at Christabel's Ball, with Charlie Watson in Watendlath, with Warren in Paris, and someone cried in her ear: 'Had it not been thus this would never have come about.'

'But what?' she cried.

But she could not see the event. She struggled, her heart full of love and fear. Adam, approaching her, tried to speak to her but was prevented. John waved to her a despairing hand before he vanished from sight. But she could do nothing. She was held, as one is in dreams, impotent, with no power in her limbs to move. Suddenly the old cruel figure of Mrs Ponder, Jennifer's servant, appeared. She was on her knees searching Judith's private papers.

'NOW you will have to leave the house!' she cried, raising her malignant face.

'But I will not!' Judith answered.

And she had not. That was one thing upon which she could look back with pleasure, that in spite of all the odiousness and spying, in spite of Jennifer's lazy treachery, she had faced Mrs Ponder to the end, seeing the hateful woman at last out of the house. But what had Mrs Ponder to do with John? Ah, she remembered the little scene when that vile woman had thrown John's rabbit out of window. Was that, too, one link in the chain? Had every event, however slight, its inevitable result? But she must do something about John. She must not allow him to slip into tragedy as his father, Francis, had done. She must do something about John, and then she looked up to see Margaret coming across the grass towards her. She was now thirty-four years of age and a fine strongly built woman with a broad carriage, a calm open countenance and great quietness and repose in all her movements.

'She has grown,' Judith thought, 'like Adam and Adam like her, as many married people do when they have lived much together and love one another.' As she thought this a spasm of the old jealousy bit her as it might be a little animal jumping from the grass, but she brushed it away with her hand.

Margaret was wearing a simple grey muslin with panniers of white taffeta placed at the edges. In the bosom of her dress she had a white rose. Her dark hair was brushed back on either side, parted in the middle. She was carrying her hat in her hand. She brought peace and assurance with her.

'I like this woman,' Judith thought, as though she were seeing her for the first time. 'I am friends with her at last.'

The children had tired of their game and had run into the house. The sun was very slowly sinking, and the golden glow moved, travelling from place to place, softening the mountains with a purple flush while the sky faded slowly from bright blue into a translucent amber. Soon there will be a world of grey and silver and the hill will be dark, chill and strong. But that is not yet. The two women have half an hour to talk, the running stream the only sound in the world save their voices.

'You will not be cold, Mother?' Margaret asked, laying her broad strong hand on Judith's black dress.

'Oh no, my dear. And see that the grass is not damp for you.'

Margaret laughed. 'I have so many petticoats,' she said, 'I could sit in a stream and not be wet.'

Her voluminous grey dress spread out on the green grass and the light transmuted it.

'Have you seen John?' Judith asked.

'No; he has been away all day,' Margaret answered, sighing. 'He seems dreadfully unhappy. He has been so for months. He would talk to Adam at one time, but lately he has avoided him too, and Adam loves him so much. Elizabeth says that he will not talk to her either.'

'Yes—he is as his father was.' Judith beat her small hands impatiently on her lap. 'I can catch hold of NOTHING.'

'Adam thinks,' Margaret began, 'that it all began from the day when someone near here told him about his father and mother. He had a shock then that has weakened him like water, and it is of no use to say that he OUGHT not, that I would not be like that, that I would not let the past touch me. We are all different, and it seems to me that the Herries who ARE weak are weaker than any others, as though someone had said once: "If you are born a Herries and refuse to have common-sense you shall suffer as no one else suffers. Have common-sense or die." Adam has just enough common-sense to save him.'

'Well, he is only half a Herries, my dear,' Judith said briskly. 'His father was only half a Herries and I am only by nature quarter a one, for my father was a wanderer and a vagabond and so was my mother. And here I am as warm and comfortable as a cat, thank goodness. It's more than I have deserved.'

Margaret hesitated. She found words no more easily than Adam, but there was something that she had been wanting for a long while to say, and now was a good time.

'Mother,' she began at last, slowly, in her deep rich voice, looking down at the grass. 'You do not hate me any longer, do you?'

'Hate you? Why, no, my child, I love you.'

'You did hate me once.'

Judith shook her head. 'No, I never hated you, of course. How could I when Adam loved you?—and besides all my life I must confess that I have found it very difficult to hate anyone. John's mother for a while once,

and a horrid servant she had. Walter, perhaps, at odd moments. No. But I was jealous of you, I must confess.'

'Yes, I knew it.' Margaret stroked the grass with her hand. 'And it made me terribly unhappy. But I have never been able to express myself. I am so very shy of feeling, and women are not supposed to have any feelings. It is not thought nice.'

'In my young day,' Judith said, nodding her head vigorously, 'women had plenty of feeling and showed it. I don't know what's come over the world. Women are not supposed to have legs any more, and children are found in gooseberry bushes. Stuff!'

'And you are not jealous any more?'

'No. All my fires have died down. I sit and look on. But I love you, my dear. I do indeed. Adam has been the passion of all my life since my husband died, but a time came when I saw that someone else must do the things for him that I had done—and more things than I could ever do. How fortunate I have been that it was a woman like you, not one of these coarse painted creatures or one of these niminy-piminies all affectation, or one of those good perfect creatures like the woman in Mr Dickens' David Copperfield. What was her name? Agnes. But, of course, Adam would have chosen well. He would have had a whipping from me if he had not.'

'I have wanted to tell you,' Margaret said slowly, 'how grateful I am to you, how dearly I love you. I cannot say things, but I thought that once I must tell you--'

She leant up and put her arms around Judith. The two women kissed, and Judith laid her hand for a moment on Margaret's broad forehead.

'God bless you and keep you in all His ways, dear daughter. And now,' she went on quite sharply, 'I must go in. The sun will soon be down. How nice! I shall read Mrs Gaskell's Cranford over the fire. They say it is all about old ladies who are frightened by cows--like Mrs Potter at Threlkeld. Give me your arm, my dear. My right foot has gone fast asleep.'

A little later she was sitting in front of the parlour fire, her feet propped up on a worsted stool, a thick woollen shawl round her shoulders, and large spectacles on the end of her small nose. Her trouble was that her nose was TOO small. The spectacles WOULD slip off! It was only of late that her eyes had begun to fail her. She was reading Cranford with many chuckles.

'How true this is! We are just the same here round Uldale. "In the first place, Cranford is in possession of the Amazons--all the holders of houses, above a certain rent, are women. If a married couple come to settle in the town, somehow the gentleman disappears; he is either fairly frightened to death by being the only man in the Cranford evening parties, or he is accounted for by being with his regiment, his ship, or closely engaged in business all the week in the great neighbouring commercial town of Drumble, distant only twenty miles on a railroad. In short, whatever does become of the gentlemen, they are not at Cranford; . . . but every man cannot be a surgeon. For keeping the trim gardens full of choice flowers without a weed to speck them; for frightening away little boys who look wistfully at the said flowers through the railings; for rushing out at the geese that occasionally venture into the gardens if the gates are left open; for deciding all questions of literature and politics without troubling themselves with unnecessary reasons or arguments; for obtaining clear and correct knowledge of everybody's affairs in the parish; for keeping their neat maidservants in admirable order; for kindness (somewhat dictatorial) to the poor, and real tender good offices to each other whenever they are in distress--the ladies of Cranford are quite sufficient.'"

Judith laid the book down on her lap and considered.

'How very excellent! That is exactly Miss Poole and Janet and Mary Darlington and Mrs Withers and Mrs Spooner. We are a world of women. Why? Why is Dorothy so important? She is not very clever nor is she at all beautiful, but she has a kind of kingdom. Now I NEVER had a kingdom--'

The door opened. The little maid Eliza, her face twisted from its rosy simplicity with surprise, horror, alarm, excitement and general sense of drama, whispered something.

'What do you say, Eliza?' Judith asked, turning round and pushing her spectacles back on to her nose.

'Sir Walter Herries, ma'am.'

Walter! Her book dropped to the floor. She stayed, for a moment, listening as though she expected to hear some dreadful sound, but all that came to her was the cheerful shrill voice of someone singing in the kitchen. Then, sitting up very straight, she said:

'Ask Sir Walter to come in.'

A moment later he was standing beside the sofa, very stiffly bowing. He was dressed for riding and carried his hat in his hand. His hair was grey now (he was sixty-two) and he was clean-shaven, which was most unusual and gave him an odd babyish appearance. His red face was purple-veined, but he was not so stout as when Judith had last seen him. He was untidy, as though he had no one to look after him. Judith, against her wish, felt sorry for him.

'Well, Walter, how are you? Won't you sit down? Been poisoning any of our cows lately? How are the little Peaches? Humphrey, the stableman, found one of them in our gooseberry bushes not long ago.'

Walter sat down. He spread his legs, looked gravely at her; she noticed that his mouth was not very steady and that his hands shook.

'You are looking well, Judith,' he said.

'I am very well, thank you.' She took off her spectacles. She did not intend that he should say that her sight was going. Then sharply, as though to convey to him that she had not all day to waste:

'Why am I honoured?'

'A damned pretty place you've got,' he said, looking about him. 'Everything very fresh and charming.'

'Well--well. That's not what you've come to say.'

'No, it isn't. Sharp as ever you were!'

'Nor have you come to pay me compliments. Do you mind that window? If so, pray close it.' (For the window was open. Judith, unlike her contemporaries, loved fresh air.)

'No matter, thank you.' He hummed and hawed, then began a long rambling statement.

She could not make out what he was after. He had a lot to say about the past. Was it not foolish that they had wasted so much of their lives in quarrelling? He had been a young hot-headed fool, had done many things that he now regretted. Looking back, his ill-temper seemed to him now to have been very aimless, motiveless. But it was his father who, from the time he was a baby, had persuaded him that his mother had been insulted, and then Jennifer and Francis--well, Judith would agree that their conduct . . .

'I will agree to nothing,' Judith said.

But he did not appear to hear her. He went rambling on. He was afraid that he'd taught Uhland the same doctrine. He saw now what a mistake he had made. He saw now that he had been mistaken in many things.

'Well, I'm glad of that anyway,' said Judith. 'But there is no use to go back on the past. If you are asking me to forget and forgive, Walter, frankly I cannot. Too much harm has been done-- Francis, Jennifer, Reuben, and Jennifer's children. My own life, too . . .' She coughed. She could not but be sorry for him a little. There were spots on his waistcoat, and his stock was badly tied. 'But what do you WANT, Walter? What have you come here for?'

He hesitated, looked at her as though he were begging her to help him. Then he said an extraordinary thing.

'Hatred, Judith, is a very rare quality in men. One seldom meets it.'

She did not know what to say.

'Very rare,' she answered drily.

'I have never hated you. My mother never hated anybody. Jennifer never hated anyone. You yourself have never hated.'

'Well?'

'What I intend to say is--I am clumsy at expressing myself--but out of all this past quarrelling, not very real, you understand, there has come much unhappiness.' He paused, rubbed his cheek with his hand. 'I myself am not a happy man. All my own fault, I admit it. I have lost my daughter quite through my own fault. There is something bad in our blood which, if it is indulged--'

517

He stared at her in quite a fuddled way as though he had been drinking, which it was likely that he had. But what was his meaning? What was his intention? For what had he come? She remembered the scene in this very room when she had slapped his face. He was not the kind of man either to condone or forget.

'Hatred, Judith,--real hatred--is a sort of madness.'

'Well?'

He went on again, finding words very difficult.

'You see . . . you know . . . you must understand . . . Upon my word, I am extremely clumsy--you must forgive me--but my boy-- Uhland--'

'Yes--Uhland?' she said, more softly, because now, as always when he spoke of his son, there was a new and moving note in his voice.

'I had great hopes for Uhland. I may be a man who has made a mess of his life. When I am sober I am ready to make such an admission-- but Uhland was to be different. He had a heavy handicap' (his voice was gathering ardour now that Uhland was his topic) 'his lameness--the sense that he was unlike the others. And then his mother was not strong, and I was not the wisest father. I was anxious to indulge him, too anxious perhaps, and he was unusual, unlike other boys--'

He paused again, and gently, looking at him almost as though she were his friend, Judith said:

'Yes, Walter, I understand. In that at least I have always understood you.'

Encouraged, he went on:

'I am another man when I am in my cups. I will be quite honest with you. I have spoiled many things by my follies, but Uhland I have always kept apart. I saw from the beginning that he was by himself, alone. He has never cared for anyone except your Adam. He has never, I fear, cared in the least for myself, and the knowledge that he did not made me wilder, wilder than perhaps I would otherwise have been. But what I would point out is that all our quarrels, yours and mine and our parents' before us--the events in the life of your own father so many years ago--have found a kind of resting-place in poor Uhland's nature. He was born with a grudge and all his instincts have been twisted. In a fashion he is a scapegoat for the errors of the rest of us.' He stopped once more, wiped his mouth with his hand.

She was, in spite of herself, deeply touched. This was a different Walter from any that she had ever seen. She felt behind his precise, artificial, clumsy speech almost an agony of apprehension, and her own apprehension that she had been so conscious of all day rose to meet his.

She almost cried out:

'Oh, Walter, what is it? What has happened?'

Enemies though they had been all their lives, they were now almost allies.

He went on, staring at her as though that assisted him.

'Uhland has grown ever more strange. Our house is not an agreeable place. I will not pretend that it is agreeable, but of late Uhland's conduct has frightened me greatly--'

'Uhland's conduct?'

'Yes.' He found now the greatest difficulty in choosing his words. 'He is, I fear, most unhappy, but he will speak to no one. He shuts himself in his room. He walks over the house. The servants are afraid to remain where he is. And for myself, I think he hates me.'

She said nothing. He went on more swiftly.

'But it is not of myself that I wanted to speak to you. I came . . . I came because--' He said urgently, leaning towards her: 'You have John staying with you?'

'Yes,' she said.

'You know, of course, that from the time of his childhood Uhland has always especially hated John.'

'Yes,' she said.

'It has been a sort of madness in him. I fear, I greatly fear that I was myself originally responsible for that. It seemed to me in those days unfair--unfair that John should be so handsome while my son--'

'Yes, I know, I know,' Judith said quickly.

'Then I implore you, Judith--I beg of you--send John back to London immediately. Immediately. Uhland knows that he is here. He has, during the last week, been very odd in his behaviour. He talks--he was talking last night--as though that old grudge had reached some kind of climax. We are, all of us, responsible for the past, I more than any, and if anything were to happen--'

'But what could happen?'

'There have been many acts of violence in our family,' he went on. 'It is as though there were an element of violence in our blood . . . No. This is perhaps foolish, unreal. We are, I suppose, the most sober and sensible family in England, and just because of that when we are not sensible--'

He got up and she could see that he was greatly agitated.

'Never mind our family,' he said. 'Damn the family! This is urgent, personal to ourselves. I implore you, send John back to London tomorrow.'

She nodded. She looked up and gave him her hand for the first time for many years.

'Yes, Walter. You are right. Thank you for coming. It could not have been easy. John shall return to London. In fact this is no new thing. I have been aware of it for many years. John has been under some kind of shadow all his life, as his father was before him. I will see that he goes tomorrow.'

Walter held her hand, looked at her, bowed, then said almost defiantly:

'I have not come here to confess my sins, Judith. I shall be tomorrow as I was yesterday. I shall find myself a fool, I don't doubt, for coming to visit you. But for an hour at least I see sense. Goodbye. I can find my own way out.'

Judith sat on, her hands folded in front of her, looking into the fire, wondering as to which would be the best way to persuade John. This, had she known it, was a waste of energy, for John had heard everything, standing among some flowerpots, his hands scratched unwittingly by the nails of rose-briars fastened to the wall. He had returned from his ride and had seen Walter's horse tied to the gate. A quarter of an hour before he had seen both Walter and Uhland riding down the road from Ireby. He had come round the wing of the house towards the front door when, very clearly through the open window, he had heard the words in Walter's thick ropy voice: 'You know, of course, that from the time of his childhood Uhland has always especially hated John.'

So he stayed there, his body pressed against the wall, his eyes staring out into a sky that swam in frosty September light with one blazing diamond star. He heard everything. He heard Walter say: 'If anything were to happen--', and Judith later: 'Yes, Walter. You are right . . . John has been under some kind of shadow . . .'

So it had come to this! 'Under some kind of shadow! Under some kind of shadow.' And they planned to smuggle him away to London lest anything should happen . . . anything should happen.

He went back to the stable and got out his horse Barnabas. A small terrier, very devoted to him, Mumps by name, little more than a puppy, came rushing across the cobbles when he saw Barnabas let out again. He had thought that the fun was over for the day, but apparently it was not. John went quickly by the gate that bordered the orchard. This brought him straight into the village street and he knew that he would be now ahead of Walter. The sun was just sinking, and hills, fields, pasture and stream lay in a mirror of light; you could fancy that if you swung, lazily, god-like in the sky, you would look down and see your Olympian features reflected in this sea of gold. Almost at once, just out of the village, at the dip in the road before it turned left to Peterfield, he found Uhland, waiting for his father, while his horse cropped the grass.

He knew that he had very little time before Walter came up, and, guiding his horse quite close to Uhland's, he said softly:

'I think that we must end this. It has gone on long enough--and by ourselves where no one can disturb us.'

It was as though because of their connexion through so many years they had grown to understand one another like the closest and dearest friends, for Uhland did not appear startled, nor did he ask 'End what?' or 'What has been long enough?' He simply drew his horse a little away from John's and nodded his head.

'Well--if you wish it. As to ending it--' Then he said sharply in his cold rather thin voice: 'What is it you want?'

'That we should have it out, the two of us, once and for all-- alone.'

They both heard the tap-tap of a horse on the road. It would be, likely, Walter.

'Yes, I agree.'

They were like two schoolboys arranging a rendez-vous for a fight; from the beginning there had been something childlike and something eternal too in their relationship.

Uhland went on, as though to himself: 'Yes, I have had enough of this. I must get rid of this.' He said coldly: 'Well--what do you propose?'

'Tomorrow. I will meet you somewhere.'

Uhland paused. They could see Walter coming down the hill.

'Yes. What do you say to the house opposite Calva in Skiddaw Forest? Tomorrow afternoon at four?'

'Yes. I'll be there.'

John turned his horse and a moment later passed Walter without a word or any greeting.

CLIMAX TO A LONG SEQUENCE

II SKIDDAW FOREST

On the following day, Uhland, waking very early in his tower, lighted his candle and began to read in a brown stubby volume. It was a translation of Vasari's Lives of the Italian Painters. After a while he came to this: 'Whereupon having taken this buckler with him to Florence without telling Leonardo whose it was, Ser Piero asked him to paint something upon it. Leonardo having taken one day this buckler in his hands, and seeing it twisted, ill-made and clumsy, straightened it by the fire, and having given it to a turner, from the rough and clumsy thing that it was, caused it to be made smooth and equal; and afterwards, having covered it with gesso and having prepared it after his own method, he began to think of what he might paint on it, that should be able to terrify all who should come upon it, producing the same effect as once did the head of Me-dusa. Leonardo therefore, to this end, carried to a room into which no one entered save himself, slow-worms, lizards, field-crickets, snakes, moths, grasshoppers, bats and other kinds of such-like animals, out of the number of which, variously put together, he evolved a most horrible and terrifying creature, which poisoned the air with its breath, and turned it into flame; and he repre-sented it coming out of a dark and jagged rock, belching poison from its open throat, and fire from its eyes, and smoke from its nostrils, in so strange a manner that it seemed altogether a monstrous and horrible thing; and such pains did he take in executing it, that although the smell of the dead animals in the room was very noisome, it was not perceived by Leonardo, so great was the passion that he bore towards his art . . .'

'So great was the passion that he bore towards his art,' Uhland repeated to himself and closed the book and blew out his candle to let the moth-like colour of the early morning strengthen in the room. So it was to be a great artist, such would he have done had he had the opportunity and the power. He had neither, only the longing. He had done nothing with his life, which now was over. He was certain that it was over and that this was the last time that he would see the early light spread about the room. But today he would release something from within himself that had been there since he was conceived. If he could live after that was released-- ah! then perhaps he would become an artist.

He always had a headache now when he woke in the morning, a pain that pressed on his forehead like iron, and his eyes for the first hour were misted so that he had read the Vasari with great difficulty, and his lame leg hurt him sorely. But this morning when later he bathed and dressed he felt a glow, a warmth, a deep and burning excitement. That miserable coward had at last faced up to him. He would see him standing in front of him. They would be alone, removed from all the world. He would strike him in the face and see what he would do. This was the moment for which all his life he had been longing, to revenge himself upon the whole world for making him twisted and a cripple, all those people who had watched him as he walked, all the kind Herries relations who had despised and pitied him. Today he would revenge himself upon all his family--the crowd of them, so pleased with themselves and their strong bodies and the children they had begotten, so scornful of anyone unlike themselves . . . and the fellow had dared-- had dared-- to marry his sister!

All morning he limped about the house thinking of a thousand absurd things--how his grandfather Will, now, Heaven be praised, dust and ashes, had looked at him across the dining-table in Hill Street as though he said: 'This poor misshapen creature--how can he be MY grandson?' How Amery had invited him to ride with him, adding: 'You CAN ride, can't you?' How he had slipped on the stair at the Fortress, and Archdeacon Rodney's young son had muttered (but Uhland had heard him): 'Poor devil!' How Sylvia had looked at his leg and then blushed when he caught her--all, all, all pitying him, despising him, scorning him! Leonardo had filled his room with newts and toads and lizards and from them had constructed a figure so horrible . . . There was power! Ah! there was power indeed! And today he would be revenged on them all. He would make that figure, seen all his days as the type of all that he himself despised and hated, cringe and shake and fall--a strange fire ran in his veins so that he felt almost

as though his limp were gone and he as strong as any of them.

With the exception of his own place and the servants' quarters, his father's room was the only one in all the Fortress now that was cared for. The rest was tumbling to ruin. The walls were strong, but dust lay everywhere, and all the other rooms were damp-smelling and foetid. But he went everywhere as though he were saying goodbye to it all, a happy, glad goodbye. They called it the Fortress first in admiration, now in jest and mockery. So with this damned country: they thought that they were building a Fortress, eaten up with conceit they were, but one day it would be like this house, rotten and a jest to all the world. Pity he couldn't live to see that day . . .

Later, with his gun over his shoulder, he went in to say farewell to his father.

Sir Walter Herries, Bart, was playing backgammon with his housekeeper, a thin painted woman called Mrs Throstle. Mrs Throstle enjoyed bright colours and was expecting friends from Keswick, so she was dressed in a worsted poplin of bright yellow and wore the most elaborate sleeves in the prevailing fashion, ruffed muslin with coloured ribbons at the wrist. She had coral bracelets. Over all this her sharp face peered anxiously at the board, for she was a mean woman, and they were playing for high stakes. Or so they seemed to her. But she always came out right in the end, because if she won she won, and if she lost she went through Herries' pockets at night after he slept and took what there was. But there was not much these days because everything was going to rack and ruin.

She was discontented, too, because Herries would not drink at present. He was sober and cross and peevish. He had struck her last night for saying that Uhland was a lame duck. She hated Uhland, as indeed did all the servants.

Walter, very soberly dressed, gave only half his attention to the game. He had been worried for weeks about Uhland, and his visit to Judith yesterday had done little to relieve him. Indeed, it had added to his discontent, for the Uldale house had looked so bright and shining. He had liked Judith too, that neat, capable, strong old woman, and all the silly enmity over which he had spent so much of his energy seemed to have blown into thin air. But enmity, hatred and all uncharitableness are never wasted, as he was to find out before many days were over.

He looked up at the door opening and hungered with love for his son. He saw that he was dressed for going out and had a gun over his shoulder; at once he was alarmed with a strange interior fear, the room seemed to fill with smoke before his eyes; his hand trembled, and he knocked the backgammon board off the table.

'There now!' said Mrs Throstle. 'And I was winning too!'

'Clear out!' said Uhland sharply. 'I want to speak to my father.'

Mrs Throstle rose, trembling. She was terrified of Uhland; one look at his contemptuous face and she shook all over. She gathered herself together, touched her coral bracelets indignantly, tossed her head and went. The round backgammon counters lay on the dirty carpet, but Walter stared at his son.

'Going out?' he asked.

'Yes, Father.'

'Shooting?'

'Maybe.'

Walter rose heavily, stretched his arms and yawned. 'I think I'll come too. Fresh air will do me good.'

'No, Father. I'm going alone today.'

Uhland looked at his father and felt, to his own surprise, a certain tenderness. He could remember--he did at this moment vividly remember--old, old days at Westaways when everything had been so rich, many people about, the house shining with colour, and his father bursting with health and self-satisfaction. But his father had wasted himself on emptiness, had let everything dribble through his hands like grain falling idly through the air. Grain falling--it lay now, in layers of dust, thick upon the floor. They had done nothing with their lives, either of them, and he saw for perhaps the first time that if he had returned some of his father's love things might have been otherwise. His father had had no return for either his love or his hate. A dry, wasted man . . .

He did what of his own free will he had never done before--limped up and put his hand on his father's shoulder.

'Better I go alone,' he said. 'I'm in a sulky temper.'

Walter was so deeply moved by his son's gesture that he said angrily: 'You are always in a sulky temper.' He leaned his big heavy body towards his son's. He touched the gun.

'Going shooting?' he asked again.

'Maybe,' answered Uhland. 'Goodbye then.' He moved towards the door.

'When are you returning?'

'Oh, any time. Don't count on it,' and he went out, his backward glance from the door showing him his father bending his great stern towards the floor that he might pick up the backgammon counters.

He rode down the hill and then slowly along the ridge of the Fell towards Peter's House. He had plenty of time to be at Skiddaw House by four. It was a day in which everything seemed restrained, as though the sun were longing to break out but was held back by a strong hand. He passed an orchard where the pear trees were a bright yellow, and then in the distance he saw how the yellow hills were already autumnal, the heather resting on them in a rosy shadow from place to place. He had always been alive to beauty, although he resented it often because he felt that it, like the rest of the world, mocked at any cripple; now today the shadowed sun, the bright yellow of the leaves, the distant hills, were all part of his own purpose. They knew what would happen, and it was strange to him that they should all be able to see ahead of him, certain of the event before it had occurred.

'Everything is arranged then,' he thought. 'It is quite settled what I shall do. Every past incident contributes to this. I am what I have been made. And yet I could turn back if I wished. I would cheat God if God there be. I am greater than God, because now if I wished I could ride up Ireby Hill again and go in quietly and play backgammon with my father.' He stayed his horse for a moment, and had the fantastic thought that 'just to show them' he would ride back. But he could not; of course, he could not. Old 'Rogue' Herries; his father's words when he was very little: 'Don't you hate that conceited young cousin of yours, Uhland?'; Rodney's young son muttering 'Poor devil!' . . . no, fragment after fragment had with infinite patience been brought together, all that he might ride to Skiddaw House to meet John Herries. And once again at the thought of that meeting his blood was hot.

Jane Bellairs was the only one in the house to see John go. She had two great devotions in her life--one for her great-great-aunt Judith, the other for her uncle John. She eliminated, as did her brothers and sisters, the degrees of greatness from Judith, and called her quite simply (and very proudly) 'my aunt'.

'But, dear, she cannot be your aunt,' tiresome Mrs Munberry in Keswick had years ago said to her. 'She is far too elderly. You mean great-aunt.'

But Jane had simply thought Mrs Munberry a foolish old witch, with her grey hair and sharp eyebrows. For all the children Judith was ageless. She had lived, of course, for ever, and would live for ever. She was like God, only more easily loved. But Uncle John was Jane's especial property. When he was absent in London, Jane not only prayed for him night and morning but also talked to him when she was alone, asked him whether she could fetch him anything, and thought about him before she slept, because she was certain that he was lonely. This idea that he must be lonely had come to her at a very early age when, rocking her doll by the fire in the parlour, she had looked up and seen him staring out of window.

She had given him her doll to care for, and also, although he did not perhaps know it, herself at the same time. The others laughed at her for her devotion, especially Veronica, who was a good hearty girl with no nonsense about her. But Jane did not mind when they laughed. She had long grown accustomed to having her own private life, a life that no one understood but Aunt

Judith. Her mother least of all, for Dorothy would perpetually be saying: 'Dreaming again, Jane. Where's your work, child?' and Jane would pick up her piece of worsted on which she was embroidering a red rose or a ship with sails and, with a small sigh that nobody heard, pricking her forefinger and biting her lip, would set about it. She was, however, as Dorothy frequently declared, the easiest of all the children, for when she lost her temper she was quiet, not noisy like the others, and could amuse herself quite happily all the day long. Although she was nearly fourteen years of age now she was very slight and small.

'That child will never grow,' Dorothy exclaimed, and Judith replied: 'My dear, don't be foolish. I'm eighty and have never grown an inch since I was eight.'

And now she was the only one of all the family to see John go. All morning she had been painting a picture. This was her favourite pursuit, and here too the others laughed at her because she did not paint easy things like cottages and cows and the sun, very red with rays like wires, setting on a mountain, but things much too difficult for her, like the Queen in her Palace, the whale swallowing Jonah, and Noah seeing dry land. Yesterday on her walk she had seen some horses drinking from a pond, and this morning she had been drawing a great white horse swimming. Beyond the pond there were mountains, and for some reason (she did not know why) it was winter and the pond was black with ice. She covered the pond with purple paint. This painting was to be for John and, before dinner, she looked for him everywhere to give it to him. She found him coming from the stable, leading his horse Barnabas, and the small dog Mumps was with him. He smiled when he saw the little girl in her pink bonnet. Her dress, with its double skirt and fan-shaped corsage, made her quaint while on the other children it seemed quite natural. It was as though she were in fancy-dress.

'Hullo, Janey!' he said.

'Are you going to ride?'

'Yes.' He put his arm around her and kissed her.

'I've been up to Auntie's room and she's sleeping yet.'

Judith had not been well that morning and when she was not well all the house was quieter. Jane considered him. Should she show him her painting? He was busy because he was going riding.

Yes, she would. She MUST show him.

'I've done a painting and it's for you.'

'Let's see.' He bent down, while Barnabas and Mumps stood patiently waiting. All he saw was that some kind of animal was sitting on a floor of purple paint. But he guessed that the animal was a horse.

'That's a grand horse,' he said, pinching her cheek.

'Yes, and it's swimming in a pond all frozen with ice, and then it will ride up the mountain.'

'What a splendid horse! Is that for me?'

'Yes.'

He kissed her and held her for a moment close to him. Then he put the painting very carefully in his riding-coat pocket.

'Goodbye, my darling.'

'Where are you riding to?'

'Oh, only a little way.'

'Will you be back before I go to bed?'

'Yes, sweetheart.'

'Will you read Nicholas Nickleby?'

'Yes, if there's time enough.'

She stood in the gateway waving to him until he was out of sight. At the corner before the houses of the village hid him he turned on his horse and waved back to her. She ran into the house and wondered what there would be for dinner.

When, beyond the village, he was riding by Langlands he noticed an orchard and how yellow the leaves of the pear trees were. That made his heart beat, and the thick grass under the trees, the spikes of some of the sharper grasses, were already brown at the tips. There had been frost every morning of late. Then, as he turned towards Over Water, he realized that Mumps was running most confidently at his side, his little black eyes sparkling, his mouth open, stopping for quick snatched moments to sniff at a smell, his whole person expressing extreme content and happiness.

He must not have Mumps with him on this ride, so he pulled Barnabas up and said sharply:

'Go home, Mumps! Go home!'

Mumps stopped and looked at him as though he had just received the surprise of his life, as though he could not, in fact, believe his ears.

'Go home, Mumps! I mean it.' And he flourished his whip. Barnabas also exchanged a look with Mumps, saying: 'Yes. This is genuine.'

Mumps ran forward, pretending that he had discovered so rich a smell that John must be pleased, and being pleased, would soften his heart. Then he stood, with one paw raised, intently listening. Then when that was of no avail he sat down and scratched his underparts. Then, that accomplished, he looked up at John pleadingly. All of no value. The stern order was repeated, so, after one more imploring stare, he surrendered and slunk down the road, his tail between his legs. Round the bend, he reconsidered the matter. He saw that his master was slowly riding on, so, slowly, he followed, maintaining a tactful distance.

When John had Over Water on his right and was approaching Orthwaite Hall, he heard a bell ringing, the kind of bell that rings from the belfry of a manor-house calling the servants to a meal. It came beautifully through the honey-misted air. 'It is as though,' he thought, 'some giant were holding back the sun.' Thin patches of sunlight lay on the fields, and on the hills the heather spread in clouds of rosy shadow. All was dim, and the little sheet of water was like a buckler on whose surface someone had been breathing, silver under cobweb, without bounds, raised in air above the soil.

'It's funny,' he thought. 'Aunt Judith has always said that she could see Over Water from the windows of the house. Of course she could not. She must have the neck of a giraffe.' And yet he himself had often thought that he saw Over Water from those windows-- a mirage. But how friendly a little piece of water it was! All his life he had loved it--his whole life long.

Then, with a sharp stab of anticipation, he was aware of what he was about. Somewhere already in this misty countryside Uhland Herries was riding. They might meet on the way. He was somewhere near, shadow behind shadow--and the bell, still ringing, echoed in the air: 'This--Time--is--the--Last. This--Time--is--the--Last.' He was conscious of an awful temptation to turn back. Perspiration beaded his forehead. Why should he go on--to his death maybe? This lovely land that all his life he had adored; why should everything have been spoilt for him so long by one person to whom he had never done any harm? No. He must recognize that Uhland was only a symbol. Life would have been for him always a place of fears and terrors even though Uhland had never been born. What did the ordinary man--men like Garth and Uncle Will and old James--know about such a life, know how it was to wake in the night because you heard a sound, to turn in the street and look back over your shoulder, to watch a picture lest it should drop from the wall, to hear a mouse scratch in the wainscot so that your heart thumped, to expect with every post bad news, to fight, all your life long, shadows, shadows, shadows? . . .

Oh, to be done with it, to throw fear out of your heart like a dirty rag, and then perhaps he would be like Adam, so quiet and sure, a little ironical about life but never afraid of it, with a heart so unalarmed that it could spend itself on love of others. He thought then that he heard a horse's hoofs knocking on the road behind him, and he turned sharply. But there was no one. The bell had ceased to ring. At last, today, it would be over. He would settle with Uhland for ever. THAT fear at least should be killed.

He rode on, past Peter's House, up on to the path across the Fell leading to the road that climbed under Dead Crag up steeply past Dash Waterfall. On his right were the Caldbeck Fells humped against the sky and stained now with every colour, the rose and purple of the heather, silver grey where the grass was thin, a bright and burning green of fields between walls, and down the side of one fell splashes of white quartz ran like spilt milk.

He looked about him to see whether anywhere there was another rider. He could see for a great distance now, to the right to the sweep of the Bassenthwaite Woods, to the left where the dark wine-stained sea of heather, grass and bare soil ran in a flood to the feet of the Caldbeck Fells, breaking, as it began to climb, into patches of field, a farm with a white wall, cows and sheep grazing. But no human being moved in all the landscape. Under Dead Crag, before he began to climb, he thought of the ravens for which the Crag was famous. He looked up to where the jagged edge cut the sky, and two birds, as though in answer to a call, floated out like black leaves, circled silently in the still air. The only sound was made by the Dash that tumbled with fierce gestures from the height above. It was full and strong, which was strange when there had been so little rain.

He was sorry that he had not been able to see Aunt Judith before he left, and yet it was perhaps as well. She had sent down word that she would like to see him in her room after her three o'clock dinner, and of course he knew what it was that she wanted--to persuade him at once to return to London. He wondered what reason she would have given: something about Elizabeth, he supposed, and at the thought of Elizabeth his heart seemed to stop its beat. If he did not return from this ride . . . if he did not return . . . Never to see her again . . . He climbed the steep road.

When Uhland reached Orthwaite Hall and looked across Over Water the bell had ceased to ring. Then suddenly it began again, softly, steadily, persistently: 'Going--going--gone . . .'

Uhland looked at the Tarn, and then turning to the hills saw a thick tangle of mist like the ends of a woman's mantilla stray loosely over the tops. If the mists were coming down that would be serious. Many a man had been lost for hours between Calva and Skiddaw when the mist fell. The House would be hard to find, and, as though he had made a bet with some contestant, he was pledged to reach the place by four. The sun that had been shining so warmly when John half an hour before had been there, now was withdrawing. The light still lay in patches on the fields and the moor; down the Caldbeck Fells the shadow slipped, leaving the glow bare behind it as the skirts of a woman might fall.

But Uhland was aware now of a great impatience. Nothing should cheat him of this meeting. He longed to have John close to him, to see him flinch, above all to put to the final test all that those years and years of shadowing had anticipated. He urged on his horse, hearing the bell follow him as he rode up towards Dead Crag and the shining tumble of the Dash. He looked up at the steep road that ran up under the Crag and saw three birds circling like black leaves above the line of rock.

'Those must be ravens,' he thought, and remembered how, when he was a very small child, he had heard men tell of the ravens that haunted Dead Crag, and how, years ago, after the 'Forty-Five Rebellion', they had flown above the corpses of men, crying and calling in a vindictive triumph. He looked about him, down to the Bassenthwaite Woods that were now black like iron, then across to the sequence of fell-tops, but he could see no other rider.

'Is he behind me or before me?' he thought, and again that hot excitement as of wine pouring through his body exalted him. He felt a sort of grandeur that he had never known before. His lameness did not handicap him now. He was as good as anyone, and better, for he was on his way to dominate and conquer that supercilious, disdainful fool whom he would have down on his knees before the day was over.

But when he had almost reached the top of the road and the waters of the Dash were loud in his ears, he saw that the mist was beginning to pour like smoke from behind the hills. It came in eddies and whirls of movement although there was no wind. Greedily it ate up the farms, the fields, rose for a moment as though beaten by the sun, then fell again. When he was actually on the height he saw it advancing from every side. He pushed his horse forward and a moment later felt its cold fingers on his cheek. The whole world was blotted out.

The first thing that John heard when he started away from the Dash was the eager, excited breathing of a dog. He looked back and saw Mumps, his tongue out, happily racing towards him. The dog knew that now there was nothing to be done. Too late now to order him to go back. He felt a strange comfort as though this were a sign from Fell House.

He was soon lost in the spaces of Skiddaw Forest. There was no forest here; there had never perhaps been trees; the name was used in the old Scottish hunting sense of a place for game. John knew slightly General Sir Henry Wyndham whose land this was, and his keeper Donald Grant, who lived at the House, his present destination. The House was one of the loneliest dwelling-places in all the British Isles, the only building from Threlkeld to Dash. John knew also that, at this moment, Grant was in Scotland, his family with him. He had heard only the week before that the House was closed.

He could not anywhere in the whole world be more alone than he now was. A chill, in contrast with the warm valley below, was in the air, and the patches of heather, the sharp green of the grass where the bilberries had been, the grey boulders, all had lost the brilliance of their colour. He looked back once before he went on and saw the Solway lit with a shaft of sunlight that glittered and trembled under the line of Criffel and his companions. He was leaving that shining world and with every step of his horse was advancing into danger. On his right the flanks of Skiddaw began to extend and he could see the cairn that marked its

peak against the sky. Calva was on his left. A moment later he saw the bounds of his journey's end, on the right Lonskill Crag, and on the left, extraordinarily black and angry, the sharp line of Foul Crag, Blencathra's edge. Between them, far away, in sunlight like the smile of another world, was the ridge of Helvellyn. Sunlight behind him, sunlight before him, but his own country dark, shadowed, without form, guarded by hostile crags. He knew that under Lonskill was the House, and at the thought that he was now so near to it a shudder that he could not control took him. Soon he would come to the Caldew river, and, crossing that, he would move into his fate, a fate that had been advancing upon him since the day of his birth and before whose menace he had been always helpless.

It was then that he noticed the mist. It came on the right from Skiddaw, on the left from Calva. It tossed and rolled, crept almost to his feet. Was Uhland in front of him or behind? And, even as he asked himself, the whole world was blotted out.

CLIMAX TO A LONG SEQUENCE

III IN A DARK HOUSE

When Uhland felt the wet mist close in he was conscious of an almost desperate irritation. He was of so morbid and irritable a temperament that he had always been unusually susceptible to weather, to places, to trees and hills. He did not, as did John and Adam, feel that this country was in any case beloved, that, whatever it chose to do, it was to be accepted and welcomed as an ally. It had seemed to him all his life bent on his frustration, and, like others of his kind, he discounted lovely days but recorded all the disappointments and, as they seemed to him, the malignancies.

The fellow, he now contemptuously thought, would take this mist as an excuse: 'I could not find the House. When the mist came on I turned back'--and it seemed to Uhland that there would never be an opportunity again. If he missed this he missed his power over the man. He would hate him no longer but would henceforth hate himself, and, more than that, be choked till he died with this passion of which he could not rid himself.

He rode a little way and could not tell whether he were going forward or back. He had been often in such mists before, but had never been baffled and blinded as he now was, and, as always when it was damp, his lame leg began to ache, as angry as he was at this frustration.

He stopped to see whether he could hear the Caldew. It must be somewhere near, but he had never in his life known such a silence as had now fastened about him. The absence of any sound or movement closed in upon his ears like the beat of a drum. He moved on again, and as one often does in mist, thought that someone was close behind him. It would be just like that fellow to stab or shoot him in the back, an easy way once and for all to rid himself of his enemy, and, although Uhland was not afraid, it would be the last fitting irony of the injustice that he had all his life suffered under to be stabbed in the dark and dropped into space like carrion. He listened. Behind him something moved, pebbles were displaced, or there was a soft crunching of the grass.

'Herries, are you there?' he cried, and his own voice, the voice that he had always despised and hated, came back clogged with wet mist. 'Herries, are you there?'

The scene was fantastic, for at his feet and just in front of him little fragments of ground were exposed, were closed, and were exposed again. The mist immediately surrounding him was so thick that it was like fog and so wetting that he was already soaked through and through his clothes. It cleared at the top of Calva, and the round shoulder of the hill sprang out like a live thing on his left. It was so clear that he could see the patches of bright green and bare boulders lit with a chill iridescence as though in moonlight. Calva frowned at him, then raced under mist again, leaving only a fragment like a bare arm lying nonchalantly in space.

His horse struck pebbles, and then he heard the slow stealthy murmur of the Caldew. Well, he was moving forward, for not far beyond was the rising hill on which the House stood. Behind the House was a wood, and if Wyndham's keeper should be at home they could finish this affair among the trees. No one would see them on such a day.

There should be a little wooden bridge over the Caldew. He pulled in his horse, jumped off and peered around him. Now, if John Herries was really behind him, would be the time for him to come at him, and perhaps they would struggle there where they stood and end it once and for all.

He spoke again: 'Now, Herries, I'm on foot . . . Are you there?' There was no answer. If Herries WERE there he was sitting motionless on his horse, and Uhland fancied that he could SEE a horse there in the mist, and on it a gigantic figure, motionless, waiting. He stumbled and almost fell over the rocks into the stream. With an oath he pulled himself back and began to find his way along the bank. Now he had lost the horse, for the mist was around him like a wall, but the horse whinnied, and at the same moment he discovered the wooden bridge. He went back and led the horse safely across. Now he knew where he was, for at once the ground began to rise. He came to a gate, opened it, leading the horse through.

It was at this point that it was exactly as though someone stood in his path. For a moment he COULD

not move, and he felt as though a great hand were pressed against his chest.

'Let me through, damn you,' he said, and stumbled and fell. His lame leg often failed him, but now it was over a rock that he had fallen. He had cut his hand, and his body pressed into the wet soil, just as though someone were on his back holding him down. The soil was filthy, soaking, deep in mire. His cheeks were muddy and the knees of his breeches heavy with water. He pushed backwards and was suddenly freed, as light as air, the mist thinning so that, as he got on to his feet again, he saw the House only a little way above him, swimming in air like a ship in the sea. He moved forward, leading the horse, unlatched the gate, passed through a small tangled garden of cabbages and currant bushes. His feet grated on a gravel path, and he saw that in one of the windows of the House a candle was shining.

Uhland's thought had not been far out. John, as the mist enfolded him, had felt stir in him that weak boneless animal, so long so hated a companion, who whimpered: 'Here is a way of escape. You can say that you were lost, had to turn back.' He stopped his horse and stayed there, listening and considering. At once an odd memory came to him, odd because he had not thought of it for years, and now it touched him as though there were suddenly a warm, strong hand on his shoulder. He remembered how once, when they were little children, Aunt Judith had told them a story of their grandfather, David Herries; how he had run away with their grandmother, years, years ago when she was a girl, and fleeing with her from Wasdale up Stye Head had been pursued by an uncle or someone of the kind--and then by the Tarn, in swirling mist, Grandfather David and the uncle had fought while Grandmother Herries watched, and Grandfather David had killed the other. It had sounded then a grand story, like a story out of a book, unrelated in any way to the warm fires and old armchairs of Uldale. Now it was real. The mist that at this moment swirled about him had swirled about David Herries then, and David Herries had won. It was almost as though someone rode beside him, smiling at him as they went. So then he rode forward, but nevertheless the memory of an old story could not kill the struggle within himself. 'Turn back! Turn back!' the boneless creature said. 'You know that you are afraid. You know that when you are face to face with him that old terror will be too strong for you, and at the first word from that voice you'll run.'

And the other companion at his side seemed to whisper: 'Go on! You have nothing to fear. All your life you have been fighting shadows, and today at last you will discover what shadows they have been.'

Yes, that was true. It had begun in his very babyhood when in his cot he had seen how the reflections from the fire had made fearful shapes on the wall. Then his nurse, old Mrs Ponder, how he had shivered as he heard her heavy step on the stair, and her voice as she said, 'Now, Mr John. I dare you to move!' and he had stood, his heart thumping, transfixed; then the day when she had thrown his rabbit out of window. The day, too, when he had first seen Uhland, Uhland limping down the Keswick street, and that pale face had turned towards him and something in him had bent down and hidden away. The evening, too, when with Adam he had seen Walter sitting his horse, silently, on the hill. But Walter Herries had never meant much to him; the dread of his whole life had been concentrated in Uhland, and it was of no use for others to say, 'But this is phantasmal. There is no reality here.' For his father, too, had found the real world a prison, and, year after year, had allowed his mother to be mistress . . .

He threw up his head. 'I am revenging my father,' he thought, 'and my son, when he is born, will be fine if I am brave now.' For he felt, as many men with imagination have done, that with the vision they are given they can see that no men are apart, that History has no Time, and that all souls struggle for victory together.

So, greatly strengthened and as though suddenly he were seeing his destiny for the first time, he pushed through the mist as someone in a cellar pushes through wet cobwebs.

He now heard the running of the Caldew, and at the same moment thought that Uhland was just behind him. He stopped Barnabas and was aware of a multitude of noises. There was the murmur of the stream, the thin breathing of the little dog, and, it seemed to him, a multitude of whispering voices. Also dimly there sounded music in the air. Since he was a boy he had known that hereabouts was the place in Cumberland for finding the Musical Stones--certain stones and boulders which, when cut, gave out musical notes when you struck them. At the Museum in Keswick there was a good set of these stones, and Mr Cunningham at Caldbeck had a set on which he and his sons played many tunes. They beat them with a leather- covered hammer. Often as children Adam and he had come up to these parts and searched for them, and he had once had a stone that gave out a great ringing sound like an organ note. He had heard that in ancient days the Romans here had used them in their houses for gongs. This memory came to him now and pleased him. There was certainly some kind of music in the air. He waited. Maybe Uhland was also there waiting, but it was hard to see in the mist. If so this would be a good place to end it.

At last he said out loud: 'Is anyone there?' and again, 'Who's there?' But there was no answer.

He dismounted from Barnabas to find the wooden bridge across the stream, and at once Mumps found it for him, going in front of him and looking back to see whether he were following. After that, it was easy to mount the rising ground, and soon, leading Barnabas, he passed through the gate, along the little garden, and up to the door of the House. The mist floated about the walls in smoking wreaths. He could see dimly the wood. He found, as he had expected, that the door was locked. There was no one there. He went to the window on the right of the door and to his surprise it was slightly open. Then he tied Barnabas to the garden wall, pushed up the lower pane and easily vaulted into the room. It was so dark that for a while he stood there accustoming his eyes to it, and the mist poured in through the open window as though all the outer world were on fire. After a time he stumbled about, knocking his knees against a chair and the edge of a table. He found the fireplace, and on the mantel his hand closed on a candle. He struck a match from a box in his inner pocket and lit it. He waited, listening. He opened the door and went into the passage.

'Is anyone in the house?' he called.

There was no answer. He heard some hens running. Then he went back into the room, and almost immediately after there were steps on the pebble path outside.

Standing back against the mantel he heard the steps go to the door, he heard the lock shaken, then back to the window, a pause, and Uhland had climbed into the room.

As they faced one another the room at once became of great importance, and when Uhland closed the window behind him the candle, that had been blowing wildly, steadied itself and seemed to watch thereafter with a piercing eye. There was very little in the room. A deal table, and on it a bright green mat and some pallid wax fruit under a dusty glass cover. On the mantelpiece were two large china dogs with bright red spots like a rash on their bodies, a clock that pointed to five minutes to four although it was not going. In the corner there was a grandfather clock that leaned forward drunkenly, on the walls a large highly-coloured print of the opening of the Great Exhibition and an engraving of the Duke of Wellington covered with yellow dampspots. There was a wheel-back armchair with a patchwork cushion and in the corner a child's rocking-horse. In another corner there was a spinning-wheel. The floor was of brick. In the window there was a dead plant in a pot.

Uhland set his gun against the wall and sat down. His leg hurt him confoundedly. He rested his arms on the table, and stared at John. As he looked he was reassured. He had thought that perhaps now when they met at last he would find that there was nothing to be done, nothing to be said. All this chase and pursuit for so long had been a chimera. He would not be rid of the mad impatience and restlessness in his heart by any contact with this poor fool. He would just look at him contemptuously and let him go. But it was not so. The very sight of John started his rage. John had taken off his riding-coat. He wore a narrow blue tie over which his shirt collar was folded, and his shirt had an inset-breast of the finest linen. He wore a waistcoat of dark blue patterned with tiny dark red flowers. He was not a dandy, but everything about him was exquisitely clean and well-fitting. His features, pale, keen, sensitive, gave him an air of great aloofness and high breeding without, however, any conceit or arrogance, and he seemed, in some way, in spite of his years, still a boy--for his figure was slim as a boy's and his air as delicate and untouched by life as a boy's of seventeen might be.

Uhland knew that he himself was muddied, wet, and that his hand was stained with blood. There was mud on his cheek. Yes, he would spoil some of that beauty and aloofness before he left that house, and once again the blood began to beat, hot and insistent, in his veins.

He tapped with his fingers on the bare table.

'I'm here,' he said. 'What do you want to say?'

'I want to say this.' John found to his disgust that his hands were trembling. He held them tight against his sides. 'I want to ask you a question. Why for years now have you followed me--in London, here in Cumberland--everywhere? I have never done you any harm that I know.'

'I fancy,' said Uhland, 'that I may go where I please. Who says that I have been following you?'

'You know that you have, and that you have done it because it offends me. It must cease from now on.'

Uhland paused. Then he repeated softly: 'It must cease . . . But why?'

'Because I say that it must.'

'You talk like a schoolboy,' Uhland replied. 'We are grown men. Of course I go where I please and do what I please. You are a coward, you know. You are the son of a coward, you were born a coward, you will be a coward until you die. Otherwise you would have faced up to me years ago.'

'No,' said John. 'I could not because you are a cripple.'

At that word Uhland's fingers ceased to beat on the table. A little shiver ran through his body.

'That makes a good excuse for you,' he said at last quietly. 'Now listen to me for a moment. It is quite true that I have always hated you. Your family is a disgrace. Your father allowed your mother to be a man's mistress for many years. I daresay the fellow paid him to keep quiet. Then your father was challenged to a duel and ran away. Then, because there was nothing else for him to do, he shot himself in London. Well, it has not been nice for the rest of us to have such relations at our very gates. It was very painful for my father. From the very first you gave yourself airs, you mocked at my lameness, you spread scandal about my father's manner of life. You were always--although you did nothing but walk about Keswick in your grand clothes--a vain fool. The very sight of you was an irritation, but an irritation that pleased me because you were,

and are, so miserable a coward that a very look from me made you quake. And then you had the damned impertinence to marry my sister.'

'We will leave her out of this,' John said.

'Oh no, we will not. That is a score that I have been waiting a long while to pay . . . Why, look!' he suddenly cried, with a mocking laugh. 'You are shaking now!'

'Yes,' John said, and he drew a little kitchen chair to the table and sat down. 'I will sit down. I am trembling, as you say, but that is because you always affect me so. A sort of disgust that I cannot control.'

But, as he spoke, he knew that it was more than disgust, it was fear from the disgust. Now if ever was the moment to which all his life had led. If he failed now, everything would be lost--his father, Elizabeth, their child. And he did not know that it would not be lost, for something within him--the traitor to himself that had been born with him--was urging him to run. 'Run! Run! Climb out of that window and run for your life.' His limbs were moving with a power that was not his own at all. He had to hold his feet against the brick floor. The fight within himself was so arduous that he could scarcely think of, or even see, Uhland. It was something more than Uhland, and something worse.

'If I move I'm lost,' he thought. He fixed his eyes on the pallid, deathly wax fruit. He fixed his eyes but he could not fix his heart. Ah, if only he could rise and throw himself on Uhland, that would be an escape as well as the other, but the man was a cripple, a damned cripple--

'I see,' said Uhland. 'I fill you with disgust. But it's yourself you're disgusted with. Because I found you out years ago. You've cheated the others, who think you a mighty fine fellow. I've shown you to yourself. Every time that I've been near you you've felt what you are. You have at least the grace to be ashamed . . .'

Then an odd thing occurred. Uhland stretched one of his arms out along the table, and his hand lay there, almost under John's eyes. It was a lean white hand, the knuckles red, and on the back of it thin hairs faintly yellow. The nails were long and dead. The hand seemed to John to curve and twist on the table, like a thing in a nightmare, and, when it was close to him, he was suddenly strengthened. Was it that hand that he had always been fearing? Was this the ghost? Was this all? His eyes cleared. The room was formed and plain. The spinning-wheel was real, the Duke looked at him with grave, stern eyes. His legs were no longer trembling.

'Well,' he said in a clear strong voice that had no quaver, 'whatever the past has been, I am afraid of you no longer. You should have done more with your life than to spend it over one man, in especial if he's the poor creature you think me. I am afraid of you no more, so you can follow me no more. Nor shall you insult my father and mother again. You may be lame or not lame. After those insults your lameness is of no account, and before we leave this house you are down on your knees--on your knees. When you please. Choose your time. We can be here all night if you wish.'

Would his courage last? Was this a true lasting thing that he felt? For the first time he looked Uhland straight in the face.

Uhland withdrew his hand. He now was trembling, but with anger, the choking wild anger that so constantly came to him from the sense of his own ostracism. It was as though, at John's repeated 'lameness', all the world laughed, and a little crowd of sympathizers inside himself massed together and begged him to avenge them.

'You coward!' he cried in that odd shrill voice that should have been, if fate had been fair, rich, deep and generous. 'Why, you are afraid of your own shadow! You shall stay here--do you hear?-- and you shall not move! Stay there without moving until I bid you, and then it is you who shall be on your knees, and beg and pray, and beg--' He half rose, leaning forward on his arms, his thin muddied face staring into John's.

And John could not move. He would have risen and he could not. Something within him was melting, loosening . . . in another moment it would be too late for ever.

It seemed that an hour passed. It was only a moment. Then, his head bent as though he were putting forth all his strength, at the instant when his power seemed gone, he pushed over the table.

It fell with a crash, the wax fruit with it, and the glass shattering on the brick floor.

His eyes shining, he stood back to the wall. He would not touch the man! He would not touch the man! But all fear was gone. He was strong with his whole strength--

'Come on, Uhland. Down!' he cried, laughing. 'I won't touch you. On your knees and then off with you. Back home--'

He saw Uhland stand. He marked every part of him, his hair thin on the top, the mud on his cheek, his damp stock, the round buttons of his coat. He saw Uhland take his gun from the wall. He thought, 'Elizabeth!' Uhland fired.

At the noise the little dog on the path outside began to bark. He barked running up and down outside the closed door. Then he began to whimper, again and again scratching at the door. The room was filled with smoke and mist. Slowly it cleared. Uhland stood for a long while with the gun in his hand, but at last he leant it carefully against the wall and went over to the empty fireplace. He bent down and looked at the body. John lay there, his face hidden in his arm. Very gently Uhland turned him over, unfastened his waistcoat, felt for his heart. John was dead.

'Well, that is the end,' he thought.

He felt no relief; only an increased grudge of injustice. He felt sick, too, with that accustomed nausea that had so often attacked him. He sat in the wheel-back chair, licking his dry lips with his tongue. The whole aim of his life was gone, and what it had been he had now no idea. He was sorry for no one but himself, and even about himself he felt now a bitter, savage irony. All those days and years for nothing. He had had a right to be in a rage, but how purposeless rage was! He was the victim of the grossest injustice, but what a poor, muddy, shabby victim! He felt an especial rage with his nausea. To be sick now would be the last indignity. But he would not be sick. At least he could prevent that. And this was all the long pursuit had come to . . . nothing . . . sickness . . . and his hand was bleeding again. He looked about the room. He knew what he wanted. A piece of paper. He got up and limped here and there, almost stumbling once over John's body. There was no paper anywhere, and why to God was that dog outside whimpering? He blundered against the clock, and it lurched as though it tapped him on the shoulder. No paper anywhere. He knelt down, with difficulty, because his knees were stiff. Then he got up again. No, he would try first the riding-coat. In the inside pocket he found a paper and drew it out. It was once folded. What the devil was this? a crude painting, a sea of purple and some animal, a horse, a cow. But the reverse side was blank.

He sat down at the table and, taking a pencil from his pocket, wrote:

To all whom it may concern.

This is to say that John Herries of Fell House, Uldale, and I, Uhland Herries of High Ireby, met here at Skiddaw House by appointment. After a discussion we quarrelled, and I shot John Herries, he being undefended. After, I shot myself.

Uhland Herries.
September 23rd, 1854

He laid the paper on the table, then unfastened his stock and laid that beside it.

He went to his gun, loaded it, placed the muzzle inside his mouth and fired.

END OF PART III

Part Four

Mother and Son

'Eighty-five! Is she, by God!' said Captain O'Brien, putting up his eyeglass.

'Yes,' said Veronica, smiling. 'But you mustn't swear. You swear dreadfully, Captain O'Brien, and I don't think it's at all nice.'

'Do I, by God?' said the Captain. 'I mean to say, Miss Veronica, I'd no idea . . . 'pon my soul, I must get a hold on myself. Is it our turn? Damn the game! Always getting in the way . . . What I mean to say--'

'Yes, I suppose it is our turn. What do you think, Captain O'Brien? Shall we have war with France? Louis Napoleon is VERY dangerous, isn't he? But of course we've got the Volunteers.'

'Ho! the Volunteers!' shouted the Captain in derision. 'The Volunteers! That's good. Damned useful they'll be. But I tell you what, Miss Veronica.' But it WAS his turn. Amabel, who was playing (most reluctantly) with the Reverend Mr Hall, a bony, black-bearded clergyman from Penrith, had missed her hoop.

The occasion was a garden-party given by 'Madame' to her friends and neighbours on an afternoon of the summer of '59. Most fortunately it was a lovely day--fortunate because in August you never could be sure, the most treacherous month of the year in these districts. But today was lovely indeed, as Mrs O'Brien said over and over to anyone who would listen to her. 'Most lovely! Most fortunate! Who would have supposed? And such a lovely garden!'

The old house was gentle and benign under the small ivory clouds that floated in shreds and patches on the summer sky. The lawn was a smooth stainless green. The part of it that spread under the cherry-coloured wall had been laid out for croquet. Near the Gothic temple a tent had been set up for tea; the ser-vants were coming backwards and forwards from the house.

Chairs were arranged under the wing of the house near the croquet- lawn, and in the shade of the trees by the Temple there were more chairs, two or three, placed beside Madame's. To these, people were led up in turns to talk to her--'Not for too long, you understand,' Dorothy explained. 'So as not to tire her, you know. But she enjoys everything. She was never better in her life. Yes, eighty-four last Christmas. Most extraordinary! But she has always enjoyed the best of health! She does delight in a talk! Everything interests her!'

'A very pretty scene!' Judith thought happily. Although she was in the shade, the sun warmed her through the trees. She was wearing the black dress with the white lace at her throat and wrists that had been for so many years now her costume, but around her shoulders was the beautiful Cashmere shawl that Adam had given to her last Christmas, a shawl light, soft and bright, embroidered in silk with a heavy knotted silk fringe at its edge. On her head she wore a cap of white lace and, every once and again, she held over her head a black parasol. Against her chair rested her famous cane. Her face now had the pallor of ivory, but the cheeks were stouter than they used to be. Her eyes shone with a startling brilliance. She missed nothing. On her breast she wore a locket that contained Adam's picture. 'A very pretty scene!' but nevertheless she thought the crinolines ridiculous. They were not, perhaps, quite so absurd for young girls like Veronica and Jane, but Dorothy now! Yes, Dorothy was monstrous. She was a woman of fifty-one and had grown very stout. Her crinoline was vast and very heavy. It was of Chinese gauze and had twelve flounces. Her sleeves also had many flounces, and they looked as though a number of horns had been stuck one within another. Her bertha had ruches, embroideries in profusion, and she wore on her shoulders a Scottish plaid which the Empress Eugénie had made the fashion after her visit to her maternal home. A graceful woman might do something with all this--but a woman of Dorothy's figure! And when she moved in the house all the furniture was in constant peril!

The girls were pretty; at any rate Veronica in white, with her bonnet far back on her head, showing her really beautiful dark hair almost to the crown; and darling Jane, so fair, so slender, although no one thought her pretty in comparison with Veronica, was, in Judith's eyes, bewitching.

As the figures moved across the lawn, in their wide swinging dresses, white, rose and blue, the sun shining down so benevolently, no sounds save the click of the mallets and the balls, the murmur of voices, the clink of the china as the servants (Lucy and Emily--SUCH good girls) arranged the tea, Judith felt a deep, satisfying content. The only thing was that Margaret was not so well. Her child was due very soon now, but Doctor Bettany said not for a week, he thought. But she had not been well this morning. Adam was anxious. Strange to have, after all these years of marriage, their first child! And Margaret was not so young any longer.

Ah, here was that tiresome, silly Mrs Osmaston. Mrs Osmaston was thin, withered and weary. She had had so many children that nothing remained of her but a bone or two, a nervous cough and an interest in gossip. She was neither kind nor unkind, discreet nor indiscreet. The only two facts certain about her were-- one, that she had been a mother many many times, and two, that she was exceedingly stupid. She was afraid of Judith, who, she was sure, mocked at her when her back was turned. No one in the world ought to be both so old and so vigorous. There she was, a magazine on her lap, and she had been reading without glasses.

'Oh, what is it you have been reading, dear Madame Paris?' Mrs Osmaston asked, seating herself with care in the garden chair. Her crinoline was of the latest fashion, that is, its steel hoops were lowered so that they did not begin immediately below the bodice but only at the knees, and in this way the dress fitted under the hips and only began to grow wider below the knees. This scarcely suited Mrs Osmaston's thin figure, but she was very proud of it and thought herself smarter than any other woman present. And WHAT she thought of Dorothy Bellairs! Oh, but she would entertain the family circle when she arrived home this evening! (She could not see, fortunately, the Shade of her great-grandmother-in-law, who, a swearing, horsy, good-natured Ghost, looked out from the Gothic Temple, remembering how she once had drunk tea on this very lawn, and wondered, in her hearty indecent fashion, at this ridiculous Ghost of a descendant-in-law.)

'Yes, what is it you have been reading, dear Madame Paris?'

'Interesting,' said Judith, picking up the Quarterly Review. 'There are some comments on Mr Tennyson's Idylls of the King.' She read: "The chastity and moral elevation of this volume, its essential and profound though not didactic Christianity, are such as perhaps cannot be matched throughout the circle of English literature in conjunction with an equal power.' She paused and gave Mrs Osmaston a sharp look. Then she continued, a little lower down:

'He has had to tread upon ground which must have been slippery for any foot but his. We are far from knowing that either Lancelot or Guinevere would have been safe even for mature readers, were it not for the instinctive purity of his mind and the high skill of his management . . .'

Judith looked Mrs Osmaston full in the face and casting the Quarterly upon the grass, repeated: 'Chastity and moral elevation! Stuff! Did you ever hear such humbug and hypocritical nonsense, Mrs Osmaston?'

Mrs Osmaston, who had just been preparing to say that she thought it one of the most beautiful critical utterances she had ever listened to, sent her Adam's apple up and down in so swift a necessity for reversal of judgement. She gasped like a fish suddenly raised from the water.

'Oh yes . . . indeed, yes . . . very absurd. I have not yet read Mr Tennyson's Idylls.'

Judith wished that she had not been so impulsive. The last thing that she wished was to make Mrs Osmaston unhappy. The older she grew the greater need she saw in the world for general kindness and charity, and the harder she found it to suffer fools gladly. That was why life was always difficult, amusing and exciting.

She knew that now, simply because of this little incident, Mrs Osmaston would go away and talk, like a hen scratching in a backyard. Judith could hear her. 'Not softened in the least by that awful tragedy of five years ago. You would have thought that such a TERRIBLE thing . . .'

Not softened! Judith's heart and gaze left the garden and the figures moving across the lawn, and she was caught up again, as she so constantly was, into that dreadful afternoon and evening . . . Yes, five years ago . . . when, lying in bed, she had heard first that John had ridden out, no one knew whither, and how then, with a frightened pathetic foreboding, she had lain there listening to every sound, and at last she could bear it no longer but had got up and come downstairs. And she and Dorothy had sat there, waiting, listening. Then the opening of the gate, the rap on the door, the news that his body was outside . . .

And after that, old though she was, she had held everything together. There had been a wild, mad, hysterical letter from Walter; Elizabeth had come, a lovely fragile ghost, and in February of the next year had borne a boy, here at Fell House, whom she had named Benjamin. There had been Jane, too, who for a while had seemed to be mentally unsettled. The poor child had fancied that there was something that she might have done, might have held him there, prevented him from riding . . .

The excitement in the neighbourhood had gone on and on and on . . . It was only, they all said, what they might have expected. There had always been a strain of madness in the Herries. Didn't old Herries in the eighteenth century sell his mistress at a Fair, kill his first wife with unkindness, and marry a gipsy for his second? Hadn't Madame always been crazy, clever though she was? And all the sorry, stale business of Francis and Jennifer came up again, over and over, and then all the drunkenness and evil living at the Fortress, and Uhland of course was mad--everyone knew--but to shoot his cousin who was defenceless, there on Skiddaw, miles from anywhere--and the little dog had been whimpering like a human being when they found the bodies.

But somehow, by sheer strength of personality, Judith had dominated it all and beaten it down. Now at last the full value and force of her character was seen. For one thing so many of them liked her. She had done so many kindnesses, she was no respecter of persons, the same to one as to another, and yet she was dignified and commanding. She was the more commanding in that she no longer went about, and only visitors to the house saw her, and not many of THEM. But when they had visited her they always returned home with wonderful stories. Everyone obeyed her as though she were a General in an army, and yet everyone loved her. She thought of everyone and everything, and yet could rap you over the knuckles with a sharp word. She didn't care who it was that she rapped. The whole County was proud of her, admired her, talked of her without end, told every sort of tale about her. She was a legend.

And here was Adam coming towards them! She knew everything that was passing through his mind. She saw his quick glance at Mrs Osmaston, his loving look at herself. She smiled back, saying at the same time: 'Well, to my mind there's far too much nowadays of making small children feel that they're born in sin. Do not you think so, Mrs Osmaston?' She liked the beard that he had grown in the last year. It suited him; he looked well, solid and muscular, not stout as she had once feared that he would be. How dearly she loved the half-humorous half-cynical brightness of his eyes. He suffered fools no more gladly than she--in fact, she thought comfortably, they grew more like one another every day. But she could not persuade him to wear his party clothes. He would wear his sack coat and round hard hat, and the checks of his trousers were so VERY pronounced. All his clothes hung about him loosely, and there was Captain O'Brien with his great moustaches and tightly fitting fawn trousers so EXTREMELY elegant. She did hope that Veronica would not fall in love with him nor with young Mr Eustace, the curate, who with his fluffy hair and surprised gaze resembled a chicken just out of the egg!

'How do you do, Mr Paris?' said Mrs Osmaston a little stiffly; she was no more comfortable with the son than she was with the mother. And why did he wear such very ill-fitting clothes? He also wrote for the London magazines, which made him very dangerous, for you never knew that he might not put you into something!

Adam sat very close to his mother, his big square body protecting her tiny one. He exchanged, in a whisper, one quick word with her.

'I have just been in to see Margaret, Mother. She really is not so well. Do you think that I should send James for Bettany? He is over at Greystoke, you know.'

She nodded her head.

'Yes, dear, I should. Just as well.'

Adam bowed to Mrs Osmaston (sarcastically, she felt) and strode towards the house.

Ah, now, Judith thought, they are moving to the tent for tea. She had an impulse of impatience to run across the lawn that she might see that everything was right. But of course she could run no longer. But Lucy was a GOOD girl and Dorothy had sense. And one good thing--she could now rid herself of Mrs Osmaston.

'Tea, Mrs Osmaston,' she said. 'I see they are going to the tent for tea. Mr Hattick,' she cried, her voice wonderfully sweet and clear, 'will you take Mrs Osmaston to tea?'

Mr Hattick was a stout red-faced manufacturer from Birmingham who had bought a place on Bassenthwaite Lake, a very common man. The County was still undecided whether to cut him or no, but he had been kind to Judith and presented Timothy with a fine bay, and if he was kind that was enough. And now it would be good for Mrs Osmaston that she should be taken into tea by Mr Hattick.

She was watching them moving across the lawn with much amusement when an awful thing occurred. Amabel suddenly appeared, and in her voice were the notes of excited surprise and exceeding pleasure.

'Oh, Aunt Judith--what do you think? Miss Martineau has come!'

Harriet Martineau! Of all appalling things! And now, when she was already a little tired and was thinking that she would go in presently and see how Margaret was . . .

Alas, Judith did not care for Miss Martineau, and had often congratulated herself that Ambleside was far distant from Uldale. She recognized that she was exceedingly wise, immensely learned, and possibly the greatest woman now alive in England, but Judith did not care for so much learning. She had never herself had much education, she was not a Positivist, she detested the thought of mesmerism, and she envied the way in which Miss Martineau milked her own cows and ploughed her own fields. Moreover, Miss Martineau never ceased to talk--about Comte, about America, about her marvellous Cure, about her weak heart, about her pigs and cows, about her novels (Judith thought Deerbrook a very silly book), about Mr Atkinson, about her Guide to the Lakes. Miss Martineau spoke always of the Lakes as though they were her own creation and would not have existed had it not been for her. She PATRONIZED the Lakes. In addition Harriet was all for women taking man's place; Judith did not see how they could possibly do so. They were very nice as they were: pretty Veronica twining Captain O'Brien around her little finger, and Margaret indoors about to present the world with a dear little baby. Harriet wanted women 'to rise up and take their proper place in the world'. As though, Judith thought indignantly, they had not their proper place already. And this was all very bad for Amabel, who said that she did not care for men and would like to be in Parliament. In Parliament! Women in Parliament! You might as well make doctors of them. Amabel adored Harriet Martineau, and was always hoping that she would be invited to stay at the Knoll.

But worst of all was Harriet's trumpet. Judith had, in spite of herself, a little scorn for deaf people because her own hearing was so extremely good. But a trumpet! ... And Miss Martineau was so proud of it. Moreover, in a most irritating fashion, she would remove it in the middle of one of Judith's sentences. Malicious people said that she always did that if she thought that something was coming that she did not wish to hear. However, here she was-- in no time at all she was striding towards them. 'Is it a woman or a man,' an old lady once said of her to William Howitt, 'or what sort of animal is it? said I to myself; there she came--stride, stride, stride--great heavy shoes, stout leather leggings on, and a knapsack on her back--they say she mows her own grass, and digs her own cabbages and taturs!'

She was decently enough dressed today, with no ridiculous crinoline (that is in her favour, thought Judith), large boots certainly, and a thing like a Scotsman's bonnet on her head, and one of the fashionable Scottish plaids over her shoulders. In her right hand she held her trumpet; Amabel, listening to her every word, was beside her, and Adam, coming from the house, was not far behind.

'Well, well, well, Madame Paris, and how are you? I have been for the night in Caldbeck and am to be this evening in Keswick. I am giving an address on Domestic Economy as you have doubtless seen by the papers. And I have brought you my Letters on the Laws of Man's Nature and Development. It was published as far back as '51, you know, but Mrs Leeds told me that she was sure that you had not read it, and I thought that I would have your opinion. And here are some peaches straight from my garden. I said to myself, "Madame Paris shall have those peaches because she is a woman I admire. She should have been a man and represented us in Parliament."'

'Indeed I should not,' Judith answered indignantly, and then discovering that she was speaking into the air when she should have spoken into the trumpet, seized that instrument and shouted down into it: 'Indeed I would not have been a man for any money!'

'Would you not?' said Miss Martineau complacently and with a look of kindness at the old lady (for she liked those bright eyes and that independence, for she was as good-hearted and free of meanness as she was egoistic and free of sensitiveness). 'Well, I had no notion that you had a party.'

'Yes,' said Judith, catching the trumpet again. 'They are in the tent having tea. You had better go and have some.'

'Indeed I will not,' said Harriet, laughing. 'I have come to see YOU and I cannot stop more than a moment. My enlargement of the heart, you know, forbids me to stay long on a visit. Old Colonel Albany in Keswick insists on a talk. He says that he has several criticisms to make on my Suggestions for the Future Government of India. Criticism indeed! I shall like to hear what he has to say. All these old Colonels are the same. It has needed a woman to tell them the truth about their own affairs.' She kicked one leg in front of her and thrust her trumpet almost into Judith's eye.

'Now tell me what YOU think about India.'

'I, my dear?' Judith shook her head. 'Why, I have no thoughts about anything. I live in the past and not the sort of past that interests YOU, Miss Martineau. My past is all pin-cushions, lavender-water and parasols. I assure you there was never anyone with less opinions.'

'Don't you believe her, Miss Martineau,' said Adam, laughing. 'She is a mountain of opinions. There never was anyone with so many.'

But Miss Martineau had caught only the word 'mountain'.

'Mountain! That's what I said to Coleridge once--'

'Ah, you knew Coleridge,' Adam said eagerly. She caught that and it pleased her.

'Yes. I talked to him only once. Not that I can say that his career is anything but a warning. All that transcendental conversation, you know, was all nonsense. Nothing but nonsense--'

'Yes, but,' Adam shouted down the trumpet, 'what was he like? Tell us what he was like.'

'Oh, very fine--a perfect picture of an old poet. Neatly dressed in black as I remember, with perfectly white hair. And what I especially recollect was his underlip that quivered with a very touching expression of weakness--very touching indeed. The face was neither thin nor pale as I remember it, but the eyes! No, I must declare, although in my opinion his poetry will not be remembered and as to his philosophy--I cannot express the scorn I have for his philosophy--but I never SAW such eyes. The GLITTER! The amazing GLITTER, and shining so that one was nearly afraid to look at them! All the same, the glitter was only opium, you know, nothing but opium.'

'The father of my little Hartley,' Judith thought, smiling to herself--and in some strange way now, at this moment, while the late afternoon sun threw long purple shadows over the grass, and, behind the temple, the trees, whose leaves were tenderly touched with orange, massed like a solid cloud against the line of faint and silver hills, the thick dreaming figure of the poet seemed to wander towards them across the lawn.

The girls, moving like dancers, came smiling from the tent. In the clear still air the rich unctuous voice of the Reverend Mr Hall could be heard saying: 'Ah, but, Miss Bellairs, you misunderstand me. It is against the rule of my cloth to have a bet with you, but nevertheless . . .'

'Mr Coleridge! Mr Coleridge!' Adam could have cried. 'Come and sit with us and we will assure you that your poetry will never die!'

But Miss Martineau must be moving on. She was pleased that that sensible-looking child (Amabel) gazed at her with such evident devotion. Maybe she would invite her to stay at the Knoll. Her heart was warm and kind, and it was not HER fault that she knew such a terrible deal about so many very different things. But, as she wished goodbye to Judith, she thought: 'I should like to become an old lady like that.' Then she stamped away to her carriage.

She was hardly gone when Will Leathwaite appeared and, standing solidly and quietly beside Adam, said: 'The doctor is come, Mr Adam.'

'I'll be with you,' said Judith.

He gave her his arm. Veronica came running towards them.

'Aunt Judith, can I help you?'

'No, my dear, thank you. It is growing chilly for me. You must be hostess, Veronica, my dear.'

They went into the house together, she leaning on Adam's arm, Will Leathwaite following them like a bodyguard. It was splendid to have Leathwaite: he was as obstinate as he was devoted, as scornful of what he did not understand as he was faithful to all that he loved. He loved Adam and all that Adam comprehended, but only BECAUSE Adam comprehended.

'Will tolerates me,' Judith said to Adam, laughing.

'Will loves you.'

'Only because I'm your mother.'

'And what better reason could he have, pray?'

Stopping for a moment in the hall she said: 'Ah, there are Harriet's peaches and her book. I shall eat the peaches and not read the book. She's a kind soul, but I never wish to listen to what SHE wishes to tell me. Adam, I'm weary and shall go to bed.'

It was then that, looking up, they saw the doctor coming down the stairs towards them, and in that one glance the world was changed for both of them. Gone were Miss Martineau's book and peaches, crinolines swaying in the sunshine, pleasant lawns and rose-coloured garden walls. Adam jumped to the stairs and caught the doctor's arm.

'Bettany, what is it?'

'Labour has begun,' Bettany said gravely.

'Well, well?'

'It will be difficult. You can do nothing, Paris. Best stay down here.'

But Judith at once took charge.

'Yes, Adam. Wait in the parlour. All will be perfectly well. I am sure of it. Remember Margaret is a strong woman. There, there, Adam.' She leaned up to him and kissed his cheek. 'Don't be nervous. There is nothing that you can do. Women understand these things. Come with me, Doctor. Is there anything further you require?'

Then there came to all of them a sound from above, half-moan, half-cry. It seemed to break the silence, the indifference of the house as a rough hand tears tissue paper.

'Oh, my God!' Adam whispered.

But they were gone. He was alone. He summoned all his fortitude and turned with firm step to the parlour. Will Leathwaite was standing by the hall door.

'Is the mistress bad, sir?' he asked.

'Yes--no--I don't know, Will. But the labour pains have begun. Would you go into the garden and tell Mrs Bellairs quietly? Don't draw attention to it, you know. Ask her to come in to my mother.'

Leathwaite went. In the parlour Adam sat down on the old familiar sofa with the rosy apples. Nothing was changed, for Judith had forbidden any change. There was the spinet, there was the Chinese wallpaper, the silhouettes above the fireplace of David and Sarah Herries. Only Dorothy's needlework-box spoke something alien. Without knowing what he was doing he had it in his hands, and all his life after he was to remember it--with its polished walnut wood and satin-wood edge, the painted flowers on the top and sides, and inside it a tray painted pink, the wooden bobbins wound with coloured silks, the pin-cushion, the miniature hand mirror, the folding memorandum tablet in a morocco case, the needle-cushion of red and green wool with yellow beads, and a star-shaped piece of boxwood. The red and green needle-cushion he took between his hands and turned about and about a thousand times.

He had known nothing like this since Caesar Kraft had, on the day of the Chartist meeting, fallen dead at his feet. That had been one of the great crises of his life, because at that moment when Kraft had died in his arms he had resigned for ever all his life's hopes of Men's Brotherhood, of some movement that would catch the whole world up into some heavenly universal understanding and sympathy. Resigning those hopes, he had turned to his mother and to Margaret, the two persons in the world whom he supremely loved. His nature had developed a certain cynicism about the world in general. Men were not destined to understand one another and therefore, not understanding, also would not love. Love was to be found rather in the relationship with one or two individuals and in service to them. So he had lived for his mother and Margaret, and in a lesser degree for John and Elizabeth. John's death had once again set him back, for if so fearful a thing could happen so causelessly what was God about? He understood then that there was real evil in the world, that a battle was always in progress, and that one selfish, cruel act led to many more. One bad thought even had incalculable results. He understood from watching so small an entity as his own family that a battle between good and evil was even there always in progress. His was an age that believed quite definitely in good and evil, in God and the Devil, and in so far as Adam shared that belief, Adam was a man of his period.

With Margaret, after that scene in the bedroom here at Uldale one Christmas, his relation had grown ever richer and richer. He discovered that true love between two persons means a mutual interaction of beautiful, gay and noble discoveries. Both must be fine persons if love is to be full and progressive, and unless it is progressive it is not alive. He learnt that Margaret was far nobler that he, richer in unselfishness, in uncalculating generosity, in ever-growing charity, but as she rose higher she carried him with her. Love was this and only this: a companionship that was grander in trust, in humour, in understanding with every day.

He sat there, his broad legs widely spread, fingering the furniture of the needlework-box, the little wooden bobbins, the boxwood, the needle-cushion of red and green. He was maddened by his inaction. He walked about the room, sat down again. Once Dorothy looked in.

'How is she?' he said eagerly. 'Can I not go up?'

'Oh, well enough. The doctor is doing everything possible. No, better not go up just now, Adam. Margaret is wonderful. Her courage . . .'

Yes, Margaret was wonderful. But if she were to go now . . . A hundred scenes rushed in front of him-- Margaret lying in bed, her hair spread about the pillow, waiting for him; Margaret singing some German song as she went about her work; Margaret sitting opposite him, sewing; Margaret listening as he read her some article or criticism or one of his fairy-stories that he loved to write and was so shy of showing to anybody. All quarrels and disputes were forgotten, or if remembered had an added colour and glow because of their intimacy. He crushed the needle-cushion out of shape, he jumped up and shook his fist at the ceiling, then creeping on tiptoe to the door like a child, he opened it and listened. There was not a sound in the house. Where were they all? Were all the guests gone? The hall was in a half-light, but Leathwaite stepped out of the dusk.

'It's warmer in the library,' said Will confidentially, and then relapsed for a moment into Cumberland. 'The spumkey fire's burning fine--and I've told Jeames to give the mare watter and a teate o' hay for he was driving her fast to t'doctor. But t'doctor was on t'road anyway. Lucky thing that!'

He drew near to Adam as though to protect him, and Adam put his hand on his shoulder. They whispered in the hall like two conspirators.

'Will--how is she, do you think? It's been a terrible long time.'

'It's a' reet, Mr Adam. It's a' reet. Dinna fash yersel' now.'

They stood close together, shoulder to shoulder.

'I don't know what I'd do without you, Will,' Adam said. 'If I were to lose her--'

The two men exchanged a handshake.

'It's not that she's pampered,' Will explained. 'Now some ither lass, delicate, but t'Mistress--she's strong as a horse.'

Adam went into the parlour again and it comforted him that Will was outside, as it were on guard. Will always fell into broad Cumberland when he was deeply agitated, but showed his agitation in no other fashion.

The minutes passed; the clock struck the half-hour. Adam's forehead now was damp with perspiration. It was like him to do as he was told. They would come for him when they wanted him, but his agony gripped his stomach as though he were taking part in HER agony, as though he were inside her and she inside him. The room was dark now. He did not think to light the candles. He stood in the darkness, his hands pressed the one into the other, the nails digging into the flesh.

In the hall Lucy had lit the gas and saw Leathwaite drawn up stiffly outside the parlour door.

'Eh!' she cried and started. 'I didna see ye.' Then hummed, looking at him:

The lasses lap up 'hint their lads,
Some stridin' an' some sydeways;
An' some there were that wished their lot
Had been what Ann's, the bryde was,
    Ay, oft that day.

'Hist!' he whispered indignantly. 'Can't you be still?'

But she tossed her head, smiled back at him and walked slowly up the stairs, the taper in her hand.

Doctor Bettany almost knocked her over, hurrying his little fat body--all fobs and cravat--down to the hall.

As he passed Leathwaite he cried: 'It's a girl! A fine girl!'

'The Lord be praised!' said Leathwaite piously.

Bettany strode up to Adam and wrung his hand. 'A girl, Paris. A grand girl!'

'Yes--but my wife?'

'All's well. You may see her for a moment--only a moment, mind.'

As Adam tore up the staircase a slow smile lit up Leathwaite's eyes and mouth. Then, feeling in his pocket for his tobacco, he turned towards the kitchen, sharing with Adam the position of the happiest man in Cumberland.

PART IV

SAYERS VERSUS HEENAN

One of the most remarkable scenes that the London Bridge terminus ever witnessed occurred in the very early morning of Tuesday, April 17th, 1860. The darkness of the early April day was illuminated only by some pallid and evil-smelling gas-lamps. The platform, the offices behind the platform, and the street outside the station were thronged with a pushing, swearing, laughing, spitting, drinking, smoking throng, all men, all happy, all strung to a key of an intense excitement. They had assembled that they might be carried by the special monster train to Farnborough to behold in the fields near by the great fight between Tom Sayers, Champion of Great Britain, and John Heenan the American. Impossible to say who were there and who not in that thick semi-darkness smelling of damp hay and train-smoke and escaping gas, unwashed bodies and morning air. At any rate there were fish-porters from Billingsgate, butchers from Newgate Market, pugilists of course, poets and journalists of course, dandies as well, celebrated statesmen, and even, so it was afterwards said, some eminent divines.

Most striking at the first showing was the amazing variety of smell-- decaying vegetables, mildewed umbrellas, fumes of vile tobacco and stale corduroy suits--but nobody minded, nobody cared, everyone was happy. Clothes are of an amazing variety; there are the friends of sport, quite naturally in the majority; there may be a white neckcloth and black broadcloth, but the cut is unmistakable; hard- featured men, spare-limbed, fond of burying their hands deep in their coat-pockets and never in their trousers. Some are in fine plush galligaskins, top-boots, fur caps, and have sticks with crutches and a thong at the end. There is the 'swell', with his long surtout, double-breasted waistcoat, accurately folded scarf, peg-top trousers, eyeglasses, umbrella and drooping moustache. And there is the dandy with lofty heels to his varnished boots, great moustache and whiskers, ponderous watchchain bearing coins and trinkets, starched choking all-round collar and wonderful breezy necktie, and, lastly, there is a certain number of quiet, severe, retiring gentlemen in tremendous top-hats, dignified black with one pearl or diamond in the black necktie, sucking as likely as not the heads of their heavy canes.

The small group of Herries gentlemen going down to enjoy together the great event had members, it appeared, in all these different classes, for Garth, now purple-faced and corpulent (although he was but fifty years of age), might because of his horsy appearance be making straight for Tattersall's. His brother Amery was something of a dandy and wore an eyeglass. Barnabas Newmark (Phyllis' youngest boy, now about thirty, and known to all his friends as Barney) was altogether the 'swell', with his double-breasted waistcoat of crimson and his trousers of the loudest checks (but, as was characteristic of the Newmark strain, he was, in spite of himself, a little behind the time, coloured waistcoats having just gone out). Lord Rockage (Roger, who had succeeded his father two years earlier) was stout, very fair in colour, with light blue eyes. He was dressed gravely as became his position and sucked reflectively the marble head of his cane. (But he was not reflecting. He was thinking of nothing at all.) The remaining Herries was young Ellis, Will's son. He was now a boy of seventeen and strikingly resembled his father, thin of body with the high Herries cheek-bones and prominent nose, serious, reserved and fully conscious of his duty to the world.

Garth, Arnery and young Barney were taking sips of brandy from a silver flask and were as merry as merry could be. Garth was for ever recognizing friends and acquaintances.

'Hullo, Sawyer!' he cried to a stout red-faced gentleman in tremendous checks. 'What did I tell you? Didn't I say you'd have a bid for Satan before you'd been on him half an hour? I told you what to do. Just to keep jogging on him to qualify and you'd get all you wanted.'

'We tried him, Mr Herries,' Mr Sawyer said in a deep melancholy voice, 'yesterday morning against Polly-Anne and beat her by more than a length.'

'There! What did I tell you? . . . Well, how'll the fight be?'

'I've known Tom,' said Mr Sawyer, more gloomy than ever, 'since he was a lad high as my boot. Why, I knew him when he was a bricklayer at Brighton. Why, God Almighty can't beat him!'

'Heenan is five inch taller than Sayers,' said Garth, 'and three stone heavier.'

'Why, blast my soul,' said Mr Sawyer, 'he won't bloody well get near him. There's no one on this bleeding firmament as quick as Tom is.'

It was not more than a shed under whose shelter they were all crowding, and the noise was now terrific, the back-slapping tremendous, the drinking ferocious and the oaths Rabelaisian.

"Pon my soul,' said Rockage vacantly, 'there's a lot of fellers crowdin' about. And there'll not be a Fight perhaps after all. Wish I was in bed, 'pon my soul I do.'

Ellis looked at him with exactly that look of cold superiority that had been his father's in HIS youth. But he was not feeling superior. He was conscious of a deep and burning excitement and of pleasure in the scene. But he would not show it. He was by temperament intensely cautious and by training suspicious, and, mingled with these two strains, there was an odd element of personless, rather noble philanthropy. He was already persuading his guardians, his mother, Stephen Newmark and Amery Herries, that he would like to assist the Institute for Necessitous Orphans in Wigmore Street, and the Home for Irish Immigrants in Penelope Place. He liked to do good with his money on condition that he need not encounter those whom he benefited.

'Odd fish!' Amery had said to his sister-in-law Sylvia. 'Damn' generous so long as he don't have to be personal. He'd give anything to a charity and quite a bit to an Italian organ-grinder, but he seems to me to have no heart at all--no feeling for individuals, you know.'

'Wish I were an Italian organ-grinder,' Sylvia had said with a sigh, for although they lived now in two poky little rooms near Victoria Station, they were always quite hopelessly in debt.'

So Ellis now felt a cold distaste for all the humanity surging about him, but had someone on the platform begged from him he would have plunged his hand into his pocket and given him a handful of silver on condition that he did not speak to him after. He had come down from Eton last Christmas, although only seventeen, and, after the summer, was to go into the City, in his father's firm of Herries & Herries. He had all his father's genius for turning one penny into two, but he was more deeply concerned than Will had been with the magnificent power of his family. He was, indeed, even at this early age, family mad. The Herries were the greatest family in England; even at Eton, where he had encountered heirs of all the ages and heirs with quite as genuine a belief in their inheritances as his own, he had never wavered. Howards, Buckinghams, Beaminsters, Warwicks, Cecils--they had all, in his own mind, bowed before the Herries. His closest friend at Eton had been young Beaminster, whose mother, then a woman of thirty-eight or so, was afterwards the famous and hideous old Duchess of Wrexe. Beaminster said to him once:

'Someone, Ellis, told me the other day that your great-grandfather was a sort of highwayman fellow who married a gipsy.'

'Quite,' said Ellis, stretching his long thin neck, 'and now see what we are!'

So today he felt that this fight was arranged principally for the benefit of the Herries: it was America versus Herries. He looked upon the crowd: they were all off to Farnborough to see Herries whack America. It was high time America learnt a lesson; it was not the last time that a Herries would be conscious of such a need.

The bell sounded and they all crowded into the railway carriage. There was no ceremony about places, and Rockage discovered to his disgust that a great 'labouring-man' as he termed him, in galligaskins and a fur cap, already far away in liquor, with a black bottle in one hand and a vast ham sandwich in the other, was spreading all over him, and even before the train had started had planted a large red hand on his own elegant stout knee.

'Here, my good fellow,' Rockage said, trying to move his leg away. But he was wedged remorselessly

and, as was his fate constantly in life, no one heard what he said.

Garth Herries and Barney Newmark had secured places together by the window. Just before the train started Garth touched Barney's hand: 'By God, young Barney, look there!'

On the platform a great scramble for places was going on. Everyone was good-natured as, in England, everyone is unless it is felt that injustice is being done. There were shouts and cries, bodies were pushed forward through crowded doors by other bodies, there was laughter and singing. A tall broad-shouldered man with a high top-hat, a rather shabby stock, white hair longer than the fashion and straggling white moustaches, waited quietly apart from the struggle. He had a body that must once have been full and strong. It seemed now to have shrunken, under the black clothes. His shoulders were bowed. At the last moment he walked forward and, without any effort, entered a carriage.

'By heaven!' said Garth. 'I thought he was coming in here.'

'Why?' said Barney. 'Who was it?'

'Walter Herries!'

'What?' whispered Barney in a voice of awed interest. 'You don't say!' He peered out of window, but the train was already moving. He looked across to Ellis who was at the opposite end of the carriage. 'Imagine if he had come in here!' he excitedly whispered. 'What a family scene!'

'Yes, poor devil.'

'What did he look like? They say he was all cut up by his son's death. A pretty little murder that was. What do you think, Garth? Was Uhland Herries mad?'

'Mad as a hatter. Young Harry Trent was up North last year and he thought he'd call on Walter--out of curiosity, you know. Besides he was some sort of relation of Jennifer Herries--John's mother. His father was her cousin or something. Well, he DID call, and he says he never had such an hour. Gloomy house on the top of a hill. I've stayed there in the old days. They call it the Fortress. But it's all gone to ruin, and there was Walter Herries in a dirty dressing-gown drinking with an old woman. Harry says he was very courteous, walked about and tried to do the honours. And then he took him up to Uhland's room. He'd kept it just as it was when Uhland was alive--cold windy place at the top of the tower they have there. And Harry says he began a long wandering thing about Uhland, said it was all his own fault because it was he taught Uhland to hate John Herries or some such nonsense. Harry says he suggested Walter should get out a bit, do some shooting or hunting or something, but Walter just said that he hadn't the heart . . . Poor devil! Hope we don't stumble on him at Farnborough. Wonder what he's doing down here!'

But the train was now in the country. It was yet dark, the land shadowy about them, but with the running into air and space the hissing spluttering gas in its grimy glass covering seemed at once incongruous and even itself ashamed. They had not gone far when Garth called out: 'Why, Collins! What are you doing here?'

A large handsome fellow with a high, broad head, plenty of brown hair, very gay in a brown velvet coat, white waistcoat and brown pantaloons, was sitting next to Ellis. He jumped up, regardless of Herries, showing himself a man of great size and strength, and wrung Garth's hand.

'Herries, by God! So it is.'

Garth introduced him to the other members of the family. 'Mr Mortimer Collins, a friend of mine. One of the most promising poets in England; one of the most important editors in England too.'

'Now stop your codding, Herries. How are you, sir? How do you do, sir? Fine day we're going to have. I've come all the way from Plymouth, gentlemen, to see this fight, and by God if the "Blues" interfere I'll know the reason why.'

'He's a friend of Adam Paris,' Garth explained, 'and editor of the Plymouth Mail. Christopher North said he was the best young poet in England--did he not, Collins? All *I* know is that he's wiser about dogs than anyone I've ever met and he can tell a pretty girl when he sees one--can't you, Collins?'

All the carriage looked at Collins with great interest, but Collins was not at all abashed, laughed and ran his hand through his brown hair and began to talk at a tremendous rate.

How was Paris? Clever fellow although lazy. Always had his mind elsewhere, and he'd been running off when he ought to be working. Always talking of Cumberland, but Collins could understand that. Collins thought Cumberland a grand place. He'd paid a visit to the poet Wordsworth once--in '48, it was--and Wordsworth had looked like 'an old Roman Senator dressed as an English farmer'. First- rate the Lake Country! Everyone lived to be a hundred there. But who cared about Cumberland this morning? He'd have walked from John o' Groats to Land's End to see this fight. Why, he'd known Tom Sayers since he was a lad. He saw his first fight with Abe Crouch in '49, and although Crouch was two stone the heavier, Sayers smashed his face to pulp. And he'd seen him fight Jack Grant of Southwark for two hours and a half and just beat him. That had been a GRAND fight!

He was so jolly in his general enthusiasm and the way in which he took the whole carriage into his confidence that they all felt very friendly even though he WAS a poet. Barney Newmark was especially taken with him because he had always had a notion that he himself might be a bit of a writer. In fact those books Miss Rich of Manchester and Fox and Grapes (which were declared at the time to be quite as good as Whyte-Melville) and, of more importance still, the Chapters from the Life of an English Family might never have been written had it not been for his friendship, begun at

this meeting, with Collins. Nor, in all probability, would some of the best passages in Sweet Anne Page have been quite what they were had Collins never known Barney.

But now they were approaching Farnborough and excitement ran mountains high. Two gentlemen were so thoroughly drunk that it was little of the fight that they would see. (In fact they never got farther that day than the Farnborough pub). The train drew up and everyone swarmed out. Once outside, a frenzy seemed to seize the world. Light was in the sky, the grass was fresh to the feet, the trees in their first spring green, overhead (Collins noticed it because he was a poet) larks were soaring and singing. And he was the only one, maybe, in all those thousands who did notice it, for, from every side, multitudes were pouring (the crowd was afterwards estimated at three thousand persons), men climbing the hedges, leaping the walls, running over the grass, racing, laughing, shouting. The meadow that was to witness the great scene had been cunningly chosen, surrounded by ditches and double hedges that it might be difficult for the authorities to take anyone by surprise. Already there had appeared in The Times a little notice:

THE FORTHCOMING PRIZE FIGHT

Hertford, Saturday

This afternoon Colonel Archibald Robertson, Chief Constable of the Herfordshire Police Force, made application to the justices assembled in petty session at Hertford for a warrant to apprehend Thomas Sayers, the 'Champion of England', and John Heenan, the American pugilist, in order that they might be bound over to keep the peace . . .

It happened that Amery and Ellis were separated, as they approached the meadow, from the rest of their party. They could see just in front of them the broad gesticulating figure of Collins, Garth laughing and Rockage picking his way as carefully as a hen in a hothouse. Amery felt his arm tapped and turned to see Walter Herries at his side. He said afterwards it was one of the most awful moments of his life. It was not only that he had Ellis with him, that, so far as he knew, the two step-brothers had never met in their lives before, but something in Walter Herries' appearance caught at his heart. He was not an emotional fellow, Amery. He had all the caution of his kind of Herries, and then some more, but he had not set eyes on Walter for many years. When he had seen him last he had been stout, jolly, blustering, self-confident, ready to shout any man down, but now he stood beside him as though he were bewildered, lost, and as even Amery, with all his fear of exaggeration, put it, 'he had aged a century'.

'Why, Walter!' he said.

'How are you, Amery?' Walter said gravely. 'I trust you are well.'

'Very, thanks. I thought you were in Cumberland!'

'Cumberland? No. Business has brought me South, and I thought that by coming here I might recover something--might recover something--' He looked at Ellis without any recognition, and Ellis looked at him. There was nothing else for it.

'This is Ellis, Walter. I don't know whether--'

Walter held out his gloved hand to his brother.

'Indeed?' They shook hands. A strange emotion seized them all. For an instant they were so isolated that they alone might have inhabited the globe. Then Walter walked forward by himself as though he had already forgotten that the others existed. It was from that moment of meeting, Amery said afterwards, that young Ellis, he thought, got all his peculiar notions about the family-- his sense above all that the family must not be 'queer'. No one knew, no one ever was to know, what Ellis had thought about the terrible Uhland-John scandal. He must have heard about it again and again, child though he was at the time, for all the Herries in London were for ever discussing it. The papers had had, of course, plenty about it, and every decent normal Herries had felt it a dreadful slur on the family. Young Ellis had been undoubtedly conscious of this, had, in all probability, brooded on it. For he was simply the most normal Herries who ever lived; all the Herries' dislike of queerness, poetry, public immorality, all the Herries' distrust of the Arts, of anything un-English, of odd clothes and eccentric talk, met its climax in Ellis. The wandering ghost of the old Rogue and all his family found at last their match in Will's younger son. If indeed there had been for years growing in him a hatred of the unusual, of the 'sport', the 'misfit', how he must have hated the Uhland scandal! But perhaps he did not realize this disgust of his fully until the moment when he saw this figure of his own brother, dishevelled, unhappy, alone, at a gathering so particularly normal, British and Herries as this one. In any case this is certain--that after this day he never mentioned poor John or Uhland or Walter if he could help it. You could not offend him more than by any allusion to them.

All his later troubles and the troubles of Vanessa and Benjamin, and of the other Herries connected with them, dated perhaps from this meeting at Farnborough with his brother. It is not fanciful to imagine so. And that meeting, it is also not altogether fanciful to imagine, became inevitable when, nearly a hundred and fifty years before, Francis Herries rode, with his children, for the first time up Borrowdale.

Amery and Ellis soon joined Rockage, Garth, Barney and Collins at the ringside. Garth, of course, had friends who were in the inner circles of Pugilism, so he had seen to it that his little company had fine places, and Mortimer Collins was with them by the right of the Press. The arena was a twenty-four foot one. Behind the ropes a great multitude was pressed, body against body, and on every face was that mingled gaze of joy, expectation, anxiety and a sort of childish innocence as though no one present were more than eight years old.

For Barney Newmark, compounded as he was of escape from all the repressions of his early youth (his father, it may be said, was deeply disappointed in his youngest son, who seemed to him to have neither reverence for the things that mattered nor any discipline of character), of imagination and sheer joy of living, this scene with the early morning sun overhead, the turf at his feet, the ardent eager crowd, the brilliant green of the prepared Ring, the excitement of the event, and above all his personal adoration of Tom Sayers, made up the supreme morning of his life. (And, perhaps, never again would he know anything so good.) He had never seen Sayers, but had read every scrap about him since he could remember. And he had never heard anything but good, because Sayers was a grand fellow-- serious of mind, modest and unassuming, utterly fearless, generous and good-living. To do the Herries justice--men like Garth and Ormerod and Rodney-- he was the kind of Englishman they WANTED to create. They felt indeed that they had created him, and would not have been at all surprised had it been discovered that he had a drop of Herries in him somewhere. It might be that every man in that crowd felt that he had created him just as he had created this England that was beginning once again, after years of uncertainty, to dominate the whole world. Nelson, the Duke, Tom Sayers--they were all Herries men.

So Barney waited, his heart beating in his ears, his mouth a little open, and his hand resting on Collins' broad shoulder.

'That's the great Tom Oliver,' said Collins.

'Oh, where?' gasped Barney, and was pointed out an aged and grizzled gentleman superintending the last details, testing the ropes, looking up at the sky, consulting with other important gentlemen, inspecting anxiously his watch. For there was not a man in the crowd who was not aware that at any moment the authorities might arrive and the Fight be 'off'. And if that occurred this multitude of amiable citizens would be changed in one brief moment into a howling mob of savages!

It was seven-twenty by Barney's watch. A great sigh of excitement went into the air. Sayers had thrown his hat into the ring and a moment later followed it. So this was his hero! For a second of time Barney was disappointed. Sayers was no classical beauty. His face at first sight was ordinary, that of a quiet commonplace stable-man or agricultural labourer. He seemed slight in figure although he had great shoulders, but nothing, it seemed, of a chest. Nothing extraordinary, for a moment thought Barney. Heenan's hat followed, and a second later Heenan was inside. Then when he stripped a murmur of admiration followed, for this was surely the most magnificent human being God had ever made. Heenan was six feet two inches in height, Sayers but five feet eight, so that the American towered over his opponent. Moreover, Heenan was a beauty. The sun, growing ever more powerful, shone on his shoulders; his chest was superb, his face handsome and distinguished. Sayers looked an ordinary hard little middleweight, which was what by weight he really was. Moreover, he was eight years older than Heenan.

So that when Sayers stripped Barney drew a deep breath of alarm. How could this stocky grave little fellow hope to approach that giant? The thing was absurd, and he heard comment all around him expressing the same fear. 'The match is a horse to a hen,' said a wrinkled dark man beside him. A big stout gentleman in a very high hat swore with many oaths that 'Heenan would knock Sayers into a cocked hat in ten minutes,' and someone else cried out: 'Tom may beat him, but may I be fried in hell if he can eat him.'

Collins seemed to understand Barney's alarm, for he turned to him and said: 'All right. Don't you worry. It's not that Tom's so quick--Charlie Buller was quicker and so were Langham and Ned Donally--but you wait till you see the force he uses--and his timing! There's never been such timing since the world began! It's the way he moves that saves him. You watch!'

And Barney did watch. He saw Sayers look at his man, then nod as much as to say 'I can manage that'. Then they tossed and a groan went round: 'Tom's lost the toss,' and a large crowd of Americans in Heenan's corner shouted with glee. Sayers now must take the lower ground, but Barney's hope rose again when he saw him stand in so perfect an attitude, tapping the ground with his left foot, his arms down, his head well back, and a smile on his face.

'Oh, God, make him win!' Barney whispered to himself. 'He must win! He MUST win!'

They shook hands and then, as they moved round, each man to his right in order to avoid the other's right hand, they laughed at each other, as cheery and friendly a laugh as you could see anywhere on a lovely spring morning.

They sparred, closed, and Sayers got down easily. Their seconds sponged them down, gave them water to rinse their mouths with, and they came up again. It was plain that Sayers was absolutely confident. He had beaten big men before--size was nothing to him. Heenan led and led again, but always missed; then he got one on his opponent's mouth, and Sayers reeled. Sayers returned but was banged on the forehead and went down in his own corner, whereupon the Americans whooped their delight.

And it was now that the great crowd became part of the fight. Wives, mistresses, children were forgotten. All the trades and all the labours, the small shop, the wide curve of the field as the horses ploughed it, the window at the Club, with the last private scandal, the hiss of the white wave at the boat's keel as it swept from the shore, the call on the bare windy 'top' as the sheepdog ran to his master's bidding, the gossip under lamplight at the village wall, the last climb into the dark wood before the lovers found their longed for security, all aches and pains and ills, triumph and failure, all bitterness and jealousy, all were lost and forgotten as though they had never been. Every man was drawn into that Ring and fought for a victory that seemed just then to be a whole life's aim. Garth forgot his last quarrel with Sylvia when for the thousandth time she had wept and he had sworn, Amery thought nothing of that 'pretty good thing' in Railway Shares that Ormerod had told him of, Rockage forgot his cows down in Wiltshire, Ellis forgot his dignity, and Collins thought nothing of his ambitions that he hoped would bring him from Plymouth and establish him in London as the finest writer of his time. Barney? Barney was part of Sayers' very soul. He had always BEEN Sayers. Every blow that Sayers dealt was Barney's--every knock that Sayers got he felt on his own heart.

Only Walter--standing not far from his relations--remained in a world that would not set him free. He watched because something was going to happen. His loneliness would be terminated and he would return to a moving, breathing life from which, since that moment when they had told him that Uhland was dead, he had been always excluded. He bent forward, watching intently, but it was neither Sayers nor Heenan that he was seeing.

Four times Sayers was down, and every time that he fell all England fell with him. Once Heenan got in a severe right, once trying to avoid the sun he slipped, and once Heenan with a terrible left altogether floored him. Nevertheless, Tom's footwork was marvellous, in and out, in and out, avoiding that long arm and always on the retreat when a blow threatened him, so that the force of it was lessened.

Collins was in an ecstasy. 'Oh, look at his feet!' he cried. 'Look at his feet! Oh, the darling! There's beauty! There's movement!' He was beside himself with excitement, gripping Barney's arm, rolling his head to the rhythm of the fighting, stamping with his feet on the ground. Nevertheless, the sun was bothering Sayers (he tried continually to get Heenan to change his ground but always failed), he was now severely marked and had an awful cut over his eyebrow.

Would he last? Many voices, shaking with excitement, the words coming anyhow, could be heard saying that Tom was a beaten man. 'The American's too big for him.' 'He's taken a size too large for him!'

Barney caught Mortimer Collins' arm and in a piteous whisper said: 'He isn't beat, is he? Oh, he can't be! He can't be!'

'You must wait,' said Collins between his teeth. 'He hasn't begun.'

It was then that Walter Herries suddenly began to feel deep down in his loneliness that everything would be different for him henceforth if only Sayers won. Uhland could not return, but life would begin again. That strange cessation of time that for five years now he had endured would lapse. It was as though he waited for a door to open, and, even as, years before, Georges Paris had staked his future on the result of a wrestle on a hill-top in Cumberland, so now Walter Herries held his breath and waited.

'Now!' suddenly cried Collins. 'Do you see that?'

Heenan had sent out a smashing blow which Sayers had avoided, and then, jumping right back, Sayers had landed a terrific hit on the American's eye. It was one of those sliding upward hits, almost splitting Heenan's cheek.

And now Sayers was growing happy. You could see it in his quiet confident gaze, the hint of a smile that played about his bruised lips.

'I've got him now! I've got him now!' Barney whispered, his nails digging into the palms of his hands in his excitement. Indeed, it seemed that Sayers had. Stopping a hard lead with his forearm he dealt a harder one, then suddenly, as though inspired by the kindly heavens, launched out with such a thunderbolt that it seemed as though Heenan's nose must be crushed in. The tremendous fellow was all but lifted off his legs; the Americans in his corner gave a kind of 'Oh!' of wonder, and how the rest of the world shouted, Herries and all! Even Ellis cried: 'Bravo, Sayers! Bravo, my man!' just as though he had been an honest hardworking gardener in the Herries employ.

But for five foot eight to raise six foot two from the ground was no minor feat. Yes, Tom Sayers for all his quiet peace-loving friendly countenance could hit.

Again in the seventh round Sayers struck Heenan another fearful blow which sent the blood gushing from Heenan's nose; so weak and tottering was the American that he grabbed at Sayers' body and they hugged, although Sayers got in some nice body blows before they fell together.

And Barney, in his innocence, thought it all over. The American couldn't stand any more of that; another little tap and he'd be gone, put to sleep for the rest of his natural.

'Oh, he's got him! he's got him!' he cried, enchanted, dancing up and down on his two feet like a little boy, and even Walter, not far away, began to feel as though a great weight were lifting from him.

'I think Sayers is winning,' he said very gravely to a man with a broken nose, standing beside him.

'I wouldn't be so sure,' said the man with the broken nose. 'Why isn't Tom hitting more with his right?'

Barney, in fact, was increasingly aware now from the atmosphere around him that something was going wrong. What it was he couldn't tell. Everything SEEMED to be all right. To look at Sayers you would-n't suppose that he had an anxiety in the world. His face, that would have been solemn as a churchwarden's had it not been for the twinkling crowsfeet about his eyes, was expressionless and innocent. He had the earnest and serious gaze of a student of Mr Darwin or Mr Huxley. But something was wrong.

'What is it?' Barney whispered to Collins.

'It's his arm, his right arm,' Collins whispered back. 'I think he's broken it.'

Barney always said afterwards that, of the three or four most dramatic crises in his life, that moment when Sayers broke his arm in his fight with Heenan (or a tendon as it turned out after--a happening quite as disastrous in the circumstances as a broken arm could be) was the most thrilling. Life seemed to stop: the world was held in a frozen mask, the air like ice, and no sound in the universe. Exaggerated it sounded later, but that's how it was just then.

And now it was that Barney Newmark loved Sayers, loved Sayers as he loved himself plus the love that he had just then for Miss Nellie Blossom of the Adelphi plus the love that he had for his mother, brother, and sisters, and his French bulldog Louis. All the different loves of his life were concentrated in that little stocky man when he saw him holding his right arm across his chest in the orthodox position as though nothing were the matter, relying now altogether on his feet for his defence and his left for attack, although it had always been his right that had won him his victories.

And then the beautiful thing happened, for Sayers grinned, grinned as though he were greeting an old crony, and Heenan, although his face was marked as though it had been slashed with sabre-cuts (for knuckles could cut into the flesh as gloves cannot do), grinned back. Indeed so completely was Sayers master of himself that, sending Heenan down with a horrible smasher, he used the twenty- five seconds that he might have had for resting in going over and peering into Heenan's face to see what it was like when they had wiped the blood off it. He might get some useful information that way.

Next there was a terrific round: one of the historic rounds in the history of British boxing, when they fought for a quarter of an hour and were, both of them, so badly exhausted at the end of it that they had to be carried to their corners by their respective seconds.

It was after this round that a new element entered into the fight. Heenan was now a fearful sight, for his face looked as though it were gashed with deep wounds. He was bleeding dreadfully, and one of his eyes was completely closed. The gathering of men, who felt as though they, too, had been fighting all this while, began, spiritually, to move in a new world, or rather in a very old primitive one. The tenseness was frightful. Men drew deep breaths and groaned in agony of spirit, stranger held stranger by the shoulder as though he would never let him go. Sweat was beaded thickly on Garth's forehead. Amery could not stand still but kept beating with his fist on another man's shoulder. The betting was now frantic. The Americans kept up a continual roar from their corner, and a strange rhythmical stir seemed to beat through all that multitude, the mass of human beings rising and falling with every movement of the two fighters.

They, indeed, seemed less seriously concerned than anyone else, for once Heenan picked Sayers off his legs and threw him, and then there they were both laughing at one another, and it was a strange sight to see that great American with one eye closed and his cheek in strips laughing as though this was good fun--although a trifle rough perhaps!

Indeed only once in all this time did Sayers show a sign of anger, and that was when he spat some blood and the American laughed. He was stung with that and rushed at Heenan, sent him reeling with a left, and then another and then another! When he hit him a fourth blow Heenan staggered; had Sayers had his right arm he might, indeed, have finished the whole thing with a knockout. Of one blow on Heenan's ribs The Times correspondent afterwards said: 'It sounded all over the meadow as if a box had been smashed in'. On the other hand, had Heenan been clever with his right the match might ere this have ended the American way!

It was now that a sort of madness seemed to swing down upon that meadow. Not an ignoble madness either, for here were these two men, heroes if ever heroes were, laughing like boys at play, and one of them with his face a pulp, blinded, so that he struck his second in mistake for his opponent, and the other had been fighting for an hour with one arm useless, a mass of bruises and fearfully swollen. Nor was their Cause ignoble, for they were showing to all the world that their countries had strength and courage, restraint and control, fairness of mind and an honest cheerfulness, manifesting these qualities indeed a great deal more plainly than their countries often did!

And now all the Herries (save Walter only) were shouting like mad: even Ellis was crying 'Go on, sir! Well done, sir! Very fine indeed!' and with him were shouting many other Herries, the old Rogue with his saturnine humour, and stout David, his son--the best wrestler in Cumberland--and old Pomfret waving a bottle, and young Reuben in defence of the bear, young Francis rising slowly to face his invisible enemy, and poor John winning a victory in the loneliness of Skiddaw. They were fighting to be free, as every man in that crowd was fighting to be free--with every blow that Sayers struck, with every reply of the mighty blinded Heenan, three thousand men drove with them to freedom.

But the spirit of madness grew more powerful. Sayers was weakening, Heenan blinded. They had been fighting for over two hours, and in the rear of the crowd policemen--the hated 'Blues'-- were trying to break their way. Once Heenan caught Sayers, closed, and hit him when on the ground. What a yell of 'Foul!' went up

then, and the Americans roared back 'No foul!' and the umpire said that all was well because 'the blow was struck in the heat of fighting'. Would Sayers last? WOULD Sayers last? Barney himself now was weak at the knees, his mouth was dry, his eyes burning. He had been fighting, it seemed to him, week upon week. As for a moment he leaned forward, his head rested on Collins' shirt. It was soaked with the sweat of his body. And Walter, in his place, was shaking. He did not know it. He knew neither where he was nor how he had got there--only it seemed to him that Uhland was fighting there in the Ring, and that the moment would come when he would turn to him, crying out:

'Father, you must come and help me. I'm nearly beaten'--a cry that Walter had all his life waited for in vain.

Then, suddenly, came the climax. Heenan had Sayers' head under his left arm when in a corner. He was too weak to do anything but lean on the stake and hold on to Sayers as though trying to strangle him. He said after--and it was likely enough it was true--that he was too blind to know what he did.

Sayers did all he could to free his head, but could not; with his left he got in a blow or two. But Heenan twisted round so that Tom's neck was hard against the upper rope and then he leaned on it. Poor Tom was black in the face and it was plain that he could not breathe.

Then came pandemonium; men were fighting and yelling. 'Foul!' 'Foul!' 'Foul!' The umpire called out 'Cut the rope!' The ringside was broken and the crowd poured in, hemming the fighters round so that they could only stand up against one another. Each hit the other and they both fell down--there, prone, at the feet of their admirers.

The police stopped the fight.

They had fought for two hours and twenty minutes. The result was a draw. The last great contest of fisticuffs on English soil.

Walter moved in a dream. On a wall in front of him that seemed always to be receding, a great cock with a crimson crest was crowing. It crowed and crowed.

A little common man in a fur cap kept pace beside him.

'Well, Guv'nor, that wor' grand. I call that GRAND!'

'Thank you,' said Walter. 'I enjoyed it greatly'--and went back to the Fortress.

SHE VISITS THE FORTRESS FOR THE LAST TIME

Elizabeth, forty-seven but looking oddly like a young girl in distress, confused in fact by her inexperience, stood one very wet morning beside Judith's bed and stared at the old lady with, if the truth is known, a good deal of irritation. At her side, the cause of her worry, stood her son Benjamin, now aged seven.

'It isn't,' said Elizabeth, in a clear sweet voice, 'as though he didn't know he'd done wrong, Aunt Judith. He knows perfectly well. Besides, Timothy beat him when he found out the truth. But he doesn't care in the least.'

Judith in her lace cap, mittens on her little hands, her face smiling and serene, the article in The Times about Mr Lincoln and the North and what the Americans had better do next open on her lap, knew two things--one, that Elizabeth wished her to be very serious in order that Benjamin should be impressed, and the other, that she thought it high time that Elizabeth gave up her widow's cap and black silk dress. Poor John had been gone nearly eight years now, and gentle colours, silver grey, dove colour, rose, suited Elizabeth so very well. Moreover, Elizabeth would be all the happier if she married. Mr Morant of Brough was eager to marry her. She was wasted as a widow, and Benjamin was altogether too much for her. Judith was smiling because she was thinking of the other children who had been too much for their relations. She had been too much for David Herries. Adam had at one time been too much for herself. Barney Newmark had been too much for Phyllis and Stephen. But Benjamin was a little different, for in this present time children, whatever they thought in secret, had outwardly to conform. All over England children were conforming, saying 'Yes, Papa' and 'No, Mama', looking up to their parents as to God, believing (apparently) all that they were told about both the creation of the world and the creation of themselves (the first in six days exactly, the second in a gooseberry bush), above all observing Sunday with the ritual and solemnity of a Sacred Order.

All this was correct, Judith supposed, although it had not been so when she was young, but she was now a very old woman and must not expect the world to stand still. (The only question was: was it perhaps going back? But how could one ask that when Britain was triumphant among the nations?)

It was Sunday that had been young Benjamin's trouble. He was quite unlike Adam as a child, for although Adam had been independent and gone his own way he had given no one any trouble except when he had disappeared for a whole day without warning. Moreover, he always listened to reason. But Benjamin would never listen to anyone, and this was the stranger when you considered that he was the son of John, who had always listened to everyone too much. It was perhaps because of John's tragedy that everyone had been over-indulgent to Benjamin in his babyhood. Poor little infant, born only a few months after his father had been brutally murdered, murdered by the child's own uncle! Could anyone have a more pitiful start in life? Had Ben-

jamin been a delicate, sensitive soul everyone would have approved and everyone would have been satisfied. But, so odd are the workings of nature, that that was the very last thing that Benjamin turned out to be! He was plump, healthy and merry. No one had ever known him to cry. He laughed all day. He did not of course know as yet of his father's tragedy, but it was feared that when he did know it would not affect him very greatly. It was not that he was cruel, nor that he was heartless, but he had none of the right and proper feelings. At Uldale, Veronica and Jane made much of him. Dorothy petted him, even Tim paid him attentions. They all thought him a sweet little child, for he was round and rosy and had large yellow curls on the top of his head. But he yielded to none of their blandishments. Jane was the only one who could do anything with him, and she not very much. It was not that he was hard or selfish. He was everybody's friend, would give everything that he possessed away to anybody (they had to stop him giving his toys, marbles, sweets to the village children); no, the awful thing was that he had no morals!

That seems a hard thing to say about a child who was only just seven, but what they meant by it was that he had no idea at all of the difference between right and wrong. The first occasion had been when he had stolen the piece of sandalwood out of Dorothy's needlework-box. She had missed it; they had searched everywhere for it. Benjamin had been challenged, had denied that he had it, and then it had been found on his person. Timothy had whipped him, Elizabeth had explained to him what a dreadful thing a lie was, but he had remained cheerful and unrepentant through it all. But unrepentant was the wrong word. He was simply unaware that he should not tell a lie if to tell a lie was of benefit to him. He laughed like anything when Dorothy, in her vast crinoline, tried to instruct him.

Of course he was very young at the time, and Dorothy elaborately expounded to Elizabeth that very small children never knew the difference between right and wrong. They were born in sin and only later became the children of Grace. But whether Benjamin would ever be a child of Grace seemed to Elizabeth, who knew him better than the others, a sadly uncertain question.

He was for ever in hot water, and at last he committed his worst crime: he dropped a handsome silver riding-whip of Timothy's into a deep empty well at the back of the stables. On this occasion he at once confessed. He said that he wanted to see how far it would fall. He was whipped, sent to bed without supper, lectured. He minded nothing, would not say that he was sorry, and at last was brought up to Judith to see whether she could do anything with him. He looked at the old lady in the big bed and thought how small she was. His round and chubby figure smiled all over at the old lady, and the old lady smiled back at him. This, thought Elizabeth in despair, was not at all what she had wanted.

'It makes it so much worse, Aunt Judith,' she said, 'that it should be Sunday.'

'I don't know, my dear. Do you think that it does?' She drew off her mittens and then with her slender white fingers used a silver knife to peel a large rosy apple. She had always for breakfast a cup of coffee and an apple, a meal that everyone thought eccentric.

Benjamin watched the peeling of the apple with wide-eyed excitement. Would she be able to strip the whole apple without breaking the skin?

'You see, Elizabeth dear,' Judith went on in her very small voice that had a touch of tartness in it like a good preserve. 'I'm nearly ninety years of age, you know, and though I've got all my faculties, thank God, still I do live a great deal in the past. It's very hard for me to tell very often which IS the past and which the present. You see, for one thing I've lived in this bedroom much of my life--always coming back to it. It was very much the same when I was a little girl as it is now. Of course the wallpaper's changed. It used to have blue Chinese pagodas on it. Very pretty it was. But that tallboy is the same, and this blue tester over my bed, and these charming acanthus leaves carved on the wood . . . What was I saying? Oh yes, about Sunday. Well, you see, living so much in the past I don't understand this not allowing children to amuse themselves of a Sunday. Of course they get into mischief. There is nothing else for them to do.'

This was not at all what Elizabeth wanted. And the old lady was becoming very garrulous now. Moreover, Benjamin, fascinated by the apple, had drawn ever closer and closer to the bed and had completely forgotten that he had come there to be scolded. He was grinning with all his might and, unconsciously, his small chubby AND grubby fist was stretched towards Judith.

'There! would you like a piece?' She cut off a section with the silver knife. 'Now what do you say?'

'Thank you, Aunt Judith.'

'They all call me Aunt Judith. Isn't it charming? And I'm ninety years old. Well, well . . .' She put on her silver-rimmed spectacles. 'That's the only thing, Elizabeth, that's beginning to fail me. I can't see to read newspaper print as I did. Ah! there's another poem about the poor Prince Consort, although he's been dead six months. And as to Mr Lincoln--the Times man says that if he would only--' She was aware that Elizabeth wanted something of her. She stared at Benjamin severely over her spectacles.

'Your mother is very unhappy about you, Benjamin, because you will not say you are sorry to Timothy. You are seven now and quite old enough to know that you mustn't throw other people's things down wells.'

He smiled at her.

'I'll say I'm sorry,' he said.

'But are you sorry?'

'No.'

'But are you not sorry to make others unhappy? And do you not see that the whip belonged to Timothy? What would you say if Timothy took your soldiers and threw them in the road?'

'He can have all my soldiers,' said Benjamin.

'You see, Aunt Judith,' Elizabeth said in despair, 'it is quite impossible to make him realize.'

A new tone came into Judith's voice, that same tone with which once she had spoken to Will at Stone Ends, once to Mrs Ponder, and more than once to Walter.

'Benjamin,' and he was suddenly grave, looking up into her face. 'Will you please go at once to Timothy and make your apologies? Without waiting another minute, please.'

'Yes, Aunt Judith,' he said, and instantly left the room.

'There, you see,' Judith said, greatly pleased. 'All that is needed is a little firmness.'

Elizabeth shook her head, smiled, shook her head again.

'I don't know. He's such a funny boy. He'll be going to school presently--that's, I suppose, what he needs. But I am so frightened for him. He seems to have no idea at all as to what is wrong. He plays with the servants just as though they were not servants at all. He is so restless. Jane tries to teach him, but he will never settle to his books.'

'There, my dear,' said Judith comfortably. 'Come and sit down for a little. Benjamin has his own idea of right and wrong just as I had when I was a little girl. He is generous and loving, is he not? And he is happy too.'

Elizabeth sat down beside the bed.

'Aunt Judith, I'm not tiring you?'

'Tiring me! Oh dear, no. Why, it is only the beginning of the day. I can do with so very little sleep now, or perhaps it is that I sleep most of the time--'

'There is another thing,' Elizabeth began.

'Yes, dear, tell me.'

'I am most unhappy about father. Oh, I know that it would be of no use to go and see him. He would not see me, I suppose, if I did go. We have talked of it before and decided that it would be of no use. But now I hear that he has a really dreadful woman there, a Mrs Pangloss--a terrible creature who bullies him and of whom he is afraid. Father afraid! Why, when I lived with him you would say that he would never be afraid . . . But it is terrible to sit here and know that he is shut up in that horrible house with that woman. I don't know what I should do, but it makes me so unhappy--thinking of it--being sorry for him.'

Judith stared in front of her. Then suddenly she clapped her hands.

'I know!' she cried. 'I'll go myself and see him!'

'Oh no, Aunt Judith! No, no! Why, it's a dreadful day! It's a deluge--and you haven't been farther than the garden for months.'

'That doesn't say that I couldn't if I wanted to. I'm lazy, that's all. It's an excellent idea. I have wanted to speak to Walter-- poor Walter. Yes, it is all over, our quarrel--quite finished, and it has brought misery enough on everybody. Yes, I'll go and see Walter, An excellent idea!'

There was a knock on the door. Dorothy, Margaret, Adam and the three-year-old Vanessa all entered. Every member of the family paid a visit of a few minutes every morning. This had become a ceremony as almost everything to do with Judith had now something of the ceremonial about it. Not that she wanted it to be so. All that she wanted was that she should feel that she was in touch with everybody. She loved them all, man, woman and child--and she also wished to know exactly what they were all about.

Dorothy was dressed for going out. She was in the very newest fashion--a brown 'pork-pie' but with a dark red feather, a chignon, and her crinoline raised several inches from the ground, revealing that her stout feet were encased in miniature Hessian boots. This was the first time that Judith had seen these and at once she burst out laughing.

'Oh, Dorothy, my dear. What HAVE you got on?'

She sat up in bed, leaning forward, settling her spectacles exactly on her nose that she might see the better.

Dorothy blushed, but she was as phlegmatic and good-natured as she was stout.

'Very handsome I call it. And I am wearing an American Cage for the first time. You've always complained that my crinolines are too large.'

'I don't know, I'm sure,' said Judith, 'why with your figure you should run such risks.' Then, to Vanessa: 'Come here, my darling, and see what I've got for you. Give me that little silver box from the table, Adam.'

Vanessa promised to be a very beautiful child. She had hair as dark as Jennifer's had once been, and large dark serious eyes. She had Margaret's broad calm forehead and something of Adam's humorous, almost sarcastic twinkle. When she had been a baby sitting quietly on her mother's lap she would unexpectedly look at you inviting you to agree that the world, although pleasant, was quite absurd. She already adored her father, and he worshipped her. She had a lovely little body, slim and straight. Baby though she was, she carried herself with a beautiful easy natural gesture, bearing her head high and looking all the world in the face.

As a child she was no trouble at all. Adam had insisted that she should be called Vanessa.

'There was once a Vanessa, a lovely lady. And there was an Irish Dean--and there were some letters . . .'

'Oh, you mean Swift!' said Dorothy, who was as literal as any Herries. 'All the same it's a very odd name.'

'My grandmother,' said Adam, 'was called Mirabell, and that was a man's name out of a play by Congreve.'

'Yes,' said Dorothy. 'But I don't see why because your grandmother was odd you should be.'

'Don't you?' said Adam gravely. 'I do.'

'I do wish, Adam,' said Judith as he brought her the little silver box, 'that you wouldn't wear that hideous sack coat. You are too stout for it.'

'Yes, Mother,' he said, smiling. 'But it's comfortable.'

(And, oh, how she loved him! When he approached the bed, bent down and kissed her, her whole body thrilled and it was all she could do not to put her arms around him and hold him tight to her. But not with all those women in the room. Oh dear, no!)

'There, darling.' She took two sugared almonds out of the box. This was a daily ritual.

'Thank you, Grandmother.' Adam lifted the little girl up, and for a moment the three of them, grandmother, son and grandchild, were caught together into a loving relationship that no one else in the whole world shared.

'And now,' said Judith comfortably, 'I am going to get up. Send Lucy to me, somebody, and tell James to bring the carriage round. You can go in the barouche to Keswick, Dorothy. I am going up to Ireby to see how poor Cousin Walter is doing.'

She knew that this would be a bombshell and she enjoyed greatly the effect of it.

'What!' Dorothy cried as though she had just heard that the end of the world had come. 'Going out! On a day like this! When you haven't been out for months! To the Fortress! Why, you're crazy, Aunt Judith!'

And even Margaret, who thought now that everything that Adam's mother did was wise, said: 'Oh, but, Mother--surely that is incautious! Listen to the rain!'

'Thank you, my dear. My mind is quite made up.'

Adam, who knew that the more his mother was opposed the more determined she was, said, 'Well, then, Mother, if you go up there, I go with you.'

'Certainly not. What should I want you for? It is quite time I had a little air. Now it is settled. Go along, all of you.'

'But, Aunt Judith--' Dorothy, who was in truth deeply distressed, broke in. 'You can't--'

'Nobody says can't to me!' Judith answered. 'No one ever has, and no one ever will.'

'But Doctor Bettany--'

'Doctor Bettany doesn't know everything. It will do me a great deal of good. And there is something I must say to Walter Herries.'

'But you know what that house is. And there is some horrible woman there now. She will be rude to you and--'

'No one is ever rude to me. At any rate after the first minute. My mind is quite made up, so it's of no use your talking, Dorothy. Now I want one word alone with Adam, if you don't mind.'

Elizabeth, who had been listening in great distress, stayed behind the other two.

'Aunt Judith, PLEASE. If it is for my sake, I beg you not to go. I would never have said anything if I had thought you would have such an idea--'

'That is quite all right, my dear,' Judith said, smiling at her. 'Your father cannot eat me. I am too old an old lady for anyone to be rude to me. The drive will do me good. Now, go and see that Benjamin isn't getting into mischief. Jane will be teaching him his lesson.'

She was left alone with Adam.

'Mother, is it wise? Walter is very odd, they say, and the house in terrible disorder. At least let me go with you. I can remain outside in the carriage.'

He sat on the edge of the bed. She laid her hand in his large brown one.

'Is it not strange?' she said. 'Do you remember, Adam? In this very room I undressed you and bathed you and you asked all kinds of ridiculous questions. And now see what you are! You are still untidy as you were then, and you have that same brown gipsy colour. And you are not as stout as I feared you would be--'

He sighed. Then he looked at her whimsically. 'Aye, I'm brown and heavy but not fat, and I'm not a dandy--and what I am as well is a failure!'

'Oh no, Adam! Oh no!'

'Now come, Mother. You had great hopes of me, hadn't you? And I've disappointed all of them.'

'Of course not,' she said fiercely. 'All that I hoped for you when you were a baby was that you would be a farmer and live in Watendlath. That, I suppose, was the mistake of my life--that I did not go to Watendlath. But it doesn't matter now. That is the best of being old-- nothing matters very much. It is very pleasant to sit outside and watch.'

He laughed. 'YOU watch! Why, you are in the middle of everything! No one does a thing in this house but you know it--' He paused, then added slowly: 'We are rather a multitude here. Let me see, not mentioning the servants there are--you, Dorothy, Veronica, Tim, Amabel, Jane, Elizabeth, Benjamin, Margaret, Vanessa and myself. Eleven of us.'

'And not one too many!' she said sharply. 'Now, Adam, I know what you are going to say. You are not to mention buying that land you were speaking of. We have plenty of money. The house is large. There is room for everybody.'

He looked at her with that deprecating shy glance that he had always used with her, since he was a baby, when he had something to confess.

'I have bought it, Mother. The thing was settled yesterday.'

She took her hand from his. All that old anger that rose in her when she was circumvented, all that old distress and alarm that she always felt whenever he was going away, seized her. She began to tremble all over. She glared at him through her spectacles. She pushed

The Times away from her so violently that it fell on to the floor.

'Now listen, Mother,' he began, speaking quickly. 'I am forty- seven years of age. I have tried everything and failed at everything. Once I tried to do something for my fellow men and THAT failed. Then I tried to write, and although that did not exactly fail it has never come to anything at all. Mortimer Collins was right when he abused me one night and said that I failed at everything because I could not STICK at anything. As soon as I was settled anywhere I wanted to run away. I have THAT from you, Mother. You know that I have. Only I haven't the character that you have, nor am I so unselfish. You would have been a wanderer all your days had you not thought so much of others. But I-- except for you and Margaret, Kraft and John--I've loved no one but myself! But John's death shocked me. Kraft's death shocked me once and John's completed it. I must settle. If I do not now, I never shall--and there is only one place where I CAN settle. On my own piece of ground in this country. Then I fancy that I still can do something. They all say that I can write-- Dickens said so, and Yates and Collins. I shall never write anything that matters MUCH, but it will be something. It is not that I shall be far away. The piece of ground above Manesty that I have bought is no distance. I shall come here constantly. But I must have my own place, and Vanessa must have HER home to grow up in. There are too many women in this house, nor is it fair for Margaret.'

'I am sure dear Margaret is very happy,' Judith broke in.

'Yes, she is happy, but not so happy as she would be in her own home. You MUST see it, Mother. You who are so wise and so sensible . . .'

She saw it. She had always had the capacity to see other people's point of view. But this was the end--the END.

She had only a few more years to live. Adam was all that she had in the world. If Adam left her . . . All that she said was:

'Pick up The Times for me, will you, dear? I think that it is MOST ridiculous that Germany should wish to have a Navy. I saw a very funny picture in Punch last week--'

He bent down and kissed her, and when he felt her body tremble, he put his arms round her. But he said no more. He knew that she would realize this was best for himself and Margaret, and that when she had realized that she would never say another word on the matter.

Nor did she. All the while that Lucy was dressing her she scarcely spoke. When the dressing was finished she sat down in a chair.

'Lucy, did I not hear that you are engaged to be married?'

'Yes, Madame.'

'I hope he is a good man.'

'Very good, Madame. He helps Mr Boulter, the butcher, in Keswick.'

'Oh yes . . . I hope he is sober.'

'He never touches a drop, Madame.'

'Well, I trust that you will be very happy. We shall be sorry to lose you.'

'Thank you, Madame.'

Veronica came in and helped her downstairs.

'Thank you, my dear. How pretty you are looking today!'

'It's terrible weather. Do you think you ought to go out, Aunt Judith?'

'I don't think--I know,' she answered. 'Now you can tell James that I am ready.'

James Bennett, son of Bennett Senior (now with God), a stout sturdy fellow and practically speechless, arrived with a very large umbrella to shelter her over the garden-path. She was settled in the carriage with rugs and a foot-warmer. She waved out of the window to Veronica and Jane in the doorway, and Margaret, Benjamin and Vanessa in an upper window.

But, so soon as the carriage had started, she fell into a fit of melancholy--indeed saw herself, a poor little aged worn-out not- wanted creature, lying at the very bottom of the sort of damp dark insect-ridden well into which Benjamin had thrown Timothy's whip. Such a mood was very rare with her. Now for a quarter of an hour she thoroughly indulged herself.

In the first place the weather helped, for it was one of the worst days of rain and storm that the year had yet seen. From the eastern sky the rain swung in a solid sheet--you could see it, slanting, as though in the folds of some thin grey stuff blown by the wind against the horses' heads. It hissed through the air and all the ground was running with water; you could see through the window rivulets of rain bubbling on the grass, and the rain leaping on the roadway; the wind drove it across the land from Solway in gusts of lines and spirals and curves.

'Dear, dear,' Judith thought. 'What a day to choose to come out in after months indoors.' She wondered what impulse had decided her on this visit; she was so very comfortable indoors, and this announcement of Adam's had swallowed Walter completely as though he never had been.

It was as though her whole life through she had been trying to catch Adam and he had always eluded her. Of course he loved her, but not as she loved him, for she must share him with Margaret and Vanessa. Margaret was an excellent woman and Vanessa a sweet baby, but after all they were not his mother. Here to her own surprise and disgust she felt a tear trickle down her cheek. She took her handkerchief and wiped it indignantly away. It was years since she had shed tears; not indeed since John's death, and then only when she was alone. But when you were old your body was feeble,

boast as you might to others. You could not be sure of commanding it.

This decision of Adam's was dreadful. He said that he would see her often, but he would not. Once he was away there on the hills above Derwentwater his visits to her would be fewer and fewer. She cared of course for the others--for dear Jane especially--but they were not inside her heart as Adam was. And she was not--although she would not admit it--at home in this new world that was growing up around her, a world of material riches and prosperity, a world in which the men seemed to be divided from the women so that an elaborate sort of hypocrisy sprang up between them when they met. Dorothy was shocked--or thought it proper to be shocked--if you talked of cows calving or sheep lambing. Jane and Amabel were quite resigned to being old maids, it seemed. The countryside was covered with old maids, and yet, on the other hand, all the girls in the County thought of nothing but marriage, only they must not say so and indeed must pretend that they had no notion of the barbarous practices that marriage involved. It had been very different in Judith's youth, and she had a sudden picture of herself and Georges and Emma Furze in London and the things that they would discuss and that other people would do!

'If it goes on much longer like this,' Judith had said to Dorothy the other day, 'there will be no more babies, for parents will be ashamed of creating them!'

She disliked too a kind of religion that was beginning to be prevalent, a religion that Dorothy took an interest in and that even the beautiful Veronica pretended to admire. It came, she believed, from Oxford, and Mr Hall and Mr Eustace were its local prophets. It consisted, so far as Judith could discover, in talking in a high affected voice, bowing and scraping in church and professing the saintly life. She believed that Mr Hall WAS perhaps a Saint--she knew that he gave everything away and lived entirely on potatoes--but Mr Eustace with his shrill voice and ogling eyes revolted her. She had been given to read a novel that, so she was told, portrayed the ideal saintly character of this religious movement--The Heir of Redclyffe by Miss Charlotte Mary Yonge--but she had found it mawkish and unreal and had wanted to throw it into the fire. In all this she was of course very ignorant; she knew nothing at all about the Oxford Movement, but it all helped to make her feel, when she was depressed, that she had lived far too long and had wandered into a world that was not hers.

However, she was not often depressed and she did not intend to be long depressed now. She dried her eyes, blew her nose and tried to pretend that she was as independent of Adam as she was of everyone else in the world. If he WISHED to go and live on a patch of ground above Derwentwater, why, let him go! How absurd of her, when she should be thinking of her approaching End, to be disturbed by what ANYONE wished to do! Nevertheless the pretence was not very successful. The very thought of Adam, smiling, untidy in his sack coat, so ludicrously absentminded, so clever (as she thought him), so well-read and wise and learned but so exceedingly modest about it . . . she had only to think of him to bring him right into the carriage beside her! And so, after all, it might be when he was living on Cat Bells! He could not REALLY be very far away from her!

The carriage was now driving through the storm up the hill to Ireby. She must prepare herself for the encounter with Walter. This meeting with him was in fact no new idea. She had had it in mind ever since the awful catastrophe of John's death. She must tell him, before she died, that their quarrel was ended, that she forgave him everything--yes, even the deaths of Francis and Reuben-- and she must try to console him a little and try if he would not perhaps see Elizabeth and his grandson.

As Bennett, down whose cape the water was now pouring in a vicious stream, whipped the poor horses up the hill, the carriage met the full force of the storm. The wind tugged at the windows, the rain lashed them, and she rose to the vigour of it. 'This is the way I like it,' she thought. Something in her bones, that had crept into them when old Squire Tom carried her the first day of her life through the snowstorm, excited her now. She pushed her nose against the window to see whether she had arrived, but could realize nothing because the wet blur of the rain was so thick. Then the carriage stopped; Bennett got down from his seat. With difficulty he opened the carriage door and then had to push his chest right inside to avoid the wind. His rough red cheek, fresh with rain, was close against Judith.

'Well, are we there, James?'

'Yes, Madame.'

'What do we do now?'

'Well, Madame . . . best for me t'pull t'bell while you stay inside t'carriage.'

'Pull it then.'

She could see dimly through the window now and thought how desolate the Fortress had become. The building was dark, naked and repellent. The stone seemed to have blackened under rain as though it had been smoked. The wood behind the house moaned and wailed. A pile of earth stood near the flagged path in the garden as though in preparation for a grave, and all the plants were beaten down with the wind. A tree somewhere rocked and screamed. She could see so dimly that she could not be sure what she saw. She could fancy that figures moved in and out through the rain, and especially her fancy, the growing faintness of the sight of her old age, made her imagine that the shape of a woman in black cloak or shawl moved out from the trees and stood motionless, staring at the carriage.

Suddenly she disliked so greatly staying in the carriage alone that she picked herself up, found her cane, adjusted her bonnet and climbed down into the rain,

then walked with great assurance up the flagged path and joined Bennett.

She heard the bell pealing through the house as though the place were empty and deserted. She could smell the wet stale smell of laurels and elder bushes. Then the door opened and a slatternly girl poked her head through. Just then there was a gust of wind so violent that Judith, slight as she was, was blown into the house.

She stood in the hall and the girl gaped at her.

'You'd better close the door,' Judith said gently. 'It is terrible weather, isn't it?'

The girl's hair had been blown across her cheek, and she stared at Judith as though she were an apparition.

'I think I'll sit down,' Judith said, and so she did on a hard straight-backed oak chair with arms that she remembered well from the old Westaways house. A cat came into the hall, mewing . . .

'Who might you be wanting?' asked the girl.

'Would you tell Sir Walter Herries that Madame Paris from Uldale would like to see him for a moment?'

The cat came over to her and rubbed against her leg. She bent down and stroked it, then with her two gloved hands resting on her cane leaned forward and waited.

She did not have to wait long, for a door swung back and there stood before her a great fat woman in a mob cap. 'This,' she thought, 'must be the Mrs Pangloss of whom I have heard,' and noticed with great dislike her face red as a ham, her thick bare neck, her big uncontrolled bosom, her long peering nose and other more unagreeable features. Her personal, almost passionate, love of cleanliness made a woman such as this very unpleasing to her.

The hall was dark and the woman stared about her.

'Well?' she said, glaring at the girl. 'What are you standing there for? Haven't I told you--?'

'There's someone--' said the girl.

The woman turned to Judith.

'Yes?' she said. 'What can I do for you?'

'I was wondering,' said Judith, 'whether I might see Sir Walter Herries for a moment. Pray forgive my sitting down, but I am not so young as I once was.' She smiled.

The woman at once recognized her. She said: 'Oh yes? Indeed! Well, I fear that Sir Walter is not very well today and is unable to see anyone.'

'I am sorry to hear that. Perhaps if I were to see him for a moment only--'

'Impossible, I'm afraid.'

The woman stood staring as the maid had done. Judith was so famous a figure that this visit was astonishing. The woman's slow brain doubtless was moving through a maze of questions. What did old 'Madame' want? Did this threaten her own power here? Was there some plot hostile to herself?

'Would you at least,' said Judith patiently, 'tell Sir Walter that I am here?'

'Mustn't disturb him.'

'It is of importance that I should see him--great importance.'

'Excuse me,' said the woman more insolently, as though she had made up her mind that Judith was not to be feared. 'Another day perhaps, but today. Sir Walter is not to be disturbed. I'm in charge here. I'll tell him that you inquired.'

The door to the left of the staircase opened and Walter appeared. He was in slippers and a faded snuff-coloured dressing-gown. At first he could not see who was there. Then, almost knocking against the chair, he stumbled back.

'Why, Judith!' he cried.

She held out her hand.

'I am delighted to see you, Walter. Your house-keeper said that you were indisposed, but I shall not keep you long. Can you give me five minutes with you alone?'

He plainly did not know what to do, and she was so sorry for him and felt so strong an impulse to carry him off there and then from under the sharp nose of Mrs Pangloss that any old enmity there might ever have been fell, dead, once and for all.

The woman did not move.

'Why, certainly,' Walter said. 'I have not been well. Mrs Pangloss was correct. This is Mrs Pangloss, my housekeeper.'

Judith gave a little bow.

The woman said angrily: 'Now you know what the doctor said--that you wasn't to see anyone, no matter who it was, and you'll catch your death away from the fire, you know you will. Sorry, ma'am, it's the doctor's orders, and another day when he's more himself it won't matter, I'm sure--but I have to see to his health. If I don't, nobody does.'

Here, however, Walter plucked up courage; it must have shamed him that Judith of all people should have seen him thus.

'Very well, Mrs Pangloss. You are acting for the best, I am sure, but now that Madame Paris has come all this way on such a day . . . Pray ask Alice to light a fire in the library. That will save you the stairs, Judith. Allow me to give you an arm.'

Mrs Pangloss stood there, looking at them. She never moved and, after they had gone, stood staring at the spot where they had been.

The room into which Walter led Judith had already a fire burning in the grate and a rich brooding odour of spirits about it. A decanter and two tumblers, one half filled with something that was, Judith thought, gin and water, stood on a table. This, she realized at once, had been Mrs Pangloss' sanctum that morning. Otherwise it was desolate enough. A picture of a hunting scene hung crooked on a nail and there was a screen with pictures of boxing scenes pasted on to it. Very little else. Walter settled Judith in an armchair whose grey and disordered stuffing protruded from the seat. A window looked out on to the soaked and neglected garden. The wind whistled behind the wallpaper. Walter sat down on a hard chair near Judith. She was greatly distressed at the change in him. She had last seen him three years before, riding in Keswick, and on horseback, wrapped in a high riding-coat, he had had something of his old carriage and even, she thought, arrogance. Now he had a rugged grey beard, his cheeks had fallen, and as he sat with his old dressing-gown huddled about him he looked more than his seventy years.

'If that woman was rude to you,' he said abruptly, 'I shall dismiss her.'

'Not at all,' said Judith cheerfully. 'She said you were not well and should see nobody.'

'She's a good creature in her way,' he went on. 'She means well by me--the only one who does.'

'Now, Walter, that's nonsense. We all mean well by you if you will let us.'

'Fine words, Judith, fine words.' He drew the dressing-gown closer about him. 'I'm always cold now. This house is damp. You wouldn't think so when I built it, but the damp's come in just as everything else has gone out. What have you come for?' he asked bluntly. 'We've been meeting like this all our lives, but our meetings never come to anything.' Then as though he had said nothing: 'How old are you now?'

'I? I'm nearly eighty-eight.'

'Eighty-eight! Wonderful! And still able to get about.'

'Well, I don't get about much now, you know. There is plenty to do in the house.'

'Yes; got your fingers on everything, I suppose, just as you used to. What have you come to see ME for?' he asked again.

'I have come for two reasons, Walter. First, I want you to know that our old feud is over. At least on my side. You must not think that I am angry or feel any enmity. The past is dead. At any rate our quarrel is dead.'

He rubbed his finger against his stubbly cheek. 'The past is never dead,' he said. 'You know that as well as I do. When you come to our age we live in the past. It is all I do live in. Back--back-- to when my son was alive, when he could walk into this room just as anyone did and say "Good morning". Not that he cared for me, of course--he never did that--but he was there. He was in this house. I could hear him moving over stairs. You could tell his walk, you know, because he limped. Uhland was lame from birth, you know, Judith, and that is what made him bitter--that and my telling him when he was a baby that he had an injustice, being lame. And so he had an injustice, poor boy, and cleverer than anyone in the County. That is why he thought poorly of me. He could see I had no brains, never had any. But it's too late now. The harm's been done, done years and years ago, before we were born.'

He would have continued to talk forever. Indeed he had forgotten her, but she was so deeply touched that she rose a little in her chair, leaned over and took his hand. Even as she did so, she thought: 'Twenty years ago! If you had told me that I would ever feel so tenderly! But what does it matter now? We are both so old!'

He let her hand hold his, which was hot and dry to the touch.

'Listen, Walter!' she said. 'That is what I have come to say. You must not think that you are alone in regretting the past. That old quarrel has done us all much harm, but I feel that--that--that catastrophe eight years ago--it was terrible, tragic--but John and Uhland by dying rid us all of an enmity, something bad in the blood, that must not come back again. John left a son, you know--a grandson whom you have never seen--and it would be wicked, WICKED, if his life was spoilt by it. It seems to me now when I am old that we cannot do anything without affecting someone else, and one bad, selfish cruel thing can spread and spread into the lives of people we never see . . . I want you now to be friends with us all, to see Elizabeth and your grandchild . . . to help us all so that his life at least shall suffer no effects from all that past trouble. Let Elizabeth come . . .

She had not been sure that he had heard anything that she had said, but at the repetition of Elizabeth's name his body trembled and shook, he caught his hand from hers and sprang to his feet.

'No, no!' he cried, swaying on his feet and gesticulating with his hands as though he were beating someone away from him. 'She's no daughter of mine and you shan't come round me with all your talk. She left me, and good riddance. She married my boy's murderer. Oh yes, she did! Don't you tell me now! Do you suppose that he didn't taunt him with his lameness, and she too? Uhland knew. Uhland heard what they said, the two of them. Now you can go, and pretty quick too, and don't let me catch you here again . . . And put some coal on the fire before you go,' he said, his voice suddenly dropping. 'This room's as cold as hell. Hell's cold--not warm as they say. This is MY house, and no enemy of my boy is going to sit in it.'

He stood looking at her, shaking, his legs wavering. 'Well, you are an old woman,' he said, sitting down again. 'You can stay if you like, but don't talk such nonsense. You ought to know better at your age.'

'Very well,' she said quietly. 'I'll stay, Walter, but not if you're rude and violent. We do no good by shouting at one another.'

'No, I suppose we do not,' he said, nodding his head. 'I tell you what it is, Judith. I'm not used to company. A while ago I went to London. You didn't know that, did you? And I saw a Fight--a fine Fight it was too, but the man I wanted to win didn't win, and so I

came home to be by myself. I said, "Now if you win, everything will be all right. Uhland will come back." But he didn't win, and so what was the use in seeing anybody any more? So I came home, and I'm not very good company. You must forgive me.'

She saw that there was nothing more to be said just then about Elizabeth. Nevertheless something had been achieved by her visit. They sat close together now like two old cronies.

'You see, Walter, I'm very old--very old indeed. I may die at any time. Not that I mind dying, but I wouldn't wish to leave any bad feeling behind me when I go. When you are as old as I am, bad feeling seems so very stupid--and I hope it won't continue into another generation. Your grandfather, David, used to tell me many stories about my father. Fancy! He has been dead now almost a hundred years! But David Herries used to say that he thought all the trouble in our branch of the family started when my father as a young man sold his mistress at a Fair in a temper. You've heard the old story. It's a legend, they say now, but it was all true enough, I believe. My father was a good man but he had a hot temper. That is perhaps what Uhland had too--but now those stories are all so old and so long ago and there is a new generation growing up. Dear little Vanessa, my granddaughter, such a pretty child. And Benjamin, your grandson--a very lively high-spirited boy. I don't want them to be in any family quarrel when they grow up. The world is more sensible now than when I was a girl--too sensible, I sometimes think, with people like Mr Gladstone and so much church on Sundays. Of course I think young people ought to go to church, but not as a duty. I'm rambling on, but what I really mean is that I want Vanessa and Benjamin to grow up without any hatred. Hatred is silly--waste of time and temper.'

She had talked on, but it seemed that he had listened to none of it. He only sat there staring in front of him, scratching his cheek. She was trying to reconcile him with the stout, cheerful, bullying man she had once known. How could Jennifer and the others have feared him as they did? He had never had any brains, only some instincts, and so he had collapsed under the pressure of events. You must have either intelligence or spiritual faith to stand up against life. When you had both you could be a conqueror. Jennifer had never had any brains, so she had gone the same way.

'Well, I must go now. Will you help me to my carriage?'

She rose a little unsteadily. When she stood beside him her little body was at his height, he sitting.

She kissed him.

Then, to her distress, she saw slow unmeaning tears trickle down his cheek. He did not try to stop them. He did not perhaps know that he was crying. Gently she stroked his rough unbrushed hair, speaking to him as though he were a child.

'There, there, Walter . . . Things are not so bad, my dear. I will come again and see you. I am glad that we are friends at last. If you want anything, you have only to send to Uldale. There, there, Walter. Remember that we are all your friends. You are not alone any more. Uldale is no distance, you know.'

He rose slowly, looked about him in a bewildered fashion, then very courteously offered her his arm and conducted her to her carriage.

ON CAT BELLS: ESCAPE FROM ECSTASY

Adam, turning on his side, caught the light from the window. The morning clouds, fiery with gold, were piling up above Walla Crag. HIS field--the field of all his life with its five little trees and its arch of sloping green-- rolled into the glow; then, as though with a sigh of satisfaction, held the light; the little trees stood up and stretched their morning limbs. He looked at the field, thought that it was late (but they had not returned from Ambleside until one this morning), looked over his shoulder and saw that Margaret was yet deeply sleeping, then stretched out his brown hand to the bedside table and found Barney Newmark's letter.

There was light enough now to read by. Barney described Thackeray's funeral:

'. . . You would have been moved, Adam, although you thought the man proud and sensitive. So perhaps he was, but he had reason to be. Maybe he was the loneliest man I have ever met. One of the kindliest too. I could not but remember the first time I ever went to his house--his table covered, not with books and papers as you might think, but with compasses and pencils, bits of chalk and India ink, and little square blocks of box- wood. He was drawing, not writing. There were no signs of the author in the room, only the appliances of the draughtsman, and when we chatted he would rather talk about drawings than about books. And in what a kind, generous way, putting his hand on my arm, he said: "Well: and how can I be of any service to you?"

'And then there I was at Harlesden and a labourer going to his work said, quite casually: "You must make haste if you want to see him buried." It was a bright December day, everything shining and glittering, a dense black crowd waiting by the grave, and then the hearse-- quite a common one, one of those plain, dull, black- painted boxes upon wheels without feathers or any ornament, drawn by only two horses: two or three car- riages following, and then the straggling mourners-- Dickens looking defiant as though he would like to knock someone down, Cruikshank, Millais, Louis Blanc, and the Punch people--you know, Mark Lemon, Leech and Tenniel--a lot more. The eight men could scarcely carry the coffin--he was a giant, wasn't he? Then the short ceremony--thank heaven it IS so short!--and the mourners elbowing their way through the crowd to take a last look. And wasn't this an irony? There was a heavy prosaic policeman by the grave and as we filed past he said to the man in front of me: "Now don't be in a hurry; follow each other to the right, and you will all see comfortably." Would not Thackeray himself have liked that. The younger men of course are saying that he is already old-fashioned, but I myself think . . .'

Adam did not just then discover what it was that Barney thought. He put down the letter and lay for a while looking out across the Lake to Walla Crag. Thackeray was dead and he himself was forty- eight, and his mother, amazing woman, was eighty-nine; the Americans were fighting one another, and Bismarck was bullying the Danes; he must widen the vegetable-patch beyond the trees to the right of the house, and today he would start his fairy story--the one that had been in his head for more than a year now--and young Benjamin was riding over for the day and night from Uldale. It was the last week of his holiday before he returned to school--and here he was, he, Adam Paris, who had done nothing with his life as yet at all, but was happy, happy, happy . . . here in this January of 1864, in his own cot- tage that he had helped to build with his own hands under the brow of the hill, and Margaret his wife lying beside him, and their child cradled in her arm (for in the night, when they had returned, she had wakened, climbed out of her cot and demanded to come to them). Well, well . . . and Thackeray was dead, dead and buried.

He stretched out his hand again, this time for a volume of a novel. The novel was called The Ordeal of Richard Feverel; it was written by a young man, George Meredith. Although it had been published some four years or so, he had only now heard of it. An unusual book! Fantastically written but new--new in thought, in style and in audacity. And Thackeray was old-fashioned. Thackeray was dead. He rolled over and laid his arm very lightly but protectively over Margaret. They had sailed all the perilous seas now and were in harbour, through passion (but Margaret had never been very passionate), through that strange period of isolation the one from the other, when they knew one another too well and yet not nearly well enough. (That had been ended by the scene at Uldale that Christmas-time.) Then through the wonderful stage of renewed passion and a heightened glorious intimacy. (This stage had included Caesar Kraft's death and the end of Adam's 'Brotherhood' ambitions.) Then, back in Cumberland, out of passion and into this, the real glory of every mar- riage that can attain it, a confidence, a trust, an intimacy so great and deep and calm that it was like Derwent- water there beyond the window.

She would never QUITE understand him. There was a vein of cynicism running through his nature that was quite foreign to her. Nor would she ever under- stand his restlessness. Once she had his love and the

550

love of their child, and KNEW that she had them, nothing could ever disturb her again--except, of course, losing either himself or Vanessa. Always when he left her, even for an hour or two, a little wrinkle lined her calm brow. She was not REALLY happy again until he had returned. But she was no longer possessive as she had once been. That was because she was sure of him now.

At that thought he moved a little restlessly. Did he want her to be sure of him? Did any man want his wife to be sure of him, and was not every wife unhappy unless she WAS sure? That was perhaps one of the eternal misunderstandings in marriage. And in this his mother completely understood him. In every way his mother understood him, shared his restlessness, his longings, his disappointments in himself, knew him as no one else did. He and she were wanderers constrained by the circumstances of life to be stay-at-homes. Had he not married Margaret what a useless, worthless wanderer he would have been! Like his old legendary grandfather! Yes, he had been lucky to marry a woman like Margaret, so good and loyal, faithful and true. Once he would have been wearied and irritated by too much goodness and fidelity.

He got out of bed very quietly and went down to the yard behind the house for Will to sluice him down.

Although it was early January and mortal cold, he did not shrink from the sluicing. The yard was hidden from the world save for the little wood on the rise of the ground. No windows looked on it, and it was sheltered from the winds. Will was already there, cleaning the boots and hissing away at them like a hostler. He straightened himself when he saw Adam and stood up, grinning, his yellow forelock straggling over his forehead, his eyes as blue, direct and unflinching as those of an honest and fearless child, his body balanced easily on its strong legs.

'I'm late this morning, Will.'

'Aye. You was late last night.'

'Lovely day.'

Will looked up. The sky was blue and laced everywhere with little clouds that still had tints of amber and rose.

'Cold this morning,' Adam said.

He looked at Will with great affection. The whole day started wrongly if he did not have a brief talk alone with Will at the beginning of it, for his relation with Will was that of man to man, rid of all the uncertainties, sudden crises, sudden darknesses that haunt like ghosts the relation of the sexes. In a way Will understood him better than did either his mother or Margaret. In a way Will loved him better than did either of the women, for it was a love completely unselfish, that asked nothing in return, that was disturbed by no moods or reticences. When Adam was in a temper or caught into some creative distance far from all human agency or had a cold or a headache or felt his liver, Margaret was disturbed as though she were in danger of losing something (al-

though she had learnt to conceal this disturbance, Adam knew that it was there and it irritated him), but Will was unchanged. Let Adam have what mood he wished, Will loved him just the same. He could be jealous, and was often confoundedly obstinate and pig-headed, but his loyalty, devotion, trustworthiness never varied a hair's breadth.

Two wooden buckets filled with cold water stood side by side. Adam threw off his shirt and breeches, then shivered as the cold air struck his bare flesh.

'Quick, Will. Quick, you devil!'

Will took up one bucket in his two arms and with a heave threw the water over Adam. Then the other. Then quickly he caught a rough towel that was hanging on the back of the kitchen door, seized Adam and rubbed him with great violence, hissing furiously.

Adam ran into the kitchen and stood naked in front of the roaring fire. Now he was glorious. He was in fine condition. Drops of water clung to his beard and his hairy chest. His flesh was firm and strong. His heart beat like a good steady hammer. He took deep breaths. Will watched the operation with high satisfaction.

'You know, Will,' Adam said, stretching out his bare arms, 'my mother has told me that her father used to have his man swill him down at Rosthwaite where he lived, in just this way. He was a queer character, he was. My mother has a heap of tales about him from his son, her stepbrother. He was years older than she was--David Herries, I mean. And now she's nearing ninety. Takes you back a long time, doesn't it?'

'Aye,' said Will. 'It does that. We're born and we're wed and we're dead before we know. 'Tis odd when you think of it, Mr Adam, that folk make the fuss they do when they're dead so quick. About little things, I mean. Now there was that man from Seathwaite last evening. Was in here with a long tale about a cow he'd lost. I told him not to fret and he was furious, as though I'd stolen the damned cow myself. Mary will be in likely. I can hear her coming.' This was the old woman from the farm halfway to Grange. She came every day as help.

Adam pulled on his shirt and breeches and went upstairs.

Later he was sitting in his room waiting to begin his fairy story. This room--not very large--was square, papered a dull rather shabby red, and the two windows looked full on to the Lake and Walla Crag. The wall opposite the windows was lined with shelves, and there were his books, not a great collection, some four or five hundred in all.

They were, moreover, a mixed lot, in no sort of order. A faded row of little blue volumes of the Iliad and Odyssey had for companions Pickwick in its shilling parts (the covers of some of the numbers disgracefully torn), Rogers' Italy with the handsome illustrations,

Arthur Young's Travels in France and Leigh Hunt's Story of Rimini. There were thirty volumes of the 'English Poets', ten of Chaucer, Sir Charles Grandison and Tristram Shandy. On the table at his side were two volumes of Richard Feverel, Huxley's Man's Place in Nature, and The Woman in White. By itself on the other side of him was a fresh brilliant copy in green and gold of Barney Newmark's first novel*--Dandy Grimmett--in three volumes.

* Dandy Grimmett, by Barnabas Newmark: 3 vols, Suller & Thorne 1863.

'They have bound young Barney very handsomely,' he thought. (He still looked on Barney as an infant although he was now nearly thirty-four years of age.) He felt a pang of envy, regret, sadness. There was young Barney, of whom no one had thought very much, publishing his first novel and some of it not bad either, especially the racing scenes, the fight (plainly taken from Sayers and Heenan), and the last chapter when old Dandy, dying, is brought back to his rooms in London and hears the carriages rolling to the theatres, the cries of the newsboys, and the thick heavy ticking of the clock on the marble mantelpiece. He's been influenced by Thackeray, of course--not doing anything new like this young man Meredith. But is it important to be new? Nothing is new but superficials. He can paint a scene that is real. He knows his world . . . Damned clever sketch of his father, old Stephen. He'd deny it, of course . . .'

His mind went floating away to the lake that lay in the morning sun like a snake's skin, grey and rippled, convulsed, it seemed, with little shudders. The sunlight hung above it on the flanks of the hill as though afraid to descend. He pushed open the window and looked out, heard the stream running at the back of the house, smelt the dead bracken, the gritty flakiness of the dead earth, and saw a snowdrop, solitary and beautiful, bend its stem in the breeze.

He heard Vanessa calling. His heart warmed. It was all he could do not to go out to her, but he knew that once he had left that room incident after incident would occur to prevent his return to it, as though a malicious Fate were determined for ever to hold him back from doing anything. With a sigh he closed the window and went back to the table. He picked up a number of London Society that had just arrived and read from the serial story:

'"Nor need you wish to do so, Miss Fleming" said Jane quickly. "Nor, if you were thrown on the world, would you ever be what Milly and I are now. We have had unusual advantages from our cradles, and with great natural aptitude, have improved them to the uttermost."'

He sighed again. 'Great natural aptitude . . .' 'Improved them to the uttermost.' No, people did not talk like that. Why were novels so silly?

But this seemed to encourage him. HE was going to write a fairy story. He sat down resolutely, drew the paper in front of him and wrote in his firm strong hand:

THE DWARF WITH THE PURPLE COMB*

He sat, looking out of window, biting the feather of his quill. Then he was off and away!

Once upon a time there was a King who had five lovely daughters. The names of the five Princesses were Hazel, Rosamond, Amaryllis, Mellicent and Mary. Mary was the youngest and she was not given so grand a name as the others because the King, her father, had wanted to have a son and was so grievously disappointed when the Doctor told him that the baby was a girl that he shut himself into his bedroom for four and a half days and refused to see anybody, even the Queen. He lived all that time on bread and water. So at least it was said. But Fortunatus, the son of the Woodcutter in the Forest near by, saw the Palace gardener climb on a ladder and hand through the King's bedroom window a gold tray that had on it a gingerbread cake, a roast goose, a Christmas pudding and a dish with oranges, plums and apricots.

Fortunatus told his father, the Woodcutter, what he had observed, and his father said that he must never mention it to anyone or he would lose his head. Mary, who was the loveliest child ever seen-- she had hair as dark as the ravens and a smile so sweet that everyone at the Court loved her--was always punished when her sisters did anything wrong. For example, one fine morning Princess Rosamond was given a beautiful dress by her Fairy Godmother (it was her birthday). The dress was made of tissue and silver and it had buttons of green jade, a collar of emeralds, and the sleeves were decorated with the feathers of the Bird of Paradise. When Princess Mellicent saw this beautiful dress she was so angry because HER Fairy Godmother had given her on HER birthday only a needlework- case. So she took the gold scissors from her needlework-case and when Princess Rosamond was practising the piano in the Green Drawing-room she went into her sister's bedroom and cut the beautiful dress into shreds.

Now when this was discovered and Mellicent had confessed to what she had done, Mary was put to stand in the corner of the Audience Chamber with her face to the wall so that everyone who passed by could see her.

It happened then one fine morning that Fortunatus, the Woodcutter's son, was sent by his father to the Palace with a wheelbarrow full of logs for the Royal fireplaces, and, peeping in (for he was a very inquisitive boy) at the door of the Audience Chamber, he saw the lovely little Princess standing with her face to the wall . . .

* The Dwarf with the Purple Comb, And other Stories; by Adam Paris, Harris & Sons, 1865.

Little Vanessa ran down the path and up the road. It was time for Benjamin to be coming, and from the corner where the stream ran from the tops straight like a silver arrow into the Lake you could watch the higher bend of the road. She danced about, clapping her hands because it was cold.

She was wearing a dress of green and black checked taffeta, which was the new material. She was immensely proud of it and had begged to be allowed to wear it because Benjamin was coming. She was already tall for her age, carried herself to her full height, and now, when she was dancing, every movement was natural in its grace as the silver pattern of the stream, the dull amber of the dead bracken and the bare wood whose trees were flushed in the distance like an evening sky against the grey Lake filmed with ice. Skiddaw and Blencathra were powdered with snow, and hard round clouds like snowballs hung above their lines. Vanessa's mind was intently fixed on Benjamin. Although he was over four years older she thought that he was a perfect companion. She was even then an excellent listener; her curiosity was acute, and she could never be told enough about anything if someone wanted to tell her. Benjamin told her the most extraordinary things. Everything that happened at Uldale was of absorbing interest to her, and she spent so much of her time with grown-up people-- her mother and father, Will, and Mary from the farm-- that although she was entirely a child and in many things still a baby, she understood the LIVES of grown-up people, knew why they did things and could IMAGINE their world. Her grandmother--the old lady who was as smart as a pin, all white and black (and the very WHITEST of white!) with her cap, her ivory cane, her shoes with the silver buckles, who was so kind, amusing, understanding, but could, all in a moment, be so sharp and commanding (very like the Queen of England)--was to Vanessa simply the most miraculous person in the world, composed of magic, fire, ice, diamonds. There she was in her room, older than anyone had ever been, but more acquainted with all that Vanessa was thinking than anyone save her mother. Then there was Aunt Jane, the nicest of all the Aunts. Aunt Veronica who was beautiful, Aunt Amabel who could throw a ball like a boy. Uncle Timothy who was so big that he could take the whole of you in his hand if he wished, Aunt Dorothy who was always busy, James the coachman, Daniel the stableman, Martha the cook--and so on, so

on--a whole WORLD was in Uldale. One could never have enough of it.

And Benjamin was her Uldale storyteller. She would like him to go on for hours telling her things, but he could never be still, never stay in one place more than five minutes. And Vanessa thought this unusual, because his mother, Aunt Elizabeth, was so quiet. She would sit all evening in the same corner of the sofa reading a book-- only often, as Vanessa had noticed, she was not reading, but would put down her book and sit staring in front of her. Benjamin had no father, which, Vanessa thought, was terribly sad for him.

Ah! there Benjamin was! He came trotting round the corner on Albert, his pony (named after the Prince Consort, who had died the very month that Uncle Timothy gave it him). Mumps the dog was running at the side. Mumps loved Benjamin, and even now, when he was ten years old or more, would never leave Benjamin's side could he help it. The boy saw Vanessa and waved his riding-whip. When he came up to her he burst out laughing. His round, plump face was crimson with the cold air and the exercise, and his funny small nose needed wiping.

'You're wearing a new dress!' he shouted.

'Yes,' she said, still dancing. 'And there's ice on the Lake. It will be frozen perhaps tomorrow--enough to skate on.'

They went up the path to the cottage, and as soon as Benjamin was off the pony he felt in his coat-pocket and produced a large, very sticky chunk of toffee.

'Have some!' he said, trying to break it.

'Did Uncle Timothy give it you?'

'No. I stole it from the kitchen. Mother said I wasn't to have any because I was sick last time from eating so much, so I had to get it from the kitchen, and Martha nearly caught me.'

Benjamin always puzzled Vanessa in this way, because he was for ever doing things that he was told not to do. When he was caught he never lied nor did he seem in the least to mind punishment, but it appeared that you had only to make a rule for him to want to break it.

However, she took some of the toffee and, with their mouths full, they went round to the back to put the pony up and see Will. When they were in the back-yard Benjamin turned a somersault. He had just learned to do it. 'There's a boy at school called Turnip,' he explained. 'And he can do it and he said I couldn't, so now I can.'

'What a funny name to have!' she remarked.

'They call him that because his REAL name is Turner--see?' Benjamin said, turning head over heels again.

In the living-room of the cottage Adam had few books, but he had been given two things out of the parlour at Uldale and these he prized over all his other possessions--one was the old spinet with roses painted on its lid, the other the music-box with the Queen in her green dress and the King in his amber coat. When Judith, growing too old to argue violently with Dorothy, saw that big heavy new furniture was coming into the parlour do what she would, she insisted that Adam should have the spinet for his cottage. She would have given him the sofa with the red apples also had she not felt a superstition. Her hand had rested on that when she had made her great decision . . .

Adam's living-room had not much furniture. There were the wax flowers that he had bought Margaret at the Pantheon. The square carpet had eight groups of flowers on a light pink ground. There were three carved mahogany chairs with needlework seats and backs. There was a chiffonnier bookcase, brown and gold with marquetry panels. These things had been presents from various members of the family. Carey Rockage's wife had given him two cornucopias, Will Herries the bookcase. On the walls against some very variegated wallpaper was a watercolour called 'The Lady of the House', an engraving of Watendlath, and a Baxter print, 'Dippers and Nest'. In one corner of the room was Vanessa's joy, a Peepshow of the Central Hall at the Great Exhibition. Over the mantelpiece was hung a Sand Picture, 'Saddle Horse', by James Zobel. Barney Newmark had given him this one Christmas. So the room was an odd jumble, and he didn't care for anything in it save the music-box and the spinet. But it was in this room and among these things that he experienced a little scene with young Benjamin. He had reached a point in his fairy story where the Dwarf had tapped on the Princess Mary's window. The Palace Garden was flooded with moonlight. She came to the window, and, standing on top of the ladder, he whispered to her that, if she would come with him, he would take her to the orchard and there, hidden in the ground at the roots of an old apple tree, he would find for her the Purple Comb . . .

At that point everything had ceased. He could see no more the Princess, the Dwarf, young Fortunatus. All had vanished, the Lake rippled under its silver shading of ice, and Blencathra had the bloom of a plum. Soon it would be time for the meal. He was hungry, so, rubbing his hands, he went into the living-room. A moment later Benjamin came in.

'Uncle Adam,' he asked, 'can you wrestle?'

'No,' he said.

'Try,' said Benjamin, and without a moment's warning he pushed himself on to Adam. He butted his stomach with his round head, tried to bring his arms together around Adam's broad thighs, twisted his small legs round Adam's thick ones. He put a ferocious energy into this, blowing and grunting, straining every muscle in his body. For a moment he made Adam rock. Adam could feel the muscles of the boy's leg strung to their utmost against his calf. The two small hands tore at his waistcoat. A button flew off. The hands groped inside his shirt, pinched his flesh.

'Hi!' he called out. 'That's enough! You're hurting!'

'I'll do it! I'll do it!' Benjamin gasped. 'I'll bring you down!'

Adam, laughing, put out his arms, caught the boy to him with a bear's hug, then swung him into the air and held him there.

'Now what will you do?'

Benjamin kicked. Then he was rolled on to the floor, lay there for a moment panting.

'Things look funny from here,' he observed. He got up. 'I haven't it right yet. There's a trick you do with your left leg. Next time I shall manage it.' His hair was dishevelled, his cheeks crimson, his shirt open. He grinned.

'You have torn one of my buttons off,' Adam said.

'Oh, that's all right. Aunt Margaret will sew it on for you.'

He came close to Adam, leaned against him, looked up at him, smiling, but with a strange mature glance.

Adam said: 'Are you liking school? I hear that you were in all kinds of trouble the last term. Why was that?'

Benjamin nodded.

'I can't help it, Uncle Adam. If anyone tells me to do anything I don't want to do it.'

'Why's that?'

'I don't know. I expect it's because my uncle killed my father. There isn't another boy in the whole school whose uncle killed his father.'

The words came out quite easily, with no sense of self- consciousness, no unhappiness--a clear statement of simple fact. To Adam those words were like thunder in his ears. The floor seemed to rock. He didn't know that the boy had any notion of the way that his father had died. They had, all of them, for years been in a conspiracy to prevent any allusion to it before the boy, and although at first it had seemed a vain hope that he should not hear, as the years passed they all thought that they had succeeded, for when Benjamin spoke of his father it was quite naturally. He seemed to believe that he had died of some illness just like any other man.

Benjamin nodded.

'You thought I didn't know. I have known for years and years and years. First a farmer at Peter's House told me. I know just what they did. They rode through the mist to Skiddaw House. They had arranged it all, and my uncle shot my father and then shot himself. And my father hadn't a gun. So you see I'm different from all the other boys, and I'll be different all my life.'

Adam did not know what to say. He moved off and looked out of window. Then he turned round.

'Your father,' he said, 'was a very fine man and I loved him. He always did the right thing and so must you.'

Benjamin answered quickly, as though he were speaking in someone's defence.

'I love my father more than anyone, and if I had been there with him I would have taken the gun from my uncle and shot him, and all my life I'll kill men like my uncle who are beasts and cowards. I don't care. I'm not afraid of anyone, and I'll never do something just because someone tells me . . .' His voice suddenly was the voice of a small boy. 'I'll be like Robin Hood. He was an outlaw and I'll be an outlaw. I have a band of outlaws under me at school and we're not afraid of anybody.'

To Adam there came a quick picture of a wood, a pool, a man on a white horse and himself dancing in defiance of that rider's whip . . .

He came across the floor to Benjamin and put his arm around him.

'I was like that myself once and now I'm an old gentleman who writes fairy stories. The great thing,' he went on, holding the boy close to him, 'is not to be bitter against life because of what happened to your father. Don't allow things that have happened in the past, Benjamin, to spoil your life. The past is past. They are ghosts, all those dead men.'

'My father is not a ghost,' Benjamin said. 'I have his picture and a riding-whip he had and his hairbrushes. I took the hairbrushes out of Mama's room and I've hidden them. No one knows where they are but me. And one day I shall meet someone like my uncle and I will shoot him just as he shot my father, except that he shall have a gun, so that it's fair.'

Adam shook his head. 'That's no good,' he said. 'Because a wrong was done once, to do another wrong doesn't make things better.'

'Look here, Uncle,' Benjamin said. 'I can make a somersault. I THINK I can make two now. Here! Look!' and he turned two somersaults, one after the other, in the space between the chairs and the table. He tumbled straight into old Mary who was helping Margaret to bring in the meal.

Had Benjamin affected him? When they were sitting after the meal quietly watching the sunlight stain the flowers of the carpet, the gilt of the bookcase, and strike, as though maliciously, the simpering self-importance of 'The Lady of the House', he felt a curious and abnormal ecstasy of perception. It seemed to him that his senses were all tingling with an extra activity.

Margaret, opposite him, was making a basket cover in old silk patchwork. On a ground of dark green she was forming a kaleidoscope pattern of glittering scraps--flakes of crimson, sea- green, primrose, hyacinth blue, the rose of apple orchards, the gold of corn. On the grey stuff of the lap of her dress the fragments of silk lay scattered, her look so serenely safe and happy that it caught at his heart. Once and again she would glance up at him and smile. Vanessa and Benjamin were stretched on the floor, their heads together, looking at a book of Japanese drawings. From where he sat he could see the brilliant figures of birds and men in blue and crimson carrying burdens over bridges and the wide expanse of purple seas. Everything was colour and everything was peace. Tiny details seemed to wear a heightened significance, the buttons on Vanessa's dress, freckles on Benjamin's snub nose, the needlework pattern on the chairs.

He was filled with a kind of immortal ecstasy. This he had achieved. Through all the disappointments and failures of his life he had caught this and held it--love, fatherhood, security. The patch of ground upon which his feet were set was his, this hill, the silver birch gleaming in the sun beyond the window, the stream of music he could hear, this Cumberland that all his life long he had worshipped, and beyond it England, the hills running to the sea, the valleys running to the South, all this land that, now that he had his home, flowed to the North, South, East and West. Running from his door to all the seas, his for ever and ever, although his realization of it lasted only for a moment.

His happiness caught him at the throat. His eyes were blinded. He moved in his chair, and Margaret looked across at him and smiled.

Then Benjamin glanced up at them and sprang to his feet.

'I want to go out! Come along, Vanessa! I'll race you!'

They opened the doors and ran out into the garden.

It was as though he had himself spoken. He felt suddenly that his security was dangerous. He did not want it. He was bound, a prisoner. Somewhere, a small child, he was running, running, escaping, shouting, and his mother was with him. Panting, they raced up the hill to see the sun rise. The woods fell below them, the Tarn was dark, and he could hear the sheep rustling past him up the dark path. His mother was a gipsy and he was her gipsy son. He could see the lights from the painted carts--a horse neighed . . . waving his arms and shouting he breasted the hill . . .

He woke as though he had been sleeping, and saw Margaret choosing the colours from the fragments of silk, holding a scrap of rose against the light to see how it would do . . .

'I'll be back, Meg,' he said.

He went to the door and almost ran from the house. He began to climb through the dead bracken above his stone wall. As he mounted he heard the voices of the children from the garden, a cart was creaking down the road that was already a white ribbon. The Lake rose and he saw that the sun had veined it with patterns of light, here there were pools of grey and ashen pallor and there deep shadows of saffron--all confined by the hills, Skiddaw, Saddleback, Walla Crag. As he climbed, the Lake and the hills climbed with him. The air was cold like a whip, but so fresh that it struck his cheeks as the water had done when Will sluiced him that morning.

Then he began to run, he called aloud, he shouted. He stumbled and fell over the stones and thought how old Rackstraw had told him once: 'Clouds and stones! Stones and clouds! That's what this country is!'

His breathing hurt him like a knife, for he was no child now but a stout middle-aged man with a beard and middle-aged habits of comfort and laziness. But he liked the catch at his lungs, the bruise on his knee where the stone had hit him. He climbed, stumbling, waving his arms, turning to catch the Lake and the hills with him and draw them up. He did not know that he was climbing like a madman, climbing as he had never climbed that hill before, because he was part of the hill, the wind, the sun. He hurled himself over the last boulders and flung himself on the strong, resilient turf, lying there at full length, his arms spread out, his chest heaving. Why should he ever return? Something wild and authentic in his blood beat in his brain. Margaret, Vanessa, his mother, they were nothing to him because he was not himself, Adam Paris, but something beyond himself, beyond time, the past, the present and all that was to come.

He lay on the turf, the soil was in his beard, his hands dug into the short sweet grass, the grit of the land, chilled, hardened with a frost that had outlived the midday sun. He stood up. Below him was Derwentwater to the east, Newlands to the west veiled now in the shadow of the lengthening day. He saw Catchedicam to the left of Helvellyn top, and southwards was Langdale Pike o' Stickle. Why should he ever return? He started to run again on a surface so buoyant that it seemed to run with him. Up the easy slope of Maiden Moor, Scafell and Gable coming to meet him between Eel Crag and Dale Head. Why should he ever return? Borrowdale and Grange were below and now the Pillar was in view between Dale Head and Hindscarth. He might race on for ever--Hindscarth and Robinson, then down to Buttermere across to Ennerdale, over to Waswater, to Eskdale and the sea!

He was a wandering man, a lost man, a man at last his own master!

He shouted. 'Oh, hoi! Oh, hoi!' All the hills echoed him as it seemed to him, and the waters of a thousand streams roared about his ears.

He flung out his arms and embraced the world . . .

Folly! He sat down, hugging his knees. He brushed the soil from his beard. He pulled up his trousers to see whether his knee were bleeding. It was not. He could barely see the scratch. Two sheep came wandering towards him and stood a little way off him, watching. Then, reassured, began to graze again. The sun was gone; it fell swiftly behind the hills on these January days. Helvellyn burned in a haze of rosy smoke, and all the air was frosty as though the ice had suddenly thickened on the Lake below and the hills around him. Maiden Moor, Robinson were breathing in gusts of cold thickened air. The sky paled to become the white field of one solitary star that glittered, a spark of frosted fire. Dusk and a great silence enwrapped the world.

He started home. The thought of home was comforting. Margaret sitting by the fire, and he would tell Benjamin and Vanessa a story . . .

He started down the slope, singing as he went.

A DAY IN THE LIFE OF A VERY OLD LADY

She rose and then sank again, sank and rose, on a great billowy cloud of softest down. The movement was so exquisite, and she was herself so lazy, that she abandoned herself completely, although there were, she knew, a thousand things that she ought to be doing. Everything, far and near, was of a dazzling white save only Adam's nose that was purple and dripping with cold. Had she the energy she would tell him that he must blow it. There was the cloud available and it would irritate her, did she allow herself to be irritated, that he did not make use of so convenient a remedy. But she would not permit herself to be irritated. She was altogether too happy. As she rocked she sang softly to herself a song that Emma Furze had taught her, but she would not sing loudly lest she should wake Georges who was snoring on a cloud near by. How well she knew that snore--it was part of her whole life--and although she did not care for snores in general, Georges' snore was her own property and he must sleep long, here in Watendlath, for yesterday had been the clipping and he would be weary.

Moreover, just round the corner was the whole family--Dorothy, Tim, Veronica, Amabel and dear Jane. They were busy at some game. She could not quite see them, but she knew what they were about. Practising at archery, as indeed they must, for in a week's time there was the contest in Keswick and Veronica had a chance of a prize. It was winter, but in visions such as this all seasons were confused. How lovely she looked, Veronica, her body stretched, her bow held straight from her arms, her beautiful head thrown back! But Jane would be clumsy. If she were not careful they would laugh and then Jane would blush, pretending not to mind, but hurt at her clumsiness . . . and she would call from her cloud, as so often she had done before, 'Jane! Jane! I want you!' simply to save her.

Things began to press in upon her consciousness. A great white bird, the sunlight glittering in silver on its sweeping wings, flew slowly above her head, and the white blossom fell, at a touch of the warm breeze, there across the lawn in the orchard, the petals hovering, wavering . . . hovering, wavering! The sheep, their fleece stained with red, were pressing up the road at Watendlath, and Charlie Watson, motionless on his horse, watched them go. There was something that she must say to Charlie Watson, and so, raising herself from her cloud, she called softly 'Charlie! Charlie!'

The sky was blinded with a white radiance. The great bird, shaking showers of brilliance from its wings, beat upwards towards the sun. The radiance was so bright that she put her hand before her eyes, crying out with joy at so much loveliness, then heard--close beside here--Jane's eager laughing voice.

'Wake up, Aunt Judith! Look at the snow! It has fallen in the night! There never was such a beautiful day!'

She turned her head, rubbed her eyes, then reached for her spectacles. Putting them on she caught, in one sweep, the whole of the real world, for Jane had drawn back the blinds and, from her bed, she could see the flanks of Skiddaw glistening in crystal snow, and snow heaped on the windowsill. Above it all, there was a burning blue sky and the sun blazed over all the room. Jane stood there with the basin of water, the sponge, the soap, the towel, the silver brushes, the ivory comb, and, on a table not far away, breakfast was waiting.

'Well, my dear,' she said with a little sigh of happiness. 'I've had a very good night, thank you. I woke once and heard it strike three and that was the only time. Dear me, what a splendid sunshine! And how are you, Jane dear? I hope you slept well. I dreamt you were practising archery with Veronica.'

'I have had a very good night, thank you,' said Jane, and at once she began, with a dexterity and neatness that Judith adored (she would allow no one but Jane to perform these offices), to hold the basin, to see that the sponge was not too full, and then, when the washing was concluded, to bring the round mirror with the green wood and the gilt doves, so that Judith might see clearly to brush her silver hair.

'Mary will be in shortly to set the fire. There are plenty of logs, I told James yesterday.'

'What is there for breakfast?'

The tray was brought to the bed and carefully arranged.

'I chose those two brown eggs myself. And there is the damson preserve.'

'Dear me, how pleasant!'

'Adam is coming over today, you know.'

'As though I could forget, my dear.'

'He is bringing Vanessa.'

'Of course, of course,' Judith said, quite crossly. They would treat her--even dear Jane did this--as though she found it difficult to remember things. She remembered everything-- EVERYTHING. It was true that it seemed to her as though Georges and Charlie Watson were still in the room. Past and Present were one and the same. Jane herself would discover that one day. But because she, Judith, was ninety-five years of age (she had had her birthday a week or two ago) was no reason why they should think her helpless. It was true that she could not, any longer, walk very much, but for the rest she was as active and alive as any of them. She took off the top of one of her eggs and said:

'How is everybody? How is Timothy's cold?'

'Bad. But he doesn't mind. He has ridden off to Orpen Farm to see about the Hunt tomorrow. With the snow like this it will be difficult, but it will thaw this afternoon, I dare say. It never lies long here.'

Judith enjoyed her breakfast. Every morning as she drank her tea and ate her toast and preserve, she considered her state. She was no hypochondriac, but from a kind of outside consideration she summoned her forces. Had she a headache? Did her eyes smart? How was her throat which, a day or two ago, had been a little sore? How was that sharp pain in the right elbow? And the soreness just above the left knee? Was her stomach (which Dorothy thought it most indelicate ever to mention) preparing to upset her or was it lazy and good-natured today? (She saw her stomach as a kind of cat, sometimes full of warm milk and purring, sometimes in the worst of tempers, always selfish.)

But how was the Captain of her Ragged Army, her Heart? Everything depended on her Heart. While she felt that her stomach was definitely hostile, didn't care a rap about her, her Heart, she considered, was on her side, disliked extremely to distress her, would not miss a beat and then beat twice in a hurry if he could help it. Her Heart was a Gentleman who was making the best of it in very difficult circumstances.

Although she held this review every morning she never spoke to anyone about it. She could indeed carry on a perfect domestic conversation with Jane at the very moment when she was saying inside herself: 'Well, Knee, are you wishing to be tiresome today? You are very quiet just now, but I dare say you've got something up your sleeve for later on.'

And, behind all this, was her terrific pride at reaching her present age. Every morning when she woke to find herself alive she made another triumphant notch on the slate of her mind. It soon might be--it might be indeed at any moment--that she would slip into a stage of semi-consciousness when living would be nothing but a dreaming preparation for Death. When that came she would not be able to reckon her triumph, so now she would make the most of it. On November 28th last, her ninety-fifth birthday, she had had messages, letters, gifts, from Herries all over the country--from Ellis and his mother, Janet and Roger at Grosset, Stephen Newmark, Phyllis, Barnabas, Katherine (who had married Colonel Winch of Forrest Hatch, Salisbury), Emily, from Garth and Amery and Sylvia, from the Ormerods at Harrogate and the Cards at Bournemouth, from all the Witherings near Carlisle--yes, from Herries and Herries all the country over. They had all been kind and generous, but she knew what it was that they had all been thinking. She must reach her Hundredth Birthday! At all costs SHE MUST LIVE TO BE A HUNDRED!

Not for many, many years--not in fact since old Maria Herries who had been born on the day of the Battle of Naseby--had any Herries come so near to a Hundred. Great-Aunt Maria had missed it, and they were all disappointed even now, after all this time, that she had done so.

But Judith was their pride and their hope. True that she had not always been their pride, true that her father had been a disgrace, that she herself had married a rascal of a Frenchman who had died shamefully in a drunken scramble, that she had lived like a farmer's wife in the country, that she had had an illegitimate son, but that was all long ago. She had become a famous person, a legend. All over the country Herries said: 'Oh yes, we are a strong stock, live to a great age. There's old Madame now, ninety something, and commands a houseful of women up in Cumberland as though she were twenty. Wonderful old lady! She'll reach her Century, you may be sure. Nothing can stop her.'

Judith knew that they were saying this and she was proud of it. Of course it was foolish, but then the Herries WERE foolish--foolish and rather charming, in their childishness. When she felt well, as on a morning like this present one, she thought that she could live until two hundred. Why not? What was to stop her? There WERE days when she was infinitely weary and longed for it all to be over. But as soon as the bad days passed she forgot them.

Today her mind was as clear as a crystal. She remembered everything. Timothy's cold, the calf that had been born two nights before, the new maid Hannah from Seathwaite, the proposal that Captain Forster of Runner Hall, near Penrith, had made to Veronica a week ago (would she accept him? She was thirty-one years of age and had she not been so beautiful would have been long thought an old maid), a chair that Dorothy had bought for her in Carlisle (it was of hand-carved walnut and its seat was covered in maroon plush; Judith had thought it hideous but did not wish to hurt Dorothy's feelings), Adam's visit, a present of a miniature set in Bristol jet ware (teapot, sugar-box and cream-jug) that she had for Vanessa. Jane had found it in Keswick and it was exactly what Vanessa loved . . . all these things she had in mind while Jane talked and the snow glittered, the sun flooded the room, and the damson preserve tasted most excellent . . .

Afterwards she had her bath, warm and delicious, while the logs blazed and the large tortoiseshell cat purred on the rug; then Jane helped her to dress and at last she was seated in her armchair near the fire ready for the Visits.

'I think, Jane dear, I'll be able to go downstairs a little this afternoon!'

What a picture she made, Jane thought, in her black silk with her snow-white cap, the lace at her throat and wrists, the thin long gold chain that hung almost to her waist, her black shoes with the glittering buckles!

'Yes, dear, I think you can on such a lovely day.' It was at this moment when she was not so well, just before the Visits, that she had to pull herself together, to drag herself up out of that other world, the Watendlath world where Georges and Charlie laughed and rode, where Christabel and Jennifer quarrelled before a fantasy of masked figures, where an old man with a long white beard stroked his nose . . . On her bad days that past was more real than any present. But not today. She was all alert, and when Dorothy, followed by Amabel, entered with their 'Isn't it a beautiful day, Aunt Judith?' and Dorothy began at once, as was her custom, with a cheerful 'tit-tat-tat-tit' of conversation (her manner with very old people) Judith was all alive.

Dorothy was wearing a new dress, the upper skirt caught up almost to the hips and the back of the skirt descending in a straight sloping line from the waist to the ground. The upper skirt was of brown silk and the lower of bright blue taffeta. This suited her stoutness better than the old exaggerated crinoline. Judith knew at once what the new dress meant.

'You are going into Keswick, my dear?'

'Yes. Veronica is coming with me. WHAT do you think? Veronica intends to accept Captain Forster!'

Here was news indeed! One less of the great virginal army! And Captain Forster was not so bad. On the stout side and not very clever, but devoted, with a charming place, money enough, a kind heart. Veronica should have been in London. She might then have married ANYBODY. But she was lazy. There was something of Jennifer in her blood. She had told Judith once that the only man she had ever really loved had been a farmer from Buttermere way. That had been only her fun. Of course Veronica would never think of such a thing! But why not? Had not Charlie Watson been a farmer?

Never mind. Here was Captain Forster--plump, clean, adoring.

'Are you certain?'

'Well, she hasn't confessed it in so many words. But he is to be at the Osmastons'. I am SURE that she means to accept him.'

Amabel, who was always dressed severely and thought men contemptible, tossed her head.

'What she can see in that fat man!'

'Well, dear,' said Dorothy complacently, 'it is she that is going to marry him, not you.'

'Yes, thank heaven.'

They talked for a little, then Dorothy said:

'We will leave you now because I think Elizabeth wants a word. She is unhappy about Benjamin.'

'What has he been doing?'

Dorothy sighed.

'What hasn't he been doing? He had a fight in the village last evening with Marston's boy, and his report from Rugby has come. It is terrible, really terrible. You must speak to him, Aunt Judith. You are the only one who can do anything with him.'

They went and Elizabeth came in.

Elizabeth was fifty-four and as beautiful now as she had been at twenty. She wore a grey dress, her fair hair flat on the top and gathered into a large bun at the back of her head, a golden glory even in that so hideous fashion. She had the air of remoteness that had been hers ever since John's death. She was not priggish nor superior in this. She joined in everything that went on, laughed, sang, played games, hunted (she was still a splendid horsewoman), but nothing could bring her into the real current of life that the others shared. She loved her son, she loved Judith, she loved Jane, but even they, even Benjamin, were shades compared with John. When he was killed she received a blow that was mortal, and Judith, seeing her, knew that the Herries battle was not yet over, and that the consequences of old long-ago histories had still their own history to make.

But because of her own story she understood Elizabeth as did none of the others. Her own Georges had suffered sudden death, as had John, and for ten years after it she, too, had been herself a dead woman. She had had the fears for Adam that Elizabeth now had for Benjamin, but she had been spared because fate had chosen John for its mark instead of Adam. All the more reason that she should help Elizabeth now.

Elizabeth, sitting close beside her, began at once.

'Aunt Judith, we have had Benjamin's report, and it is dreadful.'

'What does it say, my dear?'

'It says that we must take him away if he does not improve. They acknowledge that he is clever but he will not work, he obeys nobody. He is always fighting.'

'Well, my dear, he is a healthy boy and has to let himself go, I suppose.'

Elizabeth shook her head.

'Yes, but he will obey nobody and he does not care. When I speak to him he only smiles. He is not cruel nor selfish. In fact, as you know, there never was a more generous boy. It is not that he is absent-minded. He throws himself altogether into anything that he is doing. But there is something WILD in him. He says he wants to be a gipsy!'

'A gipsy!'

'Yes. He wants to go away in a caravan and eat roasted hedgehogs. Then . . . there is another thing . . .'

She hesitated. 'Two afternoons ago I saw him kissing Hannah; in the passage under the backstairs. Of course it was nothing. He is only a child--he is not yet fourteen and he is tremendously honest. He conceals nothing. He says that he bet her a shilling that he would kiss her . . . I am in despair. He is so merry, always laughing and doing things for others--but he will listen to nobody!'

'He kissed Hannah, did he?' said Judith, thinking how different he was from his father John. And from her own Adam too.

'Yes,' went on Elizabeth. 'I am sure, too, that it is my fault. Aunt Judith, I have been wrong not to FORCE my way into Ireby. But I hated it so that time I went . . .'

(Two years before Elizabeth had gone to the Fortress, had asked for her father, had suffered a fearful scene with Mrs Pangloss who had refused her entry.)

'You know that I have written again and again and he has never answered. But if I had gone and refused to be beaten by that horrible woman and stayed with father whatever she did, I feel that Benjamin would respect me more. He never speaks either of his father or his grandfather. I don't know even now whether he knows . . . whether he knows . . .'

She broke down, hid her head in her hands, then suddenly knelt at Judith's feet, burying her head in Judith's lap. The old lady gently stroked her hair. Even on her very alert days she had moments of slipping off into a dream. Now with her hand on Elizabeth's hair she saw the room filled with sparkling snow: whorls of dancing crystal filled the air, which was shot with splinters of golden sun. The windows had faded and a great sea of virgin snow, upon whose breast waves of iridescence quietly formed, broke and formed again, spread from the hills' horizon to her very feet. She was herself as light as a snowflake, and it seemed to her that she had to exert especial power not to float away on the current of that white loveliness and never be seen again . . . Was this Death--and if it was so, why did men fear it? So sweet, so friendly, so just . . .

'. . . You see, Aunt Judith,' Elizabeth's voice came like a soft key closing a door, and the room swam back, the bed with the hangings, the ugly chair that Dorothy had given her (oh, why had she forgotten to thank her just now?), the sparkling buckles on her own shoes. 'I seem to have no will-power any longer. I do things with everyone else, but my real self is not here. It is away with John. It is as though he were always whispering to me things that I ought to do--be more firm with Benjie, live with father and make him more comfortable. I had will-power once, but John's death did something to me. Grief doesn't break your heart as the novels say, but it takes your character away. I don't GRIEVE for John. I am sure that he is happier now than he ever was here. But I am not alive. When you lost your husband did you feel at all the same?'

'Yes, dear, I did. Just as you describe. For nearly ten years I lived with the Rockages in Wiltshire and I had no real life at all; but it comes back in the end. Nothing can kill you. Nothing.'

Elizabeth rose from her knees and stood before the fire, her long slim body irradiated by the leaping light, her soft grey dress like a cloud against the sparkling logs.

'Aunt Judith,' she said. 'Do you believe in God?'

'I don't know.'

'You are not certain?'

'My dear, I have been a pagan all my life long. I know now that everyone is very religious, and if you don't go to church on Sunday it's very wrong, but in my young days it wasn't so. Going to church is just a fashion, I think. At one time it's the thing and at another it's not. My husband thought it foolish to believe in anything you couldn't see, but a great friend of mine, Reuben Sunwood, was as sure of God as I am of this room. For myself, now I am so very old, there SEEMS to be another world--but that may be my old age and my body failing. On some days, you know, my hearing is bad and I cannot see very well. Then I seem to be in another world. But I don't know. When one loves someone very much one seems to go beyond bodily things. When one's in a bad temper or loses one's spectacles or the servants are tiresome it's different.' She rapped her fingers impatiently on her spectacle- case.

'Dear Elizabeth, you must pull yourself together a little more. It is quite right what you say. Benjamin needs more discipline. Send him to me, my dear. This morning. In the afternoon I'm often sleepy.'

Elizabeth bent down and kissed the dry, withered cheek. How VERY old Aunt Judith was! It was wrong to trouble her, but then she liked to be troubled.

'If I can find him I'll send him to you now.'

When she was alone in the room again she gave a little sigh of satisfaction. She liked to be alone, and she liked also to be in the centre of things. She was happy this morning because neither her heart nor her stomach troubled her, because it was a beautiful day and because, old though she was, they still wished to consult her. The world was whirring around her! Veronica would marry Captain Forster, Benjamin was naughty, Adam would soon be here . . . She arranged her spectacles on her nose, picked up from the table at her side a number of the Spectator and read its opinion of Mr Longfellow's Hiawatha, an old poem now but still criticized with reverence: 'Mr Longfellow's Hiawatha is one of the really permanent contributions to modern literature, and no other genius known to us would have been in any way equal to the work. It is not the grasp of imagination, so much as the grace and sweep of a peculiarly majestic FANCY--a fancy like the impulsive fancy of children . . . How bright and playful is the picture of the lower animals with the little Indian prophet . . . But it is not only in the details, it is in the whole spirit of the poem--the fanciful joy and beauty, the equally fanciful weirdness and gloom--that we enjoy the touch of a master hand.'

Well, that was very nice for Mr Longfellow. But she was not sure. The writer used the word 'fanciful' a great many times. That was perhaps a warning. In any case she could not read for very long in these days--Jane read to her every afternoon--a lengthy poem, read aloud . . . No, she thought she would not bother with Hiawatha.

There was a knock on the door, and Benjamin came in. He was shooting up; he was no longer the small chubby child. He would not be a handsome man, although he had fine clear eyes, a splendid colour, and a strong stocky body. As usual he seemed to be enjoying a joke of some kind. She could see that he knew that he had come to be scolded and was endeavouring to be grave.

'Is that you, Benjie? Come over here where I can see you.'

He came and stood beside the chair in the attitude of straitened attention that children must observe before their elders. His cheeks were flushed with the cold and his hair was in disorder. He tried to arrange it with his hand. He looked her in the face, giving her all his mind, not as Adam had so often done when he was small, thinking of something else.

'Now, Benjie, I have sent for you because they tell me that your report has come from Rugby and it is shocking. They say that you will be sent away if you do not behave better. Your mother is very unhappy. What have you to say?'

What had he to say? How very, VERY old Aunt Judith was! And so small and so tidy. There came from her a pleasant scent of exquisite cleanliness and the smell of some flower, a carnation perhaps. But what must it be like to be as old as that? Why, her father had been born at the very beginning of the eighteenth century! There wasn't a boy at Rugby who had a relation as old as this! Something to be proud of. He pulled himself together and tried to attend. He always attended to the thing in hand, and the thing in hand at the moment was that Aunt Judith was going to scold him about his report. He didn't mind. He liked her. He liked everybody.

'I am very sorry, Aunt Judith.'

She kicked one shoe impatiently.

'Yes, but that is not enough. You must do something about it. You are a big boy now and threaten to be a disgrace to us all.'

She looked at him and her heart melted within her. She worshipped small boys, and although Benjie was very different from her own Adam, he had Adam's independence. She adored independence.

'Why are you so naughty?'

'There are so many rules and they teach you such silly things.'

It was the tradition in England that all children obeyed absolutely their parents, did nothing that their parents didn't wish them to do, were preparing, one and all, to be the heroes and heroines of the future. But Benjie seemed unaware of the tradition.

'You know you belong to a very fine family,' she began, 'and, when you grow up, everyone will expect you to make your family proud of you.'

'I know. They are always talking about the family, but I don't see why I should think about the family. I'm myself, aren't I?'

'Yes, but--'

'When you were a little girl you ran away. Your father was always against the family. My grandfather shot himself in London and my father was killed, when he couldn't defend himself, by my uncle. I'm not like the rest of the family. I'm different and I'll always be different. Mother and Aunt Veronica and Aunt Amabel and Ellis and Cousin Amery--THEY are the family. But I'm different. I'm by myself.'

Her heart began to beat furiously. Her eyes dimmed. She could have caught the boy to her and kissed him. And with that odd exaltation (so bad for her heart) was fear also. Would this battle NEVER be ended? She seemed for an instant to behold her father, whom she had never seen, standing, erect, triumphant, against the snow . . .

She beat down her emotion and in a voice that trembled a little said: 'Yes, but, Benjie, you must understand that being different is NOT amusing--not amusing at all. It seems to you, I daresay, very splendid to stand up now and say "I'm different", but I'm a very old woman and have had great experience and I can tell you that the world does not like people to be different, and especially our family does not. You can't know yet how powerful the world is and how RIGHT the world is too, because if everyone was independent and refused to suit themselves to the world's rules, nothing would ever be done. My father learnt that, I have learnt it, your grandfather learnt it. You HAVE to do as you are told unless you want to fight all your life long.'

'I do like to fight,' he broke in eagerly. 'You see, Aunt Judith, I think it's stupid to do things just because other people do them.'

'Yes, but do you never think of others? You must see how selfish it is always to have your own way. You can see how unhappy you make your mother--'

'But I don't WANT to make her unhappy. I don't want to make anyone sorry for what I do. They needn't be, only half the time they are glad they are sorry.'

She had nothing to say. She was on his side, so terribly on his side, and yet it would never do if he were disgraced at Rugby . . .

'Well, then,' she said as though some silent comprehending confidence had passed between them. 'You must promise me to do your best for the sake of those who love you--for your mother's sake and mine. Will you promise?'

He smiled, staring straight into her eyes. She really was a DEAR old lady and he was proud of her because she had lived to so great an age. He nodded.

'All right, Aunt Judith. I'll try.'

'And you won't fight?'

'Well, I don't know . . . I can't promise if another boy goes for me--'

'You won't be the first in any case?'

'It's so hard often to tell who IS the first. You see--' But this was too technical.

'Kiss me then. And I shall expect a good report next term.'

He kissed her. How dry her cheek was! Towards the door he turned.

'There's one thing,' he said. 'Why do I never see my grandfather?'

'Your grandfather?'

'Yes. Up at the Fortress.'

'He is very ill and sees nobody. He was very unkind to your mother once, you know.'

'Yes, but that was years ago. You can't go on remembering things for ever, can you? I shall go one day and see him.'

Then he came back to her chair and, grinning, said: 'Aunt Judith, would you like to see my ferret?'

'A ferret? Oh, I don't like ferrets.'

'You would this one. It's grand. James gave it me.'

'Very well. You can bring it one day.'

He nodded and went humming out.

The talk had affected her deeply. She took off her spectacles, wiped her eyes, put them on again. Her heart was beating oddly. It was not good for her to be agitated, but what was she to do when all the old questions, so long answered and dismissed, came surging up again?

When Jane brought her her dinner she found her greatly excited. She had her favourite dinner--fried sole, apple-pudding--but now she did not care. The talk with Benjamin had, although it was so short, exhausted her: old terrors and alarms would surround her and hem her in, did she allow them.

'I don't think I'll come down this afternoon after all, Jane dear. I'm a trifle tired.'

'You have seen too many people, that's what it is,' Jane said firmly. She had the air a little, as she arranged the silver dish containing the apple-pudding in front of Judith, of a witch or a fairy, someone from another and slightly inhuman world. She was growing into that especial product of the British Isles, the queer old maid, someone enterprising, eccentric, kindly, and very much alone. Jane would be eccentric, she would suddenly snap her fingers, dress quaintly (she was wearing now a funny old black velvet jacket), roll her bread at a mealtime into little pellets, talk to herself, but she had a heart as rich and warm as any fairy godmother. She loved Judith with a passion that was almost unholy. Although she was religious, virtuous and indeed prudish, she would have committed any crime for Judith, married anyone, killed anyone, stolen from anyone. So now she realized that Judith was weary and had added in a moment, as old people do, twenty years to her age. An hour ago she had been seventy, now she was ninety, soon, if one were not careful, she would be a hundred and ten.

'Yes, I don't think I'll go down . . . Jane, what do YOU think of Benjamin?'

'He is a fine boy. I love him!'

'Yes, yes, of course!' She knocked her silver spoon against the plate. 'We all love him, but I am afraid that he is a very naughty boy.'

'Oh, he has fights, but so do all proper boys.'

'Jane, why don't you marry someone?'

Jane blushed. She said almost in a whisper: 'I don't like men-- not in that way.'

'Dear, dear!' said Judith. (She was beginning to recover.) 'It was a very nice way. Everyone is so prudish now that they are ashamed to talk of going to bed with a man. It's perfectly natural. Nothing to be ashamed of. But although they won't speak of it they think of nothing else. It's all the same whoever it is-- Mrs Osmaston, Helen Withering, Mrs James Anstruther. How shall we marry our daughters? We must put our girls to bed with a man the first possible opportunity, do everything we can, dress them so as to accentuate their figures, throw them at every man we see, everything to marry them-- but speak of what happens when they ARE married-- oh, dear me, no!'

Jane disliked it when Judith talked like this. She did wish that she wouldn't.

'Now, there's Dorothy! In SUCH a flutter this morning because Veronica is going to marry. She'd marry Amabel to ANYBODY if only somebody would have her, but a pestle and mortar is the only thing Amabel will ever marry. Yes--well, that pudding was very good. I think I'll have my nap now so as to be ready for Adam.'

When Adam came she was quite ready for him. Her nap had refreshed her. The afternoon sun shone into the room like the reflection from a pale cloud of gold. The eaves were dropping with the heat of the sun and, when her spectacles were on, she could see blue shadows on Skiddaw. There was a strange mountain lightness over everything, and the logs in the fireplace were crimson with heat, and crackled like mad. As soon as Adam came in, sat beside her, took her hand, they were enclosed as though there were no one else in the world.

She wanted to talk about the Trades Unions. She had had a letter from Horace Newmark, who was in business in Manchester. 'He is as proud of all the chimneys as though they were bluebells,' she said. 'He says Manchester is nothing but smoke and dirt and it's grand. It's making England what it is, the mistress of the world. Stuff! Who wants to be mistress of the world? So like a Herries!'

Two years before, a man called Broadhead in Sheffield had, it was proved, paid for men who had rebelled against his Union to be murdered, and had paid out of the funds of the Union of which he was secretary. The tyranny of 'rattening' whereby noxious workers' tools were destroyed, women were blinded, men were shot at, was prevalent, and in Manchester, among the brick-makers, the clay which offending brick-makers were to use was sometimes stuffed with thousands of needles in order to maim the hands of those who worked on it. But the investigations into these crimes had proved, too, that many of the conditions of work were iniquitous and had remained unaltered since the days of Elizabeth.

Judith was greatly interested. 'What do you think, Adam? What about these Trades Unions?'

'I think they are necessary. The more England becomes an industrial country--and she IS now the first industrial country in the world--the greater the power of the working-man. He will rule England one day, mark my words, and I hope he'll be wise enough to know what to do with the power when he has it. That was the trouble with the Chartists. They weren't wise enough nor clever enough. But in fifty years' time there'll be few big families left. Everything will be shared--and quite right too.'

'I don't know,' Judith said. 'England was very nice once when there were no railways and no chimneys. Isn't it strange? I've been in a sedan-chair and saw a boy hung in the streets of London. Yes, and bears were baited, and I've danced at Vauxhall. I feel sleepy. It's the fire. Where is Vanessa?'

'Vanessa is downstairs with Benjamin.'

'And how is Cat Bells?'

'Cat Bells is covered with snow.'

'And how is dear Margaret?'

'Margaret sent her love and is coming soon to see you. She is baking today and Will is helping her.'

'It all sounds very pleasant. And how are you yourself?'

'I am very well.'

'And the book?'

'Nearly finished.'

'It's not a fairy story this time.'

'No, it's about two boys at the North Pole.'

'What do you know about the North Pole? You've never been there.'

'No. That's why I know so much about it.'

'But how can you write about what you've never seen?'

'There are two sorts of writers, Mother, just as there are two sorts of Herries. One sort believes in facts, the other sort believes in things behind the facts.'

'The books I like best,' she answered, 'are those that have both sorts in them.'

'For instance?'

'Jane is reading me a very amusing story called Under Two Flags. It's silly, of course--not like real life at all--but most enjoyable. And then there's Alice in Wonderland. And then there's Mr Huxley's Man's Place in Nature.'

Adam laughed. 'Mother, what a ridiculous mixture!'

'They all come to the same thing in the end.'

'What thing?'

'The world is made up both of fancy and reality, I suppose. Oh dear, I don't know . . . Adam, now that I cannot move from this house I can see how NICE England is.'

He smiled.

'Yes. I know you say "Foolish old woman at her age to love anything with a passion." But I am not senile. The moment I'm senile, Adam, you shall drop a pill into my chicken-broth and finish me off. No, I am very wide awake, and I can see that all my life I've loved England. Why do you not write a book about England?'

'How would YOU do it, Mother?'

'Oh, I would put in everything--men sowing the fields, the horses ploughing, old ladies selling sweets in the village shop, Mr Disraeli with his oily hair and Mr Gladstone with his collar, Horace's Manchester chimneys, all the Herries thinking THEY'VE made England, my father riding up Borrowdale, the snow on Skiddaw, the apple-pudding I had at dinner, sheep on a hill, the man lighting the lamps in Hill Street--and you, Adam, running by Charlie's horse in Watendlath, at Chartist meetings in London, writing stories at Cat Bells . . .' She broke off, her finger to her lip. 'That gives me an idea-- I have an idea!'

'What idea?'

'No matter. I shall tell you when it has got further on. Dear me, I've talked such a deal today. One day I talk; another day not a word. Sometimes I sleep all day. I'm ninety-five, you know.'

'Yes, I know. You're always telling me.'

She took his arm and, quickly, shyly caught his hand and kissed it.

'My whole life has been you and Georges.'

'You said it was England.'

'You ARE both England to me. We are sunk in the country, you and I, up to our necks. That's why I am so strong. Do you know, Adam, I have never had a day's illness in my life? Even when I was bearing you I was only ill for an hour or two--ugh!--that was horrid. There was an elephant . . .'

He drew his chair closer, bent over her and put his arm round her.

'Are you sure you are not tired?'

'No, indeed . . . I was a little but I had a nap. I can go to sleep whenever I wish. Oh yes, I remember! Benjamin! Adam, what do you think of Benjamin?'

'A grand boy--brave, generous. He will do fine things.'

'I am not so sure. He has had a dreadful report from Rugby.'

'All the best boys have.'

'Yes, but he was in here this morning and I scolded him, and he said that he didn't care because he was different from other boys, different because of his father and his grandfather.'

Adam nodded. 'Yes, he told me that once too. But that's all right. It's only that he feels wild sometimes. Why, I feel wild myself at times, Mother. A year or two ago I went mad and ran up Cat Bells--thought I would never come back.'

She smiled. 'I am delighted that you are wild still sometimes. I thought you were so contented that you'd never be wild again. If I had the strength I'd climb out of the window now just as I did when I was a child. Is Vanessa wild?' she asked.

He sighed. 'Vanessa is an angel. But I am sometimes troubled. She is so generous, so trusting, and believes in everyone.'

'Well, there is no harm in that as a beginning.'

'No, but she must suffer . . . Oh well, we all suffer. She adores Benjie. He is her God at present.'

'Can I see her?'

'Yes. I will go and fetch her.'

He went quickly from the room. She thought-- Benjamin, Vanessa, the new generation, and I shall be gone . . . soon I shall be gone. How strange and how familiar that thought that this room, her old companion, would continue with Skiddaw beyond the window, the snow falling, and she not here to see it, to move the chairs, dust the china, put a log on the fire . . . She looked at the table where was the parcel of the miniature teaset. She'll like that, she thought. She had always adored giving presents. Adam came in, bringing Vanessa with him. Vanessa was ten and tall for her age. She was wearing a dress of red taffeta, and her little skirt stood out stiffly. She had beautiful legs and arms, and her head with its black hair was carried with a wonderful dignity for so young a child. She came and made a curtsy, then she kissed the old lady, then waited patiently, smiling.

'I have a present for you, my dear.'

Vanessa's whole body was transformed with joy. You could see that her heart was beating with excitement; she compressed her lips so that she should not burst out into indecorous cries.

'Yes . . . Bring me that parcel, darling.'

She brought it very carefully. It was unwrapped. She knelt down on the floor so that she could see the wonder. She picked up each tiny piece, the teapot, the cups, the saucers, and held them, one by one, against the light.

'Oh!' she said slowly. 'It is the loveliest . . . Oh, Aunt Judith! . . . I never thought . . . I never expected . . .' Then she reached out for her father's hand. He pulled her to her feet. Even now, with all her joy, she controlled herself. She remembered how old Aunt Judith was, she kissed her tenderly and with great care. Then she stared at the precious things as though she would never take her eyes away.

THE FORTRESS

'Do you like them?'

'LIKE them!' She curtsied again, then turned to the window as though her feelings were so great that she must hide them. Once again the three of them had the sense that they were enclosed, away from all the world, rapt into a private communion of happiness.

'I must show them to Benjie,' she said.

Judith nodded. 'Yes, show them to Benjie. And come again and say goodnight before you go.'

'I will be off too,' Adam added. 'I will help her to carry the tea- things.'

'Yes,' said his mother, her sharp eyes staring with some secret excitement. 'And send Jane to me if you can find her. My idea! My idea! I must go on with my idea!'

She tapped impatiently on the silk of her dress.

'Tell Jane I want her at once. AT ONCE-- whatever she may be at!'

Jane arrived, quite breathless. She had been washing Dorothy's bitch Maria, an old and sulky spaniel who was washed every Thursday, come what might: and today was Thursday, Dorothy was in Keswick, and there was no one else . . .

'I've left Hannah to finish her!'

'Now sit down and get your breath.'

'What is it, Aunt Judith? Adam says you have an idea.'

'Yes, I have . . . Look in that wardrobe near the window, and among those bundles of letters you will find a manuscript book in a dark-green leather cover. Yes--that fat one . . . Now you have it? There's not a word in it, is there? No, I thought not. Francis gave it to me years ago on a birthday. He thought the dark-green leather handsome. Now bring the little writing bureau closer. That's it. Near the fire so that you will be warm and will hear what I say. Excellent. Have you a pen that suits you? Now listen, my dear. I was talking to Adam about England. You know old ladies talk and talk until they are quite exhausted. I have often noticed it--the older you are the more you talk. Dear Penny- feather at Keswick was like that. Her last years you could NOT stop her . . . a constant flow. Well, now I intend to talk to some purpose. Adam and I said we love England and so we do. Then I had an idea. You know I never saw either my father or my mother, but my half-brother David--he was old enough to be my father, you know--would often, before he died, poor man, tell me stories of them. He liked to take me for a walk, or we would ride to Bassenthwaite or Caldbeck or to the Dash, and all the way there and back he would tell me about the old days and my father.

'Now I think that I should write it down--or rather that YOU should, Jane dear. I may die at any moment. Oh yes, I may--of course I may--and what a pity! All this lost for ever. No one knows it but I. And that was a very odd life my father lived in Borrowdale. David told me that he remembered exactly the night they first arrived in Keswick. No, but wait. You shall write it down. Do not you think it a good idea, Jane?'

The old lady was so eager and excited that it would have been cruelty to prevent her. But Jane did not wish to prevent her. She was herself greatly interested in that world and in that very strange man, her great-great- grandfather. How very curious that the FATHER of Aunt Judith sitting there so comfortably before the fire should be her own great-great-grandfather! It was like stepping on to a magic carpet and swinging back into another fairy- world. So she took her pen and began to write in the dark-green leather book.

'Now tell me, dear, if I go too fast. Well, you'd better begin in this way. "I, Judith Paris, was born at Rosthwaite in the valley of Borrowdale, Cumberland, on November 28th, in the Year of Our Lord 1774 . . ." There! Have you got that? That's a good solid begin- ning, I think, rather like Macaulay's History. Now to continue. "I never knew my dear father and mother because they both died on the day I was born, and had I not been found and rescued from the cold by Squire Gauntry of Stone Ends, who happened to be riding past that day and heard me crying, I should undoubtedly have perished."

'Have you got that, Jane?' She peered over her spectacles on the very edge of her nose. 'Let me see, my dear. Yes, you write very nicely. Am I going too fast for you?'

'Not at all, Aunt Judith. How very interesting this will be!'

'I hope so. I certainly think it may. Well, to con- tinue. "It is not, however, my own history about which I write, but rather about some of the early days that my father spent in the valley of Borrowdale. My father himself lived to a good age, and I myself am now a very old woman, so that I am a link with the long-ago past. I have heard very much of what happened in those long- ago times from my half-brother David Herries. David Herries was my father's son by his first wife, and he was fifty-five when I was born, so that I could have been his granddaughter. He was very famous as a young man as a boxer and wrestler and runner. He had great strength as a younger man, but when I knew him he had grown stout and was living very happily with his family at Uldale, where I also was living. He would take me for walks and rides, and it was then that he would tell me these stories.

'"He told me that he remembered exactly the night that he first arrived in Keswick. He could remember every detail, and so do I, even at this distance of time. How he was in the inn at Keswick in a big canopied bed with his sisters Mary and Deborah. The canopy that ran round the top of the bed was a faded green and had a gold thread in it. There were fire-dogs by the fire with mouths like grinning dragons. And he remembered that a woman was sitting warming herself in front of the fire, a woman he hated. Then his father came in and thought he was sleeping. He remembered that his father was wearing a beautiful coat of a claret colour and a chestnut wig, and there were red roses on his grey silk waistcoat. He remembered, too, that his father said something to the woman by the fire that made her very angry, and she began to talk in a loud, heated voice.'"

Jane went on, and in that clear little voice like a bell Judith refashioned this old world to her, describing the inn and the servants running hither and thither with candles, some relations who had a meal with them, and how David's uncle wanted to make him drink wine and he would not. Then the dark mysterious night-ride to Borrowdale, and how he sat on the horse in front of his father and how proud he was, and his father asked him whether he were frightened, and he answered bravely that he was never frightened where his father was. How then they came to a house on a little hill and David ran forward and was in the house first, and there were two shining suits of armour in the hallway.

'There,' said Judith suddenly. 'I am tired. That will be enough for today. I think you shall help me to bed.'

'Oh, Aunt Judith,' said Jane. 'That IS interesting!'

But Aunt Judith was weary. She had suddenly collapsed, her head nodded, she yawned and yawned and was almost helpless in Jane's hands as she undressed her. It was dark now beyond the window; a faint powdery blue framed the silent masses of snow; some stars, lonely in that cold sky, were like sparks blown up from a fire. Jane drew the cherry-coloured curtains. She saw that Judith was propped up with pillows and two candles lit by her side (how tiny and soft her body had been--like a child's), then she left the room to return with some tea, a small sponge-cake and some raspberry jam in a blue glass saucer. Then, most unfortunately, Aunt Judith lost her temper. It had been a tiring day, there had been something too exciting about that dropping back into the past--the past that was not only the past, but the present and future as well.

So she lost her temper over the sponge cake. It was a plum cake that she had wanted. Dorothy only yesterday had promised her a plum cake.

'But, Aunt Judith, it is not good for you. Doctor Bettany said that plum cake was too rich--'

'Doctor Bettany never said anything of the kind.'

'But indeed he did!'

'So I am a liar! Thank you, dear Jane. I am glad I know.'

'No, of course not. But you know that last time you were upset--'

'I was not upset!' She was trembling, her eyes were filled with hot tears of anger. She was in a rage, so that for tuppence she would have taken the teatray and thrown it and its contents all over the room. How dare Jane say that she was a liar! And she hated this soft soppy sponge cake! They thought they could do what they liked with her! She was so good to them all, and yet they tried to starve her! After listening all day to their troubles they could so ill-treat her!

She took the sponge cake and with a shaking hand threw it into the middle of the floor.

At the same moment Adam and Vanessa came in to say goodbye, and with them were Dorothy and Veronica back from their party. But Judith did not care. She was not ashamed. They should see whether they could bully her.

'You promised me plum cake!' she cried to Dorothy.

'Oh, I am so sorry! . . . Aunt Judith, Veronica is engaged to be married! Captain Forster--'

'I don't care! You think you can do what you like with me, all of you, just because I am an old woman--'

But the sight of Veronica's beautiful happy face was too much for her.

'Oh, well . . . Come here, my dear, and give me a kiss! There! That's right! Don't spill the tea-things! What did he say to you? Did he go down on his knees? Were you very gracious? . . .'

A long while after as it seemed to her, the room dark save for the flicker from the fire, she lay there, very happy, on the edge of sleep. It had been a wonderful day. She had never left that room, but all the world had come into it. The elderly Dorothy, Adam, Elizabeth, with all their personal histories hot about them, and the young, Veronica engaged to be married, dear Jane so sweet and good, and the children, Vanessa and Benjamin. All the generations! They had come to her for advice and help and to tell her what they were doing. They had wanted to know what she thought. They could not get on without her.

She herself had welcomed the sun, eaten delightful food, read a little, given a present, discussed serious matters like God and the Trades Unions with Adam and Elizabeth, sunk back into the past, thought of Georges and Warren and Adam as a baby, and then gone behind that again to her own childhood and dear David, and then back beyond that to a hundred and forty years ago when her father had been a young man and worn a claret-coloured coat--all this without leaving her room, all within a day. And she was ninety-five. All the Herries all over England were waiting to see her grow to a hundred!

Well, she would. Nothing was going to stop her! How could she possibly disappoint such a great number of kind relations?

So, in that happy thought, she slipped away and once again was rocking on that billowing cloud of softest down. She rose and then sank again, sank and rose . . . Georges was sleeping near to her. He was snoring with that snore so familiar to her that it was also hers. All about them the world was of a dazzling white, shining with a million crystals.

She rose and then sank again, sank and rose . . .

AT VICTORINE'S

In London, a boy aged fifteen stood on an October afternoon pressing his nose to the window of a house in Hill Street. This boy was young Benjamin Herries.

This was the day, the evening, the night of his life, for on this day, October 14th, 1870, he was to become a man.

It had all happened in the most surprising manner, and the cause of it had been the death, one evening while he was drinking his tea, of old Stephen Newmark. Everyone had been expecting him to die for years, but with that priggish obstinacy characteristic of him he had refused to go, degenerating into a tiresome silent old gentleman with a female nurse of whom, in the opinion of the family, he was much too fond.

Poor Phyllis had predeceased him by some years; as he was not a Herries no one had very much interest in his attaining a great age. He died in the act of pronouncing one of his almost hourly anathemas on Mr Disraeli.

Most unexpectedly it was decided that young Benjamin must be present at his funeral. It seemed that Stephen had a great regard for Elizabeth and had declared that 'he would do something for her boy one day'. So Benjamin had been sent for from Rugby (where he still survived, much to his own astonishment); Lady Herries had invited him to stay in Hill Street for the funeral, and here he was.

The funeral, two days before, had been great fun. Everything was great fun for Benjamin, and he could not be expected to feel much grief for Stephen Newmark, whom he had rarely seen. Moreover, he noticed that Stephen's children were not greatly downcast, and his own close friend Barney made no pretence of sorrow.

'The Governor never liked me,' he confided to Benjamin on the way to the funeral. 'He disapproved of me altogether and never even looked at my novels. I don't blame him for that, but I'm not going to be a crocodile about it. I leave that to sister Emily.'

Lady Herries, who was now a rather ancient and (in Benjamin's opinion) a very silly lady, did the honours with much satisfaction, and Ellis Herries, already a man of importance in the world of affairs, was dignified and solemn. Benjamin had got considerable pleasure out of his days in town. He had never really stayed in London before.

He had had a number of projects. Why should he return to Rugby? He thought of being a stowaway in some vessel chartered for the West Indies or (his old cherished dream) joining some gipsies somewhere. He took a liking to an Italian organ-grinder, with whom he talked in Berkeley Square, and fancied that he might buy a barrel-organ. But his principal notion was that, if he could get money enough, he would escape to France and, in some way, slip into Paris and enjoy a bit of the Siege. He had followed, with eager excitement, the Franco-Prussian War from its commencement. He had cut out from the illustrated papers pictures of the Emperor, Bismarck, MacMahon, Palikao, Bazaine, Frossard, the young Prince Imperial, and many of the Empress. He was in love with the Empress; he would be delighted to die for her. He wanted nothing but to run on some mission for her, be shot in the discharge of it and fall dying at her feet. He could not understand why his companions at Rugby were on the whole so indifferent.

Then, with the catastrophe at Sedan, his whole soul was on fire. He learnt every detail of the battle by heart. He knew the exact positions of Bazeilles and Balan, of the Donchery bridge, where were the Villa Beurmann, Illy, and the fatal spot where the Prussian Guards crossed the Givonne. He was sure that, had he been in command, he would not have fallen into so complete a trap, and the moment when the Emperor, old and sick, cried out 'The firing must be stopped at all costs!' was, for him, a real agonizing piece of personal experience.

He hated and detested the Prussians; he adored the French, and Barney, listening to him, was amazed that so young and jolly a boy could feel so intensely. When he read how the Empress, escaping from Paris, hailed a cab and was recognized by a street urchin, he drew a deep breath as though he himself had only just missed a great peril.

And now that Paris was invested it was for him as though he himself shared the siege. When he heard how, on October 7th, Gambetta escaped from Paris in a balloon he shouted 'Hurray!' and gave all his pocket-money towards a dormitory feast in its celebration. However, here he was now in London, and his own immediate affairs demanded a lot of attention. Tomorrow he was to return to Rugby, and he had a sad feeling that he WOULD return instead of making use of this magnificent opportunity of adventure. Indeed, had it not been for his mother and Aunt Judith, he would have certainly tried the stowaway adventure. But they would grieve, although why they should he could not understand. But women were queer and these two women he did not wish to hurt. Moreover, Aunt Judith was so VERY old. He had better wait until she was gone.

Then, this very morning, after breakfast, Barney had arrived at Hill Street and, pulling Benjamin aside, had whispered to him that he intended that evening to take Ellis and himself out to dinner. 'Not a word to a soul,' he confided. 'Emily and the others would make a terrible row if they knew. But we must do something. These last days have been too gloomy for anything.'

So Benjamin stood at the window, all ready dressed, waiting for Barney to arrive.

It was the bewitching hour when the lamp-lighter has gone his way and the lamps star the streets like nectarines. A faint wisp of fog--having in it to Benjie's excited nostrils a slight sniff of gunpowder (he was thinking possibly of Paris); from beyond the window came magical sounds of London, the clop-clop of a horse, the rattle of wheels, feet mysteriously echoing, the distant plaintive murmur of a barrel-organ. On the top of area steps belonging to the house opposite a housemaid was entertaining, for a moment, a policeman. A brougham was waiting a few doors away and down the steps came a stout, pompous, old gentleman, pilloried in starch, a red shaven face and a white waistcoat and white gloves that seemed to Benjie too big for him. The fog increased a little, the lamps spread into a hazy iridescence, some old man in a large and battered high hat came slowly down, ringing a bell and calling out something in a melancholy voice, a carriage rolled by with two footmen in cocked hats standing up at the back of it--and always that soft rumble of sound as of a fat, comfortable nurse singing lullaby to her children.

His excitement was intense; it was all that he could do not to jump about the room, turn his favourite somersault. But Lady Herries or Emily Newmark might come in at any moment. He thought them safe and secure in the great cold draughty drawing room upstairs. But you never could be sure. Grown-up people were always creeping about and opening doors unexpectedly, like that old beast 'Turker' Evans, head of his House at Rugby. His thoughts were oddly jumbled. It was a pity that Ellis was coming; it would be very much pleasanter without him. Not that he disliked Ellis, or he would not did he not patronize him. Of course Ellis was YEARS older, a grown-up man who did business every day in the City. And he was very kind. He had given Benjie ten shillings only yesterday, but, for some dim obscure reason, Benjie would rather not have taken it. Ellis did not really like him--not REALLY, as Barney and Adam Paris and Thornton Minor and James at Uldale liked him. And then again, looking out at the lamps and the misty street, suppose there was no God as Barney said. Barney had sprung this astonishing piece of news upon him at the funeral.

'Of course there's no God,' he had said, as though he were sure of it.

'Well, what is there then?' Benjamin asked.

'Nothing at all,' Barney had answered gaily. 'We're nothing but monkeys, old boy. You are old enough now to read Darwin. He'll tell you.'

What an astonishing idea! Then all this going to church and saying your prayers, that had been going on for hundreds of years, meant nothing at all. There was no gigantic old man with a white beard sitting on a cloud and listening! His mother and Aunt Jane and the others were all taken in! A stupendous thought! But he had only Barney's word for it, and you could never be sure whether Barney meant what he said!

Oh! there was the organ-grinder coming round the corner! He could just see him in the dim light, and there, joy of joys, from the opposite side was the muffin-man approaching! There MUST be a God, or why should there be muffin-men and organ-grinders? Would the organ-grinder have a monkey? The door opened and Lady Herries entered. She was a little, faded, old woman now, and Benjamin was certain that she painted her cheeks. He thought she looked ridiculous, her dress bunched up behind and her rather scanty hair dressed in a cascade of curls at the back of her head. She was, of course, in the deepest black and she walked with small mincing steps.

'Why, Benjamin! Dear me! Why has William not lit the gas! All alone! Emily was asking for you! Come and tell me what you have been doing. Ellis tells me that you and he are going to have dinner at some quiet place with Barnabas.'

'Yes,' said Benjamin. 'Won't it be fun?'

'I don't think this is quite the time to talk of fun, Benjamin dear. It has all been very distressing. However, you are too young yet to realize what death means.'

The front door banged. That must be Barney. They went into the hall, and there, praise be, Barney was, looking very smart in his evening dress and high black hat. He was growing stout, and looked like a very amiable clown, Benjie always thought. Chalk his face white and give him a red nose and he would be a perfect clown!

They all went upstairs to the drawing room, which was as cold as a mausoleum. They stood in a group beside the sulky peevish fire and talked in low grave voices.

Emily Newmark, a heavy stout woman in tremendous black, joined them. It is a temptation for every generation to deride any world that was fifty years its predecessor: Judith, Veronica, Elizabeth, Jane--these were, in their own kind and character, women to be proud of. They were generous, humorous, courageous and idealistic without priggishness. No period that was their background could conceivably be a period to be mocked. But Emily Newmark was frankly a pity, and was one, among others, responsible for providing our satirists with a living. She believed that Politics and the Services were the only polite careers, and the Land and the Funds the only springs of wealth that could be called decent. She was a snob and a toady. If a gentleman smoked in front of a lady he was insulting that lady's morals. She was always ready to be insulted. She looked absurd in her gathered flounces, draped skirts, and hair-plaits at the back of her head, but thought she was magnificent. She approved of the Queen in retirement and was preparing to be shocked by the Prince of Wales. (She WANTED to be shocked.) She considered ALL foreigners (including--very much including--Americans) false, obscene, dangerous and unwashed. (Her own ablutions were neither so constant nor so thorough as you would suppose.)

She approved of archery, croquet and painting in water-colours for young girls, but thought that that was enough excitement for them. She was an exceeding prude with a passionate private curiosity in sexual matters. She believed in good works, Missions to the Heathen, and patronizing visits to the slums. She was, in fact, ALL wrong, being hypocritical, snobbish, unkind to servants, a worshipper of wealth and a devout believer in a god whom she had created entirely after her own image. She was not a typical woman of her period--only typical of the section of it that was the easiest for after-generations to caricature.

She disapproved, of course, entirely of her brother Barney; she thought his novels 'horrid' with their racing, gambling, and loose women. Sometimes he brought men like Mortimer Collins to the Newmark home, and they smoked and drank together in Barney's sanctum. Now that both Phyllis and Stephen were gone, that Horace lived in Manchester, that Mary was dead, and Katherine married, Emily took charge of the Newmark remnants, Phyllis (named after her mother) who was a weak character, Barney who was not, and Stephen who was a lazy ne'er-do-well. She thought that she dominated all three, but Phyllis agreed with her in order that she might get what she wanted--new hats, novels from the library and a succession of silly young men; Stephen stole money from her, and Barney laughed at her. But Emily, in her blind self-satisfaction, arrogant patriotism and hypocritical prudery, learnt nothing. She had, however, her effect on others . . .

She had her effect on this particular and very important evening, for had she not entered the Hill Street drawing room just when she did she might not have exasperated Barney to his point of later recklessness.

'What's this I hear, Barney?' she cried. 'You are surely staying indoors this evening?'

'I am not,' said Barney.

'Well, of course,' and her voice was of a sepulchral gloom, 'it is not for me to say, but father has only been buried two days--'

'Father won't mind,' Barney said. 'He has other things to think of.'

Emily had but just sat down on the sofa. She rose.

'I will not hear such blasphemy. Nor shall this poor child. Benjamin, come with me.'

'Benjie is my guest tonight,' Barney remarked. 'He is to share my humble chop in some decent quiet place where we can think reverently of the past and pray hopefully for the future.'

Emily was aghast. She was truly and honestly aghast. This seemed to her a horrible thing. She broke into a flood of oratory in which their poor father, their poor mother, their poor sister Mary, all looked down from heaven in an agony of distress, in which childhood and vice, innocence and nasty men of the world, insults to herself and Lady Herries, all confusedly figured.

'Ellis will at least support me in this.'

'Ellis is coming with us,' said Barney.

She burst into tears.

'Oh, dammit, I can't stand this!' Barney cried. 'Come along, Benjie.' And Benjie rather sheepishly followed him out.

Down in the hall they found Ellis.

Ellis, waiting, looking up to the staircase, down which they were descending, had then the oddest hallucination. He was not an imaginative man, but, staring in the rather dim gaslight, he saw this: Barney had vanished. Benjamin, not a boy but a man of mature years, had halted on the stairs. Behind him stood a very beautiful lady in a white evening cloak with a high white collar. There was a Chinese clock at the turn of the stairs, a tall, thin clock brilliant in gilded lacquer. He noticed the time on its round face. It was twelve-thirty exactly. He was conscious of a violent, suffocating rage, and he heard his own voice, high, shrill, convulsed: 'Get out, both of you! Get out! Get out!'

As quickly as it came, it was gone.

There was no clock. Benjie jumped the last two steps.

'Hullo, Ellis!' he cried.

This only meant that Ellis was tired and had a headache. When one had a headache one did not know what one was seeing or what one was hearing. These last few days had been trying, with so many members of the family in and out of the house. But he always felt a little queer with Benjamin, never quite at his ease. He was not perhaps comfortable with small boys, and you could never be sure whether they were not laughing at you. But it was more than that. Ever since that day, ten years back, of the Heenan and Sayers fight, he had had an almost nauseating impression of Walter Herries. He could see him now, wandering, lost, drunk, you might have said, a disgusting old man, and also his own half-brother. He hated to think that he had any link with him. And here was the man's grandson. They said that Walter's life in Cumberland was a disgrace. That horrid man's son had murdered this boy's father. Everything that was abnormal, fantastic, revolting--cruelty and illicit passion and madness--were in the strain of that branch of the family. And he was himself mixed in it, he who loved everything to be proper and sane and wholesome and virtuous. He had a passion for virtue! But old Walter and he had the same father. He would have cut all that off as he would have cut off a diseased arm, and so he would have been able to do were it not for this boy. The boy seemed normal and decent enough. But he was young yet. You could not tell what the future would be. And just as something in that branch disgusted him, so something attracted him. He had insisted that the boy should be invited to Hill Street. He tried to be friendly with the boy, but he was not clever at friendliness, poor Ellis. He wanted to be so many things that nature prevented him from being.

'All right,' said Barney. 'Shall we go?'

They found a cab in Berkeley Square and, on the way, Barney enlarged to Benjamin on the delights of London life.

'You shall have a night out, young 'un. We'll have dinner at Duke's. No, be quiet, Ellis. It's my evening. What are you, Benjie? Fifteen? Dammit, you look seventeen anyway.' He'd like to give the boy a week. He'd take him to the Café Riche, Sally Sutherland's, Kate Hamilton's, Rose Young's, Mott's. Cafés were open all night. Pity he hadn't been with Barney at the fight between King and Heenan, driving across London Bridge three in the morning with a pork pie in your pocket. Mott's, too, where old Freer kept guard. None of your tradesmen let in there--not that Barney minded tradesmen. 'You're in the City, Ellis, yourself, aren't you, my boy?' But still a gentleman was a gentleman when it came to eating together. It was at Mott's you could have seen 'Skittles', famous for her ponies, or lovely Nelly Fowler. And Kate Hamilton's--well, Benjie was still at school so he'd say no more. But you should have seen a raid at Kate's--carpets turned up, boards--under which bottles and glasses were hidden--raised, all in the twinkling of an eye.

Or the 'Pie', where you were positively bound to have a row before the night was up and where you tipped the Kangaroo so that he shouldn't knock you down.

Barney wasn't a bad fellow; he was warm-hearted, generous, a famous friend, but tonight three things drove him on--the thought of his sister Emily, Ellis' air of wanting 'to be a sport' and wanting, too, to go home to his comfortable bed, and Benjie's excitement. He really loved the boy that night as he sat there, a proper little gentleman, his high hat tilted a trifle, his lips parted with his eagerness, his fresh colour, his sparkling eyes, his laugh, his readiness to trust anyone, his impulse to throw himself into whatever adventure was forward. 'I'll look after him,' he thought. 'I'll see that he comes to no harm.'

Duke's, near St Alban's Place, was half-hotel, half-hostelry. In the bedrooms the beds were cleanly enough, and most of the residents slept in them all day because they were out and about all night. A number of the residents may be said to have never been sober.

Excellent joints could be had for dinner, and the best of eggs and bacon any time of day or night, but the establishment DID exist mainly for drinking--no one pretended other. Brandy-and-soda, rum and milk all day, sherry and bitters before breakfast, and a glass of brandy for tea.

A later generation might have thought Duke's eating room a little on the stuffy side. Everything was a trifle close, smelly, thick with tobacco and brandy fumes, linen and under-linen not quite clean, a strange air of rooms littered with feathers from an old bed, warm with the odour of unwashed bodies, cats furtively picking at fish-bones on a sanded floor, and the Chairman banging with his hammer on the table in the smoke-thickened distance. Stuffy! That was the word for the night-life of the London of the 'sixties.

But for Benjamin, Duke's room was Paradise. He gazed with eyes of wonder and admiration at old Charles, the presiding deity, who shuffled about in a tiny snuff-coloured tail suit and slippers, who-- Barney told him--was never known to sleep, for at any moment of day or night he was ready to assist a drunken gentleman from a cab, or part two combatants. There were two chuckers-out, Jerry and Tom-- men, it seemed, of almost legendary strength. It was nothing, Barney said, to see a long wooden coffin come down the stairs into the middle of the diners. One of the gentlemen had died upstairs, of delirium tremens. No one thought anything of it at all.

Dinner went well enough. Ellis was quiet. He seemed even to be enjoying himself and watched a young swell with an eyeglass and long moustaches drink one brandy and soda after another. 'Marvellous, isn't it?' he said in his precise careful voice. 'Can't think how he does it!'

But it was here and now that Benjamin had the first brandy and soda of his life. He had tried gin up in Cumberland, but had not liked it. Cherry-brandy had been an adventure at Rugby. But this brandy and soda was different. It may be said, in a way, to have changed his whole life. He was ready for it. In many ways he was old, very old; in others he was a baby. But the recklessness, the urge to do something simply because it was forbidden, the bravado that led him again and again to challenge anybody at anything, the absence in him, not of a sense of good and bad, but altogether of a sense of right and wrong, all these were pledged by him that night in that glass of brandy and soda. As he drank it down he may be said to have whispered to his familiar spirit the words that were to be his Creed all his days: 'I'll do what I want. I'll see all that I can see. I'll love and enjoy with all my heart. I'll do no one harm but nothing shall stop my adventure.'

To be fair to Barney it was true that Benjie LOOKED seventeen. There was something in his hard blue eye, in his confident carriage and his air of assurance that made him seem, even then, mature. But he was not; in one meaning of the word, he would never be. After that brandy and soda he was ready for anything and he thought that it would be amusing to tease Ellis.

Ellis was twelve years older. He was staying in Ellis' house, and Ellis had been kind to him. For all these reasons he should have been polite to Ellis. But he was happy, he was reckless, he liked old Ellis even though he WAS a bit of a woman and even though Ellis didn't like him. So, on their way to the 'Paragon', he broke out:

'I say, Ellis--what relation are you to me really? Ought I to call you Uncle?'

'No, of course not. What an idea!'

'But WHAT are you? My grandfather is your brother, ain't he?'

'My half-brother,' Ellis answered stiffly.

'Oh, so you're my half-great-uncle! What a funny thing to be to anybody!'

'All right,' said Ellis, yet more stiffly. 'We'll forget it!'

'Oh, I shan't forget it! I say, Barney, isn't that funny? To be someone's half-great-uncle?'

He hadn't a notion that Ellis was minding. All life was rosy and golden. Never, never had he been so happy before. He loved Barney and would do anything in the world for him. The streets were a glory of light and splendour. Wouldn't it be fine to be going to the Opera in the Haymarket--and then, all in a moment, they are out of Piccadilly and walking down a street where the gas is flaring over coarse scraps of meat, where linen-drapers are still, at this hour, invaded by poorly dressed women wanting pennyworths of needles or farthingsworths of thread, where there are little open dens, reeking with the odour of fried fish and sausages, where a lady in a mob-cap is instructing a sailor in the mysteries of the famous dance 'Dusty Bob and Black Sal', where a huge Negro, his teeth gleaming white under the gaslight and his brown chest bare, is turning somersaults for pennies!

Then, as suddenly, they were in broad lighted streets again and passing through the wide painted doors of the 'Paragon'.

'We'll walk about,' said Barney. 'We can see just as well from here.'

Benjie had never been to a real theatre before. It was a while before he could take all the dazzling brilliance into his system. First the stage with its blaze of light held him. A group of young women in low green bodices and wide skirts were dancing while two gentlemen in evening dress, one at each corner of the stage, waved flags. A large box, protruding over the stage, contained a crowd of gentlemen, very elegant and noisy, smoking cigars and leaning over to shout encouragement to the girls. At the back of the theatre everyone was walking about, talking and laughing. There were little tables at which ladies and gentlemen were drinking. Men stood up in the pit and shouted at one another.

'Hullo, Connie!' Barney said. 'Never thought I'd see you here.'

'Oh, didn't you? Well, where were you last Friday night? I was waiting an hour and a half and wouldn't have had no supper at all if a gentleman hadn't taken pity on me. Nice treatment, I call it!'

Benjie thought that, save for his mother and Veronica, he had never seen anyone so beautiful. She was fair with bright blue eyes, ringlets and a dress the colour of primroses, gathered into great festoons at the back. She was angry, anyone could see, but Barney was not at all discomforted, only more like a clown than ever, his hat on one side of his head, grinned and stared over his shoulder to see who else might be there. Benjamin feared that she was about to do something desperate, she looked so angry, but her eyes fell on himself. She smiled, a lovely, entrancing smile.

'Hullo, baby,' she said. 'Where's your mother?'

He smiled back, and murmured something with proper bashfulness.

'Isn't he a pet? What's your name, dear?'

But Barney was, in an instant, the guardian. He put his hand on Benjie's shoulder.

'Now then, Connie, enough of that.'

Her voice was soft. She stared at Benjie as though she could eat him.

'All right,' she said quietly, 'I shan't hurt him.'

There were two chairs near to them. She sat down in one and motioned Benjie to the other.

'There! Now we are at a proper distance. Is he your guardian or something?'

'No,' said Benjie.

'What's your name then?'

'Benjamin Herries.'

'Well I never! Do you often come here?'

'It's the first time,' said Benjie.

'But not your last, I'll be sworn. Here! you want a flower in your buttonhole. Take this.'

She had two small white roses at her waist. She took out one and gave it him. Very proudly he stuck it in his buttonhole.

'You're the prettiest boy I've EVER seen!' She drew her chair a little closer. 'Like to come and see me one day?'

'I should very much,' said Benjie. 'Only you see--' He was about to say that tomorrow he would return to school, but that seemed to him childish, so he altered it to 'I don't live in London.'

'Where do you live then?'

'In Cumberland.'

'Where's that?'

'Up in the North.'

'Oh, never mind where you live. Here, see, I'll give you my card and then--'

But it seemed that Ellis, who had been standing awkwardly by himself, was now remonstrating, in great excitement, with Barney, for Barney broke out:

'Come on, young Benjamin. We'll go and visit the Captain. Ta-ta, Connie. See you again.'

Benjamin had to go. He had just not courage enough to demand that he should stay, but as Ellis and Barney turned ahead of him, the lovely Connie, coming so close to him that his nose was suffocated in some scent that seemed to contain a whole garden of flowers, caught his neck in her fair hand and kissed him.

He ran after the others, his heart hammering, his cheeks flaming, and his mouth tasting of some sweet powder. Who had ever dreamt that life could be like this?

PART IV

They went behind the stage to a large room in which ladies (performers evidently) were drinking with bearded and high-hatted gentlemen, while a funny little man in a very light waistcoat and bushy side-whiskers claimed Barney as his most intimate friend, bowed gravely to Ellis, and asked them all to have a drink.

But Benjie saw and heard nothing. He sat in a dream of happiness. Oh! what a lovely lady! How kind, how generous, how amusing! It was always his first thought when he met anyone whom he liked that he wanted to make his new friend a present. What could he give her in return for his rose? He had the ten shillings that Ellis had bestowed on him--or, at least, he had some of it. He could buy her flowers or fruit. Barney would tell him where she lived. He would go to visit her . . . Into the middle of these charming dreams Ellis gruesomely plunged.

'Benjamin, we are going home, you and I.'

'Going home?' he gasped.

'Yes. You must not be up late. You are returning to Rugby tomorrow. I myself am tired.'

'But of course I am not going home!'

He hated Ellis, who had the sad long face of a horse pining for its stable.

'This is no proper place for you,' he said.

'Why not?'

'Well--it's plain--you are only a boy--Places like this--'

To do Ellis justice, this was one of the most difficult things that he had ever had to do. He did not wish to preach, to improve others; on the contrary, his desire was that he should be a jolly companion, a merry wit, a Prince of Good Fellows. But nature is too strong for us. Good fellows are not made, they are born. His capacity for finding life shocking was abnormally large. It was not his fault that it was so. It was simply his destiny. He did not want to spoil Benjamin's fun; he only thought it dreadful that Benjamin should be finding this fun at all.

'You are to come with me,' he said, his voice trembling. He looked out of place, absurd, in that room.

Benjie saw it and, unhappily, Benjie laughed.

'You don't know how funny you look, Ellis!'

Then Ellis hated him. One thing he could not forgive--mockery that seemed to him unjust. It was his misfortune that all mockery of which he was the victim seemed to him unjust.

He caught Barney's arm.

'Benjamin and I are going home.'

Most regrettably Barney was by now drunk enough to find seriousness a farce and gloomy faces a pantomime. He roared with laughter.

'I say--don't be so sad, Ellis, old buck. Why, dammit--oh lor! look at your face--'

'We are going home,' Ellis, pale, tortured, terrified of a public scene, repeated.

'Well, I'M not,' Benjamin cried. 'I'm not, am I, Barney?'

'No, of course you're not. Here, Captain, this is my young friend, VERY young friend. Never been to a Green Room before, never seen a pretty girl.'

'Shame! Shame!' Ellis cried in the best transpontine manner. He caught Benjie's arm.

'You are coming with me!'

'I'm not,' said Benjie, struggling to be free.

Two girls laughed. A gentleman with enormous side-whiskers, holding a glass of champagne rather uncertainly, came forward.

'What's the matter?' he said.

'Let me go!' Benjie said indignantly, wrenching himself from Ellis' hold.

Ellis let him go, and in that moment hated his half-great-nephew with all the hatred that a shy, self-conscious, awkward man feels for anyone who makes him the centre of a scene. Lowering his head, picking up his hat, he slipped away.

Benjamin was invited to sit at a table. Several ladies talked to him. Somebody said: 'You can have four monkeys to one if you like.'

'Put it down,' said someone else.

'By Gad,' some voice cried, 'if you can put me on to a good thing, Gordon, I'll be eternally grateful.'

He drank some champagne. He felt a little sleepy. The ladies were kind to him, but they were nothing, nothing at all because Connie had kissed him. Then he heard the Captain, the gentleman with the flowing whiskers and very light waistcoat, say:

'What about Victorine's, Barney, old boy?'

'I'm agreeable,' said Barney.

'What about the boy?'

'I'll look after him. We shan't be long.'

Benjamin found himself accompanying the Captain, who confided to him as they went into the street:

'I've got a boy just your age. What are you? Seventeen?'

'Yes,' said Benjie, lying proudly. 'And a half.'

He felt about forty, or what he supposed that forty would feel. Nothing excited him like something new--something he had never done before, the company of someone whom he had never seen before, a new place, a new trick, a new risk, a new danger. Now, feeling like a knight of old, he strode through the streets, trying to keep pace with his two friends so that they should not discover how short his steps were. He did a little trot, then a long step, then a little trot again. Where were they going? Would Connie be there? Victorine's! That sounded exciting. They came at length to a barren waste surrounded with railings. In the centre of the waste was an equestrian statue. Here were oyster rooms, public-houses, night-houses. Here was Jerry Fry's Coffee House and there a small theatre with a large lady in black tights painted on a crimson ground over the doorway. A four-wheeler, lonely and disconsolate, wandered from darkness into darkness.

They turned into a narrow, intensely dark street, found their way cautiously down a kind of tunnel.

571

'Here we are,' said Barney.

Behind the door, through a little window, two jani-
tors were watching. They recognized both Barney and
the Captain; the door swung back. As they passed in,
the barren waste of Leicester Square seemed to follow
them, bringing with it the 'Shades', one of the wildest
eating-houses in London, where the spoons and forks
were marked 'Stolen from the Shades' as a delicate hint
to its patrons, and the 'Tableaux Vivants', a festive hall
almost next door to Victorine's, where, for a shilling,
you could listen to more filth within half an hour than in
any other place in London.

'Victorine's', however, seemed as respectable as a
church-service. Barney, Benjie and the Captain seated
themselves in a corner and brandy and sodas were ordered from a benevolent-looking old man with a hare-
lip and snow-white hair. It was not a very big room. In
the far corner was a billiard-table at which several gentlemen were playing. The centre of the room was
cleared for dancing and there was a shabby piano decorated with two dusty ferns in pots wrapped in green
paper; at the piano a large ringleted lady in a crimson
dress was playing. Two staircases vanished into upper
regions. Several ladies were drinking at little tables with
several gentlemen. But the great glory of the place was
Victorine herself, a huge woman weighing over twenty
stone, who sat at a raised desk near the piano. It was
said that she drank champagne all day and all night. Her
countenance was hideous, for her nose was flat, she had
a scar across her upper lip and a number of chins. Her
little eyes were wrapped in fat.

Benjie gazed at her with excited fascination. Her
bodice was cut very low and her enormous bosom
shook with every movement. He had never seen anyone so ugly and he felt that he would like to talk to her.
The gentlemen at the tables embraced the ladies, and
one stout female balanced herself precariously on a
stout gentleman's knee. Benjie was always a great observer; he missed very little, and was capable of a
detached non-moral attitude that permitted him to see
life steadily and, unless his own emotions were aroused,
with great fairness.

His emotions were not aroused now except that he
was greatly enjoying himself--for had not Connie kissed
him and given him a white rose? He was still, in the
back of his mind, considering what sort of a present he
should give her. He had better wait, perhaps. Christmas-time he would be in funds.

Then Victorine noticed them and beckoned Barney
over to her. After a while he returned and said to Benjamin:

'Ma wants to speak to you. She won't eat you.
Come along.'

Benjamin went over to her, feeling rather self-
conscious as he crossed the floor, but he was ready for
any adventure. He stood on the raised platform beside

her, laughing. She spoke in a deep husky voice. She
held out a large dirty hand.

'How are you?' she asked.

'Very well, thank you, ma'am,' said Benjie.

'How do you like my place?'

'I think it's very nice,' said Benjie.

'First time you've been here, isn't it?' she asked
him, suddenly bending towards him, and he thought
that he had never known anything so terrifying as that
great round soiled, misshapen face with its little eyes, its
flat nose, its grotesque mouth coming so close to his
own.

'Yes, it's the first time.'

'You can see for yourself how quiet it is.' Her little
eyes stared into his. 'There isn't a quieter house in London. It's these -- -- -- who come with their -- -- --
interference who make all the trouble. Take my word
for it.'

It was astonishing to him, the quiet friendly manner in which she used words of a terrifying impropriety.
They were not, it is sad to say, new to him, because boys
at Rugby, or anywhere else, understand many words that
would frighten Billingsgate. Not that they had ever
done Benjie any harm, these words. They were simply
counters in a normal day's play.

'You see,' Madame Victorine continued, her voice
lower than ever, her manner extremely confidential, 'I
am a mother to all the boys and girls who come here.
You wouldn't believe all that I do for them. Saved their
lives again and again. Mother I am and Mother they call
me. I'm a widow, you know,' she added unexpectedly.
'My late husband was a Captain in the Army and he died
in the West Indies of a yellow fever.'

'I am sorry,' Benjie said. He could think of nothing
else to say.

'Yes. It was a tragedy.' There was a tear in her eye.
Her vast bosom heaved. He thought that she was going
to cry, but instead, to his great surprise, she banged with
her fist on the desk and yelled in a voice of thunder,
'Here, you dirty ----. Get out of here! Didn't I tell you
last Thursday not to show your ---- face in my place
again? Here, Cormey, put him out! Knock his ---- face
in if there's an argument!'

Benjie turned to see a very mild-looking little man,
bearded, in a dirty sack-coat and pepper-and-salt trousers talking with a big man in his shirtsleeves. The little
man gave one glance round the room and vanished
through the door. At the same moment Barney came
and rescued Benjie, bringing him back to their table.

Barney was never so drunk that he did not know
what he was doing. Now he preached Benjie a little
sermon. 'You see, my boy, I've brought you here to
show you life a bit. But never do anything you'd be
ashamed of your mother knowing. You're young yet,
but how are you to know what to avoid if you don't
look round a bit?'

'I say, Barney,' said Benjamin. 'I want to give that lady a present. I'm going back to Rugby tomorrow so there isn't much time. Do you think you could give her something from me? I'll pay you back when I get my pocket-money. I've got a bit now that Ellis gave me, and with two weeks' pocket-money--'

'Here you are, my boy,' said Barney, diving confusedly into his pocket.

He produced two golden sovereigns.

'I don't know what you are talking about, but if it's money you're wanting--'

Two sovereigns!

'Oh, I say! But, Barney, I shan't have two pounds for months!'

'Oh, never mind! Keep them.'

'No. If I give her something, you see, I want it to be with my own money--'

He kept a sovereign. With luck he could pay that back by Christmas. A sovereign! He could buy her something fine--a scarf, a pin, a brooch . . . And it was then that the fun began. Over the silver image of his divine Connie he saw, rising as it were from the floor, a thick-set squat fellow, very hairy, very unkempt, very drunk. He wandered, as though he were describing with his feet a geometric figure, towards one of the little tables, raised a glass of champagne stationed there in front of a gentleman and drank from it. At the same time, grinning amiably, he knocked off the hat of the gentleman. Then, turning, he began to orate to the room:

'In the name of our Queen, of Mr Disraeli and little Lottie Heever, down with the French! Down, I say, with the French! Are they eating dogs in Paris? Poodle dogs? And is elephant their one luxury? Right and right again! To hell with the French!'

But he proceeded no further, for the two strong men, who had been watching the billiards, were across the room, had the man by the legs and were trundling him towards the door. At the same time the gentleman whose drink had been abstracted--stout, plethoric, with a beard of the colour of jet--cried something in a kind of frenzy and rushed towards one of the staircases. Benjie, looking in that direction, saw that two young ladies, most scantily dressed, were peering over the stair-rail. One of them, seeing the bearded gentleman, vanished with a scream, the gentleman after her.

Then everything happened together. The victim of the strong men wriggled from his captors and, his trousers tumbling towards his knees (for the strong men had burst his buttons), lurched towards the piano; there were shouts and cries from the upper floor which drew Madame Victorine, panting, upwards; some gentlemen ran in from the billiard table; the lady at the piano stayed with her back to it, cursing at the height of a shrill soprano; a large tortoiseshell cat crept from nowhere and began to feed eagerly upon a sandwich that had dropped; a table fell, glasses and bottles crashing with it; and the Captain, who had been dancing very solemnly

with a stout lady in green, left her where she was and reeled (for he was very drunk) towards Barney.

'Here,' said Barney. 'We must be out of this.'

And then a fantastic thing occurred. At the end of the room there was a long mirror hung with yellow and green papers. Reflected in the centre of this mirror was the old waiter with the white hair and the hare-lip. He seemed to Benjie to swell and lengthen. As he grew in size, another figure, long and thin, spread out behind him, caught him from the back, in the neck, and began to twist his head round. The mirror grew ever more unusual, for now it was swinging, slowly swinging on its nail, and the two men reflected in it increased to three, to four, to five. They all struggled together, and behind them and around them the room swayed with them, tables and chairs, Madame's desk, the coloured portraits of the Queen and the Prince Consort, the piano, overturned tables, all swaying, swinging, swaying again.

Someone threw one of the flowerpots and it struck the mirror in its centre: a great crack like a spider's web struck the bodies, faces, furniture . . . Someone turned out the gas.

It was then, in that strange darkness, smelling of spirits, dust and tobacco, filled with cries and shouts, that Benjie felt a great exultation and a wild spirit of enterprise.

'Here! Benjie! Where are you?' he heard Barney crying.

But nothing could stop him. He plunged forward into the darkness, tumbled over a recumbent body, was up again, had found the piano, was enveloped by large female arms. Some woman held him to her. She was crying, sobbing.

'Oh dear, oh dear! . . . And I had a nice supper at home waiting . . .' And then, in a whisper over Benjie's head, 'Mr Archer, are you there? Are you there, Mr Archer! Oh dear, and if it hadn't been for the five shillings he promised me--'

'It's all right,' Benjie said, feeling real wet warm tears dropping on his cheek and, in sympathy, patting with his hand what was, he imagined, a huge naked arm. 'Only a moment and they'll have the lights--'

But the lady murmured, sobbing as she spoke, 'Don't you move, Charlie, my darling. You'll be killed for certain if you move a step--'

She planted a wet kiss on his cheek. She began to croon in a drunken kind of lullaby, her vast arms now tight about him, and then surprisingly, in the middle of her crooning, in a sharp businesslike voice as though she were giving an order at a shop: 'Where are you, Mr Archer? I'm here, Mr Archer, by the piano.'

He ducked his head, slipped to his knees and had escaped. Everything was wild now. Fighting was on all sides. He could hear blows struck, bodies thudding to the floor. Women were screaming, it seemed, from earth and air. Someone again embraced him. This time it was a man--someone fat, paunchy and smelling dreadfully of brandy. They were entangled, intermingled, dragging along the ground together. The man said no word but breathed desperately. He had Benjie by the slack of his breeches, and Benjie had his fist in a handful of beard. The mirror must have fallen, for there was a great crash of shattering glass. Benjie, laughing, shouting he knew not what, tore at the beard, was released like a shot from a catapult, and half flew, half fell through a door, clutched at a wall to save himself and was caught by some hand. He looked up and saw that it was Barney, Barney hatless, his neckerchief torn, but Barney quite sober.

'Thank God!' He held Benjie as though he'd never let him go. 'Here's a piece of luck. Come on, my lad. It's the lock-up for us if we are not speedy.'

A moment later they were in the deserted street, surveyed by an orange-tinted moon and two gas-lamps. Dead silence. Dead, dead silence. A little breeze rose from the pavement and fluttered on their faces. Victorine's was gone. Everything in and around Victorine's was gone. Ahead of them was the desolate waste of Leicester Square with the equestrian statue.

'Walk! Walk!' said Barney. 'Can you walk all right? Have you got your legs?'

'Oh, I'm all right,' said Benjie grandly. 'Are you all right, Barney?'

'Hush!' said Barney, who now that he had found Benjie was, all in a moment, drunk again. 'Hush! We'll wake Emily.'

Benjie's head ached, he thought that he had lost a tooth, his right leg hurt a trifle. But he felt at his buttonhole. Miraculous! The white rose was still there! How had it escaped? Was that not of itself a triumph? He was dizzy with happiness, adventure, maturity, first love, the wine of battle, the ether of recklessness, the full, complete, uncensored actuality of life.

'Barney, I've still got my rose!'

But Barney was striding on ahead. Benjie did a long step, a trot or two, a step again.

With a sudden alarm he felt in his pocket. Yes, the sovereign was there. What would he buy for her? A scarf, a chain, a pin, a brooch? . . .

He did a long step, a trot or two, a step again.

BATTLE WITH PANGLOSS

Elizabeth, walking through the dusky afternoon up the hill to Fell House, was stopped by a little man like a ferret riding a large bay mare. She knew at once who it was--Glose, the handy-man at the Fortress, her father's handy-man--and, as always when anyone or anything connected with Ireby confronted her, she shivered with apprehension. Glose, who had sharp beady eyes and was always a trifle drunk, thought, as he looked at her: 'That's a pretty piece, although she HAS got grey hair.'

It was generally acknowledged up at the Fortress that Walter Herries' daughter, even though she was nearly sixty, was the most beautiful lady in the County. They liked to tell old Ma Pangloss so, when they dared.

'She'll be back one of these days and send you packing, Mrs Pangloss, MADAM,' said a lively carroty-haired girl from Braithwaite who had just received her notice, 'and then we'll have a lady who IS a lady'.

Elizabeth had a dark crimson coat with a silver-grey fur collar turned up above her slender neck, and she wore on her grey hair a feather toque with flame-coloured feathers. She was protected from the chill October wind by a thin veil. The twists and bands in which her hair was arranged at the back under the little feathered hat held lovely lights and shadows, so Glose thought. He was something of a poet where women were concerned, and afterwards in the kitchen at Ireby he declared:

'She had on a little hat all flaming feathers, and her hair was silver, you understand, and she has the figure of a girl of twenty, old as she is. Very pretty with the dusk coming on and the leaves blowing down, all the colour of her little hat.'

He was an Irishman, vagrant and worthless. He was in gaol for trying to knife a man in Keswick three months later.

But he had a letter for Mrs Herries. He was riding up to Fell House. He touched his cap, leaned down and gave her the letter.

Her hand trembled as she read it by the pale light of the saffron sky above the hill. It was written in a hand so shaky that it was difficult to decipher.

DEAR ELIZABETH--I am ill and would like to see you.--Your affectionate father,
WALTER HERRIES

That was all.

'Thank you,' she said to Glose. 'I will see to it.' She walked quickly up the hill. She was in a turmoil of emotion, but once in the house she told no one anything. She had always been quiet, reserved, by herself; her mother, who had learnt, through suffering, restraint, had taught her.

She peeped in to say goodnight to Judith, but the old lady was sleeping. Had she been awake Elizabeth might have said something, for although Judith was now ninety-eight and was being preserved as though constructed of egg-shell china, every noise, shock, sudden news kept from her, yet, inside this elegant glass case, she lived, Elizabeth fancied, an exceedingly alive and conscious existence. Judith knew more about Walter than anyone else at Uldale. It was she who had seen him last, who had known him longest. To her, Elizabeth might have spoken. But to Dorothy, who was now as fat as a tub and as contented as a pork pie, Elizabeth said not a word. Otherwise there was only Jane, for Veronica had been Mrs Forster now for two years, and Amabel had, of all mad things, gone to be a student at the Ladies' College at Hitchin. She had been there two years and was now at Cambridge, whither the College had just removed under the name of Girton. Ridiculous of Amabel, who was now between thirty and forty! She said, of all things, that she intended to study medicine!

So there were, besides Dorothy, Judith and Elizabeth, only Timothy (who showed no signs of marrying: he was fat, red-faced, cheerful-- a proper Squire) and Jane. Elizabeth might have said something to Jane. She did not. Jane was such a dear old spinster, already ringleted and shawled, her face sweet and anxious and kind under her pale-gold hair, her small body INTENSELY virginal. No, she would be of little use.

Of course Elizabeth must go to Ireby, and this time she would remain. From the moment that she received the note and read it in the gathering shadow of the autumn dusk she knew that there was only one thing that she must do. But oh! how she didn't want to! Her quiet, reserved, cloistered life, saturated with the memory and actual presence of John, devoted to Benjamin and Aunt Judith, was exactly right at Uldale. She was young no longer. She was nearing sixty. She shrank in every vein and pulse of her body from the roughness, violence, hateful rudeness that going to Ireby meant.

So she fortified herself with Adam and Margaret. On the morning after receiving her father's letter she told Dorothy quietly that she was going to stay at Cat Bells for a night or two.

'Are you sure that they want you, Elizabeth dear?' said Dorothy. 'Adam is just finishing his book, I believe.'

'I don't think that they will mind,' Elizabeth said. And they did not.

On that first evening, sitting by the fire after Vanessa had gone to bed, hearing Will softly singing as he occupied himself with something in the kitchen close by, Adam tranquilly smoking his pipe, they talked it all over.

The two women had a great regard for one another. Margaret had broadened into a maternal and seemingly placid woman, more German now perhaps in type than English. Her love for Adam was so strong that she could not sit with him five minutes without snatching a private glance at him to see that all was well. She knew that he loved her but she knew also, as nine out of every ten wives come to know, that she had not captured all of him; a certain wildness in him had escaped her. He was her friend and she was his, but she knew also that soon he would get up, knock his pipe against the stone of the fireplace, mutter something and slip off to Will--and that then for an hour at least those two deep voices would rumble on beyond the wall, and that they would both be happy together with a kind of happiness that neither of them could find with a

woman. So she was glad to have Elizabeth then. They were two quiet, elderly women, sitting together by the fire; they were like hundreds of thousands of other elderly women sitting beside the fire that evening all over England--and the lives of those women contained sufficient courage, unselfishness and loving devotion to fill a Calendar of Saints.

Margaret, beneath her reserve, was frightened. There were many things in the Herries family that she did not understand, and what she understood least of all was that some of them were so very different from others! That you should have Garth and Amery, the Archdeacon of Polchester, Will and Ellis, Judith and Adam, poor John, crazy Uhland and his father, all of the same stock and closely related, seemed to her sober German imagination extravagantly improbable. Yet it was so, and she had long ago realized that the mad strain in the Herries family was not for her. She shrank from it with all her quiet strength because it was that element in her husband--although Adam of course was not crazy!-- that prevented him from being entirely hers, and it had been that same element in his mother that had given her all her young married sorrows.

Now she was set, with all the determination of which she was capable, to keep the wildness from Vanessa! Vanessa as yet was as good and obedient and loving as a child could possibly be, but she was impulsive, fantastically generous, and--most perilous of all!-- worshipped, increasingly with every year of her growth, Benjamin Herries. Now Margaret was Elizabeth's friend, but in her heart she was afraid of Elizabeth's son. Young Benjamin was wild; they said that he did wild things in London. He was eighteen years of age, and in another term he would be leaving Rugby. Then, Margaret supposed, he would come to live at Ireby and would be terribly close to Cat Bells. Margaret had to confess that when she was in the boy's company she could not but like him. He looked you straight in the face with his clear blue eye, he was merry, honest, open-handed, the friend of all the world. But he was wild. Margaret was sure that he had no principles, and although Adam sometimes laughed at principles yet he respected them as a good man should. Margaret was no narrow condemner of her fellow but she had acquired the prejudices of her time. She believed in righteousness, and for her own beloved daughter she would fight like a fish-wife if need be.

Vanessa would be beautiful--of that there was no question--and she must be guarded against Benjamin, but how she was to be guarded poor Margaret had no idea. Adam only laughed when she spoke to him of it.

And now Elizabeth was going back to that horrible place at Ireby with that drunken old wretch her father and the loose women he had with him. She was going back into all that craziness and wildness and bad living, and she intended to remain there. That quiet, frail woman, with her gentle face, shy, retiring way, so perfect and refined an English lady, thought Margaret, would live in a world that must revolt and disgust her at every turn. And, if she did remain, Benjamin would of course come to her there; he was heir, Margaret supposed, to that place, and any money the old man might have if, indeed, his dissipations had left him any. And Benjamin at Ireby meant Benjamin very near to Vanessa. At the thought of her child so peacefully sleeping in the upper room her whole protective fighting maternity was at arms. She felt inclined to cry out to Elizabeth, although she loved and admired her:

'Go away! Please, please go away and let neither your son nor yourself ever return.'

But they sat talking calmly; only once Margaret said:

'Do you think, Elizabeth dear, that it is WORTH going? Can you do anything for him? Is his life not too settled? Can it ever be your life?'

And Elizabeth answered, looking at Margaret:

'I know it's my duty, Margaret.'

Margaret shivered with some quick sense of chill and discomfort. Her German blood gave her an unusual sensitiveness to intangible influences. Many past events touched her moment's consciousness, and future events, linked to these, hung like clouds about her vision. It was as though the cheerful fire-lit room were, at that instant, fogged with smoke.

Elizabeth slept little that night and in the morning she shrank from what she was going to do as she had never shrunk from anything in her life before. After all, she was returning to the house where, it seemed to her excited fancy, Uhland's footstep must have left everywhere an imprint of blood. That was not a melodramatic exaggeration. John's death had been bloody, and, although his murderer had been her own brother, that did not make his ghost more stainless. In every room, at every turn, there would be memories, agonizing thoughts, vain, wretched recriminations. But nevertheless, she had no hesitation as to what her duty was.

Two things made the journey easier for her. One was the luxuriant splendour of the day. In October this country is often a fantastic dream, and on this especial morning the fragment of this world contained by the sky, the hills, the water, was a glory. Last night there had been the first frost and the lawn glittered in a dancing firefly extravagance under a pale autumnal mist. She stood in the doorway of the cottage and looked out to the Lake and Walla Crag. Near her was a mulberry tree; there were roses, chrysanthemums, currant bushes; someone was drawing water, and the smoke from the cottage chimney went up in a gay, fluttering pennon of thin colour. A squirrel watched her from a branch. She could see into the living room with the bright-blue cups on the white cloth, rough pottery with a pattern of flowers. All this world at her hand was clear and distinct with a hard edge to it. Then, in the space of the lawn, of a leaping jump, terrestial existence was cut off and mirage began.

The blue cold sky ranged like a sea infinitely high and remote from change: the tops of the larch and birch and fir suddenly, if they were high enough, struck a hard stainless light and were edged like cut paper, but so soon as the feathering vapours of mist rolled curtain-like across the scene colour so rich and varied began that the sky seemed to belong to another infinitely remote existence, unactual and a planet away.

The mist was neither ascending nor descending in clouds; it was not thick enough for form, it only caught the sunlight and transmuted it, and that sunlight, joyfully enclosed, glowed within, an imprisoned fire.

It is the quality of this country that with a structure of rock, naked fell and dark grim water, it has the power of breaking into an opulence of light and colour. So the Lake that could be cold as driving snow, harsh like shadowed steel, fierce with white foam as a bird's feathers are blown angrily by storm, now was streaked and veined with shadows of the grape that trembled, as though a hand gently stroked its surface. This trembling was not cold nor wind-swept, but burned with the sun-filled mist. Above these purple shadows the hillsides were orange clouds, orange in their brighter spaces, but like smouldering, glowing embers where vapour enshrouded them. An isolated field, a blazing tree, a strip of bracken against the dark plum-coloured islands, shone out like the gilt of missals, damascened, exotic, flaming to the eye where all else was mystery, but the mist above the gold was as dim as the white ash of burnt wood.

Because the sky was decisive with its virgin chastity of eggshell blue, the misted land in contrast took all the colours of purple, topaz, orange, and laid them under washes of pale gold. And yet, with all this dimness the hills were strong, striking deep into the Lake and, where they topped the mist, hard-ridged against the chill sky. And on Skiddaw there was a sudden flame-shaped crest.

Nothing but words of colour could describe this colour, but its final delight for Elizabeth was that it was friendly. The Lake, the cottage, the chrysanthemums, the sparkling lawn, wished her well. She could feel the warm quiver in the air, could think without extravagance that the sun laughed with pleasure as it struck again and again through the mist to touch with the point of its shaking lance the purple shadowy waters, the flaming autumn trees, the sharp dark ridge of Blencathra. She drew in a deep breath of the frosted air as she saw Walla Crag riding into the orange vapour like the bow of a Viking ship. The breath was as though she had leant her forehead against the pure cold of a newly riven stone . . .

And the second thing was that Will Leathwaite drove her to Ireby.

She could not have had a more perfect defence in perilous country. But before she went she had a moment with Vanessa. Vanessa came dancing on to the lawn, flinging her long arms out, running across the frosty grass, breathing in the air that stung the throat like peppermint. Her dark hair was in ringlets, her white strong neck bare. 'She will have big strong breasts,' thought Elizabeth, 'she will be very tall. I never saw a child carry her head with such majesty, and yet she is dancing about the lawn like a little pony.' She was going down with Will to Grange to fetch the carriage. They had to keep it in Grange. As she came nearer to Elizabeth the curve of her face from cheek to chin, still the face of a child innocent, open-eyed, fearless, gave promise of an almost startling beauty. You looked again to see whether that curve could be as perfect in shadowed line, in proportion and purity as you had at first supposed. And it was. Her eyes, lit now with happiness, were direct, unequivocal, so honest that they put you on your guard. What base part of myself am I going to betray here? you must ask yourself.

But Elizabeth knew that Vanessa was no perfect paragon. Her impulsiveness was always taking her into trouble; she had a temper. She was irritated often by stupid people; like her father and grandmother, she did not suffer fools gladly. Her mother was always checking her for answering back her elders (which no child was allowed to do), but, as Vanessa said, it was her father's fault because he encouraged her.

She was compassionate and generous, but not at all sentimental. At a time when both young men and young women 'gushed' and the world was on the whole more insincere than usual, Vanessa laughed. She laughed, it is to be feared, at Dorothy Bellairs, and Captain Forster who had married Veronica, and Mrs Ponsonby and a good many more. In fact Vanessa was not perfect at all. Margaret often shook her head over her.

'I am going down to Grange with Will. We'll be back in a twinkle!'

'Vanessa!' said Margaret.

'Well, but, Mama, twinkle is quite a proper word!'

'And as soon as you are back, Vanessa, you sit down to the German.'

'Oh, bother the German on this lovely day! I'm sorry, Mama; isn't it a pity that I don't like the German language better?'

She came to Elizabeth and said goodbye.

'Please, how is Benjamin?'

'Very well. He plays in the football team this term, and you know Rugby is very famous for football.'

'Yes. I am so glad.'

'Now, Vanessa, Will's waiting.'

'When you write to him will you tell him, please, that I asked?'

'Of course I will.'

'Now, Vanessa.'

Elizabeth thought it rather strange that Adam and Margaret should allow their girl when she was only fourteen to go off alone with Will--but then all the family at Uldale, except Judith, thought that Adam treated Will with far too great a familiarity. Servants were servants, and however good and valuable Will might be (certainly he was a MOST trustworthy man), still it was intended that a member of one Class should not be too intimate with a member of another Class. Emily Newmark, when she heard of it in London, tossed her head. 'Oh, well, we are none of us surprised. Adam Paris was a Chartist for years and would have burnt us all in our beds had he had the chance. Of course he WOULD make friends with a common working-man.'

However, when Elizabeth was seated beside Will in the little carriage and they were driving towards Bassenthwaite she could not feel that he WAS 'a common working-man'. He was simply Will Leathwaite, and like most Cumbrian and Westmorland men, sons of Statesmen who have owned their own land for hundreds of years and been servants to none, he held his head high, said nought, and feared no man. But the great thing that Will Leathwaite was was comforting. He was a man of tremendous prejudices, prejudices often based on nothing at all, and he disliked more people that he liked, but if he DID take you under his wings, then he would see that you were protected. There was nothing he wouldn't do for you, no danger, no strife of tongues (a thing that he greatly disliked) that he wouldn't face. His loyalty was absolute. He had long regarded Elizabeth Herries with a tender protective affection because of John Herries' death. Further than that, she was a member of the Herries clan. He did not think much of several Herries whom he had met, but his friend and master Adam was a Herries and that was enough for him. So Elizabeth was under his wing. As he sat there, staring in front of him, saying 'Gee-up', cracking his whip, his brow wrinkled a little above his very clear blue eyes, his rebellious lock of hair tumbling out across his forehead from under his old high hat, he said very little--but she KNEW that he was protecting her.

In actual fact he was wondering what he would do when they reached Ireby. He did not want to leave the elderly, delicate lady all alone there. There was every kind of bad story about the Fortress, and that Mrs Pangloss was a holy terror. HE could deal with her-- he would like to see any old fat whale of a woman get the better of him--but a lady like Mrs John Herries, so quiet and soft-spoken, what chance would SHE have?

At last when they were driving along the far end of Bassenthwaite Lake, he said: 'See here now, Mrs Herries. I don't like leaving you all alone, by yourself as it were, at the Fortress. Please pardon me, Mrs Herries, if I am saying what I shouldn't.'

By now, poor lady, she was dreadfully frightened, and her hands were trembling inside her muff, but Will must not know that.

'No, Will. You can say anything you like, of course. But I shan't need anyone. Sir Walter is my father, you know.'

This made it very difficult for Will, who considered that to warn a daughter against her own father was not at all man's work. Nevertheless, something had to be done. So he thought, looking straight in front of him between the ears of old Bartholomew the horse.

'Yes, Mrs Herries,' he said at last. 'I do hope you'll forgive me, ma'am, meaning nothing but good intentions and doing as Mr Adam would wish me to do, seeing that you are one of the family, ma'am.' He cleared his throat, gave a crack with his whip, set back his broad shoulders. 'You see, Mrs Herries, your father isn't so young as he once was, and there's a woman--Pangloss, they call her--who's no good whatever if the half they say is true. And a lady like you and a woman like her . . . I thought if I was to wait half an hour or so and you wave a handkerchief or some such article out of the window to say that she hadn't done you no kind of harm--'

'She won't harm me, thank you, Will,' Elizabeth said. 'It's very kind of you, and I've met Mrs Pangloss. I know that she isn't a very nice woman. But I'm not afraid, you know. My father himself has written to me to come and see him, so there is nothing to fear.'

'Yes, Mrs Herries, I quite understand, ma'am,' said Will. Nevertheless, he made a private resolve that he would not drive away until he was well assured that all was safe for the poor dear lady.

When they had driven slowly up Ireby Hill and the Fortress came at last into view, Elizabeth drew a deep breath of astonishment. She had seen the chimneys and the two towers, of course, every day from Uldale, but she had never, since her rebuff six years ago, been up that hill. She could not believe what she saw. How could someone as strong, as commanding, as powerful as her father had been, have allowed what had once been his pride to drop into this decay? She had seen the degradation begin in him long before her flight, but the house itself, ugly and forbidding as it was, had been proud, well cared for, the gardens kept, every kind of life and bustle about the place. And now!

She made Will stop the carriage round the bend of the trees so that they could not be seen from the house. In this part the veils of mist were thicker than above Derwentwater, and both Uldale and Skiddaw were invisible. The sun burnt strongly enough for the clouds of vapour to be faintly stained with rose, and here, as on the islands of the Lake, the upper mist was grey above the rose like the ashes of dying fires. But the top of the hill, the trees, the house, were chill and clear, crowning the shrouded valley; their detail was lined with sharpness against the cold bare sky. Elizabeth could see everything, how the trees had grown until they seemed to be throttling one another, how the garden was overgrown with weeds, grass had sprung up between the stones of the garden path, a shutter had swung off a hinge before one of the lower windows, there was an empty pane in the top window of the right- hand tower, stones had tumbled from the wall. There was something especially deserted today in the house outlined against so pale and bare a sky. As she looked it seemed to her that the house moved, its walls bulging outwards then sagging in again--an illusion of light.

She caught Will's arm.

'Is there not someone moving in the garden?'

'I don't see no one,' said Will.

'There--moving into the trees--a woman in black. No, it is my imagination. There is no one--not a soul . . .'

She put up her hand to her throat; this was so pitiful, this home of her youth where there had been so much life, now picked bare like a bone, or, to see it the other way, strangled with climbing triumphing vegetation.

'Leave the carriage here,' she said. 'I'll walk to the door. Bring my bag.'

She pulled her coat more closely about her, for it was cold up here, arranged her veil and walked quickly up the road through the gate, up the garden path.

She did not dare to hesitate for a moment lest she should lose all her courage, but it was a reassurance to hear Will's heavy certain tread behind her. Then she rang the bell and it pealed in the air as bells peal through empty houses. She looked around.

'No one has tended this garden. Look at those poor chrysanthemums. I feel as though someone were watching us.'

'Maybe it's the Pangloss woman from behind the window.'

She rang again and while the bell was still echoing the door opened. To her surprise a little girl, very ragged and tattered, wearing a woman's bonnet, was standing there. Elizabeth had thought out her plan of campaign and, taking her bag from Will, she walked into the hall and on into the small room beyond, which, in the old days, had been the gun-room. She knew it very well of course. But now it was quite different: the walls bare save for an old hunting-scene picture; there was a screen with boxing pictures pasted on it, and she remembered that this had been once an ornament of one of the spare bedrooms. There were the ashes of a fire in the grate and a stuffy stale smell of spirits in the air. She put her bag down and stood in front of the fireplace.

She saw that the child, who had large goggly eyes, was in the doorway staring at her.

'What's your will?' the child asked.

It was plain that she had not seen for a long time so grand a lady, for her gaze was rapt by the little dark green bonnet, the green coat with the velvet collar that Elizabeth was wearing.

'Will you please tell Sir Walter Herries that his daughter, Mrs John Herries, is here and would like to see him?'

The child said nothing but only gaped.

Elizabeth came over to her. She took her mottled red hand in her glove.

'Poor little thing . . . You are shivering with cold. Listen, my dear. Will you find Sir Walter for me and then say that his daughter has come to see him?'

The child vanished; the house was still. A mouse scratched behind the wainscot. She was glad that Will was waiting in the road outside. The door flung open and there stood a fat blowzy woman with a red round face, wearing a faded blue calico dress.

'I beg your pardon, madam,' she said, speaking very quickly. 'The girl shouldn't have shown you in here. This is private.'

All Elizabeth's fear had vanished at the sight of this woman, and she was so deeply filled with pity for her father that she could think of nothing else.

'It is not private to me,' she answered smiling. 'I am Mrs John Herries, Sir Walter's daughter, and I lived in this house for several years. So you see I know it well. We have met before.'

'Yes, and Sir Walter is not well enough to see any-one.'

'I know that my father is not well because he wrote to me, telling me so and asking me to come and see him.'

'Oh, did he? Excuse me for doubting your word, but he's not able to write to anyone.'

Elizabeth found the note and handed it to her. This brought them nearer to one another.

Mrs Pangloss read it very slowly, word by word.

'Silly old fool!' Elizabeth heard her mutter. Her great bosom heaved with indignation, but the letter had its effect.

'Well, I'm sorry, Mrs Herries, I'm very sorry, I'm sure. You're his daughter, as you say, and have a right--although for all the trouble his relations have taken all these years he might have been dead and buried, poor old man, for all they cared. What he WOULD have done if it hadn't been for strangers taking care of him it's pitiful to think. However, perhaps you'll call another day, Mrs Herries, if it isn't a trouble. He isn't quite himself today--he's past eighty, you know, Mrs Herries--and it's the doctor's orders that he isn't to be disturbed by no one--not his nearest and dearest.'

Elizabeth walked back to the fireplace.

'I'm sorry,' she said, 'but I'm afraid, Mrs Pangloss, I can't do that. You see, I've come to stay. I have brought my bag. I intend to remain here.'

Mrs Pangloss gasped. Colour slowly mounted into her cheeks and changed them from red into a faintly streaked purple.

'Remain?' she brought out at last in a husky whisper.

'Yes. I have been far too long away. I should have come back years ago and would have done so, had I thought that my father wished for me. Now it is plain from this letter that he does. So will you take me to him, please?'

They stared at one another. This very slender elderly lady was, it seemed, nothing to be afraid of, for Mrs Pangloss changed her tone.

'No, Mrs Herries, I'm afraid I can't. Very sorry, but there it is. Doctor's orders, you see, IS doctor's orders, and those were the doctor's very words. "I trust you to see, Mrs Pangloss, that nobody disturbs him, not on any account WHATEVER--no account WHATEVER. I wouldn't like to be answerable for consequences," he said. Those were the doctor's very words.'

'When was the doctor here last?' Elizabeth asked.

'Well, I'm sure, Mrs Herries, I don't see that it's any business of yours, but if you WANT to know--well, yesterday afternoon.'

'What doctor did you call in?'

'Now really and truly, Mrs Herries, you are going too far! Here you are, his only child, the only one left to him, poor old gentleman, and you living for years as you might say right at his very door and never so much as asking--'

Elizabeth's delicate face flushed and her eyes flashed--really flashed so that a light, indignant, proud, struck the thick heavy features of Mrs Pangloss. So, many, many years before, a young Buck in Islington had also been struck!

'I wrote several times,' she said, 'but received no answer. I understand now why I did not. I came once myself--perhaps you have forgotten, Mrs Pangloss? I did not wish to remind you because you were exceedingly rude and vulgar on that occasion. I admit that after seeing the kind of woman into whose hands my father had fallen I ought to have left it there, but I was anxious not to drive myself in upon him . . . I was always hoping for a letter--'

'Oh yes,' Mrs Pangloss broke in. 'I can have you up for libel for that, Mrs Herries! I can indeed--"kind of woman" indeed--"kind of woman!"--and I the only one all these years who's been good to him. And THAT settles it! I'm a trifle wearied of having all his relations coming round poking their noses in, and it's got to stop! A year or two ago it was that old French Madame who should have been in her grave years back if she'd had any proper decency--and her mother nothing better than a road-gipsy if all they say is true. And now YOU coming worrying! Well, you've no right here, Mrs Herries--no right at all--and I'll thank you to be off!'

She had worked herself into a splendid temper and, shaking with an anger that had been plainly fortified with both gin and brandy, she advanced several paces into the room.

That was the very thing that Elizabeth desired. It was not very dignified perhaps, but dignity, on such an occasion, must be forgotten. She walked swiftly to the door and then, once outside, ran up the wide staircase, along a passage, up another stair, and through the door into the room that had always been her father's bed-room.

Thank God, it still was! Yes, and there was the same big four-poster with the yellow saffron hangings that, as a tiny child at Westaways, she had looked at with awe and terror, the picture of a hunt with gentlemen in red coats, over the stone mantelpiece, the two old chairs covered in green silk that she so well recollected, a walnut ring-stand, the mahogany cheval glass, the white sheepskin hearthrug, a mahogany washstand with marble top and two rosewood pole-screens--all articles that seemed to be part of her very life.

And he, her father, was in the four-poster. From the door she could see only the peaked nightcap but, at the first step forward, he roused himself.

'Who's that!' he called out. 'Alice, you bitch, I told you to bring me a drink. Hours back I told you.'

She came up to the bed. And this was her father whom she had last seen, on the evening before her flight, corpulent, rosy, covered with clothes even too strikingly elegant, master--as he thought--of his world. Now under the nightcap there was untidy grey hair, drawn cheeks with a week's grey stubble; his open nightshirt showed the bones of his throat as sharp and pointed as those of a plucked bird. For him, too, it must have been a striking vision--this very elegant lady with her grey hair, her little green bonnet and her long green coat fitting perfectly her tall slender body. He did not recognize her. He raised himself on his elbow.

'Why, what the devil--?' he said.

She stood close to the bed, smiling.

'Father, don't you know me? You wrote to me and I've come. Elizabeth. I should have come years ago.'

'Elizabeth!' he sat up, and at the same time, with trembling hands, pushed his nightcap straight on his head and pulled his nightshirt about his skinny neck. 'Are you Elizabeth? Dear me! Yes, I wrote that I was ill. But I should not receive you here. Go into another room a moment, my dear, while I dress--'

'No, Father; I've come to stay. You must--'

But she said no more, for Mrs Pangloss, bursting in, had interrupted her.

'If this isn't SHAMEFUL!' she cried. 'I can have the Courts on you for this, madam. There he was just in his first sleep of the morning and me keeping all the house quiet so that it shouldn't be broken--'

But Walter, sitting up and grinning, said:

'Alice, you old washerwoman, this is my daughter. She has come to pay me a visit.'

'Yes,' cried Mrs Pangloss with a ripe round oath, for she was now too angry to care what she said (and had also, in the brief interval between the scene downstairs and this, fortified herself with more brandy). 'As she's come so she'll go. I'm mistress here, and the sooner she knows it the better. Forcing herself into a gentleman's bedroom, even if he is her own father!'

Elizabeth had crossed to the window which looked on the road and, glancing down, saw the thick solid body of Will Leathwaite stationed patiently by the gate. He looked up, saw her; she waved her hand.

Turning into the room again, she said:

'Now, Mrs Pangloss, have this perfectly clear. It is not of the slightest use for you to rant and swear. I am Sir Walter's daughter, he has asked for me--here I am and here I stay--and you leave within the hour.'

At the audacity of this Mrs Pangloss for a moment could not reply at all. She gasped and stuttered. Then, in jerks, the words came.

'Me! . . . within the hour! You to order me . . . You!' She strode to the door, flung it wide and called: 'Harry! Harry! Where are you? Come here a moment! I want you!'

Walter, meanwhile, found it extremely amusing. He sat there, propped up by pillows, his eyes moving from the one to the other, grinning with his bare gums (his teeth were in a glass by the bed) and mumbling: 'THAT'S done it! THAT'S a pretty thing! Now for a tumble!'

A moment later there arrived a heavy slouching man in corduroys, black rough hair over his eyes. He looked exceedingly sheepish, as well he might. Here was his master in bed in his nightcap, and Pangloss in one of her tantrums, and there, near the window, a beautiful lady in green. He was further embarrassed by the fact that the little girl (the child of himself and Mrs Pangloss) had crept after him (for although he beat her when drunk, she adored him as truly as she hated her mother) and, sucking her thumb, her old woman's bonnet on the back of her head, looked in.

Throughout the scene he kept muttering: 'Get away, Lucy . . . 'Tisn't no place for you . . . Go on or I'll larrup yer,' but the child paid no heed, and he, Harry Borden, restlessly shifted from heel to heel.

Mrs Pangloss turned to him. 'Now, Harry, you listen to me. This lady has been asked to go. Master has asked her. I've asked her. If she won't go, well--YOU shall ask her!'

Elizabeth went back to the window. She could see from there all the soft sprawling shoulders of Blencathra above the tops of the golden trees. The whole world swam in light this lovely morning. Inside the room the sun fell in coins and saucers of gold upon the faded ragged carpet. She felt the autumn sun, knew that Will was in the road below, and was conscious of a cheerfulness and high spirits that had not been here for many a day. She thought: 'Benjamin would enjoy this.'

'Well, Mrs Herries, ma'am, will you have the decency to go? You came uninvited--the sooner you go the better for all parties.'

'I did not come uninvited,' Elizabeth answered quietly. 'And I am certainly remaining.'

'You are not! You are not!' Mrs Pangloss found a glory of liquor at her heart and the fury of a righteous woman monstrously wronged in her head. 'If you won't go out you shall be put out! I'm in charge here, and so you shall know. Harry, if this lady won't go, you'll please LEAD her--'

But the ludicrous little scene was interrupted from the bed.

'Alice! Do you know to whom you are speaking? And who told you to bring Harry Borden into my bedroom? And I want my drink--I'm sure it's well past eleven--and The Times newspaper of yesterday. You'll fetch me my drink, Alice, and give a poke to the fire before you go.'

But Mrs Pangloss, all control lost, strode to the bed, stood over the old man and screamed at him. Words poured from her. She flooded the room with her life story, her virtues as a child, her nobility as a young woman, the criminal errors of Husband One, the positive loathsomeness of Husband Two, her patience in bearing great suffering, a struggle with Husband Two that had nearly lost her an eye, her self-sacrifice in coming to the Fortress, her devotion, generosity in guarding and caring for a gentleman . . . But, most unexpectedly, Walter rose to the occasion.

'Clear out, Alice. Clear out. I'm sick to death of you. I've been sick of you for years. There's been nothing but mess and filth here, and I'm too old to put up with you any longer. An old man wants his comforts, and you've always thought of yourself, you nasty old woman. And what are you thinking of, talking like that in front of my daughter? I asked my daughter to come and I'm glad she's here. So you be off this afternoon. Mrs Herries will pay you what is due to you. Harry can drive you in the cart. And tell the old hag downstairs to send up my drink. I'm parched.'

The poor woman was amazed. She was stuffed after all only with sawdust, and perhaps, Elizabeth, watching from the window, thought, she had a real affection for him. The look in her face of dismay and chagrin was not only brought there by drink and ill-temper. She stared through her stupid tear-filled eyes. She put out her hand as though she would appeal. 'You don't want me any more? . . . After all I've done for you?'

'I'm sick to death of you, I tell you. I'm sick enough anyway, but I'll spend my remaining days in peace. There, there! . . . I can't bear women to cry. Mrs Herries shall pay you what's due and Harry shall drive you in the cart . . .'

The catastrophe had been so sudden that she could only look about her, turning her head now this way, now that, large fat tears coursing down her cheeks.

She must care for him or she would not so abruptly surrender, Elizabeth thought. She felt an impulse of pity.

But the woman turned to her, her words almost lost between anger and tears:

'It's you that have done this, Mrs Herries, and I shan't forget it either.'

Then, blowing her nose and wiping her eyes with a large check handkerchief, she went to the door.

'Come, Harry,' she said. 'They shall suffer for this.'

'Don't forget the drink,' Walter called after her.

When she was gone Elizabeth opened for a brief moment the window, and leaned out.

'Thank you, Will,' she called, waving her hand. 'There is no need to wait. Please tell Mr Paris that I am remaining.'

Will nodded and started down the road to the carriage.

She closed the window and came to the bed. She took off her bonnet and folded her veil.

'There are a number of things will need doing in this house,' she said.

He looked at her rather piteously.

'You'll be kind to me, won't you? I'm a very old man.'

THE HUNDREDTH BIRTHDAY

As the great day of November 28th, 1874, approached ever more nearly it may be said without very much exaggeration that all the Herries all over England held their breath. Would she do it? Could she last the course? Were they once more in their history to touch the Hundred? Or would she perhaps fail them just before reaching the post? A little chill, a window left carelessly open, a hot-water bottle neglected, the wrong food, a sudden shock . . .

Barney Newmark, who had been staying in Cumberland recently with Adam, declared: 'Pooh! She is as tough as an old hen! Not that I speak disrespectfully, for a nicer, jollier old lady you never saw. I had half an hour with her and her brain's as clear as a bell. She's got eyes like a child's. Of course, she's OLD. What do you expect at ninety-nine? She looks frail. She was always a pocket- edition but, dammit, she's sporting! AND got a temper! But sweet- natured, you know, wants everyone to be happy. They all worship her and I don't wonder!'

In August she caught a cold and the news went right through England. Lady Herries in Hill Street (she detested Judith) gave a sniff and said the vain old woman had lived quite long enough, and for once Ellis became quite heated and said she had no right to speak so. She was an honour to all of them and it would be splendid did she live to her Hundred. Garth and Sylvia, pigging it in a little alley off Victoria Street, were genuinely concerned when they heard of the cold. 'Oh, she MUST live to a Hundred. She MUST,' Sylvia cried passionately.

'Perhaps she'll leave us something,' Garth said gloomily. Then added: 'I say, old girl, I lost on that damned horse yesterday. You'll have to pawn that ring again.'

Emily Newmark remarked virtuously that the Lord knoweth His Own Time. What He Giveth He taketh away; but Barney said:

'By gad, Emily, you'd weary a saint.'

All over the country it was the same. In Wiltshire, Carey, coming in from riding, was told by his mother and cried: 'Oh lor! I hope she isn't beat at the post! A cold, do you say? Damn' dangerous at ninety-nine.' Down at Bournemouth, where Jennifer's brother Robert had founded a little family (Robert himself was dead and his son Bradley reigned in his stead), they were greatly concerned, and Ruth, a pretty girl of twenty-two, thought of writing to Dorothy with a cure for colds that a Bournemouth doctor had given her. The Ormerods in London DID write to Dorothy, and Horace Newmark, now extremely wealthy in Manchester, thought of running up to see the old lady.

However, all was well. Judith quickly recovered.

'Nothing the matter with her whatever,' Dorothy wrote to Sylvia. 'Of course it's very touching that everyone should be so deeply concerned, but Jane and I are QUITE capable of looking after her. And WHAT do you think? Timothy is engaged at last, to a Miss Greenacre of Taunton Hall, near Grasmere. She seems a nice girl-- quite a beauty but manners a little haughty. Timothy says she'll make a good mother. I trust he won't be disappointed.'

The truth was that the Herries were very ready for a public demonstration of their position. A century or so back they had been nothing at all--and now look at them! A Peerage in Wiltshire (Carey intended to stand for Parliament at the next election); Ellis, young though he was, one of the richest and most important men in the City; Barney Newmark, a famous Novelist (famous ENOUGH anyway); Adam Paris, a well-known writer (well known at least to all the REAL readers of literature); Horace Newmark, one of the richest men in the North of England; Rodney, Archdeacon of Polchester, and his son, a most oncoming Captain in the Navy; Lady Herries in Hill Street, a leader of fashion; the Witherings, and the Bellairs at Uldale, among the first County families of the North; and Judith Paris herself, REALLY famous so that all kinds of people asked after her. Mr Disraeli had known her, Dickens and Thackeray in their day had heard of her, the Bishop of Polchester often asked Rodney about her, and as to the North itself--why, everyone knew her and everyone was proud of her!

So they were determined to make this Birthday of hers a Herries demonstration, just to show the world what a Herries could do were he or she so minded! No other family in England, so far as was known, contained so famous an old lady.

Many of them intended to be present at Uldale for the event. As the day drew near, Dorothy, Timothy and Jane, who were the managers and presenters of the Ceremony, had great difficulty in arranging for what Timothy called the 'horse-boxes'. Where were all the Herries to be put? Fell House itself would have to entertain for the night--Veronica, Captain Forster, Amabel, Lady Herries, Adam, Margaret, Ellis and Vanessa. Quite a problem! Jane and Amabel must share, Margaret and Vanessa; Forster, Ellis and Adam would have to take one of the big attic rooms. The Witherings, who would drive over, could put up Garth, Sylvia and Amery, old friends of theirs. Horace and Barney could manage in the village. Will Herries, the naval son of Rodney, his wife and sister Dora were found rooms in the Peter's House Farm. There were two distant cousins--Rose Ormerod and Sophia Fanchard--who were to stay in Bassenthwaite, and, lastly, Ruth and Richard, the grandchildren of Robert, Jennifer's brother, were young enough and lively enough not to care where they were. The two little rooms over the stables would do for them. How fortunate that Elizabeth and Benjamin were now settled at the Fortress! That left more room for everyone.

When this was all settled there arose the question of the Orders of the Day. It was decided that the procession to Judith's room with the gifts and the little speeches should take place in the morning: that would be less tiring for her. Then there should be a grand dinner at two o'clock. In the afternoon everyone should go their own sweet way, and in the evening there was to be a Ball to which everyone of any importance in the neighbourhood was to be invited.

This all settled, two great questions remained--one, the state of the weather, and two, the state of Judith's health. Were it to pour all day--to come down a regular 'posh' as so easily it might-- why, then we must all put up with it, smile, and say that we liked rain rather than not. Nevertheless, it would be provoking. All the afternoon the house would be unpleasantly crowded, for these Southerners were not accustomed to Cumberland rain and had not acquired the good Cumberland habit of going out in all weathers. Tempers would be strained and it would be annoying to overhear, as one undoubtedly would: 'Of course in the Lakes it always rains.' . . . 'My dear, what do you suppose you came for? Here it never STOPS raining.'

The other question--of Judith's health--was the most serious of all. Of late she had had her bad days: how at her age could you not expect it? She was often dreamy, far away, lost in some other world. Sometimes she was cross and peevish when her digestion worried her. Sometimes she was very deaf and could hear nothing, although Dorothy always declared that she could hear perfectly and affected this deafness simply to give herself a rest. But her heart was her real trouble: any excitement was bad for her, but how could she enjoy her Hundredth Birthday WITHOUT excitement?

And to make everything worse, she insisted upon taking the greatest personal interest in everything. She wanted to know exactly who was coming, WHERE everyone was staying, what everyone would do. Her brain was often of an astonishing clarity. 'My dear, don't be a fool,' she would say to Dorothy. 'Of course, the Herries woman must have a room to herself.' Or 'Dora? That's Rodney's girl. I remember. Her brother was at the opening of the Exhibition. In the Navy. A prig.'

It was a delight to her that Adam, Margaret and Vanessa were to sleep at Fell House. It was a long time since they had done so. It became clear, as the day approached, that almost all her anticipation was centred round Adam. It was HIS coming, that HE should be present at her Hundredth Birthday, that gave her the keenest pleasure. Had she had the strength she would have gone herself to see the attic where they were putting Adam and Forster.

'Is the wardrobe large enough? Adam is very untidy, you know, Jane. He throws his clothes all about. Is there a nice cheval glass?'

But of course she could not move farther than to the armchair by the fire. If she had one of her bad days she must not leave her bed and they must make their speeches as quickly as possible.

But on the great morning of the Twenty-Eighth all was well. It was neither a good day nor a bad day as to weather, but at least it was not raining. Clouds shaped like ram's horns twisted above the hills, whiter than other grey clouds behind them. It might be that they held snow, for it was cold enough. The larch trees were pale gold--like gold beaten very thin--against a background of rolling hills, grey and thick like flannel, and from this vast sprawling bed a point on Blencathra, palely lit, stuck up like an old man's nose. Nevertheless it was not a bad day.

By nine o'clock of the morning they thronged the downstairs and passages. The Ceremony was to be at ten. All the women were in their loveliest dresses, and there was no question but that Veronica outshone them all. Matrimony had improved her. She knew-- and dear Robert, her husband, knew--that she was to have a child; as yet there was no sign of this, but the knowledge of it (for now she loved her Robert dearly) gave her an added colour and excitement. Her dress, too, admirably suited her, with its corsage like a cavalryman's tunic, the draped back, the innumerable narrow flounces. At the back of her head her dark hair was piled in masses of curls, and she wore a little hat, very small indeed, pushed forward over her forehead. The colour of her dress was rose. She wore broad ribbons of rose on her hat. So she was the queen of the party, and Robert Forster was intensely proud of her. No one else was beautiful (Elizabeth had not yet arrived from the Fortress). Lady Herries was painted and affected, Sylvia's dress had too many flounces to suit her age, Dorothy, was too stout, Amabel too masculine, Jane was just a dear old maid, Rose Ormerod was a pretty little thing, Ruth Cards--grand-niece of Jennifer--was by far the most charming of the younger ones. She had a slight

slender figure like a boy's, and the skirts of her jacket, projecting over her bustle, made her look like a boy in fancy dress. She and her brother Richard were rather new events in the life of the Herries. No one had seen them before. They won approval.

Of the men it may be said that Timothy was the most impressive, for he was host; he was large, stout and jolly, and he was but recently engaged to that stiff, haughty-looking girl in a purple dress, Violet Greenacre. He was of the type that the Herries admired, for he looked as though he would stand no nonsense and would live for ever. Barney was in splendid form, laughing with everyone. The Herries liked him because, although he WAS an author, he did not, thank God, look like one! Ellis was grave, dignified and, as usual, alone. They thought him haughty, stuck-up, and did not know that he, in his heart, was longing to be jolly, genial, generous as Timothy was, but didn't in the least know how.

And what of Judith upstairs?

She did not know, she told Jane, whether she had had a good night or no. She THOUGHT that she had slept well, but she could not in fact be certain because it was hard to tell when she was sleeping or when she wasn't.

She was, however, very cheerful, drank her tea and enjoyed her egg. OF COURSE she would get up! She had, it soon appeared, thought out everything. The armchair was to be just here, near the fire but not too near, the small table at her side for her silver spectacle-case, her needle-case, a spare handkerchief and a silver-topped bottle of smelling-salts. She knew the Ceremony was to be at ten o'clock and she was glad that it would be early, because then 'she could have a nice time after talking to one and another'. Dressed, in her chair, she seemed, thought Jane, very small and very beautiful. Judith had never been beautiful, but it may be true to say that she approached more nearly to beauty on this her Hundredth Birthday than ever she had done before.

Her white lace cap had the brilliance of a jewel, the soft folds of her black silk dress shone in the firelight, her cane was at her hand, and on her black shoes were the diamond buckles that she wore only on very great occasions. The white lace at her wrists emphasized the fragility of her hands. Her only ring was the plain gold one that Georges had given her. Around her neck was the long thin gold chain that ended with a small gold watch in a pocket at her waist.

But it was her snow-white hair (once so brilliantly flaming) and the small face crowned by it that caught any observer's attention. That small face was wrinkled across the forehead and at the corners of the eyes and was pale ivory in colour--yet its outlines were as firm as ever they had been. The mouth had not the weak indecision of the mouths of so many old people. The lips were firm, now parting in a smile, now ironic, now commanding and sometimes bitter, for all old ladies are bitter sometimes. The eyes, though, were never bitter.

Their light was astonishingly bright for so long a history, shining, penetrating, merry, questioning and, above all, loving: never weak nor sentimental unless she suffered unexpectedly some childish disappointment, when she could look like a little girl not out of the nursery.

It would be idle to pretend that she was not feeling the fullest satisfaction in this her great day. What is more, she felt that she deserved every bit of it. Very few people lived to be a Hundred and it needed a lot of doing! She was proud of herself and proud of England. She had been thinking a great deal about England during this last year, not with any weak sentiment nor any boastful patriotism. She thought, it is true, of the Queen because she was another woman like herself and had suffered a bereavement just as she once had, but she did not otherwise think of any special events or persons--neither of Mr Gladstone nor of Mr Disraeli, nor of Oxford undergraduates breaking stones in the road for Mr Ruskin, nor of Cardinal Manning advising the Irish working-man to be temperate, nor of the Monday Pops, nor of the famous new Ladies' Golf Club at Westward Ho, nor of the great bicycling race from Bath to London. Even in the mornings now when Jane read her the newspaper she did not listen very much and often fell asleep.

The England that preoccupied her now was her own personal England which seemed, when she looked at it, to spread all about her, a bright, coloured, lovely country, infinitely gentle and infinitely kind. The England of the wild life at Stone Ends, of Uncle Tom Gauntry and Emma Furze, of the fireworks at the Lake's edge, of that moment in the hall at Stone Ends when Georges had proposed to her, of mornings and evenings and nights at Watendlath with the Tarn black under the hill, the fresh smell of the new bracken, the early-morning calling of the cows, the sight of Georges coming up the path with the crimson bird in the cage, Braund Fell and Armboth, Rosthwaite and Stockley Bridge. The England of London, of the cobbles and the sedan chairs, the Ball at poor Christabel's, Mrs Ponder and the Southey's and Jennifer, the hour at Rosthwaite with Warren. The England (her happiest England of all) of Watendlath and young Adam and Charlie (dying so foolishly after of a little silly chill), of Adam above Hawkshead laughing at Walter, running up the hill with her to see the sun rise . . .

And later than that England did not seem to go. After that many things had happened to England, she supposed, and Adam had grown, married, and had a child; the hills, her beloved hills, had darkened and been lit again by the sun, had taken on every colour and been blinded by the rain--but in this later England movement had ceased. Someone called Judith had lived there, but the real Judith by then had slipped away. And yet the real Judith was still here and Adam was here. He was coming this very morning to see her have her Hundredth Birthday. She had every reason to be happy.

She smiled at Jane, who was seeing that everything in the room was right.

'I think England is very nice, dear,' Judith said.

'What, darling?' said Jane, who thought that she had not heard aright, but that Judith had been talking about her breakfast.

But Judith did not bother to repeat. However, she said something else.

'Will Walter be coming?' she asked.

Jane was startled. 'Oh no, dear. Poor Walter is much too feeble. But Elizabeth and Benjie are coming, of course.'

'Walter!' thought Jane; 'what an idea!' He was now quite a foolish, brainless old man, and although Elizabeth had done wonders so that the Fortress was now clean and alive and wholesome again, the thought of Walter coming into the middle of this happy Birthday was most distressing.

'That's a pity,' said Judith.

'What, dear?' asked Jane, who was busy all over the room, as she loved to be, dealing with trifles.

'I said "That's a pity,"' said Judith. 'You are growing a little deaf, Jane dear. I've noticed it before.'

Jane said nothing.

'It's a pity, because Walter and I once had a quarrel and I should like to tell him that it's ended.'

'He knows that,' said Jane. 'The last time you ever went out you drove up to the Fortress and made it up. Don't you remember?'

'Of course I remember. But today would be a nice day to end it all up--a very nice day. Is Adam come yet?'

She had asked that already fifty times. Jane went to the window.

'Why, yes. There he is now. Driving up.'

Judith smiled.

'Very good. I'm very glad.'

Meanwhile downstairs, Adam, Margaret and Vanessa had arrived and mingled with the family. Vanessa's beauty startled everyone. Many of them had never seen her, and for others she had been still a child. Now, although she was only fifteen, her slender height, her rich colouring, her black ringleted hair behind her little dark blue hat, her girl's dress with the white flounces, the bustle only just pronounced enough to give her waist its perfect shape, her modesty and quietness mingled with the evidence, almost impossible to control, of tremendous happiness and high spirits, created a great impression.

'That's a stunning girl!' said Captain Will to his sister Dora. 'She's Madame's grand-daughter, you know. Yes, her mother's a German. Her father married a German. That's him--that brown-faced bearded fellow over there. Writes fairy stories, books for boys-- that sort of thing.'

Adam and Barney were delighted to see one another.

'I say!' cried Barney, 'that girl of yours is growing into a Beauty. 'Pon my word, she is! Regular Beauty!'

Adam laughed, pleased and proud.

'She's as good as she's beautiful, my boy.'

'Not TOO good, I hope,' said Barney. 'Don't like 'em too good, you know.'

But it was Ellis who was stricken as though by lightning. Standing by himself, near the staircase, hating it all, wishing it over, wishing that his mother would not make a fool of herself, intensely proud at the same time, saying to himself: 'You couldn't find such a set of people in the whole of England,' proud of his relations and despising them, longing to be friends with them all, hating it if any of them came up to speak to him; it was Ellis who, seeing Vanessa for the first time in his life, as she waited a little shyly behind her father, just out of the crowd, received a blow at the heart from which all his life he was never to recover. It was not that he fell in love with her at first sight; it was, more simply, that he had never known what life was before, that he moved, at the instant, into a new world of colour, light, sound. He stood there, staring. He gazed and gazed. He did not know who she might be. He turned and found Garth, already a little gay with morning brandy, at his side.

Tell me, Garth, who is that?'

'Who is what, my boy?' said Garth, who had already borrowed a considerable amount of money from Ellis and intended to borrow a lot more.

'Why, there--over there! That young girl with the black hair--in the blue hat.'

Garth followed his directing hand.

'Oh, that! Why, she's Adam Paris' daughter, the old lady's grand- daughter . . . Damn' pretty child, if you ask me.'

Ellis said no more. He stood back against the wall, gazing.

There then occurred the great sensation of the day. The clocks pointed to twenty minutes to ten, and the party from the Fortress had not yet arrived.

Dorothy was distressed, anxious. She moved about like a great green whale, saying to everyone: 'Very strange! Elizabeth is so punctual! I hope that nothing has occurred. Very strange indeed! I hope that Walter has not died, this morning of all times!'

There was a stir by the door. They HAD arrived. All was well. Dorothy hurried forward. The door opened and Elizabeth, bringing the cold November air in a gust with her, came in. Leaning on her arm, looking about him in an interested but rather aimless fashion, was her father, Walter Herries.

Walter Herries! The news went round the company in a flash. Walter Herries, who was, they all supposed, a doddering old idiot whom Elizabeth had splendidly rescued from destruction and was now nobly devoting her remaining years to succouring! Walter Herries, once the villain of the Herries piece, now a harmless old imbecile-- actually he had come to Judith's Birthday!

It was a real sensation that gave way presently to a grave and general satisfaction. This was well. This was indeed most fitting! The Feud that had distressed for so long all the Herries, that had had its climax in a terrible tragedy, was now, on this splendid occasion, to be finally closed. This was Elizabeth's doing, Elizabeth who had suffered more deeply from that Feud than any other. Could anything be more proper? Soon everyone was delighted. A chair was found for Walter in the parlour and down on it he sat, looking kindly about him, smiling, seeming quite happy, yet plainly without any idea as to where he was.

'Elizabeth's smartened him up!' said Lady Herries to Amery. He looked indeed quite elegant with his snow-white beard, a handsome blue frock-coat and a dark blue neckerchief.

And that brown-faced, healthy-looking young man with the bright blue eyes was Benjamin, Elizabeth's boy. Yes, the son of poor John . . . A bit of a rascal . . . He had left Rugby now and was looking after his grandfather's land, or SHOULD be . . . But they said he couldn't stick to anything, was a great anxiety to his mother. Yes, he was eighteen or nineteen, just kicking his heels . . .

Benjamin himself heard none of these whispers nor would he have cared if he HAD heard. He was enjoying himself outrageously as he always did enjoy everything. Where was Vanessa? His first thought was for Vanessa. What a rum lot of old codgers these relations were! How ridiculous old Lady Herries in her paint and powder! Garth he could see had already been at the bottle. By Jove, was not Veronica a picture? THERE was a woman! Beautiful figure and what a pair of eyes! What fun bringing Grandfather into the middle of all this! It had been the old man's own idea. In a lucid interval he had grasped that Judith was having a grand birthday. He had hunted round and found a brooch that had belonged to his wife, a pretty little gold thing with three pearls and a ruby. He would give her that and he would present it himself. He explained to Elizabeth that he and Judith had not been the best of friends-- but that was all over now, quite finished. Much too sensible a woman to cherish a grudge. And his excitement had been tremendous. He had got out of bed himself at about four that morning to find a box to put the pearls in. He sat in the parlour now, clutching the box in his hand, patiently waiting until he should offer it. Rum old boy, thought Benjamin, rejoicing in his own youth and strength; but he rather liked him. He was just like a child, and Benjie played draughts with him most evenings. Not that the old boy could play.

He just moved the counters about, but it gave him pleasure. And there the old man sat, clutching his parcel.

However, Benjie had not come there to look at his grandfather. He moved about looking for Vanessa. And then, of course, he knocked against Ellis, the last man in the world he wanted to see.

He had encountered Ellis only briefly since that rowdy night in London four years ago. He was aware, without any question, that that evening had made a breach between himself and Ellis. Not that they were ever the kind to get on well together, Ellis so solemn and proper, and himself--well, NOT so solemn and proper! But he could not know with what profound distaste Ellis now regarded him nor the deep shudder of disapproval with which Ellis had seen Walter's entrance. What did they want to bring that old man for? He had a wild fantastic notion that it had been done in some way to insult himself. As with all egoists and men unsure of themselves, like all men sensitive to an unpopularity that they would give their lives to alter, most things in life seemed to Ellis to be directed against himself. This doddering, wandering old man was his brother! Did they not know that? Well, then . . .

It would be, he suddenly thought, just like young Benjamin to have arranged this--maliciously, simply to distress him. Ever since that night at the 'Paragon', Ellis had thought of Benjamin as wild, malicious, reckless--all the things that he hated!

'Hullo, Ellis!' said Benjamin.

They made a strange contrast, Ellis, long-nosed, pale-faced, grave, in his official dark clothes; Benjie, snub-nosed, brown-faced, in a long brown sack-coat and a dark red tie caught with a gold ring.

'How do you do, Benjamin?' said Ellis, offering his hand.

'Have a good journey up?'

'So-so. Cold, you know.'

'Yes, I suppose. Well, we'll be moving up to the old lady shortly. Quite a gathering of the clans, ain't it?'

'Quite,' said Ellis.

Benjie moved off. He had no intention of wasting his precious life over Ellis!

WHERE was Vanessa? He tumbled into Adam. Dear old Adam, the man he liked best in the world and Vanessa's father!

'Why, Adam! Isn't this grand? I say, where's Vanessa?'

'Somewhere,' said Adam, who was rejoicing in every minute of this great day that was to do his mother honour. 'How are you, young Benjie?'

'So-so,' said Benjie, dropping his voice and grasping Adam's arm. 'I say, this sort of thing makes a fellow restless. Ever feel restless?'

'Sometimes,' said Adam.

'Well, I feel restless up at the Fortress. If it weren't for mother I wouldn't stay.'

'Why, where would you go to?'

'I don't know. The sea perhaps. Or America.'

'Take my advice,' said Adam, 'and stay at home. There's no place like home.'

'You didn't always think so?'

'No.'

'Nor do I. When I'm your age, Adam, I'll settle, but as it is--'

He went off, laughing, poking Barney in the ribs, bowing ceremoniously to Lady Herries whom he detested, seeing little Ruth Cards for the first time in his life and thinking. That's a pretty girl. I wonder if she'd mind being kissed.' He did in fact kiss someone a moment later, for he wandered through the green-baize door at the back of the hall and there, in the passage leading to the kitchens, was Hannah, carrying a tray.

'Why, Hannah!' he cried.

'Master Benjie!' She smiled. They all adored him.

'Here, give me a kiss! No, there isn't a moment to lose! Here, I'll hold the tray!'

'No, Master Benjie, you're not to!'

But he put his arms round her, held her close to him, kissed her full on the lips. Then, laughing, ran off.

But where, oh, where was Vanessa?

All the clocks struck ten. Everyone began to move upstairs. There had been a change in the arrangements. A very handsome volume in blue leather and gold had been provided, and in it every member of the Herries family who could be found had signed his or her name, agreeing that they from the bottom of their hearts congratulated Judith on her Hundredth Birthday and wished her health and prosperity.

It had been Barney's idea, a very pretty one. It had been intended that Adam should present this, but after Walter's unexpected arrival it had been thought that it would be excellent if Walter, the senior of them all, should make the Presentation. At first there had been some difficulty. He wanted to give his OWN present. He had come all that way to give his OWN present . . .

'But so you shall, dear,' Elizabeth whispered. 'You shall give them both. Only this is from all of us and the other is your special one . . .'

But he wanted to give his OWN present! However, at last he had consented to hold the blue leather book in one hand and his own precious little box in the other. Elizabeth guiding him, they headed the Procession up the stairs.

And up the stairs they all crowded, laughing, joking, excited, feeling that this was really a GREAT Herries occasion, that, as it were, the eyes of all England were upon them.

On the way up Barney said one thing to Amery in a chuckling whisper:

'Very fitting, you know, old Walter making the Presentation. Closes the Feud. He and Judith were enemies for years. That's the end of THAT!'

At the same moment Benjie caught sight of Vanessa just ahead of him. He brushed forward, almost, in his haste, knocking someone over. He did not know (nor would he have cared if he HAD known) that that someone was Ellis.

'I say! Vanessa! Vanessa! Where HAVE you been?'

She turned. She was a stair or two higher. Her face was lit with delight as she turned her head and saw him.

'Oh, Benjie! I've been looking for you everywhere!'

Ellis stared at her. The staircase seemed to rock beneath him.

'Hush!' Timothy said. 'We go in now, three at a time. Sir Walter, you're first. Thank you. Elizabeth, if you wouldn't mind!'

Judith sat looking at the door, Jane standing beside the chair. She was quite calm, very dignified, extremely proud and happy.

The door opened and Walter entered, led forward by Elizabeth.

Jane gasped.

'Oh, Aunt Judith--it's Walter Herries!'

But to Judith it seemed perfectly natural.

'There, Jane, I said he would come. How extremely attentive of him!'

Walter had no idea of anything save that it was Judith's birthday and he was giving her a present. But he realized, as he wandered, gazing about him, across the floor, that that was Judith sitting in the chair. He knew Judith well enough. He had known her all his life. But why was he in a bedroom? He stopped, midway, and looked at the bed.

'Walter,' said Judith, smiling. 'How are you?'

That brought him to himself. This was, in any case, Judith, and this was her birthday. He found himself by the chair. Elizabeth was beside him.

'Well, Judith,' he said, his eyes still roving about the room. 'They tell me it's your birthday, so I've come and I've brought you a present.'

He pushed the little parcel into her lap and dropped the blue book. Elizabeth picked it up and put it into his hand again.

'Father, dear. You know what you are to say. You are to give Aunt Judith this. It's from all of us, and you are to say that all our names are here and that we all wish her a lovely birthday and many more birthdays.'

'A lovely birthday and many more birthdays,' said Walter, dropping the volume into her lap. Then, quite of his own accord, he bent forward and kissed her. Elizabeth had to steady him because his knees were very shaky.

Judith was delighted and greatly touched. She took her handkerchief from the table and wiped her eyes.

'Thank you indeed, Walter. Thank you, thank you. I am very glad you have come, because once we were not friends, were we? And now we are. I want to be friends with everyone today. And most especially with you, Walter.'

Walter began eagerly: 'And you must open MY present, Judith.'

With very firm fingers Judith undid the parcel.

'Oh, isn't that pretty? ISN'T that pretty? Do you see it, Jane? A lovely brooch! Walter, how VERY good of you--'

'Yes,' he said, immensely satisfied. 'It's a very pretty thing. I've had it a long time . . .' His eyes began to wander. 'Uhland would have come today, only--only--I don't know why--but--'

Elizabeth gently took his arm.

'Now, Father, you must make way for the others.' She led him to the window.

And Judith, now with her eyes bright and eager, was staring at the door. The great moment of her life had come. Adam would be next. Surely, surely Adam MUST be next!

She saw that they had all crowded to the door, and, all their faces smiling, were staring in.

A figure detached itself from the crowd. Grinning all over his face, moving his heavy body in his own rambling, comfortable way, Adam came forward.

At the sight of her son Judith's eyes and mouth broke into the loveliest smile that any member of the Herries family, here present, had ever seen.

NOW her Hundredth Birthday was indeed a Triumph!

THE END

VANESSA

FOR ERIK PALMSTIERNA
IN FRIENDSHIP

A Prefatory Letter

My dear Erik,

I take the greatest pleasure in dedicating this final novel in the Herries series to yourself because during those last years our friendship has been one of the best things I possess.

With that pleasure I must contrast a very real sense of loss. I am, as I write the last lines of Vanessa, saying goodbye to work that has been, for the last six years, my constant preoccupation. It cannot interest my readers that Judith, Benjie, Vanessa and the others have appeared to me such real and constant friends, but now, as they vanish down the wind, I feel a true and personal loneliness.

But I should like to thank those readers who have also found them friends, and to urge upon one or two critics that long novels are no new thing, and have been always in the tradition of the English novel.

Yet more boldly I would say that in this present case these four Herries novels are intended to be read as one novel, and I hope that some day there will be a reader who will both live long enough and be idle enough to read them so? But one ambition of mine is realized. Some of those who love and know Cumberland have found in these pages a tribute to that country which has pleased them.

Affectionately,
Hugh Walpole

'Therefore, like as May month flowereth and flourisheth in many gardens, so in like wise let every man of worship flourish his heart in this world, first unto God, and next unto the joy of them that he promised his faith unto; for there was never worshipful man nor worshipful woman, but they loved one better than another: and worship in arms may never be foiled, but first reserve the honour to God, and secondly the quarrel must come of thy lady: and such love I call virtuous love.'

Sir Thomas Malory

Part One

The Rascal

At the sight of her son Judith's eyes and mouth broke into the loveliest smile that any member of the Herries family, there present, had ever seen. It was Judith Paris' hundredth birthday. The Family was making a Presentation.

Adam bent down and kissed her. Her tiny, trembling hand rested on the velvet collar of his coat then lay against his cheek. Her triumph was complete; her exceeding happiness overflowed so that, laughing though she was, tears rolled down her cheeks.

Afterwards, at the luncheon downstairs, Adam was to make the speech, but when the time came, the one that he made was very feeble. Everyone (except of course Adam's wife, Margaret, and Adam's young daughter, Vanessa) agreed that he was no speaker; the speech of the occasion came, oddly enough, from Amery Herries, of whom no one had expected very much. There were more speeches at the dinner later in the day--Timothy, Barney Newmark, Carey Rockage, Captain Will Herries, all spoke--but it was Amery who was afterwards recalled.

'Damned good speech, d'you remember?' years later one Herries would say to another. 'At old Madame's Hundredth Birthday party up in Cumberland . . . Best speech ever I heard in my life.'

Adam was a failure. He never could say anything in public, even long ago in his Chartist days. More than that, he was thinking of his mother, the old lady upstairs, all the time. And more than that again, he couldn't sound the right Herries note. He was only QUARTER Herries anyway, and he simply wasn't able

to think of them in the grand historical light that all the family, expectant round the luncheon table, desired.

But Amery could. He thought of them all (including himself) in precisely the grand manner.

All Adam said was:

'I am sure we are all very happy to be here today for my mother's hundredth birthday. You'll forgive me, I know, if I don't say very much. Not very good at expressing my feelings. Yes--well--I know what you're all feeling. We're all very proud of my mother and we all ought to be. She's like the Queen--nothing can beat her. I don't need to tell you how good she is. Of course I know that better than the rest of you--naturally I would. There's no one like her anywhere. I ask you all to drink her health.'

And so they did--with the greatest enthusiasm. Nevertheless there was a feeling of disappointment, for he had said nothing about the Family--not a word. It was expected of him. After all, even though he WAS illegitimate, his father had been of Herries blood. They knew, they had always known, that Adam Paris failed at anything that he tried. What could you expect of a fellow who had once been a Chartist and approved of these Trades Unions, was always on the wrong side, against Disraeli, in favour of tiresome agitators like Mr Plimsoll? (They disliked any and every agitator. They disapproved of agitation.)

But Amery made everything right again with HIS speech. He didn't look his sixty-five years, so spare of figure and straight in the back; he had not run to seed like poor Garth, who led, it was feared, a most improvident and dissolute life. Amery's speech was short but entirely to the point:

'Only a word. I won't take more than a minute. But I do want to say that my friend Adam is quite right--this IS a great occasion for all of us! There is not, I venture to say, another family in England with so remarkable a lady at the head of it as Madame whom we are gathered together to honour. It is not only that she has reached her hundredth year--although that is an achievement in itself--but that she has reached it with such vigour, such health, such courage! It is interesting to remember that nearly a hundred and fifty years ago her father, as a young man, rode pack-horse into this district, a stranger and almost you might say homeless. There were, I suppose, members of our family scattered about England at that time, but no one, I fear, had ever heard of any of them. Now, sitting round this table today we have one of England's most famous novelists-- spare your blushes, Barney Newmark--the widow of one of England's most prominent financiers--I bow to you, Lady Herries--whose son is following worthily in his father's footsteps--I drink to the City, Ellis--the son of one of England's leading Divines, the gallant Captain here--one of the most active members, I'm told, of the House of Peers--never been there myself, but that's what they tell me, Carey, my son--and one of the loveli-est women in the whole of England, Mrs Robert Forster--I bow towards you, Veronica!

'I promised that I would be short, so I will not point out to you how unusual a family ours is. You know it already.' (Loud and happily complacent laugh-ter.) 'We ARE a remarkable family. Why should we not say so? We have done, we are doing something for England. England, glorious England, Mistress of the World as she deserves to be.' (He was going on to say something about foreigners but remembered just in time that Madame's husband had been a Frenchman and that Adam had married a German.) 'So here's to Madame and here's to England and here's to the Herries family! May they all three live, prosper, and help the world along the way that it should go!'

What cheers, what enthusiasm, what excitement! He had said exactly what they were all longing for someone to say--the one thing needed to make the day a perfect success!

Judith's granddaughter, Adam's daughter, little Vanessa Paris, aged fifteen, sat between her mother and father and was so happily excited that she found it diffi-cult to keep still. Some of the ladies thought that it was not quite correct that she should be there. In 1874 the golden rule was that children should be seen (at inter-vals) and never heard. She was Madame's granddaughter and it was proper that she should have been present at the moving ceremony when the presen-tation was made to the old lady, but the right thing then was for her mother to send her back to Cat Bells where she lived. Nevertheless Lady Herries agreed with Emily Newmark that the child was tall for her age, was cer-tainly pretty in her blue dress, and behaved with decorum. 'It's only to be hoped,' Lady Herries said with foreboding, 'that indulgence like this won't spoil her.

But what can you expect? Her mother's a German. Adam Paris can have no idea of how to bring up a child. I never allowed,' Lady Herries added, 'Ellis any liberties, and no mother could wish for a more perfect son.'

Vanessa, of course, neither knew nor cared what anyone was saying. She trusted the whole world and everything and everyone in it. She loved everybody and especially her mother, her father, her grandmother, Aunt Jane Bellairs, Benjamin, Will Leathwaite (how she wished that he was here and could see all that was going on! She was storing everything up to tell him when she was home again).

From where she sat she could watch everything that Benjamin did and said. For the rest she was sharply observant. She noticed the large and very hideous yel-low brooch that Lady Herries wore on her meagre bosom, the beautiful colour of Aunt Elizabeth's hair (many of the ladies were her aunts, although not strictly so in chronology), the way that fat Garth Herries swal-lowed his wine and smacked his lips at intervals, the funny way that Aunt Jane (who had just come down from upstairs and reported that Madame was doing SPLENDIDLY--not the LEAST tired by all the fuss) made little pellets of her bread, Aunt Amabel's suspi-cious manner of eating as though she suspected poison in every mouthful, and the shy frightened air of Ellis. (She supposed that THAT was because his mother was watching him!)

Of them all there were two who especially inter-ested her. One was Benjamin, whom she loved with all her heart, and the other was a lady whose name she did not know, whom she had never seen before, who ap-peared to her the perfection of grace and beauty.

First Benjamin, whom she knew so well that he was like part of herself. She had loved him from the first moment of seeing him when, himself between six and seven, and she somewhere about two, he had made her first sticky and afterward sick with toffee that he had made against orders at the kitchen fire. Her first mem-ory of him was connected with disobedience; so she had known him ever after, always against the law, always doing things of which she shouldn't approve, but she kept sacred to the death every secret confided to her. She would never betray him; she would always love him for ever and ever. It was as simple as that. She knew with that intuitive quickness given to children that her mother did not approve of him. She knew more--that no one approved of him. He lived up at the Fortress with his mother, the lovely Elizabeth, and his grandfa-ther, old broken-down Sir Walter, and it was supposed that Benjamin looked after the estate. In a way, as Vanessa knew, he did. In his own way. He would work like a saint and a hero for a week, really work and with good solid common sense. Then he would have a mad spell, disappear for days to the sorrow and grief of his mama. He told Vanessa that he simply couldn't help it. 'Must breathe fresh air,' he said. He never told anyone where he went. He was already, as Vanessa knew, 'suspect' by the Family. He had been a failure at Rugby: there were stories of scandalous doings in Town. 'He's going to be no good.' 'The makings of a fine Rascal,' and, as always with the Herries family when speaking of someone of whom they disapproved, their voices took on a sort of ceremonial ring, a kind of chanting sound. 'But what can you expect? His grandfather shot himself, and his uncle murdered his father. What an inheritance! And look at his other grandfather!-- up at the Fortress-- what a life he's led! Nothing better now than an idiot!'

No, poor Benjie has no chance at all, they decide with satisfaction. Nevertheless they could not help but like him--when they were with him. Of course it was different when their backs were turned. But in his company it was difficult not to smile. He was so merry, so gay, always laughing. So generous too. 'No one's enemy but his own,' Barney Newmark, who liked him greatly, said-- and poor old Garth Herries, who had been no one's enemy but his own to such an extent that he was a complete wreck and ruin, sighed sadly in reply.

Vanessa was aware of much of this, although no one had ever told her. She was always hot in Benjie's defence, no matter what the charge might be. When someone accused him it was as though she herself were accused; she was conscious at such times of a strange pain in her heart--a feeling of tenderness, sympathy, and apprehension. Now, as she looked across the table at him, she knew that he had no need of her sympathy. He was at his very gayest. He was not large--he would be rather a small man--but his shoulders were broad, his head round, bullet-shaped, his colour red and brown like a healthy pippin, his nose snub, his blue eyes bright and sparkling. If all the Herries were like horses, as someone had said, then Benjie was like a racy little pony, ready for anything and especially mischief. 'He's wild and, I'm sure, wicked. In fact I KNOW he's wicked,' Lady Herries said. 'And Ellis doesn't like him at all. But what can you expect with such a family history?' Then dropping her voice and looking into Emily Newmark's eyes with that intimate confidence felt by one upright woman for another: 'Women! Of course--I hear that already . . .'

Nevertheless he was happy, he loved his beautiful mother, he feared no man, he was generous, almost everything--even the tiniest things-- gave him pleasure. What if he did find women enchanting, forgot to pay his debts, possessed no sense of class at all so that a tramp was exactly the same to him as a Herries, found it difficult to work at a thing for more than a week at a time, took no thought for the morrow, saw a joke in everything?--there he was, enjoying life to the uttermost, which was more than could be said for some of the other Herries seated round the table.

As to the very beautiful lady whom Vanessa so greatly admired, her name was Rose Ormerod.

After the luncheon Vanessa flung her arms round her father and kissed him.

'Happy, my darling?'

'Oh yes. Oh yes, I've never been so happy--'

'That's right. I didn't make much of a speech, did I, my pet?'

'Oh yes, Papa! It was much better than the other one because you were thinking of Grandmamma.'

'Thank you, darling. So I was. But I'm not good at speeches. That's a fact.' She laid her cheek against his. Then, remembering, straightened up.

'Papa, may I go for a walk with Benjie? He's asked me to.'

Adam hesitated. Then, taking her small white hand between his, he said:

'All right.'

He could trust her with Benjamin. And yet--

She clapped her hands and ran off, crying: 'Yes, Benjie, I can. Papa says I can.' She ran into Ellis Herries and looked up laughing. 'I beg your pardon.' She put her hand for a moment on his sleeve.

His thin anxious face looked down at her.

'My fault, I'm sure. It's--it's a nice day, isn't it?'

'Yes, it is.' She stood there, waiting, but longing to get off to Benjie. It was good manners, though, if a gentleman wished to talk to you, to wait while he did so.

Ellis Herries was tall, thin and pale. She noticed that he had a little brown mole in the middle of his left cheek.

'A very happy party we're having,' he said in his stiff anxious voice. He always spoke as though he were afraid that the words he used would betray him, laugh at him behind his back, as it were.

'Oh, it IS nice!' She smiled, felt that she had done her duty, and ran off.

When they walked out on to the road they saw that they had but an hour before dark. Frost was sharpening the air. They mounted straight on to the moor and moved swiftly through a moth-grey world where mountains were gigantic and the turf was crisping under their feet. The house stood behind them like a lighted ship. The candles were burning in every room. Vanessa had sometimes to run to keep up with Benjamin, but in any case she ran because she was so happy, deeply excited and enchanted to be alone with him. Soon they slowed down, stood on a hillock and looked over to Scotland.

'There's Criffel,' he said, pointing.

'I can't see it,' Vanessa said.

'No, but it's there all the same.' He took her hand. 'I approve of you in that fine hat. Where did you find the feather?'

'Mama bought the hat in Keswick.'

He stood close to her.

'You are almost as tall as I am, Vanessa. You are going to be very tall.'

'Papa says I am. Will you never be taller, Benjie?'

'No, I hope not. You see, it's very useful to be short.'

'Useful?'

'Yes--if there's a row you can crawl under tables or hide behind a curtain or creep into the clock. I remember once in London--' He stopped.

Vanessa's innocence must be protected.

'Oh, do tell me about London!'

'One day, when you've been there. It wouldn't mean anything to you if you don't know the places.'

They walked on. They were both strong, sturdy, filled with health and excitement.

Benjamin flung out his arms.

'Don't you love this country? But of course you do. We belong to it. There'll never be any other country for either of us. Your father once told me that when he was a boy he had a tutor called Rackstraw who knew more about this country than anyone. He said it was all stones and clouds. One stone wall running up a hill, one sky with the clouds pouring over it, and you're happy. It's so old. There are Romans' bones under your foot. It's so strong-- Border fights and Picts and Scots. It's so wide and smells so good. Don't you like the smell of dry bracken, of the trees, of the stream water when you lie flat and drink it? Which hill do you like best?'

'Cat Bells,' said Vanessa promptly.

'Oh, I mean a real hill. Skiddaw has wings, Saddleback's like a shark, Gable is a helmet . . .' He stopped suddenly, put his arms round her and kissed her. 'Oh, Vanessa, I do love you!'

'And I love you,' she said, a little breathless.

'Will you marry me when you grow up?'

'Of course I will,' she said, laughing.

They walked on, more slowly, he keeping his arm around her.

'Well, you'd better not. Everyone disapproves of me.'

'What does that matter?'

Her trust touched him most deeply.

'Would you marry me if your father and mother forbade it?'

That was an awful question. She stopped to consider it.

'Yes,' she said.

'Oh, you darling! But I won't allow you to marry me. Ask anyone. No woman ought to marry me. I couldn't be faithful.'

'You would be,' said Vanessa, 'if we had children.'

'Will you like to have children?' he asked her, wondering what she would say.

'Of course. But you can't help it. God brings you a baby. You wake up in the morning and find it lying there beside you. That must be wonderful. Mama says that God knows just when you want one.'

'So you believe in God?'

Vanessa laughed. 'Why, of course. What a silly question, Benjie! Everybody does.'

'Everybody doesn't--' He pulled up. He must not disturb her.

'Of course everyone does!' she answered indignantly. 'Why, who made everything if God didn't? God's everywhere. Will Leathwaite says that when he has been swearing too much God gives him the rheumatism just to remind him.'

Benjie thought some other topic wiser.

'Well--but if I was in disgrace with everyone, had done something shameful and no one would speak to me, would you still marry me?'

'Of course I would.'

'But if you yourself thought it shameful?'

'I shouldn't think anything YOU did shameful,' she answered.

'If I killed someone as my uncle killed my father?'

She stood, puzzled, staring into the grey cold landscape.

'Yes,' she said, nodding her head. 'I would know why you did it. There would be some reason that I should understand.'

He caught her hands in his.

'Will you promise me that whatever happens you will always stand by me?'

'Yes, I promise.'

'Always and for ever?'

'Yes.'

'Whatever I did?'

'Yes.'

'I'll remind you of that one day.' He turned round. 'Now we'll go back to all the cats and monkeys,' he said.

They were both quiet returning. They had to go arm in arm, very close together, because it was growing dark. For a brief while there was a faint orange glow over Skiddaw like the reflection of a distant fire; the air grew with every moment more frosty.

Once as they were nearing the house he said:

'Don't you hate Ellis? I do. AND his old pig of a mother.'

In the hall, standing for a moment to accustom herself to the lights and splendour after the half-dark, Vanessa found her father. He had been standing there, waiting for her, hearing the voices and laughter all over the house, the distant click of billiard balls, someone singing to the piano sentimental songs like Drink to me only and My hero, my Troubadour, Elizabeth coming back from the Fortress where she had deposited poor old Walter, quite in pieces. She had put him to bed. He had fallen almost at once to sleep; all he had said, she told Adam, just before he went off to sleep, was: 'Wake me when Uhland comes in.' Very touching, but, as she said, a comfort for him to think that Uhland was still alive. Sometimes, Elizabeth confessed, she thought that he was and she could hear the tap-tap of his lame leg mounting to his tower . . . Then along the passage from the kitchen came bursting Barney Newmark and Garth and Timothy, stout, noisy, and triumphant. Why triumphant? Had they been kissing the maids? But the Herries men got like that very easily if things were going well and there were no ghosts about.

In the middle of all this Adam waited anxiously for his little daughter. His wife, Margaret, was sitting in the parlour trying to be on terms with Lady Herries and that fascinating Rose Ormerod from Harrogate (she wasn't beautiful, Adam decided--not to be compared with Elizabeth or Veronica--her nose was a little crooked, she had a faint, a very faint moustache on her upper lip. It was her colour, dark, black, crimson, like a gipsy: and then she was silent--she spoke very rarely, only smiled and used her eyes). Poor Margaret would not be happy in there; he knew how anxious SHE was about Vanessa! When he told her that the child had gone for a walk with Benjamin she gave a little cry of dismay.

'Oh, Adam! You should not have allowed her!'

'Pooh, my dear! Benjamin's safe!'

'No, he isn't! You know he isn't! And Vanessa's growing!'

'She is only fifteen.'

He had calmed her a little, but his own fears had increased. What was he to do about this? He knew that Vanessa loved Benjamin with all the fire, loyalty, ignorance of an adoring child. Benjamin's reputation was bad, very bad. And yet he liked him. He could not help it. He had always had a weakness for sinners . . . But Benjamin and his own child! No, no!

As the darkness strengthened about the house his alarm grew. He was about to get his coat and go after them when in they came, Vanessa glowing with colour, her eyes shining, her body so alive that it could not keep still.

He told her that she was to come up and say goodnight to her grandmother.

'We must not stay for more than a moment. She is in bed and tired, of course, after such a fatiguing day. It's something to be a hundred, you know!'

Vanessa was at once subdued and still. She lived so entirely, at present, in her interest in other people that, in a moment, she became what they wanted her to be. That is if she loved them. She was quite otherwise, it is to be feared, with one or two--Aunt Amabel, for instance, whom she couldn't abide, and Timothy's fiancée, who had aggravated her by talking to her in baby language.

Judith's bedroom seemed now a mysterious place, quite different from the bright sunlit room of the morning, crowded with happy faces, and the old lady sitting so erect in her chair, smiling as they brought her their presents.

The curtains were drawn now, the room dark save for the fire and the dim lamplight beside the bed. That old four-poster with its dark hangings appeared like a little room in itself. Aunt Jane was moving softly about.

When Adam and Vanessa appeared in the doorway she put her fingers to her lips.

She went over to the bed, leant over.

'Aunt Judith! Aunt Judith!'

'Yes, my dear,' said a very lively voice. 'What is it?'

'Adam and Vanessa are here to say goodnight.'

'Turn up the lamp.' Judith sat up, put out her hand for her spectacles, and, her eyes as sharp behind them as a bird's, said: 'That's right. Very kind of you, Adam. Come over here, my dears.'

They crossed the room, and Jane put the crimson armchair for Adam. Vanessa stood close to him, her hand on his shoulder.

The old lady seemed a little breathless. She was wearing a cap as white as snow with the sun on it, and over her shoulders Jane laid a thick white cashmere shawl. Her little face was drawn and lined, waxen in the lamplight. It was her eyes and hands that were alive, and her enchanting, humorous, slightly ironical smile.

'So I'm a hundred at last!' she said with a sigh of satisfaction. 'That's something, Adam, isn't it?'

'Indeed it is, Mother.'

'Yes, and a VERY nice day it's been.'

'You're not tired?'

'Well--a little. Yes, a little tired. My heart'--she put her hand to her breast--'jumps. There's nothing odd about that though. It's been jumping for a hundred years. It was never so steady as it ought to be.'

Vanessa smiled.

'Have you had a happy day, my darling?' She put her hand out and took Vanessa's. How hot and dry it was, Vanessa thought--burning bones under parchment, and at the touch of it the child had a moment's realization of what it was to be old, to be a hundred years old, to be burnt up with life and all the things that you had seen and done!

'It was nice,' Judith said, 'poor old Walter coming. Very nice. He's sadly broken up, I'm afraid. Sadly aged.' She spoke with tenderness, satisfaction, and triumph. She had beaten Walter at last. She was older than he and yet here she was as lively as you like and he a poor old man who had to be led about, weak in the head, uncertain where he was!

Yet she herself was suddenly weary. She lay back on her pillow, her spectacles falling to the edge of her nose.

'I hope everyone is happy,' she murmured.

'Very happy, Mother dearest,' Adam answered, catching a command from Jane's watchful eye. 'You must go to sleep now. You will be fresh as anything tomorrow.'

'Yes, dear,' Judith murmured.

Vanessa bent forward and kissed her. Then Adam, moved by the deepest emotion, tears rising to his eyes, kissed her, felt her hand lift for a moment and touch his cheek in the old familiar way.

Before they had stolen from the room she was, it seemed, asleep.

The first Ball of Vanessa's life!

Was Ball too grand a word to give to it? There was for orchestra Mrs Blader from Troutbeck at the piano; Mr Murdy of Keswick, violin; old Mr Bayliss of Keswick, 'cello. There was perhaps in all thirty couples, and the dining-room, cleared, within the hour following dinner, miraculously of its table and chairs, had a perfect floor. It had often been tested. The room looked lovely, Vanessa thought, with the gleaming, glittering candelabra, the candles in their silver candlesticks, the coloured paper streamers slung from corner to corner against the ceiling. It was colours everywhere, dresses-- pink, white, blue, orange--billowing and surging as the dancers moved, necks and shoulders bare, jewels sparkling; almost everyone to Vanessa seemed beautiful-- even old Lady Herries, although she was absurdly painted and had a neck like a writhing chicken, had diamonds in her hair that must, Vanessa thought, be worth a fortune.

Three of the women were beautiful beyond compare--Elizabeth Herries who was fifty-nine years of age but had the arms and shoulders of a girl; and Veronica, now proudly Mrs Forster, 'a queen of a woman, by Gad,' Will Herries murmured somewhat unwisely to his wife, who was a good woman but no beauty. The third was Ruth Cards, who went shortly after this to live in the wilds of Northumberland and but seldom left them.

At first Vanessa had felt a devastating shyness. At dinner she had been very quiet. She was wearing her first grand evening dress and only she and her mother knew what consultations there had been with Miss Kew of Keswick, how often they had paid visits to Miss Kew's stuffy little room near St John's, how important it had been that it should be HALF grown-up--Miss Kew had been alarmed: girls of fifteen did not go to Balls, but then of course this was a family affair, a little different . . . nevertheless, as Miss Kew confided to her brother, Mrs Paris was a German woman--'Such things might be well in Germany' just as though she had said Shanghai!

So they had planned between them something very original, the neck and shoulders bare--'Miss Vanessa has such beautiful shoulders'-- the skirt full, but not TOO full. A pale pink silk and round her slender neck her only piece of jewellery, a necklace of crystal beads that her father had brought her from London.

At dinner she was certain that they must ALL be saying: 'And what is THIS child doing here?' All day she had been so happy that she had not given herself a thought, but at dinner Garth Herries had been on the one side of her and Ellis on the other.

Rose Ormerod was Garth's other companion and very quickly he surrendered to her as apparently all men did. He did not speak to Vanessa once. And Ellis! Well, Ellis was very strange. He stared at her in the oddest way. He spoke to her confusedly as though he were afraid of her. He said: 'I hope you are enjoying yourself,' and then later: 'I do hope, most sincerely, that you are enjoying yourself.' He made her embarrassed. It was he perhaps who made her self-conscious. He looked at her shoulders and hands, and once he said, in a strangled fashion as though food were choking him 'I hope you will give me a dance.' Very bravely she asked him once whether he liked to live in London. 'Oh yes, indeed yes. Very pleasant. Lived there all my life, you know.'

She coloured; she felt that it had been a very silly question; she looked about her to find her father, but he was sitting on the same side of the table as herself.

Then, at first, no one asked her to dance. She sat on a little sofa with her mother, feeling that everyone must be looking at her bare shoulders, not very far, if the truth must be known, from tears. It had been a lovely day, but she had no right to be here. She thought that, in a little while, she would whisper something to her mother and slip away to bed . . .

It was Benjie who came to her rescue. The most beautiful waltz had just begun and he charged down upon them, had her on her feet before she knew, and then they were lost in Paradise.

She was a lovely dancer. She had danced all her life, danced up and down the parlour at Cat Bells while her father whistled the tunes, danced by the Lake in Manesty, danced in the kitchen with Will, had had dancing lessons in Keswick at Mr Kew's (brother to Miss Kew) dancing class. She was a dancer by all the light of her nature.

'That child dances well,' said Lady Herries to Rose Ormerod. 'Very pretty.'

'That child will be a beautiful woman,' said Miss Ormerod. The two were passing them at the moment. Miss Ormerod's intense gaze followed them round the room. In a second of time Vanessa's misery had been changed to timeless, priceless delight. They did not speak. Benjamin also loved dancing. He knew at once whether his partner was worthy of him. Already many a young woman had found herself, after a round or two, sitting to her own surprise on the sofa, and Benjie beside her, charming but static.

'You dance better than anyone else in the room, Vanessa.'

'Oh, do I?' Vanessa whispered. 'Oh, Benjie, do I really?'

He did not tell her that he had said that to many a partner in the past. He knew that he would say it to thousands in the future. But tonight he meant every word of it. When the dance was over and they were sitting on the stairs she confided to him how unhappy she had been at dinner.

'You will often be unhappy again,' he instructed her. 'Everyone is so. Dinners are the devil. You never know whom you will get. It's a game, you see, Vanessa, and the worse ninny you have beside you the better the game is. Flatter them. That's the way. Everyone likes to be flattered. You can't put it on too thick. And do it as though you meant it. Then you'll discover you DO mean it, for the moment anyway.'

'What do you flatter them about?' she asked.

'Oh, you'll soon discover their weak point. Everyone has them. Ask them first what they like best--games or travelling or adding up sums in a stuffy office as Ellis does. After that, all you've got to do is listen. Nobody wants you to do anything but listen, no men anyway. Women are different. They like you to tell them that they are beautiful or clever. And why shouldn't they? We all get enough of the other thing. Parties are meant to cheer you up and make you feel for a moment that all the things the people who know you best think about you aren't true.'

'Well,' said Vanessa, 'whatever happens now it won't matter. I've had one lovely dance.'

But she need not have been afraid. Soon Amery came to ask her, then Will Herries, then young Richard Cards, then Carey Rockage and, at last, Ellis.

She gave them all places on her flowery programme. She swung round the room in an ecstasy. 'Isn't this lovely?' she murmured to Amery.

Amery, who was anxious about his brother Garth, now rather drunk and quarrelsome in the parlour, answered at first absent-mindedly, then realized that he was moving with a grace and charm that he hadn't known for years. 'By Gad,' he thought, 'I'm more of a dancer than I knew I was,' and wondered whether if he had been more gay in his past and his brother less gay, it wouldn't have been better for both of them! 'Poor Sylvia!' he thought, seeing Garth's wife, painted, raddled, and weary as she bumped round with Rockage, who was no dancer. 'She's had a rotten life!' He was suddenly charitable to everyone. This charming child, light as a fairy--by Jove, she was bewitching! Why had he known nothing like this? He had married late, and it hadn't lasted long. There had been others of course--Doris, whom he had had to keep so long after he was tired of her, and Alice Mason, who'd smashed all his china one night in a fit of temper, and the Frenchwoman, Marguerite Calvin, whose father's debts he had paid. Had he had much in return? No, not very much. As he felt Vanessa's hand on his arm he sighed. What was the use? He would be just the same tomorrow.

Vanessa, to her own great amusement, began at once to put Benjie's advice into practice with all these gentlemen. It worked like a miracle. Amery talked to her about money, horses, and the Family. Will Herries talked to her about the Navy, the sea, the West Indies, Glebeshire, dogs, Polchester, the sea, the Family. Young Richard (whom she liked greatly) talked about books (Middlemarch, Mrs Browning, Hawley Smart), gardening, riding, and the Family, and Carey talked about the place in Wiltshire, the weather, the weather, the weather, the place in Wiltshire, and the Family. She

found that they soon forgot that they were talking to a child. She found that they all wanted comforting, consoling, reassuring, and so learnt one very useful never-to-be-forgotten lesson about Men. She discovered, too that all of them, except young Richard, felt that in one way or another an injustice had been done. They hadn't had fair treatment. Someone was to blame. Carey Rockage in especial was like a blinded bewildered animal whom unseen persecutors were prodding with pitch-forks.

'Oh, I AM so sorry!' she found herself saying over and over again.

And Ellis? Ellis was another matter. She had noticed that he watched her. Often, feeling that someone's eye was upon her, she saw that it was his. When their dance came it was 'Sir Roger', and he asked her whether she would mind sitting with him instead. She DID mind because she loved 'Sir Roger' and something in her was afraid of a long talk with Ellis, but she followed him meekly out into the hall and to a top corner of the stairs.

Here the sounds of the music were very dim, the house was still, and she thought of her darling grand-mother, not far away, deep in sleep. It was as though for a moment something drew her into that bedroom. She stood there, looking at the dim light by the bed.

'Are you asleep, Grandmamma?' she seemed to say.

'Yes, dear. I'm sleeping beautifully,' the answer came. She put her hand on Ellis' thin arm. 'Did you hear anything? Anyone call?'

'No,' he said.

There seemed to her a sound of light steps along the passage above them. Then she was compelled to give all her attention to Ellis. He forced her to do so. She did not know how old he was (he was in fact close on thirty-two), but he seemed to her both very old and very young.

He was unhappy, she was sure, and, like her grandmother, she could not bear that anyone should be unhappy. So, wanting to console him, she felt older than he. He was not exactly plain; he was distinguished in his thin, pale, quiet way; very serious; he scarcely ever smiled. But when he did his smile was rather beautiful. It lit up his thin face and his colourless eyes. It was as though he were pleading to be liked. He wants feeding up, she thought. His eyes were sometimes a little mad.

For a while he could do nothing but stammer out disconnected sentences. Then, following Benjie's advice, she asked him questions, about London, the City, theatres, and what he did in his spare time.

'I haven't any spare time,' he assured her. 'You see, my father had so many affairs in the City, and it all devolves upon me. I like it, you know. The City is a very agreeable place, it is indeed. Yes.' Then he said, staring at her with all his eyes: 'You must come one day, Cousin Vanessa, and stay with my mother and myself in Hill Street.'

'Thank you,' she said. 'I should love to go to London. I have never been to a theatre or a circus, and oh! how I should like to see the Queen!'

'The Queen is very much in retirement,' he said solemnly, as though he kept her in his pocket, 'but the Prince of Wales and the Princess are often to be seen driving.'

Then there was another awkward pause, until he broke out:

'I do hope you will come, Cousin Vanessa. Our house is not very gay, but if you came it would be--' He choked in his throat. 'Will you, please, not forget me? Will you think of me sometimes?'

'Of course I will think of you, Cousin Ellis,' she answered, laughing because she felt, for some strange reason, uncomfortable.

'Will you indeed? That will make me very happy . . . I have not many friends,' he added. 'My own fault of course. I am shy. You may not have guessed it, but I am very shy indeed.'

She certainly HAD guessed it--not only was he shy but he made others who were with him shy too. Then the music, to her relief, began again.

'Oh, we must go!' she cried, jumping up.

'You promise to think of me?' he asked again urgently. 'I shall think of you often--very often indeed.'

When she was with them all again she sat for a while among the ladies and was aware of something that she had never thought of before (she was making so many discoveries tonight!), namely, that this family to which she belonged contained the real benefactors of the human race. Dorothy Bellairs, Veronica, Emily Newmark, even Sylvia Herries--they were all the same! If it were not for them the Poor, the Unprotected, almost everyone in fact who wasn't Herries, would perish. Vanessa had a strange picture of all the cottage women of England seeing through their window the arrival in a carriage and pair of Dorothy, Veronica, Emily, Sylvia. These ladies were armed magnificently against the cold, their hands were in muffs, the high collars of their coats reached to their bonnets. Majestically they moved down the cottage path, John, James, William following behind with basket on arm. Then the cottage woman hastens, straightens her apron, puts the children in their places, arranges grandfather by the fire, hurries to the door.

'Good afternoon, my lady.'

'Oh, good afternoon, Mrs Cottage Woman. How are you this afternoon?' The seat of the chair is dusted, even the cottage clock, the cottage cat, the cottage table are deferential. Glory has descended upon the cottage woman!

Vanessa had never thought of this before. The life that they enjoyed at Cat Bells was so very different; she had never had on every side of her so many Herries women. She had never, never realized that were it not for the Ladies of England the Poorer Classes would fade away. She had never known that there WERE any Poorer Classes.

Even Veronica! Beautiful, lovely Aunt Veronica!

'Oh, well, I told her . . . that if she didn't drink the soup . . . WOULD give it to her worthless old father . . .'

And Rockage's wife: 'They complained about the drains, but Carey explained to them . . .'

She turned it all over in her mind while she was dancing with young Richard.

Afterwards, when they were talking, she asked him:

'Are you glad you're partly a Henries?'

'Glad?' he said, turning round and smiling.

'Yes. Is it better being a Henries than being a Jones or Smith?'

(While she spoke she thought: What IS happening to me? I've never thought of these things before.)

'Well, don'tcherknow,' said Richard slowly, 'there IS something fine in being one of the oldest families--'

'But ARE we one of the oldest? I mean, aren't the Jones and the Smiths just as old really?'

'I suppose they are. It's being English that counts.'

'Is it better to be English than German or French?'

Richard, who had no notion that Vanessa's mother was a German, answered with no hesitation at all:

'By Gad, yes--I should jolly well think it is.' So that settled it.

As the evening went on she was aware that she had seen but little of Benjamin. She went to look for him and found him in the billiard room dancing solemnly up and down with Barney Newmark, both of them swaying a little as they moved.

Vanessa--quite suddenly a child again--stood hesitating in the doorway, and Benjamin, looking up, saw two Vanessas, both lovely, both darlings, both the beloved of his heart. But he was never so much a gentleman as when he had drunk too much, so he disengaged himself from Barney and gave a courtly bow.

'Sit down, Vanessa, and I will fetch you some lemonade.'

She stood there, bitterly disappointed. She had often seen gentlemen who drank too much, but never Benjamin. She saw that his hair was ruffled, his eyes shining, and that he swayed on his feet, but she knew also that she loved him as dearly as ever, that her impulse was to go to him, smooth his hair, straighten his tie . . .

'No, thank you,' she said.

He came up to her and took her hand. He saw that she was frightened.

'Come and we'll dance, Vanessa,' he said.

'I am afraid that this one is engaged,' she answered, looking over his shoulder at Barney Newmark, who was gently singing to himself. She hurried away, leaving Benjamin staring after her.

In the dining-room again she danced once more with Amery and soon she was happy. How could she help it? Everyone was so happy around her. The musicians played like mad, the candles shone like stars, the noise filled the room so that it was like a paper bag on the point of bursting. The waltz was a lovely tune. They began to sing to it. The 'Blue Danube'. Oh! the 'Blue Danube'! How lovely! One was not on earth but swinging, swaying in an azure heaven, limitless, lit with radiance. The wide, full dresses eddied and billowed, the naked shoulders and arms were gleaming, there was that gentle undertone of music rocking, rocking . . .

Wait! What's the matter? The music had stopped! With a surge the room has reasserted itself, the candles have lost their radiance, everyone is silent, standing looking . . .

Vanessa, near to the door, saw that Aunt Jane, white-faced, shaking, Rockage's arm around her, was speaking. Amery turned to the child.

'How sad! How tragic! Madame! . . . dead!' Then realizing that it was Vanessa: 'Your grandmother . . .'

The silence that followed was so strange. Life had fled from the house.

'Yes, in her sleep . . . Jane went up five minutes ago . . . Quite quietly . . . in her sleep . . . They have sent for Doctor Bettany.'

As they stared, conscious, every one of them, of the precariousness of this moment of existence, of the folly of their pretences of safety, thinking at the same time of the figure of the morning, so upright, so grand in her pleasure and happiness, all this only a moment ago, they themselves, perhaps, before the morning . . .

But she was A Hundred! She had reached her Hundred! Nothing could deprive her of that. A great age. Best of all to go quietly in your sleep . . . A wonderful woman!

But beyond the windows the snow has begun to fall. Are there figures there on the frosty road? Old Herries, with the scar on his cheek, upright on his horse as when, so many years ago, he had ridden up to that same gate to tell his son that his wife had run away; stout David, young again, riding on the wind to his beloved hills; Georges, waiting now for Judith who had been in spite of his many infidelities, his only love; Charlie Watson waiting too, after so long an uncomplaining patience; poor Warren with that one hour of happiness to remember--and for those silent motionless watchers was there a sudden opening of the gates, a running out of a little figure, happy, daring, triumphant, a moment's stare up and down the road, and then a cry?

'Georges! Georges! . . . Charlie! Warren! . . . Father!'

Vanessa felt an arm around her as Adam drew her away with him, murmuring:

'Don't cry, my darling. It was the happiest way. Quietly--without any fuss--while we were all dancing.'

FOUNTAIN AT THE ROADSIDE

Walter Herries died in April 1880.

For the last five years of his life he was unaware of all that was happening in the world and perfectly happy. His daughter Elizabeth nursed him with infinite kindness and care and he was an infant in her hands. The Fortress, during those years, was a very quiet place. Benjamin, Elizabeth's son, managed the estate, which was not now large in extent--two farms and a cottage or two in Lower Ireby were the full extent of it.

He managed it, that is to say, when he was there. For much of that period he was away; he visited the East, was said to have left his young mark on Shanghai and to have invaded the sanctities of Indian temples, to have assisted pirates in the South Seas and to have been knifed within an inch of his life in Sarawak: it was whispered even that he had five Chinese wives, numberless Asiatic concubines. He returned, however, looking very much as he went--brown, stubby, solid, cheerful, and without a conscience. 'I care for nobody, no, not I, and nobody cares for me' was said, by all his friends and relations, to be his daily song.

He did, however, care for his mother, and after his third return in '79 swore that he would settle down and become the Cumberland squire. He loved Cumberland with passion and he had a good head on his shoulders, so that, for a while, he was successful. Everyone liked him; for a brief time it seemed that he might be the most popular man in Cumberland. But soon stories were everywhere. He could not, it appeared, see a woman without kissing her, could not tell the truth (was it possible that his acquaintances had no humour?), had no social sense at all, so that he invited farmers' wives to meet Mrs Osmaston and took a shepherd with him to supper at Uldale. He was also, it was said, an atheist and openly defended Bradlaugh. He visited London frequently and never returned thence without a scandal hanging to his tail. It was said that the lowest ground in that city was HIS ground, that he drank, gambled, spent a fortune over horses and cheeked his relations. How many of these stories came from Hill Street, from old Lady Herries and her son Ellis, who both hated him, no one could say, but certain it was that he was himself responsible for many of them because he never denied anything and never admitted anything, cherished no grudges, accused no one and told anyone who asked him that yes, it must be true if everyone said so; he had no morals, he supposed; he would like to have some; they must be useful things, but he simply didn't know where they were to be found.

On the other hand everyone was forced to admit that, as he grew older, he did not look dissipated. His colour was of the healthiest, his body of the toughest, his eyes bright and glowing. When he bathed in the

Lake or a mountain stream in the summer with young Osmaston or Timothy Bellairs or Robert Forster it could be seen that his limbs were brown and supple as though he lived for ever in the open air. He was never drunk now as many of his neighbours were; smutty stories never appealed to him in the least, and if girls were the worse for his friendliness nobody knew of it for a fact. It was said that he walked vast distances over the hills and alone. Nobody ever saw him out of spirits or out of temper. He was generous to a fault. With all this nobody really knew him and nobody trusted him. 'He's a rascal,' said the Herries in London, in Bournemouth, in Harrogate, in Manchester, in Carlisle, 'and he'll come to no good.' In fact they longed, many of them, that he SHOULD come to no good as quickly as possible.

His only friends among his relations were Aunt Jane at Uldale, Adam Paris and his daughter Vanessa, Barney Newmark, and Rose Ormerod at Harrogate, who always said she'd marry him tomorrow if he asked her.

His one saving grace, they all said, was that he loved his mother-- loved her, they added, quite selfishly because he left her whenever he pleased and for months she had not a line from him. It was not hard, they added, for him to love his mother, for she was the sweetest and gentlest of ladies and gave him everything that he wanted.

It was also added that he possessed that strange and mysterious quality known as 'charm'--which meant that when you were with him you could not help but like him and that, as soon as his back was turned, you wondered whether he had meant a word that he said.

He happened to be at home when his grandfather died. Walter was sleeping late on a spring afternoon, and his room was bathed in sunshine. Wrapped in a padded crimson dressing-gown, his long white hair falling over his face as he slept, he seemed a bundle of clothes topped by a wig. Then he looked up, blinked at the sunlight, called for his son Uhland, saw him come slowly tap- tapping with his stick across the floor to him, grinned joyfully at the long-expected sight, and died--or, if you prefer it, went from the room, leaning on his son's arm, happy as he had not been for many a day.

That night, when the old man had been decently laid out on the four- poster in the room upstairs, Elizabeth and her son sat in the little parlour off the hall and talked. The evening was very warm and a window was open. The trees faintly rustled; there came the occasional late fluting of a bird; the scent of early spring flowers, dim and cool with the night, hung about the room.

Benjamin sat opposite his mother, his legs stretched wide, and thought how beautiful she still was, how dearly he loved her, how selfish and restless he was, how quiet and unselfish was she! Elizabeth's beauty had always been shy, delicately coloured, fragile. She was a Herries only in her strength of will and a certain opposition to new ideas. She had never cared for ideas but always for persons--and then for very few persons. As she looked across at her son she thought: 'He is all that I have left. I know that he loves me and I know that I have no power over him.' Then she raised her hand ever so slightly as though she were touching someone who bent above her chair. John Herries, her husband, had been dead for more than twenty years to everyone but herself. It was not sentiment nor vague superstition nor longing that made her aware that he was always alive at her side. It was plain fact--and as it was her own concern, her own experience, it was of no importance that others should say that this was absurd, or weak, or against facts. She worried no one else about the matter, not even her son.

Benjamin loved her so dearly that evening, thought she looked so lovely in her full black dress, felt so intensely how lonely she would be, that he was ready to do anything for her--except sacrifice anything that threatened his liberty. Everything threatened his liberty.

'So your long service is over, Mother. How wonderful you were to him! Everyone marvelled at it. I'm terribly proud of you.'

She looked at him, smiled (and with perhaps a touch of affectionate irony):

'And now, Benjie, I suppose you'll go away again?'

'Oh no, Mother. Of course not! Leave you now!'

'Well, perhaps not just now--but soon. Jane is coming to stay later. And Vanessa. Vanessa is coming tomorrow for a week.'

He looked up sharply.

'Vanessa!'

'Yes. You didn't know that she was here this evening? It was quite by chance. She had ridden over to Uldale. She had stayed the night with the Grigsbys. She came up to ask how everyone was. I told her the news, and like the darling she is she said that she would come tomorrow. Adam is away at Kendal, so it suits very well.'

'Oh, I'm glad!' He drummed his heels into the carpet.

'You know, of course, that she loves you?'

'And I love her.'

Elizabeth smiled. 'You say that very easily, Benjie.'

'Well, you know how it is.' He got up and stood in front of the fireplace. 'We've loved one another all our lives. Whatever else happens she always comes first. There's no one in the world to put beside her. But she's too fine for me to marry her. You know she is. No one knows it better than you do.'

He came and sat at her feet, his hand resting on her knee.

'How too fine?'

'You know what everyone says of me; that I'm no good, that I spoil everything I touch--a rascal, a vagabond, all the rest. And it's true, I suppose. I'm no man to marry anyone.'

She stroked his hair gently.

'Is it true what they say?'

'You know me better than anyone else, Mother--or rather you and Vanessa do. I don't think about myself. I take myself as I am. But I know that I can't stick--to anyone or anything. It grows worse as I'm older. I want to do a thing--and I do it!'

'Is there any harm in that--if you don't do bad things?'

'But perhaps I do--things that you call bad. I can't tell. I don't think that I know the difference between right and wrong. Or rather my ideas of right and wrong are different from other people's. I'm too interested in everything to stop and think. I think when it's too late.'

He laughed and looked up into her face.

'I'm a bad lot--but I love you and Vanessa with all my heart.'

'Yes--but not enough to do things for us?'

'Anything you like. Tell me to fetch you something from Peking now and I'll go and get it. But I can't be tied, I can't be told what to do, I can't be preached at by anybody.'

'Perhaps,' Elizabeth said quietly, 'if you married Vanessa that would steady you.'

He shook his head vehemently.

'Vanessa is so good and so fine. She isn't strait-laced. She's wise and tolerant, but she's high-minded. She believes in God, you know, Mother.'

'And don't you?'

'You know that I don't. Not as she does. Not as she does. I may be wrong. I dare say I am. But I MUST be honest. I don't SEE things that way. I'm ignorant. I don't know any more than the next fellow and I want the next fellow to believe as he sees, but I must be allowed to see for myself. I can't SEE God anywhere. The things that people believe are fine for them but nonsense to me. To me as I am now. I've got all my life in front of me and everything to learn. God may be proved to me yet. I hope He will be.'

'Proved!' Elizabeth laid her cheek for a moment against his, 'God can't be proved, Benjie. He must be felt.'

'Yes, I suppose so. That may come to me one day. Meanwhile--a heathen and a vagabond can't marry Vanessa.'

She thought for a little and then said: 'Have you talked of these things to Vanessa?'

'No. I don't want to hurt her.'

'I don't think you would hurt her. She's very wise and very tolerant She doesn't want everyone's experience to be hers. Her father isn't religious in her way, but she understands him perfectly. So she may you.'

'Oh, she understands me, as much as she knows of me. But I know things about myself that I'd be ashamed for her to know. I'm not ashamed of MYSELF, Mother. I'd like to be different--settled, no-

ble, unselfish. Or would I? I can't tell. I'm not proud of myself, but I'm not ASHAMED of myself either. I'm simply what I am. All the same I don't see why I should burden someone else with the care of me. That at least I can do. Save others from troubling about me.'

'Yes,' said Elizabeth. 'But if someone loves you they want to trouble. They can't help but trouble.'

He flung his arms around her and kissed her.

'Funny I should be your son. The luck's all with me.'

Next day Vanessa came. She was now nearly twenty-one years of age. Her beauty had a quality of surprise in it. She was tall and slender. Her face was young for her age, much younger than her carriage, which was mature and controlled. She moved with such grace that you thought, as you watched her, that she was fully assured. Then when you saw her eyes and mouth, her perpetual gaiety, the sudden change of mood, the constant excitement, her stirred animation, you felt that life had not yet touched her. She was like her father in sweetness of expression but unlike him in her alertness, so that she seemed to miss nothing that went on around her. She was immensely kind, but could be sharp and irritated by slowness and stupidity and most of all by any pomposity or show of self-conceit. That is, except in the case of those whom she loved, when she simply could not criticize. For example, she loved Timothy Bellairs at Uldale and he WAS a trifle pompous.

Her hair was very dark but her colouring rather pale, unless she were excited by something. She blushed very easily, which exasperated her. When she moved she was like a queen, but often when she talked or joined with others in a game or a sport she was childish and impetuous. She was intensely loyal, obstinate, for-giving, so warm-hearted that her father often feared for her, but of late she had been learning many things about human nature. She was no fool where people were con-cerned.

Her mother had died in the autumn of '77 and since then she had lived with her father and Will on Cat Bells. They had been always devoted friends, she and her father, but now, after losing both his mother and his wife, Adam seemed to turn to Vanessa with an urgency that had something almost desperate about it. He re-mained always humorous, kindly, a little cynical, half in his fairy stories (he tried his hand at a number of things--books for boys, biographies of Nelson and Walter Raleigh, even two novels, but they were all fairy stories), half in the wild, loose, stormy Cumberland life that was in his blood and bones. Everyone liked him, nobody knew him. Many people laughed at him in an easy gen-erous fashion. Vanessa alone understood him. She understood him because she had (although as yet she did not realize it) very much of her grandmother's char-acter. Adam, of course, knew that. He saw his mother in his daughter again and again: her kindness, generosity, sudden flashes of temper and irritation and a constant exasperation at belonging to the Herries family.

'We don't belong, my dear,' he said one day.

'We belong enough,' she answered in a flash of prophetic perception, 'to have to fight them for the rest of our lives.'

Another thing. He knew that Vanessa loved Benjamin. It made Adam unhappy whenever he thought of it. He was himself fond of Benjie, but oh! he did not want him to marry Vanessa! Margaret's last words had been: 'Adam, you mustn't let Vanessa marry Benjamin', and he had answered: 'She must be free'.

But oh no! oh no! he did not want her to marry Benjamin! They never discussed it. That was their one silence.

Walter was buried in Ireby churchyard and, ironically, not far from the grave of Jennifer Herries, into which he once so long ago had terrified her. At the funeral, besides Elizabeth, Benjie, and Vanessa, there were Adam, Veronica and her husband, Timothy and his wife, and dear Aunt Jane. Also a few neighbours.

It was a cold windy day, one of those days when you realize how true it is that Cumberland is composed only of cloud and stone: lovely iridescent stone with green and rosy shadows but rising in pillars of smoke to meet the cloud, and the cloud coming down, to settle like blocks and boulders of stone on the soil until, with the wind in your ears, you do not know which is stone and which is cloud. The little church tugged at the wind like a cloud striving to be free, and the clouds rolled in the sky as though some giant hurled rocks at his enemy.

They all stood, blown about, in the little churchyard, and poor old Walter, a capital example of the waste of energy that hatred involves, was dropped into the ground.

That same evening Vanessa and Elizabeth had a talk. Elizabeth had done all she could with the house. Her taste had never been aesthetic and she had dressed the cold bare bones of the place with heavy, very heavy, material. The big bleak rooms she had filled with large sofas, heavy carpets, big chairs, all in the manner of their period, which, if it was not a very beautiful manner, was comfortable.

She had crowds of things partly because everyone she knew did the same, partly because she hoped thus to escape the stoniness, the melancholy, the ghostliness of the place. She could not escape it. The rooms that were empty and shut up--the rooms in the two towers for instance--were heavy with ghosts. Not only she knew it. Everyone in the countryside knew it. Voices and steps were heard. Pale faces looked from behind windows, dogs barked, and parrots screeched. The Fortress, in fact, was not to surrender to a confusion of cornucopias, steel and brass fire-irons, japanned coal boxes, tables covered with beadwork, satin walnut chairs, and wax flowers under glass shades. Nevertheless in the few rooms that she herself inhabited her presence warmed and comforted. There were fires, Cumberland servants who adored her, flowers and books.

But Vanessa, in spite of the flowers, shivered. She had her father's taste, her grandmother's passion for order and arrangement. How, thought Vanessa, can Elizabeth, who is so beautiful, endure this hideous place? She did not realize that Elizabeth could endure anywhere so long as John, her husband, was with her.

Benjamin had gone that evening to see a farmer in Braithwaite. He would not be back until the following afternoon, so the two women had the house to themselves. They sat close together over a roaring fire and tried not to listen to the wind, which found the Fortress the happiest hunting ground it knew. Although Elizabeth was sixty-five and Vanessa only twenty-one they understood one another very well. They believed very much in the same things and they both loved the same man.

That evening, in fact, was a crisis for Vanessa, and in the course of it she set her feet resolutely along the path that was to lead her so very far.

'What are you going to do, Elizabeth, now?' Vanessa asked.

'Do, my dear? Why, go on as before.'

'Won't this house be very lonely for you?'

'I am used to it, you know. I'm an old woman now and like a quiet life.'

'Benjamin will be with you. That's one good thing.'

'Oh no, he won't!' Elizabeth smiled. 'He'll come and go as he's always done.'

'Oh, but he must,' Vanessa answered vigorously. 'He can't leave you all alone here. He has plenty to do, loves the country. He has wandered enough.'

'You know that he has not,' Elizabeth answered. 'He will never have wandered enough. He might settle down if you married him. Otherwise, never.'

She had spoken quietly but, as both women knew, it was a challenge of the deepest import.

There was a long silence, then Vanessa said slowly:

'Benjie has not asked me to marry him.'

'No. That is because he is afraid--afraid of himself. He loves you more than anyone in the world and does not want to make you unhappy.'

'Yes,' Vanessa said at last. 'He might make me unhappy, but I would not mind, I think.' After a pause she went on: 'You see, Elizabeth, I have Benjie in my blood. I have always had. I'm quite shameless about it--to myself, I mean. What is the use of being otherwise? I would rather be miserable with Benjie than happy with anyone else. And perhaps I should not be miserable. I understand him very well.'

She waited, but Elizabeth said nothing.

'We are very alike in some ways. I want my liberty quite as much as he does his. My great-grandmother was a gipsy, my great- grandfather a vagabond, my father illegitimate. And Benjie--' She broke off.

'Thinks he is a vagabond too,' Elizabeth went on, 'because of his father. You needn't fear, Vanessa darling, to talk about it. Here we are in the house that is filled with it. Sometimes I wake in my bed and hear the tap of Uhland's stick on the floor. I was impetuous, too, once, my dear. I ran away and married John. I had courage for anything in those days; but I know now that every impetuous step, every blow in anger, can mean tragedy for the next generation. There is no end to the consequences. They are never done.'

'Perhaps it isn't what we do,' said Vanessa, 'but something in ourselves. A strain that won't let us alone. You know, Elizabeth, that when I go over and stay with Veronica there's so much Herries stolidness and convention that I feel, I'm sure, just as Judith did when she ran away to Paris. That's where I understand Benjie. And sometimes when I'm with Timothy, although I'm very fond of him, I could whip him. I could really. He WON'T see things and is proud of not seeing them. He believes in Gladstone but has never heard of Rossetti.'

'Rossetti, dear?' asked Elizabeth.

'Yes--well, never mind. He writes poetry and paints.'

'Oh yes,' said Elizabeth. 'I'm sure I've heard the name--'

'I expect you have. But that doesn't matter. The point is that I would understand if Benjie wanted to go away by himself. I think it's silly of married people always to be together.'

'And then there's religion,' Elizabeth said. 'Benjie declares that he doesn't believe in God, foolish boy.'

'Many people say they don't believe in God,' Vanessa answered, speaking as though she were sixty and Elizabeth twenty. 'I don't think Father does, not as I do. But if you love someone those things settle themselves. I could never be as Timothy and Violet are, keeping the children in awe of them, never allowing them an idea of their own. Why, they have to come to the dining-room and bow, poor little things, after every meal! And Tim's only three, but I know he's going to be an artist. He's always drawing things. And when I spoke of it to his father the other day he was as shocked as if I'd said Tim was going to be an actor.'

'Well,' said Elizabeth, 'that wouldn't be a nice thing for little Tim to grow up into.'

'I don't know,' said Vanessa. 'There are the Bancrofts anyway. They have luncheon with the Prince of Wales.'

'Come here, dear, and give me a kiss,' Elizabeth said. 'I'd rather have you for a daughter than anyone in the world.'

Then came the last day of April, the day before Vanessa returned to Cat Bells. After dinner that night there was a large full moon. The air was warm and the moonlight filled all the garden with silver dust so that one seemed to walk on white powdery surf, now rising on a wave of quicksilver, then passing into an ebb of luminous grey. The hills were thin like silver tissue. Benjie, governed as ever by his mood, by the food that he had eaten, the wine that he had drunk, thinking Vanessa perfect in her dark dress that below the narrow waist broke out into bows and frills and trimmings, swearing that no neck and arms in all the world were so lovely as hers, seemed to see her as though this were for the first time, a new Vanessa to whom he had but just been introduced, so that under his breath he must murmur: 'This is the loveliest in all the world. All my life I have been waiting for this.'

At first she would not go out with him, as though something warned her. She stood by the fire, laughing, talking about anything, nothing. She had had a letter from Rose Ormerod, who was having a gay time in London.

'No, but you must listen to this, Benjie.'

'I don't want to listen. I don't like her. I can't think why she is your friend.'

'But she likes YOU! In this letter she says: "If you see Benjie give him my love, my LOVE, mind." And she means it.'

'Oh, she gives everyone her love--far too many people.'

'She has been having a beautiful visit. Lady Herries gave a dinner party. Very sticky, she says. And she went to the Haymarket Theatre and saw Money. A silly old play, she says, but Marion Terry was lovely as Clara Douglas, and Mr Bancroft was Sir Frederick, and Mrs Bancroft, Lady Franklyn, and--'

'What DO I care who they were? This is the last night of April. Tomorrow is the first of May. It is as warm as summer--silly to have a fire--and the moon is the largest--'

'Oh yes, and she went to Mr Alma-Tadema's studio to see the pictures he's sending to the Academy, and one is called "Fredegonda", and it shows an angry Queen looking out of a window at her husband--'

'Please, Vanessa.'

She looked at him and saw that he was unhappy. She nodded.

'All right. I'll come out.'

She went upstairs to fetch a shawl. Benjie, while he waited, wondered what he was going to do. This was the moment that for years he had determined to avoid. He must not marry Vanessa. He must not marry anyone. At the thought of marriage something within him warned him. But Vanessa--Vanessa . . . He shivered. Outside in the garden it was warmer than in the firelit room. The house was always cold, do what you would with it. Vanessa--Vanessa . . . Why had he been such a fool as to stay? He had an impulse to go round to the stable, fetch his horse, and ride off. Ride off anywhere-- not seeing her again until she was safely married to someone else. But would that end it? All his life, however far away he had been, he had been tied to her, tied by her goodness, her beauty, her love for himself--and by all that was best in him. His best? A very poor thing. He had never thought so humbly of himself as at that moment when she came towards him, saying: 'I'm ready. How lovely the moonlight is!'

They walked into the garden arm in arm. Originally Walter Herries had planned a series of garden walks and a succession of little waterfalls, dropping stage after stage into a lily-covered pond. Now there were the sad ruins of these things, tangled shrubberies, little winding and melancholy paths, the doubtful splash of water and a weedy pool. Over the ruins the moon rode throwing its silver in a conceited largesse, penetrating the uttermost tangle of the trees.

'I have just finished a very amusing book,' said Vanessa, who felt as though the moon were scornfully wishing her a disastrous destiny, like the old witches her great-grandfather had known.

'What is it called?' asked Benjamin, wondering for how long he could resist to kiss Vanessa.

'Travels with a Donkey.'

'What a silly name!' The muscle on his arm suddenly jumped at the touch of Vanessa's hand. 'Who wrote it?'

'His name is Stevenson. I have never heard of him before, have you?'

'No. Never.'

'He writes well.' Vanessa almost whispered as they stepped into a pool of moonlight. 'Very precious, as though he'd licked every word on his tongue first before he stuck it down. Oh, look at the moon insulting Blencathra. There! Stand here! You can just see it between the trees.'

Benjie took her in his arms and kissed her with a ferocity that Ouida--a novel by whom Vanessa had recently been enjoying-- describes somewhere 'as the lovely tiger's grandeur and the abandoned wildness of the jungle'. Benjie had never kissed Vanessa before save almost as a brother. This was the first time in her life that Vanessa had ever been passionately kissed. She found it entrancing. They stayed for a long while without moving. The shawl fell from Vanessa's shoulders, but she felt no cold. The pressure of Benjie's strong hand on her shoulder was surely the thing that since the day of her birth she had longed for. Her hand touched Benjie's hair as though he were her child. He kissed her eyes, which was another thing that no one had ever done to her before. They separated. He bent down and picked up her shawl.

'This is something,' he said breathlessly, 'that I have been longing to do for years. And now we'll talk if you don't mind.'

They walked hand in hand.

'I am going away tomorrow morning and will not see you again until someone has married you.'

'I can wait,' she answered confidently. 'I will marry you any time.'

'You are not like the modern maiden, are you, Vanessa? If their young man proposes to them they faint with astonishment although they have planned nothing else all their lives.'

'No. Why should I be astonished? I always knew that we would be married one day.'

'We are not going to be married,' Benjie answered, taking his hand from hers and walking by himself. 'I ought not to have kissed you. After tonight we shall not be alone together again until you are safe. I love you as truly as any man ever loved anyone, and that is why we are not going to be married.'

Vanessa laughed and took his hand again.

'I am not a child, Benjie. I know that you are afraid of marriage-- and perhaps you would be right if it were anyone else, but we are different. We know one another so well. I shall never marry anyone else.'

'Now listen.' He put his arm around her and drew her close to him. 'You must not try to shake me, Vanessa. Really you must not. You say you know me, but it isn't true. You don't know me. Everyone is right about me. I'm no good by any standards but my own. I should make you terribly unhappy, and that I won't do. No, I will not. I will not. Other women--well, that's their affair. But you-- you've got to have a wonderful life, be a queen, have everyone worship you, adore you, have splendid children, a husband whom everyone looks up to . . .'

She interrupted him, laughing.

'But I don't want that kind of husband! I don't want to be a Queen! I don't want to be admired. I want to be free quite as much as you do. You talk as though it were my ambition to be head of the Herries family, live in Hill Street and give parties like old Lady Henries. Of course I ENJOY parties and it will be fun to go to London one day, but without you I don't want ANYTHING!'

'Oh Lord! How can I get you to understand? Don't you see, Vanessa, that I'm no good? Really no good. One day I'm this, another day I'm that. If I see a pretty woman I want to kiss her. If I want to gamble I gamble. I'm no sooner in a place than I want to go somewhere else. My mother and yourself are the only two people I love. I have hurt my mother many times already, but you I won't hurt--'

'But, Benjie,' she broke in, 'I don't think you COULD hurt me! I should understand whatever you did.'

'You don't know.' He spoke angrily, breaking again away from her. 'You don't know ANYTHING about life, Vanessa. You don't know the things I've done, the company I've kept. If I could say to you, "Vanessa, I've sown my wild oats and now I'm going to settle down, go to church on Sunday, read Tennyson with you in the evening--"'

'But, Benjie, how absurd you are! I don't WANT to read Tennyson, and if you don't wish to go to church you needn't! Father never goes to church. And as to the rest, what you have done is no business of mine. I'm sure I'm no saint myself. I know that Timothy and Violet think me often disgraceful and are afraid that I shall harm the children. Look at Grandmother! SHE wasn't a saint although she was one of the finest women who ever lived AND one of the bravest. And her father! He's a kind of legend for lawlessness and roguery. I think we should suit one another very well. And as to the relations and all they say about you--what do they matter? A stuffy lot! That's what they are!'

He shook his head. 'That's not the point, Vanessa. You may say what you like, but you are good and I'm not--that is by all that anyone means by good. You talk of Judith's father. I expect he was a fine fellow. I often think of him and wish I'd known him. I like that man. I could have been his friend, I know. But the truth is he made everyone unhappy who trusted him. And so shall I. I can't help it. It's something inside me. And I won't make you unhappy. I love you too much. It would be the one sin for me. I don't care about the rest, but THAT I'll avoid, so help me God!'

They had walked down to the weeded pool which lay now, like a foolish white face, dirtied and soiled, at their feet.

Vanessa spoke, but more gravely because she was feeling that her whole future life was to depend on the next ten minutes. What did she see? The man as he was? Perhaps . . . But herself in relation to all that he might be? She did not yet know life enough for that.

'Benjie, listen, I am not asking you against your will to marry me. I don't WANT you to marry me. We have been friends all our lives and we can go on as we are. But if you want to marry somebody, then it had better be me. I'm sure you will never meet anyone again who knows you so well.' She put her hand again in his. 'Do you remember that time--Grandmother's hundredth birthday--the day she died?'

'Yes, of course I remember.'

'We went for a walk, and I told you that I would never marry anyone but you and that I would wait as long as you liked. I was only a child then. I'm a woman now. But it is the same. It hasn't changed. I don't see how it can. No one can ever be to either of us what we are to one another. As to risks, life's made for them. I'm not afraid.'

She felt his hand tremble as it clutched hers.

'Listen, Vanessa. You MUST listen. If I don't make you understand now you never will. You say you are not afraid of life, but that is because you don't know. How can you? You have been sheltered always. Your father worships you as he ought to. Everyone loves you. You have never been treated unkindly, never had to put up with slights, never made an enemy. You hear people say: "Oh, Benjamin Herries, he's a bad lot, he's a rascal!" But they are only words. You've never seen me DO the things, SAY the things that they mean. I am at my best--a poor best but still my best-- when I'm with you because I love you and I'm not a bad fellow if I'm in a good temper, not bored, able to get away when I want to. We've seen one another at long intervals. We've loved to be together and they have been grand times because we were free. But to LIVE with me--that's another thing. I'm no man's good company for long. I've got old Rogue Herries' devil in me, I think. Sometimes I fancy I'm the old Rogue himself come again. And if that's nonsense--and I'm sure I don't know what's nonsense and what isn't in this ridiculous world-- at least I'm like him in that I'm my own worst enemy, can see what's right to do and never do it, curse my best friend and all the rest. Oh, mind you, I'm not pitying myself or even condemning myself. I'm not bad as men go. I enjoy every minute of the day unless I've got the toothache or lose money at cards or some woman won't look at me. And even those things are interesting. But I'm not the man for you. You're as far above me as that moon is above this silly-faced pond and, do me justice, I've always known it.'

He had spoken swiftly, the words pouring out, his face serious, mature, almost grim, as though he were resolving that this once in his life at least the honest truth should come from him.

'All that you have said, Benjie, I know,' Vanessa answered. 'I may be a fool as you say, protected from harm and all the rest. But Father has never treated me as a child. We've been companions for years and talked freely about everything. When I stay with Veronica and Robert Forster's drunk, as he is sometimes, I can see some of the things marriage can be. You may be nasty when you're drunk, but not half as nasty as Robert is. Of course I know that marriage isn't all fun. It isn't for anybody. Only I think that you and I would be often happy together if we were married because we know one another so well. We'd be unhappy too, but I don't always want to be happy. That would be dull. When we fought we'd know that we still loved one another. If you left me I'd know that you would come back.'

'No, I might not,' he said in a low voice. 'I might never come back. Loving you as much as I do now, I might still say: "No, I can't stand this." And I'd be off-- and perhaps never return.'

'Oh, Benjie, would you?'

They were standing now by the gate that led into the road. The road stretched in front of them, and beyond it the country fell to the valley like a sheet of shadowed snow.

'Oh, would you?' She was thinking. She turned, as though she had resolved a problem, and looked up at him, smiling. 'Then I'd be a grass widow. They say that they have a glorious life.'

Both laughing, they walked out into the road and at once were encompassed by a field of dazzling stars above them, sparkling and dancing as though they knew that tomorrow was the first of May and the beginning of a new summer world.

'You know, Vanessa,' Benjie said, looking over to Skiddaw, 'that I have an odd fancy. It isn't really mine. Some old shepherd told me some tale once. There's Skiddaw Forest where--where my father died. Of course it's often in my thoughts. When you stand below Skiddaw House and look over to Skiddaw you can see sometimes, just before the hill rises, a dark patch that looks like the opening of a cave. It is only a trick of light. There's no cave there, but when I was a boy I often walked there and I used to fancy that it was the opening to a great subterranean hall, a gigantic place, you know, that ran right under the mountain. I told myself tales about it. I fancied that all the men who had loved this place returned there, had great feasts there, jolly splendid affairs, with singing and drinking, everything that was fine. All of them grand comrades, whoever they were, farmers and shepherds, huntsmen, squires and parsons--any man to whom this piece of country is the best in the world. Perhaps on a night like this there they all are singing and laughing, happy as grigs--old Rogue Herries and my grandfather, my father and my uncle, John Peel and Wordsworth and Southey, little Hartley, "auld Will" Ritson of Wasdale, James Jackson of Whitehaven, Ewan Clark, John Rooke, thousands on thousands more--I used to fancy on a still day that I could hear them laughing and singing. A great hall, you know, Vanessa, where they could wrestle and run, ride their horses, shout their songs, tell their stories . . . That's where I'd like to be, Vanessa. I could do without women there. I wouldn't want to roam the world. I'd need no other company--' He broke off. 'Yes, I'd want you, I think. Wherever I was, whatever I'd be doing.'

They turned up the road and stopped at a little water trough where from a rudely carved dolphin's head water trickled into a small basin. The thin drip of the water was the only sound.

'Why don't you say,' he murmured, '"Benjie, you're a bad lot. We'll meet no more?" It would be better for you.'

'I can't say that,' she answered, leaning close to him, 'because I love you.'

The pause that followed marked both their lives. It had a sanctity, an intimacy that went beyond all their experience. They kissed again, but quietly now, gently meeting in complete oneness.

At last he said:

'Be kind to me, Vanessa. I've tried to do the best. Maybe I'll change. Mother said that loving you might do it for me. Give me a chance.'

He waited, then went on.

'My darling--let us be engaged, here and now, for two years. This is the last day of April 1880. In April 1882, I'll come to you and ask you if you are still of the same mind. If you are--if I can trust myself--we'll be married. If, before then, you think otherwise you shall tell me. And in the two years we will tell nobody, not a word to a soul. I shall be twenty-seven then, and if I'm no good at that age I shall never be any good. Give me that chance.'

Vanessa looked in front of her, then at last turned on him, smiling.

'Yes, if that's what you'd like, Benjie.'

'Not a word to anyone.'

She waited again.

'I have always told Father everything--'

'No. Even your father. I'm on probation. If he knew he might not understand.'

'Very well. Here's my hand on it.'

They held hands, looking one another in the eyes.

'It's a poor bargain for you,' he said. 'Mind, if ever you want to be free of me you have only to tell me--'

'I shall never want to be free,' Vanessa said proudly.

'All the men under Skiddaw heard you say that,' he answered. 'And they think me a poor lot for asking you.'

'Ah, they don't know you as I do,' she answered.

As they walked up to the house she held her head high, feeling the proudest woman in England.

And Benjie, for once in his life, was humble.

HERRIES DRAWING-ROOM

Vanessa paid the first visit of her life to London in the spring of 1882.

Old Lady Herries had, during the last two years, invited her repeatedly to stay in Hill Street, but the trouble had been that her father refused to go with her and Vanessa would not leave him.

Adam was obdurate and Vanessa was obdurate.

'No, my dear, I won't go. I hope never to see London again. I am sixty-six and entitled at last to my own way. London would upset me. I know I'm nothing at all, but London would make me feel less than nothing. I'm quite contented where I am. But of course you must go. It's time that they saw you and fell down before you. It's always been the custom that the family in London should see the Cumberland branch once and again and realize how superior it is. Your grandmother took me up when I was a boy and they all fell flat before her--so they shall before you.'

Vanessa refused. She did not want to go, she did not wish to see London, they would all think her an absurd country cousin and mock at her. With her father at her side she could mock back at them, but alone she would not dare to open her mouth. (None of these were, of course, real reasons. She longed to see London and she was afraid of no one.) He wished her to go because he was afraid that they were growing, as he described it, 'inside one another'.

For the last two years Vanessa had been strange. She was, it seemed, quite content to be alone with her father and, except for visits to Elizabeth at the Fortress and to Uldale, saw nobody. She seemed happy enough, but there were times when she appeared abstracted, lost, far away. Once or twice he wondered whether Benjie Herries had anything to do with this. Benjie had been out of England for most of the two years, deserting, everyone said, his mother most shamefully. Could it be that Vanessa still cared for him. Adam put the thought violently away from him. He had an affection for Benjie, but the fellow was a wanderer, a wastrel, would come, Adam very much feared, to no kind of good. And yet some wildness that there was in Adam attracted him to the man. He might have been, had things gone otherwise, just such himself. And Vanessa had some wildness in her too. Was it that that kept the men of the county away from her? No one doubted that she was better looking than any other girl in the North of England. And she was gentle with them, gave herself no airs. But she was alone. Save for her father, Elizabeth, and little Jane Bellairs at Uldale, she had no friends. Oh yes, and the children at Uldale--she adored THEM, especially young Tim.

But there it was; she had no friends of her own age, had no gaieties, did not appear to wish for any. It was not good for her. She must go to London.

And at last she yielded. He could not tell the reason. A letter came from Lady Herries. She looked across the table at Adam and said: 'Very well, Papa; I'll go.'

Then, when it was all arranged, he did not want her to go. He realized that he would be most damnably lonely. He was sure that, after this visit, she would never be the same again. She was still, in spite of her twenty-three years, very much of a child. She could be surprisingly naïve and impetuous. She seemed at one moment to judge human nature most wisely and then she would trust someone for no reason at all. She reminded him constantly of her grandmother in her simple directness to everyone, her lack of all affectation, her complete ignoring of class differences, her generosity and warmth both of heart and temper. But she was unlike Judith in that she had many reserves and no wish to dominate anybody. In those things she resembled himself. Oh, he would be all right, he supposed. There was plenty to do--his writing, his garden, the hills of which he never wearied; he was still, in spite of his sixty-six years, strong enough to walk over Stye Head into Eskdale and so to the sea, or over Watendlath to Grasmere. He had old Will Leathwaite for company. But he would miss her--miss her damnably. There was no one else he cared for now but Will. He was growing old. He continued to write--he could not help himself--but it was poor, secondary stuff. Not at all what he had meant

once to do. Why, Dickens had told him once that he would be the equal of them all. But Dickens was warm-hearted, generous, with his variegated waistcoats and passion for theatricals. A great man: no one like him now. Him and Wordsworth, that arrogant but child-hearted little man whose genius seemed now to cover all the country like a soft sunny cloud, impregnating the air, calling the scent from the flowers, echoed in the birds' call. Dickens and Wordsworth--simple men both of them--while today these Merediths and Swinburnes and Rossettis . . . He picked up the Poems and Ballads from the table, read a line or two, turned away with a sigh. Very clever. You could not call Wordsworth clever, thank God.

And so she went. It was arranged very easily, because Mrs Osmaston was travelling to London at the same time. Mrs Osmaston was a good serious woman who would bore Vanessa considerably. That would teach her, Adam thought quite fiercely, to leave her old father!

She went: and Adam discovered, not for the first time in his history, the tactful beauties in Will Leathwaite's character. Will had all the Cumbrian gift of showing his affection without mentioning it. He scolded and grumbled and protested as he had always done. In the evening they played backgammon together, and Will invariably won.

'You have the most damnable luck,' Adam swore at him.

'Aye,' said Will, 'I have. And I play nicely too.'

Four days after her departure Adam received a letter, the first that he had ever had from his dear daughter.

'My dearest Papa,' it began.

'A letter from my daughter,' he said to Will, who was sprawling against the doorpost, his hands in his pockets. He was fat now, red in the face and grizzled in the hair. It was in his eyes that you saw his youth, for their blue was as clear, gay, and sparkling as though they were fresh from their Maker.

'Aye,' he said. 'That's grand. Hope she's enjoying herself. Not too much, you know. She's better than anything London can give her.'

Adam, after glancing through, read Will her letter. Will never stirred. His eyes, shining, luminous, and in some fashion rather sardonic, were fixed on his friend-- as though he said: 'Yes. She's spreading her wings. You'll find I'm the only stay-by. We're a pair of left-overs. And who cares?'

The letter was:

MY DEAREST PAPA--I don't know how to begin I've so much to tell you. The journey was very long of course, the carriage smelt of escaping gas and oh, it was cold the last part! My feet were frozen. We couldn't see to read but it would not have been so bad had Mrs Osmaston not chattered so! She is SO contented,

SO fortunate, has so perfect a husband, such LOVELY children (you know little Mary and James Osmaston--not lovely at all!) but the worst is that she loves all the world. Her charity is too general to be personal. We are all God's children in a kind of celestial nursery. Well, I must get on.

Here I am two days in Hill Street and I MUST say that I am enjoying it. I find them very kind. Do you know that Lady Herries is seventy-eight? She is immensely proud of it and all our relations are proud of it too. If you live long enough in our family you are always looked up to whatever you may be or do. It is when you are young that you must be careful. She paints of course prodigiously and wears the brightest colours. Bustles have come in again you know, and she likes a sash and a bow at the waist! But I must not mock for she is really kind and wants me to be happy. So does Ellis. He is grave and nervous. He is dreadfully afraid of doing the wrong thing. He is exceedingly wealthy everyone tells me and ought to be married. I am very sorry for him because he does not know how to be careless and happy. Rose Ormerod says that he is always his own Governess and that no sooner does he do a thing than the Governess tells him he should not. Hill Street is a kind of Temple for the family. They come here and worship the god of the clan--a three-faced god, one face Queen Victoria, one face Commerce, and one face the Herries features, high cheekbones, noble foreheads, and a cold eye. They are very different though. Barney Newmark, old Amery and his son Alfred, Rose and her brother Horace, Emily Newmark. These are the principal ones who come to the house. Captain Will Herries and his wife are in town. Also the Rockages. I think they like me. I amuse them and perhaps shock them. I like Barney the best. He laughs at everyone. The house is very large and very cold, but of course you know it and I should imagine that it has not altered at all in thirty years. Very cold, full of noise from pipes and cisterns, masses of furniture, statues and little fires that burn up the chimney. There is the great Charles, too. Charles is the butler and he is so large that it is always warmer when he is in the room with one. He is very gracious and would be perfect if his eyes were not so glassy.

Just imagine! We have been to the theatre both nights! The first night was Romeo and Juliet with Mr Irving and Miss Ellen Terry. Shall I whisper to you, dear Papa, that I was a little disappointed? Mr Irving is better when he is not making love. In the balcony scene he stood behind such a ridiculous little tree that it was difficult not to laugh. When he makes love it is not the REAL THING. He has thought it all out beforehand. Miss Terry is LOVELY. Oh, how beautiful and charming! But she, too, acts better when she is NOT with Mr Irving. With the NURSE she is perfection. I liked Mr Terriss as Mercutio but the best of all is Mrs Stirling as the Nurse although propriety makes them cut out all her

BEST lines. The scenery is almost too good to be true I think. You admire the moonlight when you ought to be LOST with the lovers. At least that is what I felt.

Will you be very ashamed of me when I tell you that I enjoyed the second evening more? The piece was The Manager at the Court Theatre. This was Barney's party and I think Ellis was a little ashamed at LAUGHING at a Farce. But he could not help himself. There is an actress in this piece called Lottie Venne who is PERFECT and Mr Clayton SPLENDID! I laughed so much that Rose, who was with us, said Mr Clayton played twice as well as usual!

Of course I have not seen very much of London yet. Rose and I are to have a morning's shopping tomorrow. There is to be a grand party in Hill Street next week and Madame Trebelli of the Opera is to sing. I have ridden in a hansom-cab and found it very exciting.

And now I must go to bed. I have been writing this in my room and I am so cold that there is an icicle on the end of my nose! Do you miss me? I do hope so, but also I hope that you are not lonely. Give Will my love and the children at Uldale if you see them. If I ALLOW myself I shall be homesick, but that will never do. Last night I dreamt that you and I walked to Robinson and met five sheep who turned into the five Miss Clewers from Troutbeck! Have you seen Elizabeth? Is her cold quite gone now? I am hoping there will be a letter from you tomorrow--Your very loving daughter,
VANESSA

'That's grand,' said Will and went off to his work.

No one could guess from Vanessa's letter, nor indeed from anything that she herself said or thought, that her arrival in London was the sensation of the year for her relations. Afterwards, among them all, 1882 was remembered as the year 'when Vanessa first came to town'. And this for two reasons. One was the natural astonishment at her beauty, for which they were quite unprepared, although some of them recollected that 'she had been a damned pretty child at old Madame's Hundredth Birthday'.

By chance it happened that the fashion of the moment suited Vanessa: the dresses looped up behind, crossed with fringed draperies rather in the manner of the heavy window curtains of the time, the waists very narrow (and Vanessa had, all her life, a marvellous waist), the top portion of the costume following as closely as possible the lines of the corset, flaring out below the hips in frills and bows and trimmings. The violent colours just then popular also suited her dark hair and soft skin. The dress that she wore at her first Herries party, dark blue with an edging of scarlet, white lace frills at the throat and wrists, was long remembered.

She arrived with only a dress or two and they of Keswick make, but Adam had insisted that she must 'dress like a peacock in London' and gave her money to do it with. They were the first grand costumes of her life, and Rose Ormerod saw to it that they were fine. Her beauty staggered them all, the more that she seemed to be perfectly unaware of it. And they saw immediately that here was a family asset.

This raw naïve girl from Cumberland might marry anybody. There was no limit to the possibilities. Old Amery said to his son Alfred (Amery had married late in life a parson's infant fresh from the schoolroom: she presented him with Alfred in '62 and incontinently died) after his first sight of Vanessa in the Hill Street drawing-room: 'That girl will be a Duchess--bet you a "monkey",' These possibilities gave her at once a great importance in their eyes-- one more factor in the rise of Herries power!

And here that queer old Lady Herries, known familiarly as 'the witch of Hill Street', comes into the story. No one in London knew anything about that old woman save that she was useful as an entertainer and adored her son. When Will Herries had married her she had been a buxom, silly, empty-headed woman of no character and less common sense. She had given Will a son, and that was the only sensible thing she'd ever been known to do. But as Ellis grew to manhood her love for him created in her a kind of personality. People must always admire in this world any strong, undeviating, unfaltering devotion: for one thing it is rare, for another it appears unselfish although it may have all its roots in selfishness. This example was the more admired because Ellis was, most certainly, not everybody's money. Only was anybody's money, in fact, because he had himself such a profusion of that admirable commodity. They led, those two, in the Hill Street house, a life of extraordinary loneliness. In spite of the dinners, receptions, conversaziones, balls and theatre parties, they had no friends, nor did they communicate, so far as anyone could see, with one another. Old Lady Herries broke into frequent rages with her son and to these he listened with a grave and unaccommodating silence. Abroad she talked of him incessantly, his brilliance in the City, his nobility, his love for his fellow-men. At home she often told him he was stupid, ungrateful, and cold. Her extravagances grew with her age, her paint, gay colours, fantastic screams of laughter. She was a sight with her trimmings, fichus, shawls, her little hats perched high on her old head, her fingers covered with rings, bands and twists of hair, dyed, and interwoven with strands of ribbon and sprays of foliage. It remained, however, that she won respect because it was known that, selfish in everything else, clinging to life like a tigress, she would die for her son at any moment if the call came.

On the night of Vanessa's arrival, when the house was as silent as the moon, Ellis visited his mother in her bedroom. Sitting up in bed she looked the old, shrivelled, lonely, exhausted monkey that she really was. Ellis stood gravely beside her bed and said:

'Well, Mama, it is as I thought. Vanessa is the only woman whom I will ever marry.'

Lady Herries blinked her eyes. For eight years now, ever since the Hundredth Birthday in Cumberland, he had told her this. She did not care for Vanessa; she had thought Adam a country yokel, old Judith a mountebank. Moreover the girl's mother was a German. But if Ellis wanted anything he was to have it. God, she thought--she believed in a God made exactly in the image of herself--must be of the same opinion.

She could not deny that she had been struck by the girl's beauty. She had both the scorn and jealousy of beauty felt by many women who have fought life's battle without that great advantage. But this girl was exceptional. Raw, untrained, straight from the country: nevertheless with care and attention the girl could undoubtedly be turned into something. She had long made it a practice to refuse, at first, any request that Ellis might make of her, because she never lost hope that he might one day become more urgent in his prayers. She knew, in her heart, that this was one of the many hopes that would never be fulfilled.

So now she said: 'Nonsense. The girl's straight from a farm or a dairy or whatever it is. She's got no breeding.'

'She has perfect breeding,' Ellis said, and left her.

Next morning, considering the matter, she determined to make the girl devoted to her. Assuming, as do many old people, that she would live for ever, it was important that when Ellis married his wife they should continue to live in Hill Street. To lose Ellis was, of course, not to be thought of, but Vanessa might influence him. In her grinning, chattering way she did her best to be charming. It was not difficult to win Vanessa's affections if sincerity was there, and Lady Herries was, in this, sincere. Before three days were out the old woman felt that for the first time in her life someone cared for her. For the first time in her life she herself cared for someone other than her son. But truly everything was enchantment to Vanessa. She never saw London again as she saw it in those early days.

Everything about London was a miracle. The first morning she walked out she saw an old crossing-sweeper who stood at the corner of Berkleley Square and Charles Street dressed in an old faded scarlet hunting coat, given him, Barney told her, by Lord Cork, Master of the Buckhounds. That old man, with his broom, in his scarlet coat, seemed to her delighted eyes the very symbol of London, its incongruity, unexpected romance, humanity and pathos. There was an Indian crossing-sweeper, too, who stood with his broom outside the Naval and Military Club. There were the many Punch and Judy shows, the poor, dark, melancholy Italian sellers of cheap statuettes, and the old hurdy-gurdy man with his monkey.

Hyde Park was her chief delight. Lady Herries liked to drive in the afternoon, and so they paraded in a grand victoria, the old woman sitting with a back like a poker, gay as the rainbow, while Simon the coachman, in a multi-coloured livery, in figure like a sealion, drove, as though he were acting in a pageant, his magnificent horses.

But it was all like a pageant, the small phaetons with their high- stepping horses, the pony chaises conveying ladies of fashion, the victorias, the smart buggies driven by men about town, and the quiet-looking little broughams containing, it was supposed, all sorts of mysterious occupants!

This was a fine and warm April, and in the evening, between five and seven, everyone took the air in the Park. It was, it seemed, a world of infinite leisure where no one had anything to do but to see and be seen. On the other hand, there was nothing extravagant or forced in the display. No one, it appeared, wished to stagger anyone else. Everyone's position was too sure and certain. Rotten Row was, in fact, for more sophisticated eyes than Vanessa's, a superb affair.

In every way London was a magnificent show. The omnibuses alone gave it an air, for painted red, or royal blue, or green, they were always handsome and individual, with their strong horses and their swaggering, accomplished drivers who had, with the flick of their whips, the air of conjurers about to produce rabbits out of their greatcoats.

The horses indeed were wonderful, Vanessa thought, never needing the whip, the drivers' cheerful hiss all the encouragement they wanted. They were, she thought, both fiery and gentle, a glorious combination. The doors, the straw on the floor, these things were gone. The omnibuses were now the final word in the modern science of travel. But best of all were the hansom-cabs, the splendid horses driven by the most elegant cabmen who wore glossy hats and had flowers in their buttonholes. On the first day that Barney took Vanessa down Piccadilly and Westminster in a hansom-cab, she sat, her hands clasped, her eyes shining, her smart little hat perched on her dark hair, Queen, it seemed to her, of all Fairyland.

Finally London then was a town of constant surprises. You never knew what at any moment would turn up. Every building had life and character of its own, little crooked houses next to big straight ones, sudden little streets--dark, twisted, and eccentric--leading to calm dignified squares, fantastic statues, glittering fountains, shops blazing with splendour, hostelries that had not altered for hundreds of years. Everywhere colour, leisure, and, in this first superficial view, light-hearted happiness.

In that first week she spent her days with Lady Herries (Ellis was in the City all day), Rose Ormerod, and her brother Horace. The power that Rose had over Vanessa from the beginning came from her jollity, her

kindness, her humour, her warm-heartedness. Rose had also other qualities which appeared later in their friendship. Horace, her brother, had a job as secretary to some big benevolent society. He was rosy-cheeked, square-shouldered, spoke well of everyone, was the friend of all the world. He was a little naïve. He talked frankly about himself. He was modest.

'I'm nothing exceptional, you know, Vanessa. I don't suppose you think I am. What I say is--why not see the best in everyone? It's easy enough if you try. People have a hard enough time. Why shouldn't we all make it pleasant for one another? I must confess that I find life a good thing.'

He was very jolly, had a hearty laugh, seemed generous and genial to everyone. There was something faintly episcopal about him as though he were in training to be a bishop. Rose was sometimes a little sarcastic about her brother, but then she was sarcastic about everyone.

Vanessa was happy, but underneath this exciting London adventure one consuming thought possessed her. Where was Benjie?

This was April 1882. The time had come when Benjie would demand the conclusion to the vow that they had made by the water dolphin of Ireby. Perhaps because she had seen him so seldom in these two years the thought of him by now completely possessed her. If she had loved him two years ago it was by this time as though he were part of her very flesh. She was neither romantic nor sentimental in her idea of him. She saw him as he was just as she saw herself as she was. Would he come? Where was he? He had written to her, on some dozen occasions, little letters, from Burma, China, India, North America. In these he had not said much, and yet she knew that he needed her, that he was thinking of her as she of him. Would he come? London brought him nearer. When the first sharp excitement of her visit paled a little she began to look for him, in the Park, the streets, the theatre. Often she thought that she saw his small stocky figure, dark face, often fancied that she recognized the quick determined step with which he walked. Would he come, and, if April passed without him, what would she do? Was he faithless, volatile, careless, as they all said of him? Could she trust that he was faithful at least to her? Would he, oh, would he come? She spoke of him, of course, to no one, not even to Rose.

And then, in the second week of her visit, she began to be embarrassed by Ellis. She liked Ellis. She understood him better than others did. Most of all she was sorry for him. She wanted, as she so often wanted with people, to make him happy. There was something about his spare, grave figure that touched her heart. He was so ALONE. He wanted, she was sure, to be jolly with everyone but did not know how to set about it. She saw in him sometimes an eagerness as though he said: 'Now this time I shall be lucky and find touch.'

But always his shyness, his fear of a rebuff, checked him. As Lady Herries became more confidential the old lady poured out to Vanessa the truth about Ellis as she saw it, his goodness, kindliness of heart, diffidence. 'He can't chatter away,' Lady Herries said indignantly, 'like Barney Newmark or Horace Ormerod; but he has ten times their brains.'

Vanessa supposed that he had. He must be very clever to remain so silent for so long.

As the days passed she had an odd impression that he was approaching her ever nearer and nearer. He was not in reality; he always sat at a distance from her and when he walked with her seemed deliberately to take care that he should not by accident touch her. And yet she was ever more and more conscious of his body, his high cheekbones, the pale skin pulled tightly over them, his sharp-pointed nose, very Herries, with nostrils open, slightly raw, sensitive; his thin mouth, his high shoulder blades, his spare slim hands, his long legs that seemed always so lonely and desolate inside his over-official London clothes. He was very tall and walked as though he had a poker down his back. He was distinguished certainly with his top hat, his shining black tie, collar and cuffs almost too starched and gleaming, his pale gloves, his neatly rolled umbrella with its gold top. People looked after him and wondered who he might be, just as once they had wondered about his father. His pale thin face peered out anxiously at the world over his high collar. When he spoke you felt that his words were important although they seldom were so. He had a nervous little cough and often he blinked with his eyes.

One fine spring day he took a holiday from the City and in the company of Horace and Rose and Vanessa walked in the Park. Very soon Vanessa found herself sitting alone with him while Rose and Horace talked to friends. She was wearing her most beautiful frock, rose and white, the pleated and flounced skirt with tucked panniers over the hips, the bodice cut high in the neck, long and pointed at the waistline. The wide skirt, the modified bustle, the little hat with roses, the different shades of rose in the dress itself, all these things were remembered by her when many times afterwards she recalled that costume as one of the loveliest of her life and the one that she was wearing when Ellis first proposed marriage.

He plunged at once like a man flinging himself with the courage of despair into icy water.

'Vanessa, I must tell you. I can avoid it no longer. I love you with all my soul. Please—please—will you marry me?'

It was then, although his seat was apart from hers, that she felt as if the moment, which for days had been approaching, had arrived. He seemed to have flung his body on to hers; she felt his thin hands at her neck, his bony cheek against hers, she could feel his heart wildly, furiously beating. She looked and saw that he had not moved. He was sitting, staring in front of him at the carriages, the riders, the colours, the sun; his gloved hands were folded on the gold knob of his umbrella.

She wanted then, as never before in her life, to be kind.

'Ellis! Marry you! But I don't want to marry anybody!'

(That was untrue. She wanted, oh, how she wanted, to marry Benjie!)

He had recovered himself a little.

'I know that it must be a shock to you, dear Vanessa. I recognize that. I must give you time. But you must not think that it is any sudden idea of mine. I have had no other thought since I first saw you, years ago, in Cumberland. That time—we were downstairs at Uldale. From that moment I knew that only you of everyone in the world could be my wife.'

She laid her hand for a moment on his knee.

'I am proud that you should think of me like that,' she said slowly, 'but I'm afraid I can't. Ellis, I like you very much, but I don't want to be married—really I don't. I couldn't leave my father. It wouldn't be kind to him now he is all alone.'

(How stupid and stiff her words were! She wanted to be good to him, to say something that would take that wistful, forlorn look from his eyes.)

'Your father could come and live with us.'

'I'm afraid he could never live in London. He is miserable now if he is away from Cumberland.'

'If you could—if you could—love me a little, Vanessa. I would wait. I would be very patient. Perhaps you could love me a little—'

She must be honest.

'No. I don't love you, Ellis. Love is very rare, isn't it? I like you so much—'

'Well, then,' he caught her up eagerly, 'that will perhaps turn into love. If you stay with us a little while. My mother likes you so much. I have never known her like anyone so much before. I can be very patient. I will give you as much time as you like—'

'I am afraid time will not alter it,' she answered gently. 'Friendship and love are so different—'

But he did not seem to hear. He went on eagerly.

'I will give you everything you can want. There's nothing you can ask for that you shan't have. I will never interfere with you. Only let me love you and serve you. I am not a man who has many friends. You have noticed that perhaps. I have been always shy in company, but with you beside me I feel that I could do anything. You are so good, so beautiful—'

Now the little scene was becoming dreadful to her. His intensity, his earnestness shamed her as though she had been caught in some misconduct.

'Ellis, dear. Listen. I don't love you. I'm afraid I never shall. We would be both of us most unhappy. Let us be friends, better and better friends, and you will find someone who WILL love you, who will make you so very happy—'

Words that every lady has used to every disconsolate lover! She knew it. She had not conceived that she could be so stupid. But, it seemed, he had not heard her. Rose and Horace gaily approached them, Horace laughing, greeting all the world as a jolly brother.

'Never mind, Vanessa,' Ellis said quietly. 'I will ask you again. It is a shock, of course. I am afraid that I was very sudden.'

'We do apologize,' cried Rose. 'That was Colonel Norton. I haven't seen him for an age. We were only gone a minute.'

It seemed to Vanessa that they had been an hour away.

When, alone in her room that night, she was dressing for dinner, she most unexpectedly had a fit of crying. She did not often cry, although young ladies thought nothing of it. But now, sitting in front of the glass, twisting her hair into ringlets, she found that the tears made ridiculous splashes on the pincushion, which was fat and round like a large white toad with a bright pink eye. She was crying, she discovered, because that Ellis should love her made her want Benjie so terribly. Oh, if it had been Benjie who had said those words in the Park! But it was not. It was Ellis. Then she found that she was crying because she felt, for the first time in her life, lonely and needed her father. She seemed to see him in the glass facing her, his brown beard, his soft rather ironical, rather sleepy eyes, his broad shoulders, rough coat . . . She thought that tomorrow morning, as early as possible, she would take the train to Cumberland . . .

Her tears were quickly dried because she was, she saw in the glass, so long and lanky. Now Rose might cry very prettily because she was slight and delicate in spite of her dark colour. But Vanessa was too tall for tears. She stood up in her skirt, all flounces and frills, raised her arms, threw up her head. Because Ellis had proposed to her was no reason for tears!

Then she laughed. The day before she had paid a visit with Rose to one of Rose's friends, a Mrs Pettinger. Mrs Pettinger's husband was an artist, and their little house in Pimlico had shone with the new aestheticism. The walls had Morris wallpapers, everywhere there were Japanese fans, bamboo tables, lilies in tall thin glasses, Japanese prints. Also two drawings by Mr Whistler which, privately, Vanessa had thought very beautiful. Privately, because Rose had confided to her that she found them absurd.

'Why, anyone could do that!' she said. 'I could. Just take your pencil and draw a few lines up and down. You have to stand a mile away to see what they're about.'

What made her laugh was the contrast between the room that she was in now and Mrs Pettinger's house. It seemed symbolically to be the contrast that she felt between her love for Benjie and Ellis' proposal. Her large cold bedroom had not, she supposed, been changed in detail for thirty years. Especially did she notice, as though seeing them for the first time, two armchairs of light oak carved with floral decorations and upholstered with dark-green velvet having a floral pattern. When you sat down in one of them it clung to you as though asserting its righteousness. Then the frame of Tonbridge-ware that contained a picture of a little girl outside a church made in seaweed, the Coalport toilet service, the dressing-table and mirror trimmed with glazed linen and muslin, the mahogany bedstead, the needlework bell-pulls. Yes, she thought, sitting down on the green velvet armchair, there were two worlds, as her father had always told her. Sitting there, without moving, staring before her, thinking of her mother, her father, Benjie, all those whom she loved, she moved naturally, simply into another world that had been, all her life, as real to her as the plush chair on which she was sitting. There was no effort, no conscious act of the will. An inner life flowed like a strong stream beneath all external things. This life had its own history, its own progress, its own destiny. She never spoke of it nor tried to explain it. It needed no explanation. Sometimes the two lives met, the two streams flowed together, but whereas the external life had its checks, its alarms, its vanities, and empty disappointments, this inner life flowed steadily, was always there. Yes, two worlds in everything. How to connect them? The Saints, she supposed, were those who had learnt the answer, men and women in whose lives one life always interpenetrated the other. But she, Vanessa, was no saint. She could only, at certain moments, be conscious of an awareness, an illumination, that irradiated everything so that in that brilliant light both things and people had suddenly their proper values.

Sitting on her plush chair she had now such a moment . . .

In the days that followed, Ellis behaved to her exactly as he had always done. It was as though their little conversation in the Park had never been. She obtained increasingly from the Herries family both instruction and amusement. Old Amery greatly amused her with his intimate stories of high places, of the adventures, for example, of King William of the Netherlands, one of whose ladies broke all the crockery in his palace during one of her tempers, of some Italian prince in Paris who disguised himself as an organ-grinder for a whole month that he might station himself outside his lady-love's door, of young Lord So-and-so who, rejected by his mistress, put a large black band on his hat, went to his rooms, and committed suicide by cutting his wrist open with a razor, remembering first to place a slop pail by the chair that there might be no mess. Young Alfred amused her because he would tolerate anyone who promised to be notable. She liked Captain Will with his breezy manner of finding the sea the only possible place, and yet now he never went there. The Rockages were redolent of the country. Carey himself, although he was tidy enough, seemed to carry good Wiltshire mud on his boots, and little Lady Rockage walked as though she were ready to spring on to a horse's back at any moment. She soon knew them all and liked them all with the single exception of Emily, Barney's sister, who was pious but not charitable, prudish with an unpleasant inquisitiveness, and a mischief-maker for the best of motives.

She found them all most strangely alike in some basic way. They had no pose, made no attempts to assert themselves, took everything for granted. For them all, the Herries were the backbone of England, and England was the only country in the world that mattered at all. It was Barney Newmark, however, who best explained the family position to her, sitting beside her on the occasion of the splendid Herries party in Hill Street when Mme Trebelli sang and Signor Pesto played so enthusiastically the violin.

Vanessa liked Barney best of them all. Rose, of course, excepted. Barney was now fifty-two, stout, fresh-coloured, and carelessly dressed but not untidy. He looked a little Bohemian but not very; you would not know that he was a writer, said Vanessa. That was a period when writers LOOKED like writers. He took life very lightly, laughed at everyone and everything, but behind that was, she thought, a disappointed man. He had published a dozen novels and lived comfortably on the proceeds. She had read several of them. They were not very good and not very bad. They were like the books of other authors. But he never spoke of his novels, laughed scornfully when they were mentioned to him. She felt, however, that he would like it very much if someone else praised them. At their first meeting in London she said what she could. At once he stopped her.

'Dear Vanessa. Thank you very much. And now we need never mention them again, need we? No friends of mine can read my novels. That is a sign of their friendship.' Very different, had she but known it, from the man who once at a prize-fight had clasped Mortimer Collins by the shoulder!

They sat now in a corner of the big drawing-room and watched the splendid affair. The room was very crowded. It looked for the first time alive, for the heavy furniture was gone and, save for the palms, ferns and flowers packed into the corners, round the piano, in front of the great marble fireplace, only human beings filled it. The ladies wore their jewels, their shoulders gleamed under the gaslight, everyone was splendid, dignified, assured and, it appeared, happy. Vanessa would never have had courage to penetrate the throng, but almost at once she saw Barney, who carried her off

into a corner, saying: 'Now I shall be the proudest man here for five minutes, before you are discovered, you know. Soon there will be so many proud men that you won't be able to breathe.'

She was very happy alone with him. She would like to stay thus throughout the evening.

'Tell me who everyone is, Barney dear,' she said.

He pointed out a few. 'That dignified cleric is the Bishop of London. That fine fellow there is Mr Bancroft.'

'And oh, who is that darling old man?'

That darling old man looked like a ship's captain. He had a grey beard, grey hair erect and curly through which he often ran his hands, a florid complexion, clear eyes. He was the finest man in the room.

'That is Mr Madox Brown,' said Barney.

'And that lovely lady?'

'That lovely lady is Mrs Samuel Maguire, and her husband gives her a diamond every morning with her coffee.'

'And that very dark man?'

'That is Isaac Lowenfeld, the financier. He once blacked gentlemen's shoes in Constantinople. Jews are coming in. The Prince of Wales likes them, and why should he not? I like them myself. They have the best hearts, the best brains and the staunchest religion in London.'

She noticed two young men with high white foreheads, long pale hair and a very languishing manner.

'And those?'

'Those are the aesthetes. They look at a lily for breakfast, worship china teacups and lisp in poetry. I don't like 'em myself. They are not my kind. But they have their uses.'

'Everyone is here then? Lady Herries will be pleased.'

'Yes, it is a success because soon the room will be so crowded that no one can move, so noisy that no one will hear anyone else, and so hot that several young ladies will faint.'

She soon found members of the Herries family here and there.

'There is Emily. How nice and healthy Captain Will looks! I think Alfred is over-dressed.'

'Yes, we are all here,' said Barney. 'A great satisfaction to all of us. A fine family. And yet we are not of the first rank. Oh, I don't mean in history. We are, I suppose, as old as any family in England. But we are not, and never shall be, like the Chichesters, the Medleys. Nor like the Beaminsters, the Cecils, the Howards. Although in fact we ARE a kind of relation of the Howards. But we're not like the new democrats either, people like the Ruddards, the Denisons. All very poor kind of talk this, but it's important, the social history of England, partly because it's history, partly because in another fifty years' time there won't be any social history. There, do you see that little woman in black with that jade pendant--with the hard mouth and the small nose? That's the Duchess of Wrexe. That's her daughter, Adela Beaminster, with her. Well, she walks as though she owned the world, every scrap of it. Contrast her with Lady Herries. Oh, I know SHE isn't a Herries really, but she's acquired ALL the Herries characteristics. The wives of Herries men always do. That's what I mean. We are upper middle class. We belong in the country, small Squires, maiden ladies in places like Bournemouth and Harrogate, houses like Uldale for example. That's where WE are. For the last hundred years we've been rising or seeming to. Will made a heap of money and Ellis is making more. Then there are the Rockages, a small pocket-nobility. But we are not first class in anything. We write--well, as I do. We are parsons and one of us becomes an Archdeacon. We make money in the City but can't TOUCH Lowenfeld. We entertain, but when we bring off a party like this it's a kind of accident. Not that we see ourselves like that. We think there's nobody to touch us, but that's because we have no imagination. That's why we are of real importance in the country. If there's ever a revolution in England it's the Herries and others like them who will save us all. Even as we begin to die out the lower ranks take our places and become just like us. We are filled up from below, but we never RISE any higher. We have our good points--we are not acquisitive, we are not greedy, we are kind if we are not attacked, generous even; we never lose our heads, we adore our country although we criticize it. We never have to speak foreign languages, we revel in our abominable climate, on the whole we are contented.'

'But?--' asked Vanessa.

'We have one great weakness. We are terrified of anything out of the normal. If we see it we fight and slay it. Unhappily there is a strain of the artist in our family. It breaks out again and again. Then we are shamed, disgraced, humiliated. We have never learnt how to assimilate it. That is why if we breed an artist he is always second-rate. The family is too strong for him. That is why we fight among ourselves and why some of us, if we are courageous enough not to come to terms, are so unhappy. Oh, you needn't look at me, my dear. I HAVE come to terms. I couldn't fight it out. That is why I am what I am. I am always hoping that we shall breed an artist who, because he is forced to fight, becomes a GREAT artist. Why have the English the finest poets in the world? Because the other members of the family have always done their best to kill them. Why was your grandmother so splendid? Because she never capitulated.'

'Father always says that she declared that she DID capitulate,' said Vanessa.

'Capitulate? She? Think of her! Capitulate? Not she! If she were in this room tonight she'd blow out the Duchess of Wrexe like a farthing dip!'

'And have you altogether capitulated, Barney?'

'Yes, my dear. Entirely. I'm no good at all. But I tell you who HASN'T capitulated. That's Benjie!'

At the unexpected sound of his name the lights blurred, the voices faded.

'No,' said Barney, 'but if he doesn't they'll drum him out of the field. You watch them. It will be a fight worth beholding!'

And now the room was crammed indeed. The roar of conversation, like the break of the tide on shingle with here a whisper, here a grating clatter of pebbles, here a resounding hiss, made private talk impossible, so Barney, pleased with his analysis of his relations, stood up and looked about him while Vanessa watched Mr Madox Brown roaring at the Bishop of London, and the lovely Mrs Williamson (who was reputed to bathe in milk every morning) listening kindly to one of the young aesthetes, who twisted and bent like a reed in a gale.

She caught fragments of conversation. 'I heard Trebelli at Sims Reeves' concert in February. No, he couldn't appear, so we had Trebelli and Santley instead. Oh, of course Trebelli's the best contralto in the world. But to tell you the honest truth I enjoyed better Santley's "Vicar of Bray"--irresistible. Quite irresistible . . .'

'Oh, but Bradlaugh! . . .'

'And then, my love, WHAT do you think? She went to the pastrycook's round the corner and HERSELF fetched a dozen cream buns in a paper bag . . .'

'Yes, but what I say is that they could keep Jumbo here perfectly well, doncherknow, if they wanted to--really wanted to. What I mean is, that Jumbo is important for the country, for the TOURISTS, doncherknow--something for them to go to the Zoo and look at. What I mean is, we all feel it PERSONALLY . . .'

'Very UNKIND of Punch, I think. Poor Mr Irving--to print his picture and then quote "Romeo! Romeo! Wherefore are THOU Romeo?" That's too personal in my opinion. All the same he is NOT the young, ardent lover . . .'

'Yes, but what Russell wants is to buy out the Irish landlords and present the holdings to the tenants! Simple! I should think so! If Gladstone would only say what he means . . .'

'And so, darling, Henry said to him, "That lady is intended evidently for a Chinese"--trying to be witty, poor man, and the large man with the teeth whom he'd NEVER seen before said furiously, "And why, pray? That lady is my sister." And oh, wasn't Henry clever? He answered at once, "Why, because she has such exquisitely small feet."'

It was Vanessa's first London party, and, standing there, waiting before she should be drawn into the middle of it, she knew, as her grandmother had known on just such another occasion, that something in her responded to this with excitement and eagerness. It was as though, a vagabond and wanderer, peering in through a window at a splendid feast, she exclaimed to herself: 'I can do this as well as anyone. I know all the tricks.' She would never truly belong to it, but it was a part that she could play as well as anyone there. The personal drama had seized her. The drama of London, the Park with the brilliant sunlit figures, the old crossing- sweeper with the scarlet coat, Ellen Terry laughing into the wicked eyes of old Mrs Stirling, Mr Conway rebuking his errant daughter, Gladstone in his high collar thundering at the House, old Lady Herries fixing, with trembling hands, the jewels about her throat, the melancholy wail of the hurdy-gurdy two streets away, the Prince of Wales talking to Mr Lowenfeld, the 'greenery-yallery' young men yearning over a Japanese print, the carts packed with flowers arriving in the early morning at Covent Garden, Gambetta drinking his morning coffee in Paris, and that picturesque brigand Arabi ordering an execution in Egypt, an account that she had read only last week in a paper of a Professor who had invented 'little electric lamps of wires of platinum inside glass bulbs,' Ellis loving her and Horace Ormerod's friendliness, and Rose's adventurousness, Barney's kindness, and, behind it all, sitting in the hut at the top of the Cat Bells garden, watching the thin spidery rain veil the Lake in webs of lawn while fragments of blue sky, as bright as speedwells, flashed and vanished and flashed again. Her mind was a jumble of this kind; at the back of the jumble was the deep unceasing preoccupation. Would Benjie come before the month was out? Would he keep his word? Was there nothing that could still this burning ceaseless preoccupation of hers? And, if he cared no longer for her, could she make her life without him? She could! She could! She was not so weak, so helpless! But her throat was dry at the thought! Her hand touched her breast to check the wild beating of her heart.

She was discovered. Rose and Horace discovered her. They led her into the throng and at once her own life was broken into little scattered fragments. She had no life. She was nothing but a laughing, smiling, murmuring adjunct to all the other laughs, smiles, murmurs.

She was introduced to Mr Madox Brown. They sat down together near the piano. At first he said nothing, pushing his strong brown hand through his curly hair, muttering a little, looking as though he wanted to escape. Then something happened. SHE did not know what it was. In actual fact it was his sudden realization of her beauty. He never saw her again, but many times after he would growl:

'One night at one of those damned musical parties I came on a girl . . . you never saw anyone so lovely. Quite unconscious of it too.'

He became gentle and most friendly. He told her about his son. 'He died seven years ago. There never WAS anyone so talented. Only nineteen when he died. One day, when he was dying and I sitting at his bedside, he smiled and said I smelt of tobacco. I said, "All right. I'll not smoke again until you're better." I never SHALL smoke again. Never. Paint? Write? He could do any-

thing. And sweet-natured. Oliver was the only genius I've known. No one else. Not GENIUS. Genius is something from another world. Nothing to do with this shabby one.'

He asked her where she came from.

She told him, Cumberland.

'Oh yes, Wordsworth and all that.'

Looking at her he said:

'You have beautiful eyes. Forgive an old painter's impertinence, my dear. I always begin with the eyes, you know. Paint the eyes of the central figure first and that gives tone to the picture. I begin at the top left hand of the canvas and go straight down to the bottom. And what do YOU do?'

'I can't paint,' she answered, laughing. 'I can't do anything.'

'You don't need to,' he told her.

They could have become great friends had life arranged it.

Then she was alone with Rose, sitting behind a gigantic pessimistic palm. They were clearing the space about the piano. Trebelli was going to sing. What, she thought, was Rose's power over her? Why was she so fond of her? Rose was like a carnation, set deep in colour, slight, with a wine-dark air. Not beautiful, for her eyes were too large for her small face, her nose a little snub, and her mouth, Vanessa must confess, rather hard. Her eyes laughed, danced, sparkled, but her mouth was always a little cold, a little cruel. If you judged people by their eyes, then Rose was a dear sweet girl, but if by their mouth, then Rose was nothing of the kind. She said once to Vanessa:

'Horace and I are both completely hard and self-seeking!'

'Oh no!' protested Vanessa.

'Oh yes, we are! The only difference between us is that I look at myself in the glass and know EXACTLY what I am. Horace looks greedily into other people's faces for his reflection and woe betide you if it isn't a pleasant one.' She added: 'We are both adventurers. We have scarcely a penny to our name. I'm the Becky Sharp in Thackeray's stupid novel except that I'm sometimes sentimental. After I've been sentimental I'm so angry with everyone that I could commit murder. I dare say I shall one day. Probably my husband. First I must get one. I'm twenty-seven, you know.'

She talked a great deal about herself, and this Vanessa found delightful, but Rose's real attraction for her was that she knew life so thoroughly. Girls who were Vanessa's contemporaries knew nothing about life at all. They were not supposed to know and, what was more, they really did not know. Most of them married without the slightest idea of what came next, with the simple result that, for the rest of their days, they were a little melancholy and looked at all men, except clergymen, with a faint distrust. The women on the other hand, like Rose, for whom life (including men) had no secrets, were like gipsies who pitch their caravans at their own risk. The female world looked on them with suspicion, and the male world frequently presumed further than slight acquaintance warranted.

Rose had by this time told Vanessa everything she knew, and Vanessa, because she possessed certain beliefs, fidelities and a strong sense of humour, was not at all shocked. She hoped nevertheless that Rose would be married soon. It would be wiser.

Rose, on her side, loved Vanessa. She might be herself a lost angel--and she was a great deal more lost than Vanessa realized-- but she adored a good angel with a sense of humour. She admired passionately in Vanessa all the qualities that she did not herself possess. She was no fool about human nature. She knew quite well that even from her mercenary point of view the virtues pay better in the end than the vices.

So they sat together behind the pessimistic palm and talked about those present. Rose knew something about everyone. She knew just what to tell Vanessa, amusing things but not cruel ones. She kept her cruel ones for other audiences.

Then, touching Vanessa's hand, she said: 'There, I think, is the man I am going to marry.'

'Oh, where?' cried Vanessa. 'Rose, dear, do you mean it.'

'I THINK that I mean it. That man with the eyeglass, the pale whiskers, the beautiful figure.'

Vanessa looked. He was certainly very handsome.

'Oh, who is he?'

'He is Captain Fred Wycherley. He is in the Army and is very rich.'

'Oh, Rose dear, I am so glad! Has he proposed to you? Do you love him very much?'

'No, he has not proposed, but I think within the week he will. I don't love him, of course. It would never do for me to love my husband: it would give him too much power over me. But he is agreeable, amusing. I think we shall understand one another.'

Before they could say any more Trebelli began to sing. She had an extremely powerful voice and sang as though she were commanding a regiment. She was made, it appeared, of brass from head to foot.

After the singing everyone began to move about again and Vanessa was introduced to a number of people. Among them was a stout, round gentleman with fair hair and the face of a very good-natured pig, whose eyes beamed with kindliness. This, she discovered, was Lord John Beaminster, a son of the Duchess of Wrexe. He spoke in jerks, smiling upon her as though he had known her all her life.

'Very hot, these parties,' he said.

'Yes,' she said, copying Barney. 'The hotter they are the more successful they are.'

'Do you care for music?'

'Yes, sometimes.'

'That woman has deafened my eardrum. All the opera women shout. Do you like the opera?'

'I've never been in my life,' said Vanessa. 'I live in the country.'

'Oh, in the country, do you? Wouldn't want to live there. All right for a day or two. What part?'

'Up in Cumberland.'

'Doesn't it rain there?'

'Yes, when it wants to, but nobody minds the rain.'

'I do, unless I'm shooting or hunting, you know.' He smiled as though they had reached the most delightful intimacy. 'Oh, that damned feller's going to play the fiddle.'

It was then that as she looked beyond him towards the door, as though something had compelled her, the miracle of her whole life occurred. Beaminster was saying something to her. The violin began to wail. The shining shoulders of some woman at her side spread, as it appeared, into an infinite distance.

In the doorway, looking about him with a friendly grin, stood Benjie Herries.

She did not move. Beaminster, seeing a friend, said, with a bow: 'Excuse me one moment.'

Then Benjie seemed to drive, like a swimmer breasting the tide, straight towards her. She saw people greet him. She heard (for he was very near to her now) Will Herries exclaim:

'Hullo, Benjie! Where have you come from?'

She did not move until his hand was on her sleeve. She heard him say: 'Come out of this. Outside.'

She went with him down the room. In the passage above the stairs there was no one. From the room within, the violin went on and on like a voice speaking only for them.

She stood up against the wall, staring at him, feeling that at any moment she might cry, unable to speak because her heart beat so fiercely, hammering her body as though it must throw her down. But there was no need to speak, no time for it.

'You thought that I wasn't coming back. Didn't you? You thought that I had forgotten. Quick, Vanessa, tell me--do you love me? Do you love me as much as two years ago? Is there anyone else? If so, where is he? I'll kill him. Quick. Tell me. I have run all the way from Brindisi. If you knew how I've run! Tell me. Tell me. Do you love me? Are you going to marry me? Can I go in there now and tell them all? Quick. Don't waste a moment! Do you love me?'

'Benjie, wait! Of course I do. I thought you'd never come! I've been longing--'

But she did not finish her sentence. He kissed her, patting her shoulder, her arm, laying his cheek against hers. Then he caught her hand in his.

'Now come! At once! We must tell everyone! We mustn't lose a moment!'

He pulled her with him to the door. The voice of the violin came towards them, dancing over the crowd, the flowers, the palms.

Seated by the door was an old lady, blazing with diamonds, listening to the music through an ear-trumpet.

'Excuse me--' said Benjie.

'Hush! hush!' said everyone near the door. The violin rose into a thin, long, vibrating note. Then ceased.

The old lady, turning to a man beside her, said:

'And NOW it ought to be time for supper.' Then, looking up: 'Why, it's Benjamin Herries! I thought you were in China, young man.'

Benjie wrung her hand as though she were the friend of his heart.

'I was, Lady Mullion. I was--only yesterday. Let me introduce you to Miss Vanessa Paris. We are going to be married--'

'Going to be what?' she asked, her round red face ignorantly beaming.

He took the ear-trumpet, and, in a voice loud enough for all the world to hear, shouted: 'We are going to be married.'

'Oh, is that all?' said the old lady. 'I thought there'd been an accident. And now I do HOPE we are going down to supper.'

THE SEASHORE

Timothy Bellairs took his wife and family that summer to an old house, Low Dene, in the village of Gosforth, which was situated ten miles from Wastwater and a little more than three miles from Seascale on the coast.

Young Tim, now aged five, had not lately been very well; one cold had followed the other. Sea air would do the children good, and he would have found some place ON the sea had it not been for Mrs Bellairs, who disliked the sea and all its works. So a compromise was effected.

Low Dene was one of those large, rambling, untidy houses of which at that time the country offered many examples. They were especially suited to the large families that good English parents thought it proper to create. The house was in a hollow under the hill to the right of the village; fields ran to the edge of the big scrambling garden; there was a croquet lawn, a wood, shrubberies, a stream, everything that children desired. The place belonged to a retired Indian colonel whose children were now grown. He had gone with his wife and four daughters to Brighton, where he hoped to marry the daughters and recapture some of his own youth. It was one of those houses which here are furnished and there are not. The drawing-room, some of the bedrooms, were crowded with large and small impedimenta, so crowded that you could scarcely move without disabling a china figure, upsetting an Indian idol, or flinging a wool mat to the floor. On the other hand most of the passages, some of the bedrooms, the bathroom, had no covering to the bare boards, the wind whistled through the thin faded wallpapers, the piano was altogether out of tune, every fireplace smoked, the gas hissed, the cistern groaned, there was an odd smell of dog in every room, and draughts played in every corner. In spite of these things the house had an air of cosiness and comfort--why, it would be difficult to say. It was, maybe, because a large family had grown up in it and their games, quarrels, intimacies, pleasures had sunk into the brick, permeated the boards of the passages, helped to stain curtains and wallpapers into their faded homely colours.

Timothy, his wife, and children were well pleased. Fell House, Uldale, was the joy and boast of Timothy's heart, but it was pleasant for a while to escape its responsibilities. Timothy was lazy although he disguised the laziness with true English aplomb. As to the children this was the happiest summer of their young lives. Discipline was relaxed; their father condescended to walk with them, there was the Farm at the top of the hill, the fields with the haymaking, the mysterious wood, the sea, and above all Vanessa.

It was Timothy who had invited Vanessa to stay with them. Mrs Bellairs had objected, although in her sleepy, limited fashion she rather liked Vanessa. They had both been deeply shocked--as had Herries up and down the country--when they heard of her engagement to Benjamin Herries. They had thought at first that they would never speak to Vanessa again. But Timothy had as true an affection for her as he had for anyone in the world. In his stout slow body there was little rancour, no spitefulness, temper only with his own children. He was negative in all his emotions except his family pride. He thought that he had the finest house, the finest wife, the finest children in the world, and perhaps, deep in his heart, he loved his children and had an affection for his wife. But it was not the fashion for either husbands or parents to be demonstrative. He was now forty-five years of age, laziness and corpulency made him virtuous, but he had still an eye for a pretty woman, and Vanessa's beauty, although he might not speak of it (for Mrs Bellairs could be a jealous woman), gave him the greatest pleasure to look upon. He would stare and stare at her with something of the same emotion with which he would gaze upon a fine shoulder of mutton freshly come to table. Nevertheless he cared for Vanessa. He would, at a push, do more for her than for anyone.

Discussing the tragic Vanessa-Benjie affair in the large family bed at Uldale, he declared that Vanessa should be invited to come with them to Gosforth. Mrs Bellairs groaned and lamented, but knew that if he had decided on something it was decided. They were both lazy people, but she was lazier than he. His point was that they might influence Vanessa. She had been carried off her feet by the London atmosphere. (He had the greatest contempt for London. He knew that he would not shine if he went there.) Let her spend a week or two with them in the country and they would soon show her her silly mistake.

'And her father?' murmured Mrs Bellairs.

'Let him come too,' said Timothy, who tolerated Adam but scorned him because he did nothing with his time but write books. 'The house is big enough.'

However, Adam refused. He might come over for a day or two.

Timothy, his wife, his sister Jane, now an old maid of forty-two, the children, Mrs Clopton the nurse, Agnes the young maid, Jim Wilson the coachman, Peter the dog, all moved over to Low Dene in the large family chariot.

Vanessa arrived there two days later.

The real reason of Vanessa's visit was that she wished to escape from Benjie, whom she had been seeing almost every day for the last three months.

It was not that she loved Benjie less: it was that she loved him more, and this love had plunged her into a turmoil of problems, excitements, and distresses not only about him but about herself as well.

She had never, until now, known any very close and intimate relation with anyone save her father and mother. Her life had always moved on certain fixed and stable laws. Her own faults and failings, which were many--impetuous feeling, hasty temper, neglect of obvious duties--had all, when tested by a few principles, been clearly faults and failings. There had never been any question about what she OUGHT to do. Simply she had been wicked and failed.

But she was as honest as anyone alive, both with herself and everyone else, and, after a week with Benjie, she saw that neither right nor wrong conduct would ever be so clear and simple again.

That she had been carried off her feet by Benjie's return and proposal did not at all blind her to the fact that no one else had. She realized immediately at the first half-hour in the party at Hill Street that no one anywhere was going to approve of the engagement--no, not even Rose. 'She is throwing herself away,' she could hear everyone saying. Benjie's charm and light-heartedness when he was happy affected many when he was with them, and during that final week in London he was very charming indeed, but, returning to Cumberland, she found that even Elizabeth was doubtful. 'It is what I have always wanted,' Elizabeth said. 'And oh, my dear, I do hope he will make you happy!'

And her father? He kissed her and told her that her happiness was dearer to him than anything else on earth. She was a woman now. She knew where her happiness lay.

She simply said: 'I have loved him all my life.' He said no more, but she noticed in him after this a constant anxiety, an extra tenderness, and in herself, a certain reticence that had not been there before. Their relationship was for the first time in their lives a little clouded.

Benjie came up to the Fortress and lived there quietly with his mother. At first he was happy with an exuberance, a generosity to all the world, that showed him at his very best. Everyone noticed the change in him.

'I think,' Elizabeth confided to Vanessa after a week or two, 'that it will be as I hoped. You are going to change him altogether.' He told her again and again how, during those last months abroad, her image, his adoration of her, obsessed him more and more completely. On his journey home his impatience was a fever. At the sight of her at last in that silly drawing-room he nearly died! They must be married immediately. She was quite ready. She did not want to wait. Let them be married tomorrow!

Then it was he, Benjie, who postponed it. One afternoon, walking again in the garden at the Fortress, all the old doubts came forward. He was not good enough for her. Everyone was right. He would make her unhappy. When she knew him better she would hate him. She calmed him. She laughed at him. She told him once again that she had known him all her life, that she was not blind nor ignorant about men, that they must trust one another and take what came. She was so certain of her own deep, unchangeable love that they need have no fear. He asked her, in a kind of despair, why did she love him as she did. Soon against her will she was asking herself that question. What was Benjie's power over her? She loved him because he alone in all the world drew everything out of her: she loved him as a woman, as a mother, as a sister, as a friend and a companion. He was honest, generous, gay, independent, brave. He was also careless, selfish, casual, forgetful, always surrendering to the mood of the moment, hating to be tied. But that he adored her no one could doubt. He knew, his mother knew, even the men and women about the place knew that, with all his faults, this love for Vanessa was true, staunch, unyielding. Had his character been as fine as his love they would be happy for evermore!

The wildness in him was quite untamed. She knew that and reckoned with it, but to watch it working at a distance and to have it in close daily communion with herself were two quite different things.

He could conceal nothing that was in his mind, and soon he attacked what he called her 'childishness'. He attacked her religion. He told her again and again that he did not want her to change in the least and tried to change her. 'You know that there can't be a God, Vanessa. In your heart you must know it. You are a wise woman. You read and think. Well, then, ask yourself. How CAN there be a God and life be as it is? If there is one He ought to be deuced ashamed of Himself, that's all I can say.'

She disliked intensely to talk about her religion. She had never done so with anyone save her mother and Elizabeth. Her father had always respected that reticence. But quietly and with humour she answered Benjie's indignation. 'We go by our experience, I suppose, Benjie dear. God is as real to me as you are. Of course I don't know WHY life is as it is. I am a very ignorant woman, and Mr Darwin's monkeys are beyond my scope. But a hundred thousand monkeys wouldn't alter the truth that I love you, nor would they change my love of God either. Don't worry about it, Benjie. Let us be what we are.'

Then soon there was another thing. She had never known before what physical love was. She had never been close to Benjie so constantly. She had never conceived her own weakness. One fine day they had ridden out to Borrowdale and, sitting in the sun under some trees above Rosthwaite, they had talked. She knew that everyone thought it very disgraceful that they went about together without a chaperon. Even her father had shyly spoken to her of it. She had laughed and said that he need have no fears. But now, quite suddenly, she realized that he was right to be afraid. It was as though she and Benjie were caught up into a hot burning cloud of light. The world turned so that both sound and vision were obliterated. For a fearful dumb blind moment she was almost lost. Then by the grace of God she escaped into sight and sound again.

Next day she said, 'Benjie, why should we wait? Let us marry soon.'

But there was her father. She could not endure to leave him. It is true that she would be at the Fortress, not far away, but the thought of his lonely days, his sitting at his table writing, looking up out of window, thinking of her, wanting her, was intolerable. He told her with a smile that he would be quite happy. He had Will, he had his work and garden. She knew that he was doing his best. He did not take her in at all. Then in June he fell ill. He caught a cold, suffered from rheumatism, had to go to bed for a while. When he was better Benjie, who had been wonderful during Adam's sickness, coming constantly to visit him, laughing, cheering him up, reading to him, suffered from all his old scruples again.

'Vanessa, give me up! I'll go away and never come back! I'm not worth all your sacrifice. I'm not worth anyone's sacrifice.'

But he loved her more than ever and he was more charming than ever. He was, during those weeks in July, unselfish, thoughtful, considered her in everything. But they decided that they would wait until the spring. 'You will know then finally, once and for all, whether I am worth it.'

'I know it now,' she said gently. 'Nothing can change.'

But she perceived by now that, beyond any doubt, it was something he knew about himself that stirred all his self-depreciation. That, because he knew himself so

well and loved her so dearly, he was determined to do this one decent honest thing--not to ruin her life.

But what was it that he knew about himself? He was not, in his attitude to anyone else, self-depreciatory. Far from it. 'Take me as I am; as I take you,' was his attitude to the world. Only he would not spoil Vanessa's life for her.

'But of course you will not spoil it.'

'You don't know me.'

'I take the risk,' she answered.

By the end of July she felt that she must, for a little while, be at a distance from him. This indecision and hesitation could not go on. It was making them both sensitive, moody, self-conscious. So she went to Gosforth.

When she had been a day there her spirit was quieted, her gaiety returned.

Gosforth itself, small quiet village that it was, contained all the past. In the churchyard there was a cross of red sandstone which represented a figure chained beneath a serpent dropping upon him poison. This was a Christian cross and yet it had on it a heathen symbol. No one could tell its age, but many Vikings, she understood, had been half Christian, half heathen. She liked to think that this had been a Viking cross. Then there was Gosforth Hall near the church, the very house where Bishop Nicolson in the seventeenth century, as a young archdeacon, courted Barbara Copley. Near the Hall was a holy well where there had been once a mediaeval chapel, and half a mile from the Hall was the Dane's Camp, and farther from that again the King's Camp, at Laconby. Many of the old houses in the neighbourhood, like Ponsonby Hall and Sella Park, were packed with history, while not far away was Calder Abbey.

In the middle of all this concentration of Time slept the perfect English countryside. There was often sunshine that August and sweeping shafts of it fell across the cornfields, warming the colours into red gold, falling at the feet of the dark shadows of the woods. It was pastoral everywhere, while on windless days the silence, made more musical by the creaking of a cart, dogs barking, the call of the farmer to his horse, seemed to carry all the summer scents of flowers and corn and trees and pile them about you so that on the hot lawn you need not stir but gather, without motion, everything into your heart.

Yet how strangely even in this country of cornfield, wood and hedgerow still the mountains dominated. At every point, from every rise, Black Combe, thrusting its head like a lazy friendly whale into the sea, held your eye. From Black Combe's top you could hold in your grasp the Isle of Man, the Scottish and Welsh coasts with Snowdon greeting you, while landwards were Lancashire and the Yorkshire Fells.

To the right from a little hill above the house you could salute the Screes and in your mind's eye follow them as they rushed with all their power to bury their foundations deep in the heart of the black lake. Standing on her hill Vanessa would watch the clouds hurrying like smoke to invade the serried tops, then to spill themselves in storm or to break into pavilions snow-white or crimson with fire, or to shred and scatter into strands of gold and crimson. And she liked to sense, as she felt the motionless peace of the cornfields below them, catching the sun and throwing it up to her again, that above those hills the wind was raging and that their shining, slanting surface glistened with hardness, and the stone walls, straight as a sword, ran to the skyline over ground that was rough and peaty and free. All history was in this small patch of ground, and all nature too, shadowed by the triumphant wing of the great Eagle to whose kingly progress History was but a day.

In the house and out of it there were the children. They were sternly disciplined. Mrs Clopton, a tall dark woman with heavy eyebrows and a faint moustache, was a Tartar. She was not unkind, but she thrived on her despair of human nature. She hoped for the best but gloried in her constant disappointment. Her God--she was a deeply religious woman--was the real God of the Israelites, revengeful, on the watch for every blunder, cruel in His punishments. Oddly the children liked her; they were proud of her. She had no need to punish; a look, a word from her was sufficient. Not that they were perfect children. They made their own lives in their world of perpetual discipline. They learnt their Collects on Sunday, said 'Yes, Mama' and 'No, Mama', never spoke when with their elders unless spoken to, but once by themselves, the official eye removed from them, they were free, natural, and often naughty. It was as though they understood the terms under which they lived and made their plans accordingly. Violet was delicate--fair-haired, slender, blue-eyed and was already making her poor health her pleasant advantage.

But Tim was Vanessa's darling. He was fair and slender like Violet, but strong and wiry. She saw that he was an artist born and that nothing would stop him. He drew unconsciously without any deliberate awareness. He noticed the shapes and colours of clouds, the patterns of leaves, the path that the wind made through the corn, a snail's shiny track on the lawn, the purple shadows on the flanks of Black Combe. He was already at odds with Herries common sense.

His father would darken the doorway.

'Tim, what are you doing?'

'Making a picture, Papa.'

'Let me see.'

Then after a pause:

'Now what is this?'

'A ship with pirates, Papa.'

'Pirates! Pirates! What do you know about pirates?'

'Aunt Essie told us, Papa.'

'And you call this a ship?'

'I don't know ships very well and--'

'Well, wait until you do. Wasting your time like this! What have I often told you?'

'Not to waste my time, Papa.'

'Exactly. Now put away that rubbish.'

The children worshipped Vanessa. For half an hour before they went to bed she was allowed to tell them stories. Mrs Clopton listened in stern astonishment. There was nothing of which she disapproved so thoroughly as stories, but, while her needles clicked, she found herself attending: fairy palaces rose above her head, the Crystal Lake was at her feet and a White Horse of incomparable splendour strode the ice-bound hills.

'Time for their bed, Miss Vanessa.'

But, over her solitary supper, she wondered, against her will: 'What did the Princess find behind the secret door? Did the dwarf climb out of the cellar? Why was the Green Necklace the King's most treasured possession?'

Best of all there was the sea. On fine days they drove there in the victoria. The sand stretched in a floor of mother-of-pearl to the line of trembling white. On the horizon the Isle of Man hung between sea and sky. Timothy slept, Mrs Bellairs talked, the children were busy with their fantasies, Mrs Clopton read her Bible, Vanessa thought of Benjamin.

On a sunny afternoon, staring dreamily at the incoming tide, she saw him coming towards her.

At first she was delighted, then she was angry, then delighted again. She wanted NOT to be pleased! He was for ever breaking his word. They had agreed that they would not meet for three weeks. And why had he not written to her to tell her that he was coming? Or had he perhaps ridden over and tomorrow was returning? Or did he intend? . . . The children had seen him and began to run towards him, then stopped, remembering their elders. They loved, however, Benjie better than anyone else in the world--far better indeed. No one, not even Aunt Vanessa nor Aunt Jane nor any other, could create for them a world and then live contentedly inside it as Benjie could.

'Uncle Benjie! Uncle Benjie!' Tim cried and woke up his father. Mrs Bellairs disapproved of Benjamin completely. She was terrified lest he should contaminate the children. She SAID this, but in actual fact when he was in her company she always surrendered to him. Had she been honest with herself she would have acknowledged that to be so vicious and yet so amiable touched the adventurous woman in her. Although stout and forty, completely the British matron, there hid somewhere within her a girl who longed to see what the other half of the world was like. This girl was slowly starving to death. Once and again she received sustenance: Benjie more than any other kept her alive.

Nevertheless he WAS dangerous to the children with all the horrible things he had seen and done, the dreadful women he must know. Moreover, had they not invited Vanessa to stay for the sole purpose of showing her how shocking, how impossible Benjie was?

But what were you to do when in a moment he was down on his knees in the sand helping Tim with his castle, which the child had already decorated with a pink shell, the green stopper of a ginger- beer bottle, and a piece of red rag tied to a stick?

And WHAT were you to do when, smiling all over his face, sand on his trousers, waving a child's spade, he came over to you crying:

'Just think, Violet, I've come all the way from the Fortress on a bicycle.'

'On a bicycle!' She sat up, settled her bustle, arranged the large yellow brooch neatly on her bosom and stared with what she trusted was a mixture of disapprobation and dignity.

'Now don't look like that, Violet! You know you are glad I have come. One might think I was Cetewayo by your disapproval. I'm not going to poison the children or tell them naughty stories. I MAY tell you a few later on, but to be honest with you I've come to see Vanessa, the lady to whom I'm engaged, and nobody else . . . Yes, I've come on a bicycle! I bought it in Carlisle last week.'

'Where is it?' asked Mrs Bellairs, speaking as though he had brought with him the late-lamented Jumbo from the Zoo.

'It is at my lodging.'

'Your lodging? Then you are going to stay here?'

'For a day or two--as long as Vanessa will put up with me.'

'Well, we can't offer you a bed at Low Dene if that's what you want. There are rooms enough but no servants. I'm sorry, but you should have told us you were coming.'

Benjie laughed. 'But, my dear Violet, why will you not understand? I have not come to see YOU. Of course if you appear sometimes I shall be glad to talk to you and to listen to what you have to say. If you are VERY good I will tell you a story or two about Port Said. But I have not the slightest interest in either yourself or Low Dene just now. I prefer the company of Mrs Halliday and Rosemary Cottage.'

'And WHO is Mrs Halliday?'

'A retired gentlewoman with a beautiful daughter, who, an hour ago, lured me with a card in the window which said that a bedroom was to let on moderate terms. Rosemary Cottage has a sea view, the beautiful daughter was in the parlour tending the plants. Within five minutes terms were arranged, and my bicycle is now occupying all the space in the front hall.'

'Very well. If you are satisfied. But I'm sure you might leave Vanessa alone for a little. You do not mean to say that you've come thirty miles today on that bicycle?'

'No. I stayed last night in Whitehaven and transacted a little piece of business.'

'I see.' She rose with great dignity, patted her bosom, shook her dress so that the frills and ruches settled in their proper places, and said:

'Timothy, it is time we were returning. Come, children. The air is chill.'

But the victoria had to be ordered, and Benjie was able to secure a moment alone with Vanessa.

'Why have you come?' Vanessa asked him. 'Three weeks was our bargain.'

'I know. I could not help it. I had to show you the bicycle.'

'No, but I am angry. Really I am. You should not have come.'

'You haven't written, Vanessa.'

'I have only been here four days.'

'Yes, but FOUR DAYS! An intolerable time. But see how tactful I am. I am here at Rosemary Cottage. There is Mrs Halliday's beautiful daughter. I am quite happy, and we need not meet at all.'

'You know that we shall meet.'

'Let the others go in front.' He caught her hand. 'Vanessa. We must stop this nonsense. We must be married immediately. I mean it. I cannot live even four days without you.'

'Tomorrow you will say something quite different. I cannot trust you from one day to another.'

'No, I know. That is why we must be married immediately. Next month. I have told my mother. There is nothing against it.'

'There has never been anything against it,' she answered. 'Only your own indecision.' Then she laughed. 'Oh, Benjie, I am so glad to see you! I have been wanting you every minute I have been here!'

'If,' he said, 'we walk up through those sand-dunes no one can see us.'

Between the sand dunes they kissed as though they had been parted for years.

When he had seen them all drive off in the victoria he walked to his lodging, singing. Everything was settled at last. His own indecision was ended. After all, was he not changed? Did he not adore Vanessa? He knew that he did! How beautiful, how very, very beautiful she had looked in the simple blue dress with the high dark collar, the white frill at the throat, the little gold brooch that he had given her, her hair brushed from her splendid forehead, she kneeling there on the sand watching Tim's castle. No one was so lovely, no one so good and true, no one loved him so dearly! The wildness was gone from his nature. They would settle at the Fortress, soon there would be children, boys like Tim, girls better than Violet; the garden should blossom with the rose, the Fortress should burn with light and heat . . .

He was approaching Rosemary Cottage. It stood by itself, its feet almost in the sand dunes, a small windblown desolate garden looking on to the sandy track.

As he approached it he ceased to sing. The sun was setting: shadows crept over the sea and a mist veiled the little moon.

Before he entered he hesitated. Something about this place checked his high spirits. Vanessa seemed far away. A little wind, suddenly rising, blew the sand in thin spirals among the strong tufted grass.

In the sitting-room the lamp was already lit and a meal spread on the table--a ham, a dish of stewed fruit, cheese.

Mrs Halliday appeared in the doorway.

'Shall I bring the eggs and tea now?' she asked. She was a spare desolate woman in a black silk dress. He noticed that she had no eyebrows and wore mittens on her hands.

'Thank you,' he said. He pulled off his boots, changing them for slippers, found in his bag a novel by Ouida, pulled out his pipe. She reappeared with the tea and eggs.

'I trust you have no objection to smoking in here?' he asked, looking up at her with a smile.

'Oh, none at all, Mr--' She paused. 'I beg your pardon. I did not catch your name before. Pray forgive me.'

'Oh, certainly. My name is Herries.'

'Thank you. I am a little deaf in one ear.' She waited as though she expected him to speak.

'That tea looks splendid.' He moved to the table. I am exceedingly hungry.'

'I am very glad, I am sure.' She waited, then went on. 'I do hope we shall satisfy you. My daughter and I are not accustomed to having lodgers. We have been in this place barely a month.'

'Oh yes?' He cut the bread.

'Yes. We come from Warwickshire. My husband was a gentleman of means. He was carried off with a severe fever six months ago.'

'Oh, I AM sorry,' said Benjie. 'What brought you, then, to this district?'

'I have a son who has taken a farm in the Buttermere direction. He always was fond of the country, but was of course in very different circumstances when my poor husband was alive.' She paused, gave a dry little cough. 'He passed away with great suddenness. His affairs were sadly involved. He was ruined by one whom he thought his friend.'

'Oh dear, I AM sorry,' Benjie said. But he had been startled by the extreme vindictiveness of that last sentence. Up to then she had spoken so very quietly.

'Yes, and so after that my daughter and I have had to do what we can . . . Thank you, Mr Herries. I hope that you have everything that you need.'

'Oh yes, thank you.'

She left the room. What an extremely quiet woman she was! It was not only that she spoke quietly, the words coming from between her thin lips reluctantly, but her movements were quiet, almost stealthy.

She had been in the room before he noticed it. Had he been anyone but Benjie he would have said at once that he did not like her, but his charity was all-embracing, at any rate until he had full and sufficient reason for a stern decision. But as he ate his ham and his eggs he felt uncomfortable. He thought that perhaps tomorrow he would make a move. He had half an impulse to get up and see whether his bicycle was safe in the hall. At any rates it was stuffy in here. The room was too full of things, china dogs, pale yellow daguerreotypes, large seashells, little tables covered with plush fastened with bright gilt nails. There was a smell in the room as though the windows had not been opened for a very long time--a smell, was it of seaweed, of stale scent, musty and clinging? Ah well, he was an ancient mariner, he had travelled the world over and known every discomfort. He would not be disturbed by a musty smell and a china dog or two. Nevertheless he disliked intensely a large daguerreotype of a pale severe gentleman in black cloth whose cold eyes followed him wherever he moved. Possibly Mrs Halliday would not object to moving THAT picture in the morning!

There was a knock on the door; he said 'Come in!' and the daughter entered.

'Mother wished me to see whether you needed anything,' she said.

'Not at all,' he answered. 'Everything is excellent, thank you.'

The girl stood against the table looking at him.

She was certainly not beautiful, not even pretty. She was thin like her mother and very fair. Her colour was so pale as to be almost white; her large eyes were blue-grey. She looked at him and smiled faintly. No, she was not pretty but there was something striking about her. It was true that she was thin, but her very fragility seemed to claim your protection.

He smiled back at her.

'Do you like it here?' he asked her.

'No,' she said. 'I do not.' She came nearer to him and laid her hand on the cloth. He noticed at once what a beautiful hand she had, finely formed, with slender fingers. Her hand moved towards the teapot while still she looked at him.

He had a mad impulse to put out his hand towards hers.

He jumped up from the table.

'I shan't want anything else tonight, thank you,' he said, turning his back to her abruptly as he filled his pipe.

The world does not grow less mysterious as it grows older, and it is one of its more striking but less incalculable secrets that human love when it is strong enough defies physical distance. This was not the first time nor the last in their history that Vanessa, as now, riding in the victoria through the dark summer hedges to Low Dene, was quite suddenly aware that Benjie was in danger. Benjie was so often in danger, whether spiritual, mental, or physical, that there must have been many occasions when Vanessa was unaware. There is also the perfectly plausible theory that Victorian women were exceptionally sensible to chills because they wrapped up so much. In any case Vanessa, sitting in the victoria, perfectly happy, feeling that at last she was on a relationship with Benjie that was safe and secure, began to shiver. They were turning into the long straggling Gosforth street. The sky in front of them was a pale translucent green in whose bright waters some trembling silver stars were glittering.

'Why! you are shivering, my dear!' said Mrs Bellairs. 'Wrap this round you! I do trust that you haven't caught a chill!'

Young Tim was sitting beside her, and his hot damp fist was enclosed in her gloved hand. In his fist, as she knew, were several shells and a piece of golden seaweed. She had the obscure and unreasonable fancy that it was through his hot little fist that she caught the sense that Benjie was in danger. How could he be in danger? He had left her only half an hour before to walk, happy and singing, to his lodging. Rosemary Cottage! There COULD be nothing wrong about Rosemary Cottage. Nevertheless they were both of a strange ancestry, she and Benjie. Francis Herries fighting in the frosty air, Mirabell bending over her lover's body on the Carlisle stones, Francis Herries looking at a picture on the wall in a London lodging for the last time, John--his son--calling through the mist in Skiddaw Forest: 'Is anyone there?', Judith, released at last, running into the road joyfully to greet her friends--these are only moments in a contemporary history where facts are important only as pointers, and where the significance is only externally material, and where Time has no significance at all.

'Thank you, Violet,' said Vanessa, gratefully accepting the Shetland shawl. 'It IS cold after the sun sets.' At the same moment she had a most incongruous thought--that it was so LIKE Timothy and Violet to christen their children with their own names!

She was uneasy all that evening and, next morning, a little talk that she had with Aunt Jane only increased that uneasiness.

It was a blazing summer day and they sat out on the lawn while the children, under the stern eye of Mrs Clopton, knocked the croquet balls about. Vanessa had on her knee a novel by Rhoda Broughton, and Aunt Jane had on hers a novel by Mrs Alexander. Aunt Jane had a dear little face that would soon be covered with wrinkles. Her ringlets, her shawl (even in this warm weather), the spectacles that she used when reading, her little apprehensive starts as though she expected that at

any moment a bear would jump out on her from the shrubbery, a round silver biscuit tin from which she would produce suddenly sweet biscuits for the children when Mrs Clopton wasn't looking, her extreme delicacy about other people's feelings, her willing slavery to the wishes of other people, her single- hearted devotion to those whom she loved, none of these attributes concealed from Vanessa the fact that, in spite of her modesty, reserve and deep religious beliefs, she knew a great deal more about life and men and women than did either Timothy or Violet.

Vanessa had not often an opportunity of being alone with her. She was constantly busy on other people's business. Timothy especially was always providing her with occupations. She was, when others were present, very silent, and her brother and sister-in-law would have been amazed had they realized the things that she perceived and pondered. They were certain that she adored them and considered them perfect human beings. In the first of these they were correct or nearly correct (she loved people in her own way, which was not at all theirs), in the second they were altogether wrong.

The little conversation that Vanessa now had with her was punctuated with Mrs Clopton's sharp: 'Now, Master Tim, don't dirty your stockings!' and 'Let your brother have the ball now, Miss Violet', and 'What did I tell you? You must look where you are going.'

From the field above the garden came the voices of the haymakers.

'Benjie has come to stay in Seascale, Aunt Jane,' said Vanessa.

'Yes, dear, I know. That's very nice for you.'

'And we are going to be married in the autumn.'

Aunt Jane took off her spectacles.

'I'm glad of that too. I think you have been engaged quite long enough.'

'Why do you think that?' Vanessa asked quietly.

'Oh, my dear, I know nothing about marriage of course, but Benjie, I always say, is not at all an ordinary man. I would never expect YOU to marry an ordinary man, Vanessa dear. You have too much of your grandmother in you. But when a man is NOT an ordinary man I always say that it is better that he should be married.'

'Of course Benjie's not an ordinary man. But then nobody is ordinary if you know them well enough.'

'Quite so. That's what Mrs Alexander, whose book I am finding it extremely difficult to read, does not appear to have discovered. All her characters are so VERY ordinary.'

Vanessa hesitated. Then she went on:

'Aunt Jane, I am going to ask you something. You are so very wise. You have known both Benjie and me since we were babies. Why is it, do you think, that when we are together we so often misunderstand one another?'

'That is just what I mean about marriage,' said Jane. 'People always misunderstand one another. But the point about marriage is that if you go on long enough together you arrive at an understanding. Once you are married you are bound together. I believe all married people find the connexion very irritating for a long while, and if they were not married they would separate. But being married they cannot, and so, at last, the understanding arrives. I put it very badly of course. I am not clever as your grandmother was. But there it is. That's what marriage does.'

'We must not be engaged too long, Benjie and I,' Vanessa said, as though she were speaking to herself. 'There is something dangerous about waiting.'

'There is something dangerous, my dear, about every human relationship. That is God's intention. People would never learn anything if there were not plenty of danger about. That is what your grandmother always said.'

'Oh, how I wish she were still alive!' Vanessa cried. 'She would have helped me. I know nothing about life at all--nothing about Benjie either, I sometimes think, although I've been with him all my life. How can we know anything about men? We are never alone with them; all they do is concealed from us; when they are with us they never tell us the truth.'

'Yes, dear, you are quite right,' said Jane. 'I often think that women today are far too sheltered. Not that I like the girls that your Miss Broughton writes about. That is surely going TOO far. But when your grandmother was a girl, as she often told me, women were far more free. I dare say they will be again one day, but as it is just now they have to spend all their time guessing.'

'Aunt Jane,' Vanessa said, staring at the rising field, the sunlight that soaked the lawn, 'I'm frightened. I feel that one wrong slip and Benjie will be carried away into some place where I can't reach him. I love him so terribly, but I am only CLOSE to him at moments. He's here. He's gone. And when he is gone I am so helpless . . .'

Jane smiled. 'Don't be frightened, my dear. Trust God. He knows so very much more than we do. Remember always that Benjie has a tragic history behind him, his father, his grandfather . . . You know, don't you, that I was the last person to talk to his father on that dreadful day? He was leading his horse from the stable. Of course I was only a little girl then, but I have always thought that perhaps I could have stopped him if I had known what to do or say, I loved him when I was a child more than I loved anyone, and I have been haunted all my life since by the thought that I failed him. But what I say is,' she went on more cheerfully, 'that if we do right as far as we can it's all we can do. Life's a dangerous thing, my dear, and you can't escape the danger by staying in bed all day or making other people act FOR you. Don't expect things to be easy. Why should they be? God doesn't arrange the universe

only for me--nor for you either. To listen to the way the people talk in this novel of Mrs Alexander's you'd think that every time they have a toothache God ought to be ashamed of Himself . . .' She nodded to herself, picked up her book. 'I'm at page one hundred and fifty-three and that's as far as I shall go. I always like to finish a book if I can; when the writer's taken so much trouble it seems only right; but THIS time I simply can't be bothered. Mrs Alexander will never know, so there's no harm done.'

For one reason or another this little talk left Vanessa--who as a rule was sensible enough and level-headed--in a kind of panic. That was the quality that Aunt Jane had, that when she DID talk she always suggested so much more than she said. Her honesty forbade her to offer false consolations. If people did not inquire what she thought she was too thorough a lady to tell them, but if they DID ask her they must accept the consequences. Vanessa now had the conviction that Aunt Jane thought her love for Benjie a disaster!

She endured three days of a distress and apprehension altogether new to her experience. For much of this the child that she still was responsible. These were perhaps the last days of immaturity, those days when persons and events have still the size and colours of nursery hours, moments when we are left alone in a room where the flickering firelight throws gigantic shadows on the wall, when the clock's tick is a menace, and the twig snapping on the windowsill threatens the approach of some dreadful stranger!

She had three days of nightmare--and was transported into Paradise!

Timothy, as befitted a Bellairs, liked society if it was proper enough, and at the houses in the neighbourhood--Muncaster and Ponsonby and others--there was plenty. It was still the fashion, if you went out to dinner, to take a footman with you to assist at the meal; there were elaborate croquet parties and magnificent picnics.

So one fine day Timothy and his wife set off to Muncaster, and Vanessa went with the nurse and children to the sea. They had not been settled on the shore five minutes before Benjie was with them. He and Vanessa started to walk across the long, shining sands.

It was a day of perfect peace. Chroniclers may define that moment as the final peaceful one in English country life--a moment of historic tranquillity when the cornfields lay placid beneath the sun, the hedgerows slept, woods were untrodden, and every village sheltered under its immemorial elm while the villagers slumbered off their beer on the parochial bench. At the final moment, then, before the trumpet of the new world sounded, Benjamin and Vanessa crossed Seascale sands!

She knew at once that he was disturbed. There had been something, then, in her own unrest.

She said at once: 'Benjie, what is it?'

He caught her arm with his hand and pressed her against his side so that they might walk like one man. She was taller than he. She was wearing a small, rather masculine hat ornamented with blue flowers. She held her parasol high over her head. She was smiling, she was happy. She could feel his hand within her arm against her heart. All her fears were fled.

'There is nothing the matter except that I love you. And that IS the matter, for we must be married in a month's time. I can wait no longer. I am bad through and through. I am without a redeeming point, but I have told you all that so often that I shall never mention it again.'

'Certainly we will be married in a month's time. Tomorrow if you like! I have been dreadfully unhappy these three days. I can't tell you why, but as I was driving back the other evening I had a sudden fear that something had happened to you. That cottage--what did you call it? Where you are staying. I have been dreaming of it, crawling with spiders and earwigs. I have been thinking that if we are not married at once we never will be married. And Aunt Jane frightened me.'

'What has Aunt Jane been saying?' he asked quickly.

'Oh, nothing--dear Aunt Jane! She loves us both, I know. But she is afraid for us. I know she is. She thinks there is dangerous blood in our veins. She wants to see us SAFE.'

'She's right!' he said fiercely. 'We must be SAFE-- or someone will part us, something will happen!'

They were standing at the sea edge, on a floor of mother-of-pearl. The incoming tide drew thin lines of white as with a pencil on the shore and beyond the line the sea heaved without breaking, as gently as a sigh.

'No,' she said. 'I think that NOTHING can part us. I don't mean because we love one another. I can imagine that you might come to hate me or I would be so proud that I would never see you again, but still we would not be parted. It has been like that all our lives.'

Then she added, as though to herself: 'That is my worst fault, my pride.'

He turned and looked at her as though he were seeing her newly.

'What do you mean, Vanessa--your pride?'

'I would endure anything, I think,' she answered, 'or so I feel. I would show what I was suffering to nobody, but it would remain inside me. I could not let it out, I cannot let things go--words that someone said years ago, little things that people have done. No one knows that I remember them, but I never forget. They do something to me. I hate my pride. I would like to be free as you are, Benjie--every day a new day--'

'No, Vanessa darling,' he broke in. 'Not like me. If there were two of us, both like me, oh, what a time we would have! You are the only one in all the world who influences me! That is why you are to marry me, teach me, change me.'

'I don't think I can teach anyone.' She sighed. 'I don't know why it is, but I would rather leave people alone, leave them as they are. Father is like that too. Mother used to be constantly distressed at how bad people were. Not that she blamed them. She was too kind. But it bewildered her. Right was so right and wrong was so wrong. I have no conscience for other people, I think--not even for you, Benjie.'

He asked her again for the thousandth time: 'Why do you love me, Vanessa? Everyone tells you not to.'

'I love you,' she answered, 'as I shall always love you, because you are part of me, because you are all that I have in the world, because without you I am always lonely, because I am not alive without you. There!' she said, turning round and laughing, looking at him too with infinite tenderness, with a kind of brooding devotion as though she could not look at him enough, could not have him close enough to her. 'Now--are you satisfied?'

For a moment he was silent, then he took her hand and kissed it.

'God helping me,' he said, 'you shall not regret it.' Then, characteristically, added as they turned to walk back: 'Although I don't believe in Him, I expect Him to help me, you see.'

They discussed details. He had written to Elizabeth the night before. They would be married in Ireby church, a very quiet wedding.

'There is only Adam,' Benjie said. 'I hate to think how he will miss you. We will do everything we can. You can go and stay with him whenever you wish, and he shall stay with us.'

'He will be happy if I am,' she answered. 'And he is well now-- stronger than for a long while.' But nevertheless she knew leaving him would be terrible. They must think of a plan . . . some way . . .

As they neared the children two women passed them. Benjie raised his hat.

'Do you know them?' she asked.

'Yes,' he said, laughing. 'That is the enchantress of Rosemary Cottage. Two enchantresses. Mrs Halliday and her lovely daughter Marion.'

Driving home, with Violet on her lap while Mrs Clopton told her stories of the heathen in Africa and all that was being done to improve their minds, she was thinking in an ecstasy of happiness:

'We are safe! We are safe! In a month we shall be married. Nothing can touch us now.'

In the morning the old postman, bent and twisted like a gnome, brought her a letter. It was from her father.

DEAREST VAN--I am not very well--nothing serious--but I think perhaps you had better come home-- Your loving

FATHER

FALL OF THE HOUSE OF ULDALE

Adam Paris hovered through the whole of that autumn between life and death. His sickness began, it appeared, with some mysterious poisoning, was followed by pneumonia, and left him with a heart so weak that every excitement, every sudden movement, was a danger.

So he was told not to move, not to suffer excitement. In the early days of January he was permitted to walk a little, supported on Will Leathwaite's stout arm, in the garden. During those months Vanessa scarcely left his side; even Benjamin was almost forgotten by her.

Whatever else Adam might be, he was always a philosopher. By January 1883 he was sixty-seven years of age--sixty-seven was three years from three score and ten. To die at that age was no very terrible misfortune. He did not want to die. He did not want to leave Cumberland, nor Will, nor Vanessa. Every day held some adventure, some charm, some beauty. But he most certainly did not care to linger on an invalid, a trouble and anxiety to everyone about him. He knew that had it not been for his illness Vanessa would now be married, and although he did not wish, had never wished, that Benjamin should marry her, he wanted to see her settled before he went. Moreover, he had now perceived that it was Benjamin and Benjamin alone whom she must have, and he made the best of it.

If anybody could make anything settled and secure out of Benjamin, it was Vanessa. So great an opinion had he of her wisdom, common sense and fidelity that he thought that she might.

During those long trying days of convalescence he kept a Journal-- not a very regular one, not a very original one, but he put into it his honest opinions, some of his experience. These were some pages of it:

. . . A long and dangerous illness is an odd enough thing, I find. It is a commonplace that it seems to you, when you are in good health, incredible that you should ever die, and that when you are very ill you do not care a hang whether you die or no. Nature has arranged that very cleverly. But now that I am growing stronger again I find that I want to live for the smallest, most insignificant reasons. I have, for example, a new dog that Benjie gave me the other day, a rough clumsy kind of terrier. I have called him Tux after Rousseau's animal--the one that the Duchess of Luxembourg gave him. I have always liked Prince de Conti and the Luxembourg for their niceness to Rousseau, who must have been, just then, as tiresome and sensitive a creature as God ever made--but the queer thing and the enduring thing about Rousseau is that he had in him something of Everyman.

He would have felt, I am sure, just as I did yesterday when Timothy and Violet came up from Uldale to pay me a visit. So very well-meaning, so extremely irritating! However, in one thing I am luckier than he. I have no Thérèse for them to patronize! But I felt just as he did about presents. Timothy gave me a shawl 'to keep my knees warm' as though the whole of the Herries family were presenting me with a medal. However, it is quite natural that he should think me a fool who all his life has wasted his time over nothing! And I had my ambitions once, too, but ambitions when you get to my age are cheap affairs. Would I have been a happier man had I been Gladstone or Dizzy or Dickens? Sour grapes perhaps to say that I would not. It is natural that I should like now to clap my hand on the table and say: 'Yes, I have added THAT to the world's achievements, a law or a poem, a picture or a character.' But my illness has left me altogether indifferent. My dear mother, I suppose, went the wrong way for both of us when she stayed at Uldale instead of escaping the family and going to Watendlath. She always said that it was the mistake of her life. Had she gone I would have been a farmer, never seen a relation, never lived in London, never married Margaret, never had Vanessa for a daughter. What I would have missed! But I might, I fancy, have been a stronger man, a more determined character, and I would certainly have had more of this country, the sight and smell and sound of it. But I would have been always a dreamer who never pursued his dreams far enough. There can be no man but is dissatisfied with his life when he looks back on it. What a confusion of shreds and patches, of starting first here and then there, of one blind move after another--walking at night along a dark road and thinking every tree a hobgoblin! But I was never much of an adventurer, too easily disheartened, too ready to be an idealist without suffering for my ideals, far too ready to shrink away into myself if I met a rebuff. A failure, I suppose, trying to conceal my failure with a certain cynicism, and yet on the whole what a happy life I have had. I have known three glorious women-- my wife, my daughter, and my mother--one or two magnificent men-- Dickens, Caesar Kraft, Will, and in my babyhood, Reuben Sunwood. I have been given the perception of beauty in art and in nature and, although my own writing has been less than nothing in its result, I have had, in the pursuit of it, some glorious visions. Best of all, I have never been betrayed by my own failure into thinking man a poor affair. I have never come to thinking human nature a bad blunder, although in my Chartist days I met some poor specimens. Nor, thank God, have I ever suffered a fool gladly, least of all myself.

The whole pageant of life has been, and is, of an extraordinary interest. I can see now clearly enough that Time is nothing, that each and every man is tested with the same tests and rises or falls according to what he learns. Learning is everything. But for what? I have never been sure of any kind of personal immortality. As my mother used to say: 'I don't FEEL it and so I don't BELIEVE it.' But Margaret was sure and Vanessa is sure and they are both wiser than I. There is a great deal of the pagan in me, as there was in my mother. We inherit that, I suppose. But even with my paganism I wonder that the world should be so beautiful and men often so fine and courageous if there is nothing more than this brief experience. I have touched some grand moments too: my first sight of Margaret in that little room off the Seven Dials, Dickens' hand on my shoulder, the day when I finished my first story, walks with Will, the day when in a kind of panic I ran away from Margaret up Cat Bells here, hours with books, sunrises and sunsets, even yesterday when looking from this window I saw the hills rosy and the Lake a misty blue. Do these mountains of perception mean nothing at all? I don't know, and up to a week or so ago in all those months of illness I certainly did not care. One night in September I was sure I would be dead before morning and everyone else was sure too. I was quite clearheaded and quite indifferent-- yes, even to Will and Vanessa. But I remember that I felt intolerably wise, that I thought that I had discovered the secret. Will turned me over in bed that I might lie easier and I muttered: 'Well, THAT'S it. Why didn't I discover that before?' But what I had discovered I haven't now the least idea. Nothing is certain except love, love of anything or anybody that takes you beyond yourself. This may be, for all I know, a proof of God. It's as good a one as anything the parsons can give you. 'For what we have received let us be truly thankful . . .'

January 9th, 1883

Benjie came up yesterday afternoon and we had a talk. I never saw a man look so healthy. He is a gipsy for colour and hard as iron. Nothing seems to fatigue him and nothing bores him. What is best about him is that he is an individual. He is like no one else at all: you never know where you have him, or at least I don't. If you think him happy he isn't. Behind his merriment (and I must say I like it when he throws his head back and laughs as a boy laughs) there is a strain of melancholy. That he loves Vanessa there is no mistaking, but I am certain that he has misgivings about their marriage. He is right when he says he can't stick to anything. He is always against the law, whatever the law happens to be, and in that he is, I suppose, like my romantic grandfather and the Frenchman my mother married. He is of their world and so all against the Herries world, which is altogether anti-individualist. I couldn't help thinking yesterday as I listened to him that that may be the fight the whole earth is slipping into--the type against the individual. All the troubles in our family have come from the individual refusing to conform. Do I want Vanessa to be engaged in that kind of battle? No, indeed I do not. Nor do I want her to marry a type-

Herries either. The truth is, I suppose, that I love her so much that I shall never find anyone good enough for her!

Benjie yesterday was in a queer state of indecision. He came, I fancy, that I should make his mind up for him, but about what? He never said. He asked me the absurdest questions all covering something deeper that he never owned up to. Should he go to a Ball at Greystoke? Yes, I said, if he wanted to. Oh, he'd be sick of it in half an hour and do something outrageous. There's some woman and her daughter whom he met in the summer at Seascale have come to live in Keswick. Should he go and call on them? Why, yes, I said, if he liked them. But he didn't like them. Well, then, don't go. They had been friendly to him in Seascale and so on and so on. Vanessa had gone to Uldale, and I could see that he was deeply disappointed and yet was relieved. Nevertheless how charming he can be! I never knew anyone better with Will. He gets behind that man's defences in a moment. He knows by instinct what are Will's reticences. He is on a level with him completely, no patronage and no sycophancy either. His heart is good, but he is so restless and so impulsive that he is in trouble before he knows where he is. He is like a wild man who has never been tamed, and then, in a flash, a perfect courteous gentleman. Can Vanessa tame him? I believe that he fears himself that she cannot, and trembles lest he should do her a wrong. Like him I must, and fear for the future I must too. How I wish that my mother were alive! She would understand him as no other. She was the daughter of one wild man and tamed another--but my mother was unique. There will never be another like her again.

When he was gone I was tired enough and Will helped me to bed. That pain just over my heart returned like an old familiar friend. Odd how a pain, to which you are accustomed, seems in a fashion friendly. I could feel its fingers pinching my flesh, then pressing heavily, constricting the muscles, and as I laboured for breath I could almost hear its voice: 'Now we are together again, you and I. Is not our intimacy pleasant?' I could not altogether own that it was, and yet I could have almost replied: 'Yes, but don't press too hard, old fellow. Spare me what you can.'

And now this morning, this bright frosted January morning, I am well and the pain is forgotten. How quickly the past is over! How dim the pain of five minutes before! Yes, and the pleasure too! I can remember how often on a fine day, walking or sitting lazily in my boat on the Lake, the beauty has been so intense that I have longed to catch it in my fingers, hold it, wrap it up, put it away for safety. And in a moment it is gone. A rosy cloud turns grey, there is a whisper on the water, the shadow envelops the hill and THAT beauty is lost! But the intensity of the realization is caught at least. My friend Jean-Jacques, of whom for some reason I have been thinking much in these last weeks, speaks of that. I haven't the Confessions with me but the passage goes a little like this: 'The movement and the counter-movement of the water, the stirrings, rising, falling, gave me pleasure in mere existence. No need to think, to live at that moment was enough! Letting my boat go where it would, I would abandon myself to reverie. I was completely under Thy power, Nature! No wicked men to interpose themselves between us! Yes, all is a perpetual movement on earth. Nothing is constant. Our affections change and alter. Everything is in front or behind. We recall the past to which we are now indifferent or anticipate a future that may never come. Nothing solid for our hearts! But the soul may find a state solid enough on which it may repose with no thought of the past, no fear for the future--and so long as such a state endures he who experiences it may speak of bliss . . .'

Once on a day I knew that passage by heart, I think: now it comes to me only in fragments. Poor Rousseau, demon-haunted, finding no spot where his foot might rest. How in those days when the Confessions were so actual to me, I hated Voltaire and the vile Grimm and the false Madame d'Epinay!

But after all I suppose that his troubles were of his own making. There would have been no genius had there been no sickness. But I think at my age I hate most in this life the jealousy and rage of men against one another. How trivial and worthless our plottings when we are here for so short a time. How easy, you would say, for Man to tolerate his brother. And yet how I myself detested old Walter, so that I would lie awake and think how I might injure him. And then at the last that poor, weak, crying old man to be fed with a spoon and have his mouth wiped! I swear that if I recover from this I will never be angry again. And yet it has been, I dare say, that I have not been angry enough in life, have not known indignation enough. I have hated injustice, but men are too often like birds in a cage. They would not be there if they could escape, and the cage is not of their own designing. This wandering along on paper has passed an hour--and now for The Story of an African Farm that they are all praising. New militant woman eager for her rights! If the world is to be full of them, as I suspect it will be, I shall not be sorry to have gone . . .

FELL HOUSE, ULDALE, April 3rd, 1883

. . . so three days ago Vanessa and I moved to Fell House for a week or two. I am a very great deal better, can take a walk by myself and am not so utterly dependent on Will as I have been--how patient, tolerant, and sensible he's been no words can say, but I recognize sufficiently that two moments in my life have been supremely lucky--one when as a small boy I watched Will win a race through Keswick, the other when as Victoria returned crowned from Westminster I tumbled up against Caesar Kraft. The love of one man for another

is an odd thing: it is bare of sex and yet does in certain moods surpass the love of woman. Maybe I have never been a sexual man. Looking back now I can see that it was not virtue kept me free in my youth but a certain fastidiousness that I got, as I got so much else, from my mother. I sometimes think that had I been the child of a street-woman and, say, a card-sharper, I could have been something of a writer. But no matter now. Never was anything of less importance. All the same, being what I am, I doubt whether any relationship could be finer than mine with Will. And it has been his fineness, not mine. Complete unselfishness, unsparing devotion, and a deep, always by me perceptible, emotion under it all. With all that it has been always humorous, mixed with plenty of plain speaking. I cannot see that it has had any falseness in it anywhere. And, although I have no belief in immortality, it is hard for me, I confess, to imagine a state when Will and I will not be together and consciously together. Such a relationship as ours goes far beyond the body and, maybe, survives the body. There is this at least about it that it makes you think well of your fellow-men. It makes me wonder sometimes whether any country but England (and sometimes I wonder any county but Cumberland) could produce such a man as Will. He is altogether Cumbrian in his honesty, reticence, obstinacy. But this of course is nonsense. There are men like him, I don't doubt, all the world over. My grandfather had such a one. Quixote found one, Montaigne had one; thank God the world is full of them.

Well, after this sentiment which no eye will ever see but my own, here is the other side of the shield. The only other visitor here but ourselves is Phyllis Newmark's boy, Philip Rochester. Rochester, whom she married some thirty years ago, has something, I fancy, to do with railways and has amassed a nice fortune. Barney, I know, dislikes him and always calls him a humbug. As for Master Philip, I have seldom disliked a young man so much. He is thin and willowy, talks in a piping voice about the 'Inevitability of Sin' and that 'Art is the only Moralist'. It happens that in this very week's Punch there is a little piece which I shall have great pleasure in showing him. It is apt enough to copy into this Journal:

TO BE SOLD, the whole of the Stock-in-Trade, Appliances, and Inventions of a Successful Aesthete, who is retiring from business. This will include a large stock of faded lilies, dilapidated sunflowers, and shabby peacocks' feathers, several long-haired wigs, a collection of incomprehensible poems, and a number of impossible pictures. Also, a valuable Manuscript Work, entitled Instruction to Aesthetes, containing a list of aesthetic catch-words, drawings of aesthetic attitudes, and many choice secrets of the craft. Also, a number of well-used dadoes, sad-coloured draperies, blue and white china, and brass fenders. To shallow- pated young men with no education, who are anxious to embark in a profitable business which requires no capital but impudence, and involves no previous knowledge of anything, this presents an unusual opportunity. No reasonable offer refused. Apply in the first instance to Messrs SUCKLEMORE and SALLOWACK, Solicitors, Chancery Lane.

A trifle sledge-hammer but it has got Mr Philip exactly. I wouldn't mind the young man's effeminacy, his ridiculous clothes, and his languor, were it not that he considers himself the Prince of the World. The scorn that he feels AND expresses for everyone in his house is nauseating. Everyone but Vanessa, whom he condescends to admire, and talks of 'a perfect du Maurier' and how he wishes that Whistler could paint her. He would apparently make the attempt himself (for he paints the most atrocious daubs) 'had he the time'. Had he the time! When he never gets up before ten, wanders about the house like a misplanted lily, pecks at the piano and studies himself in the looking-glass. His morals would be, I have no doubt, revolting had he any blood in his poor body. He speaks of his 'soul-mates and the tyranny of the marriage laws' and such disgusting nonsense. I should shudder whenever the children approached him, but they, unlike his elders, find him a kind of clown. Amazingly, Timothy and Violet are both rather impressed, and Vanessa, in her goodness of heart, is kind to him. How my mother would have dealt with him!

April 8th

It is perhaps my illness, but whatever the reason I cling to this old house as never before. My mother's presence is everywhere, but, beyond that, the house itself for ever speaks to me as though this were the last time it would ever shelter me, as though I were the last human link it will ever have with all the life that is gone. And that is true enough. There is no one else alive but myself who knew it as it was. When I first came here Francis and Jennifer were living, David and Sarah were remembered and had seen old Rogue Herries himself ride up, looking for his wandering wife. David, Jennifer, my own mother died under its roof. Violet has done all she can to ruin it, as the house very well knows. How easy and pleasant to have left some of it as it was--at least the little parlour that my mother so dearly loved. I can yet see it as it was when I was a child--the old spinet with the roses painted on the lid, the famous music box that was played for me when I was good, with the King in his amber-coloured coat and the Queen in her green dress. Then the carpet, upon which I sprawled with John, that had the pictures of the great Battle, cannons firing and horses rising on their haunches; the Chinese wallpaper with pagodas of blue and white, temples, bridges, and flowers. Best of all the sofa, the stuff of which was decorated with apple trees and red apples. How well I remember that room and the way the clock with the gold mandarin would strike the hour, coughing a little between the strokes.

All gone now and also the things from my mother's bedroom, the red chairs, the four-poster bed. All gone, all gone, the house tonight seems to echo around me. And instead so many ugly things, mahogany wardrobes like coffins set up on end, attempts here and there to be in the fashion with imitation Morris wallpapers, sham Burne-Jones tapestry in the drawing-room--but the dining-room how awful with its circular cellarette, the vast Sheffield soup tureen, the sideboard with its malignant and obscene carved ends, the lacquered knife-tray, the needlework bell-pulls that Timothy tugs at so furiously when he is impatient, the sheep-faced mahogany clock--and all these things both Violet and Timothy think so handsome! Yes, I can hear the old house groaning through all its brickwork. I am the only one who knows how deeply ashamed it feels!

April 15th

I must write tonight to banish some of this intolerable melancholy that has seized me. There is a real Cumberland wind wailing about the house, as though it had lost a thousand children. How sharp and strong it must be on the Tops! Almost impossible to keep your feet with the black heavy clouds driving furiously like chariots above you, and all the streams preparing for rain . . . I have not been so well these last days and I have an assurance in my breast that my time now is short. I had my evening meal in my room and Vanessa came up to talk to me. I was allowed a fire and by the light of two candles we chatted, comfortably, easily, like the old friends we are. Why was it that I had so dreary a sense that this was to be our last talk? Nonsense, of course, and in the morning, as has happened so often before, feeling well again I shall laugh at my past terrors. But as I sat opposite over the fire I put out my hand to touch her dress as though I were frightened to lose her, and she drew her chair over to mine. She was cheerful and nonsensical as she often is, laughing at Phil Rochester who had been reading her some of his poems, one called 'The Lovers Last Cry' which was, I gathered, especially comical. Benjie is staying in Keswick. She is sure that he has some attraction there and takes it quite calmly. All she said about THAT was:

'When we marry and are together, I'll make him happy, I know.'

And to that I said:

'You'll have to beat him once a week. He says so himself.'

How I hate to leave her no one knows but me! She talked about herself, a thing that she very seldom does.

629

'I find that I'm intolerant, Papa. Intolerant and impatient.'

'Very well,' I said. 'Those are not bad things to be.'

'I was so angry with Timothy tonight that I could have smacked him. He was so extremely self-satisfied. I think all men are except yourself. Why should he talk as though he had MADE England?'

'That's a Herries habit,' I answered.

'Yes, but it's also something masculine. We were talking about Moody and Sankey and the Salvation Army and he said that such things weren't English. Englishmen never show their emotions, he said, and THAT'S why England is what it is. What he meant was, "*I* never show my emotions and THAT'S why England is what it is."'

'There's something in what he says,' I answered.

'Oh, well, I wanted to scream and beat that hideous Indian gong in the hall. Then he said that The Story of an African Farm is a disgusting book and ought to be burnt. When I asked him about it I discovered that he had only read the first chapter. And then after that he was going to say something about Benjie, but Violet stopped him.'

'Altogether a very pleasant meal,' I said.

'But why are we so different, you and I, from Timothy and Violet?'

'Two halves of the whole,' I told her. 'Life isn't complete without both of us.'

I could see that in reality she was deeply dissatisfied with herself. She is maturing, and I am sure that this long uncertain time with Benjie is affecting her seriously, although she is too proud to say anything about it.

She sat close to me, holding my hand, her splendid noble head raised high, looking into the fire.

'Well, I'm a perverse creature,' she said, nodding. 'I seem to have no control over myself at all.'

'But you HAVE,' I assured her. 'You see you didn't bang the table and you didn't beat the gong.'

'No, but I can't be rational, the thing that all nice women ought to be. I laugh when I should be serious, I'm angry when there's nothing at all to be angry about. I'm not at all proper in my feelings either. Violet thinks it dreadful to mention the word adultery. She positively said the other day that the Commandments in church made her quite shy. She thinks it dreadful to be seen with a French novel. Oh! I do hope I'm not going to be a prig!'

I laughed at that.

'Why, no, I should say the very opposite.'

'No, but, Papa, virtuous about other people being NOT virtuous! . . . In fact I hate myself tonight. Everything is wrong but you.'

She kissed me, laid her cheek against mine, made a fuss of me, told me again and again how she loved me, asked me to forgive her for all the trouble she had been to me. Never was she more sweet, never more my friend and companion. Before she went she turned at the door and blew me a kiss with her hand, laughing and saying: 'And now I'm going to the drawing-room to listen to Timothy telling us out of The Times what HE would do if he were Gladstone.'

Tomorrow we are going for a drive.

This is the end of Adam's Journal. They were the last words that he ever wrote. . .

He lay in bed for a while, rather wide-awake, watching the shadows from the fire leap on the wall, hearing the wind scream about the house, tug at the windowpanes, belabour the trees and hammer the tendrils of the vines against the glass. He thought of the cottage at Cat Bells, how cosy, warm with life and human affections. He had brought there many of his mother's things, her books, some pictures, the account she dictated to Jane of her early days, bound in a fat, green-leather volume, the presentation that they made her on that fatal Hundredth Birthday. Vanessa would have these things and would pass them on, pass them on to her children and Benjie's, and they to theirs, and so it would go on and on, until at length it might be that it would only be through Judith's green book that anyone knew that once a man sold a woman at a Fair or fought for his beloved on Stye Head . . . He was growing sleepy. He laid his head on his breast inside his shirt as though to say goodnight to his heart and request it, as a favour, to keep quiet for an hour or two. He did not want to wake sharply to that grinding pain, that squeezing of the muscles between two inhuman fingers, that beating and struggling for breath . . . He was falling asleep and a stout man was riding on a horse and he a little boy as bare as your hand danced to annoy him and the stout man raised his whip . . .

He awoke. What had roused him he did not know. He sat up, resting on his arm. He was so deeply accustomed now to find himself woken at night by pain that that was his first thought: 'Where is the pain this time? Which part of me is misbehaving?' But there was no pain. His heart beat calmly and his back did not ache. He had no neuralgia across his forehead. The room was intensely dark. Many hours must have passed since he fell asleep, for the fire had been strong. Now there was no glimmer of dying log or fading coal. The wind was roaring like a beating lively voice in the darkness but, listening, he heard something beyond the wind—a small chattering whispering voice. Was there someone in the room? No, it sounded like several voices, human and yet not human. He raised his head, sniffing. A moment later he was out of bed. Somewhere something was on fire. He opened the door and a belly of smoke blew towards him. He cried out: 'Fire! Fire!' and ran back into the room. It was then that the strange stillness of everything struck him. The house slept like the dead, he heard clocks ticking and somewhere a snore.

He pulled on a dressing-gown, and again, calling out 'Fire! Fire!', ran into the passage. His first thought was of Vanessa. He knew that her room was on the floor above his and, covering his mouth with his arm, turned towards the stairs, but even as he did so the passage to the left leading to the servants' quarters began--as it seemed to his excited imagination--to tremble, and a moment later through the green-baize door there shot a tongue of fire exactly like a vindictive criminal struggling to be free. A second later the flame shot upwards and little tongues began to lick the green baize, and a thin line of light, clear as day, shone between the hinges and the wall. At the same time the smoke rising in the same direction began to roll in thick grey waves, and the voices that it contained grew louder and angrier. What was strange was that the rest of the house, his room, the staircase from the hall, was cold, quiet, aloof, and even as he turned to the stair leading to the other floor he heard the cuckoo-clock that was at the corner of the hall below begin to sound the ridiculous bird's voice: 'Cuckoo! Cuckoo! Cuckoo!'

Still calling out and wondering in a mad irritation why nobody had been aroused by all this commotion, he stumbled up the stairs but, halfway up them, was met by another curling strand of smoke that seemed to issue from the wall on his left. For some reason that smoke bewildered him. It increased very rapidly, seeming to come from below him and to encircle him, to beat about his head, to come even from within himself, from his heart and lungs. He should now have been outside Vanessa's door, but he did not know where he was, for his eyes were blinded and weeping with the bitter and acrid thickness that now began to fill his mouth and heart and lungs.

He knocked his knees against a box or a chair, heard something fall somewhere and, turning his head, saw below him spurts and whirls of flame and a light that had a ferocity in it and a gigantic sense of power. He called out again and thought that some voice answered him, but he spoke against a wall, almost as though some enemy held a cloth over his mouth to deaden his cries. He thought: 'But this is absurd! Where are they all? What are they doing?' Called again and again: 'Vanessa! Vanessa! Wake up! Fire! Fire!' He moved to the right where he thought that her room must be, but now was caught in a perfect fog of smoke. His feet struck some more stairs and he remembered that above this floor were the attics. If he could reach those he could fling open the windows, for even his mad anxiety for Vanessa was countered by his agony for breath. His lungs were choked, he could not see and, although his brain was clear, his limbs refused to obey him. At that same moment pain leapt on to him, pain moving in the centre of the smoke. An iron hand crushed his breast. The fingers pressed and pressed. He fell on to his knees. 'A moment,' he thought. 'This pain will pass and I shall be able to move again.' But it did not. The giant hand turned and turned, so that he could see his poor heart crushed, screwed round and then squeezed until the pain seemed to draw his very eyeballs down into his stomach.

His last conscious thought was of Vanessa. 'Vanessa,' he murmured, 'Vanessa.' He rolled over and lay there, prone, while the eddies of smoke--strong, careless, singing a song--rose, saluted the wind, filling every cranny.

Vanessa had been long in a dreamless sleep when she awoke to the sound of a loud banging on her door. Even as she opened her eyes Violet and Timothy rushed in, behind them a strange glare and everywhere in the air a crackling, murmuring, buzzing frenzy.

She did not need their cry: 'Vanessa! Get up! The whole house is on fire!'

In an instant everything was visible and clear to her. She seemed in that moment of springing out of bed to have time to notice everything--the calm undisturbed paraphernalia of the bedroom, her clothes across the chair, the yellow sofa that she always thought so ugly, the long looking-glass in which were reflected Timothy and Violet, Timothy with a riding coat over his nightshirt, Violet in a bright blue dressing-gown, and behind them that sinister glitter veiled with sudden mists. The air stank of smoke. She heard a dog bark.

Violet pulled at her arm.

'It's terrible! It's terrible!' she continued to cry. 'The whole house is on fire!'

And Timothy, running back, called:

'The children! The children! Get the children!'

But her own thought was at once for her father. She thought of nothing and nobody else. She put on her dressing-gown and slippers with a single gesture and ran out. She saw them flocking down the stairs--Philip, Timothy, Violet, the children. The stairs were still untouched. You seemed from the lower stairs to plunge into darkness while on the first floor the baize door was a sheet of flame and all around her the smoke rose like water, flooding forward, eddying back again. She ran down the first flight and crossed at once into her father's room. It was empty. At that same moment she thought that through the crackle of the fire she heard a cry from above her: 'Vanessa!' She listened, and even as she did so saw Timothy's head and shoulders above the lower banister.

'Father!' she cried. 'He is not in his room!'

Timothy shouted back. 'Come down! The whole place is falling down. It's all right--everyone's out. Yes, Adam too. He is on the lawn!'

She turned back once more into his room, saw the bed disordered, caught--without knowing what she did, obeying some blind instinct-- things from the table, his Journal, a book, his gold watch; then ran out to meet in full force a towering column of smoke that rose in front of her like some genie. Gasping, her hand over her face, she ran forward, was down the stairs, through the door, and, in an instant, in a wild, chill, blowing world, the wind screaming above her, voices everywhere, shouts and cries, some child's wail, the neighing of horses, and faces white like paste in the blinding light of the fire.

She ran from figure to figure, not recognizing them at all as persons, for they also seemed to be running, moving in some kind of dance through the wind.

She called again and again:

'Father! Father! Where are you?' She pulled at some man's arm: 'My father! Is he here? Have you seen him?' and some figure that she did not know, someone holding a clock and a picture, cried, as though in an ecstasy. 'The house! The house! The roof will be in!'

Then she ran into Leathwaite. He cried before she could speak:

'Miss Vanessa! The master! He's not here!'

They turned together and ran towards the house which was now all bright with flame and alive in every part, while from its heart there came a beat like a drum and above it arms of fire strained up to the ebony sky, starred with the pigeons from the loft, flying into the light as though splashed with bright water, then vanishing into darkness.

Will dashed through the door. She would have gone after him but some man's hand held her, gripping her shoulder. 'You mustn't go, Miss Vanessa,' someone shouted in her ear as though she were deaf. 'It's not safe--' and then called, 'Will! Will! Come back! Everyone's out!'

She struggled. 'Let me go! What do you mean? They are not all out. My father is there--'

A moment later Will's face, strangely unreal, appeared at a window. He shouted to them.

'He's not here! I'm in his room!' And then, after looking into the room again: 'I can't go back! The fire's too strong!'

'Jump!' several voices cried, and a woman screamed. He climbed out on to the windowsill, let his legs dangle, caught his arm in something and fell.

And, at once, as things happen in dreams, inconsequent, without reason, Vanessa saw that Benjie was beside her. She heard his voice, as from an infinite distance, explaining that he had come back from Keswick that evening, been roused and at once ridden down. 'Oh, thank God you're safe, Vanessa,' he said, hurried from her as figures do in dreams, was back again, his arm round her, crying, 'It's all right. Will's broken a leg. No one else is harmed. Everyone's safe.'

She tore herself away from him.

'No, no, Benjie! Don't you see? Father's in there! Father's there!'

She ran forward. He pulled her back.

'Don't be mad. No one can live in there! The roof is falling!'

She fought him, she struck his face.

'Let me go! Let me go! We must find him!'

He held her with all his strength, pressing her against him. The ground was covered with people; the horses that they had taken from the stable trampled and neighed. With a great gesture, as though in a frenzy of exultation, the flames flung up their arms, the roof crashed.

The house gave up its life.

WILD NIGHT IN THE HILLS

There was at that time in the hills between Derwentwater and Cummock a very lonely farm called Hatchett's Fosse.

To this farm Benjamin Herries rode some three days after Adam Paris' burial at Ireby.

Adam's charred and almost unrecognizable body had been found when at last the fire had died sufficiently for safe search to be made. The red brick walls of Fell House still stood, blackened and scorched but enduring. But these walls were a shell. Nothing else remained. The wind that night had been so ferocious that in any circumstances there could have been small hope of saving the house, but everything had contributed to aggravating the disaster: the ancient fire-engine at Braithwaite broke down on the road. There was nothing at the house itself, no protection of any kind. The horses and animals were saved. No life was lost but Adam's. A little furniture, some pictures, were rescued. That was all. Fell House, Uldale, was no more.

The death of Adam Paris shocked the whole countryside. He had not been widely known. He was held to be a 'shy sort of man' but he was liked. He was said to be kindly, friendly, generous. No one had anything against him. He was old Madame's son, even though he had been born on the wrong side of the blanket, and he wrote books. But more than any of these, he was the father of Vanessa, whose beauty was renowned from Silloth to Kendal. Everyone knew how she had loved him, and there was something deeply real and true in the sympathy that rose now on every side of her. Cumberland people are reputed by those who know them little to be too blunt of tongue for complacent comfort, but any man in trouble will be lucky if he has Cumbrian friends near to him. They have not been masters of their own soil for hundreds of years without learning what courtesy means, and courtesy is not in this part of England another name for heartlessness.

But Vanessa was stricken down in these first days beyond any possibility of help. With Jane Bellairs and Will she went back to Cat Bells and there she stayed, seeing nobody. On the day before the funeral she saw Benjie. He knew at once that she could not just then bear either to see him or talk to him.

She spoke in a low voice, looking beyond him at the door as though she expected someone to come in.

'I don't blame you, Benjie. You did what you thought right, but you should not have held me back.'

'Vanessa, HOW could I have let you go? The roof fell in a moment later. You would have been killed as well as Adam. What good would that have been?'

'I had rather have been killed. To think that he was alone in there! That nobody but myself and Will thought of him!'

He saw that at present there was nothing to be done. He kissed her. She made no movement, no response. She said in a low voice:

'The awful thing is that I heard him calling me. From some other part of the house. But Timothy told me he was out. I will never forgive Timothy and I will never forgive myself.'

When he went home things were no better. His mother had been unwell for some months, and the night of the fire with its tragic consequences was a shock from which it was unlikely that she would recover. The destruction of Fell House was a dreadful thing to her. She had been there so often. John, her husband, had been born there; he had walked out of there to his death. More than that, this appeared to her to be a revenge from the past. Her father had built the Fortress to triumph over Fell House. It had seemed at his death that he was defeated; but he had NOT been defeated. This was the last unexpected triumph of the Fortress, a house that she had always hated and now detested. She seemed to hear her brother Uhland tapping with his stick night and day about the passages. How satisfied he must be! These vindictive people were stronger in death than they had been in life and there was no end to their malevolence. She had loved Adam, and her heart ached now for Vanessa. She was old, alone with ghosts. No one could help her.

Benjie, her son, it seemed, least of all. She had been very patient with his selfishness, but now at last she was exasperated. He seemed to her hard and callous. For once her intuition failed her. She did not know that he was suffering more deeply than she. On the day after Adam's funeral he came into her bedroom and said:

'I can't bear this, Mother. I must go away for a day or two.'

'What can't you bear?' she asked him quietly.

'Vanessa,' he broke out in a kind of storm of indignation, 'thinks that I was responsible for Adam's death.'

She thought that he was indignant with Vanessa, but had she been well and strong she would have known that the indignation was with himself.

'She is suffering from shock,' she answered. 'You must be patient and wait.'

'Wait! Wait!' he burst out. 'For what? Everything is changed, Mother. It will never be the same again.'

The farmer at Hatchett's Fosse was Fred Halliday, the son of the woman with whom Benjie had stayed at Seascale.

Some months back Benjie, riding along Main Street, saw Mrs Halliday and her daughter Marion looking at him from across the street. His first impulse had been to move on, but something had prevented him. He did not like them, he did not wish to see them again; nevertheless he rode over and spoke to them. They were to stay in Keswick for a while. Mrs Halliday had notions of opening a boarding house there. Still with that strange mingling of attraction and repulsion, he had met them a number of times. Mrs Halliday was definitely repugnant to him: she whined, she crept, she was genteel, she was vindictive. The girl spoke little, had little colour in her voice or movements, but she had some power over him. He kissed her and hated himself for doing so. She appeared to expect his distaste; indeed she said to him once:

'How you dislike me!'

But she did not seem at all to resent this except that, in her still, motionless way, she resented everything. Her pale skin, thin anaemic body, quiet, almost stealthy movements, stirred him as though he were attracted by his own exact opposite. She did not speak to his mind nor his heart, but his senses. When he touched her--and always it seemed that it was by her volition and not his-- he felt no tenderness nor affection, but a sensual inquisitiveness as though something persuaded him to explore further--as though some sensual secret were hidden there which would, when discovered, excite and surprise him.

He did not know--and he did not care--whether she liked him or no. She appeared to like no one, to have no life beside that of sudden little movements, unexpected advances and withdrawals. One evening he met her in the dusk walking down the hill behind St John's Church. He talked to her and then embraced her passionately. She eagerly returned his embraces. He went home in a mood of bitter revulsion against himself. He had met her brother several times in Keswick. Fred Halliday was a big, broad, red-faced hearty man, quite unlike his mother and sister, who laughed at everything, drank a good deal, and was friend of all the world. And yet it was true that nobody in Keswick liked him. He was not trusted, and it was said that when drunk he was very quarrelsome and abusive.

Not a very worthy family for Benjie to be friendly with, but then it was always like that with him. When he was jolly, as at most times he was, anyone would do to be jolly with. At this period of his life almost anyone was good enough to pass the time of day with. Who was he to be a judge? Except for his mother and Vanessa no one alive mattered. He was proud of not caring. Life was not important and one man resembled another. He loved Vanessa, who was much too good for him, and if women liked to be kissed, why, he liked to kiss them! In spite of his escapades he had never yet got any woman into trouble. His luck in that had held. He would not hurt anyone for the world.

But as he rode out to Hatchett's Fosse he was not sure that he did not want to hurt everybody. Fred Halliday had often invited him to come and see the farm; he had never thought that he would really go. But now anywhere would do, anywhere away from his own unhappiness, his sense that he had lost Vanessa for ever and that he deserved to have lost her.

The morbid side of his character had grown stronger during this past year. Although he loved the place, this Cumberland country always increased the strain of superstition so deeply ingrained in his character. Away from his home he was as other men and could consort with them on equal terms, but at the Fortress and in the country around him he felt sometimes like a man caught in a trap. On the one hand was the small lonely house in Skiddaw Forest where his father had been murdered; on the other--and only a step away-- the great cavern beneath Skiddaw where all the spirits of the true men lived and rejoiced for ever. Surely fantastic nonsense as food for a healthy man's brain! But in this Benjie was not healthy, nor are most imaginative men free of certain dreams, omens, and apprehensions. These two contrasted things were for him perhaps only symbols, but they brought with them a conviction that, whenever he returned to this country, he was not his own free master. And yet he must return! He could not keep away from it. He could not remain in it when he was there. And were his instincts altogether wrong? Had he not, in this last year, been twice prevented from marrying Vanessa, once by her father's illness and now by this cursed fire? The Men under Skiddaw would receive him in their company IF he could reach them, but, like a man in a dream, he was held back. Who could dare to deny that the past was more powerful than the present and that you must fight like the devil or the moment you were born you were done for! That old ancestor of his, Francis Herries, might still have something to say!

All this was, of course, only a part of Benjie's mind. None of the men who knew him as he roamed the world would credit him with THIS kind of imagination! But he was compounded of stiff incongruities-- proud and yet humble, faithful and yet most unfaithful, wandering but steadfast--and at this time he was still young with most of his soul-making ahead of him.

So as he rode down Bassenthwaite and on towards Braithwaite he felt only an urgent need of escape: escape from the senseless waste of Adam's death, from all the grief that that was causing (he had an eager sensitiveness to the unhappiness of others); escape from his mother, whom he knew that he should not be leaving; but above all escape from Vanessa, whom he loved now when he was sure that he had lost her, with a deeper sense of frustration than ever before.

Then he raised his head, looked up at the stormy sky and swore. 'Well, THIS has settled the business.

She is better, far better, without me. She'll know that at last.'

But even while he said this he felt that they were inseparable, that however their lives went they would be bound together for ever-- yes, even when he was secure and singing with the Men under Skiddaw he would be thinking of her!

As he began slowly to climb Whinlatter he felt the wind tugging at him. On the day following the fire the wind had folded its arms and stolen away as though the purpose of its coming were accomplished. Then, as is often the case in the late spring, it sprang up again and rushed about the country in flurries of excitement, blowing the daffodils silly, making the young leaves tremble and the young sheep skip, and flashing quivers of light like turning glass across the streams. The colours were all delicate--faint shadowed plum, a gold so pale that it was almost white under cloud, a wet virginal green of the young bracken. And field after field, up and up the hillsides, was silver-grey.

This afternoon, though, quite another mood was in the air, spring was forgotten. It happens sometimes here that the hills, as though an order had been given, suddenly dominate all the scene. The pastoral fields, the farms, the roads, towns, villages shrink together into nothingness and the hills step forward, spread their shoulders, swell their chests out, raise their heads and begin to march. If you listen you can almost hear the tramping. It is at such times that you can understand Benjie's fantasy of his men under the mountain, for it is no fantasy just then. Lie down on the turf and listen with your ear to the ground and you can catch the echo of the voices, a rumble of a drinking song and laughter like the cracking of a drum's skin. At such a moment when the hills take power there is a sense of menace in the air. The sky is disturbed with a furious confusion, great sweeps of cloud smoking along with a wind behind them that is personal in its strength. The old pictures of Aeolus blowing the four winds from his mouth is true now. You can see him standing behind the hills, his strong legs spread across the sea, his broad naked shoulders stretched above his vigorous lungs. The wind and the hills act in unison. The hills, that are in actual measurement so slight, take on themselves additional properties that belong to the great mountains of the world. With white mist flanking them and black funnels of cloud eddying above their heads, they seem as powerful as Everest. Their power is menacing. They seem to crowd together in conclave: 'Now shall we step forward and crush out of existence these little fields, cowering hamlets, tiny midgets of humans?' You can watch them as they bend their heads together and twitch their shoulders with the impatience of a group of boys waiting for the word of release. The wind is enchanted with the sport promised. It goes swinging from arm to arm of the hills, crying: 'Now let us go! Now we are off!' and it sweeps whirlwinds of rain now here, now there, making it sting the earth like a hail of small shot, then raising it again in sheets of steel as though all the heavens were letting down their defensive gates. A great game that leads to no ill because the power here is friendly. They have not learnt any deep vindictiveness. This square of earth is kind to the men who settle, for a moment, upon its surface. The Genius here is benevolent.

Such a storm of wind without rain rose about Benjie as he climbed Whinlatter. The water of Bassenthwaite below him that had been a field of grey shadows as he rode beside it was now, when he looked down upon it, trembling with white waves that gleamed with an almost phosphorescent glow under the blackness of Skiddaw. The clouds were so low that when he was at the highest point of the Pass they skirted him on every side, shifting from place to place with long sweeps of spidery grey. It was bitterly cold and he had to lower his head, pulling up the collar of his riding coat.

He knew that with Lorton Fell on his right, before he turned off down to Swinside, his path branched away to the left. The farm was just here somewhere, in a hollow between Grisedale Pike and Hobcarton. He directed his horse across the rough turf, moving very slowly under the sting of the wind. To his right he looked down on to the flat plain that stretched to the Border with fields like squares of a chessboard and trees and houses like dolls' furniture. The wind raced over this flat country with a shrill whistling exultation; thin patches of white broke the grey sky above the sea. It was raining above St Bees.

It would be difficult to find this place, and if the mist came down, impossible. He might wander here for hours. He cursed himself for coming, and had an impulse to turn back. In certain moods this driving wind and cold sharp air would have exalted him, but not today, for he was sick with his own self-distrust and disapproval. Nothing grand about him today to answer the grandeur of the elements. Why should he not turn back and wait patiently for Vanessa to recover? How impulsive he had been to have taken her present mood as permanent! And how selfish he had been to ride away from her at the very moment when, in her heart, she needed him! He half turned his horse's head. He would go back. Then, as he looked round him, he saw the farm, a little to his right in the fold of the hill, a bare meagre place with a few bent trees and a stone wall. The first drops of rain stung his cheek. He rode on.

When he reached the farm two dogs ran out, wildly barking: he heard Fred's voice cursing them and then saw the big stout man filling the doorway.

He gave a shout when he saw who it was.

'Hullo, Herries! What a surprise!'

He came to meet him, his face beaming.

'You've come for the night, I hope?'

'Yes,' said Benjie. 'If you'll have me.'

'Of course I'll have you. Couldn't be better.'

They led the horse round to the stable at the back of the house, Halliday talking all the time.

'My mother and sister are staying here and some friends of ours are coming up from Lorton this evening, so you've struck the right moment. It's going to be a wild night. The wind's blowing great guns. Come along in and get warm.'

Benjie went in, hung up his hat and coat, passed into an inner room that seemed half kitchen, half living-room. Sitting beside a roaring fire were Mrs Halliday and her daughter.

At the moment when he saw them, the large smoke-stained fireplace, the window that looked out on to a little scrambling path where a cluster of primroses was hiding, two canaries in a cage, and a large sheepdog lying in front of the fire with his nose on his paws, his mood changed. This was jolly, cheerful, friendly. They were all friends of his. Other friends were coming. They would make a night of it. He had closed a door, a heavy silent-swinging door like one that guards a cathedral, upon all that other world where his friends were burnt, those whom he loved blamed him and, worst of all, where he blamed himself. Here he loved no one and no one loved him. It was not a world of hurting, haunting intimacies. He would be happy. So, as always when he was happy, he wanted to do things for everybody, drew a chair to the fire and chattered like a boy, threw back his head and roared with laughter, his rather ugly face with friendliness and generosity in all its wrinkles. And the two women quietly answered or asked questions while Fred Halliday leaned his bulk against the kitchen dresser and, with a smile on his face, watched them.

Benjie had all the London gossip: of the success that Iolanthe was and the other piece that the German Reeds were running, The Mountain Heiress, where Corney Grain was a solicitor and sang a wonderful song called 'Our Mess', and that Goring Thomas' Esmeralda at the Lane, where Mr Carl Rosa had a month's opera season, contained, they say, some pretty songs but that Mme Georgina Burns couldn't act for toffee.

Mrs Halliday said that the matter with the London theatre today was that it was too expensive, not comfortable enough, and that most of the plays were silly. In fact, with a few well-chosen words, she demolished the London theatre. And Benjie said, oh, he didn't know. That was a little severe, wasn't it, and that one went to the theatre to be jolly, didn't one, and that he'd go a long way to hear Corney Grain sing 'Our Mess'. Then they discussed the Budget, which had been introduced a week or two before by Mr Childers. Certainly had forestalled the Conservatives, who had been intending to come out as Champions of Economy, but Gladstone knew two of that. Everyone talking of Economy now. Yes, said Mrs Halliday, the great thing was of course to BE economical, but easier to say than to do. Benjie, nodding his head profoundly, agreed that that WAS the problem!

Then they discussed books, and Benjie said that he did hope that Miss Marion didn't read French novels, and Miss Marion said that she sometimes did and thought them very amusing, much nearer to real life than silly writers like Rhoda Broughton and Ouida. She liked poetry, though. Did Mr Herries read poetry? No, Mr Herries didn't. A writer like Tennyson took such a long time to say what he wanted to. No, Miss Halliday did NOT agree. Poetry could do something that nothing else could do. Wouldn't Mr Herries agree to that? And, yes, he thought on the whole that he DID agree to that!

So they talked in the pleasantest fashion and the time flew by while the wind roared outside and the rain that had swept up from the sea beat against the window frames. Fred Halliday had some excellent beer and Benjie drank plenty of it. The fire, the beer, the pleasant easy talk all comforted and reassured him. Yes, the door, with its heavy leather curtain, had swung to; all sounds from the outer world were deadened. Mrs Halliday, he thought, was a more agreeable woman than he supposed. She sat there knitting a stocking most domestically. Her face was grave, but after all, not repellent at all. The glow from the fire softened her rather gaunt features.

Once and again she smiled, baring her teeth with her upper lip, almost as though she were about to whistle.

And as to the girl he felt once more, and increasingly as the beer warmed him, that he would like to touch her. He must be kind to her, poor child, for she could not have much happiness in her life. He began to wonder whether she had not finer feelings, more sensitive tastes than her mother and brother could satisfy. She read French, she liked poetry. Not that she had any pride. No one could be quieter about her accomplishments. Once or twice he caught her looking at him, her pale eyes staring at him, and he felt then a little embarrassment, as though he should be ashamed of his brown face and strong body when she herself was so delicate. At the thought of her delicacy some sensuous nerve in him was touched. She was so slight, so fragile, that in his arms she would be powerless, must submit to anything that he wished. Not that he would hurt her. He would not hurt anybody in the world.

The shrill clock on the mantelpiece struck seven and, a moment later, the door was flung open and Halliday came in, bringing three men with him. These men had taken their coats off in the passage; two of them were youngish, had rough corduroy trousers with long black coats containing deep pockets. One of the two was little and wiry, with bright red hair and a small, shaggy, red beard; the other was broad, strong, very dark with bright, glancing, restless eyes and a close-clipped black moustache. He was a handsome fellow. These two men might be both between thirty and forty in age. The third, as Benjie immediately learned, was the father

of these two. He was tall and thin, dressed in a long black coat with wide tails and black trousers. His hair was grey and sparse; he had little eyes and above them a very high domed forehead. He looked something like a schoolmaster.

Halliday introduced them to Benjie. Their name, he discovered, was Endicott; Thomas the elder one, George and Robert the two sons. They all sat down by the fire. Thomas Endicott had rather a shrill piercing voice, small in compass and high-pitched. He spoke with care as though, with difficulty, he had learned how to be cultured. The voices of the two younger men were rough. Robert, the little red-haired fellow, spoke with an effeminate note; he was restless and given to gestures. George's voice was deep but without any Cumbrian accent. They seemed friendly. They knew the two women and were old acquaintances, it appeared, of Halliday. Endicott the elder talked to Benjie, a little pompously and always with that slow carefulness as though he would choose the right word and never on any account drop an 'h'. Oh no, they did not live at Lorton. He himself resided in Whitehaven. Yes, oh yes, his wife and her sister lived with him. This boy George here, oh! he was a rascal, could settle to nothing, had been in the Army for a bit, hadn't he, George? Could put his hand to anything, a fine boxer; oh yes, a splendid footballer if he kept in condition--but a rascal. Wouldn't settle to anything, would he, George? They all laughed, and George smiled at Benjie in friendly fashion, as much as to say: 'I like you. I've taken to you. We shall be friends.'

Oh yes, and Robert was a wanderer too. He would go from place to place selling things, go round Fairs, you know, all over the country. What you would call a pedlar in the old days. Didn't mind what he did any more than George.

Oh, they were a wandering family. That's what his wife always complained of. Yes, an old Border family. Nothing much to boast of a hundred years ago-- smugglers and worse, so he heard.

'As a matter of fact, Mr Herries,' he said, 'I have been wanting to meet you. We're almost related in a kind of way. There was a girl in our family years ago married one of your ancestors, well known in the Borrowdale district. Rogue Herries he was called.'

'What!' cried Benjie. 'Rogue Herries! Why!--'

'Aye, there were two brothers, George and Anthony Endicott, mad Tony they called him. Their sister married a man called Starr and these two had a daughter. It was her old Herries married.'

Why, that was Judith's mother! Benjie was indeed amazed; what with the beer and the warmth of the kitchen everything seemed to him now wonderful and jolly and all that it should be. Here they were, these three nice fellows, and their ancestress was Judith's mother. Judith's mother, Vanessa's great-grandmother-- but at that thought the leather-curtained door, that had for a moment swung back, was closed again. No thought of Vanessa. Vanessa was far away.

'Aye,' said Thomas Endicott. 'Funny how small the world is. I've often thought I'd like to meet one of you, although maybe those ancestors of ours are nothing to be proud of.'

'Proud of them!' cried Benjie. 'I should think I am! Francis Herries you're speaking of, was a great man, a grand fighter, and a man of his hands.'

'Aye,' said Thomas Endicott slowly. 'There are plenty of stories of him in Borrowdale. He sold his woman at a Fair once, they tell.'

'And a good thing too!' Benjie cried. 'What do you say, Mrs Halliday? If you're tired of a woman and someone else wants her? Why not sell her? Fair exchange, you know.'

But Mrs Halliday only smiled and went on knitting.

Then they had supper, a very good supper too, ham and beef and chicken, a big apple tart, rum butter and cheese and plenty of cakes. Halliday produced a wine, a good warming Burgundy, and while they ate and chattered and laughed the wind tore at the house as though it would tumble it over. But the house was strong, very old, Halliday told them.

'There was a man murdered here once,' Halliday said. 'In the 'forties it was. His wife and daughter murdered him for his money. Cut his head open with a hatchet and he bled all over this very floor.'

After supper they all helped to clear the table and then they sang songs. There was an old piano there, not strictly in tune but what did that matter? They roared out the songs and banged the piano and laughed and stood with their arms round one another's shoulders.

Soon Benjie knew that he was very merry, very merry indeed. Not drunk; oh no, not drunk at all, but as happy as a grig. He had never had a better evening. What splendid fellows they were, and especially George! His hand rested on George's shoulder. He must see George again, must see George often. This was the kind of evening he enjoyed. Yes; he would like to do something for him, put George in the way of a job if he wanted one. And George looked at him as though he liked him. He didn't say much, but he smiled and pushed out his chest when he sang and poured beer down his throat.

The ladies said goodnight. It was time for them to retire.

'We shall see you in the morning,' said Mrs Halliday. 'What a wild night it is, to be sure!'

Some time later Benjie thought that he must go to the door for a moment to cool his head. He slipped out, opened the front door, and was almost tumbled off his feet by the wind. The world was raging outside, the rain sweeping through the air in whipping fury. With great difficulty he closed the door again and turned back to see the girl standing there quite close to him. There was a dim reflection of light from the upper floor. The voices of the men singing came raucously from the inner room.

'Why, Marion!' he said.

'I am just going up to bed.'

'It was so hot in there I came out for a breath of air.'

'Yes, I know. I was hot too.'

Her hand was touching his. He caught it, then putting his arms around her, kissed her. She kissed him passionately in return, her lips clinging to his as though they would never leave them. When he held her in his arms, so slight and slender was she that he was afraid of hurting her.

'I'm hurting you,' he whispered.

'I like you to hurt me,' she whispered back, then gently freeing herself, said 'Goodnight' and ran up the stairs.

Oh, well, he shouldn't have done that. But she was so close to him. She was in his arms before he realized it. Kissing a girl-- nothing in it. It was natural to kiss a girl. There was something about her . . . not that he liked her . . . He stood for a moment leaning against the wall in the dark passage, and felt an odd chagrin, an almost desperate loneliness, an impulse to leave the house at once, fetch his horse from the stable and ride home . . .

But he went back into the room, joining the chorus with them as he entered it.

Now that the women were gone, gaiety and friendliness rose a note higher. This was what life should be, men together with care thrown out of the window, plenty to drink, a wild night outside, all friends together. They might have known one another all their lives. Father Endicott was not such a schoolmaster as you might suppose. He possessed, in fact, a grand fund of bawdy stories. Very funny they were. That one about the old farmer's wife of Esthwaite and the two simple young men and the lady from London. There was nothing about old Cumberland life that he didn't know, the life that was going now so fast with all the tourists in the summer and the railways everywhere. A pity, a pity! Those were the good old days when Lizzie O'Branton, the witch, jumped out of her coffin at her funeral and rode away on a broomstick, and Mrs Machell of Penrith would drive her ghostly carriage whenever a 'helm' wind was blowing, when the 'need fire' charmed the cattle, when the song was sung at the shearing. Here they broke out all together:

Heigh O! Heigh O! Heigh O!
And he that doth this health deny.
Before his face I him defy.
He's fit for no good company,
So let this health go round.

Good fun, too, when they had the public whippings, or the hangings in Carlisle or the witch-drownings.

'Changed times,' said old Endicott sadly. 'All the fine spirit gone.'

But THEIR spirit was not gone. It increased with every drop they drank. The table was pushed aside and George and Benjie tried a 'wrastle'. They took off their coats, waistcoats, and shoes and went to it. Solemnly they circled round and round trying for a hold. But Benjie was no very great wrestler and soon George had 'buttocked' him and, throwing him, tumbled over him. They crashed to the floor and then lay there, panting, one on the other. For they were not drunk, oh no, not drunk at all, but it was comfortable there on the floor and Benjie had his arm round George's neck, looked up at the whitewashed ceiling, pulled George's hair, said, laughing, 'I like you, George. We're friends, we are,' and George's hand rested on Benjie's back and he said nothing at all. Old Endicott played a polka on the piano and they danced heavily, clumsily, staggering about the room, and Benjie cried:

'There's a fine place under Skiddaw, George, where well go when we're dead and we'll dance and sing for ever and ever.'

'Aye,' said George. 'Aye. That'll be grand.'

In all the merry evening there was only one unpleasant incident, which Benjie could never after properly recall.

He said something to little red-bearded Robert, and Robert took offence. The little man was dancing with rage and screaming out:

'You're a liar, I tell you. A damned bloody liar!'

'Call me a liar?' shouted Benjie.

'Aye, and I will too. Who do you think I am?'

'Why!' cried Benjie. 'I'll tell you who you are. You're a funny little man, that's who you are!'

'I was here in this country before any of you were born. Aye, and I was too, selling laces and silver boxes, visiting the witches in Borrowdale--'

'Shut your mouth, Robert,' cried George. 'Who wants to listen to your lies? Why, man--'

'Lies, are they?' The little man was screaming, dancing up and down until to Benjie's dazzled eyes he seemed a dozen little men with peaked caps on their heads, riding through the kitchen on the wind and rain. But the little man wanted to fight, and the others, roaring with laughter, held his arms and they knocked the lamp over. The room was dark save for the firelight. Oh, but the little man's red beard shone and he was angry! And Benjie embraced him, pulled his beard, gave him a friendly kick on the pants, and he went and sat in a corner by the fireplace, waving his hands and making shadows of rabbits on the wall with his fingers.

Later, Benjie found himself with a candle wandering on his way to bed. Halliday showed him where his room was, a little whitewashed room at the top of the house. Halliday helped him into bed.

And later than that, as he lay looking at the ceiling and smiling, the door opened. The girl stood there, a candle in her hand, wearing a dressing-gown with a wool collar over her nightdress.

He sat up on his elbow and looked at her. She closed the door very softly and came over to him. She smiled and said:

'The wind's died down. Everyone's sleeping.'

He could only stare at her. She took off her dressing-gown and carefully laid it on the chair. Then she blew out the candle, climbed into bed and lay down beside him.

INSIDE THE FORTRESS

It was early in the wet and stormy weather of that year when Vanessa came to stay with Elizabeth at the Fortress.

Elizabeth had been seriously ill ever since the fire at Fell House in April. No one could say exactly where the trouble was. It was what was known as a 'decline'. She was weak, instantly tired by any exertion; her features now had the delicacy of a thin rose-tinted shell. Her hair was snow-white, her figure still slim and erect, but ghost-like in its fragility. She walked a little from room to room: although she leaned on a stick she was still tall. She was kind and gracious to everyone, but most of her, as Mrs Harwen, the cook-housekeeper, said, was 'otherwhither'.

'It's my opinion,' John Harwen, the handyman about the place and Mrs Harwen's little hostler-like spouse, remarked, 'That the difference between her living and her dead is so slight that you'll not notice it. After she's gone she'll still be here, so to speak.'

'We've enough ghosts in this house already,' said Mrs Harwen.

Benjie had not been home since June. No one knew where he was. No one had heard from him. Elizabeth had through many years practised herself to be patient about these absences, but now it was another matter. For she knew that she had not long to live and she had only one desire in her heart--that Benjie and Vanessa should be married before she went.

She had not seen very much of Vanessa. The girl had stayed first with Timothy in Eskdale, where he had thoughts of buying a house (for he had decided not to rebuild Fell House), then had returned to Cat Bells, where Will and the old cook had looked after her.

In July she visited Elizabeth, who saw at once that here now was a woman of self-command, deep reserves and a very fine courage. Vanessa was cheerful, talked freely about her father, seemed indeed to wish to talk of him, recalling days and moments and words and phrases; saying: 'Papa always felt that' or 'Papa never troubled to be angry--he said it was waste of time.' But his death, Elizabeth saw, had made a fundamental change in Vanessa, had brought out certain qualities that were latent before, and had checked others.

She was not so impetuous: her heart was as warm but it was guarded now against shock.

Just before she went she said:

'And what about Benjie?'

Elizabeth told her that she had not heard, that she had no idea where he was.

'It's a shame!' Vanessa cried indignantly. 'You wanting him--'

'Yes,' said Elizabeth quietly. 'I am not going to live much longer, my dear, and I MUST see him. But no one knows where he is.'

'I think,' said Vanessa lowly, 'that perhaps I am partly to blame. He came to see me--after the fire. I was not myself. I didn't want Benjie or anyone. I wanted to be left alone. So he went away.'

'We'll be independent of him,' said Elizabeth gently.

Then Vanessa asked if she might come and stay. Elizabeth's pale cheek flushed.

'Oh, Vanessa dearest, do you mean it? Will you really come? How happy I shall be!'

Early in September Vanessa came. No one knew what that was to her, the first time that she looked from the long windows of the Fortress down to the valley where, very clearly, in the pale colourless moving air, the walls of Fell House were still standing. She had been dreading this moment from the instant when she made her proposal of a visit to Elizabeth. She had not seen the place since the day of the funeral. But she knew that it had to be faced, that everything had to be faced. She had learnt many things since April and one of them was that the only way to make anything of life was to fit, resolutely, with courage, into the patterns that life, in change after change, presented. To attempt to force life into YOUR pattern was to challenge disaster. You must accept EVERYTHING and turn it to good.

So she stood there that morning in her black dress, her hands clenched at her sides, the house silent about her with that dull brooding silence that seemed the Fortress' special property. In the valley the four bare walls stood, the moors climbing above them as though they already recognized that here was a spot that now they would soon reclaim, as, one day, they would reclaim everything.

Tears rolled down Vanessa's cheeks, but she made no sound. For a moment she cried within herself: 'Oh, I cannot endure this! I CANNOT endure it!' and this was followed by the strong response: 'I CAN endure it! I can endure anything!'

The hardest thing to bear was that she had not at present recovered her father for herself. When someone dearly loved passes away there is a period when everything is blurred. The personality has broken up into a thousand pieces, something here, something there, but the radiant heart is absent. Slowly the friend returns, never-- if feeling has been true--to be lost again.

Elizabeth, watching her, felt at first the girl's deep loneliness. There they were alike. She, too, was lonely, had been for years, but that is a lesson that women learn and it is one of the principal bonds between them. Vanessa was only setting out on a road that Elizabeth knew by heart, of which she was even proud. At the same time they were not a gloomy pair. They laughed, drove out in the landau, had visitors, read together, played piquet and backgammon. Elizabeth's extreme weakness was what Vanessa needed. She needed, more than she had ever conceived that she would, someone to care for. It was the strongest need of her nature and would always be, as it had been her grandmother's. That was why she wanted Benjie more with every day that passed. Now that Adam was gone she had nobody else but Benjie. And, as Elizabeth needed him too, these two, although they seldom mentioned him, thought of him all the time.

But there were other things growing in Vanessa, as Elizabeth one day discovered.

A Mrs Marrable from Rosthwaite called. Now the Marrable family, its colour, personality, and circumstances, would make a very fit subject of study for anyone interested in English family life in the eighties. Mr John Marrable had interests in China. He was now retired, wore a black beard, smoked a kind of Oriental hookah, and was to be seen for the most part in green-and-red worsted carpet slippers walking up and down the glass-covered passage on the outside of his Rosthwaite house. Mrs Marrable was round, stout, full-bosomed, and her skirt so beflounced and beribboned that she was all bits and pieces. John Marrable was severe and extremely self-satisfied. Mrs Marrable very talkative, serious-minded, but gay with that nervous gaiety peculiar to wives who expect their husbands to enter at any moment in the worst of all possible tempers. The Marrables had five children, four girls and a boy; they lived entirely up to the later caricatured notion of Victorian manners in that the four Miss Marrables had been completely sacrificed to their brother Edward, for whom everything had been done. The result of doing everything for Edward was that he had turned out very badly indeed, being sent down from Cambridge for grossly insulting a Proctor and then, while supposedly following his father's Chinese interests in London, mixing in the lowest society and incurring a multitude of debts. Meanwhile the four Miss Marrables, who were not beauties, waited patiently at home for someone to marry them, were bullied by their father and grew ever more plain of feature. One of them, the third in age, Lettice, Vanessa had liked, been kind to; the result of this was that Lettice Marrable worshipped her with a passion that was made up of religion, sexual hunger, and a devastating loneliness. Lettice Marrable's adoration for Vanessa had its consequences.

In any case for the moment here Mrs Marrable was, taking tea with Elizabeth and Vanessa in the drawing-room of the Fortress. She chattered on for a long time in the eager, apprehensive, incoherent manner that was especially hers, and as she talked a large locket jumped about on her stout bosom like a thing imprisoned and mad for freedom.

'Yes, thank you, we have heard from Ned. His present enthusiasm is for Miss Mary Anderson. He goes to see her every evening in Ingomar, although every evening is of course the dear fellow's exaggeration. The play is a failure, he tells us, but Miss Anderson is lovelier than ever.'

'Why don't you take the girls up to London, Mrs Marrable, for a jaunt, and go and see her?'

'Take the girls up to London! My dear Miss Paris! With things in China as bad as they are! No. Mr Marrable says we must economize in every possible direction, and we are thinking of cutting down the landau. He tells the girls that we must all make sacrifices and he is quite right. Ned went with some friends to Hurlingham last weekend and seems really to have enjoyed himself, and he actually saw the Duke of Cambridge riding down a side street on a bicycle the other day! I agree with Mr Marrable that our Royal Family should keep up their position. Do not you, Mrs Herries? And Mr Marrable says that with all this odd behaviour of France in China there is no knowing where we shall all be and we look to the Royal Family to keep us all together. Although Ned writes in his letter that the Prince of Wales really DOES encourage some very light-hearted behaviour. Now is it right? What I mean, Miss Paris, is that we all look up to the Royal Family. What kind of example is he setting our girls? And that reminds me. They tell me that Miss Nettleship, the daughter of Doctor Nettleship, is going up to Girton. Now I don't know what YOU think, Miss Paris, but my opinion is--and Mr Marrable's too--that all these things that girls are wanting to do are the GREATEST mistake. More than that, they are unwomanly--the very word that Mr Marrable used this morning.'

'What things?' asked Vanessa, smiling.

Now it happened that that smile which Vanessa had intended in all friendliness irritated Mrs Marrable. She had had a trying day. John Marrable had come down to breakfast with a cold and had been very severe with everyone. She was anxious about Ned's doings in London, and Mrs Martin of Keswick had asked for her bill (a thing that nobody in Keswick ever dreamt of doing unless seized by some sudden insanity). Moreover, neither she nor Mr Marrable really approved of Vanessa. It was true, of course, that she was a great beauty, but was she quite nice? It was said of her that she had some very odd opinions, and unusual she certainly must be to engage herself to that rascal of a son of Mrs Herries, who, poor woman, was popular with everyone, partly because she did no harm and partly because everyone had the luxury of pitying her.

Mrs Marrable did not approve of Vanessa although she could not deny but that black suited her, she was a very lovely girl, she was kind to Lettice, and belonged to one of the best families in Cumberland. This smile, however, hinted at broad views, was patronizing, and the drive back to Rosthwaite would be very long. She wished now that she had brought one of the girls to bear her company . . .

'What things?' cried Mrs Marrable, a little sharply. 'Why, anything that takes a woman away from the home where she belongs. All this gadding about, doing as men do--it isn't natural and you know it isn't, Miss Paris.'

'Why isn't it natural?' asked Vanessa. She was suddenly weary of Mrs Marrable. She wished that she would go. Mrs Marrable's bright green dress was most unsuited to her figure.

'Why isn't it natural?' Mrs Marrable had a maddening habit of repeating everything that the last speaker had said. 'Why, my dear Miss Paris, what did Nature intend women for? Marriage and the home. Marriage and the home.'

'But if they don't get married?' Vanessa continued, not very wisely. 'There are more women than men in this country. Many more. What are they to do? What do they do? Sit at home, twiddle their thumbs, and look out of window for a husband.'

This was unwise of her because it was exactly what the Miss Marrables spent their time in doing, as Mrs Marrable very well knew. She bridled in every limb.

'Well, if they do sit at home it is better in my opinion than that they should unsex themselves. Why, they are actually doctors, some of them! It is MY opinion, Miss Paris, that that Doctor Garrett Anderson they are always talking about should be put in prison!'

Elizabeth, who was watching Vanessa rather anxiously, saw her straighten her tall body and throw back her head.

'Another cup, Mrs Marrable?'

'Oh no, thank you, Mrs Herries. I positively must be going.'

'Why should she be put in prison?' asked Vanessa.

'Well, really, Miss Paris,' Mrs Marrable said, patting her locket and smiling rather nervously, 'I wonder you can ask such a question! But you, of course, are of the younger generation. We older ones wonder sometimes where the world is going to!'

'No, but, Mrs Marrable,' Vanessa persisted, 'I truly want to know. WHY should Doctor Garrett Anderson be put in prison?'

This was plainly intended as a challenge and Mrs Marrable took it as such.

'I consider her a wicked woman and a dangerous influence. I read an article about her only the other day. Do you know that she once actually read a paper on "The Limits of Parental Authority"? Do you happen to know, Miss Paris, that she actually supports the fantastic idea that women should have a vote? A vote indeed! If that is not against Nature I don't know what is! And do you know,' and here Mrs Marrable dropped her voice to an awful trembling hush, 'that she took the part of the fallen women in opposing an excellent Act of Parliament demanding their supervision?--yes, and she and her friends positively succeeded in having the Act repealed.'

'If women do not protect fallen women I scarcely see who will. Certainly not men.'

'Protect! Protect! My dear Miss Paris! And you quite a young girl! One naturally dislikes discussing such a matter at all, but people seem to discuss everything nowadays. All I can say is that if you approve this condonation of gross immorality I--I--I'm most surprised!'

'Let that be as it may, Mrs Marrable,' Vanessa said. 'I know a few things also about Doctor Anderson. She is one of the bravest and finest women alive in the world today. In fact, with the exception of Florence Nightingale, there is not a finer. I also could tell you one or two things about her that perhaps you don't know. Have you ever thought of the conditions women lived under when Doctor Anderson was a girl? A married woman was scarcely a human being. She had no rights, no property, nothing. Did you ever read Miss Leigh Smith's Brief Summary of the Most Important Laws Concerning Women?'

'No, indeed I have not,' said Mrs Marrable, panting with nervousness and annoyance.

'Well then, you should. It was written long ago and is still excellent reading. Do you know that when Elizabeth Garrett wanted to be a doctor she could not find a physician in England to whom she could be apprenticed? Do you know that she worked all day at the Middlesex Hospital, where there were no antiseptics and anaesthetic was scarcely used? That needed some courage, did it not? Do you know that the whole medical profession tried to stop her, that they got up a memorial against her, that London University when she tried to matriculate was closed to women? Do you know that she had to fight every step of the way and that when at last with Sophia Jex-Blake she started the School of Medicine for Women a howl went up through the whole of England? And all for why? Because, Mrs Marrable, at last women in England have grown tired of sitting still and looking out of the window for husbands! They want to have a life of their own, they want to be independent, as one day, please God, they shall be!'

Elizabeth had never seen Vanessa like this before. Her voice rang across the room as though she challenged the world. With her shoulders back and her eyes flashing she looked as though she would like to crush Mrs Marrable to powder. In fact at that moment she hated that good, kindly, and quite unoffending woman.

Unoffending but not unoffended! She was so deeply offended that she would never forget--never forget and never forgive. She was not, in her life and circumstance, a happy enough woman to forgive. Like all women who have a grievance which they refuse to admit, she made her friends take the blame. Vanessa was to be blamed for ever and ever.

The lady got up to go, smoothing her bosom and arranging her wide and voluminous skirt.

'Thank you, Mrs Herries, for a most delightful afternoon.'

'I am so glad that you came, Mrs Marrable.'

She carried it off. She shook her fingers playfully at Vanessa. 'When you are my age, Miss Paris,' she said, 'you will see the danger of these things.'

'Oh dear,' said Vanessa after her departure. 'How intolerable of me! And how unexpected! It was the very last thing I thought of doing. And in your house too.'

'You were rather vehement,' said Elizabeth. 'I have never seen you like that before.'

'No, but I am afraid you will see me like that again. I have a terrible temper and it flies up before I know that it's there. You are wise, Elizabeth. Tell me what I shall do about it.'

'No. I don't think you lost your temper, dear. You were indignant. That's all. And I agreed with every word that you said.'

Nevertheless, going to bed that night, Vanessa was very unhappy. Something was wrong, and what was wrong was that her spirit was weighed down with an intolerable loneliness. With every day that passed she realized more bitterly the agony of her father's loss. She had been wrong, perhaps, to build her life so entirely around him. It was the caring for him, the watching that he should be happy, the comfort of knowing that they loved one another--these things, gone, left in her utter desolation. Dear Elizabeth . . . but Elizabeth was now almost out of the world and did not need her. Nobody needed her, nobody anywhere.

And at that she faced the other trouble besides her father's loss. She wanted Benjie: she wanted to be married to Benjie, to care for him, understand him, comfort him, make him happy. And Benjie was away, would perhaps never return.

'That's amusing,' she thought as she lay down in bed. 'Here was I railing at Mrs Marrable about women's independence and I myself the least independent woman in the world!'

Two days later a telegram came:
'Arriving tonight. Benjie.'

Elizabeth ran to the door, flung it open, called out 'Vanessa! Vanessa!' and Vanessa came running down the stairs, thinking that Elizabeth was ill.

'Oh, what is it?'

But Elizabeth caught her hand.

'He's coming--tonight. That's all he says. It's sent from Liverpool.'

Vanessa took the telegram.

'Tonight! Oh, Elizabeth, I am so glad! He'll take the train to Carlisle, I shouldn't wonder, and then drive. He says nothing about being met.'

All day preparations were made, roses in his bedroom, Mrs Harwen roasting two ducks, the silver polished, the garden paths brushed, and everything at the end of it as dead around the house as it was at the beginning.

It was four in the afternoon. Tea had been just brought in. The hills beyond the windows lay like dark purple prehistoric animals bathing in a sea of orange mist. You could see them sprawling, burying their snouts, heaving their scaly backs, while below, all about the valley, the mist, like bales of wool, rolled from field to field.

Vanessa, holding Elizabeth close to her, stared at the hills.

'Benjie thinks there are men under Skiddaw,' she said. 'Dead men. A kind of Cumbrian Valhalla.'

But Elizabeth had not heard. She looked exceedingly frail today. Excitement was bad for her heart. She trembled a little, leaning against Vanessa's strong side.

'This house,' she said, 'whatever you do to it, it refuses to live. It was conceived in hatred, my dear. It has always hated everybody and everything just as poor Uhland did. It is this place should have been burnt, not Fell House. Look at this room. Look at the roses! I have put them here, there, everywhere. They are dropping with uneasiness. Nothing good will ever happen in this place. Benjie is bringing some bad news. I know it.'

Vanessa led her back to the sofa.

'Now lie down, Elizabeth darling. I'll bring you your tea. Don't THINK about Benjie until he's here. What bad news COULD there be?'

She was herself triumphant. She felt that she was able to deal with ANY situation that Benjie might offer. Were he in trouble through some foolishness she would stand by him. There was nothing that he could confess, as she had told him years ago, that she would not share with him. And then at last, after all these postponements, they would be married. There was nothing now to prevent it save the old obstacle of Benjie's scruples, which came, as she knew well, because he loved her so much. Now when he saw that her sorrow had only made her the more resolved, he would be as eager as she.

She went about the house, singing. She petted Mrs Harwen, who in any case adored her, went several times

to Benjie's room to see that everything was right, put Elizabeth to bed.

'He will be late. He has thirty miles to drive, you know. He shall come up to you the moment he arrives.'

It was after ten when he came. She was standing at her window and saw the lights of the carriage, heard the crunch of the wheels on the road, heard the driver shout 'Whoa!' to his horses, then, with a recognition that drove her heart against her ribs, the well-known timbre of Benjie's voice.

'All right, driver. I'll get someone to help you with the box.'

He came up the path, saw the light in her window, and looked up.

'Hulloa, Vanessa. Is that you?' he called out.

'Yes. I'll come down.'

As their hands clasped she knew that he loved her as dearly as ever. She was so happy that she could have flung her arms around his neck, but all she did was to say, smiling her quiet steady smile:

'Elizabeth has gone to bed. She's longing to see you.'

Old Harwen helped the driver in with the luggage. Benjie took off his coat, nodded to her, and saying, 'I'll see Mother a moment and come down,' he ran up the stairs.

It was something in his voice and look that frightened her. WHAT was it? He did not look well, but he would be tired, of course, after his journey. It was not that. As he spoke, he had avoided her eyes.

She went into the dining-room where some supper was laid out for him. She told Mrs Harwen to bring in the soup in ten minutes. Then she stood there under the gas that hissed very faintly above her head and tried to calm her fear.

Something was the matter. Had she not said that nothing that he could tell her would alarm her? Now, face to face with him, she was not sure. She felt herself quite inexperienced. She had thought that she could deal with him, but what did she REALLY know about men? Perhaps he was going to tell her that he did not love her any more. No, she knew that it was not that. That first gaze into one another's eyes had told her that they still belonged to one another just as they had always done. What else could it be? Had he done anything disgraceful? She would share that with him, whatever it might be. She moved restlessly about the room, moving the things upon the table, seeing that the bowl of red and yellow roses was in the centre, arranging knives and forks.

Mrs Harwen came in with the soup tureen.

'Yes, Mrs Harwen, I think he'll be down in a minute now.'

'And you'll ring for the meat and vegetables, Miss Vanessa?'

'Yes. He must be hungry.'

'Yes, Miss. It's a couple of ducks--and an apple tart to follow.'

She walked to the window. Why did this house always fill her with apprehension? Her anxiety was needless. He was tired after his journey. After five minutes with her he would be his old self.

The door opened and he came in. He smiled at her, sat down and began to eat: she drew a chair to the table near to him.

'How well you are looking, Vanessa,'

He had not seen her since the week of the fire. They were both conscious of that, she thought. That is why he is uneasy and will not look at me; but her fear increased.

'Where have you been, Benjie, all this time? Are you hungry? Is the toast dry? I told Mrs Harwen not to make it before she heard you arriving.'

'I've come from Liverpool.' He looked at her and smiled, a pathetic smile as though he longed to be friends with her and for some reason must not be. The childishness so often apparent in him--one of his strongest appeals to women because he was quite unconscious of it--caught her heart, making her ache to take him in her arms and comfort him.

He was terribly unhappy: that was certain.

'And where have you been besides Liverpool?'

'Oh, abroad. In June I went to Germany. I thought that I'd like to see Bismarck. Not to speak to him, of course--simply to have a sight of the old man. And I did. He was driving one day in Berlin in an open carriage. It was strange, you know, Vanessa, because when I was a boy at Rugby in 1870 I hated the Prussians--I would have done anything to help the French-- nearly ran away to Paris to share in the Siege. But when I saw the old boy riding through Berlin I cheered like the others.'

'What did he look like?'

'Oh, just an old man. But he sat up straight and bowed. Very striking eyes.'

Mrs Harwen came in with the ducks.

'Hulloa! Mrs Harwen! How are you?'

'Very well, thank you, sir, and I hope you're the same?'

'Oh, I'm well enough! Two ducks! I can't eat two ducks!'

'I thought if one wasn't tender you could try the other, sir.'

'Thanks. But I'm not hungry.'

'There's an apple tart to follow, sir.'

'No. Not for me tonight. I'll have it cold tomorrow.'

He carved the duck, ate a little of it, then pushed his plate aside.

'I'm not hungry, Vanessa.'

'Oh, you ought to be after that long journey.'

'No, I'm not . . . Mother's not very well, I'm afraid.'

'No, she has grown much weaker lately. I'm afraid she can't live much longer, Benjie.'

His face seemed to be shadowed. The constraint between them grew deeper with every moment.

'No, I can't eat.' He got up. 'Let's go into the other room. There's something I must say to you.'

He opened the door for her and she went out, crossing the passage, down the stairs, into the little room off the hall that had been poor old Walter's sanctum.

There was a fire there and yet the room was cheerless. They sat down in the old leather armchairs opposite one another.

'Don't you hate this house?' he asked her.

'I don't like it. It is impossible to make it comfortable.'

'Old Walter sees to that,' he answered grimly. There followed an awful pause. At last she could endure it no longer.

'Benjie, what's the matter?'

'Nothing. Oh yes, there is. Of course there is.'

'Well, tell me. Don't be a coward about it.' She hesitated. 'Is it that you don't love me any longer?'

He, too, hesitated. Then he answered, looking her at last straight in the face:

'I love you more than ever.'

A wave of joy, burning with splendid warmth, swept over her. She was, for an instant, submerged by it, blind, deaf, conscious of her joy as though she were alone in space, the beautiful glass-green wave arching above her head.

'I'm glad of that,' she said at last, 'because I also love you more than ever.' She went on: 'Father's death has left me with only you. I have no one else to care for, no one else to care for ME. When you were away so long I thought I could not endure it--not if it went on much longer. I find that I cannot live without someone to love, and as there is only you, Benjie--'

'Don't!' he broke in with a cry. 'Vanessa, don't!'

He had sprung to his feet. A panic of apprehension caught her. Something terrible had happened. She held the arm of the chair with her hand.

'What is it?'

'It's this. We can't be married. We can never be married.'

She waited for the next word.

'We can't be married because--because'--he turned away from her, staring at the window--'because I was married last week.'

He had rehearsed this moment to himself all day, and for many days past. He had not known what he would do, nor what she would do either. He had thought of everything--every possibility but one.

He had not thought that, after what seemed to him an age of silence, she would murmur:

'Oh, poor Benjie. Oh, what a dreadful thing!'

She had thought first of himself. She had guessed instantly that he was in some bad, inescapable tangle. He could have fallen at her feet and kissed her hands for her perception.

'We should have married last year,' she said. 'That would have saved both of us.'

He turned and looked at her with a deep sombre gaze as though he were fixing her for ever in his mind, just as she was, now that he had lost her. Then he knelt down, at her feet, bowed his head: she held his hand. Neither of them spoke for a long time.

He got up and sat in the chair again.

'I must tell you about it,' he said. 'You must know everything.'

'Yes, tell me,' she answered.

'After the fire when I came to see you, you were upset. I thought that you blamed me for your father's death. I'm so ready to be blamed. I'm blamed so often. But I don't care. I don't care perhaps enough--unless it is you who blame me. So I rode off in a temper. You remember that in Seascale last year I stayed in rooms with a widow and her daughter?'

Vanessa, looking at him with eyes that were so unhappy but so resolutely determined not to flinch that he could not face them, nodded.

'Yes, I remember. I saw them walking one day on the beach.'

'Yes. Well--a mother and daughter called Halliday--I didn't like them--not either of them. I was thinking only of you, Vanessa, that summer--you were obsessing me. Nevertheless I kissed the girl, disliked her more than ever, and kissed her again.'

He flashed a look at her, then dropped his glance and went on, looking at the floor.

'You and I would have been married, of course, that autumn, had it not been for Adam's illness. Fate. Call it what you like. Perhaps really the best thing. In any case the widow and her daughter came to live in Keswick.'

'Tell me,' Vanessa said, 'what she looks like. I saw her only for a moment at Seascale. Is she beautiful? WHAT is she?'

'No, she is not. She is not beautiful, she is not clever. My eyes have been open from the first. She held me like one of one's pet cheap temptations--those you are always ashamed of, never resist, never confess to anyone . . . I must be fair to her, Vanessa. Whatever happens I must be fair. But you will see in a moment what she is like.'

Vanessa drew a deep, trembling breath. Her hands were folded in her lap. Benjie stared at them as though hypnotized, noticing how white they were against the black dress. He thought that he could tell the rest of the story better were he holding her hand, but he did not move.

'Yes, I must be fair to her. She knew that she had some attraction for me. She was, I think, determined from the very beginning that I should marry her, but really because, I am afraid, she loved-- loves--me.'

'Yes,' said Vanessa.

'Thinking of you always, loving you more every day, yet I went to see the two of them in Keswick. I must speak of something difficult, Vanessa. It is this. The more I saw you the more I loved you--and with my body as well as the rest of me. I have always wanted my body to have power. I have liked to see it travelling about the world, getting experience, eating, drinking, strong, vigorous. I have always thought that most people do not give their bodies all the chances. Well, that spring you were occupied with Adam, of course, and I would leave you, restless and unsatisfied. Both of us were, I think. But I was doubly unsatisfied--because I wanted you so badly and because I was so unworthy of you.'

She murmured: 'That has been where the mistake was.'

'Oh, don't misunderstand me, Vanessa. I don't go about the world thinking I am unworthy of people. Of nobody else. Only you. But the one thing I must not do, I tell myself, is to spoil your life. I mustn't. I mustn't, I tell myself--and then--I do . . .

'So I went to see them. Then a day or two after the fire I rode out to Halliday's farm--the brother, you know. I stayed there the night. I drank too much. The girl slept with me.'

He waited. There was a mouse scratching somewhere. They both raised their heads together, and Vanessa thought, as she had often done before, that she heard one of the dogs that Uhland used to keep in his room howling from the Tower. Somewhere a dog WAS howling, and at that moment she realized a hatred for that girl such as she had never felt before for anyone.

'Next day,' Benjie went on, 'I came back to the Fortress. I stayed for a while, then I went off with Halliday and two of his friends called Endicott shooting. I met the girl again. She was quiet, most respectable, as though now she had got what she wanted. I am sure her mother knew. I think her brother knew too. I was extremely unhappy. I wanted to come to you and ask that we might be married at once, but I was ashamed and afraid--you are the only human being I have ever been afraid of, Vanessa. I went abroad to Germany.

'When I came back the girl, her mother, and brother were in London. The girl came to see me and told me that she was going to have a child--my child, she said. I don't know whether that was the truth or no. That was a month ago. Will you believe me, Vanessa, when I tell you that I loved you during all this time more than ever?'

'Yes,' said Vanessa. 'I believe you.'

'The girl said that of course now I would marry her. The mother said the same. The brother the same.

I was not frightened of them in the least. I have never been afraid of anyone or anything except your despising me or doing you harm. But also, in spite of all that I have done, I have never got a woman into trouble. I tell you that I didn't know, I don't know now, whether I was responsible in this case. I want to be fair to her in every way, but I cannot be certain of her virtue. They were all three quite friendly and quite frank. The girl said that she had always loved me, always meant to marry me. The brother said that of course it would not be pleasant for my mother if she knew of this. I agreed with that. Ill as she was it would probably kill her. But I think that my mind was entirely on you. Although I loved you so dearly I might do this again. I have never had any trust in myself. It is only myself that I blame, but from my birth, as I have always told you, there has been some strain in me that I could never trust, as there was in my father, my grandfather. And I have always been honest with you. I would have had to tell you of this, and when you knew that this was to be my child--would you marry me? Would you, Vanessa? Would you have married me knowing this?'

He waited with passionate eagerness for her answer, leaning forward, looking into her face.

At last she said:

'No. Perhaps I would not.'

He nodded his head. 'I thought not. "This ends it," I thought. All this struggle about you that I have had for years. You will be free. Perhaps you will hate me and so be clear of me, then after a while you will marry somebody splendid. One day, long after, you will acknowledge that I was right. That's what I thought. So I married her--last week in Liverpool.'

A long, long silence followed.

At last Vanessa said:

'Do you care for her? Are you fond of her in any way at all?'

'No--not in any way at all.'

Then she said:

'Thank you for telling me so honestly.' And then again, after another pause: 'This will be terrible for Elizabeth.'

'Yes,' he answered.

She got up and went over to him and laid her hand against his cheek.

'You must do all you can for her.'

He caught her hand fiercely; kissed it again and again.

'What are we to do? I can't live without seeing you.'

She shook her head.

'No. Of course we must not meet. That would be too difficult for both of us.'

She bent down and kissed him.

'How foolish we both have been, Benjie dear.' She held him close to her like a mother her son. At that moment, with his head against her breast, she realized with the utmost clarity the desolation of her loneliness. She kissed him again, then drew herself from his grasp.

'Goodnight, Benjie darling. I'll go back to Cat Bells in the morning. You won't write or anything, will you? It will be much better.'

'I'll do anything you say.'

At the door she turned back.

'I don't know whether it's right. Very wrong perhaps. But although we mustn't meet or write, if you're in trouble--real, serious trouble--you must tell me.'

'I'll tell you,' he said.

Then she went out.

THE DUCHESS OF WREXE'S BALL

One day in November 1884 Barney Newmark went in to drink a cup of tea with his sister, Phyllis Rochester, in her pleasant little house in Eaton Place.

He chose this afternoon because he knew that his brother-in-law, Clarence Rochester, was at Brighton. He did not like Clarence at all--he thought him a humbug. And Clarence did not like Barney--he thought him an obscene, conceited libertine. Phyllis, who cared deeply for Barney and had grown accustomed to Clarence, kept the balance between them.

Phyllis, who was now a buxom woman of sixty-three (all the Newmarks of this generation were stout), loved her comforts and adored her eccentric son Philip. So long as she had plenty of the little cakes, jams, and preserved fruits that she preferred and so long as Philip lived with her in Eaton Place she had no alarms. She had a charming complexion, and Clarence was away as often as not. Her one fear had been lest Philip should marry. But now it did not seem likely. Philip did not like women.

Barney today was in an excellent temper. He had that morning finished his novel, a novel in which Newmarket, Boulogne, and Scottish shooting parties were his principal backgrounds, where everything was very light and careless and the principal scene was a baccarat-cheating scandal. Like the majority of novelists he enjoyed, for a day or two following a novel's conclusion, an extraordinary sense of freedom and light-heartedness. Unlike most novelists these happy days were not followed by an intense gloom. He knew the thing was of no value at all. He told everybody so. He wrote to make money. He was none of your Merediths, Zolas, or Shorthouses. He couldn't write a novel like-- what was its name?-- that John Inglesant to save his life. Nor did he want to. So long as a fellow or two got his novel from a library he was perfectly satisfied--and so were his publishers.

Between the brother and sister sitting together having tea in the pleasant little drawing-room there was a strong resemblance. They were both stout, jolly, and easily amused. Barney was the best of fellows when alone with his sister. They were both glad that Clarence was at Brighton. The room was very warm, heavily curtained, and crammed with knick-knacks. There were china dogs, china shepherds and shepherdesses, china mandarins. There was even a large china copy of a Chinese temple with little bells that tinkled when there was a draught, and of this Phyllis was inordinately proud. There were photographs everywhere. Four photographs of Mary Anderson, two of Ellen Terry, three of Mr Terriss, photographs of Ellis and Garth and Emily Newmark (very forbidding) and Barney (riding a horse) and Vanessa and Carey Rockage. There were numberless little tables, all heavily loaded, a great many little chairs and a basket near the fire in which a fat pug called Charles was now wheezing. The two round tea tables were covered with cakes, pastries, muffins, piles of buttered toast.

'Good Heavens, Phil,' Barney cried, 'how many people are you expecting?'

'Nobody except you.'

'Why all the food?'

'Oh, I like to have plenty to eat. And Philip may come in.'

'Oh, may he? And what is he doing today?'

'He has gone to an Art Exhibition with Samuel Roscoe.'

'Oh, has he?'

To change the subject--which might be an unpleasant one--Phyllis asked:

'And what's the news?'

'I finished my novel this morning.'

'Oh, did you? What is it called?'

'Neck or Nothing.'

'What a clever title! I don't know how you think of all these things.'

'No, nor do I. I have been helping John Beaminster to choose a horse.'

'Oh, have you?' Phyllis was greatly interested. The Beaminsters were always exciting. 'Did he tell you anything about his mother?'

'No. What should he tell me?'

'Oh, I don't know, but I do think it is so extraordinary her being shut up in that Portland Place house all these years. Do you remember when she came to that party that Ellis gave a year or two ago?'

'Of course I remember.'

'Well, they say she hadn't been out of doors for years before that. Then for a week or two she was seen everywhere. Then she went back again and has shut herself up ever since.'

'That was the party,' said Barney slowly, 'when Benjie suddenly appeared. Do you remember? And that night he was engaged to Vanessa.'

Phyllis, shaking her head, choosing with great care the richest of several little cakes, answered indignantly:

'Oh, don't mention Benjie to me! I have finished with him for ever and so has everybody! I consider him a murderer!'

'Oh, come now,' said Barney, smiling.

'Well, isn't he? He killed his mother by throwing Vanessa over and marrying that horrible woman.'

'You don't know that she's horrible. You've never seen her.'

'No, but other people have. Alfred was up that way with a friend the other day and thought he'd call. They had the most dreadful visit. Benjie would do nothing but swear, and the house was a pig sty and the baby howling. Alfred said that the woman was awful! As thin as a pole and cross-eyed.'

'Oh no, not that!' said Barney, laughing.

'Well, there was something odd about her eyes, Alfred said. And she hardly spoke a word.'

'I like Benjie,' Barney said. 'I always have and I always will. There was something behind that business we don't know.'

'Nothing to Benjie's credit, you can be sure,' said Phyllis. 'Poor Vanessa. So beautiful and buried up there. She's only been to London once since it happened. She stayed with Rose for a week, you remember, and I never saw anyone more lovely. Very nice she was too. Philip was in a passion over her.'

'You needn't pity Vanessa,' said Barney sharply. 'She needs no one's pity.'

'Oh no, of course not!' Here again seemed a dangerous subject, so Phyllis, finding safety in general affairs, asked:

'And what do they say about General Gordon?'

'There is little news since Stewart's murder. Wolseley is moving up the Nile.'

'Do you think Gladstone has made a mistake?'

'Possibly. He'll hear of it if he has.'

'Some people say that Gordon is mad.'

'Mad people do most of the things in this world. That, my dear Phil, is what our family will never learn.'

'I sometimes think Emily is mad. What do you think she came in here raging about yesterday?'

'I NEVER think about Emily.'

'She wants to close the Alhambra and have all the women who go there put in prison.'

'Emily will be improperly assaulted one day by a Salvation Army worker. Then she will learn something.'

The maid opened the door and said: 'Miss Ormerod and Mr Ormerod.'

Rose and Horace came in and were eagerly welcomed.

Rose looked charming indeed, in one of the Scottish plaid costumes that were then most fashionable, and her hat tilted over her hair arranged in a bun was so small as to be almost invisible. 'Where,' thought Phyllis, 'does she get the money to buy her clothes from?'

Horace, red-faced, amiable and enthusiastic, was like a successful clergyman on holiday. His vibrating enthusiasm made Barney very cynical. 'I always believe well of human nature,' Barney said, 'until Horace Ormerod comes along.'

Horace rubbed his hands together, beamed, pushed his spectacles (he had been wearing spectacles for a year or two) back on to his short nose and cried: 'Well, this is splendid indeed! Rose and I were walking in the Park and I said to her, "We'll take a hansom and see if Phil has some tea for us!" Splendid day! Fresh and bright! I never felt better in my life!'

Barney said: 'I'm glad of that, Horace. We need cheering, with so many of our fellows without employment and the City in a scare and Egypt in a muddle!'

'Nonsense! Nonsense! You WILL look on the black side of things! I have it on the best of authority that the City is doing very well indeed. And as to Egypt, you trust Gladstone. He did the right thing in sending Gordon. You can take it from me!'

'I don't take it from you!' said Barney. 'How do you know?'

'What I always say,' said Horace, 'is that you can trust Old England. She always does the right thing in the end. I hate this pessimism. It's men like you, Barney, who do all the harm. But of course you're a novelist, live in your imagination and that sort of thing.'

'Now, Horace,' Rose interrupted, 'don't be tiresome. Barney knows more about everything than you do. But I know something that HE doesn't know!'

They were eager for information.

'Vanessa arrived at Hill Street this morning for a long visit!'

'No!' cried Barney. 'Vanessa! How splendid!'

'Yes. I saw Alfred in the Park, and HE had seen Ellis in the City. Our dear Vanessa is with us again, and it shan't be our fault if she doesn't stay for months.'

Phyllis nodded.

'Ellis will be glad,' she said.

'And Ellis' ma will be glad,' Rose went on. 'And I have come in only for a moment because I am going to Hill Street to see her.'

An hour later Rose was in Hill Street.

'I will tell Miss Paris,' the butler said, leaving her alone in the big cold drawing-room.

Old Lady Herries was now eighty years of age and spent most of her time in bed where, rumour had it, she arranged her pearls, rubies and diamonds on the counterpane, played games with them and counted them over and over again. But because she was in bed and Ellis for most of the day in the City, the house was more like a mortuary than a living-place. The drawing-room was decorated in mustard yellow, the curtains had heavy folds of it, the chairs and sofas were wrapped in it. On the mantelpiece was a clock of yellow-and-white marble. The marble statues that had been there ever since

Will Herries first bought the house glimmered whitely under the gas. Rose shivered.

'WHAT a house! But now that Vanessa has come they will entertain again. Now that Benjie is out of the way they will think there is hope for Ellis. Is there? Vanessa is lonely enough, poor darling, to try anything, and she has always had a kind of maternal feeling for Ellis.'

Ellis came in.

Rose did not dislike Ellis. She thought him absurd and pathetic. She was also blind neither to his baronetcy nor to his wealth. At one time she had thought that she might herself marry him, but her clear common sense soon showed her that she did not attract him in the least.

'He has no eyes for anyone but Vanessa.'

Now when he came in she was compelled to admit that he looked distinguished, and not really his forty-two years. Or rather he might be any age. His body was slim and erect. His closely fitting black clothes and high sharp-pointed collar gave him distinction. He was Sir Ellis Herries, Bart, all right and a ridiculous physical copy of his father. A very hideous painting of his father hung on the left side of the fireplace. Yes, ludicrously alike, but the real Ellis, Rose (who was no poor judge of character) well knew, was nervous, highly strung, sensitive, unbalanced as his father had never been.

But now as she shook hands Rose liked him, for today he was radiant with happiness. When Ellis was happy you were touched because his hold on his joy seemed so precarious. He was like a man who, to his own surprise, looks to be, for once, winning a game. In the end he will in all probability lose it, but this unusual, unexpected chance gains you to his side.

'I came in only for a moment,' Rose said. 'Alfred told me that Vanessa had arrived. I couldn't wait to see her.'

'Vanessa,' said Ellis, speaking in his precise careful voice, 'is, I am happy to say, under our roof again. She will be delighted to see you.'

'But this is splendid. None of us knew that she was coming.'

'No. WE did not know until last week. She has been staying with Carey in Wiltshire.'

'How is she looking?'

'Oh, very well. Very well indeed. But here she is. Vanessa, my dear, here is Rose to see you.'

They flung themselves into one another's arms while Ellis stood benevolently by, stroking his chin and smiling.

'But, DEAR Rose! How sweet of you to come so soon!'

'Well, of course! But why not a line to anyone that you were coming?'

'I truly did not know, did I, Ellis? You see Carey and May quite suddenly were invited to Panshanger and they thought they should go. They wanted me to stay on until they returned, but--well, I fancied a little London gaiety.'

They sat down on the sofa together.

'And now, young ladies,' said Ellis in his best paternal fashion, 'I shall leave you. I am sure you have a great deal to talk over. Dinner at seven, Vanessa.'

'Oh Lord!' Rose cried, looking at her watch. 'And it is six now.'

'No, no,' said Vanessa eagerly, 'Come up with me when I dress. It is so LOVELY to see you. And are you not engaged yet to Captain What's-his-name and what other gentlemen are there and have you seen dear Barney? How is Horace? How, in fact, are all the Herries?'

They noticed at once changes in one another, as was natural after a year's separation. The difference that Vanessa saw in Rose was the same difference that her grandmother had once noticed in this same room years ago in Sylvia Herries--a slight, oh, so very slight, fading of the natural bloom, a heightening of the artificial colour, a little hardening of the voice, the eye a trifle more anxious. The Scottish plaid was extremely pretty, with its red and grey, and the little hat was a beauty--very expensive clothes. Rose looked altogether very expensive. Upon what in reality did she and her brother live?

And Rose saw at once that Vanessa was a girl no longer. She was even for a moment or two afraid of her. Had she lost her? But very soon she realized the thing that she would realize again so often--that once Vanessa was your friend it was not easy to lose her.

Vanessa's dress was dove-grey, her dark hair brushed back from her forehead. Her hand caught Rose's and held it.

'Rose, I want to have FUN! I want to see people, plenty and plenty. I want to go to the theatre. There is Mary Anderson as Juliet, isn't there? and Mr Wilson Barrett as Hamlet, and Gilbert and Sullivan and Mrs John Wood. I've been studying the papers. Lady Herries has asked May and Carey to come and stay so that May can chaperon me. They are coming from Panshanger the day after tomorrow. I want to see everybody and do everything.'

'And everyone wants to see you. You are much the most beautiful woman in London. Mrs Langtry is nothing at all in comparison.'

Vanessa smiled, very happy.

'I want to be beautiful just for a week or two--after that I don't care in the least. I want everyone to think me lovely, to say, "Oh, who is THAT lovely girl?" In fact, Rose dear, I want some encouragement. I've been fighting things by myself--without any help from anyone.'

'I know, dear, I know,' Rose said, stroking her hand. There was something feverish, she thought, in Vanessa's tone, something unlike her natural restraint.

'Yes, Timothy and Violet have been very good to me. I stayed there for months in the house they've bought in Eskdale. Lovely. Not far from the sea, with the mountains behind them. But of course I couldn't TALK to them. And there was another thing--'

She broke off, then, holding Rose's hand more tightly, went on:

'This is something I want to say and then we will never mention it again. About Benjie. I know that everyone is against him, that they think he treated me badly, that he made a wretched mess of everything, which is what they have always hoped for. Now, Rose dear, I want you to make them understand--ALL of them--that I will not hear one word against Benjie. That I will never speak again to anyone who attacks him when I'm there. Barney is the only one I'll talk to about him. Barney is his friend, I know. Will you make them all understand that?'

'Of course,' Rose hesitated. 'Vanessa, what is it? What happened? What made him do it?'

'No, Rose, I can't tell even you. It's his affair. We don't meet. We don't write. But I understand what he did. I'm his friend, and not one word shall be said against him in my presence.'

Rose felt her hand tremble, she saw that her eyes were misty. She put her arms round her and kissed her.

'And now, Rose darling,' said Vanessa cheerfully, 'tell me about yourself? How are you? When are you to be married? That hat and costume are lovely!'

'Yes, very nice,' said Rose. 'But not paid for, my dear. Never mind me. Horace and I live in a little house in Shepherd Market. Well, to tell you the truth they are four rooms over a grocer's. We got them cheap from old Lady Martindale, who lost her money at cards and had to decamp at a moment's notice. They are the very best address and are cosy even if they are small. For the rest I have debts, and gentlemen who admire me and ladies who don't, just like any other lady--and I shall marry the first decent man who proposes to me, whoever he is.'

'And Horace?'

'Oh, Horace is getting along fast on the simple plan of refusing to know anyone save those who will be useful to him. He smiles on everyone and has a genius for not seeing those he doesn't want to see. And now, dear, let us go to your room. I am longing to know what you are going to wear.'

So they went upstairs.

Vanessa dined alone with Ellis and Miss Mabel Fortescue, the lady who now 'ran' the Hill Street house. Miss Fortescue reminded Vanessa at once of Miss Murdstone, and she herself would have felt not unlike David Copperfield had she not quickly seen that the situation was serious and she must rather be Betsey Trotwood. So from the very beginning she was firm with Miss Fortescue. Really remarkable, her resemblance to Miss Murdstone. She had the stiff poker back, the dark complexion and black hair, the heavy eyebrows that nearly met over a large nose, and Vanessa was certain that in her bedroom were the 'two uncompromising hard black boxes, with her initials on the lids in hard brass nails'.

Ellis thought the world of her--'Most efficient woman, Vanessa. Excellently behaved. Knows just how to treat my mother.' Then waking in the early morning hours to hear the London sparrows cheep beyond the window, Vanessa discovered two other things.

'Miss Fortescue hated me at sight. And hopes to marry Ellis.'

The dinner was a very agreeable one: Ellis was so happy and when he was happy he was childlike. Vanessa knew, too, that he was happy because she was there, and it was so long since she had been cared for in this way. Timothy and Violet took her for granted. Aunt Jane loved her but thought her still ten years old. So also Will Leathwaite. Carey and May were fond of her, but liked their dogs and horses still better. She was, she discovered, HUNGERING for affection, and placing her foot in London had as it were set all her world alight. That afternoon, going for a walk, the window of a florist in Piccadilly had been ablaze with chrysanthemums; down Bond Street into Piccadilly had come the carriages, shining in the November sun, the coachmen stout and splendid, the horses sleek, the harness glittering, and from a distance, through the walls of the houses, the echo of a barrel-organ, heard as it always should be, a street or two away. She had thrown up her head and sniffed the air, sharp and horsy and honeyed with the sun. London! She adored London! She could manage without Cumberland, clouded with unhappy memories, for a while. Then against this background there was first Rose, who loved her, and now Ellis, who loved her too. Ellis was improved. He was intelligent. He talked about Gladstone and Gordon, about the 'New Radicalism' that was interesting itself in the conditions of housing and the happiness of the poorer classes, about the Trades Unions, about the abolishing of the Income Tax, about the provisions of the Electric Lighting Act, about the Redistribution Bill, about all these serious things, sensibly, with inside knowledge. His tact with her was extraordinary, for he was not by nature a tactful man. He studied her without appearing to. He was affectionate, but with the affection of a brother. She knew of course that he loved her, but he did not embarrass her with any implied emotion.

After dinner she went upstairs to visit Lady Herries. She saw at once a great change in her. Some of the stories they told about her were true, for she was sitting up in bed and on a white shawl on her lap were rings, bracelets, and necklaces. She played with them like a

child, holding them up to the light, rubbing them with her fingers, laying one against the other.

Nevertheless she appeared quite sensible. She was enchanted to see Vanessa.

Her great pleasure was to talk about people. Staying in her room as she did, she brought the world around her, speculating, gathering stories, chuckling over scandals and foibles.

'You will find London very much changed, my dear. Money is the only thing, getting it and losing it. If you have money you can go anywhere. That is why London is much more amusing and not nearly so remarkable as it used to be.'

She talked about the family.

'Alfred, Amery's boy, will make a fortune. He's in with all the Jews. His nose gets sharper every day. Dora, old Rodney's daughter, has such a pretty child, Cynthia. Dora married Freddie Beauchamp. Do you remember him? A thin man with a long nose. They live in London now, and Cynthia will marry well. Very well, I shouldn't wonder. Then Barney has made quite a name for himself-- amusing books he writes--but he has some very odd friends. However, that doesn't matter if he's a success. Then Phyllis' boy, Philip--you remember him?--a little affected but very clever. He's quite a friend of Mr Oscar Wilde. I'm glad Carey and May are coming. Their two girls, Maud and Helen, are VERY plain, poor things, but of course they have never done anything but ride horses, so what can you expect? They will improve as they grow older.'

She chattered on, moving the jewels about on the white shawl, sometimes talking to herself:

'Now THAT won't do! If Carey and May come on Friday I must put off Miss Blades. She comes and reads to me, my dear. A very nice woman with the funniest stories about everyone . . . I will not have that fish three days running. I must tell Miss Fortescue.'

Then quite unexpectedly she fell asleep, letting her head, with its tousled white hair, fall on the pillow, opening her mouth and snoring.

Vanessa soon discovered that she was to be a gathering point for all the family. They had been longing for something of the kind. Hill Street sprang to life, and Ellis was rejuvenated. May Rockage was a simple creature whose heart was in the country with her horses, her dogs, and her two girls. But she had a hearty power of enjoyment and, although she dressed badly, laughed like a man and was extremely innocent of the world, she became very quickly an excellent companion for Vanessa.

Vanessa threw herself into the family interests. Soon she knew all their secrets, their fears, their ambitions, and their odd little ways.

First of all there was Rose, who, she declared to Vanessa, was going 'the primrose path'. She had two or three gentlemen friends, a Captain Rackrent, horsy and raffish, a Mr Marchbanks, who was some sort of a publisher and encouraged young men to write as much like the French as possible, and a Mr Easy, who was like a Jew but said he was not one, Assyrian, purple-bearded and, Rose said, very rich. He had something to do with the Theatre. Rose said that he proposed marriage to her every week--and she added, 'One day when the bailiffs are drinking beer in the parlour--the awful thing will happen--I shall marry him.'

Cynthia, Rodney's granddaughter, was the prettiest, most fairylike creature. She at once fell down at Vanessa's feet and worshipped. Her hair was spun gold, her eyes the tenderest blue, her little figure exquisite; wearing a tiny hat perched on a golden bun, her dress gathered into loops behind her, her bosom clearly defined, she was something to make men tremble. She was sweet and tender and loving but, Vanessa thought, quite ruthlessly determined to make the best marriage possible. All the girls were sweet, tender, and loving, and all the girls were determined to be well married. 'You would think,' said Rose, 'to listen to these infants talk that they didn't know what men were made of. But they DO know. They know very well indeed.'

Barney's set were writers, painters, horsy men, theatrical men, and men about town. All these men--including Barney--had feminine friends who were never obtruded. Once Vanessa, going with Rose unexpectedly to Barney's rooms, found an elegant creature seated on his sofa, mending his stockings. She was delightful, and most maternal to Barney. Her name was Miss Montefiore, an actress 'resting between engagements'.

Then Vanessa was forced, against her will, to see something of Emily Newmark. Vanessa did not like Emily, but had to confess that she did good in the world. She was for ever 'rescuing' people, 'unfortunate women', drunkards, young pickpockets and foreigners--Chinamen, Negroes, lost and strayed Scandinavians. Her only interest in people was that they could be 'rescued'. She lectured Vanessa, patronized her, and was sometimes unexpectedly human, bursting into tears and saying that she was 'misjudged'.

Old Amery, tottering and bewildered, thought only of his son Alfred. That sharp young man was always adding up figures and subtracting them again. He came to Ellis once a week with schemes. Ellis said that many of these were clever. Alfred would get on.

A very odd world, too, was that of young Philip, Phyllis' boy. The young men, Philip's friends, looked and were ridiculous, but they lived up to their gospel. They wrote little stories, painted little pictures, and treated all the Arts as their own especial property. They arrived from Oxford in increasing numbers. They lisped, they languished. They thought Mr Whistler, Mr Wilde, French poets, and the art of Japan all 'too utterly beautiful'.

In short the Herries were everywhere. Into every corner of London life they drove their strong determined wedge of common sense. Even Philip, with his absurdities, had common sense. England was now at the top of the world, was at a stage of material success and triumph that exactly suited the Herries character. No member of the family ever boasted or wondered or explained. They simply went everywhere, into the Beaminster house in Portland Place, into the theatres and restaurants, into the churches and lecture halls, into the Kensington drawing-rooms, into the City, into the slums and did their good work. No Herries was at the TOP of anything. No Herries (with the exception of Ellis) accumulated great wealth, cared for property, dominated politics or the Arts or the Church or the Army. They simply were everywhere and influenced everything.

Vanessa, however, soon discerned that her arrival was for all of them a dramatic event. At certain times in their history a combination of circumstances produced an Event to which all the family, gladly and joyfully, reacted. Their hatred of the eccentric, the queer, the abnormal made them respond ecstatically to anything that allowed them to display that hatred. It had been so in the old days of the Rogue, in the quarrels about the famous Fan, in the dreadful scandal of Uhland, and now it was so in the affairs of Benjamin, Vanessa, and Ellis. Benjie was their rogue, their scapegoat. Vanessa was, at this moment, their heroine. What had happened in the North about her engagement? No one knew. Would she marry Ellis and become not only the most beautiful but also one of the richest women in London? Why had she come to Hill Street if not to marry Ellis? Her presence made that winter one of the most exciting in their lives.

And Vanessa let herself go. She was there to forget all the past. She must make a world for herself in which she could be independent--never, never would she depend on anyone again. She went everywhere, to balls and theatres and Hurlingham and concerts and immensely long, elaborate dinner parties.

She and May travelled down to Brighton in the ten o'clock Pullman, lunched at Mutton's, where Barney and Alfred joined them, watched the dowagers in the carriages, the girls in the dogcarts, the invalids in the both-chairs, the babies in the goat-chaises, men on bicycles. They went on the electric railways in Madeira Road, visited the Aquarium, listened to the band in the Birdcage and had dinner at a fine hotel. A glorious day! Brighton in November, sunshine, sea air. What an enchanting world!

Vanessa went to the House and heard Mr Gladstone speak on the Maamstrasna Murders question, and when Mr O'Connor rose and called the speech 'the lamest, weakest and most halting I have ever heard', and young Mr Stanhope shouted out, "That's what the ferret said when the lion roared', she could have clapped her hands in her delight because that was exactly what SHE thought!

She went of course to Romeo and Juliet at the Lyceum and thought Mary Anderson so lovely that she never troubled about the acting. She saw Mrs John Wood in Young Mrs Winthrop and laughed herself into tears. When Mrs Wood meets her husband, from whom she has been divorced, they do nothing but wink! Oh, WHAT a wink! In fact all London went to see this not very good little play because of Mrs Wood's wink.

She was sad when Henry Fawcett died, thrilled by what Mr Ruskin had to say to his friends at Oxford, read William Black's Judith Shakespeare, wanted to go to a Spiritualist meeting but could find no one to accompany her, gazed at Mrs Langtry at a party, ate oysters and pheasant, drove so often in hansoms that she thought nothing at all about it, and enjoyed Mr Corney Grain in the German Reeds' entertainment. 'Nothing,' as Emily Newmark said to her severely, 'nothing but a life of idle pleasure.'

In that winter Vanessa caught a sense of London that she was never after to lose, its smells and odours, flowers and horses and fogs, its incongruities, its shabbiness, as for instance when you passed, on the way into the Underground, the faded photographs, smirking from the wall, of old burlesque actresses, Planché's ghost hovering around them, or when in some of the smaller theatres the smell of beer, the dim rose coverings of the stalls, the dirty globes of gas, the white spots of plaster between the flaking gilt, the past, mournful, pathetic, strangled the struggling present. But everywhere and in every case London was homely--homely in the clack- clack of the horses, in the scattered rumbling of the omnibuses, in the barrel-organs and the German bands, in the sudden flashing splendour of the Guard riding up St James's from the Palace, in the gentlemen's servants taking the air, in the elegant dandies of the Row, in the melancholy street-singers, the lingering notes of the church bells, in the fogs that, yellow and sulky, crept from street to street, in the comfortable laziness of afternoon tea, in the high collar of Mr Gladstone, the radiance of the Jersey Lily, the dignity and humanity of the Prince, and, above all, in that stout little regal figure, never forgotten, sitting somewhere behind the walls of plain-faced Buckingham Palace or bird-haunted Windsor, receiving an Indian prince, being sharp with Mr Gladstone or smiling at her grandchildren. All this was London and London was all this.

One further thing that winter dominated the Town: the thought of Gordon. This great victory of common sense, this triumph of plain reality--was it threatened by that figure, fanatical, heroic, and alone, fearlessly erect among his enemies? Could it be--and it was a question forced again and again upon the Herries through all their history--that common sense was not enough, that there were other things, dangerous, mysterious things of the spirit that could spring upon you and defeat you did you too long disregard them? Is there another world with which we have refused to reckon?

After the disaster of Abu Hamed there was silence. On the day that Herbert Stewart started across the desert there was a message: 'Khartoum all right. 14.12.84. C. G. Gordon.'

After that, silence again.

On the 22nd of January, the day on which London learned of the battle of Abu Klea, Ellis proposed to Vanessa the second time.

They were about to go up to bed. The candles with their heavy silver snuffers stood there waiting. May Rockage had said goodnight and started up the stairs, the great drawing-room with its yellow hangings stayed patiently for their departure. Ellis touched Vanessa's arm.

'Vanessa--one moment.'

She turned to him, smiling, then knew at once what he was going to say. He was very nervous, he put his hand to his throat, looked at her with a beseeching smile.

'I have been good, have I not? You have been happy during these weeks here?'

'Very happy, Ellis.'

'Your presence here has been a joy to all of us. My mother has been a different being, and I--I must tell you--I have never been so happy in all my life before.'

'I'm very glad. You have been wonderfully good to me.'

'How could one help being? But I cannot wait any longer. I must ask you once more. It is a long time, is it not, since the last occasion in the Park. Vanessa, will you marry me?'

Before she could answer he went on with a trembling eager passion that touched her and made her long to be kind to him.

'Listen. I implore you not to answer before you have thought it over. I know how much older I am. I know that you do not love me. But you like me. You are friendly, aren't you? I can feel that you are friendly.'

'Of course I am friendly, Ellis. And more than that. But--'

'Well, then, that's all I ask. Indeed it is. I ask nothing more. If you will marry me everything shall be as you wish. I know that money makes no appeal to you, but perhaps power--the power to do good, to help others, to put wrong things right--may mean a little. You are so good, you have so wonderful a character, that you SHOULD be able to influence your generation. I will help you to do that-- under your guidance. And we are friends. We have known one another for a long time and surely can now trust one another completely. Think it over, Vanessa. Do not answer me now. Please, please not now. But think of it . . . Goodnight.'

And before she could speak he was gone

In her room that night she did indeed think of it. Ellis, during these two months, had been so kind, so unselfish and so wise--they had been such good friends--he had talked about so many things with so much understanding--that she had come to care for him as once would have appeared impossible. She did not love him. But with the impetuous certainty both of her youth and past events she was sure that love was over for her, would never return. Or, rather, she loved as she had always done. Benjie was as truly now in her heart as he had always been. But she must never think of him, neither now nor in any possible future time. So love being over was this not perhaps the nest best thing?

Men had in these London weeks gathered round her. Two had proposed to her, and in the very moments of their proposal she had realized that the very thought of any man but Benjie in THAT world of romantic passion was fantastically unreal. Well, this was not romantic passion. But Ellis was the only one save Rose who belonged to her childhood and youth. She had known him so long that he was part of all that early life. And he wanted to be cared for, and SHE wanted, now more than anything else in the world, to bestow her care on someone.

Was it also not true that she could do good in the world with the power that his money would give her? She was still very young in many things and believed that to do good to your fellows was not so very difficult. She did not want to make them better, only to make them happy. Was this not, perhaps, her duty? She knelt down and prayed, passing as she always did into a world of comfort and security. God was more real to her than Ellis, more real to her than Benjie . . . But tonight she heard no reassuring voice. She rose from her knees in a struggle of bewilderment, for, coming she knew not whence, a wildness that sometimes seized her, descended on her. She did not want to be here. Her spirit was caught away into a fantastic air of wind and rain, of streams running wildly, of clouds tearing at the turf, of the sea tossing at the foot of the hill. Her blood was not tamed. Cold January night though it was, she threw up her window and, beyond the reddened haze of the gigantic town, she saw Skiddaw's dividing lines, the serried edge of Blencathra, and within the rhythm of a solitary hansom's clatter was the whisper of the running water against the shining boulder and the bark of the dog beyond the sloping hill. She thought of Judith. She thought of her father. She thought of Will Leathwaite's slow smile.

She closed the window. No. Oh no, she COULD not marry Ellis!

* * *

A few days later came the invitation to the Duchess of Wrexe's Ball, February 18th.

This Ball had been talked of all through the winter. Very very seldom was there a big function at the Portland Place house, but when they DID have a show-- well, it WAS a show! The old Duchess must have some reason for this event. Perhaps her eldest son Richard was at last to marry. Or maybe John--or Adela. But the Duchess herself of course would not appear. Somewhere hidden in the dark confines of the Portland Place house, unseen by all save a few intimates who played cards with her, her physician and the family, she plotted

and planned. This Ball was to be a protest, some people said, against the new world that she detested, the Jewish financiers, the American heiresses come to search for titled husbands, the South Americans, the Theatre, and the rest. The Ball would be exceedingly exclusive. The Prince and Princess would be present.

It was very quickly an interesting question as to who among the Herries had been invited. Quite a number--Ellis, Vanessa, Carey, May, Barney, little Cynthia and her mother. It was characteristic of the family that so soon as it was known that there would be several of them there, everyone was satisfied. There was no individual jealousy. Granted that the Herries were sufficiently represented, that was all that was necessary. There was no flavour of snobbery either. It was important that members of the family should be present because it would be for the general good of English Society. Anything anywhere was better for having a mixture of Herries in it. Barney was invited because of his friendship with Johnnie Beaminster. Little Cynthia had achieved quite a friendship with Lady Adela. Moreover, the Herries were the type of English of which the Duchess approved--not Upper Ten, of course, but good sound English stock with practically no foreign mixture. The snobbery, in fact, was ENGLISH, not HERRIES. Barney commented on this. 'The English will always be snobs because they care about caste. But it's a fine sort of snobbery as the world is at present. Keeps the right people at the top. One day when the whole world is democratic and cares more for doing things than being them, it will all seem most ridiculous. Then England will become a third-rate Power and everyone will be happier than they've been for centuries.'

They were having an artistic hour at the Winter Exhibition of the Royal Society of Painters in Water Colours, Vanessa and Barney, Horace and Rose. Very delightful, Vanessa thought the pictures. Mr Birket Foster's grand 'West Highlands' made her feel quite sick for home, and Sir John Gilbert's 'Retreat' was splendid, Mr Watson's 'Bathers' Pool' was enchanting, and Du Maurier's 'Last Look at Whitby' so very clever. But best of all Mr Goodwin's 'Strayed Sheep', so homely and English with its cawing rooks and gentle colours.

'Oh, Horace, DO look at the pictures! What have we come here for!'

But Horace's thoughts were on England.

'Really, Barney! England a third-rate Power! What about our Empire?' Everyone was beginning to beat on the word Empire as though it were the family gong.

'Our Empire! Who says it's ours? It's ours for the moment. One day it will be off on its own.'

'Politics are SO tiresome,' said Rose. 'Doesn't that man over there look like the Claimant? He's been appearing at a music hall. Yes, dear, I think the pictures are sweetly pretty.' She wandered off, her arm through

Vanessa's. 'Vanessa darling, do you think Ellis would lend me fifty pounds if I were to ask him?'

'Oh, Rose, I shouldn't. Can't you get it in any other way?'

'Not without being under painful obligations. Oh, do look at Horace watching the door so that if anyone useful comes in he can snatch at them!'

'Rose, dear, are you in a fix?'

'Yes, I am--about ten fixes.'

'Perhaps I can help. How much do you truly need?'

'About twelve hundred pounds. But twenty would help.'

'I think I can manage that.'

'Oh, you are good to me!' Rose was charming when she was grateful. She looked so pretty, so young, so sincere. She WAS sincere. She loved to be grateful--but to the right people.

Vanessa, thinking about this and other things, discovered that the family had come to regard her as Ellis' private conscience. When anyone wanted anything of Ellis, an opinion, an invitation, a tip from the City, Vanessa was the oracle. She could do with him, they said, anything that she liked. She knew that she could.

Then a little incident occurred. One afternoon when he had just returned from the City and they were discussing the evening plans, Ellis cut his hand. He was sharpening a pencil, the knife slipped. It was a bad gash, blood flowed, he turned ashen. She rang the bell for Buller, the butler, and helped Ellis to a chair, staunching the blood with his handkerchief, which soon was soaked. Very white, he leaned back against her, her arm around him. She thought that he would faint. Smiling very wanly he kissed her cheek. She did not move. His slender body in her arm, his confident reliance on her, his touching submission, made her feel as though he were her child. As she waited for Buller to come she thought that when Ellis depended on her for comfort she could do anything for him. At that moment she loved him. He said something, and she bent forward to catch his words. Her cheek touched his.

'I think I am going to faint.'

'Buller will be here in a moment.'

Her arm tightened about him. She just heard him sigh.

'Oh, Vanessa, how I love you!'

Then Buller came in, advancing as he always did like a churchwarden to whom the morning's money offerings had proved disappointing.

'Sir Ellis has cut his hand badly. Get brandy, Buller, and something to bandage it with.'

She sat there, with Ellis in her arms. Miss Fortescue appeared in the doorway, then hurried forward.

'Oh, Sir Ellis, what HAVE you done?'

'Only a slight cut, Miss Fortescue. Buller has gone for some brandy.'

Miss Fortescue looked at them darkly.

'How that woman does hate me!' Vanessa thought.

As January drew to a close and February began there were only two topics in the London world: General Gordon and the Beaminster Ball. About the first it was said on the one side that an awful mistake had been made, on the other that exactly the right thing had been done. About the Ball it was said that it would be the grandest ever given.

On the 24th of January the steamers started up the Nile on an advance on Khartoum; on February 6th it was known that Khartoum had fallen and the relief force had been too late. Meanwhile, having satisfied himself that Khartoum was wholly in the Mahdi's hands, Sir Charles Wilson had turned his steamers and gone downstream. Then for ten days England remained in suspense. On the 16th of February a telegram was published from Wolseley saying that Gordon had been killed.

Vanessa came down to breakfast on that morning to find family prayer over and Ellis standing with The Times shaking in his hand.

'A crime!' he cried, with an odd shrill voice that she had never heard before. The most monstrous crime! Gladstone will never be forgiven for this! Never! Never! Never!'

She thought for a moment that she had to do with a madman. His pale eyes were shining, his hands jerking the newspaper as though they would tear it. They were alone, for Carey and May had not yet come down and Miss Fortescue had meals in her own fierce fastnesses.

'What is it? What has happened?'

'Gordon has been murdered! We have basely deserted him. Left the bravest Saint and Hero to go to his death alone! England will be shamed before all the world!'

'Gordon murdered! Gordon killed!'

'Yes, yes; there is the telegram!'

It seemed in thousands of homes that morning as though a veil of darkness fell over the world. Nothing could be clearer, simpler than that splendid figure, selfless, a missionary thinking only of his God, fearless; it was told of him how he had gone through all the campaign in China, his only weapon a cane, of how he had thought always of everyone but himself in the Sudan. It seemed now that the blackest treachery, the meanest political chicanery had betrayed him. There were other colours in the real picture, and it says something for the accused that, through all those weeks of almost insane vituperation, they never attempted to dim the saintliness, the courage, the selflessness. But Gordon's death was, perhaps, the first warning cloud on a horizon that had been now for a whole decade stainlessly blue.

That terrible news had also its private personal repercussions.

Ellis dropped the paper to the floor, sat down by the table, then, speaking now quietly, said:

'I feel as though I had myself betrayed him. Why do we all wait and trust to a kind of luck? Why are we all so cowardly? Vanessa, I am bitterly ashamed.'

His hand trembled against the tablecloth.

'I never thought that it would happen,' he said. 'I was afraid sometimes, but Gladstone was so sure. We have come to think that Gladstone always has God in his pocket. That they have intimate talks together and Gladstone tells God what to do. Well, this time God has not listened.'

Ellis was always best when he forgot himself. He had a kind of almost fanatical pure-mindedness at such times. Then something robbed him of his self-consciousness, his fears, his absurd egotisms. He would now have thrown his money, his physical cowardice, his fear of offending public opinion, even his Herries blood out of the window could he, by doing so, have saved Gordon. He had a kind of grandeur.

He and Vanessa were very close at that moment. He took her hand.

'Oh, Vanessa!' he sighed. 'You and I--if only together we could help it to be a better world!'

Then Carey and May came in and the world was at once a more mundane place. After breakfast Vanessa went upstairs to find old Lady Herries in tears.

'Oh, poor General Gordon! All alone! Such a good man! Those savages! And Gladstone worse than any of them!'

Then as though she realized that Ellis downstairs must be very unhappy, her last word to Vanessa was:

'Be kind to Ellis, won't you, my dear?'

We quickly forget. Two days later, although Gordon's death was the only topic, the tragedy had become impersonal. No one any longer thought it was possible to have died at his side. Not even perhaps quite desirable. What WAS desirable was to have Mr Gladstone's head on a charger.

Vanessa went to the Beaminster Ball in a turmoil of varying emotions. There was, of course, her dress, the loveliest that she had ever had. It was a white dress, with a red rose fastened at the narrow waist its only ornament. The bodice fitted very tightly to the figure. She wore long white gloves and carried a beautiful white fan of ostrich feathers, a present from Lady Herries. Her only ornament was a diamond brooch, bequeathed her by Judith, fastened on her right shoulder. The effect of her dark hair and all this cloud of dazzling whiteness was very splendid, but, Ellis thought as he glanced at her, it was the softness of her eyes, the charm and kindliness of her eagerness, her youth, her excitement, her happiness that made her so brilliant, so unlike anyone else. For tonight she WAS happy. She could have taken all London into her arms and embraced it. Her mind was set on the future, the life that she would make for herself, the friendliness of all the world. She was aware of her beauty and delighted that she was beautiful. She had never BELIEVED that a dress could be so marvellous a fit! She would see the Prince and Princess! How good and kind of Ellis to give her all this happiness! She let her gloved hand rest on Ellis' coat as the carriage rolled on through the lighted streets and she heard men calling as though it were for her that they were crying some message. She sat very straight, her head forward, taking all this life into her heart and intending to give it out again with all the fullness of which she was capable. Benjie was never out of her mind, but tonight he was in the back of her consciousness. One day she would be with him again, quietly, confidently, his friend. Perhaps after all it had been for the best. This was the safer way.

They halted. They were in a stream of carriages that stretched down Portland Place. Then on either side of the red carpet was a crowd of sightseers whom a large policeman kept in order. Vanessa and May passed up the steps, into the hall. Looking up for a moment before she turned to the right to the cloakroom Vanessa saw a line of footmen in red coats and velvet knee-breeches on either side of the great staircase. Dimly she heard the echoes of the band.

As she arranged her hair before the looking-glass she heard May's whisper: 'Oh, you do look lovely, Vanessa darling!'

Ellis and Carey were waiting for them and slowly they mounted the staircase. At the top Adela Beaminster, blazing in diamonds, received them.

'Lord and Lady Rockage!'

'Sir Ellis Herries!'

'Miss Vanessa Paris!'

They passed on into the ballroom. It was one of the famous rooms in London with its white walls and gold ceiling, and on the white walls were hanging the Lelys, the Van Dycks, the other famous Beaminster portraits. The far end of the great room where the band played was banked with masses of white flowers. Although so many people were standing about there was plenty of dancing space. The roar of voices rolled in waves from wall to wall.

She stood at first with May, extremely happy, quite contented to watch. Decorations were worn, the dresses of the women were superb. How ridiculous of her to have been proud of her own! She had never seen in one place so many beautiful women. The air sparkled with diamonds. A tall thin woman near her was wearing a tiara that focused all the light to itself, that made, in truth, her plain pale face shadowed like a mask. Vanessa unfolded her fan and stood, waving it slowly, smiling as though she could never have enough of this lovely scene.

She was not, however, to be left alone for long. Soon one man came up to her and then another. During these months in London she had made many friends and was in fact very much better known than she had any idea of. A Captain Verrier, who had been sending her flowers, who had taken her and May on one occasion to Hurlingham, asked her to dance. She adored to waltz--surely there was no experience in life so perfect! He talked to her, but she answered him only in monosyllables. When the music stopped and they had moved into a long narrow room beyond the ballroom and sat down, he said to her:

'I don't think you heard a word I said when we were dancing.'

'No. I love dancing so much, it seems a pity to talk.'

'I'm sorry, because I said some very amusing things.'

'You can tell them me now, Captain Verrier.'

'You know, to look at you, Miss Paris, one would imagine that you had never been to a Ball before.'

'I never have--a Ball like this. When will the Prince and Princess come?'

'Oh, later on. About midnight, I expect.'

'And is the Duchess sitting in her room upstairs all this time?'

'Yes. Like a field-marshal. And her generals deliver dispatches.'

'I saw her once. She came to a party in Hill Street.'

'Yes. She went out for a little while some years ago. But she soon went in again. She found that her importance was lessened as soon as she became visible.'

Then he began to make love to her. Laughing, she stopped him.

'Are you asking me to marry you?'

He was embarrassed.

'Well, no, not exactly. You see--'

'I should make a very bad mistress, I am afraid. I can imagine nothing more uncomfortable.'

'Oh no. You misunderstand me. I only meant--'

'I like you very much, and I am very glad we are friends.'

'You are not offended?'

'Oh dear, no. Why should I be? Only why don't you marry? There are so many nice girls who are longing to be married--'

'Well, you see, I haven't a penny. Only my pay--'

They discussed his affairs, and Vanessa was very maternal.

After that she was dancing all the time. She found everyone delightful. Some tried to make love to her, some confided their troubles to her, some laughed and behaved like schoolboys, some were extremely pompous, one asked her to go to India with him.

'India!' she cried. 'What should I do in India?' He was not sure, except that she would make him very happy.

Then something occurred which, on looking back afterwards, affected, she found, strongly her later behaviour that night. Barney appeared and with him a charming, shy young man.

'Vanessa,' Barney said, 'here is a cousin of yours. An unknown cousin. Be kind to him.'

The boy, who looked about nineteen, was slender and tall with fair hair and bright, ingenuous blue eyes.

'I'm not a good dancer,' he said, blushing furiously. 'Shall we sit this out? I think that you will be more comfortable that way.' She discovered that his name was Adrian Cards and that he was at New College, Oxford. He was a younger brother of the Ruth and Richard Cards who had, years ago, been present at Judith's Hundredth Birthday. He was a great-nephew of Jennifer Cards, Benjie's grandmother.

At first he was very shy, but no one could be shy for long with Vanessa. He began to pour out his heart. He had many enthusiasms. Literature. No, he did not like the Aesthetes much. They still read Swinburne, but were not he and Tennyson a little--well, pontifical? The earlier Browning, but not these 'Inn Albums' and things. Pater, yes. The Renaissance was wonderful. He had met Pater. A Society called 'The Passionate Pilgrims' had invited him, and there he had sat, cross-legged, looking rather like a Chinaman. He had seen Matthew Arnold and often Jowett. You could see Miss Rhoda Broughton out walking. But he was all, she discovered, for philanthropy! Toynbee Hall, W. T. Stead. They had started a Mission in Bethnal Green that he visited. Oh, Miss Paris, he did hope that she would not think him a prig. He was not that. He rowed in his College boat. He didn't like saints, he did not wish to improve people's SOULS--no, but their BODIES! Oh, Miss Paris! Did she KNOW of the distress and unemployment? Did she realize that last month four thousand men came to the Mayor in Birmingham and asked for work, that they were starving and could scarcely stand? Had she heard of the Industrial Remuneration Conference, of all the things that the Trades Unions were doing? There was a Mr Bernard Shaw who had read a brilliant paper, and Mr John Burns had warned them all of what England would be in another thirty years! He was burning with it all, words poured from him, while the splendour and almost fantastic pageantry of the evening passed backwards and forwards in front of them.

Then he checked himself with a most charming smile.

'You have been so sympathetic! I am ashamed of my preaching. But you are staying with Cousin Ellis, are you not? I can't help thinking of all he might do with his money if he liked! Can't you influence him, Miss Paris?'

'Don't call me Miss Paris,' she said. 'We are cousins, you know. My name is Vanessa.'

'Oh, thank you. And MY name is Adrian.'

'Yes, Barney told me.'

'Cannot you influence him? The things he could do! If only you could persuade him just once to go to Bethnal Green.'

She told him that she had very little influence with anyone.

'Someone as beautiful as you are must have influence! Oh, I beg your pardon! Have I been impertinent?' He broke off and then with the same eagerness he asked her about Cumberland. He had never been there. Ruth had told him how lovely it was! She often spoke of Madame. What a marvellous old lady she must have been! And how sad that the house at Uldale had been burnt down!

'Oh, your father--' He was always rushing in and then out again!

'No, I like to talk of my father. He was the best man who ever lived!' She began to tell him things about Adam and Cat Bells and Uldale. She told him about Hesket and Caldbeck, of John Peel and the Herdwick sheep and the best-cured hams in the world. They had there the largest water-wheel and the smallest parish in England. Of the grand old farmers and their splendid ploughing, of an old lady she knew who had eighteen children and was ninety today, of how if you asked an old ploughman, strong as the horse he was leading, how old he was, he'd say 'Ah's nobbut eighty!' of how they would sing 'Old Towler' under the fellside, of Tom Pearson, the wrestler, who could dance a better step-dance than any woman, of the 'Ivinson' grey tweed, the strongest in the world--and, as she talked, all Skiddaw broke into the London house, clouds came down over the gold ceiling, and the bleating of the sheep was louder than the band!

She had missed a dance with someone or other. She rose and held out her hand.

'You'll come and see me, Adrian? Come tomorrow to Hill Street, tea time.'

'Yes, I will,' he said fervently.

But when she was dancing again she knew that something had happened to her. The wildness was upon her again, but now it was full of fear and warning. She must not return to Cumberland! She must make her life in another fashion. Where Benjie was, danger lay. That boy was right. It was being shown to her clearly that, at the side of Ellis she should help the world. The two of them together-- what could they not do? Ellis had told her that he was waiting for her to help him. Already in these weeks in London they had grown close together. At the thought of all they could do for the world her cheeks burned, her heart beat high.

She had been living without any thought of all the unhappiness, the poverty! The things that Ellis and she might do together! . . .

There was a pause. Everyone moved to the right and left. The Prince and Princess had arrived.

They walked up the room, bowing and smiling, stopping once and again to speak to a friend, while the women curtsied and the band blared. It was a glorious moment. He looked so kindly and she so beautiful. England was safe for ever and ever: the peoples of the world were bowing. A hero had died for his country in the Sudan. Here and there were a ruffian or two to be taught their place and duty! The Beaminster portraits smiled down their loyalty and patriotism, the jewels blazed, England lay like a cloak at the royal feet, and the Empire did obeisance.

'Oh! to do something splendid!' Vanessa's heart cried.

It was Ellis who took her in to supper. He was quiet, stealing glances at her once and again. She seemed to be carried high on some wave of exaltation. She looked at him so kindly that when they moved away and sat down together in a distant corner where from the hall below they could hear them summoning the carriages, he said, now for the third time:

'Vanessa, will you marry me?'

She, staring beyond him into an imagined world, nodded her head, saying:

'Yes, Ellis dear--if you want me.'

Part Two

THE HUSBAND

JUBILEE

Early in June of the great year 1887 Ellis and Vanessa went one evening to hear Albani in Lucia and, waiting in the portico of the Opera House, were caught by a breeze that, in spite of the warm evening, made Ellis its victim.

In the following days he paid no attention to his chill, sternly from morn to eve pursuing his City adventures. On the eighteenth of June there was a grand party in Hill Street, a Jubilee party, with Royalty and Colonel Cody. Next day Ellis was threatened with pneumonia. On the morning of the supreme Tuesday he was as hopelessly a prisoner as any poor wretch in Vine Street.

It was a tragedy. Ellis and Vanessa had seats in the Abbey; for months Ellis had looked forward and, in his odd way, half child, half man of importance, he had come to feel (as perhaps many other Herries were feeling) that the Jubilee was created only that he should sit with the loveliest woman in London and give his approbation to his Queen's Thanksgiving.

He lay there, his cheeks mottled, his nose sharp and white, his thin body stretched like a corpse, his eyes rheumy with cold and bitter disappointment. Vanessa refused to go to the Abbey without him. She would watch the Procession from Piccadilly with Rose and Barney and young Adrian. When she came in to say goodbye she felt so vividly his own bitterness that she cried: 'Ellis, I won't go. I'll stay here with you. Rose will tell me all about it, and besides the heat is fearful or will be soon. Ellis, I'll stay.'

He longed to agree that she should. He would not miss it so grievously if she also missed it, and the thought that she had given this up for him would be a salve to that intolerable unceasing doubt, the doubt that she loved him.

But he was not so selfish; no, no, he was not so selfish. So, in a voice thick with cold, drawing the bed-clothes close to his chin, he murmured: 'Absurd! How absurd you are, my darling! You had better not kiss me. Go and enjoy yourself!'

He knew that when she was gone he would repeat to himself again and again: 'She offered to stay. One word from me and she would have stayed.'

How beautiful she was! He watched her hungrily. Her dress with its full bustle, rose-coloured, fitted her tall graceful body with exquisite symmetry. No woman in London wore clothes as Vanessa did; the little hat, perched on her dark hair, was wreathed with rosebuds. The parasol that she carried was rose. Two roses, dark and rich like the summer weather, were at her waist. She was a Queen, he thought. Had we gone to the Abbey she would have been lovelier than any other woman there. 'The beautiful Lady Herries . . .' and he would have been with her, the proudest man in England.

'Give me some more of those drops, dear, before you go.'

She thought the big bare room chill and stuffy. Beyond the window the sun blazed on the street; very faintly from the far distance came the sound of a band. She could see a flag gently moving in the morning breeze from an opposite house. She was all impatience to be gone. She might be a grand lady now who must never forget her dignity, but for nothing at all she would dance down Hill Street waving her parasol. How terrible had he said: 'Yes, dear. Remain!' How terrible not to see the kings and the princes, not to hear the blare of the bands, not to see the colour and the excited happy faces of the people, not to wave to the Queen! She was so sorry for his disappointment that tears filled her eyes as she smoothed his thin hair with her hand, straightened the bedclothes, laid the books and The Times close to him! How old he looked when he was ill! How old and how at the same time like an ugly disappointed little boy! How near and how intimate to him she was, and how far away and separate! How kind and tender she wished to be to him! And how her very heart contracted in her breast when he made love to her! How grateful for all his kindness, how deeply irritated, against her will, by his unceasing care of her!

She sat in the chair beside his bed, holding his hot dry hand.

'You will take care not to be in the sun.'

'Oh yes, there is a large awning over our stand.'

He was moved by a sudden spasm of irritation and kicked up his knees beneath the bedclothes.

'It is too bad. It is really too bad. To happen just now! In another week I could have gone!'

'I know, I know, dear. Oh, why did we go to that silly Opera? . . . Ellis, let me stay! I'll go with Rose this evening and see the illuminations . . . After all it is going to be so hot, most uncomfortable, I expect, and a procession is always so quickly over . . .'

He sighed. How wonderful if it had been she who was ill and he had been given the opportunity of sacrificing himself! At once he was ashamed of such a thought. His love for Vanessa prompted him to strange wicked desires. He who would give her anything in the world, to wish anything so wicked! He choked, coughed, drank a little water, smiled with wan bravery.

'What you must think me! As though I could be so selfish! Enjoy yourself, my dearest, and tell me about it . . .'

He picked up Walter Besant's novel, laid it pathetically on the bedclothes. 'I shall count the minutes until your return.'

Afterwards in the sun and splendour she felt as though she had escaped, by a miracle, from prison.

Early though it was, the streets were thronged and the stands already crowded, but she had only to slip down Berkeley Square and in at a back door, be conducted by an extremely polite young footman through a drawing-room and so out to the stand where Rose already was.

When she settled herself and looked about her she uttered a cry of childlike delight. The sky was an unbroken blue, the full green of the trees of the Green Park was soft and deep and luminous like a sunlit cloud. From her seat she could watch the hovering flutter of the flags, the massed colour of clothes, the splashes of scarlet that broke the pearl-grey of the London stone. All this colour was translated by the sunlight into something trembling and unsubstantial as though lit by some unseen fire. There was a brooding silence scored like a sheet of music with the clatter of a horse's hoofs, the echo of distant band music rising and falling on the slight morning breeze. Above the buildings flags drifted against the blue as though under the impulse of some secret rhythm. The front of the stand was banked with flowers.

She sat there, her gloved hands clasped, her lips parted, her eyes shining. At that moment, if she had been ordered, she would have died for her country, for the Queen, for any cause that needed her. For a very little thing she would have burst into tears.

Rose, who looked very exotic with her dark colour, her red dress, was as deeply excited as Vanessa.

'This is all very foolish,' she said. 'By this afternoon I shall be ashamed of myself. No matter, I like being ashamed of myself.' Rose read from her programme:

Her Majesty will be accompanied on horseback by the following Princes placed in the order of their relationship to Her Majesty:

Grandsons and Grandsons-in-Law of Her Majesty		
HIH the Grand Duke Serge of Russia	HRH the Prince Albert Victor of Wales, KG	HRH the Prince William of Prussia, KG
HRH the Prince Henry of Prussia, GCB	HRH the Prince George of Wales, KG	HRH the Hereditary Grand Duke of Hesse
His Highness the Hereditary Prince of Saxe-Meiningen	His Highness the Prince Christian Victor of Schleswig-Holstein	His Serene Highness the Prince Louis of Battenberg, KCB
Sons-in-Law of Her Majesty		
HRH the Prince Christian of Schleswig-Holstein, KG	His Imperial and Royal Highness the Crown Prince of Germany, KG	HRH the Grand Duke of Hesse, KG
Sons of Her Majesty		
HRH the Duke of Connaught and Strathearn, KG	HRH The Prince of Wales, KG	HRH Duke of Edinburgh, KG

She talked without ceasing, waving her hands, half rising from her seat, turning to look for friends. Did Vanessa know that people were paying twenty-five pounds for a good place? That nearly three hundred books of gold leaf had been used for decorating the State Coach, that there was still living a survivor of George III's Jubilee, an old lady in Gloucestershire, that the Pope is so pleased at the Jubilee that he wants England to re-establish relations with the Vatican, that so much gas was to be used in the illuminations, that? . . .

She said:

'Oh, Vanessa, I am so happy!'

She caught Vanessa's hand, then drew away again whispering:

'No, I won't spoil your fun. Don't listen to me. It isn't true. I'm too excited to know what I am saying.'

Vanessa turned to her.

'Rose, what has happened? What have you done?'

'Nothing. Nothing. I didn't mean what I said.' Then abruptly again she broke out:

'You know that Horace is engaged?'

'No. When? To whom?'

'A few nights ago--at the Ball at the Reform Club. A Miss Lindsay. A nice little girl. With money of course. And he will treat her abominably.'

'You'll be alone, Rose. You won't like that even though Horace isn't the most--'

'No. Yes. Well, perhaps.'

'Rose, you are going to do something foolish. What is it? Tell me. I insist on your telling me.'

Their lives had been bound together. Ever since that day of Judith's Hundredth Birthday when Vanessa, looking across the luncheon table, had seen her, wanted her for a friend, loved her, there had been a bond which Rose's recklessness, her risks and mistakes and gradual descent from safety into danger, had only strengthened.

'Vanessa, you will always love me, always, always, whatever I do?'

So also Benjie had claimed. She had fulfilled her promise. She laid her hand on Rose's arm.

'Rose, don't do anything without telling me. You must not. It is not fair to me. We have been friends so long and have helped one another so often. Promise me! Promise me!'

'Look! There is someone riding up the street. He is seeing that everything is clear. Doesn't he look grand with his feathers?'

'Rose, tell me. What are you doing? Not Fred Wycherley? You told me--'

'Vanessa, darling--it is all right. Really it is. I was excited. I'm always doing something silly. Look! how the stands are filling up! Why don't Barney and Adrian come? They are missing everything--'

'But it isn't Wycherley? Promise me that it isn't Wycherley--with his wife and those two children--'

'No, of course it isn't Fred. Oh, do look at that woman in that bonnet! There, to the right! Did you ever SEE such a thing?'

At that moment Barney and Adrian Cards arrived.

Adrian, who, young as he was, was now in the Foreign Office, who wrote articles for the magazines on religion, economics, French poetry, who loved Vanessa with such open devotion that everyone thought it charming, sat on one side of her, Barney, who was now very stout, on the other.

'Here we are!' said Barney. 'I have just seen Timothy and Violet and their offspring.' (Timothy had brought his family with him permanently to London.)

'I have also seen Phyllis and Rochester struggling for breath in Northumberland Avenue, Amery, son Alfred, and the new plain wife nestling under the lions in Trafalgar Square, so I have not done so badly by the family. How is poor Ellis?'

'Oh, Barney,' said Vanessa, 'he was crying with disappointment. He had been SO looking forward--'

'Yes. It's a shame. Poor Ellis.' But he was not thinking of poor Ellis as he leant his fat body forward and drank in delightedly the scene, except perhaps, without any unkindness, to relish his own fun the more because Ellis' catastrophe made him realize that he too might have caught a cold and been prevented. He pushed out his chest, stretched his stout arms a little, wondered how little Daisy McPhail (the present lady of his apartments) was getting on somewhere along the Mall (he had loved her now for three months and still found her good company), considered (as all novelists consider) whether he would be able to describe this heat, colour, movement, expectation on paper, looked at Vanessa and marvelled yet once again at her beauty ('But this life with Ellis is telling on her, and I don't wonder'); leaned yet farther forward to gaze down Piccadilly and saw, a little to the right, only a row or two away, Benjamin Herries.

'By Heaven--'

'What is it?' Rose asked--and he could feel that she was trembling with some agitation deeper than any Jubilee warranted.

'Nothing.' He had pulled himself in. 'Only that everything is so jolly. WHAT a day! Doesn't that old lady have luck with her weather?' (WAS it Benjie? Yes, certainly. He had half turned. He had seen then.) Barney suddenly was assured that Benjie had seen Vanessa from the moment of her first entry. The little man, square-backed, brown as a berry, in some fashion independent, alone like a hill-man who had come down to study for a moment, the people of the plain, sat erect, his chin resting on the handle of his stick, the most significant thing about him his living, questing, eager eyes.

'A bandit!' Barney thought. 'For tuppence he'd hold a gun at the lot of us!'

Benjie half turned again and gave Barney a nod, slight, humorous, secret.

'His eye never leaves Vanessa. But Vanessa must not see him. Lucky that Ellis is locked away in Hill Street!'

And again, like any novelist, he considered that here was a situation, old and hackneyed though it might be, that would make a chapter or two: Benjie, Ellis, Vanessa--all of them so much more real than anything that Barney could do on paper. And he summed up for judgement the half-written efforts of his present work, Julia Paddock . . . Poor thing, how she wilted and died before the sharp indifference of actual life!

'Look here, Adrian, change places with me, will you? I'm a bit deaf in this right ear. Creeping senility, you know.'

They changed places, Adrian seated now between Vanessa and Rose. Barney's broad body would, with decent luck, hide Benjie from Vanessa.

Young Adrian talked of the People's Palace which Besant's All Sorts and Conditions of Men had started as popular philanthropy. Vanessa was on a Committee. Mr Besant had come to tea in Hill Street. A nice, booming, self-confident, bustling kind of man.

'Oh, don't let's think of committees!' cried Vanessa. 'This is so much nicer. I'm not very good at committees, Adrian. My thoughts wander.'

He was only twenty-two years of age, and Vanessa was the love of his whole life. He had the imagination of the abnormal, but with it the common sense and balance of the normal. He was, in fact, closer to Will and Ellis and Timothy and old Pomfret than to Francis and John and Adam. He would never commit suicide nor dream his life away. His philanthropy, idealism, poetry, would be practical, definite things. He was the straight, normal Herries at its best. So, looking at Vanessa, he worshipped her without any thought of contact. She was the greatest lady he would ever know, the kindest, the loveliest. And how glorious to be beside her today when she was like a child in her pleasure! He had seen her of late so often as the hostess sitting at the end of her table at those endless dinner parties in Hill Street, curtsying to Royalty, talking to Ambassadors, moving down the room with all eyes upon her . . . Now, for an hour, she was close to him, friend with friend. Not that she was ever affected or grand. The world in which for two years now she had moved had not touched her, but, as he had often noticed, when Ellis was not there, she was free, spontaneous, self-forgetful . . .

'Oh! they are coming!' she cried. 'They are coming! I can hear the bands!'

Distant music broke across the heat and light as though somewhere a door had opened. All individuality was lost; colours, blue, crimson, green, hung like painted cloths about an empty-room, for here in the sunlight there was a bare space which only one figure could fill. The empty room waited for that entrance; the door would be opened and soon, for the briefest instant, a small stout old lady would be borne forward, would stay for a moment, looking about her while the colour, the music, the sunlight made a canopy over her; then, with a little bow, she would retire and all would be ended. A bell would ring, a trumpet blare, the door would close.

A kind of sanctification fell upon those people. They turned, their eyes straining down that long pathway between the banks of colour, a pathway so oddly bare. There was a fear of a last instant's frustration. Would a thunderbolt fall, the final trumpets for Judgement sound, and so--after the agonized anticipation--that royal carriage with the little bowing figure never appear? The sky, the trees, the flags, the splashes of crimson, all a painted prepared pattern for that instant

of completion that even yet might not occur. Vanessa, looking upwards for a moment, saw three birds, dark and remote, slowly fly across the blue. At the sight of the first advancing soldier, glittering in the sun, his black horse moving with dignified austerity, she turned to Barney and whispered:

'My father met my mother for the first time on the Queen's Coronation Day.'

She wanted to evoke Adam. She wanted him there with his kind, sleepy smile and that touch of his hand on her arm . . . Then she forgot everything but the Procession. Thicker and thicker they came. The pathway that had been so bare sparkled now with silver and gold. She was drawn down into a medley of colours, sounds, and, pressing close upon her, that clear clop-clop of the horses' hoofs like the ringing of little hammers on stone. Men were detached from the river of movement; a figure, the back straight as a board, the thighs stiff, one gauntleted hand raised, would become real against fantasy. You believed suddenly that it breathed, it touched its bearded cheek with its gauntlet: the rider and the horse stood out above the flood as though the trumpets had summoned it. The three Kings were in closed carriages--very disappointing of them. The cheering increased. Now, glittering with gold, an open carriage could be seen, and then, in an instant, the air broke into cheering, the caparisoned horses, the outriders, the scarlet and the gold swung into being before the green clouded trees. The Queen, her parasol raised, in a dress of black and white, passed by. One horseman, in a silver helmet and shining cuirass, seemed her especial guardian--the Crown Prince of Germany. The door closed.

'Oh!' said Vanessa. 'How lovely that was!'

The soldiers were still marching, the drums and trumpets sounding, but the ordinary real world had assumed its place again. She heard someone behind her say: 'The twenty-sixth, remember. I'll have the carriage and we'll go straight down.'

She sat there watching for a while, happy, tranquil, remembering things to tell Ellis, suddenly thinking of Will Leathwaite in the cottage on Cat Bells. He would be going out that evening to see the bonfires and he would think of her as he always did when anything of interest happened.

'Didn't you love that, Rose? Didn't you think her splendid?'

But Rose was gone. How strange!

'Adrian, did you see Rose go?'

'Yes, she slipped away just after the Queen passed. She didn't want to disturb you.'

'Oh, I wanted to tell her--' Vanessa looked back to see whether she might yet catch her. People were rising, moving about, already many seats were empty.

Then, turning to the right, looking over Barney's head, she saw Benjie.

He was staring at her, standing up in his place. They looked at one another. He raised his hat, bowed, gave her one more long stare; then, turning his back, climbed up the wooden benches and disappeared.

She had invited Barney and Adrian to luncheon and they returned to the house with her, but, before she joined them, before she went in to see Ellis, she stood, without moving, in the middle of the floor of her bedroom, gazing in front of her. She had but a moment. Ellis, in the next room, knew that she had returned but, with the sunlight streaming about her, still wearing her hat and gloves, she stayed there, lost.

Benjie! She had not seen him for close on four years, but in that momentary glance it had been as it had always been. They had not separated. They COULD not separate. Marriage altered nothing, distance altered nothing; she must confess to herself what indeed she had never denied--that Benjie and herself could not be parted. He had looked as he always looked. His London clothes, his tall hat and dark coat could not change him, his apartness, his humorous defiance, his challenge to the world. He had been, apparently, alone. Had he been aware of her for a long while? Had he intended to speak to her? Was he staying in London? Was he here permanently, perhaps with his wife and boy? Or had he parted from his wife? Or was he on his way abroad? How strange that out of all the thousands who had watched the Procession they two should have been so close together. He could not have known where she would sit. Or had he perhaps met Barney the day before and asked him? Would he call at Hill Street or would he keep his part of their bargain? During these four years he had never written to her, nor sent a message. As she took off her hat and slowly drew off her gloves she knew that she would at that moment give everything--name, reputation, happiness--for one word with him.

Her body shivered. She knelt down for an instant beside her bed, pressing her hands against her eyes. Oh, how she wished that she had not seen him! Oh, how glad, how glad she was that she had! The sunlight fell hot upon her head like a caress. She bathed her face and hands and went through into Ellis' room.

Ellis lay there, his long hands with their prominent knuckles on the counterpane, and he looked at her steadily, following her with his eyes as she moved as a painted portrait does.

She came to the bed, sat down, took his hand and began to tell him all about everything. 'The colour, Ellis! You can't imagine it! The trees of the Park made everything so much brighter, and then the splashes of scarlet and the grey buildings and all the flowers. We had beautiful places, better than the Abbey. We could see both ways down Piccadilly and had a view of the Queen's carriage for ever so long. Rose was there. She was rather restless. I do hope she isn't getting into

trouble again. And Barney and Adrian, Barney is really disgracefully fat. He said he'd seen Timothy and Violet and Amery and his son.'

'Did you see anyone else you knew?'

She realized at once that Ellis was hostile, that something had happened here in her absence. HAD Benjie called? Had he written? Had Barney been up to see Ellis already and told him? Oh, but he would not! That was not Barney's way. Had someone else seen Benjie about London and told Ellis? Since their marriage Ellis had never uttered Benjie's name . . .

She answered quickly:

'No one to speak to. We left before the Procession was over to escape the crowd. And we did. The Square was quite empty. Not a soul about. But the crush in the streets was dreadful, and what the heat must have been . . .'

He interrupted in that small cold voice always used by him when he was offended (he was very proud of it: he thought it was calculated to strike terror into any heart).

'Some letters came for you while you were away.'

So that was it! There was a letter for her in some hand that he suspected. She had noticed of late that he looked at the writing on the envelopes of her letters with an eager curiosity which he always thought that he hid.

'Miss Fortescue brought them in,' he went on. 'She thought that you were still here.'

('She KNEW that I was NOT here,' Vanessa thought indignantly.)

The letters were in a little pile on a table near the door. She went across, picked them up, then turned and smiled at Ellis. 'Well,' she said, 'what has disturbed you, Ellis? Something has made you unhappy.'

He said at once, his voice shaking:

'One of those letters is from Benjamin Herries.'

(Was it so? Then he had written to tell her that he was coming to London? He had written to make an appointment?)

She looked quickly. There was no letter from Benjie. One, in a man's hand, was from Keswick, but, as she knew at once, it was from a Doctor Harris there who had written asking if she would subscribe to some sports to be held in August at Threlkeld. She did not dare even glimpse at her own fierce disappointment. She was NOT disappointed. It was MUCH better that Benjie should not write, should never write, never see her, never speak to her . . .

She came quietly to the bedside and gave Ellis the letter.

'There is nothing from Benjie. This, I suppose, is the letter you meant. Read it.'

He looked quickly at the letters, then pushed them towards her.

'No, no. Of course I will not read them. I am very ashamed. Please, please forgive me. If you knew how I have been suffering!'

'It has done your cold good anyway,' she thought, 'having something else to think about.'

Her anger and indignation, of which she was always afraid because they were so strong when they were aroused, stirred in her eyes. She did not ask herself whether her disappointment assisted her anger.

'Please read them, Ellis, if you want to. I have no secrets from you whatever.' (Had she not?)

He looked up at her abjectly, a look that she detested, in human beings, in animals, in anyone or anything that should have pride.

'Please, please forgive me. The handwriting was like. I thought that he might be coming to London for the Jubilee. I have been lying here all these hours longing for you . . . You are so beautiful today . . . I love you so terribly. I cannot grow used to it. I used to think that in time it would become part of life, ordinary, but it does not. It is stronger every day because it is never satisfied. It is not your fault. But you don't love me. You never loved me.'

That was just. That was true. At once she felt tender towards him because of that injustice. He was like a small son who had asked for a present that she could not give him, and so she put her arms around him and comforted him. She sat down beside him and took his hand again.

'Ellis, dear, we all care for one another in different ways. That is everybody's trouble. I think perhaps I am not passionate in the way you mean. Many women are not. But we are such splendid friends. More every day. Let us be thankful for that. And don't begin to suspect things. Let's trust one another. If we do not we shall torture one another. We have been married for over two years and have trusted one another perfectly. Ask me always if anything makes you uneasy; suspicion in marriage is horrible. It's worthy of neither of us.'

He moved towards her, put his thin arms round her, laid his head on her breast.

'Love me! Love me! Love me!'

She tried to comfort him; her relief when at last he moved away made her feel ashamed. Today something new had entered their married life, something not quite new. Rather a forgotten acquaintance who unexpectedly arrives and says that now, from henceforth, he will live in the house.

She kissed him and stood up.

'I must go down to Barney and Adrian. They are waiting for luncheon. I will come up afterwards.'

He lay staring at the door long after she had left the room.

And even then this day was not done with her. When Adrian and Barney were gone she went upstairs again and read Besant's novel aloud until Ellis slept. Then she went down to the drawing-room. She had done what she could with it. There was a portrait of her by Whistler in a white dress standing against a dull gold wallpaper, holding a fan. She had not filled the room with odds and ends as many of her friends liked to do. It had now a silver-grey wallpaper, there were many flowers about, there was a deep purple Persian carpet, but the place was not alive. It would never live, it would never be home to her. The two tall windows were open--a pale blue light shadowed the houses. The sky was pale with the evening heat. There was holiday everywhere, shouts and cries, distant bands, and the flags moving lazily in the gentle summer breeze. There was that scent of burning that a very hot day in London leaves behind it, and the odour of flowers, roses, carnations, and the dry dusty fragrance of geranium leaves. She turned back into the long dusky room that was like a cool deserted cave. She walked up and down, knowing that life, after two years of comparative quiescence, had in a moment taken another turn. Everything from this hour was different. Tonight there was to be a family dinner party. Ellis had insisted that his illness should make no change. Rose and Horace, Phyllis, Clarence Rochester and Philip, Barney, Amery and his son and new daughter-in-law, Timothy and Violet and Aunt Jane, Carey and May Rockage, pretty Cynthia, Rodney's grand-daughter, and her husband Peile Worcester, Adrian . . . they were all coming. No one but the Family. What an odd mixed lot they were, and yet how alike--even the wives of other stock. They moved forward in one body, not to the outer world important and yet affecting the world by their quiet insistence on normality, confidence, the domestic virtues, patriotism, deep suspicion of the foreigner, belief in the Church, Tennyson, the Houses of Parliament, the Royal Family (with reservations about the Prince of Wales, Barney's mistresses, Rose's reputation, Jews-- unless they were very rich--and one or two things more).

They had been very kindly to Vanessa. Old Lady Herries before she died last year had said: 'My dear, never fight the family. I know you often want to, but it isn't worth it. They always win in the end.'

But did they? Had not Judith defeated them, and Uhland and even her own father? The battle continued. She had not, herself, surrendered. And Benjie? Oh, WHERE was he? Was he quite close to her somewhere in London? She had the maddest impulse to go to Barney's rooms in Duke Street. He would know, she was sure. She went to the door, opened it, and listened. The house was as still as the inside of a drum. Only the beating of her heart seemed to thud down the passages. Then there was something else. Someone was coming up the stairs.

She went back into the drawing-room with the wildest thought that it might be Benjie. What would she do? How could she defend both herself and him? She stood, one hand pressed to her breast, staring at the door. But, when it opened, it was Finch, the new butler, a man she did not like because she was sure that he was in league with Miss Fortescue, a fat red-faced man with sandy hair.

He had a note on the salver.

'A letter for you, my lady. A boy has just left it. He said that he was told that there was no answer.'

She saw at once that it was in Rose's hand, and as soon as Finch was gone, opened it, reading it there where she stood.

DEAREST--I could not tell you this morning. I went to the Procession with a wild hope that something would occur, that I should break a leg or be strangled by the crowd. Nothing DID occur, so by the time that you get this I shall be on my way to France with Fred. Insane. I know it. I think that we both of us know it. But I would not care if it were not for you. But you said that you would love me whatever I did. Remember-- your love is all that I shall have in a year's time.

ROSE

The note fell from her hand to the ground. She bent down and picked it up. A foreboding, dusky and cold like the room, crept to her side and touched her hand.

THE FLITTING

Benjie Herries, a week or two after Jubilee Day, walked up the hill on a lovely summer evening towards the Fortress. He had been playing cricket with the young men of Ireby village. On his shoulder he was carrying his son Tom, aged three years, and beside him was Bob Rantwood, a famous poacher, drunkard and ne'er-do-well, one of Benjie's best friends. A sunny haze covered all the world. In the village there had been much motion, the long wagon drawn by its splendid team of horses, the chatter at the little inn with its coloured prints, its gay pictures of hunters and horses, and a grand flower-and-fruit piece that was the landlord's especial joy, left there by some travellers to pay a debt more than a hundred years ago, the flagged passage, and beyond the bottle-green windows the clear blue of the summer sky. Mrs Enderby's shop with the liquorice, bull's-eyes, bootlaces and a portrait of the Prince of Wales, the long fields rising to the grey hills, the deep oaks, the bleatings of sheep, the brilliant leaves of the copper beech, the scent of clover and bean blossom.

He was at peace and not at peace; he had enjoyed the game, the comradeship (for they liked him), the taste and sound of Cumbrian air and soil, but Rantwood unsettled him. He had poached with him many a time, knew all about salmon and trout poaching, the 'draughting' and 'poling'. Lovely nights he had had with Rantwood draughting a river, or, by himself, guiding his poles, knowing exactly where there is a spile or a crook. The thrill, in mild weather, to find a spot where the fish are spawning, or on a dark night to see the dawn steal over the fan-shaped hill, to hear the moorhen plunge! Or, draughting with Rantwood, trailing the net slowly down the river, stoning the water to frighten the salmon into the net--or best of all on a moonlight night, when an old coat had been soaked with paraffin, the thrill of the moment when this improvised torch is lit and the men with him, sticks in hand, plunge into the water . . .

Rantwood, like most poachers, was a discontented, cursing, but most amiable fellow. Nothing was ever right with him. He would swear at the game laws by the hour together, 'gloweran' aboot' like a madman, and then he would laugh, throw his thick arms around, and call Benjie, for whom he had warm friendship but no reverence, 'thoo girt daft cauf, thoo'.

He was always restless, always wanting to be somewhere where he was not--and so was Benjie. But Benjie knew what was now the matter with him. He should not have gone to London, should not have seen Vanessa . . .

Three days he had stayed there. He had not especially enjoyed his visit although he had done all the things that would, he thought, amuse him. He had visited Earl's Court and seen 'Buffalo Bill' Cody's Wild West Show, had travelled on the Underground Railway and been stifled by the sulphur and smoke from the engine, the fumes from the oil lamp, the reeking pipes of his fellow-travellers. He had visited the Gaiety Bar and talked to the magnificent ladies who served him, had spent several hours in the Argyle Music Hall, admired the Chairman who with such militant authority banged the table with his gavel, and wondered at the amount of liquor he could consume.

He had wandered the streets and like any country yokel stared at the illuminations, had watched London Society display its elegance in Hyde Park, had been pleased with the superb procession of curricles, landaus, victorias, the powdered footmen, the silk stockings, the yellow plush; had found a beautiful lady at the Alhambra, gone with her to her room in Portland Street, but once there, after half an hour's most elegant conversation, had politely left her. He had been, in fact, the loneliest of men. That seat from which he had viewed the Procession (a pretty penny he had paid for it!) had been his ruin. He had gone to London on a sudden impulse, resolving to visit no member of the family. It had been the cruellest fate (the kind of check to his virtue that fate was for ever dealing out to him) that Vanessa should be sitting there almost at his side! For two hours he had watched her. Every detail of her dress, every movement had been absorbed by him. It was not her loveliness that had struck him to the heart, but his intimacy with her so that he knew instantly, at the first sight of her, that nothing was altered, that his four years' exile from her had hindered nothing.

He had made no attempt to speak to her. Weak, irresolute as he was, he would keep his word--at least, for a little longer. But he returned to Cumberland a haunted man.

He shifted young Tom a little, liking to feel the warmth of those small confident fingers against his neck. A funny freak of chance that Tom should have in him some kindred blood with the second wife of Vanessa's great-grandfather. After Vanessa he loved Tom--the only two in the world whom he loved.

'All the family have cleared out of the country,' he said aloud, following his thoughts. 'I'm the last here. We were all over the County a while ago.'

'Aye,' said Rantwood, who was pursuing his own thoughts. Would Herries ask him in for a drink? He had a thirst all right. But Mrs Herries--she didn't like him. Nor he her--whimsey-whumsey kind of female.

'My great-great-grandfather rode into Keswick one night from Doncaster. That's how it all started. We were all over the place once. Oh, I've told you before. And now we're all away again.' He looked over the hedge down the valley where the summer evening breathed tranquilly under a stainless sky. Around them the insects were humming and on the other side of the hedge a brook sang beneath the willows. Voices cried through the stillness with a dying fall. As though he spoke aloud: 'I am walking up this hill and soon I will be gone. I have done my best. I have kept my vow, but soon I shall be wandering again. I can neither be free of this country nor settle in it, and when I am away I shall remember just such an evening as this, the meadow falling into dusk, and all the names that I love-- Blencathra, Uldale (almost all the bricks of the house are gone now: soon there will be nothing but the turf and the sheep cropping it), Bassenthwaite, Ireby--beautiful names like the words of a vow, a vow that I have kept but can keep no longer. I hate this house I am coming to. I have always hated it. I hate this woman in the house. I have always hated her, and one day soon I shall take young Tom and we will walk away and never come back. The last Herries . . . but the place will be always in my bones. I shall never tread on such turf again nor drink such running water nor see such lithe walls running into the sky nor hear such friendly voices. But I have lived long enough away from Vanessa, and although I never speak to her again I must see her once between one day and another day.'

'That was a good catch I made to get Will Davidson,' he said aloud.

'Aye,' said Rantwood. 'Thoo can play at cricket a' reet.'

'Well, goodnight to you, Bob.' He turned in at the gate.

'I mun slacken my thirst wi' watter,' Rantwood thought discontentedly, starting down the hill.

Inside the house even on this summer evening it was damp. They had come down to live only in three rooms and the kitchen. An old woman, Mrs Cumming, was the present successor to all the in-and-out females who had done service in that place. The room at the top of the first stair-flight that had once been the drawing-room with the fine gilt chairs, the naked goddesses, the rosy cupids on the ceiling, was now the general living-room. All that remained of Walter's splendours was the long mirror with the gilded frame, and reflected in this Benjie now stood with his little son. His shirt wide open showed his brown chest, his neck firmly set, his head like a hard apple, the twinkling kindly eyes alive and eager, his small restless body upon which clothes seemed always an excrescence, Benjamin Herries, rogue, good fellow, a 'deep' chap, a good-for-nothing, the kindest man in the county, the suddenest- tempered, 'a man all by himself', a jolly man, a man of his word, a man you couldn't trust, a gentleman, a vagabond, a wise man, a fool-- just as your personal experience happened to be.

And his small son stood beside him, like his father because he had the brown colour and the sparkling eyes, a child always laughing, filled already with secret plans and plays of his own, never wanting company, never afraid, never asking anyone to help him.

The mirror also reflected the room, which was a scramble and a confusion, littered with fishing rods, guns, a woman's dress, a child's playthings, a table with the remains of a meal, and a sofa with a hole in it.

'Vanessa,' said Benjie, looking into the mirror.

Later, to the light of a smoking lamp, Mr and Mrs Herries enjoyed their evening meal together, old Mrs Cumming clattering in on her clogs bringing the beef and gooseberry pudding, banging them down on the table, going out with a toss of the head because she and Mrs Herries had but now crossed swords in the kitchen.

Mrs Herries was the thinnest woman in all Cumberland and her face was of a faintly green pallor. But she was the same reserved passive woman she had ever been. In years she was still a girl, but her features were of that ageless cast belonging to women who have matured when very young and live on their passions. Benjie was always kind to her; that he hated her was not her fault. He knew that she had been many times unfaithful to him, but she was no more personal to him than her pale reflection in the mirror might be. It was amazing to him that they had stayed together in this horrible house for three years, but his vow had kept him, he supposed. He had shown Vanessa that he could be faithful. This woman had at least done that for him; so he was kind to her, smiled across the table at her and told her he had made thirty runs in the cricket game.

He ate his beef, seeing that the long gilt mirror was loose on its nail and swayed ever so slightly, so that the room rocked too a little. The two high windows were open and the place was suffused with the summer evening heat, with the odour of the roses that rioted about the garden. A moon, tip-tilted on the edge of one small cloud lit from within like cotton wool around a lantern, drunkenly grinned through the window.

'Mrs Cumming can't cook meat, that's one thing certain,' he said, smiling at his wife.

'No, she can't,' the late Miss Halliday agreed, 'But we never get a decent servant here.'

'We pay them plenty,' said Benjie, who from land, from money left him by Elizabeth, was not so badly off.

'They won't come here. They are afraid of you.'

'What! that I'll go to bed with them? You know that I've been faithful to you since our wedding day.'

(He had, marvel of marvels! Or no--to put it better, he had been faithful to Vanessa.)

'That doesn't interest me,' Mrs Herries said. 'You know you're free to do what you like. Oh, it isn't you. They would know how to deal with you if you started anything. No, it's the house.'

'Ghosts?' said Benjie,

'What you like to call them. Mrs Cumming was talking about it tonight--steps up and down the passage, a dog whining. You've heard the dog yourself up there in the Tower. Someone tapping with a stick. And that woman in black wandering about the garden.'

'Do you believe in spirits, then?' he asked her.

'Spirits!' she answered impatiently. 'These gooseberries aren't half cooked. Well, what are you to think? Those friends of my brother's, YOUR friends, those Endicott men, they've seen things time and again. But there's something queer about this house.'

'Yes, from the moment the first stone was laid. My grandfather spoilt it with his obstinacy. If you see a thing isn't going to turn out well you should give it up. No good going on if the signs are against you.'

She sat leaning forward, her sharp-peaked chin resting on her hands. He noticed that she was regarding him with great attention tonight. He felt that something was in the wind.

'Ghosts!' He smiled. 'I saw one in London the other day--a beauty. She was tall like a lily, carried herself like a queen, she was dressed like a rose and a had dark, dark hair. It makes you think of a ghost like that when you see a room in the mess this is in. Why don't you tidy things a bit, Marion; keep things in order more?'

'Ah! What's the use? You're never in, and nothing would ever stay neat in this house. Three years I've had of it--'

'You're a strange woman.' They regarded one another in friendly fashion. 'You've never had any liking for the boy, and he's a fine little chap too. It has meant nothing to you, being a mother.'

'No, nothing at all,' she answered. 'Women mean nothing to me, no, nor children. But men--ah! that's another story! And you, Benjie, more than any. I want to be in your arms as badly as ever I did the first time I saw you. But what's the use? Why you've stayed with me all this time I can't imagine . . . Well, I must wash the dishes. I won't have that sneak of a woman in the house after tonight. She goes tomorrow.'

'Why, what has she been doing?'

She was standing up, her hands on her hips, staring at him as though she would never see him again.

'I like you like that with your shirt open. You're brown all over like a foreigner. Where did you get that skin from?'

'Who knows where one gets anything from? That's the mystery. Where we come from, who made us what we are, what we make ourselves into, where we are going to. And we've lived three years together, Marion, and are as far apart as ever we were.'

'Yes,' she said. 'It's all the body, what it looks like, what its clothes are. I'm not your beautiful ghost like a rose, tall as a lily. But see the rose's nose crooked and give her a black eye, and where's your love for her then?'

'I'm not so sure,' said Benjie. 'I'm not so sure.'

'But I am! It's only because you've a brown skin and are strong and haven't an ugly mark on your body that I'm in love with you. But what's the use? You don't care for me and never did. And you're the only man I've never tired of. Most men are the same after you've known them once.'

She said all this in a quiet, dispassionate voice. Was it because of her own unresting physical passion that he had once on a day been caught by her? Maybe. But that didn't matter now. It was not her fault. A pity that she didn't care about young Tom, though. That might have been something of a bond between them.

'Well, I mustn't stay talking here. That woman's stealing the spoons, I wouldn't wonder.' She went out, carrying the beef with her.

He wandered out into the garden.

Moonlight on a summer's night is a most impermanent thing. Everything is new born, but only for a moment, and when the silvery world rises it is like a dream that, even while you are enchanted, you know that you must not trust. The flowers on such a night are ghosts that at a touch will vanish away, and water, shining under the moon, belongs to no earthly stream. This garden had never yielded to any man's will. Flowers had died when you cared for them and waxed abundant when you neglected them. The moonlight poured out now from under the trees like a flood that, at the beckoning of a cloud, would be withdrawn. Only the trees stood firm, waiting the moment when they would advance, cover the ground, swallow the house and resume their kingdom. Man had never been wanted here, especially man filled with the spirit of obstinacy, revenge, and pride.

Was there some dark figure moving under the trees? He stood there watching. It was easy to imagine, with all that you had heard, that a tall woman in black, now in moonlight, now in grey shadow, moved, hesitated, moved again. He walked forward, the plants crowding about him; then he turned to the stone steps that ran to the higher ground at the side of the house. He had always disliked these steps. His mother had told him that for some reason they had always frightened her. Uhland had tap-tapped down them with his stick, Walter's drunken friends had sprawled against them and fallen from top to bottom like the helpless fools that they were. Now they were washed white in the moonlight and you could see the tufts of grass like black bunches of fingers pressing up between the broken flagstones. Here, standing halfway up, he was exactly under Uhland's stair and he could fancy that behind that dark window Uhland was standing and behind him perhaps old Rogue Herries. The two of them watching the third in that sequence. He stretched his arms. He whistled a tune. He might be of their family, but he was not of their destinies. He was fit and well and strong; he had a son and he loved a woman, he had friends and a hundred miles of country that he would not exchange, with its clouds and stones, for all the sunny kingdoms of the world. He looked down on that moonlit garden. He could hear the water falling from one pool to another. An owl hooted. WAS not that a woman who moved from tree to tree? He whistled his tune, kicked the loose stones from under his foot and went in to see that his child was comfortably sleeping on this hot night.

Tom slept in a corner of his own bedroom, a room in Uhland's Tower, once used by Walter as a guest room. It was sparsely furnished, his bed, Tom's small one, a large tin bath, a dressing-table, his hunting prints and the faded painting of the old Elizabethan Herries that had once hung in Borrowdale. A fierce, frowning old boy with no nonsense about him! The carpet had holes, the cupboard where Benjie kept his clothes creaked with every wind, but tonight it was transformed with the moonlight and the scent of the roses. Although the window was open the room was very hot, and the child had thrown off the bedclothes and lay, his nightshirt ruffled to his chest, his little legs drawn up, one fist--clutching a small wooden horse--still clenched.

Benjie stood there, looking at him. This was his son, and not a bad son either. Pity he had that Halliday blood which was no good at all in his veins, but Benjie flattered himself that his own Herries blood could beat the Halliday mixture. Vanessa had as yet no child. That anaemic husband of hers would never give her one-- and, perhaps, one day Tom would know her and love her and get his idea of women from her.

Poor Benjie sighed. He was really ashamed of himself for having a son at all. He was no sort of father for a boy to have, and he knew already what a man, who is no great hero and has done a shameful thing or two in his time, can feel when a small boy thinks him perfect. 'Well, he won't think me perfect long, and I can teach him to shoot and ride and not be afraid of anyone . . . Still, he ought to have some sort of mother to care for him.'

Then he undressed. He could not find a nightshirt so he slept naked, curling up his legs as his child had done. Father and son slept side by side and the clouds came up over the moon, drenching the room with darkness.

Tom always woke very early and came into his father's bed. He would lie, his small head against his father's chest, looking at the trees beyond the window, waiting until his father should wake. He talked to his horse, named Caesar, telling him about the things that they would do that day, bacon for breakfast, a visit to the village, and, if very lucky, a ride to Bassenthwaite. He didn't PROMISE Caesar these delights. He had learnt already that it did not do to expect ANYTHING, that one was left alone when one least expected it, or worst of all, handed over to Mrs Cumming with her constant: 'Now don't be a worrit' or 'Keep quiet, do'. He was accustomed to being without his father for days at a time, and, although his mother was never unkind to him, he knew quite well that she did not care for him. Only once had she been really angry with him, and that was when, coming into a room unexpectedly, he had seen her sitting on a fat man's knee. She had slapped him severely although he did not know what wrong he had done, and then the fat man had given him sixpence. The only fear that he had was that, when his father went away, he would never come back again. He discussed this often with Caesar, and Caesar reassured him. OF COURSE his father would come back. But when he was in bed with his father he clutched him very tightly, his arm on his breast or his neck. That comforted him greatly.

At last the grand moment arrived when his father opened his eyes, grinned, yawned, stretched his arms, played a game or two. Then he watched his father splash in the tin bath, after which he was himself plunged into the same. His father helped him with his clothes, fastening his buttons, brushing his hair, and tying his boots. This was a lovely morning, as fresh as a bird's wing, and between the trees you could see Blencathra's shoulder resting against the faint early summer blue. His father whistled and sang, which showed that he was happy this morning; then, hand in hand, they went down to breakfast together.

The big untidy room was bright with sunshine, but there was no breakfast; no cloth was on the table, and, although it was by now half past eight, no sign nor sound of Mrs Herries.

Then Mrs Cumming came clopping in, carrying a plate of bacon in one hand and a dented silver coffee pot in the other.

'Where's Mrs Herries?' asked Benjie.

'Mrs Herries is gone,' said Mrs Cumming, her eyes staring with a fat, half-sleepy curiosity.

'Gone?'

'Aye. Mr Ewart's trap come and fetch her seven this morning. She told me they was driving into Carlisle and she left me a letter.'

She felt in the pocket of her cotton dress and produced it; she gave him a stare and went out.

He held the letter in his hand, but, before he opened it, settled Tom in his place, cut the bread, gave him some bacon and poured out the coffee. Tom wriggled until he was comfortable, set Caesar up on the table in front of his place and set to.

The letter was as follows:

DEAR BENJAMIN--I have gone away with Charlie Ewart and shall never return. He has been pressing me for a long time. I'd have told you last night, but what's the use? There's nothing to be said. You don't want me, you never have after the first night or two. I did a wrong thing in the first place to force you to it as I did, but Mother pressed me and I was in love with you. I wonder we've stayed together as long as we have and I must say you've always been very patient, your nature being what it is. We haven't had what you could really call a cross word all these years. All the same we haven't been happy, either of us. I wish I could have felt more for the boy. I'm sure I've tried, but it isn't in my nature. I wasn't meant to have children and if I can help it shan't ever have another.

You'll be much better without me; I haven't a gift for keeping things straight and tidy. What Charlie Ewart sees in me I can't think, and I don't suppose we shall be together long although he says different. You can divorce me if you want to but I don't want any money from you and I'll never be married again. Well, good-bye, Benjie. One thing I'm glad of, that I shan't have to live in the Fortress any more. It's a place would make a cat sick--Your sincere friend,

Marion

Benjie read the letter through three times, then he gave his son some more bacon. 'Well, that settles it,' he said aloud. As though the sunshine penetrated his heart he felt a great joy and gladness. He was free again; he had been set free. He had kept his vow and now, without any act on his part, he was liberated. Charlie Ewart! That thin, shanky, lop-eared farmer! Poor Marion! He was so sorry for her that had she at that moment appeared in the doorway he would, in spite of his disappointment at her return, have been kind and con-

siderate. But, thank Heaven, there was no need to be kind and considerate any more!

He went into the passage and called Mrs Cumming.

'Mrs Cumming, Mrs Herries has gone to London. I am going also and I want you to order Sam Bender round with the trap in an hour's time. I'll catch the train from Carlisle. I'm taking the boy with me. I don't know when I'll be back, but I'll write from London.'

So that was the end of the Fortress. He would sell the damned place and be done with it for ever. He would be in London and Vanessa would be in London. He had done what he could, and it was not his fault that now he was free to go where he would.

Poor Marion! Charlie Ewart! Well, well . . .

He went to his room and packed a few things, Tom going hand in hand with him everywhere. He dressed Tom in his best suit and his grey summer jacket.

'We are going to London,' he said. 'You, I and Caesar.'

While he was sitting waiting for the trap, he talked to his son.

'We're going away, Tom, and I don't expect we'll ever live in this house again. Years and years ago a man rode into this country with his son and went to live in a little house the other side of Keswick. He had a brother living in Keswick too. And as the years went by his son had a wife, and they went and lived in a house down in the valley there which was burnt in a fire later on. There were many of our family in the country, but, one by one, they died and went away until you and I are the only ones left. And now we're going away too. But that's not the end of it. You and I have got this country in our blood. You don't know what that means now, but you will one day. Everything you ever do will be affected by this country, and however far you travel you'll never find any other country so beautiful nor any other that's in your bones as this one is. You'll come back to it. Be sure of that. But I hope you won't come back to this house, because it was built in a bad temper and hasn't been any good to anybody.'

Tom seemed to understand. 'The funny thing is,' thought Benjie, 'that one remembers after the things that one was told although one was too young at the time. I remember things that Adam told me about birds and wrestling. Very rum that.'

'You've got to be a better man than I've been, Tom,' he added. 'And I hope you'll stay in one place sometimes. You never learn anything if you're always moving. But you'll be all right so long as you're never afraid of anyone. There's nothing to be afraid of really.'

It wasn't like him to preach, but the warm sun was comforting and he felt so happy and cheerful that he had to be talking to someone.

They took a last look at the place together, the Cumberland stone, the overgrown garden, the two cross-faced towers. A dog was whining somewhere and little flakes of plaster fell from the ceiling of the living-room.

Then Sam Bender came with his trap and took them both away.

VIOLET BELLAIRS IS PREVENTED

When Timothy Bellairs and Violet his wife had been established in London a year or so they became the centre of social exchange for the London members of the Herries family.

Hill Street was of course the Temple: all the splendour and sanctification were in Hill Street. Only Vanessa of all the Herries entertained the Prince and Princess to tea (although it was said that the Prince HAD paid pretty little Cynthia a visit at her pretty little house in Charles Street); only Vanessa invited Archbishop Benson to luncheon; only Vanessa was on friendly personal terms with Mr Chamberlain.

During these years Hill Street was the Temple. But neither Ellis nor Vanessa cared for gossip. At least Vanessa enjoyed it but appeared to consider some things spiteful when they were only amusing. Now Violet Bellairs was quite different from this. A Cumberland country cousin, she had become very speedily a most entertaining London hostess. She was not, of course, very clever: you could laugh at her to her face and she seldom perceived it. She had no talent for the Arts, thought Oscar Wilde an actor, and supposed that Robert Elsmere was written by a clergyman, and had only just heard of young Mr Kipling. But it was not for the Arts that any Herries went to Onslow Square. They went, quite frankly, to hear about the other Herries. You could always tell when any scandal was afoot because Violet, her stout body enclosed within the brightest colours, her red face beaming, her hat elegant with a stuffed bird, her eager, friendly voice with its 'Well, how are you? Haven't seen you for an age!' was to be seen everywhere--at Charles Street, in Barney's bachelor rooms in Duke Street, in Phyllis' overcrowded drawing-room, even in the cold and gloomy place in Kensington where old Emily Newmark held her prayer meetings.

Violet was always in the best of spirits, kind and friendly to everyone, leaving a trail of scandal behind her. She DID enjoy a gossip, she freely confessed, and liking, quite naturally, to be the centre of any company, if she had no thrilling tale to tell she invented one. Her husband, who was fat and sleepy, spent his days in the Conservative Club and his evenings at Jimmie's or the Alhambra or where you please. He was no trouble to her at all.

Violet, like so many women who married Herries men, became more Herries than the Herries. She was patriotic, strictly moral and all for the law. Nevertheless any human failing made her happy because she was never censorious, but treated a 'mishap' as a town crier treats a lost dog--rang her bell, felt kindly towards the dog but hoped that it would not be found before the whole town had had time to observe that it was lost. Her best women friends among the Herries were old Phyllis Rochester, Cynthia Worcester, Alfred's wife (Amery's daughter-in-law) and (again oddly enough) old Emily Newmark.

She had, of course, many many friends quite outside the Herries circle, but they were not of quite the same importance to her. As she often said: 'Our family holds together. There's not another family like it in England for that.'

It happened that, early in September 1889, Violet was very busy. It had not been a dull summer, for first there had been Mrs Maybrick (dreadful woman: why was she not hung?), and then those terrible Dock Strikers who, week after week, poor abandoned creatures, went about demanding their Rights, starving and altogether behaving disgracefully. It was not, however, either Mrs Maybrick or the Strikers who gave her so agreeable a week or two at the beginning of this September. It was a real Herries sensation-- WHAT was happening in Hill Street?

Two years earlier, a week or two after the Jubilee, the question had been--what WILL happen in Hill Street? for Benjamin Herries had come to Town, leading his son by the hand, and one of those family crises so greatly beloved by the Herries promised to be on the way. Then, to everyone's surprise--to the surprise of old Garth, old Amery, young Alfred, heavy Emily, dear little Cynthia, even the stout Barney himself--NOTHING occurred. Benjie called on none of them. He spent an evening or two with Barney; he never went NEAR Hill Street. So far as anyone could tell, he neither wrote to Vanessa nor spoke to her. Everything had been the more dramatic in that summer of 1887 because of the dreadful (but rather delightful) Rose scandal. She had escaped to Paris with Captain Fred Wycherley, leaving Mrs Wycherley, poor thing, and two young children in London. ('Did you expect him to take them with him?' Barney asked ironically.) More than that, she met Carey Rockage in the Rue de Rivoli one September day and laughed and joked with him as though nothing had occurred.

Carey was in a fine way because May, his wife, and Maud, his elder daughter, were at a hotel not two streets distant. How fearful if Rose should suggest that she should call! But Rose (who was looking both young and pretty, Carey thought) suggested nothing of the kind.

'I know you have May and Maud with you, Carey. You were at the Opéra-Comique last night. If you are making a domestic parade one day and meet Fred and myself, we shall expect to be cut, you know. So don't worry. Only, if out on a little bit of evening fun on your own, Carey, remember that Fred has his spies everywhere. He'll give you a tip or two as to the best places if you ask him! He's the kindest of creatures!' She went off, laughing, swinging her bustle. Poor Rose. She had been always a coarse woman. Horace, her brother, married last autumn and it was understood that he did not wish Rose's name to be mentioned. Simply because of the awkwardness that it caused to others. Looking more like a Bishop than ever, he let it be understood that he was devoted to Rose. 'Which of us is above reproach?' he inquired of Barney, 'What I mean, old fellow, is that charity is the finest of the virtues. For my part I look at the good qualities in my fellow-men. Who am I to judge? And Rose has loved Fred Wycherley for years.'

Nevertheless it could not be expected that Miss Ada Lindsay that was, a plain pale-faced girl, twenty-one years of age to Horace's thirty when he married her, coming as she did straight from a wealthy but Christian family in Kensington, would care to hear such things mentioned. What Ada herself thought of it nobody knew because she seldom spoke. No one knew what her thoughts were about anything--including Horace.

However, the really interesting side to Rose's disgrace was that it was well known in all Herries circles that there was a deep difference of opinion concerning it in Hill Street. Ellis was disgusted, Vanessa would not listen to a word against Rose. Cynthia Worcester was known to be devoted to Vanessa, to worship her in fact, but even she confessed that if Vanessa was going to 'bite her nose off like that all about nothing' she would think twice about visiting Hill Street again. All that she had said was that Rose had got at last what she wanted, and Vanessa had turned on her, scolded her in front of Ellis as though she were ten years old.

It was plain then that Vanessa's own views on morals were a little queer. Had they not always been queer? After all, had not Judith Paris been her grandmother, Rogue Herries her great-grandfather? Had not her own father been illegitimate and her mother a German? No one meant any of this unkindly. Vanessa was so beautiful, so generous and socially so resplendent that one could forgive her almost anything; nevertheless she belonged to the quarter from which the dangerous winds were for ever blowing, those winds that had for centuries disturbed the peace and order of the right-living, right-thinking Herries.

Benjie, however, was a disappointment. He did nothing spectacular. Nobody saw him. They said that his wife in Cumberland had run away from him after he had beaten her to jelly, that he drank like a fish and consorted with abandoned women. But these things were but rumour and Barney stoutly denied all of them. In the winter of '87 he left London for what destination no one knew.

It was in the spring of '88 that everyone began to say that things were not well in Hill Street. On the surface everything was very well indeed. Vanessa went everywhere and Ellis was often at her side, looking as

proud as a peacock. Everyone LOVED Vanessa; how could you help it, so kind and generous and simple-hearted as she was? Nevertheless she made few friendships. Cynthia complained that 'there was always a barrier', but old Phyllis Rochester said that Cynthia was 'socially jealous'. Did Vanessa give herself airs? Surely not. She was the same to everyone, knew no social distinctions, and had been seen one day by Emily Newmark sitting on the top of a bus and chatting to the driver. Her only close friend was young Adrian Cards. She certainly spoilt that young man, who, because he was in the Foreign Office, looked after a Boys' Club in the East End and wrote for Mr Henley, thought himself quite out of the ordinary. OF COURSE no one suggested that Vanessa was in love with him, but it was agreed that he visited Hill Street a great deal more often than Ellis cared for, and he helped Vanessa with her many charities.

Ellis was, in fact, the mystery. What went on behind that cold reserved official manner of his? He loved Vanessa madly: ever MORE madly as the time went on. He behaved to her in public with a really exaggerated courtesy and deference, but it began to be said that in private he was impossibly jealous. How do these things become known? Miss Fortescue (who, as everyone was aware, did not like Vanessa) told a thing or two, and there was that occasion when Alfred and his wife were lunching at Hill Street. Ellis had left the table abruptly and had not appeared again. Very odd. They all shook their heads over it. Then, in the late spring of '89, Benjie Herries once more reappeared in London. He lived in two rooms in Soho Square with his little boy. Poor little boy! That was the first thing that everyone said. Benjie did not now conceal himself as he had done on the earlier occasion. He paid calls on everyone-- including Vanessa--and aroused the greatest interest. They all surrendered to his charm while he was WITH them. He looked peculiar, wearing clothes of a rough tweed, sometimes the new knickerbockers, but for the most part loose baggy trousers. His tie was generally a deep red in colour and enclosed in a gold ring, and this colour with his dark skin gave him the nickname of 'the little gipsy'. They told one another, however, with a rather reluctant satisfaction, that you could never mistake him for anything but a gentleman. He was always at his ease, laughed like a boy, was worshipped by any Herries children who happened to be about. He made no effort to win the affections of his relations: they could take him or leave him, and for a while they certainly took him. After June there was an exodus from London: Cynthia and her husband went to Ostend; Timothy and his family to Eastbourne; Alfred and his wife to Brighton.

Old Emily of course remained, and it was from her one must suppose that the story spread--the story that one night at the Alhambra, Benjie was engaged in a disgraceful scuffle, knocked a man down and spent the night in a police station. There HAD been a scuffle, that was certain, but Barney said that it had been extremely creditable to Benjie. Some drunken ruffian had insulted the lady in Benjie's company and Benjie had knocked him down. But what was Benjie doing at the Alhambra with a lady and what sort of a lady was she?

Then in August came the great news that Benjie had paid a call at Hill Street and been forbidden the house for evermore by Ellis. This was from Miss Fortescue.

Well, now, what do you think of that? Somebody said that Ellis had slapped Benjie's face, someone else that Vanessa had had to rush in between the two men and separate them. No one knew what had happened because nobody was present. Ellis and Vanessa left town to pay a series of visits. They stayed with the Rockages in Wiltshire, and with Horace Newmark-- Barney's brother--now an old man of seventy in his grand house near Manchester.

It was reported that Vanessa was serene and happy, but that Ellis was 'queer'. What do you mean by queer? Well, May Rockage was bound to confess that she didn't like the look in Ellis' eye. He seemed unhappy if Vanessa left him even for a moment. Pathetic to see how he adored her, and Vanessa looked after him as though he were her son, but he was restless and Carey confessed that 'he didn't seem normal', the most alarming thing that any one Herries could say about another. All the old family scandals were revived, the misbehaviour of the ancient Rogue, the old quarrel at Christabel's ball, the suicide of Francis, and of course the dreadful affair of poor John and the crazy Uhland. Was the family never to be allowed to sit down quietly by its fireside and enjoy its domesticity, serve the country and worship its Maker? What was this crazy spirit that refused to leave them alone? Benjie was as bad as the old Rogue, and the sooner he left the country for good the better.

Early in September most of the Herries were back in London again; Vanessa was at Hill Street, Amery and Alfred in Tavistock Square, Timothy and Violet in Onslow Square, and Emily remained in Tutton Street, South Kensington.

So one fine September afternoon Violet thought that she would go and see what everyone was thinking. She took her son, young Timothy, aged now twelve, with her. Timothy was a beautiful boy; she refused to cut his hair, which fell in gold ringlets to his broad white collar. For parties or calls he was dressed in a black velvet suit. He was the pride of his mother's heart. It is sad to have to record that at this period of his life he detested his mother. He was not allowed to go to school, but shared his sister's governess. He was washed and dressed and brushed morning, noon and evening. He loathed his long hair, his velvet suit, the comments of his mother's friends; he was mocked at and shouted after by little street boys; he cried himself to sleep at nights because of their insults. The only thing in the world for which he cared was to draw and

paint; this he must do in secret because his father, whom he rarely saw, laughed at such nonsense and his mother showed his drawings to her friends. He had to drive in an open carriage in the Park with his mama, he had to sit on a chair in ladies' drawing-rooms and be commented on as though he were something in a circus. His settled resolve was to run away as soon as the proper moment occurred. Barney Newmark was his only friend. Barney had said to Timothy: 'What the devil do you dress the poor child up like that for? It's cruelty to children, poor little beggar,' and Violet, hearing of this, never forgave him.

On this particular afternoon in Cynthia Worcester's drawing-room, he was not altogether out of place. Two young poets were present, a lady dressed in blue velvet and peacock's feathers, and Mr Oscar Wilde. Mr Wilde was very kind to him, sat beside him in a corner and told him a story about a young Prince who ran away from his father's kingdom and became a bell ringer in a church with a wonderfully high tower. One day when the Prince was ringing the bells, a swallow flew into the tower and rested on his shoulder. The swallow had damaged its wing, so the Prince took it back with him to the cottage where he was living . . .

At this point the ladies demanded that Mr Wilde should entertain them, so the tall heavy man with the grave eyes and the beautiful voice had reluctantly to leave young Tim, who never afterwards forgot him.

Two more men and a girl came in. There was a great chatter. Violet admired Cynthia's looks but she must say she couldn't admire the way that she did her drawing-room with the pale grey wallpaper, some flowers in a white vase, a Japanese screen, one little table with some odd-looking thin books upon it--nothing else. No photographs! No cosy coverings to her room, no fans pinned to the wall, or shelves with cups and saucers and large blue plates. However, Cynthia LOVED a good talk and was just jealous enough of Vanessa to enjoy a story or two. You could not find two types more exactly opposite than Cynthia--so small and fair, with such very light-blue eyes--and Vanessa-- tall, dark, 'one of Du Maurier's women', or as Horace Ormerod liked to say impressively, '"A daughter of the gods divinely fair"--fair in the sense of beautiful, you know.' So that there was just enough difference between the two for Cynthia not to object to a little scandal . . . no harm, only to ask where Benjie was, had anyone seen him, did Cynthia know what Ellis, when he was staying down in Wiltshire . . . ?

So that Violet was pleased when the two young men and the girl came in, because now it would be perfectly easy to have a little chat with Cynthia without disturbing the others. Smiling happily upon everyone as though she would say, 'Now I know I'm a large woman and when I move it is a little upsetting, but I like you all immensely and you must none of you be disturbed,' she drew her chair closer to Cynthia's.

'Cynthia darling--what BEAUTIFUL teacups! Where did you find them? Everything you have is always so lovely. Listen, dear.' She dropped her voice. 'HAVE you heard what Benjie has been doing? They tell me that Ellis . . .'

But something was wrong. For once Cynthia did not appear to be attending.

She said: 'Yes, Violet dear, how interesting!' but her sharp blue eyes were fastened on the heavy frock-coated man with the pale jowl, the friendly smile, the heavily lidded eyes, who, standing in front of the fireplace, talked with a self-confidence that awed Violet although privately she thought it a little vulgar.

One of the young men said something with a titter about the Queen. All the patriotic Herries in Violet (acquired by marriage) was affronted. Smiling very brightly she said:

'The Queen! Surely we must be proud to HAVE such a Queen. Young man, you are disloyal.' (Shaking her finger at him playfully.)

'Violet is really dreadful when she's coy,' thought Cynthia, and for the first time (because she was not interested in children) wondered whether it was not rather a shame that poor child on the sofa (to whom one of ladies was now talking) should be dressed as a doll.

Mr Wilde said: 'The Queen? Do you know, madam, what Thackeray once wrote about our Queen?'

'No,' said Violet, 'Something fine, I'm sure.'

'Very fine,' said Mr Wilde, looking at her with so kindly an expression that she wondered whether she would not invite him to luncheon. 'He wrote, as nearly as I recollect, something like this: "I salute the sovereign; the good mother; the accomplished lady; the enlightened friend of art."'

'How very fine--and how true!' said Violet.

'Not true at all, madam. The Queen has not been a good mother, she is not accomplished, and she has not been a friend to art in any fashion whatever.'

Everyone laughed, Violet felt most uncomfortable.

'We owe to her in fact the present interest in the Arts. An Englishman is only an artist when those in authority despise the Arts.'

'What about Queen Elizabeth?' said Cynthia, laughing.

'Do you imagine that Elizabeth was an artist or cared for the Arts? She wanted to be entertained and made love to, and because the Arts then were part of a man's daily life, to tempt a man to make love to you was to rouse the artist in him. The Arts today can only exist by separating themselves from daily life. That is why the real artists today are never successful lovers, live from hand to mouth and wander the streets. Very different from the life of our Queen.'

'You are forgetting Mr Kipling,' said Violet, who had been persuaded only a week or two ago to read Soldiers Three.

'Mr Kipling believes in the Empire,' said Mr Wilde, smiling.

'Do we not all believe in the Empire?' asked Violet, pleased that she was holding her own in this very intellectual conversation.

'Do you know what Tennyson wrote for the Jubilee?'

'A very splendid poem, I remember,' said Violet. 'He wrote:

'Fifty years of ever-broadening Commerce!
Fifty years of ever-brightening Science!
Fifty years of ever-widening Empire!'

Everyone laughed, but Violet did not see that there was anything to laugh at. Uncomfortable without knowing why, she waited a minute or two and then attempted Cynthia again:

'Do tell me, Cynthia darling. Have you been to Hill Street since they came back from the country? How did you think Vanessa was looking?'

'No, I haven't seen Vanessa for weeks.'

'It seems that Ellis has been behaving so very strangely--not sleeping, they say, and absurdly jealous. Phyllis had a letter from May Rockage . . .'

Everyone was laughing. The young man with the flowing black tie on the sofa had been drawing a picture for Timothy, and here was Timothy actually himself drawing something!

'It's a ship! It's a ship!' he cried excitedly.

One of the other young men jumped up and began to recite dramatically:

'Spirit of Beauty! Tarry still awhile.
 They are not dead, thine ancient votaries,
 Some few there are to whom thy radiant smile
  Is better than a thousand victories,
 Though all the nobly slain of Waterloo

Rise up in wrath against them! Tarry still, there are a few
 Who for thy sake would give their manlihood
  And consecrate their being. I at least
 Have done so, made thy lips my daily food,
  And in thy temples found a goodlier feast
 Than this starved age can give me, spite of all
 Its new-found creeds so sceptical and so dogmatical.'

'A very good poem,' said Mr Wilde, 'whoever wrote it. Its fault is that it contains a philosophy. Poetry has nothing to do with philosophy, but only with feeling.'

'You had a philosophy when you wrote it, Oscar,' said one of the young men.

'Yes, and got rid of it by writing about it. Any philosophy is foolish if you look it in the face. Christ hid His face, you remember, to cover the foolishness of His disciples. And that is why He loved John, because John had no philosophy--only feeling.'

'What very bad taste,' Violet thought, 'to talk about Christ in that ordinary fashion.'

Nevertheless it was now that she was disturbed by an odd sensation. There was something in this room that deprived her of her desire for gossip. It was not that she thought the Arts important; the young men looked most unhealthy, and Mr Wilde's complexion was anything but hearty. Nor was she ashamed of wishing to talk about the family, but there was something here before which personalities seemed unimportant. She felt frustrated, prevented. Even Cynthia, whom she knew so well, was different. The things of which these men talked were not in Violet's mind beautiful, and yet beauty was in the air. Perhaps after all her drawing-room in Onslow Square was a little overcrowded. The flowers in the white vase were a pretty colour . . .

It was almost as though someone had laid a hand on her mouth. She was most uncomfortable and thought at the first opportunity she would make an excuse and go.

One of the young men had, it seemed, but just returned from Paris and had seen there a performance of Othello.

'The absurdity about Othello,' Cynthia said, 'is that he should be upset so easily by so trivial a matter. A magnificent general, the strongest man in the State, and a little strawberry-spotted handkerchief--'

'You are wrong, dear lady,' said Mr Wilde. The tragedy of Othello is not Desdemona. She is only one element in his downfall. We know, when he appears before the Senate, that he is poised above an abyss. He knows, we know, the Senate knows, that this new command is his last chance. He would have been recalled from Cyprus and Cassio given his place had there been no wife, no jealousy, no murder. Before the play begins he has reached the moment that comes to every man when the journey downhill has started. I have always seen Othello played as though he were a king of men in the majesty of purple triumph, with the trumpets sounding about him. That is wrong; he has the bitter knowledge that the glory is already in the past. It is of the past that he speaks to Desdemona, not the future. He comes to the Senate, leading Desdemona by the hand, and despair is already seated in his eyes. Great success demands great failure.' He laughed, smiling at them all. 'I am already preparing for the day when I shall know St Helena, and perhaps Calvary. I hope I shall not complain, because the only artist who can count himself fortunate is he who has learnt the value of great failure. When Othello pierced his breast with his sword and remembered Aleppo his soul cried triumphantly: "Now my experience is complete. I thank the Gods!" For Othello was undoubtedly a great artist.'

'You are making him out to be as self-conscious as yourself, Oscar,' said one of the young men.

'Not to be self-conscious is not to be conscious at all,' Mr Wilde answered.

'And not to be conscious at all--well, that is to be "Ruskin".'

Everyone laughed, although again Violet saw nothing funny in the remark. Mr Ruskin, whose name was constantly in the paper, was most certainly of a greater importance than Mr Wilde. To be important was, apparently, with these young men, to be mocked at. The Queen, Lord Tennyson, Mr Kipling, Thackeray, Mr Ruskin . . . it was some comfort to her to recollect that she admired them all. She wanted to remain and she wanted to go. Something stirred in her. The house in Onslow Square, Timothy, the general trend and colour of her daily life--she was suddenly dissatisfied with them all. Family gossip, for a moment, seemed stupid and worthless.

But this was absurd. She resented her disloyalty to herself. She got up to go.

'Do tell me, Mr Wilde,' she said, 'one or two interesting new poets to read.'

He regarded her with so kindly a glance that once again she wondered whether she would not invite him to luncheon.

'I am afraid there ARE no new poets,' he answered her. 'But then there never have been. The best poets are old from the beginning. Mr Dowson there is a poet, and a very old one indeed, although he only left Oxford a year or so ago.' He indicated one of the young men on the sofa.

'I will remember.' She nodded graciously to the young man. 'Come, Timothy. Well, Cynthia, it has been most delightful. You must come to luncheon one day soon, dear, and perhaps you will bring Mr Wilde with you.'

But in the carriage she was indignant. Whatever had possessed her to be affected by two or three young men who were so irreverent and common? And how stupid of her to have determined to have a word or two with Cynthia. It was a lovely afternoon; she would drive to Kensington and see old Emily, who always loved a gossip and was certain to know the latest thing about Vanessa and Ellis.

Timothy was silent as he always was when exposed in public. But he was not unhappy. He thought longingly of the large heavy man who had begun to tell him a story and the other pale-faced man who had drawn things for him, who had not laughed at his own drawing of a ship but on the contrary had liked it so well that he had shown it to his friend.

The weather brought out the bicycles. What Timothy longed for more than any of the world's treasures was a bicycle. As a very small infant at Uldale he had seen Mr Rander, the clergyman from Ireby, ride a penny-farthing, and that glorious entrancing vehicle with its high front wheel and tiny back wheel had seemed to him the height of possible adventure. Now first Mr Stanley and then Mr Dunlop had provided safety and reasonableness. Everyone was beginning to bicycle. Timothy, sitting stiffly opposite his mama wishing that his hands were as large as umbrellas that they might cover his velvet suit, thought of the kind gentleman who had told him a story, and then with longing eyes looked out on the driver of the omnibus, yet more fervently on the driver of the hansom, but most passionately of all upon the bicyclist. It was the bicycle that must be--not, he hoped, so far distantly--his engine of escape!

'Now here we are at Miss Newmark's,' said Violet to her little son, speaking with some severity. She was still uncomfortable, still felt the touch of an unknown hand upon her mouth . . .

Here at any rate there would be no hindrance to a nice heart-to-heart gossip. But, as always when she was ill at ease, she was severe with her children, and now she spoke impatiently to Timothy and told Hunter, the coachman, that she might be a long time, she might not, she did not know, she could not tell, all this in the severe irritable voice that the Herries always use when they are nervous.

She had no need to be nervous as she stood, holding Timothy's hand outside the gloomy plague-stricken door of Miss Newmark's Kensington home. She had been here so very often before and called the door 'plague-stricken' because the paint had faded and blistered until the surface represented a chart for one of the more sinister Oriental diseases. Above the door was a top hat made of iron and painted a faded green. The lower part of the house had once belonged to a hatter. Violet had often noticed how, when she called upon Emily on a sunny day, there was always a gloomy sky in Emily's street. Very odd--as though the houses in Emily's street were mountains! It was the same today. Just as Parker, Emily's viperish maid, opened the door, the first drop of rain fell. Parker had been with Emily for twenty years and hated and despised all her fellow human beings without any exception whatever, save only her mistress. She could not be said to love her mistress, because she was part of her, bone of her bone and flesh of her flesh, and both Parker and Emily were above any kind of personal vanity. But Parker was of importance at this moment in the Herries family affairs because she was on speaking terms with Miss Fortescue from Hill Street. Miss Fortescue, who as a child had lived in a family of Second Adventists, visited Emily frequently and had many a chat with Parker before she left the house. These little social contacts have made history before now.

Violet and Timothy climbed the steep dark stairs and heard the thunder roll beyond the walls.

'I said it was going to thunder,' said Violet. All the way up the staircase Timothy gazed with a terrified eye at the series of pictures from the Bible decorating the wall. He hated to come to this house for many reasons, but chiefly because of these pictures, which represented all the more dreadful scenes in Old Testament history-- the murder of Abel, the destruction of the Cities of the Plain, the Flood, the Serpent in the Wilderness, the Plagues of the Egyptians. He wanted to hurry past, but his mother held him always tightly by the hand; her movements were slow and solemn. He wanted not to look, but was compelled. There was in one picture a fat snake with a flicking tongue, which writhed its coils around a shrieking woman and her child. That snake was remembered by Timothy all his life long.

'Mrs Bellairs and Master Bellairs, Miss Newmark.' So Parker always announced them in tones of the deepest dissatisfaction. She called her mistress 'Miss Newmark' on every occasion. They both preferred it.

In spite of the gloomy and uncertain light of the drawing-room, Violet saw at once that there were other visitors. Emily, now a large and heavy woman with hair of steely grey, a slight grey moustache on her upper lip, dressed always in black and having the oddest resemblance at times both in voice and features to her very different brother Barney, came forward and greeted them.

'Miss Pope. Mr Pope. Mrs Glass,' she said, introducing a pale young woman, a young man and a stout round lady wearing an old-fashioned bonnet, a very large bustle and a cashmere shawl.

On all ordinary occasions when Violet paid Emily a visit the same procedure was followed: first Timothy was put into a corner of a sofa and given a large illustrated Bible to look at and then the two ladies drew up to the fire (or the window if it were summer) and gossiped away the fortunes and happiness of every Herries in England. But today things were different. The lady in the shawl, Mrs Glass, said almost at once to Timothy: 'Oh, the pretty dear! Come and talk to me, my dear, and tell me where you got your lovely curls from.'

The room was littered with properties, sacred and reminiscent: Bibles, huge sea-shells, family albums, and volumes of poetry of a pious nature. These things gave the room the homely comfort which it needed. But today there was no homely comfort. Although the curtains were drawn and the gas lit, the thunderstorm could very distinctly be heard.

'I'll ring for some fresh tea,' said Emily.

'Oh no,' said Violet. 'I have had some tea with Cynthia'--then wished that she had not mentioned Cynthia, because Emily disapproved of her even more than she did of Vanessa. But today the mention of Cynthia roused no response. Emily seemed absent-minded. The three visitors were talking together, making a fuss of Timothy, who was struggling with a vast fragment of ancient and desiccated seed-cake.

Violet sighed, then patted Emily's knee.

'Well, how are you, my dear? I thought that I must just drive round and see how you were. For one thing Phillis has had a letter from May Rockage that would, I was certain, interest you. Vanessa and Ellis have been staying with them, you know, and it seems from what May says that Ellis's jealousy is becoming QUITE abnormal. She says that if Vanessa leaves the room for a single moment he begins--'

'There you are, Miss Pope!' Emily suddenly interrupted. 'Just what you said! A thunderstorm! Now isn't that strange after Mr Euclid's sermon last Sunday evening? Did he not foretell this very thing? God will thunder forth from His Heavens that we may be warned of the Wrath to come! Those were his very words. Violet, I've told you again and again that you should go to St Hilary's of a Sunday. Yes, and bring your husband with you. It would do him a world of good . . . Listen to that thunder! God speaking to us if ever He did and yet we will not listen . . . I beg your pardon, Violet . . . What were you saying about May Rockage?'

But here the pale young woman, Miss Pope, interrupted. She had, Violet thought, a HYSTERICAL face, for set like little fires in that pallor were her large burning eyes. She had a quiet, rather pleasing voice; her long, thin hands were clasped together as she spoke, and her body trembled slightly.

'Miss Newmark, you must come next time with my brother and myself. Really you must! You cannot imagine how affecting it was! The dock directors are monstrous. They could not behave as they do had they seen some of the sights that Edward and I see every day. They refuse to agree to the payment of sixpence an hour. Sixpence an hour! They would give a dog more! Dr Liddon's fund for the women and children is being wonderfully supported and that shows what the public feeling is! You should go down to the docks, Miss Newmark! They are empty. The Corn Exchange and the Coal Exchange are practically empty. You should have heard how Mr Burns and Mr Tillett were cheered last week, by big City men themselves. I cannot sleep, Miss Newmark, thinking of the women and children-- the starving children--'

Violet thought that she was about to cry, and oh! how uncomfortable that would be!

Emily said: 'God is working for them. The day will come when these wicked oppressors will be punished as they deserve.' Her voice was gentle. She was touched as Violet had never seen her before. Really, with the thunder outside and this emotion inside, the atmosphere of the room was quite embarrassing, but soon the three on the sofa with Timothy began to talk eagerly together once more.

'Have you seen Vanessa since she returned, Emily?' Violet asked.

'No, my dear.'

'I do hope that everything is all right in Hill Street. You know that Benjie is in London again . . .'

'We should go through the streets,' Emily cried, 'with Christ at our head and FORCE the world to listen. I suggest, Miss Pope, that you go and see Mr Euclid and suggest something of the kind to him. I know that you would find him sympathetic. We don't ask God's help enough. That's what *I* think! We try with our own

feeble hands to build up His kingdom. We can do nothing of ourselves.'

'You are right, Miss Newmark,' said the young man in a voice unexpectedly deep and manly. He got up. 'Would you mind--should we not offer up a prayer now to Almighty God and ask Him to help these poor brothers and sisters of ours? Where two or three are gathered together . . .'

He went down on his knees, almost upsetting the table as he did so. The three ladies did the same and Violet was also compelled to do so, although she felt extremely awkward.

'O Lord!' said Mr Pope, 'we Thy humble servants gathered by chance together speak to Thee with one voice for our unhappy brothers and sisters. We have sinned in our selfishness. We have not asked for Thy guidance. Show us, dear Lord, in Thine own good time how these, our suffering brothers and sisters, may be rightly helped and taken out of their undeserved misery, and open the hearts of the wicked taskmasters that they may incline towards mercy and know that without Thee the temple that they build rests on sand. Show us what to do, O Lord, and give us strength so that without fear we may go forward in Thy good work to Thy glory, world without end, Amen.'

'Amen,' said everyone.

Then Emily repeated the Lord's Prayer.

When they rose from their knees they showed no shyness at all, but began eagerly to talk together.

For the second time that afternoon Violet felt that a hand had been laid on her mouth,

There was nothing to do but go.

'Come, Timothy! . . . Well, Emily,' she broke in upon their talk, 'we must be on our way. Do let me know in what way I can help. I had no idea that the poor people were suffering so. It does seem too bad indeed.'

She embraced Emily, bowed to the others and departed.

In the carriage again, as she turned towards home, she felt vexed and uneasy. There had been something very queer abroad this afternoon. Now, as they drove through the streets, the lamps seemed to blow in the breeze that had sprung up, everyone was moving swiftly as though bent on some secret mission. Her mind hung about Vanessa. Vanessa was in great trouble. She was sure of it. It was as though the lights, the passers-by, the air of the September evening thickening as though with a film of thin smoke about the roofs and chimneys- -all these formed a clouded mirror in whose glass she saw pictures shaping. Real trouble. Not something at a distant remove, about which it would be amusing to gossip. Her heart was moved, she could not tell why. She made Timothy sit beside her, wrapping the carriage rug round him, then put her arm about him drawing him closer to her. She would go and see Vanessa tomorrow . . .

PART II

Vanessa was in trouble. And then these poor people at the Docks . . .

'How much is there in your money box, Timothy?'

'I don't know, Mama. About three shillings, I think.'

'Wouldn't it be nice to give it to those poor women who can't give their children enough to eat?'

'Yes, Mama.'

But he thought: 'Now it will be longer than ever to buy the bicycle.'

'We must be kind to everyone,' said his mother, kissing him.

A JOURNAL AND SOME LETTERS

Barney Newmark kept for many years a Journal. In 1896 he squeezed out of it what he felt to be some of the more interesting passages and made a volume of reminiscences which failed to attract much attention,* but for the purposes of a family chronicle some extracts from the original diaries are of interest. It was their misfortune, from the ordinary reader's point of view, that they dealt with private persons rather than public, family incidents rather than general affairs. He had always kept them for his own amusement and in that at least he had the advantage of some of his contemporaries.

* Some Memories, by Barnabus Newmark. Hatcher and Thorburn, 1896.

February 4th, 1890

. . . I could not conceive what he wanted me there for. I came to the house, I'll confess, in spite of my advanced years, rather like a naughty schoolboy ordered to the headmaster's study. He has of course never liked me. That is in fact putting it mildly. I date his positive antagonism from that evening long ago when he went with me and young Benjie on an evening out, went reluctant and returned disgusted. With the years his dislike has grown to a kind of horror. I stand for everything that he most abominates--a writer of cheap novels, irreligious, a lover of horses and women, a gambler, a drunkard. That I have been none of these things very desperately has given him only the greater displeasure. Had I gone to the dogs he could have pitied me. As it is I have kept my head just sufficiently above water to be still a danger. Vanessa's persistent loyalty to me has only aggravated the trouble. This is the first time that he has asked to see me for at least twenty years. The odd thing is that I have always rather liked him. He has an integrity that I can admire. Then I understand so well his desire to win affection and his inability to do so,

his shyness, his rectitude of conduct, his honesty. But is not his rectitude at last threatened? After yesterday I am inclined to think so.

I arrived at Hill Street punctually at four o'clock. Orders had been given that I was to be taken straight to his private Cave and I was conveyed up dark stairs and along sombre passages as though I were either a criminal or a spy--both, perhaps.

He was not there when I arrived and I had time to look about me in what is surely one of the gloomiest little rooms in London-- bookcases filled with those dreary volumes of Journals and Papers marked with little white paper labels, a bald bust of some dead Roman, a large stern writing-table with silver writing things and an immaculate blotter, a grim, grizzling little fire and two leather armchairs. Poor Ellis! Many is the time, I am sure, that he has paced that little room, wondering why things are wrong when he is himself so right, shrinking from a world that he would give his soul to placate, lonely and bewildered, suspicious and uneasy.

I was not there very long. He came in, said: 'Well, Barney, how are you?' asked me to sit down, seated himself opposite me, and then, tapping his fingers together, looked all round and about him with a kind of distressed dismay on his features that was both pathetic and funny.

We hung about for a long time without coming to the point. He said that it was a long while since we had met, that it was a pity, that he understood that Allsopp's brewery was in difficulties, that the shortage of gold made separate bank reserves very difficult, that it was high time the Treasury dealt with the Coinage question, and so on and so on. He asked me whether I was writing anything just now in that tone in which people who despise novels speak to novelists--as you might inquire of a coiner whether he has been doing well lately.

I made some suitable reply and then silence fell. I had no intention of helping him out. It was his affair, not mine.

Then suddenly it came:

Would I use my influence to persuade Benjie Herries to leave England?

So that was it? I stared and said nothing. He was extremely uncomfortable. He got up and began to walk the room. I must understand that he had nothing against the fellow. He disliked him, of course. He would be perfectly frank with me. He had always disliked him. He dare say that he was well enough from his own point of view, but I would have to admit that he had never been a credit to the family--very much the opposite in fact. His life, quite frankly, had been something of a scandal. That was Benjie's private affair. The last thing that Ellis wanted to do was to interfere with anyone's private life, but his continued residence here in London was distressing to many of us, and he, Ellis, as head of the family in London, had felt for a considerable time that something ought to be done. He wished me to understand that he brought no kind of personal charge and he hoped that I would regard this conversation as most strictly confidential. I broke in there that of course he understood that I was Benjie's friend. I also asked him did he wish me to tell Benjie that he had spoken to me?

To which he answered in great distress, Oh no! of course not! The last thing that he wanted was any quarrel with Benjie. It was unfortunate, most unfortunate, that some time ago he had been compelled to ask Benjie not to pay any more visits in Hill Street. He regretted it, regretted it greatly, but on his last visit he had been so outrageous in some of his views and had behaved most insultingly to Miss Fortescue--'My wife's lady housekeeper,' he added, poor dear, as though he didn't know that *I* know exactly all that Miss Fortescue is and how thoroughly Vanessa has always detested her.

But really, he went on, the point was simply this. He did not wish to detain me. He knew that I was an extremely busy man. Did I think that I could persuade Benjie that a residence abroad would be more suitable, more suitable in every way . . . more suitable in every way? . . . While he was speaking my mind ran over past family history. How odd this perpetual desire in our family for one member to rid himself of another! Old Francis the Rogue and his brother, Jennifer and Christabel, Walter and Jennifer, John and Uhland--as though it is a law with us that one half of us shall always aggravate the other to madness! Yes, to madness! As I watched Ellis, with his pale face, long restless hands, pacing up and down the room, it seemed to me that there was a kind of insanity, born of brooding unhappiness and perhaps jealousy--born anyway of a tormented unsatisfied love--not so far away!

I replied, quietly enough, that I certainly could not ask Benjie to leave the country. I could not agree with him that Benjie was a scandal. He was sometimes in London, sometimes abroad; he had his own friends, lived his own life. I could not see that he did harm to anyone.

At that Ellis became more agitated. Oh, indeed! And what had I to say to his fight at the Alhambra and a night in Vine Street? What had I to say to . . . Here, with a great effort, he pulled himself up. He must repeat that he had no charges against Benjie. It was only for his own good, for his own good and the general good . . . Did I think--Here he paused, seemed to be greatly agitated. Did I think that a sum of money? . . . He was prepared to offer . . .

At that I rose from my stiff leather chair.

'Look here Ellis,' I said. 'This goes no further of course. It ends here. But you don't know what you're saying. You send for me and suggest to me that I should bribe a friend of mine for no reason whatever to leave the country, go into exile. He has a son, you know, a fine little boy. Frankly I shall forget that we ever had this conversation. It is not worthy of you.'

I went to the door. He followed me and looked at me for a moment with such malevolence that it was a new Ellis, one I had never seen before.

'Oh, of course,' he said. 'You are his friend. I might have known . . . GOOD afternoon'

And that was all. I was out of the house almost as soon as I was in it. As I walked away I thought that I had never known a queerer business. How could he have supposed for a moment that I would have listened to anything of the kind? And to what a pitch of brooding and suspicion he must have come to send for ME, whom he has always so greatly disliked! At first I was so angry that I felt like turning back and punching his head. Then the pathos of the man himself came to me. And after that real fear and anxiety for Vanessa. I have known for some while that things are not going well with her, but she keeps up so brave a front that none of us can tell what is really happening to her. Is she meeting Benjie? Does Ellis know of something hidden from the rest of us? Of one thing I am sure--that she will be honest and straightforward in all her dealings; but all last night the thought of her enclosed behind those walls with Ellis for her companion and Fortescue in attendance--well, frankly it spoilt my evening. But I have put everything concerned with this little incident down here exactly as it occurred. The facts may be useful one day. I am Benjie's friend, Vanessa's friend, even--who knows?--Ellis' friend. A nuisance for an old, selfish, comfort-loving bachelor who hates to be disturbed. All day today I have been tempted to go and see Vanessa. But no. It is better that I avoid Hill Street for a time. The nuisance is that tonight when I should have been getting on with my novel I haven't been able to think of a thing. Quite impossible to get Vanessa and Ellis out of my head!

From Vanessa Herries to Rose Ormerod at 27 Rue Montaigne, Paris

September 6th, 1850

MY DEAREST ROSE--I have the whole evening to myself--Ellis has gone out to some meeting and I have done what I love better than anything else in the world, gone to bed, had some supper on a tray and now can write you a long letter without fear of any interruption.

After you left on Wednesday I was very unhappy. We had so short a time together and said so little although we both wanted to say so much. I was unhappy too because I knew that you were. You could not disguise it from me. All your brave talk about your loving to be alone and Fred's having been so generous in his settlement and your finding it such a relief to have done with men for ever--none of it deceived me in the least. The very fact that we had to meet as furtively as we did in Miss Mercer's rooms speaks volumes! You and I furtive! Doesn't that of itself show that there is something very wrong? Why not have come to Hill Street? Ellis would not have eaten you. You never used to be afraid of anyone. And although you pretended that it was for MY sake. Well, I can deal with Ellis, you know. I haven't lived with him all these years for nothing! It struck me suddenly tonight with a kind of terror that for the first time in all our married life I have, in this one week, concealed two things from him--one my meeting with you, the other, well, I will tell you of the other in a moment.

But now, Rose, listen. Let me tell you here sitting alone in my room, loving you very dearly, something that I could not when we were together. The association with Fred Wycherley has been dreadfully bad for you. You know it better than I. I was shocked at the change and more shocked still at your own consciousness of it. You saw also a change in me. Yes, it is true. I know now this about life--that, far more than I had ever supposed, we affect one another. To live with another is to have to fight for your own integrity morning and night. I suppose if you love someone enough you lose your own integrity and find another much finer. But if you don't . . . You know, Rose, when leaning on that hideous mantelpiece at Miss Mercer's you looked over your shoulder and said: 'Vanessa, men don't mind what they turn their women into', I knew and you knew where you have got to in these last years. Rose darling, oh darling darling Rose, let this life go. Leave Paris. Settle somewhere in England where it isn't too dull. You have some money, you have intelligence enough not to need the kind of life Fred gave you. I suppose you don't hunger for Cumberland all day and every day as I do, but why not try it for a while? Try Eskdale or Coniston or Ullswater for a month or two. They are lovely in the autumn. The Cumbrians are kindly uninquisitive folk. Why not bring that Mlle Mathieu with you whom you like? I don't know. Making plans for others is never any good, but if you were to tell me that I was to have a week on Cat Bells beginning tomorrow, I think I'd just go crazy with joy! But Ellis is frightened of Cumberland. He thinks I'll go wild there, leave him for a gipsy or something. Yes, after all these years of my good proper social behaviour he still fears it. More now than ever. Which brings me to the other thing. I nearly told you on Wednesday. I tell you now because you are the only one I can tell. I won't even say that it's a secret. If Ellis asks me tomorrow morning: 'Have you seen Benjie Herries?' I shall say yes and tell him all (or almost all) about it. But if he doesn't ask me . . .

This is all it is, my grand secret. Since 1887 I have seen Benjie a few times and spoken with him, but never by arrangement. I saw him at the Jubilee Procession. I saw him once at the Theatre. On neither occasion did we exchange a word. Last week on a lovely afternoon I had been visiting Cynthia, I sent the carriage back and walked in the Park. I was wandering down one of the paths, thinking how old I was getting (I am thirty-one, you know), frightened as old married ladies will be at the way that life was passing, when I looked up and there was Benjie with his little boy walking straight into me! Well, what were we to do? We couldn't, all things considered, just pass one another with a stiff bow! I had never seen his little boy. But in any case we could not stop to reason. We have been friends since we were babies. He belongs to all my life, all of it that I love the most passionately. We-- oh well, why explain anything to you? There we were and both of us so happy at meeting that we could only look at one another, without words. It was, as it always is when we are together, as though we had never parted. We sat down on a bench, the little boy beside me. We had then the happiest hour of our lives. We did not mind who saw us. People were passing all the time. If Ellis had come by, I would not have cared. What was there to be ashamed of? Even Ellis must admit that all this time we have done our duty, never tried to see one another, never written. We love one another of course. We have always loved one another. I have no doubt that if we had married as we meant to, we would have been very unhappy, but happiness and unhappiness have nothing to do with love. If Ellis asks me--as he will one day--do you love Benjie, of course I will say yes. I will never lie to him or to anyone. We thought of none of this, not of Ellis nor the family nor anyone at all but ourselves. He told me about his life, that he was lonely, that Tom his boy--who is six now--is going soon to a little day school in Bloomsbury; I told him a little about Hill Street--not everything. But we didn't talk very much as I remember. We were simply so happy to be together again. Then we walked a little way and parted. We made an arrangement to meet in Barney's rooms. He was to be there and I was to come as though by accident. But in the evening when I was home again I knew that it would not do. I wrote him a letter saying that we must not meet again and I know that I was right. Nothing stands still. At every meeting it would be harder to part and what would the end of it be? But, Rose--never forget it--Benjie has been wonderful during these years. With his character and nature to keep away as he has done, to help me by keeping away--no man has ever done anything finer.

Well, there it is. So we go on, the three of us, doing our best. The queer thing is that since that meeting, Ellis, although he can't possibly know of it, has been increasingly uneasy and suspicious. He isn't well, is working too hard and has dreadful headaches. Then there is Miss Fortescue, who hates me, of course, and would do me harm if she could. Poor Ellis--if only he would be content with what we have. All these years we have been friends. When he is happy we are SUCH good friends and life goes so calmly, but lately I have been afraid. He behaved so strangely last year in Wiltshire that everyone noticed it. His love frightens me often and is becoming every week less tranquil. Can I manage all this? Of course I can. I have never been beaten by anything yet, but marriage isn't easy when it's dramatic--or perhaps it is I who hate scenes. HOW I hate them! Their childishness and extravagance . . .

Rose, darling, goodnight. Come away from Paris. Come home. I saw Horace yesterday and his silent wife. He was VERY cheerful and bright and breezy--Your most loving

VANESSA

Part of a letter from Mrs Timothy Bellairs to Miss Lavinia Newmark, Constance Court, near Manchester.

June 25th, 1891

. . . I do hope that your father is better. Of course at his age one must expect a day in bed now and again. Timothy has been complaining of lumbago and I insisted on his staying in bed last week. As you may imagine, no one has been talking of anything but the Baccarat Case. Poor Sir William! I am quite SURE that he did not intend cheating and I really think that some of them showed great vindictiveness. Mrs Lycett Green is quite a friend of May Rockage you know, and Timothy has often met Lord Coventry at his Club. Of course the Prince's appearance in the witness box was THE sensation and everyone thinks that he came out of it very well and that it was most unnecessary of The Times to say what it did! It is all a great pity and very bad for the working classes, who are inclined in any case to be troublesome just now. Timothy says that that man Burns is a danger to the country and ought to be in gaol. I suppose you haven't heard of poor Vanessa's illness. So unlike her to be ill and nobody QUITE knows what the matter has been. They say all sorts of things, but I refuse to listen to gossip, especially of the family variety. . .

Barney Newmark's Journal.

February 18th, 1892

I haven't entered anything in this Journal for weeks, but yesterday afternoon deserves a record. Stephen Bertrand, the novelist, came in most unexpectedly to see me. And then who should enter directly after but dear Horace Ormerod? It was really entertaining to see them together. Horace I knew had come for some purpose. He would never waste his time on me unless he wanted something. Bertrand had met him once or twice before and was pleased to see him again, as well he might be, for no human alive could better satisfy his passion for innocent copy! I could see Bertrand's round, obese little body hurrying home that he

might not waste a moment before putting Horace's self-revelations into his notebook! And how Horace gratified him! He was nervous a little, I suppose, of Bertrand's cold penetrating eye and talked therefore twice as much as ordinary! His healthy rosy face beamed with complacency; his honest, clean, and incipiently stout person vibrated with energy. His friendly eyes shone behind their glasses. With jolly deprecation he told us how good he found life to be, how easy it was to be generous, how simple to see the best in everyone! 'Have you seen Valentine lately?' Bertrand asked rather cruelly. Valentine at the time of the success two or three years back had been a great friend of Horace, who liked to be intimate with one of the most promising poets of the day. THEN one thought that he would be John Lane's proudest boast, that Dowson, Lionel Johnson and the rest were not in the race compared with him! But alas, the bottle and the ladies have been too much for poor Valentine! No one is a greater adept than Horace at dropping a failure gracefully! There were, I swear, tears behind his glasses as he cried:

'Poor Valentine! I wish I could do something for him. He's his own worst enemy, I fear. I did have a word with him some six months ago, but he has become oddly embittered, poor fellow.'

This was joy indeed to Bertrand, who most skilfully led poor Horace on until I could not bear it any longer and had to interfere. When Bertrand was gone Horace said complacently:

'Nice fellow, Bertrand. I must invite him to lunch at the Club. He seems to know everybody and that last novel of his had quite a success, hadn't it?'

I told him that it had.

'What was it called?'

I told him.

'I must remember and read it before he comes to luncheon. You novelists are all so sensitive!'

Funnily enough, on reflection, I felt a strong resemblance between Bertrand and Horace, although I must confess that I like Bertrand the better of the two. Both are equally complacent, Horace because he is a fool and Bertrand because he is pleased with his gifts, with his penetration into human motives, with his cold, clear eye, with his horror of sentiment. But both are sentimentalists, Bertrand perhaps the greater of the two. Bertrand cannot understand that he is disliked (as I fear that he is) and attributes it to the fear of his fellow human beings for the naked truth. Bertrand is the kindest of men and Horace one of the unkindest, yet Bertrand is held to be cruel and Horace, although a fool, good-natured. Bertrand means no unfriendliness when he puts his acquaintances into his books. Indeed he thinks they are lucky fellows to be used for so fine a work of art! 'The artist,' he says, 'thinks only of his art', and forgets that his friends, and still more his friends' friends, think only of their reputations. And this is odd because Bertrand himself thinks a great deal of his own reputation. But I like Bertrand and give him free leave to make any use of me that he pleases!

But now to the point, Horace's point. Violet Bellairs and Horace have become great friends of late. They have many things in common. Violet, it seems, often appeals to Horace for help in her troubles. Here is the latest! Young Timothy (a very decent kid who will be an artist one day) has, it appears, been indulging a secret friendship with Tom, Benjie's boy! Where they first met, or how, I don't know. It has been a complete and most dreadful surprise to Timothy's poor mother! Tim is fourteen and Tom under eight, so you would not suppose that Tim was in great danger! But Tom is already--according to Horace (who by the way has never set eyes on the child)--a young ruffian and a moral danger to any companion. This letter was discovered by Violet Bellairs in the pocket of one of her young son's jackets. Horace left it with me and I copy it here verbatim, spelling and all:

DEAR TOM--Mother is going out tomorrow afternoon and it's a harfholiday. The old cat is in bed with inflewensa so i can meat you the same place--Your loving

TIM

I at once inquired of Horace whether 'the old cat' was Tim's mother, but it seems not. She is apparently Violet's governess, and I at once said that Violet deserved all she got if she wouldn't send Tim to a decent school like any other boy. 'Oh, well,' said Horace, who never defends his friends whole-heartedly unless everyone around him is doing the same, 'Violet thinks Tim's delicate.'

'She only thinks he's delicate because she's tried to make him so,' I burst out, 'with his curls and all. The kid's a fighter and with a will of his own. He'll be a grand artist one day. But what's the matter anyway if Tim does make a friend of young Tom?'

Oh, then Horace broke out, forgetting all his natural caution. Benjie was a danger to everyone. They were all coming to feel it. I, poor fool, was the only one left to stand by him. He was contaminating the family reputation. Ellis had done with him long ago. Alfred hated him. Cynthia wouldn't have him in the house, and now, through his nasty little boy, Benjie was perverting Violet's child. Only I and of course Vanessa . . . and everyone knew that Vanessa was in love with him even though she DIDN'T see him . . .

At that I did gloriously what I haven't done for years, I lost my temper. I lost it so that I took Horace by his fat shoulders and shook him so that his glasses rolled on his fat nose. All my long dislike of Horace was at last expressed. I called him every name I could think of, obscene words that Horace's soul would shudder at; I told him what I thought of him, that he was false, sycophantic, mean, treacherous. (Only one side of Horace after all, for he is not a whit worse than the rest of us, only naïver.) I told him that I was Benjie's friend and that Benjie was worth all the family put together (which Benjie isn't, of course), I told him that he was not fit to breathe in Vanessa's presence and that if I ever heard him utter a word against Vanessa again I'd murder him. I'm sure he thought that I would. I never saw a man look more frightened. So I threw him out of the room, washed my face and hands and laughed a little. But it is truly no laughing matter. The thing grows. It is instinctive. Benjie is some wild half- human animal to them and Vanessa DOES love him. And Ellis' brain begins to turn. Well, God help them all, say I, and myself no less than the rest. But how the troubles in this world come from chatter! Fools like Horace and Violet!--and perhaps ruin to nobler men because there are parrots on the trees. Could we but keep silent for a little while and let men work out their own salvation without comment. Too much ever to hope for!

A letter from Benjamin Herries to Vanessa Herries.

TOLEDO,
Spain,
April 6th, 1893

Vanessa, will you ever see this? For the first time I am breaking my vow and now I shall continue to break it, for my endurance has been tested too sharply. This goes to Barney. I have told him to let you have it. I expect no answer but I am hungering for one-- only one line to tell me that you understand the sort of fate that follows me, a ridiculous fate that I cannot escape and shall no longer try to, by God! This last time was too much! As though it wasn't enough that Cynthia should be there, but Alfred and his wife as well! I had not drunk a drop that evening. You may believe it, Vanessa. I have never lied to you yet. I came into the place as sober as a church. The woman who was with me was a poor thing I used to know, hadn't seen for years, found that afternoon longing for a meal in a decent restaurant, quietly, with a friend. Well, the Café Riche is decent enough, isn't it? We were having our meal as quietly as two churchwardens all sober in our corner. I saw Cynthia come in with a man. Then a little later Alfred and his wife. We had nearly finished when Fanny Church (the girl with me) caught my arm, begged me to pay my bill and go. There was a man at the other side of the room of whom she was terrified. She had been his mistress once, it seemed, and he had treated her damnably--a heavy man with a black beard. Before I could do anything he had seen us and come to our table. He paid no attention to me, but, smiling at Fanny, said he was glad to see her again and where had she been all this time and wouldn't she tell him where she was living?

She was trembling all over, poor girl, looking at me to protect her, and I, very quietly and most politely, asked him to go. He asked me who the devil I was and did I know that I was interfering with his friends, his VERY old friends. Then he put his hand on her arm. What could I do then but knock him down? Wouldn't any man have done the same? He was a big man and he fell heavily and a table went over. Of course there was a row. I waited quietly, told him that I would pay for the damage, left my card and went out with Fanny. That was all. But quite enough of course. Cynthia and Alfred had all the evidence they wanted.

But the SECOND public row, Vanessa! After all these years of discipline. Was there ever anyone born more unlucky? Well, this is the end. I can do no more. I was never made for this hypocrisy nor were YOU made for that life in Hill Street. Tom is at a good school, that's one comfort, and I am finished for ever with London and that farce of civilization and the damned family and their chatter and my trying to be what I'm not. I'm finished for ever with everything but loving you. I shall write sometimes and tell you how I love you, for I am a boy no longer. If you do not answer me it will make no difference. I cannot believe any longer that you are happy, for I know that you are not. I shall always let you hear where I am, one way or another, and one day, if it is all too much for you, come to me. In this black town I am at peace again. The walls go sheer down to the plain. As I look from my window I can see the gipsies moving off along the narrow street, and in the Cathedral it is so cool and dark that you can stay there by the hour and hear no man's chatter. I have a room in an inn; my room is high up. Everything is grand here, the gold in the Cathedral, the wind against the wall, the sound of water falling as it does in Cumberland. One thing already makes me think of you. In a little church at the end of my street there is a picture painted years ago, they say--pictor ignotus--of a Black Centaur pawing the ground, his head up, while over the hill there goes a Procession carrying the Host. I don't know its meaning, bringing Christ to the Heathen or some such thing, but the Centaur is noble. His head is up, he is ready for what may come, and he made me think of you because of that dream you used to tell me of--the horse that strikes the mountain with his hooves, springing from the water. I WILL not be dismayed, Vanessa! That little London is behind me. I have only Tom and you in the world, but YOU know and I know that as long as life lasts we will go on finding the meaning of it, loving one another although we never meet again, not fearing anything, not despising life until we KNOW that it is worthless, which it is not and never will be. I have tried hard all these years to do as you say. YOU know how I have tried--but I will be tied down no longer. They think, Cynthia and Alfred and Ellis and the rest, that life is a cow to be milked--but it is rather the Centaur on to whose back I will leap. One day you

will ride with me. When you see Barney tell him to write to me once a week about Tom. That's a good school, they say, and I liked the man when I saw him. There's someone playing music in the inn room and I'm going down.

You won't despise me I know, or believe anything they say. You are part of me and the law is we must NOT despise ourselves. Give my love to dear Violet and Timothy and Barney's sweet sister Emily. Oh God! but I'm glad I'm done with London!--Your loving, loving

BENJIE

A letter from Vanessa Herries to Barney Newmark in Rome.

March 13th, 1894

MY DEAR BARNEY--The moment I received your telegram I went down to the school. Fortunately Ellis was away on a visit to old Horace for three days. I went down, taking Lettice Marrable with me. You don't know who she is, do you? She is a girl from Cumberland whom I have brought to Hill Street as my secretary--a kind of counter to Miss Fortescue. She is an odd girl, would like to dress like a man, has all this new craze for tennis, breeches, women's freedom-- all a result of the frightful way she has been kept down all her life at home. However, you won't want me to waste your time with HER except that she is the most loyal, faithful, attached creature who ever lived and a great comfort to me. We went by train to Salisbury and drove over to the school. The headmaster, Mr Collins, was exceedingly kind. I took the greatest fancy to him, his wild black beard, his black eyes so lively behind his glasses, and his evident friendship and loyalty to Benjie. He took me to the Infirmary where Tom was. He HAS been very ill, but is much better. He lay there as white as paper, but he has Benjie's smile, hasn't he? I had only ever met him once before--in the Park a long time ago-- but he remembered me and told me about the book the nurse was reading to him--a Talbot Baines Reed--and he was greatly amused by Lettice's hard straw hat and the sort of golfing suit she wears! He likes funny things, Mr Collins says. He asked me had I seen Tim, Violet's boy? He showed me a letter Tim had written him in secret. Awkward for me, wasn't it? He was too white-faced for me to say it was wrong for himself and Tim to write to one another. I said nothing. In fact, dear Barney, ALL my ideas of the difference between right and wrong are fast vanishing! Which brings me to this. You must send me Benjie's address, tell me where he is. I had a letter last year from Toledo. I did not answer it. I have not written a line to him since he left England, although YOU know how I have wanted to! But I can keep it up no longer. I must send him word about Tom, right or wrong. He worships his father of course. He said to me over and over again: 'When is he coming? He hasn't been here for a long time!' For the Easter holiday he is going, as you know, to the Quintires again at Longbridge Deveril. He says it is nice there, they are kind to him, pleasant girls who tell him stories. They write them themselves, he says, which seems to him marvellous. They have a magazine among themselves and oh! Tom said, wouldn't they be lucky if they could get Tim to draw pictures for it! He is a warm-hearted little boy. I wished, coming back in the train, that I had one like that of my own. Lettice slipped some money under his pillow. I saw her do it, and it's good of her because she hasn't a penny! But he's all right, Barney, and I like that master. For myself what shall I tell you? Nothing. You're in Rome and London is far away. We have been to Charley's Aunt and The Second Mrs Tanqueray. We have had a party. Cynthia has had a party. I have had a letter from Will Leathwaite, from Cat Bells. Barney, Cat Bells! Cat Bells! Cat Bells! . . . No more of that. Shall I tell you about clothes? Sleeves are very wide, waists narrower than ever. Skirts are long and trailing. My arm aches with holding mine up. Everybody is wanting to be rich. If you are rich enough you can go anywhere. Alfred gets richer every day. But this is not what you want in Rome. I have read a beautiful book by a man called Yeats, The Celtic Twilight. Have you heard of him? But of course you have. Ibsen is the fashion. Ellis--but I will not weary you with my silly troubles. Am I happy? No, Barney, I am not. Is anyone happy? Possibly no one. Are we all being gay and merry? Very gay and merry indeed. Send me Benjie's address--Your loving

VANESSA

Extracts from Barney Newmark's Journal.

April and May 1895

COPLEY BECK, DUDDON VALLEY.

. . . This letter. What am I to do about it? Ellis has not spoken to me for years, thinks I am altogether on Benjie's side and must know that Benjie is in England. I showed him the letter at once and asked him what I should do. It is a number of days old, forwarded with some bills and papers from Duke Street--and we have been walking from Seascale to Boot, from Boot here-- that's two days. Vanessa is probably in Cumberland by now. She gives a Keswick hotel as an address. But Benjie swears that she can have no idea that he is even in England, much less that he is walking up here with me. But is Ellis likely to believe that? Can I prevent them meeting, do I even want to? I put it to Benjie on his conscience. 'My conscience says that I am to see her,' he answered, and his silly brown face lit up with such happiness at the thought that I would be a thief

robbing a blind man to prevent him. Why should I stop their half-hour? She has the Marrable she- male with her, she tells me, and she is surely enough for anyone as guard! Ellis need never know--WILL never know! Benjie is even now, as I write, standing out on the sward, looking at the lambs, the water jumping the rocks of Harter Fell in a thundercloud and the sun striking like a sword on the fresh green of the larch. He is standing there kicking stones with his foot, giving little leaps. For a small man, he is a packet of vitality, but it is happiness that makes him leap! To see her, out of the blue, without arrangement on his part . . . by divine accident! He will go over to the little hotel at Dungeon Ghyll for a day. Vanessa and the Marrable girl can stay the night there or drive over from Ambleside. Could anything be more discreet? And I'm tired of Ellis. He has been considerably rude to me for years and he is making Vanessa unhappy. That's enough for me . . .

. . . Benjie and I have been talking for hours about the Wilde affair. Benjie sees her tomorrow and can think of nothing else, so I talk to divert him. But poor Oscar! What a muddle of vanity, British hypocrisy, snobbery and false judgement. As to the crime itself I say nothing. It has not, thank God, been one of my temptations, but as I have always yielded to every temptation I HAVE had, if that had been one of them I might have yielded to it. How do I know? Anyway it is more mental than criminal, I suspect. But this I do know: that Oscar is always at his best with very simple childish people. He is himself a child with his vanity, heartlessness, kindness, generosities and self-confidence. I always disliked him when he was showing off, but put him with children or stupid kindly men or warm-hearted impulsive women and he is lovable indeed. Men like Whistler or Charles Brookfield or Carson really terrify him at heart, as children are frightened when, sent for by unwise parents to show off to their elders, they suddenly see the cold eye of a guest speculatively fixed upon them. This remains at least, that never even in hypocritical England has there been such a revolting show of hypocrisy as this--and it will put Art and Letters in England back for twenty years . . .

. . . Well, we are back again, and Benjie is out walking in the rain and dark by himself. I have had a happy afternoon walking for two and a half hours with the Marrable girl. We landed at last, after climbing Wrynose, back at Blea Tarn and sat there patiently. I never saw it more beautiful with the trees coming down black as thunder to the very edge, Wordsworth's 'Solitary's' cottage white in the sun and the sky pale yellow behind the Pikes. I was interested too, for she told me enough about Ellis to fill a volume. Vanessa's patience with him must be a marvellous thing, and even Lettice Marrable who hates him, pities him too. It must be a weird household now with the monstrous Fortescue, Ellis half mad with a vague torturing jealousy that has no facts at all to justify it, and this odd, masculine country girl who worships Vanessa. 'I would DIE for her!' she cries, looking into the green water of the Tarn.

'Now would you?' I ask her cynically. 'Easily said.' Then look at her and feel that she really would!

What will be the end of it?

Of what Vanessa and Benjie said to one another I know nothing. I asked nothing. I was told nothing. Vanessa is better than ever. She is surely the grand lady. To see her walk across a room is a benefit to humanity. But she is a child too. When she saw Benjie there she simply laughed, took his arm and walked off with him. I don't think I ever before realized so sharply that, behind all this present fuss and bother, there is the fact that they have been friends all their lives long. That makes a difference, of course.

I said: 'Miss Marrable, shall we take a stroll?' And so we did. WHAT a plain girl! But I can't help liking her.

Part of a letter from Violet Bellairs to Cynthia Worcester.

September 9th, 1896

... We have been with the Rockages a week now. I can't say that it's a comfortable house--horses and dogs morning and night, and Carey is so far behind with The Times--which he intends to read every night but goes to sleep over--that he is still discussing the Jameson Raid. It has been the hottest summer ever known here and the children feel it. Timothy is being very difficult. Carey agrees with me that this painting nonsense must be knocked out of him! I never knew anyone talk so much about CRICKET as Carey does. It's Ranjitsinhji for every meal, or whether Cambridge or Oxford bowled balls that WEREN'T balls in the University Match! Men are too strange and I've simply given up trying to understand them. Timothy WILL read this nasty new paper the Daily Mail. I think it's the HALFPENNY that appeals to him. He always LOVES to get something for nothing. I hear that Benjie Herries is in Africa and has married a Negress. Thank heaven that friendship between his boy and Timothy was nipped in the bud. Did you ever know anything so horrible as the baby-farming murder? I hear that the Dyer woman actually ...

From Master Tom Herries to Timothy Bellairs.

LONGBRIDGE,
DEVERIL
September, 9th, 1896

DEAR TIM--I will bicycle over on Tuesday and be JUST INSIDE the farm gate by Locker Wood at half past three--Your loving

T.

ELLIS IN PRISON

On that warm evening in July 1897 Timothy Bellairs senior left Ellis soon after dinner and went home. He was going to bed; he had a touch of lumbago and would catch it in time.

'He looks a lot more than his sixty years,' Ellis thought with some satisfaction. And he did. He had grown terribly stout. It would have been better for his health had he stayed in Cumberland.

The house was still as the tomb after Timothy's departure--and why was it never really warm even on these summer evenings? Or was it Ellis who was never warm? After seeing Timothy off, he stood in the hall listening to the silence. Vanessa was at the theatre with the Worcesters, and he had promised her to go to bed early because all day he had had one of his terrible headaches. It was she who had suggested that he should invite old Timothy to have dinner with him, because Timothy was no trouble but would chatter on and on about anything or nothing. So he had done; about the Jubilee, very different from the '87 affair--not many people in the streets and the Queen so feeble, poor old lady, that it had almost killed her; all the same, WHAT a country England was! The Review at Spithead made you feel that: no other country could touch us for a Navy! Still, the country hadn't the style it used to have with cohorts of young men on bicycles and these halfpenny papers. Fine poem, Kipling's 'Recessional'. (He recited some of it as though Ellis had never heard it before!) Made you feel proud to be a Briton AND a Herries! He could remember when he was a boy in Cumberland ... And Salisbury had said that Africa was created to be the plague of the Foreign Office. Some truth there! They had better watch President Krüger. (He spoke with scorn of Krüger as though the Herries family had decided in conclave that Krüger was a rat and ought to be stamped on.) Well, we are getting on, getting on ... Sixty last birthday, and yet it seemed only yesterday when old Madame--Judith Paris--had threatened him with the cane she always carried, for stealing gooseberries out of the Uldale garden. Pity that place was burned down! Fine place. And there was something about Cumberland which ... But Ellis did not like to hear about Cumberland, and changed the conversation. Well, he must be getting home. This damnable lumbago . . . Driving with Violet yesterday in the Park. Did Ellis know that Alfred had bought one of these motor-cars, and only last year, wasn't it, they had changed the law about a man walking in front with a red flag? Pity in his opinion they HAD changed the law. How were you to protect the public with these things charging all over the place? However, they would never do away with the carriage, thank Heaven. Sensible people would always prefer the horse to those stinking, screaming engines that nobody could control. Well, well, it was a changing world and time he went home. Violet wasn't quite the woman she had been. A bit puffy in the chest and they were not quite happy about Timothy, who was at Cambridge now and not settling down as he should. Always wanting to go to Paris and paint! Ridiculous notion for a gentleman's son.

Well, well, goodnight to you, Ellis. Give my love to Vanessa. Still the handsomest woman in London . . .

Why was the house so silent? When would Vanessa be back from the theatre? It was of no use to go to bed. He never slept until she came to say goodnight to him, and she knew that, and was good about returning early. Good? Was Vanessa good? As usual, so soon as he began to think of her his heart thumped in his thin bony breast, and that other man, taller than he, with the handkerchief wrapped round his head, stole out of the wall and stood beside him. WHY was the house so silent? The servants must be moving about somewhere. Miss Fortescue must be in her room. He climbed the stairs to his study, the other figure keeping pace with him. The room was cold. The bust of Cicero watched him with its blind lidless eyes. Could you watch anyone if you were blind? Why, most certainly. His shadow with the handkerchief bound about its head was blind and yet, with ceaseless preoccupation, it watched him.

He began to pace the room as now so many, many times a day he paced it. The distance that he must cover was not of great extent AND how well he knew it! So far to the writing-table where he would pause and arrange, rearrange, arrange again the silver writing things. Then, half turn, four paces to the wall where there hung an excellent engraving of that fine picture, 'Christ Leaving the Praetorium'. Christ, so gentle, so kindly, His hands bound in front of Him, the crowd pressing forward, the stout muscle-swelling guards restraining them. One guard Ellis had come to know well, a broad, cheerful, helmeted fellow looking over his shoulder at Ellis and, Ellis thought, in some friendly way warning him. Warning him of what? Well, and then, half turn again and down the room until you reached the door. This door, which was painted an ugly light brown, had for a handle a round cold white knob. Ellis always touched this knob, grasped it indeed with his warm fingers, for its chill indifferent hardness comforted him; it stilled his beating heart. He thought of it sometimes when he was in the City or the Park or at the Play. That cold white knob, so gloriously indifferent! What did IT care

whether he were torn with jealousy, whether Vanessa loved him? . . . But of course Vanessa did not love him. That was the first fact. He stopped, as a thousand times he had stopped in the middle of that floor, and marshalled the facts that, when seen in an ordinary row, would make him a sensible clear-headed man.

It only needed that they should be properly marshalled, and he saw them like little children (cretins perhaps) with large round white heads like the doorknob, all sitting in a line, their white fleshy hands folded, waiting to be marshalled.

Bald-headed Fact One. Vanessa did not love him, had never loved him, would never love him.

Bald-headed Fact Two. He loved Vanessa with a burning, devouring fire. (It was literally that. In a cavity behind his ribs this fire was burning. He could see the flames leap and fall and leap again.)

Bald-headed Fact Three. He was jealous without reason. Jealousy. Dreadful. Like catching a disease that turned your bones to water. Intermittent. It was most devilish in this--that it left you for five, ten minutes, so that, within that space, you saw quite clearly and wondered how you ever could BE jealous. See! See! No reason. Vanessa has never been faithless to you. She is honest, is fond of you, has been very, very good to you for more than a dozen years. And then, the more savage for its brief absence, the jealousy returns, just distorting everything so that the wallpaper is tinged with green and the cat moves to its platter of milk with private purpose in its eyes.

Bald-headed Fact Four. That he is no longer any good in the City. That his business powers have left him. That young Alfred who has come into the Firm is already taking his place. He must see to this. He is losing money.

Bald-headed Fact Five. His body. That he cannot sleep. That he has headaches. That he is suspicious of everyone. That he is drinking. That his body is hot at one moment and cold the next. That he sleeps with Vanessa when she does not wish it, which is what no gentleman should do. That the Family--Violet and Cynthia and Alfred and Emily and the effeminate Philip--are watching him just as he is watching them and everyone else. Cat and Mouse. Mouse and Cat.

Bald-headed Fact Six. That he thinks much about the past. His father who wanted him to love him, but he could not; his poor old mother; his shyness and awkwardness and longing to be liked; the first moment when, on old Madame's Hundredth Birthday, he had seen Vanessa. Shadows, shadows of the Past. That Cumberland which he hated and feared. Always trying to lure him back to it again so that it might set its fingers about his throat and hold him there while the mocking rain poured down on his upturned face and the stone walls crowded him in and the clouds came lower and lower . . . All the ghosts of the Past. Old Herries, poor Francis who shot himself, John who was murdered, mad Uhland.

Bald-headed Fact Seven. That this beastly, threatening world had as its representative that brown, ragamuffin, dissolute gipsy whom Vanessa loved. Had always loved. They had been children together.

Bald-headed Fact Eight. That when all the Facts were seated quietly in the row he would see how unreal they were, would see that he was Sir Ellis Herries, third Baronet, a wealthy decent citizen of Queen Victoria, much honoured by his friends, thought well of in the City, possessing the handsomest woman in London for his wife, the kindest, the truest, most popular. There was, he would see, no reason at all for agitation. All was well. He had reason to be happy. He must go about and show people that he meant them well, that he was a likeable good man, that the hospitality for which his house was famous was practised because he wished them well, because he liked them and wished them well . . .

Someone was in the room. He started as though a gun had been let off in his ear. Oh! it was Miss Fortescue.

'I beg your pardon, Sir Ellis. I thought you had gone to bed. I came to put these papers ready for you in the morning.'

Miss Fortescue was now, in appearance, completely the sinister remorseless figure of one of Mr Wilkie Collins' savage women. She was hard, black (hair, eyes, eyebrows), efficient, and humourless. Nevertheless, she was no villainess. She was sentimental, read with passion and admiration the novels of Ouida, Miss Braddon, and that comparatively new writer Mr Hall Caine. She was lonely and romantic and had, from the first moment of seeing him, decided that Ellis also was lonely and romantic. She was not in love with him; she had loved, so many times, so many heroes in fiction that no man in everyday life could satisfy her. But she had from the first considered her master as her child, to be protected, guarded, aided. Vanessa's beauty had always irritated her. She thought her kindliness a posture, for she was convinced that she had married Ellis for his money while in secret she had loved another--which was quite in agreement with her reading. She also by temperament distrusted Vanessa's general friendliness, her high spirits, her generosities. This was not a world in which women could let themselves go. There was danger, as her novels told her, on every side. She kept her romanticism and sentiment for her reading and for one or two human beings--Ellis, her ancient mother who lived at Canterbury, and an ailing brother. It had, however, taken many years for her dislike and distrust of Vanessa to grow into hatred-- that true and unalterable hatred that can come to any human being who has never known passion nor independence nor compliments. In daily life she was an excellent practical woman. She gave no joy to the house in Hill Street but she managed it perfectly. Vanessa always admitted that all the burdens were taken from her shoulders. She added that she would willingly sweep the floors and make the beds were Miss Fortescue removed. She had never asked for her removal because, as the years advanced, it became more and more evident that Ellis would be a lost man without her.

She stood now, her black dress sweeping the floor in iron folds, the high puffs of her sleeves made, it seemed, of steel.

Her pale cheeks might, had she been another woman, have betrayed her excitement. The moment for which, during many long, unjust, weary years, she had been waiting, had arrived.

He had paused in his walk and seemed to be listening. Then he realized her.

'I thought you had gone to bed,' he said.

'Yes, Sir Ellis. I am just going. But there is one thing--'

'Yes?' he said, more at ease and comfortable now that the silence was broken and that the tall figure with the handkerchief on its head had slipped into the wall again. He sat down in one of the armchairs, picking up aimlessly a Society paper that was lying there. He opened it, turning over the pages, looking at the illustrations. There was a supplement illustrating the Spithead Review.

She stood near to him, her hands folded.

'You have often told me,' she said, 'that if there was anything that I thought you ought to know, I should tell you.'

'Certainly,' he answered. 'Yes, Miss Fortescue.'

'Something has come to my ears that I think you should know.' This was like a scene in one of Miss Braddon's novels. She recognized every step and movement. She was (a luxury seldom allowed her) herself a figure in one of her beloved stories. At the same time this was real life. The room was real; the persons concerned were real. She was the sort of woman who might poison an acquaintance, with no malice at all, simply that she might justify her own reading. Neverthless there was malice, true revenge for beauty, wealth, power, that she had never enjoyed.

'I learnt today from an unquestioned source that a little more than two years ago Lady Herries spent a whole day, practically alone, with Mr Benjamin Herries in Cumberland. Probably she has already told you of this; if she has not, I think it right that you should know. It is exactly information of this kind that you have said to me that you WISH to know.'

He asked her: 'Where did you learn this, Miss Fortescue?'

'A sister of Miss Marrable's is in London. She told Miss Emily Newmark, who this afternoon told me. Both Lady Herries and Mr Herries, who are of course well known in the district, were seen in a compromising position at a hotel called the Dungeon Ghyll Hotel.'

He was shaking from head to foot, but all that Miss Fortescue saw was that his hand trembled against the paper and his foot tapped the floor.

'It is a long while ago.'

'Yes; but it can be completely substantiated by reliable witnesses if you wish it.'

Incredible that, loving Vanessa as he did, he should not have sprung from his chair and banished Miss Fortescue from the house for ever, but at her first word he had moved from the world where things are as they are, to the world, long familiar to him, where men are seen as shadows and a mist-like smoke reveals only monsters of distrust.

'Where and when do you say this occurred?'

'Just over two years ago. At a hotel called the Dungeon Ghyll Hotel in Cumberland.'

He waited a long time; then he said:

'It is of no importance. Lady Herries, I think, spoke to me about it.' He looked at her. 'You misunderstood me if you thought that I wished to hear such things. I know that you always wish to help me, but I have complete confidence in Lady Herries.'

She cleared her throat, a small, dry, mechanical sound.

'I thought it my duty; I cannot bear to see you deceived. Whatever I do, I do out of loyalty to you. You are the only interest that I have and you have taken me on many occasions into your confidence.'

'Yes, yes,' he said. 'But I do not wish you to speak of Lady Herries to me. That is not your province.'

'I understand,' she answered. 'If I have done wrong, please forgive me. I considered the matter and thought that it was better that you should hear of it from me than from someone--someone less loyal.'

He took the paper and began to read.

'Goodnight,' she said, and went.

He read very seriously with knitted brows the Society paper. He read every word.

The sight of London divested of its boards and bunting was too distressing to my aesthetic soul, so I came down to Medmenham Abbey Hotel for a few days' perfect rest, where the flags are not scarlet and blue but violet and purple, and where they rest not against crimson cotton, but on a tender background of green leaves. It is quite beautiful down here, the only drawback to its complete charm being its distance from the railway station. I have a passion for flying from my fellow-creatures, so that they can flee after me; but when it is a question of a four-mile drive after an hour's journey with a change of trains at Bourne End, their pursuing ardour seems to cool. However, Mr Playfair, whose marriage was such a blow to me last year, and who is living in the neighbourhood to write a book, offers to supply the social deficiencies of my existence, and Florrie's husband has comforted me with the loan of his punt, which looks absolutely beautiful with new blue and white cushions, so I expect I shall get on very well, and by my calm acquiescence in my solitary state excite the suspicions of my unworthy family. I have seen only two dresses worthy of the name since I came here, and they were both my own; one of light drab homespun with a mauve batiste shirt, with a turndown linen collar and a black necktie, which does duty with a white linen skirt, crowned with a pale-green mushroom-shaped hat, trimmed with a mass of shaded green wings. Now I must go out and see if I can get Mr Playfair to agree with me as to the charms of this latter.'

Of all of this he read every word; he read it all twice over, murmuring aloud some of the sentences: 'A tender background of green leaves' . . . 'I have a passion for flying from my fellow-creatures' . . . 'Mr Playfair, whose marriage was such a blow to me' . . . 'Florrie's husband has comforted me' . . . 'The suspicions of my unworthy family' . . . 'A pale-green mushroom-shaped hat' . . . 'A mass of shaded green wings' . . . 'If I can get Mr Playfair to agree with me'.

'Mr Playfair, Mr Playfair, Mr Playfair,' he repeated, looking at the shaded eyes of Cicero. Although he read the whole of this passage with such intensity and although some of the sentences from it were to remain with him for the rest of his life, he was not, at the moment, in the least aware of anything that he had been reading. He put the paper down, got his hat, and went out.

It was after ten o'clock, and the streets were quiet. Berkeley Square was very still, the leaves of the trees rustling faintly in an evening breeze, the clop-clop of a hansom's horse sounding once and again from Piccadilly. At this hour London streets and houses take on themselves a listening, watching air. They resume their own proper purposeful life which has been disguised during the day by the rushing torrent of human beings; with their lighted windows they watch the traffic of the world that moves without sound, their chimneys and doorways re-establish communication one with another. Like cats they can see in the dark.

Ellis walked, his tall body bent, his head with its high black hat a little forward, his hands clasped behind his back. He passed into the light of Piccadilly, then back again into thin-shadowed streets. His companion walked with him. It is the condition of the disease of jealousy that love, self-pity and hatred move forward together. The victim can be cured, in a moment, by a word, only to be the more diseased by another. He moves always in double form, for while he sees clearly his own madness he at the same time embraces it with eager conviction. He cries out for relief from his torture and at the same time refuses to allow himself to be relieved. Every word, every sound is a significant portent, and yet he is aware how insignificant these words can, in the final truth, prove themselves.

He accepts greedily evidence that he knows to be no evidence at all.

With Ellis this was the climax to years of unsatisfied desire--a climax, the night, the trees, the houses, the lighted windows, thundered into his ears, and yet he knew also that the facts were in themselves almost nothing. Two years ago. In all the time since then Vanessa had been kind, honest, attentive. If, at any moment, he had said to her: 'Vanessa, have you seen Benjie Herries?' he knew that she would at once have replied: 'Yes--in Cumberland on such a day.' Thousands upon thousands of times in these twelve years he had longed to ask her this question and yet never once had he dared to do so. Since the day of the '87 Jubilee, when he had spoken to her of the letter, he had scarcely mentioned Herries, but in blind, secret, surreptitious ways he had spied upon her. That had been disgraceful. It had been disgraceful that he had permitted Miss Fortescue to speak to him tonight, but it is a symptom of jealousy that the noblest of men may commit disgraceful acts as a chaste woman will utter obscenities in delirium. And Ellis was not the noblest of men. He had, all his life, been lonely, mistrustful, caught in a web that he could not break.

This remained: Vanessa had spent a day with Herries and had not told him. She had spent one day--why not others? She had deceived him in this. Then she had deceived him often. But she had not deceived him because he had not asked her. She had not lied. She had, he knew, never lied to him--but is it not a lie when a woman sees her lover in secret? Was Herries her lover? It was at that agonizing moment, a moment that had visited him often before but never with such tyranny as now, that he looked about him and saw that the starlit sky, the houses, the deserted street, were coloured a faint green. 'A tender background of green leaves.' 'A pale-green mushroom-shaped hat.' 'A mass of shaded green wings.' This faint green light trembled like the mist of a cloud of greenflies, touching the steps before dark walls, the white posters of the evening papers outside the closed and barred newspaper shop, the bent figure of an old woman in a battered straw hat picking something from the gutter, the light of a gas lamp.

A hansom clattered past. A bell from some church sounded the hour. Trembling with a terrible chilling heat, Ellis turned homewards.

He was half undressed when he heard Vanessa come in. As though he were a man with a thousand ears he had been listening ever since he entered his room for those sounds. His door was just ajar. He knew what he would hear. The closing of the hall door, the soft voice of the butler, Vanessa's softer one, a little pause. Then 'Goodnight', the butler's 'Goodnight, my lady', then the sweep of her long dress as she climbed the stairs. Then the opening of her own door, its shutting.

After that he undressed feverishly, but was extremely careful to fold his clothes, to place his studs in their silver box, to brush his scanty hair. Over his nightdress he drew on his dark grey dressing-gown, went into the passage, listened, then knocked.

She knew of course his knock. He heard her say: 'Come in.'

She was sitting in front of her mirror, a white wrap over her shoulders, brushing her long dark hair which fell to her waist. As he came in she looked at him over her shoulder, smiling.

'I thought you would be asleep. I came in as quietly as I could.'

He stood by the door staring at her; seeing her in the lamplight with that dark flood of hair, the white wrap over the loose white robe, her smile so friendly and simple, he felt so furious a storm of jealousy sweep over him that he lowered his eyes as though, in actuality, he had been overwhelmed by a tremendous arching wave of blinding deafening water.

At last he moved across the room and sat in a chair near the bed. She continued to brush her hair, talking happily. 'We went to The Prisoner of Zenda after all. Peile had seen it before, but as he never remembers anything THAT didn't matter. It was new to the rest of us. George Alexander and Fay Davis, you know. Miss Davis is handsome, but WHAT a stick of a part, and Alexander never can forget the clothes he's wearing. The house was full, but of course it was only revived last week. I saw Johnny Beaminster and, oh yes, Alice Parlington. You remember--you danced with her at the Devonshire Ball. She was Isabella of Spain or something. Well, she asked about you and wants us to go to dinner one night . . .'

She moved into her dressing-room. For a long while he sat there, staring in front of him. She returned and got into bed, giving him a light kiss on his forehead as she passed him.

'What sort of an evening have you had? Was old Timothy a terrible bore? I thought of you when Alexander was an hour or more kissing Flavia's hand. I was most dreadfully bored, but comforted myself with thinking that you were equally bored at home. Cynthia looked so pretty, but I am sure she is harming herself with her tiny waist. It is smaller every time I see her. And the smaller her waist grows the more intellectual she becomes. Ibsen is her only wear. Elizabeth Robins and Janet Achurch her only actresses. She was so horrified when she found that I hadn't read Esther Waters that I thought she'd fall out of the box, and yet she puts up with Peile Worcester who can hardly spell his own name. She loves him, I really believe . . .' She stopped. She was aware that he had not spoken since he had entered the room. She sat up, resting her head on her hand.

'What is it, Ellis? Aren't you well? Is your head still bad?'

She put out her hand and touched his forehead.

'Why, you're in a fever. Let me--'

'No,' he said. 'Don't do anything. I want to speak to you.'

She saw then that he was trembling from head to foot and, as always when someone near her was suffering, she forgot everything save that distress. She got out of bed, put on the white wrap and went towards the door.

'You're ill. You're shaking all over. Wait, while I--'

He looked across the room at her.

'No, please. There's something I must say. Go back to bed.'

She did so. She knew that something had occurred while she was at the theatre. She had now for so many years been prepared for some crisis that never arrived. How many times there had been a preface like this: Ellis in misery, dumb with some hidden trouble, beginning to speak, turning away like a child afraid, and because he was always a child to her she always comforted him, not asking what his trouble was, but consoling him. Men seemed to her completely inarticulate in any real distress--her father, Benjie, Ellis, they were all the same. They could not speak when they had something important to say, and when there was nothing they chattered interminably. She had been tired, wearied with her day, the gossip, the heat of the theatre, but now she forgot herself, wondering only, as she had wondered so often before, what she could do to soothe him.

Then he said, not looking at her:

'I heard this evening that two years ago you were alone in Cumberland with Herries--alone for a whole day, seen in a compromising position.'

So THAT was it! Two years ago. Ridiculous. A compromising position. That angered her. She drew back into the bed like a child who has been hurt.

'It is quite true that I was with Benjie in Cumberland one afternoon two years ago. The "compromising position" part of it is insulting. You remember, I went to Cumberland for a week. I had no idea that Benjie was there, of course. When we found that we were so near, we met. If you had asked me I would have told you.'

'Then you admit it?'

'Admit what?'

'That you met him secretly, spent the day with him alone, and told me nothing afterwards.'

'I met him certainly. We were alone for part of the time. I would have told you had you asked me.'

She looked at him, forgetting very quickly her own anger because the fuss was about so little, was so unimportant. Once sure of that, her earlier sensation swept back--that here was something small, childlike, suffering, and that she must comfort him. She moved nearer to

him. She put out her hand and let it rest very gently on his shoulder.

'Ellis dear, there is no mystery, no adultery, nothing sensational. Miss Fortescue, I suppose, told you--tonight while I was at the theatre. The "compromising position" could be only hers. Now listen, Ellis. I have seen Benjie perhaps half a dozen times since our marriage--and we have been married over twelve years--so that's not bad, is it? I have spoken to him twice alone, once in the Park, once in Cumberland. I gave no promise not to speak to him. If you had ever asked me I would have told you. You must remember that Benjie and I have been friends all our lives. I know that some of the family don't like him, that you don't like him, but when you have known someone always--you see them differently.'

She had broken off abruptly, the tone of her voice had changed, her hand had withdrawn from his shoulder, because suddenly in the middle of a sentence she saw that he, not hearing what she was saying to him, was staring at her and that his stare was crazy. Two people living together with some ill-adjustment often find that they go with slow measured steps for a long period and that then quite suddenly, and for no apparent cause, as though someone caught them in the small of their backs and jerked them forward, they are hurled into a precipitous and often catastrophic descent. It is only afterwards, on looking back, that they can see that this sudden jerk forward had the beginning of its impetus in those very first slow steps.

It was so with Vanessa now. She looked at Ellis and saw a grotesque. Under the shade of the lamp a man with a high domed forehead and a lean peaked nose was sitting. This man wore a grey dressing-gown and a nightdress that was open at the neck so that two protruding bones, pink in the lamplight, gave him a hen's neck. His bare ankles, too, were pink and sharply boned. This thin bony man with his long body looped together in the chair had two eyes that looked at Vanessa but did not see her, looked beyond her at the room but did not see that either, saw something that frightened and angered them, something that no one else saw. This separate and apart vision--which is what the sane man means when he calls his brother insane--gave the figure in the chair an aspect of loneliness, isolation. Put this man in a crowded theatre and he would be quite alone, put him in a solitary cell and he would have company.

Vanessa saw life very simply. She had some of the good sense and quiet of her father, some of the good sense and love of action of her grandmother. She was entirely sane about all things. That she was also a poet, because of the country blood in her veins, affected not at all her relations with her fellows. She had lived with Ellis for more than twelve years and had needed all her patience, sanity, humour, and common sense. Any woman, living with a man who loves her, whom she herself does not love, needs all these things, day by day and week by week. But she had learnt that you can care for a man without loving him and obtain satisfaction of your need--so she cared for Ellis. But behind her care there had grown and grown the fear that one day the situation would be too difficult for her. As she always herself said, she hated scenes, melodramas, floods of tears, self-pityings, shrieks, and beatings of the breast. She did not know how to behave in such a world. Her father and mother had been quiet people and she was a quiet person, although as with her grandmother there was a wild passionate life at the core of her nature. She had also a strong sense of the ridiculous both in herself and in others.

But now, looking at Ellis, she had no sense of the ridiculous. There was something here both real and terrible. Instinctively, as she always did in a crisis, she thought of her father. 'Help me through this,' she said, as she had done when she was a little child on Cat Bells.

She suspected that Ellis was going to scream.

'He will rouse the whole house.' She even remembered that Miss Fortescue would not yet be asleep and that her room was not far away. However, Ellis did not scream. He said very quietly:

'You are a liar. Herries has been your lover for years.'

(Even as he said it he knew that it was not true. A very quiet little animal squatting inside his head observed rather wearily: 'THAT you know is not true.')

'Ellis, let us talk sense.' Vanessa held her hands tightly together under the bedclothes. 'You are fifty-four. I shall soon be thirty-eight. We have lived together for years and you know that I have never lied to you, not in the smallest, most unimportant matter. I have never been Benjie's lover nor anyone's lover. You must trust me as I trust you, otherwise we must separate.'

He leant forward towards her: her impulse was to shrink back, but courage in this dangerous moment for which, she felt now, she had for years been preparing, was of more importance than any other quality. So she sat up, put out her hand and picked up the white silk wrap from the chair on the other side of the bed; then with it warmly around her, her hair falling darkly about her, leaning forward, her hands clasped on her raised knees, she said, very quietly:

'Ellis, listen. We are too old not to be sensible about this. We matter too much to one another to have scenes. Besides, I hate scenes. You mustn't be unhappy and there is no reason--'

'No reason!' he broke in. His thin hand shot forward and caught her upraised knee. 'No reason when you have made me unhappy for years--not loving me, pretending, taking people in, but not me. Do you hear?--never me! Do you hear? Do you hear? I've had enough of it. You drive me mad with your unkindness! You--your lover . . .'

All drama verges on the ridiculous, and especially English drama. Vanessa had once, years ago, in the Park, felt Ellis' physical contact although he had not touched her. When her protective affection was aroused Ellis' body was there for her to comfort. But when he was angry or sexually passionate she hated his touch. One hand had closed about her knee, the other was on her breast; his face was close to hers, his body stretching up to the bed. If this scene was ludicrous she was too angry to notice it.

'You are hurting me,' she said.

He threw himself on the bed, his body convulsed, trembling, thrusting against hers. He tore open her nightdress; with his knees on the bed, his arms around her body, his hands bruising her, he pushed her down into the bed. Then his hands moved to her neck: panting, murmuring unintelligible words, he twisted her head round into the pillow. His hysteria gave him great strength; she began to wonder, in a quite detached way, whether he would kill her, and she had no power at all to resist. She tried to conserve her strength, for his hands now were so tightly about her neck that she could not breathe except in little gasps of pain. A black cloud, scattered with spots of intense light, pushed against her vision.

She thought: 'This is absurd', and anger, fear of death, pain were all mingled in the dark wavering cloud.

The pressure of his hands relaxed. His body, without moving, lay heavily on hers. He was crying. She listened, as it seemed for a long time, to his sobs. At last, very wearily, she turned. He slowly raised himself, slipped off the bed. She lifted herself painfully and saw that he was kneeling on the floor, his head bowed, hidden in the bed, his body shaken with sobs.

For a long while there was no other sound in the room. At last she rose, went into the dressing-room, bathed her face and hands, stood there for a while wondering what she would do. When she came back he was still there, his body bent low, his face buried in his hands, crying.

She touched his shoulder.

'You will catch cold, Ellis.' She took her white cloak and wrapped it round him, but as her hands came into contact with his body he trembled. She went back into bed and waited for him to recover.

THE GREAT TIMOTHY SCANDAL

'Yes, that is the cruel moment, when you really begin to feel old,' said Barney, nodding his head and settling his fat body more comfortably in his chair. 'I am sixty-eight, you know, Vanessa, in this year of grace eighteen hundred and ninety-eight--close on seventy--

and I had no sense of age at all until last week when Nevinson took me to a Fabian Reception. There we were all walking about, already in the New Century, and every macaroon was a hard little Fact and every cup of tea an admonition not to be silly. Well, I like to be silly. In the coming century no one is going to be silly. It will be motor-cars, telephones, and all our food will be in little pills. If it weren't for things like the Klondike madness and the German Emperor and Sarah Grand I should know that the Fairy-Tale World was gone for ever. I've lived all my life in it, you know--charming world where everything had a meaning, when we believed in Faith, Hope, and Charity, assisted by Watts, when we really meant to be good even if we were not, when our children said "Sir" and "Ma'am", when we thought the Albert Memorial lovely, and were certain that it was our duty to convert every unhappy Black Man to trousers and the worship of our Sovereign. Why, in the coming century I wouldn't wonder if we don't believe in the Empire any more! I wouldn't be surprised if even adultery becomes a scientific fact rather than a moral crime. But I liked the old world. It was MY world. My silly novels amused it (or a small fragment of it), I could lead my own life without interference so long as I didn't shock anyone in public, I could eat and drink as much as I liked. I remember, Vanessa, when I was a lad, going to the fight between Sayers and Heenan, the last great fight in England it was. It was just an adventure then, but I can see now that it was the end of an epoch. Epochs are always ending, I suppose; it doesn't matter unless you're seventy. Well, I've had a good life. I can grow as fat as I like. Nobody cares any more.'

'I care,' said Vanessa, smiling across the table at him. They were having tea alone together in Hill Street.

'While I'm getting fatter you're getting thinner.'

'Am I? I'm thirty-nine this year, you know.'

He looked at her intently. He loved her very dearly, more now than any other woman in the world.

'You haven't been very merry lately, Vanessa,' he said. 'I haven't heard you laugh as you used to do for a long time.'

'I'm not very merry,' she answered, getting up and walking about the room, her long black-and-white dress trailing behind her. She turned round, came over to him and stood beside him.

'Barney--what are the family saying?'

'The family?'

'Yes--Violet, Cynthia, Alfred--all of them.'

'Saying about what?'

'Us--Ellis. This house.'

He didn't answer at first, then he said slowly:

'Nothing much.'

'Oh! They are! In the last few months they've been closing in-- nearer and nearer. For one thing Miss Fortescue's going must have been enough to start them--' She drew a chair close to him and sat down.'

'I can't keep quiet any longer. Something must be done. I've never been beaten by anything before, and I said that THIS shouldn't beat me either. Two other bad things have happened to me in my life--once when my father died, once when Benjie and I--oh, well, that's past history. Each time I held my head up and said: "I can manage this"--and manage it I did. My married life hasn't been easy, you know, but there have always been all kinds of little things to help it along. Life, I'm sure, isn't MEANT to be too tragic and I've had great consolation in feeling that I was dressing up--PRETENDING to be a grand hostess, you know. Grandmother had a devil of pride inside her and so have I had, and all the time that I was longing to run away to Cumberland and be my real self I have felt as though she and father knew about this game that I was playing and wanted me to do my best at it. Then there's been Ellis. I did him a terrible injustice in marrying him when I didn't love him. The only thing I could do in return was to be kind to him, protect him, be his friend . . . I'm not boasting, Barney, but I truly have played the game all these years. Now I can play it no longer. I'm beaten.'

Barney took her hand in his.

'What's happened, my dear?'

'Last July Ellis and I had a dreadful scene. Miss Fortescue told him one evening that I had been alone with Benjie two years before in Cumberland. You know--that day at Dungeon Ghyll. In itself that was nothing, but Ellis had been wretchedly jealous long before, as you know. This was the climax. I was in bed and he almost strangled me--a ridiculous scene, and it ended in his crying all night, imploring me to forgive him, going to sleep at last in my arms. For weeks after that he was abject. He dismissed Miss Fortescue, as you know, and for a time I thought that I could manage him. That was July. This is February. I know now that I'll never be able to manage him again.'

She paused. Barney felt her hand tremble in his.

'What is it?' he asked.

'Ellis is mad. He has been mad for months. Oh, only at times. We have parties here, he goes to the City. So far as I know no one except Lettice Marrable suspects anything. The servants may. I don't know . . . You can't think, Barney, how pitiful it is! If I could help him neither you nor anyone else should know anything, but I CAN'T help him. It is I who aggravate him. I would give him anything, anything he asks if it would help him. Nothing can help him. I don't know whether to go or stay. But one day it will be too much for me and I shall go. The worst of it is that now, although I am so sorry for him, I don't feel even kind. If I had loved him I would stay with him for ever, but the dreadful thing now . . . the dreadful thing . . .' She turned her head. 'I hate him. I fear him. I have never been afraid of anyone or anything, but now the very sound of his step . . .'

She began to cry. Barney had never seen her cry before.

'I am middle-aged. I have loved one man all my life with my whole heart and he has loved me. Why should I lose everything? What have I done?'

Very quickly she recovered herself. She walked to the window and he waited. When she returned she was quite calm again.

'Listen, Barney. You are to say nothing of this to anybody. Only . . . if it gets too difficult . . . I shall ask you to help me. It may be better soon. He has been quite normal for the last month. Very quiet. Very submissive. Poor Ellis! Listen! He's coming . . . I know his step now, even when I don't hear it.'

Ellis came in. But he was not alone: on either side of him walked a lady, and Barney remembered afterwards with amusement that the first sight that he had of his two relations, Miss Vera Trent and Miss Winifred Trent, was this entry, guarding and protecting Ellis.

For they were, it seemed, distant cousins. Ellis, quietly and with much courtesy, explained it. 'Henry Cards--he had a wife back in the eighteenth century, Lucilla. I can remember, dear Miss Trent, my father speaking of her. My father was born in 1770--it seems odd, doesn't it?--and Lucilla died about 1780, I think. She painted very charming watercolours. I shouldn't wonder if there are not one or two still about somewhere. Henry and Lucilla had two sons. One of them, Prosper, was Jennifer's father, my dear Vanessa. Well, Prosper married a Miss Amelia Trent, and our two cousins descend from her younger brother. Now what does that make you to us, Miss Trent? About second cousin twice removed, does it not? Still, there's always a strong family feeling, a very strong family feeling . . .'

Everyone laughed. The butler brought in fresh tea. Who were these two ladies? Vanessa had the sense that they had been in this house all their lives and had known Ellis for ever. However, it appeared not. They had never visited Hill Street. Their carriage had driven up just as Ellis had arrived from the City. They had met on the doorstep. Oh! they must apologize, but the fact is that they had lived all their lives in Bournemouth. Such a charming place, and a hundred years ago there was nothing at all but the sea waves, the sand, a tree or two! Yes, they loved Bournemouth. Vanessa interrupted. That was where Jennifer's father and mother had lived, was it not? Yes, indeed, Doctor Trent of those days had been a close friend of Mr and Mrs Cards. Mrs Cards had been SO proud of Bournemouth, so proud that she used to speak and write of the town as a fashionable watering-place when it was really only a house or two. Doctor Trent and Mr and Mrs Cards had been among its earliest inhabitants. Oh yes, they remembered all about the beautiful Jennifer! At one time it was thought that she would become the Duchess of Wrexe. She was actually engaged to the Duke for a brief while, they believed . . .

They chattered on, most happily. They were both tall and elderly women and remarkably alike. They were slim and had soft grey hair under their large black hats. They wore black feather boas, black silk dresses very long in the skirts; each lady had a big bunch of imitation Parma violets pinned to her breast and wore a very thin gold chain. Their faces resembled those of placid, extremely kindly sheep, but behind the mildness, Vanessa decided, there was a strong and possibly relentless determination. It certainly appeared that they had made complete appropriation of Ellis. They sat one on either side of him and, although they smiled at Vanessa and listened with deference to Barney, it was Ellis whom they admired. Their voices were soft with that comforting murmur that belongs to a distant mowing machine on a summer day. They took off their gloves; each wore two or three rings, thickly studded with diamonds, on the fingers. They were alike in almost every particular; the only difference perhaps being that Miss Vera was a little the more severe and determined of the two, Miss Winifred the softer and more melting. They were greatly interested in all the Herries relations--Alfred and his wife, Horace and HIS wife, Emily, Phyllis' son Philip, old Horace in Manchester, the Rockages in Wiltshire and their girls Maud and Helen, Cynthia and Peile Worcester. They seemed to have the fullest information about all of them. Vanessa noticed that they made no mention of Benjie or Rose and that they shook their heads over Timothy at Cambridge. Yesterday, it appeared, they had paid a call on Violet. With all their comments and questions they were kind and hushed. They behaved, Vanessa thought, as though they were nurses in a sickroom.

Barney watched all this in amazement. He found that he could not tear himself away. How dramatic a transition! A moment before Vanessa had been telling him the most awful things, speaking, he could not doubt, with the most absolute sincerity, and now here they were all drinking tea together, these two old maids like two cows in a field, and Ellis, calm, benign, dignified, smiling and courteous! Had Vanessa been imagining her terrors? No, he knew her too well. She was the least hysterical of women. He would not wonder but that the tears that she had just now shed were the first since her childhood. As he saw her now so quiet and so lovely in her black-and-white dress, laughing, looking after the two old women as though they were her first care in the world, smiling up at Ellis, her broad unruffled brow, her large dark eyes that had never lost the frankness, the eagerness of her earlier simplicity, her dignity as hostess, her natural friendliness as one human being with another, he thought: 'Well, I'm damned if she can't manage this. It's not so bad as she said.'

When he got up to go, Ellis most courteously went all the way downstairs with him, bending his long neck to hear what Barney had to say, rather as an Ambassador listens with the utmost attention to a diplomatic visitor.

'Hullo! That's a new clock you've got!' Barney said, at the turn of the stairs. It was a long thin clock of gilded red Chinese lacquer.

'Yes,' said Ellis. 'Vanessa saw it somewhere and liked it.'

'Of course he hates me,' Barney thought. 'We both know that. Still, he's behaving very well.'

Finally, in the street, he shook his head. Ellis was not mad. He, Barney, knew a madman when he saw one!

When the ladies were gone Vanessa praised them. Ellis walked about the room and praised them too. How quiet, intelligent, and well-behaved! He had feared that the women in England were lost, with their clubs, their passion for 'this Bridge', their bicycle riding, their indecent novels, their conceit. He understood that there were in London alone thirty clubs for ladies. What did ladies want with clubs? What--

He stopped, went to a table and fidgeted with a small silver box, a paper knife, a book. He picked up the book, put it down.

'Vanessa, I did not care for that hat you were wearing yesterday.'

The room was rather dimly lit, the fire low. Her nerves had been shaken by her little talk with Barney, and as she got up and went across to him she felt an impulse, so strong that she wondered whether she would be able to conquer it, to tell him that she could endure this no longer, that she must leave the house, London, all the life that had, so ridiculously, been built up around her . . . leave the house, at once, without a moment's delay . . .

'What hat?' she asked.

'The one you were wearing yesterday. The one with the--green birds' wings.' He seemed to have difficulty in speaking the last words.

She was standing close to him. Her agitation fell from her because his eyes were so weary that she was suddenly filled with pity.

'Oh, Ellis, you're tired. Go and lie down until dinner. Or stay here. I'll read to you.'

'No. But you understand, Vanessa? Please don't wear that hat again.'

She laughed and was frightened. His hand was shaking against the dark stuff of his trousers.

'It's quite new. Yesterday was the first time I had worn it. I thought you would like it.'

'Then you must change its colour. You know that . . . green . . . I don't like it as a colour.'

She tried to speak easily. 'Certainly. You shall never see the hat again.'

He put his hand out and touched her forehead. All her strength was needed not to move away, so she came closer to him.

'How cool your forehead is! Mine is always burning.'

She put her hand through his arm and drew him to the sofa. She helped him to lie down, arranging the cushions, but he said, as though he were half asleep: 'No, sit here--close to me.'

She sat down and he laid his head on her lap. He closed his eyes. The creeping whisper of the fire, the steady determined tick of the large gold clock on the mantelpiece filled the long, shadowy room. She sat there without moving. Her childhood--the friendly figures of her father, Will Leathwaite, Elizabeth, Aunt Jane, her grandmother--the places, the Cat Bells garden with the little sturdy wood, the stream, the line of the hill above the cottage, lovely days at Uldale, the seashore at Seascale, the purple shadows of Skiddaw, sunlit brilliant clouds of snow on Blencathra, the main street of Keswick, someone riding by on a horse, the scarlet coach from Kendal, the friendliness, the small gardens of daffodils and primulas, the grey steeple of St John's above the green fields running to the Lake's edge, the hillsides flaming with bracken, the Herdwicks moving their thick sturdy bodies slowly in front of the shepherd . . . her father, her father waving his hand to her from his writing-table as she passed along the garden path, her father with his soft lazy eyes, his loving ironical glance, his hand resting on Will's shoulder . . .

Tears stole down her cheek. Without moving, yet she felt that she was hastening, against her will, down a dark path away from everything in life that was loving and good into a house dark and chill, with doors that would be locked behind her. How dearly she loved life! How hard she had tried to do what was right, and now she was nearly forty, frightened like a small child, and lonely! . . . She had never known that it was possible for anyone to be as lonely as she was. What was she to do?

And Benjie? She had, in these hard minutes, kept him away from her, but now, heart and mind opened, too weak any longer to resist, she threw out her arms, he came running, running to her. She clasped him to her, felt his face pressed close to hers, his heart beat against her breast.

The Chinese clock on the stairs struck. The gold clock followed it. For an hour she had not moved and Ellis, pallid as a dead man, lay with his head on her lap.

Then the Great Timothy Scandal sprang upon her. It was an excellent moment for a family excitement. There was but little in May 1898 for anyone to discuss. A small coal strike, a war between the United States and Spain, the death of poor old Mr Gladstone, the Dreyfus case, the low spirits of the Liberal Party. In none of these things did the Herries take a very extravagant interest. Cynthia redecorated her little house and gave an evening party for the Ibsen enthusiasts, Alfred introduced everywhere an astonishingly uncouth South African who was said to be worth millions, Emily discovered a Prophet from Shoreditch. The Season began and huge evening receptions rolled from house to house. The West End was populated with coachmen, footmen and men with grave diplomatic countenances hired for the evening. Every kind of carriage and every kind of horse glittered and shone. The window boxes blazed with geraniums. The Opera sparkled with diamonds. There was so much money that everyone despised it and would do anything, invite anybody, go anywhere, to obtain more. Morals were as loose as usual and manners beginning to crumble. Woman was no longer subservient to Man, and the Empire was at its apogee.

The Herries took all this for granted as every other English family was taking it for granted. The Herries concluded that everything would last for ever just as it was. Emily's Prophet said uncomfortable things, and Cynthia, Violet, Mrs Alfred, went to a meeting to hear him. They found him very sweet with his deep black eyes and flowing black hair. Melba sang at the Opera. Also at one of Vanessa's parties. A man called Conrad published a book called Tales of Unrest, but no member of the Herries family read it. Several ladies and gentlemen rode in electric cabs. Violet wore an evening dress with a high collar encircled with four rows of pearls. Lettice Marrable was seen bicycling in a pair of knickerbockers. For some while, however, inside this dazzling world the Herries circle had been moving quietly. There had been no family sensation. Something strange was happening in Hill Street although Vanessa appeared as usual and Ellis was stiff, courtly, and boring as usual. Rose, it was said, was drinking herself to death in Paris. Nothing had been heard of Benjie. One topic of interest was the career of the two Miss Trents, who went everywhere and were constantly at Hill Street. That, however, was not a scandal--far from it. Two quieter, gentler ladies could not be found anywhere.

The Great Timothy Scandal, then, burst brilliantly and, small though its cause, it brought in its sequence changes to many people. It struck Vanessa on a sunny May day when, coming back after a drive in the Park with Cynthia, when they had both been very gay and talked much nonsense, Lettice Marrable threw the news at the quiet tea-table. Cynthia always regarded Miss Marrable as a kind of aboriginal savage: her little hard hats, her manlike tunic, short skirt, her brusque masculine tone and quite extraordinary masculine attitudes, her public smoking of cigarettes, her abilities at tennis and golf, her passionate desire that women should sit in Parliament, all these things filled Cynthia with a wondering amaze. She was never weary of looking at her, although she did not care to be seen with her in public.

Lettice Marrable now came in and said:

'Timothy Bellairs has run away to Paris with Tom, Benjie Herries' boy. Violet has just heard. Timothy had a letter written from Paris. Violet is in a terrible way and says that Tom has perverted Timothy or some word like that. Timothy senior has left for Paris. If he sees Benjie he is going to shoot him. They are all talking at Violet's now. I've just come from there. Horace and

the Miss Trents and Carey Rockage . . . Benjie Herries is to be horsewhipped whenever he's found. Oh, you never saw anything so funny in your life as Horace threatening to whip Benjie--WHEN he finds him! And the real joke is that Tom is only fourteen. He must have run away from school up to town and met Tim here. Anyway they are both safe in Paris.'

Cynthia said: 'I wish I was.'

Vanessa said: 'But it is ridiculous of Violet to blame anyone but herself. Tim has wanted to be a painter since he was a baby. It is nothing to do with Benjie at all.'

After that with every hour the affair grew. It seemed that Benjie WAS in Paris and that the two boys stayed with him. Then came news of a meeting between old Timothy and Benjie. Old Timothy gave it him, it was generally understood, 'hot and strong'. What really happened no one knew because no third person was present: it was difficult, however, for the Herries to believe that Timothy gave anyone anything 'hot and strong'. He was sixty-one, suffered from his heart, was as fat as a barrel. Moreover he was amiably minded.

It appeared that Benjie's attitude was that, as regarded his own boy, if he wanted to leave school and see the world, he should do so. Benjie was the same at his age. As for Timothy, he was twenty-one and ought to know his own mind. As a matter of fact he always HAD known his own mind, and it was only the stupid conventionality of his parents that held him back. It was said that at this point old Timothy called Benjie 'a damned blackguard' and that Benjie did not resent the insult as any gentleman would have done, but offered Timothy a cigarette. It was further said that the interview between Timothy and his son was extremely painful. Young Timothy declared that now that he was in Paris he was going to stay there and that Tom Herries had had nothing whatever to do with it. They had been friends all their lives, he and Tom; Tom hated his school and wanted to be with his father. By this time it was generally admitted that Benjie was the Devil. He had always been the Devil. It was time the family were rid of him.

Would Benjie come to London and face his accusers? It was understood that, with a shrug of his shoulders, he said that of course he would come to London, although he had no idea what he was to be accused of.

He came to London.

A meeting, as famous in its own small way as Christabel's Ball or Walter's historic visit to the Christmas party at Uldale, took place on the second of June at the Rockland Club between these gentlemen: Carey Rockage, Timothy Bellairs, Alfred Herries, Horace Ormerod, Barney Newmark and Benjamin Herries, Esquire.

The best evidence of what actually occurred is to be found in Barney's Journal (the Journals are all in the family archives at Centor Park, bound in faded red leather, behind glass, in the library. Judith Paris' book and the earlier eighteenth-century papers are in the same bookshelf, equally protected and equally unread).

DUKE STREET, W. June 2nd, 1898

I will try to put down as briefly as possible what occurred today at Rockland's, a matter purely of family interest but important perhaps one day to young Tim and to Tom.

I met Benjie at the Criterion for lunch. I hadn't seen him for a considerable time, but there he was, just the same as ever, brown with health, cocky as a robin--very like a robin. He has just that bright, roguish, adventurous, don't-care-a-damn kind of eye and, although he's stocky, his lack of height (always a sore point with him) gives him a birdlike appearance. He looked, I'll confess, a bit odd because he wasn't wearing a hat; he had a soft nondescript collar with his usual dark red tie in its gold ring, and his clothes were a sort of wine-coloured tweed. He is always scrupulously clean, though. Benjie's careless but at the same time spruce, and his brown cheeks, bright eyes, stiff close-cropped wiry hair, hands that look as hard as iron, taut, springy body--all these, with the very kindly wrinkles about his eyes and his extremely engaging smile, prejudice you in his favour if you're an ordinary man on two legs and not a hypocrite like Horace or a prig like Ellis.

Anyway there he was, saying 'Hullo, Barney!' just as though we'd met yesterday, and walking into the big room at the Criterion as though he owned the place and at the same time found it very absurd.

As usual he ate very little. He didn't talk much either. He couldn't understand what they wanted to see him about. 'I'm not a boy, you know. I'm forty-three. I haven't harmed the family so far as I can see. They seem to think that I've lured Tim to Paris and that I may ruin his body and soul--using young Tom as a decoy. Damnable nonsense! Tim's a fine painter. I don't know much about it, but he's started away at Lucien's, which is, I believe, one of the best of those places, and old Lucien himself thinks highly of him. Tim's crazy about these men I don't understand--Gauguin, Van Gogh, Cezanne--but I'm ready to tell him he's right. How do you and I know? We may have taste but we don't care enough really to know. You can only know about Art if you happen both to love it and have a trained taste. Anyway, there he is and Tom's learning languages. He's got a passion for them and his great idea is to train for a War Correspondent. "What'll you do if there's never a war again?" I asked him. "Oh, there'll always be one somewhere," he said, and I expect he's right. He can put things down on paper pretty smartly for his age. Well, there they are, a decent pair of kids. What's the trouble? *I* had nothing to do with it. What do they want ME to do?'

'As I understand it,' I answered, 'they want you to tell Tim to return to his parents. They think you've got some unholy influence over him.'

'Unholy be damned!' said Benjie. 'I've never had the smallest influence over anyone.'

'If you refuse they'll expel you with bell, book, and candle.'

'Expel me from what?'

'The family circle.'

'A fat lot *I* care!'

So after luncheon we went along. Rockland's is, I have always thought, the stupidest and slowest Club in London. It is just right for elderly Herries like Timothy and Carey Rockage and old Horace when he comes down from Manchester. It is small and dingy, and the room where they waited for us smelt of whisky and stale cigar-smoke. The windows looked as though they hadn't been cleaned for months. Timothy and Carey belong to grander Clubs of course, and when they want to show off they go to them, but for a real family bust-up Rockland's is the place. They were all waiting for us in an upstairs card room which we had to ourselves. When we came in it struck me at once how large physically we were compared with Benjie and how physically unfit. Carey, Timothy, Horace and myself are all stout men and Alfred is pasty. Benjie could have taken the lot of us on and thrown us all out of window! However, he was not in the least aggressive. He smiled at everyone as though he loved them and if no one smiled back that was not HIS fault! Oddly enough as I looked round the room I felt, although I'd come there of course as Benjie's friend and supporter, an acute sympathy with all of them. I understood exactly how they felt. With the exception of Horace they are all decent men, and in my opinion the decent normal Herries man is about as decent as any Englishman anywhere. He is brave, loyal, patriotic, God-fearing, good to his women and generous to all men. Simply he hasn't any imagination. A little imagination and they would understand that Benjie's type is permanent. You can't get rid of it by cursing and abusing it. You've got somehow to make terms with it. Put it in gaol, exile it, and it will always return. When men like Carey and old Timothy have learnt how to assimilate men like Benjie, the Herries family will rule the world--until then it will be always second-rate. But, of course, that assimilation will never occur. So there will be always tales to tell, poets formed out of rebellion, and wars between nations. But I understood how they felt about Benjie. You could see, as they looked at his country clothes and his round head with its sharp little eyes and his sturdy little legs, that he was the personification of disorder to them! And they were right.

Old Timothy, as the principal sufferer, took charge, and, standing in front of the fireplace, with his legs spread, he outlined the case. Unfortunately he was both lengthy and pompous. He said the same thing over and over again. What it came to was that he wanted his son back, that Benjie had tempted him to

Paris and must therefore bring him back to London again. There was nothing personal in this. He spoke as though Benjie were the kind of man with whom he could not possibly HAVE any personal relations.

When Timothy had finished at last, Benjie answered quietly that he had NOT tempted young Tim to Paris, that Tim was of age, and that, although of course it was a pity that he and his father did not agree, it was nevertheless the boy's own affair. 'In fact,' said Benjie, beaming round on all of them, 'I cannot see what I have to do with it or why you have asked me to meet you here.'

At that everyone wanted to speak at once. It was interesting to me to see the strong likeness that springs up between the men of our family when we are together. Alfred with his sharp nose that is always a little shiny, his high cheekbones and short black curly hair can hardly be said to resemble short-armed, short-legged, paunchy Carey who is the perfect Country Gentleman, or Timothy who is a kind of hundred-times-cleaned-scrubbed-and-brushed pillowcase, or myself who am just fat, careless and, alas, now purple-veined about the nostrils. And yet alike we all are, alike we always have been. Is it our English beef and cabbage that has made us so? Or our politics? Or the Battle of Hastings, 1066? Or insular security?

There in any case we all were, leaning forward like one man wanting to tell Benjie what we thought of him. Carey, who always speaks as though the thick Wiltshire soil had through the years crept up and swallowed his tonsils, had his word. He spoke as an English peer who has the crops, the family, and the British reputation among foreigners all to protect at once.

'Why we have asked you here,' he said, 'is because we feel, rightly or wrongly, that you are responsible for Timothy's boy's behaviour. The lad has caused his mother and father much pain. He has carried on a clandestine correspondence with your boy, it seems, for a long time past and of that we feel that you must have been--ah-- cognizant.' (Here I caricature old Carey's style a bit.) 'THEREFORE, therefore we have asked you to meet us. We are representing here today the family in London. I need not emphasize to you the grief that this has caused the lad's mother, nor the necessity we all feel that her boy--her only boy--should be restored to her. The lad is a good lad--fundamentally a good lad-- and we feel that he must have been under some most unfortunate influence to persuade him--'

'Rot!' Benjie broke in. 'Never was greater nonsense. Tim's been pleading since he was in that unfortunate velvet suit that his mother always made him wear, to be allowed to be a painter. There isn't one of us here who understands anything about Art, including Barney, even if he does write novels. Why the devil,' he went on, suddenly attacking Timothy, 'couldn't you have let the boy try his hand? It's none of my business or was none until I was dragged into it like this, but no one is responsible for Tim's running off to Paris except his parents--and that's the truth!'

This was from every point of view a most unfortunate speech, and after it there was no hope at all of saving anybody's bacon. I had tried to advise Benjie at luncheon that he must go slow, placate the old boys, show them that he meant them no harm. But it was of course hopeless from the start. The very sight of their London clothes, the air they had not only of owning the Rockland (to which they were thoroughly welcome) but the whole of England, annoyed him, exasperated him. However, it might not have been so bad had it not been for his allusion to Art. Now none of them--not Timothy, nor Carey, nor Alfred, nor Horace--cared a damn about pictures, but they hated to be told that they knew nothing about them. Carey said to me long afterwards: 'It was the arrogance of it, you know--telling us we don't know a picture when we see one! Why, damn it, a picture is a picture, isn't it? A feller has eyes, hasn't he?'

When Benjie had finished Carey rapped out:

'Are you going to bring young Tim back to London or not?'

'Certainly not,' said Benjie.

Horace broke in:

'Oh, but, Benjie, I'm sure that Carey misunderstands you! What you mean to say is that you will do all you can in the circumstances--'

Benjie jumped to his feet.

'I mean nothing of the sort!' (He really loathed Horace.) 'I consider it a piece of damnedest impertinence, all of you sitting round here as though you were in judgement on me. I only came to show you that I didn't care a damn for any of you! You can all go to hell for all I care!'

Both Carey and Alfred, who were hot-tempered, jumped to their feet and I thought for a moment that there would be a bit of a fight. Alfred is tall and wiry; Carey, although his arms are so short, has shoulders like a coal-heaver and is strong for his sixty-odd years. Benjie stood there, almost touching them, waiting for anything that might come. Horace was nervously pushing at his glasses in a way that he has when he is frightened (Rose used to imitate this very well), Timothy threw out his stomach as a sort of vanguard of protection.

But this was where I came in. I took Benjie by the arm and led him out of the group.

'We're not in the Klondike,' I remarked (or something equally cheap). 'Benjie doesn't see that he has any responsibility for Tim's being in Paris and I don't see that he has either. Feeling no responsibility, he doesn't see that he can do anything about it. And that's the end of it.'

I could see them looking at us and classing us together. All writers are queer to men like Carey and Timothy, and at that time, with the Wilde trial still fresh in their minds, queerer than queer. It was perhaps some feeling about the Wilde business that made them the more intolerant of Benjie although they all knew that Benjie was normal enough. The fact remains that the Wilde trial made many people in England think, for a long time, that all writers, painters, musicians, were freaks and dangerous freaks. So there we were, the 'little gipsy', the rogue of the family, and the loose-living, novel-writing eccentric. We were damned together.

'That's not the end of it,' said Carey at last. 'We don't want to be unfair, Benjie, but the fact is that we've had about enough of you. For years now you've been upsetting everyone. Even as a boy you were a family scandal. You've been mixed up in two public brawls already and now there's this business. It is the feeling of all of us that we wish to have nothing more to do with you. And if you're a gentleman we trust you'll respect our feeling.'

Then it was I who figured in the scene. I lost my temper. Never mind what I said. It's of no importance. But as I once told Horace what I thought of him, so now I told Timothy, Carey, and Alfred. I enjoyed myself for at least five minutes.

When, scant of breath (for I'm nearly seventy and my heart is not as good as it was), I had ended, it was Benjie who drew me away.

He smiled at them all. 'Goodbye, friends and relations,' he said. 'I shan't bother any of you again.' (He liked a little theatricality at times. It stirred his sense of colour.)

So, his arm through mine, we went out together.

VANESSA IN PRISON

Hysteria is the only word for the emotional state in which the Herries family now indulged. It is little exaggeration to say that as London once saw Jack the Ripper behind every area step, so now the Herries saw Benjie.

In 1898 and 1899, as afterwards in 1913 and 1914, London itself became hysterical. A mad craze for wealth and pleasure, an extravagance of display, a fantastic exhibitionism of non-morality raged everywhere. Diamonds and politics from Africa, an international plutocracy from the Holy Land, a pride and arrogance and self-confidence, a recklessness of materialism, the beginning of the breaking down of all barriers of caste and exclusive traditions: these things marked these years, the last defiant 'Ta-ra-ra-boom-de-ay' before the drums beat in the figures and the problems of the new world.

The Kaiser waved his theatrical arm in Potsdam, old Krüger sat in his kitchen reading his Bible, in London jumping signs for the first time illuminated the night sky and frightened the horses, The Belle of New York and The Gay Lord Quex shocked the religious, vast audiences swallowed gladly the wild tales of de

Rougemont; Kipling frightened two hemispheres by threatening to die of pneumonia; the cry was everywhere, 'Let 'em all come!'

In the week of the Rockland meeting young Timothy caught pneumonia in Paris, nearly died of it and refused to see either his father or mother when they hurried over to him. But Violet saw Benjie. She could not deny that he was quiet and courteous. He was eager that she should see her son: it was Timothy who refused to allow her to enter his room. She returned to London like an insane woman. It was perhaps that she felt in her heart that she had herself been to blame in the first place. She was an old woman. She was a tiresome woman. Her passion for chatter had grown into a garrulousness that bored the world; her grievances were so many that she was herself confused by their number. She said that 'everything had begun' on an awful day when old Emily Newmark had prayed over her and Oscar Wilde had laughed at her. Violet--her daughter--married in 1897 a Colonel Caldecott. The house in Onslow Square was the stiller and emptier for old Violet's ceaseless chatter.

Bore though everyone found her, it became the accepted fact that Benjie had stolen her son from her and ruined her life. Respectable people like the Rockages and the Worcesters and the Alfred Herries were, in sober fact, terrified of what Benjie might do next. The Worcesters and the Alfreds now had young children--Cynthia had two girls, Alfred a boy and a girl; who knew but that Benjie might kidnap them and hold them for ransom?

He was seen in London and the whole Herries world shuddered. The situation was developed by the part that Adrian Cards played in it. He went everywhere--and he was now a man of importance in the London world, an Under-Secretary and a writer of witty articles ('Very malicious', Alfred and Horace thought him)--saying that Benjie Herries was the best of fellows and that his relations were ridiculous people. The Herries--the Worcesters, Alfred, Violet and old Timothy, the Rockages--felt that everywhere Adrian went they were mocked. They knew of course the reason of his championship of Benjie. It was, as they assured everyone, because of his passion for Vanessa. He went with Vanessa everywhere. She was, at last, after years of good behaviour, forgetting her position, her duty to Ellis. All that wildness that MUST be in her blood when you remember her grandmother and great-grandfather, was at last coming out. It was true that Ellis must be very trying. But could she not remember what she owed to her position? There, too, Benjie's influence could be traced. After the scene at the Rockland Club, Benjie was banished from all decent male society, and yet Vanessa was known to have said that all the Herries men, except Barney, had behaved like fools in that affair.

It was true, Vanessa was at last angry. For thirteen years she had behaved, both in public and in private, as she ought to behave. Now she was beginning not to care whether she behaved or no. For she was increasingly unhappy, frightened and indignant. She was moving swiftly, with a crazy husband at her side, no close woman friend except Lettice Marrable in the world, a sense of deep injustice burning within her, to a climax.

The two ladies, Miss Vera and Miss Winifred Trent, helped to precipitate it. 'What is reality? This mirror is real because I can touch the silver tracing on the woodwork of the frame, but I stand, looking into it, brushing my hair, and Ellis is suddenly standing behind me. Ellis is not real. Then is the mirror not real any longer? Ellis is listening behind the door? I open it and the carpet on the stairs is real, the ticking from the Chinese clock is real, but is there not the sudden sharp click of a closing door, the very crack of the finger of unreality? And through all this I am a woman who longs to love and be loved in return. I am nearing forty and my life is more than half gone. I have no children, no one-- since my father died--to whom I might freely give my whole heart. Only Benjie and Rose--both disgraced, both exiles . . . Is that, then, at last MY reality, my hunger for love, my HUNGER, my HUNGER . . . in a woman who is nearly forty surely THAT cannot be real? . . . The Miss Trents have called. As they call now every day.'

'Dear Vanessa. We drove round to see how you and dear Ellis are. HOW is Ellis? Is his headache better?'

'Yes,' says Vanessa. 'Tonight we are going to The Canary. They say that it is a most amusing play.'

They look at her, inspect her with their large, soft and yet most resolute gaze. Everyone is watching her just as Ellis never ceases to watch her.

'If I don't get out of this I shall go mad, just as Ellis is . . .'

Yet, with all this, she could not prevent herself from enjoying to the full any fun that came her way. She went out and about with Adrian, Barney, Cynthia. She had plenty of the great world, for the Duchess of Devonshire was less formidable with her than with any other woman in London, she watched Lady Londonderry's passion for power with all the more sympathy because she had never herself known the passion, and she helped Lady de Grey turn the Opera from a shabby squalling business into a splendid tiaraed pageant. Of all the grand ladies Lady Dorothy Nevill was to her taste the most delightful; she never tired of her daintiness, her humour, her anecdotes, her resolute vulgarities, and her eager curiosity about human nature. No one who came to Hill Street thought that there was anything but peace and plenty there. Only the Family knew and the Family didn't say. It was the business of the Family to inform the world in general that anything Herries was right. Vanessa was the Family public pride and of the utmost importance to them all.

Adrian was Lady Dorothy Nevill's especial pet, and he and Vanessa went together very often to the house in Charles Street.

'You're not in love with the young man, are you, my dear?' she asked.

'Not the least little bit,' said Vanessa, laughing.

'Not that it matters,' said Lady Dorothy, tossing her little head with its marvellous auburn wig, shaking her many beads and necklets and amulets. 'You're not like these modern girls with all their paintin' and powderin'. How men can kiss them I can't understand. What Dizzy if HE were alive . . .'

Vanessa had friends everywhere, girls in shops, young men from the East End in whom Adrian was interested, writers famous like Henry James and Kipling, obscure like young Mr Smith who brought her the tattered manuscript of his novel to read or Mr Brown who had written an Epic on the Armada, actresses and actors like Irving, Ellen Terry, Forbes-Robertson and young men who walked on at the Lyceum. All were alike to her. She had no pose, no arrogances, no prejudices. So life whirled on the outside while within steadily the drama grew more intolerable.

Insanity is of all things the most pathetic, the most piteous, the most intangible. Everyone WITHIN the house knew that Ellis was insane. The servants nodded their heads together and watched him as children watch a strange and unaccountable animal. They developed a kind of pride in him. They marvelled that towards the outside world he was 'always all right'. Seriously, with an almost magisterial dignity, saying very little, listening to his guests with a sort of absorbed gravity (he was not listening; he was watching the figures BEHIND the figures), he played his part. With Finch the butler, Mrs Martin the cook, the two men-servants, the housemaids, Lettice Marrable, he was the master of the house, betraying himself to them only by the twitching of his fingers, the way in which he would look over their shoulders, the sudden impatient 'Very well, very well' or a sharp 'Is that door closed? I can hear someone moving upstairs.'

The servants had for both their master and mistress a new and rather touching kindliness. They were very well treated, were paid excellent wages. Vanessa they adored. (Even Finch, who, after Miss Fortescue's departure, robbed right and left, drank the best wine and so had a real friendliness to his employers.) They were kind, did their duties, but they waited . . . Something would happen soon . . . They might all be murdered in their beds . . . This made them feel privileged.

Vanessa herself wondered, often enough, whether there were not two Ellises. He was very often, when alone with her, so quiet and rational that it was almost as though the old friendly days were back again. When he slept beside her he moaned in his sleep and she drew him to her, stroked his forehead, felt as though she were protecting him against an evil demon. Yet, with this, she suffered an appalling fear of him that, do what she would, always increased. Perhaps one night he would kill her. She was always prepared for that. She would not, she thought, mind very greatly. Oddly, pity and fear went hand in hand together. She, too, waited for the next step . . .

Then one day in June 1898 she received a letter saying that Will Leathwaite was dead.

She had just come in from a drive and stood in the hall, the letter in her hand. It was from Mrs Newson, who had looked after the cottage and Will for some years--a very decent woman. It simply said that Will had been ailing for some time past, hadn't cared for his food, complained of his legs. Mrs Newson had gone to Grange to see a friend and, returning about seven of the evening, found Will dying in his chair by the fire.

'I thought you'd like to know, my lady, that it was your father's name he kept saying before he died, over and over. I don't rightly think he was ever the same man after your father died. But he was tranquil up to the last, and a finer-looking man not to be found anywhere I always said. And no trouble at all, not to no one.'

She stood there, lost in the past. Will was gone: now everyone was gone. She remembered her father's description of Will winning the race at Keswick years and years ago, how he pounded up the hill to the Druids' Circle, and young Adam, himself only a boy, riding in front of Will's father on the family mare, yelled encouragement. And then how Will had come up to Adam one Christmas Day and asked if he did not want a servant. Will's love for Adam had been the best that one human being can find for another: its character was paternal, protective, selfless, and also gay, simple, unsycophantic, man to man, brother to brother. It had been perhaps the finest thing in her father's life, Vanessa thought, looking back. Was there not always antagonism in every sex relation? But in this perfect charity, honesty, and--above all, best of all-- equality . . .

There was no Past when you experienced a love like this, for Adam and Will would go on for ever, for ever racing up the Keswick hill, for ever meeting, the snow sun-glittering at their feet, the blue smoke rising in the silent air, for ever one waiting the other's return, for ever that exchange of glance, sure and trustful, for ever that touch of hand on hand . . . In all this changing, bewildering, unstable world the one sure and certain proof that there is something eternal in man's soul; that, once in a lifetime, one touches, deep in the heart, evidence of immortality.

The letter fell to the ground: she heard the Chinese lacquered clock strike the half-hour with its sententious solemn purr. The clock's voice resembled Horace's. Will's death increased her loneliness. She had not seen him for so long a time and yet he had been behind her-- they two together thinking of Adam.

She picked up the letter and saw that Ellis was standing near to her and looking at her. Why did she never hear his step these days?

'Oh, Ellis!' she cried. 'Will Leathwaite is dead!'

Ridiculously, tears stole down her cheek behind her veil.

'Will Leathwaite?' he asked.

'Yes. Father's servant. You've seen him--a big fair-haired man with blue eyes.'

She had trained herself never to mention anything in connexion with Cumberland, but at this moment she was thinking of Will, not of Ellis.

He nodded, looked at her without speaking, and walked upstairs.

A few days later a very unaccountable thing occurred. He came to her in her room where she was reading, and timidly, as though he were asking a favour, said:

'Vanessa, let us go to Cumberland for a week--to your cottage on Derwentwater.'

He stood in front of her, very tall, very pale and rigid, as though she had ordered him in front of her to be scolded.

'To Cumberland?' She was so deeply astonished that she dropped the book. 'But, Ellis, you hate Cumberland!'

'No--who told you that?'

'Nobody, of course. Only yourself.'

'When have I said that I hated Cumberland?'

'Not HATED. But disliked it. The rain--and you don't like the North--'

'Who told you that I hated Cumberland?'

She got up and walked away. His eyes frightened her. He bent down and picked up the book. 'Why do they bind books in green? It is such an ugly colour.' Then, in rather a shrill voice: 'I don't hate Cumberland. Of course not. It will be very agreeable. I need a holiday.'

She came back to him, smiling.

'That IS good of you, Ellis. Of course I shall love to go.'

And they went. On the evening of her arrival she could not believe that she was there. In the living-room there were all her father's things just as they had always been. His books--the little blue volumes of the Iliad and the Odyssey--the tattered shilling parts of Pickwick, the English Poets, Sir Charles Grandison and Tristram Shandy, Barney's novels, Dandy Grimmett and the rest.

And all the old beloved things, part of her very life: the two cornucopias, Zobel's sand picture, 'The Saddle Horse', the old watercolour, 'The Lady of the House', the Baxter print 'Dippers and Nest', the Peepshow of the Central Hall at the Great Exhibition, above all, the spinet from Uldale with the roses painted on the lid, and the music box with the King in his amber coat and the Queen in her green dress.

As she stood at the window, with all these beloved things around her, she held her hands tightly together lest she should show her emotion. The last evening light touched the hills: Skiddaw's twin peaks lay like islands in a clear cold silver above bars of fleecy cloud, and the ridge of Blencathra was black against the white-washed sky. Between the trees the water of the Lake, struck by the trail of a tiny boat, fell into darker and darker shadow. The wood pigeons murmured from the wood. Some ghostly sheep wandered, just as they had so often done, slowly up the road. This was her home. How foolish she had been to be so long an exile from it! And as she watched, the years fell away from her. Twenty of those years were suddenly gone. She raised her arms above her head and, smiling, saw herself, another very different woman, moving slowly up the staircase of some grand house, hearing the names called, the distant band—Lady Herries, a middle-aged woman with a dull, stiff husband, still beautiful but soon not to be very interesting, to be nothing more than a London hostess who knew everyone, whom everyone knew, who mattered to no one, to whom no one mattered. Her body seemed to her young again; she would hear her father call her name, Benjie would be riding over from Uldale, all life was before her . . . All life before her? She shivered. It was behind her. She was in prison with Ellis.

But in the following days she could not keep down her joy. She had come home. What is it that makes in a certain square of ground every blade of grass, every hovering uncertain cloud, every note in a bird's song one's own? She had heard often enough, in London, scorn of this country, its rain, its ponds, its little hills, old Wordsworth and his daffodils, Coleridge and his opium, reading parties from Cambridge. She had had often to hold herself back from a ridiculous personal protest as though the scoffers had insulted herself. She had wondered why Lettice and Timothy and Violet, who had lived so long here, had had no personal feeling. She had heard Timothy thank his stars that he had done with the 'beastly climate'. She had asked Lettice whether she did not want to go back. 'Go back? All the unhappiest part of my life was there. I never want to see the place again.' She knew for herself that if her childhood had been one long misery still she must return . . . and return . . .

There was something deeper here, some inheritance that was mingled with all the truest, most importunate things in life. Her love of this place was her key to the connexion between the two worlds. 'Only connect . . .' 'Only connect . . .' The whole problem for man and for woman was here. They move as in a game of blind-man's- buff from figure to figure turned, twisted, bewildered. Guess rightly and the light floods in . . .

As she stood at the window, the world beyond it sinking into darkness, she knew with sudden certainty that to find the key of connexion was man's only business on this earth. All else was folly beside it. And the key for her, as it had been for her father, her grandmother, her great-grandfather, was here--like a pot of gold hidden in this square of ground. For Benjie too perhaps? She had, in that instant, one of those illuminating flashes of revelation, that once and again are granted the Hoodman Blind. God the Invisible and man exploring; she smiled as she thought of the ironies of Barney or Benjie or Rose if she told them of her naïveté.

'I looked out of the window as the world grew dark and knew that there are two worlds, that they are linked together, and that it is God's purpose that we should find the connexion. All beauty is for that. I must have courage, honesty, and I must rid myself of my Blind Man's Hood, my egotism . . . I must test life by no experience but my own. For you, dear Barney, God is an exploded superstition. That is YOUR experience. You are right to hold honestly by it. But for myself, standing at this window, I have another guide. Credit my honesty and I will credit yours. Let us be tolerant to one another.'

As she turned back into the lighted room she had a moment of almost blinding happiness. Her troubles faded. What matter if she were close on forty, if she loved Benjie whom she could never be with any more? What was her fear of Ellis? All the values of life were for a moment altered. She had courage for anything.

She needed that courage in the days that followed.

They were sitting quietly after supper, she reading a novel, he a newspaper. He said, still looking at his paper:

'Vanessa, when we return to London, I shall wish you to see a doctor.'

'A doctor?'

'Yes,' he said, leaning forward and laying his long bony hands on his knees. 'I have been long coming to the conclusion that you are not well. I came up here with you that I might observe you a little. In London it is so difficult. So many people to interfere. We do not see enough of one another. My suspicions--my suspicions,' he repeated the word softly, 'are quite confirmed.'

'What suspicions? I am perfectly well, Ellis dear.'

'Ah, so you think,' he went on quietly. 'That, I fear, is part of the disease.'

'Disease?' she broke in. Her heart was hammering. She looked quickly about among the old familiar things in the room to reassure herself. 'Why, I was never better in my life, and especially since I have come up here.'

'There, there. You mustn't get excited. Excitement is bad for both of us. I have said nothing until I could be certain. I did not wish to alarm you. I have myself for some while been none too well, but now I am quite recovered--quite recovered,' he repeated, nodding his head. 'But now that I have mentioned it, you can speak to me without fear. There is no one listening. At least I think not.' He got up, went very cautiously to the door and listened, then to the windows, pulling back the curtains for a moment. He walked on tiptoe.

'Listen, Vanessa. For a long time we have not been happy. Oh, I know that it has not been altogether your fault. For a time I was accompanied everywhere by someone. Very unagreeable and difficult to account for, but now that he is gone again--and I took care not to bother you with his intrusion--I realize that your care of me during these last years, in addition to all your social duties, has been too much for your strength, your mental strength. And then it is hereditary, no doubt. Your grandmother . . . You will need great quiet in the future, and an able doctor--perhaps retirement into the country to some soothing place . . .' He stopped to listen. 'You heard nothing? The city is so noisy and restless. Always something moving.'

She picked up her book. Her hands were trembling, but she answered quietly:

'There is nothing the matter with me, Ellis.' Forcing herself, she looked up at him and smiled. 'We have both been tired a little by London. That is why this week in the country was such a good idea.'

He bent down, patted her shoulder, kissed her forehead.

'There, there. You must not disturb yourself. I will see to it.' He straightened himself and tiptoed to the door. He listened, looking anxiously into the wall. 'And now I think I will go up to bed. Don't worry. Worry is bad for you. Quiet, quiet. We must all have quiet.'

She lay awake for hours that night, wondering what she should do. In the large bed that they shared he slept the peace of the insane just. He breathed like a child, never stirring. She beat herself into common sense. Panic was so near that, all the night through, she kept it off only by using her utmost strength. She could run away, leave him never to return, but that would mean defeat and cowardice. If she left him it would not be long before he would be put somewhere, in some awful, silent house, faced with dark silent windows, inhabited by poor sufferers like himself. She must not go until the last test of endurance had been reached. But this new twist of his brain was so awful that she refused to face it. If he, mad though he was, thought HER mad, might not others also think so? Had the strain of these last years been too much for her? Had there been something hysterically unreal in her manner? In the darkness of the room she saw the Misses Trent, in their large black hats, their trailing gowns, standing close together watching her. 'Yes,' she heard one of them say to Ellis. 'You are right. Vanessa has been behaving very strangely . . .' But then her common sense returned. She had never been more sane in her life than she was now. She

could deal with this as she had dealt with everything that preceded it. She turned on her side and slept.

Then, after one happy hour, she realized to the full the danger that she was in. That day, the seventeenth of June 1898, was stamped, in its tiniest detail, on her memory for ever.

In the afternoon she drove to Rosthwaite. A lady, Mrs Merriman, who lived in Borrowdale, gave a party for some of the children from Grange, Rosthwaite, Seatoller, and invited Vanessa. They all knew her here. She was one of themselves and had it not been for her silent, pale-faced, alarming husband they would have asked her everywhere. They hoped, now that she had returned to her real home, that she would often come and, although they did not say so, without her husband. They knew that she was a grand lady in London, but Cumberland people take things naturally. Everyone is on a level, and if anyone behaves grandly they look foolish and are to be pitied. Vanessa of course did not behave grandly at all. No one could be more simple, and on this afternoon in Rosthwaite she sat on the floor and allowed the babies to climb all over her, played musical chairs with breathless excitement and then, to the cracked piano, sang songs for them and afterwards played for them to dance. Mrs Merriman, who was thin and pale, had an invalid husband and more children than she wanted, had been inclined to be jealous at first of this woman with her lovely clothes, her beauty, her life in the great world. 'She has everything. How unfair it is.' But soon she was not sure that she had everything. There was something, she told her husband, pathetic about Vanessa. 'She played with the children as though she could not bear to let them go. She told me that coming back here was heaven to her. She went to the window and looked out at the hill like a starving woman. "Well, why don't you come here more often, Lady Herries?" I asked her. "After all, it's your home. We are all delighted to have you here." "Oh, how I wish I could!" she said. I wouldn't wonder if she's not happy with her husband. I'm sure I shouldn't be. He really frightened me, he was so stiff and solemn. I never saw a woman carry herself so beautifully, and such lovely dark hair as she's got and such a kind expression. But I'm certain she's not happy. Lovely dark hair with not a grey thread, although she can't be far off forty. No airs at all, although the Prince and Princess often come to her house, I believe. You know, Philip, I felt like a mother to her. There's something makes me feel that she needs someone to love her. Oh, I know you'll call me romantic. But I can't help it. She's the most beautiful woman I've ever seen and simply sweet with the children. You could tell her anything, I'm sure.'

When the children were having tea Vanessa slipped out, crossed the road, the bridge, and looked at the solid, comfortable little Victorian house with its sloping lawn, its trim garden, the house built on the very spot where her great-grandfather had once lived. She stood there, listening to the running water, feeling the afternoon sun on her face, wondering where that old wild man now was. He, too, had stood here, looking at the hills, feeling the sun on his face, waiting for his wife to return. It had been wild then: the bare rock, the tumbling water, the valley beyond uncouth and deserted. The sun had shone on his purple coat and silver braid. She felt intimately close to him. Once again time was not. Was it fancy that a hand rested on her shoulder, comforting her? Of course it was fancy.

Here was the trim garden and on the lawn two garden chairs, a small mowing machine, a watering pot. An old bent gardener was clipping the roses. Two bicyclists passed down the road, and then a scarlet coach filled with tourists. But, after the coach was gone, silence tumbled back again, the hills, clear and defined in the sunshine, cut the cloudless sky. The gardener pushed the mowing machine, and the soft dreamy whirr filled the world with summer peace. As she turned to the bridge she whispered 'Goodbye'. Was it fancy that a figure in a purple coat watched her go?

'And now, children, we must all thank Lady Herries for helping to make our afternoon such a pleasant one.'

They all thanked her in shrill treble voices. They ran into the road to see the splendid lady in her rose-coloured coat get into the carriage, and one baby cried because it was not allowed to go with her. She kissed Mrs Merriman.

'Come back soon,' Mrs Merriman said.

'Yes, I will,' said Vanessa.

Ellis locked the door. Vanessa looked up from her book at the sound of the turning key. Why had he locked the door? She had thought that he had gone up to bed. The little clock with the painted moon and stars (as a baby she had been lifted again and again to count them) pointed to quarter to eleven. Mrs Newson and her husband slept on the far side of the cottage. They would hear nothing. She continued to read. This was a very clever book of short stores; it was written by a woman who must be simply too clever to do any of the ordinary things that ordinary women did. The stories were in the manner that was becoming popular; they had no beginning. One story called 'The Haystack' started with this sentence: 'Oh, but dripping is so cheap . . . and it's really not bad when you get used to it.' Nor had they any conclusion. 'The Haystack' ended: 'Yes, but half a crown--that was altogether too much for such a second-rate article.' They were depressing stories. London in the rain, hateful boarding houses, shabby men making love, the British Museum Reading Room, someone wringing a chicken's neck outside the kitchen window. They were very feminist. Men figured as poor creatures, mean, faithless, and greedy. But oh! what cleverness! What observation! Nothing escaped this

lady's eye; the yellow stain on the tablecloth where mustard had been spilled at the last meal, the tear in the cheap umbrella, the shabby feather in the outworn hat . . . . Vanessa knew, as she read, that one thing that was the matter with herself was that she was not clever at all. Neither clever nor witty. She could not remember that she had ever said a brilliant thing in her life. Rose, Cynthia, Lady Dorothy Nevill--what clever things they were always saying! 'I'm a bore,' thought Vanessa. 'The woman who wrote this book wouldn't endure me for five minutes.'

But why had he locked the door? He came and sat down opposite to her. The clothes that he was wearing, a dark brown cloth intended for the country, did not suit him nor did they look like country clothes. Wherever he might be, he wore always the deep sharp collar that belonged to the Gladstone caricatures, and that did not suit him either because his throat was so thin, his Adam's apple so large. She noticed tonight for the first time that the back of his pale long hand was freckled.

He sighed, then said:

'It was not kind of you, Vanessa, to have me watched all this afternoon.'

She looked at him steadily, determining that tonight at least she would not be afraid. They were returning to London tomorrow and then something must be done. For her own safety, for his, something must be done.

'What DO you mean, Ellis? No one was watching you.'

'Ah, come, Vanessa. Why lie to me? I don't blame you, not at all. I know that you are not yourself. But it is wrong of you to embarrass me. And such an unpleasant man. I stood here for half an hour while he watched me outside the window. He never moved until I came myself to the window; then he vanished into that green bush beyond the flowerbed. Then when I returned to the fireplace, pretending not to notice him, he came to the window again. A long thin man in a green coat. I fancied that I had seen him before.'

She got up and came over to him, seeming very tall in that small room.

'Ellis dear, let's go to bed. You know that I haven't had you watched. Why should I? Now come to bed.'

'Oh, I'm not vexed, my dear. Not at all vexed. I said to myself, "If he hadn't got that green coat I really should not mind. He could watch me as long as he pleased. But I dislike green as a colour and his eyes were most unpleasant." When I went out into the garden he was gone. Then he came back again. He pressed his face to the windowpane. All the same you would dislike it if I had YOU watched, you know. You wouldn't like it at all. In fact, lately, I've had it in my mind because, being as you are, it isn't safe for you to go about alone.' He sighed, deeply, deeply as though in dreadful distress. The truth is that we are neither of us well. Life has been a failure for both of us. It is better for us to end it.'

She looked about the room to reassure herself with the old homely comfort of the familiar things--the spinet, the books, the music box, the pictures. She walked to the window, then from the far side of the table said: 'Ellis, give me that key. You have locked the door. Give me that key.'

'No, my dear, certainly not. Because you had me watched this afternoon is reason enough. We have not been happy for a long time; indeed I have never been happy. I cannot remember a time when I was happy. Nor are you happy. So here, very quietly, while there is no one about, is a very good opportunity to finish all this tiresome business. I feel it my duty. I have hesitated for some time, but now my duty is quite clear.'

He fumbled in his inside coat pocket and brought from it a large kitchen knife with a thick brown handle.

'You will feel nothing,' he said smiling. 'It will be no more than a cut on the finger. And then I will follow you. I can't possibly express to you how agreeable it will be to be tired no longer, to have no more headaches. For both of us it will be a relief, I am sure--'

He held the knife in one hand and stroked its edge, very gently, with the other. The little clock struck eleven.

'This is the silliest scene,' she thought, 'I have ever been in. So unreal that all the things in the room have become unreal too.' She thought also: 'But this ends everything. At last, thank Heaven, this ends everything.'

'I have thought it all out,' he said. 'Sit in that chair, Vanessa. Close your eyes. You'll feel nothing at all.' He was very close to her now, but she did not move.

'Ellis, give me the key. Put down that knife. Go to bed. You are behaving like a baby. Put that knife down on that table.'

'Perhaps I will,' he said, looking at her very cunningly. 'Perhaps I will not. But it won't matter, because nothing you can say will alter my decision. And how absurd of you not to do as I wish! But you have never done as I wish. A pale-green mushroom hat that you are always wearing. You know that I dislike it. And yet day after day you persist in wearing it.' He murmured: 'A mass of shaded green wings. A mass of shaded green wings. That's what Mr Playfair said.'

He threw out his hand and caught her arm.

'Come to the chair, Vanessa. Come to the chair. That is the easiest way.'

He looked up at her like a beseeching child. His eyes were filled with tears.

'Dear Vanessa. How I love you! How unhappy we are!'

His arm encircled her body . . . His head fell forward and rested on her breast. The knife tumbled to

the floor. She led him back to the armchair, he submitting like a child.

'Please, Ellis, give me the key,' she said.

Tears pouring down his cheeks, he fumbled for the key, found it, gave it her.

'Another time,' he sobbed. 'Perhaps another time will be better. I meant it for the best . . .' Then, as she moved away, he caught her hand: 'Don't leave me. Don't leave me. I am afraid of being alone.'

She knelt down beside him, comforting him as she had done so often before. But, in her heart, she knew that this was for the last time.

ESCAPE INTO DANGER

They had to leave very early next morning to catch the train for London. Vanessa, who had not slept at all, stood at the lawn's edge and found that the world was rolling in rosy smoke. It would be a hot day. The smoke lifted from the Lake even as she looked, as someone lifts the covers from a bed: the Lake shivered, trembling, at the touch of the sun that itself also dared as yet only to breathe upon the water, but to breathe like God, strongly, confidently (in spite of so very many disappointments) and with the very tenderness of love. The colour flew upwards from the hills and broke into petals of rose against the sky that would soon be drenched with sun. All the hills waited--Cat Bells, Robinson, Gable, Scafell, the Langdales, Helvellyn, Blencathra--they all waited for their illumination high, high above these madmen who today are one thing and tomorrow another.

This would be a horrible journey--and so it was.

'Perhaps,' said Ellis, when they were halfway down England, 'you would like my Times?' He spoke to a stout fellow in a suit of loud checks who had been, ever since Penrith, staggered by Vanessa's beauty. For she wore a small toque, a spotted veil, her rose-coloured coat; behind the veil, the man in the checks was, with beating heart, assured, breathed the only woman for whom all his life he had been searching. He had money, he had rude health, a kind wife and a mistress in Carlisle, but he had not, he had never, never had, the Beauty for which he longed.

'Thank you, sir. Very kind of you. Hooley's bankruptcy means the end of the cycling boom. Mark my word.'

The fields rushed up to the window and all the houses bobbed and curtsied in the sun. Vanessa sat there, her clever book of stories on her lap, and fought down her terrors. She had not slept, and Ellis, who now looked like a Prime Minister, a director of a railway company or the real author of Robert Elsmere, had last night wished to cut her throat with a knife with a brown handle. He had, as usual, wept leaning against her breast.

He would never weep against her breast again, for her duty there was ended. Once she had loved him as a mother her child, then she had pitied him because he was sick, now she was a weary, angry woman resolved on escape. Next week they were giving a Ball in Hill Street, a very grand Ball indeed, and that should be the last. That should be the end, for her, of Ellis, Hill Street, London . . . One need not, one must not, be stuck so deep in a quagmire of ludicrous danger . . . ludicrous kitchen knives, Ellis' tears and tiptoe to the window, Ellis' man in the green bush beyond the window, Ellis' moaning in his sleep, poor Ellis . . . 'To find some life that is neither false nor dangerous . . .' Letting her head fall, she slept at last, dreaming that the babies in Rosthwaite pulled her with eager hands up the hill to the water falling with such cool certainty down the face of the rock. Standing waiting for her there was Benjie.

At Hill Street was a letter for her from Rose. Next day she went to see her. Rose was living in two very small dingy rooms off Baker Street. She met Vanessa defiantly, as though to say: 'I know you will find me changed and you can say, if you wish, that you never want to see me again.' Yes, Rose WAS changed. Her cheeks were painted, the puffed shoulders of her dress absurdly exaggerated, her waist too small for any comfort, her eyes unhappy. Her room was untidy, clothes thrown about, a dusty piano open with a bright green hat ornamented with a bird of paradise plume flung down on the keys.

A strange thought struck Vanessa. 'This is the world into which, very shortly, I may be moving.'

But oh! it was wonderful to be loved again! She could not believe that she had endured all these years without it! She was like a woman starved as, sitting with Rose on the shabby hole-and-corner sofa, she heard what Rose chose to tell her (a sort of fairy story in which every gentleman was kind, money sprang from the carpet, and life was one long victory).

At the end of it Vanessa said:

'I'm glad you're so happy.'

And Rose said:

'Life's hell. Don't believe a word I've said, Vanessa.'

They discovered very quickly that life just then was bad for both of them. Vanessa did not tell Rose that Ellis had wanted to cut her throat with a kitchen knife, but she DID give her to understand that the end of Hill Street had arrived at last and that Rose must be prepared . . .

There came in upon them without a word of warning the most dreadful man--Major Featherstone-Haigh. The Major was short, purple in the face, smelt of brandy, called Vanessa 'My dear' and looked at Rose as though he owned her--which, at that moment, he probably did.

Vanessa went back to Hill Street. She went back to Hill Street to find Miss Vera and Miss Winifred Trent waiting for her in the drawing-room. Standing in her room, before she went down to them, she knew a moment of fear worse than any that had preceded it. She stood, motionless, her head up as though she were listening. Then with quick nervous movements she took off her white soft-feathered toque, her veil, her long gloves. She listened again. It was a hot thundery day and her windows were wide open. A hansom clop-clopped down Hill Street; she looked out and saw a man crying his flowers which blazed in a cloud of colour on his barrow--roses, carnations, lilies. Below the windows of the houses the window boxes shone with bright blue, with scarlet, with flaunting yellows. At the end of the street was a barrel-organ that played again and again an old air from Trovatore. Light, colour, music: but inside the house it was cold and dark as it always was. Her dress was white and black, the shoulders very puffed, the waist very small. She looked at herself in the long silver mirror. She seemed to herself hideous, her pale face beneath the dark hair, her long white neck, her full bosom; her height was ridiculous. She hated the way that she carried her head, stiff, pompous, 'as though I were for ever at the top of the stairs, receiving. Thank Heaven, it is ended. In a week or two, in one way or another, it will be over. I will never receive anyone any more. Death, perhaps.' It did not seem impossible, for there was Ellis loose about the house, and the house so still, and those two old women in their long trailing black waiting for her in the drawing-room.

At that moment, looking at herself in the mirror with disgust as at someone for whom everything was over, someone moving in a crazy house cold as the grave, a lunatic its master, she had almost, for the first time, lost all her courage. Rose lost, Benjie somewhere wandering, no one else . . . Then also she remembered her grandmother, that small indomitable woman with the white hair and ivory cane who lived to be a hundred, who had faced everything because she knew how to be indifferent to life whilst adoring it, 'She did--so can I.' She went down to the two ladies.

'Ah, dear Vanessa, how nice to see you again. And how are you?'

'Very well indeed, thank you.'

They both kissed her, and as they did so it was as though they were graciously inviting her to stay for an hour or so in her own drawing-room. They were extremely quiet. When they moved, their long black dresses scarcely rustled. They appeared also to have a secret understanding. They had moreover the power to make you feel that you could not take a step without their permission. Finch brought in the tea, and it seemed likely for a moment that Miss Vera Trent would instruct him where the table should be placed. Their voices were what Barney once called 'boneless'.

'We have already seen dear Ellis,' said Miss Winifred.

'He says that his holiday has done him good,' said Miss Vera.

'But we advised him to be careful during these hot weeks in London,' said Miss Winifred. 'The worst thing possible for his headaches. How is he, do you think, Vanessa?'

'Oh, very well,' said Vanessa brightly. 'We had such lovely weather in Cumberland.'

'You did?' said Miss Winifred. 'Now isn't that delightful? Cumberland when it is FINE must be indeed charming.'

'And for you--to return to your old home again-- how delightful!' said Miss Vera. 'There is no place quite the same as one's childhood's home.'

'And what have you been doing?' asked Vanessa. 'What are the family scandals? Whom have you seen?'

'Oh, we lead quiet lives, you know,' said Miss Winifred. 'We had tea one day with dear Cynthia. May and her girls were in London for a week. And poor Violet-- not at all well, I fear, and now that both children--' She broke off. The Misses Trent were nothing if not tactful, and, after all, Vanessa most strangely defended that horrible man who had lured poor Violet's boy--

They both looked at her together, a strange look, a look full of some knowledge that at present they would keep to themselves. Miss Vera said, smiling, raising her hand on which her diamond rings sparkled, to help herself to a little cake: 'And what is this that Ellis tells us, dear Vanessa, about your own health? Rather a sad report, I fear.'

'My health?' said Vanessa. 'Why, it was never better.'

Miss Vera shook her finger. 'Now that is not at all what dear Ellis tells us. He insists that you see a doctor. Altogether over- fatigued, he says, and I am sure that I don't wonder with all that you do. And then this great Ball next week to which Winifred and I are so greatly looking forward. But after it Ellis thinks that a quiet time in the country--'

Her anger rose. She was suddenly aware that she hated these two women as she had never hated anyone in her life before. 'I think that I am the best judge of that,' she said quietly. 'I am perfectly well.'

The door opened and she saw that Ellis had come in. The two ladies rose and moved to either side of him. He greeted them with a grave smile.

Surely, they must be aware of his strangeness, his eyes are never still nor do they see the things at which they are looking, and he walks now like a cat with padded feet . . .

All three looked at her. Then Ellis said:

'A little tea, my dear. Thundery weather.'

They all sat down.

One more move needed to complete the preparation. Next day meeting Barney at Cynthia's he put in her hand a note. It was from Benjie.

18 Half Moon Street.

DEAR VANESSA--I am here and shall be so for some weeks. If I may not see you I may at least be happy because I am near you.

B.

The last Ball ever given by Vanessa and Ellis in Hill Street was a brilliant success. Vanessa, in a dress of white satin and with diamonds in her hair, stood at the top of the stairs. She saw, as though it were a mechanical toy wound up for her amusement, the figures appear around the bend of the staircase--one two, one two, one two--the ladies' heads erect, bosoms thrust forward, trains draped over their arms, jewels glittering, a scent of powder and roses and the heat of the London June evening . . .

'Lord and Lady Danesborough.'
'Sir James and Lady Ford.'
'Mr Forbes-Robertson.'
'Lady Carteris.'
'Lord John Beaminster.'
'Lady Adela Beaminster.'
'Miss Rachel Beaminster.'
'Mr Timothy Herries.'
'Miss Vera Trent.'
'Miss Winifred Trent.'
'Lady Dorothy Nevill.'
'Sir Henry and Miss Nevill and Lady Wade.'
'Madame Sarah Bernhardt.'
'Mr and Mrs Peile Worcester.'
'Lord Clancarty.'
'Mr Henry James.'
'Mr Edmund Gosse.'
'Mr and Mrs Colvin.'
'Lady Sarah Meux.'
'Monsieur Felix Brun.'
'Mr Yale Ross.'
'Lady Carloes.'
'Mr Robert Hichens.'
'Sir Roderick Seddon.'
'The Honourable Lionel Talmache.'
'Mr Adrian Cards.'
'Lady Lettice Forjambe.'
'Mr and Mrs Humphrey Ward.'
'Sir Peter and Lady Thornby.'
'Miss Mary Thornby.'
'Lady Eustace.'
'Miss Pamela Eustace.'
'Mrs Clifford.'

'Mr Barnabas Newmark.'
'Lord and Lady Rockage.'
'Miss Veasey.'
'Mr and Mrs Ormerod.'
'Lady Cynthia Lamb.'
'Mr and Mrs Frederick Macmillan.'
'Mrs Grant Bingham.'
'Mr Herbert Beerbohm Tree.'
'Mr Pendle Smith.'
'Mrs Langtry.'
'General Fortescue and Mrs Fortescue.'
'Mr Max Beerbohm.'
'Miss Carlyon.'
'Mr Ross.'
'Mr Tumer.'
'Mrs Fortescue Brown.'
'Mr Brookfield.'
'Mrs Craigie.'
'Mr Charles Wyndham.'

She reflected: 'It must be midnight. The actors and actresses are arriving.' She glanced back and saw that the long room was now filled to overflowing with dancers.

'Mr Bertrand.'
'Lady Garvice.'
'Miss Garvice.'
'Mr Galleon.'
'Lady Torring.'
'Mr and Mrs Frost.'

Barney, a little later, found himself in a corner with Bertrand the novelist.

'I suppose,' Bertrand said, 'you think I'm here to pour scorn on my fellow-creatures.'

'No, not especially,' said Barney. 'Any more than anyone else.'

'As a matter of fact,' said Bertrand, 'I love my fellow-creatures. I think we are all absurd, of course. And tonight I feel something sinister in the air.'

'Sinister?' asked Barney.

'Yes. I can't explain it except that I think London IS sinister just now. Have you read Hichens' Londoners, or don't you read your fellow-novelists?'

'Not very often,' said Barney.

'Neither do I. But Hichens' book is clever madness—too long, but not really exaggerated. We are all mad.' He looked around him. 'Do you see that little man over there talking to Mrs Langtry?' He pointed to a small, very dapper gentleman, with bright observant eyes, who was talking with exceeding animation and a good deal of un-English gesticulation.

'That is Felix Brun. He lives only for the social history of Europe. He knows all the moves, the undercurrents, the plots, and plotters. Whenever he appears in London, you can be sure that there is a change coming. I met him a week or two ago at the Rede Gallery where he had come to look at Ross' portrait of the old Duchess of Wrexe—a very fine painting,

by the way. He was very interesting. Like myself, he has no illusions.'

'You must have been a fine gloomy pair,' Barney said, laughing.

'Oh, not gloomy at all. Why be gloomy? It has been dull, this long sleepy prosperity. Brun agrees with me that things are breaking up.'

'What things?' Barney asked. He was looking at Ellis, who, standing near to him, alone, had in his eyes so fixed a gaze, and in his pose so odd an air of waiting for someone, that he interested Barney.

'What things?' repeated Bertrand. 'Oh, all this. The conviction that we are the finest people in the world, superior to everything and everybody. The conviction that we rule the world and it is right that we should. Brun says that England's day as ruler of the world is over.'

'That must give you great satisfaction.'

'No—why should it? We do some things very well, but we have no taste, no subtlety, no sensitiveness to what other people are feeling, and our Imperial ambitions are revolting. I am going to live in France.'

Beaminster brought up to Vanessa a very beautiful girl.

'This is my niece Rachel, Vanessa. You were at her Ball the other day. She has not been out long enough yet to be blasé. She thinks you are the most wonderful woman in London.'

Vanessa looked with great pleasure at the girl in front of her. Miss Rachel Beaminster, granddaughter of the old Duchess of Wrexe. Vanessa had gone in May to a very grand Ball in Portland Place given for this child's coming-out. The girl was tall and thin, with dark hair and beautiful eyes, a little gauche and a little foreign. Her mother had been a Russian actress, and the old Duchess had, Vanessa was told, never forgiven her son for his mésalliance. But the importance of this meeting for Vanessa was that this girl might be herself—herself twenty years ago.

'I do hope you're enjoying yourself.'

'Oh yes, Lady Herries. It's a lovely Ball.'

'Plenty of partners?'

The girl smiled and became at once transformed; her happiness took away that little awkwardness and you felt pleasure, excitement, anticipation beat through her body.

'Plenty. I could dance all night.'

'I have known your uncle a long time. He is one of my oldest friends.'

'Oh, Uncle John? Isn't he a dear? I should have been terrified of everything had it not been for him.'

Yes, and she might be, Vanessa thought, with that awful old grandmother and stiff, forbidding Adela for an aunt and prim, pompous Richard for an uncle!

'It's so wonderful,' Rachel said, 'seeing Sarah Bernhardt. Uncle John is taking me next week to one of her plays at the Lyric. She looks kinder, more simple—'

'Would you like to meet her?' asked Vanessa.

'Oh yes! Can I? You see, my mother was an actress--'

'Come along and I'll introduce you. Tell her about your mother.'

They went across to where the great woman was listening, with eyes half closed, to M. Brun.

Vanessa presented the girl and was pleased to see with what ease and simplicity the child behaved. She turned and, for a moment before she was caught again, watched the room, swinging under the lights to the rhythm and symmetry of the waltzes. The music softly beat into her ears: 'The last time--the last time--the last time . . .'

What if there should be a scene? What if Ellis should commit some awful indiscretion? He was looking strange tonight. Surely others had noticed it besides herself. She talked, she laughed, she walked with uplifted head. Many said afterwards that she had never seemed more splendid than at this Ball, more easily the mistress of her world. 'And for her age still such a beauty,' said little Brun. 'What is she? Nearly forty? She must be.' He remarked to Bertrand: 'An interesting family, these Herries. So typically English and yet with a strain of something--'

'And we'll have fires out of the Grand Duke's Wood,' quoted Bertrand.

'Fires out of the wood?'

'Yes--a quotation from one of the other Herries-- the mad ones, you know.'

'Ah, there have been mad ones then?'

'Oh, plenty. There are several scandals at the moment.'

'Ah,' said Brun. 'That's what makes you English so interesting. You are madder than any other people and yet so conventional. Impossible to understand, you turn and rend your madmen while they are alive and yet are so proud of them after they are dead.'

'That,' said Bertrand, who was suddenly bored with little Brun (he tired of people very quickly--of himself also), 'is why we are so conceited. We have so much common sense that when our poets have written their poetry we kill them. Except Wordsworth and Tennyson of course. But they were mad very young and got over it.'

After that Bertrand sat by himself for a while and collected notes for his notebook. He watched Madame Bernhardt act and Henry James unravel sentences of benignity from his beard, Mrs Langtry raise her lovely arm, bishops grow genial, politicians indiscreet and all the most beautiful girls in London manoeuvre for husbands. Then he noticed his host, who listened at first with grave intensity to a stout lady in a bright green dress, and then, when she left him, stood as though bewildered, staring about him.

'By Jove, the old boy's trembling from head to foot,' he said to himself. 'He'll have a fit or something.'

Ellis backed to the wall. He straightened himself against it. Then Bertrand saw that he felt the wall with the palm of his hand; he moved his hand up and down against the surface, and in his eyes was the most unhappy gaze that Bertrand had ever seen in a human countenance. Then Bertrand saw that two tall elderly ladies came up to him, stood on either side of him, talking to him. With his hand through the arm of one of them, Ellis moved away. Bertrand wrote in his notebook that night:

'But the strangest thing this evening was the terror of my host. A very commonplace dull man, you would say, but the dullest of us may become interesting when, lost in the bush, he hears the tom-toms of the approaching cannibals.'

The Ball reached its apogee. There was a superb and nearly riotous set of Lancers. Everyone had had supper. The summer morning was breaking beyond the windows. The carriages drove away. Finch, downstairs, entertained the footmen and the maids with his splendid imitations of the more important guests.

Vanessa, reaching her room at last, locked the door. A few minutes later there was a knock. She stood motionless, listening. The knock was several times repeated. Then silence.

As the small brown silver-faced clock that she had brought with her from Cat Bells struck eleven, she awoke. She had told them not to call her; now she rang the bell, looked at her letters, the newspaper, drank her coffee. Through and behind it all was a sense of crisis. And yet why? She had given last night one of the most successful Balls of the season; no hitch, no misadventure. And today there was no reason why anything should happen. Something SOON must be done, but immediately, today . . .

The sun poured into the room. The paper told her that there was a new successful play at the Court--His Excellency the Governor--and that her friend, Irene Vanbrugh, one of the women whom for her generous spirit, unaffected good nature and cheerful courage she liked best in London, had made a great success in it. She read of a hat that sounded a miracle of loveliness:

A daring little toque of turquoise straw, jet pins with very big heads, white wings and a black velvet rosette in front. She also read: The Louis Seize bow is almost ubiquitous. We meet it on hats, it is a charming head-dress for evening wear, it occurs in almost every embroidery, every appliqué of lace, it airs itself in the lace curtains, on our walls, everywhere.

'There shall be no Louis Seize bows on MY walls,' she thought, half asleep, and then remembered, with the sharpness of a knife cutting through tissue paper, an unexpected little incident of the evening before. Just after she had come up from supper Ellis appeared at her elbow and with him a stout roughly bearded man. All that Ellis had said was that this was a friend of his, a Doctor Playfair. She had talked with the man for five minutes. What had they discussed? Bernhardt's season at the Lyric, the Spanish-American War, Gladstone's funeral, Cecil Rhodes--anything, nothing? He had seemed a well-informed, pleasant enough man. As soon as his back was turned she had forgotten him. She had not thought of him again until now when, suddenly, she seemed to see him in the room here with her--his untidy brown beard speckled with grey, his white waistcoat that fitted ill over his paunch, his heavy bowed shoulders, but, above all, his thick glasses behind which his large grey eyes had stared at her without blinking. How he had stared! She had not at the time thought of it, for, by now, she was accustomed that people should stare at her. But how he had stared! She fancied now that there had been some especial emphasis in Ellis' introduction . . .

She must get away! Oh! at once! at once! Somewhere, anywhere. Was she perhaps nervously overstrung? This trembling, this beating of the heart . . . Had people been thinking her ill and not cared to tell her? WAS her mind affected by this last horrible year? She jumped out of bed, went to the mirror. Nothing ailed her. She was in the full vigorous possession of her brain, her will, her heart. She had never been more conscious of true bodily strength, of real and absolute sanity. She had been imagining the doctor . . . There had been nothing intended, nothing sinister--but with Ellis now from minute to minute you never knew . . . you never knew . . .

She had luncheon alone and afterwards drove to the Rede Art Gallery in Bond Street, where she had arranged to meet Barney. They had agreed that they must see Yale Ross' portrait of the Duchess of Wrexe. He was waiting for her inside the Gallery and she thought to herself: 'What a nice wide-awake amusing face he has for an old man of nearly seventy! How pleasant it is always to see him! What a friend he has always been to both Benjie and myself!'

They went together and looked at the portrait. It was certainly brilliant. The old woman sat, leaning a little forward, holding a black ebony cane, in a high carved chair. The most striking thing in her pose was the way in which her dry claw-like fingers clutched her cane. Her dress was black and the only colour against it was the dull green of a jade pendant. The colour of her face was almost dead white and the skin was drawn so tightly over the veins that a sigh, a breath, you felt, would snap it. She looked indomitable, remorseless,

proud, nor was there a shadow of humour in her mouth (which was cruel) and her eyes (which were cold). On either side of the chair were two green and white dragons, grotesques with large flat feet and open mouths. A tapestry of dull figured gold filled the background.

'Theatrical, brilliant, and most uncomplimentary,' Vanessa said.

'She wouldn't think so,' said Barney. 'I'm told she's delighted with the picture. And she IS theatrical--her life, I mean. She shuts herself up in Portland Place so that she may be a figure. If she went out and about she would be simply an old and tiresome woman who had outlived her time. As it is people think that she pulls all the strings.'

Vanessa thought of the young girl, Rachel, to whom she had spoken last night.

'That girl has character,' she said. 'It would be a tussle between the two of them if they fought.'

They found a quiet corner. The little room with its cool light, its gleaming pictures, its silence, was most refreshing.

'Now tell me, Barney, quite honestly, have you noticed anything strange in me lately?'

'No. Nothing. Of course not. I never saw you more beautiful, more completely mistress of yourself, than last night. Everyone said the same.'

'Thank you, my dear. And now listen.'

Vanessa told him everything; of the journey to Cumberland, the incident of the knife, Ellis' remarks about her health, the two old women in the house, the few minutes with the doctor. Barney was horrified.

'At least that settles it. Something must be done at once--at once.'

'Yes, but what? I cannot--no, I cannot--endure another week of this. And it is not right for Ellis either. We are not safe and he is not safe.'

Barney stared in front of him. 'This is dreadful. I knew that things were bad, but not like this.'

'How much does anyone else know?'

'Well, we--the family--have realized that something was wrong with Ellis for a long time. But only vaguely. I have only known what you told me and others have guessed a little perhaps, but so long as everything was all right on the surface they have accepted it. They don't WANT, you see, that there should be anything public. There have been enough Herries scandals.'

Vanessa went on:

'And it is all my fault. The sin was my marrying Ellis in the first place when it was Benjie whom I loved. I thought of myself rather than Ellis. But there was this strain, perhaps, in him from the beginning . . . I can't DEAL with it, Barney. My courage is gone, and I thought once that I had enough for anything. But how can I leave him like this, defenceless, without anybody, in that awful world of his own? If you saw how unhappy he sometimes looks, the way that he cries, the

BITTERNESS of his weeping! How lonely one must be!'

She trembled and put one gloved hand on Barney's knee to steady herself.

'Oh, Barney, WHAT am I to do?'

'Wait,' Barney said. 'Let's be sensible about this. Under the cold eyes of the old Duchess. What would SHE do? Lock Ellis up in a Portland Place cellar and feed him on bread and water. No my dear, I'm not laughing. This is serious enough for anything, but forgive me if I'm thinking about you first. You have to be protected, you know. Let's be practical. Ellis is dangerous, poor chap. And there are the two old women. And that doctor last night.'

She asked him, dropping her voice:

'Can they do anything? I mean if they really tried to get me away into the country. Oh, I don't mean murder me. But shut me up, isolate me?'

'Oh no--not while Benjie and I are about. That is only a crazy idea of Ellis'. He honestly believes it, I shouldn't wonder. He may have persuaded the two old ladies that at least you are tired, overstrung. But you MUST leave him--for the time, anyway.'

'And precipitate everything,' she went on quickly. 'If I go and refuse to return there will be no question about Ellis--everyone will know.'

'Will they? I wonder. You will be blamed of course.' He looked at her. 'Vanessa, will you mind blame, criticism? You have had very little in your life, haven't you? Everyone has loved you. It will be different. You won't be the splendid Lady Herries any more . . .'

'Oh, that! That is nothing. But there IS something else . . .'

Some people had come into the Gallery. She lowered her voice.

'I don't think, Barney, that I can go on any longer without seeing Benjie. I've had thirteen years of it, you know. I love him as deeply as ever I did--more deeply, I think. He is alone, has been for years. I know that it is wrong. I've no illusions about that at all. I'm very old-fashioned about God, my friends tell me, but of this I'm sure--that to live with Benjie would be a sin and that somewhere, sometime, I should suffer and rightly suffer. If I sinned it would be deliberately, one thing against another. But I think NOW that perhaps to sin and be punished is better than to live and die without loving anyone.'

When Vanessa talked like this she seemed to Barney so touchingly childish that he wanted to pat her hand and say: There! There! my dear. I'll go with you and tell them it wasn't your fault. I'll see that you're not punished.' Sin! Good Heavens! WHAT a word! And the things that HE had done, the fine times he had had, and here he was nearing seventy and as hale and hearty . . .

'Well, that may be, my dear--or it may not be. Sin seems to me a vague word. If you're right and there's

some old tyrant waiting to see you slip and punish you, why, then I'd defy him and tell him to do his worst. Let's be practical. Go off with Benjie, well and good. But there are two things to consider. One is the social part of it. Probably that seems unimportant to you, but it isn't so nice in practice. Men and women can be very nasty when they see someone enjoying a freedom they haven't themselves the courage for.'

'Yes,' said Vanessa, and thought of Rose.

'And there's another thing. What about Benjie? How old is he now? Forty something, isn't he? You aren't either of you very young any longer. Benjie's a rover. He IS a bit of the gipsy they call him. He loves you, I know. That has been the finest, by far the finest, thing in his life. I think if you've courage enough you can bring it off. But you'll need all the courage you've got.'

She stood up, pulling down her veil, standing there in her pale dress of grey and silver, for a moment, as desolate and lonely as he'd ever seen her.

'I know,' she said. 'I'm in a muddle, aren't I? Father always used to say that I was a careless little fool--not those words, you know, but that's what it amounted to. And yet for so long I've been so careful--so absurdly careful.

As they went out she said:

'I wish we hadn't talked under the eyes of that dreadful old woman, Barney.'

As they went down the stairs Barney caught her hand.

'Remember, Vanessa, that I'm here whenever you want me. Always, whatever you decide.'

'Yes,' she said, smiling back at him. 'You, Benjie, Rose, Adrian, Lettice. Five. In the whole world. Well, I suppose there are many people would be grateful for so many.' She added, as she got into her carriage: 'And I AM grateful! You're a friend worth having, Barney.'

They dined alone, very late, she and Ellis, and at once she saw that the crisis was upon her. Ellis had some plan that was not to wait long for its explanation. Living with him, as she had done in these last years, she had learnt something of the strange country in which he was now lodging. She knew that his brain always moved along a single path, or rather the paths lay side by side like railway tracks and he might jump at any second from one to another, but that he was conscious ONLY of the one that he was, at that moment, treading. Tonight she was very close to him; she could see clearly the character of the world in which he moved, its grey uncertain darkness so that you went stumbling, hitting your shins against sharp edges like razors, or of a sudden putting your hand on a cold soft substance, a gelatinous mass on whose surface spiders wove webs. And then at such contacts you screamed. What could you do other, alone as you were, wrapped in darkness, driving forward but with no knowledge of your destination?

She understood, too, how bewildering were the sudden flares of light--like the up-blazing in some works when, conducted around by the manager, he explains the moving of some minute wheel--both of you lit by the glare of Hell. That was Ellis' world, and these flares of hot flaming light were all he had to guide him. They might be a hat with a mass of green wings, the name of Playfair, a man looking through the window, the swinging of a mirror for no cause, the whistle of a train, a book read late at night when the house is silent--these and such as these were all he had to light his path. But pursue his path he must, and would with an absorbed intensity. One track--one purpose. The burning molten substances flares to heaven, and the track and purpose are changed--changed but as intensely pursued.

She knew tonight that some intention completely absorbed him and that that intention concerned herself. Because she knew this she had a kind of prevision of what was coming. At least she was quite certain that this very evening would see the finish of all her business here. She even knew, as she smiled at Finch and said: 'No, no more asparagus, thank you, Finch', that this was the last time that she would sit at this table, the last time at least for many a day . . . One might return. She speculated about that. To what did one not return? The same tests were repeated again and again. She felt that there was neither time nor space tonight but that together she, her father, grandmother, great-grandfather, Will Leathwaite, Rose, Benjie's wife, anyone you please, all in the same moment stood up to be tested while the Eagle flew across the sun . . .

Just before she rose from the table to lead the way up to the drawing-room, she had the hallucination, staring at the wallpaper under the candlelight, that it would be for ever thus--she and Ellis facing one another over the broken fruit skins and half- emptied glasses, her father swinging her to and fro above the grass of the Cat Bells lawn, old David falling at the news of the Bastille, older Herries standing at his door waiting for his wife, Rose and Major Featherstone-Haigh, all the Herries, nay, all the world transfixed into immobility while God cries from His judgement seat: 'Now!' The candles blew in the wind, a picture swung very, very slightly on its cord, and it was Ellis, not God, who said 'Now!'

'Now, Vanessa, we will go upstairs. There is something I must tell you.'

So highly pitched was her sensibility that when they were alone together in the drawing-room and the door closed behind them, she felt like an animal entrapped. There was, in fact, good reasonable common sense here, for you could not one evening allow your husband to attempt to cut your throat without, after that, finding other evenings with him rather dangerous. The door was not, this time, locked. Finch and the young footman were within calling distance. She had

always hated this room. She had done what she could with it, taken down the yellow hangings, allowed Whistler to paint her portrait, spread rugs, bought roses, carnations, lilies--but Whistlers, rugs, roses, carnations, lilies COULD not prevent that this room was still the yellow drawing-room that, even though only last night it had swung with a maze of happy figures under the crystal candelabra, was dead like a mausoleum and cold as Hell must be for those who love the warmth.

He made her sit down beside him on the sofa. He patted her hand and his hand was warm and dry.

'Are you tired, Vanessa?' He spoke to her with infinite consideration.

'Not in the least.'

'Not after last night's festivities?'

'No. I slept until eleven.'

'What have you done today?'

'Oh, nothing very much. I went to the Rede Gallery to see Ross' portrait of the old Duchess that everyone is talking of.'

'Did anyone go with you?'

'Yes, Barney.'

'Ah . . . Barney . . . Everyone agrees that last night's was a most successful Ball.'

'I think it was. Really Finch and the servants did excellently. Finch may have his faults, but he knows his business.'

'Did you notice last night,' Ellis asked her, 'how those who were not invited came and laughed at us? It disturbed me greatly, but I said nothing to anybody. They gathered in groups, I was afraid at one time there would be trouble.'

'No one came who was not invited.'

'Oh yes. You are quite wrong. There were many there who had no right to be present. I thought at one time that I would have them driven out of the house. But that would have made a scene. Neither of us wished for that. Everything must be done quietly.'

She moved a little away. She looked at the clock. It was five minutes to ten. The servants would go to bed early tonight.

'Well,' he went on cheerfully, patting his knee with his hand, 'we must be thankful that all went off well. It is the last Ball that we shall give for a long time, because tomorrow I am going to send you into the country.'

'And where are you sending me?' she asked, smiling.

'There is a Doctor Playfair. At least I call him that. I am not sure at the moment whether that is his right name. He has a place-- in Gloucestershire, I think. But I have it all written down. I am sure that it is Gloucestershire.'

She began to speak.

'But why--'

He put up his hand. 'Now, Vanessa, please. I have one of my headaches tonight--spiders in the brain, you know. That is exactly what Doctor Playfair said when I told him about my headaches, "Like spiders in the brain?" he asked. "Exactly," I replied, "and behind the eyes." He understood as though it had been his own experience, and when I spoke to him this morning about you--he had had five minutes' conversation with you last night--'

'I remember,' said Vanessa. 'A large heavy man with spectacles and an untidy beard.'

'Exactly. Doctor Playfair. He called to see me this morning. At this house in Gloucestershire--I THINK he said Gloucestershire--you will find every comfort. It is very quiet there. There are woods. Only the other patients--'

Vanessa laughed. 'This is all nonsense, of course, about my wanting a rest. But even if it were not, do you really suppose, Ellis, that I would leave you all alone here?'

'Ah, that is what I had intended to tell you. I shall NOT be alone. Vera and Winifred will for the future live here. This will be their home.'

So THAT was it! At the same instant as she realized with a flash of discovery that her responsibility was ended--and HOW strange THAT revelation was, liberating her, she suddenly saw, from years of bondage--a horror of being caught seized her. Those two old women! Did she not act immediately she would never escape. How they would hold her she did not know, but hold her they would! So many things came to her at the same instant and with these a new view of Ellis as though he had become twice as dangerous and twice as far removed. Through all the insanity of this last year she had thought at least that he needed her; now, with that spoken sentence, she saw that he did not need her. Those two old women had taken her place . . . But there were three against her now instead of one.

'Vera and Winifred? To make this their home? But that's preposterous. You are joking, Ellis. You--'

'It is arranged,' he answered, smiling and patting her knee. 'Very satisfactory. You will rest in the country and they will see that I am comfortable while you are away. I shall shut up part of the house. I am very tired of parties and I shall see no one--only Doctor Playfair and one or two old friends. The house will be thoroughly cleaned, swept from top to bottom. The windows need cleaning. They have grown darker every day.'

He came very close to her. He put his hand on her forehead.

'See how hot your forehead is! You have been ill for a long, long time. That is why I have myself been so very uneasy. Doctor Playfair agrees that what you need is quiet. And what I need is quiet. We will have shutters on the windows and someone will see to the doors. They have been far too noisy.'

He got up. 'Tomorrow afternoon,' he said, 'you shall go down to Gloucestershire.' He stood, looking down at her.

'Poor dear, poor dear!' He kissed her forehead. 'Go to bed now. Rest is what you want. I shall be in my room for a while. I have most important work--very important work indeed.'

When he was gone she sat there thinking. Her first impulse was for immediate flight. But where? Rose. Yes, Rose. Then she thought: 'No. This will be cowardice. And besides this may be all Ellis' imagination. How do I know that this absurd idea about Winifred and Vera is not invented by him? And this ridiculous notion about my going into the country. Of course he cannot MAKE me go. I must talk to him again. Just now I said nothing. I must talk to Barney. Perhaps HE will see Ellis. In any case I can't leave him like this without knowing the truth, the facts . . .'

Then she thought of Benjie. She was in a turmoil of weariness, fear, indignation. The appalling element in it was her own isolation, and she saw now that, for months, she had been becoming more isolated; everything had been closing in upon her, shutting her off.

It came to her like a cry. She would see Benjie. About her future now she was reckless. She had done her utmost, she had fought battle after battle, and now she would fight no more. The thought that half an hour from now she might be with Benjie, have, at last, after all this long waiting, his love again . . . simply to see him, to hear his voice, to escape from this fantasy of the last years so easily . . . the room swam before her eyes.

She ran up to her room, found a hat and cloak, waited on the landing, listening, reached the hall in safety (no sound in all the house but the ticking of the clocks), opened the door and, at the end of Hill Street, found a hansom. She gave the man the number in Half Moon Street. Benjie would, in all probability, be out. Would she wait in his rooms for him? The old stock situation of the Society melodrama . . . As the hansom turned into Half Moon Street, which was only a minute's distance from Hill Street, she tried to think what she would do, but she could not. She was ringing the bell before she came to any decision. A grave elderly manservant opened the door.

'Is Mr Herries at home?' she asked.

He did not seem in the least surprised to see her.

'If you will come in a moment, madam, I will see. What name, madam?'

'Lady Herries.'

'Very good, my lady, if you would not mind waiting.'

He disappeared around the corner of the stairs. Almost at once he appeared again, saying:

'Yes, Mr Herries is in. Will you come up, please?'

Benjie was at the door of his room. She went in and he followed her, closing the door behind him. He stared at her as though a cloud of angels had floated down to him from the ceiling.

'Vanessa!'

'Yes. This is just like a play, isn't it?' She was trembling but was determined that he should not see it.

At the very sight of him she was so happy that she could only smile, stare back at him, then, with fumbling hands, take off her hat.

'Here,' he said. 'Take this chair. It is the only comfortable one. Oh, my God, Vanessa! If you knew how many times I've sat here imagining just this: saying to myself, "And now the bell will ring and Humphries will come to the door and he will say 'Lady Herries', and I . . ."'

'That's in the play too.' She steadied her hands, holding them tightly together. 'But there is nothing dramatic in this, Benjie. I have come only for five minutes. But that isn't true either. It IS dramatic, I suppose. You must give me advice. Tell me what to do.'

He sat down in the chair on the other side of the fireplace, his small body balanced forward, staring and staring and staring.

She saw that he was looking splendid, as brown and hard as a russet apple, spare, taut, not changed. Oh, not changed in the least these twenty years!

'I shouldn't have done this, I suppose,' she went on. 'At least--I don't know. There's no SHOULDN'T any more. The fact is, quite simply, that Ellis is proposing to send me away to a private asylum in the country tomorrow . . . It has been tonight a situation that I couldn't face by myself any longer. You know about Ellis? You have heard something?'

'My God!' Benjie shouted, springing up. 'Send YOU away? Send you to an asylum?'

'Yes. Quietly, Benjie dear. We have got to be sensible about this. The fact is that Ellis has been out of his mind for the last year or more. Twice he has tried to kill me, and still I held on. It has been miserable, tragic . . . I don't want to talk about that part of it. That is past. But I must do something now, now, at once. You know Winifred and Vera Trent?'

Benjie nodded.

'They have taken charge of him. I think they intended to from the first. Oh, I don't mean that it is they who have planned to get me out of the house. I don't think they had the least idea of it. That is only Ellis' crazy notion. But it has come to this--that tonight, an hour ago, Ellis told me that they were from now on to live in the house, I was to be sent into the country, most of the house to be shut up. I don't know how much is Ellis' fantasy, how much is truth, but I DID know, as he went on talking, that I could stand no more, I have been alone in this thing too long. And so--I came to see you.'

'Oh, Vanessa!' he sighed. 'At last!'

She nodded, smiling.

'Yes--at last. I have wasted my whole life. I can't go on without you any longer.'

He came over to her, knelt down beside her and took her hand. He sat on the floor, resting his head against her, her hand pulsing against his. They stayed for a long time quietly, without speaking, feeling as at every long-separated meeting they had always done--that there had never been any parting.

Then he became practical. He asked her every sort of question and she told him everything. For the first time in all these many years she poured everything from her heart, her unresting love for himself, her increasing loneliness, the friendship that she and Ellis had had for the first few years, the influence of Miss Fortescue, Ellis' headaches, the day of the Jubilee when he had first made her uneasy, the night when he had attacked her, and then detail after detail to the last Cumberland visit.

'But now--even now--I would not go were it not for those two old women. How I hate them! Oh, Benjie, how I hate them! But it isn't that; it is that my responsibility is over.'

He nodded.

'You have always been dreadfully conscientious, Vanessa. And now you are coming to me--for ever and ever and ever, amen.'

'Yes. I talked to Barney about it this afternoon.'

'And what did HE say?'

'He pointed out that the world would be shocked, Violet would close her doors to me, I should no more be asked to Grosset.'

'Yes, that's true. And shall you mind?'

'I don't know--a little, perhaps. What I DO know is that I am doing wrong. I shall suffer for it in one way or another. I suppose that, without realizing it, I have been thinking of this for a long time. I am not a fool about it. I know the delight-- and I know the punishment.'

'Punishment!' he cried. 'There will be no punishment! We shall be happy for ever!'

She smiled, shaking her head.

'Of course nobody is happy for ever.' She put her hand under his chin, turning his face up towards hers. 'Benjie, are you SURE you want me? Are you certain? I'm middle-aged, you know. You're middle-aged too, but for a man it is quite different. Are you SURE that you want me--still--after all this time?'

'Sure? Sure? Why, Vanessa, I love you more than I did twenty years ago. Loving you has been the only good thing in me--that, and caring for Tom. Are YOU sure,' he went on, 'that YOU want me? I'm not much, you know, Vanessa. Apart from you I'm nothing at all. With you I may still do something.'

'Yes, I'm sure,' she said quietly.

'It is true, too, what Barney said. We shall be cut, you know. Wherever we live someone will be unkind. And as to the relations! Yet another scandal in the Herries history!'

'Oh yes.' She nodded her head. 'I understand just how things will be.' (Again, for a flashing instant, she thought of Rose.) 'I understand everything, I think,' she went on. 'I'm not a child now. I have seen how things go. Often and often I have been tempted to come to you. You must have known that! But I was wrong when I married Ellis, and his needing me--or my thinking that he did--kept me there. And then,' she added after a moment, 'to fly in the face of God. I know those are only words to you, but it is true reality to me. But if I can make you happy--isn't that something? You see, I've never made anyone happy since my father died. No one. Isn't that awful? If I had made MYSELF happy it would have been a little, but not even that. Until tonight. Until now. Now I am so happy that there MUST be something right in it somewhere. Don't you think so?'

'I don't know about God. I think that's a tall word. But here and now we are going to do the best we can by one another. Until your God separates us we'll stay together just as years ago we meant to do.'

After a while they discussed the immediate plan.

'Tonight I'm returning to Hill Street,' Vanessa said. 'I must see Ellis once more and know what is fact and what isn't. I can't leave him until I know.'

'Then I am coming back with you,' Benjie said.

'To Hill Street?'

'Certainly. I must see that you are safe. If Ellis has gone to bed and is asleep, well and good. What time is it? Nearly twelve. He ought to be asleep. If he is not, I will talk to him. Don't be frightened. There shall be none of my famous fights. But I don't leave you until you are safe.'

She agreed. She wished now to hide nothing. If Ellis in reality intended to carry out his crazy plan it was right that she should be no longer alone. And she felt a feverish impatience that this absurd business should be settled once and for all. And she could not face Ellis alone again that night.

They walked round to Hill Street. In that clear air they heard Big Ben strike midnight as she opened the door with her key. They went up to the drawing-room. Ellis was standing there in front of the big marble fireplace.

Benjie spoke at once.

'I beg your pardon, Ellis, for coming at this impossible hour. Vanessa came round to me tonight to tell me that you intended to send her into the country tomorrow--to some doctor's. Well, Vanessa and I are very old friends, you know. We have obeyed your wishes all these years and kept apart, but when Vanessa told me this we thought it better that we should both see you. We can talk about it tomorrow if you prefer, but in that case Vanessa will go to a hotel for the night.'

Vanessa said: 'Ellis, after our talk tonight I couldn't stay here alone. For both our sakes--'

But Ellis, without moving and very quietly, waved his hand at the door.

'Would you mind,' he said to Benjie, 'coming farther into the room? They may be listening outside.'

Benjie came forward.

'Thank you.' Ellis looked at him very severely. 'I thought I told you that you were never to enter my house again?'

'Yes,' said Benjie. 'You did, and I wouldn't have come had it not been for Vanessa. Frankly, Ellis, she's frightened. You shouldn't have talked about that nonsense about sending her into the country.'

'That is perfectly correct,' said Ellis. 'She is going to Doctor Playfair's.'

'Well--she is not,' said Benjie. 'Nothing of the kind. You must see, Ellis, that she can't live with you any longer after this. I didn't want her to come back here tonight at all, but she said she must know whether you MEANT what you said. It seems that you do.'

Vanessa had been standing, her hand up to the white cloak with the high white collar that she was wearing. She had been looking into Ellis' face, trying to find there some appeal to herself for help, some kindliness. If at that moment he had turned and gone to her, blindly asking her, as he used to do, that she should help him, she would, even now, have stayed . . .

But he did not seem in the least unusual. There was no sign of madness in him anywhere, and after that one sentence to Benjie about the door there was, in this scene, NO queerness. There was no QUEERNESS, but there was hatred.

'You see, Ellis,' Vanessa said, 'I have realized that you don't need me anymore. We haven't been happy together for a long time, have we? And as you don't need me we had better separate.'

'That is our affair,' he said. 'We can settle that tomorrow. If you were well, Vanessa, I'd have something to say to you for bringing this dirty ruffian here. As it is, Herries, get out and keep out.'

'Come on, Vanessa,' Benjie said. 'Let's go.'

She took a step forward to Ellis.

'Ellis. Don't you see how impossible it is?--'

He moved forward to her. Benjie stepped between them, then, taking her arm, he drew her away.

With quick steps Ellis followed them. He passed them as though he did not see them and ran down the stairs. In the hall he turned.

In a high, shrill, convulsed voice he cried:

'Get out, both of you! Get out! Get out!'

At the same moment the Chinese clock struck the half-hour. Benjie, halfway down the stairs, put his hand on Vanessa's shoulder. They waited. He did not know what Ellis would do. But the scene ended very quietly. Ellis did not move. Vanessa and Benjie walked out of the house.

They found a hansom in Piccadilly.

'And now where?' Benjie asked.

'I'll go to Rose,' Vanessa answered.

She was trembling and he put his arm round her, holding her close to him. Benjie gave the address to the cabman.

Part Three

The Lover

HAPPINESS IN RAVENGLASS

One fine September afternoon of that momentous year 1899, Mrs Runcing of Olive Bank, Ravenglass, came to tea with Mrs Jocelyn of Sea View Cottage. It was a most beautiful day, and the sun caressed the sea, the sea caressed the shore, and the birds rising in little flocks from the island hovered against the quivering sky like blown petals, silver-grey, and as the wing turned, of glittering metal. The cry of the gulls made the lazy sky lazier.

The two ladies sat at the window of Sea View Cottage and drank their tea.

'I'm using this room,' Mrs Jocelyn explained, 'because of my lodgers. I'm not sure that I don't like it quite as well as the other.'

A lady and gentleman rode past on a tandem bicycle. The gentleman rang his bell.

'What's that, dear?' an odd, croaking, half-strangled voice asked from within the room.

'Only a bicycle, Mother.'

On the farther side of the fireplace, almost hidden with shawls, was old Mrs Burgess, Mrs Jocelyn's mother. Mrs Burgess was ninety-two and, except that she was never warm, was a wonder for her age. She was as lively and spiteful and selfish and scandal-mongering as though she had been a young thing of twenty. There was nothing that happened from Barrow to Whitehaven in which she did not take an interest, and most especially, of course, in anything that had to do with love and--most particularly--illicit love. She was a Puritan and had all the eager questing spirit of the Puritan. Her curiosity it was that had kept her alive and would, it seemed, keep her alive for evermore.

Her daughter, Hester Jocelyn, was in every way her opposite: a little, warm-blooded, impetuous, charitable, kind-hearted woman whose husband had, ten years earlier, run away with an actress to South America. She

had not loved him very much, but her loneliness was often worst at three in the morning when she could not sleep-- quite terrible, yet she was cheerful, busy, charitable and infinitely patient with her horrid old mother. Something of a heroine perhaps.

Mrs Runcing, her visitor, was nothing of a heroine: a long bony woman with three daughters whom she would sell her eyes to marry. She threw them at the men of the district as you throw darts at a dartboard. As with so many women of their time, they had been trained to nothing, taught nothing. Their father thought them too tiresome for words, their mother hated them because no one would have them and yet loved them because they were hers. The poor Miss Runcings!

'Things look bad in South Africa,' said Mrs Runcing. 'Henry says we shall have war for certain. It's all the fault of that wicked old Krüger. And so you like your lodgers, Hetty dear?' She laid rum butter thickly on her bread. She was a greedy woman.

'Like them!' said Mrs Jocelyn. 'I should think so! No one could help it. Mr Herries is as gay a gentleman as you'd find anywhere, always singing and laughing. No trouble at all. But Mrs Herries is my favourite. She's a LOVELY lady--so kind and thoughtful, and so friendly. It's nice to see a married pair so happy--and not young either. I've never had visitors I've taken to so.'

There was a pause. Mrs Jocelyn looked up.

'What is it, Cecilia? You've something on your mind.'

Mrs Runcing paused yet longer, then, dropping her voice, said: 'Hetty, there's something you ought to know.'

Mrs Jocelyn moved uneasily. She knew well this opening of her friend's and always it meant no good.

'Know? What ought I to know?'

'It's just like you, Hetty. The last in the place to be aware of what everyone is saying.'

'WHAT is everyone saying?'

'About Mrs Herries. She isn't Mrs Herries at all. She's Lady Herries--and she and Mr Herries are no more married than . . . than you and I are!'

'Cecilia, what ARE you saying?' Mrs Jocelyn got up from the window, 'Now I won't have it! You've always got some story about someone, Cecilia. It's too bad. It's a shame.'

'Oh, is it! Always got some story, have I? That's a nice thing to say to an old friend. I'm telling you out of kindness. It's been the talk here for days and you ought to know it.'

There was an excited movement of the shawls from the back of the room.

'I'm sure Mr and Mrs Herries are married. I don't care what anyone says.'

'Well, you're wrong for once. Mrs Herries is Lady Herries, wife of Sir Ellis Herries in London. She ran away from him last year, with this Mr Herries.'

'What's that you are saying, Cecilia?' the old lady from the fireplace croaked. 'Not married, you say? Not married? Well, I never! Well, I never did! Not married!'

'Of course they're not married. The affair made a sensation last year in London. And more than that, they've been lovers for years and years. Everybody knows them. The Herries are Cumberland people or, anyway, they've been in Cumberland for centuries. There was an old Mr Herries lived here in Ravenglass years ago, they say, and this Mr Herries has a house near Bassenthwaite Lake. Lady Herries was brought up on Derwentwater. She was a great lady in London for years. I call it a piece of downright impertinence for them to come back to this part of the country where everyone knows them. Disgusting, I call it. But they say there's been one scandal after another in that family. Years and years ago there was a Mr Herries who was a holy terror, and some fifty years back one of the Herries murdered another one somewhere by Keswick. It's a disgrace their coming to Ravenglass. They should be ashamed to show their faces!'

Mrs Runcing had not intended to be so violent, but, as often before, when denouncing the vices of others her own virtues grew in colour and strength. As others went down she herself went up, and the higher she went the better she felt.

Little Mrs Jocelyn had turned very pale. At last she said:

'I don't care whether they're married or not. They shall stay here as long as they like!'

'Hetty!' Here was a thing for a decent Christian woman to say!

'I don't care! I mean it!'

'Think of what people will say!'

And there was a croak from the fireplace: 'Not married . . . in this house!'

Then, beyond the half-open window, they heard a step on the gravel path. Both women turned and looked. Vanessa was coming up from the sea.

'All I know,' said Mrs Jocelyn, almost sobbing with emotion, 'is that that's the finest lady I've ever met. She's welcome to this roof as long as she wishes.'

Vanessa was walking, her head back to the sea breeze, her dress blown against her legs. Her face was warm with colour. She had grown a little stouter in this last year, her bosom fuller, and, carrying herself thus strongly, she moved like a woman who was happy, free and self-confident.

This seemed to Mrs Runcing, whose own bosom, do what she would, was never what it ought to be, insulting.

'You'd think she had nothing to be ashamed of,' she said.

'Neither she has,' answered Mrs Jocelyn indignantly. 'They're happy, aren't they? And that's more than most people manage to be. I expect her husband was horrible.'

Mrs Runcing set her lips. 'You'll be sorry, Hetty,' she said. 'Encouraging immorality. You'll see how people will talk . . .'

Meanwhile Vanessa had gone into the little sitting-room on the other side of the passage, taken off her straw hat, and sat down by the window to wait for Benjie. He had gone fishing. In an hour's time he would return, they would sit reading, talking, the veils of light would fall over the sea, the stars would come out, the cries of the birds would die away; after supper they would take a last walk, then, tired and happy, return, light the lamp, play chess, go up the crooked staircase to bed.

She sat there, dreaming.

More than a year had passed and still God had not let loose His thunderbolts. She had known a period of perfect unrestrained happiness. She looked back, first to the time at Eastbourne, then to the months in France, then to the wonderful glorious experience of coming home to Cumberland. What troubles had there been? In Eastbourne she had been cut by Mrs Harbin, a friend of Violet's. Alfred and his wife had met her in the hotel lounge and that had been a little uncomfortable. On the other hand Adrian, at one time, Rose at another, Barney at another, had stayed with them. The news from London had at first been a little distressing. The talk had been, she understood, terrific. The sympathy had gone, universally, to Ellis. Winifred and Vera Trent had gone to live in Hill Street and, so far as Vanessa could discover, Ellis had been quite tranquil, had enjoyed the sympathy and had allowed it generally to be understood that he was able to bear his misfortunes like a gentleman. Often--and this was perhaps her severest trouble-- she asked herself whether she had imagined all that queerness. But no: the scene in Cumberland, the frenzies and tears in Hill Street had been real enough, but how much of it had been histrionic, an attempt on

Ellis' side to catch her sympathy, a passion for melo-drama?

Strangely the question of Ellis' insanity was no longer the main one. She knew now, in the light of these last months, that for years she had been living in prison. It was only now that she understood how solemn, how unhumorous, how dreary that Hill Street life had been, what a DREARY creature she herself had become! Everything in it had been false, the social fuss, the hours that she had spent with people for whom she did not care, the shamness of her interests. She thought of the balls, the receptions, the silly games, the sillier country houses and race meetings and baccarat; her weak good nature, her amiability, her own stupidity, she told herself, had kept her there long, long after she should have left it.

And Benjie? She smiled as she lay back in her chair looking at the long dune like the back of a whale over whose brown surface little waves broke in edges of white and silver. Benjie was not perfect. She had never supposed that he would be. There had been the night at Eastbourne when she had entered their bedroom to discover him kissing the chambermaid. Twice, once at Eastbourne, once in Paris, he had left her for two days without warning. Sometimes he was out of temper, sometimes (but very seldom) he was drunk. He knew some very queer people, although he was scrupulous about the company he introduced her to. Once he had declared that he must go immediately to Italy to meet a man in Siena. Tom, who, although he was only still a boy, had much wisdom, had settled that little business. Tom, by good fortune, thought Vanessa the most wonderful woman in the world.

Vanessa, on her side, was not always perfect. Far from it. She was impatient, suffered fools badly (and some of Benjie's friends were very foolish), sometimes nagged Benjie, sometimes (as she well knew) bored him with her naïveté, her religion, her obstinacy. But they had been saved, both of them, by their splendid comradeship. Because they had been friends all their lives long that business of compromise, so difficult in the first year of marriage, had been quite natural for both of them. They loved for every kind of reason, but chiefly because they knew one another so well, and admired and laughed at, for the most part, the same things. The wildness in Benjie Vanessa understood because, in her own way, she had the same wildness. They must both be free. They stayed together only because they loved one another. The troubles that they had were on the surface because the base of their relationship was firm, unshakeable. They were honest, but not so honest that they were for ever challenging weaknesses. OF COURSE they were weak, mistaken, faulty in this way or that. They took these things for granted. Because Benjie kissed the chambermaid it did not mean that he did not love Vanessa. He loved ONLY Vanessa. He had loved Vanessa only, all his life long.

But the best of their relationship was its gaiety. Vanessa found that she had not been gay for thirteen years but now, like a language once learnt and long unpractised, living with the natives again, back it returned.

Love, if it is to be worth anything, must be honest, trusting, humorous, protective, far-seeing. With them both it was all these things.

And under its influence Vanessa grew and developed. It had been her danger always that because of her great simplicity of nature she would become tiresome company. Her mother and father had both been very simple people and it was possible that they had bored a good many persons. Vanessa, in her London years, had learnt superficial variety--that is, she had been trained to adapt herself to a great many different characters--but her lack of subtlety sometimes revealed her. Bertrand, the novelist, whose eye was so sharp that its rather fishy, sleepy indifference often deceived the innocent, said that the only women who were interesting were the good ones who wanted to be bad, that no women were so dull as the bad women who wanted to be good. The bad ones who were content to be bad were, he said, amusing companions, but they were all the same--know one and you knew all.

Now Vanessa had, in London, been a good woman determined to be unprejudiced and open-minded. She defended Rose because she loved her, but also a little to show that she was above censorship. She had never REALLY known the kind of life that a woman like Rose was leading. Her father, Barney, her husband, Lettice Marrable--from none of these did she get the real sense of it. But after a year with Benjie she knew. They talked together like two schoolboys without any reticences whatever. She was now TRULY aware of the humour, the generosity, the comradeship, the dirty untidy tragedy of the 'vicious' world. She knew that it was NOT vicious--simply a place inhabited by the uncontrolled, the needy, the weak, the greedy and, above all, the lonely. That the very last thing that it called for was superior patronage, and that those who lived in it did not wish, for the most part, for any sympathy from anybody.

So Vanessa grew wise. She learnt now to be patient, tolerant and unpriggish. This continuous love that burnt steadily from hour to hour, from day to day, warmed her heart so that it was impossible NOT to be generous. It is only the disappointed, starved, and robbed who are jealous and unfair.

Waiting now for Benjie she had on her lap and read from time to time Judith's old green-bound book. She had rescued it from her father's room at Uldale on the night of the fire. Judith, in her old age, had dictated it to Aunt Jane, and in Aunt Jane's clear spidery hand it was as fresh as though written last week. There was a piece about Ravenglass.

It seemed that, in the spring of 1737, Judith's father, Rogue Herries, had ridden over with his son David to spend a night or two with his brother Harcourt Herries, an old bachelor who had lived for many years in Ravenglass.

'David used to tell us,' Judith's book said, 'of that visit to Ravenglass as one of the striking incidents in his life because of the quarrel that he had with his father there. He would describe to us the ride over Stye Head on horseback, how gloomy his father was on that ride, suffering from one of his "demons", how they came into Ravenglass in the evening, clattering over the cobbles, smelling the sea, and hearing the gulls. Then there was Uncle Harcourt, who was a very precise old bachelor and wouldn't have a woman in his house, and he wore, David remembered, a wonderful ring on his finger with a green stone, and a rose-coloured skirted coat. After supper Uncle Harcourt talked of the London of Queen Anne, where he had been as a boy, of the Sacheverell Riots, of the Thames barge the Folly, and the coffee houses, and of how he had seen Mrs Rogers as Berenice.

'Uncle Harcourt was a fervent Jacobite and gave the toast of "The King over the water", breaking his wine glass after it, and he recited to them Pope's Elegy to the Memory of an Unfortunate Lady. Then David's father lost his temper, took David out to sea and ordered him to strip for a beating as a punishment for some fancied misdemeanour. David refused and said that he was no longer a child, and that was the beginning of a new relationship between them. This,' Judith went on, 'was one of David's favourite stories and, as a little girl, while I listened I could see it all as vividly as though I had been there--the London of Queen Anne, and the little bachelor declaiming Pope, and David and his father standing by the sea.'

'And here I am,' thought Vanessa, 'in this same place as though time never had been. Little Uncle Harcourt might walk in at this door any moment. I knew Judith so well and she lived in the same house with the man whose uncle saw the Sacheverell Riots. In London now they have the telephone and there are these new "moving pictures" and Alfred Herries has a motor-car. Time does not separate any of us, but rather our stupidities, selfishness, and fears. Judith, if she were here, would scold me for moralizing. She always hated it. But, on the other hand, she would be glad that I am happy and would altogether approve of my running away from Ellis . . .'

She heard the hall door open and close, a quick step, and Benjie had come in. 'They say that when you live with anyone their features become so familiar that you can't see them any more. Well, I can see Benjie all right, his bright eyes with the humorous crows' feet at the corners, his brown hands, the part of his forehead that grows white above the brown just below his hair; I know how his arms fasten about me and how strong is his kiss on my lips. It is all as new as though it had never happened until now, and my heart beats at the sound of his step as though now for the first time he was about to tell me that he loved me.'

He went up and washed. Mrs Jocelyn brought in the supper, and after they had eaten they sat close together by the window.

'I've been reading Judith's book, Benjie,' Vanessa said. 'The part about Ravenglass. It seemed as though time hadn't passed at all and little Harcourt Herries might be walking in on us with his green ring and rose-coloured coat. My great-grandfather was born in William III's reign, and Alfred has a motor-car. So soon as I am back in this part of the country time doesn't exist. We none of us die here--'

'Take a step,' Benjie said lazily, 'and you are at Gosforth; another, and it's Ennerdale. Then over the hill to Buttermere, Honister, Borrowdale. Yes, we're back in our own country, Vanessa. Bold of us, perhaps. The old boatman wasn't so friendly today. He knows we're living in sin.'

She did not answer. They had been living in sin for a year and she was not yet aware of it. Was it now, when she had returned to her own people, that she WOULD be aware?

'I've had a letter from that man Alington. He advises me to go in for those Australian mines--at once, without losing a minute. Shall I?'

She looked at him quietly. 'No, I don't think so.' Everyone was speculating. The fever in London had spread everywhere, and Gold Mines glittered on every doorstep. 'You promised me, you know. We don't know enough about it. We have enough. We don't want to be rich, either of us.'

'Don't we?' She saw that he was restless. 'I'm not sure that I don't. I've never been rich. I wouldn't mind the sensation.'

She put out her hand and caught his.

'You're restless--what is it?'

'It's South Africa for one thing. It looks bad--or good if you like. A war would be fun. We haven't had one for ages. Tom would go as a war correspondent if he weren't so young.'

'Well, YOU'RE too old to go. That's one comfort.'

'Oh no, I'm not,' he answered quickly.

'You're forty-four.'

'What's that? No age at all. And I'm as fit as a fiddle.'

'Let's not talk of it.' She stilled her fear. 'I'm so happy. Don't spoil it.'

'If there WAS a war,' he said, 'it would be only for a week or two. I'd be back in no time--with a VC probably and all the Family greeting me like a hero.'

He drew his chair closer to her and leant his head on her shoulder.

'Vanessa, you're not tired of me yet?'

'No, I'm not tired of you.'

'How happy we've been and are!' He sighed. 'Why can't everyone find love like this? It seems so simple when you get it. I suppose that somewhere there's the right person for everyone--one for each--but they don't meet. Do you find there's something a little pathetic in two people of our age loving one another so? We ought to be young--we ought to be twenty--as we might have been had I not been such a fool. And I'm still a fool, Vanessa. It may break out any time.'

She laid her hand against his cheek.

'We used to say long ago that nothing could separate us. Nothing has. Nothing can now.'

'Yes--death,' he answered.

'You know that I don't think so.'

'Without our bodies? Shall we love still? You without your hair, your eyes, without the warm touch of your hand against my cheek? When I can see you smile no longer nor the way that you put your hand up to your hair, nor hear your voice. And I! I'll be a poor ghost, Vanessa--'

'What of your Valhalla under the hill, the men singing?'

'Ah, you won't be there! And I'll be such a wild ghost, flying from Top to Top, haunting old women down the chimney, stealing the butter from the dairy, pinching the young women. I love you for every conceivable reason, Vanessa, but without your body I shouldn't know you. I'd be as restless as I used to be. I'd never find you. I'd go searching from ghost to ghost . . . And you'd be so good. You'd be in favour in Heaven, one of the guardian angels. They'd have no use for me, I'm afraid, and whatever job they set me to do I'd do it wrong.'

She kissed him.

'I'd find you. Wherever you went I'd go too.'

'Are you sure,' he asked her, 'that you never miss London? Not Ellis, of course, nor Hill Street--but all your friends and the good times you had with all the nobs. Don't you MIND being a disgrace and something to make virtuous ladies shudder over?'

'I've never been so happy in all my life,' she said, her voice very low. 'I seem to have reached middle age quite emptily--as though I'd been born yesterday. There was my childhood--that was happy. And now there's this. Nothing between.'

'And now there's this,' he repeated contentedly.

They were aware that the door opened. They both turned together, thinking that it was Mrs Jocelyn who had come to say goodnight. The lamp was burning dimly and in the half-light they saw the oddest figure in the doorway. It was old Mrs Burgess, wrapped in a multitude of shawls, leaning on her stick; she stood there, her old brown wrinkled face pushed forward like the head of a tortoise. She stared at them, they could see, as though she could never satisfy her curiosity. Then she vanished.

'What did SHE want?' Benjie asked. He got up and went to the door. 'What cheek! To come in without knocking--'

'She's half crazy, poor old thing,' Vanessa said. 'Mrs Jocelyn says that she ought to be in her bed, but they can't keep her there.'

'What did she want? She looked at us as though she'd never seen us before.'

They played their game of chess and went up to bed. Long after Benjie was asleep in Vanessa's arms she lay there awake. He slept like a child, his hand on her breast. She lay there, forcing herself resolutely, quite calmly, to a new courage. Instinct, light words lightly spoken, some shadow like the finger of a cloud on a sunlit hill, told her that it would be needed.

She was right. It WAS needed. Next day Benjie had moved into his savage state. That was how she always put it to herself. It was as though he reverted into some old wild existence where the rules, objects, dangers, joys of life were all quite different from this one. He seemed physically to change. He could not stay in the same spot from one tick of the clock to another. He moved about the room as though he were unclothed, his brown finely muscled body moving naked through tall grass, his eyes shiningly alert for the enemy. As often as not he did not hear what you said to him, he snapped back replies, he suddenly started walking down the road saying that he did not know when he would return.

The happy thing was that Vanessa understood this transformed state to perfection. She was aware of it often in herself but, being a woman and therefore having all her eggs in one basket (which was Benjie), Benjie could satisfy her wildest longings. She could not satisfy Benjie's. Nor did she try. When this restlessness came on him she let him go free.

But now there was more serious trouble. His words about South Africa had clutched her heart. Was there going to be war? If so, then Benjie would be off . . . Nothing could keep him . . . He would revel in it. He would be killed, perhaps. People were killed in wars . . .

Today was the eighteenth of September, and it seemed that, on the sixteenth, the Transvaal had replied to the British proposals of starting the argument all over again by proposing to revert to a joint Commission. There was something sinister in the tone underlying the Boer phrases.

What was it all about? For a long while she had not taken it with any seriousness. It was all due, it seemed, to Krüger's fear of Rand dominion of his country. It all went back to the old Gold Rushes into the Rand. Rather naturally, Vanessa considered, Krüger thought that to give franchise to the Rand population must entirely alter Boer rule. He was honest, perhaps, in wishing to keep the Transvaal an agricultural country. On the other hand, the British Government must protect its subjects. But ought those subjects to be in that country at all? Didn't it look as though a small, resolute, independent people were to be bullied and affronted by a big Power when all that the little people wanted was freedom to live as they wished on their own soil? On the other hand, COULD Great Britain allow her own sons to be persecuted, ill-treated, mishandled, and say nothing?

It seemed, Vanessa thought with a sigh, one of those questions that had so clearly two sides to it. And the Boers were thick-headed, obstinate, stupid, hypocritical perhaps . . . On the other hand, it WAS their country! Or wasn't it? She soon, however, abandoned the wider, more public question for the private personal one. If there was a war, Benjie would go . . . If Benjie went . . . She pulled herself to her full height, clasping her hands behind her head, staring in front of her. The stiffest job of her whole life was approaching her.

Then a very absurd thing occurred. Coming into the house one morning she encountered old Mrs Burgess, who was shuffling along in flat slippers, trailing shawls about her and making that odd wheezy noise peculiarly her own. She saw Vanessa and, thrusting her old head forward, hissed some word. Then, with yellow convulsive hands, drawing her shawls tightly about her, she slip-slopped into her fastness.

Vanessa did not know what the word was, but it was evidently intended to express moral horror and indignation. She asked Mrs Jocelyn to come and speak to her. She told her of it. She liked Mrs Jocelyn extremely.

'Sit down, Mrs Jocelyn,' Vanessa said. 'Let's sit together by the window.' They sat down. 'Now I'm not wrong, am I, in supposing that your mother has learnt that Mr Herries and I are not married?'

Mrs Jocelyn nervously rubbed her hands together.

'No, Mrs Herries. That's correct.'

'I should have told you before. I'm not Mrs Herries. I'm Lady Herries. I left my husband last year.'

'Oh yes . . .' said Mrs Jocelyn nervously.

'I should have told you. I did not mean to conceal anything. I would have told you at once if you had asked me, but I really did not feel that it was anyone's business but our own. Now I suppose you would like us to go. I quite understand and I do hope you'll forgive us for putting you into this unpleasant position. We have been so happy here and you have been so very good to us.'

Mrs Jocelyn was a sentimental and emotional little woman. Her eyes glittered with tears as she looked out of the window. Many things made her cry: the music of a band in the street, reading of a deed of heroism in the newspaper, details of a wedding, the more moving portions of almost any novel. But although she was emotional, she had the strength (and sometimes the obstinacy) of Mr Krüger himself.

'Oh no, Lady Herries,' she said. 'Please don't think of going. A friend told us, a week or so ago. It appears that you and Mr Herries are well known in Cumberland and Westmorland. You come from these parts, do you not? So of course the people here have talked about you. But please pay no attention. Mother is a very old lady and not always accountable. It doesn't matter at all. Really it doesn't.'

Vanessa smiled.

'Thank you, Mrs Jocelyn, for saying that. We'll never forget it. But of course we mustn't stay here. It would be wrong for us to make it awkward for you in any way.'

'It doesn't make it awkward,' said Mrs Jocelyn with tremendous energy. 'I hope you won't think it impertinent, but my knowing you, Lady Herries, has been the nicest thing that has ever happened to me. I don't know, of course, what reasons you had for leaving your husband, but I'm sure they were very good ones. There were times in the past when I quite easily might have left Mr Jocelyn, although now that he isn't here I wouldn't like to say anything against him. I'm sorry, of course, that you and Mr Herries can't be married, but as you can't you can't, and that's all there is to it.'

Vanessa was very much moved.

'I'm afraid that isn't all there is to it,' she said. 'I have done something that is wrong. I did it knowing that it was wrong, and the fact that we are both happy doesn't make it any more right. But I did it deliberately and I will take what comes. All the same it's not fair that anyone else should be involved, especially anyone as kind and good as you are.'

'I'm neither kind nor good,' Mrs Jocelyn replied. 'I'm often most unkind to my mother, I'm afraid. And as to being good, I'm too old now, I suppose, to be anything else very much, but when I was younger there were times when I would have run away from Mr Jocelyn most gladly if there had been anyone to run away with.'

She got up and added, smiling rather timidly:

'I've not had many friends and my life hasn't been very exciting, but when I HAVE a friend--well, there it is. If you were to go away I should be very unhappy. And don't mind Mother. I'll see that she doesn't worry you.'

Vanessa went with her to the door and kissed her.

'Then we'll stay,' she said.

On October 9th the Boers delivered their ultimatum. For three weeks after this neither Benjie nor Vanessa spoke of the only subject in their minds.

Under the eyes of a watchful and gossiping Ravenglass they spent quiet days, bicycling to Wastwater and Black Combe, seeing the shadows turn the flanks of the Screes to purple and the bracken flame in Eskdale. Then Vanessa had a letter from Adrian.

DEAREST VANESSA--How are things going with you? Here we talk nothing but the War. General opinion is that it will be over before Christmas and everyone--except your humble servant--is turning himself into a soldier as quickly as possible that he may see something of the fun before it is finished. I am not so sure. It seems to me that we are already everywhere on the defensive. I lie low and say nothing, for the general feeling is that it is all a great lark--a sort of polo game in which even the poorest may join. I listened to Chamberlain defending the Government for three long hours and what he DID say was all right--but how about all the things he didn't?

What is certain is that we are now beholding the end of the Victorian Era. Do you remember young Violet complaining to you and me once how, when the maid was busy elsewhere, she must sit indoors all a fine afternoon because she must not go out alone? Haven't you, at your own Balls, seen the chaperons sitting in weary rows hour after hour? I prophesy that you will never see those chaperons again and that Alfred's girl will, in another fifteen years or so, be smoking a cigarette as she enjoys her luncheon alone at the Criterion.

The Family, by the way, is amusing. They take the War of course as their own affair. Krüger is a kind of Benjie who has insulted them all personally. It is 'OUR War'--Horace especially is full of club- martial ardour. Carey is going out in some capacity or another although he's sixty-three or so. Also Peile Worcester and--would you believe it?--Philip is being sent out by some paper, I am generally despised because I say that the Government must be carried on and if *I* go who will remain?

And Benjie? What is he going to do? If he goes, don't worry. Benjie will always survive things like wars. They were made for him, not he for them. Write and tell me . . .

Then Benjie had a letter from Paris. Tom, young though he was, had hitched himself on to some French newspaper man and was already on the sea. Tim had thrown over his painting and come home to enlist.

'You see,' Benjie said, staring at her as though he were taking her image into his very heart. 'I've got to go.'

'Yes,' said Vanessa, smiling. 'Of course you have.'

Their last night in Ravenglass they did not sleep. They lay in one another's arms while the rain lashed the windows and the wind screamed along the sea. A bird, in the early morning, beat its wings against the pane.

'You mustn't be lonely,' Benjie said over and over again. 'I shall be back almost before I've gone. I shall think of you all the time. You mustn't be lonely. You mustn't be lonely.'

As the light wove grey webs upon the wall he said, stroking her cheek:

'When I loved you a year ago, Vanessa, I didn't know what love was. This year has taught me.'

'And I love you,' she answered simply, 'more every day. I thought it couldn't grow; I didn't know . . . I didn't believe . . .'

She began to cry--a ridiculous thing, she thought, a woman of forty crying. But this once when there was no one to see . . . He kissed her tears. He had lain so often in her arms like a boy. Now he held her like a man and she was a child.

They were both very merry that morning. She would not come with him to London. She saw him drive off in the old cab; she waved her hand, laughing, while all Ravenglass watched from behind its windows.

Then she walked, her head bent to the wind, and did not return till it was dark.

THE KOPJE

She went back to Cat Bells.

Was not that perhaps a piece of impertinence? Everyone in the neighbourhood thought so. But she was not at all disturbed by the thoughts of her neighbours. She said to Mrs Newson on the evening of her arrival:

'You know, Mrs Newson, that I've left my husband.'

'Yes--so I've heard, my lady.'

'And since that time Mr Benjamin Herries and I have lived as man and wife. He has gone out to South Africa.'

'Yes, my lady. I hope he'll come back safe.'

'So do I,' said Vanessa, smiling. 'But I want you to tell me if you and your husband would rather get some other position. I shall be glad to help you until you are suited.'

Mrs Newson, who was a stout short woman with red checks and grey hair, paused. Then slowly delivered her mind.

'It's like this, my lady. It wouldn't be fair to say that me and Robert haven't talked this over. We have. We don't think it right in general for a woman to live with a man she's not married to. I wouldn't do it myself, nor would Robert. But you see, you're different. Folks can say what they like, but you're our own, so to speak. The last thing Will Leathwaite said to me while he was sensible enough to say anything was you was a grand lady and I wasn't to forget it. In Cumberland we're slow but sure, and me and Robert think you must have had good reasons for what you done, and there's no place can be to us what this cottage is after being here so long, so we'll be staying if it's all the same to you, my lady.'

After a week she could not have been more private, she thought, had she lived in a nunnery. No one came to see her; she went to see no one. She walked, read, followed with passionate interest every detail of the war. Gradually the peace of that place stole about her and enfolded her. Her father, her mother, Will, seemed to keep her company. The fell that rose above the roof of the cottage was burnished with the dying bracken; the herons sailed majestically against the sky. The little field circled with its toy-like trees on the slope above Lodore caught the morning light with such confident tranquillity that its curve, like the bowl of a cup, filled, emptied, filled again as though obeying happily its commander.

She bicycled over to the Fortress and looked down into the Uldale valley. There was a church there now and sheep were grazing where Fell House had been. The Fortress, she heard, was let to a Mr Swanwick. Children were playing in the garden, a bicycle leant against the door, two dogs ran to the gate and barked at her.

She thought day and night of Benjie. His earlier training as one of the much-bemocked Volunteers years before helped him now and he had sailed for South Africa early in November. She took a hurried journey to London, stayed there with him for two nights, seeing no one else but Barney, and returned to Cumberland. Then, some weeks later, she received her first letter.

MY DARLING--This must be only a short note. I shall soon have a chance, I hope, of a long letter. The worst part of the voyage was its monotony. From the moment we left London we were shut off from all news. To be without news for a fortnight at a time like this-- you can imagine what hell it is! We thought we'd learn something at Madeira. Not a word. We were all inoculated against enteric and I to my shame took it badly. We had cinematograph men on board, but I don't myself think THAT will ever come to much! The machinery is so cumbrous that if they want to take anything that moves it is gone before their machines are ready. Then at last we sighted a sail and were so close that, when they put a board up with some news on it, we could read it easily. What they told us was: 'Three battles. Boers defeated'--and then didn't we cheer? After that no more news till we sighted Robben Island. THEN there was news all right! . . . But you will know it all by this time and much more.

What else can I tell you but that I love you, love you, my darling? I carry you with me. You are never absent from me for a single moment, your courage, your goodness, your loyalty to a poor old devil whom no one has a good word for. But haven't they? The world has changed, Vanessa. Everyone is to me like a brother. No member of the Herries family here to tell the world what I really am--all damned good fellows--and, old though I am, I'm as lively as the youngest and will make

you proud of me before I'm done. So cheer up, my sweetest, and believe in me as you have always done. Tomorrow, I believe, we are off again--whither I don't know. I'm as impatient as a flea on a hot plate. Impatient also for your first letter. Tell me EVERYTHING--how the stream runs down through the garden, what you do every hour of the day, are the Newsons good to you? Have you had a look at the Fortress?

They are calling me. I must go--Your loving and devoted and eternally faithful

B.

A fortnight passed and there was another letter, a long one. Part of it was as follows:

. . . It was a bit of a battle. How can I make you see it? Looking back I can see a green hill, kopje, almost blood colour, and then grass-green veldt. The trains stopped and poured khaki into the veldt. Funny to see the confused mass, then order forming out of it, then the line of tiny dots, then a thicker line, more and more lines, then a mass of khaki. First the dots were at the base, almost lost in the brown of the hill, then altogether lost, then suddenly against the skyline. Away on the right the Imperial Light Horse. Then our guns thudded, and, thud came the answer. Then the shells. Thin whirr, screaming cry. Ball after ball of white smoke struck the kopje, then little balloons of shrapnel from our guns; then the guns pealing faster and faster. Just as our own order to move came, down crashed the rain. You never saw anything like it, Vanessa. It drove through macintoshes like blotting paper. The earth underfoot melted while you looked at it into mud and the mud turned to water. Everything was blotted out in the cloud of swirling water, but the guns thundered and doggedly we pushed ahead.

Soon we were in it--my first battle, you know. What did I feel? I can't tell you--except that the ridges we must conquer seemed endless. Up one there was another! I wasn't afraid. The bugles and the pipes stirred your blood. And then I was caught into the noise. Officers shouting, swearing, cursing; all of us stumbling, falling, jumping, killing--and then, like a maniac's desired dream there at our feet the Boer camp and the Boers galloping out of it!

As I started down the hill, though, something struck me. Don't be frightened. It turned out to be nothing--a slight scratch--but my face was buried in mud, all the world seemed to crash over my head and when at last I raised myself and wiped the mud from my eyes I seemed to be transfixed by a small kopje not far off. It stared at me, I at it. Brown-red in colour, it was shaped like a pig with horns. It seemed to move, to wriggle as though it wanted to scratch its back. I was dazed of course, and didn't rightly know for a moment where I was, but I thought it moved towards me, wagging its ears. Then the scene cleared. I stood up. I was all right and ran down the hill. . .

Afterwards it was cold and drizzling. Some of the prisoners joined us and we were all most friendly. Decent chaps the Boers really-- fine fellows with their beards and corduroys, with a grand dignity, some of them. There's been a lot of looting and you see men with the weirdest clothes. And you should watch the guns scatter at a shell. See the legs of the horses leap! You never imagined such nimbleness . . .

And who do you think has turned up? George Endicott, a friend of my wife's brother. A wild chap but I always liked him and now here he is in my own regiment. Small world, isn't it? Young Tom's shut up in Mafeking. Carey Rockage is in Ladysmith. Are you well, my darling, and keeping up your spirits? You seem to be always with me. Last night I talked to you . . .

She held on, but the strain began to tell. The loneliness of her days and nights frightened her. She became restless. She wanted to be doing something, something for the war, something, through others, for Benjie.

After the Black Week, the 10th-16th of December: Stormberg, Magersfontein, Tugela River, the feeling of the whole country changed. What was this that had happened to England? While the rest of the world looked on, jeering, hostile, longing for our humiliation-- here was the most shameful time for us since the Indian Mutiny. Lord Roberts was appointed to the chief command, and Kitchener of Khartoum was to go with him. The appointment roused a storm of new energy. The gay, light-hearted jesting was over. This was a job that the country must settle. The colonies offered new contingents, a great call went out for yeomanry, and the new infantry volunteers flamed into being. The City of London would raise and equip a regiment entirely at its own expense. Everywhere there were new khaki uniforms. From all parts of the country, shipyard men, squires' sons, farmers' sons, artisans, and clerks poured into the new forces. Nothing spectacular any more. Had they but known it, that Black Week killed spectacular warfare for ever. Nothing to catch the eye was tolerated. Scarlet fled, never to return to the battlefield. A new patience, a fresh endurance, no more the reckless charge, but 'the infinitely painful crawl through the long, long day'.

For Vanessa those first months in the new year became an agony. She heard now from Benjie at the longest intervals. This country, for the first time in her life, failed her. The old beloved names-- Skiddaw and Scafell, the running Derwent, the ridge of Blencathra, the slow ripple of the quiet Lake meant nothing. The valleys held no peace and the running water no music.

Her ostracism now terribly distressed her. It was a time when she wanted to have part and lot with all her fellow-beings, but on Cat Bells she was like a prisoner. Her loneliness became a horror; she could not sleep. She walked restlessly, tried to read and could not. She grew thin and pale. The Newsons heard her talking to herself, and once Mrs Newson found her crying, her head in her hands.

'Don't cry, my lady. It will be all right. 'Twill be over soon, they all say.'

Then at the beginning of April she had a brief letter from Benjie that frightened her. He had been ill in hospital; he was better, but things moved slowly. It would be all right, of course, but the Boers were obstinate fellows and Tom in Mafeking made it anxious work . . . But he was all right . . . She wasn't to worry . . . That letter was too much for her. She came to London.

She went to a little hotel called 'The Clarence', off Baker Street. A lady in the train told her of it and she thought: 'How funny! I have never stayed by myself in a hotel before!' As soon as she was in the hansom driving to the hotel she was happy. She was nearer to Benjie; she was in touch with human beings again. She had not minded at all when Mrs Hope of Portinscale cut her in the Keswick street, when Mrs Merriman, who had before been so kind to her in Rosthwaite, gave her a sharp little bow and hurried down the Borrowdale Road. No, no, she had not minded . . . She had been prepared for it. She had taken it gaily. Nevertheless, how different these things were without Benjie! Loneliness had returned, not the old spiritual loneliness of the life at Hill Street, but physical, material loneliness, hearing no voice, touching no hand, receiving no kiss. Now she was in the middle of life again. She noticed how many motors there were now; all the traffic was speedier and pedestrians were speedier too. One good thing--these new motor-cars would soon kill that London plague, the cab tout who had run at the side of your hansom pestering to serve you. She had a rich grand sense, after the silence of those Cumberland months, of plunging into a roaring new world ready to welcome her. Well, the Family would not be ready to welcome her. But she need not see them--only Barney and Adrian and Rose. And perhaps Cynthia--she had not, in the old days, been so violently shocked! It would be pleasant to have tea with Cynthia again in her pretty room, to hear the gossip, to ask about the theatres and to catch, even though from a distance, the tone and colour of that world to which she had once belonged! She sat upright in her hansom staring through the glass in front of her like a young girl free for the first time!

'The Clarence' was odd enough. A very large lady, her hair puffed out over elaborate pads, her shoulders very high, her waist almost invisible beneath her swelling bosom, her costume sweeping the floor, received Vanessa in an affected manner and directed a minute and rather shabby pageboy to show her to her room. This was dingy, with a view of chimney pots, a large portrait of Queen Victoria and a general gurgling of water pipes to give it character and life. The hotel smelt of fog and dead geraniums. At the head of the stairs was a large tank in which goldfish were swimming. The walls were everywhere very thin. As Vanessa changed her dress she heard from the next room a protesting voice:

'But, Mama, why not?'

'Because Mother thinks it better not, dear.'

'But Mama--'

'Now, Cecily. Mother knows best. He is not a young man who can possibly mean anything seriously. He has not a penny besides his Army pay.'

'But, Mama--'

The intimacy of this conversation terrified Vanessa, and when next afternoon Adrian came to visit her, and they sat in a room crowded with palms and dimmed by windows with blue and red glass, Vanessa told him that this was the most virtuous hotel in London. No indiscretion could be committed without everyone in the hotel being aware of it.

She was gay, merry, full of eagerness to enter life again.

'I must get something to do, Adrian. It was dreadful in Cumberland. I simply moped. I must work, help, tire myself to death until Benjie returns.'

She was aware of a certain awkwardness in Adrian. She remembered unexpectedly that evening, years ago, when Adrian had been led up to her at the Ball, his eagerness, his vitality, his impulsive determination to help the world. He was as kind, as affectionate as ever, but he was now a Government servant, the HERRIES Government servant. His clothes were exquisite, his manner that of one who had to carry a good many public burdens on his shoulders. Was he writing anything? No, he had little time he was afraid. H. D. Traill's death had distressed him greatly; he had given him a good deal of reviewing in Literature. Had she read Fleury's Louis XV Intime? A most interesting work with a very striking portrait of La Pompadour. And Dr Barry's Arden Massiter, quite good as novels go. A little overwritten. And a very amusing little book, Lambkin's Remains. The writer signed himself H. B. He was the author of The Bad Child's Book of Beasts. 'You remember, Vanessa.'

But Vanessa, alas, did not remember. She had never heard of Dr Barry and was not sure whether she had met Mr Traill or no.

'Perhaps he came to one of our parties.'

Oh no, Traill never went to parties. But Vanessa was trembling for news.

'Adrian, tell me about Hill Street.'

Adrian's pale, still very youthful countenance coloured.

'Oh, no one goes there now. Winifred and Vera keep Ellis quite a prisoner. He likes it, I believe. He's queer, of course. They say he makes paper boats and has toy engines. He doesn't go to the City any more. Alfred has everything in his hands. But they say Ellis is quite happy.'

Did Vanessa imagine it or was there a new note in Adrian's voice? Was he a little, a very little, superior? Why did he seem to patronize? Vanessa's imagination. And then he must hate this hotel.

'It's a horrid hotel, isn't it?' she said.

'Yes. Beastly. But you want it quiet, don't you? I mean--you don't want to run up against any of the family.'

'Oh no--except Barney, of course.'

'Dear old Barney--he's getting pretty aged. He plays bridge all his evenings.'

'Bridge?'

Why, of course!' Adrian expressed surprise. 'Where HAVE you been? Don't they play it in Cumberland? London's crazy about it--has been for ages.'

There was a pause. Mrs Mont, the proprietress, came into the room and looked around. It was odd to see her balance her enormous bosom on two such very small feet! She patted her great head of hair and stared at the pair of them.

'Has she already heard about me?' Vanessa wondered.

'Oh yes--and do tell me about the others. Carey's shut up in Ladysmith, Benjie told me. And Cynthia's husband--he's in Natal, isn't he? Adrian!--Cynthia--how does she feel about me? Do you think I could go and see her? Would she mind? She used to be very broadminded . . .'

There was an awkward pause. Adrian coughed, stroking the side of his nose in a manner common to many of the Herries men.

At last he spoke: 'Look here, Vanessa. There's something I ought to say. You're such a sport, you're so wise, I know you'll understand perfectly. But the whole family has taken this awfully badly. They can't get over it. You see--they admired you so much and they were so proud of Hill Street. And then--if it had been anyone but Benjie, whom they've disapproved of for years! And then there have been so many family scandals! It didn't matter so much perhaps years ago when they weren't anyone particularly, but now they are respected everywhere. Alfred's a great man in the City, and Cynthia thinks herself Queen of London. She does really. You'd be amused if you saw her. Already she's bringing her two girls up most awfully carefully. They're nice little girls too. She wants them to marry Dukes. What I mean is--there's me and there's Barney--but the others-- well, I'm afraid you mustn't expect them to change. They won't. They are more respectable than you've any idea of. They can't endure Benjie and they think you-- they think you were unkind to Ellis.'

'I see,' said Vanessa quietly. 'Thank you for telling me, Adrian.'

'Oh, that's all right. I say, isn't there rather a queer smell in here? It may be my fancy.'

He got up.

'Well, I must be off. Got some work to do. You tell me, Vanessa, if there's anything I can do. We'll go out one night. We'll do a play. The one at the St James's isn't bad--The Man of Forty. Alexander and Fay Davis.'

'Thank you, Adrian.' She stood looking at him with a wise and rather maternal smile. She could not resist saying: 'You won't be ashamed to be seen out with me, will you, Adrian?'

He blushed, looking like a boy of eighteen.

'My God, no! Why, what do you think, Vanessa? *I* haven't any prejudices. I'll be proud!'

But, a little later, sitting in her bedroom and listening to the gurgles of the water pipes, she was not so sure.

Then, next day, when old Barney came to see her, she learnt more about the Family. Barney was seventy, stout, rather untidy. There were pouches under the eyes, his cheeks were puffed out, giving him a childish pouting expression, but the eyes themselves were full of sparkle, humour, kindliness, and his grey hair, though it was untidy, was strong and wiry. He had a paunch, but he walked on his thick legs sturdily, his back straight, his head up, and always that slightly mocking boy-out-for-a-lark expression at his mouth's corners as though he found life more of a joke than ever. And yet you could, if you knew the Family, tell that he was old Emily's brother and pompous, long-buried Newmark's son. He found life a joke indeed because there had been originally enough of the solemn Herries there for him to see how ridiculous it could be.

Sitting again in the room with the palms and the coloured glass, this teatime was very different from the one of yesterday. Vanessa was one of Barney's REAL devotions. As he saw her now, seated very quietly, a middle-aged woman whose hair was turning grey, in this shabby hotel, and thought how barely two years ago he had seen her with her white satin and diamonds leading the cotillion in the Hill Street drawing-room, satin and diamonds seemed to him very vulgar things. But did she mind this shabby hotel, he wondered? Was she still satisfied with her bargain?

'Adrian came to tea yesterday,' she told him. 'I thought him a little--well, a little superior. Has he become so, or is it only with me because I'm a black sheep now, or did I imagine it?'

'Oh, Adrian's a little more Herries than he was--that's all. The Foreign Office might have been invented by our family--it's so exactly what we most approve of.'

He looked at her anxiously, rather as though he were her father.

'You're happy, Vanessa?'

'Well, I'm rather lonely, Barney, at the moment. I miss Benjie, you see--and I want work, something to do. Can you find me something? I must be busy.'

'Yes, I think I can find something. There's a Mrs Cundlip who's a friend of mine. She has a working party. They make things for the soldiers three afternoons a week. She and her friends live very quietly in Kensington. They don't gossip and they are nice kind women. I think you'd like it.'

'Oh, Barney, thank you! You ARE a dear!'

He was touched by her gratitude. Poor Vanessa, she MUST have been lonely! He told her more of the Family. Cynthia was now the star. Worcester was doing very well in South Africa. He was to join Roberts' staff. May Rockage was in London, doing war work, and desperately trying to find husbands for her girls. Horace was rather chastened. His silent wife had developed into a grim woman who frightened him. Alfred's two children were nice little things. Richard Cards--Adrian's older brother--was now living in London. He had married rather late and had two children. Barney gave very much the same account of Hill Street as Adrian had done. No one saw Ellis and it was generally known that he was eccentric. Barney did not tell Vanessa the general opinion that her flight had turned Ellis' brain. Winifred and Vera Trent never left him. And that was that. Vanessa understood quite clearly that the Family would have nothing to do with her . . .

In another day or two she went to call on Mrs Cundlip, found her a kindly simple woman with a son at the Front and a plain energetic daughter with a passion for the clergy.

Whether Mrs Cundlip and her friend knew Vanessa's story or no, they gave no sign of interest in it. Indeed they seemed never to gossip and had, as a group, a curiously impersonal air as thought they were part of the quiet Kensington scene like the trees in the Gardens, the nurses with their perambulators, the solid policeman at the gates, the decorous shoppers in the High Street. Vanessa found them a comfort. She worked in the gentle Kensington drawing- room hung with watercolours of Switzerland and Italy and thought of Benjie and tried to be happy. As the days passed she found that increasingly she was afraid of a chance encounter with one of the Family. She remained in her unpleasant hotel because it was so safe. None of them would ever come there. When she shopped or went to the theatre her apprehension was always alive. It would hurt her, she knew now, to be cut by Cynthia or May. WOULD May cut her?--that kind, simple countrywoman in whose house she had so often stayed? But May had her girls now to think of. Old Violet Bellairs was very ill and never left her bed. The younger Violet who had married a Colonel belonged, Vanessa heard, to a very fast set (in revenge for her constricted youth) who played bridge all day and all night. And Lettice Marrable? Lettice was secretary now to a branch in Manchester of

Women's Suffrage. She wrote very lovingly to Vanessa and said that she would come to see her as soon as she had time to visit London. She was very busy and talked in her letter about The Cause as though there were but one in all the world.

So there they all were.

Then one sunny afternoon early in May, Vanessa tumbled almost into Horace's arms in the Army and Navy Stores. There was no way of avoiding it! There was Horace, red-faced, stout, benignant behind his glasses, buying soap. He stepped back unexpectedly, almost trod on Vanessa, said, 'I beg your pardon' with his customary episcopal courtesy and saw who it was. His plump cheeks were scarlet.

'Vanessa!' he said.

'How are you, Horace?' she replied, holding out her hand and smiling.

They shook hands and she noticed that at once he moved with her a little out of earshot.

'I'm so glad to see you, Horace. You're looking very well.'

'Yes, I'm very well, thanks.'

'I can see you're busy. So am I.'

She smiled at him very gaily. Oh yes, it WAS pleasant to see one of the Family even though it were only Horace, with his high white forehead, large spectacles and protruding chin! For the first time in her life she LIKED Horace.

'Oh yes--indeed yes . . . very busy . . .' he stuttered, looking nervously about him. No one was near him, no one was looking at him. He coughed. 'Very agreeable to see you, Vanessa. Are you long in London?'

'Yes, for some time, I think.' She looked him straight between the glasses. 'Benjie is in South Africa, you know.'

'Oh yes, indeed. I had heard . . .' (Why wasn't he a Bishop? Not that she had anything against Bishops. Often the noblest of men, but Horace's benevolence needed an apron.)

Now that he was assured that no one was observing them he was more at his ease. He began to talk with some of his old eager but, in some odd way, calculated friendliness. He spoke of the nobility of our men at the Front, of Britain's showing the world, of everyone doing what they could, of human nature being at its best in times of stress. He became more practical, revealing himself, as he had always liked to do, at the very centre of affairs. He had just been lunching with a most interesting man--name of Yerkes--the projector of the new electric Underground. He confidently prophesied that we should all be living at least fifty miles out of London owing to electrified trains--we should think nothing of it, nothing of it at all; said what a nuisance half-sovereigns were--he had nearly given one just now as a tip instead of a sixpence; that all the best horses had gone to South Africa, so that the omnibuses were sadly suffering. He talked as though he were delivering an address to a gathering of charity children, Vanessa

thought, but he meant to be kindly. It had always been Horace's trouble that he meant so well, but had weaknesses, insincerities, tempers and absent-mindedness like the rest of us. Then he saw some ladies approaching and, raising his hat, hurried away.

'The gentleman has forgotten his soap,' the shopman said.

'He will come back for it, I'm sure,' said Vanessa.

She was very tired. It would have been nice of Horace if he had invited her to take a cup of tea. But certainly that was too much to expect. Her arm ached. She was suffering from what was known as 'skirt wrist'.

A night or two later she had a horrible dream. She dreamt that she was on a vast green plain, bounded by hills spotted with small black patches. She had lost her way and then saw coming towards her the kopje that Benjie had mentioned in one of his first letters. It was coloured red, as Benjie had said, and shaped like a pig. It came wriggling after her, flapping large naked red ears. It covered the ground with extraordinary speed. She began to run but made no advance. It came nearer and nearer; she could smell its fetid breath and see, on its back, tufts of hair. The thing rolled in its movement. It had no face, only the flapping ears. 'This is my punishment,' she thought in her despair. 'I knew that I could not escape it.' She screamed for Benjie and woke.

After that night she seemed always to be tired. The loneliness that she had felt in Cumberland returned. Both Adrian and Barney were kind, but they were busy people; the ladies in Kensington were most pleasant, but they did not invite her to their houses; she grew no nearer in intimacy to any of them, nor did she wish to. After that dream she was haunted with fear for Benjie. It was a fortnight now since she had heard from him, and his last letter had seemed to her dispirited, disappointed. With increasing unrest she looked every day at the casualties in the newspaper. She told herself that she must be calm and brave, that thousands of other women were suffering as she was, but it became soon impossible for her to be impersonal. There seemed to be no one in the world but Benjie. It was not only that he might be killed, but that his restlessness, his passion for liberty, must be fed my this adventure, that the longer he was away from her the easier it would be for him to remain away.

She suffered as all women do who love a man but are tied to him by no official bond. She had no hold on him at all but his love for her, and he might love other women as he loved her. When he was there she knew that he loved her, but now she was tortured by the very indefiniteness of their relationship, although at its heart it was anything but indefinite.

Then, on the eighteenth of May, sitting in her bedroom, reading, she heard a timid knock on the door.

'Come in!' she said.

The blowsy good-natured chambermaid, Kate by name, put her head in through the door.

'Excuse me, mum,' she said, 'but I thought you'd like to know. They're saying as Mafeking's been relieved!'

'Oh no!' Vanessa cried, jumping up.

'Yes, mum. Ain't it grand? Relieved yesterday, they say!'

Her first thought was for Tom. How delighted Benjie would be! And then that it would mean that the war would be soon ended, very soon perhaps. And, after that, that now England could hold her head up again, the long period of doubt and failure was over. She was so happy that, in a moment, all her troubles seemed to be ended. Everyone would be happy! Everyone WAS happy!

At dinner in the hotel that evening even the old waiter in his dirty dicky could scarcely carry the plates for joy. Two old ladies who had never before spoken to her said: 'Isn't it excellent? SUCH good news! We are so glad!' as though it had all been done for their especial benefit.

At the table next to hers a schoolgirl with her mother was in a state of almost frenzied excitement. She had, it seemed, been allowed to come down to dinner in celebration of the great event. She was a plain little girl, wearing the hideous khaki-coloured dress then considered patriotic for schoolgirls. She was talking of some elder girl who was allowed to wear a red, white, and blue costume, with a regimental clasp in front. The 'thing' at school was to pin on to yourself many penny buttons decorated with the heads of generals, and one girl was the envy of all the others because she had found somewhere a regular saucer with the picture of Baden-Powell and went everywhere with this pinned to her chest.

As Vanessa listened she thought, 'I'd like to have a little girl of my own. Would it be unfair to her that Benjie and I are not married? Father was illegitimate and never minded. Is it worse for a girl? Would *I* have minded? Nothing that Father had done would have seemed to me wrong.' Soon she would be too old to have children. She had missed that as she had missed other things. But she had not missed love . . . Benjie would soon be back now, and Tom. She would love Tom with all her heart, be a splendid friend to him and, in her old age, stand by him, help his wife when he married. For Tom was unusual like all the other unusual Herries-- wild at the heart, wanting often to be free of everyone; hard men for a woman to understand were these Herries!

She would go out and share in everybody's happiness. In Baker Street she boarded an omnibus, but when they reached Oxford Circus they could go no farther. She climbed down and plunged into pandemonium. She stayed for a while in a shop door and let the crowd surge past her. First, looking upwards it was as though the sky itself had gone mad. From nowhere out of nothing (for there had been little warning) the fa-

çades had created their illumination. Electric light was still rare and, at its greatest peak of grandeur, could not have rivalled the magic of those gas jets. Their wonder was that they were swayed by those little winds that came and went, running in blue-and-gold ripples like water against the grey surface, seeming for a moment to be blown out and then, with a sense of mischievous laughter, bursting into life again, as though by their own happy agency they had relighted themselves. They ran in waves of trembling light, hesitated, vanished and, with new energy, ran again. The sky was alive with beauty.

Beneath it what a world--as though a new race inhabited the earth! Men in evening dress, hats on the back of their heads, cocked sideways, evening capes flying, danced arm in arm with the ladies of the East End. These women who were to go down in history, dressed in black satin, wore great hats crowned with ostrich plumes; and so they danced, their fine bosoms swelling, the flounces of their long dresses swinging from their tiny waists, petticoats whitely revealed and vanishing. Their own gentlemen for that night at least were in 'high dress' with mother-of-pearl on their flat caps, trousers tight to the knee, flapping round the ankles. They changed hats with their Donahs, moving in the 'double- shuffle' in an ecstasy of joy. The East End came West that night, and the West was glad.

And the noise! Everyone was shouting, singing, turning rattles, blowing the coiled paper springs, screaming down pink-and-white tuppenny trumpets gay with silvery angels' hair. You were 'killing Krüger with your mouth'. You were singing 'Duke's son, cook's son, son of a belted Earl'. You were shouting 'W'ERE did you get that 'at?', 'Wot price old Krüger!', 'Git yer 'air cut!' You were singing:

Hark! I hear the bugle calling,
And I can no longer stay.
Goodbye, Dolly, I must leave you.
Goodbye, Dolly Gray!

That night the British Army was worshipped. It was to be worshipped again, but in another sterner spirit, when tuppenny trumpets and mother-of-pearl could not meet a far more menacing enemy.

The soldier and the sailor were the heroes, and the 'Little Englander' was the villain of the piece. Close to Vanessa a girl, waving her arms, screamed: 'Down with Lloyd George!' and behold his image was flung deep under the dancing shoes of that multitude. And there is a god in a monocle, with an orchid in his buttonhole-- 'Three cheers for Joe!' 'Not for Joseph!' 'Good old Joe!' Labour? One man named Keir Hardie has boldly walked into the House with a cloth cap on his head. So much for Labour. Squeakers and ticklers and corncrakes have, that evening, little consciousness of a new world that very soon will be demanding very different instruments . . .

Vanessa for a while was safe in her doorway, but soon the crowd was wilder. Hansoms appearing from the very bowels of the earth discharged young men in evening dress; something other than tea is the draught of the Town; here there is a fight between a cabman and a fare, there a policeman has seized some gesticulating figure, raised him above the crowd, then, as though abandoning the hopeless charge, dropped him back into the crowd again.

Vanessa has been swung from her doorstep. It is best to go with the crowd. Someone has linked arms with her and she is swayed down Regent Street, all the shouts, songs, cries seeming to catch a sudden rhythm so that it is as though the very sky itself were singing. At the edge of Piccadilly Circus the surge forward is arrested and you see a rising, falling pattern of life--not individual life now but something made up of the windy, swaying lights, tumbling bursts of sound, the very buildings swinging, it seemed, in the uncertain glare.

A woman grasped her arm: with her other hand she wielded a toy trumpet, her straw hat at the back of her padded hair. Vanessa turned and looked. It was Rose.

'Hooray! Hooray!' she cried, waving the trumpet. 'Hooray for Joe! Hooray--' She said confidently to Vanessa: 'Come on, dear! Let's give him a cheer!'

'Rose,' Vanessa said, bending her body sideways to avoid the pressure of a stout perspiring gentleman with a tickler. 'Don't you know me?'

Rose stared. 'Vanessa!' She threw her arms around her, scratching the back of her neck with her trumpet. Her straw hat, falling, disappeared. 'Oh, Vanessa--my darling! my darling!'

Vanessa realized that Rose had been too splendidly celebrating victory. At the moment she could realize nothing further, for the impulse of the crowd swept them both off their feet. It appeared not unlikely that there and then they would find death in one another's arms, bells clanging in their ears, somewhere the trumpets of a distant band, the smell of sweating bodies, broadcloth, patchouli, against their nostrils and, against the sky, grey walls like rocks on whose surfaces flickered in the wind the jets of blue, green, red, thrown up from the tossing dark pool at their feet. It was then confusion. The fountain of the Circus stood out above the singing waters. Heads rose and fell like despairing drowning mariners. Fastened firmly in the midst was the rock of a towering hansom up whose side figures were climbing. Beyond that again an effigy with a tangled beard, a battered high hat, jerked as though in agony against the lights--Krüger moving to his bonfire.

Then the waters parted. Waves of human beings slumped like falling walls. The effigy was moving forward, followed by a great cheering procession, men waving their hats, women screaming, and under the confusion--above it, outside and within it--the steady pulse of The Soldiers of the Queen, into whose tune at last all the scattered sounds and voices were gathered.

Driven back at the corner of Shaftesbury Avenue, Vanessa suddenly discovered that, a wide porch of a restaurant protecting her, she was free. Miraculously, still holding to her arm was Rose.

'Oh, where is he?' Rose cried. 'The Captain! The Captain gone! He swore he wouldn't leave me. Oh, Vanessa, I'm lost--I don't know where he lives. He's got my little green bag, my little bag . . .'

They stood in the shelter of the porch against the wall, shoulder to shoulder. Rose cried out as though she were demented. A lock of false hair had detached itself from the disordered pile and tickled her mouth. There was a small scratch on her cheek from which blood was trickling. Altogether a battered Rose.

She looked at Vanessa, and as she looked her wildness fell from her.

'Oh, Vanessa, I've drunk too much. Take me home. I don't care if I never see the Captain again.'

Very slowly they moved up Shaftesbury Avenue; then, turning at the first opening, found themselves in a little dark street, deserted, melancholy, shutting off like a curtain the lights, the singing, the press of the surging crowd.

'Where's your hat, dear?' Vanessa asked. She took out her handkerchief and wiped Rose's cheek. Rose began to cry.

'Oh, you must think me dreadful. Fancy your meeting me like this after all this time. But it was all the Captain's fault, and my bag had all my money in it.'

Vanessa, her hand through Rose's arm, led her from little street to little street. Near Oxford Street they found a hansom.

'Now, Rose, where are you living?'

Rose stared. 'I don't know . . . Oh yes, Three Orcutt Street. That's where I was living three days ago, before I met the Captain.'

'Well--is that where you want to go?'

'Yes. You'll come with me, Vanessa? I'm not drunk really. I only had a drop in the Captain's room.'

In the hansom Rose leant her head against Vanessa's bosom and sobbed.

'Mafeking! Mafeking! I wish to God I had never heard of Mafeking or the Captain either.' In a grim little street they stopped at a grim little house.

'No. Don't come in. My room isn't very grand.' She was quite sober now, looking like a dishevelled child afraid of a scolding. 'But you'll come and see me tomorrow? Or I'll come and see YOU. May I?'

Vanessa told her the address of the hotel. Once more Rose flung her arms about her neck and passionately kissed her.

'It all feels different, meeting you. Like old times.' She wiped her eyes. 'I've lost my hat. I don't know what Mrs Blaker will think if she sees me. She doesn't think much of me anyway. Goodnight, darling.'

Later up to Vanessa's bedroom came the shouts and cries of a city madly rejoicing. Some kind of a triumph. A passionate impulse of compassion caught her heart, compassion for the world, for Rose, for all lonely and misguided creatures. The kopje could not frighten her now.

Indeed, indeed it could not. Two weeks later there was a telegram forwarded from Cumberland. Benjie had lost an arm and was being sent home at once.

She sat, with the telegram in her hand, staring in front of her. She was so happy that she could scarcely breathe lest the telegram should prove unreal. Then she knelt down by her bed and thanked God.

YOUNG TOM IN NEWLANDS

Young Tom Herries, sitting one summer evening on a slope below Dale Head, the peak which closes the Newlands Valley, watched the sky. It had for some while fascinated him and distracted him from the second volume of Hardy's The Woodlanders, which lay on the turf beside him. He was always known as Young Tom, but even in years he was not so young any longer, for he was now seventeen years of age, but in character, in a subtle intuition of motive and feeling, in self-command, he had never been young. In looks he was something like his father, dark, short and thick with a round hard head and short wiry hair. He had also some of his father's geniality and all of his warmth of heart.

But he was different from him altogether in his self-control, in his patience, in his consideration for others. His early flight to Paris with Timothy, the free life there spent always in the company of his elders, his experiences in South Africa, his acquaintance with all the ways of humankind, bad, good, sensual, virtuous, foolish, wise, had helped him to come to terms with real life long before the common time. But, with this, there was something young in him that made folk, the country people, the townspeople, all who knew him, speak of him as Young Tom. He WAS young in this: that unlike his father he took all his responsibilities with extreme seriousness. His principal responsibility was to his father and to Vanessa. He loved them both, but he knew his father too well to think him in any way wonderful. He felt to his father as he would to a younger brother whose faults he knew by heart but whom he loved and

guarded the more for those faults, but Vanessa he worshipped.

He had been living with them now in this little house in the Vale of Newlands for six months, and the longer he lived with them the deeper did his devotion to Vanessa grow. He was thinking of her now as he lay on his back, his arms behind his head, looking at the sky. She seemed to him of another kind altogether from any women he had ever known, and he had known some very strange ones. Her love for him, which she had felt since she had visited him a little boy ill at school, made her more natural with him, perhaps, than she was with anyone else. They were very often alone together and then she talked to him as though she were a girl of his own age. She poured out all her heart to him: she told him more than she had ever told Benjie. She told him everything: of her childhood, her love for her father, her life in London with Ellis, her love for Tom's father--and they discussed, for hours together, Benjie's character, his sweetness, irresponsibility, restlessness, honesty, infidelities. When Benjie was drunk (rare occasions but unfortunate) Tom managed him to a marvel. When Benjie disappeared, Tom reassured Vanessa until he appeared again. Tom sometimes rated his father as though their positions were reversed. Benjie never resented it. He was as proud of his son as he could be. Tom himself, of course, was far from perfect. He was obstinate and sometimes sulked. He was given to fits of melancholy that he inherited from his own Herries strain, and then he would go away by himself and brood. There were many causes for these, but the chief of them was that he had always meant, since he was a tiny boy, to be a great writer and he thought now that he would never be even a good one. His early devotion to Timothy had been stirred the more by his saying to himself that Tim would be a great painter and he would be a great writer. Now Tim was, if not a great painter, a very good one. He was in Paris selling his pictures. He was known everywhere as a promising and unusual artist. But Tom, although he was a fair journalist, was no more. He talked to Vanessa again and again about this; he showed her his attempts. She was too honest and knew the value that he put on her honesty too well to encourage him.

'What is it,' he said to her in despair, 'that I can't get?'

'It is something, I suppose, that doesn't come by asking for it. Never mind, Tom. You began so young. You're only seventeen now! There are so many writers. You will do something better in another way.'

Now, thinking of The Woodlanders, he felt a sort of rage against fate. Yes, he was only seventeen--there was plenty of time--and yet he did not lie to himself. THIS thing would never be his. And WHAT was it? Hardy, Tom thought, was a peasant, he had scarcely moved from his countryside: he already knew far more about the wide world than Hardy could know. Hardy often made his characters talk in stilted, unnatural sentences; his books were filled with ridiculous coincidences--but here in these pages was life, the life that so many polished sophisticated writers missed altogether. Tom looked at the scene around him and his spirits fell into quiet.

For the last fortnight there had been perfect weather in Cumberland. By day the sun had shone, veiled with mist sufficient to give hill and water their rightful size. It was a late year and so the larch still stood in patterns of green flame against the smoky shadows of yew and fir, the stems of the young bracken were pellucid as are the throats of pale-green glasses. And with the sunny mist, over the green flats, up the stony sides of the fells, above the glittering chattering runnels of water, there was now thin shadow, now a breadth of light, all warm, kindly, beneficent; as a generous man's hand strokes his dog's shoulder, so God bent down from His cloud and caressed His world.

Tom, lying on his back, wondered that now the sky could be so quiet and so pure when so often he had watched clouds battling in armies for supremacy, seen one fierce cloud-captain drag another by his hair, watched the surge upward, from the hinder-parts of the Tops, of whirling frenzied clouds, angrily purple, and the thick grey sullen banks of storm mount and spread until all the world was covered with them and rain fell in spears of steel upon the earth. Now the sky was pale like the inside of a pearl shell; light was translucent and softer than down. Cat Bells and Dale Head, Robinson and Maiden Moor were bathed in a peace that seemed eternal, and towards the dip where Lobstone Band hid its rocky tors, a carpet of purple shadow hung above the little fields that welcomed the evening.

Near him Herdwick sheep were browsing--the bravest little sheep in England and the most adaptable. Their wool may be harsh, but so faithful in spirit are they that all their lives they will not move far from the place where they were born, not because they are unenterprising, but because here for generations their ancestors have been and here, like proper Cumbrians, their heart is set. So, with the old forest trees, the fir, the oak, the birch, with the stones and boulders that they can, if they will, so closely resemble, with the running water and the flying clouds, they obey the law.

Soon the stars would come out, breaking the green of the evening sky, and a young crescent moon would rise, and all night long the light would last, paler than ivory, quieter than sleep. The air was scented with the newly cut hay from a field nearby, with the first honeysuckle, with the summer heat drawn from grass and fern. Birds winged slowly, making the silence vocal. The line of the hills grew with every moment sharper as the shining sky paled.

Tom's thoughts turned to his own future. This had been a fine holiday, but it could not last for ever. He loved this country as he loved none other, but soon he must go back into the world again. He had for so long now been a man--ever since he was fourteen--that he had not a boy's light indifference of waiting until life should begin for him. He had been kicked about in Paris, he had endured a historic siege like the other men with him, and time would not wait. For six months, too, he had been ostracized. No one came to see them at Cold Fell. His mother's cottage was only ten minutes away over the hill. It was let to a painter and his family, but that long slow slope of Cat Bells cut the three of them from the world as though they were on a separate planet. Sometimes, when he rode into Keswick, he was looked at almost as though he had a deformity. He minded in spite of himself. What did it matter that his father and Vanessa were not married? They WOULD be married if only that crazy old lunatic in London would die. They loved one another more faithfully than many a married pair, and, stroking the back of The Woodlanders with his hand, he thought to himself that the writer of that book would understand if he were here and would come to see them and be their friend. There was something terribly wrong with the world when people as good as his father and Vanessa could be exiled simply because some old clergyman had not blessed them. He knew, though, that it all went further than this, that people thought it impertinent of his father to come back and live with his woman here in the very spot where they were so well known, and that there had been scandals before, old scandals of a hundred and fifty years ago that everyone in these valleys knew, scandals that had lost nothing in constant telling.

His young heart was passionately in sympathy with all the outlaws. It was enough for someone to be in disgrace for Tom to be on his side, so long as the outlaw was not cruel nor mean nor a coward. At his age it seemed very easy for the world to be wrong and for all the good men to be outlaws. And he was, like his father, a born champion of lost causes.

He heard voices and, sitting up, saw his father coming towards him and with him a large rough untidy-looking man. Benjie, when he saw his son, waved his one arm and, as they came up, introduced his companion.

'Tom, this is Mr George Endicott, an old friend of mine.' Then, reaching his hand up to the big man's shoulder, he said: 'George, this is my boy, Tom. I don't think you've seen him before. Tom, Endicott was with me in Africa. This boy, you know, George, was all through the Mafeking siege.'

The man, Tom thought, was one of the strongest and wildest he had ever seen. He looked like part of the countryside, belonging to the stones and bracken like the Herdwick sheep.

He wore no hat, his face was of a brick-red colour, and his shirt was wide open, showing a brown chest with a pelt of black hair. His body was solid like a stone, but he moved lightly on his feet, making no sound. He had only nodded at Tom and then passed straight up the fell, swinging his arms.

'Tom, look here. I'm glad I saw you. When you go down tell them I shan't be back tonight.'

'When will you be back?'

'Oh, tomorrow likely. Endicott has come over from Whitehaven. We're going for a tramp.'

Benjie looked shamefaced. He knew that Tom knew that he had gone from the house without telling Vanessa.

'All right,' Tom said shortly, and without another word, picking up his book, he started down the hill. He hated it when his father was ashamed, when Vanessa was disappointed, when rough ill-looking men from God-knows-where took his father off to drink and fool with girls and not to return for days perhaps. His father was fine, his father was the best man he knew--but why must he make Vanessa unhappy?

Cold Fell had changed not at all in the last hundred years, with its whitewashed front, its narrow passages and low-ceilinged rooms, the rough cobbling before the door, the slope down the hill where the hens were and the broad fields that crossed the stream and the valley, the cows now clustered for the cool under a large oak, the sheep browsing on the fell slope. Great sweeping shadows of gold covered the valley, and the sun, low now above the hill, struck through the thick leafage of the oak. The river, shrunk though it was now, could be heard very clearly chattering over its stones, so still was the air.

Vanessa was standing in the doorway when Tom came up.

'Have you seen your father, Tom?'

'Yes.' Tom put his arm round her and kissed her. He did not kiss anyone easily, but he liked to kiss Vanessa--her skin was so cool and so firm. Her hair was greying but her cheek had a girl's freshness. 'Yes. He's away for the night.'

She said nothing but went in.

Later they had their supper in the porch. An old woman called Mrs Williams came every day and 'did' for them. But Benjie and Vanessa cooked, and they, all three of them, did the house, looked after the piece of garden at the back. Tom went into Keswick for the shopping. For six months Vanessa had scarcely stirred from the valley. She looked now like a woman who had always lived in the country, her hair very simply brushed back, parted in the middle, leaving her fine brow clear and broad. She wore a plain blue cotton dress, shorter by a great deal than the prevailing fashion. Her waist was not pinched nor were her shoulders puffed. She looked her age, but her body had strengthened. With her height, her broad shoulders, her firm big breasts, she was a woman who would be noticed anywhere, and all her life she had carried herself superbly.

They had cold chicken and Cumberland ham, a salad, a cold apple tart, and a cheese. A fine supper on a summer evening with the murmur of the river coming up to them and the air as sweet as honey.

Vanessa, leaning her arms on the table, looked out to the valley.

'You know, Tom, I think Benjie might have told me.'

'He was afraid to. He had a man with him.'

'A man?--what man?'

'His name was Enderby, or Enderley--something like that.'

'Endicott. George Endicott. I know him. He is an old friend of Benjie's. He met him first when he met your mother. He was a friend of your uncle's.'

'What kind of man is he?'

'Oh, all right, I dare say. Rough, wild, always on the tramp.'

'Father said he was with him in Africa.'

'I wouldn't mind,' she went on, after a pause, 'if only he'd tell me when he's going, but he slips out of the house as though he were ashamed.'

'He IS ashamed,' said Tom.

'The trouble is that each time I say to myself: "Perhaps this time he won't come back." Judith, my grandmother, used to talk to me sometimes when I was a girl about HER married life. She's often told me that her husband--he was a Frenchman--would go off just like that, only he would be away for months. The difference was, though, that Judith was married. I'm not. I've no hold on your father except that we love one another. That's the only hold any woman ought to want, but women are funny. I've never known a woman, Tom, who was really sure of a man. Men belong to a different world, and you can't be sure, from minute to minute, that they won't have a new idea in their head. Women are too serious about everything. They can't take things lightly. It isn't that I doubt your father. We've loved one another all our lives--but I've nothing else now. I've put all my eggs in one basket.'

'You've got me,' Tom said proudly.

'Yes. You're very faithful. You'll make a splendid husband one day.'

Tom saw that she was struggling not to be unhappy; he saw how deeply disappointed she was and, with an intuition wonderful for a boy, knew that she was dreading the long lonely summer night. He wanted terribly to help her.

'I know what it is in Father,' he said. 'It isn't anything to do with you and me. He wants to be free sometimes. He told me once that there's bad blood in us. My great-uncle killed my grandfather in Skiddaw Forest and my great-grandfather killed himself. You know all that. And I think sometimes it all comes over my father-- a kind of superstition about the past. Of course the past can't do anything to you REALLY, can it? But you have to fight it sometimes perhaps. So he goes away and fights and then comes back to you again. That's HOW I explain it!' he ended.

She got up and kissed him.

'The truth is, Tom dear, that I've never been a very sensible woman. I haven't enough humour. If I could only see how funny things are it would be a lot easier. When the Queen died I was unhappy for weeks. Why should I have been? I'd never known her, but I couldn't get used to her not being there. It's always been the same if I've loved anyone. You take life lightly, Tom, and people easily. It's the only way.'

'I'm rather serious-minded too, I expect,' said Tom. 'Tim's always said so. Tim used to say that I ought to have been an old nurse with families of other people's children to look after.' He laughed. 'Don't you worry. Father will be back tomorrow.' He got up and patted her on the shoulder, then moved about taking the plates and dishes into the house.

Vanessa sat there, her chin propped on her hands, staring in front of her.

Three days passed and Benjie had not returned, nor had any word come from him. This was the longest time that he had ever been away from Vanessa since her flight from Hill Street. The hours were quiet, stealthy, and packed with a secret significance. She did not know that time could be so long, and on the third day she found herself walking down the valley towards the hills, standing and looking about her, starting with an agitated excitement at the figure of a shepherd, thinking that stones were men and that every sound in the air was Benjie's voice. Tom's care of her, which he tried to make unconcerned and indifferent, irritated her. She came back to the house on the afternoon of the fourth day, driven by absurd fear. Benjie had been planning this for months past; he was weary of her and had not the courage to tell her so. Some woman somewhere had entrapped him and, as he had always been faithless, so now he proved it to her for ever. She was intensely humiliated. 'I have never been able to hold anyone to myself; there is something in me charmless, dull, wearying; everything that I touch falls away from me.' She was even haunted by the dazzling, dominating figure of her grandmother who, with her head up, stamping her ivory cane, could rule the world if she wished, but she, Vanessa, who had had beauty and all the world to charm, had been able to hold no one. Women between thirty and forty often know an especial terror and apprehension, for youth has gone; if they have had children they are being abandoned by them, men are searching for younger faces, and old age, that demands more wisdom for the subduing of its terrors from women than from men, already leers, like a cocksure arrogant old man, over the fence. Women have greater courage wherewith to meet spiritual loneliness than men have, but their capacity for spiritual experience is also greater.

She came back to the house, its floors flooded with the June sun as though to taunt her, and said passionately to Tom: 'He is never coming back. I can make my mind up to it.'

Tom said something. She turned on him furiously with one of her old tempers. 'What do you know about it? You are only a boy!'

Then she burst out of the house again and walked swiftly away from the hills. She was in a mood for anything. That old, scared, irrational Herries blood for ever mixing in the personal Herries history beat now in her brain. Why not end it? Her life had been a failure from beginning to end. Her father had died when she might have saved him, she had married a man without loving him and he had gone crazy from it, she had risked everything for another Herries who was notorious for his instability and lightness. But even now, in this passion of fear and unhappiness, she would not blame Benjie. No, it was herself--her dullness and heaviness of spirit. 'Why have I not managed life better? What is lacking, has always been lacking in me?' She came to the little church and, scarcely knowing that she did so, finding the door open, entered.

She had often, in the last six months, visited this little place and had grown to love it. Behind its wall, guarded by its trees, hills mounting to every side of it and one of the loveliest small rivers in England at its back, quiet, restrained and confident, it held something in its heart greater than change or fashion. Everything was simple, the whitewashed walls, the altar, the pews, the birds that nestled in its roof, the scents that filled it from the summer fields, and the unceasing rhythm of the river.

Very unhappy, Vanessa knelt and prayed: 'God, in this quiet place, help me to find my courage again. I knew, when I did wrong, that I would suffer, but if it be possible allow me not to suffer without anyone to help me. It is not right that I should ask You anything, for I have not yet repented of the wrong that I did. I know that You ask me to be honest, and so I say that if there was that wrong to do again I would do it again. I feel that I acted against a law and against my conscience, but I did it deliberately. God, don't take Benjie away from me. Let me care for him and watch over him and share his life later when we will need somebody. If You are my Father as, in this quiet place, I feel You to be, do as my own father would have done, and let me be good to someone I love. Don't take Benjie from me. I know him better than anyone else does. I can care for him more than anyone else can. Let me be punished in any other way, but not by losing Benjie. You have placed this church here that we should make our requests in it. This is my only prayer--let me keep Benjie . . .'

She found that she was saying aloud, her hands clenched, her eyes staring at the little altar on which was a glass bowl filled with red and white roses: 'Don't take Benjie away from me! Don't take Benjie away from me!'

The strain of her intensity snapped. She rose from her knees and sat on the hard bench. She heard a bird singing, the water swinging by, and the voice of a shepherd as he crossed the grass by the church wall, talking to another.

'Well, goodnight.'

'Goodnight.'

She knew the man by his voice and with that familiarity all the outer world swung in. She heard Barney in London saying: 'Why, no, Vanessa dear, if it makes you happy to believe in such things . . .'

She saw the Prince and Princess entering in procession into the Hill Street drawing-room . . . She was in a theatre and Bernhardt was speaking . . . Then, someone saying: 'God? Oh, God died long ago. Didn't you know?'

But the church filled with light. She heard the sheep with their gentle sleepy rustle pass beyond the wall. A fragrance of flowers and new-mown hay seemed to be carried, by the sweet, persistent note of the bird, into the church again. She knew with a sudden delighted conviction that for herself at least this presence was true. Some wise power entered into her and, falling on her knees again and hiding her face in her hands, she was pervaded, through and through, with intimate kindliness. That intimacy! To be lonely no more! 'Only connect . . .' The connexion was there, her hands were held, her bent head blessed. Time was lost. The bird continued its song as the shadows came down upon the mountains.

When she came into the house again Tom was there in the passage.

'It's all right,' he said (a little shyly, for she had been angry when she went away). 'Father's back. He's upstairs and he's awfully tired, for he's walked miles.'

She went up into the low-ceilinged bedroom and there was Benjie, lying, stripped to his trousers, on the bed, his arms behind his head. He grinned but didn't move. She saw the stump of his arm where the flesh had been joined in a sharp red line, the deep brown of his bare chest, taut and spare as a boy's, his hair tumbled over his forehead, his impudent ashamed grin, and she was drowned in a wave of triumphant happiness. But she must not show it. She must be calm, sarcastically humorous as a wise woman would be, indifferent as though whether he went or came meant little to her. So she stood where she was and looked at him.

'So you're back?'

'Yes.' Then as she still didn't move, with his bright eyes fastened on her face he said: 'Haven't you a kiss for me?'

'No, I haven't. Why did you go off without telling me?'

'Oh, I don't know. That man Endicott came over from Whitehaven. He wanted a walk.'

'I see. You never thought, I suppose, how anxious Tom and I would be.'

'Why should you be anxious? You knew I'd come back.'

'Four days is a long time without a word from you.' She gave him one long look, then turned to the door. 'I suppose I'd better get you something to eat. You'll be hungry.'

'Yes--famished.' He looked at her, smiling. He put out his arm. 'Here, Vanessa. Come here. Don't be so cross with me. I haven't seen you for four days.'

'I'm not cross.' She came over to the bed and stood there. He put his bare arm round her waist, then drew her down. She knelt by the bed and they embraced. Then she rested her head on his body, he stroking her hair.

'Benjie, it wasn't kind . . . four whole days . . . I was in a panic. Tom and I are all alone here. Nobody comes, and if you're away the days drag. I've been watching the hills all day.'

He turned on his side, drew her on to the bed, put his hand inside her cotton dress that it might rest on her heart. Her hand stroked his back, rejoicing in the strong muscles, the smooth skin warm and fresh like the summer evening. Through the open window she could hear the bird singing and the running water as she had done in the church. He settled himself comfortably against her.

'Now I'll tell you all about it. Quite truthfully. George Endicott turned up and as soon as I saw him I wanted to go off. He wasn't here more than a minute. You were in the back of the house. I said "Hullo, George," and he said, "Hullo." I asked him where he had come from and he said "Whitehaven". I asked him whether he wanted a walk and he said "Yes" and there we were. I HAD to go off when I saw him, Vanessa. I HAD to. I'd have told you, only I knew you'd want to know WHERE I was going and how long I'd be, and I didn't know where and I didn't know how long.'

'I wouldn't,' she murmured. (But she knew that she would.)

'Then we went up the Fell and saw young Tom and I told him. It was pretty late by then, but we got on to Robinson and then at dusk on Honister. It isn't dusk, you know--there's a white light in the sky. There was a new moon, too. We found a cave on the other side of Honister. Endicott said that in the old days, years ago, his great-grandfather used the cave when they were smuggling. They were bad lots, you know--as bad as they make 'em. When we came to the cave there were two others there--a man and a girl. The girl had red hair and was pretty in a way. They didn't say much, but they were cooking a hare and they let us share their meal.

'Then we all curled up and went to sleep and I was as happy, Vanessa, as I've ever been in my life. I didn't care for you or Tom or anybody or anything. It was just like that--I'm telling you honestly. I was free and the air was fine and warm. I'd drunk their whisky and eaten their meat and beyond the cave there was the misty moonlight over the hills. I was a free man and I didn't want ever to be tied again. Well, I went to sleep and, after a time, I woke to find the girl had come over and was lying close to me, right up against me she was, with her arm around me. There she lay all night. I didn't do a thing to her. I didn't even kiss her. I'm telling you honestly, mind. I'd tell you just the same if there'd been anything, I'm not being virtuous about it. I might have done a lot of things but I just didn't. In the morning we set off again, the four of us. We were together the next three days. We went down into Eskdale, then over to Coniston, on to Helvellyn, along the Saddleback. This morning we separated, and here I am. It was grand, I tell you, Vanessa--lovely days and fine nights, not saying much, any of us. George wanted me to come back to Whitehaven and stay with him a bit, but by this morning you'd all come over me again, Vanessa. I HAD to see you. I didn't feel free any longer. I didn't WANT to be free. So I kissed the red-haired girl for the first time, gave George a kick, and here I am. I know I did wrong not to tell you, but if I'd told you I wouldn't have had such a good time somehow. You've got to forgive me and believe me too. I've never told you a lie yet.'

She sat up on the bed, her arm around him. This was something of a crisis between them and she wanted to say what was best and wisest.

'Yes, Benjie, that's all right. I know you must be free. Haven't I always said so?'

'Yes, you've always SAID so,' he answered, laughing and stroking her cheek.

'Have I prevented you? Have I ever stopped you?' she asked.

'Don't be so serious, darling. Take it lightly. I've only been for a walk--and here I am.'

'That's easy to say,' she answered. 'Does no man EVER understand these things? Every time you go off I can't be sure you'll ever come back again. Oh yes, I feel safe enough now--now that you are here and close to me--but when you are gone I say to myself, why should he come back? I've no hold on him. He may be tired of me, hiding it from me.'

Tired of you? I love you more than I ever did. Why, Vanessa, I've loved you all my life! How could I NOT come back? I'll always return--'

'Ah yes, you think so!' she answered quickly. 'But I've seen you change your mind so often about so many things! If I were younger, gayer! But sometimes I seem to myself so dull, so heavy! Women are faithful if they're given a chance--it's the thing they like best to be! But men--when they've got what they want, they want something else. Then,' she went on, 'it's lonely when you're away. For six months here we've seen nobody. When you're with me I don't WANT to see anyone, but when you're away every minute is an hour. It wouldn't be if I knew you'd be back at such and such a time. But when you haven't said a word--'

He sat up. 'Look here, Vanessa. Let's have a child! Then you wouldn't doubt any more--'

'Oh no,' she answered slowly. 'That would be wrong--'

'Why wrong? Your father didn't mind because he was illegitimate.'

'I think he did. It made a difference to his life.'

'If only Ellis would die!' He beat the bed with his hand. 'Now don't be hypocritical about that, Vanessa. You know it would be much better if he should die. He's old, he's crazy. Life can't be any fun for him.'

But he was afraid of alluding to Ellis. A shadow crept into her eyes. He hated that she should think of the past.

'Look, Vanessa! I have to go off sometimes. Sometimes I'm restless beyond bearing. I think of my father, my mad uncle, my grandfather. There are days when I hate myself, my ancestry, all the past and the present together. Then you can't help me--nobody can. But never doubt that you're the love of my whole life, Vanessa. If ever any man in the world loved anyone, I love you! Why, even now I couldn't be away three days from you without running back! But there's this country, every fell-side, every stream, every stone wall, is in my blood! Why, you know that as well as I! Wasn't it crazy of us to come back here where everyone knows us and all our family history? But could we help it? Of course not! No man escapes the past, nor the fields where he was as a boy if that poison is in his blood. With some of us it is, with some of us it isn't. What do Timothy or Violet or Ellis care for this country? That's why they'll never understand us nor why we do what we do! We are the gipsies, with the smell of the ground always in our nostrils. That's our history, mixed up with the country, with Cumberland, with England.'

He stretched himself and yawned.

'Lord! I'm a poet! And I'm famished too! I could eat a whole sheep!'

He held her tightly in his arm, kissing her again and again.

'Darling, don't be sad, don't be too serious. I'm yours for ever and ever. You're the one thing I'll never leave. You and this country here. And I'll be good next time--I'll tell you before I go. And I didn't make love to the red-haired girl. Remember that! Vanessa, sweetheart, darling sweetheart, don't you KNOW that you've got me for ever and ever? Have you no sense? Can't you TELL a thing like that?'

A little later, going down to prepare the food, she found Tom making, very seriously, an omelette.

'Father's frightfully hungry,' he said. Then he saw how happy she was. He sighed as though a great burden were lifted from him. She kissed him.

'I'm sorry I was angry this afternoon,' she said. Then, as she began to make the meal, she added: 'I'm afraid, Tom dear, that we both take life too seriously.'

An hour later, in front of the cottage, the moon, cherry-tinted in a white sky, rising above the hill, they had the best meal of their lives.

STORM COMING UP

'Time, of course,' said Mr Benbow who was, during September, taking the work of the Vicar of Newlands, 'does not exist. There IS no time.' He was, he had always been, of a mathematical mind, but he did not know, as he said this, raising his glass of beer and looking at the charming sun through its smoky depths, the strange things that his simple sentence provoked.

Here, in the September sunshine, sitting with Benjie and Vanessa outside their white house (he was a man who cared nothing for social conventions), he killed history. There was no past. Upon this square of ground, over which the Eagle was magnificently sailing, even as he spoke, across the spine of hill that rose in front of them, Francis Herries, his small son tight against his breast, rode over the wild land, not pastured now, sweeping in unchecked confusion down Borrowdale to the small house under the moon, with its shining suits of armour. 'Take me to the Fair with you,' Mrs Press cried. 'No, I will not,' he answered, while Margaret his wife lay sick in the room above.

Keswick waited basking in the sun while the coach rolled in from Kendal, and old Pomfret, a little drunken, looked out of his study window. At the same moment David, at Uldale, heard of the fall of the Bastille and cursed his son, Jennifer walked tapping with her slippers up the road to the Fortress, and Judith's boy, naked by the Tarn, mocked the big man on the white horse. In his London rooms Francis, David's son, sick of life, blew his brains out while young Tom Macaulay talked with old Rogers in Hatchard's bookshop. Judith saw the big woman count the lumps of sugar in the Paris café, and young Will raced up to the Druids' Circle while Adam cheered him on. 'It's war then,' said Judith, nodding her bonnet at Walter, and, even as she spoke, the flames leapt upon Uldale and her son fell fighting the choking fumes. The carriages moved slowly at Will's funeral, and Sayers with a broken arm faced unflinchingly the blinded Heenan.

'Thank you very much, Miss Martineau,' said Judith, shouting down the ear-trumpet, one eye on the tea tent, and John called through the mists of Skiddaw for his enemy. 'Yes, it's too late,' said Benjie, bowing his head; 'I'm married already,' and Vanessa turned, in the long drawing-room, thinking that she heard Ellis' step on the stair. The Chinese clock strikes, and old Emily has offered up a prayer while young Tom, his hand for a moment on Vanessa's shoulder, says: 'He'll be back soon. He'll be back soon, Vanessa.'

Behind these figures, mingling with them, giving them their meaning and sharing in their destinies, fog swallows up Carlisle to hide Prince Charlie's men, Keswick receives Mr Gray and the young gentlemen from Cambridge who hope to have a word with Mr Southey while on their reading party, the Reform Bill rides in with a cheering mob behind it, trees fall, the roads are bound with stone walls, figures from here, there, everywhere, buy lead pencils, picnic on Skiddaw, whose green slopes young Mr Keats and sturdy Sir Walter find adventurous. A Macclesfield paper advertises for workers: 'Wanted, between 4,000 and 5,000 persons between the ages of 7 and 21 years.' Thick bellies of smoke veil the Midland sky. Disraeli sees the war of the two nations; Mr Joseph Hebergam, aged seventeen, works from five in the morning until eight at night with a break of thirty minutes at noon. 'Bravo! Bravo!' cry Will and Horace and the Vicar of Little Rodney-on-the-Marsh, 'England rules the world', while a man or two, with pens in their hands--Shelley, Carlyle, Dickens, Ruskin, Morris--speak of 'a Golgotha of souls and bodies buried alive'. The Herries are rising, the lights of London grow brighter, the fields of middle England are lost in smoke, slowly, slowly men are pushing up from under ground, are meeting, are banding together, demanding their share, pulling down the Park railings, putting up bright little red houses, chasing the Squire's wife out of the cottages, pushing into Westminster Hall, driving the South African millionaires out of Park Lane, running here, running there, from coast to coast with their children behind them, dancing on Primrose Hill, standing in rows of shiny black as, at last, the old Queen passes . . .

And still on that square of ground, over which the Eagle is hovering, nothing has changed. The coach rolls in to Keswick square, the shepherd searches the mist under Helvellyn for his wandering sheep, the sun falls from Seatoller on to the silent blue of Buttermere and, under Gable, the Tarn sleeps like a rusted shield.

'There is no time,' said Mr Benbow. 'Time is an anachronism. At this moment Caesar falls on the steps of the Capitol and David challenges his giant enemy.'

At this moment, too, Cynthia Worcester brought her two little girls on a visit to Cumberland. Strange how the Herries were drawn back, again and again, to this patch of ground. But in Cynthia's case it was perhaps Vanessa rather than Cumberland that drew her. Cynthia had never set an eye on Vanessa since the flight from Hill Street. She had not seen her but had stepped into her place--or very nearly. Peile Worcester was not, of course, as rich as Ellis; they could not, in their house in Charles Street, entertain as Vanessa had done in Hill Street. On the other hand, they were cleverer than Vanessa. Vanessa had not been clever--kind, gentle, generous, most beautiful to look upon, but NOT, oh, most certainly not clever.

Cynthia was as pretty as a rosebud (a flower to which she had been often compared) and ALSO as clever as a monkey. She had always been INSIDE the Arts as Vanessa had never attempted to be. Indeed, so far was Cynthia now inside that her set embalmed her like a fly in amber. But everyone came to her afternoons, her evenings--Mr Bernard Shaw, the Sidney Webbs and Mr H. G. Wells; while on the other side there were the aesthetes, Mr Sidney Colvin at the Museum, young Mr Binyon, a wild young man who had sailed before the mast and swept the floor in a bar, Mr Masefield, and, above all, the Homer, the Milton (who knew, perhaps the Shakespeare of our day?), honey-voiced Mr Stephen Phillips. The politicians came too--Cynthia had no Party politics: Sir Henry Campbell-Bannerman dined at her table as well as Mr Balfour. Even the new Labour candidate for Barnard Castle, Mr Arthur Henderson, came to tea . . .

Cynthia had taken Vanessa's place. She was the social head of the family now, and the younger generation, Alfred's children, Maurice and Clara, Carey's girls, cousins from Manchester and cousins from Bournemouth, Philip and his odd effeminate friends, young Violet and her stupid husband--they recognized it and submitted to it.

Nevertheless (as is always the case in every family history) some things were not quite right. Cynthia was not as happy as she ought to be. She possessed just enough imagination to wish her position a little different. HER struggle between Prose and Poetry was, of course, all on the side of Prose. There was never any doubt as to which party she belonged to. Of the world of Judith, of Rose, of Vanessa she would never even glimpse the borders: nevertheless the world where she was was not quite good enough. Peile Worcester was not quite good enough, their income was not quite good enough, their two lovely obedient little girls were not quite good enough. In fact, in this September of 1903, Cynthia was supremely discontented, her rosebud mouth curled down at the ends; she, one afternoon, startled Mr Phillips almost out of his life by saying that today she really didn't want to listen to Marpessa, and she lost her temper altogether with Horace when he informed her that 'in his own small way he grew with every increasing year more and more of an optimist'. She could not ABIDE Horace, she decided, with his high domed forehead, his mild eyes naked of eyebrows, his plump rosy cheeks, and his way of being able to help anyone in the world out of any trouble so long as he personally got the glory of it.

After her rudeness to Horace (for which she was sincerely sorry, for she was a kind-hearted little thing) she took herself in hand. What was the matter with her? Two things. One, her husband. The other, that she longed to see Vanessa again. She must get away from Peile for a while and she must see Vanessa, if only for a moment. With a start of surprise, staring into her mirror, she discovered that, in all probability, she cared for and admired Vanessa more than anyone else in the world. Vanessa had of course done a dreadful thing.

Had she run away with anyone but Benjie Herries! Nevertheless Cynthia, feeling as she did at the moment about Peile, thought that running away from one's husband was not so extraordinary a business. Only it was a thing that a Herries must never do, because the eyes of the world were on the Herries family, they stood for domesticity, patriotism, and virtuous common sense. That was why Vanessa's affair had been so truly awful!

The matter with Peile was that he never changed. He was exactly the same as he had been when she married him, EXACTLY the same, and all the things for which she had loved him then were precisely the things that exasperated her now!

He had not changed in looks; he was as good-looking as ever. He did not appear a day older (how she wished he did!) with his crinkly fair hair, his fair short moustache, his splendid figure, his immaculate clothes. He was an English Gentleman in excelsis. He had today precisely the same complaints against the English middle classes that he had had when he married her. THEN they had seemed to her charming, and she had agreed with every one of them, for the Herries belonged to the Upper Middle Classes and thought therefore that almost everything that the Middle Middle Classes did was a pity. Peile's complaints and sarcasms now were just what they had always been but were more, far more, vehemently expressed, because he was older now and had all the Englishman's touching faith that the older you grew the more important your opinions were.

At this particular moment there were a number of things that made the Middle Middle Classes especially offensive to Peile. Business was bad. The country had not yet recovered from the effects of that stupid mismanaged war. How ironical to remember the cheering crowds lining the street as the CIVs marched past, or the shocking vulgar manifestations of Mafeking night! Then there was the Whitaker-Wright affair that had been dragging on for years, and only in March had the Public Prosecutor seen fit to prosecute. There was Chamberlain's absurd loan of thirty-five million pounds to South Africa. THERE was a nice burden for the Upper Middle Class (on whom now ALL the taxes were falling!) to pay! There were the unemployed walking about the streets with their collecting boxes. There was Brodrick's ridiculous 'Phantom Army Corps' of which young Winston Churchill so rightly made fun. There was this demand on the part of the Lower Middle Classes for cheap food--and they were getting it too, mostly in tins, of course, but nevertheless eating lobster and asparagus, peas and apricots, as though these things were their right instead of a luxury. There was the horrible 'Art and Craft' furniture with which the Lower Middle Classes were encumbering their homes, dreadful cheap confusions of memories of William Morris and vulgar German Kunst, A typist whom Alfred had engaged actually owned a mechanical piano- player, bought of course on hire-purchase. There was this new passion on the part of the Lower Middle Classes for learning things, for buying cheap books about atheism and how to put a bicycle together. There were their odd forms of entertainment and exercise--walking races to Brighton. There had been the other day a race to Brighton for waitresses! There was a sudden craze for swimming the Channel; and schools for quite inferior children were mad about hockey teams, just like the school attended by his own girls. There was this crazy ugly music by Richard Strauss that had not a tune in it, and this vulgar new halfpenny paper, the Daily Mirror, for women. There was the sordid excitement over the Moat Farm Murder, and there was this fearful increase in motor vehicles, so that a law was to be passed ordering them to be numbered and some 'test of efficiency' for the driver . . .

It was not that Peile was a snob. He did not think himself better than anyone else, or only so very, very little better, but anyone could see that this new power in the Lower Middle Classes, their crazy desire for the best of things and intolerable fashion of making themselves heard through the daily Press, through Leagues and Unions and meetings and speeches was doing old England no good, was in fact fast dragging her down from her grand position as Mistress of the World. Something must be done about it, and the Upper Middle Classes were the people to do it: it was their right and their duty. Peile did not know WHAT everyone was about! The country going to wrack and ruin and nobody cared. What was Alfred doing, and old Barney and older Horace in Manchester? Why, simply nothing at all!

It was after Cynthia had endured months and months of this at every meal and for an hour or so every night in the quiet of the matrimonial chamber that she decided to take the girls for a holiday to Cumberland.

She simply told Peile one evening and, next morning, departed.

Arrived in Keswick, she looked for rooms, preferring these to a hotel, and found them--most charming ones--on the right side of the road that ran down to the lake. She spent half an hour putting the rooms' things away into a cupboard--trays from India, china figures from Manchester, bead mats, two large coloured portraits and three huge sea-shells. Mrs Colbourne the landlady was a little astonished, but there was something about Cynthia, so tiny but so charming, with such lovely hair, such lovely eyes, and a manner that had just the right mixture of kindliness and authority. Mrs Colbourne, who was a widow and came from near Liverpool (had she been a Cumbrian she would not have been so quickly melted), surrendered to Cynthia entirely, giving the governess special food (for she had a delicate stomach), sitting up one night when Rosalind had a cough that might become pneumonia (you never can tell), and hiring a pony trap from her friend Mr

Lewthwaite at especial terms for Cynthia's especial use. In those few days she used it in fact a great deal. She became a familiar sight in Keswick, sitting up driving, her little back like a ramrod, and a veil concealing her lovely features. The citizens of Keswick are not very easily impressed--they have too many visitors--but the Hon Mrs Peile Worcester, driving her pony cart, her two lovely little girls sitting as stiff as Royalty behind with their governess, Miss King, was a sight that they did not for a while forget.

Then, after four extremely happy days, there came a peremptory letter from Peile. He was not well. He had been in bed all day. He had a temperature. The doctor thought that it might be serious. He demanded her instant return.

She did not return instantly, however. She waited a day. She went with her two little girls and called on Vanessa. The pony trap arrived at the church. There they all three dismounted and walked across the meadows to the white house. Having tea by the house door were Vanessa, Benjie, and Tom. At first Cynthia thought it was the farmer and his wife. It was one of those lovely September days when, above the turning bracken, the sun lies in happy content from shoulder to shoulder of the hills and all the little streams flash with light. Perhaps one small cloud, dark as a mulberry, hangs motionless like a hawk above the glittering valley and, for a moment, the sun slips behind its shelter. Then at that instant all is sombre--the hill, the streams, the little running walls, as though a vast curving wing from the protecting Eagle shadowed the world. Then the sun is free of the cloud, and light leaps up from the heart of the soil.

It was such a day, but very warm: Benjie was in his shirt sleeves, the sleeve of his one arm rolled up; his neck was bare. He was wearing corduroy riding breeches, and Vanessa in a sun bonnet had a cotton dress--white scattered with blue flowers.

After another look Cynthia saw that it was indeed Vanessa: she ran forward with a little cry. The two women embraced.

Two days after her return to London, Cynthia wrote to May Rockage. This is part of the letter:

. . . But of course I wasn't going to miss Vanessa, the very thing I'd come up there for. So we drove over, the girls and I, to the funny little valley where they live. Peile was very annoyed when he heard that I took the girls. Very annoyed indeed, especially as he has a sore throat and thinks himself on the point of death. (He's better tonight. Nothing but a bad cold. Aren't husbands absurd?) But the girls enjoyed themselves. They went off quite alone with Benjie's boy, Tom. He's nineteen now, Vanessa told me, and MOST serious as though he was eighty. But of course he had all that time in Paris and South Africa, which makes him more grown-up. Anyway I knew the children were quite safe with him. I think both of them have fallen in love with him. They've talked of nothing else since. Benjie was nice. I should say Vanessa's calmed him down. Of course he LOOKS rough. He might have been a tramp or gipsy or anything, and he's brown as a berry. But he's always a gentleman even if he hasn't always behaved like one.

But, May dear, here's the great news. Vanessa is going to have a baby. Any time. It might have come while we were there having tea! She doesn't attempt to conceal it. Really I was rather afraid what the girls would think, but they're too young, thank Heaven, to know anything about it. Miss King is EXCELLENT at answering awkward questions. When I went up with Vanessa to her room (SUCH a small room, with white-washed walls and smelling of hay), she told me that they hadn't meant to have one--a baby I mean-- but there it is, and of course it will be illegitimate, which is a pity. Isn't it funny how we CAN'T keep illegitimacy out of the family, and yet I'm sure most of us are as proper as can be? When I was with Vanessa I couldn't help feeling I'd made a mistake and it would have been much better to have run away in a caravan with a gipsy instead of all these silly London parties. Benjie and Vanessa seemed so VERY happy. But of course as soon as I was in London again I knew it would never have done. I'd NEVER be happy in a caravan roasting hedgehogs and telling people's fortunes. But what IS there about Vanessa? Of course she's still beautiful even as she is and dressed like a cottage woman with a sun bonnet. But her features are lovely, so NOBLE without being a bit superior. She has the grandest eyes, the finest fore-head, the kindest mouth of any woman I've ever seen. I've always adored her, even though I WAS a little jeal-ous of her in London. She's just as quiet as she always was. She sits there, her hands on her lap, and you feel you could tell her anything. She isn't clever of course--I mean she never SAYS anything that's clever--but you can trust her absolutely, which you can't do with many women. She asked about Ellis, but I couldn't tell her much except that he's quite happy looked after by those two awful old women. I asked her whether she were happy and she said she was. I think she is--part of the time. But I caught her looking at Benjie as though she expected him to go off at any moment. Not that she lets HIM see that. She's too wise. She knows that men want to FEEL they're free even though they're not really. I asked her whether she were anxious about the baby. She's forty-four you know and it's her first. But she said no. She said she didn't mind dying so long as Benjie was there. But I don't know WHAT he'd do without her. He may be wild and all the rest, but if any man ever loved a woman Benjie loves Vanessa. And it was all so quiet there, with the sun on the fields and the sheep grazing and the noise of running water. If Maud and Helen are coming up next week to town do let me know. Peile says . . .

'A storm's coming up,' said Benjie, looking back towards Keskadale and Buttermere Hause. The sky was a stainless blue, but over Whiteless Pike little shreds of cloud like tags of cotton wool floated and gathered. A low whispering wind stirred the dying bracken.

'I'm coming with you,' Vanessa said. As she said it she thought: 'Now this is foolish of me. This is what I determined not to do-- not to force myself on him. He doesn't want me. He will be so much happier by him-self. And yet I'm determined. What is it? Is it the child? I can't bear these days to let him out of my sight.'

'Better not,' Benjie said. 'There's a storm coming. And I'm out for a long walk--Hindscarth, Robinson, over Red Pike to Ennerdale. You'll never do it, Van, as you are. It wouldn't be safe.'

How well she knew him when he thought that someone was laying a hand on him to constrain him-- herself, anyone--like a hare who, with ears pricked, hears the hunter treading the long grass. But she was deter-mined. All her cautious ways of dealing with him were gone. She could not ENDURE a whole day and night just now without him. If she had asked him to stay he would have stayed--but reluctantly, behaving all day as though she had tethered him with a rope to a stone! How well she knew him! As though it were herself who was resenting it.

'I can't help it,' she said, smiling, her head up, her hands on her broad hips. 'I must come, Benjie. It will be all right. Wenlock says that it won't be yet. I never felt better in my life.'

He looked at her and she knew what he was think-ing: 'This big broad woman stands over me like a gaoler. Why did I tie myself up? Can't even go off for a walk by myself!'

And yet, all these months, since they had known that there was to be a child, he had been exquisitely tender for her, taking every trouble, thinking of her, watching over her as he never would have done for anyone five years ago. Oh! he had grown. Living with her, loving her, had taught him something. Had taught HER something too--should have taught her not to worry him, to let him go off free! But he ought not to want to go for a night and a day now, when, in spite of what the doctor had said, he knew that the child MIGHT be born . . . and she alone with Tom in the house. The child MIGHT be born . . . it was mad of her to insist that she must go with him. And yet she DID insist.

'I'm coming,' she said obstinately.

'Look here.' He did not look at her, but slanted his eyes, bright, lively, shining in his brown face, away from her, looking at the walls of the house, the sheep crop-ping, the wind stirring in the bracken. 'Look here, I've told you. There's a storm coming. I must have a walk. I've been cooped up for weeks. ('Oh no, you haven't,'

Vanessa thought. 'Last week you were away for two nights.') I'll be back tomorrow morning. It's madness for you to think of coming. Look here. Walk to the end of the lane with me. Then come back.'

'No, I'm coming,' she answered obstinately. She went in to get some things. As she was collecting them she thought: 'What is making me do this? And why, at moments like this, do we almost hate one another? I would give him anything, anything in the world. I would die for him. It wouldn't be hard at all. But now the more he wants me not to come with him the more I'm coming. And when it's like this it seems as though we had always been fighting one another, all our lives long. And yet soon--when we are agreed again--it will seem as though we had never had a fight in our lives worth mentioning.'

When she came down in her short skirt and with her stick and rucksack she looked in at the lower room to say goodbye to Tom. He was seated at the table, his square arm firmly planted, his honest determined eyes bent on a book. He sprang up.

'Why, where are you going?'

'I'm going with Benjie for a walk.'

The look came into his eyes that she knew so well--of fear and love and motherly anxiety.

'Oh, but you shouldn't! Not now. What's father doing to let you?--'

She smiled the old ironical mischievous smile that she had had as a child, a smile just like Adam's.

'He doesn't want me to. He's very cross about it, in fact.'

'Well, of course he is. Oh, Van, you mustn't.'

She caught him to her and kissed him.

'Dear Tom! You're going to have an awful life--always upsetting yourself about other people.'

She went outside. Benjie never said a word, but he was as sulky as a scolded schoolboy. They set off. She waved to Tom who was watching at the window, who would be, she knew, anxious and miserable all day.

'I don't care,' she thought defiantly. 'They're only men. They haven't the least idea what a woman wants. It will be good for me, this exercise. I never felt better in my life.' She walked, her head up, striding, a smile on her lips, and Benjie stepped along at her side, whistling, kicking pebbles. Only as they crossed the beck and she jumped from a stone to the bank he said:

'You're a fool, Van, you know. But on your own head be it.' Then he seemed better. He could never be sulky for long. Any little thing interrupted his mood. 'Look, Van! Look at that hawk! Like a stone on the sky! Ah! it's dropped--a fieldmouse, I expect. Here. Take my hand. This fence is a bit steep.'

Then all was well again; they were as close together as though they were one body, moving through the air, treading the turf so lightly, brushing the bracken as they began to climb. She looked back on the little stream before they left it. It played lingeringly about its gleaming stones as though loath to leave them, and the stones, too, seemed to cling to the water, stopping it, having excited murmurous chats with it, then, as though trying a last strategy, exercising in a tiny dance with flurries of silver lines and circles. All about the stream the scene was 'calm as a resting wheel' and the air so clean that trees and hill lines seemed stamped on the atmosphere like a seal on blue paper. The September day was exceptionally warm, but everywhere was the finger of decay, the leaves gold and dun and then of a sudden brightly green as though defiant of approaching death. At a cottage above the right bank of the stream a woman called to a shepherd striding uphill, two dogs at his heel: 'Well, anudder time . . .' Her voice rang out in the still air like a cry.

'Oh, how happy I am!' Vanessa thought, 'and ten minutes back I was nervous, uncertain, anxious. I only want Benjie to be happy and then everything in me is tranquil.' She remembered, as they pressed past a big boulder and began to tread the turf and to feel the wind, touched with the salt of the sea, in their faces, her London life. How dead and gone that seemed! But Cynthia's visit had stirred her strangely. She had accepted her ostracism almost gladly--she had suffered so little--but she had been moved, deeply moved that Cynthia had brought her children. Yes, and had allowed Tom to take them off across the valley. Tom had thought little Mary the most beautiful creature he had ever beheld. He had spoken of her again and again. He was to go shortly to London. He was to be given a trial on the Standard newspaper, a job that dear old Barney had found for him. How would the Family receive him? Peile and Alfred and Horace . . . Would May and Carey invite him to Wiltshire? After all, it was not HIS fault, poor boy, that his father had disgraced himself! And Society was more tolerant now. Every kind of queer person was admitted. When she had married Ellis the conventions had been rigid, as though you belonged to a Regiment, and any social or moral offence was as bad as desertion. She did not care for herself--HER case was socially hopeless and would be more so after the birth of a child--but she DID want Tom to have a good time!

Benjie took her arm to help her up a steep place. At his touch warmth poured through her body. It was always so. She had had, in her life, so little experience, but she had always heard that, when passion was gone, the best that a married pair could hope for was a kind of compromising friendship. But still, after all these years, Benjie's body was lovely to her. She would lie awake at night, while he slept, her hand on his thigh, and know that his vigour, his warmth, the freshness of his skin, the strength of his bones was unique for her and always would be. Now she understood fidelity--spiritual fidelity. Yes, that she had always understood, but when it was aided by the body how undefeated it must be! She understood now the tragedy of the marriage in which physical things were disharmonized. Easy for others to argue that it must be endured, but the touch, the kiss, the stroke of the hand, the meeting of the cheek against cheek, the personal flavour of the flesh, how much of spiritual contact went with these physical things--they were the very gateway of the spirit!

So, on the brow of the hill, she said that they would sit down for a moment and they did so. He put his arm around her and she drew his head to her breast. She felt almost a faintness of ecstasy here in this high air, with the smell of bracken and short stiff grass and the sea wind. Far below them she saw a little figure of a man leading his horse, and she thought of him, the year going past him, rousing his horses, driving his plough through flint and marl, the peewit wheeling above him, kestrels soaring, his eyes always so patient, so wise about so many things, walking as his forefathers had done in all the old ways. The child leapt in her womb and, with that lovely sense of new life, her eyes grew bright with comfort and she smiled.

They moved on again. She asked Benjie:

'I suppose now you think you know me better than anyone else in the world?'

'Yes, I think I do.'

'Yes, now. Father knew me; Rose--poor Rose-- knew me . . . Don't you know me so well, Benjie, that it's dull?'

'Dull?'

'Yes. I never can surprise you any more. You always know what I'm going to do.'

'I know you as though you were part of myself--the better part. You ARE part of myself. You always have been.'

'A part you often want to be rid of.'

'No, not often. Sometimes. Every man is like that.' He stopped and looked at her. 'Sure you're all right? Not tired?'

'Splendid. I could walk a hundred miles.'

'You know, when you said you were coming with me I hated you for a moment. I could have run off and never come back. That's what I felt like.'

'Yes, I knew you did.'

'Aren't you wise? You resent nothing. You forgive everything.'

'Yes,' she said, laughing. 'I'm placid--like a cow.'

'No. Oh no!' He struck his stick against a stone. 'You've a fearful temper. You can be so angry that the air quivers. But you never resent. You forgive and pass on. Every day you're finer.'

'Am I? That's because I love you.'

'Yes, and I love YOU! I love you! I love you! I love you!' he called. 'Do you hear the echo? It comes from that rift of rock.' Then, looking about him, sniffing the air, he went on: 'I was right about the storm, Van. It's coming. Do you see those clouds?'

Over Newlands a fleet of small, ragged clouds were slowly gathering, as though with purpose, as though marshalled. The sun shone brightly, but the air was colder and the wind now was busy along the ground, whistling in an undertone.

She didn't care about the storm. It would be nothing. She took her last look at the valley, so small but packed with history. In the time of Elizabeth, the German company had worked the mines in Newlands: there had been the Goldscope lead mines worked at the beginning of the nineteenth century. At Stair there had been the woollen mills--all that energy and human life, lovemaking and childbearing, foreign tongues, and Elizabeth's sharp eye fixed on her profits--and now the little valley bathed in silence, the small farms, the enclosed fields, the hawks and kestrels, the shepherd calling his dogs, the farmer ploughing the stiff field . . .

'Benjie, this is the only place in the world for us! The only spot . . . and for my father, my grandmother, her father . . .'

'Yes,' he answered. 'I can't tear away from it. Try as I may I can't. Everything passes--on the surface everything passes. But underneath, Van, you land on the rock, you give a cry of delight, you defend yourself against attack, and then, in a moment, you're gone to join the others under Skiddaw perhaps. We SEEM to change but we don't.'

She stopped, leaning on her stick.

'Yes, God gives you your moment of experience-- to overcome fear.'

'Oh, you and your God!' he said, laughing. 'Hasn't science taught you anything yet, Vanessa?'

'Science I don't know . . .'

He looked at her curiously. 'Then God does exist for you, Van? Just as I do?'

'Yes, if one's brave enough to believe in Him,' she said shyly, 'It needs courage like everything else. We never talk about Him, Benjie. Why? Because I'm afraid that you'll laugh, and YOU'RE afraid--what are you afraid of? Of looking too far. What does everyone say? That Huxley and Darwin have settled the whole question, so why argue? And they leave it like that because it's easier, because it's dangerous to look any further. I shouldn't have the courage if I were not driven to it, but I think God has tormented me all my life. Tormented isn't the right word perhaps. Moved restlessly in and around me. YOU say that that is superstition. I say that there's no other choice for me. I HAVE to be aware that you are there; I know your step, your voice, your frown. So I'm aware that God is there. I didn't ask for it. I'm not better or worse than you or anyone else because of it. It's simply a fact.'

She had not for a very long time discussed such things with him. He knew that she prayed, that much of the tranquillity that was always increasing in her came from some inner experience, the only thing that she did not share with him. Once he had been jealous of it, angry with her because of it. Now he loved her so much that he only wanted her to be happy. Perhaps? . . . Who knows? . . .

'It's a great thing to conquer fear,' he said. 'Anyone who does that is a kind of god.'

Even as he spoke the storm broke on them. Benjie knew the dangers of this piece of country. Robinson and Hindscarth had rough faces with much scree, and the ghylls into Buttermere had loose and falling rock with water suddenly, and sodden turf on the fell-side. A nasty ground for mist. But, at the moment, he could think of nothing but the wind which, quite suddenly, leapt from the ground, rushed forward from the hillside and tore up the valley. The clouds boiled from behind the hill, and the sun was obscured. The moss, heather, bracken that had been so brightly lit lost all colour.

'Are you all right?' he shouted to Vanessa.

'Yes, yes, I'm all right,' she answered.

Could they reach the bend of the hill they would have shelter. The storm was so furious that it could not last, he thought, but how strange was this sudden roaring of waters! The rain had begun to fall in slanting whips of steel, but the becks and mountain rivulets had not had time to absorb it; yet in his ears it was as though all the thundering waters of the world had been unloosed! It was as though a spirit with inky hair strode the fell and passed, blowing a great horn summoning his army! They could see the rain sweeping from the farthest horizon in curtains of gauze, blowing, bending, but never breaking.

'Turn your back to it!' he cried to Vanessa. 'Get your breath! There'll be a rock soon that we can shelter against.'

She turned, her skirts blown against her legs, her hair in her eyes and, at that same moment, with a little gasp of pain, felt a strong hand clutch her vitals, squeeze them, let them go. She bent her head. The stab of pain passed. She hurried, pressing through the storm so swiftly that Benjie cried:

'Come on! That's the spirit! We'll find shelter beyond the brow.'

They were both soaked through their coats, but a sort of ecstasy seized Benjie. This was what he loved, all the hills bared by the wind, all the streams exulting because they would be strong and vehement again, rain and wind at their full power and the sky black with cloud. If Vanessa were not beaten by it! But there she was, her head up, striding forward, striking the earth with her stick! He ran, he jumped the stones, he sang! Then, through the rain, the mist surged forward. It rose, broke to show dark fell and shining rock, closed again with fingers on your eyes, lifted from the ground a little to reveal the short grass tugging to escape the soil . . .

Vanessa was gone. . . He shouted.

'Van! Van! Vanessa! Where are you?'

The mist broke and he saw one jet-black cloud, and towards it everything, fell and gleaming stone and line of hill, seemed to strain.

He saw Vanessa standing, her hand to her heart. He caught up with her.

'Are you all right?'

Her face was grey in that half-light, but as she answered him the mist came down again, hiding her.

But she was glad that he could not see her, for she was about to die. She knew it as certainly as though the tall figure, grey-cloaked with grave assured eyes, stood in the mist, his curving silver-gleaming scythe in his hand. Her knees bent, her head was bowed on her breast. So appalling was the pain that death held no terrors, nor her loneliness. Strange that her one thought about death for years had been that Benjie must be with her when it came. And now it was here, and she hoped that Benjie would not see her, but would pass on, striking his iron-tipped stick on the stone, and she would drop there where she was and die, alone, hidden in mist . . . She did not want anyone to see her die.

So fearful was the pain that she could not keep back a moan, and then another. But only her own heart heard. The wind screamed in her ear, and the mist, wet like a thin soaked towel, pressed on her eyes and nose and mouth. Dimly through her pain she thought how silly it had been that, only ten minutes before, she had been talking so confidently about God. God was not here. She was animal, only fighting for endurance and to die without cowardice . . .

Then the pain was so fierce that she thought of nothing, neither the storm nor any company. She knelt on the sodden turf, her head back, her teeth set, hands clenched. She fancied that, from a great distance, she heard Benjie calling, and a sudden warming thought as though it were the very last that she would have in this world came to her of his sweetness, jollity, kindliness. Nothing in this world mattered so much as kindliness . . . that men should be kind to one another because they suffered, one and all, and life was short . . .

The pain passed. It withdrew as though a figure that had been bending over her had moved away.

She looked up and saw that the mist had broken, leaving a round cup like a room suddenly revealed, a room furnished with a gleaming rock like a ship's stern. The pain was gone: she would not die yet. The child should be born. Not rain nor wind should defeat her, and she rose from her knees and breasted the wind, moving forward. The mist cleared still further and she saw Benjie moving back to her.

'It's all right,' he shouted. 'There's a farm here just on the bend. Where the trees are.'

She took his arm.

'Isn't the wind strong? It almost beat me to my knees.'

He had noticed nothing, and she now brought all her resources to the business of meeting the pain again when it returned. For return it would. She could hear it afar off as though faintly the thin warning of a distant horn.

When they came to the trees they were rocking and groaning like mad things. The mist was shredded now, blowing in crazy tears and tatters over a landscape that was all fell scattered with stone and rock. The scene was immemorial and had changed in nothing since, maybe, Roman trumpets had echoed there from distance to distance.

It was a little white farmhouse, very simple, with a small beck rushing furiously at its side, the whole world filled with wind and rain. Benjie knocked on the door, two dogs barked, then a woman opened it and looked out. The wind rushed in and they followed it, coming into a clean and bright kitchen. It was low-roofed; there were legs of cured mutton and hams hanging from the smoky rafters. On a shelf nearby there were pots and jars, little yellow cheeses, dried herbs. By the ingle there was an old white-haired man, another younger man with broad shoulders and a bull-neck standing up, the woman who had opened the door, and a pretty girl in a blue gown busy at the table.

They were very cordial and friendly, made Vanessa and Benjie come to the fire to dry themselves. Yes, they had a spare room for the night if the storm kept on. The old man was loquacious; he had light blue eyes like flowers.

'Aye,' he said. 'We're verra oot o't warld--seven mile fra a shop, eight mile fra a church--an' hard roads.'

He was proud of their isolation. The housewife asked them if they were hungry. Benjie said indeed he was. She began to be busy cooking eggs and Cumberland ham.

Vanessa sat there, her knees close together, looking into the fire, waiting for the next pain to come. She wondered how soon she might go up to bed, take her things off: Benjie had noticed nothing. He was exceedingly happy, had taken off his boots and stockings, coat and waistcoat, and sat there, smiling at them all. He told them how he had lost his arm in Africa in the war. The old man had a long story to tell about sheep--'terrible wark' sometimes. The young man had a newspaper a week old. 'A newspaper! Aye--we mun gang a lang ways to get yan o' thame here.' Benjie laughed and chattered, loving the sound of the storm beyond the house, the smell of the frying eggs and ham. His twinkling eyes rested on the girl. WHAT a pretty girl! Dark, slim, and a cheeky upturned nose such as he preferred. He smiled at her and she shyly smiled back again . . .

Later Vanessa said: 'Benjie, I am tired. I think I'll go to bed.'

'Supper's nearly ready. You must be starved. I know I am.'

'I'm not hungry,' she answered. 'I think I'll go up.'

She stood, her hand pressed to her side. He looked at her anxiously but she smiled back at him. The girl went up with her to show her the room.

The storm died down. Benjie had his supper, the woman and girl waiting on him. It was now, in a place like this with simple, friendly people, that he felt at his best. In his shirt and trousers he sat there, eating, drinking big cups of tea, laughing, telling them about South Africa and other parts of the world where he had been. Once and again he smiled at the girl and she glanced back at him, their eyes meeting, holding one another, parting quickly. The storm had died away and beyond the kitchen window a flood of primrose light laced with the tree branches spread above the bare fell.

'Hurray! The storm is over!' Benjie said.

The girl had gone. He could hear her moving on the floor above. He got up.

'I'll go and see how my wife is,' he said. But, even as he spoke, the wind came again, raging in a fury about the house, banging at the house door, rattling the windows. All the trees screamed and the colour ebbed from the sky, leaving it white.

'That was sudden,' he said, turning round. 'I thought it had died.'

He saw a scurry of leaves blow against the pane and flatten. Some stayed pressed against the window.

''Twill be a wild neet,' the old man said calmly.

Benjie climbed the crooked stairs that smelt of mice and whitewash. At the top was the girl just coming down. There was a ghostly light from the passage window. He caught the girl with his arm and she surrendered to him at once, pressing closely against him as though she were hungry to be loved, which indeed she was. He held her tight, kissing her eyes, her cheeks, her mouth. Then, behind the pleasure and strength and warm happiness that wrapped him in, he heard a deep breath as of someone close at his elbow. Looking past the girl he saw Vanessa at the doorway. Her hair fell about her shoulders and she had caught a patchwork quilt around her; the colours were bizarre--blue, crimson, orange, green--and above it her eyes, fixed as though fastened on some desperate resolution, stared at him. She said something, but the wind was shaking the window. All the house seemed to be quivering. The girl was as though she had never been, and as he reached Vanessa's side he said:

'Vanessa, it was nothing . . . Vanessa darling . . .'

She looked at him, tried to smile, but her mouth shook. He heard her murmur, 'I'm very ill . . . Tell the woman to come . . .'

So, as nearly ninety years ago Judith Paris, her grandmother, had borne an illegitimate child in the heart of storm and confusion, did Vanessa now.

Sally, daughter of Benjamin Herries and Vanessa Herries, was born at eleven-thirty on the night of September 21st, 1903, at Randle Farm in Cumberland.

PERFECT LOVE

Vanessa sat on the slope of the hill behind the white farm watching for Tom's coming.

Sally, now nearly three years of age, sprawled beside her. Vanessa had a book on her lap but she was not reading. It was a cold sunny May afternoon. The scene was so still that it was like a painted canvas--or a bowl with flowers, for the hills circled her in but flowers were everywhere--crab blossom, speedwell blue as a jewel, anemones. In the garden behind the farm the primroses were still in yellow clumps, violets, celandines, and pansies. Soon the blue hyacinths would be full-blown. But the bowl that held the flowers was harsh with the tang of winter. The higher hills were thinly powdered with snow and the rocks so black that they glittered in the May sun like steel, and the little coppice beyond the stream yet seemed to tremble as though it could not be sure that winter was truly over.

Sally was not a pretty child but she, too, was a flower. She was small, spare, taut. Her hair had a red shadow in its brown, and she was always pale, but not with the pallor of ill-health. She was the strongest child. Nothing ever ailed her. When she cried it was from ill-temper. She had a most determined will, hated to be frustrated, knew her own way and intention always. But she never sulked, loved where she loved, hated where she hated, stood no nonsense, refused to be either flattered or petted and thought her mother the beginning and end of all things.

The love of this baby for her mother was astonishing. It had been so from the very beginning, and Vanessa, sitting there in the sun, felt a supreme content. Three human beings loved her--Benjie, Tom and Sally. They would not love her for ever perhaps. Benjie still moved towards her and then away from her again. Tom, although he was the most faithful of men, had his own life now and much of it she could not share. Sally would grow up and leave her. But at this moment, in this pellucid air, happy in this bowl of flowers, she thanked God for all that He had given her.

'Am I still frightened?' she asked herself. For, since her childhood, she had had to battle with fear. She had, all her life, given her heart to someone of whom she could not be certain and that was perhaps the reason that she loved him so dearly. Would the time ever come when she would be CERTAIN of Benjie? He was fifty-one now, she nearing forty-seven, but the old alarms returned, day after day, as they had always done. When he went would he return?

Nevertheless in the years since Sally's birth she had known greater happiness than ever before. They had been shut off from all the world; the friends they had made had been farmers, shepherds, wandering men. They had had almost no communication with London. An occasional letter from old Barney, Adrian, once from Cynthia. Benjie had been twice abroad, once to Italy, once to Spain, but had not stayed in London on either occasion. Anything that they knew of the outer life was from Tom. When he came he told them all the news, journalistic, social, family. He was happy on his newspaper; the family were kind to him, and he was deeply, hopelessly in love with Mary, Cynthia's girl, who was still only a child but, Tom said (he confessed only to Vanessa), the love of his life . . .

Time had passed with incredible swiftness. They were forgotten, Vanessa said, not only by the world but by time as well. They were contented.

But for how long would this endure? Still she never woke of a morning without wondering whether before night Benjie would not leave her. He loved her--of course he loved her--but the restlessness was there in his blood as it had ever been. One day he would go, and he would be lured farther and farther, always intending to return, never returning . . . What she had suffered during his two adventures out of England no one would ever know. She had, by now, trained herself to the complete hiding of her fear. She gave him no sign . . .

Somewhere a dog barked and at the same moment she saw that a trap had drawn up at the gate behind the church. Someone climbed out. It was Tom.

'Sally! Sally!' she cried. 'It's Tom!' She was as excited as a child.

Sally screamed: 'Tom! Tom! Tom!'

She picked Sally up and ran down the slope to the farm.

They hurried along the green sward, she carrying the child in the crook of her arm. She waved with the other hand, Tom waved back. A moment later they were all together.

Tom was short and sturdy. He had Adam's figure before he became stout and he had Adam's quietness and certainty. You knew always exactly where you were with him. Some people would think him dull as they had thought Adam. Other people found that he was to be trusted beyond most men and that, once his loyalty and affection were engaged, nothing could cause them to waver again. A dull quality, loyalty, and an unimaginative! But valuable to some people who believe in knowing where they are.

He was not dull to Vanessa. For one thing he loved her, as he showed with every look, every movement. For another he was their herald from the outer world. As they sat that evening round the table he had a thousand things to tell them. He had taken Adrian to one of these wrestling matches, now so popular. There had been a dinner party at Cynthia's. He had met Edmund Gosse, who had told funny stories about George Eliot.

'I haven't the least notion who Edmund Gosse is, darling,' Vanessa said.

Barney had been ill with rheumatism. But the most sensational piece of news was that Maud and Helen, Carey's girls, had become desperate Suffragettes.

Really desperate. They wanted to break into the Houses of Parliament. They had marched in a procession carrying banners. Their mother was dreadfully distressed.

About journalism there were many exciting things. It was rumoured that Harmsworth, now Lord Northcliffe, intended to purchase The Times. Everything in Fleet Street was changing. Men were dismissed from their jobs at a moment's notice. No one was safe any longer.

'Oh, it's nice here!' he said at last. 'It's so quiet. There's such a good smell.'

'How long have you got?' Benjie asked.

'A fortnight.' He wanted to walk. He wanted to go over to Haweswater and spend two days in Eskdale.

'I'll go with you,' said Benjie.

'Oh, that will be grand!' Tom said.

But Vanessa was sure that he wanted to go alone. There was something not quite intimate between himself and his father-- something a little uneasy.

And that night as Benjie was undressing he said to Vanessa:

'Tom doesn't want me with him.'

He was pulling off his shirt, a little awkwardly with his one arm. His face flushed, his hair tousled, looking at her over the top of his shirt before he dragged it over his head, he seemed to her suddenly pathetic a little, and her love went out to him with an unexpected fierce rush of emotion. She was sitting before the glass brushing her hair. She turned, the brush in her hand. He, standing bare to the waist, looked back at her. They exchanged a long deep gaze. The room was lit with candles that blew in the breeze from the open window, and their shadows were gigantic on the white wall.

They stayed, transfixed, looking at one another. Then at last, with a deep breath as though he were experiencing some extraordinary new emotion, he came over to her. He put his hand on her shoulder, then moved it to her neck and so held her, her gaze still upon him. Her eyes filled with tears; her heart was hammering. It was as though he had never made love to her before, as though at last he were about to say to her the words for which she had so long been aching.

He knelt down and enfolded her with his arm, his head on her breast. With light gentle fingers she stroked his hair, staring in front of her, all the room dimmed because her eyes were dim. A ridiculous clock that had a note, Benjie always said, like an angry parrot, told the hour, but the sound was an infinite distance away. What had happened? What was then this tumultuous fiery rush of joy at her heart?

'What is it?' she said at last. 'Benjie--darling--tell me. Are you unhappy about Tom?'

He did not answer. He held her only the more tightly. At last he said:

'It's like this, Van . . . It's as though I had never seen you before.'

He got up and stood there, looking at her.

'You'll catch cold with the window open.'

But he did not move; only stood there staring at her.

'Isn't it odd, Van? I'm falling in love with you all over again.'

She finished brushing her hair, although it was difficult because her hands trembled. She slipped on her nightdress and got into bed.

He always wore at night an open shirt that came no farther than the knees. For a moment he was naked and, looking at him in the candlelight, she thought how wonderfully he had preserved his body. For a man of past fifty he had an astonishing spareness and hardness. No fat. Nothing slack. And, as always, he looked as though he never wore clothes, as though his flesh were always exposed to the wind and sun. He stretched himself like an animal, raised his arm above his head, swelled out his brown chest. But he never took his bright, blue, fearless eyes from her face. She had never seen such eyes in any other man. They were so childlike, honest, dependable. But he was not a child and he was not dependable . . .

She expected that her own emotion would recede. It had been but a moment, born perhaps of her maternal longing over him because he was disappointed in Tom. But the emotion did not recede. She clasped her hands under the bedclothes and tried to beat down her joy. Like many another woman she was afraid of it lest it should lead her to expect too much and bring soon some disappointment that would be almost unbearably bitter--that she would remember afterwards, when the joy was forgotten.

'I mustn't love him too much,' she told herself, as so many, many times she had told herself before. He blew out the candles and lay down beside her. She knew at once by his touch on her breast that tonight he was very gentle. He scarcely touched her and yet she was thrilled by his proximity as she had never been before. They kissed and it was a kiss far deeper than passion. They did not stir, only their two hearts beating the one against the other, but this kiss was different from any other that they had ever exchanged. It was radiant with awe and wonder and reverence at something quite beyond and outside themselves.

At last he said: 'What has happened, Van? I have never loved anyone as I do you tonight.' His hand found hers and now they lay, very quietly, side by side, hand in hand. She turned on her side, laying her cheek against his.

'How still it is! Only the running water!'

He stroked her arm with his hand, very gently, as though he were afraid lest he should hurt her.

'Van, this is heaven. I have never loved you before as I do tonight.'

'Nor I you, Benjie.'

'We'll never forget this.'

'No. Never, never.'

'I seem to understand at this moment what life ought to be.' She sighed with a deep, yearning happiness. 'I'm not afraid any more. I don't care now what happens. We have never been together like this before . . .'

'No. Never. I wonder why . . .'

They turned to meet one another in a passionate embrace.

And, with the morning, nothing was changed. She knew immediately that he was still moving in this new relationship. She saw that Tom was at once aware of it and that he came in an instant more closely to his father. Benjie was quiet. In ordinary he conveyed a sense of restlessness, of wanting to move from the place where he was to some other place. But this morning, after they had breakfasted, he stood in front of the farm looking at the green field, the hills, the flowers, as though he had never seen them before.

'Come for a stroll,' he said to Vanessa, and they went. But, as they walked, they scarcely spoke. They went side by side, and for Vanessa it was as though they were not walking but rather were held, in some burning cloud, alone, away from man and time and destiny. What had happened? Was it not impossible that at their age, after they had lived so long together, known one another so intimately, there could be a new relationship between them? Friendship, comradeship, yes; but a new emotion, a new passion? Surely it was impossible?

Only at the end of this walk, before they went into the house, he turned to her and said again:

'Vanessa, what has happened to us? Are we in love for the first time?'

Day followed day, week followed week; the summer passed and autumn was smoke and flame, smoke of the clouds, flame of the bracken. With November the rains fell. There was clouded light over the dales and the wind currents were as vexed and troubled as the twists and turns of a stream. A black whirlwind of cloud would rush across the tops, discharging its waters as though from a gigantic tub impatiently overset by a celestial housemaid: you would wake to a morning of universal dark; the very fire burnt dimly and the rain fell with the tramp of armies; or the wet mists would blow from Robinson, from Cat Bells, thin and airy, carrying with them all the scene, a bare hillside lit by a sudden splash of shining rock, a herd of sheep stalwart under the chill stone walls, houses of stone raised into air by the web of vapour. Or it would rain quite solemnly like a clergyman of the old school preaching into eternity, or a writer of stories for whom two hundred years are but as a day, and then nothing lovelier in the world could be seen than that quick break before dusk when a pulse of gold beats through the dark and the sun creeps from under the blanket of cloud and everything is lit with radiance for a short breathless while. In these valleys and hills rain is as beautiful as fair weather and more various, and it is rain always broken by sudden breathtaking surprises. Only in this weather and perhaps only in this country can you see what the ebon flank of a cloud may be above a misty hill, or how purple--richer than grape-bloom--can cover a fell after tempest, or the white shadow, whiter than ivory and thin like glass, that strokes the field under a pale young stormy moon.

Men who write of these things are always defeated by them, so rare and strange is their beauty, but in their hearts an eternal homesickness is created so that they are never either safe or happy again in any land where it is dry and the sun is for ever shining.

Throughout the summer, the autumn, the winter, this miracle remained for Benjie and Vanessa. Many writers for hundreds of years have written about first love, and some writers (but not so very many) have spoken of the happiness of married comradeship. But life is never settled nor arranged, nor does it behave as it ought, by the laws of the written word, to do. Many men and women would behave nobly were they given the perfect conditions and circumstances, but there is always toothache, a broken promise, a jealousy, an unreasonable desire. Only once in a lifetime perhaps a Beethoven Symphony arrives punctually and, in a lighted room, two friends forget that there is such a tyranny as Time. And, even then, sentiment may steal the prize.

Vanessa and Benjie had good fortune. Not by their own desire, and, in any case, they did not know where to look for it. It came to them and they knew what perfect love can be.

During this winter they were never parted. Their happiness was too deep and soundless for them to fear it. For Vanessa it was as though God kept them in continual company. Her ideas of God were, of course, very simple; she felt His radiance as though she moved from morning to night in sunlight. For Benjie it was simpler still. He wanted to be near Vanessa; he did not know why she irritated him no more, why he was restless no longer. He did not search for reasons. He only knew that body, soul, and spirit, he was complete.

One starlit night after Christmas they climbed the hill and sat down together. The sky was quite clear. It was as though they were wrapped in Stardust. A little way above them the snow began. It was bitterly cold, but he wrapped his large shepherd's cloak around both of them and, because there was no wind, they took no hurt.

'It would not be bad, Van,' he said, 'if we were to die now, both of us together.'

Then, as she did not answer, he went on: 'That is what all lovers have always said. But YOUNG lovers. Lovers in their first ecstasy. We are very OLD lovers.'

'I don't feel old,' she answered at last. 'When shall we begin to feel old?'

'Oh, I suppose--with sickness, separation . . .'

'We will never be separated now,' she said quickly.

He held her to him, under the cloak, more closely.

'I don't trust life even now. I think you're the only thing in the whole world I trust. There never was anyone so trustworthy as you are.'

She laughed. 'Yes, that's why I'm dull--for everyone except you and Tom.'

'No. You're not dull. They didn't think you dull in London. But you're shy. You can't show people what you are. You're courageous enough about THINGS. You'd stand up to anything. But you're shy of human beings. Only in these last three months have even I known what you are.'

'For the first time since my father died,' she said. 'I'm not afraid.'

Five weeks later the letter came.

It came, as catastrophic letters often come, with an almost maidenly quietness. Vanessa opened it, looking over the table to Benjie, and laughing at something that he had just said. This was the letter:

Hill Street, London, W.
February 8th, 1907

DEAR VANESSA--You will, I am sure, be extremely surprised to receive a letter from me--surprised and not altogether pleased, I fear, but Vera and I have, for some weeks now, discussed the matter and have at last decided that this letter must be written. The matter is quite simply this. For some while now--ever since last summer in fact--Ellis has been seriously ailing. He has not, of course, been strong mentally for a very long time past. That you know. But his bodily conditions have been surprisingly good: he has eaten and slept well, and, within his own mental world, has really lived with content under our care. We have done our best. It has not always been easy, but of that I wish here to say nothing. Last summer we took Ellis to Harrogate as perhaps you heard at the time. We found a small and comfortable house where we could enjoy privacy and where, at the same time, my sister (whose rheumatism has for some time been trying) and Ellis could receive medical attention.

It was during our stay in Harrogate that the change took place. He has long been given, as you must have heard, to childish pursuits. He enjoys playing with dolls, soldiers, and trains. We have always, under excellent Doctor Lancaster's advice, humoured him in this and one day in Harrogate Vera bought him a doll to give him pleasure. So soon as he saw it it reminded him of you. I must tell you that he had not, so far as my sister and I were aware, once mentioned your name during all these years. But on this occasion, on Vera's presenting him with the doll, he said at once: 'Why, this is Vanessa come back again!' At first he seemed extremely happy at his fancy, but my sister and I noticed that from this moment he began to be less well. His headaches, which you will perhaps remember, returned. His temperature was often above normal. He was restless. Many of the things that had amused him seemed to amuse him no

longer. He is of course, not young any more-- sixty-four years of age--and his recurrent fever made us anxious. Whatever you may feel about my sister and myself you must remember, Vanessa, that we have both for a very long time now been most deeply and sincerely attached to your husband. Throughout this last winter he has been most unwell and now for several weeks has not left his bed. Doctor Lancaster says that it is difficult to say that there is anything organically wrong, but he fears that he has not long to live. We feel, Vera and I, that if this is indeed so, we must do everything to make the last months of his life happy. We are two childless women and in these years at Hill Street we have come to feel for Ellis as though he were our son. I hope you will forgive my saying this, but the whole situation is-- and has always been--so very strange!

And now to come to the point of this letter (it has not been an easy one to write). It is that, continually, during these last weeks Ellis has begged for your return. He has, it seems, a clear memory of the events that led up to your departure, but his mental decay has wiped from his recollection all bitterness and anger. He is as gentle and submissive as the child that so often he seems to be. 'I want Vanessa!' he cries and, again and again: 'When is Vanessa coming? Why does Vanessa not come?'

In these circumstances my sister and I feel it right that you should know how things stand. It is not easy for us to take this step. We can not pretend that we approved, or now approve, of the action that you took. But it is not for us to judge and we can only assure you that if you return to Hill Street for the few remaining weeks of Ellis' life (Doctor Lancaster tells us that it cannot be much more) you will hear no single word of reproach from us and we will regard you as the mistress of this house in every way. Your place just now, Vanessa, is with your husband, whatever the past has been. You have it in your power to give him this last happiness. We feel that we would never forgive ourselves if we did not acquaint you with the facts--Yours sincerely,

WINIFRED TRENT

Vanessa read the letter. Benjie, watching her from the other side of the table, saw at once that something of the uttermost seriousness had occurred.

'What is it?' he asked, coming across to her.

She gave him the letter. He read it slowly, sometimes repeating some of the words aloud.

'But this is monstrous!' he said at last. His face was flushed with anger, and also with the beginning of a terrible fear.

She sat down, staring in front of her, then held out her hand for the letter and read it through again.

'Yes,' she said. 'I have always known that the punishment would come. It HAD to come--to make things just.'

'Now--look, Van.' He sat down beside her. 'You are not to consider this for a moment; what the old witch suggests, I mean. Go to London. I'll come with you. Go to Hill Street. Pay him a visit. We'll stay in London if you like and you shall go often and see him-- anything else is preposterous.'

She shook her head.

'He wants me back. I never would have left him if he had wanted me. But he didn't. Now he does. He's dying.'

Benjie with an effort to be calm--one of the hardest things he had attempted for many a day (for this WAS preposterous; this was a plot, Hill Street all madmen and witches)--put his hand on hers, which was trembling, and summoned all his wisdom:

'Listen, Van. He doesn't want you. He can't. He doesn't know what he wants. It's some plot to get you back there again. The two old women are tired of their job, I shouldn't wonder. They think it would be a fine thing for you to take it on again. He CAN'T want you with his dolls and his trains.'

'No. I don't like Vera and Winifred--but they're honest. They have no imagination and no humour, but they're honest and they've been angels to Ellis. When I wrote to Vera three years ago--you remember--to ask her to persuade Ellis to divorce me, her letter wasn't kind but it was honest and plucky. I don't like them, but there are no lies in this letter.'

She turned round and stared at him. She looked, he thought, quite suddenly an ageing woman. Her confidence and happiness had left her.

'This is awful,' she said at last. 'Terrible. The worst thing that could happen. To go back to that house, that life . . . to leave you. Oh!' she cried, her hand on her breast. 'I don't think I can! I don't think I can!'

'Of course you can't--and, I tell you, there's no need to. We'll go to London. We'll see Ellis . . .'

But she shook her head. She had recovered her courage.

'Of course I must go--and you know it, Benjie. There can be no other way. What would I feel now if, after that letter, I didn't go? How could I go on living with you as we have been living? Oh, I knew it was too good to last! Something HAD to happen . . . these last six months--we've had a new life--and it was too fine, too wonderful to be allowed much of. It's unfair, it's unfair. That one mistake I made so long ago, to be punished for it so many times!' Then she cried out in a kind of agony: 'That house, Benjie! I can't STAND that house!'

Then he was really frightened and because he was frightened he was angry. He got up roughly, knocking his chair over.

'Look here Van--if you leave me now because two crazy old women write a letter--if you leave me after all that has happened to us these last months--you'll lose me. I can't keep up without you now. I'm not young any more. I could have done without you once, perhaps, but not now . . . You owe me more than you owe Ellis.'

'No, I don't,' she interrupted. 'I ruined Ellis' life. I've made you happy, I made him unhappy.'

'It was his own fault. He made you marry him.' (He did not remember that it had been HIS fault.)

'No, he did not. I need not have married him . . .' Then she turned and caught his arm. 'Benjie, there's Sally! There's Sally!'

'You see,' he cried triumphantly. 'You see how impossible it is. Of course you can't leave Sally. She's your child, isn't she?'

'No . . . No . . . Of course, I would have to have Sally with me. I would insist on that. I would make my terms--'

Then he swore at her. 'Damn you, Vanessa, am *I* nothing? What about me? You think of your crazy husband, you think of your baby. But I'm to be left out of it. Anything can happen to me--' He was not going to plead for himself. He looked at her and saw that her mind was made up. This was the law: Vanessa's character being what it was, this was fate.

He saw that and saw, also, for himself a future so intolerable that he closed his eyes and bowed his head.

Then they drew together and clung together, without a word. Both knew that in this there was no alternative.

TIMOTHY BELLAIRS PAYS SOME VISITS

Old Barney Newmark died quite suddenly in his sleep in the autumn of 1909. The Family were sorry because they had approved of Barney's fame as a novelist. It was not, perhaps, very great and he belonged to a very different generation from the present. The obituaries were kind; he had been a genial fellow, always in London, friendly and cheerful with everyone. He was spoken of as the 'Hawley Smart of his period'. The Referee wrote: 'Mr Newmark could write of horses and pretty women with a grace and humour that exceeded any of his contemporaries.' But the paragraph that pleased the Family was one in The Daily Telegraph: 'Mr Newmark, whose loss was so widely deplored last week, was of course a member of the famous Herries family, so well known in so many directions. Lord Rockage, who owns in Wiltshire one of the finest houses in England, is a member of it; Mr Alfred Herries, the well-known financier, another; Mr Timothy Bellairs, whose picture "Mme Rochambert" created a sensation in last year's Salon, another. The Hon Mrs Peile Worcester, whose parties in Charles Street have long been famous, is a member of the family, and another member, Mr

Horace Newmark, who died not so long ago, was known for many years as "the Monarch of Manchester". The Herries family is very well known in the North of England, most especially in Cumberland and the Border country. One of the most remarkable women of an earlier generation in the North was Madame Paris, also a member of the famous family. She has become almost a legend in Cumberland and Westmorland, I believe. Mr Newmark's delightful friendly, easy, and merry novels belonged to a time when the art of fiction was scarcely as seriously considered as it is today. This has been a sad year for English letters, mourning as we do both Meredith and Swinburne. Mr Newmark would have been the first to deprecate any comparison between two such giants and his own agreeable novels. Nevertheless he will be missed and for a long time to come.'

This was very pleasant. It had been for the Herries family a year of definite accomplishment. They had lived down the misadventures of the South African War and the disgrace of Vanessa's elopement (both events, in their view, of equal family importance). The Edwardian period, with its gracious (if materially minded) monarch, its common sense, its proper appreciation of money, its fostering of the upper middle class (even though the lower orders WERE behaving immodestly), its enthusiasm for Empire, its general applause for the solider English virtues, exactly suited the Herries: wildness, immorality, gambling, these things, when they appeared, became almost at once socially rationalized. The Family had no objection to immorality when it was photographed at a weekend house party during the shooting season. Private behaviour was no matter so long as it appeared publicly decent, and this was not hypocrisy on the Herries' part. It was simply that they cared for England, guarded her reputation most zealously. And this was natural, for England was Herries and Herries were England . . .

At last they could sit back for a moment and see that all was well. Family feuds (ridiculous, all about nothing--a fan, a green vase, a house on a hill) were things of the past. One possible scandal, the unspeakable Rose--poor Horace Ormerod's sister--had, luckily, been hidden by the grime of mean streets. Vanessa was living once again most properly with her husband; even Barney's death was not so bad a thing, for he had outlived his reputation and had been inclined at times to say oddly sarcastic things about the Family.

England had never seemed more secure, more prosperous, more certain of the grandeur of her great destiny--and as England was, so were the Herries.

It happened that Timothy Bellairs, the painter, came over to London for Barney's funeral. The old boy had been good to him in times past. Barney and Benjie (and of course young Tom) were the only members of the Family for whom he cared. He had lived so long in Paris that he did not feel Herries any longer. Or did he? He came over to London to find out.

He was a tall thin man with very light blue eyes and hair the colour of pale corn. He wore a small pointed beard. He had a way of watching you while you talked, of agreeing with you but causing you to wonder whether he did not think you a terrible fool. His voice was gentle and he had a charming smile. He appeared detached and impersonal. He had in fact only two passions--one was for painting, the other for one or two individuals. He was capable of iron fidelity. Benjie and Tom were two of his devotions, although he had not seen either of them for a very long time. Another was a stout and extremely cynical lady who shared his bed and board in Paris.

Attending Barney's funeral he observed the Family.

Vanessa was there. He had not seen her for many years but, knowing her story and of her return to Ellis nearly three years ago, he watched her with especial interest. Her grey hair under the black hat, the pale face beneath the veil--these gave her a greater appearance of age than he had expected. But her carriage (he watched her as, attended by a little thin woman, she walked up the aisle to her seat) was very fine. She was a big woman, full- breasted, large-shouldered and, he thought, as he saw her before she turned into her seat, apart from everyone else there. 'She has learnt how to play her role.'

Tom was with him and whispered some names. That was Horace, that stout fellow in glasses, with plump cheeks, the full Herries chin and an air of self-conscious benevolence. 'Barney hated him,' Tom whispered. Cynthia swept up, Peile Worcester in attendance. Very smart, Timothy thought, with her beautifully fitting black and Parma violets--not thinking about Barney, though.

An extremely thin tall gentleman, wearing pince-nez, his black clothes rigid as though cut from wood, 'very Herries' in feature, moved to his seat as though he were taking his place as chairman of a board meeting.

'That's Alfred.'

A fat cheerful gentleman and a very fat cheerful lady hurried up the aisle, showering benevolence on all around them. 'Sidney and Mary--Horace's son from Manchester.'

Then old Carey Rockage, bent with rheumatism, May thin and short- sighted, with the two suffragette daughters who strode forward looking about them with an air of resentment.

Timothy's sister, who had married a Colonel and lived in Surbiton, was not present. Vanessa was by far the most interesting person in that church to Timothy. He thought of Barney.

'Good old boy. He had a fine life. Did what he wanted, enjoyed every moment of it.' When he remembered Barney's mistresses it amused him that the Family should come, in such numbers, to pay him the last compliments. 'They wouldn't do the same for Benjie,' he thought, feeling the touch of Tom's shoulder against his. But Barney, in some clever fashion of his own, had never openly outraged the conventions. No member of the Family had ever been brought face to face with his mistresses, while in poor Benjie's case every rebellion had been as open as it could be! And then, just as the service was about to start, Benjie walked up the aisle. He walked slowly, his brown face and bright blue eyes unconcerned, the empty sleeve of his jacket pinned to his breast. He was wearing a loose dark suit--so far he had submitted to convention-- but he looked, as he always looked in public, apart, as though he were of another country, an exile and a rebellious one. 'He looks more than that,' Tim thought. 'He looks worn and strained. He's too thin.'

Had he seen Tom and Timothy he would undoubtedly have stopped and sat with them, but, his head up, seeing nobody, he walked straight ahead. 'He said he wasn't coming,' Tom whispered.

He passed the seat where Vanessa was. Some instinct seemed to tell him. He stopped for a moment, then turned and found a place on the other side of the aisle beside stout Sidney and Mary Newmark. It amused Timothy to observe the startled and frightened look that they gave him.

So old Barney Newmark, accorded by the Family full honours, joined (perhaps thankfully) the Rogue and David, Judith and young John, and was, beyond question, glad of their company.

Timothy had not as yet paid Benjie a proper visit. Tom, who shared lodgings with his father in Tite Street, told Tim that Benjie was in one of his bad moods.

'He'll tell you all about it when you go. He's very unhappy--but he'll tell you. Only you'd better wait till he chooses his day.'

Meanwhile Timothy was painting Mary Worcester's picture. He had seen, at once, that this was a thing that he had to do. She was the loveliest child he had ever beheld. She was going to be a real beauty. The modelling of her face was exquisite, her colour perfect, everything delicate, gentle, dark hair, dark eyes, already a sense of poise and movement. But, he decided very quickly, she was stupid and dull. Her voice was lovely in tone, soft and resonant, but she had nothing to say. Her eyes were large and full; she had a way of using them so that they rested on you as though they found you enchanting. But she did not find you enchanting. She was not thinking about you at all. She was only sixteen and had been kept, at home, closely guarded, but even then Timothy thought, she surely had SOME ideas about something! It seemed that she had not.

Her mother, whose little figure was still perfect but was betrayed by her too bony neck and eyes that were older than her complexion allowed for, said about her beautiful daughter that: 'You've no idea how intelligent that child is! Now Rosalind says just what's in her head and nine times out of ten it's nonsense, as I tell her-- but MARY! No one knows what that child's thinking!'

Cynthia also unburdened herself to Timothy about Vanessa:

'Of course it's awful for her. We all realize that. She came back nearly three years ago thinking that Ellis had only a week or two to live. And now there he is quite strong and hearty! Of course he's mad as a hatter, but quite nice and gentle, I believe. He's simply Vanessa's slave, poor thing. And isn't it odd! Vera and Winifred Trent used to hate her, but since Vera died last year Winifred adores her. I must say Vanessa always had the power of making people fond of her. I always have loved her in spite of what she did. What is it about Vanessa? Perhaps you'll find out, Timothy. Because she's really dull and has no sense of humour at all. I must say she's very sporting. Right or wrong, Benjie's the love of her life and there they both are, eating their hearts out. Between you and me I wonder Benjie doesn't creep into Hill Street and poison Ellis. What's the good of his living? He's quite hopeless mentally, you know. Of course Vanessa's got Sally with her. She insisted on that. Her little girl and Benjie's. It always seems funny to me when Ellis, poor thing, has always been so proper and moral, that Vanessa's illegitimate child should be in his house under his roof. And I believe he's passionately fond of the child. Altogether very queer. Vanessa doesn't go out into society at all, but she likes people to go and see her. I go sometimes although Peile doesn't much like my doing it and I confess the place gives me the shudders.'

'Does she see Benjie?' Timothy asked.

'Oh yes, sometimes. There's nothing improper of course. The fact is, Timothy, they are the only example I know anywhere of real love. It's gone on all their lives and they're as much in love as ever they were. She's quite tamed Benjie. He used to be as wild as anything. It's a bit hard on him, isn't it? Separated from his child, too, but I believe he thinks it the right thing for Vanessa to do. They're an odd pair altogether.'

It happened that on the afternoon following the funeral Cynthia was giving a small children's party. For a brief while Timothy observed the ceremony; not for long--he detested children unless they were paintable. He was extremely sharp at catching character from face, voice, and movement. He had a number of young Herries under his eye (the coming upholders of the Herries tradition) and quickly decided that only one of them was beautiful (Mary Worcester of course) and only one charming--little Sally, Vanessa's daughter. He wondered for a moment that 'a little bastard' should be allowed in among all the true-born offspring, but decided that this was the Herries way of showing Vanessa that they had forgiven her.

The Herries children were: first Mary and Rosalind Worcester (Mary a gracious and lovely hostess; Rosalind clutching her friend little Ada Newmark--Horace's grandchild, the daughter of stout Sidney and stout Mary--and going off with her into a corner); the aforesaid Ada and her brother Gordon; Maurice and Clara, Alfred's children, plain, with good manners, but wanting the best for themselves. Mary, Rosalind, Ada, Gordon, Maurice and Clara: little ordinary Herries, all that they should be. It was amusing, he thought, as he watched, to notice the way in which these Herries children took command of the other children who were not Herries. Took command quite confidently, without arrogance or tiresome conceit, but quite as though it must be. And yet, with the notable exception of Mary, they were not very beautiful nor certainly were they brilliant. The Herries, he reflected, were never first class unless they were mad. 'I am not first class because I am not mad. Benjie, although he has never done anything with his life except love Vanessa, has something first class about him. A first-class passion for something outside oneself can make one first class. I have a passion for my Art. Why am I not first class? Because there is just enough Herries in me to prevent my escape from myself.'

Then he saw little Sally and went and talked to her. She was an odd-looking child, small with straight uncurling brown hair and a pale face. But she was all alive. She sat on a sofa and her eyes were everywhere, eager, merry, and very intelligent. She did not join in anything until she was invited, but she suffered from no self-consciousness. Little coloured balloons were handed round (they were to be blown across a tablecloth). Clara, Alfred's child, preferred the colour of Sally's balloon to her own and said so. Sally at once gave her hers, but Tim thought that she, at the same time, looked at her with a little baby irony as much as to say: 'You're like that, are you, even at your age'--a very elderly look for a child of six. 'But then,' thought Timothy, 'it will be odd if she isn't queer, born as she was and brought up in Hill Street.'

Next day he went and visited Benjie. London was very interesting to him. It was so long since he had stayed here. This was a great year for mechanical progress. The virtue of single planes advanced in a sudden leap the history of flying. In July, Blériot had crossed the Channel. In October there was a flying week at Blackpool and Mr Farman surprised everyone by flying for half an hour in wild and gusty weather.

But the great change in London was the advance of motor-cabs. Hitherto motoring had been mainly for the well-to-do. Now it was discovered that cabs could be made both cheaply and strongly. The new cabs, fitted with taximeters, were comfortable, safe, and the old uncertainty of the proper fare for the tiresome and truculent old cabby was gone. Only a little while before,

motors had been the property of the rich: now, quite suddenly, they were everywhere. The whole aspect of the London streets was changed. It signified perhaps the final advent to assured power and importance of the middle classes.

Timothy felt this most emphatically during his evening expeditions about the town. He went everywhere: to the White City, to a first night at Wyndham's, or the Haymarket, or the St James's, to a dinner at the Savage Club, to the National Sporting Club, to the London Sketch Club, to a Sunday night at the New Lyric, and everywhere it was the same--the English Middle Class was now triumphant, subservient to nothing and nobody. The reign of the Autocrats in England was over. Sargent painted his Jew millionaires, Wells and Bennett invigorated the novel with their portraits of lower middle-class life. The word 'respectable' had no longer any especial significance in English life. The ordinary man ruled England and he was determined to find pleasure where he could and hold to it. The ordinary man ruled England, and Herries were the ordinary man.

He found Benjie in three rooms of the upper part of a house in Tite Street, Chelsea. When he came in, Benjie was walking up and down. He was wearing an old grey jacket, grey flannel trousers, and a faded red tie. Tim was struck, more than ever, by his spareness, the fierceness of his blue eyes. He noticed that his hair was turning grey at the temples. He looked as though he had been lost in the desert and rescued in the nick of time. After half an hour's talk Tim felt that Benjie would, on the whole, have preferred that the rescue had not take place.

The room was very bare, but it had a broad bright window filled with scurrying clouds and a cold blue sky. Very shortly it would be dark. In the window was a long deal table with Vanessa's photograph (a very old one), a book which Tim picked up and found to be Hudson's Purple Land, some writing paper, a pen, and a long truculent-looking ruler. On the walls there was nothing save over the fireplace two grinning masks made of some dark wood. There were two shabby armchairs.

Tim knew Benjie well. In the very old days when he had gone over to Paris with Tom, Benjie had been his saviour. He had protected him against the Family, Tim, who was faithful, would stick to Benjie always because of that, were there no other reason. But there WERE other reasons, plenty of them. He liked Benjie because he was honest, generous, courageous, and his own worst enemy. Benjie had one charming quality, and a very rare one it is. He always, whatever his own personal melodramas, wanted to hear about the adventures of his friends. This was not from self-conscious duty nor from a desire to be kind. He was truly interested.

So Timothy told him--about Mlle Thérèse, his stout but charming mistress, about his new flat, about the portrait he was painting of the two little girls of the

Minister of Finance, about his picking up a charming Berthe Morisot for almost nothing, of English writers whom he had met in Paris--Somerset Maugham and Arnold Bennett ('both interested in painting--very odd'), about this and that.

'And you?' he asked at last

'Oh--I?' Benjie sat on the deal table, swinging his legs, 'I go on-- as you see.'

Tim was aware, at that moment, just as a rather slatternly white- haired woman brought in the tea, that he was encountering some experience so deep and poignant that he was frightened of it. He was frightened of very little; he was certainly not frightened of Benjie. But there was something here that belonged to that rarest of all worlds--the world of absolute and positive experience. 'Because,' he thought, 'we all live one skin deep at the most. We do not, most of us, know that we can go deeper.'

So to ease things he himself talked.

'I've been observing the Family. I haven't seen it, you know, for a long time. Coming along very nicely, I should say. It ostracized me once and now it welcomes me because I'm a moderate success. I'm not exactly prejudiced in its favour. But we've settled down. All the quarrels are over. All the same there are a few rebels left, but they're not so grand as they used to be.' Then he said an incautious thing. 'But I tell you what, Benjie-- your daughter's going to be a rebel. You should have seen her with the rest of them. It persists, the divine strain. How I wish I had more of it!'

Benjie jumped to the floor.

'You've seen Sally--where? when?'

'Oh, yesterday--at a children's party at Cynthia's.'

'Did you talk to her? She's remarkable, isn't she? Unusual?'

'Yes, I talked to her a little. I loathe children's parties, you know. Certainly she's unusual. I was saying so.'

'I see her, you know.' Benjie came and sat down close to him, bending eagerly forward. 'Quite often. In fact I can see her as often as I like so long as I never go to the house. Odd situation, isn't it?'

'Very,' said Timothy, terribly touched by his friend's emotion, thinking, too, of the old Benjie who had been a wandering kind of rascal with no very constant attachment.

'Have you been to see Vanessa, Tim?'

'No, not yet. Do you think she would like to see me?'

'Of course she would. And you must go soon. Then come and tell me about it.'

'Tell you about it?'

'Yes. Vanessa and I meet sometimes. Not too often or it would be unbearable. But I never enter the house of course. And I don't ask her about the house. When we are together in fact we don't talk very much. Talking seems to waste the time. The only one who

told me much about what it was like inside was old Barney. And now he's gone. Adrian goes there, but Adrian's a prig. The rest of the family don't see much of me, you know.'

'I see,' said Timothy. 'Of course I'll go if she won't think it impertinent.'

'Oh no, she'll love it. Especially if you tell her you've been here. You'll have to repeat every word of our conversation, you know.'

Tim said slowly: 'It's all damned hard on you.'

Benjie answered quickly: 'It's far worse for her. You see, the bad part of it is that we were having such a marvellous time just before he wanted her. And we thought it was only for a month or two. Now it's been close on three years, and God knows how much longer!'

'Well, if you want my opinion,' Timothy broke out, 'I think the whole thing's preposterous! There are you, two people in the prime of life, loving one another, and on the other side Ellis who's too mad to know whether she's there or no.'

'You're wrong,' Benjie said quietly. 'Know? Why, she's his very life! He worships her. If she left him it would be like leaving a helpless child, and worse than that, because she married him. She only left him because he DIDN'T want her. No, there's no other way-- until Ellis dies. She would never be happy for a moment if she came away. Not that she's happy as it is, but she's got Sally.'

'And you?' Tim asked.

'Oh, I? Don't mind about me. Don't think I'm being noble either. I'm not. I curse like hell. I'd hate him if--if he were normal. As it is one can't hate anyone in the affair, more's the pity. Oh, I'm all right. I go abroad sometimes. There's Tom here for company and he's so kind that I could kill him. I'm working at a job too. I go to a travel agency every day and advise people about foreign parts. Sometimes I go wild for a day or two. I've got some awful friends, you know. But I'm never wild for long nor away for long. I come slinking back because Vanessa's here.'

'I'm glad you love her so much,' Tim said. 'Anyone's in luck to have the chance of the real thing.'

'Love her?' He threw his head back. 'Did you ever know our real story, Tim? No. Well, I'm not going to bore you with it. But we loved one another from childhood. We meant to marry. First her father died--was burnt in the fire at Uldale. That stopped it. Then-- imagine it!--I married someone else! Fantastic? Not at all. My cursed imbecility that has made me do the wrong thing at the wrong time all my life. But listen. However wild I've been, however caught she's been--caught in a trap, because that's what her marriage to Ellis was-- we've never ceased to love one another for a single moment. At the very instant of making love to another woman I've always known it was only Vanessa I loved. And the best time we ever had was just before we parted. And now we'll never be free of one another--I doubt if death can part us. And yet when I say that, how ridiculous, how sentimental! Hasn't every lover always said the same? But we are such OLD lovers! It goes far beyond the body--beyond--into what? Is it simply association, all that we have been through together? Vanessa isn't very clever. She isn't any longer very beautiful. But she's LOVELY, Tim. She never falters, she never lets you down, she has a childish pleasure in tiny things, she's generous, loyal, and although she thinks she's a coward, she never flinches at anything. And yet it's only a little for her character that I love her. One doesn't love people for their character, does one? Or only a little. Why? Why? Why are Vanessa and I bound together? Is she right, do you think? Is there a spiritual life that outlasts the bodily? Will Vanessa and I go on together, never apart, loving one another? . . . Sometimes when I sit alone in here at night, hearing the mouse in the wall and seeing those masks grin, knowing that she's there and I here--such a little distance--I begin to believe that I can pull her spirit in here with me, her body there in Hill Street. I could swear that she comes in, sits with her head against my knee as she used to do in Cumberland--is this mad, Tim, do you think? Am I going queer a bit? Do I LOOK queer?'

'No, Benjie, not in the least. Only it's bad for both of you, I should think, separated like this and yet so near to one another. Lord! I wish I loved someone like that, though! Or do I? It's a terrible strain. One can't work if one's always wanting someone . . .'

He waited a while, then he said abruptly:

'Do you ever read history, Benjie?'

'History? No. Oh, I've read Macaulay and a bit of Froude--'

'You SHOULD read history. There's nothing so interesting. History or biography. A nation or a family or an individual--it's all the same. The point is that men's values are all wrong. The things that they THINK are happening aren't happening at all. Do you remember Tolstoi's Anna Karénina and the racecourse scene? Everyone THOUGHT that the racing was the important thing. It wasn't in the least. It was the struggle in the hearts of Anna and Karénin and Vronsky. Yes, and in thousands of other souls that day. Little temptations to meanness, lusts, sacrifices. Small tests, tests as small as a pin--but soul histories are the only histories. Write an account of a family or a county and find out where the crises of the human spirit lie. See how it meets all the tests, is beaten, is victorious, encounters its two chief enemies, greed and fear, is encouraged to extend into something wider, grander, nobler than itself. Shakespeare knew that that was the only kind of history. What are the stories of his six great kings but soul histories? What does he care for national history? It is Richard in his tent, Henry praying before the battle, the old king dying in Westminster . . . I'm not religious, you know. I can't swear to heaven, I don't know whether there are pearly gates. And I'm not

given to preaching. But I do know that you've got the only thing that matters, Benjie. You can feed your soul with an unselfish passion. You're not starving it. You should see old Monet painting. He's like an eagle beating his wings for joy that he's free, gross, fat old man that he is! To escape beyond oneself! To lose one's soul because one's beyond fear, and so to save it. That's the history of the endeavour of every man and woman born on this earth. The only thing that gives us grandeur, fleas on a cinder as we are!'

Benjie smiled.

'I've never heard you talk like that before.'

'No. I'm growing old. I've faced up to the fact that I shall never be the painter I hoped to be, never meet the woman I hoped to meet. We all do. I'm just of the age. I hold my tongue. I haven't talked like this for an age. The French are a cynical people, you know. All the same it's a marvel to me that men can refuse so obstinately to think of the only things that really matter. We'll suffer for it. We're bound to. Well, I must go.'

He raised his long thin body, pulled at his pale corn-coloured beard, stretched his arms and yawned.

'You're going to see Vanessa, aren't you?'

'Yes--tomorrow.'

'And you'll come and see me again?'

'I'll come and see you again.'

When he was gone Benjie sat down and wrote to Vanessa.

Next day Tim went to Hill Street. An old butler with face like a muffin, plump, boneless, without shape, received him and led him upstairs. In the long drawing-room Vanessa was entertaining Mary Newmark, wife of Sidney, old Horace's son. Mary Newmark was fat in a bright, cheerful way. She wore a dress of shining blue and she had a large hat with blue feathers. Under the hat her face, like a gigantic strawberry, beamed on the world. Beside her Vanessa, who was dressed in black, looked very quiet. But Tim was surprised. He had expected her to be grave and a little ceremonious. Not at all. She was extremely human. He could see that she was bored with Mary Newmark, who quite clearly had no idea of it. Mary was one of those women who, without any arrogance, feel that their presence is a benefit to all concerned. She was also convinced that any statement, any opinion on her part, was of the first importance.

Tim saw that Vanessa was surprised to see him and greatly pleased. Mary Newmark was flustered a little; artists were to her strange creatures: moreover Timothy lived in Paris. She was plainly determined to be kind to him whatever he might have done.

'No, don't send for more tea,' he said. 'This is splendid. If it's stewed I like it stewed.'

'I was telling Vanessa,' Mary Newmark began, 'that Sidney and I disapprove totally of the Suffragettes.'

'Why?' asked Timothy.

'The proper place for women is the home. I don't want a vote. What would I do with one?'

As Timothy was about to speak she shook a finger at him.

'Now, Mr Bellairs, I know you're an artist and have, I'm sure, all sorts of queer ideas. But if women don't look after their homes, who will?'

'Perhaps the men will,' said Timothy.

'Men!' said Mary Newmark gaily. 'Would you like to know what I think about men?'

'Very much,' said Timothy.

'Men are children. Nothing but children. They never grow up. Once learn that about a man and you never have any more trouble.'

'Well, then, isn't it wrong if men are only children that they should have all the say in governing the country? If women are so much wiser--'

'Ah, that's just it,' said Mary Newmark with complete self-confidence. 'Women ARE much cleverer, but their proper place is behind the scenes, influencing the men. Sidney doesn't know it, but there's not a thought in his head that doesn't come from me.' She beamed on the world. 'I've no use at all for all this modern nonsense, nor has Sidney. Modern books, modern pictures, modern women--I don't mean anything personal, Mr Bellairs. I'm sure you paint very nice pictures--very pleasant, I'm sure, but what was good enough for my mother is good enough for me. What modern writers have we to compare with Charles Dickens? Answer me that now.'

'It would be a great pity, wouldn't it,' said Timothy, 'if we had Dickens over and over again? One Dickens, yes--but a hundred Dickenses!'

'Well, I don't know, I'm sure. I've certainly read David Copperfield over and over--my favourite bits, you know. Sidney reads aloud to me in the evenings in Manchester.'

The door opened and Sally came in. She stood for a moment, hesitating and smiling. Then she came forward.

'Say how do you do to Mrs Newmark, darling.'

'How do you do?' said Sally.

'And to Mr Bellairs. You met him the other day, you know.'

'How do you do?' said Sally, grinning.

Mary Newmark drew Sally forward and spoke to her in the voice she considered suitable to children, a voice she also used for little dogs.

'Well, darling? And what have you been doing today?'

'I've done my lessons and I've been for a walk.'

'That's a good little girl. And where did you go for a walk?'

'I went in Kensington Gardens.'

'And what did you see there?'

'Oh, nothing particular.'

Mrs Newmark pinched her cheek, a thing that she considered children adored.

'And what lessons have you done today?'

This was frightful. Vanessa intervened.

'At present she has lessons with me. I'm not a very good teacher, I'm afraid.'

There was silence. Sally was looking at Mrs Newmark with a smile that in some undefined way she felt to be sarcastic. A strange child, with her peaked face and dark brown hair. She was suddenly uncomfortable. The house was so very silent and the painter not very friendly. Moreover, there was Ellis somewhere and at any moment he might break in. How unpleasant that would be! Whenever she was uncomfortable she moved on. She moved on now.

'I'm afraid I must be going, Vanessa dear. It HAS been delightful. You must come and see us before we go back to Manchester. Goodbye, Mr Bellairs. Don't become TOO modern in your painting!' She kissed Sally and sailed away. Halfway down the stairs she stopped a moment to listen whether she could hear Ellis moving about. There was no sound anywhere.

After she had gone they all three sat on the sofa together. Timothy had at once noticed that there was a strong and deep alliance between the mother and the child. When Sally moved and spoke it was as though Vanessa moved and spoke with her. Now Sally sat beside her mother; they sat hand in hand. They made no allusion at all to Mrs Newmark. Their feelings about her were identical. They were all three very happy and confidential together.

'Now, darling, you must go to bed.'

Sally got up from the sofa. She sighed.

'Don't you wish you hadn't to go to bed?' she asked Timothy.

'I love my bed,' he answered. 'It's the best place there is.'

She looked at him sharply to see whether he were speaking the truth. She decided that he was.

'When I'm older I shall go to bed only once a week--every Friday.'

'Why Friday?'

'Because Saturday's a nice day and Thursday's a nice day, but Friday's horrid.'

She lifted her face to be kissed.

'I'll come up and see you, darling,' Vanessa said.

She walked away rather sadly. At the door she looked back and smiled.

Vanessa looked at the door for a moment after it closed. Then she turned back.

'It was extraordinarily nice of you to come and see me.'

There was something young about her, Timothy thought, and eager. She was not dull as he had half expected to find her. She had lived, he knew, for years in lonely country but she was not dowdy. Her wide clear forehead, her grey hair parted in the middle, the severity of her black dress, her breadth and height, gave her massiveness, but he had an unexpected conviction that she was younger than he, years and years younger.

'It's very strange,' Vanessa said, 'but I've never set eyes on you since you were a small boy. I can see you now sitting up in an open carriage dressed like little Lord Fauntleroy and hating it.'

'Yes, I did hate it. And I'm afraid I hated my mother too for making a show of me.'

'No--but when you were such wonderful friends with Tom and Benjie . . . it's absurd that we should never have met! You were with Benjie yesterday!' she added quickly.

'Yes. How did you know?'

'I had a letter from him this morning, telling me about your visit. He writes and tells me if anything especially nice has happened. How was he? How was he looking?'

'Rather thin, I thought. No spare flesh.'

'No. I saw him last a fortnight ago. I wish he'd eat more. He doesn't look after himself.'

And then, in front of him, her face in a moment aged. She was sitting quietly, her hands folded on her lap, but he felt that behind her serenity she was enduring to the limit of everything: one burden more and she would break. He was a man who found life in general amusing and absurd rather than dramatic, but he was very sharply aware of the drama now being played in front of him--this long chill room, the house beyond it where Ellis was playing at soldiers or nursing a doll, Benjie in Tite Street, and all the Family moving like figures in a wavering tapestry as a frame to the scene. Vanessa, he thought, must be fifty or more and yet he had, at that moment, as urgent a longing to help her to escape as though she were a lovely girl of twenty!

'Benjie tells me,' she went on, 'that he talked about me--about us. Do--do you think--Do you think that it is all getting to be more than he can stand? I mean--oughtn't I perhaps to MAKE him go away, to insist on it? Perhaps, away from me, he would find someone--'

'There's nothing you can do. He will never be able to go away. He will never find someone else.'

'I don't want him to go away, you know.' She smiled again. 'I think I'd die if he did. Oh, don't fancy that I'm pitying myself. I have him and Tom--and Sally of course. Don't you like Sally?'

'I do indeed. She's very unusual.'

'Yes, she is, isn't she? And--I'm telling you everything because you have been Benjie's friend so long and of course that makes you mine. Ellis . . . I have grown fond of him. No one could help it. He needs me, and he is so docile and so affectionate. So different from what he was. But of course it's not a good house for Sally to grow up in. It's not healthy here, although she's too young to understand things and behaves to Ellis as though he were her brother. I thought at first that I would keep them apart, but Sally made that impossible. She goes to him quite naturally, never seems to think it

strange that an old man of sixty-six should play with dolls and soldiers. Perhaps she knows more than we think. Children may be much wiser than we suppose.'

'You are all, it seems to me,' said Timothy, 'behaving very finely.'

'Oh no, we're not! I don't see how we could behave otherwise. And I myself am not fine at all. Often I long for Ellis to die. Sometimes I feel that I CANNOT keep away from Benjie any longer. You see, we thought that it would only be for a month or two. Already it has been nearly three years . . .' She hesitated, looking down at her lap. 'The hardest part of it has been that in Cumberland, just before we separated, Benjie and I were happier than ever before.'

'I know. Benjie told me.'

'Oh, did he tell you? I'm so very glad.' She went on: 'You must think this all very sentimental, Timothy. Two old people like Benjie and me both pouring out our hearts to you.'

'Only false things are sentimental,' Timothy said. 'And this isn't false, Vanessa. Your grandmother, Judith Paris, wouldn't have thought so. I gather that she was anything but sentimental.'

'No--she wouldn't have thought it false. I so often think of her and sometimes feel as if she were here helping us both. I still have a tiny tea-set she gave me when I was a little girl, and it seems only yesterday that I climbed on to her bed and kissed her.'

There was a pause. He got up to go.

'I must be moving on. I'm so glad that we have met, and if there is anything I can do, Vanessa, I always will. You can count on me. I've got every weakness except infidelity.'

'Yes. Benjie always says that you are one of the most faithful people in the world.'

Before he went he said, rather shyly:

'Look here! Don't let this be too much of a strain on you. One can only stand so much, you know. Oughtn't you to go out more?'

'Go out?'

'Yes, be gay a little--go to theatres and see the sights.'

'Oh, I do go out. And I've had so much of that in the past. But it's all right. I'm perfectly happy.'

With that brave challenge in his ears he left the house, but for several days he could not get her out of his mind.

When he had gone, Vanessa went up to say good-night to Sally. She was in bed waiting. Vanessa sat on the bed and Sally lay within her arm, very contentedly, her eyes smiling.

'Mummy, Mrs Newmark IS a funny lady!' (It was like Sally to have the surname quite clearly and accurately.)

'In what way funny, darling?'

'She thinks children silly. They aren't, are they?'

'Sometimes.'

'Well, not like THAT, anyway.'

Soon she was asleep.

Then Vanessa went to Ellis. The upper part of the house had now been made into a suite for him. He had a sitting-room, bedroom and bathroom of his own. The sitting-room was large, with high windows looking out on to chimney pots and sky. On the table was a large bowl with chrysanthemums (he loved flowers). Near the flowers was a big wooden fort with guns and soldiers. In one armchair an elaborate doll, dressed in blue silk, was lolling.

Ellis himself was sitting, when she came in, very busy with one of those puzzles the point of which is that little black balls should roll into little silver holes. He was bending over this, shaking it, holding it very still, shaking it again. He looked very old. His thin hair was white now, his shoulders very bent. He had the almost waxen cleanliness of a patient who is constantly washed and brushed by others.

'Oh, Vanessa!' he cried, when he saw her. 'I'm so glad you've come. I've been trying to do this for ever so long. As soon as one's in another rolls out.'

She sat down beside him and took the puzzle. He watched her as she manipulated it, with the eager attention of a dog who is waiting for you to throw a ball.

Soon all the little black balls were in the little silver holes. He clapped his hands.

'Oh, that's lovely! Now shake it! Now I'll see if I can do it!'

She sat there quietly beside him.

He put the puzzle down.

'I'm very hungry,' he said.

'Your dinner will be coming very soon, dear.'

'What do you think it will be?'

'I don't know. Something nice.'

'Marmalade pudding?'

'Perhaps.'

'Oh, I hope so.' He sighed, laying his head against his hand. She put her arm around him.

'Did you have a nice drive?' she asked him.

'We saw some soldiers.'

'Was there a band?'

'No. There wasn't a band. I wish we could have a band--here in this room. Wouldn't it make a fine noise?' He sighed again. 'My head aches.'

'It's the weather, Ellis dear. It's been very close all day. My head's been aching all day.'

'Has it?' He put his hand up and stroked her forehead and then her cheek. He loved to do that. At first she had shrunk from it. His hand was dry and hot and his fingernails very white, like a dead man's nails. But now it moved her strangely when he made any demonstration. And once, years and years ago, he had wanted to kill her! How queer!

With the abrupt restlessness that was characteristic of him he got up and fetched the doll from the chair.

'I've dressed and undressed her three times today,' he said. 'She doesn't seem to mind.' He gave her to Vanessa. 'Will you play for me tonight, Vanessa?'

In the corner of the room was a small piano. Vanessa did not play very well--only old and simple things, old songs, hymns tunes, waltzes. He loved her to play. He could sit for hours watching her.

'Yes, of course, dear. I'll come up when I've had my dinner.'

He was delighted.

'Oh, how nice! Play the one with mice in the can.'

'Yes, I'll play that one.'

'And the one with armies marching.'

'Yes, dear.'

She put her arm around him and he lay back against her with his eyes closed.

After a while Winifred Trent came in. She was very thin and her pale long face was covered with wrinkles.

'I think dinner is ready, Vanessa. I'll stay with Ellis while he has his.'

A gong sounded from below. Winifred Trent said every evening this same sentence.

'Thank you, Winifred.' Vanessa got up. She kissed Ellis and went downstairs.

The dining-room seemed very large and empty. Rodd, the butler with a face like a muffin, waited on her.

'Sole, my lady?'

'Thank you, Rodd.'

She sat staring in front of her. Suddenly she smiled. Benjie had enjoyed Timothy's visit. He would be happier today.

'Brussels sprouts, my lady?'

'Thank you, Rodd.'

After Ellis was in bed she would write to Benjie and tell him about Timothy's visit.

WHITE WITH SWANS

One night early in 1912, Vanessa woke and was assured that she was about to die. She was conscious of no especial pain, only a scantness of breath and a general faintness. Dimly, as though she were many miles away, she realized that the early morning light, very cold and thin, laid ghostly shadows on the floor. She heard a sparrow twitter.

But so certain was she that the end had come that she felt that she must write something to Benjie, saying goodbye, telling him to be good to Sally . . . but she found that she had no wish to make the slightest movement. She lay there, her eyes fixed on the ceiling upon whose dark surface some strange light, thin and bright like a lustre bowl, seemed to hover. Her brain was quite clear. For months past she had known that her energy was leaving her as water trickles from a cistern. Until less than three years ago (she could fix the time exactly, for the change had come when Timothy Bellairs, the painter, had paid her a visit and, turning to her, had said: 'Don't let this be too much of a strain on you') her resistance had been equal to the struggle. But after that day (she remembered that when Timothy had gone she had been up and said goodnight to Sally, had visited Ellis and dined downstairs alone, and Rodd had said 'Brussels sprouts, my lady') something had snapped. Her nobility had gone, she supposed. Lying now, about to pass away altogether from this silly business, she could summarize the past clearly and without sentiment. Her nobility had gone. She no longer, after that day, wanted to play her part. What she wanted was for Ellis to die and then, for herself, that she should go to Benjie and never again, for one single moment, night or day, leave him.

She seemed after this (it was as though she were now speaking to God Himself, for life was over and He would understand) to be without scruples and yet to be tied with scruples. She was now quite shameless and, in intention, had already left Ellis and was somewhere safe in Cumberland with Benjie, but in fact of course she did nothing of the kind.

For three more years she did as she had already done; nursed Ellis, played her part, ached (oh God, how her heart had ached!) for Benjie, and there it was. But whereas in the first three years she had acted as she did because she thought it right, in the second three she acted as she did because she had to. She could not leave Ellis because he was so helpless, but her heart became a strange confusion of disgust and misery and longing and sheer exhausted weariness.

The effort was becoming always more frightful, and not only for herself but also for Benjie. For one whole year he went abroad. They wrote and met when he was in London. They poured their very souls into their letters. But the longing became too great. He returned, thin as a stick, new lines of age and perhaps of bitterness in his face. During this last year they met more and more often, but always as though, at the very moment of meeting, they must part. As for Ellis, nothing ailed him, and Vanessa was his very life. Then Winifred Trent died. Six months ago a chill had carried her off. Before she died she said to Vanessa: 'You've been wonderful,' and Vanessa, although she had grown to be fond of Winifred Trent, had a terrible impulse to tell Winifred Trent a number of coarse truths . . .

After that strength had ebbed from her. She woke weary; she went to bed too tired to sleep. And Ellis grew stronger and stronger in the body. He liked her to play to him on the little piano by the hour. Well, now she was going to die and the whole thing would be over. She thought of Benjie and Sally and Tom, and summoned them to her side.

To Benjie she said: 'My darling, my beloved, this can't separate . . .'

To Tom: 'Thank you for looking after me, Tom dear. Mary Worcester isn't worth it . . .'

And to Sally: 'Don't forget me. Have a good life, darling . . .'

Then it seemed to her that her heart ceased to beat. She thought of God as very near to her. She clasped her hands and began the Lord's Prayer . . .

A moment later apparently Janet, the maid, came in, carrying the tea, drawing the blinds. So she had not died!

She lay there, drank her tea.

'What kind of day is it, Janet?'

'Nice and bright, my lady.'

Then Janet said:

'You don't look very well this morning, my lady. Have your breakfast in bed. Do now.'

(Janet had from the first, two years ago, been very friendly, maternal, and comforting.)

'Oh no, Janet. I must get up. I didn't sleep very well.'

'What a shame! I should stay the morning in bed, my lady.'

And she did. She was surprised at herself. Sally came in to say goodbye to her before departing to her school in Kensington. She had her luncheon with Ellis in his room.

But, after this, the obsession remained with her that she had not long to live.

One evening she was gay: that is, she went with Cynthia, Philip Rochester and Horace Ormerod to the first night of a new play. It was Tuesday, March 5th-- Cynthia's birthday--and they had a very charming dinner first at Claridge's. Cynthia was very coy about her age, Horace hearty and hopeful, and Philip--who painted his face so cleverly that you wouldn't notice it unless you were a woman--was most witty at the expense of all his nearest and dearest.

'But I thought you liked Humphrey Bell!' Cynthia said, when Philip had just intimated that Humphrey cheated at cards and beat his mistresses.

'Oh, so I do! I ADORE Humphrey! He's a perfect pet! I know he wouldn't mind a WORD I've been saying!'

'Well, I'm not so sure,' observed Cynthia.

How very old, Vanessa thought, Philip was! He was all Dowsonish and Wildeish. And how long ago was that buried age with its glittering surface and tinkling music box echoes! The time when she had been a hostess and driven in the Park, had tea with Mrs Langtry in that extraordinarily cosy drawing-room, breathing that lovely lady's good-nature and kindness of heart. It had been a cosy, good-natured time--yes, and an enterprising one too! Now-- what was the matter?--everyone was restless, uneasy; nothing seemed secure. She herself felt shabby, an old owl not used to the light. She sat in the back of the box with Horace, feeling a little faint, longing for Cumberland and Benjie and the Newlands farm . . .

The play seemed to answer some of her questions. It was called Milestones and was by Arnold Bennett and Edward Knoblock. The little Royalty Theatre contained that night many celebrated persons. The customary first-night remark was made that if a bomb were dropped on the theatre . . . In fact, all the customary first- night remarks were made. Mr Knoblock was discerned sitting in a box with his sister. Famous persons were observed, commented upon. But it was not, as it happened, a first night quite like other first nights. It was, in itself, a Milestone. This passing of time, this blindness of each generation to the significant things, the battle between the helpless imaginative and the confident unimaginative.

'Why, these are Herries!' Vanessa thought. 'These are our very selves!'

And then Haidée Wright's brilliant passionate Aunt was simply Judith Paris come to life. She seemed to Vanessa to be living there on the stage in front of her. She was eternal, immortal, as Judith was. That little figure, her voice trembling with her vitality and courage, dominated not only the theatre but the world beyond it. 'So Judith still dominates us all.' In the last Act an actress made a great success. She was extremely beautiful, and Vanessa, who had never seen her before, searched her programme. Her name was Gladys Cooper. There was something in her self- confidence and scorn of sentiment that spoke of the future. 'Will Sally be like that? Not so beautiful of course, but brave, scornful of anything that seems to her unreal?' Everyone in the theatre that night was thinking a little as Vanessa. How time passes and we don't know it! We are at the mercy of forces greater than ourselves. What if these forces grow stronger than we? What if we become their slaves? A wind of insecurity blew through the theatre that night. The actors seemed like figures in a Morality.

In the second interval, Cynthia and Philip went out to greet some friends. In the back of the box, Vanessa and Horace talked. Vanessa had never liked Horace before, but tonight he touched her sympathy. His wife had died in the preceding year. He said that he was very lonely. This big heavy man with the protruding chin, the shining forehead, the gleaming glasses, was suddenly a small and very unprotected schoolboy.

'I suppose it's my own fault,' he said. 'I'm sure I've always done my best, looked on the bright side, been cheerful very often when I really didn't feel it, but people don't want you to be cheerful and kind and jolly. They like you much better if you're sour and cynical. The fact is, I know it, people get bored with me. There was a woman once, Vanessa, whom I loved to distraction. I'd have done anything for her. For a month or so it was like heaven--it was really. I thought she loved me passionately. One weekend she went to Eastbourne and wrote me two of the most wonderful letters. Beautiful

they were. And then, one night, she was to dine with me in my flat. I was all ready and waiting. I'd ordered the most beautiful little dinner. But instead of coming herself she sent a letter--a short, curt note saying that she was afraid she couldn't see me any more. She was very sorry. She had thought about it and decided that it wasn't right her seeing me and so on. But I knew that THAT wasn't the reason. It was simply that she was bored with me. And yet I'd always done my best.'

'You'd spoilt her, I expect,' said Vanessa.

'No. I'd done what any other man would have done. She found me a bore. Yes, it's very strange. People like you if you're cruel and malicious. I've never been cruel in my life to anyone.'

'Would you mind, Horace,' Vanessa said, 'getting me a glass of water? I feel rather faint.'

When he returned with one he had something he wanted to say. It was about Rose. He had seen Rose that very afternoon.

'Oh, Rose!' Vanessa exclaimed. 'Quick, Horace, tell me! I have written to her and had no answer. Once a letter from Madrid, a short one, telling me nothing.'

'I've seen her from time to time,' Horace said. 'Of course it's been very painful. But she was always determined that you shouldn't see her. It's been the one thing that she resolved. She was ashamed . . .'

'Oh no,' Vanessa cried. 'She shouldn't have been. I'm her friend. Quick, Horace, they're coming back. Where is she now? Is she in London?'

'Yes, that's why I told you. She's very ill. She's going to have a serious operation. This is her address. I've written it down.'

(Poor old Horace. Not such a bad fellow--or at any rate not so bad in old age and loneliness, much more bearable in misfortune.)

Cynthia and Philip came into the box. Vanessa had the address. She thought, as the curtain went up-- 'They've forgiven me. They consider me respectable again. But Rose they have pushed down and down . . .'

On the following afternoon she found her way to the street in Bloomsbury. It was a fine March day with gay light clouds hurrying like ballerinas across the chimney pots. The pigeons fluttered on the steps of the Museum, and there was a sniff of spring in the air.

Rose's room was at the very top of the thin grey house and, halfway up, Vanessa felt once more her faintness, had to pause while the stairs slowly rose and fell and a grimy window bent anxiously towards her. At last she was there. She knocked on the door and went in. Rose was sitting, a shawl over her shoulders, before a grumbling, sulky fire. The room was stuffy and had the smell of a not very clean blanket.

'Oh! Vanessa!' Rose cried out.

Vanessa bent down and they embraced as though they would never let one another go. Rose cried a little, wiping her eyes with a rather soiled handkerchief. Then she brightened. She was fearfully thin and her complexion was a pale and dry yellow. She was wearing a shabby blue skirt and faded silver slippers. She held Vanessa's hand.

'At last I told Horace that you might come and see me. I wouldn't hear of it before. But my number's up at last and I had to have one last glimpse of you before I met St Peter.'

'I've tried to see you--'

'Yes, I know. I've been abroad. Here, let's have a look at you!'

She took Vanessa by the shoulder and held her off so that she might see her.

'This bloody gas! It isn't very gay, is it? But we don't run to electric light here yet. Well, my dear, you don't look any too grand yourself, if I may say so. You're a fine big woman, of course--always were. But you look as though you hadn't had any sleep for a month.'

'I haven't been sleeping very well, but never mind me. What about yourself? What's the matter, Rose darling?'

'Oh, the wages of sin. As a matter of fact it's cancer and that's the plain truth. Old Furry-Face the doctor says, "Only a little internal trouble. We'll have you right in no time." But *I* know. You can't cheat me. I'm starving to death and I'm sick of it. Horace has been a brick, though. He's paying for the nursing home, insists on it although I tell him any old ditch will do to die in.'

'But, Rose, you're wrong. I'm sure you are! After all, they know--'

'Wrong my foot! You can't kid me. Now look here, my dear, now you ARE here! I want to know everything. How ARE you? How's Benjie? How much longer are you going on in this ridiculous way?'

Vanessa told her something of her life, ending up: 'You see, we thought that it wouldn't be so long. It's been five years.'

'And Benjie and you eating your hearts out! Well, I think it's a bit of sentimental tosh! Giving yourself up heart, soul and body to someone who'd be just as happy with any nurse--'

'No,' Vanessa said. 'You're wrong there. I might have left him, perhaps, if he hadn't needed me. Because it hasn't been fair on Benjie. But he DOES need me. Every year it has been more impossible to leave him.'

'And now you're killing yourself! Oh, I know! It's draining all the strength out of you. I can see it. And here we are, the two of us! You've done the virtuous thing. I've done the other! Not much to choose . . .'

They talked about old times. Rose never let Vanessa's hand go. Her clutch was hot and feverish.

'You needn't be afraid, Vanessa. It's all over. There's no drunken Major coming in. Even my taste for drink has gone. I was in Madrid three years. Yes, a

Professor kept me--a very nice little man he was, with a curly black beard and a wife he couldn't stand the sight of. I was fond of him. I truly was. That's a funny thing. In spite of the life I've led I haven't got tired of wanting to be fond of men--really fond of them, mend their clothes, put their buttons on, that sort of thing. Then I get tired of them. Domestic one minute, restless the next. But virtue's got nothing to do with it. I've never felt more virtuous than when I've been doing my worst . . . There was a young fellow from College once went off with me. Pretty well broke his mother's heart, too. We went on a trip to Scotland. We stopped at Keswick. I wanted to have a look at it, and there it was, same as ever--St John's spire and the square with the clock. We went down to the Lake the night we arrived and I can hear the water lapping against the jetty now. And Friar's Crag. We went on to Friar's Crag and the boy talked about Ruskin. Well, you never saw a more virtuous pair than we were that trip, reading Shelley and wondering whether there was a God and picking flowers . . . and I suppose I never did a wickeder thing than taking that young man away. Funny, isn't it? This morality! Very vexed question, if you ask me!'

After a while she asked Vanessa:

'Why do you love Benjie so, Vanessa? I've never loved anyone like that. You're the only one I've loved all my life long and you're a woman. Why do you love him so?'

'Oh, I don't know,' said Vanessa. 'He's everything I want in a man. You should ask rather why he loves me. I often tell him he should have a gay, lively woman, witty, and quick to see things. There's ONE reason I love him, I think. I can see his jokes. It used to be terrible in the old days in Hill Street when I didn't see a joke and had to pretend I did. But Benjie and I find one another amusing. We're comic to one another. That's a good reason for love.'

They fell into silence. Vanessa thought that Rose had fallen asleep. At last it was time for her to go.

'Rose darling--are you looked after here? Is there anyone to care for you?'

'Oh yes, it isn't so bad. The woman's quite decent. And I'm going to the nursing home tomorrow. You'll come and see me there, won't you?'

Vanessa promised. She looked back at the door and saw Rose's eyes-- hungry, shining, feverish--fixed upon her. She went slowly away.

She visited Rose every day in the nursing home. A week later Rose had her operation and three days after that she died. She was worn out, the doctor said. Injudicious living in the past . . . yes . . . sad . . . but, as a matter of fact, there would have been no hope. She could not have recovered.

Vanessa was happy for her sake. That was the way that she would have wished it.

Meanwhile the Family watched Vanessa with curiosity. She went round paying visits on everybody exactly as though she were going away somewhere.

Cynthia and May Rockage (who was in London just then) and stout Mary Newmark, putting their heads together, decided that she was going off with Benjie again. She was gay, light-hearted and extraordinarily kind. She said some odd things. She said to Cynthia: 'I can't get that play Milestones out of my head. Do you remember the girl in the last Act saying, "Please remember that we're in the year 1912"? Isn't it funny to think that for Sally, one day, 1912 will be as old-fashioned as 1812? Doesn't it make you feel queer?'

'Not in the least,' said Cynthia.

'Oh, well, then--doesn't it seem odd to you that my grandmother probably said, "Please remember that we're in the year 1812"?'

'Not in the least. Your grandmother lived to be a hundred.'

'Oh, I know. That isn't what I mean. What I mean is that people are more important than time. What I mean is that my father, who was a darling, once said in his garden on Cat Bells: "Look, Vanessa! There's the squirrel again!" That, my relationship to him, our love for one another, all of it comes back as I think of that sentence: it isn't dead, it isn't gone. He's alive because we loved one another. 1812, 1912 doesn't mean anything at all. What we think is life is nothing--the secret life has quite another history. Am I being very stupid?'

'No, dear,' said Cynthia, who was only half listening, because there were some new and extremely beautiful photographs of her daughter Mary that she was examining. 'You're being very clever-- too clever for me I'm afraid.'

('One half of our family will NEVER understand what the other half is after--never, never, never!' Vanessa thought.)

'Aren't these good?' said Cynthia. 'I don't want to be the fond mother, but really Mary is going to be a beauty.'

'Yes, she is,' said Vanessa eagerly, glad that Cynthia was happy and at the same time wishing, in spite of herself, that Sally was taller and had a brighter complexion.

'Do you think, Cynthia, that there is something true in what the old man said at the end of Milestones?'

'What did he say, dear?' asked Cynthia, holding one of the photographs at an odd angle and smiling at it.

'Don't you remember? He said women of today aren't what they used to be. They're hard. They've none of the old charm. They're unsexed. Are Sally and Mary going to be hard? They ARE different from us. I've noticed it. Sally isn't afraid of anything and she doesn't like to show her feelings. She's rather like a boy sometimes. Won't it be dreadful if all the women are like men and all the men--?'

'Like Philip,' Cynthia concluded. 'Why do you think so much about the future, Vanessa? The present is so very agreeable. Peile hasn't been in a bad temper for weeks. Everything is so comfortable and settled.'

'Settled? Do you think so?' said Vanessa.

Later, the Family recalled the strangeness of Vanessa during these weeks. They had, perhaps, none of them ever really known her. She became again rather beautiful. Her pallor suited her grey hair, and her eyes were still lovely, soft, gentle, and generous. No, they had none of them really known her. There was something wild in the middle of her gentleness. You might call her timid because she disliked quarrelling, high words. Yet she had a temper, she could be most courageous. She had been, by all Herries standards, grossly immoral, living for years with a man to whom she was not married, and yet she was religious as none of them were. She had succeeded in holding a man's devotion for a whole lifetime, and a most difficult man too. And yet she was not a woman of the type, you would suppose, for Benjie. For five years she had performed a task that was, they all admitted, an exceedingly hard one. They admired her now although they had once criticized her so severely. But she was outside them all--a stranger in the end. 'There have been always odd ones in the family,' Mary Newmark said complacently. 'As Sidney says, "We're different from ordinary families."'

Vanessa meanwhile paid a visit to her doctor.

'Is there anything wrong with me? I'd like to know.'

He examined her.

'You have been under a great strain. You're very tired. Can't you go abroad for a while and have a proper rest?'

'No,' said Vanessa. 'I can't, I'm afraid.'

'Well, you aren't looking after yourself properly--'

'Is anything organically wrong?'

'No. You're nearly fifty-three, though, and should take care of yourself. A chill or an extra strain--any little thing--might be serious.'

She smiled. They were very old friends,

'Thank you. I'll try and take care.'

Then the day came (she had known that it was coming) when she could not leave Benjie. They had been having tea in his room as they did about once a fortnight. ('How old we're getting!' she said to Benjie once. 'No one thinks it immoral for us to be alone any more.') She got up to go. She could not. She stared at him helplessly.

'What is it?' he asked, getting up and coming to her.

'Oh, I don't know!' She tried to smile, but her mouth trembled. 'Suppose that this should be the last time!'

'What do you mean--the last time?'

'It's always been like that lately--harder to part.'
She drew away from him. 'Oh, I was forgetting! I
brought you something.'

She went to the deal table and picked something
up. 'I thought I'd like you to have this.'

'What is it? You're always giving me things.'

She undid the paper wrapper.

'This is Judith's book. You know, the one we used
to read out of in Cumberland.' She held it up, with its
faded green cover. 'I thought I'd like YOU to have it
now.'

'Why? But you are so fond of it!'

'Yes--but if anything happened . . . You know,
Benjie, I've always thought it such a pity that someone
shouldn't publish it; it's so lively and amusing.'

'People aren't interested. We aren't a very remarkable family.'

'Aren't we?' said Vanessa. 'I think we are.'

He kissed her. 'All right. I'll look after it for you.
Write your name in it--your name and mine.'

She went to the table and sat down. She wrote:
'For Benjie with love from Vanessa Herries and Judith
Paris. March 29th, 1912.'

'I feel as though she were in the room with us
now.'

He laughed. He was standing behind her, his hand
on her shoulder.

'Ghosts! What a child you are, Van! Once we're
gone we're gone!'

He felt her shiver.

'What's the matter?' he asked. 'Are you cold?'

'No.' She turned round, looked up into his face,
her hands on his chest. 'Don't say that, Benjie. I can't
endure to think that death--physical death--can separate
us. After all--who knows?--it may be only after that that
we're really together. When two people have loved one
another so long and so truly as we have, isn't it absurd
to think that a little thing--a cold, a stumble in the street,
oh! anything--can separate us for ever?'

'Well,' he said, looking down at her with great tenderness, 'life is absurd, my darling--absurd, meaningless,
cruel.'

She lowered her eyes. He felt her tremble again.

'Perhaps I'm wrong,' he said, putting his arm round
her, holding her to him. 'I don't know any more than
the next fellow. It's ridiculous to dogmatize. But if
there's a God and He's kept us apart for five years as a
cat tortures a mouse, why, then I say as many a man has
said before me--'

He stopped. She was crying. He knelt down beside her.

'Oh, my darling, don't cry! After all, we've got one
another. We've had years of one another. That's something. And this can't go on for ever. It mustn't. It
shan't. It gets harder every day. It's killing both of us . .
. Darling, look up! Think of the happy times! Think of
the night in Newlands when Tom arrived from London!

And even now--the hours we have, the way our love
grows stronger and stronger . . .'

He knelt, holding her, while she sobbed against his
shoulder. He caught some words.

'I'm so tired . . . I love you so much . . .'

She rose, wiping her eyes. 'There! At my age!
Wait. I'll wash my face in your bedroom!'

While she was gone he stood there in perplexity.
Tonight he could not endure that she should leave him
and return to that house, to that dark house, that insane
house . . .

This could not go on as it was. They had both endured it too long. He must think of some way.

She came back smiling, but he saw that she was
dreadfully weary.

'Come with me to the King's Road until I get a
cab.'

At the door they embraced, clinging to one another
with an almost dreadful desperation.

'I wish I'd seen Tom,' she said. 'Say goodbye to
him for me.'

'Of course. But you'll be seeing him next week.'

'Oh yes. It was so good of him to take Sally out
the other day. She DID enjoy it so!'

They went down the long stairs hand in hand. He
walked beside her with the defiant boyish adventurous
air that was so especially his, his hat cocked a little to the
side, his empty sleeve, a flower in his coat.

In the King's Road they saw a cab, but she said:

'Let's walk a little farther. There'll be another.'
The only thing that she said was: 'What do you think?
Carey and May are going to America in April. Adventurous for old things like them, isn't it? They're going in
this wonderful new ship, the Titanic.'

'We'll go to America one day!' he said.

In Sloane Square she found a cab and got in. He
stood looking after it until it turned the corner.

It was a quiet, still evening with little clouds of
peach blossom floating serenely across a gentle sky.
The traffic moved as in a dream and she stopped the
cab by the Ritz (she wanted to go to Hatchard's bookshop), got out and walked. Influenced as she always
was by the world about her, all humankind seemed, in
this evening hush, to be amiable and friendly. She
thought of the Family, that they had all been good to
her after their lights, Cynthia and Mary and May and
Alfred, Horace and Adrian; two old bachelor brothers,
George and Stephen Cards, who, having come to live in
London, had been especially good to her, leaving flowers at Hill Street and inviting her to their funny little
dinners. All the feuds were over. Into what kind of
world would Sally, Mary and Rosalind and Maurice grow
up? The Family had risen now above the old jealousies
and causeless rivalries. She felt that she herself had
done her part in the mysterious weaving of God's shuttle by her return to Ellis. Her love and Benjie's had not
been wasted. Nothing was wasted, no goodness, no
kindness, no little unheeded courtesy.

She lost, for a moment, under that peach-blossom sky, consciousness of her own small personal history and so was happy. But she was tired. She sat down on one of Mr Hatchard's chairs as they fastened up for her a book, Carnival, by some new young man. Adrian had told her that she must certainly read it. Then, as she went out into the street again, she was conscious of a small, stabbing pain in her side. As she was aware of it she knew also a sudden mysterious foreboding as though someone had whispered in her ear: 'This is what you have been waiting for. You will need now all your courage.' She put her hand to her side as though to reassure herself.

At home again she went up to Sally's room and found her sitting at her table biting her pencil over arithmetic. She sprawled over the table, the perfect schoolgirl in her dark blue dress, ink on her cheek and her hair ruffled, drumming her heels on the floor.

'I'm no good at sums, darling,' Vanessa said, sitting down beside her and loving her with a passionate desire to draw her into her arms and never let her go again. But she knew well that Sally did not care for demonstrations.

'Oh, that's all right, Mummy,' Sally said. 'I'll do the beastly things. It's in our blood, I expect, not to be good at sums.' Then she added casually: 'I'm playing for the First at Hockey on Saturday.'

Vanessa knew that this had been, during the last two months, Sally's besetting ambition, but she only said:

'Oh, are you, darling? I'm so glad.'

'Yes.' Sally pushed the book away and looked at her mother. 'You DO look sweet! Who gave you the violets?'

'Your father.'

'Good.' She thought a moment. Then she went on: 'Mummy, ought I to mind about being illegitimate?'

'Why, dear?'

'Well, Mabel Staines said today that she wouldn't be illegitimate for anything, and that her mother wanted to ask me to tea but wouldn't when Mabel told her.'

'I shouldn't worry about it, Sally dear,' Vanessa said.

'Oh, I don't worry!' Sally said cheerfully. 'I told her that her mother could keep her old tea. I rather like being illegitimate. I'm different from the other girls.'

'Do most of the girls know?' asked Vanessa.

'I don't think so. They're all quite decent anyway.' Then she looked at her mother again. 'Mummy, you're tired. You want some tea. I'll get some.'

'No, dear, thank you. I've had some.'

Then Sally did what was rare with her. She threw her arms round Vanessa's neck and hugged her. She rubbed her cheek against her mother's.

'I'll look after you when you're older, and you're the only one I WILL look after.'

'Will you, darling?'

'Yes, you shall have everything you want. I'll make money for you and keep you.'

'What'll you make money with?'

'Oh, I don't know--be a secretary or a market gardener or something.'

'Perhaps you'll marry?'

'Indeed I shan't. I think boys and men are awful. All except Tom and Daddy and Ellis.' Then she dropped her voice confidentially. 'Ellis came in here crying a little while ago. He'd broken a green vase they put flowers in. I told him not to worry.'

(Extraordinary, Vanessa thought, how Sally takes everything for granted!)

'I must go up to him.'

Sally gave her a long and very wet kiss.

'Darling Mummy, I do love you so!' she murmured.

'And I love you,' Vanessa said.

She went up to Ellis and found him, quite contented, playing cards. There was a very simple Patience that Vanessa had taught him. As he played he murmured to himself. 'That's the Red Queen. Now where's the next one. What comes after nine, Vanessa?' he asked as she came in.

'Ten,' she said.

'No, the other way.'

'Eight comes before nine.'

'Eight. Eight. Eight,' he said.

He had grown, in the last few weeks, to look very old. His face was wizened, very wrinkled. He looked like a pathetic old monkey.

'Play the piano,' he said, smiling at her.

She sat down at the piano, and as she played 'Annie Laurie' and 'Drink to me only' she felt the pain at her side like a knife. He came and stood beside her, humming out the tune. Then he drew a chair and sat there, all huddled up, nursing his knees.

He was like a little gnome, and with his dead white fingernails he tapped on his knee.

Soon she stopped.

'I'm tired tonight,' she said.

'Yes, I'm tired too,' he said and laid his head on her lap. She stroked his white hair as he liked her to do. Poor Ellis! Would it not be kinder? . . . Then, at the thought which sometimes came to her like a messenger falsely tempting her, she put her arms round his thin body and held him close to her.

But she was too weary to go on. She kissed him and left him, he looking after her with his pathetic wondering eyes.

She went to bed. She was brought some food, but could not eat it. When, at last, to her great relief, she was left alone, she propped her pillows up and wrote a letter to Benjie. Then she lay down to sleep. She could not sleep. Out of a cave of darkness where a dragon slumbered, she moved (carefully lest she should rouse the dragon). She thought that she would read, and she opened a book that was on the little table. It was a volume of Rossetti's poems and, to pain now stabbing her with every breath, she read some verses:

Although the lattice had dropped loose
   There was no wind; the heat
Being so at rest that Amelotte
Heard far beneath the plunge and float
   Of a hound swimming in the moat.

Some minutes since, two rooks had toiled
   Home to the nests that crowned
Ancestral ash-trees. Through the glare
Beating again, they seemed to tear
   With that thick caw the woof o' the air.

But else, 'twas at the dead of noon
   Absolute silence: all
From the raised bridge and guarded sconce
To green-clad places of pleasaunce
   Where the long lake was white with swans.

She let the book fall and lay back that she might struggle the better with her painful breathing. What was the matter with her? She was ill. She felt the heat rising, as in dry dusty wafts from the desert, through her body, and this heat seemed to be mingled with the clear, sharp picture in the poem that she had just been reading. She herself leant out from some high window on a day of fierce heat and in the general stillness she could hear the sudden cool splash of the hound, and then the caw of the rooks tearing the still air, and then, turning her weary head, she saw the lake, like a mirror in a green wall, and over its glassy green-reflected light the swans, whiter than sunny snow, floated. Ah, this heat and this coldness! This stillness behind whose surface heat beat like a drum! And the swans became horses, great white horses struggling through the lake that now was black; out of the icy water the horses struggled up on to the flank of the icy frozen hills and their hoofs rang against the ice! As the splendid white horses drew breath with pain, so she fought for hers. Everything moved and shifted. She was a child running across the Cat Bells lawn to greet her father, the house was burning, flames rose mountain-high, as high as Skiddaw, and she was burning too.

But Benjie came and caught her up with his one arm and they rode on the white horse over Skiddaw, Blencathra, over Helvellyn and the Pikes, sailed above Scafell and so out to sea, to the magical island on the horizon, and below them all Wastwater was a lake set in a green wall, and the white swans, with a grand remote dignity, floated on its surface . . .

At some moment, she could not tell when, she saw the crumpled face of Rodd, the butler, bending over her.

'No, Rodd,' she whispered from an infinite distance. 'I'm not very well. I don't think I'll get up today.'

Rodd went upstairs to see the nurse who tended Ellis. She was a big bony woman with a serious kindly face. She had a faint moustache and grey eyes that were both practical and gentle. Her name was Milligan.

'Nurse, her ladyship is very unwell. I don't like the look of her at all.'

The nurse went down. Vanessa recognized her and smiled at her.

'I'm not very well,' she said. 'I have a bad pain in my side. I don't think I'll get up, if you don't mind.'

'It's pneumonia,' Milligan said to Rodd. 'I'll get Doctor Lancaster at once.'

Doctor Lancaster came. Vanessa was very ill.

Later in the morning Rodd telephoned to Cynthia. Cynthia had, a moment before, been telephoning about bridge and she was annoyed because she could not, that afternoon, secure the four that she wanted. It was stupid of Anne Fellowes to bother, on that afternoon of all afternoons, about her old husband just because he had only been home from China a week. 'When he's been home another fortnight she won't bother,' she thought. She put down the receiver and wondered whom she should ask. The bell rang.

'Well,' she said, in that little voice exactly like ice knocking against a glass, a voice that was warning enough to anyone who was sensitive. 'Oh, is that you, Rodd?' she said.

'Yes, madam,' said Rodd, who was not at all sensitive. 'It's her ladyship, madam. She's very ill. Pneumonia, Doctor Lancaster said. We were wondering whether you could come to Hill Street.'

Half an hour later she was in Hill Street. As she came into the room she heard a strange sound of recurrent short breaths, something inhuman and cruel. Vanessa did not recognize her, but murmured: 'The white swans. Benjie! Benjie! Look at the swans!'

On the following morning Benjie was roused, at about half past seven, from a deep sleep by the ringing of the telephone. When he went to it he heard to his surprise Cynthia's voice:

'Benjie, is that you?'

'Yes,' he said, shivering a little in his pyjamas.

'I'm at Hill Street. I think you'd better come as soon as possible.'

'Hill Street?' he repeated, bewildered.

'Yes. It's Vanessa. She's terribly ill. Double pneumonia.'

'I'll come at once,' he answered quietly.

He was aware that Tom was in the room.

'Father's what is it?'

'It's Vanessa. She's very ill. Double pneumonia.'

'Oh no! Oh no!' Tom cried.

'Yes. I must go at once.'

He felt nothing except that he must get to Vanessa. He must get to Vanessa and save her.

He found a cab, rang in a frenzy the bell, rushed into the house and up the stairs. On the first landing he saw Cynthia.

'Oh, Benjie!' she cried and stopped. Then, the tears streaming down her face, she said: 'Vanessa's dead!'

He did not see her. He stood in the long drawing-room like a man lost, his eyes wandering from wall to wall. He was not thinking at all.

He felt a touch on his arm and, turning, saw at his side an old, wizened, bent, and wrinkle-faced man who looked up at him with questioning eyes. Moving from some infinite cold distance he came close to this strange figure. Then, with no shock of surprise, he realized that it was Ellis. From this same room Ellis had once driven him out. Now he said, in a trembling voice:

'Where is Vanessa?'

Benjie led him to the sofa and the old man sat down beside him, close to him, shivering a little.

'Vanessa's all right,' he said.

'No. But why isn't she here? Why hasn't she come upstairs? I want her to play the piano.'

He put his arm round the old man. 'We must both be patient,' he said.

'Yes, I'll be patient,' Ellis said and sat there, staring in front of him, waiting . . .

Afterwards Cynthia gave him a letter.

'It is for you, Benjie. Vanessa had written on the envelope that it was to be given to you after she was gone.' Cynthia, who had loved Vanessa, looked at him as though she would like to achieve with him some new and affectionate relation, but she discovered at once that she did not know him at all, that he looked 'foreign', and that he scarcely saw her. He took the letter and walked out of the house.

He read it in his own room.

MY DARLING--I'm writing this in bed. Perhaps you will never read it, but I am writing because I feel unwell tonight and for weeks now have had a foreboding that I might die without seeing you. This is probably nothing except my being very tired, as I have been now for a long time. But in any case it is like talking to you, and is better than that in some ways because I can say some things that I might be shy to say to your face, well though I know you--or perhaps because I do know you so well.

What I want most to say is that if I were to die very suddenly and you not see me, you are never to feel afterwards that our love has been wasted. It has been the most wonderful and glorious thing in both our lives,

hasn't it? It has been everything to me, not only because of our love, but because it has shown me that there is something in life far deeper than anything physical or material. I have sometimes thought that the separation of these last years has been the best thing that could have happened, because we have been separated and yet in every important way have been closer together than ever we were. I have wished so often that I could have been a different kind of woman for you--I suppose every woman wishes that for the man she loves. I would have liked to be brilliant, witty, the kind of woman clever men describe in their books. I have been unfortunate, I sometimes think, because I have been a woman between two periods. Forty years ago women knew what they were supposed to be and do. In fact there was no choice for most of them. In times to come when Sally is grown up, women, I expect, will be free, equal with men, afraid of nothing. I have not, I'm sure, made a success of my life, and yet I feel that I have, because I won and KEPT your love, and Sally and Tom love me too. I won't say anything about religion, because I know that it bores you, but think sometimes of me that I had no more doubt that God exists than I have of your love for me. People nowadays seem to think that anyone who believes in God is a hypocrite, TRYING to believe because it is more comfortable, but it ISN'T so. There are many people who are not stupid nor false who feel God close to them quite as practically as they feel the people they know close to them. I express this very badly and I don't want you to think I am influencing you--only when I am gone remember that this was the greatest TRUE fact in my life. Perhaps you will come to feel one day that there may be some other life that goes on side by side with, or rather INSIDE, the physical one. I feel that just now everyone is bewildered, unhappy and restless. It wasn't always so, I am sure. People will understand God one day perhaps in a new fashion when they have been unsatisfied and restless long enough.

But I didn't mean this letter to be a sermon. I only meant to thank you, again and again, for loving me so much and so long. Don't be sad if I go. Perhaps I shall be more with you than I have been. Who knows? Do you really think that our love, after all it has been through, can be killed by physical death? I am sure that it cannot. Think often of all the happy times we have had, especially in Newlands. That is our country. That is where I will always be closest to you. It has been our country for nearly two hundred years and perhaps before that. Every stone and tree there is a witness that life is worth living, however hard it is, beautiful and terrible and comic and disappointing and rewarding. Go and climb Robinson or stand by the Watendlath Tarn and think of Judith and remember old Herries in Borrowdale. I KNOW that nothing is lost, that everything lives, that there is no death, whatever people say.

You will care for Sally, won't you? She is very high-spirited and determined, and I sometimes think that she is the first FEARLESS Herries, the first one to rise above all the jealousy and fear and greediness that there has been so long. Perhaps the world that is coming will be full of Sallies! And give Tom all the love that you can. He will miss me, I think, more than anyone. He has such a warm heart and all his happiness is bound up in other people. Forgive me for all the times that you have thought me sentimental and stupid and slow to see things. But I know you have and will. Remember that our love isn't ended, that it will never end, that nothing can destroy it now--Your most loving and devoted

VANESSA

If you have a chance, see poor Ellis sometimes.

Part Four

The Ghost

I THE FLAME

Three weeks after the outbreak of war several of the Herries family dined at Alfred's fine house in Drummond Street.

It was a kind of farewell dinner, because Tom, Maurice--Alfred's son--and Gordon--the son of Sidney and Mary Newmark--would be shortly departing for the Front. There were present Alfred himself, Benjie (who, in two days' time, was leaving for Russia), Tom, Mary Worcester (now twenty-one years of age and a frantic beauty), Rosalind (her sister), Maurice and Clara (Alfred's children), Gordon and Ada, with Sidney and Mary Newmark (their parents)--and Sally, who was not quite eleven, but was allowed to stay up on this one occasion because it might be a long time before she had dinner with Benjie and Tom again.

There were twelve of the family in all.

Dinner was finished. Tom, Maurice and Gordon, looking very young and innocent in uniform, were sipping Alfred's brandy with the quiet air of practised connoisseurs.

Alfred got up to make a speech. The Herries family had always been rather fond of making speeches. Alfred especially enjoyed it. He was a practised hand at making speeches in the City and proving in his cold, restrained voice that everything was absolutely for the best so long as he and his fellow-directors were in charge.

Tonight, however, his voice was not quite cold, not quite restrained. His long nose and thin horse-like face looked down at them with a kind of anxious tenderness, and he looked especially at Maurice, his son, whose face was round and rosy, whose tastes were for the Arts rather than figures, who was unlike him in everything.

And he was doing for the first time in his life, perhaps, an artistic thing. He held in one long, bony hand a thin, beautifully chased silver candlestick. Up its slender stem ran a pattern of leaves and branches.

'I'm not going to make a long speech,' he said. 'But I must say something. Here we all are as a family, all together, wishing one another well. It hasn't always been so, you may remember. At one time, in the days of our grandfathers and grandmothers, there was some trouble, as I dare say you know. But now we are all united, a symbol, I like to think, of England itself--all united to fight the greatest enemy the world has ever known--Prussian militarism. Whatever else you may say about our family, no one can deny that, on the whole, we have always stood for England's best interests. One of our ancestors helped to defend Carlisle against Prince Charlie and the Scots. Benjie here lost an arm in South Africa, and in countless other ways we have backed our country. And now we are doing it again. She has never needed us as she needs us now, but because we believe she is in the right we are giving all we have, our sons, our money, our lives. Ahem! yes . . . well . . . It was Maurice's idea that we should do some little thing tonight that we should all remember when we are separated later on, and that when we remember it we should remember one another . . . Yes . . . I have, left me by my father, a pair of old candlesticks. They belonged, I believe, to an ancestor of ours, Harcourt Herries, who lived in Cumberland in the eighteenth century, and before him to an old Elizabethan Herries who had something to do with the mines in Keswick. Well, that's past history and this is present history, and it was Maurice's idea that we should link up past and present, that we should pass this candle round, each one of us standing up in his or her turn, holding the lighted candle and wishing the rest of us good luck.

'Well . . . ahem . . . that's all, I think. Except that Sally here, the youngest, shall be the one to light it.'

It was done as he said. Sally--standing on a chair because she was so small--lit it and round it went. The electric light was switched out and round the little flame went, very clear and bright and steady. Everyone wished everyone else good luck.

It was a frosty, sparkling morning and the guns were still. Two hours after midnight there had been a fearful bombardment. On and on went that shattering malignant thunder. Then it ended. There was a perfect cloud of silence everywhere over the desolate country. Tom was ordered to see how the land, now remorselessly altered, might look. New mounds, new pits. Four or five of the raiders lay stretched out, abandoned and desolate; one a stout officer with a snub nose and part of his face gone, another a dark squat-shaped boy who lay, his head on his arm, his wide dark eyes staring at the sky. The raid had been well planned. Tom returned. The light was strengthening, but the air was thin like stretched paper and most bitterly cold. He looked out over a land that might have been trampled by dinosaurs. The country was quite deserted save for one or two snipers at the sap-head. No sound anywhere, but he knew that all about him thousands of men were concealed. Desolation and silence . . . He went into his dug-out and began a letter to Sally.

DARLING LITTLE SALLY--I've got half an hour to myself and everything's as quiet as the top of Cat Bells. They raided us last night and for an hour or two there was a terrible din. We lost some men, I'm afraid. It's a cold and frosty morning, which is heaps better than the mud and rain. I'm all right, feeling very well in fact. Do you remember the dinner at Alfred's when you lit the candle, and do you remember his saying that we were proud, as proper, right-minded Herries, of defending the world against Prussian Militarism? I suppose we were right at the time to feel like that, and it's still nice to think of that lighted candle going round the table, isn't it? But how long ago that all seems now, and how our point of view has altered!

I haven't had any sleep for twenty-fours hours, but last time I DID sleep I dreamt of Vanessa. It was scarcely like a dream. She seemed to be sitting beside me holding my hand and wearing the clothes she used to wear in Newlands--just as I would wake sometimes in the morning and find her sitting on my bed. Doesn't she seem PEACEFUL now in all this trouble? Do you remember how calm she used to be when something went wrong, and the way she smiled? . . .

He broke off and stared in front of him, smiling at the thought of Vanessa. Then he went on:

The thing I hate most here is being sent out to reconnoitre positions and getting lost. It's awful. Perhaps it's raining, and through the mist you see lights trembling on the horizon, or you think you do. Then, out of nowhere, someone says, as though they were fearfully angry, 'Get down!' and you find yourself in a barrage. Then you run for your life, the wet clay clinging to your legs like hands. Then you're lost again--in darkness. You go up and you go down, not knowing what is hill and what isn't. Perhaps some rifles suddenly open on you. You run and crouch, and slip and crouch and run-- always lost, always alone and dirty and cold, like a nightmare after we'd eaten too much as kids.

How are you? Are you doing well at school? Remember there are the three of us--you and I and Father --or four with Vanessa. Never forget Vanessa, darling, will you? Of course I know you won't. Have you heard from Father in Russia? I haven't for ages. Have you seen Mary? Did you ask her to write to me? She promised to but she hasn't yet. DON'T FORGET THIS. It's very important. Do you write to Father regularly? You must, even though he seems so far away. I think he's in Galicia somewhere. Isn't this funny? It's lying on the table beside me. Someone left it:

PLEASE!

Will you help your lad at the Front and all other lads, in a very simple way, and will you give your friends the chance to help as well?

Do it Thus!

Fill in THIS POSTCARD with your name and address, and post it back to us. We will then send you a number of bookmarkers . . .

Bookmarkers! You don't know how funny that sounds here. And lads! Don't you hate the word 'lads'?

Well, darling, keep up your spirits and behave just as though everything were all right. I'm fine myself and perhaps I'll get a spot of leave soon. Don't forget to write to Father and don't forget to ask Mary to write to me. Tell me what she was wearing when you saw her last. That's important--Your most loving brother,

TOM

The candle, stuck in a bottle with a collar of grease, flared up. The flame was bright, pure, steady, of gold.

'There's a flame!' cried Benjie.

The Retreat had begun and with the rest of the Otriad he had been flung into the little town of O----. It was a place of dust, whirling clouds of dust, dust in your eyes and mouth and nose. This dust was blown by the wind and behind the thin spirals of it a hot sun blazed. Everywhere there was the Russian soldier, the Russian soldier apathetic like a cow but humorous and touching also. He was everywhere, in the streets, on the dirty staircases, crowding the tumbled untidy rooms; the Russian soldier and the dust.

'I never want to see either of them again,' thought Benjie.

But he had cried out at the sudden flame. It was evening and, after the dust storms and the hot malignant sun, the pale blue of the sky and the cool air were friendly. The members of the Otriad were lying or walking or sitting in the half-ruined building into which Molozov, their chief, had turned them. Benjie found this place intolerable. It was a long room with a naked gleaming floor and an apparently endless succession of looking-glasses. This gleaming empty reflection was broken with an infernal clatter through the open window of horses, soldiers and carts that rattled on the cobbles. There was a smell everywhere of dust and dung.

He went to see if he could be of any use with the wounded. Going out originally in August 1914 with two journalists who were friends of his, he kicked his heels in Moscow for some weary months and at last only found adventure by joining, after a week or two in a Moscow hospital, a Red Cross unit attached to the Ninth Army. They had been sent to Galicia and, after some apparent victories, had begun a retreat. He would never forget the moment of that change of fortune. He and several soldiers had gone, under the charge of a rather feckless Englishman called Trenchard, to the forest to bury the dead. This was not his own Otriad. He had come over with two of his own unit to pay this Otriad a visit. It had been pleasant to find another Englishman here, although no two men could have been found more different than Benjie with his short thick figure, his off-hand but commanding independent personality, and this untidy, seemingly foolish Englishman who would wander about singing Early One Morning in a cracked voice or, quite unexpectedly, looking so wretched that you thought he would burst into tears. Benjie was told that he had been engaged to a pretty, charming nurse in his Otriad who had thrown him over.

Benjie was to return that same evening to his own Otriad. But he did not. Under the trees of the forest he was looking at a dead man--a man who had been dead some three weeks perhaps. This man was all right until you came to his face. His strong blue-grey trousers were in splendid condition and he had good stout boots. Out of the top of one boot a tin spoon protruded. But he had no face, only a grinning skull, and in and out of the mouth and eye sockets little black creatures like ants were crawling. It was all very peaceful there. The sanitars began to dig a grave. Some quietly smoked cigarettes. Then a sanitar observed that the bursting of the shrapnel that had been dim and distant all day now sounded much closer. That was the beginning of the Retreat . . .

But it was at the town of O---- that he saw the sudden flame. He had been for nearly a week now with this Otriad that was not his own. He had begun to know them all--Molozov, the stocky square- shouldered Chief who would say over and over again: "There's no method . . . no system . . . nothing at all . . . By God, THERE'S a pretty girl!" Nikitin, a doctor who had a charming intellectual face; a surgeon, Alexei Petrovitch Semyonov, a striking-looking fellow, very thickset and muscular with a strange square-cut beard of so fair a colour that in some lights it seemed almost white. A man of very strong personality and great self-confidence. There was the pretty Sister, Marie Ivanovna, and the feckless untidy Englishman, Trenchard. He made friends with them and liked them, but they were nevertheless all shadows on a screen to him who had his constant, secret preoccupations.

He found work to do in the vast room at O----. This was a strange place. It had been the theatre of the town. It was lit now with candles stuck into bottles, and in this dim and wavering light the doctors did their work. The busy silence was broken with patient plaintive cries of 'Oh, Steritza! Oh, Steritza!' or 'Borjé moi! Borjé moi!' and then the sharp official questions, 'What regiment? What division? Shrapnel or bullet?'

And across the stage at the back of the room was still hanging, wavering in the draught, the painted backcloth of some old play. This amused Benjie by its incongruity, for there was a picture of a market-place in a town all very gaily painted, and down the marble stairs flower-girls with legs like bolsters came merrily tripping while soldiers in scarlet and blue drank with their girls at little tables.

Meanwhile the real soldiers cried out in their agony 'Oh! Oh! Oh! . . . Oh! Borjé moi . . . Borjé moi!' as Nikitin and Semyonov probed for bullets under the uncertain flame of the candles, and a soldier in delirium sang a song about gathering the corn, in a shrill broken voice.

The dominating square-bearded man, Semyonov, had stopped his work for a moment and stood, his arms folded, looking on, beside Benjie.

'You seem to stand this pretty well,' he said. 'If it isn't impertinent--how old are you?'

'Just gone sixty,' said Benjie.

'Yes. You look fit. Lose your arm in this War?'

'No. In the Boer War.'

'Bad luck.'

'Oh, I'm used to it.'

'What do you think of us--the Russians, I mean?' Semyonov asked.

'Oh, you're plucky--marvellous. I never saw such courage. But you're a bit muddled high up, aren't you?'

'Yes. Hopeless. Everyone's robbing and cheating and spying and betraying. It's a mess of a war altogether. When do you think it will end?'

'Never, I should think,' said Benjie.

'I agree. Why don't you people do something on the other Front?'

'We're doing our best, I believe,' said Benjie.

'I believe you are. But they're beginning to be impatient over here.' He turned angrily, and Benjie thought he had never seen a more determined aggressive profile. 'There's that bloody fellow- countryman of yours messing things up again. Never saw a more useless fellow in my life.'

'Oh, you mean Trenchard,' Benjie said.

'Yes. I wish to God he'd get back to his own country.'

It was then that a candle, close at Benjie's elbow, flared. It was low down in its socket. In the spurt of light Benjie thought that he saw Vanessa. She stood quietly there, smiling at Trenchard, who was nervously bandaging the knee of a large patient-eyed soldier. She smiled at him, then turned her eyes to Benjie's. They drank in one another's happiness. Oh! how glad he was to see her again! But she was not there. Only the flame, bright, pure, steady.

And Sally, seeing it, said to Mary Worcester: 'Look, Mary! That light in the sky!'

Sally and Mary were looking out from behind the blinds in Cynthia's house in Eaton Place. Cynthia had taken the house six months ago. It was small, compact, could be worked with four servants. Everyone must make sacrifices now.

Ellis had died two months after Vanessa. He had been lost, bewildered; he had cried a great deal and would sit for hours, his knees hunched up, staring like an old sick monkey at the closed piano. They had found him there one morning huddled up in the chair dead. So had passed away the son of Will's old age and great hopes.

After his death Sally had gone to live with her father and Tom, and then, when war broke out, Cynthia had taken her. Although she was now, at the beginning of 1916, over twelve years of ago, she did not grow. She did not herself mind.

'I'm like my great-grandmother. She didn't grow, but nobody cared.'

She never worried in the least about her own personal appearance, as, in fact, her great-grandmother had done. How many, many times Judith Paris had wished that her legs were longer, but Sally Herries didn't care a damn!

She was, Mary thought, regrettably tomboyish. She didn't care how she looked, how she sat, what clothes she wore. She might be made to look rather striking with her brown hair and pale face. She said she simply could not bother. She was, at her present stage, direct and honest to a terrible degree. Loyal and warm-hearted, if she liked anyone. Unfortunately she did not like Mary nor did Mary like her. Mary considered that Sally was envious of her great beauty and, further, that she was jealous of her because her adored Tom thought Mary a queen and a goddess.

In the first of these there was no truth at all. Sally DID think Mary the most beautiful woman in the world. She also thought her the coldest and most selfish, and for this reason she resented Tom's quite hopeless passion. For Mary would never dream of marrying a poor journalist like Tom. She was extremely ambitious. On the other hand, she was neither so cold nor so hard-hearted as Sally supposed her. The true basic reason for Sally's dislike of Mary, however, was that Mary had no feeling about Vanessa. Vanessa was the principal abiding fact in Sally's life. There never had been, there never would be again, anyone like Sally's mother. Sally was neither sentimental nor gushing, but deep in her nature lived intense emotion. All this, as yet, was given to the memory of her mother. She adored Tom, she liked her father, but they also were part of Vanessa.

Now, for Mary, when someone was dead someone was dead. Moreover, she had not seen Vanessa very often and remembered her only as a large rather calm lady with a broad white forehead and grey hair parted in an old-fashioned way. Also Vanessa had lived with a man not her husband and of this Sally was the result. Mary was conventional. She liked people to do the proper things. So why SHOULD she be passionate about Vanessa? Twice she had spoken rather slightingly to Sally about her mother--only in a joke of course, but Mary's sense of humour was not very delicate. She was neither witty nor quick-witted. Like other beautiful women, her beauty was all she needed.

But, ironically, she had, if she had known it, something of the beauty that Vanessa had had as a young woman. She was tall, dark, full-breasted. She had been told that she carried herself like a queen and never forgot it. It was her tragedy, perhaps, that she was moving into an age when carrying yourself like a queen would be no longer an asset.

Sally knelt on a chair beside Mary and stared, from behind the blind, at a dark and dead London. No light showed anywhere. Only on the horizon there had flashed a sudden finger of light.

'A flame in the sky!' Sally cried.

'It's a searchlight,' said Mary.

Rosalind, a plain-faced, good-natured girl, was seated at the table within the room, knitting. They had all been knitting, making chest-protectors. The Ladies' Committee for which they worked wanted body-belts, Warleigh leggings, gas masks, pneumonia jackets and operation shirts. Sally hated to knit and so did Mary. Rosalind enjoyed it.

'Take care you don't show any light,' she said mildly, for the penalty of failing to conform was actually One Hundred Pounds or six months' imprisonment. People were making blinds from old curtains and women's skirts.

'Oh, that's all right!' Sally came back to the table. 'I suppose I must do my beastly algebra. Oh dear, there's never any peace these days!'

At first the War had been fun, then it had been a bore, now it was rather terrible. Many girls at school had lost their fathers and brothers, and when it came to your best friend (whose name was Charlotte Greene) having to leave because her father was killed and there was no money in the family any more--why, then you positively realized it. Tom had been home on leave twice, and last time he had been pale-faced, nervous and oddly silent. But the worst was Maurice, Alfred's son, who, two nights before he went back, alone with Sally in his father's dining-room had, quite unexpectedly, burst into tears. He had been joking but a moment before.

'I don't want to go back! I don't want to go back!' he had cried.

Sally had plenty of common sense. She never lost her head, but if at that moment it had been suggested that she should return to France instead of Maurice, she would at once have agreed to go.

She stood by the table thinking of her father (so far away in Russia, with only his one arm), of Tom who wrote such splendid letters, of poor Maurice and of Gordon Newmark, who did not seem to mind a bit and had won the DSO. Standing there, thinking, it seemed to Sally as though, across a dark stretch of water, there was a black marshy land and down its length spread a vast scaly dragon, flame issuing from its jaws.

'You funny little thing!' said Mary, who, drawn to her full height, was looking very beautiful in front of the blind. 'What are you thinking about?'

But Sally pushed past her and, on the other side of the blind, stared into the dark. Even as she looked a flame of light shot up into the sky.

'THAT was a flash!' said Maurice Herries.

This was from one of the gas-projectors from the hill behind them. They were hurling opened cylinders of gas on to the enemy position some thousand yards away. Maurice shivered. Time was short. He ordered the morning rum issue to be taken round the platoons. Then suddenly there began a procession of 'whizz-bangs'.

Maurice stood there wishing that he might 'stop one' before he had to go over the top. It was that cold, terrifying moment half an hour before the dawn when everything is clear and unmistakable like hell. 'In another forty minutes I may be dead. In another forty minutes I may be sticking my bayonet into a Boche's belly, deep, deep, as though into butter. In forty minutes I may be mad with pain, my sight gone, my body crippled for life . . .'

Many men did not think of those things. Maurice was a poet. He thought Shakespeare, Blake and Gerard Manley Hopkins the three greatest men in the world. He loathed the mud and the filth and the smells and Berkley Cannon, his best friend, dying in his arms, and he loved the comradeship, the good humour, the courage and friendly simplicity of common men, the moments of ecstasy . . . and he hated this pause before action, hated it as he had never hated anything in his life before.

He wondered whether a Boche attack had forestalled their own. 'Perhaps they have learned our plans and will shatter our huddled groups before we leave our lines.'

Then the flame! It stabbed the sky. First the roar was one blow as on a great sheet of iron, then after a pause another, then a pause again and another. Then one continuous throbbing thunder. The shells screamed and a pillar of fire leaned up the wall of the dim uncertain sky. 'Our barrage,' Maurice thought. 'Zero hour.'

Maurice shouted to his little group, they jumped out of the trench and stumbled forward. Now came the moment that he always dreaded, when the group broke and one straggled forward singly, one little mannikin in a world of malignant danger. Through the noise as of cannon-balls rolling down sheets of iron, there was the phut! phut! of rifle bullets. And there to the right are heads of Boches in a shell hole shooting. Trotter, a giant of a man, one of the jolliest, most carefree and kindest, staggers, seems to leap on his feet, crashes down. 'No, there is no chance for us tumbling through this mud with these fellows shooting at us,' and he and Conklin, Bush and two others have slithered down into a shell hole and are firing over the top of it. Conklin's face is smashed in. We have got two of the Boches but more are running up. The sky is lightening, and the roar of the guns, and now the German guns, thunders on-- but by this time it is familiar, belonging to a world that one knows, that is part of one, that is almost friendly.

Then Maurice 'stopped one'. There was an impact on his right shoulder as though a big stone had hit him. No pain. He slipped down into the bottom of the shell hole and, staring upwards, was aware now that the sky was much lighter and, to his great surprise, that he was alone there except for Conklin who, his smashed face in the mud, huddled at his feet. His shoulder, his arm, his hand were soaking wet, but still there was no pain. He did not want to move. He was quite happy. A faint, a very faint blue was stealing into the sky, and some small clouds, like rosy petals, seemed to his eye to be dancing, gently and carefully, against the blue.

The thundering noise withdrew, and in front of his eyes, which he soon must close, a small and delicate flame wavered. The flame of the candle that Sally had lit! He smiled. He would write a poem about it, this small candleflame that neither the wind of the great guns nor the delicate fleeciness of the morning clouds could put out. Pity that his father hated him to write poetry, thought all books a mistake, wanted him to add up sums in the City. He would never add up sums, but he would write poems to the glory of England as Rupert Brooke had done, or about old ships like Flecker . . . He would carry on the glory of the Family, would go and live in Cumberland, near the sea, in the valleys of which old Benjie Herries had told him. A face bent close to his. Someone moved him and a flame of pain licked his heart. He cried out and the flame moved up, spreading, glorious, golden, blotting out, with its light, the whole world. There were two flames . . .

The two flames burnt steadily, illuminating the mirror, lighting the dressing-table, the pictures on the walls, of 'Queen Victoria receiving the News of her Accession' and 'Dignity and Impudence', the narrow bed and the small shining table beside it.

'The electric light's fused,' said Gordon Newmark, looking in at the door.

'I know,' said Tom. 'I've found some candles.' He sat in front of the mirror, brushing his hair with his two old battered silver brushes.

'Hurry up, you blighter,' Gordon said.

'All right. I won't be a minute.'

Gordon Newmark was broad and tall and the pink of self-confidence. Tom seemed gentle, small, submissive beside him. Tom was thirty-two and Gordon twenty-one, but Gordon had won the DSO, loved the War--'best time I'm ever likely to have, old boy'--and was home now on leave as a kind of conqueror, patronizing, in a jolly friendly way, all the family, especially his old father and mother and his sister Ada, who all adored him. He was, if he had known it, the recurrent Herries type, the type of old Pomfret, of Prosper-- Jennifer's father, of Rodney--Cynthia's grandfather, and especially of Walter--Tom's great-grandfather. But he didn't know it. He didn't care. He was the triumphant, riding, roughshod, bullying Herries. But the type had softened, emasculated a bit. He thought old Benjie a dissolute old rogue and Tom a 'soft 'un' and Maurice Herries 'a decent sort of ass who writes poems'; his type was as far from the other as ever, in the family history, it had been, but the two did not quarrel any more. Life was beginning to move too swiftly; you had too much to do to bother about quarrels. The Herries didn't fight any more. But Gordon felt, all the same, a sort of friendly scorn as he saw Tom struggling into his clothes. Under the light of the candles Tom's face was serious, care-worn, too kindly to be aggressive. 'That's all he'll ever be,' Gordon thought, 'a sort of second-rate journalist. Thinks too much about other people. Almost a woman--about his old father, his kid sister, his father's mistress who died. I'd worry!' thought Gordon, who hoped that night to pick up a pretty girl somewhere . . . you needn't be too particular these days when you'd be returning in a week's time to be killed maybe . . . But Tom didn't want a girl. He was sweet on Mary Worcester. Poor old Tom! He hadn't a dog's chance with that beautiful swollen-headed female!

Tom blew out the candles. They groped their way down the dark staircase. Tom still stuck to the rooms in Tite Street. In the dark King's Road they found a taxi, and through a town of pitch they plunged until the friendly arms of the Carlton Grill received them. Then they went to the Alhambra to see The Bing Boys for the twentieth time, sang If you were the only girl in the world with other of their slightly intoxicated fellows and roared at George Robey whenever he lifted his eyebrows.

Afterwards they found a dingy door in Soho and behind it a yet dingier nightclub known as 'The Five Pennies'. Tom had not wanted to go. 'Leave' was offering no attractions. He wanted to be back in France, although he didn't like that either. Mary tortured him. She liked him, he thought. Sometimes he fancied that she more than liked him, but he knew in his heart that he had no chance with her, and knowing it loved her only the more desperately. He had loved her always. He was chaste, having had no sexual experience whatever, and this chastity seemed, just now, to separate him from everybody. Men, all men, seemed to be caught into a passionate longing for sexual intercourse--any intercourse with anyone . . . It was a hunger, the only solace for the filth, the fear, the cold, the wounds, the long drawn-out tension of this fantastic trial. And he? He thought always of Vanessa and of Mary. Of his father and Sally and his friends as well, but Vanessa and Mary were always with him, one of the kindest, gentlest, most understanding of mothers, the other the loveliest, divinest of goddesses. And he could touch neither: one was a ghost, the other a dream . . .

As he sat in the small, fearfully hot and indecently smelling room of 'The Five Pennies' he screwed his courage to the sticking point. His life seemed just now to be running on hard lines, but it was worse for others. Worse for poor Maurice, for instance, who had lost his arm, worse for hundreds, for thousands of fine men. He would stick it, but he wished that he had Gordon's hardy indifference--Gordon who was, at this moment, talking to two women with a carefree gaiety that made him seem the only really happy person in the room. A girl came and sat beside Tom. He ordered her a drink; drink was being served in coffee cups. He watched Gordon a little anxiously. He knew that these places just now were haunted by 'crows', women who made their men friends drunk, took them on somewhere and robbed them of everything they had. But Gordon was no fool. He knew a thing or two.

The girl at Tom's table was tired. She complained, through the raucous jazz music, in a weary little voice, of the violence and callousness of men. Men didn't seem to care. They weren't kind any more. Generous, yes, but not kind. Life wasn't really gay although everyone pretended that it was. Food was awful. Why, fancy, eggs were a luxury food. Fancy eggs being a luxury! Butter was half a crown a pound and a chicken cost thirteen bob! Why, fancy a chicken costing . . . So she went on, repeating everything twice.

Suddenly, into the middle of the jazz, the laughter, the movement of the dancers, a voice broke. A tall swaying officer had pushed into the middle of the floor, he was brushing the dancers aside. He was drunk, of course. And he cried out in a shrill scream:

'Blast this bloody war! To hell with it! Blast this bloody war! To hell with the bloody war! To hell . . .'

767

Two waiters caught hold of him and led him away. People laughed.

'You see,' said the girl. 'That's just what I say. What I mean to say is that nobody really enjoys things much. And they aren't kind any more. If you were a woman you'd agree with me. And the women aren't kind either. What I mean to say is, it's affected everybody, and how we're ever to get back to the way we were--'

'We'll never get back,' said Tom.

He was watching a man near him who held up, with a rather unsteady hand, a lighter. He pushed at his cigarette with it. The little flame burnt bravely, with a fine uprightness. Then it went out.

KALEIDOSCOPE

II TRIUMPHAL ARCH

In the early days of 1917 Sally Herries had a strange experience. It was at Cynthia's house in Eaton Place.

Altogether life was strange at this time, strange and yet familiar. Sally was over thirteen years of age, went to school every day, did on the whole what she was told, was calm and quiet and collected, but suffered, at unexpected moments, extraordinary and poignant longings for her mother--also, but less poignantly, for her father and for Tom.

She had only a few friends, but in this dark uncertain world that now surrounded everyone friendships were not important. Some of the girls at school she liked, but they had all now their own especial interests-- the ways in which they were helping the War, brothers, fathers at the Front, food that had become important because it was rationed, the personal experiences of air raids or the second-hand experiences of emotionalists, rumour and story and gossip; it seemed that all these things kept one apart from the ordinary relationships of ordinary life. Sally did not care. At Eaton Place she was quite alone. Mary and Rosalind were too old, Peile a silly (but kindly) old man, Cynthia infinitely distant.

But HOW fantastic a world it was! That moment after dusk when all the world was dark, the first experience of an air raid with the alarm, the silence, the distant firing, the expectancy (not at all frightening--pleasurable, like being at the theatre just before the curtain went up), the rumours, the stories that people told, the anxieties about Tom, about Gordon, the many women wearing black, the tales that reached even her ears of the funny ways that soldiers and their girlfriends had in places like Trafalgar Square after dark . . .

She was aware that her family were behaving very finely. She herself caught some of the family pride. It was really true, she felt, that but for her family England and the War would be lost. When she went to other people's houses--the houses of the parents of her friends--she heard many very despairing remarks. It would make no difference, they said, that America had severed diplomatic relations with Germany. America would not be able to be in time, we would all be defeated before America could do anything. Someone told a story about going into a tear-shell factory and weeping tears enough to fill a jug. People recounted horrible details of wounds and suffering and lonely agonies. Sally tried not to listen but she HAD to . . . Her imagination was vivid. She saw these dreadful things as though they were happening in front of her. She grew older very quickly. People said that we were bound to be beaten. All the glory was gone. We were led by idiotic Generals, our politicians were impossible fools. People said that it would be better if we made terms with the Germans. Let THEM have the glory!

'Oh no!' Sally cried out in the house of kind Mrs Mickleham, the mother of Connie Mickleham who was so clever at algebra. 'That would be wicked!' And for once she burst into tears and ran from the room.

But INSIDE the family it was ALL quite different. No one dreamt of anything but complete victory. We would go on for ever and ever but victory must certainly be ours.

It was now that the Herries were seen at their very best. Their normality, their common sense, the absence of GRAB in their natures, their non-property qualities, so to speak, their courage, their indifference to facts that they refused to realize, enabled them to become completely patriotic. They loved their country because their country depended on them and while THEY were there all must be well.

Maurice came home without an arm and sat, with a white face, staring into distance. They were sorry for him but disregarded him. Gordon came home, filled with the War. It was glorious. When the Americans came in we would soon sweep the dirty Boche back to Berlin. He had extraordinary stories about the dirtiness of the Boche, his meanness, cruelty, cowardice and savagery. The Herries on one side, the Germans on the other. Who could doubt of the result?

It was on one March evening that Sally had her funny little adventure.

She had been doing her schoolwork in her cold little room at the top of the house and remembered that her geography book was in the dining-room. She came downstairs for it. The house was still and plunged into that eerie dusk that seemed now to be always the atmosphere of rooms and passages. She reached the hall that had only a light at the farthest end, near the kitchen stairs. She walked forward to the dining-room door and saw that a man was hiding, close up against the wall, behind the umbrella stand. He was a little man with spectacles, a rather dirty face, and he was in uniform.

As she saw him he whispered, but without moving from the wall to which he seemed to be fastened, 'If yer say a word I'll throttle yer.'

It was all part of the general strangeness, the half-light, the silent streets, the sense of the War, prowling like a large cat almost at one's very door, of Benjie somewhere in Russia, of Tom underground in France eating plum and apple jam to the light of a single candle, of that man weeping a bucket of tears in the factory, of Maurice without an arm, that this little man should be pinned against the wall of the house in Eaton Place.

She saw that he was very frightened and she wanted to give him something. She gave him half a crown that she was saving to buy something for Tom with.

He said 'Gawd bless yer, miss', and in another moment had opened the hall door and slipped away, letting into the house a blast of cold biting air before the door closed. She stood there wondering. What had he wanted? Had he come to steal? He looked very unhappy. He was a piece of the War. She had encountered the War. She continued quickly to grow up.

Her father, crossing a small snow-covered square in Petrograd, heard a strange sound. He was walking with a little black-bearded Jew, Konrad Mathias. Mathias had just said: 'It is between personality and non-personality. Everything comes down to that. Am I, Konrad Mathias, an individual with a history, an important history like no one else's, or am I a little gas, a little acid, a little water, dissipated at the prick of a pin? . . . Do you see? Am I Konrad Mathias? Am I? Am I?'

'I should think you probably are,' Benjie had said, looking at a church dome, a brilliant green against the burning blue of the sky. The snow sparkled at his feet. 'I like this,' he said. 'The green, the blue, the sparkling snow. It stirs me--not the acid and water in me, I think. Or is it?'

'No, no!' Little Mathias, in his black woolly fur cap, jumped on the snow.

'Well, I don't know,' Benjie said. 'The individual can't be very important. If the world goes topsy-turvy the individual starves and is very quickly gas and water again. There's a revolution in South America and Mr Smith in London loses his job. His child dies because it hasn't enough nourishment. It's the revolution that matters. Certainly not Mr Smith.'

'Oh, you're wrong,' Mathias cried. 'What if he does lose his job? He's losing it or gaining it all the time. Everyone in a lifetime meets his personal crisis whether there's a revolution or not. Birth, love, death, economic struggle, falling out of love with one's wife, seeing a pretty girl round the corner, having a suspicion there's a God, then deciding there isn't. Always the same crisis turning up for everybody. The hoops of the circus--you must jump through them. That's fate. The way you

jump. That's free will and is the only thing that matters. It's the individual who is always different. How will you meet this? A toothache, syphilis, cancer, a sudden bit of success. That's history.'

'Then you believe in God?'

'Of course I do. Only He doesn't interfere. He sets the scene. You play your part. I've been about the world a lot. It's everywhere the same. Are you a realist or a romantic? If you're the first it will be the dates, the scientific facts, the large movements, the cold truth that will seem to you to be important. If you're the second it will be the things behind the facts--what each man does with his soul.'

'You think man has a soul?'

'A spiritual life? Of course. It's the only thing that squares the facts.'

'Is there a life after death, do you think?' Benjie asked more eagerly than he had intended.

'Life? Death? There's always death. Every man is living and dying all the time. But PHYSICAL death--that's not important. Men are so thoughtless. And they worry about the wrong things.'

'So you think the old world is finished?'

'Of course it is. And the new one will take a long while settling itself. But that doesn't matter. Men will have their personal histories just the same. Why, take myself! I'm fifty-five--a Jew of no importance whatever. But I was afraid for years, afraid of everything and everyone. Thought people despised me. And I was greedy too. Now I'm not often afraid and not greedy. That's more important than a revolution. Not because I am important, mind you-- no more and no less than the next man--but it's important to God that I should get a move on. More important than that Napoleon should win Austerlitz or Rasputin be murdered.'

'But Rasputin's death has affected millions.'

'No. Only provided situations for men to meet. They'd meet them in one fashion or another in any case.'

It was then that Benjie heard the noise. It was like the sharp cracking of twigs. The scene was very peaceful. At the end of the square was the canal and along the side of it a cab was slowly crawling, the isvostchik, in his fat clothes, bunched up on the seat. Some birds flew slowly across the blue. Some church bells were ringing. It was about three in the afternoon.

A moment later it was as though the blue sky had burst and poured confusion on to the earth. Down the path by the canal a mob of people, shouting, crying, came pouring, and on to the square from the other end rolled a lorry, piled high with soldiers, bristling with rifles. The lorry stayed still. A man came running from the canal. He ran a little way into the square, outlined very sharply against the snow. He stopped and looked back at the people. Then from the lorry there came a noise like the clearing of a throat, and the man ran a step, stood, crumpled at the knees, fell, raised himself, fell flat, wriggled like a worm and lay still.

Benjie had known many bad moments in his life but none so bad as this one--for there he was, isolated, alone in all that gleaming, glittering colour. He must run for miles, it seemed, before he could reach security. But Mathias was already running. An absurd notion came to Benjie that it would be undignified to run. He walked slowly, his hand in his pocket. But now many people were running into the square, and as they did so a red light rose like a fan above the houses and spread into the blue.

He walked slowly and as he went repeated to himself like a man in a dream, aloud: 'This is Revolution. This is Revolution.' Then he saw the square flooded with people. They were shouting: 'To the Nevski!' 'No, no, to the Duma!'

He was carried with the crowd . . .

And it was now September. Tom on leave, walking down Piccadilly, heard the air-raid warning. Instinctively he hurried his step and then slowed down again. For what did it matter?

He had come from half an hour with the lovely Mary. On his way there he had thought: 'Well, now, tonight I'll ask her. She will be sorry for me, perhaps, moved because next week I return to France. She will think "Oh, poor boy". And she will be kind.' As he had walked towards Eaton Place his love--that had been part of him for so long now, that had gained so terribly in intensity out there where every homeward vision shone with a mystical light--his love had dried and constricted his heart so that it was a shrivelling little ball in his body. Away, beyond the houses, not far distant, somewhere hanging in the pale September sky was his hope. He would say:

'Mary, I have loved you so long. Let me go back with just this to remember! I may not return. Be kind to me.' A weak, cowardly sort of prayer, but he was beyond all pride now. He wanted her so. His thoughts were lascivious and pure, of the body and the soul, all things together. Oh! if she would only be kind!

And she had been kind--kind and abstracted. Her eyes had rested on him without seeing him, and then she had been suddenly aware that she must do something about this poor man who had loved her since she was a child and was so good and patient and so tiresome. And next week he would return to France and would suffer horrors, perhaps, would be frightened and tired and lonely.

Comprehension came into her eyes. She saw Tom. She wanted to be good to him. She asked him questions about the Front.

But he knew that it was only kindness. He refused a second cup of tea and went.

So he did not mind now if there were an air raid. The omnibuses seemed to hasten, and soon, as he neared the Circus, the streets were quite empty. This was the week when there were almost daily air raids. They said that people's nerves were beginning to go, and Tom remembered how a friend had told him that, two nights ago, he had walked down a street in Pimlico during a raid and that it had been naked, empty, shining, but that behind every window people were playing pianos.

No pianos here. Nothing but the Circus, bare as though set for a scene in a theatre. The firing came nearer and flashes lit the sky. Light hit the Circus and sprang away. But nothing happened. The all-clear sounded. He went on a bus back to Chelsea.

During the remaining days of his leave he found that he could endure no one but Sally. For the first time he was afraid that his nerve was breaking. He was so TIRED of it--sick to death of it all, he was. And worst was the chatter. He lunched with Alfred and listened to Gordon. He lunched with Cynthia and listened to poor old Peile. He heard that Sir Henry Wilson was sold to the French, that £100,000,000 had been spent on gas, that German cruisers were lying off Harwich, that . . . Oh, what did it matter? Everything was unreal now. Life itself was unreal, the physical processes of the body, the putting on of a collar, brushing one's teeth . . .

He went to entertainments, heard Beecham conduct Figaro, saw a farce, was made miserable by a musical comedy. All these were unreal.

But Sally was real. He had always loved her with that patient, unchanging, unfaltering devotion that was so especially his. He delighted in the growth that he saw in her. Although she was so young she had great common sense, courage and much humour. And, in one way or another, she constantly reminded him of Vanessa. She had Vanessa's integrity.

On the last evening before his return they talked.

'I wish I was going with you, Tom,' Sally said.

'Do you?' he laughed. 'You wouldn't like it.'

'No, of course I shouldn't. The girls at school all wanted to go once, were dying for the time when they'd be grown up enough to be nurses or something, but now they're not so keen. I don't want to go for any adventurous reason. Only to help.'

'You do help,' he said, 'by staying quietly here and being good-humoured and patient.'

'How long do you think it will last, Tom?'

'Oh, I don't know.' He was holding her small but strong hand in his. 'I've given up prophesying.'

'Do you think that after all we may be beaten?' Her voice sank into an awed whisper.

'No. The Germans won't last as long as we will--not now the Americans have come in.'

'Yes--but the Russians won't fight any more now, will they?' She seemed to be looking into great distances. 'I wonder how Daddy is?'

'Oh, he'll be all right wherever he is,' said Tom.

'When I grow up I hope I shan't forget all I feel now. Don't you, Tom? It would be awful if when we're older we all forgot how horrid it all is and let there be another war.'

She sat on the edge of his chair and put her arms round his neck.

She produced a present, a scarf that she had knitted.

'It isn't very good. I'm not clever with my fingers and, to tell you the truth, I'd have hated the bother if it had been for anyone else.'

So he went back again, trying not to think of Mary. But he didn't think of anyone much. He was terribly tired, not in the body but in the head. And he dreaded the noise. It would be almost better to be dead, because then at least there would be quiet.

And Maurice, the son of Alfred, the son of Amery (thin-legged, dyspeptic, high-stocked, over-large Adam's apple), the son of Durward (of Rocklington Hall; stout, plethoric, fine calves), the son of Pelham (stubborn, hot-tempered), the son of Grandison (exceedingly stout, dewlapped like a bull, intimate with St John), son of Robert (stout, good-natured sot, gambler and humorist, a friend of Charles II), son of Robert who first brought distinction on the family by breeding bullocks in Wiltshire and marrying a Scottish heiress--(he was son of the Herries who came to watch German miners in Borrowdale in his Queen's service, that cross- grained bitter fellow whose portrait hung in the Herries house in Rosthwaite and later at the Fortress)--well, what of Maurice?

Not very much. 'A poor reward for all the trouble I've taken,' his father would think, looking at him. 'What if he HAS lost an arm? So have lots of other fellows, and worse, blinded, tubes in their stomach, mice in the brain--and there he sits, doing nothing but stare or read or listen to high-class music on the gramophone. Can hardly believe he's my son. Rotten pessimist too. No patriotism. I believe he likes the Germans better than the English.'

So Alfred told him one day at lunch:

'My God, Maurice, I believe you'd rather be a German than an Englishman.'

Maurice gave him a queer look.

'I'd rather be anything than a Herries,' he said.

For by this time in the spring of 1918 he was very, very tired of his family. It was May and the Billing-Maud Allan case was amusing everyone at the Courts. That the case was poisonously hysterical startled nobody. The Family--Alfred, Gordon, Cynthia--alluded darkly to perversion. 'We must sweep these abnormalities from our national life,' wheezed old Horace. 'It's a splendid thing for England that this cancer should be revealed.' But he confided privately to Maurice: 'I know what you're feeling, my boy. To tell you the truth,

I'm not as optimistic as I used to be. But one has to put a brave face on things.'

'Why?' asked Maurice.

Horace didn't exactly know. He supposed that he had always been determined to see the bright side of things. All his life it had been the same. After all it wasn't life that was important but the way that you dealt with it. Some writer had said that somewhere, and he thought that it was very true. He wheezed in his chair (his heart was bad) and looked bravely, through rheumy eyes, into Maurice's face.

'I've been laughed at all my life,' he said. 'I've wanted people to like me and they've only laughed at me. I've thought I've done my best, but I can see now that I've failed. My sister went on the streets and died there, and everyone's found me a bore.' He sat there; a thick heavy tear trickled on to his fat cheek and stayed there. He brushed it away.

'All the same,' he said, 'even if I've made a mess of things, what I say is true all the same. It's better to be cheerful and it needs a lot of obstinacy. Cheer up, Maurice. You might have lost both your legs, you know.'

But Maurice couldn't cheer up. His father, his sister, all the Herries save little Sally, drove him mad. He thought perhaps that he was going mad. There were times when the guns sounded so loudly in his ears that he could hear nothing else. He would sit in his bedroom and try to read Joyce or T. S. Eliot or D. H. Lawrence. Beautiful, wonderful things their books had in them. They told the truth at last. For centuries writers had been lying about life, but now no honest writer need ever deceive again. Lawrence seemed to him a kind of young god, fighting all the hypocrisies, the prejudices, the falsities of mankind, and fighting all alone, his back to the wall. He had been persecuted by the damned interfering authorities simply because he protested against this bloody war. And then, when Maurice thought of the authorities (he saw them as a fat, red-tabbed crimson-faced officer screaming at some trembling private . . .), he would get up and walk about his room, and the stump of his arm would ache and the guns would sound in his ears and strange fierce lights would flash over the dressing-table and crimson the eiderdown on his bed.

There came a night when he thought that he would end it. He woke at an early hour of grey dawn and a voice said, quite clearly, in his ear: 'Come on. Put an end to this. You've had enough of it. You're never going to be any good at anything. Never. Life is endless.'

So, as though obedient to a command, he got out of bed and wondered what he would do. Should he go down to the kitchen and turn on the gas? That seemed a long business and would need a lot of arranging. He had a penknife. Should he cut an artery? A messy affair. Should he throw himself from his bedroom window? That might not finish him. He walked up and down, followed, it seemed to him, by this persuasive voice.

'Go on, you're no good. You're spoilt and finished. Better get out of it . . .'

At last he sat down in the chair by the ash-strewn fire and burst into tears. He cried and cried as though he never would stop. Then he fell asleep in the chair where he was.

A poor affair. Nothing fine about it anywhere. He had a job those last months in the Ministry of Information and so he walked, alone and unattended save by his private demon, from one place to another . . .

About half past ten on Monday morning, November 11th, Benjie went into Hatchard's bookshop. While waiting there he was accosted by a stout pale-faced gentleman who said to him: 'I say--the Armistice is signed.'

'Oh, is it?' said Benjie, bought his book and walked into Piccadilly. There was no sign anywhere of excitement--the buses rolled along, people passed on their business, a young man stood with his eyes seriously fixed on Mr Jackson's appetizing window.

Benjie had moved from Chelsea after his return from Russia and had rooms now in Ryder Street. As he was about to turn into Jermyn Street he spoke to an old man with newspapers.

'Is it true,' he asked, 'that the Armistice is signed?'

'Can't say, sir, I'm sure,' the old man answered, rubbing his nose with the back of his hand.

'Very strange,' Benjie thought. 'This is the moment for which we have all been passionately waiting and no one cares, no one cares at all.'

Entering his flat he saw Sally and Tom sitting together on the sofa.

'Hullo!' he said. 'What are you two doing here?'

'Tom found me in Piccadilly,' Sally explained.

'Why aren't you at school?'

'There's mumps. We were all sent off this morning.' Then she added: 'Tom says the Armistice is signed.'

The valet of the flats came out of Benjie's bedroom with a suit over his arm.

'Bailey,' Benjie said, 'the Armistice is signed.'

'Indeed, sir,' said Bailey. 'I'm very glad, I'm sure. A great relief to everyone. Will you be in to luncheon?'

'Yes--no. Look here, we'll go and celebrate somewhere.'

He looked at both of them.

'Are you sure it's true?' he asked Tom.

'Oh yes--quite sure. The paper had it in an hour ago.'

'This is all wrong,' Benjie thought. He went to the window and glanced down into Ryder Street. No one was stirring.

He looked back at them. 'One day in Russia,' he said, 'about a week after the March Revolution, I got caught in the crowd. We all marched singing through the streets. Everybody was singing. It was the most marvellous thing . . . Well, why aren't we singing? The greatest and most horrible war in history is over.'

'I suppose we can't realize it,' said Tom. 'And we're all rather tired.'

'Yes, we're all rather tired,' Benjie thought, 'and we're going to be tired for years and years. Perhaps nobody will have the energy to sing again.'

'All the same,' he added aloud, 'it's something that men aren't going to be killed any more. That's something.'

At that moment they heard the maroons going off and the silver clock on the mantelpiece struck in its thin surprised tone eleven o'clock. They all went to the window and saw people pouring into the street. From every door they seemed to be coming. Men, without hats, rushed out, waving their arms. Flinging the window open, Benjie could hear distant shouting.

'Come on,' he said. 'Let's go out and see the sights.'

After that they were part of a vast, wild, cheering and yet oddly unexcited crowd. That at least was what Benjie felt, as though all these people said to him with one voice (not a loud voice--almost a whisper): 'It is right for us to be excited. We've won a great war, but life is changed. We can never be quite so light-hearted and careless again. Once, not so very long ago, on Mafeking night, we all went mad. But we shan't go mad now. We have to behave as though we were gloriously happy. But we are not. By tonight we may be drunk a little and make a noise, but it doesn't mean anything.'

Nevertheless, with Sally close at his side, he could not but feel that something was accomplished. Another phase of history, another phase of his own life, was closed. His adventurous days were over and so too, maybe, were the adventurous days of the world. It would be all cold mechanism now--mechanism, science, a remorseless progress.

He had a sudden longing for Vanessa and at that same moment Sally said: 'How I wish that Mother was here!' He pressed her arm close to him. So long as Sally was alive things would not be mechanical. She was too individual for that.

They had pushed their way to Trafalgar Square, but here they were brought to a standstill. A thick unbroken mass of humanity. Men were shouting and singing, girls waving. But Benjie felt that everyone was waiting for something. That moment of singing in Petrograd would not be recovered here. It would never be recovered. It had been a moment of extravagant idealistic hope.

'There should be a Triumphal Arch,' he thought. 'Here in front of the lions. And everyone should march away under it, swearing as they passed beneath it that never again would men hate, plunder, be greedy . . . Never again!' He smiled. Not bad nonsense for an old cynic like himself. That was the sort of thing that old

Horace would say. Alfred and Gordon and the others would have a fine time tonight. They at least would be happy, for they had won the War and were Lords of the Earth.

But not perhaps for long. The battle was not over yet between the Maurices and the Gordons, the Cynthias and the Vanessas.

'Come on,' he said. 'We'll go to the Berkeley and have a feed.'

A thin rain had begun to fall. There was no Triumphal Arch. As they pushed their way slowly Benjie saw a soldier, motionless, staring, unshifted by the crowd. 'Perhaps he's thinking that now he won't be killed. He won't have to go back to that hell. That's something anyway.'

He thought constantly of Vanessa. If she were here how happy she would be that he was safe now, and that Tom was safe. She would be happy for all the women all over the world.

All the women! Yes, that was something.

But there was no Triumphal Arch.

SALLY AND TOM

Cynthia gave Gordon Newmark a theatre party on his thirtieth birthday (he was thirty on February 4th, 1925) and Sally and old Horace Ormerod and Rosalind and Adrian came too. Cynthia (who was now over sixty, although you would never think it unless you looked at her neck), had a weakness for Gordon and hoped that, with judicious management, he might be induced to marry her daughter Rosalind. Rosalind was a good girl, had the best character in the world, and, although she was on the plain side and was now over thirty, would make a good wife for Gordon. Gordon once might have married her, for he was just the kind of man to appreciate good solid wearing qualities in a wife, but after the deaths of old Sidney and Mary Newmark (they died within a week or two of one another) it was discovered that their children, Gordon and Ada, would have large fortunes. Gordon was, of course, in his grandfather's business but made his headquarters in London. He was of another generation from old Horace Newmark, who thought that there was no city in the world to equal Manchester. Gordon was good-looking, with clear-cut features (a little too clear-cut perhaps) and that fashion that cropped up again and again in Herries businessmen of wearing clothes that looked too immaculate to be human. He was an agreeable well-mannered fellow, proud of his own looks, his D S O, his business ability, his family and his 'I like a man with no nonsense about him'--one of his favourite sayings. He intended a little later to go into politics and he would have a peerage before he finished. But first he must marry, and Cynthia hoped that in spite of his money, his profile and his self-confidence he might marry Rosalind.

For alas, neither Mary nor Rosalind was yet married. It was too extraordinary! Mary was still lovely, but for some reason young men didn't propose to her. They came up to her, looked at her with wonder in their eyes and went away again. The fact was that, thirty years earlier, when Vanessa ruled Hill Street, Mary would have been exactly what everyone wanted--beautiful, dignified, graceful, and not too clever. Now the young men (who after all had served their country) wanted something more lively.

So Cynthia had her troubles. Peile was aged and, although his figure was still good, this new post-War world appeared to have struck him dumb with amazement. It had been, at one time, the middle classes that had seemed to him astonishing. He had appealed to his Herries relations to save the country. But the job had been, it seemed, altogether too much for his relatives. So now, standing on his thin aristocratic legs, looking at the Income Tax and the closing of the great houses of England and the young women who looked like boys and the young men who looked like girls, he could only stare and stutter and gasp.

So he was not of very much use to Cynthia, who, from the house in Eaton Place, did what she could, looking now like a rather pretty little pig, with her hair a little too yellow, her cheeks a little too pink, her skirts a little too short, and her neck (in spite of all she could do) a little too wrinkled.

She had invited Sally to the theatre party because she had invited old Horace. She had had no intention of asking Horace, but one afternoon when he had called on her and had sat there looking so old and pathetic, her heart (which was still kindly when she gave it an opportunity) was moved to say: 'Well, Horace, you must come to the theatre with us. Come next week. We are going to that play that everyone is talking about--by a new young man whose name I forget. They say he's extraordinarily clever and only left school last year.' Horace, who was now nearing seventy, had purple streaks on either side of his nose, an unwieldy stomach, and a cheery smile that was habit rather than intention (and so seemed to Cynthia terribly pathetic), said eagerly that he'd love to come. He was free practically any night next week.

('What a bore!' thought Cynthia. 'Whatever did I ask him for?')

Having done so she must also invite Sally, for the strange thing was (one of the many strange things about Sally) that she was attached to Horace; she was kind to him and never showed him that sharp tongue and penetrating criticism only too apparent with others. Sally would look after Horace. It was a pity that Gordon did not like Sally. That, however, would throw Gordon all the more into Rosalind's company, and she, Cynthia, could be amused by Adrian, who was elegant, witty, drily cynical, and knew the private behaviour of everyone.

So they went to The Vortex. They met at the theatre because the play began early, and instead of dinner before they would have supper at the Savoy Grill afterwards. Sally was the first to arrive and Gordon the second. Each was annoyed at seeing the other.

'Who else is coming?' asked Gordon.

'Horace.'

'Horace? Oh Lord, what a bore!'

'Why?' said Sally.

'Oh, well, he's a bit comic,' said Gordon.

'Comic?' said Sally. 'So's everyone. I am--you are.'

Gordon said nothing but he was greatly annoyed. HE comic? You might call him anything you like--everyone with personality has detractors--but comic? He looked at Sally with great distaste. Her hair, which had now lost its carroty shade and was a plain dark brown, was bobbed in the new fashion. With a few more inches and a little more colour she would not have been so bad. She was slim, her eyes and mouth were bright, alive--too alive, perhaps, for he hated young girls to look sarcastic. She was unlike other girls and that he also disliked. The height of good form, he thought, was that you should not attract attention in a crowd. Of course if you were a BEAUTIFUL woman, that was another matter. No one could call Sally Herries beautiful, and there she was, thinking no end of herself, secretary to some old Jew (she worked because she liked it, not because she had to), living in the most independent manner with another girl, illegitimate (although of course in these days no one minded that) and, worst of all, Benjie Herries' daughter. Now that Gordon considered himself the head of the Herries family and responsible for its good behaviour, he greatly regretted Benjie, who, in spite of his being seventy and having only one arm, often behaved outrageously and had some dreadful friends.

So Gordon ('Who IS that handsome man?' someone, standing near him in the foyer, asked her companion. 'What splendid features! He looks like an actor.') and Sally stood there disliking one another exceedingly. The others arrived and they all went in. Soon the curtain went up, and the young author of the play, himself playing the lead, began to tell the other characters exactly what he thought of them.

Cynthia, as she listened, became more and more uncomfortable. What a VERY queer collection of people! The mother, with her cropped hair, her painted face, her passion for cigarettes and cocktails, was of course nothing like Cynthia, and it made it all the queerer that the part should be acted by nice Miss Lilian Braithwaite, whom Cynthia knew well, a charming woman with nothing very modern about her. No, the mother on the stage was nothing like Cynthia, who was received everywhere, and by the young people especially, with the greatest warmth. She so often said: 'I don't feel a day more than thirty', and it was true, she did not, unless her neuritis bothered, or chance had forced upon her a succession of late nights. No, she did not resemble this woman in any way nor did any of the friends of Mary or Rosalind resemble the girl with the Eton crop, played by Miss Molly Kerr, or the dreadful young man whom Noel Coward presented so vigorously. When the curtain went down she turned to Adrian.

'Well I never--what an extraordinary lot of people!'

Adrian, whose eyelids were always a little weary like Mr Pater's Monna Lisa's, said: 'Oh, do you think so? There are lots like them nowadays!'

'Surely not!'

He waited a little. Then he said:

'When I see this sort of thing, I think of Vanessa. I never forget her as I saw her first at a ball. She was dressed in white, with her dark hair piled on the top of her head. I have never seen anything so beautiful before or since.'

'Poor Vanessa!' said Cynthia. 'How terrible she would think all of this!'

'Not at all,' Adrian said sharply. 'She was too simple to be frightened off by external differences. She would be shy, of course, and think that she was being stupid, but she would make friends with that boy and girl in no time. There's been nobody like her since she died.'

'Oh, do you think so? Well, if you come to that, nobody's like anybody, are they? But I can't agree with you, Adrian. Vanessa would be miserable in a world like this. She wouldn't know how to adapt herself.'

'She wouldn't try to,' said Adrian rather crossly. 'She'd just be natural. Of course some people would find her dull. Some people always did. But others--she'd be just what they are always looking for now and can't find.'

('Adrian's getting a bore,' Cynthia thought. 'And old--a fussy old Foreign Office bachelor.')

Sally took Horace for a stroll.

'Are you enjoying yourself, Horace dear?' she asked him.

'Oh, I should just think I am!' he answered her in his full philanthropic voice. 'I enjoy everything. When you get to my age, my dear, you'll realize how true it is what Stevenson once said: "We all ought to be as happy as kings."'

'Your tie's up at the back of your collar,' Sally said critically. 'What a whacking lie if Stevenson ever did say that. And you know you don't mean it, Horace. Even though you've been pretending to be jolly all your life you needn't pretend it now with me.'

'But I AM enjoying the play,' he said a little sheepishly. 'I don't go so often to the theatre nowadays, you know. I like a jaunt. I'm a lonely old widower and a bit of fun does me good.'

774

Behind his red cheeks and large round glasses and protruding chin there was fear: fear of illness, fear of being laughed at, fear of solitude at the last and, above all, fear of being left behind. Sally knew that it was true, that the world found Horace a dreadful bore, that men at the Club slipped away as he approached, that young men laughed at him and that all his relations despised him. She was fond of him because she knew all these things.

'Lonely! Of course you're not!' she said cheerfully. 'Look here, come and have tea with Margaret and me tomorrow afternoon. I've got an afternoon off. My old Jew's going down to Brighton.'

'Oh, thank you, my dear.' Horace's glasses beamed. 'I should enjoy it immensely. I like your friend Margaret.'

'Margaret's a pet,' said Sally.

'And when is your father returning from South Africa?'

'Oh, any day now.'

'And Tom--how's Tom getting on?'

'Very well indeed. He writes some of the leaders now.'

That's fine,' said Horace, looking proudly about him. Here he was with a splendid girl--a true representative of the young generation-- and she had asked him to tea, and Cynthia, one of the smartest women in London, had invited him to the theatre, and he belonged to one of the most prominent families in England. He forgot, in his sudden exuberance, the faded gloom of his rooms in Jermyn Street, the surly indifference of his manservant, and the rude manner with which Alfred had turned his back on him a few days ago.

He had always said: 'I don't know what it is, but there's a sort of inner happiness in me which nothing can destroy.' It wasn't quite true any longer and he had never realized that his consciousness of it had been, in the past, one of the principal reasons for his unpopularity, but it was true enough at the moment for him to look at all the men near him with a certain kindly condescension as though they had all just fallen into the water and he was there, with a strong manly hand, ready to pull them out again.

Cynthia and Adrian joined them.

('Why is it,' Sally had once asked Tom, 'that all the members of our family move about as though they had just opened public buildings?')

'I think the play's absurd,' said Cynthia. 'I never saw such people!'

'Oh, do you?' said Sally. 'There are lots of them about. I'm rather like it myself.'

She wasn't and she knew that she wasn't, but it pleased her to irritate Cynthia.

At that moment Adrian brought up a man. 'Cynthia, this is a friend of mine at the Foreign Office-- Arnold Young.'

The man was perhaps about five-and-twenty, slim, tall, fair-haired. He had a weak chin, a mouth with hu-mour and bright blue eyes. He looked weak and amiable, as though he needed caring for and would be charming if you cared for him.

Sally looked at him and her heart was moved. He instantly smiled. 'You were rather like a choir boy,' he told her afterwards, 'who was bored to death with the sermon.'

The bell rang and they turned into the passage.

'Do you like this play?' the young man asked Sally.

'Oh, frightfully!'

'Isn't Noel Coward marvellous?'

'Simply marvellous.'

And just as they reached the stalls he said to her:

'I say--I hope we meet again somewhere.'

They must have met somewhere again very shortly after this, because, about a week later, Sally had this conversation with Tom.

Tom, who was a concrete Conservative, still inhabited the rooms in Tite Street.

Tom was now forty-one years of age. He was heavily built but not stout, short and square-shouldered, with a pale, anxious, extremely kindly face. Many years of journalism had not changed him. He was dressed in a black coat, black tie, striped dark trousers always. He played golf a little, and in the summer tennis a little. He liked his work but was not enthusiastic about it. He had only two passions--Cumberland and the few people he loved--Vanessa, his father, Mary and Sally. Over these four (Vanessa's ghost was certainly one of them) he watched and worried until they would sometimes scream with annoyance. He knew this and now did all he could to hide his care for them. He pretended to be quite indifferent as to whether they came or went. He was even a little afraid of letting Vanessa's ghost know how often he thought of her! Because he cared for his father less than for the others he irritated him the least. Besides, in these days, Benjie was often abroad. But Mary and Sally were simply his whole world. When they snapped at him, as they frequently did, he would slowly flush and blame himself for being so tiresome. Curiously, in relation to the rest of the world he was rather indifferent. Men in Fleet Street both respected and liked him. He was not clever enough to rouse their jealousy and he was always ready to do someone a turn, not from sentiment but simply because he was good-natured.

But that world hardly existed for him. He would have been a better journalist if it had. When he could snatch a night or two he would hurry up to Cumberland. There was a farm between Grange and Cat Bells where he always had a bedroom. Then he would walk, generally alone. He knew the Tops like his London bedroom wallpaper.

Sally loved him and bullied him. It exasperated her that year after year he should long for Mary Worcester who would never marry him. With glee she told him one day that people said that she was going to marry the young Duke of Wrexe.

'Funny, isn't it? History repeats itself. Our great-grandmother was engaged for a while to the Duke of Wrexe of her day. The lovely Jennifer--lovely and stupid like Mary.'

However, the young Duke of Wrexe married an American girl.

'Why do you tease me about Mary, Sally?' Tom asked her once. 'I never mention her.'

'Why do you go on year after year when it's hopeless! I want you to marry a nice good girl and make me an aunt.'

'You wouldn't like it if I did,' he said truthfully.

On this particular day when Sally had tea with him in Tite Street she did not tease him. She was very affectionate. He loved her dearly when she was kind. All the best in her came out. Her eternal qualities of courage and honesty were transmuted when she was kind into a true nobility. When she was not kind she seemed sometimes hard and selfish.

But today she looked at him with eyes of love. She sat on the edge of his armchair, swinging her legs, his arm round her.

'When's Father coming home?'

'Any time now.'

'I wonder what he's been doing in South Africa. I hope he's been behaving himself. Every year I think he's getting too old to misbehave any more, but he doesn't. Vanessa managed him, but no one else ever has.' She waved her arms. 'I love him! He's such a pet with his little ruddy face and his sharp eyes and his one arm and his eagerness to fall into any scrap that's coming! He'll startle us all yet and shock the family once again before he's done.'

She looked at Tom meditatively.

'Tom, I'm going to tell you something. You'll probably hate it. I'm in love--for the first time in my life.'

His arm clutched her a little more tightly. His heart began to hammer and he told himself: 'Now be careful. Don't show her that you mind. Don't show her that you're anxious. She's a modern girl. She won't stand being warned or advised.' He was able to say very quietly:

'Who with, Sally darling?'

She stroked his head.

'That's right, my pet. You're taking it well. He's a man in the Foreign Office. He's a friend of Adrian's and his name is Arnold Young.'

'Oh yes? I don't think I've met him.'

(Inside he was saying to himself: 'Now I shall have to protect Sally without her knowing it and see that he treats her right. She thinks she knows everything about life, like all girls now, but she doesn't.')

'No, you wouldn't have. Well, he's tall and got a lovely figure and he's very fair with blue eyes. On the other hand, he has no chin and wants looking after. He

has a mother who plays bridge, morning, noon and night.'

'Does he know you're in love with him? Where did you meet him?'

'I met him when I went to The Vortex with Cynthia. I don't think he knows I'm in love with him. We've only met twice. I'm very rude to him. I've never been in love before and it's a funny feeling.'

'Would you like to marry him?'

'Yes, I think so--if he asked me. Of course all Margaret's friends think marriage is rot nowadays. As long as you don't have a baby there's no point about marriage, they say. But I don't quite agree. It's all very well going away with a man for a weekend, but I think it would be nice to LOOK AFTER Arnold, run his home for him and everything. I expect I'm old-fashioned. Margaret says I am.'

'Is he a decent fellow?' Tom asked. 'I mean has he got a mistress somewhere or anything like that?'

'Oh no,' said Sally. 'He doesn't seem to care for girls. He's terribly under his mother's influence. That's the worst thing about him. But he isn't one of those, you know, or anything like that. Not a bit nancy. I don't say he's very fine or grand or wonderful. I'm just in love with him, that's all--here in the pit of the stomach!'

Then to Tom's astonishment she put her arms round his neck, kissed him and laid her cheek against his. She hardly ever kissed him.

'Do you know,' she said, 'we're all by ourselves--Vanessa, Father, you and I. Misfits. Still, we don't have a bad time.'

She began to roam round the room. Looking up, on a shelf above her head she saw an old green book. She stood on her toes and brought it down. She looked into it. It was a large fat book filled with rather faded writing in an old-fashioned female hand.

'What's this?' she asked.

'Oh, don't you know? That's some recollections Judith Paris wrote when she was an old lady--or rather she dictated them.'

'How marvellous! May I read them?'

'You'd better not take them away. Father asked me to take care of them for him.'

'Why--are they shocking?'

'Not in the least. But Judith gave them to Adam, Vanessa's father, and Vanessa gave them to Father.'

'Oh, but listen, Tom! They go back ever so far--almost to the beginning of the eighteenth century.'

'Yes; Judith lived to be a hundred, you know.'

'Oh, let me take them! I'll be frightfully careful.'

He hesitated. 'Well, if you're FEARFULLY careful--'

'Of course I will. I must go now.' She came to him and kissed him. 'Dear old Tom. I don't want to be sloppy, but you ARE a darling.'

He held her with his hand on her arm.

'Sally. Look here. I know you hate my being serious, but--well, what I mean is you haven't got anyone but me, in a way. Father isn't here and he wouldn't be much use. Vanessa told me to look after you.'

She smiled.

'Well--what is it?'

'You will be careful, won't you? I know girls know everything these days. Since the War they don't care WHAT they do. But-- you'll be careful, won't you? Tell me if you want any help about anything. Are you sure he's a decent fellow?'

'Of course he is. I can look after myself.'

After she was gone Tom walked about the room sighing. She looked such a baby. She was such a good sort. He loved her so dearly. But there you were. It wasn't the thing now to show your feelings. He had such a lot. Had he only been able to write! He sat down and soon was lost in a book of Santayana's. Now THERE was a writer!

On a day in April Adrian gave a luncheon party at his rooms in Lincoln's Inn. He invited Sally, Maurice, Maurice's young woman, Arnold Young, Miss Culloden, the well-known novelist, and her friend Miss James.

Sally hadn't known that Arnold was to be there. She had not seen him for three weeks. Adrian had asked her very casually and she had thought that very possibly she would be the only guest besides Maurice and Emily Tempest, to whom he was engaged. When she saw Miss Culloden she was afflicted with the shyness that she inherited from her mother. She was always sorry when she was shy, because shyness made her rude and abrupt in self-defence. Sally had read none of Miss Culloden's books. She read very little and for the most part the authors whom her friend Margaret admired--Lawrence and Aldous Huxley. She had attempted Women in Love and Ulysses and found them very tiresome. Then one evening she had found an old faded copy of Rider Haggard's She tucked away on a shelf. Scornfully she had begun it, and Margaret, coming in at one in the morning, had found her, curled up in a corner of the sofa, entranced.

'Whatever are you reading?' said Margaret. And then, when she saw, all she said was: 'My God!'

So Sally did not know what her real taste in books was. But she did know that she had read nothing by Miss Culloden.

Miss Culloden was a large cheerful friendly woman who reminded Sally of one of those broad-backed white horses at the circus, who go patiently round and round while ladies spring on to them and off them again. Miss James was her little friend who went with her everywhere and 'brought her out' on the subject of her works. Sally could not conceive why Adrian had invited her, for Adrian's taste in the Arts was severe, but it afterwards appeared that Miss Culloden had met him somewhere and had insisted on being invited. That was why the party today was mainly 'Family'. No celebrated persons. Miss Culloden was the life and soul. She was one of those fortunate writers (very rare) who are completely satisfied with everything--their own works, their publishers, their public and everything concerning them.

'You remember, Molly,' said Miss James, 'there was that chapter about Venice in Grapes and Thistles--one of your best bits, I always thought.'

Adrian changed the conversation to Sargent, who was recently dead.

'Everyone said at the time,' said Miss James 'that the artist in Models for Sale was intended for Sargent.'

'Well, he wasn't,' said Miss Culloden very firmly. 'He was a composite portrait.'

'I remember you were very anxious at the time,' said Miss James.

'Well, I'd have hated Sargent's feelings to be hurt. People are terribly sensitive. They're hurt if they think they're IN a book and they're hurt if they're not.'

After a while Miss Culloden surveyed the table. 'You're quite a family party, aren't you? Netta and I feel honoured at being made one of you like this. Oh yes, I know what I wanted to say. I was hearing about a marvellous member of your family the other day, an old lady who lived to be a hundred. And she'd actually seen Napoleon just before Waterloo, and knew Disraeli and all sorts of famous people. Wouldn't she be wonderful for a novel? I wonder if you'd all mind if I wrote a book about her one day?'

'I don't think she actually SAW Napoleon,' Adrian said. 'She was Sally's great-grandmother--'

'Was she REALLY?' Miss Culloden beamed upon Sally. 'Oh, how splendid! Now do tell me!'

'If you ever DARE to put her in a book,' Sally said, her voice trembling, 'I'll bring an action.'

Everyone was uncomfortable. That was just like the girl, Adrian thought, to take the old fool seriously. You never knew what she WOULD be serious over! But of course with Benjie for a father . . .

However, Miss Culloden didn't mind in the least, but thought: 'What a strange, unusual little girl! I'll see more of her.'

Adrian changed the conversation yet once again and asked Miss Culloden whether she had been to the theatre. Had she seen No, No, Nanette?

'Yes, indeed--and it's simply splendid--' she began.

But Sally was miserable. There she was, making a fool of herself before Arnold. She could remember when she was seven or six or some absurd age that Vanessa had warned her about her tempers. She could see Vanessa standing by the window in the room at Hill Street, the room with the two yellow globes and the picture with 'Miss Muffet and the Spider'. Yes, Vanessa was there, wanting not to laugh, wanting to be stern and severe, but Sally had made a face and Vanessa had laughed . . .

'--and if Miss Herries EVER forgives me,' Miss Culloden was saying, 'I shall ask her one day--'

Everyone was looking at Sally as though they expected her to do something, so she smiled at Miss Culloden, hating herself, one of those horrible smiles that you fastened on to your mouth as a dentist fastens on a gag.

And not only was Vanessa standing there, but now also Judith Paris, for, in the last few weeks, Sally had absorbed that old green book into her very blood and bones. She knew it almost by heart and it was agony to her when it stopped, stopped at one of its most thrilling moments when Judith was remembering the terrible quarrel about the fan at Christabel's Ball. Why, conceive it! Here was Sally and there at her very elbow was Judith who, going on a jaunt with her French husband to the 'Elephant and Castle', had worn a dress--'a jaquette of pale silver-coloured silk and the bodice and under-dress were of dark wine colour: I wore a hat of light straw and my shoes had silver buckles'. There was Judith in her old age dictating to her great-great-niece Jane Bellairs, who, a sweet old maiden lady with ringlets, had died as recently as 1905, and here was she, Sally, in 1925, feeling that Judith was in the very room with her, the hat of light straw perched on her red hair . . .

'I'm sure you are wrong, dear,' Miss James was saying in her firm even voice that was like a ruler drawing lines on a piece of white paper. 'It wasn't until Love in a Garret that America really took you to its heart. I remember so well your telling me that the Americans were fickle and that you were not going to allow yourself to be persuaded by the success of one book into thinking that it would last. You told me, I remember, that Sir Philip Gibbs said--'

'Oh, God! this is awful!' Adrian thought. He looked at Maurice, who was one of the discontented members of the family. 'A legacy of the War' Cynthia called Maurice, and it was certainly true that he had lost an arm and written a little book about Blake and got himself engaged, when he had no money at all, to a young woman who painted ladies with green hair and the oddest legs, all things--in the opinion of Cynthia and Alfred and Gordon--that might be classed together as a 'pity'.

'Oh, these awful women!' thought Adrian. 'What CAN Maurice be thinking of them?'

He had a high opinion of Maurice, who had bought a Matisse in Paris very cheap, and had had tea with James Joyce. But he was wrong about Maurice, who liked Miss Culloden very much. She reassured him. Obviously to her the world was not a bloody, menacing place in which everything and everybody was going to hell. He liked her, whereas he loathed Gordon, who also believed in life. But then Gordon believed in life because Gordon was such a wonderful fellow, and Miss Culloden believed in life because she was naturally happy, like a lark in the sky . . .

When the party was breaking up, Arnold said to Sally: 'Can I take you anywhere? I've got a car.'

Sally's heart leapt for joy.

'Yes, you can,' she said. 'Anywhere you like. I haven't got to be at the office till four.' She was so happy that, on bidding farewell, she looked up at Miss Culloden and said, smiling (this time with real if rather childlike sincerity):

'Please forgive me if I was rude.'

'Rude, my dear!' cried Miss Culloden. 'Why, you're too sweet for anything! Now you must come and have lunch with me, you really must--and I promise not to say a word about your great-aunt or whatever she was. Now what day can you come?' She produced a small silver-edged notebook. 'I'm talking to the Soroptimists on Tuesday and there's Marie Lowndes on Wednesday. Thursday I'm going out to Surbiton. Now what about Friday? Friday's quite all right. There's only the Tallboys Club Committee in the afternoon . . . Now WHAT about Friday?'

So Sally was engaged for Friday.

In the little car (which was bright red in colour and VERY smart) Sally said: 'Where are we going?'

'Anywhere you like.'

'Haven't you any work or anything?'

'Oh yes, but I MUST talk to you.'

'Well, let's go to the National Gallery and look at the Sargents.'

Side by side on a settee alone in the room, looking at one lovely woman after another, Sally said:

'I like Mrs Charles Hunter's hat.' Then she added: 'They're all quite unreal, aren't they?'

'Yes,' said Arnold. 'He despised women. The only thing he admired about them was their clothes. You can see how he hated his sitters. His hatred is real in the pictures even if nothing else is.'

'Yes,' said Sally, who, sitting there very meekly, wishing that her legs were a little longer and that altogether she was built on a larger scale, was nevertheless a great deal happier than any girl of her generation thought it fitting to be.

'Will you marry me?' Arnold said suddenly.

'Yes,' Sally said. 'I'd love to.'

'I'm terribly glad,' Arnold said. 'I loved you from the first moment I saw you.'

As he said this Sally thought that he'd never wanted looking after so badly as now. She longed to put her arm round him. All she said was:

'You know I'm illegitimate.'

'What on earth does that matter?'

'Have you any money, Arnold darling?'

'Well, not a lot. There's what I get in the Foreign Office and my mother makes me an allowance.'

'Your mother doesn't like me,' Sally said quickly.

'She will when she knows you, darling.'

'No, she never will. She thinks I'm Bohemian and she's heard things about Father. She knows Father and

Mother weren't married. These things matter to HER and always will.'

A shadow seemed to pass very swiftly over Arnold's face. (Poor dear! he certainly DID need looking after!)

'She wants you to marry a fine girl of a noble family. Her generation are LIKE that.'

'Well, your family's all right. It's one of the best in England.'

'I know, dear--but don't let's be snobbish. The point about our family is that there are the right ones and the wrong ones. There always have been. Cynthia Worcester and Alfred and Gordon are the right ones--but my father and I are the wrong ones, I'm afraid.'

'What nonsense you're talking, Sally darling. You're splendid! You're wonderful! And my mother isn't going to say whom I'm going to marry! It's my life, not hers!' It was the bravest thing Arnold had ever said.

'Well, you go and talk to her,' Sally said, laying her hand for a moment on his. 'I won't be engaged until you've talked to her, but I do love you frightfully and I think I always will.'

There, in that public room, in front of all the Sargent ladies, they kissed, and as he felt Sally's small body tremble against his he swore to himself that he would defy a thousand mothers . . .

'Oh, of course,' young Mr Elton was saying, 'if you prefer to read people like Galsworthy and Barrie--'

'Why shouldn't I?' said Mary Worcester. 'I don't, if you want to know. But why shouldn't I?'

'Because they're false as hell,' said young Mr Elton. Then he saw that his audience was despicable, made his adieus and departed.

'I suppose I'd better be going too,' said Tom.

'I don't think Mother will be in now. She's playing bridge and SAID she'd be back, but with bridge you never know . . .'

Tom stood in the middle of the charming little drawing-room, which in the fashion of the moment had only one French picture on its walls--a late and not-at-all-good Utrillo--a bronze by Dobson on the mantelpiece, and very little else.

Then, hiding his fear, he spoke the words that, for almost all his life, had been trembling on his lips. Why now? Was it less hopeless than ever? Certainly not. Mary, who in these days was often depressed, was very depressed indeed at the moment. An extremely agreeable handsome young man, who would have been an excellent escort to all kinds of places, had found her, like all the other agreeable young men, most appallingly dull. She didn't WANT to be dull. She was ready to admire their painters, their poets, their morals, their cynicism, their atheism, although in her heart she found all these things unpleasant, but it was of no use. They found her a bore and practically said so. She was thirty-two. Life was ghastly.

Nevertheless the words came pouring from Tom's lips.

'Mary, I can't help it. I've wanted to say this so often. You know I have. Won't you marry me? I've loved you all my life. It mightn't turn out so badly. I've got a rise. I'm doing leaders on the paper now, and there are articles too I write for the weeklies. It isn't such a bad income and, if you married me, I believe I could do ever so much better still. I would look after you--I would care for you--'

He stopped because the words choked him. He looked away from her at the Dobson bronze, a figure with thighs so enormous and a head so small that it filled him, at this moment, with terror.

Mary looked at him with great kindness. She patted the grey sofa with her hand.

'Tom, come and sit down.' He came and sat down. 'You know I can't.'

'Why not? No one has loved you so long nor so faithfully--'

'Yes, I know. But there are other things beside fidelity. One thing is that I don't love you. You know that I don't. That isn't my fault or yours. Another is that I'm frightfully stupid. If I lived with you I'd bore you terribly. Another is that I must marry someone with money. And another--perhaps the most important--is that I never would marry any member of our family.'

He came closer to her and she allowed him to take her hand.

'Then there's another. You're TOO good, you're TOO faithful. I couldn't bear anyone who loved me as you do. I know I'm not worth it, but it isn't that. No one's worth it. But I like people who are independent of me, who don't give a damn whether I'm nice to them or no. If I snap at you it's as though I struck you. You wince. But I DO like you. I don't mean that. Only to live with you--never, dear Tom.'

She hesitated, then went on:

'You see, you're old-fashioned. You believe in God and kindness and charity and all the old things. How you can, I can't think! It's a rotten world run by stupid people. It may come right again one day, although not in our time, I expect. You're like old Horace in that, except that you really DO believe in the things you say. You're like Vanessa, who was, I'm sure, the finest woman who ever lived, but she simply doesn't BELONG to our time.'

'You're not to say a word--' began Tom.

'There you are, you see? You won't face the facts. You never do. I didn't know Vanessa very well, but I DO think she was splendid-- much finer than any of us are! But she seems old-fashioned now-- she was Victorian--and you're a bit Victorian too.'

There was a long pause. Then he said:

'What do you mean--you wouldn't marry one of the family?'

'Just what I say! I hate and loathe our family! Either we're prigs or we're mad. We are so damnably English whatever we are. Mother's all right, I suppose, but look at Father and Rosalind and Alfred and Gordon--and poor Maurice who's as cracked as can be; and there was Ellis who was mad for years; and Rose, Horace's sister, who died in the gutter. And if you go back it's just the same. Your grandfather was murdered by your great-uncle, and before that there was a Herries shot himself in London, and there was the crazy Herries in the eighteenth century. And in between the others have all been dull and self-satisfied and self-righteous. I shall marry someone or other just to get away. But I won't marry to stay.'

Tom answered slowly: 'You're wrong, Mary. Whether we've been mad or sane we've been alive. You may laugh at England, but it's the finest--Oh, don't let's talk about the family! What does it matter? I'm only half Herries! The family can't make any difference! And I won't fuss over you, Mary, really I won't. You shall have your own life. You shan't see more of me than you want to! We get on together. We have for years. You like being with me. If you married me--'

She sighed. 'It's a shame,' she said at last. 'I'm glad you've told me, though, because--now that you see that it's hopeless perhaps you'll find someone else. I've wanted for years to tell you how hopeless it is. Of course I like you and like being with you--sometimes. But I'm not worth it--not worth your kind of devotion, Tom. And you'd regret it like anything. I shall get fat and plain and peevish. I haven't an idea in my head, only scraps of other people's ideas. And I want money. It's the only thing that can save me. With money I can make things do, perhaps. Without it--'

'If you loved me,' he said at last, 'would any of these other things have mattered?'

'Once they wouldn't. But now--it isn't love I want but money and comfort and safety.'

He got up. She liked him at that moment very much. She got up and held out her hand.

'Goodbye, Tom dear,' she said.

'Goodbye,' he answered and left her.

He went back to Tite Street, sat in his room, his head between his hands, thinking. This was awful. Mary's refusal had made no difference to his love for her. How could it when it was part of his very being? But now he had got to make terms with it, he thought. He must manage his life henceforth so that this dead hope did not spread like a cancer into all his energies. For, until today, there had always been a hope--for years and years that hope had been a light in his room. Now he must manage without it.

He was so desperately tired that he slept in his chair, his head forward on his breast.

He woke to find that the light had been switched on and his father was standing there. He rubbed his eyes, for he was only half awake, and Benjie was like a figure in a dream, standing in a rough heather-coloured overcoat and holding on a chain a very alert, eye-shining, panting rough-haired terrier.

'Good God!' Tom cried, lumping up.

'Yes,' said Benjie smiling. 'Here I am.'

'Why didn't you send a wire?'

'Well, you see, Tom, I didn't know when I'd arrive. As it is I've been in the New Forest a whole week wandering about. That's where I bought this.'

The dog, its tongue out and its brilliant deep brown eyes almost jumping from its head, strained at the hold. The colour of its coat was black and tan, with a fine rough white patch across the neck.

'Why didn't you write from the New Forest?' asked Tom.

'Oh Lord, I don't know! Don't badger me. My bags are in the other room. Isn't this a nice overcoat? I won it in a bet on the boat. Luckily the other fellow was just my size. Heavens! but I'm tired!'

He took his coat off. He was thinner and browner than ever, thought Tom, and his eyes had the same desperate brightness as the dog's. He went and poured himself out a whisky and soda. He sat on the edge of the deal table, swinging his thin legs, his little animal-like face cocked a bit over his glass. Tom had noticed that the very first thing he had looked at across the room was a large photograph of Vanessa.

'Any news?'

'Sally's engaged.'

'What!' Benjie sprang off the table. 'Sally! My little Sally! Heavens! Who to?'

'A fellow called Young--Arnold Young. He's in the Foreign Office.'

Benjie was excited. He came over to Tom, holding up his glass with his one hand.

'What's he like?'

'Oh, he's all right, I suppose. Sally thinks so. But he's just the sort of chap Sally would pick up--a bit weak, I should think, and wants looking after.'

'Any money?'

'Got a rich mother, and I should think she's bloody from what Sally says. Nor does she like Sally. She goes about everywhere, I believe, saying that there's no engagement and it's preposterous and so on.'

'Why, what has she got against my Sally?'

'Oh, I don't know.'

'Born out of wedlock, scamp of a father--that sort of thing?'

'I don't know. I haven't seen her.'

Then, very like Benjie, he drove the thing right out of his mind. He had released the dog, who now bounded all over the room, sometimes prancing on four legs at once like a young lamb, and examining everything.

'What's it's name?'

'Sam.'

'It's a shame to keep a dog like that in London.'

'I shan't keep it in London. I'm going up to Cumberland.'

'Oh, I say, are you really!' Tom's eyes shone.

Benjie put his glass down and rested his hand on Tom's shoulder.

'Like to come too?'

'Wouldn't I, though!'

'Could you get off?'

'Yes, for a bit, I think.'

Benjie looked at him critically, then drew him closer until shoulder touched shoulder.

'You're not looking any too fine.'

'Oh, I'm all right.'

Father and son gave one another a glance and each smiled.

'What's the matter? Mary turned you down?'

'Yes. How did you know?'

'Oh, I guessed. I'm a bit lonely too. South Africa was all right-- interesting seeing it again after all these years. But it would have been better if Vanessa had been there.' Then he added cheerfully: 'I say--Mary's damned dull, you know.'

Tom shook his head.

'You don't understand how it is.'

'Oh, don't I?' He laughed. 'You bet I do! I've been in love with the same woman fifty years. How about that?' For a brief moment he held Tom closely to him.

'Come on and eat.'

'What about the dog?' asked Tom.

'Oh, he'll come too. I know a place where they don't mind dogs.'

Meanwhile on that same evening another member of the family was carrying on the Herries history a further stage. Arnold had taken Sally out to the theatre--to Mr Lonsdale's play Spring Cleaning. Sally enjoyed the play, although she thought it old-fashioned. They were having supper at 'The Gargoyle', they were dancing a little, talking a little. They were, both of them, terribly in love.

'Yes,' said Sally. 'I think all these plays about how wicked we are seem very Victorian--East Lynne, you know. There's The Vortex and Fallen Angels and the one tonight. All the young men are-- well, you know, and the young women have monocles and Eton crops. Everyone drinks and they go to bed with one another in the bathroom. Just as they did in Mrs Henry Wood's day--'

'Well, aren't we all like that just now? Look round you, my pet, and observe.'

'There are just about forty million people,' said Sally, 'who've never heard of "The Gargoyle" or Noel

Coward. They don't sleep together in the bathroom nor do their young men powder their faces.'

'What do they do then?' asked Arnold.

'They go to football matches, read the News of the World and sleep cosily with their wives and husbands.'

He drove her to her door. Then he asked her whether he might come in for a moment. She hesitated, for Margaret was away. But then she nodded. The sitting-room that she shared with Margaret had a very comfortable sofa, a long well-filled bookcase, a gas stove, and posters by Mr McKnight Kauffer pinned to the walls. Over the mantelpiece there was a watercolour by Charles Holmes of a black hill with a shaft of sunlight breaking on it and illuminating a field that shone with the brilliance of a missal.

'That's nice,' said Arnold. 'Where is it?'

'It's Stonethwaite Valley in Cumberland.'

There was also an old photograph of Vanessa. She was standing, her hand on a chair; her dress had the puffed sleeves and the small waist of the period. But she did not look absurd. She looked very charming indeed.

'Who's that?' Arnold asked.

'That's my mother.'

'By Jove, she was a beauty.'

'Yes, wasn't she?'

On the sofa she gathered him into her thin childish arms.

'Oh, Arnold,' she said. 'I want you to be happy!'

(She was not aware that more than a hundred years before in a ragged deserted house in Borrowdale, Judith Paris had said the same words. But Judith had not loved Vanessa's grandfather.)

He strained up to her, putting his arm up to hold her round boyish head as in a cup.

'And so do I you.' He kissed her, holding her so closely to him that their two hearts seemed to beat as one.

'Well, you can make me happy--frightfully happy--'

'Yes, darling?' Sally said, stroking his hair.

'Let me stay here tonight.'

She drew away from him, placing her hand firmly on his arm. She sat back against the corner of the sofa and looked at him.

'Well, really, Arnold!' She was suddenly frightened, frightened in a way that a modern girl with all her knowledge of life should never be.

He began to speak eagerly.

'See here, Sally. There's nothing so very dreadful. I know how to look after you. Why shouldn't we have a good time? Everyone else does. You don't believe in God or hell-fire or any of that old junk, do you?' He laughed rather nervously. He was not a practised seducer. He had never seduced anyone before. He did not feel that he was trying to seduce Sally. He simply, he thought, loved her so madly that he wanted to be as close to her as possible.

'I don't believe in hell-fire,' she said slowly. 'But I'm not sure about God. My mother believed in God.'

'Of course. So does mine. All their generation did, but ours doesn't. We're simply some sort of chemical mixture. There's no future or past or anything, so why shouldn't we enjoy ourselves? We'll only be young once, and perhaps before we're much older there'll be another war like the last and we'll all be blown to bits.'

'I think it would be nicer,' Sally said slowly, 'to wait till we're married. If we have everything now there won't be anything new to experience later on.'

'Yes, but don't you see, Sally? As we are going to be married it doesn't matter anticipating it a bit, does it?'

She knelt on the sofa, turning her little body towards him, holding his head between her hands, looking at him very seriously.

'Arnold--we ARE going to be married, aren't we?'

'But of course we are!' He moved his soft cheek against her hand.

'Yes, but what if your mother goes on hating me?'

'She doesn't hate you. She doesn't know you.'

'No, she WON'T know me! Now tell me--it's true, isn't it?--she told you that our engagement is absurd, that I'm no good and my father's no good and that she won't have her darling wee pet of an Arnold marrying a little bastard.'

'No, of course not, darling. How absurd you are!' She jumped back from him, sprang to her feet. She stood there, small, pale-faced, but dominating.

'Now listen, Arnold! She DOES say that. You know it and I know it! And I'll tell you something--I'm as good as anyone in England, as proud, as independent. I had the grandest mother anyone ever had. There never has been, and there never will be again, anyone as fine as Vanessa. And I don't want your damned charity. And your mother can be as superior as she likes, I'm not going on to my knees and imploring, but her--'

He was in a dreadful state. He had never loved her so much as at that moment. He had in fact (and this was true) never loved anyone before.

'Sally, my sweet, my pet. We'll be married when you like. Tomorrow if you wish. Anything you say--' He caught her with his arms, carried her back to the sofa, and they lay there, close together, saying nothing, he kissing her mouth, her eyes, her hair.

And she thought: 'How terribly I love him. I'd give him anything. Why not be kind while one may?' As his body trembled in her arms she was infinitely touched. Oh, darling Arnold, darling, darling Arnold! Judith had loved a man outside marriage, and her own mother . . . She was herself illegitimate . . . and in these days, when everyone was free . . . He was right . . . Who knew how long their happiness might last?

Why should she not be kind? Why should she not give anything she could that would make him happy? She sighed, touched his cheek.

'All right, Arnold darling,' she said. 'You can stay.'

MEN AT WAR

On this evening of May 3rd, 1926, Benjie took the dog Sam out for a little exercise. He had, only the day before, returned from Morocco and found that he was plunged into a world of turmoil. Tom, who was pale and tired and plainly overworked, said that by next morning we might find ourselves plunged into Revolution. 'Revolution,' said Benjie; 'how absurd!' But to himself, perhaps, more than to anyone else in London it did not seem absurd, for he carried, always present with him, that picture of a ragged mob crossing a bridge, of the skaters vanishing, of a sudden rifle shot, of a square frozen and bare under a shining sun but quivering with danger, and, most tremendous of all, a multitude of people singing as though Paradise had come. And had Paradise come? Not at all. Murder, destruction, and the slow agonizing beginning of a new world . . . So here it might be also.

But what, he inquired, had been happening? Tom entered into a slow and tortuous explanation. The Secretary of the Miners' Federation, Arthur Cook, had made the trouble. After the Samuel Commission had recommended reduction in pay, Arthur Cook had replied: 'Not a cent off the pay, not a minute on the day', and all the miners of England had repeated his words with emphasis. The Government had announced the withdrawal of the subsidy, and on April 23rd the owners had delivered an ultimatum. Cook had not liked the terms of the ultimatum, his men had appealed for help to the Trades Union Congress, and that body, in its turn, had put the question of a General Strike to a ballot of its unions.

No one supposed that the Trades Union Congress really WANTED a General Strike--of course they didn't--but they thought that mild Mr Baldwin would capitulate. However, mild Mr Baldwin gave a puff or two at his pipe and DIDN'T capitulate. (It happened that the Government had been making their preparations ever since 1925.) Well, then, on this very Monday, members of the Association of Printers' Assistants working for the Daily Mail had demanded the withdrawal of a leading article entitled 'For King and Country', and the men on the Daily Mirror had objected to a news article directing anti-strike volunteers to recruiting stations in the London area. The General Council Committee thought that they would go and have a talk with Mr Baldwin, but when they went to see him he was not there. They were greatly surprised.

At midnight the General Strike was to begin. On the evening of the Monday, Benjie took Sam for a little walk. It was a fine night, and he went to Hyde Park, thinking that it would be a good occasion for himself and Sam (who was in excellent spirits) to listen to the Marble Arch orators. They would surely be at their best at such a crisis and most amusingly violent. But the gates at Hyde Park Corner were closed. A cordon of police was stationed there, and the policemen said, quietly and coldly as though they were thinking of something else: 'Move on there, please!'

He joined the crowd pressed against the railings, and in this crowd no one spoke--only they gazed. Very odd, thought Benjie, on this fine May evening, and the strike not yet declared, to see Hyde Park a camp. Inside the railings there were fleets of lorries and huts and tents rising. No one spoke: only Sam barked at a chow tethered by a blue cord to the arm of a lady. Benjie looked at the lady and saw that she was fair. Her figure was as slim as fashion dictated figures should be (to Benjie's constant chagrin, for he liked figures to be plump). She was wearing a little blue hat, her hair was pale gold, and she had the face of an innocent, rather bewildered child. Her chow was aloof and dignified. Sara, at the end of his lead, strained towards it. Benjie raised his hat.

'The Government seems to have got in first,' he said.

'Oh yes,' she answered in a voice that was all music. 'Isn't it splendid of them?'

It had been difficult, with his one arm, to raise his hat and control Sam at the same time. His movement had for a moment jerked Sam on to his hind feet. She smiled at that. After all he was seventy-one, but no one would know it. He was spare and tough as he had been at forty.

'What is going to happen, do you think?' she asked him.

They walked away together. Half an hour later she had given him her address. She had rooms, it appeared, on the Chelsea Embankment. Her name, it seemed, was Miss Grace Mortimer.

He took her, that same evening, out to supper.

When he reached his own place at three or four o'clock the following morning he was aware of a deep and bitter unhappiness. He sat on his bed in his shirt, staring at his own abasement. He was not abased because he had been friendly to Miss Mortimer. He had done no harm to the pretty lady, to whom sudden meetings with strange gentlemen were no novel affair. She had been charming, had talked of her father, a General, now deceased, had shrugged her bare shoulders at the way the world was going, had thanked him for his generous gift, had begged him to come and have tea with her on the following afternoon. He had not told her that he was over seventy, and he was certain that she had not supposed him a day more than fifty. He had been ashamed of nothing that he had done, and yet he was most utterly ashamed.

At that hour of the morning with the chilly room hostile and the town preparing in a ghastly silence for the coming day's warfare, he was as lonely an old man as

the world contained. Sam was sleeping in his basket near the window, comfortable and indifferent.

'Vanessa! Vanessa! I want you, I want you! Where are you? Why aren't you here to keep me company in this damnable world?'

Then he got off to bed, pulled his shirt over his head, did his exercises. Afterwards he lay sleepless, seeing the lorry, projecting rifles like a hedgehog, hearing the wild shouts beneath the window, starting at that sudden flame on the horizon of a burning building . . . He had never loved London so dearly as in those hours.

When daylight came he was still ashamed and abashed. He was saying to himself, as he had said so often before, that he was finished with women, but that statement did not lessen his abasement. He lay in bed, his head resting on his arm, wondering what was happening to the world and hating and despising himself. Here was the country tumbling into ruin and he doing nothing about it, but worse than that, here was he himself a hale and hearty old man who did nothing but wander about the world, sigh for a woman long dead, and appease his appetites in any selfish easy way that appeared to him. He was not convicted of sin. He did not feel a sinner who must hurry to repentance; but he WAS convicted of waste, of sterility.

He had achieved some kind of relation with his son, it was true, but in spite of their greater friendliness Tom still bored him. Tom wanted to mother him, and oh, God! he hated to be mothered!

And then there was Sally. Before he had left for Morocco he had taken Sally to the theatre. He could see that she was unhappy, but she wouldn't tell him anything. Just like these modern children; got no confidence in their parents. There was a gulf fixed between his generation and theirs. She was unhappy. This young man of hers was no good. Benjie didn't like him, a weak backboneless kind of fellow, the sort of man women wanted to help. He was making Sally miserable, and Benjie's heart ached for her. He wanted, in fact, to be allowed to love someone--yes, although he was past seventy. He was damnably lonely and no use to anyone. Perhaps after all there was something in what Vanessa said. There was somewhere another, a secret life, and if you didn't find it you were 'left' when you were old. Oh, but he was not going to whine! He didn't care if he WAS alone. Everyone was alone if it came to that. He had better be up and doing, see what was happening to this crazy world.

While he was dressing Tom came in.

'Look here,' said Benjie. 'How can I make myself useful?'

'Oh, easily. They want volunteers for every kind of thing. You can take that car of yours and drive people to their offices. Everyone's walking. It's a sight, I can tell you. Outside the Foreign Office it's packed with people waiting to enrol. They've enlisted a hundred thousand in the Volunteer Service Corps already. They're going to supply two million gallons of milk a day from Hyde Park. It's marvellous! England's middle class counts for something in a crisis.'

'Yes, that's what Russia hadn't got,' said Benjie. He added, smiling: 'Our family will be pleased. I bet they're all busy serving the country. Any fighting yet?' Benjie asked.

'No, I don't think so. But I dare say there will be. I've got to go down to Limehouse.'

Benjie looked out of the window. Not a soul was to be seen. He went out. Everyone was walking. He came to Birdcage Walk and found it packed with cars, crawling along four abreast. He discovered that the gates of Charing Cross railway station were locked. No one seemed to know quite what to do. It was a new world, a new life, but beneath the uncertainty he was aware of a strong united determination. He seemed to feel it in the very stones of the street. 'The Strike hasn't got a chance,' he thought. He decided that he would get his car from the garage and be of some use. He climbed on to a pirate omnibus driven by a very bright but determined young man in knickerbockers. Two young men standing beside him were going down to Dover to assist in the unloading of ships. He thought that he would offer to go with them, but an unwonted shyness stopped him. He saw an omnibus that had been in the wars, standing derelict surrounded by a large, gazing, meditative crowd. He noticed a big advertisement on its boards: 'Maurice Moscovitch: The Great Lover.'

The great lover! Well, he was done with women and all the silly, sterile, messy things in his life, and then he saw a girl near to him, swaying uncomfortably as the bus moved. A pretty girl looking defenceless and a little frightened. He wondered whether she would not like his assistance. A fat, rather breathless man near him said: 'This bloody Strike's being helped by the bloody Germans. Give you my word! Syndicate of German financiers. I happen to know. They're landing bullion on the East Coast from a small ship.'

Instantly Benjie's temper, which was easily moved, was up. Silly damned liar! He'd like to tell him so. He nearly did, but got off at the top of Knightsbridge instead. Yes, he got off and walked straight into Gordon Newmark.

'Hullo!' said Gordon. 'Why, it's Benjie!'

'Yes,' said Benjie. 'It is!'

'Isn't this splendid!' said Gordon. 'We'll show them, the dirty tykes. No one knew what England was capable of until now.'

He was swelled with elation, triumph, pride and satisfaction. His handsome face (Benjie always thought that he looked like a horse that was one of the best and smartest performers in the most famous of circuses) was carved into a proper model of all that the English ruling classes should be.

'Here!' cried Gordon. 'What are you doing to help?'

'What ought I to do?' Benjie asked modestly.

'Go down to the Mansion House. They'll soon enrol you there and tell you what to do.'

'I will,' said Benjie. 'Thanks very much.'

At the same moment his daughter Sally was saying to her employer, Mr Bimberg:

'No, thank you, Mr Bimberg. I can get home quite all right this afternoon.'

Mr Bimberg was plump, bald and very neatly dressed. She had been quite comfortable with him for a long time now, but of late--within the last few months--he had taken, it seemed, a new interest in her. He put his soft round hand on her arm, he patted her shoulder. A pity, because the job suited her.

But this morning she was too deeply involved in her own private history to consider the outside world very deeply. She was fighting with all the strength that she had to keep dreadful terror at bay. As she sat taking down Mr Bimberg's letters her thoughts were wild. Arnold had not kept his appointment last night. She had waited and waited. He had arranged to take her to The Best People that they might together admire the fine art of Miss Olga Lindo. She had sat in her evening frock (she had worn it only twice before) for a whole hour. How horrible that hour had been! Sally was tutored to conceal her emotions, but after that agony of suspense she had burst into tears, torn off her frock and lain on her bed. He might come. Something had kept him. Ten. Eleven. Midnight. But why had he not telephoned? In the morning there would be a letter. But there was no letter. Choking her independence, she had telephoned. He had left the house half an hour before. So, her head up, looking gravely at Mr Bimberg, she had taken down his letters.

At lunchtime, alone in the room, she had telephoned again. Arnold answered her. Her heart hammering, her voice a little breathless in spite of herself, she said:

'Arnold, whatever happened last night?' (She would forgive him whatever his excuse might be.)

'Oh, my dear, I'm too frightfully sorry.'

'No--but whatever was it? I waited and waited.'

She knew that he hesitated.

'Darling, I'll explain everything. It wasn't my fault. Really it wasn't.'

'But what WAS it?' Her knees were trembling. She steadied herself with her hand on a chair.

'I can't explain here.'

'But why didn't you telephone?'

'I couldn't. It was impossible where I was.'

'But where were you?'

'Don't be so difficult, sweet. You know how difficult it is on a telephone.'

'But we can't leave it like this. I waited and waited. It was awful. How soon can I see you?'

Again he hesitated. Then he said:

'All right. I'll come along to your place about six.'

'You WILL come?'

'Of course I will.'

A little reassured she sat there, thinking. She did not go out to lunch, but stayed there without moving. She ought not to have told him that she cared. It was the doctrine of her friends that a girl never showed that she cared for a man. She could hear Margaret saying: 'So of course I told him that if he wanted to go he could. *I* didn't mind. So off he went, and I rang up Archie and we had a grand time at Ciro's. OF COURSE he came round the next day . . .'

But she wasn't quite like that. She had been Arnold's mistress for nearly a year and that did make a difference, didn't it? It made a difference in every kind of way, because Arnold now had everything he wanted while she . . . she wanted more and more. Not physical things, but for him to WANT her and to need her, to depend on her . . . The physical thing was nothing, and yet it was everything because, after it happened, Sally was his mother, his sister, his friend, his companion, while Arnold was still only Sally's lover and that not so warmly as once he had been. He should have married her. It was not perhaps very fine of him to fear so abjectly his mother, and yet Sally understood that too. SHE was not afraid of his mother, but it was natural that Arnold should be. For he was afraid of a great many things, which was partly the reason of Sally's love for him because she wanted to shelter and protect him.

As the afternoon went on her fears grew again. WHY had he not come?

'Yes,' said Mr Bimberg. 'You had really better let me drive you home.'

'Oh no, thank you, Mr Bimberg.'

'You'll have to walk all the way, you know.'

'I'm not going very far.' (Which was untrue.)

He looked at her with his round eyes like rather damp marbles. She thought that he was going to touch her. She stood her ground. But he did not. He sighed and ambled away.

The streets were very strange. Crowds of people were walking, all rather quickly and rather silently. Was this Revolution, the kind of thing that had happened in Russia? She did not care in the least if it were. She only cared about Arnold. They all walked together like an army obeying orders. She began to be conscious of something corporate in this movement. She saw an omnibus, ran for it, stood packed in a confusion of legs and bodies, had her penny collected by a very pleasant red-faced man in a brown suit, jumped off again, stood in a side street listening to the sudden silence as though she expected to hear a gun fired or to see a flare of light against the sky. WAS this Revolution? Would there be fighting and barricades? Perhaps Arnold would need her more if there was fighting--and she had a curious quick picture of herself as a small child, looking up from her book in the Hill Street house, seeing Ellis in the doorway and hearing him say: 'Sally, do come and play soldiers . . .' She looked at her wristwatch and hurried on.

'I mustn't show him that I care,' she thought. 'I must be quite indifferent. I KNOW that he wants me. He CAN'T do without me.'

When she reached the flat Arnold was already there, standing in front of the fireplace. When she saw him she loved him so dreadfully that it was all she could do not to hurry into his arms. But she did not. She went into her room, took off her small brown hat, gave her cropped hair a shake, waited for a moment staring at, but not seeing, the photograph of her mother on the mantelpiece. Then she came in, sat down, lit a cigarette and said:

'Well, you're a beauty, Arnold. Whatever did you let me down for like that last night?'

He did not move towards her, and there was a constricted movement at her heart as though a cold finger had touched it. But she looked at him quietly, noticed his tie of blue and red stripes, his pale long hands, his eager, easily startled eyes. Yes, she knew him so very well.

'Look here, darling,' he began. 'I'm most awfully sorry about last night.'

'No--but what WAS it? Of course I'd have understood if something had kept you, but even then you should have phoned, shouldn't you?'

She knew that her voice slipped into a sharper pitch, not from anger but from fear.

'Oh yes, I should. I meant to. But you see I was at home--'

'Well, you've GOT a telephone in your house, haven't you?'

'Yes. Of course. Don't be facetious, Sally . . .' He came forward a few steps, hesitated, then plunged.

('Why,' thought Sally to herself, 'he's just like a piece of seaweed, yellow, and if you pressed any part of him with your finger it would go "pop".' At the same time she wanted to take him and smooth his hair, calm his fears, give him a present, offer him a drink, lie down on the outside of the bed with him, draw his head to her breast and listen to a catalogue of his troubles. At the same time she also wanted to throw the book on the table--she even saw the title, Jacob's Room--at his head and stamp on his toes. She always said that he wore shoes with too shiny a toe.)

These things passed through her mind and like odds and ends caught up with a shower were drowned in the one and only insistent drumming consciousness:

'He's come to tell me something. He's not going to see me any more.'

'The fact is, Sally, I had an awful row with my mother last night.'

'Oh, did you? What about?' (But she knew quite well what about.)

'About you. She says that I have to choose.'

'Choose?'

'Yes. Between you and her.'

Sally stared at him and saw the seaweed, gold with dark brown fronds swaying in a sea pool, swaying indeterminately while the breeze ruffled the water of the pool into little angry protests.

'Oh, I see. She's told you that before.'

He went back to the fireplace, hanging his head at the gritty little fire and kicking the fender with his shoe.

'Yes, I know.' He turned round and faced her. 'Look here, Sally. I'm no good. You've got to give me up. I can't stand it. I've had more than a year of it, facing Mother. It's more than my being afraid of her. It's like being afraid of oneself. Oh! I can't explain these things, but I'm sort of inside her. Part of me thinks just as she does--I've loved you frightfully, I do love you frightfully now, but all the time I'm wanting to be right with Mother again. I thought, perhaps, she'd get over it. I thought she'd get used to the idea. But she doesn't. She hates it more and more.'

'WHY does she hate me?' Sally asked in a small sharp voice.

'Oh, it isn't YOU that she hates! I think she'd make a fuss about my marrying anyone. She doesn't want to lose me. Of course that's all wrong and very selfish, but in a way I understand it. I don't really want to lose her either. All the same she'd get over that-- because she's really an awfully good sort--if you . . . if you--' He hesitated. 'You see, Sally, she's heard a lot about your father and she says that there's one side of your family that's mad and it always has been. Of course that's all rot--'

'It isn't all rot at all,' Sally interrupted. 'If you look at it from one point of view it's true, I suppose.'

'Mother isn't conventional exactly, but--'

'Does she know,' Sally interrupted, 'that I'm your mistress?'

'No, she doesn't.' He squared his shoulders. His face was so white and miserable that something in Sally cried: 'I hate both these women who are making you so unhappy. Pay no attention to either of them.' And something else in her cried: 'You're a wretched weak creature and I'm a fool to have bothered over you for a single moment.'

'To tell you the truth, Sally, I'd be afraid for her to know. She's old-fashioned about those things. And it wouldn't make it better if she did know.'

'She'd see me as the designing siren, I suppose,' Sally said. 'Well, perhaps I have been.' Then, after a pause, she asked: 'What exactly did happen last night?'

'I was dressed and just going out to you when she came into my room. She asked me where I was going and I told her. She made a most awful scene. Oh, it went on for hours! She cried. She wouldn't let me telephone or anything.'

'I see,' said Sally. 'And then?'

'Oh, then--at last--'

'You promised to give me up?'

He nodded his head.

He began a torrent of explanation. She cut him short.

'All right, Arnold. I understand perfectly.'

She went up to him, kissed him gently on the forehead, held out her hand.

'Goodbye, my dear.'

'No, but Sally--' He tried to catch her in his arms. Quietly she moved away from him, stood looking at him for a moment, then said:

'Now cut along. We've had a lovely time and I don't blame you a little bit.'

He was going to speak again but, looking at her, decided not to. He picked up his hat and coat and went out.

Into his small room at the Mansion House, Benjie was aware just as the clock struck seven of the intrusion of panic. A stout General with very bright red tabs on his shoulders was shouting down the telephone: 'Oh, but, look here, the thing's absurd! Give the feller a kick in the pants and tell him to clear out. What do you say? I can't hear . . . very bad at Camden Town? Well, tell Ritchie to cut along . . . Hullo! hullo! are you there, Ward? Well, why couldn't you say so? Can you hear me? Hullo! hullo!'

Benjie, his gaze idly fixed on the General's large posterior, wondered for the first time whether after all the Herries would manage to hold the fort. Everyone seemed to him to be Herries down here, and he himself, in these few days, had become civilized Herries too. He had enrolled countless men and women, urging them to do their utmost for King and Country, and as, with serious and patient faces, they had promised him to do so, he had thought: 'By God, this country is all right. The heart of this old country is sound', almost as though he had been Cynthia or Alfred or Gordon or Adrian or even old Horace, who, the night before at Cynthia's, had beamed sentimentally through his glasses and, like a bishop pronouncing the blessing, had said: 'This will go down in history. England has proved herself.' It WOULD go down in history, but he was not sure whether it would be quite in the fashion that his family had desired. What was happening beyond this quiet and dignified room?

The Government in its British Gazette proclaimed that it was maintaining with complete success all the vital services of supply-- light, food and power. Communications were improving every day. On the other hand, fifty London General omnibuses had not returned to their depot last night; at Middlesbrough some women and boys had held up a train; a motor-bus had been set on fire in East London; shops were being looted in Edinburgh; and Mr Saklatvala had been sentenced to two months' imprisonment. On this very morning the British Gazette announced that they had discovered that the General Council had issued a new order to 'paralyse and break down the supply of food and the necessaries of life'. How far would this spread? Every day increased the danger. He did not know that at any moment returning through Piccadilly he might not see the appearance of the lorry bristling like a hedgehog, the pieces of red cloth tied to the rifles, the windows of the Ritz smashed with machine-gun fire. 'They don't know. They haven't had the experience, any of them. They are blind to everything. Their whole social order has crumbled to pieces under their very eyes and they are not aware of it. This machinery--the machinery they've been used to so long--may vanish in a moment's temper . . . They don't know it. They haven't seen it . . .'

'By God!' the General was shouting into the telephone, 'tell them they've GOT to or it will be worse for them. This isn't Russia, you know.'

No, it wasn't Russia. The Herries were here. There had been no Herries in Russia. All the same . . .

'Coming along, Herries?' the General said, his face beaming. 'I told the bastards where THEY got off. Coming my way? I'll drive you.'

So he sat in the back of the car with the General and discovered as, with throngs of pedestrians on every side of them, they pushed their way towards Trafalgar Square, that this fine stout kindly officer was happier than ever he had been in his life before.

'This is what I've been wanting, Herries. Teach the blighters a lesson. I'll be damned glad myself if it does come to real trouble. Give us an excuse to be rid of a few of them. That feller Saklatvala--I'd string him up on a lamp-post if I had MY way. By God, I've never been so proud of my country as I am tonight.'

So the Herries were saying. They'd all like to string Saklatvala up on a lamp-post. Old Judith Paris, he remembered, had written in her book somewhere of seeing a boy hanged outside a butcher's shop. She hadn't liked it. But then she'd always been a queer one. And the Herries were right. Civilization had got to be kept on its feet. But suppose the old world was gone. Gone for ever and ever? Suppose on that evening when the whole world had burst out singing (he had sung like the others) they had sung the old world out of existence? Why, then WHERE would the Herries be?

The town seemed to him sinister tonight. It had started to rain and soon it was a downpour. Through the rain the town was walking home. In the heart of the crowd the motor-cars, loaded with people-- shopgirls, secretaries, elderly women, old men like himself-- ploughed the way. The lights flared and the darkness stifled the lights. The whole town seemed on the move as though the order had been given to abandon it, and everyone was fleeing for safety. And yet they were not fleeing. That was the very last thing that they were doing. These people were defending the town, nobly, gallantly, without a thought for themselves. But what about the enemy? HE knew how silent a thin street could be, and behind every window a concealed rifle. HE knew how men could gather, in secret, in silence, and then, at a spoken word, the familiar places--so old,

so safe, so complacent--would be filled with death. This was no melodrama. Efficient, historical fact. One machine gun at the Oxford Circus end of Regent Street, where they now were, and that crowd would turn in upon itself, would scream, cry aloud, bodies crushed into the mud, and the rain pouring down . . . Oh, he was an old man! What had happened to his nerve?

'And that, my dear feller,' the General was saying, 'is the way I'D deal with them!'

At the top of Portland Place, where several roads meet, there was a complete confusion. Under torrential rain a mass of cars, coming from different directions, faced one another like angry herds of cattle. Horns hooted, men shouted, nothing could move. A policeman, his black cape shining in the rain, appeared as it seemed from the bowels of the earth, waving his hand. He came right up to the General's car, placing his hand on the bonnet, and Benjie saw his face, his blue eyes, his cheeks wet with the rain, and a clear, unflinching, unhesitating power of direction and order in his every movement. He seemed a giant from some other planet, impersonal and inhuman. He called out, waved his hand, and at once the disorder was composed into order: the cars separated and divided. Benjie was reassured. 'That man wasn't in Russia,' he thought. But just before his own car moved on he saw a girl, almost slipping, recovering, placing her hand for an instant against the window. It was Sally.

'Here. Let me out. Goodnight, General. See you tomorrow.'

A moment later he had caught his girl's arm.

'Hi! Sally! What are you doing here?'

The rain was driving in their faces, and the collar of her waterproof was drawn up. He held on to her arm, but he could feel that she was resisting him. They had moved away from the roar and confusion and stopped under a lamp. She looked up at him.

'Hullo, Father!' she said. 'What a coincidence!'

'The lamplight,' he thought, 'is making her look like this, and the rain. By God! something has happened to her, though. She's as though she were walking in her sleep.' Then she woke up. He felt her arm tremble under his hand, and her small pale face under the light little hat from which the rain was dripping hardened into that look of angry determination that was often exactly his own.

'I must get on,' she said. 'I'm late.'

'Where are you going?'

'Oh--I've got an engagement with a friend.'

Then her lower lip began to tremble. He saw that she was on the edge of tears. He put his arm round her.

'You haven't any engagements my dear,' he said. 'Nor have I. I'll take you home.'

She had ceased to resist.

'All right,' she said. 'I don't care.'

They walked back to Oxford Street and not a word was spoken. Then they found an omnibus that was driven by quite an elderly party with a white moustache and was crowded with rowdy young men who were going off on some job.

'They say there's been terrible fighting in Camberwell tonight,' an elderly lady said.

'We'll protect you, ma'am,' the young men shouted. 'Lenin shan't get you.'

When they were in Sally's room and had taken off their wet things they sat opposite one another on either side of the fire.

'Margaret coming in?' Benjie asked.

'No, I don't think so,' Sally said. Then she added: 'I've nothing to give you to eat, Father. There isn't a scrap in the place.'

'That doesn't matter.' He pulled out his pipe, crossed his thin legs, leaned back. He was weary. This was a life, when all was said and done, for an old man of seventy-one, and, fit though he was, his back ached and his legs told him that they had done enough for one day.

'Look here, Sally--that was all my eye about your going anywhere. You didn't know where you were going.'

She didn't answer him.

'What's the matter?'

Still she didn't answer him, but sat up straight in her chair, her hands crossed over her knees.

'Why don't you let me take you out and give you a meal?'

'Oh, it's all right, thanks.'

He said at last: 'I wish to God Vanessa was here.' He went on to cover the silence:

'You know, Sally, we ought to see more of one another. I've been a bit shy, I dare say, but it's been my fault that I've never, in all my life, been able to get on any very sound terms with anyone except your mother. Light come and light go. And now I'm paying for it. All the same,' he said, 'you and I and Tom--we've only got one another now. You've got your young man, I suppose.'

'He's gone,' she said.

'What do you mean--he's gone?'

'Oh, he left me three or four days ago. His mother didn't like me.'

'Oh, so that's it,' said Benjie softly.

There was a long silence.

'Well, my dear,' Benjie said at last, 'I shouldn't worry about him too much. You'll find someone much better.'

'Oh, I dare say,' said Sally.

'He was frightened of his mother, wasn't he?'

'He was very fond of her. He hoped for a long time that she would get used to me. But she didn't.'

'Was it partly,' Benjie asked, 'because you had a bad lot for a father?'

'It was all of us. You and I and Vanessa and Judith Paris and your father being shot. Right away back. She seemed to know all about us. Now if I had been Rosalind or Mary it would have been all right.'

'I see,' said Benjie. 'Sins of the fathers. Very unfair, I always think.'

'She didn't know I was sleeping with Arnold,' said Sally in a dull toneless voice. 'That would only have made it worse.'

'He was a bit of a cad, I should say,' Benjie remarked. 'All the same I'm glad he didn't marry you.'

'No, he wasn't a cad at all. I understand him perfectly.'

'You'll get over it, my dear. One gets over everything. (All the same, he thought, I've never got over being without Vanessa.) I've come to the conclusion there's a lot to be said for marriage. Oh, I know, your generation don't think so, and I know that Vanessa had the hell of a time with Ellis. All the same I can see now that it would have been very pleasant if your mother and I had been married. It's the best arrangement society's discovered yet.'

'I didn't care,' Sally said, 'whether I was married to Arnold or not. I wanted to look after him. I wanted--I wanted--'

Her voice broke. She tried to recover herself, beating her hand against her knee. Her mouth moved and quivered and shook. Then she began to cry.

Benjie went over to her.

'Here, Sally--don't cry. It's all right. You've got your life in front of you. Darling--Sally darling.'

He knelt down beside her, putting his arm round her.

'These days--I didn't know anything could be so bad . . . I didn't know I could miss anyone so much. I thought I knew enough not to be hurt by anything. He was so sweet . . . He loved me . . . he did really . . .'

'There, Sally, it will be all right. Really it will. It's been my fault. I haven't been with you as I ought to be. We'll stick together now. You can tell me anything. I've been very lonely too . . . Hellish . . .'

He drew her with him to the other chair, a big roomy one. He sat back and, with his arm around her, wrapped her into his embrace. She was folded up in his arm like a child. She was so small that he could hold her easily. Her hand was clenched inside his. She dried her eyes and with little convulsive sobs told him everything: how Arnold had not taken her to the theatre, of their last meeting, of how, next day, she had not known what she was doing, had wandered about in the crowds, had worked for Bimberg mechanically, had not slept at all for three nights--and tonight she had not known, she had thought that perhaps now that everything was over it would be better . . .

He held her more tightly, feeling her quiver against his heart.

'I know. We all go through it. It doesn't matter what generation we belong to, how much we think we know. It doesn't make any difference . . .'

He thought of that last talk with Vanessa in his room, the agony and distress of letting her go. He was ashamed of his casual life, his neglect of his promise--'I swear, Vanessa, I'll never let her go again.'

A long time after, Sally got up from her chair, went into her room and washed her face and hands.

She stood looking at him, and smiled.

'You're rather a pet,' she said. 'You've been awfully nice to me.'

'What shall we do?' he asked. 'Go out and have a meal?'

'Oh no. I don't think I could eat anything.'

'Let's see how the Strike's going.' He went to the wireless and turned it on. Someone was speaking. 'Why, it's old Baldwin!' Benjie said.

Mr Baldwin was saying:

'The Government is not fighting to lower the standard of living of the miners. That suggestion is being spread abroad. It is not true. No honest person can doubt that my whole desire is to maintain the standard of living of every worker.'

Then after a while there were the sonorous tones of Lord Oxford:

'The real victims of a general strike are what is called the common people. We should have lost all self-respect if we were to allow any section of the community, at its own will and for whatever motives, to bring to a standstill the industrial and social life of the nation. That would be to acquiesce in the substitution for Free Government of a Dictatorship. This the British People will never do.'

The voice died away. Sally's eyes were closing.

'Go on. Go to bed,' said Benjie.

He went with her into her bedroom and, with a little sigh, without taking off even her slippers, she lay down on the bed. He lay down beside her, taking her in his arm again. In a moment, her head against his waistcoat, she was asleep, and he lay there, looking with his sharp, ironical eyes at the ceiling, happier than he had been for many a year.

BELOVED MOUNTAIN

'And now,' said Tom, 'as we cross the bridge you'll see how beautiful it is!'

'And I hope to God she will,' he thought, for he was convinced now that the visit, the visit to which he had looked forward with such eagerness, would prove a terrible failure. Sally had invited herself: he would never have dared, of himself, to ask her. He had taken his three weeks' holiday late this year--it was now early in November 1928--and, as always, had come up to Cumberland. He wanted to be nowhere else. It was lovelier with every visit. He had taken rooms in a house, Bella Vista, on the road from Grange to Manesty, and settled in there, very happy with Mrs Zanazzi, his hostess, and Miss Zanazzi her daughter, and his books, walking every day, sometimes a long tramp, when he would be away in Eskdale, or by Esthwaite, or Patterdale for the night. He was forty-four now and used to being alone. His father was in Spain. He had friends in London, but no one whom he wished to have with him.

And then Sally had written, saying that she would come and stay with him for a week, Sally who had been so strange and hard for so long, who had scarcely seen him, who had had nothing to say to him when they were together.

He had been terribly excited. Mrs Zanazzi had arranged that Sally should have the best bedroom in the house, the room with the view out over the shelving fields to Skiddaw and the Lake.

They would have a glorious week. He and Sally would recover one another again. He knew how unhappy she was and, if he were very careful and did not show her in any way that he wanted to help her, he might give her something that she needed. Oh yes! how VERY careful he would be!

So he had gone to the station full of eager expectation. She wouldn't think much of his small Austin, but he would explain to her that it was better to have a small car in this country; so often the bridges were narrow and the roads little more than lanes . . .

When he saw her come from the train he had gone eagerly forward.

'Hullo, Tom!' she had said, and, at once (so sensitive he was) he had known that there was no change, that she was hundreds of miles away from him, that she didn't care for him, that she didn't know why she had come.

And the drive in the Austin had been terrible. She had shown no interest in anything. When he had asked her about London and had she been to parties and how was old Bimberg and Cynthia and Maurice and Margaret, she had assured him, 'Oh yes' and 'Oh no' and 'Everything's just the same'.

'And now,' he said, 'as we cross the bridge you'll see how beautiful it is!'

To himself it was exquisite. The brilliant autumn colouring was gone. Everything was silver-grey. There had been much rain and the Lake had flooded; the stream ran under the bridge in tumbling curves and circles, watched gravely by the dark hills while the last pale leaves clung to the trees; the fields were faintly green, floating in the last light of the autumn day towards the Lake like green smoke gently stirred by the wind.

He did not know that as Sally looked out she was caught by a quick apprehension. 'Something awful is going to happen. Why did I come? Whatever made me write and ask to come?' Tom's kind and serious face, his short heavy body bent a little forward at the wheel, his eagerness to make her happy . . . Oh, why was Tom always the same, why was he not some heavenly messenger who had swung down in a silver aeroplane and whispered to her: 'You have had enough of this. You have had more than two years of if. I will catch you up and we will fly, like the golden Eagle, into coloured clouds and a foaming brilliant sea'? But Tom was no heavenly messenger, and like green smoke those sleepy fields rolled into the Lake.

A pale ivory twilight lay over the landscape when Sally looked from her window. She could distinguish no detail, only overhead, above the dark shadows of clustering trees, the sky broke into spaces of dim ghostly light as though a moon were somewhere hiding. When she heard running water something caught at her heart. Since her babyhood she had never been in this country, but now it was as though something familiar were returning to her; the smell of wet leaves, the sky that revealed nothing and yet seemed a world of motion and movement, the queer windy whisper in the air, dark shapes on the horizon that were, she knew, the mountains, these things were all familiar to her and unique. No country of hill and field where she had been was like this one, and yet she could see nothing but shadow and, when a dog barked, it was a voice welcoming her, reproaching her for being so long away.

After supper when she sat opposite Tom in the sitting-room she smiled,

'I like being here, Tom,' she said. 'It's as though I'd been here before.'

'Well you have. You were born not far away from here.'

'I know. In a farm, in a storm. Mother nearly died getting to the farm. She often told me.'

'The funny thing is,' Tom said, 'that we came into this country two hundred years ago--old Rogue Herries riding a horse with his small son in front of him. Then we grew and multiplied like the Israelites. We covered the country. And now we've died away again. There are none of us here any more. But it's caught one after another of us, set its seal on us, made us influence others. Perhaps, although we haven't any of us been important, we've altered England's history by coming here. That's what a small piece of country can do.'

'You ought to write about it, Tom,' she said, laughing and thinking that he was nicer here, sitting back, smoking his pipe, than he was anywhere else.

'I can't. That's what's so damnable.' He picked up an orange- covered book on a table near him. 'Listen to this, Sally.'

He read:

'So she let her book lie unburied and dishevelled on the ground, and watched the vast view, varied like an ocean floor this evening with the sun lightening it and the shadows darkening it. There was a village with a church tower among elm trees; a grey domed manor house in a park; a spark of light burning on some glasshouse; a farmyard with yellow corn stacks. The fields were marked with black tree clumps and beyond the fields stretched long woodlands, and there was the gleam of a river, and then hills again. In the far distance Snowdon's crags broke white among the clouds; she saw the far Scottish hills and the wild tides that swirl about the Hebrides. She listened for the sound of gun-firing out at sea. No--only the wind blew. There was no war today. Drake had gone; Nelson had gone. "And there," she thought, letting her eyes, which had been looking at these far distances, drop once more to the land beneath her, "was my land once; that Castle between the downs was mine; and all that moor running to the sea was mine". Here the landscape (it must have been some trick of the fading light) shook itself, heaped itself, let all this encumbrance of houses, castles, and woods slide off its tent-shaped sides. The bare mountains of Turkey were before her. It was blazing noon. She looked straight at the baked hillside. Goats cropped the sandy tufts at her feet. An eagle soared above her. The raucous voice of old Rustum, the gipsy, croaked in her ears, "What is your antiquity and your race, and your possessions compared with this? What do you need with four hundred bedrooms and silver lids on your dishes, and housemaids dusting?"'

'Whatever's that?' asked Sally.

'It's Orlando, by Virginia Woolf. Just out.'

'I don't understand a word of it. What's it mean?'

'It means what it says. You must forget things like space and time.'

'How can you?'

'You can if you like to go far enough. Do you remember in Judith's book, little Harcourt Herries reciting Pope to Francis and David at Ravenglass? Well, he's still reciting it. He's still moved by the beauty of it as I'm moved now by the beauty of this.'

'That's nonsense,' said Sally.

'Yes, if you like to think so.'

They sat in silence, quite happy, coming closer to one another with every tick of the clock.

'I'm beginning,' said Tom, 'to see why we are all so restless and unhappy. It's an awful time really. No one seems to be sure of anything any more--religion, economics, politics. So many people out of jobs. Why, look at you and me and Father. I lost Mary, you lost Arnold, Father lost Vanessa. And so in a way everyone we know seems to have lost something. But then, as the gipsy says in Orlando, "What do you need with four hundred bedrooms and silver lids on your dishes?" You don't need them if you discover the other world. Do you think I'm talking rot?'

'I don't understand a word that you're saying.'

'Well, I'm a failure, a complete and absolute failure. I wanted to be a good writer. I wanted to marry Mary. I adored Vanessa and she died. I wanted you and Father to need me--and you don't. Nobody needs me. So I'm a good example of times like these. I've been unhappy and restless for years. But lately I've been finding out that there's a world that has nothing to do with my needs, nothing to do with space and time, a world that has been showing me points of light for years like the sun flashing on a window, but I haven't seen . . . If I could LIVE in that world, Sally, it wouldn't matter how much a failure I myself was because it's so beautiful, so timeless and so alive that personal failure is of no importance at all.'

'It all sounds very vague to me,' said Sally, but looking at him with curiosity. It was so odd to see Tom with his heavy body, thick shoulders, quiet ways, bursting like this into fantasy.

'But I too can be fantastic,' she thought, realizing suddenly why it was that, through all these years, she had never been really intimate with Margaret. 'I too can be fantastic,' and, looking into the fire, she let her mind wander back over the past year, which had, in truth, been as nasty and spiteful a year as she had ever known. Later, lying in bed, unable to sleep, she reviewed it and discovered that it had already altered its colours under the influence of this place. Like the families in Genesis, Margaret led to Olive Stane and Olive Stane to Miss Bourchier and Miss Bourchier to Freddie Tallent and Freddie to Freda and Freda to William Blake and William Blake (so VERY unlike the poet!) to Mrs Carslake-King and Mrs Carslake-King to stout, solid and feminist Mrs Brent. At the stopping place of Mrs Brent, Sally considered herself as a feminist. She had not been a very good one. Why? It had seemed, after the tragedy of Arnold, the natural thing to consider men feeble and conceited and exasperating creatures. There was, if you were to believe them, a regular war of the sexes. All the men stood up for one another and were most unfair about it, and all the women stood up for one another and were not unfair about it. Some of the women were grand--Olive Stane and Miss Bourchier for instance. They had wit, humour, generosity, courage. What did they lack? They lacked nothing perhaps, but spent their time altogether too much in London literary sets, never really meeting anyone but one another, although they thought they did.

And so, not one of them reached the first class. As writers they were clever and no more, as politicians they were not effective, as women they left men cold and frightened.

So Sally, who had never really been at home with them because she was not clever enough, admired them and left them. She went for a while to parties, but this life she soon abandoned. She disliked to be made love to in an absent-minded way, which was what the young men did; she disliked to be drunk; she disliked not to know the name of the hostess who was entertaining her. She disliked to drink gin dressed (for it was, that night, an Infant Party) as a babe-in-arms. She disliked people to take it for granted that unless she was Lesbian she was uninteresting. Nevertheless she did not make the mistake of supposing that the whole of her generation

were worthless. On the contrary, she found among them enough courage, honesty and common sense to save Europe were someone really worthwhile to get hold of it. Only there was not, it appeared, anyone worthwhile. Lenin was dead and Mussolini was in Italy.

So, unable to be intellectual, and weary of parties, she fell back on the Family. There were not many just now, of her own generation. There were two distant cousins, Phyllis and Anstey Veasey. Their great-grandfather had been the younger brother of Anna Veasey, who had married Warren, Adam Paris' father. Their own father was a Judge and they lived, in considerable splendour, in Connaught Place. They were amusing, full of vitality and very sure of themselves. Then there were two girls, Mabel and Jessie Rossiter, relations of Adrian's, who lived with a widowed mother in Chelsea. They were nice girls but extremely serious, believing in Bertrand Russell and determining, as soon as they had children, to encourage them in complete freedom of expression.

No, so far as Sally was concerned, her only friends in the Family were poor old Horace and Maurice.

Maurice's marriage was unhappy, but just now everything about him was unhappy. He could not forget the War. He could not translate his experience of it into indifference and a kind of shoulder-shrugging tolerance as did so many of his contemporaries. Sally did what she could for him and he loved her.

No, she decided, turning over restlessly on her bed (which was comfortable because Mrs Zanazzi knew how to please her guests), everything for ages had been awful except her father. There the relationship begun on the week of the Strike had bloomed. They were friends now and always would be. They enjoyed their times together, they understood one another, they cared for one another. And it was Benjie who, just before he had gone away to Spain, had suggested that she should go up to Cumberland and stay with Tom.

'You'll find it's like going home,' he had said.

Two things still troubled her, though. One was that she could not forget Arnold. He had married a Miss Thurston. Their pictures had been in the papers. That was all that Sally knew. But surely by now she, a sensible modern girl who would stand no nonsense, would have rid herself of his presence. But she could not. He still haunted her at every turn. Little things that he had said, done, looked, been . . .

And the other ghost was Vanessa. It was, she supposed, because she had been so unhappy that she had thought of her mother so constantly. But it had been more than thought. In London she had been constantly expecting that her mother would appear. She had even at times run up the long dark staircase to her rooms, thinking-- in spite of all common sense and practical wisdom--that Vanessa would be there, waiting for her. This was a ghost that had no sense in it at all.

So, lying restlessly on her comfortable bed, she decided that things in general had been altogether rotten.

Was there something in what Tom had said that evening about finding another world? Was that what everyone was wanting? Was this other world . . . and, so wondering, she fell asleep.

In the days that followed, the country opened up on every side of her. Miss Zanazzi was a great walker and climber. What she said was: 'There's no end to all of this, Miss Herries. You can go to the same spot every day for a year and it's always different. The changing clouds and the light, I suppose.' She explained to her that every part of the country had its own personality: Wastwater and Wasdale were savage, Windermere polite, Ullswater a fortress, Buttermere a fairytale, and every hill a separate character. Of course Scotland was bigger and finer, but the charm of this country was that it was so close together. With every step the view changed and the colours altered. 'It's mysterious, Miss Herries. You'll never come to the end of it.'

She went with Tom to Rosthwaite and saw the little hill where old Rogue Herries' house had been. There was a sturdy little stone house there now. They went to Uldale and saw the green field, on the edge of the moor, next to the church (that had not been there in the old days) where David's house had been, where Judith had grown up, where Adam had died. They climbed Ireby hill and looked over the wall at the Fortress and saw an old lady come to the dining-room window and stare at them.

'Uhland still walks there. I'm sure he does,' said Tom.

They walked up the road from Bella Vista and looked at the cottage on Cat Bells.

'Who lives there now?' Sally asked, and Tom told her that it was a novelist, none of whose books Sally had ever read.

'What a shame!' said Sally.

'Oh, I don't know,' said Tom. 'If he's happy--only I wish he hadn't painted his garage door blue.'

So everything was gone and yet everything remained. They went up from Rosthwaite to Watendlath and visited John Green's House where Judith had lived with her French husband. The sun was shining on a birch tree, and they noticed, as Dorothy Wordsworth once had noticed before them, how 'it glanced in the wind like a flying sunshiny shower', Tom found the place in the Journal that evening and read from it:

'It was yielding to the gusty wind with all its tender twigs. The sun shone upon it, and it glanced in the wind like a flying sunshiny shower. It was a tree in shape, with stem and branches, but it was like a Spirit of water. The sun went in, and it resumed its purplish appearance, the twigs still yielding to the wind. The other birch trees that were near it looked bright and cheerful, but it was a creature by its own self among

them . . . We went through the wood. It became fair. There was a rainbow which spanned the lake from the island-house to the foot of Bainriggs. The village looked populous and beautiful. Catkins are coming out; palm trees budding; the alder, with its plum-coloured buds.'

'Now isn't that lovely?' said Tom. 'As fine as any poem by her brother. But how does she do it? There's hardly a word of more than two syllables. I suppose it's partly that she was so honest-- no humbug--and partly that she found everything beautiful from the village to the smallest twig of the birch.'

But Sally was thinking of Judith in Watendlath:

'Do you remember how she saw her husband coming down the path, after he had been away so long, with the bright bird in the cage? It's as though it happened while we were there.'

'Do you see?' said Tom triumphantly. 'I told you that Time's a fallacy. Live here long enough and you'll see that that's true.'

She felt that the process going on within her was mysterious. It was, as Benjie had told her, that she felt as though she had come home. 'I belong here. All my friends are here--and Tom is really a darling.' For the first time she began to forget Arnold.

But the days were passing and soon she must return to Mr Bimberg. They decided that they would do one grand expedition before she returned to London. But it was late in the year for grand expeditions, and Miss Zanazzi warned them: 'The weather can be funny this time of year. Mists, you know, and there might even be some snow. It's turning colder.'

It was. One night there was a furious gale and the wind tore up the valley, whipping the trees on the right of the house, lashing the windows with rain, screaming with an exultation that Sally found splendid as it galloped up the mountainside.

The streams began to beat like drums and, behind the uproar, it seemed to Sally that men were shouting, calling, crying aloud. Yet, next morning, a shining and placid peace lay over the country. A frost glittered on the chrysanthemums and a long stretch of purple lay above the faint browns and greens, staining the bare trees and spreading on the hillsides in a thin grape-coloured cloud.

'How lovely!' Sally thought. 'It is as still as a dream.'

So they decided to make their expedition next day. Tom would drive the Austin to Seathwaite, leave it there, and then they would go up Stye Head, climb Scafell and be back for supper.

Next morning the sky was flurried with little white clouds and the air was sharply cold. Miss Zanazzi told them that the glass was going down, but she thought that they would be safe for the day. They started out in splendid spirits.

As they began to walk from Seathwaite, Tom said:

'You know, Sally, I think this has been the happiest week of my life.'

Sally, who disliked very much to express her feelings, said:

'Well, that's all right.' But she added, because she could not help herself: 'We'll come up here together again, won't we?--just the two of us. And perhaps Father.'

'Oh, Father knows every inch of it. He loves it more than I do.'

Tom chattered away. He wasn't tiresome any more and Sally realized that people who need affection are natural and easy once they have got it. They are embarrassing only because they are starved. 'I don't believe I'll ever be annoyed by him again,' she thought.

They crossed the little Stockley Bridge. They had been hemmed in by Glaramara on the left and Base Brown on the right, and now the sharp precipices of Great End filled up the valley in front. It was here that Sally had the first perception that she was moving into an uncertain world.

'You'd think,' Tom said, 'that you're looking at the same hill all the time, Great End. Well, you're not--halfway between Seathwaite and Seatoller it's Lingmell you've been looking at.'

The tops did indeed appear to be different with every step, and soon after leaving Seathwaite all the civilized state of man dropped out of existence. Sour Milk Gill was a raging torrent, and the wind that blew in between crevices of rock and boulder frothed it to a spume. They were shut in by a barricade of hills, Glaramara on the left and Base Brown on the right.

'Base Brown,' Sally said. 'What a horrid name!' She was conscious of a return of the apprehension that she had felt on her drive from the station the first day. It was as though a wall of grey menacing stone rose in front of her and on the other side of it was Margaret throwing a book on to the sofa and crying: 'Well, of all the tosh!' and Humphrey Bell, the novelist, who could not forget that the War had personally insulted him and was therefore most blameworthy (as though the War were an absconding solicitor!) . . . and the wooden barricades in Piccadilly Circus, and Olive Stane saying: 'Oh, I'll make it a Gin and It', and poor old Horace leading her so proudly in to dinner at the Piccadilly Grill, and the shimmering rug with purple trees and dark green birds on Cynthia's dining-room floor, and Adrian giving her tea in his lovely flat with the Duncan Grant landscape that had a barn in it of so deep an amber-red, and the green Elk of Carl Milles, and Unamuno's Quixote open on the table, and the old blind man in Piccadilly with the cup and his fat body and patient, patient face.

'And now we climb,' said Tom. 'Not much of one. That's Taylor Gill on the right. I've never seen it so fierce.'

She was both frightened and exhilarated. Everything seemed fierce and angry. The wind rose as they rose. In an incredibly short time the Borrowdale valley was far below, and at the far end of it over Skiddaw and Blencathra a grim wall of grey cloud was mounting but, miraculously, from some unseen place, a tongue of sunlight struck the valley, quivering across it like a searchlight.

At the top they were on a long boggy flat through which a stream ran. Lingmell was in front of them and Scafell Pike to the left of it.

Now they were truly in no-man's-land. A bird flew slowly, mournfully over their heads, but otherwise there was no sign of life at all. Sally saw that Tom was now completely happy, and in his happiness he had a strong family likeness to Benjie and Vanessa when THEY were happy. The true Tom appeared as he never appeared in London. His body did not seem thick and clumsy now. Sally was surprised at the easy agility with which he moved. In London, when he was in a room, you always watched with anxiety lest he should knock something over. Every teacup was in peril from him, but now you felt that he could shoulder a mountain with safety. He began to sing slightly out of tune, and soon Sally began to sing too. Really this was a splendid day.

They reached Stye Head Tarn and, as they did so, a pale sun, dim and veiled, burst the grey paper tissue of the clouds and shivered with a queer iridescent shimmer on the black surface of the little Tarn.

It was very cold, but they found shelter behind a rock on the slope of Green Gable, looked down to the Tarn across the flat, and ate their luncheon. This was the very wildest scenery that Sally had ever beheld. There were of course many places of far greater splendour and terror in the world, but the intimacy and closeness of this place made it personal, as though it had a quality of fairy tale--one of the old stories when the hero reaches at last his perilous destiny, and from the dark rock, the shaggy tree, the awful enemy emerges. And yet, with this peril there was also friendliness. Gable with its great rounded top is the least hostile of all mountains, and the whole plateau with its stream and tarn is kind because it has been there for so long and is so sure of its passive power.

'It was just above here,' Tom said, 'by the other tarn that David fought his duel.' As he spoke a ripple of light ran across the Tarn. Everything sprang to life as though it answered him, then fell into a waiting silence again.

It was too cold to remain long where they were and, after they had eaten, they walked slowly up the slope to Esk House. Here, when Sally looked down into Eskdale, she gave a cry. The valley was sombre today and for many an observer would have seemed little more than a tumble of rock and rough grass falling away to the sea, but at that moment, more than any other, Sally felt that she had come home. On every side of her the hills rose darkly to a dark sky and there was a strength in all those uncouth forms, a strength and patience, a wildness controlled, that seemed to her lovelier than anything that she had ever known. She caught Tom's arm and held it. 'I feel as though I could never be unhappy again,' she said.

Then they started slowly to climb the Scafell Pike track. The wind was rising, murmuring from top to top, and the faint illumination of the pale sun vanished suddenly as though at a word of command. The heavy sky seemed to move down in a lower band above their heads.

'I thought I felt a flake of snow on my cheek,' Sally said.

'Oh, that's all right. It won't come to anything. Not at this time of year,' Tom answered. 'We'll soon be at the top.'

They turned slightly to the right up a green slope which was not difficult, although beyond them the eastern buttress of the Pike had a grim look.

Tom glanced at his wristwatch. It was later than he had supposed; you grew, through the summer, accustomed to Summer Time and fancied that the light would last for ever. There should, for a long while yet, be enough, but it was a dark day and, in the last half-hour, had grown very swiftly darker.

Instinctively he hurried his steps and Sally called out: 'It's all right, isn't it? We've got plenty of time, haven't we?' She had to shout, for the wind whistled in the air.

'Quite all right,' Tom called cheerfully.

She wondered whether she should suggest that they should turn back. Something would have frightened her had she not been determined against any sort of fright. Where Tom could go she could, and she knew that these were little hills and that, in summer, the slopes of Scafell were like a picnic party. Nevertheless she had spent her life in the town; this was the first day she had ever had on the Tops and her feet ached: if she stopped for a moment the wind cut her with its cold, and again she felt some lingering flakes of snow against her cheek. But more than these things it was the changed aspect of the scene that alarmed her. The hills appeared to have doubled their size, and instead of that entire intimacy they had drawn apart, lifting black shoulders and ragged edges against a sky that seemed now to be alive with dark motion, piles of cloud with the dead whiteness of dried bones running before grey unsubstantial vapour. Still, where Tom could go she could.

He stopped for her and held out his hand.

'We'll go back if you like,' he said.

'Oh no--we're near the top, aren't we?'

'Very near--and then we can run down in five minutes.'

When the Pillar and Steeple came into view Tom, who had often climbed this before, although always in fine weather, knew that the rest of the way would be rough.

'Look here, Sally. Perhaps we'd better go back.'

'Oh no. Let's do it now we're here.'

The path now was a confusion of rough stones and the wind seemed to meet them from every quarter. A scurry came up from the valley and with it a whirl of light wet snow.

Then, a moment later, from no quarter at all as it seemed, a blinding storm came upon them. There was snow in it and a wet mist, and it appeared to Tom that from below them, on either side, a boiling vapour of mist rushed, edging up.

They were near the top, he supposed, but he could see nothing. He caught Sally close to him. It was as though they both of them stood on air. If there was ground it rocked under their feet, and the gale lashed their faces like the sharp whip of stinging twigs.

With his arm round her he shouted: 'I say, this is awful. We must find shelter somewhere. This will soon be over.'

The trouble was that it had become suddenly unknown country. He knew that on the one side of the Pike it was easy descent but on the other it was rock and precipice. They moved forward together, step by step, stumbling over the stones. The wind was ferocious, and the sleet came in waves as though it were timed and obeyed a certain rhythm.

Sally stumbled, she caught his arm, then put her hand up to his wet cheek.

'I wanted to be sure you were there. It's the cold--it takes your breath.'

He must shelter her somewhere until this gust was over, but he feared the whirling dusk that was now so thick and clinging that he was like a blind man who, sightless, yet knows his room is turning about him. He felt that all round them was a world of rock; stones that would seem minute enough in daylight now were gigantic. It was as though one single rock moved with them, maliciously keeping them company.

'Look here, Sally,' he said. 'What do you think we had best do? I don't know where we're going. If I could tell which way the wind's blowing, but it seems to be coming in every direction at once. If we could touch grass we'd be all right, but the fact is I'm afraid of striking the rocks on the other side.'

She scarcely heard him. She was ready for anything, but this icy wind was beyond any experience that she had ever had. The cold seemed to grip and shake her; she had never known before what it was to lose faith in her own power of resistance, but her knees were cut with the cold, her head was buffeted and her hands were gone.

She realized that they were beginning to descend, and the wind now leapt up from below, tugging at their feet.

They turned the edge of a rock and the gale fell. Bending down Tom saw that the rock was arched. He groped round it and found that within the curve there was shelter.

He manoeuvred her into its hollow. 'Look here. Rest your back against the rock here. Now bend your knees up. You can't feel the wind now.'

The relief was blessed, for the roar had died, her face was no longer torn with the cold, and she could feel her hands again. He knelt in front of her.

'Thank God. You'll be all right there till the storm's over. I don't suppose it will last long. It doesn't as a rule when it gets up as suddenly as that.'

She pulled at his arm.

'Come in too.'

'No. There isn't room. I'll stay here for a moment. Any second the mist can blow away and I'll see where we are.'

She held on to his arm.

'Tom, you're grand--as though you'd been in storms all your life. You are a brick to look after me.'

She'd never before praised him for looking after her. Well, that was something. He had his back to the gale and it was as though a thudding door of ice beat upon it. He turned sideways, lying up partly against her. So they waited, her hand on his knee.

He thought: 'Now I can do something. I'll see that she's all right. We'll be laughing at this in half an hour.'

Then the sleet changed to snow. There was a thin bright whiteness in the air; in spite of its thinness the general scene was no clearer. Nothing was more visible, but now the touch of the storm was soft and clinging while the wind moaned through the web with a singing, whining cry.

They waited. Time passed.

A long time later Tom put his hand on Sally's. It was icily cold. He bent forward and touched her cheek. She whispered, in a voice strangely unlike hers: 'It's fearfully cold, Tom.'

He took off his waterproof and his coat, then his thick woollen jersey.

'Look here. You've got to put this on.'

She acquiesced, and he knew at once that she was already sleepy with the cold, for, in her own self, she would have eagerly resisted.

But, as he held her against himself, he felt her whole body slacken. He pulled the jersey over her head, then laid his coat over her, thrusting her hands into its pockets. Lastly he took the waterproof and wrapped it round her legs. He saw that she was curled up well within the shelter of the rock. Her head fell forward and he knew that she was asleep . . .

He waited. His eyes stared into the dancing thickness that now had, it seemed, a rosy light at its heart. Then the cold bit him; he felt its teeth at his breast and a warm breath against his nostrils as though out of the storm an animal had crept to him for shelter . . .

Circles, crimson at the edge with centres of dazzling white, floated, hung, fell slowly and rose like telephone wires seen from a train. With a terrific effort he rose to his feet, tottered, balanced himself against the rock.

'Sally!' he whispered. 'Are you all right, Sally?' But of course she was all right. He smiled. Then he moved. He must move or he would sleep.

He stumbled into the light. For now the world broke into a dazzling brightness. He stepped forward to greet it. Soft hands caressed his cheeks and someone stroked his eyes.

Oh! Beloved Mountain! This place of light and splendour for which all his life long he had been waiting. Beloved Mountain that took him now with the warm strong caressing grasp of a friend.

Everywhere about him, from the height and the depth, voices greeted him. A light, more splendid than any that he had ever known, dazzled his closing eyes. He ran forward and fell.

Later a shepherd, looking for his sheep, found Sally sleeping under the rock.

FAMILY DINNER

Two events of the first importance occurred during the spring of 1930 in the Herries family: one was the marriage on April 3rd at St Margaret's, Westminster, of Miss Mary Worcester to the Marquis of Paignton, the other was Alfred's removal to a very fine and spacious house in Hampstead. The two events were celebrated by the dinner that Alfred gave in the second week of May.

Lord Paignton was thirty-eight years of age when he invited Mary to be his Marchioness, and Mary was thirty-seven, so there was, as Adrian said, 'nothing of the virginal about it'. All the same Paignton was a very 'virginal' man. He had proposed to other ladies on other occasions and had twice been engaged, but none of these young women had been serious enough for him. He was himself intensely serious-minded as was right and proper in the future Duke of Wendover. He was famous for his conversational opening gambit: 'If you are at all interested in my opinion of the matter . . .' He had excellent views on Tariffs, Russia, Unemployment, the Pound Sterling, Agriculture, and Why Our Churches are Empty Today. But the interesting thing about him, Adrian thought, was that he was marrying Mary for her brains rather than her looks.

She still HAD looks of a statuary, marble kind and he would, Adrian thought, be just the man to admire her poise, her immobility and air of watching repose. But no, her brain was the lure. 'I'm marrying the most intelligent woman in England,' he told his friends at the Bendish, a little club in St James's Street where gatherings were held of so solemn a character that it was said that a waiter there hung himself because he hadn't seen anyone smile for five years.

'Does he think her clever because she never says anything?' Adrian wondered. But it did not matter. The Herries were pleased, although by this time they were so firmly the backbone of England that nothing either here or there could make any difference. Cynthia was now entirely swallowed up in the waters of bridge, and was so weary with her long, long efforts to find a husband for Mary that, when at last Mary found a husband for herself, she had very little to say about it.

Rosalind had married a Major Brigstock, a good fellow who luckily believed the Herries the finest family in the world, and Peile had died two years ago from influenza, so Cynthia thought now of nothing at all but Contract, her two Pekinese--Tang and Ming--and her figure, which was by this time as thin and sharp as a needle.

Alfred bought the house in Hampstead because money was very uncertain and he thought it not a bad thing to have it in property. He also saw quite clearly that very soon now the West End would be nothing but shops, and anyone who had to live in London would be ashamed to be seen south of St John's Wood. He had also a very charming house near Sunningdale and, although he was sixty-eight this year, played a good game of golf every weekend. He was a dry self-satisfied old man with supreme confidence in himself and a contempt for anyone who was not practical. But he could be generous and, when his liver was in good order, could tell a funny story. He was now deeply disappointed with his son, Maurice, who settled down to nothing, thought that he could write poetry, and led a cat-and-dog life with his wife. On the other hand his girl, Clara, had married a rich American, Borden Wadsworth, and entertained regally in Chicago.

His only trouble had been that he liked women around him. Men as companions were only useful for golf and an exchange of opinions about the money market. Quite recently this lack in his life had been strangely supplied. A woman called Abigail Hill, a single lady of forty or so, occupied the position of his best friend. The true story of Abigail Hill was a most interesting one and her influence on the whole Herries family already promised to be remarkable. She was a tall, gaunt, extremely fashionable woman who had lived, it appeared, for many years at Eastbourne with an old invalid father. He, dying, had left her a large sum of money. She had come to London and had taken a large flat at the Marble Arch end of Park Lane. Here she entertained, and with excellent taste. She was, apparently, cynical and plain-spoken. She won a reputation for her caustic remarks. But, cynical or no, she became attached to old Alfred and he to her.

No one suggested for a moment that there was anything lyrical in their association. They were quite simply good friends and, whenever he gave a dinner party, it became natural to find her there as hostess. She furnished the Hampstead house for him and did it magnificently. She was modern and not too modern. This was a good time, because of the growing distress in Europe and America, for 'picking up' things cheaply, and Alfred's pictures and furniture were worth seeing. He, like the other Herries before him, cared little or nothing for property as such. It was beneath a Herries' dignity to think that he or she was valuable because of possessions. All Alfred wanted was that he should be suitably surrounded. Abigail Hill saw that it was so.

In a short time she had made her mark on every member of the family. She played bridge with Cynthia, talking cynically with Adrian, flattered Gordon, soothed Maurice and even bothered to have tea with poor old Horace. The only members of the family with whom she could do nothing at all were Benjie and Sally. She complained of them to Alfred.

'They're too sentimental for anything. They don't seem like your relations.'

'Benjie's always been a bad lot,' Alfred said, 'and his daughter takes after him.'

Nevertheless they were invited to the dinner party because Abigail said that what was needed was a little variety. 'You're all a little monotonous in the lump,' she said, 'and as a matter of fact I rather like Benjie even though he detests me.'

Adrian was engaged and therefore a young Frenchman and his sister, children of a French financier of importance to Alfred, were invited. They were the only two present who were not of the family circle, and only at the last moment was it discovered that the Frenchman, Raymond Herriot, was blind--blinded in the War.

'That's uncomfortable,' Alfred said. 'I wish we hadn't asked them.'

'I believe he's no trouble at all,' Abigail answered. 'He goes about quite a lot.'

The dinner party consisted of Alfred, Miss Hill, Gordon, Maurice and his wife, Tim Bellairs the painter, now living in London, Phyllis and Anstey Veasey, Mary and Lord Paignton, Cynthia, Rosalind (her husband the Major was away in Ireland), Raymond and Mlle Herriot, Sally and Benjie.

Yes, quite a party.

Sally had given up her rooms and lived with her father ever since Tom's death. They got on splendidly. Now as she drove him up to Hampstead in her small bright-red Midget he thought of her with most loving affection. Tom's death had wrought a deep change in her. It was strange, when you thought of it, that Tom had longed all his life to do something for those he loved, and in his death, which had seemed accidental, gratuitous, he had at last won his desire. Well, perhaps nothing was gratuitous, accidental . . .

But with Sally it was the three great unhappinesses of her life-- her mother's death, her misadventure with Arnold, and Tom's death-- that made her what she now was, and Benjie, looking at her, knowing her courage, common sense, humour and kindness, wondered whether ever in England before there had been created a generation so fine and intelligent as this one of Sally's. 'Only we can't tell yet. We can't tell for another twenty years.'

Assembled in Alfred's grand drawing-room, panelled, the splendid possessor of three lovely Canalettos, they found that they were the last of the party,

'Yes, this IS the Family!' Benjie thought, sarcastically, for whenever he encountered them en masse he disliked them, felt that they disliked him and would be relieved if he left them for ever. He could never be with the Family without, at the same time, feeling rather ashamed of himself, and that made him both shy and angry. For they had succeeded. As a family (for they had only the slenderest connexion with the Scottish Herries) in 1730 they had been nothing, in 1780 a little something, in 1820 people were aware of them, in 1850 they counted, in 1900 they were prominent, and now in 1930 they were everywhere . . . And yet for him now as he looked at them, the romantic period of their history was closing. They no longer fought, struggled, were jealous, cruel . . . Cynthia, Alfred, Mary, Gordon, Rosalind . . . They had become part of England, and future history would be made of struggles elsewhere and of another kind.

'We've been interesting for just two hundred years,' he thought. 'Sally and Maurice and the Veasey children may make history, but it will be a new chapter.'

For he was old enough now to be a philosopher and have a perspective. And, physically, he was in splendid condition for an old boy who had led a life, had only one arm and was seventy-five years of age.

They marched into the dining-room. The long shining table was lit by tall candles in high silver candlesticks. Over the mantelpiece was a fine picture by John of a peasant in a blue cloak standing against a background of dark hills.

Benjie threw his eye around him. He was himself sitting between Phyllis Veasey and a grave dark girl with charming intelligent eyes whose name he did not know.

'Who is it on the other side of me?' he asked Phyllis under cover of the opening babble of conversation.

'French,' said Phyllis. 'A Mademoiselle Herriot. That's her brother over there next to Sally. He's blind.'

He looked across and saw, next to Abigail Hill, a young man with black hair and a strong watchful face. He was watchful because he was blind. His brown eyes gazed with a steady absorbed look in front of him and, instead of appearing sightless, had a penetration that seemed to go beyond all things physical to rest calmly

on a world where everything was quiet, profound and real . . .

'Vanessa's world,' Benjie thought.

Phyllis Veasey began at once to talk. She found it difficult to keep still. She was gay, bright, like a coloured bird who had just risen from the water and must shake the sparkling drops from its wings.

She had been reading a very long book called Kristin Lavransdatter.

'I'm afraid you don't read much, Cousin Benjie.'

'No, not very much. I never have. I'm an old man and want to see everything I can before my time's up. I like a man called Hudson who writes about birds.'

'Well, Kristin Lavransdatter's miles long. I like long books, don't you? You go on and on and on. I got this one from the Book Society.'

'What's the Book Society?'

'Oh, five writers tell you what to read.'

'Why five?'

'Oh, I don't know. Five's better than one. Not so prejudiced.'

'I should have thought five times as prejudiced. Anyway, what do you want anyone to tell you what to read for? Why don't you decide for yourself?'

'Oh, there isn't any time and one wants to read what other people are reading.'

'The girl's an idiot,' thought Benjie crossly. He found that his temper rose just as quickly as ever it had done in spite of his seventy-five years. So he turned to Mlle Herriot and found, to his relief, that she talked perfect English. For his own French was nothing to be proud of.

'Don't we seem odd to you,' he asked her; 'an English family all dining together inside the security of one's own fortress?'

'In what way--odd?' She had a most charming smile, gay and gentle. And, at that same moment, he realized that young Herriot, turning to Sally, had the same smile.

'Well, the French and English never really understand one another, do they? And never will. You are so realistic. We so sentimental. Now we don't look sentimental, all of us in this room. But I assure that we are. We believe devoutly in our fairy stories--the splendour of England, that hearts are more than coronets, although we are the most snobbish people on earth, and that the Herries family is unique in the world for its qualities of good sense, patriotism and fine breeding.'

'But I think England IS splendid--and France too. You see, I also am romantic. I think, too, that England has her faults, her stupidities, and France too. Now is not that a safe answer?'

'Very safe,' he said, smiling. 'That is your brother-- on the other side to the left, sitting next to my daughter?'

'Yes. Oh, is that your daughter? What an amusing face she has! And how intelligent! She is more alive than anyone else here.' Then she hurried on lest he should think that she was paying obvious compliments. 'My brother, Raymond, was blinded in the War. He is the most splendid man I know. His blindness hardly handicaps him at all. He lives in Berlin. He is working with a group of other young men for international understanding.'

'Not an easy job,' said Benjie.

'No,' Mlle Herriot said eagerly. 'But most interesting. He gets on with the Germans splendidly. His blindness seems to help him. He says that people accept from him, because he is blind, more than they would from others.'

'Perhaps it would be better if some more of us were blind. We might see farther.'

Just then he caught Sally's eyes and they smiled at one another. He could see that she was very happy. She was. She had not looked forward with great pleasure to this party. Big dinners were out of fashion now, family groups were out of fashion, and old Alfred and Abigail were not, in Sally's view, an interesting pair.

She had left Bimberg long ago, and now (because work she must) was helping the famous Lady Connington in an effort to rouse the people of England to an interest in the League of Nations. Benjie was not rich, nor had she inherited anything from Ellis who, in a will written shortly after Vanessa's flight, had left his wealth first to the Miss Trents, and at their death to charities. Lady Connington was a fool, and the League was not, at times, very encouraging. It attracted so many half-baked nitwits. Nevertheless, Sally was staunch to it. It was, Mr Rack-Bunden told her, 'the only thing there is. Without it our civilization is ruined. We go tottering into the abyss.' So Sally held on to the League, went about the country in her MG speaking for it, and explained to Sheffield and Newark and Doncaster what Gandhi's theory was and what was happening in China .
. .

She had felt, in fact, after Tom's death that she must try and do some good somewhere. Do something for him in return, as it were. She had long ago understood that among her friends the worst thing that anyone could say about anyone else was that he or she was trying to do good. It was simply too 'shy-making', in the phrase of the moment. At the same time she realized that many of them did a great deal of good in a humorous, cynical, and 'Don't you dare to remind me of it' manner. She hid her motives; she tried to pretend that Lady Connington and the League satisfied her. She was exceedingly lonely. Here she was, twenty-six years of age, and she had achieved nothing whatever except to be considered, by a stupid, ignorant woman, not good enough for a weak, helpless young man. She had lost her mother, her lover and her brother. She was beginning to wonder, in spite of her twentieth-century materialism, whether there was not a curse on her father and herself. They were, both of them, so plainly isolated, by themselves, not wanted.

So she had not looked forward to the dinner. Abigail Hill did not like her; Alfred thought that she encouraged Maurice in his discontents; Gordon disliked her; the Veaseys were afraid of her.

And then, when, after five minutes, a few words with Gordon, her neighbour on her left, had convinced her that their hatred of one another was entirely mutual, she turned to her other companion. He turned also with eyes that seemed to stare with a gentle, almost indecent obstinacy into her heart. They did, indeed, make her heart suddenly beat with a confusing rapidity. She did not know him. She had never seen him before. Why did he stare at her so? And then she saw that his hands moved round his plate, touched, very quickly, the knives and forks. Then that his duck had been cut into small pieces before it was brought to him. She knew now why his eyes so unwinkingly stared.

'You must forgive me,' she heard him say (his English was good, but it had a pleasing accent). 'I am blind, and so am unable to be sure whether you want to talk with me or not. I don't even know whether you are looking my way.'

She touched his sleeve with her hand.

'I am looking your way and I want to talk.'

'Bien. Thank you very much. I don't often go to dinner parties because I'm afraid of being tiresome. Or, rather, I did not. But now my life in Berlin includes a good deal of--what do you say?-- sociability, so I am getting over my shyness.'

'Oh, do you live in Berlin?' asked Sally.

'Yes. I was blinded in the War. At Verdun. I was in hospital for two years and did not know what to do with myself. And then in '25 a very brilliant man, a Swiss, a Monsieur Holthois, formed an International Group with members in all the principal cities in Europe--also in America. His purpose was no more than for internationally-minded people of every country to be in constant communication--see each other often, you know. We are all patriots, but internationalists as well--not so difficult as you suppose. Our only rules are that we deliberately discuss everything--are not afraid to--and that we see one another's point of view and that we allow no difference of opinion to separate us. We are growing very fast, and I am the principal French representative in Berlin. But, dear me, I talk only of myself. Tell me about YOU. What are you called? Who are you? Married or single? What do you look like? You see, you must help me.'

'Yes,' said Sally, rather breathlessly. 'I want to. My name is Sally Herries. I'm twenty-six years of age and not married. I help Lady Connington about the League of Nations, or try to, but I'm not much use, I'm afraid. My father is sitting on the other side of the table. He and I live together. My mother died when I was only nine, but I've never forgotten her. She was the finest person I've ever known. Then my only brother was killed in Cumberland in 1928--we were caught in a storm on a mountain, and he kept me warm by wrapping his clothes round me, and he fell over a rock and was stunned and died of the cold.'

'I'm very sorry,' said Raymond Herriot.

'Yes, so you see there's nothing very special about ME?'

'Would you please tell me,' he asked, dropping his voice a little, 'if you do not think it impertinent, what you look like?'

'Of course.' She laughed. 'Shall I be honest? I'd better be, because other people would tell you the truth if I didn't. I'm short and small. I've got dark-brown hair--short, you know--a sallow complexion which I try to brighten up a bit, a snub nose and not a very pretty mouth. On the other hand, my eyes are nice. I've quite good hands and very small feet--only my legs are too short.'

'Thank you,' he said.

She did not know whether she had been impertinent and too familiar or too hasty. She had never had an experience like this before. She felt that she would tell him anything.

'One thing you have not said. You have a beautiful voice.'

'My voice isn't bad,' she answered recklessly, 'when I'm in a good mood. I have an awful temper. I get that from Father, and then, when I lose it, my temper I mean, my voice has a nasty edge to it.' She added, thinking that it was time to get away from the personal: 'What a wonderful thing to do! To work like that in Berlin! I do envy you.'

'Come and work there too,' he said earnestly.

'Oh, do you think I could?'

'Why not?' Then he added: 'I feel as though we were meant to meet tonight. Please let this not be our last meeting.'

'Oh no!' Sally said. 'Oh no! We'll meet as often as you like!'

It was after that that her eyes met Benjie's and they smiled.

By this time everyone was very gay. Alfred's wines were excellent, and that spirit of self-confidence that always developed when members of the family were for a time together was now most happily universal.

Dessert came and Alfred made a little speech (he liked to make speeches).

'I welcome you all to my new house and I hope you will be very often here. It may seem ostentatious for an old man like me to have a new house, but it is intended for the Family as much as for myself. I don't know whether some of you remember,' he went on. 'It is a long time ago but it is very vivid to myself. At the beginning of the War, before Gordon and Maurice went to the Front, some of you had dinner with me, and Sally here, who was only a child then, lit a candle which we passed from one to another. I must say that I think there has been something that has held us all together

through all the hard times, and will, I am convinced, hold us together still.

'I would like to say how pleased I am that on this occasion we should have with us two friends from that splendid country so grandly our ally then and now. I drink to the health of glorious France.'

Everyone stood up and drank.

Then young Herriot replied. He said only a few words:

'I must thank you very much on behalf of my country and my sister and myself. We are all proud of the countries to which we belong: it is, I think, that pride, one of the finest things in human nature--but with it there must go something as fine--pride in the whole world, a desire to see the whole world one, so that so dreadful a thing as war can never return to the world again.'

Then there was a very regrettable episode--one of those episodes for ever recurring in the Herries history. Young Anstey Veasey had been drinking. He was a nice young fellow. Everyone agreed about that afterwards. What he did any one of his generation might have done. Luckily the little affair was very soon over. Fifty years ago there would have been more lasting consequences; a hundred years ago perhaps a family feud as in the famous ancient story of poor Christabel and the fan. But now--well, now in the twentieth century the Herries temper had mellowed, the hysterical element in it had been taught discipline.

What occurred was that young Veasey cried out:

'It's all very well for you fellows who had all the fun to say that there's to be no war--but what about us? Are we never to have any adventure again? Oh, I know what all you older people say--that the last war was horrible and the next one will be worse. But how do we know? You had some pretty good times in the War. I've heard lots of fellows say it was the best time in their lives. Of course men were killed and wounded, but we've all got to die some time, and after all it's the greatest adventure can happen to anybody. I don't think another war would be such a bad thing when all's said and done. It would clear up some of the mess the world's in anyway. After all, you can't stop men fighting. It's their nature to fight, and I think a jolly old scrap with the Russians or someone would do a lot of good.'

He was, of course, only a boy who had had too much to drink, and his silly nonsense should have passed unnoticed.

But what happened was that before anyone else could speak Maurice had sprung to his feet.

'It's a damnable lie!' he cried out. He stood there, white-faced, his thin nervous body trembling, his voice pitched high. 'I say it's a lie! My God, is this what we went through all that hell for? Only a few years and already there are fools daring to talk that blasphemy. We suffered--we suffered, millions of us, men, women and children suffered. We went through hell day after day, month after month, year after year. Our lives have been wrecked. We've lost everything, friends, faith, belief in God . . . We've been ruined, been damned . . . The only hope we've ever had is that at least what we suffered has made it impossible for anyone to suffer that way again. And now, now--already--it's coming back, and men dare to say they want it back--and all we've been through has been no good. Anyone, any-one--who helps another war is damned. They're enemies of their fellow-men--the cruellest--'

He stopped short and, to everyone's horror, burst into tears. He stood there, his hand in front of his face, sobbing. Then, with a gesture of his hand, his head down, be turned and hurried from the room.

There was a moment's silence then. Rosalind got up and went after him.

'I say,' said young Anstey, 'I'm most awfully sorry--'

Paignton broke in: 'If anyone cares to hear what I think--'

Conversation became general. It was very unpleas-ant, of course, and especially because there were those present who were not English and because Maurice was Alfred's son.

But all the concentrated common sense of the Family rose like a calming breeze. They knew nowa-days--Alfred and Cynthia and Gordon and Mary--how to deal with that sort of hysteria. Poor Maurice! It was natural enough that he should feel as he did, but at his age he should really have learnt to control his emotions--one of the first and most important lessons.

Soon everyone was easy again. Rosalind returned and said that Maurice had gone.

'He's been having his headaches,' she explained.

'Poor boy!' Alfred said. 'You'd think that after all these years his nerves would be in better control. I think of sending him to Vienna. There's a doctor there . . .'

Later, in a corner of the drawing-room under the enchanting Canaletto that showed the gondolas like butterflies, the figures of rose and silver in their masks crossing the bridge, Sally had some last words with Raymond Herriot. His sister was saying her farewells to Alfred.

They were partly concealed from the others by the folds of a curtain of dark shadowed gold. He put out his hand and touched her sleeve. Then his hand rested firmly on her arm.

'It is,' he said, 'how do you say?--up to you, our next meeting.'

'I will meet you whenever and wherever you like,' she answered.

'Well, then--why not tomorrow? Would you come and have tea, perhaps, with my sister and me? We are at Brown's Hotel.'

'Yes. Of course I will.'

'Bien. And then one day perhaps you will come to Berlin?'

'Yes, if you would like me to.'

'Yes, I would like you to.' His face broke into a beautiful smile. 'I have a perfect picture of you in my mind--already.'

'You must ask your sister,' Sally answered.

'I don't need to ask anyone.' Then very abruply he said: 'Now, how old do you suppose I am?'

'Oh--' She moved a little closer to him. 'I should say--thirty- five.'

'Yes--thirty-six. And still a bachelor. Strange, is it not?'

'I don't know. I'm not married either.'

'Yes, that is very strange. But you are ten years younger.'

She said nothing.

With that quiet gentle voice that she found ex-tremely charming he asked her: 'That is not too great a difference in years--between us?'

'No. Of course not.'

She could not help herself. She put out her hand and caught his. He held hers and then, raising it, kissed it.

She sat beside her father, driving the car, staring in front of her.

'Did you enjoy it?' he asked her.

'Yes, Father--most awfully.'

'Pity Maurice had that outburst. I hate to see a man cry. Poor chap. If I had my way, I'd give young Anstey a good leathering. Rotten manners with Herriot there!'

'Lots of his generation think like that.'

'Do they? More fools they.' He looked at her. 'You seemed to get on well with that young Frenchman.'

'Yes. I'm going to tea with him and his sister to-morrow.'

Then she added:

'He thinks I might help him in their work in Ber-lin.'

'Oh, does he? Would you like to?'

'Yes, I think I would.'

He sighed, but so gently that Sally did not hear him. So that was Sally's destiny. Just what she wanted, someone with her own notions, someone for her to look after. But blind? And a Frenchman?

Sally would manage it. She'd found what she wanted. And so the last link was broken. He would be alone now--the last of the bad Herries. They were all good now . . .

Cumberland.

It was as though the Derwent suddenly broke in a torrent across Piccadilly and Glaramara rose towering above the Ritz.

He put his hand on Sally's knee.

'He looks a fine fellow,' he said, 'if you want to know what I think about it. And when you're married I shall take the next train for Keswick.'

Sally laughed.

'Father, how ridiculous! I don't know that he even likes me.'

'No, but I do. Look out! You nearly had that taxi.'

When later she kissed him goodnight she was quite especially affectionate, and, after she had gone to bed, he sat for a long while looking at Vanessa's photograph.

'Sentimental,' he said, knocking his pipe out on the fender. 'That's what I've become! All the same--Vanessa would have approved of that man. He's her sort.'

COUNTRY FAIR

Sally Herries was engaged to Raymond Herriot just before Christmas 1930. They were married in London at a register office on the 14th of November, 1931.

In February 1932 Benjie paid them a visit in Berlin. He stayed with them for a fortnight and had a grand time. The more he saw of young Herriot the better he liked him, and Sally's happiness was founded on excellent reason. The only thing that distressed him was that she might become TOO international. She had, in a few weeks, the troubles of Germany at her fingertips. She knew what Schleicher wanted, what Hitler said, and what the German Princes were doing. She also knew why the middle-class German was starving. At the same time she understood to a marvel what were the difficulties of M. Herriot (no relation at all of her husband's). She understood the ambitions of Mussolini, the restlessness of the Japanese, the confusion of the Chinese, why America would be Democratic before the end of the year and just how far the Five Year Plan had collapsed.

'You know,' said Benjie when he had listened to a great deal of discussion, 'I'm so old now that none of these things seem to me of the least importance.' He patted Sally on the shoulder, 'When you are busy making the new world don't forget there's such a place as Cumberland.'

'There you are, you see,' Sally said. 'How can you say that the state of the world isn't important? How can Cumberland be happy if there isn't enough to eat?'

'Temporary questions, temporary questions,' Benjie murmured. 'There's something more important.'

'What is?' She put her arm around his neck. He was such a fine old man, so sturdy on his legs, so irascible and jolly and indignant and easily placated, so strong and healthy for his years.

'I don't know--and I don't care, as long as I know that SOMETHING is--'

He kissed her. They were saying farewell. It was in the Kurfürstendamm on a Sunday evening. They had been seeing Jannings' new film Tempest with the new actress Anna Sten. She had excited Benjie and he would have given anything to be able to kiss her adorable and most mysterious almond eyes. 'But I don't kiss women any more,' he told Sally. 'Or hardly ever. Old men of my age should look and not touch.'

He was catching the night train to the Hook, and in the train he felt for a while very melancholy. The last link was gone. Not only was he alone now, but the romantic history of the Herries family was closed and finished. He would go back to Cumberland and never leave it till he died. He hated to feel lonely, so he thought of Vanessa. He opened a novel that he had been told was good--The Fountain, by Charles Morgan. He was very quickly interested in it although he seldom read novels. 'Sort of book Vanessa would like,' he thought.

In the summer he did a ridiculous thing. He bought a caravan. He had been staying for some days near Canterbury and he saw this thing. It looked very handsome, for it was painted a deep crimson and the curtains of the little windows were pink and white. It contained, he discovered, every possible requirement and was remarkably cheap because its owner had just been declared bankrupt. He found that his motor-car could be attached to it very comfortably. He bought it there and then. Afterwards he had the difficult task of explaining its advantages to John Holly. Holly was his man, chauffeur, cook, bottle-washer, general factotum, friend and perpetual grumbler, who had been with him now for several years. He was a small spindle-shanked man whose appearance was never as smart as Benjie wished. He had a passion for engines, dogs and women. He was sober and industrious, but an abominable gossip and a Bolshevik in politics. He was no respecter of persons.

'Gor blimey! What do you want a bloody caravan for?'

'To live in.'

'To live in? You can't live in a caravan in London.'

'We aren't going to live in London any more, John. We shall probably never see it again. We are going up to Cumberland to stay.'

'Oh, well, you can take my notice. I'm not going to live in the country.'

'All right. You can go as soon as you like.'

'I damned well would go it if weren't for the dog.'

'There you are, you see. It's much better for Sam to live in the country. You're always saying he doesn't get enough exercise.'

Sam, although he was no longer young, behaved like a puppy still. Holly adored him.

'A caravan! My God! We WILL look a couple of pretties!'

Before his departure for Cumberland, Benjie went round and said goodbye to the Family. They were none of them sorry to see him go, as he very well knew. Only Horace perhaps regretted him, which was ironic, because Benjie had for so long detested Horace. However, Sally had cared for him, and now at the age of seventy-four he put up, on the whole, a very brave show.

He was as optimistic as ever and even quoted 'God's in His heaven: All's right with the world'.

'Everything possible is wrong with it,' said Benjie, 'and we're two old derelicts who ought to have been dead long ago.'

'I'm remarkably well,' Horace said, 'except for a twinge of rheumatism. I'll come up and visit you in Cumberland one day.'

'I'm damned if you will,' thought Benjie. However, he shook him warmly by the hand.

Cynthia's Pekinese barked at him until he was deafened (he detested toy dogs), Alfred showed him round the Hampstead garden, Gordon slapped him on the back, Adrian, who was now a weary dyspeptic pessimist, said to him:

'I'll be sorry not to see you about, Benjie. I've always admired you, you know.'

'Admired me? Good God--why?'

'You've always gone your way. I might have done once. And then you make me think of Vanessa, the only woman I ever really loved.'

They weren't so bad, he thought, when he'd said goodbye to all of them. He had fought them all his life and was glad to be rid of them, but he saw quite clearly their integrity, their wholesome common sense, their loyalty to their own beliefs.

'There have to be the imaginative and the unimaginative, but they'll never understand one another. And that's that.'

August this year was luckily a dry fine month. Everyone was astonished--as everyone in England always is when holidays are fine-- astonished and a little indignant, as though England were posing slightly. The caravan was most amusing. Benjie, Holly, and Sam all slept in the little cupboard behind the general living-room unless the nights were dry, when Holly and Sam slept out of doors. But they got on very well. They were all quiet and unemotional sleepers.

There was a great deal of traffic and general holiday rejoicing. Holly, as was the way of his kind, was extremely proud of the caravan in the presence of strangers and very indignant about it to Benjie.

'Blasted old inculus' (he meant 'incubus'). 'It wobbles like an old fat woman.' But he talked to everyone-- farmers, hotel girls, motor-cyclists and the AA officials.

'Ought to have one,' Benjie heard him say. 'Everyone will be having them soon. They say we all got to economize. Well, what about it? Most economic thing going.'

When they were north of Doncaster, Benjie's spirits rose higher and higher. For one thing, he'd never felt better in his life.

'What do you think of me for seventy-seven?' he would ask John. He would be doing his exercises, half stripped on a sunny morning outside the caravan, while Sam sniffed for rabbits under the hedge.

'Take care you don't catch no cold,' John would say. 'And another thing. Don't let no women see you. They'll think we're nudists.' Then, with a reluctant and cynical smile he would add: 'You've got a fine brown skin--like the gipsies. I'm a gipsy now myself, I reckon, but I can't get that brown colour. Lived too much in towns.'

On the whole they found that farmers, proprietors of fields, publicans and sinners were all very agreeable to them. A very good thing, for Benjie's temper was up in a minute.

'I give what I get--always have. Give me sauce and you'll know it.'

Then, when they came to Kendal, it was just like going home. There's a brow of the hill between Kendal and Windermere when the waters of the Lake are suddenly revealed. It is as though a door were unlocked. Benjie caught Holly's shoulder. 'Look at that, John, and thank your Maker.'

'Here, look out--I'll be driving into the hedge.'

'Well, stop the damned thing.'

All three of them got out and looked at the Promised Land.

'The only woman I ever loved lived with me there. I was born there. My children were born there.'

'What!' said Holly, astonished, 'Only loved one woman in your life? A gay old man like you? Glad I can't say the same.'

But Benjie didn't answer.

They came into Keswick on a fine summer's afternoon and attracted a good deal of attention, but they didn't stop there. They found that on the following day, September 3rd, were the Braithwaite Games, so Benjie said that they should pitch their caravan in a field nearby. They found a nice green one under the beneficent shadow of Grisedale and Grasmoor. They found a farmer too, a little bouncing man with a red face.

At first he was very angry and then he was very friendly. He told them to clear out and Benjie spoke his mind. Holly, watching them, found it amusing to see two little men so furious.

'What I want to know,' Benjie remarked, 'is why you can't keep a civil tongue in your head. We aren't doing any harm to your blasted field. I'll pay you properly, if that's your trouble.'

'Aye,' said the farmer, 'but I don't want your money or your company either.'

Then he smiled. Benjie was standing, with his hat off, his blue eyes fiery as though he wanted nothing better than a hand-to-hand encounter.

'It's a nice day,' the farmer said. 'You can stay if you like--and I don't want your money either.'

They shook hands and finally sat down on the steps of the caravan and had a chat.

And next morning it came down a regular posh. Not only did it pour, but the wind blew, and not only did the wind blow, but it blew from every possible direction. The whole world was a turmoil of wind and water. But Braithwaite people are not easily discouraged. Have they not the finest village hall for entertainments in the County? No, they are not the people to be defeated. Benjie in a mackintosh and Sam with his stiff short hair blown sideways and one ear over one eye (all the work of the wind) went along to see how things were progressing. They discovered that the tea tent had just been blown down for the third time. Everyone was in a state of mind. As the Mid-Cumberland Herald afterwards neatly put it: 'All morning wind and rain conspired to make conditions as unpleasant as possible. While the caterers were manfully struggling to erect a marquee in which to feed the spectators, and had to give up after the third attempt, the would- be spectators were debating in their own minds whether to attend or not. The secretary and committee were wondering what the patrons would do.'

Benjie and Sam assisted for a while and then, feeling that they were wet enough for anything, went back to the caravan. Here, for the rest of the morning, while the rain beat and the wind blew, Benjie wrote to Sally and entertained Sam.

Sam had never grown up. He had not changed in the slightest since Benjie first had him; the white and brown curls of his coat were as charming as ever, his brown eyes as alive and his body as packed with quivering and alert eagerness. A small rubber ball was everything that he needed to turn life from a dull sombre business into a matter of quicksilver daring and adventure.

The caravan apartment was small and loaded with cooking things, clothes, a rifle, a broken-down armchair, a radio and a number of books. In and out of this confusion Benjie and Sam enjoyed an entertainment that had surprise for motive and confusion for its atmosphere. As the ball bounced man and dog rushed for it together. Benjie was, after many years of practice, up to every kind of guile, but Sam knew all the tricks. He stood, the stump of his tail erect and quivering, his eyes on fire, his nose twitching, his right foreleg trembling! Had you shouted in his ear that the Last Trumpet was at hand it would have been no matter. Benjie, his arm raised, held the ball: he feinted towards the cooking stove and Sam's body swung in that direction but his eyes did not shift. He knew, too, of that. When the ball bounced his teeth snapped, he sprang and Benjie grabbed. Books fell, tins rattled, clothes swung in mid-air. Benjie was on his belly groping under the chair while Sam, in no way deceived in this manoeuvre, knowing well that Benjie had the ball set in his hand,

stayed, his legs parted, his eyes burning, his complete soul (for he had one) concentrated . . .

Meanwhile the rain lashed the caravan, sweeping across the field in sheeted splendour.

'Not bad for seventy-seven!' Benjie cried to Holly, who, standing disdainful in his yellow ulster, saw his master with his shirt open, on his knees, and dust on his cheeks.

'Gawd, what weather!' Holly said.

Nevertheless in the afternoon they ventured and had their reward. Cumberland people are not to be shaken by the weather and there was a good crowd. The weather in fact shook its head and decided to improve. The rain when it did come was a deluge, but in between the sun shone and the colours came out like a picture show. The clouds rushed like mad things across the sky. The sun fell, as though the light had been spilled from a bucket, on to Skiddaw and at once the purple glow of the heather on its flanks spread like a living shadow from shoulder to shoulder while above and below it the green turf almost hurt the eye with its brightness. Then, on the other side of the valley you might see (if you had time to notice) the dark clouds piling up over the tops and swinging through Coledale Pass like an army. On the clouds came and a minute later the rain poured down. The army marched on to invade Keswick and out the sun came again. If you cared to watch you could time the showers and run for shelter.

In the heavens it was all life and movement and on the ground the same stir and constant change.

Benjie drew a deep breath of satisfaction. When he saw Mr Bowe, the secretary, who for weeks past had been saying to all and sundry, 'Now, whatever you do you mustn't miss Braithwaite', hastening hither and thither to see that everything was up to time, his own excitement was intense. He was home again; he was among friends again; he was breathing the air that was, by right of birth, his own. He knew exactly what they were all feeling and wanting and hoping, and he felt and wanted and hoped with them. The clouds were his and the grass was his and the surrounding watching hills.

In a noisy crowd the bookies shouted their odds. In spite of the rain the booths with sweets and apples and ginger-beer drove their trade. Dogs were everywhere, and children and anxious parents, farmers and Keswick citizens and men from Cockermouth and Bassenthwaite, from Under Skiddaw and Threlkeld and Grange and Portinscale.

Soon everything was in motion. In the centre of the field were the wrestlers, the twelve-stoners and the ten-stoners, moving slowly round and round one another with a heavy foot-treading solemnity. Round and round they would go, arms out, broad backs straining; they would seem thus like nothing so much as dreamers who find that meditation on the Deity, the character of the soil they tread, the end of their mysterious destinies, can be obtained best by this slow motion and steady contemplation. Western mystics with their proper sacred ceremonies--and then suddenly there is a start, a jerk, they are locked in one another's arms like lovers, a face stares to the sky, a vast leg stiffens, there is a fall.

'Aye, it will be Blakeney's for sartain,' a farmer beside Benjie prophesied to him gravely.

'Why Blakeney?'

'Didn't ye know? Three times nine and a half stone world champion-- aye. He's a lad . . .'

Round the circle of the field the flat-racers were already arranging themselves.

But it was the Puppy Trail that made Benjie's heart beat. In his excitement he dragged Holly by the arm, for that man of a mechanical world was gazing about him with an urban civilized scorn for these poor countrymen who knew nothing better than, on a wet day, to strip almost to the buff and circle slowly round and round on a sodden field.

Benjie might be seventy-seven, but he ran as well as anyone, climbed the low wall and hurried into the next field to see the start of the Trail. At the sight of the men holding the hounds in leash, at the sight of those same hounds straining, yelping, pulling, he sniffed the air as though he were an old hound himself. The last hound trail he had seen he had been with Vanessa over Loweswater way. It had been a glorious day, he remembered, so hot that they had sheltered together under a thick tree for the cool. Afterwards they had had their tea there, and the shadows, moving to the sound of the running beck at their side, had slowly covered the slope of the hill. Then the first stars had come out and, as they had walked together to the road, they had heard from the tent the softened buzzing of the band . . .

Now, as he waited, the sun flashed between the showers, the two trail runners with their 'pads' of old stockings and their aniseed bottles came running in, someone dashed down the flag and the hounds were off. Up the hill, over the wall, across the field and they were lost to view.

After they were gone there was a strange silence, a vacuum, a sense of 'How shall we fill in the time until they're back again?' Some with field glasses climbed the slope, others stood in clusters discussing results--was it to be Starlight or Saturn or Meg?

They turned back for a brief while to watch the wrestling. As Benjie stopped before the wall he felt his shoulder gripped. Against him, at his shoulder, was a strong old man roughly dressed in corduroys, black-haired, bent a little in the back. It was George Endicott.

Benjie stared, feeling that now at this very moment he was wrestling with George on that parlour floor while on the staircase above the woman stood with the candle, waiting, listening . . . that moment that had twisted wrongly his whole life. He had not seen Endicott for ten years.

'George!'

'Funny to see you here. Thought you were dead.'

'And you.'

'Come and have a drink.' It was as though they had never parted. It was his last struggle. He was old and Endicott was old, but there was time yet, old though they were, for the ancient shabbiness, wildness, waste, to return. George had still his black eyes, his loose mouth, that animal lurch of his shoulders. Benjie had never gone away with George yet but that one thing had led to another and so, step by step, into a craziness that ended in darkness. Odd how, at the sight of George, that other world crowded in, all the women he had kissed, the silly toasts he had drunk, the fights he had fought, yes, and further back through that, striking back to some old scene when a woman had been sold in a tent and on a starlit night swords had flashed, and on the Carlisle wall, befogged, he had seen the Devil . . . Had he or had he not? Was this the last touch of that wild hand on his shoulder?

It seemed that it was, for, smiling he said:

'No, George, thank you.'

'What?' said George. 'Too old for drinking?'

'Oh, I'll drink with you some time, but I'm waiting for the hounds to come back.'

George's dark eyes covered him. They studied him from head to toe.

'You look fit.'

'Yes, very fit, thanks. Only a stiffness in my right leg once and again. Are you staying round here?'

'No. I'm moving on to Carlisle tonight. Like to come?'

'What are you doing there?'

'Eh, I don't know. Meeting a man about a dog, you know.'

There flamed up in him one final tempting impulse. He was lonely. He had thought, this morning, that it was happiness enough wandering the country with John and Sam. But he didn't know . . . It would be good to be with George again, to move, ancient though he was, into that old world without law, without order, without discipline.

Then he shook his head.

'Afraid I can't.'

'Sure?'

'Yes. Can't get away.'

'So long then. See you some time.'

George vanished and Benjie turned back to see where Holly was, almost as though he needed protection.

He felt an intense relief as though a weight that had hampered him for years past were gone. A relief-- and a loneliness--for he was old and, in the final stage of life, with every added year our fellows recede from us further.

He waited on the edge of the hill, watching for the first sight of the hounds. To John at his side he explained the mysteries. 'You must be careful laying your trail. You've got to watch out that it isn't too dangerous for the hounds, loose scree or falling boulders, and your curve mustn't have too small a radius because a clever hound will pick up the scent on the far side and cut off a troublesome corner. There are hounds who'll be half a mile ahead of the others again and again simply by cutting off corners. And you've got to watch out for men stopping them on the course, giving them meat or something. Once you have betting, men will do anything. All the same it's the prettiest thing in the world, this and sheepdog trials. You've come to the right country, John.'

'Well--so you say--'

Then, suddenly, there was a shout. Over the top of Barrow the hounds had been sighted. Against the dark green slopes you could see the light-coloured bodies moving now in spots of colour, hidden by trees and then, in a moment, all in a line along the fell path.

'There they are!' 'I can see Starlight!' 'Meg's in front.' 'Nay, that's Saturn!'

Now they had all vanished behind a knoll. There was a breathless pause and then a great shout as two hounds appeared abreast.

"'Tis Starlight!'

'Nay--Saturn! Saturn! Saturn!'

'Yes, 'tis Starlight all right!'

Then down, down the hill they came all together over the hedge on to the roadway. At the last fence Saturn was over first, Starlight just behind him.

'By God! a grand finish!' someone shouted.

But the hullabaloo was now fearful, for all the trainers, with signals perfectly understood by their hounds, let them know, with plenty of time to spare, where the finishing point may be. The shrieks, yells, howls, whistles can be heard a mile away, and some farmer driving his cart up a country lane catches the din on the breeze and will say:

'Yes. Yon's t'hound trail at Braithwaite.'

Starlight and Saturn were up the field together, and had either slackened victory would have been to the other. Did they slacken? Not they. It was one of the best finishes for years--and Saturn has it, two lengths ahead of Starlight, and Granite close behind him.

The rain came, the rain cleared. A lovely mellow light covered the earth. It was the final of the twelve-stone wrestling--Bob Greatouse of Arradfoot had been beaten in the final of the twelve- stone by Blakeney the champion, but the other Greatouse of Arradfoot was in the final of the ten-stone. He was wrestling Pickthall of Cleator Moor. All men held their breath. The two figures went round and round. There was a clinch. Everyone said 'Ah!' Pickthall was thrown with a back-heel . . . Round and round again. Another 'Ah!' Pickthall was thrown again, this time with a twist off the breast and a back-heel. Arradfoot could be proud that night.

Benjie was talking, he did not know to whom. Everyone was friendly. Someone asked him whence he had come.

'Oh, from the South.'

And where would he be going to?

'I'm going nowhere. I'm staying here.'

'Aye, Nowt t'matter wi' Coomberland.'

He turned back and looked up to Barrow.

Yes, he was staying. He'd come home.

THE EAGLE

During the following weeks Benjie made a number of friends. He was of course quickly recognized, the wild young Herries who had grown up with his mother at Ireby, married beneath him, disappeared and then returned with a woman not his wife, shut himself up for years in Newlands.

In the old days you might have disapproved or not disapproved according to your own uprightness of character. But now he was no longer a danger. They called him 'an old rascal' but his teeth were drawn now. He was a character with his one arm, his short- cropped grey curly hair, face like a russet apple, bright blue eyes. And he liked to wear blue shirts and dark-red ties. So he went about the district with his caravan and his man and his dog.

'Yes, he's a rascal,' they'd say, but he never did any harm to anyone. He had a fiery temper and knocked a man down in Cockermouth in spite of his seventy-seven years, but for the most part he was ready to be friendly.

Moreover he was a Herries, and the Herries, although they'd been queer, had been fond of the district for two hundred years.

And Judith Paris was still remembered everywhere--Madame with her white hair and grand manner and walking stick.

'Glad you've come back,' they said to Benjie, and they were.

There came a day in October at last when he thought he would pitch his caravan in a field by Rosthwaite. He had avoided this for weeks; some superstitious feeling had kept him away, as though that ride from Keswick to Rosthwaite and his sitting down there at the spot where the Herries house had once been under the shadow of Watendlath, had some kind of deep spiritual significance for him. He didn't believe much in deep spiritual significances, but there came times when a man stopped, like Balaam's ass, at a shadow on the path. He had been everywhere else-- Uldale and Ireby and Cat Bells and Newlands and

Seascale and Gosforth and Ravensglass--all the places that kept anything of Vanessa in their atmosphere--but he had held back from Rosthwaite.

'When I get there I'm closing the chapter.' He didn't know, but he thought it likely that he would end his days in Borrowdale. 'And then that's the finish. No Herries here any more.'

But at last, on a lovely October day, he decided to move on to Rosthwaite. First he had luncheon at the Keswick Hotel, by invitation, with two Keswick residents--Mr Glossop and Mr Blane. Mr Glossop was a bachelor, a large stout cheery man in very baggy knickerbockers. He lived in St John's in the Vale and was reputed to be wealthy. Mr Blane was married, had three children and a small income. He had been a Civil Servant in India, had retired, and suffered from a very uncertain digestion. It was natural that Glossop should be an optimist and Blane a pessimist, but Benjie was interested to realize, as luncheon continued, how very much less certain he was of his opinions than were these two much younger men. He neither knew so certainly nor cared so deeply.

As they walked into the hotel Glossop was waving his arms and crying out cheerily: 'What a day! What a grand day! How are you, Mrs Wivell? Pretty good? That's right . . . No, Herries, as I was saying, this Government seems to be doing wonderfully well. Of course we know that people complain about the Means Test, but what I say is this . . .'

Later at luncheon Mr Blane looked at Mr Glossop with his rather dim yellow-shadowed eyes and remarked, nervously crumbling his bread:

'Really, Glossop, how you dare! Why, we're on the edge of the pit, the whole lot of us. Hasn't sterling gone down eight points this very week? Isn't France at her wits' end to balance her budget? Haven't those poor fellows from all parts of the country been marching through the rain all this week on London? Isn't Germany making ready to fight Poland and shan't we be compelled because of Locarno to join in? Really, Glossop, I'd be surprised if I didn't know you. Don't be taken in by him, Mr Herries. His spirits go down to zero the minute he has the toothache--'

'Ha! Bah!' said Glossop. 'You're a defeatist, Blane, that's what you are! One would think that a little bit of discomfort means the ruin of the universe! Why, after the Napoleonic Wars they had thirty years of distress and a much worse distress than anything we're experiencing. You just wait until after the American election. You'll be surprised how quickly things settle themselves and trade's booming again! Why, Davis from America is over here consulting with MacDonald this very week, and I see that today's Express says . . .'

So it went on and Benjie's mind wandered. He pulled himself together to say once:

'I've got a girl in Berlin working on international affairs.'

'And what does she tell you?' said Glossop, beaming.

'Well, she doesn't tell me anything.'

And then a little later he remarked:

'Of course if they can teach Doyle to defend himself he'll make some of those Americans look silly. He's a natural fighter.'

But he couldn't really attend. Mr Blane cried:

'Well, I simply can't understand you, Glossop. There you are, fiddling while Rome is burning.' He added, 'We're bewildered, that's what we all are. Don't feel safe any more.'

And Benjie thought: 'That's his generation--afraid. Sally's isn't.'

He remarked: 'Sam had a great fight yesterday in Penrith. One of those nasty Aberdeens some fat woman was carrying round with her. He just about bit its ear off.'

And after luncheon he could not fix his mind on serious matters. It was as though this going out to Rosthwaite were all-absorbing. They went with him through the town to where his caravan was pitched between the Art School and Crosthwaite Church. All the way along Mr Glossop was heartily greeting his friends.

'How are you, Mrs Fox?' and then in parenthesis, 'Mrs Fox of Fawe Park--American--charming woman', or 'Fine day, Mrs Johnson. How's the boy getting on at Cambridge?' or 'How do, Todd', or 'How are you, Lewin?' as a clergyman passed them on a bicycle. While on the other hand Mr Blane recognized no one, nor did he see the charm of the old tower nor the break between the houses which showed the sunlit hills rolling through the mortar and brick, nor the white cloud like a gigantic bird's nest perched between the breasts of Skiddaw. He saw nothing, for, defeated once again by the malignant obstinacy of his greed, he had eaten Cumberland ham at luncheon, the richest ham in the world and for him the most destructive. Already he saw pain and discomfort approaching him down the road . . .

Before Benjie sat with Holly in the front of the motor that pulled the caravan (and Sam on his knee) he shouted to Mr Blane:

'Try five-minute exercises with your colon like that fellow I read about in a book the other day. Nothing like it for the digestion.' But Mr Blane didn't think that funny. He assumed a rather sinister air.

As they sputtered off along Main Street, Benjie was cross.

'Having a joke with some men about their digestion is as serious as joking about their religion.'

'That's all right,' said Holly, 'if your stomach's behaving proper. You've got a stomach like an ostrich. I've always said so.'

As usual, they were a sensation in the town, and today, under the blue sky, the red caravan with all the handles to the doors highly polished was a fine sight.

Benjie, his hat cocked on one side, a late rosebud in his buttonhole, was a throw-back, as he himself had observed, to Britannia seated on her throne in the old circus processions.

'You know, Holly,' he said, 'two hundred years ago on a dark night a very wicked ancestor of mine rode out into Borrowdale just as we're doing.'

He was thinking a lot about Francis Herries just then, for a fortnight ago he had read Judith's book once again right through. Times weren't so good, with investments down as they were. It was true that now that Sally was settled his needs were small, but he had wondered whether, after all, Judith's book mightn't be worth publishing. After reading it he decided that it would be sacrilege. But the whole world of that book was very present to him. When you were as old as he was time vanished and had no meaning.

Holly had no interest whatever in the Herries family, but he WAS interested in scandal.

'What way was he wicked?' he asked.

'Oh, the usual way.'

'Wine, women and song! Oh, boy!' said Holly.

'There's no need to be American, John,' Benjie remarked. 'They're fine people and their own language suits them, but you're English.'

'You bet,' Holly said. 'No damned foreigners for me.'

When they reached the Ashness gate Benjie made him pull up. He got out and looked across the Lake. There was not a ripple on the water, which was coloured so faintly blue that it was almost white, to the Manesty bank. Here the trees, the chesnuts, the maples, the larches flamed on the water's edge. They seemed in actual fact to be burning. You might fancy that, across the still water, you heard the branches crackle in the blaze. From the darkest crimson, through amber, orange, the rich yellow of a canary's wing, to the faint gold pallor of Chinese lacquer, they were massed against the red cloud of bracken that covered the fell. To the right the cloud that had been a bird's nest on Skiddaw had grown until it enveloped the peaks in a tumbled mass that glittered like frozen snow. There was no sound nor breath of stirring.

'It's a fine day,' he said, climbing back beside Holly.

'And it'll rain tomorrow, I bet you,' said Holly.

With every yard of ground--past the Lodore Hotel, the Borrowdale, Grange Bridge, the Bowder Stone, down the hill into the valley-- Benjie's spirits rose. The outer world slipped behind them. The old valley was still shut in even as in ancient days, when its citizens had, as the legend went, tried to build a wall to enclose the cuckoo. Glaramara and Grey Knotts and Brandreth were the advance guard; Gable, Scafell, Great End, Bowfell were still guardians at the close, as for so many hundreds of years they had been. The valley was as still as the Lake had been, and above the green fields, to the right at the side of the streams, the leaves in orange and crimson lifted their glory to the blue.

'Where are we going?' asked Holly. 'Does this valley lead to anywhere?'

'No. It does not. We're stopping for the night near the place where that same ancestor of mine built a house.'

'Kind of lost sort of place, this valley,' said Holly.

Where the path leads off the high road up to Watendlath they halted. Here there was a little stone bridge that crossed a stream flecked now with the blue of the sky, and just above it was a solid little stone house.

'Is that the place your ancestor built?'

'No. That's not the house, but it's the spot. Two ladies lived there, but now it's sold. There's nobody in it, I fancy, just now.'

After some trouble they found a spot on the level below the house where the caravan could remain.

When they were settled Benjie lit a pipe, and taking with him that day's Times which he had procured in Keswick, Judith's book at which he thought he would have another look, and Casson's Wise Kings of Borrowdale (an old friend of his that he had not seen for many a year but had found today in Chaplin's shop), he seated himself comfortably on the step of the caravan while Sam pursued idyllic scents on the border of the stream.

He had only to raise his eyes, he reflected, and there was old Rogue Herries riding up the path with the little boy in his arms . . . The boy runs forward and flings open the door . . .

He opened Judith's book at the beginning and read:

'I, Judith Paris, was born at Rosthwaite in the valley of Borrowdale, Cumberland, on the 28th of November in the Year of Our Lord 1774 . . .' He skipped a little, but old Aunt Jane's feminine mid-Victorian hand was wonderfully clear. 'I have heard very much of what happened in those long-ago times from my half-brother David Herries. David Herries was my father's son by his first wife, and he was fifty-five when I was born, so that I could have been his granddaughter . . . He told me that he remembered exactly the night that he first arrived in Keswick. He could remember every detail, and so do I, even at this distance of time. How he was in the inn at Keswick in a big canopied bed with his sisters Mary and Deborah. The canopy that ran round the top of the bed was a faded green and had a gold thread in it. There were fire-dogs by the fire with mouths like grinning dragons. And he remembered that a woman was sitting warming herself in front of the fire, a woman he hated. Then his father came in and thought he was sleeping. He remembered that his father was wearing a beautiful coat of claret colour and a chestnut wig, and there were red roses on his grey silk waistcoat. . .'

Benjie skipped a page or two. He came to the ride through Borrowdale. 'David was wide awake now and knew that his father was happily drunk. He sang a song that was popular with children then. David had played it as a game:

'Lady Queen Anne who sits in her stand,
And a pair of green gloves upon her hand.
As white as a lily, as fair as a swan,
The fairest lady in a' the land.

'They rode on and suddenly the clouds broke and a moon sailed out and the sky was covered with stars. Then they moved up the little hill and it was all very quiet. It all seemed very wonderful to David, who had never seen mountains before, and of course they were very large in the moonlight.

'Then they stopped and someone said:

'"That is the house on the left of us."

'They went on through a thick group of trees and now they were outside a rough stone wall guarding a courtyard where grass was growing. David remembered that he was sadly disappointed in his first view of the house, for it looked so small under the hill. Then some dogs ran out, barking, and his father put him to the ground and he ran forward and was first into the house. In the hall, which through the open door was moonlit, he saw two shining suits of armour . . .'

'It's all very vivid,' thought Benjie; 'if I try hard enough I can see it just as it was and the boy running across the courtyard.' The air was so still that it was not difficult to fancy that there were figures standing listening, and that the old house was still there with the moon shining in on the suits of armour.

The fresh air made him feel sleepy. The past was so much more real to him than the present, as it is perhaps to all old people. The things that the two men had discussed at luncheon were dim and shadowy.

'It may be,' he thought, 'that it is only when you are old that you see things in their true perspective. The world seems to be crumbling but it has crumbled so often before, changing into a new shape that will appear as solid to another generation as its earlier form seemed to the older people. But I'm no philosopher. I've been better at doing things than thinking them.' And his life crowded up into his consciousness, all of it moving at the same time. He was with Barney and Ellis at the music hall and a lady gave him a white rose, he asked Vanessa to marry him in the moonlight in the Fortress garden, he wrestled with Endicott; once again, misery at his heart, he told Vanessa that he was married, and once again he stood by the Chinese clock while Ellis shouted at them from below; he was in Newlands and there came the most wonderful moment of his life when

Vanessa, brushing her hair, turned and looked at him . . .

He would go no further. But how strange that all these things should be still so alive and other things that had nothing to do with his heart--Africa and Spain and (the greatest moment in his life apart from Vanessa) the sunlit day in Petrograd when they had marched, singing, into the new world. Why, he thought, were the only things that counted in a man's life, when you looked back, the things that touched his spirit--if he had one?

Was it true, as Vanessa believed, that there was a secret life, progressive, unceasing, all-important?

Holly had come to the caravan door, a frying-pan in his hand.

'John, do you think there's a secret life?'

'Will you have your eggs scrambled or fried?' John asked, disregarding, as he so often did, Benjie's mad way of asking questions that meant nothing.

Benjie turned back to the scene. It was growing cold. As fire dies into ash so the sky was fading into grey. He was very happy. His memories and this country made him so.

He opened Casson's thin green book, but could scarcely see to read.

I bid ye mourn not for the death of beauty.
For, though the Springtide fades from
                              Cumberland,
Her streams and tarns, there is eternal spring
In heaven. And, on my island where I live,
I dream that heaven is very like this land,
Mountains and lakes and rivers undecaying,
And simple woodlands and wild cherry flowers.
At least I know no better. But weep not.
For, though this land is but the shadow of heaven,
It yet is heaven's shadow.

He was almost asleep. His pipe fell from his hand. It was so small a country--this green valley, up the Pass into the hollow guarded by Gable, and the Scafells with dark Wastwater to one side, lonely Ennerdale to another, Eskdale, and, to the south the Pikes and Langdale, Esthwaite and Windermere and Coniston. One turn of the hand to the north, and in close company Grasmere and Rydal, Ullswater, and so, towards the Border, Derwentwater, Buttermere, Crummock . . . a land that the sweep of a bird might in a flash of the sun cover with its shadow. England itself, from these little hills and lakes, through the dark space of the Midlands, in a moment of time, over field and stream and sloping hill to the sea . . .

The Eagle's wing embraced it. The White Horse, striking upward from the dark water, climbed the icy hill. The Eagle free, the White Horse triumphant, the same Eagle, the same Horse as in captivity, now lost themselves in a larger liberty, in a purpose far grander than their individual struggle . . .

Was he asleep? He thought he heard Holly's voice: 'You'll get cold out there. Supper's nearly ready.' But he rested his head against the upper step. He sighed with happiness because all the struggle was over. No one was afraid any longer. Vanessa was all right. Tom was all right. Sally, who knew no fear, was building the new world. And he himself was at home where he had always wanted to be.

He turned his head, smiling, and sleepily murmured, as in the past he had so often done: 'Goodnight, Vanessa.'

Over this country, when the giant Eagle flings the shadow of his wing, the land is darkened. So compact is it that the wing covers all its extent in one pause of the flight. The sea breaks on the pale line of the shore; to the Eagle's proud glance waves run in to the foot of the hills that are like rocks planted in green water.

From Whinlatter to Black Combe the clouds are never still. The Tarns like black unwinking eyes watch their chase, and the colours are laid out in patterns on the rocks and are continually changed. The Eagle can see the shadows rise from their knees at the base of Scafell and Gable, he can see the black precipitous flanks of the Screes washed with rain and the dark purple hummocks of Borrowdale crags flash suddenly with gold.

So small is the extent of this country that the sweep of the Eagle's wing caresses all of it, but there is no ground in the world more mysterious, no land at once so bare in its nakedness and so rich in its luxury, so warm with sun and so cold in pitiless rain, so gentle and pastoral, so wild and lonely; with sea and lake and river there is always the sound of moving water, and its strong people have their feet in the soil and are independent of all men.

During the flight of the Eagle two hundred years are but as a day--and the life of a man, as against all odds he pushes towards immortality, is eternal . . .

THE END

CPSIA information can be obtained at www.ICGtesting.com
Printed in the USA
BVOW02s1442290114

343405BV00007B/273/P